COMPLETE WORKS

OF

William Shakespeare

WITH
A LIFE OF THE POET,
BY CHARLES SYMMONS, D.D.

A GLOSSARY
AND
FIFTY EMBELLISHMENTS

Complete In One Volume

6 Highbury Corner, London N5 1RD
Manufactured under arrangement with
Ottenheimer Publishers, Inc.

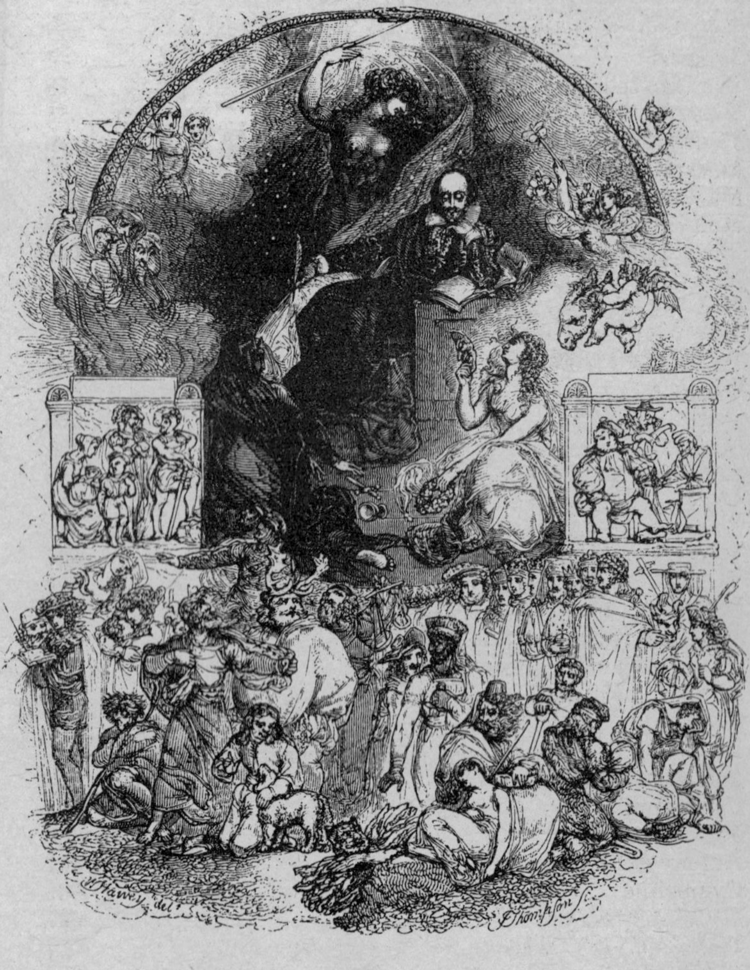

YES, MASTER OF THE HUMAN HEART! WE OWN
THY SOVEREIGN SWAY; AND BOW BEFORE THY THRONE:
AT THY COMMAND THE VARIED TUMULT ROLLS:
NOW PITY MELTS, NOW TERROR CHILLS OUR SOULS.
NOW, AS THOU WAVEST THY WIZARD-ROD, ARE SEEN
THE FAYS AND ELVES QUICK GLANCING O'ER THE GREEN:
AND, AS THE MOON HER PERFECT ORB DISPLAYS,
THE LITTLE PEOPLE SPARKLE IN HER RAYS.
THERE, MID THE LIGHTNING'S BLAZE, AND WHIRLWIND'S HOWL,
ON THE SCATH'D HEATH THE FATAL SISTERS SCOWL:
OR, AS HELL'S CALDRON BUBBLES O'ER THE FLAME,
PREPARE TO DO "A DEED WITHOUT A NAME."
THESE ARE THY WONDERS, NATURE'S DARLING BIRTH!
AND FAME EXULTING BEARS THY NAME O'ER EARTH.

SYMMONS.

CONTENTS

THE
LIFE OF WILLIAM SHAKSPEARE.

BY CHARLES SYMMONS, D.D.

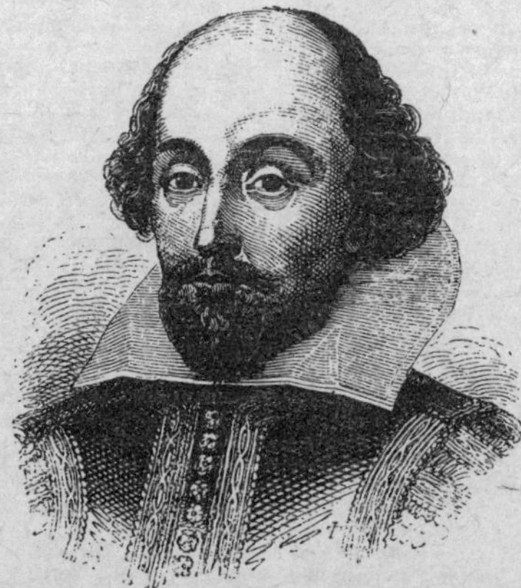

Wherever any extraordinary display of human intellect has been made, there will human curiosity, at one period or the other, be busy to obtain some personal acquaintance with the distinguished mortal whom Heaven had been pleased to endow with a larger portion of its own etherial energy. If the favoured man walked on the high places of the world; if he were conversant with courts; if he directed the movements of armies or of states, and thus held in his hand the fortunes and the lives of multitudes of his fellow-creatures, the interest, which he excites, will be immediate and strong: he stands on an eminence where he is the mark of many eyes; and dark and unlettered indeed must be the age in which the incidents of his eventful life will not be noted, and the record of them be preserved for the instruction or the entertainment of unborn generations. But if his course were through the vale of life: if he were unmingled with the factions and the contests of the great: if the powers of his mind were devoted to the silent pursuits of literature—to the converse of philosophy and the Muse, the possessor of the etherial treasure may excite little of the attention of his contemporaries; may walk quietly, with a veil over his glories, to the grave; and, in other times, when the expansion of his intellectual greatness has filled the eyes of the world, it may be too late to inquire for his history as a man. The bright track of his genius indelibly remains; but the trace of his mortal footstep is soon obliterated for ever. Homer is now only a name—a solitary name, which assures us, that, at some unascertained period in the annals of mankind, a mighty mind was indulged to a human being, and gave its wonderful productions to the perpetual admiration of men, as they spring in succession in the path of time. Of Homer himself we actually know nothing; and we see only an arm of immense power thrust forth from a mass of impenetrable darkness, and holding up the hero of his song to the applauses of never-dying fame. But it may be supposed that the revolution of, perhaps, thirty centuries has collected the cloud which thus withdraws the father of poesy from our sight. Little more than two centuries has elapsed since William Shakspeare conversed with our tongue, and trod the self-same soil with ourselves; and if it were not for the records kept by our Church in its registers of births, marriages, and burials, we should at this moment be as personally ignorant of the "sweet swan of Avon" as we are of the old minstrel and rhapsodist of Meles. That William Shakspeare was born in Stratford upon Avon; that he married and had three children; that he wrote a certain number of dramas; that he died before he had attained to old age, and was buried in his native town, are positively the only facts, in the personal history of this extraordinary man, of which we are certainly possessed; and, if we should be solicitous to fill up this bare and most unsatisfactory outline, we must have recourse to the vague reports of unsubstantial tradition, or to the still more shadowy inferences of lawless and vagabond conjecture. Of this remarkable ignorance of one of the most richly endowed with intellect of the human species, who ran his mortal race in our own country, and who stands separated from us by no very great intervention of time, the causes may not be difficult to be ascertained. William Shakspeare was an actor and a writer of plays; in neither of which characters, however he might excel in them, could he be lifted high in the estimation of his contemporaries. He was honoured, indeed, with the friendship of nobles, and the patronage of monarchs: his theatre was frequented by the wits of the metropolis; and he associated with the most intellectual of his times. But the spirit of the age was against him; and, in opposition to it, he could not become the subject of any general or comprehensive interest. The nation, in short, knew little and cared less about him. During his life, and for some years after his death, inferior dramatists outran him in the race of popularity; and then the flood of puritan fanaticism swept him and the stage together into temporary oblivion. On the restoration of the monarchy and the theatre, the school of France perverted our taste, and it was not till the last century was somewhat advanced that William Shakspeare arose again, as it were, from the tomb, in all his proper majesty of light. He then became the subject of solicitous and learned inquiry: but inquiry was then too late; and all that it could recover, from the ravage of time, were only a few human fragments, which could scarcely be united into a man. To these causes of our personal ignorance of the great bard of England, must be added his own strange indifference to the celebrity of genius. When he had produced his admirable works, ignorant or heedless of their value, he abandoned them with perfect indifference to oblivion or to fame. It surpassed his thought that he could grow into the admiration of the world; and, without any reference to the curiosity of future ages, in which he could not conceive himself to possess an interest, he was contented to die in the arms of obscurity, as an unlaurelled burgher of a provincial town. To this combination of causes are we to attribute the scantiness of our materials for the Life of William Shakspeare. His works are in myriads of hands: he constitutes the delight of myriads of readers: his renown is coextensive with the civilization of man; and, striding across the ocean from Europe, it occupies the wide region of transatlantic empire: but he is himself only a shadow which disappoints our grasp; an undefined form which is rather intimated than discovered to the keenest searchings of our eye. Of the little however, questionable or certain, which can be told of him we must now proceed to make the best use in our power, to write what by courtesy may be called his life; and we have only to lament that the result of our labour must greatly disappoint the curiosity which has been excited by the grandeur of his reputation. The slight narrative of Rowe, founded on the information obtained, in the beginning of the last century, by the inquiries of Betterton, the famous actor, will necessarily supply us with the greater part of the materials with which we are to work.

William Shakspeare, or Shakspere, (for the floating orthography of the name is properly attached to the one or the other of these varieties) was baptized in the church of Stratford upon Avon, as is ascertained by the parish register, on the 26th of April 1564; and he is said to have been born on the 23d of the same month, the day consecrated to the tutelar saint of England. His parents, John and Mary Shakspeare, were not of equal ranks in the community; for the former was only a respectable tradesman, whose ancestors cannot be traced into gentility, whilst the latter belonged to an ancient and opulent house in the county of Warwick, being the youngest daughter of Robert Arden of Wilmecote. The family of the Ardens (or Ardernes, as it is written in all the old deeds,) was of considerable antiquity and importance, some of them having served as high sheriffs of their county, and two of them (Sir John Arden and his nephew, the grandfather of Mrs. Shakspeare), having enjoyed each a station of honour in the personal establishment of Henry VII. The younger of these Ardens was made, by his sovereign, keeper of the park of Aldercar and bailiff of the lordship of Codnore. He obtained, also, from the crown a valuable grant in the lease of the manor of Yoxsal in Staffordshire, consisting of more than 4,600 acres, at a rent of 42*l*. Mary Arden did not come dowerless to her plebeian husband, for she brought to him a small freehold estate called Asbies, and the sum of 6*l*. 13*s*. 4*d*. in money. The freehold consisted of a house and fifty-four acres of land; and, as far as it appears, it was the first piece of landed property which was ever possessed by the Shakspeares. Of this marriage the offspring was four sons and four daughters; of whom Joan (or, according to the orthography of that time, Jone,) and Margaret, the eldest of the children, died one in infancy and one at a somewhat more advanced age; and Gilbert, whose birth immediately succeeded to that of our Poet, is supposed by some not to have reached his maturity, and by others to have attained to considerable longevity. Joan, the eldest of the four remaining children, and named after her deceased sister, married William Hart, a hatter in her native town; and Edmund, the youngest of the family, adopting the profession of an actor, resided in St. Saviour's parish in London; and was buried in St. Saviour's Church on the last day of December 1607, in his twenty-eighth year. Of Anne and Richard, whose births intervened between those of Joan and Edmund, the parish register tells the whole history, when it records that the former was buried on the 4th of April 1579, in the eighth year of her age, and the latter on the 4th of February 1612-13, when he had nearly completed his thirty-ninth.

In consequence of a document, discovered in the year 1770, in the house in which, if tradition is to be trusted, our Poet was born, some persons have concluded that John Shakspeare was a Roman Catholic, though he had risen, by the regular gradation of office, to the chief dignity of the corporation of Stratford, that of high bailiff; and, during the whole of this period, had unquestionably conformed to the rites of the Church of England. The asserted fact seemed not to be very probable; and the document in question, which, drawn up in a testamentary form and regularly attested, zealously professes the Roman faith of him in whose name it speaks, having been subjected to a rigid examination by Malone, has been pronounced to be spurious. The trade of John Shakspeare, as well as his religious faith, has recently been made the subject of controversy. According to the testimony of Rowe, grounded on the tradition of Stratford, the father of our Poet was a dealer in wool, or, in the provincial vocabulary of his country, a wool-driver; and such he has been deemed by all the biographers of his son, till the fact was thrown into doubt by the result of the inquisitiveness of Malone. Finding, in an old and obscure MS. purporting to record the proceedings of the bailiff's court in Stratford, our John Shakspeare designated as a glover, Malone insults over the ignorance of poor Rowe, and assumes no small degree of merit to himself as the discoverer of a long sought and a most important historic truth. If he had recollected the remark of the clown in the Twelfth Night*, that "a sentence is but a cheverel glove to a good wit. How quickly the wrong side may be turned outwards!" he would, doubtless, have pressed the observation into his service, and brought it as an irresistible attestation of the veracity of his old MS.

Whatever may have been the trade of John Shakspeare, whether that of wool-merchant or of glover, it seems, with the little fortune of his wife, to have placed him in a state of easy competence. In 1569 or 1570, in consequence partly of his alliance with the Ardens, and partly of his attainment of the prime municipal honours of his town, he obtained a concession of arms from the herald's office, a grant, which placed him and his family on the file of the gentry of England; and, in 1574, he purchased two houses, with gardens and orchards annexed to them, in Henley Street in Stratford. But before the year 1578, his prosperity, from causes not now

* Act iii. sc. 1.

ascertainable, had certainly declined; for in that year, as we find from the records of his borough, he was excused, in condescension to his poverty, from the moiety of a very moderate assessment of six shillings and eightpence, made by the members of the corporation on themselves; at the same time that he was altogether exempted from his contribution to the relief of the poor. During the remaining years of his life, his fortunes appear not to have recovered themselves; for he ceased to attend the meetings of the corporation hall, where he had once presided; and, in 1586, another person was substituted as alderman in his place, in consequence of his magisterial inefficiency. He died in the September of 1601, when his illustrious son had already attained to high celebrity; and his wife, Mary Shakspeare, surviving him for seven years, deceased in the September of 1608, the burial of the former being registered on the eighth and that of the latter on the ninth of this month, in each of these respective years.

On the 30th of June 1564, when our Poet had not yet been three months in this breathing world, his native Stratford was visited by the plague; and, during the six succeeding months, the ravaging disease is calculated to have swept to the grave more than a seventh part of the whole population of the place. But the favoured infant reposed in security in his cradle, and breathed health amid an atmosphere of pestilence. The Genius of England may be supposed to have held the arm of the destroyer, and not to have permitted it to fall on the consecrated dwelling of his and Nature's darling. The disease, indeed, did not overstep his charmed threshold; for the name of Shakspeare is not to be found in the register of deaths throughout that period of accelerated mortality. That he survived this desolating calamity of his townsmen, is all that we know of William Shakspeare from the day of his birth till he was sent, as we are informed by Rowe, to the free-school of Stratford; and was stationed there in the course of his education, till, in consequence of the straitened circumstances of his father, he was recalled to the paternal roof. As we are not told at what age he was sent to school, we cannot form any estimate of the time during which he remained there. But if he was placed under his master when he was six years old, he might have continued in a state of instruction for seven or even for eight years; a term sufficiently long for any boy, not an absolute blockhead, to acquire something more than the mere elements of the classical languages. We are too ignorant, however of dates in these instances to speak with any confidence on the subject; and we can only assert that seven or eight of the fourteen years, which intervened between the birth of our Poet in 1564 and the known period of his father's diminished fortune in 1578, might very properly have been given to the advantages of the free-school. But now the important question is to be asked—What were the attainments of our young Shakspeare at this seat of youthful institution? Did he return to his father's house in a state of utter ignorance of classic literature? or was he as far advanced in his school-studies as boys of his age (which I take to be thirteen or fourteen) usually are in the common progress of our public and more reputable schools? That his scholastic attainments did not rise to the point of learning, seems to have been the general opinion of his contemporaries; and to this opinion I am willing to assent. But I cannot persuade myself that he was entirely unacquainted with the classic tongues; or that, as Farmer and his followers labour to convince us, he could receive the instructions, even for three or four years, of a school of any character, and could then depart without any knowledge beyond that of the Latin accidence. The most accomplished scholar may read with pleasure the poetic versions of the classic poets; and the less advanced proficient may consult his indolence by applying to the page of a translation of a prose classic, when accuracy of quotation may not be required: and on evidences of this nature is supported the charge which has been brought, and which is now generally admitted, against our immortal bard, of more than school-boy ignorance. He might, indeed, from necessity apply to North for the interpretation of Plutarch; but he read Golding's Ovid only, as I am satisfied, for the entertainment of its English poetry. Ben Jonson, who must have been intimately conversant with his friend's classic acquisitions, tells us expressly that, "He had small Latin and less Greek." But, according to the usual plan of instruction in our schools, he must have traversed a considerable extent of the language of Rome, before he could touch even the confines of that of Greece. He must in short have read Ovid's Metamorphoses, and a part at least of Virgil, before he could open the grammar of the more ancient, and copious, and complex dialect. This I conceive to be a fair statement of the case in the question respecting Shakspeare's learning. Beyond controversy he was not a scholar; but he had not profited so little by the hours, which he had passed in school, as not to be able to understand the more easy Roman authors without the assistance of a translation. If he himself had been asked, on the subject, he might have parodied his own Falstaff and have answered, "Indeed I am not a Scaliger or a Budæus, but yet no blockhead, friend." I believe also that he was not wholly unacquainted with the popular languages of France and Italy. He had abundant leisure to acquire them; and the activity and the curiosity of his mind were sufficiently strong to urge him to their acquisition. But to discuss this much agitated question would lead me beyond the limits which are prescribed to me; and, contenting myself with declaring that, in my opinion, both parties are wrong, both they who contend for our Poet's learning, and they who place his illiteracy on a level with that of John Taylor, the celebrated water-poet, I must resume my humble and most deficient narrative. The classical studies of William Shakspeare, whatever progress he may or may not have made in them, were now suspended; and he was replaced in his father's house, when he had attained his thirteenth or fourteenth year, to assist with his hand in the maintenance of the family. Whether he continued in this situation whilst he remained in his single state, has not been told to us, and cannot therefore at this period be known. But in the absence of information, conjecture will be busy; and will soon cover the bare desert with unprofitable vegetation. Whilst Malone surmises that the young Poet passed the interval, till his marriage, or a large portion of it, in the office of an attorney, Aubrey stations him during the same term at the head of a country school. But the surmises of Malone are not universally happy; and to the assertions of Aubrey I am not disposed to attach more credit than was attached to them by Anthony Wood, who knew the old gossip and was competent to appreciate his character. It is more probable that the necessity, which brought young Shakspeare from his school, retained him with his father's occupation at home, till the acquisition of a wife made it convenient for him to remove to a separate habitation. It is reasonable to conclude that a mind like his, ardent, excursive, and "all compact of imagination," would not be satisfied with entire inactivity; but would obtain knowledge where it could, if not from the stores of the ancients, from those at least which were supplied to him by the writers of his own country.

In 1582, before he had completed his eighteenth year, he married Anne Hathaway, the daughter, as Rowe informs us, of a substantial yeoman in the neighbourhood of Stratford. We are unacquainted with the precise period of their marriage, and with the church in which it was solemnized, for in the register of Stratford there is no record of the event; and we are made certain of the year, in which it occurred, only by the baptism of Susanna, the first produce of the union, on the 26th of May 1583. As young Shakspeare neither increased his fortune by this match, though he probably received some money with his wife, nor raised himself by it in the community, we may conclude that he was induced to it by inclination, and the impulse of love. But the youthful poet's dream of happiness does not seem to have been realized by the result. The bride was eight years older than the bridegroom: and whatever charms she might possess to fascinate the eyes of her boy-lover, she probably was deficient in those powers which are requisite to impose a durable fetter on the heart, and to hold "in sweet captivity" a mind of the very highest order. No charge is intimated against the lady: but she is left in Stratford by her husband during his long residence in the metropolis; and on his death, she is found to be only slightly and, as it were, casually remembered in his will. Her second pregnancy, which was productive of twins, (Hamnet and Judith, baptized on the 2d of February 1584-5,) terminated her pride as a mother; and we know nothing more respecting her than that, surviving her illustrious consort by rather more than seven years, she was buried on the 8th of August 1623, being, as we are told by the inscription on her tomb, of the age of sixty-seven. Respecting the habits of life, or the occupation of our young Poet by which he obtained his subsistence, or even the place of his residence, subsequently to his marriage, not a floating syllable has been wafted to us by tradition for the gratification of our curiosity; and the history of this great man is a perfect blank till the occurrence of an event, which drove him from his native town, and gave his wonderful intellect to break out in its full lustre on the world. From the frequent allusions in his writings to the elegant sport of falconry, it has been suggested that this, possibly, might be one of his favorite amusements: and nothing can be more probable, from the active season of his life, and his fixed habitation in the country, than his strong and eager passion for all the pleasures of the field. As a sportsman, in his rank of life, he would naturally become a poacher; and then it is highly probable that he would fall into the acquaintance of poachers; and, associating with them in his idler hours, would occasionally be one of their fellow marauders on the manors of their rich neighbours. In one of these licentious excursions on the grounds of Sir Thomas Lucy of Charlecote, in the immediate vicinity of Stratford, for the purpose as it is said of stealing his deer, our young bard was detected; and, having farther irritated the knight by affixing a satirical ballad on him to the gates of Charlecote, he was compelled to fly before the enmity of his powerful adversary, and to seek an asylum in the capital. Malone, who is prone to doubt, wishes to question the truth of this whole narrative, and to ascribe the flight of young Shakspeare from his native country to the embarrassment of his circumstances, and the persecution of his creditors. But the story of the deer-stealing rests upon the uniform tradition of Stratford, and is confirmed by the character of Sir T. Lucy, who is known to have been a rigid preserver of his game; by the enmity displayed against his memory by Shakspeare in his succeeding life; and by a part of the offensive ballad itself, preserved by a Mr. Jones of Tarbick, a village near to Stratford, who obtained it from those who must have been acquainted with the fact, and who could not be biased by any interest or passion to falsify or misstate it. Besides the objector, in this instance, seems not to be aware that it was easier to escape from the resentment of an offended proprietor of game than from the avarice of a creditor: that whilst the former might be satisfied with the removal of the delinquent to a situation where he could no longer infest his parks or his warrens, the latter would pursue his debtor wherever bailiffs could find and writs could attach him. On every account, therefore, I believe the tradition, recorded by Rowe, that our Poet retired from Stratford before the exasperated power of Sir T. Lucy, and found a refuge in London, not possibly beyond the reach of the arm, but beyond the hostile purposes of his provincial antagonist.

The time of this eventful flight of the great bard of England cannot now be accurately determined: but we may somewhat confidently place it between the years 1585 and 1588; for in the former of these we may conclude him to have been present with his family at the baptism of his twins, Hamnet and Judith; and than the latter of them we cannot well assign a later date for his arrival in London, since we know that before 1592 he had not only written two long poems, the Venus and Adonis and the Rape of Lucrece, but had acquired no small degree of celebrity as an actor and a dramatic writer.

At this agitating crisis of his life, the situation of young Shakspeare was certainly, in its obvious aspect, severe and even terrific. Without friends to protect or assist him, he was driven, under the frown of exasperated power, from his profession; from his native fields; from the companions of his childhood and his youth; from his wife and his infant offspring. The world was spread before him, like a dark ocean, in which no fortunate isle could be seen to glitter amid the gloomy and sullen tide. But he was blessed with youth and health: his conscience was unwounded, for the adventure for which he suffered, was regarded, in the estimation of his times, as a mere boy's frolick, of not greater guilt than the robbing of an orchard; and his mind, rich beyond example in the gold of heaven, could throw lustre over the black waste before him, and could people it with a beautiful creation of her own. We may imagine him, then, departing from his home, not indeed like the great Roman captive as he is described by the poet—

> Fertur pudicæ conjugis osculum,
> Parvosque natos, ut capitis minor,
> Ab se removisse, et virilem
> Torvus humi posuisse vultum, &c.

but touched with some feelings of natural sorrow, yet with an unfaltering step, and with hope vigorous at his heart. It was impossible that he should despair; and if he indulged in sanguine expectation, the event proved him not to be a visionary. In the course of a few years, the exile of Stratford became the associate of wits, the friend of nobles, the favorite of monarchs; and in a period, which still left him not in sight of old age, he returned to his birthplace in affluence, with honour, and with the plaudits of the judicious and the noble resounding in his ears.

His immediate refuge in the metropolis was the stage; to which his access, as it appears, was easy. Stratford was fond of theatrical representations, which it accommodated with its town or guildhall; and had frequently been visited by companies of players when our Poet was of an age, not only to enjoy their performances but to form an acquaintance with their members. Thomas Greene, who was one of their distinguished actors, has been considered by some writers as a kinsman of our author's; and though he, possibly, may have been confounded by them with another Thomas Greene, a barrister, who was unquestionably connected with the Shakspeares, he was certainly a fellow townsman of our fugitive bard's; whilst Heminge and Burbage, two of the leaders of the company in question, belonged either to Stratford or to its immediate neighbourhood. With the door of the theatre thus open to him, and under the impulse of his own theatrical bias, (for however in after life he may have lamented his degradation as a professional actor, it must be concluded that he now felt a strong attachment to the stage,) it is not wonderful that young Shakspeare should solicit this asylum in his distress; or that he should be kindly received by men who knew him, and some of whom were connected, if not with his family, at least with his native town. The company to which he united himself, was the Earl of Leicester's or the Queen's; which had obtained the royal license in 1574. The place of its performances, when our Poet became enrolled among its members, was the Globe on the Bankside; and its managers subsequently purchased the theatre of Blackfriars (the oldest theatre in London), which they had previously rented for some years; and at these two theatres, the first of which was open in the centre for summer representations and the last covered for those of winter, were acted all the dramatic productions of Shakspeare. That he was at first received into the company in a very subordinate situation may be regarded not merely as probable, but as certain: that he ever carried a link to light the frequenters of the theatre, or ever held their horses, must be rejected as an absurd tale, fabricated, no doubt, by the lovers of the marvellous, who were solicitous to obtain a contrast in the humility of his first to the pride of his subsequent fortunes. The mean and servile occupation, thus assigned to him, was incompatible with his circumstances, even in their present afflicted state: and his relations and connexions, though far from wealthy, were yet too remote from absolute poverty, to permit him to act for a moment in such a degrading situation. He was certainly, therefore, immediately admitted within the theatre; but in what rank or character cannot now be known. This fact, however, soon became of very little consequence; for he speedily raised himself into consideration among his new fellows by the exertions of his pen, if not by his proficiency as an actor. When he began his career as a dramatic writer; or to what degree of excellence he attained in his personation of dramatic characters, are questions which have been frequently agitated without any satisfactory result. By two publications, which appeared toward the end of 1592, we know, or at least we are induced strongly to infer that at that period, either as the corrector of old or as the writer of original dramas, he had supplied the stage with a copiousness of materials. We learn also from the same documents that, in his profession of actor, he trod the boards not without the acquisition of applause. The two publications, to which I allude, are Robert Greene's "Groatsworth of Wit bought with a Million of Repentance," and Henry Chettle's "Kind Hart's Dream." In the former of these works, which was published by Chettle subsequently to the unhappy author's decease, the writer, addressing his fellow dramatists, Marlowe, Peele, and Lodge, says, "Yes! trust them not" (the managers of the theatre); "for there is an upstart crow, beautified with our feathers, that, with his tiger's heart wrapt in a player's hide, supposes he is as well able to bombast out a blank verse as the best of you; and, being an absolute Johannes Fac-totum, is in his own conceit the only Shake-scene in a country." As it could not be doubtful against whom this attack was directed, we cannot wonder that Shakspeare should be hurt by it: or that he should expostulate on the occasion rather warmly with Chettle as the editor of the offensive matter. In consequence, as it is probable, of this expression of resentment on the part of Shakspeare, a pamphlet from the pen of Chettle called "Kind Hart's Dream" issued from the press before the close of the same year (1592), which had witnessed the publication of Greene's posthumous work. In this pamphlet, Chettle acknowledges his concern for having edited any thing which had given pain to Shakspeare, of whose character and accomplishments he avows a very favorable opinion. Marlowe, as well as Shakspeare, appears to have been offended by some passages in this production of poor Greene's: and to both of these great dramatic poets Chettle refers in the short citation which we shall now make from his page: "With neither of them that take offence was I acquainted, and with one of them" (concluded to be Marlowe, whose moral character was unhappily not good) "I care not if I never be. The other" (who must necessarily be Shakspeare) "whom at that time I did not so much spare as since I wish I had; for that, as I have moderated the hate of living authors, and might have used my own discretion, (especially in such a case, the author being dead), that I did not I am as sorry as if the original fault had been my fault: because myself have seen his demeanor no less civil than he is excellent in the quality he professes. Besides divers of worship have reported his uprightness of dealing, which argues his honesty; and his facetious grace in writing, that approves his art." Shakspeare was now twenty-eight years of age; and this testimony of a contemporary, who was acquainted with him, and was himself an actor, in favour of his moral and his professional excellence, must be admitted as of considerable value. It is evident that he had now written for the stage; and before he entered upon dramatic composition we are certain that he had completed, though he had not published, his two long and laboured poems of Venus and Adonis, and the Rape of Lucrece. We cannot, therefore, date his arrival in the capital later than 1588, or, perhaps, than 1587; and the four or five years which interposed between his departure from Stratford and his becoming the object of Greene's malignant attack, constituted a busy and an important period of his life. Within this term he had conciliated the friendship of the young Thomas Wriothesly, the liberal, the high-souled, the romantic Earl of Southampton; a friendship which adhered to him throughout his life; and he had risen to that celebrity, as a poet and a dramatist, which placed him with the first wits of the age, and subsequently lifted him to the notice and the favour of Elizabeth and James, as they successively sate upon the throne of England.

At the point of time which our narrative has now reached, we cannot accurately determine what dramatic pieces had been composed by him: but we are assured that they were of sufficient excellence to excite the envy and the consequent hostility of those who, before his rising, had been the luminaries of the stage. It would be gratifying to curiosity if the feat were possible, to adjust with any precision the order in which his wonderful productions issued from his brain. But the attempt has more than once been made, and never yet with entire success. We know only that his connexion with the stage continued for about twenty years (though the duration even of this term cannot be settled with precision) and that, within this period he composed either partially, as working on the ground of others, or educing them altogether from his own fertility, thirty-five or (if that wretched thing, Pericles, in consequence of Dryden's testimony in favour of its authenticity, and of a few touches of THE GOLDEN PEN being discoverable in its last scenes, must be added to the number) thirty-six dramas; and that of these it is probable that such as were founded on the works of preceding authors were the first essays of his dramatic talent; and such as were more perfectly his own, and are of the first sparkle of excellence, were among the last. While I should not hesitate, therefore, to station "Pericles," the three parts of "Henry VI." (for I cannot see any reason for throwing the first of these parts from the protection of our author's name), "Love's Labour Lost," "The Comedy of Errors," "The Taming of the Shrew," "King John," and "Richard II.," among his earliest productions, I should, with equal confidence, arrange "Macbeth," "Lear," "Othello," "Twelfth Night," and "The Tempest," with his latest, assigning them to that season of his life, when his mind exulted in the conscious plenitude of power. Whatever might be the order of succession in which this illustrious family of genius sprang into existence, they soon attracted notice, and speedily compelled the homage of respect from those who were the most eminent for their learning, their talents, or their rank. Jonson, Selden, Beaumont, Fletcher, and Donne were the associates and the intimates of our Poet: The Earl of Southampton was his especial friend: the Earls of Pembroke and of Montgomery were avowedly his admirers and patrons: Queen Elizabeth distinguished him with her favour; and her successor, James, with his own hand, honoured the great dramatist with a letter of thanks for the compliment paid in Macbeth to the royal family of the Stuarts.

The circumstance which first brought the two lords of the stage, Shakspeare and Jonson, into that embrace of friendship which continued indissoluble, as there is reason to believe, during the permission of mortality, is reported to have been the kind assistance given by the former to the latter, when he was offering one of his plays (Every Man in his Humour) for the benefit of representation. The manuscript, as it is said, was on the point of being rejected and returned with a rude answer, when Shakspeare, fortunately glancing his eye over its pages, immediately discovered its merit; and, with his influence, obtained its introduction on the stage. To this story some specious objections have been raised; and there cannot be any necessity for contending for it, as no lucky accident can be required to account for the inducement of amity between two men of high genius, each treading the same broad path to fame and fortune, yet each with a character so peculiarly his own that he might attain his object without wounding the pride or invading the interests of the other. It has been generally believed that the intellectual superiority of Shakspeare excited the envy and the consequent enmity of Jonson. It is well that of these asserted facts no evidences can be adduced. The friendship of these great men seems to have been unbroken during the life of Shakspeare; and, on his death, Jonson made an offering to his memory of high, just, and appropriate panegyric. He places him above not only the modern but the Greek dramatists; and he professes for him admiration short only of idolatry. They who can discover any penuriousness of praise in the surviving poet must be gifted with a very *peculiar* vision of mind. With the flowers, which he strewed upon the grave of his friend, there certainly was not blended one poisonous or bitter leaf. If, therefore, he was, as he is represented to have been by an impartial and able judge, (Drummond of Hawthornden) "a great lover and praiser of himself; a contemner and scorner of others; jealous of every word and action of those about him, &c. &c.," how can we otherwise account for the uninterrupted harmony of his intercourse with our bard than by supposing that the frailties of his nature were overruled by that preeminence of mental power in his friend which precluded competition; and by his friend's sweetness of temper and gentleness of manners, which repressed every feeling of hostility. Between Shakspeare and Thomas Wriothesly, the munificent and the noble Earl of Southampton, distinguished in history by his inviolable attachment to the rash and the unfortunate Essex, the friendship was permanent and ardent. At its commencement, in 1593, when Shakspeare was twenty-nine years of age, Southampton was not more than nineteen; and, with the love of general literature, he was particularly attached to the exhibitions of the theatre. His attention was first drawn to Shakspeare by the poet's dedication to him of the "Venus and Adonis," that "first heir," as the dedicator calls it, "of his invention;" and the acquaintance, once begun between characters and hearts like theirs, would soon mature into intimacy and friendship. In the following year (1594) Shakspeare's second poem, "The Rape of Lucrece," was addressed by him to his noble patron in a strain of less distant timidity: and we may infer from it that the poet had then obtained a portion of the favour which he sought. That his fortunes were essentially promoted by the munificent patronage of Southampton cannot reasonably be doubted. We are told by Sir William Davenant, who surely possessed the means of knowing the fact, that the peer gave at one time to his favoured dramatist the magnificent present of a thousand pounds.

Of the degree of patronage and kindness extended to Shakspeare by the Earls of Pembroke and Montgomery, we are altogether ignorant: but we know, from the dedication of his works to them by Heminge and Condell, that they had distinguished themselves as his admirers and friends. That he numbered many more of the nobility of his day among the homagers of his transcendent genius, we may consider as a specious probability. But we must not indulge in conjectures, when we can gratify ourselves with the reports of tradition, approaching very nearly to certainties. Elizabeth, as it is confidently said, honoured our illustrious dramatist with her especial notice and regard. She was unquestionably fond of theatric exhibitions; and, with her literary mind and her discriminating eye, it is impossible that she should overlook; and that, not overlooking, she should not appreciate the man, whose genius formed the prime glory of her reign. It is affirmed that, delighted with the character of Falstaff as drawn in the two parts of Henry IV., she expressed a wish to see the gross and dissolute knight under the influence of love; and that the result of our Poet's compliance, with the desire of his royal mistress, was "The Merry Wives of Windsor." Favoured, however, as our Poet seems to have been by Elizabeth, and notwithstanding the fine incense which he offered to her vanity, it does not appear that he profited in any degree by her bounty. She could distinguish and could smile upon genius: but unless it were immediately serviceable to her personal or her political interests, she had not the soul to reward it. However inferior to her in the arts of government and in some of the great characters of mind might be her Scottish successor, he resembled her in his love of letters, and in his own cultivation of learning. He was a scholar, and even a poet: his attachment to the general cause of literature was strong; and his love of the drama and the theatre was particularly warm. Before his accession to the English throne he had written, as we have before noticed, a letter, with his own hand, to Shakspeare, acknowledging, as it is supposed, the compliment paid to him in the noble scenes of Macbeth; and scarcely had the crown of England fallen upon his head, when he granted his royal patent to our Poet and his company of the Globe; and thus raised them from being the Lord Chamberlain's servants to be the servants of the King. The patent is dated on the 19th of May 1603, and the name of William Shakspeare stands second on the list of the patentees. As the demise of Elizabeth had occurred on the 24th of the preceding March, this early attention of James to the company of the Globe may be regarded as highly complimentary to Shakspeare's theatre, and as strongly demonstrative of the new sovereign's partiality for the drama. But James's patronage of our Poet was not in any other way beneficial to his fortunes. If Elizabeth were too parsimonious for an effective patron, by his profusion on his pleasures and his favorites, James soon became too needy to possess the means of bounty for the reward of talents and of learning. Honour, in short, was all that Shakspeare gained by the favour of two successive sovereigns, each of them versed in literature, each of them fond of the drama, and each of them capable of appreciating the transcendency of his genius.

It would be especially gratifying to us to exhibit to our readers some portion at least of the personal history of this illustrious man during his long residence in the capital;—to announce the names and characters of his associates, a few of which only we can obtain from Fuller; to delineate his habits of life; to record his convivial wit; to commemorate the books which he read; and to number his compositions as they dropped in succession from his pen. But no power of this nature is indulged to us. All that active and efficient portion of his mortal existence, which constituted considerably more than a third part of it, is an unknown region, not to be penetrated by our most zealous and intelligent researchers. It may be regarded by us as a kind of central Africa, which our reason assures us to be glowing with fertility and alive with population; but which is abandoned in our maps, from the ignorance of our geographers, to the death of barrenness, and the silence of sandy desolation. By the Stratford register we can ascertain that his only son, Hamnet, was buried in the twelfth year of his age, on the 11th of August 1596; and that, after an interval of nearly eleven years; his eldest daughter, Susanna, was married to John Hall, a physician, on the 5th of June 1607. With the exception of two or three purchases made by him at Stratford, one of them being that of New Place, which he repaired and ornamented for his future residence, the two entries which we have now extracted from the register, are positively all that we can relate with confidence of our great Poet and his family, during the long term of his connexion with the theatre and the metropolis. We may fairly conclude, indeed, that he was present at each of the domestic events, recorded by the register: that he attended his son to the grave, and his daughter to the altar. We may believe also, from its great probability, even on the testimony of Aubrey, that he paid an annual visit to his native town; whence his family were never removed, and which he seems always to have contemplated as the resting place of his declining age. He probably had nothing more than a lodging in London, and this he might occasionally change: but in 1595 he is said to have lived somewhere near to the Bear-Garden in Southwark.

In 1606, James procured from the continent a large importation of mulberry trees, with a view to the establishment of the silk manufactory in his dominions; and, either in this year or in the following, Shakspeare enriched his garden at New Place with one of these exotic, and at that time very rare trees. This plant of his hand took root, and flourished till the year 1752, when it was destroyed by the barbarous axe of one Francis Gastrell, a clergyman, into whose worse than Gothic hands New Place had most unfortunately fallen.

As we are not told the precise time, when Shakspeare retired from the stage and the metropolis to enjoy the tranquillity of life in his native town, we cannot pretend to determine it. As he is said, however, to have passed some years in his establishment at New Place, we may conclude that his removal took place either in 1612 or in 1613, when he was yet in the vigour of life, being not more than forty-eight or forty-nine years old. He had ceased, as it is probable, to tread the stage as an actor at an earlier period; for in the list of actors, prefixed to the Volpone of B. Jonson, performed at the Globe theatre, and published in 1605, the name of W. Shakspeare is not to be found. However versed he might be in the science of acting, (and that he was versed in it we are assured by his directions to the players in Hamlet) and however well he might acquit himself in some of the subordinate characters of the drama, it does not appear that he ever rose to the higher honours of his profession. But if they were above his attainment, they seem not to have been the objects of his ambition; for by one of his sonnets* we find that he lamented the fortune which had devoted him to the stage, and that he considered himself as degraded by such a public exhibition. The time was not yet come when actors were to be the companions of princes; when their lives, as of illustrious men, were to be written; and when statues were to be erected to them by public contribution!

The amount of the fortune, on which Shakspeare retired from the busy world, has been the subject of some discussion. By Gildon, who forbears to state his authority, this fortune is valued at 300*l.* a year; and by Malone, who, calculating our Poet's real property from authentic documents, assigns a random value to his personal, it is reduced to 200*l.* Of these two valuations of Shakspeare's property, we conceive that Gildon's approaches the more nearly to the truth: for if to Malone's conjectural estimate of the personal property, of which he professes to be wholly ignorant, be added the thousand pounds, given by Southampton, (an act of munificence of which we entertain not a doubt) the precise total, as money then bore an interest of 10*l.* per cent., of the three hundred pounds a year will be made up. On the smallest of these incomes, however, when money was at least of five times its present value, might our Poet possess the comforts and the liberalities of life: and in the society of his family, and of the neighbouring gentry, conciliated by the amiableness of his manners and the pleasantness of his conversation, he seems to have passed his few remaining days in the enjoyment of tranquillity and respect. So exquisite, indeed, appears to have been his relish of the quiet, which was his portion within the walls of New Place, that it induced a complete oblivion of all that had engaged his attention, and had aggrandized his name in the preceding scenes of his life. Without any regard to his literary fame, either present or to come, he saw with perfect unconcern some of his immortal works brought, mutilated and deformed, in surreptitious copies, before the world; and others of them, with an equal indifference to their fate, he permitted to remain in their unrevised or interpolated MSS. in the hands of the

* See Sonnet cxi.

theatric prompter. There is not, probably, in the whole compass of literary history, such another instance of a proud superiority to what has been called by a rival genius,

"The last infirmity of noble minds,"

as that which was now exhibited by our illustrious dramatist and poet. He seemed

"As if *he* could not or *he* would not find,
How much *his* worth transcended all *his* kind*."

With a privilege, rarely indulged even to the sons of genius, he had produced his admirable works without any throes or labour of the mind: they had obtained for him all that he had asked from them,—the patronage of the great, the applause of the witty, and a competency of fortune adequate to the moderation of his desires. Having fulfilled or, possibly, exceeded his expectations, they had discharged their duty; and he threw them altogether from his thought; and whether it were their destiny to emerge into renown, or to perish in the drawer of a manager; to be brought to light in a state of integrity, or to *revisit the glimpses of the moon with a thousand mortal murders on their head*, engaged no part of his solicitude or interest. They had given to him the means of easy life, and he sought from them nothing more. This insensibility in our Author to the offspring of his brain may be the subject of our wonder or admiration: but its consequences have been calamitous to those who in after times have hung with delight over his pages. On the intellect and the temper of these ill fated mortals it has inflicted a heavy load of punishment in the dullness and the arrogance of commentators and illustrators—in the conceit and petulance of Theobald; the imbecility of Capell; the pert and tasteless dogmatism of Steevens; the ponderous littleness of Malone and of Drake. Some superior men, it is true, have enlisted themselves in the cause of Shakspeare. Rowe, Pope, Warburton, Hanmer, and Johnson have successively been his editors; and have professed to give his scenes in their original purity to the world. But from some cause or other, which it is not our present business to explore, each of these editors, in his turn, has disappointed the just expectations of the public: and, with an inversion of Nature's general rule, the little men have finally prevailed against the great. The blockheads have hooted the wits from the field; and attaching themselves to the mighty body of Shakspeare, like barnacles to the hull of a proud man of war, they are prepared to plough with him the vast ocean of time; and thus, by the only means in their power, to snatch themselves from that oblivion to which Nature had devoted them. It would be unjust, however, to defraud these gentlemen of their proper praise. They have read for men of talents; and, by their gross labour in the mine, they have accumulated materials to be arranged and polished by the hand of the finer artist. Some apology may be necessary for this short digression from the more immediate subject of my biography. But the three or four years, which were passed by Shakspeare in the peaceful retirement of New Place are not distinguished by any traditionary anecdote deserving of our record; and the chasm may not improperly be supplied with whatever stands in contiguity with it. I should pass in silence, as too trifling for notice, the story of our Poet's extempore and jocular epitaph on John Combe, a rich townsman of Stratford, and a noted money-lender, if my readers would not object to me that I had omitted an anecdote which had been honoured with a place in every preceding biography of my author. As the circumstance is related by Rowe, "In a pleasant conversation among their common friends, Mr. Combe told Shakspeare, in a laughing manner, that he fancied he intended to write his epitaph if he happened to outlive him; and since he could not know what might be said of him when he was dead, he desired it might be done immediately: upon which Shakspeare gave him these four verses:

Ten in the hundred lies here ingraved:
'Tis a hundred to ten his soul is not saved.
If any man ask, who lies in this tomb:
Ho! Ho! quoth the devil, 'tis my John a Combe.

But the sharpness of the satire is said to have stung the man so severely that he never forgave it." By Aubrey the story is differently told: and the lines in question, with some alterations, which evidently made them worse, are said to have been written after Combe's death. Steevens and Malone discredit the whole tale. The two first lines, as given to us by Rowe, are unquestionably not Shakspeare's; and that any lasting enmity subsisted between these two burghers of Stratford is disproved by the respective wills of the parties, John Combe bequeathing five pounds to our Poet, and our Poet leaving his sword to John Combe's nephew and residuary legatee, John Combe himself being at that time deceased. With the two commentators abovementioned, I am inclined, therefore, on the whole, to reject the story as a fabrication; though I cannot, with Steevens, convict the lines of malignity; or think, with him and with Malone, that the character of Shakspeare, on the supposition of his being their author, could require any laboured vindication to clear it from stain. In the anecdote, as related by Rowe, I can see nothing but a whimsical sally, breaking from the mind of one friend, and of a nature to excite a good-humoured smile on the cheek of the other. In Aubrey's hands, the transaction assumes a somewhat darker complexion; and the worse verses, as written after the death of their subject, may justly be branded as malevolent, and as discovering enmity in the heart of their writer. But I have dwelt too long upon a topic which, in truth, is undeserving of a syllable; and if I were to linger on it any longer, for the purpose of exhibiting Malone's reasons for his preference of Aubrey's copy of the epitaph to Rowe's, and his discovery of the propriety and beauty of the single Ho in the last line of Aubrey's, as Ho is the abbreviation of Hobgoblin, one of the names of Robin Good-fellow, the fairy servant of Oberon, my readers would have just cause to complain of me as sporting with their time and their patience.

On the 9th of July 1614, Stratford was ravaged by a fire, which destroyed fifty-four dwelling-houses besides barns and out-offices. It abstained, however, from the property of Shakspeare: and he had only to commiserate the losses of his neighbours.

With his various powers of pleasing; his wit and his humour; the gentleness of his manners; the flow of his spirits and his fancy; the variety of anecdote with which his mind must have been stored; his knowledge of the world, and his intimacy with man, in every gradation of the society, from the prompter of a playhouse to the peer and the sovereign, Shakspeare must have been a delightful—nay, a fascinating companion; and his acquaintance must necessarily have been courted by all the prime inhabitants of Stratford and its vicinity. But over this, as over the preceding periods of his life, brood silence and oblivion; and in our total ignorance of his intimacies and friendships, we must apply to our imagination to furnish out his convivial board where intellect presided, and delight with admiration gave the applause.

On the 2d of February 1615-16, he married his youngest daughter, Judith, then in the thirty-first year of her age, to Thomas Quiney, a vintner in Stratford; and on the 25th of the succeeding month he executed his will. He

* Epitaph on a Fair Maiden Lady, by Dryden.

was then, as it would appear, in the full vigour and enjoyment of life; and we are not informed that his constitution had been previously weakened by the attack of any malady. But his days, or rather his hours, were now all numbered; for he breathed his last on the 23d of the ensuing April, on that anniversary of his birth which completed his fifty-second year. It would be gratifying to our curiosity to know something of the disease, which thus prematurely terminated the life of this illustrious man: but the secret is withheld from us; and it would be idle to endeavour to obtain it. We may be certain that Dr. Hall, who was a physician of considerable eminence, attended his father-in-law in his last illness; and Dr. Hall kept a register of all the remarkable cases, with their symptoms and treatment, which in the course of his practice had fallen under his observation. This curious MS., which had escaped the enmity of time, was obtained by Malone: but the recorded cases in it most unfortunately began with the year 1617; and the preceding part of the register, which most probably had been in existence, could no where be found. The mortal complaint, therefore, of William Shakspeare is likely to remain for ever unknown; and, as darkness had closed upon his path through life, so darkness now gathered round his bed of death, awfully to cover it from the eyes of succeeding generations.

On the 25th of April 1616, two days after his decease, he was buried in the chancel of the church of Stratford; and at some period within the seven subsequent years (for in 1623 it is noticed in the verses of Leonard Digges) a monument was raised to his memory either by the respect of his townsmen, or by the piety of his relations. It represents the Poet with a countenance of thought, resting on a cushion and in the act of writing. It is placed under an arch, between two Corinthian columns of black marble, the capitals and bases of which are gilt. The face is said, but, as far as I can find, not on any adequate authority, to have been modelled from the face of the deceased; and the whole was painted to bring the imitation nearer to nature. The face and the hands wore the carnation of life: the eyes were light hazel; the hair and beard were auburn: a black gown, without sleeves, hung loosely over a scarlet doublet. The cushion in its upper part was green: in its lower crimson; and the tassels were of gold colour. This certainly was not in the high classical taste; though we may learn from Pausanias that statues in Greece were sometimes coloured after life; but as it was the work of contemporary hands, and was intended, by those who knew the Poet, to convey to posterity some resemblance of his lineaments and dress, it was a monument of rare value; and the tastelessness of Malone, who caused all its tints to be obliterated with a daubing of white lead, cannot be sufficiently ridiculed and condemned. Its material is a species of free-stone; and as the chisel of the sculptor was most probably under the guidance of Doctor Hall, it bore some promise of likeness to the mighty dead. Immediately below the cushion is the following distich:—

Judicio Pylium; genio Socratem; arte Maronem
Terra tegit; populus mœret; Olympus habet.

On a tablet underneath are inscribed these lines:—

Stay, passenger, why dost thou go so fast?
Read, if thou canst, whom envious death has placed
Within this monument—Shakspeare; with whom
Quick Nature died; whose name doth deck the tomb
Far more than cost: since all that he hath writ
Leaves living art but page to serve his wit:

and the flat stone, covering the grave, holds out, in very irregular characters, a supplication to the reader, with the promise of a blessing and the menace of a curse:

Good Friend! for Jesus' sake forbear
To dig the dust inclosed here.
Blest be the man that spares these stones;
And cursed be he that moves my bones.

The last of these inscriptions may have been written by Shakspeare himself under the apprehension of his bones being tumbled, with those of many of his townsmen, into the charnel-house of the parish. But his dust has continued unviolated, and is likely to remain in its holy repose till the last awful scene of our perishable globe. It were to be wished that the two preceding inscriptions were more worthy, than they are, of the tomb to which they are attached. It would be gratifying if we could give any faith to the tradition, which asserts that the bust of this monument was sculptured from a cast moulded on the face of the departed poet; for then we might assure ourselves that we possess one authentic resemblance of this preeminently intellectual mortal. But the cast, if taken, must have been taken immediately after his death; and we know neither at whose expense the monument was constructed; nor by whose hand it was executed; nor at what precise time it was erected. It may have been wrought by the artist, acting under the recollections of the Shakspeare family, into some likeness of the great townsman of Stratford: and on this probability, we may contemplate it with no inconsiderable interest. I cannot, however, persuade myself that the likeness could have been strong. The forehead, indeed, is sufficiently spacious and intellectual: but there is a disproportionate length in the under part of the face: the mouth is weak; and the whole countenance is heavy and inert. Not having seen the monument itself, I can speak of it only from its numerous copies by the graver; and by these it is possible that I may be deceived. But if we cannot rely on the Stratford bust for a resemblance of our immortal dramatist, where are we to look with any hope of finding a trace of his features? It is highly probable that no portrait of him was painted during his life; and it is certain that no portrait of him, with an incontestable claim to genuineness, is at present in existence. The fairest title to authenticity seems to be assignable to that which is called the Chandos portrait, and is now in the collection of the Duke of Buckingham at Stowe.

It is well that we are better acquainted with the rectitude of his morals, than with the symmetry of his features. To the integrity of his heart; the gentleness and benignity of his manners, we have the positive testimony of Chettle and Ben Jonson; the former of whom seems to have been drawn by our Poet's good and amiable qualities, from the faction of his dramatic enemies; and the latter, in his love and admiration of the man, to have lost all his natural jealousy of the successful competitor for the poetic palm. I have already cited Chettle: let me now cite Jonson, from whose pages much more of a similar nature might be adduced. "I loved," he says in his 'Discoveries,' "I loved the man, and do honour his memory, on this side idolatry as much as any. He was, indeed, honest, of an open and free nature; had an excellent fancy, brave notions, and gentle expressions," &c. &c. When Jonson apostrophizes his deceased friend, he calls him, "My gentle Shakspeare," and the title of "the sweet swan of Avon," so generally given to him, after the example of Jonson, by his contemporaries, seems to have been given with reference as much to the suavity of his temper as to the harmony of his verse. In their dedication of his works to the Earls of Pembroke and Montgomery, his fellows, Heminge and Condell, profess that their great object in their publication was "only to keep the memory of so worthy a friend and fellow alive as was our Shakspeare:" and their preface to the public appears evidently to have been dictated by their personal and affectionate attachment to their departed friend. If we wish for any further evidence in the support of the moral character of Shakspeare, we may find it in the friendship of Southampton; we may extract it from the pages of his immortal works. Dr. Johnson, in his much over-praised Preface, seems to have taken a view, very different from ours, of the morality of our author's scenes. He says, "His (Shakspeare's) first defect is that to which may be imputed most of the evil in books or in men. He sacrifices virtue to convenience; and is so much more careful to please than to instruct that he seems to write without any moral purpose. From his writings, indeed, a system of moral duty may be selected," (indeed!) "but his precepts and axioms drop casually from him:" (Would the preface-writer have wished the dramatist to give a connected treatise on ethics like the offices of Cicero?) "he makes no just distribution of good or evil, nor is always careful to show in the virtuous a disapprobation of the wicked; he carries his persons indifferently through right and wrong; and at the close dismisses them without further care, and leaves their examples to operate by chance. This fault the barbarity of the age cannot extenuate! for it is always a writer's duty to make the world better, and justice is a virtue independent on time or place." Why this commonplace on justice should be compelled into the station in which we here most strangely find it, I cannot for my life conjecture. But absurd as it is made by its association in this place, it may not form an improper conclusion to a paragraph which means little, and which, intending censure, confers dramatic praise on a dramatic writer. It is evident, however, that Dr. Johnson, though he says that a system of moral duty may be selected from Shakspeare's writings, wished to inculcate that his scenes were not of a moral tendency. On this topic, the first and the greater Jonson seems to have entertained very different sentiments—

——" Look, how the father's face

(says this great man)

Lives in his issue; even so the race
Of Shakspeare's mind, and manners, brightly shines
In his well-turned and true filed lines."

We think, indeed, that his scenes are rich in sterling morality, and that they must have been the effusions of a moral mind. The only crimination of his morals must be drawn from a few of his sonnets; and from a story first suggested by Antony Wood, and afterwards told by Oldys on the authority of Betterton and Pope. From the Sonnets* we can collect nothing more than that their writer was blindly attached to an unprincipled woman, who preferred a young and beautiful friend of his to himself. But the story told by Oldys presents something to us of a more tangible nature; and as it possesses some intrinsic merit as a story, and rests, as to its principal facts, on the authority of Wood, who was a native of Oxford and a veracious man, we shall not hesitate, after the example of most of the recent biographers of our Poet, to relate it, and in the very words of Oldys. "If tradition may be trusted, Shakspeare often baited at the Crown Inn or Tavern in Oxford, on his journey to and from London. The landlady was a beautiful woman and of a sprightly wit; and her husband, Mr. John Davenant, (afterwards mayor of that city) a grave, melancholy man, who, as well as his wife, used much to delight in Shakspeare's pleasant company. Their son, young Will Davenant (afterwards Sir William Davenant) was then a little schoolboy, in the town, of about seven or eight years old; and so fond also of Shakspeare that, whenever he heard of his arrival, he would fly from school to see him. One day, an old townsman, observing the boy running homeward almost out of breath, asked him whither he was posting in that heat and hurry. He answered, to see his *god*-father, Shakspeare. There is a good boy; said the other; but have a care that you don't take God's name in vain! This story Mr. Pope told me at the Earl of Oxford's table, upon occasion of some discourse which arose about Shakspeare's monument, then newly erected in Westminster Abbey."

* See Son. 141. 144. 147. 151 152

On these two instances of his frailty, under the influence of the tender passion, one of them supported by his own evidence, and one resting on authority which seems to be not justly questionable, depend all the charges which can be brought against the strict personal morality of Shakspeare. In these days of peculiarly sensitive virtue, he would not possibly be admitted into the party of the saints: but, in the age in which he lived, these errors of his human weakness did not diminish the respect, commanded by the probity of his heart; or the love, conciliated by the benignity of his manners; or the admiration exacted by the triumph of his genius.

The Will of Shakspeare, giving to his youngest daughter, Judith, not more than three hundred pounds, and a piece of plate, which probably was valuable, as it is called by the testator, "My broad silver and gilt bowl," assigns almost the whole of his property to his eldest daughter, Susanna Hall, and her husband; whom he appoints to be his executors. The cause of this evident partiality in the father appears to be discoverable in the higher mental accomplishments of the eldest daughter; who is reported to have resembled him in her intellectual endowments, and to have been eminently distinguished by the piety and the Christian benevolence which actuated her conduct. Having survived her estimable husband fourteen years, she died on the 11th of July 1649; and the inscription on her tomb, preserved by Dugdale, commemorates her intellectual superiority and influence of religion upon her heart. This inscription, which we shall transcribe, bears witness also, as we must observe, to the piety of her illustrious father.

Witty above her sex; but that's not all:
Wise to salvation was good Mistress Hall.
Something of Shakspeare was in *that*; but *this*
Wholly of him, with whom she now's in bliss.
Then, passenger, hast ne'er a tear
To weep with her, that wept with all:
That wept, yet set herself to cheer
Them up with comforts cordial.
Her love shall live, her mercy spread
When thou hast ne'er a tear to shed.

Judith, his younger daughter, bore to her husband, Thomas Quiney, three sons; Shakspeare, who died in his infancy, Richard and Thomas, who deceased, the first in his 21st year, the last in his 19th, unmarried and before their mother; who, having reached her 77th year, expired in February 1661-2—being buried on the 9th of that month. She appears either not to have received any education, or not to have profited by the lessons of her teachers, for to a deed, still in existence, she affixes her mark.

We have already mentioned the dates of the birth, marriage, and death of Susanna Hall. She left only one daughter, Elizabeth, who was baptized on the 21st of February 1607-8, eight years before her grandfather's decease, and was married on the 22nd of April 1626, to Mr. Thomas Nash, a country gentleman, as it appears, of independent fortune. Two years after the death of Mr. Nash, who was buried on the 5th of April 1647, she married on the 5th of June 1649, at Billesley in Warwickshire, Sir John Barnard, Knight, of Abington, a small village in the vicinity of Northampton. She died, and was buried at Abington, on the 17th of February 1669-70; and, as she left no issue by either of her husbands, her death terminated the lineal descendents of Shakspeare. His collateral kindred have been indulged with a much longer period of duration; the descendents of his sister, Joan, having continued in a regular succession of generations even to our days; whilst none of them, with a single exception, have broken from that rank in the community in which their ancestors, William Hart and Joan Shakspeare united their unostentatious fortunes in the year 1599. The single exception to which we allude is that of Charles Hart, believed, for good reasons, to be the son of William the eldest son of William and Joan Hart, and consequently the grand-nephew of our poet. At the early age of seventeen, Charles Hart, as lieutenant in Prince Rupert's regiment, fought at the battle of Edgehill; and, subsequently betaking himself to the stage, he became the most renowned tragic actor of his time. "What Mr. Hart delivers," says Rymer, (I adopt the citation from the page of Malone) "every one takes upon content: their eyes are prepossessed and charmed by his action before aught of the poet's can approach their ears; and to the most wretched of characters he gives a lustre and brilliancy, which dazzles the sight that the deformities in the poetry cannot be perceived." "Were I a poet," (says another contemporary writer) "nay a Fletcher or a Shakspeare, I would quit my own title to immortality so that one actor might never die. This I may modestly say of him (nor is it my particular opinion, but the sense of all mankind) that the best tragedies on the English stage have received their lustre from Mr. Hart's performance: that he has left such an impression behind him, that no less than the interval of an age can make them appear again with half their majesty from any second hand." This was a brilliant eruption from the family of Shakspeare: but as it was the first, so it appears to have been the last; and the Harts have ever since, as far at least as it is known to us, "pursued the noiseless tenor of their way," within the precincts of their native town on the banks of the soft-flowing Avon*.

Whatever is any degree associated with the personal history of Shakspeare is weighty with general interest. The circumstance of his birth can impart consequence even to a provincial town; and we are not unconcerned in the past or the present fortunes of the place, over which hovers the glory of his name. But the house in which he passed the last three or four years of his life, and in which he terminated his mortal labours, is still more engaging to our imaginations, as it is more closely and personally connected with him. Its history, therefore, must not be omitted by us; and if, in some respects, we should differ in it from the narrative of Malone, we shall not be without reasons sufficient to justify the deviations in which we indulge. New Place, then, which was not thus first named by Shakspeare, was built in the reign of Henry VII., by Sir Hugh Clopton, Kt., the younger son of an old family resident near Stratford, who had filled in succession the offices of Sheriff and of Lord Mayor of London. In 1563 it was sold by one of the Clopton family to William Bott; and by him it was again sold in 1570 to William Underhill, (the purchaser and the seller being both of the rank of esquires) from whom it was bought by our Poet, in 1597. By him it was bequeathed to his daughter, Susanna Hall; from whom it descended to her only child, Lady Barnard. In the June of 1643, this Lady, with her first husband Mr. Nash, entertained, for nearly three weeks, at New Place, Henrietta Maria, the queen of Charles I., when, escorted by Prince Rupert and a large body of troops, she was on her progress to meet her royal consort, and to proceed with him to Oxford. On the death of Lady Barnard without children, New Place was sold in 1675, to Sir Edward Walker, Kt., Garter King at Arms; by whom it was left to his only child, Barbara, married to Sir John Clopton, Kt., of Clopton in the parish of Stratford. On his demise, it became the property of a younger son of his, Sir Hugh Clopton, Kt., (this family of the Cloptons seems to have been peculiarly prolific in the breed of knights), by whom it was repaired and decorated at a very large expense. Malone affirms that it was pulled down by him, and its place supplied by a more sumptuous edifice. If this statement were correct, the crime of its subsequent destroyer would be greatly extenuated; and the hand which had wielded the axe against the hallowed mulberry tree, would be absolved from the second act, imputed to it, of sacrilegious violence. But Malone's account is, unquestionably, erroneous. In the May of 1742, Sir Hugh entertained Garrick, Macklin, and Delany under the shade of the Shakspearian mulberry. On the demise of Sir Hugh in the December of 1751, New Place was sold by his son-in-law and executor, Henry Talbot, the Lord Chancellor Talbot's brother, to the Rev. Francis Gastrell, Vicar of Frodsham in Cheshire; by whom, on some quarrel with the magistrates on the subject of the parochial assessments, it was razed to the ground, and its site abandoned to vacancy. On this completion of his outrages against the memory of Shakspeare, which his unlucky possession of wealth enabled him to commit, Francis Gastrell departed from Stratford, hooted out of the town, and pursued by the execrations of its inhabitants. The fate of New Place has been rather remarkable. After the demolition of the house by Gastrell, the ground, which it had occupied, was thrown into the contiguous garden, and was sold by the widow of the clerical barbarian. Having remained during a certain period, as a portion of a garden, a house was again erected on it; and, in consequence also of some dispute about the parish assessments, that house, like its predecessor, was pulled down; and its site was finally abandoned to Nature, for the production of her fruits and her flowers: and thither may we imagine the little Elves and Fairies frequently to resort, to trace the footsteps of their beloved poet, now obliterated from the vision of man; to throw a finer perfume on the violet; to unfold the first rose of the year, and to tinge its cheek with a richer blush; and, in their dances beneath the full-orbed moon, to chant their harmonies, too subtle for the gross ear of mortality, to the fondly cherished memory of their darling, THE SWEET SWAN OF AVON.

* By intelligence, on the accuracy of which I can rely, and which has only just reached me, from the birthplace of Shakspeare, I learn that the family of the Harts, after a course of lineal descents during the revolution of two hundred and twenty-six years, is now on the verge of extinction; an aged woman, who retains *in single blessedness* her maiden name of Hart, being at this time (Nov. 1825) its sole surviving representative. For some years she occupied the house of her ancestors, in which Shakspeare is reported to have first seen the light; and here she obtained a comfortable subsistence by showing the antiquities of the venerated mansion to the numerous strangers who were attracted to it. Being dispossessed of this residence by the rapaciousness of its proprietor, she settled herself in a dwelling nearly opposite to it. Here she still lives; and continues to exhibit some reliques, not reputed to be genuine, of the mighty bard, with whom her maternal ancestor was nourished in the same womb. She regards herself also as a dramatic poet; and, in support of her pretensions, she produces the rude sketch of a play, uninformed, as it is said, with any of the vitality of genius. For this information I am indebted to Mr. Charles Fellows of Nottingham; who, with the characteristic kindness of his most estimable family, sought for the intelligence which was required by me, and obtained it.

*** For the complete Life of Shakspeare, by Dr. Symmons, with some Remarks upon his Dramatic Writings, the Reader is referred to Singer's Edition, with Notes, in 10 vols.

TEMPEST.

PERSONS REPRESENTED.

ALONZO, *King of* Naples.
SEBASTIAN, *his Brother.*
PPOSPERO, *the rightful Duke of* Milan.
ANTONIO, *his Brother, the usurping Duke of* Milan.
FERDINAND, *Son to the King of* Naples.
GONZALO, *the honest old Counsellor of* Naples.
ADRIAN, FRANCISCO, } *Lords.*
CALIBAN, *a savage and deformed Slave.*
TRINCULO, *a Jester.*
STEPHANO, *a drunken Butler.*
Master of a Ship, Boatswain, and Mariners.
MIRANDA, *Daughter to* Prospero.
ARIEL, *an airy Spirit.*
IRIS, CERES, JUNO, Nymphs, Reapers, } *Spirits.*
Other Spirits attending on Prospero.

SCENE—*The Sea, with a Ship; afterwards an uninhabited Island.*

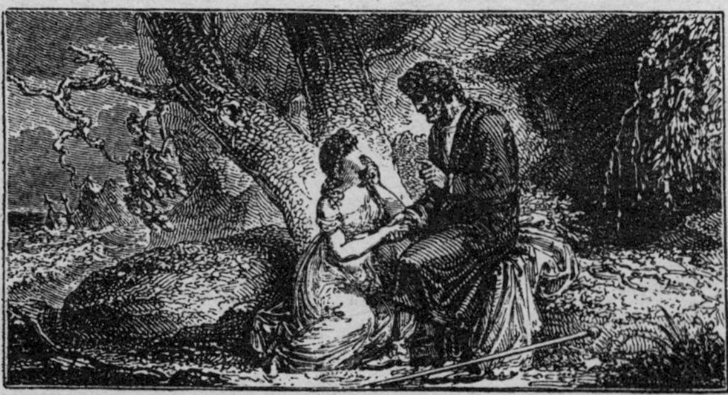

ACT I.

SCENE I. *On a Ship at Sea.*

A Storm, with Thunder and Lightning.

Enter a Shipmaster *and a* Boatswain.

Mast. BOATSWAIN,—

Boats. Here, master: what cheer?

Mast. Good: speak to the mariners: fall to 't yarely, or we run ourselves aground: bestir, bestir. [*Exit.*

Enter Mariners.

Boats. Heigh, my hearts; cheerly, cheerly, my hearts; yare, yare: Take in the top-sail; Tend to the master's whistle.—Blow till thou burst thy wind, if room enough!

Enter ALONZO, SEBASTIAN, ANTONIO, FERDINAND, GONZALO, *and others.*

Alon. Good boatswain, have care. Where's the master? Play the men.

Boats. I pray now, keep below.

Ant. Where is the master, boatswain?

Boats. Do you not hear him? You mar our labour; keep your cabins: you do assist the storm.

Gon. Nay, good, be patient.

Boats. When the sea is. Hence! What care these roarers for the name of king? To cabin: silence: trouble us not.

Gon. Good; yet remember whom thou hast aboard.

Boats. None that I more love than myself. You are a counsellor; if you can command these elements to silence, and work the peace of the present, we will not hand a rope more; use your authority. If you cannot, give thanks you have lived so long, and make yourself ready in your cabin for the mischance of the hour, if it so hap.—Cheerly, good hearts.—Out of our way, I say. [*Exit.*

Gon. I have great comfort from this fellow: methinks, he hath no drowning mark upon him; his complexion is perfect gallows. Stand fast, good fate, to his hanging! make the rope of his destiny our cable, for our own doth little advantage! If he be not born to be hanged, our case is miserable. [*Exeunt.*

Re-enter Boatswain.

Boats. Down with the topmast; yare; lower, lower; bring her to try with main course. [*A cry within.*] A plague upon this howling! they are louder than the weather, or our office.—

Re-enter SEBASTIAN, ANTONIO, *and* GONZALO.

Yet again? what do you here? Shall we give o'er, and drown? Have you a mind to sink?

Seb. A pox o' your throat, you bawling, blasphemous, uncharitable dog!

Boats. Work you, then.

Ant. Hang, cur, hang! you whoreson, insolent noise-maker, we are less afraid to be drowned than thou art.

Gon. I'll warrant him from drowning; though the ship were no stronger than a nutshell, and as leaky as an unstanched wench.

Boats. Lay her a-hold, a-hold; set her two courses; off to sea again, lay her off.

Enter Mariners, *wet.*

Mar. All lost! to prayers, to prayers! all lost! [*Exeunt.*

Boats. What, must our mouths be cold?

Gon. The king and prince at prayers! let us assist them,
For our case is as theirs.

Seb. I am out of patience.
Ant. We are merely cheated of our lives by drunkards.—
This wide-chapped rascal;——'Would, thou might'st lie drowning,
The washing of ten tides!
Gon. He'll be hanged yet;
Though every drop of water swear against it,
And gape at wid'st to glut him.
[*A confused noise within.*] Mercy on us!—We split, we split!—Farewell, my wife and children!—Farewell, brother!—We split, we split, we split.—
Ant. Let's all sink with the king. [*Exit.*
Seb. Let's take leave of him. [*Exit.*
Gon. Now would I give a thousand furlongs of sea for an acre of barren ground; long heath, brown furze, any thing: The wills above be done! but I would fain die a dry death. [*Exit.*

SCENE II.

The Island, before the Cell of Prospero.

Enter Prospero *and* Miranda.

Mira. If by your art, my dearest father, you have
Put the wild waters in this roar, allay them:
The sky, it seems, would pour down stinking pitch,
But that the sea, mounting to the welkin's cheek,
Dashes the fire out. O, I have suffer'd
With those that I saw suffer! a brave vessel,
Who had no doubt some noble creatures in her,
Dash'd all to pieces. O, the cry did knock
Against my very heart! Poor souls! they perish'd.
Had I been any god of power, I would
Have sunk the sea within the earth, or e'er
It should the good ship so have swallowed, and
The freighting souls within her.
Pro. Be collected;
No more amazement: tell your piteous heart,
There's no harm done.
Mira. O, woe the day!
Pro. No harm.
I have done nothing but in care of thee,
(Of thee, my dear one! thee, my daughter!) who
Art ignorant of what thou art, nought knowing
Of whence I am; nor that I am more better
Than Prospero, master of a full poor cell,
And thy no greater father.
Mira. More to know
Did never meddle with my thoughts.
Pro. 'Tis time,
I should inform thee further. Lend thy hand,
And pluck my magick garment from me.—So;
[*Lays down his mantle.*
Lie there my art.—Wipe thou thine eyes; have comfort.
The direful spectacle of the wreck, which touch'd
The very virtue of compassion in thee,
I have with such provision in mine art
So safely order'd, that there is no soul—
No, not so much perdition as an hair,
Betid to any creature in the vessel
Which thou heard'st cry, which thou saw'st sink. Sit down;
For thou must now know further.
Mira. You have often
Begun to tell me what I am; but stopp'd
And left me to a bootless inquisition;
Concluding, *Stay, not yet.*—
Pro. The hour's now come;
The very minute bids thee ope thine ear;
Obey, and be attentive. Canst thou remember
A time before we came unto this cell?
I do not think thou canst; for then thou wast not
Out three years old.
Mira. Certainly, sir, I can.
Pro. By what? by any other house, or person?
Of any thing the image tell me, that
Hath kept with thy remembrance.
Mira. 'Tis far off;
And rather like a dream than an assurance
That my remembrance warrants: Had I not
Four or five women once, that tended me?
Pro. Thou had'st, and more, Miranda: But how is it,
That this lives in thy mind? What seest thou else
In the dark backward and abysm of time?
If thou remember'st aught, ere thou cam'st here,
How thou cam'st here, thou may'st.
Mira. But that I do not.
Pro. Twelve years since, Miranda, twelve years since,
Thy father was the duke of Milan, and
A prince of power.
Mira. Sir, are not you my father?
Pro. Thy mother was a piece of virtue, and
She said—thou wast my daughter; and thy father
Was duke of Milan; and his only heir
A princess;—no worse issued.
Mira. O, the heavens!
What foul play had we, that we came from thence?
Or blessed was 't, we did?
Pro. Both, both, my girl:
By foul play, as thou say'st, were we heaved thence;
But blessedly holp hither.
Mira. O, my heart bleeds
To think o' the teen that I have turn'd you to,
Which is from my remembrance! Please you, further.
Pro. My brother, and thy uncle, call'd Antonio—
I pray thee, mark me,—that a brother should
Be so perfidious!—he whom, next thyself,
Of all the world I loved, and to him put
The manage of my state; as, at that time,
Through all the signiories it was the first,
And Prospero the prime duke; being so reputed
In dignity, and, for the liberal arts,
Without a parallel; those being all my study,
The government I cast upon my brother,
And to my state grew stranger, being transported,
And rapt in secret studies. Thy false uncle—
Dost thou attend me?
Mira. Sir, most heedfully.
Pro. Being once perfected how to grant suits,
How to deny them; whom to advance, and whom
To trash for over-topping; new created
The creatures that were mine; I say, or chang'd them,
Or else new-form'd them: having both the key
Of officer and office, set all hearts i' th' state
To what tune pleased his ear; that now he was
The ivy, which had hid my princely trunk,
And suck'd my verdure out on 't.—Thou attend'st not.
Mira. O good sir, I do.
Pro. I pray thee, mark me.
I thus neglecting worldly ends, all dedicate
To closeness, and the bettering of my mind
With that, which, but by being so retir'd,
O'er-prized all popular rate, in my false brother
Awak'd an evil nature: and my trust,
Like a good parent, did beget of him
A falsehood, in its contrary as great
As my trust was; which had, indeed, no limit,
A confidence sans bound. He being thus lorded,
Not only with what my revenue yielded,
But what my power might else exact,—like one,
Who having, unto truth, by telling of it,
Made such a sinner of his memory,
To credit his own lie,—he did believe
He was indeed the duke; out of the substitution,
And executing the outward face of royalty,
With all prerogative:—Hence his ambition
Growing,—Dost hear?
Mira. Your tale, sir, would cure deafness.
Pro. To have no screen between this part he play'd
And him he play'd it for, he needs will be
Absolute Milan: Me, poor man!—my library

Was dukedom large enough; of temporal royalties
He thinks me now incapable: confederates
(So dry he was for sway) with the king of Naples,
To give him annual tribute, do him homage;
Subject his coronet to his crown, and bend
The dukedom, yet unbow'd, (alas, poor Milan!)
To most ignoble stooping.

Mira. O the heavens!

Pro. Mark his condition, and the event; then tell me,
If this might be a brother.

Mira. I should sin
To think but nobly of my grandmother:
Good wombs have borne bad sons.

Pro. Now the condition.
This king of Naples, being an enemy
To me inveterate, hearkens my brother's suit;
Which was, that he in lieu o' the premises,—
Of homage, and I know not how much tribute,—
Should presently extirpate me and mine
Out of the dukedom; and confer fair Milan,
With all the honours, on my brother: Whereon,
A treacherous army levied, one midnight
Fated to the purpose, did Antonio open
The gates of Milan; and, i' the dead of darkness,
The ministers for the purpose hurried thence
Me, and thy crying self.

Mira. Alack, for pity!
I, not rememb'ring how I cried out then,
Will cry it o'er again; it is a hint,
That wrings mine eyes to 't.

Pro. Hear a little further,
And then I'll bring thee to the present business
Which now 's upon us; without the which, this story
Were most impertinent.

Mira. Wherefore did they not
That hour destroy us?

Pro. Well demanded, wench;
My tale provokes that question. Dear, they durst not;
(So dear the love my people bore me) nor set
A mark so bloody on the business; but
With colours fairer painted their foul ends.
In few, they hurried us aboard a bark;
Bore us some leagues to sea; where they prepar'd
A rotten carcass of a boat, not rigg'd,
Nor tackle, sail, nor mast; the very rats
Instinctively had quit it: there they hoist us,
To cry to the sea that roar'd to us; to sigh
To the winds, whose pity, sighing back again,
Did us but loving wrong.

Mira. Alack! what trouble
Was I then to you!

Pro. O! a cherubim
Thou wast, that did preserve me! Thou didst smile,
Infused with a fortitude from heaven,
When I have deck'd the sea with drops full salt;
Under my burden groan'd; which rais'd in me
An undergoing stomach, to bear up
Against what should ensue.

Mira. How came we ashore?

Pro. By Providence divine.
Some food we had, and some fresh water, that
A noble Neapolitan, Gonzalo,
Out of his charity, (who being then appointed
Master of this design,) did give us; with
Rich garments, linens, stuffs, and necessaries,
Which since have steaded much; so, of his gentleness,
Knowing I loved my books, he furnish'd me,
From my own library, with volumes that
I prize above my dukedom.

Mira. 'Would, I might
But ever see that man!

Pro. Now I arise:—
Sit still, and hear the last of our sea-sorrow.
Here in this island we arrived; and here
Have I, thy schoolmaster, made thee more profit
Than other princes can, that have more time
For vainer hours, and tutors not so careful.

Mira. Heavens thank you for 't! and now, I pray you, sir,
(For still 'tis beating in my mind,) your reason
For raising this sea-storm?

Pro. Know thus far forth.—
By accident most strange, bountiful fortune,
Now my dear lady, hath mine enemies
Brought to this shore: and by my prescience
I find my zenith doth depend upon
A most auspicious star; whose influence
If now I court not, but omit, my fortunes
Will ever after droop.—Here cease more questions:
Thou art inclin'd to sleep; 'tis a good dulness,
And give it way;—I know thou canst not choose.— [MIRANDA *sleeps*.
Come away, servant, come: I am ready now;
Approach, my Ariel; come.

Enter ARIEL.

Ari. All hail, great master! grave sir, hail; I come
To answer thy best pleasure; be 't to fly,
To swim, to dive into the fire, to ride
On the curl'd clouds; to thy strong bidding, task
Ariel, and all his quality.

Pro. Hast thou, spirit,
Perform'd to point the tempest that I bade thee?

Ari. To every article.
I boarded the king's ship; now on the beak,
Now in the waist, the deck, in every cabin,
I flam'd amazement: Sometimes, I'd divide,
And burn in many places; on the top-mast,
The yards, and bowsprit, would I flame distinctly,
Then meet, and join: Jove's lightnings, the precursors
O' the dreadful thunder-claps, more momentary
And sight out-running were not: The fire, and cracks
Of sulphurous roaring, the most mighty Neptune
Seem'd to besiege, and make his bold waves tremble,
Yea, his dread trident shake.

Pro. My brave spirit!
Who was so firm, so constant, that this coil
Would not infect his reason?

Ari. Not a soul
But felt a fever of the mad, and play'd
Some tricks of desperation: All, but mariners,
Plung'd in the foaming brine, and quit the vessel,
Then all a-fire with me: the king's son, Ferdinand,
With hair up-staring, (then like reeds, not hair,)
Was the first man that leap'd; cried, *Hell is empty, And all the devils are here.*

Pro. Why, that's my spirit!
But was not this nigh shore?

Ari. Close by, my master.

Pro. But are they, Ariel, safe?

Ari. Not a hair perish'd;
On their sustaining garments not a blemish,
But fresher than before: and as thou bad'st me,
In troops I have dispersed them 'bout the isle:
The king's son have I landed by himself;
Whom I left cooling of the air with sighs,
In an odd angle of the isle, and sitting,
His arms in this sad knot.

Pro. Of the king's ship,
The mariners, say, how thou hast disposed,
And all the rest o' the fleet?

Ari. Safely in harbour
Is the king's ship; in the deep nook, where once
Thou call'dst me up at midnight to fetch dew
From the still-vex'd Bermoothes, there she's hid:
The mariners all under hatches stow'd;
Whom, with a charm join'd to their suffer'd labour,
I have left asleep; and for the rest o' the fleet,
Which I dispers'd, they all have met again;
And are upon the Mediterranean flote,

Bound sadly home for Naples;
Supposing that they saw the king's ship wreck'd,
And his great person perish.
Pro. Ariel, thy charge
Exactly is perform'd; but there's more work:
What is the time o' the day?
Ari. Past the mid season.
Pro. At least two glasses: The time 'twixt six and now,
Must by us both be spent most preciously.
Ari. Is there more toil? Since thou must give me pains,
Let me remember thee what thou hast promis'd,
Which is not yet perform'd me.
Pro. How now? moody?
What is 't thou canst demand?
Ari. My liberty.
Pro. Before the time be out? no more.
Ari. I pray thee
Remember, I have done thee worthy service;
Told thee no lies, made no mistakings, serv'd
Without or grudge or grumblings: thou did'st promise
To bate me a full year.
Pro. Dost thou forget
From what a torment I did free thee?
Ari. No.
Pro. Thou dost; and think'st
It much, to tread the ooze of the salt deep;
To run upon the sharp wind of the North;
To do me business in the veins o' the earth,
When it is bak'd with frost.
Ari. I do not, sir.
Pro. Thou liest, malignant thing! Hast thou forgot
The foul witch, Sycorax, who, with age, and envy,
Was grown into a hoop? hast thou forgot her?
Ari. No, sir.
Pro. Thou hast: where was she born? speak; tell me.
Ari. Sir, in Argier.
Pro. O, was she so? I must,
Once in a month, recount what thou hast been,
Which thou forget'st. This damn'd witch, Sycorax,
For mischiefs manifold, and sorceries terrible
To enter human hearing, from Argier,
Thou know'st, was banish'd; for one thing she did,
They would not take her life: Is not this true?
Ari. Ay, sir.
Pro. This blue-ey'd hag was hither brought with child,
And here was left by the sailors: Thou, my slave,
As thou report'st thyself, was then her servant:
And, for thou wast a spirit too delicate
To act her earthy and abhorr'd commands,
Refusing her grand hests, she did confine thee,
By help of her more potent ministers,
And in her most unmitigable rage,
Into a cloven pine; within which rift
Imprison'd, thou did'st painfully remain
A dozen years; within which space she died,
And left thee there; where thou did'st vent thy groans,
As fast as mill-wheels strike: Then was this island,
(Save for the son that she did litter here,
A freckled whelp, hag-born) not honour'd with
A human shape.
Ari. Yes; Caliban, her son.
Pro. Dull thing, I say so; he, that Caliban,
Whom now I keep in service. Thou best know'st
What torment I did find thee in: thy groans
Did make wolves howl, and penetrate the breasts
Of ever-angry bears: it was a torment
To lay upon the damn'd, which Sycorax
Could not again undo; it was mine art,
When I arriv'd, and heard thee, that made gape
The pine, and let thee out.
Ari. I thank thee, master.
Pro. If thou more murmur'st, I will rend an oak,
And peg thee in his knotty entrails, till
Thou hast howl'd away twelve winters.
Ari. Pardon, master:
I will be correspondent to command,
And do my spriting gently.
Pro. Do so; and after two days
I will discharge thee.
Ari. That's my noble master!
What shall I do? say what? what shall I do?
Pro. Go make thyself like to a nymph o' the sea;
Be subject to no sight but mine; invisible
To every eyeball else. Go, take this shape,
And hither come in 't: hence, with diligence.
[*Exit* ARIEL.
Awake, dear heart, awake! thou hast slept well;
Awake!
Mira. The strangeness of your story put
Heaviness in me.
Pro. Shake it off: come on;
We'll visit Caliban, my slave, who never
Yields us kind answer.
Mira. 'Tis a villain, sir,
I do not love to look on.
Pro. But, as 'tis,
We cannot miss him: he does make our fire,
Fetch in our wood; and serves in offices
That profit us. What ho! slave! Caliban!
Thou earth, thou! speak.
Cal. [*within.*] There's wood enough within.
Pro. Come forth, I say; there's other business for thee;
Come forth, thou tortoise! when?

Re-enter ARIEL, *like a Water-nymph.*

Fine apparition! My quaint Ariel,
Hark in thine ear.
Ari. My lord, it shall be done. [*Exit.*
Pro. Thou poisonous slave, got by the devil himself
Upon thy wicked dam, come forth!

Enter CALIBAN.

Cal. As wicked dew as e'er my mother brush'd
With raven's feather from unwholesome fen
Drop on you both! a south-west blow on ye,
And blister you all o'er!
Pro. For this, be sure, to-night thou shalt have cramps,
Side-stitches that shall pen thy breath up; urchins
Shall, for that vast of night that they may work,
All exercise on thee: thou shalt be pinch'd
As thick as honey-combs, each pinch more stinging
Than bees that made them.
Cal. I must eat my dinner.
This island's mine, by Sycorax my mother,
Which thou tak'st from me. When thou camest first,
Thou strok'dst me, and mad'st much of me; would'st give me
Water with berries in 't; and teach me how
To name the bigger light, and how the less,
That burn by day and night: and then I lov'd thee,
And shew'd thee all the qualities o' the isle,
The fresh springs, brine pits, barren place, and fertile;
Cursed be I that did so!—All the charms
Of Sycorax, toads, beetles, bats, light on you!
For I am all the subjects that you have,
Which first was mine own king: and here you sty me
In this hard rock, whiles you do keep from me
The rest of the island.
Pro. Thou most lying slave,
Whom stripes may move, not kindness: I have used thee,
Filth as thou art, with human care; and lodg'd thee

In mine own cell, till thou didst seek to violate
The honour of my child.

Cal. O ho, O ho!—'Would, it had been done!
Thou didst prevent me; I had peopled else
This isle with Calibans.

Pro. Abhorred slave!
Which any print of goodness will not take,
Being capable of all ill! I pitied thee,
Took pains to make thee speak, taught thee each hour
One thing or other; when thou didst not, savage,
Know thine own meaning, but would'st gabble like
A thing most brutish, I endow'd thy purposes
With words that made them known: But thy vile race,
Though thou didst learn, had that in't which good natures
Could not abide to be with; therefore wast thou
Deservedly confin'd into this rock,
Who hadst deserv'd more than a prison.

Cal. You taught me language; and my profit on't
Is, I know how to curse: the red plague rid you,
For learning me your language!

Pro. Hag-seed, hence!
Fetch us in fuel: and be quick, thou wert best,
To answer other business. Shrug'st thou, malice?
If thou neglect'st, or dost unwillingly
What I command, I'll rack thee with old cramps;
Fill all thy bones with aches; make thee roar,
That beasts shall tremble at thy din.

Cal. No, 'pray thee!—
I must obey: his art is of such power, [*Aside.*
It would control my dam's god, Setebos,
And make a vassal of him.

Pro. So, slave; hence!
[*Exit* CALIBAN.

Re-enter ARIEL *invisible, playing and singing;* FERDINAND *following him.*

ARIEL'S Song.

Come unto these yellow sands,
And then take hands:
Court'sied when you have, and kiss'd,
(The wild waves whist)
Foot it featly here and there;
And, sweet sprites, the burden bear.
Hark, hark!
[*Bur.*] Bowgh, wowgh. [*Dispersedly.*
The watch-dogs bark:
[*Bur.*] Bowgh, wowgh. [*Dispersedly.*
Hark, hark! I hear
The strain of strutting chanticlere
Cry, Cock-a-doodle-doo.

Fer. Where should this musick be; i' the air, or the earth?
It sounds no more; and sure it waits upon
Some god of the island. Sitting on a bank,
Weeping again the king my father's wreck,
This musick crept by me upon the waters;
Allaying both their fury, and my passion,
With its sweet air: thence I have follow'd it,
Or it hath drawn me rather:—But 'tis gone.
No, it begins again.

ARIEL sings.

Full fathom five thy father lies;
Of his bones are coral made;
Those are pearls that were his eyes:
Nothing of him that doth fade,
But doth suffer a sea-change
Into something rich and strange.
Sea-nymphs hourly ring his knell:
[*Burden,* ding-dong.
Hark! now I hear them,—ding-dong, bell.

Fer. The ditty does remember my drown'd father:—
This is no mortal business, nor no sound
That the earth owes:—I hear it now above me.

Pro. The fringed curtains of thine eye advance,
And say, what thou seest yond'.

Mira. What is't? a spirit?
Lord, how it looks about! Believe me, sir,
It carries a brave form:—but 'tis a spirit.

Pro. No, wench; it eats and sleeps, and hath such senses
As we have, such: This gallant, which thou seest,
Was in the wreck; and but he's something stain'd
With grief, that's beauty's canker, thou might'st call him
A goodly person: he hath lost his fellows,
And strays about to find them.

Mira. I might call him
A thing divine; for nothing natural
I ever saw so noble.

Pro. It goes on, I see, [*Aside.*
As my soul prompts it:—Spirit, fine spirit! I'll free thee
Within two days for this.

Fer. Most sure, the goddess
On whom these airs attend!—Vouchsafe, my prayer
May know, if you remain upon this island;
And that you will some good instruction give,
How I may bear me here; My prime request,
Which I do last pronounce, is, O you wonder!
If you be maid, or no?

Mira. No wonder, sir;
But, certainly a maid.

Fer. My language! heavens!—
I am the best of them that speak this speech,
Were I but where 'tis spoken.

Pro. How! the best?
What wert thou, if the king of Naples heard thee?

Fer. A single thing, as I am now, that wonders
To hear thee speak of Naples; he does hear me;
And, that he does, I weep: myself am Naples;
Who with mine eyes, ne'er since at ebb, beheld
The king my father wreck'd.

Mira. Alack, for mercy!

Fer. Yes, 'faith, and all his lords; the duke of Milan,
And his brave son, being twain.

Pro. The duke of Milan,
And his more braver daughter, could control thee,
If now 'twere fit to do't:—At the first sight
[*Aside.*
They have chang'd eyes;—Delicate Ariel,
I'll set thee free for this!—A word, good sir;
I fear you have done yourself some wrong; a word.

Mira. Why speaks my father so ungently? This
Is the third man that e'er I saw; the first
That e'er I sigh'd for: pity move my father
To be inclin'd my way!

Fer. O, if a virgin,
And your affection not gone forth, I'll make you
The queen of Naples.

Pro. Soft, sir; one word more.—
They are both in either's powers: but this swift business
I must uneasy make, lest too light winning
[*Aside.*
Make the prize light.—One word more; I charge thee,
That thou attend me: thou dost here usurp
The name thou ow'st not; and hast put thyself
Upon this island, as a spy to win it
From me, the lord on't.

Fer. No, as I am a man.

Mira. There's nothing ill can dwell in such a temple:
If the ill spirit have so fair a house,
Good things will strive to dwell with't.

Pro. Follow me.—[*To* FERD.
Speak not you for him; he's a traitor.—Come.
I'll manacle thy neck and feet together;
Sea-water shalt thou drink, thy food shall be
The fresh-brook muscles, wither'd roots, and husks,
Wherein the acorn cradled: Follow.

Fer. No;

I will resist such entertainment, till
Mine enemy has more power. [*He draws.*

Mira. O dear father,
Make not too rash a trial of him, for
He's gentle, and not fearful.

Pro. What, I say,
My foot my tutor!—Put thy sword up, traitor;
Who mak'st a show, but dar'st not strike, thy conscience
Is so possess'd with guilt: come from thy ward;
For I can here disarm thee with this stick,
And make thy weapon drop.

Mira. 'Beseech you, father!

Pro. Hence; hang not on my garments.

Mira. Sir, have pity;
I'll be his surety.

Pro. Silence! one word more
Shall make me chide thee, if not hate thee. What!
An advocate for an impostor? hush!
Thou think'st, there are no more such shapes as he,
Having seen but him and Caliban: Foolish wench!
To the most of men this is a Caliban,
And they to him are angels.

Mira. My affections
Are then most humble; I have no ambition
To see a goodlier man.

Pro. Come on; obey: [*To* FER.
Thy nerves are in their infancy again,
And have no vigour in them.

Fer. So they are:
My spirits, as in a dream, are all bound up.
My father's loss, the weakness which I feel,
The wreck of all my friends, or this man's threats,
To whom I am subdued, are but light to me,
Might I but through my prison once a day
Behold this maid: all corners else o' the earth
Let liberty make use of: space enough
Have I in such a prison.

Pro. It works:—Come on,—
Thou hast done well, fine Ariel!—Follow me.— [*To* FERD. *and* MIR.
Hark, what thou else shalt do me. [*To* ARIEL.

Mira. Be of comfort;
My father is of a better nature, sir,
Than he appears by speech: this is unwonted,
Which now came from him.

Pro. Thou shalt be as free
As mountain winds: but then exactly do
All points of my command.

Ari. To the syllable.

Pro. Come, follow: speak not for him. [*Exeunt.*

ACT II.

SCENE I. *Another Part of the Island.*

Enter ALONZO, SEBASTIAN, ANTONIO, GONZALO, ADRIAN, FRANÇISCO, *and others.*

Gon. 'Beseech you, sir, be merry: you have cause
(So have we all) of joy; for our escape
Is much beyond our loss: our hint of woe
Is common; every day, some sailor's wife,
The masters of some merchant, and the merchant,
Have just our theme of woe: but for the miracle,
I mean our preservation, few in millions
Can speak like us: then wisely, good sir, weigh
Our sorrow with our comfort.

Alon. 'Pr'ythee, peace.

Seb. He receives comfort like cold porridge.

Ant. The visitor will not give him o'er so.

Seb. Look, he's winding up the watch of his wit; by and by it will strike.

Gon. Sir,——

Seb. One:——Tell.

Gon. When every grief is entertain'd, that's offer'd,
Comes to the entertainer—

Seb. A dollar.

Gon. Dolour comes to him, indeed; you have spoken truer than you purposed.

Seb. You have taken it wiselier than I meant you should.

Gon. Therefore, my lord,—

Ant. Fie, what a spendthrift is he of his tongue!

Alon. I pr'ythee spare.

Gon. Well, I have done: But yet—

Seb. He will be talking.

Ant. Which of them, he, or Adrian, for good wager, first begins to crow?

Seb. The old cock.

Ant. The cockrel.

Seb. Done: The wager?

Ant. A laughter.

Seb. A match.

Adr. Though this island seem to be desert,—

Seb. Ha, ha, ha!

Ant. So, you've pay'd.

Adr. Uninhabitable, and almost inaccessible,—

Seb. Yet,

Adr. Yet—

Ant. He could not miss it.

Adr. It must needs be of subtle, tender, and delicate temperance.

Ant. Temperance was a delicate wench.

Seb. Ay, and a subtle; as he most learnedly delivered.

Adr. The air breathes upon us here most sweetly.

Seb. As if it had lungs, and rotten ones.

Ant. Or, as 'twere perfumed by a fen.

Gon. Here is every thing advantageous to life.

Ant. True; save means to live.

Seb. Of that there's none, or l ttle.

Gon. How lush and lusty the grass looks? how green?

Ant. The ground, indeed, is tawny.

Seb. With an eye of green in 't.

Ant. He misses not much.

Seb. No; he doth but mistake the truth totally.

Gon. But the rarity of it is (which is indeed almost beyond credit)—

Seb. As many vouch'd rarities are.

Gon. That our garments, being, as they were, drenched in the sea, hold, notwithstanding, their freshness, and glosses; being rather new dy'd, than stain'd with salt water.

Ant. If but one of his pockets could speak, would it not say, he lies?

Seb. Ay, or very falsely pocket up his report.

Gon. Methinks, our garments are now as fresh as when we put them on first in Africk, at the marriage of the king's fair daughter Claribel to the king of Tunis.

Seb. 'Twas a sweet marriage, and we prosper well in our return.

Adr. Tunis was never graced before with such a paragon to their queen.

Gon. Not since widow Dido's time.

Ant. Widow? a pox o' that! How came that widow in? Widow Dido!

Seb. What if he had said, widower Æneas too? good lord, how you take it!

Adr. Widow Dido, said you? you make me study of that: she was of Carthage, not of Tunis.

Gon. This Tunis, sir, was Carthage.

Adr. Carthage?

Gon. I assure you, Carthage.

Ant. His word is more than the miraculous harp.

Seb. He hath raised the wall and houses too.

Ant. What impossible matter will he make easy next?

Seb. I think, he will carry this island home in his pocket, and give it his son for an apple.

Ant. And sowing the kernels of it in the sea, bring forth more islands.

Gon. Ay?

Ant. Why, in good time.

Gon. Sir, we were talking that our garments seem now as fresh as when we were at Tunis at the marriage of your daughter, who is now queen.

Ant. And the rarest that e'er came there.

Seb. 'Bate, I beseech you, widow Dido.

Ant. O, widow Dido; ay, widow Dido.

Gon. Is not, sir, my doublet as fresh as the first day I wore it? I mean, in a sort.

Ant. That sort was well fish'd for.

Gon. When I wore it at your daughter's marriage?

Alon. You cram these words into mine ears, against
The stomach of my sense: 'Would, I had never
Married my daughter there! for, coming thence,
My son is lost; and, in my rate, she too,
Who is so far from Italy remov'd,
I ne'er again shall see her. O thou mine heir
Of Naples and of Milan, what strange fish
Hath made his meal on thee!

Fran. Sir, he may live;
I saw him beat the surges under him,
And ride upon their backs; he trod the water,
Whose enmity he flung aside, and breasted
The surge most swoln that met him: his bold head
'Bove the contentious waves he kept, and oar'd
Himself with his good arms in lusty stroke
To the shore, that o'er his wave-worn basis bow'd,
As stooping to relieve him: I not doubt,
He came alive to land.

Alon. No, no, he's gone.

Seb. Sir, you may thank yourself for this great loss;
That would not bless our Europe with your daughter,
But rather lose her to an African;
Where she, at least, is banish'd from your eye,
Who hath cause to wet the grief on 't.

Alon. 'Pr'ythee, peace.

Seb. You were kneel'd to, and importun'd otherwise
By all of us; and the fair soul herself
Weigh'd, between loathness and obedience, at
Which end o' the beam she'd bow. We have lost your son,
I fear, for ever: Milan and Naples have
More widows in them of this business' making,
Than we bring men to comfort them: the fault's
Your own.

Alon. So is the dearest of the loss.

Gon. My lord Sebastian,
The truth you speak doth lack some gentleness,
And time to speak it in: you rub the sore,
When you should bring the plaster.

Seb. Very well.

Ant. And most chirurgeonly.

Gon. It is foul weather in us all, good sir,
When you are cloudy.

Seb. Foul weather?

Ant. Very foul.

Gon. Had I a plantation of this isle, my lord,—

Ant. He'd sow it with nettle-seed.

Seb. Or docks or mallows.

Gon. And were the king of it, What would I do?

Seb. 'Scape getting drunk, for want of wine.

Gon. I' the commonwealth I would by contraries
Execute all things: for no kind of traffick
Would I admit; no name of magistrate;
Letters should not be known; riches, poverty,
And use of service, none; contract, succession,
Bourn, bound of land, tilth, vineyard, none:
No use of metal, corn, or wine, or oil:
No occupation; all men idle, all;
And women too; but innocent and pure:
No sovereignty:—

Seb. And yet he would be king on 't.

Ant. The latter end of his commonwealth forgets the beginning.

Gon. All things in common nature should produce
Without sweat or endeavour: treason, felony,
Sword, pike, knife, gun, or need of any engine,
Would I not have; but nature should bring forth,
Of its own kind, all foizon, all abundance,
To feed my innocent people.

Seb. No marrying 'mong his subjects?

Ant. None, man; all idle; whores, and knaves.

Gon. I would with such perfection govern, sir,
To excel the golden age.

Seb. 'Save his majesty!

Ant. Long live Gonzalo!

Gon. And, do you mark me, sir?—

Alon. Pr'ythee, no more: thou dost talk nothing to me.

Gon. I do well believe your highness; and did it to minister occasion to these gentlemen, who are of such sensible and nimble lungs, that they always use to laugh at nothing.

Ant. 'Twas you we laugh'd at.

Gon. Who in this kind of merry fooling am nothing to you; so you may continue, and laugh at nothing still.

Ant. What a blow was there given?

Seb. An it had not fallen flat-long.

Gon. You are gentlemen of brave mettle: you would lift the moon out of her sphere, if she would continue in it five weeks without changing.

Enter ARIEL *invisible, playing solemn Musick.*

Seb. We would so, and then go a bat-fowling.

Ant. Nay, good my lord, be not angry.

Gon. No, I warrant you; I will not adventure my discretion so weakly. Will you laugh me asleep, for I am very heavy?

Ant. Go sleep, and hear us.

[*All sleep but* ALON. SEB. *and* ANT.

Alon. What, all so soon asleep! I wish mine eyes
Would, with themselves, shut up my thoughts: I find,
They are inclin'd to do so.

Seb. Please you, sir,
Do not omit the heavy offer of it:
It seldom visits sorrow; when it doth,
It is a comforter.

Ant. We two, my lord,
Will guard your person, while you take your rest,
And watch your safety.

Alon. Thank you: Wondrous heavy.

[ALONZO *sleeps. Exit* ARIEL.

Seb. What a strange drowsiness possesses them!

Ant. It is the quality o' the climate.

Seb. Why
Doth it not then our eyelids sink? I find not
Myself dispos'd to sleep.

Ant. Nor I; my spirits are nimble.
They fell together all, as by consent;
They dropp'd, as by a thunder-stroke. What might,
Worthy Sebastian?—O, what might?—No more;—
And yet, methinks, I see it in thy face,
What thou should'st be: the occasion speaks thee; and
My strong imagination sees a crown
Dropping upon thy head.

Seb. What, art thou waking?

Ant. Do you not hear me speak?

Seb. I do; and, surely,
It is a sleepy language; and thou speak'st
Out of thy sleep: What is it thou didst say?
This is a strange repose, to be asleep
With eyes wide open; standing, speaking, moving,
And yet so fast asleep.

Ant. Noble Sebastian,
Thou let'st thy fortune sleep—die rather; wink'st
Whiles thou art waking.

Seb. Thou dost snore distinctly;
There's meaning in thy snores.

Ant. I am more serious than my custom: you
Must be so too, if heed me; which to do,
Trebles thee o'er.

Seb. Well; I am standing water.

Ant. I'll teach you how to flow.
Seb. Do so: to ebb,
Hereditary sloth instructs thee.
Ant. O,
If you but knew how you the purpose cherish,
Whiles thus you mock it! how, in stripping it,
You more invest it! Ebbing men, indeed,
Most often do so near the bottom run,
By their own fear, or sloth.
Seb. 'Pr'ythee, say on:
The setting of thine eye, and cheek, proclaim
A matter from thee; and a birth, indeed,
Which throes thee much to yield.
Ant. Thus, sir:
Although this lord of weak remembrance, this
(Who shall be of as little memory,
When he is earth'd,) hath here almost persuaded
(For he's a spirit of persuasion, only
Professes to persuade) the king, his son's alive;
'Tis as impossible that he's undrown'd,
As he that sleeps here, swims.
Seb. I have no hope
That he's undrown'd.
Ant. O, out of that no hope,
What great hope have you! no hope, that way, is
Another way so high a hope, that even
Ambition cannot pierce a wink beyond,
But doubts discovery there. Will you grant, with me,
That Ferdinand is drown'd?
Seb. He's gone.
Ant. Then tell me,
Who's the next heir of Naples?
Seb. Claribel.
Ant. She that is queen of Tunis; she that dwells
Ten leagues beyond man's life; she that from Naples
Can have no note, unless the sun were post,
(The man i' the moon's too slow), till new-born chins
Be rough and razorable: she, from whom
We were all sea-swallow'd, though some cast again;
And, by that, destin'd to perform an act,
Whereof what's past is prologue; what to come,
In yours and my discharge.
Seb. What stuff is this?—How say you?
'Tis true, my brother's daughter's queen of Tunis;
So is she heir of Naples; 'twixt which regions
There is some space.
Ant. A space whose every cubit
Seems to cry out, *How shall that Claribel*
Measure us back to Naples?—Keep in Tunis,
And let Sebastian wake!—Say, this were death
That now hath seiz'd them; why, they were no worse
Than now they are: There be, that can rule Naples,
As well as he that sleeps; lords, that can prate
As amply, and unnecessarily,
As this Gonzalo; I myself could make
A chough of as deep chat. O, that you bore
The mind that I do! what a sleep were this
For your advancement! Do you understand me?
Seb. Methinks, I do.
Ant. And how does your content
Tender your own good fortune?
Seb. I remember,
You did supplant your brother Prospero.
Ant. True:
And, look, how well my garments sit upon me;
Much feater than before: My brother's servants
Were then my fellows, now they are my men.
Seb. But, for your conscience—
Ant. Ay, sir; where lies that? if it were a kybe,
'Twould put me to my slipper; but I feel not
This deity in my bosom: twenty consciences,
That stand 'twixt me and Milan, candied be they,
And melt, ere they molest! Here lies your brother,
No better than the earth he lies upon,
If he were that which now he's like, that's dead;
Whom I, with this obedient steel, three inches of it,
Can lay to bed for ever: whiles you, doing thus,
To the perpetual wink for aye might put
This ancient morsel, this sir Prudence, who
Should not upbraid our course. For all the rest,
They'll take suggestion, as a cat laps milk;
They'll tell the clock to any business that
We say befits the hour.
Seb. Thy case, dear friend,
Shall be my precedent; as thou got'st Milan,
I'll come by Naples. Draw thy sword; one stroke
Shall free thee from the tribute which thou pay'st;
And I the king shall love thee.
Ant. Draw together:
And when I rear my hand, do you the like,
To fall it on Gonzalo.
Seb. O, but one word.
[*They converse apart.*

Musick. Re-enter ARIEL, *invisible.*

Ari. My master through his art foresees the danger
That you, his friends, are in: and sends me forth,
(For else his projects die,) to keep them living.
[*Sings in* GONZALO'S *ear.*

While you here do snoring lie,
Open-ey'd conspiracy
His time doth take:
If of life you keep a care,
Shake off slumber, and beware:
Awake! awake!

Ant. Then let us both be sudden.
Gon. Now, good angels, preserve the king!
[*They wake.*
Alon. Why, how now, ho! awake! Why are you drawn?
Wherefore this ghastly looking?
Gon. What's the matter?
Seb. Whiles we stood here securing your repose,
Even now, we heard a hollow burst of bellowing
Like bulls, or rather lions; did it not wake you?
It struck mine ear most terribly.
Alon. I heard nothing.
Ant. O, 'twas a din to fright a monster's ear;
To make an earthquake! sure it was the roar
Of a whole herd of lions.
Alon. Heard you this, Gonzalo?
Gon. Upon mine honour, sir, I heard a humming,
And that a strange one too, which did awake me:
I shak'd you, sir, and cry'd; as mine eyes open'd,
I saw their weapons drawn:—there was a noise,
That's verity: 'Best stand upon our guard;
Or that we quit this place: let's draw our weapons.
Alon. Lead off this ground; and let's make further search
For my poor son.
Gon. Heavens keep him from these beasts!
For he is, sure, i' the island.
Alon. Lead away.
Ari. Prospero my lord shall know what I have done. [*Aside.*
So, king, go safely on to seek thy son. [*Exeunt.*

SCENE II. *Another Part of the Island.*

Enter CALIBAN, *with a burden of Wood.*

A noise of Thunder heard.

Cal. All the infections that the sun sucks up
From bogs, fens, flats, on Prosper fall, and make him
By inch-meal a disease! His spirits hear me,
And yet I needs must curse. But they'll nor pinch,
Fright me with urchin shows, pitch me i' the mire,
Nor lead me, like a firebrand, in the dark
Out of my way, unless he bid them; but
For every trifle are they set upon me:
Sometimes like apes, that moe and chatter at me,
And after, bite me; then like hedgehogs, which

Lie tumbling in my bare-foot way, and mount
Their pricks at my foot-fall: sometime am I
All wound with adders, who, with cloven tongues,
Do hiss me into madness:—Lo! now! lo!

Enter TRINCULO.

Here comes a spirit of his; and to torment me,
For bringing wood in slowly: I'll fall flat;
Perchance he will not mind me.

Trin. Here's neither bush nor shrub, to bear off any weather at all, and another storm brewing; I hear it sing i' the wind: yond' same black cloud, yond' huge one, looks like a foul bumbard that would shed his liquor. If it should thunder, as it did before, I know not where to hide my head: yond' same cloud cannot choose but fall by pailfuls.—What have we here? a man or a fish? Dead or alive? A fish: he smells like a fish; a very ancient and fish-like smell; a kind of, not of the newest, Poor-John. A strange fish! Were I in England now, (as once I was,) and had but this fish painted, not a holiday-fool there but would give a piece of silver: there would this monster make a man; any strange beast there makes a man: when they will not give a doit to relieve a lame beggar, they will lay out ten to see a dead Indian. Legg'd like a man! and his fins like arms! Warm o'my troth! I do now let loose my opinion, hold it no longer; this is no fish but an islander, that hath lately suffered by a thunderbolt. [*Thunder.*] Alas! the storm is come again: my best way is to creep under his gaberdine; there is no other shelter hereabout: Misery acquaints a man with strange bedfellows. I will here shroud, till the dregs of the storm be past.

Enter STEPHANO, *singing; a Bottle in his Hand.*

Ste. *I shall no more to sea, to sea,*
Here shall I die ashore;—

This is a very scurvy tune to sing at a man's funeral:
Well, here's my comfort. [*Drinks.*

The master, the swabber, the boatswain, and I,
The gunner, and his mate,
Lov'd Mal, Meg, and Marian, and Margery,
But none of us car'd for Kate:
For she had a tongue with a tang,
Would cry to a sailor, Go, hang:
She lov'd not the savour of tar nor of pitch,
Yet a tailor might scratch her where'er she did itch:
Then to sea, boys, and let her go hang.

This is a scurvy tune too: But here's my comfort. [*Drinks.*

Cal. Do not torment me: O!

Ste. What's the matter? Have we devils here? Do you put tricks upon us with savages, and men of Inde? Ha! I have not 'scap'd drowning, to be afeard now of your four legs; for it hath been said, As proper a man as ever went on four legs, cannot make him give ground: and it shall be said so again, whilst Stephano breathes at nostrils.

Cal. The spirit torments me: O!

Ste. This is some monster of the isle, with four legs; who hath got, as I take it, an ague: Where the devil should he learn our language? I will give him some relief, if it be but for that: If I can recover him, and keep him tame, and get to Naples with him, he's a present for any emperor that ever trod on neat's-leather.

Cal. Do not torment me, pr'ythee;
I'll bring my wood home faster.

Ste. He's in his fit now; and does not talk after the wisest. He shall taste of my bottle: if he have never drunk wine afore, it will go near to remove his fit: if I can recover him, and keep him tame, I will not take too much for him: he shall pay for him that hath him, and that soundly.

Cal. Thou dost me yet but little hurt; thou wilt
Anon, I know it by thy trembling:
Now Prosper works upon thee.

Ste. Come on your ways; open your mouth; here is that which will give language to you, cat; open your mouth: this will shake your shaking, I can tell you, and that soundly: you cannot tell who's your friend: open your chaps again.

Trin. I should know that voice: It should be —But he is drowned; and these are devils: O! defend me!—

Ste. Four legs, and two voices; a most delicate monster! His forward voice now is to speak well of his friend; his backward voice is to utter foul speeches, and to detract. If all the wine in my bottle will recover him, I will help his ague: Come,——Amen! I will pour some in thy other mouth.

Trin. Stephano,—

Ste. Doth thy other mouth call me? Mercy! mercy! This is a devil, and no monster: I will leave him; I have no long spoon.

Trin. Stephano!—If thou beest Stephano, touch me, and speak to me; for I am Trinculo: —be not afeard,—thy good friend Trinculo.

Ste. If thou beest Trinculo, come forth; I'll pull thee by the lesser legs; if any be Trinculo's legs, these are they. Thou art very Trinculo, indeed: How cam'st thou to be the siege of this moon-calf? Can he vent Trinculos?

Trin. I took him to be killed with a thunder-stroke:—But art thou not drowned, Stephano? I hope now, thou art not drowned. Is the storm over-blown? I hid me under the dead moon-calf's gaberdine, for fear of the storm: And art thou living, Stephano? O Stephano, two Neapolitans 'scap'd!

Ste. Pr'ythee do not turn me about; my stomach is not constant.

Cal. These be fine things, an if they be not sprites.
That's a brave god, and bears celestial liquor:
I will kneel to him.

Ste. How did'st thou 'scape? How cam'st thou hither? swear by this bottle, how thou cam'st hither. I escaped upon a butt of sack, which the sailors heaved over-board, by this bottle! which I made of the bark of a tree, with mine own hands, since I was cast a-shore.

Cal. I'll swear, upon that bottle, to be thy true subject; for the liquor is not earthly.

Ste. Here; swear then how thou escap'dst.

Trin. Swam a-shore, man, like a duck; I can swim like a duck, I'll be sworn.

Ste. Here, kiss the book: Though thou canst swim like a duck, thou art made like a goose.

Trin. O Stephano, hast any more of this?

Ste. The whole butt, man; my cellar is in a rock by the sea-side, where my wine is hid. How now, moon-calf? how does thine ague?

Cal. Hast thou not dropped from heaven!

Ste. Out o' the moon, I do assure thee: I was the man in the moon, when time was.

Cal. I have seen thee in her, and I do adore thee; My mistress showed me thee, and thy dog, and bush.

Ste. Come, swear to that: kiss the book: I will furnish it anon with new contents: swear.

Trin. By this good light, this is a very shallow monster:—I afeard of him?—a very weak monster:—The man i' the moon?—a most poor credulous monster: Well drawn, monster, in good sooth.

Cal. I'll show thee every fertile inch o' the island;
And kiss thy foot: I pr'ythee be my god.

Trin. By this light, a most perfidious and drunken monster; when his god's asleep, he'll rob his bottle.

Cal. I'll kiss thy foot; I'll swear myself thy subject.

Ste. Come on then; down, and swear.

Trin. I shall laugh myself to death at this puppy-headed monster: A most scurvy monster! I could find in my heart to beat him,—

Ste. Come, kiss.

Trin. —but that the poor monster's in drink: An abominable monster!

Cal. I'll shew thee the best springs; I'll pluck thee berries:
I'll fish for thee, and get thee wood enough.
A plague upon the tyrant that I serve!
I'll bear him no more sticks, but follow thee,
Thou wondrous man.

Trin. A most ridiculous monster; to make a wonder of a poor drunkard.

Cal. I pr'ythee, let me bring thee where crabs grow;
And I with my long nails will dig thee pig-nuts;
Shew thee a jay's nest, and instruct thee how
To snare the nimble marmozet: I'll bring thee
To clust'ring filberds, and sometimes I'll get thee
Young sea-mells from the rock: Wilt thou go with me?

Ste. I pr'ythee now, lead the way, without any more talking.—Trinculo, the king and all our company else being drowned, we will inherit here.—Here; bear my bottle. Fellow Trinculo, we'll fill him by and by again.

Cal. *Farewell, master; farewell, farewell.*
[*Sings drunkenly.*

Trin. A howling monster; a drunken monster.

Cal. *No more dams I'll make for fish;*
Nor fetch in firing
At requiring,
Nor scrape trenchering, nor wash dish;
'Ban 'Ban, Ca—Caliban,
Has a new master—get a new man.
Freedom, hey-day! hey-day, freedom! freedom, hey-day, freedom!

Ste. O brave monster! lead the way.
[*Exeunt.*

ACT III.

SCENE I. *Before* Prospero's *Cell.*

Enter FERDINAND, *bearing a Log.*

Fer. There be some sports are painful; and their labour
Delight in them sets off: some kinds of baseness
Are nobly undergone; and most poor matters
Point to rich ends. This my mean task would be
As heavy to me, as 'tis odious; but
The mistress, which I serve, quickens what's dead,
And makes my labours pleasures: O, she is
Ten times more gentle than her father's crabbed;
And he's composed of harshness. I must remove
Some thousands of these logs, and pile them up,
Upon a sore injunction: My sweet mistress
Weeps when she sees me work; and says, such baseness
Had ne'er like executor. I forget;
But these sweet thoughts do even refresh my labours;
Most busy-less when I do it.

Enter MIRANDA; *and* PROSPERO *at a distance.*

Mira. Alas, now, pray you,
Work not so hard: I would, the light'ning had
Burnt up those logs, that you are enjoin'd to pile!
Pray, set it down, and rest you: when this burns,
'Twill weep for having wearied you: my father
Is hard at study; pray now, rest yourself;
He's safe for these three hours.

Fer. O most dear mistress,
The sun will set, before I shall discharge
What I must strive to do.

Mira. If you'll sit down,
I'll bear your logs the while: 'Pray, give me that;
I'll carry it to the pile.

Fer. No, precious creature:
I'd rather crack my sinews, break my back,
Than you should such dishonour undergo,
While I sit lazy by.

Mira. It would become me
As well as it does you: and I should do it
With much more ease, for my good will is to it,
And your's it is against.

Pro. Poor worm! thou art infected;
This visitation shews it.

Mira. You look wearily.

Fer. No, noble mistress; 'tis fresh morning with me,
When you are by at night. I do beseech you,
(Chiefly, that I might set it in my prayers,)
What is your name?

Mira. Miranda:—O my father,
I have broke your hest to say so!

Fer. Admir'd Miranda!
Indeed, the top of admiration; worth
What's dearest to the world! Full many a lady
I have ey'd with best regard; and many a time
The harmony of their tongues hath into bondage
Brought my too diligent ear: for several virtues
Have I liked several women; never any
With so full soul, but some defect in her
Did quarrel with the noblest grace she ow'd,
And put it to the foil: But you, O you,
So perfect, and so peerless, are created
Of every creature's best.

Mira. I do not know
One of my sex; no woman's face remember,
Save, from my glass, mine own; nor have I seen
More that I may call men, than you, good friend,
And my dear father: how features are abroad,
I am skill-less of; but, by my modesty,
(The jewel in my dower,) I would not wish
Any companion in the world but you;
Nor can imagination form a shape,
Besides yourself, to like of: but I prattle
Something too wildly, and my father's precepts
I therein do forget.

Fer. I am, in my condition,
A prince, Miranda; I do think, a king;
(I would, not so!) and would no more endure
This wooden slavery, than to suffer
The flesh-fly blow my mouth.—Hear my soul speak;—
The very instant that I saw you, did
My heart fly to your service; there resides,
To make me slave to it; and, for your sake,
Am I this patient log-man?

Mira. Do you love me?

Fer. O heaven, O earth, bear witness to this sound,
And crown what I profess with kind event,
If I speak true; if hollowly, invert
What best is boded me, to mischief! I,
Beyond all limit of what else i' the world,
Do love, prize, honour you.

Mira. I am a fool,
To weep at what I am glad of.

Pro. Fair encounter
Of two most rare affections! Heavens rain grace
On that which breeds between them!

Fer. Wherefore weep you?

Mira. At mine unworthiness, that dare not offer
What I desire to give; and much less take,
What I shall die to want: But this is trifling;
And all the more it seeks to hide itself,
The bigger bulk it shews. Hence, bashful cunning!
And prompt me, plain and holy innocence!
I am your wife, if you will marry me;
If not, I'll die your maid: to be your fellow
You may deny me; but I'll be your servant,
Whether you will or no.

Fer. My mistress, dearest,
And I thus humble ever.

Mira. My husband then?

Fer. Ay, with a heart as willing
As bondage e'er of freedom: here's my hand.

Mira. And mine, with my heart in 't: And now farewell,
Till half an hour hence.
Fer. A thousand! thousand!
[*Exeunt* FER. *and* MIR.
Pro. So glad of this as they, I cannot be,
Who are surprised with all; but my rejoicing
At nothing can be more. I'll to my book;
For yet, ere supper time, must I perform
Much business appertaining. [*Exit.*

SCENE II. *Another Part of the Island.*

Enter STEPHANO *and* TRINCULO; CALIBAN *following with a Bottle.*

Ste. Tell not me;—when the butt is out, we will drink water; not a drop before: therefore bear up, and board 'em: Servant-monster, drink to me.

Trin. Servant-monster? the folly of this island! They say, there's but five upon this isle: we are three of them; if the other two be brained like us, the state totters.

Ste. Drink, servant-monster, when I bid thee; thy eyes are almost set in thy head.

Trin. Where should they be set else? he were a brave monster indeed, if they were set in his tail.

Ste. My man-monster hath drowned his tongue in sack: for my part, the sea cannot drown me: I swam, ere I could recover the shore, five-and-thirty leagues, off and on, by this light.—Thou shalt be my lieutenant, monster, or my standard.

Trin. Your lieutenant, if you list; he's no standard.

Ste. We'll not run, monsieur monster.

Trin. Nor go neither: but you'll lie, like dogs; and yet say nothing neither.

Ste. Moon-calf, speak once in thy life, if thou beest a good moon-calf.

Cal. How does thy honour? Let me lick thy shoe:
I'll not serve him, he is not valiant.

Trin. Thou liest, most ignorant monster; I am in case to justle a constable: Why, thou debosh'd fish thou, was there ever man a coward, that hath drunk so much sack as I to-day? Wilt thou tell a monstrous lie, being but half a fish, and half a monster?

Cal. Lo, how he mocks me! wilt thou let him, my lord?

Trin. Lord, quoth he!—that a monster should be such a natural!

Cal. Lo, lo, again! bite him to death, I pr'ythee.

Ste. Trinculo, keep a good tongue in your head; if you prove a mutineer, the next tree— The poor monster's my subject, and he shall not suffer indignity.

Cal. I thank my noble lord. Wilt thou be pleas'd
To hearken once again the suit I made thee?

Ste. Marry will I: kneel, and repeat it; I will stand, and so shall Trinculo.

Enter ARIEL, *invisible.*

Cal. As I told thee
Before, I am subject to a tyrant;
A sorcerer, that by his cunning hath
Cheated me of this island.
Ari. Thou liest.
Cal. Thou liest, thou jesting monkey, thou!
I would, my valiant master would destroy thee:
I do not lie.

Ste. Trinculo, if you trouble him any more in his tale, by this hand, I will supplant some of your teeth.

Trin. Why, I said nothing.

Ste. Mum then, and no more.—[*To Caliban.*] Proceed.

Cal. I say, by sorcery he got this isle;
From me he got it. If thy greatness will
Revenge it on him—for, I know, thou dar'st;
But this thing dare not.
Ste. That's most certain.
Cal. Thou shalt be lord of it, and I'll serve thee.

Ste. How now shall this be compassed? Canst thou bring me to the party?

Cal. Yea, yea, my lord; I'll yield him thee asleep,
Where thou may'st knock a nail into his head.
Ari. Thou liest, thou canst not.
Cal. What a pied ninny's this? Thou scurvy patch!
I do beseech thy greatness, give him blows,
And take his bottle from him: when that's gone,
He shall drink nought but brine: for I'll not shew him
Where the quick freshes are.

Ste. Trinculo, run into no further danger: interrupt the monster one word further, and, by this hand, I'll turn my mercy out of doors, and make a stock-fish of thee.

Trin. Why, what did I? I did nothing: I'll go further off.

Ste. Didst thou not say he lied?

Ari. Thou liest.

Ste. Do I so? take thou that. [*Strikes him.*] As you like this, give me the lie another time.

Trin. I did not give the lie: Out o' your wits, and hearing too?——A pox o' your bottle! this can sack, and drinking do. A murrain on your monster, and the devil take your fingers!

Cal. Ha, ha, ha!

Ste. Now, forward with your tale. Pr'ythee stand further off.

Cal. Beat him enough: after a little time,
I'll beat him too.
Ste. Stand further. Come, proceed.
Cal. Why, as I told thee, 'tis a custom with him
I' the afternoon to sleep: there thou may'st brain him,
Having first seiz'd his books; or with a log
Batter his skull, or paunch him with a stake,
Or cut his wezand with thy knife: Remember,
First to possess his books; for without them
He's but a sot, as I am, nor hath not
One spirit to command: They all do hate him,
As rootedly as I: Burn but his books;
He has brave utensils, (for so he calls them,)
Which, when he has a house, he'll deck withal.
And that most deeply to consider, is
The beauty of his daughter; he himself
Calls her a nonpareil: I ne'er saw woman,
But only Sycorax my dam, and she;
But she as far surpasseth Sycorax,
As greatest does least.
Ste. Is it so brave a lass?
Cal. Ay, lord; she will become thy bed, I warrant,
And bring thee forth brave brood.

Ste. Monster, I will kill this man: his daughter and I will be king and queen; (save our graces!) and Trinculo and thyself shall be viceroys:—Dost thou like the plot, Trinculo?

Trin. Excellent.

Ste. Give me thy hand; I am sorry I beat thee; but while thou livest, keep a good tongue in thy head.

Cal. Within this half hour will he be asleep;
Wilt thou destroy him then?
Ste. Ay, on mine honour.
Ari. This will I tell my master.
Cal. Thou mak'st me merry: I am full of pleasure;
Let us be jocund: Will you troll the catch
You taught me but while-ere?

Ste. At thy request, monster, I will do reason, any reason: Come on, Trinculo, let us sing. [*Sings.*

Flout 'em, and skout 'em; and skout 'em, and flout 'em;
Thought is free.

Cal. That's not the tune.

[ARIEL *plays the tune on a Tabor and Pipe.*

Ste. What is this same?

Trin. This is the tune of our catch, played by the picture of No-body.

Ste. If thou beest a man, shew thyself in thy likeness: if thou beest a devil, take 't as thou list.

Trin. O, forgive me my sins!

Ste. He that dies, pays all debts: I defy thee:— Mercy upon us!

Cal. Art thou afeard?

Ste. No, monster, not I.

Cal. Be not afeard; the isle is full of noises,
Sounds, and sweet airs, that give delight, and hurt not.
Sometimes a thousand twangling instruments
Will hum about mine ears; and sometimes voices,
That, if I then had wak'd after long sleep,
Will make me sleep again; and then in dreaming,
The clouds, methought, would open, and shew riches
Ready to drop upon me; that, when I wak'd,
I cry'd to dream again.

Ste. This will prove a brave kingdom to me, where I shall have my musick for nothing.

Cal. When Prospero is destroyed.

Ste. That shall be by and by: I remember the story.

Trin. The sound is going away: let's follow it, and after, do our work.

Ste. Lead, monster; we'll follow.—I would, I could see this taborer: he lays it on.

Trin. Wilt come? I'll follow, Stephano.

[*Exeunt.*

SCENE III. *Another Part of the Island.*

Enter ALONZO, SEBASTIAN, ANTONIO, GONZALO, ADRIAN, FRANCISCO, *and others.*

Gon. By'r lakin, I can go no further, sir;
My old bones ache; here's a maze trod, indeed,
Through forth-rights, and meanders! by your patience,
I needs must rest me.

Alon. Old lord, I cannot blame thee,
Who am myself attach'd with weariness,
To the dulling of my spirits: sit down, and rest.
Even here I will put off my hope, and keep it
No longer for my flatterer: he is drown'd,
Whom thus we stray to find: and the sea mocks
Our frustrate search on land: Well, let him go.

Ant. I am right glad that he's so out of hope.

[*Aside to* SEBASTIAN.

Do not, for one repulse, forego the purpose
That you resolv'd to effect.

Seb. The next advantage
Will we take thoroughly.

Ant. Let it be to-night:
For, now they are oppress'd with travel, they
Will not, nor cannot, use such vigilance,
As when they are fresh.

Seb. I say, to-night: no more.

Solemn and strange Musick; and PROSPERO *above, invisible. Enter several strange Shapes, bringing in a Banquet; they dance about it with gentle actions of salutation; and inviting the King, &c. to eat, they depart.*

Alon. What harmony is this? my good friends, hark!

Gon. Marvellous sweet musick!

Alon. Give us kind keepers, heavens! What were these?

Seb. A living drollery: Now I will believe
That there are unicorns: that, in Arabia
There is one tree, the phœnix' throne; one phœnix
At this hour reigning there.

Ant. I'll believe both;
And what does else want credit, come to me,
And I'll be sworn 'tis true: Travellers ne'er did lie,
Though fools at home condemn them.

Gon. If in Naples
I should report this now, would they believe me?
If I should say, I saw such islanders,
(For, certes, these are people of the island),
Who, though they are of monstrous shape, yet, note,
Their manners are more gentle-kind, than of
Our human generation you shall find
Many, nay, almost any.

Pro. Honest lord,
Thou hast said well; for some of you there present
Are worse than devils. [*Aside.*

Alon. I cannot too much muse,
Such shapes, such gesture, and such sound, expressing
(Although they want the use of tongue) a kind
Of excellent dumb discourse.

Pro. Praise in departing.

[*Aside.*

Fran. They vanish'd strangely.

Seb. No matter, since
They have left their viands behind; for we have stomachs.—
Will 't please you taste of what is here?

Alon. Not I.

Gon. Faith, sir, you need not fear: When we were boys,
Who would believe that there were mountaineers,
Dew-lapp'd like bulls, whose throats had hanging at them,
Wallets of flesh? or that there were such men,
Whose heads stood in their breasts? which now we find
Each putter-out on five for one, will bring us
Good warrant of.

Alon. I will stand to, and feed,
Although my last: no matter, since I feel
The best is past:—Brother, my lord the duke,
Stand to, and do as we.

Thunder and Lightning. Enter ARIEL *like a Harpy claps his wings upon the table, and, by a quaint device, the Banquet vanishes.*

Ari. You are three men of sin, whom destiny
(That hath to instrument this lower world,
And what is in 't,) the never-surfeited sea
Hath caused to belch up; and on this island
Where man doth not inhabit; you 'mongst men
Being most unfit to live. I have made you mad;

[*Seeing* ALON. SEB. *&c. draw their swords.*

And even with such like valour, men hang and drown
Their proper selves. You fools! I and my fellows
Are ministers of fate; the elements
Of whom your swords are temper'd, may as well
Wound the loud winds, or with bemock'd-at stabs
Kill the still-closing waters, as diminish
One dowle that's in my plume; my fellow ministers
Are like invulnerable: if you could hurt,
Your swords are now too massy for your strengths,
And will not be uplifted; But, remember,
(For that's my business to you,) that you three
From Milan did supplant good Prospero;
Expos'd unto the sea, which hath requit it,
Him, and his innocent child: for which foul deed
The powers, delaying, not forgetting, have
Incens'd the seas and shores, yea, all the creatures,
Against your peace: Thee, of thy son, Alonzo,
They have bereft; and do pronounce by me,
Ling'ring perdition (worse than any death
Can be at once,) shall step by step attend
You, and your ways; whose wraths to guard you from
(Which here, in this most desolate isle, else falls
Upon your heads,) is nothing, but heart's sorrow,
And a clear life ensuing.

He vanishes in Thunder: then, to soft musick, enter the Shapes again, and dance with mops and mowes, and carry out the table.

Pro. [*Aside.*] Bravely the figure of this harpy hast thou
Perform'd, my Ariel; a grace it had, devouring:
Of my instruction hast thou nothing 'bated,
In what thou had'st to say: so, with good life,
And observation strange, my meaner ministers
Their several kinds have done: my high charms work,
And these, mine enemies, are all knit up
In their distractions: they now are in my power:
And in these fits I leave them, whilst I visit
Young Ferdinand, (whom they suppose is drown'd),
And his and my loved darling.
[*Exit* PROSPERO *from above.*

Gon. I' the name of something holy sir, why stand you
In this strange stare?

Alon. O, it is monstrous! monstrous!
Methought, the billows spoke, and told me of it;
The winds did sing it to me; and the thunder,
That deep and dreadful organ-pipe, pronounc'd
The name of Prosper; it did bass my trespass.
Therefore my son i' the ooze is bedded; and
I'll seek him deeper than e'er plummet sounded,
And with him there lie mudded. [*Exit.*

Seb. But one fiend at a time,
I'll fight their legions o'er.

Ant. I'll be thy second.
[*Exeunt* SEB. *and* ANT.

Gon. All three of them are desperate; their great guilt,
Like poison given to work a great time after,
Now 'gins to bite the spirits: I do beseech you
That are of suppler joints, follow them swiftly,
And hinder them from what this ecstasy
May now provoke them to.

Adr. Follow, I pray you.
[*Exeunt.*

ACT IV.

SCENE I. *Before* PROSPERO'S *Cell.*

Enter PROSPERO, FERDINAND, *and* MIRANDA.

Pro. If I have too austerely punish'd you,
Your compensation makes amends; for I
Have given you here a thread of mine own life,
Or that for which I live; whom once again
I tender to thy hand: all thy vexations
Were but my trials of thy love, and thou
Hast strangely stood the test: here, afore Heaven,
I ratify this my rich gift. O Ferdinand,
Do not smile at me, that I boast her off,
For thou shalt find she will outstrip all praise,
And make it halt behind her.

Fer. I do believe it,
Against an oracle.

Pro. Then, as my gift, and thine own acquisition,
Worthily purchas'd, take my daughter: But
If thou dost break her virgin knot before
All sanctimonious ceremonies may
With full and holy rite be minister'd,
No sweet aspersion shall the heavens let fall
To make this contract grow; but barren hate,
Sour-ey'd disdain, and discord, shall bestrew
The union of your bed with weeds so loathly,
That you shall hate it both: therefore, take heed,
As Hymen's lamps shall light you.

Fer. As I hope
For quiet days, fair issue, and long life,
With such love as 'tis now; the murkiest den,
The most opportune place, the strong'st suggestion
Our worser Genius can, shall never melt
Mine honour into lust; to take away
The edge of that day's celebration,
When I shall think, or Phœbus' steeds are founder'd,
Or night kept chain'd below.

Pro. Fairly spoke;
Sit then, and talk with her, she is thine own.—
What, Ariel; my industrious servant Ariel!

Enter ARIEL.

Ari. What would my potent master? here I am.

Pro. Thou and thy meaner fellows your last service
Did worthily perform; and I must use you
In such another trick: go, bring the rabble,
O'er whom I give thee power, here, to this place:
Incite them to quick motion; for I must
Bestow upon the eyes of this young couple
Some vanity of mine art; it is my promise,
And they expect it from me.

Ari. Presently?

Pro. Ay, with a twink.

Ari. Before you can say, *Come*, and *go*,
And breathe twice; and cry, *so, so;*
Each one, tripping on his toe,
Will be here with mop and mowe:
Do you love me, master? no.

Pro. Dearly, my delicate Ariel: Do not approach,
Till thou dost hear me call.

Ari. Well I conceive. [*Exit.*

Pro. Look, thou be true; do not give dalliance
Too much the rein; the strongest oaths are straw
To the fire i' the blood: be more abstemious,
Or else, good night, your vow!

Fer. I warrant you, sir;
The white-cold virgin snow upon my heart
Abates the ardour of my liver.

Pro. Well.—
Now come, my Ariel; bring a corollary,
Rather than want a spirit; appear, and pertly.—
No tongue; all eyes; be silent. [*Soft musick.*

A Masque. Enter IRIS.

Iris. Ceres, most bounteous lady, thy rich leas
Of wheat, rye, barley, vetches, oats, and peas:
Thy turfy mountains, where live nibbling sheep,
And flat meads thatch'd with stover, them to keep;
Thy banks with peonied and lilied brims,
Which spungy April at thy hest betrims,
To make cold nymphs chaste crowns; and thy broom groves,
Whose shadow the dismissed bachelor loves,
Being lass-lorn; thy pole-clipt vineyard;
And thy sea-marge, steril, and rocky-hard,
Where thou thyself dost air: The queen o'the sky,
Whose watery arch, and messenger, am I,
Bids thee leave these; and with her sovereign grace,
Here on this grass-plot, in this very place,
To come and sport: her peacocks fly amain;
Approach, rich Ceres, her to entertain.

Enter CERES.

Cer. Hail, many-colour'd messenger, that ne'er
Dost disobey the wife of Jupiter;
Who, with thy saffron wings, upon my flowers
Diffusest honey-drops, refreshing showers:
And with each end of thy blue bow dost crown
My bosky acres, and my unshrubb'd down.
Rich scarf to my proud earth: Why hath thy queen
Summon'd me hither, to this short-grass'd green?

Iris. A contract of true love to celebrate;
And some donation freely to estate
On the bless'd lovers.

Cer. Tell me, heavenly bow,
If Venus, or her son, as thou dost know,
Do now attend the queen? since they did plot
The means, that dusky Dis my daughter got,
Her and her blind boy's scandal'd company
I have forsworn.

Iris. Of her society
Be not afraid: I met her deity

Cutting the clouds towards Paphos; and her son
Dove-drawn with her: here thought they to have done
Some wanton charm upon this man and maid,
Whose vows are, that no bed-rite shall be paid
Till Hymen's torch be lighted: but in vain;
Mars's hot minion is return'd again;
Her waspish-headed son has broke his arrows,
Swears he will shoot no more, but play with sparrows,
And be a boy right out.

Cer. Highest queen of state,
Great Juno comes; I know her by her gait.

Enter JUNO.

Juno. How does my bounteous sister? Go with me,
To bless this twain, that they may prosperous be,
And honour'd in their issue.

SONG.

Juno. *Honour, riches, marriage-blessing,*
Long continuance, and increasing,
Hourly joys be still upon you!
Juno sings her blessings on you.

Cer. *Earth's increase, and foison plenty;*
Barns and garners never empty;
Vines, with clust'ring bunches growing;
Plants, with goodly burden bowing;
Spring come to you, at the farthest,
In the very hand of harvest!
Scarcity and want shall shun you;
Ceres' blessing so is on you.

Fer. This is a most majestic vision, and
Harmonious charmingly: May I be bold
To think these spirits?

Pro. Spirits, which by mine art
I have from their confines call'd to enact
My present fancies.

Fer. Let me live here ever;
So rare a wonder'd father, and a wife,
Make this place Paradise.

[JUNO *and* CERES *whisper, and send* IRIS *on employment.*

Pro. Sweet now, silence:
Juno and Ceres whisper seriously;
There's something else to do; hush, and be mute,
Or else our spell is marr'd.

Iris. You nymphs, call'd Naiads, of the wand'ring brooks,
With your sedg'd crowns, and ever harmless looks,
Leave your crisp channels, and on this green land
Answer your summons; Juno does command:
Come, temperate nymphs, and help to celebrate
A contract of true love; be not too late.

Enter certain Nymphs.

You sun-burn'd sicklemen, of August weary,
Come hither from the furrow, and be merry;
Make holy-day: your rye-straw hats put on,
And these fresh nymphs encounter every one
In country footing.

Enter certain Reapers, properly habited: they join with the Nymphs in a graceful dance; towards the end of which PROSPERO *starts suddenly, and speaks; after which, to a strange, hollow, and confused noise, they heavily vanish.*

Pro. [*Aside.*] I had forgot that foul conspiracy
Of the beast Caliban, and his confederates,
Against my life; the minute of their plot
Is almost come.—[*To the Spirits.*] Well done;—avoid;—no more.

Fer. This is strange: your father's in some passion
That works him strongly.

Mira. Never till this day,
Saw I him touch'd with anger so distemper'd.

Pro. You do look, my son, in a mov'd sort,
As if you were dismay'd: be cheerful, sir:
Our revels now are ended: these our actors,
As I foretold you, were all spirits, and
Are melted into air, into thin air:
And, like the baseless fabrick of this vision,
The cloud-capp'd towers, the gorgeous palaces,
The solemn temples, the great globe itself,
Yea, all which it inherit, shall dissolve;
And, like this insubstantial pageant faded,
Leave not a rack behind: We are such stuff
As dreams are made of, and our little life
Is rounded with a sleep.—Sir, I am vex'd;
Bear with my weakness; my old brain is troubled.
Be not disturb'd with my infirmity:
If you be pleas'd, retire into my cell,
And there repose; a turn or two I'll walk,
To still my beating mind.

Fer. Mira. We wish your peace. [*Exeunt.*

Pro. Come with a thought:—I thank you:—Ariel, come.

Enter ARIEL.

Ari. Thy thoughts I cleave to: What's thy pleasure?

Pro. Spirit,
We must prepare to meet with Caliban.

Ari. Ay, my commander: when I presented Ceres,
I thought to have told thee of it; but I fear'd,
Lest I might anger thee.

Pro. Say again, where didst thou leave these varlets?

Ari. I told you, sir, they were red-hot with drinking;
So full of valour, that they smote the air
For breathing in their faces; beat the ground
For kissing of their feet: yet always bending
Towards their project: then I beat my tabor,
At which, like unback'd colts, they prick'd their ears,
Advanc'd their eyelids, lifted up their noses,
As they smelt music; so I charm'd their ears,
That, calf-like, they my lowing follow'd, through
Tooth'd briers, sharp furzes, pricking goss, and thorns,
Which enter'd their frail shins: at last I left them
I' the filthy mantled pool beyond your cell,
There dancing up to the chins, that the foul lake
O'er-stunk their feet.

Pro. This was well done, my bird:
Thy shape invisible retain thou still:
The trumpery in my house, go, bring it hither,
For stale to catch these thieves.

Ari. I go, I go. [*Exit.*

Pro. A devil, a born devil, on whose nature
Nurture can never stick; on whom my pains,
Humanely taken, all, all lost, quite lost;
And as, with age, his body uglier grows,
So his mind cankers: I will plague them all,

Re-enter ARIEL, *loaden with glistering Apparel, &c.*

Even to roaring:—Come, hang them on this line.

PROSPERO *and* ARIEL *remain invisible. Enter* CALIBAN, STEPHANO, *and* TRINCULO; *all wet.*

Cal. Pray you tread softly, that the blind mole may not
Hear a foot fall: we now are near his cell.

Ste. Monster, your fairy, which, you say, is a harmless fairy, has done little better than play'd the Jack with us.

Trin. Monster, I do smell all horse-piss; at which my nose is in great indignation.

Ste. So is mine. Do you hear, monster? if I should take a displeasure against you; look you,—

Trin. Thou wert but a lost monster.

Cal. Good my lord, give me thy favour still:
Be patient, for the prize I'll bring thee to
Shall hood-wink this mischance; therefore, speak softly,
All's hush'd as midnight yet.

Trin. Ay, but to lose our bottles in the pool,—

Ste. There is not only disgrace and dishonour in that, monster, but an infinite loss.

Trin. That's more to me than my wetting: yet this is your harmless fairy, monster.

Ste. I will fetch off my bottle, though I be o'er ears for my labour.

Cal. 'Pry'thee, my king, be quiet: Seest thou here,
This is the mouth of the cell: no noise, and enter:
Do that good mischief, which may make this island
Thine own for ever, and I, thy Caliban,
For aye thy foot-licker.

Ste. Give me thy hand: for I do begin to have bloody thoughts.

Trin. O king Stephano! O peer! O worthy Stephano! look, what a wardrobe here is for thee!

Cal. Let it alone, thou fool: it is but trash.

Trin. O, ho, monster; we know what belongs to a frippery:—O king Stephano!

Ste. Put off that gown, Trinculo; by this hand, I'll have that gown.

Trin. Thy grace shall have it.

Cal. The dropsy drown this fool! what do you mean,
To dote thus on such luggage? Let it alone,
And do the murder first: if he awake,
From toe to crown he'll fill our skins with pinches;
Make us strange stuff.

Ste. Be you quiet, monster.—Mistress line, is not this my jerkin? Now is the jerkin under the line: now, jerkin, you are like to lose your hair, and prove a bald jerkin.

Trin. Do, do: We steal by line and level, and't like your grace.

Ste. I thank thee for that jest; here's a garment for't: wit shall not go unrewarded, while I am king of this country: *Steal by line and level,* is an excellent pass of pate; there's another garment for't.

Trin. Monster, come, put some lime upon your fingers, and away with the rest.

Cal. I will have none on't: we shall lose our time,
And all be turn'd to barnacles, or to apes
With foreheads villanous low.

Ste. Monster, lay-to your fingers; help to bear this away, where my hogshead of wine is, or I'll turn you out of my kingdom: go to, carry this.

Trin. And this.

Ste. Ay, and this.

A noise of Hunters heard. Enter divers Spirits in shape of hounds, and hunt them about; PROSPERO *and* ARIEL *setting them on.*

Pro. Hey, *Mountain*, hey!

Ari. *Silver!* there it goes, *Silver!*

Pro. *Fury! Fury!* there, *Tyrant*, there! hark! hark! [CAL. STE. *and* TRIN. *are driven out.*
Go, charge my goblins that they grind their joints
With dry convulsions; shorten up their sinews
With aged cramps; and more pinch-spotted make them,
Than pard, or cat o' mountain.

Ari. Hark, they roar.

Pro. Let them be hunted soundly: At this hour
Lie at my mercy all mine enemies:
Shortly shall all my labours end, and thou
Shalt have the air at freedom: for a little,
Follow, and do me service. [*Exeunt.*

ACT V.

SCENE I. *Before the Cell of* PROSPERO.

Enter PROSPERO *in his magic robes, and* ARIEL.

Pro. Now does my project gather to a head:
My charms crack not; my spirits obey; and time
Goes upright with his carriage. How's the day?

Ari. On the sixth hour; at which time, my lord,
You said our work should cease.

Pro. I did say so,
When first I rais'd the tempest. Say, my spirit,
How fares the king and his followers?

Ari. Confin'd together
In the same fashion as you gave in charge;
Just as you left them, sir; all prisoners
In the lime grove which weather-fends your cell:
They cannot budge, till your release. The king,
His brother, and yours, abide all three distracted;
And the remainder mourning over them,
Brim-ful of sorrow, and dismay; but chiefly
Him you term'd, sir, *The good old lord, Gonzalo;*
His tears run down his beard, like winter's drops
From eaves of reeds: your charm so strongly works them,
That if you now beheld them, your affections
Would become tender.

Pro. Dost thou think so, spirit?

Ari. Mine would, sir, were I human.

Pro. And mine shall.
Hast thou, which art but air, a touch, a feeling
Of their afflictions? and shall not myself,
One of their kind, that relish all as sharply,
Passion as they, be kindlier mov'd than thou art?
Though with their high wrongs I am struck to the quick,
Yet, with my nobler reason, 'gainst my fury,
Do I take part: the rarer action is
In virtue than in vengeance: they being penitent,
The sole drift of my purpose doth extend
Not a frown further: Go, release them, Ariel;
My charms I'll break, their senses I'll restore,
And they shall be themselves.

Ari. I'll fetch them, sir. [*Exit.*

Pro. Ye elves of hills, brooks, standing lakes, and groves;
And ye, that on the sands with printless foot
Do chase the ebbing Neptune, and do fly him
When he comes back; you demy-puppets, that
By moon-shine do the green-sour ringlets make,
Whereof the ewe not bites; and you, whose pastime
Is to make midnight-mushrooms; that rejoice
To hear the solemn curfew; by whose aid
(Weak masters though you be) I have be-dimm'd
The noon-tide sun, call'd forth the mutinous winds,
And 'twixt the green sea and the azur'd vault
Set roaring war: to the dread rattling thunder
Have I given fire, and rifted Jove's stout oak
With his own bolt: the strong-bas'd promontory
Have I made shake; and by the spurs pluck'd up
The pine, and cedar: graves, at my command,
Have wak'd their sleepers; op'd and let them forth,
By my so potent art: But this rough magick
I here abjure: and, when I have required
Some heavenly music, (which even now I do,)
To work mine end upon their senses, that
This airy charm is for, I'll break my staff,
Bury it certain fathoms in the earth,
And, deeper than did ever plummet sound,
I'll drown my book. [*Solemn musick.*

Re-enter ARIEL: *after him,* ALONSO, *with a frantic gesture, attended by* GONZALO; SEBASTIAN *and* ANTONIO *in like manner, attended by* ADRIAN *and* FRANCISCO: *They all enter the circle which* PROSPERO *had made, and there stand charmed; which* PROSPERO *observing, speaks.*

A solemn air, and the best comforter
To an unsettled fancy, cure thy brains,
Now useless, boil'd within thy skull! There stand,
For you are spell-stopp'd.——
Holy Gonzalo, honourable man,
Mine eyes, even sociable to the shew of thine,
Fall fellowly drops.—The charm dissolves apace;
And as the morning steals upon the night,
Melting the darkness, so their rising senses
Begin to chase the ignorant fumes that mantle
Their clearer reason.—O my good Gonzalo,
My true preserver, and a loyal sir
To him thou follow'st; I will pay thy graces
Home, both in word and deed.—Most cruelly
Didst thou, Alonso, use me and my daughter:

Thy brother was a furtherer in the act;—
Thou'rt pinch'd for't now, Sebastian.—Flesh and blood,
You brother mine, that entertain'd ambition,
Expell'd remorse and nature; who with Sebastian
(Whose inward pinches therefore are most strong,)
Would here have kill'd your king; I do forgive thee,
Unnatural though thou art!—Their understanding
Begins to swell; and the approaching tide
Will shortly fill the reasonable shores,
That now lie foul and muddy. Not one of them,
That yet looks on me, or would know me:— Ariel,
Fetch me the hat and rapier in my cell;
[*Exit* ARIEL.
I will dis-case me, and myself present,
As I was sometime Milan:—quickly, spirit;
Thou shalt ere long be free.

ARIEL *re-enters, singing, and helps to attire* PROSPERO.

Ari. *Where the bee sucks, there suck I;*
In a cowslip's bell I lie:
There I couch when owls do cry.
On the bat's back I do fly,
After summer, merrily:
Merrily, merrily, shall I live now,
Under the blossom that hangs on the bough.

Pro. Why, that's my dainty Ariel; I shall miss thee;
But yet thou shalt have freedom: so, so, so—
To the king's ship, invisible as thou art:
There shalt thou find the mariners asleep
Under the hatches; the master, and the boatswain,
Being awake, enforce them to this place;
And presently, I pr'ythee.
Ari. I drink the air before me and return
Or e'er your pulse twice beat. [*Exit* ARIEL.
Gon. All torment, trouble, wonder, and amazement
Inhabits here: Some heavenly power guide us
Out of this fearful country!
Pro. Behold, sir king,
The wronged duke of Milan, Prospero:
For more assurance that a living prince
Does now speak to thee, I embrace thy body;
And to thee and thy company, I bid
A hearty welcome.
Alon. Whe'r thou beest he, or no,
Or some enchanted trifle to amuse me,
As late I have been, I not know: thy pulse
Beats, as of flesh and blood; and, since I saw thee,
The affliction of my mind amends, with which,
I fear, a madness held me: this must crave
(An if this be at all) a most strange story.
Thy dukedom I resign; and do entreat
Thou pardon me my wrongs:—But how should Prospero
Be living, and be here?
Pro. First, noble friend,
Let me embrace thine age; whose honour cannot
Be measur'd, or confin'd.
Gon. Whether this be,
Or be not, I'll not swear.
Pro. You do yet taste
Some subtilties o' the isle, that will not let you
Believe things certain:—Welcome, my friends all:—
But you, my brace of lords, were I so minded,
[*Aside to* SEB. *and* ANT.
I here could pluck his highness' frown upon you,
And justify you traitors: at this time
I'll tell no tales.
Seb. The devil speaks in him. [*Aside.*
Pro. No:—
For you, most wicked sir, whom to call brother
Would even infect my mouth, I do forgive
Thy rankest fault; all of them; and require
My dukedom of thee, which, perforce, I know,
Thou must restore.
Alon. If thou beest Prospero,
Give us particulars of thy preservation:
How thou hast met us here, who three hours since
Were wreck'd upon this shore; where I have lost
(How sharp the point of this remembrance is!)
My dear son Ferdinand.
Pro. I am woe for't, sir.
Alon. Irreparable is the loss; and Patience
Says, it is past her cure.
Pro. I rather think,
You have not sought her help; of whose soft grace,
For the like loss, I have her sovereign aid,
And rest myself content.
Alon. You the like loss?
Pro. As great to me, as late; and portable
To make the dear loss, have I means much weaker
Than you may call to comfort you; for I
Have lost my daughter.
Alon. A daughter?
O heavens! that they were living both in Naples,
The king and queen there! that they were, I wish
Myself were mudded in that oozy bed
Where my son lies. When did you lose your daughter?
Pro. In this last tempest. I perceive, these lords
At this encounter do so much admire,
That they devour their reason; and scarce think
Their eyes do offices of truth, their words
Are natural breath; but, howsoe'er you have
Been justled from your senses, know for certain,
That I am Prospero, and that very duke
Which was thrust forth of Milan; who most strangely
Upon this shore where you were wreck'd, was landed,
To be the lord on't. No more yet of this;
For 'tis a chronicle of day by day,
Not a relation for a breakfast, nor
Befitting this first meeting. Welcome, sir;
This cell's my court: here have I few attendants,
And subjects none abroad; pray you, look in.
My dukedom, since you have given me again,
I will requite you with as good a thing;
At least, bring forth a wonder, to content ye,
As much as me my dukedom.

The entrance of the Cell opens, and discovers FERDINAND *and* MIRANDA *playing at chess.*

Mira. Sweet lord, you play me false.
Fer. No, my dearest love,
I would not for the world.
Mira. Yes, for a score of kingdoms you should wrangle,
And I would call it fair play.
Alon. If this prove
A vision of the island, one dear son
Shall I twice lose.
Seb. A most high miracle!
Fer. Though the seas threaten, they are merciful:
I have curs'd them without cause.
[FER. *kneels to* ALON.
Alon. Now all the blessings
Of a glad father compass thee about!
Arise, and say how thou cam'st here.
Mira. O! wonder!
How many goodly creatures are there here!
How beauteous mankind is! O brave new world,
That has such people in't!
Pro. 'Tis new to thee.
Alon. What is this maid, with whom thou wast at play?
Your eld'st acquaintance cannot be three hours:
Is she the goddess that hath sever'd us,
And brought us thus together?
Fer. Sir, she's mortal;
But, by immortal Providence, she's mine;
I chose her, when I could not ask my father
For his advice; nor thought I had one: she

Is daughter to this famous duke of Milan,
Of whom so often I have heard renown,
But never saw before; of whom I have
Received a second life, and second father
This lady makes him to me.
Alon. I am hers;
But O, how oddly will it sound, that I
Must ask my child forgiveness!
Pro. There, sir, stop:
Let us not burden our remembrances
With heaviness that's gone.
Gon. I have inly wept,
Or should have spoke ere this. Look down, you gods,
And on this couple drop a blessed crown;
For it is you, that have chalk'd forth the way
Which brought us hither!
Alon. I say, Amen, Gonzalo!
Gon. Was Milan thrust from Milan, that his issue
Should become kings of Naples? O, rejoice
Beyond a common joy; and set it down
With gold on lasting pillars: In one voyage
Did Claribel her husband find at Tunis;
And Ferdinand, her brother, found a wife
Where he himself was lost; Prospero his dukedom,
In a poor isle; and all of us, ourselves,
When no man was his own.
Alon. Give me your hands: [*To* FER. *and* MIRA.
Let grief and sorrow still embrace his heart,
That doth not wish you joy!
Gon. Be't so! Amen!

Re-enter ARIEL, *with the* Master *and* Boatswain *amazedly following.*

O look, sir, look, sir! here are more of us!
I prophesied, if a gallows were on land,
This fellow could not drown:—Now, blasphemy,
That swear'st grace o'erboard, not an oath on shore?
Hast thou no mouth by land? What is the news?
Boats. The best news is, that we have safely found
Our king, and company: the next our ship,—
Which, but three glasses since, we gave out split,—
Is tight and yare, and bravely rigg'd, as when
We first put out to sea.
Ari. Sir, all this service
Have I done since I went. [*Aside.*
Pro. My tricksy spirit!
Alon. These are not natural events; they strengthen,
From strange to stranger:—Say, how came you hither?
Boats. If I did think, sir, I were well awake,
I'd strive to tell you. We were dead of sleep,
And (how, we know not,) all clapp'd under hatches,
Where, but even now, with strange and several noises
Of roaring, shrieking, howling, gingling chains,
And more diversity of sounds, all horrible,
We were awak'd; straightway at liberty:
Where we, in all her trim, freshly beheld
Our royal, good, and gallant ship; our master
Cap'ring to eye her: On a trice, so please you,
Even in a dream, were we divided from them,
And were brought moping hither.
Ari. Was't well done? [*Aside.*
Pro. Bravely, my diligence. Thou shalt be free.
Alon. This is as strange a maze as e'er men trod:
And there is in this business more than nature
Was ever conduct of: some oracle
Must rectify our knowledge.
Pro. Sir, my liege,
Do not infest your mind with beating on
The strangeness of this business: at pick'd leisure,
Which shall be shortly, single I'll resolve you
(Which to you shall seem probable) of every
These happen'd accidents: till when, be cheerful,
And think of each thing well.—Come hither, spirit; [*Aside.*
Set Caliban and his companions free:
Untie the spell. [*Exit* ARIEL.] How fares my gracious sir?
There are yet missing of your company
Some few odd lads, that you remember not.

Re-enter ARIEL, *driving in* CALIBAN, STEPHANO, *and* TRINCULO, *in their stolen apparel.*

Ste. Every man shift for all the rest, and let no man take care for himself; for all is but fortune:—Coragio, bully-monster, Coragio!
Trin. If these be true spies which I wear in my head, here's a goodly sight.
Cal. O Setebos, these be brave spirits, indeed!
How fine my master is! I am afraid
He will chastise me.
Seb. Ha, ha;
What things are these, my lord Antonio!
Will money buy them?
Ant. Very like; one of them
Is a plain fish, and, no doubt, marketable.
Pro. Mark but the badges of these men, my lords,
Then say, if they be true:—This mis-shapen knave,
His mother was a witch; and one so strong
That could control the moon, make flows and ebbs,
And deal in her command, without her power:
These three have robb'd me; and this demi-devil
(For he's a bastard one) had plotted with them
To take my life: two of these fellows you
Must know, and own; this thing of darkness I
Acknowledge mine.
Cal. I shall be pinch'd to death.
Alon. Is not this Stephano, my drunken butler?
Seb. He is drunk now: Where had he wine?
Alon. And Trinculo is reeling ripe: Where should they
Find this grand liquor that hath gilded them?—
How cam'st thou in this pickle?
Trin. I have been in such a pickle, since I saw you last, that, I fear me, will never out of my bones: I shall not fear fly-blowing.
Seb. Why, how now, Stephano?
Ste. O, touch me not; I am not Stephano, but a cramp.
Pro. You'd be king of the isle, sirrah?
Ste. I should have been a sore one then.
Alon. This is as strange a thing as e'er I look'd on. [*Pointing to* CALIBAN.
Pro. He is as disproportion'd in his manners,
As in his shape:—Go, sirrah to my cell;
Take with you your companions; as you look
To have my pardon, trim it handsomely.
Cal. Ay, that I will; and I'll be wise hereafter,
And seek for grace: What a thrice double ass
Was I, to take this drunkard for a god,
And worship this dull fool?
Pro. Go to; away!
Alon. Hence, and bestow your luggage where you found it.
Seb. Or stole it, rather.
[*Exeunt* CAL. STE. *and* TRIN.
Pro. Sir, I invite your highness, and your train,
To my poor cell: where you shall take your rest
For this one night; which (part of it) I'll waste
With such discourse, as I not doubt, shall make it
Go quick away: the story of my life,
And the particular accidents, gone by,
Since I came to this isle: And in the morn,
I'll bring you to your ship, and so to Naples,
Where I have hope to see the nuptial
Of these our dear-belov'd solemnized;
And thence retire me to my Milan, where
Every third thought shall be my grave.

Alon. I long
To hear the story of your life, which must
Take the ear strangely.
Pro. I'll deliver all;
And promise you calm seas, auspicious gales,
And sail so expeditious, that shall catch
Your royal fleet far off.—My Ariel,—chick,—
That is thy charge; then to the elements
Be free, and fare thou well!—[*Aside.*] Please you, draw near. [*Exeunt.*

EPILOGUE.

SPOKEN BY PROSPERO.

Now my charms are all o'erthrown,
And what strength I have's mine own,
Which is most faint: now, 'tis true,
I must be here confin'd by you,
Or sent to Naples: Let me not,
Since I have my dukedom got,
And pardon'd the deceiver, dwell
In this bare island, by your spell;
But release me from my bands,
With the help of your good hands.
Gentle breath of yours my sails
Must fill, or else my project fails,
Which was to please: Now I want
Spirits to enforce, art to enchant;
And my ending is despair,
Unless I be reliev'd by prayer;
Which pierces so, that it assaults
Mercy itself, and frees all faults.
As you from crimes would pardon'd be,
Let your indulgence set me free.

TWO GENTLEMEN OF VERONA.

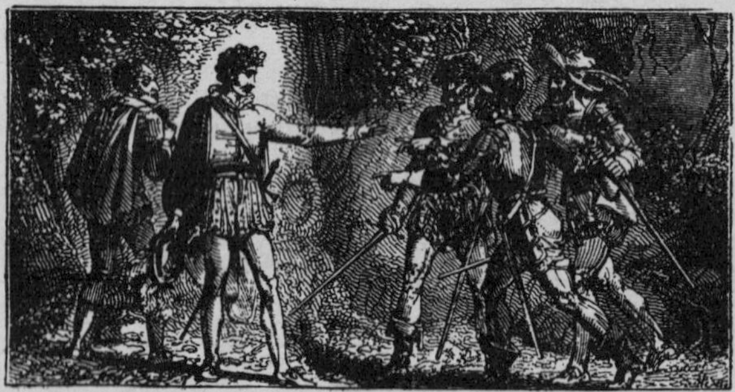

PERSONS REPRESENTED.

DUKE of MILAN, *Father to* Silvia.
VALENTINE, PROTEUS, } *Gentlemen of Verona.*
ANTONIO, *Father to* Proteus.
THURIO, *a foolish Rival to* Valentine.
EGLAMOUR, *Agent for* Silvia *in her escape.*
SPEED, *a clownish Servant to* Valentine.
LAUNCE, *Servant to* Proteus.
PANTHINO, *Servant to* Antonio.
Host, *where Julia lodges in Milan.*
Outlaws.

JULIA, *a Lady of Verona, beloved by* Proteus.
SILVIA, *the Duke's Daughter, beloved by Valentine.*
LUCETTA, *Waitingwoman to* Julia.

Servants, Musicians.

SCENE—*Sometimes in* VERONA; *sometimes in* MILAN; *and on the frontiers of* MANTUA.

ACT I.

SCENE I. *An open Place in Verona.*

Enter VALENTINE *and* PROTEUS.

Val. CEASE to persuade, my loving Proteus;
Home-keeping youth have ever homely wits:
Wer't not, affection chains thy tender days
To the sweet glances of thy honour'd love,
I rather would entreat thy company,
To see the wonders of the world abroad,
Than living dully sluggardiz'd at home,
Wear out thy youth with shapeless idleness.
But, since thou lov'st, love still, and thrive therein,
Even as I would, when I to love begin.
Pro. Wilt thou begone? Sweet Valentine, adieu!
Think on thy Proteus, when thou, haply, seest
Some rare note-worthy object in thy travel:
Wish me partaker in thy happiness,
When thou dost meet good hap; and, in thy danger,
If ever danger do environ thee,
Commend thy grievance to my holy prayers,
For I will be thy beadsman, Valentine.
Val. And on a love-book pray for my success.
Pro. Upon some book I love, I'll pray for thee.
Val. That's on some shallow story of deep love,
How young Leander cross'd the Hellespont.
Pro. That's a deep story of a deeper love;
For he was more than over shoes in love.
Val. 'Tis true; for you are over boots in love,
And yet you never swam the Hellespont.
Pro. Over the boots? nay, give me not the boots.
Val. No, I will not, for it boots thee not.
Pro. What?
Val. To be in love, where scorn is bought with groans;
Coy looks, with heart-sore sighs; one fading moment's mirth,

With twenty watchful, weary, tedious nights:
If haply won, perhaps a hapless gain;
If lost, why then a grievous labour won;
However, but a folly bought with wit,
Or else a wit by folly vanquished.

Pro. So, by your circumstance, you call me fool.

Val. So, by your circumstance, I fear, you'll prove.

Pro. 'Tis love you cavil at; I am not Love.

Val. Love is your master, for he masters you:
And he that is so yoked by a fool,
Methinks should not be chronicled for wise.

Pro. Yet writers say; As in the sweetest bud
The eating canker dwells, so eating love
Inhabits in the finest wits of all.

Val. And writers say, As the most forward bud
Is eaten by the canker ere it blow,
Even so by Love the young and tender wit
Is turn'd to folly; blasting in the bud,
Losing his verdure even in the prime,
And all the fair effects of future hopes.
But wherefore waste I time to counsel thee,
That art a votary to fond desire?
Once more adieu: my father at the road
Expects my coming, there to see me shipp'd.

Pro. And thither will I bring thee, Valentine.

Val. Sweet Proteus, no; now let us take our leave.
To Milan, let me hear from thee by letters,
Of thy success in love, and what news else
Betideth here in absence of thy friend;
And I likewise will visit thee with mine.

Pro. All happiness bechance to thee in Milan!

Val. As much to you at home! and so, farewell!
[*Exit* VALENTINE.

Pro. He after honour hunts, I after love.
He leaves his friends, to dignify them more;
I leave myself, my friends, and all for love.
Thou, Julia, thou hast metamorphos'd me;
Made me neglect my studies, lose my time,
War with good counsel, set the world at nought:
Made wit with musing weak, heart sick with thought.

Enter SPEED.

Speed. Sir Proteus, save you: Saw you my master?

Pro. But now he parted hence, to embark for Milan.

Speed. Twenty to one then, he is shipp'd already;
And I have play'd the sheep, in losing him.

Pro. Indeed a sheep doth very often stray,
An if the shepherd be a while away.

Speed. You conclude that my master is a shepherd then, and I a sheep?

Pro. I do.

Speed. Why then, my horns are his horns, whether I wake or sleep.

Pro. A silly answer, and fitting well a sheep.

Speed. This proves me still a sheep.

Pro. True; and thy master a shepherd.

Speed. Nay, that I can deny by a circumstance.

Pro. It shall go hard, but I'll prove it by another.

Speed. The shepherd seeks the sheep, and not the sheep the shepherd; but I seek my master, and my master seeks not me: therefore I am no sheep.

Pro. The sheep for fodder follow the shepherd, the shepherd for food follows not the sheep; thou for wages followest thy master, thy master for wages follows not thee: therefore thou art a sheep.

Speed. Such another proof will make me cry baa.

Pro. But dost thou hear? gav'st thou my letter to Julia?

Speed. Ay, sir; I, a lost mutton, gave your letter to her, a laced mutton; and she, a laced mutton, gave me, a lost mutton, nothing for my labour.

Pro. Here's too small a pasture for such a store of muttons.

Speed. If the ground be overcharged, you were best stick her.

Pro. Nay, in that you are astray; 'twere best pound you.

Speed. Nay, sir, less than a pound shall serve me for carrying your letter.

Pro. You mistake; I mean the pound, a pinfold.

Speed. From a pound to a pin? fold it over and over,
'Tis threefold too little for carrying a letter to your lover.

Pro. But what said she? did she nod.
[SPEED *nods*.

Speed. I.

Pro. Nod, I! why, that's noddy.

Speed. You mistook, sir; I say, she did nod: and you ask me, if she did nod; and I say, I.

Pro. And that set together is—noddy.

Speed. Now you have taken the pains to set it together, take it for your pains.

Pro. No, no, you shall have it for bearing the letter.

Speed. Well, I perceive I must be fain to bear with you.

Pro. Why, sir, how do you bear with me?

Speed. Marry, sir, the letter very orderly; having nothing but the word, noddy, for my pains.

Pro. Beshrew me, but you have a quick wit.

Speed. And yet it cannot overtake your slow purse.

Pro. Come, come, open the matter in brief: What said she?

Speed. Open your purse, that the money and the matter may be both at once delivered.

Pro. Well, sir, here is for your pains: What said she?

Speed. Truly, sir, I think you'll hardly win her.

Pro. Why? Could'st thou perceive so much from her?

Speed. Sir, I could perceive nothing at all from her; no, not so much as a ducat for delivering your letter: And being so hard to me that brought your mind, I fear she'll prove as hard to you in telling your mind. Give her no token but stones, for she's as hard as steel.

Pro. What, said she nothing?

Speed. No, not so much as—*take this for thy pains*. To testify your bounty, I thank you, you have testern'd me; in requital whereof, henceforth carry your letters yourself: and so, sir, I'll commend you to my master.

Pro. Go, go, begone, to save your ship from wreck;
Which cannot perish, having thee aboard,
Being destined to a drier death on shore:—
I must go send some better messenger;
I fear my Julia would not deign my lines,
Receiving them from such a worthless post.
[*Exeunt*.

SCENE II. *The same. Garden of* Julia's *House.*

Enter JULIA *and* LUCETTA.

Jul. But say, Lucetta, now we are alone,
Would'st thou then counsel me to fall in love?

Luc. Ay, madam; so you stumble not unheedfully.

Jul. Of all the fair resort of gentlemen,
That every day with parle encounter me,
In thy opinion, which is worthiest love?

Luc. Please you, repeat their names, I'll show my mind
According to my shallow simple skill.

Jul. What think'st thou of the fair Sir Eglamour?

Luc. As of a knight well-spoken, neat and fine;
But, were I you, he never should be mine.

Jul. What think'st thou of the rich Mercatio?

Luc. Well of his wealth; but of himself, so, so.

Jul. What think'st thou of the gentle Proteus?

Luc. Lord, lord! to see what folly reigns in us!

Jul. How now! what means this passion at his name?

Luc. Pardon, dear madam; 'tis a passing shame,
That I, unworthy body as I am,
Should censure thus on lovely gentlemen.

Jul. Why not on Proteus, as of all the rest?

Luc. Then thus,——of many good I think him best.

Jul. Your reason?

Luc. I have no other but a woman's reason;
I think him so, because I think him so.

Jul. And would'st thou have me cast my love on him?

Luc. Ay, if you thought your love not cast away.

Jul. Why, he of all the rest hath never mov'd me.

Luc. Yet he of all the rest, I think, best loves ye.

Jul. His little speaking shows his love but small.

Luc. Fire, that's closest kept, burns most of all.

Jul. They do not love that do not show their love.

Luc. O, they love least, that let men know their love.

Jul. I would, I knew his mind.

Luc. Peruse this paper, madam.

Jul. *To Julia.*—Say, from whom?

Luc. That the contents will show.

Jul. Say, say; who gave it thee?

Luc. Sir Valentine's page; and sent, I think, from Proteus:
He would have given it you, but I, being in the way,
Did in your name receive it; pardon the fault, I pray.

Jul. Now, by my modesty, a goodly broker!
Dare you presume to harbour wanton lines?
To whisper and conspire against my youth?
Now, trust me, 'tis an office of great worth,
And you an officer fit for the place.
There, take the paper, see it be return'd;
Or else return no more into my sight.

Luc. To plead for love deserves more fee than hate.

Jul. Will you be gone?

Luc. That you may ruminate. [*Exit.*

Jul. And yet, I would, I had o'erlook'd the letter.
It were a shame to call her back again,
And pray her to a fault for which I chid her.
What fool is she, that knows I am a maid,
And would not force the letter to my view!
Since maids, in modesty, say *No*, to that
Which they would have the profferer construe, *Ay*.
Fie, fie, how wayward is this foolish love,
That, like a testy babe, will scratch the nurse,
And presently, all humbled, kiss the rod!
How churlishly I chid Lucetta hence,
When willingly I would have had her here!
How angerly I taught my brow to frown,
When inward joy enforc'd my heart to smile!
My penance is, to call Lucetta back,
And ask remission for my folly past:—
What ho! Lucetta!

Re-enter LUCETTA.

Luc. What would your ladyship?

Jul. Is it near dinner time?

Luc. I would it were:
That you might kill your stomach on your meat,
And not upon your maid.

Jul. What is't you took up
So gingerly?

Luc. Nothing.

Jul. Why didst thou stoop then?

Luc. To take a paper up that I let fall.

Jul. And is that paper nothing?

Luc. Nothing concerning me.

Jul. Then let it lie for those that it concerns.

Luc. Madam, it will not lie where it concerns,
Unless it have a false interpreter.

Jul. Some love of your's hath writ to you in rhyme.

Luc. That I might sing it, madam, to a tune:
Give me a note: your ladyship can set.

Jul. As little by such toys as may be possible:
Best sing it to the tune of *Light o' love.*

Luc. It is too heavy for so light a tune.

Jul. Heavy? belike it hath some burden then.

Luc. Ay: and melodious were it, would you sing it.

Jul. And why not you?

Luc. I cannot reach so high.

Jul. Let's see your song:—How now, minion?

Luc. Keep tune there still, so you will sing it out:
And yet, methinks, I do not like this tune.

Jul. You do not?

Luc. No, madam; it is too sharp.

Jul. You, minion, are too saucy.

Luc. Nay, now you are too flat,
And mar the concord with too harsh a descant:
There wanteth but a mean to fill your song.

Jul. The mean is drown'd with your unruly base.

Luc. Indeed, I bid the base for Proteus.

Jul. This babble shall not henceforth trouble me.
Here is a coil with protestation!
[*Tears the letter.*
Go, get you gone; and let the papers lie:
You would be fingering them, to anger me.

Luc. She makes it strange; but she would be best pleas'd
To be so anger'd with another letter. [*Exit.*

Jul. Nay, 'would, I were so anger'd with the same!
O hateful hands, to tear such loving words!
Injurious wasps! to feed on such sweet honey,
And kill the bees, that yield it, with your stings!
I'll kiss each several paper for amends.
And here is writ—*kind Julia;*—unkind Julia!
As in revenge of thy ingratitude,
I throw thy name against the bruising stones,
Trampling contemptuously on thy disdain.
Look, here is writ—*love wounded Proteus;*—
Poor wounded name! my bosom, as a bed,
Shall lodge thee, till thy wound be throughly heal'd;
And thus I search it with a sovereign kiss.
But twice, or thrice, was Proteus written down:
Be calm, good wind, blow not a word away,
Till I have found each letter in the letter,
Except mine own name; that some whirlwind bear
Unto a ragged, fearful, hanging rock,
And throw it thence into the raging sea!
Lo, here in one line is his name twice writ,—
Poor forlorn Proteus, passionate Proteus,
To the sweet Julia;—that I'll tear away;
And yet I will not, sith so prettily
He couples it to his complaining names:
Thus will I fold them one upon another;
Now kiss, embrace, contend, do what you will.

Re-enter LUCETTA.

Luc. Madam,
Dinner is ready, and your father stays.

Jul. Well, let us go.

Luc. What, shall these papers lie like tell-tales here?

Jul. If you respect them, best to take them up.

Luc. Nay, I was taken up for laying them down:
Yet here they shall not lie, for catching cold.

Jul. I see you have a month's mind to them.

Luc. Ay, madam, you may say what sights you see;
I see things too, although you judge I wink.

Jul. Come, come, will't please you go?
[*Exeunt.*

SCENE III.

The same. A Room in Antonio's *House.*

Enter ANTONIO *and* PANTHINO.

Ant. Tell me, Panthino, what sad talk was that,
Wherewith my brother held you in the cloister?
Pant. 'Twas of his nephew, Proteus, your son.
Ant. Why, what of him?
Pant. He wonder'd, that your lordship
Would suffer him to spend his youth at home;
While other men, of slender reputation,
Put forth their sons to seek preferment out:
Some, to the wars, to try their fortune there;
Some, to discover islands far away;
Some, to the studious universities.
For any, or for all these exercises,
He said, that Proteus, your son, was meet;
And did request me, to importune you,
To let him spend his time no more at home,
Which would be great impeachment to his age,
In having known no travel in his youth.
Ant. Nor need'st thou much importune me to that
Whereon this month I have been hammering.
I have consider'd well his loss of time;
And how he cannot be a perfect man,
Not being try'd and tutor'd in the world:
Experience is by industry achiev'd,
And perfected by the swift course of time:
Then, tell me, whither were I best to send him?
Pant. I think, your lordship is not ignorant,
How his companion, youthful Valentine,
Attends the emperor in his royal court.
Ant. I know it well.
Pant. 'Twere good, I think, your lordship sent him thither:
There shall he practise tilts and tournaments,
Hear sweet discourse, converse with noblemen;
And be in eye of every exercise,
Worthy his youth and nobleness of birth.
Ant. I like thy counsel: well hast thou advised:
And, that thou may'st perceive how well I like it,
The execution of it shall make known;
Even with the speediest expedition
I will despatch him to the emperor's court.
Pant. To-morrow, may it please you, Don Alphonso,
With other gentlemen of good esteem,
Are journeying to salute the emperor,
And to commend their service to his will.
Ant. Good company; with them shall Proteus go:
And, in good time,—now will we break with him.

Enter PROTEUS.

Pro. Sweet love! sweet lines! sweet life!
Here is her hand, the agent of her heart:
Here is her oath for love, her honour's pawn:
O, that our fathers would applaud our loves,
To seal our happiness with their consents!
O heavenly Julia!
Ant. How now? what letter are you reading there?
Pro. May't please your lordship, 'tis a word or two
Of commendations sent from Valentine,
Deliver'd by a friend that came from him.
Ant. Lend me the letter; let me see what news.
Pro. There is no news, my lord; but that he writes
How happily he lives, how well belov'd
And daily graced by the emperor;
Wishing me with him, partner of his fortune.
Ant. And how stand you affected to his wish?
Pro. As one relying on your lordship's will,
And not depending on his friendly wish.
Ant. My will is something sorted with his wish;
Muse not that I thus suddenly proceed;
For what I will, I will, and there an end.
I am resolv'd, that thou shalt spend some time
With Valentinus in the emperor's court;
What maintenance he from his friends receives,
Like exhibition thou shalt have from me.
To-morrow be in readiness to go:
Excuse it not, for I am peremptory.
Pro. My lord, I cannot be so soon provided;
Please you, deliberate a day or two.
Ant. Look, what thou want'st, shall be sent after thee:
No more of stay; to-morrow thou must go.—
Come on, Panthino; you shall be employed
To hasten on his expedition.
[*Exeunt* ANT. *and* PANT.
Pro. Thus have I shunn'd the fire for fear of burning;
And drench'd me in the sea, where I am drown'd:
I fear'd to shew my father Julia's letter,
Lest he should take exceptions to my love;
And with the vantage of mine own excuse
Hath he excepted most against my love.
O, how this spring of love resembleth
The uncertain glory of an April day;
Which now shows all the beauty of the sun,
And by and by a cloud takes all away!

Re-enter PANTHINO.

Pant. Sir Proteus, your father calls for you;
He is in haste, therefore, I pray you go.
Pro. Why, this it is! my heart accords thereto;
And yet a thousand times it answers, no.
[*Exeunt.*

ACT II.

SCENE I. Milan. *A Room in the* Duke's *Palace.*

Enter VALENTINE *and* SPEED.

Speed. Sir, your glove.
Val. Not mine; my gloves are on.
Speed. Why then this may be yours, for this is but one.
Val. Ha! let me see: ay, give it me, it's mine:—
Sweet ornament that decks a thing divine!
Ah Silvia! Silvia!
Speed. Madam Silvia! madam Silvia!
Val. How now, sirrah?
Speed. She is not within hearing, sir.
Val. Why, sir, who bade you call her?
Speed. Your worship, sir; or else I mistook.
Val. Well, you'll still be too forward.
Speed. And yet I was last chidden for being too slow.
Val. Go to, sir; tell me, do you know madam Silvia?
Speed. She that your worship loves?
Val. Why, how know you that I am in love?

Speed. Marry, by these special marks: First, you have learned, like Sir Proteus, to wreath your arms like a male-content: to relish a love-song, like a robin-red-breast; to walk alone, like one that had the pestilence; to sigh, like a school-boy that had lost his A B C; to weep, like a young wench that had buried her grandam; to fast, like one that takes diet; to watch, like one that fears robbing; to speak puling, like a beggar at Hollowmas. You were wont, when you laugh'd, to crow like a cock; when you walked, to walk like one of the lions; when you fasted, it was presently after dinner; when you looked sadly, it was for want of money; and now you are metamorphosed with a mistress, that, when I look on you, I can hardly think you my master.

Val. Are all these things perceived in me?
Speed. They are all perceived without you.
Val. Without me? They cannot.

Speed. Without you! nay, that's certain, for, without you were so simple, none else would: but you are so without these follies, that these follies are within you, and shine through you like the water in an urinal; that not an eye, that sees you, but is a physician to comment on your malady.

Val. But, tell me, dost thou know my lady Silvia?

Speed. She that you gaze on so, as she sits at supper?

Val. Hast thou observed that? even she I mean.

Speed. Why, sir, I know her not.

Val. Dost thou know her by my gazing on her, and yet know'st her not?

Speed. Is she not hard-favour'd, sir?

Val. Not so fair, boy, as well favour'd.

Speed. Sir, I know that well enough.

Val. What dost thou know?

Speed. That she is not so fair, as (of you) well-favour'd.

Val. I mean, that her beauty is exquisite, but her favour infinite.

Speed. That's because the one is painted, and the other out of all count.

Val. How painted? and how out of count?

Speed. Marry, sir, so painted to make her fair, that no man counts of her beauty.

Val. How esteem'st thou me? I account of her beauty.

Speed. You never saw her since she was deformed.

Val. How long hath she been deform'd?

Speed. Ever since you loved her.

Val. I have loved her ever since I saw her; and still I see her beautiful.

Speed. If you love her, you cannot see her.

Val. Why?

Speed. Because love is blind. O, that you had mine eyes; or your own eyes had the lights they were wont to have, when you chid at Sir Proteus for going ungartered!

Val. What should I see then?

Speed. Your own present folly, and her passing deformity: for he, being in love, could not see to garter his hose; and you, being in love, cannot see to put on your hose.

Val. Belike, boy, then you are in love; for last morning you could not see to wipe my shoes.

Speed. True, sir; I was in love with my bed: I thank you, you swinged me for my love, which makes me the bolder to chide you for yours.

Val. In conclusion, I stand affected to her.

Speed. I would you were set, so, your affection would cease.

Val. Last night she enjoined me to write some lines to one she loves.

Speed. And have you?

Val. I have.

Speed. Are they not lamely writ?

Val. No, boy, but as well as I can do them:—
Peace, here she comes.

Enter SILVIA.

Speed. O excellent motion! O exceeding puppet! now will he interpret to her.

Val. Madam and mistress, a thousand good-morrows.

Speed. O, 'give you good even! here's a million of manners. [*Aside.*

Sil. Sir Valentine and servant, to you two thousand.

Speed. He should give her interest; and she gives it him.

Val. As you enjoin'd me, I have writ your letter,
Unto the secret nameless friend of yours;
Which I was much unwilling to proceed in,
But for my duty to your ladyship.

Sil. I thank you, gentle servant: 'tis very clerkly done.

Val. Now trust me, madam, it came hardly off;
For, being ignorant to whom it goes,
I writ at random, very doubtfully.

Sil. Perchance you think too much of so much pains?

Val. No, madam, so it stead you, I will write,
Please you command, a thousand times as much:
And yet,—

Sil. A pretty period! Well, I guess the sequel;
And yet I will not name it:—and yet I care not;—
And yet take this again;—and yet I thank you;
Meaning henceforth to trouble you no more.

Speed. And yet you will; and yet another yet. [*Aside.*

Val. What means your ladyship? do you not like it?

Sil. Yes, yes; the lines are very quaintly writ:
But since unwillingly, take them again;
Nay, take them.

Val. Madam, they are for you.

Sil. Ay, ay; you writ them, sir, at my request;
But I will none of them; they are for you:
I would have had them writ more movingly.

Val. Please you, I'll write your ladyship another.

Sil. And, when it's writ, for my sake read it over:
And, if it please you, so; if not, why, so.

Val. If it please me, madam! what then?

Sil. Why if it please you, take it for your labour;
And so good-morrow, servant. [*Exit* SILVIA.

Speed. O jest unseen, inscrutable, invisible,
As a nose on a man's face, or a weathercock on a steeple!
My master sues to her; and she hath taught her suitor,
He being her pupil, to become her tutor.
O excellent device! was there ever heard a better?
That my master, being scribe, to himself should write the letter?

Val. How now, sir? what are you reasoning with yourself?

Speed. Nay, I was rhyming; 'tis you that have the reason.

Val. To do what?

Speed. To be a spokesman from madam Silvia.

Val. To whom?

Speed. To yourself: why she woos you by a figure.

Val. What figure?

Speed. By a letter, I should say.

Val. Why, she hath not writ to me?

Speed. What need she, when she hath made you write to yourself? Why, do you not perceive the jest?

Val. No, believe me.

Speed. No believing you indeed, sir: But did you perceive her earnest?

Val. She gave me none, except an angry word.

Speed. Why, she hath given you a letter.

Val. That's the letter I writ to her friend.

Speed. And that letter hath she deliver'd, and there an end.

Val. I would, it were no worse.

Speed. I'll warrant you, 'tis as well:
For often have you writ to her; and she, in modesty,
Or else for want of idle time, could not again reply;
Or fearing else some messenger, that might her mind discover,
Herself hath taught her love himself to write unto her lover.
All this I speak in print; for in print I found it.—
Why muse you, sir? 'tis dinner-time.

Val. I have dined.

Speed. Ay, but hearken, sir; though the chameleon Love can feed on the air, I am one that am nourished by my victuals, and would fain have meat; O, be not like your mistress; be moved, be moved. [*Exeunt.*

SCENE II. Verona. *A Room in* Julia's *House.*

Enter PROTEUS *and* JULIA.

Pro. Have patience, gentle Julia.

Jul. I must, where is no remedy.

Pro. When possibly I can, I will return.

Jul. If you turn not, you will return the sooner:
Keep this remembrance for thy Julia's sake. [*Giving a ring.*

Pro. Why then we'll make exchange; here, take you this.

Jul. And seal the bargain with a holy kiss.
Pro. Here is my hand for my true constancy;
And when that hour o'er-slips me in the day,
Wherein I sigh not, Julia, for thy sake,
The next ensuing hour some foul mischance
Torment me for my love's forgetfulness!
My father stays my coming: answer not:
The tide is now: nay, not thy tide of tears;
That tide will stay me longer than I should;
[*Exit* JULIA.
Julia, farewell.—What! gone without a word!
Ay, so true love should do: it cannot speak;
For truth hath better deeds than words to grace it.

Enter PANTHINO.

Pant. Sir Proteus, you are staid for.
Pro. Go; I come, I come:—
Alas! this parting strikes poor lovers dumb.
[*Exeunt.*

SCENE III. *The same. A Street.*

Enter LAUNCE, *leading a Dog.*

Laun. Nay, 'twill be this hour ere I have done weeping; all the kind of the Launces have this very fault; I have received my proportion, like the prodigious son, and am going with sir Proteus to the Imperial's court. I think, Crab my dog be the sourest-natured dog that lives: my mother weeping, my father wailing, my sister crying, our maid howling, our cat wringing her hands, and all our house in a great perplexity, yet did not this cruel-hearted cur shed one tear: he is a stone, a very pebble stone, and has no more pity in him than a dog: a Jew would have wept to have seen our parting; why, my grandam having no eyes, look you, wept herself blind at my parting. Nay, I'll show you the manner of it: This shoe is my father:—no, this left shoe is my father;—no, no, this left shoe is my mother;—nay, that cannot be so neither;—yes, it is so, it is so; it hath the worser sole; This shoe, with the hole in it, is my mother; and this my father: A vengeance on't! there 'tis: now, sir, this staff is my sister; for, look you, she is as white as a lily, and as small as a wand: this hat is Nan, our maid; I am the dog:—no, the dog is himself, and I am the dog;—oh, the dog is me, and I am myself: Ay, so, so. Now come I to my father; *Father, your blessing;* now should not the shoe speak a word for weeping; now should I kiss my father; well, he weeps on:—now come I to my mother, (O that she could speak now!) like a wood woman;—well, I kiss her;—why there 'tis; here's my mother's breath up and down: now come I to my sister; mark the moan she makes: now the dog all this while sheds not a tear, nor speaks a word; but see how I lay the dust with my tears.

Enter PANTHINO.

Pan. Launce, away, away, aboard; thy master is shipped, and thou art to post after with oars. What's the matter? why weepest thou, man? Away, ass; you will lose the tide, if you tarry any longer.
Laun. It is no matter if the ty'd were lost; for it is the unkindest ty'd that ever any man ty'd.
Pan. What's the unkindest tide?
Laun. Why, he that's ty'd here; Crab, my dog.
Pan. Tut, man, I mean thou'lt lose the flood; and, in losing the flood, lose thy voyage; and, in losing thy voyage, lose thy master; and, in losing thy master, lose thy service; and, in losing thy service,—Why dost thou stop my mouth?
Laun. For fear thou should'st lose thy tongue.
Pan. Where should I lose my tongue?
Laun. In thy tale.
Pan. In thy tail?
Laun. Lose the tide, and the voyage, and the master, and the service: And the tide!—Why, man, if the river were dry, I am able to fill it with my tears; if the wind were down, I could drive the boat with my sighs.
Pan. Come, come away, man; I was sent to call thee.
Laun. Sir, call me what thou darest.
Pan. Wilt thou go?
Laun. Well, I will go. [*Exeunt.*

SCENE IV. Milan. *A Room in the* Duke's *Palace.*

Enter VALENTINE, SILVIA, THURIO, *and* SPEED

Sil. Servant—
Val. Mistress?
Speed. Master, Sir Thurio frowns on you.
Val. Ay, boy, it's for love.
Speed. Not of you.
Val. Of my mistress then.
Speed. 'Twere good you knocked him.
Sil. Servant, you are sad.
Val. Indeed, madam, I seem so.
Thu. Seem you that you are not?
Val. Haply, I do.
Thu. So do counterfeits.
Val. So do you.
Thu. What seem I, that I am not?
Val. Wise.
Thu. What instance of the contrary?
Val. Your folly.
Thu. And how quote you my folly?
Val. I quote it in your jerkin.
Thu. My jerkin is a doublet.
Val. Well, then, I'll double your folly.
Thu. How?
Sil. What, angry, Sir Thurio? do you change colour?
Val. Give him leave, madam; he is a kind of chameleon.
Thu. That hath more mind to feed on your blood, than live in your air.
Val. You have said, sir.
Thu. Ay, sir, and done too, for this time.
Val. I know it well, sir; you always end ere you begin.
Sil. A fine volley of words, gentlemen, and quickly shot off.
Val. 'Tis indeed, madam; we thank the giver.
Sil. Who is that, servant?
Val. Yourself, sweet lady; for you gave the fire: Sir Thurio borrows his wit from your ladyship's looks, and spends what he borrows, kindly in your company.
Thu. Sir, if you spend word for word with me, I shall make your wit bankrupt.
Val. I know it well, sir: you have an exchequer of words, and, I think, no other treasure to give your followers; for it appears by their bare liveries, that they live by your bare words.
Sil. No more, gentlemen, no more; here comes my father.

Enter DUKE.

Duke. Now, daughter Silvia, you are hard beset.
Sir Valentine, your father's in good health:
What say you to a letter from your friends
Of much good news?
Val. My lord, I will be thankful
To any happy messenger, from thence.
Duke. Know you Don Antonio, your countryman?
Val. Ay, my good lord, I know the gentleman
To be of worth, and worthy estimation,
And not without desert so well reputed.
Duke. Hath he not a son?
Val. Ay, my good lord; a son, that well deserves
The honour and regard of such a father.
Duke. You know him well?
Val. I knew him as myself; for from our infancy
We have convers'd, and spent our hours together:
And though myself have been an idle truant,
Omitting the sweet benefit of time,

To clothe mine age with angel-like perfection;
Yet hath Sir Proteus, for that's his name,
Made use and fair advantage of his days;
His years but young, but his experience old;
His head unmellow'd, but his judgment ripe;
And, in a word, (for far behind his worth
Come all the praises that I now bestow),
He is complete in feature, and in mind,
With all good grace to grace a gentleman.

Duke. Beshrew me, sir, but, if he make this good,
He is as worthy for an empress' love,
As meet to be an emperor's counsellor.
Well, sir; this gentleman is come to me,
With commendation from great potentates;
And here he means to spend his time a while:
I think, 'tis no unwelcome news to you.

Val. Should I have wish'd a thing, it had been he.

Duke. Welcome him then according to his worth.
Silvia, I speak to you; and you, Sir Thurio:—
For Valentine, I need not 'cite him to it:
I'll send him hither to you presently. [*Exit Duke.*

Val. This is the gentleman, I told your ladyship,
Had come along with me, but that his mistress
Did hold his eyes lock'd in her crystal looks.

Sil. Belike, that now she hath enfranchis'd them
Upon some other pawn for fealty.

Val. Nay, sure, I think, she holds them prisoners still.

Sil. Nay, then he should be blind; and, being blind,
How could he see his way to seek out you?

Val. Why, lady, love hath twenty pair of eyes.

Thu. They say, that love hath not an eye at all.

Val. To see such lovers, Thurio, as yourself;
Upon a homely object love can wink.

Enter PROTEUS.

Sil. Have done, have done; here comes the gentleman.

Val. Welcome, dear Proteus!—Mistress, I beseech you,
Confirm his welcome with some special favour.

Sil. His worth is warrant for his welcome hither,
If this be he you oft have wish'd to hear from.

Val. Mistress, it is: sweet lady, entertain him
To be my fellow-servant to your ladyship.

Sil. Too low a mistress for so high a servant.

Pro. Not so, sweet lady; but too mean a servant
To have a look of such a worthy mistress.

Val. Leave off discourse of disability:—
Sweet lady, entertain him for your servant.

Pro. My duty will I boast of, nothing else.

Sil. And duty never yet did want his meed;
Servant, you are welcome to a worthless mistress.

Pro. I'll die on him that says so, but yourself.

Sil. That you are welcome?

Pro. No; that you are worthless.

Enter Servant.

Ser. Madam, my lord your father would speak with you.

Sil. I'll wait upon his pleasure. [*Exit* Serv.
Come, Sir Thurio,
Go with me:—Once more, new servant, welcome:
I'll leave you to confer of home affairs;
When you have done, we look to hear from you.

Pro. We'll both attend upon your ladyship.
[*Exeunt* SILVIA, THURIO, *and* SPEED.

Val. Now, tell me, how do all from whence you came?

Pro. Your friends are well, and have them much commended.

Val. And how do yours?

Pro. I left them all in health.

Val. How does your lady? and how thrives your love?

Pro. My tales of love were wont to weary you;
I know you joy not in a love-discourse.

Val. Ay, Proteus, but that life is alter'd now;
I have done penance for contemning love;
Whose high imperious thoughts have punish'd me
With bitter fasts, with penitential groans,
With nightly tears, and daily heart-sore sighs;
For, in revenge of my contempt of love,
Love hath chas'd sleep from my enthralled eyes,
And made them watchers of mine own heart's sorrow.
O, gentle Proteus, love's a mighty lord;
And hath so humbled me, as, I confess,
There is no woe to his correction.
Nor, to his service, no such joy on earth!
Now, no discourse, except it be of love;
Now can I break my fast, dine, sup, and sleep,
Upon the very naked name of love.

Pro. Enough; I read your fortune in your eye:
Was this the idol that you worship so?

Val. Even she; and is she not a heavenly saint?

Pro. No; but she's an earthly paragon.

Val. Call her divine.

Pro. I will not flatter her.

Val. O, flatter me; for love delights in praises.

Pro. When I was sick, you gave me bitter pills;
And I must minister the like to you.

Val. Then speak the truth by her; if not divine,
Yet let her be a principality,
Sovereign to all the creatures on the earth.

Pro. Except my mistress.

Val. Sweet, except not any,
Except thou wilt except against my love.

Pro. Have I not reason to prefer mine own?

Val. And I will help thee to prefer her too:
She shall be dignified with this high honour,—
To bear my lady's train; lest the base earth
Should from her vesture chance to steal a kiss,
And, of so great a favour growing proud,
Disdain to root the summer-swelling flower,
And make rough winter everlastingly.

Pro. Why, Valentine, what braggardism is this?

Val. Pardon me, Proteus: all I can, is nothing
To her, whose worth makes other worthies nothing;
She is alone.

Pro. Then let her alone.

Val. Not for the world: why, man, she is mine own;
And I as rich in having such a jewel,
As twenty seas, if all their sand were pearl,
The water nectar, and the rocks pure gold.
Forgive me, that I do not dream on thee,
Because thou seest me dote upon my love.
My foolish rival, that her father likes,
Only for his possessions are so huge,
Is gone with her along; and I must after,
For love, thou know'st, is full of jealousy.

Pro. But she loves you?

Val. Ay, and we are betroth'd;
Nay, more, our marriage hour,
With all the cunning manner of our flight,
Determin'd of: how I must climb her window;
The ladder made of cords; and all the means
Plotted; and 'greed on, for my happiness.
Good Proteus, go with me to my chamber,
In these affairs to aid me with thy counsel.

Pro. Go on before; I shall inquire you forth:
I must unto the road, to disembark
Some necessaries that I needs must use;
And then I'll presently attend you.

Val. Will you make haste?

Pro. I will.— [*Exit* VAL.
Even as one heat another heat expels,
Or as one nail by strength drives out another,
So the remembrance of my former love
Is by a newer object quite forgotten.
Is it her mien, or Valentinus' praise,
Her true perfection, or my false transgression,
That makes me, reasonless, to reason thus?

She's fair; and so is Julia, that I love:
That I did love, for now my love is thaw'd;
Which, like a waxen image 'gainst a fire,
Bears no impression of the thing it was.
Methinks, my zeal to Valentine is cold;
And that I love him not, as I was wont:
O! but I love his lady too, too much;
And that's the reason I love him so little.
How shall I dote on her with more advice,
That thus without advice begin to love her?
'Tis but her picture I have yet beheld,
And that hath dazzled my reason's light;
But when I look on her perfections,
There is no reason but I shall be blind.
If I can check my erring love, I will;
If not, to compass her I'll use my skill. [*Exit.*

SCENE V. *The same. A Street.*

Enter SPEED *and* LAUNCE.

Speed. Launce! by mine honesty, welcome to Milan.

Laun. Forswear not thyself, sweet youth; for I am not welcome. I reckon this always—that a man is never undone, till he be hanged; nor never welcome to a place, till some certain shot be paid, and the hostess say, welcome.

Speed. Come on, you mad-cap, I'll to the alehouse with you presently; where, for one shot of five pence thou shalt have five thousand welcomes. But, sirrah, how did thy master part with madam Julia?

Laun. Marry, after they closed in earnest, they parted very fairly in jest.

Speed. But shall she marry him?

Laun. No.

Speed. How then? shall he marry her?

Laun. No, neither.

Speed. What, are they broken?

Laun. No, they are both as whole as a fish.

Speed. Why then, how stands the matter with them?

Laun. Marry, thus; when it stands well with him, it stands well with her.

Speed. What an ass art thou! I understand thee not.

Laun. What a block art thou, that thou canst not?
My staff understands me.

Speed. What thou say'st?

Laun. Ay, and what I do too: look thee, I'll but lean, and my staff understands me.

Speed. It stands under thee, indeed.

Laun. Why, stand under and understand is all one.

Speed. But tell me true, will't be a match?

Laun. Ask my dog: if he say, ay, it will; if he say, no, it will; if he shake his tail, and say nothing, it will.

Speed. The conclusion is then, that it will.

Laun. Thou shalt never get such a secret from me, but by a parable.

Speed. 'Tis well that I get it so. But, Launce, how say'st thou, that my master is become a notable lover?

Laun. I never knew him otherwise.

Speed. Than how?

Laun. A notable lubber, as thou reportest him to be.

Speed. Why, thou whoreson ass, thou mistakest me.

Laun. Why, fool, I meant not thee; I meant thy master.

Speed. I tell thee, my master is become a hot lover.

Laun. Why, I tell thee, I care not though he burn himself in love. If thou wilt go with me to the alehouse, so; if not, thou art a Hebrew, a Jew, and not worth the name of a Christian.

Speed. Why?

Laun. Because thou hast not so much charity in thee, as to go to the ale with a Christian. Wilt thou go?

Speed. At thy service. [*Exeunt.*

SCENE VI. *The same. An Apartment in the Palace*

Enter PROTEUS.

Pro. To leave my Julia, shall I be forsworn;
To love fair Silvia, shall I be forsworn;
To wrong my friend, I shall be much forsworn;
And even that power, which gave me first my oath,
Provokes me to this threefold perjury.
Love bade me swear, and love bids me forswear:
O sweet suggesting love, if thou hast sinn'd,
Teach me, thy tempted subject, to excuse it.
At first I did adore a twinkling star,
But now I worship a celestial sun.
Unheedful vows may heedfully be broken;
And he wants wit, that wants resolved will
To learn his wit to exchange the bad for better.—
Fie, fie, unreverend tongue! to call her bad,
Whose sovereignty so oft thou hast preferr'd
With twenty thousand soul-confirming oaths.
I cannot leave to love, and yet I do;
But there I leave to love, where I should love.
Julia I lose, and Valentine I lose;
If I keep them, I needs must lose myself;
If I lose them, thus find I by their loss,
For Valentine, myself; For Julia, Silvia.
I to myself am dearer than a friend;
For love is still most precious in itself:
And Silvia, witness heaven, that made her fair!
Shews Julia but a swarthy Ethiope.
I will forget that Julia is alive,
Rememb'ring that my love to her is dead;
And Valentine I'll hold an enemy,
Aiming at Silvia as a sweeter friend.
I cannot now prove constant to myself,
Without some treachery used to Valentine:—
This night, he meaneth with a corded ladder
To climb celestial Silvia's chamber-window;
Myself in counsel, his competitor:
Now presently I'll give her father notice
Of their disguising, and pretended flight;
Who, all enrag'd, will banish Valentine;
For Thurio, he intends, shall wed his daughter:
But, Valentine being gone, I'll quickly cross,
By some sly trick, blunt Thurio's dull proceeding.
Love, lend me wings to make my purpose swift,
As thou hast lent me wit to plot this drift! [*Exit.*

SCENE VII. Verona. *A Room in* Julia's *House.*

Enter JULIA *and* LUCETTA.

Jul. Counsel, Lucetta; gentle girl, assist me!
And, e'en in kind love, I do conjure thee,—
Who art the table wherein all my thoughts
Are visibly character'd and engrav'd,—
To lesson me; and tell me some good mean,
How, with my honour, I may undertake
A journey to my loving Proteus.

Luc. Alas! the way is wearisome and long.

Jul. A true-devoted pilgrim is not weary
To measure kingdoms with his feeble steps;
Much less shall she, that hath love's wings to fly;
And when the flight is made to one so dear,
Of such divine perfection, as Sir Proteus.

Luc. Better forbear, till Proteus make return.

Jul. O, know'st thou not, his looks are my soul's food?
Pity the dearth that I have pined in,
By longing for that food so long a time.
Didst thou but know the inly touch of love,
Thou would'st as soon go kindle fire with snow,
As seek to quench the fire of love with words.

Luc. I do not seek to quench your love's hot fire;
But qualify the fire's extreme rage,
Lest it should burn above the bounds of reason.

Jul. The more thou dam'st it up, the more it burns;
The current, that with gentle murmur glides,
Thou know'st, being stopp'd, impatiently doth rage;
But, when his fair course is not hindered,
He makes sweet musick with th' enamel'd stones,

Giving a gentle kiss to every sedge
He overtaketh in his pilgrimage;
And so by many winding nooks he strays,
With willing sport to the wild ocean.
Then let me go, and hinder not my course:
I'll be as patient as a gentle stream,
And make a pastime of each weary step,
Till the last step have brought me to my love;
And there I'll rest, as, after much turmoil,
A blessed soul doth in Elysium.

Luc. But in what habit will you go along?

Jul. Not like a woman; for I would prevent
The loose encounters of lascivious men:
Gentle Lucetta, fit me with such weeds
As may beseem some well reputed page.

Luc. Why then your ladyship must cut your hair.

Jul. No, girl; I'll knit it up in silken strings,
With twenty odd-conceited true-love knots:
To be fantastic may become a youth
Of greater time than I shall show to be.

Luc. What fashion, madam, shall I make your breeches?

Jul. That fits as well, as—"tell me, good my lord,
"What compass will you wear your farthingale?"
Why, even what fashion thou best lik'st, Lucetta.

Luc. You must needs have them with a cod-piece, madam.

Jul. Out, out, Lucetta; that will be ill favour'd.

Luc. A round hose, madam, now's not worth a pin,
Unless you have a cod-piece to stick pins on.

Jul. Lucetta, as thou lovest me, let me have
What thou think'st meet, and is most mannerly:
But tell me, wench, how will the world repute me,
For undertaking so unstaid a journey?
I fear me, it will make me scandaliz'd.

Luc. If you think so, then stay at home, and go not.

Jul. Nay, that I will not.

Luc. Then never dream on infamy, but go.
If Proteus like your journey, when you come,
No matter who's displeas'd, when you are gone:
I fear me, he will scarce be pleas'd withal.

Jul. That is the least, Lucetta, of my fear:
A thousand oaths, an ocean of his tears,
And instances of infinite of love,
Warrant me welcome to my Proteus.

Luc. All these are servants to deceitful men.

Jul. Base men, that use them to so base effect!
But truer stars did govern Proteus' birth:
His words are bonds, his oaths are oracles;
His love sincere, his thoughts immaculate;
His tears, pure messengers sent from his heart;
His heart as far from fraud, as heaven from earth.

Luc. Pray heaven, he prove so, when you come to him!

Jul. Now, as thou lov'st me, do him not that wrong,
To bear a hard opinion of his truth;
Only deserve my love, by loving him;
And presently go with me to my chamber,
To take a note of what I stand in need of,
To furnish me upon my longing journey.
All that is mine I leave at thy dispose,
My goods, my lands, my reputation;
Only, in lieu thereof despatch me hence;
Come, answer not, but to it presently;
I am impatient of my tarriance. [*Exeunt.*

ACT III.

SCENE I.

Milan. *An Anti-room in the* Duke's *Palace.*

Enter DUKE, THURIO, *and* PROTEUS.

Duke. Sir Thurio, give us leave, I pray, awhile;
We have some secrets to confer about.——
[*Exit* THURIO.
Now, tell me, Proteus, what's your will with me?

Pro. My gracious lord, that which I would discover,
The law of friendship bids me to conceal:
But, when I call to mind your gracious favours
Done to me, undeserving as I am,
My duty pricks me on to utter that
Which else no worldly good should draw from me.
Know, worthy prince, Sir Valentine, my friend,
This night intends to steal away your daughter;
Myself am one made privy to the plot.
I know you have determined to bestow her
On Thurio, whom your gentle daughter hates;
And should she thus be stolen away from you,
It would be much vexation to your age.
Thus, for my duty's sake, I rather chose
To cross my friend in his intended drift,
Than, by concealing it, heap on your head
A pack of sorrows, which would press you down,
Being unprevented, to your timeless grave.

Duke. Proteus, I thank thee for thine honest care;
Which to requite, command me while I live.
This love of theirs myself have often seen,
Haply, when they have judged me fast asleep;
And oftentimes have purpos'd to forbid
Sir Valentine her company, and my court:
But, fearing lest my jealous aim might err,
And so unworthily disgrace the man,
(A rashness that I ever yet have shunn'd),
I gave him gentle looks; thereby to find
That which thyself hast now disclos'd to me.
And, that thou may'st perceive my fear of this,
Knowing that tender youth is soon suggested,
I nightly lodge her in an upper tower,
The key whereof myself have ever kept;
And thence she cannot be convey'd away.

Pro. Know, noble lord, they have devised a mean
How he her chamber-window will ascend,
And with a corded ladder fetch her down;
For which the youthful lover now is gone,
And this way comes he with it presently;
Where, if it please you, you may intercept him.
But, good my lord, do it so cunningly,
That my discovery be not aimed at;
For love of you, not hate unto my friend,
Hath made me publisher of this pretence.

Duke. Upon mine honour, he shall never know
That I had any light from thee of this.

Pro. Adieu, my lord; Sir Valentine is coming.
[*Exit.*

Enter VALENTINE.

Duke. Sir Valentine, whither away so fast?

Val. Please it your grace there is a messenger
That stays to bear my letters to my friends,
And I am going to deliver them.

Duke. Be they of much import?

Val. The tenor of them doth but signify
My health, and happy being at your court.

Duke. Nay, then no matter; stay with me a while;
I am to break with thee of some affairs,
That touch me near, wherein thou must be secret.
'Tis not unknown to thee that I have sought
To match my friend, Sir Thurio, to my daughter.

Val. I know it well, my lord; and, sure, the match
Were rich and honourable; besides, the gentleman
Is full of virtue, bounty, worth, and qualities
Beseeming such a wife as your fair daughter:
Cannot your grace win her to fancy him?

Duke. No, trust me; she is peevish, sullen, froward,
Proud, disobedient, stubborn, lacking duty;
Neither regarding that she is my child,
Nor fearing me as if I were her father:
And, may I say to thee, this pride of hers,
Upon advice, hath drawn my love from her;
And, where I thought the remnant of mine age
Should have been cherish'd by her childlike duty,

I now am full resolv'd to take a wife,
And turn her out to who will take her in:
Then let her beauty be her wedding-dower;
For me and my possessions she esteems not.

Val. What would your grace have me to do in this?

Duke. There is a lady, sir, in Milan, here,
Whom I affect; but she is nice, and coy,
And nought esteems my aged eloquence:
Now, therefore, would I have thee to my tutor,
(For long agone I have forgot to court:
Besides, the fashion of the time is chang'd);
How, and which way, I may bestow myself,
To be regarded in her sun-bright eye.

Val. Win her with gifts, if she respect not words;
Dumb jewels often, in their silent kind,
More than quick words, do move a woman's mind.

Duke. But she did scorn a present that I sent her.

Val. A woman sometimes scorns what best contents her:
Send her another; never give her o'er;
For scorn at first makes after-love the more.
If she do frown, 'tis not in hate of you,
But rather to beget more love in you:
If she do chide, 'tis not to have you gone;
For why, the fools are mad if left alone.
Take no repulse, whatever she doth say:
For, *get you gone*, she doth not mean, *away;*
Flatter, and praise, commend, extol their graces,
Though ne'er so black, say, they have angels' faces.
That man that hath a tongue, I say, is no man,
If with his tongue he cannot win a woman.

Duke. But she, I mean, is promis'd by her friends
Unto a youthful gentleman of worth;
And kept severely from resort of men,
That no man hath access by day to her.

Val. Why then I would resort to her by night.

Duke. Ay, but the doors be lock'd, and keys kept safe,
That no man hath recourse to her by night.

Val. What lets, but one may enter at her window?

Duke. Her chamber is aloft, far from the ground;
And built so shelving that one cannot climb it
Without apparent hazard of his life.

Val. Why then, a ladder quaintly made of cords,
To cast up with a pair of anchoring hooks,
Would serve to scale another Hero's tower,
So bold Leander would adventure it.

Duke. Now, as thou art a gentleman of blood,
Advise me where I may have such a ladder.

Val. When would you use it? pray, sir, tell me that.

Duke. This very night; for love is like a child,
That longs for every thing that he can come by.

Val. By seven o'clock I'll get you such a ladder.

Duke. But, hark thee; I will go to her alone;
How shall I best convey the ladder thither?

Val. It will be light, my lord, that you may bear it
Under a cloak that is of any length.

Duke. A cloak as long as thine will serve the turn?

Val. Ay, my good lord.

Duke. Then let me see thy cloak;
I'll get me one of such another length.

Val. Why, any cloak will serve the turn, my lord.

Duke. How shall I fashion me to wear a cloak?—
I pray thee, let me feel thy cloak upon me.—
What letter is this same? What's here?—*To Silvia!*
And here an engine fit for my proceeding?
I'll be so bold to break the seal for once. [*reads.*

My thoughts do harbour with my Silvia nightly:
And slaves they are to me that send them flying:
O, could their master come and go as lightly,
Himself would lodge where senseless they are lying.
My herald thoughts in thy pure bosom rest them;
While I, their king, that thither them importune,
Do curse the grace that with such grace hath bless'd them,
Because myself do want my servants' fortune:
I curse myself, for they are sent by me,
That they should harbour where their lord should be.
What's here?
Silvia, this night I will enfranchise thee!
'Tis so; and here's the ladder for the purpose.—
Why, Phaeton (for thou art Merop's son,)
Wilt thou aspire to guide the heavenly car,
And with thy daring folly burn the world?
Wilt thou reach stars because they shine on thee?
Go, base intruder! over-weening slave!
Bestow thy fawning smiles on equal mates:
And think, my patience, more than thy desert,
Is privilege for thy departure hence:
Thank me for this, more than for all the favours
Which, all too much, I have bestow'd on thee.
But if thou linger in my territories
Longer than swiftest expedition
Will give thee time to leave our royal court,
By heaven, my wrath shall far exceed the love
I ever bore my daughter, or thyself.
Begone, I will not hear thy vain excuse,
But, as thou lov'st thy life, make speed from hence. [*Exit* DUKE.

Val. And why not death, rather than living torment?
To die, is to be banish'd from myself;
And Silvia is myself: banish'd from her,
Is self from self; a deadly banishment!
What light is light, if Silvia be not seen?
What joy is joy, if Silvia be not by?
Unless it be to think that she is by,
And feed upon the shadow of perfection,
Except I be by Silvia in the night,
There is no music in the nightingale;
Unless I look on Silvia in the day,
There is no day for me to look upon:
She is my essence; and I leave to be,
If I be not by her fair influence
Foster'd, illumin'd, cherish'd, kept alive.
I fly not death, to fly his deadly doom;
Tarry I here, I but attend on death;
But, fly I hence, I fly away from life.

Enter PROTEUS *and* LAUNCE.

Pro. Run, boy, run, run, and seek him out.

Laun. So-ho! so-ho!

Pro. What seest thou?

Laun. Him we go to find; there's not a hair on's head, but 'tis a Valentine.

Pro. Valentine?

Val. No.

Pro. Who then? his spirit?

Val. Neither.

Pro. What then?

Val. Nothing.

Laun. Can nothing speak? master, shall I strike?

Pro. Whom wouldst thou strike?

Laun. Nothing.

Pro. Villain, forbear.

Laun. Why, sir, I'll strike nothing: I pray you—

Pro. Sirrah, I say, forbear: Friend Valentine, a word.

Val. My ears are stopp'd, and cannot hear good news,
So much of bad already hath possess'd them,

Pro. Then in dumb silence will I bury mine,
For they are harsh, untunable, and bad.

Val. Is Silvia dead?

Pro. No, Valentine.

Val. No Valentine, indeed, for sacred Silvia!—
Hath she forsworn me?

Pro. No, Valentine,

Val. No Valentine, if Silvia have forsworn me!—
What is your news?
Laun. Sir, there's a proclamation that you are vanish'd.
Pro. That thou art banished, O, that's the news:
From hence, from Silvia, and from me, thy friend.
Val. O, I have fed upon this woe already,
And now excess of it will make me surfeit.
Doth Silvia know that I am banished?
Pro. Ay, ay; and she hath offer'd to the doom,
(Which, unrevers'd, stands in effectual force,)
A sea of melting pearl, which some call tears:
Those at her father's churlish feet she tender'd;
With them, upon her knees, her humble self;
Wringing her hands, whose whiteness so became them,
As if but now they waxed pale for woe:
But neither bended knees, pure hands held up,
Sad sighs, deep groans, nor silver-shedding tears,
Could penetrate her uncompassionate sire;
But Valentine, if he be ta'en, must die.
Besides, her intercession chaf'd him so
When she for thy repeal was suppliant,
That to close prison he commanded her,
With many bitter threats of 'biding there.
Val. No more; unless the next word that thou speak'st,
Have some malignant pow'r upon my life:
If so, I pray thee, breathe it in mine ear,
As ending anthem of my endless dolour.
Pro. Cease to lament for that thou canst not help,
And study help for that which thou lament'st.
Time is the nurse and breeder of all good.
Here if thou stay, thou canst not see thy love;
Besides, thy staying will abridge thy life.
Hope is a lover's staff; walk hence with that,
And manage it against despairing thoughts.
Thy letters may be here, though thou art hence;
Which, being writ to me, shall be deliver'd
Even in the milk-white bosom of thy love.
The time now serves not to expostulate:
Come, I'll convey thee through the city gate;
And, ere I part with thee, confer at large
Of all that may concern thy love affairs:
As thou lov'st Silvia, though not for thyself,
Regard thy danger, and along with me.
Val. I pray thee, Launce, an if thou seest my boy,
Bid him make haste, and meet me at the north gate.
Pro. Go, sirrah, find him out. Come, Valentine.
Val. O my dear Silvia! hapless Valentine!
[*Exeunt* VALENTINE *and* PROTEUS.

Laun. I am but a fool, look you; and yet I have the wit to think, my master is a kind of a knave: but that's all one, if he be but one knave. He lives not now, that knows me to be in love: yet I am in love; but a team of horse shall not pluck that from me; nor who 'tis I love, and yet 'tis a woman: but what woman, I will not tell myself; and yet 'tis a milk-maid: yet 'tis not a maid, for she hath had gossips: yet 'tis a maid, for she is her master's maid, and serves for wages. She hath more qualities than a water-spaniel,—which is much in a bare christian. Here is the cate-log [*Pulling out a paper*] of her condition. Imprimis, *She can fetch and carry.* Why, a horse can do no more; nay, a horse cannot fetch, but only carry; therefore is she better than a jade. Item, *She can milk;* look you, a sweet virtue in a maid with clean hands.

Enter SPEED.

Speed. How now, signior Launce? what news with your mastership?
Laun. With my master's ship? why it is at sea.
Speed. Well, your old vice still, mistake the word:
What news then in your paper?
Laun. The blackest news that ever thou heard'st.
Speed. Why, man, how black?
Laun. Why, as black as ink.
Speed. Let me read them.
Laun. Fie on thee, jolt-head; thou canst not read.
Speed. Thou liest, I can.
Laun. I will try thee: Tell me this; Who begot thee?
Speed. Marry, the son of my grandfather.
Laun. O illiterate loiterer! it was the son of thy grandmother: this proves that thou canst not read.
Speed. Come, fool, come: try me in thy paper.
Laun. There: and saint Nicholas be thy speed!
Speed. Imprimis, *She can milk.*
Laun. Ay, that she can.
Speed. Item, *She brews good ale.*
Laun. And therefore comes the proverb,—Blessing of your heart, you brew good ale.
Speed. Item, *She can sew.*
Laun. That's as much as to say, can she so?
Speed. Item, *She can knit.*
Laun. What need a man care for a stock with a wench, when she can knit him a stock.
Speed. Item, *She can wash and scour.*
Laun. A special virtue; for then she need not be washed and scoured.
Speed. Item, *She can spin.*
Laun. Then may I set the world on wheels, when she can spin for her living.
Speed. Item, *She hath many nameless virtues.*
Laun. That's as much as to say, bastard virtues; that, indeed, know not their fathers, and therefore have no names.
Speed. *Here follow her vices.*
Laun. Close at the heels of her virtues.
Speed. Item, *She is not to be kissed fasting, in respect of her breath.*
Laun. Well, that fault may be mended with a breakfast: Read on.
Speed. Item, *She hath a sweet mouth.*
Laun. That makes amends for her sour breath.
Speed. Item, *She doth talk in her sleep.*
Laun. It's no matter for that, so she sleep not in her talk.
Speed. Item, *She is slow in words.*
Laun. O villain, that set this down among her vices! To be slow in words, is a woman's only virtue: I pray thee, out with't; and place it for her chief virtue.
Speed. Item, *She is proud.*
Laun. Out with that too; it was Eve's legacy, and cannot be ta'en from her.
Speed. Item, *She hath no teeth.*
Laun. I care not for that neither, because I love crusts.
Speed. Item, *She is curst.*
Laun. Well, the best is, she hath no teeth to bite.
Speed. Item, *She will often praise her liquor.*
Laun. If her liquor be good, she shall: if she will not, I will; for good things should be praised.
Speed. Item, *She is too liberal.*
Laun. Of her tongue she cannot; for that's writ down she is slow of: of her purse she shall not; for that I'll keep shut; now of another thing she may; and that cannot I help. Well, proceed.
Speed. Item, *She hath more hair than wit, and more faults than hairs, and more wealth than faults.*
Laun. Stop there; I'll have her; she was mine, and not mine, twice or thrice in that last article: Rehearse that once more.
Speed. Item, *She hath more hair than wit.*—
Laun. More hair than wit,—it may be; I'll prove it: The cover of the salt hides the salt, and therefore it is more than the salt; the hair that covers the wit, is more than the wit; for the greater hides the less. What's next?
Speed. *And more faults than hairs.*—
Laun. That's monstrous: O, that that were out!

Speed. *And more wealth than faults.*

Laun. Why, that word makes the faults gracious: Well, I'll have her: and if it be a match, as nothing is impossible,—

Speed. What then?

Laun. Why, then will I tell thee, that thy master stays for thee at the north-gate.

Speed. For me?

Laun. For thee! ay; who art thou? he hath staid for a better man than thee.

Speed. And must I go to him?

Laun. Thou must run to him, for thou hast staid so long, that going will scarce serve the turn.

Speed. Why didst not tell me sooner? 'pox of your love-letters! [*Exit.*

Laun. Now will he be swinged for reading my letter: An unmannerly slave, that will thrust himself into secrets! I'll after, to rejoice in the boy's correction. [*Exit.*

SCENE II.

The same. A Room in the Duke's *Palace.*

Enter DUKE *and* THURIO; PROTEUS *behind.*

Duke. Sir Thurio, fear not, but that she will love you,
Now Valentine is banish'd from her sight.

Thu. Since his exile she hath despised me most,
Forsworn my company, and rail'd at me,
That I am desperate of obtaining her.

Duke. This weak impress of love is as a figure
Trenched in ice; which with an hour's heat
Dissolves to water, and doth lose his form.
A little time will melt her frozen thoughts,
And worthless Valentine shall be forgot.—
How now, Sir Proteus? Is your countryman,
According to our proclamation, gone?

Pro. Gone, my good lord.

Duke. My daughter takes his going grievously.

Pro. A little time, my lord, will kill that grief.

Duke. So I believe; but Thurio thinks not so.—
Proteus, the good conceit I hold of thee,
(For thou hast shown some sign of good desert),
Makes me the better to confer with thee.

Pro. Longer than I prove loyal to your grace,
Let me not live to look upon your grace.

Duke. Thou know'st, how willingly I would effect
The match between Sir Thurio and my daughter.

Pro. I do, my lord.

Duke. And also, I think, thou art not ignorant
How she opposes her against my will.

Pro. She did, my lord, when Valentine was here.

Duke. Ay, and perversely she persevers so.
What might we do, to make the girl forget
The love of Valentine, and love Sir Thurio?

Pro. The best way is to slander Valentine
With falsehood, cowardice, and poor descent;
Three things that women highly hold in hate.

Duke. Ay, but she'll think that it is spoke in hate.

Pro. Ay, if his enemy deliver it:
Therefore it must, with circumstance, be spoken
By one, whom she esteemeth as his friend.

Duke. Then you must undertake to slander him.

Pro. And that, my lord, I shall be loath to do:
'Tis an ill office for a gentleman;
Especially against his very friend.

Duke. Where your good word cannot advantage him,
Your slander never can endamage him;
Therefore the office is indifferent,
Being entreated to it by your friend.

Pro. You have prevail'd, my lord: if I can do it,
By aught that I can speak in his dispraise,
She shall not long continue love to him.
But say, this weed her love from Valentine,
It follows not that she will love Sir Thurio.

Thu. Therefore, as you unwind her love from him,
Lest it should ravel, and be good to none,
You must provide to bottom it on me:
Which must be done, by praising me as much
As you in worth dispraise Sir Valentine.

Duke. And, Proteus, we dare trust you in this kind;
Because we know, on Valentine's report,
You are already love's firm votary,
And cannot soon revolt and change your mind.
Upon this warrant shall you have access,
Where you with Silvia may confer at large;
For she is lumpish, heavy, melancholy,
And, for your friend's sake, will be glad of you;
Where you may temper her, by your persuasion,
To hate young Valentine, and love my friend.

Pro. As much as I can do, I will effect:—
But you, Sir Thurio, are not sharp enough;
You must lay lime, to tangle her desires,
By wailful sonnets, whose composed rhymes
Should be full fraught with serviceable vows.

Duke. Ay, much is the force of heaven-bred poesy.

Pro. Say, that upon the altar of her beauty
You sacrifice your tears, your sighs, your heart:
Write till your ink be dry; and with your tears
Moist it again; and frame some feeling line,
That may discover such integrity:—
For Orpheus' lute was strung with poet's sinews;
Whose golden touch could soften steel and stones,
Make tigers tame, and huge leviathans
Forsake unsounded deeps to dance on sands.
After your dire-lamenting elegies,
Visit by night your lady's chamber window
With some sweet consort; to their instruments
Tune a deploring dump; the night's dead silence
Will well become such sweet complaining grievance.
This, or else nothing, will inherit her.

Duke. This discipline shews, thou hast been in love.

Thu. And thy advice this night I'll put in practice.
Therefore, sweet Proteus, my direction-giver,
Let us into the city presently
To sort some gentlemen well skill'd in musick:
I have a sonnet, that will serve the turn,
To give the onset to thy good advice.

Duke. About it, gentlemen.

Pro. We'll wait upon your grace till after supper:
And afterward determine our proceedings.

Duke. Even now about it; I will pardon you. [*Exeunt.*

ACT IV.

SCENE I. *A Forest, near* Mantua.

Enter certain Out-laws.

1 *Out.* Fellows, stand fast; I see a passenger.

2 *Out.* If there be ten, shrink not, but down with 'em.

Enter VALENTINE *and* SPEED.

3 *Out.* Stand, sir, and throw us that you have about you;
If not, we'll make you sit, and rifle you.

Speed. Sir, we are undone! these are the villains
That all the travellers do fear so much.

Val. My friends,—

1 *Out.* That's not so, sir; we are your enemies.

2 *Out.* Peace; we'll hear him.

3 *Out.* Ay, by my beard, will we; for he is a proper man.

Val. Then know, that I have little wealth to lose;
A man I am, cross'd with adversity:
My riches are these poor habiliments,
Of which if you should here disfurnish me,
You take the sum and substance that I have.

2 *Out.* Whither travel you?
Val. To Verona.
1 *Out.* Whence came you?
Val. From Milan.
3 *Out.* Have you long sojourned there?
Val. Some sixteen months; and longer might have staid,
If crooked fortune had not thwarted me.
1 *Out.* What, were you banish'd thence?
Val. I was.
2 *Out.* For what offence?
Val. For that which now torments me to rehearse:
I kill'd a man, whose death I much repent;
But yet I slew him manfully in fight,
Without false vantage, or base treachery.
1 *Out.* Why, ne'er repent it, if it were done so;
But were you banish'd for so small a fault?
Val. I was, and held me glad of such a doom.
1 *Out.* Have you the tongues?
Val. My youthful travel therein made me happy;
Or else I often had been miserable.
3 *Out.* By the bare scalp of Robin Hood's fat friar,
This fellow were a king for our wild faction.
1 *Out.* We'll have him; sirs, a word.
Speed. Master, be one of them;
It is an honourable kind of thievery.
Val. Peace, villain!
2 *Out.* Tell us this: Have you any thing to take to?
Val. Nothing but my fortune.
3 *Out.* Know, then, that some of us are gentlemen,
Such as the fury of ungovern'd youth
Thrust from the company of awful men:
Myself was from Verona banish'd,
For practising to steal away a lady,
An heir, and near allied unto the duke.
2 *Out.* And I from Mantua, for a gentleman,
Whom, in my mood, I stabbed unto the heart.
1 *Out.* And I, for such like petty crimes as these.
But to the purpose,—(for we cite our faults,
That they may hold excus'd our lawless lives,)
And, partly, seeing you are beautify'd
With goodly shape; and by your own report
A linguist; and a man of such perfection,
As we do in our quality much want;—
2 *Out.* Indeed, because you are a banish'd man,
Therefore, above the rest, we parley to you:
Are you content to be our general?
To make a virtue of necessity,
And live, as we do, in this wilderness?
3 *Out.* What say'st thou? wilt thou be of our consort?
Say ay, and be the captain of us all;
We'll do thee homage, and be rul'd by thee,
Love thee as our commander and our king.
1 *Out.* But if thou scorn our courtesy, thou diest.
2 *Out.* Thou shalt not live to brag what we have offer'd.
Val. I take your offer, and will live with you;
Provided that you do no outrages
On silly women, or poor passengers.
3 *Out.* No, we detest such vile base practices.
Come, go with us, we'll bring thee to our crews,
And shew thee all the treasure we have got;
Which, with ourselves, all rest at thy dispose.
[*Exeunt.*

SCENE II. Milan. *Court of the Palace.*

Enter PROTEUS.

Pro. Already have I been false to Valentine,
And now I must be as unjust to Thurio.
Under the colour of commending him,
I have access my own love to prefer;
But Silvia is too fair, too true, too holy,
To be corrupted with my worthless gifts.
When I protest true loyalty to her,
She twits me with my falsehood to my friend;
When to her beauty I commend my vows,
She bids me think, how I have been forsworn
In breaking faith with Julia whom I lov'd:
And, notwithstanding all her sudden quips,
The least whereof would quell a lover's hope,
Yet, spaniel-like, the more she spurns my love,
The more it grows and fawneth on her still.
But here comes Thurio; now must we to her window,
And give some evening musick to her ear.

Enter THURIO, *and Musicians.*

Thu. How now, Sir Proteus? are you crept before us?
Pro. Ay, gentle Thurio; for, you know that love
Will creep in service where it cannot go.
Thu. Ay, but, I hope, sir, that you love not here.
Pro. Sir, but I do; or else I would be hence.
Thu. Who? Silvia?
Pro. Ay, Silvia,—for your sake.
Thu. I thank you for your own. Now, gentlemen,
Let's tune, and to it lustily a while.

Enter Host, *at a distance; and* JULIA *in boy's clothes.*

Host. Now, my young guest! methinks, you're allycholly; I pray you, why is it?
Jul. Marry, mine host, because I cannot be merry.
Host. Come, we'll have you merry: I'll bring you where you shall hear musick, and see the gentleman that you ask'd for.
Jul. But shall I hear him speak?
Host. Ay, that you shall.
Jul. That will be musick. [*Musick plays.*
Host. Hark! hark!
Jul. Is he among these?
Host. Ay: but peace, let's hear 'em.

SONG.

Who is Silvia? What is she,
That all our swains commend her?
Holy, fair, and wise is she;
The heavens such grace did lend her,
That she might admired be.
Is she kind, as she is fair?
For beauty lives with kindness:
Love doth to her eyes repair,
To help him of his blindness;
And, being help'd, inhabits there.
Then to Silvia let us sing,
That Silvia is excelling;
She excels each mortal thing,
Upon the dull earth dwelling:
To her let us garlands bring.

Host. How now? are you sadder than you were before?
How do you, man? the musick likes you not.
Jul. You mistake; the musician likes me not.
Host. Why, my pretty youth?
Jul. He plays false, father.
Host. How? out of tune on the strings?
Jul. Not so; but yet so false that he grieves my very heart-strings.
Host. You have a quick ear.
Jul. Ay, I would, I were deaf! it makes me have a slow heart.
Host. I perceive, you delight not in musick.
Jul. Not a whit, when it jars so.
Host. Hark, what fine change is in the musick!
Jul. Ay; that change is the spite.
Host. You would have them always play but one thing?
Jul. I would always have one play but one thing. But, host, doth this Sir Proteus, that we talk on, often resort unto this gentlewoman?
Host. I tell you what Launce, his man, told me, he loved her out of all nick.
Jul. Where is Launce?
Host. Gone to seek his dog; which, to-morrow, by his master's command, he must carry for a present to his lady.
Jul. Peace! stand aside! the company parts.

Pro. Sir Thurio, fear not you! I will so plead,
That you shall say, my cunning drift excels.
Thu. Where meet we?
Pro. At saint Gregory's well.
Thu. Farewell. [*Exeunt* THU. *and Musicians.*

SILVIA *appears above, at her window.*

Pro. Madam, good even to your ladyship.
Sil. I thank you for your musick, gentlemen:
Who is that, that spake?
Pro. One, lady, if you knew his pure heart's truth,
You'd quickly learn to know him by his voice.
Sil. Sir Proteus, as I take it.
Pro. Sir Proteus, gentle lady, and your servant.
Sil. What is your will?
Pro. That I may compass yours.
Sil. You have your wish; my will is even this,—
That presently you hie you home to bed.
Thou subtle, perjur'd, false, disloyal man!
Think'st thou, I am so shallow, so conceitless,
To be seduced by thy flattery,
That hast deceiv'd so many with thy vows?
Return, return, and make thy love amends.
For me,—by this pale queen of night I swear,
I am so far from granting thy request,
That I despise thee for thy wrongful suit;
And by and by intend to chide myself,
Even for this time I spend in talking to thee.
Pro. I grant, sweet love, that I did love a lady;
But she is dead.
Jul. 'Twere false, if I should speak it;
For, I am sure, she is not buried. [*Aside.*
Sil. Say, that she be; yet Valentine, thy friend,
Survives; to whom, thyself art witness,
I am betroth'd: And art thou not asham'd
To wrong him with thy importunacy?
Pro. I likewise hear, that Valentine is dead.
Sil. And so suppose am I; for in his grave,
Assure thyself, my love is buried.
Pro. Sweet lady, let me rake it from the earth.
Sil. Go to thy lady's grave, and call hers thence;
Or, at the least, in hers sepulchre thine.
Jul. He heard not that. [*Aside.*
Pro. Madam, if your heart be so obdurate,
Vouchsafe me yet your picture for my love,
The picture that is hanging in your chamber;
To that I'll speak, to that I'll sigh and weep:
For, since the substance of your perfect self
Is else devoted, I am but a shadow;
And to your shadow will I make true love.
Jul. If 'twere a substance, you would, sure, deceive it,
And make it but a shadow, as I am. [*Aside.*
Sil. I am very loath to be your idol, sir;
But, since your falsehood shall become you well
To worship shadows, and adore false shapes,
Send to me in the morning, and I'll send it:
And so good rest.
Pro. As wretches have o'ernight,
That wait for execution in the morn.
[*Exeunt* PROTEUS; *and* SILVIA *from above.*
Jul. Host, will you go?
Host. By my hallidom, I was fast asleep.
Jul. 'Pray you, where lies Sir Proteus?
Host. Marry, at my house: Trust me, I think, 'tis almost day.
Jul. Not so; but it hath been the longest night
That e'er I watch'd, and the most heaviest.
[*Exeunt.*

SCENE III. *The same.*

Enter EGLAMOUR.

Egl. This is the hour that madam Silvia
Entreated me to call and know her mind:
There's some great matter she'd employ me in.—
Madam, madam!

SILVIA *appears above, at her window.*

Sil. Who calls?
Egl. Your servant, and your friend;
One that attends your ladyship's command.
Sil. Sir Eglamour, a thousand times good-morrow.
Egl. As many, worthy lady, to yourself.
According to your ladyship's impose,
I am thus early come, to know what service
It is your pleasure to command me in.
Sil. O Eglamour, thou art a gentleman,
(Think not, I flatter, for I swear, I do not),
Valiant, wise, remorseful, well accomplish'd.
Thou art not ignorant, what dear good-will
I bear unto the banish'd Valentine;
Nor how my father would enforce me marry
Vain Thurio, whom my very soul abhorr'd.
Thyself hast lov'd; and I have heard thee say,
No grief did ever come so near thy heart,
As when thy lady and thy truelove died,
Upon whose grave thou vow'dst pure chastity.
Sir Eglamour, I would to Valentine,
To Mantua, where, I hear, he makes abode;
And, for the ways are dangerous to pass,
I do desire thy worthy company,
Upon whose faith and honour I repose.
Urge not my father's anger, Eglamour,
But think upon my grief, a lady's grief;
And on the justice of my flying hence,
To keep me from a most unholy match,
Which heaven and fortune still reward with plagues.
I do desire thee, even from a heart
As full of sorrows as the sea of sands,
To bear me company, and go with me:
If not, to hide what I have said to thee,
That I may venture to depart alone.
Egl. Madam, I pity much your grievances;
Which since I know they virtuously are placed,
I give consent to go along with you;
Recking as little what betideth me,
As much I wish all good befortune you.
When will you go?
Sil. This evening coming.
Egl. Where shall I meet you?
Sil. At friar Patrick's cell,
Where I intend holy confession.
Egl. I will not fail your ladyship:
Good-morrow, gentle lady.
Sil. Good-morrow, kind Sir Eglamour.
[*Exeunt.*

SCENE IV. *The same.*

Enter LAUNCE, *with his Dog.*

When a man's servant shall play the cur with him, look you, it goes hard: one that I brought up of a puppy; one that I saved from drowning, when three or four of his blind brothers and sisters went to it! I have taught him—even as one would say precisely, Thus I would teach a dog. I was sent to deliver him, as a present to mistress Silvia, from my master; and I came no sooner into the dining-chamber, but he steps me to her trencher, and steals her capon's leg. O, 'tis a foul thing, when a cur cannot keep himself in all companies! I would have, as one should say, one that takes upon him to be a dog indeed, to be, as it were, a dog at all things. If I had not had more wit than he, to take a fault upon me that he did, I think verily he had been hanged for't: sure as I live, he had suffer'd for't; you shall judge. He thrusts me himself into the company of three or four gentleman-like dogs, under the duke's table: he had not been there (bless the mark) a pissing while; but all the chamber smelt him. *Out with the dog*, says one; *What cur is that?* says another; *Whip him out*, says the third; *Hang him up*, says the duke. I, having been acquainted with the smell before, knew it was Crab; and goes me to the fellow that whips the dogs: *Friend*, quoth I, *you mean to whip the dog? Ay, marry, do I*, quoth he. *You do him the more wrong*, quoth I; *'twas I did the thing you wot of.* He makes me no more ado, but whips me out of the chamber. How many masters would do this for their servant? Nay, I'll be sworn, I have sat in the stocks for puddings he hath stolen, otherwise he had been executed: I have stood on the pillory for geese he hath killed, otherwise he had suffered for't: thou think'st not of this now!—Nay, I remember the trick you served me, when I took my leave of madam Silvia: did not I bid thee still mark me, and do as I do? When didst thou see me heave up my leg, and make water against a gentlewoman's farthingale? didst thou ever see me do such a trick?

Enter PROTEUS *and* JULIA.

Pro. Sebastian is thy name? I like thee well,
And will employ thee in some service presently.
Jul. In what you please;—I will do what I can.
Pro. I hope, thou wilt.—How now, you whoreson peasant! [*To* LAUNCE.
Where have you been these two days loitering?
Laun. Marry, sir, I carried mistress Silvia the dog you bade me.
Pro. And what says she to my little jewel?
Laun. Marry, she says, your dog was a cur; and tells you, currish thanks is good enough for such a present.
Pro. But she received my dog?
Laun. No, indeed, did she not: here have I brought him back again.
Pro. What, didst thou offer her this from me?
Laun. Ay, sir; the other squirrel was stolen from me by the hangman's boys in the market-place: and then I offered her mine own; who is a dog as big as ten of yours, and therefore the gift the greater.
Pro. Go, get thee hence, and find my dog again,
Or ne'er return again into my sight.
Away, I say: Stay'st thou to vex me here?
A slave, that, still an end turns me to shame.
[*Exit* LAUNCE.
Sebastian, I have entertained thee,
Partly, that I have need of such a youth,
That can with some discretion do my business,
For 'tis no trusting to yon foolish lowt;
But, chiefly for thy face and thy behaviour:
Which (if my augury deceive me not)
Witness good bringing up, fortune, and truth:
Therefore know thou, for this I entertain thee.
Go presently and take this ring with thee,
Deliver it to madam Silvia:
She loved me well deliver'd it to me.
Jul. It seems you loved her not, to leave her token:
She's dead, belike.
Pro. Not so; I think, she lives.
Jul. Alas!
Pro. Why dost thou cry, alas?
Jul. I cannot choose but pity her.
Pro. Wherefore should'st thou pity her?
Jul. Because, methinks, that she lov'd you as well
As you do love your lady Silvia:
She dreams on him that has forgot her love;
You dote on her that cares not for your love.
'Tis pity, love should be so contrary:
And thinking on it makes me cry, alas!
Pro. Well, give her that ring, and therewithal
This letter;—that's her chamber.—Tell my lady,
I claim the promise for her heavenly picture.
Your message done, hie home unto my chamber,
Where thou shalt find me sad and solitary.
[*Exit* PROTEUS.
Jul. How many women would do such a message?
Alas, poor Proteus, thou hast entertained
A fox, to be the shepherd of thy lambs:
Alas, poor fool! why do I pity him
That with his very heart despiseth me?
Because he loves her, he despiseth me;
Because I love him, I must pity him.
This ring I gave him, when he parted from me,
To bind him to remember my good-will:
And now am I (unhappy messenger!)
To plead for that, which I would not obtain;
To carry that, which I would have refus'd;
To praise his faith, which I would have disprais'd.
I am my master's true confirmed love;
But cannot be true servant to my master,
Unless I prove false traitor to myself.
Yet I will woo for him: but yet so coldly,
As, heaven, it knows, I would not have him speed.

Enter SILVIA, *attended.*

Gentlewoman, good day! I pray you be my mean
To bring me where to speak with madam Silvia.
Sil. What would you with her, if that I be she?
Jul. If you be she, I do entreat your patience
To hear me speak the message I am sent on.
Sil. From whom?
Jul. From my master, Sir Proteus, madam.
Sil. O!—he sends you for a picture?
Jul. Ay, madam.
Sil. Ursula, bring my picture there.
[*Picture brought.*
Go, give your master this: tell him from me,
One Julia, that his changing thoughts forget,
Would better fit his chamber than this shadow.
Jul. Madam, please you peruse this letter.—
Pardon me, madam; I have unadvis'd
Deliver'd you a paper that I should not;
This is the letter to your ladyship.
Sil. I pray thee let me look on that again.
Jul. It may not be; good madam, pardon me.
Sil. There, hold.
I will not look upon your master's lines:
I know, they are stuff'd with protestations,
And full of new-found oaths; which he will break
As easily as I do tear his paper.
Jul. Madam, he sends your ladyship this ring.
Sil. The more shame for him that he sends it me;
For, I have heard him say a thousand times,
His Julia gave it him at his departure:
Though his false finger hath profan'd the ring,
Mine shall not do his Julia so much wrong.
Jul. She thanks you.
Sil. What say'st thou?
Jul. I thank you, madam, that you tender her:
Poor gentlewoman! my master wrongs her much.
Sil. Dost thou know her?
Jul. Almost as well as I do know myself:
To think upon her woes, I do protest,
That I have wept a hundred several times.
Sil. Belike, she thinks that Proteus hath forsook her.
Jul. I think, she doth, and that's her cause of sorrow.
Sil. Is she not passing fair?
Jul. She hath been fairer, madam, than she is:
When she did think, my master lov'd her well,
She, in my judgment, was as fair as you;
But since she did neglect her looking-glass,
And threw her sun-expelling mask away,
The air hath starv'd the roses in her cheeks,
And pinch'd the lily-tincture of her face,
That now she is become as black as I.
Sil. How tall was she?
Jul. About my stature: for, at Pentecost,
When all our pageants of delight were play'd,
Our youth got me to play the woman's part,
And I was trimm'd in madam Julia's gown,
Which served me as fit, by all men's judgment,
As if the garment had been made for me;
Therefore, I know, she is about my height.
And, at that time, I made her weep a good,
For I did play a lamentable part:
Madam, 'twas Ariadne, passioning
For Theseus' perjury, and unjust flight;
Which I so lively acted with my tears,
That my poor mistress, moved therewithal,
Wept bitterly; and, would I might be dead,
If I in thought felt not her very sorrow!
Sil. She is beholden to thee, gentle youth!—
Alas, poor lady! desolate and left!—
I weep myself, to think upon thy words.

Here, youth, there is my purse; I give thee this
For thy sweet mistress' sake, because thou lov'st her.
Farewell. [*Exit* SILVIA.
Jul. And she shall thank you for't, if e'er you know her.—
A virtuous gentlewoman, mild, and beautiful.
I hope my master's suit will be but cold,
Since she respects my mistress' love so much.
Alas, how love can trifle with itself!
Here is her picture: Let me see; I think,
If I had such a tire, this face of mine
Were full as lovely as is this of hers:
And yet the painter flatter'd her a little,
Unless I flatter with myself too much.
Her hair is auburn, mine is perfect yellow:
If that be all the difference in his love,
I'll get me such a colour'd periwig.
Her eyes are gray as glass; and so are mine:
Ay, but her forehead's low, and mine's as high.
What should it be, that he respects in her,
But I can make respective in myself,
If this fond love were not a blinded god?
Come, shadow, come, and take this shadow up,
For 'tis thy rival. O thou senseless form,
Thou shalt be worship'd, kiss'd, lov'd, and ador'd;
And, were there sense in this idolatry,
My substance should be statue in thy stead.
I'll use thee kindly for thy mistress' sake,
That us'd me so; or else by Jove I vow,
I should have scratch'd out your unseeing eyes,
To make my master out of love with thee.
[*Exit.*

ACT V.

SCENE I. *The same. An Abbey.*

Enter EGLAMOUR.

Egl. The sun begins to gild the western sky;
And now it is about the very hour
That Silvia, at friar Patrick's cell should meet me.
She will not fail; for lovers break not hours,
Unless it be to come before their time;
So much they spur their expedition.

Enter SILVIA.

See, where she comes: Lady, a happy evening!
Sil. Amen, amen! go on, good Eglamour!
Out at the postern by the abbey wall;
I fear I am attended by some spies.
Egl. Fear not: the forest is not three leagues off;
If we recover that, we are sure enough. [*Exeunt.*

SCENE II.

The same. A Room in the Duke's *Palace.*

Enter THURIO, PROTEUS, *and* JULIA.

Thu. Sir Proteus, what says Silvia to my suit?
Pro. O, sir, I find her milder than she was;
And yet she takes exceptions at your person.
Thu. What, that my leg is too long?
Pro. No; that it is too little.
Thu. I'll wear a boot, to make it somewhat rounder.
Pro. But love will not be spurr'd to what it loaths.
Thu. What says she to my face?
Pro. She says it is a fair one.
Thu. Nay, then the wanton lies; my face is black.
Pro. But pearls are fair; and the old saying is,
Black men are pearls in beauteous ladies' eyes.
Jul. 'Tis true; such pearls as put out ladies' eyes;
For I had rather wink than look on them.
[*Aside.*
Thu. How likes she my discourse?
Pro. Ill, when you talk of war.
Thu. But well, when I discourse of love and peace?
Jul. But better indeed, when you hold your peace. [*Aside.*
Thu. What says she to my valour?
Pro. O, sir, she makes no doubt of that.
Jul. She needs not, when she knows it cowardice. [*Aside.*
Thu. What says she to my birth?
Pro. That you are well deriv'd.
Jul. True, from a gentleman to a fool. [*Aside.*
Thu. Considers she my possessions?
Pro. O, ay; and pities them.
Thu. Wherefore?
Jul. That such an ass should owe them.
[*Aside.*
Pro. That they are out by lease.
Jul. Here comes the duke.

Enter DUKE.

Duke. How now, Sir Proteus? how now, Thurio?
Which of you saw Sir Eglamour of late?
Thu. Not I.
Pro. Nor I.
Duke. Saw you my daughter?
Pro. Neither.
Duke. Why, then she's fled unto that peasant Valentine;
And Eglamour is in her company.
'Tis true, for friar Laurence met them both,
As he in penance wander'd through the forest:
Him he knew well, and guess'd that it was she;
But, being mask'd, he was not sure of it:
Besides, she did intend confession
At Patrick's cell this even: and there she was not:
These likelihoods confirm her flight from hence.
Therefore, I pray you, stand not to discourse,
But mount you presently; and meet with me
Upon the rising of the mountain foot
That leads towards Mantua, whither they are fled:
Despatch, sweet gentlemen, and follow me.
[*Exit.*
Thu. Why, this it is to be a peevish girl,
That flies her fortune when it follows her:
I'll after; more to be reveng'd on Eglamour,
Than for the love of reckless Silvia. [*Exit.*
Pro. And I will follow, more for Silvia's love,
Than hate of Eglamour that goes with her. [*Exit.*
Jul. And I will follow more to cross that love,
Than hate for Silvia, that is gone for love..
[*Exit.*

SCENE III. *Frontiers of* Mantua. *The Forest.*

Enter SILVIA, *and* Out-laws.

Out. Come, come;
Be patient, we must bring you to our captain.
Sil. A thousand more mischances than this one
Have learn'd me how to brook this patiently.
2 *Out.* Come, bring her away.
1 *Out.* Where is the gentleman that was with her?
3 *Out.* Being nimble-footed, he hath outrun us,
But Moyses and Valerius follow him.
Go thou with her to the west end of the wood,
There is our captain: we'll follow him that's fled;
The thicket is beset, he cannot 'scape.
1 *Out.* Come, I must bring you to our captain's cave:
Fear not; he bears an honourable mind,
And will not use a woman lawlessly.
Sil. O Valentine, this I endure for thee!
[*Exeunt.*

SCENE IV. *Another part of the Forest.*

Enter VALENTINE.

Val. How use doth breed a habit in a man!
This shadowy desert, unfrequented woods,
I better brook than flourishing peopled towns:
Here can I sit alone, unseen of any,
And, to the nightingale's complaining notes,
Tune my distresses, and record my woes.

O thou that dost inhabit in my breast,
Leave not the mansion so long tenantless;
Lest, growing ruinous, the building fall,
And leave no memory of what it was!
Repair me with thy presence, Silvia;
Thou gentle nymph, cherish thy forlorn swain!—
What halloing, and what stir, is this to-day?
These are my mates, that make their wills their law,
Have some unhappy passenger in chase:
They love me well; yet I have much to do
To keep them from uncivil outrages.
Withdraw thee, Valentine; who's this comes here? [*Steps aside.*

Enter PROTEUS, SILVIA, *and* JULIA.

Pro. Madam, this service I have done for you,
(Though you respect not aught your servant doth)
To hazard life, and rescue you from him
That would have forced your honour and your love.
Vouchsafe me, for my meed, but one fair look;
A smaller boon than this I cannot beg,
And less than this, I'm sure, you cannot give.
Val. How like a dream is this I see and hear!
Love, lend me patience to forbear a while. [*Aside.*
Sil. O miserable, unhappy that I am!
Pro. Unhappy were you, madam, ere I came;
But, by my coming, I have made you happy.
Sil. By thy approach thou mak'st me most unhappy.
Jul. And me, when he approacheth to your presence. [*Aside.*
Sil. Had I been seized by a hungry lion,
I would have been a breakfast to the beast,
Rather than have false Proteus rescue me.
O, heaven be judge, how I love Valentine,
Whose life's as tender to me as my soul;
And full as much (for more there cannot be)
I do detest false perjur'd Proteus:
Therefore begone, solicit me no more.
Pro. What dangerous action, stood it next to death,
Would I not undergo for one calm look?
O, 'tis the curse in love, and still approv'd,
When women cannot love where they're belov'd.
Sil. When Proteus cannot love where he's belov'd.
Read over Julia's heart, thy first best love,
For whose dear sake thou didst then rend thy faith
Into a thousand oaths; and all those oaths
Descended into perjury, to love me.
Thou hast no faith left now, unless thou hadst two,
And that's far worse than none; better have none
Than plural faith, which is too much by one:
Thou counterfeit to thy true friend!
Pro. In love,
Who respects friend?
Sil. All men but Proteus.
Pro. Nay, if the gentle spirit of moving words
Can no way change you to a milder form,
I'll woo you like a soldier, at arms' end;
And love you 'gainst the nature of love, force you.
Sil. O heaven!
Pro. I'll force thee yield to my desire.
Val. Ruffian, let go that rude uncivil touch;
Thou friend of an ill fashion.
Pro. Valentine!
Val. Thou common friend, that's without faith or love,
(For such is a friend now), treacherous man!
Thou hast beguil'd my hopes; nought but mine eye
Could have persuaded me: Now I dare not say
I have one friend alive; thou would'st disprove me.
Who should be trusted now, when one's right hand
Is perjur'd to the bosom? Proteus,
I am sorry I must never trust thee more,
But count the world a stranger for thy sake.
The private wound is deepest: O time most accurst!
'Mongst all foes, that a friend should be the worst!
Pro. My shame and guilt confound me.—
Forgive me, Valentine: if hearty sorrow
Be a sufficient ransom for offence,
I tender it here; I do as truly suffer,
As e'er I did commit.
Val. Then I am paid;
And once again I do receive thee honest:—
Who by repentance is not satisfied,
Is nor of heaven, nor earth; for these are pleas'd;
By penitence th' Eternal's wrath's appeas'd:—
And, that my love may appear plain and free,
All that was mine in Silvia, I give thee.
Jul. O me, unhappy! [*Faints.*
Pro. Look to the boy.
Val. Why, boy! why, wag! how now? what is the matter? Look up; speak.
Jul. O good sir, my master charg'd me to deliver a ring to Madam Silvia; which, out of my neglect, was never done.
Pro. Where is that ring, boy!
Jul. Here 'tis: this is it. [*Gives a ring.*
Pro. How! let me see: why this is the ring I gave to Julia.
Jul. O, cry you mercy, sir, I have mistook; this is the ring you sent to Silvia. [*Shows another ring.*
Pro. But, how cam'st thou by this ring? at my depart, I gave this unto Julia.
Jul. And Julia herself did give it me;
And Julia herself hath brought it hither.
Pro. How! Julia!
Jul. Behold her that gave aim to all thy oaths,
And entertain'd them deeply in her heart:
How oft hast thou with perjury cleft the root?
O Proteus, let this habit make thee blush!
Be thou asham'd, that I have took upon me
Such an immodest raiment; if shame live
In a disguise of love:
It is the lesser blot modesty finds,
Women to change their shapes, than men their minds.
Pro. Than men their minds? 'tis true: O heaven! were man
But constant, he were perfect: that one error
Fills him with faults; makes him run through all the sins:
Inconstancy falls off, ere it begins:
What is in Silvia's face, but I may spy
More fresh in Julia's, with a constant eye?
Val. Come, come, a hand from either:
Let me be blest to make this happy close?
'Twere pity two such friends should be long foes.
Pro. Bear witness, heaven, I have my wish for ever.
Jul. And I mine.

Enter Out-laws, *with* DUKE *and* THURIO.

Out. A prize, a prize, a prize!
Val. Forbear, forbear, I say; it is my lord the duke.
Your grace is welcome to a man disgrac'd,
Banished Valentine.
Duke. Sir Valentine!
Thu. Yonder is Silvia; and Silvia's mine.
Val. Thurio, give back, or else embrace thy death;
Come not within the measure of my wrath:
Do not name Silvia thine: if once again,
Verona shall not hold thee. Here she stands,
Take but possession of her with a touch;—
I dare thee but to breathe upon my love.
Thu. Sir Valentine, I care not for her, I;
I hold him but a fool, that will endanger
His body for a girl that loves him not:
I claim her not, and therefore she is thine.
Duke. The more degenerate and base art thou,
To make such means for her as thou hast done,
And leave her on such slight conditions.—
Now, by the honour of my ancestry,

I do applaud thy spirit, Valentine,
And think thee worthy of an empress' love.
Know then, I here forget all former griefs,
Cancel all grudge, repeal thee home again.—
Plead a new state in thy unrivall'd merit,
To which I thus subscribe,—Sir Valentine,
Thou art a gentleman, and well deriv'd;
Take thou thy Silvia, for thou hast deserv'd her.

Val. I thank your grace; the gift hath made me happy.
I now beseech you, for your daughter's sake,
To grant one boon that I shall ask of you.

Duke. I grant it for thine own, whate'er it be.

Val. These banish'd men, that I have kept withal,
Are men endued with worthy qualities;
Forgive them what they have committed here,
And let them be recall'd from their exile:
They are reformed, civil, full of good,
And fit for great employment, worthy lord.

Duke. Thou hast prevail'd: I pardon them, and thee;
Dispose of them, as thou know'st their deserts.
Come, let us go; we will include all jars
With triumphs, mirth, and rare solemnity.

Val. And, as we walk along, I dare be bold
With our discourse to make your grace to smile:
What think you of this page, my lord?

Duke. I think the boy hath grace in him; he blushes.

Val. I warrant you, my lord; more grace than boy.

Duke. What mean you by that saying?

Val. Please you, I'll tell you as we pass along,
That you will wonder what hath fortuned.—
Come, Proteus, 'tis your penance but to hear
The story of your loves discovered:
That done, our day of marriage shall be yours;
One feast, one house, one mutual happiness.
[*Exeunt.*

MERRY WIVES OF WINDSOR.

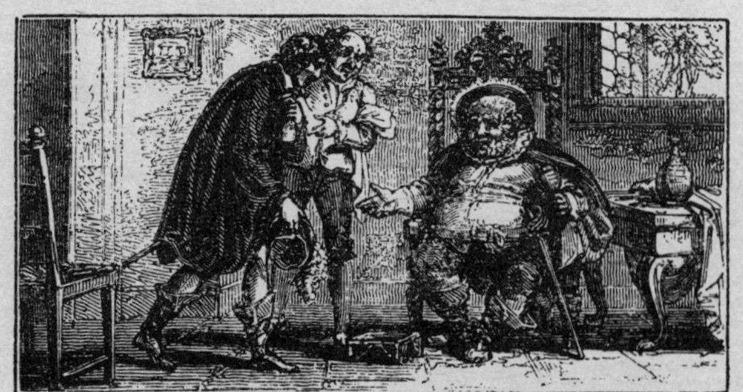

PERSONS REPRESENTED.

SIR JOHN FALSTAFF.
FENTON.
SHALLOW, *a country Justice.*
SLENDER, *Cousin to* Shallow.
MR. FORD, } *two Gentlemen dwelling at* Windsor.
MR. PAGE, }
WILLIAM PAGE, *a Boy, Son to* Mr. Page.
SIR HUGH EVANS, *a Welsh Parson.*
DR. CAIUS, *a French Physician.*
Host *of the Garter Inn.*
BARDOLPH, *Follower of* Falstaff.
PISTOL, } *Followers of* Falstaff.
NYM, }
ROBIN, *Page to* Falstaff.
SIMPLE, *Servant to* Slender.
RUGBY, *Servant to* Dr. Caius.

MRS. FORD.
MRS. PAGE.
MRS. ANNE PAGE, *her Daughter, in love with* Fenton.
MRS. QUICKLY, *Servant to* Dr. Caius.

Servants to Page, Ford, *&c.*

SCENE—Windsor, *and the Parts adjacent.*

ACT I.

SCENE I. Windsor. *Before* Page's *House.*

Enter JUSTICE SHALLOW, SLENDER, *and* SIR HUGH EVANS.

Shal. SIR Hugh, persuade me not: I will make a Star-chamber matter of it: if he were twenty Sir John Falstaffs, he shall not abuse Robert Shallow, esquire.

Slen. In the county of Gloster, justice of peace, and *coram.*

Shal. Ay, cousin Slender, and *Cust-alorum.*

Slen. Ay, and *ratolorum* too; and a gentleman born, master parson; who writes himself *armigero;* in any bill, warrant, quittance, or obligation, *armigero.*

Shal. Ay, that I do; and have done any time these three hundred years.

Slen. All his successors, gone before him, have done't; and all his ancestors, that come after him, may: they may give the dozen white luces in their coat.

Shal. It is an old coat.

Eva. The dozen white louses do become an old coat well; it agrees well, passant: it is a familiar beast to man, and signifies—love.

Shal. The luce is the fresh fish; the salt fish is an old coat.

Slen. I may quarter, coz?

Shal. You may, by marrying.

Eva. It is marring, indeed, if he quarter it.

Shal. Not a whit.

Eva. Yes, pe'r-lady; if he has a quarter of your

coat, there is but three skirts for yourself, in my simple conjectures: but that is all one: If Sir John Falstaff have committed disparagements unto you, I am of the church, and will be glad to do my benevolence, to make atonements and compromises between you.

Shal. The Council shall hear it; it is a riot.

Eva. It is not meet the Council hear a riot; there is no fear of Got in a riot: the Council, look you, shall desire to hear the fear of Got, and not to hear a riot; take your vizaments in that.

Shal. Ha! o' my life, if I were young again, the sword should end it.

Eva. It is petter that friends is the sword, and end it: and there is also another device in my prain, which, peradventure, prings goot discretions with it: There is Anne Page, which is daughter to master George Page, which is pretty virginity.

Slen. Mistress Anne Page? She has brown hair, and speaks small like a woman.

Eva. It is that fery person for all the 'orld, as just as you will desire; and seven hundred pounds of monies, and gold, and silver, is her grandsire, upon his death's bed (Got deliver to a joyful resurrections!) give, when she is able to overtake seventeen years old: it were a goot motion, if we leave our pribbles and prabbles, and desire a marriage between master Abraham and mistress Anne Page.

Shal. Did her grandsire leave her seven hundred pound?

Eva. Ay, and her father is make her a petter penny.

Shal. I know the young gentlewoman; she has good gifts.

Eva. Seven hundred pounds, and possibilities, is good gifts.

Shal. Well, let us see honest master Page: Is Falstaff there?

Eva. Shall I tell you a lie? I do despise a liar, as I do despise one that is false; or, as I despise one that is not true. The knight, Sir John, is there; and, I beseech you, be ruled by your well-willers. I will peat the door [*knocks*] for master Page. What, hoa! Got pless your house here!

Enter PAGE.

Page. Who's there?

Eva. Here is Got's plessing, and your friend, and justice Shallow: and here young master Slender; that, peradventures, shall tell you another tale, if matters grow to your likings.

Page. I am glad to see your worships well: I thank you for my venison, master Shallow.

Shal. Master Page, I am glad to see you; Much good do it your good heart! I wished your venison better; it was ill kill'd:—How doth good mistress Page?—and I love you always with my heart, la; with my heart.

Page. Sir, I thank you.

Shal. Sir, I thank you; by yea and no, I do.

Page. I am glad to see you, good master Slender.

Slen. How does your fallow greyhound, sir? I heard say, he was out-run on Cotsale.

Page. It could not be judg'd, sir.

Slen. You'll not confess, you'll not confess.

Shal. That he will not;—'tis your fault, 'tis your fault:—'Tis a good dog.

Page. A cur, sir.

Shal. Sir, he's a good dog, and a fair dog; Can there be more said? he is good, and fair.—Is Sir John Falstaff here?

Page. Sir, he is within; and I would, I could do a good office between you.

Eva. It is spoke as a christians ought to speak.

Shal. He hath wrong'd me, master Page.

Page. Sir, he doth in some sort confess it.

Shal. If it be confess'd, it is not redress'd: is not that so, master Page? He hath wrong'd me; indeed he hath;—at a word, he hath;—believe me;—Robert Shallow, esquire, saith he is wrong'd.

Page. Here comes Sir John.

Enter SIR JOHN FALSTAFF, BARDOLPH, NYM, *and* PISTOL.

Fal. Now, master Shallow, you'll complain of me to the king?

Shal. Knight, you have beaten my men, killed my deer, and broke open my lodge.

Fal. But not kiss'd your keeper's daughter?

Shal. Tut, a pin! this shall be answer'd.

Fal. I will answer it straight;—I have done all this:—That is now answer'd.

Shal. The Council shall know this.

Fal. 'Twere better for you, if it were known in counsel: you'll be laugh'd at.

Eva. *Pauca verba*, Sir John, good worts.

Fal. Good worts! good cabbage.—Slender, I broke your head: What matter have you against me?

Slen. Marry, sir, I have matter in my head against you; and against your coney catching rascals, Bardolph, Nym, and Pistol. They carried me to the tavern, and made me drunk, and afterwards picked my pocket.

Bar. You banbury cheese!

Slen. Ay, it is no matter.

Pist. How now, Mephostophilus?

Slen. Ay, it is no matter.

Nym. Slice, I say! *pauca, pauca;* slice! that's my humour.

Slen. Where's Simple, my man?—can you tell, cousin?

Eva. Peace: I pray you! Now let us understand: There is three umpires in this matter, as I understand: That is—master Page, *fidelicet*, master Page; and there is myself, *fidelicet*, myself; and the three party is, lastly and finally, mine host of the Garter.

Page. We three, to hear it, and end it between them.

Eva. Fery goot: I will make a prief of it in my note-book; and we will afterwards 'ork upon the cause with as great discreetly as we can.

Fal. Pistol, ——

Pist. He hears with ears.

Eva. The tevil and his tam; what phrase is this, *He hears with ear?* Why, it is affectations.

Fal. Pistol, did you pick master Slender's purse?

Slen. Ay, by these gloves, did he (or I would, I might never come in mine own great chamber again else), of seven groats in mill-sixpences, and two Edward shovel-boards, that cost me two shilling and twopence a-piece of Yead Miller, by these gloves.

Fal. Is this true, Pistol?

Eva. No; it is false, if it is a pick-purse.

Pist. Ha! thou mountain-foreigner!—Sir John,
and master mine,
I combat challenge of this latten bilbo:
Word of denial in thy labras here;
Word of denial; froth and scum, thou liest.

Slen. By these gloves, then 'twas he.

Nym. Be avised, sir, and pass good humours: I will say, *marry, trap*, with you, if you run the nuthook's humour on me; that is the very note of it.

Slen. By this hat, then he in the red face had it: for though I cannot remember what I did when you made me drunk, yet I am not altogether an ass.

Fal. What say you, Scarlet and John?

Bard. Why, sir, for my part, I say, the gentleman had drunk himself out of his five sentences.

Eva. It is his five senses: fie, what the ignorance is!

Bard. And being fap, sir, was, as they say, cashier'd; and so conclusions pass'd the careires.

Slen. Ay, you spake in Latin then too; but 'tis no matter: I'll ne'er be drunk whilst I live again, but in honest, civil, godly company, for this trick: If I be drunk, I'll be drunk with those that have the fear of God, and not with drunken knaves.

Eva. So Got 'udge me, that is a virtuous mind.

Fal. You hear all these matters denied, gentlemen; you hear it.

Enter MISTRESS ANNE PAGE, *with wine;* MISTRESS FORD *and* MISTRESS PAGE *following.*

Page. Nay, daughter, carry the wine in; we'll drink within. [*Exit* ANNE PAGE.

Slen. O heaven! this is mistress Anne Page.

Page. How now, mistress Ford?

Fal. Mistress Ford, by my troth, you are very well met: by your leave, good mistress. [*kissing her.*

Page. Wife, bid these gentlemen welcome:—Come, we have a hot venison pasty to dinner; come, gentlemen, I hope we shall drink down all unkindness.

[*Exeunt all but* SHAL. SLENDER, *and* EVANS.

Slen. I had rather than forty shillings I had my book of Songs and Sonnets here:—

Enter SIMPLE.

How now, Simple! where have you been? I must wait on myself, must I? You have not *The Book of Riddles* about you, have you?

Sim. *Book of Riddles!* why, did you not lend it to Alice Shortcake upon Allhallowmas last, a fortnight afore Michaelmas?

Shal. Come, coz; come, coz; we stay for you. A word with you, coz: marry this, coz: There is, as 'twere, a tender, a kind of tender, made afar off by Sir Hugh here;—Do you understand me?

Slen. Ay, sir, you shall find me reasonable; if it be so, I shall do that that is reason.

Shal. Nay, but understand me.

Slen. So I do, sir.

Eva. Give ear to his motions, master Slender: I will description the matter to you, if you be capacity of it.

Slen. Nay, I will do as my cousin Shallow says: I pray you, pardon me; he's a justice of peace in his country, simple though I stand here.

Eva. But this is not the question; the question is concerning your marriage.

Shal. Ay, there's the point, sir.

Eva. Marry, is it; the very point of it; to mistress Anne Page.

Slen. Why, if it be so, I will marry her upon any reasonable demands.

Eva. But can you affection the 'oman? Let us command to know that of your mouth, or of your lips; for divers philosophers hold that the lips is parcel of the mouth;—Therefore, precisely, can you carry your good will to the maid?

Shal. Cousin Abraham Slender, can you love her?

Slen. I hope, sir,—I will do as it shall become one that would do reason.

Eva. Nay, Got's lords and his ladies, you must speak possitable, if you can carry her your desires towards her.

Shal. That you must: Will you, upon good dowry, marry her?

Slen. I will do a greater thing than that, upon your request, cousin, in any reason.

Shal. Nay, conceive me, conceive me, sweet coz; what I do is to pleasure you, coz: Can you love the maid?

Slen. I will marry her, sir, at your request; but if there be no great love in the beginning, yet heaven may decrease it upon better acquaintance, when we are married, and have more occasion to know one another: I hope upon familiarity will grow more contempt: but if you say, *marry her,* I will marry her, that I am freely dissolved, and dissolutely.

Eva. It is a fery discretion answer; save the faul' is in the 'ort dissolutely: the 'ort is, according to our meaning, resolutely;—his meaning is good.

Shal. Ay, I think my cousin meant well.

Slen. Ay, or else I would I might be hanged, la.

Re-enter ANNE PAGE.

Shal. Here comes fair mistress Anne:—Would I were young for your sake, mistress Anne!

Anne. The dinner is on the table; my father desires your worships' company.

Shal. I will wait on him, fair mistress Anne.

Eva. Od's plessed will! I will not be absence at the grace.

[*Exeunt* SHALLOW *and* SIR H. EVANS.

Anne. Will't please your worship to come in, sir?

Slen. No, I thank you, forsooth, heartily; I am very well.

Anne. The dinner attends you, sir.

Slen. I am not a-hungry, I thank you, forsooth: Go, sirrah, for all you are my man, go, wait upon my cousin Shallow [*Exit* SIMPLE]. A justice of peace sometime may be beholden to his friend for a man:—I keep but three men and a boy yet, till my mother be dead: But what though? yet I live like a poor gentleman born.

Anne. I may not go in without your worship: they will not sit till you come.

Slen. I'faith, I'll eat nothing; I thank you as much as though I did.

Anne. I pray you, sir, walk in.

Slen. I had rather walk here, I thank you: I bruised my shin the other day with playing at sword and dagger with a master of fence, three veneys for a dish of stewed prunes; and, by my troth, I cannot abide the smell of hot meat since. Why do your dogs bark so? be there bears i' the town?

Anne. I think there are, sir; I heard them talked of.

Slen. I love the sport well; but I shall as soon quarrel at it as any man in England:—You are afraid if you see the bear loose, are you not?

Anne. Ay, indeed, sir.

Slen. That's meat and drink to me now: I have seen Sackerson loose twenty times; and have taken him by the chain: but, I warrant you, the women have so cried and shriek'd at it, that it pass'd:—but women, indeed, cannot abide 'em; they are very ill-favour'd rough things.

Re-enter PAGE.

Page. Come, gentle master Slender, come; we stay for you.

Slen. I'll eat nothing; I thank you, sir.

Page. By cock and pye, you shall not choose, sir: come, come.

Slen. Nay, 'pray you, lead the way.

Page. Come on, sir.

Slen. Mistress Anne, yourself shall go first.

Anne. Not I, sir; pray you, keep on.

Slen. Truly, I will not go first, truly, la: I will not do you that wrong.

Anne. I pray you, sir.

Slen. I'll rather be unmannerly than troublesome: you do yourself wrong, indeed, la. [*Exeunt.*

SCENE II. *The same.*

Enter SIR HUGH EVANS *and* SIMPLE.

Eva. Go your ways, and ask of Doctor Caius' house, which is the way: and there dwells one mistress Quickly, which is in the manner of his nurse, or his dry nurse, or his cook, or his laundry, his washer, and his wringer.

Simp. Well, sir.

Eva. Nay, it is petter yet:——give her this letter; for it is a 'oman that altogether's acquaintance with mistress Anne Page; and the letter is, to desire and require her to solicit your master's desires to mistress Anne Page: I pray you, be gone. I will make an end of my dinner; there's pippins and cheese to come. [*Exeunt.*

SCENE III. *A Room in the Garter Inn.*

Enter FALSTAFF, Host, BARDOLPH, NYM, PISTOL, *and* ROBIN.

Fal. Mine host of the Garter,—

Host. What says my bully-rook? Speak scholarly, and wisely.

Fal. Truly, mine host, I must turn away some of my followers.

Host. Discard, bully Hercules; cashier; let them wag; trot, trot.

Fal. I sit at ten pounds a week.

Host. Thou'rt an emperor, Cæsar, Keiser, and Pheezar, I will entertain Bardolph; he shall draw, he shall tap: said I well, bully Hector?

Fal. Do so, good mine host.

Host. I have spoke; let him follow: Let me see thee froth, and lime: I am at a word; follow. [*Exit* Host.

Fal. Bardolph, follow him; a tapster is a good trade: an old cloak makes a new jerkin; a withered servingman, a fresh tapster: Go; adieu.

Bard. It is a life that I have desired; I will thrive. [*Exit* BARD.

Pist. O base Gongarian wight! wilt thou the spigot wield?

Nym. He was gotten in drink: Is not the humour conceited? His mind is not heroick, and here's the humour of it.

Fal. I am glad I am so acquit of this tinderbox; his thefts were too open: his filching was like an unskilful singer, he kept not time.

Nym. The good humour is, to steal at a minute's rest.

Pist. Convey, the wise it call: Steal! foh; a fico for the phrase!

Fal. Well, sirs, I am almost out at heels.

Pist. Why then let kibes ensue.

Fal. There is no remedy; I must coney-catch; I must shift.

Pist. Young ravens must have food.

Fal. Which of you know Ford of this town?

Pist. I ken the wight; he is of substance good.

Fal. My honest lads, I will tell you what I am about.

Pist. Two yards, and more.

Fal. No quips now, Pistol; indeed I am in the waist two yards about; but I am now about no waste; I am about thrift. Briefly, I do mean to make love to Ford's wife; I spy entertainment in her; she discourses, she carves, she gives the leer of invitation: I can construe the action of her familiar style, and the hardest voice of her behaviour, to be English'd rightly is, *I am Sir John Falstaff's.*

Pist. He hath studied her well, and translated her well; out of honesty into English.

Nym. The anchor is deep: will that humour pass?

Fal. Now, the report goes, she has all the rule of her husband's purse; she hath legions of angels.

Pist. As many devils entertain; and, *To her, boy,* say I.

Nym. The humour rises; it is good; humour me the angels.

Fal. I have writ me here a letter to her; and here another to Page's wife; who even now gave me good eyes too, examined my parts with most judicious eyliads: sometimes the beam of her view gilded my foot, sometimes my portly belly.

Pist. Then did the sun on dunghill shine.

Nym. I thank thee for that humour.

Fal. O, she did so course o'er my exteriors with such a greedy intention, that the appetite of her eye did seem to scorch me up like a burning glass! Here's another letter to her: she bears the purse too: she is a region in Guiana, all gold and bounty. I will be cheater to them both, and they shall be exchequers to me; they shall be my East and West Indies, and I will trade to them both. Go, bear thou this letter to mistress Page; and thou this to mistress Ford: we will thrive, lads, we will thrive.

Pist. Shall I Sir Pandarus of Troy become,
And by my side wear steel? then, Lucifer take all!

Nym. I will run no base humour; here, take the humour-letter; I will keep the 'haviour of reputation.

Fal. Hold, sirrah [*to* ROB.], bear you these letters tightly;
Sail like my pinnace to these golden shores.—
Rogues, hence avaunt! vanish like hailstones, go;
Trudge, plod away, o' the hoof; seek shelter, pack!
Falstaff will learn the humour of this age,
French thrift, you rogues; myself, and skirted page. [*Exeunt* FALSTAFF *and* ROBIN.

Pist. Let vultures gripe thy guts! for gourd and fullam holds,
And high and low beguile the rich and poor:
Tester I'll have in pouch, when thou shalt lack,
Base Phrygian Turk!

Nym. I have operations in my head, which be humours of revenge.

Pist. Wilt thou revenge?

Nym. By welkin, and her star!

Pist. With wit, or steel?

Nym. With both the humours, I:
I will discuss the humour of this love to Page.

Pist. And I to Ford shall eke unfold,
How Falstaff, varlet vile,
His dove will prove, his gold will hold,
And his soft couch defile.

Nym. My humour shall not cool: I will incense Page to deal with poison; I will possess him with yellowness, for the revolt of mien is dangerous: that is my true humour.

Pist. Thou art the Mars of malcontents: I second thee; troop on. [*Exeunt.*

SCENE IV. *A Room in* Dr. Caius's *House.*

Enter Mrs. QUICKLY, SIMPLE, *and* RUGBY.

Quick. What; John Rugby!—I pray thee, go to the casement, and see if you can see my master, master Doctor Caius, coming: if he do, i'faith, and find any body in the house, here will be an old abusing of God's patience, and the king's English.

Rug. I'll go watch. [*Exit* RUGBY.

Quick. Go; and we'll have a posset for't soon at night, in faith, at the latter end of a sea-coal fire. An honest, willing, kind fellow, as ever servant shall come in house withal; and, I warrant you, no tell-tale, nor no breed-bate: his worst fault is, that he is given to prayer; he is something peevish that way: but nobody but has his fault;—but let that pass. Peter Simple, you say, your name is?

Sim. Ay, for fault of a better.

Quick. And master Slender's your master?

Sim. Ay, forsooth.

Quick. Does he not wear a great round beard, like a glover's paring knife?

Sim. No, forsooth: he hath but a little wee face, with a little yellow beard; a Cain-coloured beard.

Quick. A softly-sprighted man, is he not?

Sim. Ay, forsooth: but he is as tall a man of his hands, as any is between this and his head; he hath fought with a warrener.

Quick. How say you?—O, I should remember him; Does he not hold up his head, as it were? and strut in his gait?

Sim. Yes, indeed, does he.

Quick. Well, heaven send Anne Page no worse fortune? Tell master parson Evans, I will do what I can for your master: Anne is a good girl, and I wish—

Re-enter RUGBY.

Rug. Out, alas! here comes my master.

Quick. We shall all be shent: Run in here, good young man; go into this closet. [*Shuts* Simple *in the closet.*] He will not stay long.—

What, John Rugby! John, what, John, I say!—Go, John, go inquire for my master; I doubt, he be not well, that he comes not home:—*and down, down, adown-a, &c.* [*Sings.*

Enter Doctor Caius.

Caius. Vat is you sing? I do not like dese toys: Pray you, go and vetch me in my closet *un boitier verd;* a box, a green-a box; Do intend vat I speak? a green-a box.

Quick. Ay, forsooth, I'll fetch it you. I am glad he went not in himself; if he had found the young man, he would have been horn-mad. [*Aside.*

Caius. Fe, fe, fe, fe! ma foi, il fait fort chaud. Je m'en vais a la Cour,—la grande affaire.

Quick. Is it this, sir?

Caius. Ouy; mette le au mon pocket; *Depeche,* quickly:—Vere is dat knave Rugby?

Quick. What, John Rugby! John!

Rug. Here, sir.

Caius. You are John Rugby, and you are Jack Rugby; Come, take-a your rapier, and come after my heel to de court.

Rug. 'Tis ready, sir, here in the porch.

Caius. By my trot, I tarry too long:—Od's me! *Qu'ay-j'oublie?* dere is some simples in my closet, dat I vill not for the varld I shall leave behind.

Quick. Ah me! he'll find the young man there, and be mad.

Caius. *O diable, diable!* vat is in my closet?—Villany? *larron!* [*Pulling* Simple *out.*] Rugby, my rapier.

Quick. Good master, be content.

Caius. Verefore shall I be content-a?

Quick. The young man is an honest man.

Caius. Vat shall de honest man do in my closet? dere is no honest man dat shall come in my closet.

Quick. I beseech you, be not so flegmatick; hear the truth of it: He came of an errand to me from parson Hugh.

Caius. Vell.

Sim. Ay, forsooth, to desire her to——

Quick. Peace, I pray you.

Caius. Peace-a your tongue:—Speak-a your tale.

Sim. To desire this honest gentlewoman, your maid, to speak a good word to mistress Anne Page for my master, in the way of marriage.

Quick. This is all, indeed, la; but I'll ne'er put my finger in the fire, and need not.

Caius. Sir Hugh send-a you?—Rugby, *baillez* me some paper:—Tarry you a little-a while. [*Writes.*

Quick. I am glad he is so quiet: if he had been thoroughly moved, you should have heard him so loud, and so melancholy;—But notwithstanding, man, I'll do your master what good I can: and the very yea and the no is, the French Doctor, my master,—I may call him my master, look you, for I keep his house; and I wash, wring, brew, bake, scour, dress meat and drink, make the beds, and do all myself;—

Sim. 'Tis a great charge, to come under one body's hand.

Quick. Are you advis'd o' that? you shall find it a great charge: and to be up early, and down late;—but notwithstanding (to tell you in your ear; I would have no words of it;) my master himself is in love with mistress Anne Page: but notwithstanding that,—I know Anne's mind,—that's neither here nor there.

Caius. You jack'nape; give-a dis letter to Sir Hugh, by gar, it is a shallenge: I vill cut his troat in de park; and I vill teach a scurvy jack-a-nape priest to meddle or make:—you may be gone; it is not good you tarry here:—by gar, I vill cut all his two stones; by gar, he shall not have a stone to trow at his dog. [*Exit* Simple.

Quick. Alas, he speaks but for his friend.

Caius. It is no matter-a for dat:—do not you tell-a me dat I shall have Anne Page for myself?—by gar, I vill kill de Jack priest; and I have appointed mine host of *de Jarterre* to measure our weapon:—by gar, I vill myself have Anne Page.

Quick. Sir, the maid loves you, and all shall be well: we must give folks leave to prate: What, the good-jer!

Caius. Rugby, come to the court vit me;—By gar, if I have not Anne Page, I shall turn your head out of my door:—Follow my heels, Rugby. [*Exeunt* Caius *and* Rugby.

Quick. You shall have An fools-head of your own. No, I know Anne's mind for that: never a woman in Windsor knows more of Anne's mind than I do; nor can do more than I do with her, I thank heaven.

Fent. [*Within.*] Who's within there, ho?

Quick. Who's there, I trow? Come near the house, I pray you.

Enter Fenton.

Fen. How now, good woman: how dost thou?

Quick. The better, that it pleases your good worship to ask.

Fent. What news? how does pretty mistress Anne?

Quick. In truth, sir, and she is pretty, and honest, and gentle; and one that is your friend, I can tell you that by the way; I praise heaven for it.

Fent. Shall I do any good, thinkest thou? Shall I not lose my suit?

Quick. Troth, sir, all is in his hands above: but notwithstanding, master Fenton, I'll be sworn on a book, she loves you:—Have not your worship a wart above your eye?

Fent. Yes, marry, have I; what of that?

Quick. Well, thereby hangs a tale;—good faith, it is such another Nan:—but, I detest, an honest maid as ever broke bread:—We had an hour's talk of that wart;—I shall never laugh but in that maid's company! But, indeed, she is given too much to allicholly and musing: But for you—Well, go to.

Fent. Well, I shall see her to-day: Hold, there's money for thee; let me have thy voice in my behalf: if thou seest her before me, commend me—

Quick. Will I? i'faith, that we will: and I will tell your worship more of the wart, the next time we have confidence: and of other wooers.

Fent. Well, farewell; I am in great haste now. [*Exit.*

Quick. Farewell to your worship.—Truly, an honest gentleman; but Anne loves him not; for I know Anne's mind as well as another does: Out upon't! what have I forgot? [*Exit.*

ACT II.

SCENE I. *Before* Page's *House.*

Enter Mistress Page, *with a letter.*

Mrs. Page. What! have I 'scaped love-letters in the holy-day time of my beauty, and am I now a subject for them? Let me see? [*Reads.*

Ask me no reason why I love you; for though love use reason for his precisian, he admits him not for his counsellor; You are not young, no more am I; go to then, there's sympathy; you are merry, so am I; Ha! ha! then there's more sympathy: you love sack, and so do I; would you desire better sympathy? Let it suffice thee, mistress Page (at the least, if the love of a soldier can suffice), that I love thee. I will not say, pity me, 'tis not a soldier-like phrase; but I say, love me. By me,

Thine own true knight,
By day or night.
Or any kind of light,
With all his might
For thee to fight,

John Falstaff.

What a Herod of Jury is this!—O wicked, wicked world!—one that is well nigh worn to pieces with age, to show himself a young gallant! What an unweighed behaviour hath this Flemish drunkard picked (with the devil's name) out of my conversation, that he dares in this manner assay me? Why, he hath not been thrice in my company!—What should I say to him?—I was then frugal of my mirth:—heaven forgive me!—Why, I'll exhibit a bill in the parliament for the putting down of fat men. How shall I be revenged on him? for revenged I will be, as sure as his guts are made of puddings.

Enter Mistress FORD.

Mrs. Ford. Mistress Page! trust me, I was going to your house.

Mrs. Page. And, trust me, I was coming to you. You look very ill.

Mrs. Ford. Nay, I'll ne'er believe that: I have to show to the contrary.

Mrs. Page. 'Faith, but you do, in my mind.

Mrs. Ford. Well, I do then; yet, I say, I could show you to the contrary: O, mistress Page, give me some counsel!

Mrs. Page. What's the matter, woman?

Mrs. Ford. O woman, if it were not for one trifling respect, I could come to such honour!

Mrs. Page. Hang the trifle, woman; take the honour: What is it?——dispense with trifles;—what is it?

Mrs. Ford. If I would but go to hell for an eternal moment, or so, I could be knighted.

Mrs. Page. What?—thou liest!—Sir Alice Ford!——These knights will hack; and so thou should'st not alter the article of thy gentry.

Mrs. Ford. We burn day-light; here, read, read;—perceive how I might be knighted.—I shall think the worse of fat men, as long as I have an eye to make difference of men's liking: And yet he would not swear; praised women's modesty: and gave such orderly and well behaved reproof to all uncomeliness, that I would have sworn his disposition would have gone to the truth of his words: but they do no more adhere and keep place together, than the hundredth psalm to the tune of *Green sleeves.* What tempest, I trow, threw this whale, with so many tuns of oil in his belly, ashore at Windsor? How shall I be revenged on him? I think, the best way were to entertain him with hope, till the wicked fire of lust have melted him in his own grease.—Did you ever hear the like?

Mrs. Page. Letter for letter; but that the name of Page and Ford differs!—To thy great comfort in this mystery of ill opinions, here's the twin-brother of thy letter: but let thine inherit first; for, I protest, mine never shall. I warrant he hath a thousand of these letters, writ with blank space for different names, (sure more), and these are of the second edition: He will print them out of doubt: for he cares not what he puts into the press, when he would put us two. I had rather be a giantess, and lie under mount Pelion. Well, I will find you twenty lascivious turtles, ere one chaste man.

Mrs. Ford. Why, this is the very same; the very hand, the very words: What doth he think of us?

Mrs. Page. Nay, I know not: It makes me almost ready to wrangle with mine own honesty. I'll entertain myself like one that I am not acquainted withal; for, sure, unless he know some strain in me, that I know not myself, he would never have boarded me in this fury.

Mrs. Ford. Boarding, call you it? I'll be sure to keep him above deck.

Mrs. Page. So will I; if he come under my hatches, I'll never to sea again. Let's be revenged on him; let's appoint him a meeting; give him a show of comfort in his suit; and lead on with a fine-baited delay, till he hath pawn'd his horses to mine Host of the Garter.

Mrs. Ford. Nay, I will consent to act any villainy against him, that may not sully the chariness of our honesty. O, that my husband saw this letter! it would give eternal food to his jealousy.

Mrs. Page. Why, look, where he comes; and my good man too: he's as far from jealousy, as I am from giving him cause; and that, I hope, is an unmeasurable distance.

Mrs. Ford. You are the happier woman.

Mrs. Page. Let's consult together against this greasy knight: Come hither. [*They retire.*

Enter FORD, PISTOL, PAGE, *and* NYM.

Ford. Well, I hope it be not so.

Pist. Hope is a curtail dog in some affairs:
Sir John affects thy wife.

Ford. Why, sir, my wife is not young.

Pist. He woos both high and low, both rich and poor,
Both young and old, one with another, Ford:
He loves the gally-mawfry; Ford, perpend.

Ford. Love my wife?

Pist. With liver burning hot: Prevent, or go thou,
Like Sir Actæon he, with Ring-wood at thy heels:
O, odious is the name!

Ford. What name, sir?

Pist. The horn, I say: Farewell.
Take heed; have open eye; for thieves do foot by night:
Take heed, ere summer comes, or cuckoo birds do sing.—
Away, Sir comporal Nym—
Believe it, Page; he speaks sense. [*Exit* PIST.

Ford. I will be patient; I will find out this.

Nym. And this is true. [*To* PAGE.] I like not the humour of lying. He hath wronged me in some humours; I should have borne the humoured letter to her: but I have a sword, and it shall bite upon my necessity. He loves your wife; there's the short and the long. My name is corporal Nym; I speak, and I avouch. 'Tis true:—my name is Nym, and Falstaff loves your wife.—Adieu! I love not the humour of bread and cheese; and there's the humour of it. Adieu. [*Exit* NYM.

Page. The humour of it, quoth'a! here's a fellow frights humour out of his wits.

Ford. I will seek out Falstaff.

Page. I never heard such a drawling, affecting rogue.

Ford. If I do find it, well.

Page. I will not believe such a Cataian, though the priest of the town commended him for a true man.

Ford. 'Twas a good sensible fellow: Well.

Page. How now, Meg?

Mrs. Page. Whither go you, George?—Hark you.

Mrs. Ford. How now, sweet Frank? why art thou melancholy?

Ford. I melancholy! I am not melancholy.—Get you home, go.

Mrs. Ford. 'Faith, thou hast some crotchets in thy head now.—Will you go, mistress Page?

Mrs. Page. Have with you.—You'll come to dinner, George?—Look, who comes yonder: she shall be our messenger to this paltry knight. [*Aside to* MRS. FORD.

Enter MISTRESS QUICKLY.

Mrs. Ford. Trust me, I thought on her: she'll fit it.

Mrs. Page. You are come to see my daughter Anne?

Quick. Ay, forsooth; And, I pray, how does good mistress Anne?

Mrs. Page. Go in with us, and see; we have an hour's talk with you.

[*Exeunt* MRS. PAGE, MRS. FORD, *and* MRS. QUICKLY.

Page. How now, master Ford?

Ford. You heard what this knave told me; did you not?

Page. Yes; and you heard what the other told me?

Ford. Do you think there is truth in them?

Page. Hang'em, slaves! I do not think the knight would offer it: but these that accuse him in his intent towards our wives, are a yoke of his discarded men; very rogues, now they be out of service.

Ford. Were they his men?

Page. Marry, were they.

Ford. I like it never the better for that.—Does he lie at the Garter?

Page. Ay, marry, does he. If he should intend this voyage towards my wife, I would turn her loose to him; and what he gets more of her than sharp words, let it lie on my head.

Ford. I do not misdoubt my wife; but I would be loath to turn them together: a man may be too confident: I would have nothing lie on my head; I cannot be thus satisfied.

Page. Look, where my ranting host of the Garter comes: there is either liquor in his pate, or money in his purse, when he looks so merrily.—How now, mine host?

Enter HOST *and* SHALLOW.

Host. How now, bully-rook? thou'rt a gentleman: cavalero-justice, I say.

Shal. I follow, mine host, I follow.—Good even, and twenty, good master Page! Master Page, will you go with us? we have sport in hand.

Host. Tell him, cavalero-justice; tell him, bully-rook.

Shal. Sir, there is a fray to be fought, between Sir Hugh the Welsh priest, and Caius the French doctor.

Ford. Good mine host o' the Garter, a word with you.

Host. What say'st thou, bully-rook?

[*They go aside.*

Shal. Will you [*to* PAGE] go with us to behold it? my merry host hath had the measuring of their weapons; and, I think he hath appointed them contrary places: for, believe me, I hear the parson is no jester. Hark, I will tell you what our sport shall be.

Host. Hast thou no suit against my knight, my guest-cavalier?

Ford. None, I protest: but I'll give you a pottle of burnt sack to give me recourse to him, and tell him, my name is Brook; only for a jest.

Host. My hand, bully: thou shalt have egress and regress; said I well? and thy name shall be Brook: It is a merry knight.—Will you go, Cavaliers?

Shal. Have with you, mine host.

Page. I have heard, the Frenchman hath good skill in his rapier.

Shal. Tut, sir, I could have told you more: In these times you stand on distance, your passes, stoccadoes, and I know not what: 'tis the heart, master Page: 'tis here, 'tis here. I have seen the time, with my long sword, I would have made you four tall fellows skip like rats.

Host. Here, boys, here, here! shall we wag?

Page. Have with you:—I had rather hear them scold than fight.

[*Exeunt* HOST, SHAL. *and* PAGE.

Ford. Though Page be a secure fool, and stands so firmly on his wife's frailty, yet I cannot put off my opinion so easily; She was in his company at Page's house; and, what they made there, I know not. Well, I will look further into't: and I have a disguise to sound Falstaff: If I find her honest, I lose not my labour; if she be otherwise, 'tis labour well bestowed.

[*Exit.*

SCENE II. *A Room in the Garter Inn.*

Enter FALSTAFF *and* PISTOL.

Fal. I will not lend thee a penny.

Pist. Why, then the world's mine oyster,
Which I with sword will open.—
I will retort the sum in equipage.

Fal. Not a penny. I have been content, sir, you should lay my countenance to pawn: I have grated upon my good friends for three reprieves for you and your coach-fellow Nym; or else you had looked through the grate like a geminy of baboons. I am damned in hell, for swearing to gentlemen my friends, you were good soldiers, and tall fellows: and when mistress Bridget lost the handle of her fan, I took't upon mine honour, thou hadst it not.

Pist. Didst thou not share? hadst thou not fifteen pence?

Fal. Reason, you rogue, reason: Think'st thou, I'll endanger my soul *gratis?* At a word, hang no more about me, I am no gibbet for you:—go.—A short knife and a throng;—to your manor of Pickthatch, go.—You'll not bear a letter for me, you rogue! you stand upon your honour!—Why, thou unconfinable baseness, it is as much as I can do to keep the terms of my honour precise. I, I, I myself sometimes, leaving the fear of heaven on the left hand, and hiding mine honour in my necessity, am fain to shuffle, to hedge, and to lurch; and yet, you, rogue, will ensconce your rags, your cat-a-mountain looks, your red-lattice phrases, and your bold-beating oaths, under the shelter of your honour! You will not do it, you?

Pist. I do relent; what would'st thou more of man.

Enter ROBIN.

Rob. Sir, here's a woman would speak with you.

Fal. Let her approach.

Enter MISTRESS QUICKLY.

Quick. Give your worship good-morrow.

Fal. Good-morrow, good wife.

Quick. Not so, an't please your worship.

Fal. Good maid, then.

Quick. I'll be sworn; as my mother was, the first hour I was born.

Fal. I do believe the swearer: What with me?

Quick. Shall I vouchsafe your worship a word or two?

Fal. Two thousand, fair woman; and I'll vouchsafe thee the hearing.

Quick. There is one Mistress Ford, sir;—I pray, come a little nearer this ways:—I myself dwell with master doctor Caius.

Fal. Well, on: Mistress Ford, you say,——

Quick. Your worship says very true: I pray your worship, come a little nearer this ways.

Fal. I warrant thee, nobody hears:—mine own people, mine own people.

Quick. Are they so? Heaven bless them, and make them his servants!

Fal. Well: mistress Ford:—what of her?

Quick. Why, sir, she's a good creature. Ford, lord! your worship's a wanton: Well, heaven forgive you, and all of us, I pray!

Fal. Mistress Ford:—come, mistress Ford,—

Quick. Marry, this is the short and the long of it: you have brought her into such a canaries as 'tis wonderful. The best courtier of them all, when the court lay at Windsor, could never have brought her to such a canary. Yet there has been knights, and lords, and gentlemen, with their coaches; I warrant you, coach after coach, letter after letter, gift after gift; smelling so sweetly (all musk), and so rushling, I warrant you, in silk and gold; and in such alligant terms; and in such wine and sugar of the best, and the fairest, that would have won any woman's heart; and, I warrant you, they could never get an eye-wink of her.—I had myself twenty angels given me this morning: but I defy all angels (in any such sort, as they say), but in the way of honesty:—and, I warrant you, they could never get her so much as sip on a cup with the proudest of them all: and yet there has been earls, nay, which is more, pensioners; but, I warrant you, all is one with her.

Fal. But what says she to me? be brief, my good she Mercury.

Quick. Marry, she hath received your letter; for the which she thanks you a thousand times: and she gives you to notify, that her husband will be absence from his house between ten and eleven.

Fal. Ten and eleven?

Quick. Ay, forsooth; and then you may come and see the picture, she says, that you wot of; master Ford, her husband, will be from home. Alas! the sweet woman leads an ill life with him; he's a very jealousy man; she leads a very frampold life with him, good heart.

Fal. Ten and eleven: Woman, commend me to her; I will not fail her.

Quick. Why, you say well: But I have another messenger to your worship: Mrs. Page hath her hearty commendations to you too;—and let me tell you in your ear, she's as fartuous a civil modest wife, and one (I tell you) that will not miss you morning nor evening prayer, as any is in Windsor, whoe'er be the other: and she bade me tell your worship, that her husband is seldom from home; but she hopes, there will come a time. I never knew a woman so dote upon a man; surely, I think you have charms, la; yes, in truth.

Fal. Not I, I assure thee; setting the attraction of my good parts aside, I have no other charms.

Quick. Blessing on your heart for't!

Fal. But, I pray thee, tell me this: has Ford's wife, and Page's wife, acquainted each other how they love me?

Quick. That were a jest, indeed!—they have not so little grace, I hope:—that were a trick indeed! But Mistress Page would desire you to send her your little page of all loves; her husband has a marvellous infection to the little page; and, truly, master Page is an honest man. Never a wife in Windsor leads a better life than she does; do what she will, say what she will, take all, pay all, go to bed when she list, rise when she list, all is as she will; and, truly, she deserves it: for if there be a kind woman in Windsor, she is one. You must send her your page; no remedy.

Fal. Why, I will.

Quick. Nay, but do so then: and, look you, he may come and go between you both; and, in any case, have a nay word, that you may know one another's mind, and the boy never need to understand any thing; for 'tis not good that children should know any wickedness: old folks, you know, have discretion, as they say, and know the world.

Fal. Fare thee well: commend me to them both: there's my purse; I am yet thy debtor.—Boy, go along with this woman.—This news distracts me! [*Exeunt* QUICKLY *and* ROBIN.

Pist. This punk is one of Cupid's carriers:—
Clap on more sails; pursue, up with your fights;
Give fire; she is my prize, or ocean whelm them
all! [*Exit* PISTOL.

Fal. Say'st thou so, old Jack? go thy ways, I'll make more of thy old body than I have done. Will they yet look after thee? Wilt thou, after the expense of so much money, be now a gainer? Good body, I thank thee: Let them say, 'tis grossly done; so it be fairly done, no matter.

Enter BARDOLPH.

Bard. Sir John, there's one master Brook below would fain speak with you, and be acquainted with you: and hath sent your worship a morning's draught of sack.

Fal. Brook is his name?

Bard. Ay, sir.

Fal. Call him in: [*Exit* BARDOLPH.] Such Brooks are welcome to me, that o'erflow such liquor. Ah! ah! mistress Ford and mistress Page, have I encompass'd you? go to; *via!*

Re-enter BARDOLPH, *with* FORD *disguised.*

Ford. Bless you, sir.

Fal. And you, sir: Would you speak with me?

Ford. I make bold to press with so little preparation upon you.

Fal. You're welcome; What's your will? Give us leave, drawer. [*Exit* BARDOLPH.

Ford. Sir, I am a gentleman that have spent much; my name is Brook.

Fal. Good master Brook, I desire more acquaintance of you.

Ford. Good Sir John, I sue for yours: not to charge you; for I must let you understand, I think myself in better plight for a lender than you are: the which hath something embolden'd me to this unseason'd intrusion; for they say, if money go before, all ways do lie open.

Fal. Money is a good soldier, sir, and will on.

Ford. Troth, and I have a bag of money here troubles me: if you will help me to bear it, Sir John, take all, or half, for easing me of the carriage.

Fal. Sir, I know not how I may deserve to be your porter.

Ford. I will tell you, sir, if you will give me the hearing.

Fal. Speak, good master Brook; I shall be glad to be your servant.

Ford. Sir, I hear you are a scholar,—I will be brief with you;——and you have been a man long known to me, though I had never so good means, as desire, to make myself acquainted with you. I shall discover a thing to you, wherein I must very much lay open mine own imperfection: but, good Sir John, as you have one eye upon my follies, as you hear them unfolded, turn another into the register of your own; that I may pass with a reproof the easier, sith you yourself know, how easy it is to be such an offender.

Fal. Very well, sir; proceed.

Ford. There is a gentlewoman in this town, her husband's name is Ford.

Fal. Well, sir.

Ford. I have long loved her, and, I protest to you, bestowed much on her; followed her with a doting observance; engrossed opportunities to meet her; fee'd every slight occasion, that could but niggardly give me sight of her; not only bought many presents to give her, but have given largely to many, to know what she would have given: briefly, I have pursued her, as love hath pursued me; which hath been on the wing of all occasions. But whatsoever I have merited, either in my mind or in my means, meed, I am sure, I have received none; unless experience be a jewel: that I have purchased at an infinite rate; and that hath taught me to say this:

Love like a shadow flies, when substance love pursues;
Pursuing that that flies, and flying what pursues.

Fal. Have you received no promise of satisfaction at her hands?

Ford. Never.

Fal. Have you importuned her to such a purpose?

Ford. Never.

Fal. Of what quality was your love then?

Ford. Like a fair house, built upon another man's ground, so that I have lost my edifice, by mistaking the place where I erected it.

Fal. To what purpose have you unfolded this to me?

Ford. When I have told you that, I have told you all. Some say, that though she appear honest to me, yet, in other places, she enlargeth her mirth so far, that there is shrewd construction made of her. Now, Sir John, here is the heart of my purpose: You are a gentleman of excellent breeding, admirable discourse, of great admittance, authentick in your place and person, generally allowed for your many warlike, courtlike, and learned preparations.

Fal. O, sir!

Ford. Believe it, for you know it:—There is money; spend it, spend it, spend more; spend all I have; only give me so much of your time in exchange of it, as to lay an amiable siege to the honesty of this Ford's wife: use your art of wooing, win her consent to you; if any man may, you may as soon as any.

Fal. Would it apply well to the vehemency of your affection, that I should win what you would enjoy? Methinks you prescribe to yourself very preposterously.

Ford. O, understand my drift! she dwells so securely on the excellency of her honour, that the folly of my soul dares not present itself; she is too bright to be looked against. Now, could I come to her with any detection in my hand, my desires had instance and argument to commend themselves; I could drive her then from the ward of her purity, her reputation, her marriage-vow, and a thousand other her defences, which now are too strongly embattled against me: What say you to't, Sir John?

Fal. Master Brook, I will first make bold with your money; next give me your hand; and last, as I am a gentleman, you shall, if you will, enjoy Ford's wife.

Ford. O good sir!

Fal. Master Brook, I say you shall.

Ford. Want no money, Sir John, you shall want none.

Fal. Want no mistress Ford, master Brook, you shall want none. I shall be with her (I may tell you), by her own appointment; even as you came in to me, her assistant, or go-between, parted from me: I say, I shall be with her between ten and eleven; for at that time the jealous rascally knave, her husband, will be forth. Come you to me at night; you shall know how I speed.

Ford. I am blest in your acquaintance. Do you know Ford, sir?

Fal. Hang him, poor cuckoldly knave! I know him not:—yet I wrong him to call him poor; they say, the jealous wittolly knave hath masses of money; for the which his wife seems to me well-favoured, I will use her as the key of the cuckoldly rogue's coffer; and there's my harvest-home.

Ford. I would you knew Ford, sir; that you might avoid him, if you saw him.

Fal. Hang him, mechanical salt-butter rogue! I will stare him out of his wits; I will awe him with my cudgel; it shall hang like a meteor o'er the cuckold's horns: master Brook, thou shalt know, I will predominate o'er the peasant, and thou shalt lie with his wife.—Come to me soon at night:—Ford's a knave, and I will aggravate his style: thou, master Brook, shalt know him for a knave and cuckold:—come to me soon at night. [*Exit.*

Ford. What a damned Epicurean rascal is this!—My heart is ready to crack with impatience.—Who says this is improvident jealousy? —My wife hath sent to him, the hour is fixed, the match is made. Would any man have thought this?—See the hell of having a false woman! my bed shall be abused, my coffers ransacked, my reputation gnawn at; and I shall not only receive this villanous wrong, but stand under the adoption of abominable terms, and by him that does me this wrong. Terms! names! ——Amaimon sounds well; Lucifer, well; Barbason, well; yet they are devils' additions, the names of fiends: but cuckold! wittol cuckold! the devil himself hath not such a name. Page is an ass, a secure ass; he will trust his wife, he will not be jealous: I will rather trust a Fleming with my butter, parson Hugh the Welshman with my cheese, an Irishman with my aqua-vitæ bottle, or a thief to walk my ambling gelding, than my wife with herself: then she plots, then she ruminates, then she devises: and what they think in their hearts they may effect, they will break their hearts but they will effect. Heaven be praised for my jealousy!—Eleven o'clock the hour—I will prevent this, detect my wife, be revenged on Falstaff, and laugh at Page. I will about it; better three hours too soon, than a minute too late. Fie, fie, fie! cuckold! cuckold! cuckold! [*Exit.*

SCENE III. *Windsor Park.*

Enter CAIUS *and* RUGBY.

Caius. Jack Rugby.

Rug. Sir.

Caius. Vat is de clock, Jack?

Rug. 'Tis past the hour, sir, that Sir Hugh promised to meet.

Caius. By gar, he has save his soul, dat he is no come: he has pray his Pible vell, dat he is no come: by gar, Jack Rugby, he is dead already, if he be come.

Rug. He is wise, sir; he knew your worship would kill him, if he came.

Caius. By gar, de herring is no dead, so as I vill kill him. Take your rapier, Jack; I vill tell you how I vill kill him.

Rug. Alas, sir, I cannot fence.

Caius. Villany, take your rapier.

Rug. Forbear; here's company.

Enter HOST, SHALLOW, SLENDER, *and* PAGE.

Host. 'Bless thee, bully doctor.

Shal. Save you, master doctor Caius.

Page. Now, good master doctor!

Slen. Give you good-morrow, sir.

Caius. Vat be all you, one, two, tree, four, come for?

Host. To see thee fight, to see thee foin, to see thee traverse, to see thee here, to see thee there; to see thee pass thy punto, thy stock, thy reverse, thy distance, thy montant. Is he dead, my Ethiopian? is he dead, my Francisco? ha, bully! What says my Æsculapius? my Galen! my heart of elder? ha! is he dead, bully Stale? is he dead?

Caius. By gar, he is de coward Jack-priest of de vorld; he is not show his face.

Host. Thou art a Castilian, king-urinal! Hector of Greece, my boy!

Caius. I pray you, bear vitness that me have stay six or seven, two, tree hours for him, and he is no come.

Shal. He is the wiser man, master doctor: he is a curer of souls, and you a curer of bodies; if you should fight, you go against the hair of your professions; is it not true, master Page?

Page. Master Shallow, you have yourself been a great fighter, though now a man of peace.

Shal. Bodykins, master Page, though I now be old, and of the peace, if I see a sword out, my finger itches to make one: though we are justices, and doctors, and churchmen, master Page, we have some salt of our youth in us; we are the sons of women, Master Page.

Page. 'Tis true, master Shallow.

Shal. It will be found so, master Page. Master doctor Caius, I am come to fetch you home. I am sworn of the peace; you have showed yourself a wise physician, and Sir Hugh hath shown himself a wise and patient churchman: you must go with me, master doctor.

Host. Pardon, guest justice:—A word, monsieur Muck-water.

Caius. Muck-vater; vat is dat?

Host. Muck-water, in our English tongue, is valour, bully.

Caius. By gar, then I have as much muck-vater as de Englishman:—Scurvy jack-dog priest; by gar, me vil cut his ears.

Host. He will clapper-claw thee tightly, bully.

Caius. Clapper-de-claw! vat is dat?

Host. That is, he will make thee amends.

Caius. By gar, me do look, he shall clapper-de-claw me; for, by gar, me vill have it.

Host. And I will provoke him to't, or let him wag.

Caius. Me tank you for dat.

Host. And moreover, bully,—But first, master guest, and master Page, and eke cavalero Slender, go you through the town to Frogmore. [*Aside to them.*

Page. Sir Hugh is there, is he?

Host. He is there: see what humour he is in; and I will bring the doctor about by the fields: will it do well?

Shal. We will do it.

Page, Shal. and Slen. Adieu, good master doctor. [*Exeunt* PAGE, SHAL. *and* SLEN.

Caius. By gar, me vill kill de priest; for he speak for a jack-an-ape to Anne Page.

Host. Let him die: but, first, sheath thy impatience; throw cold water on thy choler: go about the fields with me through Frogmore: I will bring thee where Mrs. Anne Page is, at a farmhouse a feasting; and thou shalt woo her: Cry'd game, said I well?

Caius. By gar, me tank you for dat: by gar, I love you: and I shall procure-a you de good guest, de earl, de knight, de lords, de gentlemen, my patients.

Host. For the which, I will be thy adversary towards Anne Page; said I well?

Caius. By gar, 'tis good; vell said.

Host. Let us wag then.

Caius. Come at my heels, Jack Rugby. [*Exeunt.*

ACT III.

SCENE I. *A Field near Frogmore.*

Enter SIR HUGH EVANS *and* SIMPLE.

Eva. I pray you now, good master Slender's serving-man, and friend Simple by your name, which way have you looked for master Caius, that calls himself *Doctor of Physick?*

Sim. Marry, sir, the pittie-ward, the park-ward, every way; old Windsor way, and every way but the town way.

Eva. I most fehemently desire you, you will also look that way.

Sim. I will, sir.

Eva. 'Pless my soul! how full of cholers I am, and trempling of mind!—I shall be glad, if he have deceived me:—how melancholies I am!—I will knog his urinals about his knave's costard, when I have good opportunities for the 'ork:—'pless my soul! [*Sings.*

To shallow rivers, to whose falls
Melodious birds sing madrigals;
There will we make our peds of roses,
And a thousand fragrant posies.
To shallow ———

'Mercy on me! I have a great dispositions to cry.

Melodious birds sing madrigals;—
When as I sat in Pabylon.——
And a thousand vagram posies.
To shallow———

Sim. Yonder he is coming this way, Sir Hugh.

Eva. He's welcome:——

To shallow rivers, to whose falls——

Heaven prosper the right!—What weapons is he?

Sim. No weapons, sir: There comes my master, master Shallow, and another gentleman from Frogmore, over the stile, this way.

Eva. Pray you, give me my gown; or else keep it in your arms.

Enter PAGE, SHALLOW, *and* SLENDER.

Shal. How now, master parson? Good morrow, good Sir Hugh. Keep a gamester from the dice, and a good student from his book, and it is wonderful.

Slen. Ah, sweet Anne Page!

Page. Save you, good Sir Hugh.

Eva. 'Pless you from his mercy sake, all of you!

Shal. What! the sword and the word! do you study them both, master parson?

Page. And youthful still, in your doublet and hose, this raw rheumatic day?

Eva. There is reasons and causes for it.

Page. We are come to you, to do a good office, master parson.

Eva. Fery well: What is it?

Page. Yonder is a most reverend gentleman, who belike, having received wrong by some person, is at most odds with his own gravity and patience, that ever you saw.

Shal. I have lived fourscore years and upward; I never heard a man of his place, gravity, and learning, so wide of his own respect.

Eva. What is he?

Page. I think you know him; master doctor Caius, the renowned French physician.

Eva. Got's will, and his passion of my heart! I had as lief you would tell me of a mess of porridge.

Page. Why?

Eva. He has no more knowledge in Hibocrates and Galen,—and he is a knave besides; a cowardly knave, as you would desires to be acquainted withal.

Page. I warrant you, he's the man should fight with him.

Slen. O sweet Anne Page!

Shal. It appears so, by his weapons:—Keep them asunder;—here comes doctor Caius.

Enter HOST, CAIUS, *and* RUGBY.

Page. Nay, good master parson, keep in your weapon.

Shal. So do you, good master doctor.

Host. Disarm them, and let them question; let them keep their limbs whole, and hack our English.

Caius. I pray you, let-a me speak a word vit your ear: Verefore vill you not meet-a me?

Eva. Pray you, use your patience: In good time.

Caius. By gar, you are de coward, de Jack dog, John ape.

Eva. Pray you, let us not be laughing-stogs to other men's humours; I desire you in friendship, and I will one way or other make you amends:—I will knog your urinals about your knave's cogscomb, for missing your meetings and appointments.

Caius. Diable!—Jack Rugby,—mine *Host de Jarterre*, have I not stay for him, to kill him? have I not, at de place I did appoint?

Eva. As I am a Christians soul, now, look you, this is the place appointed; I'll be judgment by mine host of the Garter.

Host. Peace, I say Guallia and Gaul, French and Welsh; soul-curer and body-curer.

Caius. Ay, dat is very good! excellent!

Host. Peace, I say; hear mine host of the Garter. Am I politick? am I subtle? am I a Machiavel? Shall I lose my doctor? no; he gives me the potions, and the motions. Shall I lose my parson? my priest, my Sir Hugh? no; he gives me the pro-verbs and the no-verbs. —Give me thy hand, terrestrial; so:—Give me thy hand, celestial; so.——Boys of art, I have deceived you both; I have directed you to wrong places: your hearts are mighty, your skins are whole, and let burnt sack be the issue.

--Come, lay their swords to pawn:—Follow me, lad of peace; follow, follow, follow.

Shal. Trust me, a mad host:—Follow, gentlemen, follow.

Slen. O, sweet Anne Page!

[*Exeunt* SHAL. SLEN. PAGE, *and* Host.

Caius. Ha! do I perceive dat? have you make-a de sot of us? ha, ha!

Eva. This is well; he has made us his vlouting-stog.—I desire you, that we may be friends; and let us knog our prains together, to be revenge on this same scall, scurvy, cogging companion, the host of the Garter.

Caius. By gar, vit all my heart; he promise to bring me vere is Anne Page: by gar, he deceive me too.

Eva. Well, I will smite his noddles:—Pray you, follow. [*Exeunt.*

SCENE II. *The Street in Windsor.*

Enter MISTRESS PAGE *and* ROBIN.

Mrs. Page. Nay, keep your way, little gallant; you were wont to be a follower, but now you are a leader: Whether had you rather lead mine eyes, or eye your master's heels?

Rob. I had rather, forsooth, go before you like a man, than follow him like a dwarf.

Mrs. Page. O you are a flattering boy; now, I see you'll be a courtier.

Enter FORD.

Ford. Well met, mistress Page: Whither go you?

Mrs. Page. Truly, sir, to see your wife: Is she at home?

Ford. Ay; and as idle as she may hang together, for want of company: I think, if your husbands were dead, you two would marry.

Mrs. Page. Be sure of that,—two other husbands.

Ford. Where had you this pretty weather-cock?

Mrs. Page. I cannot tell what the dickens his name is my husband had him of: What do you call your knight's name, sirrah?

Rob. Sir John Falstaff.

Ford. Sir John Falstaff!

Mrs. Page. He, he; I can never hit on's name. There is such a league between my good man and he!—Is your wife at home, indeed?

Ford. Indeed she is.

Mrs. Page. By your leave, sir;—I am sick, till I see her. [*Exeunt* MRS. PAGE *and* ROBIN.

Ford. Has Page any brains? hath he any eyes? hath he any thinking? Sure, they sleep; he hath no use of them. Why, this boy will carry a letter twenty miles, as easy as a cannon will shoot point blank twelve score. He pieces-out his wife's inclination; he gives her folly motion and advantage: and now she's going to my wife, and Falstaff's boy with her. A man may hear this shower sing in the wind!—and Falstaff's boy with her!—Good plots!—they are laid; and our revolted wives share damnation together. Well; I will take him; then torture my wife, pluck the borrowed veil of modesty from the so-seeming mistress Page, divulge Page himself for a secure and wilful Actæon; and to these violent proceedings all my neighbours shall cry aim. [*Clock strikes.*] The clock gives me my cue, and my assurance bids me search; there I shall find Falstaff: I shall be rather praised for this, than mocked; for it is as positive as the earth is firm, that Falstaff is there: I will go.

Enter PAGE, SHALLOW, SLENDER, Host, SIR HUGH EVANS, CAIUS, *and* RUGBY.

Shal. Page, &c. Well met, master Ford.

Ford. Trust me a good knot: I have good cheer at home; and, I pray you all, go with me.

Shal. I must excuse myself, master Ford.

Slen. And so must I, sir; we have appointed to dine with mistress Anne, and I would not break with her for more money than I'll speak of.

Shal. We have lingered about a match between Anne Page and my cousin Slender, and this day we shall have our answer.

Slen. I hope, I have your good will, father Page.

Page. You have, master Slender; I stand wholly for you:—but my wife, master doctor, is for you altogether.

Caius. Ay, by gar; and de maid is love-a me; my nursh-a Quickly tell me so mush.

Host. What say you to young master Fenton? he capers, he dances, he has eyes of youth, he writes verses, he speaks holyday, he smells April and May: he will carry't; he will carry't; 'tis in his buttons; he will carry't.

Page. Not by my consent, I promise you. The gentleman is of no having: he kept company with the wild Prince and Poins; he is of too high a region, he knows too much. No, he shall not knit a knot in his fortunes with the finger of my substance: if he take her, let him take her simply; the wealth I have waits on my consent, and my consent goes not that way.

Ford. I beseech you, heartily, some of you go home with me to dinner: besides your cheer, you shall have sport; I will show you a monster.——Master doctor, you shall go;—so shall you, master Page;—And you, Sir Hugh.

Shal. Well, fare you well:—we shall have the freer wooing at master Page's.

[*Exeunt* SHALLOW *and* SLENDER.

Caius. Go home, John Rugby; I come anon.

[*Exit* RUGBY.

Host. Farewell, my hearts: I will to my honest knight Falstaff, and drink canary with him.

[*Exit* Host.

Ford. [*Aside.*] I think, I shall drink in pipewine first with him; I'll make him dance. Will you go, gentles?

All. Have with you, to see this monster.

[*Exeunt.*

SCENE III. *A Room in* Ford's *House.*

Enter MRS. FORD *and* MRS. PAGE.

Mrs. Ford. What, John! what Robert!

Mrs. Page. Quickly, quickly: Is the buck-basket—

Mrs. Ford. I warrant:—What, Robin, I say.

Enter Servants with a basket.

Mrs. Page. Come, come, come.

Mrs. Ford. Here, set it down.

Mrs. Page. Give your men the charge; we must be brief.

Mrs. Ford. Marry, as I told you before, John and Robert, be ready here hard by in the brew-house; and when I suddenly call you, come forth, and (without any pause, or staggering) take this basket on your shoulders: that done, trudge with it in all haste, and carry it among the whitsters in Datchet mead, and there empty it in the muddy ditch, close by the Thames' side.

Mrs. Page. You will do it?

Mrs. Ford. I have told them over and over; they lack no direction: Be gone, and come when you are called. [*Exeunt* Servants.

Mrs. Page. Here comes little Robin.

Enter ROBIN.

Mrs. Ford. How now, my eyas-musket? what news with you?

Rob. My master Sir John is come in at your back door, mistress Ford; and requests your company.

Mrs. Page. You little Jack-a-lent, have you been true to us?

Rob. Ay, I'll be sworn: My master knows not of your being here; and hath threatened to put me into everlasting liberty, if I tell you of it; for, he swears, he'll turn me away.

Mrs. Page. Thou art a good boy; this secrecy

of thine shall be a tailor to thee, and shall make thee a new doublet and hose.—I'll go hide me.

Mrs. Ford. Do so:—Go tell thy master, I am alone. Mistress Page, remember you your cue. [*Exit* ROBIN.

Mrs. Page. I warrant thee; if I do not act it, hiss me. [*Exit* MRS. PAGE.

Mrs. Ford. Go to then: we'll use this unwholesome humidity, this gross watry pumpion;—we'll teach him to know turtles from jays.

Enter FALSTAFF.

Fal. Have I caught thee, *my heavenly jewel?* Why, now let me die, for I have lived long enough; this is the period of my ambition: O this blessed hour!

Mrs. Ford. O sweet Sir John!

Fal. Mistress Ford, I cannot cog, I cannot prate, mistress Ford. Now shall I sin in my wish: I would thy husband were dead: I'll speak it before the best lord, I would make thee my lady.

Mrs. Ford. I your lady, Sir John! alas, I should be a pitiful lady.

Fal. Let the court of France show me such another; I see how thine eye would emulate the diamond: Thou hast the right arched bent of the brow, that becomes the ship-tire, the tire-valiant, or any tire of Venetian admittance.

Mrs. Ford. A plain kerchief, Sir John: my brows become nothing else; nor that well neither.

Fal. By the lord, thou art a traitor to say so: thou would'st make an absolute courtier; and the firm fixture of thy foot would give an excellent motion to thy gait, in a semi-circled farthingale. I see what thou wert, if fortune thy foe were not: nature is thy friend: Come, thou canst not hide it.

Mrs. Ford. Believe me, there's no such thing in me.

Fal. What made me love thee? let that persuade thee, there's something extraordinary in thee. Come, I cannot cog, and say thou art this and that, like a many of these lisping hawthorn buds, that come like women in men's apparel, and smell like Bucklersbury in simple time; I cannot: but I love thee; none but thee; and thou deservest it.

Mrs. Ford. Do not betray me, sir; I fear you love mistress Page.

Fal. Thou might'st as well say, I love to walk by the Counter-gate; which is as hateful to me as the reek of a lime-kiln.

Mrs. Ford. Well, heaven knows how I love you; and you shall one day find it.

Fal. Keep in that mind; I'll deserve it.

Mrs. Ford. Nay, I must tell you, so you do; or else I could not be in that mind.

Rob. [*within.*] Mistress Ford, mistress Ford! here's mistress Page at the door, sweating and blowing, and looking wildly, and would needs speak with you presently.

Fal. She shall not see me; I will ensconce me behind the arras.

Mrs. Ford. Pray you, do so; she's a very tattling woman.— [FALSTAFF *hides himself.*

Enter MISTRESS PAGE *and* ROBIN.

What's the matter? how now?

Mrs. Page. O mistress Ford, what have you done? You're shamed, you are overthrown, you are undone for ever.

Mrs. Ford. What's the matter, good mistress Page?

Mrs. Page. O well-a-day, mistress Ford! having an honest man to your husband, to give him such cause of suspicion!

Mrs. Ford. What cause of suspicion?

Mrs. Page. What cause of suspicion? Out upon you! how am I mistook in you!

Mrs. Ford. Why, alas! what's the matter?

Mrs. Page. Your husband's coming hither, woman, with all the officers in Windsor, to search for a gentleman, that, he says, is here now in the house, by your consent, to take an ill advantage of his absence: You are undone.

Mrs. Ford. Speak louder.—[*Aside.*]—'Tis not so, I hope.

Mrs. Page. Pray heaven it be not so, that you have such a man here; but 'tis most certain your husband's coming with half Windsor at his heels, to search for such a one. I come before to tell you: if you know yourself clear, why I am glad of it: but if you have a friend here, convey, convey him out. Be not amazed: call all your senses to you; defend your reputation, or bid farewell to your good life for ever.

Mrs. Ford. What shall I do?—There is a gentleman, my dear friend; and I fear not my own shame, so much as his peril: I had rather than a thousand pound, he were out of the house.

Mrs. Page. For shame, never stand, *you had rather,* and *you had rather;* your husband's here at hand, bethink you of some conveyance: in the house you cannot hide him.—O, how have you deceived me!—Look, here is a basket; if he be of any reasonable stature, he may creep in here; and throw foul linen upon him, as if it were going to bucking: Or, it is whiting-time, send him by your two men to Datchet mead.

Mrs. Ford. He's too big to go in there: What shall I do?

Re-enter FALSTAFF.

Fal. Let me see't; let me see't! O let me see't! I'll in, I'll in; follow your friend's counsel:—I'll in.

Mrs. Page. What! Sir John Falstaff! Are these your letters, knight?

Fal. I love thee, and none but thee; help me away: let me creep in here; I'll never.

[*He goes into the basket; they cover him with foul linen.*

Mrs. Page. Help to cover your master, boy: Call your men, mistress Ford:—You dissembling knight!

Mrs. Ford. What, John, Robert, John! [*Exit* Robin! *Re-enter* Servants.] Go take up these clothes here, quickly; where's the cowl-staff? look, how you drumble: carry them to the laundress in Datchet mead; quickly, come.

Enter FORD, PAGE, CAIUS, *and* SIR HUGH EVANS.

Ford. Pray you, come near: If I suspect without cause, why then make sport at me, then let me be your jest; I deserve it.—How now? whither bear you this?

Serv. To the laundress, forsooth.

Mrs. Ford. Why, what have you to do whither they bear it? You were best meddle with buck-washing.

Ford. Buck? I would I could wash myself of the buck! Buck! buck! buck? Ay, buck? I warrant you, buck; and of the season too, it shall appear. [*Exeunt* Servants *with the basket.*] Gentlemen, I have dreamed to-night; I'll tell you my dream. Here, here, here be my keys: ascend my chambers, search, seek, find out: I'll warrant we'll unkennel the fox:—Let me stop this way first:—So, now uncape.

Page. Good master Ford, be contented; you wrong yourself too much.

Ford. True, master Page.—Up, gentlemen; you shall see sport anon: follow me, gentlemen. [*Exit.*

Eva. This is fery fantastical humours and jealousies.

Caius. By gar, 'tis no de fashion of France: it is not jealous in France.

Page. Nay, follow him, gentlemen, see the issue of his search.

[*Exeunt* EVANS, PAGE, *and* CAIUS.

Mrs. Page. Is there not a double excellency in this?

Mrs. Ford. I know not which pleases me better, that my husband is deceived, or Sir John.

Mrs. Page. What a taking was he in, when your husband asked who was in the basket!

Mrs. Ford. I am half afraid he will have need of washing; so throwing him into the water will do him a benefit.

Mrs. Page. Hang him, dishonest rascal! I would all of the same strain were in the same distress.

Mrs. Ford. I think my husband hath some special suspicion of Falstaff's being here; for I never saw him so gross in his jealousy till now.

Mrs. Page. I will lay a plot to try that: And we will yet have more tricks with Falstaff; his dissolute disease will scarce obey this medicine.

Mrs. Ford. Shall we send that foolish carrion, mistress Quickly, to him, and excuse his throwing into the water; and give him another hope, to betray him to another punishment?

Mrs. Page. We'll do it; let him be sent for to-morrow eight o'clock to have amends.

Re-enter FORD, PAGE, CAIUS, *and* SIR HUGH EVANS.

Ford. I cannot find him: may be the knave bragged of that he could not compass.

Mrs. Page. Heard you that?

Mrs. Ford. Ay, ay, peace:—You use me well, master Ford, do you?

Ford. Ay, I do so.

Mrs. Ford. Heaven make you better than your thoughts!

Ford. Amen.

Mrs. Page. You do yourself mighty wrong, master Ford.

Ford. Ay, ay; I must bear it.

Eva. If there be any pody in the house, and in the chambers, and in the coffers, and in the presses, heaven forgive my sins at the day of judgment.

Caius. By gar, nor I too; dere is no bodies.

Page. Fie, fie, master Ford! are you not ashamed? What spirit, what devil suggests this imagination? I would not have your distemper in this kind for the wealth of Windsor Castle.

Ford. 'Tis my fault, master Page: I suffer for it.

Eva. You suffer for a pad conscience: your wife is as honest a 'omans as I will desires among five thousand, and five hundred too.

Caius. By gar, I see 'tis an honest woman.

Ford. Well;—I promised you a dinner:—Come, come, walk in the park: I pray you, pardon me; I will hereafter make known to you, why I have done this.—Come, wife;—Come, mistress Page; I pray you, pardon me; pray heartily, pardon me.

Page. Let's go in, gentlemen; but, trust me, we'll mock him. I do invite you to-morrow morning to my house to breakfast; after, we'll a birding together; I have a fine hawk for the bush: Shall it be so?

Ford. Any thing.

Eva. If there is one, I shall make two in the company.

Caius. If there be one or two, I shall make-a de turd.

Eva. In your teeth; for shame.

Ford. Pray you go, master Page.

Eva. I pray you now remembrance to-morrow, on the lousy knave, mine host.

Caius. Dat is good; by gar, vit all my heart.

Eva. A lousy knave; to have his gibes, and his mockeries. [*Exeunt.*

SCENE IV. *A Room in* Page's *House.*

Enter FENTON *and* MISTRESS ANNE PAGE.

Fent. I see, I cannot get thy father's love;
Therefore, no more turn me to him, sweet Nan.

Anne. Alas! how then?

Fent. Why, thou must be thyself.
He doth object, I am too great of birth;
And that, my state being gall'd with my expense,
I seek to heal it only by his wealth:
Besides these, other bars he lays before me,——
My riots past, my wild societies;
And tells me, 'tis a thing impossible
I should love thee, but as a property.

Anne. May be, he tells you true.

Fent. No, heaven so speed me in my time to come!
Albeit, I will confess, thy father's wealth
Was the first motive that I woo'd thee, Anne;
Yet, wooing thee, I found thee of more value
Than stamps in gold, or sums in sealed bags;
And 'tis the very riches of thyself
That now I aim at.

Anne. Gentle master Fenton,
Yet seek my father's love: still seek it, sir:
If opportunity and humblest suit
Cannot attain it, why then—Hark you hither.
[*They converse apart.*

Enter SHALLOW, SLENDER, *and* MRS. QUICKLY.

Shal. Break their talk, mistress Quickly; my kinsman shall speak for himself.

Slen. I'll make a shaft or a bolt on't: slid, 'tis but venturing.

Shal. Be not dismay'd.

Slen. No, she shall not dismay me: I care not for that,—but that I am afeard.

Quick. Hark ye; master Slender would speak a word with you.

Anne. I come to him.—This is my father's choice.
O, what a world of vile ill-favour'd faults
Looks handsome in three hundred pounds a year!
[*Aside.*

Quick. And how does good master Fenton? Pray you, a word with you.

Shal. She's coming; to her, coz. O boy, thou hadst a father!

Slen. I had a father, mistress Anne;—my uncle can tell you good jests of him:—Pray you, uncle, tell mistress Anne the jest, how my father stole two geese out of a pen, good uncle.

Shal. Mistress Anne, my cousin loves you.

Slen. Ay, that I do; as well as I love any woman in Gloucestershire.

Shal. He will maintain you like a gentlewoman.

Slen. Ay, that I will, come cut and long tail, under the degree of a 'squire.

Shal. He will make you a hundred and fifty pounds jointure.

Anne. Good master Shallow, let him woo for himself.

Shal. Marry, I thank you for it; I thank you for that good comfort. She calls you, coz: I'll leave you.

Anne. Now, master Slender.

Slen. Now, good mistress Anne.

Anne. What is your will?

Slen. My will? od's heartlings, that's a pretty jest indeed! I ne'er made my will yet, I thank heaven; I am not such a sickly creature, I give heaven praise.

Anne. I mean, master Slender, what would you with me?

Slen. Truly, for mine own part, I would little or nothing with you: Your father, and my uncle, have made motions; if it be my luck, so: if not, happy man be his dole! They can tell you how things go, better than I can: You may ask your father; here he comes.

Enter PAGE *and* MISTRESS PAGE.

Page. Now, master Slender:—Love him, daughter Anne.—
Why, how now! what does master Fenton here?
You wrong me, sir, thus still to haunt my house:
I told you, sir, my daughter is dispos'd of.

Fent. Nay, master Page, be not impatient.

Mrs. Page. Good master Fenton, come not to my child.

Page. She is no match for you.

Fent. Sir, will you hear me?

Page. No, good master Fenton.
Come, master Shallow; come, son Slender; in:—
Knowing my mind, you wrong me, master Fenton.

[*Exeunt* PAGE, SHALLOW, *and* SLENDER.

Quick. Speak to mistress Page.

Fent. Good mistress Page, for that I love your daughter
In such a righteous fashion as I do,
Perforce, against all checks, rebukes, and manners,
I must advance the colours of my love,
And not retire: Let me have your good will.

Anne. Good mother, do not marry me to yond' fool.

Mrs. Page. I mean it not; I seek you a better husband.

Quick. That's my master, master doctor.

Anne. Alas, I had rather be set quick i' the earth,
And bowl'd to death with turnips.

Mrs. Page. Come, trouble not yourself: Good master Fenton,
I will not be your friend, nor enemy.
My daughter will I question how she loves you,
And as I find her, so am I affected;
'Till then, farewell, sir:—she must needs go in;
Her father will be angry.

[*Exeunt* MRS. PAGE *and* ANNE.

Fent. Farewell, gentle mistress; farewell, Nan.

Quick. This is my doing, now:—Nay, said I, will you cast away your child on a fool, and a physician? Look on master Fenton:—this is my doing.

Fent. I thank thee; and I pray thee, once to-night
Give my sweet Nan this ring: There's for thy pains. [*Exit.*

Quick. Now heaven send thee good fortune! A kind heart he hath: a woman would run through fire and water for such a kind heart. But yet, I would my master had mistress Anne; or I would master Slender had her; or, in sooth, I would master Fenton had her: I will do what I can for them all three; for so I have promised, and I'll be as good as my word; but speciously for master Fenton. Well, I must of another errand to Sir John Falstaff from my two mistresses: What a beast am I to slack it! [*Exit.*

SCENE V. *A Room in the Garter Inn.*

Enter FALSTAFF *and* BARDOLPH.

Fal. Bardolph, I say,—

Bard. Here, sir.

Fal. Go fetch me a quart of sack; put a toast in't. [*Exit* BARD.] Have I lived to be carried in a basket, like a barrow of butcher's offal; and to be thrown into the Thames? Well; if I be served such another trick, I'll have my brains ta'en out, and butter'd, and give them to a dog for a new year's gift. The rogues slighted me into the river with as little remorse as they would have drowned a bitch's blind puppies, fifteen i' the litter: and you may know by my size, that I have a kind of alacrity in sinking; if the bottom were as deep as hell, I should down. I had been drowned, but that the shore was shelvy and shallow; a death that I abhor; for the water swells a man; and what a thing should I have been, when I had been swelled! I should have been a mountain of mummy.

Re-enter BARDOLPH, *with the wine.*

Bard. Here's mistress Quickly, sir, to speak with you.

Fal. Come, let me pour in some sack to the Thames water; for my belly's as cold, as if I had swallowed snow-balls for pills to cool the reins. Call her in.

Bard. Come in, woman.

Enter MRS. QUICKLY.

Quick. By your leave; I cry you mercy: Give your worship good-morrow.

Fal. Take away these chalices: Go brew me a pottle of sack finely.

Bard. With eggs, sir?

Fal. Simple of itself; I'll no pullet-sperm in my brewage.—[*Exit* BARDOLPH.]—How now?

Quick. Marry, sir, I come to your worship from mistress Ford.

Fal. Mistress Ford! I have had ford enough; I was thrown into the ford: I have my belly full of ford.

Quick. Alas the day! good heart, that was not her fault; she does so take on with her men; they mistook their erection.

Fal. So did I mine, to build upon a foolish woman's promise.

Quick. Well, she laments, sir, for it, that it would yearn your heart to see it. Her husband goes this morning a birding; she desires you once more to come to her between eight and nine: I must carry her word quickly: she'll make you amends, I warrant you.

Fal. Well, I will visit her: Tell her so; and bid her think what a man is: let her consider his frailty, and then judge of my merit.

Quick. I will tell her.

Fal. Do so. Between nine and ten say'st thou?

Quick. Eight and nine, sir.

Fal. Well, be gone: I will not miss her.

Quick. Peace be with you, sir! [*Exit.*

Fal. I marvel, I hear not of master Brook; he sent me word to stay within; I like his money well. O, here he comes.

Enter FORD.

Ford. Bless you, sir!

Fal. Now, master Brook? you come to know what hath passed between me and Ford's wife?

Ford. That, indeed, Sir John, is my business.

Fal. Master Brook, I will not lie to you; I was at her house the hour she appointed me.

Ford. And how sped you, sir!

Fal. Very ill-favouredly, master Brook.

Ford. How so, sir? Did she change her determination?

Fal. No, master Brook; but the peaking cornuto, her husband, master Brook, dwelling in a continual 'larum of jealousy, comes me in the instant of our encounter, after we had embraced, kissed, protested, and, as it were, spoke the prologue of our comedy; and at his heels a rabble of his companions, thither provoked and instigated by his distemper, and, forsooth, to search his house for his wife's love.

Ford. What, while you were there?

Fal. While I was there.

Ford. And did he search for you, and could not find you?

Fal. You shall hear. As good luck would have it, comes in one mistress Page; gives intelligence of Ford's approach; and, by her invention, and Ford's wife's distraction, they conveyed me into a buck-basket.

Ford. A buck-basket?

Fal. By the Lord, a buck-basket: rammed me in with foul shirts and smocks, socks, foul stockings, and greasy napkins; that, master Brook, there was the rankest compound of villanous smell, that ever offended nostril.

Ford. And how long lay you there?

Fal. Nay, you shall hear, master Brook, what I have suffered to bring this woman to evil for your good. Being thus crammed in the basket, a couple of Ford's knaves, his hinds, were called forth by their mistress, to carry me in the name of foul clothes to Datchet-lane: they took me on their shoulders; met the jealous knave their master in the door; who asked them once or twice what they had in their basket: I quaked for fear, lest the lunatic knave would have searched it; but Fate, ordaining he should be a cuckold, held his hand. Well, on went he for a search, and away went I for foul clothes. But mark the sequel, master Brook: I suffered the pangs of three several deaths: first, an intolerable fright, to be detected with a jealous rotten bellwether: next, to be compassed like a good bilbo, in the circumference of a peck, hilt to point, heel to head: and then, to be stopped in, like a strong distillation, with stinking clothes that fretted in their own grease: think of that,—a man of my kidney,—think of that; that am as subject to heat as butter; a man of continual dissolution and thaw; it was a miracle to 'scape suffocation. And in the height of this bath, when I was more than half stewed in grease, like a Dutch dish, to be thrown into the Thames, and cooled, glowing hot, in that surge, like a horse-shoe; think of that;—hissing hot,—think of that, master Brook.

Ford. In good sadness, sir, I am sorry that for my sake you have suffered all this. My suit then is desperate; you'll undertake her no more.

Fal. Master Brook, I will be thrown into Ætna, as I have been into Thames, ere I will leave her thus. Her husband is this morning gone a birding: I have received from her another embassy of meeting; 'twixt eight and nine is the hour, master Brook.

Ford. 'Tis past eight already, sir.

Fal. Is it? I will then address me to my appointment: Come to me at your convenient leisure, and you shall know how I speed; and the conclusion shall be crowned with your enjoying her: Adieu. You shall have her, master Brook; master Brook, you shall cuckold Ford. [*Exit.*

Ford. Hum! ha! is this a vision? is this a dream? do I sleep? Master Ford, awake; awake, master Ford; there's a hole made in your best coat, master Ford. This 'tis to be married! this 'tis to have linen, and buck-baskets!—Well, I will proclaim myself what I am: I will now take the lecher; he is at my house: he cannot 'scape me; 'tis impossible he should; he cannot creep into a halfpenny purse, nor into a pepper-box: but, lest the devil that guides him should aid him, I will search impossible places. Though what I am I cannot avoid, yet to be what I would not, shall not make me tame: if I have horns to make one mad, let the proverb go with me, I'll be horn mad. [*Exit.*

ACT IV.

SCENE I. *The Street.*

Enter MRS. PAGE, MRS. QUICKLY, *and* WILLIAM.

Mrs. Page. Is he at master Ford's already, think'st thou?

Quick. Sure, he is by this; or will be presently: but truly, he is very courageous mad, about his throwing into the water. Mistress Ford desires you to come suddenly.

Mrs. Page. I'll be with her by and by; I'll but bring my young man here to school: Look, where his master comes; 'tis a playing-day, I see.

Enter SIR HUGH EVANS.

How now, Sir Hugh? no school to-day?

Eva. No; master Slender is let the boys leave to play.

Quick. Blessing of his heart!

Mrs. Page. Sir Hugh, my husband says, my son profits nothing in the world at his book; I pray you, ask him some questions in his accidence.

Eva. Come hither, William; hold up your head; come.

Mrs. Page. Come on, sirrah; hold up your head; answer your master, be not afraid.

Eva. William, how many numbers is in nouns?

Will. Two.

Quick. Truly, I thought there had been one number more; because they say, od's nouns.

Eva. Peace your tattlings. What *is fair*, William?

Will. *Pulcher.*

Quick. Poulcats! there are fairer things than poulcats, sure.

Eva. You are a very simplicity 'oman; I pray you peace. What is *lapis*, William?

Will. A stone.

Eva. And what is a stone, William?

Will. A pebble.

Eva. No, it is *lapis;* I pray you remember in your prain.

Will. *Lapis.*

Eva. That is good, William. What is he, William, that does lend articles?

Will. Articles are borrowed of the pronoun and be thus declined, *Singulariter, nominativo, hic hæc, hoc.*

Eva. *Nominativo, hig, hag, hog;* pray you, mark: *genitivo, hujus:* Well, what is your *accusative case?*

Will. *Accusativo, hinc.*

Eva. I pray you, have your remembrance, child; *Accusativo, hing, hang, hog.*

Quick. Hang hog, is Latin for bacon, I warrant you.

Eva. Leave your prabbles, 'oman. What is the focative case, William?

Will. O—*vocativo*, O.

Eva. Remember, William; focative is *caret.*

Quick. And that's a good root.

Eva. 'Oman, forbear.

Mrs. Page. Peace.

Eva. What is your *genitive case plural,* William?

Will. *Genitive case?*

Eva. Ay.

Will. *Genitivo,—horum, harum, horum.*

Quick. 'Vengeance of *Jenny's* case! fie on her!—never name her, child, if she be a whore.

Eva. For shame, 'oman.

Quick. You do ill to teach the child such words: he teaches him to hick and to hack, which they'll do fast enough of themselves; and to call horum:—fie upon you!

Eva. 'Oman, art thou lunatics? hast thou no understandings for thy cases, and the numbers of the genders? Thou art as foolish christian creatures as I would desires.

Mrs. Page. Pr'ythee hold thy peace.

Eva. Shew me now, William, some declensions of your pronouns.

Will. Forsooth, I have forgot.

Eva. It is *ki, kæ, cod;* if you forget your *kies,* your *kæs,* and your *cods,* you must be preeches. Go your ways, and play, go.

Mrs. Page. He is a better scholar than I though he was.

Eva. He is a good sprag memory. Farewell, mistress Page.

Mrs. Page. Adieu, good Sir Hugh. [*Exit* SIR HUGH.] Get you home, boy.—Come, we stay too long. [*Exeunt.*

SCENE II. *A Room in* Ford's *House.*

Enter FALSTAFF *and* MRS. FORD.

Fal. Mistress Ford, your sorrow hath eaten up my sufferance: I see, you are obsequious in your love, and I profess your requital to a hair's breadth: not only, mistress Ford, in the simple office of love, but in all the accoutrement, complement, and ceremony of it. But are you sure of your husband now?

Mrs. Ford. He's a birding, sweet Sir John.

Mrs. Page. [*within.*] What hoa, gossip Ford! what hoa!

Mrs. Ford. Step into the chamber, Sir John. [*Exit* FALSTAFF.

Enter MRS. PAGE.

Mrs. Page. How now, sweetheart? who's at home beside yourself?

Mrs. Ford. Why, none but mine own people.

Mrs. Page. Indeed?

Mrs. Ford. No, certainly;—speak louder. [*Aside.*

Mrs. Page. Truly, I am so glad you have nobody here.

Mrs. Ford. Why?

Mrs. Page. Why, woman, your husband is in his old lunes again: he so takes on yonder with my husband; so rails against all married mankind; so curses all Eve's daughters, of what complexion soever; and so buffets himself on the forehead, crying, *Peer out, peer out!* that any madness, I ever yet beheld, seemed but tameness, civility, and patience, to this his distemper he is in now: I am glad the fat knight is not here.

Mrs. Ford. Why, does he talk of him?

Mrs. Page. Of none but him; and swears, he was carried out, the last time he searched for him, in a basket: protests to my husband he is now here; and hath drawn him and the rest of their company from their sport, to make another experiment of his suspicion: but I am glad the knight is not here; now he shall see his own foolery.

Mrs. Ford. How near is he, mistress Page?

Mrs. Page. Hard by; at street end; he will be here anon.

Mrs. Ford. I am undone!—the knight is here.

Mrs. Page. Why, then you are utterly shamed, and he's but a dead man. What a woman are you?—Away with him, away with him, better shame than murder.

Mrs. Ford. Which way should he go? how should I bestow him? Shall I put him into the basket again?

Re-enter FALSTAFF.

Fal. No, I'll come no more i' the basket: May I not go out, ere he come?

Mrs. Page. Alas, three of master Ford's brothers watch the door with pistols, that none shall issue out; otherwise you might slip away ere he came. But what make you here?

Fal. What shall I do?—I'll creep up into the chimney.

Mrs. Ford. There they always used to discharge their birding-pieces: Creep into the kiln-hole.

Fal. Where is it?

Mrs. Ford. He will seek there on my word. Neither press, coffer, chest, trunk, well, vault, but he hath an abstract for the remembrance of such places, and goes to them by his note: There is no hiding you in the house.

Fal. I'll go out then.

Mrs. Page. If you go out in your own semblance, you die, Sir John. Unless you go out disguised,—

Mrs. Ford. How might we disguise him?

Mrs. Page. Alas the day, I know not. There is no woman's gown big enough for him; otherwise, he might put on a hat, a muffler, and a kerchief, and so escape.

Fal. Good hearts, devise something: any extremity, rather than a mischief.

Mrs. Ford. My maid's aunt, the fat woman of Brentford, has a gown above.

Mrs. Page. On my word, it will serve him; she's as big as he is: and there's her thrum'd hat, and her muffler too: Run up, Sir John.

Mrs. Ford. Go, go, sweet Sir John: mistress Page and I will look some linen for your head.

Mrs. Page. Quick, quick; we'll come dress you straight: put on the gown the while. [*Exit* FALSTAFF.

Mrs. Ford. I would my husband would meet him in this shape: he cannot abide the old woman of Brentford; he swears, she's a witch; forbade her my house, and hath threatened to beat her.

Mrs. Page. Heaven guide him to thy husband's cudgel; and the devil guide his cudgel afterwards!

Mrs. Ford. But is my husband coming?

Mrs. Page. Ay, in good sadness, is he; and talks of the basket too, howsoever he hath had intelligence.

Mrs. Ford. We'll try that; for I'll appoint my men to carry the basket again, to meet him at the door with it, as they did last time.

Mrs. Page. Nay, but he'll be here presently: let's go dress him like the witch of Brentford.

Mrs. Ford. I'll first direct my men, what they shall do with the basket. Go up, I'll bring linen for him straight. [*Exit.*

Mrs. Page. Hang him, dishonest varlet! we cannot misuse him enough.

We'll leave a proof, by that which we will do,
Wives may be merry, and yet honest too:
We do not act that often jest and laugh;
'Tis old but true, *Still swine eat all the draff.* [*Exit.*

Re-enter MRS. FORD, *with two* Servants.

Mrs. Ford. Go, sirs, take the basket again on your shoulders; your master is hard at door; if he bid you set it down, obey him, quickly, despatch. [*Exit.*

1 *Serv.* Come, come, take it up.

2 *Serv.* Pray heaven, it be not full of the knight again.

1 *Serv.* I hope not; I had as lief bear so much lead.

Enter FORD, PAGE, SHALLOW, CAIUS, *and* SIR HUGH EVANS.

Ford. Ay, but if it prove true, master Page, have you any way then to unfool me again?—Set down the basket, villain: Somebody call my wife:——You, youth in a basket, come out here!—O, you panderly rascals! there's a knot, a ging, a pack, a conspiracy against me: Now, shall the devil be shamed. What! wife, I say! come, come forth; behold what honest clothes you send forth to bleaching.

Page. Why, this passes! Master Ford, you are not to go loose any longer; you must be pinioned.

Eva. Why, this is lunatics! this is mad as a mad dog!

Shal. Indeed, master Ford, this is not well; indeed.

Enter MRS. FORD.

Ford. So say I too, sir.—Come hither, mistress Ford; mistress Ford, the honest woman, the modest wife, the virtuous creature, that hath the jealous fool to her husband!—I suspect without cause, mistress, do I?

Mrs. Ford. Heaven be my witness, you do, if you suspect me in any dishonesty.

Ford. Well said, brazen-face; hold it out.——Come forth, sirrah. [*Pulls the clothes out of the basket.*

Page. This passes!

Mrs. Ford. Are you not ashamed? let the clothes alone.

Ford. I shall find you anon.

Eva. 'Tis unreasonable! will you take up your wife's clothes? Come away.

Ford. Empty the basket, I say.

Mrs. Ford. Why, man, why?

Ford. Master Page, as I am a man, there was one conveyed out of my house yesterday in this basket: Why may he not be there again? In my house I am sure he is: my intelligence is true; my jealousy is reasonable: Pluck me out all the linen.

Mrs. Ford. If you find a man there, he shall die a flea's death.

Page. Here's no man.

Shal. By my fidelity, this is not well, master Ford; this wrongs you.

Eva. Master Ford, you must pray, and not

follow the imaginations of your own heart: this is jealousies.

Ford. Well, he's not here I seek for.

Page. No, nor no where else, but in your brain.

Ford. Help to search my house this one time; if I find not what I seek, show no colour for my extremity, let me for ever be your table-sport; let them say of me, As jealous as Ford, that searched a hollow walnut for his wife's leman. Satisfy me once more; once more search with me.

Mrs. Ford. What hoa, mistress Page! come you, and the old woman down; my husband will come into the chamber.

Ford. Old woman! What old woman's that?

Mrs. Ford. Why, it is my maid's aunt of Brentford.

Ford. A witch, a quean, an old cozening quean! Have I not forbid her my house? She comes of errands, does she? We are simple men; we do not know what's brought to pass under the profession of fortune telling. She works by charms, by spells, by the figure, and such daubery as this is; beyond our element; we know nothing. ——Come down, you witch, you hag you; come down, I say.

Mrs. Ford. Nay, good, sweet husband;—good gentlemen, let him not strike the old woman.

Enter FALSTAFF *in women's clothes, led by* MRS. PAGE.

Mrs. Page. Come, mother Pratt, come, give me your hand.

Ford. I'll *prat* her:——Out of my door, you witch! [*beats him*] you rag, you baggage, you polecat, you ronyon! out! out! I'll conjure you, I'll fortune-tell you. [*Exit* FALSTAFF.

Mrs. Page. Are you not ashamed? I think you have killed the poor woman.

Mrs. Ford. Nay, he will do it;—'Tis a goodly credit for you.

Ford. Hang her, witch!

Eva. By yea and no, I think, the 'oman is a witch indeed: I like not when a 'oman has a great peard: I spy a great peard under her muffler.

Ford. Will you follow, gentlemen? I beseech you, follow; see but the issue of my jealousy; if I cry out thus upon no trail, never trust me when I open again.

Page. Let's obey his humour a little further: Come, gentlemen.

[*Exeunt* PAGE, FORD, SHALLOW, *and* EVANS.

Mrs. Page. Trust me, he beat him most pitifully.

Mrs. Ford. Nay, by the mass that he did not; he beat him most unpitifully, methought.

Mrs. Page. I'll have the cudgel hallowed, and hung o'er the altar; it hath done meritorious service.

Mrs. Ford. What think you? May we, with the warrant of woman-hood, and the witness of a good conscience, pursue him with any further revenge?

Mrs. Page. The spirit of wantonness is, sure, scared out of him; if the devil have him not in fee-simple, with fine and recovery, he will never, I think, in the way of waste, attempt us again.

Mrs. Ford. Shall we tell our husbands how we have served him?

Mrs. Page. Yes, by all means; if it be but to scrape the figures out of your husband's brains. If they can find in their hearts, the poor unvirtuous fat knight shall be any further afflicted, we two will still be the ministers.

Mrs. Ford. I'll warrant they'll have him publickly shamed: and, methinks, there would be no period to the jest, should he not be publickly shamed.

Mrs. Page. Come to the forge with it then, hape it: I would not have things cool.

[*Exeunt.*

SCENE III. *A room in the Garter Inn.*

Enter Host *and* BARDOLPH.

Bard. Sir, the Germans desire to have three of your horses: the duke himself will be to-morrow at court, and they are going to meet him.

Host. What duke should that be comes so secretly? I hear not of him in the court: Let me speak with the gentlemen; they speak English?

Bard. Ay, sir, I'll call them to you.

Host. They shall have my horses: but I'll make them pay, I'll sauce them: they have had my house a week at command; I have turned away my other guests: they must come off: I'll sauce them; Come. [*Exeunt.*

SCENE IV. *A Room in Ford's House.*

Enter PAGE, FORD, MRS. PAGE, MRS. FORD, *and* SIR HUGH EVANS.

Eva. 'Tis one of the pest discretions of a 'oman as ever I did look upon.

Page. And did he send you both these letters at an instant?

Mrs. Page. Within a quarter of an hour.

Ford. Pardon me, wife: Henceforth do what thou wilt;
I rather will suspect the sun with cold,
Than thee with wantonness: now doth thy honour stand,
In him that was of late an heretic,
As firm as faith.

Page. 'Tis well, 'tis well; no more.
Be not as extreme in submission,
As in offence;
But let our plot go forward: let our wives
Yet once again, to make us public sport,
Appoint a meeting with this old fat fellow,
Where we may take him, and disgrace him for it.

Ford. There is no better way than that they spoke of.

Page. How! to send him word they'll meet him in the park at midnight! fie, fie; he'll never come.

Eva. You say, he has been thrown into the rivers; and has been grievously peaten, as an old 'oman; methinks there should be terrors in him, that he should not come; methinks his flesh is punished, he shall have no desires.

Page. So think I too.

Mrs. Ford. Devise but how you'll use him when he comes,
And let us two devise to bring him thither.

Mrs. Page. There is an old tale goes, that Herne the hunter,
Sometime a keeper here in Windsor forest,
Doth all the winter time, at still midnight,
Walk round about an oak, with great ragg'd horns;
And there he blasts the tree, and takes the cattle;
And makes milch-kine yield blood, and shakes a chain
In a most hideous and dreadful manner:
You have heard of such a spirit; and well you know,
The superstitious idle-headed eld
Received, and did deliver to our age,
This tale of Herne the hunter for a truth.

Page. Why, yet there want not many, that do fear
In deep of night to walk by this Herne's oak;
But what of this?

Mrs. Ford. Marry, this is our device;
That Falstaff at that oak shall meet with us,
Disguised like Herne, with huge horns on his head.

Page. Well, let it not be doubted but he'll come,
And in this shape: When you have brought him thither,
What shall be done with him? what is your plot?

Mrs. Page. That likewise have we thought upon, and thus:

Nan Page my daughter, and my little son,
And three or four more of their growth, we'll dress
Like urchins, ouphes, and fairies, green and white,
With rounds of waxen tapers on their heads,
And rattles in their hands; upon a sudden,
As Falstaff, she, and I, are newly met,
Let them from forth a saw-pit rush at once
With some diffused song; upon their sight,
We two in great amazedness will fly:
Then let them all encircle him about,
And, fairy-like, to-pinch the unclean knight;
And ask him, why, that hour of fairy revel,
In their so sacred paths he dares to tread,
In shape profane.

Mrs. Ford. And till he tell the truth,
Let the supposed fairies pinch him sound,
And burn him with their tapers.

Mrs. Page. The truth being known,
We'll all present ourselves: dishorn the spirit,
And mock him home to Windsor.

Ford. The children must
Be practised well to this, or they'll ne'er do't.

Eva. I will teach the children their behaviours; and I will be like a Jack-an-apes also, to burn the knight with my taber.

Ford. That will be excellent. I'll go buy them vizards.

Mrs. Page. My Nan shall be the queen of all the fairies,
Finely attired in a robe of white.

Page. That silk will I go buy;—and in that time
Shall master Slender steal my Nan away,
And marry her at Eton. [*Aside.*] Go send to Falstaff straight.

Ford. Nay, I'll to him again in name of Brook:
He'll tell me all his purpose: Sure, he'll come.

Mrs. Page. Fear not you that: Go get us properties,
And tricking for our fairies.

Eva. Let us about it: It is admirable pleasures, and fery honest knaveries.

[*Exeunt* PAGE, FORD, *and* EVANS.

Mrs. Page. Go, mistress Ford,
Send quickly to Sir John, to know his mind.

[*Exit* MRS. FORD.

I'll to the doctor; he hath my good will,
And none but he, to marry with Nan Page.
That Slender, though well landed, is an idiot;
And he my husband best of all affects:
The doctor is well money'd, and his friends
Potent at court; he, none but he, shall have her,
Though twenty thousand worthier come to crave her. [*Exit.*

SCENE V. *A Room in the Garter Inn.*

Enter Host *and* SIMPLE.

Host. What would'st thou have, boor? what, thick-skin? speak, breathe, discuss; brief, short, quick, snap.

Sim. Marry, sir, I come to speak with Sir John Falstaff from master Slender.

Host. There's his chamber, his house, his castle, his standing-bed, and truckle-bed; 'tis painted about with the story of the prodigal, fresh and new: Go, knock and call; he'll speak like an *anthropophaginian* unto thee: Knock, I say.

Sim. There's an old woman, a fat woman, gone up into his chamber; I'll be so bold as stay, sir, till she come down: I come to speak with her, indeed.

Host. Ha! a fat woman! the knight may be robbed: I'll call.—Bully knight! Bully Sir John? speak from thy lungs military: Art thou there? it is thine host, thine Ephesian, calls.

Fal. [*above.*] How now, mine host?

Host. Here's a Bohemian-Tartar tarries the coming down of thy fat woman: Let her descend, bully, let her descend; my chambers are honourable: Fye! privacy? fye!

Enter FALSTAFF.

Fal. There was, mine host, an old fat woman even now with me; but she's gone.

Sim. Pray you, sir, was't not the wise woman of Brentford?

Fal. Ay, marry, was it, muscle-shell; What would you with her?

Sim. My master, sir, my master Slender, sent to her, seeing her go through the streets, to know, sir, whether one Nym, sir, that beguiled him of a chain, had the chain, or no.

Fal. I spake with the old woman about it.

Sim. And what says she, I pray, sir?

Fal. Marry, she says, that very same man that beguiled master Slender of his chain, cozened him of it.

Sim. I would I could have spoken with the woman herself; I had other things to have spoken with her too, from him.

Fal. What are they? let us know.

Host. Ay, come; quick.

Sim. I may not conceal them, sir.

Fal. Conceal them, or thou diest.

Sim. Why, sir, they were nothing but about mistress Anne Page; to know if it were my master's fortune to have her, or no.

Fal. 'Tis, 'tis his fortune.

Sim. What, sir?

Fal. To have her,—or no: Go; say the woman told me so.

Sim. May I be so bold to say so, sir?

Fal. Ay, Sir Tyke; who more bold?

Sim. I thank your worship: I shall make my master glad with these tidings. [*Exit* SIMPLE.

Host. Thou art clerkly, thou art clerkly, Sir John: Was there a wise woman with thee?

Fal. Ay, that there was, mine host; one that hath taught me more wit than ever I learned before in my life: and I paid nothing for it neither, but was paid for my learning.

Enter BARDOLPH.

Bard. Out, alas, sir! cozenage! mere cozenage!

Host. Where be mine horses? speak well of them, varletto.

Bard. Run away with the cozeners: for so soon as I came beyond Eton, they threw me off, from behind one of them, in a slough of mire; and set spurs, and away, like three German devils, three Dr. Faustuses.

Host. They are gone but to meet the duke, villain: do not say they be fled; Germans are honest men.

Enter SIR HUGH EVANS.

Eva. Where is mine host?

Host. What is the matter, sir?

Eva. Have a care of your entertainments: there is a friend of mine come to town, tells me, there is three cousin germans, that has cozened all the hosts of Readings, of Maidenhead, of Colebrook, of horses and money. I tell you for good-will, look you: you are wise, and full of gibes and vlouting-stogs; and it is not convenient you should be cozened: Fare you well. [*Exit.*

Enter DOCTOR CAIUS.

Caius. Vere is mine *Host de Jarterre.*

Host. Here, master doctor, in perplexity, and doubtful dilemma.

Caius. I cannot tell vat is dat: but it is tell-a me, dat you make grand preparations for a duke *de Jarmany:* by my trot, dere is no duke, dat the court is know to come; I tell you for good vill: adieu. [*Exit.*

Host. Hue and cry, villain, go:—assist me, knight; I am undone:—fly, run, hue and cry, villain! I am undone!

[*Exeunt* Host *and* BARDOLPH.

Fal. I would all the world might be cozened; for I have been cozen'd and beaten too. If it should come to the ear of the court, how I have been transformed, and how my transformation hath been washed and cudgeled, they would melt me out of my fat, drop by drop, and liquor fishermen's boots with me; I warrant they would whip me with their fine wits, till I were as crestfallen as a dried pear. I never prospered since I forswore myself at *Primero*. Well, if my wind were but long enough to say my prayers, I would repent.—

Enter MRS. QUICKLY.

Now! whence come you?

Quick. From the two parties forsooth.

Fal. The devil take one party, and his dam the other, and so they shall be both bestowed! I have suffered more for their sakes, more than the villanous inconstancy of man's disposition is able to bear.

Quick. And have not they suffered? Yes, I warrant, speciously one of them; mistress Ford, good heart, is beaten black and blue, that you cannot see a white spot about her.

Fal. What tell'st thou me of black and blue! I was beaten myself into all the colours of the rainbow, and I was like to be apprehended for the witch of Brentford; but that my admirable dexterity of wit, my counterfeiting the action of an old woman deliver'd me, the knave constable had set me i' the stocks, i' the common stocks, for a witch.

Quick. Sir, let me speak with you in your chamber; you shall hear how things go; and I warrant, to your content. Here is a letter will say somewhat. Good hearts, what ado here is to bring you together! Sure, one of you does not serve heaven well, that you are so crossed.

Fal. Come up into my chamber. [*Exeunt.*

SCENE VI. *Another Room in the Garter Inn.*

Enter FENTON *and* Host.

Host. Master Fenton, talk not to me; my mind is heavy, I will give over all.

Fent. Yet hear me speak: Assist me in my purpose,
And, as I am a gentleman, I'll give thee
A hundred pound in gold, more than your loss.

Host. I will hear you, master Fenton; and I will, at the least, keep your counsel.

Fent. From time to time I have acquainted you
With the dear love I bear to fair Anne Page;
Who, mutually hath answer'd my affection
(So far forth as herself might be her chooser),
Even to my wish: I have a letter from her
Of such contents as you will wonder at;
The mirth whereof so larded with my matter,
That neither, singly, can be manifested,
Without the show of both;—wherein fat Falstaff
Hath a great scene: the image of the jest
[*Showing the letter.*
I'll show you here at large. Hark, good mine host:
To-night at Herne's oak, just 'twixt twelve and one,
Must my sweet Nan present the fairy queen;
The purpose why is here: in which disguise,
While other jests are something rank on foot,
Her father hath commanded her to slip
Away with Slender, and with him at Eton
Immediately to marry: she hath consented:
Now, sir,
Her mother, even strong against that match,
And firm for doctor Caius, hath appointed
That he shall likewise shuffle her away,
While other sports are tasking of their minds,
And at the deanery, where a priest attends,
Straight marry her: to this her mother's plot
She, seemingly obedient, likewise hath
Made promise to the doctor;—Now thus it rests:
Her father means she shall be all in white;
And in that habit, when Slender sees his time
To take her by the hand, and bid her go,
She shall go with him:—her mother hath intended,
The better to denote her to the doctor
(For they must all be mask'd and vizarded),
That, quaint in green she shall be loose enrob'd,
With ribands pendant, flaring 'bout her head;
And when the doctor spies his vantage ripe,
To pinch her by the hand, and, on that token,
The maid hath given consent to go with him.

Host. Which means she to deceive? father or mother?

Fent. Both, my good host, to go along with me:
And here it rests,—that you'll procure the vicar
To stay for me at church, 'twixt twelve and one,
And, in the lawful name of marrying,
To give our hearts united ceremony.

Host. Well, husband your device; I'll to the vicar:
Bring you the maid, you shall not lack a priest.

Fent. So shall I ever more be bound to thee;
Besides, I'll make a present recompence.
[*Exeunt.*

ACT V.

SCENE I. *A Room in the Garter Inn.*

Enter FALSTAFF *and* MRS. QUICKLY.

Fal. Pr'ythee, no more prattling;—go.——I'll hold: This is the third time; I hope good luck lies in odd numbers. Away, go; they say, there is divinity in odd numbers, either in nativity, chance, or death.—Away.

Quick. I'll provide you a chain; and I'll do what I can to get you a pair of horns.

Fal. Away, I say; time wears: hold up your head and mince. [*Exit* MRS. QUICKLY.

Enter FORD.

How now, master Brook? Master Brook, the matter will be known to-night, or never. Be you in the Park about midnight, at Herne's oak and you shall see wonders.

Ford. Went you not to her yesterday, sir, as you told me you had appointed?

Fal. I went to her, master Brook, as you see, like a poor old man: but I came from her, master Brook, like a poor old woman. That same knave, Ford, her husband, hath the finest mad devil of jealousy in him, master Brook, that ever governed frenzy. I will tell you.—He beat me grievously in the shape of a woman; for in the shape of man, master Brook, I fear not Goliath with a weaver's beam; because I know also, life is a shuttle. I am in haste; go along with me; I'll tell you all, master Brook. Since I plucked geese, played truant, and whipped top, I knew not what it was to be beaten, till lately. Follow me: I'll tell you strange things of this knave Ford: on whom to-night I will be revenged, and I will deliver his wife into your hand.—Follow: Strange things in hand, master Brook! follow. [*Exeunt.*

SCENE II. *Windsor Park.*

Enter PAGE, SHALLOW, *and* SLENDER.

Page. Come, come; we'll couch i' the castle-ditch, till we see the light of our fairies—Remember, son Slender, my daughter.

Slen. Ay, forsooth; I have spoke with her, and we have a nay word how to know one another. I come to her in white, and cry, *mum;* she cries, *budget;* and by that we know one another.

Shal. That's good too: But what needs either your *mum*, or her *budget;* the white will decipher her well enough.—It hath struck ten o'clock.

Page. The night is dark; light and spirits will become it well. Heaven prosper our sport! No man means evil but the devil, and we shall know him by his horns. Let's away; follow me. [*Exeunt.*

SCENE III. *The Street in Windsor.*

Enter MRS. PAGE, MRS. FORD, *and* DR. CAIUS.

Mrs. Page. Master doctor, my daughter is in green; when you see your time, take her by the hand, away with her to the deanery, and dispatch it quickly: Go before into the park; we two must go together.

Caius. I know vat I have to do; Adieu.

Mrs. Page. Fare you well, sir. [*Exit* CAIUS.] My husband will not rejoice so much at the abuse of Falstaff, as he will chafe at the doctor's marrying my daughter: but 'tis no matter; better a little chiding, than a great deal of heart-break.

Mrs. Ford. Where is Nan now, and her troop of fairies? and the Welsh devil, Hugh?

Mrs. Page. They are all couched in a pit hard by Herne's oak, with obscured lights; which at the very instant of Falstaff's and our meeting, they will at once display to the night.

Mrs. Ford. That cannot choose but amaze him.

Mrs. Page. If he be not amazed, he will be mocked; if he be amazed, he will every way be mocked.

Mrs. Ford. We'll betray him finely.

Mrs. Page. Against such lewdsters, and their lechery,
Those that betray them do no treachery.

Mrs. Ford. The hour draws on; To the oak, to the oak! [*Exeunt.*

SCENE IV. *Windsor Park.*

Enter SIR HUGH EVANS *and* Fairies.

Eva. Trib, trib, fairies; come; and remember your parts; be pold, I pray you; follow me into the pit; and when I give the watch-'ords, do as I pid you; Come, come; trib, trib. [*Exeunt.*

SCENE V. *Another part of the Park.*

Enter FALSTAFF *disguised, with a buck's head on.*

Fal. The Windsor bell hath struck twelve; the minute draws on: Now, the hot-blooded gods assist me:—Remember, Jove, thou wast a bull for thy Europa; love set on thy horns—O powerful love! that in some respects, makes a beast a man; in some other, a man a beast.—You were also, Jupiter, a swan, for the love of Leda;—O, omnipotent love! how near the god drew to the complexion of a goose?—A fault done first in the form of a beast;—O Jove, a beastly fault! and then another fault in the semblance of a fowl; think on't, Jove; a foul fault.—When gods have hot backs, what shall poor men do? For me, I am here a Windsor stag; and the fattest, I think, i' the forest: send me a cool rut-time, Jove, or who can blame me to piss my tallow? Who comes here? my doe?

Enter MRS. FORD *and* MRS. PAGE.

Mrs. Ford. Sir John? art thou there, my deer, my male deer?

Fal. My doe with the black scut?—Let the sky rain potatoes; let it thunder to the tune of *Green Sleeves;* hail kissing-comfits, and snow eringoes; let there come a tempest of provocation, I will shelter me here. [*Embracing her.*

Mrs. Ford. Mistress Page is come with me, sweetheart.

Fal. Divide me like a bribe-buck, each a haunch: I will keep my sides to myself, my shoulders for the fellow of this walk, and my horns I bequeath your husbands. Am I a woodman? ha! Speak I like Herne the hunter?—Why, now is Cupid a child of conscience; he makes restitution. As I am a true spirit, welcome! [*Noise within.*

Mrs. Page. Alas! What noise?

Mrs. Ford. Heaven forgive our sins!

Fal. What should this be?

Mrs. Ford. } *Mrs. Page.* } Away, away. [*They run off.*

Fal. I think, the devil will not have me damned, lest the oil that is in me should set hell on fire; he would never else cross me thus.

Enter SIR HUGH EVANS, *like a satyr;* MRS. QUICKLY, *and* PISTOL; ANNE PAGE, *as the Fairy Queen, attended by her brother and others, dressed like fairies, with waxen tapers on their heads.*

Quick. Fairies, black, gray, green, and white,
You moon-shine revellers, and shades of night,
You orphan-heirs of fixed destiny,
Attend your office, and your quality.——
Crier Hobgoblin, make the fairy o-yes.

Pist. Elves, list your names; silence, you airy toys.
Cricket, to Windsor chimneys shalt thou leap:
Where fires thou find'st unrak'd, and hearths unswept,
There pinch the maids as blue as bilberry:
Our radiant queen hates sluts, and sluttery.

Fal. They are fairies; he that speaks to them shall die:
I'll wink and couch: No man their works must eye. [*Lies down upon his face.*

Eva. Where's *Pede?*—Go you, and where you find a maid,
That, ere she sleep, has thrice her prayers said,
Raise up the organs of her fantasy,
Sleep she as sound as careless infancy;
But those as sleep, and think not on their sins,
Pinch them, arms, legs, backs, shoulders, sides, and shins.

Quick. About, about;
Search Windsor Castle, elves, within and out:
Strew good luck, ouphes, on every sacred room:
That it may stand till the perpetual doom,
In state as wholesome, as in state 'tis fit;
Worthy the owner, and the owner it.
The several chairs of order look you scour
With juice of balm, and every precious flower:
Each fair instalment, coat, and several crest,
With loyal blazon, evermore be blest!
And nightly, meadow-fairies, look, you sing,
Like to the Garter's compass, in a ring:
The expressure that it bears, green let it be,
More fertile-fresh than all the field to see;
And, *Hony soit qui mal y pense,* write,
In emerald tufts, flowers purple, blue and white;
Like sapphire, pearl, and rich embroidery, }
Buckled below fair knighthood's bending knee; }
Fairies use flowers for their charactery. }
Away; disperse: But, 'till 'tis one o'clock,
Our dance of custom, round about the oak
Of Herne the hunter, let us not forget.

Eva. Pray you, lock hand in hand; yourselves in order set:
And twenty glowworms shall our lanterns be,
To guide our measure round about the tree.
But, stay; I smell a man of middle earth.

Fal. Heaven defend me from that Welsh fairy! lest he transform me to a piece of cheese!

Pist. Vile worm, thou wast o'erlook'd even in thy birth.

Quick. With trial fire touch me his finger-end;
If he be chaste, the flame will back descend,
And turn him to no pain; but if he start,
It is the flesh of a corrupted heart.

Pist. A trial, come.

Eva. Come, will this wood take fire?
[*They burn him with their tapers.*

Fal. Oh, oh, oh!

Quick. Corrupt, corrupt, and tainted in desire!
About him fairies; sing a scornful rhyme:
And as you trip, still pinch him to your time.

Eva. It is right; indeed he is full of lecheries and iniquity.

SONG.

Fye on sinful fantasy!
Fye on lust and luxury!
Lust is but a bloody fire,
Kindled with unchaste desire,

Fed in heart; whose flames aspire,
As thoughts do blow them, higher and higher.
Pinch him, fairies, mutually;
Pinch him for his villany;
Pinch him, and burn him, and turn him about,
Till candles, and starlight, and moonshine be out.

During this song, the fairies pinch Falstaff. Doctor Caius *comes one way, and steals away a fairy in green;* Slender *another way, and takes off a fairy in white; and* Fenton *comes, and steals away* Mrs. Anne Page. *A noise of hunting is made within. All the fairies run away.* Falstaff *pulls off his buck's head, and rises.*

Enter Page, Ford, Mrs. Page, *and* Mrs. Ford. *They lay hold on him.*

Page. Nay, do not fly: I think, we have watch'd you now;
Will none but Herne the hunter serve your turn?

Mrs. Page. I pray you, come; hold up the jest no higher:—
Now, good Sir John, how like you Windsor wives?
See you these, husband? do not these fair yokes
Become the forest better than the town?

Ford. Now, sir, who's a cuckold now?—Master Brook, Falstaff's a knave, a cuckoldy knave; here are his horns, master Brook: And, master Brook, he hath enjoyed nothing of Ford's but his buck-basket, his cudgel, and twenty pounds of money, which must be paid to Master Brook: his horses are arrested for it, master Brook.

Mrs. Ford. Sir John, we have had ill luck, we could never meet. I will never take you for my love again, but I will always count you my deer.

Fal. I do begin to perceive that I am made an ass.

Ford. Ay, and an ox too; both the proofs are extant.

Fal. And these are not fairies? I was three or four times in the thought, they were not fairies: and yet the guiltiness of my mind, the sudden surprise of my powers, drove the grossness of the foppery into a received belief, in despite of the teeth of all rhyme and reason, that they were fairies. See now, how wit may be made a Jack-a-lent, when 'tis upon ill employment!

Eva. Sir John Falstaff, serve Got, and leave your desires, and fairies will not pinse you.

Ford. Well said, fairy Hugh.

Eva. And leave you your jealousies too, I pray you.

Ford. I will never mistrust my wife again, till thou art able to woo her in good English.

Fal. Have I laid my brain in the sun, and dried it, that it wants matter to prevent so gross o'er-reaching as this? Am I ridden with a Welsh goat too? Shall I have a coxcomb of frize? 'tis time I were choked with a piece of toasted cheese.

Eva. Seese is not good to give putter; your pelly is all putter.

Fal. Seese and putter! Have I lived to stand at the taunt of one that makes fritters of English? This is enough to be the decay of lust and late walking through the realm.

Mrs. Page. Why, Sir John, do you think, though we would have thrust virtue out of our hearts by the head and shoulders, and have given ourselves without scruple to hell, that ever the devil could have made you our delight?

Ford. What, a hodge-pudding? a bag of flax?

Mrs. Page. A puffed man?

Page. Old, cold, withered, and of intolerable entrails?

Ford. And one that is as slanderous as Satan?

Page. And as poor as Job?

Ford. And as wicked as his wife?

Eva. And given to fornications, and to taverns, and sack, and wine, and metheglins, and to drinkings, and swearings and starings, pribbles and prabbles?

Fal. Well, I am your theme; you have the start of me; I am dejected; I am not able to answer the Welsh flannel; ignorance itself is a plummet o'er me: use me as you will.

Ford. Marry, sir, we'll bring you to Windsor, to one master Brook, that you have cozened of money, to whom you should have been a pander: over and above that you have suffered, I think, to repay that money will be a biting affliction.

Mrs. Ford. Nay, husband, let that go to make amends;
Forgive that sum, and so we'll all be friends.

Ford. Well, here's my hand; all's forgiven at last.

Page. Yet be cheerful, knight: thou shalt eat a posset to-night at my house; where I will desire thee to laugh at my wife, that now laughs at thee: Tell her, master Slender hath married her daughter.

Mrs. Page. Doctors doubt that: If Anne Page be my daughter, she is, by this, doctor Caius' wife. [*Aside.*

Enter Slender.

Slen. Whoo! ho! ho! father Page!

Page. Son! how now? how now, son? have you despatched?

Slen. Despatched!—I'll make the best in Gloucestershire know on't; 'would, I were hanged, la, else.

Page. Of what, son?

Slen. I came yonder at Eton to marry mistress Anne Page, and she's a great lubberly boy. If it had not been i' the church, I would have swinged him, or he should have swinged me. If I did not think it had been Anne Page, would I might never stir, and 'tis a post-master's boy.

Page. Upon my life then you took the wrong.

Slen. What need you tell me that? I think so, when I took a boy for a girl: If I had been married to him, for all he was in woman's apparel, I would not have had him.

Page. Why, this is your own folly. Did not I tell you, how you should know my daughter by her garments?

Slen. I went to her in white, and cry'd *mum;* and she cry'd *budget*, as Anne and I had appointed; and yet it was not Anne, but a postmaster's boy.

Eva. Jeshu! Master Slender, cannot you see but marry boys?

Page. O, I am vexed at heart: What shall I do?

Mrs. Page. Good George, be not angry: I knew of your purpose; turned my daughter into green; and, indeed, she is now with the doctor at the deanery, and there married.

Enter Caius.

Caius. Vere is mistress Page? By gar, I am cozened: I ha' married *un garcon*, a boy; *un paisan*, by gar, a boy; it is not Anne Page: by gar, I am cozened.

Mrs. Page. Why, did you take her in green?

Caius. Ay, be gar, and 'tis a boy; be gar, I'll raise all Windsor. [*Exit* Caius.

Ford. This is strange! Who hath got the right Anne?

Page. My heart misgives me: Here comes master Fenton.

Enter Fenton *and* Anne Page.

How now, master Fenton?

Anne. Pardon, good father! good my mother, pardon!

Page. Now, mistress! how chance you went not with master Slender?

Mrs. Page. Why went you not with master doctor, maid?

Fent. You do amaze her: Hear the truth of it.
You would have married her most shamefully,

Where there was no proportion held in love.
The truth is, she and I, long since contracted,
Are now so sure that nothing can dissolve us.
The offence is holy that she hath committed:
And this deceit loses the name of craft,
Of disobedience, or unduteous title;
Since therein she doth evitate and shun
A thousand irreligious cursed hours,
Which forced marriage would have brought upon her.

Ford. Stand not amaz'd; here is no remedy:—
In love, the heavens themselves do guide the state;
Money buys lands, and wives are sold by fate.

Fal. I am glad, though you have ta'en a special stand to strike at me, that your arrow hath glanced.

Page. Well, what remedy? Fenton, heaven give thee joy!
What cannot be eschew'd, must be embrac'd.

Fal. When night-dogs run, all sorts of deer are chas'd.

Eva. I will dance and eat plums at your wedding.

Mrs. Page. Well, I will muse no further:—master Fenton,
Heaven give you many, many merry days!
Good husband, let us every one go home,
And laugh this sport o'er by a country fire;
Sir John and all.

Ford. Let it be so:—Sir John,
To master Brook you yet shall hold your word;
For he to-night shall lie with mistress Ford.

[*Exeunt.*

TWELFTH NIGHT; OR, WHAT YOU WILL.

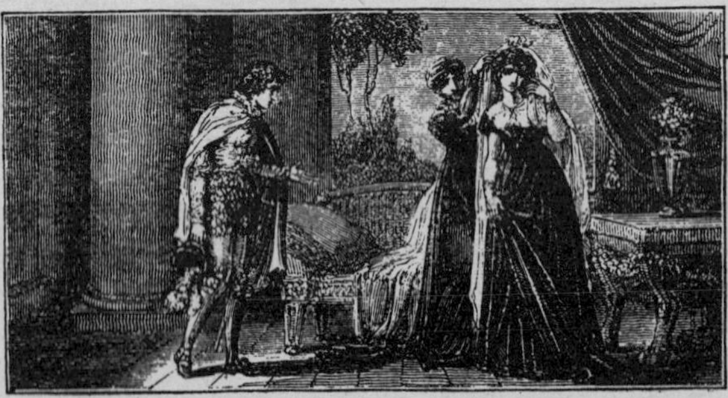

PERSONS REPRESENTED.

ORSINO, *Duke of* Illyria.
SEBASTIAN, *a young Gentleman, Brother to* Viola.
ANTONIO, *a Sea Captain, friend to* Sebastian.
A Sea Captain, *Friend to* Viola.
VALENTINE, } *Gentlemen attending on the Duke.*
CURIO, }
SIR TOBY BELCH, *Uncle of* Olivia.
SIR ANDREW AGUE-CHEEK.
MALVOLIO, *Steward to* Olivia.
FABIAN, } *Servants to* Olivia.
Clown, }

OLIVIA, *a rich Countess.*
VIOLA, *in love with the Duke.*
MARIA, Olivia's *Woman.*

Lords, Priests, Sailors, Officers, Musicians, and other Attendants.

SCENE—*a City in* Illyria; *and the Sea Coast near it.*

ACT I.

SCENE I. *An Apartment in the* Duke's *Palace.*

Enter Duke, CURIO, Lords; *Musicians attending.*

Duke. IF musick be the food of love, play on,
Give me excess of it; that, surfeiting,
The appetite may sicken, and so die.——
That strain again;—it had a dying fall:
O, it came o'er my ear like the sweet south,
That breathes upon a bank of violets,
Stealing, and giving odour.—Enough; no more;
'Tis not so sweet now as it was before.
O spirit of love, how quick and fresh art thou!
That notwithstanding thy capacity
Receiveth as the sea, nought enters there,
Of what validity and pitch soever,
But falls into abatement and low price,
Even in a minute! so full of shapes is fancy,
That it alone is high-fantastical.

Cur. Will you go hunt, my lord?

Duke. What, Curio?

Cur. The hart.

Duke. Why, so I do, the noblest that I have:
O, when mine eyes did see Olivia first,
Methought, she purg'd the air of pestilence;
That instant was I turn'd into a hart;
And my desires, like fell and cruel hounds,
E'er since pursue me.—How now? what news from her?

Enter VALENTINE.

Val. So please my lord, I might not be admitted,
But from her handmaid do return this answer:
The element itself, till seven years heat,
Shall not behold her face at ample view;
But, like a cloistress, she will veiled walk,
And water once a day her chamber round
With eye-offending brine: all this, to season
A brother's dead love, which she would keep fresh,
And lasting, in her sad remembrance.

Duke. O, she, that hath a heart of that fine frame,
To pay this debt o love but to a brother

How will she love, when the rich golden shaft
Hath kill'd the flock of all affections else
That live in her! when liver, brain, and heart,
These sovereign thrones, are all supplied, and fill'd
(Her sweet perfections) with one self king!
Away before me to sweet beds of flowers;
Love-thoughts lie rich, when canopied with bowers. [*Exeunt.*

SCENE II. *The Sea Coast.*

Enter VIOLA, Captain, *and* Sailors.

Vio. What country, friends, is this?
Cap. Illyria, lady.
Vio. And what should I do in Illyria?
My brother he is in Elysium.
Perchance he is not drown'd:—What think you, sailors?
Cap. It is perchance that you yourself were saved.
Vio. O my poor brother! and so, perchance, may he be.
Cap. True, madam: and, to comfort you with chance,
Assure yourself, after our ship did split,
When you, and that poor number saved with you,
Hung on our driving boat, I saw your brother,
Most provident in peril, bind himself
(Courage and hope both teaching him the practice)
To a strong mast, that lived upon the sea.
Where, like Arion on the dolphin's back,
I saw him hold acquaintance with the waves,
So long as I could see.
Vio. For saying so, there's gold:
Mine own escape unfoldeth to my hope,
Whereto thy speech serves for authority,
The like of him. Know'st thou this country?
Cap. Ay, madam, well; for I was bred and born
Not three hours travel from this very place.
Vio. Who governs here?
Cap. A noble duke, in nature,
As in his name.
Vio. What is his name?
Cap. Orsino.
Vio. Orsino! I have heard my father name him:
He was a bachelor then.
Cap. And so is now,
Or was so very late: for but a month
Ago I went from hence; and then 'twas fresh
In murmur (as you know, what great ones do,
The less will prattle of), that he did seek
The love of fair Olivia.
Vio. What's she?
Cap. A virtuous maid, the daughter of a count
That died some twelvemonth since; then leaving her
In the protection of his son, her brother,
Who shortly also died: for whose dear love
They say she hath abjur'd the company
And sight of men.
Vio. O, that I serv'd that lady:
And might not be delivered to the world,
Till I had made mine own occasion mellow,
What my estate is.
Cap. That were hard to compass;
Because she will admit no kind of suit,
No, not the duke's.
Vio. There is a fair behaviour in thee, captain;
And though that nature with a beauteous wall
Doth oft close in pollution, yet of thee
I will believe, thou hast a mind that suits
With this thy fair and outward character.
I pray thee, and I'll pay thee bounteously,
Conceal me what I am; and be my aid
For such disguise as, haply, shall become
The form of my intent. I'll serve this duke;
Thou shalt present me as an eunuch to him,
It may be worth thy pains; for I can sing,
And speak to him in many sorts of musick,
That will allow me very worth his service.
What else may hap, to time I will commit;
Only shape thou thy silence to my wit.
Cap. Be you his eunuch, and your mute I'll be:
When my tongue blabs, then let mine eyes not see!
Vio. I thank thee: Lead me on. [*Exeunt.*

SCENE III. *A Room in* Olivia's *House.*

Enter SIR TOBY BELCH *and* MARIA.

Sir To. What a plague means my niece, to take the death of her brother thus? I am sure, care's an enemy to life.

Mar. By my troth, Sir Toby, you must come in earlier o'nights; your cousin, my lady, takes great exceptions to your ill hours.

Sir To. Why, let her except before excepted.

Mar. Ay, but you must confine yourself within the modest limits of order.

Sir To. Confine? I'll confine myself no finer than I am: these clothes are good enough to drink in, and so be these boots too; an they be not, let them hang themselves in their own straps.

Mar. That quaffing and drinking will undo you: I heard my lady talk of it yesterday; and of a foolish knight, that you brought in one night here, to be her wooer.

Sir To. Who, Sir Andrew Ague-cheek?

Mar. Ay, he.

Sir To. He's as tall a man as any's in Illyria.

Mar. What's that to the purpose?

Sir To. Why, he has three thousand ducats a year.

Mar. Ay, but he'll have but a year in all these ducats; he's a very fool and a prodigal.

Sir To. Fye, that you'll say so! he plays o' the viol-de-gambo, and speaks three or four languages word for word without book, and hath all the good gifts of nature.

Mar. He hath, indeed,—almost natural: for, besides that he's a fool, he's a great quarreller; and, but that he hath the gift of a coward to allay the gust he hath in quarrelling, 'tis thought among the prudent, he would quickly have the gift of a grave.

Sir To. By this hand they are scoundrels, and substractors, that say so of him. Who are they?

Mar. They that add moreover, he's drunk nightly in your company.

Sir To. With drinking healths to my niece; I'll drink to her, as long as there is a passage in my throat, and drink in Illyria: He's a coward, and a coystril, that will not drink to my niece, till his brains turn o' the toe like a parish-top. What, wench? Castiliano volto; for here comes Sir Andrew Ague-face.

Enter SIR ANDREW AGUE-CHEEK.

Sir And. Sir Toby Belch! how now, Sir Toby Belch?

Sir To. Sweet Sir Andrew!

Sir And. Bless you, fair shrew.

Mar. And you too, sir.

Sir To. Accost, Sir Andrew, accost.

Sir And. What's that?

Sir To. My niece's chamber-maid.

Sir And. Good mistress Accost, I desire better acquaintance.

Mar. My name is Mary, sir.

Sir And. Good mistress Mary Accost,——

Sir To. You mistake, knight: accost, is, front her, board her, woo her, assail her.

Sir And. By my troth, I would not undertake her in this company. Is that the meaning of accost?

Mar. Fare you well, gentlemen.

Sir To. An thou let part so, Sir Andrew, 'would thou might'st never draw sword again.

Sir And. An you part so, mistress, I would I might never draw sword again. Fair lady, do you think you have fools in hand?

Mar. Sir, I have not you by the hand.

Sir And. Marry, but you shall have; and here's my hand.

Mar. Now, sir, thought is free: I pray you, bring your hand to the buttery-bar, and let it drink.

Sir And. Wherefore, sweetheart? what's your metaphor?

Mar. It's dry, sir.

Sir And. Why, I think so; I am not such an ass, but I can keep my hand dry. But what's your jest?

Mar. A dry jest, sir.

Sir And. Are you full of them?

Mar. Ay, sir; I have them at my fingers' ends: marry, now I let go your hand, I am barren. [*Exit* MARIA.

Sir To. O knight, thou lack'st a cup of canary: When did I see thee so put down?

Sir And. Never in your life, I think; unless you see canary put me down: Methinks, sometimes I have no more wit than a christian, or an ordinary man has: but I am a great eater of beef, and, I believe, that does harm to my wit.

Sir To. No question.

Sir And. An I thought that, I'd forswear it. I'll ride home to morrow, Sir Toby.

Sir To. *Pourquoy*, my dear knight?

Sir And. What is *pourquoy?* do or not do? I would I had bestowed that time in the tongues, that I have in fencing, dancing, and bear-baiting: O, had I but followed the arts!

Sir To. Then hadst thou had an excellent head of hair.

Sir And. Why, would that have mended my hair?

Sir To. Past question; for thou seest it will not curl by nature.

Sir And. But it becomes me well enough, does't not?

Sir To. Excellent; it hangs like flax on a distaff; and I hope to see a housewife take thee between her legs and spin it off.

Sir And. 'Faith, I'll home to-morrow, Sir Toby: your niece will not be seen; or, if she be, it's four to one she'll none of me: the count himself, here hard by, woos her.

Sir To. She'll none o' the count; she'll not match above her degree, neither in estate, years, nor wit; I have heard her swear it. Tut, there's life in't, man.

Sir And. I'll stay a month longer. I am a fellow o' the strangest mind i' the world; I delight in masques and revels sometimes altogether.

Sir To. Art thou good at these kickshaws, knight?

Sir And. As any man in Illyria, whatsoever he be, under the degree of my betters; and yet I will not compare with an old man.

Sir To. What is thy excellence in a galliard, knight?

Sir And. 'Faith, I can cut a caper.

Sir To. And I can cut the mutton to't.

Sir And. And, I think I have the back-trick, simply as strong as any man in Illyria.

Sir To. Wherefore are these things hid? wherefore have these gifts a curtain before them? are they like to take dust, like mistress Mall's picture? why dost thou not go to church in a galliard, and come home in a coranto? My very walk should be a jig; I would not so much as make water, but in a sink-a-pace. What dost thou mean? is it a world to hide virtues in? I did think, by the excellent constitution of thy leg, it was formed under the star of a galliard.

Sir And. Ay, 'tis strong, and it does indifferent well in a flame-coloured stock. Shall we set about some revels?

Sir To. What shall we do else? were we not born under Taurus?

Sir And. Taurus? that's sides and heart.

Sir To. No, sir; it is legs and thighs. Let me see thee caper; ha! higher: ha, ha!—excellent! [*Exeunt.*

SCENE IV. *A Room in the* Duke's *Palace.*

Enter VALENTINE, *and* VIOLA *in man's attire.*

Val. If the Duke continue these favours towards you, Cesario, you are like to be much advanced; he hath known you but three days, and already you are no stranger.

Vio. You either fear his humour, or my negligence, that you call in question the continuance of his love: Is he inconstant, sir, in his favours?

Val. No, believe me.

Enter DUKE, CURIO, *and* Attendants.

Vio. I thank you. Here comes the count.

Duke. Who saw Cesario, ho?

Vio. On your attendance, my lord; here.

Duke. Stand you awhile aloof.—Cesario,
Thou know'st no less but all; I have unclasp'd
To thee the book even of my secret soul:
Therefore, good youth, address thy gait unto her;
Be not deny'd access, stand at her doors,
And tell them, there thy fixed foot shall grow,
Till thou have audience.

Vio. Sure, my noble lord,
If she be so abandon'd to her sorrow
As it is spoke, she never will admit me.

Duke. Be clamorous, and leap all civil bounds,
Rather than make unprofited return.

Vio. Say, I do speak with her, my lord; what then?

Duke. O, then unfold the passion of my love,
Surprise her with discourse of my dear faith:
It shall become thee well to act my woes;
She will attend it better in thy youth,
Than in a nuncio of more grave aspect.

Vio. I think not so, my lord.

Duke. Dear lad, believe it:
For they shall yet belie thy happy years
That say, thou art a man: Diana's lip
Is not more smooth and rubious; thy small pipe
Is as the maiden's organ, shrill and sound,
And all is semblative a woman's part.
I know thy constellation is right apt
For this affair:—Some four or five attend him;
All, if you will; for I myself am best,
When least in company:—Prosper well in this,
And thou shalt live as freely as thy lord,
To call his fortunes thine.

Vio. I'll do my best
To woo your lady: yet [*Aside*], a barful strife!
Whoe'er I woo, myself would be his wife. [*Exeunt.*

SCENE V. *A Room in* Olivia's *House.*

Enter MARIA *and* Clown.

Mar. Nay, either tell me where thou hast been, or I will not open my lips so wide as a bristle may enter, in way of thy excuse: my lady will hang thee for thy absence.

Clo. Let her hang me: he that is well hanged in this world needs to fear no colours.

Mar. Make that good.

Clo. He shall see none to fear.

Mar. A good lenten answer: I can tell thee where that saying was born, of, I fear no colours.

Clo. Where, good mistress Mary?

Mar. In the wars; and that may you be bold to say in your foolery.

Clo. Well, God give them wisdom, that have it; and those that are fools, let them use their talents.

Mar. Yet you will be hanged for being so long absent: or, to be turned away, is not that as good as a hanging to you?

Clo. Many a good hanging prevents a bad marriage; and, for turning away, let summer bear it out.

Mar. You are resolute then?

Clo. Not so neither; but I am resolved on two points.

Mar. That, if one break, the other will hold; or, if both break, your gaskins fall.

Clo. Apt, in good faith; very apt! Well, go

thy way; if Sir Toby would leave drinking, thou wert as witty a piece of Eve's flesh as any in Illyria.

Mar. Peace, you rogue, no more o' that; here comes my lady: make your excuse wisely, you were best. [*Exit.*

Enter OLIVIA *and* MALVOLIO.

Clo. Wit, and't be thy will, put me into good fooling! Those wits, that think they have thee, do very oft prove fools; and I, that am sure I lack thee, may pass for a wise man: For what says Quinapalus? Better a witty fool, than a foolish wit.——God bless thee, lady!

Oli. Take the fool away.

Clo. Do you not hear, fellows? Take away the lady.

Oli. Go to, you're a dry fool; I'll no more of you: besides you grow dishonest.

Clo. Two faults, madonna, that drink and good counsel will amend: for give the dry fool drink, then is the fool not dry; bid the dishonest man mend himself; if he mend, he is no longer dishonest; if he cannot, let the botcher mend him: Any thing that's mended, is but patched: virtue, that transgresses, is but patched with sin: and sin, that amends, is but patched with virtue: If that this simple syllogism will serve, so; if it will not, what remedy? As there is no true cuckold but calamity, so beauty's a flower:— the lady bade take away the fool; therefore, I say again, take her away.

Oli. Sir, I bade them take away you.

Clo. Misprision in the highest degree!—Lady, *Cucullus non facit monachum;* that's as much as to say, I wear not motley in my brain. Good madonna, give me leave to prove you a fool.

Oli. Can you do it?

Clo. Dexterously, good madonna.

Oli. Make your proof.

Clo. I must catechise you for it, madonna: Good my mouse of virtue, answer me.

Oli. Well, sir, for want of other idleness, I'll 'bide your proof.

Clo. Good madonna, why mourn'st thou?

Oli. Good fool, for my brother's death.

Clo. I think his soul is in hell, madonna.

Oli. I know his soul is in heaven, fool.

Clo. The more fool you, madonna, to mourn for your brother's soul being in heaven.—Take away the fool, gentlemen.

Oli. What think you of this fool, Malvolio? doth he not mend?

Mal. Yes; and shall do, till the pangs of death shake him: Infirmity, that decays the wise, doth ever make the better fool.

Clo. God send you, sir, a speedy infirmity, for the better increasing your folly! Sir Toby will be sworn that I am no fox; but he will not pass his word for twopence that you are no fool.

Oli. How say you to that, Malvolio?

Mal. I marvel your ladyship takes delight in such a barren rascal; I saw him put down the other day with an ordinary fool that has no more brain than a stone. Look you now, he's out of his guard already; unless you laugh and minister occasion to him, he is gagged. I protest I take these wise men, that crow so at these set kind of fools, no better than the fools' zanies.

Oli. O, you are sick of self-love, Malvolio, and taste with a distempered appetite. To be generous, guiltless, and of free disposition, is to take those things for bird-bolts, that you deem cannon-bullets: There is no slander in an allowed fool, though he do nothing but rail; nor no railing in a known discreet man, though he do nothing but reprove.

Clo. Now Mercury endue thee with leasing, for thou speakest well of fools!

Re-enter MARIA.

Mar. Madam, there is at the gate, a young gentleman, much desires to speak with you.

Oli. From the count Orsino, is it?

Mar. I know not, madam; 'tis a fair young man, and well attended.

Oli. Who of my people hold him in delay?

Mar. Sir Toby, madam, your kinsman.

Oli. Fetch him off, I pray you; he speaks nothing but madman: Fie on him! [*Exit* MARIA.] Go you, Malvolio; if it be a suit from the count, I am sick, or not at home; what you will to dismiss it. [*Exit* MALVOLIO.] Now you see, sir, how your fooling grows old, and people dislike it.

Clo. Thou hast spoke for us, madonna, as if thy eldest son should be a fool: whose skull Jove cram with brains, for here he comes, one of thy kin, has a most weak *pia mater.*

Enter SIR TOBY BELCH.

Oli. By mine honour, half drunk.—What is he at the gate, cousin?

Sir To. A gentleman.

Oli. A gentleman! what gentleman?

Sir To. 'Tis a gentleman here—A plague o' these pickle-herrings!—How now, sot?

Clo. Good Sir Toby,——

Oli. Cousin, cousin, how have you come so early by this lethargy?

Sir To. Lechery! I defy lechery: There's one at the gate.

Oli. Ay, marry; what is he?

Sir To. Let him be the devil, an he will, I care not: give me faith, say I. Well, it's all one. [*Exit.*

Oli. What's a drunken man like, fool?

Clo. Like a drown'd man, a fool, and a madman: one draught above heat makes him a fool; the second mads him; and a third drowns him.

Oli. Go thou and seek the coroner, and let him sit o' my coz; for he's in the third degree of drink; he's drown'd; go, look after him.

Clo. He is but mad yet, madonna; and the fool shall look to the madman. [*Exit* Clown.

Re-enter MALVOLIO.

Mal. Madam, 'yond young fellow swears he will speak with you. I told him you were sick; he takes on him to understand so much, and therefore comes to speak with you: I told him you were asleep; he seems to have a foreknowledge of that too, and therefore comes to speak with you. What is to be said to him, lady? he's fortified against any denial.

Oli. Tell him, he shall not speak with me.

Mal. He has been told so: and he says, he'll stand at your door like a sheriff's post, and be the supporter of a bench, but he'll speak with you.

Oli. What kind of man is he?

Mal. Why, of man kind.

Oli. What manner of man?

Mal. Of very ill manner; he'll speak with you, will you or no.

Oli. Of what personage and years is he?

Mal. Not yet old enough for a man, nor young enough for a boy; as a squash is before 'tis a peascod, or a codling when 'tis almost an apple: 'tis with him e'en standing water, between boy and man. He is very well favoured, and he speaks very shrewishly; one would think, his mother's milk were scarce out of him.

Oli. Let him approach: Call in my gentlewoman.

Mal. Gentlewoman, my lady calls. [*Exit.*

Re-enter MARIA.

Oli. Give me my veil; come, throw it o'er
 my face;
We'll once more hear Orsino's embassy.

Enter VIOLA.

Vio. The honourable lady of the house, which is she?

Oli. Speak to me, I shall answer for her: Your will?

Vio. Most radiant, exquisite, and unmatchable beauty,—I pray you, tell me, if this be the lady of the house, for I never saw her: I would be loath to cast away my speech; for, besides that it is excellently well penn'd, I have taken great pains to con it. Good beauties, let me sustain no scorn; I am very comptible, even to the least sinister usage.

Oli. Whence came you, sir?

Vio. I can say little more than I have studied, and that question's out of my part. Good gentle one, give me modest assurance, if you be the lady of the house, that I may proceed in my speech.

Oli. Are you a comedian?

Vio. No, my profound heart: and yet, by the very fangs of malice, I swear, I am not that I play. Are you the lady of the house?

Oli. If I do not usurp myself, I am.

Vio. Most certain, if you are she, you do usurp yourself; for what is yours to bestow, is not yours to reserve. But this is from my commission: I will on with my speech in your praise, and then shew you the heart of my message.

Oli. Come to what is important in't: I forgive you the praise.

Vio. Alas, I took great pains to study it, and 'tis poetical.

Oli. It is the more like to be feigned; I pray you, keep it in. I heard you were saucy at my gates; and allowed your approach, rather to wonder at you than to hear you. If you be not mad, be gone; if you have reason, be brief: 'tis not that time of moon with me, to make one in so skipping a dialogue.

Mar. Will you hoist sail, sir? here lies your way.

Vio. No, good swabber: I am to hull here a little longer.—Some mollification for your giant, sweet lady.

Oli. Tell me your mind.

Vio. I am a messenger.

Oli. Sure, you have some hideous matter to deliver, when the courtesy of it is so fearful. Speak your office.

Vio. It alone concerns your ear. I bring no overture of war, no taxation of homage; I hold the olive in my hand: my words are as full of peace as matter.

Oli. Yet you began rudely. What are you? what would you?

Vio. The rudeness, that hath appear'd in me, have I learn'd from my entertainment. What I am, and what I would, are as secret as maidenhead: to your ears, divinity; to any other's, profanation.

Oli. Give us the place alone; we will hear this divinity. [*Exit* MARIA.] Now, sir, what is your text?

Vio. Most sweet lady,——

Oli. A comfortable doctrine, and much may be said of it. Where lies your text.

Vio. In Orsino's bosom?

Oli. In his bosom? In what chapter of his bosom?

Vio. To answer by the method, in the first of his heart.

Oli. O, I have read it; it is heresy. Have you no more to say?

Vio. Good madam, let me see your face.

Oli. Have you any commission from your lord to negotiate with my face? you are now out of your text: but we will draw the curtain, and shew you the picture. Look you, sir, such a one as I was, this presents:—Is't not well done? [*Unveiling.*

Vio. Excellently done, if God did all.

Oli. 'Tis in grain, sir; 'twill endure wind and weather.

Vio. 'Tis beauty truly blent, whose red and white
Nature's own sweet and cunning hand laid on:
Lady, you are the cruel'st she alive,
If you will lead these graces to the grave,
And leave the world no copy.

Oli. O, sir, I will not be so hard-hearted; I will give out divers schedules of my beauty: It shall be inventoried; and every particle and utensil labelled to my will: as, item, two lips indifferent red; item, two gray eyes, with lids to them; item, one neck, one chin, and so forth. Were you sent hither to praise me?

Vio. I see you what you are: you are too proud;
But, if you were the devil, you are fair.
My lord and master loves you; O, such love
Could be but recompens'd, though you were crown'd
The nonpareil of beauty!

Oli. How does he love me?

Vio. With adorations, with fertile tears,
With groans that thunder love, with sighs of fire.

Oli. Your lord does know my mind, I cannot love him:
Yet I suppose him virtuous, know him noble,
Of great estate, of fresh and stainless youth;
In voices well divulg'd, free, learn'd, and valiant,
And, in dimension, and the shape of nature,
A gracious person: but yet I cannot love him;
He might have took his answer long ago.

Vio. If I did love you in my master's flame,
With such a suffering, such a deadly life,
In your denial I would find no sense,
I would not understand it.

Oli. Why, what would you?

Vio. Make me a willow cabin at your gate,
And call upon my soul within the house;
Write loyal cantons of contemned love,
And sing them loud even in the dead of night;
Holla your name to the reverberate hills,
And make the babbling gossip of the air
Cry out, Olivia! O, you should not rest
Between the elements of air and earth,
But you should pity me.

Oli. You might do much: What is your parentage?

Vio. Above my fortunes, yet my state is well:
I am a gentleman.

Oli. Get you to your lord;
I cannot love him: let him send no more;
Unless, perchance, you come to me again,
To tell me how he takes it. Fare you well:
I thank you for your pains: spend this for me.

Vio. I am no fee'd post, lady; keep your purse;
My master, not myself, lacks recompense.
Love make his heart of flint, that you shall love;
And let your fervour, like my master's, be
Plac'd in contempt! Farewell, fair cruelty. [*Exit.*

Oli. What is your parentage?
Above my fortunes, yet my state is well:
I am a gentleman.—I'll be sworn thou art,
Thy tongue, thy face, thy limbs, actions, and spirit,
Do give thee five-fold blazon;—Not too fast:—soft! soft!
Unless the master were the man.—How now?
Even so quickly may one catch the plague?
Methinks, I feel this youth's perfections,
With an invisible and subtle stealth,
To creep in at mine eyes. Well, let it be.—
What, ho, Malvolio!—

Re-enter MALVOLIO.

Mal. Here, madam, at your service.

Oli. Run after that same peevish messenger,
The county's man: he left this ring behind him,
Would I, or not; tell him, I'll none of it.
Desire him not to flatter with his lord,
Nor hold him up with hopes! I am not for him:
If that the youth will come this way to-morrow,
I'll give him reasons for't. Hie thee, Malvolio.

Mal. Madam, I will. [*Exit.*

Oli. I do I know not what: and fear to find
Mine eye too great a flatterer for my mind.
Fate, show thy force: ourselves we do not owe;
What is decreed, must be; and be this so!
[*Exit.*

ACT II.

SCENE I. *The Sea Coast.*

Enter ANTONIO *and* SEBASTIAN.

Ant. Will you stay no longer? nor will you not, that I go with you?

Seb. By your patience, no: my stars shine darkly over me; the malignancy of my fate might, perhaps, distemper yours; therefore I shall crave of you your leave, that I may bear my evils alone: It were a bad recompense for your love, to lay any of them on you.

Ant. Let me yet know of you, whither you are bound.

Seb. No, 'sooth, sir; my determinate voyage is mere extravagancy. But I perceive in you so excellent a touch of modesty, that you will not extort from me what I am willing to keep in; therefore it charges me in manners the rather to express myself. You must know of me, then, Antonio, my name is Sebastian, which I called Rodorigo: my father was that Sebastian of Messaline, whom, I know, you have heard of: he left behind him myself, and a sister, both born in an hour. If the heavens had been pleased, 'would we had so ended! but, you, sir, altered that; for, some hour before you took me from the breach of the sea, was my sister drowned.

Ant. Alas, the day!

Seb. A lady, sir, though it was said she much resembled me, was yet of many accounted beautiful: but, though I could not, with such estimable wonder, overfar believe that, yet thus far I will boldly publish her, she bore a mind that envy could not but call fair: she is drowned already, sir, with salt water, though I seem to drown her remembrance again with more.

Ant. Pardon me, sir, your bad entertainment.

Seb. O, good Antonio, forgive me your trouble.

Ant. If you will not murder me for my love, let me be your servant.

Seb. If you will not undo what you have done, that is, kill him whom you have recovered, desire it not. Fare ye well at once; my bosom is full of kindness; and I am yet so near the manners of my mother, that upon the least occasion more, mine eyes will tell tales of me. I am bound to the count Orsino's court: farewell. [*Exit.*

Ant. The gentleness of all the gods go with thee!
I have many enemies in Orsino's court,
Else would I very shortly see thee there:
But, come what may, I do adore thee so,
That danger shall seem sport, and I will go. [*Exit.*

SCENE II. *A Street.*

Enter VIOLA; MALVOLIO *following.*

Mal. Were not you even now with the countess Olivia?

Vio. Even now, sir; on a moderate pace I have since arrived but hither.

Mal. She returns this ring to you, sir; you might have saved me my pains, to have taken it away yourself. She adds moreover, that you should put your lord into a desperate assurance she will none of him: And one thing more; that you be never so hardy to come again in his affairs, unless it be to report your lord's taking of this. Receive it so.

Vio. She took the ring of me!—I'll none of it.

Mal. Come, sir, you peevishly threw it to her; and her will is, it should be so returned: if it be worth stooping for, there it lies in your eye; if not, be it his that finds it. [*Exit.*

Vio. I left no ring with her: What means this lady?
Fortune forbid my outside have not charm'd her!
She made good view of me; indeed, so much,
That, sure, methought her eyes had lost her tongue,
For she did speak in starts distractedly.
She loves me, sure; the cunning of her passion
Invites me in this churlish messenger.
None of my lord's ring! why, he sent her none.
I am the man;—If it be so, (as 'tis),
Poor lady, she were better love a dream.
Disguise, I see, thou art a wickedness,
Wherein the pregnant enemy does much.
How easy is it for the proper-false
In women's waxen hearts to set their forms!
Alas, our frailty is the cause, not we;
For, such as we are made of, such we be.
How will this fadge? My master loves her dearly;
And I, poor monster, fond as much on him;
And she, mistaken, seems to dote on me:
What will become of this! As I am man,
My state is desperate for my master's love;
As I am woman, now alas the day!
What thriftless sighs shall poor Olivia breathe?
O time, thou must untangle this, not I;
It is too hard a knot for me to untie. [*Exit.*

SCENE III. *A Room in* Olivia's *House.*

Enter SIR TOBY BELCH, *and* SIR ANDREW AGUE-CHEEK.

Sir To. Approach, Sir Andrew: not to be a-bed after midnight, is to be up betimes; and *diluculo surgere*, thou know'st,——

Sir And. Nay, by my troth, I know not: but I know to be up late, is to be up late.

Sir To. A false conclusion; I hate it as an unfilled can: To be up after midnight, and to go to bed then, is early; so that to go to bed after midnight, is to go to bed betimes. Do not our lives consist of the four elements?

Sir And. 'Faith, so they say; but, I think, it rather consists of eating and drinking.

Sir To. Thou art a scholar; let us therefore eat and drink.—Marian, I say!—a stoop of wine!

Enter Clown.

Sir And. Here comes the fool, i'faith.

Clo. How now, my hearts? Did you never see the picture of we three?

Sir To. Welcome, ass, now let's have a catch.

Sir And. By my troth, the fool has an excellent breast. I had rather than forty shillings I had such a leg; and so sweet a breath to sing, as the fool has. In sooth, thou wast in very gracious fooling last night, when thou spokest of Pigrogromitus, of the Vapians passing the equinoctial of Queubus; 'twas very good, i'faith. I sent thee sixpence for thy leman: Hadst it?

Clo. I did impeticos thy gratillity; for Malvolio's nose is no whipstock: My lady has a white hand, and the Myrmidons are no bottle-ale houses.

Sir And. Excellent! Why, this is the best fooling, when all is done. Now, a song.

Sir To. Come on; there is sixpence for you; let's have a song.

Sir And. There's a testril of me too: if one knight give a ——

Clo. Would you have a love-song, or a song of good life?

Sir To. A love-song, a love-song.

Sir And. Ay, ay; I care not for good life.

SONG.

Clo. O *mistress mine, where are you roaming?*
O, stay and hear; your true love's coming,
That can sing both high and low:
Trip no further, pretty sweeting;
Journeys end in lovers' meeting,
Every wise man's son doth know.

Sir And. Excellent good, i'faith!

Sir To. Good, good.

Clo. *What is love? 'tis not hereafter;*
Present mirth hath present laughter;
What's to come is still unsure:
In delay there lies no plenty;
Then come kiss me, sweet-and-twenty,
Youth's a stuff will not endure.

Sir And. A mellifluous voice, as I am true knight.

Sir To. A contagious breath.

Sir And. Very sweet and contagious, i'faith.

Sir To. To hear by the nose, it is dulcet in contagion. But shall we make the welkin dance indeed? Shall we rouse the night-owl in a catch, that will draw three souls out of one weaver? shall we do that?

Sir And. An you love me, let's do't: I am dog at a catch.

Clo. By'r lady, sir, and some dogs will catch well.

Sir And. Most certain: let our catch be, *Thou knave.*

Clo. *Hold thy peace, thou knave,* knight? I shall be constrain'd in't, to call thee knave, knight.

Sir And. 'Tis not the first time I have constrain'd one to call me knave. Begin, fool; it begins, *Hold thy peace.*

Clo. I shall never begin, if I hold my peace.

Sir And. Good, i' faith! Come, begin.
[*They sing a catch.*

Enter MARIA.

Mar. What a caterwauling do you keep here! If my lady have not called up her steward, Malvolio, and bid him turn you out of doors, never trust me.

Sir To. My lady's a Cataian, we are politicians; Malvolio's a Peg-a-Ramsey, and *Three merry men we be.* Am not I consanguineous? am I not of her blood? Tilley valley, lady! *There dwelt a man in Babylon, lady, lady!*
[*Singing.*

Clo. Beshrew me, the knight's in admirable fooling.

Sir And. Ay, he does well enough, if he be disposed, and so do I too; he does it with a better grace, but I do it more natural.

Sir To. *O, the twelfth day of December,*—
[*Singing.*

Mar. For the love o'God, peace.

Enter MALVOLIO.

Mal. My masters, are you mad? or what are

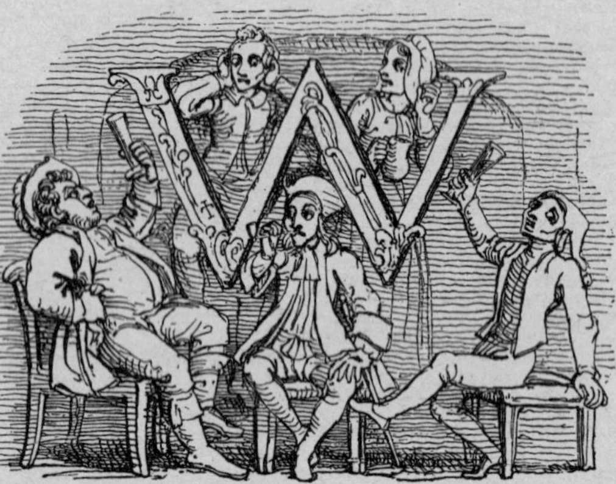

you? Have you no wit, manners, nor honesty, but to gabble like tinkers at this time of night? Do you make an alehouse of my lady's house, that ye squeak out your coziers' catches without any mitigation or remorse of voice? Is there no respect of place, persons, nor time, in you?

Sir To. We did keep time, sir, in our catches. Sneck up!

Mal. Sir Toby, I must be round with you. My lady bade me tell you, that though she harbours you as her kinsman, she's nothing allied to your disorders. If you can separate yourself and your misdemeanors, you are welcome to the house; if not, an it would please you to take leave of her, she is very willing to bid you farewell.

Sir To. *Farewell, dear heart, since I must needs be gone.*

Mar. Nay, good Sir Toby.

Clo. *His eyes do shew his days are almost done.*

Mal. Is't even so?

Sir To. *But I will never die.*

Clo. Sir Toby, there you lie.

Mal. This is much credit to you.

Sir To. *Shall I bid him go?* [*Singing.*

Clo. *What an if you do?*

Sir To. *Shall I bid him go, and spare not?*

Clo. *O no, no, no, no, you dare not.*

Sir To. Out o'time? sir, ye lie.—Art any more than a steward? Dost thou think, because thou art virtuous, there shall be no more cakes and ale?

Clo. Yes, by Saint Anne: and ginger shall be hot i'the mouth too.

Sir To. Thou'rt i'the right.—Go, sir, rub your chain with crums:—A stoop of wine, Maria!

Mal. Mistress Mary, if you prized my lady's favour at any thing more than contempt, you would not give means for this uncivil rule; she shall know of it, by this hand. [*Exit.*

Mar. Go shake your ears.

Sir And. 'Twere as good a deed as to drink when a man's a hungry, to challenge him to the field; and then to break promise with him, and make a fool of him.

Sir To. Do't, knight: I'll write thee a challenge; or I'll deliver thy indignation to him by word of mouth.

Mar. Sweet Sir Toby, be patient for to-night; since the youth of the count's was to-day with my lady, she is much out of quiet. For monsieur Malvolio, let me alone with him: if I do not gull him into a nay-word, and make him a common recreation, do not think I have wit enough to lie straight in my bed: I know, I can do it.

Sir To. Possess us, possess us; tell us something of him.

Mar. Marry, sir, sometimes he is a kind of Puritan.

Sir And. O, if I thought that, I'd beat him like a dog.

Sir To. What, for being a Puritan? thy exquisite reason, dear knight?

Sir And. I have no exquisite reason for't, but I have reason good enough.

Mar. The devil a Puritan that he is, or any thing constantly but a time pleaser; an affectioned ass, that cons state without book, and utters it by great swarths: the best persuaded of himself, so crammed, as he thinks, with excellencies, that it is his ground of faith, that all, that look on him, love him; and on that vice in him will my revenge find notable cause to work.

Sir To. What wilt thou do?

Mar. I will drop in his way some obscure epistles of love; wherein, by the colour of his beard, the shape of his leg, the manner of his gait, the expressure of his eye, forehead, and complexion, he shall find himself most feelingly personated: I can write very like my lady, your niece; on a forgotten matter we can hardly make distinction of our hands.

Sir To. Excellent! I smell a device.

Sir And. I have't in my nose too.

Sir To. He shall think, by the letters that thou wilt drop, that they come from my niece, and that she is in love with him.

Mar. My purpose is, indeed, a horse of that colour.

Sir And. And your horse now would make him an ass.

Mar. Ass, I doubt not.

Sir And. O, 'twill be admirable.

Mar. Sport royal, I warrant you: I know, my physick will work with him. I will plant you two, and let the fool make a third, where he shall find the letter; observe his construction of it. For this night, to bed; and dream on the event. Farewell. [*Exit.*

Sir To. Good night, Penthesilea.

Sir And. Before me, she's a good wench.

Sir To. She's a beagle, true bred, and one that adores me; What o' that?

Sir And. I was adored once too.

Sir To. Let's to bed, knight.—Thou hadst need send for more money.

Sir And. If I cannot recover your niece, I am a foul way out.

Sir To. Send for money, knight; if thou hast her not i' the end, call me Cut.

Sir And. If I do not, never trust me, take it how you will.

Sir To. Come, come; I'll go burn some sack, 'tis too late to go to bed now: come, knight; come, knight. [*Exeunt.*

SCENE IV. *A Room in the* Duke's *Palace.*

Enter DUKE, VIOLA, CURIO, *and others.*

Duke. Give me some musick:—Now, good morrow, friends:—
Now, good Cesario, but that piece of song,
That old and antique song we heard last night;
Methought, it did relieve my passion much,
More than light airs and recollected terms,
Of these most brisk and giddy-paced times:——
Come, but one verse.

Cur. He is not here, so please your lordship, that should sing it.

Duke. Who was it?

Cur. Feste, the jester, my lord: a fool, that the lady Olivia's father took much delight in: he is about the house.

Duke. Seek him out, and play the tune the while. [*Exit* CURIO.—*Musick.*
Come hither, boy; if ever thou shalt love,
In the sweet pangs of it, remember me:
For, such as I am, all true lovers are;
Unstaid and skittish in all motions else,
Save, in the constant image of the creature
That is belov'd.—How dost thou like this tune?

Vio. It gives a very echo to the seat
Where Love is thron'd.

Duke. Thou dost speak masterly:
My life upon't, young though thou art, thine eye
Hath stay'd upon some favour that it loves;
Hath it not, boy?

Vio. A little, by your favour.

Duke. What kind of woman is't?

Vio. Of your complexion.

Duke. She is not worth thee then. What years, i'faith?

Vio. About your years, my lord.

Duke. Too old, by heaven; Let still the woman take
An elder than herself; so wears she to him,
So sways she level in her husband's heart.
For, boy, however we do praise ourselves,
Our fancies are more giddy and unfirm,
More longing, wavering, sooner lost and worn,
Than women's are.

Vio. I think it well, my lord.

Duke. Then let thy love be younger than thyself,
Or thy affection cannot hold the bent:
For women are as roses; whose fair flower,
Being once display'd, doth fall that very hour.

Vio. And so they are: alas, that they are so;
To die, even when they to perfection grow!

Re-enter CURIO *and* Clown.

Duke. O fellow, come, the song we had last night:—
Mark it, Cesario; it is old, and plain:
The spinsters and the knitters in the sun,
And the free maids that weave their thread with bones,
Do use to chant it; it is silly sooth,
And dallies with the innocence of love,
Like the old age.

Clo. Are you ready, sir?

Duke. Ay; pr'ythee, sing. [*Musick.*

SONG.

Clo. *Come away, come away, death,*
And in sad cypress let me be laid;
Fly away, fly away, breath;
I am slain by a fair cruel maid.
My shroud of white, stuck all with yew,
O, prepare it;
My part of death no one so true
Did share it.
Not a flower, not a flower sweet,
On my black coffin let there be strown;
Not a friend, not a friend greet
My poor corpse, where my bones shall be thrown:
A thousand thousand sighs to save,
Lay me, O, where
Sad true-lover never find my grave,
To weep there.

Duke. There's for thy pains.

Clo. No pains, sir; I take pleasure in singing, sir.

Duke. I'll pay thy pleasure then.

Clo. Truly, sir, and pleasure will be paid one time or another.

Duke. Give me now leave to leave thee.

Clo. Now, the melancholy god protect thee; and the tailor make thy doublet of changeable taffata, for thy mind is a very opal—I would have men of such constancy put to sea, that their business might be every thing, and their intent every where; for that's it, that always makes a good voyage of nothing.—Farewell. [*Exit* Clown.

Duke. Let all the rest give place.——
[*Exeunt* CURIO *and Attendants.*
Once more, Cesario,
Get thee to yon' same sovereign cruelty:

Tell her, my love, more noble than the world,
Prizes not quantity of dirty lands;
The parts that fortune hath bestow'd upon her,
Tell her, I hold as giddily as fortune;
But 'tis that miracle, and queen of gems,
That nature pranks her in, attracts my soul.
Vio. But, if she cannot love you, sir?
Duke. I cannot be so answer'd.
Vio. 'Sooth, but you must.
Say, that some lady, as, perhaps, there is,
Hath for your love as great a pang of heart
As you have for Olivia: you cannot love her;
You tell her so; Must she not then be answer'd?
Duke. There is no woman's sides
Can bide the beating of so strong a passion
As love doth give my heart: no woman's heart
So big, to hold so much; they lack retention.
Alas, their love may be call'd appetite,—
No motion of the liver, but the palate,—
That suffer surfeit, cloyment, and revolt;
But mine is all as hungry as the sea,
And can digest as much: make no compare
Between that love a woman can bear me,
And that I owe Olivia.
Vio. Ay, but I know,—
Duke. What dost thou know?
Vio. Too well what love women to men may owe:
In faith they are as true of heart as we.
My father had a daughter lov'd a man,
As it might be, perhaps, were I a woman,
I should your Lordship.
Duke. And what's her history?
Vio. A blank, my lord: She never told her love,
But let concealment, like a worm i' the bud,
Feed on her damask cheek: she pin'd in thought;
And, with a green and yellow melancholy,
She sat, like patience on a monument,
Smiling at grief. Was not this love, indeed?
We men may say more, swear more; but, indeed,
Our shows are more than will; for still we prove
Much in our vows, but little in our love.
Duke. But died thy sister of her love, my boy?
Vio. I am all the daughters of my father's house,
And all the brothers too;—and yet I know not:—
Sir, shall I to this lady?
Duke. Ay, that's the theme.
To her in haste; give her this jewel; say,
My love can give no place, bide no denay.
[*Exeunt.*

SCENE V. Olivia's *Garden.*

Enter SIR TOBY BELCH, SIR ANDREW AGUE-CHEEK, *and* FABIAN.

Sir To. Come thy ways, signior Fabian.

Fab. Nay, I'll come; if I lose a scruple of this sport, let me be boiled to death with melancholy.

Sir To. Wouldst thou not be glad to have the niggardly rascally sheep-biter come by some notable shame?

Fab. I would exult, man: you know, he brought me out of favour with my lady, about a bear-baiting here.

Sir To. To anger him, we'll have the bear again; and we will fool him black and blue:—Shall we not, Sir Andrew?

Sir And. An we do not, it is pity of our lives.

Enter MARIA.

Sir To. Here comes the little villain:—How now, my nettle of India?

Mar. Get ye all three into the box-tree: Malvolio's coming down this walk: he has been yonder i' the sun, practising behaviour to his own shadow, this half hour: observe him, for the love of mockery; for, I know, this letter will make a contemplative idiot of him. Close, in the name of jesting! [*The men hide themselves.*] Lie thou there; [*throws down a letter.*] for here comes the trout that must be caught with tickling. [*Exit* MARIA.

Enter MALVOLIO.

Mal. 'Tis but fortune; all is fortune. Maria once told me, she did affect me: and I have heard herself come thus near, that, should she fancy, it should be one of my complexion. Besides, she uses me with a more exalted respect, than any one else that follows her. What should I think on't?

Sir To. Here's an overweening rogue!

Fab. O, peace! Contemplation makes a rare turkey-cock of him; how he jets under his advanced plumes!

Sir And. 'Slight, I could so beat the rogue:—

Sir To. Peace, I say.

Mal. To be count Malvolio;—

Sir To. Ah, rogue!

Sir And. Pistol him, pistol him.

Sir To. Peace, peace!

Mal. There is example for't; the lady of the Strachy married the yeoman of the wardrobe.

Sir And. Fie on him, Jezebel!

Fab. O, peace! now he's deeply in; look, how imagination blows him.

Mal. Having been three months married to her, sitting in my state,—

Sir To. O, for a stone-bow, to hit him in the eye!

Mal. Calling my officers about me, in my branched velvet gown; having come from a day-bed, where I left Olivia sleeping.

Sir To. Fire and brimstone!

Fab. O, peace, peace!

Mal. And then to have the humour of state: and after a demure travel of regard,—telling them I know my place, as I would they should do theirs,—to ask for my kinsman Toby:

Sir To. Bolts and shackles!

Fab. O, peace, peace, peace! now, now.

Mal. Seven of my people, with an obedient start, make out for him; I frown the while; and, perchance, wind up my watch, or play with some rich Jewel. Toby approaches; court'sies there to me:

Sir To. Shall this fellow live?

Fab. Though our silence be drawn from us with cars, yet peace.

Mal. I extend my hand to him thus, quenching my familiar smile with an austere regard of control:

Sir To. And does not Toby take you a blow o'the lips then?

Mal. Saying, *Cousin Toby, my fortunes having cast me on your niece, give me this prerogative of speech:*—

Sir To. What, what?

Mal. *You must amend your drunkenness.*

Sir To. Out, scab.

Fab. Nay, patience, or we break the sinews of our plot.

Mal. *Besides, you waste the treasure of your time with a foolish knight;*

Sir And. That's me, I warrant you.

Mal. *One Sir Andrew:*

Sir And. I knew, 'twas I; for many do call me fool.

Mal. What employment have we here? [*Taking up the letter.*

Fab. Now is the woodcock near the gin.

Sir To. O, peace! and the spirit of humours intimate reading aloud to him!

Mal. By my life, this is my lady's hand: these be her very *C's*, her *U's*, and her *T's*; and thus makes she her great *P's*. It is, in contempt of question, her hand.

Sir And. Her *C's*, her *U's*, and her *T's*: Why that?

Mal. [*reads*] *To the unknown beloved, this, and my good wishes:* her very phrases!—By your leave, wax.—Soft!—and the impressure her Lucrece, with which she uses to seal: 'tis my lady: To whom should this be?

Fab. This wins him, liver and all.

Mal. [*reads*] *Jove knows, I love:*
But who?
Lips do not move,
No man must know.

No man must know.—What follows? the numbers altered!—*No man must know*:—If this should be thee, Malvolio?

Sir To. Marry, hang thee, brock!

Mal. *I may command, where I adore:*
But silence, like a Lucrece knife,
With bloodless stroke my heart doth gore;
M, O, A, I, *doth sway my life.*

Fab. A fustian riddle!

Sir To. Excellent wench, say I.

Mal. M, O, A, I, *doth sway my life.*—Nay, but first, let me see,—let me see,—let me see.

Fab. What a dish of poison hath she dressed him!

Sir To. And with what wing the stannyel checks at it!

Mal. *I may command where I adore.* Why, she may command me; I serve her, she is my lady. Why, this is evident to any formal capacity. There is no obstruction in this;—And the end,—What should that alphabetical position portend? if I could make that resemble something in me,—Softly,—*M, O, A, I.*—

Sir To. O, ay, make up that:—he is now at a cold scent.

Fab. Sowter will cry upon't, for all this, though it be as rank as a fox.

Mal. M,—Malvolio:—*M,*—why, that begins my name.

Fab. Did not I say, he would work it out? the cur is excellent at faults.

Mal. M, But then there is no consonancy in the sequel; that suffers under probation: *A* should follow, but *O* does.

Fab. And *O* shall end, I hope.

Sir To. Ay, or I'll cudgel him, and make him cry, O.

Mal. And then *I* comes behind.

Fab. Ay, an you had an eye behind you, you might see more detraction at your heels, than fortunes before you.

Mal. *M, O, A, I*;—This simulation is not as the former:—and yet, to crush this a little, it would bow to me, for every one of these letters are in my name. Soft; here follows prose.—*If this fall into thy hand, revolve. In my stars I am above thee; but be not afraid of greatness: Some are born great, some achieve greatness, and some have greatness thrust upon them. Thy fates open their hands; let thy blood and spirit embrace them. And, to inure thyself to what thou art like to be, cast thy humble slough, and appear fresh. Be opposite with a kinsman, surly with servants: let thy tongue tang arguments of state; put thyself into the trick of singularity: She thus advises thee, that sighs for thee. Remember who commended thy yellow stockings; and wished to see thee ever cross-gartered: I say, remember. Go to; thou art made, if thou desirest to be so; if not, let me see thee a steward still, the fellow of servants, and not worthy to touch fortune's fingers. Farewell. She that would alter services with thee, The fortunate-unhappy.*

Day-light and champian discovers not more: this is open. I will be proud, I will read politick authors, I will baffle Sir Toby, I will wash off gross acquaintance, I will be point-de-vice, the very man. I do not now fool myself, to let imagination jade me; for every reason excites to this, that my lady loves me. She did commend my yellow stockings of late, she did praise my leg being cross-gartered; and in this she manifests herself to my love, and, with a kind of injunction, drives me to these habits of her liking. I thank my stars, I am happy. I will be strange, stout, in yellow stockings, and cross-gartered, even with the swiftness of putting on. Jove, and my stars be praised!—Here is yet a postscript. *Thou canst not choose but know who I am. If thou entertainest my love, let it appear in thy smiling; thy smiles become thee well: therefore in my presence still smile, dear my sweet, I pr'ythee.* Jove, I thank thee.—I will smile; I will do every thing that thou wilt have me. [*Exit.*

Fab. I will not give my part of this sport for a pension of thousands to be paid from the Sophy.

Sir To. I could marry this wench for this device.

Sir And. So could I too.

Sir To. And ask no other dowry with her, but such another jest.

Enter MARIA.

Sir And. Nor I neither.

Fab. Here comes my noble gull-catcher.

Sir To. Wilt thou set thy foot o' my neck?

Sir And. Or o' mine either?

Sir To. Shall I play my freedom at tray-trip, and become thy bond-slave?

Sir And. I'faith, or I either?

Sir To. Why, thou hast put him in such a dream, that, when the image of it leaves him, he must run mad.

Mar. Nay, but say true: does it work upon him?

Sir To. Like aqua-vitæ with a midwife.

Mar. If you will then see the fruits of the sport, mark his first approach before my lady: he will come to her in yellow stockings, and 'tis a colour she abhors; and cross-gartered, a fashion she detests; and he will smile upon her, which will now be so unsuitable to her disposition, being addicted to a melancholy as she is, that it cannot but turn him into a notable contempt: if you will see it, follow me.

Sir To. To the gates of Tartar, thou most excellent devil of wit!

Sir And. I'll make one too. [*Exeunt.*

ACT III.

SCENE I. Olivia's *Garden.*

Enter VIOLA, *and* Clown, *with a tabor.*

Vio. Save thee, friend, and thy musick: Dost thou live by thy tabor?

Clo. No, sir, I live by the church.

Vio. Art thou a churchman?

Clo. No such matter, sir; I do live by the church; for I do live at my house, and my house doth stand by the church.

Vio. So thou may'st say, the king lies by a beggar, if a beggar dwell near him: or, the church stands by thy tabor, if thy tabor stand by the church.

Clo. You have said, sir.—To see this age!—A sentence is but a cheveril glove to a good wit; How quickly the wrong side may be turned outward!

Vio. Nay, that's certain; they, that dally nicely with words, may quickly make them wanton.

Clo. I would, therefore, my sister had had no name, sir.

Vio. Why, man?

Clo. Why, sir, her name's a word; and to dally with that word, might make my sister wanton: But, indeed, words are very rascals, since bonds disgraced them.

Vio. Thy reason, man?

Clo. Troth, sir, I can yield you none without words; and words are grown so false, I am loath to prove reason with them.

Vio. I warrant, thou art a merry fellow, and carest for nothing.

Clo. Not so, sir, I do care for something: but

in my conscience, sir, I do not care for you: if that be to care for nothing, sir, I would it would make you invisible.

Vio. Art not thou the lady Olivia's fool?

Clo. No, indeed, sir; the lady Olivia has no folly: she will keep no fool, sir, till she be married; and fools are as like husbands, as pilchards are to herrings, the husband's the bigger; I am, indeed, not her fool, but her corrupter of words.

Vio. I saw thee late at the count Orsino's.

Clo. Foolery, sir, does walk about the orb, like the sun; it shines every where. I would be sorry, sir, but the fool should be as oft with your master, as with my mistress: I think I saw your wisdom there.

Vio. Nay, an thou pass upon me, I'll no more with thee. Hold, there's expenses for thee.

Clo. Now Jove, in his next commodity of hair, send thee a beard!

Vio. By my troth, I'll tell thee; I am almost sick for one: though I would not have it grow on my chin. Is thy lady within?

Clo. Would not a pair of these have bred, sir?

Vio. Yes, being kept together, and put to use.

Clo. I would play lord Pandarus of Phrygia, sir, to bring a Cressida to this Troilus.

Vio. I understand you, sir; 'tis well begg'd.

Clo. The matter, I hope, is not great, sir, begging but a beggar; Cressida was a beggar. My lady is within, sir. I will con-strue to them whence you come; who you are, and what you would, are out of my welkin: I might say, element; but the word is over-worn. [*Exit.*

Vio. This fellow's wise enough to play the fool;
And, to do that well, craves a kind of wit:
He must observe their mood on whom he jests,
The quality of persons, and the time;
And, like the haggard, check at every feather
That comes before his eye. This is a practice,
As full of labour as a wise man's art:
For folly, that he wisely shows, is fit;
But wise men, folly-fallen, quite taint their wit.

Enter SIR TOBY BELCH, *and* SIR ANDREW AGUE-CHEEK.

Sir To. Save you, gentleman.

Vio. And you, sir.

Sir And. *Dieu vous garde, monsieur.*

Vio. *Et vous aussi; votre serviteur.*

Sir And. I hope, sir, you are; and I am yours.

Sir To. Will you encounter the house? my niece is desirous you should enter, if your trade be to her.

Vio. I am bound to your niece, sir: I mean, she is the list of my voyage.

Sir To. Taste your legs, sir, put them to motion.

Vio. My legs do better understand me, sir, than I understand what you mean by bidding me taste my legs.

Sir To. I mean, to go, sir, to enter.

Vio. I will answer you with gait and entrance. But we are prevented.

Enter OLIVIA *and* MARIA.

Most excellent accomplish'd lady, the heavens rain odours on you!

Sir And. That youth's a rare courtier! *Rain odours!* well.

Vio. My matter hath no voice, lady, but to your own most pregnant and vouchsafed ear.

Sir And. *Odours, pregnant,* and *vouchsafed.*—I'll get 'em all three ready.

Oli. Let the garden door be shut, and leave me to my hearing.

[*Exeunt* SIR TOBY, SIR ANDREW, *and* MARIA.

Give me your hand, sir.

Vio. My duty, madam, and most humble service.

Oli. What is your name?

Vio. Cesario is your servant's name, fair princess.

Oli. My servant, sir! 'Twas never merry world,
Since lowly feigning was call'd compliment;
You are servant to the count Orsino, youth.

Vio. And he is yours, and his must needs be yours;
Your servant's servant is your servant, madam.

Oli. For him, I think not on him: for his thoughts,
'Would they were blanks, rather than fill'd with me!

Vio. Madam, I come to whet your gentle thoughts
On his behalf:—

Oli. O, by your leave, I pray you;
I bade you never speak again of him:
But, would you undertake another suit,
I had rather hear you to solicit that,
Than musick from the spheres.

Vio. Dear lady,——

Oli. Give me leave, 'beseech you: I did send,
After the last enchantment you did here,
A ring in chase of you; so did I abuse
Myself, my servant, and, I fear me, you;
Under your hard construction must I sit,
To force that on you, in a shameful cunning,
Which you knew none of yours: What might you think?
Have you not set mine honour at the stake,
And baited it with all the unmuzzled thoughts
That tyrannous heart can think? To one of your receiving
Enough is shown; a cypress, not a bosom,
Hides my heart: So let me hear you speak.

Vio. I pity you.

Oli. That's a degree to love.

Vio. No, not a grise; for 'tis a vulgar proof,
That very oft we pity enemies.

Oli. Why, then, methinks, 'tis time to smile again;
O world, how apt the poor are to be proud!
If one should be a prey, how much the better
To fall before the lion, than the wolf?
[*Clock strikes.*
The clock upbraids me with the waste of time.—
Be not afraid, good youth, I will not have you:
And yet, when wit and youth is come to harvest,
Your wife is like to reap a proper man:
There lies your way, due west.

Vio. Then westward-hoe:
Grace and good disposition 'tend your ladyship!
You'll nothing, madam, to my lord by me?

Oli. Stay:
I pr'ythee, tell me, what thou think'st of me.

Vio. That you do think, you are not what you are.

Oli. If I think so, I think the same of you.

Vio. Then think you right; I am not what I am.

Oli. I would you were as I would have you be!

Vio. Would it be better, madam, than I am,
I wish it might; for now I am your fool.

Oli. O, what a deal of scorn looks beautiful
In the contempt and anger of his lip!
A murd'rous guilt shows not itself more soon
Than love that would seem hid: love's night is noon.
Cesario, by the roses of the spring,
By maidhood, honour, truth, and every thing,
I love thee so, that, maugre all thy pride,
Nor wit, nor reason, can my passion hide.
Do not extort thy reasons from this clause,
For, that I woo, thou therefore hast no cause:
But, rather, reason thus with reason fetter!
Love sought is good, but given unsought, is better.

Vio. By innocence I swear, and by my youth,
I have one heart, one bosom, and one truth,
And that no woman has; nor never none
Shall mistress be of it, save I alone.

And so adieu, good madam; never more
Will I my master's tears to you deplore.

Oli. Yet come again: for thou, perhaps, may'st move
That heart, which now abhors, to like his love.
[*Exeunt.*

SCENE II. *A Room in* Olivia's *House.*

Enter SIR TOBY BELCH, SIR ANDREW AGUE-CHEEK, *and* FABIAN.

Sir And. No, faith, I'll not stay a jot longer.

Sir To. Thy reason, dear venom, give thy reason.

Fab. You must needs yield your reason, Sir Andrew.

Sir And. Marry, I saw your niece do more favours to the count's serving man, than ever she bestowed upon me: I saw 't i' the orchard.

Sir To. Did she see thee the while, old boy? tell me that.

Sir And. As plain as I see you now.

Fab. This was a great argument of love in her toward you.

Sir And. 'Slight! will you make an ass o' me?

Fab. I will prove it legitimate, sir, upon the oaths of judgment and reason.

Sir To. And they have been grand jury-men, since before Noah was a sailor.

Fab. She did show favour to the youth in your sight, only to exasperate you, to awake your dormouse valour, to put fire in your heart, and brimstone in your liver: You should then have accosted her; and with some excellent jests, fire-new from the mint, you should have banged the youth into dumbness. This was looked for at your hand, and this was baulked: the double gilt of this opportunity you let time wash off, and you are now sailed into the north of my lady's opinion; where you will hang like an icicle on a Dutchman's beard, unless you do redeem it by some laudable attempt, either of valour, or policy.

Sir And. And 't be any way, it must be with valour; for policy I hate: I had as lief be a Brownist as a politician.

Sir To. Why then, build me thy fortunes upon the basis of valour. Challenge me the count's youth to fight with him; hurt him in eleven places; my niece shall take note of it: and assure thyself, there is no love-broker in the world can more prevail in man's commendation with woman, than report of valour.

Fab. There is no way but this, Sir Andrew.

Sir And. Will either of you bear me a challenge to him?

Sir To. Go, write it in a martial hand; be curst and brief; it is no matter how witty, so it be eloquent, and full of invention: taunt him with the licence of ink: if thou *thou'st* him some thrice, it shall not be amiss; and as many lies as will lie in thy sheet of paper, although the sheet were big enough for the bed of Ware in England, set 'em down; go, about it. Let there be gall enough in thy ink; though thou write with a goose-pen, no matter: About it.

Sir And. Where shall I find you?

Sir To. We'll call thee at the *cubiculo:* Go.
[*Exit* SIR ANDREW.

Fab. This is a dear manakin to you, Sir Toby.

Sir To. I have been dear to him, lad; some two thousand strong, or so.

Fab. We shall have a rare letter from him: but you'll not deliver it.

Sir To. Never trust me then! and by all means stir on the youth to an answer. I think, oxen and wainropes cannot hale them together. For Andrew, if he were opened, and you find so much blood in his liver as will clog the foot of a flea, I'll eat the rest of the anatomy.

Fab. And his opposite, the youth, bears in his visage no great presage of cruelty.

Enter MARIA.

Sir To. Look where the youngest wren of nine comes.

Mar. If you desire the spleen, and will laugh yourselves into stitches, follow me: yon' gull Malvolio is turned heathen, a very renegado; for there is no Christian, that means to be saved by believing rightly, can ever believe such impossible passages of grossness. He's in yellow stockings.

Sir To. And cross-gartered?

Mar. Most villanously; like a pedant that keeps a school i' the church.—I have dogged him, like his murderer: He does obey every point of the letter that I dropped to betray him. He does smile his face into more lines, than are in the new map, with the augmentation of the Indies: you have not seen such a thing as 'tis; I can hardly forbear hurling things at him. I know, my lady will strike him; if she do, he'll smile, and take't for a great favour.

Sir To. Come, bring us, bring us where he is.
[*Exeunt.*

SCENE III. *A Street.*

Enter ANTONIO *and* SEBASTIAN.

Seb. I would not, by my will, have troubled you;
But, since you make your pleasure of your pains,
I will no further chide you.

Ant. I could not stay behind you; my desire,
More sharp than filed steel, did spur me forth;
And not all love to see you (though so much
As might have drawn one to a longer voyage),
But jealousy what might befall your travel,
Being skilless in these parts; which, to a stranger,
Unguided and unfriended, often prove
Rough and unhospitable: My willing love,
The rather by these arguments of fear,
Set forth in your pursuit.

Seb. My kind Antonio,
I can no other answer make, but, thanks,
And thanks, and ever thanks: Often good turns
Are shuffled off with such uncurrent pay:
But, were my worth, as is my conscience, firm,
You should find better dealing. What's to do?
Shall we go see the reliques of this town?

Ant. To-morrow, sir; best, first, go see your lodging.

Seb. I am not weary, and 'tis long to night;
I pray you, let us satisfy our eyes
With the memorials, and the things of fame,
That do renown this city.

Ant. 'Would, you'd pardon me;
I do not without danger walk these streets:
Once, in a sea-fight, 'gainst the Count his galleys,
I did some service; of such note, indeed,
That, were I ta'en here, it would scarce be answer'd.

Seb. Belike, you slew great number of his people.

Ant. The offence is not of such a bloody nature;
Albeit the quality of the time, and quarrel,
Might well have given us bloody argument.
It might have since been answer'd in repaying
What we took from them; which, for traffick's sake,
Most of our city did: only myself stood out:
For which, if I be lapsed in this place,
I shall pay dear.

Seb. Do not then walk too open.

Ant. It doth not fit me. Hold, sir, here's my purse:
In the south suburbs, at the Elephant,
Is best to lodge: I will bespeak our diet,
Whiles you beguile the time, and feed your knowledge,
With viewing of the town; there shall you have me.

Seb. Why I your purse?

Ant. Haply, your eye shall light upon some toy

You have desire to purchase; and your store,
I think, is not for idle markets, sir.

Seb. I'll be your purse-bearer, and leave you for
An hour.

Ant. To the Elephant.—

Seb. I do remember.

[*Exeunt.*

SCENE IV. Olivia's *Garden.*

Enter OLIVIA *and* MARIA.

Oli. I have sent after him: He says he'll come;
How shall I feast him? what bestow on him?
For youth is bought more oft, than begg'd, or borrow'd.
I speak too loud.——
Where is Malvolio?—he is sad, and civil,
And suits well for a servant with my fortunes;—
Where is Malvolio?

Mar. He's coming, madam; but in very strange manner. He is sure possessed, madam.

Oli. Why, what's the matter? does he rave?

Mar. No, madam, he does nothing but smile: your ladyship were best to have some guard about you, if he come; for sure, the man is tainted in his wits.

Oli. Go call him hither.—I'm as mad as he,
If sad and merry madness equal be.—

Enter MALVOLIO.

How now, Malvolio?

Mal. Sweet lady, ho, ho. [*Smiles fantastically.*

Oli. Smil'st thou?
I sent for thee upon a sad occasion.

Mal. Sad, lady? I could be sad: This does make some obstruction in the blood, this cross-gartering: But what of that, if it please the eye of one, it is with me as the very true sonnet is: *Please one, and please all.*

Oli. Why, how dost thou, man? what is the matter with thee?

Mal. Not black in my mind, though yellow in my legs: It did come to his hands, and commands shall be executed. I think, we do know the sweet Roman hand.

Oli. Wilt thou go to bed, Malvolio?

Mal. To bed? ay, sweet-heart; and I'll come to thee.

Oli. God comfort thee! Why dost thou smile so, and kiss thy hand so oft?

Mar. How do you, Malvolio?

Mal. At your request? Yes; Nightingales answer daws.

Mar. Why appear you with this ridiculous boldness before my lady?

Mal. *Be not afraid of greatness:*—'Twas well writ.

Oli. What meanest thou by that, Malvolio?

Mal. *Some are born great,*—

Oli. Ha?

Mal. *Some achieve greatness,*—

Oli. What say'st thou?

Mal. *And some have greatness thrust upon them.*

Oli. Heaven restore thee!

Mal. *Remember who commended thy yellow stockings;*—

Oli. Thy yellow stockings?

Mal. *And wished to see thee cross-gartered.*

Oli. Cross-gartered?

Mal. *Go to: thou art made, if thou desirest to be so;*—

Oli. Am I made?

Mal. *If not, let me see thee a servant still.*

Oli. Why, this is very midsummer madness.

Enter Servant.

Ser. Madam, the young gentleman of the count Orsino's is returned; I could hardly entreat him back: he attends your ladyship's pleasure.

Oli. I'll come to him. [*Exit* Servant.] Good Maria, let this fellow be looked to. Where's my cousin Toby? Let some of my people have a special care of him; I would not have him miscarry for the half of my dowry.

[*Exeunt* OLIVIA *and* MARIA.

Mal. Oh, ho! do you come near me now? no worse man than Sir Toby to look to me? This concurs directly with the letter: she sends him on purpose, that I may appear stubborn to him; for she incites me to that in the letter. *Cast thy humble slough,* says she; *be opposite with a kinsman, surly with servants,—let thy tongue tang with arguments of state,—put thyself into the trick of singularity;*—and, consequently, sets down the manner how; as, a sad face, a reverend carriage, a slow tongue, in the habit of some sir of note, and so forth. I have limed her; but it is Jove's doing, and Jove make me thankful! And, when she went away now, *Let this fellow be looked to:* Fellow! not Malvolio, nor after my degree, but fellow. Why, every thing adheres together; that no dram of a scruple, no scruple of a scruple, no obstacle, no incredulous or unsafe circumstance,—What can be said? Nothing that can be, can come between me and the full prospect of my hopes. Well, Jove, not I, is the doer of this, and he is to be thanked.

Re-enter MARIA, *with* SIR TOBY BELCH *and* FABIAN.

Sir To. Which way is he, in the name of sanctity? If all the devils in hell be drawn in little, and Legion himself possessed him, yet I'll speak to him.

Fab. Here he is, here he is:—How is't with you, sir? how is't with you, man?

Mal. Go off: I discard you; let me enjoy my private; go off.

Mar. Lo, how hollow the fiend speaks within him! did not I tell you?—Sir Toby, my lady prays you to have a care of him.

Mal. Ah, ha! does she so?

Sir To. Go to, go to; peace, peace, we must deal gently with him; let me alone. How do you, Malvolio? ho wis't with you? What, man! defy the devil; consider, he's an enemy to mankind.

Mal. Do you know what you say?

Mar. La you, an you speak ill of the devil, how he takes it at heart! 'Pray God, he be not bewitched!

Fab. Carry his water to the wise woman.

Mar. Marry, and it shall be done to-morrow morning, if I live. My lady would not lose him for more than I'll say.

Mal. How now, mistress?

Mar. O lord!

Sir To. 'Pr'ythee, hold thy peace; this is not the way: Do you not see, you move him; let me alone with him.

Fab. No way but gentleness; gently, gently: the fiend is rough, and will not be roughly used.

Sir To. Why, how now, my bawcock? how dost thou, chuck?

Mal. Sir?

Sir To. Ay, biddy come with me. What, man! 'tis not for gravity to play at cherry-pit with Satan: Hang him, foul collier!

Mar. Get him to say his prayers; good Sir Toby, get him to pray.

Mal. My prayers, minx?

Mar. No, I warrant you, he will not hear of godliness.

Mal. Go, hang yourselves all! you are idle shallow things: I am not of your element; you shall know more hereafter. [*Exit.*

Sir To. Is't possible?

Fab. If this were played upon a stage now, I could condemn it as an improbable fiction.

Sir To. His very genius hath taken the infection of the device, man.

Mar. Nay, pursue him now; lest the device take air, and taint.

Fab. Why, we shall make him mad, indeed.

Mar. The house will be the quieter.

Sir To. Come, we'll have him in a dark room, and bound. My niece is already in the belief that he is mad; we may carry it thus, for our pleasure, and his penance, till our very pastime, tired out of breath, prompt us to have mercy on him: at which time, we will bring the device to the bar, and crown thee for a finder of madmen. But see, but see.

Enter SIR ANDREW AGUE-CHEEK.

Fab. More matter for a May morning.

Sir And. Here's the challenge, read it; I warrant there's vinegar and pepper in't.

Fab. Is't so saucy?

Sir And. Ay, is it, I warrant him: do but read.

Sir To. Give me. [*Reads.*] *Youth, whatsoever thou art, thou art but a scurvy fellow.*

Fab. Good, and valiant.

Sir To. *Wonder not, nor admire not in thy mind, why I do call thee so, for I will show thee no reason for't.*

Fab. A good note: that keeps you from the blow of the law.

Sir To. *Thou comest to the lady Olivia, and in my sight she uses thee kindly: but thou liest in thy throat, that is not the matter I challenge thee for.*

Fab. Very brief, and exceeding good sense-less.

Sir To. *I will waylay thee going home; where if it be thy chance to kill me,—*

Fab. Good.

Sir To. *Thou killest me like a rogue and a villain.*

Fab. Still you keep o' the windy side of the law: Good.

Sir To. *Fare thee well: And God have mercy upon one of our souls! He may have mercy upon mine; but my hope is better, and so look to thyself. Thy friend, as thou usest him, and thy sworn enemy.——* ANDREW AGUE-CHEEK.

Sir To. If this letter move him not, his legs cannot: I'll give't him.

Mar. You may have very fit occasion for't; he is now in some commerce with my lady, and will by and by depart.

Sir To. Go, Sir Andrew; scout me for him at the corner of the orchard, like a bum-bailiff: so soon as ever thou seest him, draw; and, as thou drawest, swear horrible; for it comes to pass oft, that a terrible oath, with a swaggering accent sharply twanged off, gives manhood more approbation than ever proof itself would have earned him. Away.

Sir And. Nay, let me alone for swearing. [*Exit.*

Sir To. Now will not I deliver his letter: for the behaviour of the young gentleman gives him out to be of good capacity and breeding; his employment between his lord and my niece confirms no less: therefore this letter, being so excellently ignorant, will breed no terror in the youth, he will find it comes from a clodpole. But, sir, I will deliver his challenge by word of mouth; set upon Ague-cheek a notable report of valour; and drive the gentleman (as I know his youth will aptly receive it) into a most hideous opinion of his rage, skill, fury, and impetuosity. This will so fright them both, that they will kill one another by the look, like cockatrices.

Enter OLIVIA *and* VIOLA.

Fab. Here he comes with your niece: give them way, till he take leave, and presently after him.

Sir To. I will meditat the while upon some horrid message for a challenge.

[*Exeunt* SIR TOBY, FABIAN, *and* MARIA.

Oli. I have said too much unto a heart of stone,
And laid my honour too unchary out:
There's something in me, that reproves my fault;
But such a headstrong potent fault it is,
That it but mocks reproof.

Vio. With the same 'haviour that your passion bears,
Go on my master's griefs.

Oli. Here, wear this jewel for me, 'tis my picture;
Refuse it not, it hath no tongue to vex you:
And, I beseech you, come again to-morrow,
What shall you ask of me that I'll deny,
That, honour sav'd, may upon asking give?

Vio. Nothing but this, your true love for my master.

Oli. How with mine honour may I give him that
Which I have given to you?

Vio. I will acquit you.

Oli. Well, come again to-morrow: Fare thee well;
A fiend, like thee, might bear my soul to hell. [*Exit.*

Re-enter SIR TOBY BELCH *and* FABIAN.

Sir To. Gentleman, God save thee.

Vio. And you, sir.

Sir To. That defence thou hast, betake thee to't: of what nature the wrongs are thou hast done him, I know not; but thy intercepter, full of despight, bloody as the hunter, attends thee at the orchard end: dismount thy tuck, be yare in thy preparation, for thy assailant is quick, skilful, and deadly.

Vio. You mistake, sir; I am sure no man hath any quarrel to me; my remembrance is very free and clear from any image of offence done to any man.

Sir To. You'll find it otherwise, I assure you: therefore, if you hold your life at any price, betake you to your guard; for your opposite hath in him what youth, strength, skill, and wrath, can furnish man withal.

Vio. I pray you, sir, what is he?

Sir To. He is knight, dubbed with unhatched rapier, and on carpet consideration; but he is a devil in private brawl: souls and bodies hath he divorced three; and his incensement at this moment is so implacable, that satisfaction can be none but by pangs of death and sepulchre: hob, nob, is his word; give't, or take't.

Vio. I will return again into the house, and desire some conduct of the lady. I am no fighter. I have heard of some kind of men, that put quarrels purposely on others, to taste their valour: belike, this is a man of that quirk.

Sir To. Sir, no; his indignation derives itself out of a very competent injury; therefore, get you on, and give him his desire. Back you shall not to the house, unless you undertake that with me, which with as much safety you might answer him: therefore on, or strip your sword stark naked; for meddle you must, that's certain, or forswear to wear iron about you.

Vio. This is as uncivil, as strange. I beseech you, do me this courteous office, as to know of the knight what my offence to him is; it is something of my negligence, nothing of my purpose.

Sir To. I will do so. Signior Fabian, stay you by this gentleman till my return. [*Exit* SIR TOBY.

Vio. 'Pray you, sir, do you know of this matter?

Fab. I know the knight is incensed against you, even to a mortal arbitrement; but nothing of the circumstance more.

Vio. I beseech you what manner of man is he?

Fab. Nothing of that wonderful promise, to read him by his form, as you are like to find him in the proof of his valour. He is indeed, sir, the most skilful, bloody, and fatal opposite that you could possibly have found in any part of Illyria: Will you walk towards him? I will make your peace with him, if I can.

Vio. I shall be much bound to you for't: I am one, that would rather go with sir priest, than sir knight: I care not who knows so much of my mettle. [*Exeunt.*

Re-enter SIR TOBY, *with* SIR ANDREW.

Sir To. Why, man, he's a very devil; I have not seen such a firago. I had a pass with him, rapier, scabbard, and all, and he gives me the stuckin, with such a mortal motion, that it is inevitable; and on the answer, he pays you as surely as your feet hit the ground they step on: They say, he has been fencer to the Sophy.

Sir And. Pox on't, I'll not meddle with him.

Sir To. Ay, but he will not now be pacified: Fabian can scarce hold him yonder.

Sir And. Plague on't; an I thought he had been valiant and so cunning in fence, I'd have seen him damned ere I'd have challenged him. Let him let the matter slip, and I'll give him my horse, gray Capilet.

Sir To. I'll make the motion: stand here, make a good show on't; this shall end without the perdition of souls: Marry, I'll ride your horse as well as I ride you. [*Aside.*

Re-enter FABIAN *and* VIOLA.

I have his horse [*to* FAB.] to take up the quarrel; I have persuaded him, the youth's a devil.

Fab. He is as horribly conceited of him; and pants, and looks pale, as if a bear were at his heels.

Sir To. There's no remedy, sir: he will fight with you for his oath's sake: marry, he hath better bethought him of his quarrel, and he finds that now scarce to be worth talking of: therefore draw, for the supportance of his vow; he protests, he will not hurt you.

Vio. Pray God defend me! A little thing would make me tell them how much I lack of a man. [*Aside.*

Fab. Give ground, if you see him furious.

Sir To. Come, Sir Andrew, there's no remedy; the gentleman will, for his honour's sake, have one bout with you: he cannot by the duello avoid it: but he has promised me, as he is a gentleman and a soldier, he will not hurt you. Come on; to't.

Sir And. 'Pray God, he keep his oath! [*Draws.*

Enter ANTONIO.

Vio. I do assure you, 'tis against my will. [*Draws.*

Ant. Put up your sword:—If this young gentleman
Have done offence, I take the fault on me;
If you offend him, I for him defy you. [*Drawing.*

Sir To. You, sir? why, what are you?

Ant. One, sir, that for his love dares yet do more
Than you have heard him brag to you he will.

Sir To. Nay, if you be an undertaker, I am for you. [*Draws.*

Enter Two Officers.

Fab. O good Sir Toby, hold; here come the officers.

Sir To. I'll be with you anon. [*To* ANTONIO.

Vio. Pray, sir, put up your sword, if you please. [*To* SIR ANDREW.

Sir And. Marry, will I, sir;—and, for that I promised you, I'll be as good as my word: He will bear you easily; and reins well.

1 *Off.* This is the man; do thy office.

2 *Off.* Antonio, I arrest thee at the suit
Of count Orsino.

Ant. You do mistake me, sir.

1 *Off.* No, sir, no jot: I know your favour well.
Though now you have no sea-cap on your head.—
Take him away; he knows, I know him well.

Ant. I must obey.—This comes with seeking you;
But there's no remedy; I shall answer it.
What will you do? Now my necessity
Makes me to ask you for my purse: It grieves me
Much more, for what I cannot do for you,
Than what befalls myself. You stand amaz'd;
But be of comfort.

2 *Off.* Come, sir, away.

Ant. I must entreat of you some of that money.

Vio. What money, sir?
For the fair kindness you have show'd me here,
And, part, being prompted by your present trouble,
Out of my lean and low ability
I'll lend you something: my having is not much;
I'll make division of my present with you:
Hold, there is half my coffer.

Ant. Will you deny me now?
Is't possible, that my deserts to you
Can lack persuasion? Do not tempt my misery,
Lest that it make me so unsound a man,
As to upbraid you with those kindnesses
That I have done for you.

Vio. I know of none;
Nor know I you by voice, or any feature:
I hate ingratitude more in a man,
Than lying, vainness, babbling, drunkenness,
Or any taint of vice, whose strong corruption
Inhabits our frail blood.

Ant. O heavens themselves!

2 *Off.* Come, sir, I pray you go.

Ant. Let me speak a little. This youth that you see here,
I snatch'd one half out of the jaws of death;
Reliev'd him with such sanctity of love,——
And to his image, which, methought did promise
Most venerable worth, did I devotion.

1 *Off.* What's that to us? The time goes by; away.

Ant. But, O, how vile an idol proves this god!—
Thou hast, Sebastian, done good feature shame.—
In nature there's no blemish, but the mind;
None can be call'd deform'd, but the unkind:
Virtue is beauty; but the beauteous-evil
Are empty trunks, o'erflourished by the devil.

1 *Off.* The man grows mad; away with him.
Come, come, sir.

Ant. Lead me on. [*Exeunt* Officers *with* ANT.

Vio. Methinks, his words do from such passion fly,
That he believes himself; so do not I.
Prove true, imagination, O, prove true,
That I, dear brother, be now ta'en for you!

Sir To. Come hither, knight; come hither, Fabian; we'll whisper o'er a couple or two of most sage saws.

Vio. He nam'd Sebastian; I my brother know
Yet living in my glass; even such, and so,
In favour was my brother; and he went
Still in this fashion, colour, ornament,
For him I imitate: O, if it prove,
Tempests are kind, and salt waves fresh in love! [*Exit.*

Sir To. A very dishonest paltry boy, and more a coward than a hare: his dishonesty appears, in leaving his friend here in necessity, and denying him; and for his cowardship, ask Fabian.

Fab. A coward, a most devout coward, religious in it.

Sir And. 'Slid, I'll after him again, and beat him.

Sir To. Do, cuff him soundly, but never draw thy sword.

Sir And. An I do not,— [*Exit.*

Fab. Come, let's see the event.

Sir To. I dare lay any money, 'twill be nothing yet. [*Exeunt.*

ACT IV.

SCENE I. *The Street before* Olivia's *House.*

Enter SEBASTIAN *and* Clown.

Clo. Will you make me believe that I am not sent for you?

Seb. Go to, go to, thou art a foolish fellow;
Let me be clear of thee.

Clo. Well held out, i'faith! No, I do not know you; nor I am not sent to you by my lady, to bid you come speak with her; nor your name is not master Cesario; nor this is not my nose neither.—Nothing, that is so, is so.

Seb. I pr'ythee, vent thy folly somewhere else;
Thou know'st not me.

Clo. Vent my folly! He has heard that word of some great man, and now applies it to a fool. Vent my folly! I am afraid this great lubber, the world, will prove a cockney.—I pr'ythee now, ungird thy strangeness, and tell me what I shall vent to my lady; Shall I vent to her, that thou art coming?

Seb. I pr'ythee, foolish Greek, depart from me:
There's money for thee; if you tarry longer,
I shall give worse payment.

Clo. By my troth, thou hast an open hand:—These wise men that give fools money, get themselves a good report after fourteen years' purchase.

Enter SIR ANDREW, SIR TOBY, *and* FABIAN.

Sir And. Now, sir, have I met you again? there's for you. [*Striking* SEBASTIAN.

Seb. Why, there's for thee, and there, and there:
Are all the people mad? [*Beating* SIR ANDREW.

Sir To. Hold, sir, or I'll throw your dagger o'er the house.

Clo. This will I tell my lady straight; I would not be in some of your coats for two-pence. [*Exit* Clown.

Sir To. Come on, sir; hold. [*Holding* SEBASTIAN.

Sir And. Nay, let him alone; I'll go another way to work with him; I'll have an action of battery against him, if there be any law in Illyria: though I struck him first, yet it's no matter for that.

Seb. Let go thy hand.

Sir To. Come, sir, I will not let you go. Come, my young soldier, put up your iron: you are well fleshed; come on.

Seb. I will be free from thee. What would'st thou now?
If thou dar'st tempt me further, draw thy sword. [*Draws.*

Sir To. What, what! Nay, then I must have an ounce or two of this malapert blood from you. [*Draws.*

Enter OLIVIA.

Oli. Hold, Toby; on thy life, I charge thee, hold.

Sir To. Madam!

Oli. Will it be ever thus? Ungracious wretch,
Fit for the mountains and the barbarous caves,
Where manners ne'er were preach'd! out of my sight!
Be not offended, dear Cesario:——
Rudesby, begone!—I pr'ythee, gentle friend,
[*Exeunt* SIR TOBY, SIR ANDREW, *and* FABIAN.
Let thy fair wisdom, not thy passion, sway
In this uncivil and unjust extent
Against thy peace. Go with me to my house;
And hear thou there how many fruitless pranks
This ruffian hath botch'd up, that thou thereby
May'st smile at this: thou shalt not choose but go;
Do not deny: Beshrew his soul for me,
He started one poor heart of mine in thee.

Seb. What relish is in this? how runs the stream?
Or I am mad, or else this is a dream:—
Let fancy still my sense in Lethe steep;
If it be thus to dream, still let me sleep!

Oli. Nay, come, I pr'ythee: 'Would, thou'dst be rul'd by me!

Seb. Madam, I will.

Oli. O, say so, and so be! [*Exeunt.*

SCENE II. *A Room in* Olivia's *House.*

Enter MARIA *and* Clown.

Mar. Nay, I pr'ythee, put on this gown, and this beard; make him believe, thou art Sir Topas the curate; do it quickly: I'll call Sir Toby the whilst. [*Exit* MARIA.

Clo. Well, I'll put it on, and I will dissemble myself in't; and I would I were the first that ever dissembled in such a gown. I am not tall enough to become the function well; nor lean enough to be thought a good student: but to be said, an honest man, and a good housekeeper, goes as fairly as to say, a careful man, and a great scholar. The competitors enter.

Enter SIR TOBY BELCH *and* MARIA.

Sir To. Jove bless thee, master parson.

Clo. *Bonos dies*, Sir Toby: for as the old hermit of Prague, that never saw pen and ink, very wittily said to a niece of king Gorboduc, *That, that is, is:* so I, being master parson, am master parson: For what is that, but that? and is, but is?

Sir To. To him, Sir Topas.

Clo. What, hoa, I say;—Peace in this prison!

Sir To. The knave counterfeits well: a good knave.

Mal. [*in an inner chamber.*] Who calls there?

Clo. Sir Topas the curate, who comes to visit Malvolio the lunatic.

Mal. Sir Topas, Sir Topas, good Sir Topas, go to my lady.

Clo. Out, hyperbolical fiend! how vexest thou this man? talkest thou nothing but of ladies?

Sir To. Well said, master parson.

Mal. Sir Topas, never was man thus wronged: good Sir Topas, do not think I am mad: they have laid me here in hideous darkness.

Clo. Fie, thou dishonest Sathan! I call thee by the most modest terms; for I am one of those gentle ones, that will use the devil himself with courtesy: Say'st thou, that house is dark?

Mal. As hell, Sir Topas.

Clo. Why, it hath bay windows transparent as barricadoes, and the clear stories towards the south-north are as lustrious as ebony; and yet complainest thou of obstruction?

Mal. I am not mad, Sir Topas: I say to you, this house is dark.

Clo. Madman, thou errest: I say, there is no darkness, but ignorance; in which thou art more puzzled than the Egyptians in their fog.

Mal. I say, this house is as dark as ignorance, though ignorance were as dark as hell; and I say, there was never man thus abused: I am no more mad than you are; make the trial of it in any constant question.

Clo. What is the opinion of Pythagoras concerning wild-fowl?

Mal. That the soul of our grandam might haply inhabit a bird.

Clo. What thinkest thou of his opinion?

Mal. I think nobly of the soul, and no way approve his opinion.

Clo. Fare thee well: Remain thou still in darkness: thou shalt hold the opinion of Pythagoras, ere I will allow of thy wits: and fear to kill a woodcock, lest thou dispossess the soul of thy grandam. Fare thee well.

Mal. Sir Topas, Sir Topas,—

Sir To. My most exquisite Sir Topas!

Clo. Nay, I am for all waters.

Mar. Thou might'st have done this without thy beard and gown; he sees thee not.

Sir To. To him in thine own voice, and bring me word how thou findest him; I would, we were well rid of this knavery. If he may be conveniently delivered, I would he were; for I am now so far in offence with my niece, that I cannot pursue with any safety this sport to the upshot. Come by and by to my chamber. [*Exeunt* SIR TOBY *and* MARIA.

Clo. *Hey Robin, jolly Robin,*
Tell me how thy lady does. [*Singing.*

Mal. Fool,—

Clo. *My lady is unkind, perdy.*

Mal. Fool,—

Clo. *Alas, why is she so?*

Mal. Fool, I say;—

Clo. *She loves another*—Who calls, ha?

Mal. Good fool, as ever thou wilt deserve well at my hand, help me to a candle, and pen, ink, and paper; as I am a gentleman, I will live to be thankful to thee for't.

Clo. Master Mavolio!

Mal. Ay, good fool.

Clo. Alas, sir, how fell you besides your five wits?

Mal. Fool, there was never man so notoriously abused: I am as well in my wits, fool, as thou art.

Clo. But as well? then you are mad, indeed, if you be no better in your wits than a fool.

Mal. They have here propertied me: keep me in darkness, send ministers to me, asses, and do all they can to face me out of my wits.

Clo. Advise you what you say; the minister is here,—Malvolio, Malvolio, thy wits the heavens restore! endeavour thyself to sleep, and leave thy vain bibble babble.

Mal. Sir Topas,——

Clo. Maintain no words with him, good fellow. —Who, I, sir? not I, sir. God b'wi'you, good Sir Topas.—Marry, amen.—I will, sir, I will.

Mal. Fool, fool, fool, I say,—

Clo. Alas, sir, be patient. What say you, sir? I am shent for speaking to you.

Mal. Good fool, help me to some light, and some paper; I tell thee, I am as well in my wits as any man in Illyria.

Clo. Well-a-day,—that you were, sir!

Mal. By this hand, I am: Good fool, some ink, paper, and light, and convey what I will set down to my lady; it shall advantage thee more than ever the bearing of letter did.

Clo. I will help you to't. But tell me true, are you not mad, indeed? or do you but counterfeit?

Mal. Believe me, I am not; I tell thee true.

Clo. Nay, I'll ne'er believe a madman till I see his brains. I will fetch you light, and paper, and ink.

Mal. Fool, I'll requite it in the highest degree: I pr'ythee, begone.

Clo. *I am gone, sir,*
And anon, sir,
I'll be with you again,
In a trice;
Like to the old vice,
Your need to sustain;

Who with dagger of lath,
In his rage and his wrath,
Cries ah, ha! to the devil:
Like a mad lad,
Pare thy nails, dad,
Adieu, goodman drivel. [*Exit.*

SCENE III. Olivia's *Garden.*

Enter SEBASTIAN.

Seb. This is the air: that is the glorious sun;
This pearl she gave me, I do feel't and see't:
And though 'tis wonder that enwraps me thus,
Yet 'tis not madness. Where's Antonio then?
I could not find him at the Elephant:
Yet there he was; and there I found this credit,
That he did range the town to seek me out.
His counsel now might do me golden service:
For though my soul disputes well with my sense,
That this may be some error, but no madness,
Yet doth this accident and flood of fortune
So far exceed all instance, all discourse,
That I am ready to distrust mine eyes,
And wrangle with my reason, that persuades me
To any other trust, but that I am mad,
Or else the lady's mad; yet, if 'twere so,
She could not sway her house, command her followers,
Take, and give back affairs, and their dispatch,
With such a smooth, discreet, and stable bearing,
As, I perceive, she does: there's something in't
That is deceivable. But here comes the lady.

Enter OLIVIA *and a* Priest.

Oli. Blame not this haste of mine: if you mean well,
Now go with me, and with this holy man,
Into the chantry by: there, before him,
And underneath that consecrated roof,
Plight me the full assurance of your faith;
That my most jealous and too doubtful soul
May live at peace: He shall conceal it,
Whiles you are willing it shall come to note;
What time we will our celebration keep
According to my birth.—What do you say?

Seb. I'll follow this good man, and go with you;
And, having sworn truth, ever will be true.

Oli. Then lead the way, good father:——And heavens so shine,
That they may fairly note this act of mine! [*Exeunt.*

ACT V.

SCENE I. *The Street before* Olivia's *House.*

Enter Clown *and* FABIAN.

Fab. Now, as thou lovest me, let me see his letter.

Clo. Good master Fabian, grant me another request.

Fab. Any thing.

Clo. Do not desire to see this letter.

Fab. That is, to give a dog, and in recompense desire my dog again.

Enter DUKE, VIOLA, *and* Attendants.

Duke. Belong you to the lady Olivia, friends?

Clo. Ay, sir; we are some of her trappings.

Duke. I know thee well: How dost thou, my good fellow?

Clo. Truly, sir, the better for my foes, and the worse for my friends.

Duke. Just the contrary; the better for thy friends.

Clo. No, sir, the worse.

Duke. How can that be?

Clo. Marry, sir, they praise me, and make an ass of me; now my foes tell me plainly I am an ass: so that by my foes, sir, I profit in the knowledge of myself; and by my friends I am abused: so that, conclusions to be as kisses, if your four negatives make your two affirmatives, why, then the worse for my friends, and the better for my foes.

Duke. Why, this is excellent.

Clo. By my troth, sir, no; though it please you to be one of my friends.

Duke. Thou shalt not be the worse for me; there's gold.

Clo. But that it would be double dealing, sir, I would you could make it another.

Duke. O, you give me ill counsel.

Clo. Put your grace in your pocket, sir, for this once, and let your flesh and blood obey it.

Duke. Well I will be so much a sinner to be a double dealer; there's another.

Clo. *Primo, secundo, tertio,* is a good play; and the old saying is, the third pays for all; the *triplex,* sir, is a good tripping measure; or the bells of St. Bennet, sir, may put you in mind One, two, three.

Duke. You can fool no more money out of me at this throw: if you will let your lady know, I am here to speak with her, and bring her along with you, it may awake my bounty further.

Clo. Marry, sir, lullaby to your bounty, till I come again. I go, sir; but I would not have you to think, that my desire of having is the sin of covetousness; but, as you say, sir, let your bounty take a nap, I will awake it anon. [*Exit* Clown.

Enter ANTONIO *and* Officers.

Vio. Here comes the man, sir, that did rescue me.

Duke. That face of his I do remember well;
Yet, when I saw it last, it was besmear'd
As black as Vulcan, in the smoke of war:
A bawling vessel was he captain of,
For shallow draught, and bulk unprizable:
With which such scathful grapple did he make
With the most noble bottom of our fleet,
That very envy, and the tongue of loss,
Cry'd fame and honour on him.—What's the matter?

1 *Off.* Orsino, this is that Antonio
That took the Phœnix and her fraught, from Candy:
And this is he that did the Tiger board,
When your young nephew Titus lost his leg:
Here in the streets, desperate of shame and state,
In private brabble did we apprehend him.

Vio. He did me kindness, sir; drew on my side;
But, in conclusion, put strange speech upon me,
I know not what 'twas, but distraction.

Duke. Notable pirate! thou salt-water thief!
What foolish boldness brought thee to their mercies,
Whom thou, in terms so bloody, and so dear,
Hast made thine enemies?

Ant. Orsino, noble sir,
Be pleas'd that I shake off these names you give me;
Antonio never yet was thief, or pirate,
Though, I confess, on base and ground enough,
Orsino's enemy. A witchcraft drew me hither:
That most ingrateful boy there, by your side,
From the rude sea's enrag'd and foamy mouth
Did I redeem: a wreck past hope he was:
His life I gave him, and did thereto add
My love, without retention or restraint,
All his in dedication: for his sake,
Did I expose myself, pure for his love,
Into the danger of this adverse town;
Drew to defend him, when he was beset;
Where being apprehended, his false cunning
(Not meaning to partake with me in danger),
Taught him to face me out of his acquaintance,
And grew a twenty-years-removed thing,
While one would wink; denied me mine own purse,
Which I had recommended to his use
Not half an hour before.

Vio. How can this be?

Duke. When came he to this town?

Ant. To-day, my lord; and for three months before
(No interim, not a minute's vacancy),
Both day and night did we keep company.

Enter OLIVIA *and* Attendants.

Duke. Here comes the countess; now heaven walks on earth.——
But for thee, fellow, fellow, thy words are madness:
Three months this youth hath tended upon me;
But more of that anon.——Take him aside.

Oli. What would my lord, but that he may not have,
Wherein Olivia may seem serviceable?—
Cesario, you do not keep promise with me.

Vio. Madam?

Duke. Gracious Olivia,——

Oli. What do you say, Cesario?——Good my lord,——

Vio. My lord would speak, my duty hushes me.

Oli. If it be ought to the old tune, my lord,
It is as fat and fulsome to mine ear,
As howling after musick.

Duke. Still so cruel?

Oli. Still so constant, lord.

Duke. What! to perverseness? you uncivil lady,
To whose ingrate and unauspicious altars
My soul the faithfull'st offerings hath breath'd out,
That e'er devotion tender'd! What shall I do?

Oli. Even what it please my lord, that shall become him.

Duke. Why should I not, had I the heart to do it,
Like to the Egyptian thief, at point of death,
Kill what I love; a savage jealousy,
That sometime savours nobly?—But hear me this:
Since you to non-regardance cast my faith,
And that I partly know the instrument
That screws me from my true place in your favour,
Live you, the marble-breasted tyrant, still;
But this your minion, whom, I know, you love,
And whom, by heaven, I swear, I tender dearly,
Him will I tear out of that cruel eye,
Where he sits crowned in his master's spite.—
Come, boy, with me; my thoughts are ripe in mischief:
I'll sacrifice the lamb that I do love,
To spite a raven's heart within a dove. [*Going.*

Vio. And I, most jocund, apt, and willingly,
To do you rest, a thousand deaths would die. [*Following.*

Oli. Where goes Cesario?

Vio. After him I love,
More than I love these eyes, more than my life,
More, by all mores, than e'er I shall love wife:
If I do feign, you witnesses above,
Punish my life, for tainting of my love!

Oli. Ah me, detested! how am I beguil'd!

Vio. Who does beguile you? who does do you wrong?

Oli. Hast thou forgot thyself? Is it so long?—
Call forth the holy father. [*Exit an Attendant.*

Duke. Come away. [*To* VIOLA.

Oli. Whither, my lord?—Cesario, husband, stay.

Duke. Husband?

Oli. Ay, husband; Can he that deny?

Duke. Her husband, sirrah?

Vio. No, my lord, not I.

Oli. Alas, it is the baseness of thy fear,
That makes thee strangle thy propriety:
Fear not, Cesario, take thy fortunes up;
Be that thou know'st thou art, and then thou art
As great as that thou fear'st.—O, welcome, father!

Re-enter Attendant *and* Priest.

Father, I charge thee, by thy reverence,
Here to unfold (though lately we intended
To keep in darkness, what occasion now
Reveals before 'tis ripe), what thou dost know,
Hath newly past between this youth and me.

Priest. A contract of eternal bond of love,
Confirm'd by mutual joinder of your hands,
Attested by the holy close of lips,
Strengthened by interchangement of your rings;
And all the ceremony of this compact
Seal'd in my function, by my testimony:
Since when, my watch hath told me, toward my grave
I have travell'd but two hours.

Duke. O, thou dissembling cub! what wilt thou be,
When time hath sow'd a grizzle on thy case?
Or will not else thy craft so quickly grow,
That thine own trip shall be thine overthrow?
Farewell, and take her; but direct thy feet,
Where thou and I henceforth may never meet.

Vio. My lord, I do protest,—

Oli. O, do not swear;
Hold little faith, though thou hast too much fear.

Enter SIR ANDREW AGUE-CHEEK, *with his head broke.*

Sir And. For the love of God, a surgeon; send one presently to Sir Toby.

Oli. What's the matter?

Sir And. He has broke my head across, and has given Sir Toby a bloody coxcomb too: for the love of God, your help: I had rather than forty pound, I were at home.

Oli. Who has done this, Sir Andrew?

Sir And. The count's gentleman, one Cesario: we took him for a coward, but he's the very devil incardinate.

Duke. My gentleman, Cesario?

Sir And. Od's lifelings, here he is:—You broke my head for nothing; and that that I did, I was set on to do't by Sir Toby.

Vio. Why do you speak to me? I never hurt you:
You drew your sword upon me, without cause;
But I bespake you fair, and hurt you not.

Sir And. If a bloody coxcomb be a hurt, you have hurt me; I think you set nothing by a bloody coxcomb.

Enter SIR TOBY BELCH, *drunk, led by the* Clown.

Here comes Sir Toby halting, you shall hear more: but if he had not been in drink, he would have tickled you othergates than he did.

Duke. How now, gentleman? how is't with you?

Sir To. That's all one; he has hurt me, and there's the end on't.—Sot, didst see Dick surgeon, sot?

Clo. O he's drunk, Sir Toby, an hour agone; his eyes were set at eight i' the morning.

Sir To. Then he's a rogue, and a passy-measures pavin; I hate a drunken rogue.

Oli. Away with him: Who hath made this havock with them?

Sir And. I'll help you, Sir Toby, because we'll be dressed together.

Sir To. Will you help?—An ass-head, and a coxcomb, and a knave? a thin-faced knave, a gull?

Oli. Get him to bed, and let his hurt be look'd to. [*Exeunt* Clown, SIR TOBY, *and* SIR ANDREW.

Enter SEBASTIAN.

Seb. I am sorry, madam, I have hurt your kinsman;
But, had it been the brother of my blood,
I must have done no less, with wit and safety.
You throw a strange regard upon me, and
By that I do perceive it hath offended you;
Pardon me, sweet one, even for the vows
We made each other but so late ago.

Duke. One face, one voice, one habit, and two persons;
A natural perspective, that is, and is not.

Seb. Antonio! O, my dear Antonio,
How have the hours rack'd and tortur'd me,
Since I have lost thee.

Ant. Sebastian are you?

Seb. Fear'st thou that, Antonio?

Ant. How have you made division of yourself?—
An apple, cleft in two, is not more twin
Than these two creatures. Which is Sebastian?

Oli. Most wonderful!

Seb. Do I stand there? I never had a brother;
Nor can there be that deity in my nature,
Of here and every where. I had a sister,
Whom the blind waves and surges have devour'd:—
Of charity, what kin are you to me? [*To* VIOLA.
What countryman? what name? what parentage?

Vio. Of Messaline: Sebastian was my father;
Such a Sebastian was my brother too,
So went he suited to his watery tomb:
If spirits can assume both form and suit,
You come to fright us.

Seb. A spirit I am, indeed;
But am in that dimension grossly clad,
Which from the womb I did participate.
Were you a woman, as the rest goes even,
I should my tears let fall upon your cheek,
And say—Thrice welcome, drowned Viola!

Vio. My father had a mole upon his brow.

Seb. And so had mine.

Vio. And died that day when Viola from her birth
Had number'd thirteen years.

Seb. O, that record is lively in my soul!
He finished, indeed, his mortal act,
That day that made my sister thirteen years.

Vio. If nothing lets to make us happy both,
But this my masculine usurp'd attire,
Do not embrace me, till each circumstance
Of place, time, fortune, do cohere, and jump,
That I am Viola: which to confirm,
I'll bring you to a captain in this town,
Where lie my maiden weeds; by whose gentle help
I was preserv'd, to serve this noble count:
All the occurrence of my fortune since
Hath been between this lady, and this lord.

Seb. So comes it, lady, you have been mistook: [*To* OLIVIA.
But nature to her bias drew in that.
You would have been contracted to a maid;
Nor are you therein, by my life, deceived,
You are betroth'd both to a maid and man.

Duke. Be not amaz'd; right noble is his blood.—
If this be so, as yet the glass seems true,
I shall have share in this most happy wreck:
Boy, thou hast said to me a thousand times, [*To* VIOLA.
Thou never should'st love woman like to me.

Vio. And all those sayings will I over-swear;
And all those swearings keep as true in soul,
As doth that orbed continent the fire
That severs day from night.

Duke. Give me thy hand;
And let me see thee in thy woman's weeds.

Vio. The captain, that did bring me first on shore,
Hath my maid's garments: he, upon some action,
Is now in durance, at Malvolio's suit,
A gentleman and follower of my lady's.

Oli. He shall enlarge him:—Fetch Malvolio hither:
And yet, alas, now I remember me,
They say, poor gentleman, he's much distract.

Re-enter Clown, *with a letter.*

A most extracting frenzy of mine own
From my remembrance clearly banish'd his.—
How does he, sirrah?

Clo. Truly, madam, he holds Belzebub at the stave's end, as well as a man in his case may do; he has here writ a letter to you, I should have given it you to-day morning; but as a madman's epistles are no gospels, so it skills not much when they are delivered.

Oli. Open it, and read it.

Clo. Look then to be well edified, when the fool delivers the madman:—*By the lord, madam,—*

Oli. How now! art thou mad?

Clo. No, madam, I do but read madness: an your ladyship will have it as it ought to be, you must allow *vox*.

Oli. 'Pr'ythee, read i' thy right wits.

Clo. So I do, madonna; but to read his right wits, is to read thus: therefore perpend, my princess, and give ear.

Oli. Read it you, sirrah. [*To* FABIAN.

Fab. [Reads.] *By the Lord, madam, you wrong me, and the world shall know it: though you have put me into darkness, and given your drunken cousin rule over me, yet have I the benefit of my senses as well as your ladyship. I have your own letter that induced me to the semblance I put on; with the which I doubt not but to do myself much right, or you much shame. Think of me as you please. I leave my duty a little unthought of, and speak out of my injury. The madly-used* Malvolio.

Oli. Did he write this?

Clo. Ay, madam.

Duke. This savours not much of distraction.

Oli. See him delivered, Fabian; bring him hither. [*Exit* FABIAN.
My lord, so please you, these things further thought on,
To think me as well a sister as a wife,
One day shall crown the alliance on't, so please you,
Here at my house, and at my proper cost.

Duke. Madam, I am most apt to embrace your offer.—
Your master quits you [*To* VIOLA]; and, for your service done him,
So much against the mettle of your sex,
So far beneath your soft and tender breeding,
And since you call'd me master for so long,
Here is my hand; you shall from this time be
Your master's mistress.

Oli. A sister?—you are she.

Re-enter FABIAN, *with* MALVOLIO.

Duke. Is this the madman?

Oli. Ay, my lord, this same:
How now, Malvolio?

Mal. Madam, you have done me wrong,
Notorious wrong.

Oli. Have I, Malvolio? no.

Mal. Lady, you have. 'Pray you, peruse that letter:
You must not now deny it is your hand,
Write from it, if you can, in hand, or phrase;
Or say 'tis not your seal, nor your invention:
You can say none of this: Well, grant it then,
And tell me, in the modesty of honour,
Why you have given me such clear lights of favour;
Bade me come smiling, and cross-garter'd to you,
To put on yellow stockings, and to frown
Upon Sir Toby, and the lighter people:
And, acting this in an obedient hope,
Why have you suffer'd me to be imprison'd,
Kept in a dark house, visited by the priest,
And made the most notorious geck, and gull,
That e'er invention play'd on? tell me why.

Oli. Alas, Malvolio, this is not my writing,
Though, I confess, much like the character:
But, out of question, 'tis Maria's hand.
And now I do bethink me, it was she
First told me, thou wast mad; then cam'st in smiling,
And in such forms which here were presuppos'd
Upon thee in the letter. 'Pr'ythee, be content:
This practice hath most shrewdly pass'd upon thee;
But, when we know the grounds and authors of it,
Thou shalt be both the plaintiff and the judge
Of thine own cause.

Fab. Good madam, hear me speak;
And let no quarrel, nor no brawl to come,
Taint the condition of this present hour,
Which I have wonder'd at. In hope it shall not,
Most freely I confess, myself, and Toby,
Set this device against Malvolio here,
Upon some stubborn and uncourteous parts
We had conceiv'd against him: Maria writ
The letter, at Sir Toby's great importance;
In recompense whereof, he hath married her.
How with a sportful malice it was follow'd,
May rather pluck on laughter than revenge;
If that the injuries be justly weigh'd,
That have on both sides past.

Oli. Alas, poor fool! how have they baffled thee!

Clo. Why, *some are born great, some achieve greatness, and some have greatness thrown upon them.* I was one, sir, in this interlude; one Sir Topas, sir; but that's all one:—*By the Lord, fool, I am not mad.*—But do you remember? *Madam, why laugh you at such a barren rascal? an you smile not, he's gagg'd:* And thus the whirligig of time brings in his revenges.

Mal. I'll be revenged on the whole pack of you. [*Exit.*

Oli. He hath been most notoriously abus'd.

Duke. Pursue him, and entreat him to a peace:—
He hath not told us of the captain yet;
When that is known and golden time convents,
A solemn combination shall be made
Of our dear souls.—Mean time, sweet sister,
We will not part from hence.—Cesario, come,
For so you shall be, while you are a man;
But, when in other habits you are seen,
Orsino's mistress, and his fancy's queen.
[*Exeunt.*

SONG.

Clo. *When that I was and a little tiny boy,*
With hey, ho, the wind and the rain,
A foolish thing was but a toy,
For the rain it raineth every day.

But when I came to man's estate,
With hey, ho, the wind and the rain,
'Gainst knaves and thieves men shut their gate,
For the rain it raineth every day.

But when I came, alas! to wive,
With hey, ho, the wind and the rain,
By swaggering could I never thrive,
For the rain it raineth every day.

But when I came unto my bed,
With hey, ho, the wind and the rain,
With toss-pots still had drunken head,
For the rain it raineth every day.

A great while ago the world begun,
With hey, ho, the wind and the rain,
But that's all one, our play is done,
And we'll strive to please you every day.
[Exit.

MEASURE FOR MEASURE.

PERSONS REPRESENTED.

VICENTIO, *Duke of* Vienna.
ANGELO, *Lord Deputy in the Duke's absence.*
ESCALUS, *an ancient Lord, joined with* Angelo *in the Deputation.*
CLAUDIO, *a young Gentleman.*
LUCIO, *a Fantastick.*
Two other like Gentlemen.
VARRIUS, *a Gentleman, Servant to the Duke.*
Provost.
THOMAS, } *Two Friars.*
PETER, }
A Justice.
ELBOW, *a simple Constable.*
FROTH, *a foolish Gentleman.*
Clown, *Servant to* Mrs. Over-done.
ABHORSON, *an Executioner.*
BARNARDINE, *a dissolute Prisoner.*

ISABELLA, *Sister to* Claudio.
MARIANA, *betrothed to* Angelo.
JULIET, *beloved by* Claudio.
FRANCISCA, *a Nun.*
MISTRESS OVER-DONE, *a Bawd.*

Lords, Gentlemen, Guards, Officers, and other Attendants.

SCENE—Vienna.

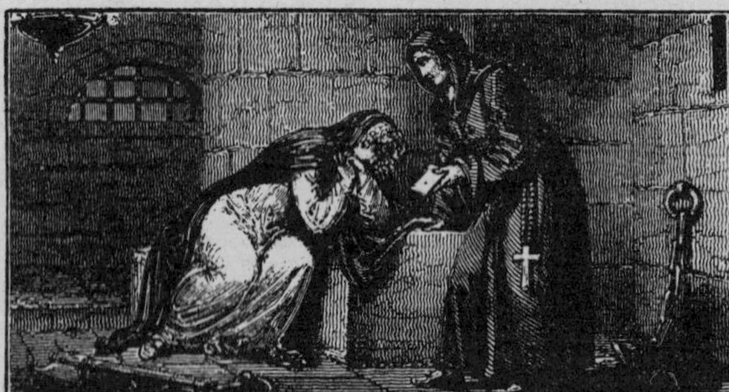

ACT I.

SCENE I. *An Apartment in the* Duke's *Palace.*

Enter Duke, ESCALUS, Lords, *and Attendants.*

Duke. ESCALUS,—
Escal. My lord.
Duke. Of government the properties to unfold,
Would seem in me to affect speech and discourse;
Since I am put to know, that your own science
Exceeds, in that, the lists of all advice
My strength can give you: Then no more remains
But that to your sufficiency, as your worth is able,
And let them work. The nature of our people,
Our city's institutions, and the terms
For common justice, you are as pregnant in,
As art and practice hath enriched any
That we remember: There is our commission,
From which we would not have you warp.—
Call hither,
I say, bid come before us Angelo.—
[*Exit an Attendant.*
What figure of us think you he will bear?
For you must know, we have with special soul
Elected him our absence to supply;
Lent him our terror, drest him with our love;
And given his deputation all the organs
Of our own power: What think you of it?
Escal. If any in Vienna be of worth
To undergo such ample grace and honour,
It is lord Angelo.

Enter ANGELO.

Duke. Look, where he comes.
Ang. Always obedient to your grace's will,
I come to know your pleasure.
Duke. Angelo,
There is a kind of character in thy life,
That, to the observer doth thy history
Fully unfold: Thyself and thy belongings
Are not thine own so proper, as to waste
Thyself upon thy virtues, them on thee.
Heaven doth with us, as we with torches do;
Not light them for themselves: for if our virtues
Did not go forth of us, 'twere all alike
As if we had them not. Spirits are not finely
touch'd,
But to fine issues: nor nature never lends
The smallest scruple of her excellence,
But, like a thrifty goddess, she determines
Herself the glory of a creditor,
Both thanks and use. But I do bend my speech
To one that can my part in him advertise;
Hold therefore.—Angelo;
In our remove, be thou at full ourself;
Mortality and Mercy in Vienna
Live in thy tongue and heart: Old Escalus,
Though first in question, is thy secondary:
Take thy commission.
Ang. Now, good my lord,
Let there be some more test made of my metal,
Before so noble and so great a figure
Be stamp'd upon it.
Duke. No more evasion:
We have with a leaven'd and prepared choice
Proceeded to you; therefore take your honours.
Our haste from hence is of so quick condition,
That it prefers itself, and leaves unquestion'd
Matters of needful value. We shall write to you,
As time and our concernings shall importune,
How it goes with us: and do look to know
What doth befall you here. So, fare you well:
To the hopeful execution do I leave you
Of your commissions.

Ang. Yet, give leave, my lord,
That we may bring you something on the way.
Duke. My haste may not admit it;
Nor need you on mine honour have to do
With any scruple: your scope is as mine own;
So to enforce or qualify the laws,
As to your soul seems good. Give me your hand;
I'll privily away: I love the people,
But do not like to stage me to their eyes:
Though it do well, I do not relish well
Their loud applause, and *aves* vehement;
Nor do I think the man of safe discretion,
That does affect it. Once more, fare you well.
Ang. The heavens give safety to your purposes!
Escal. Lead forth, and bring you back in happiness.
Duke. I thank you: Fare you well. [*Exit.*
Escal. I shall desire you, sir, to give me leave
To have free speech with you; and it concerns me
To look into the bottom of my place:
A power I have; but of what strength and nature
I am not yet instructed.
Ang. 'Tis so with me:—Let us withdraw together,
And we may soon our satisfaction have
Touching that point.
Escal. I'll wait upon your honour.
[*Exeunt.*

SCENE II. *A Street.*

Enter LUCIO *and two* Gentlemen.

Lucio. If the duke, with the other dukes, come not to composition with the king of Hungary, why, then all the dukes fall upon the king.

1 Gent. Heaven grant us its peace, but not the king of Hungary's!

2 Gent. Amen.

Lucio. Thou concludest like the sanctimonious pirate, that went to sea with the ten commandments, but scraped one out of the table.

2 Gent. Thou shalt not steal?

Lucio. Ay, that he razed.

1 Gent. Why, 'twas a commandment to command the captain and all the rest from their functions; they put forth to steal: There's not a soldier of us all, that, in the thanksgiving before meat, doth relish the petition well that prays for peace.

2 Gent. I never heard any soldier dislike it.

Lucio. I believe thee; for, I think, thou never wast where grace was said.

2 Gent. No? a dozen times at least.

1 Gent. What? in metre?

Lucio. In any proportion, or in any language.

1 Gent. I think, or in any religion.

Lucio. Ay! why not? Grace is grace, despite of all controversy: As for example; Thou thy self art a wicked villain, despite of all grace.

1 Gent. Well, there went but a pair of shears between us.

Lucio. I grant; as there may between the lists and the velvet: Thou art the list.

1 Gent. And thou the velvet: thou art good velvet: thou art a three-pil'd piece, I warrant thee: I had as lief be a list of an English kersey, as be pil'd, as thou art pil'd, for a French velvet. Do I speak feelingly now?

Lucio. I think thou dost; and, indeed, with most painful feeling of thy speech: I will, out of thine own confession, learn to begin thy health; but, whilst I live, forget to drink after thee.

1 Gent. I think, I have done myself wrong; have I not?

2 Gent. Yes, that thou hast; whether thou art tainted or free.

Lucio. Behold, behold, where madam Mitigation comes! I have purchased as many diseases under her roof, as come to—

2 Gent. To what, I pray?

1 Gent. Judge.

2 Gent. To three thousand dollars a-year.

1 Gent. Ay, and more.

Lucio. A French crown more.

1 Gent. Thou art always figuring diseases in me: but thou art full of error; I am sound.

Lucio. Nay, not as one would say, healthy; but so sound, as things that are hollow; thy bones are hollow: impiety has made a feast of thee.

Enter Bawd.

1 Gent. How now? Which of your hips has the most profound sciatica?

Bawd. Well, well; there's one yonder arrested, and carried to prison, was worth five thousand of you all.

1 Gent. Who's that, I pray thee?

Bawd. Marry, sir, that's Claudio, signior Claudio.

1 Gent. Claudio to prison! 'tis not so.

Bawd. Nay, but I know, 'tis so; I saw him arrested; saw him carried away; and which is more, within these three days his head's to be chopped off.

Lucio. But, after all this fooling, I would not have it so: Art thou sure of this?

Bawd. I am too sure of it: and it is for getting madam Julietta with child.

Lucio. Believe me, this may be: he promised to meet me two hours since; and he was ever precise in promise-keeping.

2 Gent. Besides, you know, it draws something near to the speech we had to such a purpose.

1 Gent. But most of all, agreeing with the proclamation.

Lucio. Away; let's go learn the truth of it.
[*Exeunt* LUCIO *and* Gentlemen.

Bawd. Thus, what with the war, what with the sweat, what with the gallows, and what with poverty, I am custom-shrunk. How now? what's the news with you?

Enter Clown.

Clo. Yonder man is carried to prison.

Bawd. Well: what has he done?

Clo. A woman.

Bawd. But what's his offence?

Clo. Groping for trouts in a peculiar river.

Bawd. What is there a maid with child by him?

Clo. No; but there's a woman with maid by him: You have not heard of the proclamation, have you?

Bawd. What proclamation, man?

Clo. All houses in the suburbs of Vienna must be pluck'd down.

Bawd. And what shall become of those in the city?

Clo. They shall stand for seed: they had gone down too, but that a wise burgher put in for them.

Bawd. But shall all our houses of resort in the suburbs be pull'd down?

Clo. To the ground, mistress.

Bawd. Why, here's a change, indeed, in the commonwealth! What shall become of me?

Clo. Come, fear not you; good counsellors lack no clients: though you change your place, you need not change your trade; I'll be your tapster still. Courage; there will be pity taken on you: you that have worn your eyes almost out in the service, you will be considered.

Bawd. What's to do here, Thomas Tapster? Let's withdraw.

Clo. Here comes signior Claudio, led by the provost to prison: and there's madam Juliet.
[*Exeunt.*

SCENE III. *The same.*

Enter Provost, CLAUDIO, JULIET, *and* Officers; LUCIO, *and two* Gentlemen.

Claud. Fellow, why dost thou show me thus to the world?
Bear me to prison, where I am committed.
Prov. I do it not in evil disposition,
But from lord Angelo by special charge.

Claud. Thus can the demi-god, Authority,
Make us pay down for our offence by weight.—
The words of heaven;—on whom it will, it will;
On whom it will not, so; yet still 'tis just.

Lucio. Why, how now, Claudio? whence comes this restraint?

Claud. From too much liberty, my Lucio, liberty;
As surfeit is the father of much fast,
So every scope by the immoderate use
Turns to restraint: Our natures do pursue,
(Like rats that ravin down their proper bane)
A thirsty evil; and when we drink, we die.

Lucio. If I could speak so wisely under an arrest, I would send for certain of my creditors: And yet, to say the truth, I had as lief have the foppery of freedom, as the morality of imprisonment.—What's thy offence, Claudio?

Claud. What, but to speak of would offend again.

Lucio. What is it? murder?

Claud. No.

Lucio. Lechery?

Claud. Call it so.

Prov. Away, sir; you must go.

Claud. One word, good friend:—Lucio, a word with you. [*Takes him aside.*

Lucio. A hundred, if they'll do you any good.—
Is lechery so look'd after?

Claud. Thus stands it with me:—Upon a true contract,
I got possession of Julietta's bed;
You know the lady; she is fast my wife,
Save that we do the denunciation lack
Of outward order: this we came not to,
Only for propagation of a dower
Remaining in the coffer of her friends;
From whom we thought it meet to hide our love,
Till time had made them for us. But it chances,
The stealth of our most mutual entertainment,
With character too gross is writ on Juliet.

Lucio. With child, perhaps?

Claud. Unhappily, even so.
And the new deputy now for the duke,—
Whether it be the fault and glimpse of newness;
Or whether that the body public be
A horse whereon the governor doth ride,
Who, newly in the seat, that it may know
He can command, lets it straight feel the spur:
Whether the tyranny be in his place,
Or in his eminence that fills it up,
I stagger in:—But this new governor
Awakes me all the enrolled penalties,
Which have, like unscour'd armour, hung by the wall
So long, that nineteen zodiacs have gone round,
And none of them been worn; and, for a name,
Now puts the drowsy and neglected act
Freshly on me:—'tis surely, for a name.

Lucio. I warrant, it is: and thy head stands so tickle on thy shoulders, that a milk-maid, if she be in love, may sigh it off.—Send after the duke, and appeal to him.

Claud. I have done so, but he's not to be found.
I pr'ythee, Lucio, do me this kind service:
This day my sister should the cloister enter,
And there receive her approbation:
Acquaint her with the danger of my state;
Implore her, in my voice, that she make friends
To the strict deputy; bid herself assay him;
I have great hope in that: for in her youth
There is a prone and speechless dialect,
Such as moves men; beside, she hath prosperous art
When she will play with reason and discourse,
And well she can persuade.

Lucio. I pray, she may: as well for the encouragement of the like, which else would stand under grievous imposition; as for the enjoying of thy life, who I would be sorry should be thus foolishly lost at a game of tick-tack. I'll to her.

Claud. I thank you, good friend Lucio.

Lucio. Within two hours,——

Claud. Come, officer, away. [*Exeunt.*

SCENE IV. *A Monastery.*

Enter Duke *and* Friar Thomas.

Duke. No: holy father; throw away that thought;
Believe not that the dribbling dart of love
Can pierce a complete bosom: why I desire thee
To give me secret harbour, hath a purpose
More grave and wrinkled than the aims and ends
Of burning youth.

Fri. May your grace speak of it?

Duke. My holy sir, none better knows than you
How I have ever loved the life remov'd;
And held in idle price to haunt assemblies,
Where youth, and cost, and witless bravery keeps.
I have deliver'd to lord Angelo
(A man of stricture, and firm abstinence)
My absolute power and place here in Vienna,
And he supposes me travell'd to Poland;
For so I have strew'd it in the common ear,
And so it is receiv'd: Now, pious sir,
You will demand of me, why I do this?

Fri. Gladly, my lord.

Duke. We have strict statutes, and most biting laws,
(The needful bits and curbs for headstrong steeds,)
Which for these fourteen years we have let sleep;
Even like an o'ergrown lion in a cave,
That goes not out to prey: Now, as fond fathers,
Having bound up the threat'ning twigs of birch,
Only to stick it in their children's sight,
For terror, not to use; in time the rod
Becomes more mock'd than fear'd: so our decrees,
Dead to infliction, to themselves are dead;
And liberty plucks justice by the nose;
The baby beats the nurse, and quite athwart
Goes all decorum.

Fri. It rested in your grace
To unloose this tied-up justice, when you pleas'd:
And it in you more dreadful would have seem'd,
Than in lord Angelo.

Duke. I do fear, too dreadful:
Sith 'twas my fault to give the people scope,
'Twould be my tyranny to strike, and gall them
For what I bid them do: For we bid this be done,
When evil deeds have their permissive pass,
And not the punishment. Therefore, indeed, my father,
I have on Angelo impos'd the office;
Who may, in the ambush of my name, strike home,
And yet my nature never in the sight,
To do it slander: And to behold his sway,
I will, as 'twere a brother of your order,
Visit both prince and people: therefore, I pr'ythee,
Supply me with the habit, and instruct me
How I may formally in person bear me
Like a true friar. More reasons for this action,
At our more leisure shall I render you;
Only this one:—Lord Angelo is precise;
Stands at a guard with envy; scarce confesses
That his blood flows, or that his appetite
Is more to bread than stone: Hence shall we see,
If power change purpose, what our seemers be.
[*Exeunt.*

SCENE V. *A Nunnery.*

Enter Isabella *and* Francisca.

Isab. And have you nuns no further privileges?

Fran. Are not these large enough?

Isab. Yes, truly: I speak not as desiring more;
But rather wishing a more strict restraint
Upon the sisterhood, the votarists of saint Clare.

Lucio. Ho! Peace be in this place! [*Within.*

Isab. Who's that which calls?

Fran. It is a man's voice: Gentle Isabella,
Turn you the key, and know his business of him;
You may, I may not; you are yet unsworn:
When you have vow'd, you must not speak with men,
But in the presence of the prioress:
Then, if you speak, you must not show your face;
Or, if you show your face, you must not speak.
He calls again; I pray you, answer him.
[*Exit* FRANCISCA.

Isab. Peace and prosperity! Who is't that calls?

Enter LUCIO.

Lucio. Hail, virgin, if you be; as those cheek-roses
Proclaim you are no less! Can you so stead me,
As bring me to the sight of Isabella,
A novice of this place, and the fair sister
To her unhappy brother Claudio?

Isab. Why her unhappy brother? let me ask;
The rather, for I now must make you know
I am that Isabella, and his sister.

Lucio. Gentle and fair, your brother kindly greets you:
Not to be weary with you, he's in prison.

Isab. Woe me! for what?

Lucio. For that, which, if myself might be his judge,
He should receive his punishment in thanks:
He hath got his friend with child.

Isab. Sir, mock me not:—your story.

Lucio. 'Tis true, I would not,—though 'tis my familiar sin
With maids to seem the lapwing, and to jest,
Tongue far from heart,—play with all virgins so:
I hold you as a thing ensky'd, and sainted;
By your renouncement, an immortal spirit;
And to be talk'd with in sincerity,
As with a saint.

Isab. You do blaspheme the good, in mocking me.

Lucio. Do not believe it. Fewness and truth, 'tis thus:
Your brother and his lover have embrac'd:
As those that feed grow full; as blossoming time,
That from the seedness the bare fallow brings
To teeming foison; even so her plenteous womb
Expresseth his full tilth and husbandry.

Isab. Some one with child by him?—My cousin Juliet?

Lucio. Is she your cousin?

Isab. Adoptedly; as school-maids change their names,
By vain though apt affection.

Lucio. She it is.

Isab. O let him marry her!

Lucio. This is the point.
The duke is very strangely gone from hence;
Bore many gentlemen, myself being one,
In hand, and hope of action; but we do learn
By those that know the very nerves of state,
His givings out were of an infinite distance
From his true-meant design. Upon his place,
And with full line of his authority,
Governs lord Angelo; a man, whose blood
Is very snow-broth; one who never feels
The wanton stings and motions of the sense;
But doth rebate and blunt his natural edge
With profits of the mind, study and fast.
He (to give fear to use and liberty,
Which have, for long, run by the hideous law,
As mice by lions,) hath pick'd out an act,
Under whose heavy sense your brother's life
Falls into forfeit: he arrests him on it;
And follows close the rigour of the statute,
To make him an example: all hope is gone,
Unless you have the grace by your fair prayer
To soften Angelo: And that's my pith
Of business 'twixt you and your poor brother.

Isab. Doth he so seek his life?

Lucio. Has censur'd him
Already; and, as I hear, the provost hath
A warrant for his execution.

Isab. Alas! what poor ability's in me
To do him good?

Lucio. Assay the power you have.

Isab. My power! Alas! I doubt,—

Lucio. Our doubts are traitors,
And make us lose the good we oft might win,
By fearing to attempt: Go to lord Angelo,
And let him learn to know, when maidens sue,
Men give like gods; but when they weep and kneel,
All their petitions are as freely theirs
As they themselves would owe them.

Isab. I'll see what I can do.

Lucio. But speedily.

Isab. I will about it straight;
No longer staying but to give the mother
Notice of my affair. I humbly thank you:
Commend me to my brother: soon at night
I'll send him certain word of my success.

Lucio. I take my leave of you.

Isab. Good sir, adieu.
[*Exeunt.*

ACT II.

SCENE I. *A Hall in* Angelo's *House.*

Enter ANGELO, ESCALUS, *a* Justice, Provost, Officers, *and other Attendants.*

Ang. We must not make a scare crow of the law,
Setting it up to fear the birds of prey,
And let it keep one shape, till custom make it
Their perch, and not their terror.

Escal. Ay, but yet
Let us be keen, and rather cut a little,
Than fall, and bruise to death: Alas! this gentleman,
Whom I would save, had a most noble father,
Let but your honour know,
(Whom I believe to be most strait in virtue),
That, in the working of your own affections,
Had time coher'd with place, or place with wishing,
Or that the resolute acting of your blood
Could have attain'd the effect of your own purpose,
Whether you had not sometime in your life
Err'd in this point which now you censure him,
And pull'd the law upon you.

Ang. 'Tis one thing to be tempted, Escalus,
Another thing to fall. I not deny,
The jury, passing on the prisoner's life,
May, in the sworn twelve, have a thief or two
Guiltier than him they try: What's open made to justice,
That justice seizes. What know the laws,
That thieves do pass on thieves? 'Tis very pregnant,
The jewel that we find, we stoop and take it,
Because we see it; but what we do not see,
We tread upon, and never think of it.
You may not so extenuate his offence,
For I have had such faults; but rather tell me,
When I, that censure him, do so offend,
Let mine own judgment pattern out my death,
And nothing come in partial. Sir, he must die.

Escal. Be it as your wisdom will.

Ang. Where is the provost?

Prov. Here, if it like your honour.

Ang. See that Claudio
Be executed by nine to-morrow morning:
Bring him his confessor, let him be prepared;
For that's the utmost of his pilgrimage.
[*Exit* Provost.

Escal. Well, heaven forgive him; and forgive us all!
Some rise by sin, and some by virtue fall:
Some run from brakes of vice, and answer none;
And some condemned for a fault alone.

Enter ELBOW, FROTH, Clown, Officers, *&c.*

Elb. Come, bring them away: if these be

good people in a common-weal, that do nothing but use their abuses in common houses, I know no law; bring them away.

Ang. How now, sir! What's your name? and what's the matter?

Elb. If it please your honour, I am the poor duke's constable, and my name is Elbow; I do lean upon justice, sir, and do bring in here before your good honour two notorious benefactors.

Ang. Benefactors! Well: what benefactors are they? are they not malefactors?

Elb. If it please your honour, I know not well what they are; but precise villains they are, that I am sure of; and void of all profanation in the world, that good christians ought to have.

Escal. This comes off well; here's a wise officer.

Ang. Go to: What quality are they of? Elbow is your name? Why dost thou not speak, Elbow?

Clo. He cannot, sir? he's out at elbow.

Ang. What are you, sir?

Elb. He, sir? a tapster, sir; parcel-bawd; one that serves a bad woman; whose house, sir, was, as they say, plucked down in the suburbs: and now she professes a hot-house, which, I think, is a very ill house too.

Escal. How know you that?

Elb. My wife, sir, whom I detest before heaven and your honour,—

Escal. How! thy wife?

Elb. Ay, sir; whom, I thank heaven, is an honest woman,—

Escal. Dost thou detest her therefore?

Elb. I say, sir, I will detest myself also, as well as she, that this house, if it be not a bawd's house, it is a pity of her life, for it is a naughty house.

Escal. How dost thou know that, constable?

Elb. Marry, sir, by my wife; who, if she had been a woman cardinally given, might have been accused in fornication, adultery, and all uncleanliness there.

Escal. By the woman's means?

Elb. Ay, sir, by mistress Over-done's means: but as she spit in his face, so she defied him.

Clo. Sir, if it please your honour, this is not so.

Elb. Prove it before these varlets here, thou honourable man, prove it.

Escal. Do you hear how he misplaces? [*To* ANGELO.

Clo. Sir, she came in great with child; and longing (saving your honour's reverence), for stew'd prunes: sir, we had but two in the house, which at that very distant time stood, as it were, in a fruit-dish, a dish of some three pence: your honours have seen such dishes; they are not China dishes, but very good dishes.

Escal. Go to, go to: no matter for the dish, sir.

Clo. No, indeed, sir, not of a pin; you are therein in the right: but, to the point: As I say, this mistress Elbow being, as I say, with child, and being great belly'd, and longing, as I said, for prunes; and having but two in the dish, as I said, master Froth here, this very man having eaten the rest, as I said, and, as I say, paying for them very honestly;—for, as you know, master Froth, I cou'd not give you three pence again.

Froth. No, indeed.

Clo. Very well: you being then, if you be remember'd, cracking the stones of the aforesaid prunes.

Froth. Ay, so I did, indeed.

Clo. Why, very well: I telling you then, if you be remember'd, that such a one, and such a one, were past cure of the thing you wot of, unless they kept very good diet, as I told you.

Froth. All this is true.

Clo. Why, very well then.

Escal. Come, you are a tedious fool: to the purpose,—What was done to Elbow's wife, that he hath cause to complain of? Come me to what was done to her.

Clo. Sir, your honour cannot come to that yet.

Escal. No, sir, nor I mean it not.

Clo. Sir, but you shall come to it, by your honour's leave: And, I beseech you, look into master Froth here, sir; a man of fourscore pound a year; whose father died at Hallowmas: —Was't not at Hallowmas, master Froth?

Froth. All-hollond eve.

Clo. Why, very well; I hope here be truths: He, sir, sitting, as I say, in a lower chair, sir: 'twas in the *Bunch of Grapes*, where, indeed, you have a delight to sit: Have you not?

Froth. I have so; because it is an open room, and good for winter.

Clo. Why, very well, then:—I hope here be truths.

Ang. This will last out a night in Russia,
When nights are longest there: I'll take my leave,
And leave you to the hearing of the cause;
Hoping, you'll find good cause to whip them all.

Escal. I think no less; Good morrow to your lordship. [*Exit* ANGELO.
Now, sir, come on: What was done to Elbow's wife, once more?

Clo. Once, sir? there was nothing done to her once.

Elb. I beseech you, sir, ask him what this man did to my wife.

Clo. I beseech your honour, ask me.

Escal. Well, sir: What did this gentleman to her?

Clo. I beseech you, sir, look in this gentleman's face:—Good master Froth, look upon his honour; 'tis for a good purpose: Doth your honour mark his face?

Escal. Ay, sir, very well.

Clo. Nay, I beseech you, mark it well.

Escal. Well, I do so.

Clo. Doth your honour see any harm in his face?

Escal. Why, no.

Clo. I'll be supposed upon a book, his face is the worst thing about him: Good then; if his face be the worst thing about him, how could master Froth do the constable's wife any harm? I would know that of your honour.

Escal. He's in the right: Constable, what say you to it?

Elb. First, an it like you, the house is a respected house: next, this is a respected fellow; and his mistress is a respected woman.

Clo. By this hand, sir, his wife is a more respected person than any of us all.

Elb. Varlet, thou liest; thou liest, wicked varlet: the time is yet to come, that she was ever respected with man, woman, or child.

Clo. Sir, she was respected with him before he married with her.

Escal. Which is the wiser here? Justice, or Iniquity? Is this true?

Elb. O thou caitiff! O thou varlet! O thou wicked Hannibal! I respected with her, before I was married to her? If ever I was respected with her, or she with me, let not your worship think me the poor duke's officer:—Prove this, thou wicked Hannibal, or I'll have mine action of battery on thee.

Escal. If he took you a box o' th' ear, you might have your action of slander too.

Elb. Marry, I thank your good worship for it; What is't your worship's pleasure I should do with this wicked caitiff?

Escal. Truly, officer, because he has some offences in him, that thou wouldst discover if thou couldst, let him continue in his courses till thou know'st what they are.

Elb. Marry, I thank your worship for it:— Thou seest, thou wicked varlet now, what's come upon thee; thou art to continue now, thou varlet; thou art to continue.

Escal. Where were you born, friend? [*To* FROTH.

Froth. Here in Vienna, sir.
Escal. Are you of fourscore pounds a year?
Froth. Yes, and't please you, sir.
Escal. So.—What trade are you of, sir? [*To the* Clown.
Clo. A tapster; a poor widow's tapster.
Escal. Your mistress's name?
Clo. Mistress Over-done.
Escal. Hath she had any more than one husband?
Clo. Nine, sir; Over-done by the last.
Escal. Nine!—Come hither to me, master Froth. Master Froth, I would not have you acquainted with tapsters; they will draw you, master Froth, and you will hang them: Get you gone, and let me hear no more of you.
Froth. I thank your worship: for mine own part, I never come into any room in a taphouse, but I am drawn in.
Escal. Well; no more of it, master Froth: farewell. [*Exit* FROTH.]—Come you hither to me, master tapster; what's your name, master tapster?
Clo. Pompey.
Escal. What else?
Clo. Bum, sir.
Escal. 'Troth, and your bum is the greatest thing about you: so that, in the beastliest sense, you are Pompey the great. Pompey, you are partly a bawd, Pompey, howsoever you colour it in being a tapster. Are you not? come, tell me true; it shall be the better for you.
Clo. Truly, sir, I am a poor fellow, that would live.
Escal. How would you live, Pompey? by being a bawd? What do you think of the trade, Pompey? is it a lawful trade?
Clo. If the law would allow it, sir?
Escal. But the law will not allow it, Pompey; nor it shall not be allowed in Vienna.
Clo. Does your worship mean to geld and spay all the youth in the city?
Escal. No, Pompey.
Clo. Truly, sir, in my poor opinion, they will to't then: If your worship will take order for the drabs and the knaves, you need not to fear the bawds.
Escal. There are pretty orders beginning, I can tell you: It is but heading and hanging.
Clo. If you head and hang all that offend that way but for ten year together, you'll be glad to give out a commission for more heads. If this law hold in Vienna ten year, I'll rent the fairest house in it, after three pence a bay: if you live to see this come to pass, say, Pompey told you so.
Escal. Thank you, good Pompey: and, in requital of your prophecy, hark you,—I advise you, let me not find you before me again upon any complaint whatsoever, no, not for dwelling where you do; If I do, Pompey, I shall beat you to your tent, and prove a shrewd Cæsar to you; in plain dealing, Pompey, I shall have you whipt: so for this time, Pompey, fare you well.
Clo. I thank your worship for your good counsel: but I shall follow it as the flesh and fortune shall better determine.
Whip me? No, no; let carman whip his jade;
The valiant heart's not whipt out of his trade. [*Exit.*
Escal. Come hither to me, master Elbow; come hither, master Constable. How long have you been in this place of constable?
Elb. Seven year and a half, sir.
Escal. I thought, by your readiness in the office, you had continued in it some time: You say, seven years together?
Elb. And a half, sir.
Escal. Alas! it hath been great pains to you! They do you wrong to put you so oft upon't: Are there not men in your ward sufficient to serve it?
Elb. Faith, sir, few of any wit in such matters: as they are chosen, they are glad to choose me for them; I do it for some piece of money, and go through with all.
Escal. Look you, bring me in the names of some six or seven, the most sufficient of your parish.
Elb. To your worship's house, sir?
Escal. To my house: Fare you well. [*Exit* ELBOW.] What's o'clock, think you?
Just. Eleven, sir.
Escal. I pray you home to dinner with me.
Just. I humbly thank you.
Escal. It grieves me for the death of Claudio;
But there's no remedy.
Just. Lord Angelo is severe.
Escal. It is but needful:
Mercy is not itself that oft looks so;
Pardon is still the nurse of second woe:
But yet,—Poor Claudio!—There's no remedy.
Come, sir. [*Exeunt.*

SCENE II. *Another Room in the same.*

Enter Provost *and a* Servant.

Serv. He's hearing of a cause; he will come straight.
I'll tell him of you.
Prov. 'Pray you, do. [*Exit* Servant.] I'll know
His pleasure: may be, he will relent: Alas,
He hath but as offended in a dream!
All sects, all ages smack of this vice; and he
To die for it!—

Enter ANGELO.

Ang. Now, what's the matter, provost?
Prov. Is it your will Claudio shall die to-morrow?
Ang. Did I not tell thee, yea? hadst thou not order?
Why dost thou ask again?
Prov. Lest I might be too rash:
Under your good correction, I have seen,
When, after execution, judgment hath
Repented o'er his doom.
Ang. Go to; let that be mine:
Do you your office, or give up your place,
And you shall well be spar'd.
Prov. I crave your honour's pardon.—
What shall be done, sir, with the groaning Juliet?
She's very near her hour.
Ang. Dispose of her
To some more fitter place; and that with speed.

Re-enter Servant.

Serv. Here is the sister of the man condemn'd,
Desires access to you.
Ang. Hath he a sister?
Prov. Ay, my good lord: a very virtuous maid,
And to be shortly of a sisterhood,
If not already.
Ang. Well, let her be admitted. [*Exit* Servant.
See you, the fornicatress be remov'd;
Let her have needful, but not lavish, means;
There shall be order for it.

Enter LUCIO *and* ISABELLA.

Prov. Save your honour! [*Offering to retire.*
Ang. Stay a little while.—[*To* ISAB.] You are welcome: What's your will?
Isab. I am a woful suitor to your honour,
Please but your honour hear me.
Ang. Well; what's your suit?
Isab. There is a vice, that most I do abhor,
And most desire should meet the blow of justice;
For which I would not plead, but that I must;
For which I must not plead, but that I am
At war, 'twixt will, and will not.
Ang. Well: the matter?
Isab. I have a brother is condemn'd to die:
I do beseech you, let it be his fault,
And not my brother.
Prov. Heaven give thee moving graces!
Ang. Condemn the fault, and not the actor of it!

Why, every fault's condemn'd, ere it be done:
Mine were the very cipher of a function,
To fine the faults, whose fine stands in record,
And let go by the actor.
Isab. O just, but severe law!
I had a brother then.—Heaven keep your honour! [*Retiring.*
Lucio. [*To* Isab.] Give't not o'er so: to him again, entreat him:
Kneel down before him, hang upon his gown;
You are too cold: if you should need a pin,
You could not with more tame a tongue desire it:
To him, I say.
Isab. Must he needs die?
Ang. Maiden, no remedy.
Isab. Yes; I do think that you might pardon him,
And neither heaven, nor man, grieve at the mercy.
Ang. I will not do't.
Isab. But can you, if you would?
Ang. Look, what I will not, that I cannot do.
Isab. But might you do't, and do the world no wrong,
If so your heart were touch'd with that remorse
As mine is to him?
Ang. He's sentenc'd: 'tis too late.
Lucio. You are too cold. [*To* Isabella.
Isab. Too late? why, no; I, that do speak a word,
May call it back again: Well, believe this,
No ceremony that to great ones 'longs,
Not the king's crown, nor the deputed sword,
The marshal's truncheon, nor the judge's robe,
Become them with one half so good a grace,
As mercy does. If he had been as you,
And you as he, you would have slipt like him;
But he, like you, would not have been so stern.
Ang. 'Pray you, begone.
Isab. I would to heaven I had your potency,
And you were Isabel! should it then be thus?
No; I would tell what 'twere to be a judge,
And what a prisoner.
Lucio. Ay, touch him: there's the vein. [*Aside.*
Ang. Your brother is a forfeit of the law,
And you but waste your words.
Isab. Alas! alas!
Why, all the souls that were, were forfeit once;
And He that might the vantage best have took,
Found out the remedy: How would you be,
If he, which is the top of judgment, should
But judge you as you are? O, think on that;
And mercy then will breathe within your lips,
Like man new made.
Ang. Be you content, fair maid;
It is the law, not I, condemns your brother:
Were he my kinsman, brother, or my son,
It should be thus with him;—he must die to-morrow.
Isab. To-morrow? O, that's sudden! Spare him, spare him:
He's not prepar'd for death! Even for our kitchens
We kill the fowl of season: shall we serve heaven
With less respect than we do minister
To our gross selves? Good, good my lord, bethink you:
Who is it that hath died for this offence?
There's many have committed it.
Lucio. Ay, well said.
Ang. The law hath not been dead, though it hath slept:
Those many had not dar'd to do that evil,
If the first man that did the edict infringe
Had answer'd for his deed: now, 'tis awake;
Takes note of what is done; and, like a prophet,
Looks in a glass, that shows what future evils,
(Either now, or by remissness new-conceiv'd,
And so in progress to be hatch'd and born),
Are now to have no successive degrees,
But, where they live, to end.
Isab. Yet show some pity.
Ang. I show it most of all, when I show justice;
For then I pity those I do not know,
Which a dismiss'd offence would after gall;
And do him right, that, answering one foul wrong,
Lives not to act another. Be satisfied;
Your brother dies to-morrow: be content.
Isab. So you must be the first, that gives this sentence:
And he, that suffers: O, it is excellent
To have a giant's strength; but it is tyrannous
To use it like a giant.
Lucio. That's well said.
Isab. Could great men thunder
As Jove himself does, Jove would ne'er be quiet,
For every pelting, petty officer,
Would use his heaven for thunder; nothing but thunder.——
Merciful heaven!
Thou rather, with thy sharp and sulphurous bolt,
Split'st the unwedgeable and gnarled oak,
Than the soft myrtle:—But man, proud man!
Drest in a little brief authority:
Most ignorant of what he's most assur'd,
His glassy essence,—like an angry ape,
Plays such fantastick tricks before high heaven,
As make the angels weep; who, with our spleens,
Would all themselves laugh mortal.
Lucio. O, to him, to him, wench: he will relent;
He's coming, I perceive't.
Prov. 'Pray heaven, she win him!
Isab. We cannot weigh our brother with our-self:
Great men may jest with saints: 'tis wit in them;
But, in the less, foul profanation.
Lucio. Thou'rt in the right, girl; more o' that.
Isab. That in the captain's but a cholerick word,
Which in the soldier is flat blasphemy.
Lucio. Art advis'd o' that? more on 't.
Ang. Why do you put these sayings upon me?
Isab. Because authority, though it err like others,
Hath yet a kind of medicine in itself,
That skins the vice o' the top: Go to your bosom;
Knock there, and ask your heart, what it doth know
That's like my brother's fault: if it confess
A natural guiltiness, such as is his,
Let it not sound a thought upon your tongue
Against my brother's life.
Ang. She speaks, and 'tis
Such sense, that my sense breeds with it.—Fare you well.
Isab. Gentle my lord, turn back.
Ang. I will bethink me:—Come again to-morrow.
Isab. Hark, how I'll bribe you: Good my lord, turn back.
Ang. How! bribe me?
Isab. Ay, with such gifts, that heaven shall share with you.
Lucio. You had marr'd all else.
Isab. Not with fond shekels of the tested gold,
Or stones, whose rates are either rich, or poor,
As fancy values them: but with true prayers,
That shall be up at heaven, and enter there,
Ere sun-rise; prayers from preserved souls,
From fasting maids, whose minds are dedicate
To nothing temporal.
Ang. Well: come to me
To-morrow.
Lucio. Go to; it is well away. [*Aside to* Isabel.
Isab. Heaven keep your honour safe!
Ang. Amen:
For I am that way going to temptation, [*Aside.*
Where prayers cross.
Isab. At what hour to-morrow
Shall I attend your lordship?

Ang. At any time 'fore noon.
Isab. Save your honour!
[*Exeunt* LUCIO, ISABELLA, *and* Provost.
Ang. From thee; even from thy virtue!—
What's this? what's this? Is this her fault, or mine?
The tempter, or the tempted, who sins most? Ha!
Not she; nor doth she tempt: but it is I,
That lying by the violet, in the sun,
Do, as the carrion does, not as the flower,
Corrupt with virtuous season. Can it be,
That modesty may more betray our sense
Than woman's lightness? Having waste ground enough,
Shall we desire to raze the sanctuary,
And pitch our evils there? O, fy, fy, fy!
What dost thou? or, what art thou, Angelo?
Dost thou desire her foully, for those things
That make her good? O, let her brother live:
Thieves for the robbery have authority,
When judges steal themselves. What? do I love her,
That I desire to hear her speak again,
And feast upon her eyes? What is't I dream on?
O cunning enemy, that, to catch a saint,
With saints dost bait thy hook! Most dangerous
Is that temptation, that doth goad us on
To sin in loving virtue: never could the strumpet,
With all her double vigour, art and nature,
Once stir my temper; but this virtuous maid
Subdues me quite;—Ever, till now,
When men were fond, I smil'd, and wonder'd how! [*Exit.*

SCENE III. *A Room in a Prison.*

Enter Duke, *habited like a Friar, and* Provost.

Duke. Hail to you, Provost! so, I think you are.
Prov. I am the provost: What's your will, good friar?
Duke. Bound by my charity, and my bless'd order,
I come to visit the afflicted spirits
Here in the prison: do me the common right
To let me see them; and to make me know
The nature of their crimes, that I may minister
To them accordingly.
Prov. I would do more than that, if more were needful.

Enter JULIET.

Look, here comes one; a gentlewoman of mine,
Who falling in the flames of her own youth,
Hath blister'd her report: She is with child;
And he that got it, sentenc'd: a young man
More fit to do another such offence,
Than die for this.
Duke. When must he die?
Prov. As I do think, to-morrow.—
I have provided for you; stay a while, [*To* JULIET.
And you shall be conducted.
Duke. Repent you, fair one, of the sin you carry?
Juliet. I do; and bear the shame most patiently.
Duke. I'll teach you how you shall arraign your conscience,
And try your penitence, if it be sound,
Or hollowly put on.
Juliet. I'll gladly learn.
Duke. Love you the man that wrong'd you?
Juliet. Yes, as I love the woman that wrong'd him.
Duke. So then, it seems, your most offenceful act
Was mutually committed?
Juliet. Mutually.
Duke. Then was your sin of heavier kind than his.
Juliet. I do confess it, and repent it, father.
Duke. 'Tis meet so, daughter: But lest you do repent,
As that the sin hath brought you to this shame,—
Which sorrow is always toward ourselves, not heaven;
Showing, we'd not spare heaven as we love it,
But as we stand in fear,—
Juliet. I do repent me, as it is an evil;
And take the shame with joy.
Duke. There rest.
Your partner, as I hear, must die to-morrow,
And I am going with instruction to him.—
Grace go with you! *Benedicite!* [*Exit.*
Juliet. Must die to-morrow! O, injurious love,
That respites me a life, whose very comfort
Is still a dying horror!
Prov. 'Tis pity of him. [*Exeunt.*

SCENE IV. *A Room in* Angelo's *House.*

Enter ANGELO.

Ang. When I would pray and think, I think and pray
To several subjects: heaven hath my empty words;
Whilst my invention, hearing not my tongue,
Anchors on Isabel: Heaven in my mouth,
As if I did but only chew his name;
And in my heart, the strong and swelling evil
Of my conception: The state, whereon I studied,
Is like a good thing, being often read,
Grown fear'd and tedious; yea, my gravity,
Wherein (let no man hear me) I take pride,
Could I, with boot, change for an idle plume,
Which the air beats for vain. O place! O form!
How often dost thou with thy case, thy habit,
Wrench awe from fools, and tie the wiser souls
To thy false seeming? Blood, thou still art blood!
Let's write good angel on the devil's horn,
'Tis not the devil's crest.

Enter Servant.

How now, who's there?
Serv. One Isabel, a sister,
Desires access to you.
Ang. Teach her the way.
[*Exit* Servant.
O heavens!
Why does my blood thus muster to my heart;
Making both it unable for itself,
And dispossessing all the other parts
Of necessary fitness?
So play the foolish throngs with one that swoons;
Come all to help him, and so stop the air
By which he should revive: and even so
The general, subject to a well-wish'd king,
Quit their own part, and in obsequious fondness
Crowd to his presence, where their untaught love
Must needs appear offence.

Enter ISABELLA.

How now, fair maid?
Isab. I am come to know your pleasure.
Ang. That you might know it, would much better please me,
Than to demand what 'tis. Your brother cannot live.
Isab. Even so?—Heaven keep your honour!
[*Retiring.*
Ang. Yet may he live awhile; and it may be,
As long as you, or I: Yet he must die.
Isab. Under your sentence?
Ang. Yea.
Isab. When, I beseech you? that in his reprieve,
Longer, or shorter, he may be so fitted,
That his soul sicken not.
Ang. Ha! Fye, these filthy vices! It were as good
To pardon him, that hath from nature stolen
A man already made, as to remit
Their saucy sweetness, that do coin heaven's image
In stamps that are forbid: 'tis all as easy
Falsely to take away a life true made,

As to put metal in restrained means,
To make a false one.

Isab. 'Tis set down so in heaven, but not in earth.

Ang. Say you so? then I shall pose you quickly.
Which had you rather, That the most just law
Now took your brother's life; or, to redeem him,
Give up your body to such sweet uncleanness,
As she that he hath stain'd?

Isab. Sir, believe this,
I had rather give my body than my soul.

Ang. I talk not of your soul: Our compell'd sins
Stand more for number than accompt.

Isab. How say you?

Ang. Nay, I'll not warrant that; for I can speak
Against the thing I say. Answer to this;—
I, now the voice of the recorded law,
Pronounce a sentence on your brother's life:
Might there not be a charity in sin,
To save this brother's life?

Isab. Please you to do't,
I'll take it as a peril to my soul,
It is no sin at all, but charity.

Ang. Pleas'd you to do't, at peril of your soul,
Were equal poise of sin and charity.

Isab. That I do beg his life, if it be sin,
Heaven, let me bear it! you granting of my suit,
If that be sin, I'll make it my morn prayer
To have it added to the faults of mine,
And nothing of your answer.

Ang. Nay, but hear me:
Your sense pursues not mine: either you are ignorant,
Or seem so, craftily; and that's not good.

Isab. Let me be ignorant, and in nothing good,
But graciously to know I am no better.

Ang. Thus wisdom wishes to appear most bright,
When it doth tax itself: as these black masks
Proclaim an enshield beauty ten times louder
Than beauty could display'd.—But mark me;
To be received plain, I'll speak more gross:
Your brother is to die.

Isab. So.

Ang. And his offence is so, as it appears
Accountant to the law upon that pain.

Isab. True.

Ang. Admit no other way to save his life,
(As I subscribe not that, nor any other,
But in the loss of question), that you, his sister,
Finding yourself desir'd of such a person,
Whose credit with the judge, or own great place,
Could fetch your brother from the manacles
Of the all-binding law; and that there were
No earthly mean to save him, but that either
You must lay down the treasures of your body
To this supposed, or else to let him suffer;
What would you do?

Isab. As much for my poor brother, as myself;
That is, Were I under the terms of death,
The impression of keen whips I'd wear as rubies,
And strip myself to death, as to a bed
That longing I have been sick for, ere I'd yield
My body up to shame.

Ang. Then must your brother die.

Isab. And 'twere the cheaper way:
Better it were, a brother died at once,
Than that a sister, by redeeming him,
Should die for ever.

Ang. Were not you then as cruel as the sentence
That you have slander'd so?

Isab. Ignomy in ransom, and free pardon,
Are of two houses: lawful mercy is
Nothing akin to foul redemption.

Ang. You seem'd of late to make the law a tyrant;
And rather prov'd the sliding of your brother
A merriment than a vice.

Isab. O pardon me, my lord; it oft falls out,
To have what we'd have, we speak not what we mean:
I something do excuse the thing I hate,
For his advantage that I dearly love.

Ang. We are all frail.

Isab. Else let my brother die,
If not a feodary, but only he,
Owe, and succeed by weakness.

Ang. Nay, women are frail too.

Isab. Ay, as the glasses where they view themselves;
Which are as easy broke as they make forms.
Women!—Help, heaven! men their creation mar
In profiting by them. Nay, call us ten times frail;
For we are soft as our complexions are,
And credulous to false prints.

Ang. I think it well:
And from this testimony of your own sex,
(Since, I suppose, we are made to be no stronger
Than faults may shake our frames) let me be bold;—
I do arrest your words; Be that you are,
That is, a woman; if you be more, you're none;
If you be one (as you are well express'd
By all external warrants), show it now,
By putting on the destin'd livery.

Isab. I have no tongue but one: gentle my lord,
Let me entreat you speak the former language.

Ang. Plainly conceive, I love you.

Isab. My brother did love Juliet; and you tell me,
That he shall die for it.

Ang. He shall not, Isabel, if you give me love.

Isab. I know, your virtue hath a licence in't,
Which seems a little fouler than it is,
To pluck on others.

Ang. Believe me, on mine honour,
My words express my purpose.

Isab. Ha! little honour to be much believ'd,
And most pernicious purpose!—seeming, seeming!—
I will proclaim thee, Angelo; look for't:
Sign me a present pardon for my brother,
Or, with an outstretch'd throat, I'll tell the world
Aloud, what man thou art.

Ang. Who will believe thee, Isabel?
My unsoil'd name, the austereness of my life,
My vouch against you, and my place i' the state,
Will so your accusation overweigh,
That you shall stifle in your own report,
And smell of calumny. I have begun;
And now I give my sensual race the rein:
Fit thy consent to my sharp appetite;
Lay by all nicety, and prolixious blushes,
That banish what they sue for; redeem thy brother
By yielding up thy body to my will;
Or else he must not only die the death,
But thy unkindness shall his death draw out
To lingering sufferance: answer me to-morrow,
Or, by the affection that now guides me most,
I'll prove a tyrant to him: As for you,
Say what you can, my false o'erweighs your true. [*Exit.*

Isab. To whom shall I complain? Did I tell this,
Who would believe me? O perilous mouths,
That bear in them one and the selfsame tongue,
Either of condemnation or approof!
Bidding the law make court'sy to their will;
Hooking both right and wrong to the appetite,
To follow as it draws! I'll to my brother:
Though he hath fallen by prompture of the blood,
Yet hath he in him such a mind of honour,
That had he twenty heads to tender down
On twenty bloody blocks, he'd yield them up,
Before his sister should her body stoop
To such abhorr'd pollution.
Then, Isabel, live chaste, and, brother, die:
More than our brother is our chastity.
I'll tell him yet of Angelo's request,
And fit his mind to death, for his soul's rest. [*Exit.*

ACT III.

SCENE I. *A Room in the Prison.*

Enter Duke, Claudio, *and* Provost.

Duke. So, then you hope of pardon from lord Angelo?
Claud. The miserable have no other medicine,
But only hope:
I have hope to live, and am prepar'd to die.
Duke. Be absolute for death; either death or life,
Shall thereby be the sweeter. Reason thus with life,—
If I do lose thee, I do lose a thing
That none but fools would keep: a breath thou art,
(Servile to all the skiey influences),
That dost this habitation, where thou keep'st,
Hourly afflict: merely, thou art death's fool;
For him thou labour'st by thy flight to shun,
And yet runn'st toward him still: Thou art not noble;
For all the accommodations that thou bear'st,
Are nurs'd by baseness: Thou art by no means valiant;
For thou dost fear the soft and tender fork
Of a poor worm: Thy best of rest is sleep,
And that thou oft provok'st; yet grossly fear'st
Thy death, which is no more. Thou art not thyself;
For thou exist'st on many a thousand grains
That issue out of dust: Happy thou art not;
For what thou hast not, still thou striv'st to get;
And what thou hast, forget'st: Thou art not certain;
For thy complexion shifts to strange affects,
After the moon: If thou art rich, thou art poor;
For, like an ass, whose back with ingots bows,
Thou bear'st thy heavy riches but a journey,
And death unloads thee: Friend hast thou none;
For thine own bowels, which do call thee sire,
The mere effusion of thy proper loins,
Do curse the gout, serpigo, and the rheum,
For ending thee no sooner: Thou hast nor youth, nor age;
But, as it were, an after-dinner's sleep,
Dreaming on both; for all thy blessed youth
Becomes as aged, and doth beg the alms
Of palsied eld; and when thou art old, and rich,
Thou hast neither heat, affection, limb, nor beauty,
To make thy riches pleasant. What's yet in this
That bears the name of life? Yet in this life
Lie hid more thousand deaths; yet death we fear,
That makes these odds all even.
Claud. I humbly thank you.
To sue to live, I find, I seek to die:
And seeking death, find life: Let it come on.

Enter Isabella.

Isab. What, ho! Peace here; grace and good company!
Prov. Who's there? come in; the wish deserves a welcome.
Duke. Dear sir, ere long I'll visit you again.
Claud. Most holy sir, I thank you.
Isab. My business is a word or two with Claudio.
Prov. And very welcome. Look, signior, here's your sister.
Duke. Provost, a word with you.
Prov. As many as you please.
Duke. Bring me to hear them speak, where I may be conceal'd,
Yet hear them. [*Exeunt* Duke *and* Provost.
Claud. Now, sister, what's the comfort?
Isab. Why, as all comforts are, most good indeed:
Lord Angelo, having affairs to heaven,
Intends you for his swift embassador,
Where you shall be an everlasting leiger:
Therefore your best appointment make with speed;
To-morrow you set on.
Claud. Is there no remedy?
Isab. None, but such remedy, as to save a head,
To cleave a heart in twain.
Claud. But is there any?
Isab. Yes, brother, you may live;
There is a devilish mercy in the judge,
If you'll implore it, that will free your life,
But fetter you till death.
Claud. Perpetual durance?
Isab. Ay, just, perpetual durance; a restraint,
Though all the world's vastidity you had,
To a determined scope.
Claud. But in what nature?
Isab. In such a one as (you consenting to't)
Would bark your honour from that trunk you bear,
And leave you naked.
Claud. Let me know the point.
Isab. O, I do fear thee, Claudio; and I quake,
Lest thou a feverous life should'st entertain,
And six or seven winters more respect
Than a perpetual honour. Dar'st thou die?
The sense of death is most in apprehension;
And the poor beetle that we tread upon,
In corporal sufferance finds a pang as great
As when a giant dies.
Claud. Why give you me this shame?
Think you I can a resolution fetch
From flowery tenderness? If I must die,
I will encounter darkness as a bride,
And hug it in mine arms.
Isab. There spake my brother; there my father's grave
Did utter forth a voice! Yes, thou must die:
Thou art too noble to conserve a life
In base appliances. This outward-sainted deputy,—
Whose settled visage and deliberate word
Nips youth i' the head, and follies doth enmew,
As falcon doth the fowl,—is yet a devil;
His filth within being cast, he would appear
A pond as deep as hell.
Claud. The princely Angelo?
Isab. O, 'tis the cunning livery of hell,
The damned'st body to invest and cover
In princely guards! Dost thou think, Claudio,
If I would yield him my virginity,
Thou might'st be freed?
Claud. O, heavens! it cannot be.
Isab. Yes, he would give it thee, from this rank offence,
So to offend him still: This night's the time
That I should do what I abhor to name,
Or else thou diest to-morrow.
Claud. Thou shalt not do't.
Isab. O, were it but my life,
I'd throw it down for your deliverance
As frankly as a pin.
Claud. Thanks, dear Isabel.
Isab. Be ready, Claudio, for your death to-morrow.
Claud. Yes.—Has he affections in him,
That thus can make him bite the law by the nose,
When he would force it? Sure it is no sin;
Or of the deadly seven it is the least.
Isab. Which is the least?
Claud. If it were damnable, he being so wise,
Why, would he for the momentary trick,
Be perdurably fin'd?—O Isabel!
Isab. What says my brother?
Claud. Death is a fearful thing.
Isab. And shamed life a hateful.
Claud. Ay, but to die, and go we know not where;
To lie in cold obstruction, and to rot:
This sensible warm motion to become
A kneaded clod; and the delighted spirit

To bathe in fiery floods, or to reside
In thrilling regions of thick-ribbed ice;
To be imprison'd in the viewless winds,
And blown with restless violence round about
The pendent world; or to be worse than worst
Of those, that lawless and uncertain thoughts
Imagine howling!—'tis too horrible!
The weariest and most loathed worldly life,
That age, ach, penury, and imprisonment
Can lay on nature, is a paradise
To what we fear of death.

Isab. Alas! alas!

Claud. Sweet sister, let me live:
What sin you do to save a brother's life,
Nature dispenses with the deed so far,
That it becomes a virtue.

Isab. O, you beast!
O, faithless coward! O, dishonest wretch!
Wilt thou be made a man out of my vice?
Is't not a kind of incest, to take life
From thine own sister's shame? What should I think?
Heaven shield, my mother play'd my father fair?
For such a warped slip of wilderness
Ne'er issued from his blood. Take my defiance:
Die; perish! might but my bending down
Reprieve thee from thy fate, it should proceed:
I'll pray a thousand prayers for thy death,
No word to save thee.

Claud. Nay, hear me, Isabel.

Isab. O, fye, fye, fye!
Thy sin's not accidental, but a trade:
Mercy to thee would prove itself a bawd:
'Tis best that thou diest quickly. [*Going.*

Claud. O hear me, Isabella.

Re-enter Duke.

Duke. Vouchsafe a word, young sister, but one word.

Isab. What is your will?

Duke. Might you dispense with your leisure, I would by and by have some speech with you: the satisfaction I would require, is likewise your own benefit.

Isab. I have no superfluous leisure; my stay must be stolen out of other affairs; but I will attend you awhile.

Duke. [*To* CLAUDIO, *aside.*] Son, I have overheard what hath past between you and your sister. Angelo had never the purpose to corrupt her; only he hath made an essay of her virtue, to practise his judgment with the disposition of natures: she having the truth of honour in her, hath made him that gracious denial which he is most glad to receive: I am confessor to Angelo, and I know this to be true; therefore prepare yourself to death: Do not satisfy your resolution with hopes that are fallible: to-morrow you must die; go to your knees, and make ready.

Claud. Let me ask my sister pardon. I am so out of love with life, that I will sue to be rid of it.

Duke. Hold you there: Farewell.

[*Exit* CLAUDIO.

Re-enter Provost.

Provost, a word with you.

Prov. What's your will, father?

Duke. That now you are come, you will be gone: Leave me awhile with the maid; my mind promises with my habit, no loss shall touch her by my company.

Prov. In good time. [*Exit* Provost.

Duke. The hand that hath made you fair, hath made you good: the goodness, that is cheap in beauty, makes beauty brief in goodness; but grace, being the soul of your complexion, should keep the body of it ever fair. The assault that Angelo hath made to you, fortune hath convey'd to my understanding; and, but that frailty hath examples for his falling, I should wonder at Angelo. How would you do to content this substitute, and to save your brother?

Isab. I am now going to resolve him: I had rather my brother die by the law, than my son should be unlawfully born. But O, how much is the good duke deceived in Angelo! If ever he return, and I can speak to him, I will open my lips in vain, or discover his government.

Duke. That shall not be much amiss: Yet, as the matter now stands, he will avoid your accusation; he made trial of you only.—Therefore, fasten your ear on my advisings; to the love I have in doing good, a remedy presents itself. I do make myself believe, that you may most uprighteously do a poor wronged lady a merited benefit; redeem your brother from the angry law; do no stain to your own gracious person; and much please the absent duke, if peradventure, he shall ever return to have hearing of this business.

Isab. Let me hear you speak further; I have spirit to do any thing that appears not foul in the truth of my spirit.

Duke. Virtue is bold, and goodness never fearful. Have you not heard speak of Mariana the sister of Frederick, the great soldier, who miscarried at sea?

Isab. I have heard of the lady, and good words went with her name.

Duke. Her should this Angelo have married; was affianced to her by oath, and the nuptial appointed: between which time of the contract, and limit of the solemnity, her brother Frederick was wrecked at sea, having in that perish'd vessel the dowry of his sister. But mark, how heavily this befell to the poor gentlewoman: there she lost a noble and renowned brother, in his love toward her ever most kind and natural; with him the portion and sinew of her fortune, her marriage dowry; with both, her combinate husband, this well-seeming Angelo.

Isab. Can this be so? Did Angelo so leave her?

Duke. Left her in tears, and dry'd not one of them with his comfort; swallowed his vows whole, pretending, in her, discoveries of dishonour: in few, bestowed her on her own lamentation, which she yet wears for his sake; and he, a marble to her tears, is washed with them, but relents not.

Isab. What a merit were it in death, to take this poor maid from the world! What corruption in this life, that it will let this man live!—But how out of this can she avail?

Duke. It is a rupture that you may easily heal: and the cure of it not only saves your brother, but keeps you from dishonour in doing it.

Isab. Show me how, good father.

Duke. This forenamed maid hath yet in her the continuance of her first affection; his unjust unkindness, that in all reason should have quenched her love, hath, like an impediment in the current, made it more violent and unruly. Go you to Angelo: answer his requiring with a plausible obedience; agree with his demands to the point: only refer yourself to this advantage,—first, that your stay with him may not be long; that the time may have all shadow and silence in it; and the place answer to convenience: this being granted in course, now follows all. We shall advise this wronged maid to stead up your appointment, go in your place; if the encounter acknowledge itself hereafter, it may compel him to her recompense: and here, by this, is your brother saved, your honour untainted, the poor Mariana advantaged, and the corrupt deputy scaled. The maid will I frame, and make fit for his attempt. If you think well to carry this as you may, the doubleness of the benefit defends the deceit from reproof. What think you of it?

Isab. The image of it gives me content already; and, I trust, it will grow to a most prosperous perfection.

Duke. It lies much in your holding up: Haste you speedily to Angelo; if for this night he entreat you to his bed, give him promise of satisfaction. I will presently to St. Luke's; there, at the moated grange, resides this dejected Mariana: At that place call upon me; and dispatch with Angelo, that it may be quickly.

Isab. I thank you for this comfort: Fare you well, good father. [*Exeunt severally.*

SCENE II. *The Street before the Prison.*

Enter Duke, *as a Friar; to him* ELBOW, Clown, *and* Officers.

Elb. Nay, if there be no remedy for it, but that you will needs buy and sell men and women like beasts, we shall have all the world drink brown and white bastard.

Duke. O, heavens! what stuff is here?

Clo. 'Twas never merry world, since of two usuries, the merriest was put down, and the worser allow'd, by order of law, a furr'd gown to keep him warm; and furr'd with fox and lamb-skins too, to signify, that craft, being richer than innocency, stands for the facing.

Elb. Come your way, sir:—Bless you, good father friar.

Duke. And you, good brother father: What offence hath this man made you, sir?

Elb. Marry, sir, he hath offended the law: and, sir, we take him to be a thief too, sir; for we have found upon him, sir, a strange picklock, which we have sent to the deputy.

Duke. Fye, sirrah; a bawd, a wicked bawd!
The evil that thou causest to be done,
That is thy means to live: Do thou but think
What 'tis to cram a maw, or clothe a back,
From such a filthy vice: say to thyself,—
From their abominable and beastly touches
I drink, I eat, array myself, and live.
Canst thou believe thy living is a life,
So stinkingly depending? Go, mend, go, mend.

Clo. Indeed, it does stink in some sort, sir; but yet, sir, I would prove——

Duke. Nay, if the devil have given thee proofs for sin,
Thou wilt prove his. Take him to prison, officer;
Correction and instruction must both work,
Ere this rude beast will profit.

Elb. He must before the deputy, sir; he has given him warning: the deputy cannot abide a whoremaster: if he be a whoremonger, and comes before him, he were as good go a mile on his errand.

Duke. That we were all, as some would seem to be,
Free from our faults, as faults from seeming free!

Enter LUCIO.

Elb. His neck will come to your waist, a cord, sir.

Clo. I spy comfort; I cry, bail: Here's a gentleman, and a friend of mine.

Lucio. How now, noble Pompey? What, at the heels of Cæsar? Art thou led in triumph? What, is there none of Pygmalion's images, newly made woman, to be had now, for putting the hand in the pocket and extracting it clutch'd? What reply? Ha? What say'st thou to this tune, matter, and method? Is't not drown'd i' the last rain? Ha? What say'st thou, trot? Is the world as it was, man? Which is the way? Is it sad, and few words? Or how? The trick of it?

Duke. Still thus, and thus! still worse!

Lucio. How doth my dear morsel, thy mistress? Procures she still? Ha?

Clo. Troth, sir, she hath eaten up all her beef, and she is herself in the tub.

Lucio. Why, 'tis good; it is the right of it; it must be so: Ever your fresh whore, and your powder'd bawd: an unshunn'd consequence; it must be so: Art going to prison, Pompey?

Clo. Yes, 'faith, sir.

Lucio. Why, 'tis not amiss, Pompey: Farewell: Go; say, I sent thee thither. For debt, Pompey? Or how?

Elb. For being a bawd, for being a bawd.

Lucio. Well, then imprison him: If imprisonment be the due of a bawd, why, 'tis his right: Bawd is he, doubtless, and of antiquity too; bawd-born. Farewell, good Pompey: Commend me to the prison, Pompey; You will turn good husband now, Pompey; you will keep the house.

Clo. I hope, sir, your good worship will be my bail.

Lucio. No, indeed, will I not, Pompey; it is not the wear. I will pray, Pompey, to increase your bondage: if you take it not patiently, why your mettle is the more: Adieu, trusty Pompey.—Bless you, friar.

Duke. And you.

Lucio. Does Bridget paint still, Pompey? Ha?

Elb. Come your ways, sir; come.

Clo. You will not bail me then, sir?

Lucio. Then, Pompey? nor now.—What news abroad, friar? What news?

Elb. Come your ways, sir; come.

Lucio. Go,—to kennel, Pompey, go:

[*Exeunt* ELBOW, Clown, *and* Officers.

What news, friar, of the duke?

Duke. I know none: Can you tell me of any?

Lucio. Some say, he is with the emperor of Russia; other some, he is in Rome: But where is he, think you?

Duke. I know not where: But wheresoever, I wish him well.

Lucio. It was a mad fantastical trick of him, to steal from the state, and usurp the beggary he was never born to. Lord Angelo dukes it well in his absence; he puts transgression to't.

Duke. He does well in't.

Lucio. A little more lenity to lechery would do no harm in him: something too crabbed that way, friar.

Duke. It is too general a vice, and severity must cure it.

Lucio. Yes, in good sooth, the vice is of a great kindred; it is well ally'd: but it is impossible to extirp it quite, friar, till eating and drinking be put down. They say, this Angelo was not made by man and woman, after the downright way of creation: Is it true, think you?

Duke. How should he be made then?

Lucio. Some report a sea-maid spawn'd him:—Some that he was begot between two stockfishes:—But it is certain, that when he makes water his urine is congeal'd ice; that I know to be true: and he is a motion ungenerative, that's infallible.

Duke. You are pleasant, sir; and speak apace.

Lucio. Why, what a ruthless thing is this in him, for the rebellion of a cod-piece, to take away the life of a man? Would the duke, that is absent, have done this? Ere he would have hang'd a man for the getting a hundred bastards, he would have paid for the nursing of a thousand: He had some feeling of the sport; he knew the service, and that instructed him to mercy.

Duke. I never heard the absent duke much detected for women; he was not inclined that way.

Lucio. O, sir, you are deceived.

Duke. 'Tis not possible.

Lucio. Who? not the duke? yes, your beggar of fifty;—and his use was, to put a ducat in her clack-dish: the duke had crotchets in him: He would be drunk too; that let me inform you.

Duke. You do him wrong, surely.

Lucio. Sir, I was an inward of his: A shy fellow was the duke: and I believe, I know the cause of his withdrawing.

Duke. What, I pr'ythee, might be the cause?

Lucio. No,—pardon;—'tis a secret must be lock'd within the teeth and the lips: but this I can let you understand,—The greater file of the subject held the duke to be wise.

Duke. Wise? why, no question but he was.

Lucio. A very superficial, ignorant, unweighing fellow.

Duke. Either this is envy in you, folly, or mistaking; the very stream of his life, and the business he hath helmed, must, upon a warranted need, give him a better proclamation. Let him be but testimonied in his own bringings forth, and he shall appear to the envious, a scholar, a statesman, and a soldier: Therefore, you speak unskilfully; or, if your knowledge be more, it is much darkened in your malice.

Lucio. Sir, I know him, and I love him.

Duke. Love talks with better knowledge, and knowledge with dearer love.

Lucio. Come, sir, I know what I know.

Duke. I can hardly believe that, since you know not what you speak. But, if ever the duke return (as our prayers are he may), let me desire you to make your answer before him: If it be honest you have spoke, you have courage to maintain it: I am bound to call upon you; and, I pray you, your name?

Lucio. Sir, my name is Lucio; well known to the duke.

Duke. He shall know you better, sir, if I may live to report you.

Lucio. I fear you not.

Duke. O, you hope the duke will return no more; or you imagine me too unhurtful an opposite. But, indeed, I can do you little harm; you'll forswear this again.

Lucio. I'll be hang'd first: thou art deceived in me, friar. But no more of this: Canst thou tell if Claudio die to-morrow, or no?

Duke. Why should he die, sir?

Lucio. Why? for filling a bottle with a tundish. I would, the duke, we talk of, were return'd again: this ungenitur'd agent will unpeople the province with continency; sparrows must not build in his house-eaves, because they are lecherous. The duke yet would have dark deeds darkly answered; he would never bring them to light: 'would, he were return'd! Marry, this Claudio is condemn'd for untrussing. Farewell, good friar; I pr'ythee, pray for me. The duke, I say to thee again, would eat mutton on Fridays. He's now past it; yet, and I say to thee, he would mouth with a beggar, though she smelt brown bread and garlick: say, that I said so. Farewell. [*Exit.*

Duke. No might nor greatness in mortality
Can censure 'scape; back-wounding calumny
The whitest virtue strikes: What king so strong,
Can tie the gall up in the slanderous tongue?
But who comes here?

Enter ESCALUS, Provost, Bawd, *and* Officers.

Escal. Go, away with her to prison.

Bawd. Good my lord, be good to me; your honour is accounted a merciful man: good my lord.

Escal. Double and treble admonition, and still forfeit in the same kind? This would make mercy swear, and play the tyrant.

Prov. A bawd of eleven years continuance, may it please your honour.

Bawd. My lord, this is one Lucio's information against me: mistress Kate Keep-down was with child by him in the duke's time, he promised her marriage; his child is a year and a quarter old, come Philip and Jacob: I have kept it myself; and see how he goes about to abuse me.

Escal. That fellow is a fellow of much licence:—let him be called before us.—Away with her to prison: Go to; no more words. [*Exeunt* Bawd *and* Officers.] Provost, my brother Angelo will not be alter'd, Claudio must die to-morrow: let him be furnished with divines, and have all charitable preparation: if my brother wrought by my pity, it should not be so with him.

Prov. So please you, this friar hath been with him, and advised him for the entertainment of death.

Escal. Good even, good father.

Duke. Bliss and goodness on you!

Escal. Of whence are you?

Duke. Not of this country, though my chance is now
To use it for my time: I am a brother
Of gracious order, late come from the see,
In special business from his holiness.

Escal. What news abroad i' the world?

Duke. None, but that there is so great a fever on goodness, that the dissolution of it must cure it: novelty is only in request; and it is as dangerous to be aged in any kind of course, as it is virtuous to be constant in any undertaking. There is scarce truth enough alive, to make societies secure; but security enough, to make fellowships accurs'd: much upon this riddle runs the wisdom of the world. This news is old enough, yet it is every day's news. I pray you, sir, of what disposition was the duke?

Escal. One, that, above all other strifes, contended especially to know himself.

Duke. What pleasure was he given to?

Escal. Rather rejoicing to see another merry, than merry at any thing which professed to make him rejoice: a gentleman of all temperance. But leave we him to his events, with a prayer they may prove prosperous; and let me desire to know how you find Claudio prepared. I am made to understand, that you have lent him visitation.

Duke. He professes to have received no sinister measure from his judge, but most willingly humbles himself to the determination of justice: yet had he framed to himself, by the instruction of his frailty, many deceiving promises of life; which I, by my good leisure, have discredited to him, and now is he resolved to die.

Escal. You have paid the heavens your function, and the prisoner the very debt of your calling. I have labour'd for the poor gentleman, to the extremest shore of my modesty; but my brother justice have I found so severe, that he hath forced me to tell him, he is indeed —justice.

Duke. If his own life answer the straitness of his proceeding, it shall become him well; wherein, if he chance to fail, he hath sentenced himself.

Escal. I am going to visit the prisoner: Fare you well.

Duke. Peace be with you!

[*Exeunt* ESCALUS *and* Provost.

He, who the sword of heaven will bear,
Should be as holy as severe;
Pattern in himself to know,
Grace to stand, and virtue go;
More nor less to others paying,
Than by self-offences weighing.
Shame to him, whose cruel striking
Kills for faults of his own liking!
Twice treble shame on Angelo,
To weed my vice, and let his grow!
O, what may man within him hide,
Though angel on the outward side!
How may likeness, made in crimes,
Mocking, practice on the times,
To draw with idle spiders' strings
Most pond'rous and substantial things!
Craft against vice I must apply:
With Angelo to-night shall lie
His old betrothed, but despised;
So disguise shall, by the disguis'd,
Pay with falsehood false exacting,
And perform an old contracting. [*Exit.*

ACT IV.

SCENE I. *A Room in* Mariana's *House.*

MARIANA *discovered sitting; a* Boy *singing.*

SONG.

Take, oh take those lips away,
That so sweetly were forsworn;
And those eyes, the break of day,
Lights that do mislead the morn:
But my kisses bring again,
bring again,
Seals of love, but seal'd in vain,
seal'd in vain.

Mari. Break off thy song, and haste thee quick away;
Here comes a man of comfort, whose advice
Hath often still'd my brawling discontent.—
[*Exit* Boy.

Enter Duke.

I cry you mercy, sir; and well could wish
You had not found me here so musical:
Let me excuse me, and believe me so,—
My mirth it much displeas'd, but pleas'd my woe.

Duke. 'Tis good: though musick oft hath such a charm,
To make bad, good, and good provoke to harm.
I pray you, tell me, hath any body inquired for me here to-day? much upon this time have I promis'd here to meet.

Mari. You have not been inquired after: I have sat here all day.

Enter ISABELLA.

Duke. I do constantly believe you:—The time is come, even now. I shall crave your forbearance a little; may be, I will call upon you anon, for some advantage to yourself.

Mari. I am always bound to you. [*Exit.*

Duke. Very well met, and welcome.
What is the news from this good deputy?

Isab. He hath a garden circummur'd with brick,
Whose western side is with a vineyard back'd;
And to that vineyard is a planched gate,
That makes his opening with this bigger key:
This other doth command a little door,
Which from the vineyard to the garden leads;
There have I made my promise to call on him,
Upon the heavy middle of the night.

Duke. But shall you on your knowledge find this way?

Isab. I have ta'en a due and wary note upon't;
With whispering and most guilty diligence,
In action all of precept, he did show me
The way twice o'er.

Duke. Are there no other tokens
Between you 'greed, concerning her observance?

Isab. No, none, but only a repair i' the dark;
And that I have possess'd him, my most stay
Can be but brief: for I have made him know,
I have a servant comes with me along,
That stays upon me; whose persuasion is,
I come about my brother.

Duke. 'Tis well borne up.
I have not yet made known to Mariana
A word of this:—What, ho! within! come forth!

Re-enter MARIANA.

I pray you, be acquainted with this maid;
She comes to do you good.

Isab. I do desire the like.

Duke. Do you persuade yourself that I respect you?

Mari. Good friar, I know you do; and have found it.

Duke. Take then this your companion by the hand,
Who hath a story ready for your ear:
I shall attend your leisure; but make haste;
The vaporous night approaches.

Mari. Will't please you walk aside?
[*Exeunt* MARIANA *and* ISABELLA.

Duke. O place and greatness, millions of false eyes
Are stuck upon thee! volumes of report
Run with these false and most contrarious quests
Upon thy doings? thousand 'scapes of wit
Make thee the father of their idle dream,
And rack thee in their fancies?—Welcome! How agreed?

Re-enter MARIANA *and* ISABELLA.

Isab. She'll take the enterprise upon her, father,
If you advise it.

Duke. It is not my consent,
But my entreaty too.

Isab. Little have you to say,
When you depart from him, but, soft and low,
Remember now my brother.

Mari. Fear me not.

Duke. Nor, gentle daughter, fear you not at all:
He is your husband on a pre-contract:
To bring you thus together, 'tis no sin;
Sith that the justice of your title to him
Doth flourish the deceit. Come, let us go;
Our corn's to reap, for yet our tilth's to sow.
[*Exeunt.*

SCENE II. *A Room in the Prison.*

Enter Provost *and* Clown.

Prov. Come hither, sirrah: Can you cut off a man's head?

Clo. If the man be a bachelor, sir, I can: but if he be a married man, he is his wife's head, and I can never cut off a woman's head.

Prov. Come, sir, leave me your snatches, and yield me a direct answer. To-morrow morning are to die Claudio and Barnardine: Here is in our prison a common executioner, who in his office lacks a helper: if you will take it on you to assist him, it shall redeem you from your gyves; if not, you shall have your full time of imprisonment, and your deliverance with an unpitied whipping; for you have been a notorious bawd.

Clo. Sir, I have been an unlawful bawd, time out of mind; but yet I will be content to be a lawful hangman. I would be glad to receive some instruction from my fellow partner.

Prov. What ho, Abhorson! Where's Abhorson, there?

Enter ABHORSON.

Abhor. Do you call, sir?

Prov. Sirrah, here's a fellow will help you to-morrow in your execution: If you think it meet, compound with him by the year, and let him abide here with you; if not, use him for the present, and dismiss him: He cannot plead his estimation with you; he hath been a bawd.

Abhor. A bawd, sir? Fye upon him, he will discredit our mystery.

Prov. Go to, sir; you weigh equally; a feather will turn the scale. [*Exit.*

Clo. Pray, sir, by your good favour (for, surely, sir, a good favour you have, but that you have a hanging look), do you call, sir, your occupation a mystery?

Abhor. Ay, sir; a mystery.

Clo. Painting, sir, I have heard say, is a mystery; and your whores, sir, being members of my occupation, using painting, do prove my occupation a mystery: but what mystery there should be in hanging, if I should be hang'd, I cannot imagine.

Abhor. Sir, it is a mystery.

Clo. Proof.

Abhor. Every true man's apparel fits your thief: If it be too little for your thief, your true man thinks it big enough; if it be too big for your thief, your thief thinks it little enough: so every true man's apparel fits your thief.

Re-enter Provost.

Prov. Are you agreed?

Clo. Sir, I will serve him; for I do find, your hangman is a more penitent trade than your bawd; he doth oftener ask forgiveness.

Prov. You, sirrah, provide your block and your axe, to-morrow four o'clock.

Abhor. Come on, bawd; I will instruct thee in my trade; follow.

Clo. I do desire to learn, sir; and, I hope, if you have occasion to use me for your own turn, you shall find me yare; for, truly, sir, for your kindness, I owe you a good turn.

Prov. Call hither Barnardine and Claudio:
[*Exeunt* Clown *and* ABHORSON.
One has my pity; not a jot the other,
Being a murderer, though he were my brother.

Enter CLAUDIO.

Look, here's the warrant, Claudio, for thy death:
'Tis now dead midnight, and by eight to-morrow
Thou must be made immortal. Where's Barnardine?

Claud. As fast lock'd up in sleep, as guiltless labour
When it lies starkly in the traveller's bones:
He will not wake.

Prov. Who can do good on him?
Well, go, prepare yourself. But hark, what noise?
[*Knocking within.*
Heaven give your spirits comfort! [*Exit* CLAUDIO.] By and by:—
I hope it is some pardon, or reprieve,
For the most gentle Claudio.—Welcome, father.

Enter DUKE.

Duke. The best and wholesomest spirits of the night
Envelope you, good Provost! Who call'd here of late?

Prov. None, since the curfew rung.

Duke. Not Isabel?

Prov. No.

Duke. They will then, ere 't be long.

Prov. What comfort is for Claudio?

Duke. There's some in hope.

Prov. It is a bitter deputy.

Duke. Not so, not so; his life is parallel'd
Even with the stroke and line of his great justice;
He doth with holy abstinence subdue
That in himself, which he spurs on his power
To qualify in others: were he meal'd
With that which he corrects, then were he tyrannous;
But this being so, he's just.—Now are they come.—
[*Knocking within.*—Provost *goes out.*
This is a gentle provost: Seldom when
The steeled gaoler is the friend of men.—
How now? What noise? That spirit's possess'd with haste,
That wounds the unsisting postern with these strokes.

Provost *returns, speaking to one at the door.*

Prov. There he must stay, until the officer
Arise to let him in; he is call'd up.

Duke. Have you no countermand for Claudio yet,
But he must die to-morrow?

Prov. None, sir, none.

Duke. As near the dawning, Provost, as it is,
You shall hear more ere morning.

Prov. Happily,
You something know; yet, I believe, there comes
No countermand; no such example have we:
Besides, upon the very siege of justice,
Lord Angelo hath to the publick ear
Profess'd the contrary.

Enter a Messenger.

Duke. This is his lordship's man.

Prov. And here comes Claudio's pardon.

Mess. My lord hath sent you this note; and by me this further charge, that you swerve not from the smallest article of it, neither in time, matter, or other circumstance. Good-morrow; for, as I take it, it is almost day.

Prov. I shall obey him. [*Exit* Messenger.

Duke. This is his pardon; purchas'd by such sin, [*Aside.*
For which the pardoner himself is in:
Hence hath offence his quick celerity,
When it is borne in high authority:
When vice makes mercy, mercy's so extended,
That for the fault's love, is the offender friended.—
Now, sir, what news?

Prov. I told you: Lord Angelo, be-like, thinking me remiss in mine office, awakens me with this unwonted putting on: methinks, strangely; for he hath not used it before.

Duke. 'Pray you, let's hear.

Prov. [Reads.] *Whatsoever you may hear to the contrary, let Claudio be executed by four of the clock; and, in the afternoon, Barnardine: for my better satisfaction, let me have Claudio's head sent me by five. Let this be duly performed; with a thought, that more depends on it than we must yet deliver. Thus fail not to do your office, as you will answer it at your peril.*
What say you to this, sir?

Duke. What is that Barnardine, who is to be executed in the afternoon?

Prov. A Bohemian born; but here nursed up and bred: one that is a prisoner nine years old.

Duke. How came it that the absent duke had not either deliver'd him to his liberty, or executed him? I have heard, it was ever his manner to do so.

Prov. His friends still wrought reprieves for him: And, indeed, his fact, till now in the government of Lord Angelo, came not to an undoubtful proof.

Duke. Is it now apparent?

Prov. Most manifest, and not denied by himself.

Duke. Hath he borne himself penitently in prison? How seems he to be touch'd?

Prov. A man that apprehends death no more dreadfully, but as a drunken sleep: careless, reckless, and fearless of what's past, present, or to come; insensible of mortality, and desperately mortal.

Duke. He wants advice.

Prov. He will hear none: he hath evermore had the liberty of the prison; give him leave to escape hence, he would not: drunk many times a day, if not many days entirely drunk. We have very often awaked him, as if to carry him to execution, and show'd him a seeming warrant for it: it hath not moved him at all.

Duke. More of him anon. There is written in your brow, Provost, honesty and constancy: if I read it not truly, my ancient skill beguiles me; but in the boldness of my cunning, I will lay myself in hazard. Claudio, whom here you have a warrant to execute, is no greater forfeit to the law than Angelo who hath sentenced him: To make you understand this in a manifested effect, I crave but four days respite; for the which you are to do me both a present and a dangerous courtesy.

Prov. 'Pray, sir, in what?

Duke. In the delaying death.

Prov. Alack! how may I do it? having the hour limited; and an express command, under penalty, to deliver his head in the view of Angelo? I may make my case as Claudio's, to cross this in the smallest.

Duke. By the vow of mine order, I warrant you, if my instructions may be your guide. Let this Barnardine be this morning executed, and his head borne to Angelo.

Prov. Angelo hath seen them both, and will discover the favour.

Duke. O, death's a great disguiser: and you may add to it. Shave the head, and tie the beard; and say, it was the desire of the penitent to be so bared before his death: You know, the course is common. If any thing fall to you upon this, more than thanks and good fortune, by the saint whom I profess, I will plead against it with my life.

Prov. Pardon me, good father; it is against my oath.

Duke. Were you sworn to the duke, or to the deputy?

Prov. To him, and to his substitutes.

Duke. You will think you have made no offence, if the duke avouch the justice of your dealing?

Prov. But what likelihood is in that?

Duke. Not a resemblance, but a certainty. Yet since I see you fearful, that neither my coat, integrity, nor my persuasion, can with ease attempt you, I will go further than I meant, to pluck all fears out of you. Look you, sir, here is the hand and seal of the duke. You know the character, I doubt not; and the signet is not strange to you.

Prov. I know them both.

Duke. The contents of this is the return of the duke; you shall anon overread it at your pleasure; where you shall find, within these two days he will be here. This is a thing that Angelo knows not: for he this very day receives letters of strange tenor; perchance, of the duke's death; perchance, entering into some monastery; but, by chance, nothing of what is writ. Look, the unfolding star calls up the shepherd. Put not yourself into amazement, how these things should be: all difficulties are but easy when they are known. Call your executioner, and off with Barnardine's head: I will give him a present shrift, and advise him for a better place. Yet you are amazed; but this shall absolutely resolve you. Come away; it is almost clear dawn. [*Exeunt.*

SCENE III. *Another Room in the same.*

Enter Clown.

Clo. I am as well acquainted here, as I was in our house of profession: one would think it were mistress Overdone's own house, for here be many of her old customers. First, here's young master Rash; he's in for a commodity of brown paper and old ginger, ninescore and seventeen pounds; of which he made five marks, ready money: marry, then, ginger was not much in request, for the old women were all dead. Then is there here one master Caper, at the suit of master Three-pile the mercer, for some four suits of peach-colour'd satin, which now peaches him a beggar. Then have we here young Dizy, and young master Deep-vow, and master Copper-spur, and master Starve-lackey the rapier and dagger man, and young Drop-heir that kill'd lusty Pudding, and master Forthright the tilter, and brave master Shoe-tie the great traveller, and wild Half-can that stabb'd Pots, and, I think, forty more; all great doers in our trade, and are now for the Lord's sake.

Enter ABHORSON.

Abhor. Sirrah, bring Barnardine hither.

Clo. Master Barnardine! you must rise and be hang'd, master Barnardine!

Abhor. What, ho, Barnardine!

Barnar. [*Within.*] A pox o' your throats! Who makes that noise there? What are you?

Clo. Your friends, sir; the hangman: You must be so good, sir, to rise and be put to death.

Barnar. [*Within.*] Away, you rogue, away; I am sleepy.

Abhor. Tell him he must awake, and that quickly too.

Clo. 'Pray, master Barnardine, awake till you are executed, and sleep afterwards.

Abhor. Go in to him, and fetch him out.

Clo. He is coming, sir, he is coming; I hear his straw rustle.

Enter BARNARDINE.

Abhor. Is the axe upon the block, sirrah?

Clo. Very ready, sir.

Barnar. How now, Abhorson? what's the news with you?

Abhor. Truly, sir, I would desire you to clap into your prayers; for, look you, the warrant's come.

Barnar. You rogue, I have been drinking all night, I am not fitted for't.

Clo. O, the better, sir; for he that drinks all night, and is hanged betimes in the morning, may sleep the sounder all the next day.

Enter Duke.

Abhor. Look you, sir, here comes your ghostly father; Do we jest now, think you?

Duke. Sir, induced by my charity, and hearing how hastily you are to depart, I am come to advise you, comfort you, and pray with you.

Barnar. Friar, not I; I have been drinking hard all night, and I will have more time to prepare me, or they shall beat out my brains with billets: I will not consent to die this day, that's certain.

Duke. O, sir, you must: and therefore, I beseech you,
Look forward on the journey you shall go.

Barnar. I swear, I will not die to-day for any man's persuasion.

Duke. But hear you.——

Barnar. Not a word; if you have any thing to say to me, come to my ward; for thence will not I to-day. [*Exit.*

Enter Provost.

Duke. Unfit to live, or die: O, gravel heart!—
After him, fellows; bring him to the block.
[*Exeunt* ABHORSON *and* Clown.

Prov. Now, sir, how do you find the prisoner?

Duke. A creature unprepar'd, unmeet for death;
And, to transport him in the mind he is,
Were damnable.

Prov. Here in the prison, father,
There died this morning of a cruel fever
One Ragozine, a most notorious pirate,
A man of Claudio's years; his beard and head,
Just of his colour: What if we do omit
This reprobate, till he were well inclined;
And satisfy the deputy with the visage
Of Ragozine, more like to Claudio?

Duke. O, 'tis an accident that heaven provides!
Despatch it presently; the hour draws on
Prefix'd by Angelo; See, this be done,
And sent according to command; whiles I
Persuade this rude wretch willingly to die.

Prov. This shall be done, good father, presently.
But Barnardine must die this afternoon:
And how shall we continue Claudio,

To save me from the danger that might come,
If he were known alive?

Duke. Let this be done:—Put them in secret holds,
Both Barnardine and Claudio: Ere twice
The sun hath made his journal greeting to
The under generation, you shall find
Your safety manifested.

Prov. I am your free dependant.

Duke. Quick, despatch,
And send the head to Angelo. [*Exit* Provost.
Now will I write letters to Angelo,—
The provost, he shall bear them,—whose contents
Shall witness to him, I am near at home;
And that, by great injunctions, I am bound
To enter publickly: him I'll desire
To meet me at the consecrated fount,
A league below the city; and from thence,
By cold gradation and weal-balanced form,
We shall proceed with Angelo.

Re-enter Provost.

Prov. Here is the head; I'll carry it myself.

Duke. Convenient is it: Make a swift return;
For I would commune with you of such things,
That want no ear but yours.

Prov. I'll make all speed. [*Exit.*

Isab. [*Within.*] Peace, ho, be here!

Duke. The tongue of Isabel:—She's come to know,
If yet her brother's pardon be come hither:
But I will keep her ignorant of her good,
To make her heavenly comforts of despair,
When it is least expected.

Enter ISABELLA.

Isab. Ho, by your leave.

Duke. Good morning to you, fair and gracious daughter.

Isab. The better, given me by so holy a man.
Hath yet the deputy sent my brother's pardon?

Duke. He hath releas'd him, Isabel, from the world;
His head is off, and sent to Angelo.

Isab. Nay, but it is not so.

Duke. It is no other:
Show your wisdom, daughter, in your close patience.

Isab. O, I will to him, and pluck out his eyes.

Duke. You shall not be admitted to his sight.

Isab. Unhappy Claudio! Wretched Isabel!
Injurious world! Most damned Angelo!

Duke. This nor hurts him, nor profits you a jot;
Forbear it therefore; give your cause to heaven.
Mark what I say, which you shall find
By every syllable a faithful verity:
The duke comes home to-morrow;—nay, dry your eyes;
One of our convent, and his confessor,
Gives me this instance: Already he hath carried
Notice to Escalus and Angelo;
Who do prepare to meet him at the gates,
There to give up their power. If you can, pace your wisdom
In that good path that I would wish it go;
And you shall have your bosom on this wretch,
Grace of the duke, revenges to your heart,
And general honour.

Isab. I am directed by you.

Duke. This letter then to friar Peter give;
'Tis that he sent me of the duke's return:
Say, by this token, I desire his company
At Mariana's house to-night. Her cause, and yours,
I'll perfect him withal; and he shall bring you
Before the duke; and to the head of Angelo
Accuse him home, and home. For my poor self,
I am combined by a sacred vow,
And shall be absent. Wend you with this letter;
Command these fretting waters from your eyes
With a light heart; trust not my holy order,
If I pervert your course.—Who's here?

Enter LUCIO.

Lucio. Good even!
Friar, where is the Provost?

Duke. Not within, sir.

Lucio. O, pretty Isabella, I am pale at mine heart, to see thine eyes so red: thou must be patient: I am fain to dine and sup with water and bran; I dare not for my head fill my belly; one fruitful meal would set me to't: But they say the duke will be here to-morrow. By my troth, Isabel, I lov'd thy brother: if the old fantastical duke of dark corners had been at home, he had lived. [*Exit* ISABELLA.

Duke. Sir, the duke is marvellous little beholden to your reports; but the best is, he lives not in them.

Lucio. Friar, thou knowest not the duke so well as I do: he's a better woodman than thou takest him for.

Duke. Well, you'll answer this one day. Fare ye well.

Lucio. Nay, tarry; I'll go along with thee; I can tell thee pretty tales of the duke.

Duke. You have told me too many of him already, sir, if they be true; if not true, none were enough.

Lucio. I was once before him for getting a wench with child.

Duke. Did you such a thing?

Lucio. Yes, marry, did I; but was fain to forswear it; they would else have married me to the rotten medlar.

Duke. Sir, your company is fairer than honest: Rest you well.

Lucio. By my troth, I'll go with thee to the lane's end: If bawdy talk offend you, we'll have very little of it: Nay, friar, I am a kind of burr, I shall stick. [*Exeunt.*

SCENE IV. *A Room in* Angelo's *House.*

Enter ANGELO *and* ESCALUS.

Escal. Every letter he hath writ hath disvouch'd other.

Ang. In most uneven and distracted manner. His actions show much like to madness: 'pray heaven, his wisdom be not tainted! And why meet him at the gates, and re-deliver our authorities there?

Escal. I guess not.

Ang. And why should we proclaim it in an hour before his entering, that, if any crave redress of injustice, they should exhibit their petitions in the street?

Escal. He shows his reason for that: to have a despatch of complaints; and to deliver us from devices hereafter, which shall then have no power to stand against us.

Ang. Well, I beseech you, let it be proclaim'd:
Betimes i' the morn, I'll call you at your house:
Give notice to such men of sort and suit,
As are to meet him.

Escal. I shall, sir: fare you well. [*Exit.*

Ang. Good night.—
This deed unshapes me quite, makes me unpregnant,
And dull to all proceedings. A deflower'd maid!
And by an eminent body, that enforc'd
The law against it!—But that her tender shame
Will not proclaim against her maiden loss,
How might she tongue me? Yet reason dares her?—no:
For my authority bears a credent bulk,
That no particular scandal once can touch,
But it confounds the breather. He should have liv'd,

Save that his riotous youth, with dangerous sense,
Might, in the times to come, have ta'en revenge,
By so receiving a dishonour'd life,
With ransom of such shame. 'Would yet he had liv'd!
Alack, when once our grace we have forgot,
Nothing goes right; we would, and we would not. [*Exit.*

SCENE V. *Fields without the Town.*

Enter Duke *in his own habit, and* FRIAR PETER.

Duke. These letters at fit time deliver me. [*Giving letters.*
The provost knows our purpose, and our plot.
The matter being afoot, keep your instruction,
And hold you ever to our special drift;
Though sometimes you do blench from this to that,
As cause doth minister. Go, call at Flavius' house,
And tell him where I stay: give the like notice
To Valentinus, Rowland, and to Crassus,
And bid them bring the trumpets to the gate;
But send me Flavius first.
F. Peter. It shall be speeded well. [*Exit* Friar.

Enter VARRIUS.

Duke. I thank thee, Varrius; thou hast made good haste:
Come, we will walk: There's other of our friends
Will greet us here anon, my gentle Varrius. [*Exeunt.*

SCENE VI. *Street near the City Gate.*

Enter ISABELLA *and* MARIANA.

Isab. To speak so indirectly, I am loath;
I would say the truth; but to accuse him so,
That is your part: Yet I'm advis'd to do it;
He says, to 'vailfull purpose.
Mari. Be rul'd by him.
Isab. Besides, he tells me, that, if peradventure
He speak against me on the adverse side,
I should not think it strange; for 'tis a physick,
That's bitter to sweet end.
Mari. I would, friar Peter—
Isab. O, Peace; the friar is come.

Enter FRIAR PETER.

F. Peter. Come, I have found you out a stand most fit,
Where you may have such vantage on the duke,
He shall not pass you; Twice have the trumpets sounded;
The generous and gravest citizens
Have hent the gates, and very near upon
The duke is ent'ring; therefore hence, away. [*Exeunt.*

ACT V.

SCENE I. *A publick Place near the City Gate.*

MARIANA *(veil'd)*, ISABELLA, *and* PETER, *at a distance. Enter at opposite doors,* Duke, VARRIUS, Lords; ANGELO, ESCALUS, LUCIO, Provost, Officers, *and* Citizens.

Duke. My very worthy cousin, fairly met:—
Our old and faithful friend, we are glad to see you.
Ang. and Escal. Happy return be to your royal grace!
Duke. Many and hearty thankings to you both.
We have made inquiry of you; and we hear
Such goodness of your justice, that our soul
Cannot but yield you forth to publick thanks,
Forerunning more requital.
Ang. You make my bonds still greater.
Duke. O, your desert speaks loud; and I should wrong it,
To lock it in the wards of covert bosom,
When it deserves with characters of brass
A forted residence, 'gainst the tooth of time,
And razure of oblivion: Give me your hand,
And let the subject see, to make them know
That outward courtesies would fain proclaim
Favours that keep within.—Come, Escalus;
You must walk by us on our other hand;—
And good supporters are you.

PETER *and* ISABELLA *come forward.*

F. Peter. Now is your time; speak loud, and kneel before him.
Isab. Justice, O royal duke! Vail your regard
Upon a wrong'd, I'd fain have said, a maid!
O worthy prince, dishonour not your eye
By throwing it on any other object,
Till you have heard me in my true complaint,
And given me, justice, justice, justice, justice!
Duke. Relate your wrongs: In what? By whom? Be brief:
Here is Lord Angelo shall give you justice!
Reveal yourself to him.
Isab. O, worthy duke,
You bid me seek redemption of the devil:
Hear me yourself; for that which I must speak
Must either punish me, not being believ'd,
Or wring redress from you; hear me, O, hear me, here.
Ang. My lord, her wits, I fear me, are not firm:
She hath been a suitor to me for her brother,
Cut off by course of justice.
Isab. By course of justice!
Ang. And she will speak most bitterly, and strange.
Isab. Most strange, but yet most truly, will I speak:
That Angelo's forsworn; is it not strange?
That Angelo's a murderer; is't not strange?
That Angelo is an adulterous thief,
A hypocrite, a virgin-violator;
Is it not strange, and strange?
Duke. Nay, ten times strange.
Isab. It is not truer he is Angelo,
Than this is all as true as it is strange:
Nay, it is ten times true; for truth is truth
To the end of reckoning.
Duke. Away with her:—Poor soul,
She speaks this in the infirmity of sense.
Isab. O prince, I conjure thee, as thou believ'st
There is another comfort than this world,
That thou neglect me not, with that opinion
That I am touch'd with madness: make not impossible
That which but seems unlike: 'tis not impossible,
But one, the wicked'st caitiff on the ground,
May seem as shy, as grave, as just, as absolute,
As Angelo; even so may Angelo,
In all his dressings, characts, titles, forms,
Be an archvillain: believe it, royal prince,
If he be less, he's nothing; but he's more,
Had I more name for badness.
Duke. By mine honesty,
If she be mad (as I believe no other),
Her madness hath the oddest frame of sense,
Such a dependency of thing on thing,
As e'er I heard in madness.
Isab. O, gracious duke,
Harp not on that; nor do not banish reason
For inequality: but let your reason serve
To make the truth appear, where it seems hid;
And hide the false, seems true.
Duke. Many that are not mad,
Have, sure, more lack of reason.—What would you say?
Isab. I am the sister of one Claudio,
Condemn'd upon the act of fornication
To lose his head; condemn'd by Angelo:
I, in probation of a sisterhood,
Was sent to by my brother: One Lucio
As then the messenger;—
Lucio. That's I, an't like your grace:
I came to her from Claudio, and desir'd her

To try her gracious fortune with Lord Angelo,
For her poor brother's pardon.
Isab. That's he, indeed.
Duke. You were not bid to speak.
Lucio. No, my good lord;
Nor wish'd to hold my peace.
Duke. I wish you now then;
'Pray you, take note of it: and when you have
A business for yourself, pray heaven, you then
Be perfect.
Lucio. I warrant your honour.
Duke. The warrant's for yourself; take heed to it.
Isab. This gentleman told somewhat of my tale.
Lucio. Right.
Duke. It may be right; but you are in the wrong
To speak before your time.—Proceed.
Isab. I went
To this pernicious caitiff deputy.
Duke. That's somewhat madly spoken.
Isab. Pardon it:
The phrase is to the matter.
Duke. Mended again: the matter;—Proceed.
Isab. In brief,—to set the needless process by,
How I persuaded, how I pray'd, and kneel'd,
How he refell'd me, and how I reply'd;
(For this was of much length), the vile conclusion
I now begin with grief and shame to utter:
He would not, but by gift of my chaste body
To his concupiscible intemperate lust,
Release my brother; and, after much debatement,
My sisterly remorse confutes mine honour,
And I did yield to him. But the next morn betimes,
His purpose surfeiting, he sends a warrant
For my poor brother's head.
Duke. This is most likely!
Isab. O, that it were as like as it is true!
Duke. By heaven, fond wretch, thou know'st not what thou speak'st;
Or else thou art suborn'd against his honour,
In hateful practice: First, his integrity
Stands without blemish:—next, it imports no reason,
That with such vehemency he should pursue
Faults proper to himself: if he had so offended,
He would have weigh'd thy brother by himself,
And not have cut him off: Some one hath set you on;
Confess the truth, and say by whose advice
Thou cam'st here to complain.
Isab. And is this all?
Then, oh, you blessed ministers above,
Keep me in patience; and, with ripen'd time,
Unfold the evil which is here wrapt up
In countenance!—Heaven shield your grace from woe,
As I, thus wrong'd, hence unbelieved go!
Duke. I know, you'd fain be gone:—An officer!
To prison with her:—Shall we thus permit
A blasting and a scandalous breath to fall
On him so near us? This needs must be a practice.
—Who knew of your intent, and coming hither?
Isab. One that I would were here, friar Lodowick.
Duke. A ghostly father, belike:—Who knows that Lodowick?
Lucio. My lord, I know him; 'tis a meddling friar;
I do not like the man: had he been lay, my lord,
For certain words he spake against your grace
In your retirement, I had swing'd him soundly.
Duke. Words against me? This a good friar belike!
And to set on this wretched woman here
Against our substitute!—Let this friar be found.
Lucio. But yesternight, my lord, she and that friar
I saw them at the prison: a saucy friar,
A very scurvy fellow.
F. Peter. Blessed be your royal grace!
I have stood by, my lord, and I have heard
Your royal ear abus'd: First, hath this woman,
Most wrongfully accus'd your substitute;
Who is as free from touch or soil with her,
As she from one ungot.
Duke. We did believe no less.
Know you that friar Lodowick that she speaks of!
F. Peter. I know him for a man divine and holy;
Not scurvy nor a temporary medler,
As he's reported by this gentleman:
And, on my trust, a man that never yet
Did, as he vouches, misreport your grace.
Lucio. My lord, most villanously; believe it.
F. Peter. Well, he in time may come to clear himself;
But at this instant he is sick, my lord,
Of a strange fever: Upon his mere request
(Being come to knowledge that there was complaint
Intended 'gainst lord Angelo) came I hither,
To speak, as from his mouth, what he doth know
Is true, and false; and what he with his oath,
And all probation, will make up full clear,
Whensoever he's convented. First, for this woman
(To justify this worthy nobleman,
So vulgarly and personally accused);
Her shall you hear disproved to her eyes,
Till she herself confess it.
Duke. Good friar, let's hear it.
[Isabella *is carried off, guarded; and* Mariana *comes forward.*
Do you not smile at this, lord Angelo?—
O heaven! the vanity of wretched fools!—
Give us some seats.—Come, cousin Angelo;
In this I'll be impartial; be you judge
Of your own cause.—Is this the witness, friar?
First, let her show her face; and, after, speak.
Mari. Pardon, my lord; I will not show my face
Until my husband bid me.
Duke. What, are you married?
Mari. No, my lord.
Duke. Are you a maid?
Mari. No, my lord.
Duke. A widow then?
Mari. Neither, my lord?
Duke. Why, you
Are nothing then:—Neither maid, widow, nor wife?
Lucio. My lord, she may be a punk; for many of them are neither maid, widow, nor wife.
Duke. Silence that fellow; I would he had some cause
To prattle for himself.
Lucio. Well, my lord.
Mari. My lord, I do confess I ne'er was married;
And, I confess, besides, I am no maid:
I have known my husband; yet my husband knows not,
That ever he knew me.
Lucio. He was drunk then, my lord; it can be no better.
Duke. For the benefit of silence, 'would, thou wert so too.
Lucio. Well, my lord.
Duke. This is no witness for lord Angelo.
Mari. Now I come to't, my lord:
She, that accuses him of fornication,
In selfsame manner doth accuse my husband;
And charges him, my lord, with such a time,
When I'll depose I had him in mine arms,
With all the effect of love.
Ang. Charges she more than me?
Mari. Not that I know.
Duke. No? you say, your husband.
Mari. Why, just, my lord, and that is Angelo,
Who thinks, he knows, that he ne'er knew my body,
But knows, he thinks, that he knows Isabel's.

Ang. This is a strange abuse:—Let's see thy face.

Mari. My husband bids me; now I will unmask. [*Unveiling.*
This is that face, thou cruel Angelo,
Which, once thou swor'st, was worth the looking on:
This is the hand, which, with a vow'd contract,
Was fast belock'd in thine: this is the body
That took away the match from Isabel,
And did supply thee at thy garden-house,
In her imagin'd person.

Duke. Know you this woman?

Lucio. Carnally, she says.

Duke. Sirrah, no more.

Lucio. Enough, my lord.

Ang. My lord, I must confess, I know this woman;
And, five years since, there was some speech of marriage
Betwixt myself and her; which was broke off,
Partly, for that her promised proportions
Came short of composition; but, in chief,
For that her reputation was disvalued
In levity: since which time of five years,
I never spake with her, saw her, nor heard from her,
Upon my faith and honour.

Mari. Noble prince,
As there comes light from heaven, and words from breath,
As there is sense in truth, and truth in virtue,
I am affianc'd this man's wife, as strongly
As words could make up vows: and, my good lord,
But Tuesday night last gone, in his garden-house,
He knew me as a wife: As this is true
Let me in safety raise me from my knees;
Or else for ever be confixed here,
A marble monument!

Ang. I did but smile till now;
Now, good my lord, give me the scope of justice;
My patience here is touch'd: I do perceive,
These poor informal women are no more
But instruments of some more mightier member,
That sets them on: Let me have way, my lord,
To find this practice out.

Duke. Ay, with my heart;
And punish them unto your height of pleasure.—
Thou foolish friar; and thou pernicious woman,
Compact with her that's gone! think'st thou, thy oaths,
Though they would swear down each particular saint,
Were testimonies against his worth and credit,
That's seal'd in approbation?—You, lord Escalus,
Sit with my cousin; lend him your kind pains
To find out this abuse, whence 'tis deriv'd.—
There is another friar that set them on;
Let him be sent for.

F. Peter. 'Would, he were here, my lord; for he, indeed,
Hath set the women on to this complaint:
Your provost knows the place where he abides,
And he may fetch him.

Duke. Go, do it instantly.— [*Exit* Provost.
And you, my noble and well-warranted cousin,
Whom it concerns to hear this matter forth,
Do with your injuries as seems you best,
In any chastisement: I for a while
Will leave you; but stir not you, till you have well
Determined upon these slanderers.

Escal. My lord, we'll do it thoroughly.—[*Exit* Duke.] Signior Lucio, did not you say, you knew that friar Lodowick to be a dishonest person?

Lucio. *Cucullus non facit monachum:* honest in nothing, but in his clothes; and one that hath spoke most villanous speeches of the duke.

Escal. We shall entreat you to abide here till he come, and enforce them against him: we shall find this friar a notable fellow.

Lucio. As any in Vienna, on my word.

Escal. Call that same Isabel here once again; [*To an Attendant.*] I would speak with her; 'Pray you, my lord, give me leave to question; you shall see how I'll handle her.

Lucio. Not better than he, by her own report.

Escal. Say you?

Lucio. Marry, sir, I think if you handled her privately, she would sooner confess; perchance, publickly, she'll be ashamed.

Re-enter Officers, *with* ISABELLA, *the* Duke, *in the Friar's habit, and* Provost.

Escal. I will go darkly to work with her.

Lucio. That's the way; for women are light at midnight.

Escal. Come on, mistress: [*To* ISABELLA.] here's a gentlewoman denies all that you have said.

Lucio. My lord, here comes the rascal I spoke of; here with the provost.

Escal. In very good time:—speak not you to him, till we call upon you.

Lucio. Mum.

Escal. Come, sir: Did you set these women on to slander lord Angelo? they have confess'd you did.

Duke. 'Tis false.

Escal. How! know you where you are?

Duke. Respect to your great place! and let the devil
Be sometimes honour'd for his burning throne:—
Where is the duke? 'tis he should hear me speak.

Escal. The duke's in us; and we will hear you speak;
Look, you speak justly.

Duke. Boldly at least:—But O, poor souls,
Come you to seek the lamb here of the fox?
Good night to your redress. Is the duke gone?
Then is your cause gone too. The duke's unjust,
Thus to retort your manifest appeal,
And put your trial in the villain's mouth,
Which here you come to accuse.

Lucio. This is the rascal: this is he I spoke of.

Escal. Why, thou unreverend and unhallow'd friar!
Is't not enough, thou hast suborn'd these women
To accuse this worthy man; but in foul mouth,
And in the witness of his proper ear,
To call him villain?
And then to glance from him to the duke himself;
To tax him with injustice? Take him hence;
To the rack with him:—We'll touze you joint by joint,
But we will know this purpose:—What! unjust?

Duke. Be not so hot; the duke
Dare no more stretch this finger of mine, than he
Dare rack his own; his subject am I not,
Nor here provincial: My business in this state
Made me a looker-on here in Vienna,
Where I have seen corruption boil and bubble,
Till it o'errun the stew: laws for all faults;
But faults so countenanc'd, that the strong statutes
Stand like the forfeits in a barber's shop,
As much in mock as mark.

Escal. Slander to the state! Away with him to prison.

Ang. What can you vouch against him, signior Lucio?
Is this the man that you did tell us of?

Lucio. 'Tis he, my lord. Come hither, goodman bald-pate: Do you know me?

Duke. I remember you, sir, by the sound of your voice: I met you at the prison in the absence of the duke.

Lucio. O, did you so? and do you remember what you said of the duke.

Duke. Most notedly, sir.

Lucio. Do you so, sir? And was the duke a flesh-monger, a fool, and a coward, as you then reported him to be?

Duke. You must, sir, change persons with me,

ere you make that my report: you, indeed, spoke so of him; and much more, much worse.

Lucio. O thou damnable fellow! Did not I pluck thee by the nose, for thy speeches?

Duke. I protest, I love the duke, as I love myself.

Ang. Hark! how the villain would close now, after his treasonable abuses.

Escal. Such a fellow is not to be talk'd withal:—Away with him to prison:—Where is the provost?—Away with him to prison; lay bolts enough upon him:—Let him speak no more:—Away with those giglots too, and with the other confederate companion.

[*The* Provost *lays hands on the Duke.*

Duke. Stay, sir; stay a while.

Ang. What! resists he? Help him, Lucio.

Lucio. Come, sir; come, sir; come, sir; foh, sir; Why, you bald-pated, lying rascal! you must be hooded, must you? Show your knave's visage, with a pox to you! show your sheep-biting face, and be hang'd an hour! Wilt not off? [*Pulls off the Friar's hood, and discovers the* Duke.

Duke. Thou art the first knave that e'er made a duke.——
First, Provost, let me bail these gentle three:——
Sneak not away, sir; [*To* Lucio.] for the friar and you
Must have a word anon:—lay hold on him.

Lucio. This may prove worse than hanging.

Duke. What you have spoke, I pardon; sit you down.—— [*To* Escalus.
We'll borrow place of him:—Sir, by your leave: [*To* Angelo.
Hast thou or word, or wit, or impudence,
That yet can do thee office? If thou hast,
Rely upon it till my tale be heard,
And hold no longer out.

Ang. O my dread lord,
I should be guiltier than my guiltiness,
To think I can be undiscernible,
When I perceive, your grace, like power divine,
Hath look'd upon my passes: Then, good prince,
No longer session hold upon my shame,
But let my trial be mine own confession;
Immediate sentence then, and sequent death,
Is all the grace I beg.

Duke. Come hither, Mariana;—
Say, wast thou e'er contracted to this woman?

Ang. I was, my lord.

Duke. Go take her hence, and marry her instantly.—
Do you the office, friar: which consummate,
Return him here again:—Go with him, Provost.

[*Exeunt* Angelo, Mariana, Peter, *and* Provost.

Escal. My lord, I am more amazed at his dishonour,
Than at the strangeness of it.

Duke. Come hither, Isabel:
Your friar is now your prince: As I was then
Advertising, and holy to your business,
Not changing heart with habit, I am still
Attorney'd at your service.

Isab. O, give me pardon,
That I, your vassal, have employed and pain'd
Your unknown sovereignty.

Duke. You are pardon'd, Isabel:
And now, dear maid, be you as free to us.
Your brother's death, I know, sits at your heart;
And you may marvel, why I obscured myself,
Labouring to save his life; and would not rather
Make rash remonstrance of my hidden power,
Than let him so be lost: O, most kind maid,
It was the swift celerity of his death,
Which I did think with slower foot came on,
That brain'd my purpose; But, peace be with him!
That life is better life, past fearing death,
Than that which lives to fear: make it your comfort,
So happy is your brother.

Re-enter Angelo, Mariana, Peter, *and* Provost.

Isab. I do, my lord.

Duke. For this new-married man approaching here,
Whose salt imagination yet hath wrong'd
Your well-defended honour, you must pardon
For Mariana's sake: but as he adjudged your brother
(Being criminal, in double violation
Of sacred chastity, and of promise-breach,
Thereon dependent for your brother's life),
The very mercy of the law cries out
Most audible, even from his proper tongue,
An Angelo for Claudio, death for death,
Haste still pays haste, and leisure answers leisure;
Like doth quit like, and *Measure* still *for Measure.*
Then, Angelo, thy fault's thus manifested;
Which though thou would'st deny, denies thee vantage:
We do condemn thee to the very block
Where Claudio stoop'd to death, and with like haste;—
Away with him.

Mari. O, my most gracious lord,
I hope you will not mock me with a husband!

Duke. It is your husband mock'd you with a husband:
Consenting to the safeguard of your honour,
I thought your marriage fit; else imputation,
For that he knew you, might reproach your life,
And choke your good to come: for his possessions,
Although by confiscation they are ours,
We do instate and widow you withal,
To buy you a better husband.

Mari. O, my dear lord,
I crave no other, nor no better man.

Duke. Never crave him; we are definitive.

Mari. Gentle, my liege,— [*Kneeling.*

Duke. You do but lose your labour;
Away with him to death.—Now, sir, [*To* Lucio.] to you.

Mari. O, my good lord!—Sweet Isabel, take my part;
Lend me your knees, and, all my life to come,
I'll lend you all my life to do you service.

Duke. Against all sense you do importune her:
Should she kneel down, in mercy of this fact,
Her brother's ghost his paved bed would break,
And take her hence in horror.

Mari. Isabel,
Sweet Isabel, do yet but kneel by me;
Hold up your hands, say nothing, I'll speak all.
They say, best men are moulded out of faults;
And, for the most, become much more the better
For being a little bad: so may my husband.
O, Isabel! will you not lend a knee?

Duke. He dies for Claudio's death.

Isab. Most bounteous sir, [*Kneeling.*
Look, if it please you, on this man condemn'd,
As if my brother liv'd: I partly think,
A due sincerity govern'd his deeds,
Till he did look on me: since it is so,
Let him not die: My brother had but justice,
In that he did the thing for which he died:
For Angelo,
His act did not o'ertake his bad intent;
And must be buried but as an intent
That perish'd by the way: thoughts are no subjects;
Intents but merely thoughts.

Mari. Merely, my lord.

Duke. Your suit's unprofitable; stand up, I say.—
I have bethought me of another fault:—
Provost, how came it Claudio was beheaded
At an unusual hour?

Prov. It was commanded so.

Duke. Had you a special warrant for the deed?

Prov. No, my good lord; it was by private message.

Duke. For which I do discharge you of your office:
Give up your keys.
Prov. Pardon me, noble lord:
I thought it was a fault, but knew it not;
Yet did repent me, after more advice:
For testimony whereof, one in prison
That should by private order else have died,
I have reserv'd alive.
Duke. What's he?
Prov. His name is Barnardine.
Duke. I would, thou had'st done so by Claudio.—
Go, fetch him hither; let me look upon him.
[*Exit* Provost.
Escal. I am sorry, one so learned and so wise
As you, lord Angelo, have still appear'd,
Should slip so grossly, both in the heat of blood,
And lack of temper'd judgment afterward.
Ang. I am sorry, that such sorrow I procure:
And so deep sticks it in my penitent heart,
That I crave death more willingly than mercy;
'Tis my deserving, and I do entreat it.

Re-enter Provost, BARNARDINE, CLAUDIO, *and* JULIET.

Duke. Which is that Barnardine?
Prov. This, my lord.
Duke. There was a friar told me of this man:—
Sirrah, thou art said to have a stubborn soul,
That apprehends no further than this world,
And squar'st thy life according. Thou'rt condemn'd;
But, for those earthly faults, I quit them all;
And pray thee, take this mercy to provide
For better times to come:——Friar advise him;
I leave him to your hand.—What muffled fellow's that?
Prov. This is another prisoner, that I sav'd,
That should have died when Claudio lost his head;
As like almost to Claudio, as himself.
[*Unmuffles* CLAUDIO.
Duke. If he be like your brother, [*To* ISABELLA.] for his sake
Is he pardoned; And, for your lovely sake,
Give me your hand, and say you will be mine,
He is my brother too: But fitter time for that.
By this, lord Angelo perceives he's safe;
Methinks, I see a quick'ning in his eye:—
Well, Angelo, your evil quits you well:
Look that you love your wife; her worth, worth yours.—
I find an apt remission in myself:
And yet here's one in place I cannot pardon;—
You, sirrah, [*To* LUCIO.] that knew me for a fool, a coward,
One all of luxury, an ass, a madman;
Wherein have I so deserved of you,
That you extol me thus?
Lucio. 'Faith, my lord, I spoke it but according to the trick: If you will hang me for it, you may, but I had rather it would please you I might be whipp'd.
Duke. Whipp'd first, sir, and hang'd after.—
Proclaim it, provost, round about the city;
If any woman's wrong'd by this lewd fellow,
(As I have heard him swear himself, there's one
Whom he begot with child), let her appear,
And he shall marry her: the nuptial finish'd,
Let him be whipp'd and hang'd.
Lucio. I beseech your highness, do not marry me to a whore! Your highness said even now, I made you a duke; good my lord, do not recompense me in making me a cuckold.
Duke. Upon mine honour thou shalt marry her.
Thy slanders I forgive: and therewithal
Remit thy other forfeits:—Take him to prison:
And see our pleasure herein executed.
Lucio. Marrying a punk, my lord, is pressing to death, whipping, and hanging.
Duke. Sland'ring a prince deserves it.—
She, Claudio, that you wrong'd, look you restore.—
Joy to you, Mariana!—love her, Angelo;
I have confess'd her, and I know her virtue.—
Thanks, good friend Escalus, for thy much goodness:
There's more behind, that is more gratulate.
Thanks Provost, for thy care and secrecy;
We shall employ thee in a worthier place:—
Forgive him, Angelo, that brought you home
The head of Ragozine for Claudio's;
The offence pardons itself.—Dear Isabel,
I have a motion much imports your good;
Whereto if you'll a willing ear incline,
What's mine is yours, and what is yours is mine:—
So, bring us to our palace; where we'll show
What's yet behind, that's meet you all should know. [*Exeunt.*

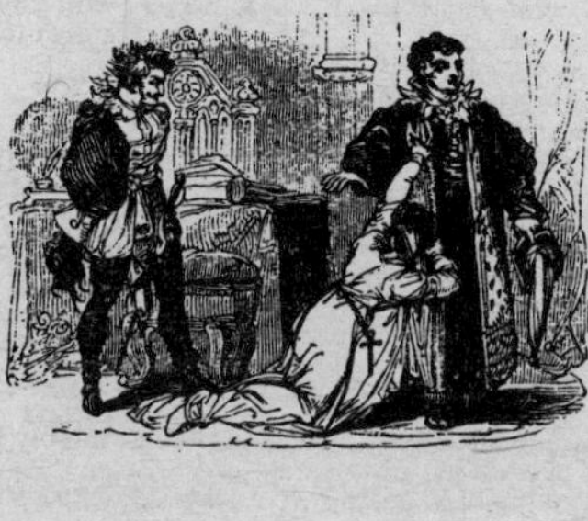

MUCH ADO ABOUT NOTHING.

PERSONS REPRESENTED.

DON PEDRO, *Prince of* Arragon.
DON JOHN, *his bastard Brother.*
CLAUDIO, *a young Lord of* Florence, *favourite to* Don Pedro.
BENEDICK, *a young Lord of* Padua, *favourite likewise of* Don Pedro.
LEONATO, *Governor of* Messina.
ANTONIO, *his Brother.*
BALTHAZAR, *Servant to* Don Pedro.
BORACHIO, CONRADE, } *Followers of* Don John.

DOGBERRY, VERGES, } *Two foolish Officers.*
A Sexton.
A Friar.
A Boy.

HERO, *Daughter to* Leonato.
BEATRICE, *Niece to* Leonato.
MARGARET, URSULA, } *Gentlewomen attending on* Hero.

Messengers, Watch, and Attendants.

SCENE—Messina.

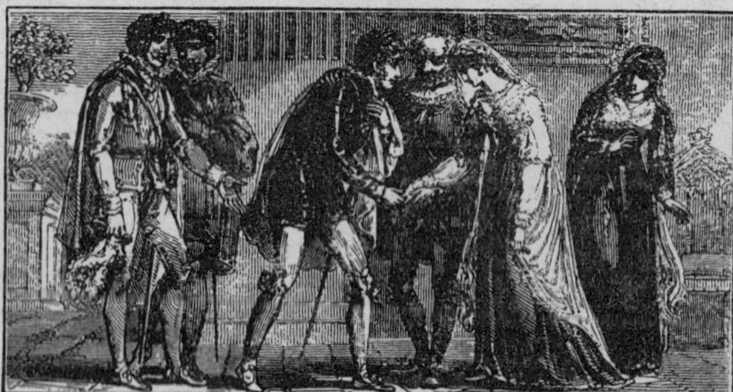

ACT I.

SCENE I. *Before* Leonato's *House.*

Enter LEONATO, HERO, BEATRICE, *and others, with a* Messenger.

Leonato. I LEARN in this letter, that Don Pedro of Arragon comes this night to Messina.

Mess. He is very near by this; he was not three leagues off when I left him.

Leon. How many gentlemen have you lost in this action?

Mess. But few of any sort, and none of name.

Leon. A victory is twice itself, when the achiever brings home full numbers. I find here, that Don Pedro hath bestowed much honour on a young Florentine, called Claudio.

Mess. Much deserved on his part, and equally remembered by Don Pedro: He hath borne himself beyond the promise of his age; doing, in the figure of a lamb, the feats of a lion: he hath, indeed, better bettered expectation, than you must expect of me to tell you how.

Leon. He hath an uncle here in Messina will be very much glad of it.

Mess. I have already delivered him letters, and there appears much joy in him; even so much, that joy could not show itself modest enough, without a badge of bitterness.

Leon. Did he break out into tears?

Mess. In great measure.

Leon. A kind overflow of kindness: There are no faces truer than those that are so washed. How much better is it to weep at joy, than to joy at weeping!

Beat. I pray you, is signior Montanto returned from the wars, or no?

Mess. I know none of that name, lady; there was none such in the army of any sort.

Leon. What is he that you ask for, niece?

Hero. My cousin means signior Benedick of Padua.

Mess. O, he is returned; and as pleasant as ever he was.

Beat. He set up his bills here in Messina, and challenged Cupid at the flight: and my uncle's fool, reading the challenge, subscribed for Cupid, and challenged him at the bird-bolt.—I pray you, how many hath he killed and eaten in these wars? But how many hath he killed? for, indeed, I promised to eat all of his killing.

Leon. 'Faith, niece, you tax signior Benedick too much; but he'll be meet with you, I doubt it not.

Mess. He hath done good service, lady, in these wars.

Beat. You had musty victual, and he hath holp to eat it: he is a very valiant trencher-man, he hath an excellent stomach.

Mess. And a good soldier too, lady.

Beat. And a good soldier to a lady:—But what is he to a lord?

Mess. A lord to a lord, a man to a man; stuffed with all honourable virtues.

Beat. It is so, indeed; he is no less than a stuffed man:—But for the stuffing,—Well, we are all mortal.

Leon. You must not, sir, mistake my niece: there is a kind of merry war betwixt signior Benedick and her: they never meet, but there is a skirmish of wit between them.

Beat. Alas, he gets nothing by that. In our last conflict, four of his five wits went halting off, and now is the whole man governed with one: so that if he have wit enough to keep himself warm, let him bear it for a difference between himself and his horse: for it is all the wealth that he hath left, to be known a reasonable creature.—Who is his companion now? He hath every month a new sworn brother.

Mess. Is it possible?

Beat. Very easily possible: he wears his faith but as the fashion of his hat, it ever changes with the next block.

Mess. I see, lady, the gentleman is not in your books.

Beat. No: an he were, I would burn my study. But, I pray you, who is his companion? Is there no young squarer now, that will make a voyage with him to the devil?

Mess. He is most in the company of the right noble Claudio.

Beat. O Lord! he will hang upon him like a disease: he is sooner caught than the pestilence, and the taker runs presently mad. God help the noble Claudio! if he have caught the Benedick, it will cost him a thousand pound ere he be cured.

Mess. I will hold friends with you, lady.

Beat. Do, good friend.

Leon. You will never run mad, niece.

Beat. No, not till a hot January.

Mess. Don Pedro is approached.

Enter DON PEDRO, *attended by* BALTHAZAR *and others,* DON JOHN, CLAUDIO, *and* BENEDICK.

D. Pedro. Good signior Leonato, you are come to meet your trouble: the fashion of the world is to avoid cost, and you encounter it.

Leon. Never came trouble to my house in the likeness of your grace: for trouble being gone, comfort should remain; but, when you depart from me, sorrow abides, and happiness takes his leave.

D. Pedro. You embrace your charge too willingly.—I think, this is your daughter.

Leon. Her mother hath many times told me so.

Bene. Were you in doubt, sir, that you asked her?

Leon. Signior Benedick, no; for then were you a child.

D. Pedro. You have it full, Benedick: we may guess by this what you are, being a man. Truly, the lady fathers herself:—Be happy, lady! for you are like an honourable father.

Bene. If Signior Leonato be her father, she would not have his head on her shoulders, for all Messina, as like him as she is.

Beat. I wonder, that you will still be talking, signior Benedick; no body marks you.

Bene. What, my dear lady Disdain! are you yet living?

Beat. Is it possible disdain should die, while she hath such meet food to feed it, as signior Benedick? Courtesy itself must convert to disdain, if you come in her presence.

Bene. Then is courtesy a turn-coat:—But it is certain, I am lov'd of all ladies, only you excepted: and I would I could find in my heart that I had not a hard heart; for, truly, I love none.

Beat. A dear happiness to women; they would else have been troubled with a pernicious suitor. I thank God, and my cold blood, I am of your humour for that; I had rather hear my dog bark at a crow, than a man swear he loves me.

Bene. God keep your ladyship still in that mind! so some gentleman or other shall 'scape a predestinate scratched face.

Beat. Scratching could not make it worse, an 'twere such a face as yours were.

Bene. Well, you are a rare parrot-teacher.

Beat. A bird of my tongue is better than a beast of yours.

Bene. I would, my horse had the speed of your tongue; and so good a continuer: But keep your way o'God's name; I have done.

Beat. You always end with a jade's trick; I know you of old.

D. Pedro. This is the sum of all, Leonato,—signior Claudio, and signior Benedick,—my dear friend Leonato, hath invited you all. I tell him, we shall stay here at the least a month; and he heartily prays, some occasion may detain us longer; I dare swear he is no hypocrite, but prays from his heart.

Leon. If you swear, my lord, you shall not be forsworn.—Let me bid you welcome, my lord, being reconciled to the prince your brother, I owe you all duty.

D. John. I thank you: I am not of many words, but I thank you.

Leon. Please it your grace lead on?

D. Pedro. Your hand, Leonato; we will go together. [*Exeunt all but* BENEDICK *and* CLAUDIO.

Claud. Benedick, didst thou note the daughter of signior Leonato?

Bene. I noted her not; but I looked on her.

Claud. Is she not a modest young lady?

Bene. Do you question me, as an honest man should do, for my simple true judgment; or would you have me speak after my custom, as being a professed tyrant to their sex?

Claud. No, I pray thee, speak in sober judgment.

Bene. Why, i'faith, methinks she is too low for a high praise, too brown for a fair praise, and too little for a great praise: only this commendation I can afford her; that were she other than she is, she were unhandsome; and being no other but as she is, I do not like her.

Claud. Thou thinkest I am in sport; I pray thee, tell me truly how thou likest her.

Bene. Would you buy her, that you inquire after her.

Claud. Can the world buy such a jewel?

Bene. Yea, and a case to put it into. But speak you this with a sad brow? or do you play the flouting Jack; to tell us Cupid is a good hare-finder, and Vulcan a rare carpenter? Come, in what key shall a man take you to go in the song?

Claud. In mine eye, she is the sweetest lady that ever I looked on.

Bene. I can see yet without spectacles, and I see no such matter: there's her cousin, an she were not possessed with a fury, exceeds her as much in beauty, as the first of May doth the last of December. But I hope, you have no intent to turn husband; have you?

Claud. I would scarce trust myself, though I had sworn the contrary, if Hero would be my wife.

Bene. Is it come to this, i'faith? Hath not the world one man, but he will wear his cap with suspicion? Shall I never see a bachelor of three-score again? Go to, i'faith; and thou wilt needs thrust thy neck into a yoke, wear the print of it, and sigh away Sundays. Look, Don Pedro is returned to seek you.

Re-enter DON PEDRO.

D. Pedro. What secret hath held you here, that you followed not to Leonato's?

Bene. I would, your grace would constrain me to tell.

D. Pedro. I charge thee on thy allegiance.

Bene. You hear, Count Claudio: I can be secret as a dumb man, I would have you think so; but on my allegiance,—mark you this, on my allegiance:—He is in love. With who?—now that is your grace's part.—Mark, how short his answer is:—With Hero, Leonato's short daughter.

Claud. If this were so, so were it uttered.

Bene. Like the old tale, my lord: it is not so, nor 'twas not so: but, indeed, God forbid it should be so.

Claud. If my passion change not shortly, God forbid it should be otherwise.

D. Pedro. Amen, if you love her; for the lady is very well worthy.

Claud. You speak this to fetch me in, my lord.

D. Pedro. By my troth, I speak my thought.

Claud. And, in faith, my lord, I spoke mine.

Bene. And, by my two faiths and troths, my lord, I spoke mine.

Claud. That I love her, I feel.

D. Pedro. That she is worthy, I know.

Bene. That I neither feel how she should be loved, nor know how she should be worthy, is the opinion that fire cannot melt out of me; I will die in it at the stake.

D. Pedro. Thou wast ever an obstinate heretick in the despite of beauty.

Claud. And never could maintain his part, but in the force of his will.

Bene. That a woman conceived me, I thank her; that she brought me up, I likewise give her most humble thanks: but that I will have a recheat winded in my forehead, or hang my bugle in an invisible baldrick, all women shall pardon me: Because I will not do them the wrong to mistrust any, I will do myself the right to trust none; and the fine is (for the which I may go the finer), I will live a bachelor.

D. Pedro. I shall see thee, ere I die, look pale with love.

Bene. With anger, with sickness, or with hunger, my lord; not with love: prove, that ever I lose more blood with love, than I will get again with drinking, pick out mine eyes with a ballad-maker's pen, and hang me up at the door of a brothel-house, for the sign of blind Cupid.

D. Pedro. Well, if ever thou dost fall from this faith, thou wilt prove a notable argument.

Bene. If I do, hang me in a bottle like a cat, and shoot at me; and he that hits me, let him be clapped on the shoulder, and called Adam.

D. Pedro. Well, as time shall try:
In time the savage bull doth bear the yoke.

Bene. The savage bull may; but if ever the sensible Benedick bear it, pluck off the bull's horns, and set them in my forehead: and let me be vilely painted; and in such great letters as they write, *Here is good horse to hire*, let them signify under my sign—*Here you may see Benedick the married man.*

Claud. If this should ever happen, thou would'st be horn-mad.

D. Pedro. Nay, if Cupid have not spent all his quiver in Venice, thou wilt quake for this shortly.

Bene. I look for an earthquake too then.

D. Pedro. Well, you will temporize with the hours. In the mean time, good signior Benedick, repair to Leonato's; commend me to him, and tell him, I will not fail him at supper; for, indeed, he hath made great preparation.

Bene. I have almost matter enough in me for such an embassage: and so I commit you—

Claud. To the tuition of God: From my house, (if I had it)—

D. Pedro. The sixth of July: Your loving friend, Benedick.

Bene. Nay, mock not, mock not: The body of your discourse is sometime guarded with fragments, and the guards are but slightly basted on neither: ere you flout old ends any further, examine your conscience, and so I leave you. [*Exit* BENEDICK.

Claud. My liege, your highness now may do me good.

D. Pedro. My love is thine to teach; teach it but how,
And thou shalt see how apt it is to learn
Any hard lesson that may do thee good.

Claud. Hath Leonato any son, my lord?

D. Pedro. No child but Hero, she's his only heir;
Dost thou affect her, Claudio?

Claud. O my lord,
When you went onward on this ended action,
I look'd upon her with a soldier's eye,
That lik'd, but had a rougher task in hand
Than to drive liking to the name of love:
But now I am return'd, and that war-thoughts
Have left their places vacant, in their rooms
Come thronging soft and delicate desires,
All prompting me how fair young Hero is,
Saying, I lik'd her ere I went to wars.

D. Pedro. Thou wilt be like a lover presently,
And tire the hearer with a book of words:
If thou dost love fair Hero, cherish it;
And I will break with her, and with her father,
And thou shalt have her: Was't not to this end,
That thou began'st to twist so fine a story?

Claud. How sweetly do you minister to love,
That know love's grief by his complexion!
But lest my liking might too sudden seem,
I would have salv'd it with a longer treatise.

D. Pedro. What need the bridge much broader than the flood?
The fairest grant is the necessity:
Look, what will serve, is fit: 'tis once, thou lov'st;
And I will fit thee with the remedy.
I know we shall have revelling to-night;
I will assume thy part in some disguise,
And tell fair Hero I am Claudio;
And in her bosom I'll unclasp my heart,
And take her hearing prisoner with the force
And strong encounter of my amorous tale:
Then, after, to her father will I break;
And, the conclusion is, she shall be thine:
In practice let us put it presently. [*Exeunt.*

SCENE II. *A Room in* Leonato's *House.*

Enter LEONATO *and* ANTONIO.

Leon. How now, brother? Where is my cousin, your son? hath he provided this musick?

Ant. He is very busy about it. But, brother, I can tell you strange news that you yet dreamed not of.

Leon. Are they good?

Ant. As the event stamps them; but they have a good cover, they show well outward. The prince and Count Claudio, walking in a thick-pleached ally in my orchard, were thus much overheard by a man of mine: The prince discovered to Claudio, that he loved my niece your daughter, and meant to acknowledge it this night in a dance; and, if he found her accordant, he meant to take the present time by the top, and instantly break with you of it.

Leon. Hath the fellow any wit, that told you this?

Ant. A good sharp fellow: I will send for him, and question him yourself.

Leon. No, no; we will hold it as a dream, till it appear itself: but I will acquaint my daughter withal, that she may be the better prepared for an answer, if peradventure this be true. Go you, and tell her of it. [*Several persons cross the stage.*] Cousins, you know what you have to do.—O, I cry you mercy, friend; you go with me, and I will use your skill:—Good cousins, have a care this busy time. [*Exeunt.*

SCENE III. *Another Room in* Leonato's *House.*

Enter DON JOHN *and* CONRADE.

Con. What the good year, my lord! why are you thus out of measure sad?

D. John. There is no measure in the occasion that breeds it, therefore the sadness is without limit.

Con. You should hear reason.

D. John. And when I have heard it, what blessing bringeth it?

Con. If not a present remedy, yet a patient sufferance.

D. John. I wonder, that thou being (as thou say'st thou art) born under Saturn, goest about to apply a moral medicine to a mortifying mischief. I cannot hide what I am: I must be sad when I have cause, and smile at no man's jests; eat when I have stomach, and wait for no man's leisure; sleep when I am drowsy, and tend to no man's business; laugh when I am merry, and claw no man in his humour.

Con. Yea, but you must not make the full show of this, till you may do it without controlment. You have of late stood out against your brother, and he hath ta'en you newly into his grace; where it is impossible you should take true root, but by the fair weather that you make yourself: it is needful that you frame the season for your own harvest.

D. John. I had rather be a canker in a hedge, than a rose in his grace; and it better fits my blood to be disdained of all, than to fashion a carriage to rob love from any; in this, though I cannot be said to be a flattering honest man, it must not be denied that I am a plain-dealing villain. I am trusted with a muzzle, and enfranchised with a clog; therefore I have decreed not to sing in my cage: If I had my mouth, I would bite; if I had my liberty, I would do my liking: in the mean time, let me be that I am, and seek not to alter me.

Con. Can you make no use of your discontent?

D. John. I make all use of it, for I use it only. Who comes here? What news, Borachio?

Enter BORACHIO.

Bora. I came yonder from a great supper; the prince, your brother, is royally entertained by Leonato; and I can give you intelligence of an intended marriage.

D. John. Will it serve for any model to build mischief on? What is he for a fool, that betroths himself to unquietness?

Bora. Marry, it is your brother's right hand.

D. John. Who? the most exquisite Claudio?

Bora. Even he.

D. John. A proper squire! And who, and who? which way looks he?

Bora. Marry, on Hero, the daughter and heir of Leonato.

D. John. A very forward March chick! How came you to this?

Bora. Being entertained for a perfumer, as I was smoking a musty room, comes me the prince and Claudio, hand in hand, in sad conference: I whipt me behind the arras; and there heard it agreed upon, that the prince should woo Hero for himself, and having obtained her, give her to count Claudio.

D. John. Come, come, let us thither; this may prove food to my displeasure: that young start-up hath all the glory of my overthrow; if I can cross him any way, I bless myself every way: You are both sure, and will assist me?

Con. To the death, my lord.

D. John. Let us to the great supper: their cheer is the greater, that I am subdued: 'Would, the cook were of my mind!—Shall we go prove what's to be done?

Bora. We'll wait upon your lordship. [*Exeunt.*

ACT II.

SCENE I. *A Hall in* Leonato's *House.*

Enter LEONATO, ANTONIO, HERO, BEATRICE, *and others.*

Leon. Was not count John here at supper?

Ant. I saw him not.

Beat. How tartly that gentleman looks! I never can see him, but I am heart-burned an hour after.

Hero. He is of a very melancholy disposition.

Beat. He were an excellent man, that were made just in the mid-way between him and Benedick: the one is too like an image, and says nothing; and the other, too like my lady's eldest son, evermore tattling.

Leon. Then half signior Benedick's tongue in count John's mouth, and half count John's melancholy in signior Benedick's face,—

Beat. With a good leg, and a good foot, uncle, and money enough in his purse, such a man would win any woman in the world,—if he could get her good will.

Leon. By my troth, niece, thou wilt never get thee a husband, if thou be so shrewd of thy tongue.

Ant. In faith, she is too curst.

Beat. Too curst is more than curst: I shall lessen God's sending that way: for it is said, *God sends a curst cow short horns;* but to a cow too curst he sends none.

Leon. So, by being too curst, God will send you no horns.

Beat. Just, if he send me no husband: for the which blessing, I am at him upon my knees every morning and evening: Lord! I could not endure a husband with a beard on his face; I had rather lie in the woollen.

Leon. You may light upon a husband that hath no beard.

Beat. What should I do with him? dress him in my apparel, and make him my waiting gentlewoman? He that hath a beard, is more than a youth: and he that hath no beard, is less than a man: and he that is more than a youth, is not for me; and he that is less than a man, I am not for him. Therefore I will even take sixpence in earnest of the bear-herd, and lead his apes into hell.

Leon. Well then, go you into hell?

Beat. No; but to the gate: and there will the devil meet me, like an old cuckold, with horns on his head, and say, *Get you to heaven, Beatrice, get you to heaven; here's no place for you maids:* so deliver I up my apes, and away to saint Peter for the heavens; he shows me where the bachelors sit, and there live we as merry as the day is long.

Ant. Well, niece, [*To* HERO.] I trust, you will be ruled by your father.

Beat. Yes, 'faith; it is my cousin's duty to make courtesy, and say, *Father, as it please you:*—but yet for all that, cousin, let him be a handsome fellow, or else make another courtesy, and say, *Father, as it please me.*

Leon. Well, niece, I hope to see you one day fitted with a husband.

Beat. Not till God make men of some other metal than earth. Would it not grieve a woman to be over-mastered with a piece of valiant dust? to make an account of her life to a clod of wayward marl? No, uncle, I'll none; Adam's sons are my brethren; and truly, I hold it as a sin to match in my kindred.

Leon. Daughter, remember what I told you: if the prince do solicit you in that kind, you know your answer.

Beat. The fault will be in the musick, cousin, if you be not woo'd in good time: if the prince be too important, tell him, there is measure in every thing, and so dance out the answer. For hear me, Hero; Wooing, wedding, and repenting, is as a Scotch jig, a measure, and a cinque-pace: the first suit is hot and hasty, like a Scotch jig, and full as fantastical; the wedding, mannerly modest, as a measure full of state and ancientry; and then comes repentance, and, with his bad legs, falls into the cinque-pace faster and faster, till he sink into his grave.

Leon. Cousin, you apprehend passing shrewdly.

Beat. I have a good eye, uncle; I can see a church by day-light.

Leon. The revellers are entering; brother, make good room.

Enter DON PEDRO, CLAUDIO, BENEDICK, BALTHAZAR; DON JOHN, BORACHIO, MARGARET, URSULA, *and others, masked.*

D. Pedro. Lady, will you walk about with your friend?

Hero. So you walk softly, and look sweetly, and say nothing, I am yours for the walk; and, especially, when I walk away.

D. Pedro. With me in your company?

Hero. I may say so, when I please.

D. Pedro. And when please you to say so?

Hero. When I like your favour; for God defend, the lute should be like the case!

D. Pedro. My vizor is Philemon's roof; within the house is Jove.

Hero. Why, then your visor should be thatch'd.

D. Pedro. Speak low, if you speak love. [*Takes her aside.*

Bene. Well, I would you did like me.

Marg. So would not I, for your own sake; for I have many ill qualities.

Bene. Which is one?

Marg. I say my prayers aloud.

Bene. I love you the better; the hearers may cry, Amen.

Marg. God match me with a good dancer!

Balth. Amen.

Marg. And God keep him out of my sight, when the dance is done!—Answer, clerk.

Balth. No more words: the clerk is answered.

Urs. I know you well enough; you are signior Antonio.

Ant. At a word, I am not.

Urs. I know you by the waggling of your head.

Ant. To tell you true, I counterfeit him.

Urs. You could never do him so ill-well, unless you were the very man: Here's his dry hand up and down; you are he, you are he.

Ant. At a word, I am not.

Urs. Come, come; do you think I do not know you by your excellent wit? Can virtue hide itself? Go to, mum, you are he: graces will appear, and there's an end.

Beat. Will you not tell me who told you so?

Bene. No, you shall pardon me.

Beat. Nor will you not tell me who you are?

Bene. Not now.

Beat. That I was disdainful,—and that I had my good wit out of the *Hundred Merry Tales*;—Well, this was signior Benedick that said so.

Bene. What's he?

Beat. I am sure, you know him well enough.

Bene. Not I, believe me.

Beat. Did he never make you laugh?

Bene. I pray you, what is he?

Beat. Why, he is the prince's jester; a very dull fool; only his gift is in devising impossible slanders: none but libertines delight in him; and the commendation is not in his wit, but in his villany; for he both pleaseth men, and angers them, and then they laugh at him, and beat him: I am sure, he is in the fleet: I would he had boarded me.

Bene. When I know the gentleman, I'll tell him what you say.

Beat. Do, do: he'll but break a comparison or two on me; which, peradventure, not marked, or not laughed at, strikes him into melancholy; and then there's a partridge' wing saved, for the fool will eat no supper that night. [*Musick within.*] We must follow the leaders.

Bene. In every good thing.

Beat. Nay, if they lead to any ill, I will leave them at the next turning.

[*Dance. Then exeunt all but* DON JOHN, BORACHIO, *and* CLAUDIO.

D. John. Sure, my brother is amorous on Hero, and hath withdrawn her father to break with him about it: The ladies follow her, and but one vizor remains.

Bora. And that is Claudio: I know him by his bearing.

D. John. Are not you signior Benedick?

Claud. You know me well; I am he.

D. John. Signior, you are very near my brother in his love: he is enamoured on Hero; I pray you, dissuade him from her, she is no equal for his birth: you may do the part of an honest man in it.

Claud. How know you he loves her?

D. John. I heard him swear his affection.

Bora. So did I too; and he swore he would marry her to-night.

D. John. Come, let us to the banquet.

[*Exeunt* DON JOHN *and* BORACHIO.

Claud. Thus answer I in name of Benedick,
But hear these ill news with the ears of Claudio.—
'Tis certain so;—the prince woos for himself.
Friendship is constant in all other things,
Save in the office and affairs of love:
Therefore, all hearts in love use their own tongues;
Let every eye negotiate for itself,
And trust no agent: for beauty is a witch,
Against whose charms faith melteth into blood.
This is an accident of hourly proof,
Which I mistrusted not: Farewell therefore, Hero!

Re-enter BENEDICK.

Bene. Count Claudio?

Claud. Yea, the same.

Bene. Come, will you go with me?

Claud. Whither?

Bene. Even to the next willow, about your own business, count. What fashion will you wear the garland of? About your neck, like a usurer's chain? or under your arm, like a lieutenant's scarf? You must wear it one way, for the prince hath got your Hero.

Claud. I wish him joy of her.

Bene. Why, that's spoken like an honest drover; so they sell bullocks. But did you think the prince would have served you thus?

Claud. I pray you, leave me.

Bene. Ho! now you strike like the blind man; 'twas the boy that stole your meat, and you'll beat the post.

Claud. If it will not be, I'll leave you. [*Exit.*

Bene. Alas, poor hurt fowl! Now will he creep into sedges.——But, that my lady Beatrice should know me, and not know me! The Prince's fool!—Ha! it may be, I go under that title, because I am merry.—Yea; but so; I am apt to do myself wrong: I am not so reputed: it is the base, the bitter disposition of Beatrice, that puts the world into her person, and so gives me out. Well, I'll be revenged as I may.

Re-enter DON PEDRO.

D. Pedro. Now, signior, where's the count; Did you see him?

Bene. Troth, my lord, I have play'd the part of lady Fame. I found him here as melancholy as a lodge in a warren; I told him, and, I think, I told him true, that your grace had got the good will of this young lady; and I offered him my company to a willow tree, either to make him a garland, as being forsaken, or to bind him up a rod, as being worthy to be whipped.

D. Pedro. To be whipped! What's his fault?

Bene. The flat transgression of a schoolboy; who, being overjoyed with finding a bird's nest, shows it his companion, and he steals it.

D. Pedro. Wilt thou make a trust a transgression? The transgression is in the stealer.

Bene. Yet it had not been amiss, the rod had been made, and the garland too; for the garland he might have worn himself; and the rod he might have bestowed on you, who, as I take it, have stol'n his bird's nest.

D. Pedro. I will but teach them to sing, and restore them to the owner.

Bene. If their singing answer your saying, by my faith, you say honestly.

D. Pedro. The lady Beatrice hath a quarrel to you; the gentleman, that danced with her, told her, she is much wronged by you.

Bene. O, she misused me past the endurance of a block: an oak, but with one green leaf on it, would have answered her; my very visor began to assume life, and scold with her: She told me, not thinking I had been myself, that I was the prince's jester: that I was duller than a great thaw; huddling jest upon jest, with such impossible conveyance, upon me, that I stood like a man at a mark, with a whole army shooting at me: She speaks poniards, and every word stabs: if her breath were as terrible as her terminations, there were no living near her, she would infect the north star. I would not marry her, though she were endowed with all that Adam had left him before he transgressed; she would have made Hercules have turned spit; yea, and have cleft his club to make the fire too. Come, talk not of her; you shall find her the infernal Ate in good apparel. I would to God, some scholar would conjure her; for, certainly, while she is here, a man may live as quiet in hell, as in a sanctuary; and people sin upon purpose, because they would go thither: so, indeed, all disquiet, horror, and perturbation follow her.

Re-enter CLAUDIO, BEATRICE, HERO, *and* LEONATO.

D. Pedro. Look, here she comes.

Bene. Will your grace command me any service to the world's end? I will go on the slightest errand now to the Antipodes, that you can devise to send me on; I will fetch you a toothpicker now from the farthest inch of Asia; bring you the length of Prester John's foot; fetch you a hair off the great cham's beard: do you any embassage to the Pigmies, rather than hold three words' conference with this harpy: You have no employment for me?

D. Pedro. None, but to desire your good company.

Bene. O God, sir, here's a dish I love not; I cannot endure my lady Tongue. [*Exit.*

D. Pedro. Come, lady, come; you have lost the heart of signior Benedick.

Beat. Indeed, my lord, he lent it me a while; and I gave him use for it, a double heart for his single one: marry, once before, he won it of me with false dice, therefore, your grace may well say, I have lost it.

D. Pedro. You have put him down, lady, you have put him down.

Beat. So I would not he should do me, my lord, lest I should prove the mother of fools. I have brought count Claudio, whom you sent me to seek.

D. Pedro. Why, how now, count? wherefore are you sad?

Claud. Not sad, my lord.

D. Pedro. How then? Sick?

Claud. Neither, my lord.

Beat. The count is neither sad, nor sick, nor merry, nor well: but civil, count; civil as an orange, and something of that jealous complexion.

D. Pedro. I' faith, lady, I think your blazon to be true; though, I'll be sworn, if he be so, his conceit is false. Here, Claudio, I have wooed in thy name, and fair Hero is won; I have broke with her father, and his good will obtained: name the day of marriage, and God give thee joy!

Leon. Count, take of me my daughter, and with her my fortunes: his grace hath made the match, and all grace say Amen to it!

Beat. Speak, count, 'tis your cue.

Claud. Silence is the perfectest herald of joy: I were but little happy, if I could say how much. —Lady, as you are mine, I am yours: I give away myself for you, and dote upon the exchange.

Beat. Speak, cousin; or, if you cannot, stop his mouth with a kiss, and let him not speak neither.

D. Pedro. In faith, lady, you have a merry heart.

Beat. Yea, my lord: I thank it, poor fool, it keeps on the windy side of care:—My cousin tells him in his ear, that he is in her heart.

Claud. And so she doth, cousin.

Beat. Good lord, for alliance!—Thus goes every one to the world but I, and I am sunburned; I may sit in a corner, and cry, heigh ho! for a husband.

D. Pedro. Lady Beatrice, I will get you one.

Beat. I would rather have one of your father's getting: Hath your grace ne'er a brother like you? Your father got excellent husbands, if a maid could come by them.

D. Pedro. Will you have me, lady?

Beat. No, my lord, unless I might have another for working-days; your grace is too costly to wear every day:—But, I beseech your grace, pardon me: I was born to speak all mirth, and no matter.

D. Pedro. Your silence most offends me, and to be merry best becomes you; for, out of question, you were born in a merry hour.

Beat. No, sure, my lord, my mother cry'd; but then there was a star danced, and under that was I born.—Cousins, God give you joy!

Leon. Niece, will you look to those things I told you of?

Beat. I cry you mercy, uncle.—By your grace's pardon. [*Exit* BEATRICE.

D. Pedro. By my troth, a pleasant-spirited lady.

Leon. There's little of the melancholy element in her, my lord: she is never sad, but when she sleeps; and not ever sad then; for I have heard my daughter say, she hath often dreamed of unhappiness, and waked herself with laughing.

D. Pedro. She cannot endure to hear tell of a husband.

Leon. O, by no means; she mocks all her wooers out of suit.

D. Pedro. She were an excellent wife for Benedick.

Leon. O lord, my lord, if they were but a week married, they would talk themselves mad.

D. Pedro. Count Claudio, when mean you to go to church?

Claud. To-morrow, my lord: Time goes on crutches, till love have all his rites.

Leon. Not till Monday, my dear son, which is hence a just seven-night: and a time too brief too, to have all things answer my mind.

D. Pedro. Come, you shake the head at so long a breathing; but, I warrant thee, Claudio, the time shall not go dully by us; I will, in the interim, undertake one of Hercules' labours; which is, to bring signior Benedick and the lady Beatrice into a mountain of affection, the one with the other. I would fain have it a match; and I doubt not but to fashion it, if you three will but minister such assistance as I shall give you direction.

Leon. My lord, I am for you, though it cost me ten nights' watchings.

Claud. And I, my lord.

D. Pedro. And you too, gentle Hero?

Hero. I will do any modest office, my lord, to help my cousin to a good husband.

D. Pedro. And Benedick is not the unhopefullest husband that I know: thus far can I praise him; he is of a noble strain, of approved valour, and confirmed honesty. I will teach you how to humour your cousin, that she shall fall in love with Benedick:—and I, with your two helps, will so practice on Benedick, that, in despite of his quick wit and his queasy stomach, he shall fall in love with Beatrice. If we can do this, Cupid is no longer an archer; his glory shall be ours, for we are the only love-gods. Go in with me, and I will tell you my drift. [*Exeunt.*

SCENE II. *Another Room in* Leonato's *House.*

Enter DON JOHN *and* BORACHIO.

D. John. It is so: the count Claudio shall marry the daughter of Leonato.

Bora. Yea, my lord; but I can cross it.

D. John. Any bar, any cross, any impediment will be medicinable to me: I am sick in displeasure to him; and whatsoever comes athwart his affection, ranges evenly with mine. How canst thou cross this marriage?

Bora. Not honestly, my lord; but so covertly that no dishonesty shall appear in me.

D. John. Show me briefly how.

Bora. I think, I told your lordship, a year since, how much I am in the favour of Margaret, the waiting-gentlewoman to Hero.

D. John. I remember.

Bora. I can, at any unseasonable instant of the night, appoint her to look out at her lady's chamber-window.

D. John. What life is in that to be the death of this marriage?

Bora. The poison of that lies in you to temper. Go you to the prince your brother; spare not to tell him, that he hath wronged his honour in marrying the renowned Claudio (whose estimation do you mightily hold up) to a contaminated stale, such a one as Hero.

D. John. What proof shall I make of that?

Bora. Proof enough to misuse the prince, to vex Claudio, to undo Hero, and kill Leonato: Look you for any other issue?

D. John. Only to despite them, I will endeavour any thing.

Bora. Go then, find me a meet hour to draw Don Pedro and the count Claudio alone: tell them, that you know that Hero loves me; intend a kind of zeal both to the prince and Claudio, as—in love of your brother's honour, who hath made this match; and his friend's reputation, who is thus like to be cozened with the semblance of a maid,—that you have discovered thus. They will scarcely believe this without trial: offer them instances; which shall bear no less likelihood, than to see me at her chamber-window; hear me call Margaret, Hero; hear Margaret term me Claudio; and bring them to see this, the very night before the intended wedding; for, in the mean time I will so fashion the matter, that Hero shall be absent; and there shall appear such seeming truth of Hero's disloyalty, that jealousy shall be call'd assurance, and all the preparation overthrown.

D. John. Grow this to what adverse issue it can, I will put it in practice: Be cunning in the working this, and thy fee is a thousand ducats.

Bora. Be you constant in the accusation, and my cunning shall not shame me.

D. John. I will presently go learn their day of marriage. [*Exeunt.*

SCENE III. Leonato's *Garden.*

Enter BENEDICK *and a* BOY.

Bene. Boy,—

Boy. Signior.

Bene. In my chamber-window lies a book; bring it hither to me in the orchard.

Boy. I am here, already, sir.

Bene. I know that;—but I would have thee hence, and here again. [*Exit* Boy.]—I do much wonder, that one man, seeing how much another man is a fool when he dedicates his behaviours to love, will, after he hath laughed at such shallow follies in others, become the argument of his own scorn, by falling in love: And such a man is Claudio. I have known, when there was no musick with him but the drum and fife; and now had he rather hear the tabor and the pipe: I have known, when he would have walked ten mile afoot, to see a good armour; and now will he lie ten nights awake, carving the fashion of a new doublet. He was wont to speak plain, and to the purpose, like an honest man, and a soldier; and now is he turn'd orthographer; his words are a very fantastical banquet, just so many strange dishes. May I be so converted, and see with these eyes? I cannot tell; I think not: I will not be sworn, but love may transform me to an oyster; but I'll take my oath on it, till he have made an oyster of me, he shall never make me such a fool. One woman is fair; yet I am well: another is wise; yet I am well: another virtuous; yet I am well: but till all graces be in one woman, one woman shall not come in my grace. Rich she shall be, that's certain; wise, or I'll none; virtuous, or I'll never cheapen her; fair, or I'll never look on her; mild, or come not near me; noble, or not I for an angel; of good discourse, an excellent musician, and her hair shall be of what colour it please God. Ha! the prince and monsieur Love! I will hide me in the arbour. [*Withdraws.*

Enter DON PEDRO, LEONATO, *and* CLAUDIO.

D. Pedro. Come, shall we hear this musick?

Claud. Yea, my good lord:—How still the evening is,
As hush'd on purpose to grace harmony!

D. Pedro. See you where Benedick hath hid himself?

Claud. O, very well, my lord: the musick ended,
We'll fit the kid-fox with a penny-worth.

Enter BALTHAZAR, *with musick.*

D. Pedro. Come, Balthazar, we'll hear that song again.

Balth. O good my lord, tax not so bad a voice
To slander musick any more than once.

D. Pedro. It is the witness still of excellency,
To put a strange face on his own perfection:—
I pray thee, sing, and let me woo no more.

Balth. Because you talk of wooing, I will sing:
Since many a wooer doth commence his suit
To her he thinks not worthy; yet he woos;
Yet will he swear, he loves.

D. Pedro. Nay, 'pray thee, come:
Or, if thou wilt hold longer argument,
Do it in notes.

Balth. Note this before my notes,
There's not a note of mine that's worth the noting.

D. Pedro. Why these are very crotchets that he speaks;
Note, notes, forsooth, and noting! [*Musick.*

Bene. Now, *Divine air!* now is his soul ravished!—Is it not strange, that sheep's guts should hale souls out of men's bodies?—Well, a horn for my money, when all's done.

BALTHAZAR *sings.*

I.

Balth. *Sigh no more, ladies, sigh no more,*
Men were deceivers ever;
One foot in sea, and one on shore;
To one thing constant never:
Then sigh not so,
But let them go,
And be you blithe and bonny;
Converting all your sounds of woe
Into Hey nonny, nonny.

II.

Sing no more ditties, sing no mo
Of dumps so dull and heavy;
The fraud of men was ever so,
Since summer first was leavy:
Then sigh not so, &c.

D. Pedro. By my troth, a good song.

Balth. And an ill singer, my lord.

D. Pedro. Ha? no; no, 'faith; thou singest well enough for a shift.

Bene. [*Aside.*] An he had been a dog, that should have howl'd thus, they would have hanged him: and I pray God, his bad voice bode no mischief! I had as lief have heard the night-raven, come what plague could have come after it.

D. Pedro. Yea, marry; [*To* CLAUDIO.]—Dost thou hear, Balthazar? I pray thee get us some excellent musick; for to-morrow night we would have it at the lady Hero's chamber window.

Balth. The best I can, my lord.

D. Pedro. Do so: farewell. [*Exeunt* BALTHAZAR *and musick.*] Come hither, Leonato: What was it you told me of to-day? That your niece Beatrice was in love with signior Benedick?

Claud. O, ay:—Stalk on, stalk on; the fowl sits. [*Aside to* PEDRO.] I did never think that lady would have loved any man.

Leon. No, nor I neither; but most wonderful, that she should so dote on signior Benedick, whom she hath in all outward behaviours seemed ever to abhor.

Bene. Is't possible? Sits the wind in that corner? [*Aside.*

Leon. By my troth, my lord, I cannot tell what to think of it; but that she loves him with an enraged affection,—it is past the infinite of thought.

D. Pedro. May be, she doth but counterfeit.

Claud. 'Faith, like enough.

Leon. O God! counterfeit! There never was counterfeit of passion came so near the life of passion, as she discovers it.

D. Pedro. Why, what effects of passion shows she?

Claud. Bait the hook well; this fish will bite. [*Aside.*

Leon. What effects, my lord! She will sit you,—You heard my daughter tell you how.

Claud. She did, indeed.

D. Pedro. How, how, I pray you? You amaze me: I would have thought her spirit had been invincible against all assaults of affection.

Leon. I would have sworn it had, my lord; especially against Benedick.

Bene. [*Aside.*] I should think this a gull, but that the white-bearded fellow speaks it: knavery cannot, sure, hide itself in such reverence.

Claud. He hath ta'en the infection; hold it up. [*Aside.*

D. Pedro. Hath she made her affection known to Benedick?

Leon. No; and swears she never will: that's her torment.

Claud. 'Tis true indeed; so your daughter says: *Shall I*, says she, *that have so oft encounter'd him with scorn, write to him that I love him!*

Leon. This says she now when she is beginning to write to him: for she'll be up twenty times a night: and there will she sit in her smock, till she have writ a sheet of paper:—my daughter tells us all.

Claud. Now you talk of a sheet of paper, I remember a pretty jest your daughter told us of.

Leon. O!—When she had writ it, and was reading it over, she found Benedick and Beatrice between the sheet!—

Claud. That.

Leon. O! she tore the letter into a thousand halfpence; railed at herself, that she should be so immodest to write to one that she knew would flout her: *I measure him*, says she, *by my own spirit, for I should flout him, if he writ to me; yea, though I love him, I should.*

Claud. Then down upon her knees she falls, weeps, sobs, beats her heart, tears her hair, prays, curses:—*O sweet Benedick! God give me patience!*

Leon. She doth indeed; my daughter says so: and the ecstasy hath so much overborne her, that my daughter is sometime afraid she will do a desperate outrage to herself: It is very true.

D. Pedro. It were good, that Benedick knew of it by some other, if she will not discover it.

Claud. To what end? He would but make a sport of it, and torment the poor lady worse.

D. Pedro. An he should, it were an alms to hang him: She's an excellent sweet lady; and, out of all suspicion, she is virtuous.

Claud. And she is exceeding wise.

D. Pedro. In every thing but in loving Benedick.

Leon. O my lord, wisdom and blood combating in so tender a body, we have ten proofs to one, that blood hath the victory. I am sorry for her, as I have just cause, being her uncle and her guardian.

D. Pedro. I would, she had bestow'd this dotage on me; I would have daff'd all other respects, and made her half myself: I pray you, tell Benedick of it, and hear what he will say.

Leon. Were it good, think you?

Claud. Hero thinks surely, she will die: for she says, she will die if he love her not; and she will die ere she makes her love known; and she will die if he woo her, rather than she will 'bate one breath of her accustomed crossness.

D. Pedro. She doth well: if she should make tender of her love, 'tis very possible he'll scorn it; for the man, as you know all, hath a contemptible spirit.

Claud. He is a very proper man.

D. Pedro. He hath, indeed, a good outward happiness.

Claud. 'Fore God, and in my mind, very wise.

D. Pedro. He doth, indeed, show some sparks that are like wit.

Leon. And I take him to be valiant.

D. Pedro. As Hector, I assure you: and in the managing of quarrels you may say he is wise; for either he avoids them with great discretion, or undertakes them with a most christian-like fear.

Leon. If he do fear God, he must necessarily keep peace; if he break the peace, he ought to enter into a quarrel with fear and trembling.

D. Pedro. And so will he do: for the man doth fear God, howsoever it seems not in him by some large jests he will make. Well, I am sorry for your niece: Shall we go see Benedick, and tell him of her love?

Claud. Never tell him, my lord; let her wear it out with good counsel.

Leon. Nay, that's impossible: she may wear her heart out first.

D. Pedro. Well, we'll hear further of it by your daughter; let it cool the while. I love Benedick well; and I could wish he would modestly examine himself, to see how much he is unworthy to have so good a lady.

Leon. My lord, will you walk? dinner is ready.

Claud. If he do not dote on her upon this, I will never trust my expectation. [*Aside.*

D. Pedro. Let there be the same net spread for her; and that must your daughter and her gentlewoman carry. The sport will be, when they hold one an opinion of another's dotage, and no such matter; that's the scene that I would see, which will be merely a dumb show. Let us send her to call him in to dinner. [*Aside.*

[*Exeunt* DON PEDRO, CLAUDIO, *and* LEONATO.

BENEDICK *advances from the arbour.*

Bene. This can be no trick: The conference was sadly borne.—They have the truth of this from Hero. They seem to pity the lady; it seems, her affections have their full bent. Love me! why, it must be requited. I hear how I am censured: they say, I will bear myself proudly, if I perceive the love come from her; they say too, that she will rather die than give any sign of affection.—I did never think to marry:—I must not seem proud:—Happy are they that hear their detractions, and can put them to mending. They say the lady is fair; 'tis a truth, I can bear them witness: and virtuous;—'tis so, I cannot reprove it; and wise, but for loving me:—By my troth, it is no addition to her wit;—nor no great argument of her folly, for I will be horribly in love with her. I may chance have some odd quirks and remnants of wit broken on me, because I have railed so long against marriage:—But doth not the appetite alter? A man loves the meat in his youth that he cannot endure in his age: Shall quips, and sentences, and these paper bullets of the brain, awe a man from the career of his humour; No: The world must be peopled. When I said, I would die a bachelor, I did not think I should live till I were married.—Here comes Beatrice: By this day she's a fair lady: I do spy some marks of love in her.

Enter BEATRICE.

Beat. Against my will I am sent to bid you come in to dinner.

Bene. Fair Beatrice, I thank you for your pains.

Beat. I took no more pains for those thanks than you take pains to thank me; if it had been painful, I would not have come.

Bene. You take pleasure then in the message?

Beat. Yea, just so much as you may take upon a knife's point, and choke a daw withal:—You have no stomach, signior; fare you well. [*Exit.*

Bene. Ha! *Against my will I am sent to bid you come to dinner*—there's a double meaning in that. *I took no more pains for those thanks than you took pains to thank me*—that's as much as to say, Any pains that I take for you is as easy as thanks:—If I do not take pity of her, I am a villain; if I do not love her, I am a Jew: I will go get her picture. [*Exit.*

ACT III.

SCENE I. Leonato's *Garden.*

Enter HERO, MARGARET, *and* URSULA.

Hero. Good Margaret, run thee into the parlour;
There shalt thou find my cousin Beatrice
Proposing with the Prince and Claudio:
Whisper her ear, and tell her, I and Ursula
Walk in the orchard, and our whole discourse
Is all of her; say, that thou overheard'st us;
And bid her steal into the pleached bower,
Where honey-suckles, ripen'd by the sun,
Forbid the sun to enter;—like favourites,
Made proud by princes, that advance their pride
Against that power that bred it:—there will she hide her,
To listen our propose: This is thy office,
Bear thee well in it, and leave us alone.

Marg. I'll make her come, I warrant you, presently. [*Exit.*

Hero. Now, Ursula, when Beatrice doth come,
As we do trace this alley up and down,
Our talk must only be of Benedick;
When I do name him, let it be thy part
To praise him more than ever man did merit:
My talk to thee must be, how Benedick
Is sick in love with Beatrice: Of this matter
Is little Cupid's crafty arrow made,
That only wounds by hearsay. Now begin;

Enter BEATRICE, *behind.*

For look where Beatrice, like a lapwing, runs
Close by the ground, to hear our conference.

Urs. The pleasant'st angling is to see the fish
Cut with their golden oars the silver stream,
And greedily devour the treacherous bait:
So angle we for Beatrice; who even now
Is couched in the woodbine coverture:
Fear you not my part of the dialogue.

Hero. Then go we near her, that her ear lose nothing
Of the false sweet bait, that we lay for it.— [*They advance to the bower.*
No, truly, Ursula, she is too disdainful;
I know her spirits are as coy and wild
As haggards of the rock.

Urs. But are you sure,
That Benedick loves Beatrice so entirely?

Hero. So says the prince, and my new-betrothed lord.

Urs. And did they bid you tell her of it, madam?

Hero. They did entreat me to acquaint her of it;
But I persuaded them, if they lov'd Benedick,
To wish him wrestle with affection,
And never let Beatrice know of it.

Urs. Why did you so? Doth not the gentleman
Deserve as full, as fortunate a bed,
As ever Beatrice shall couch upon?

Hero. O God of love! I know he doth deserve
As much as may be yielded to a man:
But nature never fram'd a woman's heart
Of prouder stuff than that of Beatrice:
Disdain and scorn ride sparkling in her eyes,
Misprising what they look on; and her wit
Values itself so highly, that to her
All matter else seems weak: she cannot love,
Nor take no shape nor project of affection,
She is so self-endeared.

Urs. Sure, I think so;
And therefore, certainly, it were not good
She knew his love, lest she make sport at it.

Hero. Why, you speak truth: I never yet saw man,
How wise, how noble, young, how rarely featur'd,
But she would spell him backward: if fair-fac'd,
She'd swear the gentleman should be her sister;
If black, why, nature, drawing of an antick,
Made a foul blot: if tall, a lance ill-headed;
If low, an agate very vilely cut:
If speaking, why a vane blown with all winds:
If silent, why a block moved with none.
So turns she every man the wrong side out;
And never gives to truth and virtue that
Which simpleness and merit purchaseth.

Urs. Sure, sure, such carping is not commendable.

Hero. No: not to be so odd, and from all fashions,
As Beatrice is, cannot be commendable:
But who dare tell her so? If I should speak,
She'd mock me into air; O, she would laugh me
Out of myself, press me to death with wit.
Therefore let Benedick, like cover'd fire,
Consume away in sighs, waste inwardly:
It were a better death than die with mocks;
Which is as bad as die with tickling.

Urs. Yet tell her of it; hear what she will say.

Hero. No; rather I will go to Benedick,
And counsel him to fight against his passion:
And, truly, I'll devise some honest slanders
To stain my cousin with: One doth not know,
How much an ill word may empoison liking.

Urs. O, do not do your cousin such a wrong.
She cannot be so much without true judgment,
(Having so swift and excellent a wit,
As she is priz'd to have), as to refuse
So rare a gentleman as signior Benedick.

Hero. He is the only man of Italy,
Always excepted my dear Claudio.

Urs. I pray you, be not angry with me, madam,
Speaking my fancy; Signior Benedick,
For shape, for bearing, argument, and valour,
Goes foremost in report through Italy.

Hero. Indeed, he hath an excellent good name.

Urs. His excellence did earn it, ere he had it.—
When are you married, madam?

Hero. Why, every day;—to-morrow: Come, go in;
I'll show thee some attires; and have thy counsel,
Which is the best to furnish me to-morrow.

Urs. She's lim'd I warrant you; we have caught her, madam.

Hero. If it prove so, then loving goes by haps:
Some Cupid kills with arrows, some with traps. [*Exeunt* HERO *and* URSULA.

BEATRICE *advances.*

Beat. What fire is in mine ears? Can this be true?
Stand I condemn'd for pride and scorn so much?
Contempt, farewell! and, maiden pride, adieu!
No glory lives behind the back of such.
And, Benedick, love on, I will requite thee;
Taming my wild heart to thy loving hand;
If thou dost love, my kindness shall incite thee
To bind our loves up in a holy band:
For others say, thou dost deserve; and I
Believe it better than reportingly. [*Exit.*

SCENE II. *A Room in* Leonato's *House.*

Enter DON PEDRO, CLAUDIO, BENEDICK, *and* LEONATO.

D. Pedro. I do but stay till your marriage be consummate, and then I go toward Arragon.

Claud. I'll bring you thither, my lord, if you'll vouchsafe me.

D. Pedro. Nay, that would be as great a soil in the new gloss of your marriage, as to show a child his new coat, and forbid him to wear it. I will only be bold with Benedick for his company: for, from the crown of his head to the sole of his foot, he is all mirth; he hath twice or thrice cut Cupid's bowstring, and the little hangman dare not shoot at him: he hath a heart as sound as a bell, and his tongue is the clapper; for what his heart thinks, his tongue speaks.

Bene. Gallants, I am not as I have been.

Leon. So say I; methinks you are sadder.

Claud. I hope, he be in love.

D. Pedro. Hang him, truant; there's no true drop of blood in him, to be truly touch'd with love: if he be sad, he wants money.

Bene. I have the tooth-ach.

D. Pedro. Draw it.

Bene. Hang it!

Claud. You must hang it first, and draw it afterwards.

D. Pedro. What, sigh for the tooth-ach?

Leon. Where is but a humour, or a worm?

Bene. Well, every one can master a grief, but he that has it.

Claud. Yet say I, he is in love.

D. Pedro. There is no appearance of fancy in him, unless it be a fancy that he hath to strange disguises; as, to be a Dutchman to-day; a Frenchman to-morrow; or in the shape of two countries at once; as, a German from the waist downward, all slops; and a Spaniard from the hip upward, no doublet: Unless he have a fancy to this foolery, as it appears he hath, he is no fool for fancy, as you would have it appear he is.

Claud. If he be not in love with some woman, there is no believing old signs: he brushes his hat o' mornings; What should that bode?

D. Pedro. Hath any man seen him at the barber's?

Claud. No, but the barber's man hath been seen with him; and the old ornament of his cheek hath already stuffed tennis-balls.

Leon. Indeed, he looks younger than he did, by the loss of a beard.

D. Pedro. Nay, he rubs himself with civet: Can you smell him out by that?

Claud. That's as much as to say, The sweet youth's in love.

D. Pedro. The greatest note of it is his melancholy.

Claud. And when was he wont to wash his face?

D. Pedro. Yea, or to paint himself? for the which, I hear what they say of him.

Claud. Nay, but his jesting spirit; which is now crept into a lutestring, and now governed by stops.

D. Pedro. Indeed, that tells a heavy tale for him: Conclude, conclude, he is in love.

Claud. Nay, but I know who loves him.

D. Pedro. That would I know too; I warrant, one that knows him not.

Claud. Yes, and his ill conditions; and, in despite of all, dies for him.

D. Pedro. She shall be buried with her face upwards.

Bene. Yet is this no charm for the tooth-ach.—Old signior, walk aside with me: I have studied eight or nine wise words to speak to you, which these hobby-horses must not hear. [*Exeunt* BENEDICK *and* LEONATO.

D. Pedro. For my life, to break with him about Beatrice.

Claud. 'Tis even so: Hero and Margaret have by this played their parts with Beatrice; and then the two bears will not bite one another when they meet.

Enter DON JOHN.

D. John. My lord and brother, God save you.

D. Pedro. Good den, brother.

D. John. If your leisure served, I would speak with you.

D. Pedro. In private?

D. John. If it please you:—yet Count Claudio may hear; for what I would speak of concerns him.

D. Pedro. What's the matter?

D. John. Means your lordship to be married to-morrow? [*To* CLAUDIO.

D. Pedro. You know, he does.

D. John. I know not that, when he knows what I know.

Claud. If there be any impediment, I pray you, discover it.

D. John. You may think, I love you not; let that appear hereafter, and aim better at me by that I now will manifest: For my brother, I think, he holds you well; and in dearness of heart hath holp to effect your ensuing marriage: surely, suit ill spent, and labour ill bestowed!

D. Pedro. Why, what's the matter?

D. John. I came hither to tell you; and, circumstances shortened, (for she hath been too long a talking of,) the lady is disloyal.

Claud. Who? Hero?

D. John. Even she; Leonato's Hero, your Hero, every man's Hero.

Claud. Disloyal?

D. John. The word is too good to paint out her wickedness; I could say, she were worse; think you of a worse title, and I will fit her to it. Wonder not till further warrant: go but with me to-night, you shall see her chamber-window entered; even the night before her wedding-day: if you love her then, to-morrow wed her: but it would better fit your honour to change your mind.

Claud. May this be so?

D. Pedro. I will not think it.

D. John. If you dare not trust that you see, confess not that you know: if you will follow me, I will show you enough; and when you have seen more, and heard more, proceed accordingly.

Claud. If I see any thing to-night why I should not marry her to-morrow; in the congregation, where I should wed, there will I shame her.

D. Pedro. And as I wooed for thee to obtain her, I will join with thee to disgrace her.

D. John. I will disparage her no farther, till you are my witnesses: bear it coldly but till midnight, and let the issue show itself.

D. Pedro. O day untowardly turned!

Claud. O mischief strangely thwarting!

D. John. O plague right well prevented!
So will you say, when you have seen the sequel. [*Exeunt.*

SCENE III. *A Street.*

Enter DOGBERRY *and* VERGES, *with the* Watch.

Dogb. Are you good men and true?

Verg. Yea, or else it were pity but they should suffer salvation, body and soul.

Dogb. Nay, that were a punishment too good for them, if they should have any allegiance in them, being chosen for the prince's watch.

Verg. Well, give them their charge, neighbour Dogberry.

Dogb. First, who think you the most desartless man to be constable?

1 *Watch.* Hugh Oatcake, sir, or George Seacoal: for they can write and read.

Dogb. Come hither, neighbour Seacoal. God hath blessed you with a good name: to be a well favoured man is the gift of fortune; but to write and read comes by nature.

2 *Watch.* Both which, master constable,——

Dogb. You have; I knew it would be your answer. Well, for your favour, sir, why, give God thanks, and make no boast of it; and for your writing and reading, let that appear when there is no need of such vanity. You are thought here to be the most senseless and fit man for the constable of the watch; therefore bear you the lantern: This is your charge: You shall comprehend all vagrom men: you are to bid any man stand, in the prince's name.

2 *Watch.* How if he will not stand?

Dogb. Why then, take no note of him, but let him go; and presently call the rest of the watch together, and thank God you are rid of a knave.

Verg. If he will not stand when he is bidden, he is none of the prince's subjects.

Dogb. True, and they are to meddle with none but the prince's subjects:—You shall also make no noise in the streets; for, for the watch to babble and talk, is most tolerable and not to be endured.

2 *Watch.* We will rather sleep than talk; we know what belongs to a watch.

Dogb. Why, you speak like an ancient and most quiet watchman; for I cannot see how sleeping should offend; only, have a care that your bills be not stolen:—Well, you are to call at all the alehouses, and bid those that are drunk get them to bed.

2 *Watch.* How if they will not?

Dogb. Why then, let them alone till they are sober; if they make you not then the better answer, you may say, they are not the men you took them for.

2 *Watch.* Well, sir.

Dogb. If you meet a thief, you may suspect him, by virtue of your office, to be no true man: and, for such kind of men, the less you meddle or make with them, why, the more is for your honesty.

2 *Watch.* If we know him to be a thief, shall we not lay hands on him?

Dogb. Truly, by your office, you may; but I think, they that touch pitch will be defiled: the most peaceable way for you, if you do take a thief, is, to let him show himself what he is, and steal out of your company.

Verg. You have been always called a merciful man, partner.

Dogb. Truly, I would not hang a dog by my will; much more a man, who hath any honesty in him.

Verg. If you hear a child cry in the night, you must call to the nurse, and bid her still it.

2 *Watch.* How if the nurse be asleep, and will not hear us?

Dogb. Why then, depart in peace, and let the child wake her with crying: for the ewe that will not hear her lamb when it baas, will never answer a calf when he bleats.

Verg. 'Tis very true.

Dogb. This is the end of the charge. You, constable, are to present the prince's own person; if you meet the prince in the night, you may stay him.

Verg. Nay, by'r lady, that, I think, he cannot.

Dogb. Five shillings to one on't, with any man that knows the statues, he may stay him: marry, not without the prince be willing; for, indeed, the watch ought to offend no man; and it is an offence to stay a man against his will.

Verg. By'r lady, I think, it be so.

Dogb. Ha, ha, ha! Well, masters, good night: an there be any matter of weight chances, call up me: keep your fellows' counsels and your own, and good night.—Come, neighbour.

2 *Watch.* Well, masters, we hear our charge: let us go sit here upon the church-bench till two, and then all to bed.

Dogb. One word more. honest neighbours: I pray you, watch about signior Leonato's door; for the wedding being there to-morrow, there is a great coil to-night: Adieu, be vigitant, I beseech you. [*Exeunt* DOGBERRY *and* VERGES.

Enter BORACHIO *and* CONRADE.

Bora. What! Conrade,—

Watch. Peace, stir not. [*Aside.*

Bora. Conrade, I say!

Con. Here, man, I am at thy elbow.

Bora. Mass, and my elbow itched; I thought, there would a scab follow.

Con. I will owe thee an answer for that; and now forward with thy tale.

Bora. Stand thee close then under this pent-house, for it drizzles rain; and I will, like a true drunkard, utter all to thee.

Watch. [*Aside.*] Some treason, masters; yet stand close.

Bora. Therefore know, I have earned of Don John a thousand ducats.

Con. Is it possible that any villany should be so dear?

Bora. Thou shouldst rather ask, if it were possible any villany should be so rich; for when rich villains have need of poor ones, poor ones may make what price they will.

Con. I wonder at it.

Bora. That shows thou art unconfirmed: Thou knowest, that the fashion of a doublet, or a hat, or a cloak, is nothing to a man.

Con. Yes, it is apparel.

Bora. I mean, the fashion.

Con. Yes, the fashion is the fashion.

Bora. Tush! I may as well say, the fool's the fool. But seest thou not what a deformed thief this fashion is?

Watch. I know that Deformed; he has been a vile thief this seven year; he goes up and down like a gentleman: I remember his name.

Bora. Didst thou not hear somebody?

Con. No; 'twas the vane on the house.

Bora. Seest thou not, I say, what a deformed thief this fashion is? how giddily he turns about all the hot bloods, between fourteen and five and thirty? sometime, fashioning them like Pharaoh's soldiers in the reechy painting; sometime, like god Bel's priests in the old church window; sometime, like the shaven Hercules in the smirched worm-eaten tapestry, where his cod-piece seems as massy as his club?

Con. All this I see; and see, that the fashion wears out more apparel than the man: But art not thou thyself giddy with the fashion too, that thou hast shifted out of thy tale into telling me of the fashion.

Bora. Not so neither: but know, that I have to-night wooed Margaret, the lady Hero's gentlewoman, by the name of Hero; she leans me out at her mistress' chamber-window, bids me a thousand times good night,—I tell this tale vilely:—I should first tell thee, how the Prince, Claudio, and my master, planted, and placed, and possessed by my master Don Jon, saw afar off in the orchard this amiable encounter.

Con. And thought they, Margaret was Hero?

Bora. Two of them did, the Prince and Claudio; but the devil my master knew she was Margaret; and partly by his oaths, which first possessed them, partly by the dark night, which did deceive them, but chiefly by my villany, which did confirm any slander that Don John had made, away went Claudio enraged; swore he would meet her as he was appointed, next morning at the temple, and there, before the whole congregation, shame her with what he saw over-night, and send her home again without a husband.

1 *Watch.* We charge you in the prince's name, stand.

2 *Watch.* Call up the right master constable: We have here recovered the most dangerous piece of lechery that ever was known in the commonwealth.

1 *Watch.* And one Deformed is one of them; I know him, he wears a lock.

Con. Masters, masters.

2 *Watch.* You'll be made bring Deformed forth, I warrant you.

Con. Masters,—

1 *Watch.* Never speak; we charge you, let us obey you to go with us.

Bora. We are like to prove a goodly commodity, being taken up of these men's bills.

Con. A commodity in question, I warrant you. Come, we'll obey you. [*Exeunt.*

SCENE IV. *A Room in* Leonato's *House.*

Enter HERO, MARGARET, *and* URSULA.

Hero. Good Ursula, wake my cousin Beatrice, and desire her to rise.

Urs. I will, lady.

Hero. And bid her come hither.

Urs. Well. [*Exit* URSULA.

Marg. Troth, I think, your other rabato were better.

Hero. No, pray thee, good Meg, I'll wear this.

Marg. By my troth, it's not so good; and I warrant, your cousin will say so.

Hero. My cousin's a fool, and thou art another; I'll wear none but this.

Marg. I like the new tire within excellently, if the hair were a thought browner: and your gown's a most rare fashion, i'faith. I saw the duchess of Milan's gown, that they praise so.

Hero. O, that exceeds, they say.

Marg. By my troth it's but a night-gown in respect of yours: Cloth of gold, and cuts, and laced with silver; set with pearls, down-sleeves, side-sleeves, and skirts round, underborne with a blueish tinsel: but for a fine, quaint, graceful, and excellent fashion, yours is worth ten on't.

Hero. God give me joy to wear it, for my heart is exceeding heavy!

Marg. 'Twill be heavier soon by the weight of a man.

Hero. Fye upon thee! art not ashamed?

Marg. Of what, lady? of speaking honourably? Is not marriage honourable in a beggar? Is not your lord honourable without marriage? I think, you would have me say, saving your reverence,—*a husband:* an bad thinking do not wrest true speaking, I'll offend nobody: Is there any harm in—*the heavier for a husband?* None, I think, an it be the right husband, and the right wife; otherwise 'tis light, and not heavy: Ask my lady Beatrice else, here she comes.

Enter BEATRICE.

Hero. Good morrow, coz.

Beat. Good morrow, sweet Hero.

Hero. Why, how now! do you speak in the sick tune?

Beat. I am out of all other tune, methinks.

Marg. Clap us into—*Light o' love;* that goe without a burden; do you sing it, and I'll danc it.

Beat. Yea, *Light o' love,* with your heels?—then if your husband have stables enough, you'll see he shall lack no barns.

Marg. O illegitimate construction! I scorn that with my heels.

Beat. 'Tis almost five o'clock, cousin; 'tis time you were ready. By my troth I am exceeding ill:—hey ho!

Marg. For a hawk, a horse, or a husband?

Beat. For the letter that begins them all, H.

Marg. Well, an you be not turned Turk, there's no more sailing by the star.

Beat. What means the fool, trow?

Marg. Nothing I; but God send every one their heart's desire!

Hero. These gloves the count sent me, they are an excellent perfume.

Beat. I am stuffed, cousin, I cannot smell.

Marg. A maid, and stuffed! there's goodly catching of cold.

Beat. O, God help me! God help me! how long have you profess'd apprehension?

Marg. Ever since you left it: doth not my wit become me rarely?

Beat. It is not seen enough, you should wear it in your cap.—By my troth, I am sick.

Marg. Get you some of this distilled Carduus Benedictus, and lay it to your heart; it is the only thing for a qualm.

Hero. There thou prick'st her with a thistle.

Beat. Benedictus! why Benedictus? you have some moral in this Benedictus.

Marg. Moral? no, by my troth, I have no moral meaning; I meant, plain holy-thistle. You may think, perchance, that I think you are in love: nay, by'r lady, I am not such a fool to think what I list; nor I list not to think what I can; nor, indeed, I cannot think, if I would think my heart out of thinking, that you are in love, or that you will be in love, or that you can be in love: yet Benedick was such another, and now is he become a man: he swore he would never marry; and yet now, in despite of his heart, he eats his meat without grudging: and how you may be converted, I know not; but methinks, you look with your eyes as other women do.

Beat. What pace is this that thy tongue keeps?

Marg. Not a false gallop.

Re-enter URSULA.

Urs. Madam, withdraw; the prince, the count, signior Benedick, Don John, and all the gallants of the town, are come to fetch you to church.

Hero. Help to dress me, good coz, good Meg, good Ursula. [*Exeunt.*

SCENE V. *Another Room in* Leonato's *House.*

Enter LEONATO, *with* DOGBERRY *and* VERGES.

Leon. What would you with me, honest neighbour?

Dogb. Marry, sir, I would have some confidence with you, that decerns you nearly.

Leon. Brief, I pray you; for you see, 'tis a busy time with me.

Dogb. Marry, this it is, sir.

Verg. Yes, in truth it is, sir.

Leon. What is it, my good friends?

Dogb. Goodman Verges, sir, speaks a little off the matter: an old man, sir, and his wits are not so blunt, as, God help, I would desire they were; but, in faith, honest as the skin between his brows.

Verg. Yes, I thank God, I am as honest as

any man living, that is an old man, and no honester than I.

Dogb. Comparisons are odorous: *palabras*, neighbour Verges.

Leon. Neighbours, you are tedious.

Dogb. It pleases your worship to say so, but we are the poor duke's officers; but, truly, for mine own part, if I were as tedious as a king, I could find in my heart to bestow it all of your worship.

Leon. All thy tediousness on me! ha!

Dogb. Yea, and 'twere a thousand times more than 'tis; for I hear as good exclamation on your worship, as of any man in the city; and though I be but a poor man, I am glad to hear it.

Verg. And so am I.

Leon. I would fain know what you have to say.

Verg. Marry, sir, our watch to-night, excepting your worship's presence, have ta'en a couple of as arrant knaves as any in Messina.

Dogb. A good old man, sir; he will be talking; as they say, When the age is in, the wit is out; God help us! it is a world to see!—Well said, i'faith, neighbour Verges:—well, God's a good man; an two men ride of a horse, one must ride behind:—An honest soul, i'faith, sir! by my troth he is, as ever broke bread: but, God is to be worshiped: All men are not alike; alas! good neighbour!

Leon. Indeed, neighbour, he comes too short of you.

Dogb. Gifts, that God gives.

Leon. I must leave you.

Dogb. One word, sir: our watch, sir, have, indeed, comprehended two aspicious persons, and we would have them this morning examined before your worship.

Leon. Take their examination yourself, and bring it me; I am now in great haste, as it may appear unto you.

Dogb. It shall be suffigance.

Leon. Drink some wine ere you go; fare you well.

Enter a Messenger.

Mess. My lord, they stay for you to give your daughter to her husband.

Leon. I will wait upon them; I am ready.

[*Exeunt* LEONATO *and* Messenger.

Dogb. Go, good partner, go, get you to Francis Seacoal, bid him bring his pen and inkhorn to the gaol; we are now to examination these men.

Verg. And we must do it wisely.

Dogb. We will spare for no wit, I warrant you; here's that [*Touching his forehead.*] shall drive some of them to a *non com:* only get the learned writer to set down our excommunication, and meet me at the gaol. *Exeunt.*

ACT IV.

SCENE I. *The Inside of a Church.*

Enter DON PEDRO, DON JOHN, LEONATO, Friar, CLAUDIO, BENEDICK, HERO, *and* BEATRICE, *&c.*

Leon. Come, friar Francis, be brief; only to the plain form of marriage, and you shall recount their particular duties afterwards.

Friar. You come hither, my lord, to marry this lady?

Claud. No.

Leon. To be married to her, friar; you come to marry her.

Friar. Lady, you come hither to be married to this count?

Hero. I do.

Friar. If either of you know any inward impediment why you should not be conjoined, I charge you, on your souls, to utter it.

Claud. Know you any, Hero?

Hero. None, my lord.

Friar. Know you any, count?

Leon. I dare make his answer, none.

Claud. O, what men dare do! what men may do! what men daily do! not knowing what they do!

Bene. How now! Interjections? Why, then some be of laughing, as, ha! ha! he!

Claud. Stand thee by, friar:—Father, by your leave!
Will you with free and unconstrained soul
Give me this maid, your daughter?

Leon. As freely, son, as God did give her me.

Claud. And what have I to give you back, whose worth
May counterpoise this rich and precious gift.

D. Pedro. Nothing, unless you render her again.

Claud. Sweet prince, you learn me noble thankfulness.—
There, Leonato, take her back again;
Give not this rotten orange to your friend;
She's but the sign and semblance of her honour.—
Behold, how like a maid she blushes here:
O, what authority, and show of truth
Can cunning sin cover itself withal!
Comes not that blood, as modest evidence,
To witness simple virtue? Would you not swear,
All you that see her, that she were a maid,
By these exterior shows?—But she is none:
She knows the heat of a luxurious bed:
Her blush is guiltiness, not modesty.

Leon. What do you mean, my lord?

Claud. Not to be married,
Not to knit my soul to an approved wanton.

Leon. Dear my lord, if you, in your own proof
Have vanquish'd the resistance of her youth,
And made defeat of her virginity,——

Claud. I know what you would say; If I have known her,
You'll say, she did embrace me as a husband,
And so extenuate the 'forehand sin:
No, Leonato,
I never tempted her with word too large;
But, as a brother to his sister, show'd
Bashful sincerity, and comely love.

Hero. And seem'd I ever otherwise to you?

Claud. Out on thy seeming! I will write against it:
You seem to me as Dian in her orb;
As chaste as is the bud ere it be blown;
But you are more intemperate in your blood
Than Venus or those pamper'd animals
That rage in savage sensuality.

Hero. Is my lord well, that he doth speak so wide?

Leon. Sweet prince, why speak not you?

D. Pedro. What should I speak?
I stand dishonour'd, that have gone about
To link my dear friend to a common stale.

Leon. Are these things spoken? or do I but dream?

D. John. Sir, they are spoken, and these things are true.

Bene. This looks not like a nuptial.

Hero. True, O God!

Claud. Leonato, stand I here?
Is this the prince? Is this the prince's brother?
Is this face Hero's? Are our eyes our own?

Leon. All this is so; But what of this, my lord?

Claud. Let me but move one question to your daughter;
And, by that fatherly and kindly power
That you have in her, bid her answer truly.

Leon. I charge thee do so, as thou art my child.

Hero. O God, defend me! how am I beset!—
What kind of catechizing call you this?

Claud. To make you answer truly to your name.

Hero. Is it not Hero? Who can blot that name
With any just reproach?

Claud. Marry, that can Hero;
Hero itself can blot out Hero's virtue.
What man was he talk'd with you yesternight

Out at your window, betwixt twelve and one?
Now, if you are a maid, answer to this.

Hero. I talk'd with no man at that hour, my lord.

D. Pedro. Why, then are you no maiden.—Leonato,
I am sorry you must hear; Upon mine honour,
Myself, my brother, and this grieved count,
Did see her, hear her, at that hour last night,
Talk with a ruffian at her chamber-window;
Who hath, indeed, most like a liberal villain,
Confess'd the vile encounters they have had
A thousand times in secret.

D. John. Fye, fye! they are
Not to be nam'd, my lord, not to be spoke of;
There is not chastity enough in language,
Without offence, to utter them: Thus, pretty lady,
I am sorry for thy much misgovernment.

Claud. O Hero! what a Hero hadst thou been,
If half thy outward graces had been placed
About thy thoughts, and counsels of thy heart!
But, fare thee well, most foul, most fair! farewell,
Thou pure impiety, and impious purity!
For thee I'll lock up all the gates of love,
And on my eyelids shall conjecture hang,
To turn all beauty into thoughts of harm,
And never shall it more be gracious.

Leon. Hath no man's dagger here a point for me? [HERO *swoons.*

Beat. Why, how now, cousin? wherefore sink you down?

D. John. Come, let us go: these things, come thus to light,
Smother her spirits up.

[*Exeunt* DON PEDRO, DON JOHN, *and* CLAUDIO.

Bene. How doth the lady?

Beat. Dead, I think;—help, uncle;—
Hero! why, Hero!—Uncle!—Signior Benedick!
—friar?

Leon. O fate, take not away thy heavy hand!
Death is the fairest cover for her shame,
That may be wish'd for.

Beat. How now, cousin Hero?

Friar. Have comfort, lady.

Leon. Dost thou look up?

Friar. Yea; wherefore should she not?

Leon. Wherefore? Why, doth not every earthly thing
Cry shame upon her? Could she here deny
The story that is printed in her blood?—
Do not live, Hero; do not ope thine eyes:
For did I think thou wouldst not quickly die,
Thought I thy spirits were stronger than thy shames,
Myself would, on the rearward of reproaches,
Strike at thy life. Griev'd I, I had but one?
Chid I for that at frugal nature's frame?
O, one too much by thee! Why had I one?
Why ever wast thou lovely in my eyes?
Why had I not, with charitable hand,
Took up a beggar's issue at my gates;
Who smirched thus, and mired with infamy,
I might have said, *No part of it is mine,*
This shame derives itself from unknown loins?
But mine, and mine I lov'd, and mine I prais'd,
And mine that I was proud on; mine so much,
That I myself was to myself not mine,
Valuing of her: why, she—O, she is fallen
Into a pit of ink! that the wide sea
Hath drops too few to wash her clean again;
And salt too little, which may season give
To her foul tainted flesh!

Bene. Sir, sir, be patient;
For my part, I am so attir'd in wonder,
I know not what to say.

Beat. O, on my soul, my cousin is belied!

Bene. Lady, were you her bedfellow last night?

Beat. No, truly not: although, until last night
I have this twelvemonth been her bedfellow.

Leon. Confirm'd, confirm'd! O, that is stronger made,
Which was before barr'd up with ribs of iron!
Would the two princes lie? and Claudio lie?
Who lov'd her so, that, speaking of her foulness,
Wash'd it with tears? Hence from her; let her die.

Friar. Hear me a little;
For I have only been silent so long,
And given way unto this course of fortune,
By noting of the lady: I have mark'd
A thousand blushing apparitions start
Into her face; a thousand innocent shames
In angel whiteness bear away those blushes;
And in her eye there hath appear'd a fire,
To burn the errors that these princes hold
Against her maiden truth:—Call me a fool;
Trust not my reading, nor my observations,
Which with experimental seal doth warrant
The tenour of my book; trust not my age,
My reverence, calling, nor divinity,
If this sweet lady lie not guiltless here
Under some biting error.

Leon. Friar, it cannot be:
Thou seest, that all the grace that she hath left,
Is, that she will not add to her damnation
A sin of perjury; she not denies it;
Why seek'st thou then to cover with excuse
That which appears in proper nakedness?

Friar. Lady, what man is he you are accus'd of?

Hero. They know, that do accuse me; I know none:
If I know more of any man alive,
Than that which maiden modesty doth warrant,
Let all my sins lack mercy!—O my father,
Prove you that any man with me convers'd
At hours unmeet, or that I yesternight
Maintain'd the change of words with any creature,
Refuse me, hate me, torture me to death.

Friar. There is some strange misprision in the princes.

Bene. Two of them have the very bent of honour;
And if their wisdoms be misled in this,
The practice of it lives in John the bastard,
Whose spirits toil in frame of villanies.

Leon. I know not; If they speak but truth of her,
These hands shall tear her; if they wrong her honour,
The proudest of them shall well hear of it.
Time hath not yet so dried this blood of mine,
Nor age so eat up my invention,
Nor fortune made such havock of my means,
Nor my bad life reft me so much of friends,
But they shall find, awak'd in such a kind,
Both strength of limb, and policy of mind,
Ability in means, and choice of friends,
To quit me of them thoroughly.

Friar. Pause a while,
And let my counsel sway you in this case.
Your daughter here the princes left for dead;
Let her awhile be secretly kept in,
And publish it, that she is dead indeed:
Maintain a mourning ostentation;
And on your family's old monument
Hang mournful epitaphs, and do all rites
That appertain unto a burial.

Leon. What shall become of this? What will this do?

Friar. Marry, this well carried, shall on her behalf
Change slander to remorse; that is some good:
But not for that, dream I on this strange course,
But on this travail look for greater birth.
She dying, as it must be so maintain'd,
Upon the instant that she was accus'd,
Shall be lamented, pitied and excus'd,
Of every hearer: For it so falls out,
That what we have we prize not to the worth,
Whiles we enjoy it; but being lack'd and lost,
Why, then we rack the value; then we find
The virtue, that possession would not show us
Whiles it was ours:—So will it fare with Claudio:

When he shall hear she died upon his words,
The idea of her life shall sweetly creep
Into his study of imagination;
And every lovely organ of her life
Shall come apparell'd in more precious habit,
More moving-delicate, and full of life,
Into the eye and prospect of his soul,
Than when she liv'd indeed:—then shall he mourn,
(If ever love had interest in his liver),
And wish he had not so accused her;
No, though he thought his accusation true.
Let this be so, and doubt not but success
Will fashion the event in better shape
Than I can lay it down in likelihood.
But if all aim but this be levell'd false,
The supposition of the lady's death
Will quench the wonder of her infamy:
And, if it sort not well, you may conceal her
(As best befits her wounded reputation),
In some reclusive and religious life,
Out of all eyes, tongues, minds, and injuries.

Bene. Signior Leonato, let the friar advise you:
And though, you know, my inwardness and love
Is very much unto the prince and Claudio,
Yet, by mine honour, I will deal in this
As secretly, and justly, as your soul
Should with your body.

Leon. Being that I flow in grief,
The smallest twine may lead me.

Friar. 'Tis well consented; presently away;
For to strange sores strangely they strain the cure.—
Come, lady, die to live: this wedding day,
Perhaps, is but prolong'd; have patience, and endure.

[*Exeunt* Friar, HERO, *and* LEONATO.

Bene. Lady Beatrice, have you wept all this while?

Beat. Yea, and I will weep a while longer.

Bene. I will not desire that.

Beat. You have no reason, I do it freely.

Bene. Surely, I do believe your fair cousin is wrong'd.

Beat. Ah, how much might the man deserve of me, that would right her!

Bene. Is there any way to show such friendship?

Beat. A very even way, but no such friend.

Bene. May a man do it?

Beat. It is a man's office, but not yours.

Bene. I do love nothing in the world so well as you? Is not that strange?

Beat. As strange as the thing I know not: It were as possible for me to say, I loved nothing so well as you: but believe me not; and yet I lie not; I confess nothing, nor I deny nothing:—I am sorry for my cousin.

Bene. By my sword, Beatrice, thou lovest me.

Beat. Do not swear by it, and eat it.

Bene. I will swear by it, that you love me; and I will make him eat it, that says, I love not you.

Beat. Will you not eat your word?

Bene. With no sauce that can be devised to it: I protest, I love thee.

Beat. Why then, God forgive me!

Bene. What offence, sweet Beatrice?

Beat. You have staid me in a happy hour; I was about to protest, I loved you.

Bene. And do it with all thy heart.

Beat. I love you with so much of my heart, that none is left to protest.

Bene. Come, bid me do any thing for thee.

Beat. Kill Claudio.

Bene. Ha! not for the wide world.

Beat. You kill me to deny it: Farewell.

Bene. Tarry, sweet Beatrice.

Beat. I am gone, though I am here:—There is no love in you:—Nay, I pray you, let me go.

Bene. Beatrice,—

Beat. In faith, I will go.

Bene. We'll be friends first.

Beat. You dare easier be friends with me, than fight with mine enemy.

Bene. Is Claudio thine enemy?

Beat. Is he not approved in the height a villain, that hath slandered, scorned, dishonoured my kinswoman?—O, that I were a man!—What! bear her in hand until they come to take hands; and then with public accusation, uncovered slander, unmitigated rancour,—O God, that I were a man! I would eat his heart in the market place.

Bene. Hear me, Beatrice;—

Beat. Talk with a man out at a window?—a proper saying!

Bene. Nay but, Beatrice;—

Beat. Sweet Hero!—she is wronged, she is slandered, she is undone.

Bene. Beat—

Beat. Princes, and counties! Surely, a princely testimony, a goodly count-confect; a sweet gallant, surely! O that I were a man for his sake! or that I had any friend would be a man for my sake! But manhood is melted into courtesies, valour into compliment, and men are only turned into tongue, and trim ones too: he is now as valiant as Hercules, that only tells a lie, and swears it:—I cannot be a man with wishing, therefore I will die a woman with grieving.

Bene. Tarry, good Beatrice: By this hand, I love thee.

Beat. Use it for my love some other way than swearing by it.

Bene. Think you in your soul the count Claudio hath wronged Hero?

Beat. Yea, as sure as I have a thought, or a soul.

Bene. Enough, I am engaged, I will challenge him; I will kiss your hand, and so leave you: By this hand, Claudio shall render me a dear account: As you hear of me, so think of me. Go, comfort your cousin; I must say, she is dead; and so, farewell. [*Exeunt.*

SCENE II. *A Prison.*

Enter DOGBERRY, VERGES, *and* Sexton, *in gowns; and the* Watch, *with* CONRADE *and* BORACHIO.

Dogb. Is our whole dissembly appeared?

Verg. O, a stool and a cushion for the sexton.

Sexton. Which be the malefactors?

Dogb. Marry, that am I and my partner.

Verg. Nay, that's certain; we have the exhibition to examine.

Sexton. But which are the offenders that are to be examined? let them come before master constable.

Dogb. Yea, marry, let them come before me.—What is your name, friend?

Bora. Borachio.

Dogb. Pray write down—Borachio.——Yours, sirrah?

Con. I am a gentleman, sir, and my name is Conrade.

Dogb. Write down—master gentleman Conrade.—Masters, do you serve God?

Con. Bora. Yea, sir, we hope.

Dogb. Write down—that they hope they serve God:—and write God first; for God defend but God should go before such villains!—Masters, it is proved already that you are little better than false knaves; and it will go near to be thought so shortly. How answer you for yourselves?

Con. Marry, sir, we say we are none.

Dogb. A marvellous witty fellow, I assure you; but I will go about with him.—Come you hither, sirrah; a word in your ear, sir; I say to you, it is thought you are false knaves.

Bora. Sir, I say to you, we are none.

Dogb. Well, stand aside.—'Fore God, they are both in a tale: Have you writ down—that they are none?

Sexton. Master constable, you go not the way to examine; you must call forth the watch that are their accusers.

Dogb. Yea, marry, that's the eftest way:—Let the watch come forth:—Masters, I charge you, in the prince's name, accuse these men.

1 *Watch.* This man said, sir, that Don John, the prince's brother, was a villain.

Dogb. Write down—prince John a villain:—Why, this is flat perjury, to call a prince's brother—villain.

Bora. Master constable,—

Dogb. 'Pray thee, fellow, peace; I do not like thy look, I promise thee.

Sexton. What heard you him say else?

2 *Watch.* Marry, that he had received a thousand ducats of Don John, for accusing the lady Hero wrongfully.

Dogb. Flat burglary, as ever was committed.

Verg. Yea, by the mass, that it is.

Sexton. What else, fellow?

1 *Watch.* And that count Claudio did mean, upon his words, to disgrace Hero before the whole assembly, and not marry her.

Dogb. O villain! thou wilt be condemned into everlasting redemption for this.

Sexton. What else?

2 *Watch.* This is all.

Sexton. And this is more, masters, than you can deny. Prince John is this morning secretly stolen away; Hero was in this manner accused, in this very manner refused, and upon the grief of this suddenly died.—Master constable, let these men be bound, and brought to Leonato's; I will go before, and show him their examination. [*Exit.*

Dogb. Come, let them be opinioned.

Verg. Let them be in the bands—

Con. Off, coxcomb!

Dogb. God's my life! where's the sexton? let him write down—the prince's officer, coxcomb.—Come, bind them:——Thou naughty varlet!

Con. Away! you are an ass, you are an ass.

Dogb. Dost thou not suspect my place? Dost thou not suspect my years?—O that he were here to write me down—an ass;—but, masters, remember, that I am an ass; though it be not written down, yet forget not that I am an ass:—No, thou villain, thou art full of piety, as shall be proved upon thee by good witness. I am a wise fellow; and, which is more, an officer; and, which is more, a householder: and, which is more, as pretty a piece of flesh as any is in Messina; and one that knows the law, go to: and a rich fellow enough, go to; and a fellow that hath had losses; and one that hath two gowns, and every thing handsome about him:—Bring him away. O, that I had been writ down—an ass. [*Exeunt.*

ACT V.

SCENE I. *Before* Leonato's *House.*

Enter LEONATO *and* ANTONIO.

Ant. If you go on thus, you will kill yourself.
And 'tis not wisdom, thus to second grief
Against yourself.

Leon. I pray thee, cease thy counsel,
Which falls into mine ears as profitless
As water in a sieve: give not me counsel;
Nor let no comforter delight mine ear,
But such a one whose wrongs do suit with mine.
Bring me a father, that so lov'd his child,
Whose joy of her is overwhelm'd like mine,
And bid him speak of patience;
Measure his woe the length and breadth of mine,
And let it answer every strain for strain;
As thus for thus, and such a grief for such,
In every lineament, branch, shape, and form:
If such a one will smile, and stroke his beard:
Cry——sorrow, wag! and hem, when he should groan;
Patch grief with proverbs; make misfortune drunk
With candle-wasters; bring him yet to me,
And I of him will gather patience.
But there is no such man: For, brother, men
Can counsel, and speak comfort to that grief
Which they themselves not feel; but, tasting it,
Their counsel turns to passion, which before
Would give preceptial medicine to rage,
Fetter strong madness in a silken thread,
Charm ach with air, and agony with words:
No, no; 'tis all men's office to speak patience
To those that wring under the load of sorrow:
But no man's virtue, nor sufficiency,
To be so moral, when he shall endure
The like himself: therefore give me no counsel:
My griefs cry louder than advertisement.

Ant. Therein do men from children nothing differ.

Leon. I pray thee, peace: I will be flesh and blood;
For there was never yet philosopher,
That could endure the tooth-ach patiently;
However they have writ the style of gods,
And made a push at chance and sufferance.

Ant. Yet bend not all the harm upon yourself;
Make those, that do offend you, suffer too.

Leon. There thou speak'st reason: nay, I will do so;
My soul doth tell me, Hero is belied,
And that shall Claudio know, so shall the prince,
And all of them, that thus dishonour her.

Enter DON PEDRO *and* CLAUDIO.

Ant. Here comes the prince, and Claudio hastily.

D. Pedro. Good den, good den.

Claud. Good day to both of you.

Leon. Hear you, my lords,—

D. Pedro. We have some haste, Leonato.

Leon. Some haste, my lord!—well, fare you well, my lord:—
Are you so hasty now?—well, all is one.

D. Pedro. Nay, do not quarrel with us, good old man.

Ant. If he could right himself with quarreling,
Some of us would lie low.

Claud. Who wrongs him?

Leon. Marry, thou dost wrong me; thou dissembler, thou:—
Nay, never lay thy hand upon thy sword,
I fear thee not.

Claud. Marry, beshrew my hand,
If it should give your age such cause of fear.
In faith, my hand meant nothing to my sword.

Leon. Tush, tush, man, never fleer and jest at me:
I speak not like a dotard, nor a fool;
As, under privilege of age, to brag
What I have done being young, or what would do,
Were I not old: Know, Claudio, to thy head,
Thou hast so wrong'd mine innocent child and me,
That I am forc'd to lay my reverence by;
And, with gray hairs, and bruise of many days,
Do challenge thee to trial of a man.
I say, thou hast belied mine innocent child;
Thy slander hath gone through and through her heart,
And she lies buried with her ancestors:
O! in a tomb where never scandal slept,
Save this of hers, fram'd by thy villany.

Claud. My villany!

Leon. Thine, Claudio; thine, I say.

D. Pedro. You say not right, old man.

Leon. My lord, my lord,
I'll prove it on his body, if he dare;
Despite his nice fence, and his active practice,
His May of youth, and bloom of lustyhood.

Claud. Away, I will not have to do with you.

Leon. Canst thou so daff me? Thou hast kill'd my child;
If thou kill'st me, boy, thou shalt kill a man.

Ant. He shall kill two of us, and men indeed:
But that's no matter; let him kill one first;—
Win me and wear me,—let him answer me,—
Come, follow me, boy; come, boy, follow me:
Sir boy, I'll whip you from your foining fence;
Nay, as I am a gentleman, I will.

Leon. Brother,—

Ant. Content yourself: God knows, I lov'd my niece;
And she is dead, slander'd to death by villains;
That dare as well answer a man, indeed,
As I dare take a serpent by the tongue;
Boys, apes, braggarts, jacks, milksops!—

Leon. Brother Antony,—

Ant. Hold you content; What, man! I know them, yea,
And what they weigh, even to the utmost scruple:
Scambling, out-facing, fashion-mong'ring boys,
That lie, and cog, and flout, deprave and slander,
Go antickly, and show outward hideousness,
And speak off half a dozen dangerous words,
How they might hurt their enemies, if they durst,
And this is all.

Leon. But, brother Antony,—

Ant. Come, 'tis no matter;
Do not you meddle, let me deal in this.

D. Pedro. Gentlemen both, we will not wake your patience.
My heart is sorry for your daughter's death;
But, on my honour, she was charg'd with nothing
But what was true, and very full of proof.

Leon. My lord, my lord,—

D. Pedro. I will not hear you.

Leon. No?
Come, brother, away:—I will be heard:—

Ant. And shall,
Or some of us will smart for it.

[*Exeunt* LEONATO *and* ANTONIO.

Enter BENEDICK.

D. Pedro. See, see; here comes the man we went to seek.

Claud. Now, signior! what news?

Bene. Good day, my lord.

D. Pedro. Welcome, signior: You are almost come to part almost a fray.

Claud. We had like to have had our two noses snapped off with two old men without teeth.

D. Pedro. Leonato and his brother: What think'st thou? Had we fought, I doubt, we should have been too young for them.

Bene. In a false quarrel there is no true valour. I came to seek you both.

Claud. We have been up and down to seek thee; for we are high-proof melancholy, and would fain have it beaten away: Wilt thou use thy wit?

Bene. It is in my scabbard; Shall I draw it?

D. Pedro. Dost thou wear thy wit by thy side?

Claud. Never any did so, though very many have been beside their wit.—I will bid thee draw, as we do the minstrels; draw, to pleasure us.

D. Pedro. As I am an honest man, he looks pale:—Art thou sick, or angry?

Claud. What! courage, man! What though care killed a cat, thou hast mettle enough in thee to kill care.

Bene. Sir, I shall meet your wit in the career, an you charge it against me:—I pray you, choose another subject

Claud. Nay, then give him another staff: this last was broke cross.

D. Pedro. By this light, he changes more and more; I think, he be angry indeed.

Claud. If he be, he knows how to turn his girdle.

Bene. Shall I speak a word in your ear?

Claud. God bless me from a challenge!

Bene. You are a villain:—I jest not:—I will make it good how you dare, with what you dare, and when you dare:—Do me right, or I will protest your cowardice. You have killed a sweet lady, and her death shall fall heavy on you: Let me hear from you.

Claud. Well, I will meet you, so I may have good cheer.

D. Pedro. What, a feast? a feast?

Claud. I'faith, I thank him; he hath bid me to a calf's head and a capon; the which if I do not carve most curiously, say, my knife's naught.—Shall I not find a woodcock too?

Bene. Sir, your wit ambles well; it goes easily.

D. Pedro. I'll tell thee how Beatrice praised thy wit the other day: I said thou hadst a fine wit: *True,* says she, *a fine little one: No,* said I, *a great wit; Right,* says she, *a great gross one: Nay,* said I, *a good wit; Just;* said she, *it hurts nobody: Nay,* said I, *the gentleman is wise; Certain,* said she, *a wise gentleman: Nay,* said I, *he hath the tongues; That I believe,* said she, *for he swore a thing to me on Monday night, which he forswore on Tuesday morning; there's a double tongue; there's two tongues.* Thus, did she, an hour together, transshape thy particular virtues; yet, at last, she concluded with a sigh, thou wast the properest man in Italy.

Claud. For the which she wept heartily, and said, she cared not.

D. Pedro. Yea, that she did; but yet, for all that, an if she did not hate him deadly, she would love him dearly: the old man's daughter told us all.

Claud. All, all; and moreover, *God saw him when he was hid in the garden.*

D. Pedro. But when shall we set the savage bull's horns on the sensible Benedick's head?

Claud. Yea, and text underneath, *Here dwells Benedick the married man?*

Bene. Fare you well, boy; you know my mind: I will leave you now to your gossip-like humour; you break jests as braggarts do their blades, which, God be thanked, hurt not.—My lord, for your many courtesies I thank you: I must discontinue your company: your brother, the bastard, is fled from Messina: you have, among you, killed a sweet and innocent lady: For my lord Lack-beard, there, he and I shall meet; and till then, peace be with him.

[*Exit* BENEDICK.

D. Pedro. He is in earnest.

Claud. In most profound earnest; And, I'll warrant you, for the love of Beatrice.

D. Pedro. And hath challenged thee?

Claud. Most sincerely.

D. Pedro. What a pretty thing man is, when he goes in his doublet and hose, and leaves off his wit.

Claud. He is then a giant to an ape: but then is an ape a doctor to such a man.

D. Pedro. But, soft you, let be; pluck up, my heart, and be sad! Did he not say, my brother was fled?

Enter DOGBERRY, VERGES, *and the* Watch, *with* CONRADE *and* BORACHIO.

Dogb. Come, you, sir; if justice cannot tame you, she shall ne'er weigh more reasons in her balance: nay, an you be a cursing hypocrite once, you must be looked to.

D. Pedro. How now, two of my brother's men bound! Borachio, one!

Claud. Hearken after their offence, my lord!

D. Pedro. Officers, what offence have these men done?

Dogb. Marry, sir, they have committed false report; moreover, they have spoken untruths; secondarily, they are slanders: sixth and lastly, they have belied a lady; thirdly, they have verified unjust things! and, to conclude, they are lying knaves.

D. Pedro. First, I ask thee what they have

done; thirdly, I ask thee what's their offence; sixth and lastly, why they are committed; and, to conclude, what you lay to their charge?

Claud. Rightly reasoned, and in his own division; and, by my troth, there's one meaning well suited.

D. Pedro. Whom have you offended, masters, that you are thus bound to your answer? this learned constable is too cunning to be understood: What's your offence?

Bora. Sweet prince, let me go no further to mine answer; do you hear me, and let this count kill me. I have deceived even your very eyes; what your wisdoms could not discover, these shallow fools have brought to light; who, in the night, overheard me confessing to this man, how Don John, your brother, incensed me to slander the lady Hero: how you were brought into the orchard, and saw me court Margaret in Hero's garments; how you disgraced her, when you should marry her: my villany they have upon record; which I had rather seal with my death, than repeat over to my shame: the lady is dead upon mine and my master's false accusation; and, briefly, I desire nothing but the reward of a villain.

D. Pedro. Runs not this speech like iron through your blood?

Claud. I have drunk poison, whiles he utter'd it.

D. Pedro. But did my brother set thee on to this?

Bora. Yea, and paid me richly for the practice of it.

D. Pedro. He is compos'd and fram'd of treachery:—
And fled he is upon this villany.

Claud. Sweet Hero! now thy image doth appear
In the rare semblance that I loved it first.

Dogb. Come, bring away the plaintiffs: by this time our sexton hath reformed signior Leonato of the matter: And, masters, do not forget to specify, when time and place shall serve, that I am an ass.

Verg. Here, here comes master signior Leonato and the Sexton too.

Re-enter LEONATO *and* ANTONIO, *with the* Sexton.

Leon. Which is the villain? Let me see his eyes;
That when I note another man like him,
I may avoid him: which of these is he?

Bora. If you would know your wronger, look on me.

Leon. Art thou the slave, that with thy breath hast kill'd
Mine innocent child?

Bora. Yea, even I alone.

Leon. No, not so, villain; thou bely'st thyself;
Here stand a pair of honourable men,
A third is fled, that had a hand in it:—
I thank you, princes, for my daughter's death;
Record it with your high and worthy deeds;
'Twas bravely done, if you bethink you of it.

Claud. I know not how to pray your patience,
Yet I must speak: Choose your revenge yourself;
Impose me to what penance your invention
Can lay upon my sin: yet sinn'd I not,
But in mistaking.

D. Pedro. By my soul, nor I;
And yet, to satisfy this good old man,
I would bend under any heavy weight
That he'll enjoin me to.

Leon. I cannot bid you bid my daughter live,
That were impossible; but, I pray you both,
Possess the people in Messina here
How innocent she died: and, if your love
Can labour aught in sad invention,
Hang her an epitaph upon her tomb,
And sing it to her bones; sing it to-night:—
To-morrow morning come you to my house;
And since you could not be my son-in-law,
Be yet my nephew: my brother hath a daughter
Almost the copy of my child that's dead,
And she alone is heir to both of us;
Give her the right you should have given her cousin:
And so dies my revenge.

Claud. O noble sir,
Your over-kindness doth wring tears from me!
I do embrace your offer; and dispose
For henceforth of poor Claudio.

Leon. To morrow then I will expect your coming;
To-night I take my leave.—This naughty man
Shall face to face be brought to Margaret,
Who, I believe, was pack'd in all this wrong,
Hir'd to it by your brother.

Bora. No, by my soul, she was not;
Nor knew not what she did, when she spoke to me;
But always hath been just and virtuous,
In any thing that I do know by her.

Dogb. Moreover, sir (which, indeed, is not under white and black), this plaintiff here, the offender, did call me ass: I beseech you, let it be remembered in his punishment: And also, the watch heard them talk of one Deformed: they say, he wears a key in his ear, and a lock hanging by it; and borrows money in God's name; the which he hath used so long, and never paid, that now men grow hard-hearted, and will lend nothing for God's sake: 'Pray you, examine him upon that point.

Leon. I thank thee for thy care and honest pains.

Dogb. Your worship speaks like a most thankful and reverend youth; and I praise God for you.

Leon. There's for thy pains.

Dogb. God save the foundation.

Leon. Go, I discharge thee of thy prisoner, and I thank thee.

Dogb. I leave an errant knave with your worship; which, I beseech your worship, to correct yourself, for the example of others. God keep your worship; I wish your worship well; God restore you to health: I humbly give you leave to depart; and if a merry meeting may be wished, God prohibit it.—Come, neighbour. [*Exeunt* DOGBERRY, VERGES, *and* Watch.

Leon. Until to-morrow morning, lords, farewell.

Ant. Farewell, my lords: we look for you to-morrow.

D. Pedro. We will not fail.

Claud. To-night I'll mourn with Hero.
[*Exeunt* DON PEDRO *and* CLAUDIO.

Leon. Bring you these fellows on; we'll talk with Margaret,
How her acquaintance grew with this lewd fellow. [*Exeunt.*

SCENE II. Leonato's *Garden.*

Enter BENEDICK *and* MARGARET, *meeting.*

Bene. 'Pray thee, sweet mistress Margaret, deserve well at my hands, by helping me to the speech of Beatrice.

Marg. Will you then write me a sonnet in praise of my beauty?

Bene. In so high a style, Margaret, that no man living shall come over it; for, in most comely truth, thou deservest it.

Marg. To have no man come over me? why, shall I always keep below stairs?

Bene. Thy wit is as quick as the greyhound's mouth, it catches.

Marg. And yours as blunt as the fencer's foils, which hit, but hurt not.

Bene. A most manly wit, Margaret, it will not hurt a woman; and so, I pray thee, call Beatrice: I give thee the bucklers.

Marg. Give us the swords, we have bucklers of our own.

Bene. If you use them, Margaret, you must put in the pikes with a vice; and they are dangerous weapons for maids.

Marg. Well, I will call Beatrice to you, who, I think, hath legs. [*Exit* MARGARET.

Bene. And therefore will come.

The god of love, [Singing.
That sits above,
And knows me, and knows me,
How pitiful I deserve,—

I mean, in singing; but in loving,—Leander the good swimmer, Trolius the first employer of panders, and a whole book full of these quondam carpet-mongers, whose names yet run smoothly in the even road of a blank verse, why, they were never so truly turned over and over as my poor self, in love: Marry, I cannot show it in rhyme; I have tried; I can find out no rhyme to *lady* but *baby*, an innocent rhyme; for *scorn, horn*, a hard rhyme; for *school, fool*, a babbling rhyme; very ominous endings: No, I was not born under a rhyming planet, nor I cannot woo in festival terms.—

Enter BEATRICE.

Sweet Beatrice, would'st thou come when I called thee?

Beat. Yea, Signior, and depart when you bid me.

Bene. O, stay but till then!

Beat. *Then*, is spoken; fare you well now:—and yet, ere I go, let me go with that I came for, which is, with knowing what hath passed between you and Claudio.

Bene. Only foul words: and thereupon I will kiss thee.

Beat. Foul words is but foul wind, and foul wind is but foul breath, and foul breath is noisome; therefore I will depart unkissed.

Bene. Thou hast frighted the word out of his right sense, so forcible is thy wit: But, I must tell thee plainly, Claudio undergoes my challenge: and either I must shortly hear from him, or I will subscribe him a coward. And I pray thee now, tell me, for which of my bad parts didst thou first fall in love with me?

Beat. For them altogether; which maintained so politic a state of evil, that they will not admit any good part to intermingle with them. But for which of my good parts did you first suffer love for me?

Bene. *Suffer love;* a good epithet! I do suffer love, indeed, for I love thee against my will.

Beat. In spite of your heart, I think; alas! poor heart! If you spite it for my sake, I will spite it for yours; for I will never love that which my friend hates.

Bene. Thou and I are too wise to woo peaceably.

Beat. It appears not in this confession: there's not one wise man among twenty that will praise himself.

Bene. An old, an old instance, Beatrice, that lived in the time of good neighbours: if a man do not erect in this age his own tomb ere he dies, he shall live no longer in monument, than the bell rings, and the widow weeps.

Beat. And how long is that, think you?

Bene. Question!—Why, an hour in clamour, and a quarter in rheum: Therefore it is most expedient for the wise (if Don Worm, his conscience, find no impediment to the contrary), to be the trumpet of his own virtues, as I am to myself: So much for praising myself (who, I myself will bear witness, is praise-worthy), and now tell me, How doth your cousin?

Beat. Very ill.

Bene. And how do you?

Beat. Very ill too.

Bene. Serve God, love me, and mend: there will I leave you too, for here comes one in haste.

Enter URSULA.

Urs. Madam, you must come to your uncle; yonder's old coil at home: it is proved, my lady Hero hath been falsely accused, the Prince and Claudio mightily abused; and Don John is the author of all, who is fled and gone: will you come presently?

Beat. Will you go hear this news, signior!

Bene. I will live in thy heart, die in thy lap, and be buried in thy eyes; and moreover, I will go with thee to thy uncle's. [*Exeunt.*

SCENE III. *The Inside of a Church.*

Enter DON PEDRO, CLAUDIO, *and* Attendants, *with Music and Tapers.*

Claud. Is this the monument of Leonato?
Atten. It is, my lord.
Claud. [*Reads from a scroll.*]

Done to death by slanderous tongues
Was the Hero that here lies:
Death in guerdon of her wrongs
Gives her fame which never dies:
So the life, that died with shame,
Lives in death with glorious fame.

Hang thou there upon the tomb, [affixing it.
Praising her when I am dumb.—

Now, musick, sound, and sing your solemn hymn.

SONG.

Pardon, Goddess of the night,
Those that slew thy virgin knight;
For the which, with songs of woe,
Round about her tomb they go.
Midnight, assist our moan;
Help us to sigh and groan,
Heavily, heavily:

Graves, yawn, and yield your dead,
Till death be uttered,
Heavily, heavily.

Claud. Now, unto thy bones good night!
Yearly will I do this rite.
D. Pedro. Good morrow, masters; put your torches out:
The wolves have prey'd; and look, the gentle day,
Before the wheels of Phœbus, round about
Dapples the drowsy east with spots of gray:
Thanks to you all, and leave us; fare you well.
Claud. Good morrow, masters; each his several way.
D. Pedro. Come, let us hence, and put on other weeds;
And then to Leonato's we will go.
Claud. And, Hymen, now with luckier issue speeds,
Than this, for whom we render'd up this woe!
[*Exeunt.*

SCENE IV. *A Room in* Leonato's *House.*

Enter LEONATO, ANTONIO, BENEDICK, BEATRICE, URSULA, Friar, *and* HERO.

Friar. Did I not tell you she was innocent?
Leon. So are the prince and Claudio, who accus'd her
Upon the error that you heard debated:
But Margaret was in some fault for this;
Although against her will, as it appears
In the true course of all the question.
Ant. Well, I am glad that all things sort so well.
Bene. And so am I, being else by faith enforc'd
To call young Claudio to a reckoning for it.
Leon. Well, daughter, and you gentlewomen all,
Withdraw into a chamber by yourselves;
And, when I send for you, come hither, mask'd:
The prince and Claudio promis'd by this hour
To visit me:—You know your office, brother;

You must be father to your brother's daughter,
And give her to young Claudio. [*Exeunt Ladies.*

Ant. Which I will do with confirm'd countenance.

Bene. Friar, I must entreat your pains, I think.

Friar. To do what, signior?

Bene. To bind me, or undo me, one of them.—
Signior Leonato, truth it is, good signior,
Your niece regards me with an eye of favour.

Leon. That eye my daughter lent her; 'Tis most true.

Bene. And I do with an eye of love requite her.

Leon. The sight whereof, I think, you had from me,
From Claudio, and the prince: But what's your will?

Bene. Your answer, sir, is enigmatical:
But, for my will, my will is, your good will
May stand with ours, this day to be conjoined
In the estate of honourable marriage;—
In which, good friar, I shall desire your help.

Leon. My heart is with your liking.

Friar. And my help.
Here comes the prince, and Claudio.

Enter DON PEDRO, *and* CLAUDIO, *with* Attendants.

D. Pedro. Good morrow to this fair assembly.

Leon. Good morrow, prince; good morrow, Claudio.
We here attend you; are you yet determin'd
To-day to marry with my brother's daughter?

Claud. I'll hold my mind, were she an Ethiope.

Leon. Call her forth, brother, here's the friar ready. [*Exit* ANTONIO.

D. Pedro. Good morrow, Benedick: Why what's the matter,
That you have such a February face,
So full of frost, of storm, and cloudiness?

Claud. I think, he thinks upon the savage bull:—
Tush, fear not, man, we'll tip thy horns with gold,
And all Europa shall rejoice at thee;
As once Europa did at lusty Jove,
When he would play the noble beast in love.

Bene. Bull Jove, sir, had an amiable low:
And some such strange bull leap'd your father's cow,
And got a calf in that same noble feat,
Much like to you, for you have just his bleat.

Re-enter ANTONIO, *with the* Ladies *masked.*

Claud. For this I owe you: here come other reckonings.
Which is the lady I must seize upon?

Ant. This same is she, and I do give you her.

Claud. Why, then she's mine: Sweet, let me see your face.

Leon. No, that you shall not, till you take her hand
Before this friar, and swear to marry her.

Claud. Give me your hand before this holy friar;
I am your husband, if you like of me.

Hero. And when I liv'd, I was your other wife: [*Unmasking.*
And when you lov'd, you were my other husband.

Claud. Another Hero!

Hero. Nothing certainer:
One Hero died defil'd; but I do live,
And, surely as I live, I am a maid.

D. Pedro. The former Hero! Hero that is dead!

Leon. She died, my lord, but whiles her slander lived.

Friar. All this amazement can I qualify;
When, after that the holy rites are ended,
I'll tell you largely of fair Hero's death:
Mean time, let wonder seem familiar,
And to the chapel let us presently.

Bene. Soft, and fair, friar.—Which is Beatrice?

Beat. I answer to that name; [*Unmasking.*] What is your will?

Bene. Do not you love me?

Beat. Why, no, no more than reason.

Bene. Why, then your uncle, and the prince, and Claudio,
Have been deceived; for they swore you did.

Beat. Do not you love me?

Bene. Troth, no, no more than reason.

Beat. Why, then my cousin, Margaret, and Ursula,
Are much deceiv'd; for they did swear you did.

Bene. They swore that you were almost sick for me.

Beat. They swore that you were well-nigh dead for me.

Bene. 'Tis no such matter:—Then, you do not love me?

Beat. No, truly, but in friendly recompense.

Leon. Come, cousin, I am sure you love the gentleman.

Claud. And I'll be sworn upon't, that he loves her;
For here's a paper written in his hand,
A halting sonnet of his own pure brain,
Fashion'd to Beatrice.

Hero. And here's another,
Writ in my cousin's hand, stolen from her pocket,
Containing her affection unto Benedick.

Bene. A miracle! here's our own hands against our hearts!—Come, I will have thee; but, by this light, I take thee for pity.

Beat. I would not deny you; but, by this good day, I yield upon great persuasion; and, partly, to save your life, for I was told you were in a consumption.

Bene. Peace, I will stop your mouth. [*Kissing her.*

D. Pedro. How dost thou, Benedick the married man?

Bene. I'll tell thee what, prince; a college of wit-crackers cannot flout me out of my humour: Dost thou think, I care for a satire, or an epigram? No: if a man will be beaten with brains, he shall wear nothing handsome about him: In brief, since I do propose to marry, I will think nothing to any purpose that the world can say against it; and therefore never flout at me for what I have said against it; for man is a giddy thing, and this is my conclusion.—For thy part, Claudio, I did think to have beaten thee; but in that thou art like to be my kinsman, live unbruised, and love my cousin.

Claud. I had well hoped thou wouldst have denied Beatrice, that I might have cudgelled thee out of thy single life, to make thee a double dealer; which, out of question, thou wilt be, if my cousin do not look exceeding narrowly to thee.

Bene. Come, come, we are friends:—let's have a dance ere we are married, that we may lighten our own hearts, and our wives' heels.

Leon. We'll have dancing afterwards.

Bene. First, o'my word; therefore play, musick.—Prince, thou art sad: get thee a wife, get thee a wife: there is no staff more reverend than one tipp'd with horn.

Enter a Messenger.

Mess. My lord, your brother John is ta'en in flight, And brought with armed men back to Messina.

Bene. Think not on him till to-morrow, I'll devise thee brave punishments for him.—Strike up, pipers. [*Dance. Exeunt.*

MIDSUMMER-NIGHT'S DREAM.

PERSONS REPRESENTED.

THESEUS, *Duke of* Athens.
EGEUS, *Father to* Hermia.
LYSANDER, } *in love with* Hermia.
DEMETRIUS, }
PHILOSTRATE, *Master of the Revels to* Theseus.
QUINCE, *the Carpenter.*
SNUG, *the Joiner.*
BOTTOM, *the Weaver.*
FLUTE, *the Bellows-mender.*
SNOUT, *the Tinker.*
STARVELING, *the Tailor.*

HIPPOLYTA, *Queen of the* Amazons, *betrothed to* Theseus.
HERMIA, *Daughter of* Egeus, *in love with* Lysander.
HELENA, *in love with* Demetrius.

OBERON, *King of the Fairies.*
TITANIA, *Queen of the Fairies.*
PUCK, or ROBIN-GOODFELLOW, *a Fairy.*
PEAS-BLOSSOM, } *Fairies.*
COBWEB, }
MOTH, }
MUSTARD-SEED, }
PYRAMUS, } *Characters in the Interlude performed by the Clowns.*
THISBE, }
WALL, }
MOONSHINE, }
LION, }

Other Fairies attending their King and Queen.
Attendants on Theseus *and* Hippolyta.

SCENE,—Athens, *and a Wood not far from it.*

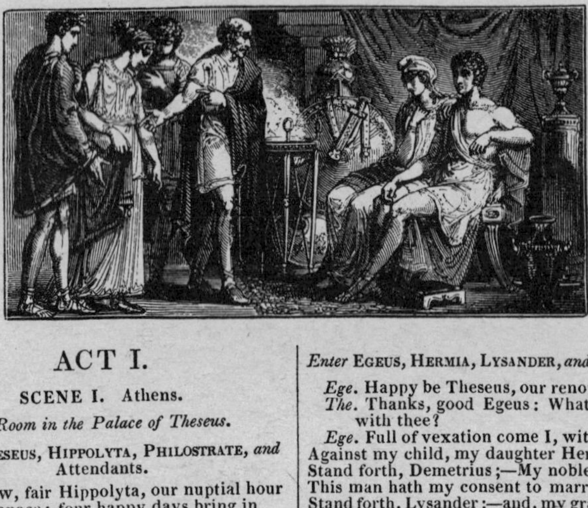

ACT I.

SCENE I. Athens.

A Room in the Palace of Theseus.

Enter THESEUS, HIPPOLYTA, PHILOSTRATE, *and* Attendants.

The. Now, fair Hippolyta, our nuptial hour
Draws on apace; four happy days bring in
Another moon: but, oh, methinks how slow
This old moon wanes! she lingers my desires,
Like to a step-dame, or a dowager,
Long withering out a young man's revenue.
Hip. Four days will quickly steep themselves in nights;
Four nights will quickly dream away the time;
And then the moon, like to a silver bow
New bent in heaven, shall behold the night
Of our solemnities.
The. Go, Philostrate,
Stir up the Athenian youth to merriments;
Awake the pert and nimble spirit of mirth;
Turn melancholy forth to funerals,
The pale companion is not for our pomp.—
[*Exit* PHILOSTRATE.
Hippolyta, I woo'd thee with my sword,
And won thy love, doing thee injuries;
But I will wed thee in another key,
With pomp, with triumph, and with revelling.

Enter EGEUS, HERMIA, LYSANDER, *and* DEMETRIUS.

Ege. Happy be Theseus, our renowned duke!
The. Thanks, good Egeus: What's the news with thee?
Ege. Full of vexation come I, with complaint
Against my child, my daughter Hermia—
Stand forth, Demetrius;—My noble lord,
This man hath my consent to marry her:—
Stand forth, Lysander;—and, my gracious duke,
This hath bewitch'd the bosom of my child:
Thou, thou, Lysander, thou hast given her rhymes,
And interchang'd love tokens with my child:
Thou hast by moon-light at her window sung,
With feigning voice, verses of feigning love;
And stol'n the impression of her fantasy
With bracelets of thy hair, rings, gauds, conceits,
Knacks, trifles, nosegays, sweet-meats; messengers
Of strong prevailment in unharden'd youth:
With cunning hast thou filch'd my daughter's heart;
Turn'd her obedience, which is due to me,
To stubborn harshness:—And, my gracious duke,
Be it so she will not here before your grace
Consent to marry with Demetrius,
I beg the ancient privilege of Athens;
As she is mine, I may dispose of her:
Which shall be either to this gentleman,

Or to her death; according to our law,
Immediately provided in that case.
The. What say you, Hermia? be advis'd, fair maid:
To you your father should be as a god;
One that compos'd your beauties; yea, and one
To whom you are but as a form in wax,
By him imprinted, and within his power
To leave the figure, or disfigure it.
Demetrius is a worthy gentleman.
Her. So is Lysander.
The. In himself he is:
But, in this kind, wanting your father's voice,
The other must be held the worthier.
Her. I would my father look'd but with my eyes.
The. Rather your eyes must with his judgment look.
Her. I do entreat your grace to pardon me.
I know not by what power I am made bold;
Nor how it may concern my modesty,
In such a presence here, to plead my thoughts:
But I beseech your grace that I may know
The worst that may befall me in this case,
If I refuse to wed Demetrius.
The. Either to die the death, or to abjure
For ever the society of men.
Therefore, fair Hermia, question your desires,
Know of your youth, examine well your blood,
Whether, if you yield not to your father's choice,
You can endure the livery of a nun;
For aye to be in shady cloister mew'd,
To live a barren sister all your life,
Chanting faint hymns to the cold fruitless moon.
Thrice blessed they, that master so their blood,
To undergo such maiden pilgrimage:
But earthlier happy is the rose distill'd,
Than that, which, withering on the virgin thorn,
Grows, lives, and dies, in single blessedness.
Her. So will I grow, so live, so die, my lord,
Ere I will yield my virgin patent up
Unto his lordship, whose unwished yoke
My soul consents not to give sovereignty.
The. Take time to pause: and by the next new moon
(The sealing-day betwixt my love and me,
For everlasting bond of fellowship),
Upon that day either prepare to die,
For disobedience to your father's will;
Or else to wed Demetrius, as he would:
Or on Diana's altar to protest,
For aye, austerity and single life.
Dem. Relent, sweet Hermia;—And, Lysander, yield
Thy crazed title to my certain right.
Lys. You have her father's love, Demetrius;
Let me have Hermia's: do you marry him.
Ege. Scornful Lysander! true, he hath my love,
And what is mine my love shall render him;
And she is mine: and all my right of her
I do estate unto Demetrius.
Lys. I am, my lord, as well deriv'd as he,
As well possess'd: my love is more than his;
My fortunes every way as fairly rank'd,
If not with vantage, as Demetrius';
And, which is more than all these boasts can be,
I am belov'd of beauteous Hermia:
Why should not I then prosecute my right?
Demetrius, I'll avouch it to his head,
Made love to Nedar's daughter, Helena,
And won her soul; and she, sweet lady, dotes,
Devoutly dotes, dotes in idolatry,
Upon this spotted and inconstant man.
The. I must confess, that I have heard so much,
And with Demetrius thought to have spoke thereof;
But, being over full of self-affairs,
My mind did lose it. But, Demetrius, come;
And come, Egeus; you shall go with me,
I have some private schooling for you both.—
For you, fair Hermia, look you arm yourself
To fit your fancies to your father's will;
Or else the law of Athens yields you up
(Which by no means we may extenuate)
To death, or to a vow of single life.—
Come, my Hippolyta; What cheer, my love?—
Demetrius, and Egeus, go along:
I must employ you in some business
Against our nuptial; and confer with you
Of something nearly that concerns yourselves.
Ege. With duty and desire we follow you.
[*Exeunt* THESEUS, HIPPOLYTA, EGEUS, DEMETRIUS, *and* Train.
Lys. How now, my love? Why is your cheek so pale?
How chance the roses there do fade so fast?
Her. Belike, for want of rain; which I could well
Beteem them from the tempest of mine eyes.
Lys. Ah me! for aught that ever I could read,
Could ever hear by tale or history,
The course of true love never did run smooth:
But, either it was different in blood;
Her. O cross! too high to be enthrall'd too low!
Lys. Or else misgraffed, in respect of years;
Her. O spite! too old to be engaged to young!
Lys. Or else it stood upon the choice of friends:
Her. O hell! to choose love by another's eye!
Lys. Or, if there were a sympathy in choice,
War, death, or sickness did lay siege to it;
Making it momentany as a sound,
Swift as a shadow, short as any dream;
Brief as the lightning in the collied night,
That, in a spleen, unfolds both heaven and earth,
And ere a man hath power to say,—Behold!
The jaws of darkness do devour it up;
So quick bright things come to confusion.
Her. If then true lovers have been ever cross'd,
It stands as an edict in destiny:
Then let us teach our trial patience,
Because it is a customary cross;
As due to love, as thoughts, and dreams, and sighs,
Wishes, and tears, poor fancy's followers.
Lys. A good persuasion; therefore, hear me, Hermia.
I have a widow aunt, a dowager
Of great revenue, and she hath no child:
From Athens is her house remote seven leagues;
And she respects me as her only son.
There, gentle Hermia, may I marry thee;
And to that place the sharp Athenian law
Cannot pursue us: If thou lov'st me then,
Steal forth thy father's house to-morrow night;
And in the wood, a league without the town,
Where I did meet thee once with Helena,
To do observance to a morn of May,
There will I stay for thee.
Her. My good Lysander!
I swear to thee, by Cupid's strongest bow;
By his best arrow with the golden head;
By the simplicity of Venus' doves;
By that which knitteth souls, and prospers loves;
And by that fire which burn'd the Carthage queen,
When the false Trojan under sail was seen;
By all the vows that ever men have broke,
In number more than ever women spoke;—
In that same place thou hast appointed me,
To-morrow truly will I meet with thee.
Lys. Keep promise, love: Look, here comes Helena.

Enter HELENA.

Her. God speed fair Helena! Whither away?
Hel. Call you me fair? that fair again unsay.
Demetrius loves your fair: O happy fair!
Your eyes are lode-stars; and your tongue's sweet air
More tuneable than lark to shepherd's ear,
When wheat is green, when hawthorn buds appear.
Sickness is catching; O, were favour so!
Yours would I catch, fair Hermia, ere I go;

My ear should catch your voice, my eye your eye,
My tongue should catch your tongue's sweet melody.
Were the world mine, Demetrius being bated,
The rest I'll give to be to you translated.
O, teach me how you look; and with what art
You sway the motion of Demetrius' heart.

Her. I frown upon him, yet he loves me still.

Hel. O, that your frowns would teach my smiles such skill!

Her. I give him curses, yet he gives me love.

Hel. O, that my prayers could such affection move!

Her. The more I hate, the more he follows me.

Hel. The more I love, the more he hateth me.

Her. His folly, Helena, is no fault of mine.

Hel. None, but your beauty; 'Would that fault were mine!

Her. Take comfort; he no more shall see my face;
Lysander and myself will fly this place.—
Before the time I did Lysander see,
Seem'd Athens as a paradise to me:
O then, what graces in my love do dwell,
That he hath turn'd a heaven unto hell!

Lys. Helen, to you our minds we will unfold:
To-morrow night when Phœbe doth behold
Her silver visage in the wat'ry glass,
Decking with liquid pearl the bladed grass
(A time that lovers' flights doth still conceal),
Through Athens' gates have we devis'd to steal.

Her. And in the wood, where often you and I
Upon faint primrose beds were wont to lie,
Emptying our bosoms of their counsel sweet,
There my Lysander and myself shall meet:
And thence, from Athens, turn away our eyes,
To seek new friends and stranger companies.
Farewell, sweet playfellow; pray thou for us,
And good luck grant thee thy Demetrius!
Keep word, Lysander; we must starve our sight
From lovers' food, till morrow deep midnight.
[*Exit* HERMIA.

Lys. I will, my Hermia.—Helena, adieu:
As you on him, Demetrius dote on you!
[*Exit* LYSANDER.

Hel. How happy some, o'er other some can be!
Through Athens I am thought as fair as she.
But what of that? Demetrius thinks not so;
He will not know what all but he do know.
And as he errs, doting on Hermia's eyes,
So I, admiring of his qualities.
Things base and vile, holding no quantity,
Love can transpose to form and dignity.
Love looks not with the eyes, but with the mind;
And therefore is wing'd Cupid painted blind;
Nor hath love's mind of any judgment taste;
Wings, and no eyes, figure unheedy haste:
And therefore is love said to be a child,
Because in choice he is so oft beguil'd.
As waggish boys in game themselves forswear,
So the boy love is perjur'd every where;
For ere Demetrius look'd on Hermia's eyne,
He hail'd down oaths, that he was only mine:
And when this hail some heat from Hermia felt,
So he dissolv'd, and showers of oaths did melt.
I will go tell him of fair Hermia's flight;
Then to the wood will he, to-morrow night,
Pursue her; and for this intelligence
If I have thanks, it is a dear expense:
But herein mean I to enrich my pain,
To have his sight thither and back again. [*Exit.*

SCENE II. *The same. A Room in a Cottage.*

Enter SNUG, BOTTOM, FLUTE, SNOUT, QUINCE, *and* STARVELING.

Quin. Is all our company here?

Bot. You were best to call them generally, man by man, according to the scrip.

Quin. Here is the scroll of every man's name, which is thought fit, through all Athens, to play in our interlude before the duke and duchess, on his wedding-day at night.

Bot. First, good Peter Quince, say what the play treats on; then read the names of the actors; and so grow to a point.

Quin. Marry, our play is—The most lamentable comedy, and most cruel death of Pyramus and Thisby.

Bot. A very good piece of work, I assure you, and a merry.—Now, good Peter Quince, call forth your actors by the scroll: Masters, spread yourselves.

Quin. Answer, as I call you,—Nick Bottom, the weaver.

Bot. Ready: Name what part I am for, and proceed.

Quin. You, Nick Bottom, are set down for Pyramus.

Bot. What is Pyramus? a lover, or a tyrant?

Quin. A lover, that kills himself most gallantly for love.

Bot. That will ask some tears in the true performing of it: If I do it, let the audience look to their eyes; I will move storms, I will condole in some measure. To the rest:—Yet my chief humour is for a tyrant: I could play Ercles rarely, or a part to tear a cat in, to make all split.

"The raging rocks,
With shivering shocks,
Shall break the locks
Of prison gates:
And Phibbus' car
Shall shine from far,
And make and mar
The foolish fates."

This was lofty!—Now name the rest of the players.—This is Ercles' vein, a tyrant's vein; a lover is more condoling.

Quin. Francis Flute, the bellows-mender.

Flu. Here, Peter Quince.

Quin. You must take Thisby on you.

Flu. What is Thisby? a wandering knight?

Quin. It is the lady that Pyramus must love.

Flu. Nay, faith, let me not play a woman; I have a beard coming.

Quin. That's all one; you shall play it in a mask, and you may speak as small as you will.

Bot. An I may hide my face, let me play Thisby too: I'll speak in a monstrous little voice;—*Thisne, Thisne—Ah, Pyramus, my lover dear; thy Thisby dear! and lady dear!*

Quin. No, no; you must play Pyramus; and, Flute, you Thisby.

Bot. Well, proceed.

Quin. Robin Starveling, the tailor.

Star. Here, Peter Quince.

Quin. Robin Starveling, you must play Thisby's mother.—Tom Snout, the tinker.

Snout. Here, Peter Quince.

Quin. You, Pyramus's father; myself, Thisby's father;—Snug, the joiner, you, the lion's part:—and, I hope, here is a play fitted.

Snug. Have you the lion's part written? pray you, if it be, give it me, for I am slow of study.

Quin. You may do it extempore, for it is nothing but roaring.

Bot. Let me play the lion too: I will roar, that I will do any man's heart good to hear me; I will roar, that I will make the duke say, *Let him roar again, Let him roar again.*

Quin. An you should do it too terribly, you would fright the duchess and the ladies, that they would shriek; and that were enough to hang us all.

All. That would hang us every mother's son.

Bot. I grant you, friends, if that you should fright the ladies out of their wits, they would have no more discretion but to hang us: but I will aggravate my voice so, that I will roar you as gently as any sucking dove; I will roar you an 'twere any nightingale.

Quin. You can play no part but Pyramus: for

Pyramus is a sweet-faced man; a proper man, as one shall see in a summer's day; a most lovely, gentleman-like man; therefore you must needs play Pyramus.

Bot. Well, I will undertake it. What beard were I best to play it in?

Quin. Why, what you will.

Bot. I will discharge it in either your straw-coloured beard, your orange-tawny beard, your purple-in-grain beard, or your French-crown-colour beard, your perfect yellow.

Quin. Some of your French crowns have no hair at all, and then you will play bare-faced.—But, masters, here are your parts: and I am to entreat you, request you, and desire you, to con them by to-morrow night; and meet me in the palace wood, a mile without the town, by moon-light; there will we rehearse: for if we meet in the city, we shall be dogg'd with company, and our devices known. In the mean time I will draw a bill of properties, such as our play wants. I pray you, fail me not.

Bot. We will meet; and there we may rehearse more obscenely, and courageously. Take pains; be perfect, adieu.

Quin. At the duke's oak we meet.

Bot. Enough; Hold, or cut bow-strings.

[*Exeunt.*

ACT II.

SCENE I. *A Wood near* Athens.

Enter a Fairy *at one door, and* Puck *at another.*

Puck. How now, spirit! whither wander you?

Fai. Over hill, over dale,
Thorough bush, thorough briar,
Over park, over pale,
Thorough flood, thorough fire.
I do wander every where,
Swifter than the moones sphere;
And I serve the fairy queen,
To dew her orbs upon the green:
The cowslips tall her pensioners be;
In their gold coats spots you see;
Those be rubies, fairy favours,
In those freckles live their savours:
I must go seek some dewdrops here,
And hang a pearl in every cowslip's ear.
Farewell, thou lob of spirits, I'll be gone;
Our queen and all her elves come here anon.

Puck. The king doth keep his revels here to-night;
Take heed the queen come not within his sight.
For Oberon is passing fell and wrath,
Because that she, as her attendant, hath
A lovely boy, stol'n from an Indian king;
She never had so sweet a changeling:
And jealous Oberon would have the child
Knight of his train, to trace the forests wild:
But she, perforce, withholds the loved boy,
Crowns him with flowers, and makes him all her joy:
And now they never meet in grove, or green,
By fountain clear, or spangled star-light sheen,
But they do square; that all their elves, for fear,
Creep into acorn cups, and hide them there.

Fai. Either I mistake your shape and making quite,
Or else you are that shrewd and knavish sprite,
Call'd Robin Good-fellow: are you not he,
That fright the maidens of the villagery:
Skim milk; and sometimes labour in the quern,
And bootless make the breathless housewife churn;
And sometime make the drink to bear no barm;
Mislead night-wanderers, laughing at their harm?
Those that Hobgoblin call you, and sweet Puck,
You do their work; and they shall have good luck:
Are not you he?

Puck. Thou speak'st aright;
I am that merry wanderer of the night.
I jest to Oberon, and make him smile,
When I a fat and bean-fed horse beguile,
Neighing in likeness of a filly foal:
And sometime lurk I in a gossip's bowl,
In very likeness of a roasted crab;
And, when she drinks, against her lips I bob,
And on her wither'd dew-lap pour the ale.
The wisest aunt, telling the saddest tale,
Sometime for three-foot stool mistaketh me:
Then slip I from her bum, down topples she,
And *tailor* cries, and falls into a cough;
And then the whole quire hold their hips, and loffe;
And yexen in their mirth, and neeze, and swear
A merrier hour was never wasted there.—
But room, Faery, here comes Oberon.

Fai. And here my mistress:—'Would that he were gone!

SCENE II.

Enter Oberon, *at one door, with his* Train, *and* Titania, *at another, with hers.*

Obe. Ill met by moon-light, proud Titania.

Tita. What, jealous Oberon? Fairy, skip hence;
I have forsworn his bed and company.

Obe. Tarry, rash wanton: Am not I thy lord?

Tita. Then I must be thy lady: But I know
When thou hast stol'n away from fairy land,
And in the shape of Corin sat all day,
Playing on pipes of corn; and versing love
To amorous Phillida. Why art thou here,
Come from the farthest steep of India?
But that, forsooth, the bouncing Amazon,
Your buskin'd mistress, and your warrior love,
To Theseus must be wedded; and you come
To give their bed joy and prosperity.

Obe. How canst thou thus, for shame, Titania,
Glance at my credit with Hippolyta,
Knowing I know thy love to Theseus?
Didst thou not lead him through the glimmering night
From Perigenia, whom he ravished?
And make him with fair Ægle break his faith,
With Ariadne, and Antiopa?

Tita. These are the forgeries of jealousy:
And never, since the middle summer's spring,
Met we on hill, in dale, forest, or mead,
By paved fountain, or by rushy brook,
Or on the beached margent of the sea,
To dance our ringlets to the whistling wind,
But with thy brawls thou hast disturb'd our sport.
Therefore the winds, piping to us in vain,
As in revenge, have suck'd up from the sea
Contagious fogs; which falling in the land,
Have every pelting river made so proud,
That they have overborne their continents:
The ox hath therefore stretch'd his yoke in vain,
The ploughman lost his sweat; and the green corn
Hath rotted, ere his youth attain'd a beard:
The fold stands empty in the drowned field,
And crows are fatted with the murrain flock;
The nine men's morris is fill'd up with mud;
And the quaint mazes in the wanton green,
For lack of tread, are undistinguishable:
The human mortals want their winter here;
No night is now with hymn or carol blest:
Therefore the moon, the governess of floods,
Pale in her anger, washes all the air,
That rheumatic diseases do abound:
And thorough this distemperature, we see
The seasons alter: hoary-headed frosts
Fall in the fresh lap of the crimson rose;
And on old Hyems' chin, and icy crown,
An odorous chaplet of sweet summer buds
Is, as in mockery, set: The spring, the summer,
The childing autumn, angry winter, change
Their wonted liveries; and the 'mazed world,

By their increase, now knows not which is which:
And this same progeny of evils comes
From our debate, from our dissension;
We are their parents and original.
Obe. Do you amend it then; it lies in you:
Why should Titania cross her Oberon?
I do but beg a little changeling boy,
To be my henchman.
Tita. Set your heart at rest,
The fairy land buys not the child of me.
His mother was a vot'ress of my order:
And, in the spiced Indian air, by night,
Full often hath she gossip'd by my side;
And sat with me on Neptune's yellow sands,
Marking the embarked traders on the flood;
When we have laugh'd to see the sails conceive,
And grow big-bellied, with the wanton wind;
Which she, with pretty and with swimming gait
Following (her womb, then rich with my young 'squire),
Would imitate; and sail upon the land,
To fetch me trifles, and return again,
As from a voyage, rich with merchandize.
But she, being mortal, of that boy did die;
And, for her sake, I do rear up her boy:
And, for her sake, I will not part with him.
Obe. How long within this wood intend you stay?
Tita. Perchance, till after Theseus' wedding-day.
If you will patiently dance in our round,
And see our moon-light revels, go with us;
If not, shun me, and I will spare your haunts.
Obe. Give me that boy, and I will go with thee.
Tita. Not for thy fairy kingdom.—Fairies, away:
We shall chide down-right, if I longer stay.
[*Exeunt* TITANIA, *and her* Train.
Obe. Well, go thy way: thou shalt not from this grove,
Till I torment thee for this injury.—
My gentle Puck, come hither: Thou remember'st
Since once I sat upon a promontory,
And heard a mermaid, on a dolphin's back,
Uttering such dulcet and harmonious breath,
That the rude sea grew civil at her song;
And certain stars shot madly from their spheres,
To hear the sea-maid's musick.
Puck. I remember.
Obe. That very time I saw (but thou could'st not),
Flying between the cold moon and the earth,
Cupid all arm'd: a certain aim he took
At a fair vestal, throned by the west;
And loos'd his love-shaft smartly from his bow,
As it should pierce a hundred thousand hearts:
But I might see young Cupid's fiery shaft
Quench'd in the chaste beams of the wat'ry moon;
And the imperial vot'ress passed on,
In maiden meditation, fancy-free.
Yet mark'd I where the bolt of Cupid fell:
It fell upon a little western flower,—
Before, milk-white; now purple with love's wound—
And maidens call it, love-in-idleness.
Fetch me that flower: the herb I show'd thee once:
The juice of it on sleeping eyelids laid,
Will make or man or woman madly dote
Upon the next live creature that it sees.
Fetch me this herb: and be thou here again,
Ere the leviathan can swim a league.
Puck. I'll put a girdle round about the earth
In forty minutes. [*Exit* PUCK.
Obe. Having once this juice,
I'll watch Titania when she is asleep,
And drop the liquor of it in her eyes:
The next thing then she waking looks upon
(Be it on lion, bear, or wolf, or bull,
On meddling monkey, or on busy ape),
She shall pursue it with the soul of love.
And ere I take this charm off from her sight
(As I can take it with another herb),
I'll make her render up her page to me.
But who comes here? I am invisible;
And I will overhear their conference.

Enter DEMETRIUS, HELENA *following him.*

Dem. I love thee not, therefore pursue me not.
Where is Lysander, and fair Hermia?
The one I'll slay, the other slayeth me.
Thou told'st me they were stol'n into this wood,
And here am I, and wood within this wood,
Because I cannot meet with Hermia.
Hence, get thee gone, and follow me no more.
Hel. You draw me, you hard-hearted adamant;
But yet you draw not iron, for my heart
Is true as steel; Leave you your power to draw,
And I shall have no power to follow you.
Dem. Do I entice you? Do I speak you fair?
Or, rather, do I not in plainest truth
Tell you—I do not, nor I cannot love you?
Hel. And even for that do I love you the more.
I am your spaniel; and, Demetrius,
The more you beat me, I will fawn on you:
Use me but as your spaniel, spurn me, strike me,
Neglect me, lose me; only give me leave,
Unworthy as I am, to follow you.
What worser place can I beg in your love,
(And yet a place of high respect with me),
Than to be used as you do use your dog?
Dem. Tempt not too much the hatred of my spirit;
For I am sick, when I do look on thee.
Hel. And I am sick, when I look not on you.
Dem. You do impeach your modesty too much
To leave the city, and commit yourself
Into the hands of one that loves you not;
To trust the opportunity of night,
And the ill counsel of a desert place,
With the rich worth of your virginity.
Hel. Your virtue is my privilege for that.
It is not night, when I do see your face,
Therefore I think I am not in the night:
Nor doth this wood lack worlds of company;
For you, in my respect, are all the world:
Then how can it be said, I am alone,
When all the world is here to look on me?
Dem. I'll run from thee, and hide me in the brakes,
And leave thee to the mercy of wild beasts.
Hel. The wildest hath not such a heart as you.
Run when you will, the story shall be chang'd;
Apollo flies, and Daphne holds the chase;
The dove pursues the griffin; the mild hind
Makes speed to catch the tiger: Bootless speed!
When cowardice pursues, and valour flies.
Dem. I will not stay thy questions; let me go:
Or, if thou follow me, do not believe
But I shall do thee mischief in the wood.
Hel. Ay, in the temple, in the town, the field,
You do me mischief. Fye, Demetrius!
Your wrongs do set a scandal on my sex:
We cannot fight for love, as men may do;
We should be woo'd, and were not made to woo.
I'll follow thee, and make a heaven of hell,
To die upon the hand I love so well.
[*Exeunt* DEM. *and* HEL.
Obe. Fare thee well, nymph: ere he do leave this grove,
Thou shalt fly him, and he shall seek thy love.

Re-enter PUCK.

Hast thou the flower there? Welcome, wanderer.
Puck. Ay, there it is.
Obe. I pray thee, give it me,
I know a bank whereon the wild thyme blows,
Where oxlips and the nodding violet grows;
Quite over-canopied with luscious woodbine,
With sweet musk-roses, and with eglantine:

There sleeps Titania, some time of the night,
Lull'd in these flowers with dances and delight;
And there the snake throws her enamel'd skin,
Weed wide enough to wrap a fairy in:
And with the juice of this I'll streak her eyes,
And make her full of hateful fantasies.
Take thou some of it, and seek through this grove:
A sweet Athenian lady is in love
With a disdainful youth: anoint his eyes;
But do it, when the next thing he espies
May be the lady: Thou shalt know the man
By the Athenian garments he hath on.
Effect it with some care, that he may prove
More fond on her, than she upon her love:
And look thou meet me ere the first cock crow.

Puck. Fear not, my lord, your servant shall do so. [*Exeunt.*

SCENE III. *Another part of the Wood.*

Enter TITANIA, *with her train.*

Tita. Come, now a roundel, and a fairy song;
Then, for the third part of a minute, hence;
Some, to kill cankers in the musk-rose buds;
Some, war with rear-mice for their leathern wings,
To make my small elves coats; and some, keep back
The clamorous owl, that nightly hoots, and wonders
At our quaint spirits; Sing me now asleep;
Then to your offices, and let me rest.

SONG.

1 Fai. *You spotted snakes, with double tongue,*
Thorny hedge-hogs, be not seen;
Newts, and blindworms, do no wrong;
Come not near our fairy queen:

CHORUS. *Philomel, with melody,*
Sing in our sweet lullaby;
Lulla, lulla, lullaby; lulla, lulla, lullaby:
Never harm, nor spell nor charm,
Come our lovely lady nigh;
So, good night, with lullaby.

II.

2 Fai. *Weaving spiders, come not here;*
Hence, you long-legg'd spinners, hence:
Beetles black, approach not near;
Worm, nor snail, do no offence.

CHORUS. *Philomel, with melody, &c.*

1 *Fai.* Hence, away; now all is well:
One, aloof, stand sentinel.
[*Exeunt* Fairies. TITANIA sleeps.

Enter OBERON.

Obe. What thou seest, when thou dost wake,
[*Squeezes the flower on* TITANIA'S *eyelids.*
Do it for thy true love take;
Love, and languish for his sake:
Be it ounce, or cat, or bear,
Pard, or boar with bristled hair,
In thy eye that shall appear
When thou wak'st, it is thy dear;
Wake, when some vile thing is near. [*Exit.*

Enter LYSANDER *and* HERMIA.

Lys. Fair love, you faint with wandering in the wood;
And to speak troth, I have forgot our way;
We'll rest us, Hermia, if you think it good,
And tarry for the comfort of the day.

Her. Be it so, Lysander: find you out a bed,
For I upon this bank will rest my head.

Lys. One turf shall serve as pillow for us both;
One heart, one bed, two bosoms, and one troth.

Her. Nay, good Lysander; for my sake, my dear,
Lie further off yet, do not lie so near.

Lys. O, take the sense, sweet, of my innocence;
Love takes the meaning, in love's conference.
I mean, that my heart unto yours is knit;
So that but one heart we can make of it:
Two bosoms interchained with an oath;
So then, two bosoms, and a single troth.
Then, by your side no bed-room me deny;
For, lying so, Hermia, I do not lie.

Her. Lysander riddles very prettily:—
Now much beshrew my manners and my pride,
If Hermia meant to say, Lysander lied.
But, gentle friend, for love and courtesy
Lie further off; in human modesty
Such separation, as, may well be said,
Becomes a virtuous bachelor and a maid:
So far be distant; and good night, sweet friend:
Thy love ne'er alter, till thy sweet life end!

Lys. Amen, amen, to that fair prayer, say I;
And then end life, when I end loyalty!
Here is my bed: Sleep give thee all his rest!

Her. With half that wish the wisher's eyes be press'd! [*They sleep.*

Enter PUCK.

Puck. Through the forest have I gone,
But Athenian found I none,
On whose eyes I might approve
This flower's force in stirring love.
Night and silence! who is here?
Weeds of Athens he doth wear:
This is he, my master said,
Despised the Athenian maid;
And here the maiden, sleeping sound,
On the dank and dirty ground.
Pretty soul! she durst not lie
Near this lack-love, this kill-courtesy.
Churl, upon thy eyes I throw
All the power this charm doth owe:
When thou wak'st, let love forbid
Sleep his seat on thy eye-lid.
So awake, when I am gone;
For I must now to Oberon. [*Exit.*

Enter DEMETRIUS *and* HELENA, *running.*

Hel. Stay, though thou kill me, sweet Demetrius.

Dem. I charge thee, hence, and do not haunt me thus.

Hel. O, wilt thou darkling leave me? do not so.

Dem. Stay, on thy peril; I alone will go.
[*Exit* DEMETRIUS.

Hel. O, I am out of breath in this fond chase!
The more my prayer, the lesser is my grace.
Happy is Hermia, wheresoe'er she lies;
For she hath blessed and attractive eyes.
How came her eyes so bright? Not with salt tears:
If so, my eyes are oftener wash'd than hers.
No, no, I am as ugly as a bear;
For beasts that meet me, run away for fear:
Therefore, no marvel, though Demetrius
Do, as a monster, fly my presence thus.
What wicked and dissembling glass of mine
Made me compare with Hermia's sphery eyne?
But who is here?—Lysander! on the ground!
Dead? or asleep? I see no blood, no wound:—
Lysander, if you live, good sir, awake.

Lys. And run through fire I will, for thy sweet sake. [*Waking.*
Transparent Helena; Nature shows her art,
That through thy bosom makes me see thy heart.
Where is Demetrius? O, how fit a word
Is that vile name to perish on my sword!

Hel. Do not say so, Lysander; say not so:
What though he love your Hermia? Lord, what though?
Yet Hermia still loves you: then be content.

Lys. Content with Hermia? No: I do repent
The tedious minutes I with her have spent.
Not Hermia, but Helena I love:
Who will not change a raven for a dove?
The will of man is by his reason sway'd;
And reason says you are the worthier maid.
Things growing are not ripe until their season:
So I, being young, till now ripe not to reason;

And touching now the point of human skill,
Reason becomes the marshal to my will,
And leads me to your eyes; where I o'erlook
Love's stories written in love's richest book.

Hel. Wherefore was I to this keen mockery born?
When, at your hands, did I deserve this scorn?
Is't not enough, is't not enough, young man,
That I did never, no, nor never can,
Deserve a sweet look from Demetrius' eye,
But you must flout my insufficiency?
Good troth, you do me wrong, good sooth, you do,
In such disdainful manner me to woo.
But fare you well: perforce I must confess,
I thought you lord of more true gentleness.
O, that a lady, of one man refus'd,
Should, of another, therefore be abus'd! [*Exit.*

Lys. She sees not Hermia!—Hermia, sleep thou there;
And never mayst thou come Lysander near!
For, as a surfeit of the sweetest things
The deepest loathing to the stomach brings;
Or, as the heresies, that men do leave,
Are hated most of those they did deceive;
So thou, my surfeit, and my heresy,
Of all be hated; but the most of me!
And all my powers, address your love and might,
To honour Helen, and to be her knight! [*Exit.*

Her. [*starting.*] Help me, Lysander, help me! do thy best,
To pluck this crawling serpent from my breast!
Ah me, for pity!—what a dream was here?
Lysander, look, how I do quake with fear:
Methought a serpent eat my heart away,
And you sat smiling at his cruel prey:—
Lysander! what, remov'd? Lysander! lord!
What, out of hearing? gone? no sound, no word?
Alack, where are you? speak, an if you hear;
Speak, of all loves; I swoon almost with fear.
No?—then I well perceive you are not nigh:
Either death, or you, I'll find immediately.
[*Exit.*

ACT III.

SCENE I.

The same. The Queen of Fairies lying asleep.

Enter QUINCE, SNUG, BOTTOM, FLUTE, SNOUT, *and* STARVELING.

Bot. Are we all met?

Quin. Pat, pat; and here's a marvellous convenient place for our rehearsal: This green plot shall be our stage, this hawthorn brake our tyring house; and we will do it in action, as we will do it before the duke.

Bot. Peter Quince,—

Quin. What say'st thou, bully Bottom?

Bot. There are things in this comedy of *Pyramus and Thisby*, that will never please. First, Pyramus must draw a sword to kill himself; which the ladies cannot abide. How answer you that?

Snout. By'rlakin, a parlous fear.

Star. I believe, we must leave the killing out, when all is done.

Bot. Not a whit; I have a device to make all well. Write me a prologue: and let the prologue seem to say, we will do no harm with our swords; and that Pyramus is not killed indeed: and, for the more better assurance, tell them, that I Pyramus am not Pyramus, but Bottom the weaver: This will put them out of fear.

Quin. Well, we will have such a prologue; and it shall be written in eight and six.

Bot. No, make it two more; let it be written in eight and eight.

Snout. Will not the ladies be afeard of the lion?

Star. I fear it, I promise you.

Bot. Masters, you ought to consider with yourselves: to bring in, God shield us! a lion among ladies, is a most dreadful thing; for there is not a more fearful wild-fowl than your lion, living; and we ought to look to it.

Snout. Therefore, another prologue must tell, he is not a lion.

Bot. Nay, you must name his name, and half his face must be seen through the lion's neck; and he himself must speak through, saying thus, or to the same defect,—Ladies, or fair ladies, I would wish you, or, I would request you, or, I would entreat you, not to fear, not to tremble: my life for yours. If you think I come hither as a lion, it were pity of my life: No, I am no such thing; I am a man as other men are:—and there, indeed, let him name his name; and tell them plainly he is Snug the joiner.

Quin. Well, it shall be so. But there is two hard things; that is, to bring the moon-light into a chamber: for you know, Pyramus and Thisby meet by moon-light.

Snug. Doth the moon shine that night we play our play?

Bot. A calendar, a calendar! look in the almanack; find out moon-shine, find out moon-shine.

Quin. Yes, it doth shine that night.

Bot. Why, then you may leave a casement of the great chamber window, where we play, open; and the moon may shine in at the casement.

Quin. Ay; or else one must come in with a bush of thorns and a lanthorn, and say, he comes to disfigure, or to present, the person of moon-shine. Then, there is another thing: we must have a wall in the great chamber; for Pyramus and Thisby, says the story, did talk through the chink of a wall.

Snug. You never can bring in a wall.—What say you, Bottom?

Bot. Some man or other must present wall: and let him have some plaster, or some loam, or some rough-cast about him, to signify wall; or let him hold his fingers thus, and through that cranny shall Pyramus and Thisby whisper.

Quin. If that may be, then all is well. Come, sit down, every mother's son, and rehearse your parts. Pyramus, you begin: when you have spoken your speech, enter into that brake, and so every one according to his cue.

Enter PUCK *behind.*

Puck. What hempen home-spuns have we swaggering here,
So near the cradle of the fairy queen?
What, a play toward? I'll be an auditor;
An actor, too, perhaps, if I see cause.

Quin. Speak, Pyramus:—Thisby, stand forth.

Pyr. *Thisby, the flowers of odious savours sweet,—*

Quin. Odours, odours.

Pyr. —— *odours savours sweet:*
So hath thy breath, my dearest Thisby dear.—
But hark, a voice! stay thou but here a while,
And by and by I will to thee appear. [*Exit.*

Puck. A stranger Pyramus than e'er play'd here! [*Aside.—Exit.*

This. Must I speak now?

Quin. Ay, marry, must you: for you must understand, he goes but to see a noise that he heard, and is to come again.

This. *Most radiant Pyramus, most lily-white of hue,*
Of colour like the red rose on triumphant brier,
Most brisky Juvenal, and eke most lovely Jew,
As true as truest horse, that yet would never tire,
I'll meet thee, Pyramus, at Ninny's tomb.

Quin. Ninus' tomb, man: Why you must not speak that yet; that you answer to Pyramus: you speak all your part at once, cues and all.—Pyramus, enter; your cue is past; it is, *never tire.*

Re-enter PUCK, *and* BOTTOM *with an ass's head.*

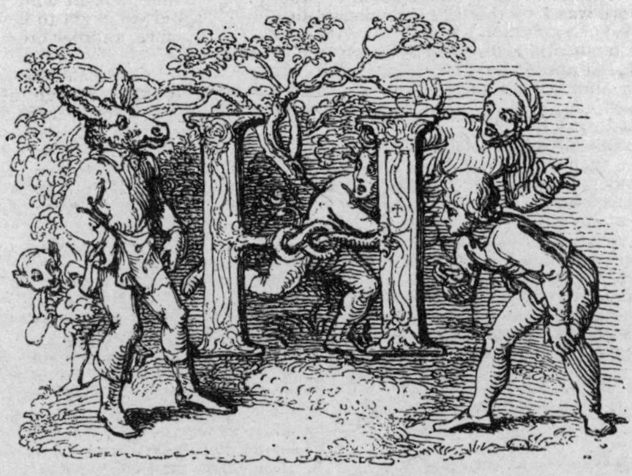

This. O,—*As true as truest horse, that yet would never tire.*

Pyr. *If I were fair, Thisby, I were only thine.*—

Quin. O monstrous! O strange! we are haunted.
Pray, masters! fly, masters! help!

[*Exeunt* Clowns.

Puck. I'll follow you, I'll lead you about a round,
Through bog, through bush, through brake, through brier;
Sometime a horse I'll be, sometime a hound,
A hog, a headless bear, sometime a fire;
And neigh, and bark, and grunt, and roar, and burn,
Like horse, hound, hog, bear, fire, at every turn.

[*Exit.*

Bot. Why do they run away? this is a knavery of them, to make me afeard.

Re-enter SNOUT.

Snout. O Bottom, thou art changed! what do I see on thee?

Bot. What do you see? you see an ass's head of your own; Do you?

Re-enter QUINCE.

Quin. Bless thee, Bottom! bless thee! thou art translated. [*Exit.*

Bot. I see their knavery! this is to make an ass of me; to fright me, if they could. But I will not stir from this place, do what they can: I will walk up and down here, and I will sing, that they shall hear I am not afraid. [*Sings.*

The ousel-cock, so black of hue,
With orange-tawney bill,
The throstle with his note so true,
The wren with little quill.

Tita. What angel wakes me from my flowery bed? [*Waking.*

Bot. *The finch, the sparrow, and the lark,*
The plain-song cuckoo gray,
Whose note full many a man doth mark,
And dares not answer, nay;—

for, indeed, who would set his wit to so foolish a bird? who would give a bird the lie, though he cry, *cuckoo*, never so?

Tita. I pray thee, gentle mortal, sing again;
Mine ear is much enamour'd of thy note,
So is mine eye enthralled to thy shape;
And thy fair virtue's force perforce doth move me,
On the first view, to say, to swear, I love thee.

Bot. Methinks, mistress, you should have little reason for that: And yet, to say the truth, reason and love keep little company together nowadays: The more the pity, that some honest neighbours will not make them friends. Nay, I can gleek upon occasion.

Tita. Thou art as wise as thou art beautiful.

Bot. Not so, neither: but if I had wit enough to get out of this wood, I have enough to serve mine own turn.

Tita. Out of this wood do not desire to go;
Thou shalt remain here, whether thou wilt or no.
I am a spirit of no common rate;
The summer still doth tend upon my state,
And I do love thee: therefore, go with me;
I'll give thee fairies to attend on thee;
And they shall fetch thee jewels from the deep:
And sing, while thou on pressed flowers dost sleep:
And I will purge thy mortal grossness so
That thou shalt like an airy spirit go.—
Peas-blossom! Cobweb! Moth! and Mustard-seed!

Enter four Fairies.

1 *Fai.* Ready.
2 *Fai.* And I.
3 *Fai.* And I.
4 *Fai.* And I.

All. Where shall we go?

Tita. Be kind and courteous to this gentleman;
Hop in his walks, and gambol in his eyes;
Feed him with apricocks and dewberries,
With purple grapes, green figs, and mulberries;
The honey bags steal from the humblebees,
And, for night tapers, crop their waxen thighs,
And light them at the fiery glowworm's eyes,
To have my love to bed, and to arise;
And pluck the wings from painted butterflies,
To fan the moonbeams from his sleeping eyes:
Nod to him, elves, and do him courtesies.

1 *Fai.* Hail, mortal!
2 *Fai.* Hail!
3 *Fai.* Hail!
4 *Fai.* Hail!

Bot. I cry your worship's mercy, heartily.—
I beseech, your worship's name?

Cob. Cobweb.

Bot. I shall desire you of more acquaintance, good master Cobweb: If I cut my finger, I shall make bold with you.—Your name, honest gentleman?

Peas. Peas-blossom.

Bot. I pray you, commend me to mistress Squash, your mother, and to master Peascod, your father. Good master Peas-blossom, I shall desire you of more acquaintance too.—Your name, I beseech you, sir?

Mus. Mustard-seed.

Bot. Good master Mustard-seed, I know your patience well: that same cowardly, giant-like ox-beef hath devoured many a gentleman of your house: I promise you, your kindred hath made my eyes water ere now. I desire you more acquaintance, good master Mustard-seed.

Tita. Come, wait upon him; lead him to my bower.
The moon, methinks, looks with a watery eye;
And when she weeps, weeps every little flower,
Lamenting some enforced chastity.
Tie up my lover's tongue, bring him silently.
[*Exeunt.*

SCENE II. *Another part of the Wood.*

Enter OBERON.

Obe. I wonder, if Titania be awak'd;
Then, what it was that next came in her eye,
Which she must dote on in extremity.

Enter PUCK.

Here comes my messenger.—How now, mad spirit?
What night-rule now about this haunted grove?

Puck. My mistress with a monster is in love.
Near to her close and consecrated bower,
While she was in her dull and sleeping hour,
A crew of patches, rude mechanicals,
That work for bread upon Athenian stalls,
Were met together to rehearse a play,
Intended for great Theseus' nuptial day.
The shallowest thick-skin of that barren sort,
Who Pyramus presented, in their sport
Forsook his scene, and entered in a brake:
When I did him at this advantage take,
An ass's nowl I fixed on his head;
Anon, his Thisbe must be answered,
And forth my mimick comes: When they him spy,
As wild geese that the creeping fowler eye,
Or russet-pated choughs, many in sort,
Rising and cawing at the gun's report,
Sever themselves, and madly sweep the sky;
So, at his sight, away his fellows fly:
And, at our stamp, here o'er and o'er one falls;
He murder cries, and help from Athens calls.
Their sense, thus weak, lost with their fears, thus strong,
Made senseless things begin to do them wrong:
For briars and thorns at their apparel snatch;
Some, sleeves; some, hats; from yielders all things catch.
I led them on in this distracted fear,
And left sweet Pyramus translated there:
When in that moment (so it came to pass),
Titania wak'd, and straightway lov'd an ass.

Obe. This falls out better than I could devise.
But hast thou yet latch'd the Athenian's eyes
With the love-juice, as I did bid thee do?

Puck. I took him sleeping,—that is finish'd too,—
And the Athenian woman by his side;
That, when he wak'd, of force she must be ey'd.

Enter DEMETRIUS *and* HERMIA.

Obe. Stand close; this is the same Athenian.

Puck. This is the woman, but not this the man.

Dem. O, why rebuke you him that loves you so?
Lay breath so bitter on your bitter foe.

Her. Now I but chide, but I should use thee worse;
For thou, I fear, hast given me cause to curse.
If thou hast slain Lysander in his sleep,
Being o'er shoes in blood, plunge in the deep,
And kill me too.
The sun was not so true unto the day,
As he to me: Would he have stolen away
From sleeping Hermia? I'll believe as soon,
This whole earth may be bor'd; and that the moon
May through the centre creep, and so displease
Her brother's noon-tide with the Antipodes.
It cannot be, but thou hast murder'd him;
So should a murderer look; so dead, so grim.

Dem. So should the murder'd look; and so should I,
Pierc'd through the heart with your stern cruelty:
Yet you, the murderer, look as bright, as clear,
As yonder Venus in her glimmering sphere.

Her. What's this to my Lysander? Where is he?
Ah, good Demetrius, wilt thou give him me?

Dem. I had rather give his carcass to my hounds.

Her. Out, dog! out, cur! thou driv'st me past the bounds
Of maiden's patience. Hast thou slain him then?
Henceforth be never number'd among men!
O! once tell true, tell true, even for my sake;
Durst thou have look'd upon him, being awake,
And hast thou kill'd him sleeping? O brave touch!
Could not a worm, an adder, do so much?
An adder did it; for with doubler tongue
Than thine, thou serpent, never adder stung.

Dem. You spend your passion on a mispris'd mood:
I am not guilty of Lysander's blood;
Nor is he dead, for aught that I can tell.

Her. I pray thee, tell me then that he is well.

Dem. An if I could, what should I get therefore?

Her. A privilege, never to see me more.—
And from thy hated presence part I so:
See me no more, whether he be dead or no.
[*Exit.*

Dem. There is no following her in this fierce vein:
Here, therefore, for a while I will remain.
So sorrow's heaviness doth heavier grow
For debt that bankrupt sleep doth sorrow owe;
Which now, in some slight measure it will pay,
If for his tender here I make some stay.
[*Lies down.*

Obe. What hast thou done? thou hast mistaken quite,
And laid the love-juice on some true-love's sight:
Of thy misprision must perforce ensue
Some true-love turn'd, and not a false turn'd true.

Puck. Then fate o'errules; that, one man holding troth,
A million fail, confounding oath on oath.

Obe. About the wood go swifter than the wind,
And Helena of Athens look thou find:
All fancy-sick she is, and pale of cheer
With sighs of love, that cost the fresh blood dear:
By some illusion see thou bring her here;
I'll charm his eyes, against she do appear.

Puck. I go, I go; look, how I go:
Swifter than arrow from the Tartar's bow.
[*Exit.*

Obe. Flower of this purple dye,
Hit with Cupid's archery,
Sink in apple of his eye!
When his love he doth espy,
Let her shine as gloriously
As the Venus of the sky.—
When thou wak'st, if she be by,
Beg of her for remedy.

Re-enter PUCK.

Puck. Captain of our fairy band,
Helena is here at hand;
And the youth, mistook by me,
Pleading for a lover's fee;
Shall we their fond pageant see?
Lord, what fools these mortals be!

Obe. Stand aside: the noise they make,
Will cause Demetrius to awake.

Puck. Then will two at once woo one;
That must needs be sport alone;
And those things do best please me,
That befall preposterously.

Enter LYSANDER *and* HELENA.

Lys. Why should you think that I should woo in scorn;
Scorn and derision never come in tears:
Look, when I vow, I weep; and vows so born
In their nativity all truth appears.
How can these things in me seem scorn to you,
Bearing the badge of faith, to prove them true?

Hel. You do advance your cunning more and more.
When truth kills truth, O devilish holy fray!
These vows are Hermia's; Will you give her o'er?
Weigh oath with oath, and you will nothing weigh:
Your vows, to her and me, put in two scales,
Will even weigh; and both as light as tales.

Lys. I had no judgment when to her I swore.

Hel. Nor none in my mind now you give her o'er?

Lys. Demetrius loves her, and he loves not you.

Dem. [*awaking.*] O Helen, goddess, nymph, perfect, divine!
To what, my love, shall I compare thine eyne?
Crystal is muddy. O, how ripe in show
Thy lips, those kissing cherries, tempting grow!
That pure congealed white, high Taurus' snow,
Fann'd with the eastern wind, turns to a crow,
When thou hold'st up thy hand: O let me kiss
This princess of pure white, this seal of bliss!

Hel. O spite! O hell! I see you all are bent
To set against me, for your merriment.
If you were civil, and knew courtesy,
You would not do me thus much injury.
Can you not hate me, as I know you do,
But you must join, in souls, to mock me too?
If you were men, as men you are in show,
You would not use a gentle lady so;
To vow, and swear, and superpraise my parts,
When, I am sure, you hate me with your hearts.
You both are rivals, and love Hermia;
And now both rivals to mock Helena:
A trim exploit, a manly enterprise,
To conjure tears up in a poor maid's eyes,
With your derision! none of noble sort
Would so offend a virgin; and extort
A poor soul's patience, all to make you sport.

Lys. You are unkind, Demetrius; be not so;
For you love Hermia: this you know, I know:
And here, with all good will, with all my heart,
In Hermia's love I yield you up my part;
And yours of Helena to me bequeath,
Whom I do love, and will do to my death.

Hel. Never did mockers waste more idle breath.

Dem. Lysander, keep thy Hermia; I will none:
If e'er I lov'd her, all that love is gone.
My heart with her but, as guest-wise, sojourn'd;
And now to Helen is it home return'd,
There to remain.

Lys. Helen, it is not so.

Dem. Disparage not the faith thou dost not know,
Lest, to thy peril, thou abide it dear.—
Look, where thy love comes; yonder is thy dear.

Enter HERMIA.

Her. Dark night, that from the eye his function takes,
The ear more quick of apprehension makes;
Wherein it doth impair the seeing sense,
It pays the hearing double recompense:—
Thou art not by mine eye, Lysander, found;
Mine ear, I thank it, brought me to thy sound.
But why unkindly didst thou leave me so?

Lys. Why should he stay, whom love doth press to go?

Her. What love could press Lysander from my side?

Lys. Lysander's love, that would not let him bide.
Fair Helena, who more engilds the night
Than all yon fiery oes and eyes of light.
Why seek'st thou me? could not this make thee know,
The hate I bare thee made me leave thee so.

Her. You speak not as you think; it cannot be.

Hel. Lo, she is one of this confederacy!
Now I percieve they have conjoin'd all three,
To fashion this false sport in spite of me.
Injurious Hermia! most ungrateful maid!
Have you conspir'd, have you with these contriv'd
To bait me with this foul derision?
Is all the counsel that we two have shar'd,
The sisters' vows, the hours that we have spent,
When we have chid the hasty-footed time
For parting us,—O, and is all forgot?
All school-days' friendship, childhood innocence?
We, Hermia, like two artificial gods,
Have with our neelds created both one flower,
Both on one sampler, sitting on one cushion,
Both warbling of one song, both in one key;
As if our hands, our sides, voices, and minds,
Had been incorporate. So we grew together,
Like to a double cherry, seeming parted;
But yet a union in partition,
Two lovely berries moulded on one stem:
So, with two seeming bodies, but one heart;
Two of the first, like coats in heraldry,
Due but to one, and crowned with one crest.
And will you rend our ancient love asunder,
To join with men in scorning your poor friend?
It is not friendly, 'tis not maidenly:
Our sex, as well as I, may chide you for it;
Though I alone do feel the injury.

Her. I am amazed at your passionate words:
I scorn you not: it seems that you scorn me.

Hel. Have you not set Lysander, as in scorn,
To follow me, and praise my eyes and face?
And made your other love, Demetrius
(Who even but now did spurn me with his foot),
To call me goddess, nymph, divine, and rare,
Precious, celestial? Wherefore speaks he this
To her he hates? and wherefore doth Lysander
Deny your love, so rich within his soul,
And tender me, forsooth, affection;
But by your setting on, by your consent?
What though I be not so in grace as you,
So hung upon with love, so fortunate;
But miserable most, to love unlov'd?
This you should pity, rather than despise.

Her. I understand not what you mean by this.

Hel. Ay, do, persever, counterfeit sad looks,
Make mows upon me when I turn my back;
Wink at each other; hold the sweet jest up:
This sport, well carried, shall be chronicled.
If you have any pity, grace, or manners,
You would not make me such an argument.
But, fare ye well: 'tis partly mine own fault;
Which death, or absence, soon shall remedy.

Lys. Stay, gentle Helena; hear my excuse;
My love, my life, my soul, fair Helena!

Hel. O excellent!

Her. Sweet, do not scorn her so.

Dem. If she cannot entreat, I can compel.

Lys. Thou canst compel no more than she entreat;
Thy threats have no more strength, than her weak prayers.—
Helen, I love thee; by my life I do:
I swear by that which I will lose for thee,
To prove him false, that says I love thee not.
Dem. I say, I love thee more than he can do.
Lys. If thou say so, withdraw, and prove it too.
Dem. Quick, come,—
Her. Lysander, whereto tends all this?
Lys. Away, you Ethiop!
Dem. No, no, he'll—Sir,
Seem to break loose; take on, as you would follow;
But yet come not: You are a tame man, go!
Lys. Hang off, thou cat, thou burr: vile thing, let loose;
Or I will shake thee from me like a serpent.
Her. Why are you grown so rude? what change is this,
Sweet love?
Lys. Thy love! out, tawny Tartar, out!
Out, loathed medicine! hated potion, hence!
Her. Do you not jest?
Hel. Yes, 'sooth: and so do you.
Lys. Demetrius, I will keep my word with thee.
Dem. I would, I had your bond; for, I perceive,
A weak bond holds you; I'll not trust your word.
Lys. What, should I hurt her, strike her, kill her dead?
Although I hate her, I'll not harm her so.
Her. What, can you do me greater harm than hate?
Hate me! wherefore? O me! what news, my love?
Am not I Hermia? Are not you Lysander?
I am as fair now as I was erewhile.
Since night you lov'd me: yet since night you left me:
Why, then you left me,—O, the gods forbid!—
In earnest shall I say?
Lys. Ay, by my life;
And never did desire to see thee more.
Therefore, be out of hope, of question, doubt,
Be certain nothing truer; 'tis no jest,
That I do hate thee, and love Helena.
Her. O me, you juggler! you canker blossom!
You thief of love! what, have you come by night,
And stol'n my heart's love from him?
Hel. Fine, i'faith!
Have you no modesty, no maiden shame,
No touch of bashfulness? What will you tear
Impatient answers from my gentle tongue?
Fie, fie! you counterfeit, you puppet you!
Her. Puppet! why so? Ay, that way goes the game.
Now I perceive that she hath made compare
Between our statures, she hath urged her height;
And with her personage, her tall personage,
Her height, forsooth, she hath prevail'd with him.—
And are you grown so high in his esteem,
Because I am so dwarfish, and so low?
How low am I, thou painted maypole? speak;
How low am I? I am not yet so low,
But that my nails can reach unto thine eyes.
Hel. I pray you, though you mock me, gentlemen,
Let her not hurt me: I was never curst;
I have no gift at all in shrewishness;
I am a right maid for my cowardice;
Let her not strike me: You, perhaps, may think,
Because she's something lower than myself,
That I can match her.
Her. Lower! hark, again.
Hel. Good Hermia, do not be so bitter with me.
I evermore did love you, Hermia,
Did ever keep your counsels, never wrong'd you;
Save that, in love unto Demetrius,
I told him of your stealth into this wood:
He follow'd you; for love, I follow'd him.
But he hath chid me hence: and threaten'd me,
To strike me, spurn me, nay, to kill me too:
And now, so you will let me quiet go,
To Athens will I bear my folly back,
And follow you no further: Let me go;
You see how simple and how fond I am.
Her. Why, get you gone: Who is't that hinders you?
Hel. A foolish heart that I leave here behind.
Her. What! with Lysander?
Hel. With Demetrius.
Lys. Be not afraid: she shall not harm thee, Helena.
Dem. No, sir; she shall not, though you take her part.
Hel. O, when she's angry, she is keen and shrewd:
She was a vixen, when she went to school;
And though she be but little, she is fierce.
Her. Little again? nothing but low and little?—
Why will you suffer her to flout me thus?
Let me come to her.
Lys. Get you gone, you dwarf,
You minimus of hind'ring knot-grass made;
You bead, you acorn.
Dem. You are too officious,
In her behalf that scorns your services:
Let her alone; speak not of Helena;
Take not her part: for if thou dost intend
Never so little show of love to her,
Thou shalt aby it.
Lys. Now she holds me not;
Now follow, if thou dar'st, to try whose right
Or thine or mine, is most in Helena.
Dem. Follow? nay, I'll go with thee cheek by jole. [*Exeunt* LYS. *and* DEM.
Her. You, mistress, all this coil is long of you:
Nay, go not back.
Hel. I will not trust you, I:
Nor longer stay in your curst company.
Your hands, than mine, are quicker for a fray;
My legs are longer though, to run away. [*Exit.*
Her. I am amaz'd, and know not what to say.
[*Exit, pursuing* HELENA.
Obe. This is thy negligence: still thou mistak'st,
Or else committ'st thy knaveries wilfully.
Puck. Believe me, king of shadows, I mistook.
Did not you tell me, I should know the man
By the Athenian garments he had on?
And so far blameless proves my enterprise,
That I have 'nointed an Athenian's eyes:
And so far am I glad it so did sort,
As this their jangling I esteem a sport.
Obe. Thou seest, these lovers seek a place to fight:
Hie, therefore, Robin, overcast the night;
The starry welkin cover thou anon
With drooping fog, as black as Acheron;
And lead these testy rivals so astray,
As one come not within another's way.
Like to Lysander sometime frame thy tongue,
Then stir Demetrius up with bitter wrong;
And sometime rail thou like Demetrius:
And from each other look thou lead them thus,
Till o'er their brows death-counterfeiting sleep
With leaden legs and batty wings doth creep:
Then crush this herb into Lysander's eye:
Whose liquor hath this virtuous property,
To take from thence all error with his might,
And make his eyeballs roll with wonted sight.
When they next wake, all this derision
Shall seem a dream, and fruitless vision;
And back to Athens shall the lovers wend
With league whose date till death shall never end.
Whiles I in this affair do thee employ,
I'll to my queen, and beg her Indian boy;
And then I will her charmed eye release
From monster's view, and all things shall be peace.

Puck. My fairy lord, this must be done with haste;
For night's swift dragons cut the clouds full fast,
And yonder shines Aurora's harbinger;
At whose approach, ghosts, wandering here and there,
Troop home to churchyards: damned spirits all,
That in cross-ways and floods have burial,
Already to their wormy beds are gone;
For fear lest day should look their shames upon,
They wilfully themselves exile from light,
And must for aye consort with black-brow'd night.

Obe. But we are spirits of another sort:
I with the Morning's love have oft made sport;
And, like a forester, the groves may tread,
Even till the eastern gate, all fiery red,
Opening on Neptune with fair blessed beams,
Turns into yellow gold his salt-green streams.
But, notwithstanding, haste; make no delay:
We may effect this business yet ere day.
[*Exit* OBERON.

Puck. Up and down, up and down,
I will lead them up and down:
I am fear'd in field and town;
Goblin, lead them up and down.
Here comes one.

Enter LYSANDER.

Lys. Where art thou, proud Demetrius? speak thou now.

Puck. Here, villain; drawn and ready. Where art thou?

Lys. I will be with thee straight.

Puck. Follow me then
To plainer ground. [*Exit* LYS. *as following the voice.*

Enter DEMETRIUS.

Dem. Lysander! speak again.
Thou runaway, thou coward, art thou fled?
Speak. In some bush? Where dost thou hide thy head?

Puck. Thou coward, art thou bragging to the stars,
Telling the bushes that thou look'st for wars,
And wilt not come? Come, recreant; come, thou child,
I'll whip thee with a rod: He is defil'd,
That draws a sword on thee.

Dem. Yea; art thou there?

Puck. Follow my voice; we'll try no manhood here. [*Exeunt.*

Re-enter LYSANDER.

Lys. He goes before me, and still dares me on;
When I come where he calls, then he is gone.
The villain is much lighter heel'd than I:
I follow'd fast, but faster he did fly;
That fallen am I in dark uneven way,
And here will rest me. Come, thou gentle day!
[*Lies down.*
For if but once thou show me thy gray light,
I'll find Demetrius, and revenge this spite.
[*Sleeps.*

Re-enter PUCK, *and* DEMETRIUS.

Puck. Ho, ho! ho, ho! Coward, why com'st thou not?

Dem. Abide me, if thou dar'st; for well I wot,
Thou runn'st before me shifting every place;
And dar'st not stand, nor look me in the face.
Where art thou?

Puck. Come hither; I am here.

Dem. Nay, then thou mock'st me. Thou shalt buy this dear.
If ever I thy face by day-light see:
Now, go thy way. Faintness constraineth me
To measure out my length on this cold bed.—
By day's approach look to be visited.
[*Lies down and sleeps.*

Enter HELENA.

Hel. O weary night, O long and tedious night,
Abate thy hours: shine comforts from the east;
That I may back to Athens by day-light,
From these that my poor company detest:—
And, sleep, that sometimes shuts up sorrow's eye,
Steal me awhile from mine own company.
[*Sleeps.*

Puck. Yet but three? Come one more;
Two of both kinds makes up four.
Here she comes, curst and sad:—
Cupid is a knavish lad,
Thus to make poor females mad.

Enter HERMIA.

Her. Never so weary, never so in woe,
Bedabbled with the dew, and torn with briers;
I can no further crawl, no further go;
My legs can keep no pace with my desires.
Here will I rest me, till the break of day,
Heaven shield Lysander, if they mean a fray!
[*Lies down.*

Puck. On the ground
Sleep sound:
I'll apply
To your eye,
Gentle lover, remedy.
[*Squeezing the juice on* LYSANDER'S *eye.*
When thou wak'st,
Thou tak'st
True delight
In the sight
Of thy former lady's eye:
And the country proverb known,
That every man should take his own,
In your waking shall be shown:
Jack shall have Jill;
Nought shall go ill;
The man shall have his mare again, and all shall be well.
[*Exit* PUCK.—DEM. HEL. *&c. sleep.*

ACT IV.

SCENE I. *The same.*

Enter TITANIA *and* BOTTOM, Fairies *attending;* OBERON *behind unseen.*

Tita. Come, sit thee down upon this flowery bed,
While I thy amiable cheeks do coy,
And stick musk-roses in thy sleek smooth head,
And kiss thy fair large ears, my gentle joy.

Bot. Where's Peas-blossom?

Peas. Ready.

Bot. Scratch my head, Peas-blossom.—Where's monsieur Cobweb?

Cob. Ready.

Bot. Monsieur Cobweb; good monsieur, get your weapons in your hand, and kill me a red-hipped humble-bee on the top of a thistle; and, good monsieur, bring me the honey-bag. Do not fret yourself too much in the action, monsieur; and, good monsieur, have a care the honey-bag break not; I would be loath to have you overflown with a honey-bag, signior.—Where's monsieur Mustard-seed?

Must. Ready.

Bot. Give me your nief, monsieur Mustard-seed. 'Pray you, leave your courtesy, good monsieur.

Must. What's your will?

Bot. Nothing, good monsieur, but to help cavalero Cobweb to scratch. I must to the barber's, monsieur; for, methinks, I am marvellous hairy about the face: and I am such a tender ass, if my hair do but tickle me, I must scratch.

Tita. What, wilt thou hear some musick, my sweet love?

Bot. I have a reasonable good ear in musick; let us have the tongs and the bones.

Tita. Or say, sweet love, what thou desir'st to eat.

Bot. Truly, a peck of provender; I could

munch good dry oats. Methinks, I have a great desire to a bottle of hay: good hay, sweet hay, hath no fellow.

Tita. I have a venturous fairy that shall seek
The squirrel's hoard, and fetch thee new nuts.

Bot. I had rather have a handful, or two, of dried peas. But, I pray you, let none of your people stir me; I have an exposition of sleep come upon me.

Tita. Sleep thou, and I will wind thee in my arms.
Fairies, be gone, and be all ways away.
So doth the woodbine, the sweet honeysuckle,
Gently entwist,—the female ivy so
Enrings the barky fingers of the elm.
O, how I love thee! how I dote on thee!
[*They sleep.*

OBERON *advances.* *Enter* PUCK.

Obe. Welcome, good Robin. Seest thou this sweet sight?
Her dotage now I do begin to pity.
For meeting her of late behind the wood,
Seeking sweet savours for this hateful fool,
I did upbraid her, and fall out with her:
For she his hairy temples then had rounded
With coronet of fresh and fragrant flowers;
And that same dew, which sometime on the buds
Was wont to swell, like round and orient pearls,
Stood now within the pretty flourets' eyes,
Like tears, that did their own disgrace bewail.
When I had, at my pleasure, taunted her,
And she, in mild terms, begg'd my patience,
I then did ask of her her changeling child;
Which straight she gave me, and her fairy sent
To bear him to my bower in fairy land.
And now I have the boy, I will undo
The hateful imperfection of her eyes.
And, gentle Puck, take this transformed scalp
From off the head of this Athenian swain;
That he awaking when the other do,
May all to Athens back again repair;
And think no more of this night's accidents,
But as the fierce vexation of a dream.
But first I will release the fairy queen.
Be, as thou wast wont to be.
[*Touching her eyes with an herb.*
See, as thou wast wont to see:
Dian's bud o'er Cupid's flower
Hath such force and blessed power.
Now, my Titania; wake you, my sweet queen.

Tita. My Oberon! what visions have I seen!
Methought I was enamour'd of an ass.

Obe. There lies your love.

Tita. How came these things to pass?
O, how mine eyes do loathe his visage now!

Obe. Silence, awhile.—Robin, take off this head.—
Titania, musick call; and strike more dead
Than common sleep, of all these five the sense.

Tita. Musick, ho! musick: such as charmeth sleep.

Puck. Now, when thou wak'st, with thine own fool's eyes peep.

Obe. Sound, musick. [*Still musick.*] Come, my queen, take hands with me,
And rock the ground whereon these sleepers be.
Now thou and I are new in amity;
And will, to-morrow midnight, solemnly,
Dance in Duke Theseus' house triumphantly,
And bless it to all fair posterity:
There shall the pairs of faithful lovers be
Wedded, with Theseus, all in jollity.

Puck. Fairy king, attend and mark;
I do hear the morning lark.

Obe. Then, my queen, in silence sad,
Trip we after the night's shade:
We the globe can compass soon,
Swifter than the wand'ring moon.

Tita. Come, my lord; and in our flight,
Tell me how it came this night,
That I sleeping here was found,
With these mortals on the ground. [*Exeunt.*
[*Horns sound within.*

Enter THESEUS, HIPPOLYTA, EGEUS, *and train.*

The. Go, one of you, find out the forester;—
For now our observation is perform'd:
And since we have the vaward of the day,
My love shall hear the musick of my hounds.—
Uncouple in the western valley; go:
Despatch, I say, and find the forester.—
We will, fair queen, up to the mountain's top,
And mark the musical confusion
Of hounds and echo in conjunction.

Hip. I was with Hercules, and Cadmus, once,
When in a wood of Crete they bay'd the bear
With hounds of Sparta; never did I hear
Such gallant chiding; for, besides the groves,
The skies, the fountains, every region near
Seem'd all one mutual cry: I never heard
So musical a discord, such sweet thunder.

The. My hounds are bred out of the Spartan kind,
So flew'd, so sanded; and their heads are hung
With ears that sweep away the morning dew;
Crook-knee'd, and dew-lapp'd like Thessalian bulls;
Slow in pursuit, but match'd in mouth like bells,
Each under each. A cry more tunable
Was never holla'd to, nor cheer'd with horn,
In Crete, in Sparta, nor in Thessaly:
Judge, when you hear.—But, soft; what nymphs are these?

Ege. My lord, this is my daughter here asleep:
And this, Lysander; this Demetrius is;
This Helena, old Nedar's Helena:
I wonder of their being here together.

The. No doubt, they rose up early, to observe
The rite of May; and, hearing our intent,
Came here in grace of our solemnity.—
But, speak, Egeus; is not this the day
That Hermia should give answer of her choice?

Ege. It is, my lord.

The. Go, bid the huntsmen wake them with their horns.

Horns, and shout within. DEMETRIUS, LYSANDER, HERMIA, *and* HELENA, *wake and start up.*

The. Good-morrow, friends. Saint Valentine is past.
Begin these wood-birds but to couple now?

Lys. Pardon, my lord.
[*He and the rest kneel to* THESEUS.

The. I pray you all, stand up.
I know you are two rival enemies;
How comes this gentle concord in the world,
That hatred is so far from jealousy,
To sleep by hate, and fear no enmity?

Lys. My lord, I shall reply amazedly,
Half 'sleep, half-waking; But as yet, I swear,
I cannot truly say how I came here:
But, as I think (for truly would I speak,—
And now I do bethink me, so it is),
I came with Hermia hither: our intent
Was to be gone from Athens, where we might be
Without the peril of the Athenian law.

Ege. Enough, enough, my lord; you have enough:
I beg the law, the law, upon his head.—
They would have stol'n away, they would, Demetrius,
Thereby to have defeated you and me:
You, of your wife, and me, of my consent;
Of my consent that she should be your wife.

Dem. My lord, fair Helen told me of their stealth,
Of this their purpose hither, to this wood;
And I in fury hither follow'd them;
Fair Helena in fancy following me.
But, my good lord, I wot not by what power
(But by some power it is), my love to Hermia,
Melted as doth the snow, seems to me now
As the remembrance of an idle gawd,

Which in my childhood I did dote upon:
And all the faith, the virtue of my heart,
The object, and the pleasure of mine eye,
Is only Helena. To her, my lord,
Was I betroth'd ere I saw Hermia:
But, like in sickness, did I loathe this food:
But, as in health, come to my natural taste,
Now do I wish it, love it, long for it,
And will for evermore be true to it.

The. Fair lovers, you are fortunately met:
Of this discourse we more will hear anon.—
Egeus, I will overbear your will;
For in the temple, by and by with us,
These couples shall eternally be knit.
And, for the morning now is something worn,
Our purpos'd hunting shall be set aside.
Away, with us, to Athens: Three and three,
We'll hold a feast in great solemnity.—
Come, Hippolyta.

[*Exeunt* THE. HIP. EGE. *and train.*

Dem. These things seem small and undistinguishable,
Like far-off mountains turned into clouds.

Her. Methinks, I see these things with parted eye,
When every thing seems double.

Hel. So methinks:
And I have found Demetrius like a jewel,
Mine own, and not mine own.

Dem. Are you sure
That we are awake? It seems to me,
That yet we sleep, we dream.—Do not you think,
The duke was here, and bid us follow him?

Her. Yea; and my father.

Hel. And Hippolyta.

Lys. And he did bid us follow to the temple.

Dem. Why then, we are awake: let's follow him;
And, by the way, let us recount our dreams.

[*Exeunt.*

As they go out, BOTTOM *awakes.*

Bot. When my cue comes, call me, and I will answer:—my next is, *Most fair Pyramus.*—Hey, ho!—Peter Quince! Flute, the bellows-mender! Snout, the tinker! Starveling! God's my life! stolen hence, and left me asleep! I have had a most rare vision. I have had a dream,—past the wit of man to say what dream it was: Man is but an ass, if he go about to expound this dream. Methought I was—there is no man can tell what. Methought I was, and methought I had,—But man is but a patched fool, if he will offer to say what methought I had. The eye of man hath not heard, the ear of man hath not seen; man's hand is not able to taste, his tongue to conceive, nor his heart to report, what my dream was. I will get Peter Quince to write a ballad of this dream: it shall be called Bottom's Dream, because it hath no bottom; and I will sing it in the latter end of a play, before the duke: Peradventure, to make it the more gracious, I shall sing it at her death. [*Exit.*

SCENE II. Athens. *A Room in* Quince's *House.*

Enter QUINCE, FLUTE, SNOUT, *and* STARVELING.

Quin. Have you sent to Bottom's house? is he come home yet?

Star. He cannot be heard of. Out of doubt, he is transported.

Flu. If he come not, then the play is marred; It goes not forward, doth it?

Quin. It is not possible: you have not a man in all Athens able to discharge Pyramus, but he.

Flu. No; he hath simply the best wit of any handicraft man in Athens.

Quin. Yea, and the best person too: and he is a very paramour, for a sweet voice.

Flu. You must say, paragon: a paramour is, God bless us, a thing of nought.

Enter SNUG.

Snug. Masters, the duke is coming from the temple, and there is two or three lords and ladies more married: if our sport had gone forward, we had all been made men.

Flu. O sweet bully Bottom! Thus hath he lost sixpence a-day during his life; he could not have 'scaped sixpence a-day: an the duke had not given him sixpence a-day for playing Pyramus, I'll be hang'd; he would have deserved it: sixpence a-day, in Pyramus, or nothing.

Enter BOTTOM.

Bot. Where are these lads? where are these hearts?

Quin. Bottom!—O most courageous day! O most happy hour!

Bot. Masters, I am to discourse wonders: but ask me not what; for, if I tell you, I am no true Athenian. I will tell you every thing, right as it fell out.

Quin. Let us hear, sweet Bottom.

Bot. Not a word of me. All that I will tell you, is, that the duke hath dined: Get your apparel together; good strings to your beards, new ribbons to your pumps; meet presently at the palace; every man look o'er his part; for, the short and the long is, our play is preferred. In any case, let Thisby have clean linen; and let not him, that plays the lion, pare his nails, for they shall hang out for the lion's claws. And, most dear actors, eat no onions, nor garlick, for we are to utter sweet breath; and I do not doubt, but to hear them say, it is a sweet comedy. No more words; away; go, away.

[*Exeunt.*

ACT V.

SCENE I. *The same.*

An Apartment in the Palace of THESEUS.

Enter THESEUS, HIPPOLYTA, PHILOSTRATE, *Lords, and Attendants.*

Hip. 'Tis strange, my Theseus, that these lovers speak of.

The. More strange than true. I never may believe
These antique fables, nor these fairy toys.
Lovers and madmen have such seething brains,
Such shaping fantasies, that apprehend
More than cool reason ever comprehends.
The lunatick, the lover, and the poet,
Are of imagination all compact:
One sees more devils than vast hell can hold;
That is, the madman: the lover, all as frantick,
Sees Helen's beauty in a brow of Egypt:
The poet's eye, in a fine frenzy rolling,
Doth glance from heaven to earth, from earth to heaven;
And, as imagination bodies forth
The forms of things unknown, the poet's pen
Turns them to shapes, and gives to airy nothing
A local habitation, and a name.
Such tricks hath strong imagination;
That, if it would but apprehend some joy,
It comprehends some bringer of that joy;
Or, in the night, imagining some fear,
How easy is a bush supposed a bear?

Hip. But all the story of the night told over,
And all their minds transfigur'd so together,
More witnesseth than fancy's images,
And grows to something of great constancy;
But, howsoever, strange and admirable.

Enter LYSANDER, DEMETRIUS, HERMIA, *and* HELENA.

The. Here come the lovers, full of joy and mirth.—
Joy, gentle friends! joy, and fresh days of love,
Accompany your hearts!

Lys. More than to us
Wait on your royal walks, your board, your bed!
The. Come now; what masks, what dances shall we have,
To wear away this long age of three hours,
Between our after supper, and bed time?
Where is our usual manager of mirth?
What revels are in hand? Is there no play,
To ease the anguish of a torturing hour?
Call Philostrate.
Philost. Here, mighty Theseus.
The. Say, what abridgment have you for this evening?
What mask? what musick? How shall we beguile
The lazy time, if not with some delight?
Philost. There is a brief, how many sports are ripe;
Make choice of which your highness will see first.
[*Giving a paper.*
The. [*Reads.*] *The battle with the Centaurs, to be sung*
By an Athenian eunuch to the harp.
We'll none of that: that have I told my love,
In glory of my kinsman Hercules.
The riot of the tipsy Bacchanals,
Tearing the Thracian singer in their rage.
That is an old device; and it was play'd
When I from Thebes came last a conqueror.
The thrice three Muses mourning for the death
Of learning, late deceas'd in beggary.
That is some satire, keen, and critical,
Not sorting with a nuptial ceremony.
A tedious brief scene of young Pyramus,
And his love Thisbe: very tragical mirth.
Merry and tragical! Tedious and brief!
That is, hot ice, and wonderous strange snow.
How shall we find the concord of this discord?
Philost. A play there is, my lord, some ten words long;
Which is as brief as I have known a play;
But by ten words, my lord, it is too long;
Which makes it tedious: for in all the play
There is not one word apt, one player fitted.
And tragical, my noble lord, it is;
For Pyramus therein doth kill himself.
Which, when I saw rehears'd, I must confess,
Made mine eyes water; but more merry tears
The passion of loud laughter never shed.
The. What are they that do play it?
Philost. Hard-handed men, that work in Athens here,
Which never labour'd in their minds till now;
And now have toil'd their unbreath'd memories
With this same play against your nuptial.
The. And we will hear it.
Philost. No, my noble lord,
It is not for you: I have heard it over,
And it is nothing, nothing in the world:
Unless you can find sport in their intents,
Extremely stretch'd, and conn'd with cruel pain,
To do you service.
The. I will hear that play;
For never any thing can be amiss,
When simpleness and duty tender it.
Go, bring them in:—and take your places, ladies.
[*Exit* PHILOSTRATE.
Hip. I love not to see wretchedness o'ercharg'd,
And duty in his service perishing.
The. Why, gentle sweet, you shall see no such thing.
Hip. He says they can do nothing in this kind.
The. The kinder we, to give them thanks for nothing.
Our sport shall be, to take what they mistake:
And what poor duty cannot do,
Noble respect takes it in might, not merit.
Where I have come, great clerks have purposed
To greet me with premeditated welcomes;
Where I have seen them shiver and look pale,
Make periods in the midst of sentences,
Throttle their practis'd accent in their fears,
And, in conclusion, dumbly have broke off,
Not paying me a welcome: Trust me, sweet,
Out of this silence, yet, I pick'd a welcome;
And in the modesty of fearful duty
I read as much, as from the rattling tongue
Of saucy and audacious eloquence.
Love, therefore, and tongue-tied simplicity,
In least speak most, to my capacity.

Enter PHILOSTRATE.

Philost. So please your grace, the prologue is addrest.
The. Let him approach. [*Flourish of trumpets.*

Enter Prologue.

Prol. *If we offend, it is with our good will.*
That you should think we come not to offend,
But with good-will. To shew our simple skill,
That is the true beginning of our end.
Consider then, we come but in despite.
We do not come as minding to content you,
Our true intent is. All for your delight,
We are not here. That you should here repent you.
The actors are at hand; and, by their show,
You shall know all, that you are like to know.
The. This fellow doth not stand upon points.
Lys. He hath rid his prologue, like a rough colt, he knows not the stop. A good moral, my lord: It is not enough to speak, but to speak true.
Hip. Indeed he hath played on this prologue like a child on a recorder; a sound, but not in government.
The. His speech was like a tangled chain; nothing impaired, but all disordered. Who is next?

Enter PYRAMUS *and* THISBE, Wall, Moonshine, *and* Lion, *as in dumb show.*

Prol. "Gentles, perchance, you wonder at this show;
"But wonder on, till truth make all things plain.
"This man is Pyramus, if you would know;
"This beauteous lady Thisby is, certain.
"This man, with lime and rough-cast, doth present
"Wall, that vile wall which did these lovers sunder:
"And through wall's chink, poor souls, they are content
"To whisper; at the which let no man wonder.
"This man, with lantern, dog, and bush of thorn,
"Presenteth moon-shine; for, if you will know,
"By moon-shine did these lovers think no scorn
"To meet at Ninus' tomb, there, there to woo.
"This grisly beast, which by name lion hight,
"The trusty Thisby, coming first by night,
"Did scare away, or rather did affright:
"And, as she fled, her mantle she did fall;
"Which lion vile with bloody mouth did stain:
"Anon comes Pyramus, sweet youth, and tall,
"And finds his trusty Thisby's mantle slain:
"Whereat with blade, with bloody blameful blade,
"He bravely broach'd his boiling bloody breast;
"And, Thisby, tarrying in mulberry shade,
"His dagger drew, and died. For all the rest,
"Let lion, moon-shine, wall, and lovers twain,
"At large discourse, while here they do remain."
[*Exeunt* Prol. THISBE, Lion, *and* Moonshine.
The. I wonder, if the lion be to speak.
Dem. No wonder, my lord: one lion may, when many asses do.
Wall. "In this same interlude it doth befall,
"That I, one Snout by name, present a wall:
"And such a wall, as I would have you think,
"That had in it a cranny'd hole, or chink,
"Through which the lovers, Pyramus and Thisby,
"Did whisper often very secretly.
"This loam, this rough-cast, and this stone doth show
"That I am that same wall; the truth is so:

"And this the cranny is, right and sinister,
"Through which the fearful lovers are to whisper."

The. Would you desire lime and hair to speak better?

Dem. It is the wittiest partition that ever I heard discourse, my lord.

The. Pyramus draws near the wall: silence!

Enter PYRAMUS.

Pyr. "O grim-look'd night! O night with hue so black;
"O night, which ever art, when day is not!
"O night, O night, alack, alack, alack,
"I fear my Thisby's promise is forgot!—
"And thou, O wall, O sweet, O lovely wall,
"That stand'st between her father's ground and mine;
"Thou wall, O wall, O sweet, and lovely wall,
"Show me thy chink, to blink through with mine eyne. [Wall *holds up his Fingers.*
"Thanks, courteous wall: Jove shield thee well for this!
"But what see I? No Thisby do I see.
"O wicked wall, through whom I see no bliss:
"Curst be thy stones for thus deceiving me!"

The. The wall, methinks, being sensible, should curse again.

Pyr. No, in truth, sir, he should not. *Deceiving me,* is Thisby's cue: she is to enter now, and I am to spy her through the wall. You shall see, it will fall pat as I told you:—Yonder she comes.

Enter THISBE.

This. "O wall, full often hast thou heard my moans,
"For parting my fair Pyramus and me:
"My cherry lips have often kiss'd thy stones:
"Thy stones with lime and hair knit up in thee."

Pyr. "I see a voice: now will I to the chink,
"To spy an I can hear my Thisby's face.
"Thisby!"

This. "My love! thou art my love, I think."

Pyr. "Think what thou wilt, I am thy lover's grace;
"And like Limander am I trusty still."

This. "And I like Helen, till the fates me kill."

Pyr. "Not Shafalus to Procrus was so true."

This. "As Shafalus to Procrus, I to you."

Pyr. "O, kiss me through the hole of this vile wall."

This. "I kiss the wall's hole, not your lips at all."

Pyr. "Wilt thou at Ninny's tomb meet me straightway?"

This. "Tide life, tide death, I come without delay."

Wall. "Thus have I, wall, my part discharged so;
"And, being done, thus wall away doth go."
[*Exeunt* Wall, PYRAMUS, *and* THISBE.

The. Now is the mural down between the two neighbours.

Dem. No remedy, my lord, when walls are so wilful to hear without warning.

Hip. This is the silliest stuff that ever I heard.

The. The best in this kind are but shadows: and the worst are no worse, if imagination amend them.

Hip. It must be your imagination then, and not theirs.

The. If we imagine no worse of them, than they of themselves, they may pass for excellent men. Here come two noble beasts in, a moon and a lion.

Enter Lion *and* Moonshine.

Lion. "You, ladies, you, whose gentle hearts do fear
"The smallest monstrous mouse that creeps on floor,
"May now, perchance, both quake and tremble here,
"When lion rough in wildest rage doth roar.
"Then know, that I, one Snug the joiner, am
"No lion fell, nor else no lion's dam:
"For if I should as lion come in strife
"Into this place, 'twere pity on my life."

The. A very gentle beast, and of a good conscience.

Dem. The very best at a beast, my lord, that e'er I saw.

Lys. This lion is a very fox for his valour.

The. True; and a goose for his discretion.

Dem. Not so, my lord; for his valour cannot carry his discretion; and the fox carries the goose.

The. His discretion, I am sure, cannot carry his valour; for the goose carries not the fox. It is well: leave it to his discretion, and let us listen to the moon.

Moon. "This lantern doth the horned moon present:"

Dem. He should have worn the horns on his head.

The. He is no crescent, and his horns are invisible within the circumference.

Moon. "This lantern doth the horned moon present:
"Myself the man i' the' moon do seem to be."

The. This is the greatest error of all the rest: the man should be put into the lantern: How is it else the man i' the moon?

Dem. He dares not come there for the candle; for, you see, it is already in snuff.

Hip. I am a weary of this moon: Would he would change!

The. It appears, by his small light of discretion, that he is in the wane: but yet, in courtesy, in all reason, we must stay the time.

Lys. Proceed, moon.

Moon. All that I have to say, is, to tell you, that the lantern is the moon; I, the man in the moon; this thorn bush, my thorn bush; and this dog, my dog.

Dem. Why, all these should be in the lantern; for they are in the moon. But silence; here comes Thisbe.

Enter THISBE.

This. "This is old Ninny's tomb: Where is my love?"

Lion. "Oh—."
[*The* Lion *roars.*—THISBE *runs off.*

Dem. Well roared, lion.

The. Well run, Thisbe.

Hip. Well shone, moon.—Truly, the moon shines with a good grace.

The. Well moused, lion.
[*The* Lion *tears* THISBE'*s Mantle and exit.*

Dem. And so comes Pyramus.

Lys. And then the moon vanishes.

Enter PYRAMUS.

Pyr. "Sweet moon I thank thee for thy sunny beams:
"I thank thee, moon, for shining now so bright.
"For, by thy gracious, golden, glittering streams,
"I trust to taste of truest Thisby's sight.
"But stay;—O spite!
"But mark;—Poor knight,
"What dreadful dole is here?
"Eyes, do you see?
"How can it be?
"O dainty duck! O dear!
"Thy mantle good,
"What, stain'd with blood?
"Approach, ye furies fell!
"O fates! come, come;
"Cut thread and thrum;
"Quail, crush, conclude, and quell!"

The. This passion, and the death of a dear friend, would go near to make a man look sad.

Hip. Beshrew my heart, but I pity the man.

Pyr. "O, wherefore, nature, didst thou lions frame?
"Since lion vile hath here deflour'd my dear:
"Which is—no, no—which was the fairest dame,
"That liv'd, that lov'd, that lik'd, that look'd with cheer.
"Come, tears, confound:
"Out, sword, and wound
"The pap of Pyramus:
"Ay, that left pap,
"Where heart doth hop:
"Thus die I, thus, thus, thus.
"Now am I dead,
"Now am I fled;
"My soul is in the sky:
"Tongue, lose thy light!
"Moon take thy flight!
"Now die, die, die, die, die."
[*Dies.—Exit* Moonshine.

Dem. No die, but an ace, for him; for he is but one.

Lys. Less than an ace, man; for he is dead; he is nothing.

The. With the help of a surgeon, he might yet recover, and prove an ass.

Hip. How chance moonshine is gone, before Thisbe comes back and finds her lover?

The. She will find him by star-light.—Here she comes; and her passion ends the play.

Enter Thisbe.

Hip. Methinks, she should not use a long one, for such a Pyramus: I hope, she will be brief.

Dem. A mote will turn the balance, which Pyramus, which Thisbe, is the better.

Lys. She hath spied him already with those sweet eyes.

Dem. And thus she moans, *videlicet.*——

This. "Asleep, my love?
"What, dead, my dove?
"O Pyramus, arise,
"Speak, speak. Quite dumb?
"Dead, dead? A tomb
"Must cover thy sweet eyes.
"These lily brows,
"This cherry nose,
"These yellow cowslip cheeks,
"Are gone, are gone:
"Lovers, make moan!
"His eyes were green as leeks.
"O sisters three,
"Come, come, to me,
"With hands as pale as milk;
"Lay them in gore,
"Since you have shore
"With shears his thread of silk.
"Tongue, not a word:—
"Come, trusty sword;
"Come, blade, my breast imbrue:
"And farewell, friends;
"Thus Thisby ends:
"Adieu, adieu, adieu." [*Dies.*

The. Moonshine and lion are left to bury the dead.

Dem. Ay, and wall too.

Bot. No, I assure you; the wall is down that parted their fathers. Will it please you to see the epilogue, or to hear a Bergomask dance, between two of our company?

The. No epilogue, I pray you: for your play needs no excuse. Never excuse; for when the players are all dead, there need none to be blamed. Marry, if he that writ it, had play'd Pyramus, and hang'd himself in Thisbe's garter, it would have been a fine tragedy: and so it is, truly; and very notably discharged. But come, your Bergomask: let your epilogue alone.
[*Here a dance of* Clowns.

The iron tongue of midnight hath told twelve:—
Lovers, to bed; 'tis almost fairy time.
I fear we shall outsleep the coming morn,
As much as we this night have overwatch'd.
This palpable-gross play hath well beguil'd
The heavy gait of night.—Sweet friends, to bed.—
A fortnight hold we this solemnity
In nightly revels, and new jollity. [*Exeunt.*

SCENE II.

Enter Puck.

Puck. Now the hungry lion roars,
And the wolf behowls the moon;
Whilst the heavy ploughman snores,
All with weary task fordone.
Now the wasted brands do glow,
Whilst the scritch-owl, scritching loud,
Puts the wretch that lies in woe,
In remembrance of a shroud.
Now it is the time of night,
That the graves all gaping wide,
Every one lets forth his sprite,
In the church-way paths to glide:
And we fairies, that do run,
By the triple Hecat's team,
From the presence of the sun,
Following darkness like a dream,
Now are frolic; not a mouse
Shall disturb this hallow'd house:
I am sent, with broom, before,
To sweep the dust behind the door.

Enter Oberon *and* Titania, *with their* Train.

Obe. Through this house give glimmering light,
By the dead and drowsy fire:
Every elf, and fairy sprite,
Hop as light as bird from brier;
And this ditty after me,
Sing and dance it trippingly.

Tita. First, rehearse this song by rote:
To each word a warbling note,
Hand in hand, with fairy grace,
Will we sing, and bless this place.

SONG AND DANCE.

Obe. Now, until the break of day,
Through this house each fairy stray.
To the best bride-bed will we,
Which by us shall blessed be;
And the issue, there create,
Ever shall be fortunate.
So shall all the couples three
Ever true in loving be:
And the blots of nature's hand
Shall not in their issue stand;
Never mole, hare-lip, nor scar,
Nor mark prodigious, such as are
Despised in nativity,
Shall upon their children be.—
With this field-dew consecrate,
Every fairy take his gate;
And each several chamber bless,
Through this palace with sweet peace:
E'er shall it in safety rest,
And the owner of it blest.
Trip away;
Make no stay;
Meet me all by break of day.
[*Exeunt* Oberon, Titania, *and* Train.

Puck. *If we shadows have offended,*
Think but this (and all is mended),
That you have but slumber'd here,
While these visions did appear.
And this weak and idle theme,
No more yielding but a dream,
Gentles, do not reprehend;
If you pardon, we will mend.
And, as I'm an honest Puck,
If we have unearned luck
Now to 'scape the serpent's tongue,
We will make amends, ere long:
Else the Puck a liar call.
So, good night unto you all.
Give me your hands, if we be friends,
And Robin shall restore amends. [*Exit.*

LOVE'S LABOUR'S LOST.

PERSONS REPRESENTED.

FERDINAND, *King of* Navarre.
BIRON, LONGAVILLE, DUMAIN, } *Lords, attending on the King.*
BOYET, MERCADE, } *Lords, attending on the Princess of* France.
DON ADRIANO DE ARMADO, *a fantastical Spaniard.*
SIR NATHANIEL, *a Curate.*
HOLOFERNES, *a Schoolmaster.*
DULL, *a Constable.*
COSTARD, *a Clown.*
MOTH, *Page to* Armado.
A Forester.

Princess *of* France.
ROSALINE, MARIA, KATHARINE, } *Ladies attending on the Princess.*
JAQUENETTA, *a country Wench.*

Officers and others, attendants on the King and Princess.

SCENE—Navarre.

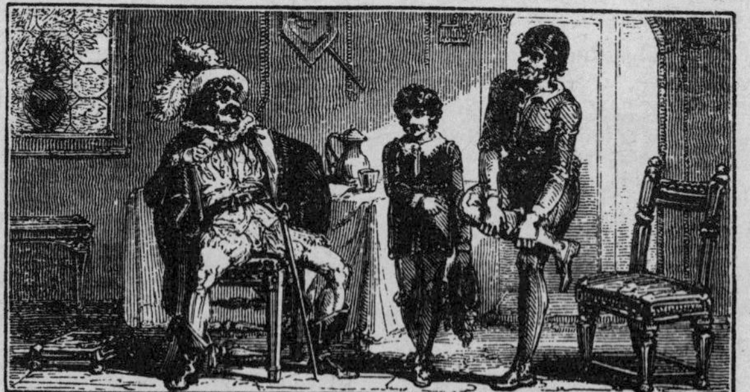

ACT I.

SCENE I. Navarre. *A Park with a Palace in it.*

Enter the King, BIRON, LONGAVILLE, *and* DUMAIN.

King. LET fame, that all hunt after in their lives,
Live register'd upon our brazen tombs,
And then grace us in the disgrace of death;
When, spite of cormorant devouring time,
The endeavour of this present breath may buy
That honour, which shall bate his scythe's keen edge,
And make us heirs of all eternity.
Therefore, brave conquerors!—for so you are,
That war against your own affections,
And the huge army of the world's desires,—
Our late edict shall strongly stand in force:
Navarre shall be the wonder of the world;
Our court shall be a little Academe,
Still and contemplative in living art.
You three, Biron, Dumain, and Longaville,
Have sworn for three years' term to live with me,
My fellow-scholars, and to keep those statutes,
That are recorded in this schedule here:
Your oaths are past, and now subscribe your names;
That his own hand may strike his honour down,
That violates the smallest branch herein:
If you are arm'd to do, as sworn to do,
Subscribe to your deep oath, and keep it too.
Long. I am resolv'd: 'tis but a three years' fast;
The mind shall banquet, though the body pine:
Fat paunches have lean pates; and dainty bits
Make rich the ribs, but bank'rout quite the wits.
Dum. My loving lord, Dumain is mortified;
The grosser manner of these world's delights
He throws upon the gross world's baser slaves:
To love, to wealth, to pomp, I pine and die;
With all these living in philosophy.
Biron. I can but say their protestation over,
So much, dear liege, I have already sworn,
That is, To live and study here three years.
But there are other strict observances:
As, not to see a woman in that term;
Which, I hope well, is not enrolled there:
And, one day in a week to touch no food;
And but one meal on every day beside;
The which, I hope, is not enrolled there:
And then, to sleep but three hours in the night,
And not be seen to wink of all the day;
(When I was wont to think no harm all night,
And make a dark night too of half the day;)
Which, I hope well, is not enrolled there:
O, these are barren tasks, too hard to keep;
Not to see ladies—study—fast—not sleep.
King. Your oath is pass'd to pass away from these.
Biron. Let me say no, my liege, an if you please;
I only swore, to study with your grace,
And stay here in your court for three years' space.
Long. You swore to that, Biron, and to the rest.
Biron. By yea and nay, sir, then I swore in jest.—
What is the end of study? let me know.
King. Why, that to know, which else we should not know.
Biron. Things hid and barr'd, you mean, from common sense?
King. Ay, that is study's godlike recompense.
Biron. Come on then, I will swear to study so,
To know the thing I am forbid to know:
As thus—To study where I well may dine,
When I to feast expressly am forbid;
Or, study where to meet some mistress fine,
When mistresses from common sense are hid:

Or, having sworn too hard-a-keeping oath,
Study to break it, and not break my troth.
If study's gain be thus, and this be so,
Study knows that, which yet it doth not know:
Swear me to this, and I will ne'er say no.

King. These be the stops that hinder study quite,
And train our intellects to vain delight.

Biron. Why, all delights are vain; but that most vain,
Which, with pain purchas'd, doth inherit pain:
As, painfully to pore upon a book,
To seek the light of truth: while truth the while
Doth falsely blind the eyesight of his look:
Light, seeking light, doth light of light beguile:
So, ere you find where light in darkness lies,
Your light grows dark by losing of your eyes.
Study me how to please the eye indeed,
By fixing it upon a fairer eye;
Who dazzling so, that eye shall be his heed,
And give him light that was it blinded by.
Study is like the heaven's glorious sun,
That will not be deep-search'd with saucy looks;
Small have continual plodders ever won,
Save base authority from others' books.
These earthly godfathers of heaven's lights,
That give a name to every fixed star,
Have no more profit of their shining nights,
Than those that walk, and wot not what they are,
Too much to know, is, to know nought but fame:
And every godfather can give a name.

King. How well he's read, to reason against reading!

Dum. Proceeded well, to stop all good proceeding!

Long. He weeds the corn, and still let's grow the weeding.

Biron. The spring is near, when green geese are a breeding.

Dum. How follows that?

Biron. Fit in his place and time.

Dum. In reason nothing.

Biron. Something then in rhyme.

Long. Biron is like an envious sneaping frost,
That bites the first-born infants of the spring.

Biron. Well, say I am; why should proud summer boast,
Before the birds have any cause to sing?
Why should I joy in an abortive birth?
At Christmas I no more desire a rose
Than wish a snow in May's new-fangled shows;
But like of each thing that in season grows.
So you, to study now it is too late,
Climb o'er the house to unlock the little gate.

King. Well, sit you out: go home Biron; adieu!

Biron. No, my good lord; I have sworn to stay with you:
And, though I have for barbarism spoke more
Than for that angel knowledge you can say,
Yet confident I'll keep what I have swore,
And bide the penance of each three years' day.
Give me the paper, let me read the same:
And to the strict'st decrees I'll write my name.

King. How well this yielding rescues thee from shame!

Biron. [*Reads.*] Item, *That no woman shall come within a mile of my court.*—Hath this been proclaim'd?

Long. Four days ago.

Biron. Let's see the penalty. [*Reads.*] *On pain of losing her tongue.*—Who devis'd this penalty?

Long. Marry, that did I.

Biron. Sweet lord, and why?

Long. To fright them hence with that dread penalty.

Biron. A dangerous law against gentility.
[*Reads.*] Item, *If any man be seen to talk with a woman within the term of three years, he shall endure such public shame as the rest of the court can possibly devise.*—

This article, my liege, yourself must break;
For, well you know, here comes in embassy
The French King's daughter, with yourself to speak,—
A maid of grace, and complete majesty,—
About surrender-up of Aquitain
To her decrepit, sick, and bed-rid father:
Therefore this article is made in vain,
Or vainly comes the admired princess hither.

King. What say you, lords? why, this was quite forgot.

Biron. So study evermore is overshot;
While it doth study to have what it would,
It doth forget to do the thing it should:
And when it hath the thing it hunteth most,
'Tis won, as towns with fire; so won, so lost.

King. We must, of force, dispense with this decree;
She must lie here on mere necessity.

Biron. Necessity will make us all forsworn
Three thousand times within these three years' space:
For every man with his affects is born:
Not by might master'd, but by special grace;
If I break faith, this word shall speak for me
I am forsworn on mere necessity.—
So to the laws at large I write my name: [*Subscribes.*
And he, that breaks them in the least degree,
Stands in attainder of eternal shame:
Suggestions are to others, as to me;
But I believe, although I seem so loath,
I am the last that will last keep his oath.
But, is there no quick recreation granted?

King. Ay, that there is: our court, you know, is haunted
With a refined traveller of Spain;
A man in all the world's new fashion planted,
That hath a mint of phrases in his brain:
One, whom the musick of his own vain tongue
Doth ravish, like enchanting harmony;
A man of compliments, whom right and wrong
Have chose as umpire of their mutiny:
This child of fancy, that Armado hight,
For interim to our studies, shall relate,
In high-born words, the worth of many a knight
From tawny Spain, lost in the world's debate.
How you delight, my lords, I know not, I;
But, I protest, I love to hear him lie,
And I will use him for my minstrelsy.

Biron. Armado is a most illustrious wight,
A man of fire-new words, fashion's own knight.

Long. Costard the swain, and he, shall be our sport;
And, so to study, three years is but short.

Enter DULL, *with a Letter, and* COSTARD.

Dull. Which is the duke's own person?

Biron. This, fellow; What would'st?

Dull. I myself reprehend his own person, for I am his grace's tharborough: but I would see his own person in flesh and blood.

Biron. This is he.

Dull. Signior Arme—Arme—commends you. There's villany abroad; this letter will tell you more.

Cost. Sir, the contempts thereof are as touching me.

King. A letter from the magnificent Armado.

Biron. How low soever the matter, I hope in God for high words.

Long. A high hope for a low having: God grant us patience!

Biron. To hear? or forbear hearing?

Long. To hear meekly, sir, and to laugh moderately; or to forbear both.

Biron. Well, sir, be it as the style shall give us cause to climb in the merriness.

Cost. The matter is to me, sir, as concerning Jaquenetta. The manner of it is, I was taken with the manner.

Biron. In what manner?

Cost. In manner and form following, sir; all those three: I was seen with her in the manor house, sitting with her upon the form, and taken following her into the park; which, put together, is, in manner and form following. Now, sir, for the manner,—it is the manner of a man to speak to a woman: for the form,—in some form.

Biron. For the following, sir?

Cost. As it shall follow in my correction; And God defend the right!

King. Will you hear this letter with attention?

Biron. As we would hear an oracle.

Cost. Such is the simplicity of man to hearken after the flesh.

King. [*Reads.*] *Great deputy, the welkin's vicegerent, and sole dominator of Navarre, my soul's earth's God, and body's fostering patron.*—

Cost. Not a word of Costard yet.

King. *So it is,*—

Cost. It may be so: but if he say it is so, he is, in telling true, but so, so.

King. Peace.

Cost. —be to me, and every man that dares not fight!

King. No words.

Cost. —of other men's secrets, I beseech you.

King. *So it is, besieged with sable-coloured melancholy, I did commend the black-oppressing humour to the most wholesome physick of thy health-giving air; and, as I am a gentleman, betook myself to walk. The time when? About the sixth hour; when beasts most graze, birds best peck, and men sit down to that nourishment which is called supper. So much for the time when: Now for the ground which; which, I mean, I walked upon: it is ycleped thy park. Then for the place where; where, I mean, I did encounter that obscene and most preposterous event, that draweth from my snow-white pen the ebon-coloured ink, which here thou viewest, beholdest, surveyest, or seest: But to the place, where,—It standeth north-north-east and by east from the west corner of thy curious-knotted garden: There did I see that low-spirited swain, that base minnow of thy mirth,*

Cost. Me.

King.—*that unletter'd small-knowing soul,*

Cost. Me.

King.—*that shallow vassal,*

Cost. Still me.

King.—*which, as I remember, hight Costard,*

Cost. O me!

King.—*sorted and consorted, contrary to thy established proclaimed edict and continent canon, with—with,—O with—but with this I passion to say wherewith,*

Cost. With a wench.

King.—*with a child of our grandmother Eve, a female; or, for thy more sweet understanding, a woman. Him I (as my ever-esteemed duty pricks me on) have sent to thee, to receive the meed of punishment, by thy sweet grace's officer, Antony Dull; a man of good repute, carriage, bearing, and estimation.*

Dull. Me, an't shall please you; I am Antony Dull.

King. *For Jaquenetta, (so is the weaker vessel called, which I apprehended with the aforesaid swain,) I keep her as a vessel of thy law's fury; and shall, at the least of thy sweet notice, bring her to trial. Thine, in all compliments of devoted and heart-burning heat of duty,* DON ADRIANO DE ARMADO.

Biron. This is not so well as I looked for, but the best that ever I heard.

King. Ay, the best for the worst. But, sirrah, what say you to this?

Cost. Sir, I confess the wench.

King. Did you hear the proclamation?

Cost. I do confess much of the hearing it, but little of the marking of it.

King. It was proclaimed a year's imprisonment, to be taken with a wench.

Cost. I was taken with none, sir; I was taken with a damosel.

King. Well, it was proclaimed damosel.

Cost. This was no damosel neither, sir; she was a virgin.

King. It is so varied too; for it was proclaimed, virgin.

Cost. If it were, I deny her virginity; I was taken with a maid.

King. This maid will not serve your turn, sir.

Cost. This maid will serve my turn, sir.

King. Sir, I will pronounce your sentence; You shall fast a week with bran and water.

Cost. I had rather pray a month with mutton and porridge.

King. And Don Armado shall be your keeper.
—My lord Biron, see him deliver'd o'er.—
And go we, lords, to put in practice that
Which each to other hath so strongly sworn.—

[*Exeunt* King, LONGAVILLE, *and* DUMAIN.

Biron. I'll lay my head to any good man's hat,
These oaths and laws will prove an idle scorn.—
Sirrah, come on.

Cost. I suffer for the truth, sir; for true it is, I was taken with Jaquenetta, and Jaquenetta is a true girl; and therefore, Welcome the sour cup of prosperity! Affliction may one day smile again, and till then, Sit thee down, sorrow!

[*Exeunt.*

SCENE II. *Another part of the same.*

Armado's *House.*

Enter ARMADO *and* MOTH.

Arm. Boy, what sign is it, when a man of great spirit grows melancholy?

Moth. A great sign, sir, that he will look sad.

Arm. Why, sadness is one and the self-same thing, dear imp.

Moth. No, no; O lord, sir, no.

Arm. How canst thou part sadness and melancholy, my tender juvenal?

Moth. By a familiar demonstration of the working, my tough senior.

Arm. Why tough senior? why tough senior?

Moth. Why tender juvenal? why tender juvenal?

Arm. I spoke it, tender juvenal, as a congruent epitheton, appertaining to thy young days, which we may nominate tender.

Moth. And I, tough senior, as an appertinent title to your old time, which we may name tough.

Arm. Pretty, and apt.

Moth. How mean you, sir? I pretty, and my saying apt? or I apt, and my saying pretty?

Arm. Thou pretty, because little.

Moth. Little pretty, because little: Wherefore apt?

Arm. And therefore apt, because quick.

Moth. Speak you this in my praise, master?

Arm. In thy condign praise.

Moth. I will praise an eel with the same praise.

Arm. What? that an eel is ingenious?

Moth. That an eel is quick.

Arm. I do say, thou art quick in answers; Thou heatest my blood.

Moth. I am answered, sir.

Arm. I love not to be crossed.

Moth. He speaks the mere contrary, crosses love not him. [*Aside.*

Arm. I have promised to study three years with the duke.

Moth. You may do it in an hour, sir.

Arm. Impossible.

Moth. How many is one thrice told?

Arm. I am ill at reckoning, it fitteth the spirit of a tapster.

Moth. You are a gentleman, and a gamester, sir.

Arm. I confess both; they are both the varnish of a complete man.

Moth. Then, I am sure, you know how much the gross sum of deuce-ace amounts to.

Arm. It doth amount to one more than two.

Moth. Which the base vulgar do call three.

Arm. True.

Moth. Why, sir, is this such a piece of study? Now here is three studied, ere you'll thrice wink: and how easy it is to put years to the word three, and study three years in two words, the dancing horse will tell you.

Arm. A most fine figure!

Moth. To prove you a cipher. [*Aside.*

Arm. I will hereupon confess, I am in love: and, as it is base for a soldier to love, so am I in love with a base wench. If drawing my sword against the humour of affection would deliver me from the reprobate thought of it, I would take desire prisoner, and ransom him to any French courtier for a new devised courtesy. I think scorn to sigh; methinks, I should outswear Cupid. Comfort me, boy: What great men have been in love?

Moth. Hercules, master.

Arm. Most sweet Hercules!—More authority, dear boy, name more; and, sweet my child, let them be men of good repute and carriage.

Moth. Samson, master: he was a man of good carriage, great carriage! for he carried the town-gates on his back, like a porter: and he was in love.

Arm. O well-knit Samson! strong jointed Samson! I do excel thee in my rapier, as much as thou didst me in carrying gates. I am in love too,—Who was Samson's love, my dear Moth?

Moth. A woman, master.

Arm. Of what complexion?

Moth. Of all the four, or the three, or the two; or one of the four.

Arm. Tell me precisely of what complexion?

Moth. Of the sea-water green, sir.

Arm. Is that one of the four complexions?

Moth. As I have read, sir; and the best of them too.

Arm. Green, indeed, is the colour of lovers: but to have a love of that colour, methinks, Samson had small reason for it. He, surely, affected her for her wit.

Moth. It was so, sir; for she had a green wit.

Arm. My love is most immaculate white and red.

Moth. Most maculate thoughts, master, are masked under such colours.

Arm. Define, define, well-educated infant.

Moth. My father's wit, and my mother's tongue, assist me!

Arm. Sweet invocation of a child; most pretty, and pathetical!

Moth. If she be made of white and red,
Her faults will ne'er be known;
For blushing cheeks by faults are bred,
And fears by pale-white shown:
Then, if she fear, or be to blame,
By this you shall not know;
For still her cheeks possess the same,
Which native she doth owe.

A dangerous rhyme, master, against the reason of white and red.

Arm. Is there not a ballad, boy, of the King and the Beggar?

Moth. The world was very guilty of such a ballad some three ages since: but, I think, now 'tis not to be found; or, if it were, it would neither serve for the writing, nor the tune.

Arm. I will have the subject newly writ o'er, that I may example my digression by some mighty precedent. Boy, I do love that country girl, that I took in the park with the rational hind Costard: she deserves well.

Moth. To be whipped; and yet a better love than my master. [*Aside.*

Arm. Sing, boy: my spirit grows heavy in love.

Moth. And that's great marvel, loving a light wench.

Arm. I say, sing.

Moth. Forbear, till this company be past.

Enter DULL, COSTARD, *and* JAQUENETTA.

Dull. Sir, the duke's pleasure is, that you keep Costard safe: and you must let him take no delight, nor no penance; but a' must fast three days a-week: For this damsel, I must keep her at the park; she is allowed for the day-woman. Fare you well.

Arm. I do betray myself with blushing.—Maid.

Jaq. Man.

Arm. I will visit thee at the lodge.

Jaq. That's hereby.

Arm. I know where it is situate.

Jaq. Lord, how wise you are!

Arm. I will tell thee wonders.

Jaq. With that face?

Arm. I love thee.

Jaq. So I heard you say.

Arm. And so farewell.

Jac. Fair weather after you!

Dull. Come, Jaquenetta, away.
[*Exeunt* DULL *and* JAQUENETTA.

Arm. Villain, thou shalt fast for thy offences, ere thou be pardoned.

Cost. Well, sir, I hope, when I do it, I shall do it on a full stomach.

Arm. Thou shalt be heavily punished.

Cost. I am more bound to you, than your fellows, for they are but lightly rewarded.

Arm. Take away this villain; shut him up.

Moth. Come, you transgressing slave; away.

Cost. Let me not be pent up, sir; I will fast, being loose.

Moth. No, sir; that were fast and loose: thou shalt to prison.

Cost. Well, if ever I do see the merry days of desolation that I have seen, some shall see—

Moth. What shall some see?

Cost. Nay, nothing, master Moth, but what they look upon. It is not for prisoners to be too silent in their words; and, therefore, I will say nothing: I thank God, I have as little patience as another man; and, therefore, I can be quiet. [*Exeunt* MOTH *and* COSTARD.

Arm. I do affect the very ground, which is base, where her shoe, which is baser, guided by her foot, which is basest, doth tread. I shall be forsworn (which is a great argument of falsehood), if I love: And how can that be true love, which is falsely attempted? Love is a familiar: love is a devil: there is no evil angel but love. Yet Samson was so tempted: and he had an excellent strength: yet was Solomon so seduced; and he had a very good wit. Cupid's butt-shaft is too hard for Hercules' club, and therefore too much odds for a Spaniard's rapier. The first and second cause will not serve my turn; the passado he respects not, the duello he regards not: his disgrace is to be called boy; but his glory is to subdue men. Adieu, valour! rust, rapier! be still, drum! for your manager is in love; yea, he loveth. Assist me, some extemporal god of rhyme, for, I am sure, I shall turn sonneteer. Devise, wit; write, pen; for I am for whole volumes in folio. [*Exit.*

ACT II.

SCENE I. *Another part of the same. A Pavilion and Tents at a distance.*

Enter the Princess *of* France, ROSALINE, MARIA, KATHARINE, BOYET, Lords, *and other* Attendants.

Boyet. Now, madam, summon up your dearest spirits;
Consider who the king your father sends;
To whom he sends; and what's his embassy:
Yourself, held precious in the world's esteem;
To parley with the sole inheritor

Of all perfections that a man may owe,
Matchless Navarre; the plea of no less weight
Than Aquitain; a dowry for a queen.
Be now as prodigal of all dear grace,
As nature was in making graces dear,
When she did starve the general world beside,
And prodigally gave them all to you.

Prin. Good lord Boyet, my beauty, though but mean,
Needs not the painted flourish of your praise;
Beauty is bought by judgment of the eye,
Not utter'd by base sale of chapmen's tongues;
I am less proud to hear you tell my worth,
Than you much willing to be counted wise
In spending your wit in the praise of mine.
But now to task the tasker,—Good Boyet,
You are not ignorant, all-telling fame
Doth noise abroad, Navarre hath made a vow,
Till painful study shall out-wear three years,
No woman may approach his silent court:
Therefore to us seemeth it a needful course,
Before we enter his forbidden gates,
To know his pleasure; and in that behalf,
Bold of your worthiness, we single you
As our best-moving fair solicitor:
Tell him, the daughter of the king of France,
On serious business, craving quick despatch,
Importunes personal conference with his grace.
Haste, signify so much; while we attend,
Like humbly-visag'd suitors, his high will.

Boyet. Proud of employment, willingly I go. [*Exit.*

Prin. All pride is willing pride, and yours is so,—
Who are the votaries, my loving lords,
That are vow-fellows with this virtuous duke?

1 *Lord.* Longaville is one.

Prin. Know you the man?

Mar. I know him, madam; at a marriage feast,
Between lord Perigort and the beauteous heir
Of Jacques Falconbridge, solemnized
In Normandy, saw I this Longaville:
A man of sovereign parts he is esteem'd;
Well fitted in the arts, glorious in arms:
Nothing becomes him ill, that he would well.
The only soil of his fair virtue's gloss
(If virtue's gloss will stain with any soil),
Is a sharp wit match'd with too blunt a will;
Whose edge hath power to cut, whose will still wills
It should none spare that come within his power.

Prin. Some merry mocking lord, belike; is't so?

Mar. They say so most, that most his humours know.

Prin. Such short-liv'd wits do wither as they grow,
Who are the rest?

Kath. The young Dumain, a well-accomplish'd youth,
Of all that virtue love for virtue lov'd;
Most power to do most harm, least knowing ill;
For he hath wit to make an ill shape good,
And shape to win grace though he had no wit.
I saw him at the duke Alençon's once;
And much too little of that good I saw,
Is my report, to his great worthiness.

Ros. Another of these students at that time
Was there with him: if I have heard a truth,
Biron they call him; but a merrier man,
Within the limit of becoming mirth,
I never spent an hour's talk withal:
His eye begets occasion for his wit;
For every object that the one doth catch,
The other turns to a mirth-moving jest;
Which his fair tongue (conceit's expositor),
Delivers in such apt and gracious words,
That aged ears play truant at his tales,
And younger hearings are quite ravished;
So sweet and voluble is his discourse.

Prin. God bless my ladies; are they all in love;
That every one her own hath garnish'd
With such bedecking ornaments of praise?

Mar. Here comes Boyet.

Re-enter BOYET.

Prin. Now, what admittance, lord?

Boyet. Navarre had notice of your fair approach;
And he, and his competitors in oath,
Were all address'd to meet you, gentle lady,
Before I came. Marry, thus much I have learnt,
He rather means to lodge you in the field
(Like one that comes here to besiege his court),
Than seek a dispensation for his oath,
To let you enter his unpeopled house.
Here comes Navarre. [*The Ladies mask.*

Enter KING, LONGAVILLE, DUMAIN, BIRON, *and* Attendants.

King. Fair princess, welcome to the court of Navarre.

Prin. Fair, I give you back again; and, welcome I have not yet: the roof of this court is too high to be yours; and welcome to the wild fields too base to be mine.

King. You shall be welcome, madam, to my court.

Prin. I will be welcome, then; conduct me thither.

King. Hear me, dear lady; I have sworn an oath.

Prin. Our lady help my lord! he'll be forsworn.

King. Not for the world, fair madam, by my will.

Prin. Why, will shall break it; will, and nothing else.

King. Your ladyship is ignorant what it is.

Prin. Were my lord so, his ignorance were wise,
Where now his knowledge must prove ignorance.
I hear your grace hath sworn-out house-keeping:
'Tis deadly sin to keep that oath, my lord,
And sin to break it:
But pardon me, I am too sudden-bold;
To teach a teacher ill beseemeth me.
Vouchsafe to read the purpose of my coming,
And suddenly resolve me in my suit. [*Gives a Paper.*

King. Madam, I will, if suddenly I may.

Prin. You will the sooner, that I were away;
For you'll prove perjur'd, if you make me stay.

Biron. Did not I dance with you in Brabant once?

Ros. Did not I dance with you in Brabant once?

Biron. I know you did.

Ros. How needless was it then
To ask the question!

Biron. You must not be so quick.

Ros. 'Tis 'long of you that spur me with such questions.

Biron. Your wit's too hot, it speeds too fast, 'twill tire.

Ros. Not till it leave the rider in the mire.

Biron. What time o' day?

Ros. The hour that fools should ask.

Biron. Now fair befall your mask!

Ros. Fair fall the face it covers!

Biron. And send you many lovers!

Ros. Amen, so you be none.

Biron. Nay, then will I be gone.

King. Madam, your father here doth intimate
The payment of a hundred thousand crowns;
Being but the one half of an entire sum,
Disbursed by my father in his wars.
But say, that he, or we (as neither have),
Receiv'd that sum; yet there remains unpaid
A hundred thousand more; in surety of the which,
One part of Acquitain is bound to us,
Although not valued to the money's worth.
If then the king your father will restore
But that one half which is unsatisfied,

We will give up our right in Aquitain,
And hold fair friendship with his majesty.
But that, it seems, he little purposeth,
For here he doth demand to have repaid
A hundred thousand crowns; and not demands,
On payment of a hundred thousand crowns,
To have his title live in Aquitain;
Which we much rather had depart withal,
And have the money by our father lent,
Than Aquitain so gelded as it is.
Dear princess, were not his requests so far
From reason's yielding, your fair self should make
A yielding 'gainst some reason, in my breast,
And go well satisfied to France again.

Prin. You do the king my father too much wrong,
And wrong the reputation of your name,
In so unseeming to confess receipt
Of that which hath so faithfully been paid.

King. I do protest, I never heard of it;
And, if you prove it, I'll repay it back,
Or yield up Aquitain.

Prin. We arrest your word:—
Boyet, you can produce acquittances,
For such a sum, from special officers
Of Charles his father.

King. Satisfy me so.

Boyet. So please your grace, the packet is not come,
Where that and other specialties are bound;
To-morrow you shall have a sight of them.

King. It shall suffice me: at which interview,
All liberal reason I will yield unto.
Mean time, receive such welcome at my hand,
As honour, without breach of honour, may
Make tender of to thy true worthiness:
You may not come, fair princess, in my gates;
But here without you shall be so receiv'd,
As you shall deem yourself lodg'd in my heart,
Though so denied fair harbour in my house.
Your own good thoughts excuse me, and farewell:
To-morrow shall we visit you again.

Prin. Sweet health and fair desires consort your grace!

King. Thy own wish wish I thee in every place! [*Exeunt* King *and his Train.*

Biron. Lady, I will commend you to my own heart.

Ros. 'Pray you, do my commendations; I would be glad to see it.

Biron. I would, you heard it groan.

Ros. Is the fool sick?

Biron. Sick at heart.

Ros. Alack, let it blood.

Biron. Would that do it good?

Ros. My Physick says, I.

Biron. Will you prick't with your eye?

Ros. No *point*, with my knife.

Biron. Now, God save thy life!

Ros. And yours from long living!

Biron. I cannot stay thanksgiving. [*Retiring.*

Dum. Sir, I pray you, a word: What lady is that same?

Boyet. The heir of Alençon, Rosaline her name.

Dum. A gallant lady! Monsieur, fare you well. [*Exit.*

Long. I beseech you a word; What is she in the white?

Boyet. A woman sometimes, an you saw her in the light.

Long. Perchance, light in the light: I desire her name.

Boyet. She hath but one for herself; to desire that were a shame.

Long. 'Pray you, sir, whose daughter?

Boyet. Her mother's, I have heard.

Long. God's blessing on your beard!

Boyet. Good sir, be not offended:
She is an heir of Falconbridge.

Long. Nay, my choler is ended.
She is a most sweet lady.

Boyet. Not unlike, sir; that may be. [*Exit* LONG.

Biron. What's her name, in the cap?

Boyet. Katharine, by good hap.

Biron. Is she wedded, or no?

Boyet. To her will, sir, or so.

Biron. You are welcome, sir; adieu!

Boyet. Farewell to me, sir, and welcome to you. [*Exit* BIRON.—*Ladies unmask.*

Mar. That last is Biron, the merry mad-cap lord;
Not a word with him but a jest.

Boyet. And every jest but a word.

Prin. It was well done of you to take him at his word.

Boyet. I was as willing to grapple, as he was to board.

Mar. Two hot sheeps, marry!

Boyet. And wherefore not ships?
No sheep, sweet lamb, unless we feed on your lips.

Mar. You sheep, and I pasture; Shall that finish the jest?

Boyet. So you grant pasture for me. [*Offering to kiss her.*

Mar. Not so, gentle beast:
My lips are no common, though several they be.

Boyet. Belonging to whom?

Mar. To my fortunes and me.

Prin. Good wits will be jangling; but, gentles, agree:
The civil war of wits were much better used
On Navarre and his book-men; for here 'tis abused.

Boyet. If my observation (which very seldom lies),
By the heart's still rhetorick, disclosed with eyes,
Deceive me not now, Navarre is infected.

Prin. With what?

Boyet. With that which we lovers entitle, affected.

Prin. Your reason?

Boyet. Why, all his behaviours did make their retire
To the court of his eye, peeping thorough desire:
His heart, like an agate, with your print impressed,
Proud with his form, in his eye pride expressed:
His tongue, all impatient to speak and not see,
Did stumble with haste in his eyesight to be;
All senses to that sense did make their repair,
To feel only looking on fairest of fair;
Methought, all his senses were lock'd in his eye,
As jewels in crystal for some prince to buy;
Who, tend'ring their own worth, from where they were glass'd,
Did point you to buy them, along as you pass'd.
His face's own margent did quote such amazes,
That all eyes saw his eyes enchanted with gazes;
I'll give you Aquitain, and all that is his,
An you give him for my sake but one loving kiss.

Prin. Come to our pavilion: Boyet is dispos'd—

Boyet. But to speak that in words, which his eye hath disclos'd:
I only have made a mouth of his eye,
By adding a tongue which I know will not lie.

Ros. Thou art an old love-monger, and speak'st skilfully.

Mar. He is Cupid's grandfather, and learns news of him.

Ros. Then was Venus like her mother; for her father is but grim.

Boyet. Do you hear, my mad wenches?

Mar. No.

Boyet. What then, do you see?

Ros. Ay, our way to be gone.

Boyet. You are too hard for me. [*Exeunt.*

ACT III.

SCENE I. *Another part of the same.*

Enter ARMADO *and* MOTH.

Arm. Warble, child, make passionate my sense of hearing.

Moth. *Concolinel*—— [*Singing.*

Arm. Sweet air! Go, tenderness of years; take this key, give enlargement to the swain, bring him festinately hither; I must employ him in a letter to my love.

Moth. Master, will you win your love with a French brawl?

Arm. How mean'st thou? brawling in French?

Moth. No, my complete master: but to jig off a tune at the tongue's end, canary to it with your feet, humour it with turning up your eyelids; sigh a note, and sing a note; sometime through the throat, as if you swallowed love with singing love; sometime through the nose, as if you snuffed up love by smelling love; with your hat penthouselike o'er the shop of your eyes; with your arms crossed on your thin belly-doublet, like a rabbit on a spit; or your hands in your pocket, like a man after the old painting; and keep not too long in one tune, but a snip and away: These are complements, these are humours; these betray nice wenches—that would be betrayed without these; and make them men of note, (do you note, men?) that most are affected to these.

Arm. How hast thou purchased this experience?

Moth. By my penny of observation.

Arm. But O,—but O,—

Moth. —the hobby-horse is forgot.

Arm. Callest thou my love, hobby-horse?

Moth. No, master; the hobby-horse is but a colt, and your love perhaps a hackney. But have you forgot your love?

Arm. Almost I had.

Moth. Negligent student! learn her by heart.

Arm. By heart, and in heart, boy.

Moth. And out of heart, master: all those three I will prove.

Arm. What wilt thou prove?

Moth. A man, if I live; and this, by, in, and without, upon the instant: By heart you love her, because your heart cannot come by her: in heart you love her, because your heart is in love with her; and out of heart you love her, being out of heart that you cannot enjoy her.

Arm. I am all these three.

Moth. And three times as much more, and yet nothing at all.

Arm. Fetch hither the swain; he must carry me a letter.

Moth. A message well sympathised; a horse to be embassador for an ass!

Arm. Ha, ha! what sayest thou?

Moth. Marry, sir, you must send the ass upon the horse, for he is very slow-gaited: But I go.

Arm. The way is but short; away.

Moth. As swift as lead, sir.

Arm. Thy meaning, pretty ingenious?
Is not lead a metal heavy, dull, and slow?

Moth. *Minime*, honest master; or rather, master, no.

Arm. I say, lead is slow.

Moth. You are too swift, sir, to say so:
Is that lead slow which is fir'd from a gun?

Arm. Sweet smoke of rhetorick!
He reputes me a cannon; and the bullet, that's he:—
I shoot thee at the swain.

Moth. Thump then, and I flee. [*Exit.*

Arm. A most acute juvenal: voluble and free of grace!
By thy favour, sweet welkin, I must sigh in thy face:
Most rude melancholy, valour gives thee place.
My herald is return'd.

Re-enter MOTH *and* COSTARD.

Moth. A wonder, master; here's a Costard broken in a shin.

Arm. Some enigma, some riddle;—come,—thy *l'envoy*;—begin.

Cost. No egma, no riddle, no *l'envoy*: no salve in the mail, sir: O, sir, plantain, a plain plantain; no *l'envoy*, no *l'envoy*, no salve, sir, but a plantain!

Arm. By virtue, thou enforcest laughter; thy silly thought, my spleen; the heaving of my lungs provokes me to ridiculous smiling; O, pardon me, my stars! Doth the inconsiderate take salve for *l'envoy*, and the word, *l'envoy*, for a salve?

Moth. Do the wise think them other? is not *l'envoy* a salve?

Arm. No, page; it is an epilogue or discourse, to make plain
Some obscure precedence that hath tofore been sain.
I will example it:
The fox, the ape, and the humble-bee,
Were still at odds, being but three.
There's the moral: Now the *l'envoy*.

Moth. I will add the *l'envoy*: Say the moral again.

Arm. The fox, the ape, and the humblebee,
Were still at odds, being but three:

Moth. Until the goose came out of door,
And stay'd the odds by adding four.
Now will I begin your moral, and do you follow with my *l'envoy*.
The fox, the ape, and the humblebee,
Were still at odds, being but three:

Arm. Until the goose came out of door,
Staying the odds by adding four.

Moth. A good *l'envoy*, ending in the goose,
Would you desire more?

Cost. The boy hath sold him a bargain, a goose; that's flat:—
Sir, your pennyworth is good, an your goose be fat.—
To sell a bargain well, is as cunning as fast and loose:
Let me see a fat *l'envoy*: ay, that's a fat goose.

Arm. Come hither, come hither: How did this argument begin?

Moth. By saying that a *Costard* was broken in a shin.
Then call'd you for the *l'envoy*.

Cost. True, and I for a plantain; Thus came your argument in;
Then the boy's fat *l'envoy*, the goose that you bought;
And he ended the market.

Arm. But tell me; how was there a Costard broken in a shin?

Moth. I will tell you sensibly.

Cost. Thou hast no feeling of it, Moth; I will speak that *l'envoy*.
I, Costard, running out, that was safely within,
Fell over the threshold, and broke my shin.

Arm. We will talk no more of this matter.

Cost. Till there be more matter in the shin.

Arm. Sirrah Costard, I will enfranchise thee.

Cost. O, marry me to one Frances:—I smell some *l'envoy*, some goose, in this.

Arm. By my sweet soul, I mean, setting thee at liberty, enfreedoming thy person; thou wert immured, restrained, captivated, bound.

Cost. True, true; and now you will be in my purgation, and let me loose.

Arm. I give thee thy liberty, set thee from durance; and, in lieu thereof, impose on thee nothing but this: Bear this significant to the country maid Jaquenetta: there is remuneration; [*Giving him money.*] for the best ward of mine honour, is, rewarding my dependents. Moth, follow. [*Exit.*

Moth. Like the sequel, I.—Signior Costard, adieu.

Cost. My sweet ounce of man's flesh! my incony Jew!— [*Exit* MOTH.

Now will I look to his remuneration. Remuneration! O, that's the Latin word for three farthings: three farthings—remuneration.—*What's the price of this inkle? a penny:—No, I'll give you a remuneration:* why, it carries it.—Remuneration!—why, it is a fairer name than French crown. I will never buy and sell out of this word.

Enter BIRON.

Biron. O, my good knave Costard! exceedingly well met.

Cost. 'Pray you, sir, how much carnation ribbon may a man buy for a remuneration?

Biron. What is a remuneration?

Cost. Marry, sir, half-penny farthing.

Biron. O, why then, three-farthings-worth of silk.

Cost. I thank your worship: God be with you!

Biron. O, stay, slave; I must employ thee:
As thou wilt win my favour, good my knave,
Do one thing for me that I shall entreat.

Cost. When would you have it done, sir?

Biron. O, this afternoon.

Cost. Well, I will do it, sir: Fare you well.

Biron. O, thou knowest not what it is.

Cost. I shall know, sir, when I have done it.

Biron. Why, villain, thou must know first.

Cost. I will come to your worship to-morrow morning.

Biron. It must be done this afternoon. Hark, slave, it is but this;—
The princess comes to hunt here in the park,
And in her train there is a gentle lady;
When tongues speak sweetly, then they name her name,
And Rosaline they call her: ask for her;
And to her white hand see thou do commend
This seal'd-up counsel. There's thy guerdon; go. [*Gives him money.*

Cost. Guerdon,—O sweet guerdon! better than remuneration; eleven-pence farthing better: Most sweet guerdon;—I will do it, sir, in print. —Guerdon—remuneration. [*Exit.*

Biron. O!—And I, forsooth, in love! I, that have been love's whip;
A very beadle to a humorous sigh;
A critick; nay, a night-watch constable;
A domineering pedant o'er the boy,
Than whom no mortal so magnificent!
This wimpled, whining, purblind, wayward boy;
This senior-junior, giant-dwarf, Dan Cupid;
Regent of love-rhymes, lord of folded arms,
The anointed sovereign of sighs and groans,
Liege of all loiterers and malcontents,
Dread prince of plackets, king of codpieces,
Sole imperator, and great general
Of trotting paritors—O my little heart!—
And I to be a corporal of his field,
And wear his colours like a tumbler's hoop!
What? I! I love! I sue! I seek a wife!
A woman, that is like a German clock,
Still a repairing; ever out of frame;
And never going aright, being a watch,
But being watch'd that it may still go right?
Nay, to be perjur'd, which is worst of all;
And, among three, to love the worst of all;
A whitely wanton with a velvet brow,
With two pitch balls stuck in her face for eyes:
Ay, and, by heaven, one that will do the deed,
Though Argus were her eunuch and her guard;
And I to sigh for her! to watch for her!
To pray for her! Go to; it is a plague
That Cupid will impose for my neglect
Of his almighty dreadful little might.
Well, I will love, write, sigh, pray, sue, and groan;
Some men must love my lady, and some Joan. [*Exit.*

ACT IV.

SCENE I. *Another part of the same.*

Enter the Princess, ROSALINE, MARIA, KATHARINE, BOYET, *Lords, Attendants, and a Forester.*

Prin. Was that the king, that spurr'd his horse so hard
Against the steep uprising of the hill?

Boyet. I know not; but, I think, it was not he.

Prin. Whoe'er he was, he show'd a mounting mind.
Well, lords, to-day we shall have our despatch;
On Saturday we will return to France.—
Then, forester, my friend, where is the bush,
That we must stand and play the murderer in?

For. Here by, upon the edge of yonder coppice;
A stand, where you may make the fairest shoot.

Prin. I thank my beauty, I am fair that shoot,
And thereupon thou speak'st, the fairest shoot.

For. Pardon me, madam, for I meant not so.

Prin. What, what? first praise me, and again say, no?
O short-liv'd pride! Not fair? alack for woe!

For. Yes, madam, fair.

Prin. Nay, never paint me now;
Where fair is not, praise cannot mend the brow.
Here, good my glass, take this for telling true; [*Giving him money.*
Fair payment for foul words is more than due.

For. Nothing but fair is that which you inherit.

Prin. See, see, my beauty will be sav'd by merit.
O heresy in fair, fit for these days!
A giving hand, though foul, shall have fair praise.—
But come, the bow:—Now mercy goes to kill,
And shooting well is then accounted ill.
Thus will I save my credit in the shoot:
Not wounding, pity would not let me do't;
If wounding, then it was to shew my skill,
That more for praise, than purpose, meant to kill.
And, out of question, so it is sometimes;
Glory grows guilty of detested crimes;
When, for fame's sake, for praise, an outward part,
We bend to that the working of the heart:
As I, for praise alone, now seek to spill
The poor deer's blood, that my heart means no ill.

Boyet. Do not curst wives hold that self-sovereignty
Only for praise' sake, when they strive to be
Lords o'er their lords?

Prin. Only for praise: and praise we may afford
To any lady that subdues a lord.

Enter COSTARD.

Here comes a member of the commonwealth.

Cost. God dig-you-den all! 'Pray you, which is the head lady?

Prin. Thou shalt know her, fellow, by the rest that have no heads.

Cost. Which is the greatest lady, the highest?

Prin. The thickest, and the tallest.

Cost. The thickest, and the tallest! it is so; truth is truth.
An your waist, mistress, were as slender as my wit,
One of these maids' girdles for your waist should be fit.
Are not you the chief woman? you are the thickest here.

Prin. What's your will, sir? what's your will?

Cost. I have a letter from monsieur Biron, to one lady Rosaline.

Prin. O, thy letter, thy letter; he's a good friend of mine:
Stand aside, good bearer.—Boyet, you can carve;
Break up this capon.

Boyet. I am bound to serve.—
This letter is mistook, it importeth none here;
It is writ to Jaquenetta.

Prin. We will read it, I swear:
Break the neck of the wax, and every one give ear.

Boyet. [Reads.] *By heaven, that thou art fair, is most infallible; true, that thou art beauteous; truth itself, that thou art lovely: More fairer than fair, beautiful than beauteous; truer than truth itself, have commiseration on thy heroical vassal! The magnanimous and most illustrate king* Cophetua *set eye upon the pernicious and indubitate beggar* Zenelophon; *and he it was that might rightly say,* veni, vidi, vici; *which to anatomize in the vulgar, (O base and obscure vulgar!)* videlicet, *he came, saw, and overcame: he came, one; saw, two; overcame, three. Who came? the king; Why did he come? to see; Why did he see? to overcome; To whom came he? to the beggar; What saw he? the beggar; Who overcame he? the beggar: The conclusion is victory; On whose side? the king's: the captive is enrich'd; On whose side? the beggar's; The catastrophe is a nuptial; On whose side? the king's?—no, on both in one, or one in both. I am the king; for so stands the comparison: thou the beggar; for so witnesseth thy lowliness. Shall I command thy love? I may: Shall I enforce thy love? I could: Shall I entreat thy love? I will. What shalt thou exchange for rags? robes; For tittles, titles; For thyself, me. Thus, expecting thy reply, I profane my lips on thy foot, my eyes on thy picture, and my heart on thy every part.*

Thine in the dearest design of industry,
DON ADRIANO DE ARMADO.

Thus dost thou hear the Nemean lion roar
'Gainst thee, thou lamb, that standest as his prey;
Submissive fall his princely feet before,
And he from forage will incline to play:
But if thou strive, poor soul, what art thou then?
Food for his rage, repasture for his den.

Prin. What plume of feathers is he, that indited this letter?
What vane? what weathercock? did you ever hear better?

Boyet. I am much deceived, but I remember the style.

Prin. Else your memory is bad, going o'er it erewhile.

Boyet. This Armado is a Spaniard, that keeps here in court;
A phantasm, a Monarcho, and one that makes sport
To the prince, and his book-mates.

Prin. Thou, fellow, a word:
Who gave thee this letter?

Cost. I told you; my lord.

Prin. To whom shouldst thou give it?

Cost. From my lord to my lady.

Prin. From which lord, to which lady?

Cost. From my lord Biron, a good master of mine,
To a lady of France, that he call'd Rosaline.

Prin. Thou hast mistaken his letter. Come, lords, away.
Here, sweet, put up this; 'twill be thine another day. [*Exit* Princess *and Train.*

Boyet. Who is the suitor? who is the suitor?

Ros. Shall I teach you to know?

Boyet. Ay, my continent of beauty.

Ros. Why, she that bears the bow.
Finely put off!

Boyet. My lady goes to kill horns; but, if thou marry,
Hang me by the neck, if horns that year miscarry.
Finely put on!

Ros. Well then, I am the shooter.

Boyet. And who is your deer?

Ros. If we choose by the horns, yourself: come near.
Finely put on, indeed!

Mar. You still wrangle with her, Boyet, and she strikes at the brow.

Boyet. But she herself is hit lower: Have I hit her now?

Ros. Shall I come upon thee with an old saying, that was a man when king Pepin of France was a little boy, as touching the hit it?

Boyet. So I may answer thee with one as old, that was a woman when queen Guinever of Britain was a little wench, as touching the hit it.

Ros. *Thou canst not hit it, hit it, hit it,* [Singing.
Thou canst not hit it, my good man.

Boyet. *An I cannot, cannot, cannot,*
An I cannot, another can.
[*Exeunt* Ros. *and* Kath.

Cost. By my troth, most pleasant! how both did fit it!

Mar. A mark marvellous well shot; for they both did hit it.

Boyet. A mark! O, mark but that mark; A mark, says my lady!
Let the mark have a prick in't, to mete at, if it may be.

Mar. Wide o'the bow hand! I'faith your hand is out.

Cost. Indeed, a' must shoot nearer, or he'll ne'er hit the clout.

Boyet. An if my hand be out, then, belike your hand is in.

Cost. Then will she get the upshot by cleaving the pin.

Mar. Come, come, you talk greasily, your lips grow foul.

Cost. She's too hard for you at pricks, sir; challenge her to bowl.

Boyet. I fear too much rubbing; Good night, my good owl. [*Exeunt* Boyet *and* Maria.

Cost. By my soul, a swain! a most simple clown!
Lord, lord! how the ladies and I have put him down!
O' my troth, most sweet jests! most incony vulgar wit!
When it comes so smoothly off, so obscenely, as it were, so fit.
Armatho o' the one side,—O, a most dainty man!
To see him walk before a lady, and to bear her fan!
To see him kiss his hand! and how most sweetly a' will swear!—
And his page o' t' other side, that handful of wit!
Ah, heavens, it is a most pathetical nit!
Sola, sola! [*Shouting within. Exit* Cost. *running.*

SCENE II. *The same.*

Enter Holofernes, Sir Nathaniel, *and* Dull.

Nath. Very reverent sport, truly; and done in the testimony of a good conscience.

Hol. The deer was, as you know, in *sanguis*,—blood; ripe as a pomewater, who now hangeth like a jewel in the ear of *cælo*,—the sky, the welkin, the heaven; and anon falleth like a crab, on the face of *terra*,—the soil, the land, the earth.

Nath. Truly, master Holofernes, the epithets are sweetly varied, like a scholar at the least; But, sir, I assure ye, it was a buck of the first head.

Hol. Sir Nathaniel, *haud credo.*

Dull. 'Twas not a *haud credo*, 'twas a pricket.

Hol. Most barbarous intimation! yet a kind of insinuation, as it were, *in via*, in way, of explication; *facere*, as it were, replication, or, rather, *ostentare*, to show, as it were, his inclination,—after his undressed, unpolished, uneducated, unpruned, untrained, or rather unlettered, or, ratherest, unconfirmed fashion,—to insert again my *haud credo* for a deer.

Dull. I said, the deer was not a *haud credo;* 'twas a pricket.

Hol. Twice sod simplicity, *bis coctus!*—O thou monster, ignorance, how deformed dost thou look!

Nath. Sir, he hath never fed of the dainties that are bred in a book; he hath not eat paper, as it were; he hath not drunk ink: his intellect is not replenished; he is only an animal, only sensible in the duller parts;
And such barren plants are set before us, that we thankful should be
(Which we of taste and feeling are) for those parts that do fructify in us more than he.
For as it would ill become me to be vain, indiscreet, or a fool,
So, were there a patch set on learning, to see him in a school:
But, *omne bene,* say I; being of an old father's mind,
Many can brook the weather that love not the wind.

Dull. You two are book-men: Can you tell by your wit,
What was a month old at Cain's birth, that's not five weeks old as yet?

Hol. Dictynna, good man Dull; Dictynna, good man Dull.

Dull. What is Dictynna?

Nath. A title to Phœbe, to Luna, to the moon.

Hol. The moon was a month old, when Adam was no more;
And raught not to five weeks, when he came to fivescore.
The allusion holds in the exchange.

Dull. 'Tis true indeed; the collusion holds in the exchange.

Hol. God comfort thy capacity! I say, the allusion holds in the exchange.

Dull. And I say the pollution holds in the exchange; for the moon is never but a month old: and I say beside, that 'twas a pricket that the princess kill'd.

Hol. Sir Nathaniel, will you hear an extemporal epitaph on the death of the deer? and, to humour the ignorant, I have called the deer the princess kill'd, a pricket.

Nath. *Perge,* good master Holofernes, *perge;* so it shall please you to abrogate scurrility.

Hol. I will something affect the letter; for it argues facility.
The praiseful princess pierc'd and prick'd a pretty pleasing pricket;
Some say, a sore; but not a sore, till now made sore with shooting.
The dogs did yell! put l to sore, then sorel jumps from thicket;
Or pricket, sore, or else sorel; the people fall a hooting.
If sore be sore, then L to sore makes fifty sores; O sore L!
Of one sore I a hundred make, by adding but one more L.

Nath. A rare talent!

Dull. If a talent be a claw, look how he claws him with a talent.

Hol. This is a gift that I have, simple, simple; a foolish extravagant spirit, full of forms, figures, shapes, objects, ideas, apprehensions, motions, revolutions: these are begot in the ventricle of memory, nourished in the womb of *pia mater;* and deliver'd upon the mellowing of occasion: But the gift is good in those in whom it is acute, and I am thankful for it.

Nath. Sir, I praise the Lord for you; and so may my parishioners; for their sons are well tutor'd by you, and their daughters profit very greatly under you: you are a good member of the commonwealth.

Hol. *Mehercle,* if their sons be ingenious, they shall want no instruction: if their daughters be capable, I will put it to them: But, *vir sapit, qui pauca loquitur:* a soul feminine saluteth us.

Enter JAQUENETTA *and* COSTARD.

Jaq. God give you good morrow, master person.

Hol. Master person,—*quasi* pers-on. And if one should be pierced, which is the one?

Cost. Marry, master schoolmaster, he that is likest to a hogshead.

Hol. Of piercing a hogshead! a good lustre of conceit in a turf of earth; fire enough for a flint, pearl enough for a swine: 'tis pretty; it is well.

Jaq. Good master parson, be so good as read me this letter; it was given me by Costard, and sent me from Don Armatho: I beseech you, read it.

Hol. *Fauste, precor gelida quando pecùs omne sub umbra*
Ruminat,—and so forth. Ah, good old Mantuan! I may speak of thee as the traveller doth of Venice:
—— *Vinegia, Vinegia,*
Chi non te vede, ei non te pregia.
Old Mantuan! old Mantuan! Who understandeth thee not, loves thee not.—*Ut, re, sol, la, mi, fa.*—Under pardon, sir, what are the contents? or, rather, as Horace says in his—What, my soul, verses?

Nath. Ay, sir, and very learned.

Hol. Let me hear a staff, a stanza, a verse: *Lege, domine.*

Nath. If love make me forsworn, how shall I swear to love?
Ah, never faith could hold, if not to beauty vowed!
Though to myself forsworn, to thee I'll faithful prove;
Those thoughts to me were oaks, to thee like osiers bowed.
Study his bias leaves, and makes his book thine eyes;
Where all those pleasures live that art would comprehend:
If knowledge be the mark, to know thee shall suffice;
Well learned is that tongue, that well can thee commend:
All ignorant that soul, that sees thee without wonder;
(Which is to me some praise, that I thy parts admire;)
Thy eye Jove's lightning bears, thy voice his dreadful thunder,
Which, not to anger bent, is musick and sweet fire.
Celestial, as thou art, oh pardon, love, this wrong,
That sings heaven's praise with such an earthly tongue!

Hol. You find not the apostrophes, and so miss the accent; let me supervise the canzonet. Here are only numbers ratified; but, for the elegancy, facility, and golden cadence of poesy, *caret.* Ovidius Naso was the man: and why, indeed, Naso; but for smelling out the odoriferous flowers of fancy, the jerks of invention? *Imitari,* is nothing: so doth the hound his master, the ape his keeper, the tired horse his rider. But, damosella virgin, was this directed to you?

Jaq. Ay, sir, from one Monsieur Biron, one of the strange queen's lords.

Hol. I will overglance the superscript. *To the snow-white hand of the most beauteous lady Rosaline.* I will look again on the intellect of the letter, for the nomination of the party writing to the person written unto:
Your ladyship's in all desired employment, BIRON.
Sir Nathaniel, this Biron is one of the votaries with the king; and here he hath framed a letter to a sequent of the stranger queen's, which, accidentally, or by the way of progression, hath

miscarried.—Trip and go, my sweet; deliver this paper into the royal hand of the king; it may concern much: Stay not thy compliment; I forgive thy duty; adieu.

Jaq. Good Costard, go with me.—Sir, God save your life!

Cost. Have with thee, my girl.

[*Exeunt* COST. *and* JAQ.

Nath. Sir, you have done this in the fear of God, very religiously; and, as a certain father saith——

Hol. Sir, tell not me of the father, I do fear colourable colours. But to return to the verses; Did they please you, sir Nathaniel?

Nath. Marvellous well for the pen.

Hol. I do dine to-day at the father's of a certain pupil of mine; where if, before repast, it shall please you to gratify the table with a grace, I will, on my privilege I have with the parents of the foresaid child or pupil, undertake your *ben venuto;* where I will prove those verses to be very unlearned, neither savouring of poetry, wit, nor invention: I beseech your society.

Nath. And thank you too: for society, (saith the text), is the happiness of life.

Hol. And, certes, the text most infallibly concludes it.—Sir, [*To* DULL.] I do invite you too; you shall not say me, nay: *pauca verba.* Away; the gentles are at their game, and we will to our recreation. [*Exeunt.*

SCENE III. *Another part of the same.*

Enter BIRON, *with a Paper.*

Biron. The king he is hunting the deer; I am coursing myself: they have pitch'd a toil; I am toiling in a pitch; pitch that defiles; defile! a foul word. Well, set thee down, sorrow! for so, they say, the fool said, and so say I, and I the fool. Well proved, wit! by the lord, this love is as mad as Ajax: it kills sheep; it kills me, I a sheep: Well proved again on my side! I will not love: if I do, hang me; i'faith, I will not. O, but her eye,—by this light, but for her eye, I would not love her; yes, for her two eyes. Well, I do nothing in the world but lie, and lie in my throat. By heaven, I do love: and it hath taught me to rhyme, and to be melancholy; and here is part of my rhyme, and here my melancholy. Well, she hath one o' my sonnets already; the clown bore it, the fool sent it, and the lady hath it: sweet clown, sweeter fool, sweetest lady! By the world, I would not care a pin if the other three were in: Here comes one with a paper; God give him grace to groan! [*Gets up into a Tree.*

Enter the King, *with a Paper.*

King. Ah me!

Biron. [*Aside.*] Shot, by heaven!—Proceed, sweet Cupid; thou hast thump'd him with thy birdbolt under the left pap:—I'faith secrets.—

King. [Reads.] *So sweet a kiss the golden sun gives not*
To those fresh morning drops upon the rose,
As thy eye-beams, when their fresh rays have smote
The night of dew that on my cheeks down flows:
Nor shines the silver moon one half so bright
Through the transparent bosom of the deep,
As doth thy face through tears of mine give light;
Thou shin'st in every tear that I do weep:
No drop but as a coach doth carry thee,
So ridest thou triumphing in my woe;
Do but behold the tears that swell in me,
And they thy glory through my grief will show:
But do not love thyself; then thou wilt keep
My tears for glasses, and still make me weep.
O queen of queens, how far dost thou excel!
No thought can think, nor tongue of mortal tell.—
How shall she know my griefs? I'll drop the paper;
Sweet leaves, shade folly. Who is he comes here? [*Steps aside.*

Enter LONGAVILLE, *with a Paper.*

What, Longaville! and reading! listen, ear.

Biron. Now, in thy likeness, one more fool, appear! [*Aside.*

Long. Ah me! I am forsworn.

Biron. Why, he comes in like a perjure, wearing papers. [*Aside.*

King. In love, I hope; Sweet fellowship in shame! [*Aside.*

Biron. One drunkard loves another of the name. [*Aside.*

Long. Am I the first that have been perjur'd so?

Biron. [*Aside.*] I could put thee in comfort; not by two, that I know:
Thou mak'st the triumviry, the corner-cap of society,
The shape of love's Tyburn that hangs up simplicity.

Long. I fear, these stubborn lines lack power to move;
O sweet Maria, empress of my love!
These numbers will I tear, and write in prose.

Biron. [*Aside.*] O, rhymes are guards on wanton Cupid's hose:
Disfigure not his slop.

Long. This same shall go.—
[*He reads the Sonnet.*
Did not the heavenly rhetorick of thine eye
('Gainst whom the world cannot hold argument),
Persuade my heart to this false perjury?
Vows, for thee broke, deserve not punishment.
A woman I forswore; but, I will prove,
Thou being a goddess, I forswore not thee:
My vow was earthly, thou a heavenly love;
Thy grace being gain'd, cures all disgrace in me.
Vows are but breath, and breath a vapour is:
Then thou, fair sun, which on my earth dost shine,
Exhal'st this vapour vow; in thee it is:
If broken then, it is no fault of mine;
If by me broke. What fool is not so wise,
To lose an oath to win a paradise?

Biron. [*Aside.*] This is the liver vein, which makes flesh a deity;
A green goose, a goddess: pure, pure idolatry.
God amend us, God amend! we are much out o' the way.

Enter DUMAIN, *with a Paper.*

Long. By whom shall I send this?—Company! stay. [*Stepping aside.*

Biron. [*Aside.*] All hid, all hid, an old infant play:
Like a demi-god here sit I in the sky,
And wretched fools' secrets heedfully o'er-eye.
More sacks to the mill! O heavens, I have my wish;
Dumain transform'd: four woodcocks in a dish!

Dum. O most divine Kate!

Biron. O most profane coxcomb! [*Aside.*

Dum. By heaven, the wonder of a mortal eye!

Biron. By earth she is but corporal; there you lie. [*Aside.*

Dum. Her amber hairs for foul have amber coted.

Biron. An amber-colour'd raven was well noted. [*Aside.*

Dum. As upright as the cedar.

Biron. Stoop, I say;
Her shoulder is with child. [*Aside.*

Dum. As fair as day.

Biron. Ay, as some days; but then no sun must shine. [*Aside.*

Dum. O that I had my wish!

Long. And I had mine! [*Aside.*

King. And I mine too, good Lord! [*Aside.*

Biron. Amen, so I had mine: Is not that a good word? [*Aside.*

Dum. I would forget her; but a fever she
Reigns in my blood, and will remember'd be.

Biron. A fever in your blood, why, then incision
Would let her out in saucers; Sweet misprision! [*Aside.*

Dum. Once more I'll read the ode that I have writ.

Biron. Once more I'll mark how love can vary wit. [*Aside.*

Dum. *On a day, (alack the day!)*
Love, whose month is ever May,
Spied a blossom, passing fair,
Playing in the wanton air:
Through the velvet leaves the wind,
All unseen, 'gan passage find;
That the lover, sick to death,
Wish'd himself the heaven's breath.
Air, quoth he, *thy cheeks may blow;*
Air, would I might triumph so!
But alack, my hand is sworn,
Ne'er to pluck thee from thy thorn:
Vow, alack, for youth unmeet;
Youth so apt to pluck a sweet.
Do not call it sin in me,
That I am forsworn for thee;—
Thee—for whom Jove would swear,
Juno but an Ethiop were;
And deny himself for Jove,
Turning mortal for thy love.—

This will I send: and something else more plain,
That shall express my true love's fasting pain.
O, would the King, Biron, and Longaville,
Were lovers too! Ill, to example ill,
Would from my forehead wipe a perjur'd note;
For none offend, where all alike do dote.

Long. Dumain, [*advancing.*] thy love is far from charity,
That in love's grief desir'st society;
You may look pale, but I should blush, I know,
To be o'erheard, and taken napping so.

King. Come, sir, [*advancing.*] you blush; as his your case is such;
You chide at him, offending twice as much:
You do not love Maria; Longaville
Did never sonnet for her sake compile;
Nor never lay his wreathed arms athwart
His loving bosom, to keep down his heart.
I have been closely shrouded in this bush,
And mark'd you both, and for you both did blush.
I heard your guilty rhymes, observ'd your fashion;
Saw sighs reek from you, noted well your passion:
Ah me! says one; O Jove! the other cries;
One, her hairs were gold, crystal the other's eyes:
You would for paradise break faith and troth; [*To* Long.
And Jove, for your love, would infringe an oath. [*To* Dumain.
What will Biron say, when that he shall hear
Faith infringed, which such a zeal did swear?
How will he scorn? how will he spend his wit?
How will he triumph, leap, and laugh at it?
For all the wealth that ever I did see,
I would not have him know so much by me.

Biron. Now step I forth to whip hypocrisy.—
Ah, good my liege, I pray thee pardon me: [*Descends from the Tree.*
Good heart, what grace hast thou, thus to reprove
These worms for loving, that art most in love?
Your eyes do make no coaches; in your tears,
There is no certain princess that appears:
You'll not be perjur'd, 'tis a hateful thing;
Tush, none but minstrels like of sonneting.
But are you not asham'd? nay, are you not,
All three of you, to be thus much o'ershot?
You found his mote; the king your mote did see:
But I a beam do find in each of three.
O, what a scene of foolery I have seen,
Of sighs, of groans, of sorrow, and of teen!
O me, with what strict patience have I sat,
To see a king transformed into a gnat!
To see great Hercules whipping a gigg,
And profound Solomon to tune a jigg,
And Nestor play at push-pin with the boys,
And critick Timon laugh at idle toys?
Where lies thy grief, O tell me, good Dumain?
And gentle Longaville, where lies thy pain?
And where my liege's? all about the breast:—
A caudle, ho!

King. Too bitter is thy jest.
Are we betray'd thus to thy over-view?

Biron. Not you by me, but I betray'd to you;
I, that am honest: I, that hold it sin
To break the vow I am engaged in;
I am betray'd, by keeping company
With moon-like men, of strange inconstancy.
When shall you see me write a thing in rhyme?
Or groan for Joan? or spend a minute's time
In pruning me? When shall you hear that I
Will praise a hand, a foot, a face, an eye,
A gait, a state, a brow, a breast, a waist,
A leg, a limb!—

King. Soft; Whither away so fast?
A true man, or a thief, that gallops so?

Biron. I post from love; good lover, let me go.

Enter Jaquenetta *and* Costard.

Jaq. God bless the king!

King. What present hast thou there?

Cost. Some certain treason.

King. What makes treason here?

Cost. Nay, it makes nothing, sir.

King. If it mar nothing neither,
The treason, and you, go in peace away together.

Jaq. I beseech your grace, let this letter be read;
Our parson misdoubts it; 'twas treason, he said.

King. Biron, read it over. [*Giving him the letter.*
Where hadst thou it?

Jaq. Of Costard.

King. Where had'st thou it?

Cost. Of Dun Adramadio, Dun Adramadio.

King. How now! what is in you? why dost thou tear it?

Biron. A toy, my liege, a toy; your grace needs not fear it.

Long. It did move him to passion, and therefore let's hear it.

Dum. It is Biron's writing, and here is his name. [*Picks up the pieces.*

Biron. Ah, you whoreson loggerhead, [*To* Costard.] you were born to do me shame.—
Guilty, my lord, guilty; I confess, I confess.

King. What?

Biron. That you three fools lack'd me fool to make up the mess:
He, he, and you, my liege, and I,
Are pick-purses in love, and we deserve to die.
O, dismiss this audience, and I shall tell you more.

Dum. Now the number is even.

Biron. True, true; we are four:—
Will these turtles be gone?

King. Hence, sirs; away.

Cost. Walk aside the true folk, and let the traitors stay. [*Exeunt* Cost. *and* Jaq.

Biron. Sweet lords, sweet lovers, O let us embrace!
As true we are, as flesh and blood can be:
The sea will ebb and flow, heaven show his face;
Young blood will not obey an old decree:
We cannot cross the cause why we were born;
Therefore, of all hands must we be forsworn.

King. What, did these rent lines show some love of thine?

Biron. Did they, quoth you? Who sees the heavenly Rosaline,
That like a rude and savage man of Inde,
At the first opening of the gorgeous east,
Bows not his vassal head; and, stricken blind,
Kisses the base ground with obedient breast?

What peremptory eagle-sighted eye
Dares look upon the heaven of her brow,
That is not blinded by her majesty?
King. What zeal, what fury hath inspir'd thee now?
My love, her mistress, is a gracious moon;
She, an attending star, scarce seen a light.
Biron. My eyes are then no eyes, nor I Biron:
O, but for my love, day would turn to night!
Of all complexions the cull'd sovereignty
Do meet, as at a fair, in her fair cheek;
Where several worthies make one dignity;
Where nothing wants; that want itself doth seek.
Lend me the flourish of all gentle tongues,—
Fye, painted rhetorick! O, she needs it not:
To things of sale a seller's praise belongs;
She passes praise; then praise too short doth blot.
A wither'd hermit, five-score winters worn
Might shake off fifty, looking in her eye:
Beauty doth varnish age, as if new-born,
And gives the crutch the cradle's infancy.
O, 'tis the sun that maketh all things shine!
King. By heaven, thy love is black as ebony.
Biron. Is ebony like her? O wood divine!
A wife of such wood were felicity.
O, who can give an oath? where is a book?
That I may swear, beauty doth beauty lack,
If that she learn not of her eye to look:
No face is fair, that is not full so black.
King. O paradox! Black is the badge of hell,
The hue of dungeons, and the scowl of night;
And beauty's crest becomes the heavens well.
Biron. Devils soonest tempt, resembling spirits of light.
O, if in black my lady's brows be deckt,
It mourns, that painting, and usurping hair,
Should ravish doters with a false aspect:
And therefore is she born to make black fair.
Her favour turns the fashion of the days;
For native blood is counted painting now;
And therefore red, that would avoid dispraise,
Paints itself black, to imitate her brow.
Dum. To look like her, are chimney-sweepers black.
Long. And since her time are colliers counted bright.
King. And Ethiops of their sweet complexion crack.
Dum. Dark needs no candles now, for dark is light.
Biron. Your mistresses dare never come in rain,
For fear their colours should be wash'd away.
King. 'Twere good, yours did; for, sir, to tell you plain,
I'll find a fairer face not wash'd to-day.
Biron. I'll prove her fair, or talk till dooms-day here.
King. No devil will fright thee then so much as she.
Dum. I never knew man hold vile stuff so dear.
Long. Look, here's thy love: my foot and her face see. [*Showing his Shoe.*
Biron. O, if the streets were paved with thine eyes,
Her feet were much too dainty for such tread!
Dum. O vile! then as she goes, what upward lies
The street should see as she walk'd overhead.
King. But what of this? Are we not all in love?
Biron. O, nothing so sure; and thereby all forsworn.
King. Then leave this chat; and, good Biron, now prove
Our loving lawful, and our faith not torn.
Dum. Ay, marry, there;—some flattery for this evil.
Long. O, some authority how to proceed;
Some tricks, some quillets, how to cheat the devil.
Dum. Some salve for perjury.
Biron. O, 'tis more than need!
Have at you then, affection's men at arms:
Consider what you first did swear unto;—
To fast,—to study,—and to see no woman;—
Flat treason 'gainst the kingly state of youth.
Say, can you fast? your stomachs are too young;
And abstinence engenders maladies.
And where that you have vow'd to study, lords,
In that each of you hath forsworn his book:
Can you still dream, and pore, and thereon look?
For when would you, my lord, or you, or you,
Have found the ground of study's excellence,
Without the beauty of a woman's face?
From women's eyes this doctrine I derive:
They are the ground, the books, the academes,
From whence doth spring the true Promethean fire.
Why, universal plodding prisons up
The nimble spirits in the arteries;
As motion, and long during action, tires
The sinewy vigour of the traveller.
Now, for not looking on a woman's face,
You have in that forsworn the use of eyes;
And study too, the causer of your vow:
For where is any author in the world,
Teaches such beauty as a woman's eye?
Learning is but an adjunct to ourself,
And where we are, our learning likewise is.
Then, when ourselves we see in ladies' eyes,
Do we not likewise see our learning there?
O, we have made a vow to study, lords:
And in that vow we have forsworn our books;
For when would you, my liege, or you, or you,
In leaden contemplation, have found out
Such fiery numbers, as the prompting eyes
Of beauteous tutors have enrich'd you with?
Other slow arts entirely keep the brain;
And therefore finding barren practisers,
Scarce show a harvest of their heavy toil:
But love, first learned in a lady's eyes,
Lives not alone immured in the brain;
But, with the motion of all elements,
Courses as swift as thought in every power;
And gives to every power a double power,
Above their functions and their offices.
It adds a precious seeing to the eye:
A lover's eyes will gaze an eagle blind;
A lover's ear will hear the lowest sound,
When the suspicious head of theft is stopp'd;
Love's feeling is more soft, and sensible,
Than are the tender horns of cockled snails;
Love's tongue proves dainty Bacchus gross in taste:
For valour, is not love a Hercules,
Still climbing trees in the Hesperides?
Subtle as sphinx; as sweet, and musical,
As bright Apollo's lute, strung with his hair;
And, when love speaks, the voice of all the gods
Makes heaven drowsy with the harmony.
Never durst poet touch a pen to write,
Until his ink were temper'd with love's sighs;
O, then his lines would ravish savage ears,
And plant in tyrants mild humility.
From women's eyes this doctrine I derive:
They sparkle still the right Promethean fire;
They are the books, the arts, the academes,
That show, contain, and nourish all the world;
Else, none at all in aught proves excellent:
Then fools you were these women to forswear;
Or, keeping what is sworn, you will prove fools.
For wisdom's sake, a word that all men love;
Or for love's sake, a word that loves all men;
Or for men's sake, the authors of these women;
Or women's sake, by whom we men are men;
Let us once lose our oaths to find ourselves,
Or else we lose ourselves to keep our oaths:
It is religion to be thus forsworn:
For charity itself fulfils the law;
And who can sever love from charity?

King. Saint Cupid, then! and, soldiers, to the field!

Biron. Advance your standards, and upon them, lords;
Pell-mell, down with them! but be first advis'd,
In conflict that you get the sun of them.

Long. Now to plain-dealing; lay these glozes by;
Shall we resolve to woo these girls of France?

King. And win them too: therefore let us devise
Some entertainment for them in their tents.

Biron. First, from the park let us conduct them thither;
Then, homeward, every man attach the hand
Of his fair mistress; in the afternoon
We will with some strange pastime solace them,
Such as the shortness of the time can shape;
For revels, dances, masks, and merry hours,
Forerun fair Love, strewing her way with flowers.

King. Away, away! no time shall be omitted,
That will be time, and may by us be fitted.

Biron. *Allons! Allons!*—Sow'd cockle reap'd no corn;
And justice always whirls in equal measure:
Light wenches may prove plagues to men forsworn;
If so, our copper buys no better treasure.
[*Exeunt*.

ACT V.

SCENE I. *Another part of the same.*

Enter HOLOFERNES, SIR NATHANIEL, *and* DULL.

Hol. *Satis quod sufficit.*

Nath. I praise God for you, sir: your reasons at dinner have been sharp and sententious; pleasant without scurrility, witty without affection, audacious without impudency, learned without opinion, and strange without heresy. I did converse this *quondam* day with a companion of the king's, who is intituled, nominated, or called, Don Adriano de Armado.

Hol. *Novi hominem tanquam te:* His humour is lofty, his discourse peremptory, his tongue filed, his eye ambitious, his gait majestical, and his general behaviour vain, ridiculous, and thrasonical. He is too picked, too spruce, too affected, too odd, as it were, too peregrinate, as I may call it.

Nath. A most singular and choice epithet.
[*Takes out his Table-book*.

Hol. He draweth out the thread of his verbosity finer than the staple of his argument. I abhor such fantastical phantasms, such insociable and point-devise companions; such rackers of orthography, as to speak doubt, fine, when he should say, doubt; det, when he should pronounce, debt: d, e, b, t; not d, e, t: he clepeth a calf, cauf; half, hauf; neighbour, *vocatur*, nebour, neigh, abbreviated, ne: This is abhominable (which he would call abominable), it insinuateth me of insanie; *Ne intelligis, domine?* to make frantic, lunatick.

Nath. *Laus Deo, bone intelligo.*

Hol. *Bone?*——*bone*, for *Bene: Priscian* a little scratch'd; 'twill serve.

Enter ARMADO, MOTH, *and* COSTARD.

Nath. *Videsne quis venit?*

Hol. *Video, et gaudeo.*

Arm. Chirra! [*To* MOTH.

Hol. *Quare* Chirra, not sirrah?

Arm. Men of peace, well encounter'd.

Hol. Most military sir, salutation.

Moth. They have been at a great feast of languages, and stolen the scraps.
[*To* COSTARD *aside*.

Cost. O, they have lived long in the alms-basket of words! I marvel, thy master hath not eaten thee for a word; for thou art not so long by the head as *honorificabilitudinitatibus:* thou art easier swallowed than a flap-dragon.

Moth. Peace; the peal begins.

Arm. Monsieur, [*To* HOL.] are you not letter'd?

Moth. Yes, yes; he teaches boys the hornbook:
What is a, b, spelt backward with a horn on his head?

Hol. Ba, *pueritia*, with a horn added.

Moth. Ba, most silly sheep, with a horn:—
You hear his learning.

Hol. *Quis, quis*, thou consonant?

Moth. The third of the five vowels, if you repeat them; or the fifth, if I.

Hol. I will repeat them, a, e, i.—

Moth. The sheep: the other two concludes it; o, u.

Arm. Now, by the salt wave of the Mediterraneum, a sweet touch, a quick venew of wit: snip, snap, quick and home; it rejoiceth my intellect: true wit.

Moth. Offered by a child to an old man; which is wit-old.

Hol. What is the figure? what is the figure?

Moth. Horns.

Hol. Thou disputest like an infant: go whip thy gig.

Moth. Lend me your horn to make one, and I will whip about your infamy *circum circa*; A gig of a cuckold's horn!

Cost. An I had but one penny in the world, thou should'st have it to buy gingerbread: hold, there is the very remuneration I had of thy master, thou half-penny purse of wit, thou pigeon-egg of discretion. O, an the heavens were so pleased, that thou wert but my bastard! what a joyful father wouldst thou make me! Go to; thou hast it *ad dunghill*, at the fingers' ends, as they say.

Hol. O, I smell false Latin; dunghill for *unguem*.

Arm. Arts-man, *præambula;* we will be singled from the barbarous. Do you not educate youth at the charge-house on the top of the mountain?

Hol. Or, *mons*, the hill.

Arm. At your sweet pleasure, for the mountain.

Hol. I do, sans question.

Arm. Sir, it is the king's most sweet pleasure and affection, to congratulate the princess at her pavilion, in the posteriors of this day; which the rude multitude call, the afternoon.

Hol. The posterior of the day, most generous sir, is liable, congruent, and measurable for the afternoon: the word is well cull'd, chose; sweet and apt, I do assure you, sir, I do assure.

Arm. Sir, the king is a noble gentleman; and my familiar, I do assure you, very good friend:—For what is inward between us, let it pass:—I do beseech thee, remember thy courtesy;—I beseech thee, apparel thy head;—and among other importunate and most serious designs,—and of great import indeed, too; but let that pass:—for I must tell thee, it will please his grace (by the world) sometime to lean upon my poor shoulder; and with his royal finger, thus, dally with my excrement, with my mustachio: but, sweet heart, let that pass. By the world, I recount no fable; some certain special honours it pleaseth his greatness to impart to Armado, a soldier, a man of travel, that hath seen the world: but let that pass.—The very all of all is,—but sweet heart, I do implore secrecy,—that the king would have me present the princess, sweet chuck, with some delightful ostentation, or show, or pageant, or antick, or firework. Now, understanding that the curate and your sweet self, are good at such eruptions, and sudden breaking out of mirth, as it were, I have acquainted you withal, to the end to crave your assistance.

Hol. Sir, you shall present before her the nine

worthies.—Sir Nathaniel, as concerning some entertainment of time, some show in the posterior of this day, to be rendered by our assistance,—the king's command, and this most gallant, illustrate, and learned gentleman,—before the princess; I say, none so fit as to present the nine worthies.

Nath. Where will you find men worthy enough to present them?

Hol. Joshua, yourself; myself, or this gallant gentleman, Judas Maccabeus; this swain, because of his great limb or joint, shall pass Pompey the great; the page, Hercules.

Arm. Pardon, sir, error: he is not quantity enough for that worthy's thumb: he is not so big as the end of his club.

Hol. Shall I have audience? He shall present Hercules in minority: his *enter* and *exit* shall be strangling a snake; and I will have an apology for that purpose.

Moth. An excellent device! so, if any of the audience hiss, you may cry: *well done, Hercules! now thou crushest the snake!* that is the way to make an offence gracious; though few have the grace to do it.

Arm. For the rest of the worthies?—

Hol. I will play three myself.

Moth. Thrice worthy gentleman!

Arm. Shall I tell you a thing?

Hol. We attend.

Arm. We will have, if this fadge not, an antick. I beseech you, follow.

Hol. *Via,* goodman Dull! thou hast spoken no word all this while.

Dull. Nor understood none neither, sir.

Hol. *Allons!* we will employ thee.

Dull. I'll make one in a dance, or so; or I will play on the tabor to the worthies, and let them dance the hay.

Hol. Most dull, honest Dull, to our sport, away. [*Exeunt.*

SCENE II. *Another part of the same. Before the* Princess's *Pavilion.*

Enter the Princess, KATHARINE, ROSALINE, *and* MARIA.

Prin. Sweet hearts, we shall be rich ere we depart,
If fairings thus come plentifully in:
A lady wall'd about with diamonds!—
Look you, what I have from the loving king.

Ros. Madam, came nothing else along with that?

Prin. Nothing but this? yes, as much love in rhyme,
As would be cramm'd up in a sheet of paper,
Writ on both sides the leaf, margent and all;
That he was fain to seal on Cupid's name.

Ros. That was the way to make his godhead wax:
For he hath been five thousand years a boy.

Kath. Ay, and a shrewd unhappy gallows too.

Ros. You'll ne'er be friends with him; he kill'd your sister.

Kath. He made her melancholy, sad, and heavy;
And so she died: had she been light, like you,
Of such a merry, nimble, stirring spirit,
She might have been a grandam ere she died:
And so may you; for a light heart lives long.

Ros. What's your dark meaning, mouse, of this light word?

Kath. A light condition in a beauty dark.

Ros. We need more light to find your meaning out.

Kath. You'll mar the light, by taking it in snuff;
Therefore, I'll darkly end the argument.

Ros. Look, what you do, you do it still i' the dark.

Kath. So do not you; for you are a light wench.

Ros. Indeed, I weigh not you; and therefore light.

Kath. You weigh me not,—O, that's you care not for me.

Ros. Great reason; for, Past cure is still past care.

Prin. Well bandied both; a set of wit well play'd.
But Rosaline, you have a favour too:
Who sent it? and what is it?

Ros. I would, you knew:
And if my face were but as fair as yours,
My favour were as great: be witness this.
Nay, I have verses too, I thank Biron:
The numbers true; and, were the numb'ring too,
I were the fairest goddess on the ground:
I am compared to twenty thousand fairs.
O, he hath drawn my picture in his letter!

Prin. Any thing like?

Ros. Much, in the letters; nothing in the praise.

Prin. Beauteous as ink; a good conclusion.

Kath. Fair as a text B in a copy-book.

Ros. 'Ware pencils! How! let me not die your debtor,
My red dominical, my golden letter:
O, that your face were not so full of O's!

Kath. A pox of that jest! and beshrew all shrows!

Prin. But what was sent to you from fair Dumain?

Kath. Madam, this glove.

Prin. Did he not send you twain.

Kath. Yes, madam; and moreover,
Some thousand verses of a faithful lover:
A huge translation of hypocrisy,
Vilely compil'd, profound simplicity.

Mar. This, and these pearls, to me sent Longaville;
The letter is too long by half a mile.

Prin. I think no less: Dost thou not wish in heart,
The chain were longer, and the letter short?

Mar. Ay, or I would these hands might never part.

Prin. We are wise girls, to mock our lovers so.

Ros. They are worse fools to purchase mocking so.
That same Biron I'll torture ere I go.
O, that I knew he were but in by the week!
How I would make him fawn, and beg, and seek;
And wait the season, and observe the times,
And spend his prodigal wits in bootless rhymes;
And shape his service wholly to my behests;
And make him proud to make me proud that jests!
So potent-like would I o'ersway his state,
That he should be my fool, and I his fate.

Prin. None are so surely caught, when they are catch'd,
As wit turn'd fool: folly, in wisdom hatch'd,
Hath wisdom's warrant, and the help of school;
And wit's own grace to grace a learned fool.

Ros. The blood of youth burns not with such excess,
As gravity's revolt to wantonness.

Mar. Folly in fools bears not so strong a note,
As foolery in the wise, when wit doth dote;
Since all the power thereof it doth apply,
To prove, by wit, worth in simplicity.

Enter BOYET.

Prin. Here comes Boyet, and mirth is in his face.

Boyet. O, I am stabb'd with laughter! Where's her grace?

Prin. Thy news, Boyet?

Boyet. Prepare, madam, prepare!—
Arm, wenches, arm! encounters mounted are
Against your peace: Love doth approach disguis'd,
Armed in arguments; you'll be surpris'd:

Muster your wits; stand in your own defence;
Or hide your heads like cowards, and fly hence.

Prin. Saint Dennis to saint Cupid! What are they,
That charge their breath against us? say, scout, say.

Boyet. Under the cool shade of a sycamore,
I thought to close mine eyes some half an hour:
When lo! to interrupt my purpos'd rest,
Toward that shade I might behold addrest
The king and his companions: warily
I stole into a neighbour thicket by,
And overheard what you shall overhear;
That, by and by, disguis'd they will be here.
Their herald is a pretty knavish page,
That well by heart hath conn'd his embassage:
Action, and accent, did they teach him there;
Thus must thou speak, and thus thy body bear;
And ever and anon they made a doubt,
Presence majestical would put him out;
For, quoth the king, *an angel shalt thou see;*
Yet fear not thou, but speak audaciously.
The boy reply'd, *An angel is not evil;*
I should have fear'd her, had she been a devil.
With that all laugh'd, and clapp'd him on the shoulder;
Making the bold wag by their praises bolder.
One rubb'd his elbow, thus; and fleer'd, and swore,
A better speech was never spoke before:
Another, with his finger and his thumb,
Cry'd *Via! we will do't, come what will come:*
The third he caper'd, and cried, *All goes well:*
The fourth turn'd on the toe, and down he fell.
With that they all did tumble on the ground,
With such a zealous laughter, so profound,
That in this spleen ridiculous appears,
To check their folly, passion's solemn tears.

Prin. But what, but what, come they to visit us?

Boyet. They do, they do; and are apparel'd thus,—
Like Muscovites, or Russians: as I guess,
The purpose is, to parle, to court, and dance:
And every one his love feat will advance
Unto his several mistress; which they'll know
By favours several, which they did bestow.

Prin. And will they so? the gallants shall be task'd:
For, ladies, we will every one be mask'd;
And not a man of them shall have the grace,
Despite of suit, to see a lady's face.—
Hold, Rosaline, this favour thou shalt wear;
And then the king will court thee for his dear;
Hold, take thou this, my sweet, and give me thine;
So shall Biron take me for Rosaline.—
And change you favours too; so shall your loves
Woo contrary, deceiv'd by these removes.

Ros. Come on then; wear the favours most in sight.

Kath. But, in this changing, what is your intent?

Prin. The effect of my intent is, to cross theirs:
They do it but in mocking merriment;
And mock for mock is only my intent.
Their several counsels they unbosom shall
To loves mistook; and so be mock'd withal,
Upon the next occasion that we meet,
With visages display'd, to talk, and greet.

Ros. But shall we dance, if they desire us to't?

Prin. No; to the death, we will not move a foot:
Nor to their penn'd speech render we no grace;
But, while 'tis spoke, each turn away her face.

Boyet. Why, that contempt will kill the speaker's heart,
And quite divorce his memory from his part.

Prin. Therefore I do it; and, I make no doubt,
The rest will ne'er come in, if he be out.
There's no such sport, as sport by sport o'erthrown;
To make theirs ours, and ours none but our own:
So shall we stay, mocking intended game;
And they, well mock'd, depart away with shame.
[*Trumpets sound within.*

Boyet. The trumpet sounds; be mask'd, the maskers come. [*The ladies mask.*

Enter the King, Biron, Longaville, *and* Dumain, *in Russian habits, and masked;* Moth, Musicians *and* Attendants.

Moth. *All hail, the richest beauties on the earth!*

Boyet. Beauties no richer than rich taffata.

Moth. *A holy parcel of the fairest dames,*
[The ladies turn their backs to him.
That ever turn'd their—backs—to mortal views!

Biron. *Their eyes,* villain, *their eyes.*

Moth. *That ever turn'd their eyes to mortal views!*
Out—

Boyet. True; *out,* indeed.

Moth. *Out of your favours, heavenly spirits, vouchsafe*
Not to behold—

Biron. *Once to behold,* rogue.

Moth. *Once to behold with your sun-beamed eyes,*
——with your sun-beamed eyes—

Boyet. They will not answer to that epithet;
You were best call it, daughter-beamed eyes.

Moth. They do not mark me, and that brings me out.

Biron. Is this your perfectness? be gone, you rogue.

Ros. What would these strangers? know their minds, Boyet:
If they do speak our language, 'tis our will
That some plain man recount their purposes:
Know what they would.

Boyet. What would you with the princess?

Biron. Nothing but peace, and gentle visitation.

Ros. What would they, say they?

Boyet. Nothing but peace, and gentle visitation.

Ros. Why, that they have; and bid them so be gone.

Boyet. She says, you have it, and you may be gone.

King. Say to her, we have measur'd many miles,
To tread a measure with her on this grass.

Boyet. They say that they have measur'd many a mile,
To tread a measure with you on this grass.

Ros. It is not so: ask them how many inches
Is in one mile: If they have measur'd many,
The measure then of one is easily told.

Boyet. If, to come hither you have measur'd miles,
And many miles; the princess bids you tell,
How many inches do fill up one mile.

Biron. Tell her, we measure them by weary steps.

Boyet. She hears herself.

Ros. How many weary steps,
Of many weary miles you have o'ergone,
Are number'd in the travel of one mile?

Biron. We number nothing that we spend for you;
Our duty is so rich, so infinite,
That we may do it still without accompt.
Vouchsafe to show the sunshine of your face,
That we, like savages, may worship it.

Ros. My face is but a moon, and clouded too.

King. Blessed are clouds, to do as such clouds do!
Vouchsafe, bright moon, and these thy stars, to shine
(Those clouds remov'd) upon our wat'ry eyne.

Ros. O vain petitioner! beg a greater matter,
Thou now request'st but moonshine in the water.

King. Then, in our measure vouchsafe but one change:
Thou bid'st me beg; this begging is not strange.

Ros. Play, musick, then: nay, you must do it soon. [*Musick plays.*
Not yet;—no dance:—thus change I like the moon.

King. Will you not dance? How come you thus estrang'd?
Ros. You took the moon at full; but now she's chang'd.
King. Yet still she is the moon, and I the man.
The musick plays; vouchsafe some motion to it.
Ros. Our ears vouchsafe it.
King. But your legs should do it.
Ros. Since you are strangers, and come here by chance,
We'll not be nice: take hands;—we will not dance.
King. Why take we hands then?
Ros. Only to part friends:—
Court'sy, sweet hearts; and so the measure ends.
King. More measure of this measure; be not nice.
Ros. We can afford no more at such a price.
King. Prize you yourselves; What buys your company?
Ros. Your absence only.
King. That can never be.
Ros. Then cannot we be bought: and so adieu;
Twice to your visor, and half once to you!
King. If you deny to dance, let's hold more chat.
Ros. In private then.
King. I am best pleas'd with that.
[*They converse apart.*
Biron. White-handed mistress, one sweet word with thee.
Prin. Honey, and milk, and sugar: there is three.
Biron. Nay then, two treys (an if you grow so nice),
Metheglin, wort, and malmsey;—Well run, dice!
There's half a dozen sweets.
Prin. Seventh sweet, adieu!
Since you can cog, I'll play no more with you.
Biron. One word in secret.
Prin. Let it not be sweet.
Biron. Thou griev'st my gall.
Prin. Gall? bitter.
Biron. Therefore meet.
[*They converse apart.*
Dum. Will you vouchsafe with me to change a word?
Mar. Name it.
Dum. Fair lady,—
Mar. Say you so? Fair lord,—
Take that for your fair lady.
Dum. Please it you,
As much in private, and I'll bid adieu.
[*They converse apart.*
Kath. What, was your visor made without a tongue?
Long. I know the reason, lady, why you ask.
Kath. O, for your reason! quickly, sir; I long.
Long. You have a double tongue within your mask,
And would afford my speechless visor half.
Kath. Veal, quoth the Dutchman; Is not veal a calf?
Long. A calf, fair lady?
Kath. No, a fair lord calf.
Long. Let's part the word.
Kath. No, I'll not be your half:
Take all, and wean it; it may prove an ox.
Long. Look, how you butt yourself in these sharp mocks!
Will you give horns, chaste lady? do not so.
Kath. Then die a calf, before your horns do grow.
Long. One word in private with you, ere I die.
Kath. Bleat softly then, the butcher hears you cry. [*They converse apart.*
Boyet. The tongues of mocking wenches are as keen
As is the razor's edge invisible,
Cutting a smaller hair than may be seen;
Above the sense of sense: so sensible
Seemeth their conference; their conceits have wings,
Fleeter than arrows, bullets, wind, thought, swifter things.
Ros. Not one word more, my maids; break off, break off.
Biron. By heaven, all dry-beaten with pure scoff!
King. Farewell, mad wenches; you have simple wits. [*Exeunt* King, Lords, MOTH, *Musick and* Attendants.
Prin. Twenty adieus, my frozen Muscovites.—
Are these the breed of wits so wonder'd at?
Boyet. Tapers they are, with your sweet breaths puff'd out.
Ros. Well-liking wits they have; gross, gross; fat, fat.
Prin. O poverty in wit, kingly-poor flout!
Will they not, think you, hang themselves to-night?
Or ever, but in visors, show their faces?
This pert Biron was out of countenance quite.
Ros. O! they were all in lamentable cases!
The king was weeping-ripe for a good word.
Prin. Biron did swear himself out of all suit.
Mar. Dumain was at my service, and his sword:
No *point*, quoth I; my servant straight was mute.
Kath. Lord Longaville said, I came o'er his heart:
And trow you, what he call'd me?
Prin. Qualm, perhaps.
Kath. Yes, in good faith.
Prin. Go, sickness, as thou art!
Ros. Well, better wits have worn plain statute-caps.
But will you hear? the king is my love sworn.
Prin. And quick Biron hath plighted faith to me.
Kath. And Longaville was for my service born.
Mar. Dumain is mine, as sure as bark on tree.
Boyet. Madam, and pretty mistresses, give ear:
Immediately they will again be here
In their own shapes; for it can never be,
They will digest this harsh indignity.
Prin. Will they return?
Boyet. They will, they will, God knows;
And leap for joy, though they are lame with blows:
Therefore, change favours; and, when they repair,
Blow like sweet roses in the summer air.
Prin. How blow? how blow? speak to be understood.
Boyet. Fair ladies, mask'd, are roses in their bud:
Dismask'd, their damask sweet commixture shown,
Are angels vailing clouds, or roses blown.
Prin. Avaunt, perplexity! What shall we do,
If they return in their own shapes to woo?
Ros. Good madam, if by me you'll be advis'd,
Let's mock them still, as well known, as disguis'd,
Let us complain to them what fools were here,
Disguis'd like Muscovites, in shapeless gear;
And wonder, what they were; and to what end
Their shallow shows, and prologue vilely penn'd,
And their rough carriage so ridiculous,
Should be presented at our tent to us.
Boyet. Ladies, withdraw; the gallants are at hand.
Prin. Whip to our tents, as roes run over land.
[*Exeunt* Princess, ROS. KATH. *and* MARIA.

Enter the King, BIRON, LONGAVILLE, *and* DUMAIN, *in their proper habits.*

King. Fair sir, God save you! Where is the princess?
Boyet. Gone to her tent: Please it your majesty,
Command me any service to her thither?

King. That she vouchsafe me audience for one word.

Boyet. I will; and so will she, I know, my lord. [*Exit.*

Biron. This fellow pecks up wit, as pigeons peas:
And utters it again when Jove doth please:
He is wit's pedler; and retails his wares
At wakes and wassels, meetings, markets, fairs:
And we that sell by gross, the Lord doth know,
Have not the grace to grace it with such show.
This gallant pins the wenches on his sleeve;
Had he been Adam, he had tempted Eve:
He can carve too, and lisp: Why, this is he,
That kiss'd away his hand in courtesy;
This is the ape of form, monsieur the nice,
That, when he plays at tables, chides the dice
In honourable terms; nay, he can sing
A mean most meanly; and, in ushering,
Mend him who can: the ladies call him, sweet;
The stairs, as he treads on them, kiss his feet:
This is the flower that smiles on every one,
To show his teeth as white as whales bone:
And consciences, that will not die in debt,
Pay him the due of honey-tongued Boyet.

King. A blister on his sweet tongue with my heart,
That put Armado's page out of his part!

Enter the Princess, *usher'd by* BOYET; ROSALINE, MARIA, KATHARINE, *and Attendants.*

Biron. See where it comes!—Behaviour, what wert thou,
Till this man show'd thee? and what art thou now?

King. All hail, sweet madam, and fair time of day!

Prin. Fair, in all hail, is foul, as I conceive.

King. Construe my speeches better, if you may.

Prin. Then wish me better, I will give you leave.

King. We came to visit you; and purpose now
To lead you to our court: vouchsafe it then.

Prin. This field shall hold me: and so hold your vow:
Nor God, nor I, delight in perjur'd men.

King. Rebuke me not for that which you provoke;
The virtue of your eye must break my oath.

Prin. You nick-name virtue: vice you should have spoke:
For virtue's office never breaks men's troth.
Now, by my maiden honour, yet as pure
As the unsullied lily, I protest,
A world of torments though I should endure,
I would not yield to be your house's guest;
So much I hate a breaking-cause to be
Of heavenly oaths, vow'd with integrity.

King. O, you have liv'd in desolation here,
Unseen, unvisited, much to our shame.

Prin. Not so, my lord; it is not so, I swear;
We have had pastimes here, and pleasant game;
A mess of Russians left us but of late.

King. How, madam? Russians?

Prin. Ay, in truth, my lord;
Trim gallants, full of courtship, and of state.

Ros. Madam, speak true:—It is not so, my lord;
My lady (to the manner of the days),
In courtesy, gives undeserving praise.
We four, indeed, confronted here with four
In Russian habit: here they stay'd an hour,
And talk'd apace; and in that hour, my lord,
They did not bless us with one happy word.
I dare not call them fools; but this I think,
When they are thirsty, fools would fain have drink.

Biron. This jest is dry to me.—Fair, gentle sweet,
Your wit makes wise things foolish; when we greet
With eyes best seeing heaven's fiery eye,
By light we lose light: Your capacity
Is of that nature, that to your huge store
Wise things seem foolish, and rich things but poor.

Ros. This proves you wise and rich; for in my eye,—

Biron. I am a fool, and full of poverty.

Ros. But that you take what doth to you belong,
It were a fault to snatch words from my tongue.

Biron. O, I am yours, and all that I possess.

Ros. All the fool mine?

Biron. I cannot give you less.

Ros. Which of the visors was it, that you wore?

Biron. Where? when? what visor? why demand you this?

Ros. There, then, that visor; that superfluous case,
That hid the worse, and show'd the better face.

King. We are descried: they'll mock us now downright.

Dum. Let us confess, and turn it to a jest.

Prin. Amaz'd, my lord? Why looks your highness sad?

Ros. Help, hold his brows! he'll swoon! Why look you pale?
Sea-sick, I think, coming from Muscovy.

Biron. Thus pour the stars down plagues for perjury.
Can any face of brass hold longer out?—
Here stand I, lady; dart thy skill at me;
Bruise me with scorn, confound me with a flout;
Thrust thy sharp wit quite through my ignorance;
Cut me to pieces with thy keen conceit;
And I will wish thee never more to dance,
Nor never more in Russian habit wait.
O! never will I trust to speeches penn'd,
Nor to the motion of a schoolboy's tongue;
Nor ever come in visor to my friend;
Nor woo in rhyme like a blind harper's song;
Taffata phrases, silken terms precise,
Three pil'd hyperboles, spruce affectation,
Figures pedantical; these summer-flies
Have blown me full of maggot ostentation:
I do forswear them, and I here protest,
By this white glove, (how white the hand, God knows!)
Henceforth my wooing mind shall be express'd
In russet yeas, and honest kersey noes:
And, to begin, wench,—so God help me, la!—
My love to thee is sound, sans crack or flaw.

Ros. *Sans* SANS, I pray you.

Biron. Yet I have a trick
Of the old rage:—bear with me, I am sick;
I'll leave it by degrees. Soft, let us see;—
Write, *Lord have mercy on us*, on those three;
They are infected, in their hearts it lies,
They have the plague, and caught it of your eyes:
These lords are visited: you are not free,
For the Lord's tokens on you do I see.

Prin. No, they are free, that gave these tokens to us.

Biron. Our states are forfeit, seek not to undo us.

Ros. It is not so; For how can this be true,
That you stand forfeit, being those that sue?

Biron. Peace; for I will not have to do with you.

Ros. Nor shall not, if I do as I intend.

Biron. Speak for yourselves, my wit is at an end.

King. Teach us, sweet madam, for our rude transgression
Some fair excuse.

Prin. The fairest is confession.
Were you not here, but even now, disguis'd?

King. Madam, I was.

Prin. And were you well advis'd?

King. I was, fair madam.

Prin. When you then were here,
What did you whisper in your lady's ear?

King. That more than all the world I did respect her.
Prin. When she shall challenge this, you will reject her.
King. Upon mine honour, no.
Prin. Peace, peace, forbear;
Your oath once broke, you force not to forswear;
King. Despise me, when I break this oath of mine.
Prin. I will; and therefore keep it:—Rosaline,
What did the Russian whisper in your ear?
Ros. Madam, he swore that he did hold me dear
As precious eyesight; and did value me
Above this world: adding thereto, moreover,
That he would wed me, or else die my lover.
Prin. God give thee joy of him! the noble lord
Most honourably doth uphold his word.
King. What mean you, madam? by my life, my troth,
I never swore this lady such an oath.
Ros. By heaven, you did; and to confirm it plain,
You gave me this: but take it, sir, again.
King. My faith, and this, the princess I did give;
I knew her by this jewel on her sleeve.
Prin. Pardon me, sir, this jewel did she wear;
And lord Biron, I thank him, is my dear:—
What; will you have me, or your pearl again?
Biron. Neither of either; I remit both twain.—
I see the trick on't:—Here was a consent,
(Knowing aforehand of our merriment),
To dash it like a Christmas comedy:
Some carry-tale, some please-man, some slight zany,
Some mumble-news, some trencher-knight, some Dick,—
That smiles his cheek in jeers; and knows the trick
To make my lady laugh, when she's dispos'd,—
Told our intents before: which once disclos'd,
The ladies did change favours; and then we,
Following the signs, woo'd but the sign of she.
Now, to our perjury to add more terror,
We are again forsworn; in will and error.
Much upon this it is:—And might not you, [*To* BOYET.
Forestall our sport, to make us thus untrue?
Do not you know my lady's foot by the squire,
And laugh upon the apple of her eye?
And stand between her back, sir, and the fire,
Holding a trencher, jesting merrily?
You put our page out: Go, you are allow'd;
Die when you will, a smock shall be your shrowd.
You leer upon me, do you? there's an eye,
Wounds like a leaden sword.
Boyet. Full merrily
Hath this brave manage, this career, been run.
Biron. Lo, he is tilting straight! Peace; I have done.

Enter COSTARD.

Welcome, pure wit! thou partest a fair fray.
Cost. O Lord, sir, they would know,
Whether the three worthies shall come in or no.
Biron. What, are there but three?
Cost. No, sir; but it is vara fine,
For every one pursents three.
Biron. And three times thrice is nine.
Cost. Not so, sir; under correction, sir; I hope, it is not so:
You cannot beg us, sir, I can assure you; sir; we know what we know:
I hope, sir, three times thrice, sir,—
Biron. Is not nine.
Cost. Under correction, sir, we know whereuntil it doth amount.
Biron. By Jove, I always took three threes for nine.
Cost. O Lord, sir, it were pity you should get your living by reckoning, sir.
Biron. How much is it?
Cost. O Lord, sir, the parties themselves, the actors, sir, will show whereuntil it doth amount: for my own part, I am, as they say, but to parfect one man,—e'en one poor man; Pompion the great, sir.
Biron. Art thou one of the worthies?
Cost. It pleased them, to think me worthy of Pompion the great: for mine own part, I know not the degree of the worthy; but I am to stand for him.
Biron. Go, bid them prepare.
Cost. We will turn it finely off, sir; we will take some care. [*Exit* COSTARD.
King. Biron, they will shame us, let them not approach.
Biron. We are shame-proof, my lord: and 'tis some policy
To have one show worse than the king's and his company.
King. I say, they shall not come.
Prin. Nay, my good lord, let me o'errule you now;
That sport best pleases, that doth least know how:
Where zeal strives to content, and the contents
Die in the zeal of them which it presents,
Their form confounded makes most form in mirth;
When great things labouring perish in their birth.
Biron. A right description of our sport, my lord.

Enter ARMADO.

Arm. Anointed, I implore so much expense of thy royal sweet breath, as will utter a brace of words.
[ARMADO *converses with the* KING, *and delivers him a paper.*
Prin. Doth this man serve God?
Biron. Why ask you?
Prin. He speaks not like a man of God's making.
Arm. That's all one, my fair, sweet, honey monarch: for, I protest, the schoolmaster is exceeding fantastical; too, too vain; too, too vain: But we will put it, as they say, to *fortuna della guerra.* I wish you the peace of mind, most royal couplement. [*Exit* ARMADO.
King. Here is like to be a good presence of worthies: He presents Hector of Troy; the swain, Pompey the great; the parish curate, Alexander; Armado's page, Hercules; the pedant, Judas Machabæus.
And if these four worthies in their first show thrive,
These four will change habits, and present the other five.
Biron. There is five in the first show.
King. You are deceiv'd, 'tis not so.
Biron. The pedant, the braggart, the hedge-priest, the fool, and the boy:—
A bare throw at novum; and the whole world again,
Cannot prick out five such, take each one in his vein.
King. The ship is under sail, and here she comes amain.
[*Seats brought for the* KING, PRINCESS, *&c.*

Pageant of the Nine Worthies.

Enter COSTARD *arm'd, for* POMPEY.

COST. *I Pompey am,*——
Boyet. You lie, you are not he.
COST. *I Pompey am,*——
Boyet. With libbard's head on knee.
Biron. Well said, old mocker; I must needs be friends with thee.
COST. *I Pompey am, Pompey surnam'd the big,*—
Dum. The great.
Cost. It is great, sir;—*Pompey surnam'd the great;*
That oft in field, with targe and shield, did make my foe to sweat;

And travelling along this coast, I here am come by chance;
And lay my arms before the legs of this sweet lass of France.
If your ladyship would say, *Thanks, Pompey*, I had done.

Prin. Great thanks, great Pompey.

Cost. 'Tis not so much worth; but, I hope, I was perfect: I made a little fault in, *great.*

Biron. My hat to a halfpenny, Pompey proves the best worthy.

Enter NATHANIEL *arm'd, for* Alexander.

Nath. *When in the world I liv'd, I was the world's commander;*
By east, west, north, and south, I spread my conquering might:
My 'scutcheon plain declares that I am Alisander.

Boyet. Your nose says, no, you are not; for it stands too right.

Biron. Your nose smells, no, in this, most tender-smelling knight.

Prin. The conqueror is dismay'd: Proceed, good Alexander.

Nath. *When in the world I liv'd, I was the world's commander;—*

Boyet. Most true, 'tis right; you were so, Alisander.

Biron. Pompey the great,——

Cost. Your servant, and Costard.

Biron. Take away the conqueror, take away Alisander.

Cost. O, sir, [*To* NATH.] you have overthrown Alisander the conqueror! You will be scraped out of the painted cloth for this: your lion, that holds his poll-ax sitting on a close-stool, will be given to A-jax: he will be the ninth worthy. A conqueror, and afeard to speak! run away for shame, Alisander. [NATH. *retires.*] There, an't shall please you; a foolish mild man; an honest man, look you, and soon dash'd! He is a marvellous good neighbour, in sooth; and a very good bowler: but, for Alisander, alas, you see how 'tis;—a little o'erparted:—But there are worthies a coming will speak their mind in some other sort.

Prin. Stand aside, good Pompey.

Enter HOLOFERNES *arm'd, for* Judas, *and* MOTH *arm'd, for* Hercules.

Hol. *Great Hercules is presented by this imp,*
Whose club kill'd Cerberus, that three-headed canus,
And, when he was a babe, a child, a shrimp,
Thus did he strangle serpents in his manus:
Quoniam, *he seemeth in minority;*
Ergo, *I come with this apology.—*
Keep some state in thy *exit*, and vanish. [*Exit* MOTH.

Hol. *Judas I am,—*

Dum. A Judas!

Hol. Not Iscariot, sir.—
Judas I am, ycleped Machabæus.

Dum. Judas Machabæus clipt, is plain Judas.

Biron. A kissing traitor:—How art thou prov'd Judas?

Hol. *Judas I am,—*

Dum. The more shame for you, Judas.

Hol. What mean you, sir?

Boyet. To make Judas hang himself.

Hol. Begin, sir; you are my elder.

Biron. Well follow'd: Judas was hang'd on an elder.

Hol. I will not be put out of countenance.

Biron. Because thou hast no face.

Hol. What is this?

Boyet. A cittern head.

Dum. The head of a bodkin.

Biron. A death's face in a ring.

Long. The face of an old Roman coin, scarce seen.

Boyet. The pummel of Cæsar's faulchion.

Dum. The carv'd-bone face on a flask.

Biron. St. George's half-cheek in a brooch.

Dum. Ay, and in a brooch of lead.

Biron. Ay, and worn in the cap of a tooth-drawer:
And now, forward; for we have put thee in countenance.

Hol. You have put me out of countenance.

Biron. False: we have given thee faces.

Hol. But you have out-fac'd them all.

Biron. An thou wert a lion, we would do so.

Boyet. Therefore, as he is, an ass, let him go.
And so adieu, sweet Jude! nay, why dost thou stay?

Dum. For the latter end of his name.

Biron. For the ass to the Jude; give it him:—Jud-as, away.

Hol. This is not generous, not gentle, not humble.

Boyet. A light for monsieur Judas: it grows dark, he may stumble.

Prin. Alas, poor Machabæus, how hath he been baited!

Enter ARMADO *arm'd, for* Hector.

Biron. Hide thy head, Achilles; here comes Hector in arms.

Dum. Though my mocks come home by me, I will now be merry.

King. Hector was but a Trojan in respect of this.

Boyet. But is this Hector?

Dum. I think, Hector was not so clean-timber'd.

Long. His leg is too big for Hector.

Dum. More calf, certain.

Boyet. No; he is best indued in the small.

Biron. This cannot be Hector.

Dum. He's a god or a painter; for he makes faces.

Arm. *The armipotent Mars, of lances the almighty,*
Gave Hector a gift,—

Dum. A gilt nutmeg.

Biron. A lemon.

Long. Stuck with cloves.

Dum. No, cloven.

Arm. Peace.
The armipotent Mars, of lances the almighty,
Gave Hector a gift, the heir of Ilion;
A man so breath'd, that certain he would fight, yea
From morn till night, out of his pavilion.
I am that flower,—

Dum. That mint.

Long. That columbine.

Arm. Sweet lord Longaville, rein thy tongue.

Long. I must rather give it the rein; for it runs against Hector.

Dum. Ay, and Hector's a greyhound.

Arm. The sweet war-man is dead and rotten; sweet chucks, beat not the bones of the buried: when he breath'd, he was a man—But I will forward with my device: Sweet royalty, [*to the* Princess.] bestow on me the sense of hearing. [BIRON *whispers* COSTARD.

Prin. Speak, brave Hector; we are much delighted.

Arm. I do adore thy sweet grace's slipper.

Boyet. Loves her by the foot.

Dum. He may not by the yard.

Arm. *This Hector far surmounted Hannibal,—*

Cost. The party is gone, fellow Hector, she is gone; she is two months on her way.

Arm. What meanest thou?

Cost. 'Faith, unless you play the honest Trojan, the poor wench is cast away: she's quick; the child brags in her belly already; 'tis yours.

Arm. Dost thou infamonize me among potentates? thou shalt die.

Cost. Then shall Hector be whipp'd, for Jaquenetta that is quick by him; and hang'd, for Pompey that is dead by him.

Dum. Most rare Pompey!

Boyet. Renowned Pompey!
Biron. Greater than great, great, great, great Pompey! Pompey the huge!
Dum. Hector trembles.
Biron. Pompey is moved:—More Ates, more Ates; stir them on! stir them on!
Dum. Hector will challenge him.
Biron. Ay, if he have no more man's blood in's belly than will sup a flea.
Arm. By the north pole, I do challenge thee.
Cost. I will not fight with a pole, like a northern man; I'll slash; I'll do it by the sword:—I pray you, let me borrow my arms again.
Dum. Room for the incensed worthies.
Cost. I'll do it in my shirt.
Dum. Most resolute Pompey!
Moth. Master, let me take you a buttonhole lower.
Do you not see, Pompey is uncasing for the combat?
What mean you? you will lose your reputation.
Arm. Gentlemen, and soldiers, pardon me;
I will not combat in my shirt.
Dum. You may not deny it; Pompey hath made the challenge.
Arm. Sweet bloods, I both may and will.
Biron. What reason have you for't?
Arm. The naked truth of it is, I have no shirt; I go woolward for penance.
Boyet. True, and it was enjoin'd him in Rome for want of linen: since when, I'll be sworn, he wore none, but a dish-clout of Jaquenetta's; and that 'a wears next his heart for a favour.

Enter MERCADE.

Mer. God save you, madam.
Prin. Welcome, Mercade;
But that thou interrupt'st our merriment.
Mer. I am sorry, madam; for the news I bring,
Is heavy in my tongue. The king your father—
Prin. Dead, for my life.
Mer. Even so; my tale is told.
Biron. Worthies, away; the scene begins to cloud.
Arm. For mine own part, I breathe free breath: I have seen the day of wrong through the little hole of discretion, and I will right myself like a soldier. [*Exeunt Worthies.*
King. How fares your majesty?
Prin. Boyet, prepare; I will away to-night.
King. Madam, not so; I do beseech you, stay.
Prin. Prepare, I say.—I thank you, gracious lords,
For all your fair endeavours; and entreat,
Out of a new-sad soul, that you vouchsafe
In your rich wisdom, to excuse, or hide,
The liberal opposition of our spirits:
If over-boldly we have borne ourselves
In the converse of breath, your gentleness
Was guilty of it.—Farewell, worthy lord!
A heavy heart bears not an humble tongue:
Excuse me so, coming so short of thanks
For my great suit so easily obtain'd.
King. The extreme parts of time extremely form
All causes to the purpose of his speed;
And often, at his very loose, decides
That which long process could not arbitrate:
And though the mourning brow of progeny
Forbid the smiling courtesy of love,
The holy suit which fain it would convince;
Yet, since love's argument was first on foot,
Let not the cloud of sorrow justle it
From what it purpos'd; since, to wail friends lost,
Is not by much so wholesome, profitable,
As to rejoice at friends but newly found.
Prin. I understand you not; my griefs are double.
Biron. Honest plain words best pierce the ear of grief;
And by these badges understand the king.
For your fair sakes have we neglected time,
Play'd foul play with our oaths; your beauty, ladies,
Hath much deform'd us, fashioning our humours
Even to the opposed end of our intents;
And what in us hath seem'd ridiculous,—
As love is full of unbefitting strains;
All wanton as a child, skipping, and vain;
Form'd by the eye, and therefore, like the eye,
Full of strange shapes, of habits, and of forms,
Varying in subjects as the eye doth roll
To every varied object in his glance:
Which party-coated presence of loose love
Put on by us, if, in your heavenly eyes,
Have misbecom'd our oaths and gravities,
Those heavenly eyes, that look into these faults,
Suggested us to make: Therefore, ladies,
Our love being yours, the error that love makes
Is likewise yours: we to ourselves prove false,
By being once false for ever to be true
To those that make us both,—fair ladies, you:
And even that falsehood, in itself a sin,
Thus purifies itself, and turns to grace.
Prin. We have receiv'd your letters, full of love;
Your favours, the ambassadors of love;
And, in our maiden council, rated them
At courtship, pleasant jest, and courtesy,
As bombast, and as lining to the time:
But more devout than this, in our respects,
Have we not been; and therefore met your loves
In their own fashion, like a merriment.
Dum. Our letters, madam, show'd much more than jest.
Long. So did our looks.
Ros. We did not quote them so.
King. Now, at the latest minute of the hour,
Grant us your loves.
Prin. A time, methinks, too short
To make a world-without-end bargain in:
No, no, my lord, your grace is perjur'd much,
Full of dear guiltiness; and, therefore this,—
If for my love (as there is no such cause)
You will do aught, this shall you do for me:
Your oath I will not trust; but go with speed
To some forlorn and naked hermitage,
Remote from all the pleasures of the world;
There stay, until the twelve celestial signs
Have brought about their annual reckoning:
If this austere insociable life
Change not your offer made in heat of blood;
If frosts, and fasts, hard lodging, and thin weeds,
Nip not the gaudy blossoms of your love,
But that it bear this trial, and last love;
Then, at the expiration of the year,
Come challenge, challenge me by these deserts,
And, by this virgin palm, now kissing thine,
I will be thine; and, till that instant, shut
My woful self up in a mourning house;
Raining the tears of lamentation,
For the remembrance of my father's death.
If this thou do deny, let our hands part;
Neither entitled in the other's heart.
King. If this, or more than this, I would deny,
To flatter up these powers of mine with rest,
The sudden hand of death close up mine eye!
Hence ever then my heart is in thy breast.
Biron. And what to me, my love? and what to me?
Ros. You must be purged too, your sins are rank;
You are attaint with faults and perjury;
Therefore, if you my favour mean to get,
A twelvemonth shall you spend, and never rest,
But seek the weary beds of people sick.
Dum. But what to me, my love? but what to me?
Kath. A wife!—A beard, fair health, and honesty;
With three-fold love I wish you all these three.
Dum. O, shall I say, I thank you, gentle wife?

Kath. Not so, my lord;—a twelvemonth and a day
I'll mark no words that smooth-fac'd wooers say:
Come when the king doth to my lady come,
Then, if I have much love, I'll give you some.
Dum. I'll serve thee true and faithfully till then.
Kath. Yet swear not, lest you be forsworn again.
Long. What says Maria?
Mar. At the twelvemonth's end,
I'll change my black gown for a faithful friend.
Long. I'll stay with patience; but the time is long.
Mar. The liker you; few taller are so young.
Biron. Studies my lady? mistress, look on me,
Behold the window of mine heart, mine eye,
What humble suit attends thy answer there:
Impose some service on me for thy love.
Ros. Oft have I heard of you, my lord Biron,
Before I saw you: and the world's large tongue
Proclaims you for a man replete with mocks;
Full of comparisons and wounding flouts;
Which you on all estates will execute,
That lie within the mercy of your wit:
To weed this wormwood from your fruitful brain;
And, therewithal, to win me, if you please
(Without the which, I am not to be won),
You shall this twelvemonth term from day to day
Visit the speechless sick, and still converse
With groaning wretches; and your task shall be,
With all the fierce endeavour of your wit,
To enforce the pained impotent to smile.
Biron. To move wild laughter in the throat of death?
It cannot be; it is impossible:
Mirth cannot move a soul in agony.
Ros. Why, that's the way to choke a gibing spirit,
Whose influence is begot of that loose grace,
Which shallow laughing hearers give to fools:
A jest's prosperity lies in the ear
Of him that hears it, never in the tongue
Of him that makes it: then, if sickly ears,
Deaf'd with the clamours of their own dear groans,
Will hear your idle scorns, continue then,
And I will have you, and that fault withal;
But, if they will not, throw away that spirit,
And I shall find you empty of that fault,
Right joyful of your reformation.
Biron. A twelvemonth? well, befall what will befall,
I'll jest a twelvemonth in an hospital.
Prin. Ay, sweet my lord; and so I take my leave. [*To the* King.
King. No, madam; we will bring you on your way.
Biron. Our wooing doth not end like an old play;
Jack hath not Jill: these ladies' courtesy
Might well have made our sport a comedy.
King. Come, sir, it wants a twelvemonth and a day.
And then 'twill end.
Biron. That's too long for a play.

Enter ARMADO.

Arm. Sweet majesty, vouchsafe me,—
Prin. Was not that Hector?
Dum. The worthy knight of Troy.
Arm. I will kiss thy royal finger, and take leave: I am a votary; I have vowed to Jaquenetta to hold the plough for her sweet love three years. But, most esteemed greatness, will you hear the dialogue that the two learned men have compiled, in praise of the owl and the cuckoo? it should have followed in the end of our show.
King. Call them forth quickly, we will do so.
Arm. Holla! approach.

Enter HOLOFERNES, NATHANIEL, MOTH, COSTARD, *and others.*

This side is Hiems, winter; this Ver, the spring; the one maintain'd by the owl, the other by the cuckoo. Ver, begin.

SONG.

I.

Spring. *When daisies pied, and violets blue,*
And lady-smocks all silver-white,
And Cuckoo-buds of yellow hue,
Do paint the meadows with delight,
The cuckoo then, on every tree,
Mocks married men, for thus sings he,
Cuckoo;
Cuckoo, cuckoo,—O word of fear,
Unpleasing to a married ear!

II.

When shepherds pipe on oaten straws,
And merry larks are ploughmen's clocks,
When turtles tread, and rooks, and daws,
And maidens bleach their summer smocks,
The cuckoo, then, on every tree,
Mocks married men, for thus sings he,
Cuckoo;
Cuckoo, cuckoo,—O word of fear,
Unpleasing to a married ear!

III.

Winter. *When icicles hang by the wall,*
And Dick *the shepherd blows his nail,*
And Tom *bears logs into the hall,*
And milk comes frozen home in pail,
When blood is nipp'd, and ways be foul,
Then nightly sings the staring owl,
To-who;
To-whit, to-who, a merry note,
While greasy Joan *doth keel the pot.*

IV.

When all aloud the wind doth blow,
And coughing drowns the parson's saw,
And birds sit brooding in the snow,
And Marian's *nose looks red and raw,*
When roasted crabs hiss in the bowl,
Then nightly sings the staring owl,
To-who;
To-whit, to-who, a merry note,
While greasy Joan *doth keel the pot.*

Arm. The words of Mercury are harsh after the songs of Apollo. You, that way; we, this way. [*Exeunt.*

MERCHANT OF VENICE.

PERSONS REPRESENTED.

DUKE *of* Venice.
Prince *of* Morocco, } *Suitors to Portia.*
Prince *of* Arragon, }
ANTONIO, *the Merchant of* Venice.
BASSANIO, *his Friend.*
SALANIO, }
SALARINO, } *Friends to* Antonio *and* Bassanio.
GRATIANO, }
LORENZO, *in love with* Jessica.
SHYLOCK, *a Jew.*
TUBAL, *a Jew, his Friend.*
LAUNCELOT GOBBO, *a Clown, Servant to* Shylock.
OLD GOBBO, *Father to* Launcelot.
SALERIO, *a Messenger from* Venice.
LEONARDO, *Servant to* Bassanio.
BALTHAZAR, } *Servants to* Portia.
STEPHANO, }

PORTIA, *a rich Heiress.*
NERISSA, *her Waiting-Maid.*
JESSICA, *Daughter to* Shylock.

Magnificoes of Venice, Officers *of the Court of Justice*, Jailer, Servants, *and other* Attendants.

SCENE,—*partly at* Venice, *and partly at* Belmont, *the Seat of* Portia, *on the Continent.*

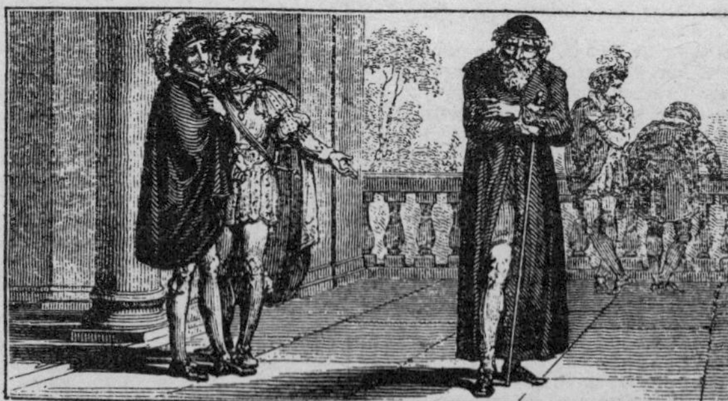

ACT I.

SCENE I. Venice. *A Street.*

Enter ANTONIO, SALARINO, *and* SALANIO.

Ant. IN sooth, I know not why I am so sad;
It wearies me; you say, it wearies you;
But how I caught it, found it, or came by it,
What stuff 'tis made of, whereof it is born,
I am to learn;
And such a want-wit sadness makes of me,
That I have much ado to know myself.
Salar. Your mind is tossing on the ocean;
There, where your argosies with portly sail,—
Like signiors and rich burghers on the flood,
Or, as it were, the pageants of the sea,—
Do overpeer the petty traffickers,
That curt'sy to them, do them reverence,
As they fly by them with their woven wings.
Salan. Believe me, sir, had I such venture forth,
The better part of my affections would
Be with my hopes abroad. I should be still
Plucking the grass, to know where sits the wind;
Peering in maps, for ports, and piers, and roads;
And every object, that might make me fear
Misfortune to my ventures, out of doubt,
Would make me sad.
Salar. My wind, cooling my broth,
Would blow me to an ague, when I thought
What harm a wind too great might do at sea.
I should not see the sandy hour-glass run,
But I should think of shallows and of flats;
And see my wealthy Andrew dock'd in sand,
Vailing her high-top lower than her ribs,
To kiss her burial. Should I go to church,
And see the holy edifice of stone,
And not bethink me straight of dangerous rocks;
Which touching but my gentle vessel's side,
Would scatter all her spices on the stream;
Enrobe the roaring waters with my silks;
And, in a word, but even now worth this,
And now worth nothing? Shall I have the thought
To think on this; and shall I lack the thought,
That such a thing, bechanc'd, would make me sad?
But, tell not me; I know, Antonio
Is sad to think upon his merchandise.
Ant. Believe me, no: I thank my fortune for it,
My ventures are not in one bottom trusted,
Nor to one place; nor is my whole estate
Upon the fortune of this present year:
Therefore, my merchandise makes me not sad.
Salan. Why then you are in love.
Ant. Fye, fye
Salan. Not in love neither? Then let's say, you are sad,
Because you are not merry: and 'twere as easy
For you, to laugh, and leap, and say, you are merry,
Because you are not sad. Now, by two-headed Janus,
Nature hath fram'd strange fellows in her time;
Some that will evermore peep through their eyes,
And laugh, like parrots at a bagpiper;
And other of such vinegar aspect,
That they'll not show their teeth in way of smile,
Though Nestor swear the jest be laughable.

Enter BASSANIO, LORENZO, *and* GRATIANO.

Salan. Here comes Bassanio, your most noble kinsman,

Gratiano, and Lorenzo: Fare you well;
We leave you now with better company.
Salar. I would have staid till I had made you merry,
If worthier friends had not prevented me.
Ant. Your worth is very dear in my regard.
I take it, your own business calls on you,
And you embrace the occasion to depart.
Salar. Good morrow, my good lords.
Bass. Good signiors both, when shall we laugh? Say, when?
You grow exceeding strange: Must it be so?
Salar. We'll make our leisures to attend on yours. [*Exeunt* SALAR. *and* SALAN.
Lor. My lord Bassanio, since you have found Antonio,
We two will leave you; but, at dinner time,
I pray you, have in mind where we must meet.
Bass. I will not fail you.
Gra. You look not well, signior Antonio;
You have too much respect upon the world:
They lose it, that do buy it with much care.
Believe me you are marvellously chang'd.
Ant. I hold the world but as the world, Gratiano;
A stage, where every man must play a part,
And mine a sad one.
Gra. Let me play the fool:
With mirth and laughter let old wrinkles come;
And let my liver rather heat with wine,
Than my heart cool with mortifying groans.
Why should a man, whose blood is warm within,
Sit like his grandsire cut in alabaster?
Sleep when he wakes? and creep into the jaundice
By being peevish? I tell thee what, Antonio,—
I love thee, and it is my love that speaks;—
There are a sort of men, whose visages
Do cream and mantle, like a standing pond;
And do a wilful stillness entertain,
With purpose to be dress'd in an opinion
Of wisdom, gravity, profound conceit;
As who should say, *I am Sir Oracle,*
And, when I ope my lips, let no dog bark!
O, my Antonio, I do know of these,
That therefore only are reputed wise,
For saying nothing; who, I am very sure,
If they should speak, would almost damn those ears,
Which, hearing them, would call their brothers fools.
I'll tell thee more of this another time:
But fish not, with this melancholy bait,
For this fool's gudgeon, this opinion.—
Come, good Lorenzo:—Fare ye well a while;
I'll end my exhortation after dinner.
Lor. Well, we will leave you then till dinner time:
I must be one of these same dumb wise men,
For Gratiano never lets me speak.
Gra. Well, keep me company but two years more,
Thou shalt not know the sound of thine own tongue.
Ant. Farewell: I'll grow a talker for this gear.
Gra. Thanks, i'faith; for silence is only commendable
In a neat'stongue dried, and a maid not vendible.
[*Exeunt* GRA. *and* LOR.
Ant. Is that any thing now?
Bass. Gratiano speaks an infinite deal of nothing more than any man in all Venice: His reasons are as two grains of wheat hid in two bushels of chaff; you shall seek all day ere you find them; and, when you have them, they are not worth the search.
Ant. Well; tell me now, what lady is this same
To whom you swore a secret pilgrimage,
That you to-day promis'd to tell me of?
Bass. 'Tis not unknown to you, Antonio,
How much I have disabled mine estate,
By something showing a more swelling port
Than my faint means would grant continuance;
Nor do I now make moan to be abridg'd
From such a noble rate; but my chief care
Is, to come fairly off from the great debts,
Wherein my time, something too prodigal,
Hath left me gag'd: To you, Antonio,
I owe the most, in money and in love;
And from your love I have a warranty
To unburthen all my plots, and purposes,
How to get clear of all the debts I owe.
Ant. I pray you, good Bassanio, let me know it;
And, if it stand, as you yourself still do,
Within the eye of honour, be assur'd,
My purse, my person, my extremest means,
Lie all unlock'd to your occasions.
Bass. In my school-days, when I had lost one shaft,
I shot his fellow of the selfsame flight
The selfsame way, with more advised watch,
To find the other forth; and, by advent'ring both,
I oft found both: I urge this childhood proof,
Because what follows is pure innocence.
I owe you much; and, like a wilful youth,
That which I owe is lost: but if you please
To shoot another arrow that self way
Which you did shoot the first, I do not doubt,
As I will watch the aim, or to find both,
Or bring your latter hazard back again,
And thankfully rest debtor for the first.
Ant. You know me well; and herein spend but time,
To wind about my love with circumstance;
And, out of doubt, you do me now more wrong,
In making question of my uttermost,
Than if you had made waste of all I have:
Then do but say to me what I should do,
That in your knowledge may by me be done,
And I am prest unto it: therefore, speak.
Bass. In Belmont is a lady richly left,
And she is fair, and, fairer than that word,
Of wondrous virtues: sometimes from her eyes
I did receive fair speechless messages:
Her name is Portia; nothing undervalued
To Cato's daughter, Brutus' Portia.
Nor is the wide world ignorant of her worth;
For the four winds blow in from every coast
Renowned suitors: and her sunny locks
Hang on her temples like a golden fleece;
Which makes her seat of Belmont, Colchos' strand,
And many Jasons come in quest of her.
O my Antonio, had I but the means
To hold a rival place with one of them,
I have a mind presages me such thrift,
That I should questionless be fortunate.
Ant. Thou know'st, that all my fortunes are at sea;
Neither have I money, nor commodity
To raise a present sum: therefore go forth,
Try what my credit can in Venice do;
That shall be rack'd, even to the uttermost,
To furnish thee to Belmont, to fair Portia.
Go, presently inquire, and so will I,
Where money is; and I no question make,
To have it of my trust, or for my sake. [*Exeunt.*

SCENE II. Belmont. *A Room in* Portia's *House.*

Enter PORTIA *and* NERISSA.

Por. By my troth, Nerissa, my little body is aweary of this great world.
Ner. You would be, sweet madam, if your miseries were in the same abundance as your good fortunes are: And yet, for aught I see, they are as sick, that surfeit with too much, as they that starve with nothing: It is no mean happiness therefore to be seated in the mean; superfluity comes sooner by white hairs, but competency lives longer.
Por. Good sentences, and well pronounced.
Ner. They would be better, if well followed.

Por. If to do were as easy as to know what were good to do, chapels had been churches, and poor men's cottages princes' palaces. It is a good divine that follows his own instructions: I can easier teach twenty what were good to be done, than be one of the twenty to follow mine own teaching. The brain may devise laws for the blood; but a hot temper leaps over a cold decree; such a hare is madness the youth, to skip o'er the meshes of good counsel the cripple. But this reasoning is not in the fashion to choose me a husband:—O me, the word choose! I may neither choose whom I would, nor refuse whom I dislike; so is the will of a living daughter curb'd by the will of a dead father: Is it not hard, Nerissa, that I cannot choose one, nor refuse none?

Ner. Your father was ever virtuous; and holy men, at their death, have good inspirations; therefore, the lottery, that he hath devised in these three chests, of gold, silver, and lead (whereof who chooses his meaning, chooses you), will, no doubt, never be chosen by any rightly, but one who you shall rightly love. But what warmth is there in your affection towards any of these princely suitors that are already come?

Por. I pray thee over-name them; and as thou namest them, I will describe them; and, according to my description level at my affection.

Ner. First, there is the Neapolitan prince.

Por. Ay, that's a colt, indeed, for he doth nothing but talk of his horse; and he makes it a great appropriation to his own good parts, that he can shoe him himself: I am much afraid, my lady his mother play'd false with a smith.

Ner. Then, is there the county Palatine.

Por. He doth nothing but frown; as who should say, *An, if you will not have me, choose;* he hears merry tales, and smiles not: I fear, he will prove the weeping philosopher when he grows old, being so full of unmannerly sadness in his youth. I had rather be married to a death's head with a bone in his mouth, than to either of these. God defend me from these two!

Ner. How say you by the French lord, Monsieur Le Bon?

Por. God made him, and therefore let him pass for a man. In truth, I know it is a sin to be a mocker; But, he! why, he hath a horse better than the Neapolitan's; a better bad habit of frowning than the count Palatine: he is every man in no man: if a throstle sing, he falls straight a capering; he will fence with his own shadow: If I should marry him, I should marry twenty husbands: if he would despise me, I would forgive him; for if he love me to madness, I shall never requite him.

Ner. What say you then to Faulconbridge, the young baron of England?

Por. You know, I say nothing to him; for he understands not me, nor I him: he hath neither Latin, French, nor Italian; and you will come into the court and swear, that I have a poor penny-worth in the English. He is a proper man's picture; but, alas! who can converse with a dumb show? How oddly he is suited! I think, he bought his doublet in Italy, his round hose in France, his bonnet in Germany, and his behaviour every where.

Ner. What think you of the Scottish lord, his neighbour?

Por. That he hath a neighbourly charity in him; for he borrowed a box of the ear of the Englishman, and swore he would pay him again, when he was able: I think, the Frenchman became his surety, and sealed under for another.

Ner. How like you the young German, the Duke of Saxony's nephew?

Por. Very vilely in the morning, when he is sober; and most vilely in the afternoon, when he is drunk: when he is best, he is a little worse than a man; and when he is worst, he is little better than a beast: an the worst fall that ever fell, I hope, I shall make shift to go without him.

Ner. If he should offer to choose, and choose the right casket, you should refuse to perform your father's will, if you should refuse to accept him.

Por. Therefore, for fear of the worst, I pray thee, set a deep glass of Rhenish wine on the contrary casket: for, if the devil be within, and that temptation without, I know he will choose it. I will do any thing, Nerissa, ere I will be married to a spunge.

Ner. You need not fear, lady, the having any of these lords; they have acquainted me with their determinations: which is indeed, to return to their home, and to trouble you with no more suit; unless you may be won by some other sort than your father's imposition, depending on the caskets.

Por. If I live to be as old as Sibylla, I will die as chaste as Diana, unless I be obtained by the manner of my father's will; I am glad this parcel of wooers are so reasonable; for there is not one among them but I dote on his very absence, and I pray God grant them a fair departure.

Ner. Do you not remember, lady, in your father's time, a Venetian, a scholar, and a soldier, that came hither in company of the Marquis of Montferrat?

Por. Yes, yes, it was Bassanio; as I think, so was he called.

Ner. True, madam; he, of all the men that ever my foolish eyes looked upon, was the best deserving a fair lady.

Por. I remember him well; and I remember him worthy of thy praise.—How now! what news?

Enter a Servant.

Serv. The four strangers seek for you, madam, to take their leave: and there is a fore-runner come from a fifth, the Prince of Morocco; who brings word, the prince, his master, will be here to-night.

Por. If I could bid the fifth welcome with so good heart as I can bid the other four farewell, I should be glad of his approach: if he have the condition of a saint, and the complexion of a devil, I had rather he should shrive me than wive me.—Come, Nerissa.—Sirrah, go before.—Whiles we shut the gate upon one wooer, another knocks at the door. [*Exeunt.*

SCENE III. Venice. *A public Place.*

Enter BASSANIO *and* SHYLOCK.

Shy. Three thousand ducats,—well.

Bass. Ay, sir, for three months.

Shy. For three months,—well.

Bass. For the which, as I told you, Antonio shall be bound.

Shy. Antonio shall become bound,—well.

Bass. May you stead me? Will you pleasure me? Shall I know your answer?

Shy. Three thousand ducats, for three months, and Antonio bound.

Bass. Your answer to that.

Shy. Antonio is a good man.

Bass. Have you heard any imputation to the contrary?

Shy. Ho, no, no, no, no;—my meaning, in saying he is a good man, is to have you understand me, that he is sufficient: yet his means are in supposition: he hath an argosy bound to Tripolis, another to the Indies; I understand moreover upon the Rialto, he hath a third at Mexico, a fourth for England,——and other ventures he hath, squander'd abroad: But ships are but boards, sailors but men: there be land-rats, and water-rats, water-thieves, and land-thieves; I mean, pirates; and then, there is the peril of waters, winds, and rocks: The man is, notwithstanding, sufficient;—three thousand ducats;—I think, I may take his bond.

Bass. Be assured you may.

Shy. I will be assured I may; and that I may be assured I will bethink me: May I speak with Antonio?

Bass. If it please you to dine with us.

Shy. Yes, to smell pork; to eat of the habitation which your prophet, the Nazarite, conjured the devil into: I will buy with you, sell with you, talk with you, walk with you, and so following; but I will not eat with you, drink with you, nor pray with you. What news on the Rialto?—Who is he comes here?

Enter ANTONIO.

Bass. This is signior Antonio.

Shy. [*Aside.*] How like a fawning publican he looks!
I hate him for he is a Christian:
But more, for that, in low simplicity,
He lends out money gratis, and brings down
The rate of usance here with us in Venice.
If I can catch him once upon the hip,
I will feed fat the ancient grudge I bear him.
He hates our sacred nation; and he rails,
Even there where merchants most do congregate,
On me, my bargains, and my well-won thrift,
Which he calls interest: Cursed be my tribe,
If I forgive him!

Bass. Shylock, do you hear?

Shy. I am debating of my present store;
And, by the near guess of my memory,
I cannot instantly raise up the gross
Of full three thousand ducats: What of that?
Tubal, a wealthy Hebrew of my tribe,
Will furnish me: But soft; How many months
Do you desire?—Rest you fair, good signior; [*To* ANTONIO.
Your worship was the last man in our mouths.

Ant. Shylock, albeit I neither lend nor borrow,
By taking, nor by giving of excess,
Yet, to supply the ripe wants of my friend,
I'll break a custom:—Is he yet possess'd,
How much you would?

Shy. Ay, ay, three thousand ducats.

Ant. And for three months.

Shy. I had forgot,—three months, you told me so.
Well then, your bond; and let me see,——But hear you;
Methought, you said, you neither lend, nor borrow,
Upon advantage.

Ant. I do never use it.

Shy. When Jacob graz'd his uncle Laban's sheep,
This Jacob from our holy Abraham was
(As his wise mother wrought in his behalf,)
The third possessor; ay, he was the third.

Ant. And what of him? did he take interest?

Shy. No, not take interest; not, as you would say,
Directly interest: mark what Jacob did.
When Laban and himself were compromis'd,
That all the eanlings which were streak'd, and pied,
Should fall as Jacob's hire; the ewes, being rank
In the end of autumn turned to the rams:
And when the work of generation was
Between these woolly breeders in the act,
The skilful shepherd peel'd me certain wands,
And in the doing of the deed of kind,
He stuck them up before the fulsome ewes;
Who, then conceiving, did in eaning time
Fall party-colour'd lambs, and those were Jacob's.
This was a way to thrive, and he was blest;
And thrift is blessing, if men steal it not.

Ant. This was a venture, sir, that Jacob serv'd for;
A thing not in his power to bring to pass,
But sway'd, and fashion'd, by the hand of heaven.
Was this inserted to make interest good?
Or is your gold and silver, ewes and rams?

Shy. I cannot tell; I make it breed as fast:—
But note me, signior.

Ant. Mark you this, Bassanio,
The devil can cite scripture for his purpose.
An evil soul, producing holy witness,
Is like a villain with a smiling cheek;
A goodly apple rotten at the heart;
O, what a goodly outside falsehood hath!

Shy. Three thousand ducats,—'tis a good round sum.
Three months from twelve, then let me see the rate.

Ant. Well, Shylock, shall we be beholden to you?

Shy. Signior Antonio, many a time and oft,
In the Rialto you have rated me
About my monies, and my usances:
Still have I borne it with a patient shrug;
For sufferance is the badge of all our tribe:
You call me—misbeliever, cut-throat dog,
And spit upon my Jewish gaberdine,
And all for use of that which is mine own.
Well then, it now appears, you need my help:
Go to then; you come to me, and you say,
Shylock, we would have monies; You say so;
You, that did void your rheum upon my beard,
And foot me, as you spurn a stranger cur
Over your threshold; monies is your suit.
What shall I say to you? Should I not say,
Hath a dog money; is it possible,
A cur can lend three thousand ducats? or
Shall I bend low, and in a bondman's key,
With 'bated breath, and whispering humbleness,
Say this,——
Fair sir, you spit on me on Wednesday last;
You spurn'd me such a day; another time
You call'd me—dog; and for these courtesies
I'll lend you thus much monies?

Ant. I am as like to call thee so again,
To spit on thee again, to spurn thee too.
If thou wilt lend this money, lend it not
As to thy friends; (for when did friendship take
A breed for barren metal of his friend?)
But lend it rather to thine enemy;
Who, if he break, thou may'st with better face
Exact the penalty.

Shy. Why, look you, how you storm!
I would be friends with you, and have your love,
Forget the shames that you have stain'd me with,
Supply your present wants, and take no doit
Of usance for my monies, and you'll not hear me:
This is kind I offer.

Ant. This were kindness.

Shy. This kindness will I show:—
Go with me to a notary, seal me there
Your single bond; and, in a merry sport,
If you repay me not on such a day,
In such a place, such sum, or sums, as are
Express'd in the condition, let the forfeit
Be nominated for an equal pound
Of your fair flesh, to be cut off and taken
In what part of your body pleaseth me.

Ant. Content, in faith; I'll seal to such a bond,
And say, there is much kindness in the Jew.

Bass. You shall not seal to such a bond for me,
I'll rather dwell in my necessity.

Ant. Why, fear not, man; I will not forfeit it;
Within these two months, that's a month before
This bond expires, I do expect return
Of thrice three times the value of this bond.

Shy. O father Abraham, what these Christians are;
Whose own hard dealings teaches them suspect
The thoughts of others! Pray you, tell me this;
If he should break his day, what should I gain
By the exaction of the forfeiture?
A pound of man's flesh, taken from a man,
Is not so estimable, profitable neither,
As flesh of muttons, beefs, or goats. I say,

To buy his favour, I extend this friendship:
If he will take it, so; if not, adieu;
And, for my love, I pray you wrong me not.

Ant. Yes, Shylock, I will seal unto this bond.

Shy. Then meet me forthwith at the notary's;
Give him direction for this merry bond,
And I will go and purse the ducats straight;
See to my house, left in the fearful guard
Of an unthrifty knave; and presently
I will be with you. [*Exit.*

Ant. Hie thee, gentle Jew.
This Hebrew will turn Christian; he grows kind.

Bass. I like not fair terms, and a villain's mind.

Ant. Come on: in this there can be no dismay,
My ships come home a month before the day. [*Exeunt.*

ACT II.

SCENE I. Belmont.

A Room in Portia's *House. Flourish of Cornets.*

Enter the Prince of Morocco, *and his Train;* PORTIA, NERISSA, *and other of her* Attendants.

Mor. Mislike me not for my complexion,
The shadow'd livery of the burnish'd sun,
To whom I am a neighbour, and near bred.
Bring me the fairest creature northward born,
Where Phœbus' fire scarce thaws the icicles,
And let us make incision for your love,
To prove whose blood is reddest, his, or mine.
I tell thee, lady, this aspect of mine
Hath fear'd the valiant; by my love, I swear,
The best-regarded virgins of our clime
Have lov'd it too: I would not change this hue,
Except to steal your thoughts, my gentle queen.

Por. In terms of choice I am not solely led
By nice direction of a maiden's eyes;
Besides, the lottery of my destiny
Bars me the right of voluntary choosing:
But, if my father had not scanted me,
And hedg'd me by his wit, to yield myself
His wife, who wins me by that means I told you,
Yourself, renowned prince, then stood as fair,
As any comer I have look'd on yet,
For my affection.

Mor. Even for that I thank you;
Therefore, I pray you, lead me to the caskets,
To try my fortune. By this scimitar,—
That slew the Sophy, and a Persian prince,
That won three fields of Sultan Solyman,—
I would out-stare the sternest eyes that look,
Out-brave the heart most daring on the earth,
Pluck the young sucking cubs from the she bear,
Yea, mock the lion when he roars for prey,
To win thee, lady: But, alas the while!
If Hercules, and Lichas, play at dice
Which is the better man, the greater throw
May turn by fortune from the weaker hand:
So is Alcides beaten by his page:
And so may I, blind fortune leading me,
Miss that which one unworthier may attain,
And die with grieving.

Por. You must take your chance;
And either not attempt to choose at all,
Or swear, before you choose,—if you choose wrong,
Never to speak to lady afterward
In way of marriage; therefore be advis'd.

Mor. Nor will not; come, bring me unto my chance,

Por. First, forward to the temple; after dinner
Your hazard shall be made.

Mor. Good fortune, then! [*Cornets.*
To make me blest, or cursed'st among men. [*Exeunt.*

SCENE II. Venice. *A Street.*

Enter LAUNCELOT GOBBO.

Laun. Certainly my conscience will serve me to run from this Jew, my master: The fiend is at mine elbow; and tempts me, saying to me, *Gobbo, Launcelot Gobbo, good Launcelot, or good Gobbo, or good Launcelot Gobbo, use your legs, take the start, run away:* My conscience says,—*no; take heed, honest Launcelot; take heed, honest Gobbo;* or, as aforesaid, *honest Launcelot Gobbo: do not run; scorn running with thy heels:* Well, the most courageous fiend bids me pack; *via!* says the fiend; *away!* says the fiend, *for the heavens; rouse up a brave mind,* says the fiend, *and run.* Well, my conscience, hanging about the neck of my heart, says very wisely to me,—*my honest friend Launcelot, being an honest man's son,*—or rather and honest woman's son; for, indeed, my father did something smack, something grow to, he had a kind of taste:—well, my conscience says, *Launcelot, budge not; budge,* says the fiend; *budge not,* says my conscience: Conscience, say I, you counsel well; fiend, say I, you counsel well: to be ruled by my conscience, I should stay with the Jew my master, who, (God bless the mark!) is a kind of devil; and, to run away from the Jew, I should be ruled by the fiend, who, saving your reverence, is the devil himself: Certainly, the Jew is the very devil incarnation; and, in my conscience, my conscience is but a kind of hard conscience, to offer to counsel me to stay with the Jew: the fiend gives the more friendly counsel: I will run, fiend; my heels are at your commandment, I will run.

Enter old GOBBO, *with a Basket.*

Gob. Master, young man, you, I pray you; which is the way to master Jew's?

Laun. [*Aside.*] O heavens, this is my true begotten father? who, being more than sand-blind, high-gravel blind, knows me not:—I will try, conclusions with him.

Gob. Master young gentleman, I pray you, which is the way to master Jew's?

Laun. Turn up on your right hand, at the next turning, but, at the next turning of all, on your left; marry, at the very next turning, turn of no hand, but turn down indirectly to the Jew's house.

Gob. By God's sonties, 'twill be a hard way to hit. Can you tell me whether one Launcelot, that dwells with him, dwell with him, or no?

Laun. Talk you of young master Launcelot?—Mark me now; [*aside.*] now will I raise the waters:—Talk you of young master Launcelot?

Gob. No master, sir, but a poor man's son; his father, though I say it, is an honest exceeding poor man, and, God be thanked, well to live.

Laun. Well, let his father be what he will, we talk of young master Launcelot.

Gob. Your worship's friend, and Launcelot, sir.

Laun. But I pray you *ergo,* old man, *ergo,* I beseech you; Talk you of young master Launcelot?

Gob. Of Launcelot, an't please your mastership.

Laun. *Ergo,* master Launcelot; talk not of master Launcelot, father; for the young gentleman (according to fates and destinies, and such odd sayings, the sisters three, and such branches of learning) is, indeed, deceased; or, as you would say, in plain terms, gone to heaven.

Gob. Marry, God forbid! the boy was the very staff of my age, my very prop.

Laun. Do I look like a cudgel, or a hovel-post, a staff, or a prop?—Do you know me, father?

Gob. Alack the day, I know you not, young gentleman: but, I pray you, tell me, is my boy (God rest his soul!) alive, or dead?

Laun. Do you not know me, father?

Gob. Alack, sir, I am sand-blind, I know you not.

Laun. Nay, indeed, if you had your eyes, you might fail of the knowing me: it is a wise father, that knows his own child. Well, old man, I will tell you news of your son: Give me your blessing: truth will come to light; murder cannot be hid long, a man's son may; but, in the end, truth will out.

Gob. Pray you, sir, stand up; I am sure, you are not Launcelot, my boy.

Laun. Pray you, let's have no more fooling about it, but give me your blessing: I am Launcelot, your boy that was, your son that is, your child that shall be.

Gob. I cannot think you are my son.

Laun. I know not what I shall think of that: but I am Launcelot, the Jew's man; and, I am sure, Margery, your wife, is my mother.

Gob. Her name is Margery, indeed: I'll be sworn, if thou be Launcelot, thou art mine own flesh and blood. Lord worship'd might he be! what a beard hast thou got! thou hast got more hair on thy chin, than Dobbin my thill-horse has on his tail.

Laun. It should seem then, that Dobbin's tail grows backward; I am sure he had more hair on his tail, than I have on my face, when I last saw him.

Gob. Lord, how art thou changed! How dost thou and thy master agree? I have brought him a present; How 'gree you now?

Laun. Well, well; but, for mine own part, as I have set up my rest to run away, so I will not rest till I have run some ground: my master's a very Jew: Give him a present! give him a halter: I am famish'd in his service; you may tell every finger I have with my ribs. Father, I am glad you are come; give me your present to one master Bassanio, who, indeed, gives rare new liveries; If I serve not him, I will run as far as God has any ground.—O rare fortune! here comes the man;—to him, father; for I am a Jew, if I serve the Jew any longer.

Enter Bassanio, *with* Leonardo, *and other Followers.*

Bass. You may do so;—but let it be so hasted, that supper be ready at the farthest by five of the clock: See these letters deliver'd; put the liveries to making; and desire Gratiano to come anon to my lodging. [*Exit a* Servant.

Laun. To him, father.

Gob. God bless your worship!

Bass. Gramercy; Would'st thou aught with me?

Gob. Here's my son, sir, a poor boy,——

Laun. Not a poor boy, sir, but the rich Jew's man; that would, sir, as my father shall specify,——

Gob. He hath a great infection, sir, as one would say, to serve——

Laun. Indeed, the short and the long is, I serve the Jew, and I have a desire, as my father shall specify,——

Gob. His master and he (saving your worship's reverence) are scarce cater-cousins:

Laun. To be brief, the very truth is, that the Jew having done me wrong, doth cause me, as my father, being I hope an old man, shall frutify unto you,——

Gob. I have here a dish of doves, that I would bestow upon your worship; and my suit is,——

Laun. In very brief, the suit is impertinent to myself, as your worship shall know by this honest old man; and, though I say it, though old man, yet poor man, my father.

Bass. One speak for both;—What would you?

Laun. Serve you, sir.

Gob. This is the very defect of the matter, sir.

Bass. I know thee well, thou hast obtain'd thy suit:
Shylock, thy master, spoke with me this day,
And hath preferr'd thee, if it be preferment,
To leave a rich Jew's service, to become
The follower of so poor a gentleman.

Laun. The old proverb is very well parted between my master Shylock and you, sir; you have the grace of God, sir, and he hath enough.

Bass. Thou speakest it well: Go, father, with thy son:—
Take leave of thy old master, and inquire
My lodging out:—Give him a livery [*To his followers.*
More guarded than his fellows: See it done.

Laun. Father, in;—I cannot get a service, no: I have ne'er a tongue in my head.—Well;—[*Looking on his palm.*] if any man in Italy have a fairer table; which doth offer to swear upon a book, I shall have good fortune. Go to, here's a simple line of life! here's a small trifle of wives: Alas, fifteen wives is nothing; eleven widows, and nine maids, is a simple coming-in for one man: and then, to 'scape drowning thrice; and to be in peril of my life with the edge of a feather-bed:—here are simple 'scapes! Well, if fortune be a woman, she's a good wench for this gear.—Father, come; I'll take my leave of the Jew in the twinkling of an eye.

[*Exeunt* Launcelot *and old* Gobbo.

Bass. I pray thee, good Leonardo, think on this:
These things being bought, and orderly bestow'd,
Return in haste, for I do feast to-night
My best-esteem'd acquaintance; hie thee, go.

Leon. My best endeavours shall be done herein.

Enter Gratiano.

Gra. Where is your master?
Leon. Yonder, sir, he walks. [*Exit* Leonardo.

Gra. Signior Bassanio,——

Bass. Gratiano!

Gra. I have a suit to you.
Bass. You have obtain'd it.

Gra. You must not deny me; I must go with you to Belmont.

Bass. Why, then you must;—But hear thee, Gratiano;
Thou art too wild, too rude, and bold of voice;—
Parts, that become thee happily enough,
And in such eyes as ours appear not faults;
But where thou art not known, why, there they show
Something too liberal;—pray thee, take pain
To allay with some cold drops of modesty
Thy skipping spirit; lest, through thy wild behaviour,
I be misconstrued in the place I go to,
And lose my hopes.

Gra. Signior Bassanio, hear me:
If I do not put on a sober habit,
Talk with respect, and swear but now and then,
Wear prayer-books in my pocket, look demurely;
Nay more, while grace is saying, hood mine eyes
Thus with my hat, and sigh, and say, amen;
Use all the observance of civility,
Like one well studied in a sad ostent
To please his grandam, never trust me more.

Bass. Well we shall see your bearing.

Gra. Nay, but I bar to-night; you shall not gage me
By what we do to-night.

Bass. No, that were pity;
I would entreat you rather to put on
Your boldest suit of mirth, for we have friends
That purpose merriment: But fare you well,
I have some business.

Gra. And I must to Lorenzo, and the rest;
But we will visit you at supper-time. [*Exeunt.*

SCENE III.

The same. A Room in Shylock's *House.*

Enter Jessica *and* Launcelot.

Jess. I am sorry, thou wilt leave my father so;
Our house is hell, and thou, a merry devil,
Didst rob it of some taste of tediousness:
But fare thee well; there is a ducat for thee.

And, Launcelot, soon at supper shalt thou see
Lorenzo, who is thy new master's guest:
Give him this letter; do it secretly,
And so farewell; I would not have my father
See me talk with thee.

Laun. Adieu!—tears exhibit my tongue.—Most beautiful pagan,—most sweet Jew! If a Christian did not play the knave, and get thee, I am much deceived: But adieu! these foolish drops do somewhat drown my manly spirit; adieu! [*Exit.*

Jess. Farewell, good Launcelot.—
Alack, what heinous sin is it in me,
To be ashamed to be my father's child!
But though I am a daughter to his blood,
I am not to his manners: O Lorenzo,
If thou keep promise, I shall end this strife;
Become a Christian, and thy loving wife. [*Exit.*

SCENE IV. *The same. A Street.*

Enter GRATIANO, LORENZO, SALARINO, *and* SALANIO.

Lor. Nay, we will slink away in supper-time;
Disguise us at my lodging, and return
All in an hour.

Gra. We have not made good preparation.

Salar. We have not spoke us yet of torch-bearers.

Salan. 'Tis vile, unless it may be quaintly order'd;
And better, in my mind, not undertook.

Lor. 'Tis now but four o'clock; we have two hours
To furnish us:—

Enter LAUNCELOT, *with a Letter.*

Friend Launcelot, what's the news?

Laun. An it shall please you to break up this, it shall seem to signify.

Lor. I know the hand; in faith, it is a fair hand;
And whiter than the paper it writ on,
Is the fair hand that writ.

Gra. Love-news, in faith.

Laun. By your leave, sir.

Lor. Whither goest thou?

Laun. Marry, sir, to bid my old master the Jew to sup to-night with my new master the Christian.

Lor. Hold here, take this:—tell gentle Jessica,
I will not fail her;—speak it privately; go.—
Gentlemen, [*Exit* LAUNCELOT.
Will you prepare you for this masque to-night?
I am provided of a torch-bearer.

Salar. Ay, marry, I'll be gone about it straight.

Salan. And so will I.

Lor. Meet me, and Gratiano,
At Gratiano's lodging some hour hence.

Salar. 'Tis good we do so.
[*Exeunt* SALAR. *and* SALAN.

Gra. Was not that letter from fair Jessica?

Lor. I must needs tell thee all; She hath directed,
How I shall take her from her father's house:
What gold, and jewels, she is furnish'd with;
What page's suit she hath in readiness.
If e'er the Jew her father come to heaven,
It will be for his gentle daughter's sake:
And never dare misfortune cross her foot,
Unless she do it under this excuse,—
That she is issue to a faithless Jew.
Come, go with me; peruse this, as thou goest:
Fair Jessica shall be my torch-bearer. [*Exeunt.*

SCENE V. *The same. Before* Shylock's *House.*

Enter SHYLOCK *and* LAUNCELOT.

Shy. Well, thou shalt see, thy eyes shall be thy judge,
The difference of old Shylock and Bassanio:—
What, Jessica!—thou shalt not gormandize,
As thou hast done with me;—What, Jessica!—
And sleep and snore, and rend apparel out;—
Why, Jessica, I say!

Laun. Why, Jessica!

Shy. Who bids thee call? I do not bid thee call.

Laun. Your worship was wont to tell me, I could do nothing without bidding.

Enter JESSICA.

Jes. Call you? What is your will?

Shy. I am bid forth to supper, Jessica:
There are my keys:—But wherefore should I go?
I am not bid for love; they flatter me:
But yet I'll go in hate, to feed upon
The prodigal Christian.—Jessica, my girl,
Look to my house:—I am right loath to go;
There is some ill a brewing towards my rest,
For I did dream of money-bags to-night.

Laun. I beseech you, sir, go; my young master doth expect your reproach.

Shy. So do I his.

Laun. And they have conspired together.—I will not say, you shall see a masque: but if you do, then it was not for nothing that my nose fell a bleeding on Black-Monday last, at six o'clock i' the morning, falling out that year on Ash Wednesday was four year in the afternoon.

Shy. What! are there masques? Hear you me, Jessica:
Lock up my doors; and when you hear the drum,
And the vile squeaking of the wry-neck'd fife,
Clamber not you up to the casements then,
Nor thrust your head into the public street,
To gaze on Christian fools with varnish'd faces;
But stop my house's ears, I mean my casements;
Let not the sound of shallow foppery enter
My sober house.—By Jacob's staff, I swear,
I have no mind of feasting forth to-night;
But I will go.—Go you before me, sirrah;
Say, I will come.

Laun. I will go before, sir.—
Mistress, look out at window for all this;
There will come a Christian by,
Will be worth a Jewess' eye.
[*Exit* LAUNCELOT.

Shy. What says that fool of Hagar's offspring, ha?

Jes. His words were, Farewell, mistress; nothing else.

Shy. The patch is kind enough; but a huge feeder.
Snail-slow in profit, and he sleeps by day
More than the wild cat; drones hive not with me;
Therefore I part with him; and part with him
To one that I would have him help to waste
His borrow'd purse.—Well, Jessica, go in;
Perhaps, I will return immediately;
Do, as I bid you,
Shut doors after you: Fast bind, fast find;
A proverb never stale in thrifty mind. [*Exit.*

Jes. Farewell; and if my fortune be not crost,
I have a father, you a daughter, lost. [*Exit.*

SCENE VI. *The same.*

Enter GRATIANO *and* SALARINO, *masqued.*

Gra. This is the pent-house, under which Lorenzo
Desir'd us to make stand.

Salar. His hour is almost past.

Gra. And it is marvel he out-dwells his hour,
For lovers ever run before the clock.

Salar. O, ten times faster Venus' pigeons fly
To seal love's bonds new made, than they are wont,
To keep obliged faith unforfeited!

Gra. That ever holds: Who riseth from a feast,
With that keen appetite that he sits down?
Where is the horse that doth untread again
His tedious measures with the unbated fire
That he did pace them first? All things that are,
Are with more spirit chased than enjoy'd.
How like a younker, or a prodigal,

The scarfed bark puts from her native bay,
Hugg'd and embraced by the strumpet wind!
How like the prodigal doth she return,
With over-weather'd ribs, and ragged sails,
Lean, rent, and beggar'd by the strumpet wind!

Enter LORENZO.

Salar. Here comes Lorenzo;—more of this hereafter.

Lor. Sweet friends, your patience for my long abode;
Not I, but my affairs have made you wait;
When you shall please to play the thieves for wives,
I'll watch as long for you then.—Approach:
Here dwells my father Jew:—Ho! who's within?

Enter JESSICA *above, in boy's clothes.*

Jes. Who are you? Tell me, for more certainty,
Albeit I'll swear that I do know your tongue.

Lor. Lorenzo, and thy love.

Jes. Lorenzo, certain; and my love, indeed;
For who love I so much? And now who knows,
But you, Lorenzo, whether I am yours?

Lor. Heaven, and thy thoughts, are witness that thou art.

Jes. Here, catch this casket; it is worth the pains.
am glad 'tis night, you do not look on me,
For I am much asham'd of my exchange:
But love is blind, and lovers cannot see
The pretty follies that themselves commit;
For if they could, Cupid himself would blush
To see me thus transformed to a boy.

Lor. Descend, for you must be my torch-bearer.

Jes. What, must I hold a candle to my shames?
They in themselves, good sooth, are too, too light.
Why, 'tis an office of discovery, love;
And I should be obscur'd.

Lor. So are you, sweet,
Even in the lovely garnish of a boy.
But come at once;
For the close night doth play the run-away,
And we are staid for at Bassanio's feast.

Jes. I will make fast the doors, and gild myself
With some more ducats, and be with you straight.
[*Exit, from above.*

Gra. Now, by my hood, a Gentile, and no Jew.

Lor. Beshrew me, but I love her heartily:
For she is wise, if I can judge of her;
And fair she is, if that mine eyes be true;
And true she is, as she hath proved herself;
And therefore, like herself, wise, fair, and true,
Shall she be placed in my constant soul.

Enter JESSICA, *below.*

What, art thou come?—On, gentlemen, away;
Our masquing mates by this time for us stay.
[*Exit with* JESSICA *and* SALARINO.

Enter ANTONIO.

Ant. Who's there?

Gra. Signior Antonio?

Ant. Fye, fye, Gratiano! where are all the rest?
'Tis nine o'clock; our friends all stay for you:—
No masque to-night; the wind is come about,
Bassanio presently will go aboard:
I have sent twenty out to seek for you.

Gra. I am glad on't; I desire no more delight,
Than to be under sail, and gone to-night.
[*Exeunt.*

SCENE VII. Belmont.

A Room in Portia's *House.—Flourish of Cornets.*

Enter PORTIA, *with the* Prince of Morocco, *and both their Trains.*

Por. Go, draw aside the curtains, and discover
The several caskets to this noble prince:—
Now make your choice.

Mor. The first, of gold, who this inscription bears:—
Who chooseth me, shall gain what many men desire.
The second, silver, which this promise carries;—
Who chooseth me, shall get as much as he deserves.
This third, dull lead, with warning all as blunt;—
Who chooseth me, must give and hazard all he hath.
How shall I know if I do choose the right?

Por. The one of them contains my picture, prince;
If you choose that, then I am yours withal.

Mor. Some god direct my judgment! Let me see,
I will survey the inscriptions back again:
What says this leaden casket?
Who chooseth me, must give and hazard all he hath.
Must give—For what? for lead? hazard for lead?
This casket threatens: Men, that hazard all,
Do it in hope of fair advantages:
A golden mind stoops not to shows of dross;
I'll then nor give, nor hazard, aught for lead.
What says the silver, with her virgin hue?
Who chooseth me, shall get as much as he decerves.
As much as he deserves?—Pause there, Morocco,
And weigh thy value with an even hand:
If thou be'st rated by thy estimation,
Thou dost deserve enough; and yet enough
May not extend so far as to the lady;
And yet to be afeard of my deserving,
Were but a weak disabling of myself.
As much as I deserve!—Why, that's the lady:
I do in birth deserve her, and in fortunes,
In graces, and in qualities of breeding;
But more than these, in love I do deserve.
What if I stray'd no further, but chose here?—
Let's see once more this saying grav'd in gold:
Who chooseth me shall gain what many men desire.
Why, that's the lady; all the world desires her.
From the four corners of the earth they come,
To kiss this shrine, this mortal breathing saint.
The Hyrcanian deserts, and the vasty wilds
Of wide Arabia, are as through-fares now,
For princes to come view fair Portia:
The watery kingdom, whose ambitious head
Spits in the face of heaven, is no bar
To stop the foreign spirits; but they come,
As o'er a brook, to see fair Portia.
One of these three contains her heavenly picture.
Is't like, that lead contains her? 'Twere damnation,
To think so base a thought: it were too gross
To rib her cerecloth in the obscure grave.
Or shall I think, in silver she's immur'd,
Being ten times undervalued to try'd gold?
O sinful thought! never so rich a gem
Was set in worse than gold. They have in England
A coin, that bears the figure of an angel
Stamped in gold; but that's insculp'd upon;
But here an angel in a golden bed
Lies all within.—Deliver me the key;
Here do I choose, and thrive I as I may!

Por. There, take it, prince, and if my form lie there,
Then I am yours. [*He unlocks the golden casket.*

Mor. O hell! what have we here?
A carrion death, within whose empty eye
There is a written scroll: I'll read the writing.

All that glisters is not gold,
Often have you heard that told:
Many a man his life hath sold.
But my outside to behold:
Gilded tombs do worms infold.
Had you been as wise as bold,
Young in limbs, in judgment old,
Your answer had not been inscroll'd:
Fare you well; your suit is cold.

Cold, indeed; and labour lost:
Then, farewell, heat; and welcome, frost.—
Portia, adieu! I have too griev'd a heart
To take a tedious leave: thus losers part. [*Exit.*

Por. A gentle riddance:——Draw the curtains, go;——
Let all of his complexion choose me so.
[*Exeunt.*

SCENE VIII. Venice. *A Street.*

Enter SALARINO *and* SALANIO.

Salar. Why, man, I saw Bassanio under sail;
With him is Gratiano gone along;
And in their ship, I am sure, Lorenzo is not.

Salan. The villain Jew with outcries rais'd the duke;
Who went with him to search Bassanio's ship.

Salar. He came too late, the ship was under sail;
But there the duke was given to understand,
That in a gondola were seen together
Lorenzo and his amorous Jessica:
Besides, Antonio certify'd the duke,
They were not with Bassanio in his ship.

Salan. I never heard a passion so confus'd,
So strange, outrageous, and so variable,
As the dog Jew did utter in the streets:
My daughter!—O my ducats!—O my daughter!
Fled with a Christian?—O my christian ducats!—
Justice! the law! my ducats, and my daughter!
A sealed bag, two sealed bags of ducats,
Of double ducats, stolen from me by my daughter!
And jewels; two stones, two rich and precious stones,
Stolen by my daughter! Justice! find the girl!
She hath the stones upon her, and the ducats!

Salar. Why all the boys in Venice follow him,
Crying,—his stones, his daughter, and his ducats.

Salan. Let good Antonio look he keep his day,
Or he shall pay for this.

Salar. Marry, well remember'd:
I reason'd with a Frenchman yesterday;
Who told me,—in the narrow seas, that part
The French and English, there miscarried
A vessel of our country, richly fraught:
I thought upon Antonio, when he told me;
And wish'd in silence that it were not his.

Salan. You were best to tell Antonio what you hear;
Yet do not suddenly, for it may grieve him.

Salar. A kinder gentleman treads not the earth.
I saw Bassanio and Antonio part:
Bassanio told him, he would make some speed
Of his return: he answer'd—*Do not so,*
Slubber not business for my sake, Bassanio,
But stay the very riping of the time;
And for the Jew's bond, which he hath of me,
Let it not enter in your mind of love:
Be merry; and employ your chiefest thoughts
To courtship and such fair ostents of love
As shall conveniently become you there:
And even there, his eye being big with tears,
Turning his face, he put his hand behind him,
And with affection wondrous sensible
He wrung Bassanio's hand, and so they parted.

Salan. I think, he only loves the world for him.
I pray thee, let us go, and find him out,
And quicken his embraced heaviness
With some delight or other.

Salar. Do we so. [*Exeunt.*

SCENE IX. Belmont.

A Room in Portia's *House.*

Enter NERISSA, *with a* Servant.

Ner. Quick, quick, I pray thee, draw the curtain straight;
The prince of Arragon hath ta'en his oath,
And comes to his election presently.

Flourish of Cornets.

Enter the Prince of Arragon, PORTIA, *and their Trains.*

Por. Behold, there stand the caskets, noble prince:
If you choose that wherein I am contain'd,
Straight shall our nuptial rites be solemniz'd;
But if you fail, without more speech, my lord,
You must be gone from hence immediately.

Ar. I am enjoin'd by oath to observe three things:
First, never to unfold to any one
Which casket 'twas I chose; next, if I fail
Of the right casket, never in my life
To woo a maid in way of marriage; lastly,
If I do fail in fortune of my choice,
Immediately to leave you and be gone.

Por. To these injunctions every one doth swear,
That comes to hazard for my worthless self.

Ar. And so have I address'd me: Fortune now
To my heart's hope!—Gold, silver, and base lead.
Who chooseth me, must give and hazard all he hath.
You shall look fairer, ere I give, or hazard.
What says the golden chest? ha! let me see:—
Who chooseth me, shall gain what many men desire.
What many men desire.—That many may be meant
By the fool multitude, that choose by show,
Not learning more than the fond eye doth teach;
Which pries not to the interior, but, like the martlet,
Builds in the weather on the outward wall,
Even in the force and road of casualty.
I will not choose what many men desire,
Because I will not jump with common spirits,
And rank me with the barbarous multitudes.
Why, then to thee, thou silver treasure-house;
Tell me once more what title thou dost bear:
Who chooseth me, shall get as much as he deserves;
And well said too: For who shall go about
To cozen fortune, and be honourable
Without the stamp of merit! Let none presume
To wear an undeserved dignity.
O, that estates, degrees, and offices,
Were not deriv'd corruptly! and that clear honour
Were purchased by the merit of the wearer!
How many then should cover, that stand bare?
How many be commanded, that command?
How much low peasantry would then be glean'd
From the true seed of honour? and how much honour
Pick'd from the chaff and ruin of the times,
To be new varnish'd? Well, but to my choice:
Who chooseth me, shall get as much as he deserves:
I will assume desert;—Give me a key for this,
And instantly unlock my fortunes here.

Por. Too long a pause for that which you find there.

Ar. What's here? the portrait of a blinking idiot,
Presenting me a schedule. I will read it.
How much unlike art thou to Portia?
How much unlike my hopes and my deservings?
Who chooseth me, shall have as much as he deserves.
Did I deserve no more than a fool's head?
Is that my prize? are my deserts no better?

Por. To offend, and judge, are distinct offices,
And of opposed natures.

Ar. What is here?

The fire seven times tried this;
Seven times tried that judgment is,
That did never choose amiss:
Some there be, that shadows kiss;
Such have but a shadow's bliss:
There be fools alive, I wis,
Silver'd o'er; and so was this.
Take what wife you will to bed,
I will ever be your head:
So begone, sir, you are sped.

Still more fool I shall appear
By the time I linger here;
With one fool's head I came to woo,
But I go away with two.—
Sweet, adieu! I'll keep my oath,
Patiently to bear my wroath.

[*Exeunt* Arragon, *and Train.*

Por. Thus hath the candle sing'd the moth.
O these deliberate fools! when they do choose,
They have the wisdom by their wit to lose.

Ner. The ancient saying is no heresy;—
Hanging and wiving goes by destiny.

Por. Come, draw the curtain, Nerissa.

Enter a Servant.

Serv. Where is my lady?

Por. Here; what would my lord?

Serv. Madam, there is alighted at your gate
A young Venetian, one that comes before
To signify the approaching of his lord:
From whom he bringeth sensible regreets;
To wit, besides commends, and courteous breath,
Gifts of rich value; yet I have not seen
So likely an ambassador of love:
A day in April never came so sweet,
To show how costly summer was at hand,
As this fore-spurrer comes before his lord.

Por. No more, I pray thee; I am half afeard,
Thou wilt say anon, he is some kin to thee,
Thou spend'st such high-day wit in praising him.—
Come, come, Nerissa; for I long to see
Quick Cupid's post, that comes so mannerly.

Ner. Bassanio, lord love, if thy will it be!
[*Exeunt.*

ACT III.

SCENE I. Venice. *A Street.*

Enter SALANIO *and* SALARINO.

Salan. Now, what news on the Rialto?

Salar. Why, yet it lives there uncheck'd, that Antonio hath a ship of rich lading wreck'd on the narrow seas; the Goodwins, I think they call the place; a very dangerous flat, and fatal, where the carcasses of many a tall ship lie buried, as they say, if my gossip report be an honest woman of her word.

Salan. I would she were as lying a gossip in that, as ever knapp'd ginger, or made her neighbours believe she wept for the death of a third husband: But it is true,—without any slips of prolixity, or crossing the plain highway of talk, —that the good Antonio, the honest Antonio,—— O that I had a title good enough to keep his name company:—

Salar. Come, the full stop.

Salan. Ha,—what say'st thou?—Why the end is, he hath lost a ship.

Salar. I would it might prove the end of his losses!

Salan. Let me say amen betimes, lest the devil cross my prayer; for here he comes in the likeness of a Jew.—

Enter SHYLOCK.

How now, Shylock? what news among the merchants?

Shy. You knew, none so well, none so well as you, of my daughter's flight.

Salar. That's certain; I, for my part, knew the tailor that made the wings she flew withal.

Salan. And Shylock, for his own part, knew the bird was fledg'd; and then it is the complexion of them all to leave the dam.

Shy. She is damn'd for it.

Salar. That's certain, if the devil may be her judge.

Shy. My own flesh and blood to rebel!

Salan. Out upon it, old carrion! rebels it at these years?

Shy. I say, my daughter is my flesh and blood.

Salar. There is more difference between thy flesh and hers, than between jet and ivory; more between your bloods, than there is between red wine and rhenish:—But tell us, do you hear whether Antonio have had any loss at sea or no?

Shy. There I have another bad match: a bankrupt, a prodigal, who dare scarce show his head on the Rialto;—a beggar, that used to come so smug upon the mart:—let him look to his bond: he was wont to call me usurer;—let him look to his bond: he was wont to lend money for a Christian courtesy;—let him look to his bond.

Salar. Why, I am sure, if he forfeit, thou wilt not take his flesh; What's that good for?

Shy. To bait fish withal: if it will feed nothing else, it will feed my revenge. He hath disgraced me, and hindered me of half a million; laughed at my losses, mocked at my gains, scorned my nation, thwarted my bargains, cooled my friends, heated mine enemies; and what's his reason? I am a Jew. Hath not a Jew eyes? hath not a Jew hands, organs, dimensions, senses, affections, passions? fed with the same food, hurt with the same weapons, subject to the same diseases, healed by the same means, warmed and cooled by the same winter and summer, as a Christian is? if you prick us, do we not bleed? if you tickle us, do we not laugh? if you poison us, do we not die? and if you wrong us, shall we not revenge? if we are like you in the rest, we will resemble you in that. If a Jew wrong a Christian, what is his humility? revenge; If a Christian wrong a Jew, what should his sufferance be by Christian example? why, revenge. The villany you teach me, I will execute; and it shall go hard, but I will better the instruction.

Enter a Servant.

Serv. Gentlemen, my master Antonio is at his house, and desires to speak with you both.

Salar. We have been up and down to seek him.

Enter TUBAL.

Salan. Here comes another of the tribe; a third cannot be matched, unless the devil himself turn Jew. [*Exeunt* SALAN. SALAR. *and* Servant.

Shy. How now, Tubal, what news from Genoa? hast thou found my daughter?

Tub. I often came where I did hear of her, but cannot find her.

Shy. Why there, there, there, there! a diamond gone, cost me two thousand ducats in Frankfort! The curse never fell upon our nation till now; I never felt it till now:—two thousand ducats in that; and other precious, precious jewels.—I would, my daughter were dead at my foot, and the jewels in her ear! 'would she were hears'd at my foot, and the ducats in her coffin! No news of them?—Why, so:—and I know not what's spent in the search: Why, thou loss upon loss! the thief gone with so much, and so much to find the thief; and no satisfaction, no revenge: nor no ill luck stirring, but what lights o' my shoulders; no sighs, but o' my breathing; no tears, but o' my shedding.

Tub. Yes, other men have ill luck too; Antonio, as I heard in Genoa,—

Shy. What, what, what? ill luck, ill luck?

Tub. —hath an argosy cast away coming from Tripolis.

Shy. I thank God, I thank God:—Is it true? is it true?

Tub. I spoke with some of the sailors that escaped the wreck.

Shy. I thank thee, good Tubal;—Good news, good news: ha! ha!—Where? in Genoa?

Tub. Your daughter spent in Genoa, as I heard, one night, fourscore ducats.

Shy. Thou stick'st a dagger in me:——I shall never see my gold again: Fourscore ducats at a sitting! fourscore ducats!

Tub. There came divers of Antonio's creditors in my company to Venice, that swear he cannot choose but break.

Shy. I am very glad of it; I'll plague him; I'll torture him; I am glad of it.

Tub. One of them showed me a ring, that he had of your daughter for a monkey.

Shy. Out upon her! Thou torturest me, Tubal: it was my turquoise; I had it of Leah, when I was a bachelor: I would not have given it for a wilderness of monkeys.

Tub. But Antonio is certainly undone.

Shy. Nay, that's true, that's very true: Go, Tubal, fee me an officer, bespeak him a fortnight before: I will have the heart of him, if he forfeit; for were he out of Venice, I can make what merchandise I will: Go, go, Tubal, and meet me at our synagogue; go, good Tubal; at our synagogue, Tubal. [*Exeunt.*

SCENE II. Belmont.

A Room in Portia's *House.*

Enter BASSANIO, PORTIA, GRATIANO, NERISSA, *and* Attendants. *The caskets are set out.*

Por. I pray you, tarry; pause a day or two,
Before you hazard; for, in choosing wrong,
I lose your company; therefore, forbear a while:
There's something tells me, (but it is not love),
I would not lose you: and you know yourself,
Hate counsels not in such a quality:
But lest you should not understand me well
(And yet a maiden hath no tongue but thought),
I would detain you here some month or two,
Before you venture for me. I could teach you,
How to choose right, but then I am forsworn;
So will I never be: so may you miss me;
But if you do, you'll make me wish a sin,
That I had been forsworn. Beshrew your eyes,
They have o'erlook'd me, and divided me;
One half of me is yours, the other half yours,——
Mine own, I would say; but if mine, then yours,
And so all yours: O! these naughty times
Put bars between the owners and their rights;
And so, though yours, not yours.—Prove it so,
Let fortune go to hell for it,—not I.
I speak too long; but 'tis to peize the time;
To eke it, and to draw it out in length,
To stay you from election.

Bass. Let me choose;
For, as I am, I live upon the rack.

Por. Upon the rack, Bassanio? then confess
What treason there is mingled with your love.

Bass. None, but that ugly treason of mistrust,
Which makes me fear the enjoying of my love:
There may as well be amity and life
'Tween snow and fire, as treason and my love.

Por. Ay, but, I fear, you speak upon the rack,
Where men enforced do speak any thing.

Bass. Promise me life, and I'll confess the truth.

Por. Well then, confess, and live.

Bass. Confess, and love,
Had been the very sum of my confession:
O happy torment, when my torturer
Doth teach me answers for deliverance!
But let me to my fortune and the caskets.

Por. Away then: I am lock'd in one of them;
If you do love me, you will find me out.—
Nerissa, and the rest, stand all aloof.—
Let musick sound, while he doth make his choice;
Then, if he lose, he makes a swanlike end,
Fading in musick: that the comparison
May stand more proper, my eye shall be the stream,
And wat'ry death-bed for him: He may win;
And what is musick then? then musick is
Even as the flourish when true subjects bow
To a new-crowned monarch; such it is,
As are those dulcet sounds in break of day,
That creep into the dreaming bridegroom's ear,
And summon him to marriage. Now he goes,
With no less presence, but with much more love,
Than young Alcides, when he did redeem
The virgin tribute paid by howling Troy
To the sea-monster; I stand for sacrifice,
The rest aloof are the Dardanian wives,
With bleared visages, come forth to view
The issue of the exploit. Go, Hercules!
Live thou, I live:—With much much more dismay
I view the fight, than thou that mak'st the fray.

Musick, whilst BASSANIO *comments on the caskets to himself.*

SONG.

1. *Tell me, where is fancy bred,*
Or in the heart, or in the head?
How begot, how nourished?
Reply, reply.

2. *It is engender'd in the eyes,*
With gazing fed; and fancy dies
In the cradle where it lies;
Let us all ring fancy's knell;
I'll begin it,——Ding, dong, bell.

All. *Ding, dong, bell.*

Bass.—So may the outward shows be least themselves;
The world is still deceiv'd with ornament.
In law, what plea so tainted and corrupt,
But, being season'd with a gracious voice,
Obscures the show of evil? In religion,
What damned error, but some sober brow
Will bless it, and approve it with a text,
Hiding the grossness with fair ornament?
There is no vice so simple, but assumes
Some mark of virtue on his outward parts.
How many cowards, whose hearts are all as false
As stairs of sand, wear yet upon their chins
The beards of Hercules, and frowning Mars;
Who, inward search'd, have livers white as milk?
And these assume but valour's excrement,
To render them redoubted. Look on beauty,
And you shall see 'tis purchas'd by the weight;
Which therein works a miracle in nature,
Making them lightest that wear most of it:
So are those crisped snaky golden locks,
Which make such wanton gambols with the wind,
Upon supposed fairness, often known
To be the dowry of a second head,
The scull that bred them, in the sepulchre.
Thus ornament is but the guiled shore
To a most dangerous sea; the beauteous scarf
Veiling an Indian beauty; in a word,
The seeming truth which cunning times put on
To entrap the wisest. Therefore, thou gaudy gold,
Hard food for Midas, I will none of thee:
Nor none of thee, thou pale and common drudge
'Tween man and man: but thou, thou meager lead,
Which rather threat'nest, than dost promise aught,
Thy paleness moves me more than eloquence,
And here choose I; Joy be the consequence!

Por. How all the other passions fleet to air,
As doubtful thoughts, and rash-embrac'd despair,
And shudd'ring fear and green-ey'd jealousy.
O love, be moderate, allay thy ecstasy,
In measure rain thy joy, scant this excess;
I feel too much thy blessing, make it less,
For fear I surfeit!

Bass. What find I here?
[*Opening the leaden casket.*
Fair Portia's counterfeit? What demi-god
Hath come so near creation? Move these eyes?
Or whether, riding on the balls of mine,
Seem they in motion? Here are sever'd lips,
Parted with sugar breath; so sweet a bar
Should sunder such sweet friends: Here in her hairs
The painter plays the spider: and hath woven
A golden mesh to entrap the hearts of men,
Faster than gnats in cobwebs: But her eyes,—
How could he see to do them? having made one,
Methinks it should have power to steal both his,
And leave itself unfurnish'd: Yet look, how far
The substance of my praise doth wrong this shadow
In underprizing it, so far this shadow
Doth limp behind the substance.—Here's the scroll,
The continent and summary of my fortune.

You that choose not by the view,
Chance as fair, and choose as true!
Since this fortune falls to you,
Be content, and seek no new.
If you be well pleas'd with this,
And hold your fortune for your bliss,
Turn you where your lady is,
And claim her with a loving kiss.
A gentle scroll: Fair lady, by your leave;
[*Kissing her.*
I come by note, to give, and to receive.
Like one of two contending in a prize,
That thinks he hath done well in people's eyes,
Hearing applause, and universal shout,
Giddy in spirit, still gazing, in a doubt
Whether those peals of praise be his or no;
So, thrice fair lady, stand I, even so;
As doubtful whether what I see be true,
Until confirm'd, sign'd, ratified by you.
Por. You see me, lord Bassanio, where I stand,
Such as I am: though, for myself alone,
I would not be ambitious in my wish,
To wish myself much better; yet, for you,
I would be trebled twenty times myself;
A thousand times more fair, ten thousand times
More rich;
That only to stand high on your account,
I might in virtues, beauties, livings, friends,
Exceed account: but the full sum of me
Is sum of something; which, to term in gross,
Is an unlesson'd girl, unschool'd, unpractis'd:
Happy in this, she is not yet so old
But she may learn; happier than this,
She is not bred so dull but she can learn;
Happiest of all, is, that her gentle spirit
Commits itself to yours to be directed,
As from her lord, her governor, her king.
Myself, and what is mine, to you, and yours
Is now converted: but now I was the lord
Of this fair mansion, master of my servants,
Queen o'er myself; and even now, but now,
This house, these servants, and this same myself,
Are yours, my lord; I give them with this ring;
Which when you part from, lose, or give away,
Let it presage the ruin of your love,
And be my vantage to exclaim on you.
Bass. Madam, you have bereft me of all words,
Only my blood speaks to you in my veins:
And there is such confusion in my powers,
As, after some oration fairly spoke
By a beloved prince, there doth appear
Among the buzzing pleased multitude:
Where every something, being blent together,
Turns to a wild of nothing, save of joy,
Express'd, and not express'd: But when this ring
Parts from this finger, then parts life from hence;
O, then be bold to say, Bassanio's dead.
Ner. My lord and lady, it is now our time,
That have stood by, and seen our wishes prosper,
To cry, good joy; Good joy, my lord, and lady!
Gra. My lord Bassanio, and my gentle lady,
I wish you all the joy that you can wish;
For, I am sure, you can wish none from me:
And, when your honours mean to solemnize
The bargain of your faith, I do beseech you,
Even at that time I may be married too.
Bass. With all my heart, so thou canst get a wife.
Gra. I thank your lordship; you have got me one.
My eyes, my lord, can look as swift as yours:
You saw the mistress, I beheld the maid;
You lov'd, I lov'd; for intermission
No more pertains to me, my lord, than you.
Your fortune stood upon the caskets there;
And so did mine too, as the matter falls:
For wooing here, until I sweat again;
And swearing, till my very roof was dry
With oaths of love: at last,—if promise last,—
I got a promise of this fair one here,
To have her love, provided that your fortune
Achiev'd her mistress.
Por. Is this true, Nerissa?
Ner. Madam, it is, so you stand pleas'd withal.
Bass. And do you, Gratiano, mean good faith?
Gra. Yes, 'faith, my lord.
Bass. Our feast shall be much honour'd in your marriage.
Gra. We'll play with them, the first boy for a thousand ducats.
Ner. What, and stake down?
Gra. No; we shall ne'er win at that sport, and stake down.——
But who comes here? Lorenzo, and his infidel?
What, and my old Venetian friend, Salerio?

Enter LORENZO, JESSICA, *and* SALERIO.

Bass. Lorenzo, and Salerio, welcome hither?
If that the youth of my new interest here
Have power to bid you welcome:—By your leave,
I bid my very friends and countrymen,
Sweet Portia, welcome.
Por. So do I, my lord;
They are entirely welcome.
Lor. I thank your honour: For my part, my lord,
My purpose was not to have seen you here;
But meeting with Salerio by the way,
He did entreat me, past all saying nay,
To come with him along.
Sale. I did, my lord,
And I have reason for it. Signior Antonio
Commends him to you. [*Gives* BASSANIO *a letter.*
Bass. Ere I ope his letter,
I pray you, tell me how my good friend doth.
Sale. Not sick, my lord, unless it be in mind;
Nor well, unless in mind: his letter there
Will show you his estate.
Gra. Nerissa, cheer yon stranger; bid her welcome.
Your hand, Salerio; What's the news from Venice?
How doth that royal merchant, good Antonio?
I know, he will be glad of our success;
We are the Jasons, we have won the fleece.
Sale. 'Would you had won the fleece that he hath lost!
Por. There are some shrewd contents in yon' same paper,
That steal the colour from Bassanio's cheek:
Some dear friend dead: else nothing in the world
Could turn so much the constitution
Of any constant man. What, worse and worse?—
With leave, Bassanio; I am half yourself,
And I must freely have the half of any thing
That this same paper brings you.
Bass. O, sweet Portia,
Here are a few of the unpleasant'st words
That ever blotted paper! Gentle lady,
When I did first impart my love to you,
I freely told you, all the wealth I had
Ran in my veins, I was a gentleman;
And then I told you true: and yet, dear lady,
Rating myself at nothing, you shall see
How much I was a braggart: When I told you
My state was nothing, I should then have told you
That I was worse than nothing: for, indeed,
I have engag'd myself to a dear friend,
Engag'd my friend to his mere enemy,
To feed my means. Here is a letter, lady;
The paper as the body of my friend,
And every word in it a gaping wound,
Issuing life-blood—But is it true, Salerio?
Have all his ventures fail'd? What, not one hit?
From Tripolis, from Mexico, and England,
From Lisbon, Barbary, and India?
And not one vessel 'scape the dreadful touch
Of merchant-marring rocks?
Sale. Not one, my lord.
Besides, it should appear, that if he had

The present money to discharge the Jew,
He would not take it: Never did I know
A creature, that did bear the shape of man
So keen and greedy to confound a man:
He plies the duke at morning, and at night;
And doth impeach the freedom of the state,
If they deny him justice: twenty merchants,
The duke himself, and the magnificoes
Of greatest port, have all persuaded with him;
But none can drive him from the envious plea
Of forfeiture, of justice, and his bond.

Jes. When I was with him, I have heard him swear,
To Tubal, and to Chus, his countrymen,
That he would rather have Antonio's flesh,
Than twenty times the value of the sum
That he did owe him: and I know, my lord,
If law, authority, and power deny not,
It will go hard with poor Antonio.

Por. Is it your dear friend, that is thus in trouble?

Bass. The dearest friend to me, the kindest man,
The best condition'd and unwearied spirit
In doing courtesies; and one in whom
The ancient Roman honour more appears,
Than any that draws breath in Italy.

Por. What sum owes he the Jew?

Bass. For me, three thousand ducats.

Por. What, no more?
Pay him six thousand, and deface the bond;
Double six thousand, and then treble that,
Before a friend of this description
Should lose a hair through my Bassanio's fault.
First, go with me to church, and call me wife:
And then away to Venice to your friend;
For never shall you lie by Portia's side
With an unquiet soul. You shall have gold
To pay the petty debt twenty times over;
When it is paid, bring your true friend along:
My maid Nerissa and myself, mean time,
Will live as maids and widows. Come, away;
For you shall hence upon your wedding-day:
Bid your friends welcome, show a merry cheer;
Since you are dear bought, I will love you dear.—
But let me hear the letter of your friend.

Bass. [Reads.] *Sweet Bassanio, my ships have all miscarried, my creditors grow cruel, my estate is very low, my bond to the Jew is forfeit; and since, in paying it, it is impossible I should live, all debts are cleared between you and I, if I might but see you at my death: notwithstanding, use your pleasure: if your love do not persuade you to come, let not my letter.*

Por. O love, despatch all business, and be gone.

Bass. Since I have your good leave to go away,
I will make haste: but, till I come again,
No bed shall e'er be guilty of my stay,
Nor rest be interposer 'twixt us twain.
[*Exeunt.*

SCENE III. Venice. *A Street.*

Enter SHYLOCK, SALANIO, ANTONIO, *and* Gaoler.

Shy. Gaoler, look to him;—Tell not me of mercy:—
This is the fool that lent out money gratis;—
Gaoler, look to him.

Ant. Hear me yet, good Shylock.

Shy. I'll have my bond; speak not against my bond;
I have sworn an oath that I will have my bond:
Thou call'dst me dog, before thou hadst a cause:
But, since I am a dog, beware my fangs:
The duke shall grant me justice.—I do wonder,
Thou naughty gaoler, that thou art so fond
To come abroad with him at his request.

Ant. I pray thee, hear me speak.

Shy. I'll have my bond; I will not hear thee speak;
I'll have my bond; and therefore speak no more.
I'll not be made a soft and dull-ey'd fool,
To shake the head, relent, and sigh, and yield
To christian intercessors. Follow not;
I'll have no speaking; I will have my bond.
[*Exit* SHYLOCK.

Salan. It is the most impenetrable cur,
That ever kept with men.

Ant. Let him alone;
I'll follow him no more with bootless prayers.
He seeks my life; his reason well I know;
I oft deliver'd from his forfeitures
Many that have at times made moan to me;
Therefore he hates me.

Salan. I am sure, the duke
Will never grant this forfeiture to hold.

Ant. The duke cannot deny the course of law;
For the commodity that strangers have
With us in Venice, if it be denied,
Will much impeach the justice of the state;
Since that the trade and profit of the city
Consisteth of all nations. Therefore, go:
These griefs and losses have so 'bated me,
That I shall hardly spare a pound of flesh
To-morrow to my bloody creditor.——
Well, gaoler, on:—'Pray God, Bassanio come
To see me pay his debt, and then I care not!
[*Exeunt.*

SCENE IV.

Belmont. *A Room in* Portia's *House.*

Enter PORTIA, NERISSA, LORENZO, JESSICA, *and* BALTHAZAR.

Lor. Madam, although I speak it in your presence,
You have a noble and a true conceit
Of god-like amity; which appears most strongly
In bearing thus the absence of your lord.
But, if you knew to whom you show this honour,
How true a gentleman you send relief,
How dear a lover of my lord your husband,
I know, you would be prouder of the work,
Than customary bounty can enforce you.

Por. I never did repent for doing good,
Nor shall not now: for in companions
That do converse and waste the time together,
Whose souls do bear an equal yoke of love,
There must be needs a like proportion
Of lineaments, of manners, and of spirit;
Which makes me think, that this Antonio,
Being the bosom lover of my lord,
Must needs be like my lord: If it be so,
How little is the cost I have bestow'd,
In purchasing the semblance of my soul
From out the state of hellish cruelty?
This comes too near the praising of myself!
Therefore, no more of it: hear other things.—
Lorenzo, I commit into your hands
The husbandry and manage of my house,
Until my lord's return; for mine own part,
I have toward heaven breath'd a secret vow,
To live in prayer and contemplation,
Only attended by Nerissa here,
Until her husband and my lord's return:
There is a monastery two miles off,
And there we will abide. I do desire you,
Not to deny this imposition;
The which my love, and some necessity,
Now lays upon you.

Lor. Madam, with all my heart;
I shall obey you in all fair commands.

Por. My people do already know my mind,
And will acknowledge you and Jessica
In place of lord Bassanio and myself.
So fare you well, till we shall meet again.

Lor. Fair thoughts, and happy hours, attend on you.

Jes. I wish your ladyship all heart's content.

Por. I thank you for your wish, and am well pleas'd
To wish it back on you: fare you well, Jessica.—
[*Exeunt* JESSICA *and* LORENZO.
Now, Balthazar,
As I have ever found thee honest, true,

So let me find thee still: Take this same letter,
And use thou all the endeavour of a man,
In speed to Padua: see thou render this
Into my cousin's hand, doctor Bellario;
And, look, what notes and garments he doth give thee,
Bring them, I pray thee, with imagin'd speed
Unto the tranect, to the common ferry
Which trades to Venice:—waste no time in words,
But get thee gone: I shall be there before thee.

Balth. Madam, I go with all convenient speed. [*Exit.*

Por. Come on, Nerissa; I have work in hand,
That you yet know not of: we'll see our husbands,
Before they think of us.

Ner. Shall they see us?

Por. They shall, Nerissa; but in such a habit,
That they shall think we are accomplished
With what we lack. I'll hold thee any wager,
When we are both accouter'd like young men,
I'll prove the prettier fellow of the two,
And wear my dagger with the braver grace:
And speak, between the change of man and boy,
With a reed voice; and turn two mincing steps
Into a manly stride; and speak of frays,
Like a fine bragging youth: and tell quaint lies,
How honourable ladies sought my love,
Which I denying, they fell sick and died;
I could not do withal:—then I'll repent,
And wish, for all that, that I had not kill'd them:
And twenty of these puny lies I'll tell,
That men shall swear, I have discontinued school
Above a twelvemonth:—I have within my mind
A thousand raw tricks of these bragging Jacks,
Which I will practise.

Ner. Why, shall we turn to men?

Por. Fye; what a question's that,
If thou wert near a lewd interpreter?
But come, I'll tell thee all my whole device
When I am in my coach, which stays for us
At the park gate; and therefore haste away,
For we must measure twenty miles to-day. [*Exeunt.*

SCENE V. *The same. A Garden.*

Enter LAUNCELOT *and* JESSICA.

Laun. Yes, truly: for, look you, the sins of the father are to be laid upon the children; therefore, I promise you, I fear you. I was always plain with you, and so now I speak my agitation of the matter: Therefore, be of good cheer; for, truly, I think, you are damn'd. There is but one hope in it that can do you any good; and that is but a kind of bastard hope neither.

Jes. And what hope is that, I pray thee?

Laun. Marry, you may partly hope that your father got you not, that you are not the Jew's daughter.

Jes. That were a kind of bastard hope, indeed; so the sins of my mother should be visited upon me.

Laun. Truly then I fear you are damn'd both by father and mother; thus when I shun Scylla, your father, I fall into Charybdis, your mother: well, you are gone both ways.

Jes. I shall be saved by my husband; he hath made me a Christian.

Laun. Truly, the more to blame he; we were Christians enough before; e'en as many as could well live, one by another: This making of Christians will raise the price of hogs; if we grow all to be pork-eaters, we shall not shortly have a rasher on the coals for money.

Enter LORENZO.

Jes. I'll tell my husband, Launcelot, what you say; here he comes.

Lor. I shall grow jealous of you shortly, Launcelot, if you thus get my wife into corners.

Jes. Nay, you need not fear us, Lorenzo; Launcelot and I are out: he tells me flatly, there is no mercy for me in heaven, because I am a Jew's daughter: and he says you are no good member of the commonwealth; for, in converting Jews to Christians, you raise the price of pork.

Lor. I shall answer that better to the commonwealth, than you can the getting up of the negro's belly: the Moor is with child by you, Launcelot.

Laun. It is much, that the Moor should be more than reason: but if she be less than an honest woman, she is, indeed, more than I took her for.

Lor. How every fool can play upon the word! I think, the best grace of wit will shortly turn into silence; and discourse grow commendable in none only but parrots.—Go in, sirrah; bid them prepare for dinner.

Laun. That is done, sir; they have all stomachs.

Lor. Goodly lord, what a wit-snapper are you! then bid them prepare dinner.

Laun. That is done too, sir; only, cover is the word.

Lor. Will you cover then, sir?

Laun. Not so, sir, neither; I know my duty.

Lor. Yet more quarrelling with occasion! Wilt thou show the whole wealth of thy wit in an instant? I pray thee, understand a plain man in his plain meaning: go to thy fellows; bid them cover the table, serve in the meat, and we will come in to dinner.

Laun. For the table, sir, it shall be served in: for the meat, sir, it shall be covered; for your coming in to dinner, sir, why, let it be as humours and conceits shall govern. [*Exit* LAUNCELOT.

Lor. O dear discretion, how his words are suited!
The fool hath planted in his memory
An army of good words: And I do know
A many fools, that stand in better place,
Garnish'd like him, that for a tricksy word
Defy the matter. How cheer'st thou, Jessica?
And now, good sweet, say thy opinion,
How dost thou like the lord Bassanio's wife?

Jes. Past all expressing: It is very meet,
The lord Bassanio live an upright life;
For, having such a blessing in his lady,
He finds the joys of heaven here on earth;
And, if on earth he do not mean it, it
Is reason he should never come to heaven.
Why, if two gods should play some heavenly match,
And on the wager lay two earthly women,
And Portia one, there must be something else
Pawn'd with the other; for the poor rude world
Hath not her fellow.

Lor. Even such a husband
Hast thou of me, as she is for a wife.

Jes. Nay, but ask my opinion too of that.

Lor. I will anon; first let us go to dinner.

Jes. Nay, let me praise you, while I have a stomach.

Lor. No, 'pray thee, let it serve for table-talk;
Then, howsoe'er thou speak'st, 'mong other things
I shall digest it.

Jes. Well, I'll set you forth. [*Exeunt.*

ACT IV.

SCENE I. Venice. *A Court of Justice.*

Enter the Duke, *the Magnificoes;* ANTONIO, BASSANIO, GRATIANO, SALARINO, SALANIO, *and others.*

Duke. What, is Antonio here?

Ant. Ready, so please your grace.

Duke. I am sorry for thee; thou art come to answer

A stony adversary, an inhuman wretch
Uncapable of pity, void and empty
From any dram of mercy.
Ant. I have heard,
Your grace hath ta'en great pains to qualify
His rigorous course; but since he stands obdurate,
And that no lawful means can carry me
Out of his envy's reach, I do oppose
My patience to his fury; and am arm'd
To suffer, with a quietness of spirit,
The very tyranny and rage of his.
Duke. Go one, and call the Jew into the court.
Salan. He's ready at the door: he comes, my lord.

Enter SHYLOCK.

Duke. Make room, and let him stand before our face.—
Shylock, the world thinks, and I think so too,
That thou but lead'st this fashion of thy malice
To the last hour of act; and then 'tis thought,
Thou'lt show thy mercy, and remorse, more strange
Than is thy strange apparent cruelty:
And where thou now exact'st the penalty,
(Which is a pound of this poor merchant's flesh,)
Thou wilt not only lose the forfeiture,
But, touch'd with human gentleness and love,
Forgive a moiety of the principal;
Glancing an eye of pity on his losses,
That have of late so huddled on his back;
Enough to press a royal merchant down,
And pluck commiseration of his state
From brassy bosoms, and rough hearts of flint,
From stubborn Turks, and Tartars, never train'd
To offices of tender courtesy.
We all expect a gentle answer, Jew.
Shy. I have possess'd your grace of what I purpose;
And by our holy Sabbath have I sworn,
To have the due and forfeit of my bond:
If you deny it, let the danger light
Upon your charter, and your city's freedom.
You'll ask me, why I rather choose to have
A weight of carrion flesh, than to receive
Three thousand ducats: I'll not answer that:
But, say, it is my humour; Is it answer'd?
What if my house be troubled with a rat,
And I be pleas'd to give ten thousand ducats
To have it baned? What, are you answer'd yet?
Some men there are love not a gaping pig;
Some, that are mad, if they behold a cat;
And others, when the bag-pipe sings i' the nose,
Cannot contain their urine; For affection,
Master of passion, sways it to the mood
Of what it likes, or loathes: Now, for your answer:
As there is no firm reason to be render'd,
Why he cannot abide a gaping pig;
Why he, a harmless necessary cat;
Why he, a woollen bag-pipe; but of force
Must yield to such inevitable shame,
As to offend, himself being offended;
So can I give no reason, nor I will not,
More than a lodg'd hate, and a certain loathing
I bear Antonio, that I follow thus
A losing suit against him. Are you answer'd?
Bass. This is no answer, thou unfeeling man,
To excuse the current of thy cruelty.
Shy. I am not bound to please thee with my answer.
Bass. Do all men kill the things they do not love?
Shy. Hates any man the thing he would not kill?
Bass. Every offence is not a hate at first.
Shy. What, wouldst thou have a serpent sting thee twice?
Ant. I pray you, think you question with a Jew:
You may as well go stand upon the beach,
And bid the main flood bate his usual height;
You may as well use question with the wolf,
Why he hath made the ewe bleat for the lamb;
You may as well forbid the mountain pines
To wag their high tops, and to make no noise,
When they are fretted with the gusts of heaven;
You may as well do any thing most hard,
As seek to soften that (than which what's harder?)
His Jewish heart:—Therefore I do beseech you,
Make no more offers, use no further means,
But, with all brief and plain conveniency,
Let me have judgment, and the Jew his will.
Bass. For thy three thousand ducats here is six.
Shy. If every ducat in six thousand ducats
Were in six parts, and every part a ducat,
I would not draw them, I would have my bond.
Duke. How shalt thou hope for mercy, rend'ring none?
Shy. What judgment shall I dread doing no wrong?
You have among you many a purchas'd slave,
Which, like your asses, and your dogs, and mules,
You use in abject and in slavish parts,
Because you bought them:—Shall I say to you,
Let them be free, marry them to your heirs?
Why sweat they under burdens? let their beds
Be made as soft as yours, and let their palates
Be season'd with such viands? You will answer,
The slaves are ours:—So do I answer you:
The pound of flesh which I demand of him,
Is dearly bought, 'tis mine, and I will have it:
If you deny me, fye upon your law!
There is no force in the decrees of Venice:
I stand for judgment: answer; shall I have it?
Duke. Upon my power, I may dismiss this court,
Unless Bellario, a learned doctor,
Whom I have sent for to determine this,
Come here to-day.
Salar. My lord, here stays without
A messenger with letters from the doctor,
New come from Padua.
Duke. Bring us the letters; Call the messenger.
Bass. Good cheer, Antonio! What, man? courage yet!
The Jew shall have my flesh, blood, bones, and all,
Ere thou shalt lose for me one drop of blood.
Ant. I am a tainted wether of the flock,
Meetest for death; the weakest kind of fruit
Drops earliest to the ground, and so let me:
You cannot better be employ'd, Bassanio,
Than to live still, and write mine epitaph.

Enter NERISSA, *dressed like a Lawyer's Clerk.*

Duke. Came you from Padua, from Bellario?
Ner. From both, my lord: Bellario greets your grace. [*Presents a Letter.*
Bass. Why dost thou whet thy knife so earnestly?
Shy. To cut the forfeiture from that bankrupt there.
Gra. Not on thy sole, but on thy soul, harsh Jew,
Thou mak'st thy knife keen: but no metal can,
No, not the hangman's axe, bear half the keenness
Of thy sharp envy. Can no prayers pierce thee?
Shy. No, none that thou hast wit enough to make.
Gra. O, be thou damn'd, inexorable dog!
And for thy life let justice be accus'd.
Thou almost mak'st me waver in my faith,
To hold opinion with Pythagoras,
That souls of animals infuse themselves
Into the trunks of men: thy currish spirit
Govern'd a wolf, who, hang'd for human slaughter,
Even from the gallows did his fell soul fleet,
And, whilst thou lay'st in thy unhallow'd dam,
Infus'd itself in thee; for thy desires
Are wolfish, bloody, starv'd, and ravenous.

Shy. Till thou canst rail the seal from off my bond,
Thou but offend'st thy lungs to speak so loud:
Repair thy wit, good youth, or it will fall
To cureless ruin.—I stand here for law.
Duke. This letter from Bellario doth commend
A young and learned doctor to our court:—
Where is he?
Ner. He attendeth here hard by,
To know your answer, whether you'll admit him.
Duke. With all my heart:—some three or four of you,
Go, give him courteous conduct to this place.—
Mean time, the court shall hear Bellario's letter.

[Clerk reads.] *Your grace shall understand, that, at the receipt of your letter, I am very sick: but in the instant that your messenger came, in loving visitation was with me a young doctor of Rome, his name is Balthasar: I acquainted him with the cause in controversy between the Jew and Antonio the merchant: we turned o'er many books together: he is furnish'd with my opinion; which, better'd with his own learning, (the greatness whereof I cannot enough commend,) comes with him, at my importunity, to fill up your grace's request in my stead. I beseech you, let his lack of years be no impediment to let him lack a reverend estimation; for I never knew so young a body with so old a head. I leave him to your gracious acceptance, whose trial shall better publish his commendation.*

Duke. You hear the learn'd Bellario, what he writes:
And here, I take it, is the doctor come.—

Enter PORTIA, *dressed like a Doctor of Laws.*

Give me your hand: Came you from old Bellario?
Por. I did, my lord.
Duke. You are welcome: take your place.
Are you acquainted with the difference
That holds this present question in the court?
Por. I am informed throughly of the cause.
Which is the merchant here, and which the Jew?
Duke. Antonio and old Shylock, both stand forth.
Por. Is your name Shylock?
Shy. Shylock is my name.
Por. Of a strange nature is the suit you follow;
Yet in such rule, that the Venetian law
Cannot impugn you, as you do proceed.—
You stand within his danger, do you not?
[*To* ANTONIO.
Ant. Ay, so he says.
Por. Do you confess the bond?
Ant. I do.
Por. Then must the Jew be merciful.
Shy. On what compulsion must I? tell me that.
Por. The quality of mercy is not strain'd;
It droppeth, as the gentle rain from heaven
Upon the place beneath: it is twice bless'd;
It blesseth him that gives, and him that takes:
'Tis mightiest in the mightiest; It becomes
The throned monarch better than his crown:
His sceptre shows the force of temporal power,
The attribute to awe and majesty,
Wherein doth sit the dread and fear of kings;
But mercy is above this sceptred sway,
It is enthroned in the hearts of kings,
It is an attribute to God himself;
And earthly power doth then show likest God's,
When mercy seasons justice. Therefore, Jew,
Though justice be thy plea, consider this,—
That in the course of justice, none of us
Should see salvation; we do pray for mercy;
And that same prayer doth teach us all to render
The deeds of mercy. I have spoke thus much,
To mitigate the justice of thy plea;
Which if thou follow, this strict court of Venice
Must needs give sentence 'gainst the merchant there.

Shy. My deeds upon my head? I crave the law,
The penalty and forfeit of my bond.
Por. Is he not able to discharge the money?
Bass. Yes, here I tender it for him in the court;
Yea, twice the sum: if that will not suffice,
I will be bound to pay it ten times o'er,
On forfeit of my hands, my head, my heart:
If this will not suffice, it must appear
That malice bears down truth. And I beseech you,
Wrest once the law to your authority:
To do a great right, do a little wrong;
And curb this cruel devil of his will.
Por. It must not be; there is no power in Venice
Can alter a decree established;
'Twill be recorded for a precedent;
And many an error, by the same example,
Will rush into the state: it cannot be.
Shy. A Daniel come to judgment! yea, a Daniel!—
O wise young judge, how do I honour thee!
Por. I pray you, let me look upon the bond.
Shy. Here 'tis, most reverend doctor, here it is.
Por. Shylock, there's thrice thy money offer'd thee.
Shy. An oath, an oath, I have an oath in heaven:
Shall I lay perjury upon my soul?
No, not for Venice.
Por. Why, this bond is forfeit;
And lawfully by this the Jew may claim
A pound of flesh, to be by him cut off
Nearest the merchant's heart:—Be merciful;
Take thrice thy money; bid me tear the bond.
Shy. When it is paid according to the tenour.—
It doth appear, you are a worthy judge;
You know the law, your exposition
Hath been most sound: I charge you by the law,
Whereof you are a well-deserving pillar,
Proceed to judgment: by my soul, I swear,
There is no power in the tongue of man
To alter me: I stay here on my bond.
Ant. Most heartily I do beseech the court
To give the judgment.
Por. Why then, thus it is.
You must prepare your bosom for his knife:
Shy. O noble judge! O excellent young man!
Por. For the intent and purpose of the law
Hath full relation to the penalty,
Which here appeareth due upon the bond.
Shy. 'Tis very true: O wise and upright judge!
How much more elder art thou than thy looks!
Por. Therefore lay bare your bosom.
Shy. Ay, his breast:
So says the bond:—Doth it not, noble judge?—
Nearest his heart, those are the very words.
Por. It is so. Are there balance here, to weigh
The flesh?
Shy. I have them ready.
Por. Have by some surgeon, Shylock, on your charge,
To stop his wounds, lest he do bleed to death.
Shy. Is it so nominated in the bond?
Por. It is not so express'd; But what of that?
'Twere good you do so much for charity.
Shy. I cannot find it; 'tis not in the bond.
Por. Come, merchant, have you any thing to say?
Ant. But little; I am arm'd, and well prepar'd.—
Give me your hand, Bassanio! fare you well!
Grieve not that I am fallen to this for you:
For herein fortune shows herself more kind
Than is her custom: it is still her use,
To let the wretched man outlive his wealth,
To view with hollow eye, and wrinkled brow,
An age of poverty; from which lingering penance
Of such a misery doth she cut me off.
Commend me to your honourable wife:
Tell her the process of Antonio's end,
Say, how I lov'd you, speak me fair in death:

And, when the tale is told, bid her be judge,
Whether Bassanio had not once a love.
Repent not you, that you shall lose your friend,
And he repents not that he pays your debt;
For, if the Jew do cut but deep enough,
I'll pay it instantly with all my heart.
Bass. Antonio, I am married to a wife,
Which is as dear to me as life itself;
But life itself, my wife, and all the world,
Are not with me esteem'd above thy life:
I would lose all, ay, sacrifice them all
Here to this devil to deliver you.
Por. Your wife would give you little thanks for that,
If she were by, to hear you make the offer.
Gra. I have a wife, whom, I protest, I love;
I would she were in heaven, so she could
Entreat some power to change this currish Jew.
Ner. 'Tis well you offer it behind her back;
The wish would make else an unquiet house.
Shy. These be the christian husbands: I have a daughter:
'Would any of the stock of Barrabas
Had been her husband, rather than a Christian! [*Aside.*
We trifle time: I pray thee, pursue sentence.
Por. A pound of that same merchant's flesh is thine;
The court awards it, and the law doth give it.
Shy. Most rightful judge!
Por. And you must cut this flesh from off his breast;
The law allows it, and the court awards it.
Shy. Most learned judge! a sentence: come, prepare.
Por. Tarry a little:—there is something else.—
This bond doth give thee here no jot of blood;
The words expressly are, a pound of flesh:
Take then thy bond, take thou thy pound of flesh;
But, in the cutting it, if thou dost shed
One drop of Christian blood, thy lands and goods
Are, by the laws of Venice, confiscate
Unto the state of Venice.
Gra. O upright judge!—Mark, Jew;—O learned judge!
Shy. Is that the law?
Por. Thyself shalt see the act:
For as thou urgest justice, be assur'd,
Thou shalt have justice, more than thou desir'st.
Gra. O learned judge! Mark, Jew;—a learned judge!
Shy. I take this offer then:—pay the bond thrice,
And let the Christian go.
Bass. Here is the money.
Por. Soft;
The Jew shall have all justice:—soft!—no haste;—
He shall have nothing but the penalty.
Gra. O Jew! an upright judge, a learned judge!
Por. Therefore prepare thee to cut off the flesh,
Shed thou no blood; nor cut thou less, nor more,
But just a pound of flesh: if thou tak'st more,
Or less than a just pound,—be it but so much
As makes it light, or heavy, in the substance,
Or the division of the twentieth part
Of one poor scruple; nay, if the scale do turn
But in the estimation of a hair,—
Thou diest, and all thy goods are confiscate.
Gra. A second Daniel, a Daniel, Jew!
Now, infidel, I have thee on the hip.
Por. Why doth the Jew pause? take thy forfeiture.
Shy. Give me my principal, and let me go.
Bass. I have it ready for thee; here it is.
Por. He hath refus'd it in the open court;
He shall have merely justice, and his bond.
Gra. A Daniel, still say I; a second Daniel!—
I thank thee, Jew, for teaching me that word.
Shy. Shall I not have barely my principal?
Por. Thou shalt have nothing but the forfeiture,
To be so taken at thy peril, Jew.
Shy. Why, then the devil give him good of it!
I'll stay no longer question.
Por. Tarry, Jew;
The law hath yet another hold on you.
It is enacted in the laws of Venice,—
If it be prov'd against an alien,
That by direct, or indirect attempts,
He seek the life of any citizen,
The party, 'gainst the which he doth contrive,
Shall seize one half his goods; the other half
Comes to the privy coffer of the state;
And the offender's life lies in the mercy
Of the duke only, 'gainst all other voice.
In which predicament, I say, thou stand'st:
For it appears by manifest proceeding,
That, indirectly, and directly too,
Thou hast contriv'd against the very life
Of the defendant: and thou hast incurr'd
The danger formerly by me rehears'd.
Down, therefore, and beg mercy of the duke.
Gra. Beg, that thou mayst have leave to hang thyself:
And yet, thy wealth being forfeit to the state,
Thou hast not left the value of a cord;
Therefore, thou must be hang'd at the state's charge.
Duke. That thou shalt see the difference of our spirit,
I pardon thee thy life before thou ask it:
For half thy wealth, it is Antonio's;
The other half comes to the general state,
Which humbleness may drive unto a fine.
Por. Ay, for the state; not for Antonio.
Shy. Nay, take my life and all, pardon not that:
You take my house, when you do take the prop
That doth sustain my house; you take my life,
When you do take the means whereby I live.
Por. What mercy can you render him, Antonio?
Gra. A halter gratis; nothing else, for God's sake.
Ant. So please my lord the duke and all the court,
To quit the fine for one half of his goods;
I am content, so he will let me have
The other half in use,—to render it,
Upon his death, unto the gentleman
That lately stole his daughter:
Two things provided more.—That, for this favour,
He presently become a Christian;
The other, that he do record a gift,
Here in the court, of all he dies possess'd,
Unto his son Lorenzo, and his daughter.
Duke. He shall do this; or else I do recant
The pardon that I late pronounced here.
Por. Art thou contented, Jew, what dost thou say?
Shy. I am content.
Por. Clerk, draw a deed of gift.
Shy. I pray you, give me leave to go from hence;
I am not well; send the deed after me,
And I will sign it.
Duke. Get thee gone, but do it.
Gra. In christening thou shalt have two godfathers;
Had I been judge, thou shouldst have had ten more;
To bring thee to the gallows, not to the font. [*Exit* SHYLOCK.
Duke. Sir, I entreat you home with me to dinner.
Por. I humbly do desire your grace of pardon;
I must away this night toward Padua,
And it is meet I presently set forth.

Duke. I am sorry that your leisure serves you not.
Antonio, gratify this gentleman;
For, in my mind, you are much bound to him.
[*Exeunt* Duke, *Magnificoes, and Train.*

Bass. Most worthy gentleman, I and my friend
Have by your wisdom been this day acquitted
Of grievous penalties; in lieu whereof,
Three thousand ducats, due unto the Jew,
We freely cope your courteous pains withal.

Ant. And stand indebted, over and above,
In love and service to you evermore.

Por. He is well paid that is well satisfied;
And I, delivering you, am satisfied,
And therein do account myself well paid;
My mind was never yet more mercenary.
I pray you, know me, when we meet again;
I wish you well, and so I take my leave.

Bass. Dear sir, of force I must attempt you further;
Take some remembrance of us, as a tribute,
Not as a fee: grant me two things, I pray you,
Not to deny me, and to pardon me.

Por. You press me far, and therefore I will yield.
Give me your gloves, I'll wear them for your sake:
And, for your love, I'll take this ring from you:—
Do not draw back your hand; I'll take no more;
And you in love shall not deny me this.

Bass. This ring, good sir,—alas, it is a trifle;
I will not shame myself to give you this.

Por. I will have nothing else but only this;
And now, methinks, I have a mind to it.

Bass. There's more depends on this, than on the value.
The dearest ring in Venice will I give you,
And find it out by proclamation:
Only for this, I pray you, pardon me.

Por. I see, sir, you are liberal in offers:
You taught me first to beg; and now, methinks,
You teach me how a beggar should be answer'd.

Bass. Good sir, this ring was given me by my wife;
And, when she put it on, she made me vow,
That I should neither sell, nor give, nor lose it.

Por. That 'scuse serves many men to save their gifts.
An if your wife be not a mad woman,
And know how well I have deserv'd this ring,
She would not hold out enemy for ever,
For giving it to me. Well, peace be with you!
[*Exeunt* Portia *and* Nerissa.

Ant. My lord Bassanio, let him have the ring;
Let his deservings, and my love withal,
Be valued 'gainst your wife's commandment.

Bass. Go, Gratiano, run and overtake him,
Give him the ring; and bring him, if thou canst,
Unto Antonio's house:—away, make haste.
[*Exit* Gratiano.
Come, you and I will thither presently;
And in the morning early will we both
Fly toward Belmont: Come, Antonio. [*Exeunt.*

SCENE II. *The same. A Street.*

Enter Portia *and* Nerissa.

Por. Inquire the Jew's house out, give him this deed,
And let him sign it; we'll away to-night,
And be a day before our husbands home:
This deed will be well welcome to Lozenzo.

Enter Gratiano.

Gra. Fair sir, you are well overtaken:
My lord Bassanio, upon more advice,
Hath sent you here this ring; and doth entreat
Your company at dinner.

Por. That cannot be:
This ring I do accept most thankfully,
And so, I pray you, tell him: Furthermore,
I pray you, show my youth old Shylock's house.

Gra. That will I do.

Ner. Sir, I would speak with you:—
I'll see if I can get my husband's ring,
[*To* Portia.
Which I did make him swear to keep for ever.

Por. Thou may'st, I warrant: We shall have old swearing,
That they did give the rings away to men;
But we'll outface them, and outswear them too.
Away, make haste; thou know'st where I will tarry.

Ner. Come, good sir, will you show me to this house? [*Exeunt.*

ACT V.

SCENE I. Belmont. *Avenue to* Portia's *House.*

Enter Lorenzo *and* Jessica.

Lor. The moon shines bright:—In such a night as this,
When the sweet wind did gently kiss the trees,
And they did make no noise: in such a night,
Troilus, methinks, mounted the Trojan walls,
And sigh'd his soul toward the Grecian tents,
Where Cressid lay that night.

Jes. In such a night,
Did Thisbe fearfully o'ertrip the dew;
And saw the lion's shadow ere himself,
And ran dismay'd away.

Lor. In such a night,
Stood Dido, with a willow in her hand,
Upon the wild sea banks, and wav'd her love
To come again to Carthage.

Jes. In such a night,
Medea gather'd the enchanted herbs
That did renew old Æson.

Lor. In such a night,
Did Jessica steal from the wealthy Jew:
And with an unthrift love did run from Venice,
As far as Belmont.

Jes. And in such a night,
Did young Lorenzo swear he lov'd her well;
Stealing her soul with many vows of faith,
And ne'er a true one.

Lor. And in such a night,
Did pretty Jessica, like a little shrew,
Slander her love, and he forgave it her.

Jes. I would out-night you, did nobody come:
But, hark, I hear the footing of a man.

Enter Stephano.

Lor. Who comes so fast in silence of the night?

Steph. A friend.

Lor. A friend? what friend? your name, I pray you, friend?

Steph. Stephano is my name; and I bring word,
My mistress will before the break of day
Be here at Belmont: she doth stray about
By holy crosses, where she kneels and prays
For happy wedlock hours.

Lor. Who comes with her?

Steph. None, but a holy hermit, and her maid.
I pray you, is my master yet return'd?

Lor. He is not, nor we have not heard from him.—
But go we in, I pray thee, Jessica,
And ceremoniously let us prepare
Some welcome for the mistress of the house.

Enter Launcelot.

Laun. Sola, sola, wo ha, ho, sola, sola!

Lor. Who calls?

Laun. Sola! did you see master Lorenzo, and mistress Lorenzo? sola, sola!

Lor. Leave hollaing, man; here.

Laun. Sola! where? where?

Lor. Here.

Laun. Tell him, there's a post come from my master, with his horn full of good news; my master will be here ere morning. [*Exit.*

Lor. Sweet soul, let's in, and there expect their coming.
And yet no matter;—Why should we go in?
My friend Stephano, signify, I pray you,
Within the house, your mistress is at hand;
And bring your musick forth into the air.—
[*Exit* STEPHANO.
How sweet the moon-light sleeps upon this bank!
Here will we sit, and let the sounds of musick
Creep in our ears; soft stillness, and the night,
Become the touches of sweet harmony.
Sit, Jessica: Look, how the floor of heaven
Is thick inlaid with patines of bright gold;
There's not the smallest orb, which thou behold'st,
But in his motion like an angel sings,
Still quiring to the young-ey'd cherubins:
Such harmony is in immortal souls;
But, whilst this muddy vesture of decay
Doth grossly close us in, we cannot hear it.—

Enter Musicians.

Come, ho, and wake Diana with a hymn;
With sweetest touches pierce your mistress' ear,
And draw her home with musick. [*Musick.*
Jes. I am never merry, when I hear sweet musick.
Lor. The reason is, your spirits are attentive:
For do but note a wild and wanton herd,
Or race of youthful and unhandled colts,
Fetching mad bounds, bellowing, and neighing loud,
Which is the hot condition of their blood;
If they but hear perchance a trumpet sound,
Or any air of musick touch their ears,
You shall perceive them make a mutual stand,
Their savage eyes turn'd to a modest gaze,
By the sweet power of musick: Therefore, the poet
Did feign that Orpheus drew trees, stones, and floods;
Since nought so stockish, hard, and full of rage,
But musick for the time doth change his nature:
The man that hath no musick in himself,
Nor is not mov'd with concord of sweet sounds,
Is fit for treasons, stratagems, and spoils;
The motions of his spirit are dull as night,
And his affections dark as Erebus:
Let no such man be trusted.—Mark the musick.

Enter PORTIA *and* NERISSA *at a distance.*

Por. That light we see is burning in my hall.
How far that little candle throws his beams!
So shines a good deed in a naughty world.
Ner. When the moon shone, we did not see the candle.
Por. So doth the greater glory dim the less:
A substitute shines brightly as a king,
Until a king be by; and then his state
Empties itself, as doth an inland brook
Into the main of waters. Musick! hark!
Ner. It is your musick, madam, of the house.
Por. Nothing is good, I see, without respect;
Methinks, it sounds much sweeter than by day.
Ner. Silence bestows that virtue on it, madam.
Por. The crow doth sing as sweetly as the lark,
When neither is attended; and, I think,
The nightingale, if she should sing by day,
When every goose is cackling, would be thought
No better a musician than the wren.
How many things by season season'd are
To their right praise, and true perfection!—
Peace, hoa! the moon sleeps with Endymion,
And would not be awak'd! [*Musick ceases.*
Lor. That is the voice,
Or I am much deceived, of Portia.
Por. He knows me, as the blind man knows the cuckoo,
By the bad voice.
Lor. Dear lady, welcome home.
Por. We have been praying for our husbands' welfare,
Which speed, we hope, the better for our words.
Are they return'd?
Lor. Madam, they are not yet;
But there is come a messenger before,
To signify their coming.
Por. Go in, Nerissa,
Give order to my servants, that they take
No note at all of our being absent hence;—
Nor you, Lorenzo:—Jessica, nor you.
[*A tucket sounds.*
Lor. Your husband is at hand, I hear his trumpet:
We are no tell-tales, madam; fear you not.
Por. This night, methinks, is but the daylight sick,
It looks a little paler; 'tis a day,
Such as a day is when the sun is hid.

Enter BASSANIO, ANTONIO, GRATIANO, *and their Followers.*

Bass. We should hold day with the Antipodes,
If you would walk in absence of the sun.
Por. Let me give light, but let me not be light;
For a light wife doth make a heavy husband,
And never be Bassanio so for me;
But God sort all!—You are welcome home, my lord.
Bass. I thank you, madam: give welcome to my friend.—
This is the man, this is Antonio,
To whom I am so infinitely bound.
Por. You should in all sense be much bound to him,
For, as I hear, he was much bound for you.
Ant. No more than I am well acquitted of.
Por. Sir, you are very welcome to our house:
It must appear in other ways than words,
Therefore, I scant this breathing courtesy.

GRATIANO *and* NERISSA *seem to talk apart.*

Gra. By yonder moon, I swear, you do me wrong;
In faith, I gave it to the judge's clerk:
Would he were gelt that had it, for my part,
Since you do take it, love, so much at heart.
Por. A quarrel, ho, already? what's the matter?
Gra. About a hoop of gold, a paltry ring
That she did give me; whose posy was
For all the world like cutler's poetry
Upon a knife, *Love me, and leave me not.*
Ner. What talk you of the posy, or the value?
You swore to me, when I did give it you,
That you would wear it till your hour of death;
And that it should lie with you in your grave:
Though not for me, yet for your vehement oaths,
You should have been respective, and have kept it,
Gave it a judge's clerk!—but well I know,
The clerk will ne'er wear hair on his face that had it.
Gra. He will, an if he live to be a man.
Ner. Ay, if a woman live to be a man.
Gra. Now, by this hand, I gave it to a youth,—
A kind of boy; a little scrubbed boy,
No higher than thyself; the judge's clerk;
A prating boy, that begg'd it as a fee;
I could not for my heart deny it him,
Por. You were to blame, I must be plain with you,
To part so slightly with your wife's first gift:
A thing stuck on with oaths upon your finger,
And riveted so with faith unto your flesh.
I gave my love a ring, and made him swear
Never to part with it; and here he stands;
I dare be sworn for him, he would not leave it,
Nor pluck it from his finger, for the wealth
That the world masters. Now, in faith, Gratiano,
You give your wife too unkind a cause of grief;
An 'twere to me, I should be mad at it.
Bass. Why, I were best to cut my left hand off,
And swear I lost the ring defending it. [*Aside.*
Gra. My lord Bassanio gave his ring away
Unto the judge that begg'd it, and, indeed,

Deserv'd it too; and then the boy, his clerk,
That took some pains in writing, he begg'd mine:
And neither man, nor master, would take aught
But the two rings.

Por. What ring gave you, my lord?
Not that, I hope, which you receiv'd of me.

Bass. If I could add a lie unto a fault,
I would deny it; but you see, my finger
Hath not the ring upon it, it is gone.

Por. Even so void is your false heart of truth.
By heaven, I will ne'er come in your bed
Until I see the ring.

Ner. Nor I in yours,
Till I again see mine.

Bass. Sweet Portia,
If you did know to whom I gave the ring,
If you did know for whom I gave the ring,
And would conceive for what I gave the ring,
And how unwillingly I left the ring,
When naught would be accepted but the ring,
You would abate the strength of your displeasure.

Por. If you had known the virtue of the ring,
Or half her worthiness that gave the ring,
Or your own honour to contain the ring,
You would not then have parted with the ring.
What man is there so much unreasonable,
If you had pleased to have defended it
With any terms of zeal, wanted the modesty
To urge the thing held as a ceremony?
Nerissa teaches me what to believe;
I'll die for't, but some woman had the ring.

Bass. No, by mine honour, madam, by my soul.
No woman had it, but a civil doctor,
Which did refuse three thousand ducats of me,
And begg'd the ring; the which I did deny him,
And suffer'd him to go displeas'd away;
Even he that had held up the very life
Of my dear friend. What should I say, sweet lady?
I was enforc'd to send it after him;
I was beset with shame and courtesy;
My honour would not let ingratitude
So much besmear it: Pardon me, good lady;
For, by these blessed candles of the night,
Had you been there, I think, you would have begg'd
The ring of me to give the worthy doctor.

Por. Let not that doctor e'er come near my house;
Since he hath got the jewel that I lov'd,
And that which you did swear to keep for me,
I will become as liberal as you:
I'll not deny him any thing I have,
No, not my body, nor my husband's bed:
Know him I shall, I am well sure of it:
Lie not a night from home; watch me, like Argus:
If you do not, if I be left alone,
Now, by mine honour, which is yet my own,
I'll have that doctor for my bedfellow.

Ner. And I his clerk; therefore be well advis'd,
How you do leave me to mine own protection.

Gra. Well, do you so: let not me take him then;
For, if I do, I'll mar the young clerk's pen.

Ant. I am the unhappy subject of these quarrels.

Por. Sir, grieve not you; You are welcome notwithstanding.

Bass. Portia, forgive me this enforced wrong;
And, in the hearing of these many friends,
I swear to thee, even by thine own fair eyes,
Wherein I see myself,——

Por. Mark you but that!
In both my eyes he doubly sees himself:
In each eye, one:—swear by your double self,
And there's an oath of credit.

Bass. Nay, but hear me:
Pardon this fault, and by my soul I swear,
I never more will break an oath with thee.

Ant. I once did lend my body for his wealth;
Which, but for him that had your husband's ring, [*To* PORTIA.
Had quite miscarried: I dare be bound again,
My soul upon the forfeit, that your lord
Will never more break faith advisedly.

Por. Then you shall be his surety: Give him this;
And bid him keep it better than the other.

Ant. Here, lord Bassanio; swear to keep this ring.

Bass. By heaven, it is the same I gave the doctor!

Por. I had it of him: pardon me, Bassanio;
For by this ring the doctor lay with me.

Ner. And pardon me, my gentle Gratiano;
For that same scrubbed boy, the doctor's clerk,
In lieu of this, last night did lie with me.

Gra. Why, this is like the mending of highways
In summer, where the ways are fair enough:
What! are we cuckolds, ere we have deserv'd it?

Por. Speak not so grossly.—You are all amaz'd:
Here is a letter, read it at your leisure;
It comes from Padua, from Bellario:
There you shall find, that Portia was the doctor;
Nerissa there, her clerk: Lorenzo here
Shall witness, I set forth as soon as you,
And but even now return'd: I have not yet
Enter'd my house.—Antonio, you are welcome;
And I have better news in store for you,
Than you expect: unseal this letter soon;
There you shall find, three of your argosies
Are richly come to harbour suddenly;
You shall not know by what strange accident
I chanced on this letter.

Ant. I am dumb.

Bass. Were you the doctor, and I knew you not?

Gra. Were you the clerk, that is to make me cuckold?

Ner. Ay; but the clerk that never means to do it;
Unless he live until he be a man.

Bass. Sweet doctor, you shall be my bedfellow;
When I am absent, then lie with my wife.

Ant. Sweet lady, you have given me life, and living;
For here I read for certain, that my ships
Are safely come to road.

Por. How now, Lorenzo?
My clerk hath some good comforts too for you.

Ner. Ay, and I'll give them him without a fee.—
There do I give to you, and Jessica,
From the rich Jew, a special deed of gift,
After his death, of all he dies possess'd of.

Lor. Fair ladies, you drop manna in the way
Of starved people.

Por. It is almost morning,
And yet, I am sure, you are not satisfied
Of these events at full: Let us go in;
And charge us there upon inter'gatories,
And we will answer all things faithfully.

Gra. Let it be so: The first inter'gatory
That my Nerissa shall be sworn on, is,
Whether till the next night she had rather stay;
Or go to bed now, being two hours to day:
But were the day come, I should wish it dark,
That I were couching with the doctor's clerk.
Well, while I live, I'll fear no other thing
So sore, as keeping safe Nerissa's ring.

[*Exeunt.*

AS YOU LIKE IT.

PERSONS REPRESENTED.

Duke, *living in exile.*
FREDERICK, *Brother to the* Duke, *and Usurper of his Dominions.*
AMIENS, JAQUES, } *Lords attending upon the* Duke *in his banishment.*
LE BEAU, *a Courtier attending upon* Frederick.
CHARLES, *his Wrestler.*
OLIVER, JAQUES, ORLANDO, } *Sons of* Sir Rowland de Bois.
ADAM, DENNIS, } *Servants to* Oliver.
TOUCHSTONE, *a Clown.*
SIR OLIVER MAR-TEXT, *a Vicar.*
CORIN, SYLVIUS, } *Shepherds.*
WILLIAM, *a country Fellow, in love with* Audrey.
A Person representing Hymen.

ROSALIND, *Daughter to the banished* Duke.
CELIA, *Daughter to* Frederick.
PHEBE, *a Shepherdess.*
AUDREY, *a country Wench.*

Lords belonging to the two Dukes; Pages, Foresters, *and other* Attendants.

The SCENE *lies, first, near* Oliver's *House; afterwards, partly in the* Usurper's *Court, and partly in the Forest of* Arden.

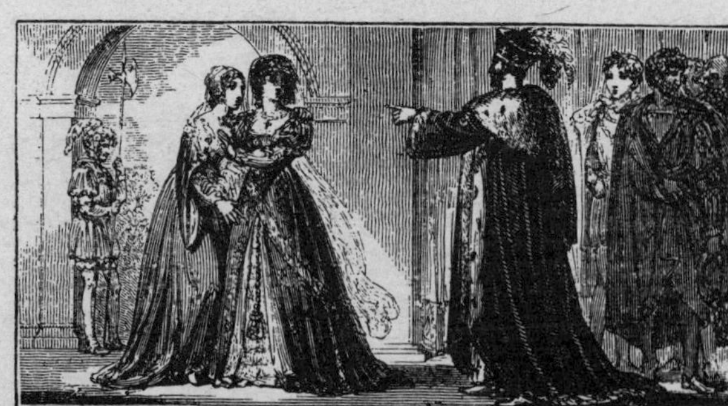

ACT I.

SCENE I. *An Orchard, near* Oliver's *House.*

Enter ORLANDO *and* ADAM.

Orl. As I remember, Adam, it was upon this fashion bequeathed me by will: But a poor thousand crowns; and, as thou say'st, charged my brother, on his blessing, to breed me well: and there begins my sadness. My brother Jaques he keeps at school, and report speaks goldenly of his profit: for my part, he keeps me rustically at home, or, to speak more properly, stays me here at home unkept: For call you that keeping for a gentleman of my birth, that differs not from the stalling of an ox? His horses are bred better; for, besides that they are fair with their feeding, they are taught their manage, and to that end riders dearly hired: but I, his brother, gain nothing under him but growth: for the which his animals on his dunghills are as much bound to him as I. Besides this nothing that he so plentifully gives me, the something that nature gave me, his countenance seems to take from me: he lets me feed with his hinds, bars me the place of a brother, and, as much as in him lies, mines my gentility with my education. This is it, Adam, that grieves me; and the spirit of my father, which I think is within me, begins to mutiny against this servitude: I will no longer endure it, though yet I know no wise remedy how to avoid it.

Enter OLIVER.

Adam. Yonder comes my master, your brother.

Orl. Go apart, Adam, and thou shalt hear how he will shake me up.

Oli. Now, sir! what make you here?

Orl. Nothing: I am not taught to make any thing.

Oli. What mar you then, sir?

Orl. Marry, sir, I am helping you to mar that which God made, a poor unworthy brother of yours, with idleness.

Oli. Marry, sir, be better employed, and be naught awhile.

Orl. Shall I keep your hogs, and eat husks with them? What prodigal portion have I spent, that I should come to such penury?

Oli. Know you where you are, sir?

Orl. O, sir, very well: here in your orchard.

Oli. Know you before whom, sir?

Orl. Ay, better than he I am before knows me. I know, you are my eldest brother; and, in the gentle condition of blood, you should so know me: The courtesy of nations allows you my better, in that you are the first-born; but the same tradition takes not away my blood, were there twenty brothers betwixt us: I have as much of my father in me, as you; albeit, I confess, your coming before me is nearer to his reverence.

Oli. What, boy!

Orl. Come, come, elder brother, you are too young in this.

Oli. Wilt thou lay hands on me, villain.

Orl. I am no villain: I am the youngest son of Sir Rowland de Bois; he was my father; and he is thrice a villain, that says, such a father begot villains: Wert thou not my brother, I would not take this hand from thy throat, till this other had pulled out thy tongue for saying so: thou hast railed on thyself.

Adam. Sweet masters, be patient; for your father's remembrance, be at accord.

Oli. Let me go, I say.

Orl. I will not, till I please: you shall hear me. My father charged you in his will to give me good education: you have trained me like a peasant, obscuring and hiding from me all gentleman-like qualities: the spirit of my father grows strong in me, and I will no longer endure it: therefore allow me such exercises as may become a gentleman, or give me the poor allottery my father left me by testament: with that I will go buy my fortunes.

Oli. And what wilt thou do? beg, when that is spent? Well, sir, get you in: I will not long be troubled with you: you shall have some part of your will: I pray you, leave me.

Orl. I will no further offend you than becomes me for my good.

Oli. Get you with him, you old dog.

Adam. Is old dog my reward? Most true, I have lost my teeth in your service.—God be with my old master! he would not have spoke such a word. [*Exeunt* ORLANDO *and* ADAM.

Oli. Is it even so? begin you to grow upon me? I will physick your rankness, and yet give no thousand crowns neither. Hola, Dennis!

Enter DENNIS.

Den. Calls your worship?

Oli. Was not Charles, the Duke's wrestler, here to speak with me?

Den. So please you, he is here at the door, and importunes access to you.

Oli. Call him in. [*Exit* DENNIS.]—'Twill be a good way; and to-morrow the wrestling is.

Enter CHARLES.

Cha. Good morrow to your worship.

Oli. Good monsieur Charles!—what's the new news at the new court!

Cha. There's no news at the court, sir, but the old news; that is, the old duke is banished by his younger brother the new duke! and three or four loving lords have put themselves into voluntary exile with him, whose lands and revenues enrich the new duke; therefore he gives them good leave to wander.

Oli. Can you tell, if Rosalind, the duke's daughter, be banished with her father.

Cha. O, no; for the duke's daughter, her cousin, so loves her,—being ever from their cradles bred together,—that she would have followed her exile, or have died to stay behind her. She is at the court, and no less beloved of her uncle than his own daughter; and never two ladies loved as they do.

Oli. Where will the old duke live?

Cha. They say, he is already in the forest of Arden, and a many merry men with him; and there they live like the old Robin Hood of England: they say, many young gentlemen flock to him every day; and fleet the time carelessly, as they did in the golden world.

Oli. What, you wrestle to-morrow before the new duke?

Cha. Marry, do I, sir; and I came to acquaint you with a matter. I am given, sir, secretly to understand, that your younger brother, Orlando, hath a disposition to come in disguis'd against me to try a fall: To-morrow, sir, I wrestle for my credit; and he that escapes me without some broken limb, shall acquit him well. Your brother is but young, and tender; and, for your love, I would be loath to foil him, as I must, for my own honour, if he come in: therefore out of my love to you, I came hither to acquaint you withal; that either you might stay him from his intendment, or brook such disgrace well as he shall run into; in that it is a thing of his own search, and altogether against my will.

Oli. Charles, I thank thee for thy love to me, which thou shalt find I will most kindly requite. I had myself notice of my brother's purpose herein, and have by underhand means laboured to dissuade him from it; but he is resolute. I'll tell thee, Charles,—it is the stubbornest young fellow of France: full of ambition, an envious emulator of every man's good parts, a secret and villanous contriver against me his natural brother; therefore use thy discretion; I had as lief thou didst break his neck as his finger: and thou wert best look to't; for if thou dost him any slight disgrace, or if he do not mightily grace himself on thee, he will practise against thee by poison, entrap thee by some treacherous device, and never leave thee till he hath ta'en thy life by some indirect means or other: for, I assure thee, and almost with tears I speak it, there is not one so young and so villanous this day living. I speak but brotherly of him: but should I anatomize him to thee as he is, I must blush and weep, and thou must look pale and wonder.

Cha. I am heartily glad I came hither to you: if he come to-morrow, I'll give him his payment: If ever he go alone again, I'll never wrestle for prize more: And so, God keep your worship. [*Exit.*

Oli. Farewell, good Charles.—Now will I stir this gamester: I hope, I shall see an end of him: for my soul, yet I know not why, hates nothing more than he. Yet he's gentle; never school'd, and yet learned; full of noble device; of all sorts enchantingly beloved; and, indeed, so much in the heart of the world, and especially of my own people, who best know him, that I am altogether misprised; but it shall not be so long; this wrestler shall clear all: nothing remains, but that I kindle the boy thither, which now I'll go about. [*Exit.*

SCENE II. *A Lawn before the* Duke's *Palace.*

Enter ROSALIND *and* CELIA.

Cel. I pray thee, Rosalind, sweet my coz, be merry.

Ros. Dear Celia, I show more mirth than I am mistress of; and would you yet I were merrier? Unless you could teach me to forget a banished father, you must not learn me how to remember any extraordinary pleasure.

Cel. Herein, I see, thou lovest me not with the full weight that I love thee: if my uncle, thy banished father, had banished thy uncle, the duke my father, so thou hadst been still with me, I could have taught my love to take thy father for mine; so would'st thou, if the truth of thy love to me were so righteously temper'd as mine is to thee.

Ros. Well, I will forget the condition of my estate, to rejoice in yours.

Cel. You know, my father hath no child but I, nor none is like to have; and, truly, when he dies, thou shalt be his heir: for what he hath taken away from thy father perforce, I will render thee again in affection; by mine honour, I will; and when I break that oath, let me turn monster: therefore, my sweet Rose, my dear Rose, be merry.

Ros. From henceforth I will, coz, and devise sports: let me see; What think you of falling in love?

Cel. Marry, I pr'ythee, do, to make sport withal: but love no man in good earnest; nor no further in sport neither, than with safety of a pure blush thou may'st in honour come off again.

Ros. What shall be our sport then?

Cel. Let us sit and mock the good housewife, Fortune, from her wheel, that her gifts may henceforth be bestowed equally.

Ros. I would, we could do so; for her benefits are mightily misplaced: and the bountiful blind woman doth most mistake in her gifts to women.

Cel. 'Tis true: for those, that she makes fair, she scarce makes honest: and those, that she makes honest, she makes very ill-favour'dly.

Ros. Nay, now thou goest from fortune's office to nature's: fortune reigns in gifts of the world, not in the lineaments of nature.

Enter TOUCHSTONE.

Cel. No? when nature hath made a fair creature, may she not by fortune fall into the fire?—Though nature hath given us wit to flout at fortune, hath not fortune sent in this fool to cut off the argument?

Ros. Indeed, there is fortune too hard for nature; when fortune makes nature's natural the cutter off of nature's wit.

Cel. Peradventure, this is not fortune's work neither, but nature's; who perceiving our natural wits too dull to reason of such goddesses, hath sent this natural for our whetstone: for always the dulness of the fool is the whetstone of his wits.—How now, wit? whither wander you?

Touch. Mistress, you must come away to your father.

Cel. Were you made the messenger?

Touch. No, by mine honour; but I was bid to come for you.

Ros. Where learned you that oath, fool?

Touch. Of a certain knight, that swore by his honour they were good pancakes, and swore by his honour the mustard was naught: now, I'll stand to it, the pancakes were naught, and the mustard was good; and yet was not the knight forsworn.

Cel. How prove you that, in the great heap of your knowledge?

Ros. Ay, marry; now unmuzzle your wisdom.

Touch. Stand you both forth now: stroke your chins, and swear by your beards that I am a knave.

Cel. By our beards, if we had them, thou art.

Touch. By my knavery, if I had it, then I were: but if you swear by that that is not, you are not forsworn: no more was this knight, swearing by his honour, for he never had any; or if he had, he had sworn it away, before ever he saw those pancakes, or that mustard.

Cel. 'Pr'ythee, who is't that thou mean'st!

Touch. One that old Frederick, your father, loves.

Cel. My father's love is enough to honour him. Enough! speak no more of him; you'll be whipp'd for taxation, one of these days.

Touch. The more pity, that fools may not speak wisely, what wise men do foolishly.

Cel. By my troth, thou say'st true: for since the little wit, that fools have, was silenced, the little foolery, that wise men have, makes a great show. Here comes Monsieur Le Beau.

Enter LE BEAU.

Ros. With his mouth full of news.

Cel. Which he will put on us, as pigeons feed their young.

Ros. Then shall we be news-cramm'd.

Cel. All the better; we shall be the more marketable. *Bon jour,* Monsieur Le Beau: What's the news?

Le Beau. Fair princess, you have lost much good sport.

Cel. Sport? Of what colour?

Le Beau. What colour, madam? how shall I answer you?

Ros. As wit and fortune will.

Touch. Or as the destinies decree.

Cel. Well said: that was laid on with a trowel.

Touch. Nay, if I keep not my rank,——

Ros. Thou losest thy old smell.

Le Beau. You amaze me, ladies: I would have told you of good wrestling, which you have lost the sight of.

Ros. Yet tell us the manner of the wrestling.

Le Beau. I will tell you the beginning, and, if it please your ladyships, you may see the end; for the best is yet to do; and here, where you are, they are coming to perform it.

Cel. Well,—the beginning, that is dead and buried.

Le Beau. There comes an old man, and his three sons,——

Cel. I could match this beginning with an old tale.

Le Beau. Three proper young men, of excellent growth and presence;——

Ros. With bills on their necks,—*Be it known unto all men by these presents,*——

Le Beau. The eldest of the three wrestled with Charles, the duke's wrestler; which Charles in a moment threw him, and broke three of his ribs, that there is little hope of life in him: so he served the second, and so the third: Yonder they lie; the poor old man, their father, making such pitiful dole over them, that all the beholders take his part with weeping.

Ros. Alas!

Touch. But what is the sport, monsieur, that the ladies have lost?

Le Beau. Why, this that I speak of.

Touch. Thus men may grow wiser every day! it is the first time that ever I heard, breaking of ribs was sport for ladies.

Cel. Or I, I promise thee.

Ros. But is there any else longs to see this broken musick in his sides? is there yet another dotes upon rib-breaking?—Shall we see this wrestling, cousin?

Le Beau. You must, if you stay here: for here is the place appointed for the wrestling, and they are ready to perform it.

Cel. Yonder, sure, they are coming: Let us now stay and see it.

Flourish. Enter DUKE FREDERICK, Lords, ORLANDO, CHARLES, *and* Attendants.

Duke F. Come on; since the youth will not be entreated, his own peril on his forwardness.

Ros. Is yonder the man?

Le Beau. Even he, madam.

Cel. Alas, he is too young: yet he looks successfully.

Duke F. How now, daughter and cousin? are you crept hither to see the wrestling?

Ros. Ay, my liege: so please you give us leave.

Duke F. You will take little delight in it, I can tell you, there is such odds in the men: In pity of the challenger's youth, I would fain dissuade him, but he will not be entreated: Speak to him, ladies; see if you can move him.

Cel. Call him hither, good Monsieur Le Beau.

Duke F. Do so; I'll not be by.

[Duke F. *goes apart.*

Le Beau. Monsieur the challenger, the princesses call for you.

Orl. I attend them, with all respect and duty.

Ros. Young man, have you challenged Charles the wrestler?

Orl. No, fair princess; he is the general challenger: I come but in, as others do, to try with him the strength of my youth.

Cel. Young gentleman, your spirits are too bold for your years: You have seen cruel proof of this man's strength: if you saw yourself with your eyes, or knew yourself with your judgment, the fear of your adventure would counsel you to a more equal enterprise. We pray you, for your own sake, to embrace your own safety, and give over this attempt.

Ros. Do, young sir; your reputation shall not therefore be misprised: we will make it our suit to the duke, that the wrestling might not go forward.

Orl. I beseech you, punish me not with your hard thoughts; wherein I confess me much guilty, to deny so fair and excellent ladies any thing. But let your fair eyes and gentle wishes go with me to my trial: wherein, if I be foiled, there is but one shamed that was never gracious; if killed, but one dead that is willing to be so;

I shall do my friends no wrong, for I have none to lament me; the world no injury, for in it I have nothing; only in the world I fill up a place, which may be better supplied when I have made it empty.

Ros. The little strength that I have, I would it were with you.

Cel. And mine, to eke out hers.

Ros. Fare you well. 'Pray heaven, I be deceived in you!

Cel. Your heart's desires be with you.

Cha. Come, where is this young gallant, that is so desirous to lie with his mother earth?

Orl. Ready, sir; but his will hath in it a more modest working.

Duke F. You shall try but one fall.

Cha. No, I warrant your grace; you shall not entreat him to a second, that have so mightily persuaded him from a first.

Orl. You mean to mock me after; you should not have mocked me before: but come your ways.

Ros. Now, Hercules be thy speed, young man!

Cel. I would I were invisible, to catch the strong fellow by the leg. [CHA. *and* ORL. *wrestle.*

Ros. O excellent young man!

Cel. If I had a thunderbolt in mine eye, I can tell who should down. [CHA. *is thrown. Shout.*

Duke F. No more, no more.

Orl. Yes, I beseech your grace; I am not yet well breathed.

Duke F. How dost thou, Charles?

Le Beau. He cannot speak, my lord.

Duke F. Bear him away. [CHARLES *is borne out.*] What is thy name, young man?

Orl. Orlando, my liege; the youngest son of Sir Rowland de Bois.

Duke F. I would, thou hadst been son to some man else.
The world esteem'd thy father honourable,
But I did find him still mine enemy:
Thou shouldst have better pleas'd me with this deed,
Hadst thou descended from another house.
But fare thee well; thou art a gallant youth;
I would, thou hadst told me of another father.
[*Exeunt* DUKE FRED. Train, *and* LE BEAU.

Cel. Were I my father, coz, would I do this?

Orl. I am more proud to be Sir Rowland's son,
His youngest son;—and would not change that calling,
To be adopted heir to Frederick.

Ros. My father lov'd Sir Rowland as his soul,
And all the world was of my father's mind:
Had I before known this young man his son,
I should have given him tears unto entreaties,
Ere he should thus have ventur'd.

Cel. Gentle cousin,
Let us go thank him, and encourage him:
My father's rough and envious disposition
Sticks me at heart.—Sir, you have well deserv'd:
If you do keep your promises in love
But justly, as you have exceeded promise,
Your mistress shall be happy.

Ros. Gentleman,
[*Giving him a chain from her neck.*
Wear this for me; one out of suits with fortune;
That could give more, but that her hand lacks means.—
Shall we go, coz.

Cel. Ay:—Fare you well, fair gentleman.

Orl. Can I not say, I thank you? My better parts
Are all thrown down; and that which here stands up,
Is but a quintain, a mere lifeless block.

Ros. He calls us back: my pride fell with my fortunes:
I'll ask him what he would:—Did you call, sir?—
Sir, you have wrestled well, and overthrown
More than your enemies.

Cel. Will you go, coz?

Ros. Have with you:—Fare you well.
[*Exeunt* ROSALIND *and* CELIA.

Orl. What passion hangs these weights upon my tongue?
I cannot speak to her, yet she urg'd conference.

Re-enter LE BEAU.

O poor Orlando! thou art overthrown;
Or Charles, or something weaker, masters thee.

Le Beau. Good sir, I do in friendship counsel you
To leave this place: Albeit you have deserv'd
High commendation, true applause, and love;
Yet such is now the duke's condition,
That he misconstrues all that you have done.
The duke is humorous; what he is, indeed,
More suits you to conceive, than me to speak of.

Orl. I thank you, sir: and, 'pray you, tell me this;
Which of the two was daughter of the duke.
That here was at the wrestling?

Le Beau. Neither his daughter, if we judge by manners;
But yet, indeed, the smaller is his daughter:
The other is daughter to the banish'd duke,
And here detain'd by her usurping uncle,
To keep his daughter company; whose loves
Are dearer than the natural bond of sisters.
But I can tell you, that of late this duke
Hath ta'en displeasure 'gainst his gentle niece;
Grounded upon no other argument,
But that the people praise her for her virtues,
And pity her for her good father's sake;
And, on my life, his malice 'gainst the lady
Will suddenly break forth.—Sir, fare you well;
Hereafter, in a better world than this,
I shall desire more love and knowledge of you.

Orl. I rest much bounden to you: fare you well! [*Exit* LE BEAU.
Thus must I from the smoke into the smother;
From tyrant duke, unto a tyrant brother:—
But heavenly Rosalind! [*Exit.*

SCENE III. *A Room in the Palace.*

Enter CELIA *and* ROSALIND.

Cel. Why, cousin; why, Rosalind;—Cupid, have mercy!—Not a word?

Ros. Not one to throw at a dog.

Cel. No, thy words are too precious to be cast away upon curs, throw some of them at me; come, lame me with reasons.

Ros. Then there were two cousins laid up; when the one should be lamed with reasons, and the other mad without any.

Cel. But is all this for your father?

Ros. No, some of it for my child's father. O, how full of briars is this working-day world!

Cel. They are but burs, cousin, thrown upon thee in holiday foolery; if we walk not in the trodden paths, our very petticoats will catch them.

Ros. I could shake them off my coat; these burs are in my heart.

Cel. Hem them away.

Ros. I would try: if I could cry hem, and have him.

Cel. Come, come, wrestle with thy affections.

Ros. O, they take the part of a better wrestler than myself.

Cel. O, a good wish upon you! you will try in time, in despite of a fall.—But, turning these jests out of service, let us talk in good earnest: Is it possible, on such a sudden, you should fall into so strong a liking with old Sir Rowland's youngest son?

Ros. The duke my father lov'd his father dearly.

Cel. Doth it therefore ensue, that you should love his son dearly? By this kind of chase, I should hate him, for my father hated his father dearly; yet I hate not Orlando.

Ros. No 'faith, hate him not, for my sake.

Cel. Why should I not? doth he not deserve well?

Ros. Let me love him for that; and do you love him, because I do:—Look, here comes the duke.

Cel. With his eyes full of anger.

Enter DUKE FREDERICK, *with* Lords.

Duke F. Mistress, dispatch you with your safest haste,
And get you from our court.

Ros. Me, uncle?

Duke F. You, cousin;
Within these ten days if that thou be'st found
So near our public court as twenty miles,
Thou diest for it.

Ros. I do beseech your grace,
Let me the knowledge of my fault bear with me;
If with myself I hold intelligence,
Or have acquaintance with mine own desires;
If that I do not dream, or be not frantic,
(As I do trust I am not,) then, dear uncle,
Never, so much as in a thought unborn,
Did I offend your highness.

Duke F. Thus do all traitors;
If their purgation did consist in words,
They are as innocent as grace itself:—
Let it suffice thee, that I trust thee not.

Ros. Yet your mistrust cannot make me a traitor:
Tell me, whereon the likelihood depends.

Duke F. Thou art thy father's daughter, there's enough.

Ros. So was I, when your highness took his dukedom;
So was I, when your highness banish'd him:
Treason is not inherited, my lord;
Or, if we did derive it from our friends:
What's that to me? my father was no traitor:
Then, good my liege, mistake me not so much,
To think my poverty is treacherous.

Cel. Dear sovereign, hear me speak.

Duke F. Ay, Celia; we stay'd her for your sake,
Else had she with her father rang'd along.

Cel. I did not then entreat to have her stay,
It was your pleasure, and your own remorse;
I was too young that time to value her,
But now I know her; if she be a traitor,
Why so am I; we still have slept together,
Rose at an instant, learn'd, play'd, eat together:
And wheresoe'er we went, like Juno's swans,
Still we went coupled, and inseparable.

Duke F. She is too subtle for thee; and her smoothness,
Her very silence, and her patience,
Speak to the people, and they pity her.
Thou art a fool: she robs thee of thy name;
And thou wilt show more bright, and seem more virtuous,
When she is gone: then open not thy lips;
Firm and irrevocable is my doom
Which I have pass'd upon her; she is banish'd.

Cel. Pronounce that sentence then on me, my liege:
I cannot live out of her company.

Duke F. You are a fool:—You, niece, provide yourself;
If you out-stay the time, upon mine honour,
And in the greatness of my word, you die.
[*Exeunt* DUKE FREDERICK *and* Lords.

Cel. O my poor Rosalind! whither wilt thou go?
Wilt thou change fathers? I will give thee mine.
I charge thee, be not thou more griev'd than I am.

Ros. I have more cause.

Cel. Thou hast not, cousin;
Pr'ythee, be cheerful: know'st thou not, the duke
Hath banish'd me, his daughter?

Ros. That he hath not.

Cel. No? hath not? Rosalind lacks then the love
Which teacheth thee that thou and I am one:
Shall we be sunder'd? shall we part, sweet girl?
No; let my father seek another heir.
Therefore, devise with me, how we may fly,
Whither to go, and what to bear with us:
And do not seek to take your change upon you,
To bear your griefs yourself, and leave me out;
For, by this heaven, now at our sorrows pale,
Say what thou canst, I'll go along with thee.

Ros. Why, whither shall we go?

Cel. To seek my uncle in the forest of Arden.

Ros. Alas, what danger will it be to us,
Maids as we are, to travel forth so far?
Beauty provoketh thieves sooner than gold.

Cel. I'll put myself in poor and mean attire,
And with a kind of umber smirch my face;
The like do you; so shall we pass along,
And never stir assailants.

Ros. Were it not better,
Because that I am more than common tall,
That I did suit me all points like a man?
A gallant curtle-axe upon my thigh,
A boar-spear in my hand; and (in my heart
Lie there what hidden woman's fear there will),
We'll have a swashing and a martial outside;
As many other mannish cowards have,
That do outface it with their semblances.

Cel. What shall I call thee, when thou art a man?

Ros. I'll have no worse a name than Jove's own page,
And therefore, look you, call me Ganymede.
But what will you be call'd?

Cel. Something that hath a reference to my state;
No longer Celia, but Aliena.

Ros. But, cousin, what if we assay'd to steal
The clownish fool out of your father's court?
Would he not be a comfort to our travel?

Cel. He'll go along o'er the wide world with me;
Leave me alone to woo him: Let's away,
And get our jewels and our wealth together;
Devise the fittest time and safest way
To hide us from pursuit that will be made
After my flight: Now go we in content,
To liberty, and not to banishment. [*Exeunt.*

ACT II.

SCENE I. *The Forest of* Arden.

Enter Duke *senior*, AMIENS, *and other* Lords, *in the dress of Foresters.*

Duke S. Now my co-mates, and brothers in exile,
Hath not old custom made this life more sweet
Than that of painted pomp? Are not these woods
More free from peril than the envious court?
Here feel we but the penalty of Adam,
The seasons' difference; as, the icy fang,
And churlish chiding of the winter's wind,
Which when it bites and blows upon my body,
Even till I shrink with cold, I smile, and say,—
This is no flattery; these are counsellors
That feelingly persuade me what I am.
Sweet are the uses of adversity;
Which, like the toad, ugly and venomous,
Wears yet a precious jewel in his head;
And this our life, exempt from public haunt,
Finds tongues in trees, books in the running brooks,
Sermons in stones, and good in every thing.

Ami. I would not change it: Happy is your grace,
That can translate the stubbornness of fortune
Into so quiet and so sweet a style.

Duke S. Come, shall we go and kill us venison?
And yet it irks me, the poor dappled fools,—
Being native burghers of this desert city,—

Should in their own confines, with forked heads
Have their round haunches gor'd.

1 *Lord.* Indeed, my lord,
The melancholy Jaques grieves at that;
And, in that kind, swears you do more usurp
Than doth your brother that hath banish'd you.
To-day, my lord of Amiens, and myself,
Did steal behind him, as he lay along
Under an oak, whose antique root peeps out
Upon the brook that brawls along this wood:
To the which place a poor sequester'd stag,
That from the hunter's aim had ta'en a hurt,
Did come to languish; and, indeed, my lord,
The wretched animal heav'd forth such groans,
That their discharge did stretch his leathern coat
Almost to bursting; and the big round tears
Cours'd one another down his innocent nose
In piteous chase; and thus the hairy fool,
Much marked of the melancholy Jaques,
Stood on the extremest verge of the swift brook,
Augmenting it with tears.

Duke S. But what said Jaques?
Did he not moralize this spectacle?

1 *Lord.* O, yes, into a thousand similes.
First, for his weeping in the needless stream;
Poor deer, quoth he, *thou mak'st a testament*
As worldlings do, giving thy sum of more
To that which had too much: Then being alone,
Left and abandon'd of his velvet friends;
'Tis right, quoth he; *this misery doth part*
The flux of company: Anon, a careless herd,
Full of the pasture, jumps along by him,
And never stays to greet him; *Ay*, quoth Jaques,
Sweep on, you fat and greasy citizens;
'Tis just the fashion: Wherefore do you look
Upon that poor and broken bankrupt there?
Thus most invectively he pierceth through
The body of country, city, court,
Yea, and of this our life; swearing, that we
Are mere usurpers, tyrants, and what's worse,
To fright the animals, and to kill them up,
In their assign'd and native dwelling-place.

Duke S. And did you leave him in this contemplation?

2 *Lord.* We did, my lord, weeping and commenting
Upon the sobbing deer.

Duke S. Show me the place;
I love to cope him in these sullen fits,
For then he's full of matter.

2 *Lord.* I'll bring you to him straight. [*Exeunt.*

SCENE II. *A Room in the Palace.*

Enter DUKE FREDERICK, Lords, *and* Attendants.

Duke F. Can it be possible that no man saw them?
It cannot be: some villains of my court
Are of consent and sufferance in this.

1 *Lord.* I cannot hear of any that did see her.
The ladies, her attendants of her chamber,
Saw her a-bed: and in the morning early,
They found the bed untreasur'd of their mistress.

2 *Lord.* My lord, the roynish clown, at whom so oft
Your grace was wont to laugh, is also missing.
Hesperia, the princess' gentlewoman,
Confesses, that she secretly o'erheard
Your daughter and her cousin much commend
The parts and graces of the wrestler
That did but lately foil the sinewy Charles;
And she believes, wherever they are gone,
That youth is surely in their company.

Duke F. Send to his brother; fetch that gallant hither;
If he be absent, bring his brother to me,
I'll make him find him: do this suddenly;
And let not search and inquisition quail
To bring again these foolish runaways. [*Exeunt.*

SCENE III. *Before* Oliver's *House.*

Enter ORLANDO *and* ADAM, *meeting.*

Orl. Who's there?

Adam. What! my young master?—O, my gentle master,
O, my sweet master, O you memory
Of old Sir Rowland! why, what make you here?
Why are you virtuous? Why do people love you?
And wherefore are you gentle, strong, and valiant?
Why would you be so fond to overcome
The bony prizer of the humorous duke?
Your praise is come too swiftly home before you.
Know you not, master, to some kind of men
Their graces serve them but as enemies?
No more do yours; your virtues, gentle master,
Are sanctified and holy traitors to you.
O, what a world is this, when what is comely
Envenoms him that bears it!

Orl. Why, what's the matter?

Adam. O unhappy youth,
Come not within these doors; within this roof
The enemy of all your graces lives:
Your brother—(no, no brother: yet the son—
Yet not the son;—I will not call him son
Of him I was about to call his father),—
Hath heard your praises; and this night he means
To burn the lodging where you use to lie,
And you within it: if he fail of that,
He will have other means to cut you off:
I overheard him, and his practices.
This is no place, this house is but a butchery;
Abhor it, fear it, do not enter it.

Orl. Why, whither, Adam, wouldst thou have me go?

Adam. No matter whither, so you come not here.

Orl. What, wouldst thou have me go and beg my food?
Or, with a base and boisterous sword, enforce
A thievish living on the common road?
This I must do, or know not what to do:
Yet this I will not do, do how I can;
I rather will subject me to the malice
Of a diverted blood, and bloody brother.

Adam. But do not so: I have five hundred crowns,
The thrifty hire I sav'd under your father,
Which I did store, to be my foster-nurse,
When service should in my old limbs lie lame,
And unregarded age in corners thrown;
Take that: and he that doth the ravens feed,
Yea, providently caters for the sparrow,
Be comfort to my age! Here is the gold;
All this I give you: Let me be your servant;
Though I look old, yet I am strong and lusty:
For in my youth I never did apply
Hot and rebellious liquors in my blood;
Nor did not with unbashful forehead woo
The means of weakness and debility;
Therefore my age is as a lusty winter,
Frosty, but kindly: let me go with you;
I'll do the service of a younger man
In all your business and necessities.

Orl. O good old man; how well in thee appears
The constant service of the antique world,
When service sweat for duty, not for meed!
Thou art not for the fashion of these times,
Where none will sweat, but for promotion;
And having that, do choke their service up
Even with the having: it is not so with thee.
But, poor old man, thou prun'st a rotten tree,
That cannot so much as a blossom yield,
In lieu of all thy pains and husbandry:
But come thy ways, we'll go along together;
And ere we have thy youthful wages spent,
We'll light upon some settled low content.

Adam. Master, go on, and I will follow thee,
To the last gasp, with truth and loyalty.—
From seventeen years till now almost fourscore
Here lived I, but now live here no more.

At seventeen years many their fortunes seek;
But at fourscore, it is too late a week;
Yet fortune cannot recompense me better,
Than to die well, and not my master's debtor.
[*Exeunt.*

SCENE IV. *The Forest of* Arden.

Enter ROSALIND *in boy's clothes*, CELIA *drest like a Shepherdess, and* TOUCHSTONE.

Ros. O Jupiter! how weary are my spirits!

Touch. I care not for my spirits, if my legs were not weary.

Ros. I could find in my heart to disgrace my man's apparel, and to cry like a woman: but I must comfort the weaker vessel, as doublet and hose ought to show itself courageous to petticoat: therefore, courage, good Aliena.

Cel. I pray you, bear with me; I cannot go no further.

Touch. For my part, I had rather bear with you, than bear you; yet I should bear no cross, if I did bear you; for, I think, you have no money in your purse.

Ros. Well, this is the forest of Arden.

Touch. Ay, now am I in Arden: the more fool I: when I was at home, I was in a better place; but travellers must be content.

Ros. Ay, be so, good Touchstone:—Look you, who comes here; a young man, and an old, in solemn talk.

Enter CORIN *and* SILVIUS.

Cor. That is the way to make her scorn you still.
Sil. O Corin, that thou knew'st how I do love her!
Cor. I partly guess; for I have lov'd ere now.
Sil. No, Corin, being old, thou canst not guess;
Though in thy youth thou wast as true a lover
As ever sigh'd upon a midnight pillow:
But if thy love were ever like to mine
(As sure I think did never man love so),
How many actions most ridiculous
Hast thou been drawn to by thy fantasy?
Cor. Into a thousand that I have forgotten.
Sil. O, thou didst then ne'er love so heartily:
If thou remember'st not the slightest folly
That ever love did make thee run into,
Thou hast not lov'd:
Or if thou hast not sat as I do now,
Wearying thy hearer in thy mistress' praise,
Thou hast not lov'd:
Or if thou hast not broke from company,
Abruptly, as my passion now makes me,
Thou hast not lov'd: O Phebe, Phebe, Phebe!
[*Exit* SILVIUS.
Ros. Alas, poor shepherd! searching of thy wound,
I have by hard adventure found mine own.

Touch. And I mine: I remember, when I was in love, I broke my sword upon a stone, and bid him take that for coming anight to Jane Smile: and I remember the kissing of her batlet, and the cow's dugs that her pretty chopp'd hands had milk'd: and I remember the wooing of a peascod instead of her; from whom I took two cods, and, giving her them again, said, with weeping tears, *Wear these for my sake.* We, that are true lovers, run into strange capers: but as all is mortal in nature, so is all nature in love mortal in folly.

Ros. Thou speak'st wiser than thou art 'ware of.

Touch. Nay, I shall ne'er be 'ware of mine own wit till I break my shins against it.

Ros. Jove! Jove! this shepherd's passion
Is much upon my fashion.
Touch. And mine; but it grows something stale with me.
Cel. I pray you, one of you question yond man,
If he for gold will give us any food;
I faint almost to death.
Touch. Holla; you, clown!
Ros. Peace, fool: he's not thy kinsman.
Cor. Who calls?
Touch. Your betters, sir.
Cor. Else they are very wretched.
Ros. Peace, I say:—
Good even to you, friend.
Cor. And to you, gentle sir, and to you all.
Ros. I pr'ythee, shepherd, if that love or gold,
Can in this desert place buy entertainment,
Bring us where we may rest ourselves, and feed:
Here's a young maid with travel much oppress'd,
And faints for succour.
Cor. Fair sir, I pity her,
And wish for her sake, more than for mine own,
My fortunes were more able to relieve her:
But I am shepherd to another man,
And do not shear the fleeces that I graze;
My master is of churlish disposition,
And little recks to find the way to heaven
By doing deeds of hospitality:
Besides, his cote, his flocks, and bounds of feed,
Are now on sale, and at our sheepcote now,
By reason of his absence, there is nothing
That you will feed on: but what is, come see,
And in my voice most welcome shall you be.
Ros. What is he that shall buy his flock and pasture?
Cor. That young swain that you saw here but erewhile,
That little cares for buying any thing.
Ros. I pray thee, if it stand with honesty,
Buy thou the cottage, pasture, and the flock,
And thou shalt have to pay for it of us.
Cel. And we will mend thy wages: I like this place,
And willingly could waste my time in it.
Cor. Assuredly, the thing is to be sold:
Go with me: if you like, upon report,
The soil, the profit, and this kind of life,
I will your very faithful feeder be,
And buy it with your gold right suddenly.
[*Exeunt.*

SCENE V. *The same.*

Enter AMIENS, JAQUES, *and others.*

SONG.

Ami. *Under the greenwood tree,*
Who loves to lie with me,
And turn his merry note
Unto the sweet bird's throat,
Come hither, come hither, come hither:
Here shall he see
No enemy,
But winter and rough weather.

Jaq. More, more, I pr'ythee, more.

Ami. It will make you melancholy, monsieur Jaques.

Jaq. I thank it. More, I pr'ythee, more. I can suck melancholy out of a song, as a weazel sucks eggs: More, I pr'ythee, more.

Ami. My voice is ragged; I know, I cannot please you.

Jaq. I do not desire you to please me, I do desire you to sing: Come, more; another stanza: Call you them stanzas?

Ami. What you will, monsieur Jaques.

Jaq. Nay, I care not for their names; they owe me nothing: Will you sing?

Ami. More at your request, than to please myself.

Jaq. Well then, if ever I thank any man, I'll thank you: but that they call compliment, is like the encounter of two dog-apes; and when a man thanks me heartily, methinks, I have given him a penny, and he renders me the beggarly thanks. Come, sing; and you that will not, hold your tongues.

Ami. Well, I'll end the song.—Sirs, cover the while; the duke will drink under this tree!—he hath been all this day to look you.

Jaq. And I have been all this day to avoid him. He is too disputable for my company: I think of as many matters as he; but I give heaven thanks, and make no boast of them. Come, warble, come.

SONG.

Who doth ambition shun, [All together here.
And loves to live i' the sun,
Seeking the food he eats,
And pleas'd with what he gets,
Come hither, come hither, come hither;
Here shall he see
No enemy,
But winter and rough weather.

Jaq. I'll give you a verse to this note, that I made yesterday in despite of my invention.

Ami. And I'll sing it.

Jaq. Thus it goes:

If it do come to pass,
That any man turn ass,
Leaving his wealth and ease,
A stubborn will to please,
Ducdame, ducdame, ducdame;
Here shall he see,
Gross fools as he,
An if he will come to me.

Ami. What's that *ducdame?*

Jaq. 'Tis a Greek invocation, to call fools into a circle. I'll go sleep if I can; if I cannot, I'll rail against all the first-born of Egypt.

Ami. And I'll go seek the duke; his banquet is prepar'd. [*Exeunt severally.*

SCENE VI. *The same.*

Enter ORLANDO *and* ADAM.

Adam. Dear master, I can go no further: O, I die for food! Here lie I down, and measure out my grave. Farewell, kind master.

Orl. Why, how now, Adam! no greater heart in thee? Live a little; comfort a little; cheer thyself a little: If this uncouth forest yield any thing savage, I will either be food for it, or bring it for food to thee. Thy conceit is nearer death than thy powers. For my sake, be comfortable; hold death awhile at the arm's end: I will here be with thee presently; and if I bring thee not something to eat, I'll give thee leave to die: but if thou diest before I come, thou art a mocker of my labour. Well said! thou look'st cheerily: and I'll be with thee quickly.—Yet thou liest in the bleak air; Come, I will bear thee to some shelter; and thou shalt not die for lack of a dinner, if there live any thing in this desert. Cheerly, good Adam! [*Exeunt.*

SCENE VII. *The same.*

A Table set out.

Enter Duke *senior,* AMIENS, Lords, *and others.*

Duke S. I think he be transform'd into a beast:
For I can no where find him like a man.

1 *Lord.* My lord, he is but even now gone hence:
Here was he merry, hearing of a song.

Duke S. If he, compact of jars, grow musical,
We shall have shortly discord in the spheres:—
Go, seek him; tell him, I would speak with him.

Enter JAQUES.

1 *Lord.* He saves my labour by his own approach.

Duke S. Why, how now, monsieur! what a life is this,
That your poor friends must woo your company?
What! you look merrily.

Jaq. A fool, a fool!——I met a fool i' the forest,
A motley fool;—a miserable world!
As I do live by food, I met a fool;
Who laid him down and bask'd him in the sun,
And rail'd on lady Fortune in good terms,
In good set terms,—and yet a motley fool.
Good-morrow, fool, quoth I: *No, sir,* quoth he,
Call me not fool, till heaven have sent me fortune:
And then he drew a dial from his poke;
And looking on it with lack-lustre eye,
Says, very wisely, *It is ten o'clock:*
Thus may we see, quoth he, *how the world wags:*
'Tis but an hour ago, since it was nine;
And after an hour more, 'twill be eleven;
And so, from hour to hour, we ripe and ripe,
And then, from hour to hour, we rot and rot,
And thereby hangs a tale. When I did hear
The motley fool thus moral on the time,
My lungs began to crow like chanticleer,
That fools shall be so deep-contemplative;
And I did laugh, sans intermission,
An hour by his dial.—O noble fool!
A worthy fool! Motley's the only wear.

Duke S. What fool is this?

Jaq. O worthy fool!—One that hath been a courtier;
And says, if ladies be but young, and fair,
They have the gift to know it: and in his brain,—
Which is as dry as the remainder biscuit
After a voyage,—he hath strange places cramm'd
With observation, the which he vents
In mangled forms:—O, that I were a fool!
I am ambitious for a motley coat.

Duke S. Thou shalt have one.

Jaq. It is my only suit;
Provided, that you weed your better judgments
Of all opinion that grows rank in them,
That I am wise. I must have liberty
Withal, as large a charter as the wind,
To blow on whom I please; for so fools have:
And they that are most galled with my folly,
They most must laugh: And why, sir, must they so?
The *why* is plain as way to parish church:
He, that a fool doth very wisely hit,
Doth very foolishly, although he smart,
Not to seem senseless of the bob: if not,
The wise man's folly is anatomiz'd
Even by the squand'ring glances of the fool.
Invest me in my motley; give me leave
To speak my mind, and I will through and through
Cleanse the foul body of the infected world,
If they will patiently receive my medicine.

Duke S. Fye on thee! I can tell what thou wouldst do.

Jaq. What, for a counter, would I do, but good?

Duke S. Most mischievous foul sin, in chiding sin:
For thou thyself hast been a libertine,
As sensual as the brutish sting itself;
And all the embossed sores and headed evils,
That thou with licence of free foot hast caught,
Wouldst thou disgorge into the general world.

Jaq. Why, who cries out on pride,
That can therein tax any private party?
Doth it not flow as hugely as the sea,
Till that the very very means do ebb?
What woman in the city do I name,
When that I say, the city-woman bears
The cost of princes on unworthy shoulders?
Who can come in, and say, that I mean her,
When such a one as she, such is her neighbour?
Or what is he of basest function,
That says his bravery is not on my cost,
(Thinking that I mean him), but therein suits
His folly to the mettle of my speech?
There then; How, what then? Let me see wherein
My tongue hath wrong'd him: if it do him right,
Then he hath wrong'd himself; if he be free,
Why then, my taxing like a wild goose flies,
Unclaim'd of any man.—But who comes here?

Enter ORLANDO, *with his Sword drawn.*

Orl. Forbear, and eat no more.

Jaq. Why, I have eat none yet.

Orl. Nor shalt not, till necessity be serv'd.
Jaq. Of what kind should this cock come of?
Duke S. Art thou thus bolden'd, man, by thy distress;
Or else a rude despiser of good manners,
That in civility thou seem'st so empty?
Orl. You touch'd my vein at first; the thorny point
Of bare distress hath ta'en from me the show
Of smooth civility: yet I am inland bred,
And know some nurture: But, forbear, I say;
He dies, that touches any of this fruit,
Till I and my affairs are answered.
Jaq. An you will not be answered with reason,
I must die.
Duke S. What would you have? Your gentleness shall force,
More than your force move us to gentleness.
Orl. I almost die for food, and let me have it.
Duke S. Sit down and feed, and welcome to our table.
Orl. Speak you so gently? Pardon me, I pray you:
I thought that all things had been savage here;
And therefore put I on the countenance
Of stern commandment: But whate'er you are,
That in this desert inaccessible,
Under the shade of melancholy boughs,
Lose and neglect the creeping hours of time;
If ever you have look'd on better days,
If ever been where bells have knoll'd to church;
If ever sat at any good man's feast;
If ever from your eyelid wip'd a tear,
And know what 'tis to pity, and be pitied;
Let gentleness my strong enforcement be:
In the which hope, I blush, and hide my sword.
Duke S. True is it that we have seen better days;
And have with holy bell been knoll'd to church;
And sat at good men's feasts; and wip'd our eyes
Of drops that sacred pity hath engender'd:
And therefore sit you down in gentleness,
And take upon command what help we have,
That to your wanting may be minister'd.
Orl. Then, but forbear your food a little while,
Whiles, like a doe, I go to find my fawn,
And give it food. There is an old poor man,
Who after me hath many a weary step
Limp'd in pure love: till he be first suffic'd,—
Oppress'd with two weak evils, age and hunger,—
I will not touch a bit.
Duke S. Go find him out,
And we will nothing waste till you return.
Orl. I thank ye; and be bless'd for your good comfort! [*Exit.*
Duke S. Thou seest, we are not all alone unhappy:
This wide and universal theatre
Presents more woful pageants than the scene
Wherein we play in.
Jaq. All the world's a stage,
And all the men and women merely players:
They have their exits, and their entrances;
And one man in his time plays many parts,
His acts being seven ages. At first, the infant,
Mewling and puking in the nurse's arms;
And then, the whining school-boy, with his satchel,
And shining morning face, creeping like snail
Unwillingly to school: And then, the lover;
Sighing like furnace, with a woful ballad
Made to his mistress' eye-brow: Then, a soldier;
Full of strange oaths, and bearded like the pard,
Jealous in honour, sudden and quick in quarrel
Seeking the bubble reputation
Even in the cannon's mouth: And then, the justice;
In fair round belly, with good capon lin'd,
With eyes severe, and beard of formal cut,
Full of wise saws and modern instances,
And so he plays his part; The sixth age shifts
Into the lean and slipper'd pantaloon;
With spectacles on nose, and pouch on side;
His youthful hose well sav'd, a world too wide
For his shrunk shank; and his big manly voice,
Turning again toward childish treble, pipes
And whistles in his sound: Last scene of all,
That ends this strange eventful history,
Is second childishness, and mere oblivion;
Sans teeth, sans eyes, sans taste, sans every thing.

Re-enter ORLANDO, *with* ADAM.

Duke S. Welcome: Set down your venerable burden,
And let him feed.
Orl. I thank you most for him.
Adam. So had you need;
I scarce can speak to thank you for myself.
Duke S. Welcome, fall to; I will not trouble you
As yet, to question you about your fortunes:—
Give us some musick; and, good cousin, sing.

AMIENS *sings.*

SONG.

I.

Blow, blow, thou winter wind,
Thou art not so unkind
As man's ingratitude;
Thy tooth is not so keen,
Because thou art not seen,
Although thy breath be rude.
Heigh, ho! sing, heigh, ho! unto the green holly:
Most friendship is feigning, most loving mere folly:
Then, heigh, ho, the holly!
This life is most jolly.

II.

Freeze, freeze, thou bitter sky,
That dost not bite so nigh
As benefits forgot:
Though thou the waters warp,
Thy sting is not so sharp,
As friend remember'd not.
Heigh, ho! sing, heigh, ho! &c.

Duke S. If that you were the good Sir Rowland's son,—
As you have whisper'd faithfully you were;
And as mine eye doth his effigies witness
Most truly limn'd, and living in your face,—
Be truly welcome hither: I am the duke,
That lov'd your father: The residue of your fortune,
Go to my cave and tell me.—Good old man,
Thou art right welcome as thy master is:
Support him by the arm.—Give me your hand,
And let me all your fortunes understand. [*Exeunt.*

ACT III.

SCENE I. *A Room in the Palace.*

Enter DUKE FREDERICK, OLIVER, Lords, *and* Attendants.

Duke F. Not see him since? Sir, sir, that cannot be:
But were I not the better part made mercy,
I should not seek an absent argument
Of my revenge, thou present: But look to it;
Find out thy brother, wheresoe'er he is;
Seek him with candle: bring him dead or living,
Within this twelvemonth, or turn thou no more
To seek a living in our territory.
Thy lands, and all things that thou dost call thine,
Worth seizure, do we seize into our hands;
Till thou canst quit thee by thy brother's mouth,
Of what we think against thee.
Oli. O, that your highness knew my heart in this!
I never lov'd my brother in my life.
Duke F. More villain thou.—Well, push him out of doors;

And let my officers of such a nature
Make an extent upon his house and lands:
Do this expediently, and turn him going.
[*Exeunt.*

SCENE II. *The Forest.*

Enter ORLANDO, *with a Paper.*

Orl. Hang there, my verse, in witness of my love:
And thou, thrice-crowned queen of night, survey
With thy chaste eye, from thy pale sphere above,
Thy huntress' name, that my full life doth sway.
O Rosalind! these trees shall be my books,
And in their barks my thoughts I'll character;
That every eye, which in this forest looks,
Shall see thy virtue witness'd every where.
Run, run, Orlando; carve, on every tree,
The fair, the chaste, and unexpressive she.
[*Exit.*

Enter CORIN *and* TOUCHSTONE.

Corin. And how like you this shepherd's life, master Touchstone?

Touch. Truly, shepherd, in respect of itself, it is a good life; but in respect that it is a shepherd's life, it is naught. In respect that it is solitary, I like it very well; but in respect that it is private, it is a very vile life. Now in respect it is in the fields, it pleaseth me well; but in respect it is not in the court, it is tedious. As it is a spare life, look you, it fits my humour well; but as there is no more plenty in it, it goes much against my stomach. Hast any philosophy in thee, shepherd?

Cor. No more, but that I know, the more one sickens, the worse at ease he is; and that he that wants money, means, and content, is without three good friends:—That the property of rain is to wet, and fire to burn: That good pasture makes fat sheep; and that a great cause of the night, is lack of the sun: That he that hath learned no wit by nature nor art, may complain of good breeding, or comes of a very dull kindred.

Touch. Such a one is a natural philosopher. Wast ever in court, shepherd?

Cor. No, truly.

Touch. Then thou art damn'd.

Cor. Nay, I hope,——

Touch. Truly, thou art damn'd; like an ill-roasted egg, all on one side.

Cor. For not being at court? Your reason.

Touch. Why, if thou never wast at court, thou never saw'st good manners; if thou never saw'st good manners, then thy manners must be wicked; and wickedness is sin, and sin is damnation: Thou art in a parlous state, shepherd.

Cor. Not a whit, Touchstone: those, that are good manners at the court, are as ridiculous in the country, as the behaviour of the country is most mockable at the court. You told me, you salute not at the court, but you kiss your hands; that courtesy would be uncleanly, if courtiers were shepherds.

Touch. Instance, briefly; come, instance.

Cor. Why, we are still handling our ewes; and their fells, you know, are greasy.

Touch. Why, do not your courtier's hands sweat? and is not the grease of a mutton as wholesome as the sweat of a man? Shallow, shallow: A better instance, I say; come.

Cor. Besides, our hands are hard.

Touch. Your lips will feel them the sooner. Shallow, again: A more sounder instance, come.

Cor. And they are often tarr'd over with the surgery of our sheep; and would you have us kiss tar? The courtier's hands are perfumed with civet.

Touch. Most shallow man! Thou worms-meat, in respect of a good piece of flesh: Indeed!—Learn of the wise, and perpend: Civet is of a baser birth than tar; the very uncleanly flux of a cat. Mend the instance, shepherd.

Cor. You have too courtly a wit for me; I'll rest.

Touch. Wilt thou rest damn'd? God help thee, shallow man! God make incision in thee! thou art raw.

Cor. Sir, I am a true labourer; I earn that I eat, get that I wear; owe no man hate, envy no man's happiness; glad of other men's good, content with my harm: and the greatest of my pride is, to see my ewes graze, and my lambs suck.

Touch. That is another simple sin in you: to bring the ewes and the rams together, and to offer to get your living by the copulation of cattle: to be bawd to a bell-wether; and to betray a she-lamb of a twelvemonth, to a crooked-pated, old, cuckoldy ram, out of all reasonable match. If thou be'st not damn'd for this, the devil himself will have no shepherds; I cannot see else how thou shouldst 'scape.

Cor. Here comes young master Ganymede, my new mistress's brother.

Enter ROSALIND, *reading a Paper.*

Ros. *From the east to western Ind,*
No jewel is like Rosalind.
Her worth, being mounted on the wind,
Through all the world bears Rosalind.
All the pictures, fairest lin'd
Are but black to Rosalind.
Let no face be kept in mind,
But the fair of Rosalind.

Touch. I'll rhyme you so, eight years together; dinners, and suppers, and sleeping hours excepted; it is the right butter-woman's rank to market.

Ros. Out, fool!

Touch. For a taste:
If a hart do lack a hind,
Let him seek out Rosalind.
If the cat will after kind,
So, be sure, will Rosalind.
Winter-garments must be lin'd,
So must slender Rosalind.
They that reap, must sheaf and bind;
Then to cart with Rosalind.
Sweetest nut hath sourest rind,
Such a nut is Rosalind.
He that sweetest rose will find,
Must find love's prick, and Rosalind.
This is the very false gallop of verses: Why do you infect yourself with them?

Ros. Peace, you dull fool; I found them on a tree.

Touch. Truly, the tree yields bad fruit.

Ross. I'll graff it with you, and then I shall graff it with a medlar: then it will be the earliest fruit in the country: for you'll be rotten e'er you be half ripe, and that's the right virtue of the medlar.

Touch. You have said; but whether wisely or no, let the forest judge.

Enter CELIA, *reading a Paper.*

Ros. Peace!
Here comes my sister, reading; stand aside.

Cel. *Why should this desert silent be?*
For it is unpeopled? No;
Tongues I'll hang on every tree,
That shall civil sayings show.
Some, how brief the life of man
Runs his erring pilgrimage;
That the stretching of a span
Buckles in his sum of age.
Some, of violated vows
'Twixt the souls of friend and friend:
But upon the fairest boughs,
Or at every sentence' end,
Will I Rosalinda write;
Teaching all that read, to know
The quintessence of every sprite
Heaven would in little show.

Therefore heaven nature charg'd
That one body should be fill'd
With all graces wide enlarg'd:
Nature presently distill'd
Helen's cheek, but not her heart;
Cleopatra's majesty;
Atalanta's better part;
Sad Lucretia's modesty.
Thus Rosalind of many parts
By heavenly synod was devis'd;
Of many faces, eyes, and hearts,
To have the touches dearest priz'd.
Heaven would that she these gifts should have,
And I to live and die her slave.

Ros. O most gentle Jupiter!—what tedious homily of love have you wearied your parishioners withal, and never cry'd, *Have patience, good people!*

Cel. How now! back friends;—Shepherd, go off a little:—Go with him, sirrah.

Touch. Come, shepherd, let us make an honourable retreat; though not with bag and baggage, yet with scrip and scrippage.

[*Exeunt* CORIN *and* TOUCHSTONE.

Cel. Didst thou hear these verses?

Ros. O, yes, I heard them all, and more too; for some of them had in them more feet than the verses would bear.

Cel. That's no matter; the feet might bear the verses.

Ros. Ay, but the feet were lame, and could not bear themselves without the verse, and therefore stood lamely in the verse.

Cel. But didst thou hear, without wondering how thy name should be hang'd and carv'd upon these trees?

Ros. I was seven of the nine days out of the wonder, before you came; for look here what I found on a palm-tree: I never was so berhymed since Pythagoras' time, that I was an Irish rat, which I can hardly remember.

Cel. Trow you, who hath done this?

Ros. Is it a man?

Cel. And a chain, that you once wore, about his neck: Change you colour?

Ros. I pr'ythee, who?

Cel. O lord, lord! it is a hard matter for friends to meet; but mountains may be removed with earthquakes, and so encounter.

Ros. Nay, but who is it?

Cel. Is it possible?

Ros. Nay, I pray thee now, with most petitionary vehemence, tell me who it is.

Cel. O wonderful, wonderful, and most wonderful wonderful, and yet again wonderful, and after that out of all whooping?

Ros. Good my complexion! dost thou think, though I am caparison'd like a man, I have a doublet and hose in my disposition? One inch of delay more is a South-sea of discovery. I pr'ythee, tell me, who is it? quickly, and speak apace: I would thou couldst stammer, that thou might'st pour this concealed man out of thy mouth, as wine comes out of a narrow-mouth'd bottle; either too much at once, or none at all. I pr'ythee take the cork out of thy mouth, that I may drink thy tidings.

Cel. So you may put a man in your belly.

Ros. Is he of God's making? What manner of man? Is his head worth a hat, or his chin worth a beard?

Cel. Nay, he hath but a little beard.

Ros. Why, God will send more, if the man will be thankful: let me stay the growth of his beard, if thou delay me not the knowledge of his chin.

Cel. It is young Orlando; that tripp'd up the wrestler's heels, and your heart both in an instant.

Ros. Nay, but the devil take mocking; speak sad brow, and true maid.

Cel. I' faith, coz, 'tis he.

Ros. Orlando?

Cel. Orlando.

Ros. Alas the day! what shall I do with my doublet and hose?—What did he, when thou saw'st him? What said he? How look'd he? Wherein went he? What makes he here? Did he ask for me? Where remains he? How parted he with thee? and when shalt thou see him again? Answer me in one word.

Cel. You must borrow me Garagantua's mouth first: 'tis a word too great for any mouth of this age's size: To say, ay, and no, to these particulars, is more than to answer in a catechism.

Ros. But doth he know that I am in this forest, and in man's apparel? Looks he as freshly as he did the day he wrestled?

Cel. It is as easy to count atomies, as to resolve the propositions of a lover:—but take a taste of my finding him, and relish it with a good observance. I found him under a tree, like a dropp'd acorn.

Ros. It may well be call'd Jove's tree, when it drops forth such fruit.

Cel. Give me audience, good madam.

Ros. Proceed.

Cel. There lay he, stretch'd along, like a wounded knight.

Ros. Though it be pity to see such a sight, it well becomes the ground.

Cel. Cry, holla! to thy tongue, I pr'ythee; it curvets very unseasonably. He was furnish'd like a hunter.

Ros. O ominous! he comes to kill my heart.

Cel. I would sing my song without a burden: thou bring'st me out of tune.

Ros. Do you not know I am a woman? when I think, I must speak. Sweet, say on.

Enter ORLANDO *and* JAQUES.

Cel. You bring me out:—Soft! comes he not here?

Ros. 'Tis he; slink by, and note him.

[CELIA *and* ROSALIND *retire.*

Jaq. I thank you for your company; but, good faith, I had as lief have been myself alone.

Orl. And so had I; but yet, for fashion's sake, I thank you too for your society.

Jaq. God be with you; let's meet as little as we can.

Orl. I do desire we may be better strangers.

Jaq. I pray you, mar no more trees with writing love-songs in their barks.

Orl. I pray you, mar no more of my verses with reading them ill-favouredly.

Jaq. Rosalind is your love's name?

Orl. Yes, just.

Jaq. I do not like her name.

Orl. There was no thought of pleasing you, when she was christen'd.

Jaq. What stature is she of?

Orl. Just as high as my heart.

Jaq. You are full of pretty answers: Have you not been acquainted with goldsmiths' wives, and conn'd them out of rings?

Orl. Not so; but I answer you right painted cloth, from whence you have studied your questions.

Jaq. You have a nimble wit; I think it was made of Atalanta's heels. Will you sit down with me? and we two will rail against our mistress the world, and all our misery.

Orl. I will chide no breather in the world, but myself; against whom I know most faults.

Jaq. The worst fault you have, is to be in love.

Orl. 'Tis a fault I will not change for your best virtue. I am weary of you.

Jaq. By my troth, I was seeking for a fool, when I found you.

Orl. He is drown'd in the brook; look but in, and you shall see him.

Jaq. There shall I see mine own figure.

Orl. Which I take to be either a fool, or a cipher.

Jaq. I'll tarry no longer with you; farewell, good signior love.

Orl. I am glad of your departure; adieu, good monsieur melancholy.

[*Exit* JAQ.—CEL. *and* ROS. *come forward.*

Ros. I will speak to him like a saucy lacquey, and under that habit play the knave with him.—Do you hear, forester?

Orl. Very well; what would you?

Ros. I pray you, what is 't o'clock?

Orl. You should ask me, what time o' day; there's no clock in the forest.

Ros. Then there is no true lover in the forest; else sighing every minute, and groaning every hour, would detect the lazy foot of time, as well as a clock.

Orl. And why not the swift foot of time? had not that been as proper?

Ros. By no means, sir: Time travels in divers paces with divers persons: I'll tell you who time ambles withal, who time trots withal, who time gallops withal, and who he stands still withal.

Orl. I pr'ythee, who doth he trot withal?

Ros. Marry, he trots hard with a young maid, between the contract of her marriage, and the day it is solemnized: if the interim be but a se'nnight, time's pace is so hard that it seems the length of seven years.

Orl. Who ambles time withal?

Ros. With a priest that lacks Latin, and a rich man that hath not the gout; for the one sleeps easily, because he cannot study; and the other lives merrily, because he feels no pain: the one lacking the burden of lean and wasteful learning; the other knowing no burden of heavy tedious penury: These time ambles withal.

Orl. Who doth he gallop withal?

Ros. With a thief to the gallows: for though he go as softly as foot can fall, he thinks himself too soon there.

Orl. Who stays it withal?

Ros. With lawyers in the vacation: for they sleep between term and term, and then they perceive not how time moves.

Orl. Where dwell you, pretty youth?

Ros. With this shepherdess, my sister; here in the skirts of the forest, like fringe upon a petticoat.

Orl. Are you native of this place?

Ros. As the coney that you see dwells where she is kindled.

Orl. Your accent is something finer than you could purchase in so removed a dwelling.

Ros. I have been told so of many; but, indeed, an old religious uncle of mine taught me to speak, who was in his youth an in-land man; one that knew courtship too well, for there he fell in love. I have heard him read many lectures against it; and I thank God, I am not a woman, to be touch'd with so many giddy offences as he hath generally tax'd their whole sex withal.

Orl. Can you remember any of the principal evils that he laid to the charge of women?

Ros. There were none principal; they were all like one another, as half-pence are; every one fault seeming monstrous, till his fellow fault came to match it.

Orl. I pr'ythee, recount some of them.

Ros. No; I will not cast away my physick, but on those that are sick. There is a man haunts the forest, that abuses our young plants with carving Rosalind on their barks; hangs odes upon hawthorns, and elegies on brambles; all, forsooth, deifying the name of Rosalind: if I could meet that fancymonger, I would give him some good counsel, for he seems to have the quotidian of love upon him.

Orl. I am he that is so love-shaked; I pray you, tell me your remedy.

Ros. There is none of my uncle's marks upon you: he taught me how to know a man in love; in which cage of rushes, I am sure, you are not prisoner.

Orl. What were his marks?

Ros. A lean cheek; which you have not: a blue eye, and sunken; which you have not; an unquestionable spirit; which you have not: a beard neglected; which you have not;—but I pardon you for that; for, simply, your having in beard is a younger brother's revenue: Then your hose should be ungarter'd, your bonnet unbanded, your sleeve unbuttoned, your shoe untied, and every thing about you demonstrating a careless desolation. But you are no such man; you are rather point-device in your accoutrements; as loving yourself, than seeming the lover of any other.

Orl. Fair youth, I would I could make thee believe I love.

Ros. Me believe it! you may as soon make her that you love believe it; which, I warrant, she is apter to do, than to confess she does: that is one of the points in the which women still give the lie to their consciences. But, in good sooth, are you he that hangs the verses on the trees, wherein Rosalind is so admired?

Orl. I swear to thee, youth, by the white hand of Rosalind, I am that he, that unfortunate he.

Ros. But are you so much in love as your rhymes speak?

Orl. Neither rhyme nor reason can express how much.

Ros. Love is merely a madness; and, I tell you, deserves as well a dark house and a whip, as madmen do: and the reason why they are not so punished and cured, is, that the lunacy is so ordinary, that the whippers are in love too: Yet I profess curing it by counsel.

Orl. Did you ever cure any so?

Ros. Yes, one; and in this manner. He was to imagine me his love, his mistress; and I set him every day to woo me: At which time would I, being but a moonish youth, grieve, be effeminate, changeable, longing, and liking; proud, fantastical, apish, shallow, inconstant, full of tears, full of smiles; for every passion something, and for no passion truly any thing, as boys and women are for the most part cattle of this colour: would now like him, now loathe him; then entertain him, then forswear him; now weep for him, then spit at him; then I drave my suitor from his mad humour of love, to a living humour of madness; which was, to forswear the full stream of the world, and to live in a nook merely monastick: And thus I cured him; and this way will I take upon me to wash your liver as clean as a sound sheep's heart, that there shall not be one spot of love in 't.

Orl. I would not be cured, youth.

Ros. I would cure you, if you would but call me Rosalind, and come every day to my cote, and woo me.

Orl. Now, by the faith of my love, I will: tell me where it is.

Ros. Go with me to it, and I'll show it to you: and, by the way, you shall tell me where in the forest you live: Will you go?

Orl. With all my heart, good youth.

Ros. Nay, you must call me Rosalind:—Come, sister, will you go? [*Exeunt.*

SCENE III.

Enter TOUCHSTONE *and* AUDREY; JAQUES *at a distance, observing them.*

Touch. Come apace, good Audrey; I will fetch up your goats, Audrey: And how, Audrey? am I the man yet? Doth my simple feature content you?

Aud. Your features! Lord warrant us! what features?

Touch. I am here with thee and thy goats, as the most capricious poet, honest Ovid, was among the Goths.

Jaq. O knowledge ill-inhabited! worse than Jove in a thatch'd house! [*Aside.*

Touch. When a man's verses cannot be understood, nor a man's good wit seconded with the forward child, understanding, it strikes a man more dead than a great reckoning in a little room:—Truly, I would the gods had made thee poetical.

Aud. I do not know what poetical is: Is it honest in deed, and word? Is it a true thing?

Touch. No, truly; for the truest poetry is the most feigning; and lovers are given to poetry; and what they swear in poetry, may be said, as lovers, they do feign.

Aud. Do you wish then, that the gods had made me poetical?

Touch. I do, truly: for thou swear'st to me thou art honest; now, if thou wert a poet, I might have some hope thou didst feign.

Aud. Would you not have me honest?

Touch. No truly, unless thou wert hard favour'd: for honesty coupled to beauty, is to have honey a sauce to sugar.

Jaq. A material fool! [*Aside.*

Aud. Well, I am not fair; and therefore I pray the gods make me honest!

Touch. Truly; and to cast away honesty upon a foul slut, were to put good meat into an unclean dish.

Aud. I am not a slut, though I thank the gods I am foul.

Touch. Well, praised be the gods for thy foulness! sluttishness may come hereafter. But be it as it may be, I will marry thee: and to that end, I have been with Sir Oliver Mar-text, the vicar of the next village; who hath promised to meet me in this place of the forest, and to couple us.

Jaq. I would fain see this meeting. [*Aside.*

Aud. Well, the gods give us joy!

Touch. Amen. A man may, if he were of a fearful heart, stagger in this attempt; for here we have no temple but the wood, no assembly but horn-beasts. But what though? Courage! As horns are odious, they are necessary. It is said,—Many a man knows no end of his goods; right; many a man has good horns, and knows no end of them. Well, that is the dowry of his wife; 'tis none of his own getting. Horns? Even so:——Poor men alone?——No, no; the noblest deer hath them as huge as the rascal. Is the single man therefore blessed? No: as a wall'd town is more worthier than a village, so is the forehead of a married man more honourable than the bare brow of a bachelor: and by how much defence is better than no skill, by so much is a horn more precious than to want.

Enter SIR OLIVER MAR-TEXT.

Here comes Sir Oliver:—Sir Oliver Mar-text, you are well met: Will you dispatch us here under this tree, or shall we go with you to your chapel?

Sir Oli. Is there none here to give the woman?

Touch. I will not take her on gift of any man.

Sir Oli. Truly, she must be given, or the marriage is not lawful.

Jaq. [*Discovering himself.*] Proceed, proceed; I'll give her.

Touch. Good even, good master *What ye call't:* How do you, sir? You are very well met: God'ild you for your last company: I am very glad to see you:—Even a toy in hand here, sir:—Nay; pray, be cover'd.

Jaq. Will you be married, Motley?

Touch. As the ox hath his bow, sir, the horse his curb, and the falcon her bells, so man hath his desires; and as pigeons bill, so wedlock would be nibbling.

Jaq. And will you, being a man of your breeding, be married under a bush, like a beggar? Get you to church, and have a good priest that can tell you what marriage is: this fellow will but join you together as they join wainscot; then one of you will prove a shrunk panel, and, like green timber, warp, warp.

Touch. I am not in the mind but I were better to be married of him than of another: for he is not like to marry me well; and not being well married, it will be a good excuse for me hereafter to leave my wife. [*Aside.*

Jaq. Go thou with me, and let me counsel thee.

Touch. Come, sweet Audrey;
We must be married, or we must live in bawdry.
Farewell, good master Oliver!
Not—O sweet Oliver,
O brave Oliver,
Leave me not behind thee;
But—wind away,
Begone, I say,
I will not to wedding with thee.
[*Exeunt* JAQ. TOUCH. *and* AUDREY.

Sir Oli. 'Tis no matter: ne'er a fantastical knave of them all shall flout me out of my calling. [*Exit.*

SCENE IV. *The same. Before a Cottage.*

Enter ROSALIND *and* CELIA.

Ros. Never talk to me, I will weep.

Cel. Do, I pr'ythee; but yet have the grace to consider, that tears do not become a man.

Ros. But have I not cause to weep?

Cel. As good cause as one would desire; therefore weep.

Ros. His very hair is of the dissembling colour.

Cel. Something browner than Judas's: marry, his kisses are Judas's own children.

Ros. I' faith, his hair is of a good colour.

Cel. An excellent colour: your chestnut was ever the only colour.

Ros. And his kissing is as full of sanctity as the touch of holy bread.

Cel. He hath bought a pair of cast lips of Diana: a nun of winter's sisterhood kisses not more religiously; the very ice of chastity is in them.

Ros. But why did he swear he would come this morning, and comes not?

Cel. Nay, certainly, there is no truth in him.

Ros. Do you think so?

Cel. Yes: I think he is not a pick-purse, nor a horse-stealer: but for his verity in love, I do think him as concave as a cover'd goblet, or a worm-eaten nut.

Ros. Not true in love?

Cel. Yes, when he is in; but, I think he is not in.

Ros. You have heard him swear downright, he was.

Cel. *Was* is not *is:* besides the oath of a lover is no stronger than the word of a tapster; they are both the confirmers of false reckonings: He attends here in the forest on the duke your father.

Ros. I met the duke yesterday, and had much question with him. He asked me of what parentage I was; I told him, of as good as he; so he laugh'd, and let me go. But what talk we of fathers, when there is such a man as Orlando?

Cel. O, that's a brave man! he writes brave verses, speaks brave words, swears brave oaths, and breaks them bravely, quite traverse, athwart the heart of his lover; as a puny tilter, that spurs his horse but on one side, breaks his staff like a noble goose: but all's brave, that youth mounts, and folly guides:—Who comes here?

Enter CORIN.

Cor. Mistress, and master, you have oft inquired
After the shepherd that complain'd of love;
Who you saw sitting by me on the turf,
Praising the proud disdainful shepherdess
That was his mistress.

Cel. Well, and what of him?

Cor. If you will see a pageant truly play'd,
Between the pale complexion of true love,
And the red glow of scorn and proud disdain,
Go hence a little, and I shall conduct you,
If you will mark it.
Ros. O, come, let us remove;
The sight of lovers feedeth those in love:—
Bring us unto this sight, and you shall say
I'll prove a busy actor in their play. [*Exeunt.*

SCENE V. *Another part of the Forest.*

Enter SILVIUS *and* PHEBE.

Sil. Sweet Phebe, do not scorn me; do not, Phebe:
Say, that you love me not; but say not so
In bitterness. The common executioner,
Whose heart the accustom'd sight of death makes hard,
Falls not the axe upon the humbled neck,
But first begs pardon; Will you sterner be
Than he that dies and lives by bloody drops?

Enter ROSALIND, CELIA, *and* CORIN *at a distance.*

Phe. I would not be thy executioner:
I fly thee, for I would not injure thee.
Thou tell'st me, there is murder in mine eye;
'Tis pretty, sure, and very probable,
That eyes,—that are the frail'st and softest things,
Who shut their coward gates on atomies,—
Should be call'd tyrants, butchers, murderers!
Now I do frown on thee with all my heart;
And, if mine eyes can wound, now let them kill thee;
Now counterfeit to swoon; why now fall down;
Or, if thou canst not, O, for shame, for shame,
Lie not, to say mine eyes are murderers.
Now show the wound mine eye hath made in thee:
Scratch thee but with a pin, and there remains
Some scar of it; lean but upon a rush,
The cicatrice and palpable impressure
Thy palm some moment keeps; but now mine eyes,
Which I have darted at thee, hurt thee not:
Nor, I am sure, there is no force in eyes
That can do hurt.
Sil. O dear Phebe,
If ever, (as that ever may be near,)
You meet in some fresh cheek the power of fancy,
Then shall you know the wounds invisible
That love's keen arrows make.
Phe. But, till that time,
Come not thou near me: and, when that time comes,
Afflict me with thy mocks, pity me not;
As, till that time, I shall not pity thee.
Ros. And why, I pray you? [*Advancing.*] Who might be your mother,
That you insult, exult, and all at once,
Over the wretched? What, though you have beauty,
(As, by my faith, I see no more in you
Than without candle may go dark to bed,)
Must you be therefore proud and pitiless?
Why, what means this? Why do you look on me?
I see no more in you, than in the ordinary
Of nature's sale-work:—Od's my little life!
I think she means to tangle my eyes too:—
No, 'faith, proud mistress, hope not after it;
'Tis not your inky brows, your black silk-hair,
Your bugle eyeballs, nor your cheek of cream,
That can entame my spirits to your worship.—
You foolish shepherd, wherefore do you follow her,
Like foggy south, puffing with wind and rain?
You are a thousand times a properer man,
Than she a woman: 'Tis such fools as you,
That make the world full of ill-favour'd children:
'Tis not her glass, but you, that flatters her;
And out of you she sees herself more proper,
Than any of her lineaments can show her.—
But, mistress, know yourself; down on your knees,
And thank heaven fasting, for a good man's love:
For I must tell you friendly in your ear,—
Sell when you can; you are not for all markets:
Cry the man mercy; love him; take his offer;
Foul is most foul, being foul to be a scoffer.
So take her to thee, shepherd:—fare you well.
Phe. Sweet youth, I pray you chide a year together;
I had rather hear you chide, than this man woo.
Ros. He's fallen in love with her foulness, and she'll fall in love with my anger: If it be so, as fast as she answers thee with frowning looks, I'll sauce her with bitter words.—Why look you so upon me?
Phe. For no ill will I bear you.
Ros. I pray you, do not fall in love with me,
For I am falser than vows made in wine;
Besides, I like you not: If you will know my house,
'Tis at the tuft of olives, here hard by:—
Will you go, sister?—Shepherd, ply her hard:—
Come, sister:—Shepherdess, look on him better,
And be not proud: though all the world could see,
None could be so abus'd in sight as he.
Come, to our flock.
[*Exeunt* ROSALIND, CELIA, *and* CORIN.
Phe. Dead shepherd! now I find thy saw of might;
Who ever lov'd, that lov'd not at first sight?
Sil. Sweet Phebe,—
Phe. Ha! What say'st thou, Silvius?
Sil. Sweet Phebe, pity me.
Phe. Why, I am sorry for thee, gentle Silvius.
Sil. Wherever sorrow is, relief would be;
If you do sorrow at my grief in love,
By giving love, your sorrow and my grief
Were both extermin'd.
Phe. Thou hast my love; is not that neighbourly?
Sil. I would have you.
Phe. Why, that were covetousness.
Silvius, the time was, that I hated thee;
And yet it is not, that I bear thee love;
But since that thou canst talk of love so well,
Thy company, which erst was irksome to me,
I will endure; and I'll employ thee too:
But do not look for further recompense,
Than thine own gladness that thou art employ'd.
Sil. So holy, and so perfect is my love,
And I in such a poverty of grace,
That I shall think it a most plenteous crop
To glean the broken ears after the man
That the main harvest reaps; loose now and then
A scatter'd smile, and that I'll live upon.
Phe. Know'st thou the youth that spoke to me ere while?
Sil. Not very well, but I have met him oft:
And he hath bought the cottage, and the bounds,
That the old carlot once was master of.
Phe. Think not I love him, though I ask for him;
'Tis but a peevish boy:—yet he talks well;—
But what care I for words? yet words do well,
When he that speaks them pleases those that hear.
It is a pretty youth:—not very pretty:
But, sure, he's proud: and yet his pride becomes him:
He'll make a proper man: The best thing in him
Is his complexion; and faster than his tongue
Did make offence, his eye did heal it up.
He is not tall; yet for his years he's tall:
His leg is but so so: and yet 'tis well:
There was a pretty redness in his lip;
A little riper and more lusty red
Than that mix'd in his cheek; 'twas just the difference
Betwixt the constant red, and mingled damask.
There be some women, Silvius, had they mark'd him
In parcels as I did, would have gone near
To fall in love with him: but, for my part,
I love him not, nor hate him not; and yet

I have more cause to hate him than to love him:
For what had he to do to chide at me?
He said, mine eyes were black, and my hair black;
And, now I am remember'd, scorn'd at me:
I marvel, why I answer'd not again;
But that's all one; omittance is no quittance.
I'll write to him a very taunting letter,
And thou shalt bear it; Wilt thou, Silvius?

Sil. Phebe, with all my heart.

Phe. I'll write it straight;
The matter's in my head, and in my heart:
I will be bitter with him, and passing short:
Go with me, Silvius. [*Exeunt.*

ACT IV.

SCENE I. *The same.*

Enter ROSALIND, CELIA, *and* JAQUES.

Jaq. I pr'ythee, pretty youth, let me be better acquainted with thee.

Ros. They say, you are a melancholy fellow.

Jaq. I am so; I do love it better than laughing.

Ros. Those that are in extremity of either, are abominable fellows; and betray themselves to every modern censure, worse than drunkards.

Jaq. Why, 'tis good to be sad and say nothing.

Ros. Why then, 'tis good to be a post.

Jaq. I have neither the scholar's melancholy, which is emulation; nor the musician's, which is fantastical; nor the courtier's, which is proud; nor the soldier's, which is ambitious; nor the lawyer's, which is politick; nor the lady's, which is nice; nor the lover's, which is all these: but it is a melancholy of mine own, compounded of many simples, extracted from many objects; and, indeed, the sundry contemplation of my travels; which, by often rumination, wraps me in a most humorous sadness.

Ros. A traveller! By my faith, you have great reason to be sad: I fear, you have sold your own lands, to see other men's; then, to have seen much, and to have nothing, is to have rich eyes and poor hands.

Jaq. Yes, I have gained my experience.

Enter ORLANDO.

Ros. And your experience makes you sad: I had rather have a fool to make me merry, than experience to make me sad; and to travel for it too.

Orl. Good day, and happiness, dear Rosalind!

Jaq. Nay then, God be wi' you, an you talk in blank verse. [*Exit.*

Ros. Farewell, monsieur traveller: Look, you lisp, and wear strange suits; disable all the benefits of your own country; be out of love with your nativity, and almost chide God for making you that countenance you are: or I will scarce think you have swam in a gondola.—Why, how now, Orlando! where have you been all this while? You a lover?—An you serve me such another trick, never come in my sight more.

Orl. My fair Rosalind, I come within an hour of my promise.

Ros. Break an hour's promise in love? He that will divide a minute into a thousand parts, and break but a part of the thousandth part of a minute in the affairs of love, it may be said of him, that Cupid hath clapp'd him o' the shoulder, but I warrant him heart-whole.

Orl. Pardon me, dear Rosalind.

Ros. Nay, an you be so tardy, come no more in my sight: I had as lief be woo'd of a snail.

Orl. Of a snail?

Ros. Ay, of a snail; for though he comes slowly, he carries his house on his head; a better jointure, I think, than you can make a woman: Besides, he brings his destiny with him.

Orl. What's that?

Ros. Why, horns; which such as you are fain to be beholden to your wives for: but he comes armed in his fortune, and prevents the slander of his wife.

Orl. Virtue is no horn-maker; and my Rosalind is virtuous.

Ros. And I am your Rosalind.

Cel. It pleases him to call you so; but he hath a Rosalind of a better leer than you.

Ros. Come, woo me, woo me; for now I am in a holiday humour, and like enough to consent: What would you say to me now, an I were your very very Rosalind?

Orl. I would kiss, before I spoke.

Ros. Nay, you were better speak first; and when you were gravelled for lack of matter, you might take occasion to kiss. Very good orators, when they are out, they will spit; and for lovers, lacking (God warn us!) matter, the cleanliest shift is to kiss.

Orl. How if the kiss be denied?

Ros. Then she puts you to entreaty, and there begins new matter.

Orl. Who could be out, being before his beloved mistress?

Ros. Marry, that should you, if I were your mistress; or I should think my honesty ranker than my wit.

Orl. What, of my suit?

Ros. Not out of your apparel, and yet out of your suit. Am not I your Rosalind?

Orl. I take some joy to say you are, because I would be talking of her.

Ros. Well, in her person I say—I will not have you.

Orl. Then, in mine own person, I die.

Ros. No, faith, die by attorney. The poor world is almost six thousand years old, and in all this time there was not any man died in his own person, *videlicit*, in a love-cause. Troilus had his brains dashed out with a Grecian club; yet he did what he could to die before; and he is one of the patterns of love. Leander, he would have lived many a fair year, though Hero had turned nun, if it had not been for a hot midsummer night: for, good youth, he went but forth to wash him in the Hellespont, and, being taken with the cramp, was drowned; and the foolish chroniclers of that age found it was—Hero of Sestos. But these are all lies; men have died from time to time, and worms have eaten them, but not for love.

Orl. I would not have my right Rosalind of this mind; for, I protest, her frown might kill me.

Ros. By this hand, it will not kill a fly: But come, now I will be your Rosalind in a more coming-on disposition; and ask me what you will, I will grant it.

Orl. Then love me, Rosalind.

Ros. Yes, faith, will I, Fridays, and Saturdays, and all.

Orl. And wilt thou have me?

Ros. Ay, and twenty such.

Orl. What say'st thou?

Ros. Are you not good?

Orl. I hope so.

Ros. Why then, can one desire too much of a good thing?—Come, sister, you shall be the priest, and marry us.—Give me your hand, Orlando:—What do you say, sister?

Orl. 'Pray thee, marry us.

Cel. I cannot say the words.

Ros. You must begin,—— *Will you, Orlando,*—

Cel. Go to:——Will you, Orlando, have to wife this Rosalind?

Orl. I will.

Ros. Ay, but when?

Orl. Why now; as fast as she can marry us.

Ros. Then you must say,—*I take thee, Rosalind, for wife.*

Orl. I take thee, Rosalind, for wife.

Ros. I might ask you for your commission; but,—I do take thee, Orlando, for my husband: There a girl goes before the priest; and, certainly, a woman's thought runs before her actions.

Orl. So do all thoughts; they are winged.

Ros. Now tell me how long you would have her, after you have possessed her.

Orl. For ever and a day.

Ros. Say a day, without the ever: No, no, Orlando; men are April when they woo: December when they wed: maids are May when they are maids, but the sky changes when they are wives. I will be more jealous of thee than a Barbary cock-pigeon over his hen; more clamorous than a parrot against rain; more newfangled than an ape; more giddy in my desires than a monkey: I will weep for nothing, like Diana in the fountain; and I will do that when you are disposed to be merry: I will laugh like a hyen, and that when thou art inclined to sleep.

Orl. But will my Rosalind do so?

Ros. By my life, she will do as I do.

Orl. O, but she is wise.

Ros. Or else she could not have the wit to do this: the wiser, the waywarder: Make the doors upon a woman's wit, and it will out at the casement; shut that, and 'twill out at the key-hole; stop that, 'twill fly with the smoke out at the chimney.

Orl. A man that had a wife with such a wit, he might say,—*Wit, whither wilt?*

Ros. Nay, you might keep that check for it, till you met your wife's wit going to your neighbour's bed.

Orl. And what wit could wit have to excuse that?

Ros. Marry, to say,—she came to seek you there. You shall never take her without her answer, unless you take her without her tongue. O, that woman that cannot make her fault her husband's occasion, let her never nurse her child herself, for she will breed it like a fool.

Orl. For these two hours, Rosalind, I will leave thee.

Ros. Alas, dear love, I cannot lack thee two hours.

Orl. I must attend the duke at dinner; by two o'clock I will be with thee again.

Ros. Ay, go your ways, go your ways;—I knew what you would prove; my friends told me as much, and I thought no less:—that flattering tongue of yours won me:—'tis but one cast away, and so,—come, death.—Two o'clock is your hour?

Orl. Ay, sweet Rosalind.

Ros. By my troth, and in good earnest, and so God mend me, and by all pretty oaths that are not dangerous, if you break one jot of your promise, or come one minute behind your hour, I will think you the most pathetical break promise, and the most hollow lover, and the most unworthy of her you call Rosalind, that may be chosen out of the gross band of the unfaithful: therefore beware my censure, and keep your promise.

Orl. With no less religion, than if thou wert indeed my Rosalind: So, adieu.

Ros. Well, time is the old justice that examines all such offenders, and let time try: Adieu! [*Exit* ORLANDO.

Cel. You have simply misus'd our sex in your love-prate: we must have your doublet and hose pluck'd over your head, and show the world what the bird hath done to her own nest.

Ros. O coz, coz, coz, my pretty little coz, that thou didst know how many fathom deep I am in love! But it cannot be sounded; my affection hath an unknown bottom, like the bay of Portugal.

Cel. Or rather bottomless; that as fast as you pour affection in it, it runs out.

Ros. No, that same wicked bastard of Venus, that was begot of thought, conceived of spleen, and born of madness; that blind rascally boy, that abuses every one's eyes, because his own are out, let him be judge, how deep I am in love:—I'll tell thee, Aliena, I cannot be out of the sight of Orlando: I'll go find a shadow, and sigh till he come.

Cel. And I'll sleep. [*Exeunt.*

SCENE II. *Another part of the Forest.*

Enter JAQUES *and* Lords, *in the habit of Foresters.*

Jaq. Which is he that kill'd the deer?

1 *Lord.* Sir, it was I.

Jaq. Let's present him to the duke like a Roman conqueror; and it would do well to set the deer's horns upon his head, for a branch of victory:—Have you no song, forester, for this purpose?

2 *Lord.* Yes, sir.

Jaq. Sing it; 'tis no matter how it be in tune, so it make noise enough.

SONG.

1. *What shall he have that kill'd the deer?*
2. *His leather skin and horns to wear.*
   1. *Then sing him home:*

Take thou no scorn, to wear the horn; } The rest shall
It was a crest ere thou wast born; } bear this bur-
1. *Thy father's father wore it;* } den.
And thy father bore it:

All. *The horn, the horn, the lusty horn,*
Is not a thing to laugh to scorn. [Exeunt.

SCENE III. *The Forest.*

Enter ROSALIND *and* CELIA.

Ros. How say you now? Is it not past two o'clock? and here much Orlando!

Cel. I warrant you, with pure love, and troubled brain, he hath ta'en his bow and arrows, and is gone forth to sleep: Look who comes here.

Enter SILVIUS.

Sil. My errand is to you, fair youth:—
My gentle Phebe, bid me give you this: [*Giving a Letter.*
I know not the contents; but as I guess,
By the stern brow and waspish action
Which she did use as she was writing of it,
It bears an angry tenour: pardon me,
I am but as a guiltless messenger.

Ros. Patience herself would startle at this letter,
And play the swaggerer; bear this, bear all:
She says, I am not fair; that I lack manners;
She calls me proud; and, that she could not love me
Were men as rare as phœnix: Od's my will!
Her love is not the hare that I do hunt:
Why writes she so to me?—Well, shepherd, well,
This is a letter of your own device.

Sil. No, I protest, I know not the contents;
Phebe did write it.

Ros. Come, come, you are a fool,
And turn'd into the extremity of love.
I saw her hand: she has a leathern hand,
A freestone-colour'd hand; I verily did think
That her old gloves were on, but 'twas her hands;
She has a huswife's hand: but that's no matter:
I say, she never did invent this letter;
This is a man's invention, and his hand.

Sil. Sure, it is hers.

Ros. Why, 'tis a boisterous and a cruel style,
A style for challengers: why, she defies me,
Like Turk to Christian: woman's gentle brain
Could not drop forth such giant-rude invention,
Such Ethiop words, blacker in their effect
Than in their countenance:—Will you hear the letter?

Sil. So please you, for I never heard it yet;
Yet heard too much of Phebe's cruelty.

Ros. She Phebe's me: Mark how the tyrant writes.

Art thou god to shepherd turn'd, [Reads.
That a maiden's heart hath burn'd?

Can a woman rail thus?

Sil. Call you this railing?

Ros. *Why, thy godhead laid apart,*
Warr'st thou with a woman's heart?

Did you ever hear such railing?—

Whiles the eye of man did woo me,
That could do no vengeance to me—

Meaning me a beast.—

If the scorn of your bright eyne
Have power to raise such love in mine,
Alack, in me what strange effect
Would they work in mild aspect?
Whiles you chid me, I did love;
How then might your prayers move?
He, that brings this love to thee,
Little knows this love in me:
And by him seal up thy mind;
Whether that thy youth and kind
Will the faithful offer take
Of me, and all that I can make;
Or else by him my love deny,
And then I'll study how to die.

Sil. Call you this chiding?

Cel. Alas, poor shepherd!

Ros. Do you pity him? no, he deserves no pity.—Wilt thou love such a woman?—What, to make thee an instrument, and play false strains upon thee! not to be endured!—Well, go your way to her, (for I see, love hath made thee a tame snake), and say this to her;—That if she love me, I charge her to love thee: if she will not, I will never have her, unless thou entreat for her.—If you be a true lover, hence, and not a word; for here comes more company.

[*Exit* SILVIUS.

Enter OLIVER.

Oli. Good-morrow, fair ones: Pray you, if you know
Where, in the purlieus of this forest, stands
A sheep-cote, fenc'd about with olive-trees?

Cel. West of this place, down in the neighbour bottom,
The rank of osiers, by the murmuring stream,
Left on your right hand, brings you to the place:
But at this hour the house doth keep itself,
There's none within.

Oli. If that an eye may profit by a tongue,
Then I should know you by description;
Such garments, and such years: *The boy is fair,*
Of female favour, and bestows himself
Like a ripe sister; but the woman low,
And browner than her brother. Are not you
The owner of the house I did inquire for?

Cel. It is no boast, being ask'd, to say, we are.

Oli. Orlando doth commend him to you both;
And to that youth he calls his Rosalind,
He sends this bloody napkin; are you he?

Ros. I am: What must we understand by this?

Oli. Some of my shame; if you will know of me
What man I am, and how, and why, and where
This handkerchief was stain'd.

Cel. I pray you, tell it.

Oli. When last the young Orlando parted from you,
He left a promise to return again
Within an hour; and, pacing through the forest,
Chewing the food of sweet and bitter fancy,
Lo, what befell! he threw his eye aside,
And, mark, what object did present itself!
Under an oak, whose boughs were moss'd with age,
And high top bald with dry antiquity,
A wretched ragged man, o'ergrown with hair,
Lay sleeping on his back: about his neck
A green and gilded snake had wreathed itself,
Who with her head, nimble in threats approach'd
The opening of his mouth; but suddenly,
Seeing Orlando, it unlink'd itself,
And with indented glides did slip away
Into a bush: under which bush's shade
A lioness, with udders all drawn dry,
Lay couching, head on ground, with catlike watch,

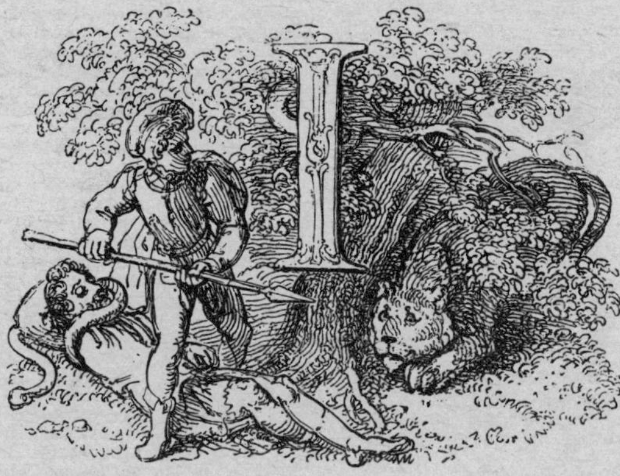

When that the sleeping man should stir; for 'tis
The royal disposition of that beast,
To prey on nothing that doth seem as dead:
This seen, Orlando did approach the man,
And found it was his brother, his elder brother.

Cel. O, I have heard him speak of that same brother;
And he did render him the most unnatural
That liv'd 'mongst men.

Oli. And well he might so do
For well I know he was unnatural.

Ros. But, to Orlando;—Did he leave him there,
Food to the suck'd and hungry lioness?

Oli. Twice did he turn his back, and purpos'd so:
But kindness, nobler ever than revenge,
And nature, stronger than his just occasion,
Made him give battle to the lioness,

Who quickly fell before him; in which hurtling
From miserable slumber I awak'd.
Cel. Are you his brother?
Ros. Was it you he rescu'd?
Cel. Was't you that did so oft contrive to kill him?
Oli. 'Twas I; but 'tis not I: I do not shame
To tell you what I was, since my conversion
So sweetly tastes, being the thing I am.
Ros. But, for the bloody napkin?—
Oli. By and by.
When from the first to last, betwixt us two,
Tears our recountments had most kindly bath'd;
As, how I came into that desert place;——
In brief he led me to the gentle duke,
Who gave me fresh array and entertainment,
Committing me unto my brother's love;
Who led me instantly unto his cave,
There stripp'd himself, and here upon his arm
The lioness had torn some flesh away,
Which all this while had bled; and now he fainted,
And cry'd, in fainting, upon Rosalind.
Brief, I recover'd him; bound up his wound;
And, after some small space, being strong at heart,
He sent me hither, stranger as I am,
To tell this story, that you might excuse
His broken promise, and to give this napkin,
Dy'd in his blood, unto the shepherd youth
That he in sport doth call his Rosalind.
Cel. Why, how now, Ganymede? sweet Ganymede? [ROSALIND *faints.*
Oli. Many will swoon when they do look on blood.
Cel. There is more in it:—Cousin—Ganymede!
Oli. Look, he recovers.
Ros. I would, I were at home.
Cel. We'll lead you thither:—
I pray you, will you take him by the arm?
Oli. Be of good cheer, youth:—You a man?—You lack a man's heart.

Ros. I do so, I confess it. Ah, sir, a body would think this was well counterfeited: I pray you, tell your brother how well I counterfeited.—Heigh ho!—

Oli. This was not counterfeit; there is too great testimony in your complexion, that it was a passion of earnest.

Ros. Counterfeit, I assure you.

Oli. Well then, take a good heart, and counterfeit to be a man.

Ros. So I do: but, i'faith, I should have been a woman by right.

Cel. Come, you look paler and paler; pray you, draw homewards:—Good sir, go with us.

Oli. That will I, for I must bear answer back—
How you excuse my brother, Rosalind.

Ros. I shall devise something: But, I pray you, commend my counterfeiting to him:—Will you go? [*Exeunt.*

ACT V.

SCENE I. *The same.*

Enter TOUCHSTONE *and* AUDREY.

Touch. We shall find a time, Audrey; patience, gentle Audrey.

Aud. 'Faith, the priest was good enough, for all the old gentleman's saying.

Touch. A most wicked Sir Oliver, Audrey, a most vile Mar-text. But, Audrey, there is a youth here in the forest lays claim to you.

Aud. Ay, I know who 'tis; he hath no interest in me in the world: here comes the man you mean.

Enter WILLIAM.

Touch. It is meat and drink to me to see a clown: By my troth, we that have good wits, have much to answer for; we shall be flouting; we cannot hold.

Will. Good even, Audrey.

Aud. God ye good even, William.

Will. And good even to you, sir.

Touch. Good even, gentle friend: Cover thy head, cover thy head; nay, pry'thee, be covered. How old are you, friend?

Will. Five-and-twenty, sir.

Touch. A ripe age: Is thy name William?

Will. William, sir.

Touch. A fair name: Wast born i' the forest here?

Will. Ay, sir, I thank God.

Touch. *Thank God;*—a good answer: Art rich?

Will. 'Faith, sir, so, so.

Touch. *So, so,* is good, very good, very excellent good:—and yet it is not; it is but so so. Art thou wise?

Will. Ay, sir, I have a pretty wit.

Touch. Why, thou say'st well. I do now remember a saying; *The fool doth think he is wise, but the wise man knows himself to be a fool.* The heathen philosopher, when he had a desire to eat a grape, would open his lips when he put it into his mouth; meaning thereby, that grapes were made to eat, and lips to open. You do love this maid?

Will. I do, sir.

Touch. Give me your hand: Art thou learned?

Will. No, sir.

Touch. Then learn this of me: To have, is to have: For it is a figure in rhetorick, that drink, being poured out of a cup into a glass, by filling the one doth empty the other: for all your writers do consent, that *ipse* is he; now you are not *ipse*, for I am he.

Will. Which he, sir?

Touch. He, sir, that must marry this woman: Therefore, you clown, abandon,—which is in the vulgar, leave,—the society,—which in the boorish is, company,—of this female,—which in the common is,—woman, which together is, abandon the society of this female; or, clown, thou perishest; or, to thy better understanding, diest; to wit, I kill thee, make thee away, translate thy life into death, thy liberty into bondage: I will deal in poison with thee, or in bastinado, or in steel; I will bandy with thee in faction; I will o'errun thee with policy; I will kill thee a hundred and fifty ways: therefore tremble, and depart.

Aud. Do, good William.

Will. God rest you merry, sir. [*Exit.*

Enter CORIN.

Cor. Our master and mistress seek you; come, away, away.

Touch. Trip, Audrey, trip, Audrey;—I attend, I attend. [*Exeunt.*

SCENE II. *The same.*

Enter ORLANDO *and* OLIVER.

Orl. Is't possible, that on so little acquaintance you should like her? that but seeing, you should love her? and, loving, woo? and, wooing, she should grant? and will you persever to enjoy her?

Oli. Neither call the giddiness of it in question, the poverty of her, the small acquaintance, my sudden wooing, nor her sudden consenting; but say with me, I love Aliena; say with her, that she loves me; consent with both, that we may enjoy each other: it shall be to your good; for my father's house, and all the revenue that was old Sir Rowland's, will I estate upon you, and here live and die a shepherd.

Enter ROSALIND.

Orl. You have my consent. Let your wedding be to-morrow: thither will I invite the duke, and all his contented followers: Go you, and prepare Aliena; for, look you, here comes my Rosalind.

Ros. God save you, brother.

Oli. And you, fair sister.

Ros. O, my dear Orlando, how it grieves me to see thee wear thy heart in a scarf.

Orl. It is my arm.

Ros. I thought thy heart had been wounded with the claws of a lion.

Orl. Wounded it is, but with the eyes of a lady.

Ros. Did your brother tell you how I counterfeited to swoon, when he showed me your handkerchief?

Orl. Ay, and greater wonders than that.

Ros. O, I know where you are:—Nay, 'tis true: there never was any thing so sudden, but the fight of two rams, and Cæsar's thrasonical brag of—I *came, saw, and overcame:* For your brother and my sister no sooner met, but they looked; no sooner looked, but they loved; no sooner loved, but they sighed; no sooner sighed, but they asked one another the reason; no sooner knew the reason, but they sought the remedy: and in these degrees have they made a pair of stairs to marriage, which they will climb incontinent, or else be incontinent before marriage: they are in the very wrath of love, and they will together; clubs cannot part them.

Orl. They shall be married to-morrow; and I will bid the duke to the nuptial. But, O, how bitter a thing it is to look into happiness through another man's eyes! By so much the more shall I to-morrow be at the height of heart-heaviness, by how much I shall think my brother happy, in having what he wishes for.

Ros. Why then, to-morrow I cannot serve your turn for Rosalind?

Orl. I can live no longer by thinking.

Ros. I will weary you no longer then with idle talking. Know of me then, (for now I speak to some purpose), that I know you are a gentleman of good conceit: I speak not this, that you should bear a good opinion of my knowledge, insomuch, I say, I know you are; neither do I labour for a greater esteem than may in some little measure draw a belief from you, to do yourself good, and not to grace me. Believe then, if you please, that I can do strange things: I have, since I was three years old, conversed with a magician, most profound in this art, and yet not damnable. If you do love Rosalind so near the heart as your gesture cries it out, when your brother marries Aliena, shall you marry her: I know into what straits of fortune she is driven; and it is not impossible to me, if it appear not inconvenient to you, to set her before your eyes to-morrow; human as she is, and without any danger.

Orl. Speakest thou in sober meanings?

Ros. By my life, I do; which I tender dearly, though I say I am a magician: Therefore put you in your best array, bid your friends; for if you will be married to-morrow, you shall; and to Rosalind, if you will.

Enter SILVIUS *and* PHEBE.

Look, here comes a lover of mine, and a lover of hers.

Phe. Youth, you have done me much ungentleness,
To show the letter that I writ to you.

Ros. I care not, if I have: it is my study,
To seem despiteful and ungentle to you:
You are there follow'd by a faithful shepherd;
Look upon him, love him; he worships you.

Phe. Good shepherd, tell this youth what 'tis to love.

Sil. It is to be all made of sighs and tears;—
And so am I for Phebe.

Phe. And I for Ganymede.

Orl. And I for Rosalind.

Ros. And I for no woman.

Sil. It is to be all made of faith and service;—
And so am I for Phebe.

Phe. And I for Ganymede.

Orl. And I for Rosalind.

Ros. And I for no woman.

Sil. It is to be all made of fantasy,
All made of passion, and all made of wishes;
All adoration, duty, and observance,
All humbleness, all patience, and impatience,
All purity, all trial, all obeisance;—
And so am I for Phebe.

Phe. And so am I for Ganymede.

Orl. And so am I for Rosalind.

Ros. And so am I for no woman.

Phe. If this be so, why blame you me to love you? [*To* ROSALIND.

Sil. If this be so, why blame you me to love you? [*To* PHEBE.

Orl. If this be so, why blame you me to love you?

Ros. Who do you speak to, *why blame you me to love you?*

Orl. To her, that is not here; nor doth not hear.

Ros. Pray you, no more of this; 'tis like the howling of Irish wolves against the moon.—I will help you, [*To* SILVIUS] if I can.—I would love you, [*To* PHEBE] if I could.—To-morrow meet me all together.—I will marry you, [*To* PHEBE] if ever I marry woman, and I'll be married to-morrow;—I will satisfy you, [*To* ORLANDO] if ever I satisfied man, and you shall be married to-morrow:—I will content you, [*To* SILVIUS] if what pleases you contents you, and you shall be married to-morrow.—As you [*To* ORLANDO] love Rosalind, meet;—as you [*To* SILVIUS] love Phebe, meet: And as I love no woman, I'll meet.—So, fare you well; I have left you commands.

Sil. I'll not fail, if I live.

Phe. Nor I.

Orl. Nor I.

[*Exeunt.*

SCENE III. *The same.*

Enter TOUCHSTONE *and* AUDREY.

Touch. To-morrow is the joyful day, Audrey; to-morrow will we be married.

Aud. I do desire it with all my heart; and I hope it is no dishonest desire, to desire to be a woman of the world. Here comes two of the banish'd duke's pages.

Enter two Pages.

1 *Page.* Well met, honest gentleman.

Touch. By my troth, well met: Come, sit, sit, and a song.

2 *Page.* We are for you: sit i'the middle.

1 *Page.* Shall we clap into't roundly, without hawking, or spitting, or saying we are hoarse; which are the only prologues to a bad voice?

2 *Page.* I'faith, i'faith; and both in a tune, like two gipsies on a horse.

SONG.

I.

It was a lover, and his lass,
With a hey, and a ho, and a hey nonino,
That o'er the green corn-field did pass,
In the spring time, the only pretty rank time,
When birds do sing, hey ding a ding, ding;
Sweet lovers love the spring.

II.

Between the acres of the rye,
With a hey, and a ho, and a hey nonino,
These pretty country folks would lie,
In spring time, &c.

III.

This carol they began that hour,
With a hey, and a ho, and a hey nonino,
How that a life was but a flower
In spring time, &c.

IV.

And therefore take the present time,
With a hey, and ho, and a hey nonino;
For love is crowned with the prime
In spring time, &c.

Touch. Truly, young gentlemen, though there was no greater matter in the ditty, yet the note was very untunable.

1 *Page.* You are deceiv'd, sir; we kept time, we lost not our time.

Touch. By my troth, yes; I count it but time lost to hear such a foolish song. God be with you: and God mend your voices! Come, Audrey. [*Exeunt.*

SCENE IV. *Another part of the Forest.*

Enter Duke *senior*, AMIENS, JAQUES, ORLANDO, OLIVER, *and* CELIA.

Duke S. Dost thou believe, Orlando, that the boy
Can do all this that he hath promised?

Orl. I sometimes do believe, and sometimes do not:
As those that fear they hope, and know they fear.

Enter ROSALIND, SILVIUS, *and* PHEBE.

Ros. Patience once more, whiles our compact is urg'd:——
You say, if I bring in your Rosalind, [*To the* Duke.
You will bestow her on Orlando here?

Duke S. That would I, had I kingdoms to give with her.

Ros. And you say, you will have her, when I bring her? [*To* ORLANDO.

Orl. That would I, were I of all kingdoms king.

Ros. You say, you'll marry me, if I be willing? [*To* PHEBE.

Phe. That will I, should I die the hour after.

Ros. But if you do refuse to marry me,
You'll give yourself to this most faithful shepherd?

Phe. So is the bargain.

Ros. You say, that you'll have Phebe, if she will? [*To* SILVIUS.

Sil. Though to have her and death were both one thing.

Ros. I have promis'd to make all this matter even.
Keep you your word, O duke, to give your daughter;—
You yours, Orlando, to receive his daughter:—
Keep your word, Phebe, that you'll marry me;
Or else, refusing me, to wed this shepherd:—
Keep your word, Silvius, that you'll marry her,
If she refuse me:—and from hence I go,
To make these doubts all even.
[*Exeunt* ROSALIND *and* CELIA.

Duke S. I do remember in this shepherd-boy
Some lively touches of my daughter's favour.

Orl. My lord, the first time that I ever saw him,
Methought he was a brother to your daughter;
But, my good lord, this boy is forest-born;
And hath been tutor'd in the rudiments
Of many desperate studies by his uncle,
Whom he reports to be a great magician,
Obscured in the circle of this forest.

Enter TOUCHSTONE *and* AUDREY.

Jaq. There is, sure, another flood toward, and these couples are coming to the ark! Here comes a pair of very strange beasts, which in all tongues are called fools.

Touch. Salutation and greeting to you all!

Jaq. Good my lord, bid him welcome: This is the motley-minded gentleman, that I have so often met in the forest: he hath been a courtier, he swears.

Touch. If any man doubt that, let him put me to my purgation. I have trod a measure; I have flattered a lady; I have been politick with my friend, smooth with mine enemy; I have undone three tailors; I have had four quarrels, and like to have fought one.

Jaq. And how was that ta'en up?

Touch. 'Faith, we met, and found the quarrel was upon the seventh cause.

Jaq. How seventh cause?—Good my lord, like this fellow.

Duke S. I like him very well.

Touch. God'ild you, sir; I desire you of the like. I press in here, sir, amongst the rest of the country copulatives, to swear, and to forswear; according as marriage binds, and blood breaks:—A poor virgin, sir, an ill-favoured thing, sir, but mine own; a poor humour of mine, sir, to take that that no man else will: Rich honesty dwells like a miser, sir, in a poor-house; as your pearl, in your foul oyster.

Duke S. By my faith, he is very swift and sententious.

Touch. According to the fool's bolt, sir, and such dulcet diseases.

Jaq. But, for the seventh cause; how did you find the quarrel on the seventh cause?

Touch. Upon a lie seven times removed:—Bear your body more seeming, Audrey:—as thus, sir, I did dislike the cut of a certain courtier's beard; he sent me word, if I said his beard was not cut well, he was in the mind it was: This is called the *Retort courteous.* If I sent him word again, it was not well cut, he would send me word, he cut it to please himself: This is called the *Quip modest.* If, again, it was not well cut, he disabled my judgment: This is call'd the *Reply churlish.* If again, it was not well cut, he would answer, I spake not true: This is call'd the *Reproof valiant.* If again, it was not well cut, he would say, I lie: This is called the *Countercheck quarrelsome:* and so to the *Lie circumstantial*, and the *Lie direct.*

Jaq. And how oft did you say, his beard was not well cut?

Touch. I durst go no further than the *Lie circumstantial*, nor he durst not give me the *Lie direct;* and so we measured swords, and parted.

Jaq. Can you nominate in order now the degrees of the lie?

Touch. O, sir, we quarrel in print, by the book; as you have books for good manners: I will name you the degrees. The first, the Retort courteous; the second, the Quip modest; the third, the Reply churlish; the fourth, the Reproof valiant; the fifth, the Countercheck quarrelsome; the sixth, the Lie with circumstance! the seventh, the Lie direct. All these you may avoid, but the lie direct; and you may avoid that too, with an *If.* I knew when seven justices could not take up a quarrel; but when the parties were met themselves, one of them thought but of an *If*, as *If you said so, then I said so;* and they shook hands, and swore brothers. Your *If* is the only peace-maker; much virtue in *If.*

Jaq. Is not this a rare fellow, my lord? he's as good at any thing, and yet a fool.

Duke S. He uses his folly like a stalking-horse, and under the presentation of that, he shoots his wit.

Enter HYMEN, *leading* ROSALIND *in woman's clothes; and* CELIA.

Still Musick.

Hym. *Then is there mirth in heaven,*
When earthly things made even,
Atone together.
Good duke, receive thy daughter,
Hymen from heaven brought her,
Yea, brought her hither;
That thou might'st join her hand with his
Whose heart within her bosom is.

Ros. To you I give myself, for I am yours:— [*To* Duke S.

To you I give myself, for I am yours.
[*To* ORLANDO.

Duke S. If there be truth in sight, you are my daughter.

Orl. If there be truth in sight, you are my Rosalind.

Phe. If sight and shape be true,
Why then,—my love, adieu!

Ros. I'll have no father, if you be not he:—
[*To* Duke S.
I'll have no husband, if you be not he:—
[*To* ORLANDO.
Nor ne'er wed woman, if you be not she:—
[*To* PHEBE.

Hym. Peace, ho! I bar confusion:
'Tis I must make conclusion
Of these most strange events:
Here's eight that must take hands,
To join in Hymen's bands,
If truth holds true contents.
You and you no cross shall part:
[*To* ORLANDO *and* ROSALIND.
You and you are heart in heart:
[*To* OLIVER *and* CELIA.
You [*To* PHEBE] to his love must accord,
Or have a woman to your lord:—
You and you are sure together,
[*To* TOUCHSTONE *and* AUDREY.
As the winter to foul weather.
Whiles a wedlock-hymn we sing,
Feed yourselves with questioning;
That reason wonder may diminish,
How thus we met, and these things finish.

SONG.

Wedding is great Juno's crown;
O blessed bond of board and bed!
'Tis Hymen peoples every town;
High wedlock then be honoured:
Honour, high honour and renown,
To Hymen, god of every town!

Duke S. O my dear niece, welcome thou art to me;
Even daughter, welcome in no less degree.

Phe. I will not eat my word, now thou art mine;
Thy faith my fancy to thee doth combine.
[*To* SILVIUS.

Enter JAQUES DE BOIS.

Jaq. de B. Let me have audience for a word or two;
I am the second son of old Sir Rowland,
That bring these tidings to this fair assembly:—
Duke Frederick, hearing how that every day
Men of great worth resorted to this forest,
Address'd a mighty power! which were on foot,
In his own conduct, purposely to take
His brother here, and put him to the sword:
And to the skirts of this wild wood he came;
Where, meeting with an old religious man,
After some question with him, was converted
Both from his enterprise, and from the world:
His crown bequeathing to his banish'd brother,
And all their lands restor'd to them again
That were with him exil'd: This to be true,
I do engage my life.

Duke S. Welcome, young man;
Thou offer'st fairly to thy brothers' wedding:
To one, his lands withheld; and to the other,
A land itself at large, a potent dukedom.
First, in this forest, let us do those ends
That here were well begun, and well begot:
And after, every of this happy number,
That have endur'd shrewd days and nights with us,
Shall share the good of our returned fortune,
According to the measure of their states.
Meantime, forget this new-fall'n dignity,
And fall into our rustick revelry:—
Play, musick;—and you, brides and bride-grooms all,
With measure heap'd in joy, to the measures fall.

Jaq. Sir, by your patience; If I heard you rightly,
The duke hath put on a religious life,
And thrown into neglect the pompous court?

Jaq. de B. He hath.

Jaq. To him will I: out of these convertites
There is much matter to be heard and learn'd.—
You to your former honour I bequeath:
[*To* Duke S.
Your patience and your virtue well deserves it:—
You [*To* ORLANDO] to a love, that your true faith doth merit:—
You [*To* OLIVER] to your land, and love, and great allies:—
You [*To* SILVIUS] to a long and well deserved bed:—
And you [*To* TOUCHSTONE] to wrangling; for thy loving voyage
Is but for two months victual'd:—So to your pleasures;
I am for other than for dancing measures.

Duke S. Stay, Jaques, stay.

Jaq. To see no pastime, I:—what you would have
I'll stay to know at your abandon'd cave. [*Exit.*

Duke S. Proceed, proceed: we will begin these rites,
And we do trust they'll end in true delights.
[*A dance.*

EPILOGUE.

Ros. It is not the fashion to see the lady the epilogue: but it is no more unhandsome, than to see the lord the prologue. If it be true, that *good wine needs no bush*, 'tis true that a good play needs no epilogue: Yet to good wine they do use good bushes; and good plays prove the better by the help of good epilogues. What a case am I in then, that am neither a good epilogue, nor cannot insinuate with you in the behalf of a good play? I am not furnished like a beggar, therefore to beg will not become me: my way is, to conjure you; and I'll begin with the women. I charge you, O women, for the love you bear to men, to like as much of this play as please you: and I charge you, O men, for the love you bear to women (as I perceive, by your simpering, none of you hate them), that between you and the women the play may please. If I were a woman, I would kiss as many of you as had beards that pleased me, complexions that liked me, and breaths that I defied not: and I am sure, as many as have good beards, or good faces, or sweet breaths, will, for my kind offer, when I make curt'sy, bid me farewell. [*Exeunt.*

ALL'S WELL THAT ENDS WELL.

PERSONS REPRESENTED.

King of France.
Duke of Florence.
BERTRAM, Count of Rousillon.
LAFEU, *an old Lord.*
PAROLLES, *a follower of* Bertram.
Several young French Lords, *that serve with* Bertram *in the* Florentine *war.*
Steward, } *Servants to the* Countess of Rousillon.
Clown, }
A Page.

Countess of Rousillon, *Mother to* Bertram.
HELENA, *a Gentlewoman protected by the* Countess.
An old Widow of Florence.
DIANA, *Daughter to the Widow.*
VIOLENTA, } *Neighbours and Friends to the Widow.*
MARIANA, }

Lords, *attending on the* King; Officers, Soldiers, *&c.* French *and* Florentine.

SCENE—*partly in* France, *and partly in* Tuscany.

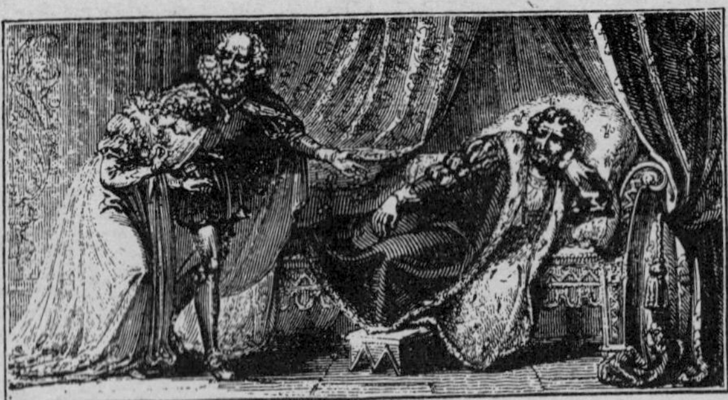

ACT I.

SCENE I. Rousillon.

A Room in the Countess's *Palace.*

Enter BERTRAM, *the* Countess of Rousillon, HELENA, *and* LAFEU, *in mourning.*

Count. IN delivering my son from me, I bury a second husband.

Ber. And I, in going, madam, weep o'er my father's death anew: but I must attend his majesty's command, to whom I am now in ward, evermore in subjection.

Laf. You shall find of the king a husband, madam;—you, sir, a father: He that so generally is at all times good, must of necessity hold his virtue to you; whose worthiness would stir it up where it wanted, rather than lack it where there is such abundance.

Count. What hope is there of his majesty's amendment?

Laf. He hath abandoned his physicians, madam; under whose practices he hath persecuted time with hope; and finds no other advantage in the process but only the losing of hope by time.

Count. This young gentlewoman had a father (O, that *had!* how sad a passage 'tis!) whose skill was almost as great as his honesty; had it stretched so far, would have made nature immortal, and death should have play for lack of work. 'Would, for the king's sake, he were living! I think it would be the death of the king's disease.

Laf. How called you the man you speak of, madam?

Count. He was famous, sir, in his profession, and it was his great right to be so: Gerard de Narbon.

Laf. He was excellent, indeed, madam; the king very lately spoke of him, admiringly, and mourningly: he was skilful enough to have lived still, if knowledge could be set up against mortality.

Ber. What is it, my good lord, the king languishes of?

Laf. A fistula, my lord.

Ber. I heard not of it before.

Laf. I would, it were not notorious.—Was this gentlewoman the daughter of Gerard de Narbon?

Count. His sole child, my lord; and bequeathed to my overlooking. I have those hopes of her good, that her education promises: her dispositions she inherits, which make fair gifts fairer; for where an unclean mind carries virtuous qualities, there commendations go with pity, they are virtues and traitors too; in her they are the better for their simpleness; she derives her honesty, and achieves her goodness.

Laf. Your commendations, madam, get from her tears.

Count. 'Tis the best brine a maiden can season her praise in. The remembrance of her father never approaches her heart, but the tyranny of her sorrows takes all livelihood from her cheek. No more of this, Helena, go to, no more; lest it be rather thought you affect a sorrow, than to have.

Hel. I do affect a sorrow, indeed, but I have it too.

Laf. Moderate lamentation is the right of the dead, excessive grief the enemy to the living.

Count. If the living be enemy to the grief, the excess makes it soon mortal.

Ber. Madam, I desire your holy wishes.

Laf. How understand we that?

Count. Be thou blest, Bertram! and succeed thy father
In manners, as in shape! thy blood, and virtue,
Contend for empire in thee; and thy goodness
Share with thy birth-right! Love all, trust a few,
Do wrong to none: be able for thine enemy
Rather in power, than use; and keep thy friend
Under thy own life's key: be check'd for silence,
But never tax'd for speech. What heaven more will,
That thee may furnish, and my prayers pluck down,
Fall on thy head! Farewell.—My lord,
'Tis an unseason'd courtier; good my lord,
Advise him.

Laf. He cannot want the best
That shall attend his love.

Count. Heaven bless him!—Farewell, Bertram. [*Exit* Countess.

Ber. The best wishes, that can be forged in your thoughts [*To* HELENA], be servants to you! Be comfortable to my mother, your mistress, and make much of her.

Laf. Farewell, pretty lady: You must hold the credit of your father.

[*Exeunt* BERTRAM *and* LAFEU.

Hel. O, were that all!—I think not on my father;
And these great tears grace his remembrance more
Than those I shed for him. What was he like?
I have forgot him: my imagination
Carries no favour in it but Bertram's.
I am undone; there is no living, none,
If Bertram be away. It were all one,
That I should love a bright particular star,
And think to wed it, he is so above me:
In his bright radiance and collateral light
Must I be comforted, not in his sphere.
The ambition in my love thus plagues itself:
The hind, that would be mated by the lion,
Must die for love. 'Twas pretty, though a plague,
To see him every hour; to sit and draw
His arched brows, his hawking eye, his curls,
In our heart's table; heart, too capable
Of every line and trick of his sweet favour:
But now he's gone, and my idolatrous fancy
Must sanctify his relicks. Who comes here?

Enter PAROLLES.

One that goes with him: I love him for his sake;
And yet I know him a notorious liar,
Think him a great way fool, solely a coward;
Yet these fix'd evils sit so fit in him,
That they take place, when virtue's steely bones
Look bleak in the cold wind: withal full oft we see
Cold wisdom waiting on superfluous folly.

Par. Save you, fair queen.

Hel. And you, monarch.

Par. No.

Hel. And no.

Par. Are you meditating on virginity?

Hel. Ay. You have some stain of soldier in you: let me ask you a question: Man is enemy to virginity; how may we barricado it against him?

Par. Keep him out.

Hel. But he assails; and our virginity, though valiant in the defence, yet is weak: unfold to us some warlike resistance.

Par. There is none; man, sitting down before you, will undermine you, and blow you up.

Hel. Bless our poor virginity from underminers, and blowers up!—Is there no military policy, how virgins might blow up men?

Par. Virginity, being blown down, man will quicklier be blown up: marry, in blowing him down again, with the breach yourselves made, you lose your city. It is not politic in the commonwealth of nature, to preserve virginity. Loss of virginity is rational increase; and there was never virgin got, till virginity was first lost. That, you were made of, is metal to make virgins. Virginity, by being once lost, may be ten times found: by being ever kept, it is ever lost: 'tis too cold a companion; away with it.

Hel. I will stand for't a little, though therefore I die a virgin.

Par. There's little can be said in't; 'tis against the rule of nature. To speak on the part of virginity, is to accuse your mothers; which is most infallible disobedience. He that hangs himself is a virgin: virginity murders itself; and should be buried in highways, out of all sanctified limit, as a desperate offendress against nature. Virginity breeds mites, much like a cheese; consumes itself to the very paring, and so dies with feeding his own stomach. Besides, virginity is peevish, proud, idle, made of self-love, which is the most inhibited sin in the canon. Keep it not: you cannot choose but lose by't: Out with't; within ten years it will make itself ten, which is a goodly increase, and the principal itself not much the worse: Away with't.

Hel. How might one do, sir, to lose it to her own liking?

Par. Let me see: Marry, ill, to like him that ne'er it likes. 'Tis a commodity will lose the gloss with lying; the longer kept, the less worth: off with't, while 'tis vendible: answer the time of request. Virginity, like an old courtier, wears her cap out of fashion; richly suited, but unsuitable: just like the brooch and toothpick, which wear not now: Your date is better in your pie and your porridge, than in your cheek: And your virginity, your old virginity, is like one of our French wither'd pears; it looks ill, it eats dryly; marry, 'tis a wither'd pear; it was formerly better; marry, yet, 'tis a wither'd pear: Will you any thing with it?

Hel. Not my virginity yet.——
There shall your master have a thousand loves,
A mother, and a mistress, and a friend,
A phœnix, captain, and an enemy,
A guide, a goddess, and a sovereign,
A counsellor, a traitress, and a dear;
His humble ambition, proud humility,
His jarring concord, and his discord dulcet,
His faith, his sweet disaster: with a world
Of pretty, fond, adoptious christendoms,
That blinking Cupid gossips. Now shall he——
I know not what he shall:—God send him well!—
The court's a learning-place:—and he is one——

Par. What one, i'faith?

Hel. That I wish well.—'Tis pity——

Par. What's pity?

Hel. That wishing well had not a body in't,
Which might be felt: that we, the poorer born,
Whose baser stars do shut us up in wishes,
Might with effects of them follow our friends,
And show what we alone must think; which never
Returns us thanks.

Enter a Page.

Page. Monsieur Parolles, my lord calls for you. [*Exit* Page.

Par. Little Helen, farewell: if I can remember thee, I will think of thee at court.

Hel. Monsieur Parolles, you were born under a charitable star.

Par. Under Mars, I.

Hel. I especially think, under Mars.

Par. Why under Mars?

Hel. The wars have so kept you under, that you must needs be born under Mars.

Par. When he was predominant.

Hel. When he was retrograde, I think, rather.

Par. Why think you so?

Hel. You go so much backward, when you fight,

Par. That's for advantage.

Hel. So is running away, when fear proposes the safety; But the composition, that your valour and fear makes in you, is a virtue of a good wing, and I like the wear well.

Par. I am so full of business, I cannot answer thee acutely: I will return perfect courtier; in the which, my instruction shall serve to naturalize thee, so thou wilt be capable of a courtier's counsel, and understand what advice shall thrust upon thee; else thou diest in thine unthankfulness, and thine ignorance makes thee away: farewell. When thou hast leisure, say thy prayers; when thou hast none, remember thy friends: get thee a good husband, and use him as he uses thee: so farewell. [*Exit.*

Hel. Our remedies oft in ourselves do lie,
Which we ascribe to heaven: the fated sky
Gives us free scope; only, doth backward pull
Our slow designs, when we ourselves are dull.
What power is it which mounts my love so high;
That makes me see, and cannot feed mine eye?
The mightiest space in fortune nature brings
To join like likes, and kiss like native things.
Impossible be strange attempts, to those
That weigh their pains in sense; and do suppose,
What hath been cannot be: Who ever strove
To show her merit, that did miss her love?
The king's disease—my project may deceive me,
But my intents are fix'd, and will not leave me. [*Exit.*

SCENE II. Paris. *A Room in the* King's *Palace.*

Flourish of Cornets. Enter the King of France, *with Letters;* Lords *and others attending.*

King. The Florentine and Senoys are by the ears;
Have fought with equal fortune, and continue
A braving war.

1 *Lord.* So 'tis reported, sir.

King. Nay, 'tis most credible; we here receive it
A certainty, vouch'd from our cousin Austria,
With caution, that the Florentine will move us
For speedy aid; wherein our dearest friend
Prejudicates the business, and would seem
To have us make denial.

1 *Lord.* His love and wisdom,
Approv'd so to your majesty, may plead
For amplest credence.

King. He hath arm'd our answer,
And Florence is denied before he comes:
Yet, for our gentlemen, that mean to see
The Tuscan service, freely have they leave
To stand on either part.

2 *Lord.* It may well serve
A nursery to our gentry, who are sick
For breathing and exploit.

King. What's he comes here?

Enter Bertram, Lafeu, *and* Parolles.

1 *Lord.* It is the count Rousillon, my good lord,
Young Bertram.

King. Youth, thou bear'st thy father's face;
Frank nature, rather curious than in haste,
Hath well compos'd thee. Thy father's moral parts
May'st thou inherit too! Welcome to Paris.

Ber. My thanks and duty are your majesty's.

King. I would I had that corporal soundness now,
As when thy father, and myself in friendship
Fast tried our soldiership! He did look far
Into the service of the time, and was
Discipled of the bravest: he lasted long;
But on us both did haggish age steal on,
And wore us out of act. It much repairs me
To talk of your good father: In his youth
He had the wit, which I can well observe
To-day in our young lords; but they may jest,
Till their own scorn return to them unnoted,
Ere they can hide their levity in honour.
So like a courtier, contempt nor bitterness
Were in his pride or sharpness: if they were,
His equal had awak'd them; and his honour,
Clock to itself, knew the true minute when
Exception bid him speak, and, at this time,
His tongue obey'd his hand: who were below him
He us'd as creatures of another place;
And bow'd his eminent top to their low ranks,
Making them proud of his humility,
In their poor praise he humbled: Such a man
Might be a copy to these younger times;
Which, follow'd well, would demonstrate them now
But goers backward.

Ber. His good remembrance, sir,
Lies richer in your thoughts, than on his tomb;
So in approof lives not his epitaph,
As in your royal speech.

King. 'Would, I were with him! He would always say,
(Methinks I hear him now; his plausive words
He scatter'd not in ears, but grafted them,
To grow there and to bear)—*Let me not live,*—
Thus his good melancholy oft began,
On the catastrophe and heel of pastime,
When it was out,—*let me not live,* quoth he,
After my flame lacks oil, to be the snuff
Of younger spirits, whose apprehensive senses
All but new things disdain; whose judgments are
Mere fathers of their garments; whose constancies
Expire before their fashions:——This he wish'd:
I, after him, do after him wish too,
Since I nor wax, nor honey, can bring home,
I quickly were dissolved from my hive,
To give some labourers room.

2 *Lord.* You are lov'd, sir;
They, that least lend it you, shall lack you first.

King. I fill a place, I know't.—How long is't, count,
Since the physician at your father's died?
He was much fam'd.

Ber. Some six months since, my lord.

King. If he were living, I would try him yet;—
Lend me an arm; the rest have worn me out
With several applications:—nature and sickness
Debate it at their leisure. Welcome, count;
My son's no dearer.

Ber. Thank your majesty. [*Exeunt. Flourish.*

SCENE III. Rousillon.

A Room in the Countess's *Palace.*

Enter Countess, Steward, *and* Clown.

Count. I will now hear: what say you of this gentlewoman?

Stew. Madam, the care I have had to even your content, I wish might be found in the calendar of my past endeavours; for then we wound our modesty, and make foul the clearness of our deservings, when of ourselves we publish them.

Count. What does this knave here? Get you gone, sirrah: The complaints I have heard of you, I do not all believe; 'tis my slowness, that I do not: for I know, you lack not folly to commit them, and have ability enough to make such knaveries yours.

Clo. 'Tis not unknown to you, madam, I am a poor fellow.

Count. Well, sir.

Clo. No, madam, 'tis not so well, that I am poor; though many of the rich are damned: But, if I may have your ladyship's good will to go to the world, Isbel the woman and I will do as we may.

Count. Wilt thou needs be a beggar?

Clo. I do beg your good will in this case.

Count. In what case?

Clo. In Isbel's case, and mine own. Service is no heritage: and, I think, I shall never have the blessing of God, till I have issue of my body; for, they say, bearns are blessings.

Count. Tell me thy reason why thou wilt marry.

Clo. My poor body, madam, requires it: I am driven on by the flesh; and he must needs go, that the devil drives.

Count. Is this all your worship's reason?

Clo. Faith, madam, I have other holy reasons, such as they are.

Count. May the world know them?

Clo. I have been, madam, a wicked creature, as you and all flesh and blood are: and, indeed, I do marry, that I may repent.

Count. Thy marriage, sooner than thy wickedness.

Clo. I am out of friends, madam; and I hope to have friends for my wife's sake.

Count. Such friends are thine enemies, knave.

Clo. You are shallow, madam; e'en great friends; for the knaves come to do that for me, which I am aweary of. He, that ears my land, spares my team, and gives me leave to inn the crop: if I be his cuckold, he's my drudge: He, that comforts my wife, is the cherisher of my flesh and blood; he, that cherishes my flesh and blood, loves my flesh and blood; he, that loves my flesh and blood, is my friend: *ergo*, he that kisses my wife, is my friend. If men could be contented to be what they are, there were no fear in marriage: for young Charbon the puritan, and old Poysam the papist, howsoe'er their hearts are severed in religion, their heads are both one, they may joll horns together, like any deer i' the herd.

Count. Wilt thou ever be a foul-mouthed and calumnious knave?

Clo. A prophet I, madam; and I speak the truth the next way.

For I the ballad will repeat,
Which men full true shall find;
Your marriage comes by destiny,
Your cuckoo sings by kind.

Count. Get you gone, sir; I'll talk with you more anon.

Stew. May it please you, madam, that he bid Helen come to you; of her I am to speak.

Count. Sirrah, tell my gentlewoman, I would speak with her; Helen I mean.

Clo. *Was this fair face the cause, quoth she,* [Singing.
Why the Grecians sacked Troy?
Fond done, done fond,
Was this king Priam's joy.
With that she sighed as she stood,
With that she sighed as she stood,
And gave this sentence then;
Among nine bad if one be good,
Among nine bad if one be good,
There's yet one good in ten.

Count. What, one good in ten; you corrupt the song, sirrah.

Clo. One good woman in ten, madam; which is a purifying o' the song: 'Would God would serve the world so all the year! we'd find no fault with the tithe-woman, if I were the parson: One in ten, quoth a'! an we might have a good woman born, but on every blazing star, or at an earthquake, 'twould mend the lottery well; a man may draw his heart out, ere he pluck one.

Count. You'll be gone, sir knave, and do as I command you?

Clo. That man should be at woman's command, and yet no hurt done!—Though honesty be no puritan, yet it will do no hurt; it will wear the surplice of humility over the black gown of a big heart.—I am going, forsooth: the business is for Helen to come hither. [*Exit* Clown.

Count. Well, now.

Stew. I know, madam, you love your gentlewoman entirely.

Count. Faith, I do: her father bequeathed her to me; and she herself, without other advantage, may lawfully make title to as much love as she finds: there is more owing her, than is paid; and more shall be paid her, than she'll demand.

Stew. Madam, I was very late more near her than, I think, she wished me! alone she was, and did communicate to herself, her own words to her own ears; she thought, I dare vow for her, they touched not any stranger sense. Her matter was, she loved your son: Fortune, she said, was no goddess, that had put such difference betwixt their two estates; Love, no god, that would not extend his might, only where qualities were level; Diana, no queen of virgins, that would suffer her poor knight to be surprised, without rescue, in the first assault, or ransome afterward: This she delivered in the most bitter touch of sorrow, that e'er I heard virgin exclaim in: which I held my duty, speedily to acquaint you withal; sithence, in the loss that may happen, it concerns you something to know it.

Count. You have discharged this honestly; keep it to yourself: many likelihoods informed me of this before, which hung so tottering in the balance, that I could neither believe, nor misdoubt; Pray you, leave me: stall this in your bosom, and I thank you for your honest care: I will speak with you further anon. [*Exit* Steward.

Enter HELENA.

Even so it was with me, when I was young:
If we are nature's, these are ours; this thorn
Doth to our rose of youth rightly belong;
Our blood to us, this to our blood is born;
It is the show and seal of nature's truth,
Where love's strong passion is impress'd in youth:
By our remembrances of days forgone,
Such were our faults;—or then we thought them none.
Her eye is sick on't; I observe her now.

Hel. What is your pleasure, madam?

Count. You know, Helen,
I am a mother to you.

Hel. Mine honourable mistress.

Count. Nay, a mother;
Why not a mother? When I said, a mother,
Methought you saw a serpent: What's in mother,
That you start at it? I say, I am your mother;
And put you in the catalogue of those
That were enwombed mine: 'Tis often seen,
Adoption strives with nature; and choice breeds
A native slip to us from foreign seeds:
You ne'er oppress'd me with a mother's groan,
Yet I express'd to you a mother's care:—
God's mercy, maiden! does it curd thy blood,
To say, I am thy mother? What's the matter,
That this distemper'd messenger of wet,
The many-colour'd Iris, rounds thine eye?
Why?——that you are my daughter?

Hel. That I am not.

Count. I say, I am your mother.

Hel. Pardon, madam;
The count Rousillon cannot be my brother:
I am from humble, he from honour'd name;
No note upon my parents, his all noble:
My master, my dear lord he is; and I
His servant live, and will his vassal die:
He must not be my brother.

Count. Nor I your mother?

Hel. You are my mother, madam; 'Would, you were
(So that my lord, your son, were not my brother,)
Indeed, my mother!—or were you both our mothers,
I care no more for, than I do for heaven,

So I were not his sister: Can't no other,
But, I your daughter, he must be my brother?

Count. Yes, Helen, you might be my daughter-in-law;
God shield, you mean it not! daughter and mother,
So strive upon your pulse: What, pale again?
My fear hath catch'd your fondness: Now I see
The mystery of your loneliness, and find
Your salt tears' head. Now to all sense 'tis gross,
You love my son; invention is asham'd,
Against the proclamation of thy passion,
To say, thou dost not: therefore, tell me true:
But tell me then, 'tis so:—for, look, thy cheeks
Confess it, one to the other: and thine eyes
See it so grossly shown in thy behaviours,
That in their kind they speak it: only sin
And hellish obstinacy tie thy tongue,
That truth should be suspected: Speak, is't so?
If it be so, you have wound a goodly clue;
If it be not, forswear't: howe'er I charge thee,
As heaven shall work in me for thine avail,
To tell me truly.

Hel. Good madam, pardon me!

Count. Do you love my son?

Hel. Your pardon, noble mistress!

Count. Love you my son?

Hel. Do not you love him, madam?

Count. Go not about; my love hath in't a bond,
Whereof the world takes note: come, come, disclose
The state of your affection; for your passions
Have to the full appeach'd.

Hel. Then, I confess,
Here on my knee, before high heaven and you,
That before you, and next unto high heaven,
I love your son:—
My friends were poor, but honest; so's my love:
Be not offended; for it hurts not him,
That he is lov'd of me: I follow him not
By any token of presumptuous suit;
Nor would I have him, till I do deserve him;
Yet never know how that desert should be.
I know I love in vain, strive against hope;
Yet, in this captious and intenible sieve,
I still pour in the waters of my love,
And lack not to lose still: thus, Indian-like,
Religious in mine error, I adore
The sun, that looks upon his worshipper,
But knows of him no more. My dearest madam,
Let not your hate encounter with my love,
For loving where you do: but, if yourself,
Whose aged honour cites a virtuous youth,
Did ever, in so true a flame of liking,
Wish chastly, and love dearly, that your Dian
Was both herself and love; O then, give pity
To her, whose state is such, that cannot choose
But lend and give, where she is sure to lose;
That seeks not to find that her search implies,
But, riddle-like, lives sweetly where she dies.

Count. Had you not lately an intent, speak truly,
To go to Paris?

Hel. Madam, I had.

Count. Wherefore? tell true.

Hel. I will tell truth; by grace itself, I swear,
You know, my father left me some prescriptions
Of rare and proved effects, such as his reading,
And manifest experience, had collected
For general sovereignty; and that he will'd me
In heedfulest reservation to bestow them,
As notes, whose faculties inclusive were,
More than they were in note: amongst the rest,
There is a remedy, approv'd, set down,
To cure the desperate languishes, whereof
The king is render'd lost.

Count. This was your motive
For Paris, was it? speak.

Hel. My lord your son made me to think of this;
Else Paris, and the medicine, and the king,
Had, from the conversation of my thoughts,
Haply, been absent then.

Count. But think you, Helen,
If you should tender your supposed aid,
He would receive it? He and his physicians
Are of a mind; he, that they cannot help him;
They, that they cannot help: How shall they credit
A poor unlearned virgin, when the schools,
Embowell'd of their doctrine, have left off
The danger to itself?

Hel. There's something hints,
More than my father's skill which was the greatest
Of his profession, that his good receipt
Shall, for my legacy, be sanctified
By the luckiest stars in heaven: and, would your honour
But give me leave to try success, I'd venture
The well-lost life of mine on his grace's cure,
By such a day, and hour.

Count. Dost thou believe't?

Hel. Ay, madam, knowingly.

Count. Why, Helen, thou shalt have my leave, and love,
Means, and attendants, and my loving greetings
To those of mine in court; I'll stay at home,
And pray God's blessing into thy attempt:
Be gone to-morrow; an be sure of this,
What I can help thee to thou shalt not miss.
[*Exeunt.*

ACT II.

SCENE I. Paris.

A Room in the King's *Palace.* *Flourish.*

Enter King, *with young* Lords *taking leave for the* Florentine *war;* BERTRAM, PAROLLES *and* Attendants.

King. Farewell, young lord, these warlike principles
Do not throw from you:—and you, my lord farewell:—
Share the advice betwixt you: if both gain all,
The gift doth stretch itself as 'tis receiv'd,
And is enough for both.

1 *Lord.* It is our hope, sir,
After well enter'd soldiers, to return
And find your grace in health.

King. No, no, it cannot be; and yet my heart
Will not confess he owes the malady
That doth my life besiege. Farewell, young lords;
Whether I live or die, be you the sons
Of worthy Frenchmen: let higher Italy
(Those 'bated, that inherit but the fall
Of the last monarchy) see, that you come
Not to woo honour, but to wed it! when
The bravest questant shrinks, find what you seek,
That fame may cry you loud: I say, farewell.

2 *Lord.* Health, at your bidding, serve your majesty!

King. Those girls of Italy, take heed of them;
They say, our French lack language to deny,
If they demand: beware of being captives,
Before you serve.

Both. Our hearts receive your warnings.

King. Farewell.—Come hither to me.
[*The King retires to a Couch.*

1 *Lord.* O my sweet lord, that you will stay behind us!

Par. 'Tis not his fault; the spark——

2 *Lord.* O, 'tis brave wars!

Par. Most admirable: I have seen those wars.

Ber. I am commanded here, and kept a coil with;
Too young, and *the next year*, and *'tis too early.*

Par. An thy mind stand to it, boy, steal away bravely.

Ber. I shall stay here the forehorse to a smock,
Creaking my shoes on the plain masonry,
Till honour be bought up, and no sword worn,
But one to dance with! By heaven, I'll steal away.

1 Lord. There's honour in the theft.

Par. Commit it, count.

2 Lord. I am your accessary; and so farewell.

Ber. I grow to you, and our parting is a tortured body.

1 Lord. Farewell, captain.

2 Lord. Sweet monsieur Parolles!

Par. Noble heroes, my sword and yours are kin. Good sparks and lustrous, a word, good metals:—You shall find in the regiment of the Spinii, one captain Spurio, with his cicatrice, an emblem of war, here on his sinister cheek; it was this very sword entrenched it: say to him I live; and observe his reports for me.

2 Lord. We shall, noble captain.

Par. Mars dote on you for his novices! [*Exeunt* Lords.] What will you do?

Ber. Stay; the king—— [*Seeing him rise.*

Par. Use a more specious ceremony to the noble lords: you have restrained yourself within the list of too cold an adieu: be more expressive to them; for they wear themselves in the cap of the time, there do muster true gait; eat, speak, and move under the influence of the most received star; and though the devil lead the measure, such are to be followed: after them, and take a more dilated farewell.

Ber. And I will do so.

Par. Worthy fellows: and like to prove most sinewy sword-men.

[*Exeunt* BERTRAM *and* PAROLLES.

Enter LAFEU.

Laf. Pardon, my lord, [*Kneeling.*] for me and for my tidings.

King. I'll fee thee to stand up.

Laf. Then here's a man
Stands, that has brought his pardon. I would, you
Had kneel'd, my lord, to ask me mercy; and
That at my bidding, you could so stand up.

King. I would, I had; so I had broke thy pate,
And ask'd thee mercy for't.

Laf. Goodfaith, across:
But, my good lord, 'tis thus; Will you be cur'd
Of your infirmity?

King. No.

Laf. O, will you eat
No grapes, my royal fox? yes, but you will,
My noble grapes, an if my royal fox
Could reach them: I have seen a medicine,
That's able to breathe life into a stone;
Quicken a rock, and make you dance canary,
With spritely fire and motion; whose simple touch
Is powerful to araise king Pepin, nay,
To give great Charlemain a pen in his hand,
And write to her a love-line.

King. What her is this?

Laf. Why, doctor she: My lord, there's one arriv'd,
If you will see her,—now, by my faith and honour,
If seriously I may convey my thoughts
In this my light deliverance, I have spoke
With one, that, in her sex, her years, profession,
Wisdom, and constancy, hath amaz'd me more
Than I dare blame my weakness: Will you see her,
(For that is her demand,) and know her business?
That done, laugh well at me.

King. Now, good Lafeu,
Bring in the admiration; that we with thee
May spend our wonder too, or take off thine,
By wond'ring how hou took'st it.

Laf. Nay, I'll fit you,
And not be all day neither. [*Exit* LAFEU.

King. Thus he his special nothing ever prologues.

Re-enter LAFEU, *with* HELENA.

Laf. Nay, come your ways.

King. This haste hath wings indeed.

Laf. Nay, come your ways:
This is his majesty, say your mind to him:
A traitor you do look like; but such traitors
His majesty seldom fears: I am Cressid's uncle,
That dare leave two together; fare you well.
[*Exit.*

King. Now, fair one, does your business follow us?

Hel. Ay, my good lord. Gerard de Narbon was
My father; in what he did profess, well found.

King. I knew him.

Hel. The rather will I spare my praises towards him;
Knowing him, is enough. On his bed of death
Many receipts he gave me; chiefly one,
Which, as the dearest issue of his practice,
And of his old experience the only darling,
He bade me store up, as a triple eye,
Safer than mine own two, more dear; I have so:
And, hearing your high majesty is touch'd
With that malignant cause wherein the honour
Of my dear father's gift stands chief in power,
I come to tender it, and my appliance,
With all bound humbleness.

King. We thank you, maiden;
But may not be so credulous of cure,—
When our most learned doctors leave us; and
The congregated college have concluded
That labouring art can never ransome nature
From her inaidable estate,—I say we must not
So stain our judgment, or corrupt our hope,
To prostitute our past-cure malady
To empiricks; or to dissever so
Our great self and our credit, to esteem
A senseless help, when help past sense we deem.

Hel. My duty then shall pay me for my pains:
I will no more enforce mine office on you;
Humbly entreating from your royal thoughts
A modest one, to bear me back again.

King. I cannot give thee less, to be call'd grateful:
Thou thought'st to help me; and such thanks I give,
As one near death to those that wish him live;
But, what at full I know, thou know'st no part;
I knowing all my peril, thou no art.

Hel. What I can do, can do no hurt to try,
Since you set up your rest 'gainst remedy:
He that of greatest works is finisher,
Oft does them by the weakest minister:
So holy writ in babes hath judgment shown,
When judges have been babes. Great floods have flown
From simple sources; and great seas have dried,
When miracles have by the greatest been denied.
Oft expectation fails, and most oft there
Where most it promises; and oft it hits,
Where hope is coldest, and despair most sits.

King. I must not hear thee; fare thee well, kind maid;
Thy pains, not us'd, must by thyself be paid:
Proffers, not took, reap thanks for their reward.

Hel. Inspired merit so by breath is barr'd:
It is not so with him that all things knows,
As 'tis with us that square our guess by shows:
But most it is presumption in us, when
The help of heaven we count the act of men.
Dear sir, to my endeavours give consent;
Of heaven, not me, make an experiment.
I am not an impostor, that proclaim
Myself against the level of mine aim;
But know I think, and think I know most sure,
My art is not past power, nor you past cure.

King. Art thou so confident? Within what space
Hop'st thou my cure?
Hel. The greatest grace lending grace,
Ere twice the horses of the sun shall bring
Their fiery torcher his diurnal ring;
Ere twice in murk and occidental damp
Moist Hesperus hath quench'd his sleepy lamp;
Or four and twenty times the pilot's glass
Hath told the thievish minutes how they pass;
What is infirm from your sound parts shall fly,
Health shall live free, and sickness freely die.
King. Upon thy certainty and confidence,
What dar'st thou venture?
Hel. Tax of impudence,—
A strumpet's boldness, a divulged shame,—
Traduc'd by odious ballads; my maiden's name
Sear'd otherwise; no worse of worst extended,
With vilest torture let my life be ended.
King. Methinks, in thee some blessed spirit doth speak;
His powerful sound, within an organ weak:
And what impossibility would slay
In common sense, sense saves another way.
Thy life is dear; for all, that life can rate
Worth name of life, in thee hath estimate:
Youth, beauty, wisdom, courage, virtue, all
That happiness and prime can happy call:
Thou this to hazard, needs must intimate
Skill infinite, or monstrous desperate.
Sweet practiser, thy physick I will try;
That ministers thine own death, if I die.
Hel. If I break time, or flinch in property
Of what I spoke, unpitied let me die;
And well deserved: Not helping, death's my fee;
But, if I help, what do you promise me?
King. Make thy demand.
Hel. But will you make it even?
King. Ay, by my sceptre, and my hopes of heaven.
Hel. Then shalt thou give me, with thy kingly hand,
What husband in thy power I will command:
Exempted be from me the arrogance
To choose from forth the royal blood of France;
My low and humble name to propagate
With any branch or impage of thy state:
But such a one, thy vassal, whom I know
Is free for me to ask, thee to bestow.
King. Here is my hand; the premises observ'd,
Thy will by my performance shall be serv'd;
So make the choice of thy own time; for I,
Thy resolv'd patient, on thee still rely.
More should I question thee, and more I must;
Though, more to know, could not be more to trust;
From whence thou cam'st, how tended on,—But rest
Unquestion'd welcome, and undoubted blest.—
Give me some help here, ho!—If thou proceed
As high as word, my deed shall match thy deed.
[*Flourish. Exeunt.*

SCENE II. Rousillon.

A Room in the Countess's *Palace.*

Enter Countess *and* Clown.

Count. Come on, sir; I shall now put you to the height of your breeding.

Clo. I will show myself highly fed, and lowly taught: I know my business is but to the court.

Count. To the court! why, what place make you special, when you put off that with such contempt? But to the court!

Clo. Truly, madam, if God have lent a man any manners, he may easily put it off at court: he that cannot make a leg, put off's cap, kiss his hand, and say nothing, has neither leg, hands, lip, nor cap; and, indeed, such a fellow, to say precisely, were not for the court: but, for me, I have an answer will serve all men.

Count. Marry, that's a bountiful answer, that fits all questions.

Clo. It is like a barber's chair, that fits all buttocks; the pin-buttock, the quatch-buttock, the brawn-buttock, or any buttock.

Count. Will your answer serve fit to all questions?

Clo. As fit as ten groats is for the hand of an attorney, as your French crown for your taffata punk, as Tib's rush for Tom's fore-finger, as a pancake for Shrove Tuesday, a morris for May-day, as the nail to his hole, the cuckold to his horn, as a scolding quean to a wrangling knave, as the nun's lip to the friar's mouth; nay, as the pudding to his skin.

Count. Have you, I say, an answer of such fitness for all questions?

Clo. From below your duke, to beneath your constable, it will fit any question.

Count. It must be an answer of most monstrous size, that must fit all demands.

Clo. But a trifle neither, in good faith, if the learned should speak truth of it: here it is, and all that belongs to't: Ask me, if I am a courtier; it shall do you no harm to learn.

Count. To be young again, if we could: I will be a fool in question, hoping to be the wiser by your answer. I pray you, sir, are you a courtier?

Clo. O Lord, sir,——There's a simple putting off;—more, more, a hundred of them.

Count. Sir, I am a poor friend of yours, that loves you.

Clo. O Lord, sir,—Thick, thick, spare not me.

Count. I think, sir, you can eat none of this homely meat.

Clo. O Lord, sir,—Nay, put me to't, I warrant you.

Count. You were lately whipped, sir, as I think.

Clo. O Lord, sir,—Spare not me.

Count. Do you cry, *O Lord, sir*, at your whipping, and *spare not me?* Indeed, your *O Lord, sir*, is very sequent to your whipping; you would answer very well to a whipping, if you were but bound to't.

Clo. I ne'er had worse luck in my life, in my —*O Lord, sir:* I see, things may serve long, but not serve ever.

Count. I play the noble housewife with the time, to entertain it so merrily with a fool.

Clo. O Lord, sir,—Why, there't serves well again.

Count. An end, sir, to your business: Give Helen this,
And urge her to a present answer back:
Commend me to my kinsmen, and my son;
This is not much.

Clo. Not much commendation to them.

Count. Not much employment for you: You understand me?

Clo. Most fruitfully; I am there before my legs.

Count. Haste you again. [*Exeunt severally.*

SCENE III. Paris. *A Room in the* King's *Palace.*

Enter Bertram, Lafeu, *and* Parolles.

Laf. They say, miracles are past; and we have our philosophical persons, to make modern and familiar things, supernatural and causeless. Hence is it, that we make trifles of terrors; ensconcing ourselves into seeming knowledge, when we should submit ourselves to an unknown fear.

Par. Why, 'tis the rarest argument of wonder, that hath shot out in our latter times.

Ber. And so 'tis.

Laf. To be relinquish'd of the artists,——

Par. So I say; both of Galen and Paracelsus.

Laf. Of all the learned and authentick fellows,—

Par. Right, so I say.

Laf. That gave him out incurable,—

Par. Why, there 'tis; so say I too.

Laf. Not to be helped,—

Par. Right: as 'twere a man assured of an—

Laf. Uncertain life, and sure death.

Par. Just, you say well; so would I have said.

Laf. I may truly say, it is a novelty to the world.

Par. It is, indeed: if you will have it in showing, you shall read it in——What do you call there?—

Laf. A showing of a heavenly effect in an earthly actor.

Par. That's it I would have said; the very same.

Laf. Why, your dolphin is not lustier: 'fore me I speak in respect——

Par. Nay, 'tis strange, 'tis very strange, that is the brief and the tedious of it; and he is of a most facinorous spirit, that will not acknowledge it to be the——

Laf. Very hand of heaven.

Par. Ay, so I say.

Laf. In a most weak——

Par. And debile minister, great power, great transcendence: which should, indeed, give us a further use to be made, than alone the recovery of the king, as to be——

Laf. Generally thankful.

Enter King, HELENA, *and* Attendants.

Par. I would have said it; you say well: Here comes the king.

Laf. Lustick, as the Dutchman says: I'll like a maid the better, whilst I have a tooth in my head: Why, he's able to lead her a coranto.

Par. *Mort du Vinaigre!* Is not this Helen?

Laf. 'Fore God, I think so.

King. Go, call before me all the lords in court.— [*Exit an* Attendant.
Sit, my preserver, by thy patient's side;
And with this healthful hand, whose banish'd sense
Thou hast repeal'd, a second time receive
The confirmation of my promis'd gift,
Which but attends thy naming.

Enter several Lords.

Fair maid, send forth thine eye: this youthful parcel
Of noble bachelors stand at my bestowing,
O'er whom both sovereign power and father's voice
I have to use: thy frank election make;
Thou hast power to choose, and they none to forsake.

Hel. To each of you one fair and virtuous mistress
Fall, when love please!—marry, to each, but one!

Laf. I'd give bay Curtal, and his furniture,
My mouth no more were broken than these boys',
And writ as little beard.

King. Peruse them well:
Not one of those but had a noble father.

Hel. Gentlemen,
Heaven hath, through me, restored the king to health.

All. We understand it, and thank Heaven for you.

Hel. I am a simple maid; and therein wealthiest,
That, I protest, I simply am a maid:——
Please it your majesty, I have done already:
The blushes in my cheeks thus whisper me,
We blush, that thou shouldst choose; but, be refus'd,
Let the white death sit on thy cheek for ever;
We'll ne'er come there again.

King. Make choice; and, see,
Who shuns thy love, shuns all his love in me.

Hel. Now, Dian, from thy altar do I fly;
And to imperial Love, that god most high,
Do my sighs stream.—Sir, will you hear my suit?

1 *Lord.* And grant it.

Hel. Thanks, sir; all the rest is mute.

Laf. I had rather be in this choice, than throw mes-ace for my life.

Hel. The honour, sir, that flames in your fair eyes,
Before I speak, too threateningly replies:
Love make your fortunes twenty times above
Her that so wishes, and her humble love!

2 *Lord.* No better, if you please.

Hel. My wish receive,
Which great love grant! and so I take my leave.

Laf. Do all they deny her? An they were sons of mine, I'd have them whipped; or I would send them to the Turk, to make eunuchs of.

Hel. Be not afraid [*To a* Lord] that I your hand should take;
I'll never do you wrong for your own sake:
Blessing upon your vows! and in your bed
Find fairer fortune, if you ever wed!

Laf. These boys are boys of ice, they'll none have her: sure, they are bastards to the English: the French ne'er got them.

Hel. You are too young, too happy, and too good,
To make yourself a son out of my blood.

4 *Lord.* Fair one, I think not so.

Laf. There's one grape yet,—I am sure, thy father drank wine.—But if thou be'st not an ass, I am a youth of fourteen; I have known thee already.

Hel. I dare not say, I take you; [*To* BERTRAM] but I give
Me, and my service, ever whilst I live,
Into your guiding power.—This is the man.

King. Why then, young Bertram, take her, she's thy wife.

Ber. My wife, my liege? I shall beseech your highness,
In such a business give me leave to use
The help of mine own eyes.

King. Know'st thou not, Bertram,
What she has done for me?

Ber. Yes, my good lord;
But never hope to know why I should marry her.

King. Thou know'st she has rais'd me from my sickly bed.

Ber. But follows it, my lord, to bring me down
Must answer for your raising? I know her well;
She had her breeding at my father's charge:
A poor physician's daughter my wife!—Disdain
Rather corrupt me ever!

King. 'Tis only title thou disdain'st in her, the which
I can build up. Strange is it, that our bloods,
Of colour, weight, and heat, pour'd all together,
Would quite confound distinction, yet stand off
In differences so mighty: If she be
All that is virtuous (save what thou dislik'st,
A poor physician's daughter), thou dislik'st
Of virtue for the name: but do not so:
From lowest place when virtuous things proceed,
The place is dignified by the doer's deed:
Where great additions swell, and virtue none,
It is a dropsied honour: good alone
Is good;—without a name, vileness is so:
The property by what it is should go,
Not by the title. She is young, wise, fair;
In these to nature she's immediate heir;
And these breed honour; that is honour's scorn,
Which challenges itself as honour's born,
And is not like the sire: Honours best thrive,
When rather from our acts we them derive
Than our fore-goers: the mere word's a slave,
Debauch'd on every tomb; on every grave,
A lying trophy, and as oft is dumb,
Where dust and damn'd oblivion is the tomb
Of honour'd bones indeed. What should be said?
If thou canst like this creature as a maid,
I can create the rest: virtue, and she,
Is her own dower: honour and wealth, from me.

Ber. I cannot love her, nor will strive to do't.

King. Thou wrong'st thyself, if thou shouldst strive to choose.

Hel. That you are well restor'd, my lord, I am glad;
Let the rest go.

King. My honour's at the stake; which to defeat,
I must produce my power: Here, take her hand,
Proud scornful boy, unworthy this good gift;
That dost in vile misprision shackle up
My love, and her desert; that canst not dream,
We, poising us in her defective scale,
Shall weigh thee to the beam; that wilt not know,
It is in us to plant thine honour, where
We please to have it grow: Check thy contempt:
Obey our will, which travails in thy good:
Believe not thy disdain, but presently
Do thine own fortunes that obedient right,
Which both thy duty owes, and our power claims;
Or I will throw thee from my care for ever,
Into the staggers and the careless lapse
Of youth and ignorance; both my revenge and hate,
Loosing upon thee in the name of justice,
Without all terms of pity: Speak; thine answer.

Ber. Pardon, my gracious lord; for I submit
My fancy to your eyes: When I consider,
What great creation, and what dole of honour,
Flies where you bid it, I find, that she, which late
Was in my nobler thoughts most base, is now
The praised of the king; who, so ennobled,
Is, as 'twere, born so.

King. Take her by the hand,
And tell her, she is thine: to whom I promise
A counterpoize; if not to thy estate,
A balance more replete.

Ber. I take her hand.

King. Good fortune, and the favour of the king,
Smile upon this contract: whose ceremony
Shall seem expedient on the now-born brief,
And be perform'd to-night: the solemn feast
Shall more attend upon the coming space,
Expecting absent friends. As thou lov'st her,
Thy love's to me religious; else, does err.

[*Exeunt* King, BERTRAM, HELENA, Lords, *and* Attendants.

Laf. Do you hear, monsieur? a word with you.

Par. Your pleasure, sir?

Laf. Your lord and master did well to make his recantation.

Par. Recantation? My lord? my master?

Laf. Ay; Is it not a language, I speak?

Par. A most harsh one; and not to be understood without bloody succeeding. My master?

Laf. Are you companion to the count Rousillon?

Par. To any count; to all counts; to what is man.

Laf. To what is count's man: count's master is of another style.

Par. You are too old, sir; let it satisfy you, you are too old.

Laf. I must tell thee, sirrah, I write man; to which title age cannot bring thee.

Par. What I dare too well do, I dare not do.

Laf. I did think thee, for two ordinaries, to be a pretty wise fellow; thou didst make tolerable vent of thy travel; it might pass: yet the scarfs, and the bannerets, about thee, did manifoldly dissuade me from believing thee a vessel of too great a burden. I have now found thee; when I lose thee again, I care not: yet art thou good for nothing but taking up; and that thou art scarce worth.

Par. Hadst thou not the privilege of antiquity upon thee,——

Laf. Do not plunge thyself too far in anger, lest thou hasten thy trial; which if—Lord have mercy on thee for a hen! So, my good window of lattice, fare thee well; thy casement I need not open, for I look through thee. Give me thy hand.

Par. My lord, you give me most egregious indignity.

Laf. Ay, with all my heart; and thou art worthy of it.

Par. I have not, my lord, deserved it.

Laf. Yes, good faith, every dram of it; and I will not bate thee a scruple.

Par. Well, I shall be wiser.

Laf. E'en as soon as thou canst, for thou hast to pull at a smack o' the contrary. If ever thou be'st bound in thy scarf, and beaten, thou shalt find what it is to be proud of thy bondage. I have a desire to hold my acquaintance with thee, or rather my knowledge; that I may say, in the default, he is a man I know.

Par. My lord, you do me most insupportable vexation.

Laf. I would it were hell-pains for thy sake, and my poor doing eternal: for doing I am past; as I will by thee, in what motion age will give me leave. [*Exit.*

Par. Well, thou hast a son shall take this disgrace off me; scurvy, old, filthy, scurvy lord!—Well, I must be patient; there is no fettering of authority. I'll beat him by my life, if I can meet him with any convenience, an he were double and double a lord. I'll have no more pity of his age, than I would have of—I'll beat him, an if I could but meet him again.

Re-enter LAFEU.

Laf. Sirrah, your lord and master's married, there's news for you; you have a new mistress.

Par. I most unfeignedly beseech your lordship to make some reservation of your wrongs: He is my good lord: whom I serve above, is my master.

Laf. Who? God?

Par. Ay, sir.

Laf. The devil it is, that's thy master. Why dost thou garter up thy arms o' this fashion? dost make hose of thy sleeves? do other servants so? Thou wert best set thy lower part where thy nose stands. By mine honour, if I were but two hours younger, I'd beat thee: methinks, thou art a general offence, and every man should beat thee. I think, thou wast created for men to breathe themselves upon thee.

Par. This is hard and undeserved measure, my lord.

Laf. Go to, sir; you were beaten in Italy for picking a kernel out of a pomegranate; you are a vagabond, and no true traveller: you are more saucy with lords, and honourable personages, than the heraldry of your birth and virtue gives you commission. You are not worth another word, else I'd call you knave. I leave you. [*Exit.*

Enter BERTRAM.

Par. Good, very good; it is so then.—Good, very good; let it be concealed a while.

Ber. Undone, and forfeited to cares for ever!

Par. What is the matter, sweet heart?

Ber. Although before the solemn priest I have sworn,
I will not bed her.

Par. What? what, sweet heart?

Ber. O my Parolles, they have married me:—
I'll to the Tuscan wars, and never bed her.

Par. France is a dog-hole, and it no more merits
The tread of a man's foot: to the wars!

Ber. There's letters from my mother; what the import is,
I know not yet.

Par. Ay, that would be known: To the wars, my boy, to the wars!
He wears his honour in a box unseen,
That hugs his kicksy-wicksy here at home;
Spending his manly marrow in her arms,
Which should sustain the bound and high curvet
Of Mars's fiery steed: To other regions!
France is a stable: we, that dwell in't, jades;
Therefore, to the war!

Ber. It shall be so; I'll send her to my house,
Acquaint my mother with my hate to her,
And wherefore I am fled; write to the king
That which I durst not speak: His present gift
Shall furnish me to those Italian fields,
Where noble fellows strike: War is no strife
To the dark house, and the detested wife.
Par. Will this capricio hold in thee, art sure?
Ber. Go with me to my chamber, and advise me.
I'll send her straight away: To-morrow
I'll to the wars, she to her single sorrow.
Par. Why, these balls bound; there's noise in it.—'Tis hard;
A young man, married, is a man that's marr'd:
Therefore away, and leave her bravely; go:
The king has done you wrong; but, hush! 'tis so. [*Exeunt.*

SCENE IV.

The same. Another Room in the same.

Enter HELENA *and* Clown.

Hel. My mother greets me kindly: Is she well?

Clo. She is not well; but yet she has her health; she's very merry; but yet she is not well: but thanks be given, she's very well, and wants nothing i'the world; but yet she is not well.

Hel. If she be very well, what does she ail, that she's not very well?

Clo. Truly, she's very well, indeed, but for two things.

Hel. What two things?

Clo. One, that she's not in heaven, whither God send her quickly! the other, that she's in earth, from whence God send her quickly!

Enter PAROLLES.

Par. Bless you, my fortunate lady!

Hel. I hope, sir, I have your good will to have mine own good fortunes.

Par. You had my prayers to lead them on: and to keep them on, have them still.—O, my knave! How does my old lady?

Clo. So that you had her wrinkles, and I her money, I would she did as you say.

Par. Why, I say nothing.

Clo. Marry, you are the wiser man; for many a man's tongue shakes out his master's undoing: To say nothing, to do nothing, to know nothing, and to have nothing, is to be a great part of your title; which is within a very little of nothing.

Par. Away, thou'rt a knave.

Clo. You should have said, sir, before a knave thou art a knave; that is, before me thou art a knave: this had been truth, sir.

Par. Go to, thou art a witty fool, I have found thee.

Clo. Did you find me in yourself, sir? or were you taught to find me? The search, sir, was profitable; and much fool may you find in you, even to the world's pleasure, and the increase of laughter.

Par. A good knave, i'faith, and well fed.—
Madam, my lord, will go away to-night;
A very serious business calls on him.
The great prerogative and rite of love,
Which, as your due, time claims, he does acknowledge;
But puts it off by a compell'd restraint;
Whose want, and whose delay, is strewed with sweets,
Which they distil now in the curbed time,
To make the coming hour o'erflow with joy,
And pleasure drown the brim.
Hel. What's his will else?
Par. That you will take your instant leave o' the king,
And make this haste as your own good proceeding,
Strengthen'd with what apology you think
May make it probable need.
Hel. What more commands he?
Par. That, having this obtain'd, you presently
Attend his further pleasure.
Hel. In every thing I wait upon his will.
Par. I shall report it so.
Hel. I pray you.—Come, sirrah, [*Exeunt.*

SCENE V. *Another Room in the same.*

Enter LAFEU *and* BERTRAM.

Laf. But, I hope, your lordship thinks not him a soldier.

Ber. Yes, my lord, and of very valiant approof.

Laf. You have it from his own deliverance.

Ber. And by other warranted testimony.

Laf. Then my dial goes not true; I took this lark for a bunting.

Ber. I do assure you, my lord, he is very great in knowledge, and accordingly valiant.

Laf. I have then sinned against his experience, and transgressed against his valour; and my state that way is dangerous, since I cannot yet find in my heart to repent. Here he comes; I pray you, make us friends, I will pursue the amity.

Enter PAROLLES.

Par. These things shall be done, sir. [*To* BERTRAM.

Laf. Pray you, sir, who's his tailor?

Par. Sir?

Laf. O, I know him well: Ay, sir; he, sir, is a good workman, a very good tailor.

Ber. Is she gone to the king? [*Aside to* PAROLLES.

Par. She is.

Ber. Will she away to-night?

Par. As you'll have her.

Ber. I have writ my letters, casketed my treasure,
Given order for our horses, and to-night,
When I should take possession of the bride,—
And, ere I do begin,——

Laf. A good traveller is something at the latter end of a dinner; but one that lies three-thirds, and uses a known truth to pass a thousand nothings with, should be once heard, and thrice beaten.—God save you, captain.

Ber. Is there any unkindness between my lord and you, monsieur?

Par. I know not how I have deserved to run into my lord's displeasure.

Laf. You have made shift to run into't, boots and spurs and all, like him that leaped into the custard; and out of it you'll run again, rather than suffer question for your residence.

Ber. It may be, you have mistaken him, my lord.

Laf. And shall do so ever, though I took him at his prayers. Fare you well, my lord; and believe this of me, There can be no kernel in this light nut; the soul of this man is his clothes: trust him not in matter of heavy consequence; I have kept of them tame, and know their natures.—Farewell, monsieur: I have spoken better of you, than you have or will deserve at my hand; but we must do good against evil. [*Exit.*

Par. An idle lord, I swear.
Ber. I think so.
Par. Why, do you not know him?
Ber. Yes, I do know him well; and common speech
Gives him a worthy pass. Here comes my clog.

Enter HELENA.

Hel. I have, sir, as I was commanded from you,
Spoke with the king, and have procur'd his leave

For present parting: only, he desires
Some private speech with you.
Ber. I shall obey his will.
You must not marvel, Helen, at my course,
Which holds not colour with the time, nor does
The ministration and required office
On my particular: prepar'd I was not
For such a business; therefore am I found
So much unsettled: This drives me to entreat you,
That presently you take your way for home;
And rather muse, than ask, why I entreat you:
For my respects are better than they seem;
And my appointments have in them a need,
Greater than shows itself at the first view,
To you that know them not. This to my mother: [*Giving a letter.*
'Twill be two days ere I shall see you; so
I leave you to your wisdom.
Hel. Sir, I can nothing say,
But that I am your most obedient servant.
Ber. Come, come, no more of that.
Hel. And ever shall
With true observance seek to eke out that,
Wherein toward me my homely stars have fail'd
To equal my great fortune.
Ber. Let that go:
My haste is very great: Farewell; hie home.
Hel. Pray, sir, your pardon.
Ber. Well, what would you say?
Hel. I am not worthy of the wealth I owe;
Nor dare I say, 'tis mine; and yet it is;
But, like a timorous thief, most fain would steal
What law does vouch mine own.
Ber. What would you have?
Hel. Something; and scarce so much:—nothing, indeed.—
I would not tell you what I would: my lord—'faith, yes;—
Strangers, and foes, do sunder, and not kiss.
Ber. I pray you stay not, but in haste to horse.
Hel. I shall not break your bidding, good my lord.
Ber. Where are my other men, monsieur?—Farewell. [*Exit* HELENA.
Go thou toward home; where I will never come,
Whilst I can shake my sword, or hear the drum:—
Away, and for our flight.
Par. Bravely, coragio! [*Exeunt.*

ACT III.

SCENE I. Florence.

A Room in the Duke's *Palace.*

Flourish. Enter the Duke *of* Florence, *attended; two* French Lords, *and others.*

Duke. So that, from point to point, now have you heard
The fundamental reasons of this war;
Whose great decision hath much blood let forth,
And more thirsts after.
1 Lord. Holy seems the quarrel
Upon your grace's part; black and fearful
On the opposer.
Duke. Therefore we marvel much, our cousin France
Would, in so just a business, shut his bosom
Against our borrowing prayers.
2 Lord. Good my lord,
The reasons of our state I cannot yield,
But like a common and an outward man,
That the great figure of a council frames
By self-unable motion: therefore dare not
Say what I think of it; since I have found
Myself in my uncertain grounds to fail
As often as I guess'd.
Duke. Be it his pleasure.
2 Lord. But I am sure, the younger of our nature,
That surfeit on their ease, will, day by day,
Come here for physick.
Duke. Welcome shall they be;
And all the honours, that can fly from us,
Shall on them settle. You know your places well;
When better fall, for your avails they fell:
To-morrow to the field. [*Flourish. Exeunt.*

SCENE II. Rousillon.

A Room in the Countess's *Palace.*

Enter Countess *and* Clown.

Count. It hath happened all as I would have had it, save, that he comes not along with her.
Clo. By my troth, I take my young lord to be a very melancholy man.
Count. By what observance, I pray you?
Clo. Why, he will look upon his boot, and sing; mend the ruff, and sing; ask questions, and sing; pick his teeth, and sing: I know a man that had this trick of melancholy, sold a goodly manor for a song.
Count. Let me see what he writes, and when he means to come. [*Opening a Letter.*
Clo. I have no mind to Isbel, since I was at court; our old ling and our Isbels o'the country are nothing like your old ling and your Isbels o'the court: the brains of my Cupid's knocked out; and I begin to love, as an old man loves money, with no stomach.
Count. What have we here?
Clo. E'en that you have there. [*Exit.*
Count. [Reads.] *I have sent you a daughter-in-law: she hath recovered the king, and undone me. I have wedded her, not bedded her; and sworn to make the* not *eternal. You shall hear, I am run away; know it, before the report come. If there be breadth enough in the world, I will hold a long distance. My duty to you.*
Your unfortunate son,
BERTRAM.

This is not well, rash and unbridled boy,
To fly the favours of so good a king;
To pluck his indignation on thy head,
By the misprizing of a maid too virtuous
For the contempt of empire.

Re-enter Clown.

Clo. O madam, yonder is heavy news within, between two soldiers and my young lady.
Count. What is the matter?
Clo. Nay, there is some comfort in the news, some comfort; your son will not be killed so soon as I thought he would.
Count. Why should he be killed?
Clo. So say I, madam, if he run away, as I hear he does: the danger is in standing to't; that's the loss of men, though it be the getting of children. Here they come, will tell you more: for my part, I only hear, your son was run away. [*Exit* Clown.

Enter HELENA *and two* Gentlemen.

1 Gent. Save you, good madam.
Hel. Madam, my lord is gone, for ever gone.
2 Gent. Do not say so.
Count. Think upon patience.—'Pray you, gentlemen,—
I have felt so many quirks of joy, and grief,
That the first face of neither, on the start,
Can woman me unto't:—Where is my son, I pray you?
2 Gent. Madam, he's gone to serve the duke of Florence:
We met him thitherward; from thence we came,
And, after some despatch in hand at court,
Thither we bend again.
Hel. Look on his letter, madam; here's my passport.

[Reads.] *When thou canst get the ring upon my finger, which never shall come off, and show me a child begotten of thy body, that I am father to, then call me husband: but in such a* then *I write a* never.
This is a dreadful sentence!
Count. Brought you this letter, gentlemen?
1 Gent. Ay, madam;
And, for the contents' sake, are sorry for our pains.
Count. I pr'ythee, lady, have a better cheer;
If thou engrossest all the griefs are thine,
Thou robb'st me of a moiety: He was my son;
But I do wash his name out of my blood,
And thou art all my child.—Towards Florence is he?
2 Gent. Ay, madam.
Count. And to be a soldier?
2 Gent. Such is his noble purpose: and, believe't,
The duke will lay upon him all the honour
That good convenience claims.
Count. Return you thither?
1 Gent. Ay, madam, with the swiftest wing of speed.
Hel. [Reads.] *Till I have no wife, I have nothing in France.*
'Tis bitter!
Count. Find you that there?
Hel. Ay, madam.
1 Gent. 'Tis but the boldness of his hand, haply, which
His heart was not consenting to.
Count. Nothing in France, until he have no wife!
There's nothing here, that is too good for him,
But only she; and she deserves a lord,
That twenty such rude boys might tend upon,
And call her hourly, mistress. Who was with him?
1 Gent. A servant only, and a gentleman
Which I have some time known.
Count. Parolles, was't not?
1 Gent. Ay, my good lady, he.
Count. A very tainted fellow, and full of wickedness.
My son corrupts a well-derived nature
With his inducement.
1 Gent. Indeed, good lady,
The fellow has a deal of that, too much,
Which holds him much to have.
Count. You are welcome, gentlemen,
I will entreat you, when you see my son,
To tell him that his sword can never win
The honour that he loses: more I'll entreat you
Written to bear along.
2 Gent. We serve you, madam,
In that and all your worthiest affairs.
Count. Not so, but as we change our courtesies.
Will you draw near?
[*Exeunt* Countess *and* Gentlemen.
Hel. *Till I have no wife, I have nothing in France.*
Nothing in France, until he has no wife!
Thou shalt have none, Rousillon, none in France,
Then hast thou all again. Poor lord! is't I
That chase thee from thy country, and expose
Those tender limbs of thine to the event
Of the none sparing war? and is it I
That drive thee from the sportive court, where thou
Wast shot at with fair eyes, to be the mark
Of smoky muskets? O you leaden messengers,
That ride upon the violent speed of fire,
Fly with false aim; move the still-piecing air,
That sings with piercing, do not touch my lord!
Whoever shoots at him, I set him there;
Whoever charges on his forward breast,
I am the caitiff, that do hold him to it;
And, though I kill him not, I am the cause
His death was so effected; better 'twere,
I met the ravin lion when he roar'd
With sharp constraint of hunger; better 'twere
That all the miseries, which nature owes,
Were mine at once: No, come thou home, Rousillon,
Whence honour but of danger wins a scar,
As oft it loses all; I will be gone:
My being here it is, that holds thee hence:
Shall I stay here to do't? no, no, although
The air of paradise did fan the house,
And angels offic'd all: I will be gone;
That pitiful rumour may report my flight,
To consolate thine ear. Come, night; end, day!
For, with the dark, poor thief, I'll steal away.
[*Exit.*

SCENE III. Florence.

Before the Duke's *Palace. Flourish.*

Enter the Duke of Florence, BERTRAM, Lords, Officers, Soldiers, *and others.*

Duke. The general of our horse thou art; and we,
Great in our hope, lay our best love and credence,
Upon thy promising fortune.
Ber. Sir, it is
A charge too heavy for my strength; but yet
We'll strive to bear it for your worthy sake,
To the extreme edge of hazard.
Duke. Then go thou forth;
And fortune play upon thy prosperous helm,
As thy auspicious mistress!
Ber. This very day,
Great Mars, I put myself into thy file:
Make me but like my thoughts; and I shall prove
A lover of thy drum, hater of love. [*Exeunt.*

SCENE IV. Rousillon.

A Room in the Countess's *Palace.*

Enter Countess *and* Steward.

Count. Alas! and would you take the letter of her?
Might you not know, she would do as she has done,
By sending me a letter? Read it again.
Stew. *I am Saint Jaques' pilgrim, thither gone;*
Ambitious love hath so in me offended,
That bare-foot plod I the cold ground upon,
With sainted vow my faults to have amended.
Write, write, that from the bloody course of war,
My dearest master, your dear son may hie;
Bless him at home in peace, whilst I from far,
His name with zealous fervour sanctify:
His taken labours bid him me forgive;
I, his despiteful Juno, sent him forth
From courtly friends, with camping foes to live,
Where death and danger dog the heels of worth:
He is too good and fair for death and me;
Whom I myself embrace, to set him free.
Count. Ah, what sharp stings are in her mildest words!——
Rinaldo, you did never lack advice so much,
As letting her pass so; had I spoke with her,
I could have well diverted her intents,
Which thus she hath prevented.
Stew. Pardon me, madam:
If I had given you this at over-night,
She might have been o'erta'en; and yet she writes,
Pursuit would be in vain.
Count. What angel shall
Bless this unworthy husband? he cannot thrive,
Unless her prayers, whom heaven delights to hear,
And loves to grant, reprieve him from the wrath
Of greatest justice.—Write, write, Rinaldo,
To this unworthy husband of his wife;
Let every word weigh heavy of her worth,
That he does weigh too light: my greatest grief,
Though little he do feel it, set down sharply.
Despatch the most convenient messenger:—

When, haply, he shall hear that she is gone,
He will return; and hope I may, that she,
Hearing so much, will speed her foot again,
Led hither by pure love: which of them both
Is dearest to me, I have no skill in sense
To make distinction:—Provide this messenger:—
My heart is heavy, and mine age is weak;
Grief would have tears, and sorrow bids me speak. [*Exeunt.*

SCENE V.

Without the Walls of Florence. *A Tucket afar off.*

Enter an old Widow *of* Florence, DIANA, VIOLENTA, MARIANA, *and other Citizens.*

Wid. Nay, come; for if they do approach the city, we shall lose all the sight.

Dia. They say, the French count has done most honourable service.

Wid. It is reported that he has taken their greatest commander; and that with his own hand he slew the duke's brother. We have lost our labour; they are gone a contrary way: hark! you may know by their trumpets.

Mar. Come, let's return again, and suffice ourselves with the report of it. Well, Diana, take heed of this French earl: the honour of a maid is her name; and no legacy is so rich as honesty.

Wid. I have told my neighbour, how you have been solicited by a gentleman his companion.

Mar. I know that knave; hang him! one Parolles: a filthy officer he is in those suggestions for the young earl.—Beware of them, Diana; their promises, enticements, oaths, tokens, and all these engines of lust, are not the things they go under: many a maid hath been seduced by them; and the misery is, example, that so terrible shows in the wreck of maidenhood, cannot for all that dissuade succession, but that they are limed with the twigs that threaten them. I hope, I need not to advise you further; but, I hope, your own grace will keep you where you are, though there were no further danger known, but the modesty which is so lost.

Dia. You shall not need to fear me.

Enter HELENA, *in the dress of a Pilgrim.*

Wid. I hope so.—Look, here comes a pilgrim; I know she will lie at my house: thither they send one another: I'll question her.—
God save you, pilgrim! Whither are you bound?

Hel. To Saint Jaques le grand.
Where do the palmers lodge, I do beseech you?

Wid. At the saint Francis here, beside the port.

Hel. Is this the way?

Wid. Ay, marry, is it.—Hark you; [*A march afar off.*
They come this way:—If you will tarry, holy pilgrim,
But till the troops come by,
I will conduct you where you shall be lodg'd;
The rather, for, I think, I know your hostess
As ample as myself.

Hel. Is it yourself?

Wid. If you shall please so, pilgrim.

Hel. I thank you, and will stay upon your leisure.

Wid. You came, I think, from France?

Hel. I did so.

Wid. Here you shall see a countryman of yours,
That has done worthy service.

Hel. His name, I pray you.

Dia. The count Rousillon; Know you such a one?

Hel. But by the ear, that hears most nobly of him;
His face I know not.

Dia. Whatsoe'er he is,
He's bravely taken here. He stole from France,
As 'tis reported, for the king had married him
Against his liking: Think you it is so?

Hel. Ay, surely, mere the truth; I know his lady.

Dia. There is a gentleman that serves the count,
Reports but coarsely of her.

Hel. What's his name?

Dia. Monsieur Parolles.

Hel. O, I believe with him,
In argument of praise, or to the worth
Of the great count himself, she is too mean
To have her name repeated; all her deserving
Is a reserved honesty, and that
I have not heard examin'd.

Dia. Alas, poor lady!
'Tis a hard bondage, to become the wife
Of a detesting lord.

Wid. Ay, right; good creature, wheresoe'er she is,
Her heart weighs sadly: this young maid might do her
A shrewd turn, if she pleas'd.

Hel. How do you mean?
May be, the amorous count solicits her
In the unlawful purpose.

Wid. He does, indeed;
And brokes with all that can in such a suit
Corrupt the tender honour of a maid:
But she is arm'd for him, and keeps her guard
In honestest defence.

Enter, with Drum and Colours, a party of the Florentine *Army,* BERTRAM, *and* PAROLLES.

Mar. The gods forbid else!

Wid. So, now they come:—
That is Antonio, the duke's eldest son;
That, Escalus.

Hel. Which is the Frenchman?

Dia. He;
That with the plume: 'tis a most gallant fellow;
I would he lov'd his wife: if he were honester,
He were much goodlier:—Is't not a handsome gentleman?

Hel. I like him well.

Dia. 'Tis pity, he is not honest: Yond's that same knave,
That leads him to these places; were I his lady,
I'd poison that vile rascal.

Hel. Which is he?

Dia. That jack-an-apes with scarfs: Why is he melancholy?

Hel. Perchance he's hurt i'the battle.

Par. Lose our drum! well.

Mar. He's shrewdly vex'd at something: Look, he has spied us.

Wid. Marry, hang you!

Mar. And your courtesy for a ring-carrier!
[*Exeunt* BERTRAM, PAROLLES, Officers, *and* Soldiers.

Wid. The troop is past: Come, pilgrim, I will bring you
Where you shall host: of enjoin'd penitents
There's four or five, to great Saint Jaques bound,
Already at my house.

Hel. I humbly thank you:
Please it this matron, and this gentle maid,
To eat with us to-night, the charge, and thanking,
Shall be for me; and, to requite you further,
I will bestow some precepts on this virgin,
Worthy the note.

Both. We'll take your offer kindly. [*Exeunt.*

SCENE VI. *Camp before* Florence.

Enter BERTRAM, *and the two* French Lords.

1 *Lord.* Nay, good my lord, put him to't; let him have his way.

2 *Lord.* If your lordship find him not a hilding, hold me no more in your respect.

1 *Lord.* On my life, my lord, a bubble.

Ber. Do you think I am so far deceived in him?

1 *Lord.* Believe it, my lord, in mine own direct knowledge, without any malice, but to speak of him, as my kinsman, he's a most notable coward, an infinite and endless liar, an hourly pro-

mise-breaker, the owner of no one good quality worthy your lordship's entertainment.

2 *Lord.* It were fit you knew him; lest, reposing too far in his virtue, which he hath not, he might, at some great and trusty business, in a main danger, fail you.

Ber. I would, I knew in what particular action to try him.

2 *Lord.* None better than to let him fetch off his drum, which you hear him so confidently undertake to do.

1 *Lord.* I, with a troop of Florentines, will suddenly surprise him; such I will have, whom, I am sure, he knows not from the enemy: we will bind and hoodwink him so, that he shall suppose no other but that he is carried into the leaguer of the adversaries, when we bring him to our tents: Be but your lordship present at his examination; if he do not, for the promise of his life, and in the highest compulsion of base fear, offer to betray you, and deliver all the intelligence in his power against you, and that with the divine forfeit of his soul upon oath, never trust my judgment in any thing.

2 *Lord.* O, for the love of laughter let him fetch his drum; he says, he has a stratagem for't: when your lordship sees the bottom of his success in't, and to what metal this counterfeit lump of ore will be melted, if you give him not John Drum's entertainment, your inclining cannot be removed. Here he comes.

Enter PAROLLES.

1 *Lord.* O, for the love of laughter, hinder not the humour of his design; let him fetch off his drum in any hand.

Ber. How now, monsieur? this drum sticks sorely in your disposition.

2 *Lord.* A pox on't, let it go; 'tis but a drum.

Par. But a drum! Is't but a drum? A drum so lost!—There was an excellent command! to charge in with our horse upon our own wings, and to rend our own soldiers.

2 *Lord.* That was not to be blamed in the command of the service; it was a disaster of war that Cæsar himself could not have prevented, if he had been there to command.

Ber. Well, we cannot greatly condemn our success: some dishonour we had in the loss of that drum; but it is not to be recovered.

Par. It might have been recovered.

Ber. It might, but it is not now.

Par. It is to be recovered: but that the merit of service is seldom attributed to the true and exact performer, I would have that drum or another, or *hic jacet.*

Ber. Why, if you have a stomach to't, monsieur, if you think your mystery in stratagem can bring this instrument of honour again into his native quarter, be magnanimous in the enterprise, and go on; I will grace the attempt for a worthy exploit: if you speed well in it, the duke shall both speak of it and extend to you what further becomes his greatness, even to the utmost syllable of your worthiness.

Par. By the hand of a soldier, I will undertake it.

Ber. But you must not now slumber in it.

Par. I'll about it this evening: and I will presently pen down my dilemmas, encourage myself in my certainty, put myself into my mortal preparation, and, by midnight, look to hear further from me.

Ber. May I be bold to acquaint his grace, you are gone about it?

Par. I know not what the success will be, my lord; but the attempt I vow.

Ber. I know, thou art valiant; and to the possibility of thy soldiership, will subscribe for thee. Farewell.

Par. I love not many words. [*Exit.*

1 *Lord.* No more than a fish loves water.—Is not this a strange fellow, my lord? that so confidently seems to undertake this business, which he knows is not to be done; damns himself to do, and dares better be damn'd than to do't.

2 *Lord.* You do not know him, my lord, as we do: certain it is, that he will steal himself into a man's favour, and, for a week, escape a great deal of discoveries; but when you find him out, you have him ever after.

Ber. Why, do you think he will make no deed at all of this, that so seriously he does address himself unto?

1 *Lord.* None in the world; but return with an invention, and clap upon you two or three probable lies: but we have almost embossed him, you shall see his fall to-night; for, indeed, he is not for your lordship's respect.

2 *Lord.* We will make you some sport with the fox, ere we case him. He was first smoked by the old lord Lafeu: when his disguise and he is parted, tell me what a sprat you shall find him; which you shall see this very night.

1 *Lord.* I must go look my twigs; he shall be caught.

Ber. Your brother, he shall go along with me.

1 *Lord.* As't please your lordship: I'll leave you. [*Exit.*

Ber. Now will I lead you to the house, and show you
The lass I spoke of.

2 *Lord.* But you say, she's honest.

Ber. That's all the fault: I spoke with her but once,
And found her wondrous cold; but I sent to her,
By this same coxcomb that we have i'the wind,
Tokens and letters which she did resend;
And this is all I have done: She's a fair creature:
Will you go see her?

2 *Lord.* With all my heart, my lord. [*Exeunt.*

SCENE VII. Florence.

A Room in the Widow's *House.*

Enter HELENA *and* Widow.

Hel. If you misdoubt me that I am not she,
I know not how I shall assure you further,
But I shall lose the grounds I work upon.

Wid. Though my estate be fallen, I was well born,
Nothing acquainted with these businesses;
And would not put my reputation now
In any staining act.

Hel. Nor would I wish you.
First, give me trust, the count he is my husband;
And, what to your sworn counsel I have spoken,
Is so from word to word; and then you cannot,
By the good aid that I of you shall borrow,
Err in bestowing it.

Wid. I should believe you:
For you have show'd me that, which well approves
You are great in fortune.

Hel. Take this purse of gold,
And let me buy your friendly help thus far,
Which I will overpay, and pay again,
When I have found it. The count he woos your daughter,
Lays down his wanton siege before her beauty,
Resolves to carry her; let her, in fine, consent,
As we'll direct her how 'tis best to bear it,
Now his important blood will nought deny
That she'll demand: A ring the county wears,
That downward hath succeeded in his house,
From son to son, some four or five descents
Since the first father wore it: this ring he holds
In most rich choice; yet, in his idle fire,
To buy his will, it would not seem too dear,
Howe'er repented after.

Wid. Now I see
The bottom of your purpose.

Hel. You see it lawful then: It is no more,
But that your daughter, ere she seems as won,

Desires this ring: appoints him an encounter;
In fine, delivers me to fill the time,
Herself most chastely absent: after this,
To marry her, I'll add three thousand crowns
To what is past already.

Wid. I have yielded:
Instruct my daughter how she shall persever,
That time and place, with this deceit so lawful,
May prove coherent. Every night he comes
With musicks of all sorts, and songs compos'd
To her unworthiness: It nothing steads us,
To chide him from our eaves: for he persists,
As if his life lay on't.

Hel. Why then, to-night
Let us assay our plot; which, if it speed,
Is wicked meaning in a lawful deed,
And lawful meaning in a lawful act;
Where both not sin, and yet a sinful fact:
But let's about it. [*Exeunt.*

ACT IV.

SCENE I. *Without the* Florentine *Camp.*

Enter first Lord, *with five or six* Soldiers *in ambush.*

1 *Lord.* He can come no other way but by this hedge' corner: When you sally upon him, speak what terrible language you will; though you understand it not yourselves, no matter; for we must not seem to understand him; unless some one among us, whom we must produce for an interpreter.

1 *Sold.* Good captain, let me be the interpreter.

1 *Lord.* Art not acquainted with him? knows he not thy voice?

1 *Sold.* No, sir, I warrant you.

1 *Lord.* But what linsy-woolsy hast thou to speak to us again?

1 *Sold.* Even such as you speak to me.

1 *Lord.* He must think us some band of strangers 'the adversary's entertainment. Now he hath a smack of all neighbouring languages; therefore we must every one be a man of his own fancy, not to know what we speak one to another; so we seem to know, is to know straight our purpose: chough's language, gabble enough, and good enough. As for you, interpreter, you must seem very politick. But couch, oh! here he comes; to beguile two hours in a sleep, and then to return and swear the lies he forges.

Enter Parolles.

Par. Ten o'clock: within these three hours 'twill be time enough to go home. What shall I say I have done? It must be a very plausive invention that carries it: They begin to smoke me; and disgraces have of late knocked too often at my door. I find my tongue is too foolhardy; but my heart hath the fear of Mars before it, and of his creatures, not daring the reports of my tongue.

1 *Lord.* This is the first truth that e'er thine own tongue was guilty of. [*Aside.*

Par. What the devil should move me to undertake the recovery of this drum; being not ignorant of the impossibility, and knowing I had no such purpose? I must give myself some hurts, and say, I got them in exploit: yet slight ones will not carry it: They will say, Came you off with so little? and great ones I dare not give. Wherefore? what's the instance? Tongue, I must put you into a butter-woman's mouth, and buy another of Bajazet's mute, if you prattle me into these perils.

1 *Lord.* Is it possible, he should know what he is, and be that he is? [*Aside.*

Par. I would the cutting of my garments would serve the turn; or the breaking of my Spanish sword.

1 *Lord.* We cannot afford you so. [*Aside.*

Par. Or the baring of my beard; and to say, it was in stratagem.

1 *Lord.* 'Twould not do. [*Aside.*

Par. Or to drown my clothes, and say, I was stripped.

1 *Lord.* Hardly serve. [*Aside.*

Par. Though I swore I leaped from the window of the citadel——

1 *Lord.* How deep? [*Aside.*

Par. Thirty fathom.

1 *Lord.* Three great oaths would scarce make that be believed. [*Aside.*

Par. I would, I had any drum of the enemy's; I would swear I recovered it.

1 *Lord.* You shall hear one anon. [*Aside.*

Par. A drum now of the enemy's!

[*Alarum within.*

1 Lord. *Throca movousus, cargo, cargo, cargo.*

All. *Cargo, cargo, villianda par corbo, cargo.*

Par. O! ransom, ransom:—Do not hide mine eyes. [*They seize him and blindfold him.*

1 Sold. *Boskos thromuldo boskos.*

Par. I know you are the Muskos' regiment.
And I shall lose my life for want of language:
If there be here German, or Dane, low Dutch,
Italian, or French, let him speak to me,
I will discover that which shall undo
The Florentine.

1 Sold. *Boskos vauvado:*——
I understand thee, and can speak thy tongue:——
Kerelybonto:——Sir,
Betake thee to thy faith, for seventeen poniards
Are at thy bosom.

Par. Oh!

1 *Sold.* O pray, pray, pray.——
Manka revania dulche.

1 Lord. *Oscorbi dulchos volivorca.*

1 *Sold.* The general is content to spare thee yet;
And, hoodwink'd as thou art, will lead thee on
To gather from thee; haply, thou mayst inform
Something to save thy life.

Par. O, let me live,
And all the secrets of our camp I'll show,
Their force, their purposes: nay, I'll speak that
Which you will wonder at.

1 *Sold.* But wilt thou faithfully?

Par. If I do not, damn me.

1 Sold. *Acordo linta.*——
Come on, thou art granted space.

[*Exit, with* Parolles *guarded.*

1 *Lord.* Go, tell the count Rousillon, and my brother,
We have caught the woodcock, and will keep him muffled,
Till we do hear from them.

2 *Sold.* Captain, I will.

1 *Lord.* He will betray us all unto ourselves;—
Inform 'em that.

2 *Sold.* So I will, sir.

1 *Lord.* Till then, I'll keep him dark, and safely lock'd. [*Exeunt.*

SCENE II.—Florence.

A Room in the Widow's *House.*

Enter Bertram *and* Diana.

Ber. They told me, that your name was Fontibell.

Dia. No, my good lord, Diana.

Ber. Titled goddess;
And worth it with addition! But, fair soul,
In your fine frame hath love no quality?
If the quick fire of youth light not your mind,
You are no maiden, but a monument:
When you are dead, you should be such a one
As you are now, for you are cold and stern;
And now you should be as your mother was,
When your sweet self was got.

Dia. She then was honest.

Ber. So should you be.

Dia. No:
My mother did but duty; such, my lord,
As you owe to your wife.

Ber. No more of that!
I pr'ythee, do not strive against my vows:

I was compell'd to her; but I love thee
By love's own sweet constraint, and will for ever
Do thee all rights of service.

Dia. Ay, so you serve us,
Till we serve you: but when you have our roses,
You barely leave our thorns to prick ourselves,
And mock us with our bareness.

Ber. How have I sworn?

Dia. 'Tis not the many oaths that make the truth;
But the plain single vow, that is vow'd true.
What is not holy, that we swear not by,
But take the highest to witness: Then, pray you, tell me,
If I should swear by Jove's great attributes,
I lov'd you dearly, would you believe my oaths,
When I did love you ill? this has no holding,
To swear by him whom I protest to love,
That I will work against him: Therefore your oaths
Are words, and poor conditions; but unseal'd;
At least, in my opinion.

Ber. Change it, change it;
Be not so holy-cruel: love is holy;
And my integrity ne'er knew the crafts
That you do charge men with: Stand no more off,
But give thyself unto my sick desires,
Who then recover: say, thou art mine, and ever
My love, as it begins, shall so persever.

Dia. I see, that men make hopes, in such affairs,
That we'll forsake ourselves. Give me that ring.

Ber. I'll lend it thee, my dear, but have no power
To give it from me.

Dia. Will you not, my lord?

Ber. It is an honour 'longing to our house,
Bequeathed down from many ancestors;
Which were the greatest obloquy i'the world
In me to lose.

Dia. Mine honour's such a ring:
My chastity's the jewel of our house,
Bequeathed down from many ancestors:
Which were the greatest obloquy i'the world
In me to lose: Thus your own proper wisdom,
Brings in the champion honour on my part,
Against your vain assault.

Ber. Here, take my ring:
My house, mine honour, yea, my life be thine,
And I'll be bid by thee.

Dia. When midnight comes, knock at my chamber window;
I'll order take, my mother shall not hear.
Now will I charge you in the band of truth,
When you have conquer'd my yet maiden bed,
Remain there but an hour, nor speak to me;
My reasons are most strong; and you shall know them,
When back again this ring shall be deliver'd:
And on your finger, in the night, I'll put
Another ring; that, what in time proceeds,
May token to the future our past deeds.
Adieu, till then; then, fail not: You have won
A wife of me, though there my hope be done.

Ber. A heaven on earth I have won, by wooing thee. [*Exit.*

Dia. For which live long to thank both heaven and me!
You may so in the end.——
My mother told me just how he would woo,
As if she sat in his heart; she says, all men
Have the like oaths: he had sworn to marry me,
When his wife's dead; therefore I'll lie with him,
When I am buried. Since Frenchmen are so braid,
Marry that will, I'll live and die a maid:
Only in this disguise, I think't no sin,
To cozen him, that would unjustly win. [*Exit.*

SCENE III. *The* Florentine *Camp.*

Enter the two French Lords, *and two or three* Soldiers.

1 *Lord.* You have not given him his mother's letter?

2 *Lord.* I have delivered it an hour since: there is something in't that stings his nature for, on the reading it, he changed almost into another man.

1 *Lord.* He has much worthy blame laid upon him, for shaking off so good a wife, and so sweet a lady.

2 *Lord.* Especially he hath incurred the everlasting displeasure of the king, who had even tuned his bounty to sing happiness to him. I will tell you a thing, but you shall let it dwell darkly with you.

1 *Lord.* When you have spoken it, 'tis dead, and I am the grave of it.

2 *Lord.* He hath perverted a young gentlewoman here in Florence, of a most chaste renown; and this night he fleshes his will in the spoil of her honour; he hath given her his monumental ring, and thinks himself made in the unchaste composition.

1 *Lord.* Now, God delay our rebellion; as we are ourselves, what things are we!

2 *Lord.* Merely our own traitors. And as in the common course of all treasons, we still see them reveal themselves, till they attain to their abhorred ends; so he that in this action contrives against his own nobility, in his proper stream o'erflows himself.

1 *Lord.* Is it not meant damnable in us, to be trumpeters of our unlawful intents? We shall not then have his company to-night.

2 *Lord.* Not till after midnight; for he is dieted to his hour.

1 *Lord.* That approaches apace; I would gladly have him see his company anatomized; that he might take a measure of his own judgments, wherein so curiously he had set this counterfeit.

2 *Lord.* We will not meddle with him till he come; for his presence must be the whip of the other.

1 *Lord.* In the mean time, what hear you of these wars?

2 *Lord.* I hear there is an overture of peace.

1 *Lord.* Nay, I assure you, a peace concluded.

2 *Lord.* What will count Rousillon do then? will he travel higher, or return again into France?

1 *Lord.* I perceive, by this demand, you are not altogether of his council.

2 *Lord.* Let it be forbid, sir! so should I be a great deal of his act.

1 *Lord.* Sir, his wife, some two months since, fled from his house; her pretence is a pilgrimage to Saint Jaques le grand; which holy undertaking, with most austere sanctimony she accomplished; and, there residing, the tenderness of her nature became as a prey to her grief; in fine, made a groan of her last breath, and now she sings in heaven.

2 *Lord.* How is this justified?

1 *Lord.* The stronger part of it by her own letters; which makes her story true, even to the point of her death: her death itself, which could not be her office to say, is come, was faithfully confirmed by the rector of the place.

2 *Lord.* Hath the count all this intelligence?

1 *Lord.* Ay, and the particular confirmations, point from point, to the full arming of the verity.

2 *Lord.* I am heartily sorry, that he'll be glad of this.

1 *Lord.* How mightily, sometimes, we make us comforts of our losses!

2 *Lord.* And how mightily, some other times, we drown our gain in tears! The great dignity, that his valour hath here acquired for him, shall at home be encountered with a shame as ample.

1 *Lord.* The web of our life is of a mingled yarn, good and ill together: our virtues would be proud, if our faults whipped them not; and our crimes would despair, if they were not cherish'd by our virtues.—

Enter a Servant.

How now? where's your master?

Serv. He met the duke in the street, sir, of

whom he hath taken a solemn leave; his lordship will next morning for France. The duke hath offered him letters of commendations to the king.

2 *Lord.* They shall be no more than needful there, if they were more than they can commend.

Enter BERTRAM.

1 *Lord.* They cannot be too sweet for the king's tartness. Here's his lordship now. How now, my lord, is't not after midnight?

Ber. I have to-night dispatched sixteen businesses, a month's length a-piece, by an abstract of success: I have conge'd with the duke, done my adieu with his nearest; buried a wife, mourned for her; writ to my lady mother, I am returning; entertained my convoy; and, between these main parcels of despatch, effected many nicer deeds; the last was the greatest, but that I have not ended yet.

2 *Lord.* If the business be of any difficulty, and this morning your departure hence, it requires haste of your lordship.

Ber. I mean the business is not ended, as fearing to hear of it hereafter: But shall we have this dialogue between the fool and the soldier?——Come, bring forth this counterfeit module; he has deceived me, like a double-meaning prophesier.

2 *Lord.* Bring him forth: [*Exeunt* Soldiers.] he has sat in the stocks all night, poor gallant knave.

Ber. No matter; his heels have deserved it, in usurping his spurs so long. How does he carry himself?

1 *Lord.* I have told your lordship already; the stocks carry him. But, to answer you as you would be understood; he weeps like a wench that had shed her milk: he hath confessed himself to Morgan, whom he supposes to be a friar, from the time of his remembrance, to this very instant disaster of his setting i'the stocks: And what think you he hath confessed?

Ber. Nothing of me, has he?

2 *Lord.* His confession is taken, and it shall be read to his face: if your lordship be in't, as I believe you are, you must have the patience to hear it.

Re-enter Soldiers, *with* PAROLLES.

Ber. A plague upon him! muffled! he can say nothing of me; hush! hush!

1 *Lord.* Hoodman comes!—*Porto tartarossa.*

1 *Sold.* He calls for the tortures; What will you say without 'em?

Par. I will confess what I know without constraint; if ye pinch me like a pasty, I can say no more.

1 Sold. *Bosko chimurcho.*

2 *Lord.* *Boblibindo chicurmurco.*

1 *Sold.* You are a merciful general:—Our general bids you answer to what I shall ask you out of a note.

Par. And truly, as I hope to live.

1 Sold. *First demand of him how many horse the duke is strong?* What say you to that?

Par. Five or six thousand; but very weak and unserviceable: the troops are all scattered, and the commanders very poor rogues, upon my reputation and credit, and as I hope to live.

1 *Sold.* Shall I set down your answer so?

Par. Do; I'll take the sacrament o'nt, how and which way you will.

Ber. All's one to him. What a past-saving slave is this!

1 *Lord.* You are deceived, my lord; this is monsieur Parolles, the gallant militarist (that was his own phrase), that had the whole theorick of war in the knot of his scarf, and the practice in the chape of his dagger.

2 *Lord.* I will never trust a man again for keeping his sword clean; nor believe he can have every thing in him, by wearing his apparel neatly.

1 *Sold.* Well, that's set down.

Par. Five or six thousand horse, I said,—I will say true,—or thereabouts, set down,—for I'll speak truth.

1 *Lord.* He's very near the truth in this.

Ber. But I con him no thanks for't, in the nature he delivers it.

Par. Poor rogues, I pray you, say.

1 *Sold.* Well, that's set down.

Par. I humbly thank you, sir: a truth's a truth, the rogues are marvellous poor.

1 Sold. *Demand of him, of what strength they are a-foot.* What say you to that?

Par. By my troth, sir, if I were to live this present hour, I will tell true. Let me see: Spurio a hundred and fifty, Sebastian so many, Corambus so many, Jaques so many; Guiltian, Cosmo, Lodowick, and Gratii, two hundred fifty each: mine own company, Chitopher, Vaumond, Bentii, two hundred and fifty each: so that the muster-file, rotten and sound, upon my life, amounts not to fifteen thousand poll; half of which dare not shake the snow from off their cassocks, lest they shake themselves to pieces.

Ber. What shall be done to him?

1 *Lord.* Nothing, but let him have thanks. Demand of him my conditions, and what credit I have with the duke.

1 *Sold.* Well, that's set down. *You shall demand of him, whether one captain Dumain be i'the camp, a Frenchman; what his reputation is with the duke, what his valour, honesty, and expertness in wars; or whether he thinks, it were not possible, with well-weighing sums of gold, to corrupt him to a revolt.* What say you to this? What do you know of it?

Par. I beseech you, let me answer to the particular of the intergatories: Demand them singly.

1 *Sold.* Do you know this captain Dumain?

Par. I know him: he was a botcher's 'prentice in Paris, from whence he was whipped for getting the sheriff's fool with child: a dumb innocent, that could not say him, nay.

[DUMAIN *lifts up his hand in anger.*

Ber. Nay, by your leave, hold your hands; though I know, his brains are forfeit to the next tile that falls.

1 *Sold.* Well, is this captain in the duke of Florence's camp?

Par. Upon my knowledge, he is, and lousy.

1 *Lord.* Nay, look not so upon me; we shall hear of your lordship anon.

1 *Sold.* What is his reputation with the duke?

Par. The duke knows him for no other but a poor officer of mine; and writ to me this other day, to turn him out o'the band: I think, I have his letter in my pocket.

1 *Sold.* Marry, we'll search.

Par. In good sadness, I do not know; either it is there, or it is upon a file, with the duke's other letters, in my tent.

1 *Sold.* Here 'tis; here's a paper. Shall I read it to you?

Par. I do not know if it be it, or no.

Ber. Our interpreter does it well.

1 *Lord.* Excellently.

1 *Sold.* Dian. *The count's a fool, and full of gold,—*

Par. That is not the duke's letter, sir; that is an advertisement to a proper maid in Florence, one Diana, to take heed of the allurement of one count Rousillon, a foolish idle boy, but for all that, very ruttish: I pray you, sir, put it up again.

1 *Sold.* Nay, I'll read it first, by your favour.

Par. My meaning in't, I protest, was very honest in the behalf of the maid: for I knew the young count to be a dangerous and lascivious boy; who is a whale to virginity, and devours up all the fry it finds.

Ber. Damnable, both sides rogue!

1 Sold. *When he swears oaths, bid him drop gold, and take it;*
After he scores, he never pays the score;
Half won, is match well made; match, and well make it;
He ne'er pays after debts, take it before;
And say, a soldier, Dian, *told thee this,*
Men are to mell with, boys are not to kiss:
For count of this, the count's a fool, I know it,
Who pays before, but not when he does owe it.
Thine, as he vow'd to thee in thine ear,
PAROLLES.

Ber. He shall be whipped through the army with this rhyme in his forehead.

2 *Lord.* This is your devoted friend, sir, the manifold linguist, and the armipotent soldier.

Ber. I could endure any thing before but a cat, and now he's a cat to me.

1 *Sold.* I perceive, sir, by the general's looks, we shall be fain to hang you.

Par. My life, sir, in any case: not that I am afraid to die; but that, my offences being many, I would repent out the remainder of nature; let me live, sir, in a dungeon, i'the stocks, or any where, so I may live.

1 *Sold.* We'll see what may be done, so you confess freely; therefore, once more to this captain Dumain: You have answered to his reputation with the duke, and to his valour: What is his honesty?

Par. He will steal, sir, an egg out of a cloister; for rapes and ravishments he parallels Nessus. He professes not keeping of oaths; in breaking them, he is stronger than Hercules. He will lie, sir, with such volubility, that you would think truth were a fool: drunkenness is his best virtue; for he will be swine-drunk; and in his sleep he does little harm, save to his bed-clothes about him; but they know his conditions, and lay him in straw. I have but little more to say, sir, of his honesty: he has every thing that an honest man should not have; what an honest man should have, he has nothing.

1 *Lord.* I begin to love him for this.

Ber. For this description of thine honesty? A pox upon him for me, he is more and more a cat.

1 *Sold.* What say you to his expertness in war?

Par. Faith, sir, he has led the drum before the English tragedians,—to belie him, I will not,—and more of his soldiership I know not; except in that country, he had the honour to be the officer at a place there call'd Mile End, to instruct for the doubling of files: I would do the man what honour I can, but of this I am not certain.

1 *Lord.* He hath out-villained villany so far, that the rarity redeems him.

Ber. A pox on him! he's a cat still.

1 *Sold.* His qualities being at this poor price, I need not ask you, if gold will corrupt him to revolt.

Par. Sir, for a *quart d'ecu* he will sell the fee-simple of his salvation, the inheritance of it: and cut the entail from all remainders, and a perpetual succession for it perpetually.

1 *Sold.* What's his brother, the other captain Dumain?

2 *Lord.* Why does he ask him of me?

1 *Sold.* What's he?

Par. Ev'n a crow of the same nest; not altogether so great as the first in goodness, but greater a great deal in evil. He excels his brother for a coward, yet his brother is reputed one of the best that is: In a retreat he outruns any lackey; marry, in coming on he has the cramp.

1 *Sold.* If your life be sav'd, will you undertake to betray the Florentine?

Par. Ay, and the captain of his horse, count Rousillon.

1 *Sold.* I'll whisper with the general, and know his pleasure.

Par. I'll no more drumming; a plague of all drums! Only to seem to deserve well, and to beguile the supposition of that lascivious young boy the count, have I run into this danger: Yet, who would have suspected an ambush where I was taken? [*Aside.*

1 *Sold.* There is no remedy, sir, but you must die: the general says, you, that have so traitorously discovered the secrets of your army, and made such pestiferous reports of men very nobly held, can serve the world for no honest use; therefore you must die. Come, headsmen, off with his head.

Par. O Lord, sir; let me live, or let me see my death!

1 *Sold.* That shall you, and take your leave of all your friends. [*Unmuffling him.*
So, look about you; Know you any here?

Ber. Good morrow, noble captain.

2 *Lord.* God bless you, captain Parolles.

1 *Lord.* God save you, noble captain.

2 *Lord.* Captain, what greeting will you to my lord Lafeu? I am for France.

1 *Lord.* Good captain, will you give me a copy of the sonnet you writ to Diana in behalf of the count Rousillon? an I were not a very coward, I'd compel it of you; but fare you well. [*Exeunt* BERTRAM, Lords, *&c.*

1 *Sold.* You are undone, captain: all but your scarf, that has a knot on't yet.

Par. Who cannot be crushed with a plot?

1 *Sold.* If you could find out a country where but women were that had received so much shame, you might begin an impudent nation. Fare you well, sir; I am for France too; we shall speak of you there. [*Exit.*

Par. Yet am I thankful: if my heart were great,
'Twould burst at this: Captain, I'll be no more;
But I will eat and drink, and sleep as soft
As captain shall: simply the thing I am
Shall make me live. Who knows himself a braggart,
Let him fear this; for it will come to pass,
That every braggart shall be found an ass.
Rust, sword! cool, blushes! and, Parolles, live
Safest in shame! being fool'd, by foolery thrive!
There's place, and means, for every man alive.
I'll after them. [*Exit.*

SCENE IV. Florence.

A Room in the Widow's *House.*

Enter HELENA, Widow, *and* DIANA.

Hel. That you may well perceive I have not wrong'd you,
One of the greatest in the Christian world
Shall be my surety; 'fore whose throne, 'tis needful
Ere I can perfect mine intents, to kneel:
Time was, I did him a desired office,
Dear almost as his life; which gratitude
Through flinty Tartar's bosom would peep forth,
And answer, thanks: I duly am inform'd,
His grace is at Marseilles; to which place
We have convenient convoy. You must know,
I am supposed dead: the army breaking,
My husband hies him home; where, heaven aiding,
And by the leave of my good lord the king,
We'll be, before our welcome.

Wid. Gentle madam,
You never had a servant, to whose trust
Your business was more welcome.

Hel. Nor you, mistress,
Ever a friend, whose thoughts more truly labour
To recompense your love: doubt not, but heaven
Hath brought me up to be your daughter's dower,
As it hath fated her to be my motive
And helper to a husband. But, O strange men!
That can such sweet use make of what they hate,
When saucy trusting of the cozen'd thoughts
Defiles the pitchy night! so lust doth play

With what it loathes, for that which is away:
But more of this hereafter:——You, Diana,
Under my poor instructions yet must suffer
Something in my behalf.

Dia. Let death and honesty
Go with your impositions, I am yours
Upon your will to suffer.

Hel. Yet, I pray you,——
But with the word, the time will bring on summer,
When briars shall have leaves as well as thorns,
And be as sweet as sharp. We must away;
Our waggon is prepar'd, and time revives us:
All's well that ends well: still the fine's the crown;
Whate'er the course, the end is the renown.
[*Exeunt.*

SCENE V. Rousillon.

A Room in the Countess's *Palace.*

Enter Countess, Lafeu, *and* Clown.

Laf. No, no, no, your son was misled with a snipt-taffata fellow there; whose villanous saffron would have made all the unbaked and doughy youth of a nation in his colour: your daughter-in-law had been alive at this hour; and your son here at home, more advanced by the king, than by that red-tailed humble-bee I speak of.

Count. I would, I had not known him! it was the death of the most virtuous gentlewoman, that ever nature had praise for creating: if she had partaken of my flesh, and cost me the dearest groans of a mother, I could not have owed her a more rooted love.

Laf. 'Twas a good lady, 'twas a good lady: we may pick a thousand salads, ere we light on such another herb.

Clo. Indeed, sir, she was the sweet-marjoram of the salad, or rather the herb of grace.

Laf. They are not salad-herbs, you knave, they are nose-herbs.

Clo. I am no great Nebuchadnezzar, sir, I have not much skill in grass.

Laf. Whether dost thou profess thyself; a knave, or a fool?

Clo. A fool, sir, at a woman's service, and a knave at a man's.

Laf. Your distinction?

Clo. I would cozen the man of his wife, and do his service.

Laf. So you were a knave at his service, indeed.

Clo. And I would give his wife my bauble, sir, to do her service.

Laf. I will subscribe for thee; thou art both knave and fool.

Clo. At your service.

Laf. No, no, no.

Clo. Why, sir, if I cannot serve you, I can serve as great a prince as you are.

Laf. Who's that? a Frenchman?

Clo. 'Faith, sir, he has an English name; but his phisnomy is more hotter in France, than there.

Laf. What prince is that?

Clo. The black prince, sir, *alias*, the prince of darkness; *alias*, the devil.

Laf. Hold thee, there's my purse: I give thee not this to suggest thee from thy master thou talkest of; serve him still.

Clo. I am a woodland fellow, sir, that always loved a great fire; and the master I speak of, ever keeps a good fire. But, sure, he is the prince of the world, let his nobility remain in his court. I am for the house with the narrow gate, which I take to be too little for pomp to enter: some, that humble themselves, may; but the many will be too chill and tender; and they'll be for the flowery way, that leads to the broad gate, and the great fire.

Laf. Go thy ways, I begin to be a-weary of thee; and I tell thee so before, because I would not fall out with thee. Go thy ways; let my horses be well looked to, without any tricks.

Clo. If I put any tricks upon 'em, sir, they shall be jades' tricks; which are their own right by the law of nature. [*Exit.*

Laf. A shrewd knave, and an unhappy.

Count. So he is. My lord, that's gone, made himself much sport out of him: by his authority he remains here, which he thinks is a patent for his sauciness; and, indeed, he has no pace, but runs where he will.

Laf. I like him well; 'tis not amiss: and I was about to tell you, since I heard of the good lady's death, and that my lord your son was upon his return home, I moved the king my master, to speak in the behalf of my daughter; which, in the minority of them both, his majesty, out of a self-gracious remembrance, did first propose: his highness hath promised me to do it: and, to stop up the displeasure he hath conceived against your son, there is no fitter matter. How does your ladyship like it?

Count. With very much content, my lord, and I wish it happily effected.

Laf. His highness comes post from Marseilles, of as able body as when he numbered thirty; he will be here to-morrow, or I am deceived by him that in such intelligence hath seldom failed.

Count. It rejoices me, that I hope I shall see him ere I die. I have letters that my son will be here to-night: I shall beseech your lordship, to remain with me till they meet together.

Laf. Madam, I was thinking, with what manners I might safely be admitted.

Count. You need but plead your honourable privilege.

Laf. Lady, of that I have made a bold charter; but, I thank my God, it holds yet.

Re-enter Clown.

Clo. O madam, yonder's my lord your son with a patch of velvet on's face: whether there be a scar under it, or no, the velvet knows; but 'tis a goodly patch of velvet: his left cheek is a cheek of two pile and a half, but his right cheek is worn bare.

Laf. A scar nobly got, or a noble scar, is a good livery of honour; so, belike, is that.

Clo. But it is your carbonadoed face.

Laf. Let us go see your son, I pray you; I long to talk with the young noble soldier.

Clo. 'Faith, there's a dozen of 'em, with delicate fine hats, and most courteous feathers, which bow the head, and nod at every man. [*Exeunt.*

ACT V.

SCENE I. Marseilles. *A Street.*

Enter Helena, Widow, *and* Diana, *with two* Attendants.

Hel. But this exceeding posting, day and night,
Must wear your spirits low: we cannot help it;
But, since you have made the days and nights as one,
To wear your gentle limbs in my affairs,
Be bold, you do so grow in my requital,
As nothing can unroot you. In happy time;——

Enter a gentle Astringer.

This man may help me to his majesty's ear,
If he would spend his power.—God save you, sir.

Gent. And you.

Hel. Sir, I have seen you in the court of France.

Gent. I have been sometimes there.

Hel. I do presume, sir, that you are not fallen
From the report that goes upon your goodness;
And therefore, goaded with most sharp occasions,
Which lay nice manners by, I put you to
The use of your own virtues, for the which
I shall continue thankful.

Gent. What's your will?

Hel. That it will please you

To give this poor petition to the king;
And aid me with that store of power you have,
To come into his presence.
Gent. The king's not here.
Hel. Not here, sir?
Gent. Not, indeed:
He hence remov'd last night, and with more haste
Than is his use.
Wid. Lord, how we lose our pains!
Hel. *All's well that ends well*, yet;
Though time seem so adverse and means unfit.—
I do beseech you, whither is he gone?
Gent. Marry, as I take it, to Rousillon;
Whither I am going.
Hel. I do beseech you, sir,
Since you are like to see the king before me,
Commend the paper to his gracious hand;
Which, I presume, shall render you no blame,
But rather make you thank your pains for it:
I will come after you, with what good speed
Our means will make us means.
Gent. This I'll do for you.
Hel. And you shall find yourself to be well thank'd,
Whate'er falls more.—We must to horse again;—
Go, go, provide. [*Exeunt.*

SCENE II. Rousillon.

The inner Court of the Countess's *Palace.*

Enter Clown *and* PAROLLES.

Par. Good Monsieur Lavatch, give my Lord Lafeu this letter: I have ere now, sir, been better known to you, when I have held familiarity with fresher clothes; but I am now, sir, muddied in fortune's moat, and smell somewhat strong of her strong displeasure.

Clo. Truly, fortune's displeasure is but sluttish, if it smell so strong as thou speakest of: I will henceforth eat no fish of fortune's buttering. 'Pr'ythee, allow the wind.

Par. Nay, you need not stop your nose, sir; I spake but by a metaphor.

Clo. Indeed, sir, if your metaphor stink, I will stop my nose; or against any man's metaphor. 'Pr'ythee, get thee further.

Par. 'Pray you, sir, deliver me this paper.

Clo. Foh, 'pr'ythee, stand away; A paper from fortune's close-stool to give to a nobleman! Look, here he comes himself.

Enter LAFEU.

Here is a pur of fortune's, sir, or of fortune's cat (but not a musk-cat), that has fallen into the unclean fishpond of her displeasure, and, as he says, is muddied withal: 'Pray you, sir, use the carp as you may; for he looks like a poor, decayed, ingenious, foolish, rascally knave. I do pity his distress in my smiles of comfort, and leave him to your lordship. [*Exit* Clown.

Par. My lord, I am a man whom fortune hath cruelly scratched.

Laf. And what would you have me to do? 'tis too late to pare her nails now. Wherein have you played the knave with fortune, that she should scratch you, who of herself is a good lady, and would not have knaves thrive long under her? There's a *quart d'ecu* for you: Let the justices make you and fortune friends; I am for other business.

Par. I beseech your honour, to hear me one single word.

Laf. You beg a single penny more: come, you shall ha't: save your word.

Par. My name, my good lord, is Parolles.

Laf. You beg more than one word then.—Cox' my passion! give me your hand:—How does your drum?

Par. O my good lord, you were the first that found me.

Laf. Was I, in sooth? and I was the first that lost thee.

Par. It lies in you, my lord, to bring me in some grace, for you did bring me out.

Laf. Out upon thee, knave! dost thou put upon me at once both the office of God and the devil? one brings thee in grace, and the other brings thee out. [*Trumpets sound.*] The king's coming, I know by his trumpets.—Sirrah, inquire further after me; I had talk of you last night: though you are a fool and a knave, you shall eat; go to, follow.

Par. I praise God for you. [*Exeunt.*

SCENE III. *The same.*

A Room in the Countess's *Palace. Flourish.*

Enter King, Countess, LAFEU, Lords, Gentlemen, Guards, *&c.*

King. We lost a jewel of her; and our esteem
Was made much poorer by it; but your son,
As mad in folly, lack'd the sense to know
Her estimation home.
Count. 'Tis past, my liege:
And I beseech your majesty to make it
Natural rebellion, done i' the blaze of youth:
When oil and fire, too strong for reason's force,
O'erbears it, and burns on.
King. My honour'd lady,
I have forgiven and forgotten all;
Though my revenges were high bent upon him,
And watch'd the time to shoot.
Laf. This I must say,——
But first I beg my pardon,—The young lord
Did to his majesty, his mother, and his lady,
Offence of mighty note; but to himself
The greatest wrong of all: he lost a wife,
Whose beauty did astonish the survey
Of richest eyes; whose words all ears took captive;
Whose dear perfection, hearts that scorn'd to serve,
Humbly call'd mistress.
King. Praising what is lost,
Makes the remembrance dear.—Well, call him hither;——
We are reconcil'd, and the first view shall kill
All repetition:—Let him not ask our pardon;
The nature of his great offence is dead,
And deeper than oblivion do we bury
The incensing relicks of it: let him approach,
A stranger, no offender; and inform him,
So 'tis our will he should.
Gent. I shall, my liege,
[*Exit* Gentleman.
King. What says he to your daughter? have you spoke?——
Laf. All that he is hath reference to your highness.
King. Then shall we have a match. I have letters sent me,
That set him high in fame.

Enter BERTRAM.

Laf. He looks well on't.
King. I am not a day of season,
For thou mayst see a sunshine and a hail
In me at once: But to the brightest beams
Distracted clouds give way; so stand thou forth,
The time is fair again.
Ber. My high-repented blames,
Dear sovereign, pardon to me.
King. All is whole;
Not one word more of the consumed time.
Let's take the instant by the forward top;
For we are old, and on our quick'st decrees
The inaudible and noiseless foot of time
Steals ere we can effect them: You remember
The daughter of this lord?
Ber. Admiringly, my liege: at first
I stuck my choice upon her, ere my heart
Durst make too bold a herald of my tongue:
Where the impression of mine eye infixing,
Contempt his scornful perspective did lend me,

Which warp'd the line of every other favour;
Scorn'd a fair colour, or express'd it stol'n;
Extended or contracted all proportions,
To a most hideous object: Thence it came,
That she, whom all men prais'd, and whom myself,
Since I have lost, have lov'd, was in mine eye
The dust that did offend it.

King. Well excus'd:
That thou didst love her, strikes some scores away
From the great compt: But love, that comes too late,
Like a remorseful pardon slowly carried,
To the great sender turns a sour offence,
Crying, that's good that's gone: our rash faults
Make trivial price of serious things we have,
Not knowing them, until we know their grave:
Oft our displeasures, to ourselves unjust,
Destroy our friends, and after weep their dust:
Our own love waking cries to see what's done,
While shameful hate sleeps out the afternoon.
Be this sweet Helen's knell, and now forget her.
Send forth your amorous token for fair Maudlin:
The main consents are had; and here we'll stay
To see our widower's second marriage-day.

Count. Which better than the first, O dear heaven, bless!
Or, ere they meet, in me, O nature, cease!

Laf. Come on, my son, in whom my house's name
Must be digested, give a favour from you,
To sparkle in the spirits of my daughter,
That she may quickly come.—By my old beard,
And every hair that's on 't, Helen, that's dead,
Was a sweet creature; such a ring as this,
The last that e'er I took her leave at court,
I saw upon her finger.

Ber. Hers it was not.

King. Now, 'pray you, let me see it; for mine eye,
While I was speaking, oft was fasten'd to 't.—
This ring was mine: and, when I gave it Helen,
I bade her, if her fortune ever stood
Necessitied to help, that by this token
I would relieve her: Had you that craft to reave her
Of what should stead her most?

Ber. My gracious sovereign,
Howe'er it pleases you to take it so,
The ring was never hers.

Count. Son, on my life,
I have seen her wear it; and she reckon'd it
At her life's rate.

Laf. I am sure, I saw her wear it.

Ber. You are deceiv'd, my lord, she never saw it:
In Florence was it from a casement thrown me,
Wrapp'd in a paper, which contain'd the name,
Of her that threw it: noble she was, and thought
I stood ingag'd: but when I had subscrib'd
To mine own fortune, and inform'd her fully,
I could not answer in that course of honour
As she had made the overture, she ceas'd,
In heavy satisfaction, and would never
Receive the ring again.

King. Plutus himself,
That knows the tinct and multiplying medicine,
Hath not in nature's mystery more science,
Than I have in this ring: 'twas mine, 'twas Helen's,
Whoever gave it you: Then if you know
That you are well acquainted with yourself,
Confess 'twas hers, and by what rough enforcement
You got it from her: she call'd the saints to surety,
That she would never put it from her finger,
Unless she gave it to yourself in bed,
(Where you have never come), or sent it us
Upon her great disaster.

Ber. She never saw it.

King. Thou speak'st it falsely, as I love mine honour;
And mak'st conjectural fears to come into me,
Which I would fain shut out: If it should prove
That thou art so inhuman,—'twill not prove so;—
And yet I know not:—thou didst hate her deadly,
And she is dead; which nothing, but to close
Her eyes myself, could win me to believe,
More than to see this ring.—Take him away.—
[Guards *seize* BERTRAM.
My fore-past proofs, howe'er the matter fall,
Shall tax my fears of little vanity,
Having vainly fear'd too little.—Away with him;—
We'll sift this matter further.

Ber. If you shall prove
This ring was ever hers, you shall as easy
Prove that I husbanded her bed in Florence,
Where yet she never was.
[*Exit* BERTRAM, *guarded.*

Enter a Gentleman.

King. I am wrapp'd in dismal thinkings.

Gent. Gracious sovereign,
Whether I have been to blame, or no, I know not;
Here's a petition from a Florentine,
Who hath, for four or five removes, come short
To tender it herself. I undertook it,
Vanquish'd thereto by the fair grace and speech
Of the poor suppliant, who by this, I know,
Is here attending: her business looks in her
With an importing visage; and she told me,
In a sweet verbal brief, it did concern
Your highness with herself.

King. [Reads.] *Upon his many protestations to marry me, when his wife was dead, I blush to say it, he won me. Now is the Count Rousillon a widower; his vows are forfeited to me, and my honour's paid to him. He stole from Florence, taking no leave, and I follow him to his country for justice: Grant it me, O king; in you it best lies; otherwise a seducer flourishes, and a poor maid is undone.*
DIANA CAPULET.

Laf. I will buy me a son-in-law in a fair, and toll for him: for this, I'll none of him.

King. The heavens have thought well on thee, Lafeu,
To bring forth this discovery.—Seek these suitors:—
Go, speedily, and bring again the count.
[*Exeunt* Gentleman, *and some* Attendants.
I am afeard, the life of Helen, lady,
Was foully snatch'd.

Count. Now, justice on the doers!

Enter BERTRAM, *guarded.*

King. I wonder, sir, since wives are monsters to you,
And that you fly them as you swear them lordship,
Yet you desire to marry.—What woman's that?

Re-enter Gentleman, *with* Widow, *and* DIANA.

Dia. I am, my lord, a wretched Florentine,
Derived from the ancient Capulet:
My suit, as I do understand, you know,
And therefore know how far I may be pitied.

Wid. I am her mother, sir, whose age and honour
Both suffer under this complaint we bring,
And both shall cease, without your remedy.

King. Come hither, count; Do you know these women?

Ber. My lord, I neither can, nor will deny
But that I know them: Do they charge me further?

Dia. Why do you look so strange upon your wife?

Ber. She's none of mine, my lord.

Dia. If you shall marry,
You give away this hand, and that is mine;

You give away heaven's vows, and those are mine;
You give away myself, which is known mine;
For I by vow am so embodied yours,
That she, which marries you, must marry me,
Either both, or none.

Laf. Your reputation [*To* BERTRAM] comes too short for my daughter; you are no husband for her.

Ber. My lord, this is a fond and desperate [creature,
Whom sometime I have laugh'd with: let your highness
Lay a more noble thought upon mine honour,
Than for to think that I would sink it here.

King. Sir, for my thoughts, you have them ill to friend,
Till your deeds gain them: Fairer prove your honour,
Than in my thought it lies!

Dia. Good my lord,
Ask him upon his oath, if he does think
He had not my virginity.

King. What say'st thou to her?

Ber. She's impudent, my lord:
And was a common gamester to the camp.

Dia. He does me wrong, my lord; if I were so,
He might have bought me at a common price:
Do not believe him: O, behold this ring,
Whose high respect, and rich validity,
Did lack a parallel; yet, for all that,
He gave it to a commoner o' the camp,
If I be one.

Count. He blushes, and 'tis it:
Of six preceding ancestors, that gem
Conferr'd by testament to the sequent issue,
Hath it been ow'd and worn. This is his wife:
That ring's a thousand proofs.

King. Methought you said,
You saw one here in court could witness it.

Dia. I did, my lord, but loath am to produce
So bad an instrument; his name's Parolles.

Laf. I saw the man to-day, if man he be.

King. Find him, and bring him hither.

Ber. What of him?
He's quoted for a most perfidious slave,
With all the spots o' the world tax'd and debosh'd:
Whose nature sickens, but to speak a truth:
Am I or that, or this, for what he'll utter,
That will speak any thing?

King. She hath that ring of yours.

Ber. I think she has: certain it is, I liked her,
And boarded her i' the wanton way of youth:
She knew her distance, and did angle for me,
Madding my eagerness with her restraint,
As all impediments in fancy's course
Are motives of more fancy; and, in fine,
Her insuit coming with her modern grace,
Subdued me to her rate: she got the ring;
And I had that, which any inferior might
At market-price have bought.

Dia. I must be patient;
You that turn'd off a first so noble wife,
May justly diet me. I pray you yet,
(Since you lack virtue, I will lose a husband),
Send for your ring, I will return it home,
And give me mine again.

Ber. I have it not.

King. What ring was yours, I pray you?

Dia. Sir, much like
The same upon your finger.

King. Know you this ring? this ring was his of late.

Dia. And this was it I gave him, being abed.

King. The story then goes false, you threw it him
Out of a casement.

Dia. I have spoke the truth.

Enter PAROLLES.

Ber. My lord, I do confess the ring was hers.

King. You boggle shrewdly, every feather starts you.——
Is this the man you speak of?

Dia. Ay, my lord.

King. Tell me, sirrah, but tell me true, I charge you,
Not fearing the displeasure of your master
(Which, on your just proceeding, I'll keep off),
By him, and by this woman here, what know you?

Par. So please your majesty, my master hath been an honourable gentleman; tricks he hath had in him, which gentlemen have.

King. Come, come, to the purpose: Did he love this woman?

Par. 'Faith, sir, he did love her; But how?

King. How, I pray you?

Par. He did love her, sir, as a gentleman loves a woman.

King. How is that?

Par. He loved her, sir, and loved her not.

King. As thou art a knave, and no knave:—
What an equivocal companion is this?

Par. I am a poor man, and at your majesty's command.

Laf. He's a good drum, my lord, but a naughty orator.

Dia. Do you know, he promis'd me marriage?

Par. 'Faith, I know more than I'll speak.

King. But wilt thou not speak all thou know'st?

Par. Yes, so please your majesty: I did go between them, as I said; but more than that, he loved her,—for, indeed, he was mad for her, and talk'd of Satan, and of limbo, and of furies, and I know not what: yet I was in that credit with them at that time, that I knew of their going to bed; and of other motions, as promising her marriage, and things that would derive me ill will to speak of, therefore I will not speak what I know.

King. Thou hast spoken all already, unless thou canst say they are married! But thou art too fine in thy evidence: therefore stand aside.—
This ring, you say, was yours?

Dia. Ay, my good lord.

King. Where did you buy it? or who gave it you?

Dia. It was not given me, nor I did not buy it.

King. Who lent it you?

Dia. It was not lent me neither.

King. Where did you find it then?

Dia. I found it not.

King. If it were yours by none of all these ways,
How could you give it him?

Dia. I never gave it him.

Laf. This woman's an easy glove, my lord; she goes off and on at pleasure.

King. This ring was mine, I gave it his first wife.

Dia. It might be yours, or hers, for aught I [know.

King. Take her away, I do not like her now;
To prison with her: and away with him.—
Unless thou tell'st me where thou hadst this ring,
Thou diest within this hour.

Dia. I'll never tell you.

King. Take her away.

Dia. I'll put in bail, my liege.

King. I think thee now some common customer.

Dia. By Jove, if ever I knew man, 'twas you.

King. Wherefore hast thou accused him all this while?

Dia. Because he's guilty, and he is not guilty
He knows I am no maid, and he'll swear to't
I'll swear I am a maid, and he knows not.
Great King, I am no strumpet, by my life;
I am either maid, or else this old man's wife.
[*Pointing to* LAFEU.

King. She does abuse our ears; to prison with her.

Dia. Good mother, fetch my bail.—Stay, royal sir; [*Exit* Widow.
The jeweller that owes the ring is sent for,
And he shall surety me. But for this lord,
Who hath abus'd me, as he knows himself,
Though yet he never harm'd me, here I quit him:

He knows himself my bed he hath defil'd;
And at that time he got his wife with child:
Dead though she be, she feels her young one kick;
So there's my riddle, One, that's dead, is quick:
And now behold the meaning.

Re-enter Widow, *with* HELENA.

King. Is there no exorcist
Beguiles the truer office of mine eyes?
Is't real that I see?

Hel. No, my good lord;
'Tis but the shadow of a wife you see,
The name, and not the thing.

Ber. Both, both: O pardon!

Hel. O, my good lord, when I was like this maid,
I found you wondrous kind. There is your ring,
And, look you, here's your letter: This it says,
When from my finger you can get this ring,
And are by me with child, &c.—This is done:
Will you be mine, now you are doubly won?

Ber. If she, my liege, can make me know this clearly,
I'll love her dearly; ever, ever dearly.

Hel. If it appear not plain, and prove untrue,
Deadly divorce step between me and you!
O, my dear mother, do I see you living?

Laf. Mine eyes smell onions, I shall weep anon:—Good Tom Drum [*To* PAROLLES], lend me a handkerchief: So, I thank thee; wait on me home, I'll make sport with thee: Let thy courtesies alone, they are scurvy ones.

King. Let us from point to point this story know,
To make the even truth in pleasure flow:—
If thou be'st yet a fresh uncropped flower,
[*To* DIANA.
Choose thou thy husband, and I'll pay thy dower;
For I can guess, that, by thy honest aid,
Thou kept'st a wife herself, thyself a maid.—
Of that, and all the progress, more and less,
Resolvedly more leisure shall express;
All yet seems well; and, if it end so meet,
The bitter past, more welcome is the sweet.
[*Flourish.*

Advancing.

The King's a beggar, now the play is done;
All is well ended, *if this suit be won,*
That you express content; which we will pay,
With strife to please you, day exceeding day;
Ours be your patience then, and yours our parts:
Your gentle hands lend us, and take our hearts.
[Exeunt.

TAMING OF THE SHREW.

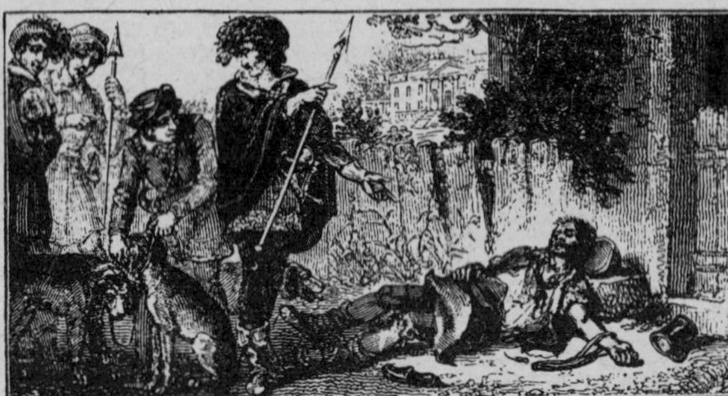

PERSONS REPRESENTED.

A Lord.
CHRISTOPHER SLY, *a drunken Tinker.*
Hostess, Page, Players, Huntsmen, *and other* Servants *attending on the* Lord.
} *Persons in the Induction.*

BAPTISTA, *a rich Gentleman of* Padua.
VINCENTIO, *an old Gentleman of* Pisa.
LUCENTIO, *Son to* Vincentio, *in love with* Bianca.
PETRUCHIO, *a Gentleman of* Verona, *a Suitor to* Katharina.
GREMIO, *Suitor to* Bianca.
HORTENSIO, *Suitor to* Bianca.
TRANIO, BIONDELLO, } *Servants to* Lucentio.
GRUMIO, CURTIS, } *Servants to* Petruchio.
Pedant, *an old fellow set up to personate* Vincentio.

KATHARINA, *the Shrew,* BIANCA, *her Sister,* } *Daughters to* Baptista.
Widow.

Tailor, Haberdasher, *and* Servants *attending on* Baptista *and* Petruchio.

SCENE—*Sometimes in* Padua; *and sometimes in* Petruchio's *House in the Country.*

INDUCTION.

SCENE I. *Before an Alehouse on a Heath.*

Enter Hostess *and* SLY.

Sly. I'LL pheeze you, in faith.

Host. A pair of stocks, you rogue!

Sly. Y'are a baggage; the Slies are no rogues; Look in the chronicles, we came in with Richard Conqueror. Therefore, *paucas pallabris;* let the world slide: *Sessa!*

Host. You will not pay for the glasses you have burst?

Sly. No, not a denier: Go by, says Jeronimy;—
Go to thy cold bed, and warm thee.

Host. I know my remedy, I must go fetch the thirdborough. [*Exit.*

Sly. Third, or fourth, or fifth borough, I'll answer him by law: I'll not budge an inch, boy; let him come, and kindly.

[*Lies down on the ground, and falls asleep.*

Wind Horns. Enter a Lord *from Hunting, with Huntsmen and Servants.*

Lord. Huntsman, I charge thee, tender well my hounds:
Brach Merriman,—the poor cur is emboss'd,
And couple Clowder with the deep-mouth'd brach.
Saw'st thou not, boy, how Silver made it good
At the hedge corner, in the coldest fault?
I would not lose the dog for twenty pound.

1 *Hunt.* Why, Belman is as good as he, my lord;
He cried upon it at the merest loss,
And twice to-day pick'd out the dullest scent:
Trust me, I take him for the better dog.

Lord. Thou art a fool; if Echo were as fleet,
I would esteem him worth a dozen such.
But sup them well, and look unto them all;
To-morrow I intend to hunt again.

1 *Hunt.* I will, my lord.

Lord. What's here? one dead, or drunk? See, doth he breathe?

2 *Hunt.* He breathes, my lord: Were he not warm'd with ale,
This were a bed but cold to sleep so soundly.

Lord. O monstrous beast, how like a swine he lies!
Grim death, how foul and loathsome is thine image!
Sirs, I will practise on this drunken man.——
What think you, if he were convey'd to bed,
Wrapp'd in sweet clothes, rings put upon his fingers,
A most delicious banquet by his bed,
And brave attendants near him when he wakes;
Would not the beggar then forget himself?

1 *Hunt.* Believe me, lord, I think he cannot choose.

2 *Hunt.* It would seem strange unto him when he wak'd.

Lord. Even as a flattering dream, or worthless fancy.
Then take him up, and manage well the jest:
Carry him gently to my fairest chamber,
And hang it round with all my wanton pictures:
Balm his foul head with warm distilled waters,
And burn sweet wood to make the lodging sweet:
Procure me musick ready when he wakes,
To make a dulcet and a heavenly sound:
And if he chance to speak, be ready straight,
And, with a low submissive reverence,
Say,—What is it your honour will command?
Let one attend him with a silver bason,
Full of rose-water, and bestrew'd with flowers;
Another bear the ewer, a third a diaper;
And say,—Will't please your Lordship cool your hands?
Some one be ready with a costly suit,
And ask him what apparel he will wear;
Another tell him of his hounds and horse,
And that his lady mourns at his disease:
Persuade him that he hath been lunatick.
And, when he says he is—, say that he dreams,
For he is nothing but a mighty lord.
This do, and do it kindly, gentle sirs:
It will be pastime passing excellent,
If it be husbanded with modesty.

1 *Hunt.* My lord, I warrant you, we'll play our part,
As he shall think, by our true diligence,
He is no less than what we say he is.

Lord. Take him up gently, and to bed with him;
And each one to his office when he wakes.—

[*Some bear out* SLY. *A trumpet sounds.*

Sirrah, go see what trumpet 'tis that sounds:—

[*Exit* Servant.

Belike, some noble gentleman; that means,
Travelling some journey, to repose him here.

Re-enter a Servant.

How now? who is it?

Serv. An it please your honour,
Players that offer service to your lordship.

Lord. Bid them come near:—

Enter Players.

Now, fellows, you are welcome.

1 *Play.* We thank your honour.

Lord. Do you intend to stay with me to-night?

2 *Play.* So please your lordship to accept our duty?

Lord. With all my heart.—This fellow I remember,
Since once he play'd a farmer's eldest son;—
'Twas where you woo'd the gentlewoman so well:
I have forgot your name; but, sure, that part
Was aptly fitted, and naturally perform'd.

1 *Play.* I think 'twas Soto that your honour means.

Lord. 'Tis very true;—thou didst it excellent.—
Well, you are come to me in happy time;
The rather for I have some sport in hand,
Wherein your cunning can assist me much.
There is a lord will hear you play to-night:
But I am doubtful of your modesties;
Lest, over-eying of his odd behaviour,
(For yet his honour never heard a play,)
You break into some merry passion,
And so offend him? for I tell you, sirs,
If you should smile, he grows impatient.

1 *Play.* Fear not, my lord; we can contain ourselves,
Were he the veriest antick in the world.

Lord. Go, sirrah, take them to the buttery,
And give them friendly welcome every one:
Let them want nothing that my house affords.—

[*Exeunt* Servant *and* Players.

Sirrah, go you to Bartholomew my page,

[*To a* Servant.

And see him dress'd in all suits like a lady:
That done, conduct him to the drunkard's chamber,
And call him—madam, do him obeisance,
Tell him from me (as he will win my love),
He bear himself with honourable action,
Such as he hath observ'd in noble ladies
Unto their lords, by them accomplished:
Such duty to the drunkard let him do,
With soft low tongue, and lowly courtesy:
And say,—What is't your honour will command,
Wherein your lady, and your humble wife,
May show her duty, and make known her love?
And then—with kind embracements, tempting kisses,
And with declining head into his bosom,—
Bid him shed tears, as being overjoy'd
To see her noble lord restored to health,
Who, for twice seven years, hath esteem'd him
No better than a poor and loathsome beggar:
And if the boy have not a woman's gift,
To rain a shower of commanded tears,
An onion will do well for such a shift:
Which in a napkin being close convey'd,
Shall in despite enforce a watery eye.
See this despatch'd with all the haste thou canst;
Anon I'll give thee more instructions.——

[*Exit* Servant.

I know the boy will well usurp the grace,
Voice, gait, and action of a gentlewoman:
I long to hear him call the drunkard husband;
And how my men will stay themselves from laughter,
When they do homage to this simple peasant.
I'll in to counsel them: haply, my presence
May well abate the over-merry spleen,
Which otherwise would grow into extremes.

[*Exeunt.*

SCENE II. *A Bedchamber in the* Lord's *House.*

SLY *is discovered in a rich night gown, with Attendants; some with apparel, others with bason, ewer, and other appurtenances. Enter* Lord, *dressed like a Servant.*

Sly. For God's sake, a pot of small ale.

1 *Serv.* Will't please your lordship drink a cup of sack?

2 *Serv.* Will't please your honour taste of these conserves?

3 *Serv.* What raiment will your honour wear to-day?

Sly. I am Christophero Sly; call not me honour, nor lordship: I never drank sack in my life; and if you give me any conserves, give me conserves of beef. Ne'er ask me what raiment I'll wear: for I have no more doublets than backs, no more stockings than legs, nor no more shoes than feet; nay, sometimes, more feet than shoes, or such shoes as my toes look through the overleather.

Lord. Heaven cease this idle humour in your honour!
O, that a mighty man of such descent,
Of such possessions, and so high esteem,
Should be infused with so foul a spirit!

Sly. What, would you make me mad? Am not I Christopher Sly, old Sly's son of Burton-heath; by birth a pedlar, by education a card-maker, by transmutation a bear-herd, and now by present profession a tinker? Ask Marian Hacket, the fat ale-wife of Wincot, if she know me not: if she say I am not fourteen pence on the score for sheer ale, score me up for the lyingest knave in Christendom. What, I am not bestraught: Here's——

1 *Serv.* O, this it is that makes your lady mourn.

2 *Serv.* O, this it is that makes your servants droop.

Lord. Hence comes it that your kindred shun your house,
As beaten hence by your strange lunacy.
O, noble lord, bethink thee of thy birth;
Call home thy ancient thoughts from banishment,
And banish hence these abject lowly dreams:
Look how thy servants do attend on thee,
Each in his office ready at thy beck.
Wilt thou have musick? hark! Apollo plays, [*Musick.*
And twenty caged nightingales do sing:
Or wilt thou sleep? we'll have thee to a couch,
Softer and sweeter than the lustful bed
On purpose trimm'd up for Semiramis.
Say, thou wilt walk; we will bestrew the ground:
Or wilt thou ride? thy horses shall be trapp'd,
Their harness studded all with gold and pearl.
Dost thou love hawking? thou hast hawks will soar
Above the morning lark: Or wilt thou hunt?
Thy hounds shall make the welkin answer them,
And fetch shrill echoes from the hollow earth.

1 *Serv.* Say, thou wilt course; thy greyhounds are as swift
As breathed stags, ay, fleeter than the roe.

2 *Serv.* Dost thou love pictures? we will fetch thee straight
Adonis, painted by a running brook;
And Cytherea all in sedges hid;
Which seem to move and wanton with her breath,
Even as the waving sedges play with wind.

Lord. We'll show thee Io, as she was a maid;
And how she was beguiled and surpris'd,
As lively painted as the deed was done.

3 *Serv.* Or Daphne roaming through a thorny wood:
Scratching her legs that one shall swear she bleeds:
And at that sight shall sad Apollo weep,
So workmanly the blood and tears are drawn.

Lord. Thou art a lord, and nothing but a lord:
Thou hast a lady far more beautiful
Than any woman in this waning age.

1 *Serv.* And, till the tears that she hath shed for thee,
Like envious floods, o'erran her lovely face,
She was the fairest creature in the world;
And yet she is inferior to none.

Sly. Am I a lord? and have I such a lady?
Or do I dream? or have I dream'd till now?
I do not sleep; I see, I hear, I speak;
I smell sweet savours, and I feel soft things:—
Upon my life, I am a lord indeed;
And not a tinker, nor Christophero Sly.—
Well, bring our lady hither to our sight;
And once again, a pot o'the smallest ale.

2 *Serv.* Will't please your mightiness to wash your hands;
[Servants *present a ewer, bason, and napkin.*
O, how we joy to see your wit restor'd!
O, that once more you knew but what you are!
These fifteen years you have been in a dream;
Or, when you wak'd, so wak'd as if you slept.

Sly. These fifteen years! by my fay, a goodly nap.
But did I never speak of all that time?

1 *Serv.* O, yes, my lord; but very idle words:—
For though you lay here in this goodly chamber,
Yet would you say, ye were beaten out of door;
And rail upon the hostess of the house;
And say, you would present her at the leet,
Because she brought stone jugs and no seal'd quarts:
Sometimes you would call out for Cicely Hacket.

Sly. Ay, the woman's maid of the house.

3 *Serv.* Why, sir, you know no house, nor no such maid,
Nor no such men as you have reckon'd up,—
As Stephen Sly, and old John Naps of Greece,
And Peter Turf, and Henry Pimpernell;
And twenty more such names and men as these,
Which never were, nor no man ever saw.

Sly. Now, Lord be thanked for my good amends!

All. Amen.

Sly. I thank thee; thou shalt not lose by it.

Enter the Page, *as a Lady, with* Attendants.

Page. How fares my noble lord?

Sly. Marry, I fare well; for here is cheer enough.
Where is my wife?

Page. Here, noble lord; What is thy will with her?

Sly. Are you my wife, and will not call me—husband;
My men should call me—lord; I am your good-man.

Page. My husband and my lord, my lord and husband;
I am your wife in all obedience.

Sly. I know it well:—What must I call her?

Lord. Madam.

Sly. Al'ce madam, or Joan madam?

Lord. Madam, and nothing else: so lords call ladies.

Sly. Madam wife, they say that I have dream'd and slept
Above some fifteen year and more.

Page. Ay, and the time seems thirty unto me;
Being all this time abandon'd from your bed.

Sly. 'Tis much;——Servants, leave me and her alone.——
Madam, undress you, and come now to bed.

Page. Thrice noble lord, let me entreat of you
To pardon me yet for a night or two;
Or, if not so, until the sun be set:
For your physicians have expressly charg'd,
In peril to incur your former malady,
That I should yet absent me from your bed:
I hope this reason stands for my excuse.

Sly. Ay, it stands so, that I may hardly tarry

so long. But I would be loath to fall into my dreams again; I will therefore tarry, in despite of the flesh and the blood.

Enter a Servant.

Serv. Your honour's players, hearing your amendment,
Are come to play a pleasant comedy,
For so your doctors hold it very meet;
Seeing too much sadness hath congeal'd your blood,
And melancholy is the nurse of frenzy,
Therefore they thought it good you hear a play,
And frame your mind to mirth and merriment,
Which bars a thousand harms, and lengthens life.

Sly. Marry, I will; let them play it: Is not a commonty a Christmas gambol, or a tumbling trick?

Page. No, my good lord; it is more pleasing stuff.

Sly. What, household stuff?

Page. It is a kind of history.

Sly. Well, we'll see't: Come, madam wife, sit by my side, and let the world slip; we shall ne'er be younger. [*They sit down.*

ACT I.

SCENE I. Padua. *A public Place.*

Enter LUCENTIO *and* TRANIO.

Luc. Tranio, since—for the great desire I had
To see fair Padua, nursery of arts,—
I am arriv'd for fruitful Lombardy,
The pleasant garden of great Italy;
And by my father's love and leave, am arm'd
With his good will, and thy good company,
Most trusty servant, well approv'd in all;
Here let us breathe, and happily institute
A course of learning, and ingenious studies.
Pisa, renowned for grave citizens,
Gave me my being, and my father first,
A merchant of great traffic through the world,
Vincentio, come of the Bentivolii.
Vincentio his son, brought up in Florence,
It shall become, to serve all hopes conceiv'd,
To deck his fortune with his virtuous deeds:
And therefore, Tranio, for the time I study,
Virtue, and that part of philosophy
Will I apply, that treats of happiness
By virtue 'specially to be achiev'd.
Tell me thy mind: for I have Pisa left,
And am to Padua come: as he that leaves
A shallow plash, to plunge him in the deep,
And with satiety seeks to quench his thirst.

Tra. *Mi perdonate*, gentle master mine,
I am in all affected as yourself.
Glad that you thus continue your resolve,
To suck the sweets of sweet philosophy.
Only, good master, while we do admire
This virtue, and this moral discipline,
Let's be no stoicks, nor no stocks, I pray;
Or so devote to Aristotle's ethicks,
As Ovid be an outcast quite abjur'd:
Balke logic with acquaintance that you have,
And practise rhetoric in your common talk:
Music and poesy use to quicken you;
The mathematics and the metaphysics,
Fall to them as you find your stomach serves you:
No profit grows where is no pleasure ta'en:—
In brief, sir, study what you most affect.

Luc. Gramercies, Tranio, well dost thou advise.
If, Biondello, thou wert come ashore,
We could at once put us in readiness;
And take a lodging fit to entertain
Such friends as time in Padua shall beget.
But stay awhile: What company is this?

Tra. Master, some show, to welcome us to town.

Enter BAPTISTA, KATHARINA, BIANCA, GREMIO, *and* HORTENSIO. LUCENTIO *and* TRANIO *stand aside.*

Bap. Gentlemen, importune me no further,
For how I firmly am resolv'd you know;
That is—not to bestow my youngest daughter,
Before I have a husband for the elder:
If either of you both love Katharina,
Because I know you well, and love you well,
Leave you shall have to court her at your pleasure.

Gre. To cart her rather: She's too rough for me:—
There, there, Hortensio, will you any wife?

Kath. I pray you, sir, [*To* BAP.] is it your will
To make a stale of me amongst these mates?

Hor. Mates, maid! how mean you that? no mates for you,
Unless you were of gentler, milder mould.

Kath. I'faith, sir, you shall never need to fear;
I wis, it is not half way to her heart:
But if it were, doubt not her cares should be
To comb your noddle with a three-legg'd stool,
And paint your face, and use you like a fool.

Hor. From all such devils, good Lord, deliver us!

Gre. And me too, good Lord!

Tra. Hush, master! here is some good pastime toward;
That wench is stark mad, or wonderful froward.

Luc. But in the other's silence I do see
Maid's mild behaviour and sobriety.
Peace, Tranio.

Tra. Well said, master; mum! and gaze your fill.

Bap. Gentlemen, that I may soon make good
What I have said,—Bianca, get you in:
And let it not displease thee, good Bianca;
For I will love thee ne'er the less, my girl.

Kath. A pretty peat! 'tis best
Put finger in the eye,—an she knew why.

Bian. Sister, content you in my discontent.—
Sir, to your pleasure humbly I subscribe;
My books, and instruments, shall be my company;
On them to look, and practise by myself.

Luc. Hark, Tranio! thou may'st hear Minerva speak. [*Aside.*

Hor. Signior Baptista, will you be so strange?
Sorry am I, that our good will effects
Bianca's grief.

Gre. Why, will you mew her up,
Signior Baptista, for this fiend of hell,
And make her bear the penance of her tongue?

Bap. Gentlemen, content ye; I am resolv'd:—
Go in, Bianca. [*Exit* BIANCA.
And for I know, she taketh most delight
In music, instruments, and poetry,
Schoolmasters will I keep within my house,
Fit to instruct her youth.—If you, Hortensio,
Or signior Gremio, you,—know any such,
Prefer them hither; for to cunning men
I will be very kind, and liberal
To mine own children in good bringing up;
And so farewell. Katharina, you may stay:
For I have more to commune with Bianca. [*Exit.*

Kath. Why, and I trust, I may go too: May I not?
What, shall I be appointed hours; as though, belike,
I knew not what to take and what to leave? Ha! [*Exit.*

Gre. You may go to the devil's dam: Your gifts are so good, here is none will hold you. Their love is not so great, Hortensio, but we may blow our nails together, and fast it fairly out; our cake's dough on both sides. Farewell. —Yet, for the love I bear my sweet Bianca, if I can by any means light on a fit man to teach her that wherein she delights, I will wish him to her father.

Hor. So will I, signior Gremio: but a word, I pray. Though the nature of our quarrel yet never brook'd parle, know now, upon advice, it toucheth us both,—that we may yet again have access to our fair mistress, and be happy rivals in Bianca's love,—to labour and effect one thing 'specially.

Gre. What's that, I pray?

Hor. Marry, sir, to get a husband for her sister.

Gre. A husband! a devil.

Hor. I say, a husband.

Gre. I say, a devil: Think'st thou, Hortensio, though her father be very rich, any man is so very a fool to be married to hell?

Hor. Tush, Gremio, though it pass your patience, and mine, to endure her loud alarums, why, man, there be good fellows in the world, an a man could light on them, would take her with all faults, and money enough.

Gre. I cannot tell; but I had as lief take her dowry with this condition,—to be whipped at the high-cross every morning.

Hor. 'Faith, as you say, there's small choice in rotten apples. But, come; since this bar in law makes us friends, it shall be so far forth friendly maintained,—till by helping Baptista's eldest daughter to a husband, we set his youngest free for a husband, and then have to't afresh.—Sweet Bianca!—Happy man be his dole! He that runs fastest, gets the ring. How say you, signior Gremio?

Gre. I am agreed: and 'would I had given him the best horse in Padua to begin his wooing, that would thoroughly woo her, wed her, and bed her, and rid the house of her. Come on.

[*Exeunt* GREMIO *and* HORTENSIO.

Tra. [*Advancing.*] I pray, sir, tell me,—Is it possible
That love should of a sudden take such hold?
Luc. O Tranio, till I found it to be true,
I never thought it possible, or likely;
But see! while idly I stood looking on,
I found the effect of love in idleness:
And now in plainness do confess to thee,—
That art to me as secret, and as dear,
As Anna to the queen of Carthage was,—
Tranio, I burn, I pine, I perish, Tranio,
If I achieve not this young modest girl:
Counsel me, Tranio, for I know thou canst;
Assist me, Tranio, for I know thou wilt.
Tra. Master, it is no time to chide you now;
Affection is not rated from the heart:
If love have touch'd you, nought remains but so,—
Redime te captum quam queas minimo.
Luc. Gramercies, lad; go forward: this contents;
The rest will comfort, for thy counsel's sound.
Tra. Master, you look'd so longly on the maid,
Perhaps you mark'd not what's the pith of all.
Luc. O yes, I saw sweet beauty in her face,
Such as the daughter of Agenor had,
That made great Jove to humble him to her hand,
When with his knees he kiss'd the Cretan strand.
Tra. Saw you no more? mark'd you not, how her sister
Began to scold; and raise up such a storm,
That mortal ears might hardly endure the din?
Luc. Tranio, I saw her coral lips to move,
And with her breath she did perfume the air;
Sacred, and sweet, was all I saw in her.
Tra. Nay, then, 'tis time to stir him from his trance.
I pray, awake, sir; If you love the maid,
Bend thoughts and wits to achieve her. Thus it stands:
Her elder sister is so curst and shrewd,
That, till the father rid his hands of her,
Master, your love must live a maid at home:
And therefore has he closely mew'd her up,
Because she shall not be annoy'd with suitors.
Luc. Ah, Tranio, what a cruel father's he!
But art thou not advis'd, he took some care
To get her cunning schoolmasters to instruct her?
Tra. Ay, marry, am I, sir; and now 'tis plotted.
Luc. I have it, Tranio.
Tra. Master, for my hand,
Both our inventions meet and jump in one.
Luc. Tell me thine first.
Tra. You will be schoolmaster,
And undertake the teaching of the maid:
That's your device.
Luc. It is: May it be done?
Tra. Not possible: For who shall bear your part,
And be in Padua here Vincentio's son?
Keep house, and ply his book; welcome his friends;
Visit his countrymen, and banquet them?
Luc. Basta; content thee, for I have it full.
We have not yet been seen in any house;
Nor can we be distinguish'd by our faces,
For man, or master: then it follows thus:—
Thou shalt be master, Tranio, in my stead,
Keep house, and port, and servants, as I should:
I will some other be; some Florentine,
Some Neapolitan, or mean man of Pisa.
'Tis hatch'd, and shall be so: Tranio, at once
Uncase thee; take my colour'd hat and cloak:
When Biondello comes, he waits on thee;
But I will charm him first to keep his tongue.
Tra. So had you need. [*They exchange habits.*
In brief then, sir, sith it your pleasure is,
And I am tied to be obedient;
(For so your father charg'd me at our parting;
Be serviceable to my son, quoth he;
Although, I think, 'twas in another sense;)
I am content to be Lucentio,
Because so well I love Lucentio.
Luc. Tranio, be so, because Lucentio loves.
And let me be a slave, to achieve that maid
Whose sudden sight hath thrall'd my wounded eye.

Enter BIONDELLO.

Here comes the rogue.—Sirrah, where have you been?
Bion. Where have I been? Nay, how now, where are you?
Master, has my fellow Tranio stol'n your clothes?
Or you stol'n his? or both? pray what's the news?
Luc. Sirrah, come hither; 'tis no time to jest,
And therefore frame your manners to the time.
Your fellow Tranio here, to save my life,
Puts my apparel and my countenance on,
And I for my escape have put on his;
For in a quarrel, since I came ashore,
I kill'd a man, and fear I was descried:
Wait you on him, I charge you, as becomes,
While I make way from hence to save my life:
You understand me?
Bion. I, sir, ne'er a whit.
Luc. And not a jot of Tranio in your mouth;
Tranio is chang'd into Lucentio.
Bion. The better for him: 'Would, I were so too!
Tra. So would I, faith, boy, to have the next wish after,—
That Lucentio indeed had Baptista's youngest daughter.
But, sirrah,—not for my sake, but your master's—I advise
You use your manners discreetly in all kind of companies:
When I am alone, why then I am Tranio;
But in all places else, your master Lucentio.
Luc. Tranio, let's go:—
One thing more rests, that thyself execute:—
To make one among these wooers: If thou ask me why,—
Sufficeth, my reasons are both good and weighty.
[*Exeunt.*

1 Serv. *My lord, you nod; you do not mind the play.*
Sly. *Yes, by Saint Anne, do I. A good matter, surely: Comes there any more of it?*
Page. *My lord, 'tis but begun.*
Sly. *'Tis a very excellent piece of work, madam lady: 'Would, 'twere done!*

SCENE II. *The same. Before* Hortensio's *House.*

Enter PETRUCHIO *and* GRUMIO.

Pet. Verona, for a while I take my leave,
To see my friends in Padua; but, of all,
My best beloved and approved friend,
Hortensio; and, I trow, this is his house:—
Here, sirrah Grumio; knock, I say.

Gru. Knock, sir! whom should I knock? is there any man has rebused your worship?

Pet. Villain, I say, knock me here soundly.

Gru. Knock you here, sir? why, sir, what am I, sir, that I should knock you here, sir?

Pet. Villain, I say, knock me at this gate,
And rap me well, or I'll knock your knave's pate.

Gru. My master is grown quarrelsome: I should knock you first,
And then I know after who comes by the worst.

Pet. Will it not be?
'Faith, sirrah, an you'll not knock, I'll wring it;
I'll try how you can *sol, fa,* and sing it.
[*He wrings* GRUMIO *by the ears.*

Gru. Help, masters, help! my master is mad.

Pet. Now, knock when I bid you: sirrah! villain!

Enter HORTENSIO.

Hor. How now?—what's the matter?—My old friend Grumio! and my good friend Petruchio!—How do you all at Verona?

Pet. Signior Hortensio, come you to part the fray?
Con tutto il core bene trovato, may I say.

Hor. *Alla nostra casa bene venuto,*
Molto honorato, signor mio Petruchio.
Rise, Grumio, rise; we will compound this quarrel.

Gru. Nay, 'tis no matter what he leges in Latin.—If this be not a lawful cause for me to leave his service.—Look you, sir, he bid me knock him, and rap him soundly, sir: Well, was it fit for a servant to use his master so; being, perhaps (for aught I see), two and thirty,—a pip out?
Whom, 'would to God, I had well knock'd at first,
Then had not Grumio come by the worst.

Pet. A senseless villain—Good Hortensio,
I bade the rascal knock upon your gate,
And could not get him for my heart to do it.

Gru. Knock at the gate?—O heavens!
Spake you not these words plain,—*Sirrah, knock me here,*
Rap me here, knock me well, and knock me soundly?
And come you now with—knocking at the gate?

Pet. Sirrah, be gone, or talk not, I advise you.

Hor. Petruchio, patience; I am Grumio's pledge:
Why, this a heavy chance 'twixt him and you;
Your ancient, trusty, pleasant servant Grumio.
And tell me now, sweet friend,—what happy gale
Blows you to Padua here, from old Verona?

Pet. Such wind as scatters young men through the world,
To seek their fortunes further than at home,
Where small experience grows. But, in a few,
Signior Hortensio, thus it stands with me:—
Antonio, my father, is deceas'd;
And I have thrust myself into this maze,
Haply to wive, and thrive, as best I may:
Crowns in my purse I have, and goods at home,
And so am come abroad to see the world.

Hor. Petruchio, shall I then come roundly to thee,
And wish thee to a shrewd ill favour'd wife?
Thou'dst thank me but a little for my counsel:
And yet I'll promise thee she shall be rich,
And very rich:—But thou'rt too much my friend,
And I'll not wish thee to her.

Pet. Signior Hortensio; 'twixt such friends as we
Few words suffice: and, therefore, if thou know
One rich enough to be Petruchio's wife,
(As wealth is burthen of my wooing dance),
Be she as foul as was Florentius' love,
Os old as Sibyl, and as curst and shrewd
As Socrates' Xantippe, or a worse,
She moves me not, or not removes, at least,
Affection's edge in me; were she as rough
As are the swelling Adriatick seas;
I come to wive it wealthily in Padua;
If wealthily, then happily in Padua.

Gru. Nay, look you, sir, he tells you flatly what his mind is: Why, give him gold enough and marry him to a puppet, or an aglet-baby; or an old trot with ne'er a tooth in her head, though she have as many diseases as two and fifty horses: why, nothing comes amiss, so money comes withal.

Hor. Petruchio, since we have stepp'd thus far in,
I will continue that I broach'd in jest.
I can, Petruchio, help thee to a wife
With wealth enough, and young, and beauteous;
Brought up as best becomes a gentlewoman;
Her only fault (and that is faults enough),
Is, that she is intolerably curst,
And shrewd, and froward; so beyond all measure,
That, were my state far worser than it is,
I would not wed her for a mine of gold.

Pet. Hortensio, peace; thou know'st not gold's effect:
Tell me her father's name, and 'tis enough;
For I will board her, though she chide as loud
As thunder, when the clouds in autumn crack.

Hor. Her father is Baptista Minola,
An affable and courteous gentleman:
Her name is Katharina Minola,
Renown'd in Padua for her scolding tongue.

Pet, I know her father, though I know not her;
And he knew my deceased father well:
I will not sleep, Hortensio, till I see her;
And therefore let me be thus bold with you,
To give you over at this first encounter,
Unless you will accompany me thither.

Gru. I pray you, sir, let him go while the humour lasts. O' my word, an she knew him as well as I do, she would think scolding would do little good upon him: She may, perhaps, call him half a score knaves or so: why, that's nothing; an he begin once, he'll rail in his rope-tricks. I'll tell you what, sir,—an she stand him but a little, he will throw a figure in her face, and so disfigure her with it, that she shall have no more eyes to see withal than a cat: You know him not, sir.

Hor. Tarry, Petruchio, I must go with thee;
For in Baptista's keep my treasure is:
He hath the jewel of my life in hold,
His youngest daughter, beautiful Bianca;
And her withholds from me, and other more
Suitors to her, and rivals in my love:
Supposing it a thing impossible,
(For those defects I have before rehears'd),
That ever Katharina will be woo'd;
Therefore this order hath Baptista ta'en;—
That none shall have access unto Bianca,
Till Katharine the curst have got a husband.

Gru. Katharine the curst!
A title for a maid, of all titles the worst.

Hor. Now shall my friend Petruchio do me grace;
And offer me, disguis'd in sober robes,
To old Baptista as a schoolmaster
Well seen in musick, to instruct Bianca:
That so I may by this device, at least,

Have leave and leisure to make love to her,
And, unsuspected, court her by herself.

Enter GREMIO; *with him* LUCENTIO *disguised, with books under his arm.*

Gru. Here's knavery! See, to beguile the old folks, how the young folks lay their heads together! Master, master, look about you: Who goes there? ha!

Hor. Peace, Grumio; 'tis the rival of my love;—
Petruchio, stand by a while.

Gru. A proper stripling, and an amorous! [*They retire.*

Gre. O, very well; I have perus'd the note.
Hark you, sir; I'll have them very fairly bound:
All books of love, see that at any hand;
And see you read no other lectures to her;
You understand me:—Over and beside
Signior Baptista's liberality,
I'll mend it with a largess:—Take your papers too,
And let me have them very well perfum'd;
For she is sweeter than perfume itself,
To whom they go. What will you read to her?

Luc. Whate'er I read to her, I'll plead for you,
As for my patron (stand you so assur'd),
As firmly as yourself were still in place:
Yea, and (perhaps) with more successful words
Than you, unless you were a scholar, sir.

Gre. O this learning; what a thing it is!

Gru. O this woodcock! what an ass it is!

Pet. Peace, sirrah.

Hor. Grumio, mum!—God save you, signior Gremio!

Gre. And you're well met, signior Hortensio. Trow you,
Whither I am going?—To Baptista Minola.
I promis'd to inquire carefully
About a schoolmaster for fair Bianca:
And, by good fortune, I have lighted well
On this young man; for learning and behaviour,
Fit for her turn; well read in poetry
And other books,—good ones, I warrant you.

Hor. 'Tis well: and I have met a gentleman,
Hath promis'd me to help me to another,
A fine musician to instruct our mistress;
So shall I no whit be behind in duty
To fair Bianca, so belov'd of me.

Gre. Belov'd of me,—and that my deeds shall prove.

Gru. And that his bags shall prove. [*Aside.*

Hor. Gremio, 'tis now no time to vent our love:
Listen to me, and if you speak me fair,
I'll tell you news indifferent good for either.
Here is a gentleman, whom by chance I met,
Upon agreement from us to his liking,
Will undertake to woo curst Katharine;
Yea, and to marry her, if her dowry please.

Gre. So said, so done, is well:
Hortensio, have you told him all her faults?

Pet. I know, she is an irksome brawling scold;
If that be all, masters, I hear no harm.

Gre. No! say'st me so, friend! What countryman?

Pet. Born in Verona, old Antonio's son:
My father dead, my fortune lives for me;
And I do hope good days, and long, to see.

Gre. O, sir, such a life, with such a wife, were strange:
But, if you have a stomach, to't o'God's name,
You shall have me assisting you in all.
But will you woo this wild cat?

Pet. Will I live?

Gru. Will he woo her? ay, or I'll hang her. [*Aside.*

Pet. Why came I hither, but to that intent?
Think you, a little din can daunt mine ears?
Have I not in my time heard lions roar?
Have I not heard the sea, puff'd up with winds,
Rage like an angry boar, chafed with sweat?
Have I not heard great ordnance in the field,
And heaven's artillery thunder in the skies?
Have I not in a pitched battle heard
Loud 'larums, neighing steeds, and trumpets' clang?
And do you tell me of a woman's tongue,
That gives not half so great a blow to the ear
As will a chestnut in a farmer's fire?
Tush! tush! fear boys with bugs.

Gru. For he fears none. [*Aside.*

Gre. Hortensio, hark!
This gentleman is happily arriv'd,
My mind presumes, for his own good, and ours.

Hor. I promis'd we would be contributors,
And bear his charge of wooing, whatsoe'er.

Gre. And so we will; provided that he win her.

Gru. I would, I were as sure of a good dinner. [*Aside.*

Enter TRANIO, *bravely apparell'd; and* BIONDELLO.

Tra. Gentlemen, God save you! If I may be bold,
Tell me, I beseech you, which is the readiest way
To the house of Signior Baptista Minola?

Gre. He that has the two fair daughters:—is't [*Aside to* TRANIO] he you mean?

Tra. Even he. Biondello!

Gre. Hark you, sir; You mean not her to——

Tra. Perhaps him and her, sir; What have you to do?

Pet. Not her that chides, sir; at any hand, I pray.

Tra. I love no chiders, sir:—Biondello, let's away.

Luc. Well begun, Tranio. [*Aside.*

Hor. Sir, a word ere you go:—
Are you a suitor to the maid you talk of, yea or no?

Tra. An if I be, sir, is it any offence?

Gre. No; if without more words, you will get you hence.

Tra. Why, sir, I pray, are not the streets as free
For me as for you?

Gre. But so is not she.

Tra. For what reason, I beseech you?

Gre. For this reason, if you'll know,——
That she's the choice love of Signior Gremio.

Hor. That she's the chosen of Signior Hortensio.

Tra. Softly, my masters! if you be gentlemen,
Do me this right,—hear me with patience.
Baptista is a noble gentleman,
To whom my father is not all unknown;
And, were his daughter fairer than she is,
She may more suitors have, and me for one.
Fair Leda's daughter had a thousand wooers;
Then well one more may fair Bianca have:
And so she shall; Lucentio shall make one,
Though Paris came in hope to speed alone.

Gre. What! this gentleman will out-talk us all.

Luc. Sir, give him head; I know he'll prove a jade.

Pet. Hortensio, to what end are all these words?

Hor. Sir, let me be so bold as to ask you,
Did you yet ever see Baptista's daughter?

Tra. No, sir; but hear I do that he hath two;
The one as famous for a scolding tongue,
As is the other for beauteous modesty.

Pet. Sir, sir, the first's for me; let her go by.

Gre. Yea, leave that labour to great Hercules;
And let it be more than Alcides' twelve.

Pet. Sir, understand you this of me, insooth;—
The youngest daughter, whom you hearken for,
Her father keeps from all access of suitors:
And will not promise her to any man,
Until the elder sister first be wed:
The younger then is free, and not before.

Tra. If it be so, sir, that you are the man
Must stead us all, and me among the rest;
An if you break the ice, and do this feat,—
Achieve the elder, set the younger free

For our access,—whose hap shall be to have her,
Will not so graceless be, to be ingrate.
Hor. Sir, you say well, and well you do conceive;
And since you do profess to be a suitor,
You must, as we do, gratify this gentleman,
To whom we all rest generally beholden.
Tra. Sir, I shall not be slack: in sign whereof,
Please ye we may contrive this afternoon,
And quaff carouses to our mistress' health;
And do as adversaries do in law,—
Strive mightily, but eat and drink as friends.
Gru. Bion. O excellent motion! Fellows, let's begone.
Hor. The motion's good indeed, and be it so;—
Petruchio, I shall be your *ben venuto*. [*Exeunt.*

ACT II.

SCENE I. *The same.*

A Room in Baptista's *House.*

Enter KATHARINA *and* BIANCA.

Bian. Good sister, wrong me not, nor wrong yourself,
To make a bondmaid and a slave of me;
That I disdain: but for these other gawds,
Unbind my hands, I'll pull them off myself,
Yea, all my raiment, to my petticoat;
Or, what you will command me, will I do,
So well I know my duty to my elders.
Kath. Of all thy suitors, here I charge thee, tell
Whom thou lov'st best; see thou dissemble not.
Bian. Believe me, sister, of all the men alive,
I never yet beheld that special face
Which I could fancy more than any other.
Kath. Minion, thou liest; Is't not Hortensio?
Bian. If you affect him, sister, here I swear,
I'll plead for you myself, but you shall have him.
Kath. O then, belike, you fancy riches more;
You will have Gremio to keep you fair.
Bian. Is it for him you do envy me so?
Nay, then you jest; and now I well perceive,
You have but jested with me all this while:
I pr'ythee, sister Kate, untie my hands.
Kath. If that be jest, then all the rest were so.
[*Strikes her.*

Enter BAPTISTA.

Bap. Why, how now, dame! whence grows this insolence?——
Bianca, stand aside:—poor girl! she weeps:—
Go ply thy needle; meddle not with her.—
For shame, thou hilding of a devilish spirit,
Why dost thou wrong her that did ne'er wrong thee?
When did she cross thee with a bitter word;
Kath. Her silence flouts me, and I'll be reveng'd. [*Flies after* BIANCA.
Bap. What, in my sight!—Bianca, get thee in.
[*Exit* BIANCA.
Kath. Will you not suffer me? Nay, now I see
She is your treasure, she must have a husband;
I must dance barefoot on her wedding-day,
And, for your love to her, lead apes in hell.
Talk not to me, I will go sit and weep,
Till I can find occasion of revenge.
[*Exit* KATHARINA.
Bap. Was ever gentleman thus griev'd as I?
But who comes here?

Enter GREMIO, *with* LUCENTIO *in the habit of a mean man*; PETRUCHIO, *with* HORTENSIO *as a Musician; and* TRANIO, *with* BIONDELLO, *bearing a Lute and Books.*

Gre. Good-morrow, neighbour Baptista.
Bap. Good-morrow, neighbour Gremio: God save you, gentlemen!
Pet. And you, good sir! Pray, have you not a daughter
Call'd Katharina, fair and virtuous?
Bap. I have a daughter, sir, call'd Katharina.
Gre. You are too blunt, go to it orderly,
Pet. You wrong me, Signior Gremio: give me leave.—
I am a gentleman of Verona, sir,
That,—hearing of her beauty and her wit,
Her affability and bashful modesty,
Her wondrous qualities, and mild behaviour,—
Am bold to show myself a forward guest
Within your house, to make mine eye the witness
Of that report which I so oft have heard.
And, for an entrance to my entertainment,
I do present you with a man of mine,
[*Presenting* HORTENSIO.
Cunning in musick, and the mathematicks,
To instruct her fully in those sciences,
Whereof, I know, she is not ignorant:
Accept of him, or else you do me wrong;
His name is Licio, born in Mantua.
Bap. You're welcome, sir; and he, for your good sake:
But for my daughter Katharine,—this I know,
She is not for your turn, the more my grief.
Pet. I see you do not mean to part with her;
Or else you like not of my company.
Bap. Mistake me not, I speak but as I find.
Whence are you, sir? what may I call your name?
Pet. Petruchio is my name; Antonio's son,
A man well known throughout all Italy.
Bap. I know him well: you are welcome for his sake.
Gre. Saving your tale, Petruchio, I pray,
Let us, that are poor petitioners, speak too:
Baccare! you are marvellous forward.
Pet. O, pardon me, Signior Gremio; I would fain be doing,
Gre. I doubt it not, sir; but you will curse your wooing.——
Neighbour, this is a gift very grateful, I am sure of it. To express the like kindness myself, that have been more kindly beholden to you than any, I freely give unto you this young scholar [*presenting* LUCENTIO], that hath been long studying at Rheims; as cunning in Greek, Latin, and other languages, as the other in musick and mathematicks: his name is Cambio: pray, accept his service.
Bap. A thousand thanks, Signior Gremio: welcome, good Cambio.—But, gentle sir [*to* TRANIO], methinks you walk like a stranger; May I be so bold to know the cause of your coming?
Tra. Pardon me, sir, the boldness is mine own;
That, being a stranger in this city here,
Do make myself a suitor to your daughter,
Unto Bianca, fair and virtuous.
Nor is your firm resolve unknown to me,
In the preferment of the eldest sister:
This liberty is all that I request,—
That, upon knowledge of my parentage,
I may have welcome 'mongst the rest that woo,
And free access and favour as the rest.
And toward the education of your daughters,
I here bestow a simple instrument,
And this small packet of Greek and Latin books:
If you accept them, then their worth is great.
Bap. Lucentio is your name? of whence, I pray?
Tra. Of Pisa, sir; son to Vincentio.
Bap. A mighty man of Pisa, by report
I know him well: you are very welcome, sir.—
Take you [*to* HOR.] the lute, and you [*to* LUC.] the set of books,
You shall go see your pupils presently.
Holla, within.

Enter a Servant.

Sirrah, lead
These gentlemen to my daughters: and tell them both,
These are their tutors; bid them use them well.
[*Exit* Servant, *with* HORTENSIO, LUCENTIO, *and* BIONDELLO.

We will go walk a little in the orchard,
And then to dinner: You are passing welcome,
And so I pray you all to think yourselves.

Pet. Signior Baptista, my business asketh haste,
And every day I cannot come to woo.
You knew my father well; and in him, me,
Left solely heir to all his lands and goods,
Which I have better'd rather than decreas'd;
Then tell me, if I get your daughter's love,
What dowry shall I have with her to wife?

Bap. After my death, the one half of my lands:
And, in possession, twenty thousand crowns.

Pet. And for that dowry, I'll assure her of
Her widowhood,—be it that she survive me,—
In all my lands and leases whatsoever:
Let specialties be therefore drawn between us,
That covenants may be kept on either hand.

Bap. Ay, when the special thing is well obtain'd,
This is,—her love; for that is all in all.

Pet. Why, that is nothing; for I tell you, father,
I am as peremptory as she proud-minded;
And where two raging fires meet together,
They do consume the thing that feeds their fury:
Though little fire grows great with little wind,
Yet extreme gusts will blow out fire and all:
So I to her, and so she yields to me;
For I am rough, and woo not like a babe.

Bap. Well mayst thou woo, and happy be thy speed!
But be thou arm'd for some unhappy words.

Pet. Ay, to the proof; as mountains are for winds,
That shake not, though they blow perpetually.

Re-enter HORTENSIO, *with his head broken.*

Bap. How now, my friend? why dost thou look so pale?

Hor. For fear, I promise you, if I look pale.

Bap. What, will my daughter prove a good musician?

Hor. I think she'll sooner prove a soldier;
Iron may hold with her, but never lutes.

Bap. Why, then thou canst not break her to the lute?

Hor. Why, no; for she hath broke the lute to me.
I did but tell her, she mistook her frets,
And bow'd her hand to teach her fingering;
When, with a most impatient devilish spirit,
Frets, call you these; quoth she: *I'll fume with them:*
And, with that word, she struck me on the head,
And through the instrument my pate made way;
And there I stood amazed for a while,
As on a pillory, looking through the lute:
While she did call me,—rascal fiddler,
And—twangling Jack; with twenty such vile terms,
As she had studied to misuse me so.

Pet. Now, by the world, it is a lusty wench;
I love her ten times more than e'er I did:
O, how I long to have some chat with her!

Bap. Well, go with me, and be not so discomfited:
Proceed in practice with my younger daughter:
She's apt to learn, and thankful for good turns.—
Signior Petruchio, will you go with us;
Or, shall I send my daughter Kate to you?

Pet. I pray you do; I will attend her here,—
[*Exeunt* BAPTISTA, GREMIO, TRANIO, *and* HORTENSIO.
And woo her with some spirit when she comes.
Say, that she rail; Why, then I'll tell her plain,
She sings as sweetly as a nightingale:
Say, that she frown; I'll say, she looks as clear
As morning roses newly wash'd with dew:
Say, she be mute, and will not speak a word;
Then I'll commend her volubility,
And say, she uttereth piercing eloquence:
If she do bid me pack, I'll give her thanks,
As though she bid me stay by her a week:
If she deny to wed, I'll crave the day
When I shall ask the banns, and when be married:
But here she comes; and now, Petruchio, speak.

Enter KATHARINA.

Good-morrow, Kate; for that's your name, I hear.

Kath. Well have you heard, but something hard of hearing;
They call me—Katharine, that do talk of me.

Pet. You lie, in faith; for you are call'd plain Kate,
And bonny Kate, and sometimes Kate the curst;
But Kate, the prettiest Kate in Christendom,
Kate of Kate-Hall, my super-dainty Kate,
For dainties are all cates: and therefore, Kate,
Take this of me, Kate of my consolation;—
Hearing thy mildness prais'd in every town,
Thy virtues spoke of, and thy beauty sounded,
(Yet not so deeply as to thee belongs),
Myself am mov'd to woo thee for my wife.

Kath. Mov'd! in good time: let him that mov'd you hither,
Remove you hence: I knew you at the first,
You were a moveable.

Pet. Why, what's a moveable?

Kath. A joint-stool.

Pet. Thou hast hit it: come, sit on me.

Kath. Asses are made to bear, and so are you.

Pet. Women are made to bear, and so are you.

Kath. No such jade, sir, as you, if me you mean.

Pet. Alas, good Kate, I will not burden thee:
For knowing thee to be but young and light,—

Kath. Too light for such a swain as you to catch;
And yet as heavy as my weight should be.

Pet. Should be? should buz.

Kath. Well ta'en, and like a buzzard.

Pet. O, slow-wing'd turtle! shall a buzzard take thee?

Kath. Ay, for a turtle; as he takes a buzzard.

Pet. Come, come, you wasp; i'faith, you are too angry.

Kath. If I be waspish, best beware my sting.

Pet. My remedy is then, to pluck it out.

Kath. Ay, if the fool could find it where it lies.

Pet. Who knows not where a wasp doth wear his sting?
In his tail.

Kath. In his tongue.

Pet. Whose tongue?

Kath. Yours, if you talk of tails; and so farewell.

Pet. What with my tongue in your tail? nay, come again,
Good Kate; I am a gentleman.

Kath. That I'll try.
[*Striking him.*

Pet. I swear I'll cuff you, if you strike again.

Kath. So may you lose your arms:
If you strike me, you are no gentleman;
And if no gentleman, why, then no arms.

Pet. A herald, Kate! O, put me in thy books.

Kath. What is your crest? a coxcomb?

Pet. A combless cock, so Kate will be my hen.

Kath. No cock of mine, you crow too like a craven.

Pet. Nay, come, Kate, come; you must not look so sour.

Kath. It is my fashion when I see a crab.

Pet. Why here's no crab; and therefore look not sour.

Kath. There is, there is.

Pet. Then show it me.

Kath. Had I a glass, I would.

Pet. What, you mean my face?

Kath. Well aim'd of such a young one.

Pet. Now, by Saint George, I am too young for you.

Kath. Yet you are wither'd.

Pet. 'Tis with cares.

Kath. I care not.

Pet. Nay, hear you, Kate: in sooth you 'scape not so.
Kath. I chafe you, if I tarry; let me go.
Pet. No, not a whit; I find you passing gentle.
'Twas told me, you were rough, and coy and sullen,
And now I find report a very liar;
For thou art pleasant, gamesome, passing courteous;
But slow in speech, yet sweet as spring-time flowers:
Thou canst not frown, thou canst not look askance,
Nor bite the lip, as angry wenches will;
Nor hast thou pleasure to be cross in talk;
But thou with mildness entertain'st thy wooers,
With gentle conference, soft and affable.
Why does the world report that Kate doth limp?
O slanderous world! Kate, like the hazel-twig,
Is straight, and slender; and as brown in hue
As hazel nuts, and sweeter than the kernels.
O, let me see thee walk: thou dost not halt.
Kath. Go, fool, and whom thou keep'st command.
Pet. Did ever Dian so become a grove,
As Kate this chamber with her princely gait?
O, be thou Dian, and let her be Kate;
And then let Kate be chaste, and Dian sportful!
Kath. Where did you study all this goodly speech?
Pet. It is extempore, from my mother-wit.
Kath. A witty mother! witless else her son.
Pet. Am I not wise?
Kath. Yes; keep you warm.
Pet. Marry, so I mean, sweet Katharine, in thy bed:
And therefore, setting all this chat aside,
Thus in plain terms:—Your father hath consented
That you shall be my wife; your dowry 'greed on;
And, will you, nill you, I will marry you.
Now Kate, I am a husband for your turn;
For, by this light, whereby I see thy beauty,
(Thy beauty, that doth make me like thee well),
Thou must be married to no man but me:
For I am he, am born to tame you, Kate:
And bring you from a wild Kate to a Kate
Conformable, as other household Kates.
Here comes your father; never make denial,
I must and will have Katharine to my wife.

Re-enter BAPTISTA, GREMIO, *and* TRANIO.

Bap. Now,
Signior Petruchio: How speed you with
My daughter?
Pet. How but well, sir? how but well?
It were impossible I should speed amiss.
Bap. Why, how now, daughter Katharine; in your dumps?
Kath. Call you me daughter? now I promise you,
You have show'd a tender fatherly regard,
To wish me wed to one half lunatic;
A mad-cap ruffian, and a swearing Jack,
That thinks with oaths to face the matter out.
Pet. Father, 'tis thus:—yourself and all the world,
That talk'd of her, have talk'd amiss of her;
If she be curst, it is for policy:
For she's not froward, but modest as the dove;
She is not hot, but temperate as the morn;
For patience she will prove a second Grissel;
And Roman Lucrece for her chastity:
And to conclude,—we have 'greed so well together,
That upon Sunday is the wedding-day.
Kath. I'll see thee hang'd on Sunday first.
Gre. Hark, Petruchio! she says she'll see thee hang'd first.
Tra. Is this your speeding? nay, then, good night our part!
Pet. Be patient, gentlemen; I choose her for myself;
If she and I be pleas'd, what's that to you?
'Tis bargain'd 'twixt us twain, being alone,
That she shall still be curst in company.
I tell you 'tis incredible to believe
How much she loves me: O, the kindest Kate!—
She hung about my neck; and kiss on kis
She vied so fast, protesting oath on oath,
That in a twink she won me to her love.
O, you are novices! 'tis a world to see,
How tame, when men and women are alone,
A meacock wretch can make the curstest shrew.—
Give me thy hand, Kate: I will unto Venice,
To buy apparel 'gainst the wedding-day:—
Provide the feast, father, and bid the guests;
I will be sure, my Katharine shall be fine.
Bap. I know not what to say: but give me your hands;
God send you joy, Petruchio! 'tis a match.
Gre. Tra. Amen, say we; we will be witnesses.
Pet. Father, and wife, and gentlemen, adieu;
I will to Venice, Sunday comes apace:——
We will have rings, and things, and fine array;
And kiss me, Kate, we will be married o' Sunday. [*Exeunt* PET. *and* KATH. *severally.*
Gre. Was ever match clapp'd up so suddenly?
Bap. 'Faith, gentlemen, now I play a merchant's part,
And venture madly on a desperate mart.
Tra. 'Twas a commodity lay fretting by you:
'Twill bring you gain, or perish on the seas.
Bap. The gain I seek is—quiet in the match.
Gre. No doubt but he hath got a quiet catch.
But now, Baptista, to your younger daughter;—
Now is the day we long have looked for;
I am your neighbour, and was suitor first.
Tra. And I am one that love Bianca more
Than words can witness, or your thoughts can guess.
Gre. Youngling! thou canst not love so dear as I.
Tra. Gray-beard! thy love doth freeze.
Gre. But thine doth fry.
Skipper, stand back; 'tis age that nourisheth.
Tra. But youth in ladies' eyes that flourisheth.
Bap. Content you, gentlemen; I'll compound this strife:
'Tis deeds must win the prize; and he of both,
That can assure my daughter greatest dower,
Shall have Bianca's love—
Say, Signior Gremio, what can you assure her?
Gre. First, as you know, my house within the city
Is richly furnished with plate and gold;
Basons, and ewers, to lave her dainty hands;
My hangings all of Tyrian tapestry:
In ivory coffers I have stuff'd my crowns;
In cypress chests my arras, counterpoints,
Costly apparel, tents, and canopies.
Fine linen, Turkey cushions boss'd with pearl,
Valance of Venice gold in needle-work,
Pewter and brass, and all things that belong
To house, or housekeeping: Then, at my farm,
I have a hundred milch-kine to the pail,
Six score fat oxen standing in my stalls,
And all things answerable to this portion.
Myself am struck in years, I must confess;
And, if I die to-morrow, this is hers,
If, whilst I live, she will be only mine.
Tra. That, only, came well in.——Sir, list to me:
I am my father's heir, and only son:
If I may have your daughter to my wife,
I'll leave her houses three or four as good,
Within rich Pisa walls, as any one
Old Signior Gremio has in Padua;
Besides two thousand ducats by the year,
Of fruitful land, all which shall be her jointure.—
What, have I pinch'd you, Signior Gremio?
Gre. Two thousand ducats by the year, of land!

My land amounts not to so much in all:
That she shall have; besides an argosy,
That now is lying in Marseilles' road;——
What, have I chok'd you with an argosy?
Tra. Gremio, 'tis known, my father hath no less
Than three great argosies; besides two galiasses,
And twelve tight galleys: these I will assure her,
And twice as much, whate'er thou offer'st next.
Gre. Nay, I have offer'd all, I have no more;
And she can have no more than all I have;—
If you like me, she shall have me and mine.
Tra. Why, then the maid is mine from all the world,
By your firm promise; Gremio is out-vied.
Bap. I must confess, your offer is the best;
And, let your father make her the assurance,
She is your own; else, you must pardon me:
If you should die before him, where's her dower?
Tra. That's but a cavil; he is old, I young.
Gre. And may not young men die, as well as old?
Bap. Well, gentlemen,
I am thus resolv'd:—On Sunday next, you know,
My daughter Katharine is to be married:
Now, on the Sunday following, shall Bianca
Be bride to you, if you make this assurance;
If not, to Signior Gremio:
And so I take my leave, and thank you both. [*Exit.*
Gre. Adieu, good neighbour.—Now I fear thee not;
Sirrah, young gamester, your father were a fool
To give thee all, and, in his waning age,
Set foot under thy table: Tut! a toy!
An old Italian fox is not so kind, my boy. [*Exit.*
Tra. A vengeance on your crafty wither'd hide!
Yet I have faced it with a card of ten.
'Tis in my head to do my master good:
I see no reason, but suppos'd Lucentio
Must get a father, call'd—suppos'd Vincentio;
And that's a wonder: fathers, commonly,
Do get their children; but, in this case of wooing,
A child shall get a sire, if I fail not of my cunning. [*Exit.*

ACT III.

SCENE I. *A Room in* Baptista's *House.*

Enter LUCENTIO, HORTENSIO, *and* BIANCA.

Luc. Fiddler, forbear; you grow too forward, sir:
Have you so soon forgot the entertainment
Her sister Katharine welcom'd you withal?
Hor. But, wrangling pedant, this is
The patroness of heavenly harmony:
Then give me leave to have prerogative;
And when in musick we have spent an hour,
Your lecture shall have leisure for as much.
Luc. Preposterous ass! that never read so far
To know the cause why musick was ordain'd?
Was it not to refresh the mind of man,
After his studies, or his usual pain?
Then give me leave to read philosophy,
And, while I pause, serve in your harmony.
Hor. Sirrah, I will not bear these braves of thine.
Bian. Why, gentlemen, you do me double wrong,
To strive for that which resteth in my choice:
I am no breeching scholar in the schools;
I'll not be tied to hours, nor 'pointed times,
But learn my lessons as I please myself.
And, to cut off all strife, here sit we down:
Take you your instrument, play you the whiles;
His lecture will be done ere you have tun'd.
Hor. You'll leave his lecture when I am in tune? [*To* BIANCA.—HORTENSIO *retires.*
Luc. That will be never!—tune your instrument.
Bian. Where left we last?
Luc. Here madam:——
Hac ibat Simois; hic est Sigeia tellus;
Hic steterat Priami regia celsa senis.
Bian. Construe them.
Luc. *Hac ibat,* as I told you before, *Simois,* I am Lucentio,—*hic est,* son unto Vincentio of Pisa,—*Sigeia tellus,* disguised thus to get your love;—*Hic steterat,* and that Lucentio that comes a wooing,—*Priami,* is my man Tranio, —*regia,* bearing my port,—*celsa senis,* that we might beguile the old pantaloon.
Hor. Madam, my instrument's in tune. [*Returning.*
Bian. Let's hear.— [HORTENSIO *plays.*
O fye! the treble jars.
Luc. Spit in the hole, man, and tune again.
Bian. Now let me see if I can construe it: *Hac ibat Simois,* I know you not;—*hic est Sigeia tellus,* I trust you not;—*Hic steterat Priami,* take heed he hear us not;—*regia,* presume not;—*celsa senis,* despair not.
Hor. Madam, 'tis now in tune.
Luc. All but the bass.
Hor. The bass is right; 'tis the base knave that jars.
How fiery and forward our pedant is!
Now for my life, the knave doth court my love:
Pedascule, I'll watch you better yet.
Bian. In time I may believe, yet I mistrust.
Luc. Mistrust it not; for, sure, Æacides
Was Ajax,—call'd so from his grandfather.
Bian. I must believe my master; else, I promise you,
I should be arguing still upon that doubt:
But let it rest.—Now, Licio, to you:—
Good masters, take it not unkindly, pray,
That I have been thus pleasant with you both.
Hor. You may go walk [*to* LUCENTIO], and give me leave awhile;
My lessons make no music in three parts.
Luc. Are you so formal, sir? well, I must wait,
And watch withal; for, but I be deceiv'd,
Our fine musician groweth amorous. [*Aside.*
Hor. Madam, before you touch the instrument,
To learn the order of my fingering,
I must begin with rudiments of art:
To teach you gamut in a briefer sort,
More pleasant, pithy, and effectual,
Than hath been taught by any of my trade:
And there it is in writing, fairly drawn.
Bian. Why, I am past my gamut long ago.
Hor. Yet read the gamut of Hortensio.
Bian. [*Reads.*] Gamut *I am, the ground of all accord.*
A re, *to plead Hortensio's passion;*
B mi, *Bianca, take him for thy lord,*
C faut, *that loves with all affection;*
D sol re, *one cliff, two notes have I;*
E la mi, *show pity, or I die.*
Call you this—gamut? tut! I like it not:
Old fashions please me best; I am not so nice,
To change true rules for odd inventions.

Enter a Servant.

Serv. Mistress, your father prays you leave your books,
And help to dress your sister's chamber up;
You know, to-morrow is the wedding-day.
Bian. Farewell, sweet masters both; I must be gone. [*Exeunt* BIANCA *and* Servant.
Luc. 'Faith, mistress, then I have no cause to stay. [*Exit.*
Hor. But I have cause to pry into this pedant;
Methinks, he looks as though he were in love:—
Yet if thy thoughts, Bianca, be so humble,
To cast thy wand'ring eyes on every stale,
Seize thee that list: If once I find thee ranging,
Hortensio will be quit with thee, by changing. [*Exit.*

SCENE II. *The same. Before* Baptista's *House.*

Enter BAPTISTA, GREMIO, TRANIO, KATHARINA, BIANCA, LUCENTIO, *and* Attendants.

Bap. Signior Lucentio, [*to* TRANIO], this is the 'pointed day
That Katharine and Petruchio should be married,
And yet we hear not of our son-in-law:
What will be said? what mockery will it be,
To want the bridegroom, when the priest attends
To speak the ceremonial rites of marriage?
What says Lucentio to this shame of ours?

Kath. No shame but mine: I must, forsooth, be forc'd
To give my hand, oppos'd against my heart,
Unto a mad-brain rudesby, full of spleen;
Who woo'd in haste, and means to wed at leisure.
I told you, I, he was a frantic fool,
Hiding his bitter jests in blunt behaviour:
And, to be noted for a merry man,
He'll woo a thousand, 'point the day of marriage,
Make friends invite them, and proclaim the banns;
Yet never means to wed where he hath woo'd.
Now must the world point at poor Katharine,
And say,—*Lo, there is mad Petruchio's wife,*
If it would please him come and marry her.

Tra. Patience, good Katharine, and Baptista too;
Upon my life, Petruchio means but well,
Whatever fortune stays him from his word:
Though he be blunt, I know him passing wise;
Though he be merry, yet withal he's honest.

Kath. 'Would, Katharine had never seen him though!

[*Exit, weeping, followed by* BIANCA *and others.*

Bap. Go, girl; I cannot blame thee now to weep;
For such an injury would vex a very saint,
Much more a shrew of thy impatient humour.

Enter BIONDELLO.

Bion. Master, master! news, old news, and such as you never heard of!

Bap. Is it new and old too? how may that be?

Bion. Why, is it not news to hear of Petruchio's coming?

Bap. Is he come?

Bion. Why, no, sir.

Bap. What then?

Bion. He is coming.

Bap. When will he be here?

Bion. When he stands where I am, and sees you there.

Tra. But, say, what:—to thine old news.

Bion. Why, Petruchio is coming, in a new hat and an old jerkin; a pair of old breeches, thrice turned; a pair of boots that have been candle-cases, one buckled, another laced; an old rusty sword ta'en out of the town armory, with a broken hilt and chapeless; with two broken points: His horse hipped with an old mothy saddle, the stirrups of no kindred: besides, possessed with the glanders, and like to mose in the chine; troubled with the lampass, infected with the fashions, full of wind-galls, sped with spavins, raied with the yellows, past cure of the fives, stark spoiled with the staggers, begnawn with the bots; swayed in the back, and shoulder-shotten; ne'er legged before; and with a half-checked bit, and a head-stall of sheep's leather; which, being restrained to keep him from stumbling, hath been often burst, and now repaired with knots: one girt six times pieced, and a woman's crupper of velure, which hath two letters for her name, fairly set down in studs, and here and there pieced with packthread.

Bap. Who comes with him?

Bion. O, sir, his lackey, for all the world caparisoned like the horse; with a linen stock on one leg, and a kersy boot-hose on the other, gartered with a red and blue list; an old hat and *The humour of forty fancies* pricked in't for a feather: a monster, a very monster in apparel; and not like a christian footboy, or a gentleman's lackey.

Tra. 'Tis some odd humour pricks him to this fashion!—
Yet oftentimes he goes but mean apparell'd.

Bap. I am glad he is come, howsoever he comes.

Bion. Why, sir, he comes not.

Bap. Didst thou not say, he comes?

Bion. Who? that Petruchio came?

Bap. Ay, that Petruchio came.

Bion. No, sir; I say, his horse comes with him on his back.

Bap. Why, that's all one.

Bion. Nay, by Saint Jamy, I hold you a penny,
A horse and a man is more than one, and yet not many.

Enter PETRUCHIO *and* GRUMIO.

Pet. Come, where be these gallants? who is at home?

Bap. You are welcome, sir.

Pet. And yet I come not well.

Bap. And yet you halt not.

Tra. Not so well apparell'd
As I wish you were.

Pet. Were it better, I should rush in thus.
But where is Kate? Where is my lovely bride?—
How does my father?—Gentles, methinks you frown:
And wherefore gaze this goodly company,
As if they saw some wondrous monument,
Some comet, or unusual prodigy?

Bap. Why, sir, you know, this is your wedding day:
First were we sad, fearing you would not come;
Now sadder, that you come so unprovided.
Fye! doff this habit, shame to your estate,
An eye-sore to our solemn festival.

Tra. And tell us, what occasion of import
Hath all so long detain'd you from your wife,
And sent you hither so unlike yourself?

Pet. Tedious it were to tell, and harsh to hear:
Sufficeth, I am come to keep my word,
Though in some part enforced to digress;
Which, at more leisure I will so excuse
As you shall well be satisfied withal.
But, where is Kate? I stay too long from her;
The morning wears, 'tis time we were at church.

Tra. See not your bride in these unreverent robes;
Go to my chamber, put on clothes of mine.

Pet. Not I, believe me; thus I'll visit her.

Bap. But thus, I trust, you will not marry her.

Pet. Good sooth, even thus; therefore have done with words;
To me she's married, not unto my clothes:
Could I repair what she will wear in me,
As I can change these poor accoutrements,
'Twere well for Kate, and better for myself.
But what a fool am I to chat with you,
When I should bid good-morrow to my bride,
And seal the title with a lovely kiss!

[*Exeunt* PET. GRU. *and* BION.

Tra. He hath some meaning in his mad attire:
We will persuade him, be it possible,
To put on better ere he go to church.

Bap. I'll after him, and see the event of this.

[*Exit.*

Tra. But, sir, to her love concerneth us to add
Her father's liking: which to bring to pass,
As I before imparted to your worship,
I am to get a man,—whate'er he be,
It skills not much; we'll fit him to our turn,—
And he shall be Vincentio of Pisa;
And make assurance, here in Padua,
Of greater sums than I have promised,
So shall you quietly enjoy your hope,
And marry sweet Bianca with consent.

Luc. Were it not that my fellow schoolmaster
Doth watch Bianca's steps so narrowly,
'Twere good, methinks, to steal our marriage;
Which once perform'd, let all the world say—no,
I'll keep mine own, despite of all the world.

Tra. That by degrees we mean to look into,
And watch our vantage in this business:
We'll overreach the gray-beard Gremio,
The narrow-prying father Minola;
The quaint musician, amorous Licio;
All for my master's sake, Lucentio.—

Re-enter GREMIO.

Signior Gremio! came you from the church?

Gre. As willingly as ere I came from school.

Tra. And is the bride and bridegroom coming home?

Gre. A bridegroom, say you? 'tis a groom, indeed,
A grumbling groom, and that the girl shall find.

Tra. Curster than she? why, 'tis impossible.

Gre. Why, he's a devil, a devil, a very fiend.

Tra. Why, she's a devil, a devil, the devil's dam.

Gre. Tut! she's a lamb, a dove, a fool to him.
I'll tell you, Sir Lucentio: When the priest
Should ask—if Katharine should be his wife,
Ay, by gogs-wouns, quoth he; and swore so loud,
That, all amaz'd, the priest let fall the book:
And, as he stoop'd again to take it up,
The mad-brain'd bridegroom took him such a cuff,
That down fell priest and book, and book and priest:
Now take them up, quoth he, *if any list.*

Tra. What said the wench, when he arose again?

Gre. Trembled and shook; for why, he stamp'd and swore,
As if the vicar meant to cozen him.
But after many ceremonies done,
He calls for wine:—*A health*, quoth he; as if
He had been aboard carousing to his mates
After a storm:—Quaff'd off the muscadel,
And threw the sops all in the sexton's face;
Having no other reason,—
But that his beard grew thin and hungerly,
And seem'd to ask him sops as he was drinking.
This done, he took the bride about the neck;
And kiss'd her lips with such a clamorous smack,
That, at the parting, all the church did echo.
I, seeing this, came thence for very shame;
And after me, I know the rout is coming:
Such a mad marriage never was before;
Hark, hark! I hear the minstrels play. [*Musick.*

Enter PETRUCHIO, KATHARINA, BIANCA, BAPTISTA. HORTENSIO, GRUMIO, *and* Train.

Pet. Gentlemen, and friends, I thank you for your pains:
I know you think to dine with me to-day,
And have prepar'd great store of wedding cheer;
But so it is, my haste doth call me hence,
And therefore here I mean to take my leave.

Bap. Is't possible, you will away to-night?

Pet. I must away to-day, before night come:—
Make it no wonder; if you knew my business,
You would entreat me rather go than stay.
And, honest company, I thank you all,
That have beheld me give away myself
To this most patient, sweet, and virtuous wife:
Dine with my father, drink a health to me;
For I must hence, and farewell to you all.

Tra. Let us entreat you stay till after dinner.

Pet. It may not be.

Gre. Let me entreat you.

Pet. It cannot be.

Kath. Let me entreat you.

Pet. I am content.

Kath. Are you content to stay.

Pet. I am content you shall entreat me stay,
But yet not stay, entreat me how you can

Kath. Now, if you love me, stay.

Pet. Grumio, my horses.

Gru. Ay, sir, they be ready; the oats have eaten the horses.

Kath. Nay, then,
Do what thou canst, I will not go to-day;
No, nor to-morrow, nor till I please myself.
The door is open, sir, there lies your way,
You may be jogging whiles your boots are green;
For me, I'll not begone till I please myself;—
'Tis like you'll prove a jolly surly groom,
That take it on you at the first so roundly.

Pet. O, Kate, content thee; pr'ythee, be not angry.

Kath. I will be angry; What hast thou to do?
Father, be quiet; he shall stay my leisure.

Gre. Ay, marry, sir; now it begins to work.

Kath. Gentlemen, forward to the bridal dinner:—
I see a woman may be made a fool,
If she had not a spirit to resist.

Pet. They shall go forward, Kate, at thy command:
Obey the bride, you that attend on her:
Go to the feast, revel and domineer,
Carouse full measure to her maidenhead,
Be mad and merry,——or go hang yourselves;
But for my bonny Kate, she must with me.
Nay, look not big, nor stamp, nor stare, nor fret;
I will be master of what is mine own:
She is my goods, my chattels; she is my house,
My household-stuff, my field, my barn,
My horse, my ox, my ass, my any thing:
And here she stands, touch her whoever dare;
I'll bring my action on the proudest he
That stops my way in Padua.——Grumio,
Draw forth thy weapon, we're beset with thieves;
Rescue thy mistress, if thou be a man:—
Fear not, sweet wench, they shall not touch thee, Kate;
I'll buckler thee against a million.
[*Exeunt* PET. KATH. *and* GRU.

Bap. Nay, let them go, a couple of quiet ones!

Gre. Went they not quickly, I should die with laughing.

Tra. Of all mad matches, never was the like!

Luc. Mistress, what's your opinion of your sister?

Bian. That being mad herself, she's madly mated.

Gre. I warrant him, Petruchio is Kated.

Bap. Neighbours and friends, though bride and bridegroom wants
For to supply the places at the table,
You know there wants no junkets at the feast.—
Lucentio, you shall supply the bridegroom's place,
And let Bianca take her sister's room.

Tra. Shall sweet Bianca practise how to bride it?

Bap. She shall, Lucentio.—Come, Gentlemen, let's go. [*Exeunt.*

ACT IV.

SENCE I. *A Hall in* Petruchio's *Country House.*

Enter GRUMIO.

Gru. Fye, fye on all tired jades! on all mad masters! and all foul ways! Was ever man so beaten? was ever man so rayed? was ever man so weary? I am sent before to make a fire, and they are coming after to warm them. Now, were not I a little pot, and soon hot, my very lips might freeze to my teeth, my tongue to the roof of my mouth, my heart in my belly, ere I should come by a fire to thaw me:—But I, with blowing the fire shall warm myself; for, considering the weather, a taller man than I will take cold. Holla! hoa! Curtis!

Enter CURTIS.

Curt. Who is that, calls so coldly?

Gru. A piece of ice: If thou doubt it, thou may'st slide from my shoulder to my heel, with no greater run but my head and my neck. A fire, good Curtis.

Curt. Is my master and his wife coming, Grumio?

Gru. O, ay, Curtis, ay: and therefore fire, fire; cast on no water.

Curt. Is she so hot a shrew as she's reported?

Gru. She was, good Curtis, before this frost: but thou know'st, winter tames man, woman, and beast; for it hath tamed my old master, and my new mistress, and myself, fellow Curtis.

Curt. Away, you three-inch fool! I am no beast.

Gru. Am I but three inches? why, thy horn is a foot; and so long am I, at the least. But wilt thou make a fire, or shall I complain on thee to our mistress, whose hand (she being now at hand) thou shalt soon feel, to thy cold comfort, for being slow in thy hot office.

Curt. I pr'ythee, good Grumio, tell me, How goes the world?

Gru. A cold world, Curtis, in every office but thine; and, therefore, fire: Do thy duty, and have thy duty; for my master and mistress are almost frozen to death.

Curt. There's fire ready: And therefore, good Grumio, the news?

Gru. Why, *Jack boy! ho boy!* and as much news as thou wilt.

Curt. Come, you are so full of conycatching:—

Gru. Why, therefore, fire; for I have caught extreme cold. Where's the cook? is supper ready, the house trimmed, rushes strewed, cobwebs swept; the serving-men in their new fustian, their white stockings, and every officer his wedding garment on? Be the jacks fair within, the jills fair without, the carpets laid, and every thing in order?

Curt. All ready; And therefore, I pray thee, news?

Gru. First, know my horse is tired; my master and mistress fallen out.

Curt. How?

Gru. Out of their saddles into the dirt; and thereby hangs a tale.

Curt. Let's ha't, good Grumio.

Gru. Lend thine ear.

Curt. Here.

Gru. There. [*Striking him.*

Curt. This is to feel a tale, and not to hear a tale.

Gru. And therefore 'tis called a sensible tale: and this cuff was but to knock at your ear, and beseech listening. Now I begin: *Imprimis*, we came down a foul hill, my master riding behind my mistress:

Curt. Both on one horse?

Gru. What's that to thee?

Curt. Why, a horse.

Gru. Tell thou the tale:——but hadst thou not crossed me, thou should'st have heard how her horse fell, and she under her horse; thou should'st have heard in how miry a place: how she was bemoiled; how he left her with the horse upon her; how he beat me because her horse stumbled; how she waded through the dirt to pluck him off me; how he swore; how she pray'd—that never pray'd before; how I cried; how the horses ran away, how her bridle was burst; how I lost my crupper;—with many things of worthy memory: which now shall die in oblivion, and thou return unexperienced to thy grave.

Curt. By this reckoning, he is more shrew than she.

Gru. Ay, and that thou and the proudest of you all shall find, when he comes home. But what talk I of this?—call forth Nathaniel, Joseph, Nicholas, Philip, Walter, Sugarsop, and the rest; let their heads be sleekly combed, their blue coats brushed, and their garters of an indifferent knit: let them curtsey with their left legs; and not presume to touch a hair of my master's horse-tail, till they kiss their hands. Are they all ready?

Curt. They are.

Gru. Call them forth.

Curt. Do you hear, ho! you must meet my master, to countenance my mistress.

Gru. Why, she hath a face of her own.

Curt. Who knows not that?

Gru. Thou, it seems; that callest for company to countenance her.

Curt. I call them forth to credit her.

Gru. Why, she comes to borrow nothing of them.

Enter several Servants.

Nath. Welcome home, Grumio.

Phil. How now, Grumio?

Jos. What, Grumio!

Nich. Fellow Grumio!

Nath. How now, old lad?

Gru. Welcome, you;—how now, you; what, you;—fellow, you;—and thus much for greeting. Now, my spruce companions, is all ready, and all things neat?

Nath. All things is ready: How near is our master?

Gru. E'en at hand, alighted by this; and therefore be not——Cock's passion, silence!——I hear my master.

Enter PETRUCHIO *and* KATHARINA.

Pet. Where be these knaves? What, no man at door,
To hold my stirrup, nor to take my horse!
Where is Nathaniel, Gregory, Philip?——

All Serv. Here, here, sir; here, sir.

Pet. Here, sir! here, sir! here, sir! here, sir!—
You logger-headed and unpolish'd grooms!
What, no attendance? no regard? no duty?—
Where is the foolish knave I sent before?

Gru. Here, sir; as foolish as I was before.

Pet. You peasant swain! you whoreson malt-horse drudge!
Did I not bid thee meet me in the park,
And bring along these rascal knaves with thee?

Gru. Nathaniel's coat, sir, was not fully made,
And Gabriel's pumps were all unpink'd i'the heel;
There was no link to colour Peter's hat,
And Walter's dagger was not come from sheathing:
There were none fine, but Adam, Ralph, and Gregory;
The rest were ragged, old, and beggarly;
Yet, as they are, here are they come to meet you.

Pet. Go, rascals, go, and fetch my supper in.— [*Exeunt some of the* Servants.
Where is the life that late I led— [Sings.
Where are those——Sit down, Kate, and welcome.
Soud, soud, soud, soud!

Re-enter Servants, *with supper.*

Why, when, I say?—Nay, good sweet Kate, be merry.
Off with my boots, you rogues, you villains; When?

It was the friar of orders grey, [Sings.
As he forth walked on his way:—

Out, out, you rogue! you pluck my foot awry:
Take that, and mend the plucking off the other.— [*Strikes him.*
Be merry, Kate:—Some water here; what, ho!
Where's my spaniel Troilus? Sirrah, get you hence,
And bid my cousin Ferdinand come hither:— [*Exit* Servant.

One, Kate, that you must kiss, and be acquainted with.—
Where are my slippers?—Shall I have some water? [*A bason is presented to him.*
Come, Kate, and wash, and welcome heartily.— [Servant *lets the ewer fall.*
You whoreson villain! will you let it fall? [*Strikes him.*

Kath. Patience, I pray you; 'twas a fault unwilling.

Pet. A whoreson, beetleheaded, flap-ear'd knave!
Come, Kate, sit down; I know you have a stomach.
Will you give thanks, sweet Kate; or else shall I?—
What is this? Mutton?

1 Serv. Ay.

Pet. Who brought it?

1 Serv. I.

Pet. 'Tis burnt; and so is all the meat:
What dogs are these!—Where is the rascal cook?
How durst you, villains, bring it from the dresser,
And serve it thus to me that love it not?
There, take it to you, trenchers, cups, and all: [*Throws the meat, &c. about the stage.*
You heedless joltheads, and unmanner'd slaves!
What, do you grumble? I'll be with you straight.

Kath. I pray you, husband, be not so disquiet;
The meat was well, if you were so contented.

Pet. I tell thee, Kate, 'twas burnt and dried away;
And I expressly am forbid to touch it,
For it engenders choler, planteth anger;
And better 'twere that both of us did fast,—
Since, of ourselves, ourselves are cholerick,—
Than feed it with such over-roasted flesh.
Be patient; to-morrow it shall be mended,
And, for this night, we'll fast for company:—
Come, I will bring thee to thy bridal chamber. [*Exeunt* PET. KATH. *and* CURT.

Nath. [*Advancing.*] Peter, didst ever see the like?

Peter. He kills her in her own humour.

Re-enter CURTIS.

Gru. Where is he?

Curt. In her chamber,
Making a sermon of continency to her:
And rails, and swears, and rates; that she, poor soul,
Knows not which way to stand, to look, to speak;
And sits as one new-risen from a dream.
Away, away! for he is coming hither. [*Exeunt.*

Re-enter PETRUCHIO.

Pet. Thus have I politickly begun my reign,
And 'tis my hope to end successfully:
My falcon now is sharp, and passing empty;
And, till she stoop, she must not be full-gorg'd,
For then she never looks upon her lure.
Another way I have to man my haggard,
To make her come, and know her keeper's call,
That is,—to watch her, as we watch these kites
That bate, and beat, and will not be obedient.
She eat no meat to-day, nor none shall eat;
Last night she slept not, nor to-night she shall not;
As with the meat, some undeserved fault
I'll find about the making of the bed;
And here I'll fling the pillow, there the bolster,
This way the coverlet, another way the sheets:—
Ay, and amid this hurly, I intend
That all is done in reverend care of her;
And, in conclusion, she shall watch all night:
And, if she chance to nod, I'll rail and brawl,
And with the clamour keep her still awake.
This is a way to kill a wife with kindness;
And thus I'll curb her mad and headstrong humour.
He that knows better how to tame a shrew,
Now let him speak; 'tis charity to shew. [*Exit.*

SCENE II. Padua. *Before* Baptista's *House.*

Enter TRANIO *and* HORTENSIO.

Tra. Is't possible, friend Licio, that Bianca
Doth fancy any other but Lucentio?
I tell you, sir, she bears me fair in hand.

Hor. Sir, to satisfy you in what I have said,
Stand by, and mark the manner of his teaching. [*They stand aside.*

Enter BIANCA *and* LUCENTIO.

Luc. Now, mistress, profit you in what you read?

Bian. What, master, read you? first resolve me that.

Luc. I read that I profess the art to love.

Bian. And may you prove, sir, master of your art!

Luc. While you, sweet dear, prove mistress of my heart. [*They retire.*

Hor. Quick proceeders, marry! Now, tell me, I pray,
You that durst swear that your mistress Bianca
Lov'd none in the world so well as Lucentio.

Tra. O despiteful love! unconstant womankind!
I tell thee, Licio, this is wonderful.

Hor. Mistake no more: I am not Licio,
Nor a musician, as I seem to be;
But one that scorn to live in this disguise,
For such a one as leaves a gentleman,
And makes a god of such a cullion:
Know, sir, that I am call'd—Hortensio.

Tra. Signior Hortensio, I have often heard
Of your entire affection to Bianca;
And since mine eyes are witness of her lightness,
I will with you,—if you be so contented,—
Forswear Bianca and her love for ever.

Hor. See, how they kiss and court.——Signior Lucentio,
Here is my hand, and here I firmly vow—
Never to woo her more; but do forswear her,
As one unworthy all the former favours
That I have fondly flatter'd her withal.

Tra. And here I take the like unfeigned oath,—
Ne'er to marry with her though she would entreat:
Fye on her! see, how beastly she doth court him.

Hor. 'Would, all the world, but he, had quite forsworn!
For me,—that I may surely keep mine oath,
I will be married to a wealthy widow,
Ere three days pass; which hath as long loved me,
As I have lov'd this proud disdainful haggard:
And so farewell, signior Lucentio.—
Kindness in women, not their beauteous looks,
Shall win my love:—and so I take my leave,
In resolution as I swore before.
[*Exit* HORTENSIO.—LUCENTIO *and* BIANCA *advance.*

Tra. Mistress Bianca, bless you with such grace
As 'longeth to a lover's blessed case!
Nay, I have ta'en you napping, gentle love;
And have forsworn you, with Hortensio.

Bian. Tranio, you jest; But have you both forsworn me?

Tra. Mistress, we have.

Luc. Then we are rid of Licio.

Tra. I' faith, he'll have a lusty widow now,
That shall be woo'd and wedded in a day.

Bian. God give him joy!

Tra. Ay, and he'll tame her.

Bian. He says so, Tranio.

Tra. 'Faith, he is gone unto the taming-school.

Bian. The taming-school! what, is there such a place?

Tra. Ay, mistress, and Petruchio is the master:
That teacheth tricks eleven and twenty long.—
To tame a shrew, and charm her chattering tongue.

Enter BIONDELLO, *running.*

Bion. O master, master, I have watch'd so long
That I'm dog-weary; but at last I spied
An ancient angel coming down the hill,
Will serve the turn.
Tra. What is he, Biondello?
Bion. Master, a mercatante, or a pedant,
I know not what; but formal in apparel,
In gait and countenance surely like a father.
Luc. And what of him, Tranio?
Tra. If he be credulous, and trust my tale,
I'll make him glad to seem Vincentio;
And give assurance to Baptista Minola,
As if he were the right Vincentio.
Take in your love, and then let me alone.
[*Exeunt* LUCENTIO *and* BIANCA.

Enter a Pedant.

Ped. God save you, sir!
Tra. And you, sir! you are welcome.
Travel you far on, or are you at the furthest?
Ped. Sir, at the furthest for a week or two:
But then up further; and as far as Rome;
And so to Tripoly, if God lend me life.
Tra. What countryman, I pray?
Ped. Of Mantua.
Tra. Of Mantua, sir?—marry, God forbid!
And come to Padua, careless of your life?
Ped. My life, sir! how, I pray? for that goes hard.
Tra. 'Tis death for any one in Mantua
To come to Padua: Know you not the cause?
Your ships are staid at Venice; and the duke
(For private quarrel 'twixt your duke and him)
Hath publish'd and proclaim'd it openly:
'Tis marvel; but that you're but newly come,
You might have heard it else proclaim'd about.
Ped. Alas, sir, it is worse for me than so;
For I have bills for money by exchange
From Florence, and must here deliver them.
Tra. Well, sir, to do you courtesy,
This will I do, and this will I advise you;
First, tell me, have you ever been at Pisa?
Ped. Ay, sir, in Pisa have I often been;
Pisa, renowned for grave citizens.
Tra. Among them, know you one Vincentio?
Ped. I know him not, but I have heard of him;
A merchant of incomparable wealth.
Tra. He is my father, sir; and, sooth to say,
In countenance somewhat doth resemble you.
Bion. As much as an apple doth an oyster, and all one. [*Aside.*
Tra. To save your life in this extremity,
This favour will I do you for his sake;
And think it not the worst of all your fortunes,
That you are like to Sir Vincentio.
His name and credit shall you undertake,
And in my house you shall be friendly lodged;—
Look, that you take upon you as you should;
You understand me, sir;—so shall you stay
Till you have done your business in the city;
If this be courtesy, sir, accept of it.
Ped. O, sir, I do; and will repute you ever
The patron of my life and liberty.
Tra. Then go with me, to make the matter good.
This, by the way, I let you understand;—
My father is here look'd for every day,
To pass assurance of a dower in marriage
'Twixt me and one Baptista's daughter here;
In all these circumstances I'll instruct you:
Go with me, sir, to clothe you as becomes you.
[*Exeunt.*

SCENE III. *A Room in* Petruchio's *House.*

Enter KATHARINA *and* GRUMIO.

Gru. No, no; forsooth; I dare not, for my life.
Kath. The more my wrong, the more his spite appears:
What, did he marry me to famish me?
Beggars, that come unto my father's door,
Upon entreaty, have a present alms;
If not, elsewhere they meet with charity:
But I,—who never knew how to entreat,—
Am starv'd for meat, giddy for lack of sleep:
With oaths kept waking, and with brawling fed:
And that which spites me more than all these wants,
He does it under name of perfect love;
As who should say,—if I should sleep, or eat,
'Twere deadly sickness, or else present death.—
I pr'ythee go, and get me some repast;
I care not what, so it be wholesome food.
Gru. What say you to a neat's foot?
Kath. 'Tis passing good; I pr'ythee let me have it.
Gru. I fear, it is too cholerick a meat:—
How say you to a fat tripe, finely broil'd?
Kath. I like it well; good Grumio, fetch it me.
Gru. I cannot tell; I fear, 'tis cholerick.
What say you to a piece of beef, and mustard?
Kath. A dish that I do love to feed upon.
Gru. Ay, but the mustard is too hot a little.
Kath. Why, then the beef, and let the mustard rest.
Gru. Nay, then I will not; you shall have the mustard,
Or else you get no beef of Grumio.
Kath. Then both, or one, or any thing thou wilt.
Gru. Why, then the mustard without the beef.
Kath. Go, get thee gone, thou false deluding slave, [*Beats him.*
That feed'st me with the very name of meat:
Sorrow on thee, and all the pack of you,
That triumph thus upon my misery!
Go, get thee gone, I say.

Enter PETRUCHIO *with a dish of meat; and* HORTENSIO.

Pet. How fares my Kate? What, sweeting, all amort?
Hor. Mistress, what cheer?
Kath. 'Faith, as cold as can be.
Pet. Pluck up thy spirits, look cheerfully upon me.
Here, love; thou see'st how diligent I am,
To dress thy meat myself, and bring it thee:
[*Sets the dish on a table.*
I am sure, sweet Kate, this kindness merits thanks.
What, not a word? Nay then, thou lov'st it not;
And all my pains is sorted to no 'proof:——
Here, take away this dish.
Kath. 'Pray you, let it stand.
Pet. The poorest service is repaid with thanks;
And so shall mine, before you touch the meat.
Kath. I thank you, sir.
Hor. Signior Petruchio, fye! you are to blame!
Come, mistress Kate, I'll bear you company.
Pet. Eat it up all, Hortensio, if thou lov'st me.— [*Aside.*
Much good do it unto thy gentle heart!
Kate, eat apace:—And now, my honey love,
Will we return unto thy father's house;
And revel it as bravely as the best,
With silken coats, and caps, and golden rings,
With ruffs, and cuffs, and farthingales, and things;
With scarfs, and fans, and double change of bravery,
With amber bracelets, beads, and all this knavery.
What, hast thou din'd? The tailor stays thy leisure,
To deck thy body with his ruffling treasure.

Enter Tailor.

Come, tailor, let us see these ornaments;

Enter Haberdasher.

Lay forth the gown.—What news with you, sir?
Hab. Here is the cap your worship did bespeak.
Pet. Why, this was moulded on a porringer;
A velvet dish;—fye, fye! 'tis lewd and filthy:

Why, 'tis a cockle, or a walnutshell,
A knack, a toy, a trick, a baby's cap;
Away with it, come, let me have a bigger.

Kath. I'll have no bigger; this doth fit the time,
And gentlewomen wear such caps as these.

Pet. When you are gentle, you shall have one too,
And not till then.

Hor. That will not be in haste. [*Aside.*

Kath. Why, sir, I trust, I may have leave to speak;
And speak I will; I am no child, no babe:
Your betters have endur'd me say my mind;
And, if you cannot, best you stop your ears.
My tongue will tell the anger of my heart;
Or else my heart, concealing it, will break:
And, rather than it shall, I will be free
Even to the uttermost, as I please, in words.

Pet. Why, thou say'st true; it is a paltry cap,
A custard-coffin, a bauble, a silken pie:
I love thee well, in that thou lik'st it not.

Kath. Love me, or love me not, I like the cap;
And it I will have, or I will have none.

Pet. Thy gown? why, ay:—Come, tailor, let us see't.
O mercy, God! what masking stuff is here?
What's this? a sleeve? 'tis like a demi-cannon:
What! up and down, carv'd like an apple-tart?
Here's snip, and nip, and cut, and slish, and slash,
Like to a censer in a barber's shop:—
Why, what, o' devil's name, tailor, call'st thou this?

Hor. I see, she's like to have neither cap nor gown. [*Aside.*

Tai. You bid me make it orderly and well,
According to the fashion, and the time.

Pet. Marry, and did; but if you be remember'd,
I did not bid you mar it to the time.
Go, hop me over every kennel home,
For you shall hop without my custom, sir:
I'll none of it; hence, make your best of it.

Kath. I never saw a better-fashion'd gown,
More quaint, more pleasing, nor more commendable;
Belike, you mean to make a puppet of me.

Pet. Why, true; he means to make a puppet of thee.

Tai. She says, your worship means to make a puppet of her.

Pet. O monstrous arrogance! Thou liest, thou thread,
Thou thimble,
Thou yard, three-quarters, half-yard, quarter, nail,
Thou flea, thou nit, thou winter cricket thou:—
Brav'd in mine own house with a skein of thread!
Away, thou rag, thou quantity, thou remnant;
Or I shall so be-mete thee with thy yard,
As thou shalt think on prating whilst thou liv'st!
I tell thee, I, that thou hast marr'd her gown.

Tai. Your worship is deceiv'd; the gown is made
Just as my master had direction:
Grumio gave order how it should be done.

Gru. I gave him no order, I gave him the stuff.

Tai. But how did you desire it should be made?

Gru. Marry, sir, with needle and thread.

Tai. But did you not request to have it cut?

Gru. Thou hast faced many things.

Tai. I have.

Gru. Face not me; thou hast braved many men; brave not me; I will neither be faced nor braved. I say unto thee,—I bid thy master cut out the gown; but I did not bid him cut it to pieces; *ergo*, thou liest.

Tai. Why, here is the note of the fashion to testify.

Pet. Read it.

Gru. The note lies in his throat, if he say I said so.

Tai. *Imprimis, a loose-bodied gown:*

Gru. Master, if ever I said loose-bodied gown, sew me in the skirts of it, and beat me to death with a bottom of brown thread: I said, a gown.

Pet. Proceed.

Tai. *With a small compassed cape:*

Gru. I confess the cape.

Tai. *With a trunk sleeve;*——

Gru. I confess two sleeves.

Tai. *The sleeves curiously cut.*

Pet. Ay, there's the villany.

Gru. Error i' the bill, sir; error i' the bill. I commanded the sleeves should be cut out, and sewed up again; and that I'll prove upon thee, though thy little finger be armed in a thimble.

Tai. This is true, that I say; an I had thee in place where, thou should'st know it.

Gru. I am for thee straight: take thou the bill, give me thy mete-yard, and spare not me.

Hor. God-a-mercy, Grumio! then he shall have no odds.

Pet. Well, sir, in brief, the gown is not for me.

Gru. You are i' the right, sir; 'tis for my mistress.

Pet. Go, take it up unto thy master's use.

Gru. Villain, not for thy life: Take up my mistress' gown for thy master's use!

Pet. Why, sir, what's your conceit in that?

Gru. O, sir, the conceit is deeper than you think for:
Take up my mistress' gown to his master's use!
O, fye, fye, fye!

Pet. Hortensio, say thou wilt see the tailor paid:— [*Aside.*
Go take it hence; be gone, and say no more.

Hor. Tailor, I'll pay thee for thy gown to-morrow.
Take no unkindness of his hasty words:
Away, I say; commend me to thy master.
[*Exit* Tailor.

Pet. Well, come, my Kate; we will unto your father's,
Even in these honest mean habiliments;
Our purses shall be proud, our garments poor;
For 'tis the mind that makes the body rich;
And as the sun breaks through the darkest clouds,
So honour peereth in the meanest habit.
What, is the jay more precious than the lark,
Because his feathers are more beautiful?
Or is the adder better than the eel,
Because his painted skin contents the eye?
O, no, good Kate; neither art thou the worse
For this poor furniture, and mean array.
If thou account'st it shame, lay it on me:
And therefore, frolick; we will hence forthwith,
To feast and sport us at thy father's house.—
Go, call my men, and let us straight to him;
And bring our horses unto Long-lane end,
There will we mount, and thither walk on foot.—
Let's see; I think, 'tis now some seven o'clock,
And well we may come there by dinner time.

Kath. I dare assure you, sir, 'tis almost two;
And 'twill be supper time, ere you come there.

Pet. It shall be seven, ere I go to horse:
Look, what I speak, or do, or think to do,
You are still crossing it.—Sirs, let 't alone:
I will not go to-day; and ere I do,
It shall be what o'clock I say it is.

Hor. Why, so! this gallant will command the sun. [*Exeunt.*

SCENE IV. Padua. *Before* Baptista's *House.*

Enter TRANIO, *and the* Pedant *dressed like* VINCENTIO.

Tra. Sir, this is the house; Please it you, that I call?

Ped. Ay, what else? and, but I be deceived,
Signior Baptista may remember me.
Near twenty years ago, in Genoa, where
We were lodgers at the Pegasus.

Tra. 'Tis well:

And hold your own, in any case, with such
Austerity as 'longeth to a father.

Enter BIONDELLO.

Ped. I warrant you: But, sir, here comes your boy;
'Twere good, he were school'd.

Tra. Fear you not him. Sirrah, Biondello,
Now do your duty throughly, I advise you;
Imagine 'twere the right Vincentio.

Bion. Tut! fear not me.

Tra. But hast thou done thy errand to Baptista?

Bion. I told him, that your father was at Venice;
And that you look'd for him this day in Padua.

Tra. Thou'rt a tall fellow; hold thee that to drink.
Here comes Baptista:—set your countenance, sir.—

Enter BAPTISTA *and* LUCENTIO.

Signior Baptista, you are happily met:—
Sir, [*to the* Pedant.]
This is the gentleman I told you of;
I pray you, stand good father to me now,
Give me Bianca for my patrimony.

Ped. Soft, son!—
Sir, by your leave: having come to Padua
To gather in some debts, my son Lucentio
Made me acquainted with a weighty cause
Of love between your daughter and himself:
And,—for the good report I hear of you;
And for the love he beareth to your daughter,
And she to him,—to stay him not too long
I am content, in a good father's care,
To have him match'd; and,—if you please to like
No worse than I, sir,—upon some agreement,
Me shall you find most ready and most willing
With one consent to have her so bestow'd;
For curious I cannot be with you,
Signior Baptista, of whom I hear so well.

Bap. Sir, pardon me in what I have to say:—
Your plainness, and your shortness, please me well.
Right true it is, your son Lucentio here
Doth love my daughter, and she loveth him,
Or both dissemble deeply their affections:
And, therefore, if you say no more than this,
That like a father you will deal with him,
And pass my daughter a sufficient dower,
The match is fully made, and all is done:
Your son shall have my daughter with consent.

Tra. I thank you, sir. Where then do you know best,
We be affied; and such assurance ta'en,
As shall with either part's agreement stand?

Bap. Not in my house, Lucentio; for, you know,
Pitchers have ears, and I have many servants:
Besides, Old Gremio is hearkening still;
And, happily, we might be interrupted.

Tra. Then at my lodging, an it like you, sir:
There doth my father lie; and there, this night,
We'll pass the business privately and well:
Send for your daughter by your servant here,
My boy shall fetch the scrivener presently.
The worst is this,—that, at so slender warning,
You're like to have a thin and slender pittance.

Bap. It likes me well:—Cambio, hie you home,
And bid Bianca make her ready straight:
And, if you will, tell what hath happened:—
Lucentio's father is arrived in Padua,
And how she's like to be Lucentio's wife.

Luc. I pray the gods she may, with all my heart!

Tra. Dally not with the gods, but get thee gone.
Signior Baptista, shall I lead the way?
Welcome! one mess is like to be your cheer:
Come, sir; we'll better it in Pisa.

Bap. I follow you.

[*Exeunt* TRANIO, Pedant, *and* BAPTISTA.

Bion. Cambio.—

Luc. What say'st thou, Biondello?

Bion. You saw my master wink and laugh upon you?

Luc. Biondello, what of that?

Bion. 'Faith, nothing; but he has left me here behind, to expound the meaning or moral of his signs and tokens.

Luc. I pray thee, moralize them.

Bion. Then thus. Baptista is safe, talking with the deceiving father of a deceitful son.

Luc. And what of him?

Bion. His daughter is to be brought by you to the supper.

Luc. And then?—

Bion. The old priest at St. Luke's church is at your command at all hours.

Luc. And what of all this?

Bion. I cannot tell; except they are busied about a counterfeit assurance: Take you assurance of her, *cum privilegio ad imprimendum solum:* to the church;—take the priest, clerk, and some sufficient honest witnesses:
If this be not that you look for, I have no more to say,
But, bid Bianca farewell for ever and a day.

[*Going.*

Luc. Hear'st thou, Biondello?

Bion. I cannot tarry: I knew a wench married in an afternoon as she went to the garden for parsley to stuff a rabbit; and so may you, sir; and so adieu, sir. My master hath appointed me to go to Saint Luke's, to bid the priest be ready to come against you come with your appendix. [*Exit.*

Luc. I may, and will, if she be so contented:
She will be pleas'd, then wherefore should I doubt?
Hap what hap may, I'll roundly go about her;
It shall go hard, if Cambio go without her.

[*Exit.*

SCENE V. *A publick road.*

Enter PETRUCHIO, KATHARINA, *and* HORTENSIO.

Pet. Come on, o' God's name; once more toward our father's.
Good Lord, how bright and goodly shines the moon!

Kath. The moon! the sun; it is not moonlight now.

Pet. I say, it is the moon that shines so bright.

Kath. I know, it is the sun that shines so bright.

Pet. Now, by my mother's son, and that's myself,
It shall be moon, or star, or what I list,
Or ere I journey to your father's house:—
Go on, and fetch our horses back again.
Evermore cross'd, and cross'd; nothing but cross'd!

Hor. Say as he says, or we shall never go.

Kath. Forward, I pray, since we have come so far,
And be it moon, or sun, or what you please:
And if you please to call it a rush candle,
Henceforth I vow it shall be so for me.

Pet. I say, it is the moon.

Kath. I know, it is the moon.

Pet. Nay, then you lie; it is the blessed sun.

Kath. Then, God be bless'd, it is the blessed sun:—
But sun it is not, when you say it is not;
And the moon changes, even as your mind.
What you will have it nam'd, even that it is;
And so it shall be so, for Katharine.

Hor. Petruchio, go thy ways; the field is won.

Pet. Well, forward, forward: thus the bowl should run,
And not unluckily against the bias.—
But soft; what company is coming here?

Enter VINCENTIO, *in a travelling dress.*

Good-morrow, gentle mistress: Where away?—

[*To* VINCENTIO.

Tell me, sweet Kate, and tell me truly too,

Hast thou beheld a fresher gentlewoman?
Such war of white and red within her cheeks!
What stars do spangle heaven with such beauty,
As those two eyes become that heavenly face?—
Fair lovely maid, once more good day to thee:—
Sweet Kate, embrace her for her beauty's sake.

Hor. 'A will make the man mad, to make a woman of him.

Kath. Young budding virgin, fair, and fresh, and sweet,
Whither away: or where is thy abode?
Happy the parents of so fair a child;
Happier the man, whom favourable stars
Allot thee for his lovely bed-fellow!

Pet. Why, how now, Kate! I hope thou art not mad;
This is a man, old, wrinkled, faded, wither'd;
And not a maiden, as thou say'st he is.

Kath. Pardon, old father, my mistaking eyes,
That have been so bedazzled with the sun,
That every thing I look on seemeth green:
Now I perceive, thou art a reverend father;
Pardon, I pray thee, for my mad mistaking.

Pet. Do, good old grandsire; and, withal, make known
Which way thou travellest: if along with us,
We shall be joyful of thy company.

Vin. Fair sir,—and you, my merry mistress,—
That with your strange encounter much amaz'd me;
My name is call'd—Vincentio; my dwelling—Pisa;
And bound I am to Padua; there to visit
A son of mine, which long I have not seen.

Pet. What is his name?

Vin. Lucentio, gentle sir.

Pet. Happily met; the happier for thy son.
And now by law, as well as reverend age,
I may entitle thee—my loving father;
The sister to my wife, this gentlewoman,
Thy son by this hath married: Wonder not,
Nor be not griev'd; she is of good esteem,
Her dowry wealthy, and of worthy birth;
Beside, so qualified as may beseem
The spouse of any noble gentleman.
Let me embrace with old Vincentio:
And wander we to see thy honest son,
Who will of thy arrival be full joyous.

Vin. But is this true? or is it else your pleasure?
Like pleasant travellers to break a jest
Upon the company you overtake?

Hor. I do assure thee, father, so it is.

Pet. Come, go along, and see the truth hereof;
For our first merriment hath made thee jealous.
[*Exeunt* PET. KATH. *and* VIN.

Hor. Well, Petruchio, this hath put me in heart.
Have to my widow; and if she be forward,
Then hast thou taught Hortensio to be untoward.
[*Exit.*

ACT V.

SCENE I. Padua. *Before* LUCENTIO'S *House.*

Enter on one side BIONDELLO, LUCENTIO, *and* BIANCA; GREMIO *walking on the other side.*

Bion. Softly and swiftly, sir; for the priest is ready.

Luc. I fly, Biondello: but they may chance to need thee at home, therefore leave us.

Bion. Nay, faith, I'll see the church o'your back; and then come back to my master as soon as I can. [*Exeunt* LUC. BIAN. *and* BION.

Gre. I marvel Cambio comes not all this while.

Enter PETRUCHIO, KATHARINA, VINCENTIO, *and* Attendants.

Pet. Sir, here's the door, this is Lucentio's house,
My father's bears more toward the market-place;
Thither must I, and here I leave you, sir.

Vin. You shall not choose but drink before you go;
I think, I shall command your welcome here,
And, by all likelihood, some cheer is toward.
[*Knocks.*

Gre. They're busy within, you were best knock louder.

Enter PEDANT *above at a window.*

Ped. What's he, that knocks as he would beat down the gate?

Vin. Is Signior Lucentio within, sir?

Ped. He's within, sir, but not to be spoken withal.

Vin. What if a man bring him a hundred pound or two, to make merry withal?

Ped. Keep your hundred pounds to yourself; he shall need none, so long as I live.

Pet. Nay, I told you, your son was beloved in Padua.—Do you hear, sir?—to leave frivolous circumstances,—I pray you, tell Signior Lucentio, that his father is come from Pisa, and is here at the door to speak with him.

Ped. Thou liest; his father is come from Pisa, and here looking out at the window.

Vin. Art thou his father?

Ped. Ay, sir; so his mother says, if I may believe her.

Pet. Why, how now, gentleman! [To VINCEN.] why, this is flat knavery, to take upon you another man's name.

Ped. Lay hands on the villain; I believe 'a means to cozen somebody in this city under my countenance.

Re-enter BIONDELLO.

Bion. I have seen them in the church together: God send 'em good shipping!—But who is here? mine old master, Vincentio? now we are undone, and brought to nothing.

Vin. Come hither, crack-hemp.
[*Seeing* BIONDELLO.

Bion. I hope I may choose, sir.

Vin. Come hither, you rogue: What, have you forgot me?

Bion. Forgot you? no, sir: I could not forget you, for I never saw you before in all my life.

Vin. What, you notorious villain, didst thou never see thy master's father, Vincentio?

Bion. What, my old, worshipful old master? yes, marry, sir; see where he looks out of the window.

Vin. Is't so, indeed? [*Beats* BIONDELLO.

Bion. Help, help, help! here's a madman will murder me. [*Exit.*

Ped. Help, son! help, Signior Baptista!
[*Exit, from the window.*

Pet. 'Pr'ythee, Kate, let's stand aside, and see the end of this controversy. [*They retire.*

Re-enter Pedant *below;* BAPTISTA, TRANIO, *and* Servants.

Tra. Sir, what are you that offer to beat my servant?

Vin. What am I, sir? nay, what are you, sir?—O immortal gods! O fine villain! A silken doublet! a velvet hose! a scarlet cloak! and a copatain hat!—O, I am undone! I am undone! while I play the good husband at home, my son and my servant spend all at the university.

Tra. How now, what's the matter?

Bap. What, is the man lunatick?

Tra. Sir, you seem a sober ancient gentleman by your habit, but your words show you a madman: Why, sir, what concerns it you, if I wear pearl and gold? I thank my good father, I am able to maintain it.

Vin. Thy father? O, villain! he is a sailmaker in Bergamo.

Bap. You mistake, sir; you mistake, sir: Pray, what do you think is his name?

Vin. His name? as if I knew not his name:

I have brought him up ever since he was three years old, and his name is—Tranio.

Ped. Away, away, mad ass! his name is Lucentio; and he is mine only son, and heir to the lands of me, Signior Vincentio.

Vin. Lucentio! O, he hath murdered his master!—Lay hold on him, I charge you, in the duke's name:—O, my son, my son!—tell me, thou villain, where is my son Lucentio?

Tra. Call forth an officer: [*Enter one with an* Officer.] carry this mad knave to the gaol:—Father Baptista, I charge you see that he be forthcoming.

Vin. Carry me to the gaol!

Gre. Stay, officer; he shall not go to prison.

Bap. Talk not, signior Gremio; I say, he shall go to prison.

Gre. Take heed, Signior Baptista, lest you be coney-catched in this business; I dare swear, this is the right Vincentio.

Ped. Swear, if thou darest.

Gre. Nay, I dare not swear it.

Tra. Then thou wert best say, that I am not Lucentio.

Gre. Yes, I know thee to be Signior Lucentio.

Bap. Away with the dotard; to the gaol with him.

Vin. Thus strangers may be haled and abused:—
O monstrous villain!

Re-enter BIONDELLO, *with* LUCENTIO, *and* BIANCA.

Bion. O, we are spoiled, and—Yonder he is; deny him, forswear him, or else we are all undone.

Luc. Pardon, sweet father. [*Kneeling.*

Vin. Lives my sweetest son?

[BIONDELLO, TRANIO, *and* Pedant *run out.*

Bian. Pardon, dear father. [*Kneeling.*

Bap. How hast thou offended?
Where is Lucentio?

Luc. Here's Lucentio,
Right son unto the right Vincentio;
That have by marriage made thy daughter mine,
While counterfeit supposes blear'd thine eyne.

Gre. Here's packing, with a witness, to deceive us all!

Vin. Where is that damned villain, Tranio,
That fac'd and brav'd me in this matter so?

Bap. Why, tell me, is not this my Cambio?

Bian. Cambio is chang'd into Lucentio.

Luc. Love wrought these miracles. Bianca's love
Made me exchange my state with Tranio,
While he did bear my countenance in the town;
And happily I have arrived at last
Unto the wished haven of my bliss:—
What Tranio did, myself enforc'd him to;
Then pardon him, sweet father, for my sake.

Vin. I'll slit the villain's nose, that would have sent me to the gaol.

Bap. But do you hear, sir? [*To* LUCENTIO.] Have you married my daughter without asking my good-will?

Vin. Fear not, Baptista; we will content you, go to: But I will in, to be revenged for this villany. [*Exit.*

Bap. And I, to sound the depth of this knavery. [*Exit.*

Luc. Look not pale, Bianca; thy father will not frown. [*Exeunt* LUC. *and* BIAN.

Gre. My cake is dough: But I'll in among the rest:
Out of hope of all,—but my share of the feast. [*Exit.*

PETRUCHIO *and* KATHARINA *advance.*

Kath. Husband, let's follow, to see the end of this ado.

Pet. First kiss me, Kate, and we will.

Kath. What, in the midst of the street?

Pet. What, art thou ashamed of me?

Kath. No, sir; God forbid:—but ashamed to kiss.

Pet. Why, then let's home again:—Come, sirrah, let's away.

Kath. Nay, I will give thee a kiss: now, 'pray thee, love, stay.

Pet. Is not this well?—Come, my sweet Kate;
Better once than never, for never too late.
[*Exeunt.*

SCENE II.

A Room in Lucentio's *House. A Banquet set out.*

Enter BAPTISTO, VINCENTIO, GREMIO, *the* Pedant, LUCENTIO, BIANCA, PETRUCHIO, KATHARINA, HORTENSIO, *and* Widow. TRANIO, BIONDELLO, GRUMIO, *and others attending.*

Luc. At last, though long, our jarring notes agree;
And time it is, when raging war is done,
To smile at 'scapes and perils overblown.—
My fair Bianca, bid my father welcome,
While I with selfsame kindness welcome thine:—
Brother Petruchio,—sister Katharina,
And thou, Hortensio, with thy loving widow,—
Feast with the best, and welcome to my house:
My banquet is to close our stomachs up,
After our great good cheer: 'Pray you, sit down;
For now we sit to chat, as well as eat.
[*They sit at table.*

Pet. Nothing but sit and sit, and eat and eat!

Bap. Padua affords this kindness, son Petruchio.

Pet. Padua affords nothing but what is kind.

Hor. For both our sakes, I would that word were true.

Pet. Now, for my life, Hortensio fears his widow.

Wid. Then never trust me if I be afeard.

Pet. You are sensible, and yet you miss my sense;
I mean, Hortensio is afeard of you.

Wid. He that is giddy, thinks the world turns round.

Pet. Roundly replied.

Kath. Mistress, how mean you that?

Wid. Thus I conceive by him.

Pet. Conceives by me!—How likes Hortensio that?

Hor. My widow says, thus she conceives her tale.

Pet. Very well mended: Kiss him for that, good widow.

Kath. He that is giddy, thinks the world turns round:——
I pray you, tell me what you meant by that.

Wid. Your husband, being troubled with a shrew,
Measures my husband's sorrow by his woe:
And now you know my meaning.

Kath. A very mean meaning.

Wid. Right, I mean you.

Kath. And I am mean indeed, respecting you.

Pet. To her, Kate!

Hor. To her, widow!

Pet. A hundred marks, my Kate does put her down.

Hor. That's my office.

Pet. Spoke like an officer:—Ha' to thee, lad.
[*Drinks to* HORTENSIO.

Bap. How likes Gremio these quick-witted folks?

Gre. Believe me, sir, they butt together well.

Bian. Head, and butt? a hasty witted body
Would say, your head and butt were head and horn.

Vin. Ay, mistress bride, hath that awaken'd you?

Bian. Ay, but not frighted me; therefore I'll sleep again.

Pet. Nay, that you shall not: since you have begun,
Have at you for a bitter jest or two.
Bian. Am I your bird? I mean to shift my bush,
And then pursue me as you draw your bow:—
You are welcome all.
[*Exeunt* BIANCA, KATHARINA, *and* Widow.
Pet. She hath prevented me.—Here, Signior Tranio,
This bird you aim'd at, though you hit her not;
Therefore, a health to all that shot and miss'd.
Tra. O, sir, Lucentio slipp'd me like his greyhound,
Which runs himself, and catches for his master.
Pet. A good swift simile, but something currish.
Tra. 'Tis well, sir, that you hunted for yourself;
'Tis thought, your deer does hold you out a bay.
Bap. O ho, Petruchio, Tranio hits you now.
Luc. I thank thee for that gird, good Tranio.
Hor. Confess, confess, hath he not hit you here?
Pet. 'A has a little gall'd me, I confess;
And, as the jest did glance away from me,
'Tis ten to one it maim'd you two outright.
Bap. Now, in good sadness, son Petruchio,
I think thou hast the veriest shrew of all.
Pet. Well, I say—no; and therefore, for assurance,
Let's each one send unto his wife;
And he, whose wife is most obedient
To come at first when he doth send for her,
Shall win the wager which we will propose.
Hor. Content:——What is the wager?
Luc. Twenty crowns.
Pet. Twenty crowns!
I'll venture so much on my hawk, or hound,
But twenty times so much upon my wife.
Luc. A hundred then.
Hor. Content.
Pet. A match; 'tis done.
Hor. Who shall begin?
Luc. That will I. Go,
Biondello, bid your mistress come to me.
Bion. I go. [*Exit.*
Bap. Son, I will be your half, Bianca comes.
Luc. I'll have no halves; I'll bear it all myself.

Re-enter BIONDELLO.

How now! what news?
Bion. Sir, my mistress sends you word
That she is busy, and she cannot come.
Pet. How! she is busy, and she cannot come!
Is that an answer?
Gre. Ay, and a kind one too:
Pray God, sir, your wife send you not a worse.
Pet. I hope, better.
Hor. Sirrah, Biondello, go, and entreat my wife
To come to me forthwith. [*Exit* BIONDELLO.
Pet. O, ho! entreat her!
Nay, then she must needs come.
Hor. I am afraid, sir,
Do what you can, yours will not be entreated.

Re-enter BIONDELLO.

Now where's my wife?
Bion. She says, you have some goodly jest in hand;
She will not come; she bids you come to her.
Pet. Worse and worse; she will not come! O vile,
Intolerable, not to be endur'd!
Sirrah, Grumio, go to your mistress;
Say, I command her come to me.
[*Exit* GRUMIO.
Hor. I know her answer.
Pet. What?
Hor. She will not come.
Pet. The fouler fortune mine; and there an end.

Enter KATHARINA.

Bap. Now, by my holidame, here comes Katharina!
Kath. What is your will, sir, that you send for me?
Pet. Where is your sister, and Hortensio's wife?
Kath. They sit conferring by the parlour fire.
Pet. Go fetch them hither; if they deny to come,
Swinge me them soundly forth unto their husbands:
Away, I say, and bring them hither straight.
[*Exit* KATHARINA.
Luc. Here is a wonder, if you talk of a wonder.
Hor. And so it is; I wonder what it bodes.
Pet. Marry, peace it bodes, and love, and quiet life,
An awful rule, and right supremacy;
And, to be short, what not, that's sweet and happy.
Bap. Now fair befall thee, good Petruchio!
The wager thou hast won; and I will add
Unto their losses twenty thousand crowns;
Another dowry to another daughter,
For she is chang'd, as she had never been.
Pet. Nay, I will win my wager better yet;
And show more sign of her obedience,
Her new-built virtue and obedience.

Re-enter KATHARINA, *with* BIANCA, *and* Widow.

See, where she comes; and brings your froward wives
As prisoners to her womanly persuasion.—
Katharine, that cap of yours becomes you not;
Off with that bauble, throw it under foot.
[KATHARINA *pulls off her cap, and throws it down.*
Wid. Lord, let me never have a cause to sigh,
Till I be brought to such a silly pass!
Bian. Fye! what a foolish duty call you this?
Luc. I would, your duty were as foolish too:
The wisdom of your duty, fair Bianca,
Hast cost me a hundred crowns since supper-time.
Bian. The more fool you for laying on my duty.
Pet. Katharine, I charge thee, tell these headstrong women
What duty they do owe their lords and husbands.
Wid. Come, come, you're mocking; we will have no telling.
Pet. Come on, I say; and first begin with her.
Wid. She shall not.
Pet. I say, she shall;—and first begin with her.
Kath. Fye, fye! unknit that threat'ning unkind brow;
And dart not scornful glances from those eyes,
To wound thy lord, thy king, thy governor:
It blots thy beauty, as frosts do bite the meads;
Confounds thy fame, as whirlwinds shake fair buds;
And in no sense is meet or amiable,
A woman mov'd, is like a fountain troubled,
Muddy, ill seeming, thick, bereft of beauty;
And, while it is so, none so dry or thirsty
Will deign to sip, or touch one drop of it.
Thy husband is thy lord, thy life, thy keeper,
Thy head, thy sovereign; one that cares for thee,
And for thy maintenance: commits his body
To painful labour, both by sea and land;
To watch the night in storms, the day in cold,
While thou liest warm at home, secure and safe;
And craves no other tribute at thy hands,
But love, fair looks, and true obedience;—
Too little payment for so great a debt.
Such duty as the subject owes the prince,
Even such a woman oweth to her husband:
And, when she's froward, peevish, sullen, sour,
And, not obedient to his honest will,
What is she, but a foul contending rebel,
And graceless traitor to her loving lord?
I am asham'd, that women are so simple

To offer war, where they should kneel for peace,
Or seek for rule, supremacy, and sway,
When they are bound to serve, love, and obey.
Why are our bodies soft, and weak, and smooth,
Unapt to toil and trouble in the world;
But that our soft conditions and our hearts
Should well agree with our external parts?
Come, come, you froward and unable worms!
My mind hath been as big as one of yours,
My heart as great; my reason, haply, more,
To bandy word for word, and frown for frown:
But now, I see, our lances are but straws;
Our strength as weak, our weakness past compare,—
That seeming to be most, which we least are.
Then vail your stomachs, for it is no boot;
And place your hands below your husband's foot:
In token of which duty, if he please,
My hand is ready, may it do him ease.

Pet. Why, there's a wench!—Come on, and kiss me, Kate.

Luc. Well, go thy ways, old lad; for thou shalt ha't.

Vin. 'Tis a good hearing, when children are toward.

Luc. But a harsh hearing when women are froward.

Pet. Come, Kate, we'll to bed:—
We three are married, but you two are sped.
'Twas I won the wager, though you hit the white; [*To* LUCENTIO.
And, being a winner, God give you good night!
[*Exeunt* PETRUCHIO *and* KATH.

Hor. Now go thy ways, thou hast tam'd a curst shrew.

Luc. 'Tis a wonder, by your leave, she will be tam'd so. [*Exeunt.*

WINTER'S TALE.

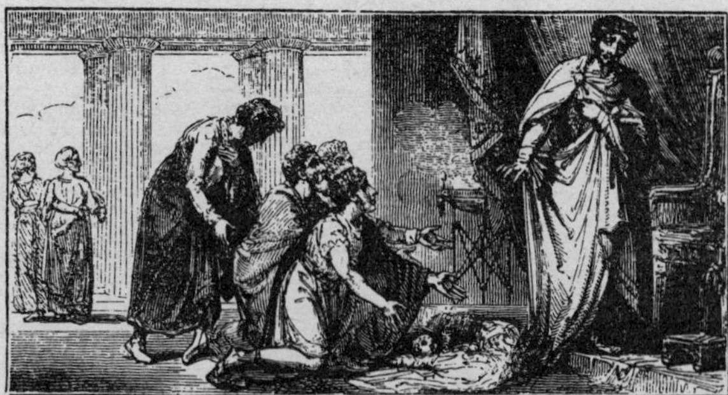

PERSONS REPRESENTED.

LEONTES, *King of* Sicilia.
MAMILLIUS, *his Son.*
CAMILLO, ANTIGONUS, CLEOMENES, DION, } Sicilian *Lords.*
Another Sicilian Lord.
ROGERO, *a* Sicilian *Gentleman.*
An Attendant *on the young* Prince Mamillius.
Officers *of a Court of Judicature.*
POLIXENES, *King of* Bohemia.
FLORIZEL, *his Son.*
ARCHIDAMUS, *a* Bohemian *Lord.*
A Mariner.
Gaoler.
An old Shepherd, *reputed Father of* Perdita.
Clown, *his Son.*
Servant *to the old Shepherd.*
AUTOLYCUS, *a Rogue.*
Time, *as Chorus.*

HERMIONE, *Queen to* Leontes.
PERDITA, *Daughter to* Leontes *and* Hermione.
PAULINA, *Wife to* Antigonus.
EMILIA, *a Lady,* Two other Ladies, } *attending the Queen.*
MOPSA, DORCAS, } *Shepherdesses.*

Lords, Ladies, *and* Attendants; Satyrs *for a Dance;* Shepherds, Shepherdesses, Guards, *&c.*

SCENE—*sometimes in* Sicilia, *sometimes in* Bohemia.

ACT I.

SCENE I.

Sicilia. *An Antichamber in* Leontes' *Palace.*
Enter CAMILLO *and* ARCHIDAMUS.

Arch. IF you shall chance, Camillo, to visit Bohemia, on the like occasion whereon my services are now on foot, you shall see, as I have said, great difference betwixt our Bohemia, and your Sicilia.

Cam. I think, this coming summer, the King of Sicilia means to pay Bohemia the visitation which he justly owes him.

Arch. Wherein our entertainment shall shame us, we will be justified in our loves: for, indeed,—

Cam. Beseech you,——

Arch. Verily, I speak it in the freedom of my knowledge: we cannot with such magnificence —in so rare—I know not what to say.——We will give you sleepy drinks: that your senses, unintelligent of our insufficience, may, though they cannot praise us, as little accuse us.

Cam. You pay a great deal too dear for what's given freely.

Arch. Believe me, I speak as my understanding instructs me, and as mine honesty puts it to utterance.

Cam. Sicilia cannot show himself over-kind

to Bohemia. They were trained together in their childhoods; and there rooted betwixt them then such an affection, which cannot choose but branch now. Since their more mature dignities, and royal necessities, made separation of their society, their encounters, though not personal, have been royally attornied, with interchange of gifts, letters, loving embassies; that they have seemed to be together, though absent; shook hands, as over a vast; and embraced, as it were, from the ends of opposed winds. The heavens continue their loves!

Arch. I think, there is not in the world either malice, or matter, to alter it. You have an unspeakable comfort of your young prince Mamillius; it is a gentleman of the greatest promise, that ever came into my note.

Cam. I very well agree with you in the hopes of him: it is a gallant child; one that, indeed, physics the subject, makes old hearts fresh: they, that went on crutches ere he was born, desire yet their life, to see him a man.

Arch. Would they else be content to die?

Cam. Yes; if there were no other excuse why they should desire to live.

Arch. If the king had no son, they would desire to live on crutches till he had one. [*Exeunt.*

SCENE II.

The same. A Room of State in the Palace.

Enter LEONTES, POLIXENES, HERMIONE, MAMILLIUS, CAMILLO, *and* Attendants.

Pol. Nine changes of the wat'ry star have been
The shepherd's note, since we have left our throne
Without a burden: time as long again
Would be fill'd up, my brother, with our thanks:
And yet we should, for perpetuity,
Go hence in debt: And therefore, like a cipher,
Yet standing in rich place, I multiply,
With one we-thank-you, many thousands more
That go before it.

Leon. Stay your thanks awhile;
And pay them when you part.

Pol. Sir, that's to-morrow.
I am question'd by my fears, of what may chance,
Or breed upon our absence: That may blow
No sneaping winds at home, to make us say,
This is put forth too truly! Besides, I have stay'd
To tire your royalty.

Leon. We are tougher, brother,
Than you can put us to't.

Pol. No longer stay.

Leon. One seven-night longer.

Pol. Very sooth, to-morrow.

Leon. We'll part the time between's then: and in that
I'll no gainsaying.

Pol. Press me not, 'beseech you, so;
There is no tongue that moves, none, none i' the world,
So soon as yours, could win me: so it should now,
Were there necessity in your request, although
'Twere needful I denied it. My affairs
Do even drag me homeward: which to hinder
Were, in your love, a whip to me; my stay,
To you a charge and trouble: to save both,
Farewell, our brother.

Leon. Tongue-tied, our queen? speak you.

Her. I had thought, sir, to have held my peace, until
You had drawn oaths from him, not to stay. You, sir,
Charge him too coldly: Tell him, you are sure,
All in Bohemia's well: this satisfaction
The by-gone day proclaim'd; say this to him,
He's beat from his best ward.

Leon. Well said, Hermione.

Her. To tell, he longs to see his son, were strong:
But let him say so then, and let him go;
But let him swear so, and he shall not stay,
We'll thwack him hence with distaffs.—
Yet of your royal presence [*To* POLIXENES] I'll adventure
The borrow of a week. When at Bohemia
You take my lord, I'll give him my commission,
To let him there a month, behind the gest
Prefix'd for his parting: yet good deed, Leontes,
I love thee not a jar o' the clock behind
What lady she her lord.—You'll stay?

Pol. No, madam.

Her. Nay, but you will?

Pol. I may not, verily.

Her. Verily!
You put me off with limber vows: But I,
Though you would seek to unsphere the stars with oaths,
Should yet say, *Sir, no going.* Verily,
You shall not go; a lady's verily is
As potent as a lord's. Will you go yet?
Force me to keep you as a prisoner,
Not like a guest; so you shall pay your fees,
When you depart, and save your thanks. How say you?
My prisoner? or my guest? by your dread verily,
One of them you shall be.

Pol. Your guest then, madam:
To be your prisoner, should import offending;
Which is for me less easy to commit,
Than you to punish.

Her. Not your gaoler then,
But your kind hostess. Come, I'll question you
Of my lord's tricks, and yours, when you were boys;
You were pretty lordlings then.

Pol. We were, fair queen,
Two lads that thought there was no more behind,
But such a day to-morrow as to-day,
And to be boy eternal.

Her. Was not my lord the verier wag o' the two?

Pol. We were as twinn'd lambs, that did frisk i' the sun,
And bleat the one at the other: what we chang'd,
Was innocence for innocence; we knew not
The doctrine of ill doing, no, nor dream'd
That any did: Had we pursued that life,
And our weak spirits ne'er been higher rear'd
With stronger blood, we should have answer'd heaven
Boldly, *Not Guilty;* the imposition clear'd,
Hereditary ours.

Her. By this we gather,
You have tripp'd since.

Pol. O my most sacred lady,
Temptations have since then been born to us: for
In those unfledg'd days was my wife a girl;
Your precious self had then not cross'd the eyes
Of my young play-fellow.

Her. Grace to boot!
Of this make no conclusion; lest you say,
Your queen and I are devils: Yet, go on;
The offences we have made you do, we'll answer;
If you first sinn'd with us, and that with us
You did continue fault, and that you slipp'd not
With any but with us.

Leon. Is he won yet?

Her. He'll stay, my lord.

Leon. At my request, he would not.
Hermione, my dearest, thou never spok'st
To better purpose.

Her. Never?

Leon. Never, but once.

Her. What? have I twice said well? when was't before?
I pr'ythee, tell me: Cram us with praise and make us
As fat as tame things: One good deed, dying tongueless,
Slaughters a thousand, waiting upon that.

Our praises are our wages: You may ride us,
With one soft kiss, a thousand furlongs, ere
With spur we heat an acre. But to the goal;—
My last good was, to entreat his stay;
What was my first it has an elder sister,
Or I mistake you: O, 'would, her name were Grace!
But once before I spoke to the purpose: When?
Nay, let me hav't; I long.

Leon. Why, that was when
Three crabbed months had sour'd themselves to death,
Ere I could make thee open thy white hand,
And clap thyself my love: then didst thou utter,
I am yours for ever.

Her. It is grace, indeed.—
Why, lo you now, I have spoke to the purpose twice:
The one for ever earn'd a royal husband;
The other, for some while a friend.

[*Giving her hand to* POLIXENES.

Leon. Too hot, too hot: [*Aside.*
To mingle friendship far, is mingling bloods.
I have *tremor cordis* on me:—my heart dances;
But not for joy,—not joy.—This entertainment
May a free face put on; derive a liberty
From heartiness, from bounty, fertile bosom,
And well become the agent: it may, I grant:
But to be paddling palms, and pinching fingers,
As now they are: and making practis'd smiles,
As in a looking-glass;—and then to sigh, as 'twere
The mort o' the deer; O, that is entertainment
My bosom likes not, nor my brows.—Mamilius,
Art thou my boy?

Mam. Ay, my good lord.

Leon. I'fecks?
Why, that's my bawcock. What, hast smutch'd thy nose?—
They say, it's a copy out of mine. Come captain,
We must be neat; not neat, but cleanly, captain:
And yet the steer, the heifer, and the calf,
Are all call'd, neat.—Still virginalling

[*Observing* POLIXENES *and* HERMIONE.
Upon his palm? How now, you wanton calf?
Art thou my calf?

Mam. Yes, if you will, my lord.

Leon. Thou want'st a rough pash, and the shoots that I have,
To be full like me: yet, they say, we are
Almost as like as eggs; women say so,
That will say any thing: But were they false
As o'er-dyed blacks, as wind, as waters; false
As dice are to be wish'd, by one that fixes
No bourn 'twixt his and mine; yet were it true
To say this boy were like me.—Come, sir page,
Look on me with your welkin eye: Sweet villain!
Most dear'st! my collop!—Can thy dam?—may't be?
Affection! thy intention stabs the centre:
Thou dost make possible, things not so held;
Communicat'st with dreams;—(How can this be?)—
With what's unreal thou coactive art,
And fellow'st nothing: Then, 'tis very credent,
Thou may'st conjoin with something; and thou dost;
(And that beyond commission, and I find it;)
And that to the infection of my brains,
And hardening of my brows.

Pol. What means Sicilia?

Her. He something seems unsettled.

Pol. How, my lord?
What cheer? how is't with you, best brother?

Her. You look,
As if you held a brow of much distraction:
Are you mov'd, my lord?

Leon. No, in good earnest.—
How sometimes nature will betray its folly,
Its tenderness, and make itself a pastime
To harder bosoms! Looking on the lines
Of my boy's face, methought I did recoil
Twenty-three years; and saw myself unbreech'd,
In my green velvet coat; my dagger muzzled,
Lest it should bite its master, and so prove,
As ornaments oft do, too dangerous.
How like, methought, I then was to this kernel,
This squash, this gentleman:—Mine honest friend,
Will you take eggs for money?

Mam. No, my lord, I'll fight.

Leon. You will? why, happy man be his dole!—My brother,
Are you so fond of your young prince, as we
Do seem to be of ours?

Pol. If at home, sir,
He's all my exercise, my mirth my matter:
Now my sworn friend, and then mine enemy;
My parasite, my soldier, statesman, all:
He makes a July's day short as December;
And, with his varying childness, cures in me
Thoughts that would thick my blood.

Leon. So stands this squire
Offic'd with me: We too will walk, my lord,
And leave you to your graver steps.—Hermione,
How thou lov'st us, show in our brother's welcome;
Let what is dear in Sicily be cheap:
Next to thyself, and my young rover, he's
Apparent to my heart.

Her. If you would seek us,
We are yours i' the garden; Shall's attend you there?

Leon. To your own bents dispose you: you'll be found,
Be you beneath the sky:—I am angling now,
Though you perceive me not how I give line.
Go to, go to! [*Aside. Observing* POL. *and* HER.
How she holds up the neb, the bill to him!
And arms her with the boldness of a wife
To her allowing husband! Gone already!
Inch-thick, knee-deep, o'er head and ears a fork'd one——

[*Exeunt* POL. HER. *and* Attendants.
Go, play, boy, play;—thy mother plays, and I
Play too; but so disgrac'd a part, whose issue
Will hiss me to my grave; contempt and clamour
Will be my knell.—Go, play, boy, play.—There have been,
Or I am much deceiv'd, cuckolds ere now;
And many a man there is, even at this present,
Now, while I speak this, holds his wife by the arm,
That little thinks, she has been sluic'd in his absence,
And his pond fish'd by his next neighbour, by
Sir Smile, his neighbour: nay, there's comfort in't,
Whiles other men have gates; and those gates open'd,
As mine, against their will: Should all despair,
That have revolted wives, the tenth of mankind
Would hang themselves. Physick for't there is none;
It is a bawdy planet, that will strike
Where 'tis predominant; and 'tis powerful, think it,
From east, west, north, and south: Be it concluded,
No barricado for a belly; know it;
It will let in and out the enemy,
With bag and baggage: many a thousand of us
Have the disease, and feel't not.—How now, boy?

Mam. I am like you, they say.

Leon. Why that's some comfort.—
What! Camillo there?

Cam. Ay, my good lord.

Leon. Go play, Mamillius; thou'rt an honest man.— [*Exit* MAMILLIUS.
Camillo, this great sir will yet stay longer.

Cam. You had much ado to make his anchor hold:
When you cast out, it still came home.

Leon. Didst note it?

Cam. He would not stay at your petitions; made
His business more material.
Leon. Didst perceive it?—
They're here with me already: whispering, rounding,
Sicilia is a so-forth: 'Tis far gone,
When I shall gust it last.—How came't, Camillo,
That he did stay?
Cam. At the good queen's entreaty.
Leon. At the queen's, be't: good, should be pertinent;
But so it is, it is not. Was this taken
By any understanding pate but thine?
For thy conceit is soaking, will draw in
More than the common blocks:—Not noted, is't,
But of the finer natures? by some severals,
Of head-piece extraordinary? lower messes,
Perchance, are to this business purblind: say.
Cam. Business, my lord? I think, most understand
Bohemia stays here longer.
Leon. Ha?
Cam. Stays here longer.
Leon. Ay, but why?
Cam. To satisfy your highness, and the entreaties
Of our most gracious mistress.
Leon. Satisfy
The entreaties of your mistress?——Satisfy?—
Let that suffice. I have trusted thee, Camillo,
With all the nearest things to my heart, as well
My chamber-councils: wherein, priestlike, thou
Hast cleans'd my bosom; I from thee departed
Thy penitent reform'd: but we have been
Deceiv'd in thy integrity, deceiv'd
In that which seems so.
Cam. Be it forbid, my lord!
Leon. To bide upon't:—Thou art not honest: or,
If thou inclin'st that way, thou art a coward;
Which hoxes honesty behind, restraining
From course requir'd: or else thou must be counted
A servant, grafted in my serious trust,
And therein negligent; or else a fool,
That seest a game play'd home, the rich stake drawn,
And tak'st it all for jest.
Cam. My gracious lord,
I may be negligent, foolish, and fearful;
In every one of these no man is free,
But that his negligence, his folly, fear,
Amongst the infinite doings of the world,
Sometime puts forth: In your affairs, my lord,
If ever I were wilful-negligent,
It was my folly; if industriously
I play'd the fool, it was my negligence,
Not weighing well the end; if ever fearful
To do a thing, where I the issue doubted,
Whereof the execution did cry out
Against the non-performance, 'twas a fear
Which oft affects the wisest: these, my lord,
Are such allow'd infirmities, that honesty
Is never free of. But, 'beseech your grace,
Be plainer with me; let me know my trespass
By its own visage: if I then deny it,
'Tis none of mine.
Leon. Have not you seen, Camillo,
(But that's past doubt: you have; or your eye-glass
Is thicker than a cuckold's horn); or heard,
(For, to a vision so apparent, rumour
Cannot be mute), or thought,—(for cogitation
Resides not in that man, that does not think it)—
My wife is slippery? If thou wilt confess,
(Or else be impudently negative,
To have nor eyes, nor ears, nor thought), then say,
My wife's a hobby-horse; deserves a name
As rank as any flax-wench, that puts to
Before her troth-plight: say it, and justify it.
Cam. I would not be a stander-by, to hear
My sovereign mistress clouded so, without
My present vengeance taken: 'Shrew my heart,
You never spoke what did become you less
Than this, which to reiterate, were sin
As deep as that, though true.
Leon. Is whispering nothing?
Is leaning cheek to cheek? is meeting noses?
Kissing with inside lip? stopping the career
Of laughter with a sigh? (a note infallible
Of breaking honesty:) horsing foot on foot?
Skulking in corners? wishing clocks more swift?
Hours, minutes? noon, midnight? and all eyes blind
With pin and web, but theirs, theirs only,
That would unseen be wicked? is this nothing?
Why then, the world, and all that's in't, is nothing;
The covering sky is nothing; Bohemia nothing;
My wife is nothing; nor nothing have these nothings,
If this be nothing.
Cam. Good my lord, be cur'd
Of this diseas'd opinion, and betimes;
For 'tis most dangerous.
Leon. Say, it be; 'tis true.
Cam. No, no, my lord.
Leon. It is: you lie, you lie:
I say, thou liest, Camillo, and I hate thee:
Pronounce thee a gross lout, a mindless slave;
Or else a hovering temporizer, that
Canst with thine eyes at once see good and evil,
Inclining to them both: Were my wife's liver
Infected as her life, she would not live
The running of one glass.
Cam. Who does infect her?
Leon. Why he, that wears her like his medal, hanging
About his neck, Bohemia: Who—if I
Had servants true about me: that bare eyes
To see alike mine honour as their profits,
Their own particular thrifts,—they would do that
Which should undo more doing: Ay, and thou,
His cup-bearer,—whom I from meaner form
Have bench'd, and rear'd to worship; who may'st see
Plainly, as heaven sees earth, and earth sees heaven,
How I am galled,—might'st bespice a cup,
To give mine enemy a lasting wink;
Which draught to me were cordial.
Cam. Sir, my lord,
I could do this: and that with no rash potion,
But with a ling'ring dram, that should not work
Maliciously like poison: But I cannot
Believe this crack to be in my dread mistress,
So sovereignly being honourable.
I have lov'd thee,——
Leon. Make't thy question, and go rot!
Dost think, I am so muddy, so unsettled,
To appoint myself in this vexation? sully
The purity and whiteness of my sheets,
Which to preserve, is sleep; which being spotted,
Is goads, thorns, nettles, tails of wasps?
Give scandal to the blood o' the prince my son,
Who, I do think is mine, and love as mine;
Without ripe moving to't? Would I do this?
Could man so blench?
Cam. I must believe you, sir;
I do: and will fetch off Bohemia for't;
Provided, that when he's remov'd, your highness
Will take again your queen, as yours at first;
Even for your son's sake; and, thereby, for sealing
The injury of tongues in courts and kingdoms
Known and allied to yours.
Leon. Thou dost advise me,
Even so as I mine own course have set down:
I'll give no blemish to her honour, none.
Cam. My lord,
Go then; and with a countenance as clear

As friendship wears at feasts, keep with Bohemia,
And with your queen: I am his cupbearer;
If from me he have wholesome beverage,
Account me not your servant.
Leon. This is all:
Do 't and thou hast the one half of my heart;
Do 't not, thou split'st thine own.
Cam. I'll do 't, my lord.
Leon. I will seem friendly, as thou hast advis'd me. [*Exit.*
Cam. O miserable lady!—But, for me,
What case stand I in? I must be the poisoner
Of good Polixenes: and my ground to do 't
Is the obedience to a master; one,
Who, in rebellion with himself, will have
All that are his, so too.—To do this deed,
Promotion follows: If I could find example
Of thousands, that had struck anointed kings,
And flourish'd after, I 'd not do 't: but since
Nor brass, nor stone, nor parchment, bears not one,
Let villany itself forswear 't. I must
Forsake the court: to do 't, or no, is certain
To me a break-neck. Happy star, reign now!
Here comes Bohemia.

Enter POLIXENES.

Pol. This is strange! methinks,
My favour here begins to warp. Not speak?——
Good-day, Camillo.
Cam. Hail, most royal sir!
Pol. What is the news i' the court?
Cam. None rare, my lord.
Pol. The king hath on him such a countenance,
As he had lost some province, and a region,
Lov'd as he loves himself: even now I met him
With customary compliment; when he,
Wafting his eyes to the contrary, and falling
A lip of much contempt, speeds from me; and
So leaves me, to consider what is breeding,
That changes thus his manners.
Cam. I dare not know, my lord.
Pol. How! dare not? do not. Do you know, and dare not
Be intelligent to me? 'Tis thereabouts;
For, to yourself, what you do know, you must;
And cannot say, you dare not. Good Camillo,
Your chang'd complexions are to me a mirror,
Which shows me mine chang'd too: for I must be
A party in this alteration, finding
Myself thus alter'd with it.
Cam. There is a sickness
Which puts some of us in distemper; but
I cannot name the disease; and it is caught
Of you that yet are well.
Pol. How! caught of me?
Make me not sighted like the basilisk:
I have look'd on thousands, who have sped the better
By my regard, but kill'd none so. Camillo,——
As you are certainly a gentleman; thereto
Clerk-like, experienc'd, which no less adorns
Our gentry, than our parents' noble names,
In whose success we are gentle,—I beseech you,
If you know aught which does behove my knowledge
Thereof to be inform'd, imprison it not
In ignorant concealment.
Cam. I may not answer.
Pol. A sickness caught of me, and yet I well!
I must be answer'd.—Dost thou hear, Camillo,
I conjure thee, by all the parts of man,
Which honour does acknowledge,—whereof the least
Is not this suit of mine,—that thou declare
What incidency thou dost guess of harm
Is creeping toward me; how far off, how near;
Which way to be prevented, if to be;
If not, how best to bear it.
Cam. Sir, I'll tell you;
Since I am charg'd in honour, and by him
That I think honourable: Therefore, mark my counsel;
Which must be even as swiftly follow'd, as
I mean to utter it; or both yourself and me
Cry, *lost*, and so good-night.
Pol. On, good Camillo.
Cam. I am appointed him to murder you.
Pol. By whom, Camillo?
Cam. By the king.
Pol. For what?
Cam. He thinks, nay, with all confidence he swears,
As he had seen 't, or been an instrument
To vice you to 't,—that you have touch'd his queen
Forbiddenly.
Pol. O, then my best blood turn
To an infected jelly; and my name
Be yok'd with his, that did betray the best!
Turn then my freshest reputation to
A savour, that may strike the dullest nostril
Where I arrive; and my approach be shunn'd,
Nay, hated too, worse than the great'st infection
That e'er was heard, or read!
Cam. Swear his thought over
By each particular star in heaven, and
By all their influences, you may as well
Forbid the sea for to obey the moon,
As or, by oath, remove, or counsel, shake
The fabrick of his folly; whose foundation
Is pil'd upon his faith, and will continue
The standing of his body.
Pol. How should this grow?
Cam. I know not: but, I am sure, 'tis safer to
Avoid what's grown, than question how 'tis born.
If therefore you dare trust my honesty,—
That lies enclosed in this trunk, which you
Shall bear along impawn'd,—away to-night.
Your followers I will whisper to the business;
And will, by twos, and threes, at several posterns,
Clear them o' the city: For myself, I'll put
My fortunes to your service, which are here
By this discovery lost. Be not uncertain:
For, by the honour of my parents, I
Have utter'd truth: which if you seek to prove,
I dare not stand by; nor shall you be safer
Than one condemn'd by the king's own mouth, thereon
His execution sworn.
Pol. I do believe thee:
I saw his heart in his face. Give me thy hand;
Be pilot to me, and thy places shall
Still neighbour mine; My ships are ready, and
My people did expect my hence departure
Two days ago.—This jealousy
Is for a precious creature: as she's rare,
Must it be great; and, as his person's mighty,
Must it be violent; and, as he does conceive,
He is dishonour'd by a man which ever
Profess'd to him, why, his revenges must
In that be made more bitter. Fear o'ershades me,
Good expedition be my friend, and comfort
The gracious queen, part of his theme, but nothing
Of his ill-ta'en suspicion! Come, Camillo;
I will respect thee as a father, if
Thou bear'st my life off hence: Let us avoid.
Cam. It is in mine authority, to command
The keys of all the posterns: Please your highness
To take the urgent hour: come, sir, away.
[*Exeunt.*

ACT II.

SCENE I. *The same.*

Enter HERMIONE, MAMILLIUS, *and* Ladies.

Her. Take the boy to you: he so troubles me,
'Tis past enduring.
1 *Lady.* Come, my gracious lord,
Shall I be your playfellow?

Mam. No, I'll none of you.
1 Lady. Why, my sweet lord?
Mam. You'll kiss me hard; and speak to me as if
I were a baby still.—I love you better.
2 Lady. And why so, my lord?
Mam. Not for because
Your brows are blacker; yet black brows they say,
Become some women best; so that there be not
Too much hair there, but in a semicircle,
Or half-moon made with a pen.
2 Lady. Who taught you this?
Mam. I learn'd it out of women's faces.—Pray now
What colour are your eyebrows?
1 Lady. Blue, my lord.
Mam. Nay, that's a mock: I have seen a lady's nose
That has been blue, but not her eyebrows.
2 Lady. Hark ye:
The queen, your mother, rounds apace: we shall
Present our services to a fine new prince,
One of these days; and then you'd wanton with us,
If we would have you.
1 Lady. She is spread of late
Into a goodly bulk: Good time encounter her!
Her. What wisdom stirs amongst you? Come, sir, now
I am for you again: Pray you, sit by us,
And tell's a tale.
Mam. Merry, or sad, shall 't be?
Her. As merry as you will.
Mam. A sad tale's best for winter:
I have one of sprites and goblins.
Her. Let's have that, sir.
Come on, sit down:—Come on, and do your best
To fright me with your sprites: you're powerful at it.
Mam. There was a man,——
Her. Nay, come, sit down; then on.
Mam. Dwelt by a church-yard;—I will tell it softly;
Yon crickets shall not hear it.
Her. Come on then,
And give 't me in mine ear.

Enter LEONTES, ANTIGONUS, Lords, *and Others.*

Leon. Was he met there? his train? Camillo with him?
1 Lord. Behind the tuft of pines I met them; never
Saw I men scour so on their way: I ey'd them
Even to their ships.
Leon. How bless'd am I
In my just censure! in my true opinion!—
Alack, for lesser knowledge! How accurs'd,
In being so blest!—There may be in the cup
A spider steep'd, and one may drink; depart,
And yet partake no venom; for his knowledge
Is not infected: but if one present
The abhorr'd ingredient to his eye; make known
How he hath drunk, he cracks his gorge, his sides,
With violent hefts:—I have drunk, and seen the spider.
Camillo was his help in this, his pander:—
There is a plot against my life, my crown;
All's true that is mistrusted:—that false villain,
Whom I employ'd, was pre-employ'd by him:
He has discover'd my design, and I
Remain a pinch'd thing; yea, a very trick
For them to play at will:—How came the posterns
So easily open?
1 Lord. By his great authority;
Which often hath no less prevail'd than so,
On your command.
Leon. I know 't too well.——
Give me the boy; I am glad you did not nurse him:
Though he does bear some signs of me, yet you
Have too much blood in him.
Her. What is this? sport?
Leon. Bear the boy hence, he shall not come about her;
Away with him:—and let her sport herself
With that she's big with; for 'tis Polixenes
Has made thee swell thus.
Her. But I'd say, he had not,
And, I'll be sworn, you would believe my saying,
Howe'er you lean to the nayward.
Leon. You, my lords,
Look on her, mark her well; be but about
To say, *she is a goodly lady,* and
The justice of your hearts will thereto add,
'Tis pity, she's not honest, honourable:
Praise her but for this her without-door form,
(Which, on my faith, deserves high speech) and straight
The shrug, the hum, or ha; these petty brands,
That calumny doth use:—O, I am out,
That mercy does; for calumny will sear
Virtue itself;—these shrugs, these hums, and has,
When you have said, she's goodly, come between,
Ere you can say she's honest: But be it known,
From him that has most cause to grieve it should be,
She's an adultress.
Her. Should a villain say so,
The most replenish'd villain in the world,
He were as much more villain: you, my lord,
Do but mistake.
Leon. You have mistook, my lady,
Polixenes for Leontes: O thou thing,
Which I'll not call a creature of thy place,
Lest barbarism, making me the precedent,
Should a like language use to all degrees,
And mannerly distinguishment leave out
Betwixt the prince and beggar!—I have said,
She's an adultress; I have said with whom:
More, she's a traitor! and Camillo is
A federary with her; and one that knows
What she should shame to know herself,
But with her most vile principal, that she's
A bed-swerver, even as bad as those
That vulgars give bold'st titles; ay, and privy
To this their late escape.
Her. No, by my life,
Privy to none of this: How will this grieve you,
When you shall come to clearer knowledge, that
You thus have publish'd me? Gentle my lord,
You scarce can right me throughly then, to say
You did mistake.
Leon. No, no; if I mistake
In those foundations which I build upon,
The centre is not big enough to bear
A school-boy's top.—Away with her to prison:
He, who shall speak for her, is afar off guilty,
But that he speaks.
Her. There's some ill planet reigns:
I must be patient, till the heavens look
With an aspect more favourable.—Good my lords,
I am not prone to weeping, as our sex
Commonly are; the want of which vain dew,
Perchance, shall dry your pities: but I have,
That honourable grief lodg'd here, which burns
Worse than tears drown: 'Beseech you all, my lords,
With thoughts so qualified as your charities
Shall best instruct you, measure me;—and so
The king's will be perform'd!
Leon. Shall I be heard? [*To the Guards.*
Her. Who is 't that goes with me?—'Beseech your highness,
My women may be with me; for, you see,
My plight requires it. Do not weep, good fools;
There is no cause: when you shall know your mistress
Has deserv'd prison, then abound in tears,

As I come out: this action, I now go on,
Is for my better grace.—Adieu, my lord:
I never wish'd to see you sorry; now,
I trust, I shall.——My women, come; you have leave.

Leon. Go, do our bidding; hence.

[*Exeunt* Queen *and* Ladies.

1 Lord. 'Beseech your highness, call the queen again.

Ant. Be certain what you do, sir; lest your justice
Prove violence; in the which three great ones suffer,
Yourself, your queen, your son.

1 Lord. For her, my lord,—
I dare my life lay down, and will do 't, sir,
Please you to accept it, that the queen is spotless
I' the eyes of heaven, and to you; I mean,
In this which you accuse her.

Ant. If it prove
She's otherwise, I'll keep my stables where
I lodge my wife; I'll go in couples with her;
Then when I feel, and see her, no further trust her;
For every inch of woman in the world,
Ay, every dram of woman's flesh, is false,
If she be.

Leon. Hold your peaces.

1 Lord. Good my lord.—

Ant. It is for you we speak, not for ourselves:
You are abus'd, and by some putter-on,
That will be damn'd for 't; 'would, I knew the villain,
I would land-damn him: Be she honour-flaw'd,—
I have three daughters; the eldest is eleven;
The second, and the third, nine, and some five;
If this prove true, they'll pay for't: by mine honour,
I'll geld them all; fourteen they shall not see,
To bring false generations; they are coheirs;
And I had rather glib myself, than they
Should not produce fair issue.

Leon. Cease; no more.
You smell this business with a sense as cold
As is a dead man's nose: I see 't, and feel 't,
As you feel doing thus; and see withal
The instruments that feel.

Ant. If it be so,
We need no grave to bury honesty;
There's not a grain of it, the face to sweeten
Of the whole dungy earth.

Leon. What! lack I credit?

1 Lord. I had rather you did lack, than I, my lord,
Upon this ground: and more it would content me
To have her honour true, than your suspicion;
Be blam'd for 't how you might.

Leon. Why, what need we
Commune with you of this? but rather follow
Our forceful instigation? Our prerogative
Calls not your counsels; but our natural goodness
Imparts this: which,—if you (or stupified,
Or seeming so in skill) cannot, or will not,
Relish as truth, like us; inform yourselves,
We need no more of your advice: the matter,
The loss, the gain, the ordering on 't, is all
Properly ours.

Ant. And I wish, my liege,
You had only in your silent judgment tried it,
Without more overture.

Leon. How could that be?
Either thou art most ignorant by age,
Or thou wert born a fool. Camillo's flight,
Added to their familiarity,
(Which was as gross as ever touch'd conjecture,
That lack'd sight only, nought for approbation,
But only seeing, all other circumstances
Made up to the deed) doth push on this proceeding:
Yet, for a greater confirmation,
(For, in an act of this importance, 'twere
Most piteous to be wild) I have despatch'd in post,
To sacred Delphos, to Apollo's temple,
Cleomenes and Dion, whom you know
Of stuff'd sufficiency: Now, from the oracle
They will bring all: whose spiritual counsel had
Shall stop, or spur me. Have I done well?

1 Lord. Well done, my lord.

Leon. Though I am satisfied, and need no more
Than what I know, yet shall the oracle
Give rest to the minds of others; such as he,
Whose ignorant credulity will not
Come up to the truth: So have we thought it good,
From our free person she should be confin'd;
Lest that the treachery of the two fled hence,
Be left her to perform. Come, follow us;
We are to speak in public: for this business
Will raise us all.

Ant. [*Aside.*] To laughter, as I take it,
If the good truth were known. [*Exeunt.*

SCENE II. *The same. The outer Room of a Prison.*

Enter PAULINA *and* Attendants.

Paul. The keeper of the prison, call to him;

[*Exit an* Attendant.

Let him have knowledge who I am,—Good lady!
No court in Europe is too good for thee,
What dost thou then in prison?—Now, good sir,

Re-enter Attendant, *with the* Keeper.

You know me, do you not?

Keep. For a worthy lady,
And one whom much I honour.

Paul. Pray you, then,
Conduct me to the queen.

Keep. I may not, madam; to the contrary
I have express commandment.

Paul. Here's ado,
To lock up honesty and honour from
The access of gentle visitors!——Is it lawful,
Pray you, to see her women? any of them?
Emilia?

Keep. So please you, madam, to put
Apart these your attendants, I shall bring
Emilia forth.

Paul. I pray now, call her.
Withdraw yourselves. [*Exeunt* Attend.

Keep. And, madam,
I must be present at your conference.

Paul. Well, be it so, pr'ythee. [*Exit* Keeper.
Here's such ado to make no stain a stain,
As passes colouring.

Re-enter Keeper, *with* EMILIA.

Dear gentlewoman, how fares our gracious lady?

Emil. As well as one so great, and so forlorn,
May hold together: On her frights and griefs
(Which never tender lady hath borne greater),
She is, something before her time, deliver'd.

Paul. A boy?

Emil. A daughter; and a goodly babe,
Lusty, and like to live: the queen receives
Much comfort in 't: says, *My poor prisoner,
I am innocent as you.*

Paul. I dare be sworn:
These dangerous unsafe lunes o' the king! beshrew them!
He must be told on 't, and he shall: the office
Becomes a woman best; I'll take 't upon me:
If I prove honey-mouth'd, let my tongue blister;
And never to my red-look'd anger be
The trumpet any more:—'Pray you, Emilia,
Commend my best obedience to the queen;
If she dares trust me with her little babe,
I'll show 't the king, and undertake to be
Her advocate to th' loudest: We do not know
How he may soften at the sight o' the child;
The silence often of pure innocence
Persuades, when speaking fails.

Emil. Most worthy madam,
Your honour, and your goodness, is so evident,

That your free undertaking cannot miss
A thriving issue; there is no lady living,
So meet for this great errand: Please your ladyship
To visit the next room, I'll presently
Acquaint the queen of your most noble offer;
Who, but to-day, hammer'd of this design;
But durst not tempt a minister of honour,
Lest she should be denied.

Paul. Tell her, Emilia,
I'll use that tongue I have: if wit flow from it,
As boldness from my bosom, let it not be doubted
I shall do good.

Emil. Now be you blest for it!
I'll to the queen: Please you, come something nearer.

Keep. Madam, if't please the queen to send the babe,
I know not what I shall incur, to pass it,
Having no warrant.

Paul. You need not fear it, sir:
The child was prisoner to the womb; and is,
By law and process of great nature, thence
Freed and enfranchis'd: not a party to
The anger of the king; nor guilty of,
If any be, the trespass of the queen.

Keep. I do believe it.

Paul. Do not you fear: upon
Mine honour, I will stand 'twixt you and danger. [*Exeunt.*

SCENE III. *The same. A Room in the Palace.*

Enter LEONTES, ANTIGONUS, Lords, *and other* Attendants.

Leon. Nor night, nor day, no rest: It is but weakness
To bear the matter thus; mere weakness, if
The cause were not in being;—part o' the cause,
She, the adultress;—for the harlot king
Is quite beyond mine arm, out of the blank
And level of my brain, plot-proof: but she
I can hook to me: Say, that she were gone,
Given to the fire, a moiety of my rest
Might come to me again.——Who's there?

1 *Attend.* My lord! [*Advancing.*

Leon. How does the boy?

1 *Attend.* He took good rest to-night.
'Tis hop'd his sickness is discharg'd.

Leon. To see,
His nobleness!
Conceiving the dishonour of his mother,
He straight declin'd, droop'd, took it deeply;
Fasten'd and fix'd the shame on 't in himself;
Threw off his spirit, his appetite, his sleep,
And downright languish'd.—Leave me solely:—go,
See how he fares. [*Exit* Attend.]—Fye, fye! no thought of him;—
The very thought of my revenges that way
Recoil upon me: in himself too mighty;
And in his parties, his alliance,—Let him be,
Until a time may serve: for present vengeance,
Take it on her. Camillo and Polixenes
Laugh at me; make their pastime at my sorrow:
They should not laugh, if I could reach them; nor
Shall she, within my power.

Enter PAULINA, *with a Child.*

1 *Lord.* You must not enter.

Paul. Nay, rather, good my lords, be second to me:
Fear you his tyrannous passion more, alas,
Than the queen's life? a gracious innocent soul;
More free, than he is jealous.

Ant. That's enough.

1 *Attend.* Madam, he hath not slept to-night; commanded
None should come at him.

Paul. Not so hot, good sir;
I come to bring him sleep. 'Tis such as you,—
That creep like shadows by him, and do sigh
At each his needless heavings,—such as you
Nourish the cause of his awaking: I
Do come with words as med'cinal as true;
Honest, as either: to purge him of that humour,
That presses him from sleep.

Leon. What noise there, ho?

Paul. No noise, my lord, but needful conference
About some gossips for your highness.

Leon. How?——
Away with that audacious lady: Antigonus,
I charg'd thee, that she should not come about me;
I knew she would.

Ant. I told her so, my lord,
On your displeasure's peril, and on mine,
She should not visit you.

Leon. What, canst not rule her?

Paul. From all dishonesty, he can: in this,
(Unless he take the course that you have done,
Commit me, for committing honour) trust it,
He shall not rule me.

Ant. Lo you now, you hear!
When she will take the rein, I let her run;
But she'll not stumble.

Paul. Good my liege, I come,—
And, I beseech you, hear me, who profess
Myself your loyal servant, your physician,
Your most obedient counsellor; yet that dare
Less appear so, in comforting your evils,
Than such as most seem yours:—I say, I come
From your good queen.

Leon. Good queen!

Paul. Good queen, my lord, good queen: I say, good queen;
And would by combat make her good, so were I
A man, the worst about you.

Leon. Force her hence.

Paul. Let him, that makes but trifles of his eyes,
First hand me: on my own accord, I'll off;
But, first, I'll do my errand.—The good queen,
For she is good, hath brought you forth a daughter;
Here 'tis; commends it to your blessing.
[*Laying down the Child.*

Leon. Out!
A mankind witch? Hence with her, out o' door:
O most intelligencing bawd!

Paul. Not so:
I am as ignorant in that, as you
In so entitling me: and no less honest
Than you are mad; which is enough, I'll warrant,
As this world goes, to pass for honest.

Leon. Traitors!
Will you not push her out? Give her the bastard:—
Thou dotard [*To* ANTIGONUS], thou art woman-tir'd, unroosted
By thy dame Partlet here:—take up the bastard;
Take 't up, I say; give 't to thy crone.

Paul. For ever
Unvenerable be thy hands, if thou
Takest up the princess, by that forced baseness
Which he has put upon 't!

Leon. He dreads his wife.

Paul. So, I would, you did; then, 'twere past all doubt,
You'd call your children yours.

Leon. A nest of traitors!

Ant. I am none, by this good light.

Paul. Nor I; nor any,
But one, that's here; and that's himself: for he
The sacred honour of himself, his queen's,
His hopeful son's, his babe's, betrays to slander,
Whose sting is sharper than the sword's; and will not
(For, as the case now stands, it is a curse
He cannot be compell'd to 't), once remove
The root of his opinion, which is rotten,
As ever oak, or stone, was sound.

Leon. A callat,

Of boundless tongue; who late hath beat her husband,
And now baits me!—This brat is none of mine;
It is the issue of Polixenes:
Hence with it; and, together with the dam,
Commit them to the fire.

Paul. It is yours;
And, might we lay the old proverb to your charge,
So like you, 'tis the worse.—Behold, my lords,
Although the print be little, the whole matter
And copy of the father: eye, nose, lip,
The trick of his frown, his forehead; nay, the valley,
The pretty dimples of his chin, and cheek; his smiles;
The very mould and frame of hand, nail, finger:—
And, thou, good goddess nature, which hast made it
So like to him that got it, if thou hast
The ordering of the mind too, 'mongst all colours
No yellow in't; lest she suspect, as he does,
Her children not her husband's!

Leon. A gross hag!—
And, lozel, thou art worthy to be hang'd,
That wilt not stay her tongue.

Ant. Hang all the husbands
That cannot do that feat, you'll leave yourself
Hardly one subject.

Leon. Once more, take her hence.

Paul. A most unworthy and unnatural lord
Can do no more.

Leon. I'll have thee burn'd.

Paul. I care not:
It is a heretick that makes the fire,
Not she which burns in't. I'll not call you tyrant;
But this most cruel usage of your queen
(Not able to produce more accusation
Than your own weak-hing'd fancy) something savours
Of tyranny, and will ignoble make you,
Yea, scandalous to the world.

Leon. On your allegiance,
Out of the chamber with her. Were I a tyrant,
Where were her life? she durst not call me so,
If she did know me one. Away with her.

Paul. I pray you, do not push me; I'll be gone.
Look to your babe, my lord; 'tis yours: Jove send her
A better guiding spirit!—What need these hands?—
You, that are thus so tender o'er his follies,
Will never do him good, not one of you.
So, so:—Farewell, we are gone. [*Exit.*

Leon. Thou, traitor, hast set on thy wife to this.—
My child? away with't!—even thou, that hast
A heart so tender o'er it, take it hence,
And see it instantly consum'd with fire;
Even thou, and none but thou. Take it up straight:
Within this hour bring me word, 'tis done
(And by good testimony), or I'll seize thy life,
With what thou else call'st thine: If thou refuse,
And wilt encounter with my wrath, say so;
The bastard brains with these my proper hands
Shall I dash out. Go, take it to the fire;
For thou sett'st on thy wife.

Ant. I did not, sir:
These lords, my noble fellows, if they please,
Can clear me in't.

1 *Lord.* We can; my royal liege,
He is not guilty of her coming hither.

Leon. You are liars all.

1 *Lord.* 'Beseech your highness, give us better credit:
We have always truly serv'd you; and beseech
So to esteem of us; And on our knees we beg
(As recompense of our dear services,
Past, and to come), that you do change this purpose;
Which, being so horrible, so bloody, must
Lead on to some foul issue: We all kneel.

Leon. I am a feather for each wind that blows:—
Shall I live on, to see this bastard kneel
And call me father? Better burn it now,
Than curse it then. But, be it; let it live:
It shall not neither.—You, sir, come you hither;
[*To* ANTIGONUS.
You, that have been so tenderly officious
With lady Margery, your midwife, there,
To save this bastard's life:—for 'tis a bastard,
So sure as this beard's gray,—what will you adventure
To save this brat's life?

Ant. Any thing, my lord,
That my ability may undergo,
And nobleness impose: at least, thus much;
I'll pawn the little blood which I have left,
To save the innocent: any thing possible.

Leon. It shall be possible: Swear by this sword,
Thou wilt perform my bidding.

Ant. I will, my lord.

Leon. Mark, and perform it; (seest thou?) for the fail
Of any point in't shall not only be
Death to thyself, but to thy lewd-tongu'd wife;
Whom, for this time, we pardon. We enjoin thee,
As thou art liegeman to us, that thou carry
This female bastard hence; and that thou bear it
To some remote and desert place, quite out
Of our dominions; and that there thou leave it,
Without more mercy, to its own protection,
And favour of the climate. As by strange fortune
It came to us, I do in justice charge thee,—
On thy soul's peril, and thy body's torture,—
That thou commend it strangely to some place,
Where chance may nurse, or end it: Take it up.

Ant. I swear to do this, though a present death
Had been more merciful.—Come on, poor babe.
Some powerful spirit instruct the kites and ravens,
To be thy nurses? Wolves, and bears, they say,
Casting their savageness aside, have done
Like offices of pity.—Sir, be prosperous
In more than this deed doth require! and blessing,
Against this cruelty, fight on thy side,
Poor thing, condemn'd to loss!
[*Exit, with the Child.*

Leon. No, I'll not rear
Another's issue.

1 *Atten.* Please your highness, posts,
From those you sent to the oracle, are come
An hour since: Cleomenes and Dion,
Being well arriv'd from Delphos, are both landed,
Hasting to the court.

1 *Lord.* So please you, sir, their speed
Hath been beyond account.

Leon. Twenty-three days
They have been absent: 'Tis good speed: foretells,
The great Apollo certainly will have
The truth of this appear. Prepare you, lords;
Summon a session, that we may arraign
Our most disloyal lady; for, as she hath
Been publicly accus'd, so shall she have
A just and open trial. While she lives,
My heart will be a burden to me. Leave me;
And think upon my bidding. [*Exeunt.*

ACT III.

SCENE I. *The same. A Street in some Town.*

Enter CLEOMENES *and* DION.

Cleo. The climate's delicate; the air most sweet;
Fertile the isle; the temple much surpassing
The common praise it bears.

Dion. I shall report,
For most it caught me, the celestial habits
(Methinks, I so should term them), and the reverence
Of the grave wearers. O, the sacrifice!
How ceremonious, solemn, and unearthly
It was i' the offering!

Cleo. But, of all, the burst
And the ear-deaf'ning voice o' the oracle,
Kin to Jove's thunder, so surpris'd my sense,
That I was nothing.

Dion. If the event o' the journey
Prove as successful to the queen,—O, be't so!—
As it hath been to us, rare, pleasant, speedy,
The time is worth the use on't.

Cleo. Great Apollo,
Turn all to the best: These proclamations,
So forcing faults upon Hermione,
I little like.

Dion. The violent carriage of it
Will clear, or end, the business: When the oracle,
(Thus by Apollo's great divine seal'd up)
Shall the contents discover, something rare,
Even then will rush to knowledge.——Go,—fresh horses;—
And gracious be the issue! [*Exeunt.*

SCENE II. *The same. A Court of Justice.*

LEONTES, Lords, *and* Officers, *appear properly seated.*

Leon. This sessions (to our great grief, we pronounce)
Even pushes 'gainst our heart: The party tried,
The daughter of a king; our wife; and one
Of us too much belov'd.—Let us be clear'd
Of being tyrannous, since we so openly
Proceed in justice; which shall have due course,
Even to the guilt, or the purgation.——
Produce the prisoner.

Offi. It is his highness' pleasure, that the queen
Appear in person here in court.—Silence!

HERMIONE *is brought in, guarded;* PAULINA *and* Ladies, *attending.*

Leon. Read the indictment.

Offi. Hermione, *queen to the worthy* Leontes, *king of* Sicilia, *thou art here accused and arraigned of high treason, in committing adultery with* Polixenes, *king of* Bohemia; *and conspiring with* Camillo *to take away the life of our sovereign lord the king, thy royal husband; the pretence whereof being by circumstances partly laid open, thou,* Hermione, *contrary to the faith and allegiance of a true subject, didst counsel and aid them, for their better safety, to fly away by night.*

Her. Since what I am to say, must be but that
Which contradicts my accusation; and
The testimony on my part, no other
But what comes from myself; it shall scarce boot me
To say, *Not guilty*: mine integrity,
Being counted falsehood, shall, as I express it,
Be so receiv'd. But thus,—If powers divine
Behold our human actions (as they do),
I doubt not then, but innocence shall make
False accusation blush, and tyranny
Tremble at patience.—You, my lord, best know
(Who least will seem to do so), my past life
Hath been as continent, as chaste, as true,
As I am now unhappy; which is more
Than history can pattern, though devis'd,
And play'd, to take spectators: For behold me,—
A fellow of the royal bed, which owe
A moiety of the throne, a great king's daughter,
The mother to a hopeful prince,—here standing
To prate and talk for life, and honour, 'fore
Who please to come and hear. For life, I prize it
As I weigh grief, which I would spare: for honour,
'Tis a derivative from me to mine,
And only that I stand for. I appeal
To your own conscience, sir, before Polixenes
Came to your court, how I was in your grace,
How merited to be so; since he came,
With what encounter so uncurrent I
Have strain'd, to appear thus: if one jot beyond
The bound of honour; or, in act, or will,
That way inclining; harden'd be the hearts
Of all that hear me, and my near'st of kin
Cry, Fye upon my grave!

Leon. I ne'er heard yet
That any of these bolder vices wanted
Less impudence to gainsay what they did,
Than to perform it first.

Her. That's true enough;
Though 'tis a saying, sir, not due to me.

Leon. You will not own it.

Her. More than mistress of,
Which comes to me in name of fault, I must not
At all acknowledge. For Polixenes,
(With whom I am accus'd) I do confess,
I lov'd him, as in honour he requir'd;
With such a kind of love as might become
A lady like me; with a love, even such,
So, and no other, as yourself commanded:
Which not to have done, I think, had been in me
Both disobedience and ingratitude,
To you, and toward your friend; whose love had spoke,
Even since it could speak, from an infant freely,
That it was yours. Now, for conspiracy,
I know not how it tastes; though it be dish'd
For me to try how: all I know of it,
Is, that Camillo was an honest man;
And, why he left your court, the gods themselves,
Wotting no more than I, are ignorant.

Leon. You knew of his departure, as you know
What you have underta'en to do in his absence.

Her. Sir,
You speak a language that I understand not:
My life stands in the level of your dreams,
Which I'll lay down.

Leon. Your actions are my dreams;
You had a bastard by Polixenes,
And I but dream'd it:—As you were past all shame
(Those of your fact are so), so past all truth:
Which to deny, concerns more than avails: for as
Thy brat hath been cast out, like to itself,
No father owning it (which is, indeed,
More criminal in thee, than it), so thou
Shalt feel our justice; in whose easiest passage,
Look for no less than death.

Her. Sir, spare your threats;
The bug, which you would fright me with, I seek.
To me can life be no commodity:
The crown and comfort of my life, your favour,
I do give lost: for I do feel it gone,
But know not how it went: My second joy,
And first-fruits of my body, from his presence
I am barr'd, like one infectious: My third comfort,
Starr'd most unluckily, is from my breast,
The innocent milk in its most innocent mouth,
Haled out to murder: Myself on every post
Proclaim'd a strumpet; with immodest hatred,
The child-bed privilege denied, which 'longs
To women of all fashion:—Lastly, hurried
Here to this place, i'the open air, before
I have got strength of limit. Now, my liege,
Tell me what blessings I have here alive,
That I should fear to die? Therefore, proceed.
But yet hear this; mistake me not;——No; life,
I prize it not a straw:—but for mine honour
(Which I would free), if I shall be condemn'd
Upon surmises; all proofs sleeping else,
But what your jealousies awake; I tell you,
'Tis rigour, and not law.—Your honours all,
I do refer me to the oracle;
Apollo be my judge.

1 Lord. This your request
Is altogether just: therefore, bring forth,
And in Apollo's name, his oracle.
[*Exeunt certain* Officers.

Her. The emperor of Russia was my father:
O, that he were alive, and here beholding
His daughter's trial! that he did but see
The flatness of my misery; yet with eyes
Of pity, not revenge!

Re-enter Officers *with* CLEOMENES *and* DION.

Offi. You here shall swear upon this sword of justice,
That you, Cleomenes and Dion, have
Been both at Delphos; and from thence have brought
This seal'd up oracle, by the hand deliver'd
Of great Apollo's priest; and that, since then,
You have not dar'd to break the holy seal,
Nor read the secrets in't.
Cleo. Dion. All this we swear.
Leon. Break up the seals, and read.
Offi. [*Reads.*] Hermione *is chaste,* Polixenes *blameless,* Camillo *a true subject,* Leontes *a jealous tyrant, his innocent babe truly begotten; and the king shall live without an heir, if that, which is lost, be not found.*
Lords. Now blessed be the great Apollo!
Her. Praised!
Leon. Hast thou read truth?
Offi. Ay, my lord; even so
As it is here set down.
Leon. There is no truth at all i' the oracle:
The sessions shall proceed; this is mere falsehood.

Enter a Servant, *hastily.*

Serv. My lord the king, the king!
Leon. What is the business?
Serv. O sir, I shall be hated to report it:
The prince your son, with mere conceit and fear
Of the queen's speed, is gone.
Leon. How! gone?
Serv. Is dead.
Leon. Apollo's angry; and the heavens themselves
Do strike at my injustice. [HERMIONE *faints.*
How now there?
Paul. This news is mortal to the queen:—Look down,
And see what death is doing.
Leon. Take her hence;
Her heart is but o'ercharg'd; she will recover.—
I have too much believ'd mine own suspicion:—
'Beseech you, tenderly apply to her
Some remedies for life.—Apollo, pardon
[*Exeunt* PAULINA *and* Ladies, *with* HERM.
My great profaneness 'gainst thine oracle!—
I'll reconcile me to Polixenes;
New woo my queen; recall the good Camillo;
Whom I proclaim a man of truth, of mercy:
For, being transported by my jealousies
To bloody thoughts and to revenge, I chose
Camillo for the minister, to poison
My friend Polixenes: which had been done,
But that the good mind of Camillo tardied
My swift command, though I with death, and with
Reward, did threaten and encourage him,
Not doing it, and being done: he, most humane,
And fill'd with honour, to my kingly guest
Unclasp'd my practice; quit his fortunes here,
Which you knew great; and to the certain hazard
Of all incertainties himself commended,
No richer than his honour:—How he glisters
Thorough my rust! and how his piety
Does my deeds make the blacker!

Re-enter PAULINA.

Paul. Woe the while!
O, cut my lace; lest my heart, cracking it,
Break too!
1 *Lord.* What fit is this, good lady?
Paul. What studied torments, tyrant, hast for me?
What wheels? racks? fires? What flaying? boiling
In leads or oils? what old, or newer torture
Must I receive; whose every word deserves
To taste of thy most worst? Thy tyranny
Together working with thy jealousies,—
Fancies too weak for boys, too green and idle
For girls of nine!—O think, what they have done,
And then run mad, indeed; stark mad! for all
Thy by-gone fooleries were but spices of it.
That thou betray'dst Polixenes, 'twas nothing;
That did but show thee, of a fool, inconstant,
And damnable ungrateful: nor was't much,
Thou would'st have poison'd good Camillo's honour,
To have him kill a king; poor trespasses,
More monstrous standing by: whereof I reckon
The casting forth to crows thy baby daughter,
To be or none, or little; though a devil
Would have shed water out of fire, ere done't:
Nor is't directly laid to thee, the death
Of the young prince, whose honourable thoughts
(Thoughts high for one so tender) cleft the heart
That could conceive, a gross and foolish sire
Blemish'd his gracious dam: this is not, no,
Laid to thy answer: But the last,—O, lords,
When I have said, cry, woe!—the queen, the queen,
The sweetest, dearest, creature's dead; and vengeance for't
Not dropp'd down yet.
1 *Lord.* The higher powers forbid!
Paul. I say, she's dead; I'll swear't: if word, nor oath,
Prevail not, go and see: if you can bring
Tincture, or lustre, in her lip, her eye,
Heat outwardly, or breath within, I'll serve you
As I would do the gods.—But, O thou tyrant!
Do not repent these things; for they are heavier
Than all thy woes can stir; therefore betake thee
To nothing but despair. A thousand knees
Ten thousand years together, naked, fasting,
Upon a barren mountain, and still winter
In storm perpetual, could not move the gods
To look that way thou wert.
Leon. Go on, go on:
Thou canst not speak too much; I have deserv'd
All tongues to talk their bitterest.
1 *Lord.* Say no more;
Howe'er the business goes, you have made fault
I' the boldness of your speech.
Paul. I am sorry for't;
All faults I make, when I shall come to know them,
I do repent: Alas, I have show'd too much
The rashness of a woman: he is touch'd
To the noble heart.—What's gone, and what's past help,
Should be past grief: Do not receive affliction
At my petition, I beseech you: rather
Let me be punish'd, that have minded you
Of what you should forget. Now, good my liege,
Sir, royal sir, forgive a foolish woman:
The love I bore your queen,—lo, fool again!—
I'll speak of her no more, nor of your children;
I'll not remember you of my own lord,
Who is lost too: Take your patience to you,
And I'll say nothing.
Leon. Thou didst speak but well,
When most the truth; which I receive much better
Than to be pitied of thee. 'Pr'ythee, bring me
To the dead bodies of my queen, and son:
One grave shall be for both; upon them shall
The causes of their death appear, unto
Our shame perpetual: Once a day I'll visit
The chapel where they lie: and tears, shed there,
Shall be my recreation: So long as
Nature will bear up with this exercise,
So long I daily vow to use it. Come,
And lead me to these sorrows. [*Exeunt.*

SCENE III. Bohemia.

A desert Country near the Sea.

Enter ANTIGONUS, *with the Child; and a* Mariner.

Ant. Thou art perfect then, our ship hath touch'd upon
The deserts of Bohemia?

Mar. Ay, my lord; and fear
We have landed in ill time: the skies look grimly,
And threaten present blusters. In my conscience,
The heavens with that we have in hand are angry,
And frown upon us.

Ant. Their sacred wills be done!—Go, get aboard;
Look to thy bark; I'll not be long, before
I call upon thee.

Mar. Make your best haste; and go not
Too far i' the land: 'tis like to be loud weather;
Besides, this place is famous for the creatures
Of prey, that keep upon't.

Ant. Go thou away:
I'll follow instantly.

Mar. I am glad at heart
To be so rid o' the business. [*Exit.*

Ant. Come, poor babe:—
I have heard (but not believ'd), the spirits of the dead
May walk again: if such thing be, thy mother
Appear'd to me last night; for ne'er was dream
So like a waking. To me comes a creature,
Sometimes her head on one side, some another;
I never saw a vessel of like sorrow,
So fill'd, and so becoming: in pure white robes,
Like very sanctity, she did approach
My cabin where I lay; thrice bow'd before me;
And, gasping to begin some speech, her eyes
Became two spouts: the fury spent, anon
Did this break from her: *Good* Antigonus,
Since fate, against thy better disposition,
Hath made thy person for the thrower-out
Of my poor babe, according to thine oath,—
Places remote enough are in Bohemia,
There weep, and leave it crying; and, for the babe
Is counted lost for ever, Perdita,
I pr'ythee, call't; for this ungentle business,
Put on thee by my lord, thou ne'er shalt see
Thy wife Paulina, *more:* and so with shrieks,
She melted into air. Affrighted much,
I did in time collect myself; and thought
This was so, and no slumber. Dreams are toys;
Yet, for this once, yea, superstitiously,
I will be squar'd by this. I do believe
Hermione hath suffer'd death: and that
Apollo would, this being indeed the issue
Of king Polixenes, it should here be laid,
Either for life, or death, upon the earth
Of its right father.—Blossom, speed thee well?
[*Laying down the Child.*
There lie; and there thy character; there these;
[*Laying down a Bundle.*
Which may, if fortune please, both breed thee, pretty,
And still rest thine.——The storm begins:—Poor wretch,
That, for thy mother's fault, art thus expos'd
To loss, and what may follow!—Weep I cannot,
But my heart bleeds; and most accurs'd am I,
To be by oath enjoin'd to this.—Farewell!
The day frowns more and more: thou art like to have
A lullaby too rough: I never saw
The heavens so dim by day. A savage clamour!—
Well may I get aboard!——This is the chase;
I am gone for ever. [*Exit, pursued by a Bear.*

Enter an old Shepherd.

Shep. I would, there were no age between ten and three-and-twenty; or that youth would sleep out the rest: for there is nothing in the between but getting wenches with child, wronging the ancientry, stealing, fighting.—Hark you now! Would any but these boiled brains of nineteen, and two-and-twenty, hunt this weather? They have scared away two of my best sheep; which, I fear, the wolf will sooner find, than the master: if any where I have them, 'tis by the sea-side, browsing on ivy. Good luck, an't be thy will; what have we here? [*Taking up the Child.*] Mercy on's, a barne; a very pretty barne! A boy or a child, I wonder? A pretty one; a very pretty one: Sure some scape: though I am not bookish, yet I can read waiting-gentlewoman in the scape. This has been some stair-work, some trunk-work, some behind-door work: they were warmer that got this, than the poor thing is here. I'll take it up for pity: yet I'll tarry till my son come; he hollaed but even now. Whoa, ho hoa!

Enter Clown.

Clo. Hilloa, loa!

Shep. What, art so near? If thou'lt see a thing to talk on when thou art dead and rotten, come hither. What ailest thou, man?

Clo. I have seen two such sights, by sea, and by land;—but I am not to say, it is a sea, for it is now the sky; betwixt the firmament and it, you cannot thrust a bodkin's point.

Shep. Why, boy, how is it?

Clo. I would, you did but see how it chafes, how it rages, how it takes up the shore! but that's not to the point: O, the most piteous cry of the poor souls! sometimes to see 'em, and not to see 'em: now the ship boring the moon with her main-mast; and anon swallowed with yest and froth, as you'd thrust a cork into a hogshead. And then for the land service,—To see how the bear tore out his shoulder-bone? how he cried to me for help, and said, his name was Antigonus, a nobleman:—But to make an end of the ship:—to see how the sea flap-dragoned it:—but, first, how the poor souls roared, and the sea mocked them;—and how the poor gentleman roared, and the bear mocked him, both roaring louder than the sea, or weather.

Shep. 'Name of mercy, when was this, boy?

Clo. Now, now; I have not winked since I saw these sights: the men are not yet cold under water, nor the bear half dined on the gentleman; he's at it now.

Shep. 'Would, I had been by, to have helped the old man!

Clo. I would you had been by the ship side, to have helped her; there your charity would have lacked footing. [*Aside.*

Shep. Heavy matters! heavy matters! but look thee here, boy. Now bless thyself; thou met'st with things dying, I with things new born. Here's a sight for thee; look thee, a bearing-cloth for a squire's child! Look thee here; take up, take up, boy; open't. So, let's see; It was told me I should be rich, by the fairies: this is some changeling:—open't: What's within, boy?

Clo. You're a made old man; if the sins of your youth are forgiven you, you're well to live. Gold! all gold!

Shep. This is fairy gold, boy, and 'twill prove so: up with it, keep it close; home, home, the next way. We are lucky, boy; and to be so still, requires nothing but secrecy,—Let my sheep go:—Come, good boy, the next way home.

Clo. Go you the next way with your findings; I'll go see if the bear be gone from the gentleman, and how much he hath eaten: they are never curst, but when they are hungry: if there be any of him left, I'll bury it.

Shep. That's a good deed; If thou may'st discern by that which is left of him, what he is, fetch me to the sight of him.

Clo. Marry, will I; and you shall help to put him i' the ground.

Shep. 'Tis a lucky day, boy; and we'll do good deeds on't. [*Exeunt.*

ACT IV.

Enter Time, *as Chorus.*

Time. I,—that please some, try all; both joy, and terror,
Of good and bad; that make, and unfold error,—
Now take upon me in the name of Time,
To use my wings. Impute it not a crime,
To me, or my swift passage, that I slide
O'er sixteen years, and leave the growth untried
Of that wide gap; since it is in my power
To o'erthrow law, and in one self-born hour
To plant and o'erwhelm custom. Let me pass
The same I am, ere ancient'st order was,
Or what is now received: I witness to
The times that brought them in; so shall I do
To the freshest things now reigning; and make stale
The glistering of this present, as my tale
Now seems to it. Your patience this allowing,
I turn my glass; and give my scene such growing,
As you had slept between. Leontes leaving
The effects of his fond jealousies; so grieving,
That he shuts up himself; imagine me,
Gentle spectators, that I now may be
In fair Bohemia; and remember well,
I mentioned a son o' the king's, which Florizel
I now name to you; and with speed so pace
To speak of Perdita, now grown in grace
Equal with wond'ring: What of her ensues,
I list not prophesy; but let Time's news
Be known, when 'tis brought forth:—a shepherd's daughter,
And what to her adheres, which follows after,
Is the argument of time: Of this allow,
If ever you have spent time worse ere now;
If never yet, that Time himself doth say,
He wishes earnestly you never may. [*Exit.*

SCENE I.

The same. A Room in the Palace of Polixenes.

Enter Polixenes *and* Camillo.

Pol. I pray thee, good Camillo, be no more importunate: 'tis a sickness, denying thee any thing; a death, to grant this.

Cam. It is fifteen years, since I saw my country: though I have, for the most part, been aired abroad, I desire to lay my bones there. Besides the penitent king, my master, hath sent for me: to whose feeling sorrows I might be some allay, or I o'erween to think so; which is another spur to my departure.

Pol. As thou lovest me, Camillo, wipe not out the rest of thy services, by leaving me now: the need I have of thee, thine own goodness hath made; better not to have had thee, than thus to want thee: thou, having made me businesses, which none without thee can sufficiently manage, must either stay to execute them thyself, or take away with thee the very services thou hast done: which if I have not enough considered, (as too much I cannot), to be more thankful to thee, shall be my study; and my profit therein, the heaping friendships. Of that fatal country, Sicilia, pr'ythee speak no more: whose very naming punishes me with the remembrance of that penitent, as thou call'st him, and reconciled king, my brother: whose loss of his most precious queen and children, are even now to be afresh lamented. Say to me, when saw'st thou the prince Florizel, my son? Kings are no less unhappy, their issue not being gracious, than they are in losing them, when they have approved their virtues.

Cam. Sir, it is three days since I saw the prince: What his happier affairs may be, are to me unknown: but I have missingly noted, he is of late much retired from court; and is less frequent to his princely exercises, than formerly he hath appeared.

Pol. I have considered so much, Camillo; and with some care; so far, that I have eyes under my service, which look upon his removedness: from whom I have this intelligence; That he is seldom from the house of a most homely shepherd: a man, they say, that from very nothing, and beyond the imagination of his neighbours, is grown into an unspeakable estate.

Cam. I have heard, sir, of such a man, who hath a daughter of most rare note: the report of her is extended more than can be thought to begin from such a cottage.

Pol. That's likewise part of my intelligence. But, I fear the angle that plucks our son thither. Thou shalt accompany us to the place: where we will, not appearing what we are, have some question with the shepherd; from whose simplicity, I think, it not uneasy to get the cause of my son's resort thither. Pr'ythee, be my present partner in this business, and lay aside the thoughts of Sicilia.

Cam. I willingly obey your command.

Pol. My best Camillo!—We must disguise ourselves. [*Exeunt.*

SCENE II. *The same.*

A Road near the Shepherd's *Cottage.*

Enter Autolycus, *singing.*

When daffodils begin to peer,——
With, heigh! the doxy over the dale,—
Why, then comes in the sweet o' the year;
For the red blood reigns in the winter's pale.
The white sheet bleaching on the hedge,—
With, hey! the sweet birds, O, how they sing!—
Doth set my pugging tooth on edge;
For a quart of ale is a dish for a king.
The lark, that tirra-lirra chants,—
With, hey! with, hey! the thrush and the jay:—
Are summer songs for me and my aunts,
While we lie tumbling in the hay.

I have served Prince Florizel, and, in my time, wore three pile; but now I am out of service:

But shall I go mourn for that, my dear?
The pale moon shines by night:
And when I wander here and there,
I then do most go right.
If tinkers may have leave to live,
And bear the sow-skin budget;
Then my account I well may give,
And in the stocks avouch it.

My traffick is sheets; when the kite builds, look to lesser linen. My father named me Autolicus; who, being as I am, littered under Mercury, was likewise a snapper up of unconsidered trifles: With die and drab, I purchased this caparison; and my revenue is the silly cheat: Gallows, and knock, are too powerful on the highway: beating, and hanging, are terrors to me; for the life to come, I sleep out the thought of it.—A prize! a prize!

Enter Clown.

Clo. Let me see;—Every 'leven wether—tods; every tod yields—pound and odd shilling: fifteen hundred shorn,—What comes the wool to?

Aut. If the springe hold, the cock's mine. [*Aside.*

Clo. I cannot do't without counters.—Let me see; what am I to buy for our sheep-shearing feast? *Three pound of sugar; five pound of currants; rice*——What will this sister of mine do with rice? But my father hath made her mistress of the feast, and she lays it on. She hath made me four-and-twenty nosegays for the shearers: three-man song-men all, and very good ones; but they are most of them means and bases: but one Puritan amongst them, and he sings psalms to hornpipes. I must have *saffron*, to colour the warden pies; *mace,—dates,*—none; that's out of my note: *nutmegs, seven; a race*, or *two of ginger; but that I may beg;—four pound of prunes, and as many of raisins o' the sun.*

Aut. O, that ever I was born!

[*Grovelling on the ground.*

Clo. I' the name of me,——

Aut. O, help me, help me! pluck but off these rags; and then, death, death!

Clo. Alack, poor soul! thou hast need of more rags to lay on thee, rather than have these off.

Aut. O, sir, the loathsomeness of them offends me more than the stripes I have received; which are mighty ones and millions.

Clo. Alas, poor man! a million of beating may come to a great matter.

Aut. I am robbed, sir, and beaten; my money and apparel ta'en from me, and these detestable things put upon me.

Clo. What, by a horse-man, or a foot-man?

Aut. A foot-man, sweet sir, a foot-man.

Clo. Indeed, he should be a foot-man, by the garments he hath left with thee: if this be a horse-man's coat, it hath seen very hot service. Lend me thy hand, I'll help thee: come, lend me thy hand. [*Helping him up.*

Aut. O! good sir, tenderly, oh!

Clo. Alas, poor soul!

Aut. O, good sir, softly, good sir: I fear, sir, my shoulder-blade is out.

Clo. How now? canst stand?

Aut. Softly, dear sir; [*Picks his pocket*] good sir, softly; you ha' done me a charitable office.

Clo. Dost 'lack any money? I have a little money for thee.

Aut. No, good sweet sir; no, I beseech you, sir; I have a kinsman not past three quarters of a mile hence, unto whom I was going; I shall there have money, or any thing I want: Offer me no money, I pray you; that kills my heart.

Clo. What manner of fellow was he that robbed you?

Aut. A fellow, sir, that I have known to go about with trol-my dames: I knew him once a servant of the prince; I cannot tell, good sir, for which of his virtues it was, but he was certainly whipped out of the court.

Clo. His vices, you would say; there's no virtue whipped out of the court: they cherish it, to make it stay there; and yet it will no more but abide.

Aut. Vices I would say, sir. I know this man well: he hath been since an ape-bearer; then a process-server, a bailiff; then he compassed a motion of the prodigal son, and married a tinker's wife within a mile where my land and living lies; and, having flown over many knavish professions, he settled only in rogue: some call him Autolycus.

Clo. Out upon him! Prig, for my life, prig: he haunts wakes, fairs, and bear-baitings.

Aut. Very true, sir; he, sir, he; that's the rogue, that put me into this apparel.

Clo. Not a more cowardly rogue in all Bohemia; if you had but looked big, and spit at him, he'd have run.

Aut. I must confess to you, sir, I am no fighter: I am false of heart that way; and that he knew, I warrant him.

Clo. How do you now?

Aut. Sweet sir, much better than I was; I can stand, and walk: I will even take my leave of you, and pace softly towards my kinsman's.

Clo. Shall I bring thee on the way?

Aut. No, good-faced sir; no, sweet sir.

Clo. Then fare thee well; I must go buy spices for our sheep-shearing.

Aut. Prosper you, sweet sir!—[*Exit* Clown.] Your purse is not hot enough to purchase your spice. I'll be with you at your sheep-shearing too: If I make not this cheat bring out another, and the shearers prove sheep, let me be unrolled, and my name put in the book of virtue!

Jog on, jog on, the foot-path way,
And merrily hent the stile-a:
A merry heart goes all the day,
Your sad tires in a mile-a. [Exit.

SCENE III. *The same. A* Shepherd's *Cottage.*

Enter FLORIZEL *and* PERDITA.

Flo. These your unusual weeds to each part of you
Do give a life: no shepherdess, but Flora,
Peering in April's front. This your sheep-shearing
Is as a meeting of the petty gods,
And you the queen on't.

Per. Sir, my gracious lord,
To chide at your extremes, it not becomes me;
O, pardon, that I name them: your high self,
The gracious mark o'the land, you have obscur'd
With a swain's wearing; and me, poor lowly maid,
Most goddess-like prank'd up: But that our feasts
In every mess have folly, and the feeders
Digest it with a custom, I should blush
To see you so attired; sworn, I think,
To show myself a glass.

Flo. I bless the time,
When my good falcon made her flight across
Thy father's ground.

Per. Now Jove afford you cause!
To me, the difference forges dread; your greatness
Hath not been used to fear. Even now I tremble
To think, your father, by some accident,
Should pass this way, as you did: O, the fates!
How would he look, to see his work, so noble,
Vilely bound up? What would he say? Or how
Should I, in these my borrow'd flaunts, behold
The sternness of his presence?

Flo. Apprehend
Nothing but jollity. The gods themselves,
Humbling their deities to love, have taken
The shapes of beasts upon them: Jupiter
Became a bull, and bellow'd; the green Neptune
A ram, and bleated; and the fire-rob'd god,
Golden Apollo, a poor humble swain,
As I seem now: Their transformations
Were never for a piece of beauty rarer;
Nor in a way so chaste: since my desires
Run not before mine honour; nor my lusts
Burn hotter than my faith.

Per. O but, dear sir,
Your resolution cannot hold, when 'tis
Opposed, as it must be, by the power o' the king:
One of these two must be necessities,
Which then will speak; that you must change this purpose,
Or I my life.

Flo. Thou dearest Perdita,
With these forc'd thoughts, I pr'ythee, darken not
The mirth o' the feast: Or I'll be thine, my fair,
Or not my father's: for I cannot be
Mine own, nor any thing to any, if
I be not thine: to this I am most constant,
Though destiny say, no. Be merry, gentle;
Strangle such thoughts as these, with any thing
That you behold the while. Your guests are coming:
Lift up your countenance; as it were the day
Of celebration of that nuptial, which
We two have sworn shall come.

Per. O lady fortune,
Stand you auspicious!

Enter Shepherd, *with* POLIXENES *and* CAMILLO, *disguised;* Clown, MOPSA, DORCAS, *and others.*

Flo. See, your guests approach:
Address yourself to entertain them sprightly,
And let's be red with mirth.

Shep. Fye, daughter! when my old wife liv'd, upon
This day, she was both pantler, butler, cook;

Both dame and servant: welcom'd all; serv'd all:
Would sing her song, and dance her turn: now here,
At upper end o' the table, now i' the middle;
On his shoulder, and his: her face o' fire
With labour; and the thing, she took to quench it,
She would to each one sip: You are retir'd,
As if you were a feasted one, and not
The hostess of the meeting: Pray you, bid
These unknown friends to us welcome: for it is
A way to make us better friends, more known.
Come, quench your blushes; and present yourself
That which you are, mistress o' the feast: Come on,
And bid us welcome to your sheep-shearing,
As your good flock shall prosper.

Per. Welcome, sir! [*To* POL.
It is my father's will, I should take on me
The hostess-ship o' the day:—You're welcome, sir! [*To* CAMILLO.
Give me those flowers there, Dorcas.—Reverend sirs,
For you there's rosemary, and rue; these keep
Seeming, and savour, all the winter long:
Grace, and remembrance, be to you both,
And welcome to our shearing!

Pol. Shepherdess,
(A fair one are you), well you fit our ages
With flowers of winter.

Per. Sir, the year growing ancient,—
Not yet on summer's death, nor on the birth
Of trembling winter,—the fairest flowers o' the season
Are our carnations, and streak'd gilliflowers,
Which some call nature's bastards: of that kind
Our rustick garden's barren; and I care not
To get slips of them.

Pol. Wherefore, gentle maiden,
Do you neglect them?

Per. For I have heard it said,
There is an art, which, in their piedness, shares
With great creating nature.

Pol. Say, there be;
Yet nature is made better by no mean,
But nature makes that mean: so, o'er that art,
Which, you say, adds to nature, is an art
That nature makes. You see, sweet maid, we marry
A gentler scion to the wildest stock;
And make conceive a bark of baser kind
By bud of nobler race; This is an art
Which does mend nature,—change it rather: but
The art itself is nature.

Per. So it is.

Pol. Then make your garden rich in gilliflowers,
And do not call them bastards.

Per. I'll not put
The dibble in earth to set one slip of them:
No more than, were I painted, I would wish
This youth should say, 'twere well; and only therefore
Desire to breed by me.—Here's flowers for you;
Hot lavender, mints, savory, marjoram;
The marigold, that goes to bed with the sun,
And with him rises weeping; these are flowers
Of middle summer, and, I think, they are given
To men of middle age: You are very welcome.

Cam. I should leave grazing, were I of your flock,
And only live by gazing.

Per. Out, alas!
You'd be so lean, that blasts of January
Would blow you through and through.—Now, my fairest friend,
I would, I had some flowers o' the spring, that might
Become your time of day; and yours; and yours;
That wear upon your virgin branches yet
Your maidenheads growing:—O Proserpina,
For the flowers now, that, frighted, thou let'st fall
From Dis's waggon! daffodils,
That come before the swallow dares, and take
The winds of March with beauty; violets, dim,
But sweeter than the lids of Juno's eyes,
Or Cytherea's breath; pale primroses,
That die unmarried, ere they can behold
Bright Phœbus in his strength, a malady
Most incident to maids; bold oxlips, and
The crown-imperial; lilies of all kinds,
The flower-de-luce being one! O, these I lack,
To make you garlands of; and, my sweet friend,
To strew him o'er and o'er.

Flo. What? like a corse?

Per. No, like a bank, for love to lie and play on;
Not like a corse: or if,—not to be buried,
But quick, and in mine arms. Come, take your flowers:
Methinks, I play as I have seen them do
In Whitsun' pastorals: sure, this robe of mine
Does change my disposition.

Flo. What you do,
Still betters what is done. When you speak, sweet,
I'd have you do it ever: when you sing,
I'd have you buy and sell so; so give alms;
Pray so; and, for the ordering your affairs,
To sing them too: When you do dance, I wish you
A wave o' the sea, that you might ever do
Nothing but that; move still, still so, and own
No other function: Each your doing,
So singular in each particular,
Crowns what you are doing in the present deeds,
That all your acts are queens.

Per. O Doricles,
Your praises are too large: but that your youth,
And the true blood, which fairly peeps through it,
Do plainly give you out an unstain'd shepherd;
With wisdom I might fear, my Doricles,
You woo'd me the false way.

Flo. I think, you have
As little skill to fear, as I have purpose
To put you to't.—But, come; our dance, I pray:
Your hand, my Perdita: so turtles pair,
That never mean to part.

Per. I'll swear for 'em.

Pol. This is the prettiest low-born lass, that ever
Ran on the green-sward: nothing she does, or seems,
But smacks of something greater than herself;
Too noble for this place.

Cam. He tells her something,
That makes her blood look out: Good sooth, she is
The queen of curds and cream.

Clo. Come on, strike up.

Dor. Mopsa must be your mistress: marry, garlick,
To mend her kissing with.

Mop. Now, in good time!

Clo. Not a word, a word; we stand upon our manners.—
Come, strike up. [*Musick.*

Here a Dance of Shepherds *and* Shepherdesses.

Pol. Pray, good shepherd, what
Fair swain is this, which dances with your daughter?

Shep. They call him Doricles, and he boasts himself
To have a worthy feeding: but I have it
Upon his own report, and I believe it;
He looks like sooth: He says, he loves my daughter;
I think so too; for never gaz'd the moon
Upon the water, as he'll stand, and read,

As 'twere, my daughter's eyes: and, to be plain,
I think, there is not half a kiss to choose,
Who loves another best.

Pol. She dances featly.

Shep. So she does any thing; though I report it,
That should be silent: if young Doricles
Do light upon her, she shall bring him that
Which he not dreams of.

Enter a Servant.

Serv. O master, if you did but hear the pedler at the door, you would never dance again after a tabor and pipe; no, the bagpipe could not move you: he sings several tunes, faster than you'll tell money; he utters them as he had eaten ballads, and all men's ears grew to his tunes.

Clo. He could never come better: he shall come in: I love a ballad but even too well; if it be doleful matter, merrily set down, or a very pleasant thing indeed, and sung lamentably.

Serv. He hath songs, for man, or woman, of all sizes; no milliner can so fit his customers with gloves; he has the prettiest love-songs for maids; so without bawdry, which is strange; with such delicate burdens of *dildos* and *fadings; jump her and thump her;* and where some stretch-mouth'd rascal would, as it were, mean mischief, and break a foul gap into the matter, he makes the maid to answer, *Whoop, do me no harm, good man;* puts him off, slights him, with *Whoop, do me no harm, good man.*

Pol. This is a brave fellow.

Clo. Believe me, thou talkest of an admirable conceited fellow. Has he any unbraided wares?

Serv. He hath ribands of all the colours i' the rainbow; points, more than all the lawyers in Bohemia can learnedly handle, though they come to him by the gross; inkles, caddisses, cambricks, lawns: why, he sings them over, as they were gods or goddesses; you would think, a smock were a she-angel; he so chants to the sleeve-hand, and the work about the square on't.

Clo. Pr'ythee, bring him in; and let him approach singing.

Per. Forewarn him, that he use no scurrilous words in his tunes.

Clo. You have of these pedlers, that have more in 'em than you'd think, sister.

Per. Ay, good brother, or go about to think.

Enter AUTOLYCUS, *singing.*

Lawn, as white as driven snow;
Cyprus, black as e'er was crow;
Gloves, as sweet as damask roses;
Masks for faces, and for noses;
Bugle-bracelet, necklace-amber,
Perfume for a lady's chamber:
Golden quoifs, and stomachers,
For my lads to give their dears;
Pins, and poking-sticks of steel,
What maids lack from head to heel:
Come, buy of me, come; come buy, come buy;
Buy, lads, or else your lasses cry;
Come, buy, &c.

Clo. If I were not in love with Mopsa, thou should'st take no money of me; but being enthrall'd as I am, it will also be the bondage of certain ribands and gloves.

Mop. I was promis'd them against the feast; but they come not too late now.

Dor. He hath promised you more than that, or there be liars.

Mop. He hath paid you all he promised you: may be, he has paid you more; which will shame you to give him again.

Clo. Is there no manners left among maids? will they wear their plackets, where they should bear their faces? Is there not milking-time, when you are going to bed, or kiln-hole, to whistle off these secrets; but you must be tittle-tattling before all our guests? 'Tis well, they are whispering: Clamour your tongues, and not a word more.

Mop. I have done. Come, you promised me a tawdry lace, and a pair of sweet gloves.

Clo. Have I not told thee, how I was cozened by the way, and lost all my money?

Aut. And, indeed, sir, there are cozeners abroad: therefore it behoves men to be wary.

Clo. Fear not thou, man, thou shalt lose nothing here.

Aut. I hope so, sir; for I have about me many parcels of charge.

Clo. What hast here? ballads?

Mop. 'Pray now, buy some: I love a ballad in print, a'-life; for then we are sure they are true.

Aut. Here's one to a very doleful tune, How a usurer's wife was brought to bed of twenty money-bags at a burden; and how she longed to eat adders' heads, and toads carbonadoed.

Mop. Is it true, think you?

Aut. Very true; and but a month old.

Dor. Bless me from marrying a usurer!

Aut. Here's the midwife's name to't, one mistress Taleporter; and five or six honest wives that were present: Why should I carry lies abroad?

Mop. 'Pray you now, buy it.

Clo. Come on, lay it by: And let's first see more ballads; we'll buy the other things anon.

Aut. Here's another ballad, of a fish, that appeared upon the coast, on Wednesday the fourscore of April, forty thousand fathom above water, and sung this ballad against the hard hearts of maids: it was thought, she was a woman, and was turned into a cold fish, for she would not exchange flesh with one that loved her: The ballad is very pitiful, and as true.

Dor. Is it true, think you?

Aut. Five justices' hands at it; and witnesses, more than my pack will hold.

Clo. Lay it by too: Another.

Aut. This is a merry ballad; but a very pretty one.

Mop. Let's have some merry ones.

Aut. Why, this is a passing merry one; and goes to the tune of, *Two maids wooing a man:* there's scarce a maid westward, but she sings it; 'tis in request, I can tell you.

Mop. We can both sing it; if thou'lt bear a part, thou shalt hear; 'tis in three parts.

Dor. We had the tune on't a month ago.

Aut. I can bear my part; you must know, 'tis my occupation: have at it with you.

SONG.

A. *Get you hence, for I must go;*
Where, it fits not you to know.
D. *Whither?* M. *O, whither?* D. *Whither?*
M. *It becomes thy oath full well,*
Thou to me thy secrets tell:
D. *Me too, let me go thither.*
M. *Or thou go'st to the grange, or mill:*
D. *If to either, thou dost ill.*
A. *Neither.* D. *What, neither?* A. *Neither.*
D. *Thou hast sworn my love to be:*
M. *Thou hast sworn it more to me:*
Then, whither go'st? say, whither?

Clo. We'll have this song out anon by ourselves: My father and the gentlemen are in sad talk, and we'll not trouble them: Come, bring away thy pack after me. Wenches, I'll buy for you both:—Pedler, let's have the first choice.—Follow me, girls.

Aut. And you shall pay well for 'em. [*Aside.*

Will you buy any tape,
Or lace for your cape,
My dainty duck, my dear-a?
Any silk, any thread,
Any toys for your head,

Of the new'st, and fin'st, fin'st wear-a?
Come to the pedler;
Money's a medler,
That doth utter all men's ware-a.
[*Exeunt* Clown, AUT. DORC. *and* MOPSA.

Enter a Servant.

Serv. Master, there is three carters, three shepherds, three neat-herds, three swine-herds, that have made themselves all men of hair; they call themselves saltiers: and they have a dance which the wenches say is a gallimaufry of gambols, because they are not in 't; but they themselves are o' the mind, (if it be not too rough for some, that know little but bowling), it will please plentifully.

Shep. Away! we'll none on't; here has been too much homely foolery already:—I know, sir, we weary you.

Pol. You weary those that refresh us: Pray, let's see these four threes of herdsmen.

Serv. One three of them, by their own report, sir, hath danced before the king; and not the worst of the three, but jumps twelve foot and a half by the squire.

Shep. Leave your prating; since these good men are pleased, let them come in; but quickly now.

Serv. Why, they stay at door, sir. [*Exit.*

Re-enter Servant, *with twelve Rusticks habited like Satyrs. They dance, and then exeunt.*

Pol. O, father, you'll know more of that hereafter.—
Is it not too far gone?—'Tis time to part them.—
He's simple, and tells much. [*Aside.*]—How now, fair shepherd?
Your heart is full of something, that does take
Your mind from feasting. Sooth, when I was young,
And handed love, as you do, I was wont
To load my she with knacks: I would have ransack'd
The pedler's silken treasury, and have pour'd it
To her acceptance; you have let him go,
And nothing marted with him: if your lass
Interpretation should abuse; and call this
Your lack of love, or bounty: you were straited
For a reply, at least, if you make a care
Of happy holding her.

Flo. Old sir, I know
She prizes not such trifles as these are:
The gifts, she looks from me, are pack'd and lock'd
Up in my heart; which I have given already,
But not deliver'd.—O, hear me breathe my life
Before this ancient sir, who, it should seem,
Hath sometime lov'd: I take thy hand; this hand,
As soft as dove's down, and as white as it;
Or Ethiopian's tooth, or the fann'd snow,
That's bolted by the northern blasts twice o'er.

Pol. What follows this?
How prettily the young swain seems to wash
The hand, was fair before!—I have put you out:—
But to your protestation; let me hear
What you profess.

Flo. Do, and be witness to 't.

Pol. And this my neighbour too?

Flo. And he, and more
Than he, and men; the earth, the heavens, and all:
That,—were I crown'd the most imperial monarch,
Thereof most worthy; were I the fairest youth
That ever made eye swerve; had force, and knowledge,
More than was ever man's,—I would not prize them,
Without her love: for her, employ them all;
Commend them, and condemn them, to her service,
Or to their own perdition.

Pol. Fairly offer'd.

Cam. This shows a sound affection.

Shep. But, my daughter,
Say you the like to him?

Per. I cannot speak
So well, nothing so well; no, nor mean better:
By the pattern of my own thoughts I cut out
The purity of his.

Shep. Take hands, a bargain;——
And, friends unknown, you shall bear witness to 't:
I give my daughter to him, and will make
Her portion equal his.

Flo. O, that must be
I' the virtue of your daughter: one being dead,
I shall have more than you can dream of yet;
Enough then for your wonder: But, come on,
Contract us 'fore these witnesses.

Shep. Come, your hand;——
And, daughter, yours.

Pol. Soft, swain, a while, 'beseech you;
Have you a father?

Flo. I have: But what of him?

Pol. Knows he of this?

Flo. He neither does, nor shall.

Pol. Methinks, a father
Is, at the nuptial of his son, a guest
That best becomes the table. 'Pray you, once more;
Is not your father grown incapable
Of reasonable affairs? is he not stupid
With age, and altering rheums? Can he speak? hear?
Know man from man? dispute his own estate?
Lies he not bed-rid? and again does nothing,
But what he did being childish?

Flo. No, good sir;
He has his health, and ampler strength, indeed,
Than most have of his age.

Pol. By my white beard,
You offer him, if this be so, a wrong
Something unfilial: Reason, my son
Should choose himself a wife; but as good reason,
The father (all whose joy is nothing else
But fair posterity) should hold some counsel
In such a business.

Flo. I yield all this;
But, for some other reasons, my grave sir,
Which 'tis not fit you know, I not acquaint
My father of this business.

Pol. Let him know 't.

Flo. He shall not.

Pol. Pr'ythee, let him.

Flo. No, he must not.

Shep. Let him, my son; he shall not need to grieve
At knowing of thy choice.

Flo. Come, come, he must not:—
Mark our contract.

Pol. Mark your divorce, young sir,
[*Discovering himself.*
Whom son I dare not call; thou art too base
To be acknowledg'd: Thou a sceptre's heir,
That thus affect'st a sheep-hook!—Thou, old traitor,
I am sorry, that, by hanging thee, I can but
Shorten thy life one week.—And thou, fresh piece
Of excellent witchcraft; who, of force, must know
The royal fool thou cop'st with;——

Shep. O, my heart!

Pol. I'll have thy beauty scratch'd with briars, and made
More homely than thy state.—For thee, fond boy,—
If I may ever know, thou dost but sigh,
That thou no more shalt see this knack, (as never
I mean thou shalt), we'll bar thee from succession;
Not hold thee of our blood, no, not our kin,
Far than Deucalion off:—Mark thou my words;

Follow us to the court.—Thou churl, for this time,
Though full of our displeasure, yet we free thee
From the dead blow of it.—And you, enchantment,—
Worthy enough a herdsman; yea, him too,
That makes himself, but for our honour therein,
Unworthy thee,—if ever, henceforth, thou
These rural latches to his entrance open,
Or hoop his body more with thy embraces,
I will devise a death as cruel for thee,
As thou art tender to 't. [*Exit.*

Per. Even here undone!
I was not much afeard: for once, or twice,
I was about to speak; and tell him plainly,
The selfsame sun, that shines upon his court,
Hides not his visage from our cottage, but
Looks on alike.—Will 't please you, sir, be gone? [*To* FLORIZEL.
I told you, what would come of this: 'Beseech you,
Of your own state take care: this dream of mine,—
Being now awake, I'll queen it no inch further,
But milk my ewes, and weep.

Cam. Why, how now, father?
Speak, ere thou diest.

Shep. I cannot speak, nor think,
Nor dare to know that which I know.—O, sir, [*To* FLORIZEL.
You have undone a man of fourscore three,
That thought to fill his grave in quiet: yea,
To die upon the bed my father died,
To lie close by his honest bones: but now
Some hangman must put on my shroud, and lay me
Where no priest shovels-in dust.—O cursed wretch! [*To* PERDITA.
That knew'st this was the prince, and would'st adventure
To mingle faith with him.—Undone! undone!
If I might die within this hour, I have liv'd
To die when I desire. [*Exit.*

Flo. Why look you so upon me?
I am but sorry, not afeard! delay'd,
But nothing alter'd: What I was, I am:
More straining on, for plucking back; not following
My leash unwillingly.

Cam. Gracious my lord,
You know your father's temper: at this time
He will allow no speech,—which, I do guess,
You do not purpose to him;—and as hardly
Will he endure your sight as yet, I fear:
Then, till the fury of his highness settle,
Come not before him.

Flo. I not purpose it.
I think, Camillo.

Cam. Even he, my lord.

Per. How often have I told you, 'twould be thus?
How often said, my dignity would last
But till 'twere known?

Flo. It cannot fail, but by
The violation of my faith; And then
Let nature crush the sides o' the earth together,
And mar the seeds within!—Lift up thy looks:—
From my succession wipe me, father! I
Am heir to my affection.

Cam. Be advis'd.

Flo. I am; and by my fancy: if my reason
Will thereto be obedient, I have reason;
If not, my senses, better pleas'd with madness,
Do bid it welcome.

Cam. This is desperate, sir.

Flo. So call it; but it does fulfil my vow;
I needs must think it honesty. Camillo,
Not for Bohemia, nor the pomp that may
Be thereat glean'd; for all the sun sees, or
The close earth wombs, or the profound seas hide
In unknown fathoms, will I break my oath
To this my fair belov'd: Therefore, I pray you,
As you have ever been my father's honour'd friend,
When he shall miss me (as, in faith, I mean not
To see him any more), cast your good counsels
Upon his passion: Let myself and fortune,
Tug for the time to come. This you may know,
And so deliver;—I am put to sea
With her, whom here I cannot hold on shore;
And, most opportune to our need, I have
A vessel rides fast by, but not prepar'd
For this design. What course I mean to hold,
Shall nothing benefit your knowledge, nor
Concern me the reporting.

Cam. O, my lord,
I would your spirit were easier for advice,
Or stronger for your need.

Flo. Hark, Perdita.——[*Takes her aside.*
I'll hear you by and by. [*To* CAMILLO.

Cam. He's irremovable,
Resolv'd for flight: Now were I happy, if
His going I could frame to serve my turn;
Save him from danger, do him love and honour;
Purchase the sight again of dear Sicilia,
And that unhappy king, my master, whom
I so much thirst to see.

Flo. Now, good Camillo,
I am so fraught with curious business, that
I leave out ceremony. [*Going.*

Cam. Sir, I think,
You have heard of my poor services, i' the love
That I have borne your father?

Clo. Very nobly
Have you deserv'd: it is my father's musick,
To speak your deeds; not little of his care
To have them recompens'd as thought on.

Cam. Well, my lord,
If you may please to think I love the king;
And, through him, what is nearest to him, which is
Your gracious self; embrace but my direction,
(If your more ponderous and settled project
May suffer alteration) on mine honour
I'll point you where you shall have such receiving
As shall become your highness; where you may
Enjoy your mistress (from the whom, I see,
There's no disjunction to be made, but by,
As heavens forefend! your ruin): marry her;
And (with my best endeavours, in your absence)
Your discontenting father strive to qualify,
And bring him up to liking.

Flo. How, Camillo,
May this, almost a miracle, be done?
That I may call thee something more than man,
And, after that, trust to thee.

Cam. Have you thought on
A place, whereto you'll go?

Flo. Not any yet:
But as the unthought-on accident is guilty
To what we wildly do; so we profess
Ourselves to be the slaves of chance, and flies
Of every wind that blows.

Cam. Then list to me:
This follows,—if you will not change your purpose,
But undergo this flight;—Make for Sicilia;
And there present yourself, and your fair princess
(For so, I see, she must be), 'fore Leontes;
She shall be habited, as it becomes
The partner of your bed. Methinks, I see
Leontes, opening his free arms, and weeping
His welcomes forth: asks thee, the son, forgiveness,
As 'twere i' the father's person: kisses the hands
Of your fresh princess: o'er and o'er divides him
'Twixt his unkindness and his kindness; the one
He chides to hell, and bids the other grow,
Faster than thought, or time.

Flo. Worthy Camillo,
What colour for my visitation shall I
Hold up before him?

Cam. Sent by the king your father
To greet him, and to give him comforts. Sir,

The manner of your bearing towards him, with
What you, as from your father, shall deliver,
Things known betwixt us three, I'll write you down:
The which shall point you forth at every sitting,
What you must say; that he shall not perceive,
But that you have your father's bosom there,
And speak his very heart.

Flo. I am bound to you:
There is some sap in this.

Cam. A course more promising
Than a wild dedication of yourselves
To unpath'd waters, undream'd shores; most certain,
To miseries enough: no hope to help you;
But as you shake off one, to take another:
Nothing so certain as your anchors; who
Do their best office, if they can but stay you
Where you'll be loath to be: Besides, you know,
Prosperity's the very bond of love;
Whose fresh complexion and whose heart together
Affliction alters.

Per. One of these is true:
I think, affliction may subdue the cheek,
But not take in the mind.

Cam. Yea, say you so?
There shall not, at your father's house, these seven years,
Be born another such.

Flo. My good Camillo,
She is as forward of her breeding, as
She is i' the rear of birth.

Cam. I cannot say, 'tis pity
She lacks instructions; for she seems a mistress
To most that teach.

Per. Your pardon, sir, for this;
I'll blush you thanks.

Flo. My prettiest Perdita.——
But, O, the thorns we stand upon!—Camillo,—
Preserver of my father, now of me;
The medicine of our house!—how shall we do?
We are not furnish'd like Bohemia's son;
Nor shall appear in Sicilia——

Cam. My lord,
Fear none of this: I think, you know, my fortunes
Do all lie there: it shall be so my care
To have you royally appointed, as if
The scene you play, were mine. For instance, sir,
That you may know, you shall not want,—one word. [*They talk aside.*

Enter AUTOLYCUS.

Aut. Ha, ha! what a fool honesty is! and trust, his sworn brother, a very simple gentleman! I have sold all my trumpery; not a counterfeit stone, not a riband, glass, pomander, brooch, table-book, ballad, knife, tape, glove, shoe-tie, bracelet, horn-ring, to keep my pack from fasting; they throng who should buy first; as if my trinkets had been hallowed, and brought a benediction to the buyer: by which means, I saw whose purse was best in picture; and, what I saw, to my good use, I remembered. My clown (who wants but something to be a reasonable man) grew so in love with the wenches' song, that he would not stir his pettitoes, till he had both tune and words, which so drew the rest of the herd to me, that all their other senses stuck in ears: you might have pinch'd a placket, it was senseless; 'twas nothing, to geld a codpiece of a purse; I would have filed keys off, that hung in chains: no hearing, no feeling, but my sir's song, and admiring the nothing of it. So that, in this time of lethargy, I picked and cut most of their festival purses: and had not the old man come in with a whoobub against his daughter and the king's son, and scared my choughs from the chaff, I had not left a purse alive in the whole army.

[CAMILLO, FLORIZEL, *and* PERDITA *come forward.*

Cam. Nay, but my letters by this means being there
So soon as you arrive, shall clear that doubt.

Flo. And those that you'll procure from king Leontes——

Cam. Shall satisfy your father.

Per. Happy be you!
All, that you speak, shows fair.

Cam. Who have we here? [*Seeing* AUTOLYCUS.
We'll make an instrument of this; omit
Nothing, may give us aid.

Aut. If they have overheard me now,——why hanging. [*Aside.*

Cam. How now, good fellow? Why shakest thou so? Fear not, man; here's no harm intended to thee.

Aut. I am a poor fellow, sir.

Cam. Why, be so still; here's nobody will steal that from thee: Yet, for the outside of thy poverty, we must make an exchange: therefore, discase thee instantly (thou must think, there's necessity in 't), and change garments with this gentleman: Though the pennyworth, on his side, be the worst, yet hold thee, there's some boot.

Aut. I am a poor fellow, sir:—I know ye well enough. [*Aside.*

Cam. Nay, pr'ythee, despatch: the gentleman is half flayed already.

Aut. Are you in earnest, sir?—I smell the trick of it. [*Aside.*

Flo. Despatch, I pr'ythee.

Aut. Indeed, I have had earnest; but I cannot with conscience take it.

Cam. Unbuckle, unbuckle.—
[FLO. *and* AUTOL. *exchange garments.*
Fortunate mistress,—let my prophecy
Come home to you!—you must retire yourself
Into some covert: take your sweetheart's hat,
And pluck it o'er your brows; muffle your face;
Dismantle you: and as you can, disliken
The truth of your own seeming; that you may
(For I do fear eyes over you) to shipboard
Get undescried.

Per. I see, the play so lies,
That I must bear a part.

Cam. No remedy.—
Have you done there?

Flo. Should I now meet my father,
He would not call me son.

Cam. Nay, you shall have
No hat:—Come, lady, come.—Farewell, my friend.

Aut. Adieu, sir.

Flo. O Perdita, what have we twain forgot?
Pray you, a word. [*They converse apart.*

Cam. What I do next, shall be to tell the king [*Aside.*
Of this escape, and whither they are bound;
Wherein, my hope is, I shall so prevail,
To force him after: in whose company
I shall review Sicilia; for whose sight
I have a woman's longing.

Flo. Fortune speed us!—
Thus we set on, Camillo, to the sea-side.

Cam. The swifter speed, the better.
[*Exeunt* FLO. PER. *and* CAM.

Aut. I understand the business, I hear it: To have an open ear, a quick eye, and a nimble hand, is necessary for a cut-purse; a good nose is requisite also, to smell out work for the other senses. I see, this is the time that the unjust man doth thrive. What an exchange had this been, without boot? what a boot is here, with this exchange? Sure, the gods do this year connive at us, and we may do any thing *extempore*. The prince himself is about a piece of iniquity; stealing away from his father, with his clog at his heels: If I thought it were not a piece of honesty to acquaint the king withal, I would do 't: I hold it the more knavery to conceal it; and therein am I constant in my profession.

Enter Clown *and* Shepherd.

Aside, aside;—here is more matter for a hot brain: Every lane's end, every shop, church, session, hanging, yields a careful man work.

Clo. See, see; what a man you are now! there is no other way, but to tell the king, she's a changeling, and none of your flesh and blood.

Shep. Nay, but hear me.

Clo. Nay, but hear me.

Shep. Go to then.

Clo. She being none of your flesh and blood, your flesh and blood has not offended the king: and, so, your flesh and blood is not to be punished by him. Show those things you found about her: those secret things, all but what she has with her: This being done, let the law go whistle; I warrant you.

Shep. I will tell the king all, every word, yea, and his son's pranks too: who, I may say, is no honest man neither to his father, nor to me, to go about to make me the king's brother-in-law.

Clo. Indeed, brother-in-law was the farthest off you could have been to him: and then your blood had been the dearer, by I know how much an ounce.

Aut. Very wisely; puppies! [*Aside.*

Shep. Well; let us to the king; there is that in this fardel, will make him scratch his beard.

Aut. I know not what impediment this complaint may be to the flight of my master.

Clo. 'Pray heartily, he be at palace.

Aut. Though I am not naturally honest, I am so sometimes by chance:—Let me pocket up my pedler's excrement. [*Takes off his false beard.*] How now, rusticks? whither are you bound?

Shep. To the palace, an it like your worship.

Aut. Your affairs there? what? with whom? the condition of that fardel, the place of your dwelling, your names, your ages, of what having, breeding, and any thing that is fitting to be known, discover.

Clo. We are but plain fellows, sir.

Aut. A lie; you are rough and hairy: Let me have no lying; it becomes none but tradesmen, and they often give us soldiers the lie: but we pay them for it with stamped coin, not stabbing steel; therefore they do not give us the lie.

Clo. Your worship had like to have given us one, if you had not taken yourself with the manner.

Shep. Are you a courtier, an't like you, sir?

Aut. Whether it like me, or no, I am a courtier. Seest thou not the air of the court, in these enfoldings? hath not my gait in it, the measure of the court? receives not thy nose court-odour from me? reflect I not on thy baseness, court-contempt? Think'st thou, for that I insinuate, or toze from thee thy business, I am therefore no courtier? I am courtier, cap-a-pe; and one that will either push on, or pluck back thy business there: whereupon I command thee to open thy affair.

Shep. My business, sir, is to the king.

Aut. What advocate hast thou to him?

Shep. I know not, an't like you.

Clo. Advocate's the court-word for a pheasant; say you have none.

Shep. None, sir; I have no pheasant, cock, nor hen.

Aut. How bless'd are we, that are not simple men!
Yet nature might have made me as these are,
Therefore I'll not disdain.

Clo. This cannot be but a great courtier.

Shep. His garments are rich, but he wears them not handsomely.

Clo. He seems to be the more noble in being fantastical; a great man, I'll warrant; I know, by the picking on's teeth.

Aut. The fardel there? what's i'the fardel? Wherefore that box?

Shep. Sir, there lies such secrets in this fardel, and box, which none must know but the king; and which he shall know within this hour, if I may come to the speech of him.

Aut. Age, thou hast lost thy labour.

Shep. Why, sir?

Aut. The king is not at the palace; he is gone aboard a new ship to purge melancholy, and air himself: For, if thou be'st capable of things serious, thou must know, the king is full of grief.

Shep. So 'tis said, sir; about his son, that should have married a shepherd's daughter.

Aut. If that shepherd be not in hand-fast, let him fly; the curses he shall have, the tortures he shall feel, will break the back of man, the heart of monster.

Clo. Think you so, sir?

Aut. Not he alone shall suffer what wit can make heavy, and vengeance bitter; but those that are germane to him, though removed fifty times, shall all come under the hangman: which though it be great pity, yet it is necessary. An old sheep-whistling rogue, a ram-tender, to offer to have his daughter come into grace! Some say, he shall be stoned; but that death is too soft for him, say I: Draw our throne into a sheep-cote! all deaths are too few, the sharpest too easy.

Clo. Has the old man e'er a son, sir, do you hear, an't like you, sir?

Aut. He has a son, who shall be flayed alive; then, 'nointed over with honey, set on the head of a wasps' nest; then stand, till he be three quarters and a dram dead: then recovered again with aqua-vitæ, or some other hot infusion: then, raw as he is, and in the hottest day prognostication proclaims, shall he be set against a brick wall, the sun looking with a southward eye upon him; where he is to behold him, with flies blown to death. But what talk we of these traitorly rascals, whose miseries are to be smiled at, their offences being so capital? Tell me (for you seem to be honest plain men) what you have to the king: being something gently considered, I'll bring you where he is aboard, tender your persons to his presence, whisper him in your behalf; and, if it be in man, besides the king, to effect your suits, here is man shall do it.

Clo. He seems to be of great authority: close with him, give him gold; and though authority be a stubborn bear, yet he is oft led by the nose with gold: show the inside of your purse to the outside of his hand, and no more ado: Remember stoned, and flayed alive.

Shep. An't please you, sir, to undertake the business for us, here is that gold I have: I'll make it as much more; and leave this young man in pawn, till I bring it you.

Aut. After I have done what I promised?

Shep. Ay, sir.

Aut. Well, give me the moiety:—Are you a party in this business?

Clo. In some sort, sir: but though my case be a pitiful one, I hope I shall not be flayed out of it.

Aut. O, that's the case of the shepherd's son:—Hang him, he'll be made an example.

Clo. Comfort, good comfort: we must to the king, and show our strange sights; he must know, 'tis none of your daughter nor my sister; we are gone else. Sir, I will give you as much as this old man does, when the business is performed; and remain, as he says, your pawn, till it be brought you.

Aut. I will trust you. Walk before toward the sea-side; go on the right hand; I will but look upon the hedge, and follow you.

Clo. We are blessed in this man, as I may say, even blessed.

Shep. Let's before, as he bids us; he was provided to do us good.

[*Exeunt* Shepherd *and* Clown.

Aut. If I had a mind to be honest, I see, fortune would not suffer me; she drops booties in my mouth. I am courted now with a double occasion; gold, and a means to do the prince my master good; which, who knows how that may turn back to my advancement? I will bring these two moles, these blind ones, aboard him: if he think it fit to shore them again, and that the complaint they have to the king concerns him nothing, let him call me rogue, for being so far officious: for I am proof against that title, and what shame else belongs to't: To him I will present them, there may be matter in it. [*Exit.*

ACT V.

SCENE I. Sicilia.

A Room in the Palace of Leontes.

Enter LEONTES, CLEOMENES, DION, PAULINA, *and others.*

Cleo. Sir, you have done enough, and have perform'd
A saintlike sorrow: no fault could you make,
Which you have not redeem'd; indeed, paid down
More penitence, than done trespass: at the last,
Do, as the heavens have done; forget your evil:
With them, forgive yourself.

Leon. Whilst I remember
Her and her virtues, I cannot forget
My blemishes in them; and so still think of
The wrong I did myself: which was so much,
That heirless it hath made my kingdom; and
Destroy'd the sweet'st companion that e'er man
Bred his hopes out of.

Paul. True, too true, my lord:
If, one by one, you wedded all the world,
Or, from the all that are, took something good,
To make a perfect woman; she, you kill'd,
Would be unparallel'd.

Leon. I think so. Kill'd!
She I kill'd? I did so: but thou strik'st me
Sorely, to say I did; it is as bitter
Upon thy tongue, as in my thought: Now, good now,
Say so but seldom.

Cleo. Not at all, good lady:
You might have spoken a thousand things that would
Have done the time more benefit, and grac'd
Your kindness better.

Paul. You are one of those,
Would have him wed again.

Dion. If you would not so,
You pity not the state, nor the remembrance
Of his most sovereign dame; consider little,
What dangers, by his highness' fail of issue,
May drop upon his kingdom, and devour
Incertain lookers on. What were more holy,
Than to rejoice, the former queen is well?
What holier, than,—for royalty's repair,
For present comfort and for future good,—
To bless the bed of majesty again
With a sweet fellow to't?

Paul. There is none worthy,
Respecting her that's gone. Besides, the gods
Will have fulfill'd their secret purposes:
For has not the divine Apollo said,
Is't not the tenour of his oracle,
That king Leontes shall not have an heir,
Till his lost child be found? which, that it shall,
Is all as monstrous to our human reason,
As my Antigonus to break his grave,
And come again to me; who, on my life,
Did perish with the infant. 'Tis your counsel,
My lord should to the heavens be contrary,
Oppose against their wills.—Care not for issue:
[*To* LEONTES.
The crown will find an heir: Great Alexander
Left his to the worthiest; so his successor
Was like to be the best.

Leon. Good Paulina,—
Who hast the memory of Hermione,
I know, in honour,—O, that ever I
Had squar'd me to thy counsel!—then even now,
I might have look'd upon my queen's full eyes;
Have taken treasure from her lips,——

Paul. And left them
More rich, for what they yielded.

Leon. Thou speak'st truth.
No more such wives; therefore, no wife: one worse,
And better us'd, would make her sainted spirit
Again possess her corps; and, on this stage
(Where we offenders now appear), soul-vex'd,
Begin, *And why to me?*

Paul. Had she such power,
She had just cause.

Leon. She had; and would incense me
To murder her I married.

Paul. I should so:
Were I the ghost that walk'd, I'd bid you mark
Her eye; and tell me, for what dull part in't
You chose her: then I'd shriek, that even your ears
Should rift to hear me; and the words that follow'd
Should be, *Remember mine.*

Leon. Stars, very stars,
And all eyes else dead coals:—fear thou no wife,
I'll have no wife, Paulina.

Paul. Will you swear
Never to marry, but by my free leave?

Leon. Never, Paulina; so be bless'd my spirit!

Paul. Then, good my lords, bear witness to his oath.

Cleo. You tempt him over-much.

Paul. Unless another,
As like Hermione as is her picture,
Affront his eye.

Cleo. Good madam,—

Paul. I have done.
Yet, if my lord will marry,—if you will, sir,
No remedy, but you will: give me the office
To choose you a queen: She shall not be so young
As was your former: but she shall be such,
As, walk'd your first queen's ghost, it should take joy
To see her in your arms.

Leon. My true Paulina,
We shall not marry, till thou bidd'st us.

Paul. That
Shall be, when your first queen's again in breath;
Never till then.

Enter a Gentleman.

Gent. One that gives out himself prince Florizel,
Son of Polixenes, with his princess (she
The fairest I have yet beheld), desires access
To your high presence.

Leon. What with him? he comes not
Like to his father's greatness: his approach,
So out of circumstance, and sudden, tells us,
'Tis not a visitation fram'd, but forc'd
By need, and accident. What train?

Gent. But few,
And those but mean.

Leon. His princess, say you, with him?

Gent. Ay; the most peerless piece of earth, I think,
That e'er the sun shone bright on.

Paul. O Hermione,
As every present time doth boast itself
Above a better, gone; so must thy grave
Give way to what's seen now. Sir, you yourself
Have said, and writ so (but your writing now
Is colder than that theme), *She had not been,*
Nor was not to be equall'd;—thus your verse
Flow'd with her beauty once; 'tis shrewdly ebb'd,
To say, you have seen a better.

Gent. Pardon, madam:
The one I have almost forgot (your pardon);

The other, when she has obtain'd your eye,
Will have your tongue too. This is such a creature;
Would she begin a sect, might quench the zeal
Of all professors else: make proselytes
Of who she but bid follow.

Paul. How? not women?

Gent. Women will love her, that she is a woman
More worth than any man; men, that she is
The rarest of all women.

Leon. Go, Cleomenes;
Yourself, assisted with your honour'd friends,
Bring them to our embracement.—Still 'tis strange,

[*Exeunt* CLEOMENES, Lords, *and* Gentlemen.

He thus should steal upon us.

Paul. Had our prince
(Jewel of children) seen this hour, he had pair'd
Well with this lord; there was not full a month
Between their births.

Leon. 'Pry'thee, no more; thou know'st,
He dies to me again, when talk'd of: sure,
When I shall see this gentleman, thy speeches
Will bring me to consider that, which may
Unfurnish me of reason.—They are come.——

Re-enter CLEOMENES, *with* FLORIZEL, PERDITA, *and* Attendants.

Your mother was most true to wedlock, prince;
For she did print your royal father off,
Conceiving you; Were I but twenty-one,
Your father's image is so hit in you,
His very air, that I should call you brother,
As I did him: and speak of something, wildly
By us perform'd before. Most dearly welcome!
And your fair princess, goddess!—O, alas!
I lost a couple, that 'twixt heaven and earth
Might thus have stood, begetting wonder, as
You, gracious couple, do! and then I lost
(All mine own folly) the society,
Amity too, of your brave father; whom,
Though bearing misery, I desire my life
Once more to look upon.

Flo. By his command
Have I here touch'd Sicilia: and from him
Give you all greetings, that a king, at friend,
Can send his brother: and, but infirmity
(Which waits upon worn times) hath something seiz'd
His wish'd ability, he had himself
The lands and waters twixt your throne and his
Measur'd, to look upon you; whom he loves
(He bade me say so) more than all the sceptres,
And those that bear them, living.

Leon. O, my brother,
(Good gentleman!) the wrongs, I have done thee, stir
Afresh within me; and these thy offices,
So rarely kind, are as interpreters,
Of my behind-hand slackness!—Welcome hither,
As is the spring to the earth. And hath he too
Expos'd this paragon to the fearful usage
(At least, ungentle) of the dreadful Neptune,
To greet a man, not worth her pains; much less
The adventure of her person?

Flo. Good my lord,
She came from Libya.

Leon. Where the warlike Smalus,
That noble honour'd lord, is fear'd, and lov'd?

Flo. Most royal sir, from thence; from him, whose daughter
His tears proclaim'd his, parting with her: thence
(A prosperous south-wind friendly) we have cross'd,
To execute the charge my father gave me,
For visiting your highness: My best train
I have from your Sicilian shores dismiss'd;
Who for Bohemia bend, to signify
Not only my success in Libya, sir,
But my arrival, and my wife's, in safety,
Here where we are.

Leon. The blessed gods
Purge all infection from our air, whilst you
Do climate here! You have a holy father,
A graceful gentleman; against whose person,
So sacred as it is, I have done sin:
For which the heavens, taking angry note,
Have left me issueless; and your father's bless'd
(As he from heaven merits it) with you,
Worthy his goodness. What might I have been,
Might I a son and daughter now have look'd on,
Such goodly things as you?

Enter a Lord.

Lord. Most noble sir,
That, which I shall report, will bear no credit,
Were not the proof so nigh. Please you, great sir,
Bohemia greets you from himself, by me;
Desires you to attach his son; who has
(His dignity and duty both cast off)
Fled from his father, from his hopes, and with
A shepherd's daughter.

Leon. Where's Bohemia? speak.

Lord. Here in the city; I now came from him.
I speak amazedly; and it becomes
My marvel, and my message. To your court
Whiles he was hast'ning (in the chase, it seems,
Of this fair couple), meets he on the way
The father of this seeming lady, and
Her brother, having both their country quitted
With this young prince.

Flo. Camillo has betray'd me;
Whose honour, and whose honesty, till now
Endur'd all weathers.

Lord. Lay't so to his charge;
He's with the king your father.

Leon. Who? Camillo?

Lord. Camillo, sir; I spake with him: who now
Has these poor men in question. Never saw I
Wretches so quake: they kneel, they kiss the earth;
Forswear themselves as often as they speak;
Bohemia stops his ears, and threatens them
With divers deaths in death.

Per. O, my poor father!—
The heaven sets spies upon us, will not have
Our contract celebrated.

Leon. You are married?

Flo. We are not, sir, nor are we like to be;
The stars, I see, will kiss the valleys first:—
The odds for high and low's alike.

Leon. My lord,
Is this the daughter of a king?

Flo. She is,
When once she is my wife.

Leon. That once, I see, by your good father's speed,
Will come on very slowly. I am sorry,
Most sorry, you have broken from his liking,
Where you were tied in duty: and as sorry,
Your choice is not so rich in worth as beauty,
That you might well enjoy her.

Flo. Dear, look up:
Though fortune, visible an enemy,
Should chase us with my father; power no jot
Hath she, to change our loves.—'Beseech you, sir,
Remember since you ow'd no more to time
Than I do now: with thought of such affections,
Step forth mine advocate; at your request,
My father will grant precious things as trifles.

Leon. Would he do so, I'd beg your precious mistress,
Which he counts but a trifle.

Paul. Sir, my liege,
Your eye hath too much youth in't: not a month
'Fore your queen died, she was more worth such gazes
Than what you look on now.

Leon. I thought of her,
Even in these looks I made.—But your petition

[*To* FLORIZEL.

Is yet unanswer'd; I will to your father:
Your honour not o'erthrown by your desires,

I am a friend to them, and you: upon which errand
I now go toward him; therefore, follow me,
And mark what way I make: Come, good my lord. [*Exeunt.*

SCENE II. *The same. Before the Palace.*

Enter AUTOLYCUS *and a* Gentleman.

Aut. 'Beseech you, sir, were you present at this relation?

1 *Gent.* I was by at the opening of the fardel, heard the old shepherd deliver the manner how he found it; whereupon, after a little amazedness, we were all commanded out of the chamber; only this, methought, I heard the shepherd say, he found the child.

Aut. I would most gladly know the issue of it.

1 *Gent.* I make a broken delivery of the business;—But the changes I perceived in the king, and Camillo, were very notes of admiration: they seemed almost, with staring on one another, to tear the cases of their eyes; there was speech in their dumbness, language in their very gesture; they looked, as they had heard of a world ransomed, or one destroyed: A notable passion of wonder appeared in them: but the wisest beholder, that knew no more but seeing, could not say, if the importance were joy, or sorrow: but in the extremity of the one, it must needs be.

Enter another Gentleman.

Here comes a gentleman, that, happily, knows more:
The news, Rogero?

2 *Gent.* Nothing but bonfires: The oracle is fulfilled; the king's daughter is found: such a deal of wonder is broken out within this hour, that ballad-makers cannot be able to express it.

Enter a third Gentleman.

Here comes the lady Paulina's steward; he can deliver you more.—How goes it now, sir? this news, which is called true, is so like an old tale, that the verity of it is in strong suspicion: Has the king found his heir?

3 *Gent.* Most true; if ever truth were pregnant by circumstance: that, which you hear, you'll swear you see, there is such unity in the proofs. The mantle of queen Hermione:—her jewel about the neck of it: The letters of Antigonus, found with it, which they know to be his character:—the majesty of the creature, in resemblance of the mother;—the affection of nobleness, which nature shows above her breeding,—and many other evidences, proclaim her, with all certainty, to be the king's daughter. Did you see the meeting of the two kings?

2 *Gent.* No.

3 *Gent.* Then have you lost a sight, which was to be seen, cannot be spoken of. There might you have beheld one joy crown another; so, and in such manner, that it seemed, sorrow wept to take leave of them; for their joy waded in tears. There was casting up of eyes, holding up of hands; with countenance of such distraction, that they were to be known by garment not by favour. Our king, being ready to leap out of himself for joy of his found daughter; as if that joy were now become a loss, cries, *O, thy mother, thy mother!* then asks Bohemia forgiveness: then embraces his son-in-law; then again worries he his daughter, with clipping her; now he thanks the old shepherd, which stands by, like a weather-bitten conduit of many kings' reigns. I never heard of such another encounter, which lames report to follow it, and undoes description to do it.

2 *Gent.* What, pray you, became of Antigonus, that carried hence the child?

3 *Gent.* Like an old tale still; which will have matter to rehearse, though credit be asleep, and not an ear open: He was torn to pieces with a bear; this avouches the shepherd's son; who has not only his innocence (which seems much) to justify him, but a handkerchief, and rings of his, that Paulina knows.

1 *Gent.* What became of his bark, and his followers?

3 *Gent.* Wrecked, the same instant of their master's death: and in the view of the shepherd: so that all the instruments, which aided to expose the child, were even then lost, when it was found. But, O, the noble combat, that, 'twixt joy and sorrow, was fought in Paulina! She had one eye declined for the loss of her husband; another elevated that the oracle was fulfilled: She lifted the princess from the earth; and so locks her in embracing, as if she would pin her to her heart, that she might no more be in danger of losing.

1 *Gent.* The dignity of this act was worth the audience of kings and princes; for by such was it acted.

3 *Gent.* One of the prettiest touches of all, and that which angled for mine eyes (caught the water, though not the fish) was, when at the relation of the queen's death, with the manner how she came to it (bravely confessed, and lamented by the king), how attentiveness wounded his daughter: till, from one sign of dolour to another, she did, with an *alas!* I would fain say, bleed tears; for, I am sure, my heart wept blood. Who was most marble there changed colour; some swooned, all sorrowed: if all the world could have seen it, the woe had been universal.

1 *Gent.* Are they returned to the court?

3 *Gent.* No: the princess, hearing of her mother's statue, which is in the keeping of Paulina,—a piece many years in doing, and now newly performed by that rare Italian master, Julio Romano; who had he himself eternity, and could put breath into his work would beguile nature of her custom, so perfectly he is her ape: he so near to Hermione hath done Hermione, that, they say, one would speak to her, and stand in hope of answer: thither with all greediness of affection, are they gone; and there they intend to sup.

2 *Gent.* I thought, she had some great matter there in hand; for she hath privately, twice or thrice a day, ever since the death of Hermione, visited that removed house. Shall we thither, and with our company piece the rejoicing?

1 *Gent.* Who would be thence, that has the benefit of access? every wink of an eye, some new grace will be born: our absence makes us unthrifty to our knowledge. Let's along. [*Exeunt* Gentlemen.

Aut. Now, had I not the dash of my former life in me, would preferment drop on my head. I brought the old man and his son aboard the prince; told him, I heard them talk of a fardel, and I know not what: but he at that time, over-fond of the shepherd's daughter (so he then took her to be), who began to be much sea-sick, and himself little better, extremity of weather continuing, this mystery remained undiscovered. But 'tis all one to me: for had I been the finder-out of this secret, it would not have relished among my other discredits.

Enter Shepherd *and* Clown.

Here come those I have done good to against my will, and already appearing in the blossoms of their fortune.

Shep. Come, boy; I am past more children; but thy sons and daughters will be all gentlemen born.

Clo. You are well met, sir: You denied to fight with me this other day, because I was no gentleman born: See you these clothes? say, you see them not, and think me still no gentleman born: you were best say, these robes are not gentlemen born. Give me the lie; do; and try whether I am not now a gentleman born.

Aut. I know you are now, sir, a gentleman born.

Clo. Ay, and have been so any time these four hours.

Shep. And so have I, boy.

Clo. So you have:—but I was a gentleman born before my father: for the king's son took me by the hand, and called me, brother; and then the two kings called my father, brother; and then the prince, my brother, and the princess, my sister, called my father, father; and so we wept: and there was the first gentleman-like tears that ever we shed.

Shep. We may live, son, to shed many more.

Clo. Ay; or else 'twere hard luck, being in so preposterous estate as we are.

Aut. I humbly beseech you, sir, to pardon me all the faults I have committed to your worship, and to give me your good report to the prince my master.

Shep. 'Pr'ythee, son, do; for we must be gentle now we are gentlemen.

Clo. Thou wilt amend thy life?

Aut. Ay, an it like your good worship.

Clo. Give me thy hand: I will swear to the prince, thou art as honest a true fellow as any is in Bohemia.

Shep. You may say it, but not swear it.

Clo. Not swear it, now I am a gentleman? Let boors and franklins say it, I'll swear it.

Shep. How if it be false, son?

Clo. If it be ne'er so false, a true gentleman may swear it, in the behalf of his friend:—And I'll swear to the prince, thou art a tall fellow of thy hands, and that thou wilt not be drunk; but I know, thou art no tall fellow of thy hands, and that thou wilt be drunk; but I'll swear it: and I would, thou would'st be a tall fellow of thy hands.

Aut. I will prove so, sir, to my power.

Clo. Ay, by any means prove a tall fellow: If I do not wonder, how thou darest venture to be drunk, not being a tall fellow, trust me not. —Hark! the kings and the princes, our kindred, are going to see the queen's picture. Come, follow us: we'll be thy good masters. [*Exeunt.*

SCENE III.

The same. A Room in Paulina's *House.*

Enter LEONTES, POLIXENES, FLORIZEL, PERDITA, CAMILLO, PAULINA, Lords, *and* Attendants.

Leon. O grave and good Paulina, the great comfort
That I have had of thee!
Paul. What, sovereign sir,
I did not well, I meant well: All my services,
You have paid home: but that you have vouchsaf'd
With your crown'd brother, and these your contracted
Heirs of your kingdoms, my poor house to visit,
It is a surplus of your grace, which never
My life may last to answer.
Leon. O Paulina,
We honour you with trouble: But we came
To see the statue of our queen: your gallery
Have we pass'd through, not without much content
In many singularities; but we saw not
That which my daughter came to look upon,
The statue of her mother.
Paul. As she liv'd peerless,
So her dead likeness, I do well believe,
Excels whatever yet you look'd upon,
Or hand of man hath done; therefore I keep it
Lonely, apart: But here it is: prepare
To see the life as lively mock'd, as ever
Still sleep mock'd death: behold; and say, 'tis well.
[PAUL. *undraws a Curtain, and discovers a Statue.*

I like your silence, it the more shows off
Your wonder: But yet speak;—first, you, my liege,
Comes it not something near?
Leon. Her natural posture!—
Chide me, dear stone; that I may say, indeed,
Thou art Hermione: or, rather, thou art she,
In thy not chiding; for she was as tender
As infancy and grace.—But yet Paulina,
Hermione was not so much wrinkled, nothing
So aged, as this seems.
Pol. O, not by much.
Paul. So much the more our carver's excellence;
Which lets go by some sixteen years, and makes her
As she liv'd now.
Leon. As now she might have done,
So much to my good comfort, as it is
Now piercing to my soul. O, thus she stood,
Even with such life of majesty (warm life,
As now it coldly stands), when first I woo'd her!
I am asham'd: Does not the stone rebuke me,
For being more stone than it?—O royal piece,
There's magic in thy majesty; which has
My evils conjur'd to remembrance; and
From thy admiring daughter took the spirits,
Standing like stone with thee!
Per. And give me leave;
And do not say, 'tis superstition, that
I kneel, and then implore her blessing.—Lady,
Dear queen, that ended when I but began,
Give me that hand of yours, to kiss.
Paul. O, patience;
The statue is but newly fix'd, the colour's
Not dry.
Cam. My lord, your sorrow was too sore laid on;
Which sixteen winters cannot blow away,
So many summers dry: scarce any joy
Did ever so long live; no sorrow,
But kill'd itself much sooner.
Pol. Dear my brother,
Let him, that was the cause of this have power
To take off so much grief from you, as he
Will piece up in himself.
Paul. Indeed, my lord,
If I had thought, the sight of my poor image
Would thus have wrought you (for the stone is mine),
I'd not have show'd it.
Leon. Do not draw the curtain.
Paul. No longer shall you gaze on't; lest your fancy
May think anon, it moves.
Leon. Let be, let be.
'Would, I were dead, but that, methinks, already—
What was he, that did make it?—See, my lord,
Would you not deem, it breath'd? and that those veins
Did verily bear blood?
Pol. Masterly done:
The very life seems warm upon her lip.
Leon. The fixture of her eye has motion in't,
As we are mock'd with art.
Paul. I'll draw the curtain;
My lord's almost so far transported, that
He'll think anon, it lives.
Leon. O sweet Paulina,
Make me to think so twenty years together;
No settled senses of the world can match
The pleasure of that madness. Let't alone.
Paul. I am sorry, sir, I have thus far stirr'd you: but
I could afflict you further.
Leon. Do, Paulina;
For this affliction has a taste as sweet
As any cordial comfort.—Still, methinks,
There is an air comes from her: What fine chisel
Could ever yet cut breath? Let no man mock me,
For I will kiss her.

Paul. Good my lord, forbear:
The ruddiness upon her lip is wet;
You'll mar it, if you kiss it; stain your own
With oily painting: Shall I draw the curtain?
Leon. No, not these twenty years.
Per. So long could I
Stand by, a looker on.
Paul. Either forbear,
Quit presently the chapel; or resolve you
For more amazement: If you can behold it,
I'll make the statue move indeed; descend,
And take you by the hand; but then you'll think
(Which I protest against), I am assisted
By wicked powers.
Leon. What you can make her do,
I am content to look on: what to speak,
I am content to hear; for 'tis as easy
To make her speak as move.
Paul. It is requir'd,
You do awake your faith: Then all stand still;
Or those, that think it is unlawful business
I am about, let them depart.
Leon. Proceed;
No foot shall stir.
Pol. Musick; awake her: strike.— [*Musick.*
'Tis time; descend; be stone no more: approach,
Strike all that look upon with marvel. Come:
I'll fill your grave up: stir; nay, come away;
Bequeath to death your numbness, for from him
Dear life redeems you.—You perceive, she stirs:
[HERMIONE *comes down from the Pedestal.*
Start not: her actions shall be holy, as,
You hear, my spell is lawful: do not shun her,
Until you see her die again; for then
You kill her double: Nay, present your hand:
When she was young, you woo'd her; now, in age,
Is she become the suitor.
Leon. O, she's warm! [*Embracing her.*
If this be magick, let it be an art
Lawful as eating.
Pol. She embraces him.
Cam. She hangs about his neck;
If she pertain to life, let her speak too.
Pol. Ay, and make't manifest where she has liv'd,
Or, how stol'n from the dead?
Paul. That she is living,
Were it but told you, should be hooted at
Like an old tale; but it appears, she lives,
Though yet she speak not. Mark a little while.—
Please you to interpose, fair madam; kneel,
And pray your mother's blessing.—Turn, good lady;
Our Perdita is found.
[*Presenting* PERDITA *who kneels to* HERM.
Her. You gods, look down,
And from your sacred vials pour your graces
Upon my daughter's head!—Tell me, mine own,
Where hast thou been preserv'd? where liv'd? how found
Thy father's court? for thou shalt hear, that I,—
Knowing by Paulina, that the oracle
Gave hope, thou wast in being,—have preserv'd
Myself to see the issue.
Paul. There's time enough for that;
Lest they desire, upon this push to trouble
Your joys with like relation. Go together,
You precious winners all; your exultation
Partake to every one. I, an old turtle,
Will wing me to some wither'd bough: and there
My mate, that's never to be found again,
Lament till I am lost.
Leon. O peace, Paulina;
Thou should'st a husband take by my consent,
As I by thine, a wife: this is a match,
And made between's by vows. Thou hast found mine:
But how is to be question'd: for I saw her,
As I thought, dead; and have in vain, said many
A prayer upon her grave: I'll not seek far
(For him, I partly know his mind), to find thee
An honourable husband:—Come, Camillo,
And take her by the hand: whose worth and honesty,
Is richly noted; and here justified
By us, a pair of kings.—Let's from this place.—
What?—Look upon my brother:—both your pardons,
That e'er I put between your holy looks
My ill suspicion.—This your son-in-law,
And son unto the king (whom heavens directing),
Is troth-plight to your daughter.—Good Paulina,
Lead us from hence; where we may leisurely
Each one demand, and answer to his par
Perform'd in this wide gap of time, since first
We were dissever'd: Hastily lead away.
[*Exeunt.*

COMEDY OF ERRORS.

PERSONS REPRESENTED.

SOLINUS, Duke *of* Ephesus.
ÆGEON, *a Merchant of* Syracuse.
ANTIPHOLUS *of* Ephesus, ANTIPHOLUS *of* Syracuse, *twin brothers and sons to* Ægeon *and* Æmilia, *but unknown to each other.*
DROMIO *of* Ephesus, DROMIO *of* Syracuse, *twin Brothers and* Attendants *on the two* Antipholuses.
BALTHAZAR, *a Merchant.*
ANGELO, *a Goldsmith.*
A Merchant, *friend to* Antipholus *of* Syracuse.
PINCH, *a Schoolmaster and a Conjurer.*
ÆMILIA, *Wife to* Ægeon, *an Abbess at* Ephesus.
ADRIANA, *Wife to* Antipholus *of* Ephesus.
LUCIANA, *her sister.*
LUCE, *her servant.*
A Courtezan.

Gaoler, Officers, *and other* Attendants.

SCENE—Ephesus.

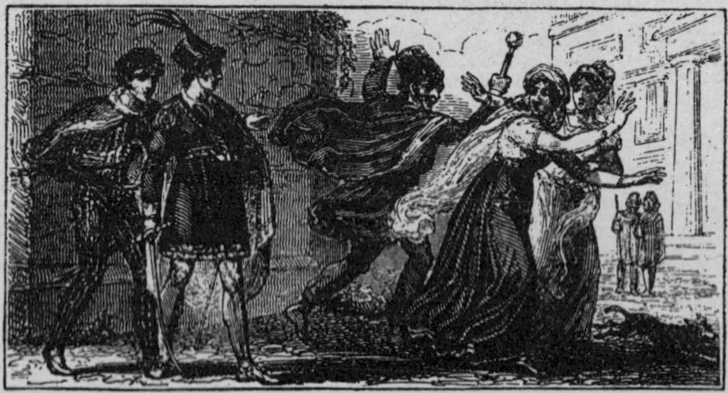

ACT I.

SCENE I. *A Hall in the* Duke's *Palace.*

Enter Duke, ÆGEON, Gaoler, Officer, *and other* Attendants.

Ægeon. PROCEED, Solinus, to procure my fall,
And, by the doom of death, end woes and all.
Duke. Merchant of Syracusa, plead no more;
I am not partial, to infringe our laws:
The enmity and discord, which of late
Sprung from the rancorous outrage of your duke
To merchants, our well-dealing countrymen,—
Who, wanting gilders to redeem their lives,
Have seal'd his rigorous statutes with their bloods,
Excludes all pity from our threatening looks.
For, since the mortal and intestine jars
'Twixt thy seditious countrymen and us,
It hath in solemn synods been decreed,
Both by the Syracusans and ourselves,
To admit no traffick to our adverse towns:
Nay, more,
If any, born at Ephesus, be seen
At any Syracusan marts and fairs,
Again, If any Syracusan born,
Come to the bay of Ephesus, he dies,
His goods confiscate to the duke's dispose:
Unless a thousand marks be levied,
To quit the penalty, and to ransom him.
Thy substance, valued at the highest rate,
Cannot amount unto a hundred marks;
Therefore, by law thou art condemn'd to die.
Æge. Yet this my comfort; when your words are done,
My woes end likewise with the evening sun.
Duke. Well, Syracusan, say, in brief, the cause
Why thou departed'st from thy native home;
And for what cause thou cam'st to Ephesus.
Æge. A heavier task could not have been imposed,
Than I to speak my griefs unspeakable:
Yet, that the world may witness, that my end
Was wrought by nature, not by vile offence,
I'll utter what my sorrow gives me leave.
In Syracusa was I born: and wed
Unto a woman, happy but for me,
And by me too, had not our hap been bad.
With her I liv'd in joy; our wealth increas'd,
By prosperous voyages I often made
To Epidamnum, till my factor's death;
And he (great care of goods at random left)
Drew me from kind embracements of my spouse:
From whom my absence was not six months old,
Before herself (almost at fainting, under
The pleasing punishment that women bear),
Had made provision for her following me,
And soon and safe, arrived where I was.
There she had not been long, but she became
A joyful mother of two goodly sons;
And, which was strange, the one so like the other,
As could not be distinguished but by names.
That very hour, and in the selfsame inn,
A poor mean woman was delivered
Of such a burden, male twins, both alike:
Those, for their parents were exceeding poor,
I bought, and brought up to attend my sons.
My wife, not meanly proud of two such boys,
Made daily motions for our home return:
Unwilling I agreed; alas! too soon.
We came aboard:
A league from Epidamnum had we sail'd,
Before the always wind-obeying deep
Gave any tragick instance of our harm:
But longer did we not retain much hope;
For what obscured light the heavens did grant
Did but convey unto our fearful minds
A doubtful warrant of immediate death;
Which, though myself would gladly have embrac'd,
Yet the incessant weepings of my wife,
Weeping before for what she saw must come,

And piteous plainings of the pretty babes,
That mourn'd for fashion, ignorant what to fear,
Forc'd me to seek delays for them and me.
And this it was,—for other means was none.—
The sailors sought for safety by our boat,
And left the ship, then sinking ripe, to us:
My wife, more careful for the latter-born,
Had fasten'd him unto a small spare mast,
Such as sea-faring men provide for storms;
To him one of the other twins was bound,
Whilst I had been like heedful of the other.
The children thus dispos'd, my wife and I,
Fixing our eyes on whom our care was fix'd,
Fasten'd ourselves at either end the mast;
And floating straight, obedient to the stream,
Were carried towards Corinth, as we thought.
At length the sun, gazing upon the earth,
Dispers'd those vapours that offended us;
And, by the benefit of his wish'd light,
The seas wax'd calm, and we discovered
Two ships from far making amain to us,
Of Corinth that, of Epidaurus this:
But ere they came,—O, let me say no more!
Gather the sequel by that went before.

Duke. Nay, forward, old man, do not break off so;
For we may pity, though not pardon thee.

Æge. O, had the gods done so, I had not now
Worthily term'd them merciless to us!
For, ere the ships could meet by twice five leagues,
We were encounter'd by a mighty rock;
Which being violently borne upon,
Our helpful ship was splitted in the midst,
So that in this unjust divorce of us,
Fortune had left to both of us alike
What to delight in, what to sorrow for.
Her part, poor soul! seeming as burden'd
With lesser weight, but not with lesser woe,
Was carried with more speed before the wind;
And in our sight they three were taken up
By fishermen of Corinth, as we thought.
At length, another ship had seiz'd on us;
And knowing whom it was their hap to save,
Gave healthful welcome to their shipwreck'd guests;
And would have reft the fishers of their prey,
Had not their bark been very slow of sail,
And therefore homeward did they bend their course.—
Thus have you heard me sever'd from my bliss;
That by misfortunes was my life prolong'd,
To tell sad stories of my own mishaps.

Duke. And for the sake of them thou sorrowest for,
Do me the favour to dilate at full
What hath befall'n of them, and thee, till now.

Æge. My youngest boy, and yet my eldest care,
At eighteen years became inquisitive
After his brother; and importun'd me,
That his attendant (for his case was like,
Reft of his brother, but retain'd his name),
Might bear him company in the quest of him:
Whom whilst I labour'd of a love to see,
I hazarded the loss of whom I lov'd.
Five summers have I spent in furthest Greece,
Roaming clean through the bounds of Asia,
And, coasting homeward, came to Ephesus;
Hopeless to find, yet loath to leave unsought,
Or that, or any place that harbours men.
But here must end the story of my life;
And happy were I in my timely death,
Could all my travels warrant me they live.

Duke. Hapless Ægeon, whom the fates have mark'd
To bear the extremity of dire mishap!
Now, trust me, were it not against our laws,
Against my crown, my oath, my dignity,
Which princes, would they, may not disannul,
My soul should sue as advocate for thee.
But, though thou art adjudged to the death,
And passed sentence may not be recall'd,
But to our honour's great disparagement,
Yet will I favour thee in what I can:
Therefore, merchant, I'll limit thee this day,
To seek thy help by beneficial help:
Try all the friends thou hast in Ephesus;
Beg thou or borrow, to make up the sum,
And live; if not, then thou art doom'd to die:—
Gaoler, take him to thy custody.

Gaol. I will, my lord.

Æge. Hopeless, and helpless, doth Ægeon wend,
But to procrastinate his lifeless end. [*Exeunt.*

SCENE II. *A publick Place.*

Enter ANTIPHOLUS *and* DROMIO *of Syracuse, and a* Merchant.

Mer. Therefore, give out, you are of Epidamnum,
Lest that your goods too soon be confiscate.
This very day, a Syracusan merchant
Is apprehended for arrival here;
And, not being able to buy out his life,
According to the statute of the town,
Dies ere the weary sun set in the west.
There is your money that I had to keep.

Ant. S. Go bear it to the Centaur, where we host,
And stay there, Dromio, till I come to thee.
Within this hour it will be dinner-time:
Till that, I'll view the manners of the town,
Peruse the traders, gaze upon the buildings,
And then return, and sleep within mine inn;
For with long travel I am stiff and weary.
Get thee away.

Dro. S. Many a man would take you at your word,
And go indeed, having so good a mean. [*Exit* DRO. S.

Ant. S. A trusty villain, sir; that very oft,
When I am dull with care and melancholy,
Lightens my humour with his merry jests.
What, will you walk with me about the town,
And then go to my inn, and dine with me?

Mer. I am invited, sir, to certain merchants,
Of whom I hope to make much benefit;
I crave your pardon. Soon, at five o'clock,
Please you, I'll meet with you upon the mart:
And afterwards consort you till bed-time;
My present business calls me from you now.

Ant. S. Farewell till then: I will go lose myself,
And wander up and down, to view the city.

Mer. Sir, I commend you to your own content. [*Exit* Merchant.

Ant. S. He that commends me to mine own content,
Commends me to the thing I cannot get.
I to the world am like a drop of water,
That in the ocean seeks another drop;
Who, falling there to find his fellow forth,
Unseen, inquisitive, confounds himself:
So I, to find a mother, and a brother,
In quest of them, unhappy, lose myself.

Enter DROMIO *of* Ephesus.

Here comes the almanack of my true date,—
What now? How chance, thou art return'd so soon?

Dro. E. Return'd so soon! rather approach'd too late:
The capon burns, the pig falls from the spit:
The clock hath strucken twelve upon the bell,
My mistress made it one upon my cheek:
She is so hot, because the meat is cold;
The meat is cold, because you come not home;
You come not home, because you have no stomach;
You have no stomach, having broke your fast;
But we, that know what 'tis to fast and pray,
Are penitent for your default to-day.

Ant. S. Stop in your wind, sir; tell me this, I pray;
Where have you left the money that I gave you?

Dro. E. O,—sixpence, that I had o'Wednesday last,
To pay the saddler for my mistress' crupper;—
The saddler had it, sir, I kept it not.

Ant. S. I am not in a sportive humour now:
Tell me, and dally not, where is the money?
We being strangers here, how dar'st thou trust
So great a charge from thine own custody?

Dro. E. I pray you, jest, sir, as you sit at dinner:
I from my mistress come to you in post;
If I return, I shall be post indeed;
For she will score your fault upon my pate.
Methinks, your maw, like mine, should be your clock,
And strike you home without a messenger.

Ant. S. Come, Dromio, come, these jests are out of season;
Reserve them till a merrier hour than this:
Where is the gold I gave in charge to thee?

Dro. E. To me, sir? why you gave no gold to me.

Ant. S. Come on, sir knave, have done your foolishness,
And tell me, how thou hast dispos'd thy charge.

Dro. E. My charge was but to fetch you from the mart
Home to your house, the Phœnix, sir, to dinner:
My mistress, and her sister, stay for you.

Ant. S. Now, as I am a christian, answer me,
In what safe place you have bestow'd my money;
Or I shall break that merry sconce of yours,
That stands on tricks when I am undispos'd:
Where is the thousand marks thou hadst of me?

Dro. E. I have some marks of yours upon my pate,
Some of my mistress' marks upon my shoulders,
But not a thousand marks between you both.—
If I should pay your worship those again,
Perchance, you will not bear them patiently.

Ant. S. Thy mistress' marks! what mistress, slave, hast thou?

Dro. E. Your worship's wife, my mistress at the Phœnix;
She that doth fast, till you come home to dinner,
And prays, that you will hie you home to dinner.

Ant. S. What, wilt thou flout me thus unto my face,
Being forbid? There, take you that, sir knave. [*Strikes him.*

Dro. E. What mean you, sir? for God's sake, hold your hands!
Nay, an you will not, sir, I'll take my heels. [*Exit* DROMIO E.

Ant. S. Upon my life, by some device or other,
The villain is o'er-raught of all my money.
They say, this town is full of cozenage:
As, nimble jugglers, that deceive the eye;
Dark-working sorcerers, that change the mind;
Soul-killing witches, that deform the body;
Disguised cheaters, prating mountebanks,
And many such like liberties of sin:
If it prove so, I will be gone the sooner.
I'll to the Centaur, to go seek this slave:
I greatly fear my money is not safe. [*Exit.*

ACT II.

SCENE I. *A publick Place.*

Enter ADRIANA *and* LUCIANA.

Adr. Neither my husband, nor the slave return'd,
That in such haste I sent to seek his master!
Sure, Luciana, it is two o'clock.

Luc. Perhaps, some merchant hath invited him,
And from the mart he's somewhere gone to dinner;
Good sister, let us dine, and never fret:
A man is master of his liberty:
Time is their master; and, when they see time,
They'll go, or come: If so, be patient, sister.

Adr. Why should their liberty than ours be more?

Luc. Because their business still lies out o'door.

Adr. Look, when I serve him so, he takes it ill.

Luc. O, know, he is the bridle of your will.

Adr. There's none, but asses, would be bridled so.

Luc. Why, headstrong liberty is lash'd with woe.
There's nothing, situate under Heaven's eye,
But hath his bound, in earth, in sea, in sky:
The beasts, the fishes, and the winged fowls,
Are their males' subjects, and at their controls:
Men, more divine, the masters of all these,
Lords of the wide world, and wild watry seas,
Indued with intellectual sense and souls,
Of more pre-eminence than fish and fowls,
Are masters to their females and their lords:
Then let your will attend on their accords.

Adr. This servitude makes you to keep unwed.

Luc. Not this, but troubles of the marriage bed.

Adr. But, were you wedded, you would bear some sway.

Luc. Ere I learn love, I'll practise to obey.

Adr. How if your husband start some other where?

Luc. Till he come home again, I would forbear.

Adr. Patience, unmov'd, no marvel though she pause;
They can be meek, that have no other cause.
A wretched soul, bruis'd with adversity,
We bid be quiet, when we hear it cry;
But were we burden'd with like weight of pain,
As much, or more, we should ourselves complain:
So thou, that hast no unkind mate to grieve thee,
With urging helpless patience would'st relieve me:
But, if thou live to see like right bereft,
This fool-begg'd patience in thee will be left.

Luc. Well, I will marry one day, but to try;—
Here comes your man, now is your husband nigh.

Enter DROMIO *of* Ephesus.

Adr. Say, is your tardy master now at hand?

Dro. E. Nay, he is at two hands with me, and that my two ears can witness.

Adr. Say, didst thou speak with him? know'st thou his mind?

Dro. E. Ay, ay, he told his mind upon mine ear:
Beshrew his hand, I scarce could understand it.

Luc. Spake he so doubtfully, thou could'st not feel his meaning?

Dro. E. Nay, he struck so plainly, I could too well feel his blows; and withal so doubtfully, that I could scarce understand them.

Adr. But say, I pr'ythee, is he coming home?
It seems he hath great care to please his wife.

Dro. E. Why, mistress, sure my master is horn-mad.

Adr. Horn-mad, thou villain?

Dro. E. I mean not cuckold-mad; but, sure, he's stark mad;
When I desir'd him to come home to dinner,
He ask'd me for a thousand marks in gold:
'*Tis dinner-time*, quoth I; *My gold*, quoth he:
Your meat doth burn, quoth I; *My gold*, quoth he:
Will you come home? quoth I; *My gold*, quoth he:
Where is the thousand marks I gave thee, villain?
The pig, quoth I, *is burn'd; My gold*, quoth he:
My mistress, sir, quoth I; *Hang up thy mistress;*
I know not thy mistress; out on thy mistress!

Luc. Quoth who?

Dro. E. Quoth my master:
I know, quoth he, *no house, no wife, no mistress;*—
So that my errand, due unto my tongue,
I thank him, I bear home upon my shoulders;
For, in conclusion, he did beat me there.

Adr. Go back again, thou slave, and fetch him home.

Dro. E. Go back again, and be new beaten home?
For God's sake, send some other messenger.
Adr. Back, slave, or I will break thy pate across.
Dro. E. And he will bless that cross with other beating:
Between you I shall have a holy head.
Adr. Hence, prating peasant; fetch thy master home.
Dro. E. Am I so round with you, as you with me,
That like a football you do spurn me thus?
You spurn me hence, and he will spurn me hither:
If I last in this service, you must case me in leather. [*Exit.*
Luc. Fie, how impatience loureth in your face?
Adr. His company must do his minions grace,
Whilst I at home starve for a merry look.
Hath homely age the alluring beauty took
From my poor cheek? then he hath wasted it:
Are my discourses dull? barren my wit?
If voluble and sharp discourse be marr'd,
Unkindness blunts it, more than marble hard.
Do their gay vestments his affections bait?
That's not my fault, he's master of my state:
What ruins are in me, that can be found
By him not ruin'd? then is he the ground
Of my defeatures: My decayed fair
A sunny look of his would soon repair:
But, too unruly deer, he breaks the pale,
And feeds from home: poor I am but his stale.
Luc. Self-harming jealousy!—fie, beat it hence.
Adr. Unfeeling fools can with such wrongs dispense.
I know his eye doth homage otherwhere;
Or else, what lets it but he would be here?
Sister, you know, he promis'd me a chain;—
'Would that alone alone he would detain,
So he would keep fair quarter with his bed!
I see, the jewel, best enamelled,
Will lose his beauty: and though gold 'bides still,
That others touch, yet often touching will
Wear gold: and so no man, that hath a name,
But falsehood and corruption doth it shame.
Since that my beauty cannot please his eye,
I'll weep what's left away, and weeping die.
Luc. How many fond fools serve mad jealousy! [*Exeunt.*

SCENE II. *The same.*

Enter ANTIPHOLUS *of* Syracuse.

Ant. S. The gold, I gave to Dromio, is laid up
Safe at the Centaur; and the heedful slave
Is wander'd forth, in care to seek me out.
By computation, and mine host's report,
I could not speak with Dromio, since at first
I sent him from the mart: see, here he comes.

Enter DROMIO *of* Syracuse.

How now, sir? is your merry humour alter'd?
As you love strokes, so jest with me again.
You know no Centaur? you receiv'd no gold?
Your mistress sent to have me home to dinner?
My house was at the Phœnix? Wast thou mad,
That thus so madly thou didst answer me?
Dro. S. What answer, sir? when spake I such a word?
Ant. S. Even now, even here, not half an hour since.
Dro. S. I did not see you since you sent me hence,
Home to the Centaur, with the gold you gave me.
Ant. S. Villain, thou did'st deny the gold's receipt;
And told'st me of a mistress, and a dinner;
For which, I hope, thou felt'st I was displeas'd.
Dro. S. I am glad to see you in this merry vein:
What means this jest? I pray you, master, tell me.
Ant. S. Yea, dost thou jeer, and flout me in the teeth?
Think'st thou, I jest? Hold, take thou that, and that. [*Beating him.*
Dro. S. Hold, sir, for God's sake: now your jest is earnest:
Upon what bargain do you give it me?
Ant. S. Because that I familiarly sometimes
Do use you for my fool, and chat with you,
Your sauciness will jest upon my love,
And make a common of my serious hours.
When the sun shines, let foolish gnats make sport,
But creep in crannies, when he hides his beams.
If you will jest with me, know my aspect,
And fashion your demeanour to my looks,
Or I will beat this method in your sconce.
Dro. S. Sconce, call you it? so you would leave battering, I had rather have it a head: an you use these blows long, I must get a sconce for my head, and insconce it too; or else I shall seek my wit in my shoulders. But, I pray, sir, why am I beaten?
Ant. S. Dost thou not know?
Dro. S. Nothing, sir; but that I am beaten.
Ant. S. Shall I tell you why?
Dro. S. Ay, sir, and wherefore; for, they say, every why hath a wherefore.
Ant. S. Why, first,—for flouting me; and then, wherefore,—
For urging it the second time to me.
Dro. S. Was there ever any man thus beaten out of season?
When, in the why, and the wherefore, is neither rhyme nor reason?—
Well, sir, I thank you.
Ant. S. Thank me, sir? for what?
Dro. S. Marry, sir, for this something that you gave me for nothing.
Ant. S. I'll make you amends next, to give you nothing for something. But say, sir, is it dinner-time?
Dro. S. No, sir; I think, the meat wants that I have.
Ant. S. In good time, sir, what's that?
Dro. S. Basting.
Ant. S. Well, sir, then 'twill be dry.
Dro. S. If it be, sir, I pray you eat none of it.
Ant. S. Your reason?
Dro. S. Lest it make you choleric, and purchase me another dry basting.
Ant. S. Well, sir, learn to jest in good time;
There's a time for all things.
Dro. S. I durst have denied that, before you were so cholerick.
Ant. S. By what rule, sir?
Dro. S. Marry, sir, by a rule as plain as the plain bald pate of father Time himself.
Ant. S. Let's hear it.
Dro. S. There's no time for a man to recover his hair, that grows bald by nature.
Ant. S. May he not do it by fine and recovery?
Dro. S. Yes, to pay a fine for a periwig, and recover the lost hair of another man.
Ant. S. Why is Time such a niggard of hair, being, as it is, so plentiful an excrement?
Dro. S. Because it is a blessing that he bestows on beasts: and what he hath scanted men in hair, he hath given them in wit.
Ant. S. Why, but there's many a man hath more hair than wit.
Dro. S. Not a man of those, but he hath the wit to lose his hair.
Ant. S. Why, thou didst conclude hairy men plain dealers without wit.
Dro. S. The plainer dealer, the sooner lost:
Yet he loseth it in a kind of jollity.
Ant. S. For what reason?
Dro. S. For two; and sound ones too.
Ant. S. Nay, not sound, I pray you.
Dro. S. Sure ones then.
Ant. S. Nay, not sure, in a thing falsing.

Dro. S. Certain ones then.

Ant. S. Name them.

Dro. S. The one, to save the money that he spends in tiring; the other, that at dinner they should not drop in his porridge.

Ant. S. You would all this time have proved, there is no time for all things.

Dro. S. Marry, and did, sir; namely, e'en no time to recover hair lost by nature.

Ant. S. But your reason was not substantial; why, there is no time to recover.

Dro. S. Thus I mend it: Time himself is bald, and therefore, to the world's end, will have bald followers.

Ant. S. I knew, 'twould be a bald conclusion: But soft! who wafts us yonder!

Enter ADRIANA *and* LUCIANA.

Adr. Ay, ay, Antipholus, look strange and frown;
Some other mistress hath thy sweet aspects,
I am not Adriana, nor thy wife.
The time was once, when thou unurg'd would'st vow
That never words were musick to thine ear,
That never object pleasing in thine eye,
That never touch well welcome to thy hand,
That never meat sweet savour'd in thy taste,
Unless I spake, look'd, touch'd, or carv'd to thee.
How comes it now, my husband, oh, how comes it,
That thou art then estranged from thyself?
Thyself I call it, being strange to me,
That, undividable, incorporate,
And better than thy dear self's better part.
Ah, do not tear away thyself from me;
For know, my love, as easy may'st thou fall
A drop of water in the breaking gulf,
And take unmingled thence that drop again,
Without addition, or diminishing,
As take from me thyself, and not me too.
How dearly would it touch thee to the quick,
Should'st thou but hear I were licentious?
And that this body, consecrate to thee,
By ruffian lust should be contaminate?
Would'st thou not spit at me, and spurn at me,
And hurl the name of husband in my face,
And tear the stain'd skin off my harlot brow,
And from my false hand cut the wedding ring,
And break it with a deep divorcing vow?
I know thou canst; and therefore, see, thou do it.
I am possess'd with an adulterate blot;
My blood is mingled with the crime of lust:
For, if we two be one, and thou play false,
I do digest the poison of thy flesh,
Being strumpeted by thy contagion.
Keep then fair league and truce with thy true bed;
I live disstain'd, thou undishonoured.

Ant. S. Plead you to me, fair dame? I know you not:
In Ephesus I am but two hours old,
As strange unto your town, as to your talk:
Who, every word by all my wit being scann'd,
Want wit in all one word to understand.

Luc. Fie, brother! how the world is chang'd with you:
When were you wont to use my sister thus?
She sent for you by Dromio home to dinner.

Ant. S. By Dromio?

Dro. S. By me?

Adr. By thee: and this thou didst return from him,—
That he did buffet thee, and, in his blows
Denied my house for his, me for his wife.

Ant. S. Did you converse, sir, with this gentlewoman?
What is the course and drift of your compact?

Dro. S. I, sir? I never saw her till this time.

Ant. S. Villain, thou liest; for even her very words
Didst thou deliver to me on the mart.

Dro. S. I never spake with her in all my life.

Ant. S. How can she thus then call us by our names,
Unless it be by inspiration?

Adr. How ill agrees it with your gravity,
To counterfeit thus grossly with your slave,
Abetting him to thwart me in my mood?
Be it my wrong, you are from me exempt,
But wrong not that wrong with a more contempt.
Come, I will fasten on this sleeve of thine:
Thou art an elm, my husband, I a vine:
Whose weakness, married to thy stronger state,
Makes me with thy strength to communicate:
If aught possess thee from me, it is dross,
Usurping ivy, briar, or idle moss:
Who, all for want of pruning, with intrusion
Infect thy sap, and live on thy confusion.

Ant. S. To me she speaks: she moves me for her theme:
What, was I married to her in my dream?
Or sleep I now, and think I hear all this?
What error drives our eyes and ears amiss?
Until I know this sure uncertainty,
I'll entertain the offer'd fallacy.

Luc. Dromio, go bid the servants spread for dinner.

Dro. S. O, for my beads! I cross me for a sinner.
This is the fairy land;—O, spite of spites;—
We talk with goblins, owls, and elvish sprites;
If we obey them not, this will ensue,
They'll suck our breath, or pinch us black and blue.

Luc. Why prat'st thou to thyself, and answer'st not?
Dromio, thou drone, thou snail, thou slug, thou sot!

Dro. S. I am transformed, master, am not I?

Ant. S. I think, thou art, in mind, and so am I.

Dro. S. Nay, master, both in mind, and in my shape,

Ant. S. Thou hast thine own form.

Dro. S. No, I am an ape.

Luc. If thou art chang'd to aught, 'tis to an ass.

Dro. S. 'Tis true; she rides me, and I long for grass.
'Tis so, I am an ass; else it could never be,
But I should know her as well as she knows me.

Adr. Come, come, no longer will I be a fool,
To put the finger in the eye and weep,
Whilst man, and master, laugh my woes to scorn.—
Come, sir, to dinner; Dromio, keep the gate:—
Husband, I'll dine above with you to-day,
And shrive you of a thousand idle pranks;
Sirrah, if any ask you for your master,
Say, he dines forth, and let no creature enter.—
Come, sister:—Dromio, play the porter well.

Ant. S. Am I in earth, in heaven, or in hell?
Sleeping or waking? mad, or well advis'd?
Known unto these, and to myself disguis'd!
I'll say as they say, and persever so,
And in this mist at all adventures go.

Dro. S. Master, shall I be porter at the gate!

Adr. Ay; and let none enter, lest I break your pate.

Luc. Come, come, Antipholus, we dine too late. [*Exeunt.*

ACT III.

SCENE I. *The same.*

Enter ANTIPHOLUS *of* Ephesus, DROMIO *of* Ephesus, ANGELO, *and* BALTHAZAR.

Ant. E. Good signior Angelo, you must excuse us all:
My wife is shrewish when I keep not hours:
Say, that I linger'd with you at your shop,
To see the making of her carkanet,
And that to-morrow you will bring it home.

But here's a villain, that would face me down
He met me on the mart; and that I beat him,
And charg'd him with a thousand marks in gold;
And that I did deny my wife and house:—
Thou drunkard, thou, what didst thou mean by this?

Dro. E. Say what you will, sir, but I know what I know:
That you beat me at the mart, I have your hand to show:
If the skin were parchment, and the blows you gave were ink,
Your own handwriting would tell you what I think.

Ant. E. I think, thou art an ass.

Dro. E. Marry, so it doth appear
By the wrongs I suffer, and the blows I bear.
I should kick, being kick'd; and, being at that pass,
You would keep from my heels, and beware of an ass.

Ant. E. You are sad, signior Balthazar: 'Pray God, our cheer
May answer my good will, and your good welcome here.

Bal. I hold your dainties cheap, sir, and your welcome dear.

Ant. E. O, signior Balthazar, either at flesh or fish,
A table full of welcome makes scarce one dainty dish.

Bal. Good meat, sir, is common; that every churl affords.

Ant. E. And welcome more common; for that's nothing but words.

Bal. Small cheer, and great welcome, makes a merry feast.

Ant. E. Ay, to a niggardly host, and more sparing guest;
But though my cates be mean, take them in good part;
Better cheer may you have, but not with better heart.
But, soft; my door is lock'd; Go bid them let us in.

Dro. E. Maud, Bridget, Marian, Cicely, Gillian, Jen'!

Dro. S. [*within.*] Mome, malt-horse, capon, coxcomb, idiot, patch!
Either get thee from the door, or sit down at the hatch:
Dost thou conjure for wenches, that thou call'st for such store,
When one is one too many? Go, get thee from the door.

Dro. E. What patch is made our porter? My master stays in the street.

Dro. S. Let him walk from whence he came, lest he catch cold on's feet.

Ant. E. Who talks within there? ho, open the door.

Dro. S. Right, sir, I'll tell you when, an you'll tell me wherefore.

Ant. E. Wherefore? for my dinner; I have not din'd to-day.

Dro. S. Nor to-day here you must not; come again, when you may.

Ant. E. What art thou, that keep'st me out from the house I owe?

Dro. S. The porter for this time, sir, and my name is Dromio.

Dro. E. O villain, thou hast stolen both mine office and my name;
The one ne'er got me credit, the other mickle blame.
If thou had'st been Dromio to-day in my place,
Thou would'st have chang'd thy face for a name, or thy name for an ass.

Luce. [*within.*] What a coil is there? Dromio, who are those at the gate?

Dro. E. Let my master in, Luce.

Luce. 'Faith, no; he comes too late:
And so tell your master.

Dro. E. O Lord, I must laugh:—
Have at you with a proverb.—Shall I set in my staff?

Luce. Have at you with another: that's,—When? can you tell?

Dro. S. If thy name be call'd Luce, Luce, thou hast answer'd him well.

Ant. E. Do you hear, you minion? you'll let us in, I hope?

Luce. I thought to have ask'd you.

Dro. S. And you said, no.

Dro. E. So, come, help; well struck; there was blow for blow.

Ant. E. Thou baggage, let me in.

Luce. Can you tell for whose sake?

Dro. E. Master, knock the door hard.

Luce. Let him knock till it ake.

Ant. E. You'll cry for this, minion, if I beat the door down.

Luce. What needs all that, and a pair of stocks in the town?

Adr. [*within.*] Who is that at the door, that keeps all this noise?

Dro. S. By my troth, your town is troubled with unruly boys.

Ant. E. Are you there, wife? you might have come before.

Adr. Your wife, sir knave! go, get you from the door.

Dro. E. If you went in pain, master, this knave would go sore.

Ang. Here is neither cheer, sir, nor welcome; we would fain have either.

Bal. In debating which was best, we shall part with neither.

Dro. E. They stand at the door, master; bid them welcome hither.

Ant. E. There is something in the wind, that we cannot get in.

Dro. E. You would say so, master, if your garments were thin.
Your cake here is warm within; you stand here in the cold:
It would make a man mad as a buck, to be so bought and sold.

Ant. E. Go, fetch me something, I'll break ope the gate.

Dro. S. Break any breaking here, and I'll break your knave's pate.

Dro. E. A man may break a word with you, sir; and words are but wind;
Ay, and break it in your face, so he break it not behind.

Dro. S. It seems, thou wantest breaking; Out upon thee, hind!

Dro. E. Here is too much, out upon thee! I pray thee, let me in.

Dro. S. Ay, when fowls have no feathers, and fish have no fin.

Ant. E. Well, I'll break in; Go borrow me a crow.

Dro. E. A crow without feather; master, mean you so?
For a fish without a fin, there's a fowl without a feather:
If a crow help us in, sirrah, we'll pluck a crow together.

Ant. E. Go, get thee gone, fetch me an iron crow.

Bal. Have patience, sir: O, let it not be so;
Herein you war against your reputation,
And draw within the compass of suspect
The unviolated honour of your wife.
Once this; your long experience of her wisdom,
Her sober virtue, years, and modesty,
Plead on her part some cause to you unknown;
And doubt not, sir, but she will well excuse
Why at this time the doors are made against you.
Be rul'd by me; depart in patience,
And let us to the Tiger all to dinner:
And, about evening, come yourself alone,
To know the reason of this strange restraint.
If by strong hand you offer to break in,

Now in the stirring passage of the day,
A vulgar comment will be made on it;
And that supposed by the common rout
Against your yet ungalled estimation,
That may with foul intrusion enter in,
And dwell upon your grave when you are dead:
For slander lives upon succession;
For ever housed, where it once gets possession.

Ant. E. You have prevail'd; I will depart in quiet,
And, in despite of mirth, mean to be merry.
I know a wench of excellent discourse,—
Pretty and witty; wild, and, yet too, gentle;—
There will we dine: this woman that I mean,
My wife (but, I protest, without desert),
Hath oftentimes upbraided me withal;
To her will we to dinner.—Get you home,
And fetch the chain; by this, I know, 'tis made:
Bring it, I pray you, to the Porcupine;
For there's the house; that chain will I bestow
(Be it for nothing but to spite my wife)
Upon mine hostess there: good sir, make haste:
Since mine own doors refuse to entertain me,
I'll knock elsewhere, to see if they'll disdain me.

Ang. I'll meet you at that place, some hour hence.

Ant. E. Do so; this jest shall cost me some expense. [*Exeunt.*

SCENE II. *The same.*

Enter Luciana, *and* Antipholus *of* Syracuse.

Luc. And may it be that you have quite forgot
A husband's office? shall, Antipholus, hate,
Even in the spring of love, thy love springs rot?
Shall love, in building, grow so ruinate?
If you did wed my sister for her wealth,
Then, for her wealth's sake, use her with more kindness:
Or, if you like elsewhere, do it by stealth;
Muffle your false love with some show of blindness:
Let not my sister read it in your eye;
Be not thy tongue thy own shame's orator;
Look sweet, speak fair, become disloyalty;
Apparel vice like virtue's harbinger:
Bear a fair presence, though your heart be tainted;
Teach sin the carriage of a holy saint:
Be secret-false; What need she be acquainted?
What simple thief brags of his own attaint?
'Tis double wrong, to truant with your bed,
And let her read it in thy looks at board:
Shame hath a bastard fame, well managed;
Ill deeds are doubled with an evil word.
Alas, poor women! make us but believe,
Being compact of credit, that you love us;
Though others have the arm, show us the sleeve;
We in your motion turn, and you may move us.
Then, gentle brother, get you in again;
Comfort my sister, cheer her, call her wife:
'Tis holy sport, to be a little vain,
When the sweet breath of flattery conquers strife.

Ant. S. Sweet mistress (what your name is else, I know not,
Nor by what wonder you do hit on mine),
Less, in your knowledge, and your grace, you show not,
Than our earth's wonder; more than earth divine.
Teach me, dear creature, how to think and speak;
Lay open to my earthy gross conceit,
Smother'd in errors, feeble, shallow, weak,
The folded meaning of your words' deceit.
Against my soul's pure truth why labour you,
To make it wander in an unknown field?
Are you a god? would you create me new?
Transform me then, and to your power I'll yield.
But if that I am I, then well I know,
Your weeping sister is no wife of mine,
Nor to her bed no homage do I owe;
Far more, far more, to you do I decline.
O, train me not, sweet mermaid, with thy note,
To drown me in thy sister's flood of tears;
Sing, siren, for thyself, and I will dote:
Spread o'er the silver waves thy golden hairs,
And as a bed I'll take thee, and there lie;
And, in that glorious supposition, think
He gains by death, that hath such means to die:—
Let love, being light, be drowned if she sink!

Luc. What, are you mad, that you do reason so?

Ant. S. Not mad, but mated; how, I do not know.

Luc. It is a fault that springeth from your eye.

Ant. S. For gazing on your beams, fair sun, being by.

Luc. Gaze where you should, and that will clear your sight.

Ant. S. As good to wink, sweet love, as look on night.

Luc. Why call you me love? call my sister so.

Ant. S. Thy sister's sister.

Luc. That's my sister.

Ant. S. No;
It is thyself, mine own self's better part;
Mine eye's clear eye, my dear heart's dearer heart;
My food, my fortune, and my sweet hope's aim,
My sole earth's heaven, and my heaven's claim.

Luc. All this my sister is, or else should be.

Ant. S. Call thyself sister, sweet, for I aim thee:
Thee will I love, and with thee lead my life;
Thou hast no husband yet, nor I no wife:
Give me thy hand.

Luc. O, soft, sir, hold you still;
I'll fetch my sister, to get her good will. [*Exit* Luc.

Enter, from the House of Antipholus *of* Ephesus, Dromio *of* Syracuse.

Ant. S. Why, how now, Dromio? where runn'st thou so fast?

Dro. S. Do you know me, sir? am I Dromio? am I your man? am I myself?

Ant. S. Thou art Dromio, thou art my man, thou art thyself.

Dro. S. I am an ass, I am a woman's man, and besides myself.

Ant. S. What woman's man? and how besides thyself?

Dro. S. Marry, sir, besides myself, I am due to a woman: one that claims me, one that haunts me, one that will have me.

Ant. S. What claim lays she to thee?

Dro. S. Marry, sir, such claim as you would lay to your horse; and she would have me as a beast: not that, I being a beast, she would have me; but that she, being a very beastly creature, lays claim to me.

Ant. S. What is she?

Dro. S. A very reverend body; ay, such a one as a man may not speak of, without he say, sir-reverence: I have but lean luck in the match, and yet she is a wondrous fat marriage.

Ant. S. How dost thou mean, a fat marriage?

Dro. S. Marry, sir, she's the kitchen-wench, and all grease; and I know not what use to put her to, but to make a lamp of her, and run from her by her own light. I warrant, her rags, and the tallow in them, will burn a Poland winter: if she lives till doomsday, she'll burn a week longer than the whole world.

Ant. S. What complexion is she of?

Dro. S. Swart, like my shoe, but her face nothing like so clean kept: For why? she sweats, a man may go over shoes in the grime of it.

Ant. S. That's a fault that water will mend.

Dro. S. No, sir, 'tis in grain; Noah's flood could not do it.

Ant. S. What's her name?

Dro. S. Nell, sir;—but her name and three

quarters, that is, an ell and three quarters, will not measure her from hip to hip.

Ant. S. Then she bears some breadth?

Dro. S. No longer from head to foot, than from hip to hip: she is spherical, like a globe; I could find out countries in her.

Ant. S. In what part of her body stands Ireland?

Dro. S. Marry, sir, in her buttocks; I found it out by the bogs.

Ant. S. Where Scotland?

Dro. S. I found it by the barrenness; hard, in the palm of the hand.

Ant. S. Where France?

Dro. S. In her forehead; arm'd and reverted, making war against her heir.

Ant. S. Where England?

Dro. S. I look'd for the chalky cliffs, but I could find no whiteness in them: but I guess, it stood in her chin, by the salt rheum that ran between France and it.

Ant. S. Where Spain?

Dro. S. 'Faith, I saw it not; but I felt it hot in her breath.

Ant. S. Where America? the Indies?

Dro. S. O, sir, upon her nose, all o'er embellish'd with rubies, carbuncles, sapphires, declining their rich aspect to the hot breath of Spain; who sent whole armadas of carracks to be ballast at her nose.

Ant. S. Where stood Belgia, the Netherlands?

Dro. S. O, sir, I did not look so low. To conclude, this drudge, or diviner, laid claim to me; call'd me Dromio; swore, I was assur'd to her; told me what privy marks I had about me, as the mark of my shoulder, the mole in my neck, the great wart on my left arm, that I, amazed, ran from her as a witch: and, I think, if my breast had not been made of faith, and my heart of steel, she had transform'd me to a curtail-dog, and made me turn i' the wheel.

Ant. S. Go, hie thee presently, post to the road;
And if the wind blow any way from shore,
I will not harbour in this town to-night.
If any bark put forth, come to the mart,
Where I will walk, till thou return to me.
If every one knows us, and we know none,
'Tis time, I think, to trudge, pack, and be gone.

Dro. S. As from a bear a man would run for life,
So fly I from her that would be my wife. [*Exit.*

Ant. S. There's none but witches do inhabit here;
And therefore 'tis high time that I were hence.
She that doth call me husband, even my soul
Doth for a wife abhor: but her fair sister,
Possess'd with such a gentle sovereign grace,
Of such enchanting presence and discourse,
Hath almost made me traitor to myself:
But, lest myself be guilty to self-wrong,
I'll stop my ears against the mermaid's song.

Enter ANGELO.

Ang. Master Antipholus?

Ant. S. Ay, that's my name.

Ang. I know it well, sir: Lo, here is the chain;
I thought to have ta'en you at the Porcupine:
The chain unfinish'd made me stay thus long.

Ant. S. What is your will, that I shall do with this?

Ang. What please yourself, sir; I have made it for you.

Ant. S. Made it for me, sir! I bespoke it not.

Ang. Not once, nor twice, but twenty times you have:
Go home with it, and please your wife withal;
And soon at supper-time I'll visit you,
And then receive my money for the chain.

Ant. S. I pray you, sir, receive the money now,
For fear you ne'er see chain, nor money, more.

Ang. You are a merry man, sir; fare you well. [*Exit.*

Ant. S. What I should think of this, I cannot tell;
But this I think, there's no man is so vain,
That would refuse so fair an offer'd chain.
I see, a man here needs not live by shifts,
When in the streets he meets such golden gifts.
I'll to the mart, and there for Dromio stay;
If any ship put out, then straight away. [*Exit.*

ACT IV.

SCENE I. *The same.*

Enter a Merchant, ANGELO, *and an* Officer.

Mer. You know, since Pentecost the sum is due,
And since I have not much importun'd you;
Nor now I had not, but that I am bound
To Persia, and want gilders for my voyage:
Therefore make present satisfaction,
Or I'll attach you by this officer.

Ang. Even just the sum, that I do owe to you,
Is growing to me by Antipholus:
And, in the instant that I met with you,
He had of me a chain; at five o'clock,
I shall receive the money for the same:
Pleaseth you walk with me down to his house,
I will discharge my bond, and thank you too.

Enter ANTIPHOLUS *of* Ephesus, *and* DROMIO *of* Ephesus *from the Courtezan's.*

Off. That labour may you save; see where he comes.

Ant. E. While I go to the goldsmith's house, go thou
And buy a rope's end; that will I bestow
Among my wife and her confederates,
For locking me out of my doors by day.—
But soft, I see the goldsmith:—get thee gone:
Buy thou a rope, and bring it home to me.

Dro. E. I buy a thousand pound a year! I buy a rope! [*Exit* DROMIO.

Ant. E. A man is well holp up, that trusts to you.
I promised your presence, and the chain;
But neither chain, nor goldsmith, came to me:
Belike, you thought our love would last too long,
If it were chain'd together; and therefore came not.

Ang. Saving your merry humour, here's the note,
How much your chain weighs to the utmost carrat;
The fineness of the gold, and chargeful fashion;
Which doth amount to three odd ducats more
Than I stand debted to this gentleman;
I pray you, see him presently discharg'd,
For he is bound to sea, and stays but for it.

Ant. E. I am not furnish'd with the present money;
Besides, I have some business in the town:
Good signior, take the stranger to my house,
And with you take the chain, and bid my wife
Disburse the sum on the receipt thereof;
Perchance, I will be there as soon as you.

Ang. Then you will bring the chain to her yourself?

Ant. E. No! bear it with you, lest I come not time enough.

Ang. Well, sir, I will: Have you the chain about you?

Ant. E. An if I have not, sir, I hope you have:
Or else you may return without your money.

Ang. Nay, come, I pray you, sir, give me the chain;
Both wind and tide stays for this gentleman,
And I, to blame, have held him here too long.

Ant. E. Good lord, you use this dalliance, to excuse
Your breach of promise to the Porcupine:
I should have chid you for not bringing it.
But like a shrew, you first begin to brawl.

Mer. The hour steals on; I pray you, sir, despatch.

Ang. You hear, how he importunes me; the chain—

Ant. E. Why, give it to my wife, and fetch your money.

Ang. Come, come, you know, I gave it you even now;
Either send the chain, or send by me some token.

Ant. E. Fie! now you run this humour out of breath:
Come, where's the chain? I pray you, let me see it.

Mer. My business cannot brook this dalliance:
Good sir, say, whe'r you'll answer me, or no;
If not, I'll leave him to the officer.

Ant. E. I answer you! What should I answer you?

Ang. The money, that you owe me for the chain.

Ant. E. I owe you none, till I receive the chain.

Ang. You know, I gave it you half an hour since.

Ant. E. You gave me none; you wrong me much to say so.

Ang. You wrong me more, sir, in denying it:
Consider, how it stands upon my credit.

Mer. Well, officer, arrest him at my suit.

Off. I do; and charge you in the duke's name, to obey me.

Ang. This touches me in reputation:
Either consent to pay this sum for me,
Or I attach you by this officer.

Ant. E. Consent to pay thee that I never had!
Arrest me, foolish fellow, if thou dar'st.

Ang. Here is thy fee; arrest him, officer;
I would not spare my brother in this case,
If he should scorn me so apparently.

Off. I do arrest you, sir; you hear the suit.

Ant. E. I do obey thee, till I give thee bail:—
But, sirrah, you shall buy this sport as dear
As all the metal in your shop will answer.

Ang. Sir, sir, I shall have law in Ephesus,
To your notorious shame, I doubt it not.

Enter DROMIO *of* Syracuse.

Dro. S. Master, there is a bark of Epidamnum,
That stays but till her owner comes aboard,
And then, sir, bears away: our fraughtage, sir,
I have convey'd aboard; and I have bought
The oil, the balsamum, and aqua-vitæ.
The ship is in her trim; the merry wind
Blows fair from land: they stay for nought at all,
But for their owner, master, and yourself.

Ant. E. How now? a madman! Why thou peevish sheep;
What ship of Epidamnum stays for me?

Dro. S. A ship you sent me to, to hire waftage.

Ant. E. Thou drunken slave, I sent thee for a rope;
And told thee to what purpose, and what end.

Dro. S. You sent me, sir, for a rope's end as soon:
You sent me to the bay, sir, for a bark.

Ant. E. I will debate this matter at more leisure,
And teach your ears to list me with more heed.
To Adriana, villain, hie thee straight:
Give her this key, and tell her in the desk,
That's cover'd o'er with Turkish tapestry,
There is a purse of ducats: let her send it;
Tell her, I am arrested in the street,
And that shall bail me: hie thee, slave; be gone.
On, officer, to prison till it come.

[*Exeunt* Mer. ANG. Officer, *and* ANT. E.

Dro. S. To Adriana! that is where we din'd,
Where Dowsabel did claim me for her husband:
She is too big, I hope, for me to compass.
Thither I must, although against my will,
For servants must their masters' minds fulfill.

[*Exit.*

SCENE II. *The same.*

Enter ADRIANA *and* LUCIANA.

Adr. Ah, Luciana, did he tempt thee so?
Might'st thou perceive austerely in his eye
That he did plead in earnest, yea or no?
Look'd he or red, or pale; or sad, or merrily?
What observation mad'st thou in this case,
Of his heart's meteors tilting in his face?

Luc. First, he denied you had in him no right.

Adr. He meant, he did me none; the more my spite.

Luc. Then swore he, that he was a stranger here.

Adr. And true he swore, though yet forsworn he were.

Luc. Then pleaded I for you.

Adr. And what said he?

Luc. That love I begg'd for you, he begg'd of me.

Adr. With what persuasion did he tempt thy love?

Luc. With words, that in an honest suit might move.
First, he did praise my beauty: then my speech.

Adr. Did'st speak him fair?

Luc. Have patience, I beseech.

Adr. I cannot, nor I will not, hold me still;
My tongue, though not my heart, shall have his will.
He is deformed, crooked, old, and sere.
Ill-fac'd, worse-bodied, shapeless every where;
Vicious, ungentle, foolish, blunt, unkind;
Stigmatical in making, worse in mind.

Luc. Who would be jealous then of such a one?
No evil lost is wail'd when it is gone.

Adr. Ah! but I think him better than I say,
And yet would herein others' eyes were worse:
Far from her nest the lapwing cries away;
My heart prays for him, though my tongue do curse.

Enter DROMIO *of* Syracuse.

Dro. S. Here, go; the desk, the purse; sweet now, make haste.

Luc. How hast thou lost thy breath?

Dro. S. By running fast.

Adr. Where is my master, Dromio? is he well?

Dro. S. No, he's in tartar limbo, worse than hell:
A devil in an everlasting garment hath him,
One, whose hard heart is button'd up with steel;
A fiend, a fairy, pitiless and rough;
A wolf, nay worse, a fellow all in buff;
A back-friend, a shoulder-clapper, one that countermands
The passages of alleys, creeks, and narrow lands;
A hound that runs counter, and yet draws dry-foot well;
One that, before the judgment, carries poor souls to hell.

Adr. Why, man, what is the matter?

Dro. S. I do not know the matter; he is 'rested on the case.

Adr. What, is he arrested? tell me at whose suit.

Dro. S. I know not at whose suit he is arrested, well;
But he's in a suit of buff, which 'rested him, that can I tell:
Will you send him, mistress, redemption, the money in the desk?

Adr. Go, fetch it, sister.—This I wonder at,

[*Exit* LUCIANA.

That he, unknown to me, should be in debt:
Tell me, was he arrested on a band?

Dro. S. Not on a band, but on a stronger thing;
A chain, a chain; do you not hear it ring?

Adr. What, the chain?

Dro. S. No, no, the bell: 'tis time that I were gone.
It was two ere I left him, and now the clock strikes one.

Adr. The hours come back! that did I never hear.

Dro. S. O yes, If any hour meet a sergeant, a' turns back for very fear.

Adr. As if time were in debt! how fondly dost thou reason?

Dro. S. Time is a very bankrupt, and owes more than he's worth to season.
Nay, he's a thief too: Have you not heard men say,
That time comes stealing on by night and day?
If he be in debt, and theft, and a sergeant in the way,
Hath he not reason to turn back an hour in a day?

Enter LUCIANA.

Adr. Go, Dromio; there's the money, bear it straight;
And bring thy master home immediately.—
Come, sister: I am press'd down with conceit;
Conceit, my comfort, and my injury.
[*Exeunt.*

SCENE III. *The same.*

Enter ANTIPHOLUS *of* Syracuse.

Ant. S. There's not a man I meet, but doth salute me
As if I were their well acquainted friend;
And every one doth call me by my name.
Some tender money to me, some invite me;
Some other give me thanks for kindnesses;
Some offer me commodities to buy:
Even now a tailor call'd me in his shop,
And show'd me silks that he had bought for me,
And, therewithal, took measure of my body.
Sure, these are but imaginary wiles,
And Lapland sorcerers inhabit here.

Enter DROMIO *of* Syracuse.

Dro. S. Master, here's the gold you sent me for: What, have you got the picture of old Adam new apparell'd?

Ant. S. What gold is this? what Adam dost thou mean?

Dro. S. Not that Adam, that kept the paradise, but that Adam, that keeps the prison: he that goes in the calf's-skin that was kill'd for the prodigal: he that came behind you, sir, like an evil angel, and bid you forsake your liberty.

Ant. S. I understand thee not.

Dro. S. No? why, 'tis a plain case: he that went like a base-viol, in a case of leather; the man, sir, that, when gentleman are tired, gives them a fob, and 'rests them; he, sir, that takes pity on decayed men, and gives them suits of durance; he that sets up his rest to do more exploits with his mace than a morris-pike.

Ant. S. What? thou mean'st an officer?

Dro. S. Ay, sir, the sergeant of the band; he that brings any man to answer it, that breaks his band: one that thinks a man always going to bed, and says, *God give you good rest.*

Ant. S. Well, sir, there rest in your foolery. Is there any ship puts forth to-night? may we be gone?

Dro. S. Why, sir, I brought you word an hour since, that the bark Expedition put forth to-night? and then were you hindered by the sergeant, to tarry for the hoy Delay; here are the angels that you sent for, to deliver you.

Ant. S. The fellow is distract, and so am I;
And here we wander in illusions;
Some blessed power deliver us from hence!

Enter a Courtezan.

Cour. Well met, well met, master Antipholus.
I see, sir, you have found the goldsmith now;
Is that the chain, you promis'd me to-day?

Ant. S. Satan, avoid! I charge thee tempt me not!

Dro. S. Master, is this mistress Satan?

Ant. S. It is the devil.

Dro. S. Nay, she is worse, she is the devil's dam; and here she comes in the habit of a light wench; and thereof comes, that the wenches say, *God damn me*, that's as much as to say, *God make me a light wench.* It is written, they appear to men like angels of light: light is an effect of fire, and fire will burn; *ergo*, light wenches will burn; Come not near her.

Cour. Your man and you are marvellous merry, sir. Will you go with me? We'll mend our dinner here.

Dro. S. Master, if you do, expect spoon-meat, or bespeak a long spoon.

Ant. S. Why, Dromio?

Dro. S. Marry, he must have a long spoon, that must eat with the devil.

Ant. S. Avoid then, fiend! what tell'st thou me of supping?
Thou art, as you are all, a sorceress:
I conjure thee to leave me, and be gone.

Cour. Give me the ring of mine you had at dinner,
Or, for my diamond, the chain you promis'd;
And I'll be gone, sir, and not trouble you.

Dro. S. Some devils ask but the paring of one's nail,
A rush, a hair, a drop of blood, a pin,
A nut, a cherry-stone: but she, more covetous,
Would have a chain.
Master, be wise; and if you give it her,
The devil will shake her chain, and fright us with it.

Cour. I pray you, sir, my ring, or else the chain;
I hope, you do not mean to cheat me so.

Ant. S. Avaunt, thou witch! Come, Dromio, let us go.

Dro. S. Fly pride, says the peacock: Mistress, that you know. [*Exeunt* ANT. *and* DRO.

Cour. Now, out of doubt, Antipholus is mad,
Else would he never so demean himself:
A ring he hath of mine worth forty ducats,
And for the same he promis'd me a chain!
Both one, and other, he denies me now.
The reason that I gather he is mad
(Besides this present instance of his rage),
Is a mad tale, he told to-day at dinner,
Of his own doors being shut against his entrance.
Belike, his wife, acquainted with his fits,
On purpose shut the doors against his way.
My way is now, to hie home to his house,
And tell his wife, that, being lunatick,
He rush'd into my house, and took perforce
My ring away: This course I fittest choose;
For forty ducats is too much to lose. [*Exit.*

SCENE IV. *The same.*

Enter ANTIPHOLUS *of* Ephesus, *and an* Officer.

Ant. E. Fear me not, man, I will not break away;
I'll give thee, ere I leave thee, so much money
To warrant thee, as I am 'rested for.
My wife is in a wayward mood to-day:
And will not lightly trust the messenger,
That I should be attach'd in Ephesus:
I tell you, 'twill sound harshly in her ears.—

Enter DROMIO *of* Ephesus, *with a rope's end.*

Here comes my man; I think, he brings the money.
How now, sir? have you that I sent you for?

Dro. E. Here's that, I warrant you, will pay them all.

Ant. E. But where's the money?

Dro. E. Why, sir, I gave the money for the rope.

Ant. E. Five hundred ducats, villain, for a rope?

Dro. E. I'll serve you, sir, five hundred at the rate.

Ant. E. To what end did I bid thee hie thee home?

Dro. E. To a rope's end, sir: and to that end am I return'd.

Ant. E. And to that end, sir, I will welcome you. [*Beating him.*

Off. Good sir, be patient.

Dro. E. Nay, 'tis for me to be patient: I am in adversity.

Off. Good now, hold thy tongue.

Dro. E. Nay, rather persuade him to hold his hands.

Ant. E. Thou whoreson, senseless villain!

Dro. E. I would, I were senseless, sir, that I might not feel your blows.

Ant. E. Thou art sensible in nothing but blows, and so is an ass.

Dro. E. I am an ass indeed; you may prove it by my long ears. I have served him from the hour of my nativity to this instant, and have nothing at his hands for my service, but blows: when I am cold, he heats me with beating: when I am warm, he cools me with beating: I am waked with it, when I sleep: raised with it, when I sit; driven out of doors with it, when I go from home; welcomed home with it, when I return: nay, I bear it on my shoulders, as a beggar wont her brat; and, I think, when he hath lamed me, I shall beg with it from door to door.

Enter ADRIANA, LUCIANA, *and the* Courtezan, *with* PINCH, *and others.*

Ant. E. Come, go along; my wife is coming yonder.

Dro. E. Mistress, *respice finem*, respect your end; or rather the prophecy, like the parrot, *Beware the rope's end.*

Ant. E. Wilt thou still talk? [*Beats him.*

Cour. How say you now? is not your husband mad?

Adr. His incivility confirms no less.—
Good doctor Pinch, you are a conjurer;
Establish him in his true sense again,
And I will please you what you will demand.

Luc. Alas, how fiery and how sharp he looks!

Cour. Mark, how he trembles in his ecstasy!

Pinch. Give me your hand, and let me feel your pulse.

Ant. E. There is my hand, and let it feel your ear.

Pinch. I charge thee, Satan, hous'd within this man,
To yield possession to my holy prayers,
And to thy state of darkness hie thee straight;
I conjure thee by all the saints in heaven.

Ant. E. Peace, doting wizard, peace; I am not mad.

Adr. O, that thou wert not, poor distressed soul!

Ant. E. You minion, you, are these your customers?
Did this companion with a saffron face
Revel and feast it at my house to-day,
Whilst upon me the guilty doors were shut,
And I denied to enter in my house?

Adr. O, husband, God doth know, you din'd at home,
Where 'would, you had remain'd until this time,
Free from these slanders, and this open shame!

Ant. E. Din'd at home! thou villain, what say'st thou?

Dro. E. Sir, sooth to say, you did not dine at home.

Ant. E. Were not my doors lock'd up, and I shut out?

Dro. E. Perdy, your doors were lock'd, and you shut out.

Ant. E. And did not she herself revile me there?

Dro. E. Sans fable, she herself revil'd you there.

Ant. E. Did not her kitchen maid rail, taunt, and scorn me?

Dro. E. Certes, she did; the kitchen-vestal scorn'd you.

Ant. E. And did not I in rage depart from thence?

Dro. E. In verity, you did;—my bones bear witness,
That since have felt the vigour of his rage.

Adr. Is't good to sooth him in these contraries?

Pinch. It is no shame; the fellow finds his vein,
And, yielding to him, humours well his frenzy.

Ant. E. Thou hast suborn'd the goldsmith to arrest me.

Adr. Alas, I sent you money to redeem you,
By Dromio here, who came in haste for it.

Dro. E. Money by me? heart and good-will you might,
But, surely, master, not a rag of money.

Ant. E. Went'st not thou to her for a purse of ducats?

Adr. He came to me, and I deliver'd it.

Luc. And I am witness with her, that she did.

Dro. E. God and the rope-maker, bear me witness,
That I was sent for nothing but a rope!

Pinch. Mistress, both man and master is possess'd;
I know it by their pale and deadly looks:
They must be bound, and laid in some dark room.

Ant. E. Say, wherefore didst thou lock me forth to-day,
And why dost thou deny the bag of gold?

Adr. I did not, gentle husband, lock thee forth.

Dro. E. And, gentle master, I receiv'd no gold;
But I confess, sir, that we were lock'd out.

Adr. Dissembling villain, thou speak'st false in both.

Ant. E. Dissembling harlot, thou art false in all;
And art confederate with a damned pack,
To make a loathsome abject scorn of me:
But with these nails I'll pluck out these false eyes,
That would behold in me this shameful sport.

[PINCH *and his* Assistants *bind* ANT. *and* DRO.

Adr. O, bind him, bind him, let him not come near me.

Pinch. More company;—the fiend is strong within him.

Luc. Ah me, poor man, how pale and wan he looks!

Ant. E. What, will you murder me? Thou gaoler, thou,
I am thy prisoner; wilt thou suffer them
To make a rescue?

Off. Masters, let him go;
He is my prisoner, and you shall not have him.

Pinch. Go, bind this man, for he is frantic too.

Adr. What wilt thou do, thou peevish officer?
Hast thou delight to see a wretched man
Do outrage and displeasure to himself?

Off. He is my prisoner; if I let him go,
The debt he owes, will be requir'd of me.

Adr. I will discharge thee, ere I go from thee:
Bear me forthwith unto his creditor,
And, knowing how the debt grows, I will pay it.
Good master doctor, see him safe convey'd
Home to my house.—O most unhappy day!

Ant. E. O most unhappy strumpet!

Dro. E. Master, I am here enter'd in bond for you.

Ant. E. Out on thee, villain! wherefore dost thou mad me?

Dro. E. Will you be bound for nothing? be mad,
Good master; cry, the devil.—

Luc. God help, poor souls, how idly do they talk!

Adr. Go bear him hence.—Sister, go you with me.—

[*Exeunt* PINCH *and* Assistants *with* ANTIPHOLUS *and* DROMIO.

Say now, whose suit is he arrested at?

Off. One Angelo, a goldsmith: Do you know him?

Adr. I know the man: What is the sum he owes?

Off. Two hundred ducats.
Adr. Say, how grows it due?
Off. Due for a chain, your husband had of him.
Adr. He did bespeak a chain for me, but had it not.
Cour. When as your husband, all in rage, to-day
Came to my house, and took away my ring,
(The ring I saw upon his finger now),
Straight after, did I meet him with a chain.
Adr. It may be so, but I did never see it:—
Come, gaoler, bring me where the goldsmith is,
I long to know the truth hereof at large.

Enter ANTIPHOLUS *of* Syracuse, *with his rapier drawn, and* DROMIO *of* Syracuse.

Luc. God, for thy mercy: they are loose again.
Adr. And come with naked swords; let's call more help,
To have them bound again.
Off. Away, they'll kill us.
[*Exeunt* Officer, ADR. *and* LUC.
Ant. S. I see these witches are afraid of swords.
Dro. S. She, that would be your wife, now ran from you.
Ant. S. Come to the Centaur; fetch our stuff from thence:
I long, that we were safe and sound aboard.
Dro. S. 'Faith, stay here this night, they will surely do us no harm; you saw, they speak us fair, give us gold: methinks, they are such a gentle nation, that but for the mountain of mad flesh that claims marriage of me, I could find in my heart to stay here still, and turn witch.
Ant. S. I will not stay to-night for all the town;
Therefore away, to get our stuff aboard.
[*Exeunt.*

ACT V.

SCENE I. *The same.*

Enter Merchant *and* ANGELO.

Ang. I am sorry, sir, that I have hinder'd you;
But, I protest, he had the chain of me,
Though most dishonestly he doth deny it.
Mer. How is the man esteem'd here in the city?
Ang. Of very reverend reputation, sir,
Of credit infinite, highly belov'd,
Second to none that lives here in the city;
His word might bear my wealth at any time.
Mer. Speak softly: yonder, as I think, he walks.

Enter ANTIPHOLUS *and* DROMIO *of* Syracuse.

Ang. 'Tis so; and that self chain about his neck,
Which he forswore, most monstrously, to have.
Good sir, draw near to me, I'll speak to him.
Signior Antipholus, I wonder much
That you would put me to this shame and trouble;
And not without some scandal to yourself,
With circumstance and oaths, so to deny
This chain, which now you wear so openly:
Besides the charge, the shame, imprisonment,
You have done wrong to this my honest friend;
Who, but for staying on our controversy,
Had hoisted sail, and put to sea to-day:
This chain you had of me, can you deny it?
Ant. S. I think, I had; I never did deny it.
Mer. Yes, that you did, sir; and forswore it too.
Ant. S. Who heard me to deny it, or forswear it?
Mer. These ears of mine, thou knowest, did hear thee:
Fie on thee, wretch! 'tis pity, that thou liv'st
To walk where any honest men resort.
Ant. S. Thou art a villain to impeach me thus:
I'll prove mine honour, and mine honesty
Against thee presently, if thou dar'st stand.
Mer. I dare, and do defy thee for a villain.
[*They draw.*

Enter ADRIANA, LUCIANA, Courtezan, *and others.*

Adr. Hold, hurt him not, for God's sake; he is mad;—
Some get within him, take his sword away:
Bind Dromio too, and bear them to my house.
Dro. S. Run, master, run; for God's sake, take a house.
This is some priory;—In, or we are spoil'd.
[*Exeunt* ANTIPH. *and* DRO. *to the Priory.*

Enter the Abbess.

Abb. Be quiet, people; Wherefore throng you hither?
Adr. To fetch my poor distracted husband hence:
Let us come in, that we may bind him fast,
And bear him home for his recovery.
Ang. I knew, he was not in his perfect wits.
Mer. I am sorry now, that I did draw on him.
Abb. How long hath this possession held the man?
Adr. This week he hath been heavy, sour, sad,
And much different from the man he was;
But, till this afternoon, his passion
Ne'er brake into extremity of rage.
Abb. Hath he not lost much wealth by wreck at sea?
Buried some dear friend? Hath not else his eye
Stray'd his affection in unlawful love?
A sin, prevailing much in youthful men,
Who give their eyes the liberty of gazing.
Which of these sorrows is he subject to?
Adr. To none of these, except it be the last;
Namely, some love, that drew him oft from home.
Abb. You should for that have reprehended him.
Adr. Why, so I did.
Abb. Ay, but not rough enough.
Adr. As roughly, as my modesty would let me.
Abb. Haply, in private.
Adr. And in assemblies too.
Abb. Ay, but not enough.
Adr. It was the copy of our conference:
In bed, he slept not for my urging it;
At board, he fed not for my urging it;
Alone, it was the subject of my theme;
In company, I often glanced it;
Still did I tell him it was vile and bad.
Abb. And therefore came it, that the man was mad:
The venom clamours of a jealous woman
Poison more deadly than a mad dog's tooth.
It seems his sleeps were hinder'd by thy railing:
And therefore comes it that his head is light.
Thou say'st his meat was sauc'd with thy upbraidings:
Unquiet meals make ill digestions,
Thereof the raging fire of fever bred;
And what's a fever but a fit of madness?
Thou say'st his sports were hinder'd by thy brawls;
Sweet recreation barr'd, what doth ensue,
But moody and dull melancholy,
(Kinsman to grim and comfortless despair);
And, at her heels, a huge infectious troop
Of pale distemperatures, and foes to life?
In food, in sport, and life-preserving rest
To be disturb'd, would mad or man, or beast:
The consequence is then, thy jealous fits
Have scar'd thy husband from the use of wits.
Luc. She never reprehended him but mildly,
When he demean'd himself rough, rude, and wildly.—
Why bear you these rebukes, and answer not?
Adr. She did betray me to my own reproof.
Good people, enter, and lay hold on him.
Abb. No, not a creature enters in my house.
Adr. Then, let your servants bring my husband forth.
Abb. Neither; he took this place for sanctuary.
And it shall privilege him from your hands,

Till I have brought him to his wits again,
Or lose my labour in assaying it.

Adr. I will attend my husband, be his nurse,
Diet his sickness, for it is my office,
And will have no attorney but myself;
And therefore let me have him home with me.

Abb. Be patient; for I will not let him stir,
Till I have us'd the approved means I have,
With wholesome syrups, drugs, and holy prayers,
To make of him a formal man again:
It is a branch and parcel of mine oath,
A charitable duty of my order;
Therefore depart, and leave him here with me.

Adr. I will not hence, and leave my husband here;
And ill it doth beseem your holiness,
To separate the husband and the wife.

Abb. Be quiet, and depart, thou shalt not have him. [*Exit* Abbess.

Luc. Complain unto the duke of this indignity.

Adr. Come, go; I will fall prostrate at his feet,
And never rise until my tears and prayers
Have won his grace to come in person hither,
And take perforce my husband from the abbess.

Mer. By this, I think, the dial points at five:
Anon, I am sure, the duke himself in person
Comes this way to the melancholy vale;
The place of death and sorry execution,
Behind the ditches of the abbey here.

Ang. Upon what cause?

Mer. To see a reverend Syracusan merchant,
Who put unluckily into this bay
Against the laws and statutes of this town,
Beheaded publickly for his offence.

Ang. See, where they come; we will behold his death.

Luc. Kneel to the duke, before he pass the abbey.

Enter Duke *attended; Ægeon bare-headed; with the* Headsman *and other* Officers.

Duke. Yet once again proclaim it publicly,
If any friend will pay the sum for him,
He shall not die, so much we tender him.

Adr. Justice, most sacred duke, against the abbess!

Duke. She is a virtuous and a reverend lady;
It cannot be, that she hath done thee wrong.

Adr. May it please your grace, Antipholus, my husband,—
Whom I made lord of me and all I had,
At your important letters,—this ill day,
A most outrageous fit of madness took him;
That desperately he hurried through the street
(With him his bondman, all as mad as he),
Doing displeasure to the citizens
By rushing in their houses, bearing thence
Rings, jewels, any thing his rage did like.
Once did I get him bound, and sent him home,
Whilst to take order for the wrongs I went,
That here and there his fury had committed.
Anon, I wot not by what strong escape,
He broke from those that had the guard of him;
And, with his mad attendant and himself,
Each one with ireful passion, with drawn swords,
Met us again, and, madly bent on us,
Chas'd us away; till raising of more aid,
We came again to bind them; then they fled
Into this abbey, whither we pursued them;
And here the abbess shuts the gates on us,
And will not suffer us to fetch him out,
Nor send him forth, that we may bear him hence.
Therefore, most gracious duke, with thy command,
Let him be brought forth, and borne hence for help.

Duke. Long since, thy husband serv'd me in my wars;
And I to thee engag'd a prince's word,
When thou didst make him master of thy bed,
To do him all the grace and good I could.—
Go, some of you, knock at the abbey-gate,
And bid the lady abbess come to me;
I will determine this, before I stir.

Enter a Servant.

Serv. O mistress, mistress, shift and save yourself!
My master and his man are both broke loose,
Beaten the maids a-row, and bound the doctor,
Whose beard they have singed off with brands of fire;
And ever as it blaz'd, they threw on him
Great pails of puddled mire to quench the hair;
My master preaches patience to him, and the while
His man with scissars nicks him like a fool;
And, sure, unless you send some present help,
Between them they will kill the conjurer.

Adr. Peace, fool, thy master and his man are here;
And that is false, thou dost report to us.

Ser. Mistress, upon my life, I tell you true;
I have not breath'd almost, since I did see it.
He cries for you, and vows, if he can take you,
To scorch your face, and to disfigure you: [*Cry within.*
Hark, hark, I hear him, mistress; fly, be gone.

Duke. Come, stand by me, fear nothing: Guard with halberds.

Adr. Ah me, it is my husband! Witness you,
That he is borne about invisible:
Even now we hous'd him in the abbey here;
And now he's there, past thought of human reason.

Enter Antipholus *and* Dromio *of* Ephesus.

Ant. E. Justice, most gracious duke, oh, grant me justice!
Even for the service that long since I did thee,
When I bestrid thee in the wars, and took
Deep scars to save thy life; even for the blood
That then I lost for thee, now grant me justice.

Æge. Unless the fear of death doth make me dote,
I see my son Antipholus, and Dromio.

Ant. E. Justice, sweet prince, against that woman there.
She whom thou gav'st to me to be my wife;
That hath abused and dishonour'd me,
Even in the strength and height of injury!
Beyond imagination is the wrong,
That she this day hath shameless thrown on me.

Duke. Discover how, and thou shalt find me just.

Ant. E. This day, great duke, she shut the doors upon me,
While she with harlots feasted in my house.

Duke. A grievous fault: Say, woman, didst thou so?

Adr. No, my good lord;—myself, he, and my sister,
To-day did dine together: So befall my soul,
As this is false he burdens me withal!

Luc. Ne'er may I look on day, nor sleep on night,
But she tells to your highness simple truth!

Ang. O perjur'd woman! they are both forsworn.
In this the madman justly chargeth them.

Ant. E. My liege, I am advised what I say;
Neither disturbed with the effect of wine,
Nor heady rash, provok'd with raging ire,
Albeit, my wrongs might make one wiser mad,
This woman lock'd me out this day from dinner:
That goldsmith there, were he not pack'd with her,
Could witness it, for he was with me then;
Who parted with me to go fetch a chain,
Promising to bring it to the Porcupine,
Where Balthazar and I did dine together.
Our dinner done, and he not coming thither,
I went to seek him: in the street I met him;
And in his company, that gentleman.

There did this perjur'd goldsmith swear me down,
That I this day of him receiv'd the chain,
Which, God he knows, I saw not: for the which,
He did arrest me with an officer,
I did obey; and sent my peasant home
For certain ducats: he with none return'd.
Then fairly I bespoke the officer,
To go in person with me to my house.
By the way we met
My wife, her sister, and a rabble more
Of vile confederates: along with them
They brought one Pinch; a hungry lean-fac'd villain,
A mere anatomy, a mountebank,
A thread-bare juggler, and a fortune teller;
A needy, hollow-ey'd, sharp-looking wretch,
A living dead man: this pernicious slave,
Forsooth, took on him as a conjurer;
And, gazing in mine eyes, feeling my pulse,
And with no face, as 'twere, outfacing me,
Cries out, I was possess'd: then altogether
They fell upon me, bound me, bore me thence;
And in a dark and dankish vault at home
There left me and my man, both bound together:
Till gnawing with my teeth my bonds in sunder,
I gain'd my freedom, and immediately
Ran hither to your grace; whom I beseech
To give me ample satisfaction
For these deep shames and great indignities.

Ang. My lord, in truth, thus far I witness with him;
That he dined not at home, but was lock'd out.

Duke. But had he such a chain of thee, or no?

Ang. He had, my lord: and when he ran in here,
These people saw the chain about his neck.

Mer. Besides, I will be sworn, these ears of mine
Heard you confess, you had the chain of him,
After you first forswore it on the mart,
And, thereupon, I drew my sword on you:
And then you fled into this abbey here,
From whence, I think, you are come by miracle.

Ant. E. I never came within these abbey walls,
Nor ever didst thou draw thy sword on me:
I never saw the chain, so help me heaven!
And this is false, you burden me withal.

Duke. Why, what an intricate impeach is this!
I think, you all have drunk of Circe's cup.
If here you hous'd him, here he would have been:
If he were mad, he would not plead so coldly:—
You say, he dined at home; the goldsmith here
Denies that saying:—Sirrah, what say you?

Dro. E. Sir, he dined with her there, at the Porcupine.

Cour. He did; and from my finger snatch'd that ring.

Ant. E. 'Tis true, my liege, this ring I had of her.

Duke. Saw'st thou him enter at the abbey here?

Cour. As sure, my liege, as I do see your grace.

Duke. Why, this is strange;—Go call the abbess hither;
I think, you are all mated, or stark mad.
[*Exit an* Attendant.

Æge. Most mighty duke, vouchsafe me speak a word;
Haply I see a friend will save my life,
And pay the sum that may deliver me.

Duke. Speak freely, Syracusan, what thou wilt.

Æge. Is not your name, sir, call'd Antipholus?
And is not that your bondman Dromio?

Dro. E. Within this hour I was his bondman, sir,
But he, I thank him, gnaw'd in two my cords;
Now am I Dromio, and his man, unbound.

Æge. I am sure, you both of you remember me.

Dro. E. Ourselves we do remember, sir, by you;
For lately we were bound as you are now.
You are not Pinch's patient, are you, sir?

Æge. Why look you strange on me? you know me well.

Ant. E. I never saw you in my life, till now.

Æge. Oh! grief hath chang'd me, since you saw me last;
And careful hours, with Time's deformed hand,
Have written strange defeatures in my face:
But tell me yet, dost thou not know my voice?

Ant E. Neither.

Æge. Dromio, nor thou?

Dro. E. No, trust me, sir, nor I.

Æge. I am sure, thou dost.

Dro. E. Ay, sir? but I am sure, I do not, and whatsoever a man denies, you are now bound to believe him.

Æge. Not know my voice! O, time's extremity!
Hast thou so crack'd and splitted my poor tongue,
In seven short years, that here my only son
Knows not my feeble key of untun'd cares?
Though now this grained face of mine be hid
In sap-consuming winter's drizzled snow,
And all the conduits of my blood froze up;
Yet hath my night of life some memory,
My wasting lamp some fading glimmer left,
My dull deaf ears a little use to hear:
All these old witnesses (I cannot err),
Tell me, thou art my son Antipholus.

Ant. E. I never saw my father in my life.

Æge. But seven years since, in Syracusa, boy,
Thou know'st, we parted: but, perhaps, my son,
Thou sham'st to acknowledge me in misery.

Ant. E. The duke, and all that know me in the city,
Can witness with me, that it is not so;
I ne'er saw Syracusa in my life.

Duke. I tell thee, Syracusan, twenty years
Have I been patron to Antipholus,
During which time he ne'er saw Syracusa:
I see, thy age and dangers make thee dote.

Enter the Abbess, *with* ANTIPHOLUS Syracusan, *and* DROMIO Syracusan.

Abb. Most mighty duke, behold a man much wrong'd. [*All gather to see him.*

Adr. I see two husbands, or mine eyes deceive me.

Duke. One of these men is Genius to the other;
And so of these; Which is the natural man,
And which the spirit? Who deciphers them?

Dro. S. I, sir, am Dromio; command him away.

Dro. E. I, sir, am Dromio; 'pray, let me stay,

Ant. S. Ægeon, art thou not? or else his ghost?

Dro. S. O, my old master! who hath bound him here?

Abb. Whoever bound him, I will loose his bonds,
And gain a husband by his liberty:
Speak, old Ægeon, if thou be'st the man
That hadst a wife once call'd Æmilia,
That bore thee at a burden two fair sons:
O, if thou be'st the same Ægeon, speak,
And speak unto the same Æmilia!

Æge. If I dream not, thou art Æmilia;
If thou art she, tell me, where is that son
That floated with thee on the fatal raft?

Abb. By men of Epidamnum, he, and I,
And the twin Dromio, all were taken up;
But, by and by, rude fishermen of Corinth
By force took Dromio and my son from them,
And me they left with those of Epidamnum:
What then became of them, I cannot tell;
I, to this fortune that you see me in.

Duke. Why, here begins his morning story right;
These two Antipholuses, these two so alike,
And these two Dromioes, one in semblance,—
Besides her urging of her wreck at sea,—
These are the parents to these children,

Which accidentally are met together.
Antipholus, thou cam'st from Corinth first.

Ant. S. No, sir, not I; I came from Syracuse.

Duke. Stay, stand apart; I know not which is which.

Ant. E. I came from Corinth, my most gracious lord.

Dro. E. And I with him.

Ant. E. Brought to this town with that most famous warrior
Duke Menaphon, your most renowned uncle.

Adr. Which of you two did dine with me to-day?

Ant. S. I, gentle mistress.

Adr. And are not you my husband?

Ant. E. No, I say nay to that.

Ant. S. And so do I, yet did she call me so;
And this fair gentlewoman, her sister here,
Did call me brother:—What I told you then,
I hope, I shall have leisure to make good:
If this be not a dream I see and hear.

Ang. That is the chain, sir, which you had of me.

Ant. S. I think it be, sir; I deny it not.

Ant. E. And you, sir, for this chain arrested me.

Ang. I think I did, sir; I deny it not.

Adr. I sent you money, sir, to be your bail,
By Dromio; but I think he brought it not.

Dro. E. No, none by me.

Ant. S. This purse of ducats I receiv'd from you,
And Dromio my man did bring them me:
I see, we still did meet each other's man,
And I was ta'en for him, and he for me,
And thereupon these errors are arose.

Ant. E. These ducats pawn I for my father here.

Duke. It shall not need, thy father hath his life.

Cour. Sir, I must have that diamond from you.

Ant. E. There, take it; and much thanks for my good cheer.

Abb. Renowned duke, vouchsafe to take the pains
To go with us into the abbey here,
And hear at large discoursed all our fortunes:—
And all that are assembled in this place,
That by this sympathized one day's error
Have suffer'd wrong, go, keep us company,
And we shall make full satisfaction.—
Twenty-five years have I but gone in travail
Of you, my sons, and till this present hour;—
My heavy burden here delivered.
The duke, my husband, and my children both,
And you the calendars of their nativity,
Go to a gossip's feast, and go with me;
After so long grief, such nativity!

Duke. With all my heart, I'll gossip at this feast.
[*Exeunt* Duke, Abbess, ÆGEON, Courtezan, Merchant, ANGELO, *and* Attendants.

Dro. S. Master, shall I fetch your stuff from ship-board?

Ant. E. Dromio, what stuff of mine hast thou embark'd?

Dro. S. Your goods, that lay at host, sir, in the Centaur.

Ant. S. He speaks to me; I am your master, Dromio;
Come, go with us: we'll look to that anon:
Embrace thy brother there, rejoice with him.
[*Exeunt* ANT. S. *and* ANT. E. ADR. *and* LUC.

Dro. S. There is a fat friend at your master's house,
That kitchen'd me for you to-day at dinner;
She now shall be my sister, not my wife.

Dro. E. Methinks, you are my glass, and not my brother:
I see by you, I am a sweet-faced youth.
Will you walk in to see their gossiping?

Dro. S. Not I, sir; you are my elder.

Dro. E. That's a question: how shall we try it?

Dro. S. We will draw cuts for the senior: till then, lead thou first.

Dro. E. Nay; then thus:
We came into the world, like brother and brother:
And now let's go hand in hand, not one before another. [*Exeunt.*

MACBETH.

PERSONS REPRESENTED.

DUNCAN, *King of* Scotland.
MALCOLM, DONALBAIN, } *his Sons.*
MACBETH, BANQUO, } *Generals of the King's Army.*
MACDUFF, LENOX, ROSSE, MENTETH, ANGUS, CATHNESS, } *Noblemen of* Scotland.
FLEANCE, *Son to* Banquo.
SIWARD, *Earl of* Northumberland, *General of the English Forces.*
YOUNG SIWARD, *his Son.*
SEYTON, *an Officer attending on* Macbeth.
Son to Macduff.
An English Doctor. A Scotch Doctor.
A Soldier. A Porter. An old Man.

LADY MACBETH.
LADY MACDUFF.
Gentlewoman *attending on* Lady Macbeth.
HECATE, *and three* Witches.

Lords, Gentlemen, Officers, Soldiers, Murderers, Attendants, *and* Messengers.
The Ghost of Banquo, *and several other* Apparitions.

SCENE—*In the end of the Fourth Act, lies in* England; *through the rest of the play, in* Scotland; *and, chiefly, at* Macbeth's *Castle.*

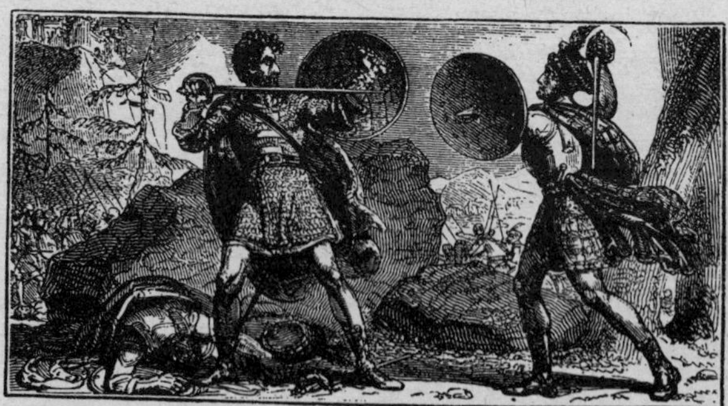

ACT I.

SCENE I.– *An open Place.*

Thunder and Lightning. Enter three Witches.

1 *Witch.* WHEN shall we three meet again,
In thunder, lightning, or in rain?
2 *Witch.* When the hurlyburly's done,
When the battle's lost and won.
3 *Witch.* That will be ere set of sun.
1 *Witch.* Where the place?
2 *Witch.* Upon the heath:
3 *Witch.* There to meet with Macbeth.
1 *Witch.* I come, Graymalkin!
All. Paddock calls:—Anon.
Fair is foul, and foul is fair:
Hover through the fog and filthy air.
[Witches *vanish.*

SCENE II. *A Camp near* Fores.

Alarum within. Enter KING DUNCAN, MALCOLM, DONALBAIN, LENOX, *with* Attendants, *meeting a bleeding* Soldier.

Dun. What bloody man is that? He can report,
As seemeth by his plight, of the revolt
The newest state.
Mal. This is the sergeant,
Who, like a good and hardy soldier, fought
'Gainst my captivity: Hail, brave friend!
Say to the king the knowledge of the broil,
As thou didst leave it.
Sold. Doubtful it stood;
As two spent swimmers, that do cling together,
And choke their art. The merciless Macdonwald
(Worthy to be a rebel; for to that
The multiplying villanies of nature
Do swarm upon him), from the western isles
Of Kernes and Gallowglasses is supplied;
And fortune, on his damned quarry smiling,
Show'd like a rebel's whore. But all's too weak:
For brave Macbeth (well he deserves that name),
Disdaining fortune, with his brandish'd steel,
Which smok'd with bloody execution,
Like valour's minion,
Carv'd out his passage, till he fac'd the slave;
And ne'er shook hands, nor bade farewell to him,
Till he unseam'd him from the nave to the chaps,
And fix'd his head upon our battlements.
Dun. O, valiant cousin! worthy gentleman!
Sold. As whence the sun 'gins his reflexion
Shipwrecking storms and direful thunders break;
So from that spring, whence comfort seem'd to come,
Discomfort swells. Mark, king of Scotland, mark:
No sooner justice had, with valour arm'd,
Compell'd these skipping Kernes to trust their heels;
But the Norweyan lord, surveying vantage,
With furbish'd arms, and new supplies of men,
Began a fresh assault.
Dun. Dismay'd not this
Our captains, Macbeth and Banquo?
Sold. Yes;
As sparrows, eagles; or the hare, the lion.

If I say sooth, I must report, they were
As cannons overcharg'd with double cracks;
So they
Doubly redoubled strokes upon the foe:
Except they meant to bathe in reeking wounds,
Or memorize another Golgotha,
I cannot tell:——
But I am faint, my gashes cry for help.

Dun. So well thy words become thee, as thy wounds;
They smack of honour both:—Go, get him surgeons. [*Exit* Soldier, *attended.*

Enter ROSSE.

Who comes here?

Mal. The worthy thane of Rosse.

Len. What a haste looks through his eyes! So should he look,
That seems to speak things strange.

Rosse. God save the king!

Dun. Whence cam'st thou, worthy thane?

Rosse. From Fife, great king.
Where the Norweyan banners flout the sky,
And fan our people cold.
Norway himself, with terrible numbers,
Assisted by that most disloyal traitor
The thane of Cawdor, 'gan a dismal conflict:
Till that Bellona's bridegroom, lapp'd in proof,
Confronted him with self-comparisons,
Point against point rebellious, arm 'gainst arm,
Curbing his lavish spirit: And, to conclude,
The victory fell on us;——

Dun. Great happiness!

Rosse. That now
Sweno, the Norways' king, craves composition;
Nor would we deign him burial of his men,
Till he disbursed, at Saint Colmes' Inch,
Ten thousand dollars to our general use.

Dun. No more that thane of Cawdor shall deceive
Our bosom interest:—Go, pronounce his death,
And with his former title greet Macbeth.

Rosse. I'll see it done.

Dun. What he hath lost, noble Macbeth hath won. [*Exeunt.*

SCENE III. *A Heath.*

Thunder. Enter the three Witches.

1 *Witch.* Where hast thou been, sister?

2 *Witch.* Killing swine.

3 *Witch.* Sister, where thou?

1 *Witch.* A sailor's wife had chestnuts in her lap,
And mounch'd, and mounch'd, and mounch'd:
—*Give me*, quoth I:
Aroint thee, witch! the rump-fed ronyon cries.
Her husband's to Aleppo gone, master o' the Tiger:
But in a sieve I'll thither sail,
And, like a rat without a tail,
I'll do, I'll do, and I'll do.

2 *Witch.* I'll give thee a wind.

1 *Witch.* Thou art kind.

3 *Witch.* And I another.

1 *Witch.* I myself have all the other;
And the very ports they blow,
All the quarters that they know
I' the shipman's card.
I will drain him dry as hay:
Sleep shall, neither night nor day,
Hang upon his pent-house lid;
He shall live a man forbid:
Weary sev'n nights, nine times nine,
Shall he dwindle, peak, and pine:
Though his bark cannot be lost,
Yet it shall be tempest toss'd.
Look what I have.

2 *Witch.* Show me, show me.

1 *Witch.* Here I have a pilot's thumb,
Wreck'd, as homeward he did come. [*Drum within.*

3 *Witch.* A drum, a drum;
Macbeth doth come.

All. The weird sisters, hand in hand,
Posters of the sea and land,
Thus do go about, about;
Thrice to thine, and thrice to mine,
And thrice again, to make up nine:
Peace!—the charm's wound up.

Enter MACBETH *and* BANQUO.

Macb. So foul and fair a day I have not seen.

Ban. How far is 't call'd to Fores?—What are these,
So wither'd, and so wild in their attire;
That look not like the inhabitants o' the earth,
And yet are on 't? Live you? or are you aught
That man may question? You seem to understand me,
By each at once her choppy finger laying
Upon her skinny lips:—You should be women,
And yet your beards forbid me to interpret
That you are so.

Macb. Speak, if you can;—What are you?

1 *Witch.* All hail, Macbeth! hail to thee, thane of Glamis!

2 *Witch.* All hail, Macbeth! hail to thee, thane of Cawdor!

3 *Witch.* All hail, Macbeth! that shalt be king hereafter.

Ban. Good sir, why do you start; and seem to fear
Things that do sound so fair?—I' the name of truth,
Are ye fantastical, or that indeed
Which outwardly ye show? My noble partner
You greet with present grace, and great prediction
Of noble having, and of royal hope,
That he seems rapt withal; to me you speak not:
If you can look into the seeds of time,
And say, which grain will grow, and which will not:
Speak then to me, who neither beg, nor fear,
Your favours, nor your hate.

1 *Witch.* Hail!

2 *Witch.* Hail!

3 *Witch.* Hail!

1 *Witch.* Lesser than Macbeth, and greater.

2 *Witch.* Not so happy, yet much happier.

3 *Witch.* Thou shalt get kings, though thou be none:
So, all hail, Macbeth, and Banquo!

1 *Witch.* Banquo, and Macbeth, all hail!

Macb. Stay, you imperfect speakers, tell me more:
By Sinel's death, I know, I am thane of Glamis;
But how of Cawdor? the thane of Cawdor lives,
A prosperous gentleman; and to be king
Stands not within the prospect of belief,
No more than to be Cawdor. Say, from whence
You owe this strange intelligence; or why
Upon this blasted heath you stop our way
With such prophetick greeting?—Speak, I charge you. [Witches *vanish.*

Ban. The earth hath bubbles, as the water has,
And these are of them:—Whither are they vanish'd?

Macb. Into the air; and what seem'd corporal, melted
As breath into the wind.—'Would, they had staid!

Ban. Were such things here, as we do speak about?
Or have we eaten of the insane root,
That takes the reason prisoner?

Macb. Your children shall be kings.

Ban. You shall be king.

Macb. And thane of Cawdor too; went it not so?

Ban. To the selfsame tune, and words. Who's here?

Enter ROSSE *and* ANGUS.

Rosse. The king hath happily receiv'd, Macbeth,
The news of thy success: and when he reads
Thy personal venture in the rebels' fight,
His wonders and his praises do contend,
Which should be thine, or his: Silenc'd with that,
In viewing o'er the rest o' the selfsame day,
He finds thee in the stout Norweyan ranks,
Nothing afeard of what thyself didst make,
Strange images of death. As thick as tale,
Came post with post; and every one did bear
Thy praises in his kingdom's great defence,
And pour'd them down before him.

Ang. We are sent,
To give thee, from our royal master, thanks;
To herald thee into his sight, not pay thee.

Rosse. And, for an earnest of a greater honour,
He bade me, from him, call thee thane of Cawdor:
In which addition, hail, most worthy thane!
For it is thine.

Ban. What, can the devil speak true?

Macb. The thane of Cawdor lives? Why do you dress me
In borrow'd robes?

Ang. Who was the thane, lives yet;
But under heavy judgment bears that life
Which he deserves to lose. Whether he was combin'd
With those of Norway, or did line the rebel
With hidden help and vantage; or that with both
He labour'd in his country's wreck, I know not;
But treasons capital, confess'd, and prov'd,
Have overthrown him.

Macb. Glamis, and thane of Cawdor;
The greatest is behind.—Thanks for your pains.—
Do you not hope your children shall be kings,
When those that gave the thane of Cawdor to me,
Promis'd no less to them?

Ban. That, trusted home,
Might yet enkindle you unto the crown,
Besides the thane of Cawdor. But 'tis strange:
And oftentimes, to win us to our harm,
The instruments of darkness tell us truths;
Win us with honest trifles, to betray us
In deepest consequence.—
Cousins, a word, I pray you.

Macb. Two truths are told,
As happy prologues to the swelling act
Of the imperial theme.—I thank you, gentlemen.—
This supernatural soliciting
Cannot be ill; cannot be good:—If ill,
Why hath it given me earnest of success,
Commencing in a truth? I am thane of Cawdor:
If good, why do I yield to that suggestion
Whose horrid image doth unfix my hair,
And make my seated heart knock at my ribs,
Against the use of nature? Present fears
Are less than horrible imaginings:
My thought, whose murder yet is but fantastical,
Shakes so my single state of man, that function
Is smother'd in surmise; and nothing is,
But what is not.

Ban. Look, how our partner's rapt.

Macb. If chance will have me king, why, chance may crown me,
Without my stir.

Ban. New honours come upon him
Like our strange garments; cleave not to their mould,
But with the aid of use.

Macb. Come what come may;
Time and the hour runs through the roughest day.

Ban. Worthy Macbeth, we stay upon your leisure.

Macb. Give me your favour:—my dull brain was wrought
With things forgotten. Kind gentlemen, your pains
Are register'd where every day I turn
The leaf to read them.—Let us toward the king.—
Think upon what hath chanc'd: and, at more time,
The interim having weigh'd it, let us speak
Our free hearts each to other.

Ban. Very gladly.

Macb. Till then, enough.—Come, friends.
[*Exeunt.*

SCENE IV. Fores. *A Room in the Palace.*

Flourish. Enter DUNCAN, MALCOLM, DONALBAIN, LENOX, *and* Attendants.

Dun. Is execution done on Cawdor? Are not
Those in commission yet return'd?

Mal. My liege,
They are not yet come back. But I have spoke
With one that saw him die: who did report,
That very frankly he confess'd his treasons;
Implor'd your highness' pardon; and set forth
A deep repentance: nothing in his life
Became him, like the leaving it; he died
As one that had been studied in his death,
To throw away the dearest thing he ow'd,
As 'twere a careless trifle.

Dun. There's no art,
To find the mind's construction in the face:
He was a gentleman on whom I built
An absolute trust.—O worthiest cousin!

Enter MACBETH, BANQUO, ROSSE, *and* ANGUS.

The sin of my ingratitude even now
Was heavy on me: Thou art so far before,
That swiftest wing of recompense is slow
To overtake thee. 'Would, thou hadst less deserv'd;
That the proportion both of thanks and payment
Might have been mine! only I have left to say,
More is thy due than more than all can pay.

Macb. The service and the loyalty I owe,
In doing it, pays itself. Your highness' part
Is to receive our duties: and our duties
Are to your throne and state, children, and servants;
Which do but what they should, by doing every thing
Safe toward your love and honour.

Dun. Welcome hither:
I have begun to plant thee, and will labour
To make thee full of growing.—Noble Banquo,
That hast no less deserv'd, nor must be known
No less to have done so, let me enfold thee,
And hold thee to my heart.

Ban. There if I grow,
The harvest is your own.

Dun. My plenteous joys,
Wanton in fulness, seek to hide themselves
In drops of sorrow.—Sons, kinsmen, thanes,
And you whose places are the nearest, know,
We will establish our estate upon
Our eldest, Malcolm; whom we name hereafter,
The prince of Cumberland: which honour must
Not, unaccompanied, invest him only,
But signs of nobleness, like stars, shall shine
On all deservers.—From hence to Inverness,
And bind us further to you.

Macb. The rest is labour, which is not us'd for you:
I'll be myself the harbinger, and make joyful
The hearing of my wife with your approach;
So, humbly take my leave.

Dun. My worthy Cawdor!

Macb. The prince of Cumberland!—That is a step,
On which I must fall down, or else o'erleap,
[*Aside.*
For in my way it lies. Stars, hide your fires!
Let not light see my black and deep desires:
The eye wink at the hand! yet let that be,
Which the eye fears, when it is done, to see.
[*Exit.*

Dun. True, worthy Banquo; he is full so valiant;
And in his commendations I am fed;
It is a banquet to me. Let us after him,
Whose care is gone before to bid us welcome:
It is a peerless kinsman. [*Flourish. Exeunt.*

SCENE V.

Inverness. *A Room in* Macbeth's *Castle.*

Enter LADY MACBETH, *reading a Letter.*

Lady M. *They met me in the day of success; and I have learned by the perfectest report, they have more in them than mortal knowledge. When I burned in desire to question them further, they made themselves —air, into which they vanished. Whiles I stood rapt in the wonder of it, came missives from the king, who all-hailed me,* Thane of Cawdor; *by which title, before, these weird sisters saluted me, and referred me to the coming on of time, with,* Hail, king that shalt be! *This have I thought good to deliver thee, my dearest partner of greatness; that thou mightest not lose the dues of rejoicing, by being ignorant of what greatness is promised thee. Lay it to thy heart, and farewell.*
Glamis thou art, and Cawdor; and shalt be
What thou art promis'd:—Yet do I fear thy nature;
It is too full o' the milk of human kindness,
To catch the nearest way: Thou would'st be great;
Art not without ambition; but without
The illness should attend it. What thou would'st highly,
That would'st thou holily; would'st not play false,
And yet would'st wrongly win; thou'd'st have, great Glamis,
That which cries, *Thus thou must do, if thou have it;*
And that which rather thou dost fear to do,
Than wishest should be undone. Hie thee hither,
That I may pour my spirits in thine ear;
And chastise with the valour of my tongue
All that impedes thee from the golden round,
Which fate and metaphysical aid doth seem
To have thee crown'd withal.——What is your tidings?

Enter an Attendant.

Attend. The king comes here to-night.
Lady M. Thou'rt mad to say it:
Is not thy master with him? who, wer't so,
Would have inform'd for preparation.
Attend. So please you, it is true; our thane is coming:
One of my fellows had the speed of him;
Who, almost dead for breath, had scarcely more
Than would make up his message.
Lady M. Give him tending,
He brings great news. The raven himself is hoarse, [*Exit* Attendant.
That croaks the fatal entrance of Duncan
Under my battlements. Come, come, you spirits
That tend on mortal thoughts, unsex me here;
And fill me, from the crown to the toe, top-full
Of direst cruelty! make thick my blood,
Stop up the access and passage to remorse;
That no compunctious visitings of nature
Shake my fell purpose, nor keep peace between
The effect, and it! Come to my woman's breasts,
And take my milk for gall, you murd'ring ministers,
Wherever in your sightless substances
You wait on nature's mischief! Come, thick night,
And pall thee in the dunnest smoke of hell!
That my keen knife see not the wound it makes;
Nor heaven peep through the blanket of the dark,
To cry, *Hold, hold!*——Great Glamis! worthy Cawdor!

Enter MACBETH.

Greater than both, by the all-hail hereafter!
Thy letters have transported me beyond
This ignorant present, and I feel now
The future in the instant.
Macb. My dearest love,
Duncan comes here to-night.
Lady. M. And when goes hence?
Macb. To-morrow,—as he purposes.
Lady M. O, never
Shall sun that morrow see!
Your face, my thane, is as a book, where men
May read strange matters:—To beguile the time,
Look like the time; bear welcome in your eye,
Your hand, your tongue: look like the innocent flower,
But be the serpent under it. He that's coming
Must be provided for: and you shall put
This night's great business into my despatch;
Which shall to all our nights and days to come
Give solely sovereign sway and masterdom.
Macb. We will speak further.
Lady M. Only look up clear;
To alter favour ever is to fear:
Leave all the rest to me. [*Exeunt.*

SCENE VI. *The same. Before the Castle.*

Hautboys. Servants *of* Macbeth *attending.*

Enter DUNCAN, MALCOLM, DONALBAIN, BANQUO, LENOX, MACDUFF, ROSSE, ANGUS, *and* Attendants.

Dun. This castle hath a pleasant seat: the air
Nimbly and sweetly recommends itself
Unto our gentle senses.
Ban. This guest of summer,
The temple-haunting martlet, does approve,
By his lov'd mansionry, that the heaven's breath
Smells wooingly here: no jutty, frieze,
Buttress, nor coigne of vantage, but this bird
Hath made his pendent bed, and procreant cradle:
Where they most breed and haunt, I have observ'd,
The air is delicate.

Enter LADY MACBETH.

Dun. See, see! our honour'd hostess!
The love that follows us, sometime is our trouble,
Which still we thank as love. Herein I teach you,
How you shall bid God yield us for your pains,
And thank us for your trouble.
Lady M. All our service,
In every point twice done, and then done double,
Were poor and single business, to contend
Against those honours deep and broad, wherewith
Your majesty loads our house: For those of old,
And the late dignities heap'd up to them,
We rest your hermits.
Dun. Where's the thane of Cawdor?
We cours'd him at the heels, and had a purpose
To be his purveyor: but he rides well:
And his great love, sharp as his spur, hath holp him
To his home before us: Fair and noble hostess,
We are your guest to-night.
Lady M. Your servants ever
Hath theirs, themselves, and what is theirs, in compt,
To make their audit at your highness' pleasure,
Still to return your own.
Dun. Give me your hand:
Conduct me to mine host; we love him highly,
And shall continue our graces towards him.
By your leave, hostess. [*Exeunt.*

SCENE VII. *The same. A Room in the Castle.*

Hautboys and Torches. Enter, and pass over the Stage, a Sewer, *and divers* Servants *with Dishes and Service. Then enter* MACBETH.

Macb. If it were done, when 'tis done, then 'twere well
It were done quickly: If the assassination
Could trammel up the consequence, and catch,
With his surcease, success; that but this blow

Might be the be-all and the end-all here,
But here, upon this bank and shoal of time,—
We'd jump the life to come.—But, in these cases,
We still have judgment here; that we but teach
Bloody instructions, which, being taught, return
To plague the inventor: This even handed justice
Commends the ingredients of our poison'd chalice
To our own lips. He's here in double trust:
First, as I am his kinsman and his subject,
Strong both against the deed; then, as his host,
Who should against his murderer shut the door,
Not bear the knife myself. Besides, this Duncan
Hath borne his faculties so meek, hath been
So clear in his great office, that his virtues
Will plead like angels, trumpet-tongued, against
The deep damnation of his taking off:
And pity, like a naked new-born babe,
Striding the blast, or heaven's cherubin, hors'd
Upon the sightless couriers of the air,
Shall blow the horrid deed in every eye,
That tears shall drown the wind.—I have no spur
To prick the sides of my intent, but only
Vaulting ambition, which o'erleaps itself,
And falls on the other—How now? what news?

Enter LADY MACBETH.

Lady M. He has almost supp'd: Why have you left the chamber?
Macb. Hath he ask'd for me?
Lady M. Know you not, he has?
Macb. We will proceed no further in this business:
He hath honour'd me of late; and I have bought
Golden opinions from all sorts of people,
Which would be worn now in their newest gloss,
Not cast aside so soon.
Lady M. Was the hope drunk,
Wherein you dress'd yourself? hath it slept since?
And wakes it now, to look so green and pale
At what it did so freely? From this time,
Such I account thy love. Art thou afeard
To be the same in thine own act and valour,
As thou art in desire? Would'st thou have that
Which thou esteem'st the ornament of life,
And live a coward in thine own esteem;
Letting I dare not wait upon I would,
Like the poor cat i' the adage?
Macb. 'Pr'ythee, peace:
I dare do all that may become a man;
Who dares do more, is none.
Lady M. What beast was 't then
That made you break this enterprise to me?
When you durst do it, then you were a man;
And, to be more than what you were, you would
Be so much more the man. Nor time, nor place,
Did then adhere, and yet you would make both:
They have made themselves, and that their fitness now
Does unmake you. I have given suck; and know
How tender 'tis to love the babe that milks me:
I would, while it was smiling in my face,
Have pluck'd my nipple from his boneless gums,
And dash'd the brains out, had I so sworn, as you
Have done to this.
Macb. If we should fail,——
Lady M. We fail!
But screw your courage to the sticking place,
And we'll not fail. When Duncan is asleep
(Whereto the rather shall his day's hard journey
Soundly invite him), his two chamberlains
Will I with wine and wassel so convince,
That memory, the warder of the brain,
Shall be a fume, and the receipt of reason
A limbeck only: When in swinish sleep
Their drenched natures lie, as in a death,
What cannot you and I perform upon
The unguarded Duncan? what not put upon
His spongy officers; who shall bear the guilt
Of our great quell?
Macb. Bring forth men-children only!
For thy undaunted mettle should compose
Nothing but males. Will it not be receiv'd,
When we have mark'd with blood those sleepy two
Of his own chamber, and us'd their very daggers,
That they have don 't?
Lady M. Who dares receive it other,
As we shall make our griefs and clamour roar
Upon his death?
Macb. I am settled, and bend up
Each corporal agent to this terrible feat.
Away, and mock the time with fairest show;
False face must hide what the false heart doth know. [*Exeunt.*

ACT II.

SCENE I. *The same. Court within the Castle.*

Enter BANQUO *and* FLEANCE, *and a* Servant, *with a Torch before them.*

Ban. How goes the night, boy?
Fle. The moon is down: I have not heard the clock.
Ban. And she goes down at twelve.
Fle. I take 't, 'tis later, sir.
Ban. Hold, take my sword;—There's husbandry in heaven,
Their candles are all out.—Take thee that too.
A heavy summons lies like lead upon me,
And yet I would not sleep: Merciful powers!
Restrain in me the cursed thoughts, that nature
Gives way to in repose:—Give me my sword;—

Enter MACBETH, *and a* Servant *with a Torch.*

Who's there?
Macb. A friend.
Ban. What, sir, not yet at rest? The king's a-bed:
He hath been in unusual pleasure, and
Sent forth great largess to your officers:
This diamond he greets your wife withal,
By the name of most kind hostess; and shut up
In measureless content.
Macb. Being unprepar'd,
Our will became the servant to defect;
Which else should free have wrought.
Ban. All's well.
I dreamt last night of the three weird sisters:
To you they have show'd some truth.
Macb. I think not of them:
Yet, when we can entreat an hour to serve,
Would spend it in some words upon that business,
If you would grant the time.
Ban. At your kind'st leisure.
Macb. If you shall cleave to my consent,—when 'tis,
It shall make honour for you.
Ban. So I lose none,
In seeking to augment it, but still keep
My bosom franchis'd, and allegiance clear,
I shall be counsel'd.
Macb. Good repose, the while!
Ban. Thanks, sir; The like to you!
[*Exit* BANQUO.
Macb. Go, bid thy mistress, when my drink is ready,
She strike upon the bell. Get thee to bed.
[*Exit* Servant.
Is this a dagger which I see before me,
The handle toward my hand? Come, let me clutch thee:——
I have thee not, and yet I see thee still.
Art thou not, fatal vision, sensible
To feeling, as to sight? or art thou but
A dagger of the mind; a false creation,
Proceeding from the heat-oppressed brain?
I see thee yet, in form as palpable
As this which now I draw.
Thou marshal'st me the way that I was going;

And such an instrument I was to use.
Mine eyes are made the fools o'the other senses,
Or else worth all the rest: I see thee still:
And on thy blade, and dudgeon, gouts of blood,
Which was not so before.—There's no such thing:
It is the bloody business which informs
Thus to mine eyes.—Now o'er the one half world
Nature seems dead, and wicked dreams abuse
The curtain'd sleeper; withcraft celebrates
Pale Hecate's offerings; and wither'd murder,
Alarum'd by his sentinel, the wolf,
Whose howl's his watch, thus with his stealthy pace,
With Tarquin's ravishing strides, towards his design
Moves like a ghost.——Thou sure and firm-set earth,
Hear not my steps, which way they walk, for fear
The very stones prate of my where-about,
And take the present horror from the time,
Which now suits with it.—Whiles I threat, he lives;
Words to the heat of deeds too cold breath gives.
[*A bell rings.*
I go, and it is done; the bell invites me.
Hear it not, Duncan; for it is a knell
That summons thee to heaven, or to hell.
[*Exit.*

SCENE II. *The same.*

Enter LADY MACBETH.

Lady M. That which hath made them drunk, hath made me bold:
What hath quench'd them, hath given me fire:—Hark!—Peace!
It was the owl that shriek'd, the fatal bellman,
Which gives the stern'st good night. He is about it:
The doors are open; and the surfeited grooms
Do mock their charge with snores: I have drugg'd their possets,
That death and nature do contend about them,
Whether they live or die.

Macb. [*Within.*] Who's there?—what, ho!

Lady M. Alack! I am afraid, they have awak'd,
And 'tis not done:—the attempt, and not the deed,
Confounds us:—Hark!—I laid their daggers ready,
He could not miss them.—Had he not resembled
My father as he slept, I had don't.—My husband?

Enter MACBETH.

Macb. I have done the deed:—Didst thou not hear a noise?

Lady M. I heard the owl scream, and the crickets cry.
Did not you speak?

Macb. When?

Lady M. Now.

Macb. As I descended?

Lady M. Ay.

Macb. Hark!—
Who lies i' the second chamber?

Lady M. Donalbain.

Macb. This is a sorry sight.
[*Looking on his hands.*

Lady M. A foolish thought, to say a sorry sight.

Macb. There's one did laugh in his sleep, and one cried, *murder!*
That they did wake each other; I stood and heard them:
But they did say their prayers, and address'd them
Again to sleep.

Lady M. There are two lodg'd together.

Macb. One cried, *God bless us!* and, *Amen,* the other;
As they had seen me, with these hangman's hands.
Listening their fear, I could not say, amen,
When they did say, God bless us.

Lady M. Consider it not so deeply.

Macb. But wherefore could not I pronounce, amen?
I had most need of blessing, and amen
Stuck in my throat.

Lady M. These deeds must not be thought
After these ways; so, it will make us mad.

Macb. Methought, I heard a voice cry, *Sleep no more!*
Macbeth does murder sleep, the innocent sleep;
Sleep, that knits up the ravell'd sleave of care,
The death of each day's life, sore labour's bath,
Balm of hurt minds, great nature's second course,
Chief nourisher in life's feast;—

Lady M. What do you mean?

Macb. Still it cried, *Sleep no more!* to all the house:
Glamis hath murder'd sleep; and therefore Cawdor
Shall sleep no more. Macbeth shall sleep no more!

Lady M. Who was it that thus cried? Why, worthy thane,
You do unbend your noble strength, to think
So brainsickly of things:—Go, get some water,
And wash this filthy witness from your hand.—
Why did you bring these daggers from the place?
They must lie there: Go, carry them; and smear
The sleepy grooms with blood.

Macb. I'll go no more:
I am afraid to think what I have done;
Look on't again, I dare not.

Lady M. Infirm of purpose!
Give me the daggers: The sleeping, and the dead,
Are but as pictures: 'tis the eye of childhood,
That fears a painted devil. If he do bleed,
I'll gild the faces of the grooms withal,
For it must seem their guilt.
[*Exit. Knocking within.*

Macb. Whence is that knocking?
How is't with me, when every noise appals me?
What hands are here! Ha! they pluck out mine eyes!
Will all great Neptune's ocean wash this blood
Clean from my hand? No; this my hand will rather
The multitudinous seas incarnardine,
Making the green—one red.

Re-enter LADY MACBETH.

Lady M. My hands are of your colour: but I shame
To wear a heart so white. [*Knock.*] I hear a knocking
At the south entry:—retire we to our chamber:
A little water clears us of this deed:
How easy is it then? Your constancy
Hath left you unattended.—[*Knocking.*] Hark! more knocking:
Get on your nightgown, lest occasion call us,
And show us to be watchers:—Be not lost
So poorly in your thoughts.

Macb. To know my deed,—'twere best not know myself. [*Knock.*
Wake Duncan with thy knocking! I would, thou could'st? [*Exeunt.*

SCENE III. *The same.*

Enter a Porter. [*Knocking within.*

Porter. Here's a knocking, indeed! If a man were porter of hell-gate, he should have old turning the key. [*Knocking.*] Knock, knock, knock: Who's there, i' the name of Belzebub? Here's a farmer, that hanged himself on the expectation of plenty: Come in time; have napkins enough about you; here you'll sweat for't. [*Knocking.*] Knock, knock: Who's there, i' the' other devil's name? 'Faith, here's an equivocator, that could swear in both the scales against either scale; who committed treason enough for God's sake, yet could not equivocate to heaven: O, come in, equivocator. [*Knocking.*] Knock, knock, knock: Who's there? 'Faith, here's an English tailor come hither, for stealing out of a French hose: Come in, tailor; here you may roast your goose. [*Knocking.*] Knock, knock: Never at quiet! What are you?—But this place is too cold for hell. I'll devil-porter it no further: I had thought to have let in some of all professions, that go the primrose way to the everlasting bonfire. [*Knocking.*] Anon, anon; I pray you, remember the porter.

[*Opens the gate.*

Enter MACDUFF *and* LENOX.

Macd. Was it so late, friend, ere you went to bed,
That you do lie so late?

Port. 'Faith, sir, we were carousing till the second cock: and drink, sir, is a great provoker of three things.

Macd. What three things does drink especially provoke?

Port. Marry, sir, nose-painting, sleep, and urine. Lechery, sir, it provokes, and unprovokes: it provokes the desire, but it takes away the performance: Therefore, much drink may be said to be an equivocator with lechery: it makes him, and it mars him; it sets him on, and it takes him off; it persuades him, and disheartens him; makes him stand to, and not stand to: in conclusion, equivocates him in a sleep, and, giving him the lie, leaves him.

Macd. I believe, drink gave thee the lie last night.

Port. That it did, sir, i' the very throat o' me: But I requited him for his lie: and, I think, being too strong for him, though he took up my legs sometime, yet I made a shift to cast him.

Macd. Is thy master stirring?—
Our knocking has awak'd him; here he comes.

Enter MACBETH.

Len. Good-morrow, noble sir!
Macb. Good-morrow, both!
Macd. Is the king stirring, worthy thane?
Macb. Not yet.
Macd. He did command me to call timely on him;
I have almost slipp'd the hour.
Macb. I'll bring you to him.
Macd. I know, this is a joyful trouble to you;
But yet, 'tis one.
Macb. The labour, we delight in, physicks pain.
This is the door.
Macd. I'll make so bold to call,
For 'tis my limited service. [*Exit* MACDUFF.
Len. Goes the king hence to-day?
Macb. He does:—he did appoint so.
Len. The night has been unruly; Where we lay,
Our chimneys were blown down: and, as they say,
Lamentings heard i' the air; strange screams of death;
And prophesying, with accents terrible,
Of dire combustion, and confus'd events.
New hatch'd to the woful time. The obscure bird
Clamour'd the livelong night: some say, the earth
Was feverous, and did shake.
Macb. 'Twas a rough night.
Len. My young remembrance cannot parallel
A fellow to it.

Re-enter MACDUFF.

Macd. O horror! horror! horror! Tongue, nor heart,
Cannot conceive, nor name thee!
Macb. Len. What's the matter?
Macd. Confusion now hath made his master-piece!
Most sacrilegious murder hath broke ope
The Lord's anointed temple, and stole thence
The life o' the building.
Macb. What is't you say? the life?
Len. Mean you his majesty?
Macd. Approach the chamber, and destroy your sight
With a new Gorgon:—Do not bid me speak;
See, and then speak yourselves.—Awake! awake!— [*Exeunt* MACB. *and* LEN.
Ring the alarum-bell: Murder! and treason!
Banquo, and Donalbain! Malcolm! awake!
Shake off this downy sleep, death's counterfeit,
And look on death itself!—up, up, and see
The great doom's image!——Malcolm! Banquo!
As from your graves rise up, and walk like sprights,
To countenance this horror! [*Bell rings.*

Enter LADY MACBETH.

Lady M. What's the business,
That such a hideous trumpet calls to parley
The sleepers of the house? speak, speak,——
Macd. O, gentle lady,
'Tis not for you to hear what I can speak:
The repetition, in a woman's ear,
Would murder as it fell——O Banquo! Banquo!

Enter BANQUO.

Our royal master's murder'd!
Lady M. Woe, alas!
What, in our house?
Ban. Too cruel, any where,——
Dear Duff, I pr'ythee, contradict thyself,
And say, it is not so.

Re-enter MACBETH *and* LENOX.

Macb. Had I but died an hour before this chance,
I had lived a blessed time; for, from this instant,
There's nothing serious in mortality:
All is but toys: renown, and grace, is dead;
The wine of life is drawn, and the mere lees
Is left this vault to brag of.

Enter MALCOLM *and* DONALBAIN.

Don. What is amiss?
Macb. You are, and do not know it:
The spring, the head, the fountain of your blood
Is stopp'd; the very source of it is stopp'd.
Macd. Your royal father's murder'd.
Mal. O, by whom?
Len. Those of his chamber, as it seem'd, had done't:
Their hands and faces were all badg'd with blood,
So were their daggers, which, unwip'd, we found
Upon their pillows:
They star'd, and were distracted; no man's life
Was to be trusted with them.
Macb. O, yet I do repent me of my fury,
That I did kill them.
Macd. Wherefore did you so?
Macb. Who can be wise, amazed, temperate, and furious,
Loyal and neutral, in a moment? No man:
The expedition of my violent love
Outran the pauser reason.—Here lay Duncan,
His silver skin lac'd with his golden blood;
And his gash'd stabs look'd like a breach in nature,
For ruin's wasteful entrance: there, the murderers,
Steep'd in the colours of their trade, their daggers
Unmannerly breech'd with gore: Who could refrain,
That had a heart to love, and in that heart
Courage, to make his love known?
Lady M. Help me hence, ho!
Macd. Look to the lady.
Mal. Why do we hold our tongues,
That most may claim this argument for ours?
Don. What should be spoken,
Here, where our fate, hid in an augre-hole,

May rush, and seize us? Let's away; our tears
Are not yet brew'd.
Mal. Nor our strong sorrow
Upon the foot of motion.
Ban. Look to the lady:—
[LADY MACBETH *is carried out.*
And when we have our naked frailties hid,
That suffer in exposure, let us meet,
And question this most bloody piece of work,
To know it further. Fears and scruples shake us:
In the great hand of God I stand; and, thence,
Against the undivulg'd pretence I fight
Of treasonous malice.
Macb. And so do I.
All. So all.
Macb. Let's briefly put on manly readiness,
And meet i' the hall together.
All. Well contented.
[*Exeunt all but* MAL. *and* DON.
Mal. What will you do? Let's not consort with them:
To show an unfelt sorrow, is an office
Which the false man does easy: I'll to England.
Don. To Ireland, I; our separated fortune
Shall keep us both the safer: where we are,
There's daggers in men's smiles: the near in blood,
The nearer bloody.
Mal. This murderous shaft that's shot,
Hath not yet lighted; and our safest way
Is, to avoid the aim. Therefore, to horse;
And let us not be dainty of leave-taking.
But shift away: There's warrant in that theft
Which steals itself, when there's no mercy left.
[*Exeunt.*

SCENE IV. *Without the Castle.*

Enter ROSSE *and an* Old Man.

Old M. Threescore and ten I can remember well:
Within the volume of which time, I have seen
Hours dreadful, and things strange: but this sore night
Hath trifled former knowings.
Rosse. Ah, good father,
Thou seest, the heavens, as troubled with man's act,
Threaten his bloody stage: by the clock, 'tis day,
And yet dark night strangles the travelling lamp:
Is it night's predominance, or the day's shame,
That darkness does the face of earth entomb,
When living light should kiss it?
Old M. 'Tis unnatural,
Even like the deed that's done. On Tuesday last,
A falcon, tow'ring in her pride of place,
Was by a mousing howl hawk'd at, and kill'd.
Rosse. And Duncan's horses (a thing most strange and certain),
Beauteous and swift, the minions of their race,
Turn'd wild in nature, broke their stalls, flung out,
Contending 'gainst obedience, as they would make
War with mankind.
Old M. 'Tis said, they ate each other.
Rosse. They did so; to the amazement of mine eyes,
That look'd upon't. Here comes the good Macduff:——

Enter MACDUFF.

How goes the world, sir, now?
Macd. Why, see you not?
Rosse. Is't known who did this more than bloody deed?
Macd. Those that Macbeth hath slain.
Rosse. Alas, the day!
What good could they pretend?
Mac. They were suborn'd
Malcolm and Donalbain, the king' stwo sons,
Are stol'n away and fled; which puts upon them
Suspicion of the deed.
Rosse. 'Gainst nature still:
Thriftless ambition, that will ravin up
Thine own life's means!—'Then 'tis most like,
The sovereignty will fall upon Macbeth.
Macd. He is already nam'd; and gone to Scone,
To be invested.
Rosse. Where is Duncan's body?
Macd. Carried to Colme-kill;
The sacred storehouse of his predecessors,
And guardian of their bones.
Rosse. Will you to Scone?
Macd. No, cousin, I'll to Fife.
Rosse. Well, I will thither.
Macd. Well, may you see things well done there;—adieu!——
Lest our old robes sit easier than our new!
Rosse. Father, farewell.
Old. M. God's benison go with you: and with those
That would make good of bad, and friends of foes! [*Exeunt.*

ACT III.

SCENE I. Fores. *A Room in the Palace.*

Enter BANQUO.

Ban. Thou hast it now, King, Cawdor, Glamis, all,
As the weird women promis'd: and, I fear,
Thou played'st most foully for't; yet it was said,
It should not stand in thy posterity;
But that myself should be the root and father
Of many kings. If there come truth from them
(As upon thee, Macbeth, their speeches shine),
Why, by the verities on thee made good,
May they not be the oracles as well,
And set me up in hope? But, hush; no more.

Senet sounded. Enter MACBETH, *as King:* LADY MACBETH, *as Queen;* LENOX, ROSSE, Lords, Ladies, *and* Attendants.

Macb. Here's our chief guest.
Lady M. If he had been forgotten,
It had been as a gap in our great feast,
And all things unbecoming.
Macb. To-night, we hold a solemn supper, sir,
And I'll request your presence.
Ban. Let your highness
Command upon me; to the which, my duties
Are with a most indissoluble tie
For ever knit.
Macb. Ride you this afternoon?
Ban. Ay, my good lord.
Macb. We should have else desir'd your good advice
(Which still hath been both grave and prosperous),
In this day's council; but we'll take to-morrow.
Is't far you ride?
Ban. As far, my lord, as will fill up the time
'Twixt this and supper: go not my horse the better,
I must become a borrower of the night,
For a dark hour, or twain.
Macb. Fail not our feast.
Ban. My lord, I will not.
Macb. We hear, our bloody cousins are bestow'd
In England, and in Ireland; not confessing
Their cruel parricide, filling their hearers
With strange invention: But of that to-morrow:
When, therewithal, we shall have cause of state,
Craving us jointly. Hie you to horse: Adieu,
Till you return at night. Goes Fleance with you?
Ban. Ay, my good lord: our time does call upon us.
Macb. I wish your horses swift, and sure of foot;

And so I do commend you to their backs.
Farewell.— [*Exit* BANQUO.
Let every man be master of his time
Till seven at night; to make society
The sweeter welcome, we will keep ourself
Till supper-time alone: while then, God be with you.
[*Exeunt* LADY MACBETH, Lords, Ladies, &c.
Sirrah, a word with you: attend those men
Our pleasure?

Atten. They are, my lord, without the palace gate.

Macb. Bring them before us.—[*Exit* Atten.]
To be thus is nothing;
But to be safely thus:—Our fears in Banquo
Stick deep; and in his royalty of nature
Reigns that, which would be fear'd:—'Tis much he dares;
And, to that dauntless temper of his mind,
He hath a wisdom that doth guide his valour
To act in safety. There is none, but he
Whose being I do fear: and, under him,
My genius is rebuk'd; as, it is said,
Mark Antony's was by Cæsar. He chid the sisters,
When first they put the name of King upon me,
And bade them speak to him; then, prophetlike,
They hail'd him father to a line of kings:
Upon my head they plac'd a fruitless crown,
And put a barren sceptre in my gripe,
Thence to be wrench'd with an unlineal hand,
No son of mine succeeding. If it be so,
For Banquo's issue have I fil'd my mind;
For them the gracious Duncan have I murder'd;
Put rancours in the vessel of my peace
Only for them; and mine eternal jewel
Given to the common enemy of man,
To make them kings; the seed of Banquo kings!
Rather than so, come, fate, into the list,
And champion me to the utterance!——Who's there?—

Re-enter Attendant, *with two* Murderers.

Now to the door, and stay there till we call.
[*Exit* Attendant.
Was it not yesterday we spoke together?

1 Mur. It was, so please your highness.

Macb. Well then, now
Have you considered of my speeches? Know,
That it was he, in the times past, which held you
So under fortune; which, you thought, had been
Our innocent self: this I made good to you
In our last conference, pass'd in probation with you,
How you were borne in hand; how cross'd; the instruments;
Who wrought with them; and all things else, that might,
To half a soul, and to a notion craz'd,
Say, Thus did Banquo.

1 Mur. You made it known to us.

Macb. I did so; and went further, which is now
Our point of second meeting. Do you find
Your patience so predominant in your nature,
That you can let this go? Are you so gospell'd
To pray for that good man, and for his issue,
Whose heavy hand hath bow'd you to the grave,
And beggar'd yours for ever?

1 Mur. We are men, my liege.

Macb. Ay, in the catalogue ye go for men;
As hounds, and greyhounds, mongrels, spaniels, curs,
Shoughs, water-rugs, and demi-wolves, are cleped
All by the name of dogs: the valued file
Distinguishes the swift, the slow, the subtle,
The house-keeper, the hunter, every one
According to the gift which bounteous nature
Hath in him clos'd; whereby he does receive
Particular addition, from the bill
That writes them all alike: and so of men.
Now, if you have a station in the file,
Not in the worst rank of manhood, say it;
And I will put that business in your bosoms,
Whose execution takes your enemy off;
Grapples you to the heart and love of us,
Who wear our health but sickly in his life,
Which in his death were perfect.

2 Mur. I am one, my liege,
Whom the vile blows and buffets of the world
Have so incens'd, that I am reckless what
I do, to spite the world.

1 Mur. And I another,
So weary with disasters, tugg'd with fortune,
That I would set my life on any chance,
To mend it, or be rid on't.

Macb. Both of you
Know, Banquo was your enemy.

2 Mur. True, my lord.

Macb. So is he mine: and in such bloody distance,
That every minute of his being thrusts
Against my near'st of life: And though I could
With bare-fac'd power sweep him from my sight,
And bid my will avouch it; yet I must not,
For certain friends that are both his and mine,
Whose loves I may not drop, but wail his fall
Whom I myself struck down: and thence it is,
That I to your assistance do make love;
Masking the business from the common eye,
For sundry weighty reasons.

2 Mur. We shall, my lord,
Perform what you command us.

1 Mur. Though our lives——

Macb. Your spirits shine through you. Within this hour at most,
I will advise you where to plant yourselves:
Acquaint you with the perfect spy o' the time,
The moment on't: for't must be done to-night,
And something from the palace; always thought,
That I require a clearness: And with him
(To leave no rubs, nor botches, in the work),
Fleance his son, that keeps him company,
Whose absence is no less material to me
Than is his father's, must embrace the fate
Of that dark hour. Resolve yourselves apart;
I'll come to you anon.

2 Mur. We are resolv'd, my lord.

Macb. I'll call upon you straight; abide within.
It is concluded:——Banquo, thy soul's flight,
If it find heaven, must find it out to-night.
[*Exeunt.*

SCENE II. *The same. Another Room.*

Enter LADY MACBETH, *and a* Servant.

Lady M. Is Banquo gone from court?

Serv. Ay, madam, but returns again to-night.

Lady M. Say to the king, I would attend his leisure
For a few words.

Serv. Madam, I will. [*Exit.*

Lady M. Nought's had, all's spent,
Where our desire is got without content:
'Tis safer to be that which we destroy,
Than, by destruction, dwell in doubtful joy.

Enter MACBETH.

How now, my lord? why do you keep alone,
Of sorriest fancies your companions making?
Using those thoughts, which should indeed have died
With them they think on? Things without remedy,
Should be without regard: what's done, is done.

Macb. We have scotch'd the snake, not kill'd it;
She'll close, and be herself; whilst our poor malice
Remains in danger of her former tooth.
But let the frame of things disjoint,
Both the worlds suffer,

Ere we will eat our meal in fear, and sleep
In the affliction of these terrible dreams
That shake us nightly: Better be with the dead,
Whom we, to gain our place, have sent to peace,
Than on the torture of the mind to lie
In restless ecstasy. Duncan is in his grave;
After life's fitful fever, he sleeps well;
Treason has done his worst: nor steel, nor poison,
Malice domestick, foreign levy, nothing,
Can touch him further!

Lady M. Come on; gentle my lord,
Sleek o'er your rugged looks; be bright and jovial
Among your guests to-night.

Macb. So shall I, love;
And so, I pray, be you: let your remembrance
Apply to Banquo: present him eminence, both
With eye and tongue: unsafe the while, that we
Must lave our honours in these flattering streams;
And make our faces vizards to our hearts,
Disguising what they are.

Lady M. You must leave this.

Mac. O, full of scorpions is my mind, dear wife!
Thou know'st, that Banquo, and his Fleance, lives.

Lady M. But in them nature's copy's not eterne.

Macb. There's comfort yet; they are assailable;
Then be thou jocund: Ere the bat hath flown
His cloister'd flight; ere, to black Hecate's summons,
The shard-borne beetle, with his drowsy hums,
Hath rung night's yawning peal, there shall be done
A deed of dreadful note.

Lady M. What's to be done?

Macb. Be innocent of the knowledge, dearest chuck,
Till thou applaud the deed. Come, seeling night,
Skarf up the tender eye of pitiful day;
And, with thy bloody and invisible hand,
Cancel, and tear to pieces, that great bond
Which keeps me pale!—Light thickens; and the crow
Makes wing to the rooky wood:
Good things of day begin to droop and drowse;
Whiles night's black agents to their preys do rouse.
Thou marvell'st at my words; but hold thee still;
Things, bad begun, make strong themselves by ill:
So, pr'ythee, go with me. [*Exeunt.*

SCENE III. *The same.*

A Park or Lawn, with a Gate leading to the Palace.

Enter three Murderers.

1 *Mur.* But who did bid thee join with us?

3 *Mur.* Macbeth.

2 *Mur.* He needs not our mistrust; since he delivers
Our offices, and what we have to do,
To the direction just.

1 *Mur.* Then stand with us.
The west yet glimmers with some streaks of day:
Now spurs the lated traveller apace,
To gain the timely inn; and near approaches
The subject of our watch.

3 *Mur.* Hark! I hear horses.

Ban. [*Within.*] Give us a light there, ho!

2 *Mur.* Then it is he; the rest
That are within the note of expectation,
Already are i' the court.

1 *Mur.* His horses go about.

3 *Mur.* Almost a mile: but he does usually,
So all men do, from hence to the palace gate
Make it their walk.

Enter BANQUO *and* FLEANCE, *a* Servant *with a Torch preceding them.*

2 *Mur.* A light, a light!

3 *Mur.* 'Tis he.

1 *Mur.* Stand to 't.

Ban. It will be rain to-night.

1 *Mur.* Let it come down.
[*Assaults* BANQUO.

Ban. O, treachery! Fly, good Fleance, fly, fly, fly;
Thou may'st revenge. O slave!
[*Dies.* FLEANCE *and* Servant *escape.*

3 *Mur.* Who did strike out the light?

1 *Mur.* Was 't not the way?

3 *Mur.* There's but one down: the son is fled.

2 *Mur.* We have lost best half of our affair.

1 *Mur.* Well, let's away, and say how much is done. [*Exeunt.*

SCENE IV. *A Room of State in the Palace.*

A Banquet prepared.

Enter MACBETH, LADY MACBETH, ROSSE, LENOX, Lords, *and* Attendants.

Macb. You know your own degrees, sit down: at first
And last, the hearty welcome.

Lords. Thanks to your majesty.

Macb. Ourself will mingle with society,
And play the humble host.
Our hostess keeps her state; but, in best time,
We will require her welcome.

Lady M. Pronounce it for me, sir, to all our friends;
For my heart speaks, they are welcome.

Enter first Murderer, *to the door.*

Macb. See, they encounter thee with their hearts' thanks:——
Both sides are even: Here I'll sit i' the midst:
Be large in mirth; anon, we'll drink a measure
The table round.—There's blood upon thy face.

Mur. 'Tis Banquo's then.

Macb. 'Tis better thee without, than he within.
Is he despatch'd?

Mur. My lord, his throat is cut; that I did for him.

Macb. Thou art the best o' the cut-throats: Yet he's good,
That did the like for Fleance: if thou didst it,
Thou art the nonpareil.

Mur. Most royal sir,
Fleance is 'scap'd.

Macb. Then comes my fit again: I had else been perfect;
Whole as the marble, founded as the rock;
As broad, and general, as the casing air:
But now, I am cabin'd, cribb'd, confin'd, bound in
To saucy doubts and fears. But Banquo's safe?

Mur. Ay, my good lord: safe in a ditch he bides,
With twenty trenched gashes on his head;
The least a death to nature.

Macb. Thanks for that:——
There the grown serpent lies; the worm, that's fled,
Hath nature that in time will venom breed,
No teeth for the present.—Get thee gone; to-morrow
We'll hear ourselves again. [*Exit* Murderer.

Lady M. My royal lord,
You do not give the cheer: the feast is sold,
That is not often vouch'd, while 'tis a making,
'Tis given with welcome: To feed were best at home;
From thence, the sauce to meat is ceremony;
Meeting were bare without it.

Macb. Sweet remembrancer!—

Now, good digestion wait on appetite,
And health on both!
Len. May it please your highness sit?
[*The Ghost of* BANQUO *rises, and sits in* MACBETH'S *place.*
Macb. Here had we now our country's honour roof'd,
Were the grac'd person of our Banquo present;
Who may I rather challenge for unkindness,
Than pity for mischance!
Rosse. His absence, sir,
Lays blame upon his promise. Please it your highness
To grace us with your royal company?
Macb. The table's full.
Len. Here's a place reserv'd, sir.
Macb. Where?
Len. Here, my good lord. What is't that moves your highness?
Macb. Which of you have done this?
Lords. What, my good lord?
Macb. Thou canst not say, I did it: never shake
Thy gory locks at me.
Rosse. Gentlemen, rise; his highness is not well.
Lady M. Sit, worthy friends:—my lord is often thus,
And hath been from his youth: 'pray you, keep seat;
The fit is momentary; upon a thought
He will again be well: If much you note him,
You shall offend him, and extend his passion;
Feed, and regard him not.—Are you a man?
Macb. Ay, and a bold one, that dare look on that
Which might appal the devil.
Lady M. O proper stuff!
This is the very painting of your fear:
This is the air-drawn dagger, which, you said,
Led you to Duncan. O, these flaws, and starts,
(Impostors to true fear), would well become
A woman's story at a winter's fire,
Authoriz'd by her grandam. Shame itself!
Why do you make such faces? When all's done,
You look but on a stool.
Macb. Pr'ythee, see there! behold! look! lo! how say you?——
Why, what care I? If thou canst nod, speak too.—
If charnel-houses, and our graves, must send
Those that we bury, back, our monuments
Shall be the maws of kites. [Ghost *disappears.*
Lady M. What! quite unmann'd in folly?
Macb. If I stand here, I saw him.
Lady M. Fye, for shame!
Macb. Blood hath been shed ere now, i' the olden time,
Ere human statute purg'd the gentle weal;
Ay, and since too, murders have been perform'd
Too terrible for the ear: the times have been,
That, when the brains were out, the man would die,
And there an end: but now, they rise again,
With twenty mortal murders on their crowns,
And push us from our stools: This is more strange
Than such a murder is.
Lady M. My worthy lord,
Your noble friends do lack you.
Macb. I do forget:—
Do not muse at me, my most worthy friends;
I have a strange infirmity, which is nothing
To those that know me. Come, love and health to all;
Then I'll sit down:——Give me some wine, fill full:
I drink to the general joy of the whole table,

Ghost *rises.*

And to our dear friend Banquo, whom we miss;
'Would, he were here! to all, and him, we thirst,
And all to all.
Lords. Our duties, and the pledge.
Macb. Avaunt! and quit my sight! Let the earth hide thee!
Thy bones are marrowless, thy blood is cold;
Thou hast no speculation in those eyes
Which thou dost glare with!
Lady M. Think of this, good peers,
But as a thing of custom: 'tis no other;
Only it spoils the pleasure of the time.
Macb. What man dare, I dare:
Approach thou like the rugged Russian bear,
The arm'd rhinoceros, or the Hyrcan tiger,
Take any shape but that, and my firm nerves
Shall never tremble: Or, be alive again,
And dare me to the desert with thy sword:
If trembling I inhabit then, protest me
The baby of a girl. Hence, horrible shadow!
[Ghost *disappears.*
Unreal mockery, hence!—Why, so;—being gone,
I am a man again.—'Pray you, sit still.
Lady M. You have displac'd the mirth, broke the good meeting,
With most admir'd disorder.
Macb. Can such things be,
And overcome us like a summer's cloud,
Without our special wonder? You make me strange
Even to the disposition that I owe,
When now I think, you can behold such sights,
And keep the natural ruby of your cheeks,
When mine are blanch'd with fear.
Rosse. What sights, my lord?
Lady M. I pray you, speak not; he grows worse and worse;
Question enrages him: at once, good night:—
Stand not upon the order of your going,
But go at once.
Len. Good night, and better health
Attend his majesty!
Lady M. A kind good night to all!
[*Exeunt* Lords *and* Attendants.
Macb. It will have blood; they say, blood will have blood;
Stones have been known to move, and trees to speak;
Augures, and understood relations have,
By magot-pies, and choughs, and rooks, brought forth
The secret'st man of blood.—What is the night?
Lady M. Almost at odds with morning, which is which.
Macb. How say'st thou, that Macduff denies his person,
At our great bidding?
Lady M. Did you send to him, sir?
Macb. I hear it by the way; but I will send:
There's not a one of them, but in his house
I keep a servant fee'd. I will to-morrow,
(And betimes I will), to the weird sisters:
More shall they speak; for now I am bent to know,
By the worst means, the worst: for mine own good,
All causes shall give way: I am in blood
Stept in so far, that, should I wade no more,
Returning were as tedious as go o'er:
Strange things I have in head, that will to hand;
Which must be acted, ere they may be scann'd.
Lady M. You lack the season of all natures, sleep.
Macb. Come, we'll to sleep: My strange and self-abuse
Is the initiate fear, that wants hard use:—
We are yet but young in deed. [*Exeunt.*

SCENE V. *The Heath. Thunder.*

Enter HECATE, *meeting the three* Witches.

1 *Witch.* Why, how now, Hecate? you look angerly.
Hec. Have I not reason, beldams, as you are,
Saucy, and overbold? How did you dare

To trade and traffick with Macbeth,
In riddles, and affairs of death;
And I, the mistress of your charms,
The close contriver of all harms,
Was never call'd to bear my part,
Or show the glory of our art?
And, which is worse, all you have done
Hath been but for a wayward son,
Spiteful, and wrathful; who, as others do,
Loves for his own ends, not for you.
But make amends now: Get you gone,
And at the pit of Acheron
Meet me i' the morning; thither he
Will come to know his destiny.
Your vessels, and your spells, provide,
Your charms, and every thing beside;
I am for the air; this night I'll spend
Unto a dismal and a fatal end.
Great business must be wrought ere noon:
Upon the corner of the moon
There hangs a vaporous drop profound;
I'll catch it ere it come to ground:
And that, distill'd by magick slights,
Shall raise such artificial sprights,
As, by the strength of their illusion,
Shall draw him on to his confusion:
He shall spurn fate, scorn death, and bear
His hopes 'bove wisdom, grace, and fear:
And you all know, security
Is mortal's chiefest enemy.
Song. [*Within.*] *Come away, come away, &c.*
Hark, I am call'd; my little spirit, see,
Sits in a foggy cloud, and stays for me. [*Exit.*
1 *Witch.* Come, let's make haste; she'll soon be back again. [*Exeunt.*

SCENE VI. Fores. *A Room in the Palace.*

Enter LENOX *and another* Lord.

Len. My former speeches have but hit your thoughts,
Which can interpret further: only, I say,
Things have been strangely borne: The gracious Duncan
Was pitied of Macbeth:—marry, he was dead:—
And the right-valiant Banquo walk'd too late;
Whom, you may say, if it please you, Fleance kill'd,
For Fleance fled. Men must not walk too late.
Who cannot want the thought, how monstrous
It was for Malcolm, and for Donalbain,
To kill their gracious father? damned fact!
How it did grieve Macbeth! did he not straight,
In pious rage, the two delinquents tear,
That were the slaves of drink, and thralls of sleep?
Was not that nobly done? Ay, and wisely too;
For 'twould have anger'd any heart alive,
To hear the men deny it. So that, I say,
He has borne all things well: and I do think,
That, had he Duncan's sons under his key,
(As, an 't please heaven, he shall not), they should find
What 'twere to kill a father; so should Fleance.
But, peace!—for from broad words, and 'cause he fail'd
His presence at the tyrant's feast, I hear,
Macduff lives in disgrace: Sir, can you tell
Where he bestows himself?
Lord. The son of Duncan,
From whom this tyrant holds the due of birth,
Lives in the English court; and is receiv'd
Of the most pious Edward with such grace,
That the malevolence of fortune nothing
Takes from his high respect: Thither Macduff
Is gone to pray the holy king, upon his aid
To wake Northumberland, and warlike Siward:
That, by the help of these, (with Him above
To ratify the work), we may again
Give to our tables meat, sleep to our nights;
Free from our feasts and banquets bloody knives;
Do faithful homage, and receive free honours,
All which we pine for now: And this report
Hath so exasperate the king, that he
Prepares for some attempt of war.
Len. Sent he to Macduff?
Lord. He did; and with an absolute, *Sir, not I,*
The cloudy messenger turns me his back,
And hums; as who should say, *You'll rue the time*
That clogs me with this answer.
Len. And that well might
Advise him to a caution, to hold what distance
His wisdom can provide. Some holy angel
Fly to the court of England, and unfold
His message ere he come; that a swift blessing
May soon return to this our suffering country
Under a hand accurs'd!
Lord. I'll send my prayers with him!
[*Exeunt.*

ACT IV.

SCENE I.

A dark Cave. In the middle, a Cauldron boiling.

Thunder. Enter the three Witches.

1 *Witch.* Thrice the brinded cat hath mew'd.
2 *Witch.* Thrice; and once the hedge-pig whin'd.
3 *Witch.* Harper cries:—'Tis time, 'tis time.
1 *Witch.* Round about the cauldron go;
In the poison'd entrails throw.——
Toad, that under coldest stone,
Days and nights hast thirty-one
Swelter'd venom, sleeping got,
Boil thou first i' the charmed pot!
All. Double, double toil and trouble;
Fire, burn; and, cauldron, bubble.
2 *Witch.* Fillet of a fenny snake,
In the cauldron boil and bake:
Eye of newt, and toe of frog,
Wool of bat, and tongue of dog,
Adder's fork, and blind-worm's sting,
Lizard's leg, and owlet's wing,
For a charm of powerful trouble,
Like a hell-broth boil and bubble.
All. Double, double toil and trouble;
Fire, burn; and, cauldron, bubble.
3 *Witch.* Scale of dragon, tooth of wolf;
Witch's mummy; maw and gulf
Of the ravin'd salt-sea shark;
Root of hemlock, digg'd i' the dark;
Liver of blaspheming Jew;
Gall of goat; and slips of yew,
Sliver'd in the moon's eclipse;
Nose of Turk, and Tartar's lips;
Finger of birth-strangled babe,
Ditch-deliver'd by a drab,
Make the gruel thick and slab:
Add thereto a tiger's chaudron,
For the ingredients of our cauldron.
All. Double, double toil and trouble;
Fire, burn; and, cauldron, bubble.
2 *Witch.* Cool it with a baboon's blood,
Then the charm is firm and good.

Enter HECATE, *and the other three* Witches.

Hec. O, well done! I commend your pains;
And every one shall share i' the gains.
And now about the cauldron sing,
Like elves and fairies in a ring,
Enchanting all that you put in.

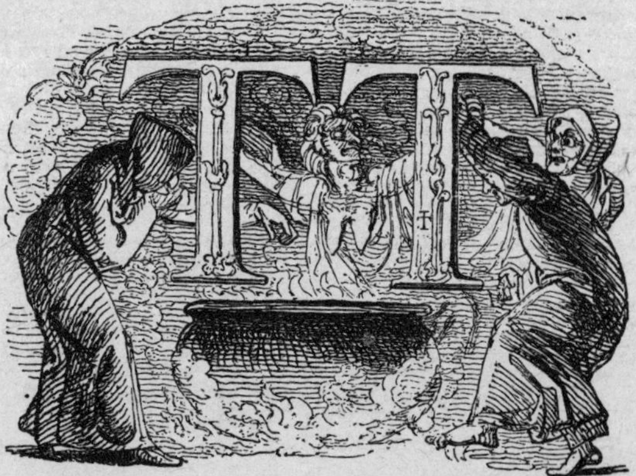

SONG.

Black spirits and white,
Red spirits and gray;
Mingle, mingle, mingle,
You that mingle may.

2 *Witch.* By the pricking of my thumbs,
Something wicked this way comes:
Open, locks, whoever knocks.

Enter MACBETH.

Macb. How now, you secret, black, and midnight hags?
What is't you do?

All. A deed without a name.

Macb. I conjure you, by that which you profess,
(Howe'er you come to know it), answer me:
Though you untie the winds, and let them fight
Against the churches; though the yesty waves
Confound and swallow navigation up;
Though bladed corn be lodg'd, and trees blown down:
Though castles topple on their warders' heads;
Though palaces, and pyramids, do slope
Their heads to their foundations; though the treasure
Of nature's germins tumble all together,
Even till destruction sicken, answer me
To what I ask you.

1 *Witch.* Speak.

2 *Witch.* Demand.

3 *Witch.* We'll answer.

1 *Witch.* Say, if thou'dst rather hear it from our mouths,
Or from our masters'?

Macb. Call them, let me see them.

1 *Witch.* Pour in sow's blood, that hath eaten
Her nine farrow; grease, that's sweaten
From the murderer's gibbet, throw
Into the flame.

All. Come, high, or low;
Thyself, and office, deftly show.

Thunder. An Apparition *of an armed Head rises.*

Macb. Tell me, thou unknown power,——

1 *Witch.* He knows thy thought;
Hear his speech, but say thou nought.

App. Macbeth! Macbeth! Macbeth! beware Macduff;
Beware the thane of Fife.—Dismiss me:—Enough. [*Descends.*

Macb. Whate'er thou art, for thy good caution, thanks;
Thou hast harp'd my fear aright:—But one word more:—

1 *Witch.* He will not be commanded: Here's another,
More potent than the first.

Thunder. An Apparition *of a bloody Child rises.*

App. Macbeth! Macbeth! Macbeth!—

Macb. Had I three ears, I'd hear thee.

App. Be bloody, bold,
And resolute; laugh to scorn the power of man,
For none of woman born shall harm Macbeth.
[*Descends.*

Macb. Then live, Macduff; What need I fear of thee?
But yet I'll make assurance double sure,
And take a bond of fate: thou shalt not live;
That I may tell pale-hearted fear, it lies,
And sleep in spite of thunder.—What is this,

Thunder. An Apparition *of a Child crowned, with a Tree in his Hand, rises.*

That rises like the issue of a king;
And wears upon his baby brow the round
And top of sovereignty?

All. Listen, but speak not.

App. Be lion-mettled, proud; and take no care
Who chafes, who frets, or where conspirers are;
Macbeth shall never vanquish'd be, until
Great Birnam wood to high Dunsinane hill
Shall come against him. [*Descends.*

Macb. That will never be;
Who can impress the forest; bid the tree
Unfix his earth-bound root? sweet bodements! good!
Rebellious head, rise never, till the wood
Of Birnam rise, and our high-plac'd Macbeth
Shall live the lease of nature, pay his breath
To time, and mortal custom.—Yet my heart
Throbs to know one thing; Tell me, (if your art
Can tell so much), shall Banquo's issue ever
Reign in this kingdom?

All. Seek to know no more.

Macb. I will be satisfied: deny me this,
And an eternal curse fall on you! Let me know:—
Why sinks that cauldron? and what noise is this?
[*Hautboys.*

1 *Witch.* Show! 2 *Witch.* Show! 3 *Witch.* Show!

All. Show his eyes, and grieve his heart;
Come like shadows, so depart.

Eight Kings appear, and pass over the Stage in order; the last with a Glass in his Hand; BANQUO *following.*

Macb. Thou art too like the spirit of Banquo; down!
Thy crown does sear mine eyeballs:—And thy hair,

Thou other gold-bound brow, is like the first:—
A third is like the former:—Filthy hags!
Why do you show me this?—A fourth?—Start, eyes!
What! will the line stretch out to the crack of doom?
Another yet?—A seventh?—I'll see no more:—
And yet the eighth appears, who bears a glass,
Which shows me many more; and some I see,
That twofold balls and treble sceptres carry:
Horrible sight!—Ay, now, I see, 'tis true;
For the blood-bolter'd Banquo smiles upon me,
And points at them for his.—What, is this so?

1 *Witch.* Ay, sir, all this is so:—But why
Stands Macbeth thus amazedly?—
Come, sisters, cheer we up his sprights,
And show the best of our delights;
I'll charm the air to give a sound,
While you perform your antique round:
That this great king may kindly say,
Our duties did his welcome pay.

[*Musick. The* Witches *dance, and vanish.*

Macb. Where are they? Gone?—Let this pernicious hour
Stand aye accursed in the calendar!
Come in, without there!

Enter LENOX.

Len. What's your grace's will?

Macb. Saw you the weird sisters?

Len. No, my lord.

Macb. Came they not by you?

Len. No, indeed, my lord.

Macb. Infected be the air whereon they ride:
And damn'd all those that trust them!—I did hear
The galloping of horse: Who was't came by?

Len. 'Tis two or three, my lord, that bring you word,
Macduff is fled to England.

Macb. Fled to England?

Len. Ay, my good lord.

Macb. Time, thou anticipat'st my dread exploits:
The flighty purpose never is o'ertook,
Unless the deed go with it: From this moment,
The very firstlings of my heart shall be
The firstlings of my hand. And even now
To crown my thoughts with acts, be it thought and done:
The castle of Macduff I will surprise;
Seize upon Fife: give to the edge o' the sword
His wife, his babes, and all unfortunate souls
That trace him in his line. No boasting like a fool:
This deed I'll do, before this purpose cool:
But no more sights!—Where are these gentlemen?
Come, bring me where they are. [*Exeunt.*

SCENE II. Fife. *A Room in* Macduff's *Castle.*

Enter LADY MACDUFF, *her* Son, *and* ROSSE.

L. Macd. What had he done, to make him fly the land?

Rosse. You must have patience, madam.

L. Macd. He had none;
His flight was madness: When our actions do not,
Our fears do make us traitors.

Rosse. You know not,
Whether it was his wisdom, or his fear.

L. Macd. Wisdom! to leave his wife, to leave his babes,
His mansion, and his titles, in a place
From whence himself does fly? He loves us not,
He wants the natural touch: for the poor wren,
The most diminutive of birds, will fight,
Her young ones in her nest, against the owl.
All is the fear, and nothing is the love;
As little is the wisdom, where the flight
So runs against all reason.

Rosse. My dearest coz',
I pray you, school yourself: But, for your husband,
He is noble, wise, judicious, and best knows
The fits o' the season. I dare not speak much further:
But cruel are the times, when we are traitors,
And do not know ourselves; when we hold rumour
From what we fear, yet know not what we fear;
But float upon a wild and violent sea,
Each way, and move.—I take my leave of you:
Shall not be long but I'll be here again:
Things at the worst will cease, or else climb upward
To what they were before.—My pretty cousin,
Blessing upon you!

L. Macd. Father'd he is, and yet he's fatherless.

Rosse. I am so much a fool, should I stay longer,
It would be my disgrace, and your discomfort:
I take my leave at once. [*Exit* ROSSE.

L. Macd. Sirrah, your father's dead;
And what will you do now? How will you live?

Son. As birds do, mother.

L. Macd. What, with worms and flies?

Son. With what I get, I mean; and so do they.

L. Macd. Poor bird! thou'dst never fear the net, nor lime,
The pitfall, nor the gin.

Son. Why should I, mother? Poor birds they are not set for.
My father is not dead, for all your saying.

L. Macd. Yes, he is dead; how wilt thou do for a father?

Son. Nay, how will you do for a husband?

L. Macd. Why, I can buy me twenty at any market.

Son. Then you'll buy 'em to sell again.

L. Macd. Thou speak'st with all thy wit; and yet i' faith,
With wit enough for thee.

Son. Was my father a traitor, mother?

L. Macd. Ay, that he was.

Son. What is a traitor?

L. Macd. Why, one that swears and lies.

Son. And be all traitors, that do so?

L. Macd. Every one that does so, is a traitor, and must be hanged.

Son. And must they all be hanged, that swear and lie?

L. Macd. Every one.

Son. Who must hang them?

L. Macd. Why, the honest men.

Son. Then the liars and swearers are fools; for there are liars and swearers enough to beat the honest men, and hang up them.

L. Macd. Now, God help thee, poor monkey!
But how wilt thou do for a father?

Son. If he were dead, you'd weep for him: if you would not, it were a good sign that I should quickly have a new father.

L. Macd. Poor prattler! how thou talk'st.

Enter a Messenger.

Mess. Bless you, fair dame! I am not to you known,
Though in your state of honour I am perfect.
I doubt, some danger does approach you nearly:
If you will take a homely man's advice,
Be not found here; hence, with your little ones.
To fright you thus, methinks, I am too savage;
To do worse to you, were fell cruelty,
Which is too nigh your person. Heaven preserve you!
I dare abide no longer. [*Exit* Messenger.

L. Macd. Whither should I fly?
I have done no harm. But I remember now
I am in this earthly world; where, to do harm,
Is often laudable; to do good, sometime,
Accounted dangerous folly: Why then, alas!
Do I put up that womanly defence,
To say, I have done no harm?——What are these faces?

Enter Murderers.

Mur. Where is your husband?

L. Macd. I hope, in no place so unsanctified,

Where such as thou may'st find him.

Mur. He's a traitor

Son. Thou ly'st, thou shag-ear'd villain.

Mur. What, you egg! [*Stabbing him.*
Young fry of treachery!

Son. He has killed me, mother;
Run away, I pray you. [*Dies.*

[*Exit* LADY MACDUFF, *crying murder, and pursued by the* Murderers.

SCENE III.

England. *A Room in the King's Palace.*

Enter MALCOLM *and* MACDUFF.

Mal. Let us seek out some desolate shade, and there
Weep our sad bosoms empty.

Macd. Let us rather
Hold fast the mortal sword; and, like good men,
Bestride our downfall'n birthdom: Each new morn,
New widows howl; new orphans cry; new sorrows
Strike heaven on the face, that it resounds
As if it felt with Scotland, and yell'd out
Like syllable of dolour.

Mal. What I believe, I'll wail;
What know, believe; and, what I can redress,
As I shall find the time to friend, I will.
What you have spoke, it may be so, perchance,
This tyrant, whose sole name blisters our tongues,
Was once thought honest: you have lov'd him well;
He hath not touch'd you yet. I am young: but something,
You may deserve of him through me; and wisdom
To offer up a weak, poor, innocent lamb,
To appease an angry god.

Macd. I am not treacherous.

Mal. But Macbeth is.
A good and virtuous nature may recoil,
In an imperial charge. But crave your pardon;
That which you are, my thoughts cannot transpose:
Angels are bright still, though the brightest fell:
Though all things foul would wear the brows of grace,
Yet grace must still look so.

Macd. I have lost my hopes.

Mal. Perchance, even there, where I did find my doubts.
Why in that rawness left you wife and child,
(Those precious motives, those strong knots of love),
Without leave taking?—I pray you,
Let not my jealousies be your dishonours,
But mine own safeties:—You may be rightly just,
Whatever I shall think.

Macd. Bleed, bleed, poor country!
Great tyranny, lay thou thy basis sure,
For goodness dares not check thee!—wear thou thy wrongs;
Thy title is affeer'd!—Fare thee well, lord:
I would not be the villain that thou think'st
For the whole space that's in the tyrant's grasp,
And the rich East to boot.

Mal. Be not offended:
I speak not as in absolute fear of you.
I think our country sinks beneath the yoke;
It weeps, it bleeds; and each new day a gash
Is added to her wounds: I think, withal,
There would be hands uplifted in my right;
And here, from gracious England, have I offer
Of goodly thousands: But, for all this,
When I shall tread upon the tyrant's head,
Or wear it on my sword, yet my poor country
Shall have more vices than it had before;
More suffer, and more sundry ways than ever,
By him that shall succeed.

Macd. What should he be?

Mal. It is myself I mean: in whom I know
All the particulars of vice so grafted,
That, when they shall be open'd, black Macbeth
Will seem as pure as snow; and the poor state
Esteem him as a lamb, being compar'd
With my confineless harms.

Macd. Not in the legions
Of horrid hell can come a devil more damn'd
In evils, to top Macbeth.

Mal. I grant him bloody,
Luxurious, avaricious, false, deceitful,
Sudden, malicious, smacking of every sin
That has a name: But there's no bottom, none,
In my voluptuousness: your wives, your daughters,
Your matrons, and your maids, could not fill up
The cistern of my lust; and my desire
All continent impediments would o'erbear,
That did oppose my will: Better Macbeth,
Than such a one to reign.

Macd. Boundless intemperance
In nature is a tyranny; it hath been
The untimely emptying of the happy throne,
And fall of many kings. But fear not yet
To take upon you what is yours: you may
Convey your pleasures in a spacious plenty,
And yet seem cold, the time you may so hoodwink.
We have willing dames enough; there cannot be
That vulture in you to devour so many
As will to greatness dedicate themselves,
Finding it so inclin'd.

Mal. With this, there grows,
In my most ill compos'd affection, such
A stanchless avarice, that, were I king,
I should cut off the nobles for their lands:
Desire his jewels, and this other's house:
And my more-having would be as a sauce
To make me hunger more: that I should forge
Quarrels unjust against the good, and loyal,
Destroying them for wealth.

Macd. This avarice
Sticks deeper; grows with more pernicious root
Than summer-seeding lust: and it hath been
The sword of our slain kings: Yet do not fear;
Scotland hath foysons to fill up your will.
Of your mere own: All these are portable,
With other graces weigh'd.

Mal. But I have none: The king-becoming graces,
As justice, verity, temperance, stableness,
Bounty, perseverance, mercy, lowliness,
Devotion, patience, courage, fortitude,
I have no relish of them; but abound
In the division of each several crime,
Acting it many ways. Nay, had I power, I should
Pour the sweet milk of concord into hell,
Uproar the universal peace, confound
All unity on earth.

Macd. O Scotland! Scotland!

Mal. If such a one be fit to govern, speak:
I am as I have spoken.

Macd. Fit to govern!
No, not to live.—O nation miserable,
With an untitled tyrant bloody-sceptred,
When shalt thou see thy wholesome days again?
Since that the truest issue of thy throne
By his own interdiction stands accurs'd,
And does blaspheme his breed?—Thy royal father
Was a most sainted king; the queen, that bore thee,
Oftener upon her knees than on her feet,
Died every day she lived. Fare thee well!
These evils, thou repeat'st upon thyself,
Have banish'd me from Scotland.—O, my breast,
Thy hope ends here!

Mal. Macduff, this noble passion,
Child of integrity, hath from my soul
Wip'd the black scruples, reconcil'd my thoughts
To thy good truth and honour. Devilish Macbeth
By many of these trains hath sought to win me

Into his power; and modest wisdom plucks me
From over-credulous haste; But God above
Deal between thee and me; for even now
I put myself to thy direction, and
Unspeak mine own detraction: here abjure
The taints and blames I laid upon myself,
For strangers to my nature. I am yet
Unknown to woman; never was forsworn;
Scarcely have coveted what was mine own;
At no time broke my faith; would not betray
The devil to his fellow; and delight
No less in truth, than life: my first false speaking
Was this upon myself: What I am truly,
Is thine, and my poor country's, to command:
Whither, indeed, before thy here-approach,
Old Siward, with ten thousand warlike men,
All ready at a point, was setting forth;
Now we'll together; And the chance, of goodness,
Be like our warranted quarrel! Why are you silent?

Macd. Such welcome and unwelcome things at once,
'Tis hard to reconcile.

Enter a Doctor.

Mal. Well; more anon.—Comes the king forth, I pray you?

Doct. Ay, sir; there are a crew of wretched souls,
That stay his cure: their malady convinces
The great assay of art; but, at his touch,
Such sanctity hath heaven given his hand,
They presently amend.

Mal. I thank you, doctor.
[*Exit* Doctor.

Macd. What's the disease he means?

Mal. 'Tis call'd the evil:
A most miraculous work in this good king;
Which often, since my here-remain in England,
I have seen him do. How he solicits heaven,
Himself best knows: but strangely visited people,
All swoln and ulcerous, pitiful to the eye,
The mere despair of surgery, he cures;
Hanging a golden stamp about their necks,
Put on with holy prayers: and 'tis spoken,
To the succeeding royalty he leaves
The healing benediction. With this strange virtue,
He hath a heavenly gift of prophecy;
And sundry blessings hang about his throne,
That speak him full of grace.

Enter Rosse.

Macd. See, who comes here?

Mal. My countryman; but yet I know him not.

Macd. My ever-gentle cousin, welcome hither.

Mal. I know him now: Good God, betimes remove
The means that make us strangers!

Rosse. Sir, Amen.

Macd. Stands Scotland where it did?

Rosse. Alas, poor country!
Almost afraid to know itself! It cannot
Be call'd our mother, but our grave: where nothing,
But who knows nothing, is once seen to smile;
Where sighs, and groans, and shrieks that rent the air,
Are made, not mark'd; where violent sorrow seems
A modern ecstasy; the dead man's knell
Is there scarce ask'd, for who; and good men's lives
Expire before the flowers in their caps,
Dying, or ere they sicken.

Macd. O, relation,
Too nice, and yet too true!

Mal. What is the newest grief?

Rosse. That of an hour's age doth hiss the speaker;
Each minute teems a new one.

Macd. How does my wife?

Rosse. Why, well.

Macd. And all my children?

Rosse. Well too.

Macd. The tyrant has not batter'd at their peace?

Rosse. No; they were well at peace when I did leave them.

Macd. Be not a niggard of your speech; How goes it?

Rosse. When I came hither to transport the tidings,
Which I have heavily borne, there ran a rumour
Of many worthy fellows that were out;
Which was to my belief witness'd the rather,
For that I saw the tyrant's power a-foot:
Now is the time of help! your eye in Scotland
Would create soldiers, make our women fight,
To doff their dire distresses.

Mal. Be it their comfort,
We are coming thither: gracious England hath
Lent us good Siward, and ten thousand men:
An older, and a better soldier, none
That Christendom gives out.

Rosse. 'Would, I could answer
This comfort with the like! But I have words,
That would be howl'd out in the desert air,
Where hearing should not latch them.

Macd. What concern they?
The general cause? or is it a fee-grief,
Due to some single breast?

Rosse. No mind, that's honest,
But in it shares some woe; though the main part
Pertains to you alone.

Macd. If it be mine,
Keep it not from me, quickly let me have it.

Rosse. Let not your ears despise my tongue for ever,
Which shall possess them with the heaviest sound
That ever yet they heard.

Macd. Humph! I guess at it.

Rosse. Your castle is surpris'd; your wife, and babes,
Savagely slaughter'd: to relate the manner,
Were, on the quarry of these murder'd deer,
To add the death of you.

Mal. Merciful heaven!—
What, man! ne'er pull your hat upon your brows;
Give sorrow words: the grief that does not speak,
Whispers the o'erfraught heart, and bids it break.

Macd. My children too?

Rosse. Wife, children, servants, all
That could be found.

Macd. And I must be from thence!
My wife kill'd too?

Rosse. I have said.

Mal. Be comforted.
Let's make us med'cines of our great revenge,
To cure this deadly grief.

Macd. He has no children.—All my pretty ones?
Did you say, all?—O, hell-kite!—All?
What, all my pretty chickens, and their dam,
At one fell swoop?

Mal. Dispute it like a man.

Macd. I shall do so;
But I must also feel it as a man:
I cannot but remember such things were,
That were most precious to me.—Did heaven look on,
And would not take their part? Sinful Macduff,
They were all struck for thee! naught that I am,
Not for their own demerits, but for mine
Fell slaughter on their souls; Heaven rest them now!

Mal. Be this the whetstone of your sword: let grief
Convert to anger; blunt not the heart, enrage it,

Macd. O, I could play the woman with mine eyes,
And braggart with my tongue!——But, gentle heaven,
Cut short all intermission; front to front,

Bring thou this fiend of Scotland, and myself;
Within my sword's length set him; if he 'scape,
Heaven forgive him too!

Mal. This tune goes manly.
Come, go we to the king: our power is ready:
Our lack is nothing but our leave: Macbeth
Is ripe for shaking, and the powers above
Put on their instruments. Receive what cheer
you may;
The night is long that never finds the day.
[*Exeunt.*

ACT V.

SCENE I. Dunsinane. *A Room in the Castle.*

Enter a Doctor *of Physick, and a waiting* Gentlewoman.

Doct. I have two nights watched with you, but can perceive no truth in your report. When was it she last walked?

Gent. Since his majesty went into the field, I have seen her rise from her bed, throw her night-gown upon her, unlock her closet, take forth paper, fold it, write upon it, read it, afterwards seal it, and again return to bed; yet all this while in a most fast sleep.

Doct. A great perturbation in nature! to receive at once the benefit of sleep, and do the effects of watching.—In this slumbry agitation, besides her walking, and other actual performances, what, at any time, have you heard her say?

Gent. That, sir, which I will not report after her.

Doct. You may, to me; and 'tis most meet you should.

Gent. Neither to you, nor any one; having no witness to confirm my speech.

Enter LADY MACBETH, *with a Taper.*

Lo you, here she comes? This is her very guise; and, upon my life, fast asleep. Observe her; stand close.

Doct. How came she by that light?

Gent. Why, it stood by her; she has light by her continually; 'tis her command.

Doct. You see her eyes are open.

Gent. Ay, but their sense is shut.

Doct. What is it she does now? Look, how she rubs her hands.

Gent. It is an accustom'd action with her, to seem thus washing her hands; I have known her continue in this a quarter of an hour.

Lady M. Yet here's a spot.

Doct. Hark, she speaks: I will set down what comes from her, to satisfy my remembrance the more strongly.

Lady M. Out, damned spot! out, I say!—One: Two: Why, then 'tis time to do't:—— Hell is murky!—Fye, my lord, fye! a soldier, and afeard? What need we fear who knows it, when none can call our power to account?—Yet who would have thought the old man to have had so much blood in him?

Doct. Do you mark that?

Lady M. The thane of Fife had a wife: Where is she now?——What, will these hands ne'er be clean?—No more o' that, my lord, no more o' that: you mar all with this starting.

Doct. Go to, go to; you have known what you should not.

Gent. She has spoke what she should not, I am sure of that: Heaven knows what she has known.

Lady M. Here's the smell of the blood still: all the perfumes of Arabia will not sweeten this little hand. Oh! oh! oh!

Doct. What a sigh is there! The heart is sorely charged.

Gent. I would not have such a heart in my bosom, for the dignity of the whole body.

Doct. Well, well, well,—

Gent. 'Pray God, it be, sir.

Doct. This disease is beyond my practice: Yet I have known those which have walked in their sleep, who have died holily in their beds.

Lady M. Wash your hands, put on your night-gown; look not so pale:—I tell you yet again, Banquo's buried; he cannot come out of his grave.

Doct. Even so?

Lady M. To bed, to bed; there's knocking at the gate. Come, come, come, come, give me your hand; What's done, cannot be undone: To bed, to bed, to bed. [*Exit* LADY MACBETH.

Doct. Will she go now to bed?

Gent. Directly.

Doct. Foul whisperings are abroad; Unnatural deeds
Do breed unnatural troubles: Infected minds
To their deaf pillows will discharge their secrets.
More needs she the divine, than the physician.—
God, God, forgive us all! Look after her;
Remove from her the means of all annoyance,
And still keep eyes upon her:—So, good night:
My mind she has mated, and amaz'd my sight:
I think, but dare not speak.

Gent. Good night, good doctor. [*Exeunt.*

SCENE II. *The Country near* Dunsinane.

Enter, with Drum and Colours, MENTETH, CATHNESS, ANGUS, LENOX, *and* Soldiers.

Ment. The English power is near, led on by
Malcolm,
His uncle Siward, and the good Macduff.
Revenges burn in them: for their dear causes
Would to the bleeding, and the grim alarm,
Excite the mortified man.

Ang. Near Birnam wood
Shall we well meet them; that way are they
coming.

Cath. Who knows, if Donalbain be with his
brother?

Len. For certain, sir, he is not: I have a file
Of all the gentry; there is Siward's son,
And many unrough youths, that even now
Protest their first of manhood.

Ment. What does the tyrant?

Cath. Great Dunsinane he strongly fortifies:
Some say, he's mad; others, that lesser hate him,
Do call it valiant fury: but, for certain,
He cannot buckle his distemper'd cause
Within the belt of rule.

Ang. Now does he feel
His secret murders sticking on his hands;
Now minutely revolts upbraid his faith-breach;
Those he commands, move only in command,
Nothing in love: Now does he feel his title
Hang loose about him, like a giant's robe
Upon a dwarfish thief.

Ment. Who then shall blame
His pester'd senses to recoil, and start,
When all that is within him does condemn
Itself for being there!

Cath. Well, march we on,
To give obedience where 'tis truly ow'd:
Meet we the medecin of the sickly weal;
And with him pour we, in our country's purge,
Each drop of us.

Len. Or so much as it needs,
To dew the sovereign flower, and drown the
weeds.
Make we our march towards Birnam.
[*Exeunt, marching.*

SCENE III. Dunsinane. *A Room in the Castle.*

Enter MACBETH, Doctor, *and* Attendants.

Macb. Bring me no more reports; let them
fly all;
Till Birnam wood remove to Dunsinane,
I cannot taint with fear. What's the boy Malcolm!
Was he not born of woman? The spirits that
know
All mortal consequents, have pronounc'd me
thus:

Fear not, Macbeth; no man that's born of woman,
Shall e'er have power on thee.——Then fly, false thanes,
And mingle with the English epicures:
The mind I sway by, and the heart I bear,
Shall never sagg with doubt, nor shake with fear.

Enter a Servant.

The devil damn thee black, thou cream-fac'd loon!
Where gott'st thou that goose look?

Serv. There is ten thousand——

Macb. Geese, villain?

Serv. Soldiers, sir.

Macb. Go, prick thy face, and over-red thy fear,
Thou lily-liver'd boy. What soldiers, patch?
Death of thy soul! those linen cheeks of thine
Are counsellors to fear. What soldiers, whey-face?

Serv. The English force, so please you.

Macb. Take thy face hence.—Seyton!—I am sick at heart,
When I behold—Seyton, I say! this push
Will cheer me ever, or disseat me now.
I have liv'd long enough; my way of life
Is fall'n into the sear, the yellow leaf:
And that which should accompany old age,
As honour, love, obedience, troops of friends,
I must not look to have; but, in their stead,
Curses, not loud, but deep, mouth-honour, breath,
Which the poor heart would fain deny, but dare not.
Seyton!—

Enter SEYTON.

Sey. What is your gracious pleasure?

Macb. What news more?

Sey. All is confirm'd, my lord, which was reported.

Macb. I'll fight, till from my bones my flesh be hack'd.
Give me my armour.

Sey. 'Tis not needed yet.

Macb. I'll put it on.
Send out more horses, skir the country round;
Hang those that talk of fear.—Give me mine armour.
How does your patient, doctor?

Doct. Not so sick, my lord,
As she is troubled with thick-coming fancies,
That keep her from her rest.

Macb. Cure her of that:
Canst thou not minister to a mind diseas'd;
Pluck from the memory a rooted sorrow;
Raze out the written troubles of the brain;
And, with some sweet oblivious antidote,
Cleanse the stuff'd bosom of that perilous stuff,
Which weighs upon the heart?

Doct. Therein the patient
Must minister to himself.

Macb. Throw physic to the dogs, I'll none of it:—
Come, put mine armour on; give me my staff:—
Seyton, send out.—Doctor, the thanes fly from me:
Come, sir, despatch:—If thou couldst, doctor, cast
The water of my land, find her disease,
And purge it to a sound and pristine health,
I would applaud thee to the very echo,
That should applaud again.—Pull't off, I say.—
What rhubarb, senna, or what purgative drug,
Would scour these English hence?—Hear'st thou of them?

Doct. Ay, my good lord; your royal preparation
Makes us hear something.

Macb. Bring it after me.——
I will not be afraid of death and bane,
Till Birnam forest come to Dunsinane. [*Exit.*

Doct. Were I from Dunsinane away and clear,
Profit again should hardly draw me here. [*Exit.*

SCENE IV.

Country near Dunsinane: *A Wood in view.*

Enter, with Drum and Colours, MALCOLM, *old* SIWARD, *and his* Son, MACDUFF, MENTETH, CATHNESS, ANGUS, LENOX, ROSSE, *and* Soldiers, *marching.*

Mal. Cousins, I hope the days are near at hand
That chambers will be safe.

Ment. We doubt it nothing.

Siw. What wood is this before us?

Ment. The wood of Birnam.

Mal. Let every soldier hew him down a bough,
And bear't before him; thereby shall we shadow
The numbers of our host, and make discovery
Err in report of us.

Sold. It shall be done.

Siw. We learn no other, but the confident tyrant
Keeps still in Dunsinane, and will endure
Our setting down befor't.

Mal. 'Tis his main hope:
For where there is advantage to be given,
Both more and less have given him the revolt;
And none serve with him but constrained things,
Whose hearts are absent too.

Macd. Let our just censures
Attend the true event, and put we on
Industrious soldiership.

Siw. The time approaches,
That will with due decision make us know
What we shall say we have, and what we owe.
Thoughts speculative their unsure hopes relate;
But certain issue strokes must arbitrate:
Towards which, advance the war.

[*Exeunt, marching.*

SCENE V. Dunsinane. *Within the Castle.*

Enter, with Drums and Colours, MACBETH, SEYTON, *and* Soldiers.

Macb. Hang out our banners on the outward walls;
The cry is still, *They come:* Our castle's strength
Will laugh a siege to scorn: here let them lie,
Till famine, and the ague, eat them up:
Were they not forc'd with those that should be ours,
We might have met them dareful, beard to beard,
And beat them backward home. What is that noise? [*A cry within, of women.*

Sey. It is the cry of women, my good lord.

Macb. I have almost forgot the taste of fears:
The time has been, my senses would have cool'd
To hear a night-shriek; and my fell of hair
Would at a dismal treatise rouse, and stir
As life were in't: I have supp'd full with horrors;
Direness, familiar to my slaught'rous thoughts,
Cannot once start me.—Wherefore was that cry?

Sey. The queen, my lord, is dead.

Macb. She should have died hereafter;
There would have been a time for such a word.—
To-morrow, and to-morow, and to-morrow,
Creeps in this petty pace from day to day,
To the last syllable of recorded time;
And all our yesterdays have lighted fools
The way to dusty death. Out, out, brief candle!
Life's but a walking shadow; a poor player,
That struts and frets his hour upon the stage,
And then is heard no more: it is a tale
Told by an idiot, full of sound and fury,
Signifying nothing.——

Enter a Messenger.

Thou com'st to use thy tongue; thy story quickly.

Mess. Gracious my lord,
I shall report that which I say I saw,
But know not how to do it.

Macb. Well, say, sir.

Mess. As I did stand my watch upon the hill,
I look'd toward Birnam, and anon, methought,
The wood began to move.

Macb. Liar and slave!

[*Striking him.*

Mess. Let me endure your wrath, if't be not so:

Within this three mile may you see it coming;
I say, a moving grove.
Macb. If thou speak'st false,
Upon the next tree shalt thou hang alive,
Till famine cling thee: if thy speech be sooth,
I care not if thou dost for me as much.—
I pull in resolution; and begin
To doubt the equivocation of the fiend,
That lies like truth: *Fear not, till Birnam wood*
Do come to Dunsinane;—and now a wood
Comes toward Dunsinane.—Arm, arm, and out!—
If this, which he avouches, does appear,
There is nor flying hence, nor tarrying here.
I 'gin to be a-weary of the sun,
And wish the estate o' the world were now undone.—
Ring the alarum-bell:—Blow, wind! come, wrack!
At least we'll die with harness on our back.
[*Exeunt.*

SCENE VI.

The same. A Plain before the Castle.

Enter, with Drums and Colours, MALCOLM, *old* SIWARD, MACDUFF, *&c. and their Army with Boughs.*

Mal. Now near enough: your leavy screens throw down,
And show like those you are:—You, worthy uncle,
Shall, with my cousin, your right noble son,
Lead our first battle: worthy Macduff, and we,
Shall take upon us what else remains to do,
According to our order.
Siw. Fare you well.—
Do we but find the tyrant's power to-night,
Let us be beaten, if we cannot fight.
Macd. Make all our trumpets speak: give them all breath,
Those clamorous harbingers of blood and death.
[*Exeunt. Alarums continued.*

SCENE VII.

The same. Another part of the Plain.

Enter MACBETH.

Macb. They have tied me to a stake; I cannot fly,
But, bearlike, I must fight the course.—What's he,
That was not born of woman? Such a one
Am I to fear, or none.

Enter young SIWARD.

Yo. Siw. What is thy name?
Macb. Thou'lt be afraid to hear it.
Yo. Siw. No; though thou call'st thyself a hotter name
Than any is in hell.
Macb. My name's Macbeth.
Yo. Siw. The devil himself could not pronounce a title
More hateful to mine ear.
Macb. No, nor more fearful.
Yo. Siw. Thou liest, abhorred tyrant; with my sword
I'll prove the lie thou speak'st.
[*They fight, and young* SIWARD *is slain.*
Macb. Thou wast born of woman.—
But swords I smile at, weapons laugh to scorn,
Brandish'd by man that's of a woman born.
[*Exit.*

Alarums. Enter MACDUFF.

Macd. That way the noise is:—Tyrant, show thy face:
If thou be'st slain, and with no stroke of mine,
My wife and children's ghosts will haunt me still.
I cannot strike at wretched kernes, whose arms
Are hir'd to bear their staves; either thou, Macbeth,
Or else my sword, with an unbatter'd edge,
I sheathe again undeeded. There thou should'st be;
By this great clatter, one of greatest note
Seems bruited: Let me find him, fortune!
And more I beg not. [*Exit. Alarum.*

Enter MALCOLM *and old* SIWARD.

Siw. This way, my lord;—the castle's gently render'd:
The tyrant's people on both sides do fight;
The noble thanes do bravely in the war;
The day almost itself professes yours,
And little is to do.
Mal. We have met with foes
That strike beside us.
Siw. Enter, sir, the castle.
[*Exeunt. Alarum.*

Re-enter MACBETH.

Macb. Why should I play the Roman fool, and die
On mine own sword? whiles I see lives, the gashes
Do better upon them.

Re-enter MACDUFF.

Macd. Turn, hell-hound, turn.
Macb. Of all men else I have avoided thee:
But get thee back, my soul is too much charg'd
With blood of thine already.
Macd. I have no words,
My voice is in my sword; thou bloodier villain
Than terms can give thee out! [*They fight.*
Macb. Thou losest labour:
As easy mayst thou the intrenchant air
With thy keen sword impress, as make me bleed:
Let fall thy blade on vulnerable crests;
I bear a charmed life, which must not yield
To one of woman born.
Macd. Despair thy charm;
And let the angel, whom thou still hast serv'd,
Tell thee, Macduff was from his mother's womb
Untimely ripp'd.
Macb. Accursed be that tongue that tells me so,
For it hath cow'd my better part of man:
And be these juggling fiends no more believ'd,
That palter with us in a double sense;
That keep the word of promise to our ear,
And break it to our hope.—I'll not fight with thee.
Macd. Then yield thee, coward,
And live to be the show and gaze o' the time.
We'll have thee, as our rarer monsters are,
Painted upon a pole; and underwrit,
Here may you see the tyrant.
Macb. I'll not yield,
To kiss the ground before young Malcolm's feet,
And to be baited with the rabble's curse.
Though Birnam wood be come to Dunsinane,
And thou oppos'd, being of no woman born,
Yet I will try the last: Before my body
I throw my warlike shield; lay on, Macduff;
And damn'd be him that first cries, *Hold, enough.*
[*Exeunt, fighting.*

Retreat. Flourish. Re-enter, with Drum and Colours, MALCOLM, *old* SIWARD, ROSSE, LENOX, ANGUS, CATHNESS, MENTETH, *and* Soldiers.

Mal. I would, the friends we miss were safe arriv'd.
Siw. Some must go off: and yet, by these I see,
So great a day as this is cheaply bought.
Mal. Macduff is missing, and your noble son.
Rosse. Your son, my lord, has paid a soldier's debt;
He only lived but till he was a man:
The which no sooner had his prowess confirm'd
In the unshrinking station where he fought,
But like a man he died.
Siw. Then he is dead?
Rosse. Ay, and brought off the field: your cause of sorrow
Must not be measur'd by his worth, for then
It hath no end.
Siw. Had he his hurts before?
Rosse. Ay, on the front.
Siw. Why then, God's soldier be he!
Had I as many sons as I have hairs,

I would not wish them to a fairer death:
And so his knell is knoll'd.

Mal. He's worth more sorrow,
And that I'll spend for him.

Siw. He's worth no more;
They say, he parted well, and paid his score:
So, God be with him!—Here comes newer comfort.

Re-enter MACDUFF, *with* MACBETH's *Head on a Pole.*

Macd. Hail, king! for so thou art: Behold, where stands
The usurper's cursed head: the time is free:
I see thee compass'd with thy kingdom's pearl,
That speak my salutation in their minds;
Whose voices I desire aloud with mine,—
Hail, king of Scotland!

All. King of Scotland, hail!
[*Flourish.*

Mal. We shall not spend a large expense of time,
Before we reckon with your several loves,
And make us even with you. My thanes and kinsmen,
Henceforth be earls, the first that ever Scotland
In such an honour nam'd. What's more to do,
Which would be planted newly with the time,—
As calling home our exil'd friends abroad,
That fled the snares of watchful tyranny;
Producing forth the cruel ministers
Of this dead butcher, and his fiendlike queen;
Who, as 'tis thought, by self and violent hands
Took off her life:—This, and what needful else
That calls upon us, by the grace of Grace,
We will perform in measure, time, and place:
So thanks to all at once, and to each one,
Whom we invite to see us crown'd at Scone.
[*Flourish. Exeunt.*

KING JOHN.

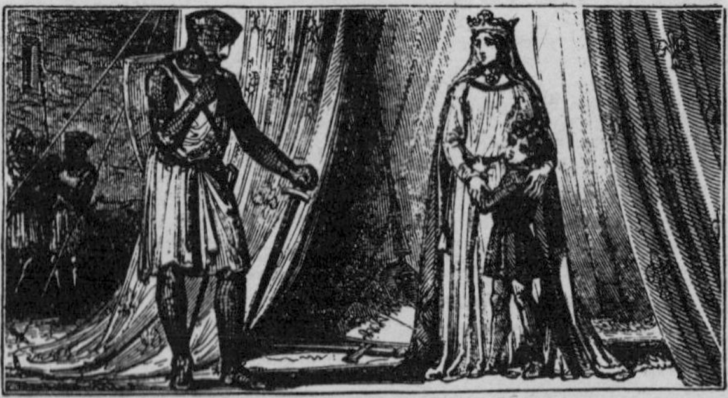

PERSONS REPRESENTED.

KING JOHN.
PRINCE HENRY, *his Son; afterwards* King Henry III.
ARTHUR, Duke of Bretagne, *Son of* Geffrey, *late* Duke of Bretagne, *the elder Brother of* King John.
WILLIAM MARESHALL, Earl of Pembroke.
GEFFREY FITZ-PETER, Earl of Essex, *chief Justiciary of* England.
WILLIAM LONGSWORD, Earl of Salisbury.
ROBERT BIGOT, Earl of Norfolk.
HUBERT DE BURGH, *Chamberlain to the* King.
ROBERT FAULCONBRIDGE, *Son of* Sir Robert Faulconbridge:
PHILIP FAULCONBRIDGE, *his Half-brother, Bastard Son to* King Richard the First.
JAMES GURNEY, *Servant to* Lady Faulconbridge.
PETER *of* Pomfret, *a Prophet.*
PHILIP, King of France.
LEWIS, *the Dauphin.*
ARCHDUKE OF AUSTRIA.
CARDINAL PANDULPH, *the Pope's Legate.*
Melun, *a French Lord.*
CHATILLON, *Ambassador from* France *to* King John.

ELINOR, *the Widow of* King Henry II. *and Mother of* King John.
CONSTANCE, *Mother to* Arthur.
BLANCH, *Daughter to* Alphonso, King of Castile, *and Niece to* King John.
LADY FAULCONBRIDGE, *Mother to the Bastard and* Robert Faulconbridge.

Lords, Ladies, Citizens *of* Angiers, Sheriff, Heralds, Officers, Soldiers, Messengers, *and other* Attendants.

SCENE,—*sometimes in* England, *and sometimes in* France.

ACT I.

SCENE I. Northampton.

A Room of State in the Palace.

Enter KING JOHN, QUEEN ELINOR, PEMBROKE, ESSEX, SALISBURY, *and others, with* CHATILLON.

K. John. Now, say, Chatillon, what would France with us?

Chat. Thus, after greeting, speaks the king of France,
In my behaviour, to the majesty,
The borrow'd majesty of England here.

Eli. A strange beginning;—borrow'd majesty!

K. John. Silence, good mother: hear the embassy.

Chat. Philip of France, in right and true behalf
Of thy deceased brother Geffrey's son,
Arthur Plantagenet, lays most lawful claim
To this fair island, and the territories;
To Ireland, Poictiers, Anjou, Touraine, Maine:
Desiring thee to lay aside the sword,
Which sways usurpingly these several titles;
And put the same into young Arthur's hand,
Thy nephew, and right royal sovereign.

K. John. What follows, if we disallow of this?

Chat. The proud control of fierce and bloody war,
To enforce these rights so forcibly withheld.
K. John. Here have we war for war, and blood for blood,
Controlment for controlment: so answer France.
Chat. Then take my king's defiance from my mouth,
The furthest limit of my embassy.
K. John. Bear mine to him, and so depart in peace:
Be thou as lightning in the eyes of France;
For ere thou canst report I will be there,
The thunder of my cannon shall be heard:
So, hence! Be thou the trumpet of our wrath,
And sullen presage of your own decay.—
An honourable conduct let him have:
Pembroke, look to't; Farewell, Chatillon.
[*Exeunt* CHATILLON *and* PEMBROKE.
Eli. What now, my son? have I not ever said,
How that ambitious Constance would not cease,
Till she had kindled France, and all the world,
Upon the right and party of her son?
This might have been prevented and made whole,
With very easy arguments of love!
Which now the manage of two kingdoms must
With fearful bloody issue arbitrate.
K. John. Our strong possession, and our right, for us.
Eli. Your strong possession, much more than your right;
Or else it must go wrong with you, and me:
So much my conscience whispers in your ear;
Which none but heaven, and you, and I, shall hear.

Enter the Sheriff *of* Northamptonshire, *who whispers* ESSEX.

Essex. My liege, here is the strangest controversy,
Come from the country to be judg'd by you,
That e'er I heard: Shall I produce the men?
K. John. Let them approach.— [*Exit* Sheriff.
Our abbies, and our priories, shall pay

Re-enter Sheriff, *with* ROBERT FAULCONBRIDGE, *and* PHILIP, *his bastard Brother.*

This expedition's charge.—What men are you?
Bast. Your faithful subject I, a gentleman,
Born in Northamptonshire; and eldest son,
As I suppose, to Robert Faulconbridge;
A soldier, by the honour-giving hand
Of Cœur-de-lion knighted in the field.
K. John. What art thou?
Rob. The son and heir to that same Faulconbridge.
K. John. Is that the elder, and art thou the heir?
You came not of one mother then, it seems.
Bast. Most certain of one mother, mighty king,
That is well known; and, as I think, one father:
But, for the certain knowledge of that truth,
I put you o'er to heaven, and to my mother;
Of that I doubt, as all men's children may.
Eli. Out on thee, rude man! thou dost shame thy mother,
And wound her honour with this diffidence.
Bast. I, madam? no, I have no reason for it;
That is my brother's plea, and none of mine;
The which if he can prove, 'a pops me out
At least from fair five hundred pound a year;
Heaven guard my mother's honour, and my land!
K. John. A good blunt fellow:—Why, being younger born,
Doth he lay claim to thine inheritance?
Bast. I know not why, except to get the land.
But once he slander'd me with bastardy:
But whe'r I be as true begot, or no,
That still I lay upon my mother's head;
But, that I am as well begot, my liege,
(Fair fall the bones that took the pains for me!)
Compare our faces, and be judge yourself.
If old Sir Robert did beget us both,
And were our father, and this son like him!—
O old Sir Robert, father, on my knee
I give heaven thanks, I was not like to thee.
K. John. Why, what a madcap hath heaven lent us here!
Eli. He hath a trick of Cœur-de-lion's face,
The accent of his tongue affecteth him:
Do you not read some tokens of my son
In the large composition of this man?
K. John. Mine eye hath well examined his parts,
And finds them perfect Richard.——Sirrah, speak,
What doth move you to claim your brother's land?
Bast. Because he hath a half-face, like my father;
With that half face would he have all my land:
A half-faced groat five hundred pound a year!
Rob. My gracious liege, when that my father liv'd,
Your brother did employ my father much;—
Bast. Well, sir, by this you cannot get my land;
Your tale must be how he employ'd my mother.
Rob. And once despatch'd him in an embassy
To Germany, there with the emperor,
To treat of high affairs touching that time:
The advantage of his absence took the king,
And in the mean time sojourn'd at my father's;
Where how he did prevail, I shame to speak:
But truth is truth; large lengths of seas and shores
Between my father and my mother lay
(As I have heard my father speak himself),
When this same lusty gentleman was got.
Upon his death-bed he by will bequeath'd
His lands to me; and took it, on his death,
That this my mother's son was none of his;
And, if he were, he came into the world
Full fourteen weeks before the course of time.
Then, good my liege, let me have what is mine,
My father's land, as was my father's will.
K. John. Sirrah, your brother is legitimate;
Your father's wife did after wedlock bear him:
And, if she did play false, the fault was hers;
Which fault lies on the hazards of all husbands
That marry wives. Tell me, how if my brother,
Who, as you say, took pains to get this son,
Had of your father claim'd this son for his?
In sooth good friend, your father might have kept
This calf, bred from his cow, from all the world;
In sooth, he might: then, if he were my brother's,
My brother might not claim him: nor your father,
Being none of his, refuse him: This concludes,—
My mother's son did get your father's heir;
Your father's heir must have your father's land.
Rob. Shall then my father's will be of no force,
To dispossess that child which is not his?
Bast. Of no more force to dispossess me, sir,
Than was his will to get me, as I think.
Eli. Whether hadst thou rather,—be a Faulconbridge,
And like thy brother, to enjoy thy land;
Or the reputed son of Cœur-de-lion,
Lord of thy presence, and no land beside?
Bast. Madam, an if my brother had my shape,
And I had his, Sir Robert his, like him:
And if my legs were too such riding-rods,
My arms such eel-skins stuff'd; my face so thin,
That in mine ear I durst not stick a rose,
Lest men should say, Look, where three farthings goes!
And, to his shape, were heir to all this land,
'Would, I might never stir from off this place,
I'd give it every foot to have this face;
I would not be sir Nob in any case.
Eli. I like thee well; wilt thou forsake thy fortune,
Bequeath thy land to him, and follow me;
I am a soldier, and now bound to France.
Bast. Brother, take you my land, I'll take my chance:

Your face hath got five hundred pounds a year;
Yet sell your face for five pence, and 'tis dear.—
Madam, I'll follow you unto the death.
Eli. Nay, I would have you go before me thither.
Bast. Our country manners give our betters way.
K. John. What is thy name?
Bast. Philip, my liege; so is my name begun;
Philip, good old Sir Robert's wife's eldest son.
K. John. From henceforth bear his name whose form thou bear'st:
Kneel thou down, Philip, but arise more great:
Arise Sir Richard, and Plantagenet.
Bast. Brother, by the mother's side, give me your hand;
My father gave me honour, yours gave land:
Now blessed be the hour by night or day,
When I was got, Sir Robert was away.
Eli. The very spirit of Plantagenet!—
I am thy grandame, Richard; call me so.
Bast. Madam, by chance, but not by truth: What though?
Something about, a little from the right,
In at the window, or else o'er the hatch:
Who dares not stir by day, must walk by night;
And have is have, however men do catch:
Near or far off, well won is still well shot;
And I am I, howe'er I was begot.
K. John. Go, Faulconbridge; now hast thou thy desire,
A landless knight makes thee a landed squire.—
Come, madam, and come, Richard; we must speed
For France, for France; for it is more than need.
Bast. Brother, adieu; Good fortune come to thee!
For thou wast got i' the way of honesty.
[*Exeunt all but the* Bastard.
A foot of honour better than I was;
But many a many foot of land the worse.
Well, now can I make any Joan a lady:——
Good den, Sir Richard,—God-a-mercy, fellow;—
And if his name be George, I'll call him Peter:
For new-made honour doth forget men's names;
'Tis too respective, and too sociable,
For your conversion. Now your traveller,—
He and his toothpick at my worship's mess;
And when my knightly stomach is suffic'd,
Why then I suck my teeth, and catechise
My picked man of countries:——*My dear sir*
(Thus, leaning on my elbow, I begin),
I shall beseech you—That is question now;
And then comes answer like an A B C-book:—
O sir, says answer, *at your best command;*
At your employment; at your service sir:——
No, sir, says question, *I, sweet sir, at yours:*
And, so, ere answer knows what question would
(Saving in dialogue of compliment;
And talking of the Alps, and Apennines,
The Pyrenean, and the river Po),
It draws towards supper in conclusion so.
But this is worshipful society,
And fits the mounting spirit, like myself:
For he is but a bastard to the time,
That doth not smack of observation:
(And so am I, whether I smack, or no);
And not alone in habit and device,
Exterior form, outward accoutrement;
But from the inward motion to deliver
Sweet, sweet, sweet poison for the age's tooth:
Which, though I will not practise to deceive,
Yet, to avoid deceit, I mean to learn;
For it shall strew the footsteps of my rising.—
But who comes in such haste, in riding robes?
What woman-post is this? hath she no husband,
That will take pains to blow a horn before her?

Enter LADY FAULCONBRIDGE *and* JAMES GURNEY.

O me! it is my mother;—How now, good lady?
What brings you here to court so hastily?
Lady F. Where is that slave, thy brother? where is he,
That holds in chase mine honour up and down?
Bast. My brother Robert? old Sir Robert's son?
Colbrand the giant, that same mighty man?
Is it Sir Robert's son, that you seek so?
Lady F. Sir Robert's son! Ay, thou unreverend boy,
Sir Robert's son! Why scorn'st thou at Sir Robert?
He is Sir Robert's son; and so art thou.
Bast. James Gurney, wilt thou give us leave awhile?
Gur. Good leave, good Philip.
Bast. Philip?—sparrow!—James,
There's toys abroad; anon I'll tell thee more.
[*Exit* GURNEY.
Madam, I was not old Sir Robert's son;
Sir Robert might have eat his part in me
Upon Good Friday, and ne'er broke his fast:
Sir Robert could do well: Marry, (to confess!)
Could he get me? Sir Robert could not do it;
We know his handy-work:—Therefore, good mother,
To whom am I beholden for these limbs?
Sir Robert never holp to make this leg.
Lady F. Hast thou conspired with thy brother too,
That for thine own gain should'st defend mine honour?
What means this scorn, thou most untoward knave?
Bast. Knight, knight, good mother,—Basilisco-like:
What! I am dubb'd; I have it on my shoulder.
But, mother, I am not Sir Robert's son;
I have disclaim'd Sir Robert, and my land;
Legitimation, name, and all is gone:
Then, good my mother, let me know my father;
Some proper man, I hope; Who was it, mother?
Lady F. Hast thou denied thyself a Faulconbridge?
Bast. As faithfully as I deny the devil.
Lady F. King Richard Cœur-de-lion was thy father;
By long and vehement suit I was seduc'd
To make room for him in my husband's bed:——
Heaven, lay not my transgression to my charge!
Thou art the issue of my dear offence,
Which was so strongly urg'd, past my defence.
Bast. Now, by this light, were I to get again,
Madam, I would not wish a better father.
Some sins do bear their privilege on earth,
And so doth yours; your fault was not your folly:
Needs must you lay your heart at his dispose,—
Subjected tribute to commanding love,—
Against whose fury and unmatched force
The awless lion could not wage the fight,
Nor keep his princely heart from Richard's hand.
He, that perforce robs lions of their hearts,
May easily win a woman's. Ay, my mother,
With all my heart I thank thee for my father!
Who lives and dares but say, thou didst not well
When I was got, I'll send his soul to hell.
Come, lady, I will show thee to my kin;
And they shall say, when Richard me begot,
If thou hadst said him nay, it had been sin:
Who says it was, he lies; I say, 'twas not.
[*Exeunt.*

ACT II.

SCENE I. France. *Before the Walls of* Angiers.

Enter, on one side, the Archduke *of* Austria, *and* Forces; *on the other,* PHILIP, King *of* France, *and* Forces; LEWIS, CONSTANCE, ARTHUR, *and* Attendants.

Lew. Before Angiers well met, brave Austria.—
Arthur, that great forerunner of thy blood,
Richard, that robb'd the lion of his heart,
And fought the holy wars in Palestine,

By this brave duke came early to his grave:
And, for amends to his posterity,
At our importance, hither is he come,
To spread his colours, boy, in thy behalf;
And to rebuke the usurpation
Of thy unnatural uncle, English John:
Embrace him, love him, give him welcome hither.

Arth. God shall forgive you Cœur-de-lion's death,
The rather, that you give his offspring life,
Shadowing their right under your wings of war:
I give you welcome with a powerless hand,
But with a heart full of unstained love:
Welcome before the gates of Angiers, duke.

Lew. A noble boy! Who would not do thee right?

Aust. Upon thy cheek lay I this zealous kiss,
As seal to this indenture of my love;
That to my home I will no more return,
Till Angiers, and the right thou hast in France,
Together with that pale, that white-fac'd shore,
Whose foot spurns back the ocean's roaring tides,
And coops from other lands her islanders,
Even till that England, hedg'd in with the main,
That water-walled bulwark, still secure
And confident from foreign purposes,
Even till that utmost corner of the west
Salute thee for her king: till then, fair boy,
Will I not think of home, but follow arms.

Const. O, take his mother's thanks, a widow's thanks,
Till your strong hand shall help to give him strength,
To make a more requital to your love.

Aust. The peace of heaven is theirs, that lift their swords
In such a just and charitable war.

K. Phi. Well then, to work; our cannon shall be bent
Against the brows of this resisting town.——
Call for our chiefest men of discipline,
To cull the plots of best advantages:—
We'll lay before this town our royal bones,
Wade to the market-place in Frenchmen's blood,
But we will make it subject to this boy.

Const. Stay for an answer to your embassy,
Lest unadvis'd you stain your swords with blood:
My Lord Chatillon may from England bring
That right in peace, which here we urge in war:
And then we shall repent each drop of blood,
That hot rash haste so indirectly shed.

Enter CHATILLON.

K. Phi. A wonder, lady!—lo, upon thy wish,
Our messenger Chatillon is arriv'd.—
What England says, say briefly, gentle lord,
We coldly pause for thee; Chatillon, speak.

Chat. Then turn your forces from this paltry siege,
And stir them up against a mightier task.
England, impatient of your just demands,
Hath put himself in arms; the adverse winds,
Whose leisure I have staid, have given him time
To land his legions all as soon as I:
His marches are expedient to this town,
His forces strong, his soldiers confident.
With him along is come the mother-queen,
An Ate, stirring him to blood and strife:
With her her niece, the Lady Blanch of Spain;
With them a bastard of the king deceas'd:
And all the unsettled humours of the land,—
Rash, inconsiderate, fiery voluntaries,
With ladies' faces, and fierce dragons' spleens,—
Have sold their fortunes at their native homes,
Bearing their birthrights proudly on their backs,
To make a hazard of new fortunes here.
In brief, a braver choice of dauntless spirits,
Than now, the English bottoms have waft o'er,
Did never float upon the swelling tide,
To do offence and scath in Christendom.
The interruption of their churlish drums
[*Drums beat.*
Cuts off more circumstance; they are at hand,
To parley, or to fight; therefore, prepare.

K. Phi. How much unlook'd for is this expedition!

Aust. By how much unexpected, by so much
We must awake endeavour for defence;
For courage mounteth with occasion:
Let them be welcome then, we are prepar'd.

Enter KING JOHN, ELINOR, BLANCH, *the* Bastard, PEMBROKE, *and Forces.*

K. John. Peace be to France; if France in peace permit
Our just and lineal entrance to our own!
If not; bleed France, and peace ascend to heaven!
Whiles we, God's wrathful agent, do correct
Their proud contempt that beat his peace to heaven.

K. Phi. Peace be to England; if that war return
From France to England, there to live in peace!
England we love; and, for that England's sake,
With burden of our armour here we sweat:
This toil of ours should be a work of thine;
But thou from loving England art so far,
That thou hast underwrought his lawful king,
Cut off the sequence of posterity,
Outfaced infant state, and done a rape
Upon the maiden virtue of the crown.
Look here upon thy brother Geffrey's face:
These eyes, these brows, were moulded out of his:
This little abstract doth contain that large,
Which died in Geffrey; and the hand of time
Shall draw this brief into as huge a volume.
That Geffrey was thy elder brother born,
And this his son; England was Geffrey's right,
And this is Geffrey's: In the name of God,
How comes it then, that thou art call'd a king,
When living blood doth in these temples beat,
Which owe the crown that thou o'ermasterest?

K. John. From whom hast thou this great commission, France,
To draw my answer from thy articles?

K. Phi. From that supernal judge, that stirs good thoughts
In any breast of strong authority,
To look into the blots and stains of right.
That judge hath made me guardian to this boy:
Under whose warrant, I impeach thy wrong;
And, by whose help, I mean to chastise it.

K. John. Alack, thou dost usurp authority.

K. Phi. Excuse; it is to beat usurping down.

Eli. Who is it, thou dost call usurper, France?

Const. Let me make answer;—thy usurping son.

Eli. Out, insolent! thy bastard shall be king;
That thou mayst be a queen, and check the world!

Const. My bed was ever to thy son as true,
As thine was to thy husband; and this boy
Liker in feature to his father Geffrey,
Than thou and John in manners; being as like,
As rain to water, or devil to his dam.
My boy a bastard! By my soul, I think,
His father never was so true begot;
It cannot be, an if thou wert his mother.

Eli. There's a good mother, boy, that blots thy father.

Const. There's a good grandam, boy, that would blot thee.

Aust. Peace!

Bast. Hear the crier.

Aust. What the devil art thou?

Bast. One that will play the devil, sir, with you,
An 'a may catch your hide and you alone.
You are the hare of whom the proverb goes,
Whose valour plucks dead lions by the beard;
I'll smoke your skin coat, an I catch you right;
Sirrah, look to 't; i' faith, I will, i' faith.

Blanch. O, well did he become that lion's robe,
That did disrobe the lion of that robe!

Bast. It lies as sightly on the back of him,
As great Alcides' shoes upon an ass:—
But, ass, I'll take that burden from your back;
Or lay on that shall make your shoulders crack.

Aust. What cracker is this same, that deafs our ears
With this abundance of superfluous breath?

K. Phi. Lewis, determine what we shall do straight.

Lew. Women and fools, break off your conference.—
King John, this is the very sum of all,—
England, and Ireland, Anjou, Touraine, Maine,
In right of Arthur do I claim of thee:
Wilt thou resign them, and lay down thy arms?

K. John. My life as soon:—I do defy thee, France.
Arthur of Bretagne, yield thee to my hand;
And, out of my dear love, I'll give thee more
Than e'er the coward hand of France can win:
Submit thee, boy.

Eli. Come to thy grandam, child.

Const. Do, child, go to it' grandam, child;
Give grandam kingdom, and it' grandam will
Give it a plum, a cherry, and a fig:
There's a good grandam.

Arth. Good my mother, peace!
I would, that I were low laid in my grave;
I am not worth this coil that's made for me.

Eli. His mother shames him so, poor boy, he weeps.

Const. Now shame upon you, whe'r she does or no!
His grandam's wrongs, and not his mother's shames,
Draw those heaven-moving pearls from his poor eyes,
Which heaven shall take in nature of a fee;
Ay, with these crystal beads heaven shall be brib'd
To do him justice, and revenge on you.

Eli. Thou monstrous slanderer of heaven and earth!

Const. Thou monstrous injurer of heaven and earth!
Call not me slanderer; thou, and thine, usurp
The dominations, royalties, and rights,
Of this oppressed boy: This is thy eldest son's son,
Infortunate in nothing but in thee;
Thy sins are visited in this poor child;
The canon of the law is laid on him,
Being but the second generation
Removed from thy sin-conceiving womb.

K. John. Bedlam, have done.

Const. I have but this to say,—
That he's not only plagued for her sin,
But God hath made her sin and her the plague
On this removed issue, plagu'd for her,
And with her plague, her sin; his injury
Her injury, the beadle to her sin;
All punish'd in the person of this child,
And all for her; A plague upon her!

Eli. Thou unadvised scold, I can produce
A will, that bars the title of thy son.

Const. Ay, who doubts that? a will! a wicked will;
A woman's will; a canker'd grandam's will!

K. Phi. Peace, lady; pause, or be more temperate:
It ill beseems this presence, to cry aim
To these ill tuned repetitions.—
Some trumpet summon hither to the walls
These men of Angiers; let us hear them speak,
Whose title they admit, Arthur's or John's.

Trumpets sound. Enter Citizens *upon the Walls.*

1 Cit. Who is it, that hath warn'd us to the walls?

K. Phi. 'Tis France, for England.

K. John. England, for itself:
You men of Angiers, and my loving subjects,—

K. Phi. You loving men of Angiers, Arthur's subjects,
Our trumpet call'd you to this gentle parle.

K. John. For our advantage;—Therefore, hear us first.——
These flags of France, that are advanced here
Before the eye and prospect of your town,
Have hither march'd to your endamagement:
The cannons have their bowels full of wrath;
And ready mounted are they, to spit forth
Their iron indignation 'gainst your walls:
All preparation for a bloody siege,
And merciless proceeding by these French,
Confront your city's eyes, your winking gates;
And, but for our approach, those sleeping stones,
That as a waist do girdle you about,
By the compulsion of their ordnance
By this time from their fixed beds of lime
Had been dishabited, and wide havock made
For bloody power to rush upon your peace.
But, on the sight of us, your lawful king,——
Who painfully, with much expedient march,
Have brought a countercheck before your gates,
To save unscratch'd your city's threaten'd cheeks,—
Behold, the French, amaz'd, vouchsafe a parle:
And now, instead of bullets wrapp'd in fire,
To make a shaking fever in your walls,
They shoot but calm words, folded up in smoke,
To make a faithless error in your ears:
Which trust accordingly, kind citizens,
And let us in, your king; whose labour'd spirits,
Forwearied in this action of swift speed,
Crave harbourage within your city walls.

K. Phi. When I have said, make answer to us both.
Lo, in this right hand, whose protection
Is most divinely vow'd upon the right
Of him it holds, stands young Plantagenet;
Son to the elder brother of this man,
And king o'er him, and all that he enjoys:
For this down trodden equity, we tread
In warlike march these greens before your town,
Being no further enemy to you,
Than the constraint of hospitable zeal,
In the relief of this oppressed child,
Religiously provokes. Be pleased then
To pay that duty, which you truly owe,
To him that owes it; namely, this young prince:
And then our arms, like to a muzzled bear,
Save in aspect, have all offence seal'd up;
Our cannons' malice vainly shall be spent
Against the invulnerable clouds of heaven;
And, with a blessed and unvex'd retire,
With unhack'd swords, and helmets all unbruis'd,
We will bear home that lusty blood again,
Which here we came to spout against your town,
And leave your children, wives, and you, in peace.
But if you fondly pass our proffer'd offer,
'Tis not the roundure of your old-fac'd walls
Can hide you from our messengers of war;
Though all these English, and their discipline,
Were harbour'd in their rude circumference.
Then, tell us, shall your city call us lord,
In that behalf which we have challeng'd it?
Or shall we give the signal to our rage,
And stalk in blood to our possession?

1 Cit. In brief, we are the king of England's subjects;
For him, and in his right, we hold this town.

K. John. Acknowledge then the king, and let me in.

1 Cit. That can we not: but he that proves the king,
To him will we prove loyal; till that time,
Have we ramm'd up our gates against the world.

K. John. Doth not the crown of England prove the king?
And, if not that, I bring you witnesses,
Twice fifteen thousand hearts of England's breed,—

Bast. Bastards, and else.
K. John. To verify our title with their lives.
K. Phi. As many, and as well born bloods as those,——
Bast. Some bastards too.
K. Phi. Stand in his face, to contradict his claim.
1 *Cit.* Till you compound whose right is worthiest,
We, for the worthiest, hold the right from both.
K. John. Then God forgive the sin of all those souls,
That to their everlasting residence,
Before the dew of evening fall, shall fleet,
In dreadful trial of our kingdom's king!
K. Phi. Amen, Amen!—Mount, chevaliers! to arms!
Bast. St. George,—that swing'd the dragon, and e'er since,
Sits on his horseback at mine hostess' door,
Teach us some fence:—Sirrah, were I at home,
At your den, sirrah [*To* Austria], with your lioness,
I'd set an ox-head to your lion's hide,
And make a monster of you.
Aust. Peace; no more.
Bast. O, tremble; for you hear the lion roar.
K. John. Up higher to the plain; where we'll set forth,
In best appointment, all our regiments.
Bast. Speed then, to take advantage of the field.
K. Phi. It shall be so;—[*To* LEWIS] and at the other hill
Command the rest to stand.—God, and our right! [*Exeunt.*

SCENE II. *The same.*

Alarums and Excursions; then a Retreat. Enter a French Herald, *with trumpets to the gates.*

F. Her. You men of Angiers, open wide your gates,
And let young Arthur, Duke of Bretagne, in;
Who, by the hand of France, this day hath made
Much work for tears in many an English mother,
Whose sons lie scatter'd on the bleeding ground:
Many a widow's husband grovelling lies,
Coldly embracing the discolour'd earth;
And victory, with little loss, doth play
Upon the dancing banners of the French;
Who are at hand, triumphantly display'd,
To enter conquerors, and to proclaim
Arthur of Bretagne, England's king, and yours.

Enter an English Herald, *with trumpets.*

E. Her. Rejoice, you men of Angiers, ring your bells;
King John, your king and England's, doth approach,
Commander of this hot malicious day!
Their armours, that march'd hence so silver-bright,
Hither return all gilt with Frenchmen's blood;
There stuck no plume in any English crest,
That is removed by a staff of France;
Our colours do return in those same hands
That did display them when we first march'd forth;
And, like a jolly troop of huntsmen, come
Our lusty English, all with purpled hands,
Dyed in the dying slaughter of their foes:
Open your gates, and give the victors way.
Cit. Heralds, from off our towers we might behold,
From first to last, the onset and retire
Of both your armies; whose equality
By our best eyes cannot be censured:
Blood hath bought blood, and blows have answer'd blows;
Strength match'd with strength, and power confronted power:
Both are alike; and both alike we like.
One must prove greatest; while they weigh so even,
We hold our town for neither; yet for both.

Enter, at one side, KING JOHN, *with his Power;* ELINOR, BLANCH, *and the* Bastard; *at the other,* KING PHILIP, LEWIS, AUSTRIA, *and* Forces.

K. John. France, hast thou yet more blood to cast away?
Say, shall the current of our right run on?
Whose passage, vex'd with thy impediment,
Shall leave his native channel, and o'erswell
With course disturb'd even thy confining shores;
Unless thou let his silver water keep
A peaceful progress to the ocean.
K. Phi. England, thou hast not sav'd one drop of blood,
In this hot trial, more than we of France;
Rather, lost more: And by this hand I swear,
That sways the earth this climate overlooks,—
Before we will lay down our just borne arms,
We'll put thee down, 'gainst whom these arms we bear,
Or add a royal number to the dead;
Gracing the scroll, that tells of this war's loss,
With slaughter coupled to the name of kings.
Bast. Ha, majesty! how high thy glory towers,
When the rich blood of kings is set on fire!
O, now doth death line his dead chaps with steel:
The swords of soldiers are his teeth, his fangs;
And now he feasts, mousing the flesh of men,
In undetermin'd differences of kings.—
Why stand these royal fronts amazed thus?
Cry, havock, kings! back to the stained field,
You equal potents, fiery-kindled spirits!
Then let confusion of one part confirm
The other's peace; till then, blows, blood, and death!
K. John. Whose party do the townsmen yet admit?
K. Phi. Speak, citizens, for England; who's your king?
1 *Cit.* The king of England, when we know the king.
K. Phi. Know him in us, that here hold up his right.
K. John. In us, that are our own great deputy,
And bear possession of our person here;
Lord of our presence, Angiers, and of you.
1 *Cit.* A greater power than we, denies all this;
And, till it be undoubted, we do lock
Our former scruple in our strong-barr'd gates:
King'd of our fears; until our fears resolv'd,
Be by some certain king purg'd and depos'd.
Bast. By heaven, these scroyles of Angiers flout you, kings;
And stand securely on their battlements,
As in a theatre, whence they gape and point
At your industrious scenes and acts of death.
Your royal presences be rul'd by me;
Do like the mutines of Jerusalem,
Be friends a while, and both conjointly bend
Your sharpest deeds of malice on this town:
By east and west let France and England mount
Their battering cannon, charged to the mouths:
Till their soul-fearing clamours have brawl'd down
The flinty ribs of this contemptuous city:
I'd play incessantly upon these jades,
Even till unfenced desolation
Leave them as naked as the vulgar air.
That done, dissever your united strengths,
And part your mingled colours once again;
Turn face to face, and bloody point to point:
Then, in a moment, fortune shall cull forth
Out of one side her happy minion;
To whom in favour she shall give the day,
And kiss him with a glorious victory.
How like you this wild counsel, mighty states?
Smacks it not something of the policy?
K. John. Now, by the sky that hangs above our heads,

I like it well;—France, shall we knit our powers,
And lay this Angiers even with the ground:
Then, after, fight who shall be king of it?
Bast. An if thou hast the mettle of a king,—
Being wrong'd, as we are, by this peevish town,—
Turn thou the mouth of thy artillery,
As we will ours, against these saucy walls:
And when that we have dash'd them to the ground,
Why, then defy each other; and, pell-mell,
Make work upon ourselves for heaven, or hell.
K. Phi. Let it be so:—Say, where will you assault?
K. John. We from the west will send destruction
Into this city's bosom.
Aust. I from the north.
K. Phi. Our thunder from the south,
Shall rain their drift of bullets on this town.
Bast. O prudent discipline! from north to south,
Austria and France shoot in each other's mouth: [*Aside.*
I'll stir them to it:—Come, away, away!
1 Cit. Hear us, great kings! vouchsafe a while to stay,
And I shall show you peace, and fair-fac'd league;
Win you this city without stroke or wound;
Rescue those breathing lives to die in beds,
That here come sacrifices for the field;
Persever not, but hear me, mighty kings.
K. John. Speak on, with favour; we are bent to hear.
1 Cit. That daughter there of Spain, the lady Blanch,
Is near to England; Look upon the years
Of Lewis the Dauphin, and that lovely maid:
If lusty love should go in quest of beauty,
Where should he find it fairer than in Blanch?
If zealous love should go in search of virtue,
Where should he find it purer than in Blanch?
If love ambitious sought a match of birth,
Whose veins bound richer blood than Lady Blanch?
Such as she is, in beauty, virtue, birth,
Is the young Dauphin every way complete:
If not complete, O say, he is not she;
And she again wants nothing, to name want,
If want it be not, that she is not he:
He is the half part of a blessed man,
Left to be finished by such a she;
And she a fair divided excellence,
Whose fulness of perfection lies in him.
O, two such silver currents, when they join,
Do glorify the banks that bound them in:
And two such shores to two such streams made one,
Two such controlling bounds shall you be, kings,
To these two princes, if you marry them.
This union shall do more than battery can,
To our fast-closed gates: for, at this match,
With swifter spleen than powder can enforce,
The mouth of passage shall we fling wide ope,
And give you entrance: but, without this match,
The sea enraged is not half so deaf,
Lions more confident, mountains and rocks
More free from motion; no, not death himself
In mortal fury half so peremptory,
As we do keep this city.
Bast. Here's a stay,
That shakes the rotten carcass of old death
Out of his rags! Here's a large mouth, indeed,
That spits forth death, and mountains, rocks, and seas;
Talks as familiarly of roaring lions
As maids of thirteen do of puppy-dogs!
What cannoneer begot this lusty blood?
He speaks plain cannon, fire, and smoke, and bounce:
He gives the bastinado with his tongue;
Our ears are cudgel'd; not a word of his,
But buffets better than a fist of France:
Zounds! I was never so bethump'd with words,
Since I first call'd my brother's father, dad.
Eli. Son, list to this conjunction, make this match;
Give with our niece a dowry large enough:
For by this knot thou shalt so surely tie
Thy now unsur'd assurance to the crown,
That yon green boy shall have no sun to ripe
The bloom that promiseth a mighty fruit.
I see a yielding in the looks of France;
Mark, how they whisper: urge them, while their souls
Are capable of this ambition:
Lest zeal, now melted, by the windy breath
Of soft petitions, pity, and remorse,
Cool and congeal again to what it was.
1 Cit. Why answer not the double majesties
This friendly treaty of our threaten'd town?
K. Phi. Speak England first, that hath been forward first
To speak unto this city: What say you?
K. John. If that the Dauphin there, thy princely son,
Can in this book of beauty read, I love,
Her dowry shall weigh equal with a queen:
For Anjou, and fair Touraine, Maine, Poictiers,
And all that we upon this side the sea
(Except this city now by us besieg'd)
Find liable to our crown and dignity,
Shall gild her bridal bed; and make her rich
In titles, honours, and promotions,
As she in beauty, education, blood,
Holds hand with any princess of the world.
K. Phi. What say'st thou, boy? look in the lady's face.
Lew. I do, my lord, and in her eye I find
A wonder, or a wondrous miracle,
The shadow of myself form'd in her eye;
Which, being but the shadow of your son,
Becomes a sun, and makes your son a shadow;
I do protest, I never lov'd myself,
Till now infixed I beheld myself,
Drawn in the flattering table of her eye. [*Whispers with* BLANCH.
Bast. Drawn in the flattering table of her eye!—
Hang'd in the frowning wrinkle of her brow!—
And quarter'd in her heart?—he doth espy
Himself love's traitor: This is pity now,
That hang'd, and drawn, and quarter'd, there should be,
In such a love, so vile a lout as he.
Blanch. My uncle's will, in this respect is mine.
If he see aught in you, that makes him like,
That any thing he sees, which moves his liking,
I can with ease translate it to my will;
Or, if you will (to speak more properly),
I will enforce it easily to my love.
Further I will not flatter you, my lord,
That all I see in you is worthy love.
Than this,—that nothing do I see in you,
(Though churlish thoughts themselves should be your judge),
That I can find should merit any hate.
K. John. What say these young ones? What say you, my niece?
Blanch. That she is bound in honour still to do
What you in wisdom shall vouchsafe to say.
K. John. Speak then, prince Dauphin; can you love this lady?
Lew. Nay, ask me if I can refrain from love;
For I do love her most unfeignedly.
K. John. Then do I give Volquessen, Touraine, Maine,
Poictiers, and Anjou, these five provinces,
With her to thee; and this addition more:
Full thirty thousand marks of English coin.—
Philip of France, if thou be pleas'd withal,

Command thy son and daughter to join hands.

K. Phi. It likes us well;—Young princes, close your hands.

Aust. And your lips too! for I am well assur'd,
That I did so, when I was first assur'd.

K. Phi. Now, citizens of Angiers, ope your gates,
Let in that amity which you have made;
For at St. Mary's chapel, presently,
The rites of marriage shall be solemniz'd.—
Is not the Lady Constance in this troop?—
I know, she is not; for this match, made up,
Her presence would have interrupted much:—
Where is she and her son? tell me, who knows.

Lew. She is sad and passionate at your highness' tent.

K. Phi. And, by my faith, this league that we have made,
Will give her sadness very little cure.—
Brother of England, how may we content
This widow lady? In her right we came;
Which we, God knows, have turn'd another way,
To our own vantage.

K. John. We will heal up all;
For we'll create young Arthur duke of Bretagne,
And earl of Richmond: and this rich fair town
We make him lord of.—Call the Lady Constance;
Some speedy messenger bid her repair
To our solemnity:—I trust we shall,
If not fill up the measure of her will,
Yet in some measure satisfy her so,
That we shall stop her exclamation.
Go we, as well as haste will suffer us,
To this unlook'd for unprepared pomp.

[*Exeunt all but the* Bastard.—*The* Citizens *retire from the Walls.*

Bast. Mad world! mad kings! mad composition!
John, to stop Arthur's title in the whole,
Hath willingly departed with a part:
And France (whose armour conscience buckled on;
Whom zeal and charity brought to the field,
As God's own soldier), rounded in the ear
With that same purpose-changer, that sly devil;
That broker, that still breaks the pate of faith;
That daily break-vow; he that wins of all,
Of kings, of beggars, old men, young men, maids,—
Who having no external thing to lose
But the word maid,—cheats the poor maid of that;
That smooth-fac'd gentleman, tickling commodity;—
Commodity, the bias of the world;
The world, who of itself is peised well,
Made to run even, upon even ground;
Till this advantage, this vile drawing bias,
This sway of motion, this commodity,
Makes it take head from all indifferency,
From all direction, purpose, course, intent:
And this same bias, this commodity,
This bawd, this broker, this all-changing word,
Clapp'd on the outward eye of fickle France,
Hath drawn him from his own determin'd aid
From a resolv'd and honourable war,
To a most base and vile-concluded peace.—
And why rail I on this commodity?
But for because he hath not woo'd me yet:
Not that I have the power to clutch my hand,
When his fair angels would salute my palm:
But for my hand, as unattempted yet,
Like a poor beggar raileth on the rich.
Well, whiles I am a beggar, I will rail,
And say,—there is no sin, but to be rich;
And being rich, my virtue then shall be,
To say,—there is no vice, but beggary:
Since kings break faith upon commodity,
Gain, be my lord! for I will worship thee!

[*Exit.*

ACT III.

SCENE I. *The same.* *The* French King's *Tent.*

Enter CONSTANCE, ARTHUR, *and* SALISBURY.

Const. Gone to be married! gone to swear a peace!
False blood to false blood join'd! Gone to be friends!
Shall Lewis have Blanch? and Blanch those provinces?
It is not so, thou hast misspoke, misheard;
Be well advis'd, tell o'er thy tale again:
It cannot be; thou dost but say, 'tis so:
I trust, I may not trust thee; for thy word
Is but the vain breath of a common man;
Believe me, I do not believe thee, man;
I have a king's oath to the contrary.
Thou shalt be punish'd for thus frighting me,
For I am sick, and capable of fears;
Oppress'd with wrongs, and therefore full of fears;
A widow, husbandless, subject to fears;
A woman, naturally born to fears;
And though thou now confess, thou didst but jest,
With my vex'd spirits I cannot take a truce,
But they will quake and tremble all this day.
What dost thou mean by shaking of thy head?
Why dost thou look so sadly on my son?
What means that hand upon that breast of thine?
Why holds thine eye that lamentable rheum,
Like a proud river peering o'er his bounds?
Be these sad signs confirmers of thy words?
Then speak again: not all thy former tale,
But this one word, whether thy tale be true.

Sal. As true, as, I believe, you think them false,
That give you cause to prove my saying true.

Const. O, if thou teach me to believe this sorrow,
Teach thou this sorrow how to make me die;
And let belief and life encounter so,
As doth the fury of two desperate men,
Which, in the very meeting, fall, and die.—
Lewis marry Blanch! O, boy, then where art thou?
France friend with England! what becomes of me?—
Fellow, be gone; I cannot brook thy sight;
This news hath made thee a most ugly man.

Sal. What other harm have I, good lady, done,
But spoke the harm that is by others done?

Const. Which harm within itself so heinous is,
As it makes harmful all that speak of it.

Arth. I do beseech you, madam, be content.

Const. If thou, that bidd'st me be content, wert grim,
Ugly, and sland'rous to thy mother's womb,
Full of unpleasing blots, and sightless stains,
Lame, foolish, crooked, swart, prodigious,
Patch'd with foul moles, and eye-offending marks,
I would not care, I then would be content;
For then I should not love thee; no, nor thou
Become thy great birth, nor deserve a crown.
But thou art fair; and at thy birth, dear boy!
Nature and fortune join'd to make thee great:
Of nature's gifts thou may'st with lilies boast,
And with the half-blown rose: but fortune, O!
She is corrupted, chang'd, and won from thee;
She adulterates hourly with thy uncle John;
And with her golden hand hath pluck'd on France
To tread down fair respect of sovereignty,
And made his majesty the bawd to theirs.
France is a bawd to fortune, and King John;
That strumpet fortune, that usurping John:—
Tell me, thou fellow, is not France forsworn?
Envenom him with words; or get thee gone,
And leave those woes alone, which I alone
Am bound to under-bear.

Sal. Pardon me, madam,
I may not go without you to the kings.

Const. Thou may'st, thou shalt, I will not go with thee:
I will instruct my sorrows to be proud;
For grief is proud, and makes his owner stout.
To me, and to the state of my great grief,
Let kings assemble; for my grief's so great,
That no supporter but the huge firm earth
Can hold it up: here I and sorrow sit;
Here is my throne, bid kings come bow to it.
[*She throws herself on the ground.*

Enter KING JOHN, KING PHILIP, LEWIS, BLANCH, ELINOR, Bastard, AUSTRIA, *and* Attendants.

K. Phi. 'Tis true, fair daughter; and this blessed day,
Ever in France shall be kept festival:
To solemnize this day, the glorious sun
Stays in his course, and plays the alchemist;
Turning, with splendour of his precious eye,
The meagre cloddy earth to glistering gold:
The yearly course, that brings this day about,
Shall never see it but a holiday.

Const. A wicked day, and not a holyday!—— [*Rising.*
What hath this day deserv'd? what hath it done;
That it in golden letters should be set,
Among the high tides, in the calendar?
Nay, rather, turn this day out of the week;
This day of shame, oppression, perjury:
Or if it must stand still, let wives with child
Pray, that their burdens may not fall this day,
Lest that their hopes prodigiously be cross'd;
But on this day, let seamen fear no wreck;
No bargains break, that are not this day made:
This day, all things begun come to ill end;
Yea, faith itself to hollow falsehood change!

K. Phi. By heaven, lady, you shall have no cause
To curse the fair proceedings of this day:
Have I not pawn'd to you my majesty?

Const. You have beguil'd me with a counterfeit,
Resembling majesty; which, being touch'd, and tried,
Proves valueless: You are forsworn, forsworn;
You came in arms to spill mine enemies' blood,
But now in arms you strengthen it with yours;
The grappling vigour and rough frown of war,
Is cold in amity and painted peace,
And our oppression hath made up this league:—
Arm, arm, you heavens, against these perjur'd kings!
A widow cries; be husband to me, heavens!
Let not the hours of this ungodly day
Wear out the day in peace; but, ere sunset,
Set armed discord 'twixt these perjur'd kings!
Hear me, O, hear me!

Aust. Lady Constance, peace.

Const. War! war! no peace! peace is to me a war.
O Lymoges! O Austria! thou dost shame
That bloody spoil: Thou slave, thou wretch, thou coward;
Thou little valiant, great in villany!
Thou ever strong upon the stronger side!
Thou fortune's champion, that does never fight
But when her humorous ladyship is by
To teach thee safety! thou art perjur'd too,
And sooth'st up greatness. What a fool art thou,
A ramping fool: to brag, and stamp, and swear,
Upon my party! Thou cold-blooded slave,
Hast thou not spoke like thunder on my side?
Been sworn my soldier? bidding me depend
Upon thy stars, thy fortune, and thy strength?
And dost thou now fall over to my foes?
Thou wear a lion's hide! doff it for shame,
And hang a calf's-skin on those recreant limbs.

Aust. O, that a man should speak those words to me!

Bast. And hang a calfs-skin on those recreant limbs.

Aust. Thou dar'st not say so, villain, for thy life.

Bast. And hang a calf's-skin on those recreant limbs.

K. John. We like not this; thou dost forget thyself.

Enter PANDULPH.

K. Phi. Here comes the holy legate of the pope.

Pand. Hail, you anointed deputies of heaven!—
To thee, King John, my holy errand is.
I Pandulph, of fair Milan cardinal,
And from Pope Innocent the legate here,
Do, in his name, religiously demand,
Why thou against the church, our holy mother,
So wilfully dost spurn; and, force perforce,
Keep Stephen Langton, chosen Archbishop
Of Canterbury, from that holy see?
This, in our 'foresaid holy father's name,
Pope Innocent, I do demand of thee.

K. John. What earthly name to interrogatories,
Can task the free breath of a sacred king?
Thou canst not, cardinal, devise a name
So slight, unworthy, and ridiculous,
To charge me to an answer, as the pope.
Tell him this tale; and from the mouth of England,
Add thus much more,—That no Italian priest
Shall tithe or toll in our dominions;
But as we under heaven are supreme head,
So under him, that great supremacy,
Where we do reign, we will alone uphold,
Without the assistance of a mortal hand:
So tell the pope; all reverence set apart,
To him and his usurp'd authority.

K. Phi. Brother of England, you blaspheme in this.

K. John. Though you, and all the kings of Christendom,
Are led so grossly by this meddling priest,
Dreading the curse that money may buy out;
And, by the merit of vile gold, dross, dust,
Purchase corrupted pardon of a man,
Who, in that sale, sells pardon from himself:
Though you, and all the rest, so grossly led,
This juggling witchcraft with revenue cherish:
Yet I, alone, alone do me oppose
Against the pope, and count his friends my foes.

Pand. Then, by the lawful power that I have,
Thou shalt stand curs'd, and excommunicate:
And blessed shall he be, that doth revolt
From his allegiance to an heretick;
And meritorious shall that hand be call'd,
Canonized, and worship'd as a saint,
That takes away by any secret course
Thy hateful life.

Const. O, lawful let it be,
That I have room with Rome to curse a while!
Good father cardinal, cry thou, amen,
To my keen curses; for, without my wrong,
There is no tongue hath power to curse him right.

Pand. There's law and warrant, lady, for my curse.

Const. And for mine too; when law can do no right,
Let it be lawful, that law bar no wrong:
Law cannot give my child his kingdom here;
For he that holds his kingdom, holds the law:
Therefore, since law itself is perfect wrong,
How can the law forbid my tongue to curse?

Pand. Philip of France, on peril of a curse,
Let go the hand of that arch-heretick;
And raise the power of France upon his head,
Unless he do submit himself to Rome.

Eli. Look'st thou pale, France? do not let go thy hand.

Const. Look to that, devil! lest that France repent,
And, by disjoining hands, hell lose a soul.

Aust. King Philip, listen to the cardinal.

Bast. And hang a calf's-skin on his recreant limbs.
Aust. Well, ruffian, I must pocket up these wrongs,
Because——
Bast. Your breeches best may carry them.
K. John. Philip, what say'st thou to the cardinal?
Const. What should he say, but as the cardinal?
Lew. Bethink you, father; for the difference
Is, purchase of a heavy curse from Rome,
Or the light loss of England for a friend:
Forego the easier.
Blanch. That's the curse of Rome.
Const. O Lewis, stand fast; the devil tempts thee here,
In likeness of a new untrimmed bride.
Blanch. The Lady Constance speaks not from her faith,
But from her need.
Const. O, if thou grant my need,
Which only lives but by the death of faith,
That need must needs infer this principle,——
That faith would live again by death of need;
O, then, tread down my need, and faith mounts up;
Keep my need up, and faith is trodden down.
K. John. The king is mov'd, and answers not to this.
Const. O, be remov'd from him, and answer well.
Aust. Do so, King Philip; hang no more in doubt.
Bast. Hang nothing but a calf's-skin, most sweet lout.
K. Phi. I am perplex'd, and know not what to say.
Pand. What canst thou say, but will perplex thee more,
If thou stand excommunicate, and curs'd?
K. Phi. Good reverend father, make my person yours,
And tell me, how you would bestow yourself.
This royal hand and mine are newly knit;
And the conjunction of our inward souls
Married in league, coupled and link'd together
With all religious strength of sacred vows;
The latest breath that gave the sound of words,
Was deep-sworn faith, peace, amity, true love,
Between our kingdoms, and our royal selves;
And even before this truce, but new before,—
No longer than we well could wash our hands,
To clap this royal bargain up of peace,
Heaven knows, they were besmear'd and over-stain'd
With slaughter's pencil; where revenge did paint
The fearful difference of incensed kings:—
And shall these hands, so lately purg'd of blood,
So newly join'd in love, so strong in both,
Unyoke this seizure, and this kind regreet?
Play fast and loose with faith? so jest with heaven,
Make such unconstant children of ourselves,
As now again to snatch our palm from palm;
Unswear faith sworn; and on the marriage bed
Of smiling peace to march a bloody host,
And make a riot on the gentle brow
Of true sincerity? O holy sir,
My reverend father, let it not be so:
Out of your grace, devise, ordain, impose
Some gentle order; and then we shall be bless'd
To do your pleasure, and continue friends.
Pand. All form is formless, order orderless,
Save what is opposite to England's love.
Therefore to arms! be champion of our church!
Or let the church, our mother, breathe her curse,
A mother's curse, on her revolting son.
France, thou may'st hold a serpent by the tongue,
A cased lion by the mortal paw,
A fasting tiger safer by the tooth,
Than keep in peace that hand which thou dost hold.
K. Phi. I may disjoin my hand, but not my faith.
Pand. So mak'st thou faith an enemy to faith;
And, like a civil war, sett'st oath to oath,
Thy tongue against thy tongue. O, let thy vow
First made to heaven, first be to heaven perform'd;
That is, to be the champion of our church!
What since thou swor'st, is sworn against thyself,
And may not be performed by thyself:
For that, which thou hast sworn to do amiss,
Is not amiss when it is truly done;
And being not done, where doing tends to ill,
The truth is then most done not doing it:
The better act of purposes mistook
Is, to mistake again: though indirect,
Yet indirection thereby grows direct,
And falsehood falsehood cures; as fire cools fire,
Within the scorched veins of one new burn'd.
It is religion, that doth make vows kept;
But thou hast sworn against religion;
By what thou swear'st, against the thing thou swear'st;
And mak'st an oath the surety for thy truth
Against an oath: The truth thou art unsure
To swear, swear only not to be forsworn;
Else, what a mockery should it be to swear?
But thou dost swear only to be forsworn:
And most forsworn, to keep what thou dost swear.
Therefore, thy latter vows, against thy first,
Is in thyself rebellion to thyself:
And better conquest never canst thou make,
Than arm thy constant and thy nobler parts
Against those giddy loose suggestions:
Upon which better part our prayers come in,
If thou vouchsafe them: but, if not, then know,
The peril of our curses light on thee;
So heavy, as thou shalt not shake them off,
But, in despair, die under their black weight.
Aust. Rebellion! flat rebellion!
Bast. Will't not be?
Will not a calf-skin stop that mouth of thine?
Lew. Father, to arms!
Blanch. Upon thy wedding day?
Against the blood that thou hast married?
What, shall our feast be kept with slaughter'd men?
Shall braying trumpets, and loud churlish drums,—
Clamours of hell,—be measures to our pomp?
O husband, hear me!—ah, alack! how new
Is husband in my mouth!—even for that name,
Which till this time my tongue did ne'er pronounce,
Upon my knee I beg, go not to arms
Against mine uncle.
Const. O, upon my knee,
Made hard with kneeling, I do pray to thee,
Thou virtuous Dauphin, alter not the doom
Fore-thought by heaven.
Blanch. Now shall I see thy love; What motive may
Be stronger with thee than the name of wife?
Const. That which upholdeth him that thee upholds,
His honour: O, thine honour, Lewis, thine honour!
Lew. I muse, your majesty doth seem so cold,
When such profound respects do pull you on.
Pand. I will denounce a curse upon his head.
K. Phi. Thou shalt not need:—England, I'll fall from thee.
Const. O fair return of banish'd majesty!
Eli. O foul revolt of French inconstancy!
K. John. France, thou shalt rue this hour within this hour.
Bast. Old time the clock-setter, that bald sexton, time,
Is it as he will? well then, France shall rue.
Blanch. The sun's o'ercast with blood: Fair day, adieu!

Which is the side that I must go withal?
I am with both: each army hath a hand;
And, in their rage, I having hold of both,
They whirl asunder, and dismember me.
Husband, I cannot pray that thou may'st win;
Uncle, I needs must pray that thou may'st lose;
Father, I may not wish the fortune thine;
Grandam, I will not wish thy wishes thrive:
Whoever wins, on that side shall I lose;
Assured loss, before the match be play'd.

Lew. Lady, with me; with me thy fortune lies.

Blanch. There where my fortune lives, there my life dies.

K. John. Cousin, go draw our puissance together,— [*Exit* Bastard.
France, I am burn'd up with inflaming wrath;
A rage, whose heat hath this condition,
That nothing can allay, nothing but blood,
The blood, and dearest valu'd blood, of France.

K. Phi. Thy rage shall burn thee up, and thou shalt turn
To ashes, ere our blood shall quench that fire:
Look to thyself, thou art in jeopardy.

K. John. No more than he that threats.—To arms let's hie! [*Exeunt.*

SCENE II. *The same. Plains near* Angiers.

Alarums; Excursions. Enter the Bastard, *with* AUSTRIA'S *Head.*

Bast. Now, by my life, this day grows wondrous hot;
Some airy devil hovers in the sky,
And pours down mischief. Austria's head, lie there:
While Philip breathes.

Enter KING JOHN, ARTHUR, *and* HUBERT.

K. John. Hubert, keep this boy:—Philip, make up:
My mother is assailed in our tent,
And ta'en, I fear.

Bast. My lord, I rescu'd her;
Her highness is in safety, fear you not:
But on, my liege: for very little pains
Will bring this labour to an happy end.
[*Exeunt.*

SCENE III. *The same.*

Alarums; Excursions; Retreat. Enter KING JOHN, ELINOR, ARTHUR, *the* Bastard, HUBERT, *and* LORDS.

K. John. So shall it be; your grace shall stay behind, [*To* ELINOR.
So strongly guarded.—Cousin, look not sad:
[*To* ARTHUR.
Thy grandam loves thee, and thy uncle will
As dear be to thee as thy father was.

Arth. O, this will make my mother die with grief.

K. John. Cousin [*To the* Bastard], away for England; haste before:
And, ere our coming, see thou shake the bags
Of hoarding abbots: imprisoned angels
Set thou at liberty: the fat ribs of peace
Must by the hungry now be fed upon:
Use our commission in his utmost force.

Bast. Bell, book, and candle shall not drive me back;
When gold and silver becks me to come on.
I leave your highness:—Grandam, I will pray
(If ever I remember to be holy)
For your fair safety: so I kiss your hand.

Eli. Farewell, my gentle cousin.

K. John. Coz, farewell.
[*Exit* Bastard.

Eli. Come hither, little kinsman; hark, a word.
[*She takes* ARTHUR *aside.*

K. John. Come hither, Hubert. O my gentle Hubert,
We owe thee much; within this wall of flesh
There is a soul counts thee her creditor,
And with advantage means to pay thy love:
And, my good friend, thy voluntary oath
Lives in this bosom, dearly cherished.
Give me thy hand. I had a thing to say,—
But I will fit it with some better time.
By heaven, Hubert, I am almost asham'd
To say what good respect I have of thee.

Hub. I am much bounden to your majesty.

K. John. Good friend, thou hast no cause to say so yet:
But thou shalt have; and creep time ne'er so slow,
Yet it shall come, for me to do thee good.
I had a thing to say,—But let it go:
The sun is in the heaven, and the proud day,
Attended with the pleasures of the world,
Is all too wanton, and too full of gawds,
To give me audience:—If the midnight bell
Did with his iron tongue, and brazen mouth,
Sound one unto the drowsy race of night;
If this same were a churchyard where we stand,
And thou possessed with a thousand wrongs;
Or if that surly spirit, melancholy,
Had bak'd thy blood, and made it heavy, thick,
(Which, else, runs tickling up and down the veins,
Making that idiot, laughter, keep men's eyes,
And strain their cheeks to idle merriment,
A passion hateful to my purposes);
Or if that thou could'st see me without eyes,
Hear me without thine ears, and make reply
Without a tongue, using conceit alone,
Without eyes, ears, and harmful sound of words;
Then, in despite of brooded watchful day,
I would into thy bosom pour my thoughts:
But ah, I will not:—Yet I love thee well;
And, by my troth, I think thou lov'st me well.

Hub. So well, that what you bid me undertake,
Though that my death were adjunct to my act,
By heaven, I'd do't.

K. John. Do not I know, thou would'st?
Good Hubert, Hubert, Hubert, throw thine eye
On yon young boy: I'll tell thee what, my friend,
He is a very serpent in my way;
And, wheresoe'er this foot of mine doth tread,
He lies before me: Dost thou understand me?
Thou art his keeper.

Hub. And I will keep him so,
That he shall not offend your majesty.

K. John. Death.

Hub. My lord?

K. John. A grave.

Hub. He shall not live.

K. John. Enough.
I could be merry now: Hubert, I love thee;
Well, I'll not say what I intend for thee;
Remember.——Madam, fare you well:
I'll send those powers o'er to your majesty.

Eli. My blessing go with thee!

K. John. For England, cousin:
Hubert shall be your man, attend on you
With all true duty.—On toward Calais, oh!
[*Exeunt.*

SCENE IV. *The same. The* French King's *Tent.*

Enter KING PHILIP, LEWIS, PANDULPH, *and* Attendants.

K. Phi. So, by a roaring tempest on the flood,
A whole armado of convicted sail
Is scatter'd and disjoin'd from fellowship.

Pand. Courage and comfort! all shall yet go well.

K. Phi. What can go well, when we have run so ill?
Are we not beaten? Is not Angiers lost?
Arthur ta'en prisoner? divers dear friends slain?
And bloody England into England gone,
O'erbearing interruption, spite of France?

Lew. What he hath won, that hath he fortified:
So hot a speed with such advice dispos'd,
Such temperate order in so fierce a cause,
Doth want example; Who hath read, or heard,
Of any kindred action like to this?

K. Phi. Well could I bear that England had this praise,
So we could find some pattern of our shame.

Enter CONSTANCE.

Look, who comes here! a grave unto a soul;
Holding the eternal spirit, against her will,
In the vile prison of afflicted breath:
I pr'ythee, lady, go away with me.

Const. Lo, now! now see the issue of your peace!

K. Phi. Patience, good lady! comfort, gentle Constance!

Const. No, I defy all counsel, all redress,
But that which ends all counsel, true redress,
Death, death:—O amiable lovely death!
Thou odoriferous stench! sound rottenness!
Arise forth from the couch of lasting night,
Thou hate and terror to prosperity,
And I will kiss thy detestable bones;
And put my eyeballs in thy vaulty brows;
And ring these fingers with thy household worms;
And stop this gap of breath with fulsome dust,
And be a carrion monster like thyself:
Come, grin on me; and I will think thou smil'st,
And buss thee as thy wife! Misery's love,
O, come to me!

K. Phi. O fair affliction, peace.

Const. No, no, I will not, having breath to cry:—
O, that my tongue were in the thunder's mouth!
Then with a passion would I shake the world
And rouse from sleep that fell anatomy,
Which cannot hear a lady's feeble voice,
Which scorns a modern invocation.

Pand. Lady, you utter madness, and not sorrow.

Const. Thou art not holy to belie me so;
I am not mad: this hair I tear is mine;
My name is Constance: I was Geffrey's wife;
Young Arthur is my son, and he is lost:
I am not mad:—I would to heaven, I were!
For then, 'tis like I should forget myself:
O, if I could, what grief should I forget!—
Preach some philosophy to make me mad,
And thou shalt be canoniz'd, cardinal:
For, being not mad, but sensible of grief,
My reasonable part produces reason
How I may be deliver'd of these woes,
And teaches me to kill or hang myself:
If I were mad, I should forget my son;
Or madly think, a babe of clouts were he:
I am not mad; too well, too well I feel
The different plague of each calamity.

K. Phi. Bind up those tresses; O, what love I note
In the fair multitude of those her hairs!
Where but by chance a silver drop hath fallen,
Even to that drop ten thousand wiry friends
Do glew themselves in sociable grief;
Like true, inseparable, faithful loves,
Sticking together in calamity.

Const. To England, if you will.

K. Phi. Bind up your hairs.

Const. Yes, that I will; and wherefore will I do it?
I tore them from their bonds; and cried aloud,
O that these hands could so redeem my son,
As they have given these hairs their liberty!
But now I envy at their liberty,
And will again commit them to their bonds,
Because my poor child is a prisoner.——
And, father cardinal, I have heard you say,
That we shall see and know our friends in heaven;
If that be true, I shall see my boy again;
For, since the birth of Cain, the first male child,
To him that did but yesterday suspire,
There was not such a gracious creature born.
But now will canker sorrow eat my bud,
And chase the native beauty from his cheek,
And he will look as hollow as a ghost;
As dim and meagre as an ague's fit;
And so he'll die; and, rising so again,
When I shall meet him in the court of heaven
I shall not know him: therefore never, never
Must I behold my pretty Arthur more.

Pand. You hold too heinous a respect of grief.

Const. He talks to me, that never had a son.

K. Phi. You are as fond of grief, as of your child.

Const. Grief fills the room up of my absent child,
Lies in his bed, walks up and down with me;
Puts on his pretty looks, repeats his words,
Remembers me of all his gracious parts,
Stuffs out his vacant garments with his form;
Then, have I reason to be fond of grief.
Fare you well: had you such a loss as I,
I could give better comfort than you do.—
I will not keep this form upon my head,
[*Tearing off her head-dress.*
When there is such disorder in my wit.
O lord, my boy, my Arthur, my fair son!
My life, my joy, my food, my all the world!
My widow-comfort, and my sorrow's cure!
[*Exit.*

K. Phi. I fear some outrage, and I'll follow her.
[*Exit.*

Lew. There's nothing in this world can make me joy;
Life is as tedious as a twice-told tale,
Vexing the dull ear of a drowsy man;
And bitter shame hath spoil'd the sweet world's taste,
That it yields nought, but shame, and bitterness.

Pand. Before the curing of a strong disease,
Even in the instant of repair and health,
The fit is strongest; evils, that take leave,
On their departure most of all show evil:
What have you lost by losing of this day?

Lew. All days of glory, joy, and happiness.

Pand. If you had won it, certainly, you had.
No, no: when fortune means to men most good,
She looks upon them with a threatening eye.
'Tis strange, to think how much King John hath lost
In this which he accounts so clearly won:
Are not you griev'd, that Arthur is his prisoner?

Lew. As heartily, as he is glad he hath him.

Pand. Your mind is all as youthful as your blood.
Now hear me speak, with a prophetic spirit;
For even the breath of what I mean to speak
Shall blow each dust, each straw, each little rub,
Out of the path which shall directly lead
Thy foot to England's throne; and, therefore, mark.
John hath seiz'd Arthur; and it cannot be,
That, whiles warm life plays in that infant's veins,
The misplac'd John should entertain an hour,
One minute, nay, one quiet breath of rest:
A sceptre, snatch'd with an unruly hand,
Must be as boisterously maintain'd as gain'd:
And he, that stands upon a slippery place,
Makes nice of no vile hold to stay him up:
That John may stand, then Arthur needs must fall;
So be it, for it cannot be but so.

Lew. But what shall I gain by young Arthur's fall?

Pand. You, in the right of Lady Blanch your wife,
May then make all the claim that Arthur did.

Lew. And lose it, life and all, as Arthur did.

Pand. How green are you, and fresh in this old world!
John lays you plots; the times conspire with you;
For he, that steeps his safety in true blood,
Shall find but bloody safety, and untrue.
This act, so evilly born, shall cool the hearts
Of all his people, and freeze up their zeal;

That none so small advantage shall step forth,
To check his reign, but they will cherish it:
No natural exhalation in the sky,
No scape of nature, no distemper'd day,
No common wind, no customed event,
But they will pluck away his natural cause,
And call them meteors, prodigies, and signs,
Abortives, presages, and tongues of heaven,
Plainly denouncing vengeance upon John.

Lew. May be, he will not touch young Arthur's life,
But hold himself safe in his prisonment.

Pand. O, sir, when he shall hear of your approach,
If that young Arthur be not gone already,
Even at that news he dies: and then the hearts
Of all his people shall revolt from him,
And kiss the lips of unacquainted change;
And pick strong matter of revolt, and wrath,
Out of the bloody fingers' ends of John.
Methinks, I see this hurly all on foot;
And, O, what better matter breeds for you,
Than I have nam'd!—The bastard Faulconbridge
Is now in England, ransacking the church,
Offending charity: If but a dozen French
Were there in arms, they would be as a call
To train ten thousand English to their side;
Or, as a little snow, tumbled about,
Anon becomes a mountain. O noble Dauphin,
Go with me to the king: 'Tis wonderful,
What may be wrought out of their discontent:
Now that their souls are topfull of offence,
For England go; I will whet on the king.

Lew. Strong reasons make strong actions; Let us go;
If you say, ay, the king will not say, no. [*Exeunt.*

ACT IV.

SCENE I. Northampton. *A Room in the Castle.*

Enter HUBERT *and two* Attendants.

Hub. Heat me these irons hot: and look thou stand
Within the arras: when I strike my foot
Upon the bosom of the ground, rush forth:
And bind the boy, which you shall find with me,
Fast to the chair: be heedful: hence, and watch.

1 *Attend.* I hope, your warrant will bear out the deed.

Hub. Uncleanly scruples! Fear not you: look to't.— [*Exeunt* Attendants.
Young lad, come forth; I have to say with you.

Enter ARTHUR.

Arth. Good morrow, Hubert.

Hub. Good morrow, little prince.

Arth. As little prince (having so great a title
To be more prince), as may be.—You are sad.

Hub. Indeed, I have been merrier.

Arth. Mercy on me!
Methinks nobody should be sad but I:
Yet, I remember, when I was in France,
Young gentlemen would be as sad as night,
Only for wantonness. By my christendom,
So I were out of prison, and kept sheep,
I should be as merry as the day is long;
And so I would be here, but that I doubt
My uncle practises more harm to me:
He is afraid of me, and I of him:
Is it my fault that I was Geffrey's son?
No, indeed, is't not; And I would to heaven,
I were your son, so you would love me, Hubert.

Hub. If I talk to him, with his innocent prate
He will awake my mercy, which lies dead:
Therefore I will be sudden, and despatch. [*Aside.*

Arth. Are you sick, Hubert? you look pale to-day:
In sooth, I would you were a little sick;
That I might sit all night, and watch with you:
I warrant, I love you more than you do me.

Hub. His words do take possession of my bosom.—
Read here, young Arthur. [*Showing a paper.*]
How now, foolish rheum! [*Aside.*
Turning dispiteous torture out of door!
I must be brief, lest resolution drop
Out at mine eyes, in tender womanish tears.—
Can you not read it? is it not fair writ?

Arth. Too fairly, Hubert, for so foul effect:
Must you with hot irons burn out both mine eyes?

Hub. Young boy, I must.

Arth. And will you?

Hub. And I will.

Arth. Have you the heart? When your head did but ake,
I knit my handkerchief about your brows
(The best I had, a princess wrought it me),
And I did never ask it you again:
And with my hand at midnight held your head;
And, like the watchful minutes to the hour,
Still and anon cheer'd up the heavy time:
Saying, What lack you? and, Where lies your grief?
Or, What good love may I perform for you?
Many a poor man's son would have lain still,
And ne'er have spoke a loving word to you;
But you at your sick service had a prince.
Nay, you may think my love was crafty love,
And call it cunning; Do, an if you will:
If heaven be pleas'd that you must use me ill,
Why, then you must.—Will you put out mine eyes?
These eyes, that never did, nor never shall,
So much as frown on you?

Hub. I have sworn to do it;
And with hot irons must I burn them out.

Arth. Ah, none, but in this iron age, would do it!
The iron of itself, though heat red-hot,
Approaching near these eyes, would drink my tears,
And quench his fiery indignation
Even in the matter of mine innocence:
Nay, after that, consume away in rust,
But for containing fire to harm mine eye.
Are you more stubborn-hard than hammer'd iron?
An if an angel should have come to me,
And told me, Hubert should put out mine eyes,
I would not have believ'd him; no tongue, but Hubert's.

Hub. Come forth. [*Stamps.*

Re-enter Attendants, *with Cords, Irons, &c.*

Do as I bid you do.

Arth. O, save me, Hubert, save me; my eyes are out,
Even with the fierce looks of these bloody men.

Hub. Give me the iron, I say, and bind him here.

Arth. Alas! what need you be so boisterous rough?
I will not struggle, I will stand stone still.
For heaven's sake, Hubert, let me not be bound!
Nay, hear me, Hubert! drive these men away,
And I will sit as quiet as a lamb;
I will not stir, nor wince, nor speak a word,
Nor look upon the iron angerly:
Thrust but these men away, and I'll forgive you,
Whatever torment you do put me to.

Hub. Go, stand within; let me alone with him.

1 *Attend.* I am best pleas'd to be from such a deed. [*Exeunt* Attendants.

Arth. Alas! I then have chid away my friend;
He hath a stern look, but a gentle heart;—
Let him come back, that his compassion may
Give life to yours.

Hub. Come, boy, prepare yourself.

Arth. Is there no remedy?
Hub. None, but to lose your eyes.
Arth. O heaven!—that there were but a mote in yours,
A grain, a dust, a gnat, a wand'ring hair,
Any annoyance in that precious sense!
Then, feeling what small things are boist'rous there
Your vile intent must needs seem horrible.
Hub. Is this your promise? go to, hold your tongue.
Arth. Hubert, the utterance of a brace of tongues
Must needs want pleading for a pair of eyes;
Let me not hold my tongue; let me not, Hubert!
Or, Hubert, if you will, cut out my tongue,
So I may keep mine eyes: O, spare mine eyes;
Though to no use, but still to look on you?
Lo, by my troth, the instrument is cold,
And would not harm me.
Hub. I can heat it, boy.
Arth. No, in good sooth; the fire is dead with grief,
Being create for comfort, to be us'd
In undeserved extremes: See else yourself;
There is no malice in this burning coal;
The breath of heaven hath blown his spirit out,
And strew'd repentant ashes on his head.
Hub. But with my breath I can revive it, boy.
Arth. And if you do, you will but make it blush,
And glow with shame of your proceedings, Hubert:
Nay, it, perchance, will sparkle in your eyes;
And, like a dog that is compell'd to fight,
Snatch at his master that doth tarre him on.
All things, that you should use to do me wrong,
Deny their office: only you do lack
That mercy, which fierce fire, and iron, extends,
Creatures of note for mercy-lacking uses.
Hub. Well, see to live; I will not touch thine eyes
For all the treasure that thine uncle owes:
Yet am I sworn, and I did purpose, boy,
With this same very iron to burn them out.
Arth. O, now you look like Hubert! all this while
You were disguised.
Hub. Peace: no more. Adieu:
Your uncle must not know but you are dead:
I'll fill these dogged spies with false reports.
And, pretty child, sleep doubtless, and secure,
That Hubert, for the wealth of all the world,
Will not offend thee.
Arth. O heaven!—I thank you, Hubert.
Hub. Silence; no more: Go closely in with me;
Much danger do I undergo for thee. [*Exeunt.*

SCENE II.

The same. A Room of State in the Palace.

Enter KING JOHN, *crowned;* PEMBROKE, SALISBURY, *and other* Lords. *The* King *takes his State.*

K. John. Here once again we sit, once again crown'd,
And look'd upon, I hope, with cheerful eyes.
Pem. This once again, but that your highness pleas'd,
Was once superfluous: you were crown'd before,
And that high royalty was ne'er pluck'd off;
The faiths of men ne'er stained with revolt;
Fresh expectation troubled not the land,
With any long'd-for change, or better state.
Sal. Therefore, to be possess'd with double pomp,
To guard a title that was rich before,
To gild refined gold, to paint the lily,
To throw a perfume on the violet,
To smooth the ice, or add another hue
Unto the rainbow, or with taper-light
To seek the beauteous eye of heaven to garnish,
Is wasteful, and ridiculous excess.
Pem. But that your royal pleasure must be done,
This act is as an ancient tale new told;
And, in the last repeating, troublesome,
Being urged at a time unseasonable.
Sal. In this, the antique and well noted face
Of plain old form is much disfigured:
And, like a shifted wind unto a sail,
It makes the course of thoughts to fetch about:
Startles and frights consideration;
Makes sound opinion sick, and truth suspected,
For putting on so new a fashion'd robe.
Pem. When workmen strive to do better than well,
They do confound their skill in covetousness:
And, oftentimes, excusing of a fault,
Doth make the fault the worse by the excuse;
As patches, set upon a little breach,
Discredit more in hiding of the fault,
Than did the fault before it was so patch'd.
Sal. To this effect, before you were new-crown'd,
We breath'd our counsel: but it pleas'd your highness
To overbear it; and we are all well pleas'd;
Since all and every part of what we would,
Doth make a stand at what your highness will.
K. John. Some reasons of this double coronation
I have possess'd you with, and think them strong;
And more, more strong (when lesser is my fear),
I shall indue you with: Mean time, but ask
What you would have reform'd, that is not well;
And well shall you perceive, how willingly
I will both hear and grant you your requests.
Pem. Then I (as one that am the tongue of these,
To sound the purposes of all their hearts),
Both for myself and them (but, chief of all,
Your safety, for the which myself and them
Bend their best studies), heartily request
The enfranchisement of Arthur; whose restraint
Doth move the murmuring lips of discontent
To break into this dangerous argument,—
If, what in rest you have, in right you hold,
Why then your fears (which, as they say, attend
The steps of wrong), should move you to mew up
Your tender kinsman, and to choke his days
With barbarous ignorance, and deny his youth
The rich advantage of good exercise?
That the time's enemies may not have this
To grace occasions, let it be our suit,
That you have bid us ask his liberty;
Which for our goods we do no further ask,
Than whereupon our weal, on you depending,
Counts it your weal, he have his liberty.
K. John. Let it be so; I do commit his youth

Enter HUBERT.

To your direction.—Hubert, what news with you?
Pem. This is the man should do the bloody deed;
He show'd his warrant to a friend of mine:
The image of a wicked heinous fault
Lives in his eye; that close aspect of his
Does show the mood of a much troubled breast;
And I do fearfully believe, 'tis done,
What we so fear'd he had a charge to do.
Sal. The colour of the king doth come and go,
Between his purpose and his conscience,
Like heralds 'twixt two dreadful battles set:
His passion is so ripe, it needs must break.
Pem. And when it breaks, I fear, will issue thence
The foul corruption of a sweet child's death.
K. John. We cannot hold mortality's strong hand:—
Good lords, although my will to give is living,
The suit which you demand is gone and dead:
He tells us, Arthur is deceas'd to-night.

Sal. Indeed, we fear'd his sickness was past cure.
Pem. Indeed, we heard how near his death he was,
Before the child himself felt he was sick:
This must be answer'd, either here, or hence.
K. John. Why do you bend such solemn brows on me?
Think you, I bear the shears of destiny?
Have I commandment on the pulse of life?
Sal. It is apparent foul-play; and 'tis shame,
That greatness should so grossly offer it:
So thrive it in your game! and so farewell.
Pem. Stay yet, Lord Salisbury; I'll go with thee,
And find the inheritance of this poor child,
His little kingdom of a forced grave.
That blood, which ow'd the breadth of all this isle,
Three foot of it doth hold; Bad world the while!
This must not be thus borne: this will break out
To all our sorrows, and ere long, I doubt.
[*Exeunt* Lords.
K. John. They burn in indignation; I repent;
There is no sure foundation set on blood;
No certain life achiev'd by others' death.——

Enter a Messenger.

A fearful eye thou hast; Where is that blood,
That I have seen inhabit in those cheeks?
So foul a sky clears not without a storm:
Pour down thy weather:—How goes all in France?
Mess. From France to England.—Never such a power
For any foreign preparation,
Was levied in the body of a land!
The copy of your speed is learn'd by them;
For, when you should be told they do prepare,
The tidings come, that they are all arriv'd.
K. John. O, where hath our intelligence been drunk?
Where hath it slept? Where is my mother's care?
That such an army could be drawn in France,
And she not hear of it?
Mess. My liege, her ear
Is stopp'd with dust; the first of April, died
Your noble mother; And, as I hear, my lord,
The Lady Constance in a frenzy died
Three days before; but this from rumour's tongue
I idly heard; if true, or false, I know not.
K. John. Withhold thy speed, dreadful occasion!
O, make a league with me, till I have pleas'd
My discontented peers!—What! mother dead?
How wildly then walks my estate in France!—
Under whose conduct came those powers of France,
That thou for truth giv'st out, are landed here?
Mess. Under the Dauphin.

Enter the Bastard *and* PETER *of* Pomfret.

K. John. Thou hast made me giddy
With these ill tidings.—Now, what says the world
To your proceedings? do not seek to stuff
My head with more ill news, for it is full.
Bast. But if you be afeard to hear the worst,
Then let the worst, unheard, fall on your head.
K. John. Bear with me, cousin; for I was amaz'd
Under the tide: but now I breathe again
Aloft the flood; and can give audience
To any tongue, speak it of what it will.
Bast. How I have sped among the clergymen,
The sums I have collected shall express.
But, as I travelled hither through the land,
I find the people strangely fantasied;
Possess'd with rumours, full of idle dreams;
Not knowing what they fear, but full of fear;
And here's a prophet, that I brought with me
From forth the streets of Pomfret, whom I found
With many hundreds treading on his heels;
To whom he sung, in rude harsh-sounding rhymes,
That ere the next Ascension-day at noon,
Your highness should deliver up your crown.
K. John. Thou idle dreamer, wherefore didst thou so?
Peter. Foreknowing that the truth will fall out so.
K. John. Hubert, away with him; imprison him;
And on that day at noon, whereon, he says,
I shall yield up my crown, let him be hang'd:
Deliver him to safety, and return,
For I must use thee.—O my gentle cousin,
[*Exit* HUBERT *with* PETER.
Hear'st thou the news abroad, who are arriv'd?
Bast. The French, my lord; men's mouths are full of it:
Besides, I met Lord Bigot, and Lord Salisbury
(With eyes as red as new-enkindled fire),
And others more, going to seek the grave
Of Arthur, who, they say, is kill'd to-night
On your suggestion.
K. John. Gentle kinsman, go,
And thrust thyself into their companies:
I have a way to win their loves again;
Bring them before me.
Bast. I will seek them out.
K. John. Nay, but make haste; the better foot before.—
O, let me have no subject enemies,
When adverse foreigners affright my towns
With dreadful pomp of stout invasion!
Be Mercury, set feathers to thy heels;
And fly, like thought, from them to me again.
Bast. The spirit of the time shall teach me speed. [*Exit.*
K. John. Spoke like a spriteful noble gentleman.—
Go after him; for he, perhaps, shall need
Some messenger betwixt me and the peers;
And be thou he.
Mess. With all my heart, my liege. [*Exit.*
K. John. My mother dead!

Re-enter HUBERT.

Hub. My lord, they say, five moons were seen to-night:
Four fixed; and the fifth did whirl about
The other four, in wondrous motion.
K. John. Five moons?
Hub. Old men, and beldams, in the streets
Do prophesy upon it dangerously:
Young Arthur's death is common in their mouths:
And when they talk of him, they shake their heads,
And whisper one another in the ear;
And he, that speaks, doth gripe the hearer's wrist;
Whilst he, that hears, makes fearful action,
With wrinkled brows, with nods, with rolling eyes.
I saw a smith stand with his hammer thus,
The whilst his iron did on the anvil cool,
With open mouth swallowing a tailor's news;
Who, with his shears and measure in his hand,
Standing on slippers (which his nimble haste
Had falsely thrust upon contrary feet),
Told of a many thousand warlike French,
That were embattailed and rank'd in Kent:
Another lean unwash'd artificer
Cuts off his tale, and talks of Arthur's death.
K. John. Why seek'st thou to possess me with these fears?
Why urgest thou so oft young Arthur's death?
Thy hand hath murder'd him: I had mighty cause
To wish him dead, but thou hadst none to kill him.
Hub. Had none, my lord! why, did you not provoke me?

K. John. It is the curse of kings to be attended
By slaves, that take their humours for a warrant
To break within the bloody house of life:
And, on the winking of authority,
To understand a law; to know the meaning
Of dangerous majesty, when, perchance, it frowns
More upon humour than advis'd respect.
Hub. Here is your hand and seal for what I did.
K. John. O, when the last account twixt heaven and earth
Is to be made, then shall this hand and seal
Witness against us to damnation:
How oft the sight of means to do ill deeds,
Makes deeds ill done! Hadest thou not been by,
A fellow by the hand of nature mark'd,
Quoted, and sign'd, to do a deed of shame,
This murder had not come into my mind:
But, taking note of thy abhorr'd aspect,
Finding thee fit for bloody villany,
Apt, liable, to be employ'd in danger,
I faintly broke with thee of Arthur's death;
And thou, to be endeared to a king,
Made it no conscience to destroy a prince.
Hub. My lord,——
K. John. Hadst thou but shook thy head, or made a pause,
When I spake darkly what I purposed;
Or turn'd an eye of doubt upon my face,
And bid me tell my tale in express words;
Deep shame had struck me dumb, made me break off,
And those thy fears might have wrought fears in me:
But thou didst understand me by my signs,
And didst in signs again parley with sin;
Yea, without stop, didst let thy heart consent,
And, consequently, thy rude hand to act
The deed, which both our tongues held vile to name.—
Out of my sight, and never see me more!
My nobles leave me; and my state is brav'd,
Even at my gates, with ranks of foreign powers;
Nay, in the body of this fleshly land,
This kingdom, this confine of blood and breath,
Hostility and civil tumult reigns
Between my conscience, and my cousin's death.
Hub. Arm you against your other enemies,
I'll make a peace between your soul and you.
Young Arthur is alive: This hand of mine
Is yet a maiden and an innocent hand,
Not painted with the crimson spots of blood.
Within this bosom never enter'd yet
The dreadful motion of a murd'rous thought,
And you have slander'd nature in my form;
Which, howsoever rude exteriorly,
Is yet the cover of a fairer mind
Than to be butcher of an innocent child.
K. John. Doth Arthur live? O, haste thee to the peers,
Throw this report on their incensed rage,
And make them tame to their obedience!
Forgive the comment that my passion made
Upon thy feature; for my rage was blind,
And foul imaginary eyes of blood
Presented thee more hideous than thou art.
O, answer not; but to my closet bring
The angry lords, with all expedient haste;
I conjure thee but slowly; run more fast.
[*Exeunt.*

SCENE III. *The same. Before the Castle.*

Enter ARTHUR, *on the Walls.*

Arth. The wall is high; and yet will I leap down:—
Good ground, be pitiful, and hurt me not!—
There's few, or none, do know me; if they did,
This ship-boy's semblance hath disguis'd me quite.
I am afraid; and yet I'll venture it.
If I get down, and do not break my limbs,
I'll find a thousand shifts to get away:
As good to die, and go, as die, and stay.
[*Leaps down.*
O me! my uncle's spirit is in these stones——
Heaven take my soul, and England keep my bones! [*Dies.*

Enter PEMBROKE, SALISBURY, *and* BIGOT.

Sal. Lords, I will meet him at Saint Edmund's-Bury;
It is our safety, and we must embrace
This gentle offer of the perilous time.
Pem. Who brought that letter from the cardinal?
Sal. The Count Melun, a noble lord of France;
Whose private with me, of the Dauphin's love,
Is much more general than these lines import.
Big. To-morrow morning let us meet him then.
Sal. Or, rather then set forward: for 'twill be
Two long days' journey, lords, or e'er we meet.

Enter the Bastard.

Bast. Once more to-day well met, distemper'd lords!
The king, by me, requests your presence straight.
Sal. The king hath dispossess'd himself of us;
We will not line his thin bestained cloak
With our pure honours, nor attend the foot
That leaves the print of blood where'er it walks;
Return, and tell him so; we know the worst.
Bast. Whate'er you think, good words, I think, were best.
Sal. Our griefs, and not our manners, reason now.
Bast. But there is little reason in your grief;
Therefore, 'twere reason, you had manners now.
Pem. Sir, sir, impatience hath its privilege.
Bast. 'Tis true: to hurt his master, no man else.
Sal. This is the prison: What is he lies here?
[*Seeing* ARTHUR.
Pem. O death, made proud with pure and princely beauty!
The earth had not a hole to hide this deed.
Sal. Murder, as hating what himself hath done,
Doth lay it open, to urge on revenge.
Big. Or, when he doom'd this beauty to a grave,
Found it too precious-princely for a grave.
Sal. Sir Richard, what think you? Have you beheld,
Or have you read, or heard? or could you think?
Or do you almost think, although you see,
That you do see? could thought, without this object,
Form such another? This is the very top,
The height, the crest, or crest unto the crest,
Of murder's arms; this is the bloodiest shame,
The wildest savag'ry, the vilest stroke,
That ever wall-ey'd wrath, or staring rage,
Presented to the tears of soft remorse.
Pem. All murders past do stand excus'd in this:
And this, so sole, and so unmatchable,
Shall give a holiness, a purity,
To the yet unbegotten sin of times,
And prove a deadly bloodshed but a jest,
Exampled by this heinous spectacle.
Bast. It is a damned and a bloody work;
The graceless action of a heavy hand,
If that it be the work of any hand.
Sal. If that it be the work of any hand?—
We had a kind of light, what would ensue:
It is the shameful work of Hubert's hand;
The practice, and the purpose, of the king:—
From whose obedience I forbid my soul,
Kneeling before this ruin of sweet life,
And breathing to his breathless excellence
The incense of a vow, a holy vow;
Never to taste the pleasures of the world,
Never to be infected with delight,
Nor conversant with ease and idleness,
'Till I have set a glory to this hand,
By giving it the worship of revenge.
Pem. Big. Our souls religiously confirm thy words.

Enter HUBERT.

Hub. Lords, I am hot with haste in seeking you:
Arthur doth live; the king hath sent for you.
Sal. O, he is bold and blushes not at death:—
Avaunt, thou hateful villain, get thee gone!
Hub. I am no villain.
Sal. Must I rob the law? [*Drawing his sword.*
Bast. Your sword is bright, sir; put it up again.
Sal. Not till I sheath it in a murderer's skin.
Hub. Stand back, Lord Salisbury, stand back, I say;
By heaven, I think, my sword's as sharp as yours:
I would not have you, lord, forget yourself,
Nor tempt the danger of my true defence;
Lest I, by marking of your rage, forget
Your worth, your greatness, and nobility.
Big. Out, dunghill! dar'st thou brave a nobleman?
Hub. Not for my life: but yet I dare defend
My innocent life against an emperor.
Sal. Thou art a murderer.
Hub. Do not prove me so;
Yet I am none: Whose tongue soe'er speaks false,
Not truly speaks; who speaks not truly, lies.
Pem. Cut him to pieces.
Bast. Keep the peace, I say.
Sal. Stand by, or I shall gall you, Faulconbridge.
Bast. Thou wert better gall the devil, Salisbury:
If thou but frown on me, or stir thy foot,
Or teach thy hasty spleen to do me shame,
I'll strike thee dead. Put up thy sword betime;
Or I'll so maul you and your toasting-iron,
That you shall think the devil is come from hell.
Big. What wilt thou do, renowned Faulconbridge?
Second a villain, and a murderer?
Hub. Lord Bigot, I am none.
Big. Who kill'd this prince?
Hub. 'Tis not an hour since I left him well:
I honour'd him, I lov'd him; and will weep
My date of life out, for his sweet life's loss.
Sal. Trust not those cunning waters of his eyes,
For villany is not without such rheum;
And he, long traded in it, makes it seem
Like rivers of remorse and innocency.
Away, with me, all you, whose souls abhor
The uncleanly savours of a slaughter-house,
For I am stifled with this smell of sin.
Big. Away, toward Bury, to the Dauphin there!
Pem. There, tell the king, he may inquire us out. [*Exeunt* Lords.
Bast. Here's a good world!—Knew you of this fair work?
Beyond the infinite and boundless reach
Of mercy, if thou didst this deed of death,
Art thou damn'd, Hubert.
Hub. Do but hear me, sir.
Bast. Ha! I'll tell thee what;
Thou art damn'd as black—nay, nothing is so black;
Thou art more deep damn'd than prince Lucifer:
There is not yet so ugly a fiend of hell
As thou shalt be, if thou didst kill this child.
Hub. Upon my soul,——
Bast. If thou didst but consent
To this most cruel act, do but despair,
And, if thou want'st a cord, the smallest thread
That ever spider twisted from her womb
Will serve to strangle thee; a rush will be
A beam to hang thee on; or would'st thou drown thyself,
Put but a little water in a spoon,
And it shall be as all the ocean,
Enough to stifle such a villain up.——
I do suspect thee very grievously.
Hub. If I in act, consent, or sin of thought
Be guilty of the stealing that sweet breath
Which was embounded in this beauteous clay,
Let hell want pains enough to torture me!
I left him well.
Bast. Go, bear him in thine arms.—
I am amaz'd, methinks; and lose my way
Among the thorns and dangers of this world.—
How easy dost thou take all England up!
From forth this morsel of dead royalty,
The life, the right, and truth of all this realm
Is fled to heaven: and England now is left
To tug and scamble, and to part by the teeth
The unowed interest of proud-swelling state.
Now, for the bare-pick'd bone of majesty,
Doth dogged war bristle his angry crest,
And snarleth in the gentle eyes of peace:
Now powers from home, and discontents at home,
Meet in one line; and vast confusion waits
(As doth a raven on a sick-fall'n beast),
The imminent decay of wrested pomp.
Now happy he, whose cloak and cincture can
Hold out this tempest. Bear away that child,
And follow me with speed; I'll to the king:
A thousand businesses are brief in hand,
And heaven itself doth frown upon the land. [*Exeunt.*

ACT V.

SCENE I. *The same. A Room in the Palace.*

Enter KING JOHN, PANDULPH *with the Crown, and* Attendants.

K. John. Thus have I yielded up into your hand
The circle of my glory.
Pand. Take again [*Giving* JOHN *the Crown.*
From this my hand, as holding of the Pope,
Your sovereign greatness and authority.
K. John. Now keep your holy word: go meet the French;
And from his holiness use all your power
To stop their marches, 'fore we are inflam'd.
Our discontented counties do revolt;
Our people quarrel with obedience;
Swearing allegiance, and the love of soul,
To stranger blood, to foreign royalty.
This inundation of mistemper'd humour
Rests by you only to be qualified.
Then pause not; for the present time's so sick,
That present medicine must be minister'd,
Or overthrow incurable ensues.
Pand. It was my breath that blew this tempest up,
Upon your stubborn usage of the Pope:
But, since you are a gentle convertite,
My tongue shall hush again this storm of war,
And make fair weather in your blustering land.
On this Ascension-day, remember well,
Upon your oath of service to the pope,
Go I to make the French lay down their arms. [*Exit.*
K. John. Is this Ascension-day? Did not the prophet
Say, that, before Ascension day at noon,
My crown I should give off? Even so I have:
I did suppose, it should be on constraint;
But, heaven be thank'd, it is but voluntary.

Enter the Bastard.

Bast. All Kent hath yielded; nothing there holds out,
But Dover castle: London hath receiv'd,
Like a kind host, the Dauphin and his powers:
Your nobles will not hear you, but are gone
To offer service to your enemy;
And wild amazement hurries up and down
The little number of your doubtful friends.

K. John. Would not my lords return to me again,
After they heard young Arthur was alive?
Bast. They found him dead, and cast into the streets;
An empty casket, where the jewel of life
By some damn'd hand was robb'd and ta'en away.
K. John. That villain Hubert told me, he did live.
Bast. So, on my soul, he did, for aught he knew.
But wherefore do you droop? why look you sad?
Be great in act, as you have been in thought;
Let not the world see fear, and sad distrust,
Govern the motion of a kingly eye:
Be stirring as the time; be fire with fire;
Threaten the threat'ner, and outface the brow
Of bragging horror: so shall inferior eyes,
That borrow their behaviours from the great,
Grow great by your example, and put on
The dauntless spirit of resolution.
Away; and glister like the god of war,
When he intendeth to become the field:
Show boldness, and aspiring confidence.
What, shall they seek the lion in his den,
And fright him there? and make him tremble there?
O, let it not be said!—Forage, and run
To meet displeasure further from the doors;
And grapple with him, ere he comes so nigh.
K. John. The legate of the pope hath been with me,
And I have made a happy peace with him;
And he hath promised to dismiss the powers
Led by the Dauphin.
Bast. O inglorious league!
Shall we, upon the footing of our land,
Send fair-play orders, and make compromise,
Insinuation, parley, and base truce,
To arms invasive? shall a beardless boy,
A cocker'd silken wanton brave our fields,
And flesh his spirit in a warlike soil,
Mocking the air with colours idly spread,
And find no check? Let us, my liege, to arms:
Perchance, the cardinal cannot make your peace;
Or if he do, let it at least be said,
They saw we had a purpose of defence.
K. John. Have thou the ordering of this present time.
Bast. Away then, with good courage; yet, I know,
Our party may well meet a prouder foe.
[*Exeunt.*

SCENE II. *A Plain, near* St. Edmund's-Bury.

Enter, in arms, LEWIS, SALISBURY, MELUN, PEMBROKE, BIGOT, *and* Soldiers.

Lew. My Lord Melun, let this be copied out,
And keep it safe for our remembrance:
Return the precedent to these lords again;
That having our fair order written down,
Both they, and we, perusing o'er these notes,
May know wherefore we took the sacrament,
And keep our faiths firm and inviolable.
Sal. Upon our sides it never shall be broken.
And, noble Dauphin, albeit we swear
A voluntary zeal, and unurg'd faith,
To your proceedings; yet, believe me, prince,
I am not glad that such a sore of time
Should seek a plaster by contemn'd revolt,
And heal the inveterate canker of one wound,
By making many: O, it grieves my soul,
That I must draw this metal from my side
To be a widow-maker; O, and there,
Where honourable rescue and defence,
Cries out upon the name of Salisbury:
But such is the infection of the time,
That, for the health and physick of our right,
We cannot deal but with the very hand
Of stern injustice and confused wrong.—
And is't not pity, O my grieved friends!
That we, the sons and children of this isle,
Were born to see so sad an hour as this;
Wherein we step after a stranger march
Upon her gentle bosom, and fill up
Her enemies' ranks (I must withdraw and weep
Upon the spot of this enforced cause),
To grace the gentry of a land remote,
And follow unacquainted colours here?
What, here?—O nation, that thou could'st remove!
That Neptune's arms, who clippeth thee about,
Would bear thee from the knowledge of thyself,
And grapple thee unto a Pagan shore;
Where these two Christian armies might combine
The blood of malice in a vein of league,
And not to spend it so unneighbourly!
Lew. A noble temper dost thou show in this;
And great affections, wrestling in thy bosom,
Do make an earthquake of nobility.
O, what a noble combat hast thou fought,
Between compulsion and a brave respect!
Let me wipe off this honourable dew,
That silverly doth progress on thy cheeks:
My heart hath melted at a lady's tears,
Being an ordinary inundation;
But this effusion of such manly drops,
This shower, blown up by tempest of the soul,
Startles mine eyes, and makes me more amaz'd
Than had I seen the vaulty top of heaven
Figur'd quite o'er with burning meteors.
Lift up thy brow, renowned Salisbury,
And with a great heart heave away this storm:
Commend these waters to those baby eyes,
That never saw the giant world enrag'd;
Nor met with fortune other than at feasts,
Full warm of blood, of mirth, of gossiping.
Come, come; for thou shalt thrust thy hand as deep
Into the purse of rich prosperity,
As Lewis himself:—so, nobles, shall you all,
That knit your sinews to the strength of mine.

Enter PANDULPH, *attended.*

And even there, methinks, an angel spake:
Look, where the holy legate comes apace,
To give us warrant from the hand of heaven;
And on our actions set the name of right,
With holy breath.
Pan. Hail, noble prince of France!
The next is this,—King John hath reconcil'd
Himself to Rome; his spirit is come in,
That so stood out against the holy church,
The great metropolis and see of Rome:
Therefore thy threat'ning colours now wind up,
And tame the savage spirit of wild war;
That, like a lion foster'd up at hand,
It may lie gently at the foot of peace,
And be no further harmful than in show.
Lew. Your grace shall pardon me, I will not back;
I am too high-born to be propertied,
To be a secondary at control,
Or useful serving-man, and instrument,
To any sovereign state throughout the world.
Your breath first kindled the dead coal of wars,
Between this chastis'd kingdom and myself,
And brought in matter that should feed this fire;
And now 'tis far too huge to be blown out
With that same weak wind which enkindled it.
You taught me how to know the face of right,
Acquainted me with interest to this land,
Yea, thrust this enterprise into my heart;
And come you now to tell me, John hath made
His peace with Rome? What is that peace to me?
I, by the honour of my marriage-bed,
After young Arthur, claim this land for mine;
And, now it is half-conquer'd, must I back,
Because that John hath made his peace with Rome?

Am I Rome's slave? What penny hath Rome borne,
What men provided, what munition sent,
To underprop this action? is 't not I,
That undergo this charge? Who else but I,
And such as to my claim are liable,
Sweat in this business, and maintain this war?
Have I not heard these islanders shout out,
Vive le roy! as I have bank'd their towns?
Have I not here the best cards for the game,
To win this easy match play'd for a crown?
And shall I now give o'er the yielded set?
No, no, on my soul, it never shall be said.

Pand. You look but on the outside of this work.

Lew. Outside or inside, I will not return
Till my attempt so much be glorified
As to my ample hope was promised
Before I drew this gallant head of war,
And cull'd these fiery spirits from the world,
To outlook conquest, and to win renown
Even in the jaws of danger and of death.— [*Trumpet sounds.*
What lusty trumpet thus doth summon us?

Enter the Bastard, *attended.*

Bast. According to the fair play of the world,
Let me have audience; I am sent to speak;——
My holy lord of Milan, from the king
I come to learn how you have dealt for him;
And, as you answer, I do know the scope
And warrant limited unto my tongue.

Pand. The Dauphin is too wilful-opposite,
And will not temporize with my entreaties;
He flatly says, he'll not lay down his arms.

Bast. By all the blood that ever fury breath'd,
The youth says well: now hear our English king;
For thus his royalty doth speak in me.
He is prepar'd; and reason too, he should:
This apish and unmannerly approach,
This harness'd masque, and unadvis'd revel,
This unhair'd sauciness, and boyish troops,
The king doth smile at; and is well prepar'd
To whip this dwarfish war, these pigmy arms,
From out the circle of his territories.
That hand, which had the strength, even at your door,
To cudgel you, and make you take the hatch;
To dive, like buckets, in concealed wells;
To crouch in litter of your stable planks;
To lie, like pawns, lock'd up in chests and trunks;
To hug with swine; to seek sweet safety out
In vaults and prisons; and to thrill, and shake,
Even at the crying of your nation's crow,
Thinking his voice an armed Englishman;—
Shall that victorious hand be feebled here,
That in your chambers gave you chastisement?
No: Know, the gallant monarch is in arms;
And like an eagle o'er his aiery towers,
To souce annoyance that comes near his nest.—
And you degenerate, you ingrate revolts,
You bloody Neroes, ripping up the womb
Of your dear mother England, blush, for shame:
For your own ladies, and pale visag'd maids,
Like Amazons, come tripping after drums;
Their thimbles into armed gauntlets change,
Their neelds to lances, and their gentle hearts
To fierce and bloody inclination.

Lew. There end thy brave, and turn thy face in peace:
We grant, thou canst outscold us: fare thee well;
We hold our time too precious to be spent
With such a brabbler.

Pand. Give me leave to speak.

Bast. No, I will speak.

Lew. We will attend to neither:—
Strike up the drums; and let the tongue of war
Plead for our interest, and our being here.

Bast. Indeed, your drums being beaten, will cry out;
And so shall you, being beaten: Do but start
An echo with the clamour of thy drum,
And even at hand a drum is ready brac'd,
That shall reverberate all as loud as thine;
Sound but another, and another shall,
As loud as thine, rattle the welkin's ear,
And mock the deep-mouth'd thunder: for at hand
(Not trusting to this halting legate here,
Whom he hath us'd rather for sport than need),
Is warlike John; and in his forehead sits
A bare-ribb'd death, whose office is this day
To feast upon whole thousands of the French.

Lew. Strike up our drums, to find this danger out.

Bast. And thou shalt find it, Dauphin, do not doubt. [*Exeunt.*

SCENE III. *The same. A Field of Battle.*

Alarums. Enter King John *and* Hubert.

K. John. How goes the day with us? O, tell me, Hubert.

Hub. Badly, I fear: How fares your majesty?

K. John. This fever, that hath troubled me so long,
Lies heavy on me: O, my heart is sick!

Enter a Messenger.

Mess. My lord, your valiant kinsman, Faulconbridge,
Desires your majesty to leave the field;
And send him word by me, which way you go.

K. John. Tell him, towards Swinstead, to the abbey there.

Mess. Be of good comfort; for the great supply,
That was expected by the Dauphin here,
Are wreck'd three nights ago on Goodwin Sands.
This news was brought to Richard but even now.
The French fight coldly, and retire themselves.

K. John. Ah me! this tyrant fever burns me up,
And will not let me welcome this good news.——
Set on towards Swinstead; to my litter straight;
Weakness possesseth me, and I am faint. [*Exeunt.*

SCENE IV. *The same. Another Part of the same.*

Enter Salisbury, Pembroke, Bigot, *and Others.*

Sal. I did not think the king so stor'd with friends.

Pem. Up once again; put spirit in the French;
If they miscarry, we miscarry too.

Sal. That misbegotten devil, Faulconbridge,
In spite of spite, alone upholds the day.

Pem. They say, King John, sore sick, hath left the field.

Enter Melun, *wounded, and led by* Soldiers.

Mel. Lead me to the revolts of England here.

Sal. When we were happy we had other names.

Pem. It is the Count Melun.

Sal. Wounded to death.

Mel. Fly, noble English, you are bought and sold;
Unthread the rude eye of rebellion,
And welcome home again discarded faith.
Seek out King John, and fall before his feet:
For, if the French be lords of this loud day,
He means to recompense the pains you take,
By cutting off your heads: Thus hath he sworn,
And I with him, and many more with me,
Upon the altar at Saint Edmund's Bury;
Even on that altar, where we swore to you
Dear amity and everlasting love.

Sal. May this be possible? may this be true?

Mel. Have I not hideous death within my view,
Retaining but a quantity of life;
Which bleeds away, even as a form of wax
Resolveth from his figure 'gainst the fire?
What in the world should make me now deceive,
Since I must lose the use of all deceit?
Why should I then be false: since it is true
That I must die here, and live hence by truth?
I say again, if Lewis do win the day,

He is forsworn, if e'er those eyes of yours
Behold another day break in the east:
But even this night,—whose black contagious breath
Already smokes about the burning crest
Of the old, feeble, and day-wearied sun,—
Even this ill night, your breathing shall expire;
Paying the fine of rated treachery,
Even with a treacherous fine of all your lives,
If Lewis by your assistance win the day.
Commend me to one Hubert, with your king;
The love of him,—and this respect besides,
For that my grandsire was an Englishman,
Awakes my conscience to confess all this.
In lieu whereof, I pray you, bear me hence
From forth the noise and rumour of the field;
Where I may think the remnant of my thoughts
In peace, and part this body and my soul
With contemplation and devout desires.

Sal. We do believe thee,—And beshrew my soul
But I do love the favour and the form
Of this most fair occasion, by the which
We will untread the steps of damned flight;
And, like a bated and retired flood,
Leaving our rankness and irregular course,
Stoop low within those bounds we have o'erlook'd,
And calmly run on in obedience,
Even to our ocean, to our great King John.——
My arm shall give thee help to bear thee hence;
For I do see the cruel pangs of death
Right in thine eye.—Away, my friends! New flight:
And happy newness, that intends old right.
[*Exeunt, leading off* MELUN.

SCENE V. *The same. The* French *Camp.*

Enter LEWIS *and his* Train.

Lew. The sun of heaven, methought, was loath to set;
But stay'd, and made the western welkin blush,
When the English measur'd backward their own ground,
In faint retire: O, bravely came we off,
When with a volley of our needless shot,
After such bloody toil, we bid good night;
And wound our tatter'd colours clearly up.
Last in the field, and almost lords of it!

Enter a Messenger.

Mess. Where is my prince, the Dauphin?
Lew. Here:—What news?
Mess. The Count Melun is slain; the English lords,
By his persuasion, are again fallen off:
And your supply, which you have wish'd so long,
Are cast away, and sunk, on Goodwin Sands.
Lew. Ah, foul shrewd news!—Beshrew thy very heart!
I did not think to be so sad to-night,
As this hath made me.—Who was he, that said,
King John did fly, an hour or two before
The stumbling night did part our weary powers?
Mess. Whoever spoke it, it is true, my lord.
Lew. well; keep good quarter, and good care to-night;
The day shall not be up so soon as I,
To try the fair adventure of to-morrow.
[*Exeunt.*

SCENE VI.

An open Place in the neighbourhood of Swinstead-Abbey.

Enter the Bastard *and* HUBERT, *meeting.*

Hub. Who's there? speak, ho! speak quickly, or I shoot.
Bast. A friend:—What art thou?
Hub. Of the part of England.
Bast. Whither dost thou go?
Hub. What's that to thee? Why may not I demand
Of thine affairs, as well as thou of mine?
Bast. Hubert, I think.
Hub. Thou hast a perfect thought:
I will, upon all hazards, well believe,
Thou art my friend, that know'st my tongue so well:
Who art thou?
Bast. Who thou wilt: an if thou please,
Thou may'st befriend me so much, as to think
I come one way of the Plantagenets.
Hub. Unkind remembrance! thou, and eyeless night,
Have done me shame:—Brave soldier, pardon me,
That any accent, breaking from thy tongue,
Should 'scape the true acquaintance of mine ear.
Bast. Come, come; sans compliment, what news abroad?
Hub. Why, here walk I, in the black brow of night,
To find you out.
Bast. Brief, then; and what's the news?
Hub. O, my sweet sir, news fitting to the night,
Black, fearful, comfortless, and horrible.
Bast. Show me the very wound of this ill news;
I am no woman, I'll not swoon at it.
Hub. The king, I fear, is poison'd by a monk:
I left him almost speechless, and broke out
To acquaint you with this evil; that you might
The better arm you to the sudden time,
Than if you had at leisure known of this.
Bast. How did he take it? who did taste to him?
Hub. A monk, I tell you; a resolved villain,
Whose bowels suddenly burst out: the king
Yet speaks, and, peradventure, may recover.
Bast. Who didst thou leave to tend his majesty?
Hub. Why know you not? the lords are all come back,
And brought prince Henry in their company;
At whose request the king hath pardon'd them,
And they are all about his majesty.
Bast. Withhold thine indignation, mighty heaven,
And tempt us not to bear above our power!——
I'll tell thee, Hubert, half my power this night,
Passing these flats, are taken by the tide,
These Lincoln washes have devoured them;
Myself, well mounted, hardly have escap'd.
Away, before! conduct me to the king;
I doubt, he will be dead, or ere I come.
[*Exeunt.*

SCENE VII. *The Orchard of* Swinstead-Abbey.

Enter PRINCE HENRY, SALISBURY, *and* BIGOT.

P. Hen. It is too late; the life of all his blood
Is touch'd corruptibly; and his pure brain
(Which some suppose the soul's frail dwelling-house),
Doth, by the idle comments that it makes,
Foretell the ending of mortality.

Enter PEMBROKE.

Pem. His highness yet doth speak: and holds belief,
That, being brought into the open air,
It would allay the burning quality
Of that fell poison which assaileth him.
P. Hen. Let him be brought into the orchard here.—
Doth he still rage? [*Exit* BIGOT.
Pem. He is more patient
Than when you left him; even now he sung.
P. Hen. O vanity of sickness! fierce extremes,
In their continuance, will not feel themselves.
Death, having prey'd upon the outward parts,
Leaves them insensible; and his siege is now
Against the mind, the which he pricks and wounds

With many legions of strange fantasies;
Which, in their throng and press to that last hold,
Confound themselves. 'Tis strange, that death should sing.——
I am the cygnet to this pale faint swan,
Who chants a doleful hymn to his own death;
And, from the organ-pipe of frailty, sings
His soul and body to their lasting rest.

Sal. Be of good comfort, prince; for you are born
To set a form upon that indigest
Which he hath left so shapeless and so rude.

Re-enter BIGOT *and* Attendants, *who bring in* KING JOHN *in a Chair.*

K. John. Ay, marry, now my soul hath elbow-room;
It would not out at windows, nor at doors.
There is so hot a summer in my bosom,
That all my bowels crumble up to dust:
I am a scribbled form, drawn with a pen
Upon a parchment; and against this fire
Do I shrink up.

P. Hen. How fares your majesty?

K. John. Poison'd,—ill fare;—dead, forsook, cast off;
And none of you will bid the winter come,
To thrust his icy fingers in my maw;
Nor let my kingdom's rivers take their course
Through my burn'd bosom; nor entreat the north
To make his bleak winds kiss my parched lips,
And comfort me with cold:—I do not ask you much,
I beg cold comfort: and you are so strait,
And so ingrateful, you deny me that.

P. Hen. O, that there were some virtue in my tears,
That might relieve you!

K. John. The salt in them is hot.—
Within me is a hell; and there the poison
Is, as a fiend, confin'd to tyrannize
On unreprievable condemned blood.

Enter the Bastard.

Bast. O, I am scalded with my violent motion,
And spleen of speed to see your majesty.

K. John. O cousin, thou art come to set mine eye:
The tackle of my heart is crack'd and burn'd;
And all the shrouds, wherewith my life should sail,
Are turned to one thread, one little hair:
My heart hath one poor string to stay it by,
Which holds but till thy news be uttered:
And then all this thou seest, is but a clod,
And module of confounded royalty.

Bast. The Dauphin is preparing hitherward:
Where, heaven he knows, how we shall answer him:
For, in a night, the best part of my power,
As I upon advantage did remove,
Were in the washes, all unwarily,
Devoured by the unexpected flood.
[*The* King *dies.*

Sal. You breathe these dead news in as dead an ear.—
My liege! my lord!—But now a king,—now thus.

P. Hen. Even so must I run on, and even so stop.
What surety of the world, what hope, what stay,
When this was now a king, and now is clay!

Bast. Art thou gone so? I do but stay behind,
To do the office for thee of revenge;
And then my soul shall wait on thee to heaven,
As it on earth hath been thy servant still.——
Now, now, you stars, that move in your right spheres,
Where be your powers? Show now your mended faiths:
And instantly return with me again,
To push destruction and perpetual shame
Out of the weak door of our fainting land:
Straight let us seek, or straight we shall be sought,
The Dauphin rages at our very heels.

Sal. It seems, you know not then so much as we;
The cardinal Pandulph is within at rest,
Who half an hour since came from the Dauphin;
And brings from him such offers of our peace
As we with honour and respect may take,
With purpose presently to leave this war.

Bast. He will the rather do it when he sees
Ourselves well sinewed to our defence.

Sal. Nay, it is in a manner done already;
For many carriages he hath despatch'd
To the seaside, and put his cause and quarrel
To the disposing of the cardinal:
With whom yourself, myself, and other lords,
If you think meet, this afternoon will post
To consummate this business happily.

Bast. Let it be so:—And you, my noble prince,
With other princes that may best be spared,
Shall wait upon your father's funeral.

P. Hen. At Worcester must his body e interr'd;
For so he will'd it.

Bast. Thither shall it then.
And happily may your sweet self put on
The lineal state and glory of the land!
To whom, with all submission, on my knee,
I do bequeath my faithful services
And true subjection everlastingly.

Sal. And the like tender of our love we make
To rest without a spot for evermore.

P. Hen. I have a kind soul, that would give you thanks,
And knows not how to do it, but with tears.

Bast. O, let us pay the time but needful woe,
Since it hath been beforehand with our griefs.—
This England never did (nor never shall)
Lie at the proud foot of a conqueror,
But when it first did help to wound itself.
Now these her princes are come home again,
Come the three corners of the world in arms,
And we shall shock them: Nought shall make us rue,
If England to itself do rest but true. [*Exeunt.*

THE LIFE AND DEATH OF
KING RICHARD THE SECOND.

PERSONS REPRESENTED.

KING RICHARD THE SECOND.
EDMUND *of* Langley, Duke of York, } *Uncles to*
JOHN *of* Gaunt, Duke of Lancaster, } *the* King.
HENRY, *surnamed* BOLINGBROKE, Duke of Hereford, *Son to* John of Gaunt; *afterwards* King Henry IV.
Duke of Aumerle, *Son to the* Duke of York.
MOWBRAY, Duke of Norfolk.
Duke of Surrey.
Earl of Salisbury. Earl Berkley.
BUSHY, }
BAGOT, } *Creatures to* King Richard.
GREEN, }
Earl of Northumberland.
HENRY PERCY, *his Son.*
Lord Ross. Lord Willoughby. Lord Fitzwater.
Bishop of Carlisle. Abbot of Westminster.
Lord Marshal; *and another* Lord.
SIR PIERCE of Exton. SIR STEPHEN SCROOP.
Captain *of a Band of* Welshmen.

Queen to King Richard.
Duchess of Gloster.
Duchess of York.
Lady *attending on the* Queen.

Lords, Heralds, Officers, Soldiers, *two* Gardeners, Keeper, Groom, *and other* Attendants.

SCENE—*dispersedly in* England *and* Wales.

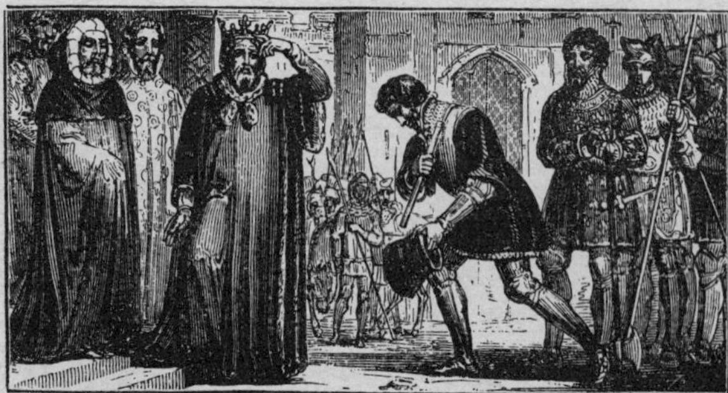

ACT I.

SCENE I. London. *A Room in the Palace.*

Enter KING RICHARD, *attended:* JOHN *of* GAUNT, *and other Nobles with him.*

K. Rich. OLD John of Gaunt, time-honour'd Lancaster,
Hast thou, according to thy oath and band,
Brought hither Henry Hereford thy bold son;
Here to make good the boisterous late appeal,
Which then our leisure would not let us hear,
Against the Duke of Norfolk, Thomas Mowbray?

Gaunt. I have, my liege.

K. Rich. Tell me moreover, hast thou sounded him,
If he appeal the duke on ancient malice;
Or worthily as a good subject should,
On some known ground of treachery in him?

Gaunt. As near as I could sift him on that argument,—
On some apparent danger seen in him,
Aim'd at your highness; no inveterate malice.

K. Rich. Then call them to our presence, face to face,
And frowning brow to brow, ourselves will hear
The accuser, and the accused, freely speak:—
[*Exeunt some* Attendants.
High stomach'd are they both, and full of ire,
In rage deaf as the sea, hasty as fire.

Re-enter Attendants, *with* BOLINGBROKE *and* NORFOLK.

Boling. Many years of happy days befall
My gracious sovereign, my most loving liege!

Nor. Each day still better other's happiness;
Until the heavens, envying earth's good hap,
Add an immortal title to your crown!

K. Rich. We thank you both: yet one but flatters us,
As well appeareth by the cause you come:
Namely, to appeal each other of high treason.—
Cousin of Hereford, what dost thou object
Against the Duke of Norfolk, Thomas Mowbray?

Boling. First, (heaven be the record to my speech!)
In the devotion of a subject's love,
Tendering the precious safety of my prince,
And free from other misbegotten hate,
Come I appellant to this princely presence.—
Now, Thomas Mowbray, do I turn to thee,
And mark my greeting well; for what I speak,
My body shall make good upon this earth,
Or my divine soul answer it in heaven;
Thou art a traitor, and a miscreant;
Too good to be so, and too bad to live:
Since, the more fair and crystal is the sky,
The uglier seem the clouds that in it fly.
Once more, the more to aggravate the note,
With a foul traitor's name stuff I thy throat

And wish (so please my sovereign), ere I move,
What my tongue speaks, my right-drawn sword may prove.

Nor. Let not my cold words here accuse my zeal:
'Tis not the trial of a woman's war,
The bitter clamour of two eager tongues,
Can arbitrate this cause betwixt us twain:
The blood is hot that must be cool'd for this:
Yet can I not of such tame patience boast,
As to be hush'd, and nought at all to say:
First, the fair reverence of your highness curbs me
From giving reins and spurs to my free speech;
Which else would post, until it had return'd
These terms of treason doubled down his throat.
Setting aside his high blood's royalty,
And let him be no kinsman to my liege,
I do defy him, and I spit at him;
Call him—a slanderous coward, and a villain:
Which to maintain, I would allow him odds;
And meet him, where I tied to run a-foot
Even to the frozen ridges of the Alps,
Or any other ground inhabitable
Where ever Englishman durst set his foot.
Mean time, let this defend my loyalty,—
By all my hopes, most falsely doth he lie.

Boling. Pale trembling coward, there I throw my gage,
Disclaiming here the kindred of the king;
And lay aside my high blood's royalty,
Which fear, not reverence, makes thee to except:
If guilty dread hath left thee so much strength,
As to take up mine honour's pawn, then stoop;
By that, and all the rights of knighthood else,
Will I make good against thee, arm to arm,
What I have spoke, or thou canst worse devise.

Nor. I take it up; and, by that sword I swear,
Which gently lay'd my knighthood on my shoulder,
I'll answer thee in any fair degree,
Or chivalrous design of knightly trial;
And, when I mount, alive may I not light,
If I be traitor, or unjustly fight!

K. Rich. What doth our cousin lay to Mowbray's charge?
It must be great, that can inherit us
So much as of a thought of ill in him.

Boling. Look, what I speak my life shall prove it true;—
That Mowbray hath receiv'd eight thousand nobles,
In name of lendings for your highness' soldiers;
The which he hath detain'd for lewd employments,
Like a false traitor, and injurious villain.
Besides I say, and will in battle prove,—
Or here, or elsewhere, to the furthest verge
That ever was survey'd by English eye,—
That all the treasons, for these eighteen years
Complotted and contrived in this land,
Fetch from false Mowbray their first head and spring.
Further I say,—and further will maintain
Upon his bad life, to make all this good,—
That he did plot the duke of Gloster's death;
Suggest his soon-believing adversaries;
And, consequently, like a traitor coward,
Sluic'd out his innocent soul through streams of blood:
Which blood, like sacrificing Abel's, cries,
Even from the tongueless caverns of the earth,
To me for justice, and rough chastisement;
And by the glorious worth of my descent,
This arm shall do it, or this life be spent.

K. Rich. How high a pitch his resolution soars!—
Thomas of Norfolk, what say'st thou to this?

Nor. O, let my sovereign turn away his face,
And bid his ears a little while be deaf,
Till I have told this slander of his blood,
How God, and good men, hate so foul a liar.

K. Rich. Mowbray, impartial are our eyes, and ears:
Were he my brother, nay, my kingdom's heir
(As he is but my father's brother's son),
Now by my sceptre's awe I make a vow,
Such neighbour nearness to our sacred blood
Should nothing privilege him, nor partialize
The unstooping firmness of my upright soul;
He is our subject, Mowbray, so art thou;
Free speech, and fearless, I to thee allow.

Nor. Then, Bolingbroke, as low as to thy heart,
Through the false passage of thy throat, thou liest!
Three parts of that receipt I had for Calais,
Disburs'd I duly to his highness' soldiers:
The other part reserv'd I by consent;
For that my sovereign liege was in my debt,
Upon remainder of a dear account,
Since last I went to France to fetch his queen:
Now swallow down that lie.——For Gloster's death,——
I slew him not; but to my own disgrace,
Neglected my sworn duty in that case.—
For you, my noble lord of Lancaster,
The honourable father to my foe,
Once did I lay in ambush for your life,
A trespass that doth vex my grieved soul:
But, ere I last receiv'd the sacrament,
I did confess it: and exactly begg'd
Your grace's pardon, and, I hope, I had it.
This is my fault: As for the rest appeal'd,
It issues from the rancour of a villain,
A recreant and most degenerate traitor:
Which in myself I boldly will defend;
And interchangeably hurl down my gage
Upon this overweening traitor's foot,
To prove myself a loyal gentleman
Even in the best blood chamber'd in his bosom:
In haste whereof, most heartily I pray
Your highness to assign our trial day.

K. Rich. Wrath-kindled gentlemen, be rul'd by me:
Let's purge this choler without letting blood:
This we prescribe, though no physician;
Deep malice makes too deep incision:
Forget, forgive; conclude, and be agreed;
Our doctors say, this is no time to bleed.—
Good uncle, let this end where it begun;
We'll calm the duke of Norfolk, you your son.

Gaunt. To be a make-peace shall become my age:
Throw down, my son, the duke of Norfolk's gage.

K. Rich. And, Norfolk, throw down his.

Gaunt. When, Harry? when?
Obedience bids, I should not bid again.

K. Rich. Norfolk, throw down; we bid; there is no boot.

Nor. Myself I throw, dread sovereign, at thy foot:
My life thou shalt command, but not my shame:
The one my duty owes; but my fair name
(Despite of death, that lives upon my grave),
To dark dishonour's use thou shalt not have.
I am disgrac'd, impeach'd, and baffled here;
Pierc'd to the soul with slander's venom'd spear;
The which no balm can cure, but his heart-blood
Which breath'd this poison.

K. Rich. Rage must be withstood:
Give me his gage:—Lions make leopards tame.

Nor. Yea, but not change their spots: take but my shame,
And I resign my gage. My dear, dear lord,
The purest treasure mortal times afford,
Is—spotless reputation; that away,
Men are but gilded loam, or painted clay,
A jewel in a ten times barr'd up chest
Is—a bold spirit in a loyal breast.
Mine honour is my life; both grow in one;
Take honour from me, and my life is done:
Then, dear my liege, mine honour let me try;
In that I live, and for that will I die.

K. Rich. Cousin, throw down your gage; do you begin.

Boling. O, God defend my soul from such foul sin!
Shall I seem crest-fallen in my father's sight?
Or with pale beggar-fear impeach my height
Before this outdar'd dastard! Ere my tongue
Shall wound mine honour with such feeble wrong,
Or sound so base a parle, my teeth shall tear
The slavish motive of recanting fear;
And spit it bleeding in his high disgrace,
Where shame doth harbour, even in Mowbray's face. [*Exit* GAUNT.

K. Rich. We were not born to sue, but to command:
Which since we cannot do to make you friends,
Be ready, as your lives shall answer it,
At Coventry, upon Saint Lambert's day;
There shall your swords and lances arbitrate
The swelling difference of your settled hate;
Since we cannot atone you, we shall see
Justice design the victor's chivalry.—
Lord Marshal, command our officers at arms
Be ready to direct these home-alarms. [*Exeunt.*

SCENE II. *The same.*

A Room in the Duke *of* Lancaster's *Palace.*

Enter GAUNT, *and* Duchess *of* Gloster.

Gaunt. Alas! the part I had in Gloster's blood
Doth more solicit me, than your exclaims,
To stir against the butchers of his life.
But since correction lieth in those hands,
Which made the fault that we cannot correct,
Put we our quarrel to the will of heaven;
Who when he sees the hours ripe on earth,
Will rain hot vengeance on offenders' heads.

Duch. Finds brotherhood in thee no sharper spur?
Hath love in thy old blood no living fire?
Edward's seven sons, whereof thyself art one,
Were as seven phials of his sacred blood,
Or seven fair branches springing from one root:
Some of those seven are dried by nature's course,
Some of those branches by the destinies cut:
But Thomas, my dear lord, my life, my Gloster,—
One phial full of Edward's sacred blood,
One flourishing branch of his most royal root,—
Is crack'd, and all the precious liquor spilt;
Is hack'd down, and his summer leaves all faded,
By envy's hand, and murder's bloody axe.
Ah, Gaunt! his blood was thine; that bed, that womb,
That mettle, that self-mould, that fashion'd thee,
Made him a man; and though thou liv'st, and breath'st,
Yet art thou slain in him: thou dost consent
In some large measure to thy father's death,
In that thou seest thy wretched brother die,
Who was the model of thy father's life.
Call it not patience, Gaunt, it is despair:
In suffering thus thy brother to be slaughter'd,
Thou show'st the naked pathway to thy life,
Teaching stern murder how to butcher thee:
That which in mean men we entitle—patience,
Is pale cold cowardice in noble breasts.
What shall I say? to safeguard thine own life,
The best way is—to 'venge my Gloster's death.

Gaunt. Heaven's is the quarrel; for heaven's substitute,
His deputy anointed in his sight,
Hath caus'd his death; the which if wrongfully,
Let heaven revenge; for I may never lift
An angry arm against his minister.

Duch. Where then, alas! may I complain myself?

Gaunt. To heaven, the widow's champion and defence.

Duch. Why then, I will. Farewell, old Gaunt.
Thou go'st to Coventry, there to behold
Our cousin Hereford and fell Mowbray fight:
O, sit my husband's wrongs on Hereford's spear,
That it may enter butcher Mowbray's breast!
Or, if misfortune miss the first career,
Be Mowbray's sins so heavy in his bosom,
That they may break his foaming courser's back,
And throw the rider headlong in the lists,
A caitiff recreant to my cousin Hereford!
Farewell, old Gaunt; thy sometime brother's wife,
With her companion grief must end her life.

Gaunt. Sister, farewell: I must to Coventry:
As much good stay with thee, as go with me!

Duch. Yet one word more;—grief boundeth where it falls,
Not with the empty hollowness, but weight:
I take my leave before I have begun;
For sorrow ends not when it seemeth done.
Commend me to my brother, Edmund York.
Lo, this is all:—Nay, yet depart not so:
Though this be all, do not so quickly go;
I shall remember more. Bid him—O, what?—
With all good speed at Plashy visit me.
Alack, and what shall good old York there see,
But empty lodgings and unfurnish'd walls,
Unpeopled offices, untrodden stones?
And what cheer there for welcome, but my groans?
Therefore commend me; let him not come there,
To seek out sorrow that dwells every where:
Desolate, desolate, will I hence, and die;
The last leave of thee takes my weeping eye. [*Exeunt.*

SCENE III.

Gosford Green, *near* Coventry. *Lists set out, and a Throne.* Heralds, *&c. attending.*

Enter the Lord Marshal, *and* AUMERLE.

Mar. My lord Aumerle, is Harry Hereford arm'd?

Aum. Yea, at all points: and longs to enter in.

Mar. The duke of Norfolk, sprightfully and bold,
Stays but the summons of the appellant's trumpet.

Aum. Why then, the champions are prepar'd, and stay
For nothing but his majesty's approach.

Flourish of Trumpets. Enter KING RICHARD, *who takes his seat on his Throne;* GAUNT, *and several* Noblemen, *who take their places. A Trumpet is sounded, and answered by another Trumpet within. Then enter* NORFOLK *in armour, preceded by a* Herald.

K. Rich. Marshal, demand of yonder champion
The cause of his arrival here in arms:
Ask him his name; and orderly proceed
To swear him in the justice of his cause.

Mar. In God's name, and the king's, say who thou art,
And why thou com'st, thus knightly clad in arms:
Against what man thou com'st, and what thy quarrel:
Speak truly, on thy knighthood, and thy oath;
And so defend thee heaven, and thy valour!

Nor. My name is Thomas Mowbray, duke of Norfolk;
Who hither come engaged by my oath,
(Which heaven defend, a knight should violate!)
Both to defend my loyalty and truth,
To God, my king, and my succeeding issue,
Against the duke of Hereford that appeals me;
And, by the grace of God, and this mine arm,
To prove him, in defending of myself,
A traitor to my God, my king, and me:
And, as I truly fight, defend me heaven! [*He takes his seat.*

Trumpet sounds. Enter BOLINGBROKE, *in armour; preceded by a* Herald.

K. Rich. Marshal, ask yonder knight in arms,
Both who he is, and why he cometh hither

Thus plated in habiliments of war;
And formally according to our law
Depose him in the justice of his cause.

Mar. What is thy name? and wherefore com'st thou hither,
Before King Richard, in his royal lists?
Against whom comest thou; and what's thy quarrel?
Speak like a true knight, so defend thee heaven!

Boling. Harry of Hereford, Lancaster, and Derby,
Am I; who ready here do stand in arms,
To prove, by heaven's grace, and my body's valour,
In lists, on Thomas Mowbray, duke of Norfolk,
That's he's a traitor, foul and dangerous,
To God of heaven, King Richard, and to me;
And, as I truly fight, defend me heaven!

Mar. On pain of death, no person be so bold,
Or daring-hardy, as to touch the lists;
Except the marshal, and such officers
Appointed to direct these fair designs.

Boling. Lord marshal, let me kiss my sovereign's hand,
And bow my knee before his majesty:
For Mowbray, and myself, are like two men
That vow a long and weary pilgrimage;
Then let us take a ceremonious leave,
And loving farewell, of our several friends.

Mar. The appellant in all duty greets your highness,
And craves to kiss your hand, and take his leave.

K. Rich. We will descend, and fold him in our arms.
Cousin of Hereford, as thy cause is right,
So be thy fortune in this royal fight!
Farewell, my blood: which if to-day thou shed,
Lament we may, but not revenge thee dead.

Boling. O, let no noble eye profane a tear
For me, if I be gored with Mowbray's spear;
As confident, as is the falcon's flight
Against a bird, do I with Mowbray fight.——
My loving lord [*To* Lord Marshal], I take my leave of you;—
Of you, my noble cousin, Lord Aumerle;—
Not sick, although I have to do with death;
But lusty, young, and cheerly drawing breath.——
Lo, as at English feasts, so I regreet
The daintiest last, to make the end most sweet;
O thou, the earthly author of my blood,— [*To* GAUNT.
Whose youthful spirit, in me regenerate,
Doth with a twofold vigour lift me up
To reach at victory above my head,—
Add proof unto mine armour with thy prayers;
And with thy blessings steel my lance's point,
That it may enter Mowbray's waxen coat,
And furbish new the name of John of Gaunt,
Even in the lusty 'haviour of his son.

Gaunt. Heaven in thy good cause make thee prosperous!
Be swift like lightning in the execution;
And let thy blows, doubly redoubled,
Fall like amazing thunder on the casque
Of thy adverse pernicious enemy:
Rouse up thy youthful blood, be valiant and live.

Boling. Mine innocency, and Saint George to thrive; [*He takes his seat.*

Nor. [*Rising.*] However heaven, or fortune, cast my lot,
There lives or dies, true to King Richard's [throne,
A loyal, just, and upright gentleman:
Never did captive with a freer heart
Cast off his chains of bondage, and embrace
His golden uncontroll'd enfranchisement,
More than my dancing soul doth celebrate
This feast of battle with mine adversary.—
Most mighty liege,—and my companion peers,—
Take from my mouth the wish of happy years:
As gentle and as jocund, as to jest,
Go I to fight; Truth hath a quiet breast.

K. Rich. Farewell, my lord; securely I espy
Virtue with valour couched in thine eye.——
Order the trial, marshal, and begin.
[*The* King *and the* Lords *return to their seats.*

Mar. Harry of Hereford, Lancaster, and Derby,
Receive thy lance; and God defend the right!

Boling. [*Rising.*] Strong as a tower in hope, I cry—amen.

Mar. Go bear this lance [*To an* Officer] to Thomas duke of Norfolk.

1 *Her.* Harry of Hereford, Lancaster, and Derby,
Stands here for God, his sovereign, and himself,
On pain to be found false and recreant,
To prove the duke of Norfolk, Thomas Mowbray,
A traitor to his God, his king, and him,
And dares him to set forward to the fight.

2 *Her.* Here standeth Thomas Mowbray, duke of Norfolk,
On pain to be found false and recreant,
Both to defend himself, and to approve
Henry of Hereford, Lancaster, and Derby,
To God, his sovereign, and to him, disloyal;
Courageously, and with a free desire,
Attending but the signal to begin.

Mar. Sound, trumpets: and set forward, combatants. [*A Charge sounded.*
Stay, the king hath thrown his warder down.

K. Rich. Let them lay by their helmets and their spears,
And both return back to their chairs again:
Withdraw with us:—and let the trumpets sound,
While we return these dukes what we decree.— [*A long flourish.*
Draw near, [*To the Combatants.*
And list, what with our council we have done.
For that our kingdom's earth should not be soil'd
With that dear blood which it hath foster'd;
And for our eyes do hate the dire aspect
Of civil wounds plough'd up with neighbours' swords;
[And for we think the eagle-winged pride
Of sky-aspiring and ambitious thoughts,
With rival-hating envy, set you on
To wake our peace, which in our country's cradle
Draws the sweet infant breath of gentle sleep;]
Which so rous'd up with boisterous untun'd drums,
With harsh resounding trumpets' dreadful bray,
And grating shock of wrathful iron arms,
Might from our quiet confines fright fair peace,
And make us wade even in our kindred's blood;—
Therefore, we banish you our territories:——
You, cousin Hereford, upon pain of death,
Till twice five summers have enrich'd our fields,
Shall not regreet our fair dominions,
But tread the stranger paths of banishment.

Boling. Your will be done: This must my comfort be,——
That sun, that warms you here, shall shine on me;
And those his golden beams, to you here lent,
Shall point on me, and gild my banishment.

K. Rich. Norfolk, for thee remains a heavier doom,
Which I with some unwillingness pronounce:
The fly-slow hours shall not determinate
The dateless limit of thy dear exile;—
The hopeless word of—never to return
Breathe I against thee, upon pain of life.

Nor. A heavy sentence, my most sovereign liege,
And all unlook'd for from your highness' mouth:
A dearer merit; not so deep a maim
As to be cast forth in the common air,
Have I deserved at your highness' hand.
The language I have learn'd these forty years,
My native English, now I must forego:
And now my tongue's use is to me no more,
Than an unstringed viol or a harp:

Or like a cunning instrument cas'd up,
Or, being open, put into his hands
That knows no touch to tune the harmony.
Within my mouth you have engaol'd my tongue,
Doubly portcullis'd, with my teeth, and lips;
And dull, unfeeling, barren ignorance
Is made my gaoler to attend on me.
I am too old to fawn upon a nurse,
Too far in years, to be a pupil now;
What is thy sentence then, but speechless death,
Which robs my tongue from breathing native breath?

K. Rich. It boots thee not to be compassionate;
After our sentence plaining comes too late.

Nor. Then thus I turn me from my country's light,
To dwell in solemn shades of endless night.
[*Retiring.*

K. Rich. Return again, and take an oath with thee.
Lay on our royal sword your banish'd hands;
Swear by the duty that you owe to heaven
(Our part therein we banish with yourselves),
To keep the oath that we administer:—
You never shall (so help you truth and heaven!)
Embrace each other's love in banishment;
Nor never look upon each other's face;
Nor never write, regreet, nor reconcile
This lowering tempest of your home-bred hate;
Nor never by advised purpose meet,
To plot, contrive, or complot any ill,
'Gainst us, our state, our subjects, or our land.

Boling. I swear.

Nor. And I, to keep all this.

Boling. Norfolk, so far as to mine enemy;—
By this time, had the king permitted us,
One of our souls had wander'd in the air,
Banish'd this frail sepulchre of our flesh,
As now our flesh is banish'd from this land:
Confess thy treasons, ere thou fly the realm;
Since thou hast far to go, bear not along
The clogging burden of a guilty soul.

Nor. No, Bolingbroke; if ever I were traitor,
My name be blotted from the book of life,
And I from heaven banish'd, as from hence!
But what thou art, heaven, thou, and I do know;
And all too soon, I fear, the king shall rue.—
Farewell, my liege:— Now no way can I stray;
Save back to England, all the world's my way.
[*Exit.*

K. Rich. Uncle, even in the glasses of thine eyes
I see thy grieved heart: thy sad aspect
Hath from the number of his banish'd years
Pluck'd four away;—Six frozen winters spent,
Return [*To* BOLING.] with welcome home from banishment.

Boling. How long a time lies in one little word!
Four lagging winters, and four wanton springs,
End in a word; Such is the breath of kings.

Gaunt. I thank my liege, that, in regard of me,
He shortens four years of my son's exile:
But little vantage shall I reap thereby;
For, ere the six years, that he hath to spend,
Can change their moons, and bring their times about,
My oil-dried lamp, and time bewasted light,
Shall be extinct with age, and endless night;
My inch of taper will be burnt and done,
And blindfold death not let me see my son.

K. Rich. Why, uncle, thou hast many years to live.

Gaunt. But not a minute, king, that thou canst give:
Shorten my days thou canst with sullen sorrow,
And pluck nights from me, but not lend a morrow:
Thou canst help time to furrow me with age,
But stop no wrinkle in his pilgrimage;
Thy word is current with him for my death;
But, dead, thy kingdom cannot buy my breath.

K. Rich. Thy son is banish'd upon good advice,
Whereto thy tongue a party verdict gave;
Why at our justice seem'st thou then to lower?

Gaunt. Things sweet to taste, prove in digestion sour.
You urg'd me as a judge; but I had rather,
You would have bid me argue like a father:—
O, had it been a stranger, not my child,
To smooth his fault I should have been more mild:
A partial slander sought I to avoid,
And in the sentence my own life destroy'd.
Alas, I look'd, when some of you should say,
I was too strict, to make mine own away;
But you gave leave to my unwilling tongue,
Against my will, to do myself this wrong.

K. Rich. Cousin, farewell;—and, uncle, bid him so;
Six years we banish him, and he shall go.
[*Flourish. Exeunt* K. RICH. *and* Train.

Aum. Cousin, farewell; what presence must not know,
From where you do remain, let paper show.

Mar. My lord, no leave take I: for I will ride,
As far as land will let me, by your side.

Gaunt. O, to what purpose dost thou hoard thy words,
That thou return'st no greeting to thy friends?

Boling. I have too few to take my leave of you,
When the tongue's office should be prodigal
To breathe the abundant dolour of the heart.

Gaunt. Thy grief is but thy absence for a time.

Boling. Joy absent, grief is present for that time.

Gaunt. What is six winters? they are quickly gone.

Boling. To men in joy; but grief makes one hour ten.

Gaunt. Call it a travel that thou tak'st for pleasure.

Boling. My heart will sigh, when I miscall it so,
Which finds it an enforced pilgrimage.

Gaunt. The sullen passage of thy weary steps
Esteem a foil, wherein thou art to set
The precious jewel of thy home return.

Boling. Nay, rather, every tedious stride I make
Will but remember me, what a deal of world
I wander from the jewels that I love.
Must I not serve a long apprenticehood
To foreign passages; and in the end,
Having my freedom, boast of nothing else,
But that I was a journeyman to grief?

Gaunt. All places that the eye of heaven visits,
Are to a wise man ports and happy havens:
Teach thy necessity to reason thus;
There is no virtue like necessity.
Think not the king did banish thee;
But thou the king: Woe doth the heavier sit,
Where it perceives it is but faintly borne.
Go, say—I sent thee forth to purchase honour,
And not—the king exil'd thee: or suppose,
Devouring pestilence hangs in our air,
And thou art flying to a fresher clime.
Look, what thy soul holds dear, imagine it
To lie that way thou go'st, not whence thou com'st:
Suppose the singing birds, musicians;
The grass whereon thou tread'st, the presence strew'd;
The flowers, fair ladies; and thy steps no more
Than a delightful measure, or a dance:
For gnarling sorrow hath less power to bite
The man that mocks at it, and sets it light.

Boling. O, who can hold a fire in his hand,
By thinking on the frosty Caucasus?
Or cloy the hungry edge of appetite,
By bare imagination of a feast?
Or wallow naked in December snow,
By thinking on fantastick summer's heat?
O, no! the apprehension of the good,
Gives but the greater feeling to the worse:

Fell sorrow's tooth doth never rankle more,
Than when it bites, but lanceth not the sore.

Gaunt. Come, come, my son, I'll bring thee on thy way:
Had I thy youth, and cause, I would not stay.

Boling. Then, England's ground, farewell; sweet soil, adieu;
My mother, and my nurse, that bears me yet!
Where'er I wander, boast of this I can,——
Though banish'd, yet a true-born Englishman. [*Exeunt.*

SCENE IV.

The same. A Room in the King's *Castle.*

Enter KING RICHARD, BAGOT, *and* GREEN; AUMERLE *following.*

K. Rich. We did observe.—Cousin Aumerle,
How far brought you high Hereford on his way?

Aum. I brought high Hereford, if you call him so,
But to the next high way, and there I left him.

K. Rich. And, say, what store of parting tears were shed?

Aum. 'Faith, none by me: except the north-east wind,
Which then blew bitterly against our faces,
Awak'd the sleeping rheum; and so, by chance,
Did grace our hollow parting with a tear.

K. Rich. What said our cousin, when you parted with him?

Aum. Farewell:
And, for my heart disdained that my tongue
Should so profane the word, that taught me craft
To counterfeit oppression of such grief,
That words seem'd buried in my sorrow's grave.
Marry, would the word farewell have lengthen'd hours,
And added years to his short banishment,
He should have had a vòlume of farewells;
But, since it would not, he had none of me.

K. Rich. He is our cousin, cousin; but 'tis doubt,
When time shall call him home from banishment,
Whether our kinsman come to see his friends.
Ourself, and Bushy, Bagot here, and Green,
Observ'd his courtship to the common people:—
How he did seem to dive into their hearts,
With humble and familiar courtesy;
What reverence he did throw away on slaves;
Wooing poor craftsmen, with the craft of smiles,
And patient underbearing of his fortune,
As 'twere, to banish their affects with him.
Off goes his bonnet to an oyster-wench;
A brace of draymen bid—God speed him well,
And had the tribute of his supple knee,
With—*Thanks, my countrymen, my loving friends;*
As were our England in reversion his,
And he our subjects' next degree in hope.

Green. Well, he is gone; and with him go these thoughts.
Now for the rebels, which stand out in Ireland:—
Expedient manage must be made, my liege;
Ere further leisure yield them further means,
For their advantage, and your highness' loss.

K. Rich. We will ourself in person to this war.
And, for our coffers—with too great a court,
And liberal largess—are grown somewhat light,
We are enforc'd to farm our royal realm;
The revenue whereof shall furnish us
For our affairs in hand: If that come short,
Our substitutes at home shall have blank charters;
Whereto, when they shall know what men are rich,
They shall subscribe them for large sums of gold,
And send them after to supply our wants;
For we will make for Ireland presently.

Enter BUSHY.

Bushy, what news?

Bushy. Old John of Gaunt is grievous sick, my lord;
Suddenly taken; and hath sent post-haste,
To entreat your majesty to visit him.

K. Rich. Where lies he

Bushy. At Ely-house.

K. Rich. Now put it, heaven, in his physician's mind,
To help him to his grave immediately!
The lining of his coffers shall make coats
To deck our soldiers for these Irish wars.—
Come, gentlemen, let's all go visit him:
'Pray God, we may make haste, and come too late! [*Exeunt.*

ACT II.

SCENE I. London. *A Room in Ely-house.*

GAUNT *on a Couch; the Duke of* YORK, *and others standing by him.*

Gaunt. Will the king come? that I may breathe my last
In wholesome counsel to his unstaied youth.

York. Vex not yourself, nor strive not with your breath;
For all in vain comes counsel to his ear.

Gaunt. O, but they say, the tongues of dying men
Enforce attention, like deep harmony:
Where words are scarce, they are seldom spent in vain.
For they breathe truth, that breathe their words in pain.
He, that no more must say, is listen'd more
Than they whom youth and ease have taught to glose;
More are men's ends mark'd, than their lives before:
The setting sun, and musick at the close,
As the last taste of sweets, is sweetest last;
Writ in remembrance, more than things long past:
Though Richard my life's counsel would not hear,
My death's sad tale may yet undeaf his ear.

York. No; it is stopp'd with other flattering sounds,
As, praises of his state: then, there are found
Lascivious metres; to whose venom sound
The open ear of youth doth always listen:
Report of fashions in proud Italy;
Whose manners still our tardy apish nation
Limps after, in base imitation,
Where doth the world thrust forth a vanity
(So it be new, there's no respect how vile),
That is not quickly buzz'd into his ears?
Then all too late comes counsel to be heard,
Where will doth mutiny with wit's regard.
Direct not him, whose way himself will choose;
'Tis breath thou lack'st, and that breath wilt thou lose.

Gaunt. Methinks, I am a prophet new inspir'd;
And thus, expiring, do foretell of him:
His rash fierce blaze of riot cannot last;
For violent fires soon burn out themselves:
Small showers last long, but sudden storms are short;
He tires betimes, that spurs too fast betimes;
With eager feeding, food doth choke the feeder:
Like vanity, insatiate cormorant,
Consuming means, soon preys upon itself.
This royal throne of kings, this sceptred isle,
This earth of majesty, this seat of Mars,
This other Eden, demi-paradise;
This fortress, built by nature for herself,
Against infection, and the hand of war;
This happy breed of men, this little world;
This precious stone set in the silver sea,
Which serves it in the office of a wall,
Or as a moat defensive to a house,
Against the envy of less happier lands;

This blessed plot, this earth, this realm, this England,
This nurse, this teeming womb of royal kings,
Fear'd by their breed, and famous by their birth,
Renowned for their deeds as far from home
(For Christian service, and true chivalry),
As is the sepulchre in stubborn Jewry,
Of the world's ransom, blessed Mary's son:
This land of such dear souls, this dear dear land,
Dear for her reputation through the world,
Is now leas'd out (I die pronouncing it),
Like to a tenement, or pelting farm:
England, bound in with the triumphant sea,
Whose rocky shore beats back the envious siege
Of watery Neptune, is now bound in with shame,
With inky blots, and rotten parchment bonds;
That England, that was wont to conquer others,
Hath made a shameful conquest of itself:
O, would the scandal vanish with my life,
How happy then were my ensuing death!

Enter KING RICHARD, *and* Queen; AUMERLE, BUSHY, GREEN, BAGOT, ROSS, *and* WILLOUGHBY.

York. The king is come: deal mildly with his youth;
For young hot colts, being rag'd, do rage the more.

Queen. How fares our noble uncle Lancaster?

K. Rich. What comfort, man? How is't with aged Gaunt?

Gaunt. O, how that name befits my composition!
Old Gaunt, indeed; and gaunt in being old:
Within me grief hath kept a tedious fast;
And who abstains from meat, that is not gaunt?
For sleeping England long time have I watch'd;
Watching breeds leanness, leanness is all gaunt:
The pleasure, that some fathers feed upon,
Is my strict fast, I mean—my children's looks;
And, therein fasting, hast thou made me gaunt:
Gaunt am I for the grave, gaunt as a grave,
Whose hollow womb inherits nought but bones.

K. Rich. Can sick men play so nicely with their names?

Gaunt. No, misery makes sport to mock itself:
Since thou dost seek to kill my name in me,
I mock my name, great king, to flatter thee.

K. Rich. Should dying men flatter with those that live?

Gaunt. No, no; men living flatter those that die.

K. Rich. Thou, now a dying, say'st—thou flatter'st me.

Gaunt. Oh! no; thou diest, though I the sicker be.

K. Rich. I am in health, I breathe, and see thee ill.

Gaunt. Now, he that made me, knows I see thee ill;
Ill in myself to see, and in thee seeing ill.
Thy deathbed is no lesser than thy land,
Wherein thou liest in reputation sick:
And thou, too careless patient as thou art,
Committ'st thy anointed body to the cure
Of those physicians that first wounded thee;
A thousand flatterers sit within thy crown,
Whose compass is no bigger than thy head;
And yet, incaged in so small a verge,
The waste in no whit lesser than thy land;
O, had thy grandsire, with a prophet's eye,
Seen how his son's son should destroy his sons,
From forth thy reach he would have laid thy shame;
Deposing thee before thou wert possess'd,
Which art possess'd now to depose thyself.
Why, cousin, wert thou regent of the world,
It were a shame to let this land by lease:
But, for thy world, enjoying but this land,
Is it not more than shame, to shame it so?
Landlord of England art thou now, not king:
Thy state of law is bondslave to the law;
And thou——

K. Rich. ——a lunatick lean-witted fool,
Presuming on an ague's privilege,
Dar'st with thy frozen admonition
Make pale our cheek; chasing the royal blood,
With fury, from his native residence.
Now by my seat's right royal majesty,
Wert thou not brother to great Edward's son,
This tongue that runs so roundly in thy head,
Should run thy head from thy unreverent shoulders.

Gaunt. O, spare me not, my brother Edward's son,
For that I was his father Edward's son;
That blood already, like the pelican,
Hast thou tapp'd out, and drunkenly carous'd:
My brother Gloster, plain well meaning soul,
(Whom fair befall in heaven 'mongst happy souls!)
May be a precedent, and witness good,
That thou respect'st not spilling Edward's blood:
Join with the present sickness that I have,
And thy unkindness be like crooked age,
To crop at once a too-long wither'd flower.
Live in thy shame, but die not shame with thee!—
These words hereafter thy tormentors be—
Convey me to my bed, then to my grave:
Love they to live, that love and honour have.
[*Exit, borne out by his* Attendants.

K. Rich. And let them die, that age and sullens have;
For both hast thou, and both become the grave.

York. 'Beseech your majesty, impute his words
To wayward sickliness and age in him:
He loves you, on my life, and holds you dear
As Harry duke of Hereford, were he here.

K. Rich. Right; you say true: as Hereford's love, so his:
As theirs, so mine; and all be as it is.

Enter NORTHUMBERLAND.

North. My liege, old Gaunt commends him to your majesty.

K. Rich. What says he now?

North. Nay, nothing; all is said:
His tongue is now a stringless instrument;
Words, life, and all, old Lancaster hath spent.

York. Be York the next that must be bankrupt so!
Though death be poor, it ends a mortal woe.

K. Rich. The ripest fruit first falls, and so doth he;
His time is spent, our pilgrimage must be:
So much for that.——Now for our Irish wars:
We must supplant those rough rug-headed kerns;
Which live like venom, where no venom else,
But only they, hath privilege to live.
And for these great affairs do ask some charge,
Towards our assistance, we do seize to us
The plate, coin, revenues, and moveables,
Whereof our uncle Gaunt did stand possess'd.

York. How long shall I be patient? Ah, how long
Shall tender duty make me suffer wrong?
Not Gloster's death, nor Hereford's banishment,
Not Gaunt's rebukes, nor England's private wrongs,
Nor the prevention of poor Bolingbroke
About his marriage, nor my own disgrace,
Have ever made me sour my patient cheek,
Or bend one wrinkle on my sovereign's face.—
I am the last of noble Edward's sons,
Of whom thy father, prince of Wales, was first;
In war, was never lion rag'd more fierce,
In peace, was never gentle lamb more mild,
Than was that young and princely gentleman:
His face thou hast, for even so look'd he,
Accomplish'd with the number of thy hours;
But, when he frown'd, it was against the French,
And not against his friends: his noble hand
Did win what he did spend, and spent not that
Which his triumphant father's hand had won:

His hands were guilty of no kindred's blood,
But bloody with the enemies of his kin.
O, Richard; York is too far gone with grief,
Or else he never would compare between.

K. Rich. Why, uncle, what's the matter?

York. O, my liege,
Pardon me, if you please; if not, I, pleas'd
Not to be pardon'd, am content withal.
Seek you to seize, and gripe into your hands,
The royalties and rights of banish'd Hereford?
Is not Gaunt dead? and doth not Hereford live?
Was not Gaunt just? and is not Harry true?
Did not the one deserve to have an heir?
Is not his heir a well deserving son?
Take Hereford's rights away, and take from time
His charters, and his customary rights;
Let not to-morrow then ensue to-day:
Be not thyself, for how art thou a king,
But by fair sequence and succession?
Now, afore God (God forbid, I say true!)
If you do wrongfully seize Hereford's rights,
Call in the letters patents that he hath
By his attorneys-general to sue
His livery, and deny his offer'd homage,
You pluck a thousand dangers on your head,
You lose a thousand well disposed hearts,
And prick my tender patience to those thoughts
Which honour and allegiance cannot think.

K. Rich. Think what you will; we seize into our hands
His plate, his goods, his money, and his lands.

York. I'll not be by the while: My liege, farewell:
What will ensue hereof, there's none can tell;
But by bad courses may be understood,
That their events can never fall out good. [*Exit.*

K. Rich. Go, Bushy, to the earl of Wiltshire straight;
Bid him repair to us to Ely-house,
To see this business: To-morrow next
We will for Ireland; and 'tis time, I trow;
And we create, in absence of ourself,
Our uncle York lord governor of England,
For he is just, and always lov'd us well.—
Come on, our queen: to-morrow must we part;
Be merry, for our time of stay is short.

[*Flourish. Exeunt* King, Queen, BUSHY, AUMERLE, GREEN, *and* BAGOT.

North. Well, lords, the duke of Lancaster is dead.

Ross. And living too; for now his son is duke.

Willo. Barely in title, not in revenue.

North. Richly in both, if justice had her right.

Ross. My heart is great; but it must break with silence,
Ere 't be disburden'd with a liberal tongue.

North. Nay, speak thy mind; and let him ne'er speak more,
That speaks thy words again, to do thee harm!

Willo. Tends that thou'dst speak, to the duke of Hereford?
If it be so, out with it boldly, man;
Quick is mine ear to hear of good towards him.

Ross. No good at all, that I can do for him;
Unless you call it good to pity him,
Bereft and gelded of his patrimony.

North. Now, afore heaven, 'tis shame, such wrongs are borne,
In him a royal prince, and many more
Of noble blood in this declining land.
The king is not himself, but basely led
By flatterers; and what they will inform,
Merely in hate 'gainst any of us all,
That will the king severely prosecute
'Gainst us, our lives, our children, and our heirs.

Ross. The commons hath be pill'd with grievous taxes,
And quite lost their hearts: the nobles hath he fin'd
For ancient quarrels, and quite lost their hearts.

Willo. And daily new exactions are devis'd;
As blanks, benevolences, and I wot not what:
But what o'God's name, doth become of this?

North. Wars have not wasted it, for warr'd he hath not,
But basely yielded upon compromise
That which his ancestors achiev'd with blows:
More hath he spent in peace, than they in wars.

Ross. The earl of Wiltshire hath the realm in farm.

Willo. The king's grown bankrupt, like a broken man.

North. Reproach, and dissolution, hangeth over him.

Ross. He hath not money for these Irish wars,
His burdenous taxations notwithstanding,
But by the robbing of the banish'd duke.

North. His noble kinsman; most degenerate king!
But, lords, we hear this fearful tempest sing,
Yet seek no shelter to avoid the storm:
We see the wind sit sore upon our sails,
And yet we strike not, but securely perish.

Ross. We see the very wreck that we must suffer;
And unavoided is the danger now,
For suffering so the causes of our wreck.

North. Not so; even through the hollow eyes of death,
I spy life peering; but I dare not say
How near the tidings of our comfort is.

Willo. Nay, let us share thy thoughts, as thou dost ours.

Ross. Be confident to speak, Northumberland:
We three are but thyself; and, speaking so,
Thy words are but as thoughts; therefore, be bold.

North. Then thus:—I have from Port le Blanc, a bay
In Brittany, receiv'd intelligence,
That Harry Hereford, Reignold Lord Cobham,
[The son of Richard earl of Arundel],
That late broke from the duke of Exeter,
His brother, archbishop late of Canterbury,
Sir Thomas Erpingham, Sir John Ramston,
Sir John Norbery, Sir Robert Waterton, and Francis Quoint,——
All these well furnish'd by the duke of Bretagne,
With eight tall ships, three thousand men of war,
Are making hither with all due expedience,
And shortly mean to touch our northern shore:
Perhaps, they had ere this; but that they stay
The first departing of the king for Ireland.
If then we shall shake off our slavish yoke,
Imp out our drooping country's broken wing,
Redeem from broking pawn the blemish'd crown,
Wipe off the dust that hides our sceptre's gilt,
And make high majesty look like itself,
Away, with me, in post to Ravenspurg:
But if you faint, as fearing to do so,
Stay, and be secret, and myself will go.

Ross. To horse, to horse! urge doubts to them that fear.

Willo. Hold out my horse, and I will first be there. [*Exeunt.*

SCENE II. *The same. A Room in the Palace.*

Enter Queen, BUSHY, *and* BAGOT.

Bushy. Madam, your majesty is too much sad:
You promis'd, when you parted with the king,
To lay aside life-harming heaviness,
And entertain a cheerful disposition.

Queen. To please the king, I did; to please myself,
I cannot do it; yet I know no cause
Why I should welcome such a guest as grief,
Save bidding farewell to so sweet a guest
As my sweet Richard: Yet, again, methinks,
Some unborn sorrow, ripe in fortune's womb,
Is coming towards me; and my inward soul

With nothing trembles: at something, it grieves,
More than with parting from my lord the king.

Bushy. Each substance of a grief hath twenty shadows,
Which show like grief itself, but are not so;
For sorrow's eye, glazed with blinding tears,
Divides one thing entire to many objects;
Like perspectives, which, rightly gaz'd upon,
Show nothing but confusion; ey'd awry,
Distinguish form: so your sweet majesty,
Looking awry upon your lord's departure,
Finds shapes of griefs, more than himself, to wail;
Which, look'd on as it is, is nought but shadows
Of what it is not. Then, thrice-gracious queen,
More than your lord's departure weep not; more's not seen:
Or if it be, 'tis with false sorrow's eye,
Which, for things true, weeps things imaginary.

Queen. It may be so; but yet my inward soul
Persuades me, it is otherwise: Howe'er it be,
I cannot but be sad; so heavy sad,
As,—though, in thinking, on no thought I think,—
Makes me with heavy nothing faint and shrink.

Bushy. 'Tis nothing but conceit, my gracious lady.

Queen. 'Tis nothing less: conceit is still deriv'd
From some fore-father grief: mine is not so;
For nothing hath begot my something grief;
Or something hath the nothing that I grieve:
'Tis in reversion that I do possess;
But what it is, that is not yet known; what
I cannot name; 'tis nameless woe, I wot.

Enter GREEN.

Green. God save your majesty!—and well met, gentlemen:—
I hope, the king is not yet shipp'd for Ireland.

Queen. Why hop'st thou so? 'tis better hope, he is;
For his designs crave haste, his haste good hope;
Then wherefore dost thou hope, he is not shipp'd?

Green. That he, our hope, might have retir'd his power,
And driven into despair an enemy's hope,
Who strongly hath set footing in this land:
The banish'd Bolingbroke repeals himself,
And with uplifted arms is safe arriv'd
At Ravenspurg.

Queen. Now God in heaven forbid!

Green. O, madam, 'tis too true; and that is worse,—
The Lord Northumberland, his young son Henry Percy,
The lords of Ross, Beaumond, and Willoughby,
With all their powerful friends, are fled to him.

Bushy. Why have you not proclaim'd Northumberland,
And all the rest of the revolted faction, traitors?

Green. We have: whereon the earl of Worcester
Hath broke his staff, resign'd his stewardship,
And all the household servants fled with him
To Bolingbroke.

Queen. So, Green, thou art the midwife to my woe,
And Bolingbroke my sorrow's dismal heir:
Now hath my soul brought forth her prodigy;
And I, a gasping new-deliver'd mother,
Have woe to woe, sorrow to sorrow join'd.

Bushy. Despair not, madam.

Queen. Who shall hinder me?
I will despair, and be at enmity
With cozening hope; he is a flatterer,
A parasite, a keeper-back of death,
Who gently would dissolve the bands of life,
Which false hope lingers in extremity.

Enter YORK.

Green. Here comes the duke of York.

Queen. With signs of war about his aged neck;
O, full of careful business are his looks!—
Uncle,
For heaven's sake, speak comfortable words.

York. Should I do so, I should belie my thoughts:
Comfort's in heaven; and we are on the earth,
Where nothing lives but crosses, care, and grief.
Your husband he is gone to save far off,
Whilst others come to make him lose at home:
Here am I left to underprop his land;
Who, weak with age, cannot support myself:——
Now comes the sick hour that his surfeit made;
Now shall he try his friends that flatter'd him.

Enter a Servant.

Serv. My lord, your son was gone before I came.

York. He was?—Why, so!—go all which way it will!——
The nobles they are fled, the commons they are cold,
And will, I fear, revolt on Hereford's side.——
Sirrah, get thee to Plashy, to my sister Gloster;
Bid her send me presently a thousand pound:—
Hold, take my ring.

Serv. My lord,, I had forgot to tell your lordship;
To-day, as I came by, I called there;
But I shall grieve you to report the rest.

York. What is it, knave?

Serv. An hour before I came, the duchess died.

York. God for his mercy! what a tide of woes
Comes rushing on this woful land at once!
I know not what to do:—I would to God
(So my untruth had not provok'd him to it),
The king had cut off my head with my brother's.—
What, are there no posts despatch'd for Ireland?—
How shall we do for money for these wars?—
Come, sister,—cousin, I would say: 'pray, pardon me.—
Go, fellow [*To the* Servant.] get thee home, provide some carts,
And bring away the armour that is there.—
[*Exit* Servant.
Gentlemen, will you go muster men? if I know
How, or which way, to order these affairs,
Thus disorderly thrust into my hands,
Never believe me. Both are my kinsmen;—
The one's my sovereign, whom both my oath
And duty bids defend; the other again,
Is my kinsman, whom the king hath wrong'd;
Whom conscience and my kindred bids to right.
Well, somewhat we must do.—Come, cousin, I'll
Dispose of you: Gentlemen, go, muster up your men,
And meet me presently at Berkley-castle.
I should to Plashy too;——
But time will not permit:—All is uneven,
And every thing is left at six and seven.
[*Exeunt* YORK *and* Queen.

Bushy. The wind sits fair for news to go to Ireland,
But none returns. For us to levy power,
Proportionable to the enemy,
Is all impossible.

Green. Besides our nearness to the king in love,
Is near the hate of those love not the king.

Bagot. And that's the wavering commons: for their love
Lies in their purses; and whoso empties them,
By so much fills their hearts with deadly hate.

Bushy. Wherein the king stands generally condemn'd.

Bagot. If judgment lie in them, then so do we,
Because we ever have been near the king.

Green. Well, I'll for refuge straight to Bristol Castle;
The earl of Wiltshire is already there.

Bushy. Thither will I with you: for little office
Will the hateful commons perform for us;

Except like curs to tear us all to pieces.—
Will you go along with us?

Bagot. No; I'll to Ireland to his majesty.
Farewell: if heart's presages be not vain,
We three here part, that ne'er shall meet again.

Bushy. That's as York thrives to beat back Bolingbroke.

Green. Alas, poor duke! the task he undertakes
Is—numb'ring sands, and drinking oceans dry:
Where one on his side fights, thousands will fly.

Bushy. Farewell at once; for once, for all, and ever.

Green. Well, we may meet again.

Bagot. I fear me, never. [*Exeunt.*

SCENE III. *The Wilds in* Glostershire.

Enter BOLINGBROKE *and* NORTHUMBERLAND, *with Forces.*

Boling. How far is it, my lord, to Berkley now?

North. Believe me, noble lord,
I am a stranger here in Glostershire.
These high wild hills, and rough uneven ways,
Draw out our miles, and make them wearisome:
And yet your fair discourse hath been as sugar,
Making the hard way sweet and delectable.
But, I bethink me, what a weary way
From Ravenspurg to Cotswold, will be found
In Ross and Willoughby, wanting your company;
Which, I protest, hath very much beguil'd
The tediousness and process of my travel:
But theirs is sweeten'd with the hope to have
The present benefit which I possess:
And hope to joy, is little less in joy,
Than hope enjoy'd: by this the weary lords
Shall make their way seem short: as mine hath done
By sight of what I have, your noble company.

Boling. Of much less value is my company,
Than your good words. But who comes here?

Enter HARRY PERCY.

North. It is my son, young Harry Percy,
Sent from my brother Worcester, whencesoever.—
Harry, how fares your uncle?

Percy. I had thought, my lord, to have learn'd his health of you.

North. Why, is he not with the queen?

Percy. No, my good lord; he hath forsook the court,
Broken his staff of office, and dispers'd
The household of the king.

North. What was his reason?
He was not so resolv'd, when last we spake together.

Percy. Because your lordship was proclaimed traitor.
But he, my lord, is gone to Ravenspurg,
To offer service to the duke of Hereford;
And sent me o'er by Berkley, to discover
What power the duke of York had levied there;
Then with direction to repair to Ravenspurg.

North. Have you forgot the duke of Hereford, boy?

Percy. No, my good lord; for that is not forgot,
Which ne'er I did remember; to my knowledge,
I never in my life did look on him.

North. Then learn to know him now; this is the duke.

Percy. My gracious lord, I tender you my service,
Such as it is, being tender, raw, and young;
Which elder days shall ripen and confirm
To more approved service and desert.

Boling. I thank thee, gentle Percy; and be sure,
I count myself in nothing else so happy,
As in a soul rememb'ring my good friends;
And, as my fortune ripens with thy love,
It shall be still thy true love's recompense:
My heart this covenant makes, my hand thus seals it.

North. How far is it to Berkley? And what stir
Keeps good old York there, with his men of war?

Percy. There stands the castle, by yon tuft of trees,
Mann'd with three hundred men, as I have heard:
And in it are the lords of York, Berkley, and Seymour;
None else of name, and noble estimate.

Enter ROSS *and* WILLOUGHBY.

North. Here come the lords of Ross and Willoughby,
Bloody with spurring, fiery-red with haste.

Boling. Welcome, my lords: I wot your love pursues
A banish'd traitor: all my treasury
Is yet but unfelt thanks, which, more enrich'd,
Shall be your love and labour's recompense.

Ross. Your presence makes us rich, most noble lord.

Willo. And far surmounts our labour to attain it.

Boling. Evermore thanks, the exchequer of the poor;
Which, till my infant fortune comes to years,
Stands for my bounty. But who comes here?

Enter BERKLEY.

North. It is my lord of Berkley, as I guess.

Berk. My lord of Hereford, my message is to you.

Boling. My lord, my answer is—to Lancaster;
And I am come to seek that name in England:
And I must find that title in your tongue,
Before I make reply to aught you say.

Berk. Mistake me not, my lord; 'tis not my meaning,
To raze one title of your honour out:—
To you, my lord, I come (what lord you will),
From the most gracious regent of this land,
The duke of York; to know, what pricks you on
To take advantage of the absent time,
And fright our native peace with self-born arms.

Enter YORK, *attended.*

Boling. I shall not need transport my words by you;
Here comes his grace in person.—My noble uncle! [*Kneels.*

York. Show me thy humble heart, and not thy knee,
Whose duty is deceivable and false.

Boling. My gracious uncle!—

York. Tut, tut!
Grace me no grace, nor uncle me no uncle:
I am no traitor's uncle; and that word—grace,
In an ungracious mouth, is but profane.
Why have those banish'd and forbidden legs
Dar'd once to touch a dust of England's ground?
But then more why;——Why have they dar'd to march
So many miles upon her peaceful bosom;
Frighting her pale-fac'd villages with war,
And ostentation of despised arms?
Com'st thou because the anointed king is hence?
Why, foolish boy, the king is left behind,
And in my loyal bosom lies his power.
Were I but now the lord of such hot youth,
As when brave Gaunt, thy father, and myself,
Rescued the Black Prince, that young Mars of men,
From forth the ranks of many thousand French;
O, then, how quickly should this arm of mine,
Now prisoner to the palsy, chastise thee,
And minister correction to thy fault!

Boling. My gracious uncle, let me know my fault;
On what condition stands it, and wherein?

York. Even in condition of the worst degree,—
In gross rebellion, and detested treason:

Thou art a banish'd man, and here art come,
Before the expiration of thy time,
In braving arms against thy sovereign.

Boling. As I was banish'd, I was banish'd Hereford;
But as I come, I come for Lancaster,
And, noble uncle, I beseech your grace,
Look on my wrongs with an indifferent eye:
You are my father, for, methinks, in you
I see old Gaunt alive; O, then, my father!
Will you permit that I shall stand condemn'd
A wand'ring vagabond; my rights and royalties
Pluck'd from my arms perforce, and given away
To upstart unthrifts? Wherefore was I born?
If that my cousin king, be king of England,
It must be granted, I am duke of Lancaster.
You have a son, Aumerle, my noble kinsman;
Had you first died, and he had been thus trod down,
He should have found his uncle Gaunt a father,
To rouse his wrongs, and chase them to the bay.
I am denied to sue my livery here,
And yet my letters patent give me leave:
My father's goods are all distrain'd, and sold;
And these, and all, are all amiss employed.
What would you have me do? I am a subject,
And challenge law: Attornies are denied me;
And therefore personally I lay my claim
To my inheritance of free descent.

North. The noble duke hath been too much abus'd.

Ross. It stands your grace upon to do him right.

Will. Base men by his endowments are made great.

York. My lords of England, let me tell you this,—
I have had feeling of my cousin's wrongs,
And labour'd all I could to do him right:
But in this kind to come, in braving arms,
Be his own carver, and cut out his way,
To find out right with wrong,—it may not be;
And you, that do abet him in this kind,
Cherish rebellion, and are rebels all.

North. The noble duke hath sworn, his coming is
But for his own: and, for the right of that,
We all have strongly sworn to give him aid;
And let him ne'er see joy, that breaks that oath.

York. Well, well, I see the issue of these arms;
I cannot mend it, I must needs confess,
Because my power is weak, and all ill left:
But, if I could, by him that gave me life,
I would attach you all, and make you stoop
Unto the sovereign mercy of the king;
But, since I cannot, be it known to you,
I do remain as neuter. So, fare you well;—
Unless you please to enter in the castle,
And there repose you for this night.

Boling. An offer, uncle, that we will accept.
But we must win your grace, to go with us
To Bristol Castle; which, they say, is held
By Bushy, Bagot, and their complices,
The caterpillars of the commonwealth,
Which I have sworn to weed, and pluck away.

York. It may be, I will go with you:—but yet I'll pause;
For I am loath to break our country's laws.
Nor friends nor foes, to me welcome you are:
Things past redress, are now with me past care. [*Exeunt.*

SCENE IV. *A Camp in* Wales.

Enter SALISBURY, *and a* Captain.

Cap. My lord of Salisbury, we have staid ten days,
And hardly kept our countrymen together,
And yet we hear no tidings from the king:
Therefore we will disperse ourselves: farewell.

Sal. Stay yet another day, thou trusty Welshman:
The king reposeth all his confidence
In thee.

Cap. 'Tis thought the king is dead: we will not stay.
The bay-trees in our country are all wither'd,
And meteors fright the fixed stars of heaven;
The pale-fac'd moon looks bloody on the earth,
And lean-look'd prophets whisper fearful change;
Rich men look sad, and ruffians dance and leap,—
The one in fear to lose what they enjoy,
The other, to enjoy by rage and war:
These signs forerun the death or fall of kings.—
Farewell; our countrymen are gone and fled,
As well assur'd, Richard their king is dead. [*Exit.*

Sal. Ah, Richard! with the eyes of heavy mind,
I see thy glory, like a shooting star,
Fall to the base earth from the firmament!
Thy sun sets weeping in the lowly west,
Witnessing storms to come, woe and unrest:
Thy friends are fled, to wait upon thy foes:
And crossly to thy good all fortune goes. [*Exit.*

ACT III.

SCENE I. Bolingbroke's *Camp at* Bristol.

Enter BOLINGBROKE, YORK, NORTHUMBERLAND, PERCY, WILLOUGHBY, ROSS: *Officers behind with* BUSHY, *and* GREEN, *prisoners.*

Boling. Bring forth these men.—
Bushy and Green, I will not vex your souls
(Since presently your souls must part your bodies),
With too much urging your pernicious lives,
For 'twere no charity: yet, to wash your blood
From off my hands, here, in the view of men,
I will unfold some causes of your death.
You have misled a prince, a royal king,
A happy gentleman in blood and lineaments,
By you unhappied and disfigured clean.
You have, in manner, with your sinful hours,
Made a divorce betwixt his queen and him;
Broke the possession of a royal bed,
And stain'd the beauty of a fair queen's cheeks
With tears drawn from her eyes with your foul wrongs.
Myself—a prince, by fortune of my birth,
Near to the king in blood; and near in love,
Till you did make him misinterpret me,——
Have stoop'd my neck under your injuries,
And sigh'd my English breath in foreign clouds,
Eating the bitter bread of banishment:
Whilst you have fed upon my signiories,
Dispark'd my parks, and fell'd my forest woods;
From my own windows torn my household coat,
Raz'd out my impress, leaving me no sign,—
Save men's opinions, and my living blood,—
To show the world I am a gentleman.
This, and much more, much more than twice all this,
Condemns you to the death:—See them deliver'd over
To execution and the hand of death.

Bushy. More welcome is the stroke of death to me,
Than Bolingbroke to England.—Lords, farewell.

Green. My comfort is,—that heaven will take our souls,
And plague injustice with the pains of hell.

Boling. My Lord Northumberland, see them despatch'd.
[*Exeunt* NORTH. *and Others, with Prisoners.*
Uncle, you say, the queen is at your house;
For heaven's sake, fairly let her be entreated:
Tell her, I send to her my kind commends;
Take special care my greetings be deliver'd.

York. A gentleman of mine I have despatch'd
With letters of your love to her at large.

Boling. Thanks, gentle uncle.—Come, lords, away:
To fight with Glendower and his complices;
Awhile to work, and, after, holiday. [*Exeunt.*

SCENE II. *The Coast of* Wales. *A Castle in view.*

Flourish: Drums and Trumpets. Enter KING RICHARD, *Bishop of* CARLISLE, AUMERLE, *and* Soldiers.

K. Rich. Barkloughly Castle call you this at hand?
Aum. Yea, my lord: How brooks your grace the air,
After your late tossing on the breaking seas?
K. Rich. Needs must I like it well; I weep for joy,
To stand upon my kingdom once again.——
Dear earth, I do salute thee with my hand,
Though rebels wound thee with their horses' hoofs:
As a long parted mother with her child
Plays fondly with her tears, and smiles, in meeting;
So, weeping, smiling, greet I thee, my earth,
And do thee favour with my royal hands.
Feed not thy sovereign's foe, my gentle earth,
Nor with thy sweets comfort his ravenous sense;
But let thy spiders, that suck up thy venom,
And heavy-gaited toads, lie in their way;
Doing annoyance to the treacherous feet,
Which with usurping steps do trample thee.
Yield stinging nettles to mine enemies:
And when they from thy bosom pluck a flower,
Guard it, I pray thee, with a lurking adder;
Whose double tongue may with a mortal touch
Throw death upon thy sovereign's enemies.—
Mock not my senseless conjuration, lords;
This earth shall have a feeling, and these stones
Prove armed soldiers, ere her native king
Shall falter under foul rebellious arms.
Bishop. Fear not, my lord; that Power, that made you king,
Hath power to keep you king, in spite of all.
The means that heaven yields must be embrac'd,
And not neglected; else, if heaven would,
And we will not, heaven's offer we refuse;
The proffer'd means of succour and redress.
Aum. He means, my lord, that we are too remiss;
Whilst Bolingbroke, through our security,
Grows strong and great, in substance and in friends.
K. Rich. Discomfortable cousin! know'st thou not,
That when the searching eye of heaven is hid
Behind the globe, and lights the lower world,
Then thieves and robbers range abroad unseen,
In murders, and in outrage, bloody here;
But when, from under this terrestrial ball,
He fires the proud tops of the eastern pines,
And darts his light through every guilty hole,
Then murders, treasons, and detested sins,
The cloak of night being pluck'd from off their backs,
Stand bare and naked, trembling at themselves?
So when this thief, this traitor, Bolingbroke,—
Who all this while hath revell'd in the night,
Whilst we were wand'ring with the antipodes,—
Shall see us rising in our throne the east,
His treasons will sit blushing in his face,
Not able to endure the sight of day,
But, self-affrighted, tremble at his sin.
Not all the water in the rough rude sea
Can wash the balm from an anointed king:
The breath of worldly men cannot depose
The deputy elected by the Lord:
For every man that Bolingbroke hath press'd,
To lift shrewd steel against our golden crown,
God for his Richard hath in heavenly pay
A glorious angel: then, if angels fight,
Weak men must fall; for heaven still guards the right.

Enter SALISBURY.

Welcome, my lord; How far off lies your power?
Sal. Nor near, nor further off, my gracious lord,
Than this weak arm: Discomfort guides my tongue,
And bids me speak of nothing but despair.
One day too late, I fear, my noble lord,
Hath clouded all thy happy days on earth:
O, call back yesterday, bid time return,
And thou shalt have twelve thousand fighting men!
To-day, to-day, unhappy day, too late,
O'erthrows thy joys, friends, fortune, and thy state;
For all the Welshmen, hearing thou wert dead,
Are gone to Bolingbroke, dispers'd, and fled.
Aum. Comfort, my liege: why looks your grace so pale?
K. Rich. But now, the blood of twenty thousand men
Did triumph in my face, and they are fled;
And, till so much blood thither come again,
Have I not reason to look pale and dead?
All souls that will be safe, fly from my side;
For time hath set a blot upon my pride.
Aum. Comfort, my liege: remember who you are.
K. Rich. I had forgot myself: Am I not king?
Awake, thou sluggard majesty! thou sleep'st.
Is not the king's name forty thousand names?
Arm, arm, my name; a puny subject strikes
At thy great glory.—Look not to the ground,
Ye favourites of a king; Are we not high?
High be our thoughts: I know, my uncle York
Hath power enough to serve our turn. But who
Comes here?

Enter SCROOP.

Scroop. More health and happiness betide my liege,
Than can my care-tun'd tongue deliver him.
K. Rich. Mine ear is open, and my heart prepar'd:
The worst is worldly loss, thou canst unfold.
Say, is my kingdom lost? why, 'twas my care;
And what loss is it, to be rid of care?
Strives Bolingbroke to be as great as we?
Greater he shall not be; if he serve God,
We'll serve him too, and be his fellow so:
Revolt our subjects? that we cannot mend;
They break their faith to God, as well as us:
Cry woe, destruction, ruin, loss, decay:
The worst is—death, and death will have his day.
Scroop. Glad am I, that your highness is so arm'd
To bear the tidings of calamity
Like an unseasonable stormy day,
Which makes the silver rivers drown their shores,
As if the world were all dissolv'd to tears;
So high above his limits swells the rage
Of Bolingbroke, covering your fearful land
With hard bright steel, and hearts harder than steel.
White-beards have arm'd their thin and hairless scalps
Against thy majesty; boys, with women's voices,
Strive to speak big, and clap their female joints
In stiff unwieldy arms against thy crown:
The very beadsmen learn to bend their bows
Of double-fatal yew against thy state;
Yea, distaff-women manage rusty bills
Against thy seat: both young and old rebel,
And all goes worse than I have power to tell.
K. Rich. Too well, too well, thou tell'st a tale so ill:
Where is the earl of Wiltshire? where is Bagot?
What is become of Bushy? where is Green?
That they have let the dangerous enemy
Measure our confines with such peaceful steps?

If we prevail, their heads shall pay for it.
I warrant, they have made peace with Bolingbroke.

Scroop. Peace have they made with him, indeed, my lord.

K. Rich. O villains, vipers, damn'd without redemption!
Dogs, easily won to fawn on any man!
Snakes, in my heart-blood warm'd, that sting my heart!
Three Judases, each one thrice worse than Judas!
Would they make peace? terrible hell make war
Upon their spotted souls for this offence!

Scroop. Sweet love, I see, changing his property,
Turns to the sourest and most deadly hate;—
Again uncurse their souls; their peace is made
With heads, and not with hands: those whom you curse,
Have felt the worst of death's destroying wound,
And lie full low, grav'd in the hollow ground.

Aum. Is Bushy, Green, and the earl of Wiltshire dead?

Scroop. Yea, all of them at Bristol lost their heads.

Aum. Where is the duke, my father, with his power?

K. Rich. No matter where; of comfort no man speak:
Let's talk of graves, of worms, and epitaphs;
Make dust our paper, and with rainy eyes
Write sorrow on the bosom of the earth.
Let's choose executors, and talk of wills:
And yet not so,—for what can we bequeath,
Save our deposed bodies to the ground?
Our lands, our lives, and all are Bolingbroke's,
And nothing can we call our own, but death;
And that small model of the barren earth,
Which serves as paste and cover to our bones.
For heaven's sake, let us sit upon the ground,
And tell sad stories of the death of kings:—
How some have been depos'd, some slain in war;
Some haunted by the ghosts they have depos'd;
Some poison'd by their wives, some sleeping kill'd;
All murder'd:—For within the hollow crown,
That rounds the mortal temples of a king,
Keeps death his court: and there the antick sits,
Scoffing his state, and grinning at his pomp;
Allowing him a breath, a little scene
To monarchize, be fear'd and kill with looks;
Infusing him with self and vain conceit,—
As if this flesh, which walls about our life,
Were brass impregnable; and humour'd thus,
Comes at the last, and with a little pin
Bores through his castle wall, and—farewell, king!
Cover your heads, and mock not flesh and blood
With solemn reverence; throw away respect,
Tradition, form, and ceremonious duty,
For you have but mistook me all this while:
I live with bread like you, feel want, taste grief,
Need friends:—Subjected thus,
How can you say to me—I am a king?

Car. My lord, wise men ne'er wail their present woes,
But presently prevent the ways to wail.
To fear the foe, since fear oppresseth strength,
Gives, in your weakness, strength unto your foe,
And so your follies fight against yourself.
Fear, and be slain; no worse can come, to fight:
And fight and die, is death destroying death;
Where fearing dying, pays death servile breath.

Aum. My father hath a power, inquire of him;
And learn to make a body of a limb.

K. Rich. Thou chid'st me well:—Proud Bolingbroke, I come
To change blows with thee for our day of doom.
This ague-fit of fear is over-blown;
An easy task it is, to win our own.——
Say, Scroop, where lies our uncle with his power?
Speak sweetly, man, although thy looks be sour.

Scroop. Men judge by the complexion of the sky
The state and inclination of the day:
So may you by my dull and heavy eye,
My tongue hath but a heavier tale to say.
I play the torturer, by small and small,
To lengthen out the worst that must be spoken:—
Your uncle York hath join'd with Bolingbroke;
And all your northern castles yielded up,
And all your southern gentlemen in arms
Upon his party.

K. Rich. Thou hast said enough.——
Beshrew thee, cousin, which didst lead me forth [*To* AUMERLE.
Of that sweet way I was in to despair!
What say you now? What comfort have we now?
By heaven, I'll hate him everlastingly,
That bids me be of comfort any more.
Go, to Flint castle; there I'll pine away;
A king, woe's slave, shall kingly woe obey.
That power I have, discharge; and let them go
To ear the land that hath some hope to grow,
For I have none:—Let no man speak again
To alter this, for counsel is but vain.

Aum. My liege, one word.

K. Rich. He does me double wrong,
That wounds me with the flatteries of his tongue.
Discharge my followers, let them hence:—Away,
From Richard's night, to Bolingbroke's fair day. [*Exeunt.*

SCENE III. Wales. *A Plain before* Flint *Castle.*

Enter, with Drum and Colours, BOLINGBROKE *and* Forces; YORK, NORTHUMBERLAND, *and Others.*

Boling. So that by this intelligence we learn,
The Welshmen are dispers'd; and Salisbury
Is gone to meet the king, who lately landed,
With some few private friends, upon this coast.

North. The news is very fair and good, my lord:
Richard, not far from hence, hath hid his head.

York. It would beseem the lord Northumberland,
To say—King Richard:—Alack the heavy day,
When such a sacred king should hide his head!

North. Your grace mistakes me; only to be brief,
Left I his title out.

York. The time hath been,
Would you have been so brief with him, he would
Have been so brief with you, to shorten you
For taking so the head, your whole head's length.

Boling. Mistake not, uncle, further than you should.

York. Take not, good cousin, further than you should.
Lest you mis-take: The heavens are o'er your head.

Boling. I know it, uncle; and oppose not
Myself against their will.—But who comes here?

Enter PERCY.

Well, Harry; what, will not this castle yield?

Percy. The castle royally is mann'd, my lord,
Against thy entrance.

Boling. Royally!
Why, it contains no king?

Percy. Yes, my good lord,
It doth contain a king: King Richard lies
Within the limits of yon lime and stone:
And with him are the Lord Aumerle, Lord Salisbury,
Sir Stephen Scroop; besides a clergyman
Of holy reverence; who, I cannot learn.

North. Belike, it is the bishop of Carlisle.

Boling. Noble lord, [*To* NORTH.
Go to the rude ribs of that ancient castle;
Through brazen trumpet send the breath of parle
Into his ruin'd ears, and thus deliver:
Harry Bolingbroke
On both his knees doth kiss King Richard's hand;
And sends allegiance, and true faith of heart,

To his most royal person: hither come
Even at his feet to lay my arms and power;
Provided that, my banishment repeal'd,
And lands restor'd again, be freely granted:
If not, I'll use the advantage of my power,
And lay the summer's dust with showers of blood,
Rain'd from the wounds of slaughter'd Englishmen:
The which, how far off from the mind of Bolingbroke
It is, such crimson tempest should bedrench
The fresh green lap of fair King Richard's land,
My stooping duty tenderly shall show.
Go, signify as much; while here we march
Upon the grassy carpet of this plain.—

[NORTHUMBERLAND *advances to the Castle, with a Trumpet.*

Let's march without the noise of threat'ning drum,
That from the castle's totter'd battlements
Our fair appointments may be well perus'd.
Methinks, King Richard and myself should meet
With no less terror than the elements
Of fire and water, when their thund'ring shock
At meeting tears the cloudy cheeks of heaven.
Be he the fire, I'll be the yielding water:
The rage be his, while on the earth I rain
My waters; on the earth, and not on him.
March on, and mark King Richard how he looks.

A Parley sounded, and answered by another Trumpet within. Flourish. Enter on the walls KING RICHARD, *the Bishop of* CARLISLE, AUMERLE, SCROOP, *and* SALISBURY.

York. See, see, King Richard doth himself appear,
As doth the blushing discontented sun
From out the fiery portal of the east;
When he perceives the envious clouds are bent
To dim his glory, and to stain the track
Of his bright passage to the occident.
Yet looks he like a king; behold, his eye,
As bright as is the eagle's, lightens forth
Controlling majesty; Alack, alack, for woe,
That any harm should stain so fair a show!

K. Rich. We are amaz'd; and thus long have we stood
To watch the fearful bending of thy knee,

[*To* NORTHUMBERLAND.

Because we thought ourself thy lawful king:
And if we be, how dare thy joints forget
To pay their awful duty to our presence?
If we be not, show us the hand of God
That hath dismiss'd us from our stewardship;
For well we know, no hand of blood and bone
Can gripe the sacred handle of our sceptre,
Unless he do profane, steal, or usurp.
And though you think, that all, as you have done,
Have torn their souls, by turning them from us,
And we are barren, and bereft of friends;——
Yet know,—my master, God omnipotent,
Is must'ring in his clouds, on our behalf,
Armies of pestilence; and they shall strike
Your children yet unborn, and unbegot,
That lift your vassal hands against my head,
And threat the glory of my precious crown.
Tell Bolingbroke (for 'yond methinks, he is),
That every stride he makes upon my land,
Is dangerous treason; He is come to ope
The purple testament of bleeding war;
But ere the crown he looks for live in peace,
Ten thousand bloody crowns of mothers' sons
Shall ill become the flower of England's face;
Change the complexion of her maid-pale peace
To scarlet indignation, and bedew
Her pastures' grass with faithful English blood.

North. The king of heaven forbid, our lord the king
Should so with civil and uncivil arms
Be rush'd upon! Thy thrice-noble cousin,
Harry Bolingbroke, doth humbly kiss thy hand;
And by the honourable tomb he swears,
That stands upon thy royal grandsire's bones;
And by the royalties of both your bloods,
Currents that spring from one most gracious head;
And by the buried hand of warlike Gaunt;
And by the worth and honour of himself,
Comprising all that may be sworn or said,—
His coming hither hath no further scope,
Than for his lineal royalties, and to beg
Enfranchisement immediate on his knees:
Which on thy royal party granted once,
His glittering arms he will commend to rust,
His barbed steeds to stables, and his heart
To faithful service of your majesty.
This swears he, as he is a prince, is just;
And, as I am a gentleman, I credit him.

K. Rich. Northumberland, say,—thus the king returns;
His noble cousin is right welcome hither;
And all the number of his fair demands
Shall be accomplish'd without contradiction:
With all the gracious utterance thou hast,
Speak to his gentle hearing kind commends.—
We do debase ourself, cousin, do we not,

[*To* AUMERLE.

To look so poorly, and to speak so fair?
Shall we call back Northumberland, and send
Defiance to the traitor, and so die?

Aum. No, good my lord; let's fight with gentle words,
Till time lend friends, and friends their helpful swords.

K. Rich. O God! O God! that e'er this tongue of mine,
That laid the sentence of dread banishment
On yon proud man, should take it off again
With words of sooth! O, that I were as great
As is my grief, or lesser than my name!
Or that I could forget what I have been!
Or not remember what I must be now!
Swell'st thou, proud heart? I'll give thee scope to beat,
Since foes have scope to beat both thee and me.

Aum. Northumberland comes back from Bolingbroke.

K. Rich. What must the king do now? Must he submit?
The king shall do it. Must he be depos'd?
The king shall be contented: Must he lose
The name of king? o'God's name, let it go:
I'll give my jewels, for a set of beads;
My gorgeous palace, for a hermitage;
My gay apparel, for an alms-man's gown;
My figur'd goblets, for a dish of wood:
My sceptre, for a palmer's walking staff;
My subjects, for a pair of carved saints;
And my large kingdom for a little grave,
A little little grave, an obscure grave:—
Or I'll be buried in the king's highway,
Some way of common trade, where subjects' feet
May hourly trample on their sovereign's head:
For on my heart they tread, now whilst I live?
And, buried once, why not upon my head?——
Aumerle, thou weep'st; My tender-hearted cousin!—
We'll make foul weather with despised tears;
Our sighs, and they, shall lodge the summer corn,
And make a dearth in this revolting land.
Or shall we play the wantons with our woes,
And make some pretty match with shedding tears?
As thus:—To drop them still upon one place,
Till they have fretted us a pair of graves
Within the earth; and, therein laid,—*There lies*
Two kinsmen, digg'd their graves with weeping eyes?
Would not this ill do well?—Well, well, I see
I talk but idly, and you mock at me.—
Most mighty prince, my Lord Northumberland,
What says King Bolingbroke? will his majesty
Give Richard leave to live till Richard die?
You make a leg, and Bolingbroke says—ay.

North. My lord, in the base court he doth attend
To speak with you; may't please you to come down?

K. Rich. Down, down, I come; like glistering Phaeton,
Wanting the manage of unruly jades.
[NORTH. *retires to* BOLING.
In the base court? Base court, where kings grow base,
To come at traitors' calls, and do them grace.
In the base court? Come down? Down, court! down, king!
For night-owls shriek, where mounting larks should sing. [*Exeunt, from above.*

Boling. What says his majesty?

North. Sorrow and grief of heart
Makes him speak fondly, like a frantick man:
Yet he is come.

Enter KING RICHARD, *and his* Attendants, *below.*

Boling. Stand all apart,
And show fair duty to his majesty.——
My gracious lord,— [*Kneeling.*

K. Rich. Fair cousin, you debase your princely knee,
To make the base earth proud with kissing it:
Me rather had, my heart might feel your love,
Than my unpleas'd eye see your courtesy.
Up, cousin, up; your heart is up, I know,
Thus, high at least [*touching his own head*], although your knee be low.

Boling. My gracious lord, I come but for mine own.

K. Rich. Your own is yours, and I am yours, and all.

Boling. So far be mine, my most redoubted lord,
As my true service shall deserve your love.

K. Rich. Well you deserve:—They well deserve to have,
That know the strong'st and surest way to get.—
Uncle, give me your hand: nay, dry your eyes;
Tears show their love, but want their remedies.—
Cousin, I am too young to be your father,
Though you are old enough to be my heir.
What you will have, I'll give, and willing too;
For do we must, what force will have us do.—
Set on towards London:—Cousin, is it so?

Boling. Yea, my good lord.

K. Rich. Then I must not say, no.
[*Flourish. Exeunt.*

SCENE IV.

Langley. *The* Duke *of* York's *Garden.*

Enter the Queen, *and two* Ladies.

Queen. What sport shall we devise here in this garden,
To drive away the heavy thought of care?

1 *Lady.* Madam, we'll play at bowls.

Queen. 'Twill make me think,
The world is full of rubs, and that my fortune
Runs 'gainst the bias.

1 *Lady.* Madam, we will dance.

Queen. My legs can keep no measure in delight.
When my poor heart no measure keeps in grief;
Therefore, no dancing, girl; some other sport.

1 *Lady.* Madam, we'll tell tales.

Queen. Of sorrow, or of joy?

1 *Lady.* Of either, madam.

Queen. Of neither, girl:
For if of joy, being altogether wanting,
It doth remember me the more of sorrow;
Or if of grief, being altogether had,
It adds more sorrow to my want of joy:
For what I have, I need not to repeat:
And what I want, it boots not to complain.

1 *Lady.* Madam, I'll sing.

Queen. 'Tis well, that thou hast cause;
But thou should'st please me better, would'st thou weep.

1 *Lady.* I could weep, madam, would it do you good.

Queen. And I could weep, would weeping do me good,
And never borrow any tear of thee.
But stay, here come the gardeners:
Let's step into the shadow of these trees.—

Enter a Gardener, *and two* Servants.

My wretchedness unto a row of pins,
They'll talk of state; for every one doth so
Against a change: Woe is forerun with woe.
[Queen *and* Ladies *retire.*

Gard. Go, bind thou up yon' dangling apricocks,
Which, like unruly children, make their sire
Stoop with oppression of their prodigal weight:
Give some supportance to the bending twigs.—
Go thou, and, like an executioner,
Cut off the heads of too fast growing sprays,
That look too lofty in our commonwealth:
All must be even in our government.——
You thus employ'd, I will go root away
The noisome weeds, that without profit suck
The soil's fertility from wholesome flowers.

1 *Serv.* Why should we, in the compass of a pale,
Keep law, and form, and due proportion,
Showing, as in a model, our firm estate?
When our sea-walled garden, the whole land,
Is full of weeds; her fairest flowers chok'd up,
Her fruit-trees all unprun'd, her hedges ruin'd,
Her knots disorder'd, and her wholesome herbs
Swarming with caterpillars?

Gard. Hold thy peace:—
He that hath suffered this disorder'd spring,
Hath now himself met with the fall of leaf:
The weeds, that his broad-spreading leaves did shelter,
That seem'd in eating him to hold him up,
Are pluck'd up, root and all, by Bolingbroke;
I mean, the earl of Wiltshire, Bushy, Green.

1 *Serv.* What, are they dead?

Gard. They are; and Bolingbroke
Hath seiz'd the wasteful king.—Oh! what pity is it,
That he had not so trimm'd and dress'd his land,
As we this garden! We at time of year
Do wound the bark, the skin of our fruit trees;
Lest, being over-proud with sap and blood,
With too much riches it confound itself:
Had he done so to great and growing men,
They might have liv'd to bear, and he to taste
Their fruits of duty. All superfluous branches
We lop away, that bearing boughs may live:
Had he done so, himself had borne the crown,
Which waste of idle hours hath quite thrown down.

1 *Serv.* What think you then, the king shall be depos'd?

Gard. Depress'd he is already; and depos'd,
'Tis doubt, he will be: Letters came last night
To a dear friend of the good duke of York's,
That tell black tidings.

Queen. O, I am press'd to death,
Through want of speaking!—Thou, old Adam's likeness, [*Coming from her concealment.*
Set to dress this garden, how dares
Thy harsh-rude tongue sound this unpleasing news?
What Eve, what serpent hath suggested thee
To make a second fall of cursed man?
Why dost thou say, King Richard is depos'd?
Dar'st thou, thou little better thing than earth,
Divine his downfal? Say, where, when, and how,
Cam'st thou by these ill tidings? speak, thou wretch.

Gard. Pardon me, madam: little joy have I,
To breathe this news; yet, what I say is true.
King Richard, he is in the mighty hold
Of Bolingbroke: their fortunes both are weigh'd:

In your lord's scale is nothing but himself,
And some few vanities that make him light;
But in the balance of great Bolingbroke,
Besides himself, are all the English peers,
And with that odds he weighs King Richard down.
Post you to London, and you'll find it so;
I speak no more than every one doth know.

Queen. Nimble mischance, that art so light of foot,
Doth not thy embassage belong to me,
And am I last that knows it? O, thou think'st
To serve me last, that I may longest keep
Thy sorrow in my breast. Come, ladies, go,
To meet at London London's king in woe.—
What, was I born to this! that my sad look
Should grace the triumph of great Bolingbroke?
Gardener, for telling me this news of woe,
I would, the plants thou graft'st, may never grow. [*Exeunt* Queen *and* Ladies.

Gard. Poor queen! so that thy state might be no worse,
I would my skill were subject to thy curse.—
Here did she drop a tear; here, in this place,
I'll set a bank of rue, sour herb of grace:
Rue, even for ruth, here shortly shall be seen,
In the remembrance of a weeping queen. [*Exeunt.*

ACT IV.

SCENE I. London. Westminster *Hall.*

The Lords *spiritual on the right side of the Throne; the* Lords *temporal on the left; the* Commons *below. Enter* BOLINGBROKE, AUMERLE, SURREY, NORTHUMBERLAND, PERCY, FITZWATER, *another* Lord, *Bishop of* CARLISLE, *Abbot of* WESTMINSTER, *and* Attendants, Officers *behind, with* BAGOT.

Boling. Call forth Bagot:——
Now, Bagot, freely speak thy mind;
What thou dost know of noble Gloster's death;
Who wrought it with the king, and who perform'd
The bloody office of his timeless end.

Bagot. Then set before my face the Lord Aumerle.

Boling. Cousin, stand forth, and look upon that man.

Bagot. My Lord Aumerle, I know, your daring tongue
Scorns to unsay what once it hath deliver'd.
In that dead time when Gloster's death was plotted,
I heard you say,—*Is not my arm of length,*
That reacheth from the restful English court
As far as Calais, to my uncle's head?
Amongst much other talk, that very time,
I heard you say, that you had rather refuse
The offer of a hundred thousand crowns,
Than Bolingbroke's return to England;
Adding withal, how blest this land would be,
In this your cousin's death.

Aum. Princes, and noble lords,
What answer shall I make to this base man?
Shall I so much dishonour my fair stars,
On equal terms to give him chastisement?
Either I must, or have mine honour soil'd
With the attainder of his sland'rous lips.——
There is my gage, the manual seal of death,
That marks thee out for hell; I say, thou liest,
And will maintain, what thou hast said, is false,
In thy heart-blood, though being all too base
To stain the temper of my knightly sword.

Boling. Bagot, forbear, thou shalt not take it up.

Aum. Excepting one, I would he were the best
In all this presence, that hath mov'd me so.

Fitz. If that thy valour stand on sympathies,
There is my gage, Aumerle, in gage to thine:
By that fair sun that shows me where thou stand'st,
I heard thee say, and vauntingly thou spak'st it,
That thou wert cause of noble Gloster's death.
If thou deny'st it, twenty times thou liest;
And I will turn thy falsehood to thy heart,
Where it was forged, with my rapier's point.

Aum. Thou dar'st not, coward, live to see that day.

Fitz. Now, by my soul, I would it were this hour.

Aum. Fitzwater, thou art damn'd to hell for this.

Percy. Aumerle, thou liest; his honour is as true,
In this appeal, as thou art all unjust:
And, that thou art so, there I throw my gage,
To prove it on thee to the extremest point
Of mortal breathing; seize it, if thou dar'st.

Aum. And if I do not, may my hands rot off,
And never brandish more revengeful steel
Over the glittering helmet of my foe!

Lord. I task the earth to the like, forsworn Aumerle;
And spur thee on with full as many lies
As may be holla'd in thy treacherous ear
From sun to sun: there is my honour's pawn;
Engage it to the trial, if thou dar'st.

Aum. Who sets me else? by heaven, I'll throw at all:
I have a thousand spirits in one breast,
To answer twenty thousand such as you.

Surrey. My Lord Fitzwater, I do remember well
The very time Aumerle and you did talk.

Fitz. 'Tis very true: you were in presence then;
And you can witness with me, this is true.

Surrey. As false, by heaven, as heaven itself is true.

Fitz. Surrey, thou liest.

Surrey. Dishonourable boy!
That lie shall lie so heavy on my sword,
That it shall render vengeance and revenge,
Till thou the lie-giver, and that lie, do lie
In earth as quiet as thy father's scull.
In proof whereof, there is my honour's pawn;
Engage it to the trial, if thou dar'st.

Fitz. How fondly dost thou spur a forward horse!
If I dare eat, or drink, or breathe, or live,
I dare meet Surrey in a wilderness,
And spit upon him, whilst I say, he lies,
And lies, and lies: there is my bond of faith,
To tie thee to my strong correction.—
As I intend to thrive in this new world,
Aumerle is guilty of my true appeal:
Besides, I heard the banish'd Norfolk say,
That thou, Aumerle, didst send two of thy men
To execute the noble duke at Calais.

Aum. Some honest Christian trust me with a gage,
That Norfolk lies: here do I throw down this,
If he may be repeal'd to try his honour.

Boling. These differences shall all rest under gage,
Till Norfolk be repeal'd: repeal'd he shall be,
And, though mine enemy, restor'd again
To all his land and signories; when he's return'd,
Against Aumerle we will enforce his trial.

Car. That honourable day shall ne'er be seen.—
Many a time hath banish'd Norfolk fought
For Jesu Christ; in glorious Christian field
Streaming the ensign of the Christian cross,
Against black pagans, Turks, and Saracens:
And, toil'd with works of war, retir'd himself
To Italy; and there, at Venice, gave
His body to that pleasant country's earth,
And his pure soul unto his captain Christ,
Under whose colours he had fought so long.

Boling. Why, bishop, is Norfolk dead?

Car. As sure as I live, my lord.
Boling. Sweet peace conduct his sweet soul to the bosom
Of good old Abraham!—Lords appellants,
Your differences shall all rest under gage,
Till we assign you to your days of trial.

Enter YORK, *attended.*

York. Great duke of Lancaster, I come to thee
From plume-pluck'd Richard; who with willing soul
Adopts thee heir, and his high sceptre yields
To the possession of thy royal hand:
Ascend his throne, descending now from him,—
And long live Henry, of that name the fourth!
Boling. In God's name, I'll ascend the regal throne.
Car. Marry, God forbid!—
Worst in this royal presence, may I speak,
Yet best beseeming me to speak the truth.
Would God, that any in this noble presence
Were enough noble to be upright judge
Of noble Richard; then true nobless would
Learn him forbearance from so foul a wrong.
What subject can give sentence on his king?
And who sits here, that is not Richard's subject?
Thieves are not judg'd, but they are by to hear,
Although apparent guilt be seen in them.
And shall the figure of God's majesty,
His captain, steward, deputy elect,
Anointed, crowned, planted many years,
Be judg'd by subject and inferior breath,
And he himself not present? O, forbid it, God,
That in a Christian climate, souls refin'd
Should show so heinous, black, obscene a deed!
I speak to subjects, and a subject speaks,
Stirr'd up by heaven, thus boldly for his king.
My lord of Hereford here, whom you call king,
Is a foul traitor to proud Hereford's king:
And if you crown him, let me prophesy,—
The blood of English shall manure the ground,
And future ages groan for this foul act;
Peace shall go sleep with Turks and infidels,
And, in this seat of peace, tumultuous wars
Shall kin with kin, and kind with kind confound:
Disorder, horror, fear, and mutiny
Shall here inhabit, and this land be call'd
The field of Golgotha, and dead men's sculls.
O, if you rear this house against this house,
It will the wofullest division prove,
That ever fell upon this cursed earth:
Prevent, resist it, let it not be so,
Lest child's child's children cry against you—woe!
North. Well have you argu'd, sir; and, for your pains,
Of capital treason we arrest you here:—
My lord of Westminster, be it your charge
To keep him safely till his day of trial.—
May't please you, lords, to grant the commons' suit.
Boling. Fetch hither Richard, that in common view
He may surrender; so we shall proceed
Without suspicion.
York. I will be his conduct. [*Exit.*
Boling. Lords, you that are here under our arrest,
Procure your sureties for your days of answer:—
Little are we beholden to your love, [*To* CAR.
And little look'd for at your helping hands.

Re-enter YORK, *with* KING RICHARD, *and* Officers *bearing the crown, &c.*

K. Rich. Alack, why am I sent for to a king,
Before I have shook off the regal thoughts
Wherewith I reign'd? I hardly yet have learn'd
To insinuate, flatter, bow, and bend my knee:—
Give sorrow leave a while to tutor me
To this submission. Yet I well remember
The favours of these men: Were they not mine?
Did they not sometime cry, all hail! to me?
So Judas did to Christ: but he, in twelve,
Found truth in all but one; I, in twelve thousand, none.
God save the king!—Will no man say, amen
Am I both priest and clerk? well then, amen.
God save the king! although I be not he:
And yet, amen, if heaven do think him me.—
To do what service am I sent for hither?
York. To do that office, of thine own good will,
Which tired majesty did make thee offer,—
The resignation of thy state and crown
To Henry Bolingbroke.
K. Rich. Give me the crown;—Here, cousin, seize the crown;
On this side, my hand; and on that side, thine.
Now is this golden crown like a deep well,
That owes two buckets filling one another;
The emptier ever dancing in the air,
The other down, unseen, and full of water:
That bucket down, and full of tears, am I,
Drinking my griefs, whilst you mount up on high.
Boling. I thought, you had been willing to resign.
K. Rich. My crown, I am; but still my griefs are mine:
You may my glories and my state depose,
But not my griefs; still am I king of those.
Boling. Part of your cares you give me with your crown.
K. Rich. Your cares set up, do not pluck my cares down.
My care is—loss of care, by old care done;
Your care is—gain of care, by new care won:
The cares I give, I have, though given away;
They tend the crown, yet still with me they stay.
Boling. Are you contented to resign the crown?
K. Rich. Ay, no;—no, ay;—for I must nothing be;
Therefore no no, for I resign to thee.
Now mark me how I will undo myself:—
I give this heavy weight from off my head,
And this unwieldy sceptre from my hand,
The pride of kingly sway from out my heart;
With mine own tears I wash away my balm,
With mine own hands I give away my crown,
With mine own tongue deny my sacred state,
With mine own breath release all duteous oaths:
All pomp and majesty I do forswear;
My manors, rents, revenues, I forego;
My acts, decrees, and statutes, I deny:
God pardon all oaths, that are broke to me!
God keep all vows unbroke, are made to thee!
Make me, that nothing have, with nothing griev'd;
And thou with all pleas'd, that hast all achiev'd!
Long mayst thou live in Richard's seat to sit,
And soon lie Richard in an earthy pit!
God save King Henry, unking'd Richard says,
And send him many years of sunshine days!—
What more remains?
North. No more, but that you read [*Offering a Paper.*
These accusations, and these grievous crimes,
Committed by your person, and your followers,
Against the state and profit of this land;
That, by confessing them, the souls of men
May deem that you are worthily depos'd.
K. Rich. Must I do so? and must I ravel out
My weav'd up follies? Gentle Northumberland,
If thy offences were upon record,
Would it not shame thee in so fair a troop,
To read a lecture of them? If thou would'st,
There should'st thou find one heinous article,—
Containing the deposing of a king,
And cracking the strong warrant of an oath,—
Mark'd with a blot, damn'd in the book of heaven:—
Nay, all of you, that stand and look upon me,
Whilst that my wretchedness doth bait myself,—
Though some of you, with Pilate, wash your hands,

Showing an outward pity; yet you Pilates
Have here deliver'd me to my sour cross,
And water cannot wash away your sin.

North. My lord, despatch; read o'er these articles.

K. Rich. Mine eyes are full of tears, I cannot see:
And yet salt water blinds them not so much,
But they can see a sort of traitors here.
Nay, if I turn mine eyes upon myself,
I find myself a traitor with the rest:
For I have given here my soul's consent,
To undeck the pompous body of a king;
Make glory base; and sovereignty, a slave;
Proud majesty, a subject; state, a peasant.

North. My lord,——

K. Rich. No lord of thine, thou haught, insulting man,
Nor no man's lord; I have no name, no title,—
No, not that name was given me at the font,—
But 'tis usurp'd:—Alack the heavy day,
That I have worn so many winters out,
And know not now what name to call myself!
O, that I were a mockery king of snow,
Standing before the sun of Bolingbroke,
To melt myself away in water-drops!—
Good king,—great king,—(and yet not greatly good),
An if my word be sterling yet in England,
Let it command a mirror hither straight;
That it may show me what a face I have,
Since it is bankrupt of his majesty.

Boling. Go some of you, and fetch a looking-glass. [*Exit an* Attendant.

North. Read o'er this paper, while the glass doth come.

K. Rich. Fiend! thou torment'st me ere I come to hell.

Boling. Urge it no more, my Lord Northumberland.

North. The commons will not then be satisfied.

K. Rich. They shall be satisfied: I'll read enough,
When I do see the very book indeed
Where all my sins are writ, and that's—myself.

Re-enter Attendant, *with a Glass.*

Give me that glass, and therein will I read.—
No deeper wrinkles yet? Hath sorrow struck
So many blows upon this face of mine,
And made no deeper wounds?—O, flattering glass,
Like to my followers in prosperity,
Thou dost beguile me! Was this face the face,
That every day under his household roof
Did keep ten thousand men? Was this the face,
That, like the sun, did make beholders wink:
Was this the face, that fac'd so many follies,
And was at last out-fac'd by Bolingbroke?
A brittle glory shineth in this face:
As brittle as the glory is the face;
[*Dashes the Glass against the ground.*
For there it is, crack'd in a hundred shivers.—
Mark, silent king, the moral of this sport,—
How soon my sorrow hath destroy'd my face.

Boling. The shadow of your sorrow hath destroy'd
The shadow of your face.

K. Rich. Say that again.
The shadow of my sorrow? Ha! let's see:—
'Tis very true, my grief lies all within;
And these external manners of lament
Are merely shadows to the unseen grief,
That swells with silence in the tortur'd soul;
There lies the substance: and I thank thee, king,
For thy great bounty, that not only giv'st
Me cause to wail, but teachest me the way
How to lament the cause. I'll beg one boon,
And then be gone, and trouble you no more.
Shall I obtain it?

Boling. Name it, fair cousin.

K. Rich. Fair cousin! I am greater than a king:
For, when I was a king, my flatterers
Were then but subjects: being now a subject,
I have a king here to my flatterer.
Being so great, I have no need to beg.

Boling. Yet ask.

K. Rich. And shall I have?

Boling. You shall.

K. Rich. Then give me leave to go.

Boling. Whither?

K. Rich. Whither you will, so I were from your sights.

Boling. Go, some of you, convey him to the Tower.

K. Rich. O, good! Convey?—Conveyers are you all,
That rise thus nimbly by a true king's fall.
[*Exeunt* K. RICH. *some* Lords, *and a* Guard.

Boling. On Wednesday next we solemnly set down
Our coronation: lords, prepare yourselves.
[*Exeunt all but the* Abbot, Bishop *of* Carlisle, *and* AUMERLE.

Abbot. A woful pageant have we here beheld.

Car. The woe's to come: the children yet unborn
Shall feel this day as sharp to them as thorn.

Aum. You holy clergymen, is there no plot
To rid the realm of this pernicious blot?

Abbot. Before I freely speak my mind herein,
You shall not only take the sacrament
To bury mine intents, but also to effect
Whatever I shall happen to devise:—
I see your brows are full of discontent,
Your hearts of sorrow, and your eyes of tears;
Come home with me to supper; I will lay
A plot, shall show us all a merry day. [*Exeunt.*

ACT V.

SCENE I. London. *A Street leading to the Tower.*

Enter Queen, *and* Ladies.

Queen. This way the king will come; this is the way
To Julius Cæsar's ill-erected tower,
To whose flint bosom my condemned lord
Is doom'd a prisoner, by proud Bolingbroke:
Here let us rest, if this rebellious earth
Have any resting for her true king's queen.

Enter KING RICHARD, *and* Guards.

But soft, but see, or rather do not see,
My fair rose wither: Yet look up; behold;
That you in pity may dissolve to dew,
And wash him fresh again with true-love tears.—
Ah, thou the model where old Troy did stand;
Thou map of honour; thou King Richard's tomb,
And not King Richard; thou most beauteous inn,
Why should hard-favour'd grief be lodg'd in thee,
When triumph is become an ale-house guest?

K. Rich. Join not with grief, fair woman, do not so,
To make my end too sudden: learn, good soul,
To think our former state a happy dream;
From which awak'd, the truth of what we are
Shows us but this; I am sworn brother, sweet,
To grim necessity; and he and I
Will keep a league till death. Hie thee to France,
And cloister thee in some religious house:
Our holy lives must win a new world's crown,
Which our profane hours here have stricken down.

Queen. What, is my Richard both in shape and mind
Transform'd and weaken'd? Hath Bolingbroke
Depos'd thine intellect? hath he been in thy heart?
The lion, dying, thrusteth forth his paw,
And wounds the earth, if nothing else, with rage
To be o'erpower'd; and wilt thou, pupil-like,
Take thy correction mildly? kiss the rod,

And fawn on rage with base humility,
Which art a lion, and a king of beasts?

K. Rich. A king of beasts, indeed: if aught but beasts,
I had been still a happy king of men.
Good sometime queen, prepare thee hence for France:
Think, I am dead; and that even here thou tak'st,
As from my death-bed, my last living leave.
In winter's tedious nights, sit by the fire
With good old folks, and let them tell thee tales
Of woful ages, long ago betid:
And, ere thou bid good night, to quit their grief,
Tell thou the lamentable fall of me,
And send the hearers weeping to their beds.
For why, the senseless brands will sympathize
The heavy accent of thy moving tongue,
And, in compassion, weep the fire out:
And some will mourn in ashes, some coal-black,
For the deposing of a rightful king.

Enter NORTHUMBERLAND, *attended.*

North. My lord, the mind of Bolingbroke is chang'd;
You must to Pomfret, not unto the Tower.——
And, madam, there is order ta'en for you:
With all swift speed you must away to France.

K. Rich. Northumberland, thou ladder wherewithal
The mounting Bolingbroke ascends my throne,—
The time shall not be many hours of age
More than it is, ere foul sin, gathering head,
Shall break into corruption: thou shalt think,
Though he divide the realm, and give thee half,
It is too little, helping him to all;
And he shall think, that thou, which know'st the way
To plant unrightful kings, wilt know again,
Being ne'er so little urg'd, another way
To pluck him headlong from the usurped throne.
The love of wicked friends converts to fear;
That fear, to hate; and hate turns one, or both,
To worthy danger, and deserved death.

North. My guilt be on my head, and there an end.
Take leave, and part; for you must part forthwith.

K. Rich. Doubly divorc'd?—Bad men, ye violate
A twofold marriage; 'twixt my crown and me;
And then, betwixt me and my married wife.—
Let me unkiss the oath 'twixt thee and me;
And yet not so, for with a kiss 'twas made.—
Part us, Northumberland: I towards the north,
Where shivering cold and sickness pines the clime;
My wife to France; from whence, set forth in pomp,
She came adorned hither like sweet May,
Sent back like Hallowmas, or short'st of day.

Queen. And must we be divided? must we part?

K. Rich. Ay, hand from hand, my love, and heart from heart.

Queen. Banish us both, and send the king with me.

North. That were some love, but little policy.

Queen. Then whither he goes, thither let me go?

K. Rich. So two, together weeping, make one woe.
Weep thou for me in France, I for thee here;
Better far off, than—near, be ne'er the near'.
Go, count thy way with sighs; I, mine with groans.

Queen. So longest way shall have the longest moans.

K. Rich. Twice for one step I'll groan, the way being short,
And piece the way out with a heavy heart.
Come, come, in wooing sorrow let's be brief,
Since, wedding it, there is such length in grief.
One kiss shall stop our mouths, and dumbly part:
Thus give I mine, and thus I take thy heart. [*They kiss.*

Queen. Give me mine own again; 'twere no good part,
To take on me to keep, and kill thy heart. [*Kiss again.*
So now I have mine own again, begone,
That I may strive to kill it with a groan.

K. Rich. We make woe wanton with this fond delay:
Once more, adieu; the rest let sorrow say. [*Exeunt.*

SCENE II.

The same. A Room in the Duke *of* York's *Palace.*
Enter YORK, *and his* Duchess.

Duch. My lord, you told me, you would tell the rest,
When weeping made you break the story off
Of our two cousins coming into London.

York. Where did I leave?

Duch. At that sad stop, my lord,
Where rude misgovern'd hands, from windows' tops,
Threw dust and rubbish on King Richard's head.

York. Then, as I said, the duke, great Bolingbroke,—
Mounted upon a hot and fiery steed,
Which his aspiring rider seem'd to know,—
With slow, but stately pace, kept on his course,
While all tongues cried—God save thee, Bolingbroke! [spake,
You would have thought the very windows
So many greedy looks of young and old
Through casements darted their desiring eyes
Upon his visage; and that all the walls,
With painted imag'ry, had said at once,—
Jesu preserve thee! welcome, Bolingbroke!
Whilst he, from one side to the other turning,
Bare-headed, lower than his proud steed's neck,
Bespake them thus,—I thank you, countrymen:
And thus still doing, thus he pass'd along.

Duch. Alas, poor Richard! where rides he the while?

York. As in a theatre, the eyes of men,
After a well grac'd actor leaves the stage,
Are idly bent on him that enters next,
Thinking his prattle to be tedious:
Even so, or with much more contempt, men's eyes
Did scowl on Richard; no man cried, God save him;
No joyful tongue gave him his welcome home:
But dust was thrown upon his sacred head;
Which with such gentle sorrow he shook off,—
His face still combating with tears and smiles,
The badges of his grief and patience,—
That had not God, for some strong purpose, steel'd
The hearts of men, they must perforce have melted,
And barbarism itself have pitied him.
But heaven hath a hand in these events;
To whose high will we bound our calm contents.
To Bolingbroke are we sworn subjects now,
Whose state and honour I for aye allow.

Enter AUMERLE.

Duch. Here comes my son Aumerle.

York. Aumerle that was;
But that is lost, for being Richard's friend;
And, madam, you must call him Rutland now:
I am in parliament pledge for his truth,
And lasting fealty to the new-made king.

Duch. Welcome, my son: Who are the violets now,
That strew the green lap of the new-come spring?

Aum. Madam, I know not, nor I greatly care not;
God knows, I had as lief be none as one.

York. Well, bear you well in this new spring of time,
Lest you be cropp'd before you come to prime.
What news from Oxford? hold those justs and triumphs?

Aum. For aught I know, my lord, they do.
York. You will be there, I know.
Aum. If God prevent it not; I purpose so.
York. What seal is that, that hangs about thy bosom?
Yea, look'st thou pale? let me see the writing.
Aum. My lord, 'tis nothing.
York. No matter then who sees it;
I will be satisfied, let me see the writing.
Aum. I do beseech your grace to pardon me;
It is a matter of small consequence,
Which for some reasons I would not have seen.
York. Which for some reasons, sir, I mean to see.
I fear, I fear,—
Duch. What should you fear?
'Tis nothing but some bond that he is enter'd into
For gay apparel, 'gainst the triumph day.
York. Bound to himself? what doth he with a bond
That he is bound to? Wife, thou art a fool.—
Boy, let me see the writing.
Aum. I do beseech you, pardon me; I may not show it.
York. I will be satisfied; let me see it, I say.
[*Snatches it, and reads.*
Treason! foul treason!—villain! traitor! slave!
Duch. What is the matter, my lord?
York. Ho! who is within there? [*Enter a* Servant.] Saddle my horse.
God for his mercy! what treachery is here!
Duch. Why, what is it, my lord?
York. Give me my boots, I say; saddle my horse:—
Now by mine honour, by my life, my troth,
I will appeach the villain. [*Exit* Servant.
Duch. What's the matter?
York. Peace, foolish woman.
Duch. I will not peace:—What's the matter, son?
Aum. Good mother, be content; it is no more
Than my poor life must answer.
Duch. Thy life answer?

Re-enter Servant, *with Boots.*

York. Bring me my boots, I will unto the king.
Duch. Strike him, Aumerle.—Poor boy, thou art amaz'd:
Hence, villain; never more come in my sight.—
[*To the* Servant.
York. Give me my boots, I say.
Duch. Why, York, what wilt thou do?
Wilt thou not hide the trespass of thine own?
Have we more sons? or are we like to have?
Is not my teeming date drunk up with time?
And wilt thou pluck my fair son from mine age,
And rob me of a mother's happy name?
Is he not like thee? is he not thine own?
York. Thou fond mad woman,
Wilt thou conceal this dark conspiracy?
A dozen of them here have ta'en the sacrament,
And interchangeably set down their hands,
To kill the king at Oxford.
Duch. He shall be none;
We'll keep him here: Then what is that to him?
York. Away,
Fond woman! were he twenty times my son,
I would appeach him.
Duch. Hadst thou groan'd for him,
As I have done, thou'dst be more pitiful.
But now I know thy mind; thou dost suspect,
That I have been disloyal to thy bed,
And that he is a bastard, not thy son:
Sweet York, sweet husband, be not of that mind;
He is as like thee as a man may be,
Not like to me, or any of my kin,
And yet I love him.
York. Make way, unruly woman. [*Exit.*
Duch. After, Aumerle: mount thee upon his horse;
Spur, post; and get before him to the king,
And beg thy pardon ere he do accuse thee.
I'll not be long behind; though I be old,
I doubt not but to ride as fast as York:
And never will I rise up from the ground,
Till Bolingbroke have pardon'd thee: Away;
Begone. [*Exeunt.*

SCENE III. Windsor. *A Room in the Castle.*

Enter BOLINGBROKE, *as King;* PERCY, *and other* Lords.

Boling. Can no man tell of my unthrifty son?
'Tis full three months since I did see him last:—
If any plague hang over us, 'tis he.
I would to God, my lords, he might be found:
Inquire at London, 'mongst the taverns there,
For there, they say, he daily doth frequent,
With unrestrained loose companions;
Even such, they say, as stand in narrow lanes,
And beat our watch, and rob our passengers;
While he, young, wanton, and effeminate boy,
Takes on the point of honour, to support
So dissolute a crew.
Percy. My lord, some two days since I saw [the prince;
And told him of these triumphs held at Oxford.
Boling. And what said the gallant?
Percy. His answer was,—he would unto the stews;
And from the commonest creature pluck a glove,
And wear it as a favour; and with that
He would unhorse the lustiest challenger.
Boling. As dissolute, as desperate: yet, through both
I see some sparkles of a better hope,
Which elder days may happily bring forth.
But who comes here?

Enter AUMERLE, *hastily.*

Aum. Where is the king?
Boling. What means
Our cousin, that he stares and looks so wildly?
Aum. God save your grace. I do beseech your majesty,
To have some conference with your grace alone.
Boling. Withdraw yourselves, and leave us here alone.— [*Exeunt* PERCY *and* Lords.
What is the matter with our cousin now?
Aum. For ever may my knees grow to the earth, [*Kneels.*
My tongue cleave to the roof within my mouth,
Unless a pardon, ere I rise, or speak.
Boling. Intended, or committed was this fault?
If but the first, how heinous ere it be,
To win thy after-love, I pardon thee.
Aum. Then give me leave that I may turn the [key,
That no man enter till my tale be done.
Boling. Have thy desire. [AUM. *locks the door.*
York. [*Within.*] My liege, beware; look to thyself;
Thou hast a traitor in thy presence there.
Boling. Villain, I'll make thee safe. [*Drawing.*
Aum. Stay thy revengeful hand;
Thou hast no cause to fear.
York. [*Within.*] Open the door, secure, foolhardy king:
Shall I, for love, speak treason to thy face?
Open the door, or I will break it open.
[BOLINGBROKE *opens the door.*

Enter YORK.

Boling. What is the matter, uncle? speak;
Recover breath; tell us how near is danger,
That we may arm us to encounter it.
York. Peruse this writing here, and thou shalt know
The treason that my haste forbids me show.
Aum. Remember, as thou read'st, thy promise past:
I do repent me; read not my name there,
My heart is not confederate with my hand.
York. 'Twas, villain, ere thy hand did set it down.—
I tore it from the traitor's bosom, king:
Fear, and not love, begets his penitence:
Forget to pity him, lest thy pity prove
A serpent that will sting thee to the heart.

Boling. O heinous, strong, and bold conspiracy!—
O loyal father of a treacherous son!
Thou sheer, immaculate, and silver fountain,
From whence this stream through muddy passages,
Hath held his current, and defil'd himself!
Thy overflow of good converts to bad;
And thy abundant goodness shall excuse
This deadly blot in thy digressing son.

York. So shall my virtue be his vice's bawd;
And he shall spend mine honour with his shame,
As thriftless sons their scraping father's gold.
Mine honour lives when his dishonour dies,
Or my sham'd life in his dishonour lies:
Thou kill'st me in his life; giving him breath,
The traitor lives, the true man's put to death.

Duch. [*Within.*] What ho, my liege! for God's sake let me in.

Boling. What shrill-voic'd suppliant makes this eager cry?

Duch. A woman, and thine aunt, great king; 'tis I.
Speak with me, pity me, open the door;
A beggar begs, that never begg'd before.

Boling. Our scene is alter'd,—from a serious thing,
And now chang'd to *The Beggar and the King.*—
My dangerous cousin, let your mother in;
I know, she's come to pray for your foul sin.

York. If thou do pardon, whosoever pray,
More sins, for this forgiveness, prosper may.
This fester'd joint cut off, the rest rests sound,
This, let alone, will all the rest confound.

Enter Duchess.

Duch. O king, believe not this hard-hearted man;
Love, loving not itself, none other can.

York. Thou frantick woman, what dost thou make here?
Shall thy old dugs once more a traitor rear?

Duch. Sweet York, be patient: Hear me, gentle liege. [*Kneels.*

Boling. Rise up, good aunt.

Duch. Not yet, I thee beseech:
For ever will I kneel upon my knees,
And never see day that the happy sees,
Till thou give joy; until thou bid me joy,
By pardoning Rutland, my transgressing boy.

Aum. Unto my mother's prayers, I bend my knee. [*Kneels.*

York. Against them both, my true joints bended be. [*Kneels.*
Ill may'st thou thrive, if thou grant any grace!

Duch. Pleads he in earnest? look upon his face;
His eyes do drop no tears, his prayers are in jest;
His words come from his mouth, ours from our breast;
He prays but faintly, and would be denied;
We pray with heart, and soul, and all beside:
His weary joints would gladly rise, I know;
Our knees shall kneel till to the ground they grow:
His prayers are full of false hypocrisy;
Ours, of true zeal and deep integrity.
Our prayers do out-pray his; then let them have
That mercy, which true prayers ought to have.

Boling. Good aunt, stand up.

Duch. Nay, do not say—stand up;
But, pardon, first; and afterwards stand up.
An if I were thy nurse, thy tongue to teach,
Pardon—should be the first word of thy speech.
I never long'd to hear a word till now;
Say, pardon, king; let pity teach thee how:
The word is short, but not so short as sweet;
No word like, pardon, for kings' mouths so meet.

York. Speak it in French, king; say, *pardonnez moy.*

Duch. Dost thou teach pardon pardon to destroy?
Ah, my sour husband, my hard-hearted lord,
That sett'st the word itself against the word!—
Speak, pardon, as 'tis current in our land:
The chopping French we do not understand.
Thine eye begins to speak, set thy tongue there;
Or, in thy piteous heart plant thou thine ear;
That, hearing how our plaints and prayers do pierce,
Pity may move thee, pardon to rehearse.

Boling. Good aunt, stand up.

Duch. I do not sue to stand,
Pardon is all the suit I have in hand.

Boling. I pardon him, as God shall pardon me.

Duch. O happy vantage of a kneeling knee!
Yet am I sick for fear: speak it again;
Twice saying pardon, doth not pardon twain,
But makes one pardon strong.

Boling. With all my heart
I pardon him.

Duch. A god on earth thou art.

Boling. But for our trusty brother-in-law, and the abbot,
With all the rest of that consorted crew,—
Destruction straight shall dog them at the heels.—
Good uncle, help to order several powers
To Oxford, or where'er these traitors are:
They shall not live within this world, I swear,
But I will have them, if I once know where.
Uncle, farewell,—and, cousin, too, adieu:
Your mother well hath pray'd, and prove you true.

Duch. Come, my old son;—I pray God, make thee new. [*Exeunt.*

SCENE IV.

Enter EXTON, *and a* Servant.

Exton. Didst thou not mark the king, what words he spake?
Have I no friend will rid me of this living fear?
Was it not so?

Serv. Those were his very words.

Exton. *Have I no friend?* quoth he; he spake it twice,
And urg'd it twice together; did he not?

Serv. He did.

Exton. And, speaking it, he wistfully look'd on me;
As who should say,—I would, thou wert the man
That would divorce this terror from my heart;
Meaning the king at Pomfret. Come, let's go;
I am the king's friend, and will rid his foe. [*Exeunt.*

SCENE V. Pomfret. *The Dungeon of the Castle.*

Enter KING RICHARD.

K. Rich. I have been studying how I may compare
This prison, where I live, unto the world:
And, for because the world is populous,
And here is not a creature but myself,
I cannot do it;—Yet I'll hammer it out.
My brain I'll prove the female to my soul;
My soul the father: and these two beget
A generation of still breeding thoughts,
And these same thoughts people this little world;
In humours, like the people of this world,
For no thought is contented. The better sort,—
As thoughts of things divine,—are intermix'd
With scruples, and do set the word itself
Against the word:
As thus,—*Come, little ones!* and then again,—
It is as hard to come, as for a camel
To thread the postern of a needle's eye.
Thoughts tending to ambition, they do plot
Unlikely wonders: how these vain weak nails
May tear a passage through the flinty ribs
Of this hard world, my ragged prison walls;
And, for they cannot, die in their own pride.
Thoughts tending to content, flatter themselves,—
That they are not the first of fortune's slaves,
Nor shall not be the last; like silly beggars,
Who, sitting in the stocks, refuge their shame,—
That many have, and others must sit there:
And in this thought they find a kind of ease,

Bearing their own misfortune on their back
Of such as have before endured the like:
Thus play I, in one person, many people,
And none contented: Sometimes am I king:
Then treason makes me wish myself a beggar,
And so I am: Then crushing penury
Persuades me, I was better when a king;
Then am I king'd again: and, by-and-by,
Think that I am unking'd by Bolingbroke,
And straight am nothing:—But, whate'er I am,
Nor I, nor any man, that but man is,
With nothing shall be pleas'd, till he be eas'd
With being nothing.—Musick do I hear?
[*Musick.*
Ha, ha! keep time:—How sour sweet musick is,
When time is broke, and no proportion kept!
So is it in the musick of men's lives.
And here have I the daintiness of ear
To check time broke in a disorder'd string;
But for the concord of my state and time,
Had not an ear to hear my true time broke.
I wasted time, and now doth time waste me.
For now hath time made me his numb'ring clock:
My thoughts are minutes; and, with sighs, they jar
Their watches on to mine eyes, the outward watch,
Whereto my finger, like a dial's point,
Is pointing still, in cleansing them from tears.
Now, sir, the sound, that tells what hour it is,
Are clamorous groans, that strike upon my heart,
Which is the bell: So sighs, and tears, and groans,
Show minutes, times, and hours:—but my time
Runs posting on in Bolingbroke's proud joy,
While I stand fooling here, his Jack o' the clock.
This musick mads me, let it sound no more;
For, though it have holpe madmen to their wits,
In me, it seems, it will make wise men mad,
Yet blessing on his heart that gives it me!
For 'tis a sign of love; and love to Richard
Is a strange brooch in this all-hating world.

Enter Groom.

Groom. Hail, royal prince!
K. Rich. Thanks, noble peer;
The cheapest of us is ten groats too dear.
What art thou? and how comest thou hither,
Where no man never comes, but that sad dog
That brings me food, to make misfortune live?
Groom. I was a poor groom of thy stable, king,
When thou wert king; who travelling towards York,
With much ado, at length have gotten leave
To look upon my sometimes royal master's face.
O, how it yearn'd my heart, when I beheld,
In London streets, that coronation day,
When Bolingbroke rode on roan Barbary!
That horse, that I so carefully have dress'd!
K. Rich. Rode he on Barbary? Tell me, gentle friend,
How went he under him?
Groom. So proudly, as if he disdain'd the ground.
K. Rich. So proud that Bolingbroke was on his back!
That jade hath eat bread from my royal hand;
This hand hath made him proud with clapping him.
Would he not stumble? Would he not fall down
(Since pride must have a fall), and break the neck
Of that proud man that did usurp his back?
Forgiveness, horse! why do I rail on thee,
Since thou, created to be aw'd by man,
Wast born to bear? I was not made a horse;
And yet I bear a burden like an ass,
Spur-gall'd, and tir'd, by jauncing Bolingbroke.

Enter Keeper, *with a Dish.*

Keep. Fellow, give place; here is no longer stay. [*To the* Groom.
K. Rich. If thou love me, 'tis time thou wert away.
Groom. What my tongue dares not, that my heart shall say. [*Exit.*
Keep. My lord, will't please you to fall to?
K. Rich. Taste of it first, as thou art wont to do.
Keep. My lord, I dare not: Sir Pierce of Exton, who
Lately came from the king, commands the contrary.
K. Rich. The devil take Henry of Lancaster, and thee!
Patience is stale, and I am weary of it.
[*Beats the* Keeper.
Keep. Help, help, help!

Enter EXTON, *and* Servants, *armed.*

K. Rich. How now? what means death in this rude assault?
Villain, thy own hand yields thy death's instrument. [*Snatching a weapon and killing one.*
Go thou, and fill another room in hell.
[*He kills another, and then* EXTON *strikes him down.*
That hand shall burn in never quenching fire,
That staggers thus my person.—Exton, thy fierce hand
Hath with the king's blood stain'd the king's own land.
Mount, mount, my soul! thy seat is up on high;
Whilst my gross flesh sinks downward here to die. [*Dies.*
Exton. As full of valour, as of royal blood:
Both have I spilt! O, 'would the deed were good!
For now the devil, that told me—I did well,
Says, that this deed is chronicled in hell.
This dead king to the living king I'll bear;—
Take hence the rest, and give them burial here.
[*Exeunt.*

SCENE VI. Windsor. *A Room in the Castle.*

Flourish. Enter BOLINGBROKE *and* YORK, *with* Lords *and* Attendants.

Boling. Kind uncle York, the latest news we hear
Is—that the rebels have consum'd with fire
Our town of Cicester in Gloucestershire;
But whether they be ta'en, or slain, we hear not.

Enter NORTHUMBERLAND.

Welcome, my lord: What is the news?
North. First, to thy sacred state wish I all happiness.
The next news is,—I have to London sent
The heads of Salisbury, Spencer, Blunt, and Kent:
The manner of their taking may appear
At large discoursed in this paper here.
[*Presenting a paper.*
Boling. We thank thee, gentle Percy, for thy pains;
And to thy worth will add right worthy gains.

Enter FITZWATER.

Fitz. My lord, I have from Oxford sent to London
The heads of Brocas and Sir Bennet Seely;
Two of the dangerous consorted traitors,
That sought at Oxford thy dire overthrow.
Boling. Thy pains, Fitzwater, shall not be forgot;
Right noble is thy merit, well I wot.

Enter PERCY, *with the* Bishop *of* Carlisle.

Percy. The grand conspirator, abbot of Westminster,
With clog of conscience, and sour melancholy,
Hath yielded up his body to the grave:
But here is Carlisle living to abide
Thy kingly doom, and sentence of his pride.
Boling. Carlisle, this is your doom:—
Choose out some secret place, some reverend room,
More than thou hast, and with it 'joy thy life;
So, as thou liv'st in peace, die free from strife:
For though mine enemy thou hast ever been,
High sparks of honour in thee have I seen.

Enter EXTON, *with* Attendants *bearing a Coffin.*

Exton. Great king, within this coffin I present
Thy buried fear: herein all breathless lies

The mightiest of thy greatest enemies,
Richard of Bordeaux, by me hither brought.

Boling. Exton, I thank thee not; for thou hast wrought
A deed of slander, with thy fatal hand,
Upon my head, and all this famous land.

Exton. From your own mouth, my lord, did I this deed.

Boling. They love not poison that do poison need,
Nor do I thee; though I did wish him dead,
I hate the murderer, love him murdered.
The guilt of conscience take thou for thy labour,
But neither my good word, nor princely favour:
With Cain go wander through the shade of night,
And never show thy head by day nor light.——
Lords, I protest, my soul is full of woe,
That blood should sprinkle me, to make me grow:
Come, mourn with me for what I do lament,
And put on sullen black incontinent:
I'll make a voyage to the Holy Land,
To wash this blood from off my guilty hand:—
March sadly after; grace my mournings here,
In weeping after this untimely bier. [*Exeunt*.

FIRST PART OF
KING HENRY THE FOURTH.

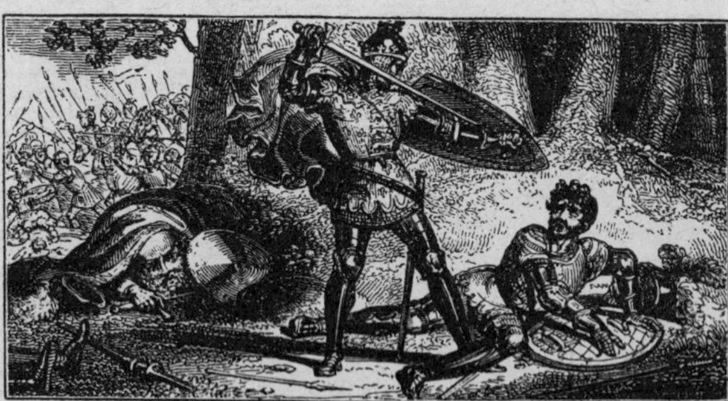

PERSONS REPRESENTED.

KING HENRY THE FOURTH.
HENRY, Prince *of* Wales, } *Sons to the* King.
Prince JOHN *of* Lancaster, }
Earl *of* WESTMORELAND, } *Friends to the* King.
SIR WALTER BLUNT, }
THOMAS PERCY, Earl *of* Worcester.
HENRY PERCY, Earl *of* Northumberland.
HENRY PERCY, *surnamed* Hotspur, *his Son*.
EDWARD MORTIMER, Earl of March.
SCROOP, Archbishop *of* York.
SIR MICHAEL, *a Friend of the* Archbishop.
ARCHIBALD, Earl *of* Douglas.
OWEN GLENDOWER.
SIR RICHARD VERNON.
SIR JOHN FALSTAFF. POINS.
GADSHILL. PETO. BARDOLPH.

LADY PERCY, *Wife to* Hotspur, *and Sister to* Mortimer.
LADY MORTIMER, *Daughter to* Glendower, *and Wife to* Mortimer.
MRS. QUICKLY, *Hostess of a Tavern in* Eastcheap.

Lords, Officers, Sheriff, Vintner, Chamberlain, Drawers, *two* Carriers, Travellers *and* Attendants.

SCENE—England.

ACT I.

SCENE I. London. *A Room in the Palace.*

Enter KING HENRY, WESTMORELAND, SIR WALTER BLUNT, *and Others*.

K. Hen. So shaken as we are, so wan with care,
Find we a time for frighted peace to pant,
And breathe short winded accents of new broils
To be commenc'd in stronds afar remote.
No more the thirsty entrance of this soil
Shall daub her lips with her own children's blood;
No more shall trenching war channel her fields,
Nor bruise her flowrets with the armed hoofs
Of hostile paces: those opposed eyes,
Which,—like the meteors of a troubled heaven,
All of one nature, of one substance bred,——
Did lately meet in the intestine shock
And furious close of civil butchery,
Shall now, in mutual, well beseeming ranks,
March all one way; and be no more oppos'd
Against acquaintance, kindred, and allies:
The edge of war, like an ill sheathed knife,
No more shall cut his master. Therefore, friends,
As far as to the sepulchre of Christ
(Whose soldier now, under whose blessed cross
We are impressed and engag'd to fight),
Forthwith a power of English shall we levy,
Whose arms were moulded in their mother's womb,
To chase these pagans, in those holy fields,
Over whose acres walk'd those blessed feet,
Which, fourteen hundred years ago, were nail'd
For our advantage, on the bitter cross.
But this our purpose is a twelve-month old,
And bootless 'tis to tell you—we will go;
Therefore we meet not now:—Then let me hear
Of you, my gentle cousin Westmoreland,
What yesternight our council did decree,
In forwarding this dear expedience.

West. My liege, this haste was hot in question,
And many limits of the charge set down
But yesternight: when, all athwart, there came
A post from Wales, loaden with heavy news;
Whose worst was,—that the noble Mortimer,
Leading the men of Herefordshire to fight

Against the irregular and wild Glendower,
Was by the rude hands of that Welshman taken,
And a thousand of his people butchered:
Upon whose dead corpse there was such misuse,
Such beastly, shameless transformation,
By those Welshwomen done, as may not be,
Without much shame, re-told or spoken of.

K. Hen. It seems then, that the tidings of this broil
Brake off our business for the Holy Land.

West. This, match'd with other, did, my gracious lord;
For more uneven and unwelcome news
Came from the north, and thus it did import.
On Holy-rood day, the gallant Hotspur there,
Young Harry Percy, and brave Archibald,
That ever valiant and approved Scot,
At Holmedon met,
Where they did spend a sad and bloody hour;
As by discharge of their artillery,
And shape of likelihood, the news was told;
For he that brought them, in the very heat
And pride of their contention did take horse,
Uncertain of the issue any way.

K. Hen. Here is a dear and true-industrious friend,
Sir Walter Blunt, new lighted from his horse,
Stain'd with the variation of each soil
Betwixt that Holmedon and this seat of ours;
And he hath brought us smooth and welcome news.
The earl of Douglas is discomfited;
Ten thousand bold Scots, two-and-twenty knights,
Balk'd in their own blood, did Sir Walter see
On Holmedon's plains: Of prisoners, Hotspur took
Mordake earl of Fife, and eldest son
To beaten Douglas, and the earls of Athol,
Of Murray, Angus, and Menteith.
And is not this an honourable spoil?
A gallant prize? ha, cousin, is it not?

West. In faith,
It is a conquest for a prince to boast of.

K. Hen. Yea, there thou mak'st me sad, and mak'st me sin
In envy that my lord Northumberland
Should be the father of so blest a son:
A son, who is the theme of honour's tongue;
Amongst a grove, the very straightest plant;
Who is sweet fortune's minion, and her pride:
Whilst I, by looking on the praise of him,
See riot and dishonour stain the brow
Of my young Harry. O, that it could be prov'd,
That some night-tripping fairy had exchang'd
In cradle-clothes our children where they lay,
And call'd mine—Percy, his—Plantagenet!
Then would I have his Harry, and he mine.
But let him from my thoughts:—What think you, coz',
Of this young Percy's pride? the prisoners,
Which he in this adventure hath surpris'd,
To his own use he keeps; and sends me word,
I shall have none but Mordake earl of Fife.

West. This is his uncle's teaching, this is Worcester,
Malevolent to you in all aspects;
Which makes him prune himself, and bristle up
The crest of youth against your dignity.

K. Hen. But I have sent for him to answer this:
And, for this cause, awhile we must neglect
Our holy purpose to Jerusalem.
Cousin, on Wednesday next our council we
Will hold at Windsor, so inform the lords:
But come yourself with speed to us again;
For more is to be said, and to be done,
Than out of anger can be uttered.

West. I will, my liege. [*Exeunt.*

SCENE II.

The same. Another Room in the Palace.

Enter HENRY, Prince *of* Wales, *and* FALSTAFF.

Fal. Now, Hal, what time of day is it, lad?

P. Hen. Thou art so fat-witted, with drinking of old sack, and unbuttoning thee after supper, and sleeping upon benches after noon, that thou hast forgotten to demand that truly which thou would'st truly know. What the devil hast thou to do with the time of the day? unless hours were cups of sack, and minutes capons, and clocks the tongues of bawds, and dials the signs of leaping-houses, and the blessed sun himself a fair hot wench in flame-colour'd taffata; I see no reason why thou should'st be so superfluous to demand the time of the day.

Fal. Indeed, you come near me now, Hal: for we, that take purses, go by the moon and seven stars; and not by Phœbus,—he, *that wandering knight so fair*. And, I pray thee, sweet wag, when thou art king,—as, God save thy grace (majesty, I should say; for grace thou wilt have none),——

P. Hen. What, none?

Fal. No, by my troth; not so much as will serve to be prologue to an egg and butter.

P. Hen. Well, how then? come, roundly, roundly.

Fal. Marry, then, sweet wag, when thou art king, let not us, that are squires of the night's body, be called thieves of the day's beauty; let us be—Diana's foresters, gentlemen of the shade, minions of the moon: And let men say, we be men of good government: being governed as the sea is, by our noble and chaste mistress the moon, under whose countenance we—steal.

P. Hen. Thou say'st well; and it holds well too; for the fortune of us, that are the moon's men, doth ebb and flow like the sea; being governed as the sea is, by the moon. As, for proof, now: A purse of gold most resolutely snatched on Monday night, and most dissolutely spent on Tuesday morning; got with swearing—lay by; and spent with crying—bring in: now, in as low an ebb as the foot of the ladder; and, by and by, in as high a flow as the ridge of the gallows.

Fal. By the Lord, thou say'st true, lad. And is not my hostess of the tavern a most sweet wench?

P. Hen. As the honey of Hybla, my old lad of the castle. And is not a buff jerkin, a most sweet robe of durance?

Fal. How now, how now, mad wag? what, in thy quips, and thy quiddities? what a plague have I to do with a buff jerkin?

P. Hen. Why, what a pox have I to do with my hostess of the tavern?

Fal. Well, thou hast called her to a reckoning, many a time and oft.

P. Hen. Did I ever call for thee to pay thy part?

Fal. No; I'll give thee thy due, thou hast paid all there.

P. Hen. Yea, and elsewhere, so far as my coin would stretch; and where it would not, I have used my credit.

Fal. Yea, and so used it, that were it not here apparent that thou art heir apparent,—But, I pr'ythee, sweet wag, shall there be gallows standing in England when thou art king? and resolution thus fobbed as it is, with the rusty curb of old father antick the law? Do not thou, when thou art king, hang a thief.

P. Hen. No; thou shalt.

Fal. Shall I? O rare! By the Lord, I'll be a brave judge.

P. Hen. Thou judgest false already; I mean, thou shalt have the hanging of the thieves, and so become a rare hangman.

Fal. Well, Hal, well; and in some sort it jumps with my humour, as well as waiting in the court, I can tell you.

P. Hen. For obtaining of suits?

Fal. Yea, for obtaining of suits: whereof the hangman hath no lean wardrobe. 'Sblood, I am as melancholy as a gib cat, or a lugged bear.

P. Hen. Or an old lion; or a lover's lute.

Fal. Yea, or the drone of a Lincolnshire bagpipe.

P. Hen. What sayest thou to a hare, or the melancholy of Moor-ditch?

Fal. Thou hast the most unsavoury similes: and art, indeed, the most comparative, rascalliest,—sweet young prince,—But, Hal, I pr'ythee, trouble me no more with vanity. I would to God, thou and I knew where a commodity of good names were to be bought: An old lord of the council rated me the other day in the street about you, sir; but I marked him not: and yet he talk'd very wisely; but I regarded him not: and yet he talk'd wisely, and in the street too.

P. Hen. Thou didst well; for wisdom cries out in the streets, and no man regards it.

Fal. O thou hast damnable iteration; and art, indeed, able to corrupt a saint. Thou hast done much harm upon me, Hal,—God forgive thee for it! Before I knew thee, Hal, I knew nothing; and now am I, if a man should speak truly, little better than one of the wicked. I must give over this life, and I will give it over; by the Lord, an I do not, I am a villain; I'll be damned for never a king's son in Christendom.

P. Hen. Where shall we take a purse tomorrow, Jack?

Fal. Where thou wilt, lad, I'll make one; an I do not, call me villain, and baffle me.

P. Hen. I see a good amendment of life in thee: from praying, to purse-taking.

Enter POINS, *at a distance.*

Fal. Why, Hal, 'tis my vocation, Hal; 'tis no sin for a man to labour in his vocation. Poins!—Now shall we know if Gadshill have set a match. O, if men were to be saved by merit, what hole in hell were hot enough for him? This is the most omnipotent villain, that ever cried, Stand, to a true man.

P. Hen. Good morrow, Ned.

Poins. Good morrow, sweet Hal. What says monsieur Remorse? What says Sir John Sack-and-Sugar? Jack, how agrees the devil and thee about thy soul, that thou soldest him on Good-friday last, for a cup of Madeira, and a cold capon's leg?

P. Hen. Sir John stands to his word, the devil shall have his bargain; for he was never yet a breaker of proverbs, he will give the devil his due.

Poins. Then art thou damned for keeping thy word with the devil.

P. Hen. Else he had been damned for cozening the devil.

Poins. But, my lads, my lads, to-morrow morning, by four o'clock, early at Gadshill: There are pilgrims going to Canterbury with rich offerings, and traders riding to London with fat purses: I have visors for you all, you have horses for yourselves; Gadshill lies to-night in Rochester; I have bespoke supper to-morrow night in Eastcheap; we may do it as secure as sleep: If you will go, I will stuff your purses full of crowns; If you will not, tarry at home, and be hanged.

Fal. Hear me, Yedward; if I tarry at home, and go not, I'll hang you for going.

Poins. You will, chops?

Fal. Hal, wilt thou make one?

P. Hen. Who, I rob? I a thief? not I, by my faith.

Fal. There's neither honesty, manhood, nor good fellowship in thee, nor thou camest not of the blood royal, if thou darest not stand for ten shillings.

P. Hen. Well, then once in my days I'll be a mad-cap.

Fal. Why, that's well said.

P. Hen. Well, come what will, I'll tarry at home.

Fal. By the Lord, I'll be a traitor then, when thou art king.

P. Hen. I care not.

Poins. Sir John, I pr'ythee, leave the prince and me alone; I will lay him down such reasons for this adventure, that he shall go.

Fal. Well, may'st thou have the spirit of persuasion, and he the ears of profiting, that what thou speakest may move, and what he hears may be believed, that the true prince may (for recreation sake) prove a false thief; for the poor abuses of the time want countenance. Farewell: you shall find me in Eastcheap.

P. Hen. Farewell, thou latter spring! Farewell, All-hallown summer! [*Exit* FALSTAFF.

Poins. Now, my good sweet honey lord, ride with us to-morrow; I have a jest to execute, that I cannot manage alone. Falstaff, Bardolph, Peto, and Gadshill, shall rob those men that we have already way-laid; yourself and I will not be there: and when they have the booty, if you and I do not rob them, cut this head from my shoulders.

P. Hen. But how shall we part with them in setting forth?

Poins. Why, we will set forth before or after them, and appoint them a place of meeting, wherein it is at our pleasure to fail; and then will they adventure upon the exploit themselves; which they shall have no sooner achieved, but we'll set upon them.

P. Hen. Ay, but, 'tis like, that they will know us, by our horses, by our habits, and by every other appointment, to be ourselves.

Poins. Tut! our horses they shall not see, I'll tie them in the wood; our visors we will change, after we leave them; and, sirrah, I have cases of buckram for the nonce, to immask our noted outward garments.

P. Hen. But, I doubt they will be too hard for us.

Poins. Well, for two of them, I know them to be as true-bred cowards as ever turned back; and for the third, if he fight longer than he sees reason, I'll forswear arms. The virtue of this jest will be, the incomprehensible lies that this same fat rogue will tell us, when we meet at supper: how thirty, at least, he fought with; what wards, what blows, what extremities he endured; and, in the reproof of this, lies the jest.

P. Hen. Well, I'll go with thee: provide us all things necessary, and meet me to-morrow night in Eastcheap, there I'll sup. Farewell.

Poins. Farewell, my lord. [*Exit* POINS.

P. Hen. I know you all, and will a while uphold
The unyok'd humour of your idleness:
Yet herein will I imitate the sun;
Who doth permit the base contagious clouds
To smother up his beauty from the world,
That, when he please again to be himself,
Being wanted, he may be more wondered at,
By breaking through the foul and ugly mists
Of vapours, that did seem to strangle him.
If all the year were playing holidays,
To sport would be as tedious as to work;
But, when they seldom come, they wish'd-for come,
And nothing pleaseth but rare accidents.
So, when this loose behaviour I throw off,
And pay the debt I never promised,
By how much better than my word I am,
By so much shall I falsify men's hopes;
And, like bright metal on a sullen ground,
My reformation, glittering o'er my fault,
Shall show more goodly, and attract more eyes,
Than that which hath no foil to set it off.
I'll so offend, to make offence a skill;
Redeeming time, when men think least I will.
[*Exit.*

SCENE III.

The same. Another Room in the Palace.

Enter KING HENRY, NORTHUMBERLAND, WORCESTER, HOTSPUR, SIR WALTER BLUNT, *and Others.*

K. Hen. My blood hath been too cold and temperate,
Unapt to stir at these indignities,

And you have found me; for, accordingly,
You tread upon my patience: but, be sure,
I will from henceforth rather be myself,
Mighty, and to be fear'd, than my condition,
Which hath been smooth as oil, soft as young down,
And therefore lost that title of respect,
Which the proud soul ne'er pays, but to the proud.

Wor. Our house, my sovereign liege, little deserves
The scourge of greatness to be used on it;
And that same greatness too which our own hands
Have holp to make so portly.

North. My lord——

K. Hen. Worcester, get thee gone, for I do see
Danger and disobedience in thine eye:
O, sir, your presence is too bold and peremptory,
And majesty might never yet endure
The moody frontier of a servant brow.
You have good leave to leave us; when we need
Your use and counsel, we shall send for you.—
[*Exit* WORCESTER.
You were about to speak. [*To* NORTH.

North. Yea, my good lord.
Those prisoners in your highness' name demanded,
Which Harry Percy here at Holmedon took,
Were, as he says, not with such strength denied
As is deliver'd to your majesty:
Either envy, therefore, or misprision
Is guilty of this fault, and not my son.

Hot. My liege, I did deny no prisoners.
But, I remember, when the fight was done,
When I was dry with rage, and extreme toil,
Breathless and faint, leaning upon my sword,
Came there a certain lord, neat, trimly dress'd,
Fresh as a bridegroom; and his chin, new reap'd,
Show'd like a stubble land at harvest home;
He was perfumed like a milliner:
And 'twixt his finger and his thumb he held
A pouncet-box, which ever and anon
He gave his nose, and took 't away again;—
Who, therewith angry, when it next came there,
Took it in snuff:—and still he smil'd, and talk'd;
And, as the soldiers bore dead bodies by,
He call'd them—untaught knaves, unmannerly,
To bring a slovenly unhandsome corse
Betwixt the wind and his nobility.
With many holiday and lady terms
He question'd me; among the rest demanded
My prisoners, in your majesty's behalf.
I then, all smarting, with my wounds being cold,
To be so pester'd with a popinjay,
Out of my grief and my impatience,
Answer'd neglectingly, I know not what;
He should, or he should not;—for he made me mad,
To see him shine so brisk, and smell so sweet,
And talk so like a waiting-gentlewoman,
Of guns, and drums, and wounds (God save the mark!)
And telling me, the sovereign'st thing on earth
Was parmaceti, for an inward bruise;
And that it was great pity, so it was,
That villanous salt-petre should be digg'd
Out of the bowels of the harmless earth,
Which many a good tall fellow had destroy'd
So cowardly; and, but for these vile guns,
He would himself have been a soldier.
This bald unjointed chat of his, my lord,
I answer'd indirectly, as I said;
And, I beseech you, let not his report
Come current for an accusation,
Betwixt my love and your high majesty.

Blunt. The circumstance consider'd, good my lord,
Whatever Harry Percy then had said,
To such a person, and in such a place,
At such a time, with all the rest re-told,
May reasonably die, and never rise
To do him wrong, or any way impeach
What then he said, so he unsay it now.

K. Hen. Why, yet he doth deny his prisoners;
But with proviso, and exception,—
That we, at our own charge, shall ransom straight
His brother-in-law, the foolish Mortimer;
Who, on my soul, hath wilfully betray'd
The lives of those that he did lead to fight
Against the great magician, damn'd Glendower;
Whose daughter, as we hear, the earl of March
Hath lately married. Shall our coffers then
Be emptied, to redeem a traitor home?
Shall we buy treason? and indent with fears,
When they have lost and forfeited themselves?
No, on the barren mountains let him starve;
For I shall never hold that man my friend,
Whose tongue shall ask me for one penny cost
To ransom home revolted Mortimer.

Hot. Revolted Mortimer!
He never did fall off, my sovereign liege,
But by the chance of war;—To prove that true,
Needs no more but one tongue for all those wounds,
Those mouthed wounds, which valiantly he took,
When on the gentle Severn's sedgy bank,
In single opposition, hand to hand,
He did confound the best part of an hour
In changing hardiment with great Glendower:
Three times they breath'd, and three times did they drink,
Upon agreement, of swift Severn's flood;
Who then, affrighted with their bloody looks,
Ran fearfully among the trembling reeds,
And hid his crisp head in the hollow bank,
Blood-stained with these valiant combatants.
Never did bare and rotten policy
Colour her working with such deadly wounds;
Nor never could the noble Mortimer
Receive so many, and all willingly:
Then let him not be slander'd with revolt.

K. Hen. Thou dost belie him, Percy, thou dost belie him;
He never did encounter with Glendower;
I tell thee,
He durst as well have met the devil alone,
As Owen Glendower for an enemy.
Art thou not ashamed? But, sirrah, henceforth
Let me not hear you speak of Mortimer:
Send me your prisoners with the speediest means,
Or you shall hear in such a kind from me
As will displease you.—My Lord Northumberland,
We license your departure with your son:—
Send us your prisoners, or you'll hear of it.
[*Exeunt* KING HENRY, BLUNT, *and* Train.

Hot. And if the devil come and roar for them,
I will not send them;—I will after straight,
And tell him so; for I will ease my heart,
Although it be with hazard of my head.

North. What, drunk with choler? stay, and pause awhile;
Here comes your uncle.

Re-enter WORCESTER.

Hot. Speak of Mortimer?
'Zounds, I will speak of him; and let my soul
Want mercy, if I do not join with him:
Yea, on his part, I'll empty all these veins,
And shed my dear blood drop by drop i' the dust,
But I will lift the down-trod Mortimer
As high i' the air as this unthankful king,
As this ingrate and canker'd Bolingbroke.

North. Brother, the king hath made your nephew mad. [*To* WORCESTER.

Wor. Who struck this heat up, after I was gone?

Hot. He will, forsooth, have all my prisoners;
And when I urg'd the ransom once again
Of my wife's brother, then his cheek look'd pale;
And on my face he turn'd an eye of death,
Trembling even at the name of Mortimer.

Wor. I cannot blame him: Was he not proclaim'd,
By Richard that dead is, the next of blood?

North. He was; I heard the proclamation:
And then it was, when the unhappy king
(Whose wrongs in us God pardon!) did set forth
Upon his Irish expedition;
From whence he, intercepted, did return
To be depos'd, and, shortly, murdered.
Wor. And for whose death, we in the world's wide mouth
Live scandaliz'd, and foully spoken of. [then
Hot. But, soft, I pray you; Did King Richard
Proclaim my brother Edmund Mortimer
Heir to the crown?
North. He did; myself did hear it.
Hot. Nay, then I cannot blame his cousin king,
That wish'd him on the barren mountains starv'd.
But shall it be, that you,—that set the crown
Upon the head of this forgetful man;
And, for his sake, wear the detested blot
Of murd'rous subornation,—shall it be,
That you a world of curses undergo;
Being the agents, or base second means,
The cords, the ladder, or the hangman rather?—
O, pardon me, that I descend so low,
To show the line, and the predicament,
Wherein you range under this subtle king.—
Shall it, for shame, be spoken in these days,
Or fill up chronicles in time to come,
That men of your nobility and power,
Did gage them both in an unjust behalf,—
As both of you, God pardon it! have done,—
To put down Richard, that sweet lovely rose,
And plant this thorn, this canker, Bolingbroke?
And shall it, in more shame, be further spoken,
That you are fool'd, discarded, and shook off
By him, for whom these shames ye underwent?
No; yet time serves, wherein you may redeem
Your banish'd honours, and restore yourselves
Into the good thoughts of the world again:
Revenge the jeering, and disdain'd contempt,
Of this proud king; who studies, day and night,
To answer all the debt he owes to you,
Even with the bloody payment of your deaths.
Therefore, I say,——
Wor. Peace, cousin, say no more:
And now I will unclasp a secret book,
And to your quick-conceiving discontents
I'll read you matter deep and dangerous;
As full of peril, and advent'rous spirit,
As to o'erwalk a current, roaring loud,
On the unsteadfast footing of a spear.
Hot. If he fall in, good night:—or sink or swim:—
Send danger from the east unto the west,
So honour cross it from the north to south,
And let them grapple:—O! the blood more stirs,
To rouse a lion, than to start a hare.
North. Imagination of some great exploit
Drives him beyond the bounds of patience.
Hot. By heaven, methinks, it were an easy leap, [moon;
To pluck bright honour from the pale-fac'd
Or dive into the bottom of the deep,
Where fathom-line could never touch the ground,
And pluck up drowned honour by the locks;
So he, that doth redeem her thence, might wear,
Without corrival, all her dignities:
But out upon this half-fac'd fellowship!
Wor. He apprehends a world of figures here,
But not the form of what he should attend.—
Good cousin, give me audience for a while.
Hot. I cry you mercy.
Wor. Those same noble Scots,
That are your prisoners,——
Hot. I'll keep them all;
By heaven, he shall not have a Scot of them:
No, if a Scot would save his soul, he shall not:
I'll keep them, by this hand.
Wor. You start away,
And lend no ear unto my purposes.—
Those prisoners you shall keep.
Hot. Nay, I will; that's flat:—
He said, he would not ransom Mortimer;
Forbad my tongue to speak of Mortimer;
But I will find him when he lies asleep,
And in his ear I'll holla—Mortimer!
Nay,
I'll have a starling shall be taught to speak
Nothing but Mortimer, and give it him,
To keep his anger still in motion.
Wor. Hear you,
Cousin; a word.
Hot. All studies here I solemnly defy,
Save how to gall and pinch this Bolingbroke:
And that same sword-and-buckler prince of Wales,—
But that I think his father loves him not,
And would be glad he met with some mischance,
I'd have him poison'd with a pot of ale.
Wor. Farewell, kinsman! I will talk to you,
When you are better temper'd to attend.
North. Why, what a wasp-tongue and impatient fool
Art thou, to break into this woman's mood;
Tying thine ear to no tongue but thine own?
Hot. Why, look you, I am whipp'd and scourg'd with rods,
Nettled, and stung with pismires, when I hear
Of this vile politician, Bolingbroke. [place?—
In Richard's time,—What do you call the
A plague upon't;—it is in Gloucestershire;—
'Twas where the madcap duke his uncle kept:
His uncle York;—where I first bow'd my knee
Unto this king of smiles, this Bolingbroke,
When you and he came back from Ravenspurg.
North. At Berkley castle.
Hot. You say true:——
Why, what a candy deal of courtesy
This fawning greyhound then did proffer me!
Look,—*when his infant fortune came to age,*
And—*gentle Harry Percy,*—and, *kind cousin,*—
O, the devil take such cozeners!——God forgive me!——
Good uncle, tell your tale, for I have done.
Wor. Nay, if you have not, to't again;
We'll stay your leisure.
Hot. I have done, i'faith.
Wor. Then once more to your Scottish prisoners.
Deliver them up without their ransom straight.
And make the Douglas' son your only mean
For powers in Scotland; which, for divers reasons,
Which I shall send you written,—be assur'd,
Will easily be granted.—You, my lord,—
[*To* NORTHUMBERLAND.
Your son in Scotland being thus employed,—
Shall secretly into the bosom creep
Of that same noble prelate, well belov'd,
The archbishop.
Hot. Of York, is't not?
Wor. True; who bears hard
His brother's death at Bristol, the Lord Scroop.
I speak not this in estimation,
As what I think might be, but what I know
Is ruminated, plotted, and set down;
And only stays but to behold the face
Of that occasion that shall bring it on.
Hot. I smell it; upon my life, it will do well.
North. Before the game's afoot, thou still let'st slip. [plot:—
Hot. Why, it cannot choose but be a noble
And then the power of Scotland, and of York,—
To join with Mortimer, ha?
Wor. And so they shall.
Hot. In faith, it is exceedingly well aim'd.
Wor. And 'tis no little reason bids us speed,
To save our heads by raising of a head;
For, bear ourselves as even as we can,
The king will always think him in our debt;
And think we think ourselves unsatisfied,
Till he hath found a time to pay us home.
And see already, how he doth begin
To make us strangers to his looks of love.

Hot. He does, he does; we'll be reveng'd on him.

Wor. Cousin, farewell:—No further go in this,
Than I by letters shall direct your course.
When time is ripe (which will be suddenly),
I'll steal to Glendower, and lord Mortimer;
Where you and Douglas, and our powers at once
(As I will fashion it), shall happily meet,
To bear our fortunes in our own strong arms,
Which now we hold at much uncertainty.

North. Farewell, good brother:—we shall thrive, I trust.

Hot. Uncle, adieu:—O, let the hours be short,
Till fields, and blows, and groans applaud our sport! [*Exeunt.*

ACT II.

SCENE I. Rochester. *An Inn Yard.*

Enter a Carrier, *with a lantern in his hand.*

1 *Car.* Heigh ho! An't be not four by the day, I'll be hanged: Charles' Wain is over the new chimney, and yet our horse not packed. What, ostler!

Ost. [*Within.*] Anon, anon.

1 *Car.* I pr'ythee, Tom, beat Cut's saddle, put a few flocks in the point: the poor jade is wrung in the withers out of all cess.

Enter another Carrier.

2 *Car.* Pease and beans are as dank here as a dog, and that is the next way to give poor jades the bots: this house is turned upside down, since Robin ostler died.

1 *Car.* Poor fellow! never joyed since the price of oats rose; it was the death of him.

2 *Car.* I think, this be the most villanous house in all London road for fleas: I am stung like a tench.

1 *Car.* Like a tench? by the mass, there is ne'er a king in Christendom could be better bit than I have been since the first cock.

2 *Car.* Why, they will allow us ne'er a jorden, and then we leak in your chimney; and your chamber-lie breeds fleas like a loach.

1 *Car.* What, ostler! come away and be hanged, come away.

2 *Car.* I have a gammon of bacon, and two razes of ginger, to be delivered as far as Charing Cross.

1 *Car.* 'Odsbody! the turkeys in my pannier are quite starved.—What, ostler!—A plague on thee! hast thou never an eye in thy head? canst not hear? An 'twere not as good a deed as drink, to break the pate of thee, I am a very villain.—Come, and be hanged:—Hast no faith in thee?

Enter GADSHILL.

Gads. Good morrow, carriers. What's o'clock?

1 *Car.* I think it be two o'clock.

Gads. I pr'ythee, lend me thy lantern, to see my gelding in the stable.

1 *Car.* Nay, soft, I pray ye; I know a trick worth two of that, i' faith.

Gads. I pr'ythee, lend me thine.

2 *Car.* Ay, when? canst tell?—Lend me thy lantern, quoth a?—marry, I'll see thee hanged first.

Gads. Sirrah carrier, what time do you mean to come to London?

2 *Car.* Time enough to go to bed with a candle, I warrant thee.—Come, neighbour Mugs, we'll call up the gentlemen; they will along with company, for they have great charge. [*Exeunt* Carriers.

Gads. What, ho! chamberlain!

Cham. [*Within.*] At hand, quoth pick-purse.

Gads. That's even as fair as—at hand, quoth the chamberlain: for thou variest no more from picking of purses, than giving direction doth from labouring; thou lay'st the plot how.

Enter Chamberlain.

Cham. Good morrow, master Gadshill. It holds current, that I told you yesternight: There's a franklin in the wild of Kent, hath brought three hundred marks with him in gold: I heard him tell it to one of his company, last night at supper; a kind of auditor; one that hath abundance of charge too, God knows what. They are up already, and call for eggs and butter: They will away presently.

Gads. Sirrah, if they meet not with Saint Nicholas' clerks, I'll give thee this neck.

Cham. No, I'll none of it: I pr'ythee, keep that for the hangman; for, I know, thou worship'st Saint Nicholas as truly as a man of falsehood may.

Gads. What talk'st thou to me of the hangman? if I hang, I'll make a fat pair of gallows: for, if I hang, old Sir John hangs with me; and, thou knowest, he's no starveling. Tut! there are other Trojans that thou dreamest not of, the which, for sport sake, are content to do the profession some grace; that would, if matters should be looked into, for their own credit sake, make all whole. I am joined with no foot land-rakers, no long-staff, sixpenny strikers; none of these mad, mustachio, purple-hued malt-worms: but with nobility, and tranquillity; burgomasters, and great oneyers; such as can hold in; such as will strike sooner than speak, and speak sooner than drink, and drink sooner than pray: And yet I lie; for they pray continually to their saint, the commonwealth; or, rather, not pray to her, but prey on her; for they ride up and down on her, and make her their boots.

Cham. What, the commonwealth their boots? will she hold out water in foul way?

Gads. She will, she will; justice hath liquored her. We steal as in a castle, cock-sure; we have the receipt of fern-seed, we walk invisible.

Cham. Nay, by my faith, I think you are more beholden to the night, than to fern-seed, for your walking invisible.

Gads. Give me thy hand: thou shalt have a share in our purchase, as I am a true man.

Cham. Nay, rather let me have it, as you are a false thief.

Gads. Go to; *Homo* is a common name to all men. Bid the ostler bring my gelding out of the stable. Farewell, you muddy knave. [*Exeunt.*

SCENE II. *The Road by* Gadshill.

Enter PRINCE HENRY, *and* POINS; BARDOLPH *and* PETO, *at some distance.*

Poins. Come, shelter, shelter: I have removed Falstaff's horse, and he frets like a gummed velvet.

P. Hen. Stand close.

Enter FALSTAFF.

Fal. Poins! Poins, and be hanged! Poins!

P. Hen. Peace, ye fat-kidneyed rascal; What a brawling dost thou keep?

Fal. Where's Poins, Hal?

P. Hen. He is walked up to the top of the hill; I'll go seek him. [*Pretends to seek* POINS.

Fal. I am accursed to rob in that thief's company: the rascal hath removed my horse, and tied him I know not where. If I travel but four foot by the squire further afoot, I shall break my wind. Well, I doubt not but to die a fair death for all this, if I 'scape hanging for killing that rogue. I have forsworn his company hourly, any time this two-and-twenty years, and yet I am bewitched with the rogue's company. If the rascal have not given me medicines to make me love him, I'll be hanged; it could not be else; I have drunk medicines.—Poins!—Hal!—a plague upon you both!—

Bardolph!—Peto!—I'll starve, ere I'll rob a foot further. An 'twere not as good a deed as drink, to turn true man, and leave these rogues, I am the veriest varlet that ever chew'd with a tooth. Eight yards of uneven ground, is threescore and ten miles afoot with me; and the stony-hearted villains know it well enough: A plague upon't, when thieves cannot be true to one another! [*They Whistle.*] Whew!—A plague upon you all! Give me my horse, you rogues; give me my horse, and be hanged.

P. Hen. Peace, ye fat-guts; lie down; lay thine ear close to the ground, and list if thou canst hear the tread of travellers.

Fal. Have you any levers to lift me up again, being down? 'Sblood, I'll not bear mine own flesh so far afoot again, for all the coin in thy father's exchequer. What a plague mean ye to colt me thus?

P. Hen. Thou liest, thou art not colted, thou art uncolted.

Fal. I pr'ythee, good Prince Hal, help me to my horse: good king's son.

P. Hen. Out, you rogue! shall I be your ostler?

Fal. Go, hang thyself in thy own heir-apparent garters! If I be ta'en, I'll peach for this. An I have not ballads made on you all, and sung to filthy tunes, let a cup of sack be my poison: When a jest is so forward, and afoot too,—I hate it.

Enter GADSHILL.

Gads. Stand.

Fal. So I do, against my will.

Poins. O, 'tis our setter: I know his voice.

Enter BARDOLPH.

Bard. What news?

Gads. Case ye, case ye; on with your visors: there's money of the king's coming down the hill; 'tis going to the king's exchequer.

Fal. You lie, you rogue; 'tis going to the king's tavern.

Gads. There's enough to make us all.

Fal. To be hanged.

P. Hen. Sirs, you four shall front them in the narrow lane; Ned Poins, and I will walk lower: if they 'scape from your encounter, then they light on us.

Peto. How many be there of them?

Gads. Some eight, or ten.

Fal. Zounds! will they not rob us?

P. Hen. What, a coward, Sir John Paunch?

Fal. Indeed, I am not John of Gaunt, your grandfather; but yet no coward, Hal.

P. Hen. Well, we leave that to the proof.

Poins. Sirrah Jack, thy horse stands behind the hedge; when thou needest him, there thou shalt find him. Farewell, and stand fast.

Fal. Now cannot I strike him, if I should be hanged.

P. Hen. Ned, where are our disguises?

Poins. Here, hard by; stand close.

[*Exeunt* P. HEN. *and* POINS.

Fal. Now, my masters, happy man be his dole, say I; every man to his business.

Enter Travellers.

1 *Trav.* Come, neighbour; the boy shall lead our horses down the hill; we'll walk afoot a while, and ease our legs.

Thieves. Stand.

Trav. Jesu bless us!

Fal. Strike; down with them; cut the villains' throats: Ah! whoreson caterpillars! bacon-fed knaves! they hate us youth: down with them; fleece them.

1 *Trav.* O, we are undone, both we and ours, for ever.

Fal. Hang ye, gorbellied knaves; Are ye undone? No, ye fat chuffs; I would, your store were here! On, bacons, on! What, ye knaves? young men must live: You are grand jurors are ye? We'll jure ye, i'faith.

[*Exeunt* FAL. *&c. driving the* Travellers *out.*

Re-enter PRINCE HENRY *and* POINS.

P. Hen. The thieves have bound the true men: Now could thou and I rob the thieves, and go merrily to London, it would be argument for a week, laughter for a month, and a good jest for ever.

Poins. Stand close, I hear them coming.

Re-enter Thieves.

Fal. Come, my masters, let us share, and then to horse before day. An the prince and Poins be not two arrant cowards, there's no equity stirring: there's no more valour in that Poins, than in a wild duck.

P. Hen. Your money.

[*Rushing out upon them.*

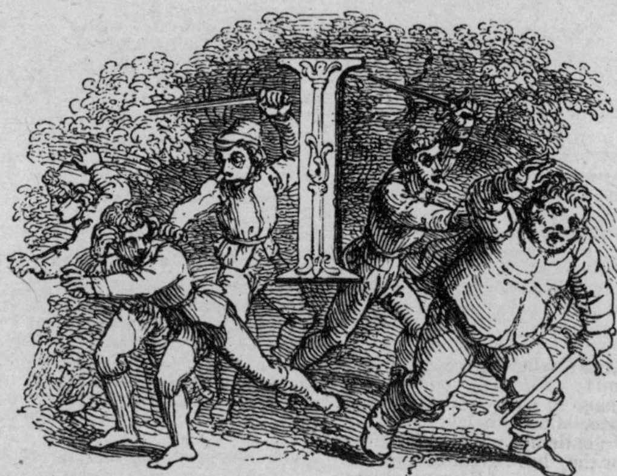

Poins. Villains.

[*As they are sharing, the* Prince *and* POINS *set upon them.* FALSTAFF, *after a blow or two, and the rest, run away, leaving their booty behind them.*

P. Hen. Got with much ease. Now merrily to horse:
The thieves are scatter'd, and possess'd with fear
So strongly, that they dare not meet each other;
Each takes his fellow for an officer.

H H

Away, good Ned. Falstaff sweats to death,
And lards the lean earth as he walks along:
Wer't not for laughing, I should pity him.
Poins. How the rogue roar'd! [*Exeunt.*

SCENE III. Warkworth. *A Room in the Castle.*

Enter HOTSPUR, *reading a Letter.*

——*But, for mine own part, my lord, I could be well contented to be there, in respect of the love I bear your house.*—He could be contented,—Why is he not then? In the respect of the love he bears our house:—he shows in this, he loves his own barn better than he loves our house. Let me see some more. *The purpose you undertake is dangerous;*—Why, that's certain; 'tis dangerous to take a cold, to sleep, to drink! but I tell you, my lord fool, out of this nettle danger, we pluck this flower, safety. *The purpose you undertake is dangerous; the friends you have named, uncertain; the time itself unsorted; and your whole plot too light, for the counterpoise of so great an opposition.*—Say you so, say you so? I say unto you again, you are a shallow, cowardly hind, and you lie. What a lack-brain is this? By the Lord our plot is a good plot as ever was laid; our friends true and constant: a good plot, good friends, and full of expectation: an excellent plot, very good friends. What a frosty-spirited rogue is this? Why, my lord of York commends the plot, and the general course of the action. 'Zounds, an I were now by this rascal, I could brain him with his lady's fan. Is there not my father, my uncle, and myself? Lord Edmund Mortimer, my lord of York, and Owen Glendower? Is there not, besides, the Douglas? Have I not all their letters, to meet me in arms by the ninth of the next month; and are they not, some of them, set forward already? What a pagan rascal is this? an infidel? Ha! you shall see now, in very sincerity of fear and cold heart, will he to the king, and lay open all our proceedings. O, I could divide myself, and go to buffets, for moving such a dish of skimmed milk with so honourable an action! Hang him! let him tell the king: We are prepared: I will set forward to-night.

Enter LADY PERCY.

How now, Kate? I must leave you within these two hours.
Lady. O my good Lord, why are you thus alone?
For what offence have I, this fortnight, been
A banish'd woman from my Harry's bed?
Tell me, sweet lord, what is't that takes from thee
Thy stomach, pleasure, and thy golden sleep?
Why dost thou bend thine eyes upon the earth;
And start so often when thou sit'st alone?
Why hast thou lost the fresh blood in thy cheeks;
And given my treasures, and my rights of thee,
To thick-ey'd musing, and curs'd melancholy?
In thy faint slumbers, I by thee have watch'd,
And heard thee murmur tales of iron wars:
Speak terms of manage to thy bounding steed;
Cry, *Courage!—to the field!* And thou hast talk'd
Of sallies, and retires; of trenches, tents,
Of palisadoes, frontiers, parapets;
Of basilisks, of cannon, culverin;
Of prisoners' ransom, and of soldiers slain,
And all the currents of a heady fight.
Thy spirit within thee hath been so at war,
And thus hath so bestirr'd thee in thy sleep,
That beads of sweat have stood upon thy brow,
Like bubbles in a late-disturbed stream:
And in thy face strange motions have appear'd,
Such as we see when men restrain their breath
On some great sudden haste. O, what portents are these?
Some heavy business hath my lord in hand,
And I must know it, else he loves me not.
Hot. What, ho! is Gilliams with the packet gone?

Enter Servant.

Serv. He is, my lord, an hour ago.
Hot. Hath Butler brought those horses from the sheriff?
Serv. One horse, my lord, he brought even now.
Hot. What horse? a roan, a crop-ear, is it not?
Serv. It is, my lord.
Hot. That roan shall be my throne.
Well, I will back him straight: O *esperance!*—
Bid Butler lead him forth into the park.
[*Exit* Servant.
Lady. But hear you, my lord.
Hot. What say'st thou, my lady?
Lady. What is it carries you away?
Hot. Why, my horse, my love, my horse.
Lady. Out, you mad-headed ape!
A weasel hath not such a deal of spleen,
As you are toss'd with. In faith,
I'll know your business, Harry, that I will.
I fear, my brother Mortimer doth stir
About his title; and hath sent for you,
To line his enterprise: But if you go——
Hot. So far afoot, I shall be weary, love.
Lady. Come, come, you paraquito, answer me
Directly to this question that I ask.
In faith, I'll break thy little finger, Harry,
An if thou wilt not tell me all things true.
Hot. Away,
Away, you trifler!—Love? I love thee not,
I care not for thee, Kate: this is no world,
To play with mammets, and to tilt with lips:
We must have bloody noses, and crack'd crowns,
And pass them current too.—Gods me, my horse!—
What say'st thou, Kate? what would'st thou have with me?
Lady. Do you not love me? do you not indeed?
Well, do not then; for since you love me not,
I will not love myself. Do you not love me?
Nay, tell me, if you speak in jest, or no.
Hot. Come, wilt thou see me ride?
And when I am o' horseback, I will swear
I love thee infinitely. But hark you, Kate;
I must not have you henceforth question me
Whither I go, nor reason whereabout:
Whither I must, I must; and, to conclude,
This evening must I leave you, gentle Kate.
I know you wise; but yet no further wise,
Than Harry Percy's wife: constant you are;
But yet a woman: and for secrecy,
No lady closer; for I well believe,
Thou wilt not utter what thou dost not know;
And so far will I trust thee, gentle Kate!
Lady. How! so far?
Hot. Not an inch further. But hark you, Kate?
Whither I go, thither shall you go too;
To-day will I set forth, to-morrow you.—
Will this content you, Kate?
Lady. It must, of force.
[*Exeunt.*

SCENE IV.

Eastcheap. *A Room in the* Boar's Head *Tavern.*

Enter PRINCE HENRY *and* POINS.

P. Hen. Ned, pr'ythee, come out of that fat room, and lend me thy hand to laugh a little.
Poins. Where hast been, Hal?
P. Hen. With three or four loggerheads, amongst three or four score hogsheads. I have sounded the very base string of humility. Sirrah, I am sworn brother to a leash of drawers; and can call them all by their Christian names, as—Tom, Dick, and Francis. They take it already upon their salvation, that, though I be but prince of Wales, yet I am the king of courtesy; and tell me flatly I am no proud Jack, like Falstaff; but a Corinthian, a lad of mettle, a good boy,—by the lord, so they call me; and when I am king of England, I shall command all the good lads in Eastcheap. They call—drinking deep, dying scarlet: and when you breathe in

your watering, they cry—hem! and bid you play it off.—To conclude, I am so good a proficient in one quarter of an hour, that I can drink with any tinker in his own language during my life. I tell thee, Ned, thou hast lost much honour, that thou wert not with me in this action. But, sweet Ned,—to sweeten which name of Ned, I give thee this pennyworth of sugar, clapp'd even now into my hand by an under-skinker; one that never spake other English in his life, than—*Eight shillings and sixpence*, and—*You are welcome;* with his shrill addition,—*Anon, anon, sir! Score a pint of bastard in the Half-moon*, or so. But, Ned, to drive away the time till Falstaff come, I pr'ythee, do thou stand in some by-room, while I question my puny drawer, to what end he gave me the sugar; and do thou never leave calling —Francis, that his tale to me may be nothing but—anon. Step aside, and I'll show thee a precedent.

Poins. Francis!

P. Hen. Thou art perfect.

Poins. Francis! [*Exit* POINS.

Enter FRANCIS.

Fran. Anon, anon, sir. Look down into the Pomegranate, Ralph.

P. Hen. Come hither, Francis.

Fran. My lord.

P. Hen. How long hast thou to serve, Francis?

Fran. Forsooth, five year, and as much as to—

Poins. [*Within.*] Francis!

Fran. Anon, anon, sir!

P. Hen. Five years! by'rlady a long lease for the clinking of pewter. But, Francis, darest thou be so valiant, as to play the coward with thy indenture, and to show it a fair pair of heels, and run from it?

Fran. O lord, sir! I'll be sworn upon all the books in England, I could find in my heart—

Poins. [*Within.*] Francis!

Fran. Anon, anon, sir.

P. Hen. How old art thou, Francis?

Fran. Let me see,—About Michaelmas next I shall be—

Poins. [*Within.*] Francis!

Fran. Anon, sir.—Pray you, stay a little, my lord.

P. Hen. Nay, but hark you, Francis: For the sugar thou gavest me,—'twas a pennyworth, was't not?

Fran. O lord, sir! I would it had been two.

P. Hen. I will give thee for it a thousand pound: ask me when thou wilt, and thou shalt have it.

Poins. [*Within.*] Francis!

Fran. Anon, anon.

P. Hen. Anon, Francis? No, Francis: but to-morrow, Francis; or, Francis, on Thursday; or, indeed, Francis, when thou wilt. But, Francis,—

Fran. My lord?

P. Hen. Wilt thou rob this leathern-jerkin, crystal-button, nott-pated, agate-ring, puke-stocking, caddis-garter, smooth-tongue, Spanish-pouch,—

Fran. O lord, sir, who do you mean?

P. Hen. Why then, your brown bastard is your only drink: for, look you, Francis, your white canvass doublet will sully: in Barbary, sir, it cannot come to so much.

Fran. What, sir?

Poins. [*Within.*] Francis!

P. Hen. Away, you rogue; Dost thou not hear them call?

[*Here they both call him; the* Drawer *stands amazed, not knowing which way to go.*

Enter Vintner.

Vint. What! stand'st thou still, and hear'st such a calling? Look to the guests within. [*Exit* FRAN.] My lord, old Sir John, with half a dozen more, are at the door; Shall I let them in?

P. Hen. Let them alone awhile, and then open the door. [*Exit* Vintner.] Poins!

Re-enter POINS.

Poins. Anon, anon, sir.

P. Hen. Sirrah, Falstaff and the rest of the thieves are at the door; Shall we be merry?

Poins. As merry as crickets, my lad. But hark ye; What cunning match have you made with this jest of a drawer? come, what's the issue?

P. Hen. I am now of all humours, that have show'd themselves humours, since the old days of goodman Adam, to the pupil age of this present twelve o'clock at midnight. [*Re-enter* FRANCIS *with wine.*] What's o'clock, Francis?

Fran. Anon, anon, sir.

P. Hen. That ever this fellow should have fewer words than a parrot, and yet the son of a woman!—His industry is—up-stairs, and down-stairs; his eloquence, the parcel of a reckoning. I am not yet of Percy's mind, the Hotspur of the north: he that kills me some six or seven dozen of Scots at a breakfast, washes his hands, and says to his wife,—*Fye upon this quiet life! I want work. O my sweet Harry*, says she, *how many hast thou killed to-day? Give my roan horse a drench*, says he; and answers, *Some fourteen*, an hour after; *a trifle, a trifle.* I pr'ythee, call in Falstaff; I'll play Percy, and that damned brawn shall play dame Mortimer his wife. *Rivo*, says the drunkard. Call in ribs, call in tallow.

Enter FALSTAFF, GADSHILL, BARDOLPH, *and* PETO.

Poins. Welcome, Jack. Where hast thou been?

Fal. A plague of all cowards, I say, and a vengeance too! marry, and amen!—Give me a cup of sack, boy.—Ere I lead this life long, I'll sew nether-stocks, and mend them, and foot them too. A plague of all cowards!—Give me a cup of sack, rogue.—Is there no virtue extant? [*He drinks.*

P. Hen. Didst thou never see Titan kiss a dish of butter? pitiful-hearted butter, that melted at the sweet tale of the sun! if thou didst, then behold that compound.

Fal. You rogue, here's lime in this sack too: There is nothing but roguery to be found in villanous man: Yet a coward is worse than a cup of sack with lime in it; a villanous coward. —Go thy ways, old Jack; die when thou wilt, if manhood, good manhood, be not forgot upon the face of the earth, then am I a shotten herring. There live not three good men unhanged in England; and one of them is fat, and grows old: God help the while! a bad world, I say! I would, I were a weaver; I could sing psalms or any thing: A plague of all cowards, I say still.

P. Hen. How now, wool-sack? what mutter you?

Fal. A king's son! If I do not beat thee out of thy kingdom with a dagger of lath, and drive all thy subjects afore thee like a flock of wild geese, I'll never wear hair on my face more. You prince of Wales!

P. Hen. Why, you whoreson round man! what's the matter?

Fal. Are you not a coward? answer me to that; and Poins there?

Poins. 'Zounds, ye fat paunch, an ye call me coward, I'll stab thee.

Fal. I call thee coward! I'll see thee damned ere I call thee coward: but I would give a thousand pound, I could run as fast as thou canst. You are straight enough in the shoulders, you care not who sees your back: Call you that backing of your friends? A plague upon such backing! give me them that will face me.—Give me a cup of sack;—I am a rogue, if I drunk to-day.

P. Hen. O villain, thy lips are scarce wiped since thou drunk'st last.

Fal. All's one for that. A plague of all cowards, still say I. [*He drinks.*

P. Hen. What's the matter?

Fal. What's the matter? there be four of us here have ta'en a thousand pound this morning.

P. Hen. Where is it, Jack? where is it?

Fal. Where is it? taken from us it is: a hundred upon poor four of us.

P. Hen. What, a hundred, man?

Fal. I am a rogue, if I were not at half-sword with a dozen of them two hours together. I have 'scap'd by miracle. I am eight times thrust through the doublet; four, through the hose; my buckler cut through and through; my sword hacked like a hand-saw, *ecce signum.* I never dealt better since I was a man: all would not do. A plague of all cowards!—Let them speak; if they speak more or less than truth, they are villains, and the sons of darkness.

P. Hen. Speak, sirs; how was it?

Gads. We four set upon some dozen,——

Fal. Sixteen, at least, my lord.

Gads. And bound them.

Peto. No, no, they were not bound.

Fal. You rogue, they were bound, every man of them; or I am a Jew else, an Ebrew Jew.

Gads. As we were sharing, some six or seven fresh men set upon us,——

Fal. And unbound the rest, and then come in the other.

P. Hen. What, fought you with them all?

Fal. All? I know not what ye call, all: but if I fought not with fifty of them, I am a bunch of radish: if there were not two or three and fifty upon poor old Jack, then I am no two-legged creature.

Poins. 'Pray God, you have not murdered some of them.

Fal. Nay, that's past praying for: for I have peppered two of them: two, I am sure, I have paid; two rogues in buckram suits. I tell thee what, Hal,—if I tell thee a lie, spit in my face, call me horse. Thou knowest my old ward;—here I lay, and thus I bore my point. Four rogues in buckram let drive at me,——

P. Hen. What, four? thou saidst but two, even now.

Fal. Four, Hal; I told thee four.

Poins. Ay, ay, he said four.

Fal. These four came all a-front, and mainly thrust at me. I made me no more ado, but took all their seven points in my target, thus.

P. Hen. Seven? why, there were but four, even now.

Fal. In buckram.

Poins. Ay, four, in buckram suits.

Fal. Seven, by these hilts, or I am a villain else.

P. Hen. Pr'ythee, let him alone; we shall have more anon.

Fal. Dost thou hear me, Hal?

P. Hen. Ay, and mark thee too, Jack.

Fal. Do so, for it is worth the listening to. These nine in buckram, that I told thee of,——

P. Hen. So, two more already.

Fal. Their points being broken,——

Poins. Down fell their hose.

Fal. Began to give me ground: But I followed me close, came in foot and hand; and, with a thought, seven of the eleven I paid.

P. Hen. O monstrous! eleven buckram men grown out of two!

Fal. But, as the devil would have it, three misbegotten knaves, in Kendal green, came at my back, and let drive at me;—for it was so dark, Hal, that thou could'st not see thy hand.

P. Hen. These lies are like the father that begets them; gross as a mountain, open, palpable. Why, thou clay-brained guts: thou knotty-pated fool; thou whoreson, obscene, greasy tallow-keech,——

Fal. What, art thou mad? art thou mad? is not the truth, the truth?

P. Hen. Why, how couldst thou know these men in Kendal green, when it was so dark thou could'st not see thy hand? come, tell us your reason; What sayest thou to this?

Poins. Come, your reason, Jack, your reason.

Fal. What, upon compulsion? No; were I at the strappado, or all the racks in the world, I would not tell you on compulsion. Give you a reason on compulsion! if reasons were as plenty as blackberries, I would give no man a reason upon compulsion, I.

P. Hen. I'll be no longer guilty of this sin: this sanguine coward, this bed-presser, this horse-back-breaker, this huge hill of flesh;——

Fal. Away, you starveling, you elf-skin, you dried neat's-tongue, bull's pizzle, you stock-fish, —O, for breath to utter what is like thee!—you tailor's yard, you sheath, you bow case, you vile standing tuck;——

P. Hen. Well, breathe awhile, and then to it again: and when thou hast tired thyself in base comparisons, hear me speak but this.

Poins. Mark, Jack.

P. Hen. We two saw you four set on four; you bound them, and were masters of their wealth.——Mark now, how plain a tale shall put you down.—Then did we two set on you four: and, with a word, outfaced you from your prize, and have it; yea, and can show it you here in the house:—and, Falstaff, you carried your guts away as nimbly, with as quick dexterity, and roared for mercy, and still ran and roared, as ever I heard bull-calf. What a slave art thou, to hack thy sword as thou hast done; and then say, it was in fight? What trick, what device, what starting hole, canst thou now find out to hide thee from this open and apparent shame?

Poins. Come, let's hear, Jack; What trick hast thou now?

Fal. By the Lord, I knew ye, as well as he that made ye. Why, hear ye, my masters: Was it for me to kill the heir apparent? Should I turn upon the true prince? Why, thou knowest, I am as valiant as Hercules: but beware instinct; the lion will not touch the true prince. Instinct is a great matter; I was a coward on instinct. I shall think the better of myself and thee, during my life; I, for a valiant lion, and thou for a true prince. But, by the Lord, lads, I am glad you have the money.——Hostess, clap to the doors; watch to-night, pray to-morrow. —Gallants, lads, boys, hearts of gold, all the titles of good fellowship come to you! What, shall we be merry? shall we have a play extempore?

P. Hen. Content;—and the argument shall be, thy running away.

Fal. Ah! no more of that, Hal, an thou lovest me.

Enter Hostess.

Host. My lord the prince,——

P. Hen. How now, my lady the hostess? what say'st thou to me?

Host. Marry, my lord, there is a nobleman of the court at door, would speak with you: he says he comes from your father.

P. Hen. Give him as much as will make him a royal man, and send him back again to my mother.

Fal. What manner of man is he?

Host. An old man.

Fal. What doth gravity out of his bed at midnight?—Shall I give him his answer?

P. Hen. 'Pr'ythee, do, Jack.

Fal. 'Faith, and I'll send him packing. [*Exit.*

P. Hen. Now, sirs; by'r lady, you fought fair; —so did you, Peto;—so did you, Bardolph: you are lions too, you ran away upon instinct, you will not touch the true prince, no,—fye!

Bard. 'Faith, I ran when I saw others run.

P. Hen. Tell me now in earnest, How came Falstaff's sword so hacked?

Peto. Why, he hacked it with his dagger; and said, he would swear truth out of England, but he would make you believe it was done in fight; and persuaded us to do the like.

Bard. Yea, and to tickle our noses with spear-grass, to make them bleed; and then to beslubber our garments with it, and to swear it was the blood of true men. I did that I did not this seven year before, I blushed to hear his monstrous devices.

P. Hen. O villain, thou stolest a cup of sack eighteen years ago, and wert taken with the manner, and ever since thou hast blushed extempore: Thou hast fire and sword on thy side, and yet thou ran'st away; What instinct hadst thou for it?

Bard. My lord, do you see these meteors? do you behold these exhalations?

P. Hen. I do.

Bard. What think you they portend?

P. Hen. Hot livers and cold purses.

Bard. Choler, my lord, if rightly taken.

P. Hen. No, if rightly taken, halter.

Re-enter FALSTAFF.

Here comes lean Jack, here comes bare-bone. How now, my sweet creature of bombast? How long is't ago, Jack, since thou sawest thine own knee?

Fal. My own knee? when I was about thy years, Hal, I was not an eagle's talon in the waist; I could have crept into an alderman's thumb-ring: a plague of sighing and grief! it blows a man up like a bladder. There's villanous news abroad: here was Sir John Bracy from your father; You must to the court in the morning. That same mad fellow of the north, Percy; and he of Wales, that gave Amaimon the bastinado, and made Lucifer cuckold, and swore the devil his true liegeman upon the cross of a Welsh hook,—What, a plague, call you him?——

Poins. O, Glendower.

Fal. Owen, Owen; the same;—and his son-in-law, Mortimer; and old Northumberland; and that sprightly Scot of Scots, Douglas, that runs o' horseback up a hill perpendicular.

P. Hen. He that rides at high speed, and with his pistol kills a sparrow flying.

Fal. You have hit it.

P. Hen. So did he never the sparrow.

Fal. Well, that rascal hath good mettle in him; he will not run.

P. Hen. Why, what a rascal art thou then, to praise him so for running?

Fal. O' horseback, ye cuckoo! but, afoot, he will not budge a foot.

P. Hen. Yes, Jack, upon instinct.

Fal. I grant ye, upon instinct. Well, he is there too, and one Mordake, and a thousand blue-caps more: Worcester is stolen away to-night; thy father's beard is turned white with the news; you may buy land now as cheap as stinking mackarel.

P. Hen. Why then, 'tis like, if there come a hot June, and this civil buffeting hold, we shall buy maidenheads as they buy hob-nails, by the hundreds.

Fal. By the mass, lad, thou sayest true; it is like, we shall have good trading that way.—But, tell me, Hal, art thou not horribly afeard? thou being heir apparent, could the world pick thee out three such enemies again, as that fiend Douglas, that spirit Percy, and that devil Glendower? Art thou not horribly afraid? doth not thy blood thrill at it?

P. Hen. Not a whit, i' faith; I lack some of thy instinct.

Fal. Well, thou wilt be horribly chid to-morrow, when thou comest to thy father: if thou love me, practise an answer.

P. Hen. Do thou stand for my father, and examine me upon the particulars of my life.

Fal. Shall I? content:—This chair shall be my state, this dagger my sceptre, and this cushion my crown.

P. Hen. Thy state is taken for a joint-stool, thy golden sceptre for a leaden dagger, and thy precious rich crown, for a pitiful bald crown!

Fal. Well, an the fire of grace be not quite out of thee, now shalt thou be moved.—Give me a cup of sack, to make mine eyes look red, that it may be thought I have wept; for I must speak in passion, and I will do it in King Cambyses' vein.

P. Hen. Well, here is my leg.

Fal. And here is my speech:—Stand aside, nobility.

Host. This is excellent sport, i' faith.

Fal. Weep not, sweet queen, for trickling tears are vain.

Host. O, the father, how he holds his countenance!

Fal. For God's sake, lords, convey my tristful [queen,
For tears do stop the flood-gates of her eyes.

Host. O rare! he doth it as like one of these harlotry players, as I ever see.

Fal. Peace, good pint-pot; peace, good tickle-brain.—Harry, I do not only marvel where thou spendest thy time, but also how thou art accompanied: for though the camomile, the more it is trodden on, the faster it grows, yet youth, the more it is wasted, the sooner it wears. That thou art my son, I have partly thy mother's word, partly my own opinion; but chiefly, a villanous trick of thine eye, and a foolish hanging of thy nether lip, that doth warrant me. If then thou be son to me, here lies the point;—Why, being son to me, art thou so pointed at? Shall the blessed sun of heaven prove a micher, and eat blackberries? a question not to be asked. Shall the son of England prove a thief, and take purses? a question to be asked. There is a thing, Harry, which thou hast often heard of, and it is known to many in our land by the name of pitch: this pitch, as ancient writers do report, doth defile; so doth the company thou keepest: for, Harry, now I do not speak to thee in drink, but in tears; not in pleasure, but in passion; not in words only, but in woes also:—And yet there is a virtuous man, whom I have often noted in thy company, but I know not his name.

P. Hen. What manner of man, an it like your majesty?

Fal. A good portly man, i' faith, and a corpulent; of a cheerful look, a pleasing eye, and a most noble carriage; and, as I think, his age some fifty, or, by'r-lady, inclining to threescore: And now I remember me, his name is Falstaff; if that man should be lewdly given, he deceiveth me; for, Harry, I see virtue in his looks. If then the tree may be known by the fruit, as the fruit by the tree, then, peremptorily I speak it, there is virtue in that Falstaff: him keep with, the rest banish. And tell me now, thou naughty varlet, tell me, where hast thou been this month?

P. Hen. Dost thou speak like a king? Do thou stand for me, and I'll play my father.

Fal. Depose me? if thou dost it half so gravely, so majestically, both in word and matter, hang me up by the heels for a rabbit-sucker, or a poulter's hare.

P. Hen. Well, here I am set.

Fal. And here I stand:—judge, my masters.

P. Hen. Now, Harry? whence come you?

Fal. My noble lord, from Eastcheap.

P. Hen. The complaints I hear of thee are grievous.

Fal. 'Sblood, my lord, they are false:—nay, I'll tickle ye for a young prince, i' faith.

P. Hen. Swear'st thou, ungracious boy? henceforth ne'er look on me. Thou art violently carried away from grace: there is a devil haunts thee, in the likeness of a fat old man: a tun of man is thy companion. Why dost thou converse with that trunk of humours, that bolting-hutch of beastliness, that swoln parcel of dropsies, that huge bombard of sack, that stuffed cloak-bag of guts, that roasted Manningtree ox with the pudding in his belly, that reverend vice, that gray iniquity, that father ruffian, that vanity in years? Wherein is he good, but to taste sack and drink it? wherein neat and cleanly, but to carve a capon and eat it? wherein cunning, but in craft? wherein crafty, but in villany? wherein villanous, but in all things? wherein worthy, but in nothing?

Fal. I would, your grace would take me with you; Whom means your grace?

P. Hen. That villanous abominable misleader of youth, Falstaff, that old white-bearded Satan.

Fal. My lord, the man I know.

P. Hen. I know, thou dost.

Fal. But to say, I know more harm in him than in myself, were to say more than I know. That he is old (the more the pity), his white hairs do witness it: but that he is (saving your reverence) a whoremaster, that I utterly deny. If sack and sugar be a fault, God help the wicked! If to be old and merry be a sin, then many an old host that I know, is damned: if to be fat be to be hated, then Pharaoh's lean kine are to be loved. No, my good lord; banish Peto, banish Bardolph, banish Poins; but for sweet Jack Falstaff, kind Jack Falstaff, true Jack Falstaff, valiant Jack Falstaff, and therefore more valiant, being as he is, old Jack Falstaff, banish not him thy Harry's company; banish plump Jack, and banish all the world.

P. Hen. I do, I will. [*A knocking heard.*

[*Exeunt* Hostess, FRANCIS, *and* BARDOLPH.

Re-enter BARDOLPH, *running.*

Bard. O, my lord, my lord; the sheriff, with a most monstrous watch, is at the door.

Fal. Out, you rogue! play out the play; I have much to say in the behalf of that Falstaff.

Re-enter Hostess, *hastily.*

Host. O Jesu, my lord! my lord!——

Fal. Heigh, heigh! the devil rides upon a fiddlestick: What's the matter?

Host. The sheriff and all the watch are at the door: they are come to search the house; Shall I let them in?

Fal. Dost thou hear, Hal? never call a true piece of gold, a counterfeit: thou art essentially mad, without seeming so.

P. Hen. And thou a natural coward, without instinct.

Fal. I deny your *major*: if you will deny the sheriff, so; if not, let him enter: if I become not a cart as well as another man, a plague on my bringing up! I hope, I shall as soon be strangled with a halter as another.

P. Hen. Go, hide thee behind the arras;—the rest walk up above. Now, my masters, for a true face, and good conscience.

Fal. Both which I have had: but their date is out, and therefore I'll hide me.

[*Exeunt all but the* Prince *and* POINS.

P. Hen. Call in the sheriff.——

Enter Sheriff *and* Carrier.

Now, master Sheriff; what's your will with me?

Sher. First, pardon me, my lord. A hue and cry
Hath follow'd certain men unto this house.

P. Hen. What men?

Sher. One of them is well known, my gracious lord,
A gross fat man.

Car. As fat as butter.

P. Hen. The man, I do assure you, is not here;
For I myself at this time have employ'd him.
And, Sheriff, I will engage my word to thee,
That I will, by to-morrow dinner time,
Send him to answer thee, or any man,
For any thing he shall be charg'd withal:
And so let me entreat you leave the house.

Sher. I will, my lord: There are two gentlemen
Have in this robbery lost three hundred marks.

P. Hen. It may be so: if he have robb'd these men,
He shall be answerable; and so, farewell.

Sher. Good night, my noble lord.

P. Hen. I think it is good morrow: Is it not?

Sher. Indeed, my lord, I think it be two o' clock. [*Exeunt* Sheriff *and* Carrier.

P. Hen. This oily rascal is known as well as Paul's. Go, call him forth.

Poins. Falstaff!—fast asleep behind the arras, and snorting like a horse.

P. Hen. Hark, how hard he fetches breath: Search his pockets. [POINS *searches.*] What hast thou found?

Poins. Nothing but papers, my lord.

P. Hen. Let's see what they be: read them.

Poins. Item, A capon, 2*s.* 2*d.*
Item, Sauce, 4*d.*
Item, Sack, two gallons, 5*s.* 8*d.*
Item, Anchovies, and sack after supper, 2*s.* 6*d.*
Item, Bread, a halfpenny.

P. Hen. O monstrous! but one halfpenny-worth of bread to this intolerable deal of sack!—What there is else, keep close; we'll read it at more advantage: there let him sleep till day. I'll to the court in the morning; we must all to the wars, and thy place shall be honourable. I'll procure this fat rogue a charge of foot; and, I know, his death will be a march of twelve-score. The money shall be paid back again with advantage. Be with me betimes in the morning; and so good morrow, Poins.

Poins. Good morrow, good my lord.

[*Exeunt.*

ACT III.

SCENE I. Bangor.

A Room in the Archdeacon's *House.*

Enter HOTSPUR, WORCESTER, MORTIMER, *and* GLENDOWER.

Mort. These promises are fair, the parties sure,
And our induction full of prosperous hope.

Hot. Lord Mortimer,—and cousin Glendower,—
Will you sit down?——
And, uncle Worcester:—A plague upon it!
I have forgot the map.

Glend. No, here it is.
Sit, cousin Percy; sit, good cousin Hotspur,
For by that name as oft as Lancaster
Doth speak of you, his cheek looks pale; and, with
A rising sigh, he wisheth you in heaven.

Hot. And you in hell, as often as he hears
Owen Glendower spoke of.

Glend. I cannot blame him: at my nativity,
The front of heaven was full of fiery shapes,
Of burning cressets; and, at my birth,
The frame and huge foundation of the earth,
Shak'd like a coward.

Hot. Why, so it would have done
At the same season, if your mother's cat had
But kitten'd, though yourself had ne'er been born.

Glend. I say, the earth did shake when I was born.

Hot. And I say, the earth was not of my mind,
If you suppose, as fearing you it shook.

Glend. The heavens were all on fire, the earth did tremble.

Hot. O, then the earth shook to see the heavens on fire,
And not in fear of your nativity.
Diseased nature oftentimes breaks forth
In strange eruptions: oft the teeming earth
Is with a kind of colick pinch'd and vex'd
By the imprisoning of unruly wind
Within her womb; which, for enlargement striving,
Shakes the old beldame earth, and topples down
Steeples, and moss-grown towers. At your birth,
Our grandam earth, having this distemperature,
In passion shook.
Glend. Cousin, of many men
I do not bear these crossings. Give me leave
To tell you once again,—that, at my birth,
The front of heaven was full of fiery shapes;
The goats ran from the mountains, and the herds
Were strangely clamorous to the frighted fields.
These signs have mark'd me extraordinary;
And all the courses of my life do show,
I am not in the roll of common men.
Where is he living,—clipp'd in with the sea
That chides the banks of England, Scotland, Wales,——
Which calls me pupil, or hath read to me?
And bring him out, that is but woman's son,
Can trace me in the tedious ways of art,
And hold me pace in deep experiments.
Hot. I think, there is no man speaks better Welsh:——
I'll to dinner.
Mort. Peace, cousin Percy; you will make him mad.
Glend. I can call spirits from the vasty deep.
Hot. Why, so can I; or so can any man:
But will they come, when you do call for them?
Glend. Why, I can teach you, cousin, to command
The devil.
Hot. And I can teach thee, coz, to shame the devil,
By telling truth; Tell truth, and shame the devil.—
If thou have power to raise him, bring him hither,
And I'll be sworn, I have power to shame him hence.
O, while you live, tell truth, and shame the devil.
Mort. Come, come,
No more of this unprofitable chat.
Glend. Three times hath Henry Bolingbroke made head
Against my power: thrice from the banks of Wye,
And sandy-bottom'd Severn, have I sent him,
Bootless home, and weather-beaten back.
Hot. Home without boots, and in foul weather too!
How 'scapes he agues, in the devil's name?
Glend. Come, here's the map: Shall we divide our right,
According to our three-fold order ta'en?
Mort. The archdeacon hath divided it
Into three limits, very equally:
England, from Trent and Severn hitherto,
By south and east, is to my part assign'd:
All westward, Wales beyond the Severn shore,
And all the fertile land within that bound,
To Owen Glendower: and, dear coz, to you
The remnant northward, lying off from Trent.
And our indentures tripartite are drawn:
Which being sealed interchangeably,
(A business that this night may execute),
To-morrow, cousin Percy, you, and I,
And my good lord of Worcester, will set forth,
To meet your father, and the Scottish power,
As is appointed us at Shrewsbury.
My father Glendower is not ready yet,
Nor shall we need his help these fourteen days:
Within that space [*To* GLEND.] you may have drawn together
Your tenants, friends, and neighbouring gentlemen.
Glend. A shorter time shall send me to you, lords,
And in my conduct shall your ladies come:
From whom you now must steal, and take no leave;
For there will be a world of water shed,
Upon the parting of your wives and you.
Hot. Methinks, my moiety, north from Burton here,
In quantity equals not one of yours:
See, how this river comes me cranking in,
And cuts me, from the best of all my land,
A huge half moon, a monstrous cantle out.
I'll have the current in this place damm'd up;
And here the smug and silver Trent shall run,
In a new channel, fair and evenly:
It shall not wind with such a deep indent,
To rob me of so rich a bottom here.
Glend. Not wind? it shall, it must; you see, it doth.
Mort. Yea,
But mark, how he bears his course, and runs me up
With like advantage on the other side;
Gelding the opposed continent as much,
As on the other side it takes from you.
Wor. Yea, but a little charge will trench him here,
And on this north side win this cape of land;
And then he runs straight and even.
Hot. I'll have it so; a little charge will do it.
Glend. I will not have it alter'd.
Hot. Will not you?
Glend. No, nor you shall not.
Hot. Who shall say me nay?
Glend. Why, that will I.
Hot. Let me not understand you then,
Speak it in Welsh.
Glend. I can speak English, lord, as well as you;
For I was train'd up in the English court:
Where, being but young, I framed to the harp
Many an English ditty, lovely well,
And gave the tongue a helpful ornament;
A virtue that was never seen in you.
Hot. Marry, and I'm glad of it with all my heart;
I had rather be a kitten, and cry—mew,
Than one of these same metre ballad-mongers:
I had rather hear a brazen canstick turn'd,
Or a dry wheel grate on an axle-tree;
And that would set my teeth nothing on edge,
Nothing so much as mincing poetry;
'Tis like the forc'd gait of a shuffling nag.
Glend. Come, you shall have Trent turn'd.
Hot. I do not care: I'll give thrice so much land
To any well deserving friend;
But, in the way of bargain, mark ye me,
I'll cavil on the ninth part of a hair.
Are the indentures drawn? shall we be gone?
Glend. The moon shines fair, you may away by night:
I'll in and haste the writer, and, withal,
Break with your wives of your departure hence:
I am afraid, my daughter will run mad,
So much she doteth on her Mortimer. [*Exit.*
Mort. Fye, cousin Percy! how you cross my father!
Hot. I cannot choose: sometimes he angers me,
With telling me of the moldwarp and the ant,
Of the dreamer Merlin and his prophecies;
And of a dragon, and a finless fish,
A clip-wing griffin, and a moulten raven,
A couching lion, and a ramping cat,
And such a deal of skimble-skamble stuff
As puts me from my faith. I tell you what,—
He held me, but last night, at least nine hours,
In reckoning up the several devils' names,
That were his lackeys: I cried, humph,—and well—go to,—
But mark'd him not a word. O, he's as tedious
As is a tir'd horse, a railing wife;
Worse than a smoky house;—I had rather live

With cheese and garlick, in a windmill, far,
Than feed on cates, and have him talk to me,
In any summer-house in Christendom.

Mort. In faith, he is a worthy gentleman;
Exceedingly well read, and profited
In strange concealments; valiant as a lion,
And wondrous affable; and as bountiful
As mines of India. Shall I tell you, cousin?
He holds your temper in a high respect,
And curbs himself even of his natural scope,
When you do cross his humour; 'faith, he does:
I warrant you, that man is not alive,
Might so have tempted him as you have done,
Without the taste of danger and reproof;
But do not use it oft, let me entreat you.

Wor. In faith, my lord, you are too wilful-blame;
And since your coming hither, have done enough
To put him quite beside his patience.
You must needs learn, lord, to amend this fault:
Though sometimes it show greatness, courage, blood,
(And that's the dearest grace it renders you),
Yet oftentimes it doth present harsh rage,
Defect of manners, want of government,
Pride, haughtiness, opinion, and disdain:
The least of which, haunting a nobleman,
Loseth men's hearts; and leaves behind a stain
Upon the beauty of all parts besides,
Beguiling them of commendation.

Hot. Well, I am school'd; good manners be your speed!
Here come our wives, and let us take our leave.

Re-enter GLENDOWER, *with the* Ladies.

Mort. This is the deadly spite that angers me,—
My wife can speak no English, I no Welsh.

Glend. My daughter weeps; she will not part with you.
She'll be a soldier too, she'll to the wars.

Mort. Good father, tell her,—that she, and my aunt Percy,
Shall follow in your conduct speedily.

[GLEND. *speaks to his Daughter in* Welsh, *and she answers him in the same.*

Glend. She's desperate here; a peevish self-will'd harlotry,
One that no persuasion can do good upon.

[LADY M. *speaks to* MORTIMER *in* Welsh.

Mort. I understand thy looks: that pretty Welsh
Which thou pourest down from these swelling heavens,
I am too perfect in; and, but for shame,
In such a parley would I answer thee.

[LADY M. *speaks.*

I understand thy kisses, and thou mine,
And that's a feeling disputation:
But I will never be a truant, love,
Till I have learn'd thy language; for thy tongue
Makes Welsh as sweet as ditties highly penn'd,
Sung by a fair queen in a summer's bower,
With ravishing division to her lute.

Glend. Nay, if you melt, then will she run mad.

[LADY M. *speaks again.*

Mort. O, I am ignorance itself in this.

Glend. She bids you on the wanton rushes lay you down,
And rest your gentle head upon her lap,
And she will sing the song that pleaseth you,
And on your eyelids crown the god of sleep,
Charming your blood with pleasing heaviness;
Making such difference 'twixt wake and sleep,
As is the difference betwixt day and night,
The hour before the heavenly harness'd team
Begins his golden progress in the east.

Mort. With all my heart I'll sit, and hear her sing:
By that time will our book, I think, be drawn.

Glend. Do so;
And those musicians that shall play to you,
Hang in the air a thousand leagues from hence;
And straight they shall be here: sit, and attend.

Hot. Come, Kate, thou art perfect in lying down: Come, quick, quick; that I may lay my head in thy lap.

Lady P. Go, ye giddy goose.

[GLENDOWER *speaks some* Welsh *words, and then the Musick plays.*

Hot. Now I perceive, the devil understands Welsh;
And 'tis no marvel, he's so humorous.
By'r-lady, he's a good musician.

Lady. P. Then should you be nothing but musical; for you are altogether governed by humours. Lie still, ye thief, and hear the lady sing in Welsh.

Hot. I had rather hear *Lady*, my brach, howl in Irish.

Lady P. Would'st thou have thy head broken?

Hot. No.

Lady P. Then be still.

Hot. Neither; 'tis a woman's fault.

Lady P. Now God help thee!

Hot. To the Welsh lady's bed.

Lady P. What's that?

Hot. Peace! she sings.

[*A* Welsh SONG *sung by* LADY M.

Hot. Come, Kate, I'll have your song too.

Lady P. Not mine, in good sooth.

Hot. Not yours, in good sooth! 'Heart, you swear like a comfit-maker's wife! Not you, in good sooth: and, As true as I live; and, as God shall mend me; and, As sure as day:
And giv'st such sarcenet surety for thy oaths,
As if thou never walk'dst further than Finsbury.
Swear me, Kate, like a lady, as thou art,
A good mouth-filling oath; and leave in sooth,
And such protest of pepper-gingerbread,
To velvet-guards, and Sunday-citizens.
Come, sing.

Lady P. I will not sing.

Hot. 'Tis the next way to turn tailor, or be redbreast teacher. An the indentures be drawn, I'll away within these two hours; and so come in when ye will. [*Exit.*

Glend. Come, come, Lord Mortimer; you are as slow,
As hot Lord Percy is on fire to go.
By this our book's drawn; we'll but seal, and then
To horse immediately.

Mort. With all my heart.

[*Exeunt.*

SCENE II. London. *A Room in the Palace.*

Enter KING HENRY, Prince of Wales, *and* Lords.

K. Hen. Lords, give us leave: the Prince of Wales and I
Must have some private conference: But be near at hand,
For we shall presently have need of you.

[*Exeunt* Lords.

I know not whether God will have it so,
For some displeasing service I have done,
That in his secret doom, out of my blood
He'll breed revengement and a scourge for me;
But thou dost, in thy passages of life,
Make me believe,—that thou art only mark'd
For the hot vengeance and the rod of heaven,
To punish my mistreadings. Tell me else,
Could such inordinate, and low desires,
Such poor, such bare, such lewd, such mean attempts,
Such barren pleasures, rude society,
As thou art match'd withal, and grafted to,
Accompany the greatness of thy blood,
And hold their level with thy princely heart?

P. Hen. So please your majesty, I would I could
Quit all offences with as clear excuse,
As well as, I am doubtless, I can purge
Myself of many I am charg'd withal:
Yet such extenuation let me beg,
As, in reproof of many tales devis'd,—

Which oft the ear of greatness needs must hear,—
By smiling pick-thanks and base newsmongers,
I may, for some things true, wherein my youth
Hath faulty wander'd and irregular,
Find pardon on my true submission.

K. Hen. God pardon thee!—yet let me wonder, Harry,
At thy affections, which do hold a wing
Quite from the flight of all thy ancestors.
Thy place in council thou hast rudely lost,
Which by thy younger brother is supplied;
And art almost an alien to the hearts
Of all the court and princes of my blood:
The hope and expectation of thy time
Is ruin'd; and the soul of every man
Prophetically does forethink thy fall.
Had I so lavish of my presence been,
So common-hackney'd in the eyes of men,
So stale and cheap to vulgar company;
Opinion, that did help me to the crown,
Had still kept loyal to possession;
And left me in reputeless banishment,
A fellow of no mark, nor likelihood.
By being seldom seen, I could not stir,
But, like a comet, I was wonder'd at:
That men would tell their children, *This is he;*
Others would say,—*Where? which is Bolingbroke?*
And then I stole all courtesy from heaven,
And dress'd myself in such humility,
That I did pluck allegiance from men's hearts,
Loud shouts and salutations from their mouths,
Even in the presence of the crowned king.
Thus did I keep my person fresh, and new;
My presence, like a robe pontifical,
Ne'er seen, but wonder'd at: and so my state,
Seldom, but sumptuous, showed like a feast;
And won, by rareness, such solemnity.
The skipping king, he ambled up and down
With shallow jesters, and rash bavin wits,
Soon kindled, and soon burn'd: carded his state;
Mingled his royalty with carping fools;
Had his great name profaned with their scorns;
And gave his countenance, against his name,
To laugh at gibing boys, and stand the push
Of every beardless vain comparative:
Grew a companion to the common streets,
Enfeoff'd himself to popularity:
That being daily swallow'd by men's eyes,
They surfeited with honey; and began
To loathe the taste of sweetness, whereof a little
More than a little is by much too much.
So, when he had occasion to be seen,
He was but as the cuckoo is in June,
Heard, not regarded; seen but with such eyes,
As, sick and blunted with community,
Afford no extraordinary gaze,
Such as is bent on sunlike majesty,
When it shines seldom in admiring eyes:
But rather drowz'd, and hung their eyelids down,
Slept in his face, and render'd such aspect
As cloudy men use to their adversaries;
Being with his presence glutted, gorg'd, and full.
And in that very line, Harry, stand'st thou:
For thou hast lost thy princely privilege,
With vile participation; not an eye
But is a-weary of thy common sight,
Save mine, which hath desir'd to see thee more;
Which now doth that I would not have it do,
Make blind itself with foolish tenderness.

P. Hen. I shall hereafter, my thrice-gracious [lord,
Be more myself.

K. Hen. For all the world,
As thou art to this hour, was Richard then
When I from France set foot at Ravenspurg;
And even as I was then, is Percy now.
Now by my sceptre, and my soul to boot,
He hath more worthy interest to the state,
Than thou, the shadow of succession:
For, of no right, nor colour like to right,
He doth fill fields with harness in the realm;
Turns head against the lion's armed jaws;
And, being no more in debt to years than thou,
Leads ancient lords, and reverend bishops on,
To bloody battles, and to bruising arms.
What never dying honour hath he got
Against renowned Douglas; whose high deeds,
Whose hot incursions, and great name in arms,
Holds from all soldiers chief majority,
And military title capital,
Through all the kingdoms that acknowledge Christ?
Thrice hath this Hotspur Mars in swathing [clothes,
This infant warrior, in his enterprises
Discomfited great Douglas; ta'en him once,
Enlarged him, and made a friend of him,
To fill the mouth of deep defiance up,
And shake the peace and safety of our throne.
And what say you to this? Percy, Northumberland,
The archbishop's grace of York, Douglas, Mor- [timer,
Capitulate against us, and are up.
But wherefore do I tell these news to thee?
Why, Harry, do I tell thee of my foes,
Which art my near'st and dearest enemy?
Thou that art like enough,—through vassal fear,
Base inclination, and the start of spleen,——
To fight against me under Percy's pay,
To dog his heels, and court'sy at his frowns,
To show how much degenerate thou art.

P. Hen. Do not think so, you shall not find it so;
And God forgive them, that have so much sway'd
Your majesty's good thoughts away from me!
I will redeem all this on Percy's head,
And, in the closing of some glorious day,
Be bold to tell you, that I am your son;
When I will wear a garment all of blood,
And stain my favours in a bloody mask,
Which, wash'd away, shall scour my shame with it.
And that shall be the day, whene'er it lights,
That this same child of honour and renown,
This gallant Hotspur, this all-praised knight,
And your unthought-of Harry, chance to meet:
For every honour sitting on his helm,
'Would they were multitudes; and on my head
My shames redoubled! for the time will come,
That I shall make this northern youth exchange
His glorious deeds for my indignities.
Percy is but my factor, good my lord,
To engross up glorious deeds on my behalf;
And I will call him to so strict account,
That he shall render every glory up,
Yea, even the slightest worship of his time,
Or I will tear the reckoning from his heart.
This, in the name of God, I promise here:
The which if he be pleas'd I shall perform,
I do beseech your majesty, may salve
The long-grown wounds of my intemperance:
If not, the end of life cancels all bands;
And I will die a hundred thousand deaths,
Ere break the smallest parcel of this vow.

K. Hen. A hundred thousand rebels die in this:— [herein.
Thou shalt have charge, and sovereign trust,

Enter BLUNT.

How now, good Blunt? thy looks are full of speed.

Blunt. So hath the business that I come to speak of.
Lord Mortimer of Scotland hath sent word,—
That Douglas, and the English rebels, met,
The eleventh of this month, at Shrewsbury:
A mighty and a fearful head they are,
If promises be kept on every hand,
As ever offer'd foul play in a state. [to-day;

K. Hen. The earl of Westmoreland set forth
With him my son, Lord John of Lancaster;
For this advertisement is five days old:—
On Wednesday next, Harry, you shall set
Forward; on Thursday, we ourselves will march:
Our meeting is Bridgnorth: and, Harry, you
Shall march through Glostershire; by which account,

Our business valued, some twelve days hence
Our general forces at Bridgnorth shall meet.
Our hands are full of business: let's away;
Advantage feeds him fat, while men delay.
[*Exeunt.*

SCENE III.

Eastcheap. *A Room in the* Boar's Head *Tavern.*

Enter FALSTAFF *and* BARDOLPH.

Fal. Bardolph, am I not fallen away vilely since this last action? do I not bate? do I not dwindle? Why, my skin hangs about me like an old lady's loose gown; I am wither'd like an old apple-john. Well, I'll repent, and that suddenly, while I am in some liking; I shall be out of heart shortly, and then I shall have no strength to repent. An I have not forgotten what the inside of a church is made of, I am a pepper-corn, a brewer's horse: the inside of a church! Company, villanous company, hath been the spoil of me.

Bard. Sir John, you are so fretful, you cannot live long.

Fal. Why, there is it:—come, sing me a bawdy song; make me merry. I was as virtuously given, as a gentleman need to be; virtuous enough: swore little; diced, not above seven times a week; went to a bawdy house, not above once in a quarter—of an hour; paid money that I borrowed, three or four times; lived well, and in good compass: and now I live out of all order, out of all compass.

Bard. Why, you are so fat, Sir John, that you must needs be out of all compass; out of all reasonable compass, Sir John.

Fal. Do thou amend thy face, and I'll amend my life: Thou art our admiral, thou bearest the lantern in the poop,—but 'tis in the nose of thee: thou art the knight of the burning lamp.

Bard. Why, Sir John, my face does you no harm.

Fal. No, I'll be sworn; I make as good use of it as many a man doth of a death's head, or a *memento mori:* I never see thy face, but I think upon hell-fire, and Dives that lived in purple; for there he is in his robes, burning, burning. If thou wert any way given to virtue, I would swear by thy face; my oath should be, By this fire: but thou art altogether given over; and wert indeed, but for the light in thy face, the son of utter darkness. When thou ran'st up Gads-hill in the night to catch my horse, if I did not think thou hadst been an *ignis fatuus*, or a ball of wildfire, there's no purchase in money. O, thou art a perpetual triumph, an everlasting bonfire-light! Thou hast saved me a thousand marks in links and torches, walking with thee in the night betwixt tavern and tavern: but the sack that thou hast drunk me, would have bought me lights as good cheap, at the dearest chandler's in Europe. I have maintain'd that Salamander of yours with fire, any time this two and thirty years; Heaven reward me for it!

Bard. 'Sblood, I would my face were in your belly!

Fal. God-a-mercy! so should I be sure to be heart-burned.

Enter HOSTESS.

How now, dame Partlet the hen? have you inquired yet, who picked my pocket?

Host. Why, Sir John! what do you think, Sir John? Do you think I keep thieves in my house? I have searched, I have inquired, so has my husband, man by man, boy by boy, servant by servant: the tithe of a hair was never lost in my house before.

Fal. You lie, hostess; Bardolph was shaved and lost many a hair: and I'll be sworn, my pocket was picked: Go to, you are a woman, go.

Host. Who I? I defy thee: I was never called so in mine own house before.

Fal. Go to, I know you well enough.

Host. No, Sir John; you do not know me, Sir John: I know you, Sir John: you owe me money, Sir John, and now you pick a quarrel to beguile me of it: I bought you a dozen of shirts to your back.

Fal. Dowlas, filthy dowlas: I have given them away to bakers' wives, and they have made bolters of them.

Host. Now, as I am a true woman, holland of eight shillings an ell. You owe money here besides, Sir John, for your diet, and by-drinkings, and money lent you, four and twenty pound.

Fal. He had his part of it; let him pay.

Host. He? alas, he is poor; he hath nothing.

Fal. How! poor? look upon his face; What call you rich? let them coin his nose, let them coin his cheeks; I'll not pay a denier. What, will you make a younker of me? shall I not take mine ease in mine inn, but I shall have my pocket picked? I have lost a seal ring of my grandfather's, worth forty mark.

Host. O Jesu! I have heard the prince tell him, I know not how oft, that the ring was copper.

Fal. How! the prince is a Jack, a sneak-cup; and, if he were here, I would cudgel him like a dog, if he would say so.

Enter PRINCE HENRY *and* POINS, *marching.* FALSTAFF *meets the* Prince, *playing on his truncheon like a fife.*

Fal. How now, lad? is the wind in that door, i' faith? must we all march?

Bard. Yea, two and two, Newgate-fashion?

Host. My lord, I pray you, hear me.

P. Hen. What sayest thou, mistress Quickly? How does thy husband? I love him well, he is an honest man.

Host. Good my lord, hear me.

Fal. 'Pr'ythee, let her alone, and list to me.

P. Hen. What sayest thou, Jack?

Fal. The other night I fell asleep here behind the arras, and had my pocket picked: this house is turned bawdy-house, they pick pockets.

P. Hen. What didst thou lose, Jack?

Fal. Wilt thou believe me, Hal? three or four bonds of forty pound a-piece, and a seal-ring of my grandfather's.

P. Hen. A trifle, some eight-penny matter.

Host. So I told him, my lord; and I said I heard your grace say so: And, my lord, he speaks most vilely of you, like a foul-mouthed man as he is; and said he would cudgel you.

P. Hen. What! he did not?

Host. There's neither faith, truth, nor womanhood in me else.

Fal. There's no more faith in thee than in a stewed prune; nor no more truth in thee, than in a drawn fox; and for womanhood, maid Marian may be the deputy's wife of the ward to thee. Go, you thing, go.

Host. Say, what thing? what thing?

Fal. What thing? why a thing to thank God on.

Host. I am no thing to thank God on, I would thou should'st know it; I am an honest man's wife: and, setting thy knighthood aside, thou art a knave to call me so.

Fal. Setting thy womanhood aside, thou art a beast to say otherwise.

Host. Say, what beast, thou knave thou?

Fal. What beast? why an otter.

P. Hen. An otter, Sir John! why an otter?

Fal. Why? she's neither fish, nor flesh; a man knows not where to have her.

Host. Thou art an unjust man in saying so; thou or any man knows where to have me, thou knave thou.

P. Hen. Thou sayest true, hostess; and he slanders thee most grossly.

Host. So he doth you, my lord; and said this other day, you ought him a thousand pound.

P. Hen. Sirrah, do I owe you a thousand pound?

Fal. A thousand pound, Hal? a million: thy love is worth a million: thou owest me thy love.

Host. Nay, my lord, he called you Jack, and said he would cudgel you.

Fal. Did I, Bardolph?

Bard. Indeed, Sir John, you said so.

Fal. Yea; if he said my ring was copper.

P. Hen. I say, 'tis copper: Darest thou be as good as thy word now?

Fal. Why, Hal, thou knowest, as thou art but man, I dare: but, as thou art prince, I fear thee, as I fear the roaring of the lion's whelp.

P. Hen. And why not, as the lion?

Fal. The king himself is to be feared as the lion: Dost thou think I'll fear thee as I fear thy father? nay, an I do, I pray God, my girdle break!

P. Hen. O, if it should, how would thy guts fall about thy knees! But, sirrah, there's no room for faith, truth, nor honesty, in this bosom of thine; it is all fill'd up with guts, and midriff. Charge an honest woman with picking thy pocket! Why, thou whoreson, impudent, embossed rascal, if there were any thing in thy pocket but tavern-reckonings, memorandums of bawdy-houses, and one poor penny-worth of sugar-candy to make thee long-winded; if thy pocket were enriched with any other injuries but these, I am a villain. And yet you will stand to it; you will not pocket up wrong; Art thou not ashamed?

Fal. Dost thou hear, Hal? thou knowest, in the state of innocency, Adam fell; and what should poor Jack Falstaff do, in the days of villany? Thou seest, I have more flesh than another man; and therefore more frailty.——You confess then, you picked my pocket?

P. Hen. It appears so by the story.

Fal. Hostess, I forgive thee: Go, make ready breakfast; love thy husband, look to thy servants, cherish thy guests: thou shalt find me tractable to any honest reason; thou seest, I am pacified.—Still? Nay, pr'ythee be gone. [*Exit* Hostess.] Now, Hal, to the news at court: for the robbery, lad, how is that answered?

P. Hen. O, my sweet beef, I must still be good angel to thee:—The money is paid back again.

Fal. O, I do not like that paying back, 'tis a double labour.

P. Hen. I am good friends with my father, and may do any thing.

Fal. Rob me the exchequer the first thing thou doest, and do it with unwashed hands too.

Bard. Do, my lord.

P. Hen. I have procured thee, Jack, a charge of foot.

Fal. I would, it had been of horse. Where shall I find one that can steal well? O for a fine thief, of the age of two and twenty, or thereabouts! I am heinously unprovided. Well, God be thanked for these rebels, they offend none but the virtuous; I laud them, I praise them.

P. Hen. Bardolph——

Bard. My lord.

P. Hen. Go bear this letter to Lord John of Lancaster,—my brother John;—this to my lord of Westmoreland.—Go, Poins, to horse, to horse; for thou, and I, have thirty miles to ride yet ere dinner time.——Jack, meet me to-morrow i'the Temple-hall at two o'clock i' the afternoon: there shalt thou know thy charge; and there receive money, and order for their furniture.
The land is burning; Percy, stands on high;
And either they, or we, must lower lie.

[*Exeunt* Prince, POINS, *and* BARDOLPH.

Fal. Rare words! brave world!——Hostess, my breakfast; come:—
O, I could wish, this tavern were my drum.

[*Exit.*

ACT IV.

SCENE I. *The rebel Camp near* Shrewsbury.

Enter HOTSPUR, WORCESTER, *and* DOUGLAS.

Hot. Well said, my noble Scot: If speaking truth,
In this fine age, were not thought flattery,
Such attribution should the Douglas have,
As not a soldier of this season's stamp
Should go so general current through the world.
By heaven, I cannot flatter; I defy
The tongues of soothers; but a braver place
In my heart's love, hath no man than yourself:
Nay, task me to the word; approve me, lord.

Doug. Thou art the king of honour:
No man so potent breathes upon the ground,
But I will beard him.

Hot. Do so, and 'tis well:—

Enter a Messenger, *with Letters.*

What letters hast thou there?—I can but thank you.

Mess. These letters come from your father,—

Hot. Letters from him! why comes he not himself?—

Mess. He cannot come, my lord; he's grievous sick.

Hot. 'Zounds! how has he the leisure to be sick,
In such a justling time? Who leads his power?
Under whose government come they along?

Mess. His letters bear his mind, not I, my lord.

Wor. I pr'ythee, tell me, doth he keep his bed?

Mess. He did, my lord, four days ere I set forth,
And at the time of my departure thence,
He was much fear'd by his physicians.

Wor. I would, the state of time had first been whole,
Ere he by sickness had been visited;
His health was never better worth than now.

Hot. Sick now! droop now! this sickness doth infect
The very life-blood of our enterprise;
'Tis catching hither, even to our camp.——
He writes me here,—that inward sickness—
And that his friends by deputation could not
So soon be drawn; nor did he think it meet,
To lay so dangerous and dear a trust
On any soul remov'd, but on his own.
Yet doth he give us bold advertisement,—
That with our small conjunction, we should on,
To see how fortune is dispos'd to us:
For, as he writes, there is no quailing now;
Because the king is certainly possess'd
Of all our purposes. What say you to it?

Wor. Your father's sickness is a maim to us.

Hot. A perilous gash, a very limb lopp'd off:—
And yet, in faith, 'tis not; his present want
Seems more than we shall find it:—Were it good,
To set the exact wealth of all our states
All at one cast? to set so rich a main
On the nice hazard of one doubtful hour?
It were not good; for therein should we read
The very bottom and the soul of hope;
The very list, the very utmost bound
Of all our fortunes.

Doug. 'Faith, and so we should;
Where now remains a sweet reversion;
We may boldly spend upon the hope of what
Is to come in:
A comfort of retirement lives in this.

Hot. A rendezvous, a home to fly unto,
If that the devil and mischance look big
Upon the maidenhead of our affairs.

Wor. But yet, I would your father had been here.
The quality and hair of our attempt
Brooks no division: It will be thought
By some, that know not why he is away,
That wisdom, loyalty, and mere dislike
Of our proceedings, kept the earl from hence;
And think, how such an apprehension
May turn the tide of fearful faction,
And breed a kind of question in our cause:

For, well you know, we of the offering side
Must keep aloof from strict arbitrement;
And stop all sight-holes, every loop, from whence
The eye of reason may pry in upon us:
This absence of your father's draws a curtain,
That shows the ignorant a kind of fear
Before not dreamt of.
Hot. You strain too far.
I, rather, of his absence make this use;—
It lends a lustre, and more great opinion,
A larger dare to our great enterprise,
Than if the earl were here: for men must think,
If we, without his help, can make a head,
To push against the kingdom; with his help,
We shall o'erturn it topsy-turvy down.—
Yet all goes well, yet all our joints are whole.
Doug. As heart can think: there is not such a word
Spoke of in Scotland, as this term of fear.

Enter SIR RICHARD VERNON.

Hot. My cousin Vernon! welcome, by my soul.
Ver. 'Pray God, my news be worth a welcome, lord.
The earl of Westmoreland, seven thousand strong,
Is marching hitherwards; with him, Prince John.
Hot. No harm: What more?
Ver. And further, I have learn'd,
The king himself in person is set forth.
Or hitherwards intended speedily,
With strong and mighty preparation.
Hot. He shall be welcome too. Where is his son,
The nimble-footed mad-cap prince of Wales,
And his comrades, that daff'd the world aside,
And bid it pass?
Ver. All furnish'd, all in arms,
All plum'd: like estridges that with the wind
Bated, like eagles having lately bath'd;
Glittering in golden coats, like images;
As full of spirit as the month of May,
And gorgeous as the sun at midsummer;
Wanton as youthful goats, wild as young bulls.
I saw young Harry,—with his beaver on,
His cuisses on his thighs, gallantly arm'd,—
Rise from the ground like feather'd Mercury,
And vaulted with such ease into his seat,
As if an angel dropp'd down from the clouds,
To turn and wind a fiery Pegasus,
And witch the world with noble horsemanship.
Hot. No more, no more; worse than the sun in March,
This praise doth nourish agues. Let them come;
They come like sacrifices in their trim,
And to the fire-ey'd maid of smoky war,
All hot, and bleeding, will we offer them:
The mailed Mars shall on his altar sit,
Up to the ears in blood. I am on fire,
To hear this rich reprisal is so nigh,
And yet not ours:—Come, let me take my horse,
Who is to bear me, like a thunderbolt,
Against the bosom of the prince of Wales:
Harry to Harry shall, hot horse to horse,
Meet, and ne'er part, till one drop down a corse.
O, that Glendower were come!
Ver. There is more news:
I learn'd in Worcester, as I rode along,
He cannot draw his power this fourteen days.
Doug. That's the worst tidings that I hear of yet.
Wor. Ay, by my faith, that bears a frosty sound.
Hot. What may the king's whole battle reach unto?
Ver. To thirty thousand.
Hot. Forty let it be;
My father and Glendower being both away,
The powers of us may serve so great a day.
Come, let us make a muster speedily:
Doomsday is near; die all, die merrily.
Doug. Talk not of dying; I am out of fear
Of death, or death's hand, for this one half year.
[*Exeunt.*

SCENE II. *A Publick Road near* Coventry.

Enter FALSTAFF *and* BARDOLPH.

Fal. Bardolph, get thee before to Coventry: fill me a bottle of sack; our soldiers shall march through; we'll to Sutton-Colfield to-night.

Bard. Will you give me money, captain?

Fal. Lay out, lay out.

Bard. This bottle makes an angel.

Fal. An if it do, take it for thy labour; and if it make twenty, take them all, I'll answer the coinage. Bid my lieutenant Peto meet me at the town's end.

Bard. I will, captain: farewell. [*Exit.*

Fal. If I be not ashamed of my soldiers, I am a soused gurnet. I have misused the king's press damnably. I have got, in exchange of a hundred and fifty soldiers, three hundred and odd pounds. I press me none but good householders, yeomen's sons: inquire me out contracted bachelors, such as had been asked twice on the bans; such a commodity of warm slaves, as had as lief hear the devil as a drum; such as fear the report of a caliver, worse than a struck fowl, or a hurt wild-duck. I pressed me none but such toasts and butter, with hearts in their bellies no bigger than pins' heads, and they have bought out their services; and now my whole charge consists of ancients, corporals, lieutenants, gentlemen of companies, slaves as ragged as Lazarus in the painted cloth, where the glutton's dogs licked his sores: and such as, indeed, were never soldiers; but discarded unjust serving-men, younger sons to younger brothers, revolted tapsters, and ostlers trade-fallen: the cankers of a calm world, and a long peace; ten times more dishonourable ragged than an old faced ancient: and such have I, to fill up the rooms of them that have bought out their services, that you would think, that I had a hundred and fifty tatter'd prodigals, lately come from swine keeping, from eating draff and husks. A mad fellow met me on the way, and told me, I had unloaded all the gibbets, and pressed the dead bodies. No eye hath seen such scare-crows. I'll not march through Coventry with them, that's flat:—Nay, and the villains march wide betwixt the legs, as if they had gives on; for indeed, I had the most of them out of prison. There's but a shirt and a half in all my company: and the half-shirt is two napkins, tacked together, and thrown over the shoulders like a herald's coat without sleeves; and the shirt, to say the truth, stolen from my host at Saint Albans, or the red-nose inn-keeper of Daintry. But that's all one; they'll find linen enough on every hedge.

Enter PRINCE HENRY *and* WESTMORELAND.

P. Hen. How now, blown Jack? how now, quilt?

Fal. What, Hal? How now, mad wag? what a devil dost thou in Warwickshire?—My good lord of Westmoreland, I cry you mercy; I thought, your honour had already been at Shrewsbury.

West. 'Faith, Sir John, 'tis more than time that I were there, and you too; but my powers are there already: The king, I can tell you, looks for us all: we must away to-night.

Fal. Tut, never fear me: I am as vigilant as a cat to steal cream.

P. Hen. I think, to steal cream indeed; for thy theft hath already made thee butter. But tell me, Jack; whose fellows are these that come after?

Fal. Mine, Hal, mine.

P. Hen. I did never see such pitiful rascals.

Fal. Tut, tut; good enough to toss; food for powder, food for powder; they'll fill a pit, as well as better: tush, man, mortal men, mortal men.

West. Ay, but, Sir John, methinks they are exceeding poor and bare; too beggarly.

Fal. 'Faith, for their poverty,—I know not where they had that: and for their bareness,—I am sure they never learn'd that of me.

P. Hen. No, I'll be sworn; unless you call three fingers on the ribs, bare. But, sirrah, make haste; Percy is already in the field.

Fal. What, is the king encamped?

West. He is, Sir John; I fear, we shall stay too long.

Fal. Well,
To the latter end of a fray, and the beginning of a feast,
Fits a dull fighter, and a keen guest. [*Exeunt.*

SCENE III. *The Rebel Camp near* Shrewsbury.

Enter HOTSPUR, WORCESTER, DOUGLAS, *and* VERNON.

Hot. We'll fight with him to-night.
Wor. It may not be.
Doug. You give him then advantage.
Ver. Not a whit.
Hot. Why say you so? looks he not for supply?
Ver. So do we.
Hot. His is certain, ours is doubtful.
Wor. Good cousin, be advis'd; stir not to-night.
Ver. Do not, my lord.
Doug. You do not counsel well;
You speak it out of fear, and cold heart.
Ver. Do me no slander, Douglas: by my life
(And I dare well maintain it with my life),
If well respected honour bid me on,
I hold as little counsel with weak fear,
As you my lord, or any Scot that lives:
Let it be seen to-morrow in the battle,
Which of us fears.
Doug. Yea, or to-night.
Ver. Content.
Hot. To-night, say I.
Ver. Come, come, it may not be.
I wonder much, being men of such great leading,
That you foresee not what impediments
Drag back our expedition: Certain horse
Of my cousin Vernon's are not yet come up:
Your uncle Worcester's horse came but to-day;
And now their pride and mettle is asleep,
Their courage with hard labour tame and dull,
That not a horse is half the half of himself.
Hot. So are the horses of the enemy
In general, journey-bated, and brought low;
The better part of ours is full of rest.
Wor. The number of the king exceedeth ours:
For God's sake, cousin, stay till all come in.
[*The Trumpet sounds a parley.*

Enter SIR WALTER BLUNT.

Blunt. I come with gracious offers from the king,
If you vouchsafe me hearing, and respect.
Hot. Welcome, Sir Walter Blunt; And 'would to God,
You were of our determination!
Some of us love you well: and even those some
Envy your great deserving, and good name;
Because you are not of our quality,
But stand against us like an enemy.
Blunt. And God defend, but still I should stand so,
So long as, out of limit, and true rule,
You stand against anointed majesty!
But, to my charge.—The king hath sent to know
The nature of your griefs; and whereupon
You conjure from the breast of civil peace
Such bold hostility, teaching his duteous land
Audacious cruelty: If that the king
Have any way your good deserts forgot,—
Which he confesseth to be manifold,—
He bids you name your griefs; and, with all speed,
You shall have your desires, with interest;
And pardon absolute for yourself, and these,
Herein misled by your suggestion.
Hot. The king is kind; and, well we know, the king
Knows at what time to promise, when to pay.
My father, and my uncle, and myself,
Did give him that same royalty he wears:
And, when he was not six and twenty strong,
Sick in the world's regard, wretched and low,
A poor unminded outlaw sneaking home,—
My father gave him welcome to the shore:
And,—when he heard him swear, and vow to God,
He came but to be duke of Lancaster,
To sue his livery, and beg his peace;
With tears of innocency, and terms of zeal,—
My father, in kind heart and pity mov'd,
Swore him assistance, and perform'd it too.
Now, when the lords, and barons of the realm
Perceiv'd Northumberland did lean to him,
The more and less came in with cap and knee;
Met him in boroughs, cities, villages;
Attended him on bridges, stood in lanes,
Laid gifts before him, proffer'd him their oaths,
Gave him their heirs as pages, follow'd him,
Even at the heels, in golden multitudes.
He presently,—as greatness knows itself,—
Steps me a little higher than his vow,
Made to my father, while his blood was poor,
Upon the naked shore at Ravenspurg:
And now, forsooth, takes on him to reform
Some certain edicts, and some strait decrees,
That lie too heavy on the commonwealth:
Cries out upon abuses, seems to weep
Over his country's wrongs; and, by this face,
This seeming brow of justice, did he win
The hearts of all that he did angle for.
Proceeded further; cut me off the heads
Of all the favourites, that the absent king
In deputation left behind him here,
When he was personal in the Irish war.
Blunt. Tut, I came not to hear this.
Hot. Then, to the point.——
In short time after, he depos'd the king;
Soon after that, depriv'd him of his life;
And, in the neck of that, task'd the whole state;
To make that worse, suffer'd his kinsman March
(Who is, if every owner were well plac'd,
Indeed his king) to be engag'd in Wales,
There without ransome to lie forfeited:
Disgrac'd me in my happy victories;
Sought to entrap me by intelligence:
Rated my uncle from the council-board;
In rage dismiss'd my father from the court;
Broke oath on oath, committed wrong on wrong;
And, in conclusion, drove us to seek out
This head of safety; and, withal, to pry
Into his title, the which we find
Too indirect for long continuance.
Blunt. Shall I return this answer to the king?
Hot. Not so, Sir Walter; We'll withdraw awhile.
Go to the king; and let there be impawn'd
Some surety for a safe return again,
And in the morning early shall mine uncle
Bring him our purposes: and so farewell.
Blunt. I would, you would accept of grace and love.
Hot. And, may be, so we shall.
Blunt. 'Pray heaven, you do!
[*Exeunt.*

SCENE IV. York.

A Room in the Archbishop's *House.*

Enter the ARCHBISHOP OF YORK, *and a* Gentleman.

Arch. Hie, good Sir Michael; bear this sealed brief,
With winged haste, to the lord marshal;
This to my cousin Scroop; and all the rest
To whom they are directed: if you knew
How much they do import, you would make haste.

Gent. My good lord,
I guess their tenor.
Arch. Like enough, you do.
To-morrow, good Sir Michael, is a day,
Wherein the fortune of ten thousand men
Must 'bide the touch: For, sir, at Shrewsbury,
As I am truly given to understand,
The king, with mighty and quick raised power,
Meets with Lord Harry: and I fear, Sir Michael,—
What with the sickness of Northumberland
(Whose power was in the first proportion),
And what with Owen Glendower's absence, thence
(Who with them was a rated sinew too,
And comes not in, o'er-ruled by prophecies),—
I fear, the power of Percy is too weak
To wage an instant trial with the king.
Gent. Why, good my lord, you need not fear; there's Douglas,
And Lord Mortimer.
Arch. No, Mortimer's not there.
Gent. But there is Mordake, Vernon, Lord Harry Percy,
And there's my lord of Worcester; and a head
Of gallant warriors, noble gentlemen.
Arch. And so there is: but yet the king hath drawn
The special head of all the land together:—
The prince of Wales, Lord John of Lancaster,
The noble Westmoreland, and warlike Blunt;
And many more cor-rivals, and dear men
Of estimation and command in arms.
Gent. Doubt not, my lord, they shall be well oppos'd.
Arch. I hope no less, yet needful 'tis to fear;
And, to prevent the worst, Sir Michael, speed:
For, if Lord Percy thrive not, ere the king
Dismiss his power, he means to visit us,—
For he hath heard of our confederacy.——
And 'tis but wisdom to make strong against him;
Therefore, make haste: I must go write again
To other friends; and so farewell, Sir Michael.
[*Exeunt severally.*

ACT V.

SCENE I. *The* King's *Camp near* Shrewsbury.

Enter King Henry, Prince Henry, Prince John *of* Lancaster, Sir Walter Blunt, *and* Sir John Falstaff.

K. Hen. How bloodily the sun begins to peer
Above yon busky hill! the day looks pale
At his distemperature.
P. Hen. The southern wind
Doth play the trumpet to his purposes:
And, by his hollow whistling in the leaves,
Foretells a tempest, and a blustering day.
K. Hen. Then with the losers let it sympathize;
For nothing can seem foul to those that win.—

Trumpet. Enter Worcester *and* Vernon.

How now, my lord of Worcester? 'tis not well,
That you and I should meet upon such terms
As now we meet: You have deceiv'd our trust;
And made us doff our easy robes of peace,
To crush our old limbs in ungentle steel;
That is not well, my lord, this is not well.
What say you to 't? will you again unknit
This churlish knot of all-abhorred war?
And move in that obedient orb again,
Where you did give a fair and natural light;
And be no more an exhal'd meteor,
A prodigy of fear, and a portent
Of broached mischief to the unborn times?
Wor. Hear me, my liege:
For mine own part, I could be well content
To entertain the lag-end of my life
With quiet hours; for, I do protest,
I have not sought the day of this dislike.
K. Hen. You have not sought for it! how comes it then?
Fal. Rebellion lay in his way, and he found it.
P. Hen. Peace, chewet, peace.
Wor. It pleas'd your majesty, to turn your looks
Of favour, from myself, and all our house;
And yet I must remember you, my lord,
We were the first and dearest of your friends.
For you, my staff of office did I break
In Richard's time; and posted day and night
To meet you on the way, and kiss your hand,
When yet you were in place and in account
Nothing so strong and fortunate as I.
It was myself, my brother, and his son,
That brought you home, and boldly did outdare
The dangers of the time: You swore to us,—
And you did swear that oath at Doncaster,—
That you did nothing purpose 'gainst the state;
Nor claim no further than your new-fall'n right,
The seat of Gaunt, dukedom of Lancaster:
To this we swore our aid. But, in short space,
It rain'd down fortune showering on your head;
And such a flood of greatness fell on you,—
What with our help; what with the absent king;
What with the injuries of a wanton time;
The seeming sufferances that you had borne;
And the contrarious winds, that held the king
So long in his unlucky Irish wars,
That all in England did repute him dead,—
And, from this swarm of fair advantages,
You took occasion to be quickly woo'd
To gripe the general sway into your hand:
Forgot your oath to us at Doncaster;
And, being fed by us, you us'd us so
As that ungentle gull, the cuckoo's bird,
Useth the sparrow: did oppress our nest;
Grew by our feeding to so great a bulk,
That even our love durst not come near your sight,
For fear of swallowing: but with nimble wing
We were enforc'd, for safety sake, to fly
Out of your sight, and raise this present head:
Whereby we stand opposed by such means
As you yourself have forg'd against yourself;
By unkind usage, dangerous countenance,
And violation of all faith and troth
Sworn to us in your younger enterprise.
K. Hen. These things, indeed, you have articulated,
Proclaim'd at market-crosses, read in churches;
To face the garment of rebellion
With some fine colour, that may please the eye
Of fickle changelings, and poor discontents,
Which gape, and rub the elbow, at the news
Of hurlyburly innovation:
And never yet did insurrection want
Such water colours, to impaint his cause;
Nor moody beggars, starving for a time
Of pellmell havock and confusion.
P. Hen. In both our armies, there is many a soul
Shall pay full dearly for this encounter,
If once they join in trial. Tell your nephew,
The prince of Wales doth join with all the world
In praise of Henry Percy: By my hopes,—
This present enterprise set off his head,—
I do not think, a braver gentleman,
More active-valiant, or more valiant-young,
More daring, or more bold, is now alive,
To grace this latter age with noble deeds.
For my part, I may speak it to my shame,
I have a truant been to chivalry;
And so, I hear, he doth account me too:
Yet this before my father's majesty,—
I am content, that he shall take the odds
Of his great name and estimation;
And will, to save the blood on either side,
Try fortune with him in a single fight.
K. Hen. And, prince of Wales, so dare we venture thee,
Albeit, considerations infinite

Do make against it:—No, good Worcester, no,
We love our people well: even those we love,
That are misled upon your cousin's part:
And, will they take the offer of our grace,
Both he, and they, and you, yea, every man
Shall be my friend again, and I'll be his:
So tell your cousin, and bring me word
What he will do:—But if he will not yield,
Rebuke and dread correction wait on us,
And they shall do their office. So, be gone;
We will not now be troubled with reply:
We offer fair, take it advisedly.
[*Exeunt* WORCESTER *and* VERNON.

P. Hen. It will not be accepted, on my life;
The Douglas and the Hotspur both together
Are confident against the world in arms.

K. Hen. Hence, therefore, every leader to his charge:
For, on their answer, will we set on them:
And God befriend us, as our cause is just!
[*Exeunt* KING, BLUNT, *and* PRINCE JOHN.

Fal. Hal, if thou see me down in the battle, and bestride me, so; 'tis a point of friendship.

P. Hen. Nothing but a colossus can do thee that friendship. Say thy prayers, and farewell.

Fal. I would it were bed-time, Hal, and all well.

P. Hen. Why, thou owest God a death. [*Exit.*

Fal. 'Tis not due yet; I would be loath to pay him before his day. What need I be so forward with him that calls not on me? Well, 'tis no matter; Honour pricks me on. Yea, but how if honour prick me off when I come on? how then? Can honour set to a leg? No. Or an arm? No. Or take away the grief of a wound? No. Honour hath no skill in surgery then? No. What is honour? A word. What is in that word, honour? What is that honour? Air. A trim reckoning!—Who hath it? He that died o'Wednesday. Doth he feel it? No. Doth he hear it? No. Is it insensible then? Yea, to the dead. But will it not live with the living? No. Why? Detraction will not suffer it:—therefore I'll none of it: Honour is a mere scutcheon, and so ends my catechism.

SCENE II. *The Rebel Camp.*

Enter WORCESTER *and* VERNON.

Wor. O, no, my nephew must not know, Sir Richard,
The liberal kind offer of the king.

Ver. 'Twere best, he did.

Wor. Then are we all undone.
It is not possible, it cannot be,
The king should keep his word in loving us;
He will suspect us still, and find a time
To punish this offence in other faults:
Suspicion all our lives shall be stuck full of eyes:
For treason is but trusted like the fox;
Who, ne'er so tame, so cherish'd, and lock'd up,
Will have a wild trick of his ancestors.
Look how we can, or sad, or merrily,
Interpretation will misquote our looks;
And we shall feed like oxen at a stall,
The better cherish'd, still the nearer death.
My nephew's trespass may be well forgot,
It hath the excuse of youth, and heat of blood;
And an adopted name of privilege,—
A hare-brain'd Hotspur, govern'd by a spleen:
All his offences live upon my head,
And on his father's;—we did train him on;
And, his corruption being ta'en from us,
We, as the spring of all, shall pay for all,
Therefore, good cousin, let not Harry know,
In any case, the offer of the king.

Ver. Deliver what you will, I'll say, 'tis so.
Here comes your cousin.

Enter HOTSPUR *and* DOUGLAS; *and* Officers *and* Soldiers, *behind.*

Hot. My uncle is return'd:—Deliver up
My lord of Westmoreland.—Uncle, what news?

Wor. The king will bid you battle presently.

Doug. Defy him by the lord of Westmoreland.

Hot. Lord Douglas, go you and tell him so.

Doug. Marry, and shall, and very willingly.
[*Exit.*

Wor. There is no seeming mercy in the king.

Hot. Did you beg any? God forbid!

Wor. I told him gently of our grievances,
Of his oath-breaking; which he mended thus,—
By now forswearing that he is forsworn:
He calls us rebels, traitors; and will scourge
With haughty arms this hateful name in us.

Re-enter DOUGLAS.

Doug. Arm, gentlemen; to arms! for I have thrown
A brave defiance in King Henry's teeth,
And Westmoreland, that was engag'd, did bear it;
Which cannot choose but bring him quickly on.

Wor. The prince of Wales stepp'd forth before the king,
And, nephew, challeng'd you to single fight.

Hot. O, 'would the quarrel lay upon our heads;
And that no man might draw short breath to-day,
But I, and Harry Monmouth! Tell me, tell me,
How show'd his tasking? seem'd it in contempt?

Ver. No, by my soul; I never in my life
Did hear a challenge urg'd more modestly,
Unless a brother should a brother dare
To gentle exercise and proof of arms.
He gave you all the duties of a man;
Trimm'd up your praises with a princely tongue;
Spoke your deservings like a chronicle;
Making you ever better than his praise,
By still dispraising praise, valued with you:
And, which became him like a prince indeed,
He made a blushing cital of himself;
And chid his truant youth with such a grace,
As if he master'd there a double spirit,
Of teaching, and of learning, instantly.
There did he pause: But let me tell the world,—
If he outlive the envy of this day,
England did never owe so sweet a hope,
So much misconstrued in his wantonness.

Hot. Cousin, I think thou art enamoured
Upon his follies; never did I hear
Of any prince, so wild, at liberty:
But, be he as he will, yet once ere night
I will embrace him with a soldier's arm,
That he shall shrink under my courtesy.——
Arm, arm, with speed:——And, fellows, soldiers, friends,
Better consider what you have to do,
Than I, that have not well the gift of tongue,
Can lift your blood up with persuasion.

Enter a Messenger.

Mess. My lord, here are letters for you.

Hot. I cannot read them now.—
O gentlemen, the time of life is short;
To spend that shortness basely, were too long,
If life did ride upon a dial's point,
Still ending at the arrival of an hour.
An if we live, we live to tread on kings;
If die, brave death, when princes die with us!
Now for our consciences,—the arms are fair,
When the intent of bearing them is just.

Enter another Messenger.

Mess. My lord, prepare: the king comes on apace.

Hot. I thank him, that he cuts me from my tale,
For I profess not talking; Only this—
Let each man do his best: and here draw I
A sword, whose temper I intend to stain
With the best blood that I can meet withal
In the adventure of this perilous day.
Now,—Esperance!—Percy!—and set on.—
Sound all the lofty instruments of war,
And by that musick let us all embrace:
For, heaven to earth, some of us never shall
A second time do such a courtesy.
[*The Trumpets sound. They embrace, and exeunt.*

SCENE III. *Plain near* Shrewsbury.

Excursions, and Parties fighting. Alarum to the Battle. Then enter DOUGLAS *and* BLUNT, *meeting.*

Blunt. What is thy name, that in the battle thus
Thou crossest me? what honour dost thou seek
Upon my head?
Doug. Know then, my name is Douglas;
And I do haunt thee in the battle thus,
Because some tell me that thou art a king.
Blunt. They tell thee true. [bought
Doug. The lord of Stafford dear to-day hath
Thy likeness: for, instead of thee, King Harry,
This sword hath ended him: so shall it thee,
Unless thou yield me as thy prisoner.
Blunt. I was not born a yielder, thou proud Scot;
And thou shalt find a king that will revenge
Lord Stafford's death.
[*They fight, and* BLUNT *is slain.*

Enter HOTSPUR.

Hot. O Douglas, hadst thou fought at Holmedon thus,
I never had triumph'd upon a Scot.
Doug. All's done, all's won; here breathless lies the king.
Hot. Where?
Doug. Here. [well:
Hot. This, Douglas? no, I know this face full
A gallant knight he was, his name was Blunt;
Semblably furnish'd like the king himself.
Doug. A fool go with thy soul, whither it goes!
A borrow'd title hast thou bought too dear.
Why didst thou tell me that thou wert a king?
Hot. The king hath many marching in his coats. [coats:
Doug. Now, by my sword, I will kill all his
I'll murder all his wardrobe, piece by piece,
Until I meet the king.
Hot. Up, and away;
Our soldiers stand full fairly for the day.
[*Exeunt.*

Other Alarums. Enter FALSTAFF.

Fal. Though I could 'scape shot-free at London, I fear the shot here; here's no scoring, but upon the pate.—Soft! who art thou? Sir Walter Blunt;—there's honour for you: Here's no vanity!—I am as hot as molten lead, and as heavy too: God keep lead out of me! I need no more weight than mine own bowels.—I have led my raggamuffins where they are peppered: there's but three of my hundred and fifty left alive; and they are for the town's end, to beg during life. But who comes here?

Enter PRINCE HENRY.

P. Hen. What, stand'st thou idle here? lend me thy sword:
Many a nobleman lies stark and stiff
Under the hoofs of vaunting enemies,
Whose deaths are unreveng'd: Pr'ythee, lend me thy sword.
Fal. O Hal, I pr'ythee give me leave to breathe a while.—Turk Gregory never did such deeds in arms, as I have done this day. I have paid Percy, I have made him sure.
P. Hen. He is, indeed; and living to kill thee. I pr'ythee, lend me thy sword.
Fal. Nay, before God, Hal, if Percy be alive, thou get'st not my sword; but take my pistol, if thou wilt.
P. Hen. Give it me: What, is it in the case?
Fal. Ay, Hal: 'tis hot, 'tis hot; there's that will sack a city.
[*The* Prince *draws out a bottle of sack.*
P. Hen. What, is't a time to jest and dally now?
[*Throws it at him, and exit.*
Fal. Well, if Percy be alive, I'll pierce him. If he do come in my way, so: if he do not, if I come in his, willingly, let him make a carbonado of me. I like not such grinning honour as Sir Walter hath: Give me life: which if I can save, so; if not, honour comes unlooked for, and there's an end. [*Exit.*

SCENE IV. *Another Part of the Field.*

Alarums: Excursions. Enter the KING, PRINCE HENRY, PRINCE JOHN, *and* WESTMORELAND.

K. Hen. I pr'ythee, [much:—
Harry, withdraw thyself; thou bleed'st too
Lord John of Lancaster, go you with him.
P. John. Not I, my lord, unless I did bleed too.
P. Hen. I do beseech your majesty, make up,
Lest your retirement do amaze your friends.
K. Hen. I will do so:
My lord of Westmoreland, lead him to his tent.
West. Come, my lord, I'll lead you to your tent. [your help:
P. Hen. Lead me, my lord? I do not need
And heaven forbid, a shallow scratch should drive
The prince of Wales from such a field as this;
Where stain'd nobility lies trodden on,
And rebels' arms triumph in massacres!
P. John. We breathe too long:—Come, cousin Westmoreland,
Our duty this way lies; for God's sake, come.
[*Exeunt* P. JOHN *and* WESTMORELAND.
P. Hen. By heaven thou hast deceiv'd me, Lancaster,
I did not think thee lord of such a spirit;
Before, I lov'd thee as a brother, John;
But now, I do respect thee as my soul. [point,
K. Hen. I saw him hold Lord Percy at the
With lustier maintenance than I did look for
Of such an ungrown warrior.
P. Hen. O, this boy
Lends mettle to us all! [*Exit.*

Alarums. Enter DOUGLAS.

Doug. Another king! they grow like Hydra's heads;
I am the Douglas, fatal to all those [thou,
That wear those colours on them.—What art
That counterfeit'st the person of a king?
K. Hen. The king himself; who, Douglas, grieves at heart,
So many of his shadows thou hast met,
And not the very king. I have two boys,
Seek Percy, and thyself, about the field:
But, seeing thou fall'st on me so luckily,
I will assay thee; so defend thyself.
Doug. I fear, thou art another counterfeit;
And yet, in faith, thou bear'st thee like a king:
But mine, I am sure, thou art, whoe'er thou be,
And thus I win thee.
[*They fight; the* King *being in danger, enter* PRINCE HENRY.
P. Hen. Hold up thy head, vile Scot, or thou art like
Never to hold it up again! the spirits
Of Shirley, Stafford, Blunt, are in my arms:
It is the Prince of Wales, that threatens thee;
Who never promiseth, but he means to pay.—
[*They fight;* DOUGLAS *flies.*
Cheerly, my lord: How fares your grace?—
Sir Nicholas Gawsey hath for succour sent,
And so hath Clifton; I'll to Clifton straight.
K. Hen. Stay, and breathe a while:—
Thou hast redeem'd thy lost opinion;
And show'd, thou mak'st some tender of my life,
In this fair rescue, thou hast brought to me.
P. Hen. O heaven! they did me too much injury,
That ever said, I hearken'd for your death.
If it were so, I might have let alone
The insulting hand of Douglas over you;
Which would have been as speedy in your end,
As all the poisonous potions in the world,
And sav'd the treacherous labour of your son.
K. Hen. Make up to Clifton, I'll to Sir Nicholas Gawsey. [*Exit* KING HENRY.

Enter HOTSPUR.

Hot. If I mistake not, thou art Harry Monmouth.

P. Hen. Thou speak'st as if I would deny my name.

Hot. My name is Harry Percy.

P. Hen. Why, then I see
A very valiant rebel of the name.
I am the prince of Wales; and think not, Percy,
To share with me in glory any more:
Two stars keep not their motion in one sphere;
Nor can one England brook a double reign,
Of Harry Percy, and the prince of Wales.

Hot. Nor shall it, Harry, for the hour is come
To end the one of us; And 'would to God,
Thy name in arms were now as great as mine!

P. Hen. I'll make it greater, ere I part from thee;
And all the budding honours on thy crest
I'll crop, to make a garland for my head.

Hot. I can no longer brook thy vanities.
[*They fight.*

Enter FALSTAFF.

Fal. Well said, Hal! to it, Hal!—Nay, you shall find no boy's play here, I can tell you.

Enter DOUGLAS; *he fights with* FALSTAFF, *who falls down as if he were dead, and exit* DOUGLAS. HOTSPUR *is wounded, and falls.*

Hot. O, Harry, thou hast robb'd me of my youth:
I better brook the loss of brittle life,
Than those proud titles thou hast won of me;
They wound my thoughts, worse than thy sword my flesh:——
But thought's the slave of life, and life time's fool;
And time, that takes survey of all the world,
Must have a stop. O, I could prophesy,
But that the earthy and cold hand of death
Lies on my tongue: No, Percy, thou art dust,
And food for—— [*Dies.*

P. Hen. For worms, brave Percy: Fare thee well, great heart!—
Ill weav'd ambition, how much art thou shrunk!
When that this body did contain a spirit,
A kingdom for it was too small a bound;
But now, two paces of the vilest earth
Is room enough:—This earth, that bears thee dead,
Bears not alive so stout a gentleman.
If thou wert sensible of courtesy,
I should not make so dear a show of zeal:—
But let my favours hide thy mangled face;
And, even in thy behalf, I'll thank myself
For doing these fair rites of tenderness.
Adieu, and take thy praise with thee to heaven!
Thy ignomy sleep with thee in the grave,
But not remember'd in thy epitaph!—
[*He sees* FALSTAFF *on the ground.*
What! old acquaintance! could not all this flesh
Keep in a little life? Poor Jack, farewell!
I could have better spar'd a better man.
O, I should have a heavy miss of thee,
If I were much in love with vanity.
Death hath not struck so fat a deer to-day,
Though many dearer, in this bloody fray:—
Embowell'd will I see thee by and by;
Till then, in blood by noble Percy lie. [*Exit.*

Fal. [*Rising slowly.*] Embowelled! if thou embowel me to-day, I'll give you leave to powder me, and eat me too, to-morrow. 'Sblood, 'twas time to counterfeit, or that hot termagant Scot had paid me scot and lot too. Counterfeit? I lie, I am no counterfeit: To die, is to be a counterfeit; for he is but the counterfeit of a man who hath not the life of a man; but to counterfeit dying, when a man thereby liveth, is to be no counterfeit, but the true and perfect image of life indeed. The better part of valour is—discretion; in the which better part, I have saved my life. 'Zounds, I am afraid of this gunpowder Percy, though he be dead: How, if he should counterfeit too, and rise? I am afraid, he would prove the better counterfeit. Therefore I'll make him sure: yea, and I'll swear I killed him. Why may not he rise as well as I? Nothing confutes me but eyes, and nobody sees me. Therefore, sirrah [*stabbing him*], with a new wound in your thigh, come you along with me.
[*Takes* HOTSPUR *on his back.*

Re-enter PRINCE HENRY *and* PRINCE JOHN.

P. Hen. Come, brother John, full bravely hast thou flesh'd
Thy maiden sword.

P. John. But, soft! whom have we here?
Did you not tell me, this fat man was dead?

P. Hen. I did; I saw him dead, breathless and bleeding,
On the ground.——
Art thou alive? or is it phantasy
That plays upon our eyesight? I pr'ythee, speak
We will not trust our eyes, without our ears:—
Thou art not what thou seem'st.

Fal. No, that's certain; I am not a double man: but if I be not Jack Falstaff, then am I a Jack. There is Percy [*throwing the body down*]: if your father will do me any honour, so; if not, let him kill the next Percy himself. I look to be either earl or duke, I can assure you.

P. Hen. Why, Percy I killed myself, and saw thee dead.

Fal. Didst thou?—Lord, lord, how this world is given to lying!—I grant you, I was down, and out of breath; and so was he: but we rose both in an instant, and fought a long hour by Shrewsbury clock. If I may be believed, so; if not, let them, that should reward valour, bear the sin upon their own heads. I'll take it upon my death, I gave him this wound in the thigh: if the man were alive, and would deny it, I would make him eat a piece of my sword.

P. John. This is the strangest tale that e'er I heard. [John.

P. Hen. This is the strangest fellow, brother
Come, bring your luggage nobly on your back:
For my part, if a lie may do thee grace,
I'll gild it with the happiest terms I have.
[*A Retreat is sounded.*
The trumpet sounds retreat, the day is ours.
Come, brother, let's to the highest of the field,
To see what friends are living, who are dead.
[*Exeunt* P. HEN. *and* P. JOHN.

Fal. I'll follow, as they say, for reward. He that rewards me, God reward him! If I do grow great, I'll grow less; for I'll purge, and leave sack, and live cleanly, as a nobleman should do
[*Exit, bearing off the Body.*

SCENE V. *Another Part of the Field.*

The Trumpets sound. Enter KING HENRY, PRINCE HENRY, PRINCE JOHN, WESTMORELAND, *and others, with* WORCESTER, *and* VERNON *prisoners.*

K. Hen. Thus ever did rebellion find rebuke.—
Ill spirited Worcester! did we not send grace,
Pardon, and terms of love to all of you?
And would'st thou turn our offers contrary!
Misuse the tenor of thy kinsman's trust?
Three knights upon our party slain to-day,
A noble earl, and many a creature else,
Had been alive this hour,
If, like a christian, thou hadst truly borne
Betwixt our armies true intelligence.

Wor. What I have done, my safety urg'd me to;
And I embrace this fortune patiently,
Since not to be avoided it falls on me.

K. Hen. Bear Worcester to the death, and Vernon too:
Other offenders we will pause upon.—
[*Exeunt* WOR. *and* VERNON, *guarded.*
How goes the field?

P. Hen. The noble Scot, Lord Douglas, when he saw
The fortune of the day quite turn'd from him,
The noble Percy slain, and all his men
Upon the foot of fear, fled with the rest;
And falling from a hill, he was so bruis'd,
That the pursuers took him. At my tent
The Douglas is; and I beseech your grace,
I may dispose of him.
K. Hen. With all my heart.
P. Hen. Then, brother John of Lancaster, to you
This honourable bounty shall belong:
Go to the Douglas, and deliver him
Up to his pleasure, ransomless, and free:
His valour, shown upon our crests to-day,
Hath taught us how to cherish such high deeds,
Even in the bosom of our adversaries.
Lan. I thank your grace for this high courtesy,
Which I shall give away immediately.
K. Hen. Then this remains,—that we divide our power.—
You, son John, and my cousin Westmoreland,
Towards York shall bend you, with your dearest speed,
To meet Northumberland and the prelate Scroop,
Who, as we hear, are busily in arms:
Myself,—and you, son Harry,—will towards Wales,
To fight with Glendower, and the earl of March.
Rebellion in this land shall lose his sway,
Meeting the check of such another day:
And since this business so fair is done,
Let us not leave till all our own be won.
[*Exeunt.*

SECOND PART OF
KING HENRY THE FOURTH.

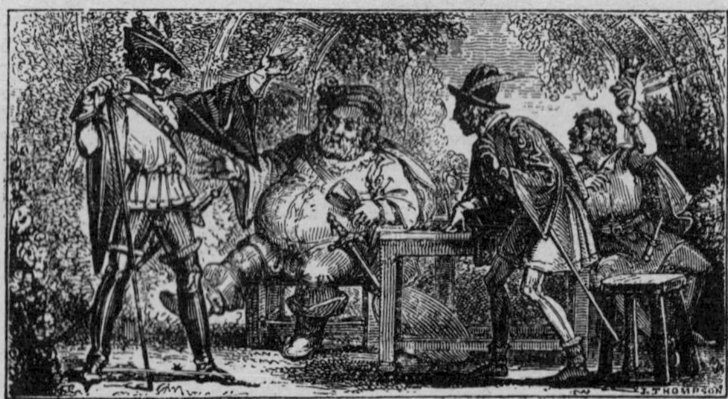

PERSONS REPRESENTED.

KING HENRY THE FOURTH.
HENRY, Prince *of* Wales, *afterwards* King Henry V.; } *his Sons.*
THOMAS, Duke *of* Clarence; } *his Sons.*
PRINCE JOHN *of* Lancaster, *afterwards* (2 Henry V.) Duke *of* Bedford; } *his Sons.*
PRINCE HUMPHREY *of* Gloster, *afterwards* (2 Hen. V.) Duke of Gloster; } *his Sons.*
EARL OF WARWICK; } *of the* King's *Party.*
EARL OF WESTMORELAND; } *of the* King's *Party.*
GOWER; HARCOURT; } *of the* King's *Party.*
Lord Chief Justice of the King's Bench.
A Gentleman *attending on the* Chief Justice.
EARL OF NORTHUMBERLAND; } *Enemies to the* King.
SCROOP, Archbishop *of* York; } *Enemies to the* King.
LORD MOWBRAY; LORD HASTINGS; } *Enemies to the* King.
LORD BARDOLPH; SIR JOHN COLEVILE; } *Enemies to the* King.
TRAVERS *and* MORTON, *Domesticks of* Northumberland.
FALSTAFF, BARDOLPH, PISTOL, *and* Page.
POINS *and* PETO, *Attendants on* Prince Henry.
SHALLOW *and* SILENCE, *Country Justices.*
DAVY, *Servant to* Shallow.
MOULDY, SHADOW, WART, FEEBLE, *and* BULLCALF, *Recruits.*
FANG *and* SNARE, *Sheriff's Officers.*
RUMOUR. *A* Porter.
A Dancer, *Speaker of the Epilogue.*

LADY NORTHUMBERLAND. LADY PERCY.
Hostess QUICKLY. DOLL TEAR-SHEET.

Lords *and other* Attendants; Officers, Soldiers, Messenger, Drawers, Beadles, Grooms, *&c.*

SCENE,—England.

INDUCTION.

Warkworth. *Before* Northumberland's *Castle.*

Enter RUMOUR, *painted full of Tongues.*

Rum. OPEN your ears; For which of you will stop
The vent of hearing, when loud Rumour speaks?
I, from the orient to the drooping west,
Making the wind my post-horse, still unfold
The acts commenced on this ball of earth:
Upon my tongues continual slanders ride;
The which in every language I pronounce,
Stuffing the ears of men with false reports.
I speak of peace, while covert enmity,
Under the smile of safety, wounds the world:
And who but Rumour, who but only I,
Make fearful musters, and prepar'd defence;
Whilst the big ear, swol'n with some other grief,
Is thought with child by the stern tyrant war,
And no such matter? Rumour is a pipe
Blown by surmises, jealousies, conjectures;

And of so easy and so plain a stop,
That the blunt monster with uncounted heads,
The still-discordant wavering multitude,
Can play upon it. But what need I thus
My well known body to anatomize
Among my household? Why is Rumour here?
I run before King Harry's victory;
Who, in a bloody field by Shrewsbury,
Hath beaten down young Hotspur, and his troops,
Quenching the flame of bold rebellion
Even with the rebels' blood. But what mean I
To speak so true at first? my office is
To noise abroad,—that Harry Monmouth fell
Under the wrath of noble Hotspur's sword;
And that the king before the Douglas' rage
Stoop'd his anointed head as low as death.
This have I rumour'd through the peasant towns
Between that royal field of Shrewsbury
And this worm-eaten hold of ragged stone
Where Hotspur's father, old Northumberland,
Lies crafty-sick: the posts come tiring on,
And not a man of them brings other news
Than they have learn'd of me; from Rumour's tongues
They bring smooth comforts false, worse than true wrongs. [*Exit.*

ACT I.

SCENE I. *The same. The Porter before the Gate.*

Enter LORD BARDOLPH.

Bard. Who keeps the gate here, ho?—Where is the earl?
Port. What shall I say you are?
Bard. Tell thou the earl,
That the Lord Bardolph doth attend him here.
Port. His lordship is walk'd forth into the orchard;
Please it your honour, knock but at the gate,
And he himself will answer.

Enter NORTHUMBERLAND.

Bard. Here comes the earl.
North. What news, Lord Bardolph? every minute now
Should be the father of some stratagem:
The times are wild; contention, like a horse
Full of high feeding, madly hath broke loose,
And bears down all before him.
Bard. Noble earl,
I bring you certain news from Shrewsbury.
North. Good, an heaven will!
Bard. As good as heart can wish:—
The king is almost wounded to the death;
And, in the fortune of my lord your son,
Prince Harry slain outright; and both the Blunts
Kill'd by the hand of Douglas: young prince John,
And Westmoreland, and Stafford, fled the field;
And Harry Monmouth's brawn, the hulk Sir John,
Is prisoner to your son: O, such a day,
So fought, so follow'd, and so fairly won,
Came not, till now, to dignify the times,
Since Cæsar's fortunes!
North. How is this deriv'd?
Saw you the field? came you from Shrewsbury?
Bard. I spake with one, my lord, that came from thence;
A gentleman well bred, and of good name,
That freely render'd me these news for true.
North. Here comes my servant, Travers, whom I sent
On Tuesday last to listen after news.
Bard. My lord, I over-rode him on the way;
And he is furnish'd with no certainties,
More than he haply may retail from me.

Enter TRAVERS.

North. Now, Travers, what good tidings come with you?
Tra. My lord, Sir John Umfrevile turn'd me back
With joyful tidings; and being better hors'd,
Outrode me. After him, came, spurring hard,
A gentleman almost forspent with speed,
That stopp'd by me to breathe his bloodied horse:
He ask'd the way to Chester; and of him
I did demand, what news from Shrewsbury.
He told me, that rebellion had bad luck,
And that young Harry Percy's spur was cold:
With that, he gave his able horse the head,
And, bending forward, struck his armed heels
Against the panting sides of his poor jade
Up to the rowel-head; and, starting so,
He seem'd in running to devour the way,
Staying no longer question.
North. Ha!——Again.
Said he, young Harry Percy's spur was cold?
Of Hotspur, coldspur? that rebellion
Had met ill luck!
Bard. My lord, I'll tell you what;—
If my young lord your son have not the day,
Upon mine honour, for a silken point
I'll give my barony: never talk of it.
North. Why should the gentleman, that rode by Travers,
Give then such instances of loss?
Bard. Who, he?
He was some hilding fellow, that had stol'n
The horse he rode on; and, upon my life,
Spoke at a venture. Look, here comes more news.

Enter MORTON.

North. Yea this man's brow, like to a title-leaf,
Foretells the nature of a tragick volume:
So looks the strond, whereon the imperious flood
Hath left a witness'd usurpation,——
Say, Morton, didst thou come from Shrewsbury?
Mor. I ran from Shrewsbury, my noble lord;
Where hateful death put on his ugliest mask,
To fright our party.
North. How doth my son, and brother?
Thou tremblest; and the whiteness in thy cheek
Is apter than thy tongue to tell thy errand.
Even such a man, so faint, so spiritless,
So dull, so dead in look, so woe-begone,
Drew Priam's curtain in the dead of night,
And would have told him, half his Troy was burn'd:
But Priam found the fire, ere he his tongue,
And I my Percy's death, ere thou report'st it.
This thou would'st say,—Your son did thus, and thus;
Your brother, thus; so fought the noble Douglas;
Stopping my greedy ear with their bold deeds:
But in the end, to stop mine ear indeed,
Thou hast a sigh to blow away this praise,
Ending with—brother, son, and all are dead.
Mor. Douglas is living, and your brother, yet:
But, for my lord your son,——
North. Why, he is dead.
See, what a ready tongue suspicion hath!
He, that but fears the thing he would not know,
Hath, by instinct, knowledge from others' eyes,
That what he fear'd is chanc'd. Yet speak, Morton;
Tell thou thy earl, his divination lies;
And I will take it as a sweet disgrace,
And make thee rich for doing me such wrong.
Mor. You are too great to be by me gainsaid:
Your spirit is too true, your fears too certain.
North. Yet, for all this, say not that Percy's dead.
I see a strange confession in thine eye:
Thou shak'st thy head, and hold'st it fear, or sin,
To speak a truth. If he be slain, say so:
The tongue offends not, that reports his death:

And he doth sin, that doth belie the dead;
Not he, which says the dead is not alive.
Yet the first bringer of unwelcome news
Hath but a losing office; and his tongue
Sounds ever after as a sullen bell,
Remember'd knolling a departing friend.

Bard. I cannot think, my lord, your son is dead.

Mor. I am sorry, I should force you to believe
That, which I would to heaven I had not seen:
But these mine eyes saw him in bloody state,
Rend'ring faint quittance, wearied and out-breath'd,
To Harry Monmouth: whose swift wrath beat down
The never daunted Percy to the earth,
From whence with life he never more sprung up.
In few, his death (whose spirit lent a fire
Even to the dullest peasant in his camp),
Being bruited once, took fire and heat away
From the best temper'd courage in his troops:
For from his metal was his party steel'd;
Which once in him abated, all the rest
Turn'd on themselves, like dull and heavy lead.
And as the thing that's heavy in itself,
Upon enforcement flies with greatest speed;
So did our men, heavy in Hotspur's loss,
Lend to this weight such lightness with their fear,
That arrows fled not swifter toward their aim,
Than did our soldiers, aiming at their safety,
Fly from the field: Then was that noble Worcester
Too soon ta'en prisoner: and that furious Scot,
The bloody Douglas, whose well labouring sword
Had three times slain the appearance of the king,
'Gan vail his stomach, and did grace the shame
Of those that turn'd their backs; and, in his flight,
Stumbling in fear, was took. The sum of all
Is,—that the king hath won; and hath sent out
A speedy power to encounter you, my lord,
Under the conduct of young Lancaster,
And Westmoreland: this is the news at full.

North. For this I shall have time enough to mourn.
In poison there is physick; and these news
Having been well, that would have made me sick,
Being sick, have in some measure made me well:
And as the wretch, whose fever-weaken'd joints,
Like strengthless hinges, buckle under life,
Impatient of his fit, breaks like a fire
Out of his keeper's arms; even so my limbs,
Weaken'd with grief, being now enrag'd with grief,
Are thrice themselves: hence therefore, thou nice crutch;
A scaly gauntlet now, with joints of steel,
Must glove this hand: and hence, thou sickly quoif;
Thou art a guard too wanton for the head,
Which princes, flesh'd with conquest, aim to hit.
Now bind my brows with iron; And approach
The ragged'st hour that time and spite dare bring,
To frown upon the enrag'd Northumberland!
Let heaven kiss earth! Now let not nature's hand
Keep the wild flood confin'd! let order die!
And let this world no longer be a stage,
To feed contention in a lingering act;
But let one spirit of the first-born Cain
Reign in all bosoms, that, each heart being set
On bloody courses, the rude scene may end,
And darkness be the burier of the dead!

Tra. This strained passion doth you wrong, my lord.

Bard. Sweet earl, divorce not wisdom from your honour.

Mor. The lives of all your loving complices
Lean on your health; the which, if you give o'er
To stormy passion, must perforce decay.
You cast the event of war, my noble lord,
And summ'd the account of chance, before you said,—
Let us make head. It was your presurmise,
That in the dole of blows your son might drop:
You knew, he walk'd o'er perils, on an edge,
More likely to fall in, than to get o'er:
You were advis'd, his flesh was capable
Of wounds, and scars; and that his forward spirit
Would lift him where most trade of danger rang'd;
Yet did you say,—Go forth; and none of this,
Though strongly apprehended, could restrain
The stiff-borne action: What hath then befallen,
Or what hath this bold enterprise brought forth,
More than that being which was like to be?

Bard. We all, that are engaged to this loss,
Knew that we ventur'd on such dangerous seas,
That, if we wrought out life, 'twas ten to one:
And yet we ventur'd, for the gain propos'd
Chok'd the respect of likely peril fear'd;
And, since we are o'erset, venture again.
Come, we will all put forth, body, and goods.

Mor. 'Tis more than time: And, my most noble lord,
I hear for certain, and do speak the truth,——
The gentle archbishop of York is up,
With well appointed powers; he is a man,
Who with a double surety binds his followers.
My lord your son had only but the corps,
But shadows, and the shows of men, to fight:
For that same word, rebellion, did divide
The action of their bodies from their souls;
And they did fight with queasiness, constrain'd,
As men drink potions; that their weapons only
Seem'd on our side, but, for their spirits and souls,
This word, rebellion, it had froze them up,
As fish are in a pond: But now the bishop
Turns insurrection to religion:
Suppos'd sincere and holy in his thoughts,
He's follow'd both with body and with mind;
And doth enlarge his rising with the blood
Of fair King Richard, scrap'd from Pomfret stones:
Derives from heaven his quarrel, and his cause;
Tells them, he doth bestride a bleeding land,
Gasping for life under great Bolingbroke;
And more, and less, do flock to follow him.

North. I knew of this before; but, to speak truth,
This present grief had wip'd it from my mind.
Go in with me; and counsel every man
The aptest way for safety, and revenge:
Get posts, and letters, and make friends with speed;
Never so few, and never yet more need.
[*Exeunt.*

SCENE II. London. *A Street.*

Enter SIR JOHN FALSTAFF, *with his* Page *bearing his Sword and Buckler.*

Fal. Sirrah, you giant, what says the doctor to my water?

Page. He said, sir, the water itself was a good healthy water: but for the party that owed it, he might have more diseases than he knew for.

Fal. Men of all sorts take a pride to gird at me: The brain of this foolish-compounded clay, man, is not able to vent any thing that tends to laughter, more than I invent, or is invented on me: I am not only witty in myself, but the cause that wit is in other men. I do here walk before thee, like a sow, that hath overwhelmed all her litter but one. If the prince put thee into my service for any other reason than to set me off, why then I have no judgment. Thou whoreson mandrake, thou art fitter to be worn in my cap, than to wait at my heels. I was never manned with an agate till now: but I will set you neither in gold nor silver, but in vile apparel, and send you back again to your master, for a jewel; the juvenal, the prince your master, whose chin is not yet fledged. I will sooner have a beard grow in the palm of my hand, than he shall get one on his cheek; and yet he will not stick to say, his face is a face-royal: God may finish it when he will, it is not a hair amiss yet: he may keep it still as a face-royal, for a barber shall never earn sixpence out of it; and yet he will be crowing, as if he had writ man ever since his father was a bachelor. He may keep his own grace, but he is almost out of mine, I can assure him.——What said master Dumbleton about the satin for my short cloak, and slops?

Page. He said, sir, you should procure him better assurance than Bardolph: he would not take his bond and yours; he liked not the security.

Fal. Let him be damned like the glutton! may his tongue be hotter!—A whoreson Achitophel! a rascally yea-forsooth knave; to bear a gentleman in hand, and then stand upon security!—The whoreson smooth-pates do now wear nothing but high shoes, and bunches of keys at their girdles; and if a man is thorough with them in honest taking up, then they must stand upon—security. I had as lief they would put ratsbane in my mouth, as offer to stop it with security. I looked he should have sent me two and twenty yards of satin, as I am a true knight, and he sends me security. Well, he may sleep in security; for he hath the horn of abundance, and the lightness of his wife shines through it: and yet cannot he see, though he have his own lantern to light him.——Where's Bardolph?

Page. He's gone into Smithfield, to buy your worship a horse.

Fal. I bought him in Paul's, and he'll buy me a horse in Smithfield: an I could get me but a wife in the stews, I were manned, horsed, and wived.

Enter the Lord Chief Justice, *and an* Attendant.

Page. Sir, here comes the nobleman that committed the prince for striking him about Bardolph.

Fal. Wait close, I will not see him.

Ch. Just. What's he that goes there?

Atten. Falstaff, an't please your lordship.

Ch. Just. He that was in question for the robbery?

Atten. He, my lord: but he hath since done good service at Shrewsbury; and, as I hear, is now going with some charge to the lord John of Lancaster.

Ch. Just. What, to York? Call him back again.

Atten. Sir John Falstaff!

Fal. Boy, tell him, I am deaf.

Page. You must speak louder, my master is deaf.

Ch. Just. I am sure he is, to the hearing of any thing good.—Go, pluck him by the elbow: I must speak with him.

Atten. Sir John,——

Fal. What! a young knave, and beg! Is there not wars? is there not employment? Doth not the king lack subjects? do not the rebels need soldiers? Though it be a shame to be on any side but one, it is worse shame to beg than to be on the worst side, were it worse than the name of rebellion can tell how to make it.

Atten. You mistake me, sir.

Fal. Why, sir, did I say you were an honest man? setting my knighthood and my soldiership aside, I had lied in my throat if I had said so.

Atten. I pray you, sir, then set your knighthood and your soldiership aside; and give me leave to tell you, you lie in your throat, if you say I am any other than an honest man.

Fal. I give thee leave to tell me so! I lay aside that which grows to me! If thou get'st any leave of me, hang me; if thou takest leave, thou wert better be hanged; You hunt counter, hence! avaunt!

Atten. Sir, my lord would speak with you.

Ch. Just. Sir John Falstaff, a word with you.

Fal. My good lord!—God give your lordship good time of day. I am glad to see your lordship abroad: I heard say, your lordship was sick: I hope, your lordship goes abroad by advice. Your lordship, though not clean past your youth, hath yet some smack of age in you, some relish of the saltness of time; and I most humbly beseech your lordship, to have a reverend care of your health.

Ch. Just. Sir John, I sent for you before your expedition to Shrewsbury.

Fal. An't please your lordship, I hear his majesty is returned with some discomfort from Wales.

Ch. Just. I talk not of his majesty:—You would not come when I sent for you.

Fal. And I hear moreover, his highness is fallen into this same whoreson apoplexy.

Ch. Just. Well, heaven mend him! I pray, let me speak with you.

Fal. This apoplexy is, as I take it, a kind of lethargy, an't please your lordship; a kind of sleeping in the blood, a whoreson tingling.

Ch. Just. What tell you me of it? be it as it is.

Fal. It hath its original from much grief; from study, and perturbation of the brain: I have read the cause of his effects in Galen; it is a kind of deafness.

Ch. Just. I think, you are fallen into the disease; for you hear not what I say to you.

Fal. Very well, my lord, very well: rather, an't please you, it is the disease of not listening, the malady of not marking, that I am troubled withal.

Ch. Just. To punish you by the heels, would amend the attention of your ears; and I care not, if I do become your physician.

Fal. I am as poor as Job, my lord; but not so patient: your lordship may minister the potion of imprisonment to me, in respect of poverty; but how I should be your patient to follow your prescriptions, the wise may make some dram of a scruple, or, indeed, a scruple itself.

Ch. Just. I sent for you, when there were matters against you for your life, to come speak with me.

Fal. As I was then advised by my learned counsel in the laws of this land-service, I did not come.

Ch. Just. Well, the truth is, Sir John, you live in great infamy.

Fal. He that buckles him in my belt, cannot live in less.

Ch. Just. Your means are very slender, and your waste is great.

Fal. I would it were otherwise; I would my means were greater, and my waist slenderer.

Ch. Just. You have misled the youthful prince.

Fal. The young prince hath misled me: I am the fellow with the great belly, and he my dog.

Ch. Just. Well, I am loath to gall a new-healed wound; your day's service at Shrewsbury hath a little gilded over your night's exploit on Gad's-hill: you may thank the unquiet time for your quiet o'erposting that action.

Fal. My lord?

Ch. Just. But since all is well, keep it so: wake not a sleeping wolf.

Fal. To wake a wolf, is as bad as to smell a fox.

Ch. Just. What! you are as a candle, the better part burnt out.

Fal. A wassel candle, my lord; all tallow: if I did say of wax, my growth would approve the truth.

Ch. Just. There is not a white hair on your face, but should have his effect of gravity.

Fal. His effect of gravy, gravy, gravy.

Ch. Just. You follow the young prince up and down, like his ill angel.

Fal. Not so, my lord; your ill angel is light;

but, I hope, he that looks upon me, will take me without weighing: and yet, in some respects, I grant, I cannot go, I cannot tell: Virtue is of so little regard in these coster-monger times, that true valour is turned bear-herd: Pregnancy is made a tapster, and hath his quick wit wasted in giving reckonings: all the other gifts appertinent to man, as the malice of this age shapes them, are not worth a gooseberry. You, that are old, consider not the capacities of us that are young: you measure the heat of our livers with the bitterness of your galls: and we that are in the vaward of our youth, I must confess, are wags too.

Ch. Just. Do you set down your name in the scroll of youth, that are written down old with all the characters of age? Have you not a moist eye? a dry hand? a yellow cheek? a white beard? a decreasing leg? an increasing belly? Is not your voice broken? your wind short? your chin double? your wit single? and every part about you blasted with antiquity? and will you yet call yourself young? Fye, fye, fye, Sir John!

Fal. My lord, I was born about three of the clock in the afternoon, with a white head, and something a round belly. For my voice,—I have lost it with hollaing, and singing of anthems. To approve my youth further, I will not: the truth is, I am only old in judgment and understanding: and he that will caper with me for a thousand marks, let him lend me the money, and have at him. For the box o' the ear that the prince gave you,—he gave it like a rude prince, and you took it like a sensible lord. I have checked him for it; and the young lion repents; marry, not in ashes, and sackcloth: but in new silk and old sack.

Ch. Just. Well, heaven send the prince a better companion!

Fal. Heaven send the companion a better prince! I cannot rid my hands of him.

Ch. Just. Well, the king hath severed you and Prince Harry: I hear, you are going with lord John of Lancaster, against the archbishop, and the earl of Northumberland.

Fal. Yea; I thank your pretty sweet wit for it. But look you pray, all you that kiss my lady peace at home, that our armies join not in a hot day! for, by the Lord, I take but two shirts out with me, and I mean not to sweat extraordinarily: if it be a hot day, an I brandish any thing but my bottle, I would I might never spit white again. There is not a dangerous action can peep out his head, but I am thrust upon it: Well, I cannot last ever: But it was always yet the trick of our English nation, if they have a good thing, to make it too common. If you will needs say, I am an old man, you should give me rest. I would to God, my name were not so terrible to the enemy as it is. I were better to be eaten to death with rust, than to be scoured to nothing with perpetual motion.

Ch. Just. Well, be honest, be honest: And God bless your expedition!

Fal. Will your lordship lend me a thousand pound, to furnish me forth?

Ch. Just. Not a penny, not a penny; you are too impatient to bear crosses. Fare you well: Commend me to my cousin Westmoreland.

[*Exeunt* Chief Justice *and* Attendant.

Fal. If I do, fillip me with a three-man beetle. —A man can no more separate age and covetousness, than he can part young limbs and lechery: but the gout galls the one, and the pox pinches the other; and so both the degrees prevent my curses.—Boy!——

Page. Sir?

Fal. What money is in my purse?

Page. Seven groats and two-pence.

Fal. I can get no remedy against this consumption of the purse: borrowing only lingers and lingers it out, but the disease is incurable.—Go bear this letter to my lord of Lancaster; this to the prince; this to the earl of Westmoreland; and this to old mistress Ursula, whom I have weekly sworn to marry since I perceived the first white hair on my chin: About it; you know where to find me. [*Exit* Page.] A pox of this gout! or, a gout of this pox! for the one, or the other, plays the rogue with my great toe. It is no matter, if I do halt; I have the wars for my colour, and my pension shall seem the more reasonable: A good wit will make use of any thing; I will turn diseases to commodity.

[*Exit.*

SCENE III. York.

A Room in the Archbishop's *Palace.*

Enter the ARCHBISHOP OF YORK, *the* LORDS HASTINGS, MOWBRAY, *and* BARDOLPH.

Arch. Thus have you heard our cause, and known our means;
And, my most noble friends, I pray you all,
Speak plainly your opinions of our hopes:—
And first, lord marshal, what say you to it?

Mowb. I well allow the occasion of our arms;
But gladly would be better satisfied,
How, in our means, we should advance ourselves
To look with forehead bold and big enough
Upon the power and puissance of the king.

Hast. Our present musters grow upon the file
To five and twenty thousand men of choice;
And our supplies live largely in the hope
Of great Northumberland, whose bosom burns
With an incensed fire of injuries.

Bard. The question then, Lord Hastings, standeth thus:—
Whether our present five and twenty thousand
May hold up head without Northumberland.

Hast. With him, we may.

Bard. Ay, marry, there's the point:
But if without him we be thought too feeble,
My judgment is, we should not step too far
Till we had his assistance by the hand:
For, in a theme so bloody-fac'd as this,
Conjecture, expectation, and surmise
Of aids uncertain, should not be admitted.

Arch. 'Tis very true, Lord Bardolph; for, indeed,
It was young Hotspur's case at Shrewsbury.

Bard. It was, my lord; who lin'd himself with hope,
Eating the air on promise of supply,
Flattering himself with project of a power
Much smaller than the smallest of his thoughts:
And so, with great imagination,
Proper to madmen, led his powers to death,
And, winking, leap'd into destruction.

Hast. But, by your leave, it never yet did hurt,
To lay down likelihoods, and forms of hope.

Bard. Yes, in this present quality of war;—
Indeed the instant action, (a cause on foot),
Lives so in hope, as in an early spring
We see the appearing buds; which to prove fruit,
Hope gives not so much warrant, as despair,
That frost will bite them. When we mean to build,
We first survey the plot, then draw the model;
And when we see the figure of the house,
Then must we rate the cost of the erection:
Which if we find outweighs ability,
What do we then, but draw anew the model
In fewer offices; or, at least, desist
To build at all? Much more, in this great work
(Which is, almost, to pluck a kingdom down,
And set another up,) should we survey
The plot of situation, and the model;
Consent upon a sure foundation;
Question surveyors; know our own estate,
How able such a work to undergo,
To weigh against his opposite; or else,
We fortify in paper, and in figures,

Using the names of men instead of men:
Like one, that draws the model of a house
Beyond his power to build it; who, half through,
Gives o'er, and leaves his part-created cost
A naked subject to the weeping clouds,
And waste for churlish winter's tyranny.

Hast. Grant that our hopes (yet likely of fair birth,)
Should be still-born, and that we now possess'd
The utmost man of expectation;
I think, we are a body strong enough,
Even as we are, to equal with the king.

Bard. What! is the king but five and twenty thousand?

Hast. To us, no more; nay, not so much, Lord Bardolph.
For his divisions, as the times do brawl,
Are in three heads: one power against the French,
And one against Glendower; perforce, a third
Must take up us: So is the unfirm king
In three divided; and his coffers sound
With hollow poverty and emptiness.

Arch. That he should draw his several strengths together,
And come against us in full puissance,
Need not be dreaded.

Hast. If he should do so,
He leaves his back unarm'd, the French and Welsh
Baying him at the heels: never fear that.

Bard. Who, is it like, should lead his forces hither?

Hast. The duke of Lancaster, and Westmoreland:
Against the Welsh, himself, and Harry Monmouth:
But who is substituted 'gainst the French,
I have no certain notice.

Arch. Let us on;
And publish the occasion of our arms.
The commonwealth is sick o. their own choice,
Their over greedy love hath surfeited:—
An habitation giddy and unsure
Hath he, that buildeth on the vulgar heart.
O thou fond many! with what loud applause
Didst thou beat heaven with blessing Bolingbroke,
Before he was what thou would'st have him be?
And being now trimm'd in thine own desires,
Thou, beastly feeder, art so full of him,
That thou provok'st thyself to cast him up.
So, so, thou common dog, didst thou disgorge
Thy glutton bosom of the royal Richard;
And now thou wouldst eat thy dead vomit up,
And howl'st to find it. What trust is in these times?
They that, when Richard liv'd, would have him die,
Are now become enamour'd on his grave:
Thou, that threw'st dust upon his goodly head,
When through proud London he came sighing on
After the admired heels of Bolingbroke,
Cry'st now, *O earth, yield us that king again,
And take thou this!* O thoughts of men accurst!
Past and to come, seem best; things present worst.

Mowb. Shall we go draw our numbers and set on?

Hast. We are time's subjects, and time bids be gone. [*Exeunt.*

ACT II.

SCENE I. London. *A Street.*

Enter Hostess; FANG, *and his* Boy, *with her; and* SNARE *following.*

Host. Master Fang, have you enter'd the action?

Fang. It is entered.

Host. Where is your yeoman? Is it a lusty yeoman? Will a' stand to't?

Fang. Sirrah, where's Snare?

Host. O lord, ay: good master Snare.

Snare. Here, here.

Fang. Snare, we must arrest Sir John Falstaff.

Host. Yea, good master Snare; I have entered him and all.

Snare. It may chance cost some of us our lives, for he will stab.

Host. Alas the day! take heed of him; he stabbed me in mine own house, and that most beastly: in good faith, a' cares not what mischief he doth, if his weapon be out: he will foin like any devil; he will spare neither man, woman, nor child.

Fang. If I can close with him, I care not for his thrust.

Host. No, nor I neither: I'll be at your elbow.

Fang. An I but fist him once; an a' come but within my vice;—

Host. I am undone by his going; I warrant you, he's an infinitive thing upon my score:—Good master Fang, hold him sure;—good master Snare, let him not 'scape. He comes continuantly to Pie-corner (saving your manhoods), to buy a saddle; and he's indited to dinner to the lubbar's head in Lumbert-street, to master Smooth's the silkman: I pray ye, since my exion is entered, and my case so openly known to the world, let him be brought in to his answer. A hundred mark is a long loan for a poor lone woman to bear: and I have borne, and borne, and borne; and have been fubbed off, and fubbed off, and fubbed off, from this day to that day, that it is a shame to be thought on. There is no honesty in such dealing; unless a woman should be made an ass, and a beast, to bear every knave's wrong.——

Enter SIR JOHN FALSTAFF, Page, *and* BARDOLPH.

Yonder he comes; and that arrant malmsey-nose knave Bardolph, with him. Do your offices, do your offices, master Fang, and master Snare; do me, do me, do me your offices.

Fal. How now? whose mare's dead? what's the matter?

Fang. Sir John, I arrest you at the suit of Mistress Quickly.

Fal. Away, varlets!—Draw, Bardolph; cut me off the villain's head; throw the quean in the channel.

Host. Throw me in the channel? I'll throw thee in the channel. Wilt thou? wilt thou? thou bastardly rogue!—Murder, murder! O thou honeysuckle villain! wilt thou kill God's officers, and the king's? O thou honey-seed rogue! thou art a honey-seed; a man-queller, and a woman-queller.

Fal. Keep them off, Bardolph.

Fang. A rescue! a rescue!

Host. Good people, bring a rescue or two.—Thou wo't, wo't thou? thou wo't, wo't thou? do, do, thou rogue! do, thou hemp-seed!

Fal. Away, you scullion! you rampallian! you fustilarian! I'll tickle your catastrophe.

Enter the Lord Chief Justice, *attended.*

Ch. Just. What's the matter? keep the peace here, ho!

Host. Good my lord, be good to me! I beseech you, stand to me!

Ch. Just. How now, Sir John? what, are you brawling here?
Doth this become your place, your time, and business?
You should have been well on your way to York.—
Stand from him, fellow; wherefore hang'st thou on him?

Host. O my most worshipful lord, an't please your grace, I am a poor widow of Eastcheap, and he is arrested at my suit.

Ch. Just. For what sum?

Host. It is more than for some, my lord: it is for all, all I have: he hath eaten me out of house and home; he hath put all my substance into that fat belly of his:—but I will have some of it out again, or I'll ride thee o'nights like the mare.

Fal. I think I am as like to ride the mare, if I have any vantage of ground to get up.

Ch. Just. How comes this, Sir John? Fye! what man of good temper would endure this tempest of exclamation? Are you not ashamed to enforce a poor widow to so rough a course to come by her own?

Fal. What is the gross sum that I owe thee?

Host. Marry, if thou wert an honest man, thyself and the money too. Thou didst swear to me upon a parcel-gilt goblet, sitting in my Dolphin-chamber, at the round table, by a sea-coal fire, upon Wednesday in Wheeson-week, when the prince broke thy head for liking his father to a singing-man of Windsor; thou didst swear to me then, as I was washing thy wound, to marry me, and make me my lady thy wife. Canst thou deny it? Did not goodwife Keech, the butcher's wife, come in then, and call me gossip Quickly? coming in to borrow a mess of vinegar; telling us, she had a good dish of prawns; whereby thou didst desire to eat some; whereby I told thee, they were ill for a green wound? And didst thou not, when she was gone down stairs, desire me to be no more so familiarity with such poor people; saying that ere long they should call me madam? And didst thou not kiss me, and bid me fetch thee thirty shillings? I put thee now to thy book-oath; deny it, if thou canst.

Fal. My lord, this is a poor mad soul; and she says, up and down the town, that her eldest son is like you: she hath been in good case, and, the truth is, poverty hath distracted her. But for these foolish officers, I beseech you, I may have redress against them.

Ch. Just. Sir John, Sir John, I am well acquainted with your manner of wrenching the true cause the false way. It is not a confident brow, nor the throng of words that come with such more than impudent sauciness from you, can thrust me from a level consideration: you have, as it appears to me, practised upon the easy-yielding spirit of this woman, and made her serve your uses both in purse and person.

Host. Yea, in troth, my lord.

Ch. Just. 'Pr'ythee, peace:—Pay her the debt you owe her, and unpay the villany you have done with her; the one you may do with sterling money, and the other with current repentance.

Fal. My lord, I will not undergo this sneap without reply. You call honourable boldness, impudent sauciness: if a man will make court'sy, and say nothing, he is virtuous: No my lord, my humble duty remembered, I will not be your suitor; I say to you, I do desire deliverance from these officers, being upon hasty employment in the king's affairs.

Ch. Just. You speak as having power to do wrong: but answer in the effect of your reputation, and satisfy the poor woman.

Fal. Come hither, hostess. [*Taking her aside.*

Enter GOWER.

Ch. Just. Now, master Gower; What news?

Gow. The king, my lord, and Harry prince of Wales
Are near at hand: the rest the paper tells.

Fal. As I am a gentleman:——

Host. Nay, you said so before.

Fal. As I am a gentleman;——Come, no more words of it.

Host. By this heavenly ground I tread on, I must be fain to pawn both my plate, and the tapestry of my dining-chambers.

Fal. Glasses, glasses, is the only drinking: and for thy walls,—a pretty slight drollery, or the story of the prodigal, or the German hunting in water-work, is worth a thousand of these bed hangings, and these fly-bitten tapestries. Let it be ten pound, if thou canst. Come, and it were not for thy humours, there is not a better wench in England. Go wash thy face, and draw thy action: Come, thou must not be in this humour with me; dost not know me? Come, come, I know thou wast set on to this.

Host. 'Pray thee, Sir John, let it be but twenty nobles; i'faith I am loath to pawn my plate, in good earnest, la.

Fal. Let it alone; I'll make other shift: you'll be a fool still.

Host. Well, you shall have it, though I pawn my gown. I hope you'll come to supper; you'll pay me all together.

Fal. Will I live?—Go with her, with her; [*To* BARDOLPH.] hook on, hook on.

Host. Will you have Doll Tear-sheet meet you at supper?

Fal. No more words; let's have her.

[*Exeunt* Hostess, BARDOLPH, Officers, *and* Page.

Ch. Just. I have heard better news.

Fal. What's the news, my good lord?

Ch. Just. Where lay the king last night?

Gow. At Basingstoke, my lord.

Fal. I hope, my lord, all's well: What's the news, my lord?

Ch. Just. Come all his forces back?

Gow. No; fifteen hundred foot, five hundred horse,
Are march'd up to my lord of Lancaster,
Against Northumberland, and the Archbishop.

Fal. Comes the king back from Wales, my noble lord?

Ch. Just. You shall have letters of me presently:
Come, go along with me, good master Gower.

Fal. My lord!

Ch. Just. What's the matter?

Fal. Master Gower, shall I entreat you with me to dinner?

Gow. I must wait upon my good lord here; I thank you, good Sir John.

Ch. Just. Sir John, you loiter here too long, being you are to take soldiers up in counties as you go.

Fal. Will you sup with me, master Gower?

Ch. Just. What foolish master taught you these manners, Sir John?

Fal. Master Gower, if they become me not, he was a fool that taught them me.—This is the right fencing grace, my lord; tap for tap, and so part fair.

Ch. Just. Now the lord lighten thee! thou art a great fool. [*Exeunt.*

SCENE II. *The same. Another Street.*

Enter PRINCE HENRY *and* POINS.

P. Hen. Trust me, I am exceeding weary.

Poins. Is it come to that? I had thought, weariness durst not have attached one of so high blood.

P. Hen. 'Faith, it does me; though it discolours the complexion of my greatness to acknowledge it. Doth it not show vilely in me to desire small beer?

Poins. Why, a prince should not be so loosely studied, as to remember so weak a composition.

P. Hen. Belike then, my appetite was not princely got; for by my troth, I do now remember the poor creature, small beer. But, indeed, these humble considerations make me out of love with my greatness. What a disgrace is it to me, to remember thy name? or to know thy face to-morrow? or to take note how many pair of silk stockings thou hast; *viz.* these and those that were the peach-colour'd ones? or to bear the inventory of thy shirts; as, one for superfluity, and one other for use?—but that the tennis-court-keeper knows better than I; for it is a low ebb of linen with thee, when thou keepest not racket there; as thou hast not done a great while, because the rest of thy low-countries have make a shift to eat up thy holland: and God knows, whether those that bawl out the ruins of thy linen, shall inherit his kingdom: but the midwives say, the children are not in the fault; whereupon the world increases, and kindreds are mightily strengthened.

Poins. How ill it follows, after you have laboured so hard, you should talk so idly? Tell me, how many good young princes would do so, their fathers being so sick as yours at this time is?

P. Hen. Shall I tell thee one thing, Poins?

Poins. Yes; and let it be an excellent good thing.

P. Hen. It shall serve among wits of no higher breeding than thine.

Poins. Go to; I stand the push of your one thing that you will tell.

P. Hen. Why, I tell thee,—it is not meet that I should be sad, now my father is sick: albeit I could tell thee (as to one it pleases me, for fault of a better, to call my friend), I could be sad, and sad indeed too.

Poins. Very hardly upon such a subject.

P. Hen. By this hand, thou think'st me as far in the devil's book, as thou, and Falstaff, for obduracy and persistency: Let the end try the man. But I tell thee,—my heart bleeds inwardly, that my father is so sick: and keeping such vile company as thou art, hath in reason taken from me all ostentation of sorrow.

Poins. The reason?

P. Hen. What would'st thou think of me, if I should weep?

Poins. I would think thee a most princely hypocrite.

P. Hen. It would be every man's thought: and thou art a blessed fellow, to think as every man thinks; never a man's thoughts in the world keeps the road-way better than thine: every man would think me a hypocrite indeed. And what accites your most worshipful thought to think so?

Poins. Why, because you have been so lewd, and so much engraffed to Falstaff.

P. Hen. And to thee.

Poins. By this light, I am well spoken of, I can hear it with my own ears: the worst that they can say of me is, that I am a second brother, and that I am a proper fellow of my hands; and those two things, I confess, I cannot help. By the mass, here comes Bardolph.

P. Hen. And the boy that I gave Falstaff: he had him from me christian; and look, if the fat villain have not transformed him ape.

Enter BARDOLPH *and* Page.

Bard. 'Save your grace!

P. Hen. And yours, most noble Bardolph!

Bard. Come, you virtuous ass [*To the* Page,] you bashful fool, must you be blushing? wherefore blush you now? What a maidenly man at arms are you become! Is it such a matter, to get a pottle-pot's maidenhead?

Page. He called me even now, my lord, through a red lattice, and I could discern no part of his face from the window: at last, I spied his eyes; and, methought he had made two holes in the ale-wife's new petticoat, and peeped through.

P. Hen. Hath not the boy profited?

Bard. Away, you whoreson upright rabbit, away!

Page. Away, you rascally Althea's dream, away!

P. Hen. Instruct, us, boy: What dream, boy?

Page. Marry, my lord, Althea dreamed she was delivered of a fire-brand; and therefore I call him her dream.

P. Hen. A crown's worth of good interpretation.—There it is, boy. [*Gives him money.*

Poins. O, that this good blossom could be kept from cankers!—Well, there is sixpence to preserve thee.

Bard. An you do not make him be hanged among you, the gallows shall have wrong.

P. Hen. And how doth thy master, Bardolph?

Bard. Well, my lord. He heard of your grace's coming to town; there's a letter for you.

Poins. Delivered with good respect.—And how doth the martlemas, your master?

Bard. In bodily health, sir.

Poins. Marry, the immortal part needs a physician: but that moves not him; though that be sick, it dies not.

P. Hen. I do allow this wen to be as familiar with me as my dog: and he holds his place: for, look you, how he writes.

Poins. [*Reads.*] John Falstaff, *knight*,——Every man must know that, as oft as he has occasion to name himself. Even like those that are kin to the king; for they never prick their finger, but they say, *There is some of the king's blood spilt: How comes that?* says he, that takes upon him not to conceive: the answer is as ready as a borrower's cap; *I am the king's poor cousin, sir.*

P. Hen. Nay, they will be kin to us, or they will fetch it from Japhet. But the letter:—

Poins. *Sir* John Falstaff, *knight, to the son of the king, nearest his father, Harry, Prince of Wales, greeting.*—Why, this is a certificate.

P. Hen. Peace!

Poins. *I will imitate the honourable Roman in brevity:*—he sure means brevity in breath; short-winded.—*I commend me to thee, I commend thee, and I leave thee. Be not too familiar with* Poins: *for he misuses thy favours so much, that he swears, thou art to marry his sister* Nell. *Repent at idle times as thou may'st, and so farewell.*

Thine, by yea and no (which is as much as to say, as thou usest him),
Jack Falstaff, *with my familiars;*
John, *with my brothers and sisters;*
and Sir John, *with all Europe.*

My lord, I will steep this letter in sack, and make him eat it.

P. Hen. That's to make him eat twenty of his words. But do you use me thus, Ned? must I marry your sister?

Poins. May the wench have no worse fortune! but I never said so.

P. Hen. Well, thus we play the fools with the time: and the spirits of the wise sit in the clouds, and mock us.—Is your master here in London?

Bard. Yes, my lord.

P. Hen. Where sups he? doth the old boar feed in the old frank?

Bard. At the old place, my lord; in Eastcheap.

P. Hen. What company?

Page. Ephesians, my lord; of the old church.

P. Hen. Sup any women with him?

Page. None, my lord, but old mistress Quickly, and mistress Doll Tear-sheet.

P. Hen. What pagan may that be?

Page. A proper gentlewoman, sir, and a kinswoman of my master's.

P. Hen. Even such kin as the parish heifers are to the town bull.—Shall we steal upon them, Ned, at supper?

Poins. I am your shadow, my lord;—I'll follow you.

P. Hen. Sirrah, you boy,—and Bardolph;—no word to your master, that I am yet come to town: There's for your silence.

Bard. I have no tongue, sir.

Page. And for mine, sir,—I will govern it.

P. Hen. Fare ye well; go. [*Exeunt* BARDOLPH

and Page.]—This Doll Tear-sheet should be some road.

Poins. I warrant you, as common as the way between Saint Alban's and London.

P. Hen. How might we see Falstaff bestow himself to-night in his true colours, and not ourselves be seen?

Poins. Put on two leather jerkins, and aprons, and wait upon him at his table as drawers.

P. Hen. From a god to a bull? a heavy descension! it was Jove's case. From a prince to a prentice? a low transformation! that shall be mine: for, in every thing, the purpose must weigh with the folly. Follow me, Ned. [*Exeunt.*

SCENE III. Warkworth. *Before the Castle.*

Enter NORTHUMBERLAND, LADY NORTHUMBERLAND, *and* LADY PERCY.

North. I pray thee, loving wife, and gentle daughter,
Give even way unto my rough affairs;
Put not you on the visage of the times,
And be, like them, to Percy troublesome.

Lady N. I have given over, I will speak no more:
Do what you will; your wisdom be your guide.

North. Alas, sweet wife, my honour is at pawn;
And, but my going, nothing can redeem it.

Lady P. O, yet, for God's sake, go not to these wars!
The time was, father, that you broke your word,
When you were more endear'd to it than now;
When your own Percy, when my heart's dear Harry,
Threw many a northward look to see his father
Bring up his powers: but he did long in vain.
Who then persuaded you to stay at home?
There were two honours lost; yours and your son's.
For your's,—may heavenly glory brighten it?
For his,—it stuck upon him as the sun
In the gray vault of heaven: and, by his light,
Did all the chivalry of England move
To do brave acts; he was, indeed, the glass
Wherein the noble youth did dress themselves.
He had no legs, that practis'd not his gait:
And speaking thick, which nature made his blemish,
Became the accents of the valiant;
For those that could speak low, and tardily,
Would turn their own perfection to abuse,
To seem like him: So that, in speech, in gait,
In diet, in affections of delight,
In military rules, humours of blood,
He was the mark and glass, copy and book,
That fashion'd others. And him,—O wondrous him!
O miracle of men!—him did you leave
(Second to none, unseconded by you),
To look upon the hideous god of war
In disadvantage; to abide a field,
Where nothing but the sound of Hotspur's name
Did seem defensible:—so you left him:
Never, O never, do his ghost the wrong,
To hold your honour more precise and nice
With others, than with him; let them alone;
The marshal, and the archbishop, are strong:
Had my sweet Harry had but half their numbers,
To-day might I, hanging on Hotspur's neck,
Have talk'd of Monmouth's grave.

North. Beshrew your heart,
Fair daughter! you do draw my spirits from me,
With new lamenting ancient oversights.
But I must go, and meet with danger there;
Or it will seek me in another place,
And find me worse provided.

Lady N. O, fly to Scotland,
Till that the nobles, and the armed commons,
Have of their puissance made a little taste.

Lady P. If they get ground and vantage of the king,
Then join you with them, like a rib of steel,
To make strength stronger; but, for all our loves,
First let them try themselves: So did your son;
He was so suffer'd: so came I a widow;
And never shall have length of life enough,
To rain upon remembrance with mine eyes,
That it may grow and sprout as high as heaven,
For recordation to my noble husband.

North. Come, come, go in with me: 'tis with my mind,
As with the tide swell'd up unto its height,
That makes a still-stand, running neither way.
Fain would I go to meet the archbishop,
But many thousand reasons hold me back:——
I will resolve for Scotland; there am I,
Till time and vantage crave my company. [*Exeunt.*

SCENE IV. London.

A Room in the Boar's Head *Tavern in* Eastcheap.

Enter Two Drawers.

1 *Draw.* What the devil hast thou brought there? apple-Johns? thou know'st, Sir John cannot endure an apple-John.

2 *Draw.* Mass, thou sayest true: The prince once set a dish of apple-Johns before him, and told him there were five more Sir Johns: and, putting off his hat, said, *I will now take my leave of these six dry, round, old withered knights.* It angered him to the heart; but he hath forgot that.

1 *Draw.* Why then, cover, and set them down: And see if thou canst find out Sneak's noise; mistress Tear-sheet would fain hear some musick. Despatch:—The room where they supped is too hot; they'll come in straight.

2 *Draw.* Sirrah, here will be the prince, and master Poins anon: and they will put on two of our jerkins, and aprons; and Sir John must not know of it: Bardolph hath brought word.

1 *Draw.* By the mass, here will be old utis: It will be an excellent stratagem.

2 *Draw.* I'll see if I can find out Sneak. [*Exit.*

Enter Hostess *and* DOLL TEAR-SHEET.

Host. I' faith, sweet heart, methinks now you are in an excellent good temperality: your pulsidge beats as extraordinarily as heart would desire; and your colour, I warrant you, is as red as any rose; But, i' faith, you have drunk too much canaries; and that's a marvellous searching wine, and it perfumes the blood ere one can say,—What's this? How do you now?

Dol. Better than I was. Hem.

Host. Why, that's well said; a good heart's worth gold. Look, here comes Sir John.

Enter FALSTAFF, *singing.*

Fal. *When Arthur first in court.*—Empty the jordan.—*And was a worthy king:* [*Exit* Drawer.] How now, mistress Doll?

Host. Sick of a calm: yea, good sooth.

Fal. So is all her sect; an they be once in a calm, they are sick.

Dol. You muddy rascal, is that all the comfort you give me?

Fal. You make fat rascals, mistress Doll.

Dol. I make them! gluttony and diseases make them; I make them not.

Fal. If the cook help to make the gluttony, you help to make the diseases, Doll: we catch of you, Doll, we catch of you; grant that, my poor virtue, grant that.

Dol. Ay, marry; our chains, and our jewels.

Fal. *Your brooches, pearls, and owches;*—for to serve bravely, is to come halting off, you know: To come off the breach with his pike bent bravely, and to surgery bravely; to venture upon the charged chambers bravely:——

Dol. Hang yourself, you muddy conger, hang yourself!

Host. By my troth, this is the old fashion; you two never meet, but you fall to some discord: you are both, in good troth, as rheumatick as two dry toasts; you cannot one bear with another's confirmities. What the good year! one must bear, and that must be you: [*To* DOLL.] you are the weaker vessel, as they say, the emptier vessel.

Dol. Can a weak empty vessel bear such a huge full hogshead? there's a whole merchant's venture of Bourdeaux stuff in him: you have not seen a hulk better stuffed in the hold.—Come, I'll be friends with thee, Jack: thou art going to the wars; and whether I shall ever see thee again, or no, there is nobody cares.

Re-enter Drawer.

Draw. Sir, ancient Pistol's below, and would speak with you.

Dol. Hang him, swaggering rascal! let him not come hither: it is the foul-mouth'dst rogue in England.

Host. If he swagger, let him not come here; no, by my faith; I must live amongst my neighbours; I'll no swaggerers: I am in good name and fame with the very best:—Shut the door;—there comes no swaggerers here: I have not lived all this while to have swaggering now:—shut the door, I pray you.

Fal. Dost thou hear, hostess?—

Host. 'Pray you, pacify yourself, Sir John; there comes no swaggerers here.

Fal. Dost thou hear? it is mine ancient.

Host. Tilly-fally, Sir John, never tell me; your ancient swaggerer comes not in my doors. I was before master Tisick, the deputy, the other day; and, as he said to me,—it was no longer ago than Wednesday last,—*Neighbour Quickly*, says he;—master Dumb, our minister, was by then;—*Neighbour Quickly*, says he, *receive those that are civil; for*, saith he, *you are in an ill name*;—now he said so, I can tell whereupon; *for*, says he, *you are an honest woman, and well thought on; therefore take heed what guests you receive: Receive*, says he, *no swaggering companions*.——There comes none here;——you would bless you to hear what he said:—no, I'll no swaggerers.

Fal. He's no swaggerer, hostess; a tame cheater, he; you may stroke him as gently as a puppy greyhound: he will not swagger with a Barbary hen, if her feathers turn back in any show of resistance.—Call him up, drawer.

Host. Cheater, call you him? I will bar no honest man my house, nor no cheater: But I do not love swaggering; by my troth, I am the worse, when one says—swagger: feel, masters, how I shake; look you, I warrant you.

Dol. So you do, hostess.

Host. Do I? yea, in very truth, do I, an 'twere an aspen leaf: I cannot abide swaggerers.

Enter PISTOL, BARDOLPH, *and* Page.

Pist. 'Save you, Sir John!

Fal. Welcome, ancient Pistol. Here, Pistol, I charge you with a cup of sack: do you discharge upon mine hostess.

Pist. I will discharge upon her, Sir John, with two bullets.

Fal. She is pistol-proof, sir; you shall hardly offend her.

Host. Come, I'll drink no proofs, nor no bullets: I'll drink no more than will do me good for no man's pleasure, I.

Pist. Then to you, mistress Dorothy; I will charge you.

Dol. Charge me? I scorn you, scurvy companion. What! you poor, base, rascally, cheating, lack-linen mate! Away, you mouldy rogue; away! I am meat for your master.

Pist. I know you, mistress Dorothy.

Dol. Away, you cut-purse rascal! you filthy bung, away! by this wine, I'll thrust my knife in your mouldy chaps, an you play the saucy cuttle with me. Away, you bottle-ale rascal! you basket-hilt stale juggler, you!—Since when, I pray you, sir?—What, with two points on your shoulder? much!

Pist. I will murder your ruff for this.

Fal. No more, Pistol; I would not have you go off here: discharge yourself of our company, Pistol.

Host. No, good captain Pistol; not here, sweet captain.

Dol. Captain! thou abominable damned cheater, art thou not ashamed to be called—captain? If captains were of my mind, they would truncheon you out, for taking their names upon you before you have earned them. You a captain, you slave! for what? for tearing a poor whore's ruff in a bawdy house?—He a captain! Hang him, rogue! He lives upon mouldy stewed prunes, and dried cakes. A captain! these villains will make the word captain as odious as the word occupy; which was an excellent good word before it was ill-sorted; therefore captains had need look to it.

Bard. 'Pray thee, go down, good ancient.

Fal. Hark thee hither, mistress Doll.

Pist. Not I: tell thee what, corporal Bardolph;—I could tear her:—I'll be revenged on her.

Page. 'Pray thee, go down.

Pist. I'll see her damned first;—to Pluto's damned lake, to the infernal deep, with Erebus and tortures vile also. Hold hook and line, say I. Down! down, dogs! down, faitors! Have we not Hiren here?

Host. Good captain Peesel, be quiet; it is very late, i' faith: I beseek you now, aggravate your choler.

Pist. These be good humours, indeed! Shall packhorses,
And hollow pamper'd jades of Asia,
Which cannot go but thirty miles a day,
Compare with Cæsars, and with Cannibals,
And Trojan Greeks? nay, rather damn them with
King Cerberus; and let the welkin roar.
Shall we fall foul for toys?

Host. By my troth, captain, these are very bitter words.

Bard. Be gone, good ancient: this will grow to a brawl anon.

Pist. Die men, like dogs; give crowns like pins; Have we not Hiren here?

Host. O' my word, captain, there's none such here. What the good-year! do you think, I would deny her? for God's sake, be quiet.

Pist. Then, feed and be fat, my fair Calipolis:
Come, give's some sack.
Si fortuna me tormenta, sperato me contenta.—
Fear we broadsides? no, let the fiend give fire:
Give me some sack;—and, sweetheart, lie thou there. [*Laying down his sword.*
Come we to full points here; and are *et ceteras* nothing?

Fal. Pistol, I would be quiet.

Pist. Sweet knight, I kiss thy nief! What! we have seen the seven stars.

Dol. Thrust him down stairs; I cannot endure such a fustian rascal.

Pist. Thrust him down stairs! know we not Galloway nags?

Fal. Quoit him down, Bardolph, like a shove-groat shilling: nay, if he do nothing but speak nothing, he shall be nothing here.

Bard. Come, get you down stairs.

Pist. What! shall we have incision? shall we imbrue?—— [*Snatching up his sword.*
Then death rock me asleep, abridge my doleful days!
Why, then, let grievous, ghastly, gaping wounds
Untwine the sisters three! Come, Atropos, I say!

Host. Here's goodly stuff toward!

Fal. Give me my rapier, boy.

Dol. I pray thee, Jack, I pray thee, do not draw.

Fal. Get you down stairs.

[*Drawing, and driving* PISTOL *out.*

Host. Here's a goodly tumult! I'll forswear keeping house, afore I'll be in these tirrits and frights. So; murder, I warrant now.——Alas, alas! put up your naked weapons, put up your naked weapons. [*Exeunt* PISTOL *and* BARDOLPH.

Dol. I pray thee, Jack, be quiet; the rascal is gone. Ah, you whoreson little valiant villain, you.

Host. Are you not hurt i' the groin? methought, he made a shrewd thrust at your belly.

Re-enter BARDOLPH.

Fal. Have you turned him out of doors?

Bard. Yes, sir. The rascal's drunk: you have hurt him, sir, in the shoulder.

Fal. A rascal! to brave me!

Dol. Ah, you sweet little rogue, you! Alas, poor ape, how thou sweat'st! Come, let me wipe thy face;—come on, you whoreson chops:—Ah, rogue! i'faith I love thee. Thou art as valorous as Hector of Troy, worth five of Agamemnon, and ten times better than the nine worthies. Ah, villain!

Fal. A rascally slave! I will toss the rogue in a blanket.

Dol. Do, if thou darest for thy heart: if thou dost, I'll canvass thee between a pair of sheets.

Enter Musick.

Page. The musick is come, sir,

Fal. Let them play;—Play, sirs;—Sit on my knee, Doll. A rascal bragging slave! the rogue fled from me like quicksilver.

Dol. I' faith, and thou followedst him like a church. Thou whoreson little tidy Bartholomew boar-pig, when wilt thou leave fighting o' days, and foining o' nights, and begin to patch up thine old body for heaven?

Enter behind PRINCE HENRY *and* POINS, *disguised like Drawers.*

Fal. Peace, good Doll! do not speak like a death's head: do not bid me remember mine end.

Dol. Sirrah, what humour is the prince of?

Fal. A good shallow young fellow: he would have made a good pantler, he would have chipped bread well.

Dol. They say, Poins has a good wit.

Fal. He a good wit? hang him, baboon! his wit is as thick as Tewkesbury mustard; there is no more conceit in him, than is in a mallet.

Dol. Why does the prince love him so then?

Fal. Because their legs are both of a bigness: and he plays at quoits well; and eats conger and fennel; and drinks off candles' ends for flap-dragons: and rides the wild mare with the boys; and jumps upon joint-stools; and swears with a good grace; and wears his boot very smooth, like unto the sign of the leg: and breeds no bate with telling of discreet stories; and such other gambol faculties he hath, that show a weak mind and an able body, for the which the prince admits him: for the prince himself is such another; the weight of a hair will turn the scales between their avoirdupois.

P. Hen. Would not this nave of a wheel have his ears cut off?

Poins. Let's beat him before his whore.

P. Hen. Look, if the withered elder hath not his poll clawed like a parrot.

Poins. Is it not strange, that desire should so many years outlive performance?

Fal. Kiss me, Doll.

P. Hen. Saturn and Venus this year in conjunction! what says the almanack to that?

Poins. And, look, whether the fiery Trigon, his man, be not lisping to his master's old tables, his note-book, his counsel-keeper.

Fal. Thou dost give me flattering busses.

Dol. Nay, truly: I kiss thee with a most constant heart.

Fal. I am old, I am old.

Dol. I love thee better than I love e'er a scurvy young boy of them all.

Fal. What stuff wilt have a kirtle of? I shall receive money on Thursday: thou shalt have a cap to-morrow. A merry song, come; it grows late, we'll to bed. Thou'lt forget me, when I am gone.

Dol. By my troth thou'lt set me a weeping, an thou sayest so: prove that ever I dress myself handsome till thy return.——Well, hearken the end.

Fal. Some sack, Francis.

P. Hen. Poins. Anon, anon, sir. [*Advancing.*

Fal. Ha! a bastard son of the king's?—And art not thou Poins his brother?

P. Hen. Why, thou globe of sinful continents, what a life dost thou lead?

Fal. A better than thou; I am a gentleman, thou art a drawer.

P. Hen. Very true, sir, and I come to draw you out by the ears.

Host. O, the Lord preserve thy good grace! by my troth, welcome to London.—Now the Lord bless that sweet face of thine! O Jesu, are you come from Wales?

Fal. Thou whoreson mad compound of majesty,—by this light flesh and corrupt blood, thou art welcome. [*Leaning his hand upon* DOLL.

Dol. How! you fat fool, I scorn you.

Poins. My lord, he will drive you out of your revenge, and turn all to a merriment, if you take not the heat.

P. Hen. You whoreson candle-mine, you, how vilely did you speak of me even now, before this honest, virtuous, civil gentlewoman?

Host. 'Blessing o' your good heart! and so she is, by my troth.

Fal. Didst thou hear me?

P. Hen. Yes; and you knew me, as you did when you ran away by Gads-hill: you knew, I was at your back; and spoke it on purpose, to try my patience.

Fal. No, no, no; not so; I did not think thou wast within hearing.

P. Hen. I shall drive you then to confess the wilful abuse; and then I know how to handle you.

Fal. No abuse, Hal, on mine honour; no abuse.

P. Hen. Not! to dispraise me; and call me—pantler, and bread-chipper, and I know not what?

Fal. No abuse, Hal.

Poins. No abuse!

Fal. No abuse, Ned, in the world; honest Ned, none. I dispraised him before the wicked, that the wicked might not fall in love with him:—in which doing, I have done the part of a careful friend, and a true subject, and thy father is to give me thanks for it. No abuse, Hal;—none, Ned, none;—no, boys, none.

P. Hen. See now, whether pure fear, and entire cowardice, doth not make thee wrong this virtuous gentlewoman to close with us? Is she of the wicked? Is thine hostess here of the wicked? Or is the boy of the wicked? Or honest Bardolph, whose zeal burns in his nose, of the wicked?

Poins. Answer, thou dead elm, answer.

Fal. The fiend hath pricked down Bardolph irrecoverable; and his face is Lucifer's privy-kitchen, where he doth nothing but roast malt-worms. For the boy,—there is a good angel about him; but the devil outbids him too.

P. Hen. For the women,——

Fal. For one of them,—she is in hell already, and burns, poor soul! For the other,—I owe her money; and whether she be damn'd for that, I know not.

Host. No, I warrant you.

Fal. No, I think thou art not; I think, thou art quit for that: Marry, there is another indictment upon thee, for suffering flesh to be eaten in thy house, contrary to the law; for the which, I think, thou wilt howl.

Host. All victuallers do so: What's a joint of mutton or two in a whole Lent?

P. Hen. You, gentlewoman,——

Dol. What says your grace?

Fal. His grace says that which his flesh rebels against.

Host. Who knocks so loud at door? look to the door there, Francis.

Enter PETO.

P. Hen. Peto, how now? what news?

Peto. The king your father is at Westminster:
And there are twenty weak and wearied posts,
Come from the north: and, as I came along,
I met, and overtook, a dozen captains,
Bare-headed, sweating, knocking at the taverns,
And asking every one for Sir John Falstaff.

P. Hen. By heaven, Poins, I feel me much to blame,
So idly to profane the precious time;
When tempest of commotion, like the south
Borne with black vapour, doth begin to melt,
And drop upon our bare unarmed heads.
Give me my sword, and cloak:—Falstaff, good night.

[*Exeunt* PRINCE HENRY, POINS, PETO, *and* BARDOLPH.

Fal. Now comes in the sweetest morsel of the night, and we must hence, and leave it unpick'd. [*Knocking heard.*] More knocking at the door?

Re-enter BARDOLPH.

How now? what's the matter?

Bard. You must away to court, sir, presently; a dozen captains stay at door for you.

Fal. Pay the musicians, sirrah. [*To the* Page.] —Farewell, hostess;—farewell, Doll.—You see, my good wenches, how men of merit are sought after: the undeserver may sleep, when the man of action is called on. Farewell, good wenches: If I be not sent away post, I will see you again ere I go.

Dol. I cannot speak;—if my heart be not ready to burst:—Well, sweet Jack, have a care of thyself.

Fal. Farewell, farewell.

[*Exeunt* FALSTAFF *and* BARDOLPH.

Host. Well, fare thee well: I have known thee these twenty-nine years, come peascod-time; but an honester, and truer-hearted man,—Well, fare thee well.

Bard. [*Within.*] Mistress Tear-sheet,——

Host. What's the matter?

Bard. [*Within.*] Bid mistress Tear-sheet come to my master.

Host. O run, Doll, run; run, good Doll.

[*Exeunt.*

ACT III.

SCENE I. *A Room in the Palace.*

Enter KING HENRY *in his Nightgown, with a* Page.

K. Hen. Go, call the earls of Surrey and of Warwick;
But, ere they come, bid them o'er-read these letters,
And well consider of them: Make good speed.—— [*Exit* Page.
How many thousand of my poorest subjects
Are at this hour asleep!—O sleep, O gentle sleep,
Nature's soft nurse, how have I frighted thee,
That thou no more wilt weigh my eyelids down,
And steep my senses in forgetfulness?
Why rather, sleep, liest thou in smoky cribs,
Upon uneasy pallets stretching thee,
And hush'd with buzzing night-flies to thy slumber;
Than in the perfum'd chambers of the great,
Under the canopies of costly state,
And lull'd with sounds of sweetest melody?
O thou dull god, why liest thou with the vile,
In loathsome beds; and leav'st the kingly couch,
A watch-case, or a common 'larum bell?
Wilt thou upon the high and giddy mast
Seal up the ship-boy's eyes, and rock his brains
In cradle of the rude imperious surge;
And in the visitation of the winds,
Who take the ruffian billows by the top,
Curling their monstrous heads, and hanging them
With deaf'ning clamours in the slippery clouds,
That, with the hurly, death itself awakes?
Canst thou, O partial sleep! give thy repose
To the wet sea-boy in an hour so rude;
And, in the calmest and most stillest night,
With all appliances and means to boot,
Deny it to a king? Then, happy low, lie down!
Uneasy lies the head that wears a crown.

Enter WARWICK *and* SURREY.

War. Many good morrows to your majesty!

K. Hen. Is it good morrow, lords?

War. 'Tis one o' clock, and past.

K. Hen. Why then, good morrow to you all, my lords,
Have you read o'er the letters that I sent you?

War. We have, my liege.

K. Hen. Then you perceive, the body of our kingdom
How foul it is; what rank diseases grow,
And with what danger, near the heart of it.

War. It is but as a body, yet, distemper'd,
Which to his former strength may be restor'd,
With good advice, and little medicine:——
My Lord Northumberland will soon be cool'd.

K. Hen. O heaven! that one might read the book of fate;
And see the revolution of the times
Make mountains level, and the continent
(Weary of solid firmness) melt itself
Into the sea! and, other times, to see
The beachy girdle of the ocean
Too wide for Neptune's hips; how chances mock,
And changes fill the cup of alteration
With divers liquors! O, if this were seen,
The happiest youth,—viewing his progress through,
What perils past, what crosses to ensue,—
Would shut the book, and sit him down and die.
'Tis not ten years gone,
Since Richard, and Northumberland, great friends,
Did feast together, and, in two years after,
Were they at wars: It is but eight years since
This Percy was the man nearest my soul;
Who like a brother toil'd in my affairs,
And laid his love and life under my foot;
Yea, for my sake, even to the eyes of Richard,
Gave him defiance. But which of you was by
(You, cousin Nevil, as I may remember,)
[*To* WARWICK.
When Richard,—with his eye brimfull of tears,
Then check'd and rated by Northumberland,—
Did speak these words, now prov'd a prophecy?
Northumberland, thou ladder, by the which
My cousin Bolingbroke ascends my throne;—
Though then, heaven knows, I had no such intent;
But that necessity so bow'd the state,
That I and greatness were compell'd to kiss:——
The time shall come, thus did he follow it,
The time will come, that foul sin, gathering head,
Shall break into corruption:—so went on,
Foretelling this same time's condition,
And the division of our amity.

War. There is a history in all men's lives,

Figuring the nature of the times deceas'd:
The which observ'd, a man may prophesy,
With a near aim, of the main chance of things
As yet not come to life; which in their seeds,
And weak beginnings, lie intreasured.
Such things become the hatch and brood of time;
And, by the necessary form of this,
King Richard might create a perfect guess,
That great Northumberland, then false to him,
Would, of that seed, grow to a greater falseness;
Which should not find a ground to root upon,
Unless on you.

K. Hen. Are these things then necessities?
Then let us meet them like necessities:—
And that same word even now cries out on us;
They say, the bishop and Northumberland
Are fifty thousand strong.

War. It cannot be, my lord;
Rumour doth double, like the voice and echo,
The numbers of the fear'd;—Please it your grace
To go to bed; upon my life, my lord,
The powers that you already have sent forth,
Shall bring this prize in very easily.
To comfort you the more, I have receiv'd
A certain instance, that Glendower is dead.
Your majesty hath been this fortnight ill;
And these unseason'd hours, perforce, must add
Unto your sickness.

K. Hen. I will take your counsel:
And, were these inward wars once out of hand,
We would, dear lords, unto the Holy Land.
[*Exeunt.*

SCENE II. *Court before Justice* Shallow's *House in* Gloucestershire.

Enter SHALLOW *and* SILENCE, *meeting;* MOULDY, SHADOW, WART, FEEBLE, BULL-CALF, *and* Servants, *behind.*

Shal. Come on, come on, come on; give me your hand, sir, give me your hand, sir: an early stirrer, by the rood. And how doth my good cousin Silence?

Sil. Good morrow, good cousin Shallow.

Shal. And how doth my cousin, your bedfellow? and your fairest daughter, and mine, my god-daughter Ellen?

Sil. Alas, a black ouzel, cousin Shallow.

Shal. By yea and nay, sir, I dare say, my cousin William is become a good scholar: He is at Oxford, still, is he not?

Sil. Indeed, sir; to my cost.

Shal. He must then to the inns of court shortly: I was once of Clement's-inn; where, I think, they will talk of mad Shallow yet.

Sil. You were called—lusty Shallow, then, cousin.

Shal. By the mass, I was called any thing; and I would have done any thing, indeed, and roundly too. There was I, and little John Doit of Staffordshire, and black George Bare, and Francis Pickbone, and Will Squele a Cotswold man,—you had not four such swinge-bucklers in all the inns of court again: and, I may say to you, we knew where the bona-robas were; and had the best of them all at commandment. Then was Jack Falstaff, now Sir John, a boy: and page to Thomas Mowbray, duke of Norfolk.

Sil. This Sir John, cousin, that comes hither anon about soldiers?

Shal. The same Sir John, the very same. I saw him break Skogan's head at the court gate, when he was a crack, not thus high: and the very same day did I fight with one Sampson Stockfish, a fruiterer, behind Gray's Inn. O, the mad days that I have spent! and to see how many of mine old acquaintance are dead!

Sil. We shall all follow, cousin.

Shal. Certain, 'tis certain; very sure, very sure: death, as the Psalmist saith, is certain to all: all shall die. How a good yoke of bullocks at Stamford fair?

Sil. Truly, cousin, I was not there.

Shal. Death is certain.—Is old Double of your town living yet?

Sil. Dead, sir.

Shal. Dead!—See, see!—he drew a good bow;—And dead!—he shot a fine shoot:—John of Gaunt loved him well, and betted much money on his head. Dead!—he would have clapped i' the clout at twelve score; and carried you a forehand shaft a fourteen and fourteen and a half, that it would have done a man's heart good to see.——How a score of ewes now?

Sil. Thereafter as they be: a score of good ewes may be worth ten pounds.

Shal. And is old Double dead!

Enter BARDOLPH, *and one with him.*

Sil. Here come two of Sir John Falstaff's men, as I think.

Bard. Good morrow, honest gentlemen! I beseech you, which is Justice Shallow?

Shal. I am Robert Shallow, sir; a poor esquire of this county, and one of the king's justices of the peace: What is your good pleasure with me?

Bard. My captain, sir, commends him to you; my captain, Sir John Falstaff; a tall gentleman, by heaven, and a most gallant leader.

Shal. He greets me well, sir; I knew him a good backsword man: How doth the good knight? may I ask, how my lady his wife doth?

Bard. Sir, pardon; a soldier is better accommodated, than with a wife.

Shal. It is well said, in faith, sir; and it is well said indeed too. Better accommodated!—it is good: yea, indeed, it is: good phrases are surely, and ever were, very commendable. Accommodated!—it comes from *accommodo:* very good; a good phrase.

Bard. Pardon me, sir; I have heard the word. Phrase, call you it? By this good day, I know not the phrase; but I will maintain the word with my sword, to be a soldierlike word, and a word of exceeding good command. Accommodated; That is, when a man is, as they say, accommodated; or, when a man is,—being,—whereby,—he may be thought to be accommodated; which is an excellent thing.

Enter FALSTAFF.

Shal. It is very just:—Look, here comes good Sir John.—Give me your good hand, give me your worship's good hand: By my troth, you look well, and bear your years very well: welcome, good Sir John.

Fal. I am glad to see you well, good master Robert Shallow:—Master Sure-card, as I think.

Shal. No, Sir John; it is my cousin Silence, in commission with me.

Fal. Good master Silence, it well befits you should be of the peace.

Sil. Your good worship is welcome.

Fal. Fye! this is hot weather.—Gentlemen, have you provided me here half a dozen sufficient men?

Shal. Marry, have we, sir. Will you sit?

Fal. Let me see them, I beseech you.

Shal. Where's the roll? where's the roll? where's the roll?—Let me see, let me see. So, so, so, so: Yea, marry, sir:—Ralph Mouldy:—let them appear as I call; let them do so, let them do so.——Let me see; Where is Mouldy?

Moul. Here, an 't please you.

Shal. What think you, Sir John? a good limbed fellow: young, strong, and of good friends.

Fal. Is thy name Mouldy?

Moul. Yea, an 't please you.

Fal. 'Tis the more time thou wert used.

Shal. Ha, ha, ha! most excellent, i' faith! things, that are mouldy, lack use: Very singular good!—In faith, well said, Sir John; very well said.

Fal. Prick him. [*To* SHALLOW.

Moul. I was pricked well enough before, an

you could have let me alone: my old dame will be undone now, for one to do her husbandry, and her drudgery: you need not to have pricked me; there are other men fitter to go out than I.

Fal. Go to; peace, Mouldy, you shall go, Mouldy, it is time you were spent.

Moul. Spent!

Shal. Peace, fellow, peace; stand aside; Know you where you are?—For the other, Sir John:—let me see;—Simon Shadow!

Fal. Ay marry, let me have him to sit under: he's like to be a cold soldier.

Shal. Where's Shadow?

Shad. Here, sir.

Fal. Shadow, whose son art thou?

Shad. My mother's son, sir.

Fal. Thy mother's son! like enough, and thy father's shadow: so the son of the female is the shadow of the male: It is often so, indeed; but not much of the father's substance.

Shal. Do you like him, Sir John?

Fal. Shadow will serve for summer,—prick him;—for we have a number of shadows to fill up the muster book.

Shal. Thomas Wart!

Fal. Where's he?

Wart. Here, sir.

Fal. Is thy name Wart?

Wart. Yea, sir.

Fal. Thou art a very ragged wart.

Shal. Shall I prick him, Sir John?

Fal. It were superfluous; for his apparel is built upon his back, and the whole frame stands upon pins: prick him no more.

Shal. Ha, ha, ha!—you can do it, sir; you can do it: I commend you well.—Francis Feeble!

Fee. Here, sir.

Fal. What trade art thou, Feeble?

Fee. A woman's tailor, sir.

Shal. Shall I prick him, sir?

Fal. You may: but if he had been a man's tailor, he would have pricked you.—Wilt thou make as many holes in an enemy's battle, as thou hast done in a woman's petticoat?

Fee. I will do my good will, sir; you can have no more.

Fal. Well said, good woman's tailor! well said, courageous Feeble! Thou wilt be as valiant as the wrathful dove, or most magnanimous mouse.—Prick the woman's tailor well, master Shallow; deep, master Shallow.

Fee. I would, Wart might have gone, sir.

Fal. I would, thou wert a man's tailor; that thou might'st mend him, and make him fit to go. I cannot put him to a private soldier, that is the leader of so many thousands: Let that suffice, most forcible Feeble.

Fee. It shall suffice, sir.

Fal. I am bound to thee, reverend Feeble.—Who is next?

Shal. Peter Bull-calf of the green!

Fal. Yea, marry, let us see Bull-calf.

Bull. Here, sir.

Fal. 'Fore God, a likely fellow!—Come, prick me Bull-calf till he roar again.

Bull. O lord! good my lord captain.—

Fal. What, dost thou roar before thou art pricked?

Bull. O lord, sir! I am a diseased man.

Fal. What disease hast thou?

Bull. A whoreson cold, sir; a cough, sir; which I caught with ringing in the king's affairs, upon his coronation-day, sir.

Fal. Come, thou shalt go to the wars in a gown; we will have away thy cold; and I will take such order, that thy friends shall ring for thee.—Is here all?

Shal. Here is two more called than your number; you must have but four here, sir;—and so, I pray you, go in with me to dinner.

Fal. Come, I will go drink with you, but I cannot tarry dinner. I am glad to see you, in good troth, master Shallow.

Shal. O, Sir John, do you remember since we lay all night in the windmill in Saint George's Fields?

Fal. No more of that, good master Shallow, no more of that.

Shal. Ha, it was a merry night. And is Jane Night-work alive?

Fal. She lives, master Shallow.

Shal. She never could away with me.

Fal. Never, never: she would always say, she could not abide master Shallow.

Shal. By the mass, I could anger her to the heart. She was then a bona-roba. Doth she hold her own well?

Fal. Old, old, master Shallow.

Shal. Nay, she must be old; she cannot choose but be old; certain, she's old; and had Robin Night-work by old Night-work, before I came to Clement's Inn.

Sil. That's fifty-five year ago.

Shal. Ha, cousin Silence, that thou hadst seen that that this knight and I have seen!—Ha, Sir John, said I well?

Fal. We have heard the chimes at midnight, master Shallow.

Shal. That we have, that we have, that we have; in faith, Sir John, we have; our watch-word was, *Hem, boys!*—Come, let's to dinner; come, let's to dinner:—O, the days that we have seen!—Come, come.

[*Exeunt* FAL. SHAL. *and* SILENCE.

Bull. Good master corporate Bardolph, stand my friend; and here is four Harry ten shillings in French crowns for you. In very truth, sir, I had as lief be hanged, sir, as go: and yet, for mine own part, sir, I do not care; but rather because I am unwilling, and, for mine own part, I have a desire to stay with my friends; else, sir, I did not care, for mine own part, so much.

Bard. Go to; stand aside.

Moul. And, good master corporal captain, for my old dame's sake, stand my friend: she has nobody to do any thing about her, when I am gone: and she is old, and cannot help herself: you shall have forty, sir.

Bard. Go to; stand aside.

Fee. By my troth, I care not:—a man can die but once;—we owe God a death:—I'll ne'er bear a base mind:—an't be my destiny, so; an't be not, so: No man's too good to serve his prince; and, let it go which way it will, he that dies this year, is quit for the next.

Bard. Well said; thou'rt a good fellow.

Fee. 'Faith, I'll bear no base mind.

Re-enter FALSTAFF, *and* Justices.

Fal. Come, sir, which men shall I have?

Shal. Four, of which you please.

Bard. Sir, a word with you:—I have three pound to free Mouldy and Bull-calf.

Fal. Go to; well.

Shal. Come, Sir John, which four will you have?

Fal. Do you choose for me.

Shal. Marry then,—Mouldy, Bull-calf, Feeble, and Shadow.

Fal. Mouldy, and Bull-calf:—For you, Mouldy, stay at home still; you are past service:—and, for your part, Bull-calf,—grow till you come unto it; I will none of you.

Shal. Sir John, Sir John, do not yourself wrong: they are your likeliest men, and I would have you served with the best.

Fal. Will you tell me, master Shallow, how to choose a man? Care I for the limb, the thewes, the stature, bulk, and big assemblance of a man! Give me the spirit, master Shallow.—Here's Wart;—you see what a ragged appearance it is: he shall charge you, and discharge you with the motion of a pewterer's hammer; come off and on, swifter than he that gibbets-on the brewer's bucket. And this same half-fac'd fellow, Shadow,—give me this man; he presents no mark to the enemy; the foe-man may with as great aim level at the edge of a penknife: And, for a retreat,—how swiftly will this Feeble, the woman's tailor, run off? O, give me the spare men, and spare me the great ones.—Put me a caliver into Wart's hand, Bardolph.

Bard. Hold, Wart, traverse: thus, thus, thus.

Fal. Come, manage me your caliver. So:—very well:—go to:—very good:—exceeding good.—O, give me always a little, lean, old, chapped, bald shot.—Well said, i' faith, Wart; thou'rt a good scab: hold, there's a tester for thee.

Shal. He is not his craft's-master, he doth not do it right. I remember at Mile-end green (when I lay at Clement's Inn,—I was then Sir Dagonet in Arthur's show), there was a little quiver fellow, and a' would manage you his piece thus: and 'a would about, and about, and come you in, and come you in: *rah, tah, tah,* would 'a say; *bounce,* would 'a say; and away again would 'a go, and again would 'a come:—I shall never see such a fellow.

Fal. These fellows will do well, master Shallow.—God keep you, master Silence; I will not use many words with you;—Fare you well, gentlemen both: I thank you: I must a dozen mile to-night.—Bardolph, give the soldiers coats.

Shal. Sir John, heaven bless you, and prosper your affairs, and send us peace! As you return, visit my house; let our old acquaintance be renewed: peradventure, I will with you to the court.

Fal. I would you would, master Shallow.

Shal. Go to; I have spoke, at a word. Fare you well. [*Exeunt* SHALLOW *and* SILENCE.

Fal. Fare you well, gentle gentlemen. On, Bardolph; lead the men away. [*Exeunt* BARDOLPH, Recruits, *&c.*] As I return, I will fetch off these justices: I do see the bottom of Justice Shallow. Lord, lord, how subject we old men are to this vice of lying! This same starved justice hath done nothing but prate to me of the wildness of his youth, and the feats he hath done about Turnbull Street; and every third word a lie, duer paid to the hearer than the Turk's tribute. I do remember him at Clement's Inn, like a man made after supper of a cheese-paring: when he was naked, he was, for all the world, like a forked radish, with a head fantastically carved upon it with a knife: he was so forlorn, that his dimensions to any thick sight were invincible: he was the very Genius of famine; yet lecherous as a monkey, and the whores called him—mandrake: he came ever in the rear-ward of the fashion; and sung those tunes to the over-scutched huswives that he heard the carmen whistle, and sware—they were his fancies, or his good-nights. And now is this Vice's dagger become a squire; and talks as familiarly of John of Gaunt, as if he had been sworn brother to him: and I'll be sworn he never saw him but once in the Tilt-yard; and then he burst his head, for crowding among the marshal's men. I saw it; and told John of Gaunt, he beat his own name; for you might have truss'd him, and all his apparel into an eelskin; the case of a treble haut-boy was a mansion for him, a court; and now has he land and beeves. Well; I will be acquainted with him, if I return: and it shall go hard, but I will make him a philosopher's two stones to me: If the young dace be a bait for the old pike, I see no reason, in the law of nature, but I may snap at him. Let time shape, and there an end. [*Exit.*

ACT IV.

SCENE I. *A Forest in* Yorkshire.

Enter the ARCHBISHOP OF YORK, MOWBRAY, HASTINGS, *and Others.*

Arch. What is this forest call'd?
Hast. 'Tis Gaultree Forest, an't shall please your grace.
Arch. Here stand, my lords; and send discoverers forth,
To know the numbers of our enemies.
Hast. We have sent forth already.
Arch. 'Tis well done.
My friends and brethren in these great affairs,
I must acquaint you that I have receiv'd
New-dated letters from Northumberland;
Their cold intent, tenour, and substance, thus:—
Here doth he wish his person, with such powers
As might hold sortance with his quality,
The which he could not levy; whereupon
He is retir'd, to ripe his growing fortunes,
To Scotland: and concludes in hearty prayers,
That your attempts may overlive the hazard,
And fearful meeting of their opposite.
Mowb. Thus do the hopes we have in him touch ground,
And dash themselves to pieces.

Enter a Messenger.

Hast. Now, what news?
Mess. West of this forest, scarcely off a mile,
In goodly form comes on the enemy:
And, by the ground they hide, I judge their number
Upon, or near, the rate of thirty thousand.
Mowb. The just proportion that we gave them out,
Let us sway on, and face them in the field.

Enter WESTMORELAND.

Arch. What well appointed leader fronts us here?
Mowb. I think, it is my lord of Westmoreland.
West. Health, and fair greeting from our general,
The prince, Lord John and duke of Lancaster.
Arch. Say on, my lord of Westmoreland, in peace;
What doth concern your coming?
West. Then, my lord,
Unto your grace do I in chief address
The substance of my speech. If that rebellion
Came like itself, in base and abject routs,
Led on by bloody youth, guarded with rage,
And countenanc'd by boys, and beggary;
I say, if damn'd commotion so appear'd,
In his true, native, and most proper shape,
You, reverend father, and these noble lords,
Had not been here, to dress the ugly form
Of base and bloody insurrection
With your fair honours. You, lord archbishop,—
Whose see is by a civil peace maintain'd;
Whose beard the silver hand of peace hath touch'd;
Whose learning and good letters peace hath tutor'd;
Whose white investments figure innocence,
The dove and very blessed spirit of peace,—
Wherefore do you so ill translate yourself,
Out of the speech of peace, that bears such grace,
Into the harsh and boist'rous tongue of war?
Turning your books to graves, your ink to blood,
Your pens to lances; and your tongue divine
To a loud trumpet, and a point of war?
Arch. Wherefore do I this?—So the question stands.
Briefly to this end:—We are all diseas'd;
And, with our surfeiting, and wanton hours,
Have brought ourselves into a burning fever,
And we must bleed for it: of which disease
Our late king, Richard, being infected, died.

But, my most noble lord of Westmoreland,
I take not on me here as a physician;
Nor do I, as an enemy to peace,
Troop in the throngs of military men:
But, rather show a while like fearful war,
To diet rank minds, sick of happiness;
And purge the obstructions, which begin to stop
Our very veins of life. Hear me more plainly.
I have in equal balance justly weigh'd
What wrongs our arms may do, what wrongs we suffer,
And find our griefs heavier than our offences.
We see which way the stream of time doth run,
And are enforc'd from our most quiet sphere
By the rough torrent of occasion:
And have the summary of all our griefs,
When time shall serve, to show in articles;
Which, long ere this, we offer'd to the king,
And might by no suit gain our audience:
When we are wrong'd, and would unfold our griefs,
We are denied access unto his person
Even by those men that most have done us wrong.
The dangers of the days but newly gone,
(Whose memory is written on the earth
With yet-appearing blood), and the examples
Of every minute's instance (present now),
Have put us in these ill beseeming arms:
Not to break peace, or any branch of it;
But to establish here a peace indeed,
Concurring both in name and quality.
West. When ever yet was your appeal denied?
Wherein have you been galled by the king?
What peer hath been suborn'd to grate on you?
That you should seal this lawless bloody book
Of forg'd rebellion with a seal divine,
And consecrate commotion's bitter edge?
Arch. My brother general, the commonwealth,
To brother born an household cruelty,
I make my quarrel in particular.
West. There is no need of any such redress;
Or, if there were, it not belongs to you.
Mowb. Why not to him, in part; and to us all,
That feel the bruises of the days before;
And suffer the condition of these times
To lay a heavy and unequal hand
Upon our honours?
West. O my good lord Mowbray,
Construe the times to their necessities,
And you shall say indeed,—it is the time,
And not the king, that doth you injuries.
Yet, for your part, it not appears to me,
Either from the king, or in the present time,
That you should have an inch of any ground
To build a grief on: Were you not restor'd
To all the duke of Norfolk's signories,
Your noble and right well remember'd father's?
Mowb. What thing in honour had my father lost,
That need to be reviv'd and breath'd in me?
The king that lov'd him as the state stood then,
Was, force perforce, compell'd to banish him:
And then, when Harry Bolingbroke, and he,—
Being mounted, and both roused in their seats,
Their neighing coursers daring of the spur,
Their armed staves in charge, their beavers down,
Their eyes of fire sparkling through sights of steel,
And the loud trumpet blowing them together;
Then, then, when there was nothing could have staid
My father from the breast of Bolingbroke,
O, when the king did throw his warder down,
His own life hung upon the staff he threw:
Then threw he down himself; and all their lives,
That by indictment, and by dint of sword,
Have since miscarried unto Bolingbroke.
West. You speak, Lord Mowbray, now you know not what:
The earl of Hereford was reputed then
In England the most valiant gentleman;
Who knows, on whom fortune would then have smil'd?
But, if your father had been victor there,
He ne'er had borne it out of Coventry:
For all the country in a general voice,
Cried hate upon him; and all their prayers, and love,
Were set on Hereford, whom they doted on,
And bless'd, and grac'd indeed, more than the king.
But this is mere digression from my purpose.—
Here come I from our princely general,
To know your griefs; to tell you from his grace,
That he will give you audience: and wherein
It shall appear that your demands are just,
You shall enjoy them; every thing set off,
That might so much as think you enemies.
Mowb. But he hath forc'd us to compel this offer;
And it proceeds from policy, not love.
West. Mowbray, you overween to take it so;
This offer comes from mercy, not from fear;
For, lo! within a ken, our army lies;
Upon mine honour, all too confident
To give admittance to a thought of fear.
Our battle is more full of names than yours,
Our men more perfect in the use of arms,
Our armour all as strong, our cause the best;
Then reason wills, our hearts should be as good:—
Say you not then, our offer is compell'd.
Mowb. Well, by my will, we shall admit no parley.
West. That argues but the shame of your offence:
A rotten case abides no handling.
Hast. Hath the Prince John a full commission,
In very ample virtue of his father,
To hear, and absolutely to determine
Of what conditions we shall stand upon?
West. That is intended in the general's name:
I muse, you make so slight a question.
Arch. Then take, my lord of Westmoreland, this schedule;
For this contains our general grievances;
Each several article herein redress'd;
All members of our cause, both here and hence,
That are insinew'd to this action,
Acquitted by a true substantial form;
And present execution of our wills
To us, and to our purposes, consign'd;
We come within our awful banks again,
And knit our powers to the arm of peace.
West. This will I show the general. Please you, lords,
In sight of both our battles we may meet:
And either end in peace, which heaven so frame!
Or to the place of difference call the swords
Which must decide it.
Arch. My lord, we will do so.
[*Exit* WEST.
Mowb. There is a thing within my bosom, tells me,
That no conditions of our peace can stand.
Hast. Fear you not that: if we can make our peace
Upon such large terms, and so absolute,
As our conditions shall consist upon,
Our peace shall stand as firm as rocky mountains.
Mowb. Ay, but our valuation shall be such,
That every slight and false-derived cause,
Yea, every idle, nice, and wanton reason,
Shall, to the king, taste of this action:
That, were our royal faiths martyrs in love,
We shall be winnow'd with so rough a wind,
That even our corn shall seem as light as chaff,
And good from bad find no partition.
Arch. No, no, my lord; Note this,—the king is weary
Of dainty and such picking grievances:
For he hath found,—to end one doubt by death

Revives two greater in the heirs of life.
And therefore will he wipe his tables clean;
And keep no tell-tale to his memory,
That may repeat and history his loss
To new remembrance: For full well he knows,
He cannot so precisely weed this land,
As his misdoubts present occasion:
His foes are so enrooted with his friends,
That, plucking to unfix an enemy,
He doth unfasten so, and shake a friend.
So that this land, like an offensive wife,
That hath enrag'd him on to offer strokes;
As he is striking, holds his infant up,
And hangs resolv'd correction in the arm
That was uprear'd to execution.

Hast. Besides, the king hath wasted all his rods
On late offenders, that he now doth lack
The very instruments of chastisement:
So that his power, like to a fangless lion,
May offer, but not hold.

Arch. 'Tis very true;—
And therefore be assur'd, my good lord marshal,
If we do now make our atonement well,
Our peace will, like a broken limb united,
Grow stronger for the breaking.

Mowb. Be it so.
Here is return'd my lord of Westmoreland.

Re-enter WESTMORELAND.

West. The prince is here at hand: Pleaseth your lordship,
To meet his grace just distance 'tween our armies?

Mowb. Your grace of York, in God's name then set forward.

Arch. Before, and greet his grace: my lord, we come. [*Exeunt.*

SCENE II. *Another Part of the Forest.*

Enter, from one side, MOWBRAY, *the* Archbishop, HASTINGS, *and Others: from the other side,* PRINCE JOHN *of* Lancaster, WESTMORELAND, Officers, *and* Attendants.

P. John. You are well encounter'd here, my cousin Mowbray:—
Good day to you, gentle lord archbishop;—
And so to you, Lord Hastings,—and to all.—
My lord of York, it better show'd with you,
When that your flock, assembled by the bell,
Encircled you, to hear with reverence
Your exposition on the holy text;
Than now to see you here an iron man,
Cheering a rout of rebels with your drum,
Turning the word to sword, and life to death.
That man, that sits within a monarch's heart,
And ripens in the sunshine of his favour,
Would he abuse the countenance of the king,
Alack, what mischiefs might be set abroach,
In shadow of such greatness! With you, lord bishop,
It is even so:—Who hath not heard it spoken,
How deep you were within the books of God?
To us, the speaker in his parliament;
To us, the imagin'd voice of God himself;
The very opener, and intelligencer,
Between the grace, the sanctities of heaven,
And our dull workings: O, who shall believe,
But you misuse the reverence of your place;
Employ the countenance and grace of heaven,
As a false favourite doth his prince's name,
In deeds dishonourable? You have taken up,
Under the counterfeited zeal of God,
The subjects of his substitute, my father;
And, both against the peace of heaven and him,
Have here up-swarm'd them.

Arch. Good my lord of Lancaster,
I am not here against your father's peace:
But, as I told my lord of Westmoreland,
The time misorder'd doth, in common sense,
Crowd us, and crush us, to this monstrous form,
To hold our safety up. I sent your grace
The parcels and particulars of our grief;
The which hath been with scorn shov'd from the court,
Whereon this Hydra son of war is born:
Whose dangerous eyes may well be charm'd asleep,
With grant of our most just and right desires:
And true obedience of this madness cur'd,
Stoop tamely to the foot of majesty.

Mowb. If not, we ready are to try our fortunes
To the last man.

Hast. And though we here fall down,
We have supplies to second our attempt;
If they miscarry, theirs shall second them:
And so, success of mischief shall be born;
And heir from heir shall hold this quarrel up,
Whiles England shall have generation.

P. John. You are too shallow, Hastings, much too shallow,
To sound the bottom of the after-times.

West. Pleaseth your grace, to answer them directly,
How far-forth you do like their articles?

P. John. I like them all, and do allow them well:
And swear here by the honour of my blood,
My father's purposes have been mistook;
And some about him have too lavishly
Wrested his meaning, and authority.—
My lord, these griefs shall be with speed redress'd;
Upon my soul, they shall. If this may please you,
Discharge your powers unto their several counties,
As we will ours: And here, between the armies,
Let's drink together friendly, and embrace;
That all their eyes may bear those tokens home,
Of our restored love, and amity.

Arch. I take your princely word for these redresses.

P. John. I give it you, and will maintain my word:
And thereupon I drink unto your grace.

Hast. Go, captain [*To an* Officer], and deliver to the army
This news of peace; let them have pay, and part:
I know, it will well please them; Hie thee, captain. [*Exit* Officer.

Arch. To you, my noble lord of Westmoreland.

West. I pledge your grace: And, if you knew what pains
I have bestow'd, to breed this present peace,
You would drink freely: but my love to you
Shall show itself more openly hereafter.

Arch. I do not doubt you.

West. I am glad of it.—
Health to my lord, and gentle cousin, Mowbray.

Mowb. You wish me health in very happy season;
For I am, on the sudden, something ill.

Arch. Against ill chances, men are ever merry;
But heaviness foreruns the good event.

West. Therefore be merry, coz: since sudden sorrow
Serves to say thus,—Some good thing comes to-morrow.

Arch. Believe me, I am passing light in spirit.

Mowb. So much the worse, if your own rule be true. [*Shouts within.*

P. John. The word of peace is render'd; Hark, how they shout!

Mowb. This had been cheerful, after victory.

Arch. A peace is of the nature of a conquest;
For then both parties nobly are subdued,
And neither party loser.

P. John. Go, my lord,
And let our army be discharged too.— [*Exit* WESTMORELAND.
And, good my lord, so please you, let our trains
March by us; that we may peruse the men
We should have cop'd withal.

Arch. Go, good Lord Hastings,
And, ere they be dismiss'd, let them march by. [*Exit* HASTINGS

P. John. I trust, my lords, we shall lie to-night together.—

Re-enter WESTMORELAND.

Now, cousin, wherefore stands our army still?

West. The leaders, having charge from you to stand,
Will not go off until they hear you speak.

P. John. They know their duties.

Re-enter HASTINGS.

Hast. My lord, our army is dispers'd already:
Like youthful steers unyok'd, they take their courses
East, west, north, south; or, like a school broke up,
Each hurries toward his home, and sporting-place.

West. Good tidings, my Lord Hastings; for the which
I do arrest thee, traitor, of high treason:—
And you, lord archbishop,—and you, Lord Mowbray,
Of capital treason I attach you both.

Mowb. Is this proceeding just and honourable?

West. Is your assembly so?

Arch. Will you thus break your faith?

P. John. I pawn'd thee none:
I promis'd you redress of these same grievances,
Whereof you did complain; which by mine honour,
I will perform with a most christian care.
But, for you, rebels,—look to taste the due
Meet for rebellion, and such acts as yours.
Most shallowly did you these arms commence,
Fondly brought here, and foolishly sent hence.—
Strike up our drums, pursue the scatter'd stray;
Heaven, and not we, hath safely fought to-day.—
Some guard these traitors to the block of death;
Treason's true bed, and yielder up of breath.
[*Exeunt.*

SCENE III. *Another Part of the Forest.*

Alarums: Excursions. Enter FALSTAFF *and* COLEVILE, *meeting.*

Fal. What's your name, sir? of what condition are you: and of what place, I pray?

Cole. I am a knight, sir; and my name is—Colevile of the dale.

Fal. Well then, Colevile is your name; a knight is your degree; and your place, the dale: Colevile shall still be your name; a traitor your degree; and the dungeon your place,—a place deep enough: so shall you still be Colevile of the dale.

Cole. Are not you Sir John Falstaff?

Fal. As good a man, as he, sir, whoe'er I am. Do ye yield, sir? or shall I sweat for you? If I do sweat, they are drops of thy lovers, and they weep for thy death: therefore rouse up fear and trembling, and do observance to my mercy.

Cole. I think, you are Sir John Falstaff; and in that thought, yield me.

Fal. I have a whole school of tongues in this belly of mine; and not a tongue of them all speaks any other word but my name. An I had but a belly of any indifferency, I were simply the most active fellow in Europe: My womb, my womb, my womb undoes me.—Here comes our general.

Enter PRINCE JOHN *of* Lancaster, WESTMORELAND, *and Others.*

P. John. The heat is past, follow no further now;—
Call in the powers, good cousin Westmoreland.—
[*Exit* WEST.
Now, Falstaff, where have you been all this while?
When every thing is ended, then you come:
These tardy tricks of yours will, on my life,
One time or other break some gallows' back.

Fal. I would be sorry, my lord, but it should be thus; I never knew yet, but rebuke and check was the reward of valour. Do you think me a swallow, an arrow, or a bullet? have I, in my poor and old motion, the expedition of thought? I have speeded hither with the very extremest inch of possibility; I have foundered nine score and odd posts: and here, travel-tainted as I am, have, in my pure and immaculate valour, taken Sir John Colevile of the dale, a most furious knight, and valorous enemy: But what of that? he saw me, and yielded; that I may justly say with the hook-nosed fellow of Rome,——I came, saw, and overcame.

P. John. It was more of his courtesy than your deserving.

Fal. I know not; here he is, and here I yield him: and I beseech your grace, let it be booked with the rest of this day's deeds; or, by the Lord, I will have it in a particular ballad else, with mine own picture on the top of it, Colevile kissing my foot: To the which course, if I be enforced, if you do not all show like gilt two-pences to me; and I, in the clear sky of fame, o'ershine you as much as the full moon doth the cinders of the element, which show like pins' heads to her; believe not the word of the noble: Therefore let me have right, and let desert mount.

P. John. Thine's too heavy to mount.

Fal. Let it shine then.

P. John. Thine's too thick to shine.

Fal. Let it do something, my good lord, that may do me good, and call it what you will.

P. John. Is thy name Colevile?

Cole. It is, my lord,

P. John. A famous rebel art thou, Colevile.

Fal. And a famous true subject took him.

Cole. I am, my lord, but as my betters are,
That led me hither: had they been rul'd by me,
You should have won them dearer than you have.

Fal. I know not how they sold themselves: but thou, like a kind fellow, gavest thyself away; and I thank thee for thee.

Re-enter WESTMORELAND.

P. John. Now, have you left pursuit?

West. Retreat is made, and execution stay'd.

P. John. Send Colevile, with his confederates,
To York, to present execution:—
Blunt, lead him hence; and see you guard him sure. [*Exeunt some with* COLEVILE.
And now despatch we toward the court, my lords;
I hear, the king my father is sore sick:
Our news shall go before us to his majesty,—
Which, cousin, you shall bear,—to comfort him;
And we with sober speed will follow you.

Fal. My lord, I beseech you, give me leave to go through Glostershire: and, when you come to court, stand my good lord, 'pray, in your good report.

P. John. Fare you well, Falstaff: I, in my condition,
Shall better speak of you than you deserve.
[*Exit.*

Fal. I would you had but the wit; 'twere better than your dukedom.—Good faith, this same young sober-blooded boy doth not love me; nor a man cannot make him laugh;—but that's no marvel, he drinks no wine. There's never any of these demure boys come to any proof: for thin drink doth so over-cool their blood, and making many fish-meals, that they fall into a kind of male green-sickness; and then, when they marry, they get wenches; they are generally fools and cowards;—which some of us should be too, but for inflammation. A good sherris sack hath a two-fold operation in it. It ascends me into the brain; dries me there all the foolish, and dull, and crudy vapours which environ it: makes it apprehensive, quick, forgetive, full of nimble, fiery, and delectable shapes; which delivered o'er to the voice (the tongue), which is the birth, becomes excellent wit. The second property of your excellent sherris is,—the warming of the blood; which, before cold and settled, left the liver white and pale, which is the badge of pusillanimity and cowardice: but the sherris warms it, and makes it course from the inwards to the parts extreme. It illumineth the face: which, as a beacon, gives warning to all the rest of this little kingdom, man, to arm: and then the vital commoners, and inland petty spirits, muster me all to their captain, the heart; who, great, and puffed up with this retinue, doth any deed of courage; and this valour comes of sherris: So that skill in the weapon is nothing, without sack; for that sets it a-work; and learning, a mere hoard of gold kept by a devil; till sack commences it, and sets it in act and use. Hereof comes it, that Prince Henry is valiant: for the cold blood he did naturally inherit of his father, he hath, like lean, steril, and bare land, manured, husbanded, and tilled, with excellent endeavour of drinking good, and good store of fertile sherris; that he is become very hot and valiant. If I had a thousand sons, the first human principle I would teach them, should be,—to forswear thin potations, and addict themselves to sack.

Enter BARDOLPH.

How now, Bardolph?

Bard. The army is discharged all, and gone.

Fal. Let them go. I'll through Glostershire; and there will I visit master Robert Shallow, esquire: I have him already tempering between my finger and my thumb, and shortly will I seal with him. Come away. [*Exeunt.*

SCENE IV. Westminster. *A Room in the Palace.*

Enter KING HENRY, CLARENCE, PRINCE HUMPHREY, WARWICK, *and Others.*

K. Hen. Now, lords, if heaven doth give successful end
To this debate that bleedeth at our doors,
We will our youth lead on to higher fields,
And draw no swords but what are sanctified.
Our navy is addressed, our power collected,
Our substitutes in absence well invested,
And every thing lies level to our wish:
Only, we want a little personal strength;
And pause us, till these rebels, now afoot,
Come underneath the yoke of government.

War. Both which, we doubt not but your majesty
Shall soon enjoy.

K. Hen. Humphrey, my son of Gloster,
Where is the prince your brother?

P. Humph. I think, he's gone to hunt, my lord, at Windsor.

K. Hen. And how accompanied?

P. Humph. I do not know, my lord.

K. Hen. Is not his brother, Thomas of Clarence, with him,

P. Humph. No, my good lord; he is in presence here.

Cla. What would my lord and father?

K. Hen. Nothing but well to thee, Thomas of Clarence.
How chance, thou art not with the prince thy brother?
He loves thee, and thou dost neglect him, Thomas;
Thou hast a better place in his affection,
Than all thy brothers: cherish it, my boy;
And noble offices thou may'st effect
Of mediation, after I am dead,
Between his greatness and thy other brethren:—
Therefore, omit him not: blunt not his love:
Nor lose the good advantage of his grace,
By seeming cold or careless of his will.
For he is gracious, if he be observ'd;
He hath a tear for pity, and a hand
Open as day for melting charity:
Yet notwithstanding, being incens'd, he's flint;
As humorous as winter, and as sudden
As flaws congealed in the spring of day.
His temper, therefore, must be well observ'd:
Chide him for faults, and do it reverently,
When you perceive his blood inclin'd to mirth:
But, being moody, give him line and scope;
Till that his passions, like a whale on ground,
Confound themselves with working. Learn this, Thomas,
And thou shalt prove a shelter to thy friends;
A hoop of gold, to bind thy brothers in;
That the united vessel of their blood,
Mingled with venom of suggestion,
(As, force perforce, the age will pour it in),
Shall never leak, though it do work as strong
As aconitum, or rash gunpowder.

Cla. I shall observe him with all care and love.

K. Hen. Why art thou not at Windsor with him, Thomas?

Cla. He is not there to-day; he dines in London.

K. Hen. And how accompanied? canst thou tell that?

Cla. With Poins, and other his continual followers.

K. Hen. Most subject is the fattest soil to weeds;
And he, the noble image of my youth,
Is overspread with them: Therefore my grief
Stretches itself beyond the hour of death:
The blood weeps from my heart, when I do shape,
In forms imaginary, the unguided days,
And rotten times, that you shall look upon,
When I am sleeping with my ancestors.
For when his headstrong riot hath no curb,
When rage and hot blood are his counsellors,
When means and lavish manners meet together,
O, with what wings shall his affections fly
Towards fronting peril and oppos'd decay!

War. My gracious lord, you look beyond him quite:
The prince but studies his companions,
Like a strange tongue: wherein, to gain the language,
'Tis needful, that the most immodest word
Be look'd upon, and learn'd: which once attain'd,
Your highness knows, comes to no further use,
But to be known, and hated. So, like gross terms,
The prince will, in the perfectness of time,
Cast off his followers: and their memory
Shall as a pattern or a measure live,
By which his grace must mete the lives of others;
Turning past evils to advantages.

K. Hen. 'Tis seldom—when the bee doth leave her comb
In the dead carrion.—Who's here? Westmoreland?

Enter WESTMORELAND.

West. Health to my sovereign? and new happiness
Added to that that I am to deliver!
Prince John, your son, doth kiss your grace's hand:
Mowbray, the bishop Scroop, Hastings, and all,
Are brought to the correction of your law;
There is not now a rebel's sword unsheath'd,
But peace puts forth her olive every where.
The manner how this action hath been borne,
Here at more leisure may your highness read;
With every course, in his particular.

K. Hen. O Westmoreland, thou art a summer bird,
Which ever in the haunch of winter sings
The lifting up of day. Look! here's more news.

Enter HARCOURT.

Har. From enemies heaven keep your majesty;
And, when they stand against you, may they fall
As those that I am come to tell you of!

The Earl Northumberland, and the Lord Bardolph,
With a great power of English, and of Scots,
Are by the sheriff of Yorkshire overthrown:
The manner and true order of the fight,
This packet, please it you, contains at large.

K. Hen. And wherefore should these good news make me sick?
Will fortune never come with both hands full,
But write her fair words still in foulest letters?
She either gives a stomach, and no food,—
Such are the poor, in health; or else a feast,
And takes away the stomach,—such are the rich,
That have abundance, and enjoy it not.
I should rejoice now at this happy news;
And now my sight fails, and my brain is giddy:—
O me! come near me, now I am much ill. [*Swoons.*

P. Humph. Comfort, your majesty!

Cla. O my royal father!

West. My sovereign lord, cheer up yourself, look up!

War. Be patient, princes; you do know, these fits
Are with his highness very ordinary.
Stand from him, give him air; he'll straight be well.

Cla. No, no; he cannot long hold out these pangs;
The incessant care and labour of his mind
Hath wrought the mure, that should confine it in,
So thin, that life looks through, and will break out.

P. Humph. The people fear me; for they do observe
Unfather'd heirs, and loathly birds of nature:
The seasons change their manners, as the year
Had found some months asleep, and leap'd them over.

Cla. The river hath thrice flow'd, no ebb between:
And the old folk, time's doting chronicles,
Say, it did so, a little time before
That our great grandsire, Edward, sick'd and died.

War. Speak lower, princes, for the king recovers.

P. Humph. This apoplex will, certain, be his end.

K. Hen. I pray you, take me up, and bear me hence
Into some other chamber: softly, 'pray.

[*They convey the* King *into an inner part of the room, and place him on a Bed.*

Let there be no noise made, my gentle friends;
Unless some dull and favourable hand
Will whisper musick to my weary spirit.

War. Call for the music in the other room.

K. Hen. Set me the crown upon the pillow here.

Cla. His eye is hollow, and he changes much.

War. Less noise, less noise.

Enter PRINCE HENRY.

P. Hen. Who saw the duke of Clarence?

Cla. I am here, brother, full of heaviness.

P. Hen. How now! rain within doors, and none abroad!
How doth the king?

P. Humph. Exceeding ill.

P. Hen. Heard he the good news yet?
Tell it him.

P. Humph. He alter'd much upon the hearing it.

P. Hen. If he be sick
With joy, he will recover without physick.

War. Not so much noise, my lords;—sweet prince, speak low;
The king your father is dispos'd to sleep.

Cla. Let us withdraw into the other room.

War. Will't please your grace to go along with us?

P. Hen. No; I will sit and watch here by the king. [*Exeunt all but* P. HENRY.
Why doth the crown lie there upon his pillow,
Being so troublesome a bedfellow?
O polish'd perturbation! golden care!
That keeps the ports of slumber open wide
To many a watchful night!—sleep with it now!
Yet not so sound, and half so deeply sweet,
As he, whose brow, with homely biggin bound,
Snores out the watch of night. O majesty!
When thou dost pinch thy bearer, thou dost sit
Like a rich armour worn in heat of day,
That scalds with safety. By his gates of breath
There lies a downy feather, which stirs not:
Did he suspire, that light and weightless down
Perforce must move.—My gracious lord!—my father!—
This sleep is sound indeed; this is a sleep,
That from this golden rigol hath divorc'd
So many English kings. Thy due, from me,
Is tears, and heavy sorrows of the blood;
Which nature, love, and filial tenderness,
Shall, O dear father, pay thee plenteously:
My due, from thee, is this imperial crown;
Which, as immediate from thy place and blood,
Derives itself to me. Lo, here it sits,— [*Putting it on his head.*
Which heaven shall guard: and put the world's whole strength
Into one giant arm, it shall not force
This lineal honour from me: This from thee
Will I to mine leave, as 'tis left to me. [*Exit.*

K. Hen. Warwick! Gloster! Clarence!

Re-enter WARWICK, *and the rest.*

Cla. Doth the king call?

War. What would your majesty? How fares your grace?

K. Hen. Why did you leave me here alone, my lords?

Cla. We left the prince my brother here, my liege,
Who undertook to sit and watch by you.

K. Hen. The prince of Wales? Where is he? let me see him:
He is not here.

War. This door is open; he is gone this way.

P. Humph. He came not through the chamber where we stay'd.

K. Hen. Where is the crown? who took it from my pillow?

War. When we withdrew, my liege, we left it here.

K. Hen. The prince hath ta'en it hence:—go, seek him out;
Is he so hasty, that he doth suppose
My sleep my death?
Find him, my lord of Warwick; chide him hither. [*Exit* WARWICK.
This part of his conjoins with my disease,
And helps to end me.—See, sons, what things you are!
How quickly nature falls into revolt,
When gold becomes her object!
For this the foolish over-careful fathers
Have broke their sleep with thoughts, their brains with care,
Their bones with industry;
For this they have engrossed and pil'd up
The canker'd heaps of strange-achieved gold;
For this they have been thoughtful to invest
Their sons with arts, and martial exercises:
When, like the bee, tolling from every flower
The virtuous sweets;
Our thighs pack'd with wax, our mouths with honey,
We bring it to the hive; and, like the bees,
Are murder'd for our pains. This bitter taste
Yield his engrossments to the ending father.—

Re-enter WARWICK.

Now, where is he that will not stay so long
Till his friend sickness hath determin'd me?

War. My lord, I found the prince in the next room,
Washing with kindly tears his gentle cheeks;
With such a deep demeanour in great sorrow,
That tyranny, which never quaff'd but blood,
Would, by beholding him, have wash'd his knife
With gentle eye-drops. He is coming hither.
K. Hen. But wherefore did he take away the crown?

Re-enter PRINCE HENRY.

Lo, where he comes.—Come hither to me, Harry:—
Depart the chamber, leave us here alone.
[*Exeunt* CLARENCE, PRINCE HUMPHREY, Lords, *&c.*
P. Hen. I never thought to hear you speak again.
K. Hen. Thy wish was father, Harry, to that thought:
I stay too long by thee, I weary thee.
Dost thou so hunger for my empty chair,
That thou wilt needs invest thee with mine honours
Before thy hour be ripe? O foolish youth!
Thou seek'st the greatness that will overwhelm thee.
Stay but a little; for my cloud of dignity
Is held from falling with so weak a wind,
That it will quickly drop: my day is dim.
Thou hast stol'n that, which after some few hours,
Were thine without offence; and, at my death,
Thou hast seal'd up my expectation:
Thy life did manifest, thou lov'dst me not,
And thou wilt have me die assured of it.
Thou hid'st a thousand daggers in thy thoughts:
Which thou hast wetted on thy stony heart,
To stab at half an hour of my life.
What! canst thou not forbear me half an hour?
Then get thee gone, and dig my grave thyself;
And bid the merry bells ring to thine ear,
That thou art crowned, not that I am dead.
Let all the tears that should bedew my hearse,
Be drops of balm, to sanctify thy head:
Only compound me with forgotten dust;
Give that, which gave thee life, unto the worms.
Pluck down my officers, break my decrees;
For now a time is come to mock at form,
Harry the fifth is crown'd;—Up, vanity!
Down, royal state! all you sage counsellors, hence!
And to the English court assemble now,
From every region, apes of idleness!
Now, neighbour confines, purge you of your scum:
Have you a ruffian, that will swear, drink, dance,
Revel the night: rob, murder, and commit
The oldest sins the newest kind of ways?
Be happy, he will trouble you no more:
England shall double gild his treble guilt;
England shall give him office, honour, might:
For the fifth Harry from curb'd licence plucks
The muzzle of restraint, and the wild dog
Shall flesh his tooth in every innocent.
O my poor kingdom, sick with civil blows!
When that my care could not withhold thy riots,
What wilt thou do, when riot is thy care?
O, thou wilt be a wilderness again,
Peopled with wolves, thy old inhabitants!
P. Hen. O, pardon me, my liege! but for my tears, [*Kneeling.*
The moist impediments unto my speech,
I had forestall'd this dear and deep rebuke,
Ere you with grief had spoke, and I had heard
The course of it so far. There is your crown;
And he that wears the crown immortally,
Long guard it yours! If I affect it more,
Than as your honour, and as your renown,
Let me no more from this obedience rise,
Which my most true and inward-duteous spirit
Teacheth this prostrate and exterior bending!
Heaven witness with me, when I here came in,
And found no course of breath within your majesty,
How cold it struck my heart! if I do feign,
O, let me in my present wildness die;
And never live to show the incredulous world
The noble change that I have purposed!
Coming to look on you, thinking you dead
(And dead almost, my liege, to think you were),
I spake unto the crown as having sense,
And thus upbraided it: *The care on thee depending,*
Hath fed upon the body of my father;
Therefore, thou, best of gold, art worst of gold.
Other, less fine in carat, is more precious,
Preserving life in med'cine potable:
But thou, most fine, most honour'd, most renown'd,
Hast eat thy bearer up. Thus, my most royal liege,
Accusing it, I put it on my head;
To try with it,—as with an enemy,
That had before my face murder'd my father,—
The quarrel of a true inheritor.
But if it did infect my blood with joy,
Or swell my thoughts to any strain of pride;
If any rebel or vain spirit of mine
Did, with the least affection of a welcome,
Give entertainment to the might of it,
Let God for ever keep it from my head!
And make me as the poorest vassal is,
That doth with awe and terror kneel to it!
K. Hen. O my son!
Heaven put it in thy mind, to take it hence,
That thou might'st win the more thy father's love,
Pleading so wisely in excuse of it.
Come hither, Harry, sit thou by my bed;
And hear, I think, the very latest counsel
That ever I shall breathe. Heaven knows, my son,
By what by-paths, and indirect crook'd ways,
I met this crown; and I myself know well,
How troublesome it sat upon my head:
To thee it shall descend with better quiet,
Better opinion, better confirmation;
For all the soil of the achievement goes
With me into the earth. It seem'd in me,
But as an honour snatch'd with boisterous hand;
And I had many living, to upbraid
My gain of it by their assistances;
Which daily grew to quarrel and to bloodshed,
Wounding supposed peace: all these bold fears,
Thou seest with peril I have answer'd:
For all my reign hath been but as a scene
Acting that argument; and now my death
Changes the mode: for what in me was purchas'd,
Falls upon thee in a more fairer sort;
So thou the garland wear'st successively.
Yet, though thou stand'st more sure than I could do,
Thou art not firm enough, since griefs are green:
And all thy friends, which thou must make thy friends,
Have but their stings and teeth newly ta'en out;
By whose fell working I was first advanc'd,
And by whose power I well might lodge a fear
To be again displac'd: which to avoid,
I cut them off; and had a purpose now
To lead out many to the Holy Land;
Lest rest, and lying still, might make them look
Too near unto my state. Therefore, my Harry,
Be it thy course, to busy giddy minds
With foreign quarrels; that action, hence borne out,
May waste the memory of the former days.
More would I, but my lungs are wasted so,
That strength of speech is utterly denied me.
How I came by the crown, O God, forgive!
And grant it may with thee in true peace live!
P. Hen. My gracious liege,
You won it, wore it, kept it, gave it me;
Then plain, and right, must my possession be:
Which I, with more than with a common pain,
'Gainst all the world will rightfully maintain.

Enter PRINCE JOHN *of* Lancaster, WARWICK, Lords, *and Others.*

K. Hen. Look, look, here comes my John of Lancaster.

P. John. Health, peace, and happiness, to my royal father!

K. Hen. Thou bring'st me happiness, and peace, son John;
But health, alack, with youthful wings is flown
From this bare, wither'd trunk: upon thy sight,
My worldly business makes a period.——
Where is my lord of Warwick?

P. Hen. My lord of Warwick!

K. Hen. Doth any name particular belong
Unto the lodging where I first did swoon?

War. 'Tis call'd Jerusalem, my noble lord.

K. Hen. Laud be to God!—even there my life must end.
It hath been prophesied to me many years,
I should not die but in Jerusalem;
Which vainly I suppos'd, the Holy Land:—
But, bear me to that chamber; there I'll lie;
In that Jerusalem shall Harry die. [*Exeunt.*

ACT V.

SCENE I. Glostershire. *A Hall in* Shallow's *House.*

Enter SHALLOW, FALSTAFF, BARDOLPH, *and* Page.

Shal. By cock and pye, sir, you shall not away to-night.——What, Davy, I say!

Fal. You must excuse me, master Robert Shallow.

Shal. I will not excuse you; you shall not be excused: excuses shall not be admitted; there is no excuse shall serve; you shall not be excused.—Why, Davy!

Enter DAVY.

Davy. Here, sir.

Shal. Davy, Davy, Davy,—let me see, Davy; let me see:—yea, marry, William cook, bid him come hither.—Sir John, you shall not be excused.

Davy. Marry, sir, thus;—those precepts cannot be served: and, again, sir,—Shall we sow the headland with wheat?

Shal. With red wheat, Davy. But for William cook:——Are there no young pigeons?

Davy. Yes, sir.——Here is now the smith's note, for shoeing, and plough-irons.

Shal. Let it be cast and paid:—Sir John, you shall not be excused.

Davy. Now, sir, a new link to the bucket must needs be had;—And, sir, do you mean to stop any of William's wages, about the sack he lost the other day at Hinckley fair?

Shal. He shall answer it:——Some pigeons, Davy; a couple of short-legged hens; a joint of mutton; and any pretty little tiny kickshaws, tell William cook.

Davy. Doth the man of war stay all night, sir?

Shal. Yes, Davy. I will use him well; A friend i' the court is better than a penny in purse. Use his men well, Davy; for they are arrant knaves, and will backbite.

Davy. No worse than they are back-bitten, sir; for they have marvellous foul linen.

Shal. Well conceited, Davy. About thy business, Davy.

Davy. I beseech you, sir, to countenance William Visor of Wincot against Clement Perkes of the hill.

Shal. There are many complaints, Davy, against that Visor; that Visor is an arrant knave on my knowledge.

Davy. I grant your worship, that he is a knave, sir: but yet, God forbid, sir, but a knave should have some countenance at his friend's request. An honest man, sir, is able to speak for himself, when a knave is not. I have served your worship truly, sir, this eight years; and if I cannot once or twice in a quarter bear out a knave against an honest man, I have but a very little credit with your worship. The knave is mine honest friend, sir; therefore, I beseech your worship, let him be countenanced.

Shal. Go to; I say, he shall have no wrong. Look about, Davy. [*Exit* DAVY.] Where are you, Sir John? Come, off with your boots.—Give me your hand, master Bardolph.

Bard. I am glad to see your worship.

Shal. I thank thee, with all my heart, kind master Bardolph:—and welcome, my tall fellow. [*To the* Page.] Come, Sir John. [*Exit* SHALLOW.

Fal. I'll follow you, good master Robert Shallow. Bardolph, look to our horses. [*Exeunt* BARDOLPH *and* Page.] If I were sawed into quantities, I should make four dozen of such bearded hermit's-staves as master Shallow. It is a wonderful thing, to see the semblable coherence of his men's spirits and his: They, by observing him, do bear themselves like foolish justices; he, by conversing with them, is turned into a justicelike serving-man; their spirits are so married in conjunction with the participation of society, that they flock together in consent, like so many wild geese. If I had a suit to master Shallow, I would humour his men, with the imputation of being near their master: if to his men, I would curry with master Shallow, that no man could better command his servants. It is certain, that either wise bearing, or ignorant carriage, is caught, as men take diseases, one of another: therefore, let men take heed of their company. I will devise matter enough out of this Shallow, to keep Prince Harry in continual laughter, the wearing-out of six fashions (which is four terns, or two actions), and he shall laugh without *intervallums.* O, it is much, that a lie, with a slight oath, and a jest, with a sad brow, will do with a fellow that never had the ache in his shoulders! O, you shall see him laugh, till his face be like a wet cloak ill laid up.

Shal. [*Within.*] Sir John!

Fal. I come, master Shallow; I come, master Shallow. [*Exit* FALSTAFF.

SCENE II. Westminster. *A Room in the Palace.*

Enter WARWICK, *and the* Lord Chief Justice.

War. How now, my lord chief Justice? whither away?

Ch. Just. How doth the king?

War. Exceeding well; his cares are now all ended.

Ch. Just. I hope, not dead.

War. He's walk'd the way of nature;
And, to our purposes, he lives no more.

Ch. Just. I would, his majesty had call'd me with him:
The service that I truly did his life,
Hath left me open to all injuries.

War. Indeed, I think, the young king loves you not.

Ch. Just. I know, he doth not; and do arm myself,
To welcome the condition of the time;
Which cannot look more hideously upon me
Than I have drawn it in my fantasy.

Enter PRINCE JOHN, PRINCE HUMPHREY, CLARENCE, WESTMORELAND, *and Others.*

War. Here come the heavy issue of dead Harry:
O, that the living Harry had the temper
Of him, the worst of these three gentlemen!
How many nobles then should hold their places,
That must strike sail to spirits of vile sort!

Ch. Just. Alas! I fear, all will be overturn'd.

P. John. Good morrow, cousin Warwick.

P. Humph. Cla. Good morrow, cousin.

P. John. We meet like men that had forgot to speak.

War. We do remember; but our argument
Is all too heavy to admit much talk.
P. John. Well, peace be with him that hath made us heavy!
Ch. Just. Peace be with us, lest we be heavier!
P. Humph. O, good my lord, you have lost a friend, indeed:
And I dare swear, you borrow not that face
Of seeming sorrow; it is, sure, your own.
P. John. Though no man be assur'd what grace to find,
You stand in coldest expectation:
I am the sorrier; 'would, 'twere otherwise.
Cla. Well, you must now speak Sir John Falstaff fair;
Which swims against your stream of quality.
Ch. Just. Sweet princes, what I did, I did in honour,
Led by the impartial conduct of my soul;
And never shall you see, that I will beg
A ragged and forestall'd remission.—
If truth and upright innocency fail me,
I'll to the king my master that is dead,
And tell him who hath sent me after him.
War. Here comes the prince.

Enter KING HENRY V.

Ch. Just. Good morrow; and heaven save your majesty!
King. This new and gorgeous garment, majesty,
Sits not so easy on me as you think.—
Brothers, you mix your sadness with some fear;
This is the English, not the Turkish, court;
Not Amurath an Amurath succeeds,
But Harry Harry: Yet be sad, good brothers,
For, to speak truth, it very well becomes you;
Sorrow so royally in you appears,
That I will deeply put the fashion on,
And wear it in my heart. Why then, be sad:
But entertain no more of it, good brothers,
Than a joint burden laid upon us all.
For me, by heaven, I bid you be assur'd,
I'll be your father and your brother too;
Let me but bear your love, I'll bear your cares.
Yet weep, that Harry's dead; and so will I:
But Harry lives, that shall convert those tears,
By number, into hours of happiness.
P. John, &c. We hope no other from your majesty.
King. You all look strangely on me;—and you most; [*To the* Chief Justice.
You are, I think, assur'd I love you not.
Ch. Just. I am assur'd, if I be measur'd rightly,
Your majesty hath no just cause to hate me.
King. No!
How might a prince of my great hopes forget
So great indignities you laid upon me?
What! rate, rebuke, and roughly send to prison
The immediate heir of England? Was this easy?
May this be wash'd in Lethe, and forgotten?
Ch. Just. I then did use the person of your father;
The image of his power lay then in me:
And, in the administration of his law,
Whiles I was busy for the commonwealth,
Your highness pleased to forget my place,
The majesty and power of law and justice,
The image of the king whom I presented,
And struck me in my very seat of judgment;
Whereon, as an offender to your father,
I gave bold way to my authority,
And did commit you. If the deed were ill,
Be you contented, wearing now the garland,
To have a son set your decrees at nought;
To pluck down justice from your awful bench;
To trip the course of law, and blunt the sword
That guards the peace and safety of your person;
Nay, more; to spurn at your most royal image,
And mock your workings in a second body.
Question your royal thoughts, make the case yours;
Be now the father, and propose a son:
Hear your own dignity so much profan'd,
See your most dreadful laws so loosely slighted,
Behold yourself so by a son disdained;
And then imagine me taking your part,
And, in your power, soft silencing your son:
After this cold considerance, sentence me;
And, as you are a king, speak in your state,
What I have done that misbecame my place,
My person, or my liege's sovereignty.
King. You are right, justice, and you weigh this well;
Therefore still bear the balance and the sword:
And I do wish your honours may increase,
Till you do live to see a son of mine
Offend you, and obey you, as I did.
So shall I live to speak my father's words;—
Happy am I, that have a man so bold,
That dares do justice on my proper son:
And not less happy, having such a son,
That would deliver up his greatness so
Into the hands of justice.—You did commit me:
For which, I do commit into your hand
The unstain'd sword that you have us'd to bear:
With this remembrance,—That you use the same
With the like bold, just, and impartial spirit,
As you have done 'gainst me. There is my hand;
You shall be as a father to my youth:
My voice shall sound as you do prompt mine ear;
And I will stoop and humble my intents
To your well practis'd, wise directions,——
And, princes all, believe me, I beseech you;—
My father is gone wild into his grave,
For in his tomb lie my affections;
And with his spirit sadly I survive,
To mock the expectation of the world;
To frustrate prophecies; and to raze out
Rotten opinion, who hath writ me down
After my seeming. The tide of blood in me
Hath proudly flow'd in vanity, till now:
Now doth it turn, and ebb back to the sea;
Where it shall mingle with the state of floods,
And flow henceforth in formal majesty.
Now call we our high court of parliament:
And let us choose such limbs of noble counsel,
That the great body of our state may go
In equal rank with the best govern'd nation;
That war, or peace, or both at once, may be
As things acquainted and familiar to us;——
In which you, father, shall have foremost hand.— [*To the* Lord Chief Justice.
Our coronation done, we will accite,
As I before remember'd, all our state:
And (God consigning to my good intents),
No prince, nor peer, shall have just cause to say,—
Heaven shorten Harry's happy life one day. [*Exeunt.*

SCENE III.

Glostershire. *The Garden of* Shallow's *House.*

Enter FALSTAFF, SHALLOW, SILENCE, BARDOLPH, *the* Page, *and* DAVY.

Shal. Nay, you shall see mine orchard: where, in an arbour, we will eat a last year's pippin of my own graffing, with a dish of carraways, and so forth;—come, cousin Silence;—and then to bed.

Fal. 'Fore God, you have here a goodly dwelling, and a rich.

Shal. Barren, barren, barren; beggars all, beggars all, Sir John:—marry, good air.—Spread Davy, spread, Davy; well said, Davy.

Fal. This Davy serves you for good uses; he is your serving-man, and your husbandman.

Shal. A good varlet, a good varlet, a very good varlet, Sir John.—By the mass, I have drunk too much sack at supper:——a good varlet. Now sit down, now sit down:—come, cousin.

Sil. Ah, sirrah! quoth-a,—we shall
Do nothing but eat, and make good cheer, [Singing.
And praise heaven for the merry year;

When flesh is cheap, and females dear,
And lusty lads roam here and there,
So merrily,
And ever among so merrily.

Fal. There's a merry heart!—Good master Silence, I'll give you a health for that anon.

Shal. Give master Bardolph some wine, Davy.

Davy. Sweet sir, sit; [*Seating* BARDOLPH *and the* Page *at another table.*] I'll be with you anon:—most sweet sir, sit.——Master page, good master page, sit: proface! What you want in meat, we'll have in drink. But you must bear; The heart's all. [*Exit.*

Shal. Be merry, master Bardolph;—and my little soldier there, be merry.

Sil. *Be merry, be merry, my wife has all;* [Singing.
For women are shrews, both short and tall:
'Tis merry in hall, when beards wag all,
And welcome merry shrove-tide.
Be merry, be merry, &c.

Fal. I did not think, master Silence had been a man of this mettle.

Sil. Who, I? I have been merry twice and once, ere now.

Re-enter DAVY.

Davy. There is a dish of leather-coats for you. [*Setting them before* BARDOLPH.

Shal. Davy,—

Davy. Your worship?—I'll be with you straight. [*To* BARD.]—A cup of wine, sir?

Sil. *A cup of wine, that's brisk and fine,*
And drink unto the leman mine; [Singing.
And a merry heart lives long-a.

Fal. Well said, master Silence.

Sil. And we shall be merry;—now comes in the sweet of the night.

Fal. Health and long life to you, master Silence.

Sil. *Fill the cup, and let it come;*
I'll pledge you a mile to the bottom.

Shal. Honest Bardolph, welcome; if thou wantest any thing, and wilt not call, beshrew thy heart.—Welcome my little tiny thief [*To the* Page]; and welcome, indeed, too.—I'll drink to master Bardolph, and to all the cavaleroes about London.

Davy. I hope to see London once ere I die.

Bard. An I might see you there, Davy,—

Shal. By the mass, you'll crack a quart together. Ha! will you not, master Bardolph?

Bard. Yes, sir, in a pottle pot.

Shal. I thank thee:—The knave will stick by thee, I can assure thee that; he will not out; he is true bred.

Bard. And I'll stick by him, sir.

Shal. Why, there spoke a king. Lack nothing: be merry. [*Knocking heard.*] Look who's at door there: Ho! who knocks? [*Exit* DAVY.

Fal. Why, now you have done me right. [*To* SILENCE, *who drinks a bumper.*

Sil. *Do me right,* [Singing.
And dub me knight:
Samingo.
Is't not so?

Fal. 'Tis so.

Sil. Is't so? Why, then say, an old man can do somewhat.

Re-enter DAVY.

Davy. An it please your worship, there's one Pistol come from the court with news.

Fal. From the court, let him come in.—

Enter PISTOL.

How now, Pistol?

Pist. God save you, Sir John!

Fal. What wind blew you hither, Pistol?

Pist. Not the ill wind which blows no man to good.—Sweet knight, thou art now one of the greatest men in the realm.

Sil. By'r lady, I think 'a be; but goodman Puff of Barson.

Pist. Puff?
Puff in thy teeth, most recreant coward base!—
Sir John, I am thy Pistol, and thy friend,
And helter-skelter have I rode to thee;
And tidings do I bring, and lucky joys,
And golden times, and happy news of price.

Fal. I pr'ythee now, deliver them like a man of this world.

Pist. A foutra for the world, and worldlings base!
I speak of Africa, and golden joys.

Fal. O base Assyrian knight, what is thy news?
Let king Cophetua know the truth thereof.

Sil. *And Robin Hood, Scarlet, and John.* [Sings.

Pist. Shall dunghill curs confront the Helicons?
And shall good news be baffled?
Then, Pistol, lay thy head in Furies' lap.

Shal. Honest gentleman, I know not your breeding.

Pist. Why then, lament therefore.

Shal. Give me pardon, sir:—If, sir, you come with news from the court, I take it, there is but two ways; either to utter them, or to conceal them. I am, sir, under the king, in some authority.

Pist. Under which king, Bezonian? speak, or die.

Shal. Under King Harry.

Pist. Harry the Fourth? or Fifth?

Shal. Harry the Fourth.

Pist. A foutra for thine office!—
Sir John, thy tender lambkin now is king;
Harry the Fifth's the man. I speak the truth:
When Pistol lies, do this; and fig me, like
The bragging Spaniard.

Fal. What? is the old king dead?

Pist. As nail in door: The things I speak are just.

Fal. Away, Bardolph; saddle my horse.—Master Robert Shallow, choose what office thou wilt in the land, 'tis thine,—Pistol, I will double charge thee with dignities.

Bard. O joyful day!—I would not take a knighthood for my fortune.

Pist. What? I do bring good news?

Fal. Carry master Silence to bed.—Master Shallow, my Lord Shallow, be what thou wilt, I am fortune's steward. Get on thy boots; we'll ride all night:—O, sweet Pistol:—Away, Bardolph. [*Exit* BARD.]—Come, Pistol, utter more to me; and, withal, devise something to do thyself good.—Boot, boot, master Shallow; I know, the young king is sick for me. Let us take any man's horses; the laws of England are at my commandment. Happy are they which have been my friends; and woe to my lord chief justice!

Pist. Let vultures vile seize on his lungs also!
Where is the life that late I led, say they:
Why, here it is; Welcome these pleasant days. [*Exeunt.*

SCENE IV. London. *A Street.*

Enter Beadles, *dragging in Hostess* QUICKLY, *and* DOLL TEAR-SHEET.

Host. No, thou arrant knave; I would I might die, that I might have thee hanged: thou hast drawn my shoulder out of joint.

1 *Bead.* The constables have deliver'd her over to me; and she shall have whipping-cheer enough, I warrant her: There hath been a man or two lately killed about her.

Dol. Nut-hook, nut-hook, you lie. Come on; I'll tell thee what, thou damned tripe-visaged rascal; an the child I now go with do miscarry, thou hadst better thou hadst struck thy mother, thou paper-faced villain.

Host. O the Lord, that Sir John were come!

he would make this a bloody day to somebody. But I pray God the fruit of her womb miscarry!

1 *Bead.* If it do, you shall have a dozen of cushions again; you have but eleven now. Come, I charge you both go with me; for the man is dead, that you and Pistol beat among you.

Doll. I'll tell thee what, thou thin man in a censer! I will have you as soundly swinged for this, you blue-bottle rogue! you filthy famished correctioner! if you be not swinged, I'll forswear half-kirtles.

1 *Bead.* Come, come, you she knight-errant, come.

Host. O, that right should thus overcome might!
Well; of sufferance comes ease.

Dol. Come, you rogue, come; bring me to a justice.

Host. Ay; come, you starved blood-hound.

Dol. Goodman death! goodman bones!

Host. Thou atomy thou!

Dol. Come, you thin thing; come, you rascal!

1 *Bead.* Very well. [*Exeunt.*

SCENE V.

A public Place near Westminster Abbey.

Enter Two Grooms, *strewing Rushes.*

1 *Groom.* More rushes, more rushes.

2 *Groom.* The trumpets have sounded twice.

1 *Groom.* It will be two o'clock ere they come from the coronation: Despatch, despatch.

[*Exeunt* Grooms.

Enter Falstaff, Shallow, Pistol, Bardolph, *and the* Page.

Fal. Stand here by me, master Robert Shallow; I will make the king do you grace: I will leer upon him, as 'a comes by; and do but mark the countenance that he will give me.

Pist. God bless thy lungs, good knight.

Fal. Come here, Pistol; stand behind me.—O, if I had had time to have made new liveries, I would have bestowed the thousand pound I borrowed of you. [*To* Shallow.] But 'tis no matter; this poor show doth better: this doth infer the zeal I had to see him.

Shal. It doth so.

Fal. It shows my earnestness of affection.

Shal. It doth so.

Fal. My devotion.

Shal. It doth, it doth, it doth.

Fal. As it were, to ride day and night; and not to deliberate, not to remember, not to have patience to shift me.

Shal. It is most certain.

Fal. But to stand stained with travel, and sweating with desire to see him; thinking of nothing else; putting all affairs else in oblivion; as if there were nothing else to be done, but to see him.

Pist. 'Tis *semper idem,* for *absque hoc nihil est:* 'Tis all in every part.

Shal. 'Tis so, indeed.

Pist. My knight, I will inflame thy noble liver,
And make thee rage.
Thy Doll, and Helen of thy noble thoughts,
Is in base durance, and contagious prison;
Haul'd thither
By most mechanical and dirty hand:—
Rouse up revenge from ebon den with fell Alecto's snake,
For Doll is in; Pistol speaks nought but truth.

Fal. I will deliver her.

[*Shouts within, and the Trumpets sound.*

Pist. There roar'd the sea, and trumpet-clangor sounds.

Enter the King *and his* Train, *the* Chief Justice *among them.*

Fal. God save thy grace, King Hal! my royal Hal!

Pist. The heavens thee guard and keep, most royal imp of fame!

Fal. God save thee, my sweet boy!

King. My lord chief justice, speak to that vain man.

Ch. Just. Have you your wits? know you what 'tis you speak?

Fal. My king, my Jove! I speak to thee, my heart!

King. I know thee not, old man: Fall to thy prayers;
How ill white hairs become a fool, and jester!
I have long dream'd of such a kind of man,
So surfeit-swell'd, so old, and so profane;
But, being awake, I do despise my dream.
Make less thy body hence, and more thy grace:
Leave gormandizing; know, the grave doth gape
For thee thrice wider than for other men:—
Reply not to me with a fool-born jest;
Presume not, that I am the thing I was:
For heaven doth know, so shall the world perceive,
That I have turned away my former self;
So will I those that keep me company.
When thou dost hear I am as I have been,
Approach me; and thou shalt be as thou wast,
The tutor and the feeder of my riots;
Till then, I banish thee, on pain of death,—
As I have done the rest of my misleaders,—
Not to come near our person by ten mile,
For competence of life, I will allow you,
That lack of means enforce you not to evil:
And, as we hear you do reform yourselves,
We will,—according to your strength, and qualities,—
Give you advancement.—Be it your charge, my lord,
To see perform'd the tenor of our word.
Set on. [*Exeunt* King, *and his* Train.

Fal. Master Shallow, I owe you a thousand pound.

Shal. Ay, marry, Sir John; which I beseech you to let me have home with me.

Fal. That can hardly be, master Shallow. Do not you grieve at this; I shall be sent for in private to him: look you, he must seem thus to the world. Fear not your advancement; I will be the man yet, that shall make you great.

Shal. I cannot perceive how; unless you give me your doublet, and stuff me out with straw. I beseech you, good Sir John, let me have five hundred of my thousand.

Fal. Sir, I will be as good as my word: this that you heard, was but a colour.

Shal. A colour, I fear, that you will die in, Sir John.

Fal. Fear no colours; go with me to dinner. Come, lieutenant Pistol;—come, Bardolph:—I shall be sent for soon at night.

Re-enter Prince John, *the* Chief Justice, Officers, *&c.*

Ch. Just. Go, carry Sir John Falstaff to the Fleet:
Take all his company along with him.

Fal. My lord, my lord,——

Ch. Just. I cannot now speak: I will hear you soon.
Take them away.

Pist. *Si fortuna me tormenta, spero me contenta.*

[*Exeunt* Fal. Shal. Pist. Bard. Page, *and* Officers.

P. John. I like this fair proceeding of the king's:
He hath intent, his wonted followers
Shall all be very well provided for;
But all are banish'd, till their conversations
Appear more wise and modest to the world.

Ch. Just. And so they are.

P. John. The king hath call'd his parliament, my lord.

Ch. Just. He hath.

P. John. I will lay odds,—that ere this year expire,
We bear our civil swords, and native fire,
As far as France: I heard a bird so sing,
Whose musick, to my thinking, pleas'd the king.
Come, will you hence? [*Exeunt.*

EPILOGUE.

Spoken by a Dancer.

FIRST, my fear; then, my court'sy; last, my speech. My fear is, your displeasure; my court'sy, my duty; and my speech to beg your pardons. If you look for a good speech now, you undo me: for what I have to say, is of mine own making; and what, indeed, I should say, will, I doubt, prove mine own marring. But to the purpose, and so to the venture.—Be it known to you (as it is very well), I was lately here in the end of a displeasing play, to pray your patience for it, and to promise you a better. I did mean, indeed, to pay you with this: which, if, like an ill venture, it come unluckily home, I break, and you, my gentle creditors, lose. Here, I promised you, I would be, and here I commit my body to your mercies: bate me some, and I will pay you some, and, as most debtors do, promise you infinitely.

If my tongue cannot entreat you to acquit me, will you command me to use my legs? and yet that were but light payment,—to dance out of your debt. But a good conscience will make any possible satisfaction, and so will I. All the gentlewomen here have forgiven me; if the gentlemen will not, then the gentlemen do not agree with the gentlewomen, which was never seen before in such an assembly.

One word more, I beseech you. If you be not too much cloyed with fat meat, our humble author will continue the story, with Sir John in it, and make you merry with fair Katharine of France: where, for any thing I know, Falstaff shall die of a sweat, unless already he be killed with your hard opinions; for Oldcastle died a martyr, and this is not the man. My tongue is weary; when my legs are too, I will bid you good night: and so kneel down before you;—but, indeed, to pray for the queen.

KING HENRY THE FIFTH.

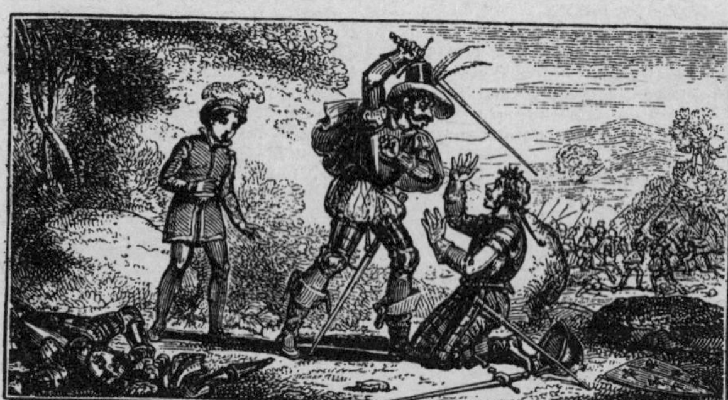

PERSONS REPRESENTED.

KING HENRY THE FIFTH.
DUKE OF GLOSTER, } *Brothers to the* King.
DUKE OF BEDFORD, }
DUKE OF EXETER, *Uncle to the* King.
EARLS OF SALISBURY, WESTMORELAND, *and* WARWICK.
ARCHBISHOP OF CANTERBURY.
BISHOP OF ELY.
EARL OF CAMBRIDGE, }
LORD SCROOP, } *Conspirators against the* King.
SIR THOMAS GREY, }
SIR THOMAS ERPINGHAM, GOWER, FLUELLEN, MACMORRIS, JAMY, *Officers in* King Henry's *Army.*
BATES, COURT, WILLIAMS, *Soldiers in the same.*
NYM, BARDOLPH, PISTOL, *formerly Servants to* Falstaff, *now Soldiers in the same.*
BOY, *Servant to them.* A Herald. Chorus.

CHARLES THE SIXTH, King *of* France.
LEWIS, *the* Dauphin.
DUKES OF BURGUNDY, ORLEANS, *and* BOURBON.
The Constable *of* France.
RAMBURES *and* GRANDPREE, *French Lords.*
Governor *of* Harfleur.
MONTJOY, *a French Herald.*
Ambassadors *to the* King *of* England.
ISABEL, Queen *of* France.

KATHARINE, *Daughter of* Charles *and* Isabel.
ALICE, *a Lady attending on the* Princess Katharine.
QUICKLY, Pistol's *Wife, an Hostess.*

Lords, Ladies, Officers, French *and* English Soldiers, Messengers, *and* Attendants.

The SCENE,—*at the beginning of the Play, lies in* England; *but afterwards wholly in* France.

Enter CHORUS.

O, FOR a muse of fire, that would ascend
The brightest heaven of invention!
A kingdom for a stage, princes to act,
And monarchs to behold the swelling scene!
Then should the warlike Harry, like himself,
Assume the port of Mars; And, at his heels,
Leash'd in like hounds, should famine, sword, and fire,
Crouch for employment. But pardon, gentles all,
The flat unraised spirit, that hath dar'd,
On this unworthy scaffold, to bring forth
So great an object: Can this cockpit hold
The vasty fields of France? or may we cram
Within this wooden O, the very casques,
That did affright the air at Agincourt?
O, pardon! since a crooked figure may
Attest, in little place, a million;
And let us, ciphers to this great accompt,

On your imaginary forces work:
Suppose, within the girdle of these walls
Are now confin'd two mighty monarchies,
Whose high upreared and abutting fronts
The perilous, narrow ocean parts asunder.
Piece out our imperfections with your thoughts;
Into a thousand parts divide one man,
And make imaginary puissance:
Think, when we talk of horses, that you see them
Printing their proud hoofs i' the receiving earth:
For 'tis your thoughts that now must deck our kings,
Carry them here and there; jumping o'er times:
Turning the accomplishment of many years
Into an hourglass; For the which supply,
Admit me chorus to this history;
Who, prologue like, your humble patience pray
Gently to hear, kindly to judge, our play.

ACT I.

SCENE I. London. *An Antichamber in the King's Palace.*

Enter the ARCHBISHOP OF CANTERBURY, *and* BISHOP OF ELY.

Cant. My lord, I'll tell you,—that self bill is urg'd,
Which in the eleventh year o' the last king's reign
Was like, and had indeed against us pass'd,
But that the scambling and unquiet time
Did push it out of further question.

Ely. But how, my lord, shall we resist it now?

Cant. It must be thought on. If it pass against us,
We lose the better half of our possession:
For all the temporal lands, which men devout
By testament have given to the church,
Would they strip from us: being valued thus,—
As much as would maintain, to the king's honour,
Full fifteen earls and fifteen hundred knights:
Six thousand and two hundred good esquires;
And to relief of lazars, and weak age,
Of indigent faint souls, past corporal toil,
A hundred alms-houses, right well supplied;
And to the coffers of the king beside,
A thousand pounds by the year: Thus runs the bill.

Ely. This would drink deep.

Cant. 'Twould drink the cup and all.

Ely. But what prevention?

Cant. The king is full of grace, and fair regard.

Ely. And a true lover of the holy church.

Cant. The courses of his youth promis'd it not.
The breath no sooner left his father's body,
But that his wildness, mortified in him,
Seem'd to die too: yea, at that very moment,
Consideration like an angel came,
And whipp'd the offending Adam out of him:
Leaving his body as a paradise,
To envelop and contain celestial spirits.
Never was such a sudden scholar made:
Never came reformation in a flood,
With such a heady current, scouring faults;
Nor never hydra-headed wilfulness
So soon did lose his seat, and all at once,
As in this king.

Ely. We are blessed in the change.

Cant. Hear him but reason in divinity,
And, all admiring, with an inward wish
You would desire, the king were made a prelate:
Hear him debate of commonwealth affairs,
You would say,—it hath been all in all his study:
List his discourse of war, and you shall hear
A fearful battle render'd you in musick:
Turn him to any cause of policy,
The Gordian knot of it he will unloose,
Familiar as his garter; that, when he speaks,
The air, a charter'd libertine, is still,
And the mute wonder lurketh in men's ears,
To steal his sweet and honeyed sentences;
So that the art and practick part of life
Must be the mistress to this theorick:
Which is a wonder, how his grace should glean it,
Since his addiction was to courses vain:
His companies unletter'd, rude, and shallow;
His hours fill'd up with riots, banquets, sports;
And never noted in him any study,
Any retirement, any sequestration
From open haunts and popularity.

Ely. The strawberry grows underneath the nettle;
And wholesome berries thrive and ripen best,
Neighbour'd by fruit of baser quality:
And so the prince obscur'd his contemplation
Under the veil of wildness; which, no doubt,
Grew like the summer grass, fastest by night,
Unseen, yet cressive in his faculty.

Cant. It must be so: for miracles are ceas'd;
And therefore we must needs admit the means,
How things are perfected.

Ely. But, my good lord,
How now for mitigation of this bill
Urg'd by the commons? Doth his majesty
Incline to it, or no?

Cant. He seems indifferent;
Or, rather, swaying more upon our part,
Than cherishing the exhibiters against us;
For I have made an offer to his majesty,—
Upon our spiritual convocation:
And in regard of causes now in hand,
Which I have open'd to his grace at large,
As touching France,—to give a greater sum
Than ever at one time the clergy yet
Did to his predecessors part withal.

Ely. How did this offer seem receiv'd, my lord?

Cant. With good acceptance of his majesty;
Save that there was not time enough to hear
(As I perceiv'd, his grace would fain have done)
The severals, and unhidden passages
Of his true titles to some certain dukedoms;
And, generally, to the crown and seat of France,
Deriv'd from Edward, his great grandfather.

Ely. What was the impediment that broke this off?

Cant. The French ambassador upon that instant
Crav'd audience: and the hour I think is come,
To give him hearing: Is it four o'clock?

Ely. It is.

Cant. Then go we in, to know his embassy;
Which I could, with a ready guess declare,
Before the Frenchman speak a word of it.

Ely. I'll wait upon you; and I long to hear it. [*Exeunt.*

SCENE II.

The same. A Room of State in the same.

Enter KING HENRY, GLOSTER, BEDFORD, EXETER, WARWICK, WESTMORELAND, *and* Attendants.

K. Hen. Where is my gracious lord of Canterbury?

Exe. Not here in presence.

K. Hen. Send for him, good uncle.

West. Shall we call in the ambassador, my liege?

K. Hen. Not yet, my cousin; we would be resolv'd,
Before we hear him, of some things of weight,
That task our thoughts, concerning us and France.

Enter the ARCHBISHOP OF CANTERBURY, *and* BISHOP OF ELY.

Cant. God, and his angels, guard your sacred throne,
And make you long become it!

K. Hen. Sure, we thank you.
My learned lord, we pray you to proceed;

And justly and religiously unfold,
Why the law Salique, that they have in France,
Or should, or should not, bar us in our claim.
And God forbid, my dear and faithful lord,
That you should fashion, wrest, or bow your reading,
Or nicely charge your understanding soul
With opening titles miscreate, whose right
Suits not in native colours with the truth;
For God doth know, how many now in health,
Shall drop their blood in approbation
Of what your reverence shall incite us to:
Therefore take heed how you impawn our person,
How you awake the sleeping sword of war;
We charge you in the name of God, take heed:
For never two such kingdoms did contend,
Without much fall of blood; whose guiltless drops
Are every one a woe, a sore complaint,
'Gainst him, whose wrongs give edge unto the swords
That make such waste in brief mortality.
Under this conjuration, speak, my lord:
And we will hear, note, and believe in heart,
That what you speak is in your conscience wash'd
As pure as sin with baptism.

Cant. Then hear me, gracious sovereign,—and you peers,
That owe your lives, your faith, and services,
To this imperial throne:—There is no bar
To make against your highness' claim to France,
But this which they produce from Pharamond,—
In terram Salicam mulieres ne succedant,
No woman shall succeed in Salique land:
Which Salique land the French unjustly gloze,
To be the realm of France, and Pharamond
The founder of this law and female bar.
Yet their own authors faithfully affirm,
That the land Salique lies in Germany,
Between the floods of Sala and of Elbe:
Where Charles the Great, having subdued the Saxons,
There left behind and settled certain French;
Who, holding in disdain the German women,
For some dishonest manners of their life,
Establish'd there this law,—to wit, no female
Should be inheritrix in Salique land;
Which Salique, as I said, 'twixt Elbe and Sala,
Is at this day in Germany call'd—Meisin.
Thus doth it well appear, the Salique law
Was not devised for the realm of France:
Nor did the French possess the Salique land
Until four hundred one and twenty years
After defunction of king Pharamond,
Idly suppos'd the founder of this law;
Who died within the year of our redemption
Four hundred twenty-six; and Charles the Great
Subdued the Saxons, and did seat the French
Beyond the river Sala, in the year
Eight hundred five. Besides, their writers say,
King Pepin, which deposed Childerick,
Did, as heir general, being descended
Of Blithild, which was daughter to King Clothair,
Make claim and title to the crown of France.
Hugh Capet also,—that usurp'd the crown
Of Charles the duke of Lorain, sole heir male
Of the true line and stock of Charles the Great,—
To fine his title with some show of truth,
(Though, in pure truth, it was corrupt and naught),
Convey'd himself as heir to the Lady Lingare,
Daughter to Charlemain, who was the son
To Lewis the emperor, and Lewis the son
Of Charles the Great. Also King Lewis the Tenth,
Who was sole heir to the usurper Capet,
Could not keep quiet in his conscience,
Wearing the crown of France, till satisfied
That fair Queen Isabel, his grandmother,
Was lineal of the Lady Ermengare,
Daughter to Charles the foresaid duke of Lorain:
By the which marriage, the line of Charles the Great
Was reunited to the crown of France.
So that, as clear as is the summer's sun,
King Pepin's title, and Hugh Capet's claim,
King Lewis his satisfaction, all appear
To hold in right and title of the female:
So do the kings of France unto this day;
Howbeit they would hold up this Salique law,
To bar your highness claiming from the female:
And rather choose to hide them in a net,
Than amply to imbare their crooked titles
Usurp'd from you and your progenitors.

K. Hen. May I, with right and conscience, make this claim?

Cant. The sin upon my head, dread sovereign!
For in the book of Numbers is it writ,—
When the son dies, let the inheritance
Descend unto the daughter. Gracious lord,
Stand for your own; unwind your bloody flag;
Look back unto your mighty ancestors;
Go, my dread lord, to your great grandsire's tomb,
From whom you claim: invoke his warlike spirit,
And your great uncle's, Edward the Black Prince;
Who on the French ground play'd a tragedy,
Making defeat on the full power of France;
Whiles his most mighty father on a hill
Stood smiling; to behold his lion's whelp
Forage in blood of French nobility.
O noble English, that could entertain
With half their forces the full pride of France;
And let another half stand laughing by,
All out of work, and cold for action!

Ely. Awake remembrance of these valiant dead,
And with your puissant arm renew their feats:
You are their heir, you sit upon their throne;
The blood and courage that renowned them,
Runs in your veins; and my thrice-puissant liege
Is in the very May-morn of his youth,
Ripe for exploits and mighty enterprises.

Exe. Your brother kings and monarchs of the earth
Do all expect that you should rouse yourself,
As did the former lions of your blood.

West. They know your grace hath cause, and means, and might;
So hath your highness; never king of England
Had nobles richer, and more loyal subjects;
Whose hearts have left their bodies here in England,
And lie pavilion'd in the fields of France.

Cant. O, let their bodies follow, my dear liege,
With blood, and sword, and fire, to win your right:
In aid whereof, we of the spirituality
Will raise your highness such a mighty sum,
As never did the clergy at one time
Bring in to any of your ancestors.

K. Hen. We must not only arm to invade the French;
But lay down our proportions to defend
Against the Scot, who will make road upon us
With all advantages.

Cant. They of those marches, gracious sovereign,
Shall be a wall sufficient to defend
Our inland from the pilfering borderers.

K. Hen. We do not mean the coursing snatchers only,
But fear the main intendment of the Scot,
Who hath been still a giddy neighbour to us;
For you shall read, that my great grandfather
Never went with his forces into France,
But that the Scot on his unfurnish'd kingdom
Came pouring, like the tide into a breach,
With ample and brimfulness of his force;
Galling the gleaned land with hot essays;
Girding with grievous siege, castles and towns;

That England, being empty of defence,
Hath shook and trembled at the ill neighbourhood.

Cant. She hath been then more fear'd than harm'd, my liege:
For hear her but exampled by herself,—
When all her chivalry hath been in France,
And she a mourning widow of her nobles,
She hath herself not only well defended,
But taken, and impounded as a stray,
The king of Scots; whom she did send to France,
To fill King Edward's fame with prisoner kings;
And make your chronicle as rich with praise,
As is the ooze and bottom of the sea
With sunken wreck and sumless treasuries.

West. But there's a saying, very old and true,—
If that you will France win,
Then with Scotland first begin:
For once the eagle England being in prey,
To her unguarded nest the weasel Scot
Comes sneaking, and so sucks her princely eggs;
Playing the mouse, in absence of the cat,
To spoil and havock more than she can eat.

Exe. It follows then, the cat must stay at home:
Yet that is but a crush'd necessity;
Since we have locks to safeguard necessaries,
And pretty traps to catch the petty thieves.
While that the armed hand doth fight abroad,
The advised head defends itself at home:
For government, though high, and low, and lower,
Put into parts, doth keep in one concent;
Congruing in a full and natural close,
Like music.

Cant. True; therefore doth heaven divide
The state of man in divers functions,
Setting endeavour in continual motion;
To which is fixed, as an aim or butt,
Obedience: for so work the honey bees;
Creatures, that, by a rule in nature, teach
The act of order to a peopled kingdom.
They have a king, and officers of sorts:
Where some, like magistrates, correct at home;
Others, like merchants, venture trade abroad;
Others, like soldiers, armed in their stings,
Make boot upon the summer's velvet buds;
Which pillage they with merry march bring home
To the tent-royal of their emperor:
Who, busied in his majesty, surveys
The singing masons building roofs of gold;
The civil citizens kneading up the honey;
The poor mechanick porters crowding in
Their heavy burdens at his narrow gate:
The sad-ey'd justice, with his surly hum,
Delivering o'er to executors pale
The lazy yawning drone. I this infer,—
That many things, having full reference
To one concent, may work contrariously;
As many arrows, loosed several ways,
Fly to one mark;
As many several ways meet in one town;
As many fresh streams run in one self sea;
As many lines close in the dial's centre;
So may a thousand actions, once afoot,
End in one purpose, and be all well borne
Without defeat. Therefore to France, my liege.
Divide your happy England into four;
Whereof take you one quarter into France,
And you withal shall make all Gallia shake.
If we, with thrice that power left at home,
Cannot defend our own door from the dog,
Let us be worried; and our nation lose
The name of hardiness, and policy.

K. Hen. Call in the messengers sent from the Dauphin.

[*Exit an* Attendant. *The* King *ascends his Throne.*

Now are we well resolv'd: and by God's help;
And yours, the noble sinews of our power,—
France being ours, we'll bend it to our awe,
Or break it all to pieces: Or there we'll sit,
Ruling, in large and ample empery,
O'er France, and all her almost kingly dukedoms:
Or lay these bones in an unworthy urn,
Tombless, with no remembrance over them:
Either our history shall, with full mouth,
Speak freely of our acts; or else our grave,
Like Turkish mute, shall have a tongueless mouth,
Not worship'd with a waxen epitaph.

Enter Ambassadors *of* France.

Now are we well prepar'd to know the pleasure
Of our fair cousin Dauphin; for, we hear,
Your greeting is from him, not from the king.

Amb. May it please your majesty, to give us leave
Freely to render what we have in charge;
Or shall we sparingly show you far off
The Dauphin's meaning, and our embassy?

K. Hen. We are no tyrant, but a Christian king;
Unto whose grace our passion is as subject,
As are our wretches fetter'd in our prisons:
Therefore, with frank and with uncurbed plainness,
Tell us the Dauphin's mind.

Amb. Thus then, in few.
Your highness, lately sending into France,
Did claim some certain dukedoms, in the right
Of your great predecessor, King Edward the Third.
In answer of which claim, the prince our master
Says,—that you savour too much of your youth;
And bids you be advis'd, there's nought in France,
That can be with a nimble galliard won;
You cannot revel into dukedoms there:
He therefore sends you, meeter for your spirit,
This tun of treasure; and, in lieu of this,
Desires you, let the dukedoms, that you claim,
Hear no more of you. This the Dauphin speaks.

K. Hen. What treasure, uncle?

Exe. Tennis-balls, my liege.

K. Hen. We are glad the Dauphin is so pleasant with us;
His present, and your pains, we thank you for:
When we have match'd our rackets to these balls,
We will, in France, by God's grace, play a set,
Shall strike his father's crown into the hazard:
Tell him, he hath made a match with such a wrangler,
That all the courts of France will be disturb'd
With chaces. And we understand him well,
How he comes o'er us with our wilder days,
Not measuring what use we made of them.
We never valu'd this poor seat of England;
And therefore, living hence, did give ourself
To barbarous license; As 'tis ever common,
That men are merriest when they are from home.
But tell the Dauphin,—I will keep my state;
Be like a king, and show my sail of greatness,
When I do rouse me in my throne of France:
For that I have laid by my majesty,
And plodded like a man for working-days;
But I will rise there with so full a glory,
That I will dazzle all the eyes of France,
Yea, strike the Dauphin blind to look on us.
And tell the pleasant prince,—this mock of his
Hath turn'd his balls to gun-stones; and his soul
Shall stand sore charged for the wasteful vengeance
That shall fly with them: for many a thousand widows
Shall this his mock mock out of their dear husbands;
Mock mothers from their sons, mock castles down;
And some are yet ungotten, and unborn,
That shall have cause to curse the Dauphin's scorn.
But this lies all within the will of God,
To whom I do appeal; And in whose name,
Tell you the Dauphin, I am coming on,

To venge me as I may, and to put forth
My rightful hand in a well hallow'd cause.
So, get you hence in peace; and tell the Dauphin,
His jest will savour but of shallow wit,
When thousands weep, more than did laugh at it.—
Convey them with safe conduct.—Fare you well.
[*Exeunt* Ambassadors.

Exe. This was a merry message.

K. Hen. We hope to make the sender blush at it. [*Descends from his Throne.*
Therefore, my lords, omit no happy hour,
That may give furtherance to our expedition:
For we have now no thought in us but France;
Save those to God, that run before our business.
Therefore, let our proportions for these wars
Be soon collected; and all things thought upon,
That may, with reasonable swiftness, add
More feathers to our wings; for, God before,
We'll chide this Dauphin at his father's door.
Therefore, let every man now task his thought,
That this fair action may on foot be brought.
[*Exeunt.*

ACT II.

Enter CHORUS.

Chor. Now all the youth of England are on fire,
And silken dalliance in the wardrobe lies;
Now thrive the armourers, and honour's thought
Reigns solely in the breast of every man:
They sell the pasture now, to buy the horse;
Following the mirror of all Christian kings,
With winged heels, as English Mercuries.
For now sits Expectation in the air;
And hides a sword, from hilts unto the point,
With crowns imperial, crowns, and coronets,
Promis'd to Harry, and his followers.
The French, advis'd by good intelligence
Of this most dreadful preparation,
Shake in their fear; and with pale policy
Seek to divert the English purposes.
O England! model to thy inward greatness,
Like little body with a mighty heart,—
What might'st thou do, that honour would thee do,
Were all thy children kind and natural!
But see thy fault! France hath in thee found out
A nest of hollow bosoms, which he fills
With treacherous crowns: and three corrupted men,—
One, Richard earl of Cambridge; and the second,
Henry Lord Scroop of Masham; and the third,
Sir Thomas Grey, knight of Northumberland,—
Have, for the gilt of France, (O guilt, indeed!)
Confirm'd conspiracy with fearful France;
And by their hands this grace of kings must die
(If hell and treason hold their promises),
Ere he take ship for France, and in Southampton.
Linger your patience on; and well digest
The abuse of distance, while we force a play.
The sum is paid; the traitors are agreed;
The king is set from London; and the scene
Is now transported, gentles, to Southampton:
There is the playhouse now, there must you sit:
And thence to France shall we convey you safe,
And bring you back, charming the narrow seas
To give you gentle pass; for, if we may,
We'll not offend one stomach with our play.
But, till the king come forth, and not till then,
Unto Southampton do we shift our scene.
[*Exit.*

SCENE I. *The same.* Eastcheap.

Enter NYM *and* BARDOLPH.

Bard. Well met, Corporal Nym.

Nym. Good morrow, Lieutenant Bardolph.

Bard. What, are ancient Pistol and you friends yet?

Nym. For my part, I care not: I say little: but when time shall serve, there shall be smiles;—but that shall be as it may. I dare not fight; but I will wink, and hold out mine iron: It is a simple one; but what though? it will toast cheese; and it will endure cold as another man's sword will: and there's the humour of it.

Bard. I will bestow a breakfast, to make you friends; and we'll be all three sworn brothers to France; let it be so, good Corporal Nym.

Nym. 'Faith, I will live so long as I may, that's the certain of it; and when I cannot live any longer, I will do as I may: that is my rest, that is the rendezvous of it.

Bard. It is certain, corporal, that he is married to Nell Quickly: and, certainly, she did you wrong; for you were troth-plight to her.

Nym. I cannot tell; things must be as they may: men may sleep, and they may have their throats about them at that time; and, some say, knives have edges. It must be as it may: though patience be a tired mare, yet she will plod. There must be conclusions. Well, I cannot tell.

Enter PISTOL *and* MRS. QUICKLY.

Bard. Here comes ancient Pistol, and his wife:—good corporal, be patient here.—How now, mine host Pistol?

Pist. Base tike, call'st thou me—host?
Now, by this hand I swear, I scorn the term;
Nor shall my Nell keep lodgers.

Quick. No, by my troth, not long: for we cannot lodge and board a dozen or fourteen gentlewomen, that live honestly by the prick of their needles, but it will be thought we keep a bawdy-house straight. [NYM *draws his sword.*] O well-a-day, Lady, if he be not drawn now! we shall see wilful adultery and murder committed. Good Lieutenant Bardolph,—good corporal, offer nothing here.

Nym. Pish.

Pist. Pish for thee, Iceland dog! thou prick-ear'd cur of Iceland!

Quick. Good Corporal Nym, show the valour of a man, and put up thy sword.

Nym. Will you shog off? I would have you solus. [*Sheathing his sword.*

Pist. *Solus*, egregious dog? O viper vile!
The *solus* in thy most marvellous face;
The *solus* in thy teeth, and in thy throat,
And in thy hateful lungs, yea, in thy maw, perdy;
And, which is worse, within thy nasty mouth!
I do retort the *solus* in thy bowels:
For I can take, and Pistol's cock is up,
And flashing fire will follow.

Nym. I am not Barbason; you cannot conjure me, I have a humour to knock you indifferently well: If you grow foul with me, Pistol, I will scour you with my rapier, as I may, in fair terms: if you would walk off, I would prick your guts a little, in good terms, as I may; and that's the humour of it.

Pist. O braggard vile, and damned furious wight!
The grave doth gape, and doting death is near;
Therefore exhale. [PISTOL *and* NYM *draw.*

Bard. Hear me, hear me what I say: he that strikes the first stroke, I'll run him up to the hilts, as I am a soldier. [*Draws.*

Pist. An oath of mickle might; and fury shall abate.
Give me thy fist, thy fore foot to me give;
Thy spirits are most tall.

Nym. I will cut thy throat, one time or other, in fair terms; that is the humour of it.

Pist. *Coupe le gorge*, that's the word?—I thee defy again.
O hound of Crete, think'st thou my spouse to get?
No; to the spital go,
And from the powdering tub of infamy
Fetch forth the lazar kite of Cressid's kind,
Doll Tear-sheet she by name, and her espouse:
I have, and I will hold, the *quondam* Quickly
For the only she; and—*Pauca*, there's enough.

Enter the Boy.

Boy. Mine host Pistol, you must come to my master,—and you, hostess;—he is very sick, and would to bed.—Good Bardolph, put thy nose between his sheets, and do the office of a warming-pan: 'faith, he's very ill.

Bard. Away, you rogue.

Quick. By my troth, he'll yield the crow a pudding one of these days: the king has killed his heart.—Good husband, come home presently.
[*Exeunt* Mrs. Quickly *and* Boy.

Bard. Come, shall I make you two friends? We must to France together; Why the devil should we keep knives to cut one another's throats?

Pist. Let floods o'erswell, and fiends for food howl on!

Nym. You'll pay me the eight shillings I won of you at betting?

Pist. Base is the slave that pays.

Nym. That now I will have; that's the humour of it.

Pist. As manhood shall compound; Push home.

Bard. By this sword, he that makes the first thrust, I'll kill him; by this sword, I will.

Pist. Sword is an oath, and oaths must have their course.

Bard. Corporal Nym, an thou wilt be friends, be friends: an thou wilt not, why then be enemies with me too. Pr'ythee, put up.

Nym. I shall have my eight shillings, I won of you at betting?

Pist. A noble shalt thou have, and present pay;
And liquor likewise will I give to thee,
And friendship shall combine, and brotherhood;
I'll live by Nym, and Nym shall live by me;
Is not this just?—for I shall suttler be
Unto the camp, and profits will accrue.
Give me thy hand.

Nym. I shall have my noble?

Pist. In cash most justly paid.

Nym. Well then, that's the humour of it.

Re-enter Mrs. Quickly.

Quick. As ever you came of women, come in quickly to Sir John: Ah, poor heart! he is so shaked of a burning quotidian tertian, that it is most lamentable to behold. Sweet men, come to him.

Nym. The king hath run bad humours on the knight, that's the even of it.

Pist. Nym, thou hast spoke the right;
His heart is fracted and corroborate.

Nym. The king is a good king: but it must be as it may; he passes some humours, and careers.

Pist. Let us condole the knight; for, lambkins, we will live. [*Exeunt.*

SCENE II. Southampton. *A Council Chamber.*

Enter Exeter, Bedford, *and* Westmoreland.

Bed. 'Fore God, his grace is bold, to trust these traitors.

Exe. They shall be apprehended by and by.

West. How smooth and even they do bear themselves!
As if allegiance in their bosoms sat,
Crowned with faith, and constant loyalty.

Bed. The king hath note of all that they intend,
By interception which they dream not of.

Exe. Nay, but the man that was his bedfellow,
Whom he hath cloy'd and grac'd with princely favours,—
That he should, for a foreign purse, so sell
His sovereign's life to death and treachery!

Trumpet sounds. Enter King Henry, Scroop, Cambbridge, Grey, Lords, *and* Attendants.

K. Hen. Now sits the wind fair, and we will aboard.
My lord of Cambridge,—and my kind lord of Masham,—
And you, my gentle knight,—give me your thoughts;
Think you not, that the powers we bear with us,
Will cut their passage through the force of France;
Doing the execution, and the act,
For which we have in head assembled them?

Scroop. No doubt, my liege, if each man do his best.

K. Hen. I doubt not that: since we are well persuaded,
We carry not a heart with us from hence,
That grows not in a fair consent with ours;
Nor leave not one behind, that doth not wish
Success and conquest to attend on us.

Cam. Never was monarch better fear'd, and lov'd,
Than is your majesty; there's not, I think, a subject,
That sits in heart-grief and uneasiness
Under the sweet shade of your government.

Grey. Even those that were your father's enemies,
Have steep'd their galls in honey; and do serve you
With hearts create of duty and of zeal.

K. Hen. We therefore have great cause of thankfulness;
And shall forget the office of our hand,
Sooner than quittance of desert and merit,
According to the weight and worthiness.

Scroop. So service shall with steeled sinews toil;
And labour shall refresh itself with hope,
To do your grace incessant services.

K. Hen. We judge no less.—Uncle of Exeter,
Enlarge the man committed yesterday,
That rail'd against our person: we consider,
It was excess of wine that set him on;
And, on his more advice, we pardon him.

Scroop. That's mercy, but too much security:
Let him be punish'd, sovereign; lest example
Breed, by his sufferance, more of such a kind.

K. Hen. O, let us yet be merciful.

Cam. So may your highness, and yet punish too.

Grey. Sir, you show great mercy, if you give him life,
After the taste of much correction.

K. Hen. Alas, your too much love and care of me
Are heavy orisons 'gainst this poor wretch.
If little faults, proceeding on distemper,
Shall not be wink'd at, how shall we stretch our eye,
When capital crimes, chew'd, swallow'd, and digested,
Appear before us?—We'll yet enlarge that man,
Though Cambridge, Scroop, and Grey,—in their dear care,
And tender preservation of our person,—
Would have him punish'd. And now to our French causes;
Who are the late commissioners?

Cam. I one, my lord;
Your highness bade me ask for it to-day.

Scroop. So did you me, my liege.

Grey. And me, my royal sovereign.

K. Hen. Then, Richard, earl of Cambridge, there is yours;—
There yours, Lord Scroop of Masham;—and, sir knight,
Grey of Northumberland, this same is yours:—
Read them; and know, I know your worthiness.—
My lord of Westmoreland,—and uncle Exeter,—
We will aboard to-night.—Why, how now, gentlemen?
What see you in those papers, that you lose
So much complexion?—look ye, how they change!
Their cheeks are paper.—Why, what read you there,

That hath so cowarded and chased your blood
Out of appearance?

Cam. I do confess my fault;
And do submit me to your highness' mercy.

Grey. Scroop. To which we all appeal.

K. Hen. The mercy, that was quick in us but late,
By your own counsel is suppress'd and kill'd:
You must not dare, for shame, to talk of mercy;
For your own reasons turn into your bosoms,
As dogs upon their masters, worrying them.—
See you, my princes, and my noble peers,
These English monsters! My lord of Cambridge here,—
You know, how apt our love was, to accord
To furnish him with all appertinents
Belonging to his honour; and this man
Hath, for a few light crowns, lightly conspir'd,
And sworn unto the practices of France,
To kill us here in Hampton: to the which,
This knight, no less for bounty bound to us
Than Cambridge is,—hath likewise sworn.—But O!
What shall I say to thee, Lord Scroop; thou cruel,
Ingrateful, savage, and inhuman creature!
Thou, that didst bear the key of all my counsels,
That knew'st the very bottom of my soul,
That almost might'st have coin'd me into gold,
Would'st thou have practis'd on me for thy use?
May it be possible, that foreign hire
Could out of thee extract one spark of evil
That might annoy my finger? 'tis so strange,
That, though the truth of it stands off as gross
As black from white, my eye will scarcely see it.
Treason, and murder, ever kept together,
As two yoke-devils sworn to either's purpose,
Working so grossly in a natural cause,
That admiration did not whoop at them:
But thou, 'gainst all proportion, didst bring in
Wonder to wait on treason, and on murder:
And whatsoever cunning fiend it was,
That wrought upon thee so preposterously,
H'ath got the voice in hell for excellence:
And other devils, that suggest by treasons,
Do botch and bungle up damnation
With patches, colours, and with forms being fetch'd
From glistering semblances of piety;
But he, that temper'd thee, bade thee stand up,
Gave thee no instance why thou should'st do treason,
Unless to dub thee with the name of traitor.
If that same demon, that hath gull'd thee thus,
Should with his lion gait walk the whole world,
He might return to vasty Tartar back,
And tell the legions—I can never win
A soul so easy as that Englishman's.
O, how hast thou with jealousy infected
The sweetness of affiance! Show men dutiful?
Why, so didst thou: Seem they grave and learned?
Why, so didst thou: Come they of noble family?
Why, so didst thou: Seem they religious?
Why, so didst thou: Or are they spare in diet;
Free from gross passion, or of mirth, or anger;
Constant in spirit, not swerving with the blood;
Garnish'd and deck'd in modest complement;
Not working with the eye, without the ear,
And, but in purged judgment, trusting neither?
Such, and so finely bolted, didst thou seem:
And thus thy fall hath left a kind of blot,
To mark the full-fraught man, and best indued,
With some suspicion. I will weep for thee;
For this revolt of thine, methinks, is like
Another fall of man.—Their faults are open,
Arrest them to the answer of the law;—
And God acquit them of their practices!

Exe. I arrest thee of high treason, by the name of Richard earl of Cambridge.

I arrest thee of high treason, by the name of Henry Lord Scroop of Masham.

I arrest thee of high treason, by the name of Thomas Grey, knight of Northumberland.

Scroop. Our purposes God justly hath discover'd;
And I repent my fault more than my death;
Which I beseech your highness to forgive,
Although my body pay the price of it.

Cam. For me,—the gold of France did not seduce;
Although I did admit it as a motive,
The sooner to effect what I intended:
But God be thanked for prevention;
Which I in sufferance heartily will rejoice,
Beseeching God and you to pardon me.

Grey. Never did faithful subject more rejoice
At the discovery of most dangerous treason,
Than I do at this hour joy o'er myself,
Prevented from a damned enterprise:
My fault, but not my body, pardon, sovereign.

K. Hen. God quit you in his mercy! Hear your sentence.
You have conspir'd against our royal person,
Join'd with an enemy proclaim'd, and from his coffers
Receiv'd the golden earnest of our death;
Wherein you would have sold your king to slaughter,
His princes and his peers to servitude,
His subjects to oppression and contempt,
And his whole kingdom into desolation.
Touching our person, seek we no revenge;
But we our kingdom's safety must so tender,
Whose ruin you three sought, that to her laws
We do deliver you. Get you therefore hence,
Poor miserable wretches, to your death:
The taste whereof, God, of his mercy, give you
Patience to endure, and true repentance
Of all your dear offences!—Bear them hence.
[*Exeunt Conspirators, guarded.*
Now, lords, for France; the enterprise whereof
Shall be to you, as us, like glorious.
We doubt not of a fair and lucky war:
Since God so graciously hath brought to light
This dangerous treason, lurking in our way,
To hinder our beginnings, we doubt not now,
But every rub is smoothed on our way.
Then, forth, dear countrymen; let us deliver
Our puissance into the hand of God,
Putting it straight in expedition.
Cheerly to sea; the signs of war advance:
No king of England, if not king of France.
[*Exeunt.*

SCENE III.

London. Mrs. Quickly's *House in* Eastcheap.

Enter PISTOL, MRS. QUICKLY, NYM, BARDOLPH *and* BOY.

Quick. Pr'ythee, honey-sweet husband, let me bring thee to Staines.

Pist. No; for my manly heart doth yearn.—
Bardolph, be blithe;—Nym, rouse thy vaunting veins.
Boy, bristle thy courage up: for Falstaff he is dead,
And we must yearn therefore.

Bard. 'Would, I were with him, wheresome'er he is, either in heaven, or in hell!

Quick. Nay, sure, he's not in hell; he's in Arthur's bosom, if ever man went to Arthur's bosom. 'A made a finer end, and went away, an it had been any christom child; 'a parted even just between twelve and one, e'en at turning o' the tide; for after I saw him fumble with the sheets, and play with flowers, and smile upon his fingers' ends, I knew there was but one way; for his nose was as sharp as a pen, and a' babbled of green fields. How now, Sir John? quoth I: what, man! be of good cheer. So 'a cried out—God, God, God! three or four times: now I, to comfort him, bid him 'a should not think of God; I hoped, there was no need to trouble himself with any such thoughts yet: So 'a bade me lay more clothes on his feet: I put my hand into the bed, and felt them, and they were as cold as any stone; then I felt to his knees, and so upward, and upward, and all was as cold as any stone.

Nym. They say, he cried out of sack.

Quick. Ay, that 'a did.

Bard. And of women.

Quick. Nay, that 'a did not.

Boy. Yes, that 'a did; and said, they were devils incarnate.

Quick. 'A could never abide carnation: 'twas a colour he never liked.

Boy. 'A said once, the devil would have him about women.

Quick. 'A did in some sort, indeed, handle women: but then he was rheumatick: and talked of the whore of Babylon.

Boy. Do you not remember, 'a saw a flea stick upon Bardolph's nose; and 'a said, it was a black soul burning in hell-fire?

Bard. Well, the fuel is gone, that maintained that fire; that's all the riches I got in his service.

Nym. Shall we shog off? the king will be gone from Southampton.

Pist. Come, let's away.—My love, give me thy lips.
Look to my chattles, and my moveables:
Let senses rule; the word is, *Pitch and Pay;*
Trust none;
For oaths are straws, men's faiths are wafer-cakes,
And hold-fast is the only dog, my duck;
Therefore, *caveto* be thy counsellor.
Go, clear thy crystals.—Yoke-fellows in arms,
Let us to France! like horse-leeches, my boys;
To suck, to suck, the very blood to suck!

Boy. And that is but unwholesome food, they say.

Pist. Touch her soft mouth, and march.

Bard. Farewell, hostess. [*Kissing her.*

Nym. I cannot kiss, that is the humour of it; but adieu.

Pist. Let housewifery appear; keep close, I thee command.

Quick. Farewell; adieu. [*Exeunt.*

SCENE IV.

France. *A Room in the* French King's *Palace.*

Enter the French King, *attended; the* Dauphin, *the* Duke of Burgundy, *the* Constable, *and Others.*

Fr. King. Thus come the English with full power upon us;
And more than carefully it us concerns,
To answer royally in our defences.
Therefore the dukes of Berry and of Bretagne,
Of Brabant, and of Orleans, shall make forth,—
And you, Prince Dauphin,—with all swift despatch,
To line, and new repair, our towns of war,
With men of courage, and with means defendant:
For England his approaches makes as fierce,
As waters to the sucking of a gulf.
It fits us then, to be as provident
As fear may teach us, out of late examples
Left by the fatal and neglected English
Upon our fields.

Dau. My most redoubted father,
It is most meet we arm us 'gainst the foe:
For peace itself should not so dull a kingdom
(Though war, nor no known quarrel, were in question),
But that defences, musters, preparations,
Should be maintain'd, assembled, and collected,
As were a war in expectation.
Therefore, I say, 'tis meet we all go forth,
To view the sick and feeble parts of France:
And let us do it with no show of fear:
No, with no more, than if we heard that England
Were busied with a Whitsun morris-dance:
For, my good liege, she is so idly king'd,
Her sceptre so fantastically borne
By a vain, giddy, shallow humorous youth,
That fear attends her not.

Con. O peace, Prince Dauphin!
You are too much mistaken in this king:
Question your grace the late ambassadors,—
With what great state he heard their embassy,
How well supplied with noble counsellors,
How modest in exception, and, withal,
How terrible in constant resolution,—
And you shall find, his vanities fore-spent
Were but the outside of the Roman Brutus,
Covering discretion with a coat of folly;
As gardeners do with ordure hide those roots
That shall first spring, and be most delicate.

Dau. Well, 'tis not so, my lord high constable,
But though we think it so, it is no matter:
In cases of defence, 'tis best to weigh
The enemy more mighty than he seems,
So the proportions of defence are fill'd;
Which, of a weak and niggardly projection,
Doth, like a miser, spoil his coat, with scanting
A little cloth.

Fr. King. Think we King Harry strong;
And princes, look, you strongly arm to meet him.
The kindred of him hath been flesh'd upon us;
And he is bred out of that bloody strain,
That haunted us in our familiar paths:
Witness our too much memorable shame,
When Cressy battle fatally was struck,
And all our princes captiv'd, by the hand
Of that black name, Edward Black Prince of Wales;
Whiles that his mountain sire,—on mountain standing,
Up in the air, crown'd with the golden sun,—
Saw his heroical seed, and smil'd to see him
Mangle the work of nature, and deface
The patterns that by God and by French fathers
Had twenty years been made. This is a stem
Of that victorious stock: and let us fear
The native mightiness and fate of him.

Enter a Messenger.

Mess. Ambassadors from Henry king of England
Do crave admittance to your majesty.

Fr. King. We'll give them present audience.
Go, and bring them.
[*Exeunt* Mess. *and certain* Lords.
You see, this chase is hotly follow'd, friends.

Dau. Turn head, and stop pursuit; for coward dogs
Most spend their mouths, when what they seem to threaten,
Runs far before them. Good my sovereign,
Take up the English short; and let them know
Of what a monarchy you are the head;
Self-love, my liege, is not so vile a sin
As self-neglecting.

Re-enter Lords, *with* Exeter *and* Train.

Fr. King. From our brother England?

Exe. From him; and thus he greets your majesty.
He wills you, in the name of God Almighty,
That you divest yourself, and lay apart
The borrow'd glories, that, by gift of heaven,
By law of nature, and of nations, 'long
To him, and to his heirs; namely, the crown,
And all wide-stretched honours that pertain,
By custom and the ordinance of times,
Unto the crown of France. That you may know,
'Tis no sinister, nor no awkward claim,
Pick'd from the worm-holes of long-vanish'd days,
Nor from the dust of old oblivion rak'd,
He sends you this most memorable line,
[*Gives a paper.*
In every branch truly demonstrative;
Willing you, overlook this pedigree;
And, when you find him evenly deriv'd
From his most fam'd of famous ancestors,

Edward the Third, he bids you then resign
Your crown and kingdom, indirectly held
From him the native and true challenger.

Fr. King. Or else what follows?

Exe. Bloody constraint; for if you hide the crown
Even in your hearts, there will he rake for it;
And therefore in fierce tempest is he coming,
In thunder, and in earthquake, like a Jove:
(That, if requiring fail, he will compel);
And bids you, in the bowels of the Lord,
Deliver up the crown; and to take mercy
On the poor souls, for whom this hungry war
Opens his vasty jaws: and on your head
Turns he the widows' tears, the orphans' cries,
The dead men's blood, the pining maidens' groans,
For husbands, fathers, and betrothed lovers,
That shall be swallow'd in this controversy.
This is his claim, his threat'ning, and my message;
Unless the Dauphin be in presence here,
To whom expressly I bring greeting too.

Fr. King. For us, we will consider of this further:
To-morrow shall you bear our full intent
Back to our brother England.

Dau. For the Dauphin,
I stand here for him; What to him from England?

Exe. Scorn, and defiance; slight regard, contempt,
And any thing that may not misbecome
The mighty sender, doth he prize you at.
Thus says my king: and, if your father's highness
Do not, in grant of all demands at large,
Sweeten the bitter mock you sent his majesty,
He'll call you to so hot an answer for it,
That caves and womby vaultages of France
Shall chide your trespass, and return your mock
In second accent of his ordnance.

Dau. Say, if my father render fair reply,
It is against my will: for I desire
Nothing but odds with England: to that end,
As matching to his youth and vanity,
I did present him with those Paris balls.

Exe. He'll make your Paris Louvre shake for it,
Were it the mistress court of mighty Europe:
And, be assured, you'll find a difference
(As we, his subjects, have in wonder found),
Between the promise of his greener days,
And these he masters now; now he weighs time,
Even to the utmost grain; which you shall read
In your own losses, if he stay in France.

Fr. King. To-morrow shall you know our mind at full.

Exe. Despatch us with all speed, lest that our king
Come here himself to question our delay;
For he is footed in this land already.

Fr. King. You shall be soon despatch'd, with fair conditions:
A night is but small breath, and little pause,
To answer matters of this consequence.
[*Exeunt.*

ACT III.

Enter CHORUS.

Chor. Thus with imagin'd wing our swift scene flies,
In motion of no less celerity
Than that of thought. Suppose, that you have seen
The well appointed king at Hampton pier
Embark his royalty; and his brave fleet
With silken streamers the young Phœbus fanning.
Play with your fancies; and in them behold,
Upon the hempen tackle, ship-boys climbing:
Hear the shrill whistle, which doth order give
To sounds confus'd: behold the threaden sails,
Borne with the invisible and creeping wind,
Draw the huge bottoms through the furrow'd sea,
Breasting the lofty surge: O, do but think,
You stand upon the rivage, and behold
A city on the inconstant billows dancing;
For so appears this fleet majestical,
Holding due course to Harfleur. Follow, follow!
Grapple your minds to sternage of this navy;
And leave your England, as dead midnight, still,
Guarded with grandsires, babies, and old women,
Either past, or not arriv'd to, pith and puissance:
For who is he, whose chin is but enrich'd
With one appearing hair, that will not follow
These cull'd and choice-drawn cavaliers to France?
Work, work, your thoughts, and therein see a siege:
Behold the ordnance on their carriages,
With fatal mouths gaping on girded Harfleur.
Suppose, the ambassador from the French comes back;
Tells Harry—that the king doth offer him
Katharine his daughter; and with her, to dowry,
Some petty and unprofitable dukedoms.
The offer likes not: and the nimble gunner
With linstock now the devilish cannon touches,
[*Alarum; and Chambers go off.*
And down goes all before them. Still be kind,
And eke out our performance with your mind.
[*Exit.*

SCENE I. *The same. Before* Harfleur.

Alarums. Enter KING HENRY, EXETER, BEDFORD, GLOSTER, *and* Soldiers, *with Scaling Ladders.*

K. Hen. Once more unto the breach, dear friends, once more;
Or close the wall up with our English dead!
In peace, there's nothing so becomes a man,
As modest stillness and humility:
But when the blast of war blows in our ears,
Then imitate the action of the tiger;
Stiffen the sinews, summon up the blood,
Disguise fair nature with hard-favour'd rage:
Then lend the eye a terrible aspect;
Let it pry through the portage of the head,
Like the brass cannon: let the brow o'erwhelm it,
As fearfully, as doth a galled rock
O'erhang and jutty his confounded base,
Swill'd with the wild and wasteful ocean.
Now set the teeth, and stretch the nostril wide;
Hold hard the breath, and bend up every spirit
To his full height!—On, on, you noble English,
Whose blood is fet from fathers of war-proof!
Fathers, that, like so many Alexanders,
Have, in these parts from morn till even fought,
And sheath'd their swords for lack of argument;
Dishonour not your mothers; now attest,
That those, whom you call'd fathers, did beget you!
Be copy now to men of grosser blood,
And teach them how to war!—And you, good yeomen,
Whose limbs were made in England, show us here
The mettle of your pasture; let us swear
That you are worth your breeding: which I doubt not;
For there is none of you so mean and base,
That hath not noble lustre in your eyes.
I see you stand like greyhounds in the slips,
Straining upon the start. The game's afoot;
Follow your spirit: and, upon this charge,
Cry—God for Harry! England! and Saint George!
[*Exeunt. Alarum, and Chambers go off.*

SCENE II. *The same.*

Forces pass over; then enter NYM, BARDOLPH, PISTOL, *and* BOY.

Bard. On, on, on, on, on! to the breach! to the breach!

Nym. 'Pray thee, corporal, stay; the knocks are too hot; and, for mine own part, I have not a case of lives: the humour of it is too hot, that is the very plain-song of it.

Pist. The plain-song is most just; for humours do abound;
Knocks go and come; God's vassals drop and die;
And sword and shield,
In bloody field,
Doth win immortal fame.

Boy. 'Would, I were in an alehouse in London! I would give all my fame for a pot of ale, and safety.

Pist. And I:
If wishes would prevail with me,
My purpose should not fail with me,
But thither would I hie.

Boy. As duly, but not as truly,
As bird doth sing on bough.

Enter FLUELLEN.

Flu. Got's plood!—Up to the preaches, you rascals! will you not up to the preaches? [*Driving them forward.*

Pist. Be merciful, great duke, to men of mould!
Abate thy rage, abate thy manly rage!
Abate thy rage, great duke!
Good bawcock, bate thy rage! use lenity, sweet chuck!

Nym. These be good humours!—your honour wins bad humours.

[*Exeunt* NYM, PISTOL, *and* BARDOLPH, *followed by* FLUELLEN.

Boy. As young as I am, I have observed these three swashers. I am boy to them all three; but all they three, though they would serve me, could not be man to me: for, indeed, three such anticks do not amount to a man. For Bardolph,—he is white-liver'd, and red-fac'd; by the means whereof, 'a faces it out, but fights not. For Pistol,—he hath a killing tongue, and a quiet sword; by the means whereof 'a breaks words, and keeps whole weapons. For Nym,—he hath heard, that men of few words are the best men; and therefore he scorns to say his prayers, lest 'a should be thought a coward: but his few bad words are match'd with as few good deeds; for 'a never broke any man's head but his own; and that was against a post, when he was drunk. They will steal any thing, and call it,—purchase. Bardolph stole a lute-case: bore it twelve leagues, and sold it for three half-pence. Nym and Bardolph are sworn brothers in filching; and in Calais they stole a fire-shovel: I knew, by that piece of service the men would carry coals. They would have me as familiar with men's pockets, as their gloves or their handkerchiefs; which makes much against my manhood, if I should take from another's pocket, to put into mine; for it is plain pocketing up of wrongs. I must leave them, and seek some better service: their villany goes against my weak stomach, and therefore I must cast it up. [*Exit* BOY.

Re-enter FLUELLEN, GOWER *following.*

Gow. Captain Fluellen, you must come presently to the mines; the duke of Gloster would speak with you.

Flu. To the mines! tell you the duke, it is not so good to come to the mines: For, look you, the mines is not according to the disciplines of the war; the concavities of it is not sufficient; for, look you, th' athversary (you may discuss unto the duke, look you,) is dight himself four yards under the countermines: by Cheshu, I think, 'a will plow up all, if there is not better directions.

Gow. The duke of Gloster, to whom the order of the siege is given, is altogether directed by an Irishman; a very valiant gentleman, i'faith.

Flu. It is Captain Macmorris, is it not?

Gow. I think it be.

Flu. By Cheshu, he is an ass, as in the 'orld: I will verify as much in his peard: he has no more directions in the true disciplines of the wars, look you, of the Roman disciplines, than is a puppy-dog.

Enter MACMORRIS, *and* JAMY, *at a distance.*

Gow. Here 'a comes; and the Scots captain, Captain Jamy, with him.

Flu. Captain Jamy is a marvellous falorous gentleman, that is certain: and of great expedition, and knowledge, in the ancient wars, upon my particular knowledge of his directions: by Cheshu, he will maintain his argument as well as any military man in the 'orld, in the disciplines of the pristine wars of the Romans.

Jamy. I say, gud-day, Captain Fluellen.

Flu. God-den to your worship, goot Captain Jamy.

Gow. How now, Captain Macmorris? have you quit the mines? have the pioneers given o'er?

Mac. By Chrish la, tish ill done: the work ish give over, the trumpet sound the retreat. By my hand, I swear, and by my father's soul, the work ish ill done; it ish give over: I would have blowed up the town, so Chrish save me, la, in an hour. O, tish ill done, tish ill done; by my hand, tish ill done!

Flu. Captain Macmorris, I peseech you now, will you vouchsafe me, look you, a few disputations with you, as partly touching or concerning the disciplines of the war, the Roman wars, in the way of argument, look you, and friendly communication; partly, to satisfy my opinion, and partly for the satisfaction, look you, of my mind, as touching the direction of the military discipline; that is the point.

Jamy. It sall be very gud, gud feith, gud captains bath: and I sall quit you with gud leve, as I may pick occasion; that sall I, marry.

Mac. It is no time to discourse, so Chrish save me, the day is hot, and the weather, and the wars, and the king, and the dukes; it is no time to discourse. The town is beseeched, and the trumpet calls us to the breach; and we talk, and, by Chrish, do nothing; 'tis shame for us all: so God sa' me, 'tis shame to stand still; it is shame, by my hand: and there is throats to be cut, and works to be done: and there ish nothing done, so Chrish sa' me, la.

Jamy. By the mess, ere theise eyes of mine take themselves to slumber, aile do gude service, or aile ligge i' the grund for it: ay, or go to death: and aile pay it as valorously as I may, that sall I surely do, that is the breff and the long: Mary, I wad full fain heard some question 'tween you 'tway.

Flu. Captain Macmorris, I think, look you, under your correction, there is not many of your nation——

Mac. Of my nation? What ish my nation? ish a villain and a bastard, and a knave, and a rascal? What ish my nation? Who talks of my nation?

Flu. Look you, if you take the matter otherwise than is meant, Captain Macmorris, peradventure, I shall think you do not use me with that affability as in discretion you ought to use me, look you; being as goot a man as yourself, both in the disciplines of wars, and in the derivation of my birth, and in other particularities.

Mac. I do not know you so good a man as myself: so Chrish save me, I will cut off your head.

Gow. Gentlemen both, you will mistake each other.

Jamy. Au! that's a foul fault. [*A Parley sounded.*

Gow. The town sounds a parley.

Flu. Captain Macmorris, when there is more better opportunity to be required, look you, I will be so bold as to tell you, I know the disciplines of war; and there is an end. [*Exeunt.*

SCENE III.

The same. Before the Gates of Harfleur.

The Governor *and some* Citizens *on the Walls; the* English Forces *below. Enter* KING HENRY *and his* Train.

K. Hen. How yet resolves the governor of the town?
This is the latest parle we will admit:
Therefore, to our best mercy give yourselves;
Or, like to men proud of destruction,
Defy us to our worst; for, as I am a soldier
(A name, that, in my thoughts, becomes me best,)
If I begin the battery once again,
I will not leave the half-achieved Harfleur
Till in her ashes she lie buried.
The gates of mercy shall be all shut up;
And the flesh'd soldier,—rough and hard of heart,—
In liberty of bloody hand, shall range
With conscience wide as hell; mowing like grass
Your fresh-fair virgins, and your flowering infants.
What is it then to me, if impious war,—
Array'd in flames, like to the prince of fiends,—
Do, with his smirch'd complexion, all fell feats
Enlink'd to waste and desolation?
What is't to me, when you yourselves are cause,
If your pure maidens fall into the hand
Of hot and forcing violation?
What rein can hold licentious wickedness,
When down the hill he holds his fierce career?
We may as bootless spend our vain command
Upon the enraged soldiers in their spoil,
As send precepts to the Leviathan
To come ashore. Therefore, you men of Harfleur,
Take pity of your town, and of your people,
Whiles yet my soldiers are in my command;
Whiles yet the cool and temperate wind of grace
O'erblows the filthy and contagious clouds
Of deadly murder, spoil, and villany.
If not, why, in a moment, look to see
The blind and bloody soldier with foul hand
Defile the locks of your shrill-shrieking daughters;
Your fathers taken by the silver beards,
And their most reverend heads dash'd to the walls;
Your naked infants spitted upon pikes;
Whiles the mad mothers with their howls confus'd
Do break the clouds, as did the wives of Jewry
At Herod's bloody hunting slaughtermen.
What say you? will you yield, and this avoid?
Or, guilty in defence, be thus destroy'd?

Gov. Our expectation hath this day an end:
The Dauphin, whom of succour we entreated,
Returns us—that his powers are not yet ready
To raise so great a siege. Therefore, dread king,
We yield our town, and lives, to thy soft mercy:
Enter our gates; dispose of us, and ours;
For we no longer are defensible.

K. Hen. Open your gates,—Come, uncle Exeter,
Go you and enter Harfleur; there remain,
And fortify it strongly 'gainst the French:
Use mercy to them all. For us, dear uncle,—
The winter coming on, and sickness growing
Upon our soldiers,—we'll retire to Calais.
To-night in Harfleur will we be your guest;
To-morrow for the march are we addrest.
[*Flourish. The* King, *&c. enter the Town.*

SCENE IV. Rouen. *A Room in the Palace.*

Enter KATHARINE *and* ALICE.

Kath. *Alice, tu as este en Angleterre, et tu parles bien le langage.*

Alice. *Un peu, madame.*

Kath. *Je te prie, m'enseignez; il faut que j'apprenne a parler. Comment appellez vous la main, en Anglois?*

Alice. *La main? elle est appellee,* de hand.

Kath. De hand. *Et les doigts?*

Alice. *Les doigts? ma foy, j' oublie les doigts; mais je me souviendray. Les doigts? je pense, qu'ils sont appelle* de fingres; *ouy,* de fingres.

Kath. *La main,* de hand; *les doigts,* de fingres. *Je pense, que je suis le bon escolier. J'ay gagne deux mots d'Anglois vistement. Comment appellez vous les ongles?*

Alice. *Les ongles? les appellons,* de nails.

Kath. De nails. *Escoutez; dites moy, si je parle bien:* de hand, de fingres, de nails.

Alice. *C'est bien dit, madame; il est fort bon Anglois.*

Kath. *Dites moy en Anglois, le bras.*

Alice. De arm, *madame.*

Kath. *Et le coude.*

Alice. De elbow.

Kath. De elbow. *Je m'en faitz la repetition de tous les mots, que vous m'avez appris des a present.*

Alice. *Il est trop difficile, madame, comme je pense.*

Kath. *Excusez moy, Alice; escoutez:* De hand, de fingre, de nails, de arm, de bilbow.

Alice. De elbow, *madame.*

Kath. *O Seigneur Dieu! je m'en oublie;* De elbow. *Comment appellez vous le col?*

Alice. De neck, *madame.*

Kath. De neck: *Et le menton?*

Alice. De chin.

Kath. De sin. *Le col,* de neck: *le menton,* de sin.

Alice. *Ouy. Sauf vostre honneur; en verite, vous prononcez les mots aussi droict que les natifs d'Angleterre.*

Kath. *Je ne doute point d'apprendre par la grace de Dieu; et en peu de temps.*

Alice. *N'avez vous pas deja oublie ce que je vous ay enseigne?*

Kath. *Non, je reciteray a vous promptement.* De hand, de fingre, de mails,—

Alice. De nails, *madame.*

Kath. De nails, de arme, de ilbow.

Alice. *Sauf vostre honneur,* de elbow.

Kath. *Ainsi dis je;* de elbow, de neck, *et* de sin; *Comment appellez vous le pieds et la robe?*

Alice. De foot, *madame; et* de con.

Kath. De foot, *et* de con? *O Seigneur Dieu! ces sont mots de son mauvais, corruptible, grosse, et impudique, et non pour les dames d'honneur d'user: Je ne voudrois prononcer ces mots devant les seigneurs de France, pour tout le monde. Il faut* de foot, *et* de con, *neant-moins. Je reciterai une autre fois ma lecon ensemble:* De hand, de fingre, de nails, de arm, de elbow, de neck, de sin, de foot, de con.

Alice. *Excellent, madame!*

Kath. *C'est assez pour une fois; allons nous a disner.* [Exeunt.

SCENE V.

The same. Another Room in the same.

Enter the French King, *the* Dauphin, Duke *of* Bourbon, *the* Constable *of* France, *and others.*

Fr. King. 'Tis certain, he hath pass'd the river Some.

Con. And if he be not fought withal, my lord,
Let us not live in France; let us quit all,
And give our vineyards to a barbarous people.

Dau. *O Dieu vivant!* shall a few sprays of us,—
The emptying of our father's luxury,
Our scions, put in wild and savage stock,

Spirt up so suddenly into the clouds,
And overlook their grafters?

Bour. Normans, but bastard Normans, Norman bastards!
Mort de ma vie! if they march along
Unfought withal, but I will sell my dukedom,
To buy a slobbery and a dirty farm
In that nook-shotten isle of Albion.

Con. *Dieu de battailes!* where have they this mettle?
Is not their climate foggy, raw, and dull?
On whom, as in despite, the sun looks pale,
Killing their fruit with frowns? Can sodden water,
A drench for sur-rein'd jades, their barley broth,
Decoct their cold blood to such valiant heat?
And shall our quick blood, spirited with wine,
Seem frosty? O, for honour of our land,
Let us not hang like roping icicles
Upon our houses' thatch, whiles a more frosty people
Sweat drops of gallant youth in our rich fields;
Poor—we may call them, in their native lords.

Dau. By faith and honour,
Our madams mock at us; and plainly say,
Our mettle is bred out; and they will give
Their bodies to the lust of English youth,
To new-store France with bastard warriors.

Bour. They bid us—to the English dancing-schools,
And teach lavoltas high, and swift corantos;
Saying our grace is only in our heels,
And that we are most lofty runaways.

Fr. King. Where is Montjoy, the herald? speed him hence;
Let him greet England with our sharp defiance.—
Up, princes; and with spirit of honour edg'd,
More sharper than your swords, hie to the field:
Charles De-la-bret, high constable of France;
You dukes of Orleans, Bourbon, and of Berry,
Alencon, Brabant, Bar, and Burgundy:
Jaques Chatillon, Rambures, Vaudemont,
Beaumont, Grandpre, Roussi, and Fauconberg,
Foix, Lestrale, Bouciqualt, and Charolois;
High dukes, great princes, barons, lords, and knights,
For your great seats, now quit you of great shames.
Bar Harry England, that sweeps through our land
With pennons painted in the blood of Harfleur!
Rush on his host, as doth the melted snow
Upon the valleys; whose low vassal seat
The Alps doth spit and void his rheum upon:
Go down upon him,—you have power enough,—
And in a captive chariot, into Rouen
Bring him our prisoner.

Con. This becomes the great.
Sorry am I, his numbers are so few,
His soldiers sick, and famish'd in their march;
For, I am sure, when he shall see our army,
He'll drop his heart into the sink of fear,
And, for achievement, offer us his ransome.

Fr. King. Therefore, lord constable, haste on Montjoy:
And let him say to England, that we send
To know what willing ransome he will give.—
Prince Dauphin, you shall stay with us in Rouen.

Dau. Not so, I do beseech your majesty.

Fr. King. Be patient, for you shall remain with us.—
Now, forth, lord constable, and princes all;
And quickly bring us word of England's fall.
[*Exeunt.*

SCENE VI. *The* English *Camp in* Picardy.

Enter GOWER *and* FLUELLEN.

Gow. How now, Captain Fluellen, come you from the bridge?

Flu. I assure you, there is very excellent service committed at the pridge.

Gow. Is the duke of Exeter safe?

Flu. The duke of Exeter is as magnanimous as Agamemnon; and a man that I love and honour with my soul, and my heart, and my duty, and my life, and my livings, and my uttermost powers: he is not (God be praised, and plessed!) any hurt in the 'orld; but keeps the pridge most valiantly, with excellent discipline. There is an ensign there at the pridge,—I think, in my very conscience, he is as valiant as Mark Antony; and he is a man of no estimation in the 'orld: but I did see him do gallant service.

Gow. What do you call him?

Flu. He is called—ancient Pistol.

Gow. I know him not.

Enter PISTOL.

Flu. Do you not know him? Here comes the man.

Pist. Captain, I thee beseech to do me favours:
The duke of Exeter doth love thee well.

Flu. Ay, I praise Got; and I have merited some love at his hands.

Pist. Bardolph, a soldier, firm, and sound of heart,
Of buxom valour, hath, by cruel fate,
And giddy fortune's furious fickle wheel,
That goddess blind,
That stands upon the rolling restless stone,—

Flu. By your patience, ancient Pistol. Fortune is painted plind, with a muffler before her eyes, to signify to you that fortune is plind: And she is painted also with a wheel; to signify to you, which is the moral of it, that she is turning, and inconstant, and variations, and mutabilities: and her foot, look you, is fixed upon a spherical stone, which rolls, and rolls, and rolls;—In good truth, the poet is make a most excellent description of fortune: fortune, look you, is an excellent moral.

Pist. Fortune is Bardolph's foe, and frowns on him;
For he hath stolen a *pix*, and hanged must 'a be.
A damned death!
Let gallows gape for dog, let man go free,
And let not hemp his windpipe suffocate:
But Exeter hath given the doom of death,
For *pix* of little price.
Therefore, go speak, the duke will hear thy voice;
And let not Bardolph's vital thread be cut
With edge of penny cord, and vile reproach:
Speak, captain, for his life, and I will thee requite.

Flu. Ancient Pistol, I do partly understand your meaning.

Pist. Why then rejoice therefore.

Flu. Certainly, ancient, it is not a thing to rejoice at; for if, look you, he were my brother, I would desire the duke to use his goot pleasure, and put him to executions; for disciplines ought to be used.

Pist. Die and be damn'd; and *figo* for thy friendship!

Flu. It is well.

Pist. The fig of Spain! [*Exit* PISTOL.

Flu. Very good.

Gow. Why, this is an arrant counterfeit rascal; I remember him now; a bawd; a cutpurse.

Flu. I'll assure you, 'a utter'd as prave 'ords at the pridge, as you shall see in a summer's day: But it is very well; what he has spoke to me, that is well, I warrant you, when time is serve.

Gow. Why, 'tis a gull, a fool, a rogue; that now and then goes to the wars, to grace himself, at his return into London, under the form of a soldier. And such fellows are perfect in great commanders' names: and they will learn you by rote, where services were done:—at such and such a sconce, at such a breach, at such a convoy; who came off bravely, who was shot, who disgraced, what terms the enemy stood on; and this they con perfectly in the phrase of war, which they trick up with new-tuned oaths: And what a beard of the general's cut, and a horrid suit of the camp, will do among foaming bottles and ale-washed wits, is wonderful to be thought on! but you must learn to know such slanders of the age, or else you may be marvellous mistook.

Flu. I tell you what, Captain Gower;—I do perceive, he is not the man that he would gladly make show to the 'orld he is; if I find a hole in his coat, I will tell him my mind. [*Drum heard.*] Hark you, the king is coming; and I must speak with him from the pridge.

Enter KING HENRY, GLOSTER, *and* Soldiers.

Flu. Got pless your majesty!

K. Hen. How now, Fluellen? camest thou from the bridge?

Flu. Ay, so please your majesty. The duke of Exeter has very gallantly maintained the pridge: the French is gone off, look you: and there is gallant and most prave passages: Marry, th' athversary was have possession of the pridge; but he is enforced to retire, and the duke of Exeter is master of the pridge; I can tell your majesty, the duke is a prave man.

K. Hen. What men have you lost, Fluellen?

Flu. The perdition of th' athversary hath been very great, very reasonable great: marry, for my part, I think the duke hath lost never a man, but one that is like to be executed for robbing a church, one Bardolph, if your majesty know the man: his face is all bubukles, and whelks, and knobs, and flames of fire; and his lips plows at his nose, and it is like a coal of fire, sometimes plue, and sometimes red; but his nose is executed, and his fire's out.

K. Hen. We would have all such offenders so cut off:—and we give express charge, that in our marches through the country, there be nothing compelled from the villages, nothing taken but paid for; none of the French upbraided, or abused in disdainful language; For when lenity and cruelty play for a kingdom, the gentler gamester is the soonest winner.

Tucket sounds. Enter MONTJOY.

Mont. You know me by my habit.

K. Hen. Well then, I know thee; What shall I know of thee?

Mont. My master's mind.

K. Hen. Unfold it.

Mont. Thus says my king:—Say thou to Harry of England, Though we seemed dead, we did but sleep; Advantage is a better soldier than rashness. Tell him, we could have rebuked him at Harfleur; but that we thought not good to bruise an injury, till it were full ripe:—now we speak upon our cue, and our voice is imperial! England shall repent his folly, see his weakness, and admire our sufferance. Bid him, therefore, consider of his ransome; which must proportion the losses we have borne, the subjects we have lost, the disgrace we have digested; which, in weight to re-answer, his pettiness would bow under. For our losses, his exchequer is too poor; for the effusion of our blood, the muster of his kingdom too faint a number; and for our disgrace, his own person, kneeling at our feet, but a weak and worthless satisfaction. To this add—defiance: and tell him, for conclusion, he hath betrayed his followers, whose condemnation is pronounced. So far my king and master; so much my office.

K. Hen. What is thy name? I know thy quality.

Mont. Montjoy.

K. Hen. Thou dost thy office fairly. Turn thee back,
And tell thy king,—I do not seek him now;
But could be willing to march on to Calais
Without impeachment: for, to say the sooth,
(Though 'tis no wisdom to confess so much
Unto an enemy of craft and vantage),
My people are with sickness much enfeebled;
My numbers lessen'd; and those few I have,
Almost no better than so many French;
Who, when they were in health, I tell thee, herald,
I thought, upon one pair of English legs
Did march three Frenchmen.—Yet, forgive me, God,
That I do brag thus!—this your air of France
Hath blown that vice in me; I must repent.
Go therefore, tell thy master, here I am;
My ransome, is this frail and worthless trunk;
My army but a weak, and sickly guard;
Yet, God before, tell him we will come on,
Though France himself, and such another neighbour,
Stand in our way. There's for thy labour, Montjoy.
Go, bid thy master well advise himself:
If we may pass, we will; if we be hinder'd,
We shall your tawny ground with your red blood
Discolour: and so, Montjoy, fare you well.
The sum of all our answer is but this:
We would not seek a battle, as we are;
Nor, as we are, we say, we will not shun it;
So tell your master.

Mont. I shall deliver so. Thanks to your highness. [*Exit* MONTJOY.

Glo. I hope, they will not come upon us now.

K. Hen. We are in God's hand, brother, not in theirs.
March to the bridge; it now draws toward night:—
Beyond the river we'll encamp ourselves;
And on to-morrow bid them march away. [*Exeunt.*

SCENE VII. *The* French *Camp, near* Agincourt.

Enter the Constable *of* France, *the* LORD RAMBURES, *the* DUKE OF ORLEANS, Dauphin, *and Others.*

Con. Tut! I have the best armour of the world.—'Would it were day!

Orl. You have an excellent armour; but let my horse have his due.

Con. It is the best horse of Europe.

Orl. Will it never be morning?

Dau. My lord of Orleans, and my lord high constable, you talk of horse and armour,—

Orl. You are as well provided of both, as any prince in the world.

Dau. What a long night is this!——I will not change my horse with any that treads but on four pasterns. *Ca, ha!* He bounds from the earth, as if his entrails were hairs; *le cheval volant*, the Pegasus, *qui a les narines de feu!* When I bestride him, I soar, I am a hawk: he trots the air; the earth sings when he touches it; the basest horn of his hoof is more musical than the pipe of Hermes.

Orl. He's of the colour of the nutmeg.

Dau. And of the heat of the ginger. It is a beast for Perseus: he is pure air and fire; and the dull elements of earth and water never appear in him, but only in patient stillness, while his rider mounts him: he is, indeed, a horse; and all other jades you may call—beasts.

Con. Indeed, my lord, it is a most absolute and excellent horse.

Dau. It is the prince of palfreys; his neigh is like the bidding of a monarch, and his countenance enforces homage.

Orl. No more, cousin.

Dau. Nay, the man hath no wit, that cannot, from the rising of the lark to the lodging of the lamb, vary deserved praise on my palfrey: it is a theme as fluent as the sea; turn the sands into eloquent tongues, and my horse is argument for them all: 'tis a subject for a sovereign to reason on, and for a sovereign's sovereign to ride on; and for the world (familiar to us, and unknown,) to lay apart their particular functions, and wonder at him. I once writ a sonnet in his praise, and began thus: *Wonder of nature,—*

Orl. I have heard a sonnet begin so to one's mistress.

Dau. Then did they imitate that which I composed to my courser; for my horse is my mistress.

Orl. Your mistress bears well.

Dau. Me well; which is the prescript praise and perfection of a good and particular mistress.

Con. *Ma foy!* the other day, methought, your mistress shrewdly shook your back.

Dau. So, perhaps, did yours.

Con. Mine was not bridled.

Dau. O! then, belike, she was old and gentle; and you rode like a Kerne of Ireland, your French hose off, and in your strait trossers.

Con. You have good judgment in horsemanship.

Dau. Be warned by me then: they that ride so, and ride not warily, fall into foul bogs; I had rather have my horse to my mistress.

Con. I had as lief have my mistress a jade.

Dau. I tell thee, constable, my mistress wears her own hair.

Con. I could make as true a boast as that, if I had a sow to my mistress.

Dau. *Le chien est retourne a son propre vomissement, et la truie lavee au bourbier:* thou makest use of any thing.

Con. Yet do I not use my horse for my mistress; or any such proverb, so little kin to the purpose.

Ram. My lord constable, the armour, that I saw in your tent to-night, are those stars, or suns, upon it?

Con. Stars, my lord.

Dau. Some of them will fall to-morrow, I hope.

Con. And yet my sky shall not want.

Dau. That may be, for you bear a many superfluously; and 'twere more honour, some were away.

Con. Even as your horse bears your praises; who would trot as well, were some of your brags dismounted.

Dau. 'Would I were able to load him with his desert! Will it never be day? I will trot to-morrow a mile, and my way shall be paved with English faces.

Con. I will not say so, for fear I should be faced out of my way: But I would it were morning, for I would fain be about the ears of the English.

Ram. Who will go to hazard with me for twenty English prisoners?

Con. You must first go yourself to hazard, ere you have them.

Dau. 'Tis midnight, I'll go arm myself. [*Exit.*

Orl. The Dauphin longs for morning.

Ram. He longs to eat the English.

Con. I think, he will eat all he kills.

Orl. By the white hand of my lady, he's a gallant prince.

Con. Swear by her foot, that she may tread out the oath.

Orl. He, is simply, the most active gentleman of France.

Con. Doing is activity; and he will still be doing.

Orl. He never did harm, that I heard of.

Con. Nor will do none to-morrow; he will keep that good name still.

Orl. I know him to be valiant.

Con. I was told that, by one that knows him better than you.

Orl. What's he?

Con. Marry, he told me so himself; and he said, he cared not who knew it.

Orl. He needs not, it is no hidden virtue in him.

Con. By my faith, sir, but it is; never any body saw it, but his lackey: 'tis a hooded valour; and, when it appears, it will bate.

Orl. Ill will never said well.

Con. I will cap that proverb with—There is flattery in friendship.

Orl. And I will take up that with—Give the devil his due.

Con. Well placed; there stands your friend for the devil: have at the very eye of that proverb, with—a pox of the devil.

Orl. You are the better at proverbs, by how much—A fool's bolt is soon shot.

Con. You have shot over.

Orl. 'Tis not the first time you were overshot.

Enter a Messenger.

Mess. My lord high constable, the English lie within fifteen hundred paces of your tent.

Con. Who hath measured the ground?

Mess. The Lord Grandpre.

Con. A valiant and most expert gentleman.—'Would it were day!—Alas, poor Harry of England!—He longs not for the dawning as we do.

Orl. What a wretched and peevish fellow is this king of England, to mope with his fat-brained followers so far out of his knowledge!

Con. If the English had any apprehension, they would run away.

Orl. That they lack; for if their heads had any intellectual armour, they could never wear such heavy head-pieces.

Ram. That island of England breeds very valiant creatures; their mastiffs are of unmatchable courage.

Orl. Foolish curs! that run winking into the mouth of a Russian bear, and have their heads crushed like rotten apples: You may as well say,—that's a valiant flea, that dare eat his breakfast on the lip of a lion.

Con. Just, just; and the men do sympathize with the mastiffs, in robustious and rough coming on, leaving their wits with their wives; and then give them great meals of beef, and iron and steel, they will eat like wolves, and fight like devils.

Orl. Ay, but these English are shrewdly out of beef.

Con. Then we shall find to-morrow—they have only stomachs to eat, and none to fight. Now is it time to arm: Come, shall we about it?

Orl. It is now two o'clock: but, let me see,—by ten,
We shall have each a hundred Englishmen. [*Exeunt.*

ACT IV.

Enter Chorus.

Chor. Now entertain conjecture of a time,
When creeping murmur, and the poring dark,
Fills the wide vessel of the universe.
From camp to camp, through the foul womb of night,
The hum of either army stilly sounds,
That the fix'd sentinels almost receive
The secret whispers of each other's watch:
Fire answers fire; and through their paly flames
Each battle sees the other's umber'd face:
Steed threatens steed, in high and boastful neighs
Piercing the night's dull ear; and from the tents,
The armourers, accomplishing the knights,
With busy hammers closing rivets up,
Give dreadful note of preparation.
The country cocks do crow, the clocks do toll,
And the third hour of drowsy morning name.
Proud of their numbers, and secure in soul,
The confident and over-lusty French
Do the low-rated English play at dice;
And chide the cripple tardy-gaited night,
Who, like a foul and ugly witch, doth limp

So tediously away. The poor condemned English,
Like sacrifices, by their watchful fires
Sit patiently and inly ruminate
The morning's danger; and their gestures sad
Investing lank-lean cheeks, and war-worn coats,
Presenteth them unto the gazing moon
So many horrid ghosts. O, now, who will behold
The royal captain of this ruin'd band,
Walking from watch to watch, from tent to tent,
Let him cry—Praise and glory on his head!
For forth he goes, and visits all his host;
Bids them good morrow, with a modest smile:
And calls them—brothers, friends, and countrymen.
Upon his royal face there is no note,
How dread an army hath enrounded him:
Nor doth he dedicate one jot of colour
Unto the weary and all-watched night;
But freshly looks, and overbears attaint,
With cheerful semblance, and sweet majesty;
That every wretch, pining and pale before,
Beholding him, plucks comfort from his looks:
A largess universal, like the sun,
His liberal eye doth give to every one,
Thawing cold fear. Then, mean and gentle all,
Behold, as may unworthiness define,
A little touch of Harry in the night:
And so our scene must to the battle fly:
Where (O for pity!) we shall much disgrace—
With four or five most vile and ragged foils,
Right ill dispos'd, in brawl ridiculous,—
The name of Agincourt: Yet, sit and see;
Minding true things, by what their mockeries be.
[*Exit.*

SCENE I. *The* English *Camp at* Agincourt.

Enter KING HENRY, BEDFORD, *and* GLOSTER.

K. Hen. Gloster, 'tis true, that we are in great danger;
The greater therefore should our courage be.—
Good morrow, brother Bedford.—God Almighty!
There is some soul of goodness in things evil,
Would men observingly distil it out;
For our bad neighbour makes us early stirrers,
Which is both healthful, and good husbandry:
Besides, they are our outward consciences,
And preachers to us all; admonishing,
That we should dress us fairly for our end.
Thus may we gather honey from the weed,
And make a moral of the devil himself.

Enter ERPINGHAM.

Good morrow, old Sir Thomas Erpingham:
A good soft pillow for that good white head
Were better than a churlish turf of France.

Erp. Not so, my liege: this lodging likes me better,
Since I may say—now lie I like a king.

K. Hen. 'Tis good for men to love their present pains,
Upon example; so the spirit is eased;
And, when the mind is quicken'd, out of doubt,
The organs, though defunct and dead before,
Break up their drowsy grave, and newly move
With casted slough and fresh legerity.
Lend me thy cloak, Sir Thomas.—Brothers both,
Commend me to the princes in our camp;
Do my good morrow to them; and, anon,
Desire them all to my pavilion.

Glo. We shall, my liege.
[*Exeunt* GLOSTER *and* BEDFORD.

Erp. Shall I attend your grace?

K. Hen. No, my good knight;
Go with my brothers to my lords of England:
I and my bosom must debate a while,
And then I would no other company.

Erp. The Lord in heaven bless thee, noble Harry! [*Exit* ERPINGHAM.

K. Hen. God-a-mercy, old heart! thou speak-est cheerfully.

Enter PISTOL.

Pist. *Qui va la?*

K. Hen. A friend.

Pist. Discuss unto me; Art thou officer;
Or art thou base, common, and popular?

K. Hen. I am a gentleman of a company.

Pist. Trailest thou the puissant pike?

K. Hen. Even so: What are you?

Pist. As good a gentleman as the emperor.

K. Hen. Then you are a better than the king.

Pist. The king's a bawcock, and a heart of gold,
A lad of life, an imp of fame;
Of parents good, of fist most valiant;
I kiss his dirty shoe, and from my heart-strings
I love the lovely bully. What's thy name?

K. Hen. Harry *le Roy*.

Pist. *Le Roy!* a Cornish name: art thou of Cornish crew?

K. Hen. No, I am a Welshman.

Pist. Knowest thou Fluellen.

K. Hen. Yes.

Pist. Tell him, I'll knock his leek about his pate,
Upon Saint Davy's day.

K. Hen. Do not you wear your dagger in your cap that day, lest he knock that about yours.

Pist. Art thou his friend?

K. Hen. And his kinsman too.

Pist. The *figo* for thee then!

K. Hen. I thank you: God be with you!

Pist. My name is Pistol called. [*Exit.*

K. Hen. It sorts well with your fierceness.

Enter FLUELLEN *and* GOWER, *severally.*

Gow. Captain Fluellen!

Flu. So! in the name of Cheshu Christ, speak lower. It is the greatest admiration in the universal 'orld, when the true and auncient prerogatifes and laws of the wars is not kept: if you would take the pains but to examine the wars of Pompey the Great, you shall find, I warrant you, that there is no tiddle taddle, or pibble pabble, in Pompey's camp; I warrant you, you shall find the ceremonies of the wars, and the cares of it, and the forms of it, and the sobriety of it, and the modesty of it, to be otherwise.

Gow. Why, the enemy is loud; you heard him all night.

Flu. If the enemy is an ass, and a fool, and a prating coxcomb, is it meet, think you, that we should also, look you, be an ass, and a fool, and a prating coxcomb; in your own conscience now?

Gow. I will speak lower.

Flu. I pray you, and beseech you, that you will.
[*Exeunt* GOWER *and* FLUELLEN.

K. Hen. Though it appear a little out of fashion,
There is much care and valour in this Welshman.

Enter BATES, COURT, *and* WILLIAMS.

Court. Brother John Bates, is not that the morning which breaks yonder?

Bates. I think it be: but we have no great cause to desire the approach of day.

Will. We see yonder the beginning of the day, but, I think, we shall never see the end of it.—Who goes there?

K. Hen. A friend.

Will. Under what captain serve you?

K. Hen. Under Sir Thomas Erpingham.

Will. A good old commander, and a most kind gentleman: I pray you, what thinks he of our estate?

K. Hen. Even as men wrecked upon a sand, that look to be washed off the next tide.

Bates. He hath not told his thought to the king?

K. Hen. No; nor it is not meet he should. For, though I speak it to you, I think, the king is but a man, as I am: the violet smells to him, as it doth to me; the element shows to him, as it doth to me; all his senses have but human conditions: his ceremonies laid by, in his nakedness he appears but a man; and though his affections are higher mounted than ours, yet, when they stoop, they stoop with the like wing; therefore when he sees reason of fears, as we do, his fears, out of doubt, be of the same relish as ours are: Yet, in reason, no man should possess him with any appearance of fear, lest he, by showing it, should dishearten his army.

Bates. He may show what outward courage he will: but, I believe, as cold a night as 'tis, he could wish himself in the Thames up to the neck; and so I would he were, and I by him, at all adventures, so we were quit here.

K. Hen. By my troth, I will speak my conscience of the king; I think, he would not wish himself any where but where he is.

Bates. Then, would he were here alone; so should he be sure to be ransomed, and a many poor men's lives saved.

K. Hen. I dare say, you love him not so ill, to wish him here alone; howsoever you speak this, to feel other men's minds: Methinks, I could not die any where so contented, as in the king's company; his cause being just, and his quarrel honourable.

Will. That's more than we know.

Bates. Ay, or more than we should seek after; for we know enough, if we know we are the king's subjects; if his cause be wrong, our obedience to the king wipes the crime of it out of us.

Will. But if the cause be not good, the king himself hath a heavy reckoning to make; when all those legs, and arms, and heads, chopped off in a battle, shall join together at the latter day, and cry all—We died at such a place; some, swearing; some, crying for a surgeon; some, upon their wives left poor behind them; some, upon the debts they owe; some, upon their children rawly left. I am afeard there are few die well, that die in battle; for how can they charitably dispose of any thing, when blood is their argument? Now, if these men do not die well, it will be a black matter for the king that led them to it; whom to disobey were against all proportion of subjection.

K. Hen. So, if a son, that is by his father sent about merchandise, do sinfully miscarry upon the sea, the imputation of his wickedness, by your rule, should be imposed upon his father that sent him: or if a servant, under his master's command, transporting a sum of money, be assailed by robbers, and die in many irreconciled iniquities, you may call the business of the master the author of the servant's damnation:—But this is not so: the king is not bound to answer the particular endings of his soldiers, the father of his son, nor the master of his servant; for they purpose not their death, when they purpose their services. Besides, there is no king, be his cause never so spotless, if it come to the arbitrement of swords, can try it out with all unspotted soldiers. Some, peradventure, have on them the guilt of premeditated and contrived murder; some, of beguiling virgins with the broken seals of perjury; some, making the wars their bulwark, that have before gored the gentle bosom of peace with pillage and robbery. Now, if these men have defeated the law, and outrun native punishment, though they can outstrip men, they have no wings to fly from God: war is his beadle, war is his vengeance; so that here men are punished, for before-breach of the king's laws, in now the king's quarrel: where they feared the death, they have borne life away; and where they would be safe, they perish: Then if they die unprovided, no more is the king guilty of their damnation, than he was before guilty of those impieties for the which they are now visited. Every subject's duty is the king's; but every subject's soul is his own. Therefore should every soldier in the wars do as every sick man in his bed, wash every mote out of his conscience: and dying so, death is to him advantage; or not dying, the time was blessedly lost, wherein such preparation was gained: and in him that escapes, it were not sin to think, that making God so free an offer, he let him outlive that day to see his greatness, and to teach others how they should prepare.

Will. 'Tis certain, every man that dies ill, the ill is upon his own head, the king is not to answer for it.

Bates. I do not desire he should answer for me; and yet I determine to fight lustily for him.

K. Hen. I myself heard the king say, he would not be ransomed.

Will. Ay, he said so, to make us fight cheerfully: but, when our throats are cut, he may be ransomed, and we ne'er the wiser.

K. Hen. If I live to see it, I will never trust his word after.

Will. 'Mass, you'll pay him then; That's a perilous shot out of an elder gun, that a poor and private displeasure can do against a monarch! you may as well go about to turn the sun to ice, with fanning in his face with a peacock's feather. You'll never trust his word after! come, 'tis a foolish saying.

K. Hen. Your reproof is something too round; I should be angry with you, if the time were convenient.

Will. Let it be a quarrel between us, if you live.

K. Hen. I embrace it.

Will. How shall I know thee again?

K. Hen. Give me any gage of thine, and I will wear it in my bonnet: then, if ever thou darest acknowledge it, I will make it my quarrel.

Will. Here's my glove, give me another of thine.

K. Hen. There.

Will. This will I also wear in my cap: if ever thou come to me and say, after to-morrow, *This is my glove*, by this hand, I will take thee a box on the ear.

K. Hen. If ever I live to see it, I will challenge it.

Will. Thou darest as well be hanged.

K. Hen. Well, I will do it, though I take thee in the king's company.

Will. Keep thy word: fare thee well.

Bates. Be friends, you English fools, be friends; we have French quarrels enough, if you could tell how to reckon.

K. Hen. Indeed, the French may lay twenty French crowns to one, they will beat us; for they bear them on their shoulders: But it is no English treason to cut French crowns; and, to-morrow, the king himself will be a clipper.

[*Exeunt* Soldiers.

Upon the king! let us our lives, our souls,
Our debts, our careful wives, our children, and
Our sins, lay on the king;—we must bear all.
O hard condition! twin-born with greatness,
Subjected to the breath of every fool,
Whose sense no more can feel but his own wringing!
What infinite heart's ease must kings neglect,
That private men enjoy?
And what have kings, that privates have not too,
Save ceremony, save general ceremony?
And what art thou, thou idle ceremony?
What kind of god art thou, that suffer'st more
Of mortal griefs, than do thy worshipers?
What are thy rents? what are thy comings in?
O ceremony, show me but thy worth!
What is thy soul of adoration?
Art thou aught else but place, degree, and form,
Creating awe and fear in other men?
Wherein thou art less happy, being fear'd,
Than they in fearing.
What drink'st thou oft, instead of homage sweet,
But poison'd flattery? O, be sick, great greatness,

And bid thy ceremony give thee cure!
Think'st thou, the fiery fever will go out
With titles blown from adulation?
Will it give place to flexure and low bending?
Canst thou, when thou command'st the beggar's knee,
Command the health of it? No, thou proud dream,
That play'st so subtly with a king's repose:
I am a king, that find thee; and I know,
'Tis not the balm, the sceptre, and the ball,
The sword, the mace, the crown imperial,
The inter-tissued robe of gold and pearl,
The farced title running 'fore the king,
The throne he sits on, nor the tide of pomp
That beats upon the high shore of this world,
No, not all these, thrice gorgeous ceremony,
Not all these, laid in bed majestical,
Can sleep so soundly as the wretched slave;
Who, with a body fill'd, and vacant mind,
Gets him to rest, cramm'd with distressful bread;
Never sees horrid night, the child of hell;
But, like a lackey, from the rise to set,
Sweats in the eye of Phœbus, and all night
Sleeps in Elysium; next day, after dawn,
Doth rise, and help Hyperion to his horse;
And follows so the ever-running year
With profitable labour, to his grave:
And, but for ceremony, such a wretch,
Winding up days with toil, and nights with sleep,
Had the fore-hand and vantage of a king.
The slave, a member of the country's peace,
Enjoys it; but in gross brain little wots,
What watch the king keeps to maintain the peace,
Whose hours the peasant best advantages.

Enter ERPINGHAM.

Erp. My lord, your nobles, jealous of your absence,
Seek through your camp to find you.
K. Hen. Good old knight,
Collect them all together at my tent:
I'll be before thee.
Erp. I shall do 't my lord. [*Exit.*
K. Hen. O God of battles! steel my soldiers' hearts!
Possess them not with fear: take from them now
The sense of reckoning of the opposed numbers:
Pluck their hearts from them not to-day, O Lord!
O not to-day! Think not upon the fault
My father made in compassing the crown!
I Richard's body have interred new;
And on it have bestow'd more contrite tears,
Than from it issued forced drops of blood.
Five hundred poor I have in yearly pay,
Who twice a day their wither'd hands hold up
Toward heaven, to pardon blood; and I have built
Two chantries, where the sad and solemn priests
Sing still for Richard's soul. More will I do:
Though all that I can do, is nothing worth;
Since that my penitence comes after all,
Imploring pardon.

Enter GLOSTER.

Glo. My liege!
K. Hen. My brother Gloster's voice?—Ay;
I know thy errand, I will go with thee:—
The day, my friends, and all things stay for me. [*Exeunt.*

SCENE II. *The* French *Camp.*

Enter Dauphin, ORLEANS, RAMBURES, *and Others.*

Orl. The sun doth gild our armour; up, my lords.
Dau. *Montez a cheval:*—My horse! *valet! lacquay?* ha!
Orl. O brave spirit!
Dau. *Via!—les eaux et la terre*——
Orl. *Rien puis? l' air et le feu*——
Dau. *Ciel!* cousin Orleans.——

Enter Constable.

Now, my lord Constable.
Con. Hark, how our steeds for present service neigh.
Dau. Mount them, and make incision in their hides;
That their hot blood may spin in English eyes,
And doubt them with superfluous courage: Ha!
Ram. What, will you have them weep our horses' blood?
How shall we then behold their natural tears?

Enter a Messenger.

Mess. The English are embattled, you French peers.
Con. To horse, you gallant princes! straight to horse!
Do but behold yon poor and starved band,
And your fair show shall suck away their souls,
Leaving them but the shales and husks of men.
There is not work enough for all our hands;
Scarce blood enough in all their sickly veins,
To give each naked curtle-ax a stain,
That our French gallants shall to-day draw out,
And sheath for lack of sport: let us but blow on them,
The vapour of our valour will o'erturn them.
'Tis positive, 'gainst all exceptions, lords,
That our superfluous lackeys, and our peasants,—
Who, in unnecessary action, swarm
About our squares of battle,—were enough
To purge this field of such a hilding foe;
Though we, upon this mountain's basis by
Took stand for idle speculation:
But that our honours must not. What's to say?
A very little little let us do,
And all is done. Then let the trumpets sound
The tucket-sonuance, and the note to mount:
For our approach shall so much dare the field,
That England shall couch down in fear, and yield.

Enter GRANDPRE.

Grand. Why do you stay so long, my lords of France?
Yon island carrions, desperate of their bones,
Ill-favour'dly become the morning field:
Their ragged curtains poorly are let loose,
And our air shakes them passing scornfully.
Big Mars seems bankrupt in their beggar'd host,
And faintly through a rusty beaver peeps.
Their horsemen sit like fixed candlesticks,
With torch-staves in their hands: and their poor jades
Lob down their heads, dropping the hides and hips;
The gum down-roping from their pale-dead eyes;
And in their pale dull mouths the gimmal bit
Lies foul with chew'd grass, still and motionless;
And their executors, the knavish crows,
Fly o'er them all, impatient for their hour.
Description cannot suit itself in words,
To demonstrate the life of such a battle
In life so lifeless as it shows itself.
Con. They have said their prayers, and they stay for death.
Dau. Shall we go send them dinners, and fresh suits,
And give their fasting horses provender,
And after fight with them?
Con. I stay but for my guard; On, to the field:
I will the banner from a trumpet take,
And use it for my haste. Come, come, away!
The sun is high, and we outwear the day. [*Exeunt.*

SCENE III. *The* English *Camp.*

Enter the English Host; GLOSTER, BEDFORD, EXETER, SALISBURY, *and* WESTMORELAND.

Glo. Where is the king?
Bed. The king himself is rode to view their battle.
West. Of fighting men they have full three score thousand.

Exe. There's five to one; besides, they all are fresh.

Sal. God's arm strike with us! 'tis a fearful odds.
God be wi' you, princes all; I'll to my charge;
If we no more meet, till we meet in heaven,
Then, joyfully,—my noble lord of Bedford,—
My dear lord Gloster,—and my good lord Exeter,
And my kind kinsman,—warriors all, adieu!

Bed. Farewell, good Salisbury; and good luck go with thee!

Exe. Farewell, kind lord; fight valiantly to-day:
And yet I do thee wrong, to mind thee of it,
For thou art fram'd of the firm truth of valour. [*Exit* SALISBURY.

Bed. He is as full of valour, as of kindness;
Princely in both.

West. O that we now had here

Enter KING HENRY.

But one ten thousand of those men in England,
That do no work to-day!

K. Hen. What's he that wishes so?
My cousin Westmoreland?—No, my fair cousin:
If we are mark'd to die, we are enough
To do our country loss; and if to live,
The fewer men, the greater share of honour.
God's will! I pray thee, wish not one man more.
By Jove, I am not covetous for gold;
Nor care I, who doth feed upon my cost;
It yearns me not, if men my garments wear;
Such outward things dwell not in my desires:
But, if it be a sin to covet honour,
I am the most offending soul alive.
No, 'faith, my coz, wish not a man from England:
God's peace! I would not lose so great an honour,
As one man more, methinks, would share from me,
For the best hope I have. O, do not wish one more:
Rather proclaim it, Westmoreland, through my host,
That he, which hath no stomach to this fight,
Let him depart; his passport shall be made,
And crowns for convoy put into his purse:
We would not die in that man's company
That fears his fellowship to die with us.
This day is call'd—the feast of Crispian:
He, that outlives this day, and comes safe home,
Will stand a tip-toe when this day is nam'd,
And rouse him at the name of Crispian.
He, that shall live this day, and see old age,
Will yearly on the vigil feast his friends,
And say—to-morrow is Saint Crispian:
Then will he strip his sleeve, and show his scars,
And say, these wounds I had on Crispin's day.
Old men forget; yet all shall be forgot,
But he'll remember, with advantages,
What feats he did that day; Then shall our names,
Familiar in their mouths as household words,—
Harry the king, Bedford and Exeter,
Warwick and Talbot, Salisbury and Gloster,—
Be in their flowing cups freshly remember'd:
This story shall the good man teach his son;
And Crispin Crispian shall ne'er go by,
From this day to the ending of the world,
But we in it shall be remembered:
We few, we happy few, we band of brothers;
For he, to-day that sheds his blood with me,
Shall be my brother; be he ne'er so vile,
This day shall gentle his condition:
And gentlemen in England, now a-bed,
Shall think themselves accurs'd, they were not here;
And hold their manhoods cheap, while any speaks,
That fought with us upon Saint Crispin's day.

Enter SALISBURY.

Sal. My sovereign lord, bestow yourself with speed;
The French are bravely in their battles set,
And will with all expedience charge on us.

K. Hen. All things are ready, if our minds be so.

West. Perish the man, whose mind is backward now!

K. Hen. Thou dost not wish more help from England, cousin?

West. God's will, my liege, 'would you and I alone,
Without more help, might fight this battle out!

K. Hen. Why, now thou hast unwish'd five thousand men;
Which likes me better, than to wish us one.—
You know your places: God be with you all!

Tucket. *Enter* MONTJOY.

Mont. Once more I come to know of thee, King Harry,
If for thy ransome thou wilt now compound,
Before thy most assured overthrow:
For, certainly, thou art so near the gulf,
Thou needs must be englutted. Besides, in mercy,
The Constable desires thee—thou wilt mind
Thy followers of repentance; that their souls
May make a peaceful and a sweet retire
From off these fields, where (wretches) their poor bodies
Must lie and fester.

K. Hen. Who hath sent thee now?

Mont. The Constable of France.

K. Hen. I pray thee, bear my former answer back;
Bid them achieve me, and then sell my bones.
Good God! why should they mock poor fellows thus?
The man, that once did sell the lion's skin
While the beast liv'd, was kill'd with hunting him.
A many of our bodies shall, no doubt,
Find native graves; upon the which, I trust,
Shall witness live in brass of this day's work:
And those that leave their valiant bones in France,
Dying like men, though buried in your dunghills,
They shall be fam'd; for there the sun shall greet them,
And draw their honours reeking up to heaven;
Leaving their earthly parts to choke your clime,
The smell whereof shall breed a plague in France.
Mark then abounding valour in our English;
That, being dead, like to the bullet's grazing,
Break out into a second course of mischief,
Killing in relapse of mortality.
Let me speak proudly;—Tell the Constable,
We are but warriors for the working-day:
Our gayness, and our gilt, are all besmirch'd
With rainy marching in the painful field;
There's not a piece of feather in our host
(Good argument, I hope, we shall not fly),
And time hath worn us into slovenry:
But, by the mass, our hearts are in the trim:
And my poor soldiers tell me—yet ere night
They'll be in fresher robes; or they will pluck
The gay new coats o'er the French soldiers' heads,
And turn them out of service. If they do this
(As, if God please, they shall), my ransome then
Will soon be levied. Herald, save thou thy labour;
Come thou no more for ransome, gentle herald;
They shall have none, I swear, but these my joints;
Which if they have as I will leave 'em to them,
Shall yield them little, tell the Constable.

Mont. I shall, King Harry. And so fare thee well:
Thou never shalt hear herald any more. [*Exit.*

K. Hen. I fear, thou'lt once more come again for ransome.

Enter the DUKE OF YORK.

York. My lord, most humbly on my knee I beg
The leading of the vaward.

K. Hen. Take it, brave York.—Now, soldiers, march away:
And how thou pleasest, God, dispose the day!
[*Exeunt.*

SCENE IV. *The Field of Battle.*

Alarums: Excursions. Enter French Soldier, PISTOL, *and* Boy.

Pist. Yield, cur.

Fr. Sol. *Je pense, que vous estes le gentilhomme de bonne qualite.*

Pist. Quality? Callino, castore me! art thou a gentleman? what is thy name? discuss.

Fr. Sol. *O seigneur Dieu!*

Pist. O, signieur Dew should be a gentleman:
Perpend my words, O signieur Dew, and mark;—
O signieur Dew, thou diest on point of fox,
Except, O signieur, thou do give to me
Egregious ransome.

Fr. Sol. *O, prennez misericorde! ayez pitie de moy!*

Pist. Moy shall not serve, I will have forty moys;
For I will fetch thy rim out at thy throat,
In drops of crimson blood.

Fr. Sol. *Est-il impossible d' eschapper la force de ton bras?*

Pist. Brass, cur!
Thou damned and luxurious mountain goat,
Offer'st me brass?

Fr. Sol. *O pardonnez moy!*

Pist. Say'st thou me so? is that a ton of moys?—
Come hither, boy; Ask me this slave in French,
What is his name.

Boy. *Escoutez; Comment estes-vous appelle?*

Fr. Sol. *Monsieur le Fer.*

Boy. He says, his name is—master Fer.

Pist. Master Fer! I'll fer him, and firk him, and ferret him:—discuss the same in French unto him.

Boy. I do not know the French for fer, and ferret, and firk.

Pist. Bid him prepare, for I will cut his throat.

Fr. Sol. *Que dit-il, monsieur?*

Boy. *Il me commande de vous dire que vous faites vous prest; car ce soldat icy est dispose tout a cette heure de couper vostre gorge.*

Pist. Ouy, couper gorge, par ma foy, pesant,
Unless thou give me crowns, brave crowns;
Or mangled shalt thou be by this my sword.

Fr. Sol. *O, je vous supplie pour l' amour de Dieu, me pardonner! Je suis gentilhomme de bonne maison: gardez ma vie, et je vous donneray deux cents escus.*

Pist. What are his words?

Boy. He prays you to save his life: he is a gentleman of a good house; and, for his ransome, he will give you two hundred crowns.

Pist. Tell him,—my fury shall abate, and I
The crowns will take.

Fr. Sol. *Petit monsieur, que dit-il?*

Boy. *Encore qu'il est contre son jurement, de pardonner aucun prisonnier; neantmoins, pour les escus que vous l'avez promis, il est content de vous donner la liberte, le franchisement.*

Fr. Sol. *Sur mes genoux, je vous donne mille remerciemens: et je m'estime heureux que je suis tombe entre les mains d'un chevalier, je pense, le plus brave, valiant, et tres distingue seigneur d' Angleterre.*

Pist. Expound unto me, boy.

Boy. He gives you, upon his knees, a thousand thanks: and he esteems himself happy that he hath fallen into the hands of (as he thinks) the most brave, valorous, and thrice-worthy signieur of England.

Pist. As I suck blood, I will some mercy show.—
Follow me, cur. [*Exit* PISTOL.

Boy. *Suivez-vous le grand capitaine.*
[*Exit* French Soldier.

I did never know so full a voice issue from so empty a heart: but the saying is true,—The empty vessel makes the greatest sound. Bardolph, and Nym, had ten times more valour than this roaring devil i' the old play, that every one may pare his nails with a wooden dagger; and they are both hanged; and so would this be, if he durst steal any thing adventurously. I must stay with the lackeys, with the luggage of our camp: the French might have a good prey of us, if he knew of it; for there is none to guard it, but boys. [*Exit.*

SCENE V. *Another Part of the field of Battle.*

Alarums. Enter Dauphin, ORLEANS, BOURBON, Constable, RAMBURES, *and Others.*

Con. *O diable!*

Orl. *O seigneur!—le jour est perdu, tout est perdu!*

Dau. *Mort de ma vie!* all is confounded, all!
Reproach and everlasting shame
Sits mocking in our plumes.—*O meschante fortune!*—
Do not run away. [*A short Alarum.*

Con. Why, all our ranks are broke.

Dau. O perdurable shame!—let's stab ourselves.
Be these the wretches that we play'd at dice for?

Orl. Is this the king we sent to for his ransome?

Bour. Shame, and eternal shame, nothing but shame!
Let us die in fight: Once more back again;
And he that will not follow Bourbon now,
Let him go hence, and, with his cap in hand,
Like a base pander, hold the chamber-door,
Whilst by a slave, no gentler than my dog,
His fairest daughter is contaminate.

Con. Disorder, that hath spoil'd us, friend us now!
Let us, in heaps, go offer up our lives
Unto these English, or else die with fame.

Orl. We are enough, yet living in the field,
To smother up the English in our throngs,
If any order might be thought upon.

Bour. The devil take order now! I'll to the throng;
Let life be short; else, shame will be too long.
[*Exeunt.*

SCENE VI. *Another Part of the Field.*

Alarums. Enter KING HENRY, *and* Forces; EXETER, *and Others.*

K. Hen. Well have we done, thrice-valiant countrymen:
But all's not done, yet keep the French the field.

Exe. The duke of York commends him to your majesty.

K. Hen. Lives he, good uncle? thrice, within this hour,
I saw him down; thrice up again, and fighting;
From helmet to the spur, all blood he was.

Exe. In which array (brave soldier) doth he lie,
Larding the plain: and by his bloody side,
(Yoke-fellow to his honour-owing wounds)
The noble earl of Suffolk also lies.
Suffolk first died, and York, all haggled over,
Comes to him, where in gore he lay insteep'd,
And takes him by the beard; kisses the gashes,
That bloodily did yawn upon his face;
And cries aloud,—*Tarry, dear cousin Suffolk!*
My soul shall thine keep company to heaven:
Tarry, sweet soul, for mine, then fly abreast;
As, in this glorious and well foughten field,
We kept together in our chivalry!
Upon these words I came, and cheer'd him up:
He smil'd me in the face, raught me his hand,
And, with a feeble gripe, says,—*Dear my lord,*
Commend my service to my sovereign.
So did he turn, and over Suffolk's neck
He threw his wounded arm, and kiss'd his lips:
And so, espous'd to death, with blood, he seal'd
A testament of noble-ending love.

The pretty and sweet manner of it forc'd
Those waters from me, which I would have stopp'd:
But I had not so much of man in me,
But all my mother came into mine eyes,
And gave me up to tears.

K. Hen. I blame you not;
For, hearing this, I must perforce compound
With mistful eyes, or they will issue too.— [*Alarum.*
But, hark! what new alarum is this same?—
The French have reinforc'd their scatter'd men:
Then every soldier kill his prisoners;
Give the word through. [*Exeunt.*

SCENE VII. *Another Part of the Field.*

Alarums. Enter FLUELLEN *and* GOWER.

Flu. Kill the poys and the luggage! 'tis expressly against the law of arms: 'tis as arrant a piece of knavery, mark you now, as can be offered in the 'orld: In your conscience now, is it not?

Gow. 'Tis certain, there's not a boy left alive; and the cowardly rascals, that ran from the battle, have done this slaughter: besides, they have burned and carried away all that was in the king's tent; wherefore the king, most worthily, hath caused every soldier to cut his prisoner's throat. O, 'tis a gallant king!

Flu. Ay, he was porn at Monmouth, captain Gower: What call you the town's name, where Alexander the pig was born?

Gow. Alexander the great.

Flu. Why, I pray you, is not pig, great? The pig, or the great, or the mighty, or the huge, or the magnanimous, are all one reckonings, save the phrase is a little variations.

Gow. I think, Alexander the great was born in Macedon; his father was called—Philip of Macedon, as I take it.

Flu. I think, it is in Macedon, where Alexander is porn. I tell you, captain,—If you look in the maps of the 'orld, I warrant, you shall find, in the comparisons between Macedon and Monmouth, that the situations, look you, is both alike. There is a river in Macedon; and there is also moreover a river at Monmouth: it is called Wye, at Monmouth: but it is out of my prains, what is the name of the other river; but 'tis all one, 'tis so like as my fingers is to my fingers, and there is salmons in both. If you mark Alexander's life well, Harry of Monmouth's life is come after it indifferent well, for there is figures in all things. Alexander (God knows, and you know), in his rages, and his furies, and his wraths, and his cholers, and his moods, and his displeasures, and his indignations, and also being a little intoxicates in his prains, did, in his ales and his angers, look you, kill his pest friend, Clytus.

Gow. Our king is not like him in that; he never killed any of his friends.

Flu. It is not well done, mark you now, to take tales out of my mouth, ere it is made an end and finished. I speak but in the figures and comparisons of it: As Alexander is kill his friend Clytus, being in his ales and his cups; so also Harry Monmouth, being in his right wits and his goot judgments, is turn away the fat knight with the great pelly-doublet: he was full of jests, and gipes, and knaveries, and mocks; I am forget his name.

Gow. Sir John Falstaff.

Flu. That is he: I can tell you, there is goot men born at Monmouth.

Gow. Here comes his majesty.

Alarum. Enter KING HENRY, *with a part of the* English Forces; WARWICK, GLOSTER, EXETER, *and Others.*

K. Hen. I was not angry since I came to France
Until this instant.—Take a trumpet, herald;
Ride thou unto the horsemen on yon hill;
If they will fight with us, bid them come down,
Or void the field; they do offend our sight:
If they'll do neither, we will come to them;
And make them skirr away, as swift as stones
Enforced from the old Assyrian slings:
Besides, we'll cut the throats of those we have;
And not a man of them, that we shall take,
Shall taste our mercy:—Go, and tell them so.

Enter MONTJOY.

Exe. Here comes the herald of the French, my liege.

Glo. His eyes are humbler than they us'd to be.

K. Hen. How now, what means this, herald? know'st thou not,
That I have fin'd these bones of mine for ransome?
Com'st thou again for ransome?

Mont. No, great king:
I come to thee for charitable licence,
That we may wander o'er this bloody field,
To book our dead, and then to bury them;
To sort our nobles from our common men;
For many of our princes (woe the while!)
Lie drown'd and soak'd in mercenary blood
(So do our vulgar drench their peasant limbs
In blood of princes); and their wounded steeds
Fret fetlock deep in gore, and, with wild rage,
Yerk out their armed heels at their dead masters,
Killing them twice. O, give us leave, great king,
To view the field in safety, and dispose
Of their dead bodies.

K. Hen. I tell thee truly, herald,
I know not, if the day be ours, or no;
For yet a many of your horsemen peer,
And gallop o'er the field.

Mont. The day is yours.

K. Hen. Praised be God, and not our strength for it!—
What is this castle call'd, that stands hard by?

Mont. They call it—Agincourt.

K. Hen. Then call we this—the field of Agincourt,
Fought on the day of Crispin Crispianus.

Flu. Your grandfather of famous memory, an 't please your majesty, and your great-uncle Edward the plack prince of Wales, as I have read in the chronicles, fought a most prave pattle here in France.

K. Hen. They did, Fluellen.

Flu. Your majesty says very true: If your majesties is remember'd of it, the Welshmen did goot service in a garden where leeks did grow, wearing leeks in their Monmouth caps; which, your majesty knows, to this hour is an honourable padge of the service; and, I do believe, your majesty takes no scorn to wear the leek upon Saint Tavy's day.

K. Hen. I wear it for a memorable honour:
For I am Welsh, you know, good countryman.

Flu. All the water in Wye cannot wash your majesty's Welsh plood out of your pody, I can tell you that: God pless it and preserve it, as long as it pleases his grace, and his majesty too!

K. Hen. Thanks, good my countryman.

Flu. By Cheshu, I am your majesty's countryman, I care not who know it; I will confess it to all the 'orld: I need not to be ashamed of your majesty, praised be God, so long as your majesty is an honest man.

K. Hen. God keep me so!—Our heralds go with him;
Bring me just notice of the numbers dead
On both our parts.—Call yonder fellow hither.
[*Points to* WILLIAMS. *Exeunt* MONTJOY *and Others.*

Exe. Soldier, you must come to the king.

K. Hen. Soldier, why wear'st thou that glove in thy cap?

Will. An't please your majesty, 'tis the gage of one that I should fight withal, if he be alive.

K. Hen. An Englishman?

Will. An't please your majesty, a rascal, that swagger'd with me last night: who, if 'a live, and ever dare to challenge this glove, I have sworn to take him a box o' the ear: or, if I can see my glove in his cap (which he swore, as he was a soldier, he would wear, if alive), I will strike it out soundly.

K. Hen. What think you, Captain Fluellen? is it fit this soldier keep his oath?

Flu. He is a craven and a villain else, an't please your majesty, in my conscience.

K. Hen. It may be his enemy is a gentleman of great sort, quite from the answer of his degree.

Flu. Though he be as goot a gentleman as the tevil is, as Lucifer and Belzebub himself, it is necessary, look your grace, that he keep his vow and his oath: if he be perjured, see you now, his reputation is as arrant a villain, and a Jack-sauce, as ever his plack shoe trod upon Got's ground and his earth, in my conscience, la.

K. Hen. Then keep thy vow, sirrah, when thou meet'st the fellow.

Will. So I will, my liege, as I live.

K. Hen. Who servest thou under?

Will. Under Captain Gower, my liege.

Flu. Gower is a goot captain; and is goot knowledge and literature in the wars.

K. Hen. Call him hither to me, soldier.

Will. I will, my liege. [*Exit.*

K. Hen. Here, Fluellen: wear thou this favour for me, and stick it in thy cap: When Alencon and myself were down together, I plucked this glove from his helm: if any man challenge this, he is a friend to Alencon and an enemy to our person; if thou encounter any such, apprehend him, an thou dost love me.

Flu. Your grace does me as great honours, as can be desired in the hearts of his subjects: I would fain see the man, that has but two legs, that shall find himself aggriefed at this glove, that is all; but I would fain see it once; an please Got of his grace, that I might see it.

K. Hen. Knowest thou Gower?

Flu. He is my dear friend, an please you.

K. Hen. Pray thee, go seek him, and bring him to my tent.

Flu. I will fetch him. [*Exit.*

K. Hen. My lord of Warwick,—and my brother Gloster,
Follow Fluellen closely at the heels:
The glove, which I have given him for a favour,
May, haply, purchase him a box o' the ear;
It is the soldier's; I, by bargain, should
Wear it myself. Follow, good cousin, Warwick:
If that the soldier strike him (as, I judge
By his blunt bearing, he will keep his word),
Some sudden mischief may arise of it;
For I do know Fluellen valiant,
And, touch'd with choler, hot as gunpowder,
And quickly will return an injury:
Follow, and see there be no harm between them.—
Go you with me, uncle of Exeter. [*Exeunt.*

SCENE VIII. *Before* King Henry's *Pavilion.*

Enter GOWER *and* WILLIAMS.

Will. I warrant it is to knight you, captain.

Enter FLUELLEN.

Flu. Got's will and his pleasure, captain, I peseech you now, come apace to the king; there is more goot toward you, peradventure, than is in your knowledge to dream of.

Will. Sir, know you this glove?

Flu. Know the glove? I know, the glove is a glove.

Will. I know this; and thus I challenge it. [*Strikes him.*

Flu. 'Sblud, an arrant traitor, as any's in the universal 'orld, or in France, or in England.

Gow. How now, sir? you villain!

Will. Do you think I'll be forsworn?

Flu. Stand away, Captain Gower; I will give treason his payment into plows, I warrant you.

Will. I am no traitor.

Flu. That's a lie in thy throat.—I charge you in his majesty's name, apprehend him; he's a friend of the duke Alencon's.

Enter WARWICK *and* GLOSTER.

War. How now, how now! what's the matter?

Flu. My lord of Warwick, here is (praised be Got for it!) a most contagious treason come to light, look you, as you shall desire in a summer's day. Here is his majesty.

Enter KING HENRY *and* EXETER.

K. Hen. How now! what's the matter?

Flu. My liege, here is a villain, and a traitor, that, look your grace, has struck the glove which your majesty is take out of the helmet of Alencon.

Will. My liege, this was my glove; here is the fellow of it: and he, that I gave it to in change, promised to wear it in his cap: I promised to strike him, if he did: I met this man with my glove in his cap, and I have been as good as my word.

Flu. Your majesty hear now (saving your majesty's manhood), what an arrant, rascally, beggarly, lowsy knave it is: I hope your majesty is pear me testimony, and witness, and avouchments, that this is the glove of Alencon, that your majesty is give me, in your conscience now.

K. Hen. Give me thy glove, soldier: Look, here is the fellow of it. 'Twas I, indeed, thou promised'st to strike; and thou hast given me most bitter terms.

Flu. An please your majesty, let his neck answer for it, if there is any martial law in the 'orld.

K. Hen. How canst thou make me satisfaction?

Will. All offences, my liege, come from the heart: never came any from mine, that might offend your majesty.

K. Hen. It was ourself thou did'st abuse.

Will. Your majesty came not like yourself: you appeared to me but as a common man; witness the night, your garments, your lowliness; and what your highness suffered under that shape, I beseech you, take it for your own fault, and not mine; for had you been as I took you for, I made no offence; therefore, I beseech your highness, pardon me.

K. Hen. Here, uncle Exeter, fill this glove with crowns,
And give it to this fellow.—Keep it, fellow;
And wear it for an honour in thy cap,
Till I do challenge it—Give him the crowns:—
And, captain, you must needs be friends with him.

Flu. By this day and this light, the fellow has mettle enough in his pelly;—Hold, there is twelve pence for you, and I pray you to serve Got, and keep you out of prawls, and prabbles, and quarrels, and dissensions, and, I warrant you, it is the petter for you.

Will. I will none of your money.

Flu. It is with a goot will; I can tell you, it will serve you to mend your shoes: Come, wherefore should you be so pashful? your shoes is not so goot: 'tis a goot silling, I warrant you, or I will change it.

Enter an English Herald.

K. Hen. Now, herald: are the dead number'd?

Her. Here is the number of the slaughter'd French. [*Delivers a Paper.*

K. Hen. What prisoners of good sort are taken, uncle?

Exe. Charles duke of Orleans, nephew to the king;
John duke of Bourbon, and Lord Bouciquault:

Of other lords, and barons, knights, and 'squires,
Full fifteen hundred, besides common men.
K. Hen. This note doth tell me of ten thousand French,
That in the field lie slain: of princes, in this number,
And nobles bearing banners, there lie dead
One hundred, twenty-six: added to these,
Of knights, esquires, and gallant gentlemen,
Eight thousand and four hundred; of the which,
Five hundred were but yesterday dubb'd knights:
So that, in these ten thousand they have lost,
There are but sixteen hundred mercenaries;
The rest are—princes, barons, lords, knights, squires,
And gentlemen of blood and quality.
The names of those their nobles that lie dead,—
Charles De-la-bret, high constable of France;
Jaques of Chatillon, admiral of France;
The master of the cross-bows, Lord Rambures;
Great-master of France, the brave Sir Guischard Dauphin;
John duke of Alencon; Antony duke of Brabant,
The brother to the duke of Burgundy;
And Edward duke of Bar: of lusty earls,
Grandpre, and Roussi, Fauconberg, and Foix,
Beaumont, and Marle, Vaudemont, and Lestrale,
Here was a royal fellowship of death!——
Where is the number of our English dead?
[Herald *presents another Paper.*
Edward the duke of York, the earl of Suffolk,
Sir Richard Ketley, Davy Gam, esquire:
None else of name; and, of all other men,
But five and twenty. O God, thy arm was here,
And not to us, but to thy arm alone
Ascribe we all.—When, without stratagem,
But in plain shock, and even play of battle,
Was ever known so great and little loss,
On one part and on the other?—Take it, God,
For it is only thine!
Exe. 'Tis wonderful!
K. Hen. Come, go we in procession to the village:
And be it death proclaimed through our host,
To boast of this, or take that praise from God,
Which is his only.
Flu. Is it not lawful, an please your majesty, to tell how many is killed?
K. Hen. Yes, captain; but with this acknowledgment,
That God fought for us.
Flu. Yes, my conscience, he did us great goot.
K. Hen. Do we all holy rites;
Let there be sung *Non nobis*, and *Te Deum*.
The dead with charity enclos'd in clay,
We'll then to Calais; and to England then;
Where ne'er from France arriv'd more happy men. [*Exeunt.*

ACT V.

Enter CHORUS.

Chor. Vouchsafe to those that have not read the story,
That I may prompt them: and of such as have,
I humbly pray them to admit the excuse
Of time, of numbers, and due course of things,
Which cannot in their huge and proper life
Be here presented. Now we bear the king
Toward Calais: grant him there; there seen,
Heave him away upon your winged thoughts,
Athwart the sea: Behold, the English beach
Pales in the flood with men, with wives, and boys,
Whose shouts and claps outvoice the deep-mouth'd sea,
Which, like a mighty whiffler fore the king,
Seems to prepare his way: so let him land;
And, solemnly, see him set on to London.
So swift a pace hath thought, that even now
You may imagine him upon Blackheath:
Where that his lords desire him, to have borne
His bruised helmet, and his bended sword,
Before him, through the city: he forbids it,
Being free from vainness and self-glorious pride;
Giving full trophy, signal, and ostent,
Quite from himself, to God. But now behold,
In the quick forge and workinghouse of thought,
How London doth pour out her citizens?
The mayor, and all his brethren, in best sort,—
Like to the senators of the antique Rome,
With the plebeians swarming at their heels,—
Go forth, and fetch their conquering Cæsar in:
As, by a lower, but by loving likelihood,
Were now the general of our gracious empress
(As, in good time, he may, from Ireland coming,
Bringing rebellion broached on his sword,
How many would the peaceful city quit,
To welcome him? much more, and much more cause,
Did they this Harry. Now in London place him;
(As yet the lamentation of the French
Invites the king of England's stay at home):
The emperor's coming in behalf of France,
To order peace between them, we omit,
And all the occurrences, whatever chanc'd,
Till Harry's back-return again to France;
There must we bring him; and myself have play'd
The interim, by remembering you—'tis past.
Then brook abridgment; and your eyes advance
After your thoughts, straight back again to France. [*Exit.*

SCENE I. France. *An* English *Court of Guard.*

Enter FLUELLEN *and* GOWER.

Gow. Nay, that's right; but why wear you your leek to-day? Saint Davy's day is past.

Flu. There is occasions and causes why and wherefore in all things: I will tell you, as my friend, Captain Gower; The rascally, scald, beggarly, lowsy, pragging knave, Pistol,—which you and yourself, and all the 'orld, know to be no petter than a fellow, look you now, of no merits,—he is come to me, and prings me pread and salt yesterday, look you, and bid me eat my leak: it was in a place where I could not breed no contentions with him; but I will be so pold as to wear it in my cap till I see him once again, and then I will tell him a little piece of my desires.

Enter PISTOL.

Gow. Why, here he comes, swelling like a turkey-cock.

Flu. 'Tis no matter for his swellings, nor his turkey-cocks.—Got pless you, ancient Pistol! you scurvy, lowsy knave, Got bless you!

Pist. Ha! art thou Bedlam? dost thou thirst, base Trojan,
To have me fold up Parca's fatal web?
Hence! I am qualmish at the smell of leek.

Flu. I peseech you heartily, scurvy, lowsy knave, at my desires, and my requests, and my petitions, to eat, look you, this leek; because, look you, you do not love it, nor your affections, and your appetites, and your digestions, does not agree with it, I would desire you to eat it.

Pist. Not for Cadwallader, and all his goats.

Flu. There is one goat for you, [*Strikes him.*] Will you be so goot, scald knave, as eat it?

Pist. Base Trojan, thou shalt die.

Flu. You say very true, scald knave, when Got's will is: I will desire you to live in the mean time, and eat your victuals; come, there is sauce for it. [*Striking him again.*] You called me yesterday mountain-squire; but I will make you to-day a squire of low degree. I pray you, fall to; if you can mock a leek, you can eat a leek.

Gow. Enough captain; you have astonished him.

Flu. I say, I will make him eat some part of my leek, or I will peat his pate four days:—Pite, I pray you; it is goot for your green wound, and your ploody coxcomb.

Pist. Must I bite?

Flu. Yes, certainly; and out of doubt, and out of questions too, and ambiguities.

Pist. By this leek, I will most horribly revenge; I eat, and eke I swear—

Flu. Eat, I pray you: Will you have some more sauce to your leek? there is not enough leek to swear by.

Pist. Quiet thy cudgel; thou dost see, I eat.

Flu. Much goot do you, scald knave, heartily. Nay, 'pray you, throw none away; the skin is goot for your proken coxcomb. When you take occasions to see leeks hereafter, I pray you, mock at them! that is all.

Pist. Good.

Flu. Ay, leeks is goot:—Hold you, there is a groat to heal your pate.

Pist. Me a groat?

Flu. Yes, verily, and in truth, you shall take it; or I have another leek in my pocket, which you shall eat.

Pist. I take thy groat, in earnest of revenge.

Flu. If I owe you any thing, I will pay you in cudgels; you shall be a woodmonger, and buy nothing of me but cudgels. God be wi' you, and keep you, and heal your pate. [*Exit.*

Pist. All hell shall stir for this.

Gow. Go, go; you are a counterfeit cowardly knave. Will you mock at an ancient tradition,—begun upon an honourable respect, and worn as a memorable trophy of predeceased valour,—and dare not avouch in your deeds any of your words? I have seen you gleeking and galling at this gentleman twice or thrice. You thought, because he could not speak English in the native garb, he could not therefore handle an English cudgel: you find it otherwise; and, henceforth, let a Welsh correction teach you a good English condition. Fare you well. [*Exit.*

Pist. Doth fortune play the huswife with me now?
News have I, that my Nell is dead i' the spital
Of malady of France;
And there my rendezvous is quite cut off.
Old I do wax; and from my weary limbs
Honour is cudgel'd. Well, bawd will I turn,
And something lean to cutpurse of quick hand.
To England will I steal, and there I'll steal:
And patches will I get unto these scars,
And swear, I got them in the Gallia wars.
[*Exit.*

SCENE II. Troyes *in* Champagne. *An Apartment in the* French King's *Palace.*

Enter, at one Door, KING HENRY, BEDFORD, GLOSTER, EXETER, WARWICK, WESTMORELAND, *and other* Lords; *at another, the* French King, QUEEN ISABEL, *the* PRINCESS KATHARINE, Lords, Ladies, *&c.* the DUKE OF BURGUNDY, *and his* Train.

K. Hen. Peace to this meeting, wherefore we are met!
Unto our brother France,—and to our sister,
Health and fair time of day:—joy and good wishes
To our most fair and princely cousin Katharine;
And (as a branch and member of this royalty,
By whom this great assembly is contriv'd),
We do salute you, duke of Burgundy;—
And, princes French, and peers, health to you all!

Fr. King. Right joyous are we to behold your face,
Most worthy brother England; fairly met:—
So are you, princes English, every one.

Q. Isa. So happy be the issue, brother England,
Of this good day, and of this gracious meeting,
As we are now glad to behold your eyes;
Your eyes, which hitherto have borne in them
Against the French, that met them in their bent,
The fatal balls of murdering basilisks:
The venom of such looks, we fairly hope,
Have lost their quality; and that this day
Shall change all griefs, and quarrels, into love.

K. Hen. To cry amen to that, thus we appear.

Q. Isa. You English princes all, I do salute you.

Bur. My duty to you both, on equal love,
Great kings of France and England! That I have labour'd
With all my wits, my pains, and strong endeavours,
To bring your most imperial majesties
Unto this bar and royal interview,
Your mightiness on both parts best can witness.
Since then my office hath so far prevail'd,
That, face to face, and royal eye to eye,
You have congreeted; let it not disgrace me,
If I demand, before this royal view,
What rub, or what impediment, there is,
Why that the naked, poor, and mangled peace,
Dear nurse of arts, plenties, and joyful births,
Should not, in this best garden of the world,
Our fertile France, put up her lovely visage?
Alas! she hath from France too long been chas'd;
And all her husbandry doth lie on heaps,
Corrupting in its own fertility.
Her vine, the merry cheerer of the heart,
Unpruned dies: her hedges even-pleached,—
Like prisoners wildly overgrown with hair,
Put forth disorder'd twigs: her fallow leas
The darnel, hemlock, and rank fumitory,
Doth root upon; while that the coulter rusts,
That should deracinate such savagery:
The even mead, that erst brought sweetly forth
The freckled cowslip, burnet, and green clover,
Wanting the scythe, all uncorrected, rank,
Conceives by idleness; and nothing teems,
But hateful docks, rough thistles, kecksies, burs,
Losing both beauty and utility.
And as our vineyards, fallows, meads, and hedges,
Defective in their natures, grow to wildness;
Even so our houses, and ourselves, and children,
Have lost, or do not learn, for want of time,
The sciences that should become our country;
But grow, like savages,—as soldiers will;
That nothing do but meditate on blood,—
To swearing and stern looks, diffus'd attire,
And every thing that seems unnatural.
Which to reduce into our former favour,
You are assembled: and my speech entreats,
That I may know the let, why gentle peace
Should not expel these inconveniences,
And bless us with her former qualities.

K. Hen. If, duke of Burgundy, you would the peace,
Whose want gives growth to the imperfections
Which you have cited, you must buy that peace
With full accord to all our just demands;
Whose tenours and particular effects
You have, enschedul'd briefly, in your hands.

Bur. The king hath heard them: to the which, as yet,
There is no answer made.

K. Hen. Well then, the peace,
Which you before so urg'd, lies in his answer.

Fr. King. I have but with a cursorary eye
O'erglanc'd the articles: pleaseth your grace
To appoint some of your council presently
To sit with us once more, with better heed
To resurvey them, we will, suddenly,
Pass our accept, and peremptory answer.

K. Hen. Brother, we shall.—Go, uncle Exeter,—
And brother Clarence,—and you, brother Gloster,
Warwick—and Huntingdon,—go with the king:
And take with you free power, to ratify,
Augment, or alter, as your wisdoms best
Shall see advantageable for our dignity,

Any thing in, or out of, our demands;
And we'll consign thereto.—Will you, fair sister,
Go with the princes, or stay here with us?

Q. Isa. Our gracious brother, I will go with them;
Haply, a woman's voice may do some good,
When articles, too nicely urg'd, be stood on.

K. Hen. Yet leave our cousin Katharine here with us;
She is our capital demand, compris'd
Within the fore-rank of our articles.

Q. Isa. She hath good leave.

[*Exeunt all but* HENRY, KATHARINE, *and her Gentlewoman.*

K. Hen. Fair Katharine, and most fair!
Will you vouchsafe to teach a soldier terms,
Such as will enter at a lady's ear,
And plead his lovesuit to her gentle heart?

Kath. Your majesty shall mock at me; I cannot speak your England.

K. Hen. O fair Katharine, if you will love me soundly with your French heart, I will be glad to hear you confess it brokenly with your English tongue. Do you like me, Kate?

Kath. *Pardonnez moy,* I cannot tell vat is—like me.

K. Hen. An angel is like you, Kate; and you are like an angel.

Kath. *Que dit il? que je suis semblable a les anges?*

Alice. *Ouy, vrayment (sauf vostre grace) ainsi dit il.*

K. Hen. I said so, dear Katharine; and I must not blush to affirm it.

Kath. *O bon Dieu! les langues des hommes sont pleines des tromperies.*

K. Hen. What says she, fair one? that the tongues of men are full of deceits?

Alice. *Ouy;* dat de tongues of de mans is be full of deceits: dat is de princess.

K. Hen. The princess is the better Englishwoman. I'faith, Kate, my wooing is fit for thy understanding: I am glad, thou canst speak no better English; for, if thou could'st, thou would'st find me such a plain king, that thou would'st think, I had sold my farm to buy my crown. I know no ways to mince it in love, but directly to say—I love you: then, if you urge me further than to say—Do you in faith? I wear out my suit. Give me your answer; i'faith, do; and so clap hands and a bargain: How say you, lady?

Kath. *Sauf vostre honneur,* me understand well.

K. Hen. Marry, if you would put me to verses, or to dance for your sake, Kate, why you undid me: for the one, I have neither words nor measure; and for the other, I have no strength in measure, yet a reasonable measure in strength. If I could win a lady at leap-frog, or by vaulting into my saddle with my armour on my back, under the correction of bragging be it spoken, I should quickly leap into a wife. Or, if I might buffet for my love, or bound my horse for her favours, I could lay on like a butcher, and sit like a jack-an-apes, never off: but, before God, I cannot look greenly, nor gasp out my eloquence, nor I have no cunning in protestation; only downright oaths, which I never use till urged, nor never break for urging. If thou canst love a fellow of this temper, Kate, whose face is not worth sun-burning, that never looks in his glass for love of any thing he sees there, let thine eye be thy cook. I speak to thee plain soldier: If thou canst love me for this, take me: if not, to say to thee—that I shall die, is true: but—for thy love, by the Lord, no; yet I love thee too. And while thou livest, dear Kate, take a fellow of plain and uncoined constancy; for he perforce must do thee right, because he hath not the gift to woo in other places: for these fellows of infinite tongue, that can rhyme themselves into ladies' favours,—they do always reason themselves out again. What! a speaker is but a prater; a rhyme is but a ballad. A good leg will fall; a straight back will stoop; a black beard will turn white: a curled pate will grow bald; a fair face will wither; a full eye will wax hollow: but a good heart, Kate, is the sun and moon; or, rather, the sun, and not the moon; for it shines bright, and never changes, but keeps his course truly. If thou would have such a one, take me: And take me, take a soldier; take a soldier, take a king: And what sayest thou then to my love? speak, my fair, and fairly, I pray thee.

Kath. Is it possible dat I should love de enemy of France?

K. Hen. No; it is not possible you should love the enemy of France, Kate: but, in loving me, you should love the friend of France; for I love France so well, that I will not part with a village of it; I will have it all mine: and, Kate, when France is mine, and I am yours, then yours is France, and you are mine.

Kath. I cannot tell vat is dat.

K. Hen. No, Kate? I will tell thee in French; which, I am sure, will hang upon my tongue like a new-married wife about her husband's neck, hardly to be shook off. *Quand j'ay la possession de France, et quand vous avez le possession de moi* (let me see, what then? Saint Dennis be my speed!)—*donc vostre est France, et vous estes mienne.* It is as easy for me, Kate, to conquer the kingdom, as to speak so much more French: I shall never move thee in French, unless it be to laugh at me.

Kath. *Sauf vostre honneur, le Francois que vous parlez est meilleur que l'Anglois lequel je parle.*

K. Hen. No, 'faith, is't not, Kate: but thy speaking of my tongue, and I thine, most truly falsely, must needs be granted to be much at one. But, Kate, dost thou understand thus much English? Canst thou love me?

Kath. I cannot tell.

K. Hen. Can any of your neighbours tell, Kate? I'll ask them. Come, I know, thou lovest me: and at night when you come into your closet, you'll question this gentlewoman about me; and I know, Kate, you will, to her, dispraise those parts in me, that you love with your heart; but, good Kate, mock me mercifully; the rather, gentle princess, because I love thee cruelly. If ever thou be'st mine, Kate, (as I have a saving faith within me, tells me,—thou shalt), I get thee with scambling, and thou must therefore needs prove a good soldier-breeder: Shall not thou and I, between Saint Dennis and Saint George, compound a boy, half French, half English, that shall go to Constantinople, and take the Turk by the beard? shall we not? what sayest thou, my fair flower-de-luce?

Kath. I do not know dat.

K. Hen. No; 'tis hereafter to know, but now to promise: do but now promise, Kate, you will endeavour for your French part of such a boy; and, for my English moiety, take the word of a king and a bachelor. How answer you, *la plus belle Katharine du monde, mon tres chere et divine deesse?*

Kath. Your *majeste* 'ave *fausse* French enough to deceive de most *sage damoiselle* dat is *en France.*

K. Hen. Now, fye upon my false French! By mine honour, in true English, I love thee, Kate: by which honour I dare not swear, thou lovest me; yet my blood begins to flatter me that thou dost, notwithstanding the poor and untempering effect of my visage. Now beshrew my father's ambition! he was thinking of civil wars when he got me; therefore was I created with a stubborn outside, with an aspect of iron, that, when I come to woo ladies, I fright them. But, in faith, Kate, the elder I wax, the better I shall appear: my comfort is, that old age, that ill layer-up of beauty, can do no more spoil upon my face; thou hast me, if thou hast me, at the worst; and thou shalt wear me, if thou wear me, better and better; And therefore tell me, most fair Katharine, will you have me? Put off your maiden blushes; avouch the thoughts of your heart with the looks of an empress; take me by the hand, and say,—Harry of England, I am thine: which word thou shalt no sooner bless mine ear withal, but I will tell thee aloud—England is thine, Ireland is thine, France is thine, and Henry Plantagenet is thine; who, though I speak it before his face, if he be not fellow with the best king, thou shalt find the best king of good fellows. Come, your answer in broken musick; for thy voice is musick, and thy English broken: therefore, queen of all, Katharine, break thy mind to me in broken English, Wilt thou have me?

Kath. Dat is, as it shall please de *roy mon pere*.

K. Hen. Nay, it will please him well, Kate; it shall please him, Kate.

Kath. Den it shall also content me.

K. Hen. Upon that I will kiss your hand, and I call you—my queen.

Kath. *Laissez, mon seigneur, laissez, laissez: ma foy, je ne veux point que vous abaissez vostre grandeur, en baisant la main d'une vostre indigne serviteure; excusez moy, je vous supplie, mon tres puissant seigneur.*

K. Hen. Then I will kiss your lips, Kate.

Kath. *Les dames, et damoiselles, pour estre baisees devant leur nopces, il n'est pas le coutume de France.*

K. Hen. Madam, my interpreter, what says she?

Alice. Dat it is not be de fashion *pour les* ladies of France,—I cannot tell what is, *baiser, en* English.

K. Hen. To kiss.

Alice. Your majesty *entendre* bettre *que moy*.

K. Hen. It is not the fashion for the maids in France to kiss before they are married, would she say?

Alice. *Ouy, vrayment.*

K. Hen. O Kate, nice customs curt'sy to great kings. Dear Kate, you and I cannot be confined within the weak list of a country's fashion: we are the makers of manners, Kate; and the liberty that follows our places, stops the mouths of all find-faults; as I will do yours, for upholding the nice fashion of your country, in denying me a kiss: therefore patiently, and yielding. [*Kissing her.*] You have witchcraft in your lips, Kate; there is more eloquence in a sugar touch of them than in the tongues of the French council; and they should sooner persuade Harry of England, than a general petition of monarchs. Here comes your father.

Enter the French King *and* Queen, BURGUNDY, BEDFORD, GLOSTER, EXETER, WESTMORELAND, *and other* French *and* English Lords.

Bur. God save your majesty! my royal cousin, teach you our princess English?

K. Hen. I would have her learn, my fair cousin, how perfectly I love her; and that is good English.

Bur. Is she not apt?

K. Hen. Our tongue is rough, coz; and my condition is not smooth: so that, having neither the voice nor the heart of flattery about me, I cannot so conjure up the spirit of love in her, that he will appear in his true likeness.

Bur. Pardon the frankness of my mirth, if I answer you for that. If you would conjure in her, you must make a circle: if conjure up love in her in his true likeness, he must appear naked, and blind; Can you blame her then, being a maid yet rosed over with the virgin crimson of modesty, if she deny the appearance of a naked blind boy in her naked seeing self? It were, my lord, a hard condition for a maid to consign to.

K. Hen. Yet they do wink, and yield; as love is blind, and enforces.

Bur. They are then excused, my lord, when they see not what they do.

K. Hen. Then, good my lord, teach your cousin to consent to winking.

Bur. I will wink on her to consent, my lord, if you will teach her to know my meaning: for maids, well summered and warm kept, are like flies at Bartholomew-tide, blind, though they have their eyes; and then they will endure handling, which before would not abide looking on.

K. Hen. This moral ties me over to time, and a hot summer; and so I will catch the fly, your cousin, in the latter end, and she must be blind too.

Bur. As love is, my lord, before it loves.

K. Hen. It is so: and you may, some of you, thank love for my blindness; who cannot see many a fair French city, for one fair French maid that stands in my way.

Fr. King. Yes, my lord, you see them perspectively, the cities turned into a maid; for they are all girdled with maiden walls, that war hath never entered.

K. Hen. Shall Kate be my wife?

Fr. King. So please you.

K. Hen. I am content; so the maiden cities you talk of, may wait on her: so the maid, that stood in the way of my wish, shall show me the way to my will.

Fr. King. We have consented to all terms of reason.

K. Hen. Is't so, my lords of England?

West. The king hath granted every article:
His daughter, first; and then, in sequel, all,
According to their firm proposed natures.

Exe. Only, he hath not yet subscribed this:—
Where your majesty demands,—That the king of France, having any occasion to write for matter of grant, shall name your highness in this form, and with this addition, in French,—*Notre tres cher filz Henry roy d'Angleterre, heritier de France;* and thus in Latin,—*Præclarissimus filius noster Henricus, rex Angliæ, et hæres Franciæ.*

Fr. King. Nor this I have not, brother, so denied,
But your request shall make me let it pass.

K. Hen. I pray you then, in love and dear alliance,
Let that one article rank with the rest:
And thereupon, give me your daughter.

Fr. King. Take her, fair son; and from her blood raise up
Issue to me: that the contending kingdoms
Of France and England, whose very shores look pale
With envy of each other's happiness,
May cease their hatred: and this dear conjunction
Plant neighbourhood and Christianlike accord
In their sweet bosoms, that never war advance
His bleeding sword 'twixt England and fair France.

All. Amen!

K. Hen. Now welcome, Kate:—and bear me witness all,
That here I kiss her as my sovereign queen. [*Flourish.*

Q. Isa. God, the best maker of all marriages,
Combine your hearts in one, your realms in one!
As man and wife, being two, are one in love,
So be there 'twixt your kingdoms such a spousal,
That never may ill office, or fell jealousy,
Which troubles oft the bed of blessed marriage,
Thrust in between the paction of these kingdoms,
To make divorce of their incorporate league;
That English may as French, French Englishmen,
Receive each other!—God speak this Amen!

All. Amen!

K. Hen. Prepare we for our marriage:—on which day,

My lord of Burgundy, we'll take your oath,
And all the peers', for surety of our leagues.—
Then shall I swear to Kate, and you to me;
And may our oaths well kept and prosp'rous be!
[*Exeunt.*

Enter CHORUS.

Thus far, with rough, and all unable pen,
Our bending author hath pursu'd the story;
In little room confining mighty men,
Mangling by starts the full course of their glory.
Small time, but, in that small, most greatly liv'd
This star of England: fortune made his sword;
By which the world's best garden he achiev'd,
And of it left his son imperial lord.
Henry the Sixth, in infant bands crown'd king
Of France and England, did this king succeed;
Whose state so many had the managing,
That they lost France, and made his England bleed:
Which oft our stage hath shown; and, for their sake,
In your fair minds let this acceptance take.
[*Exit.*

FIRST PART OF
KING HENRY THE SIXTH.

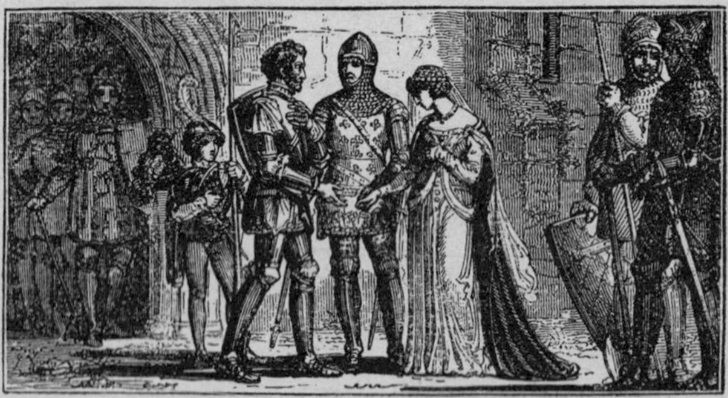

PERSONS REPRESENTED.

KING HENRY THE SIXTH.
DUKE OF GLOSTER, *Uncle to the* King, *and Protector.*
DUKE OF BEDFORD, *Uncle to the* King, *and Regent of* France.
THOMAS BEAUFORT, Duke *of* Exeter, *great Uncle to the* King.
HENRY BEAUFORT, *great Uncle to the* King, Bishop *of* Winchester, *and afterwards* Cardinal.
JOHN BEAUFORT, Earl *of* Somerset; *afterwards* Duke.
RICHARD PLANTAGENET, *eldest son of* Richard, *late* Earl *of* Cambridge; *afterwards* Duke *of* York.
EARL OF WARWICK. EARL OF SALISBURY.
EARL OF SUFFOLK.
LORD TALBOT, *afterwards* Earl *of* Shrewsbury.
JOHN TALBOT, *his* Son.
EDMUND MORTIMER, Earl *of* March.
Mortimer's Keeper, *and a* Lawyer.
SIR JOHN FASTOLFE. SIR WILLIAM LUCY.
SIR WILLIAM GLANSDALE. SIR THOMAS GARGRAVE.
Mayor *of* London.
WOODVILLE, *Lieutenant of the Tower.*
VERNON, *of the White Rose, or* York *Faction.*
BASSET, *of the Red Rose, or* Lancaster *Faction.*
CHARLES, Dauphin, *and afterwards* King *of* France.
REIGNIER, Duke *of* Anjou, *and titular* King *of* Naples.
DUKE OF BURGUNDY. DUKE OF ALENCON.
Governor *of* Paris. Bastard *of* Orleans.
Master-Gunner *of* Orleans, *and his* Son.
General *of the* French Forces *in* Bordeaux.
A French Sergeant. *A* Porter.
An old Shepherd, *Father to* Joan la Pucelle.
MARGARET, *Daughter to* Reignier: *afterwards married to* King Henry.
COUNTESS OF AUVERGNE.
JOAN LA PUCELLE, *commonly called* Joan *of* Arc.
Fiends *appearing to* La Pucelle, Lords, Warders *of the* Tower, Heralds, Officers, Soldiers, Messengers, *and several* Attendants *both on the* English *and* French.

SCENE—*partly in* England, *and partly in* France.

ACT I.

SCENE I. Westminster Abbey.

Dead March. Corpse of King Henry the Fifth *discovered, lying in state; attended on by the* DUKES OF BEDFORD, GLOSTER, *and* EXETER; *the* EARL OF WARWICK, *the* BISHOP OF WINCHESTER, Heralds, *&c.*

Bed. HUNG be the heavens with black, yield day to night!
Comets, importing change of times and states,
Brandish your crystal tresses in the sky,
And with them scourge the bad revolting stars,
That have consented unto Henry's death!
Henry the Fifth, too famous to live long!
England ne'er lost a king of so much worth.

Glo. England ne'er had a king, until his time.
Virtue he had, deserving to command:
His brandish'd sword did blind men with his beams;
His arms spread wider than a dragon's wings;
His sparkling eyes, replete with wrathful fire,
More dazzled and drove back his enemies,
Than midday sun fierce bent against their faces.

What should I say? his deeds exceed all speech:
He ne'er lift up his hand, but conquer'd.

Exe. We mourn in black; Why mourn we not in blood?
Henry is dead, and never shall revive;
Upon a wooden coffin we attend;
And death's dishonourable victory
We with our stately presence glorify,
Like captives bound to a triumphant car.
What? shall we curse the planets of mishap,
That plotted thus our glory's overthrow?
Or shall we think the subtle-witted French
Conjurers and sorcerers, that, afraid of him,
By magic verses have contriv'd his end?

Win. He was a king bless'd of the King of kings.
Unto the French the dreadful judgment day
So dreadful will not be, as was his sight.
The battles of the Lord of Hosts he fought:
The church's prayers made him so prosperous.

Glo. The church! where is it? Had not churchmen pray'd,
His thread of life had not so soon decay'd:
None do you like but an effeminate prince,
Whom, like a schoolboy, you may overawe.

Win. Gloster, whate'er we like, thou art protector;
And lookest to command the prince, and realm.
Thy wife is proud; she holdeth thee in awe,
More than God, or religious churchmen, may.

Glo. Name not religion, for thou lov'st the flesh;
And ne'er throughout the year to church thou go'st,
Except it be to pray against thy foes.

Bed. Cease, cease these jars, and rest your minds in peace!
Let's to the altar:—Heralds, wait on us:—
Instead of gold, we'll offer up our arms;
Since arms avail not, now that Henry's dead.—
Posterity, await for wretched years,
When at their mother's moist eyes babes shall suck;
Our isle be made a nourish of salt tears,
And none but women left to wail the dead.—
Henry the Fifth! thy ghost I invocate;
Prosper this realm, keep it from civil broils!
Combat with adverse planets in the heavens!
A far more glorious star thy soul will make,
Than Julius Cæsar, or bright ——

Enter a Messenger.

Mess. My honourable lords, health to you all!
Sad tidings bring I to you out of France,
Of loss, of slaughter, and discomfiture:
Guienne, Champaigne, Rheims, Orleans,
Paris, Guysors, Poictiers, are all quite lost.

Bed. What say'st thou, man, before dead Henry's corse?
Speak softly; or the loss of those great towns
Will make him burst his lead, and rise from death.

Glo. Is Paris lost? is Rouen yielded up?
If Henry were recall'd to life again,
These news would cause him once more yield the ghost.

Exe. How were they lost? what treachery was us'd?

Mess. No treachery; but want of men and money.
Among the soldiers this is mutter'd,—
That here you maintain several factions;
And, whilst a field should be despatch'd and fought,
You are disputing of your generals.
One would have ling'ring wars, with little cost;
Another would fly swift, but wanteth wings;
A third man thinks, without expense at all,
By guileful fair words peace may be obtain'd.
Awake, awake, English nobility!
Let not sloth dim your honours, new begot:
Cropp'd are the flower-de-luces in your arms;
Of England's coat one half is cut away.

Exe. Were our tears wanting to this funeral,
These tidings would call forth her flowing tides.

Bed. Me they concern; regent I am of France:—
Give me my steeled coat, I'll fight for France.—
Away with these disgraceful wailing robes!
Wounds I will lend the French, instead of eyes,
To weep their intermissive miseries.

Enter another Messenger.

2 *Mess.* Lords, view these letters, full of bad mischance,
France is revolted from the English quite;
Except some petty towns of no import:
The Dauphin Charles is crowned king in Rheims;
The bastard of Orleans with him is join'd;
Reignier, duke of Anjou, doth take his part;
The duke of Alencon flieth to his side.

Exe. The Dauphin crowned king! all fly to him!
O, whither shall we fly from this reproach?

Glo. We will not fly, but to our enemies' throats;
Bedford, if thou be slack, I'll fight it out.

Bed. Gloster, why doubt'st thou of my forwardness?
An army have I muster'd in my thoughts,
Wherewith already France is overrun.

Enter a third Messenger.

3 *Mess.* My gracious lords, to add to your laments,
Wherewith you now bedew King Henry's hearse,—
I must inform you of a dismal fight,
Betwixt the stout Lord Talbot and the French.

Win. What! wherein Talbot overcame? is't so?

3 *Mess.* O, no; wherein Lord Talbot was o'erthrown:
The circumstance I'll tell you more at large.
The tenth of August last, this dreadful lord,
Retiring from the siege of Orleans,
Having full scarce six thousand in his troop,
By three and twenty thousand of the French
Was round encompassed and set upon:
No leisure had he to enrank his men;
He wanted pikes to set before his archers;
Instead whereof, sharp stakes, pluck'd out of hedges,
They pitched in the ground confusedly,
To keep the horsemen off from breaking in.
More than three hours the fight continued;
Where valiant Talbot, above human thought,
Enacted wonders with his sword and lance.
Hundreds he sent to hell, and none durst stand him;
Here, there, and every where, enrag'd he slew:
The French exclaim'd, The devil was in arms;
All the whole army stood agaz'd on him:
His soldiers, spying his undaunted spirit,
A Talbot! a Talbot! cried out amain,
And rush'd into the bowels of the battle.
Here had the conquest fully been seal'd up,
If Sir John Fastolfe had not play'd the coward;
He being in the vaward (plac'd behind,
With purpose to relieve and follow them),
Cowardly fled, not having struck one stroke.
Hence grew the general wreck and massacre;
Enclosed were they with their enemies:
A base Walloon, to win the Dauphin's grace,
Thrust Talbot with a spear into the back;
Whom all France, with their chief assembled strength,
Durst not presume to look once in the face.

Bed. Is Talbot slain? then I will slay myself,
For living idly here, in pomp and ease,
Whilst such a worthy leader, wanting aid,
Unto his dastard foemen is betray'd.

3 *Mess.* O no, he lives; but is took prisoner,
And Lord Scales with him, and Lord Hungerford:
Most of the rest slaughter'd, or took, likewise.

Bed. His ransome there is none but I shall pay:
I'll hale the Dauphin headlong from his throne,

His crown shall be the ransome of my friend;
Four of their lords I'll change for one of ours.—
Farewell, my masters; to my task will I;
Bonfires in France forthwith I am to make,
To keep our great Saint George's feast withal:
Ten thousand soldiers with me I will take,
Whose bloody deeds shall make all Europe quake.

3 *Mess.* So you had need; for Orleans is besieg'd;
The English army is grown weak and faint:
The earl of Salisbury craveth supply,
And hardly keeps his men from mutiny,
Since they, so few, watch such a multitude.

Exe. Remember, lords, your oaths to Henry sworn;
Either to quell the Dauphin utterly,
Or bring him in obedience to your yoke.

Bed. I do remember it; and here take leave,
To go about my preparation. [*Exit.*

Glo. I'll to the Tower, with all the haste I can,
To view the artillery and munition;
And then I will proclaim young Henry king. [*Exit.*

Exe. To Eltham will I, where the young king is,
Being ordain'd his special governor?
And for his safety there I'll best devise. [*Exit.*

Win. Each hath his place and function to attend;
I am left out: for me nothing remains.
But long I will not be Jack-out-of-office;
The king from Eltham I intend to steal,
And sit at chiefest stern of public weal. [*Exit. Scene closes.*

SCENE II. France. *Before* Orleans.

Enter CHARLES, *with his* Forces; ALENCON, REIGNIER, *and Others.*

Char. Mars his true moving, even as in the heavens,
So in the earth, to this day is not known:
Late did he shine upon the English side;
Now we are victors, upon us he smiles.
What towns of any moment, but we have?
At pleasure here we lie, near Orleans;
Otherwiles, the famish'd English, like pale ghosts,
Faintly besiege us one hour in a month.

Alen. They want their porridge, and their fat bull-beeves:
Either they must be dieted like mules,
And have their provender tied to their mouths,
Or piteous they will look, like drowned mice.

Reig. Let's raise the siege; Why live we idly here?
Talbot is taken, whom we wont to fear:
Remaineth none but mad-brain'd Salisbury;
And he may well in fretting spend his gall,
Nor men, nor money, hath he to make war.

Char. Sound, sound alarum; we will rush on them.
Now for the honour of the forlorn French:—
Him I forgive my death, that killeth me,
When he sees me go back one foot, or fly. [*Exeunt.*

Alarums: Excursions: afterwards a Retreat.

Re-enter CHARLES, ALENCON, REIGNIER, *and Others.*

Char. Who ever saw the like? what men have I?—
Dogs! cowards! dastards!—I would ne'er have fled,
But that they left me 'midst my enemies.

Reig. Salisbury is a desperate homicide;
He fighteth as one weary of his life.
The other lords, like lions wanting food,
Do rush upon us as their hungry prey.

Alen. Froissard, a countryman of ours, records,
England all Olivers and Rowlands bred,
During the time Edward the Third did reign.
More truly now may this be verified;
For none but Samsons, and Goliasses,
It sendeth forth to skirmish. One to ten!
Lean raw-bon'd rascals; who would e'er suppose
They had such courage and audacity?

Char. Let's leave this town; for they are hair-brain'd slaves,
And hunger will enforce them to be more eager:
Of old I know them; rather with their teeth
The walls they'll tear down, than forsake the siege.

Reig. I think, by some odd gimmals or device,
Their arms are set, like clocks, still to strike on;
Else ne'er could they hold out so as they do.
By my consent we'll e'en let them alone.

Alen. Be it so.

Enter the Bastard *of* Orleans.

Bast. Where's the prince Dauphin? I have news for him.

Char. Bastard of Orleans, thrice welcome to us.

Bast. Methinks, your looks are sad, your cheer appall'd;
Hath the late overthrow wrought this offence?
Be not dismay'd, for succour is at hand:
A holy maid hither with me I bring,
Which, by a vision sent to her from heaven,
Ordained is to raise this tedious siege,
And drive the English forth the bounds of France.
The spirit of deep prophecy she hath,
Exceeding the nine sibyls of old Rome;
What's past, and what's to come, she can descry.
Speak, shall I call her in? Believe my words,
For they are certain and infallible.

Char. Go, call her in: [*Exit* Bastard.] But, first, to try her skill,
Reignier, stand thou as Dauphin in my place:
Question her proudly, let thy looks be stern:—
By this mean shall we sound what skill she hath. [*Retires.*

Enter LA PUCELLE, Bastard *of* Orleans, *and Others.*

Reig. Fair maid, is't thou wilt do these wondrous feats?

Puc. Reignier, is't thou that thinkest to beguile me?—
Where is the Dauphin?—come, come from behind;
I know thee well, though never seen before.
Be not amaz'd, there's nothing hid from me:
In private will I talk with thee apart:—
Stand back, you lords, and give us leave a while.

Reig. She takes upon her bravely at first dash.

Puc. Dauphin, I am by birth a shepherd's daughter,
My wit untrain'd in any kind of art.
Heaven, and our Lady gracious, hath it pleas'd
To shine on my contemptible estate:
Lo, whilst I waited on my tender lambs,
And to sun's parching heat display'd my cheeks,
God's mother deigned to appear to me;
And, in a vision full of majesty,
Will'd me to leave my base vocation,
And free my country from calamity:
Her aid she promis'd, and assur'd success:
In complete glory she reveal'd herself;
And, whereas I was black and swart before,
With those clear rays which she infus'd on me,
That beauty am I bless'd with, which you see.
Ask me what question thou canst possible,
And I will answer unpremeditated:
My courage try by combat, if thou dar'st,
And thou shalt find that I exceed my sex.
Resolve on this: Thou shalt be fortunate,
If thou receive me for thy warlike mate.

Char. Thou hast astonish'd me with thy high terms;
Only this proof I'll of thy valour make,—
In single combat thou shalt buckle with me:
And, if thou vanquishest, thy words are true;
Otherwise, I renounce all confidence.

Puc. I am prepar'd; here is my keen-edg'd sword,

Deck'd with five flower-de-luces on each side;
The which at Touraine, in Saint Katharine's churchyard,
Out of a great deal of old iron I chose forth.

Char. Then come o'God's name, I fear no woman.

Puc. And, while I live, I'll ne'er fly from a man. [*They fight.*

Char. Stay, stay thy hands; thou art an Amazon,
And fightest with the sword of Deborah.

Puc. Christ's mother helps me, else I were too weak.

Char. Whoe'er helps thee, 'tis thou that must help me:
Impatiently I burn with thy desire;
My heart and hands thou hast at once subdu'd.
Excellent Pucelle, if thy name be so,
Let me thy servant, and not sovereign, be;
'Tis the French Dauphin sueth to thee thus.

Puc. I must not yield to any rights of love,
For my profession's sacred from above:
When I have chased all thy foes from hence,
Then will I think upon a recompense.

Char. Mean time, look gracious on thy prostrate thrall.

Reig. My lord, methinks, is very long in talk,

Alen. Doubtless he shrives this woman to her smock;
Else ne'er could he so long protract his speech.

Reig. Shall we disturb him, since he keeps no mean?

Alen. He may mean more than we poor men do know:
These women are shrewd tempters with their tongues.

Reig. My lord, where are you? what devise you on?
Shall we give over Orleans, or no?

Puc. Why, no, I say, distrustful recreants!
Fight till the last gasp; I will be your guard.

Char. What she says, I'll confirm; we'll fight it out.

Puc. Assign'd am I to be the English scourge.
This night the siege assuredly I'll raise:
Expect St. Martin's summer, halcyon days,
Since I have entered into these wars.
Glory is like a circle in the water,
Which never ceaseth to enlarge itself,
Till, by broad spreading, it disperse to nought.
With Henry's death, the English circle ends;
Dispersed are the glories it included.
Now am I like that proud insulting ship,
Which Cæsar and his fortune bare at once.

Char. Was Mahomet inspired with a dove?
Thou with an eagle art inspired then.
Helen, the mother of great Constantine,
Nor yet Saint Philip's daughters, were like thee.
Bright star of Venus, fall'n down on the earth,
How may I reverently worship thee enough?

Alen. Leave off delays, and let us raise the siege.

Reig. Woman, do what thou canst to save our honours;
Drive them from Orleans, and be immortaliz'd.

Char. Presently we'll try:—Come, let's away about it:
No prophet will I trust, if she prove false.
[*Exeunt.*

SCENE III. London. *Hill before the Tower.*

Enter, at the Gates, the DUKE OF GLOSTER, *with his* Serving-men, *in blue Coats.*

Glo. I am come to survey the Tower this day;
Since Henry's death, I fear there is conveyance.—
Where be these warders, that they wait not here?
Open the gates; Gloster it is that calls.
[Servants *knock.*

1 *Ward.* [*Within.*] Who is there that knocks so imperiously?

1 *Serv.* It is the noble duke of Gloster.

2 *Ward.* [*Within.*] Whoe'er he be, you may not be let in.

1 *Serv.* Answer you so the lord protector, villains?

1 *Ward.* [*Within.*] The Lord protect him! so we answer him:
We do no otherwise than we are will'd.

Glo. Who willed you? or whose will stands, but mine?
There's none protector of the realm, but I.—
Break up the gates, I'll be your warrantize:
Shall I be flouted thus by dunghill grooms?

Servants *rush at the Tower Gates. Enter, to the Gates,* WOODVILLE, *the Lieutenant.*

Wood. [*Within.*] What noise is this? what traitors have we here?

Glo. Lieutenant, is it you, whose voice I hear?
Open the gates; here's Gloster, that would enter.

Wood. [*Within.*] Have patience, noble duke:
I may not open;
The cardinal of Winchester forbids:
From him I have express commandment,
That thou, nor none of thine, shall be let in.

Glo. Faint-hearted Woodville, prizest him 'fore me?
Arrogant Winchester? that haughty prelate,
Whom Henry, our late sovereign, ne'er could brook?
Thou art no friend to God, or to the king:
Open the gates, or I'll shut thee out shortly.

1 *Serv.* Open the gates unto the lord protector;
Or we'll burst them open, if that you come not quickly.

Enter WINCHESTER, *attended by a Train of* Servants *in tawny Coats.*

Win. How now, ambitious Humphrey? what means this?

Glo. Piel'd priest, dost thou command me to be shut out?

Win. I do, thou most usurping proditor,
And not protector of the king or realm.

Glo. Stand back, thou manifest conspirator;
Thou, that contriv'dst to murder our dead lord;
Thou, that giv'st whores indulgences to sin:
I'll canvas thee in thy broad cardinal's hat,
If thou proceed in this thy insolence.

Win. Nay, stand thou back, I will not budge a foot;
This be Damascus, be thou cursed Cain,
To slay thy brother Abel, if thou wilt.

Glo. I will not slay thee, but I'll drive thee back:
Thy scarlet robes, as a child's bearing-cloth
I'll use, to carry thee out of this place.

Win. Do what thou dar'st; I beard thee to thy face.

Glo. What, am I dar'd, and bearded to my face?—
Draw, men, for all this privileged place;
Blue-coats to tawny-coats. Priest, beware your beard;
[GLOSTER *and his men attack the* Bishop.
I mean to tug it, and to cuff you soundly:
Under my feet I stamp thy cardinal's hat;
In spite of Pope or dignities of church,
Here by the cheeks I'll drag thee up and down.

Win. Gloster, thou'lt answer this before the pope.

Glo. Winchester goose, I cry—a rope! a rope!
Now beat them hence, Why do you let them stay?
Thee I'll chase hence, thou wolf in sheep's array.
Out, tawny coats!—out, scarlet hypocrite!

Here a great Tumult. In the midst of it, Enter the Mayor *of* London, *and* Officers.

May. Fye, lords! that you, being supreme magistrates,
Thus contumeliously should break the peace!

Glo. Peace, mayor: thou know'st little of my wrongs:
Here's Beaufort, that regards nor God nor king,
Hath here distrain'd the Tower to his use.

Win. Here's Gloster too, a foe to citizens;
One that still motions war, and never peace,
O'ercharging your free purses with large fines;
That seeks to overthrow religion,
Because he is protector of the realm;
And would have armour here out of the Tower,
To crown himself king, and suppress the prince.

Glo. I will not answer thee with words, but blows. [*Here they skirmish again.*

May. Nought rests for me, in this tumultuous strife,
But to make open proclamation:—
Come, officer; as loud as e'er thou canst.

Off. *All manner of men, assembled here in arms this day against God's peace and the king's, we charge and command you, in his highness' name, to repair to your several dwelling-places; and not to wear, handle, or use, any sword, weapon, or dagger, henceforward, upon pain of death.*

Glo. Cardinal, I'll be no breaker of the law:
But we shall meet, and break our minds at large.

Win. Gloster, we'll meet; to thy dear cost, be sure:
Thy heart-blood I will have, for this day's work.

May. I'll call for clubs, if you will not away:
This cardinal is more haughty than the devil.

Glo. Mayor, farewell: thou dost but what thou may'st.

Win. Abominable Gloster! guard thy head;
For I intend to have it, ere long. [*Exeunt.*

May. See the coast clear'd, and then we will depart.—
Good God! that nobles should such stomachs bear!
I myself fight not once in forty year. [*Exeunt.*

SCENE IV. France. *Before* Orleans.

Enter, on the Walls, the Master Gunner *and his* Son.

M. Gun. Sirrah, thou know'st how Orleans is besieg'd:
And how the English have the suburbs won.

Son. Father, I know; and oft have shot at them,
Howe'er, unfortunate, I miss'd my aim.

M. Gun. But now thou shalt not. Be thou rul'd by me:
Chief master-gunner am I of this town;
Something I must do, to procure me grace:
The prince's espials have informed me,
How the English, in the suburbs close intrench'd,
Wont, through a secret grate of iron bars
In yonder tower, to overpeer the city;
And thence discover how, with most advantage,
They may vex us, with shot, or with assault.
To intercept this inconvenience,
A piece of ordnance 'gainst it I have plac'd;
And fully even these three days have I watch'd,
If I could see them. Now, boy, do thou watch,
For I can stay no longer.
If thou spy'st any, run and bring me word;
And thou shalt find me at the governor's. [*Exit.*

Son. Father, I warrant you; take you no care:
I'll never trouble you, if I may spy them.

Enter, in an upper Chamber of a Tower, the LORDS SALISBURY *and* TALBOT, SIR WILLIAM GLANSDALE, SIR THOMAS GARGRAVE, *and Others.*

Sal. Talbot, my life, my joy, again return'd!
How wert thou handled, being prisoner?
Or by what means gott'st thou to be releas'd?
Discourse, I pr'ythee, on this turret's top.

Tal. The duke of Bedford had a prisoner,
Called—the brave Lord Ponton de Santrailles;
For him I was exchang'd and ransomed.
But with a baser man of arms by far,
Once, in contempt, they would have barter'd me:
Which I, disdaining, scorn'd; and craved death
Rather than I would be so vile esteem'd.
In fine, redeem'd I was as I desir'd.
But, O! the treacherous Fastolfe wounds my heart!
Whom with my bare fists I would execute,
If I now had him brought into my power.

Sal. Yet tell'st thou not, how thou wert entertain'd.

Tal. With scoffs, and scorns, and contumelious taunts.
In open market place produc'd they me,
To be a publick spectacle to all;
Here, said they, is the terror of the French,
The scare-crow that affrights our children so.
Then broke I from the officers that led me;
And with my nails digg'd stones out of the ground,
To hurl at the beholders of my shame.
My grisly countenance made others fly;
None durst come near for fear of sudden death.
In iron walls they deem'd me not secure;
So great fear of my name 'mongst them was spread,
That they suppos'd, I could rend bars of steel,
And spurn in pieces posts of adamant:
Wherefore a guard of chosen shot I had,
That walk'd about me every minute-while;
And if I did but stir out of my bed,
Ready they were to shoot me to the heart.

Sal. I grieve to hear what torments you endur'd:
But we will be reveng'd sufficiently.
Now it is supper-time in Orleans:
Here, through this grate, I can count every one,
And view the Frenchmen how they fortify;
Let us look in, the sight will much delight thee.—
Sir Thomas Gargrave, and Sir William Glandsdale,
Let me have your express opinions,
Where is best place to make our battery next.

Gar. I think, at the north gate, for there stand lords.

Glan. And I, here, at the bulwark of the bridge.

Tal. For aught I see, this city must be famish'd,
Or with light skirmishes enfeebled.
[*Shot from the Town.* SALISBURY *and* SIR THO. GARGRAVE *fall.*

Sal. O Lord, have mercy on us, wretched sinners!

Gar. O Lord, have mercy on me, woful man!

Tal. What chance is this, that suddenly hath cross'd us?—
Speak, Salisbury: at least, if thou canst speak;
How far'st thou, mirror of all martial men?
One of thy eyes, and thy cheek's side struck off!—
Accursed tower! accursed fatal hand,
That hath contriv'd this woful tragedy!
In thirteen battles Salisbury o'ercame;
Henry the Fifth he first train'd to the wars;
Whilst any trump did sound, or drum struck up,
His sword did ne'er leave striking in the field.—
Yet liv'st thou, Salisbury? though thy speech doth fail,
One eye thou hast to look to heaven for grace:
The sun with one eye vieweth all the world.—
Heaven, be thou gracious to none alive,
If Salisbury wants mercy at thy hands!—
Bear hence his body, I will help to bury it.—
Sir Thomas Gargrave, hast thou any life?
Speak unto Talbot; nay, look up to him.
Salisbury, cheer thy spirit with this comfort;
Thou shalt not die, whiles——
He beckons with his hand, and smiles on me;
As who should say, *When I am dead and gone, Remember to avenge me on the French.*—
Plantagenet, I will; and like thee, Nero,
Play on the lute, beholding the towns burn:
Wretched shall France be only in my name.
[*Thunder heard; afterwards an Alarum.*
What stir is this? What tumult's in the heavens?
Whence cometh this alarum, and the noise?

Enter a Messenger.

Mess. My lord, my lord, the French have gather'd head?
The Dauphin, with one Joan la Pucelle join'd,—

A holy prophetess, new risen up,—
Is come with a great power to raise the siege.
[SALISBURY *groans*.

Tal. Hear, hear, how dying Salisbury doth groan!
It irks his heart, he cannot be revenged.—
Frenchmen, I'll be a Salisbury to you:—
Pucelle or puzzel, dolphin or dogfish,
Your hearts I'll stamp out with my horse's heels,
And make a quagmire of your mingled brains.—
Convey me Salisbury into his tent,
And then we'll try what these dastard Frenchmen dare. [*Exeunt, bearing out the Bodies.*

SCENE V. *The same. Before one of the Gates.*

Alarums. Skirmishings. TALBOT *pursueth the* Dauphin, *and driveth him in: then enter* JOAN LA PUCELLE, *driving* Englishmen *before her. Then enter* TALBOT.

Tal. Where is my strength, my valour, and my force?
Our English troops retire, I cannot stay them:
A woman, clad in armour, chaseth them.

Enter LA PUCELLE.

Here, here she comes:——I'll have a bout with thee;
Devil, or devil's dam, I'll conjure thee:
Blood will I draw on thee, thou art a witch,
And straightway give thy soul to him thou serv'st.

Puc. Come, come, 'tis only I that must disgrace thee. [*They fight.*

Tal. Heavens, can you suffer hell so to prevail?
My breast I'll burst with straining of my courage,
And from my shoulders crack my arms asunder,
But I will chastise this high-minded strumpet.

Puc. Talbot, farewell; thy hour is not yet come:
I must go victual Orleans forthwith.
O'ertake me, if thou canst; I scorn thy strength.
Go, go, cheer up thy hungry starved men;
Help Salisbury to make his testament:
This day is ours, as many more shall be.
[PUCELLE *enters the Town, with* Soldiers.

Tal. My thoughts are whirled like a potter's wheel;
I know not where I am, nor what I do:
A witch, by fear, not force, like Hannibal,
Drives back our troops, and conquers as she lists:
So bees with smoke, and doves with noisome stench,
Are from their hives, and houses, driven away.
They call'd us, for our fierceness, English dogs;
Now, like to whelps, we crying run away.
[*A short Alarum.*
Hark, countrymen! either renew the fight,
Or tear the lions out of England's coat:
Renounce your soil, give sheep in lions' stead:
Sheep run not half so timorous from the wolf,
Or horse, or oxen, from the leopard,
As you fly from your oft-subdued slaves.
[*Alarum. Another Skirmish.*
It will not be:—Retire into your trenches:
You all consented unto Salisbury's death,
For none would strike a stroke in his revenge.—
Pucelle is enter'd into Orleans,
In spite of us, or aught that we can do.
O, would I were to die with Salisbury!
The shame hereof will make me hide my head.
[*Alarum. Retreat. Exeunt* TALBOT *and his* Forces, *&c.*

SCENE VI. *The same.*

Enter, on the Walls, PUCELLE, CHARLES, REIGNIER, ALENCON, *and* Soldiers.

Puc. Advance our waving colours on the walls;
Rescu'd is Orleans from the English wolves:—
Thus Joan la Pucelle hath perform'd her word.

Char. Divinest creature, bright Astrea's daughter,
How shall I honour thee for this success?
Thy promises are like Adonis' gardens,
That one day bloom'd, and fruitful were the next.—
France, triumph in thy glorious prophetess?—
Recover'd is the town of Orleans:
More blessed hap did ne'er befall our state.

Reig. Why ring not out the bells throughout the town?
Dauphin, command the citizens make bonfires,
And feast and banquet in the open streets,
To celebrate the joy that God hath given us.

Alen. All France will be replete with mirth and joy,
When they shall hear how we have play'd the men.

Char. 'Tis Joan, not we, by whom the day is won;
For which, I will divide my crown with her:
And all the priests and friars in my realm
Shall, in procession, sing her endless praise.
A statelier Pyramis to her I'll rear,
Than Rhodope's, of Memphis, ever was:
In memory of her, when she is dead,
Her ashes, in an urn more precious
Than the rich-jewel'd coffer of Darius,
Transported shall be at high festivals
Before the kings and queens of France.
No longer on Saint Dennis will we cry,
But Joan la Pucelle shall be France's saint.
Come in, and let us banquet royally,
After this golden day of victory.
[*Flourish. Exeunt.*

ACT II.

SCENE I. *The same.*

Enter to the Gates, a French Sergeant, *and two* Sentinels.

Serg. Sirs, take your places, and be vigilant:
If any noise, or soldier, you perceive,
Near to the walls, by some apparent sign,
Let us have knowledge at the court of guard.

1 *Sent.* Sergeant, you shall. [*Exit* Sergeant.]
Thus are poor servitors
(When others sleep upon their quiet beds)
Constrain'd to watch in darkness, rain, and cold.

Enter TALBOT, BEDFORD, BURGUNDY, *and* Forces, *with Scaling Ladders; their Drums beating a dead March.*

Tal. Lord regent,—and redoubted Burgundy,—
By whose approach, the regions of Artois,
Walloon, and Picardy, are friends to us,—
This happy night the Frenchmen are secure,
Having all day carous'd and banqueted:
Embrace we then this opportunity;
As fitting best to quittance their deceit,
Contriv'd by art, and baleful sorcery.

Bed. Coward of France!—how much he wrongs his fame,
Despairing of his own arm's fortitude,
To join with witches, and the help of hell.

Bur. Traitors have never other company.—
But what's that Pucelle, whom they term so pure?

Tal. A maid, they say.

Bed. A maid! and be so martial!

Bur. Pray God, she prove not masculine ere long;
If underneath the standard of the French,
She carry armour as she hath begun.

Tal. Well, let them practise and converse with spirits;
God is our fortress; in whose conquering name,
Let us resolve to scale their flinty bulwarks.

Bed. Ascend, brave Talbot; we will follow thee.

Tal. Not all together: better far, I guess,

That we do make our entrance several ways;
That, if it chance the one of us do fail,
The other yet may rise against their force.

Bed. Agreed; I'll to yon corner.

Bur. And I to this.

Tal. And here will Talbot mount, or make his grave.—
Now, Salisbury! for thee, and for the right
Of English Henry, shall this night appear
How much in duty I am bound to both.

[*The* English *scale the Walls, crying, St.* George! *a* Talbot! *and all enter by the Town.*

Sent. [*Within.*] Arm, arm! the enemy doth make assault!

The French *leap over the Walls in their shirts. Enter, several ways,* BASTARD, ALENCON, REIGNIER, *half ready, and half unready.*

Alen. How now, my lords? what, all unready so?

Bast. Unready? ay, and glad we 'scap'd so well.

Reig. 'Twas time, I trow, to wake and leave our beds,
Hearing alarums at our chamber doors.

Alen. Of all exploits, since first I follow'd arms,
Ne'er heard I of a warlike enterprise
More venturous, or desperate than this.

Bast. I think, this Talbot be a fiend of hell.

Reig. If not of hell, the heavens, sure, favour him.

Alen. Here cometh Charles; I marvel how he sped.

Enter CHARLES *and* LA PUCELLE.

Bast. Tut! holy Joan was his defensive guard.

Char. Is this thy cunning, thou deceitful dame?
Didst thou at first, to flatter us withal,
Make us partakers of a little gain,
That now our loss might be ten times so much?

Puc. Wherefore is Charles impatient with his friend?
At all times will you have my power alike?
Sleeping, or waking, must I still prevail,
Or will you blame and lay the fault on me?—
Improvident soldiers! had your watch been good,
This sudden mischief never could have fall'n.

Char. Duke of Alencon, this was your default;
That, being captain of the watch to-night,
Did look no better to that weighty charge.

Alen. Had all your quarters been as safely kept,
As that whereof I had the government,
We had not been thus shamefully surpris'd.

Bast. Mine was secure.

Reig. And so was mine, my lord.

Char. And, for myself, most part of all this night,
Within her quarter, and mine own precinct,
I was employ'd in passing to and fro,
About relieving of the sentinels:
Then how, or which way, should they first break in?

Puc. Question, my lords, no further of the case,
How, or which way; 'tis sure, they found some place
But weakly guarded, where the breach was made,
And now there rests no other shift but this,—
To gather our soldiers, scatter'd and dispers'd,
And lay new platforms to endamage them.

Alarum. Enter an English Soldier, *crying a* Talbot! *a* Talbot! *They fly, leaving their Clothes behind.*

Sold. I'll be so bold to take what they have left.
The cry of Talbot serves me for a sword;
For I have loaden me with many spoils,
Using no other weapon but his name. [*Exit.*

SCENE II. Orleans. *Within the Town.*

Enter TALBOT, BEDFORD, BURGUNDY, *a* Captain, *and Others.*

Bed. The day begins to break, and night is fled,
Whose pitchy mantle over-veil'd the earth.
Here sound retreat, and cease our hot pursuit.

[*Retreat sounded.*

Tal. Bring forth the body of old Salisbury;
And here advance it in the market-place,
The middle centre of this cursed town.—
Now have I paid my vow unto his soul;
For every drop of blood was drawn from him,
There hath at least five Frenchmen died to-night.
And, that hereafter ages may behold
What ruin happen'd in revenge of him,
Within their chiefest temple I'll erect
A tomb, wherein his corpse shall be interr'd:
Upon the which, that every one may read,
Shall be engrav'd the sack of Orleans;
The treacherous manner of his mournful death,
And what a terror he had been to France.
But, lords, in all our bloody massacre,
I muse, we met not with the Dauphin's grace;
His new-come champion, virtuous Joan of Arc;
Nor any of his false confederates.

Bed. 'Tis thought, Lord Talbot, when the fight began,
Rous'd on the sudden from their drowsy beds,
They did amongst the troops of armed men,
Leap o'er the walls for refuge in the field.

Bur. Myself (as far as I could well discern,
For smoke, and dusty vapours of the night)
Am sure I scar'd the Dauphin, and his trull;
When arm in arm they both came swiftly running,
Like a pair of loving turtle-doves,
That could not live asunder day or night.
After that things are set in order here,
We'll follow them with all the power we have.

Enter a Messenger.

Mess. All hail, my lords! which of this princely train
Call ye the warlike Talbot, for his acts
So much applauded through the realm of France?

Tal. Here is the Talbot; who would speak with him?

Mess. The virtuous lady, countess of Auvergne,
With modesty admiring thy renown,
By me entreats, good lord, thou wouldst vouchsafe
To visit her poor castle where she lies;
That she may boast she hath beheld the man
Whose glory fills the world with loud report.

Bur. Is it even so? Nay, then, I see our wars
Will turn unto a peaceful comick sport,
When ladies crave to be encounter'd with.—
You may not, my lord, despise her gentle suit.

Tal. Ne'er trust me then; for, when a world of men
Could not prevail with all their oratory,
Yet hath a woman's kindness overrul'd:—
And therefore tell her, I return great thanks;
And in submission will attend on her.—
Will not your honours bear me company?

Bed. No, truly; it is more than manners will:
And I have heard it said,—Unbidden guests
Are often welcomest when they are gone.

Tal. Well then, alone, since there's no remedy,
I mean to prove this lady's courtesy.
Come hither, captain. [*Whispers.*]—You perceive my mind.

Capt. I do, my lord; and mean accordingly.

[*Exeunt.*

SCENE III. Auvergne. *Court of the Castle.*

Enter the Countess *and her* Porter.

Count. Porter, remember what I gave in charge;
And, when you have done so, bring the keys to me.

Port. Madam, I will. [*Exit.*
Count. The plot is laid: if all things fall out right,
I shall as famous be by this exploit,
As Scythian Thomyris by Cyrus' death.
Great is the rumour of this dreadful knight,
And his achievements of no less account:
Fain would mine eyes be witness with mine ears,
To give their censure of these rare reports.

Enter Messenger *and* TALBOT.

Mess. Madam,
According as your ladyship desir'd,
By message crav'd, so is Lord Talbot come.
Count. And he is welcome. What! is this the man?
Mess. Madam, it is.
Count. Is this the scourge of France?
Is this the Talbot, so much fear'd abroad,
That with his name the mothers still their babes?
I see report is fabulous and false:
I thought I should have seen some Hercules,
A second Hector, for his grim aspect,
And large proportion of his strong-knit limbs.
Alas! this is a child, a silly dwarf:
It cannot be, this weak and writhled shrimp
Should strike such terror to his enemies.
Tal. Madam, I have been bold to trouble you:
But, since your ladyship is not at leisure,
I'll sort some other time to visit you.
Count. What means he now?—Go ask him, whither he goes.
Mess. Stay, my lord Talbot; for my lady craves
To know the cause of your abrupt departure.
Tal. Marry, for that she's in a wrong belief,
I go to certify her, Talbot's here.

Re-enter Porter, *with Keys.*

Count. If thou be he, then art thou prisoner.
Tal. Prisoner! to whom?
Count. To me, blood-thirsty lord;
And for that cause I train'd thee to my house.
Long time thy shadow hath been thrall to me,
For in my gallery thy picture hangs;
But now the substance shall endure the like;
And I will chain these legs and arms of thine,
That hast by tyranny, these many years,
Wasted our country, slain our citizens,
And sent our sons and husbands captivate.
Tal. Ha, ha, ha!
Count. Laughest thou, wretch? thy mirth shall turn to moan.
Tal. I laugh to see your ladyship so fond,
To think that you have aught but Talbot's shadow,
Whereon to practise your severity.
Count. Why, art not thou the man?
Tal. I am indeed.
Count. Then have I substance too.
Tal. No, no, I am but shadow of myself:
You are deceiv'd, my substance is not here;
For what you see, is but the smallest part
And least proportion of humanity:
I tell you, madam, were the whole frame here,
It is of such a spacious lofty pitch,
Your roof were not sufficient to contain it.
Count. This is a riddling merchant for the nonce;
He will be here, and yet he is not here:
How can these contrarieties agree?
Tal. That will I show you presently.

He winds a Horn. Drums heard; then a Peal of Ordnance. The Gates being forced, enter Soldiers.

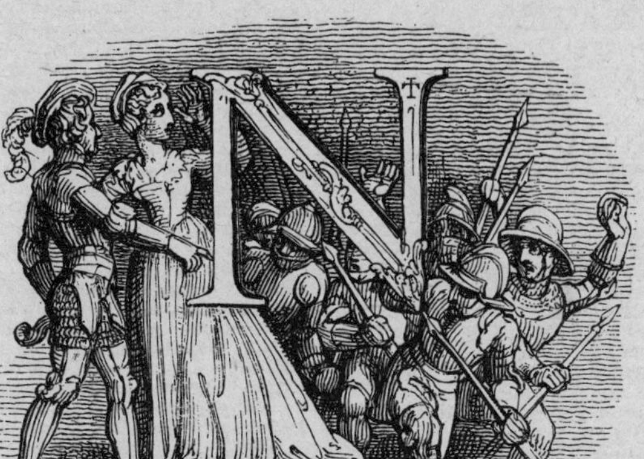

How say you, madam? are you now persuaded,
That Talbot is but shadow of himself?
These are his substance, sinews, arms, and strength,
With which he yoketh your rebellious necks;
Razeth your cities, and subverts your towns,
And in a moment makes them desolate.
Count. Victorious Talbot! pardon my abuse:
I find, thou art no less than fame hath bruited,
And more than may be gather'd by thy shape.
Let my presumption not provoke thy wrath;
For I am sorry, that with reverence
I did not entertain thee as thou art.
Tal. Be not dismay'd, fair lady; nor misconstrue
The mind of Talbot, as you did mistake
The outward composition of his body.
What you have done, hath not offended me:
No other satisfaction do I crave,
But only (with your patience) that we may
Taste of your wine, and see what cates you have;
For soldiers' stomachs always serve them well.
Count. With all my heart: and think me honoured
To feast so great a warrior in my house.
[*Exeunt.*

SCENE IV. London. *The* Temple *Garden.*

Enter the EARLS OF SOMERSET, SUFFOLK, *and* WARWICK; RICHARD PLANTAGENET, VERNON, *and another* Lawyer.

Plan. Great lords, and gentlemen, what means this silence?
Dare no man answer in a case of truth?
Suff. Within the Temple hall we were too loud:
The garden here is more convenient.

Plan. Then say at once, if I maintain'd the truth;
Or, else, was wrangling Somerset in the error?
Suff. 'Faith, I have been a truant in the law;
And never yet could frame my will to it;
And, therefore, frame the law unto my will.
Som. Judge you, my lord of Warwick, then between us.
War. Between two hawks, which flies the higher pitch,
Between two dogs, which hath the deeper mouth,
Between two blades, which bears the better temper,
Between two horses, which doth bear him best,
Between two girls, which hath the merriest eye,
I have, perhaps, some shallow spirit of judgment;
But in these nice sharp quillets of the law,
Good faith, I am no wiser than a daw.
Plan. Tut, tut, here is a mannerly forbearance:
The truth appears so naked on my side,
That any purblind eye might find it out.
Som. And on my side, it is so well apparell'd,
So clear, so shining, and so evident,
That it will glimmer through a blind man's eye.
Plan. Since you are tongue-ty'd, and so loath to speak,
In dumb significants proclaim your thoughts:
Let him, that is a true-born gentleman,
And stands upon the honour of his birth,
If he suppose that I have pleaded truth,
From off this brier pluck a white rose with me.
Som. Let him that is no coward, nor no flatterer,
But dare maintain the party of the truth,
Pluck a red rose from off this thorn with me.
War. I love no colours; and, without all colour
Of base insinuating flattery,
I pluck this white rose, with Plantagenet.
Suff. I pluck this red rose, with young Somerset;
And say withal, I think he held the right.
Ver. Stay, lords and gentlemen: and pluck no more,
Till you conclude—that he, upon whose side
The fewest roses are cropp'd from the tree,
Shall yield the other in the right opinion.
Som. Good master Vernon, it is well objected;
If I have fewest, I subscribe in silence.
Plan. And I.
Ver. Then, for the truth and plainness of the case,
I pluck this pale and maiden blossom here,
Giving my verdict on the white rose side.
Som. Prick not your finger as you pluck it off;
Lest, bleeding, you do paint the white rose red,
And fall on my side so against your will.
Ver. If I, my lord, for my opinion bleed,
Opinion shall be surgeon to my hurt,
And keep me on the side where still I am.
Som. Well, well, come on: Who else?
Law. Unless my study and my books be false,
The argument you held, was wrong in you;
[*To* SOMERSET.
In sign whereof, I pluck a white rose too.
Plan. Now, Somerset, where is your argument?
Som. Here, in my scabbard; meditating that,
Shall dye your white rose in a bloody red.
Plan. Mean time, your cheeks do counterfeit our roses;
For pale they look with fear, as witnessing
The truth on our side.
Som. No, Plantagenet,
'Tis not for fear; but anger;—that thy cheeks
Blush for pure shame, to counterfeit our roses;
And yet thy tongue will not confess thy error.
Plan. Hath not thy rose a canker, Somerset?
Som. Hath not thy rose a thorn, Plantagenet?
Plan. Ay, sharp and piercing, to maintain his truth;
Whiles thy consuming canker eats his falsehood,
Som. Well, I'll find friends to wear my bleeding roses,
That shall maintain what I have said is true,
Where false Plantagenet dare not be seen.
Plan. Now, by this maiden blossom in my hand,
I scorn thee and thy faction, peevish boy.
Suff. Turn not thy scorns this way, Plantagenet.
Plan. Proud Poole, I will; and scorn both him and thee.
Suff. I'll turn my part thereof into thy throat.
Som. Away, away, good William De-la-Poole!
We grace the yeoman, by conversing with him.
War. Now, by God's will, thou wrong'st him, Somerset;
His grandfather was Lionel, duke of Clarence,
Third son to the third Edward, king of England;
Spring crestless yeomen from so deep a root?
Plan. He bears him on the place's privilege,
Or durst not, for his craven heart, say thus.
Som. By him that made me, I'll maintain my words
On any plot of ground in Christendom:
Was not thy father, Richard, earl of Cambridge,
For treason executed in our late king's days?
And, by his treason, stand'st not thou attainted,
Corrupted, and exempt from ancient gentry?
His trespass yet lives guilty in thy blood;
And, till thou be restor'd, thou art a yeoman.
Plan. My father was attached, not attainted;
Condemn'd to die for treason, but no traitor;
And that I'll prove on better men than Somerset,
Were growing time once ripen'd to my will.
For your partaker Poole, and you yourself,
I'll note you in my book of memory,
To scourge you for this apprehension:
Look to it well; and say you are well warn'd.
Som. Ay, thou shalt find us ready for thee still:
And know us, by these colours, for thy foes;
For these my friends, in spite of thee, shall wear.
Plan. And, by my soul, this pale and angry rose,
As cognizance of my blood-drinking hate,
Will I for ever, and my faction, wear;
Until it wither with me to my grave,
Or flourish to the height of my degree.
Suff. Go forward, and be chok'd with thy ambition!
And so farewell, until I meet thee next. [*Exit.*
Som. Have with thee, Poole.—Farewell, ambitious Richard. [*Exit.*
Plan. How I am brav'd, and must perforce endure it!
War. This blot, that they object against your house,
Shall be wip'd out in the next parliament,
Call'd for the truce of Winchester and Gloster:
And, if thou be not then created York,
I will not live to be accounted Warwick.
Mean time, in signal of my love to thee,
Against proud Somerset, and William Poole,
Will I upon thy party wear this rose:
And here I prophesy,—This brawl to-day,
Grown to this faction, in the Temple garden,
Shall send, between the red rose and the white,
A thousand souls to death and deadly night.
Plan. Good master Vernon, I am bound to you,
That you on my behalf would pluck a flower.
Ver. In your behalf still will I wear the same.
Law. And so will I.
Plan. Thanks, gentle sir.
Come, let us four to dinner: I dare say,
This quarrel will drink blood another day.
[*Exeunt.*

SCENE V. *The same. A Room in the Tower.*

Enter MORTIMER, *brought in a Chair by two* Keepers.

Mor. Kind keepers of my weak decaying age.
Let dying Mortimer here rest himself.—
Even like a man new haled from the rack,
So fare my limbs with long imprisonment:
And these gray locks, the pursuivants of death,

Nestor-like aged, in an age of care,
Argue the end of Edmund Mortimer.
These eyes,—like lamps whose wasting oil is spent,—
Wax dim, as drawing to their exigent:
Weak shoulders, overborne with burd'ning grief,
And pithless arms, like to a wither'd vine
That droops his sapless branches to the ground:—
Yet are these feet—whose strengthless stay is numb,
Unable to support this lump of clay,—
Swift-winged with desire to get a grave,
As witting I no other comfort have.—
But tell me, keeper, will my nephew come?
1 *Keep.* Richard Plantagenet, my lord, will come:
We sent unto the Temple, to his chamber;
And answer was return'd that he will come.
Mor. Enough; my soul shall then be satisfied.—
Poor gentleman! his wrong doth equal mine.
Since Henry Monmouth first began to reign
(Before whose glory I was great in arms),
This loathsome sequestration have I had;
And even since then hath Richard been obscur'd,
Deprived of honour and inheritance:
But now, the arbitrator of despairs,
Just death, kind umpire of men's miseries,
With sweet enlargement doth dismiss me hence;
I would, his troubles likewise were expir'd,
That so he might recover what was lost.

Enter RICHARD PLANTAGENET.

1 *Keep.* My lord, your loving nephew now is come.
Mor. Richard Plantagenet, my friend? Is he come?
Plan. Ay, noble uncle, thus ignobly us'd,
Your nephew, late despised Richard, comes.
Mor. Direct mine arms, I may embrace his neck,
And in his bosom spend my latter gasp:
O, tell me, when my lips do touch his cheeks,
That I may kindly give one fainting kiss.—
And now declare, sweet stem from York's great stock,
Why didst thou say—of late thou wert despis'd?
Plan. First, lean thine aged back against mine arm;
And, in that ease, I'll tell thee my disease.
This day, in argument upon a case,
Some words there grew 'twixt Somerset and me:
Among which terms he us'd his lavish tongue,
And did upbraid me with my father's death;
Which obloquy set bars before my tongue,
Else with the like I had requited him:
Therefore, good uncle,—for my father's sake,
In honour of a true Plantagenet,
And for alliance' sake,—declare the cause
My father, earl of Cambridge, lost his head.
Mor. That cause, fair nephew, that imprison'd me,
And hath detain'd me, all my flow'ring youth,
Within a loathsome dungeon, there to pine,
Was cursed instrument of his decease.
Plan. Discover more at large what cause that was;
For I am ignorant, and cannot guess.
Mor. I will; if that my fading breath permit,
And death approach not ere my tale be done.
Henry the Fourth, grandfather to this king,
Depos'd his nephew Richard; Edward's son,
The first begotten, and the lawful heir
Of Edward king, the third of that descent:
During whose reign, the Percies of the north,
Finding his usurpation most unjust,
Endeavour'd my advancement to the throne:
The reason mov'd these warlike lords to this,
Was—for that (young King Richard thus remov'd,
Leaving no heir begotten of his body)
I was the next by birth and parentage;
For by my mother I derived am
From Lionel duke of Clarence, the third son
To King Edward the Third, whereas he,
From John of Gaunt doth bring his pedigree,
Being but fourth of that heroick line.
But mark; as, in this haughty great attempt,
They laboured to plant the rightful heir,
I lost my liberty, and they their lives.
Long after this, when Henry the Fifth,—
Succeeding his father Bolingbroke,—did reign,
Thy father, earl of Cambridge,—then deriv'd
From famous Edmund Langley, duke of York,—
Marrying my sister that thy mother was,
Again, in pity of my hard distress,
Levied an army; weening to redeem,
And have install'd me in the diadem:
But, as the rest, so fell that noble earl,
And was beheaded. Thus the Mortimers,
In whom the title rested, were suppress'd.
Plan. Of which, my lord, your honour is the last.
Mor. True; and thou seest, that I no issue have;
And that my fainting words do warrant death:
Thou art my heir; the rest, I wish thee gather:
But yet be wary in thy studious care.
Plan. Thy grave admonishments prevail with me:
But yet, methinks, my father's execution
Was nothing less than bloody tyranny.
Mor. With silence, nephew, be thou politick;
Strong-fixed is the house of Lancaster,
And, like a mountain, not to be remov'd.
But now thy uncle is removing hence;
As princes do their courts, when they are cloy'd
With long continuance in a settled place.
Plan. O, uncle, 'would, some part of my young years
Might but redeem the passage of your age!
Mor. Thou dost then wrong me; as the slaught'rer doth,
Which giveth many wounds, when one will kill.
Mourn not, except thou sorrow for my good;
Only, give order for my funeral;
And so farewell: and fair be all thy hopes!
And prosperous be thy life, in peace, and war!
[*Dies.*
Plan. And peace, no war, befall thy parting soul!
In prison hast thou spent a pilgrimage,
And like a hermit overpass'd thy days.—
Well, I will lock his counsel in my breast;
And what I do imagine, let that rest.—
Keepers, convey him hence; and I myself
Will see his burial better than his life.—
[*Exeunt* Keepers, *bearing out* MORTIMER.
Here dies the dusky torch of Mortimer,
Chok'd with ambition of the meaner sort:—
And, for those wrongs, those bitter injuries,
Which Somerset hath offer'd to my house,—
I doubt not, but with honour to redress:
And therefore haste I to the parliament;
Either to be restored to my blood,
Or make my ill, the advantage of my good.
[*Exit.*

ACT III.

SCENE I. *The same. The Parliament House.*

Flourish. Enter KING HENRY, EXETER, GLOSTER, WARWICK, SOMERSET, *and* SUFFOLK; *the* Bishop *of* Winchester, RICHARD PLANTAGENET, *and Others.* GLOSTER *offers to put up a Bill:* WINCHESTER *snatches it, and tears it.*

Win. Com'st thou with deep premeditated lines,
With written pamphlets studiously devis'd,
Humphrey of Gloster? if thou canst accuse,
Or aught intend'st to lay unto my charge,
Do it without invention suddenly;
As I with sudden and extemporal speech
Purpose to answer what thou canst object.

Glo. Presumptuous priest! this place commands my patience,
Or thou should'st find thou hast dishonour'd me.
Think not, although in writing I preferr'd
The manner of thy vile outrageous crimes,
That therefore I have forg'd, or am not able
Verbatim to rehearse the method of my pen:
No, prelate; such is thy audacious wickedness,
Thy lewd, pestiferous, and dissensious pranks,
As very infants prattle of thy pride.
Thou art a most pernicious usurer;
Froward by nature, enemy to peace;
Lascivious, wanton, more than well beseems
A man of thy profession, and degree;
And for thy treachery, What's more manifest?
In that thou laid'st a trap to take my life,
As well at London Bridge, as at the Tower?
Beside, I fear me, if thy thoughts were sifted,
The king, thy sovereign, is not quite exempt
From envious malice of thy swelling heart.

Win. Gloster, I do defy thee.—Lords, vouchsafe
To give me hearing what I shall reply.
If I were covetous, ambitious, or perverse,
As he will have me, How am I so poor?
Or how haps it, I seek not to advance
Or raise myself, but keep my wonted calling
And for dissension, Who preferreth peace
More than I do,—except I be provok'd?
No, my good lords, it is not that offends;
It is not that, that hath incens'd the duke:
It is, because no one should sway but he;
No one, but he, should be about the king;
And that engenders thunder in his breast,
And makes him roar these accusations forth.
But he shall know, I am as good——

Glo. As good?
Thou bastard of my grandfather?—

Win. Ay, lordly sir; For what are you, I pray,
But one imperious in another's throne?

Glo. Am I not the protector, saucy priest?

Win. And am I not a prelate of the church?

Glo. Yes, as an outlaw in a castle keeps,
And useth it to patronage his theft.

Win. Unreverent Gloster!

Glo. Thou art reverent
Touching thy spiritual function, not thy life.

Win. This Rome shall remedy.

War. Roam thither then.

Som. My lord, it were your duty to forbear.

War. Ay, see the bishop be not overborne.

Som. Methinks, my lord should be religious,
And know the office that belongs to such.

War. Methinks his lordship should be humbler;
It fitteth not a prelate so to plead.

Som. Yes, when his holy state is touch'd so near.

War. State holy, or unhallow'd, what of that?
Is not his grace protector to the king?

Plan. Plantagenet, I see, must hold his tongue;
Lest it be said, *Speak, sirrah, when you should!*
Must your bold verdict enter talk with lords?
Else would I have a fling at Winchester. [*Aside.*

K. Hen. Uncles of Gloster, and of Winchester,
The special watchmen of our English weal;
I would prevail, if prayers might prevail,
To join your hearts in love and amity.
O, what a scandal is it to our crown,
That two such noble peers as ye, should jar!
Believe me, lords, my tender years can tell,
Civil dissension is a viperous worm,
That gnaws the bowels of the commonwealth.—
[*A noise within;* Down with the tawny coats!
What tumult's this?

War. An uproar, I dare warrant,
Begun through malice of the bishop's men.
[*A noise again;* Stones! Stones!

Enter the MAYOR OF LONDON, *attended.*

May. O, my good lords,—and virtuous Henry,—
Pity the city of London, pity us!
The bishop and the duke of Gloster's men,
Forbidden late to carry any weapon,
Have fill'd their pockets full of pebble-stones;
And, banding themselves in contrary parts,
Do pelt so fast at one another's pate,
That many have their giddy brains knock'd out:
Our windows are broke down in every street,
And we, for fear, compell'd to shut our shops.

Enter, skirmishing, the Retainers *of* Gloster, *and* Winchester, *with bloody pates.*

K. Hen. We charge you, on allegiance to ourself,
To hold your slaught'ring hands, and keep the peace.
Pray, uncle Gloster, mitigate this strife.

1 *Serv.* Nay, if we be
Forbidden stones, we'll fall to it with our teeth.

2 *Serv.* Do what ye dare, we are as resolute.
[*Skirmish again.*

Glo. You of my household, leave this peevish broil,
And set this unaccustom'd fight aside.

1 *Serv.* My lord, we know your grace to be a man
Just and upright; and, for your royal birth,
Inferior to none, but his majesty:
And ere that we will suffer such a prince,
So kind a father of the commonweal,
To be disgraced by an inkhorn mate,
We, and our wives, and children, all will fight,
And have our bodies slaughter'd by thy foes.

2 *Serv.* Ay, and the very parings of our nails
Shall pitch a field, when we are dead.
[*Skirmish again.*

Glo. Stay, stay, I say!
And, if you love me, as you say you do,
Let me persuade you to forbear awhile.

K. Hen. O, how this discord doth afflict my soul!—
Can you, my lord of Winchester, behold
My sighs and tears, and will not once relent?
Who should be pitiful, if you be not?
Or who should study to prefer a peace,
If holy churchmen take delight in broils?

War. My lord protector, yield;—yield Winchester;
Except you mean, with obstinate repulse,
To slay your sovereign, and destroy the realm.
You see what mischief, and what murder too,
Hath been enacted through your enmity;
Then be at peace, except ye thirst for blood.

Win. He shall submit, or I will never yield.

Glo. Compassion on the king commands me stoop;
Or, I would see his heart out, ere the priest
Should ever get that privilege of me.

War. Behold, my lord of Winchester, the duke
Hath banish'd moody discontented fury,
As by his smoothed brows it doth appear:
Why look you still so stern, and tragical?

Glo. Here, Winchester, I offer thee my hand.

K. Hen. Fye, uncle Beaufort! I have heard you preach,
That malice was a great and grievous sin:
And will not you maintain the thing you teach,
But prove a chief offender in the same?

War. Sweet king!—the bishop hath a kindly gird.
For shame, my lord of Winchester! relent;
What, shall a child instruct you what to do?

Win. Well, duke of Gloster, I will yield to thee;
Love for thy love, and hand for hand I give.

Glo. Ay; but I, fear me, with a hollow heart.—
See here, my friends, and loving countrymen;
This token serveth for a flag of truce,
Betwixt ourselves, and all our followers:
So help me God, as I dissemble not!

Win. So help me God, as I intend it not!
[*Aside.*

K. Hen. O, loving uncle, kind duke of Gloster,

How joyful am I made by this contract!—
Away, my masters! trouble us no more;
But join in friendship, as your lords have done.
1 *Serv.* Content; I'll to the surgeon's.
2 *Serv.* And so will I.
3 *Serv.* And I will see what physick the tavern affords. [*Exeunt* Servants, Mayor, *&c.*
War. Accept this scroll, most gracious sovereign;
Which, in the right of Richard Plantagenet,
We do exhibit to your majesty.
Glo. Well urg'd, my lord of Warwick;—for, sweet prince,
And if your grace mark every circumstance,
You have great reason to do Richard right:
Especially, for those occasions
At Eltham-place I told your majesty.
K. Hen. And those occasions, uncle, were of force:
Therefore, my loving lords, our pleasure is,
That Richard be restored to his blood.
War. Let Richard be restored to his blood;
So shall his father's wrongs be recompens'd.
Win. As will the rest, so willeth Winchester.
K. Hen. If Richard will be true, not that alone,
But all the whole inheritance I give,
That doth belong unto the house of York,
From whence you spring by lineal descent.
Plan. Thy humble servant vows obedience,
And humble service, till the point of death.
K. Hen. Stoop then, and set your knee against my foot;
And, in reguerdon of that duty done,
I girt thee with the valiant sword of York:
Rise, Richard, like a true Plantagenet;
And rise created princely duke of York.
Plan. And so thrive Richard, as thy foes may fall!
And as my duty springs, so perish they
That grudge one thought against your majesty!
All. Welcome, high prince, the mighty duke of York!
Som. Perish, base prince, ignoble duke of York! [*Aside.*
Glo. Now will it best avail your majesty,
To cross the seas, and to be crown'd in France:
The presence of a king engenders love
Amongst his subjects, and his loyal friends;
As it disanimates his enemies.
K. Hen. When Gloster says the word, King Henry goes;
For friendly counsel cuts off many foes.
Glo. Your ships already are in readiness.
[*Exeunt all but* EXETER.
Exe. Ay, we may march in England, or in France,
Not seeing what is likely to ensue:
This late dissension, grown betwixt the peers,
Burns under feigned ashes of forg'd love,
And will at last break out into a flame:
As fester'd members rot but by degrees,
Till bones, and flesh, and sinews, fall away,
So will this base and envious discord breed.
And now I fear that fatal prophecy,
Which, in the time of Henry, nam'd the fifth,
Was in the mouth of every sucking babe,—
That Henry, born at Monmouth, should win all;
And Henry, born at Windsor, should lose all:
Which is so plain, that Exeter doth wish
His days may finish ere that hapless time.
[*Exit.*

SCENE II. France. *Before* Rouen.

Enter LA PUCELLE *disguised, and* Soldiers *dressed like Countrymen, with Sacks upon their Backs.*

Puc. These are the city gates, the gates of Rouen,
Through which our policy must make a breach:
Take heed, be wary how you place your words;
Talk like the vulgar sort of market-men,
That come to gather money for their corn.
If we have entrance (as, I hope, we shall),
And that we find the slothful watch but weak,
I'll by a sign give notice to our friends,
That Charles the Dauphin may encounter them.
1 *Sold.* Our sacks shall be a mean to sack the city.
And we be lords and rulers over Rouen;
Therefore we'll knock. [*Knocks.*
Guard. [*Within.*] *Qui est la?*
Puc. *Paisans, pauvres gens de France:*
Poor market-folks, that come to sell their corn.
Guard. Enter, go in; the market bell is rung.
[*Opens the Gate.*
Puc. Now, Rouen, I'll shake thy bulwarks to the ground. [PUCELLE, *&c. enter the City.*

Enter CHARLES, Bastard *of* Orleans, ALENCON, *and* Forces.

Char. Saint Dennis bless this happy stratagem!
And once again we'll sleep secure in Rouen.
Bast. Here enter'd Pucelle, and her practisants;
Now she is there, how will she specify
Where is the best and safest passage in?
Alen. By thrusting out a torch from yonder tower;
Which once discern'd, shows, that her meaning is,—
No way to that, for weakness, which she enter'd.

Enter LA PUCELLE *on a Battlement; holding out a Torch burning.*

Puc. Behold, this is the happy wedding torch,
That joineth Rouen unto her countrymen:
But burning fatal to the Talbotites.
Bast. See, noble Charles! the beacon of our friend,
The burning torch in yonder turret stands.
Char. Now shine it like a comet of revenge,
A prophet to the fall of all our foes!
Alen. Defer no time, Delays have dangerous ends;
Enter, and cry—*The Dauphin!*—presently,
And then do execution on the watch.
[*They enter.*

Alarums. *Enter* TALBOT, *and certain* English.

Tal. France, thou shalt rue this treason with thy tears,
If Talbot but survive thy treachery.—
Pucelle, that witch, that damned sorceress,
Hath wrought this hellish mischief unawares,
That hardly we escap'd the pride of France.
[*Exeunt to the Town.*

Alarum: Excursions. Enter from the Town BEDFORD, *brought in sick in a Chair, with* TALBOT, BURGUNDY, *and the* English Forces. *Then, enter on the Walls,* LA PUCELLE, CHARLES, Bastard, ALENCON, *and Others.*

Puc. Good morrow, gallants! want ye corn for bread?
I think, the duke of Burgundy will fast,
Before he'll buy again at such a rate:
'Twas full of darnel; Do you like the taste?
Bur. Scoff on, vile fiend, and shameless courtesan;
I trust, ere long, to choke thee with thine own,
And make thee curse the harvest of that corn.
Char. Your grace may starve, perhaps, before that time.
Bed. O, let no words, but deeds, revenge this treason!
Puc. What will you do, good gray-beard? break a lance,
And run a tilt at death within a chair?
Tal. Foul fiend of France, and hag of all despite,
Encompass'd with thy lustful paramours!
Becomes it thee to taunt his valiant age,
And twit with cowardice a man half dead?
Damsel, I'll have a bout with you again,
Or else let Talbot perish with this shame.

Puc. Are you so hot, sir?—Yet, Pucelle, hold thy peace;
If Talbot do but thunder, rain will follow.—
[TALBOT, *and the rest, consult together.*
God speed the parliament! who shall be the speaker?
Tal. Dare ye come forth and meet us in the field?
Puc. Belike, your lordship takes us then for fools,
To try if that our own be ours, or no.
Tal. I speak not to that railing Hecate,
But unto thee, Alencon, and the rest;
Will ye, like soldiers, come and fight it out?
Alen. Signior, no.
Tal. Signior, hang!—base muleteers of France!
Like peasant footboys do they keep the walls,
And dare not take up arms like gentlemen.
Puc. Captains, away: let's get us from the walls;
For Talbot means no goodness, by his looks.—
God be wi' you, my lord! we came, sir, but to tell you
That we are here.
[*Exeunt* LA PUCELLE, *&c. from the Walls.*
Tal. And there will we be too, ere it be long,
Or else reproach be Talbot's greatest fame!—
Vow, Burgundy, by honour of thy house,
(Prick'd on by publick wrongs, sustain'd in France),
Either to get the town again, or die:
And I,—as sure as English Henry lives,
And as his father here was conqueror;
As sure as in this late-betrayed town
Great Cœur-de-lion's heart was buried;
So sure I swear, to get the town, or die.
Bur. My vows are equal partners with thy vows.
Tal. But, ere we go, regard this dying prince,
The valiant duke of Bedford:—Come, my lord,
We will bestow you in some better place,
Fitter for sickness, and for crazy age.
Bed. Lord Talbot, do not so dishonour me:
Here will I sit before the walls of Rouen,
And will be partner of your weal, or woe.
Bur. Courageous Bedford, let us now persuade you.
Bed. Not to be gone from hence; for once I read,
That stout Pendragon, in his litter, sick,
Came to the field, and vanquished his foes:
Methinks, I should revive the soldiers' hearts,
Because I ever found them as myself.
Tal. Undaunted spirit in a dying breast!—
Then be it so:—Heavens keep old Bedford safe!—
And now no more ado, brave Burgundy,
But gather we our forces out of hand,
And set upon our boasting enemy.
[*Exeunt* BURGUNDY, TALBOT, *and* Forces, *leaving* BEDFORD, *and Others.*

Alarums: Excursions. Enter SIR JOHN FASTOLFE *and a* Captain.

Cap. Whither away, Sir John Fastolfe, in such haste?
Fas. Whither away? to save myself by flight;
We are like to have the overthrow again.
Cap. What! will you fly, and leave Lord Talbot?
Fast. Ay,
All the Talbots in the world to save my life.
[*Exit.*
Cap. Cowardly knight! ill fortune follow thee.
[*Exit.*

Retreat: Excursions. Enter, from the Town, LA PUCELLE, ALENCON, CHARLES, *&c. and exeunt flying.*

Bed. Now, quiet soul, depart when heaven please;
For I have seen our enemies' overthrow.
What is the trust or strength of foolish man?
They, that of late were daring with their scoffs,
Are glad and fain by flight to save themselves.
[*Dies, and is carried off in his Chair.*

Alarum: Enter TALBOT, BURGUNDY, *and Others.*

Tal. Lost, and recover'd in a day again!
This is a double honour, Burgundy:
Yet, heavens have glory for this victory!
Bur. Warlike and martial Talbot, Burgundy
Enshrines thee in his heart; and there erects
Thy noble deeds, as valour's monument.
Tal. Thanks, gentle duke. But where is Pucelle now?
I think, her old familiar is asleep:
Now where's the Bastard's braves, and Charles his gleeks?
What, all a-mort? Rouen hangs her head for grief,
That such a valiant company are fled.
Now will we take some order in the town,
Placing therein some expert officers;
And then depart to Paris, to the king;
For there young Harry, with his nobles, lies.
Bur. What wills Lord Talbot, pleaseth Burgundy.
Tal. But yet, before we go, let's not forget
The noble duke of Bedford, late deceas'd,
But see his exequies fulfill'd in Rouen;
A braver soldier never couched lance,
A gentler heart did never sway in court:
But kings and mightiest potentates must die;
For that's the end of human misery. [*Exeunt.*

SCENE III. *The same. The Plains near the City.*

Enter CHARLES, *the* Bastard, ALENCON, LA PUCELLE, *and* Forces.

Puc. Dismay not, princes, at this accident,
Nor grieve that Rouen is so recovered:
Care is no cure, but rather corrosive,
For things that are not to be remedied.
Let frantick Talbot triumph for a while,
And like a peacock sweep along his tail:
We'll pull his plumes, and take away his train,
If Dauphin, and the rest, will be but rul'd.
Char. We have been guided by thee hitherto,
And of thy cunning had no diffidence;
One sudden foil shall never breed distrust.
Bast. Search out thy wit for secret policies,
And we will make thee famous through the world.
Alen. We'll set thy statue in some holy place,
And have thee reverenc'd like a blessed saint;
Employ thee then, sweet virgin, for our good.
Puc. Then thus it must be; this doth Joan devise:
By fair persuasions, mix'd with sugar'd words,
We will entice the duke of Burgundy
To leave the Talbot, and to follow us.
Char. Ay, marry, sweeting, if we could do that,
France were no place for Henry's warriors;
Nor should that nation boast it so with us,
But be extirped from our provinces.
Alen. For ever should they be expuls'd from France,
And not have title to an earldom here.
Puc. Your honours shall perceive how I will work,
To bring this matter to the wished end.
[*Drums heard.*
Hark! by the sound of drum, you may perceive
Their powers are marching unto Paris-ward.

An English *March. Enter, and pass over at a distance,* TALBOT *and his* Forces.

There goes the Talbot with his colours spread;
And all the troops of English after him.

A French *March. Enter the* DUKE OF BURGUNDY *and* Forces.

Now, in the rearward, comes the duke, and his;
Fortune, in favour, makes him lag behind.
Summon a parley, we will talk with him.
[*A parley sounded.*
Char. A parley with the duke of Burgundy.

Bur. Who craves a parley with the Burgundy?
Puc. The princely Charles of France, thy countryman.
Bur. What say'st thou, Charles? for I am marching hence.
Char. Speak, Pucelle; and enchant him with thy words.
Puc. Brave Burgundy, undoubted hope of France!
Stay, let thy humble handmaid speak to thee.
Bur. Speak on; but be not over-tedious.
Puc. Look on thy country, look on fertile France,
And see the cities and the towns defac'd
By wasting ruin of the cruel foe!
As looks the mother on her lowly babe,
When death doth close his tender dying eyes,
See, see, the pining malady of France;
Behold the wounds, the most unnatural wounds,
Which thou thyself hast given her woful breast!
O, turn thy edged sword another way;
Strike those that hurt, and hurt not those that help!
One drop of blood, drawn from thy country's bosom,
Should grieve thee more than streams of foreign gore;
Return thee, therefore, with a flood of tears,
And wash away thy country's stained spots!
Bur. Either she hath bewitch'd me with her words,
Or nature makes me suddenly relent.
Puc. Besides, all French and France exclaims on thee,
Doubting thy birth and lawful progeny.
Who join'st thou with, but with a lordly nation,
That will not trust thee, but for profit's sake?
When Talbot hath set footing once in France,
And fashion'd thee that instrument of ill,
Who then, but English Henry will be lord,
And thou be thrust out, like a fugitive?
Call we to mind,—and mark but this, for proof;—
Was not the duke of Orleans thy foe?
And was he not in England prisoner?
But, when they heard he was thine enemy,
They set him free, without his ransom paid,
In spite of Burgundy, and all his friends.
See then! thou fightest against thy countrymen,
And join'st with them will be thy slaughter-men.
Come, come, return; return, thou wand'ring lord;
Charles, and the rest, will take thee in their arms.
Bur. I am vanquished: these haughty words of hers
Have batter'd me like roaring cannon shot,
And made me almost yield upon my knees.—
Forgive me, country, and sweet countrymen!
And, lords, accept this hearty kind embrace:
My forces and my power of men are yours;—
So, farewell, Talbot; I'll no longer trust thee.
Puc. Done like a Frenchman, turn, and turn again!
Char. Welcome, brave duke! thy friendship makes us fresh.
Bast. And doth beget new courage in our breasts.
Alen. Pucelle hath bravely play'd her part in this,
And doth deserve a coronet of gold.
Char. Now let us on, my lords, and join our powers;
And seek how we may prejudice the foe.
[*Exeunt.*

SCENE IV. Paris. *A Room in the Palace.*

Enter KING HENRY, GLOSTER, *and other* Lords, VERNON, BASSET, *&c.* *To them* TALBOT, *and some of his* Officers.

Tal. My gracious prince,—and honourable peers,—
Hearing of your arrival in this realm,
I have a while given truce unto my wars,
To do my duty to my sovereign;
In sign whereof, this arm—that hath reclaim'd
To your obedience fifty fortresses,
Twelve cities, and seven walled towns of strength,
Besides five hundred prisoners of esteem,—
Lets fall his sword before your highness' feet;
And, with submissive loyalty of heart,
Ascribes the glory of his conquest got,
First to my God, and next unto your grace.
K. Hen. Is this the Lord Talbot, uncle Gloster,
That hath so long been resident in France?
Glo. Yes, if it please your majesty, my liege.
K. Hen. Welcome, brave captain, and victorious lord!
When I was young (as yet I am not old),
I do remember how my father said,
A stouter champion never handled sword.
Long since we were resolved of your truth,
Your faithful service, and your toil in war;
Yet never have you tasted our reward,
Or been reguerdon'd with so much as thanks,
Because till now we never saw your face:
Therefore, stand up; and, for these good deserts,
We here create you earl of Shrewsbury;
And in our coronation take your place.
[*Exeunt* K. HEN. GLO. TAL. *and* Nobles.
Ver. Now, sir, to you, that were so hot at sea,
Disgracing of these colours that I wear
In honour of my noble lord of York,—
Dar'st thou maintain the former words thou spak'st?
Bas. Yes, sir; as well as you dare patronage
The envious barking of your saucy tongue
Against my lord the duke of Somerset.
Ver. Sirrah, thy lord I honour as he is.
Bas. Why, what is he? as good a man as York.
Ver. Hark ye; not so: in witness, take ye that.
[*Strikes him.*
Bas. Villain, thou know'st, the law of arms is such,
That, whoso draws a sword, 'tis present death;
Or else this blow should broach thy dearest blood.
But I'll unto his majesty, and crave
I may have liberty to venge this wrong;
When thou shalt see, I'll meet thee to thy cost.
Ver. Well, miscreant, I'll be there as soon as you;
And, after, meet you sooner than you would.
[*Exeunt.*

ACT IV.

SCENE I. *The same.* *A Room of State.*

Enter KING HENRY, GLOSTER, EXETER, YORK, SUFFOLK, SOMERSET, WINCHESTER, WARWICK, TALBOT, *the* Governor *of* Paris, *and Others.*

Glo. Lord bishop, set the crown upon his head.
Win. God save King Henry, of that name the sixth!
Glo. Now, governor of Paris, take your oath,
[Governor *kneels.*
That you elect no other king but him:
Esteem none friends, but such as are his friends;
And none your foes, but such as shall pretend
Malicious practices against his state:
This shall ye do, so help you righteous God!
[*Exeunt* Gov. *and his* Train.

Enter SIR JOHN FASTOLFE.

Fast. My gracious sovereign, as I rode from Calais,
To haste unto your coronation,
A letter was deliver'd to my hands,
Writ to your grace from the duke of Burgundy.
Tal. Shame to the duke of Burgundy, and thee!
I vow'd, base knight, when I did meet thee next,
To tear the garter from thy craven's leg,
[*Plucking it off.*
(Which I have done), because unworthily

Thou wast installed in that high degree.—
Pardon me, princely Henry, and the rest:
This dastard, at the battle of Patay,
When but in all I was six thousand strong,
And that the French were almost ten to one,—
Before we met, or that a stroke was given,
Like to a trusty squire, did run away;
In which assault we lost twelve hundred men;
Myself, and divers gentlemen beside,
Were there surpris'd, and taken prisoners.
Then judge, great lords, if I have done amiss;
Or whether that such cowards ought to wear
This ornament of knighthood, yea, or no.

Glo. To say the truth, this fact was infamous,
And ill beseeming any common man;
Much more a knight, a captain, and a leader.

Tal. When first this order was ordain'd, my lords,
Knights of the garter were of noble birth:
Valiant, and virtuous, full of haughty courage,
Such as were grown to credit by the wars;
Not fearing death, nor shrinking for distress,
But always resolute in most extremes.
He then, that is not furnish'd in this sort,
Doth but usurp the sacred name of knight,
Profaning this most honourable order;
And should (if I were worthy to be judge),
Be quite degraded, like a hedge-born swain
That doth presume to boast of gentle blood.

K. Hen. Stain to thy countrymen! thou hear'st thy doom:
Be packing therefore, thou that wast a knight;
Henceforth we banish thee, on pain of death.— [*Exit* FASTOLFE.
And now, my lord protector, view the letter
Sent from our uncle duke of Burgundy.

Glo. What means his grace, that he hath chang'd his style? [*Viewing the superscription.*
No more but, plain and bluntly,—*To the king?*
Hath he forgot, he is his sovereign?
Or doth this churlish superscription
Pretend some alteration in good will?
What's here?—*I have upon especial cause,*— [Reads.
Mov'd with compassion of my country's wreck,
Together with the pitiful complaints
Of such as your oppression feeds upon,—
Forsaken your pernicious faction,
And join'd with Charles, the rightful king of France.
O monstrous treachery! Can this be so;
That in alliance, amity, and oaths,
There should be found such false dissembling guile?

K. Hen. What! doth my uncle Burgundy revolt?

Glo. He doth, my lord; and is become your foe.

K. Hen. Is that the worst, this letter doth contain?

Glo. It is the worst, and all, my lord, he writes.

K. Hen. Why then, Lord Talbot there shall talk with him,
And give him chastisement for this abuse:—
My lord, how say you? are you not content?

Tal. Content, my liege? Yes; but that I am prevented,
I should have begg'd I might have been employ'd.

K. Hen. Then gather strength, and march unto him straight:
Let him perceive, how ill we brook his treason;
And what offence it is, to flout his friends.

Tal. I go, my lord; in heart desiring still,
You may behold confusion of your foes. [*Exit.*

Enter VERNON *and* BASSET.

Ver. Grant me the combat, gracious sovereign!

Bas. And me, my lord, grant me the combat too!

York. This is my servant; hear him, noble prince!

Som. And this is mine; Sweet Henry, favour him!

K. Hen. Be patient, lords; and give them leave to speak.—
Say, gentlemen, What makes you thus exclaim?
And wherefore crave you combat? or with whom?

Ver. With him, my lord; for he hath done me wrong.

Bas. And I with him; for he hath done me wrong.

K. Hen. What is that wrong whereof you both complain?
First let me know, and then I'll answer you.

Bas. Crossing the sea from England into France,
This fellow here, with envious carping tongue,
Upbraided me about the rose I wear;
Saying—the sanguine colour of the leaves
Did represent my master's blushing cheeks,
When stubbornly he did repugn the truth,
About a certain question in the law,
Argu'd betwixt the duke of York and him;
With other vile and ignominious terms:
In confutation of which rude reproach,
And in defence of my lord's worthiness,
I crave the benefit of law of arms.

Ver. And that is my petition, noble lord:
For though he seem, with forged quaint conceit,
To set a gloss upon his bold intent,
Yet know, my lord, I was provok'd by him;
And he first took exceptions at this badge,
Pronouncing—that the paleness of this flower
Bewray'd the faintness of my master's heart.

York. Will not this malice, Somerset, be left?

Som. Your private grudge, my lord of York, will out,
Though ne'er so cunningly you smother it.

K. Hen. Good lord! what madness rules in brainsick men;
When, for so slight and frivolous a cause,
Such factious emulations shall arise!—
Good cousins both, of York and Somerset,
Quiet yourselves, I pray, and be at peace.

York. Let this dissension first be tried by fight,
And then your highness shall command a peace.

Som. The quarrel toucheth none but us alone;
Betwixt ourselves let us decide it then.

York. There is my pledge; accept it, Somerset.

Ver. Nay, let it rest where it began at first.

Bas. Confirm it so, mine honourable lord.

Glo. Confirm it so? Confounded be your strife!
And perish ye, with your audacious prate!
Presumptuous vassals! are you not asham'd,
With this immodest clamorous outrage,
To trouble and disturb the king and us?
And you, my lords,—methinks, you do not well,
To bear with their perverse objections;
Much less, to take occasion from their mouths
To raise a mutiny betwixt yourselves;
Let me persuade you take a better course.

Exe. It grieves his highness;—Good my lords, be friends.

K. Hen. Come hither, you that would be combatants:
Henceforth, I charge you, as you love our favour,
Quite to forget this quarrel, and the cause.—
And you, my lords,—remember where we are;
In France, amongst a fickle wavering nation:
If they perceive dissension in our looks,
And that within ourselves we disagree,
How will their grudging stomachs be provok'd
To wilful disobedience, and rebel?
Beside, What infamy will there arise,
When foreign princes shall be certified,
That, for a toy, a thing of no regard,
King Henry's peers, and chief nobility,
Destroy'd themselves, and lost the realm of France?
O, think upon the conquest of my father,
My tender years; and let us not forego
That for a trifle, that was bought with blood!
Let me be umpire in this doubtful strife.
I see no reason, if I wear this rose, [*Putting on a red Rose.*

That any one should therefore be suspicious
I more incline to Somerset, than York:
Both are my kinsmen, and I love them both:
As well they may upbraid me with my crown,
Because, forsooth, the king of Scots is crown'd.
But your discretions better can persuade,
Than I am able to instruct or teach:
And therefore, as we hither came in peace,
So let us still continue peace and love.—
Cousin of York, we institute your grace
To be our regent in these parts of France:
And, good my lord of Somerset, unite
Your troops of horsemen with his bands of foot;—
And, like true subjects, sons of your progenitors,
Go cheerfully together, and digest
Your angry choler on your enemies.
Ourself, my lord protector, and the rest,
After some respite, will return to Calais;
From thence to England; where I hope ere long
To be presented, by your victories,
With Charles, Alencon, and that traitorous rout.
[*Flourish. Exeunt* K. HEN. GLO. SOM. WIN. SUF. *and* BASSET.

War. My lord of York, I promise you, the king
Prettily, methought, did play the orator.

York. And so he did; but yet I like it not,
In that he wears the badge of Somerset.

War. Tush! that was but his fancy, blame him not;
I dare presume, sweet prince, he thought no harm.

York. And if I wist he did,—but let it rest;
Other affairs must now be managed.
[*Exeunt* YORK, WARWICK, *and* VERNON.

Exe. Well didst thou, Richard, to suppress thy voice:
For, had the passions of thy heart burst out,
I fear we should have seen decipher'd there
More rancorous spite, more furious raging broils,
Than yet can be imagin'd or suppos'd.
But howsoe'er, no simple man that sees
This jarring discord of nobility,
This should'ring of each other in the court,
This factious bandying of their favourites,
But that it doth presage some ill event.
'Tis much, when sceptres are in children's hands;
But more, when envy breeds unkind division;
There comes the ruin, there begins confusion.
[*Exit.*

SCENE II. France. *Before* Bordeaux.

Enter TALBOT, *with his* Forces.

Tal. Go to the gates of Bordeaux, trumpeter,
Summon their general unto the wall.

Trumpet sounds a Parley. Enter, on the Walls, the General *of the* French Forces, *and Others.*

English John Talbot, captains, calls you forth,
Servant in arms to Harry king of England;
And thus he would,—Open your city gates,
Be humble to us; call my sovereign yours,
And do him homage as obedient subjects,
And I'll withdraw me and my bloody power:
But, if you frown upon this proffer'd peace,
You tempt the fury of my three attendants,
Lean famine, quartering steel, and climbing fire;
Who, in a moment, even with the earth
Shall lay your stately and air-braving towers,
If you forsake the offer of our love.

Gen. Thou ominous and fearful owl of death,
Our nation's terror, and their bloody scourge!
The period of thy tyranny approacheth.
On us, thou canst not enter, but by death:
For, I protest, we are well fortified,
And strong enough to issue out and fight:
If thou retire, the Dauphin, well appointed,
Stands with the snares of war to tangle thee:
On either hand thee there are squadrons pitch'd,
To wall thee from the liberty of flight;
And no way canst thou turn thee for redress,
But death doth front thee with apparent spoil,
And pale destruction meets thee in the face.
Ten thousand French have ta'en the sacrament,
To rive their dangerous artillery
Upon no Christian soul but English Talbot.
Lo! there thou stand'st, a breathing valiant man,
Of an invincible unconquer'd spirit:
This is the latest glory of thy praise,
That I, thy enemy, due thee withal;
For ere the glass, that now begins to run,
Finish the process of his sandy hour,
These eyes, that see thee now well coloured,
Shall see thee wither'd, bloody, pale, and dead.
[*Drum afar off.*
Hark! hark! the Dauphin's drum, a warning bell,
Sings heavy musick to thy timorous soul;
And mine shall ring thy dire departure out.
[*Exeunt* General, *&c. from the Walls.*

Tal. He fables not, I hear the enemy;—
Out, some light horsemen, and peruse their wings.—
O, negligent and heedless discipline!
How are we park'd, and bounded in a pale;
A little herd of England's timorous deer,
Maz'd with a yelping kennel of French curs!
If we be English deer, be then in blood:
Not rascal-like, to fall down with a pinch;
But rather moody-mad, and desperate stags,
Turn on the bloody hounds with heads of steel,
And make the cowards stand aloof at bay:
Sell every man his life as dear as mine,
And they shall find dear deer of us, my friends.—
God, and Saint George! Talbot, and England's right!
Prosper our colours in this dangerous fight!
[*Exeunt.*

SCENE III. *Plains in* Gascony.

Enter YORK, *with* Forces; *to him a* Messenger.

York. Are not the speedy scouts return'd again,
That dogg'd the mighty army of the Dauphin?

Mess. They are return'd, my lord; and give it out,
That he is march'd to Bordeaux with his power,
To fight with Talbot: as he march'd along,
By your espials were discovered
Two mightier troops than that the Dauphin led;
Which join'd with him, and made their march for Bordeaux.

York. A plague upon that villain Somerset;
That thus delays my promised supply
Of horsemen, that were levied for this siege!
Renowned Talbot doth expect my aid;
And I am louted by a traitor villain,
And cannot help the noble chevalier:
God comfort him in this necessity!
If he miscarry, farewell wars in France.

Enter SIR WILLIAM LUCY.

Lucy. Thou princely leader of our English strength,
Never so needful on the earth of France,
Spur to the rescue of the noble Talbot;
Who now is girdled with a waist of iron,
And hemm'd about with grim destruction:
To Bordeaux, warlike duke! to Bordeaux, York!
Else, farewell Talbot, France, and England's honour.

York. O God! that Somerset—who in proud heart
Doth stop my cornets—were in Talbot's place!
So should we save a valiant gentleman,
By forfeiting a traitor and a coward.
Mad ire, and wrathful fury, makes me weep,
That thus we die, while remiss traitors sleep.

Lucy. O, send some succour to the distress'd lord!

York. He dies, we lose; I break my warlike word;
We mourn, France smiles; we lose, they daily get;
All 'long of this vile traitor Somerset.

Lucy. Then, God take mercy on brave Talbot's soul! [since,
And on his son, young John; whom, two hours
I met in travel toward his warlike father!
This seven years did not Talbot see his son;
And now they meet where both their lives are done.

York. Alas! what joys shall noble Talbot have,
To bid his young son welcome to his grave?
Away! vexation almost stops my breath,
That sunder'd friends greet in the hour of death.—
Lucy, farewell: no more my fortune can,
But curse the cause I cannot aid the man.—
Maine, Blois, Poictiers, and Tours, are won away,
'Long all of Somerset, and his delay. [*Exit.*

Lucy. Thus, while the vulture of sedition
Feeds in the bosom of such great commanders,
Sleeping neglection doth betray to loss
The conquest of our scarce-cold conqueror,
That ever living man of memory,
Henry the Fifth:—Whiles they each other cross,
Lives, honours, lands, and all, hurry to loss. [*Exit.*

SCENE IV. *Other Plains of* Gascony.

Enter SOMERSET, *with his* Forces; *an* Officer *of* TALBOT'S *with him.*

Som. It is too late; I cannot send them now;
This expedition was by York, and Talbot,
Too rashly plotted; all our general force
Might with a sally of the very town
Be buckled with: the over daring Talbot
Hath sullied all his gloss of former honour,
By this unheedful, desperate, wild adventure:
York set him on to fight, and die in shame,
That, Talbot dead, great York might bear the name.

Off. Here is Sir William Lucy, who with me
Set from our o'ermatch'd forces forth for aid.

Enter SIR WILLIAM LUCY.

Som. How now, Sir William? whither were you sent?

Lucy. Whither, my lord? from bought and sold Lord Talbot;
Who, ring'd about with bold adversity,
Cries out for noble York and Somerset,
To beat assailing death from his weak legions.
And whiles the honourable captain there
Drops bloody sweat from his war-wearied limbs,
And, in advantage ling'ring, looks for rescue,
You, his false hopes, the trust of England's honour,
Keep off aloof with worthless emulation.
Let not your private discord keep away
The levied succours that should lend him aid,
Whiles he, renowned noble gentleman,
Yields up his life unto a world of odds:
Orleans the Bastard, Charles, and Burgundy,
Alencon, Reignier, compass him about,
And Talbot perisheth by your default.

Som. York set him on, York should have sent him aid.

Lucy. And York as fast upon your grace ex- [claims;
Swearing that you withhold his levied host,
Collected for this expedition.

Som. York lies; he might have sent and had the horse:
I owe him little duty, and less love;
And take foul scorn, to fawn on him by sending.

Lucy. The fraud of England, not the force of France,
Hath now entrapp'd the noble-minded Talbot:
Never to England shall he bear his life;
But dies, betrayed to fortune by your strife.

Som. Come, go; I will despatch the horsemen straight:
Within six hours they will be at his aid.

Lucy. Too late comes rescue; he is ta'en, or slain;
For fly he could not, if he would have fled;
And fly would Talbot never, though he might.

Som. If he be dead, brave Talbot then adieu!

Lucy. His fame lives in the world, his shame in you. [*Exeunt.*

SCENE V. *The* English *Camp, near* Bordeaux.

Enter TALBOT *and* JOHN *his* Son.

Tal. O young John Talbot! I did send for thee,
To tutor thee in stratagems of war;
That Talbot's name might be in thee reviv'd,
When sapless age, and weak unable limbs,
Should bring thy father to his drooping chair.
But,—O malignant and ill boding stars!—
Now thou art come unto a feast of death,
A terrible and unavoided danger:
Therefore, dear boy, mount on my swiftest horse;
And I'll direct thee how thou shalt escape
By sudden flight: come, dally not, begone.

John. Is my name Talbot? and am I your son?
And shall I fly? O, if you love my mother,
Dishonour not her honourable name,
To make a bastard, and a slave of me:
The world will say—He is not Talbot's blood,
That basely fled, when noble Talbot stood.

Tal. Fly, to revenge my death, if I be slain.

John. He, that flies so, will ne'er return again.

Tal. If we both stay, we both are sure to die.

John. Then let me stay; and, father, do you fly:
Your loss is great, so your regard should be;
My worth unknown, no loss is known in me.
Upon my death, the French can little boast;
In yours they will, in you all hopes are lost.
Flight cannot stain the honour you have won;
But mine it will, that no exploit have done:
You fled for vantage every one will swear;
But, if I bow, they'll say—it was for fear.
There is no hope that ever I will stay,
If, the first hour, I shrink, and run away.
Here, on my knee, I beg mortality,
Rather than life preserv'd with infamy.

Tal. Shall all thy mother's hopes lie in one tomb?

John. Ay, rather than I'll shame my mother's womb.

Tal. Upon my blessing I command thee go.

John. To fight I will, but not to fly the foe.

Tal. Part of thy father may be sav'd in thee.

John. No part of him, but will be shame in me.

Tal. Thou never hadst renown, nor canst not lose it.

John. Yes, your renowned name; Shall flight abuse it?

Tal. Thy father's charge shall clear thee from that stain.

John. You cannot witness for me, being slain,
If death be so apparent, then both fly.

Tal. And leave my followers here, to fight, and die?
My age was never tainted with such shame.

John. And shall my youth be guilty of such blame?
No more can I be sever'd from your side,
Than can yourself yourself in twain divide:
Stay, go, do what you will, the like do I;
For live I will not, if my father die.

Tal. Then here I take my leave of thee, fair son,
Born to eclipse thy life this afternoon.
Come, side by side together live and die;
And soul with soul from France to heaven fly. [*Exeunt.*

SCENE VI. *A Field of Battle.*

Alarum: Excursions, wherein TALBOT'S Son *is hemmed about, and* TALBOT *rescues him.*

Tal. Saint George and victory! fight, soldiers, fight:
The regent hath with Talbot broke his word,
And left us to the rage of France his sword.

Where is John Talbot?—pause, and take thy breath;
I gave thee life, and rescu'd thee from death.

John. O twice my father! twice am I thy son:
The life, thou gav'st me first, was lost and done;
Till with thy warlike sword despite of fate,
To my determin'd time thou gavest new date.

Tal. When from the Dauphin's crest thy sword struck fire,
It warm'd thy father's heart with proud desire
Of bold-fac'd victory. Then leaden age,
Quicken'd with youthful spleen, and warlike rage,
Beat down Alencon, Orleans, Burgundy,
And from the pride of Gallia rescu'd thee.
The ireful bastard Orleans—that drew blood
From thee, my boy; and had the maidenhood
Of thy first fight—I soon encountered;
And, interchanging blows, I quickly shed
Some of his bastard blood; and, in disgrace,
Bespoke him thus: *Contaminated, base,*
And misbegotten blood I spill of thine,
Mean and right poor; for that pure blood of mine,
Which thou didst force from Talbot, my brave boy:—
Here, purposing the Bastard to destroy,
Came in strong rescue. Speak, thy father's care;
Art thou not weary, John? How dost thou fare?
Wilt thou yet leave the battle, boy, and fly,
Now thou art seal'd the son of chivalry?
Fly, to revenge my death, when I am dead;
The help of one stands me in little stead.
O, too much folly is it, well I wot,
To hazard all our lives in one small boat.
If I to-day die not with Frenchmen's rage,
To-morrow I shall die with mickle age:
By me they nothing gain, an if I stay,
'Tis but the short'ning of my life one day:
In thee thy mother dies, our household's name,
My death's revenge, thy youth, and England's fame:
All these, and more, we hazard by thy stay;
All these are sav'd, if thou wilt fly away.

John. The sword of Orleans hath not made me smart,
These words of yours draw life-blood from my heart:
On that advantage, bought with such a shame
(To save a paltry life, and slay bright fame),
Before young Talbot from old Talbot fly,
The coward horse, that bears me, fall and die:
And like me to the peasant boys of France;
To be shame's scorn, and subject of mischance!
Surely, by all the glory you have won,
An if I fly, I am not Talbot's son:
Then talk no more of flight, it is no boot;
If son to Talbot, die at Talbot's foot.

Tal. Then follow thou thy desperate sire of Crete,
Thou Icarus; thy life to me is sweet:
If thou wilt fight, fight by thy father's side;
And, commendable prov'd, let's die in pride.
[*Exeunt.*

SCENE VII. *Another Part of the same.*

Alarum: Excursions. Enter TALBOT *wounded, supported by a* Servant.

Tal. Where is my other life? mine own is gone;—
O, where's young Talbot?—Where is valiant John?—
Triumphant death, smear'd with captivity!
Young Talbot's valour makes me smile at thee:—
When he perceiv'd me shrink, and on my knee,
His bloody sword he brandish'd over me,
And, like a hungry lion, did commence
Rough deeds of rage, and stern impatience;
But, when my angry guardant stood alone,
Tend'ring my ruin, and assail'd of none,
Dizzy-ey'd fury, and great rage of heart,
Suddenly made him from my side to start
Into the clust'ring battle of the French:
And in that sea of blood my boy did drench
His overmounting spirit; and there died
My Icarus, my blossom, in his pride.

Enter Soldiers, *bearing the Body of* JOHN TALBOT.

Serv. O my dear lord! lo, where your son is borne!

Tal. Thou antick death, which laugh'st us here to scorn,
Anon, from thy insulting tyranny,
Coupled in bonds of perpetuity,
Two Talbots, winged through the lither sky,
In thy despite shall 'scape mortality.—
O thou whose wounds become hard-favour'd death,
Speak to thy father, ere thou yield thy breath:
Brave death by speaking, whether he will, or no;
Imagine him a Frenchman, and thy foe.—
Poor boy! he smiles, methinks, as who should say—
Had death been French, then death had died to-day.
Come, come, and lay him in his father's arms:
My spirit can no longer bear these harms.
Soldiers, adieu! I have what I would have,
Now my old arms are young John Talbot's grave.
[*Dies.*

Alarums. Exeunt Soldiers *and* Servant, *leaving the two Bodies. Enter* CHARLES, ALENCON, BURGUNDY, Bastard, LA PUCELLE, *and* Forces.

Char. Had York and Somerset brought rescue in,
We should have found a bloody day of this.

Bast. How the young whelp of Talbot's, raging-wood,
Did flesh his puny sword in Frenchmen's blood!

Puc. Once I encounter'd him, and thus I said,
Thou maiden youth, be vanquish'd by a maid:
But—with a proud, majestical high scorn,—
He answer'd thus; *Young Talbot was not born*
To be the pillage of a giglot wench:
So, rushing in the bowels of the French,
He left me proudly, as unworthy fight.

Bur. Doubtless, he would have made a noble knight:
See, where he lies inhersed in the arms
Of the most bloody nurser of his harms.

Bast. Hew them to pieces, hack their bones asunder;
Whose life was England's glory, Gallia's wonder.

Char. O, no; forbear: for that which we have fled
During the life, let us not wrong it dead.

Enter SIR WILLIAM LUCY, *attended, a* French Herald *preceding.*

Lucy. Herald,
Conduct me to the Dauphin's tent; to know
Who hath obtain'd the glory of the day.

Char. On what submissive message art thou sent?

Lucy. Submission, Dauphin? 'tis a mere French word;
We English warriors wot not what it means.
I come to know what prisoners thou hast ta'en,
And to survey the bodies of the dead.

Char. For prisoners ask'st thou? hell our prison is.
But tell me whom thou seek'st?

Lucy. Where is the great Alcides of the field,
Valiant Lord Talbot, earl of Shrewsbury?
Created, for his rare success in arms,
Great Earl of Washford, Waterford, and Valence;
Lord Talbot of Goodrig and Urchinfield,
Lord Strange of Blackmere, Lord Verdun of Alton,
Lord Cromwell of Wingfield, Lord Furnival of Sheffield,
The thrice victorious lord of Falconbridge;
Knight of the noble order of Saint George,
Worthy Saint Michael, and the golden fleece;
Great mareschal to Henry the Sixth,
Of all his wars within the realm of France?

Puc. Here is a silly stately style indeed!
The Turk, that two and fifty kingdoms hath,
Writes not so tedious a style as this.—
Him, that thou magnifiest with all these titles,
Stinking and flyblown, lies here at our feet.
Lucy. Is Talbot slain; the Frenchman's only scourge,
Your kingdom's terror and black Nemesis?
O, were mine eyeballs into bullets turn'd,
That I, in rage, might shoot them at your faces!
O, that I could but call these dead to life!
It were enough to fright the realm of France:
Were but his picture left among you here,
It would amaze the proudest of you all.
Give me their bodies; that I may bear them hence,
And give them burial as beseems their worth.
Puc. I think, this upstart is old Talbot's ghost,
He speaks with such a proud commanding spirit.
For God's sake, let him have 'em; to keep them here,
They would but stink, and putrify the air.
Char. Go, take their bodies hence.
Lucy. I'll bear them hence:
But from their ashes shall be rear'd
A phœnix that shall make all France afeard.
Char. So we be rid of them, do with 'em what thou wilt.
And now to Paris, in this conquering vein:
All will be ours, now bloody Talbot's slain.
[*Exeunt.*

ACT V.

SCENE I. London. *A Room in the Palace.*

Enter KING HENRY, GLOSTER, *and* EXETER.

K. Hen. Have you perus'd the letters from the pope,
The emperor, and the earl of Armagnac?
Glo. I have, my lord; and their intent is this,—
They humbly sue unto your excellence,
To have a godly peace concluded of,
Between the realms of England and of France.
K. Hen. How doth your grace affect their motion?
Glo. Well, my good lord; and as the only means
To stop effusion of our Christian blood,
And 'stablish quietness on every side.
K. Hen. Ay, marry, uncle; for I always thought,
It was both impious and unnatural,
That such immanity and bloody strife
Should reign among professors of one faith.
Glo. Beside, my lord,—the sooner to effect,
And surer bind, this knot of amity,—
The earl of Armagnac—near knit to Charles,
A man of great authority in France—
Proffers his only daughter to your grace
In marriage, with a large and sumptuous dowry.
K. Hen. Marriage, uncle! alas! my years are young;
And fitter is my study and my books,
Than wanton dalliance with a paramour.
Yet, call the ambassadors; and, as you please,
So let them have their answers every one:
I shall be well content with any choice,
Tends to God's glory, and my country's weal.

Enter a Legate, *and two* Ambassadors, *with* WINCHESTER, *in a Cardinal's Habit.*

Exe. What! is my lord of Winchester install'd,
And call'd unto a cardinal's degree!
Then, I perceive, that will be verified,
Henry the Fifth did sometime prophesy,—
If once he come to be a cardinal,
He'll make his cap co-equal with the crown.
K. Hen. My lords ambassadors, your several suits
Have been consider'd and debated on.
Your purpose is both good and reasonable:
And, therefore, are we certainly resolv'd
To draw conditions of a friendly peace;
Which, by my lord of Winchester, we mean
Shall be transported presently to France.
Glo. And for the proffer of my lord your master,—
I have inform'd his highness so at large,
As—liking of the lady's virtuous gifts,
Her beauty, and the value of her dower,—
He doth intend she shall be England's queen.
K. Hen. In argument and proof of which contract,
Bear her this jewel, [*To the* Amb.] pledge of my affection.
And so, my lord protector, see them guarded,
And safely brought to Dover; where, inshipp'd,
Commit them to the fortune of the sea.
[*Exeunt* KING HENRY, *and* Train; GLOSTER, EXETER, *and* Ambassadors.
Win. Stay, my lord legate; you shall first receive
The sum of money, which I promised
Should be deliver'd to his holiness
For clothing me in these grave ornaments.
Leg. I will attend upon your lordship's leisure.
Win. Now, Winchester will not submit, I trow,
Or be inferior to the proudest peer.
Humphrey of Gloster, thou shalt well perceive,
That, neither in birth or for authority,
The bishop will be overborne by thee:
I'll either make thee stoop, and bend thy knee,
Or sack this country with a mutiny. [*Exeunt.*

SCENE II. France. *Plains in* Anjou.

Enter CHARLES, BURGUNDY, ALENCON, LA PUCELLE, *and* Forces, *marching.*

Char. These news, my lords, may cheer our drooping spirits:
'Tis said, the stout Parisians do revolt,
And turn again unto the warlike French.
Alen. Then march to Paris, royal Charles of France,
And keep not back your powers in dalliance.
Puc. Peace be amongst them, if they turn to us;
Else, ruin combat with their palaces!

Enter a Messenger.

Mess. Success unto our valiant general,
And happiness to his accomplices!
Char. What tidings send our scouts? I pr'ythee speak.
Mess. The English army, that divided was
Into two parts, is now conjoin'd in one;
And means to give you battle presently.
Char. Somewhat too sudden, sirs, the warning is;
But we will presently provide for them.
Bur. I trust, the ghost of Talbot is not there;
Now he is gone, my lord, you need not fear.
Puc. Of all base passions, fear is most accurs'd:—
Command the conquest, Charles, it shall be thine;
Let Henry fret, and all the world repine.
Char. Then on, my lords; And France be fortunate! [*Exeunt.*

SCENE III. *The same. Before* Angiers.

Alarums: Excursions. Enter LA PUCELLE.

Puc. The regent conquers, and the Frenchmen fly.—
Now help, ye charming spells and periapts;
And ye choice spirits that admonish me,
And give me signs of future accidents!
[*Thunder.*
You speedy helpers, that are substitutes
Under the lordly monarch of the north,
Appear, and aid me in this enterprise!

Enter Fiends.

This speedy quick appearance argues proof
Of your accustom'd diligence to me.
Now, ye familiar spirits, that are cull'd
Out of the powerful regions under earth,
Help me this once, that France may get the field,
[*They walk about, and speak not.*
O, hold me not with silence over-long!
Where I was wont to feed you with my blood,
I'll lop a member off, and give it you,
In earnest of a further benefit;
So you do condescend to help me now.—
[*They hang their heads.*
No hope to have redress?—My body shall
Pay recompense, if you will grant my suit.
[*They shake their heads.*
Cannot my body, nor blood-sacrifice,
Entreat you to your wonted furtherance?
Then take my soul; my body, soul, and all,
Before that England give the French the foil.
[*They depart.*
See! they forsake me. Now the time is come,
That France must vail her lofty-plumed crest,
And let her head fall into England's lap.
My ancient incantations are too weak,
And hell too strong for me to buckle with:
Now, France, thy glory droopeth to the dust.
[*Exit.*

Alarums. Enter French *and* English *fighting.* La Pucelle *and* York *fight hand to hand.* La Pucelle *is taken. The* French *fly.*

York. Damsel of France, I think I have you fast:
Unchain your spirits now with spelling charms,
And try if they can gain your liberty.—
A goodly prize, fit for the devil's grace!
See, how the ugly witch doth bend her brows,
As if, with Circe, she would change my shape.

Puc. Chang'd to a worser shape thou canst not be.

York. O, Charles the Dauphin is a proper man;
No shape but his can please your dainty eye.

Puc. A plaguing mischief light on Charles, and thee!
And may ye both be suddenly surpris'd
By bloody hands, in sleeping on your beds!

York. Fell, banning hag! enchantress, hold thy tongue.

Puc. I pr'ythee, give me leave to curse a while.

York. Curse, miscreant, when thou comest to the stake. [*Exeunt.*

Alarums. Enter Suffolk, *leading in* Lady Margaret.

Suff. Be what thou wilt, thou art my prisoner.
[*Gazes on her.*
O fairest beauty, do not fear, nor fly;
For I will touch thee but with reverent hands,
And lay them gently on thy tender side.
I kiss these fingers [*Kisses her hand.*] for eternal peace:
Who art thou? say, that I may honour thee.

Mar. Margaret my name; and daughter to a king,
The king of Naples, whosoe'er thou art.

Suff. An earl I am, and Suffolk am I call'd.
Be not offended, nature's miracle,
Thou art allotted to be ta'en by me:
So doth the swan her downy cygnets save,
Keeping them prisoners underneath her wings.
Yet, if this servile usage once offend,
Go, and be free again as Suffolk's friend.
[*She turns away as going.*
O, stay!—I have no power to let her pass;
My hand would free her, but my heart says—no.
As plays the sun upon the glassy streams,
Twinkling another counterfeited beam,
So seems this gorgeous beauty to mine eyes.
Fain would I woo her, yet I dare not speak:
I'll call for pen and ink, and write my mind:
Fye, De la Poole! disable not thyself;
Hast not a tongue? is she not here thy prisoner?
Wilt thou be daunted at a woman's sight?
Ay; beauty's princely majesty is such,
Confounds the tongue, and makes the senses rough.

Mar. Say, earl of Suffolk,—if thy name be so,—
What ransome must I pay before I pass?
For, I perceive, I am thy prisoner.

Suff. How canst thou tell she will deny thy suit,
Before thou make a trial of her love? [*Aside.*

Mar. Why speak'st thou not? what ransome must I pay?

Suff. She's beautiful; and therefore to be woo'd:
She is a woman; therefore to be won. [*Aside.*

Mar. Wilt thou accept of ransome, yea, or no?

Suff. Fond man! remember, that thou hast a wife:
Then how can Margaret be thy paramour?
[*Aside.*

Mar. I were best leave him, for he will not hear.

Suff. There all is marr'd; there lies a cooling card.

Mar. He talks at random; sure, the man is mad.

Suff. And yet a dispensation may be had.

Mar. And yet I would that you would answer me.

Suff. I'll win this Lady Margaret. For whom?
Why, for my king: Tush, that's a wooden thing.

Mar. He talks of wood: It is some carpenter.

Suff. Yet so my fancy may be satisfied,
And peace established between these realms.
But there remains a scruple in that too;
For though her father be the king of Naples,
Duke of Anjou and Maine, yet he is poor,
And our nobility will scorn the match. [*Aside.*

Mar. Hear ye, captain? Are you not at leisure?

Suff. It shall be so, disdain they ne'er so much:
Henry is youthful, and will quickly yield.—
Madam, I have a secret to reveal.

Mar. What though I be enthrall'd? he seems a knight,
And will not any way dishonour me. [*Aside.*

Suff. Lady, vouchsafe to listen what I say.

Mar. Perhaps, I shall be rescu'd by the French;
And then I need not crave his courtesy. [*Aside.*

Suff. Sweet madam, give me hearing in a cause—

Mar. Tush: women have been captivate ere now. [*Aside.*

Suff. Lady, wherefore talk you so?

Mar. I cry you mercy, 'tis but *quid* for *quo.*

Suff. Say, gentle princess, would you not suppose
Your bondage happy, to be made a queen?

Mar. To be a queen in bondage, is more vile,
Than is a slave in base servility:
For princes should be free.

Suff. And so shall you,
If happy England's royal king be free.

Mar. Why, what concerns his freedom unto me?

Suff. I'll undertake to make thee Henry's queen;
To put a golden sceptre in thy hand,
And set a precious crown upon thy head,
If thou wilt condescend to be my—

Mar. What?

Suff. His love.

Mar. I am unworthy to be Henry's wife.

Suff. No, gentle madam; I unworthy am
To woo so fair a dame to be his wife,
And have no portion in the choice myself.
How say you, madam; are you so content?

Mar. An if my father please, I am content.

Suff. Then call our captains, and our colours, forth:

And, madam, at your father's castle walls
We'll crave a parley to confer with him.
[Troops *come forward.*

A Parley sounded. Enter REIGNIER, *on the Walls.*

Suff. See, Reignier, see, thy daughter prisoner,
Reig. To whom?
Suff. To me.
Reig. Suffolk, what remedy?
I am a soldier, and unapt to weep,
Or to exclaim on fortune's fickleness.
Suff. Yes, there is remedy enough, my lord:
Consent (and, for thy honour, give consent),
Thy daughter shall be wedded to my king;
Whom I with pain have woo'd and won thereto;
And this her easy-held imprisonment
Hath gain'd thy daughter princely liberty.
Reig. Speaks Suffolk as he thinks?
Suff. Fair Margaret knows,
That Suffolk doth not flatter, face, or feign.
Reig. Upon thy princely warrant, I descend,
To give thee answer of thy just demand.
[*Exit, from the Walls.*
Suff. And here I will expect thy coming.

Trumpets sounded. Enter REIGNIER, *below.*

Reig. Welcome, brave earl, into our territories:
Command in Anjou what your honour pleases.
Suff. Thanks, Reignier, happy for so sweet a child,
Fit to be made companion with a king:
What answer makes your grace unto my suit?
Reig. Since thou dost deign to woo her little worth,
To be the princely bride of such a lord;
Upon condition I may quietly
Enjoy mine own, the county Maine, and Anjou,
Free from oppression, or the stroke of war,
My daughter shall be Henry's, if he please.
Suff. That is her ransome, I deliver her;
And those two counties, I will undertake,
Your grace shall well and quietly enjoy.
Reig. And I again, in Henry's royal name,
As deputy unto that gracious king,
Give thee her hand, for sign of plighted faith.
Suff. Reignier of France, I give thee kingly thanks,
Because this is in traffick of a king:
And yet, methinks, I could be well content
To be mine own attorney in this case. [*Aside.*
I'll over then to England with this news,
And make this marriage to be solemniz'd;
So, farewell, Reignier! Set this diamond safe
In golden palaces, as it becomes.
Reig. I do embrace thee, as I would embrace
The Christian prince, King Henry, were he here.
Mar. Farewell, my lord! Good wishes, praise, and prayers,
Shall Suffolk ever have of Margaret. [*Going.*
Suff. Farewell, sweet madam! But hark you, Margaret;
No princely commendations to my king?
Mar. Such commendations as become a maid,
A virgin, and his servant, say to him.
Suff. Words sweetly plac'd, and modestly directed.
But madam, I must trouble you again—
No loving token to his majesty?
Mar. Yes, my good lord; a pure unspotted heart,
Never yet taint with love, I send the king.
Suff. And this withal. [*Kisses her.*
Mar. That for thyself:—I will not so presume,
To send such peevish tokens to a king.
[*Exeunt* REIGNIER *and* MARGARET.
Suff. O, wert thou for myself!—But, Suffolk, stay;
Thou may'st not wander in that labyrinth;
There Minotaurs, and ugly treasons, lurk.
Solicit Henry with her wondrous praise:
Bethink thee on her virtues that surmount;
Mad, natural graces that extinguish art;
Repeat their semblance often on the seas,
That, when thou com'st to kneel at Henry's feet,
Thou may'st bereave him of his wits with wonder. [*Exit.*

SCENE IV. *Camp of the* Duke *of* York, *in* Anjou.

Enter YORK, WARWICK, *and Others.*

York. Bring forth that sorceress, condemn'd to burn.

Enter LA PUCELLE, *guarded, and a* Shepherd.

Shep. Ah, Joan! this kills thy father's hear outright!
Have I sought every country far and near,
And, now it is my chance to find thee out,
Must I behold thy timeless cruel death?
Ah, Joan, sweet daughter Joan, I'll die with thee!
Puc. Decrepit miser! base ignoble wretch!
I am descended of a gentler blood;
Thou art no father, nor no friend of mine.
Shep. Out, out!—My lords, an please you, 'tis not so;
I did beget her, all the parish knows:
Her mother liveth yet, can testify,
She was the first fruit of my bachelorship.
War. Graceless! wilt thou deny thy parentage?
York. This argues what her kind of life hath been;
Wicked and vile; and so her death concludes.
Shep. Fye, Joan! that thou wilt be so obstacle!
God knows, thou art a collop of my flesh;
And for thy sake have I shed many a tear:
Deny me not, I pr'ythee, gentle Joan.
Puc. Peasant, avaunt!—You have suborn'd this man,
Of purpose to obscure my noble birth.
Shep. 'Tis true, I gave a noble to the priest,
The morn that I was wedded to her mother.—
Kneel down and take my blessing, good my girl.
Wilt thou not stoop? Now cursed be the time
Of thy nativity! I would the milk
Thy mother gave thee, when thou suck'dst her breast,
Had been a little ratsbane for thy sake!
Or else, when thou didst keep my lambs a-field,
I wish some ravenous wolf had eaten thee!
Dost thou deny thy father, cursed drab?
O, burn her, burn her; hanging is too good.
[*Exit.*
York. Take her away, for she hath liv'd too long,
To fill the world with vicious qualities.
Puc. First, let me tell you whom you have condemn'd;
Not one begotten of a shepherd swain,
But issu'd from the progeny of kings;
Virtuous, and holy; chosen from above,
By inspiration of celestial grace,
To work exceeding miracles on earth.
I never had to do with wicked spirits:
But you,—that are polluted with your lusts,
Stain'd with the guiltless blood of innocents,
Corrupt and tainted with a thousand vices,—
Because you want the grace that others have,
You judge it straight a thing impossible
To compass wonders, but by help of devils.
No, misconceived? Joan of Arc hath been
A virgin from her tender infancy,
Chaste and immaculate in very thought;
Whose maiden blood, thus rigorously effus'd,
Will cry for vengeance at the gates of heaven.
York. Ay, ay;—away with her to execution.
War. And hark ye, sirs; because she is a maid,
Spare for no fagots, let there be enough:
Place barrels of pitch upon the fatal stake,
That so her torture may be shortened.
Puc. Will nothing turn your unrelenting hearts?—
Then Joan, discover thine infirmity;
That warranteth by law to be thy privilege.—
I am with child, ye bloody homicides;

Murder not then the fruit within my womb,
Although ye hale me to a violent death.
York. Now heaven forefend! the holy maid with child!
War. The greatest miracle that e'er ye wrought;
Is all your strict preciseness come to this?
York. She and the Dauphin have been juggling;
I did imagine what would be her refuge.
War. Well, go to; we will have no bastards live:
Especially, since Charles must father it.
Puc. You are deceived; my child is none of his;
It was Alencon, that enjoy'd my love.
York. Alencon! that notorious Machiavel!
It dies, an if it had a thousand lives.
Puc. O, give me leave, I have deluded you;
'Twas neither Charles, nor yet the duke I nam'd,
But Reignier, king of Naples, that prevail'd.
War. A married man! that's most intolerable.
York. Why, here's a girl! I think, she knows not well,
There were so many, whom she may accuse.
War. It's sign she hath been liberal and free.
York. And, yet, forsooth, she is a virgin pure.—
Strumpet, thy words condemn thy brat, and thee:
Use no entreaty, for it is in vain.
Puc. Then lead me hence;—with whom I leave my curse:
May never glorious sun reflex his beams
Upon the country where you make abode!
But darkness and the gloomy shade of death
Environ you; till mischief and despair,
Drive you to break your necks, or hang yourselves! [*Exit, guarded.*
York. Break thou in pieces, and consume to ashes,
Thou foul accursed minister of hell!

Enter CARDINAL BEAUFORT, *attended.*

Car. Lord regent, I do greet your excellence
With letters of commission from the king.
For know, my lords, the states of Christendom,
Mov'd with remorse of these outrageous broils,
Have earnestly implor'd a general peace
Betwixt our nation and the aspiring French:
And here at hand the Dauphin, and his train,
Approacheth, to confer about some matter.
York. Is all our travail turn'd to this effect?
After the slaughter of so many peers,
So many captains, gentlemen, and soldiers,
That in this quarrel have been overthrown,
And sold their bodies for their country's benefit,
Shall we at last conclude effeminate peace?
Have we not lost most part of all the towns,
By treason, falsehood, and by treachery,
Our great progenitors had conquer'd?—
O, Warwick, Warwick! I foresee with grief
The utter loss of all the realm of France.
War. Be patient, York: if we conclude a peace,
It shall be with such strict and severe covenants,
As little shall the Frenchmen gain thereby.

Enter CHARLES, *attended;* ALENCON, Bastard, REIGNIER, *and Others.*

Char. Since, lords of England, it is thus agreed,
That peaceful truce shall be proclaim'd in France,
We come to be informed by yourselves
What the conditions of that league must be.
York. Speak, Winchester; for boiling choler chokes
The hollow passage of my poison'd voice,
By sight of these our baleful enemies.
Win. Charles, and the rest, it is enacted thus:
That—in regard King Henry gives consent,
Of mere compassion, and of lenity,
To ease your country of distressful war,
And suffer you to breathe in fruitful peace,—
You shall become true liegemen to his crown;
And, Charles, upon condition thou wilt swear
To pay him tribute, and submit thyself,
Thou shalt be plac'd as viceroy under him,
And still enjoy thy regal dignity.
Alen. Must he be then as shadow of himself?
Adorn his temples with a coronet;
And yet, in substance and authority,
Retain but privilege of a private man?
This proffer is absurd and reasonless.
Char. 'Tis known, already, that I am possess'd
With more than half the Gallian territories,
And therein reverenc'd for their lawful king:
Shall I, for lucre of the rest unvanquish'd,
Detract so much from that prerogative,
As to be call'd but viceroy of the whole?
No, lord ambassador; I'll rather keep
That which I have, than coveting for more,
Be cast from possibility of all.
York. Insulting Charles! hast thou by secret means
Used intercession to obtain a league;
And, now the matter grows to compromise,
Stand'st thou aloof upon comparison?
Either accept the title thou usurp'st,
Of benefit proceeding from our king,
And not of any challenge of desert,
Or we will plague thee with incessant wars.
Reig. My lord, you do not well in obstinacy
To cavil in the course of this contract:
If once it be neglected, ten to one,
We shall not find like opportunity.
Alen. To say the truth, it is your policy,
To save your subjects from such massacre,
And ruthless slaughters, as are daily seen
By our proceeding in hostility:
And therefore take this compact of a truce,
Although you break it when your pleasure serves.
[*Aside to* CHARLES.
War. How say'st thou, Charles? shall our condition stand?
Char. It shall:
Only reserv'd, you claim no interest
In any of our towns of garrison.
York. Then swear allegiance to his majesty;
As thou art knight, never to disobey,
Nor be rebellious to the crown of England,
Thou, nor thy nobles, to the crown of England.—
[CHARLES, *and the rest, give tokens of fealty.*
So, now dismiss your army when ye please;
Hang up your ensigns, let your drums be still,
For here we entertain a solemn peace. [*Exeunt.*

SCENE V. London. *A Room in the Palace.*

Enter KING HENRY, *in conference with* SUFFOLK; GLOSTER, *and* EXETER *following.*

K. Hen. Your wondrous rare description, noble earl,
Of beauteous Margaret hath astonish'd me:
Her virtues, graced with external gifts,
Do breed love's settled passions in my heart:
And like as rigour in tempestuous gusts
Provokes the mightiest hulk against the tide;
So am I driven, by breath of her renown,
Either to suffer shipwreck, or arrive
Where I may have fruition of her love.
Suff. Tush! my good lord! this superficial tale
Is but a preface of her worthy praise:
The chief perfections of that lovely dame
(Had I sufficient skill to utter them),
Would make a volume of enticing lines,
Able to ravish any dull conceit.
And, which is more, she is not so divine,
So full replete with choice of all delights,
But, with as humble lowliness of mind,
She is content to be at your command;
Command, I mean, of virtuous chaste intents,
To love and honour Henry as her lord.
K. Hen. And otherwise will Henry ne'er presume.
Therefore, my lord protector, give consent,
That Margaret may be England's royal queen.
Glo. So should I give consent to flatter sin.
You know, my lord, your highness is betroth'd

Unto another lady of esteem;
How shall we then dispense with that contract,
And not deface your honour with reproach?
Suff. As doth a ruler with unlawful oaths;
Or one, that, at a triumph having vow'd
To try his strength, forsaketh yet the lists
By reason of his adversary's odds:
A poor earl's daughter is unequal odds:
And therefore may be broke without offence.
Glo. Why, what, I pray, is Margaret more than that?
Her father is no better than an earl,
Although in glorious titles he excel.
Suff. Yes, my good lord, her father is a king,
The king of Naples, and Jerusalem;
And of such great authority in France,
As his alliance will confirm our peace,
And keep the Frenchmen in allegiance.
Glo. And so the earl of Armagnac may do,
Because he is near kinsman unto Charles.
Exe. Beside his wealth doth warrant liberal dower;
While Reignier sooner will receive than give.
Suff. A dower my lords? disgrace not so your king,
That he should be so abject, base, and poor,
To choose for wealth, and not for perfect love.
Henry is able to enrich his queen,
And not to seek a queen to make him rich:
So worthless peasants bargain for their wives,
As market-men for oxen, sheep, or horse.
Marriage is a matter of more worth,
Than to be dealt in by attorneyship:
Not whom we will, but whom his grace affects,
Must be companion of his nuptial bed:
And therefore, lords, since he affects her most,
It most of all these reasons bindeth us,
In our opinions she should be preferr'd.
For what is wedlock forced, but a hell,
An age of discord and continual strife?
Whereas the contrary bringeth forth bliss,
And is a pattern of celestial peace.
Whom should we match with Henry, being a king,
But Margaret, that is daughter to a king?
Her peerless feature, joined with her birth,
Approves her fit for none, but for a king?
Her valiant courage, and undaunted spirit
(More than in women commonly is seen),
Will answer our hope in issue of a king;
For Henry, son unto a conqueror,
Is likely to beget more conquerors,
If with a lady of so high resolve,
As is fair Margaret, he be link'd in love.
Then yield, my lords; and here conclude with me,
That Margaret shall be queen, and none but she.
K. Hen. Whether it be through force of your report,
My noble lord of Suffolk; or for that
My tender youth was never yet attaint
With any passion of inflaming love,
I cannot tell; but this I am assur'd,
I feel such sharp dissension in my breast,
Such fierce alarums both of hope and fear,
As I am sick with working of my thoughts.
Take, therefore, shipping: post, my lord to France;
Agree to any covenants: and procure
That Lady Margaret do vouchsafe to come
To cross the seas to England, and be crown'd
King Henry's faithful and anointed queen:
For your expenses and sufficient charge,
Among the people gather up a tenth.
Be gone, I say; for, till you do return,
I rest perplexed with a thousand cares.—
And you, good uncle, banish all offence:
If you do censure me by what you were,
Not what you are, I know it will excuse
This sudden execution of my will.
And so conduct me, where from company,
I may revolve and ruminate my grief. [*Exit.*
Glo. Ay, grief, I fear me, both at first and last.
[*Exeunt* GLOSTER *and* EXETER.
Suff. Thus Suffolk hath prevail'd: and thus he goes,
As did the youthful Paris once to Greece;
With hope to find the like event in love,
But prosper better than the Trojan did.
Margaret shall now be queen, and rule the king;
But I will rule both her, the king, and realm.
[*Exit.*

SECOND PART OF
KING HENRY THE SIXTH.

PERSONS REPRESENTED.

KING HENRY THE SIXTH.
HUMPHREY, Duke *of* Gloster, *his Uncle.*
CARDINAL BEAUFORT, Bishop *of* Winchester, *great Uncle to the* King.
RICHARD PLANTAGENET, Duke *of* York:
EDWARD *and* RICHARD, *his Sons.*
DUKE OF SOMERSET, DUKE OF SUFFOLK, DUKE OF BUCKINGHAM, LORD CLIFFORD, *Young* CLIFFORD, *his Son.* } *of the* King's *Party.*
EARL OF SALISBURY, EARL OF WARWICK, } *of the* York *Faction.*
LORD SCALES, *Governor of the Tower.* LORD SAY.
SIR HUMPHREY STAFFORD, *and his* Brother.
SIR JOHN STANLEY.
A Sea Captain, Master, *and* Master's Mate, *and* WALTER WHITMORE.
Two Gentlemen, *Prisoners with* Suffolk.
A Herald. VAUX.
HUME *and* SOUTHWELL, *two Priests.*
BOLINGBROKE, *a Conjuror.* A Spirit *raised by him.*
THOMAS HORNER, *an Armourer.* PETER, *his Man.*
Clerk of Chatham. Mayor of St. Albans.
SIMPCOX, *an Impostor. Two* Murderers.
JACK CADE, *a Rebel:*
GEORGE, JOHN, DICK, SMITH *the Weaver*, MICHAEL, *&c. his Followers.*
ALEXANDER IDEN, *a* Kentish *Gentleman.*

MARGARET, Queen to King Henry.
ELEANOR, Duchess *of* Gloster.
MARGERY JOURDAIN, *a Witch.* Wife *to* Simpcox.

Lords, Ladies, *and* Attendants; Petitioners, Aldermen, *a* Beadle, Sheriff, *and* Officers; Citizens, Prentices, Falconers, Guards, Soldiers, Messengers, *&c.*

SCENE.—*Dispersedly in various parts of* England.

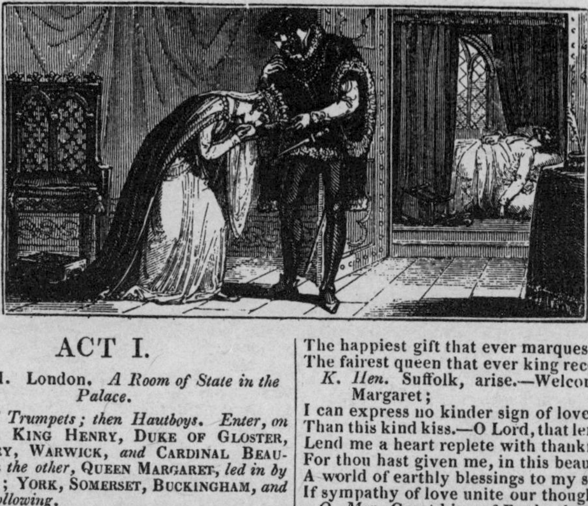

ACT I.

SCENE I. London. *A Room of State in the Palace.*

Flourish of Trumpets; then Hautboys. Enter, on one side, KING HENRY, DUKE OF GLOSTER, SALISBURY, WARWICK, *and* CARDINAL BEAUFORT; *on the other,* QUEEN MARGARET, *led in by* SUFFOLK; YORK, SOMERSET, BUCKINGHAM, *and Others, following.*

Suff. As by your high imperial majesty
I had in charge at my depart for France,
As procurator to your excellence,
To marry Princess Margaret for your grace;
So, in the famous ancient city, Tours,—
In presence of the kings of France and Sicil,
The dukes of Orleans, Calaber, Bretaigne, and Alencon, [bishops,—
Seven earls, twelve barons, twenty reverend
I have perform'd my task, and was espous'd;
And humbly now upon my bended knee,
In sight of England and her lordly peers,
Deliver up my title in the queen
To your most gracious hands, that are the substance
Of that great shadow I did represent;
The happiest gift that ever marquess gave,
The fairest queen that ever king receiv'd.

K. Hen. Suffolk, arise.—Welcome, Queen Margaret;
I can express no kinder sign of love,
Than this kind kiss.—O Lord, that lends me life,
Lend me a heart replete with thankfulness!
For thou hast given me, in this beauteous face,
A world of earthly blessings to my soul,
If sympathy of love unite our thoughts.

Q. Mar. Great king of England, and my gracious lord;
The mutual conference that my mind hath had—
By day, by night; waking, and in my dreams;
In courtly company, or at my beads,—
With you mine alder-liefest sovereign,
Makes me the bolder to salute my king
With ruder terms; such as my wit affords,
And over-joy of heart doth minister.

K. Hen. Her sight did ravish: but her grace in speech,
Her words y-clad with wisdom's majesty,
Makes me, from wondering fall to weeping joys;
Such is the fulness of my heart's content.—
Lords, with one cheerful voice welcome my love.

All. Long live Queen Margaret, England's happiness!

Q. Mar. We thank you all. [*Flourish.*

Suff. My lord protector, so it please your grace,
Here are the articles of contracted peace,
Between our sovereign and the French king
Charles,
For eighteen months concluded by consent.

Glo. [*Reads.*] Imprimis, *It is agreed between the French king, Charles, and William de la Poole, marquess of Suffolk, ambassador for Henry king of England,—that the said Henry shall espouse the lady Margaret, daughter unto Reignier king of Naples, Sicilia, and Jerusalem; and crown her queen of England, ere the thirtieth of May next ensuing.* ——Item,—*That the duchy of Anjou and the county of Maine, shall be released and delivered to the king her father——*

K. Hen. Uncle, how now?

Glo. Pardon me, gracious lord;
Some sudden qualm hath struck me to the heart,
And dimm'd mine eyes, that I can read no
further.

K. Hen. Uncle of Winchester, I pray, read on.

Win. Item,—*It is further agreed between them,—that the duchies of Anjou and Maine shall be released and delivered over to the king her father; and she sent over of the king of England's own proper cost and charges, without having dowry.*

K. Hen. They please us well.—Lord marquess,
kneel down;
We here create thee the first duke of Suffolk,
And girt thee with the sword.—
Cousin of York, we here discharge your grace
From being regent in the parts of France,
Till term of eighteen months be full expir'd.—
Thanks, uncle Winchester, Gloster, York, and
Buckingham,
Somerset, Salisbury, and Warwick;
We thank you all for this great favour done,
In entertainment to my princely queen.
Come, let us in; and with all speed provide
To see her coronation be perform'd.
[*Exeunt* King, Queen, *and* SUFFOLK.

Glo. Brave peers of England, pillars of the
state,
To you Duke Humphrey must unload his grief,
Your grief, the common grief of all the land.
What! did my brother Henry spend his youth,
His valour, coin, and people, in the wars?
Did he so often lodge in open field,
In winter's cold, and summer's parching heat,
To conquer France, his true inheritance?
And did my brother Bedford toil his wits,
To keep by policy what Henry got?
Have you yourselves, Somerset, Buckingham,
Brave York, Salisbury, and victorious Warwick,
Receiv'd deep scars in France and Normandy?
Or hath my uncle Beaufort, and myself,
With all the learned council of the realm,
Studied so long, sat in the council-house,
Early and late, debating to and fro
How France and Frenchmen might be kept in
awe?
And hath his highness in his infancy
Been crown'd in Paris, in despite of foes?
And shall these labours, and these honours,
die?
Shall Henry's conquest, Bedford's vigilance,
Your deeds of war, and all our counsel, die?
O peers of England, shameful is this league!
Fatal this marriage, cancelling your fame:
Blotting your names from books of memory:
Razing the characters of your renown:
Defacing monuments of conquer'd France;
Undoing all, as all had never been!

Car. Nephew, what means this passionate
discourse?
This peroration with such circumstance?
For France, 'tis ours; and we will keep it still.

Glo. Ay, uncle, we will keep it, if we can;
But now it is impossible we should:
Suffolk, the new-made duke that rules the roast,
Hath given the duchies of Anjou and Maine
Unto the poor king Reignier, whose large style
Agrees not with the leanness of his purse.

Sal. Now, by the death of him that died for all,
These counties were the keys of Normandy:—
But wherefore weeps Warwick, my valiant son?

War. For grief, that they are past recovery;
For, were there hope to conquer them again,
My sword should shed hot blood, mine eyes no
tears.
Anjou and Maine! myself did win them both;
Those provinces these arms of mine did conquer:
And are the cities, that I got with wounds,
Deliver'd up again with peaceful words?
Mort Dieu!

York. For Suffolk's duke—may he be suffocate,
That dims the honour of this warlike isle!
France should have torn and rent my very heart,
Before I would have yielded to this league.
I never read but England's kings have had
Large sums of gold, and dowries, with their
wives:
And our King Henry gives away his own,
To match with her that brings no vantages.

Glo. A proper jest, and never heard before,
That Suffolk should demand a whole fifteenth,
For costs and charges in transporting her!
She should have staid in France, and starv'd in
France,
Before——

Car. My lord of Gloster, now you grow too hot;
It was the pleasure of my lord the king.

Glo. My lord of Winchester, I know your
mind;
'Tis not my speeches that you do mislike,
But 'tis my presence that doth trouble you.
Rancour will out: Proud prelate, in thy face
I see thy fury: if I longer stay,
We shall begin our ancient bickerings.
Lordings, farewell; and say, when I am gone,
I prophesied—France will be lost ere long.
[*Exit.*

Car. So, there goes our protector in a rage.
'Tis known to you he is mine enemy:
Nay, more, an enemy unto you all;
And no great friend, I fear me, to the king.
Consider, lords, he is the next of blood,
And heir apparent to the English crown;
Had Henry got an empire by his marriage,
And all the wealthy kingdoms of the west,
There's reason he should be displeas'd at it.
Look to it, lords; let not his smoothing words
Bewitch your hearts; be wise, and circumspect.
What though the common people favour him,
Calling him—*Humphrey the good duke of Gloster;*
Clapping their hands, and crying with loud
voice—
Jesu maintain your royal excellence!
With—*God preserve the good duke Humphrey!*
I fear me, lords, for all this flattering gloss,
He will be found a dangerous protector.

Buck. Why should he then protect our sovereign,
He being of age to govern of himself?—
Cousin of Somerset, join you with me,
And all together—with the duke of Suffolk,—
We'll quickly hoise Duke Humphrey from his
seat.

Car. This weighty business will not brook
delay;
I'll to the duke of Suffolk presently. [*Exit.*

Som. Cousin of Buckingham, though Humphrey's pride,
And greatness of his place be grief to us,
Yet let us watch the haughty cardinal;
His insolence is more intolerable
Than all the princes in the land beside;
If Gloster be displac'd, he'll be protector.

Buck. Or thou, or I, Somerset, will be protector,
Despight Duke Humphrey, or the cardinal.
[*Exeunt* BUCKINGHAM *and* SOMERSET.

Sal. Pride went before, ambition follows him.

While these do labour for their own preferment,
Behoves it us to labour for the realm.
I never saw but Humphrey duke of Gloster
Did bear him like a noble gentleman.
Oft have I seen the haughty cardinal—
More like a soldier, than a man o' the church,
As stout, and proud, as he were lord of all,—
Swear like a ruffian, and demean himself
Unlike the ruler of a common-weal.—
Warwick, my son, the comfort of my age!
Thy deeds, thy plainness, and thy house-keeping,
Hath won the greatest favours of the commons,
Excepting none but good duke Humphrey.—
And, brother York, thy acts in Ireland,
In bringing them to civil discipline;
Thy late exploits, done in the heart of France,
When thou wert regent for our sovereign,
Have made thee fear'd, and honour'd, of the people:—
Join we together for the publick good;
In what we can to bridle and suppress
The pride of Suffolk and the cardinal,
With Somerset's and Buckingham's ambition;
And, as we may, cherish Duke Humphrey's deeds,
While they do tend the profit of the land.

War. So God help Warwick, as he loves the land,
And common profit of his country!

York. And so says York, for he hath greatest cause.

Sal. Then let's make haste away, and look unto the main.

War. Unto the main! O father, Maine is lost;
That Maine, which by main force Warwick did win,
And would have kept, so long as breath did last:
Main chance, father, you meant; but I meant Maine;
Which I will win from France, or else be slain.
[*Exeunt* WARWICK *and* SALISBURY.

York. Anjou and Maine are given to the French;
Paris is lost; the state of Normandy
Stands on a tickle point, now they are gone:
Suffolk concluded on the articles;
The peers agreed; and Henry was well pleas'd,
To change two dukedoms for a duke's fair daughter.
I cannot blame them all; What is't to them?
'Tis thine they give away, and not their own.
Pirates may make cheap pennyworths of their pillage,
And purchase friends, and give to courtesans,
Still revelling, like lords, till all be gone:
While-as the silly owner of the goods
Weeps over them, and wrings his hapless hands,
And shakes his head, and trembling stands aloof,
While all is shar'd, and all is borne away;
Ready to starve, and dare not touch his own.
So York must sit, and fret, and bite his tongue,
While his own lands are bargain'd for, and sold.
Methinks the realms of England, France, and Ireland,
Bear that proportion to my flesh and blood,
As did the fatal brand Althea burn'd,
Unto the prince's heart of Calydon.
Anjou and Maine, both given unto the French!
Cold news for me; for I had hope of France,
Even as I have of fertile England's soil.
A day will come, when York shall claim his own;
And therefore I will take the Nevils' parts,
And make a show of love to proud duke Humphrey,
And, when I spy advantage, claim the crown,
For that's the golden mark I seek to hit:
Nor shall proud Lancaster usurp my right,
Nor hold the sceptre in his childish fist,
Nor wear the diadem upon his head,
Whose church-like humours fit not for a crown.
Then, York, be still awhile, till time do serve:
Watch thou, and wake, when others be asleep,
To pry into the secrets of the state;
Till Henry, surfeiting in joys of love,
With his new bride, and England's dear bought queen,
And Humphrey with the peers be fall'n at jars:
Then will I raise aloft the milk-white rose,
With whose sweet smell the air shall be perfum'd;
And in my standard bear the arms of York,
To grapple with the house of Lancaster;
And, force perforce, I'll make him yield the crown,
Whose bookish rule hath pull'd fair England down. [*Exit.*

SCENE II. *The same.*

A Room in the Duke of Gloster's *House.*

Enter GLOSTER *and the* Duchess.

Duch. Why droops my lord, like over-ripen'd corn,
Hanging the head at Ceres' plenteous load?
Why doth the great Duke Humphrey knit his brows,
As frowning at the favours of the world?
Why are thine eyes fix'd to the sullen earth,
Gazing on that which seems to dim thy sight?
What seest thou there? King Henry's diadem,
Enchas'd with all the honours of the world?
If so, gaze on, and grovel on thy face,
Until thy head be circled with the same.
Put forth thy hand, reach at the glorious gold:—
What, is't too short? I'll lengthen it with mine;
And having both together heav'd it up,
We'll both together lift our heads to heaven;
And never more abase our sight so low,
As to vouchsafe one glance unto the ground.

Glo. O Nell, sweet Nell, if thou dost love thy lord,
Banish the canker of ambitious thoughts:
And may that thought, when I imagine ill
Against my king and nephew, virtuous Henry,
Be my last breathing in this mortal world!
My troublous dream this night doth make me sad.

Duch. What dream'd my lord? tell me, and I'll requite it
With sweet rehearsal of my morning's dream.

Glo. Methought, this staff, mine office-badge in court,
Was broke in twain, by whom, I have forgot,
But, as I think, it was by the cardinal;
And on the pieces of the broken wand
Were plac'd the heads of Edmond duke of Somerset,
And William de la Poole, first duke of Suffolk.
This was my dream, what it doth bode, God knows.

Duch. Tut, this was nothing but an argument,
That he that breaks a stick of Gloster's grove,
Shall lose his head for his presumption.
But list to me, my Humphrey, my sweet duke:
Methought, I sat in seat of majesty,
In the cathedral church of Westminster,
And in that chair where kings and queens are crown'd;
Where Henry, and dame Margaret, kneel'd to me,
And on my head did set the diadem.

Glo. Nay, Eleanor, then must I chide outright:
Presumptuous dame, ill nurtur'd Eleanor!
Art thou not second woman in the realm;
And the protector's wife, belov'd of him?
Hast thou not worldly pleasure at command,
Above the reach or compass of thy thought?
And wilt thou still be hammering treachery,
To tumble down thy husband, and thyself,
From top of honour to disgrace's feet?
Away from me, and let me hear no more.

Duch. What, what, my lord! are you so cholerick
With Eleanor, for telling but her dream?

Next time, I'll keep my dreams unto myself,
And not be check'd.

Glo. Nay, be not angry, I am pleas'd again.

Enter a Messenger.

Mess. My lord protector, 'tis his highness' pleasure,
You do prepare to ride unto Saint Albans,
Whereas the king and queen do mean to hawk.

Glo. I go—Come, Nell, thou wilt ride with us?

Duch. Yes, good my lord, I'll follow presently.

[*Exeunt* GLOSTER *and* Messenger.

Follow I must, I cannot go before,
While Gloster bears this base and humble mind,
Were I a man, a duke, and next of blood,
I would remove these tedious stumbling-blocks,
And smooth my way upon their headless necks:
And, being a woman, I will not be slack
To play my part in fortune's pageant.
Where are you there? Sir John! nay, fear not, man,
We are alone; here's none but thee, and I.

Enter HUME.

Hume. Jesu preserve your royal majesty!

Duch. What say'st thou, majesty! I am but grace.

Hume. But, by the grace of God, and Hume's advice,
Your grace's title shall be multiplied.

Duch. What say'st thou, man? hast thou as yet conferr'd
With Margery Jourdain, the cunning witch;
And Roger Bolingbroke, the conjurer?
And will they undertake to do me good?

Hume. This they have promised,—to show your highness
A spirit rais'd from depth of under ground,
That shall make answer to such questions,
As by your grace shall be propounded him.

Duch. It is enough; I'll think upon the questions:
When from Saint Albans we do make return,
We'll see these things effected to the full.
Here, Hume, take this reward; make merry, man,
With thy confederates in this weighty cause.

[*Exit* Duchess.

Hume. Hume must make merry with the duchess' gold;
Marry, and shall. But how now, Sir John Hume?
Seal up your lips, and give no words but—mum!
The business asketh silent secrecy.
Dame Eleanor gives gold, to bring the witch:
Gold cannot come amiss, were she a devil.
Yet have I gold, flies from another coast:
I dare not say, from the rich cardinal,
And from the great and new-made duke of Suffolk;
Yet I do find it so: for, to be plain,
They, knowing dame Eleanor's aspiring humour,
Have hired me to undermine the duchess,
And buz these conjurations in her brain.
They say, A crafty knave does need no broker;
Yet am I Suffolk and the cardinal's broker.
Hume, if you take not heed, you shall go near
To call them both—a pair of crafty knaves.
Well, so it stands: And thus, I fear, at last,
Hume's knavery will be the duchess' wreck;
And her attainture will be Humphrey's fall:
Sort how it will, I shall have gold for all.

[*Exit.*

SCENE III. *The same. A Room in the Palace.*

Enter PETER, *and Others, with Petitions.*

1 Pet. My masters, let's stand close; my lord protector will come this way by and by, and then we may deliver our supplications in the quill.

2 Pet. Marry, the Lord protect him, for he's a good man! Jesu bless him!

Enter SUFFOLK, *and* QUEEN MARGARET.

1 Pet. Here 'a comes, methinks, and the queen with him: I'll be the first, sure.

2 Pet. Come back, fool; this is the duke of Suffolk, and not my lord protector.

Suff. How now, fellow? would'st any thing with me?

1 Pet. I pray, my lord, pardon me! I took ye for my lord protector.

Q. Mar. [Reading the superscription.] *To my lord protector!* are your supplications to his lordship? Let me see them: What is thine?

1 Pet. Mine is, an't please your grace, against John Goodman, my lord cardinal's man, for keeping my house, and lands, and wife and all, from me.

Suff. Thy wife too? that is some wrong indeed.—What's yours?—What's here? [*Reads.*] *Against the duke of Suffolk, for enclosing the commons of Melford.*—How now, sir knave?

2 Pet. Alas, sir, I am but a poor petitioner of our whole township.

Peter. [*Presenting his petition.*] Against my master, Thomas Horner, for saying, That the duke of York was rightful heir to the crown.

Q. Mar. What say'st thou? Did the Duke of York say, he was rightful heir to the crown?

Peter. That my master was? No, forsooth: my master said, That he was; and that the king was an usurper.

Suff. Who is there? [*Enter* Servants.]—Take this fellow in, and send for his master with a pursuivant presently:—we'll hear more of your matter before the king.

[*Exeunt* Servants, *with* PETER.

Q. Mar. And as for you, that love to be protected
Under the wings of our protector's grace,
Begin your suits anew, and sue to him.

[*Tears the Petition.*

Away, base cullions!—Suffolk, let them go.

All. Come, let's be gone.

[*Exeunt* Petitioners.

Q. Mar. My lord of Suffolk, say, is this the guise,
Is this the fashion in the court of England?
Is this the government of Britain's isle,
And this the royalty of Albion's king?
What, shall King Henry be a pupil still,
Under the surly Gloster's governance?
Am I a queen in title and in style,
And must be made a subject to a duke?
I tell thee, Poole, when in the city Tours
Thou rann'st a tilt in honour of my love,
And stol'st away the ladies' hearts of France;
I thought King Henry had resembled thee,
In courage, courtship, and proportion:
But all his mind is bent to holiness,
To number *Ave-Maries* on his beads;
His champions are—the prophets and apostles;
His weapons, holy saws of sacred writ;
His study is his tilt-yard, and his loves
Are brazen images of canonized saints.
I would, the college of cardinals
Would choose him pope, and carry him to Rome,
And set the triple crown upon his head;
That were a state fit for his holiness.

Suff. Madam, be patient; as I was cause
Your highness came to England, so will I
In England work your grace's full content.

Q. Mar. Beside the haught protector, have we Beaufort,
The imperious churchman; Somerset, Buckingham,
And grumbling York: and not the least of these,
But can do more in England than the king.

Suff. And he of these, that can do most of all,
Cannot do more in England than the Nevils:
Salisbury and Warwick are no simple peers.

Q. Mar. Not all these lords do vex me half so much,

As that proud dame, the lord protector's wife.
She sweeps it through the court with troops of ladies, [wife;
More like an empress than Duke Humphrey's
Strangers in court do take her for the queen:
She bears a duke's revenues on her back,
And in her heart she scorns our poverty:
Shall I not live to be aveng'd on her?
Contemptuous base-born callat as she is,
She vaunted 'mongst her minions t'other day,
The very train of her worst wearing-gown
Was better worth than all my father's lands,
Till Suffolk gave two dukedoms for his daughter.

Suff. Madam, myself have lim'd a bush for her;
And plac'd a quire of such enticing birds,
That she will light to listen to the lays,
And never mount to trouble you again.
So, let her rest; And, madam, list to me:
For I am bold to counsel you in this.
Although we fancy not the cardinal,
Yet must we join with him, and with the lords,
Till we have brought Duke Humphrey in disgrace.
As for the duke of York, this late complaint
Will make but little for his benefit:
So, one by one, we'll weed them all at last,
And you yourself shall steer the happy helm.

Enter KING HENRY, YORK, *and* SOMERSET, *conversing with him;* DUKE *and* DUCHESS *of* GLOSTER, CARDINAL BEAUFORT, BUCKINGHAM, SALISBURY, *and* WARWICK.

K. Hen. For my part, noble lords, I care not which;
Or Somerset, or York, all's one to me.

York. If York have ill demean'd himself in France,
Then let him be denay'd the regentship.

Som. If Somerset be unworthy of the place,
Let York be regent, I will yield to him.

War. Whether your grace be worthy, yea, or no,
Dispute not that: York is the worthier.

Car. Ambitious Warwick, let thy betters speak.

War. The cardinal's not my better in the field.

Buck. All in this presence are thy betters, Warwick.

War. Warwick may live to be the best of all.

Sal. Peace, son;——and show some reason, Buckingham,
Why Somerset should be preferr'd in this.

Q. Mar. Because the king, forsooth, will have it so.

Glo. Madam, the king is old enough himself
To give his censure: these are no women's matters.

Q. Mar. If he be old enough, what needs your grace
To be protector of his excellence?

Glo. Madam, I am protector of the realm;
And, at his pleasure, will resign my place.

Suff. Resign it then, and leave thine insolence.
Since thou wert king (as who is king but thou?)
The commonwealth hath daily run to wreck:
The Dauphin hath prevail'd beyond the seas;
And all the peers and nobles of the realm
Have been as bondmen to thy sovereignty.

Car. The commons hast thou rack'd; the clergy's bags
Are lank and lean with thy extortions.

Som. Thy sumptuous buildings, and thy wife's attire,
Have cost a mass of publick treasury.

Buck. Thy cruelty in execution,
Upon offenders, hath exceeded law,
And left thee to the mercy of the law.

Q. Mar. Thy sale of offices, and towns in France,—
If they were known, as the suspect is great,—
Would make thee quickly hop without thy head.
[*Exit* GLOSTER. *The* Queen *drops her Fan.*
Give me my fan: What, minion! can you not?
[*Gives the* Duchess *a box on the ear.*
I cry you mercy, madam; Was it you?

Duch. Was't I? yea, I it was, proud Frenchwoman:
Could I come near your beauty with my nails,
I'd set my ten commandments in your face.

K. Hen. Sweet aunt, be quiet; 'twas against her will.

Duch. Against her will! Good king, look to't in time:
She'll hamper thee, and dandle thee like a baby:
Though in this place most master wear no breeches,
She shall not strike dame Eleanor unreveng'd.
[*Exit* Duchess.

Buck. Lord cardinal, I will follow Eleanor,
And listen after Humphrey, how he proceeds:
She's tickled now; her fume can need no spurs,
She'll gallop fast enough to her destruction.
[*Exit* BUCKINGHAM.

Re-enter GLOSTER.

Glo. Now, lords, my choler being overblown,
With walking once about the quadrangle,
I come to talk of commonwealth affairs.
As for your spiteful false objections,
Prove them, and I lie open to the law:
But God in mercy so deal with my soul,
As I in duty love my king and country!
But, to the matter that we have in hand:—
I say, my sovereign, York is meetest man
To be your regent in the realm of France.

Suff. Before we make election, give me leave
To show some reason, of no little force,
That York is most unmeet of any man.

York. I'll tell thee, Suffolk, why I am unmeet.
First, for I cannot flatter thee in pride:
Next, if I be appointed for the place,
My lord of Somerset will keep me here,
Without discharge, money, or furniture,
Till France be won into the Dauphin's hands.
Last time, I danc'd attendance on his will,
Till Paris was besieg'd, famish'd, and lost.

War. That I can witness; and a fouler fact
Did never traitor in the land commit.

Suff. Peace, headstrong Warwick!

War. Image of pride, why should I hold my peace?

Enter Servants *of* Suffolk, *bringing in* HORNER *and* PETER.

Suff. Because here is a man accus'd of treason:
Pray God, the duke of York excuse himself!

York. Doth any one accuse York for a traitor?

K. Hen. What mean'st thou, Suffolk? tell me: What are these?

Suff. Please it your majesty, this is the man
That doth accuse his master of high treason:
His words were these;—that Richard, duke of York,
Was rightful heir unto the English crown;
And that your majesty was an usurper.

K. Hen. Say, man, were these thy words?

Hor. An't shall please your majesty, I never said nor thought any such matter: God is my witness, I am falsely accused by the villain.

Pet. By these ten bones, my lords [*holding up his hands*], he did speak them to me in the garret one night, as we were scouring my lord of York's armour.

York. Base dunghill villain, and mechanical,
I'll have thy head for this thy traitor's speech;
I do beseech your royal majesty,
Let him have all the rigour of the law.

Hor. Alas, my lord, hang me, if ever I spake the words. My accuser is my prentice; and when I did correct him for his fault the other day, he did vow upon his knees he would be even with me: I have good witness of this; therefore, I beseech your majesty, do not cast away an honest man for a villain's accusation.

K. Hen. Uncle, what shall we say to this in law?

Glo. This doom, my lord, if I may judge.
Let Somerset be regent o'er the French,
Because in York this breeds suspicion:
And let these have a day appointed them
For single combat in convenient place;
For he hath witness of his servant's malice:
This is the law, and this Duke Humphrey's doom.

K. Hen. Then be it so. My lord of Somerset,
We make your grace lord regent o'er the French.

Som. I humbly thank your royal majesty.

Hor. And I accept the combat willingly.

Pet. Alas, my lord, I cannot fight; for God's sake, pity my case! the spite of man prevaileth against me. O, Lord have mercy upon me! I shall never be able to fight a blow: O Lord, my heart!

Glo. Sirrah, or you must fight, or else be hang'd.

K. Hen. Away with them to prison: and the day
Of combat shall be the last of the next month.—
Come, Somerset, we'll see thee sent away.
[*Exeunt.*

SCENE IV.

The same. The Duke *of* Gloster's *Garden.*

Enter MARGERY JOURDAIN, HUME, SOUTHWELL, *and* BOLINGBROKE.

Hume. Come, my masters; the duchess, I tell you, expects performance of your promises.

Boling. Master Hume, we are therefore provided: Will her ladyship behold and hear our exorcisms?

Hume. Ay; What else? fear you not her courage.

Boling. I have heard her reported to be a woman of an invincible spirit: But it shall be convenient, master Hume, that you be by her aloft, while we be busy below; and so, I pray you, go in God's name, and leave us. [*Exit* HUME.] Mother Jourdain, be you prostrate, and grovel on the earth;—John Southwell, read you; and let us to our work.

Enter Duchess, *above.*

Duch. Well said, my masters; and welcome all. To this geer; the sooner the better.

Boling. Patience, good lady; wizards know their times:
Deep night, dark night, the silent of the night,
The time of night when Troy was set on fire;
The time when screechowls cry, and ban-dogs howl,
And spirits walk, and ghosts break up their graves,
That time best fits the work we have in hand.
Madam, sit you, and fear not; whom we raise,
We will make fast within a hallow'd verge.
[*Here they perform the Ceremonies appertaining, and make the Circle;* BOLINGBROKE, *or* SOUTHWELL, *reads,* Conjuro te, &c. *It thunders and lightens terribly; then the* Spirit *riseth.*

Spir. Adsum.

M. Jourd. Asmath,
By the eternal God, whose name and power
Thou tremblest at, answer that I shall ask;
For, till thou speak, thou shalt not pass from hence.

Spir. Ask what thou wilt:—That I had said and done!

Boling. *First, of the king. What shall of him become?* [*Reading out of a Paper.*

Spir. The duke yet lives, that Henry shall depose;
But him outlive, and die a violent death.
[*As the* Spirit *speaks,* SOUTHWELL *writes the answer.*

Boling. *What fate awaits the duke of Suffolk?*

Spir. By water shall he die, and take his end.

Boling. *What shall befall the duke of Somerset?*

Spir. Let him shun castles;
Safer shall he be upon the sandy plains
Than where castles mounted stand.
Have done, for more I hardly can endure.

Boling. Descend to darkness, and the burning lake:
False fiend, avoid!
[*Thunder and Lightning.* Spirit *descends.*

Enter YORK, *and* BUCKINGHAM, *hastily, with their* Guards, *and Others.*

York. Lay hands upon these traitors, and their trash.
Beldame, I think, we watch'd you at an inch.—
What, madam, are you there? the king and commonweal
Are deeply indebted for this piece of pains;
My lord protector will, I doubt it not,
See you well guerdon'd for these good deserts.

Duch. Not half so bad as thine to England's king,
Injurious duke; that threat'st where is no cause.

Buck. True, madam, none at all. What call you this? [*Showing her the papers.*
Away with them; let them be clapp'd up close,
And kept asunder:—You, madam, shall with us:—
Stafford, take her to thee.—
[*Exit* Duchess *from above.*
We'll see your trinkets here all forth-coming;
All.—Away!
[*Exeunt* Guards, *with* SOUTH. BOLING. *&c.*

York. Lord Buckingham, methinks, you watch'd her well:
A pretty plot, well chosen to build upon!
Now, pray, my lord, let's see the devil's writ.
What have we here? [*Reads.*
The duke yet lives, that Henry shall depose;
But him outlive, and die a violent death.
Why, this is just,
Aio te, Æacida, Romanos vincere posse.
Well, to the rest:
Tell me, what fate awaits the duke of Suffolk?
By water shall he die, and take his end.—
What shall betide the duke of Somerset?
Let him shun castles;
Safer shall he be upon the sandy plains,
Than where castles mounted stand.
Come, come, my lords;
These oracles are hardly attain'd,
And hardly understood.
The king is now in progress toward Saint Albans,
With him the husband of this lovely lady:
Thither go these news, as fast as horse can carry them;
A sorry breakfast for my lord protector.

Buck. Your grace shall give me leave, my lord of York,
To be the post, in hope of his reward.

York. At your pleasure, my good lord.—Who's within there, ho!

Enter a Servant.

Invite my lords of Salisbury, and Warwick,
To sup with me to-morrow night.—Away!
[*Exeunt.*

ACT II.

SCENE I. Saint Albans.

Enter KING HENRY, QUEEN MARGARET, GLOSTER, Cardinal, *and* SUFFOLK, *with* Falconers *hollaing.*

Q. Mar. Believe me, lords, for flying at the brook,
I saw not better sport these seven years' day:
Yet, by your leave, the wind was very high;
And, ten to one, old Joan had not gone out.

K. Hen. But what a point, my lord, your falcon made,

And what a pitch she flew above the rest!—
To see how God in all his creatures works!
Yea, man and birds, are fain of climbing high.
Suff. No marvel, an it like your majesty,
My lord protector's hawks do tower so well;
They know their master loves to be aloft,
And bears his thoughts above his falcon's pitch.
Glo. My lord, 'tis but a base ignoble mind
That mounts no higher than a bird can soar.
Car. I thought as much; he'd be above the clouds.
Glo. Ay, my lord cardinal; how think you by that?
Were it not good, your grace could fly to heaven?
K. Hen. The treasury of everlasting joy!
Car. Thy heaven is on earth; thine eyes and thoughts
Beat on a crown, the treasure of thy heart;
Pernicious protector, dangerous peer,
That smooth'st it so with king and commonweal!
Glo. What, cardinal, is your priesthood grown peremptory?
Tantæne animis cœlestibus iræ?
Churchmen so hot? good uncle, hide such malice;
With such holiness can you do it?
Suff. No malice, sir; no more than well becomes
So good a quarrel, and so bad a peer.
Glo. As who, my lord?
Suff. Why, as you, my lord;
An't like your lordly lord protectorship.
Glo. Why, Suffolk, England knows thine insolence.
Q. Mar. And thy ambition, Gloster.
K. Hen. I pr'ythee, peace,
Good queen; and whet not on these furious peers,
For blessed are the peacemakers on earth.
Car. Let me be blessed for the peace I make,
Against this proud protector with my sword!
Glo. 'Faith, holy uncle, 'would, 'twere come to that! [*Aside to the* Cardinal.
Car. Marry, when thou dar'st. [*Aside.*
Glo. Make up no factious numbers for the matter,
In thine own person answer thy abuse. [*Aside.*
Car. Ay, where thou dar'st not peep: an if thou dar'st,
This evening on the east side of the grove. [*Aside.*
K. Hen. How now, my lords?
Car. Believe me, cousin Gloster,
Had not your man put up the fowl so suddenly,
We had had more sport.—Come with thy two-hand sword. [*Aside to* GLO.
Glo. True, uncle.
Car. Are you advis'd?—the east side of the grove?
Glo. Cardinal, I am with you. [*Aside.*
K. Hen. Why, how now, uncle Gloster?
Glo. Talking of hawking; nothing else, my lord.—
Now, by God's mother, priest, I'll shave your crown for this,
Or all my fence shall fail. [*Aside.*
Car. *Medice teipsum;*
Protector, see to 't well, protect yourself. } [*Aside.*
K. Hen. The winds grow high; so do your stomachs, lords.
How irksome is this musick to my heart!
When such strings jar, what hope of harmony?
I pray, my lords, let me compound this strife.

Enter an Inhabitant *of* Saint Albans, *crying,* A Miracle!

Glo. What means this noise?
Fellow, what miracle dost thou proclaim?
Inhab. A miracle! a miracle!
Suff. Come to the king, and tell him what miracle.
Inhab. Forsooth, a blind man at Saint Alban's shrine,
Within this half hour, hath receiv'd his sight;
A man, that ne'er saw in his life before.
K. Hen. Now, God be prais'd! that to believing souls
Gives light in darkness, comfort in despair!

Enter the MAYOR OF SAINT ALBANS, *and his* Brethren; *and* SIMPCOX, *borne between two Persons in a Chair; his* Wife, *and a great Multitude following.*

Car. Here come the townsmen on procession,
To present your highness with the man.
K. Hen. Great is his comfort in this earthly vale,
Although by his sight his sin be multiplied.
Glo. Stand by, my masters, bring him near the king,
His highness' pleasure is to talk with him.
K. Hen. Good fellow, tell us here the circumstance,
That we for thee may glorify the Lord.
What, hast thou been long blind, and now restor'd?
Simp. Born blind, an't please your grace.
Wife. Ay, indeed, was he.
Suff. What woman is this?
Wife. His wife, an't like your worship.
Glo. Had'st thou been his mother, thou could'st have better told.
K. Hen. Where wert thou born?
Simp. At Berwick in the North, an't like your grace.
K. Hen. Poor soul! God's goodness hath been great to thee:
Let never day nor night unhallow'd pass,
But still remember what the Lord hath done.
Q. Mar. Tell me, good fellow, cam'st thou here by chance,
Or of devotion, to this holy shrine?
Simp. God knows, of pure devotion; being call'd
A hundred times, and oftner, in my sleep
By good Saint Alban; who said,—*Simpcox, come;
Come, offer at my shrine, and I will help thee.*
Wife. Most true, forsooth; and many time and oft
Myself have heard a voice to call him so.
Car. What, art thou lame?
Simp. Ay, God Almighty help me!
Suff. How cam'st thou so?
Simp. A fall off of a tree.
Wife. A plum-tree, master.
Glo. How long hast thou been blind?
Simp. O, born so, master.
Glo. What, and would'st climb a tree?
Simp. But that in all my life, when I was a youth.
Wife. Too true; and bought his climbing very dear.
Glo. 'Mass, thou lov'dst plums well, that would'st venture so.
Simp. Alas, good master, my wife desir'd some damsons,
And made me climb, with danger of my life.
Glo. A subtle knave! but yet it shall not serve.—
Let me see thine eyes:—wink now:—now open them:—
In my opinion yet thou seest not well.
Simp. Yes, master, clear as day; I thank God, and Saint Alban.
Glo. Sayest thou me so? what colour is this cloak of?
Simp. Red, master: red as blood.
Glo. Why, that's well said: What colour is my gown of?
Simp. Black, forsooth; coal-black, as jet.
K. Hen. Why then, thou know'st what colour jet is of?
Suff. And yet, I think, jet did he never see.

Glo. But cloaks, and gowns, before this day a many.
Wife. Never, before this day, in all his life.
Glo. Tell me, sirrah, what's my name?
Simp. Alas, master, I know not.
Glo. What's his name?
Simp. I know not.
Glo. Nor his?
Simp. No, indeed, master.
Glo. What's thine own name?
Sim. Saunder Simpcox, an if it please you, master.
Glo. Then, Saunder, sit thou there, the lyingest knave
In Christendom. If thou hadst been born blind,
Thou might'st as well have known our names, as thus
To name the several colours we do wear.
Sight may distinguish of colours; but suddenly
To nominate them all, 's impossible.——
My lords, Saint Alban here hath done a miracle;
And would ye not think that cunning to be great,
That could restore this cripple to his legs?
Simp. O, master, that you could!
Glo. My masters of Saint Albans, have you not beadles in your town, and things called whips?
May. Yes, my lord, if it please your grace.
Glo. Then send for one presently.
May. Sirrah, go fetch the beadle hither straight. [*Exit an* Attendant.
Glo. Now fetch me a stool hither by and by. [*A Stool brought out.*] Now, sirrah, if you mean to save yourself from whipping, leap me over this stool, and run away.
Simp. Alas, master, I am not able to stand alone:
You go about to torture me in vain.

Re-enter Attendant, *with the* Beadle.

Glo. Well, sir, we must have you find your legs. Sirrah, beadle, whip him till he leap over that same stool.
Bead. I will, my lord.—Come on, sirrah: off with your doublet quickly.
Simp. Alas, master, what shall I do? I am not able to stand.
[*After the* Beadle *hath hit him once, he leaps over the Stool, and runs away; and the People follow, and cry,* A miracle!
K. Hen. O God, seest thou this, and bear'st so long?
Q. Mar. It made me laugh to see the villain run.
Glo. Follow the knave; and take this drab away.
Wife. Alas, sir, we did it for pure need.
Glo. Let them be whipped through every market town, till they come to Berwick, whence they came. [*Exeunt* Mayor, Beadle, Wife, *&c.*
Car. Duke Humphrey has done a miracle to-day.
Suff. True; made the lame to leap, and fly away.
Glo. But you have done more miracles than I;
You made, in a day, my lord, whole towns to fly.

Enter BUCKINGHAM.

K. Hen. What tidings with our cousin Buckingham?
Buck. Such as my heart doth tremble to unfold.
A sort of naughty persons, lewdly bent,—
Under the countenance and confederacy
Of Lady Eleanor, the protector's wife,
The ringleader and head of all this rout,—
Have practis'd dangerously against your state,
Dealing with witches, and with conjurers:
Whom we have apprehended in the fact;
Raising up wicked spirits from under ground,
Demanding of King Henry's life and death,
And other of your highness' privy council,
As more at large your grace shall understand.
Car. And so, my lord protector, by this means
Your lady is forthcoming yet at London.
This news, I think, hath turn'd your weapon's edge;
'Tis like, my lord, you will not keep your hour. [*Aside to* GLOSTER.
Glo. Ambitious churchman, leave to afflict my heart!
Sorrow and grief have vanquish'd all my powers:
And, vanquish'd as I am, I yield to thee,
Or to the meanest groom.
K. Hen. O God, what mischiefs work the wicked ones;
Heaping confusion on their own heads thereby!
Q. Mar. Gloster, see here the tainture of thy nest;
And, look, thyself be faultless, thou wert best.
Glo. Madam, for myself, to heaven I do appeal,
How I have lov'd my king and commonweal:
And, for my wife, I know not how it stands;
Sorry I am to hear what I have heard:
Noble she is; but if she have forgot
Honour, and virtue, and convers'd with such
As, like to pitch, defile nobility,
I banish her my bed, and company;
And give her, as a prey, to law, and shame,
That hath dishonour'd Gloster's honest name.
K. Hen. Well, for this night, we will repose us here:
To-morrow, toward London, back again,
To look into this business thoroughly,
And call these foul offenders to their answers;
And poise the cause in justice' equal scales,
Whose beam stands sure, whose rightful cause prevails. [*Flourish. Exeunt.*

SCENE II. London.

The Duke *of* York's *Garden.*

Enter YORK, SALISBURY, *and* WARWICK.

York. Now, my good lords of Salisbury and Warwick,
Our simple supper ended, give me leave
In this close walk, to satisfy myself,
In craving your opinion of my title,
Which is infallible to England's crown.
Sal. My lord, I long to hear it at full.
War. Sweet York, begin; and if thy claim be good,
The Nevils are thy subjects to command.
York. Then thus:—
Edward the Third, my lords, had seven sons:
The first, Edward the Black Prince, prince of Wales;
The second, William of Hatfield; and the third,
Lionel, duke of Clarence; next to whom,
Was John of Gaunt, the duke of Lancaster;
The fifth, was Edmond Langley, duke of York;
The sixth, was Thomas of Woodstock, duke of Gloster;
William of Windsor was the seventh, and last.
Edward, the Black Prince, died before his father;
And left behind him Richard, his only son,
Who, after Edward the Third's death, reign'd as king;
Till Henry Bolingbroke, duke of Lancaster,
The eldest son and heir of John of Gaunt,
Crown'd by the name of Henry the Fourth,
Seiz'd on the realm; depos'd the rightful king;
Sent his poor queen to France, from whence she came,
And him to Pomfret; where, as all you know,
Harmless Richard was murdered traitorously.
War. Father, the duke hath told the truth;
Thus got the house of Lancaster the crown.
York. Which now they hold by force, and not by right;
For Richard, the first son's heir being dead,
The issue of the next son should have reign'd.
Sal. But William of Hatfield died without an heir.
York. The third son, duke of Clarence (from whose line

I claim the crown), had issue—Philippe, a daughter,
Who married Edmund Mortimer, Earl of March;
Edmund had issue—Roger, Earl of March:
Roger had issue—Edmund, Anne, and Eleanor,

Sal. This Edmund, in the reign of Bolingbroke,
As I have read, laid claim unto the crown;
And, but for Owen Glendower, had been king,
Who kept him in captivity till he died.
But, to the rest.

York. His eldest sister, Anne,
My mother, being heir unto the crown,
Married Richard, earl of Cambridge; who was son
To Edmund Langley, Edward the Third's fifth son.
By her I claim the kingdom: she was heir
To Roger, earl of March; who was the son
Of Edmund Mortimer; who married Philippe,
Sole daughter unto Lionel, duke of Clarence:
So, if the issue of the elder son
Succeed before the younger, I am king.

War. What plain proceedings are more plain than this?
Henry doth claim the crown from John of Gaunt,
The fourth son; York claims it from the third.
Till Lionel's issue fails, his should not reign:
It fails not yet; but flourishes in thee,
And in thy sons, fair slips of such a stock.—
Then, father Salisbury, kneel we both together;
And, in this private plot, be we the first,
That shall salute our rightful sovereign
With honour of his birthright to the crown.

Both. Long live our sovereign Richard, England's king!

York. We thank you, lords. But I am not your king
Till I be crown'd; and that my sword be stain'd
With heart-blood of the house of Lancaster.
And that's not suddenly to be perform'd:
But with advice and silent secrecy,
Do you, as I do, in these dangerous days,
Wink at the duke of Suffolk's insolence,
At Beaufort's pride, at Somerset's ambition,
At Buckingham, and all the crew of them,
Till they have snar'd the shepherd of the flock,
That virtuous prince, the good duke Humphrey:
'Tis that they seek: and they, in seeking that,
Shall find their deaths, if York can prophesy.

Sal. My lord, break we off; we know your mind at full.

War. My heart assures me, that the earl of Warwick
Shall one day make the duke of York a king.

York. And, Nevil, this I do assure myself,—
Richard shall live to make the earl of Warwick
The greatest man in England but the king.
[*Exeunt.*

SCENE III. *The same. A Hall of Justice.*

Trumpets sounded. Enter KING HENRY, QUEEN MARGARET, GLOSTER, YORK, SUFFOLK, *and* SALISBURY; *the* DUCHESS OF GLOSTER, MARGERY JOURDAIN, SOUTHWELL, HUME, *and* BOLINGBROKE, *under guard.*

K. Hen. Stand forth, dame Eleanor Cobham, Gloster's wife:
In sight of God, and us, your guilt is great;
Receive the sentence of the law, for sins
Such as by God's book are adjudged to death.—
You four, from hence to prison back again;
[*To* JOURD. *&c.*
From thence, unto the place of execution:
The witch in Smithfield shall be burn'd to ashes,
And you three shall be strangled on the gallows.—
You, madam, for you are more nobly born,
Despoiled of your honour in your life,
Shall after three days open penance done,
Live in your country here, in banishment,
With Sir John Stanley, in the Isle of Man.

Duch. Welcome is banishment, welcome were my death.

Glo. Eleanor, the law, thou seest, hath judged thee;
I cannot justify whom the law condemns.—
[*Exeunt the* Duchess, *and the other* Prisoners *guarded.*
Mine eyes are full of tears, my heart of grief.
Ah, Humphrey, this dishonour in thine age
Will bring thy head with sorrow to the ground!
I beseech your majesty, give me leave to go;
Sorrow would solace, and mine age would ease.

K. Hen. Stay, Humphrey duke of Gloster: ere thou go,
Give up thy staff; Henry will to himself
Protector be: and God shall be my hope,
My stay, my guide, and lantern to my feet;
And go in peace, Humphrey, no less belov'd,
Than when thou wert protector to thy king.

Q. Mar. I see no reason, why a king of years
Should be to be protected like a child.—
God and King Henry govern England's helm:
Give up your staff, sir, and the king his realm.

Glo. My staff?—here, noble Henry, is my staff;
As willingly do I the same resign,
As e'er thy father Henry made it mine;
And even as willingly at thy feet I leave it,
As others would ambitiously receive it.
Farewell, good king: When I am dead and gone,
May honourable peace attend thy throne!
[*Exit.*

Q. Mar. Why, now is Henry king, and Margaret queen;
And Humphrey, duke of Gloster, scarce himself,
That bears so shrewd a maim; two pulls at once,—
His lady banish'd, and a limb lopp'd off.
This staff of honour raught, there let it stand,
Where it best fits to be, in Henry's hand.

Suff. Thus droops this lofty pine, and hangs his sprays;
Thus Eleanor's pride dies in her youngest days.

York. Lords, let him go.—Please it your majesty,
This is the day appointed for the combat;
And ready are the appellant and defendant,
The armourer and his man, to enter the lists,
So please your highness to behold the fight.

Q. Mar. Ay, good my lord; for purposely therefore
Left I the court, to see this quarrel tried.

K. Hen. O' God's name, see the lists and all things fit;
Here let them end it, and God defend the right!

York. I never saw a fellow worse bested,
Or more afraid to fight, than is the appellant,
The servant of this armourer, my lords.

Enter, on one side, HORNER, *and his* Neighbours, *drinking to him so much that he is drunk; and he enters bearing a staff with a sand-bag fastened to it; a drum before him: at the other side,* PETER, *with a drum and a similar staff; accompanied by* Prentices *drinking to him.*

1 *Neigh.* Here, neighbour Horner, I drink to you in a cup of sack; and fear not, neighbour, you shall do well enough.

2 *Neigh.* And here, neighbour, here's a cup of charneco.

3 *Neigh.* And here's a pot of good double beer, neighbour: drink, and fear not your man.

Hor. Let it come, i' faith, and I'll pledge you all; And a fig for Peter!

1 *Pren.* Here Peter, I drink to thee; and be not afraid.

2 *Pren.* Be merry, Peter, and fear not thy master; fight for credit of the prentices.

Peter. I thank you all: drink, and pray for me, I pray you; for, I think, I have taken my last draught in this world.—Here, Robin, an if I die, I give thee my apron; and, Will, thou shalt have my hammer:—and here, Tom, take all the money that I have.—O Lord, bless me, I pray God! for I am never able to deal with my master, he hath learnt so much fence already.

Sal. Come, leave your drinking, and fall to blows.—Sirrah, what's thy name?

Peter. Peter, forsooth.

Sal. Peter! what more?

Peter. Thump.

Sal. Thump! then see thou thump thy master well.

Hor. Masters, I am come hither, as it were, upon my man's instigation, to prove him a knave, and myself an honest man: and touching the duke of York,—will take my death, I never meant him any ill, nor the king, nor the queen: And, therefore, Peter, have at thee with a downright blow, as Bevis of Southampton fell upon Ascapart.

York. Despatch:—this knave's tongue begins to double.
Sound trumpets, alarum to the combatants.

[*Alarum. They fight, and* PETER *strikes down his Master.*

Hor. Hold, Peter, hold! I confess, I confess treason. [*Dies.*

York. Take away his weapon;—Fellow,
Thank God, and the good wine in thy master's way.

Peter. O God! have I overcome mine enemies in this presence? O Peter, thou hast prevail'd in right!

K. Hen. Go, take hence that traitor from our sight;
For, by his death, we do perceive his guilt:
And God, in justice, hath reveal'd to us
The truth and innocence of this poor fellow,
Which he had thought to have murder'd wrongfully.—
Come, fellow, follow us for thy reward.

[*Exeunt.*

SCENE IV. *The same. A Street.*

Enter GLOSTER *and* Servants, *in mourning Cloaks.*

Glo. Thus, sometimes hath the brightest day a cloud;
And, after summer, evermore succeeds
Barren winter, with his wrathful nipping cold:
So cares and joys abound, as seasons fleet.
Sirs, what's o'clock?

Serv. Ten, my lord.

Glo. Ten is the hour that was appointed me,
To watch the coming of my punish'd duchess:
Uneath may she endure the flinty streets,
To tread them with her tender-feeling feet.
Sweet Nell, ill can thy noble mind abrook
The abject people, gazing on thy face,
With envious looks, still laughing at thy shame;
That erst did follow thy proud chariot wheels,
When thou didst ride in triumph through the streets.
But, soft! I think, she comes; and I'll prepare
My tear-stain'd eyes to see her miseries.

Enter the DUCHESS OF GLOSTER, *in a white sheet, with papers pinned upon her back, her feet bare, and a taper burning in her hand;* SIR JOHN STANLEY, *a* Sheriff, *and* Officers.

Serv. So please your grace, we'll take her from the sheriff.

Glo. No, stir not, for your lives; let her pass by.

Duch. Come you, my lord, to see my open shame?
Now thou dost penance too. Look, how they gaze!
See, how the giddy multitude do point,
And nod their heads, and throw their eyes on thee!
Ah, Gloster, hide thee from their hateful looks;
And, in thy closet pent up, rue my shame,
And ban thine enemies, both mine and thine.

Glo. Be patient, gentle Nell; forget this grief.

Duch. Ah, Gloster, teach me to forget myself;
For, whilst I think I am thy married wife,
And thou a prince, protector of this land,
Methinks, I should not thus be led along,
Mail'd up in shame, with papers on my back;
And follow'd with a rabble, that rejoice
To see my tears, and hear my deep-fet groans.
The ruthless flint doth cut my tender feet;
And, when I start, the envious people laugh,
And bid me be advised how I tread.
Ah, Humphrey, can I bear this shameful yoke?
Trow'st thou, that e'er I'll look upon the world;
Or count them happy, that enjoy the sun?
No; dark shall be my light, and night my day;
To think upon my pomp shall be my hell.
Sometime I'll say, I am Duke Humphrey's wife;
And he a prince, and ruler of the land:
Yet so he rul'd, and such a prince he was,
As he stood by, whilst I, his forlorn duchess,
Was made a wonder, and a pointing stock,
To every idle rascal follower.
But be thou mild, and blush not at my shame;
Nor stir at nothing, till the axe of death
Hang over thee, as, sure, it shortly will.
For Suffolk,—he that can do all in all
With her, that hateth thee, and hates us all,—
And York, and impious Beaufort, that false priest,
Have all lim'd bushes to betray thy wings,
And, fly thou how thou canst, they'll tangle thee:
But fear not thou, until thy foot be snar'd,
Nor never seek prevention of thy foes.

Glo. Ah, Nell, forbear; thou aimest all awry;
I must offend before I be attainted:
And had I twenty times so many foes,
And each of them had twenty times their power,
All these could not procure me any scathe,
So long as I am loyal, true, and crimeless.
Would'st have me rescue thee from this reproach?
Why, yet thy scandal were not wip'd away,
But I in danger for the breach of law.
Thy greatest help is quiet, gentle Nell:
I pray thee, sort thy heart to patience;
These few days' wonder will be quickly worn.

Enter a Herald.

Her. I summon your grace to his majesty's parliament, holden at Bury the first of this next month.

Glo. And my consent ne'er ask'd herein before!
This is close dealing.—Well, I will be there.

[*Exit* Herald.

My Nell, I take my leave:—and master sheriff,
Let not her penance exceed the king's commission.

Sher. An't please your grace, here my commission stays:
And Sir John Stanley is appointed now
To take her with him to the Isle of Man.

Glo. Must you, Sir John, protect my lady here?

Stan. So am I given in charge, may't please your grace.

Glo. Entreat her not the worse, in that I pray
You use her well: the world may laugh again;
And I may live to do you kindness, if
You do it her. And so, Sir John, farewell.

Duch. What gone, my lord; and bid me not farewell?

Glo. Witness my tears, I cannot stay to speak.

[*Exeunt* GLOSTER *and* Servants.

Duch. Art thou gone too? All comfort go with thee!
For none abides with me: my joy is—death:
Death, at whose name I oft have been afear'd,
Because I wish'd this world's eternity.—
Stanley, I pr'ythee, go, and take me hence;
I care not whither, for I beg no favour,
Only convey me where thou art commanded.

Stan. Why, madam, that is to the Isle of Man;
There to be used according to your state.

Duch. That's bad enough, for I am but reproach:
And shall I then be us'd reproachfully?

Stan. Like to a duchess, and Duke Humphrey's lady,
According to that state you shall be used.
Duch. Sheriff, farewell, and better than I fare;
Although thou hast been conduct of my shame!
Sher. It is my office; and, madam, pardon me.
Duch. Ay, ay, farewell; thy office is discharg'd.—
Come, Stanley, shall we go?
Stan. Madam, your penance done, throw off this sheet,
And go we to attire you for our journey.
Duch. My shame will not be shifted with my sheet:
No, it will hang upon my richest robes,
And show itself, attire me how I can.
Go, lead the way; I long to see my prison.
[*Exeunt.*

ACT III.

SCENE I. *The Abbey at* Bury.

Enter to the Parliament, KING HENRY, QUEEN MARGARET, CARDINAL BEAUFORT, SUFFOLK, YORK, BUCKINGHAM, *and Others.*

K. Hen. I muse, my lord of Gloster is not come:
'Tis not his wont to be the hindmost man,
Whate'er occasion keeps him from us now.
Q. Mar. Can you not see? or will you not observe
The strangeness of his alter'd countenance?
With what a majesty he bears himself?
How insolent of late he is become,
How proud, how peremptory, and unlike himself?
We know the time, since he was mild and affable;
And, if we did but glance a far off look,
Immediately he was upon his knee,
That all the court admir'd him for submission:
But meet him now, and, be it in the morn,
When every one will give the time of day,
He knits his brow, and shows an angry eye,
And passeth by with stiff unbowed knee,
Disdaining duty that to us belongs.
Small curs are not regarded, when they grin:
But great men tremble, when the lion roars:
And Humphrey is no little man in England.
First, note, that he is near you in descent;
And should you fall he is the next will mount.
Me seemeth then, it is no policy,—
Respecting what a rancorous mind he bears,
And his advantage following your decease,—
That he should come about your royal person,
Or be admitted to your highness' council.
By flattery hath he won the commons' hearts;
And, when he please to make commotion,
'Tis to be fear'd, they all will follow him.
Now 'tis the spring, and weeds are shallow-rooted;
Suffer them now, and they'll o'ergrow the garden,
And choke the herbs for want of husbandry.
The reverent care, I bear unto my lord,
Made me collect these dangers in the duke.
If it be fond, call it a woman's fear;
Which fear if better reasons can supplant,
I will subscribe and say—I wrong'd the duke.
My lord of Suffolk,—Buckingham,—and York,—
Reprove my allegation, if you can;
Or else conclude my words effectual.
Suff. Well hath your highness seen into this duke;
And, had I first been put to speak my mind,
I think, I should have told your grace's tale.
The duchess, by his subornation,
Upon my life, began her devilish practices:
Or if he were not privy to those faults,
Yet by reputing of his high descent
(As next the king he was successive heir),
And such high vaunts of his nobility,
Did instigate the bedlam brain-sick duchess,
By wicked means, to frame our sovereign's fall.
Smooth runs the water where the brook is deep;
And in his simple show he harbours treason.
The fox barks not, when he would steal the lamb.
No, no, my sovereign; Gloster is a man
Unsounded yet, and full of deep deceit.
Car. Did he not, contrary to form of law,
Devise strange deaths for small offences done?
York. And did he not, in his protectorship,
Levy great sums of money through the realm,
For soldiers' pay in France, and never sent it?
By means whereof, the towns each day revolted.
Buck. Tut! these are petty faults to faults unknown,
Which time will bring to light in smooth Duke Humphrey.
K. Hen. My lords, at once: The care you have of us,
To mow down thorns that would annoy our foot,
Is worthy praise: But shall I speak my conscience?
Our kinsman Gloster is as innocent
From meaning treason to our royal person,
As is the sucking lamb, or harmless dove:
The duke is virtuous, mild; and too well given,
To dream on evil, or to work my downfall.
Q. Mar. Ah, what's more dangerous than this fond affiance!
Seems he a dove? his feathers are but borrow'd,
For he's disposed as the hateful raven.
Is he a lamb? his skin is surely lent him,
For he's inclin'd as are the ravenous wolves.
Who cannot steal a shape, that means deceit?
Take heed, my lord; the welfare of us all
Hangs on the cutting short that fraudful man.

Enter SOMERSET.

Som. All health unto my gracious sovereign!
K. Hen. Welcome, Lord Somerset. What news from France?
Som. That all your interest in those territories
Is utterly bereft you; all is lost.
K. Hen. Cold news, Lord Somerset: But God's will be done!
York. Cold news for me; for I had hope of France,
As firmly as I hope for fertile England.
Thus are my blossoms blasted in the bud,
And caterpillars eat my leaves away:
But I will remedy this gear ere long
Or sell my title for a glorious grave. [*Aside.*

Enter GLOSTER.

Glo. All happiness unto my lord the king!
Pardon, my liege, that I have staid so long.
Suff. Nay, Gloster, know, that thou art come too soon,
Unless thou wert more loyal than thou art:
I do arrest thee of high treason here.
Glo. Well, Suffolk, yet thou shalt not see me blush,
Nor change my countenance for this arrest;
A heart unspotted is not easily daunted.
The purest spring is not so free from mud,
As I am clear from treason to my sovereign:
Who can accuse me? wherein am I guilty?
York. 'Tis thought, my lord, that you took bribes of France,
And, being protector, stayed the soldier's pay;
By means whereof, his highness hath lost France.
Glo. Is it but thought so? What are they that think it?
I never robb'd the soldiers of their pay,
Nor ever had one penny bribe from France.
So help me God, as I have watch'd the night,—
Ay, night by night,—in studying good for England!
That doit that e'er I wrested from the king,
Or any groat I hoarded to my use,
Be brought against me at my trial day!
No! many a pound of mine own proper store,
Because I would not tax the needy commons,

Have I dispersed to the garrisons,
And never ask'd for restitution.
Car. It serves you well, my lord, to say so much.
Glo. I say no more than truth, so help me God!
York. In your protectorship, you did devise
Strange tortures for offenders, never heard of,
That England was defam'd by tyranny.
Glo. Why, 'tis well known, that whiles I was protector,
Pity was all the fault that was in me;
For I should melt at an offender's tears,
And lowly words were ransome for their fault.
Unless it were a bloody murderer,
Or foul felonious thief that flecc'd poor passengers,
I never gave them condign punishment:
Murder, indeed, that bloody sin, I tortur'd
Above the felon, or what trespass else.
Suff. My lord, these faults are easy, quickly answer'd:
But mightier crimes are laid unto your charge,
Whereof you cannot easily purge yourself.
I do arrest you in his highness' name;
And here commit you to my lord cardinal
To keep, until your further time of trial.
K. Hen. My lord of Gloster, 'tis my special hope,
That you will clear yourself from all suspects;
My conscience tells me, you are innocent.
Glo. Ah, gracious lord, these days are dangerous!
Virtue is chok'd with foul ambition,
And charity chas'd hence by rancour's hand;
Foul subornation is predominant,
And equity exil'd your highness' land.
I know, their complot is to have my life;
And, if my death might make this island happy,
And prove the period of their tyranny,
I would expend it with all willingness:
But mine is made the prologue to their play;
For thousands more, that yet suspect no peril,
Will not conclude their plotted tragedy.
Beaufort's red sparkling eyes blab his heart's malice,
And Suffolk's cloudy brow, his stormy hate;
Sharp Buckingham unburdens with his tongue
The envious load that lies upon his heart:
And dogged York, that reaches at the moon,
Whose overweening arm I have pluck'd back,
By false accuse doth level at my life:—
And you, my sovereign lady, with the rest,
Causeless have laid disgraces on my head;
And, with your best endeavour, have stirr'd up
My liefest liege to be mine enemy:—
Ay, all of you have laid your heads together,
Myself had notice of your conventicles,
And all to make away my guiltless life:
I shall not want false witness to condemn me,
Nor store of treasons to augment my guilt;
The ancient proverb will be well affected,—
A staff is quickly found to beat a dog.
Car. My liege, his railing is intolerable:
If those that care to keep your royal person
From treason's secret knife, and traitor's rage,
Be thus upbraided, chid, and rated at,
And the offender granted scope of speech,
'Twill make them cool in zeal unto your grace.
Suff. Hath he not twit our sovereign lady here,
With ignominious words, though clerkly couch'd,
As if she had suborned some to swear
False allegations to o'erthrow his state?
Q. Mar. But I can give the loser leave to chide.
Glo. Far truer spoke than meant: I lose indeed;—
Beshrew the winners, for they played me false!
And well such losers may have leave to speak.
Buck. He'll wrest the sense, and hold us here all day:—
Lord cardinal, he is your prisoner.
Car. Sirs, take away the duke, and guard him sure.
Glo. Ah, thus King Henry throws away his crutch,
Before his legs be firm to bear his body:
Thus is the shepherd beaten from thy side,
And wolves are gnarling who shall gnaw thee first.
Ah, that my fear were false! ah, that it were!
For, good King Henry, thy decay I fear.
[*Exeunt* Attendants, *with* GLOSTER.
K. Hen. My lords, what to your wisdoms seemeth best,
Do, or undo, as if ourself were here.
Q. Mar. What, will your highness leave the parliament?
K. Hen. Ay, Margaret; my heart is drown'd with grief,
Whose flood begins to flow within mine eyes;
My body round engirt with misery;
For what's more miserable than discontent?—
Ah, uncle Humphrey! in thy face I see
The map of honour, truth, and loyalty!
And yet, good Humphrey, is the hour to come,
That e'er I prov'd thee false, or fear'd thy faith.
What low'ring star now envies thy estate,
That these great lords, and Margaret our queen,
Do seek subversion of thy harmless life?
Thou never didst them wrong, nor no man wrong;
And as the butcher takes away the calf,
And binds the wretch, and beats it when it strays,
Bearing it to the bloody slaughter-house;
Even so, remorseless, have they borne him hence.
And as the dam runs lowing up and down,
Looking the way her harmless young one went,
And can do nought but wail her darling's loss:
Even so myself bewails good Gloster's case,
With sad unhelpful tears; and with dimm'd eyes
Look after him, and cannot do him good;
So mighty are his vowed enemies.
His fortunes I will weep; and, 'twixt each groan,
Say—*Who's a traitor*, Gloster *he is none.* [*Exit.*
Q. Mar. Free lords, cold snow melts with the sun's hot beams.
Henry my lord is cold in great affairs,
Too full of foolish pity; and Gloster's show
Beguiles him, as the mournful crocodile
With sorrow snares relenting passengers:
Or as the snake, roll'd in a flowering bank,
With shining checker'd slough, doth sting a child,
That, for the beauty, thinks it excellent.
Believe me, lords, were none more wise than I
(And yet, herein, I judge mine own wit good),
This Gloster should be quickly rid the world,
To rid us from the fear we have of him.
Car. That he should die, is worthy policy;
But yet we want a colour for his death:
'Tis meet, he be condemn'd by course of law.
Suff. But, in my mind, that were no policy:
The king will labour still to save his life;
The commons haply rise to save his life;
And we yet have but trivial argument,
More than mistrust, that shows him worthy death.
York. So that, by this, you would not have him die.
Suff. Ah, York, no man alive so fain as I.
York. 'Tis York that hath more reason for his death.—
But, my lord cardinal, and you, my lord of Suffolk,—
Say as you think, and speak it from your souls,—
Wer't not all one, an empty eagle were set
To guard the chicken from a hungry kite,
As place Duke Humphrey for the king's protector?
Q. Mar. So the poor chicken should be sure of death.
Suff. Madam, 'tis true: And wer't not madness then
To make the fox surveyor of the fold?

Who being accus'd a crafty murderer,
His guilt should be but idly posted over,
Because his purpose is not executed.
No; let him die, in that he is a fox,
By nature prov'd an enemy to the flock,
Before his chaps be stain'd with crimson blood;
As Humphrey, prov'd by reasons, to my liege.
And do not stand on quillets, how to slay him;
Be it by gins, by snares, by subtilty,
Sleeping or waking, 'tis no matter how,
So he be dead; for that is good deceit
Which mates him first, that first intends deceit.

Q. Mar. Thrice-noble Suffolk, 'tis resolutely spoke.

Suff. Not resolute, except so much were done;
For things are often spoke, and seldom meant:
But that my heart accordeth with my tongue,—
Seeing the deed is meritorious,
And to preserve my sovereign from his foe,—
Say but the word, and I will be his priest.

Car. But I would have him dead, my lord of Suffolk,
Ere you can take due orders for a priest:
Say, you consent, and censure well the deed,
And I'll provide his executioner,
I tender so the safety of my liege.

Suff. Here is my hand, the deed is worthy doing.

Q. Mar. And so say I.

York. And I: and now we three have spoke it,
It skills not greatly who impugns our doom.

Enter a Messenger.

Mess. Great lords, from Ireland am I come amain,
To signify—that rebels there are up,
And put the Englishmen unto the sword;
Send succours, lords, and stop the rage betime,
Before the wound do grow incurable;
For, being green, there is great hope of help.

Car. A breach, that craves a quick expedient stop!
What counsel give you in this weighty cause?

York. That Somerset be sent as regent thither:
'Tis meet, that lucky ruler be employ'd;
Witness the fortune he hath had in France.

Som. If York, with all his far fet policy,
Had been the regent there instead of me,
He never would have staid in France so long.

York. No, not to lose it all, as thou hast done:
I rather would have lost my life betimes,
Than bring a burden of dishonour home,
By staying there so long, till all were lost.
Show me one scar character'd on thy skin:
Men's flesh preserv'd so whole, do seldom win.

Q. Mar. Nay then, this spark will prove a raging fire,
If wind and fuel be brought to feed it with:—
No more, good York:—sweet Somerset, be still:—
Thy fortune, York, hadst thou been regent there,
Might happily have prov'd far worse than his.

York. What, worse than nought? nay, then a shame take all!

Som. And in the number, thee, that wishest shame!

Car. My lord of York, try what your fortune is,
The uncivil Kernes of Ireland are in arms,
And temper clay with blood of Englishmen:
To Ireland will you lead a band of men,
Collected choicely, from each county some,
And try your hap against the Irishmen?

York. I will, my lord, so please his majesty.

Suff. Why, our authority is his consent;
And, what we do establish, he confirms:
Then, noble York, take thou this task in hand.

York. I am content: Provide me soldiers, lords,
Whiles I take order for mine own affairs.

Suff. A charge, Lord York, that I will see perform'd.
But now return we to the false duke Humphrey.

Car. No more of him; for I will deal with him,
That, henceforth, he shall trouble us no more.
And so break off: the day is almost spent:
Lord Suffolk, you and I must talk of that event.

York. My lord of Suffolk, within fourteen days,
At Bristol I expect my soldiers;
For there I'll ship them all for Ireland.

Suff. I'll see it truly done, my lord of York.
[*Exeunt all but* YORK.

York. Now, York, or never, steel thy fearful thoughts,
And change misdoubt to resolution:
Be that thou hop'st to be; or what thou art
Resign to death, it is not worth the enjoying:
Let pale-fac'd fear keep with the mean-born man,
And find no harbour in a royal heart.
Faster than spring-time showers, comes thought on thought;
And not a thought, but thinks on dignity.
My brain, more busy than the labouring spider,
Weaves tedious snares to trap mine enemies.
Well, nobles, well, 'tis politickly done,
To send me packing with an host of men:
I fear me, you but warm the starved snake,
Who, cherish'd in your breasts, will sting your hearts.
'Twas men I lack'd, and you will give them me:
I take it kindly: yet, be well assur'd
You put sharp weapons in a madman's hands.
Whiles I in Ireland nourish a mighty band,
I will stir up in England some black storm,
Shall blow ten thousand souls to heaven or hell:
And this fell tempest shall not cease to rage
Until the golden circuit on my head,
Like to the glorious sun's transparent beams,
Do calm the fury of this mad-bred flaw.
And, for a minister of my intent,
I have seduced a headstrong Kentishman,
John Cade of Ashford,
To make commotion, as full well he can,
Under the title of John Mortimer.
In Ireland have I seen this stubborn Cade
Oppose himself against a troop of Kernes;
And fought so long, till that his thighs with darts
Were almost like a sharp-quill'd porcupine:
And, in the end being rescued, I have seen him
Caper upright like a wild Morisco,
Shaking the bloody darts, as he his bells.
Full often, like a shag-hair'd crafty Kerne,
Hath he conversed with the enemy;
And undiscover'd come to me again,
And given me notice of their villanies.
This devil here shall be my substitute;
For that John Mortimer, which now is dead,
In face, in gait, in speech, he doth resemble:
By this I shall perceive the commons' mind,
How they affect the house and claim of York.
Say, he be taken, rack'd, and tortured:
I know, no pain, they can inflict upon him,
Will make him say—I mov'd him to those arms.
Say, that he thrive (as 'tis great like he will),
Why, then from Ireland come I with my strength,
And reap the harvest which that rascal sow'd:
For, Humphrey being dead, as he shall be,
And Henry put apart, the next for me. [*Exit.*

SCENE II. Bury. *A Room in the Palace.*

Enter certain Murderers *hastily.*

1 Mur. Run to my lord of Suffolk; let him know,
We have dispatch'd the duke, as he commanded.

2 Mur. O, that it were to do!—What have we done?
Didst ever hear a man so penitent?

Enter SUFFOLK.

1 Mur. Here comes my lord.

Suff. Now, sirs, have you
Despatch'd this thing?

1 *Mur.* Ay, my good lord, he's dead.
Suff. Why, that's well said. Go, get you to my house;
I will reward you for this venturous deed.
The king and all the peers are here at hand:—
Have you laid fair the bed? are all things well,
According as I gave directions?
1 *Mur.* 'Tis, my good lord.
Suff. Away, be gone! [*Exeunt* Murderers.

Enter KING HENRY, QUEEN MARGARET, CARDINAL BEAUFORT, SOMERSET, Lords, *and Others.*

K. Hen. Go, call our uncle to our presence straight:
Say, we intend to try his grace to-day,
If he be guilty, as 'tis published.
Suff. I'll call him presently, my noble lord. [*Exit.*
K. Hen. Lords, take your places;—And, I pray you all,
Proceed no straiter 'gainst our uncle Gloster,
Than from true evidence, of good esteem,
He be approv'd in practice culpable.
Q. Mar. God forbid any malice should prevail,
That faultless may condemn a nobleman!
'Pray God, he may acquit him of suspicion!
K. Hen. I thank thee, Margaret; these words content me much.—

Re-enter SUFFOLK.

How now? why look'st thou pale? why tremblest thou?
Where is our uncle? what is the matter, Suffolk?
Suff. Dead in his bed, my lord; Gloster is dead.
Q. Mar. Marry, God forefend!
Car. God's secret judgment:—I did dream to-night,
The duke was dumb, and could not speak a word. [*The* King *swoons.*
Q. Mar. How fares my lord?—Help, lords! the king is dead.
Som. Rear up his body; wring him by the nose.
Q. Mar. Run, go, help, help!—O Henry, ope thine eyes!
Suff. He doth revive again;—Madam, be patient.
K. Hen. O heavenly God!
Q. Mar. How fares my gracious lord?
Suff. Comfort, my sovereign! gracious Henry, comfort!
K. Hen. What, doth my lord of Suffolk comfort me?
Came he right now to sing a raven's note,
Whose dismal tune bereft my vital powers;
And thinks he, that the chirping of a wren,
By crying comfort from a hollow breast,
Can chase away the first-conceived sound?
Hide not thy poison with such sugar'd words,
Lay not thy hands on me; forbear, I say,
Their touch affrights me, as a serpent's sting.
Thou baleful messenger, out of my sight!
Upon thy eyeballs murderous tyranny
Sits in grim majesty, to fright the world.
Look not upon me, for thine eyes are wounding:—
Yet do not go away;—Come basilisk,
And kill the innocent gazer with thy sight:
For in the shade of death I shall find joy:
In life, but double death, now Gloster's dead!
Q. Mar. Why do you rate my lord of Suffolk thus?
Although the duke was enemy to him,
Yet he, most christianlike, laments his death:
And for myself—foe as he was to me,
Might liquid tears, or heart-offending groans,
Or blood-consuming sighs recall his life,
I would be blind with weeping, sick with groans,
Look pale as primrose, with blood-drinking sighs,
And all to have the noble duke alive.
What know I how the world may deem of me?
For it is known we were but hollow friends;
It may be judg'd, I made the duke away:
So shall my name with slander's tongue be wounded,
And princes' courts be fill'd with my reproach.
This get I by his death: Ah me, unhappy!
To be a queen, and crown'd with infamy!
K. Hen. Ah, woe is me for Gloster, wretched man!
Q. Mar. Be woe for me, more wretched than he is.
What, dost thou turn away, and hide thy face?
I am no loathsome leper, look on me.
What, art thou, like the adder, waxen deaf?
Be poisonous too, and kill thy forlorn queen.
Is all thy comfort shut in Gloster's tomb?
Why, then dame Margaret was ne'er thy joy:
Erect his statue then, and worship it,
And make my image but an alehouse sign.
Was I, for this, nigh wreck'd upon the sea;
And twice by awkward wind from England's bank
Drove back again unto my native clime?
What boded this, but well forewarning wind
Did seem to say,—Seek not a scorpion's nest,
Nor set no footing on this unkind shore?
What did I then, but curst the gentle gusts,
And he that loos'd them from their brazen caves;
And bid them blow towards England's blessed shore,
Or turn our stern upon a dreadful rock?
Yet Æolus would not be a murderer,
But left that hateful office unto thee:
The pretty vaulting sea refus'd to drown me;
Knowing, that thou would'st have me drown'd on shore,
With tears as salt as sea through thy unkindness:
The splitting rocks cower'd in the sinking sands,
And would not dash me with their ragged sides;
Because thy flinty heart, more hard than they,
Might in thy palace perish Margaret.
As far as I could ken thy chalky cliffs,
When from the shore the tempest beat us back,
I stood upon the hatches in the storm:
And when the dusky sky began to rob
My earnest-gaping sight of thy land's view,
I took a costly jewel from my neck,—
A heart it was, bound in with diamonds,—
And threw it towards thy land;—the sea receiv'd it;
And so, I wish'd, thy body might my heart:
And even with this, I lost fair England's view,
And bid mine eyes be packing with my heart;
And call'd them blind and dusky spectacles,
For losing ken of Albion's wished coast.
How often have I tempted Suffolk's tongue
(The agent of thy foul inconstancy)
To sit and witch me, as Ascanius did,
When he to madding Dido would unfold
His father's acts, commenc'd in burning Troy?
Am I not witch'd like her? or thou not false like him?
Ah me, I can no more! Die, Margaret!
For Henry weeps that thou dost live so long.

Noise within. Enter WARWICK *and* SALISBURY. *The* Commons *press to the door.*

War. It is reported, mighty sovereign,
That good Duke Humphrey traitorously is murder'd
By Suffolk and the cardinal Beaufort's means.
The commons, like an angry hive of bees,
That want their leader, scatter up and down,
And care not who they sting in his revenge.
Myself have calm'd their spleenful mutiny,
Until they hear the order of his death.
K. Hen. That he is dead, good Warwick, 'tis too true;
But how he died, God knows, not Henry:
Enter his chamber, view his breathless corpse,
And comment then upon his sudden death.

War. That I shall do, my liege:—Stay, Salisbury,
With the rude multitude, till I return.
[WARWICK *goes into an inner Room, and* SALISBURY *retires.*

K. Hen. O thou that judgest all things, stay my thoughts:
My thoughts, that labour to persuade my soul,
Some violent hands were laid on Humphrey's life!
If my suspect be false, forgive me, God;
For judgment only doth belong to thee!
Fain would I go to chafe his paly lips
With twenty thousand kisses, and to drain
Upon his face, an ocean of salt tears;
To tell my love unto his dumb deaf trunk,
And with my fingers feel his hand unfeeling:
But all in vain are these mean obsequies:
And, to survey his dead and earthly image,
What were it but to make my sorrow greater?

The folding doors of an inner Chamber are thrown open, and GLOSTER *is discovered dead in his Bed:* WARWICK *and others standing by it.*

War. Come hither, gracious sovereign, view this body.

K. Hen. That is to see how deep my grave is made:
For, with his soul, fled all my worldly solace;
For seeing him, I see my life in death.

War. As surely as my soul intends to live
With that dread King, that took our state upon him
To free us from his Father's wrathful curse,
I do believe that violent hands were laid
Upon the life of this thrice-famed duke.

Suff. A dreadful oath, sworn with a solemn tongue!
What instance gives Lord Warwick for his vow?

War. See how the blood is settled in his face!
Oft have I seen a timely parted ghost,
Of ashy semblance, meager, pale, and bloodless,
Being all descended to the labouring heart;
Who, in the conflict that it holds with death,
Attracts the same for aidance 'gainst the enemy:
Which with the heart there cools and ne'er returneth
To blush and beautify the cheek again.
But, see, his face is black, and full of blood;
His eyeballs further out than when he liv'd,
Staring full ghastly, like a strangled man:
His hair uprear'd, his nostrils stretch'd with struggling;
His hands abroad display'd, as one that grasp'd
And tugg'd for life, and was by strength subdu'd.
Look on the sheets, his hair, you see, is sticking;
His well proportion'd beard made rough and rugged,
Like to the summer's corn by tempest lodg'd.
It cannot be, but he was murder'd here;
The least of all these signs were probable.

Suff. Why, Warwick, who should do the duke to death?
Myself, and Beaufort, had him in protection;
And we, I hope, sir, are no murderers.

War. But both of you were vow'd Duke Humphrey's foes;
And you, forsooth, had the good duke to keep:
'Tis like, you would not feast him like a friend;
And 'tis well seen he found an enemy.

Q. Mar. Then you, belike, suspect these noblemen
As guilty of Duke Humphrey's timeless death.

War. Who finds the heifer dead, and bleeding fresh,
And sees fast by a butcher with an axe,
But will suspect, 'twas he that made the slaughter?
Who finds the partridge in the puttock's nest,
But may imagine how the bird was dead,
Although the kite soar with unbloodied beak?
Even so suspicious is this tragedy.

Q. Mar. Are you the butcher, Suffolk, where's your knife?
Is Beaufort term'd a kite? where are his talons?

Suff. I wear no knife, to slaughter sleeping men;
But here's a vengeful sword, rusted with ease,
That shall be scoured in his rancorous heart,
That slanders me with murder's crimson badge:—
Say, if thou dar'st, proud lord of Warwickshire,
That I am faulty in duke Humphrey's death.
[*Exeunt* Cardinal, SOM. *and Others.*

War. What dares not Warwick, if false Suffolk dare him?

Q. Mar. He dares not calm his contumelious spirit,
Nor cease to be an arrogant controller,
Though Suffolk dare him twenty thousand times.

War. Madam, be still; with reverence may I say;
For every word you speak in his behalf,
Is slander to your royal dignity.

Suff. Blunt-witted lord, ignoble in demeanour!
If ever lady wrong'd her lord so much,
Thy mother took into her baneful bed
Some stern untutor'd churl, and noble stock
Was graft with crab-tree slip; whose fruit thou art,
And never of the Nevil's noble race.

War. But that the guilt of murder bucklers thee,
And I should rob the deathsman of his fee,
Quitting thee thereby of ten thousand shames,
And that my sovereign's presence makes me mild,
I would, false murderous coward, on thy knee
Make thee beg pardon for thy passed speech,
And say—it was thy mother that thou meant'st,
That thou thyself wast born in bastardy:
And, after all this fearful homage done,
Give thee thy hire, and send thy soul to hell,
Pernicious bloodsucker of sleeping men!

Suff. Thou shalt be waking, while I shed thy blood,
If from this presence thou dar'st go with me.

War. Away even now, or I will drag thee hence;
Unworthy though thou art, I'll cope with thee,
And do some service to Duke Humphrey's ghost.
[*Exeunt* SUFFOLK *and* WARWICK.

K. Hen. What stronger breastplate than a heart untainted?
Thrice is he armed, that hath his quarrel just;
And he but naked, though lock'd up in steel,
Whose conscience with injustice is corrupted.
[*A Noise within.*

Q. Mar. What noise is this?

Re-enter SUFFOLK *and* WARWICK, *with their Weapons drawn.*

K. Hen. Why, how now lords? your wrathful weapons drawn
Here in our presence? dare you be so bold?—
Why, what tumultuous clamour have we here?

Suff. The traitorous Warwick with the men of Bury,
Set all upon me, mighty sovereign.

Noise of a Crowd within. *Re-enter* SALISBURY.

Sal. Sirs, stand apart; the king shall know your mind.— [*Speaking to those within.*
Dread lord, the commons send you word by me,
Unless false Suffolk straight be done to death,
Or banished fair England's territories,
They will by violence tear him from your palace,
And torture him with grievous ling'ring death.
They say, by him the good Duke Humphrey died;
They say, in him they fear your highness' death;
And mere instinct of love and loyalty,—
Free from a stubborn opposite intent,
As being thought to contradict your liking,—
Makes them thus forward in his banishment.

They say, in care of your most royal person,
That, if your highness should intend to sleep,
And charge—that no man should disturb your rest,
In pain of your dislike, or pain of death;
Yet notwithstanding such a strait edict,
Were there a serpent seen, with forked tongue,
That slily glided toward your majesty,
It were but necessary you were wak'd;
Lest, being suffer'd in that harmful slumber,
The mortal worm might make the sleep eternal;
And therefore do they cry, though you forbid,
That they will guard you, whe'r you will, or no,
From such fell serpents as false Suffolk is;
With whose envenomed and fatal sting
Your loving uncle, twenty times his worth,
They say, is shamefully bereft of life.

Commons. [*Within*] An answer from the king, my lord of Salisbury.

Suff. 'Tis like the commons, rude unpolish'd hinds,
Could send such message to their sovereign:
But you, my lord, were glad to be employ'd,
To show how quaint an orator you are:
But all the honour Salisbury hath won,
Is—that he was the lord ambassador,
Sent from a sort of tinkers to the king.

Commons. [*Within.*] An answer from the king, or we'll all break in.

K. Hen. Go, Salisbury, and tell them all from me,
I thank them for their tender loving care;
And had I not been cited so by them,
Yet did I purpose as they do entreat;
For sure, my thoughts do hourly prophesy
Mischance unto my state by Suffolk's means.
And therefore—by His majesty I swear,
Whose far unworthy deputy I am,—
He shall not breathe infection in this air
But three days longer, on the pain of death.
[*Exit* SALISBURY.

Q. Mar. O Henry, let me plead for gentle Suffolk!

K. Hen. Ungentle queen, to call him gentle Suffolk.
No more, I say; if thou dost plead for him,
Thou wilt but add increase unto my wrath.
Had I but said, I would have kept my word:
But, when I swear, it is irrevocable:—
If, after three days space, thou here be'st found,
On any ground that I am ruler of,
The world shall not be ransome for thy life,—
Come, Warwick, come, good Warwick, go with me;
I have great matters to impart to thee.
[*Exeunt* K. HENRY, WARWICK, Lords, &c.

Q. Mar. Mischance, and sorrow go along with you!
Heart's discontent, and sour affliction,
Be playfellows to keep you company!
There's two of you, the devil make a third!
And threefold vengeance tend upon your steps!

Suff. Cease, gentle queen, these execrations,
And let thy Suffolk take his heavy leave.

Q. Mar. Fye, coward woman, and soft-hearted wretch!
Hast thou not spirit to curse thine enemies?

Suff. A plague upon them! wherefore should I curse them?
Would curses kill, as doth the mandrake's groan,
I would invent as bitter-searching terms,
As curst, as harsh, and horrible to hear,
Deliver'd strongly through my fixed teeth,
With full as many signs of deadly hate,
As lean-fac'd Envy in her loathsome cave:
My tongue should stumble in mine earnest words:
Mine eyes should sparkle like the beaten flint;
My hair be fix'd on end, as one distract;
Ay, every joint should seem to curse and ban:
And even now my burden'd heart would break,
Should I not curse them. Poison be their drink!
Gall, worse than gall, the daintiest that they taste!
Their sweetest shade, a grove of cypress trees!
Their chiefest prospect, murdering basilisks!
Their softest touch, as smart as lizards' stings!
Their musick, frightful as the serpent's hiss:
And boding screechowls make the concert full!
All the foul terrors in dark-seated hell—

Q. Mar. Enough, sweet Suffolk; thou torment'st thyself;
And these dread curses—like the sun 'gainst glass,
Or like an overcharged gun,—recoil,
And turn the force of them upon thyself.

Suff. You bade me ban, and will you bid me leave?
Now, by the ground that I am banish'd from,
Well could I curse away a winter's night,
Though standing naked on a mountain top,
Where biting cold would never let grass grow,
And think it but a minute spent in sport.

Q. Mar. O, let me entreat thee, cease! Give me thy hand,
That I may dew it with my mournful tears;
Nor let the rain of heaven wet this place,
To wash away my woful monuments.
O, could this kiss be printed in thy hand;
[*Kisses his hand.*
That thou might'st think upon these by the seal,
Through whom a thousand sighs are breath'd for thee!
So, get thee gone, that I may know my grief;
'Tis but surmis'd whilst thou art standing by,
As one that surfeits thinking on a want.
I will repeal thee, or, be well assur'd,
Adventure to be banished myself:
And banished I am, if but from thee.
Go, speak not to me; even now be gone.—
O, go not yet!—Even thus two friends condemn'd
Embrace, and kiss, and take ten thousand leaves,
Loather a hundred times to part than die.
Yet now farewell; and farewell life with thee!

Suff. Thus is poor Suffolk ten times banished,
Once by the king, and three times thrice by thee.
'Tis not the land I care for, wert thou hence;
A wilderness is populous enough,
So Suffolk had thy heavenly company:
For where thou art, there is the world itself,
With every several pleasure in the world;
And where thou art not, desolation.
I can no more:—Live thou to joy thy life;
Myself no joy in nought, but that thou liv'st.

Enter VAUX.

Q. Mar. Whither goes Vaux so fast? what news, I pr'ythee?

Vaux. To signify unto his majesty,
That cardinal Beaufort is at point of death:
For suddenly a grievous sickness took him,
That makes him gasp, and stare, and catch the air,
Blaspheming God, and cursing men on earth.
Sometime, he talks as if Duke Humphrey's ghost
Were by his side; sometime, he calls the king,
And whispers to his pillow as to him,
The secrets of his overcharged soul:
And I am sent to tell his majesty,
That even now he cries aloud for him.

Q. Mar. Go, tell this heavy message to the king.
[*Exit* VAUX.
Ah me! what is this world? what news are these?
But wherefore grieve I at an hour's poor loss,
Omitting Suffolk's exile, my soul's treasure?
Why only, Suffolk, mourn I not for thee,
And with the southern clouds contend in tears;
Theirs for the earth's increase, mine for my sorrows?
Now, get thee hence: The king, thou know'st, is coming?
If thou be found by me, thou art but dead.

Suff. If I depart from thee, I cannot live:
And in thy sight to die, what were it else,
But like a pleasant slumber in thy lap?
Here could I breathe my soul into the air,
As mild and gentle as the cradle babe,
Dying with mother's dug between its lips:
Where, from thy sight, I should be raging mad,
And cry out for thee to close up mine eyes,
To have thee with thy lips to stop my mouth;
So should'st thou either turn my flying soul,
Or I should breathe it so into thy body,
And then it liv'd in sweet Elysium.
To die by thee, were but to die in jest;
From thee to die, were torture more than death;
O, let me stay, befall what may befall.

Q. Mar. Away! though parting be a fretful cor'sive
It is applied to a deathful wound.
To France, sweet Suffolk: Let me hear from thee:
For wheresoe'er thou art in this world's globe,
I'll have an Iris that shall find thee out.

Suff. I go.

Q. Mar. And take my heart with thee.

Suff. A jewel, lock'd into the woful'st cask
That ever did contain a thing of worth.
Even as a splitted bark, so sunder we;
This way fall I to death.

Q. Mar. This way for me.
[*Exeunt, severally.*

SCENE III. London.

Cardinal Beaufort's *Bedchamber.*

Enter KING HENRY, SALISBURY, WARWICK, *and Others. The* Cardinal *in Bed;* Attendants *with him.*

K. Hen. How fares my lord? speak, Beaufort, to thy sovereign.

Car. If thou be'st death, I'll give thee England's treasure,
Enough to purchase such another island,
So thou wilt let me live, and feel no pain.

K. Hen. Ah, what a sign it is of evil life,
When death's approach is seen so terrible!

War. Beaufort, it is thy sovereign speaks to thee.

Car. Bring me unto my trial when you will.
Died he not in his bed? where should he die?
Can I make men live, whe'r they will or no?—
O! torture me no more, I will confess.—
Alive again? then show me where he is;
I'll give a thousand pound to look upon him.—
He hath no eyes, the dust hath blinded them.—
Comb down his hair: look! look! it stands upright,
Like lime-twigs set to catch my winged soul!—
Give me some drink; and bid the apothecary
Bring the strong poison that I bought of him.

K. Hen. O thou eternal Mover of the heavens,
Look with a gentle eye upon this wretch!
O, beat away the busy meddling fiend,
That lays strong siege unto this wretch's soul,
And from his bosom purge this black despair!

War. See, how the pangs of death do make him grin.

Sal. Disturb him not, let him pass peaceably.

K. Hen. Peace to his soul, if God's good pleasure be!
Lord cardinal, if thou think'st on heaven's bliss,
Hold up thy hand, make signal of thy hope—
He dies, and makes no sign; O God, forgive him!

War. So bad a death argues a monstrous life.

K. Hen. Forbear to judge, for we are sinners all.—
Close up his eyes, and draw the curtain close;
And let us all to meditation. [*Exeunt.*

ACT IV.

SCENE I. Kent. *The Seashore near* Dover.

Firing heard at Sea. Then enter, from a Boat, a Captain, *a* Master, *a* Master's Mate, WALTER WHITMORE, *and Others; with them* SUFFOLK, *and other* Gentlemen, *prisoners.*

Cap. The gaudy, blabbing, and remorseful day
Is crept into the bosom of the sea;
And now loud howling wolves arouse the jades
That drag the tragick melancholy night;
Who with their drowsy, slow, and flagging wings
Clip dead men's graves, and from their misty jaws
Breathe foul contagious darkness in the air.
Therefore, bring forth the soldiers of our prize;
For, whilst our pinnace anchors in the Downs,
Here shall they make their ransome on the sand,
Or with their blood stain this discolour'd shore.—
Master, this prisoner freely give I thee:—
And thou that art his mate, make boot of this;—
The other [*pointing to* SUFFOLK], Walter Whitmore, is thy share.

1 Gent. What is my ransome, master? let me know.

Mast. A thousand crowns, or else lay down your head.

Mate. And so much shall you give, or off goes yours.

Cap. What, think you much to pay two thousand crowns,
And bear the name and port of gentlemen?—
Cut both the villains' throats;—for die you shall;
The lives of those which we have lost in fight
Cannot be counterpois'd with such a petty sum.

1 Gent. I'll give it, sir; and therefore spare my life.

2 Gent. And so will I, and write home for it straight.

Whit. I lost mine eye in laying the prize aboard,
And therefore to revenge it, shalt thou die;
[*To* SUFFOLK.
And so should these, if I might have my will.

Cap. Be not so rash; take ransome, let him live.

Suff. Look on my George, I am a gentleman;
Rate me at what thou wilt, thou shalt be paid.

Whit. And so am I; my name is Walter Whitmore.
How now? why start'st thou? what, doth death affright?

Suff. Thy name affrights me, in whose sound is death.
A cunning man did calculate my birth,
And told me—that by *Water* I should die:
Yet let not this make thee be bloody minded;
Thy name is—*Gualtier*, being rightly sounded.

Whit. *Gualtier*, or *Walter*, which it is, I care not;
Ne'er yet did base dishonour blur our name,
But with our sword we wip'd away the blot;
Therefore, when merchant-like I sell revenge,
Broke be my sword, my arms torn and defac'd,
And I proclaim'd a coward through the world!
[*Lays hold on* SUFFOLK.

Suff. Stay, Whitmore; for thy prisoner is a prince,
The duke of Suffolk, William de la Pole.

Whit. The duke of Suffolk, muffled up in rags!

Suff. Ay, but these rags are no part of the duke;
Jove sometime went disguis'd, and why not I?

Cap. But Jove was never slain, as thou shalt be.

Suff. Obscure and lowly swain, King Henry's blood,
The honourable blood of Lancaster,
Must not be shed by such a jaded groom.
Hast thou not kiss'd thy hand, and held my stirrup?
Bare-headed plodded by my footcloth mule,
And thought thee happy when I shook my head?
How often hast thou waited at my cup,

Fed from my trencher, kneel'd down at the board,
When I have feasted with Queen Margaret?
Remember it, and let it make thee crest-fall'n;
Ay, and allay this thy abortive pride:
How in our voiding lobby hast thou stood,
And duly waited for my coming forth?
This hand of mine hath writ in thy behalf,
And therefore shall it charm thy riotous tongue.

Whit. Speak, captain, shall I stab the forlorn swain?

Cap. First let my words stab him, as he hath me.

Suff. Base slave! thy words are blunt, and so art thou.

Cap. Convey him hence, and on our longboat's side
Strike off his head.

Suff. Thou dar'st not for thy own.

Cap. Yes, Poole.

Suff. Poole?

Cap. Poole? Sir Poole? lord?
Ay, kennel, puddle, sink; whose filth and dirt
Troubles the silver spring where England drinks.
Now will I dam up this thy yawning mouth,
For swallowing the treasure of the realm:
Thy lips, that kiss'd the queen, shall sweep the ground;
And thou, that smil'dst at good Duke Humphrey's death,
Against the senseless winds shalt grin in vain,
Who, in contempt, shall hiss at thee again:
And wedded be thou to the hags of hell,
For daring to affy a mighty lord
Unto the daughter of a worthless king,
Having neither subject, wealth, nor diadem.
By devilish policy art thou grown great,
And, like ambitious Sylla, overgorg'd
With gobbets of thy mother's bleeding heart.
By thee, Anjou and Maine were sold to France:
The false revolting Normans, thorough thee,
Disdain to call us lord; and Picardy
Hath slain their governors, surpris'd our forts,
And sent the ragged soldiers wounded home.
The princely Warwick, and the Nevils all,—
Whose dreadful swords were never drawn in vain,—
As hating thee, are rising up in arms:
And now the house of York—thrust from the crown,
By shameful murder of a guiltless king,
And lofty proud encroaching tyranny,—
Burns with revenging fire: whose hopeful colours
Advance our half-fac'd sun, striving to shine,
Under the which is writ—*Invitis nubibus.*
The commons here in Kent are up in arms:
And, to conclude, reproach, and beggary,
Is crept into the palace of our king,
And all by thee:—Away! convey him hence.

Suff. O that I were a god, to shoot forth thunder
Upon these paltry, servile, abject drudges!
Small things make base men proud: this villain here,
Being captain of a pinnace, threatens more
Than Bargulus the strong Illyrian pirate.
Drones suck not eagles' blood, but rob bee-hives.
It is impossible, that I should die
By such a lowly vassal as thyself.
Thy words move rage, and not remorse, in me;
I go of message from the queen to France;
I charge thee, waft me safely cross the channel.

Cap. Walter,——

Whit. Come, Suffolk, I must waft thee to thy death.

Suff. *Gelidus timor occupat artus;*—'tis thee I fear.

Whit. Thou shalt have cause to fear, before I leave thee.
What, are ye daunted now? now will ye stoop?

1 *Gent.* My gracious lord, entreat him, speak him fair.

Suff. Suffolk's imperial tongue is stern and rough,
Us'd to command, untaught to plead for favour.
Far be it, we should honour such as these
With humble suit; no, rather let my head
Stoop to the block, than these knees bow to any,
Save to the God of heaven, and to my king;
And sooner dance upon a bloody pole,
Than stand uncover'd to the vulgar groom.
True nobility is exempt from fear:—
More can I bear, than you dare execute.

Cap. Hale him away, and let him talk no more.

Suff. Come, soldiers, show what cruelty ye can,
That this my death may never be forgot!
Great men oft die by vile bezonians:
A Roman sworder and banditto slave,
Murder'd sweet Tully; Brutus' bastard hand
Stabb'd Julius Cæsar; savage islanders,
Pompey the Great: and Suffolk dies by pirates.
[*Exit* SUFF. *with* WHIT. *and Others.*

Cap. And as for these whose ransome we have [set,
It is our pleasure, one of them depart:—
Therefore come you with us, and let him go.
[*Exeunt all but the first* Gentleman.

Re-enter WHITMORE, *with* Suffolk's *Body.*

Whit. There let his head and lifeless body lie.
Until the queen his mistress bury it. [*Exit.*

1 *Gent.* O barbarous and bloody spectacle!
His body will I bear unto the king:
If he revenge it not, yet will his friends:
So will the queen, that living held him dear.
[*Exit, with the Body.*

SCENE II. Blackheath.

Enter GEORGE BEVIS *and* JOHN HOLLAND.

Geo. Come, and get thee a sword, though made of a lath; they have been up these two days.

John. They have the more need to sleep now then.

Geo. I tell thee, Jack Cade the clothier means to dress the commonwealth, and turn it, and set a new nap upon it.

John. So he had need, for 'tis threadbare. Well, I say, it was never merry world in England, since gentlemen came up.

Geo. O miserable age! Virtue is not regarded in handicrafts-men.

John. The nobility think scorn to go in leather aprons.

Geo. Nay more, the king's council are no good workmen.

John. True; And yet it is said,—Labour in thy vocation; which is as much as to say, as,—let the magistrates be labouring men; and therefore should we be magistrates.

Geo. Thou hast hit it: for there's no better sign of a brave mind, than a hard hand.

John. I see them! I see them! There's Best's son, the tanner of Wingham;——

Geo. He shall have the skins of our enemies, to make dog's leather of.

John. And Dick the butcher,——

Geo. Then is sin struck down like an ox, and iniquity's throat cut like a calf.

John. And Smith the weaver:——

Geo. *Argo*, their thread of life is spun.

John. Come, come, let's fall in with them.

Drum. Enter CADE, DICK *the Butcher*, SMITH *the Weaver, and Others in great number.*

Cade. We John Cade, so termed of our supposed father,——

Dick. Or rather, of stealing a cade of herrings. [*Aside.*

Cade. — for our enemies shall fall before us, inspired with the spirit of putting down kings and princes,—Command silence.

Dick. Silence!

Cade. My father was a Mortimer.—

Dick. He was an honest man, and a good bricklayer. [*Aside.*

Cade. My mother a Plantagenet,—

Dick. I knew her well, she was a midwife.— [*Aside.*

Cade. My wife descended of the Lacies,—

Dick. She was indeed a pedler's daughter, and sold many laces. [*Aside.*

Smith. But, now of late, not able to travel with her furred pack, she washes bucks here at home. [*Aside.*

Cade. Therefore am I of an honourable house.

Dick. Ay, by my faith, the field is honourable; and there was he born, under a hedge; for his father had never a house, but the cage. [*Aside.*

Cade. Valiant I am.

Smith. 'A must needs; for beggary is valiant. [*Aside.*

Cade. I am able to endure much.

Dick. No question of that; for I have seen him whipped three market days together. [*Aside.*

Cade. I fear neither sword nor fire.

Smith. He need not fear the sword, for his coat is of proof. [*Aside.*

Dick. But, methinks, he should stand in fear of fire, being burnt i' the hand for stealing of sheep. [*Aside.*

Cade. Be brave then; for your captain is brave, and vows reformation. There shall be in England, seven half-penny loaves sold for a penny: the three-hooped pot shall have ten hoops; and I will make it felony, to drink small beer: all the realm shall be in common, and in Cheapside shall my palfry go to grass. And, when I am king (as king I will be)——

All. God save your majesty!

Cade. I thank you, good people:—there shall be no money; all shall eat and drink on my score; and I will apparel them all in one livery, that they may agree like brothers, and worship me their lord.

Dick. The first thing we do, let's kill all the lawyers.

Cade. Nay, that I mean to do. Is not this a lamentable thing, that of the skin of an innocent lamb should be made parchment? that parchment, being scribbled o'er, should undo a man? Some say, the bee stings: but I say, 'tis the bee's wax; for I did but seal once to a thing, and I was never mine own man since. How now; who's there?

Enter some, bringing in the Clerk *of* Chatham.

Smith. The clerk of Chatham: he can write and read, and cast accompt.

Cade. O monstrous!

Smith. We took him setting of boys' copies.

Cade. Here's a villain!

Smith. H'as a book in his pocket, with red letters in 't.

Cade. Nay, then he is a conjuror.

Dick. Nay, he can make obligations, and write court-hand.

Cade. I am sorry for 't: the man is a proper man, on mine honour; unless I find him guilty, he shall not die,—Come hither, sirrah, I must examine thee: What is thy name?

Clerk. Emmanuel.

Dick. They use to write it on the top of letters; —'Twill go hard with you.

Cade. Let me alone:—Dost thou use to write thy name? or hast thou a mark to thyself, like an honest plain-dealing man?

Clerk. Sir, I thank God, I have been so well brought up, that I can write my name.

All. He hath confessed: away with him; he's a villain, and a traitor.

Cade. Away with him, I say: hang him with his pen and inkhorn about his neck. [*Exeunt some with the* Clerk.

Enter MICHAEL.

Mich. Where's our general?

Cade. Here I am, thou particular fellow.

Mich. Fly, fly, fly! Sir Humphrey Stafford and his brother are hard by, with the king's forces.

Cade. Stand, villain, stand, or I'll fell thee down: He shall be encountered with a man as good as himself: He is but a knight, is 'a?

Mich. No.

Cade. To equal him, I will make myself a knight presently: Rise up Sir John Mortimer. Now have at him.

Enter SIR HUMPHREY STAFFORD, *and* WILLIAM *his Brother, with Drum and* Forces.

Staf. Rebellious hinds, the filth and scum of Kent,
Mark'd for the gallows,—lay your weapons down,
Home to your cottages, forsake this groom;—
The king is merciful, if you revolt.

W. Staf. But angry, wrathful, and inclin'd to blood,
If you go forward: therefore yield, or die.

Cade. As for these silken-coated slaves, I pass not;
It is to you, good people, that I speak,
O'er whom, in time to come, I hope to reign;
For I am rightful heir unto the crown.

Staf. Villain, thy father was a plasterer;
And thou thyself, a shearman, Art thou not?

Cade. And Adam was a gardener.

W. Staf. And what of that?

Cade. Marry, this:—Edmund Mortimer, earl of March,
Married the duke of Clarence' daughter; Did he not?

Staf. Ay, sir.

Cade. By her, he had two children at one birth.

W. Staf. That's false.

Cade. Ay, there's the question; but, I say, 'tis true:
The elder of them, being put to nurse,
Was by a beggar-woman stol'n away;
And, ignorant of his birth and parentage,
Became a bricklayer, when he came to age:
His son am I; deny it, if you can.

Dick. Nay, 'tis too true; therefore he shall be king.

Smith. Sir, he made a chimney in my father's house, and the bricks are alive at this day to testify it; therefore, deny it not.

Staf. And will you credit this base drudge's words,
That speaks he knows not what?

All. Ay, marry, will we; therefore get ye gone.

W. Staf. Jack Cade, the duke of York hath taught you this.

Cade. He lies, for I invented it myself. [*Aside.*] —Go to, sirrah, Tell the king from me, that— for his father's sake, Henry the Fifth, in whose time boys went to span-counter for French crowns,—I am content he shall reign; but I'll be protector over him.

Dick. And, furthermore, we'll have the Lord Say's head, for selling the dukedom of Maine.

Cade. And good reason; for thereby is England maimed, and fain to go with a staff, but that my puissance holds it up. Fellow kings, I tell you, that that Lord Say hath gelded the commonwealth, and made it an eunuch: and more than that, he can speak French, and therefore he is a traitor.

Staf. O gross and miserable ignorance!

Cade. Nay, answer, if you can: The Frenchmen are our enemies: go to then, I ask but this; Can he, that speaks with the tongue of an enemy, be a good counsellor, or no?

All. No, no; and therefore we'll have his head.

W. Staf. Well, seeing gentle words will not prevail,
Assail them with the army of the king.

Staf. Herald, away: and, throughout every town,
Proclaim them traitors that are up with Cade;

That those, which fly before the battle ends,
May, even in their wives' and children's sight,
Be hang'd up for example at their doors:—
And you, that be the king's friends, follow me.
[*Exeunt the Two* STAFFORDS, *and* Forces.

Cade. And you, that love the commons, follow me.—
Now show yourselves men, 'tis for liberty.
We will not leave one lord, one gentleman:
Spare none, but such as go in clouted shoon;
For they are thrifty honest men, and such
As would (but that they dare not) take our parts.

Dick. They are all in order, and march toward us.

Cade. But then are we in order, when we are most out of order. Come, march forward.
[*Exeunt.*

SCENE III. *Another Part of* Blackheath.

Alarums. The two Parties enter and fight, and both the STAFFORDS *are slain.*

Cade. Where's Dick, the butcher of Ashford?

Dick. Here, sir.

Cade. They fell before thee like sheep and oxen, and thou behavedst thyself as if thou hadst been in thine own slaughter house: therefore thus will I reward thee,—The Lent shall be as long again as it is; and thou shalt have a license to kill for a hundred lacking one, a week.

Dick. I desire no more.

Cade. And, to speak truth, thou deservest no less. This monument of the victory will I bear; and the bodies shall be dragged at my horse's heels, till I do come to London, where we will have the mayor's sword borne before us.

Dick. If we mean to thrive and do good, break open the gaols, and let out the prisoners.

Cade. Fear not that, I warrant thee. Come, let's march towards London. [*Exeunt.*

SCENE IV. London. *A Room in the Palace.*

Enter KING HENRY, *reading a supplication; the* DUKE OF BUCKINGHAM, *and* LORD SAY *with him, at a distance,* QUEEN MARGARET, *mourning over* SUFFOLK'S *Head.*

Q. Mar. Oft have I heard—that grief softens the mind,
And makes it fearful and degenerate;
Think therefore on revenge, and cease to weep.
But who can cease to weep, and look on this?
Here may his head lie on my throbbing breast:
But where's the body that I should embrace?

Buck. What answer makes your grace to the rebels' supplication?

K. Hen. I'll send some holy bishop to entreat:
For God forbid, so many simple souls
Should perish by the sword! And I myself,
Rather than bloody war shall cut them short,
Will parley with Jack Cade their general.—
But stay, I'll read it over once again.

Q. Mar. Ah, barbarous villains! hath this lovely face
Rul'd, like a wandering planet, over me;
And could it not enforce them to relent,
That were unworthy to behold the same?

K. Hen. Lord Say, Jack Cade hath sworn to have thy head.

Say. Ay, but I hope, your highness shall have his.

K. Hen. How now, madam? Still
Lamenting, and mourning for Suffolk's death?
I fear, my love, if that I had been dead,
Thou wouldest not have mourn'd so much for me.

Q. Mar. No, my love, I should not mourn, but die for thee.

Enter a Messenger.

K. Hen. How now! what news? why com'st thou in such haste?

Mess. The rebels are in Southwark; Fly, my lord!
Jack Cade proclaims himself Lord Mortimer,
Descended from the duke of Clarence' house:
And calls your grace usurper, openly,
And vows to crown himself in Westminster.
His army is a ragged multitude
Of hinds and peasants, rude and merciless;
Sir Humphrey Stafford and his brother's death
Hath given them heart and courage to proceed:
All scholars, lawyers, courtiers, gentlemen,
They call—false caterpillars, and intend their death.

K. Hen. O graceless men! they know not what they do.

Buck. My gracious lord, retire to Kenelworth,
Until a power be rais'd to put them down.

Q. Mar. Ah! were the duke of Suffolk now alive,
These Kentish rebels would be soon appeas'd.

K. Hen. Lord Say, the traitors hate thee,
Therefore away with us to Kenelworth.

Say. So might your grace's person be in danger;
The sight of me is odious in their eyes:
And therefore in this city will I stay,
And live alone as secret as I may.

Enter another Messenger.

2 Mess. Jack Cade hath gotten London Bridge; the citizens
Fly and forsake their houses:
The rascal people, thirsting after prey,
Join with the traitor; and they jointly swear,
To spoil the city, and your royal court.

Buck. Then linger not, my lord; away, take horse.

K. Hen. Come, Margaret; God, our hope, will succour us.

Q. Mar. My hope is gone, now Suffolk is deceas'd.

K. Hen. Farewell, my lord; [*To* LORD SAY.] trust not the Kentish rebels.

Buck. Trust no body, for fear you be betray'd.

Say. The trust I have is in mine innocence,
And therefore am I bold and resolute. [*Exeunt.*

SCENE V. *The same. The* Tower.

Enter LORD SCALES, *and Others, on the Walls. Then enter certain* Citizens, *below.*

Scales. How now? is Jack Cade slain?

1 Cit. No, my lord, nor likely to be slain; for they have won the bridge, killing all those that withstand them: The lord mayor craves aid of your honour from the Tower, to defend the city from the rebels.

Scales. Such aid as I can spare, you shall command;
But I am troubled here with them myself,
The rebels have assay'd to win the Tower.
But get you to Smithfield, and gather head,
And thither will I send you Matthew Gough:
Fight for your king, your country, and your lives;
And so farewell, for I must hence again.
[*Exeunt.*

SCENE VI. *The same.* Cannon Street.

Enter JACK CADE, *and his* Followers. *He strikes his Staff on London Stone.*

Cade. Now is Mortimer lord of this city. And here, sitting upon London-stone, I charge and command, that, of the city's cost, the pissing-conduit run nothing but claret wine this first year of our reign. And now, henceforward, it shall be treason for any that calls me other than —Lord Mortimer.

Enter a Soldier, *running.*

Sold. Jack Cade! Jack Cade!

Cade. Knock him down there. [*They kill him.*

Smith. If this fellow be wise, he'll never call you Jack Cade more; I think he hath a very fair warning.

Dick. My lord, there's an army gather'd together in Smithfield.

Cade. Come then, let's go fight with them: But, first, go and set London Bridge on fire; and, if you can, burn down the Tower too. Come, let's away. [*Exeunt.*

SCENE VII. *The same.* Smithfield.

Alarum. Enter on one side, CADE *and his* Company, *on the other,* Citizens, *and the* King's Forces *headed by* MATTHEW GOUGH. *They fight; the* Citizens *are routed, and* MATTHEW GOUGH *is slain.*

Cade. So, sirs:—Now go some and pull down the Savoy; others to the inns of court; down with them all.

Dick. I have a suit unto your lordship.

Cade. Be it a lordship, thou shalt have it for that word.

Dick. Only, that the laws of England may come out of your mouth.

John. Mass, 'twill be sore law then; for he was thrust in the mouth with a spear, and 'tis not whole yet. [*Aside.*

Smith. Nay, John, it will be stinking law; for his breath stinks with eating toasted cheese. [*Aside.*

Cade. I have thought upon it, it shall be so. Away, burn all the records of the realm; my mouth shall be the parliament of England.

John. Then we are like to have biting statutes, unless his teeth be pulled out. [*Aside.*

Cade. And henceforward all things shall be in common.

Enter a Messenger.

Mess. My lord, a prize, a prize! here's the Lord Say, which sold the towns in France; he that made us pay one and twenty fifteens, and one shilling to the pound, the last subsidy.

Enter GEORGE BEVIS, *with the* LORD SAY.

Cade. Well, he shall be beheaded for it ten times.—Ay, thou say, thou serge, nay, thou buckram lord! now art thou within point-blank of our jurisdiction regal. What canst thou answer to my majesty, for giving up of Normandy unto Monsieur Basimecu, the dauphin of France? Be it known unto thee, by these presence, even the presence of Lord Mortimer, that I am the besom that must sweep the court clean of such filth as thou art. Thou hast most traitorously corrupted the youth of the realm, in erecting a grammar-school: and whereas, before, our forefathers had no other books but the score and the tally, thou hast caused printing to be used; and, contrary to the king, his crown, and dignity, thou hast built a paper-mill. It will be proved to thy face, that thou hast men about thee, that usually talk of a noun, and a verb; and such abominable words, as no Christian ear can endure to hear. Thou hast appointed justices of peace, to call poor men before them about matters they were not able to answer. Moreover, thou hast put them in prison; and because they could not read, thou hast hanged them; when, indeed, only for that cause, they have been most worthy to live. Thou dost ride on a foot-cloth, dost thou not?

Say. What of that?

Cade. Marry, thou oughtest not to let thy horse wear a cloak, when honester men than thou go in their hose and doublets.

Dick. And work in their shirt too; as myself, for example, that am a butcher.

Say. You men of Kent,—

Dick. What say you of Kent?

Say. Nothing but this: 'Tis *bona terra, mala gens.*

Cade. Away with him, away with him! he speaks Latin.

Say. Hear me but speak, and bear me where you will.
Kent, in the commentaries Cæsar writ,
Is term'd the civil'st place of all this isle:
Sweet is the country, because full of riches;
The people liberal, valiant, active, wealthy;
Which makes me hope you are not void of pity.
I sold not Maine, I lost not Normandy:
Yet, to recover them, would lose my life.
Justice with favour have I always done;
Prayers and tears have mov'd me, gifts could never.
When have I aught exacted at your hands,
Kent, to maintain the king, the realm, and you?
Large gifts have I bestow'd on learned clerks,
Because my book preferr'd me to the king:
And—seeing ignorance is the curse of God,
Knowledge the wing wherewith we fly to heaven,—
Unless you be possess'd with devilish spirits,
You cannot but forbear to murder me.
This tongue hath parley'd unto foreign kings
For your behoof,—

Cade. Tut! when struck'st thou one blow in the field!

Say. Great men have reaching hands; oft have I struck
Those that I never saw, and struck them dead.

Geo. O monstrous coward! what, to come behind folks?

Say. These cheeks are pale for watching for your good.

Cade. Give him a box o'the ear, and that will make 'em red again.

Say. Long sitting to determine poor men's causes
Hath made me full of sickness and diseases.

Cade. Ye shall have a hempen caudle then, and the pap of a hatchet.

Dick. Why dost thou quiver, man?

Say. The palsy, and not fear, provoketh me.

Cade. Nay, he nods at us; as who should say, I'll be even with you. I'll see if his head will stand steadier on a pole, or no: Take him away, and behead him.

Say. Tell me, wherein I have offended most?
Have I affected wealth, or honour; speak?
Are my chests fill'd up with extorted gold?
Is my apparel sumptuous to behold?
Whom have I injur'd, that ye seek my death?
These hands are free from guiltless blood-shedding,
This breast from harbouring foul deceitful thoughts.
O, let me live!

Cade. I feel remorse in myself with his words: but I'll bridle it; he shall die, an it be but for pleading so well for his life. Away with him! he has a familiar under his tongue; he speaks not o' God's name. Go, take him away, I say, and strike off his head presently; and then break into his son-in-law's house, Sir James Cromer, and strike off his head, and bring them both upon two poles hither.

All. It shall be done.

Say. Ah, countrymen! if when you make your prayers,
God should be so obdurate as yourselves,
How would it fare with your departed souls?
And therefore yet relent, and save my life.

Cade. Away with him, and do as I command ye. [*Exeunt some, with* LORD SAY.
The proudest peer in the realm shall not wear a head on his shoulders, unless he pay me tribute; there shall not a maid be married, but she shall pay to me her maidenhead ere they have it: Men shall hold of me *in capite;* and we charge and command, that their wives be as free as heart can wish, or tongue can tell.

Dick. My lord, when shall we go to Cheapside, and take up commodities upon our bills?

Cade. Marry, presently.

All. O brave!

Re-enter Rebels, *with the heads of* LORD SAY *and his* Son-in-law.

Cade. But is not this braver?—Let them kiss one another, for they loved well, when they were alive. Now part them again, lest they consult about the giving up of some more towns in France. Soldiers, defer the spoil of the city until night: for with these borne before us, instead of maces, will we ride through the streets; and, at every corner, have them kiss.—Away! [*Exeunt.*

SCENE VIII. Southwark.

Alarum. Enter CADE, *and all his* Rabblement.

Cade. Up Fish Street! down Saint Magnus' Corner! kill and knock down! throw them into Thames!—[*A Parley sounded, then a Retreat.*] What noise is this I hear? Dare any be so bold to sound retreat or parley, when I command them kill?

Enter BUCKINGHAM, *and Old* CLIFFORD, *with* Forces.

Buck. Ay, here they be that dare and will disturb thee:
Know, Cade, we come ambassadors from the king
Unto the commons whom thou hast misled;
And here pronounce free pardon to them all,
That will forsake thee, and go home in peace.

Clif. What say ye, countrymen? will ye relent,
And yield to mercy, whilst 'tis offer'd you:
Or let a rabble lead you to your deaths?
Who loves the king, and will embrace his pardon,
Fling up his cap, and say—God save his majesty!
Who hateth him, and honours not his father,
Henry the Fifth, that made all France to quake,
Shake he his weapon at us, and pass by.

All. God save the king! God save the king!

Cade. What, Buckingham, and Clifford, are ye so brave?—And you, base peasants, do ye believe him? will you needs be hanged with your pardons about your necks? Hath my sword therefore broke through London Gates, that you should leave me at the White Hart in Southwark? I thought, ye would never have given out these arms, till you had recovered your ancient freedom; but you are all recreants, and dastards; and delight to live in slavery to the nobility. Let them break your backs with burdens, take your houses over your heads, ravish your wives and daughters before your faces; For me,—I will make shift for one; and so—God's curse 'light upon you all!

All. We'll follow Cade, we'll follow Cade.

Clif. Is Cade the son of Henry the Fifth.
That thus you do exclaim—you'll go with him?
Will he conduct you through the heart of France,
And make the meanest of you earls and dukes?
Alas, he hath no home, no place to fly to;
Nor knows he how to live, but by the spoil,
Unless by robbing of your friends, and us.
Wer't not a shame, that whilst you live at jar,
The fearful French, whom you late vanquished,
Should make a start o'er seas, and vanquish you?
Methinks, already, in this civil broil,
I see them lording it in London streets,
Crying—*Villageois!* unto all they meet.
Better ten thousand base-born Cades miscarry,
Than you should stoop unto a Frenchman's mercy.
To France, to France, and get what you have lost;
Spare England, for it is your native coast:
Henry hath money, you are strong and manly;
God on our side, doubt not of victory.

All. A Clifford! a Clifford! we'll follow the king, and Clifford.

Cade. Was ever feather so lightly blown to and fro, as this multitude? the name of Henry the Fifth hales them to a hundred mischiefs, and makes them leave me desolate. I see them lay their heads together, to surprise me; my sword make way for me, for here is no staying.—In despight of the devils and hell, have through the very midst of you! and heavens and honour be witness, that no want of resolution in me, but only my followers' base and ignominious treasons, makes me betake me to my heels. [*Exit.*

Buck. What, is he fled? go some, and follow him;
And he, that brings his head unto the king,
Shall have a thousand crowns for his reward.— [*Exeunt some of them.*
Follow me, soldiers; we'll devise a mean
To reconcile you all unto the king. [*Exeunt.*

SCENE IX. Kenelworth Castle.

Enter KING HENRY, QUEEN MARGARET, *and* SOMERSET, *on the Terrace of the Castle.*

K. Hen. Was ever king that joy'd an earthly throne,
And could command no more content than I?
No sooner was I crept out of my cradle,
But I was made a king, at nine months old:
Was never subject long'd to be a king,
As I do long and wish to be a subject.

Enter BUCKINGHAM *and* CLIFFORD.

Buck. Health, and glad tidings, to your majesty!

K. Hen. Why, Buckingham, is the traitor, Cade, surpris'd?
Or is he but retir'd to make him strong?

Enter, below, a great number of Cade's Followers, *with Halters about their Necks.*

Clif. He's fled, my lord, and all his powers do yield;
And humbly thus, with halters on their necks,
Expect your highness' doom, of life, or death.

K. Hen. Then, heaven, set ope thy everlasting gates,
To entertain my vows of thanks and praise!—
Soldiers, this day have you redeem'd your lives,
And show'd how well you love your prince and country:
Continue still in this so good a mind,
And Henry, though he be infortunate,
Assure yourselves, will never be unkind:
And so, with thanks, and pardon to you all,
I do dismiss you to your several countries.

All. God save the king! God save the king!

Enter a Messenger.

Mess. Please it your grace to be advertised,
The duke of York is newly come from Ireland;
And with a puissant and a mighty power,
Of Gallowglasses and stout Kernes,
Is marching hitherward in proud array;
And still proclaimeth, as he comes along,
His arms are only to remove from thee
The duke of Somerset, whom he terms a traitor.

K. Hen. Thus stands my state, 'twixt Cade and York distress'd:
Like to a ship, that, having scap'd a tempest,
Is straightway calm'd and boarded with a pirate:
But now is Cade driven back, his men dispers'd;
And now is York in arms to second him.—
I pray thee, Buckingham, go forth and meet him;
And ask him, what's the reason of these arms.
Tell him, I'll send Duke Edmund to the Tower;—
And, Somerset, we will commit thee thither,
Until his army be dismiss'd from him.

Som. My lord,
I'll yield myself to prison willingly,
Or unto death, to do my country good.

K. Hen. In any case, be not too rough in terms;
For he is fierce, and cannot brook hard language.

Buck. I will, my lord; and doubt not so to deal,
As all things shall redound unto your good.

K. Hen. Come, wife, let's in, and learn to govern better;
For yet may England curse my wretched reign.
[*Exeunt.*

SCENE X. Kent. Iden's *Garden.*

Enter CADE.

Cade. Fye on ambition! fye on myself; that have a sword, and yet am ready to famish! These five days have I hid me in these woods; and durst not peep out, for all the country is lay'd for me: but now I am so hungry, that if I might have a lease of my life for a thousand years, I could stay no longer. Wherefore, on a brick-wall have I climbed into this garden; to see if I can eat grass, or pick a sallet another while, which is not amiss to cool a man's stomach this hot weather. And, I think, this word sallet was born to do me good: for, many a time, but for a sallet, my brain-pan had been cleft with a brown bill; and, many a time, when I have been dry, and bravely marching, it hath served me instead of a quart-pot to drink in; and now the word sallet must serve me to feed on.

Enter IDEN, *with* Servants.

Iden. Lord, who would live turmoiled in the court,
And may enjoy such quiet walks as these?
This small inheritance, my father left me,
Contenteth me, and is worth a monarchy.
I seek not to wax great by others' waning;
Or gather wealth, I care not with what envy;
Sufficeth, that I have maintains my state,
And sends the poor well pleased from my gate.

Cade. Here's the lord of the soil come to seize me for a stray, for entering his fee-simple without leave. Ah, villain, thou wilt betray me, and get a thousand crowns of the king for carrying my head to him; but I'll make thee eat iron like an ostrich, and swallow my sword like a great pin, ere thou and I part.

Iden. Why, rude companion, whatsoe'er thou be,
I know thee not; Why then should I betray thee?
Is't not enough, to break into my garden,
And, like a thief, to come to rob my grounds,
Climbing my walls in spite of me the owner,
But thou wilt brave me with those saucy terms?

Cade. Brave thee? ay, by the best blood that ever was broached, and beard thee too. Look on me well: I have eat no meat these five days; yet, come thou and thy five men, and if I do not leave you all as dead as a door nail, I pray God, I may never eat grass more.

Iden. Nay, it shall ne'er be said, while England stands,
That Alexander Iden, an esquire of Kent,
Took odds to combat a poor famish'd man.
Oppose thy steadfast-gazing eyes to mine,
See if thou canst outface me with thy looks.
Set limb to limb, and thou art far the lesser;
Thy hand is but a finger to my fist;
Thy leg a stick, compared with this truncheon;
My foot shall fight with all the strength thou hast;
And if mine arm be heaved in the air,
Thy grave is digg'd already in the earth.
As for words, whose greatness answers words,
Let this my sword report what speech forbears.

Cade. By my valour, the most complete champion that ever I heard.—Steel, if thou turn the edge, or cut not out the burly-boned clown in chines of beef ere thou sleep in thy sheath, I beseech God on my knees, thou mayest be turned to hobnails. [*They fight;* CADE *falls.*] O, I am slain! famine, and no other, hath slain me: let ten thousand devils come against me, and give me but the ten meals I have lost, and I'd defy them all. Wither, garden; and be henceforth a burying-place to all that do dwell in this house, because the unconquered soul of Cade is fled.

Iden. Is't Cade that I have slain, that monstrous traitor?
Sword, I will hallow thee for this thy deed,
And hang thee o'er my tomb, when I am dead:
Ne'er shall this blood be wiped from thy point;
But thou shalt wear it as a herald's coat,
To emblaze the honour that thy master got.

Cade. Iden, farewell; and be proud of thy victory: Tell Kent from me, she hath lost her best man, and exhort all the world to be cowards; for I, that never feared any, am vanquished by famine, not by valour. [*Dies.*

Iden. How much thou wrong'st me, heaven be my judge.
Die, damned wretch, the curse of her that bare thee!
And as I thrust thy body in with my sword,
So wish I, I might thrust thy soul to hell.
Hence will I drag thee headlong by the heels
Unto a dunghill, which shall be thy grave,
And there cut off thy most ungracious head;
Which I will bear in triumph to the king,
Leaving thy trunk for crows to feed upon.
[*Exit, dragging out the Body.*

ACT V.

SCENE I. *The same. Fields between* Dartford *and* Blackheath.

The King's *Camp on one side. On the other, enter* YORK *attended, with Drum and Colours: his* Forces *at some distance.*

York. From Ireland thus comes York, to claim his right,
And pluck the crown from feeble Henry's head:
Ring, bells, aloud; burn, bonfires, clear and bright,
To entertain great England's lawful king.
Ah, *sancta majestas!* who would not buy thee dear?
Let them obey, that know not how to rule;
This hand was made to handle nought but gold:
I cannot give due action to my words,
Except a sword, or sceptre, balance it.
A sceptre shall it have, have I a soul;
On which I'll toss the flower-de-luce of France.

Enter BUCKINGHAM.

Whom have we here? Buckingham, to disturb me?
The king hath sent him, sure: I must dissemble.

Buck. York, if thou meanest well, I greet thee well.

York. Humphrey of Buckingham, I accept thy greeting.
Art thou a messenger, or come of pleasure?

Buck. A messenger from Henry, our dread liege,
To know the reason of these arms in peace;
Or why, thou—being a subject as I am,—
Against thy oath and true allegiance sworn,
Should'st raise so great a power without his leave,
Or dare to bring thy force so near the court.

York. Scarce can I speak, my choler is so great.
O, I could hew up rocks, and fight with flint,
I am so angry at these abject terms;
And now, like Ajax Telamonius,
On sheep or oxen could I spend my fury!
I am far better born than is the king; [*Aside.*

More like a king, more kingly in my thoughts:
But I must make fair weather yet a while,
Till Henry be more weak, and I more strong.— } *Aside.*
O Buckingham, I pr'ythee, pardon me,
That I have given no answer all this while;
My mind was troubled with deep melancholy.
The cause why I have brought this army hither,
Is—to remove proud Somerset from the king,
Seditious to his grace, and to the state.

Buck. That is too much presumption on thy part:
But if thy arms be to no other end,
The king hath yielded unto thy demand;
The duke of Somerset is in the Tower.

York. Upon thine honour, is he prisoner?

Buck. Upon mine honour, he is prisoner.

York. Then, Buckingham, I do dismiss my powers.
Soldiers, I thank you all: disperse yourselves;
Meet me to-morrow in Saint George's field,
You shall have pay, and every thing you wish.
And let my sovereign, virtuous Henry,
Command my eldest son,—nay, all my sons,
As pledges of my fealty and love,
I'll send them all as willing as I live;
Lands, goods, horse, armour, any thing I have
Is his to use, so Somerset may die.

Buck. York, I commend this kind submission:
We twain will go into his highness tent.

Enter KING HENRY, *attended.*

K. Hen. Buckingham, doth York intend no harm to us,
That thus he marcheth with thee arm in arm?

York. In all submission and humility,
York doth present himself unto your highness.

K. Hen. Then what intend these forces thou dost bring?

York. To heave the traitor Somerset from hence;
And fight against that monstrous rebel, Cade,
Who since I heard to be discomfited.

Enter IDEN, *with* CADE'S *Head.*

Iden. If one so rude and of so mean condition,
May pass into the presence of a king,
Lo, I present your grace a traitor's head,
The head of Cade, whom I in combat slew.

K. Hen. The head of Cade?—Great God, how just art thou!—
O, let me view his visage being dead,
That living wrought me such exceeding trouble.
Tell me, my friend, art thou the man that slew him?

Iden. I was, an 't like your majesty.

K. Hen. How art thou call'd? and what is thy degree?

Iden. Alexander Iden, that's my name;
A poor esquire of Kent, that loves his king.

Buck. So please it you, my lord, 'twere not amiss
He were created knight for his good service.

K. Hen. Iden, kneel down; [*He kneels.*] Rise up a knight.
We give thee for reward a thousand marks;
And will, that thou henceforth attend on us.

Iden. May Iden live to merit such a bounty,
And never live but true unto his liege!

K. Hen. See, Buckingham! Somerset comes with the queen:
Go, bid her hide him quickly from the duke.

Enter QUEEN MARGARET *and* SOMERSET.

Q. Mar. For thousand Yorks he shall not hide his head,
But boldly stand, and front him to his face.

York. How now! Is Somerset at liberty?
Then, York, unloose thy long-imprison'd thoughts,
And let thy tongue be equal with thy heart.
Shall I endure the sight of Somerset?—
False king! why hast thou broken faith with me,
Knowing how hardly I can brook abuse?
King did I call thee? no, thou art not king;
Not fit to govern and rule multitudes,
Which dar'st not, no, nor canst not rule a traitor.
That head of thine doth not become a crown;
Thy hand is made to grasp a palmer's staff,
And not to grace an awful princely sceptre.
That gold must round engirt these brows of mine;
Whose smile and frown, like to Achilles' spear,
Is able with the change to kill and cure.
Here is a hand to hold a sceptre up,
And with the same to act controlling laws.
Give place; by heaven thou shalt rule no more
O'er him, whom heaven created for thy ruler.

Som. O monstrous traitor!—I arrest thee, York,
Of capital treason 'gainst the king and crown:
Obey, audacious traitor; kneel for grace.

York. Would'st have me kneel? first let me ask of these,
If they can brook I bow a knee to man.—
Sirrah, call in my sons to be my bail;
[*Exit an* Attendant.
I know, ere they will have me go to ward,
They'll pawn their swords for my enfranchisement.

Q. Mar. Call hither Clifford; bid him come amain, [*Exit* BUCKINGHAM.
To say, that if the bastard boys of York
Shall be the surety for their traitor father.

York. O blood-bespotted Neapolitan,
Outcast of Naples, England's bloody scourge;
The sons of York, thy betters in their birth,
Shall be their father's bail: and bane to those
That for my surety will refuse the boys.

Enter EDWARD *and* RICHARD PLANTAGENET, *with* Forces, *at one side; at the other, with* Forces *also, Old* CLIFFORD *and his* Son.

See, where they come; I'll warrant they'll make it good.

Q. Mar. And here comes Clifford, to deny their bail.

Clif. Health and all happiness to my lord the king! [*Kneels.*

York. I thank thee, Clifford: say, what news with thee?
Nay, do not fright us with an angry look;
We are thy sovereign, Clifford, kneel again:
For thy mistaking so, we pardon thee.

Clif. This is my king, York, I do not mistake;
But thou mistak'st me much, to think I do:
To Bedlam with him! is the man grown mad?

K. Hen. Ay, Clifford; a bedlam and ambitious humour
Makes him oppose himself against his king.

Clif. He is a traitor; let him to the Tower,
And chop away that factious pate of his.

Q. Mar. He is arrested, but will not obey;
His sons, he says, shall give their words for him.

York. Will you not, sons?

Edw. Ay, noble Father, if our words will serve.

Rich. And if words will not, then our weapons shall.

Clif. Why, what a brood of traitors have we here!

York. Look in a glass, and call thy image so;
I am thy king, and thou a false-heart traitor.—
Call hither to the stake my two brave bears,
That, with the very shaking of their chains,
They may astonish these fell lurking curs;
Bid Salisbury, and Warwick, come to me.

Drums. Enter WARWICK *and* SALISBURY, *with* Forces.

Clif. Are these thy bears? we'll bait thy bears to death,
And manacle the bearward in their chains,
If thou dar'st bring them to the baiting-place.

Rich. Oft have I seen a hot o'erweening cur
Run back and bite, because he was withheld;
Who, being suffer'd with the bear's fell paw,
Hath clapp'd his tail between his legs, and cried:
And such a piece of service will you do,
If you oppose yourselves to match Lord Warwick.

Clif. Hence, heap of wrath, foul indigested lump,
As crooked in thy manners as thy shape!

York. Nay, we shall heat you thoroughly anon.

Clif. Take heed, lest by your heat you burn yourselves.

K. Hen. Why, Warwick, hath thy knee forgot to bow?
Old Salisbury,—shame to thy silver hair,
Thou mad misleader of thy brain-sick son!—
What, wilt thou on thy deathbed play the ruffian,
And seek for sorrow with thy spectacles?
O, where is faith? O, where is loyalty?
If it be banish'd from the frosty head,
Where shall it find a harbour in the earth?—
Wilt thou go dig a grave to find out war,
And shame thine honourable age with blood?
Why art thou old, and want'st experience?
Or wherefore dost abuse it, if thou hast it?
For shame! in duty bend thy knee to me,
That bows unto the grave with mickle age.

Sal. My lord, I have consider'd with myself
The title of this most renowned duke;
And in my conscience do repute his grace
The rightful heir to England's royal seat.

K. Hen. Hast thou not sworn allegiance unto me?

Sal. I have.

K. Hen. Canst thou dispense with heaven for such an oath?

Sal. It is great sin, to swear unto a sin;
But greater sin, to keep a sinful oath.
Who can be bound by any solemn vow
To do a murderous deed, to rob a man,
To force a spotless virgin's chastity,
To reave the orphan of his patrimony,
To wring the widow from her custom'd right;
And have no other reason for this wrong,
But that he was bound by a solemn oath?

Q. Mar. A subtle traitor needs no sophister.

K. Hen. Call Buckingham, and bid him arm himself.

York. Call Buckingham, and all the friends thou hast,
I am resolv'd for death, or dignity.

Clif. The first I warrant thee, if dreams prove true.

War. You were best to go to bed, and dream again,
To keep thee from the tempest of the field.

Clif. I am resolv'd to bear a greater storm,
Than any thou canst conjure up to-day;
And that I'll write upon thy burgonet,
Might I but know thee by thy household badge.

War. Now, by my father's badge, old Nevil's crest,
The rampant bear chain'd to the ragged staff,
This day I'll wear aloft my burgonet,
(As on the mountain top the cedar shows,
That keeps his leaves in spite of any storm),
Even to affright thee with the view thereof.

Clif. And from thy burgonet I'll rend thy bear,
And tread it under foot with all contempt,
Despight the bearward that protects the bear.

Y. Clif. And so to arms, victorious father,
To quell the rebels, and their 'complices.

Rich. Fye! charity, for shame! speak not in spite,
For you shall sup with *Jesu Christ* to-night.

Y. Clif. Foul stigmatick, that's more than thou canst tell.

Rich. If not in heaven, you'll surely sup in hell. [*Exeunt severally.*

SCENE II. Saint Albans.

Alarums: Excursions. Enter WARWICK.

War. Clifford of Cumberland, 'tis Warwick calls!
And if thou dost not hide thee from the bear,
Now,—when the angry trumpet sounds alarm,
And dead men's cries do fill the empty air,—
Clifford, I say, come forth and fight with me!
Proud northern lord, Clifford of Cumberland,
Warwick is hoarse with calling thee to arms.

Enter YORK.

How now, my noble lord? what, all a-foot?

York. The deadly handed Clifford slew my steed;
But match to match I have encounter'd him,
And made a prey for carrion kites and crows
Even of the bonny beast he lov'd so well.

Enter CLIFFORD.

War. Of one or both of us the time is come.

York. Hold, Warwick, seek thee out some other chase,
For I myself must hunt this deer to death.

War. Then, nobly, York: 'tis for a crown thou fight'st.—
As I intend, Clifford, to thrive to-day,
It grieves my soul to leave thee unassail'd. [*Exit* WARWICK.

Clif. What seest thou in me, York? why dost thou pause?

York. With thy brave bearing should I be in love,
But that thou art so fast mine enemy.

Clif. Nor should thy prowess want praise and esteem,
But that 'tis shown ignobly, and in treason.

York. So let it help me now against thy sword,
As I in justice and true right express it!

Clif. My soul and body on the action both!—

York. A dreadful lay!—address thee instantly. [*They fight, and* CLIFFORD *falls.*

Clif. *La fin couronne les œuvres.* [*Dies.*

York. Thus war hath given thee peace, for thou art still.
Peace with his soul, heaven, if it be thy will! [*Exit.*

Enter young CLIFFORD.

Y. Clif. Shame and confusion! all is on the rout:
Fear frames disorder, and disorder wounds
Where it should guard. O war, thou son of hell,
Whom angry heavens do make their minister,
Throw in the frozen bosoms of our part
Hot coals of vengeance! Let no soldier fly:
He that is truly dedicate to war,
Hath no self-love; nor he, that loves himself,
Hath not essentially, but by circumstance,
The name of valour.—O, let the vile world end. [*Seeing his dead father.*
And the premised flames of the last day
Knit earth and heaven together!
Now let the general trumpet blow his blast,
Particularities and petty sounds
To cease!—Wast thou ordain'd, dear father,
To lose thy youth in peace, and to achieve
The silver livery of advised age;
And, in thy reverence, and thy chair-days, thus
To die in ruffian battle?—Even at this sight,
My heart is turn'd to stone; and, while 'tis mine,
It shall be stony. York not our old men spares;
No more will I their babes; tears virginal
Shall be to me even as the dew to fire;
And beauty, that the tyrant oft reclaims,
Shall to my flaming wrath be oil and flax.
Henceforth I will not have to do with pity:
Meet I an infant of the house of York,
Into as many gobbets will I cut it,
As wild Medea young Absyrtus did:
In cruelty will I seek out my fame.
Come, thou new ruin of old Clifford's house; [*Taking up the Body.*

As did Æneas old Anchises bear,
So bear I thee upon my manly shoulders:
But then Æneas bare a living load,
Nothing so heavy as these woes of mine. [*Exit.*

Enter RICHARD PLANTAGENET *and* SOMERSET, *fighting, and* SOMERSET *is killed.*

Rich. So, lie thou there;—
For, underneath an alehouse paltry sign,
The Castle in Saint Albans, Somerset
Hath made the wizard famous in his death.—
Sword, hold thy temper; heart, be wrathful still:
Priests pray for enemies, but princes kill.
[*Exit.*

Alarums: Excursions. Enter KING HENRY, QUEEN MARGARET, *and Others retreating.*

Q. Mar. Away, my lord! you are slow; for shame, away!
K. Hen. Can we outrun the heavens? good Margaret, stay.
Q. Mar. What are you made of? you'll not fight, nor fly:
Now is it manhood, wisdom, and defence,
To give the enemy way: and to secure us
By what we can, which can no more but fly.
[*Alarum afar off.*
If you be ta'en, we then should see the bottom
Of all our fortunes: but if we haply scape
(As well we may, if not through your neglect),
We shall to London get; where you are lov'd;
And where this breach, now in our fortunes made,
May readily be stopp'd.

Enter young CLIFFORD.

Y. Clif. But that my heart's on future mischief set,
I would speak blasphemy ere bid you fly;
But fly you must; uncurable discomfit
Reigns in the hearts of all our present parts.
Away, for your relief! and we will live
To see their day, and them our fortune give:
Away, my lord, away! [*Exeunt.*

SCENE III. *Fields near* Saint Albans.

Alarums: Retreat. Flourish; then enter YORK, RICHARD PLANTAGENET, WARWICK, *and* Soldiers, *with Drum and Colours.*

York. Of Salisbury, who can report of him;
That winter lion, who, in rage, forgets
Aged contusions and all brush of time;
And, like a gallant in the brow of youth,
Repairs him with occasion? this happy day
Is not itself, nor have we won one foot,
If Salisbury be lost.
Rich. My noble father
Three times to-day I holp him to his horse,
Three times bestrid him, thrice I led him off,
Persuaded him from any further act:
But still, where danger was, still there I met him;
And like rich hangings in a homely house,
So was his will in his old feeble body.
But, noble as he is, look where he domes.

Enter SALISBURY.

Sal. Now, by my sword, well hast thou fought to-day;
By the mass, so did we all.—I thank you, Richard:
God knows, how long it is I have to live;
And it hath pleas'd him, that three times to-day
You have defended me from imminent death.—
Well, lords, we have not got that which we have;
'Tis not enough our foes are this time fled,
Being opposites of such repairing nature.
York. I know, our safety is to follow them;
For, as I hear, the king is fled to London,
To call a present court of parliament.
Let us pursue him, ere the writs go forth:—
What says Lord Warwick? shall we after them?
War. After them! nay, before them if we can.
Now by my faith, lords, 'twas a glorious day:
Saint Albans' battle, won by famous York,
Shall be eterniz'd in all age to come.—
Sound, drums and trumpets:—and to London all:
And more such days as these to us befall!
[*Exeunt.*

THIRD PART OF
KING HENRY THE SIXTH.

PERSONS REPRESENTED.

KING HENRY THE SIXTH.
EDWARD, Prince *of* Wales, *his* Son.
LEWIS XI. King *of* France.
DUKE OF SOMERSET, DUKE OF EXETER, EARL OF OXFORD, EARL OF NORTHUMBERLAND, EARL OF WESTMORELAND, LORD CLIFFORD, } *Lords on* King Henry's *side.*
RICHARD PLANTAGENET, Duke *of* York:
EDWARD, Earl *of* March, *afterwards* King Edward IV., EDMUND, Earl *of* Rutland, GEORGE, *afterwards* Duke *of* Clarence, RICHARD, *afterwards* Duke *of* Glocester } *his* Sons.
DUKE OF NORFOLK, MARQUIS OF MONTAGUE, EARL OF WARWICK, EARL OF PEMBROKE, } *of the* Duke *of* York's *Party.*
LORD HASTINGS, LORD STAFFORD, } *of the* Duke *of* York's *Party.*
SIR JOHN MORTIMER, SIR HUGH MORTIMER, } *Uncles to the* Duke *of* York.
HENRY, Earl *of* Richmond, *a Youth.*
LORD RIVERS, *Brother to* Lady Grey. SIR WILLIAM STANLEY. SIR JOHN MONTGOMERY. SIR JOHN SOMERVILLE. Tutor *to* Rutland. Mayor *of* York. Lieutenant *of the* Tower. *A* Nobleman. *Two* Keepers. *A* Huntsman. *A* Son *that has killed his Father.* *A* Father *that has killed his Son.*

QUEEN MARGARET.
LADY GREY, *afterwards* Queen *to* Edward IV.
BONA, *Sister to the* French Queen.

Soldiers, *and other* Attendants *on* King Henry *and* King Edward, Messengers, Watchmen, *&c.*

SCENE,—*during part of the third Act, in* France; *during all the rest of the play, in* England.

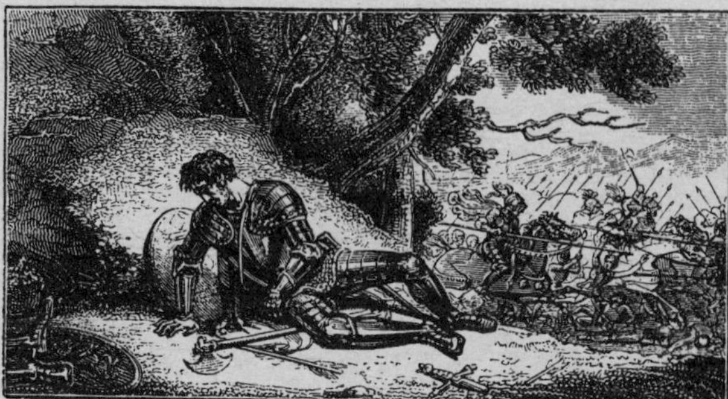

ACT I.

SCENE I. London. *The Parliament House.*

Drums. Some Soldiers *of* York's *party break in. Then, Enter the* DUKE OF YORK, EDWARD, RICHARD, NORFOLK, MONTAGUE, WARWICK, *and Others, with white Roses, in their Hats.*

War. I WONDER, how the king escap'd our hands.
York. While we pursu'd the horsemen of the north,
He slily stole away, and left his men:
Whereat the great lord of Northumberland,
Whose warlike ears could never brook retreat,
Cheer'd up the drooping army; and himself,
Lord Clifford, and Lord Stafford, all abreast,
Charg'd our main battle's front, and, breaking in,
Were by the swords of common soldiers slain.
Edw. Lord Stafford's father, duke of Buckingham,
Is either slain, or wounded dangerous:
I cleft his beaver with a downright blow;
That this is true, father, behold his blood.
[*Showing his bloody Sword.*
Mont. And, brother, here's the earl of Wiltshire's blood, [*To* YORK, *showing his.*
Whom I encounter'd as the battles join'd.
Rich. Speak thou for me, and tell them what I did.
[*Throwing down the* Duke *of* Somerset's *Head.*
York. Richard hath best deserv'd of all my sons.—
What, is your grace dead, my lord of Somerset?
Norf. Such hope have all the line of John of Gaunt!
Rich. Thus do I hope to shake King Henry's head.
War. And so do I.—Victorious prince of York,
Before I see thee seated in that throne
Which now the house of Lancaster usurps,
I vow by heaven, these eyes shall never close.
This is the palace of the fearful king,
And this the regal seat: possess it, York:
For this is thine, and not King Henry's heirs'.
York. Assist me then, sweet Warwick, and I will;
For hither we have broken in by force.
Norf. We'll all assist you; he, that flies, shall die.
York. Thanks, gentle Norfolk.—Stay by me, my lords;—
And, soldiers, stay, and lodge by me this night.
War. And, when the king comes, offer him no violence,
Unless he seek to thrust you out by force.
[*They retire.*

York. The queen this day here holds her parliament,
But little thinks we shall be of her council:
By words, or blows, here let us win our right.
Rich. Arm'd as we are, let's stay within this house.
War. The bloody parliament shall this be call'd,
Unless Plantagenet, duke of York, be king;
And bashful Henry depos'd, whose cowardice
Hath made us by-words to our enemies.
York. Then leave me not, my lords; be resolute;
I mean to take possession of my right.
War. Neither the king, nor he that loves him best,
The proudest he that holds up Lancaster,
Dares stir a wing, if Warwick shake his bells.
I'll plant Plantagenet, root him up who dares:—
Resolve thee Richard, claim the English crown.
[WARWICK *leads* YORK *to the Throne, who seats himself.*

Flourish. Enter KING HENRY, CLIFFORD, NORTHUMBERLAND, WESTMORELAND, EXETER, *and Others, with red Roses in their Hats.*

K. Hen. My lords, look where the sturdy rebel sits,
Even in the chair of state! belike, he means
(Back'd by the power of Warwick, that false peer,)
To aspire unto the crown, and reign as king.—
Earl of Northumberland, he slew thy father;—
And thine, Lord Clifford; and you both have vow'd revenge
On him, his sons, his favourites, and his friends.
North. If I be not, heavens, be reveng'd on me!
Clif. The hope thereof makes Clifford mourn in steel.
West. What, shall we suffer this? let's pluck him down:
My heart for anger burns, I cannot brook it.
K. Hen. Be patient, gentle earl of Westmoreland.
Clif. Patience is for poltroons, and such as he;
He durst not sit there, had your father liv'd.
My gracious lord, here in the parliament
Let us assail the family of York.
North. Well hast thou spoken, cousin; be it so.
K. Hen. Ah, know you not, the city favours them,
And they have troops of soldiers at their beck?
Exe. But when the duke is slain, they'll quickly fly.
K. Hen. Far be the thought of this from Henry's heart,
To make a shambles of the parliament-house!
Cousin of Exeter, frowns, words, and threats,
Shall be the war that Henry means to use.—
[*They advance to the* Duke.
Thou factious duke of York, descend my throne,
And kneel for grace and mercy at my feet:
I am thy sovereign.
York. Thou art deceiv'd, I am thine.
Exe. For shame, come down; he made thee duke of York.
York. 'Twas my inheritance, as the earldom was.
Exe. Thy father was a traitor to the crown.
War. Exeter, thou art a traitor to the crown,
In following this usurping Henry.
Clif. Whom should he follow, but his natural king?
War. True, Clifford; and that's Richard, duke of York.
K. Hen. And shall I stand, and thou sit in my throne?
York. It must, and shall be so. Content thyself.
War. Be duke of Lancaster, let him be king.
West. He is both king and duke of Lancaster:
And that the lord of Westmoreland shall maintain.
War. And Warwick shall disprove it. You forget,
That we are those, which chas'd you from the field,
And slew your fathers, and with colours spread
March'd through the city to the palace gates.
North. Yes, Warwick, I remember it to my grief;
And, by his soul, thou and thy house shall rue it.
West. Plantagenet, of thee, and these thy sons,
Thy kinsmen, and thy friends, I'll have more lives,
Than drops of blood were in my father's veins.
Clif. Urge it no more; lest that, instead of words,
I send thee, Warwick, such a messenger,
As shall revenge his death before I stir.
War. Poor Clifford! how I scorn his worthless threats!
York. Will you, we show our title to the crown?
If not, our swords shall plead it in the field.
K. Hen. What title hast thou, traitor, to the crown?
Thy father was, as thou art, duke of York;
Thy grandfather, Roger Mortimer, earl of March:
I am the son of Henry the Fifth,
Who made the Dauphin and the French to stoop,
And seiz'd upon their towns and provinces.
War. Talk not of France, sith thou hast lost it all.
K. Hen. The lord protector lost it, and not I;
When I was crown'd, I was but nine months old.
Rich. You are old enough now, and yet, methinks you lose:—
Father, tear the crown from the usurper's head.
Edw. Sweet father, do so; set it on your head.
Mont. Good brother [*To* YORK], as thou lov'st and honour'st arms,
Let's fight it out, and not stand cavilling thus.
Rich. Sound drums and trumpets, and the king will fly.
York. Sons, peace!
K. Hen. Peace thou! and give king Henry leave to speak.
War. Plantagenet shall speak first:—hear him, lords;
And be you silent and attentive too,
For he, that interrupts him, shall not live.
K. Hen. Think'st thou, that I will leave my kingly throne,
Wherein my grandsire, and my father, sat?
No: first shall war unpeople this my realm:
Ay, and their colours—often borne in France;
And now in England, to our heart's great sorrow,—
Shall be my windingsheet.—Why faint you, lords?
My title's good, and better far than his.
War. But prove it, Henry, and thou shalt be king.
K. Hen. Henry the Fourth by conquest got the crown.
York. 'Twas by rebellion against his king.
K. Hen. I know not what to say; my title's weak.
Tell me, may not a king adopt an heir?
York. What then?
K. Hen. An if he may, then am I lawful king:
For Richard, in the view of many lords,
Resign'd the crown to Henry the Fourth;
Whose heir my father was, and I am his.
York. He rose against him, being his sovereign,
And made him to resign his crown perforce.
War. Suppose, my lords, he did it unconstrain'd,
Think you, 'twere prejudicial to his crown?
Exe. No; for he could not so resign his crown,
But that the next heir should succeed and reign.
K. Hen. Art thou against us, duke of Exeter?
Exe. His is the right, and therefore pardon me.
York. Why whisper you, my lords, and answer not?

Exe. My conscience tells me he is lawful king.
K. Hen. All will revolt from me, and turn to him.
North. Plantagenet, for all the claim thou lay'st,
Think not that Henry shall be so depos'd.
War. Depos'd he shall be, in despite of all.
North. Thou art deceiv'd: 'tis not thy southern power,—
Of Essex, Norfolk, Suffolk, nor of Kent,—
Which makes thee thus presumptuous and proud,—
Can set the duke up, in despite of me.
Clif. King Henry, be thy title right or wrong,
Lord Clifford vows to fight in thy defence:
May that ground gape, and swallow me alive,
Where I shall kneel to him that slew my father!
K. Hen. O Clifford, how thy words revive my heart!
York. Henry of Lancaster, resign thy crown:—
What mutter you, or what conspire you, lords?
War. Do right unto this princely duke of York;
Or I will fill the house with armed men,
And o'er the chair of state, where now he sits,
Write up his title with usurping blood.
[*He stamps, and the* Soldiers *show themselves.*
K. Hen. My lord of Warwick, hear me but one word;—
Let me for this my lifetime, reign as king.
York. Confirm the crown to me, and to mine heirs,
And thou shalt reign in quiet while thou liv'st.
K. Hen. I am content: Richard Plantagenet,
Enjoy the kingdom after my decease.
Clif. What wrong is this unto the prince your son?
War. What good is this to England and himself?
West. Base, fearful, and despairing Henry!
Clif. How hast thou injur'd both thyself and us?
West. I cannot stay to hear these articles.
North. Nor I.
Clif. Come, cousin, let us tell the queen these news.
West. Farewell, faint-hearted and degenerate king,
In whose cold blood no spark of honour bides.
North. Be thou a prey unto the house of York,
And die in bands of this unmanly deed!
Clif. In dreadful war may'st thou be overcome!
Or live in peace, abandon'd and despis'd!
[*Exeunt* NORTH. CLIF. *and* WEST.
War. Turn this way, Henry, and regard them not.
Exe. They seek revenge, and therefore will not yield.
K. Hen. Ah, Exeter!
War. Why should you sigh, my lord?
K. Hen. Not for myself, Lord Warwick, but my son,
Whom I unnaturally shall disinherit.
But, be it as it may:—I here entail
The crown to thee, and to thine heirs for ever;
Conditionally, that here thou take an oath,
To cease this civil war, and, whilst I live,
To honour me as thy king and sovereign;
And neither by treason, nor hostility,
To seek to put me down, and reign thyself.
York. This oath I willingly take, and will perform. [*Coming from the Throne.*
War. Long live King Henry!—Plantagenet, embrace him.
K. Hen. And long live thou, and these thy forward sons!
York. Now York and Lancaster are reconcil'd.
Exe. Accurs'd be he that seeks to make them foes; [*Senet. The* Lords *come forward.*
York. Farewell, my gracious lord; I'll to my castle.
War. And I'll keep London with my soldiers.
Norf. And I to Norfolk, with my followers.
Mont. And I unto the sea, from whence I came.
[*Exeunt* YORK, *and his* SONS, WAR. NORF. MONT. Soldiers, *and* Attendants.
K. Hen. And I, with grief and sorrow, to the court.

Enter QUEEN MARGARET *and the* PRINCE OF WALES.

Exe. Here comes the queen, whose looks bewray her anger:
I'll steal away.
K. Ken. Exeter, so will I. [*Going.*
Q. Mar. Nay, go not from me, I will follow thee.
K. Hen. Be patient, gentle queen, and I will stay.
Q. Mar. Who can be patient in such extremes?
Ah, wretched man! 'would I had died a maid,
And never seen thee, never borne thee son,
Seeing thou hast prov'd sò unnatural a father!
Hath he deserv'd to lose his birthright thus?
Hadst thou but lov'd him half so well as I;
Or felt that pain which I did for him once;
Or nourish'd him, as I did with my blood;
Thou would'st have left thy dearest heart-blood there,
Rather than have made that savage duke thine heir,
And disinherited thine only son.
Prince. Father, you cannot disinherit me:
If you be king, why should not I succeed?
K. Hen. Pardon me, Margaret;—pardon me, sweet son;—
The earl of Warwick, and the duke, enforc'd me.
Q. Mar. Enforc'd thee! art thou king, and wilt be forc'd?
I shame to hear thee speak. Ah, timorous wretch!
Thou hast undone thyself, thy son, and me,
And given unto the house of York such head,
As thou shalt reign but by their sufferance.
To entail him and his heirs unto the crown,
What is it, but to make thy sepulchre,
And creep into it far before thy time?
Warwick is chancellor, and the lord of Calais;
Stern Faulconbridge commands the narrow seas;
The duke is made protector of the realm;
And yet shalt thou be safe? such safety finds
The trembling lamb, environed with wolves.
Had I been there, which am a silly woman,
The soldiers should have toss'd me on their pikes,
Before I would have granted to that act.
But thou preferr'st thy life before thine honour:
And seeing thou dost, I here divorce myself,
Both from thy table, Henry, and thy bed,
Until that act of parliament be repeal'd,
Whereby my son is disinherited.
The northern lords, that have forsworn thy colours,
Will follow mine, if once they see them spread:
And spread they shall be; to thy foul disgrace,
And utter ruin of the house of York.
Thus do I leave thee:—Come, son, let's away;
Our army's ready; Come, we'll after them.
K. Hen. Stay, gentle Margaret, and hear me speak.
Q. Mar. Thou hast spoke too much already; get thee gone.
K. Hen. Gentle son Edward, thou wilt stay with me?
Q. Mar. Ay, to be murder'd by his enemies.
Prince. When I return with victory from the field,
I'll see your grace: till then, I'll follow her.
Q. Mar. Come, son, away; we may not linger thus.
[*Exeunt* QUEEN MARGARET, *and the* Prince.
K. Hen. Poor queen! how love to me and to her son,
Hath made her break out into terms of rage!
Reveng'd may she be on that hateful duke;
Whose haughty spirit, winged with desire,
Will coast my crown, and, like an empty eagle,

Tire on the flesh of me, and of my son!
The loss of those three lords torments my heart:
I'll write unto them, and entreat them fair;—
Come cousin, you shall be the messenger.
Exe. And I, I hope, shall reconcile them all.
[*Exeunt.*

SCENE II.

A Room in Sandal Castle, *near* Wakefield, *in* Yorkshire.

Enter EDWARD, RICHARD, *and* MONTAGUE.

Rich. Brother, though I be youngest, give me leave.
Edw. No, I can better play the orator.
Mont. But I have reasons strong and forcible.

Enter YORK.

York. Why, how now, sons and brother, at a strife?
What is your quarrel? how began it first?
Edw. No quarrel, but a slight contention.
York. About what?
Rich. About that which concerns your grace, and us;
The crown of England, father, which is yours.
York. Mine, boy? not till King Henry be dead.
Rich. Your right depends not on his life, or death.
Edw. Now you are heir, therefore enjoy it now:
By giving the house of Lancaster leave to breathe,
It will outrun you, father, in the end.
York. I took an oath that he should quietly reign.
Edw. But, for a kingdom, any oath may be broken:
I'd break a thousand oaths, to reign one year.
Rich. No; God forbid, your grace should be forsworn.
York. I shall be, if I claim by open war.
Rich. I'll prove the contrary, if you'll hear me speak.
York. Thou canst not, son; it is impossible.
Rich. An oath is of no moment, being not took
Before a true and lawful magistrate,
That hath authority over him that swears:
Henry had none, but did usurp the place;
Then, seeing 'twas he that made you to depose,
Your oath, my lord, is vain and frivolous.
Therefore to arms. And, father, do but think,
How sweet a thing it is to wear a crown;
Within whose circuit is Elysium,
And all the poets feign of bliss and joy.
Why do we linger thus? I cannot rest,
Until the white rose, that I wear, be dyed
Even in the lukewarm blood of Henry's heart.
York. Richard, enough; I will be king, or die.—
Brother, thou shalt to London presently,
And whet on Warwick to this enterprise.—
Thou, Richard, shalt unto the duke of Norfolk,
And tell him privately of our intent.—
You, Edward, shall unto my lord Cobham,
With whom the Kentishmen will willingly rise:
In them I trust; for they are soldiers,
Witty, courteous, liberal, full of spirit.—
While you are thus employ'd, what resteth more,
But that I seek occasion how to rise;
And yet the king not privy to my drift,
Nor any of the house of Lancaster?

Enter a Messenger.

But, stay; What news? Why com'st thou in such post?
Mess. The queen, with all the northern earls and lords,
Intend here to besiege you in your castle:
She is hard by with twenty thousand men;
And therefore fortify your hold, my lord.
York. Ay, with my sword. What! think'st thou, that we fear them?—
Edward and Richard, you shall stay with me;—
My brother Montague shall post to London:
Let noble Warwick, Cobham, and the rest,
Whom we have left protectors of the king,
With powerful policy strengthen themselves,
And trust not simple Henry, nor his oaths.
Mont. Brother, I go; I'll win them, fear it not:
And thus most humbly I do take my leave.
[*Exit.*

Enter SIR JOHN *and* SIR HUGH MORTIMER.

York. Sir John, and Sir Hugh Mortimer, mine uncles!
You are come to Sandal in a happy hour;
The army of the queen mean to besiege us.
Sir John. She shall not need, we'll meet her in the field.
York. What, with five thousand men?
Rich. Ay, with five hundred, father, for a need.
A woman's general; What should we fear?
[*A March afar off.*
Edw. I hear their drums; let's set our men in order;
And issue forth, and bid them battle straight.
York. Five men to twenty!—though the odds be great,
I doubt not, uncle, of our victory.
Many a battle have I won in France,
When as the enemy hath been ten to one;
Why should I not now have the like success?
[*Alarum. Exeunt.*

SCENE III. *Plains near* Sandal Castle.

Alarums: Excursions. Enter RUTLAND, *and his* Tutor.

Rut. Ah, whither shall I fly to 'scape their hands?
Ah, tutor! look where bloody Clifford comes!

Enter CLIFFORD, *and* Soldiers.

Clif. Chaplain, away! thy priesthood saves thy life.
As for the brat of this accursed duke,
Whose father slew my father,—he shall die.
Tut. And I, my lord, will bear him company.
Clif. Soldiers, away with him.
Tut. Ah, Clifford! murder not this innocent child,
Lest thou be hated both of God and man.
[*Exit, forced off by* Soldiers.
Clif. How now! is he dead already? Or, is it fear,
That makes him close his eyes?—I'll open them.
Rut. So looks the pent-up lion o'er the wretch
That trembles under his devouring paws:
And so he walks, insulting o'er his prey;
And so he comes to rend his limbs asunder.—
Ah, gentle Clifford, kill me with thy sword,
And not with such a cruel threatening look.
Sweet Clifford, hear me speak before I die;—
I am too mean a subject for thy wrath,
Be thou reveng'd on men, and let me live.
Clif. In vain thou speak'st, poor boy; my father's blood
Hath stopp'd the passage where thy words should enter.
Rut. Then let my father's blood open it again;
He is a man, and, Clifford, cope with him.
Clif. Had I thy brethren here, their lives, and thine,
Were not revenge sufficient for me,
No, if I digg'd up thy forefathers' graves,
And hung their rotten coffins up in chains,
It could not slake mine ire, nor ease my heart.
The sight of any of the house of York
Is as a fury to torment my soul;
And till I root out their accursed line,
And leave not one alive, I live in hell.
Therefore—— [*Lifting his hand.*
Rut. O, let me pray before I take my death:—
To thee I pray; sweet Clifford, pity me!
Clif. Such pity as my rapier's point affords.
Rut. I never did thee harm: Why wilt thou slay me?
Clif. Thy father hath.
Rut. But 'twas ere I was born.

Thou hast one son, for his sake pity me;
Lest, in revenge thereof,—sith God is just,—
He be as miserably slain as I.
Ah, let me live in prison all my days;
And when I give occasion of offence,
Then let me die, for now thou hast no cause.

Clif. No cause?
Thy father slew my father; therefore die.
[CLIFFORD *stabs him.*

Rut. *Dii faciant, laudis summa sit ista tuæ!*
[*Dies.*

Clif. Plantagenet! I come, Plantagenet!
And this thy son's blood cleaving to my blade,
Shall rust upon my weapon, till thy blood,
Congeal'd with this, do make me wipe off both.
[*Exit.*

SCENE IV. *The same.*

Alarum. Enter YORK.

York. The army of the queen hath got the field:
My uncles both are slain in rescuing me;
And all my followers to the eager foe
Turn back, and fly, like ships before the wind,
Or lambs pursu'd by hunger-starved wolves.
My sons—God knows, what hath bechanced them:
But this I know,—they have demean'd themselves
Like men born to renown, by life, or death.
Three times did Richard make a lane to me;
And thrice cried,—*Courage, father! fight it out!*
And full as oft came Edward to my side,
With purple falchion painted to the hilt
In blood of those that had encounter'd him:
And when the hardiest warriors did retire,
Richard cried,—*Charge! and give no foot of ground!*
And cried,—*A crown, or else a glorious tomb!*
A sceptre, or an earthly sepulchre!
With this we charg'd again: but, out, alas!
We bodg'd again; as I have seen a swan
With bootless labour swim against the tide,
And spend her strength with overmatching waves. [*A short Alarum within.*
Ah, hark! the fatal followers do pursue;
And I am faint, and cannot fly their fury:
And, were I strong, I would not shun their fury:
The sands are number'd, that make up my life;
Here must I stay, and here my life must end.

Enter QUEEN MARGARET, CLIFFORD, NORTHUMBERLAND, *and* Soldiers.

Come, bloody Clifford,—rough Northumberland,—
I dare your quenchless fury to more rage;
I am your butt, and I abide your shot.

North. Yield to our mercy, proud Plantagenet.

Clif. Ay, to such mercy, as his ruthless arm,
With downright payment, show'd unto my father.
Now Phaeton hath tumbled from his car,
And made an evening at the noontide prick.

York. My ashes, as the Phœnix, may bring forth
A bird that will revenge upon you all:
And, in that hope, I throw mine eyes to heaven,
Scorning whate'er you can afflict me with.
Why come you not? what! multitudes, and fear?

Clif. So cowards fight, when they can fly no further;
So doves do peck the falcon's piercing talons;
So desperate thieves, all hopeless of their lives,
Breathe out invectives 'gainst the officers.

York. O, Clifford, but bethink thee once again,
And, in thy thought o'errun my former time:
And, if thou canst for blushing, view this face;
And bite thy tongue that slanders him with cowardice,
Whose frown hath made thee faint and fly ere this.

Clif. I will not bandy with thee word for word;
But buckle with thee blows, twice two for one.
[*Draws.*

Q. Mar. Hold, valiant Clifford! for a thousand causes,
I would prolong awhile the traitor's life:
Wrath makes him deaf: speak thou, Northumberland.

North. Hold, Clifford; do not honour him so much,
To prick thy finger, though to wound his heart:
What valour were it, when a cur doth grin,
For one to thrust his hand between his teeth,
When he might spurn him with his foot away?
It is war's prize to take all vantages;
And ten to one is no impeach of valour.
[*They lay hands on* YORK, *who struggles.*

Clif. Ay, ay, so strives the woodcock with the gin.

North. So doth the coney struggle in the net.
[YORK *is taken prisoner.*

York. So triumph thieves upon their conquer'd booty;
So true men yield, with robbers so o'ermatch'd.

North. What would your grace have done unto him now?

Q. Mar. Brave warriors, Clifford, and Northumberland,
Come make him stand upon this molehill here;
That raught at mountains with outstretched arms,
Yet parted but the shadow with his hand.—
What! was it you that would be England's king?
Was 't you that revell'd in our parliament,
And made a preachment of your high descent?
Where are your mess of sons to back you now?
The wanton Edward, and the lusty George?
And where's that valiant crookback prodigy,
Dicky, your boy, that, with his grumbling voice,
Was wont to cheer his dad in mutinies?
Or, with the rest, where is your darling Rutland?
Look, York; I stain'd this napkin with the blood
That valiant Clifford, with his rapier's point,
Made issue from the bosom of the boy:
And, if thine eyes can water for his death,
I give thee this to dry thy cheeks withal.
Alas, poor York! but that I hate thee deadly,
I should lament thy miserable state.
I pr'ythee, grieve, to make me merry, York;
Stamp, rave, and fret, that I may sing and dance.
What, hath thy fiery heart so parch'd thine entrails,
That not a tear can fall for Rutland's death?
Why art thou patient, man? thou should'st be mad;
And I, to make thee mad, do mock thee thus.
Thou would'st be fee'd, I see, to make me sport;
York cannot speak, unless he wear a crown.—
A crown for York;—and, lords, bow low to him.—
Hold you his hands, whilst I do set it on.—
[*Putting a paper Crown on his Head.*
Ay, marry, sir, now looks he like a king!
Ay, this is he that took King Henry's chair;
And this is he was his adopted heir.—
But how is it that great Plantagenet
Is crown'd so soon, and broke his solemn oath?
As I bethink me, you should not be king,
Till our King Henry had shook hands with death.
And will you pale your head in Henry's glory,
And rob his temples of the diadem,
Now in his life, against your holy oath?
O, tis a fault too too unpardonable!—
Off with the crown; and, with the crown his head;
And, whilst we breathe, take time to do him dead.

Clif. That is my office, for my father's sake.

Q. Mar. Nay, stay; let's hear the orisons he makes.

York. She wolf of France, but worse than wolves of France,
Whose tongue more poisons than the adder's tooth!
How ill beseeming is it in thy sex,
To triumph like an Amazonian trull,
Upon their woes, whom fortune captivates?
But that thy face is, visorlike, unchanging,

Made impudent with use of evil deeds,
I would assay, proud queen, to make thee blush:
To tell thee whence thou cam'st, of whom deriv'd,
Were shame enough to shame thee, wert thou not shameless.
Thy father bears the type of king of Naples,
Of both the Sicils, and Jerusalem;
Yet not so wealthy as an English yeoman.
Hath that poor monarch taught thee to insult?
It needs not, nor it boots thee not, proud queen;
Unless the adage must be verified,—
That beggars, mounted, run their horse to death.
'Tis beauty, that doth oft make women proud;
But, God he knows, thy share thereof is small:
'Tis virtue, that doth make them most admir'd;
The contrary doth make thee wonder'd at:
'Tis government, that make them seem divine;
The want thereof makes thee abominable:
Thou art as opposite to every good,
As the Antipodes are unto us,
Or as the south to the septentrion.
O, tiger's heart, wrapp'd in a woman's hide!
How could'st thou drain the life-blood of the child,
To bid the father wipe his eyes withal,
And yet be seen to bear a woman's face?
Women are soft, mild, pitiful, and flexible;
Thou stern, obdurate, flinty, rough, remorseless.
Bidd'st thou me rage, why, now thou hast thy wish:
Would'st have me weep? why, now thou hast thy will:
For raging wind blows up incessant showers.
And, when the rage allays, the rain begins.
These tears are my sweet Rutland's obsequies;
And every drop cries vengeance for his death,—
'Gainst thee, fell Clifford,—and thee, false Frenchwoman.

North. Beshrew me, but his passions move me so,
That hardly can I check my eyes from tears.

York. That face of his the hungry cannibals
Would not have touch'd, would not have stain'd with blood:
But you are more inhuman, more inexorable,—
O, ten times more,—than tigers of Hyrcania.
See, ruthless queen, a hapless father's tears:
This cloth thou dipp'dst in blood of my sweet boy,
And I with tears do wash the blood away.
Keep thou the napkin, and go boast of this:
[*He gives back the Handkerchief.*
And, if thou tell'st the heavy story right,
Upon my soul, the hearers will shed tears;
Yea, even my foes will shed fast falling tears,
And say,—Alas, it was a piteous deed!—
There, take the crown, and, with the crown, my curse;
And, in thy need, such comfort come to thee,
As now I reap at thy too cruel hand!
Hard-hearted Clifford, take me from the world;
My soul to Heaven, my blood upon your heads!

North. Had he been slaughterman to all my kin,
I should not for my life but weep with him,
To see how inly sorrow gripes his soul.

Q. Mar. What, weeping-ripe, my Lord Northumberland?
Think but upon the wrong he did us all,
And that will quickly dry thy melting tears.

Clif. Here's for my oath, here's for my father's death. [*Stabbing him.*

Q. Mar. And here's to right our gentle-hearted king. [*Stabbing him.*

York. Open thy gate of mercy, gracious God!
My soul flies through these wounds to seek out thee. [*Dies.*

Q. Mar. Off with his head, and set it on York gates;
So York may overlook the town of York.
[*Exeunt.*

ACT II.

SCENE I. *A Plain near* Mortimer's *Cross in* Herefordshire.

Drums. Enter EDWARD *and* RICHARD, *with their* Forces, *marching.*

Edw. I wonder how our princely father 'scap'd;
Or whether he be 'scap'd away, or no,
From Clifford's and Northumberland's pursuit;
Had he been ta'en, we should have heard the news;
Had he been slain, we should have heard the news;
Or, had he 'scap'd, methinks, we should have heard
The happy tidings of his good escape.
How fares my brother? why is he so sad?

Rich. I cannot joy, until I be resolv'd
Where our right valiant father is become.
I saw him in the battle range about;
And watch'd him how he singled Clifford forth.
Methought, he bore him in the thickest troop,
As doth a lion in a herd of neat:
Or as a bear encompass'd round with dogs;
Who having pinch'd a few, and made them cry,
The rest stand all aloof, and bark at him.
So far'd our father with his enemies:
So fled his enemies my warlike father;
Methinks, 'tis prize enough to be his son.
See, how the morning opes her golden gates,
And takes her farewell of the glorious sun!
How well resembles it the prime of youth,
Trimm'd like a younker, prancing to his love!

Edw. Dazzle mine eyes, or do I see three suns?

Rich. Three glorious suns, each one a perfect sun;
Not separated with the racking clouds,
But sever'd in a pale clear-shining sky.
See, see! they join, embrace, and seem to kiss,
As if they vow'd some league inviolable:
Now are they but one lamp, one light, one sun.
In this the heaven figures some event.

Edw. 'Tis wondrous strange, the like yet never heard of.
I think, it cites us, brother, to the field;
That we, the sons of brave Plantagenet,
Each one already blazing by our meeds,
Should, notwithstanding, join our lights together,
And overshine the earth, as this the world.
Whate'er it bodes, henceforward will I bear
Upon my target three fair shining suns.

Rich. Nay, bear three daughters;—by your leave I speak it,
You love the breeder better than the male.

Enter a Messenger.

But what art thou, whose heavy looks foretell
Some dreadful story hanging on thy tongue?

Mess. Ah, one that was a woful looker on,
When as the noble duke of York was slain,
Your princely father, and my loving lord.

Edw. O, speak no more! for I have heard too much.

Rich. Say how he died, for I will hear it all.

Mess. Environed he was with many foes;
And stood against them as the hope of Troy
Against the Greeks, that would have enter'd Troy.
But Hercules himself must yield to odds;
And many strokes, though with a little axe,
Hew down and fell the hardest-timber'd oak.
By many hands your father was subdu'd;
But only slaughter'd by the ireful arm
Of unrelenting Clifford, and the queen:
Who crown'd the gracious duke in high despite;
Laugh'd in his face; and, when with grief he wept,
The ruthless queen gave him, to dry his cheeks,
A napkin steeped in the harmless blood
Of sweet young Rutland, by rough Clifford slain:
And, after many scorns, many foul taunts,

They took his head, and on the gates of York
They set the same; and there it doth remain,
The saddest spectacle that e'er I view'd.

Edw. Sweet duke of York, our prop to lean upon;
Now thou art gone, we have no staff, no stay!—
O Clifford, boist'rous Clifford, thou hast slain
The flower of Europe for his chivalry;
And treacherously hast thou vanquish'd him,
For, hand to hand, he would have vanquish'd thee!—
Now my soul's palace is become a prison:
Ah, would she break from hence! that this my body
Might in the ground be closed up in rest:
For never henceforth shall I joy again,
Never, O never, shall I see more joy.

Rich. I cannot weep; for all my body's moisture
Scarce serves to quench my furnace-burning heart:
Nor can my tongue unload my heart's great burden;
For selfsame wind, that I should speak withal,
Is kindling coals, that fire all my breast,
And burn me up with flames that tears would quench.
To weep, is to make less the depth of grief;
Tears, then, for babes; blows, and revenge, for me!—
Richard, I bear thy name, I'll venge thy death,
Or die renowned by attempting it.

Edw. His name that valiant duke hath left with thee;
His dukedom and his chair with me is left.

Rich. Nay, if thou be that princely eagle's bird,
Show thy descent by gazing 'gainst the sun:
For chair and dukedom, throne and kingdom say;
Either that is thine, or else thou wert not his.

March. Enter WARWICK *and* MONTAGUE, *with* Forces.

War. How now, fair lords? What fare? what news abroad?

Rich. Great lord of Warwick, if we should recount
Our baleful news, and, at each word's deliverance,
Stab poniards in our flesh till all were told,
The words would add more anguish than the wounds.
O valiant lord, the duke of York is slain.

Edw. O Warwick! Warwick! that Plantagenet,
Which held thee dearly, as his soul's redemption,
Is by the stern Lord Clifford done to death.

War. Ten days ago I drown'd these news in tears:
And now to add more measure to your woes,
I come to tell you things since then befall'n.
After the bloody fray at Wakefield fought,
Where your brave father breath'd his latest gasp,
Tidings, as swiftly as the posts could run,
Were brought me of your loss, and his depart.
I then in London, keeper of the king,
Muster'd my soldiers, gather'd flocks of friends,
And very well appointed, as I thought,
March'd towards Saint Albans to intercept the queen,
Bearing the king in my behalf along:
For by my scouts I was advertised,
That she was coming with a full intent
To dash our late decree in parliament,
Touching King Henry's oath, and your succession.
Short tale to make,—we at Saint Albans met,
Our battles join'd, and both sides fiercely fought:
But, whether 'twas the coldness of the king,
Who look'd full gently on his warlike queen,
That robb'd my soldiers of their hated spleen;
Or whether 'twas report of her success;
Or more than common fear of Clifford's rigour,
Who thunders to his captives—blood and death,
I cannot judge: but, to conclude with truth,
Their weapons like to lightning came and went;
Our soldiers'—like the night-owl's lazy flight,
Or like a lazy thrasher with a flail,—
Fell gently down, as if they struck their friends.
I cheer'd them up with justice of our cause,
With promise of high pay, and great rewards:
But all in vain; they had no heart to fight,
And we, in them, no hope to win the day,
So that we fled; the king, unto the queen;
Lord George your brother, Norfolk, and myself,
In haste, posthaste, are come to join with you;
For in the marches here, we heard you were,
Making another head to fight again.

Edw. Where is the duke of Norfolk, gentle Warwick?
And when came George from Burgundy to England?

War. Some six miles off the duke is with the soldiers:
And for your brother,—he was lately sent
From your kind aunt, duchess of Burgundy,
With aid of soldiers to this needful war.

Rich. 'Twas odds, belike, when valiant Warwick fled:
Oft have I heard his praises in pursuit,
But ne'er, till now, his scandal of retire.

War. Nor now my scandal, Richard, dost thou hear:
For thou shalt know this strong right hand of mine
Can pluck the diadem from faint Henry's head,
And wring the awful sceptre from his fist;
Were he as famous and as bold in war,
As he is fam'd for mildness, peace, and prayer.

Rich. I know it well, Lord Warwick: blame me not;
'Tis love, I bear thy glories, makes me speak.
But, in this troublous time, what's to be done?
Shall we go throw away our coats of steel,
And wrap our bodies in black mourning gowns,
Numb'ring our Ave-Maries with our beads?
Or shall we on the helmets of our foes
Tell our devotion with revengeful arms?
If for the last, say—Ay, and to it, lords.

War. Why, therefore Warwick came to seek you out;
And therefore comes my brother Montague.
Attend me, lords. The proud insulting queen,
With Clifford, and the haught Northumberland,
And of their feather, many more proud birds,
Have wrought the easy-melting king like wax.
He swore consent to your succession,
His oath enrolled in the parliament;
And now to London all the crew are gone,
To frustrate both his oath, and what beside
May make against the house of Lancaster.
Their power, I think, is thirty thousand strong:
Now, if the help of Norfolk, and myself,
With all the friends that thou, brave earl of March,
Amongst the loving Welshmen canst procure,
Will but amount to five and twenty thousand,
Why, *Via!* to London will we march amain;
And once again bestride our foaming steeds,
And once again cry—Charge upon our foes!
But never once again turn back, and fly.

Rich. Ay, now, methinks, I hear great Warwick speak:
Ne'er may he live to see a sunshine day,
That cries—Retire, if Warwick bid him stay.

Edw. Lord Warwick, on thy shoulder will I lean;
And when thou fall'st, (as God forbid the hour!)
Must Edward fall, which peril heaven forefend!

War. No longer earl of March, but duke of York;
The next degree is, England's royal throne:
For king of England shalt thou be proclaim'd
In every borough as we pass along;
And he that throws not up his cap for joy,

Shall for the fault make forfeit of his head.
King Edward,—valiant Richard,—Montague,—
Stay we no longer dreaming of renown,
But sound the trumpets, and about our task.
Rich. Then, Clifford, were thy heart as hard as steel
(As thou hast shown it flinty by thy deeds),
I come to pierce it,—or to give thee mine.
Edw. Then strike up, drums;—God, and Saint George, for us!

Enter a Messenger.

War. How now, what news?
Mess. The duke of Norfolk sends you word by me,
The queen is coming with a puissant host;
And craves your company for speedy counsel.
War. Why then it sorts, brave warriors: Let's away. [*Exeunt.*

SCENE II. *Before* York.

Enter KING HENRY, QUEEN MARGARET, *the* PRINCE OF WALES, CLIFFORD, *and* NORTHUMBERLAND, *with* Forces.

Q. Mar. Welcome, my lord, to this brave town of York.
Yonder's the head of that arch enemy,
That sought to be encompass'd with your crown:
Doth not the object cheer your heart, my lord?
K. Hen. Ay, as the rocks cheer them that fear their wreck;—
To see this sight, it irks my very soul.—
Withhold revenge, dear God! 'tis not my fault,
Not wittingly have I infringed my vow.
Clif. My gracious liege, this too much lenity
And harmful pity, must be laid aside.
To whom do lions cast their gentle looks?
Not to the beast that would usurp their den.
Whose hand is that the forest bear doth lick?
Not his, that spoils her young before her face.
Who 'scapes the lurking serpent's mortal sting?
Not he, that sets his foot upon her back.
The smallest worm will turn, being trodden on;
And doves will peck, in safeguard of their brood.
Ambitious York did level at thy crown,
Thou smiling, while he knit his angry brows:
He, but a duke, would have his son a king,
And raise his issue, like a loving sire;
Thou, being a king, bless'd with a goodly son,
Did'st yield consent to disinherit him,
Which argued thee a most unloving father.
Unreasonable creatures feed their young:
And though man's face be fearful to their eyes,
Yet, in protection of their tender ones,
Who hath not seen them (even with those wings
Which sometime they have us'd with fearful flight),
Make war with him that climb'd unto their nest,
Offering their own lives in their young's defence?
For shame, my liege, make them your precedent!
Were it not pity that this goodly boy
Should lose his birthright by his father's fault;
And long hereafter say unto his child,—
What my great grandfather and grandsire got,
My careless father fondly gave away?
Ah, what a shame were this! Look on the boy;
And let his manly face, which promiseth
Successful fortune, steel thy melting heart,
To hold thine own, and leave thine own with him.
K. Hen. Full well hath Clifford play'd the orator,
Inferring arguments of mighty force.
But, Clifford, tell me, didst thou never hear,—
That things ill got had ever bad success?
And happy always was it for that son,
Whose father for his hoarding went to hell?
I'll leave my son my virtuous deeds behind;
And 'would, my father had left me no more!
For all the rest is held at such a rate,
As brings a thousand fold more care to keep,
Than in possession any jot of pleasure.
Ah, cousin York! 'would thy best friends did know,
How it doth grieve me that thy head is here!
Q. Mar. My lord, cheer up your spirits; our foes are nigh,
And this soft courage makes your followers faint.
You promis'd knighthood to our forward son;
Unsheath your sword, and dub him presently.—
Edward, kneel down.
K. Hen. Edward Plantagenet, arise a knight;
And learn this lesson,—Draw thy sword in right.
Prince. My gracious father, by your kingly leave,
I'll draw it as apparent to the crown,
And in that quarrel use it to the death.
Clif. Why, that is spoken like a toward prince.

Enter a Messenger.

Mess. Royal commanders, be in readiness:
For, with a band of thirty thousand men,
Comes Warwick, backing of the duke of York;
And, in the towns as they do march along,
Proclaims him king, and many fly to him:
Darraign your battle, for they are at hand.
Clif. I would, your highness would depart the field:
The queen hath best success, when you are absent.
Q. Mar. Ay, good my lord, and leave us to our fortune.
K. Hen. Why, that's my fortune too; therefore I'll stay.
North. Be it with resolution then to fight.
Prince. My royal father, cheer these noble lords,
And hearten those that fight in your defence:
Unsheath your sword, good father; cry, *Saint George!*

March. Enter EDWARD, GEORGE, RICHARD, WARWICK, NORFOLK, MONTAGUE, *and* Soldiers.

Edw. Now, perjur'd Henry, wilt thou kneel for grace,
And set thy diadem upon my head;
Or bide the mortal fortune of the field?
Q. Mar. Go, rate thy minions, proud insulting boy!
Becomes it thee to be thus bold in terms,
Before thy sovereign, and thy lawful king?
Edw. I am his king, and he should bow his keee;
I was adopted heir by his consent;
Since when, his oath is broke; for, as I hear,
You—that are king, though he do wear the crown,—
Have caus'd him, by new act of parliament,
To blot out me, and put his own son in.
Clif. And reason too;
Who should succeed the father, but the son?
Rich. Are you there, butcher?—O, I cannot speak!
Clif. Ay, crookback; here I stand to answer thee,
Or any he the proudest of thy sort.
Rich. 'Twas you that kill'd young Rutland, was it not?
Clif. Ay, and old York, and yet not satisfied.
Rich. For God's sake, lords, give signal to the fight.
War. What say'st thou, Henry, wilt thou yield the crown?
Q. Mar. Why, how now, long-tongu'd Warwick? dare you speak?
When you and I met at St. Albans last,
Your legs did better service than your hands.
War. Then 'twas my turn to fly, and now 'tis thine.
Clif. You said so much before, and yet you fled.
War. 'Twas not your valour, Clifford, drove me thence.
North. No, nor your manhood, that durst make you stay.

Rich. Northumberland, I hold thee reverently;—
Break off the parle; for scarce I can refrain
The execution of my big-swoln heart
Upon that Clifford, that cruel child-killer.
Clif. I slew thy father: Call'st thou him a child?
Rich. Ay, like a dastard, and a treacherous coward,
As thou didst kill our tender brother Rutland;
But, ere sunset, I'll make thee curse the deed.
K. Hen. Have done with words, my lords, and hear me speak.
Q. Mar. Defy them then, or else hold close thy lips.
K. Hen. I pr'ythee, give no limits to my tongue;
I am a king, and privileg'd to speak.
Clif. My liege, the wound, that bred this meeting here,
Cannot be cur'd by words; therefore be still.
Rich. Then, executioner, unsheath thy sword:
By him that made us all, I am resolv'd,
That Clifford's manhood lies upon his tongue.
Edw. Say, Henry, shall I have my right, or no?
A thousand men have broke their fasts to-day,
That ne'er shall dine, unless thou yield the crown.
War. If thou deny, their blood upon thy head;
For York in justice puts his armour on.
Prince. If that be right, which Warwick says is right,
There is no wrong, but every thing is right.
Rich. Whoever got thee, there thy mother stands;
For, well I wot, thou hast thy mother's tongue.
Q. Mar. But thou art neither like thy sire, nor dam;
But like a foul misshapen stigmatick,
Mark'd by the destinies to be avoided,
As venom toads, or lizards' dreadful stings.
Rich. Iron of Naples, hid with English gilt,
Whose father bears the title of a king,
(As if a channel should be call'd the sea),
Sham'st thou not, knowing whence thou art extraught,
To let thy tongue detect thy base-born heart?
Edw. A wisp of straw were worth a thousand crowns,
To make this shameless callet know herself—
Helen of Greece was fairer far than thou,
Although thy husband may be Menelaus;
And ne'er was Agamemnon's brother wrong'd
By that false woman, as this king by thee.
His father revell'd in the heart of France,
And tam'd the king, and made the Dauphin stoop;
And, had he match'd according to his state,
He might have kept that glory to this day:
But, when he took a beggar to his bed,
And grac'd thy poor sire with his bridal day:
Even then that sunshine brew'd a shower for him,
That wash'd his father's fortunes forth of France,
And heap'd sedition on his crown at home.
For what hath broach'd this tumult, but thy pride?
Hadst thou been meek, our title still had slept;
And we, in pity of the gentle king,
Had slipp'd our claim until another age.
Geo. But, when we saw our sunshine made thy spring,
And that thy summer bred us no increase,
We set the axe to thy usurping root:
And though the edge hath something hit ourselves,
Yet, know thou, since we have begun to strike,
We'll never leave, till we have hewn thee down,
Or bath'd thy growing with our heated bloods.
Edw. And, in this resolution, I defy thee;
Not willing any longer conference,
Since thou deny'st the gentle king to speak.—
Sound trumpets!—let our bloody colours wave!—
And either victory, or else a grave.
Q. Mar. Stay, Edward.
Edw. No, wrangling woman; we'll no longer stay;
These words will cost ten thousand lives to-day.
[*Exeunt.*

SCENE III.

A Field of Battle between Towton *and* Saxton, *in* Yorkshire.

Alarums: Excursions. Enter WARWICK.

War. Forspent with toil, as runners with a race,
I lay me down a little while to breathe:
For strokes receiv'd, and many blows repaid,
Have robb'd my strong-knit sinews of their strength,
And, spite of spite, needs must I rest awhile.

Enter EDWARD, *running.*

Edw. Smile, gentle heaven! or strike, ungentle death!
For this world frowns, and Edward's sun is clouded.
War. How now, my lord? what hap? what hope of good?

Enter GEORGE.

Geo. Our hap is loss, our hope but sad despair;
Our ranks are broke, and ruin follows us:
What counsel give you, whither shall we fly?
Edw. Bootless is flight, they follow us with wings;
And weak we are, and cannot shun pursuit.

Enter RICHARD.

Rich. Ah, Warwick, why hast thou withdrawn thyself?
Thy brother's blood the thirsty earth hath drunk,
Broach'd with the steely point of Clifford's lance:
And, in the very pangs of death, he cried,—
Like to a dismal clangor heard from far,—
Warwick, revenge! brother, revenge my death!
So underneath the belly of their steeds,
That stain'd their fetlocks in his smoking blood,
The noble gentleman gave up the ghost.
War. Then let the earth be drunken with our blood:
I'll kill my horse, because I will not fly.
Why stand we like soft-hearted women here,
Wailing our losses, whiles the foe doth rage;
And look upon, as if the tragedy
Were play'd in jest by counterfeiting actors?
Here on my knee I vow to God above,
I'll never pause again, never stand still,
Till either death hath clos'd these eyes of mine,
Or fortune given me measure of revenge.
Edw. O Warwick, I do bend my knee with thine;
And, in this vow, do chain my soul to thine.—
And, ere my knee rise from the earth's cold face,
I throw my hands, mine eyes, my heart to thee,
Thou setter up and plucker down of kings!
Beseeching thee,—if with thy will it stands,
That to my foes this body must be prey,—
Yet that thy brazen gates of heaven may ope,
And give sweet passage to my sinful soul!—
Now, lords, take leave until we meet again,
Where'er it be, in heaven, or on earth.
Rich. Brother, give me thy hand; and, gentle Warwick,
Let me embrace thee in my weary arms:—
I, that did never weep, now melt with woe,
That winter should cut off our spring-time so.
War. Away, away! Once more sweet lords, farewell.
Geo. Yet let us all together to our troops,
And give them leave to fly that will not stay;
And call them pillars, that will stand to us;
And, if they thrive, promise them such rewards

As victors wear at the Olympian games:
This may plant courage in their quailing breasts;
For yet is hope of life, and victory.—
Fore-slow no longer, make we hence amain.
[*Exeunt.*

SCENE IV. *The same. Another Part of the Field.*

Excursions. Enter RICHARD *and* CLIFFORD.

Rich. Now, Clifford, I have singled thee alone:
Suppose, this arm is for the duke of York,
And this for Rutland; both bound to revenge,
Wert thou environ'd with a brazen wall.

Clif. Now, Richard, I am with thee here alone:
This is the hand, that stabb'd thy father York;
And this the hand that slew thy brother Rutland;
And here's the heart that triumphs in their death,
And cheers these hands, that slew thy sire and brother,
To execute the like upon thyself;
And so, have at thee.
[*They fight.* WARWICK *enters;* CLIFFORD *flies.*

Rich. Nay, Warwick, single out some other chase;
For I myself will hunt this wolf to death.
[*Exeunt.*

SCENE V. *Another Part of the Field.*

Alarum. Enter KING HENRY.

K. Hen. This battle fares like to the morning's war,
When dying clouds contend with growing light;
What time the shepherd, blowing of his nails,
Can neither call it perfect day, nor night.
Now sways it this way, like a mighty sea,
Forc'd by the tide to combat with the wind;
Now sways it that way, like the selfsame sea
Forc'd to retire by fury of the wind:
Sometime, the flood prevails; and then the wind;
Now, one the better; then, another best;
Both tugging to be victors, breast to breast,
Yet neither conqueror, nor conquered:
So is the equal poise of this fell war.
Here on this molehill will I sit me down.
To whom God will, there be the victory!
For Margaret my queen, and Clifford too,
Have chid me from the battle; swearing both,
They prosper best of all when I am thence.
Would, I were dead! if God's good will were so:
For what is in this world, but grief and woe?
O God! methinks, it were a happy life,
To be no better than a homely swain;
To sit upon a hill, as I do now,
To carve out dials quaintly, point by point,
Thereby to see the minutes how they run:
How many make the hour full complete,
How many hours bring about the day,
How many days will finish up the year,
How many years a mortal man may live.
When this is known, then to divide the times:
So many hours must I tend my flock;
So many hours must I take my rest;
So many hours must I contemplate;
So many hours must I sport myself;
So many days my ewes have been with young;
So many weeks ere the poor fools will yean:
So many years ere I shall shear the fleece:
So minutes, hours, days, weeks, months, and years,
Pass'd over to the end they were created,
Would bring white hairs unto a quiet grave.
Ah, what a life were this! how sweet! how lovely!
Gives not the hawthorn bush a sweeter shade
To shepherds, looking on their silly sheep,
Than doth a rich embroider'd canopy
To kings, that fear their subjects' treachery?
O, yes it doth; a thousand fold it doth.
And, to conclude,—the shepherd's homely curds,
His cold thin drink out of his leather bottle,
His wonted sleep under a fresh tree's shade,
All which secure and sweetly he enjoys,
Is far beyond a prince's delicates,
His viands sparkling in a golden cup,
His body couched in a curious bed,
When care, mistrust, and treason wait on him.

Alarum. Enter a Son *that has killed his Father, dragging in the dead Body.*

Son. Ill blows the wind that profits no-body.—
This man, whom hand to hand I slew in fight,
May be possessed with some store of crowns:
And I, that haply take them from him now,
May yet ere night yield both my life and them
To some man else, as this dead man doth me.—
Who's this?—O God! it is my father's face,
Whom in this conflict I unawares have kill'd.
O heavy times, begetting such events!
From London by the king was I press'd forth;
My father, being the earl of Warwick's man,
Came on the part of York, press'd by his master;
And I, who at his hands receiv'd my life,
Have by my hands of life bereaved him.—
Pardon me, God, I knew not what I did!—
And pardon, father, for I knew not thee!—
My tears shall wipe away these bloody marks;
And no more words, till they have flow'd their fill.

K. Hen. O piteous spectacle! O bloody times!
Whilst lions war, and battle for their dens,
Poor harmless lambs abide their enmity.—
Weep, wretched man, I'll aid thee tear for tear;
And let our hearts, and eyes, like civil war,
Be blind with tears, and break o'ercharg'd with grief.

Enter a Father, *who has killed his Son, with the Body in his arms.*

Fath. Thou that so stoutly hast resisted me,
Give me thy gold, if thou hast any gold;
For I have bought it with a hundred blows.—
But let me see:—is this our foeman's face?
Ah, no, no, no, it is mine only son!—
Ah, boy, if any life be left in thee,
Throw up thine eye; see, see, what showers arise,
Blown with the windy tempest of my heart,
Upon thy wounds, that kill mine eye and heart!—
O, pity, God, this miserable age!—
What stratagems, how fell, how butcherly,
Erroneous, mutinous, and unnatural,
This deadly quarrel daily doth beget!—
O boy, thy father gave thee life too soon,
And hath bereft thee of thy life too late!

K. Hen. Woe above woe! grief more than common grief!
O, that my death would stay these ruthful deeds!—
O pity, pity, gentle heaven, pity!
The red rose and the white are on his face,
The fatal colours of our striving houses:
The one, his purple blood right well resembles;
The other, his pale cheeks, methinks, present!
Wither one rose, and let the other flourish!
If you contend, a thousand lives must wither.

Son. How will my mother, for a father's death,
Take on with me, and ne'er be satisfied?

Fath. How will my wife, for slaughter of my son,
Shed seas of tears, and ne'er be satisfied?

K. Hen. How will the country, for these woful chances,
Misthink the king, and not be satisfied?

Son. Was ever son, so ru'd a father's death?

Fath. Was ever father, so bemoan'd a son?

K. Hen. Was ever king, so griev'd for subjects' woe?
Much is your sorrow; mine, ten times so much.

Son. I'll bear thee hence, where I may weep my fill. [*Exit, with the Body.*

Fath. These arms of mine shall be thy windingsheet;
My heart, sweet boy, shall be thy sepulchre;
For from my heart thine image ne'er shall go.
My sighing breast shall be thy funeral bell;

And so obsequious will thy father be,
Sad for the loss of thee, having no more,
As Priam was for all his valiant sons.
I'll bear thee hence; and let them fight that will,
For I have murder'd where I should not kill.
[*Exit, with the Body.*

K. Hen. Sad-hearted men, much overgone with care,
Here sits a king more woful than you are.

Alarums: Excursions. Enter QUEEN MARGARET, PRINCE OF WALES, *and* EXETER.

Prince. Fly, father, fly! for all your friends are fled,
And Warwick rages like a chafed bull:
Away! for death doth hold us in pursuit.

Q. Mar. Mount you, my lord, towards Berwick post amain,
Edward and Richard, like a brace of greyhounds
Having the fearful flying hare in sight,
With fiery eyes, sparkling for very wrath,
And bloody steel grasp'd in their ireful hands,
Are at our backs; and therefore hence amain.

Exe. Away! for vengeance comes along with them;
Nay, stay not to expostulate, make speed;
Or else come after, I'll away before.

K. Hen. Nay, take me with thee, good sweet Exeter;
Not that I fear to stay, but love to go
Whither the queen intends. Forward; away!
[*Exeunt.*

SCENE VI. *The same.*

A loud Alarum. Enter CLIFFORD, *wounded.*

Clif. Here burns my candle out, ay, here it dies,
Which, while it lasted, gave King Henry light.
O, Lancaster! I fear thy overthrow,
More than my body's parting with my soul.
My love, and fear, glew'd many friends to thee;
And, now I fall, thy tough commixtures melt.
Impairing Henry, strength'ning mis-proud York,
The common people swarm like summer flies:
And whither fly the gnats, but to the sun?
And who shines now but Henry's enemies?
O Phœbus! hadst thou never given consent
That Phaeton should check thy fiery steeds,
Thy burning car never had scorch'd the earth:
And, Henry, hadst thou sway'd as kings should do,
Or as thy father, and his father did,
Giving no ground unto the house of York,
They never then had sprung like summer flies;
I, and ten thousand in this luckless realm,
Had left no mourning widows for our death,
And thou this day hadst kept thy chair in peace.
For what doth cherish weeds but gentle air?
And what makes robbers bold, but too much lenity?
Bootless are plaints, and cureless are my wounds;
No way to fly, nor strength to hold out flight:
The foe is merciless, and will not pity;
For at their hands I have deserv'd no pity.
The air hath got into my deadly wounds,
And much effuse of blood doth make me faint:—
Come, York, and Richard, Warwick, and the rest;
I stabb'd your fathers' bosoms, split my breast.
[*He faints.*

Alarum and retreat. Enter EDWARD, GEORGE, RICHARD, MONTAGUE, WARWICK, *and* Soldiers.

Edw. Now breathe we, lords; good fortune bids us pause,
And smooth the frowns of war with peaceful looks.—
Some troops pursue the bloody-minded queen;—
That led calm Henry, though he were a king,
As doth a sail, fill'd with a fretting gust,
Command an argosy to stem the waves.
But think you, lords, that Clifford fled with them?

War. No, 'tis impossible he should escape:
For, though before his face I speak the words,
Your brother Richard mark'd him for the grave:
And wheresoe'er he is, he's surely dead.
[CLIFFORD *groans and dies.*

Edw. Whose soul is that which takes her heavy leave?

Rich. A deadly groan, like life and death's departing.

Edw. See who it is; and now the battle's ended,
If friend, or foe, let him be gently us'd.

Rich. Revoke that doom of mercy, for 'tis Clifford;
Who not contented that he lopp'd the branch
In hewing Rutland when his leaves put forth,
But set his murdering knife unto the root
From whence that tender spray did sweetly spring,
I mean our princely father, duke of York.

War. From off the gates of York fetch down the head,
Your father's head, which Clifford placed there:
Instead whereof, let this supply the room;
Measure for measure must be answered.

Edw. Bring forth that fatal screechowl to our house,
That nothing sung but death to us and ours:
Now death shall stop his dismal threatening sound,
And his ill boding tongue no more shall speak.
[Attendants *bring the Body forward.*

War. I think his understanding is bereft:—
Speak, Clifford, dost thou know who speaks to thee?—
Dark cloudy death o'ershades his beams of life,
And he nor sees, nor hears us what we say.

Rich. O, 'would he did! and, so, perhaps he doth;
'Tis but his policy to counterfeit,
Because he would avoid such bitter taunts,
Which in the time of death he gave our father.

Geo. If so thou think'st, vex him with eager words.

Rich. Clifford, ask mercy, and obtain no grace.

Edw. Clifford, repent in bootless penitence.

War. Clifford, devise excuses for thy faults.

Geo. While we devise fell tortures for thy faults.

Rich. Thou didst love York, and I am son to York.

Edw. Thou pitied'st Rutland, I will pity thee.

Geo. Where's Captain Margaret to fence you now?

War. They mock thee, Clifford! swear as thou wast wont.

Rich. What, not an oath? nay, then the world goes hard,
When Clifford cannot spare his friends an oath:
I know by that, he's dead; And by my soul,
If this right hand would buy two hours' life,
That I in all despite might rail at him,
This hand should chop it off; and with the issuing blood
Stifle the villain, whose unstanched thirst
York and young Rutland could not satisfy.

War. Ay, but he's dead: Off with the traitor's head,
And rear it in the place your father's stands.—
And now to London with triumphant march,
There to be crowned England's royal king.
From whence shall Warwick cut the sea to France,
And ask the lady Bona for thy queen:
So shalt thou sinew both these lands together;
And having France thy friend, thou shalt not dread
The scatter'd foe, that hopes to rise again:
For though they cannot greatly sting to hurt,
Yet look to have them buz, to offend thine ears.

First, will I see the coronation:
And then to Britany I'll cross the sea,
To effect this marriage, so it please my lord.
Edw. Even as thou wilt, sweet Warwick, let it be:
For on thy shoulder do I build my seat;
And never will I undertake the thing,
Wherein thy counsel and consent is wanting.—
Richard, I will create thee duke of Gloster;—
And George, of Clarence;—Warwick, as ourself,
Shall do, and undo, as him pleaseth best.
Rich. Let me be duke of Clarence; George, of Gloster;
For Gloster's dukedom is too ominous.
War. Tut, that's a foolish observation;
Richard, be duke of Gloster: Now to London,
To see these honours in possession. [*Exeunt.*

ACT III.

SCENE I. *A Chase in the North of* England.

Enter two Keepers, *with Crossbows in their Hands.*

1 *Keep.* Under this thick grown brake we'll shroud ourselves;
For through this laund anon the deer will come;
And in this covert will we make our stand,
Culling the principal of all the deer.
2 *Keep.* I'll stay above the hill, so both may shoot.
1 *Keep.* That cannot be; the noise of thy crossbow
Will scare the herd, and so my shoot is lost.
Here stand we both, and aim we at the best:
And, for the time shall not seem tedious,
I'll tell thee what befell me on a day,
In this self place where now we mean to stand.
2 *Keep.* Here comes a man, let's stay till he be past.

Enter KING HENRY, *disguised, with a Prayerbook.*

K. Hen. From Scotland am I stol'n, even of pure love,
To greet mine own land with my wishful sight.
No, Harry, Harry, 'tis no land of thine;
Thy place is fill'd, thy sceptre wrung from thee,
Thy balm wash'd off, wherewith thou wast anointed:
No bending knee will call thee Cæsar now,
No humble suitors press to speak for right,
No, not a man comes for redress of thee;
For how can I help them, and not myself?
1 *Keep.* Ay, here's a deer whose skin's a keeper's fee:
This is the *quondam* king; let's seize upon him.
K. Hen. Let me embrace these sour adversities;
For wise men say, it is the wisest course.
2 *Keep.* Why linger we? let us lay hands upon him.
1 *Keep.* Forbear awhile; we'll hear a little more.
K. Hen. My queen, and son, are gone to France for aid;
And, as I hear, the great commanding Warwick
Is thither gone, to crave the French king's sister
To wife for Edward: If this news be true,
Poor queen, and, son, your labour is but lost;
For Warwick is a subtle orator,
And Lewis a prince soon won with moving words.
By this account, then, Margaret may win him;
For she's a woman to be pitied much:
Her sighs will make a battery in his breast;
Her tears will pierce into a marble heart;
The tiger will be mild while she doth mourn;
And Nero will be tainted with remorse,
To hear, and see, her plaints, her brinish tears.
Ay, but she's come to beg; Warwick, to give:
She, on his left side, craving aid for Henry;
He, on his right, asking a wife for Edward.
She weeps, and says—her Henry is depos'd;
He smiles, and says—his Edward is enstall'd;
That she, poor wretch, for grief can speak no more:
Whiles Warwick tells his title, smooths the wrong,
Inferreth arguments of mighty strength;
And, in conclusion, wins the king from her,
With promise of his sister, and what else,
To strengthen and support King Edward's place.
O Margaret, thus 'twill be; and thou, poor soul,
Art then forsaken, as thou went'st forlorn.
2 *Keep.* Say, what art thou, that talk'st of kings and queens?
K. Hen. More than I seem, and less than I was born to:
A man at least, for less I should not be;
And men may talk of kings, and why not I?
2 *Keep.* Ay, but thou talk'st as if thou wert a king.
K. Hen. Why, so I am, in mind; and that's enough.
2 *Keep.* But, if thou be a king, where is thy crown?
K. Hen. My crown is in my heart, not on my head;
Not deck'd with diamonds and Indian stones,
Nor to be seen: my crown is call'd content;
A crown it is, that seldom kings enjoy.
2 *Keep.* Well, if you be a king crown'd with content,
Your crown content, and you, must be contented
To go along with us: for, as we think,
You are the king, King Edward hath depos'd;
And we his subjects, sworn in all allegiance,
Will apprehend you as his enemy.
K. Hen. But did you never swear, and break an oath?
2 *Keep.* No, never such an oath, nor will not now.
K. Hen. Where did you dwell, when I was king of England?
2 *Keep.* Here in this country, where we now remain.
K. Hen. I was anointed king at nine months old;
My father and my grandfather were kings;
And you were sworn true subjects unto me:
And, tell me then, have you not broke your oaths?
1 *Keep.* No;
For we were subjects, but while you were king.
K. Hen. Why, am I dead? do I not breathe a man?
Ah, simple men, you know not what you swear.
Look, as I blow this feather from my face,
And as the air blows it to me again,
Obeying with my wind when I do blow,
And yielding to another when it blows,
Commanded always by the greater gust;
Such is the lightness of you common men.
But do not break your oaths; for, of that sin
My mild entreaty shall not make you guilty.
Go where you will, the king shall be commanded;
And be you kings; command, and I'll obey.
1 *Keep.* We are true subjects to the king, King Edward.
K. Hen. So would you be again to Henry,
If he were seated as King Edward is.
1 *Keep.* We charge you, in God's name, and in the king's,
To go with us unto the officers.
K. Hen. In God's name, lead; your king's name be obey'd:
And what God will, then let your king perform;
And what he will, I humbly yield unto.
[*Exeunt.*

SCENE II. London. *A Room in the Palace.*

Enter KING EDWARD, GLOSTER, CLARENCE, *and* LADY GREY.

K. Edw. Brother of Gloster, at Saint Albans' field
This lady's husband, Sir John Grey was slain,
His lands then seiz'd on by the conqueror:
Her suit is now, to repossess those lands;
Which we in justice cannot well deny,
Because in quarrel of the house of York
The worthy gentleman did lose his life.

Glo. Your highness shall do well to grant her suit;
It were dishonour to deny it her.

K. Edw. It were no less; but yet I'll make a pause.

Glo. Yea! is it so?
I see, the lady hath a thing to grant,
Before the king will grant her humble suit.

Clar. He knows the game; How true he keeps the wind? [*Aside.*

Glo. Silence! [*Aside.*

K. Edw. Widow, we will consider of your suit;
And come some other time to know our mind.

L. Grey. Right gracious lord, I cannot brook delay:
May it please your highness to resolve me now;
And what your pleasure is, shall satisfy me.

Glo. [*Aside.*] Ay, widow? then I'll warrant you all your lands,
And if what pleases him, shall pleasure you.
Fight closer, or, good faith, you'll catch a blow.

Clar. I fear her not, unless she chance to fall. [*Aside.*

Glo. God forbid that! for he'll take vantages. [*Aside.*

K. Edw. How many children hast thou, widow? tell me.

Clar. I think, he means to beg a child of her. [*Aside.*

Glo. Nay, whip me then; he'll rather give her two. [*Aside.*

L. Grey. Three, my most gracious lord.

Glo. You shall have four, if you'll be rul'd by him. [*Aside.*

K. Edw. 'Twere pity, they should lose their father's land.

L. Grey. Be pitiful, dread lord, and grant it then.

K. Edw. Lords, give us leave; I'll try this widow's wit.

Glo. Ay, good leave have you; for you will have leave,
Till youth take leave, and leave you to the crutch.

[GLO. *and* CLAR. *retire to the other side.*

K. Edw. Now tell me, madam, do you love your children?

L. Grey. Ay, full as dearly as I love myself.

K. Edw. And, would you not do much, to do them good?

L. Grey. To do them good, I would sustain some harm.

K. Edw. Then get your husband's lands, to do them good.

L. Grey. Therefore I came unto your majesty.

K. Edw. I'll tell you how these lands are to be got.

L. Grey. So shall you bind me to your highness' service.

K. Edw. What service wilt thou do me, if I give them?

L. Grey. What you command, that rests in me to do.

K. Edw. But you will take exceptions to my boon.

L. Grey. No, gracious lord, except I cannot do it.

K. Edw. Ay, but thou canst do what I mean to ask.

L. Grey. Why, then I will do what your grace commands.

Glo. He plies her hard; and much rain wears the marble. [*Aside.*

Clar. As red as fire! nay, then her wax must melt. [*Aside.*

L. Grey. Why stops my lord? shall I not hear my task?

K. Edw. An easy task; 'tis but to love a king.

L. Grey. That's soon perform'd, because I am a subject,

K. Edw. Why then, thy husband's lands I freely give thee.

L. Grey. I take my leave with many thousand thanks.

Glo. The match is made; she seals it with a curt'sy.

K. Edw. But stay thee, 'tis the fruits of love I mean.

L. Grey. The fruits of love, I mean, my loving liege.

K. Edw. Ay, but I fear me, in another sense.
What love, think'st thou, I sue so much to get?

L. Grey. My love till death, my humble thanks, my prayers;
That love, which virtue begs, and virtue grants.

K. Edw. No, by my troth, I did not mean such love.

L. Grey. Why, then you mean not as I thought you did.

K. Edw. But now you partly may perceive my mind.

L. Grey. My mind will never grant what I perceive
Your highness aims at, if I aim aright.

K. Edw. To tell thee plain, I aim to lie with thee.

L. Grey. To tell you plain, I had rather lie in prison.

K. Edw. Why, then thou shalt not have thy husband's lands.

L. Grey. Why, then mine honesty shall be my dower.
For by that loss I will not purchase them.

K. Edw. Therein thou wrong'st thy children mightily.

L. Grey. Herein your highness wrongs both them and me.
But, mighty lord, this merry inclination
Accords not with the sadness of my suit;
Please you dismiss me, either with ay, or no.

K. Edw. Ay; if thou wilt say ay, to my request;
No; if thou dost say no, to my demand.

L. Grey. Then, no, my lord. My suit is at an end.

Glo. The widow likes him not, she knits her brows. [*Aside.*

Clar. He is the bluntest wooer in Christendom. [*Aside.*

K. Edw. [*Aside.*] Her looks do argue her replete with modesty;
Her words do show her wit incomparable;
All her perfections challenge sovereignty:
One way, or other, she is for a king;
And she shall be my love, or else my queen.—
Say, that king Edward take thee for his queen?

L. Grey. 'Tis better said than done, my gracious lord:
I am a subject fit to jest withal,
But far unfit to be a sovereign.

K. Edw. Sweet widow, by my state I swear to thee,
I speak no more than what my soul intends;
And that is, to enjoy thee for my love.

L. Grey. And that is more than I will yield unto:
I know I am too mean to be your queen:
And yet too good to be your concubine.

K. Edw. You cavil, widow; I did mean, my queen.

L. Grey. 'Twill grieve your grace, my sons should call you—father.

K. Edw. No more than when thy daughters call thee mother.
Thou art a widow, and thou hast some children;
And, by God's mother, I, being but a bachelor,
Have other some: why, tis a happy thing
To be the father unto many sons.
Answer no more, for thou shalt be my queen.

Glo. The ghostly father now hath done his shrift. [*Aside.*

Clar. When he was made a shriver, 'twas for shift. [*Aside.*

K. Edw. Brothers, you muse what chat we two have had.

Glo. The widow likes it not, for she looks very sad.

K. Edw. You'd think it strange if I should marry her.

Clar. To whom, my lord?

K. Edw. Why, Clarence, to myself.

Glo. That would be ten days' wonder, at the least.

Clar. That's a day longer than a wonder lasts.

Glo. By so much is the wonder in extremes.

K. Edw. Well, jest on, brothers: I can tell you both,
Her suit is granted for her husband's lands.

Enter a Nobleman.

Nob. My gracious lord, Henry your foe is taken,
And brought your prisoner, to your palace gate.

K. Edw. See, that he be convey'd unto the Tower:—
And go we, brothers, to the man that took him,
To question of his apprehension.—
Widow, go you along;—Lords, use her honourable.

[*Exeunt* K. Edw. L. Grey, Clar. *and* Lord.

Glo. Ay, Edward will use women honourably.
'Would, he were wasted, marrow, bones, and all,
That from his loins, no hopeful branch may spring,
To cross me from the golden time I look for!
And yet, between my soul's desire and me
(The lustful Edward's title buried),
Is Clarence, Henry, and his son young Edward,
And all the unlook'd-for issue of their bodies,
To take their rooms, ere I can place myself:
A cold premeditation for my purpose!
Why, then I do but dream on sovereignty;
Like one that stands upon a promontory,
And spies a far-off shore where he would tread,
Wishing his foot were equal with his eye;
And chides the sea that sunders him from thence,
Saying—he'll lade it dry to have his way.
So do I wish the crown, being so far off;
And so I chide the means that keep me from it;
And so I say—I'll cut the causes off,
Flattering me with impossibilities.—
My eye's too quick, my heart o'erweens too much,
Unless my hand and strength could equal them.
Well, say there is no kingdom then for Richard;
What other pleasure can the world afford?
I'll make my heaven in a lady's lap,
And deck my body in gay ornaments,
And witch sweet ladies with my words and looks.
O miserable thought! and more unlikely,
Than to accomplish twenty golden crowns!
Why, love forswore me in my mother's womb:
And, for I should not deal in her soft laws,
She did corrupt frail nature with some bribe
To shrink mine arm up like a wither'd shrub;
To make an envious mountain on my back,
Where sits deformity to mock my body;
To shape my legs of an unequal size;
To disproportion me in every part,
Like to a chaos, or an unlick'd bear-whelp,
That carries no impression like the dam.
And am I then a man to be belov'd?
O, monstrous fault, to harbour such a thought!
Then, since this earth affords no joy to me,
But to command, to check, to o'erbear such
As are of better person than myself,
I'll make my heaven—to dream upon the crown;
And, whiles I live, to account this world but hell,
Until my misshap'd trunk that bears this head,
Be round impaled with a glorious crown.
And yet I know not how to get the crown,
For many lives stand between me and home:
And I, like one lost in a thorny wood,
That rents the thorns, and is rent with the thorns;
Seeking a way, and straying from the way;
Not knowing how to find the open air,
But toiling desperately to find it out,—
Torment myself to catch the English crown:
And from that torment I will free myself,
Or hew my way out with a bloody axe.
Why, I can smile, and murder while I smile;
And cry, content, to that which grieves my heart;
And wet my cheeks with artificial tears,
And frame my face to all occasions.
I'll drown more sailors than the mermaid shall;
I'll slay more gazers than the basilisk;
I'll play the orator as well as Nestor,
Deceive more slily than Ulysses could,
And, like a Sinon, take another Troy;
I can add colours to the cameleon;
Change shapes, with Proteus, for advantages,
And set the murd'rous Machiavel to school.
Can I do this, and cannot get a crown?
Tut! were it further off, I'll pluck it down.
[*Exit.*

SCENE III. France. *A Room in the Palace.*

Flourish. Enter Lewis, *the* French King, *and* Lady Bona, *attended; the* King *takes his State. Then enter* Queen Margaret, Prince Edward *her Son, and the* Earl of Oxford.

K. Lew. Fair Queen of England, worthy Margaret, [*Rising.*
Sit down with us; it ill befits thy state,
And birth, that thou should'st stand, while Lewis doth sit.

Q. Mar. No, mighty King of France; now Margaret
Must strike her sail, and learn awhile to serve,
Where kings command. I was, I must confess,
Great Albion's queen in former golden days:
But now mischance hath trod my title down,
And with dishonour, laid me on the ground;
Where I must take like seat unto my fortune,
And to my humble seat conform myself.

K. Lew. Why, say, fair queen, whence springs this deep despair?

Q. Mar. From such a cause as fills mine eyes with tears,
And stops my tongue, while heart is drown'd in cares.

K. Lew. Whate'er it be, be thou still like thyself,
And sit thee by our side: yield not thy neck
[*Seats her by him.*
To fortune's yoke, but let thy dauntless mind
Still ride in triumph over all mischance.
Be plain, Queen Margaret, and tell thy grief;
It shall be eas'd, if France can yield relief.

Q. Mar. Those gracious words revive my drooping thoughts,
And give my tongue-tied sorrows leave to speak.
Now, therefore be it known to noble Lewis,—
That, Henry, sole possessor of my love,
Is, of a king, become a banish'd man,
And forc'd to live in Scotland a forlorn;
While proud ambitious Edward, duke of York,
Usurps the regal title, and the seat
Of England's true anointed lawful king.
This is the cause, that I, poor Margaret,—
With this my son, Prince Edward, Henry's heir,—
Am come to crave thy just and lawful aid;
And, if thou fail us, all our hope is done:

Scotland hath will to help, but cannot help;
Our people and our peers are both misled,
Our treasure seiz'd, our soldiers put to flight,
And, as thou seest, ourselves in heavy plight.

K. Lew. Renowned queen, with patience calm the storm,
While we bethink a means to break it off.

Q. Mar. The more we stay, the stronger grows our foe.

K. Lew. The more I stay, the more I'll succour thee.

Q. Mar. O, but impatience waiteth on true sorrow:
And see, where comes the breeder of my sorrow.

Enter WARWICK, *attended.*

K. Lew. What's he, approacheth boldly to our presence!

Q. Mar. Our earl of Warwick, Edward's greatest friend.

K. Lew. Welcome, brave Warwick; What brings thee to France?
[*Descending from his State,* QUEEN MARGARET *rises.*

Q. Mar. Ay, now begins a second storm to rise;
For this is he that moves both wind and tide.

War. From worthy Edward, king of Albion,
My lord and sovereign, and thy vowed friend,
I come,—in kindness, and unfeigned love,—
First, to do greetings to thy royal person;
And, then, to crave a league of amity;
And, lastly, to confirm that amity
With nuptial knot, if thou vouchsafe to grant
That virtuous Lady Bona, thy fair sister,
To England's king in lawful marriage.

Q. Mar. If that go forward, Henry's hope is done.

War. And, gracious madam, [*To* BONA], in our king's behalf,
I am commanded, with your leave and favour,
Humbly to kiss your hand, and with my tongue
To tell the passion of my sovereign's heart;
Where fame, late entering at his heedful ears,
Hath plac'd thy beauty's image, and thy virtue.

Q. Mar. King Lewis,—and Lady Bona,—hear me speak,
Before you answer Warwick. His demand
Springs not from Edward's well meant honest love,
But from deceit, bred by necessity;
For how can tyrants safely govern home,
Unless abroad they purchase great alliance?
To prove him tyrant, this reason may suffice,—
That Henry liveth still: but were he dead,
Yet here Prince Edward stands, King Henry's son.
Look therefore, Lewis, that by this league and marriage
Thou draw not on thy danger and dishonour:
For though usurpers sway the rule awhile,
Yet heavens are just, and time suppresseth wrongs.

War. Injurious Margaret!

Prince. And why not queen?

War. Because thy father Henry did usurp;
And thou no more art prince, than she is queen.

Oxf. Then Warwick disannuls great John of Gaunt,
Which did subdue the greatest part of Spain;
And, after John of Gaunt, Henry the Fourth,
Whose wisdom was a mirror to the wisest;
And, after that wise prince, Henry the Fifth,
Who by his prowess conquered all France:
From these our Henry lineally descends.

War. Oxford, how haps it, in this smooth discourse,
You told not, how Henry the Sixth hath lost
All that which Henry the Fifth had gotten?
Methinks, these peers of France should smile at that.
But for the rest,—You tell a pedigree
Of threescore and two years; a silly time
To make prescription for a kingdom's worth.

Oxf. Why, Warwick, canst thou speak against thy liege,
Whom thou obeyedst thirty and six years,
And not bewray thy treason with a blush?

War. Can Oxford, that did ever fence the right,
Now buckler falsehood with a pedigree?
For shame, leave Henry, and call Edward king.

Oxf. Call him my king, by whose injurious doom
My elder brother, the Lord Aubrey Vere,
Was done to death? and more than so, my father,
Even in the downfall of his mellow'd years,
When nature brought him to the door of death?
No, Warwick, no; while life upholds this arm,
This arm upholds the house of Lancaster.

War. And I the house of York.

K. Lew. Queen Margaret, Prince Edward, and Oxford,
Vouchsafe, at our request, to stand aside,
While I use further conference with Warwick.

Q. Mar. Heaven grant, that Warwick's words bewitch him not!
[*Retiring with the* Prince *and* OXFORD.

K. Lew. Now, Warwick, tell me, even upon thy conscience,
Is Edward your true king? for I were loath
To link with him that were not lawful chosen.

War. Thereon I pawn my credit, and mine honour.

K. Lew. But is he gracious in the people's eye?

War. The more that Henry was unfortunate.

K. Lew. Then further,—all dissembling set aside,
Tell me for truth the measure of his love
Unto our sister Bona.

War. Such it seems,
As may beseem a monarch like himself.
Myself have often heard him say, and swear,—
That this his love was an eternal plant;
Whereof the root was fix'd in virtue's ground,
The leaves and fruit maintain'd with beauty's sun;
Exempt from envy, but not from disdain,
Unless the Lady Bona quit his pain.

K. Lew. Now, sister, let us hear your firm resolve.

Bona. Your grant, or your denial, shall be mine:—
Yet I confess, [*To* WAR.] that often ere this day,
When I have heard your king's desert recounted,
Mine ear hath tempted judgment to desire.

K. Lew. Then, Warwick, thus,—Our sister shall be Edward's;
And now forthwith shall articles be drawn
Touching the jointure that your king must make,
Which with her dowry shall be counterpois'd:—
Draw near, queen Margaret; and be a witness,
That Bona shall be wife to the English king.

Prince. To Edward, but not to the English king.

Q. Mar. Deceitful Warwick! it was thy device
By this alliance to make void my suit;
Before thy coming, Lewis was Henry's friend.

K. Lew. And still is friend to him and Margaret;
But if your title to the crown be weak,—
As may appear by Edward's good success,—
Then 'tis but reason, that I be releas'd
From giving aid, which late I promis'd.
Yet shall you have all kindness at my hand.
That your estate requires, and mine can yield.

War. Henry now lives in Scotland at his ease:
Where having nothing, nothing he can lose.
And as for you yourself, our *quondam* queen,—
You have a father able to maintain you;—
And better 'twere you troubled him than France.

Q. Mar. Peace, impudent and shameless Warwick, peace;
Proud setter-up and puller-down of kings!
I will not hence, till with my talk and tears,

Both full of truth, I make King Lewis behold
Thy sly conveyance, and thy lord's false love;
For both of you are birds of self-same feather.
[*A Horn sounded within.*

K. Lew. Warwick, this is some post to us, or thee.

Enter a Messenger.

Mess. My lord ambassador, these letters are for you;
Sent from your brother, Marquis Montague.
These from our king unto your majesty.—
And, madam, these for you; from whom I know not.
[*To* MARGARET. *They all read their Letters.*

Oxf. I like it well, that our fair queen and mistress
Smiles at her news, while Warwick frowns at his.

Prince. Nay, mark, how Lewis stamps as he were nettled:
I hope, all's for the best.

K. Lew. Warwick, what are thy news? and yours, fair queen?

Q. Mar. Mine, such as fill my heart with unhop'd joys.

War. Mine, full of sorrow and heart's discontent.

K. Lew. What! has your king married the Lady Grey?
And now, to sooth your forgery and his,
Sends me a paper to persuade me patience?
Is this the alliance that he seeks with France?
Dare he presume to scorn us in this manner?

Q. Mar. I told your majesty as much before:
This proveth Edward's love, and Warwick's honesty.

War. King Lewis, I here protest,—in sight of heaven,
And by the hope I have of heavenly bliss,—
That I am clear from this misdeed of Edward's;
No more my king, for he dishonours me;
But most himself, if he could see his shame.—
Did I forget, that by the house of York
My father came untimely to his death?
Did I let pass the abuse done to my niece?
Did I impale him with the regal crown?
Did I put Henry from his native right;
And am I guerdon'd at the last with shame?
Shame on himself! for my desert is honour.
And, to repair my honour lost for him,
I here renounce him, and return to Henry:
My noble queen, let former grudges pass,
And henceforth I am thy true servitor;
I will revenge his wrong to Lady Bona,
And replant Henry in his former state.

Q. Mar. Warwick, these words have turn'd my hate to love;
And I forgive and quite forget old faults,
And joy that thou becom'st King Henry's friend.

War. So much his friend, ay, his unfeigned friend,
That, if King Lewis vouchsafe to furnish us
With some few bands of chosen soldiers,
I'll undertake to land them on our coast,
And force the tyrant from his seat by war.
'Tis not his new-made bride shall succour him:
And as for Clarence,—as my letters tell me,
He's very likely now to fall from him;
For matching more for wanton lust than honour,
Or than for strength and safety of our country.

Bona. Dear brother, how shall Bona be reveng'd,
But by thy help to this distressed queen?

Q. Mar. Renowned prince, how shall poor Henry live,
Unless thou rescue him from foul despair?

Bona. My quarrel, and this English queen's, are one.

War. And mine, fair Lady Bona, joins with yours.

K. Lew. And mine with hers, and thine, and Margaret's.
Therefore, at last, I firmly am resolv'd,
You shall have aid.

Q. Mar. Let me give humble thanks for all at once.

K. Lew. Then England's messenger, return in post;
And tell false Edward, thy supposed king,—
That Lewis of France is sending over maskers,
To revel it with him and his new bride:
Thou seest what's past, go fear thy king withal.

Bona. Tell him, In hope he'll prove a widower shortly,
I'll wear the willow garland for his sake.

Q. Mar. Tell him, My mourning weeds are laid aside,
And I am ready to put armour on.

War. Tell him from me, That he hath done me wrong;
And therefore I'll uncrown him, ere't be long.
There's thy reward; be gone. [*Exit* Mess.

K. Lew. But, Warwick, thou,
And Oxford, with five thousand men,
Shall cross the seas, and bid false Edward battle.
And, as occasion serves, this noble queen
And prince shall follow with a fresh supply.
Yet, ere thou go, but answer me one doubt;—
What pledge have we of thy firm loyalty?

War. This shall assure my constant loyalty:—
That if our queen and this young prince agree,
I'll join mine eldest daughter, and my joy,
To him forthwith in holy wedlock bands.

Q. Mar. Yes, I agree, and thank you for your motion:—
Son Edward, she is fair and virtuous,
Therefore delay not, give thy hand to Warwick;
And, with thy hand, thy faith irrevocable,
That only Warwick's daughter shall be thine.

Prince. Yes, I accept her, for she well deserves it;
And here, to pledge my vow, I give my hand.
[*He gives his hand to* WARWICK.

K. Lew. Why stay we now? These soldiers shall be levied,
And thou, Lord Bourbon, our high admiral,
Shall waft them over with our royal fleet.—
I long, till Edward fall by war's mischance,
For mocking marriage with a dame of France.
[*Exeunt all but* WARWICK.

War. I came from Edward as embassador,
But I return his sworn and mortal foe:
Matter of marriage was the charge he gave me,
But dreadful war shall answer his demand.
Had he none else to make a stale, but me?
Then none but I shall turn his jest to sorrow.
I was the chief that rais'd him to the crown,
And I'll be chief to bring him down again:
Not that I pity Henry's misery,
But seek revenge on Edward's mockery. [*Exit.*

ACT IV

SCENE I. London. *A Room in the Palace.*

Enter GLOSTER, CLARENCE, SOMERSET, MONTAGUE, *and Others.*

Glo. Now tell me, brother Clarence, what think you
Of this new marriage with the Lady Grey?
Hath not our brother made a worthy choice?

Clar. Alas, you know, 'tis far from hence to France;
How could he stay till Warwick made return?

Som. My lords, forbear this talk; here comes the king.

Flourish. Enter KING EDWARD, *attended;* LADY GREY, *as* Queen; PEMBROKE, STAFFORD, HASTINGS, *and Others.*

Glo. And his well chosen bride.

Clar. I mind to tell him plainly what I think.

K. Edw. Now, brother of Clarence, how like you our choice,
That you stand pensive, as half malcontent?
Clar. As well as Lewis of France, or the earl of Warwick;
Which are so weak of courage, and in judgment,
That they'll take no offence at our abuse.
K. Edw. Suppose they take offence without a cause,
They are but Lewis and Warwick; I am Edward,
Your king and Warwick's, and must have my will.
Glo. And you shall have your will, because our king,
Yet hasty marriage seldom proveth well.
K. Edw. Yea, brother Richard, are you offended too?
Glo. Not I:
No; God forbid, that I should wish them sever'd
Whom God hath join'd together: ay, and 'twere pity,
To sunder them that yoke so well together.
K. Edw. Setting your scorns, and your mislike, aside,
Tell me some reason, why the Lady Grey
Should not become my wife, and England's queen:—
And you too, Somerset, and Montague,
Speak freely what you think.
Clar. Then this is my opinion,—that King Lewis
Becomes your enemy, for mocking him
About the marriage of the Lady Bona.
Glo. And Warwick, doing what you gave in charge,
Is now dishonoured by this new marriage.
K. Edw. What, if both Lewis and Warwick be appeas'd,
By such invention as I can devise?
Mont. Yet to have join'd with France in such alliance,
Would more have strengthen'd this our commonwealth
'Gainst foreign storms, than any homebred marriage.
Hast. Why, knows not Montague, that of itself
England is safe, if true within itself?
Mont. Yes; but the safer, when 'tis back'd with France.
Hast. 'Tis better using France, than trusting France:
Let us be back'd with God, and with the seas,
Which he hath given for fence impregnable,
And with their helps only defend ourselves;
In them, and in ourselves, our safety lies.
Clar. For this one speech, Lord Hastings well deserves
To have the heir of the Lord Hungerford.
K. Edw. Ay, what of that? it was my will, and grant;
And, for this once, my will shall stand for law.
Glo. And yet, methinks your grace hath not done well,
To give the heir and daughter of Lord Scales
Unto the brother of your loving bride;
She better would have fitted me, or Clarence:
But in your bride you bury brotherhood.
Clar. Or else you would not have bestow'd the heir
Of the Lord Bonville on your new wife's son,
And leave your brothers to go speed elsewhere.
K. Edw. Alas, poor Clarence! is it for a wife.
That thou art malcontent? I will provide thee.
Clar. In choosing for yourself, you showed your judgment;
Which being shallow, you shall give me leave
To play the broker in mine own behalf;
And to that end, I shortly mind to leave you.
K. Edw. Leave me, or tarry, Edward will be king,
And not be tied unto his brother's will.
Q. Eliz. My lords, before it pleased his majesty
To raise my state to title of a queen,
Do me but right, and you must all confess
That I was not ignoble of descent,
And meaner than myself have had like fortune.
But as this title honours me and mine,
So your dislikes, to whom I would be pleasing,
Do cloud my joys with danger and with sorrow.
K. Edw. My love, forbear to fawn upon their frowns:
What danger, or what sorrow can befall thee,
So long as Edward is thy constant friend,
And their true sovereign, whom they must obey?
Nay, whom they shall obey, and love thee too,
Unless they seek for hatred at my hands:
Which if they do, yet will I keep thee safe,
And they shall feel the vengeance of my wrath.
Glo. I hear, yet say not much, but think the more. [*Aside.*

Enter a Messenger.

K. Edw. Now, messenger, what letters, or what news,
From France?
Mess. My sovereign liege, no letters; and few words,
But such as I without your special pardon,
Dare not relate.
K. Edw. Go to, we pardon thee: therefore in brief,
Tell me their words as near as thou canst guess them.
What answer makes King Lewis unto our letters?
Mess. At my depart these were his very words;
Go tell false Edward, thy supposed king,—
That Lewis of France is sending over maskers,
To revel it with him and his new bride.
K. Edw. Is Lewis so brave? belike he thinks me Henry.
But what said Lady Bona to my marriage?
Mess. These were her words, utter'd with mild disdain;
Tell him, in hope he'll prove a widower shortly,
I'll wear the willow garland for his sake.
K. Edw. I blame not her, she could say little less;
She had the wrong. But what said Henry's queen?
For I have heard, that she was there in place.
Mess. *Tell him,* quoth she, *my mourning weeds are done,*
And I am ready to put armour on.
K. Edw. Belike, she minds to play the Amazon.
But what said Warwick to these injuries?
Mess. He, more incens'd against your majesty
Than all the rest, discharg'd me with these words;
Tell him from me, that he hath done me wrong,
And therefore I'll uncrown him, ere't be long.
K. Edw. Ha! durst the traitor breathe out so proud words?
Well, I will arm me, being thus forewarn'd:
They shall have wars, and pay for their presumption.
But say, is Warwick friends with Margaret?
Mess. Ay, gracious sovereign; they are so link'd in friendship,
That young Prince Edward marries Warwick's daughter.
Clar. Belike, the elder; Clarence will have the younger.
Now, brother king, farewell, and sit you fast,
For I will hence to Warwick's other daughter;
That, though I want a kingdom, yet in marriage
I may not prove inferior to yourself.—
You, that love me and Warwick, follow me.
[*Exit* CLARENCE, *and* SOMERSET *follows.*
Glo. Not I:
My thoughts aim at a further matter; I
Stay not for love of Edward, but the crown. [*Aside.*
K. Edw. Clarence and Somerset both gone to Warwick!

Yet am I arm'd against the worst can happen;
And haste is needful in this desperate case.—
Pembroke, and Stafford, you in our behalf
Go levy men, and make prepare for war;
They are already, or quickly will be landed:
Myself in person will straight follow you.
[*Exeunt* PEMBROKE *and* STAFFORD.
But, ere I go, Hastings,—and Montague,—
Resolve my doubt. You twain, of all the rest,
Are near to Warwick, by blood, and by alliance:
Tell me, if you love Warwick more than me?
If it be so, then both depart to him;
I rather wish you foes, than hollow friends;
But if you mind to hold your true obedience,
Give me assurance with some friendly vow,
That I may never have you in suspect.

Mont. So God help Montague, as he proves true!

Hast. And Hastings, as he favours Edward's cause!

K. Edw. Now, brother Richard, will you stand by us?

Glo. Ay, in despite of all that shall withstand you.

K. Edw. Why so; then am I sure of victory.
Now therefore let us hence; and lose no hour,
Till we meet Warwick with his foreign power.
[*Exeunt.*

SCENE II. *A Plain in* Warwickshire.

Enter WARWICK *and* OXFORD, *with* French *and other* Forces.

War. Trust me, my lord, all hitherto goes well;
The common people by numbers swarm to us.

Enter CLARENCE *and* SOMERSET.

But, see, where Somerset and Clarence come:—
Speak suddenly, my lords, are we all friends?

Clar. Fear not that, my lord.

War. Then, gentle Clarence, welcome unto Warwick;
And welcome, Somerset:—I hold it cowardice,
To rest mistrustful where a noble heart
Hath pawn'd an open hand in sign of love;
Else might I think, that Clarence, Edward's brother,
Were but a feigned friend to our proceedings:
But welcome, sweet Clarence; my daughter shall be thine.
And now what rests, but, in night's coverture,
Thy brother being carelessly encamp'd,
His soldiers lurking in the towns about,
And but attended by a simple guard,
We may surprise and take him at our pleasure?
Our scouts have found the adventure very easy:
That as Ulysses, and stout Diomede,
With sleight and manhood stole to Rhesus' tents,
And brought from thence the Thracian fatal steeds;
So we, well cover'd with the night's black mantle,
At unawares may beat down Edward's guard,
And seize himself; I say not—slaughter him,
For I intend but only to surprise him.—
You, that will follow me to this attempt,
Applaud the name of Henry, with your leader.
[*They all cry,* Henry!
Why, then, let's on our way in silent sort:
For Warwick and his friends, God and Saint George! [*Exeunt.*

SCENE III. Edward's *Camp, near* Warwick.

Enter certain Watchmen, *to guard the* King's *Tent.*

1 *Watch.* Come on, my masters, each man take his stand;
The king, by this, is set him down to sleep.

2 *Watch.* What, will he not to bed?

1 *Watch.* Why, no: for he hath made a solemn vow
Never to lie and take his natural rest,
Till Warwick, or himself, be quite suppress'd.

2 *Watch.* To-morrow then, belike, shall be the day,
If Warwick be so near as men report.

3 *Watch.* But say, I pray, what nobleman is that,
That with the king here resteth in his tent?

1 *Watch.* 'Tis the Lord Hastings, the king's chiefest friend.

3 *Watch.* O, is it so? But why commands the king,
That his chief followers lodge in towns about him,
While he himself keepeth in the cold field?

2 *Watch.* 'Tis the more honour, because more dangerous.

3 *Watch.* Ay; but give me worship and quietness,
I like it better than a dangerous honour.
If Warwick knew in what estate he stands,
'Tis to be doubted, he would waken him.

1 *Watch.* Unless our halberds did shut up his passage.

2 *Watch.* Ay; wherefore else guard we his royal tent,
But to defend his person from night foes?

Enter WARWICK, CLARENCE, OXFORD, SOMERSET, *and* Forces.

War. This is his tent; and see, where stand his guard.
Courage, my masters: honour now, or never!
But follow me, and Edward shall be ours.

1 *Watch.* Who goes there?

2 *Watch.* Stay, or thou diest.

[WARWICK, *and the rest, cry all*—Warwick! Warwick! *and set upon the* Guard; *who fly, crying, Arm! Arm!* WARWICK, *and the rest, following them.*

The Drum beating, and Trumpets sounding, re-enter WARWICK, *and the rest, bringing the* King *out in a Gown, sitting in a Chair;* GLOSTER *and* HASTINGS *fly.*

Som. What are they that fly there?

War. Richard, and Hastings: let them go, here's the duke.

K. Edw. The duke! why, Warwick, when we parted last,
Thou call'dst me king?

War. Ay, but the case is alter'd:
When you disgrac'd me in my embassade,
Then I degraded you from being king,
And come now to create you duke of York.
Alas! how should you govern any kingdom,
That know not how to use ambassadors:
Nor how to be contented with one wife;
Nor how to use your brothers brotherly;
Nor how to study for the people's welfare;
Nor how to shroud yourself from enemies?

K. Edw. Yea, brother of Clarence, art thou here too?
Nay, then I see, that Edward needs must down.—
Yet, Warwick, in despite of all mischance,
Of thee thyself, and all thy complices,
Edward will always bear himself as king:
Though fortune's malice overthrow my state,
My mind exceeds the compass of her wheel.

War. Then, for his mind, be Edward England's king: [*Takes off his Crown.*
But Henry now shall wear the English crown,
And be true king indeed; thou but the shadow.—
My lord of Somerset, at my request,
See that forthwith Duke Edward be convey'd
Unto my brother, archbishop of York.
When I have fought with Pembroke and his fellows,
I'll follow you, and tell what answer
Lewis, and the Lady Bona, send to him:
Now, for awhile, farewell, good duke of York.

K. Edw. What fates impose, that men must needs abide;
It boots not to resist both wind and tide.
[*Exit* K. EDW. *led out;* SOM. *with him.*

Oxf. What now remains, my lords, for us, to do,
But march to London with our soldiers?
War. Ay, that's the first thing that we have to do;
To free King Henry from imprisonment,
And see him seated in the regal throne.
[*Exeunt.*

SCENE IV. London. *A Room in the Palace.*

Enter QUEEN ELIZABETH *and* RIVERS.

Riv. Madam, what makes you in this sudden change?
Q. Eliz. Why, brother Rivers, are you yet to learn,
What late misfortune is befall'n King Edward?
Riv. What, loss of some pitch'd battle against Warwick?
Q. Eliz. No, but the loss of his own royal person.
Riv. Then is my sovereign slain?
Q. Eliz. Ay, almost slain, for he is taken prisoner;
Either betray'd by falsehood of his guard,
Or by his foe surpris'd at unawares:
And, as I further have to understand,
Is new committed to the bishop of York,
Fell Warwick's brother, and by that our foe.
Riv. These news, I must confess, are full of grief:
Yet, gracious madam, bear it as you may:
Warwick may lose, that now hath won the day.
Q. Eliz. Till then, fair hope must hinder life's decay.
And I the rather wean me from despair,
For love of Edward's offspring in my womb:
This is it that makes me bridle passion,
And bear with mildness my misfortune's cross;
Ay, ay, for this I draw in many a tear,
And stop the rising of blood-sucking sighs,
Lest with my sighs or tears I blast or drown
King Edward's fruit, true heir to the English crown.
Riv. But, madam, where is Warwick then become?
Q. Eliz. I am informed, that he comes towards London,
To set the crown once more on Henry's head:
Guess thou the rest; King Edward's friends must down.
But to prevent the tyrant's violence
(For trust not him that hath once broken faith),
I'll hence forthwith unto the sanctuary,
To save at least the heir of Edward's right;
There shall I rest secure from force, and fraud.
Come therefore, let us fly, while we may fly;
If Warwick take us, we are sure to die.
[*Exeunt.*

SCENE V.

A Park near Middleham Castle *in* Yorkshire.

Enter GLOSTER, HASTINGS, SIR WILLIAM STANLEY, *and Others.*

Glo. Now, my Lord Hastings, and Sir William Stanley,
Leave off to wonder why I drew you hither,
Into this chiefest thicket of the park.
Thus stands the case: You know, our king, my brother,
Is prisoner to the bishop here, at whose hands
He hath good usage and great liberty;
And often, but attended with weak guard,
Comes hunting this way to disport himself.
I have advertis'd him by secret means,
That if, about this hour, he make his way,
Under the colour of his usual game,
He shall here find his friends, with horse and men,
To set him free from his captivity.

Enter KING EDWARD *and a* Huntsman.

Hunt. This way, my lord; for this way lies the game.
K. Edw. Nay, this way, man; see, where the huntsmen stand.—
Now, brother of Gloster, Lord Hastings, and the rest,
Stand you thus close, to steal the bishop's deer?
Glo. Brother, the time and case requireth haste;
Your horse stands ready at the park corner.
K. Edw. But whither shall we then?
Hast. To Lynn, my lord: and ship from thence to Flanders.
Glo. Well guess'd, believe me; for that was my meaning.
K. Edw. Stanley, I will requite thy forwardness.
Glo. But wherefore stay we? 'tis no time to talk.
K. Edw. Huntsman, what say'st thou? wilt thou go along?
Hunt. Better do so, than tarry and be hang'd.
Glo. Come then, away; let's have no more ado.
K. Edw. Bishop, farewell: shield thee from Warwick's frown;
And pray that I may repossess the crown.
[*Exeunt.*

SCENE VI. *A Room in the Tower.*

Enter KING HENRY, CLARENCE, WARWICK, SOMERSET, *young* RICHMOND, OXFORD, MONTAGUE, Lieutenant *of the* Tower, *and* Attendants.

K. Hen. Master Lieutenant, now that God and friends
Have shaken Edward from the regal seat;
And turn'd my captive state to liberty,
My fear to hope, my sorrows unto joys;
At our enlargement what are thy due fees?
Lieu. Subjects may challenge nothing of their sovereigns;
But, if an humble prayer may prevail,
I then crave pardon of your majesty.
K. Hen. For what, lieutenant? for well using me?
Nay, be thou sure, I'll well requite thy kindness,
For that it made my imprisonment a pleasure:
Ay, such a pleasure as incaged birds
Conceive, when, after many moody thoughts,
At last, by notes of household harmony,
They quite forget their loss of liberty.—
But, Warwick, after God, thou set'st me free,
And chiefly therefore I thank God, and thee;
He was the author, thou the instrument.
Therefore, that I may conquer fortune's spite,
By living low, where fortune cannot hurt me;
And that the people of this blessed land
May not be punish'd with my thwarting stars;
Warwick, although my head still wear the crown,
I here resign my government to thee,
For thou art fortunate in all thy deeds.
War. Your grace hath still been fam'd for virtuous;
And now may seem as wise as virtuous,
By spying, and avoiding, fortune's malice,
For few men rightly temper with the stars:
Yet in this one thing let me blame your grace,
For choosing me, when Clarence is in place.
Clar. No, Warwick, thou art worthy of the sway,
To whom the heavens, in thy nativity,
Adjudg'd an olive branch, and laurel crown,
As likely to be blest in peace, and war;
And therefore I yield thee my free consent.
War. And I choose Clarence only for protector.
K. Hen. Warwick, and Clarence, give me both your hands:
Now join your hands, and, with your hands, your hearts,
That no dissension hinder government:
I make you both protectors of this land;
While I myself will lead a private life,
And in devotion spend my latter days,
To sin's rebuke, and my Creator's praise.

War. What answers Clarence to his sovereign's will?

Clar. That he consents, if Warwick yield consent:
For on thy fortune I repose myself.

War. Why then, though loath, yet must I be content:
We'll yoke together, like a double shadow
To Henry's body, and supply his place:
I mean, in bearing weight of government,
While he enjoys the honour, and his ease.
And, Clarence, now then it is more than needful,
Forthwith that Edward be pronounc'd a traitor,
And all his lands and goods be confiscate.

Clar. What else? and that succession be determin'd.

War. Ay, therein Clarence shall not want his part.

K. Hen. But, with the first of all your chief affairs,
Let me entreat (for I command no more)
That Margaret your queen, and my son Edward,
Be sent for, to return from France with speed:
For, till I see them here, by doubtful fear
My joy of liberty is half eclips'd.

Clar. It shall be done, my sovereign, with all speed.

K. Hen. My lord of Somerset, what youth is that,
Of whom you seem to have so tender care?

Som. My liege, it is young Henry, earl of Richmond.

K. Hen. Come hither, England's hope: If secret powers
[*Lays his Hand on his Head.*
Suggest but truth to my divining thoughts,
This pretty lad will prove our country's bliss.
His looks are full of peaceful majesty;
His head by nature fram'd to wear a crown,
His hand to wield a sceptre; and himself
Likely, in time, to bless a regal throne.
Make much of him, my lords; for this is he,
Must help you more than you are hurt by me.

Enter a Messenger.

War. What news, my friend?

Mess. That Edward is escaped from your brother,
And fled, as he hears since, to Burgundy.

War. Unsavoury news: But how made he escape?

Mess. He was convey'd by Richard duke of Gloster,
And the Lord Hastings, who attended him
In secret ambush on the forest side,
And from the bishop's huntsmen rescued him;
For hunting was his daily exercise.

War. My brother was too careless of his charge.—
But let us hence, my sovereign, to provide
A salve for any sore that may betide.
[*Exeunt* KING HENRY, WAR. CLAR. Lieut. *and* Attendants.

Som. My lord, I like not of this flight of Edward's:
For, doubtless, Burgundy will yield him help;
And we shall have more wars, before 't be long.
As Henry's late presaging prophecy
Did glad my heart, with hope of this young Richmond;
So doth my heart misgive me, in these conflicts
What may befall him, to his harm, and ours:
Therefore, Lord Oxford, to prevent the worst,
Forthwith we'll send him hence to Britany,
Till storms be past of civil enmity.

Oxf. Ay; for if Edward repossess the crown,
'Tis like, that Richmond with the rest shall down.

Som. It shall be so; he shall to Britany.
Come, therefore, let's about it speedily.
[*Exeunt.*

SCENE VII. *Before* York.

Enter KING EDWARD, GLOSTER, HASTINGS, *and* Forces.

K. Edw. Now, brother Richard, Lord Hastings, and the rest;
Yet thus far fortune maketh us amends,
And says—that once more I shall interchange
My waned state for Henry's regal crown.
Well have we pass'd, and now repass'd the seas,
And brought desired help from Burgundy:
What then remains, we being thus arriv'd
From Ravenspurg haven before the gates of York,
But that we enter, as into our dukedom?

Glo. The gates made fast!—Brother, I like not this;
For many men, that stumble at the threshold,
Are well foretold—that danger lurks within.

K. Edw. Tush, man! abodements must not now affright us:
By fair or foul means we must enter in,
For hither will our friends repair to us.

Hast. My liege, I'll knock once more, to summon them.

Enter, on the Walls, the Mayor *of* York, *and his* Brethren.

May. My lords, we were forewarned of your coming,
And shut the gates for safety of ourselves;
For now we owe allegiance unto Henry.

K. Edw. But, master mayor, if Henry be your king,
Yet Edward, at the least, is duke of York.

May. True, my good lord; I know you for no less.

K. Edw. Why, and I challenge nothing but my dukedom;
As being well content with that alone.

Glo. But, when the fox hath once got in his nose,
He'll soon find means to make the body follow.
[*Aside.*

Hast. Why, master mayor, why stand you in a doubt?
Open the gates, we are King Henry's friends.

May. Ay, say you so? the gates shall then be open'd. [*Exeunt from above.*

Glo. A wise stout captain, and persuaded soon!

Hast. The good old man would fain that all were well,
So 'twere not 'long of him: but, being enter'd,
I doubt not, I, but we shall soon persuade
Both him, and all his brothers, unto reason.

Re-enter the Mayor, *and Two* Aldermen, *below.*

K. Edw. So, master mayor: these gates must not be shut,
But in the night, or in the time of war.
What! fear not, man, but yield me up the keys;
[*Takes his Keys.*
For Edward will defend the town, and thee,
And all those friends that deign to follow me.

Drum. Enter MONTGOMERY, *and* Forces, *marching.*

Glo. Brother, this is Sir John Montgomery,
Our trusty friend, unless I be deceiv'd.

K. Edw. Welcome, Sir John! But why come you in arms?

Mont. To help King Edward in his time of storm,
As every loyal subject ought to do.

K. Edw. Thanks, good Montgomery: But we now forget
Our title to the crown! and only claim
Our dukedom, till God please to send the rest.

Mont. Then fare you well, for I will hence again;
I came to serve a king, and not a duke,—
Drummer, strike up, and let us march away.
[*A March begun.*

K. Edw. Nay, stay, Sir John, a while; and we'll debate,
By what safe means the crown may be recover'd.
Mont. What talk you of debating? in few words,
If you'll not here proclaim yourself our king,
I'll leave you to your fortune; and be gone,
To keep them back that come to succour you:
Why should we fight, if you pretend no title?
Glo. Why, brother, wherefore stand you on nice points?
K. Edw. When we grow stronger, then we'll make our claim;
Till then, 'tis wisdom to conceal our meaning.
Hast. Away with scrupulous wit! now arms must rule.
Glo. And fearless minds climb soonest unto crowns.
Brother, we will proclaim you out of hand;
The bruit thereof will bring you many friends.
K. Edw. Then be it as you will; for 'tis my right,
And Henry but usurps the diadem.
Mont. Ay, now my sovereign speaketh like himself;
And now will I be Edward's champion.
Hast. Sound, trumpet; Edward shall be here proclaim'd:—
Come, fellow-soldier, make thou proclamation.
[*Gives him a Paper. Flourish.*
Sold. [*Reads.*] *Edward the Fourth, by the grace of God, king of England and France, and lord of Ireland*, &c.
Mont. And whosoe'er gainsays king Edward's right,
By this I challenge him to single fight.
[*Throws down his gauntlet.*
All. Long live Edward the Fourth!
K. Edw. Thanks, brave Montgomery;—and thanks unto you all,
If fortune serve me, I'll requite this kindness.
Now, for this night, let's harbour here in York:
And, when the morning sun shall raise his car
Above the border of this horizon,
We'll forward towards Warwick, and his mates;
For, well I wot, that Henry is no soldier.—
Ah, froward Clarence!—how evil it beseems thee,
To flatter Henry, and forsake thy brother!
Yet, as we may, we'll meet both thee and Warwick.—
Come on, brave soldiers; doubt not of the day;
And, that once gotten, doubt not of large pay.
[*Exeunt.*

SCENE VIII. London. *A Room in the Palace.*

Enter KING HENRY, WARWICK, CLARENCE, MONTAGUE, EXETER, *and* OXFORD.

War. What counsel, lords? Edward from Belgia,
With hasty Germans, and blunt Hollanders,
Hath pass'd in safety through the narrow seas,
And with his troops doth march amain to London;
And many giddy people flock to him.
Oxf. Let's levy men, and beat him back again.
Clar. A little fire is quickly trodden out;
Which, being suffer'd, rivers cannot quench.
War. In Warwickshire I have true-hearted friends,
Not mutinous in peace, yet bold in war;
Those will I muster up:—and thou, son Clarence,
Shalt stir, in Suffolk, Norfolk, and in Kent,
The knights and gentlemen to come with thee:
Thou, brother Montague, in Buckingham,
Northampton, and in Leicestershire, shalt find
Men well inclin'd to hear what thou command'st:—
And thou, brave Oxford, wondrous well belov'd,
In Oxfordshire shalt muster up thy friends.—
My sovereign, with the loving citizens,—
Like to his island, girt in with the ocean,
Or modest Dian, circled with her nymphs,—
Shall rest in London, till we come to him.
Fair lords, take leave, and stand not to reply.—
Farewell, my sovereign.
K. Hen. Farewell, my Hector, and my Troy's true hope.
Clar. In sign of truth, I kiss your highness' hand.
K. Hen. Well-minded Clarence, be thou fortunate!
Mont. Comfort, my lord,—and so I take my leave.
Oxf. And thus [*Kissing* HENRY'S *hand.*] I seal my truth, and bid adieu.
K. Hen. Sweet Oxford, and my loving Montague,
And all at once, once more a happy farewell.
War. Farewell, sweet lords; let's meet at Coventry.
[*Exeunt* WAR. CLAR. OXF. *and* MONT.
K. Hen. Here at the palace will I rest a while.
Cousin of Exeter, what thinks your lordship?
Methinks, the power that Edward hath in field
Should not be able to encounter mine.
Exe. The doubt is, that he will seduce the rest.
K. Hen. That's not my fear, my meed hath got me fame.
I have not stopp'd mine ears to their demands,
Nor posted off their suits with slow delays;
My pity hath been balm to heal their wounds,
My mildness hath allay'd their swelling griefs,
My mercy dry'd their water-flowing tears:
I have not been desirous of their wealth,
Nor much oppress'd them with great subsidies,
Nor forward of revenge, though they much err'd:
Then why should they love Edward more than me?
No, Exeter, these graces challenge grace;
And, when the lion fawns upon the lamb,
The lamb will never cease to follow him.
[*Shout within. A* Lancaster! *A* Lancaster!
Exe. Hark, hark, my lord! what shouts are these?

Enter KING EDWARD, GLOSTER, *and* Soldiers.

K. Edw. Seize on the shame-fac'd Henry, bear him hence,
And once again proclaim us king of England.—
You are the fount that makes small brooks to flow:
Now stops thy spring; my sea shall suck them dry,
And swell so much the higher by their ebb.—
Hence with him to the Tower; let him not speak.
[*Exeunt some with* KING HENRY.
And, lords, towards Coventry bend we our course,
Where peremptory Warwick now remains:
The sun shines hot, and, if we use delay,
Cold biting winter mars our hop'd-for hay.
Glo. Away betimes, before his forces join,
And take the great-grown traitor unawares:
Brave warriors, march amain towards Coventry.
[*Exeunt.*

ACT V.

SCENE I. Coventry.

Enter, upon the Walls, WARWICK, *the* Mayor *of* Coventry, *Two* Messengers, *and Others.*

War. Where is the post that came from valiant Oxford?
How far hence is thy lord, mine honest fellow?
1 *Mess.* By this at Dunsmore, marching hitherward.
War. How far off is our brother Montague?
Where is the post that came from Montague?
2 *Mess.* By this at Daintry, with a puissant troop.

Enter SIR JOHN SOMERVILLE.

War. Say, Somerville, what says my loving son?
And, by thy guess, how nigh is Clarence now?

Som. At Southam I did leave him with his forces,
And do expect him here some two hours hence.
[*Drum heard.*

War. Then Clarence is at hand, I hear his drum.

Som. It is not his, my lord: here Southam lies:
The drum your honour hears, marcheth from Warwick,

War. Who should that be? belike, unlook'd-for friends.

Som. They are at hand, and you shall quickly know.

Drums. Enter KING EDWARD, GLOSTER, *and* Forces, *marching.*

K. Edw. Go, trumpet, to the walls, and sound a parle.

Glo. See how the surly Warwick mans the wall.

War. O, unbid spite! is sportful Edward come?
Where slept our scouts, or how are they seduc'd,
That we could hear no news of his repair?

K. Edw. Now, Warwick, wilt thou ope the city gates,
Speak gentle words, and humbly bend thy knee?
Call Edward,—king, and at his hands beg mercy,
And he shall pardon thee these outrages.

War. Nay, rather, wilt thou draw thy forces hence,
Confess who set thee up and pluck'd thee down?—
Call Warwick—patron, and be penitent,
And thou shalt still remain the duke of York.

Glo. I thought, at least, he would have said—the king;
Or did he make the jest against his will?

War. Is not a dukedom, sir, a goodly gift?

Glo. Ay, by my faith, for a poor earl to give;
I'll do thee service for so good a gift.

War. 'Twas I, that gave the kingdom to thy brother.

K. Edw. Why, then 'tis mine, if but by Warwick's gift.

War. Thou art no Atlas for so great a weight:
And, weakling, Warwick takes his gift again:
And Henry is my king, Warwick his subject.

K. Edw. But Warwick's king is Edward's prisoner:
And, gallant Warwick, do but answer this,—
What is the body, when the head is off?

Glo. Alas, that Warwick had no more forecast,
But, whiles he thought to steal the single ten,
The king was slyly finger'd from the deck!
You left poor Henry at the bishop's palace,
And, ten to one, you'll meet him in the Tower.

K. Edw. 'Tis even so; yet you are Warwick still.

Glo. Come, Warwick, take the time, kneel down, kneel down:
Nay, when? strike now, or else the iron cools.

War. I had rather chop this hand off at a blow,
And with the other fling it at thy face,
Than bear so low a sail, to strike to thee.

K. Edw. Sail how thou canst, have wind and tide thy friend;
This hand, fast wound about thy coal-black hair,
Shall, whiles the head is warm, and new cut off,
Write in the dust this sentence with thy blood,—
Wind-changing Warwick *now can change no more.*

Enter OXFORD, *with Drum and Colours.*

War. O cheerful colours! see where Oxford comes!

Oxf. Oxford, Oxford, for Lancaster!
[OXFORD *and his* Forces *enter the City.*

Glo. The gates are open, let us enter too.

K. Edw. So other foes may set upon our backs.
Stand we in good array; for they, no doubt,
Will issue out again, and bid us battle:
If not, the city, being but of small defence,
We'll quickly rouse the traitors in the same.

War. O, welcome, Oxford, for we want thy help.

Enter MONTAGUE, *with Drum and Colours.*

Mont. Montague, Montague, for Lancaster!
[*He and his* Forces *enter the City.*

Glo. Thou and thy brother both shall buy this treason
Even with the dearest blood your bodies bear.

K. Edw. The harder match'd, the greater victory;
My mind presageth happy gain, and conquest.

Enter SOMERSET, *with Drum and Colours.*

Som. Somerset, Somerset, for Lancaster!
[*He and his* Forces *enter the City.*

Glo. Two of thy name, both dukes of Somerset,
Have sold their lives unto the house of York:
And thou shalt be the third, if this sword hold.

Enter CLARENCE, *with Drum and Colours.*

War. And lo, where George of Clarence sweeps along,
Of force enough to bid his brother battle;
With whom an upright zeal to right prevails,
More than the nature of a brother's love:—
Come, Clarence, come; thou wilt, if Warwick calls.

Clar. Father of Warwick, know you what this means? [*Taking the red Rose out of his Cap.*
Look here, I throw my infamy at thee:
I will not ruinate my father's house,
Who gave his blood to lime the stones together,
And set up Lancaster. Why, trow'st thou, Warwick,
That Clarence is so harsh, so blunt, unnatural,
To bend the fatal instruments of war
Against his brother, and his lawful king?
Perhaps, thou wilt object my holy oath:
To keep that oath, were more impiety
Than Jephtha's, when he sacrific'd his daughter.
I am so sorry for my trespass made,
That, to deserve well at my brother's hands,
I here proclaim myself thy mortal foe;
With resolution, wheresoe'er I meet thee
(As I will meet thee, if thou stir abroad),
To plague thee for thy foul misleading me.
And so, proud-hearted Warwick, I defy thee,
And to my brother turn my blushing cheeks.—
Pardon me, Edward, I will make amends;
And, Richard, do not frown upon my faults,
For I will henceforth be no more unconstant.

K. Edw. Now welcome more, and ten times more belov'd,
Than if thou never hadst deserv'd our hate.

Glo. Welcome, good Clarence: this is brother-like.

War. O passing traitor, perjur'd, and unjust!

K. Edw. What, Warwick, wilt thou leave the town, and fight?
Or shall we beat the stones about thine ears?

War. Alas, I am not coop'd here for defence:
I will away towards Barnet presently,
And bid thee battle, Edward, if thou dar'st.

K. Edw. Yes, Warwick, Edward dares, and leads the way:—
Lords, to the field, Saint George and victory.
[*March. Exeunt.*

SCENE II. *A Field of Battle near* Barnet.

Alarums, and Excursions. Enter KING EDWARD, *bringing in* WARWICK *wounded.*

K. Edw. So, lie thou there: die thou, and die our fear;
For Warwick was a bug, that fear'd us all.—
Now, Montague, sit fast; I seek for thee,
That Warwick's bones may keep thine company.
[*Exit.*

War. Ah, who is nigh? come to me, friend, or foe,

And tell me who is victor, York or Warwick?
Why ask I that? my mangled body shows,
My blood, my want of strength, my sick heart shows
That I must yield my body to the earth,
And, by my fall, the conquest to my foe.
Thus yields the cedar to the axe's edge,
Whose arms gave shelter to the princely eagle,
Under whose shade the ramping lion slept;
Whose top-branch overpeer'd Jove's spreading tree,
And kept low shrubs from winter's powerful wind.
These eyes, that now are dimm'd with death's black veil,
Have been as piercing as the mid-day sun,
To search the secret treasons of the world:
The wrinkles in my brows, now fill'd with blood,
Were liken'd oft to kingly sepulchres;
For who liv'd king, but I could dig his grave?
And who durst smile, when Warwick bent his brow?
Lo, now my glory smear'd in dust and blood!
My parks, my walks, my manors that I had,
Even now forsake me; and, of all my lands,
Is nothing left me, but my body's length!
Why, what is pomp, rule, reign, but earth and dust?
And, live we how we can, yet die we must.

Enter OXFORD *and* SOMERSET.

Som. Ah, Warwick, Warwick, wert thou as we are,
We might recover all our loss again!
The queen from France hath brought a puissant power:
Even now we heard the news: Ah, could'st thou fly!

War. Why, then I would not fly.—Ah, Montague,
If thou be there, sweet brother, take my hand,
And with thy lips keep in my soul a while!
Thou lov'st me not; for, brother, if thou didst,
Thy tears would wash this cold congealed blood,
That glues my lips, and will not let me speak.
Come quickly, Montague, or I am dead.

Som. Ah, Warwick, Montague hath breath'd his last;
And, to the latest gasp, cried out for Warwick,
And said—Commend me to my valiant brother.
And more he would have said; and more he spoke,
Which sounded like a cannon in a vault,
That might not be distinguish'd; but, at last,
I well might hear deliver'd with a groan,—
O, farewell, Warwick!

War. Sweet rest to his soul!—
Fly, lords, and save yourselves: for Warwick bids
You all farewell, to meet again in heaven. [*Dies.*

Oxf. Away, away, to meet the queen's great power!
[*Exeunt, bearing off* WARWICK'S *Body.*

SCENE III. *Another Part of the Field.*

Flourish. Enter KING EDWARD *in triumph; with* CLARENCE, GLOSTER, *and the rest.*

K. Edw. Thus far our fortune keeps an upward course,
And we are graced with wreaths of victory.
But, in the midst of this bright-shining day,
I spy a black, suspicious threat'ning cloud,
That will encounter with our glorious sun,
Ere he attain his easeful western bed:
I mean, my lords,—those powers, that the queen
Hath rais'd in Gallia, have arriv'd our coast,
And, as we hear, march on, to fight with us.

Clar. A little gale, will soon disperse that cloud,
And blow it to the source from whence it came:
Thy very beams will dry those vapours up;
For every cloud engenders not a storm.

Glo. The queen is valu'd thirty thousand strong,
And Somerset, with Oxford, fled to her:
If she have time to breathe, be well assur'd,
Her faction will be full as strong as ours.

K. Edw. We are advertis'd by our loving friends,
That they do hold their course toward Tewksbury;
We having now the best at Barnet field,
Will thither straight, For willingness rids way;
And, as we march, our strength will be augmented
In every county as we go along.
Strike up the drum; cry—Courage! and away.
[*Exeunt.*

SCENE IV. *Plains near* Tewksbury.

March. Enter QUEEN MARGARET, PRINCE EDWARD, SOMERSET, OXFORD, *and* Soldiers.

Q. Mar. Great lords, wise men ne'er sit and wail their loss,
But cheerly seek how to redress their harms.
What, though the mast be now blown overboard,
The cable broke, the holding anchor lost,
And half our sailors swallow'd in the flood?
Yet lives our pilot still: Is't meet, that he
Should leave the helm, and, like a fearful lad,
With tearful eyes add water to the sea,
And give more stength to that which hath too much;
Whiles, in his moan, the ship splits on the rock,
Which industry and courage might have sav'd?
Ah, what a shame! ah, what a fault were this!
Say, Warwick was our anchor! What of that?
And Montague our top-mast; What of him?
Our slaughter'd friends the tackles; What of these?
Why, is not Oxford here another anchor?
And Somerset another goodly mast;
The friends of France our shrouds and tacklings?
And, though unskilful, why not Ned and I
For once allow'd the skilful pilot's charge?
We will not from the helm, to sit and weep;
But keep our course, though the rough wind say—no,
From shelves and rocks that threaten us with wreck.
As good to chide the waves as speak them fair.
And what is Edward, but a ruthless sea?
What Clarence, but a quicksand of deceit?
And Richard, but a ragged fatal rock?
All these the enemies to our poor bark.
Say, you can swim; alas, 'tis but a while:
Tread on the sand; why, there you quickly sink:
Bestride the rock; the tide will wash you off,
Or else you famish, that's a threefold death.
This speak I, lords, to let you understand,
In case some one of you would fly from us,
That there's no hop'd-for mercy with the brothers,
More than with ruthless waves, with sands, and rocks.
Why, courage, then! what cannot be avoided,
'Twere childish weakness to lament, or fear.

Prince. Methinks a woman of this valiant spirit
Should, if a coward heard her speak these words,
Infuse his breast with magnanimity,
And make him, naked, foil a man at arms.
I speak not this, as doubting any here:
For, did I but suspect a fearful man,
He should have leave to go away betimes;
Lest, in our need, he might infect another,
And make him of like spirit to himself.
If any such be here, as God forbid!
Let him depart, before we need his help.

Oxf. Women and children of so high a courage!
And warriors faint! why, 'twere perpetual shame.—
O, brave young prince! thy famous grandfather
Doth live again in thee; Long may'st thou live,
To bear his image, and renew his glories!

Som. And he that will not fight for such a hope,
Go home to bed, and like the owl by day,
If he arise, be mock'd and wonder'd at.

Q. Mar. Thanks, gentle Somerset:—sweet Oxford, thanks.

Prince. And take his thanks, that yet hath nothing else.

Enter a Messenger.

Mess. Prepare you, lords, for Edward is at hand,
Ready to fight; therefore be resolute.

Oxf. I thought no less: it is his policy,
To haste thus fast, to find us unprovided.

Som. But he's deceiv'd, we are in readiness.

Q. Mar. This cheers my heart, to see your forwardness.

Oxf. Here pitch our battle, hence we will not budge.

March. Enter, at a distance, KING EDWARD, CLARENCE, GLOSTER, *and* Forces.

K. Edw. Brave followers, yonder stands the thorny wood,
Which, by the heavens' assistance, and your strength,
Must by the roots be hewn up yet ere night.
I need not add more fuel to your fire,
For, well I wot, ye blaze to burn them out:
Give signal to the fight, and to it lords.

Q. Mar. Lords, knights, and gentlemen, what I should say,
My tears gainsay; for every word I speak,
Ye see, I drink the water of mine eyes.
Therefore, no more but this:—Henry, your sovereign,
Is prisoner to the foe; his state usurp'd,
His realm a slaughterhouse, his subjects slain,
His statutes cancell'd, and his treasure spent;
And yonder is the wolf, that makes this spoil.
You fight in justice: then, in God's name, lords,
Be valiant, and give signal to the fight.
[*Exeunt both* Armies.

SCENE V. *Another Part of the same.*

Alarums: Excursions: and afterwards a Retreat. Then enter KING EDWARD, CLARENCE, GLOSTER, *and* Forces; *with* QUEEN MARGARET, OXFORD, *and* SOMERSET, *Prisoners.*

K. Edw. Now, here a period of tumultuous broils.
Away with Oxford to Hammes castle straight:
For Somerset, off with his guilty head.
Go, bear them hence; I will not hear them speak.

Oxf. For my part, I'll not trouble thee with words.

Som. Nor I, but stoop with patience to my fortune. [*Exeunt* OXF. *and* SOM. *guarded.*

Q. Mar. So part we sadly, in this troublous world,
To meet with joy in sweet Jerusalem.

K. Edw. Is proclamation made,—that who finds Edward,
Shall have a high reward, and he his life?

Glo. It is: and lo, where youthful Edward comes.

Enter Soldiers, *with* PRINCE EDWARD.

K. Edw. Bring forth the gallant, let us hear him speak:
What, can so young a thorn begin to prick?
Edward, what satisfaction canst thou make,
For bearing arms, for stirring up my subjects,
And all the trouble thou hast turn'd me to?

Prince. Speak like a subject, proud ambitious York!
Suppose, that I am now my father's mouth;
Resign thy chair, and where I stand, kneel thou,
Whilst I propose the self-same words to thee,
Which, traitor, thou wouldst have me answer to.

Q. Mar. Ah, that thy father had been so resolv'd!

Glo. That you might still have worn the petticoat,
And ne'er have stol'n the breech from Lancaster.

Prince. Let Æsop fable in a winter's night;
His currish riddles sort not with this place.

Glo. By heaven, brat, I'll plague you for that word.

Q. Mar. Ay, thou wast born to be a plague to men.

Glo. For God's sake, take away this captive scold.

Prince. Nay, take away this scolding crookback rather.

K. Edw. Peace, wilful boy, or I will charm your tongue.

Clar. Untutor'd lad, thou art too malapert.

Prince. I know my duty, you are all undutiful:
Lascivious Edward,—and thou perjur'd George,
And thou misshapen Dick, I tell ye all,
I am your better, traitors as ye are:—
And thou usurp'st my father's right and mine.

K. Edw. Take that, the likeness of this railer here. [*Stabs him.*

Glo. Sprawl'st thou? take that, to end thy agony. [GLO. *stabs him.*

Clar. And there's for twitting me with perjury. [CLAR. *stabs him.*

Q. Mar. O, kill me too!

Glo. Marry, and shall. [*Offers to kill her.*

K. Edw. Hold, Richard, hold, for we have done too much.

Glo. Why should she live, to fill the world with words?

K. Edw. What! doth she swoon? use means for her recovery.

Glo. Clarence, excuse me to the king my brother:
I'll hence to London on a serious matter;
Ere ye come there, be sure to hear some news.

Clar. What? what?

Glo. The Tower, the Tower! [*Exit.*

Q. Mar. O, Ned, sweet Ned! speak to thy mother, boy!
Canst thou not speak?—O traitors! murderers!—
They, that stabb'd Cæsar, shed no blood at all,
Did not offend, nor were not worthy blame,
If this foul deed were by, to equal it.
He was a man; this, in respect, a child;
And men ne'er spend their fury on a child.
What's worse than murderer, that I may name it?
No, no; my heart will burst, an if I speak;—
And I will speak, that so my heart may burst.—
Butchers and villains, bloody cannibals!
How sweet a plant have you untimely cropp'd!
You have no children, butchers! if you had,
The thought of them would have stirr'd up remorse:
But, if ever you chance to have a child,
Look in his youth to have him so cut off.
As, deathsmen! you have rid this sweet young prince!

K. Edw. Away with her; go bear her hence perforce.

Q. Mar. Nay, never bear me hence, despatch me here;
Here sheath thy sword, I'll pardon thee my death:
What! wilt thou not?—then, Clarence, do it thou.

Clar. By heaven, I will not do thee so much ease.

Q. Mar. Good Clarence, do; sweet Clarence, do thou do it.

Clar. Didst thou not hear me swear, I would not do it?

Q. Mar. Ay, but thou usest to forswear thyself;
'Twas sin before, but now 'tis charity.
What! wilt thou not? where is the devil's butcher,
Hard-favour'd Richard? Richard, where art thou?
Thou art not here: Murder is thy alms-deed;
Petitioners for blood thou ne'er put'st back.

K. Edw. Away, I say; I charge ye, bear her hence.

Q. Mar. So come to you, and yours, as to this prince! [*Exit, led out forcibly.*
K. Edw. Where's Richard gone?
Clar. To London, all in post; and, as I guess,
To make a bloody supper in the Tower.
K. Edw. He's sudden, if a thing comes in his head. [sort
Now march we hence: discharge the common
With pay and thanks, and let's away to London,
And see our gentle queen how well she fares;
By this, I hope, she hath a son for me. [*Exeunt.*

SCENE VI. London. *A Room in the Tower.*

KING HENRY *is discovered sitting with a Book in his Hand, the* Lieutenant *attending. Enter* GLOSTER.

Glo. Good day, my lord! What, at your book so hard?
K. Hen. Ay, my good lord: My lord, I should say rather;
'Tis sin to flatter, good was little better:
Good Gloster, and good devil, were alike,
And both preposterous; therefore, not good lord.
Glo. Sirrah, leave us to ourselves: we must confer. [*Exit* Lieutenant.
K. Hen. So flies the reckless shepherd from the wolf:
So first the harmless sheep doth yield his fleece,
And next his throat unto the butcher's knife.—
What scene of death hath Roscius now to act?
Glo. Suspicion always haunts the guilty mind;
The thief doth fear each bush an officer.
K. Hen. The bird, that hath been limed in a bush,
With trembling wings misdoubteth every bush:
And I, the hapless male to one sweet bird,
Have now the fatal object in my eye,
Where my poor young was lim'd, was caught, and kill'd.
Glo. Why, what a peevish fool was that of Crete,
That taught his son the office of a fowl?
And yet, for all his wings, the fool was drown'd.
K. Hen. I Dædalus; my poor boy, Icarus;
Thy father, Minos, that denied our course;
The sun, that sear'd the wings of my sweet boy,
Thy brother Edward; and thyself, the sea,
Whose envious gulf did swallow up his life.
Ah, kill me with thy weapon, not with words!
My breast can better brook thy dagger's point,
Than can my ears that tragick history.—
But wherefore dost thou come? is 't for my life?
Glo. Think'st thou, I am an executioner?
K. Hen. A persecutor, I am sure thou art;
If murdering innocents be executing,
Why, then thou art an executioner.
Glo. Thy son I kill'd for his presumption.
K. Hen. Hadst thou been kill'd, when first thou didst presume,
Thou hadst not liv'd to kill a son of mine.
And thus I prophesy,—that many a thousand,
Which now mistrust no parcel of my fear;
And many an old man's sigh, and many a widow's,
And many an orphan's water-standing eye.—
Men for their sons, wives for their husbands' fate.
And orphans for their parents' timeless death,—
Shall rue the hour that ever thou wast born.
The owl shriek'd at thy birth, an evil sign;
The night crow cried, aboding luckless time;
Dogs howl'd, and hideous tempests shook down trees;
The raven rook'd her on the chimney's top,
And chattering pies in dismal discords sung.
Thy mother felt more than a mother's pain,
And yet brought forth less than a mother's hope;
To wit,—an indigest deformed lump,
Not like the fruit of such a goodly tree.
Teeth hadst thou in thy head, when thou wast born,
To signify,—thou cam'st to bite the world:
And, if the rest be true which I have heard,
Thou cam'st—
Glo. I'll hear no more;—Die, prophet in thy speech; [*Stabs him.*
For this, amongst the rest, was I ordain'd.
K. Hen. Ay, and for much more slaughter after this.
O God! forgive my sins, and pardon thee! [*Dies.*
Glo. What, will the aspiring blood of Lancaster
Sink in the ground? I thought it would have mounted.
See, how my sword weeps for the poor king's death!
O, may such purple tears be always shed
From those that wish the downfall of our house!
If any spark of life be yet remaining,
Down, down to hell; and say, I sent thee thither. [*Stabs him again.*
I that have neither pity, love, nor fear.—
Indeed, 'tis true, that Henry told me of;
For I have often heard my mother say,
I came into the world with my legs forward:
Had I not reason, think ye, to make haste,
And seek their ruin that usurp'd our right?
The midwife wonder'd; and the women cried,
O, Jesus bless us, he is born with teeth!
And so I was; which plainly signified—
That I should snarl, and bite, and play the dog.
Then, since the heavens have shap'd my body so,
Let hell make crook'd my mind to answer it.
I have no brother, I am like no brother:
And this word—love, which graybeards call divine,
Be resident in men like one another,
And not in me; I am myself alone.—
Clarence, beware; thou keep'st me from the light;
But I will sort a pitchy day for thee:
For I will buz abroad such prophecies,
That Edward shall be fearful of his life;
And then, to purge his fear, I'll be thy death.
King Henry, and the prince his son, are gone:
Clarence, thy turn is next, and then the rest;
Counting myself but bad, till I be best.—
I'll throw thy body in another room,
And triumph, Henry, in thy day of doom. [*Exit.*

SCENE VII. *The same. A Room in the Palace.*

KING EDWARD *is discovered sitting on his Throne; QUEEN ELIZABETH with the infant* Prince, CLARENCE, GLOSTER, HASTINGS, *and Others, near him.*

K. Edw. Once more we sit in England's royal throne,
Repurchas'd with the blood of enemies.
What valiant foemen, like to autumn's corn,
Have we mow'd down, in tops of all their pride?
Three dukes of Somerset, threefold renown'd
For hardy and undoubted champions:
Two Cliffords, as the father and the son,
And two Northumberlands; two braver men
Ne'er spurr'd their coursers at the trumpet's sound:
With them, the two brave bears, Warwick and Montague,
That in their chains fetter'd the kingly lion,
And made the forest tremble when they roar'd.
Thus have we swept suspicion from our seat,
And made our footstool of security.—
Come hither, Bess, and let me kiss my boy:—
Young Ned, for thee, thine uncles, and myself,
Have in our armours watch'd the winter's night;
Went all afoot in summer's scalding heat,
That thou might'st repossess the crown in peace;
And of our labours thou shalt reap the gain.
Glo. I'll blast his harvest, if your head were laid;
For yet I am not look'd on in the world.
This shoulder was ordain'd so thick, to heave;
And heave it shall some weight, or break my back:—
Work thou the way,—and thou shalt execute. [*Aside.*

K. Edw. Clarence, and Gloster, love my lovely queen;
And kiss your princely nephew, brothers both.

Clar. The duty, that I owe unto your majesty,
I seal upon the lips of this sweet babe.

K. Edw. Thanks, noble Clarence; worthy brother, thanks.

Glo. And, that I love the tree from whence thou sprang'st,
Witness the loving kiss I give the fruit:—
To say the truth, so Judas kiss'd his master;
And cried—all hail! when as he meant—all harm. [*Aside.*

K. Edw. Now am I seated as my soul delights,
Having my country's peace, and brothers' loves.

Clar. What will your grace have done with Margaret?
Reignier, her father, to the king of France
Hath pawn'd the Sicils and Jerusalem,
And hither have they sent it for her ransome.

K. Edw. Away with her, and waft her hence to France.
And now what rests, but that we spend the time
With stately triumphs, mirthful comick shows,
Such as befit the pleasures of the court?—
Sound, drums and trumpets!—farewell, sour annoy!
For here, I hope, begins our lasting joy.
[*Exeunt.*

LIFE AND DEATH OF

KING RICHARD THE THIRD.

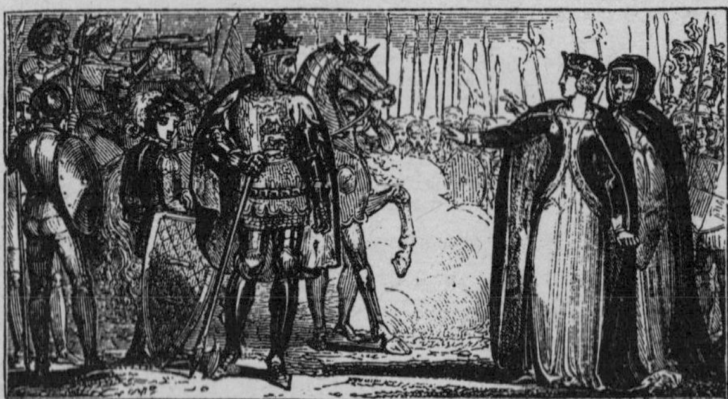

PERSONS REPRESENTED.

KING EDWARD THE FOURTH.
EDWARD, Prince *of* Wales, *afterwards* King Edward V. } *Sons to the* King.
RICHARD, Duke *of* York, } *Sons to the* King.
GEORGE, Duke *of* Clarence, } *Brothers to the* King.
RICHARD, Duke *of* Gloster, *afterwards* King Richard III. } *Brothers to the* King.
A young Son *of* Clarence.
HENRY, Earl *of* Richmond, *afterwards* King Henry VII.
CARDINAL BOURCHIER, Archbishop *of* Canterbury.
THOMAS ROTHERAM, Archbishop *of* York.
JOHN MORTON, Bishop *of* Ely.
DUKE OF BUCKINGHAM.
DUKE OF NORFOLK: EARL OF SURREY, *his Son.*
EARL RIVERS, *Brother to* King Edward's Queen.
MARQUIS OF DORSET, *and* LORD GREY, *her Sons.*
EARL OF OXFORD. LORD HASTINGS.
LORD STANLEY. LORD LOVEL.
SIR THOMAS VAUGHAN. SIR RICHARD RATCLIFF.
SIR WILLIAM CATESBY. SIR JAMES TYRREL.
SIR JAMES BLOUNT. SIR WALTER HERBERT.
SIR ROBERT BRAKENBURY, *Lieutenant of the Tower.*
CHRISTOPHER URSWICK, *a Priest. Another* Priest.
Lord Mayor *of* London. Sheriff *of* Wiltshire.

ELIZABETH, *Queen of* King Edward IV.
MARGARET, *Widow of* King Henry VI.
DUCHESS OF YORK, *Mother to* King Edward IV. Clarence, *and* Gloster.
LADY ANNE, *Widow of* Edward, Prince *of* Wales, *Son to* King Henry VI.; *afterwards married to the* Duke *of* Gloster.
A young Daughter *of* Clarence.

Lords, *and other* Attendants, *two* Gentlemen, *a* Pursuivant, Scrivener, Citizens, Murderers, Messengers, Ghosts, Soldiers, *&c.*

SCENE—England.

ACT I.

SCENE I. London. *A Street.*

Enter GLOSTER.

Glo. Now is the winter of our discontent
Made glorious summer by this sun of York;
And all the clouds, that lour'd upon our house,
In the deep bosom of the ocean buried.
Now are our brows bound with victorious wreaths;
Our bruised arms hung up for monuments;
Our stern alarums chang'd to merry meetings,
Our dreadful marches to delightful measures.
Grim-visag'd war hath smooth'd his wrinkled front;
And now,—instead of mounting barbed steeds,
To fright the souls of fearful adversaries,—
He capers nimbly in a lady's chamber,
To the lascivious pleasing of a lute.
But I,—that am not shap'd for sportive tricks,
Nor made to court an amorous looking-glass;

I, that am rudely stamp'd, and want love's majesty,
To strut before a wanton ambling nymph;
I, that am curtail'd of this fair proportion,
Cheated of feature by dissembling nature,
Deform'd, unfinish'd, sent before my time
Into this breathing world, scarce half made up,
And that so lamely and unfashionable,
That dogs bark at me, as I halt by them;—
Why I, in this weak piping time of peace,
Have no delight to pass away the time;
Unless to spy my shadow in the sun,
And descant on mine own deformity;
And therefore,—since I cannot prove a lover,
To entertain these fair well spoken days,—
I am determined to prove a villain,
And hate the idle pleasures of these days.
Plots have I laid, inductions dangerous,
By drunken prophecies, libels, and dreams,
To set my brother Clarence, and the king,
In deadly hate the one against the other:
And, if King Edward be as true and just,
As I am subtle, false, and treacherous,
This day should Clarence closely be mew'd up;
About a prophecy, which says that G
Of Edward's heirs the murderer shall be.
Dive, thoughts, down to my soul! here Clarence comes.

Enter CLARENCE, *guarded, and* BRAKENBURY.

Brother, good day: What means this armed guard,
That waits upon your grace?
Clar. His majesty,
Tendering my person's safety, hath appointed
This conduct to convey me to the Tower.
Glo. Upon what cause?
Clar. Because my name is—George.
Glo. Alack, my lord, that fault is none of yours;
He should, for that, commit your godfathers:——
O, belike, his majesty hath some intent,
That you shall be new christen'd in the Tower.
But what's the matter, Clarence? may I know?
Clar. Yea, Richard, when I know; for, I protest,
As yet I do not: But, as I can learn,
He hearkens after prophecies, and dreams;
And from the cross-row plucks the letter G,
And says—a wizard told him, that by G
His issue disinherited should be;
And, for my name of George begins with G,
It follows in his thought, that I am he:
These, as I learn, and such like toys as these,
Have mov'd his highness to commit me now.
Glo. Why, this it is, when men are rul'd by women:—
'Tis not the king, that sends you to the Tower;
My Lady Grey, his wife, Clarence, 'tis she,
That tempers him to this extremity.
Was it not she, and that good man of worship,
Antony Woodeville, her brother there,
That made him send Lord Hastings to the Tower;
From whence this present day he is deliver'd?
We are not safe, Clarence, we are not safe.
Clar. By heaven, I think, there is no man secure,
But the queen's kindred, and night-walking heralds
That trudge betwixt the king and Mistress Shore.
Heard you not, what an humble suppliant
Lord Hastings was to her for his delivery?
Glo. Humbly complaining to her deity
Got my lord chamberlain his liberty.
I'll tell you what,—I think, it is our way,
If we will keep in favour with the king,
To be her men, and wear her livery:
The jealous o'er-worn widow, and herself,
Since that our brother dubb'd them gentlewomen,
Are mighty gossips in this monarchy.
Brak. I beseech your graces both to pardon me;
His majesty hath straitly given in charge,
That no man shall have private conference,
Of what degree soever, with his brother.
Glo. Even so? an please your worship, Brakenbury,
You may partake of any thing we say:
We speak no treason, man;—We say, the king
Is wise and virtuous; and his noble queen
Well struck in years; fair, and not jealous:
We say, that Shore's wife hath a pretty foot,
A cherry lip,
A bonny eye, a passing pleasing tongue;
And that the queen's kindred are made gentlefolks:
How say you, sir? can you deny all this?
Brak. With this, my lord, myself have nought to do.
Glo. Naught to do with mistress Shore? I tell thee, fellow,
He that doth naught with her, excepting one,
Were best to do it secretly, alone.
Brak. What one, my lord?
Glo. Her husband, knave:—Wouldst thou betray me?
Brak. I beseech your grace to pardon me; and, withal,
Forbear your conference with the noble duke.
Clar. We know thy charge, Brakenbury, and will obey.
Glo. We are the queen's abjects, and must obey.
Brother, farewell: I will unto the king;
And whatsoe'er you will employ me in,—
Were it, to call King Edward's widow—sister,—
I will perform it to enfranchise you.
Mean time, this deep disgrace in brotherhood,
Touches me deeper than you can imagine.
Clar. I know it pleaseth neither of us well.
Glo. Well, your imprisonment shall not be long;
I will deliver you, or else lie for you:
Mean time, have patience.
Clar. I must perforce; farewell.
[*Exeunt* CLARENCE, BRAKENBURY, *and* Guard.
Glo. Go, tread the path that thou shalt ne'er return,
Simple, plain Clarence!—I do love thee so,
That I will shortly send thy soul to heaven,
If heaven will take the present at our hands.
But who comes here? the new deliver'd Hastings?

Enter HASTINGS.

Hast. Good time of day unto my gracious lord!
Glo. As much unto my good lord chamberlain!
Well are you welcome to this open air.
How hath your lordship brook'd imprisonment?
Hast. With patience, noble lord, as prisoners must:
But I shall live, my lord, to give them thanks,
That were the cause of my imprisonment.
Glo. No doubt, no doubt; and so shall Clarence too;
For they, that were your enemies, are his,
And have prevail'd as much on him, as you.
Hast. More pity that the eagle should be mew'd,
While kites and buzzards prey at liberty.
Glo. What news abroad?
Hast. No news so bad abroad as this at home;—
The king is sickly, weak, and melancholy,
And his physicians fear him mightily.
Glo. Now, by Saint Paul, this news is bad indeed.
O, he hath kept an evil diet long,
And over-much consum'd his royal person;
'Tis very grievous to be thought upon.
What, is he in his bed?
Hast. He is.
Glo. Go you before, and I will follow you.
[*Exit* HASTINGS.
He cannot live, I hope; and must not die,
Till George be pack'd with posthorse up to heaven.

I'll in, to urge his hatred more to Clarence,
With lies well steel'd with weighty arguments;
And, if I fail not in my deep intent,
Clarence hath not another day to live:
Which done, God take King Edward to his mercy,
And leave the world for me to bustle in!
For then I'll marry Warwick's youngest daughter:
What though I kill'd her husband, and her father?
The readiest way to make the wench amends,
Is—to become her husband, and her father:
The which will I; not all so much for love,
As for another secret close intent,
By marrying her, which I must reach unto.
But yet I run before my horse to market:
Clarence still breathes; Edward still lives, and reigns;
When they are gone, then must I count my gains. [*Exit.*

SCENE II. *The same. Another Street.*

Enter the Corpse of King Henry the Sixth, *borne in an open Coffin,* Gentlemen *bearing Halberds, to guard it; and* Lady Anne *as mourner.*

Anne. Set down, set down your honourable load,
If honour may be shrouded in a hearse,—
Whilst I a while obsequiously lament
The untimely fall of virtuous Lancaster—
Poor key-cold figure of a holy king!
Pale ashes of the house of Lancaster!
Thou bloodless remnant of that royal blood!
Be it lawful that I invocate thy ghost,
To hear the lamentations of poor Anne,
Wife to thy Edward, to thy slaughter'd son,
Stabb'd by the self-same hand that made these wounds!
Lo, in these windows, that let forth thy life,
I pour the helpless balm of my poor eyes:—
O, cursed be the hand that made these holes!
Cursed the heart, that had the heart to do it!
Cursed the blood, that let this blood from hence!
More direful hap betide that hated wretch.
That makes us wretched by the death of thee,
Than I can wish to adders, spiders, toads,
Or any creeping venom'd thing that lives!
If ever he have child, abortive be it,
Prodigious, and untimely brought to light,
Whose ugly and unnatural aspect
May fright the hopeful mother at the view;
And that be heir to his unhappiness!
If ever he have wife, let her be made
More miserable by the death of him,
Than I am made by my young lord, and thee!—
Come, now, toward Chertsey with your holy load,
Taken from Paul's to be interred there;
And, still as you are weary of the weight,
Rest you, whiles I lament King Henry's corse.
[*The Bearers take up the Corpse, and advance.*

Enter Gloster.

Glo. Stay you, that bear the corse, and set it down.
Anne. What black magician conjures up this fiend,
To stop devoted charitable deeds?
Glo. Villains, set down the corse; or, by Saint Paul,
I'll make a corse of him that disobeys.
1 *Gent.* My lord, stand back, and let the coffin pass.
Glo. Unmanner'd dog! stand thou when I command:
Advance thy halberd higher than my breast,
Or, by Saint Paul, I'll strike thee to my foot,
And spurn upon thee, beggar, for thy boldness.
[*The Bearers set down the Coffin.*
Anne. What, do you tremble? are you all afraid?
Alas, I blame you not; for you are mortal,
And mortal eyes cannot endure the devil.—
Avaunt, thou dreadful minister of hell!
Thou hadst but power over his mortal body,
His soul thou canst not have; therefore, be gone.
Glo. Sweet saint, for charity, be not so curst.
Anne. Foul devil, for God's sake, hence, and trouble us not;
For thou hast made the happy earth thy hell,
Fill'd it with cursing cries, and deep exclaims.
If thou delight to view thy heinous deeds,
Behold this pattern of thy butcheries;
O, gentlemen, see, see! dead Henry's wounds
Open their congeal'd mouths, and bleed afresh!—
Blush, blush, thou lump of foul deformity;
For 'tis thy presence that exhales this blood
From cold and empty veins, where no blood dwells:
Thy deed, inhuman and unnatural,
Provokes this deluge most unnatural.——
O God, which this blood mad'st, revenge his death!
O earth, which this blood drink'st, revenge his death!
Either, heaven, with lightning strike the murderer dead,
Or, earth, gape open wide, and eat him quick;
As thou dost swallow up this good king's blood,
Which his hell-govern'd arm hath butchered!
Glo. Lady, you know no rules of charity,
Which renders good for bad, blessings for curses.
Anne. Villain, thou know'st no law of God nor man;
No beast so fierce, but knows some touch of pity.
Glo. But I know none, and therefore am no beast.
Anne. O wonderful, when devils tell the truth!
Glo. More wonderful, when angels are so angry.—
Vouchsafe, divine perfection of a woman,
Of these supposed evils, to give me leave,
By circumstance, but to acquit myself.
Anne. Vouchsafe, diffus'd infection of a man,
For these known evils, but to give me leave,
By circumstance, to curse thy cursed self.
Glo. Fairer than tongue can name thee, let me have
Some patient leisure to excuse myself.
Anne. Fouler than heart can think thee, thou canst make
No excuse current, but to hang thyself.
Glo. By such despair, I should accuse myself.
Anne. And, by despairing, shalt thou stand excus'd;
For doing worthy vengeance on thyself,
That didst unworthy slaughter upon others.
Glo. Say, that I slew them not?
Anne. Why then, they are not dead:
But dead they are, and, devilish slave, by thee.
Glo. I did not kill your husband.
Anne. Why, then he is alive.
Glo. Nay, he is dead; and slain by Edward's hand.
Anne. In thy foul throat thou liest; Queen Margaret saw
Thy murderous falchion smoking in his blood.
The which thou once didst bend against her breast,
But that thy brothers beat aside the point.
Glo. I was provoked by her sland'rous tongue,
That laid their guilt upon my guiltless shoulders.
Anne. Thou wast provoked by thy bloody mind,
That never dreamt on aught but butcheries:
Didst thou not kill this king?
Glo. I grant ye.
Anne. Dost grant me, hedgehog? then, God grant me too,
Thou may'st be damned for that wicked deed!
O, he was gentle, mild, and virtuous.
Glo. The fitter for the King of heaven that hath him.

Anne. He is in heaven, where thou shalt never come.
Glo. Let him thank me, that holp to send him thither;
For he was fitter for that place, than earth.
Anne. And thou unfit for any place, but hell.
Glo. Yes, one place else, if you will hear me name it.
Anne. Some dungeon.
Glo. Your bed-chamber.
Anne. Ill rest betide the chamber where thou liest!
Glo. So will it, madam, till I lie with you.
Anne. I hope so.
Glo. I know so.—But, gentle Lady Anne,—
To leave this keen encounter of our wits,
And fall somewhat into a slower method;—
Is not the causer of the timeless deaths
Of these Plantagenets, Henry, and Edward,
As blameful as the executioner?
Anne. Thou wast the cause, and most accurs'd effect.
Glo. Your beauty was the cause of that effect;
Your beauty, which did haunt me in my sleep,
To undertake the death of all the world,
So, I might live one hour in your sweet bosom.
Anne. If I thought that, I tell thee, homicide,
These nails should rend that beauty from my cheeks.
Glo. These eyes could not endure that beauty's wreck,
You should not blemish it, if I stood by:
As all the world is cheered by the sun,
So I by that; it is my day, my life.
Anne. Black night o'ershade thy day, and death thy life!
Glo. Curse not thyself, fair creature; thou art both.
Anne. I would, I were, to be reveng'd on thee.
Glo. It is a quarrel most unnatural,
To be reveng'd on him that loveth thee.
Anne. It is a quarrel just and reasonable,
To be reveng'd on him that kill'd my husband.
Glo. He that bereft thee, lady, of thy husband,
Did it to help thee to a better husband.
Anne. His better doth not breathe upon the earth.
Glo. He lives, that loves you better than he could.
Anne. Name him.
Glo. Plantagenet.
Anne. Why, that was he.
Glo. The self-same name, but one of better nature.
Anne. Where is he?
Glo. Here: [*She spits at him.*] Why dost thou spit at me?
Anne. 'Would, it were mortal poison, for thy sake!
Glo. Never came poison from so sweet a place.
Anne. Never hung poison on a fouler toad.
Out of my sight! thou dost infect mine eyes.
Glo. Thine eyes, sweet lady, have infected mine.
Anne. 'Would, they were basilisks, to strike thee dead!
Glo. I would they were, that I might die at once;
For now they kill me with a living death.
Those eyes of thine from mine have drawn salt tears,
Sham'd their aspects with store of childish drops:
These eyes, which never shed remorseful tear,—
No, when my father York and Edward wept,
To hear the piteous moan that Rutland made,
When black-fac'd Clifford shook his sword at him:
Nor when thy warlike father, like a child,
Told the sad story of my father's death;
And twenty times made pause, to sob, and weep,
That all the standers-by had wet their cheeks,
Like trees bedash'd with rain:—in that sad time,
My manly eyes did scorn an humble tear;
And what these sorrows could not thence exhale,
Thy beauty hath, and made them blind with weeping.
I never sued to friend, nor enemy;
My tongue could never learn sweet soothing word;
But now thy beauty is propos'd my fee,
My proud heart sues, and prompts my tongue to speak. [*She looks scornfully at him.*
Teach not thy lip such scorn; for it was made
For kissing, lady, not for such contempt.
If thy revengeful heart cannot forgive,
Lo! here I lend thee this sharp-pointed sword;
Which if thou please to hide in this true breast,
And let the soul forth that adoreth thee,
I lay it naked to the deadly stroke,
And humbly beg the death upon my knee.
[*He lays his breast open; she offers at it with his sword.*
Nay, do not pause; for I did kill King Henry:—
But 'twas thy beauty that provoked me.
Nay, now despatch; 'twas I that stabb'd young Edward;— [*She again offers at his breast.*
But 'twas thy heavenly face that set me on.
[*She lets fall the sword.*
Take up the sword again, or take up me.
Anne. Arise, dissembler: though I wish thy death,
I will not be thy executioner.
Glo. Then bid me kill myself, and I will do it.
Anne. I have already.
Glo. That was in thy rage:
Speak it again, and even with the word,
This hand, which, for thy love, did kill thy love,
Shall, for thy love, kill a far truer love;
To both their deaths shalt thou be accessary.
Anne. I would, I knew thy heart.
Glo. 'Tis figur'd in my tongue.
Anne. I fear me, both are false.
Glo. Then never man was true.
Anne. Well, well, put up your sword.
Glo. Say then, my peace is made.
Anne. That shall you know hereafter.
Glo. But shall I live in hope?
Anne. All men, I hope, live so.
Glo. Vouchsafe to wear this ring.
Anne. To take, is not to give.
[*She puts on the ring.*
Glo. Look, how this ring encompasseth thy finger,
Even so thy breast encloseth my poor heart;
Wear both of them, for both of them are thine.
And if thy poor devoted servant may
But beg one favour at thy gracious hand,
Thou dost confirm his happiness for ever.
Anne. What is it?
Glo. That it may please you leave these sad designs
To him that hath more cause to be a mourner,
And presently repair to Crosby-place:
Where—after I have solemnly interr'd,
At Chertsey monast'ry, this noble king,
And wet his grave with my repentant tears,—
I will with all expedient duty see you:
For divers unknown reasons, I beseech you,
Grant me this boon.
Anne. With all my heart; and much it joys me too,
To see you are become so penitent.—
Tressel, and Berkley, go along with me.
Glo. Bid me farewell.
Anne. 'Tis more than you deserve:
But, since you teach me how to flatter you,
Imagine I have said farewell already.
[*Exeunt* LADY ANNE, TRES. *and* BERK.
Glo. Sirs, take up the corse.
Gent. Towards Chertsey, noble lord?
Glo. No, to White Friars; there attend my coming. [*Exeunt the rest, with the Corse.*
Was ever woman in this humour woo'd?

Was ever woman in this humour won?
I'll have her,—but I will not keep her long.
What! I, that kill'd her husband, and his father,
To take her in her heart's extremest hate;
With curses in her mouth, tears in her eyes,
The bleeding witness of her hatred by;
With God, her conscience, and these bars against me,
And I no friends to back my suit withal,
But the plain devil, and dissembling looks,
And yet to win her,—all the world to nothing!
Ha!
Hath she forgot already that brave prince,
Edward, her lord, whom I some three months since,
Stabb'd in my angry mood at Tewksbury?
A sweeter and a lovelier gentleman,—
Fram'd in the prodigality of nature,
Young, valiant, wise, and, no doubt, right royal,—
The spacious world cannot again afford:
And will she yet abase her eyes on me,
That cropp'd the golden prime of this sweet prince,
And made her widow to a woful bed?
On me, whose all not equals Edward's moiety?
On me, that halt, and am misshapen thus?
My dukedom to a beggarly denier,
I do mistake my person all this while:
Upon my life, she finds, although I cannot,
Myself to be a marvellous proper man.
I'll be at charges for a looking-glass;
And entertain a score or two of tailors,
To study fashions to adorn my body:
Since I am crept in favour with myself,
I will maintain it with some little cost.
But, first, I'll turn yon fellow in his grave;
And then return lamenting to my love.—
Shine out, fair sun, till I have bought a glass,
That I may see my shadow as I pass. [*Exit.*

SCENE III. *The same. A Room in the Palace.*

Enter QUEEN ELIZABETH, LORD RIVERS, *and* LORD GREY.

Riv. Have patience, madam, there's no doubt, his majesty
Will soon recover his accustom'd health.
Grey. In that you brook it ill, it makes him worse:
Therefore, for God's sake, entertain good comfort,
And cheer his grace with quick and merry words.
Q. Eliz. If he were dead, what would betide of me?
Grey. No other harm, but loss of such a lord.
Q. Eliz. The loss of such a lord includes all harms.
Grey. The heavens have bless'd you with a goodly son,
To be your comforter when he is gone.
Q. Eliz. Ah, he is young; and his minority
Is put unto the trust of Richard Gloster,
A man that loves not me, nor none of you.
Riv. Is it concluded he shall be protector?
Q. Eliz. It is determin'd, not concluded yet:
But so it must be, if the king miscarry.

Enter BUCKINGHAM *and* STANLEY.

Grey. Here come the lords of Buckingham and Stanley.
Buck. Good time of day unto your royal grace!
Stan. God make your majesty joyful as you have been!
Q. Eliz. The Countess Richmond, good my lord of Stanley,
To your good prayer will scarcely say—amen.
Yet, Stanley, notwithstanding she's your wife,
And loves not me, be you, good lord, assur'd,
I hate not you for her proud arrogance.
Stan. I do beseech you, either not believe
The envious slanders of her false accusers;
Or, if she be accus'd on true report,
Bear with her weakness, which, I think, proceeds
From wayward sickness, and no grounded malice.
Q. Eliz. Saw you the king to-day, my lord of Stanley?
Stan. But now, the duke of Buckingham, and I,
Are come from visiting his majesty.
Q. Eliz. What likelihood of his amendment, lords?
Buck. Madam, good hope; his grace speaks cheerfully.
Q. Eliz. God grant him health! Did you confer with him?
Buck. Ay, madam: he desires to make atonement
Between the duke of Gloster, and your brothers,
And between them and my lord chamberlain;
And sent to warn them to his royal presence.
Q. Eliz. 'Would, all were well!—But that will never be;—
I fear, our happiness is at the height.

Enter GLOSTER, HASTINGS, *and* DORSET.

Glo. They do me wrong, and I will not endure it:—
Who are they, that complain unto the king,
That I, forsooth, am stern, and love them not?
By holy Paul, they love his grace but lightly,
That fill his ears with such dissentious rumours.
Because I cannot flatter, and speak fair,
Smile in men's faces, smooth, deceive, and cog,
Duck with French nods and apish courtesy,
I must be held a rancorous enemy.
Cannot a plain man live, and think no harm,
But thus his simple truth must be abus'd
By silken, sly, insinuating Jacks?
Grey. To whom in all this presence speaks your grace?
Glo. To thee, that hast nor honesty, nor grace.
When have I injur'd thee? when done thee wrong?
Or thee?—or thee?—or any of your faction?
A plague upon you all! his royal grace,—
Whom God preserve better than you would wish!
Cannot be quiet scarce a breathing while,
But you must trouble him with lewd complaints.
Q. Eliz. Brother of Gloster, you mistake the matter;
The king, of his own royal disposition,
And not provok'd by any suitor else;
Aiming, belike, at your interior hatred,
That in your outward action shows itself,
Against my children, brothers, and myself,
Makes him to send: that thereby he may gather
The ground of your ill will, and so remove it.
Glo. I cannot tell;—The world is grown so bad,
That wrens may prey where eagles dare not perch:
Since every Jack became a gentleman,
There's many a gentle person made a Jack.
Q. Eliz. Come, come, we know your meaning, brother Gloster;
You envy my advancement, and my friends;
God grant, we never may have need of you!
Glo. Meantime, God grants that we have need of you:
Our brother is imprison'd by your means,
Myself disgrac'd, and the nobility
Held in contempt; while great promotions
Are daily given, to ennoble those
That scarce, some two days since, were worth a noble.
Q. Eliz. By Him, that rais'd me to this careful height
From that contented hap which I enjoy'd,
I never did incense his majesty
Against the duke of Clarence, but have been
An earnest advocate to plead for him.

My lord, you do me shameful injury,
Falsely to draw me in these vile suspects.
Glo. You may deny that you were not the cause
Of my Lord Hastings' late imprisonment.
Riv. She may, my lord; for——
Glo. She may, Lord Rivers?—why, who knows not so?
She may do more, sir, than denying that:
She may help you to many fair preferments;
And then deny her aiding hand therein,
And lay those honours on your high desert.
What may she not? she may,—ay, marry, may she,—
Riv. What, marry, may she?
Glo. What, marry, may she? marry, with a king,
A bachelor, a handsome stripling too:
I wis, your grandam had a worser match.
Q. Eliz. My lord of Gloster, I have too long borne
Your blunt upbraidings, and your bitter scoffs:
By heaven I will acquaint his majesty,
Of those gross taunts I often have endur'd.
I had rather be a country servant maid,
Than a great queen, with this condition—
To be so baited, scorn'd, and stormed at:
Small joy have I in being England's queen.

Enter QUEEN MARGARET, *behind.*

Q. Mar. And lessen'd be that small, God, I beseech thee!
Thy honour, state, and seat, is due to me.
Glo. What? threat you me with telling of the king?
Tell him, and spare not: look, what I have said
I will avouch, in presence of the king:
I dare adventure to be sent to the Tower.
'Tis time to speak, my pains are quite forgot.
Q. Mar. Out, devil! I remember them too well:
Thou kill'dst my husband Henry in the Tower,
And Edward, my poor son, at Tewksbury.
Glo. Ere you were queen, ay, or your husband king,
I was a packhorse in his great affairs;
A weeder-out of his proud adversaries,
A liberal rewarder of his friends;
To royalize his blood, I spilt mine own.
Q. Mar. Ay, and much better blood than his, or thine.
Glo. In all which time you, and your husband Grey,
Were factious for the house of Lancaster;—
And, Rivers, so were you:—Was not your husband
In Margaret's battle at Saint Albans slain?
Let me put in your minds, if you forget,
What you have been ere now, and what you are;
Withal, what I have been, and what I am.
Q. Mar. A murd'rous villain, and so still thou art.
Glo. Poor Clarence did forsake his father Warwick,
Ay, and forswore himself,—Which Jesu pardon!—
Q. Mar. Which God revenge!
Glo. To fight on Edward's party, for the crown:
And, for his meed, poor lord, he is mew'd up:
I would to God, my heart were flint like Edward's,
Or Edward's soft and pitiful, like mine;
I am too childish-foolish for this world.
Q. Mar. Hie thee to hell for shame, and leave this world,
Thou cacodæmon! there thy kingdom is.
Riv. My lord of Gloster, in those busy days,
Which here you urge, to prove us enemies,
We follow'd then our lord, our lawful king;
So should we you, if you should be our king.
Glo. If I should be?—I had rather be a pedler:
Far be it from my heart, the thought thereof!
Q. Eliz. As little joy, my lord, as you suppose
You should enjoy, were you this country's king:
As little joy you may suppose in me,
That I enjoy, being the queen thereof.
Q. Mar. A little joy enjoys the queen thereof;
For I am she, and altogether joyless.
I can no longer hold me patient.— [*Advancing.*
Hear me, you wrangling pirates, that fall out
In sharing that which you have pill'd from me:
Which of you trembles not, that looks on me?
If not, that, I being queen, you bow like subjects;
Yet that, by you depos'd, you quake like rebels?—
Ah, gentle villain, do not turn away!
Glo. Foul wrinkled witch, what mak'st thou in my sight?
Q. Mar. But repetition of what thou hast marr'd;
That will I make, before I let thee go.
Glo. Wert thou not banished on pain of death?
Q. Mar. I was; but I do find more pain in banishment,
Than death can yield me here by my abode.
A husband, and a son, thou ow'st to me,—
And thou a kingdom;—all of you, allegiance:
This sorrow that I have, by right is yours;
And all the pleasures you usurp, are mine.
Glo. The curse my noble father laid on thee,—
When thou didst crown his warlike brows with paper,
And with thy scorns drew'st rivers from his eyes;
And then, to dry them, gav'st the duke a clout,
Steep'd in the faultless blood of pretty Rutland;—
His curses, then from bitterness of soul
Denounc'd against thee, are all fall'n upon thee;
And God, not we, hath plagu'd thy bloody deed.
Q. Eliz. So just is God, to right the innocent.
Hast. O, 'twas the foulest deed to slay that babe,
And the most merciless, that e'er was heard of.
Riv. Tyrants themselves wept when it was reported.
Dors. No man but prophesied revenge for it.
Buck. Northumberland, then present, wept to see it.
Q. Mar. What! were you snarling all, before I came,
Ready to catch each other by the throat,
And turn you all your hatred now on me?
Did York's dread curse prevail so much with heaven,
That Henry's death, my lovely Edward's death,
Their kingdom's loss, my woful banishment,
Could all but answer for that peevish brat?
Can curses pierce the clouds, and enter heaven?—
Why, then give way, dull clouds, to my quick curses!—
Though not by war, by surfeit die your king,
As ours by murder, to make him a king!
Edward, thy son, that now is prince of Wales,
For Edward, my son, that was prince of Wales,
Die in his youth, by like untimely violence!
Thyself a queen, for me that was a queen,
Outlive thy glory, like my wretched self!
Long may'st thou live, to wail thy children's loss;
And see another, as I see thee now,
Deck'd in thy rights, as thou art stall'd in mine!
Long die thy happy days before thy death;
And, after many lengthen'd hours of grief,
Die neither mother, wife, nor England's queen!—
Rivers,—and Dorset,—you were standers by,—
And so wast thou, Lord Hastings,—when my son
Was stabb'd with bloody daggers: God, I pray him,
That none of you may live your natural age,
But by some unlook'd accident cut off!
Glo. Have done thy charm, thou hateful wither'd hag.
Q. Mar. And leave out thee? stay, dog, for thou shalt hear me.

If heaven have any grievous plague in store,
Exceeding those that I can wish upon thee,
O, let them keep it, till thy sins be ripe,
And then hurl down their indignation
On thee, the troubler of the poor world's peace!
The worm of conscience still be-gnaw thy soul!
Thy friends suspect for traitors while thou liv'st,
And take deep traitors for thy dearest friends!
No sleep close up that deadly eye of thine,
Unless it be while some tormenting dream
Affrights thee with a hell of ugly devils!
Thou elvish mark'd, abortive, rooting hog!
Thou that wast seal'd in thy nativity
The slave of nature, and the son of hell!
Thou slander of thy mother's heavy womb!
Thou loathed issue of thy father's loins!
Thou rag of honour! thou detested——

Glo. Margaret.

Q. Mar. Richard!

Glo. Ha?

Q. Mar. I call thee not.

Glo. I cry thee mercy then; for I did think,
That thou hadst call'd me all these bitter names.

Q. Mar. Why, so I did: but look'd for no reply.
O, let me make the period to my curse.

Glo. 'Tis done by me; and ends in—Margaret.

Q. Eliz. Thus have you breath'd your curse against yourself.

Q. Mar. Poor painted queen, vain flourish of my fortune!
Why strew'st thou sugar on that bottled spider,
Whose deadly web ensnareth thee about?
Fool, fool! thou whet'st a knife to kill thyself.
The day will come, that thou shalt wish for me
To help thee curse this pois'nous bunch-back'd toad.

Hast. False-boding woman, end thy frantick curse;
Lest, to thy harm, thou move our patience.

Q. Mar. Foul shame upon you! you have all mov'd mine.

Riv. Were you well serv'd, you would be taught your duty.

Q. Mar. To serve me well, you all should do me duty,
Teach me to be your queen, and you my subjects:
O, serve me well, and teach yourselves that duty.

Dors. Dispute not with her, she is lunatick.

Q. Mar. Peace, master marquis, you are malapert:
Your fire-new stamp of honour is scarce current:
O, that your young nobility could judge,
What 'twere to lose it, and be miserable!
They that stand high, have many blasts to shake them:
And, if they fall, they dash themselves to pieces.

Glo. Good counsel, marry;—learn it, learn it, marquis.

Dors. It touches you, my lord, as much as me.

Glo. Ay, and much more: But I was born so high,
Our aiery buildeth in the cedar's top,
And dallies with the wind, and scorns the sun.

Q. Mar. And turns the sun to shade!—alas! alas!—
Witness my son, now in the shade of death;
Whose bright outshining beams thy cloudy wrath
Hath in eternal darkness folded up.
Your aiery buildeth in our aiery's nest:—
O God, that seest it, do not suffer it;
As it was won with blood, lost be it so!

Buck. Peace, peace, for shame, if not for charity.

Q. Mar. Urge neither charity nor shame to me;
Uncharitably with me have you dealt,
And shamefully by you my hopes are butcher'd.
My charity is outrage, life my shame,—
And in my shame still live my sorrow's rage!

Buck. Have done, have done.

Q. Mar. O princely Buckingham, I kiss thy hand,
In sign of league and amity with thee:
Now fair befall thee, and thy noble house!
Thy garments are not spotted with our blood,
Nor thou within the compass of my curse.

Buck. Nor no one here; for curses never pass
The lips of those that breathe them in the air.

Q. Mar. I'll not believe but they ascend the sky,
And there awake God's gentle-sleeping peace.
O Buckingham, beware of yonder dog;
Look, when he fawns, he bites; and, when he bites,
His venom tooth will rankle to the death:
Have not to do with him, beware of him;
Sin, death, and hell have set their marks on him;
And all their ministers attend on him.

Glo. What doth she say, my lord of Buckingham?

Buck. Nothing that I respect, my gracious lord.

Q. Mar. What, dost thou scorn me for my gentle counsel?
And sooth the devil that I warn thee from?
O, but remember this another day,
When he shall split thy very heart with sorrow;
And say, poor Margaret was a prophetess.—
Live each of you the subjects to his hate,
And he to yours, and all of you to God's! [*Exit.*

Hast. My hair doth stand on end to hear her curses.

Riv. And so doth mine; I muse, why she's at liberty.

Glo. I cannot blame her, by God's holy mother,
She hath had too much wrong, and I repent
My part thereof, that I have done to her.

Q. Eliz. I never did her any, to my knowledge.

Glo. Yet you have all the vantage of her wrong.
I was too hot to do somebody good,
That is too cold in thinking of it now.
Marry, as for Clarence, he is well repaid:
He is frank'd up to fatting for his pains;—
God pardon them that are the cause thereof!

Riv. A virtuous and a christianlike conclusion,
To pray for them that have done scath to us.

Glo. So do I ever, being well advis'd;—
For had I curs'd now, I had curs'd myself. [*Aside.*

Enter CATESBY.

Cates. Madam, his majesty doth call for you,—
And for your grace,—and you, my noble lords.

Q. Eliz. Catesby, I come:—Lords, will you go with me?

Riv. Madam, we will attend your grace.
[*Exeunt all but* GLOSTER.

Glo. I do the wrong, and first begin to brawl.
The secret mischiefs that I set abroach,
I lay unto the grievous charge of others.
Clarence,—whom I indeed have laid in darkness,
I do beweep to many simple gulls;
Namely, to Stanley, Hastings, Buckingham;
And tell them—'tis the queen and her allies,
That stir the king against the duke my brother.
Now they believe it; and withal whet me
To be reveng'd on Rivers, Vaughan, Grey:
But then I sigh, and with a piece of scripture,
Tell them—that God bids us do good for evil:
And thus I clothe my naked villany
With old odd ends, stol'n forth of holy writ:
And seem a saint, when most I play the devil.

Enter Two Murderers.

But soft, here come my executioners.
How now, my hardy, stout resolved mates?
Are you now going to despatch this thing?

1 *Murd.* We are, my lord; and come to have the warrant,
That we may be admitted where he is.

Glo. Well thought upon, I have it here about me: [*Gives the Warrant.*
When you have done, repair to Crosby-place.
But, sirs, be sudden in the execution,
Withal obdurate, do not hear him plead;
For Clarence is well spoken, and perhaps,
May move your hearts to pity, if you mark him.

1 *Murd.* Tut, tut, my lord, we will not stand to prate,
Talkers are no good doers; be assur'd,
We go to use our hands, and not our tongues.
Glo. Your eyes drop millstones, when fools' eyes drop tears:
I like you, lads:—about your business straight;
Go, go, despatch.
1 *Murd.* We will, my noble lord.
[*Exeunt.*

SCENE IV. London. *A Room in the Tower.*

Enter CLARENCE *and* BRAKENBURY.

Brak. Why looks your grace so heavily to-day?
Clar. O, I have pass'd a miserable night,
So full of fearful dreams, of ugly sights,
That, as I am a christian faithful man,
I would not spend another such a night,
Though 'twere to buy a world of happy days;
So full of dismal terror was the time.
Brak. What was your dream, my lord? I pray you, tell me.
Clar. Methought, that I had broken from the Tower,
And was embark'd to cross to Burgundy;
And, in my company, my brother Gloster;
Who from my cabin tempted me to walk
Upon the hatches; thence we look'd toward England,
And cited up a thousand heavy times,
During the wars of York and Lancaster
That had befall'n us. As we pac'd along
Upon the giddy footing of the hatches,
Methought, that Gloster stumbled; and in falling,
Struck me, that thought to stay him, overboard,
Into the tumbling billows of the main.
O Lord! methought what pain it was to drown!
What dreadful noise of water in mine ears:
What sights of ugly death within mine eyes!
Methought, I saw a thousand fearful wrecks;
A thousand men, that fishes gnaw'd upon;
Wedges of gold, great anchors, heaps of pearl,
Inestimable stones, unvalued jewels,
All scatter'd in the bottom of the sea.
Some lay in dead men's skulls; and, in those holes
Where eyes did once inhabit, there were crept
(As 'twere in scorn of eyes) reflecting gems,
That woo'd the slimy bottom of the deep,
And mock'd the dead bones that lay scatter'd by.
Brak. Had you such leisure in the time of death,
To gaze upon these secrets of the deep?
Clar. Methought, I had; and often did I strive
To yield the ghost: but still the envious flood
Kept in my soul, and would not let it forth
To seek the empty, vast, and wand'ring air;
But smother'd it within my panting bulk,
Which almost burst to belch it in the sea.
Brak. Awak'd you not with this sore agony?
Clar. O, no, my dream was lengthen'd after life;
O, then began the tempest to my soul!
I pass'd, methought, the melancholy flood,
With that grim ferryman which poets write of,
Unto the kingdom of perpetual night.
The first that there did greet my stranger soul,
Was my great father-in-law, renowned Warwick,
Who cry'd aloud,—*What scourge for perjury*
Can this dark monarchy afford false Clarence?
And so he vanish'd: Then came wand'ring by
A shadow like an angel, with bright hair
Dabbled in blood, and he shriek'd out aloud,—
Clarence is come,—false, fleeting, perjur'd Clarence,
That stabb'd me in the field by Tewksbury;—
Seize on him, furies, take him to your torments!
With that, methought, a legion of foul fiends
Environ'd me, and howled in mine ears
Such hideous cries, that, with the very noise,
I trembling wak'd, and, for a season after,
Could not believe but that I was in hell;
Such terrible impression made my dream.
Brak. No marvel, lord, though it affrighted you!
I am afraid, methinks, to hear you tell it.
Clar. O, Brakenbury, I have done these things—
That now give evidence against my soul,—
For Edward's sake; and, see, how he requites me!—
O God! if my deep prayers cannot appease thee,
But thou wilt be aveng'd on my misdeeds,
Yet execute thy wrath on me alone:
O, spare my guiltless wife, and my poor children!—
I pray thee, gentle keeper, stay by me;
My soul is heavy, and I fain would sleep.
Brak. I will, my lord; God give your grace good rest!—
[CLARENCE *reposes himself on a Chair.*
Sorrow breaks seasons, and reposing hours,
Makes the night morning, and the noontide night.
Princes have but their titles for their glories,
An outward honour for an inward toil;
And, for unfelt imaginations,
They often feel a world of restless cares:
So that, between their titles, and low name,
There's nothing differs but the outward fame.

Enter the Two Murderers.

1 *Murd.* Ho! who's here?
Brak. What would'st thou, fellow? and how cam'st thou hither?
1 *Murd.* I would speak with Clarence, and I came hither on my legs.
Brak. What, so brief?
2 *Murd.* O, sir, 'tis better to be brief than tedious:—
Let him see our commission; talk no more.
[*A Paper is delivered to* BRAKENBURY, *who reads it.*
Brak. I am, in this, commanded to deliver
The noble duke of Clarence to your hands.
I will not reason what is meant hereby,
Because I will be guiltless of the meaning.
Here are the keys;—there sits the duke asleep:
I'll to the king; and signify to him,
That thus I have resign'd to you my charge.
1 *Murd.* You may, sir; 'tis a point of wisdom:
Fare you well. [*Exit* BRAKENBURY.
2 *Murd.* What, shall we stab him as he sleeps?
1 *Murd.* No; he'll say 'twas done cowardly, when he wakes.
2 *Murd.* When he wakes! why, fool, he shall never wake until the great judgment day.
1 *Murd.* Why, then he'll say, we stabb'd him sleeping.
2 *Murd.* The urging of that word, judgment, hath bred a kind of remorse in me.
1 *Murd.* What? art thou afraid?
2 *Murd.* Not to kill him, having a warrant for it; but to be damn'd for killing him, from the which no warrant can defend me.
1 *Murd.* I thought thou hadst been resolute.
2 *Murd.* So I am, to let him live.
1 *Murd.* I'll back to the duke of Gloster, and tell him so.
2 *Murd.* Nay, I pr'ythee, stay a little: I hope, this holy humour of mine will change; it was wont to hold me but while one would tell twenty.
1 *Murd.* How dost thou feel thyself now?
2 *Murd.* 'Faith, some certain dregs of conscience are yet within me.
1 *Murd.* Remember our reward, when the deed's done.
2 *Murd.* Come, he dies; I had forgot the reward.
1 *Murd.* Where's thy conscience now?
2 *Murd.* In the duke of Gloster's purse.
1 *Murd.* So, when he opens his purse to give us our reward, thy conscience flies out.
2 *Murd.* 'Tis no matter; let it go; there's few, or none will entertain it.

1 *Murd.* What, if it come to thee again?

2 *Murd.* I'll not meddle with it, it is a dangerous thing, it makes a man a coward; a man cannot steal, but it accuseth him; a man cannot swear, but it checks him; a man cannot lie with his neighbour's wife, but it detects him: 'Tis a blushing shame-faced spirit, that mutinies in a man's bosom; it fills one full of obstacles: it made me once restore a purse of gold, that by chance I found: it beggars any man that keeps it: it is turned out of all towns and cities for a dangerous thing; and every man that means to live well, endeavours to trust to himself, and live without it.

1 *Murd.* 'Zounds, it is even now at my elbow, persuading me not to kill the duke.

2 *Murd.* Take the devil in thy mind, and believe him not: he would insinuate with thee, but to make thee sigh.

1 *Murd.* I am strong-fram'd, he cannot prevail with me.

2 *Murd.* Spoke like a tall fellow, that respects his reputation. Come, shall we fall to work?

1 *Murd.* Take him over the costard with the hilts of thy sword, and then throw him into the malmsey butt, in the next room.

2 *Murd.* O excellent device! and make a sop of him.

1 *Murd.* Soft! he wakes.

2 *Murd.* Strike.

1 *Murd.* No, we'll reason with him.

Clar. Where art thou, keeper? give me a cup of wine.

1 *Murd.* You shall have wine enough, my lord, anon.

Clar. In God's name, what art thou?

1 *Murd.* A man, as you are.

Clar. But not, as I am, royal.

1 *Murd.* Nor you, as we are, loyal.

Clar. Thy voice is thunder, but thy looks are humble.

1 *Murd.* My voice is now the king's, my looks mine own.

Clar. How darkly, and how deadly dost thou speak!
Your eyes do menace me: Why look you pale?
Who sent you hither? Wherefore do you come?

Both Murd. To, to, to,——

Clar. To murder me?

Both Murd. Ay, ay.

Clar. You scarcely have the hearts to tell me so,
And therefore cannot have the hearts to do it.
Wherein, my friends, have I offended you?

1 *Murd.* Offended us you have not, but the king.

Clar. I shall be reconciled to him again.

2 *Murd.* Never, my lord; therefore prepare to die.

Clar. Are you call'd forth from out a world of men,
To slay the innocent? What is my offence?
Where is the evidence that doth accuse me?
What lawful quest have given their verdict up
Unto the frowning judge? or who pronounc'd
The bitter sentence of poor Clarence' death?
Before I be convict by course of law,
To threaten me with death is most unlawful.
I charge you, as you hope to have redemption
By Christ's dear blood shed for our grievous sins,
That you depart, and lay no hands on me;
The deed you undertake is damnable.

1 *Murd.* What we will do, we do upon command.

2 *Murd.* And he, that hath commanded is our king.

Clar. Erroneous vassal! the great King of kings
Hath in the table of his law commanded,
That thou shalt do no murder; Wilt thou then
Spurn at his edict, and fulfil a man's?
Take heed; for he holds vengeance in his hand,
To hurl upon their heads that break his law.

2 *Murd.* And that same vengeance doth he hurl on thee,
For false forswearing, and for murder too:
Thou didst receive the sacrament, to fight
In quarrel of the house of Lancaster.

1 *Murd.* And, like a traitor to the name of God,
Didst break that vow; and, with thy treacherous blade,
Unrip'dst the bowels of thy sovereign's son.

2 *Murd.* Whom thou wast sworn to cherish and defend.

1 *Murd.* How canst thou urge God's dreadful law to us,
When thou hast broke it in such dear degree?

Clar. Alas! for whose sake did I that ill deed?
For Edward, for my brother, for his sake:
He sends you not to murder me for this;
For in that sin he is as deep as I.
If God will be avenged for the deed,
O, know you, that he doth it publickly;
Take not the quarrel from his powerful arm;
He needs no indirect nor lawless course,
To cut off those that have offended him.

1 *Murd.* Who made thee then a bloody minister,
When gallant springing, brave Plantagenet,
That princely novice, was struck dead by thee?

Clar. My brother's love, the devil, and my rage.

1 *Murd.* Thy brother's love, our duty, and thy fault,
Provoke us hither now to slaughter thee.

Clar. If you do love my brother, hate not me;
I am his brother, and I love him well.
If you are hired for meed, go back again,
And I will send you to my brother Gloster;
Who shall reward you better for my life,
Than Edward will for tidings of my death.

2 *Murd.* You are deceiv'd, your brother Gloster hates you.

Clar. O, no; he loves me, and he holds me dear:
Go you to him from me.

Both Murd. Ay, so we will.

Clar. Tell him, when that our princely father York
Bless'd his three sons with his victorious arm,
And charg'd us from his soul to love each other,
He little thought of this divided friendship:
Bid Gloster think on this, and he will weep.

1 *Murd.* Ay, millstones; as he lesson'd us to weep.

Clar. O, do not slander him, for he is kind.

1 *Murd.* Right, as snow in harvest.—Come, you deceive yourself;
'Tis he that sends us to destroy you here.

Clar. It cannot be; for he bewept my fortune,
And hugg'd me in his arms, and swore, with sobs,
That he would labour my delivery.

1 *Murd.* Why, so he doth, when he delivers you
From this earth's thraldom to the joys of heaven.

2 *Murd.* Make peace with God, for you must die, my lord.

Clar. Hast thou that holy feeling in thy soul,
To counsel me to make my peace with God,
And art thou yet to thy own soul so blind,
That thou wilt war with God, by murd'ring me?—
Ah, sirs, consider, he, that set you on
To do this deed, will hate you for the deed.

2 *Murd.* What shall we do?

Clar. Relent, and save your souls.

1 *Murd.* Relent! 'tis cowardly, and womanish.

Clar. Not to relent, is beastly, savage, devilish.—
Which of you, if you were a prince's son,
Being pent from liberty, as I am now,
If two such murderers as yourselves came to you,—
Would not entreat for life?—
My friend, I spy some pity in thy looks;
O, if thine eye be not a flatterer,
Come thou on my side, and entreat for me,
As you would beg, were you in my distress.
A begging prince what beggar pities not?

2 *Murd.* Look behind you, my lord.
1 *Murd.* Take that, and that; if all this will not do, [*Stabs him.*
I'll drown you in the malmsey butt within. [*Exit, with the body.*
2 *Murd.* A bloody deed, and desperately despatch'd!
How fain, like Pilate, would I wash my hands
Of this most grievous guilty murder done!

Re-enter first Murderer.

1 *Murd.* How now? what mean'st thou, that thou help'st me not?
By heaven the duke shall know how slack you have been.
2 *Murd.* I would he knew, that I had saved his brother!
Take thou the fee, and tell him what I say;
For I repent me that the duke is slain. [*Exit.*
1 *Murd.* So do not I; go, coward, as thou art.—
Well, I'll go hide the body in some hole,
Till that the duke give order for his burial:
And when I have my meed, I will away;
For this will out, and then I must not stay. [*Exit.*

ACT II.

SCENE I. London. *A Room in the Palace.*

Enter KING EDWARD (*led in sick*), QUEEN ELIZABETH, DORSET, RIVERS, HASTINGS, BUCKINGHAM, GREY, *and Others.*

K. Edw. Why, so:—now have I done a good day's work;
You peers, continue this united league:
I every day expect an embassage
From my Redeemer to redeem me hence;
And now in peace my soul shall part to heaven,
Since I have made my friends at peace on earth.
Rivers, and Hastings, take each other's hand;
Dissemble not your hatred, swear your love.
Riv. By heaven, my soul is purg'd from grudging hate;
And with my hand I seal my true heart's love.
Hast. So thrive I, as I truly swear the like!
K. Edw. Take heed, you dally not before your king;
Lest he, that is the supreme King of kings,
Confound your hidden falsehood, and award
Either of you to be the other's end.
Hast. So prosper I, as I swear perfect love!
Riv. And I, as I love Hastings with my heart!
K. Edw. Madam, yourself are not exempt in this,—
Nor your son Dorset,—Buckingham, nor you;—
You have been factious one against the other.
Wife, love Lord Hastings, let him kiss your hand;
And what you do, do it unfeignedly.
Q. Eliz. There, Hastings;—I will never more remember
Our former hatred, so thrive I, and mine!
K. Edw. Dorset, embrace him,—Hastings, love lord marquis.
Dor. This interchange of love, I here protest,
Upon my part shall be inviolable.
Hast. And so swear I. [*Embraces* DORSET.
K. Edw. Now, princely Buckingham, seal thou this league
With thy embracements to my wife's allies,
And make me happy in your unity.
Buck. Whenever Buckingham doth turn his hate
Upon your grace [*To the Queen*], but with all duteous love
Doth cherish you, and yours, God punish me
With hate in those where I expect most love!
When I have most need to employ a friend,
And most assured that he is a friend,
Deep, hollow, treacherous, and full of guile,
Be he unto me! this do I beg of heaven,
When I am cold in love, to you, or yours.
[*Embracing* RIVERS, *&c.*
K. Edw. A pleasing cordial, princely Buckingham,
Is this thy vow unto my sickly heart.
There wanteth now our brother Gloster here,
To make the blessed period of this peace.
Buck. And, in good time, here comes the noble duke.

Enter GLOSTER.

Glo. Good-morrow to my sovereign king, and queen;
And, princely peers, a happy time of day!
K. Edw. Happy, indeed, as we have spent the day:—
Brother, we have done deeds of charity;
Made peace of enmity, fair love of hate,
Between these swelling wrong-incensed peers.
Glo. A blessed labour, my most sovereign liege.—
Among this princely heap, if any here,
By false intelligence, or wrong surmise,
Hold me a foe;
If I unwittingly, or in my rage,
Have aught committed that is hardly borne
By any in this presence, I desire
To reconcile me to his friendly peace:
'Tis death to me, to be at enmity;
I hate it, and desire all good men's love.—
First, madam, I entreat true peace of you,
Which I will purchase with my duteous service;—
Of you, my noble cousin Buckingham,
If ever any grudge were lodg'd between us:—
Of you, Lord Rivers,—and Lord Grey, of you,—
That all without desert have frown'd on me;—
Dukes, earls, lords, gentlemen: indeed, of all.
I do not know that Englishman alive,
With whom my soul is any jot at odds,
More than the infant that is born to-night;
I thank my God for my humility.
Q. Eliz. A holy-day shall this be kept hereafter:—
I would to God, all strifes were well compounded.—
My sovereign lord, I do beseech your highness
To take our brother Clarence to your grace.
Glo. Why, madam, have I offered love for this,
To be so flouted in this royal presence?
Who knows not that the gentle duke is dead?
[*They all start.*
You do him injury to scorn his corse.
K. Edw. Who knows not he is dead! who knows he is?
Q. Eliz. All-seeing heaven, what a world is this!
Buck. Look I so pale, Lord Dorset, as the rest?
Dor. Ay, my good lord; and no man in the presence,
But his red colour hath forsook his cheeks.
K. Edw. Is Clarence dead? the order was revers'd.
Glo. But he, poor man, by your first order died,
And that a winged Mercury did bear;
Some tardy cripple bore the countermand,
That came too lag to see him buried:—
God grant, that some, less noble, and less loyal,
Nearer in bloody thoughts, and not in blood,
Deserve not worse than wretched Clarence did,
And yet go current from suspicion.

Enter STANLEY.

Stan. A boon, my sovereign, for my service done!
K. Edw. I pr'ythee, peace; my soul is full of sorrow.
Stan. I will not rise, unless your highness hear me.
K. Edw. Then say at once, what is it thou request'st.
Stan. The forfeit, sovereign, of my servant's life;

Who slew to-day a riotous gentleman,
Lately attendant on the duke of Norfolk.
K. Edw. Have I a tongue to doom my brother's death,
And shall that tongue give pardon to a slave?
My brother kill'd no man, his fault was thought,
And yet his punishment was bitter death.
Who sued to me for him? who, in my wrath,
Kneel'd at my feet, and bade me be advis'd?
Who spoke of brotherhood? who spoke of love?
Who told me how the poor soul did forsake
The mighty Warwick, and did fight for me?
Who told me, in the field at Tewksbury,
When Oxford had me down, he rescued me,
And said, *Dear brother, live, and be a king?*
Who told me, when we both lay in the field,
Frozen almost to death, how he did lap me
Even in his garments; and did give himself,
All thin and naked, to the numb-cold night?
All this from my remembrance brutish wrath
Sinfully pluck'd, and not a man of you
Had so much grace to put it in my mind.
But when your carters, or your waiting-vassals,
Have done a drunken slaughter, and defac'd
The precious image of our dear Redeemer,
You straight are on your knees for pardon, pardon;
And I, unjustly too, must grant it you:—
But for my brother, not a man would speak,—
Nor I (ungracious) speak unto myself
For him, poor soul.—The proudest of you all
Have been beholden to him in his life;
Yet none of you would once plead for his life.—
O God! I fear, thy justice will take hold
On me, and you, and mine, and yours for this.—
Come, Hastings, help me to my closet. O,
Poor Clarence!
[*Exeunt* King, Queen, HASTINGS, RIVERS, DORSET, *and* GREY.
Glo. This is the fruit of rashness!—Mark'd you not,
How that the guilty kindred of the queen
Look'd pale, when they did hear of Clarence' death?
O! they did urge it still unto the king:
God will revenge it. Come, lords; will you go,
To comfort Edward with our company?
Buck. We wait upon your grace. [*Exeunt.*

SCENE II. *The same.*

Enter the DUCHESS OF YORK, *with a* Son *and* Daughter *of* Clarence.

Son. Good grandam, tell us, is our father dead?
Duch. No, boy.
Daugh. Why do you weep so oft? and beat your breast;
And cry—*O Clarence, my unhappy son!*
Son. Why do you look on us and shake your head,
And call us—orphans, wretches, cast-aways,
If that our noble father be alive?
Duch. My pretty cousins, you mistake me both;
I do lament the sickness of the king,
As loath to lose him, not your father's death:
It were lost sorrow, to wail one that's lost.
Son. Then, grandam, you conclude that he is dead.
The king my uncle is to blame for this:
God will revenge it; whom I will importune
With earnest prayers all to that effect.
Daugh. And so will I.
Duch. Peace, children, peace! the king doth love you well:
Incapable and shallow innocents,
You cannot guess who caus'd your father's death.
Son. Grandam, we can: for my good uncle Gloster
Told me, the king, provok'd to't by the queen,
Devis'd impeachments to imprison him:
And when my uncle told me so, he wept,
And pitied me, and kindly kiss'd my cheek;
Bade me rely on him, as on my father,
And he would love me dearly as his child.
Duch. Ah, that deceit should steal such gentle shapes,
And with a virtuous visor hide deep vice!
He is my son, ay, and therein my shame,
Yet from my dugs he drew not this deceit.
Son. Think you, my uncle did dissemble, grandam?
Duch. Ay, boy.
Son. I cannot think it. Hark! what noise is this?

Enter QUEEN ELIZABETH, *distractedly;* RIVERS, *and* DORSET, *following her.*

Q. Eliz. Ah! who shall hinder me to wail and weep?
To chide my fortune, and torment myself?
I'll join with black despair against my soul,
And to myself become an enemy.
Duch. What means this scene of rude impatience?
Q. Eliz. To make an act of tragick violence:—
Edward, my lord, thy son, our king, is dead.
Why grow the branches, when the root is gone?
Why wither not the leaves, that want their sap?—
If you will live, lament; if die, be brief;
That our swift-winged souls may catch the king's;
Or, like obedient subjects, follow him
To his new kingdom of perpetual rest.
Duch. Ah, so much interest have I in thy sorrow,
As I had title in thy noble husband!
I have bewept a worthy husband's death,
And liv'd by looking on his images:
But now two mirrors of his princely semblance
Are crack'd in pieces by malignant death;
And I for comfort have but one false glass,
That grieves me when I see my shame in him.
Thou art a widow; yet thou art a mother,
And hast the comfort of thy children left thee:
But death hath snatch'd my husband from my arms,
And pluck'd two crutches from my feeble hands,
Clarence, and Edward. O, what cause have I
(Thine being but a moiety of my grief),
To overgo thy plaints, and drown thy cries!
Son. Ah, aunt! you wept not for our father's death;
How can we aid you with our kindred tears?
Daugh. Our fatherless distress was left unmoan'd,
Your widow dolour likewise be unwept!
Q. Eliz. Give me no help in lamentation,
I am not barren to bring forth laments:
All springs reduce their currents to mine eyes,
That I, being govern'd by the wat'ry moon,
May send forth plenteous tears to drown the world;
Ah, for my husband, for my dear Lord Edward!
Chil. Ah, for our father, for our dear Lord Clarence!
Duch. Alas, for both, both mine, Edward and Clarence!
Q. Eliz. What stay had I, but Edward? and he's gone.
Chil. What stay had we, but Clarence? and he's gone.
Duch. What stays had I, but they? and they are gone.
Q. Eliz. Was never widow, had so dear a loss.
Chil. Were never orphans, had so dear a loss.
Duch. Was never mother, had so dear a loss.
Alas, I am the mother of these griefs;
Their woes are parcell'd, mine are general.
She for an Edward weeps, and so do I;
I for a Clarence weep, so doth not she:
These babes for Clarence weep, and so do I:
I for an Edward weep, so do not they:—
Alas! you three, on me threefold distress'd,
Pour all your tears, I am your sorrow's nurse,
And I will pamper it with lamentations.

Dor. Comfort, dear mother: God is much displeas'd,
That you take with unthankfulness his doing;
In common worldly things, 'tis call'd—ungrateful,
With dull unwillingness to repay a debt,
Which with a bounteous hand was kindly lent;
Much more to be thus opposite with heaven,
For it requires the royal debt it lent you.
Riv. Madam, bethink you, like a careful mother,
Of the young prince your son: send straight for him,
Let him be crown'd: in him your comfort lives:
Drown desperate sorrow in dead Edward's grave,
And plant your joys in living Edward's throne.

Enter GLOSTER, BUCKINGHAM, STANLEY, HASTINGS, RATCLIFF, *and Others.*

Glo. Sister, have comfort: all of us have cause
To wail the dimming of our shining star;
But none can cure their harms by wailing them.—
Madam, my mother, I do cry you mercy,
I did not see your grace:—Humbly on my knee
I crave your blessing.
Duch. God bless thee; and put meekness in thy breast,
Love, charity, obedience, and true duty!
Glo. Amen; and make me die a good old man!—
That is the butt-end of a mother's blessing; [*Aside.*
I marvel, that her grace did leave it out.
Buck. You cloudy princes, and heart sorrowing peers,
That bear this mutual heavy load of moan,
Now cheer each other in each other's love:
Though we have spent our harvest of this king,
We are to reap the harvest of his son.
The broken rancour of your high-swoln hearts,
But lately splinted, knit, and join'd together,
Must gently be preserv'd, cherish'd, and kept:
Me seemeth good, that, with some little train,
Forthwith from Ludlow the young prince be fetch'd
Hither to London, to be crown'd our king.
Riv. Why with some little train, my lord of Buckingham?
Buck. Marry, my lord, lest, by a multitude,
The new-heal'd wound of malice should break out;
Which would be so much the more dangerous,
By how much the estate is green and yet ungovern'd:
Where every horse bears his commanding rein,
And may direct his course as please himself,
As well the fear of harm, as harm apparent,
In my opinion, ought to be prevented.
Glo. I hope, the king made peace with all of us;
And the compact is firm, and true, in me.
Riv. And so in me; and so, I think, in all:
Yet, since it is but green, it should be put
To no apparent likelihood of breach,
Which, haply, by much company might be urg'd:
Therefore I say, with noble Buckingham,
That it is meet so few should fetch the prince.
Hast. And so say I.
Glo. Then be it so; and go we to determine
Who they shall be that straight shall post to Ludlow.
Madam, and you my mother,—will you go
To give your censures in this weighty business?
[*Exeunt all but* BUCKINGHAM *and* GLOSTER.
Buck. My lord, whoever journeys to the prince,
For God's sake, let not us two stay at home:
For, by the way, I'll sort occasion,
As index to the story we late talk'd of,
To part the queen's proud kindred from the prince.
Glo. My other self, my counsel's consistory,
My oracle, my prophet!—My dear cousin,
I, as a child, will go by thy direction.
Towards Ludlow then, for we'll not stay behind.
[*Exeunt.*

SCENE III. *The same. A Street.*

Enter two Citizens, *meeting.*

1 *Cit.* Good morrow, neighbour: Whither away so fast?
2 *Cit.* I promise you, I scarcely know myself:
Hear you the news abroad?
1 *Cit.* Yes; the king's dead.
2 *Cit.* Ill news, by'r lady; seldom comes the better:
I fear, I fear, 'twill prove a giddy world.

Enter another Citizen.

3 *Cit.* Neighbours, God speed!
1 *Cit.* Give you good morrow, sir.
3 *Cit.* Doth the news hold of good King Edward's death?
2 *Cit.* Ay, sir, it is too true; God help, the while!
3 *Cit.* Then, masters, look to see a troublous world.
1 *Cit.* No, no; by God's good grace, his son shall reign.
3 *Cit.* Woe to that land, that's govern'd by a child!
2 *Cit.* In him there is a hope of government;
That, in his nonage, council under him,
And, in his full and ripen'd years, himself,
No doubt, shall then, and till then, govern well.
1 *Cit.* So stood the state, when Henry the Sixth
Was crown'd at Paris but at nine months old.
3 *Cit.* Stood the state so? no, no, good friends, God wot;
For then this land was famously enrich'd
With politick grave counsel; then the king
Had virtuous uncles to protect his grace.
1 *Cit.* Why, so hath this, both by his father and mother.
3 *Cit.* Better it were they all came by his father;
Or, by his father there were none at all:
For emulation now, who shall be nearest,
Will touch us all too near, if God prevent it not.
O, full of danger is the duke of Gloster;
And the queen's sons, and brothers, haught and proud:
And were they to be rul'd, and not to rule,
This sickly land might solace as before.
1 *Cit.* Come, come, we fear the worst: all will be well.
3 *Cit.* When clouds are seen, wise men put on their cloaks;
When great leaves fall, then winter is at hand;
When the sun sets, who doth not look for night?
Untimely storms make men expect a dearth:
All may be well; but, if God sort it so,
'Tis more than we deserve, or I expect.
2 *Cit.* Truly, the hearts of men are full of fear:
You cannot reason almost with a man
That looks not heavily, and full of dread.
3 *Cit.* Before the days of change, still is it so:
By a divine instinct, men's minds mistrust
Ensuing danger; as, by proof, we see
The water swell before a boist'rous storm.
But leave it all to God. Whither away?
2 *Cit.* Marry, we were sent for to the justices.
3 *Cit.* And so was I; I'll bear you company.
[*Exeunt.*

SCENE IV. *The same. A Room in the Palace.*

Enter the ARCHBISHOP OF YORK, *the young* DUKE OF YORK, QUEEN ELIZABETH, *and he* DUCHESS OF YORK.

Arch. Last night, I heard, they lay at Stony-Stratford;
And at Northampton they do rest to-night:
To-morrow, or next day, they will be here.
Duch. I long with all my heart to see the prince;
I hope, he is much grown since last I saw him.

Q. Eliz. But I hear, no; they say, my son of York
Hath almost overta'en him in his growth.
York. Ay, mother, but I would not have it so.
Duch. Why, my young cousin? it is good to grow.
York. Grandam, one night, as we did sit at supper,
My uncle Rivers talk'd how I did grow
More than my brother; *Ay,* quoth my uncle Gloster,
Small herbs have grace, great weeds do grow apace:
And since, methinks, I would not grow so fast,
Because sweet flowers are slow, and weeds make haste.
Duch. 'Good faith, 'good faith, the saying did not hold
In him that did object the same to thee:
He was the wretched'st thing, when he was young:
So long a growing, and so leisurely,
That, if his rule were true, he should be gracious.
Arch. And so, no doubt, he is, my gracious madam.
Duch. I hope he is; but yet let mothers doubt.
York. Now, by my troth, if I had been remember'd,
I could have given my uncle's grace a flout,
To touch his growth, nearer than he touch'd mine.
Duch. How, my young York? I pr'ythee, let me hear it.
York. Marry, they say, my uncle grew so fast,
That he could gnaw a crust at two hours old;
'Twas full two years ere I could get a tooth.
Grandam, this would have been a biting jest.
Duch. I pr'ythee, pretty York, who told thee this?
York. Grandam, his nurse.
Duch. His nurse? why, she was dead ere thou wast born.
York. If 'twere not she, I cannot tell who told me.
Q. Eliz. A parlous boy: Go to, you are too shrewd.
Arch. Good madam, be not angry with the child.
Q. Eliz. Pitchers have ears.

Enter a Messenger.

Arch. Here comes a messenger:
What news?
Mess. Such news, my lord,
As grieves me to unfold.
Q. Eliz. How doth the prince?
Mess. Well, madam, and in health.
Duch. What is thy news?
Mess. Lord Rivers, and Lord Grey, are sent to Pomfret,
With them Sir Thomas Vaughan, prisoners.
Duch. Who hath committed them?
Mess. The mighty dukes,
Gloster and Buckingham.
Q. Eliz. For what offence?
Mess. The sum of all I can, I have disclos'd;
Why, or for what, the nobles were committed,
Is all unknown to me, my gracious lady.
Q. Eliz. Ah me, I see the ruin of my house!
The tiger now hath seiz'd the gentle hind;
Insulting tyranny begins to jut
Upon the innocent and awless throne:—
Welcome, destruction, blood, and massacre!
I see, as in a map, the end of all.
Duch. Accursed and unquiet wrangling days!
How many of you have mine eyes beheld?
My husband lost his life to get the crown;
And often up and down my sons were tost,
For me to joy, and weep, their gain and loss;
And being seated, and domestic broils
Clean overblown, themselves, the conquerors,
Make war upon themselves; brother to brother,
Blood to blood, self 'gainst self:—O, preposterous
And frantick courage, end thy damned spleen;
Or let me die to look on death no more!
Q. Eliz. Come, come, my boy, we will to sanctuary.—
Madam, farewell.
Duch. Stay, I will go with you.
Q. Eliz. You have no cause.
Arch. My gracious lady, go.
[*To the* Queen.
And thither bear your treasure and your goods.
For my part, I'll resign unto your grace
The seal I keep; And so betide to me,
As well I tender you, and all of yours!
Come, I'll conduct you to the sanctuary.
[*Exeunt.*

ACT III.

SCENE I. London. *A Street.*

The Trumpets sound. Enter the PRINCE OF WALES, GLOSTER, BUCKINGHAM, CARDINAL BOURCHIER, *and Others.*

Buck. Welcome, sweet prince, to London, to your chamber.
Glo. Welcome, dear cousin, my thoughts' sovereign:
The weary way hath made you melancholy.
Prince. No, uncle; but our crosses on the way
Have made it tedious, wearisome, and heavy:
I want more uncles here to welcome me.
Glo. Sweet prince, the untainted virtue of your years
Hath not yet div'd into the world's deceit:
No more can you distinguish of a man,
Than of his outward show; which, God he knows,
Seldom, or never, jumpeth with the heart.
Those uncles, which you want, were dangerous;
Your grace attended to their sugar'd words,
But look'd not on the poison of their hearts:
God keep you from them, and from such false friends!
Prince. God keep me from false friends! but they were none.
Glo. My lord, the mayor of London comes to greet you.

Enter the Lord Mayor, *and his* Train.

May. God bless your grace with health and happy days!
Prince. I thank you, good my lord;—and thank you all.— [*Exeunt* Mayor, *&c.*
I thought, my mother, and my brother York,
Would long ere this have met us on the way:
Fye, what a slug is Hastings! that he comes not
To tell us whether they would come, or no.

Enter HASTINGS.

Buck. And in good time, here comes the sweating lord.
Prince. Welcome, my lord: What, will our mother come?
Hast. On what occasion, God he knows, not I,
The queen your mother, and your brother York,
Have taken sanctuary: The tender prince
Would fain have come with me to meet your grace,
But by his mother was perforce withheld.
Buck. Fye! what an indirect and peevish course
Is this of hers?—Lord cardinal, will your grace
Persuade the queen to send the duke of York
Unto his princely brother presently?
If she deny,—Lord Hastings, go with him,
And from her jealous arms pluck him perforce.
Card. My lord of Buckingham, if my weak oratory
Can from his mother win the duke of York,
Anon expect him here: But if she be obdurate

To mild entreaties, God in heaven forbid
We should infringe the holy privilege
Of blessed sanctuary! not for all this land,
Would I be guilty of so deep a sin.

Buck. You are too senseless-obstinate, my lord,
Too ceremonious, and traditional:
Weigh it but with the grossness of this age,
You break not sanctuary in seizing him.
The benefit thereof is always granted
To those whose dealings have deserv'd the place,
And those who have the wit to claim the place:
This prince hath neither claim'd it, nor deserv'd it;
And therefore, in mine opinion, cannot have it:
Then, taking him from thence, that is not there,
You break no privilege nor charter there.
Oft have I heard of sanctuary men;
But sanctuary children, ne'er till now.

Card. My lord, you shall o'errule my mind for once.—
Come on, Lord Hastings, will you go with me?

Hast. I go, my lord.

Prince. Good lords, make all the speedy haste you may. [*Exeunt* Cardinal *and* HAST.
Say, uncle Gloster, if our brother come,
Where shall we sojourn till our coronation?

Glo. Where it seems best unto your royal self.
If I may counsel you, some day, or two,
Your highness shall repose you at the Tower:
Then where you please, and shall be thought most fit
For your best health and recreation.

Prince. I do not like the Tower, of any place:—
Did Julius Cæsar build that place, my lord?

Glo. He did, my gracious lord, begin that place;
Which, since, succeeding ages have re-edified.

Prince. Is it upon record? or else reported
Successively from age to age, he built it?

Buck. Upon record, my gracious lord.

Prince. But say, my lord, it were not register'd;
Methinks, the truth should live from age to age,
As 'twere retail'd to all posterity,
Even to the general all-ending day.

Glo. So wise so young, they say, do ne'er live long. [*Aside.*

Prince. What say you, uncle?

Glo. I say, without characters, fame lives long.
Thus, like the formal vice, Iniquity,
I moralize two meanings in one word. } *Aside.*

Prince. That Julius Cæsar was a famous man;
With what his valour did enrich his wit,
His wit set down to make his valour live.
Death makes no conquest of this conqueror;
For now he lives in fame, though not in life.
I'll tell you what, my cousin Buckingham.—

Buck. What, my gracious lord?

Prince. An if I live until I be a man,
I'll win our ancient right in France again,
Or die a soldier, as I liv'd a king.

Glo. Short summers lightly have a forward spring. [*Aside.*

Enter YORK, HASTINGS, *and the* Cardinal.

Buck. Now, in good time, here comes the duke of York.

Prince. Richard of York! how fares our loving brother?

York. Well, my dread lord; so must I call you now.

Prince. Ay, brother; to our grief, as it is yours:
Too late he died that might have kept that title,
Which by his death hath lost much majesty.

Glo. How fares our cousin, noble lord of York?

York. I thank you, gentle uncle. O, my lord,
You said that idle weeds are fast in growth:
The prince my brother hath outgrown me far.

Glo. He hath, my lord.

York. And therefore is he idle?

Glo. O, my fair cousin, I must not say so.

York. Then is he more beholden to you, than I.

Glo. He may command me, as my sovereign;
But you have power in me, as in a kinsman.

York. I pray you, uncle, give me this dagger.

Glo. My dagger, little cousin? with all my heart.

Prince. A beggar, brother?

York. Of my kind uncle, that I know will give;
And, being but a toy, which is no grief to give.

Glo. A greater gift than that I'll give my cousin.

York. A greater gift! O, that's the sword to it?

Glo. Ay, gentle cousin, were it light enough.

York. O then, I see, you'll part but with light gifts:
In weightier things you'll say a beggar, nay.

Glo. It is too weighty for your grace to wear.

York. I weigh it lightly, were it heavier.

Glo. What, would you have my weapon, little lord?

York. I would, that I might thank you as you call me.

Glo. How?

York. Little.

Prince. My lord of York will still be cross in talk;—
Uncle, your grace knows how to bear with him.

York. You mean, to bear me, not to bear with me:—
Uncle, my brother mocks both you and me;
Because that I am little, like an ape,
He thinks that you should bear me on your shoulders.

Buck. With what a sharp-provided wit he reasons!
To mitigate the scorn he gives his uncle,
He prettily and aptly taunts himself:
So cunning, and so young, is wonderful.

Glo. My gracious lord, will't please you pass along?
Myself, and my good cousin Buckingham,
Will to your mother; to entreat of her,
To meet you at the Tower, and welcome you.

York. What, will you go unto the Tower, my lord?

Prince. My lord protector needs will have it so.

York. I shall not sleep in quiet at the Tower.

Glo. Why, sir, what should you fear?

York. Marry, my uncle Clarence' angry ghost;
My grandam told me, he was murder'd there.

Prince. I fear no uncles dead.

Glo. Nor none that live, I hope.

Prince. An if they live, I hope, I need not fear.
But come, my lord, and, with a heavy heart,
Thinking on them, go I unto the Tower.

[*Exeunt* Prince, YORK, HASTINGS, Cardinal, *and* Attendants.

Buck. Think you, my lord, this little prating York
Was not incensed by his subtle mother,
To taunt and scorn you thus opprobriously?

Glo. No doubt, no doubt: O, 'tis a parlous boy;
Bold, quick, ingenious, forward, capable;
He's all the mother's, from the top to toe.

Buck. Well, let them rest.—
Come hither, gentle Catesby; thou art sworn
As deeply to effect what we intend,
As closely to conceal what we impart:
Thou know'st our reasons urg'd upon the way;—
What think'st thou? is it not an easy matter
To make William Lord Hastings of our mind,
For the instalment of this noble duke
In the seat royal of this famous isle?

Cate. He for his father's sake so loves the prince,
That he will not be won to aught against him.

Buck. What think'st thou then of Stanley? will not he?

Cate. He will do all in all as Hastings doth.

Buck. Well then, no more but this: Go, gentle Catesby,
And, as it were far off, sound thou Lord Hastings,
How he doth stand affected to our purpose;
And summon him to-morrow to the Tower,

To sit about the coronation.
If thou dost find him tractable to us,
Encourage him, and tell him all our reasons:
If he be leaden, icy, cold, unwilling,
Be thou so too; and so break off the talk,
And give us notice of his inclination:
For we to-morrow hold divided councils,
Wherein thyself shalt highly be employ'd.

Glo. Commend me to Lord William: tell him, Catesby,
His ancient knot of dangerous adversaries
To-morrow are let blood at Pomfret Castle;
And bid my friend, for joy of this good news,
Give mistress Shore one gentle kiss the more.

Buck. Good Catesby, go, effect this business soundly.

Cate. My good lords both, with all the heed I can.

Glo. Shall we hear from you, Catesby, ere we sleep?

Cate. You shall, my lord.

Glo. At Crosby-place, there shall you find us both. [*Exit* CATESBY.

Buck. Now, my lord, what shall we do, if we perceive
Lord Hastings will not yield to our complots?

Glo. Chop off his head, man;—somewhat we will do:—
And, look, when I am king, claim thou of me
The earldom of Hereford, and all the moveables
Whereof the king my brother was possess'd.

Buck. I'll claim that promise at your grace's hand.

Glo. And look to have it yielded with all kindness.
Come, let us sup betimes; that afterwards
We may digest our complots in some form.
[*Exeunt.*

SCENE II. *Before* Lord Hastings' *House.*

Enter a Messenger.

Mess. My lord, my lord,— [*Knocking.*

Hast. [*Within.*] Who knocks?

Mess. One from Lord Stanley.

Hast. [*Within.*] What is't o'clock?

Mess. Upon the stroke of four.

Enter HASTINGS.

Hast. Cannot thy master sleep these tedious nights?

Mess. So it should seem by that I have to say.
First, he commends him to your noble lordship.

Hast. And then,—

Mess. And then he sends you word, he dreamt
To-night the boar had rased off his helm:
Besides, he says, there are two councils held;
And that may be determin'd at the one,
Which may make you and him to rue at the other.
Therefore he sends to know your lordship's pleasure,—
If presently, you will take horse with him,
And with all speed post with him toward the north,
To shun the danger that his soul divines.

Hast. Go, fellow, go, return unto thy lord;
Bid him not fear the separated councils:
His honour, and myself, are at the one;
And, at the other, is my good friend Catesby;
Where nothing can proceed, that toucheth us,
Whereof I shall not have intelligence.
Tell him, his fears are shallow, wanting instance:
And for his dreams—I wonder, he's so fond
To trust the mockery of unquiet slumbers:
To fly the boar, before the boar pursues,
Were to incense the boar to follow us,
And make pursuit, where he did mean no chase.
Go, bid thy master rise and come to me;
And we will both together to the Tower,
Where, he shall see, the boar will use us kindly.

Mess. I'll go, my lord, and tell him what you say. [*Exit.*

Enter CATESBY.

Cate. Many good morrows to my noble lord!

Hast. Good morrow, Catesby; you are early stirring:
What news, what news, in this our tottering state?

Cate. It is a reeling world, indeed, my lord;
And, I believe, will never stand upright,
Till Richard wear the garland of the realm.

Hast. How! wear the garland? dost thou mean the crown?

Cate. Ay, my good lord.

Hast. I'll have this crown of mine cut from my shoulders,
Before I'll see the crown so foul misplac'd.
But canst thou guess that he doth aim at it?

Cate. Ay, on my life; and hopes to find you forward
Upon his party, for the gain thereof:
And, thereupon he sends you this good news,—
That, this same very day, your enemies,
The kindred of the queen, must die at Pomfret.

Hast. Indeed, I am no mourner for that news,
Because they have been still my adversaries:
But, that I'll give my voice on Richard's side,
To bar my master's heirs in true descent,
God knows, I will not do it, to the death.

Cate. God keep your lordship in that gracious mind!

Hast. But I shall laugh at this a twelvemonth hence,
That they, who brought me in my master's hate,
I live to look upon their tragedy.
Well, Catesby, ere a fortnight make me older,
I'll send some packing, that yet think not on't.

Cate. 'Tis a vile thing to die, my gracious lord,
When men are unprepar'd, and look not for it.

Hast. O, monstrous, monstrous! and so falls it out
With Rivers, Vaughan, Grey: and so 'twill do
With some men else, who think themselves as safe
As thou, and I; who, as thou know'st, are dear
To princely Richard, and to Buckingham.

Cate. The princes both make high account of you,
For they account his head upon the bridge. [*Aside.*

Hast. I know, they do; and I have well deserv'd it.

Enter STANLEY.

Come on, come on, where is your boar-spear, man?
Fear you the boar, and go so unprovided?

Stan. My lord, good morrow; and good morrow, Catesby:
You may jest on, but, by the holy rood,
I do not like these several councils, I.

Hast. My lord, I hold my life as dear as you do yours;
And never, in my life, I do protest,
Was it more precious to me than 'tis now:
Think you, but that I know our state secure,
I would be so triumphant as I am?

Stan. The lords at Pomfret, when they rode from London,
Were jocund, and suppos'd their states were sure,
And they, indeed, had no cause to mistrust;
But yet, you see, how soon the day o'ercast.
This sudden stab of rancour I misdoubt;
Pray God, I say, I prove a needless coward!
What, shall we toward the Tower? the day is spent.

Hast. Come, come, have with you.—Wot you what, my lord?
To-day, the lords you talk of are beheaded.

Stan. They, for their truth, might better wear their heads,
Than some, that have accus'd them, wear their hats.
But come, my lord, let's away.

Enter a Pursuivant.

Hast. Go on before, I'll talk with this good fellow. [*Exeunt* STAN. *and* CATESBY.
How now, sirrah? how goes the world with thee?

Purs. The better, that your lordship please to ask.

Hast. I tell thee, man, 'tis better with me now,
Than when thou met'st me last where now we meet:
Then I was going prisoner to the Tower,
By the suggestion of the queen's allies;
But now I tell thee (keep it to thyself),
This day those enemies are put to death,
And I in better state than ere I was.

Purs. God hold it, to your honour's good content!

Hast. Gramercy, fellow; There, drink that for me. [*Throwing him his purse.*

Purs. I thank your honour. [*Exit* Pursuivant.

Enter a Priest.

Pr. Well met, my lord; I am glad to see your honour.

Hast. I thank thee, good Sir John, with all my heart.
I am in your debt for your last exercise;
Come the next Sabbath, and I will content you.

Enter BUCKINGHAM.

Buck. What, talking with a priest, lord chamberlain?
Your friends at Pomfret, they do need the priest;
Your honour hath no shriving work in hand.

Hast. 'Good faith, and when I met this holy man,
The men you talk of came into my mind.
What, go you toward the Tower?

Buck. I do, my lord; but long I cannot stay there:
I shall return before your lordship thence.

Hast. Nay, like enough, for I stay dinner there.

Buck. And supper too, although thou know'st it not. [*Aside.*
Come, will you go?

Hast. I'll wait upon your lordship. [*Exeunt.*

SCENE III. Pomfret. *Before the Castle.*

Enter RATCLIFF, *with a* Guard, *conducting* RIVERS, GREY, *and* VAUGHAN, *to Execution.*

Rat. Come, bring forth the prisoners.

Riv. Sir Richard Ratcliff, let me tell thee this,—
To-day, shalt thou behold a subject die,
For truth, for duty, and for loyalty.

Grey. God keep the prince from all the pack of you!
A knot you are of damned blood-suckers.

Vaugh. You live, that shall cry woe for this hereafter.

Rat. Despatch; the limit of your lives is out.

Riv. O Pomfret, Pomfret! O thou bloody prison,
Fatal and ominous to noble peers!
Within the guilty closure of thy walls,
Richard the Second here was hack'd to death:
And, for more slander to thy dismal seat,
We give thee up our guiltless blood to drink.

Grey. Now Margaret's curse is fallen upon our heads,
When she exclaim'd on Hastings, you, and I,
For standing by when Richard stabb'd her son.

Riv. Then curs'd she Hastings, then curs'd she Buckingham.
Then curs'd she Richard:—O, remember, God,
To hear her prayers for them, as now for us!
And for my sister, and her princely sons,—
Be satisfied, dear God, with our true bloods,
Which, as thou know'st, unjustly must be spilt!

Rat. Make haste, the hour of death is expiate.

Riv. Come, Grey,—come Vaughan,—let us here embrace:
Farewell, until we meet again in heaven. [*Exeunt.*

SCENE IV. London. *A Room in the Tower.*

BUCKINGHAM, STANLEY, HASTINGS, *the* BISHOP OF ELY, CATESBY, LOVEL, *and Others, sitting at a Table;* Officers *of the* Council *attending.*

Hast. Now, noble peers, the cause why we are met
Is—to determine of the coronation:
In God's name, speak, when is the royal day?

Buck. Are all things ready for that royal time?

Stan. They are; and wants but nomination.

Ely. To-morrow then I judge a happy day.

Buck. Who knows the lord protector's mind herein?
Who is most inward with the noble duke?

Ely. Your grace, we think, should soonest know his mind.

Buck. We know each other's faces; for our hearts,—
He knows no more of mine, than I of yours;
Nor I, of his, my lord, than you of mine:
Lord Hastings, you and he are near in love.

Hast. I thank his grace, I know he loves me well;
But, for his purpose in the coronation,
I have not sounded him, nor he deliver'd
His gracious pleasure any way therein:
But you, my noble lord, may name the time;
And in the duke's behalf I'll give my voice,
Which, I presume, he'll take in gentle part.

Enter GLOSTER.

Ely. In happy time, here comes the duke himself.

Glo. My noble lords and cousins, all, good morrow:
I have been long a sleeper; but, I trust,
My absence doth neglect no great design,
Which by my presence might have been concluded.

Buck. Had you not come upon your cue, my lord,
William Lord Hastings had pronounc'd your part,—
I mean, your voice,—for crowning of the king.

Glo. Than my Lord Hastings, no man might be bolder;
His lordship knows me well, and loves me well.—
My lord of Ely, when I was last in Holborn,
I saw good strawberries in your garden there;
I do beseech you, send for some of them.

Ely. Marry, and will, my lord, with all my heart. [*Exit* ELY.

Glo. Cousin of Buckingham, a word with you. [*Takes him aside.*
Catesby hath sounded Hastings in our business;
And finds the testy gentleman so hot,
That he will lose his head, ere give consent,
His master's child, as worshipfully he terms it,
Shall lose the royalty of England's throne.

Buck. Withdraw yourself awhile, I'll go with you. [*Exeunt* GLOSTER *and* BUCKINGHAM.

Stan. We have not yet set down this day of triumph.
To-morrow, in my judgment, is too sudden;
For I myself am not so well provided,
As else I would be, were the day prolong'd.

Re-enter BISHOP OF ELY.

Ely. Where is my lord protector? I have sent
For these strawberries.

Hast. His grace looks cheerfully and smooth this morning;
There's some conceit or other likes him well,
When he doth bid good morrow with such spirit.
I think, there's ne'er a man in Christendom,

Can lesser hide his love, or hate, than he;
For by his face straight shall you know his heart.
Stan. What of his heart perceive you in his face,
By any likelihood he show'd to-day?
Hast. Marry, that with no man here he is offended;
For, were he, he had shown it in his looks.

Re-enter GLOSTER *and* BUCKINGHAM.

Glo. I pray you all, tell me what they deserve
That do conspire my death with devilish plots
Of damned witchcraft, and that have prevail'd
Upon my body with their hellish charms?
Hast. The tender love I bear your grace, my lord,
Makes me most forward in this noble presence
To doom the offenders: Whosoe'er they be,
I say, my lord, they have deserved death.
Glo. Then be your eyes the witness of their evil,
Look how I am bewitch'd; behold mine arm
Is, like a blasted sapling, wither'd up:
And this is Edward's wife, that monstrous witch,
Consorted with that harlot, strumpet Shore,
That by their witchcraft thus have marked me.
Hast. If they have done this deed, my noble lord,—
Glo. If! thou protector of this damned strumpet,
Talk'st thou to me of ifs?—Thou art a traitor:—
Off with his head: now, by Saint Paul, I swear,
I will not dine until I see the same.—
Lovel, and Catesby, look that it be done;
The rest that love me, rise and follow me.
[*Exeunt* Council, *with* GLO. *and* BUCK.
Hast. Woe! woe, for England! not a whit for me;
For I, too fond, might have prevented this:
Stanley did dream, the boar did rase his helm;
But I disdain'd it, and did scorn to fly.
Three times to-day my foot-cloth horse did stumble,
And startled, when he look'd upon the Tower,
As loath to bear me to the slaughter-house.
O, now I want the priest that spake to me:
I now repent I told the pursuivant,
As too triumphing, how mine enemies,
To-day at Pomfret bloodily were butcher'd,
And I myself secure in grace and favour.
O, Margaret, Margaret, now thy heavy curse
Is lighted on poor Hastings' wretched head.
Cate. Despatch, my lord, the duke would be at dinner;
Make a short shrift, he longs to see your head.
Hast. O momentary grace of mortal men,
Which we more hunt for than the grace of God!
Who builds his hope in air of your fair looks,
Lives like a drunken sailor on a mast;
Ready, with every nod, to tumble down
Into the fatal bowels of the deep.
Lov. Come, come, despatch; 'tis bootless to exclaim.
Hast. O, bloody Richard!—miserable England!
I prophesy the fearful'st time to thee,
That ever wretched age hath look'd upon.—
Come, lead me to the block, bear him my head;
They smile at me, who shortly shall be dead.
[*Exeunt.*

SCENE V. *The same. The Tower Walls.*

Enter GLOSTER *and* BUCKINGHAM, *in rusty armour, marvellous ill favoured.*

Glo. Come, cousin, canst thou quake, and change thy colour?
Murder thy breath in middle of a word,—
And then again begin, and stop again,
As if thou wert distraught, and mad with terror?
Buck. Tut, I can counterfeit the deep tragedian;
Speak, and look back, and pry on every side,
Tremble and start at wagging of a straw,
Intending deep suspicion: ghastly looks
Are at my service, like enforced smiles;
And both are ready in their offices,
At any time to grace my stratagems.
But what, is Catesby gone?
Glo. He is; and see, he brings the mayor along.

Enter the Lord Mayor *and* CATESBY.

Buck. Let me alone to entertain him.—Lord mayor,——
Glo. Look to the drawbridge there.
Buck. Hark, hark! a drum.
Glo. Catesby, o'erlook the walls.
Buck. Lord mayor, the reason we have sent for you,——
Glo. Look back, defend thee, here are enemies.
Buck. God and our innocence defend and guard us!

Enter LOVEL *and* RATCLIFF, *with* Hasting's *Head.*

Glo. Be patient, they are friends; Ratcliff, and Lovel.
Lov. Here is the head of that ignoble traitor,
The dangerous and unsuspected Hastings.
Glo. So dear I lov'd the man, that I must weep.
I took him for the plainest harmless creature,
That breath'd upon the earth a christian;
Made him my book, wherein my soul recorded
The history of all her secret thoughts:
So smooth he daub'd his vice with show of virtue,
That, his apparent open guilt omitted,—
I mean, his conversation with Shore's wife,—
He liv'd from all attainder of suspect.
Buck. Well, well, he was the covert'st shelter'd traitor
That ever liv'd.—Look you, my lord mayor,
Would you imagine, or almost believe,
(Were't not, that by great preservation
We live to tell it you), the subtle traitor
This day had plotted in the council-house,
To murder me, and my good lord of Gloster?
May. What! had he so?
Glo. What! think you we are Turks, or infidels,
Or that we would against the form of law,
Proceed thus rashly in the villain's death;
But that the extreme peril of the case,
The peace of England, and our persons' safety,
Enforc'd us to this execution?
May. Now, fair befall you! he deserv'd his death;
And your good graces both have well proceeded,
To warn false traitors from the like attempts.
I never look'd for better at his hands,
After he once fell in with mistress Shore.
Buck. Yet had we not determin'd he should die,
Until your lordship came to see his end;
Which now the loving haste of these our friends,
Somewhat against our meaning, hath prevented;
Because, my lord, we would have had you heard
The traitor speak, and timorously confess
The manner and the purpose of his treasons;
That you might well have signified the same
Unto the citizens, who haply, may
Misconstrue us in him, and wail his death.
May. But, my good lord, your grace's word shall serve,
As well as I had seen, and heard him speak:
And do not doubt, right noble princes both,
But I'll acquaint our duteous citizens
With all your just proceedings in this case.
Glo. And to that end we wish'd your lordship here,
To avoid the censures of the carping world.
Buck. But since you came too late of our intent,
Yet witness what you hear we did intend:
And so, my good lord mayor, we bid farewell.
[*Exit* Lord Mayor.
Glo. Go after, after, cousin Buckingham.
The mayor towards Guildhall hies him in all post:—
There, at your meetest vantage of the time,
Infer the bastardy of Edward's children:
Tell them, how Edward put to death a citizen,
Only for saying—he would make his son

Heir to the crown; meaning, indeed his house,
Which, by the sign thereof, was termed so.
Moreover, urge his hateful luxury,
And bestial appetite in change of lust;
Which stretch'd unto their servants, daughters, wives,
Even where his lustful eye, or savage heart,
Without control, listed to make his prey.
Nay, for a need, thus far come near my person:—
Tell them, when that my mother went with child
Of that insatiate Edward, noble York,
My princely father, then had wars in France;
And, by just computation of the time,
Found that the issue was not his begot;
Which well appeared in his lineaments,
Being nothing like the noble duke my father:
Yet touch this sparingly, as 'twere far off;
Because my lord, you know, my mother lives.

Buck. Doubt not, my lord; I'll play the orator,
As if the golden fee, for which I plead,
Were for myself: and so, my lord, adieu.

Glo. If you thrive well, bring them to Baynard's castle;
Where you shall find me well accompanied,
With reverend fathers, and well learned bishops.

Buck. I go; and, towards three or four o'clock,
Look for the news that the Guildhall affords.
[*Exit* BUCKINGHAM.

Glo. Go Lovel, with all speed to doctor Shaw,—
Go thou [*to* CAT.] to friar Penker;—bid them both
Meet me, within this hour, at Baynard's castle.
[*Exeunt* LOVEL *and* CATESBY.
Now will I in, to take some privy order
To draw the brats of Clarence out of sight;
And to give notice that no manner of person
Have, any time, recourse unto the princes.
[*Exit.*

SCENE VI. *A Street.*

Enter a Scrivener.

Scriv. Here is the indictment of the good lord Hastings;
Which in a set hand fairly is engross'd,
That it may be to-day read o'er in Paul's.
And mark how well the sequel hangs together:—
Eleven hours I have spent to write it over,
For yesternight by Catesby was it sent me;
The precedent was full as long a doing:
And yet within these five hours Hastings liv'd,
Untainted, unexamin'd, free, at liberty.
Here's a good world the while!—Who is so gross,
That cannot see this palpable device?
Yet who so bold, but says—he sees it not?
Bad is the world; and all will come to nought,
When such bad dealing must be seen in thought.
[*Exit.*

SCENE VII.

The same. Court of Baynard's Castle.

Enter GLOSTER *and* BUCKINGHAM, *meeting.*

Glo. How now, how now? what say the citizens?

Buck. Now by the holy mother of our Lord,
The citizens are mum, say not a word.

Glo. Touch'd you the bastardy of Edward's children?

Buck. I did; with his contract with Lady Lucy,
And his contract by deputy in France:
The insatiate greediness of his desires,
And his enforcement of the city wives;
His tyranny for trifles; his own bastardy,—
As being got, your father then in France:
And his resemblance, being not like the duke.
Withal, I did infer your lineaments,—
Being the right idea of your father,
Both in your form and nobleness of mind:
Laid open all your victories in Scotland,
Your discipline in war, wisdom in peace,
Your bounty, virtue, fair humility;
Indeed, left nothing, fitting for your purpose,
Untouch'd, or slightly handled, in discourse.
And, when my oratory grew to an end,
I bade them, that did love their country's good,
Cry,—*God save Richard, England's royal king!*

Glo. And did they so?

Buck. No, so God help me, they spake not a word;
But, like dumb statuas, or breathless stones,
Star'd on each other, and look'd deadly pale.
Which when I saw, I reprehended them;
And ask'd the mayor, what meant this wilful silence;
His answer was,—the people were not us'd
To be spoke to, but by the recorder.
Then he was urg'd to tell my tale again:
Thus saith the duke, thus hath the duke inferr'd;
But nothing spoke in warrant from himself.
When he had done, some followers of mine own,
At lower end o' the hall, hurl'd up their caps,
And some ten voices cried, *God save King Richard!*
And thus I took the vantage of those few,—
Thanks, gentle citizens, and friends, quoth I;
This general applause and cheerful shout,
Argues your wisdom, and your love to Richard:
And even here brake off and came away.

Glo. What tongueless blocks were they: Would they not speak?
Will not the mayor then, and his brethren, come?

Buck. The mayor is here at hand; intend some fear;
Be not you spoke with, but by mighty suit;
And look you get a prayer-book in your hand,
And stand between two churchmen, good my lord;
For on that ground I'll make a holy descant:
And be not easily won to our requests;
Play the maid's part, still answer nay, and take it.

Glo. I go; And if you plead as well for them,
As I can say nay to thee for myself,
No doubt we'll bring it to a happy issue.

Buck. Go, go, up to the leads; the lord mayor knocks.
[*Exit* GLOSTER.

Enter the Lord Mayor, Aldermen, *and* Citizens.

Welcome, my lord; I dance attendance here:
I think the duke will not be spoke withal.—

Enter from the Castle, CATESBY.

Now, Catesby! what says your lord to my request?

Cate. He doth entreat your grace, my noble lord,
To visit him to-morrow, or next day:
He is within, with two right reverend fathers,
Divinely bent to meditation;
And in no worldly suit would he be mov'd,
To draw him from his holy exercise.

Buck. Return, good Catesby, to the gracious duke;
Tell him, myself, the mayor, and aldermen,
In deep designs, in matter of great moment,
No less importing than our general good,
Are come to have some conference with his grace.

Cate. I'll signify so much unto him straight.
[*Exit.*

Buck. Ah, ha, my lord, this prince is not an Edward!
He is not lolling on a lewd day-bed,
But on his knees at meditation;
Not dallying with a brace of courtezans,
But meditating with two deep divines;
Not sleeping, to engross his idle body,
But praying, to enrich his watchful soul:
Happy were England, would this virtuous prince
Take on himself the sovereignty thereof:
But, sure, I fear, we shall ne'er win him to it.

May. Marry, God defend, his grace should say us nay!

Buck. I fear, he will: Here Catesby comes again:—

Re-enter CATESBY.

Now, Catesby, what says his grace?
Cate. He wonders to what end you have assembled
Such troops of citizens to come to him,
His grace not being warn'd thereof before:
He fears, my lord, you mean no good to him.
Buck. Sorry I am, my noble cousin should
Suspect me, that I mean no good to him:
By heaven, we come to him in perfect love;
And so once more return and tell his grace.
[*Exit* CATESBY.
When holy and devout religious men
Are at their beads, 'tis hard to draw them thence;
So sweet is zealous contemplation.

Enter GLOSTER, *in a Gallery above, between two* Bishops. CATESBY *returns.*

May. See, where his grace stands 'tween two clergymen!
Buck. Two props of virtue for a christian prince,
To stay him from the fall of vanity:
And, see, a book of prayer in his hand;
True ornaments to know a holy man.—
Famous Plantagenet, most gracious prince,
Lend favourable ear to our requests;
And pardon us the interruption
Of thy devotion, and right-christian zeal.
Glo. My lord, there needs no such apology;
I rather do beseech you pardon me,
Who, earnest in the service of my God,
Neglect the visitation of my friends.
But, leaving this, what is your grace's pleasure?
Buck. Even that, I hope, which pleaseth God above,
And all good men of this ungovern'd isle.
Glo. I do suspect, I have done some offence,
That seems disgracious in the city's eye;
And that you come to reprehend my ignorance.
Buck. You have, my lord; Would it might please your grace,
On our entreaties, to amend your fault!
Glo. Else wherefore breathe I in a christian land?
Buck. Know, then, it is your fault, that you resign
The supreme seat, the throne majestical,
The sceptred office, of your ancestors,
Your state of fortune, and your due of birth,
The lineal glory of your royal house,
To the corruption of a blemish'd stock:
Whilst, in the mildness of your sleepy thoughts
(Which here we waken to our country's good),
The noble isle doth want her proper limbs;
Her face defac'd with scars of infamy,
Her royal stock graft with ignoble plants,
And almost shoulder'd in the swallowing gulf
Of dark forgetfulness, and deep oblivion.
Which to recure, we heartily solicit
Your gracious self to take on you the charge
And kingly government of this your land:
Not as protector, steward, substitute,
Or lowly factor for another's gain:
But as successively, from blood to blood,
Your right of birth, your empery, your own.
For this, consorted with the citizens,
Your very worshipful and loving friends,
And by their vehement instigation,
In this just suit come I to move your grace.
Glo. I cannot tell, if to depart in silence,
Or bitterly to speak in your reproof,
Best fitteth my degree or your condition:
If, not to answer,—you might haply think,
Tongue-tied ambition, not replying, yielded
To bear the golden yoke of sovereignty,
Which fondly you would here impose on me;
If to reprove you for this suit of yours,
So season'd with your faithful love to me,
Then, on the other side, I check'd my friends.
Therefore,—to speak, and to avoid the first;
And, then in speaking, not to incur the last,—
Definitively thus I answer you.
Your love deserves my thanks; but my desert
Unmeritable, shuns your high request.
First, if all obstacles were cut away,
And that my path were even to the crown,
As the ripe revenue and due of birth;
Yet so much is my poverty of spirit,
So mighty, and so many, my defects,
That I would rather hide me from my greatness,
Being a bark to brook no mighty sea,—
Than in my greatness covet to be hid,
And in the vapour of my glory smother'd.
But God be thank'd, there is no need of me;
(And much I need to help you, if need were);
The royal tree hath left us royal fruit,
Which, mellow'd by the stealing hours of time,
Will well become the seat of majesty,
And make, no doubt, us happy by his reign.
On him I lay what you would lay on me,
The right and fortune of his happy stars,—
Which, God defend, that I should wring from him!
Buck. My lord, this argues conscience in your grace;
But the respects thereof are nice and trivial,
All circumstances well considered.
You say, that Edward is your brother's son;
So say we too, but not by Edward's wife:
For first he was contract to Lady Lucy,
Your mother lives a witness to his vow;
And afterwards by substitute betroth'd
To Bona, sister to the king of France.
These both put by, a poor petitioner,
A care-craz'd mother to a many sons,
A beauty-waning and distressed widow,
Even in the afternoon of her best days,
Made prize and purchase of his wanton eye,
Seduc'd the pitch and height of all his thoughts
To base declension, and loath'd bigamy:
By her, in his unlawful bed, he got
This Edward, whom our manners call the prince.
More bitterly could I expostulate,
Save that, for reverence to some alive,
I give a sparing limit to my tongue.
Then, good my lord, take to your royal self
This proffer'd benefit of dignity:
If not to bless us and the land withal,
Yet to draw forth your noble ancestry
From the corruption of abusing time,
Unto a lineal true-derived course.
May. Do, good my lord; your citizens entreat you.
Buck. Refuse not, mighty lord, this proffer'd love.
Cate. O, make them joyful, grant their lawful suit.
Glo. Alas, why would you heap those cares on me?
I am unfit for state and majesty:—
I do beseech you, take it not amiss;
I cannot, nor I will not yield to you.
Buck. If you refuse it,—as in love and zeal,
Loath to depose the child, your brother's son;
As well we know your tenderness of heart,
And gentle, kind, effeminate remorse,
Which we have noted in you to your kindred,
And equally, indeed, to all estates,—
Yet know, whe'r you accept our suit or no,
Your brother's son shall never reign our king;
But we will plant some other in your throne;
To the disgrace and downfall of your house.
And, in this resolution, here we leave you;
Come, citizens, we will entreat no more.
[*Exeunt* BUCKINGHAM *and* Citizens.
Cate. Call them again, sweet prince, accept their suit;
If you deny them, all the land will rue it.
Glo. Will you enforce me to a world of cares?
Well, call them again; I am not made of stone,

But penetrable to your kind entreaties,
[*Exit* CATESBY.
Albeit against my conscience and my soul.—

Re-enter BUCKINGHAM *and the rest.*

Cousin of Buckingham,—and you sage, grave men,—
Since you will buckle fortune on my back,
To bear her burden, whe'r I will, or no,
I must have patience to endure the load:
But if black scandal, or foul-fac'd reproach,
Attend the sequel of your imposition,
Your mere enforcement shall acquittance me
From all the impure blots and stains thereof;
For God he knows, and you may partly see,
How far I am from the desire of this.
May. God bless your grace! we see it, and will say it.
Glo. In saying so, you shall but say the truth.
Buck. Then I salute you with this royal title,—
Long live King Richard, England's worthy king!
All. Amen.
Buck. To-morrow may it please you to be crown'd?
Glo. Even when you please, since you will have it so.
Buck. To-morrow then we will attend your grace;
And so, most joyfully, we take our leave.
Glo. Come, let us to our holy work again.—
[*To the* Bishops.
Farewell, good cousin;—farewell, gentle friends.
[*Exeunt.*

ACT IV.

SCENE I. *Before the Tower.*

Enter on one side, QUEEN ELIZABETH, DUCHESS OF YORK, *and* MARQUIS OF DORSET; *on the other,* ANNE, DUCHESS OF GLOSTER, *leading* LADY MARGARET PLANTAGENET, Clarence's *young* Daughter.

Duch. Who meets us here?—my niece Plantagenet
Led in the hand of her kind aunt of Gloster?
Now, for my life, she's wand'ring to the Tower,
On pure heart's love, to greet the tender prince.—
Daughter, well met.
Anne. God give your graces both
A happy and a joyful time of day!
Q. Eliz. As much to you, good sister! Whither away?
Anne. No further than the Tower; and, as I guess,
Upon the like devotion as yourselves,
To gratulate the gentle princes there.
Q. Eliz. Kind sister, thanks; we'll enter all together:

Enter BRAKENBURY.

And, in good time, here the lieutenant comes.—
Master lieutenant, pray you, by your leave,
How doth the prince, and my young son of York?
Brak. Right well, dear madam: By your patience,
I may not suffer you to visit them;
The king hath strictly charg'd the contrary.
Q. Eliz. The king! who's that?
Brak. I mean, the lord protector.
Q. Eliz. The Lord protect him from that kingly title!
Hath he set bounds between their love and me?
I am their mother, who shall bar me from them?
Duch. I am their father's mother, I will see them.
Anne. Their aunt I am in law, in love their mother:
Then bring me to their sights; I'll bear thy blame,
And take thy office from thee, on my peril.
Brak. No, madam, no, I may not leave it so:
I am bound by oath, and therefore pardon me.
[*Exit* BRAKENBURY.

Enter STANLEY.

Stan. Let me but meet you, ladies, one hour hence,
And I'll salute your grace of York as mother,
And reverend looker on of two fair queens.—
Come, madam, you must straight to Westminster,
[*To the* DUCHESS OF GLOSTER.
There to be crowned Richard's royal queen.
Q. Eliz. Ah, cut my lace asunder!
That my pent heart may have some scope to beat,
Or else I swoon with this dead-killing news.
Anne. Despiteful tidings! O unpleasing news!
Dor. Be of good cheer:—Mother, how fares your grace?
Q. Eliz. O Dorset, speak not to me, get thee gone,
Death and destruction dog thee at the heels;
Thy mother's name is ominous to children:
If thou wilt outstrip death, go cross the seas,
And live with Richmond from the reach of hell.
Go, hie thee, hie thee, from this slaughter-house,
Lest thou increase the number of the dead;
And make me die the thrall of Margaret's curse,—
Nor mother, wife, nor England's counted queen.
Stan. Full of wise care is this your counsel, madam:—
Take all the swift advantage of the hours;
You shall have letters from me to my son
In your behalf, to meet you on the way:
Be not ta'en tardy by unwise delay.
Duch. O ill-dispersing wind of misery!—
O my accursed womb, the bed of death;
A cockatrice hast thou hatch'd to the world,
Whose unavoided eye is murderous!
Stan. Come, madam, come; I in all haste was sent.
Anne. And I with all unwillingness will go.—
O, would to God, that the inclusive verge
Of golden metal, that must round my brow,
Were red-hot steel, to sear me to the brain!
Anointed let me be with deadly venom;
And die, ere men can say—God save the queen!
Q. Eliz. Go, go, poor soul, I envy not thy glory!
To feed my humour, wish thyself no harm.
Anne. No! why?—When he, that is my husband now,
Came to me, as I follow'd Henry's corse;
When scarce the blood was well wash'd from his hands,
Which issu'd from my other angel husband,
And that dead saint which then I weeping follow'd;
O, when, I say, I look'd on Richard's face,
This was my wish,—*Be thou,* quoth I, *accurs'd,*
For making me, so young, so old a widow!
And, when thou wed'st, let sorrow haunt thy bed;
And be thy wife (if any be so mad),
More miserable by the life of thee,
Than thou hast made me by my dear lord's death!
Lo, ere I can repeat this curse again,
Even in so short a space, my woman's heart
Grossly grew captive to his honey words,
And prov'd the subject of mine own soul's curse:
Which ever since hath held mine eyes from rest;
For never yet one hour in his bed
Did I enjoy the golden dew of sleep,
But with his timorous dreams was still awak'd.
Besides, he hates me for my father Warwick;
And will, no doubt, shortly be rid of me.
Q. Eliz. Poor heart, adieu; I pity thy complaining.
Anne. No more than with my soul I mourn for yours.
Dor. Farewell, thou woful welcomer of glory!
Anne. Adieu, poor soul, that tak'st thy leave of it!
Duch. Go thou to Richmond, and good fortune guide thee!—
[*To* DORSET.

Go thou to Richard, and good angels tend thee!— [*To* ANNE.
Go thou to sanctuary, and good thoughts possess thee! [*To* Q. ELIZABETH.
I to my grave, where peace and rest lie with me!
Eighty odd years of sorrow have I seen.
And each hour's joy wreck'd with a week of teen.

Q. Eliz. Stay yet; look back, with me, unto the Tower.—
Pity, you ancient stones, those tender babes,
Whom envy hath immur'd within your walls!
Rough cradle for such little pretty ones!
Rude ragged nurse! old sullen playfellow
For tender princes, use my babies well!
So foolish sorrow bids your stones farewell. [*Exeunt.*

SCENE II. *A Room of State in the Palace.*

Flourish of Trumpets. RICHARD, *as King upon his throne;* BUCKINGHAM, CATESBY, *a* Page, *and Others.*

K. Rich. Stand all apart.—Cousin of Buckingham,——

Buck. My gracious sovereign.

K. Rich. Give me thy hand. Thus high by thy advice,
And thy assistance, is King Richard seated:—
But shall we wear these glories for a day?
Or shall they last, and we rejoice in them?

Buck. Still live they, and for ever let them last!

K. Rich. Ah, Buckingham, now do I play the touch,
To try if thou be current gold, indeed:—
Young Edward lives;—Think now what I would speak.

Buck. Say on, my loving lord.

K. Rich. Why, Buckingham, I say, I would be king.

Buck. Why, so you are, my thrice-renowned liege.

K. Rich. Ha! am I king? 'Tis so: but Edward lives.

Buck. True, noble prince.

K. Rich. O bitter consequence,
That Edward still should live,—true, noble prince!—
Cousin, thou wast not wont to be so dull:
Shall I be plain? I wish the bastards dead;
And I would have it suddenly perform'd.
What say'st thou now? speak suddenly, be brief.

Buck. Your grace may do your pleasure.

K. Rich. Tut, tut, thou art all ice, thy kindness freezes:
Say, have I thy consent, that they shall die?

Buck. Give me some breath, some little pause, dear lord,
Before I positively speak in this:
I will resolve your grace immediately. [*Exit* BUCKINGHAM.

Cate. The king is angry; see, he gnaws his lip. [*Aside.*

K. Rich. I will converse with iron-witted fools, [*Descends from his Throne.*
And unrespective boys: none are for me,
That look into me with considerate eyes;—
High-reaching Buckingham grows circumspect.—
Boy,——

Page. My lord.

K. Rich. Know'st thou not any whom corrupting gold
Would tempt unto a close exploit of death?

Page. I know a discontented gentleman,
Whose humble means match not his haughty mind:
Gold were as good as twenty orators,
And will no doubt tempt him to any thing.

K. Rich. What is his name?

Page. His name, my lord, is—Tyrrel.

K. Rich. I partly know the man; Go, call him hither, boy.— [*Exit* Page.
The deep-revolving witty Buckingham
No more shall be the neighbour to my counsels:
Hath he so long held out with me untir'd,
And stops he now for breath?—well, be it so.—

Enter STANLEY.

How now, Lord Stanley? what's the news?

Stan. Know, my loving lord,
The marquis Dorset, as I hear, is fled
To Richmond, in the parts where he abides.

K. Rich. Come hither, Catesby: rumour it abroad,
That Anne, my wife, is very grievous sick;
I will take order for her keeping close.
Inquire me out some mean born gentleman,
Whom I will marry straight to Clarence' daughter:—
The boy is foolish, and I fear not him.—
Look, how thou dream'st!—I say again, give out,
That Anne my queen is sick, and like to die:
About it: for it stands me much upon,
To stop all hopes, whose growth may damage me.— [*Exit* CATESBY.
I must be married to my brother's daughter,
Or else my kingdom stands on brittle glass:—
Murder her brothers, and then marry her!
Uncertain way of gain! But I am in
So far in blood, that sin will pluck on sin.
Tear-falling pity dwells not in this eye.—

Re-enter Page, *with* TYRREL.

Is thy name—Tyrrel?

Tyr. James Tyrrel, and your most obedient subject.

K. Rich. Art thou, indeed?

Tyr. Prove me, my gracious lord.

K. Rich. Dar'st thou resolve to kill a friend of mine.

Tyr. Please you; but I had rather kill two enemies.

K. Rich. Why, then thou hast it; two deep enemies,
Foes to my rest, and my sweet sleep's disturbers,
Are they that I would have thee deal upon:
Tyrrel, I mean those bastards in the Tower.

Tyr. Let me have open means to come to them,
And soon I'll rid you from the fear of them.

K. Rich. Thou sing'st sweet musick. Hark, come hither, Tyrrel;
Go, by this token:—Rise, and lend thine ear: [*Whispers.*
There is no more but so;—Say, it is done,
And I will love thee, and prefer thee for it.

Tyr. I will despatch it straight. [*Exit.*

Re-enter BUCKINGHAM.

Buck. My lord, I have consider'd in my mind
The late demand that you did sound me in.

K. Rich. Well, let that rest. Dorset is fled to Richmond.

Buck. I hear the news, my lord.

K. Rich. Stanley, he's your wife's son:—Well, look to it.

Buck. My lord, I claim the gift, my due by promise,
For which your honour and your faith is pawn'd;
The earldom of Hereford, and the moveables,
Which you have promised I shall possess.

K. Rich. Stanley, look to your wife; if she convey
Letters to Richmond, you shall answer it.

Buck. What says your highness to my just request?

K. Rich. I do remember me,—Henry the Sixth
Did prophesy, that Richmond should be king,
When Richmond was a little peevish boy.
A king!—perhaps——

Buck. My lord,——

K. Rich. How chance, the prophet could not at that time,
Have told me, I being by, that I should kill him?

Buck. My lord, your promise for the earldom,—

K. Rich. Richmond!—When last I was at Exeter,
The mayor in courtesy show'd me the castle,
And call'd it—Rouge-mont: at which name, I started;
Because a bard of Ireland told me once,
I should not live long after I saw Richmond.
Buck. My lord,——
K. Rich. Ay, what's o'clock?
Buck. I am thus bold
To put your grace in mind of what you promis'd me.
K. Rich. Well, but what is't o'clock?
Buck. Upon the stroke
Of ten.
K. Rich. Well, let it strike.
Buck. Why, let it strike?
K. Rich. Because that, like a Jack, thou keep'st the stroke
Betwixt thy begging and my meditation.
I am not in the giving vein to-day.
Buck. Why, then resolve me whe'r you will, or no.
K. Rich. Thou troublest me; I am not in the vein. [*Exeunt* KING RICHARD *and* Train.
Buck. And is it thus? repays he my deep service
With such contempt? made I him king for this?
O, let me think on Hastings; and be gone
To Brecknock, while my fearful head is on. [*Exit.*

SCENE III. *The same.*

Enter TYRREL.

Tyr. The tyrannous and bloody act is done;
The most arch deed of piteous massacre,
That ever yet this land was guilty of.
Dighton, and Forrest, whom I did suborn
To do this piece of ruthless butchery,
Albeit they were flesh'd villains, bloody dogs,
Melting with tenderness and mild compassion,
Wept like two children, in their death's sad story.
O thus, quoth Dighton, *lay the gentle babes,—*
Thus, thus, quoth Forrest, *girdling one another*
Within their alabaster innocent arms:
Their lips were four red roses on a stalk,
Which, in their summer beauty, kiss'd each other.
A book of prayers on their pillow lay;
Which once, quoth Forrest, *almost chang'd my mind;*
But, O, the devil—there the villain stopp'd:
When Dighton thus told on—*we smothered*
The most replenished sweet work of nature,
That, from the prime creation, e'er she fram'd.—
Hence both are gone with conscience and remorse,
They could not speak; and so I left them both,
To bear this tidings to the bloody king.

Enter KING RICHARD.

And here he comes:—All health, my sovereign lord!
K. Rich. Kind Tyrrel! am I happy in thy news?
Tyr. If to have done the thing you gave in charge
Beget your happiness, be happy then,
For it is done.
K. Rich. But didst thou see them dead?
Tyr. I did, my lord.
K. Rich. And buried, gentle Tyrrel?
Tyr. The chaplain of the tower hath buried them;
But where, to say the truth, I do not know.
K. Rich. Come to me, Tyrrel, soon, at after supper,
When thou shalt tell the process of their death.
Mean time, but think how I may do thee good,
And be inheritor of thy desire.
Farewell, till then.
Tyr. I humbly take my leave. [*Exit.*

K. Rich. The son of Clarence have I penn'd up close;
His daughter meanly have I match'd in marriage;
The sons of Edward sleep in Abraham's bosom,
And Anne my wife hath bid the world good night.
Now, for I know the Bretagne Richmond aims
At young Elizabeth, my brother's daughter,
And, by that knot, looks proudly on the crown,
To her go I, a jolly thriving wooer.

Enter CATESBY.

Cate. My lord,—
K. Rich. Good news or bad, that thou com'st in so bluntly?
Cate. Bad news, my lord; Morton is fled to Richmond;
And Buckingham, back'd with the hardy Welshmen,
Is in the field, and still his power increaseth.
K. Rich. Ely with Richmond troubles me more near,
Than Buckingham and his rash levied strength.
Come,—I have learn'd, that fearful commenting
Is leaden servitor to dull delay;
Delay leads impotent and snail-pac'd beggary:
Then fiery expedition be my wing,
Jove's Mercury, and herald for a king!
Go, muster men: My counsel is my shield;
We must be brief, when traitors brave the field. [*Exeunt.*

SCENE IV. *The same. Before the Palace.*

Enter QUEEN MARGARET.

Q. Mar. So, now prosperity begins to mellow,
And drop into the rotten mouth of death.
Here in these confines slily have I lurk'd,
To watch the waning of mine enemies.
A dire induction am I witness to,
And will to France; hoping, the consequence
Will prove as bitter, black, and tragical.
Withdraw thee, wretched Margaret! who comes here?

Enter QUEEN ELIZABETH *and the* DUCHESS OF YORK.

Q. Eliz. Ah, my poor princes! ah, my tender babes!
My unblown flowers, new appearing sweets!
If yet your gentle souls fly in the air,
And be not fix'd in doom perpetual,
Hover about me with your airy wings,
And hear your mother's lamentation!
Q. Mar. Hover about her; say, that right for right
Hath dimm'd your infant morn to aged night.
Duch. So many miseries have craz'd my voice,
That my woe-wearied tongue is still and mute,—
Edward Plantagenet, why art thou dead?
Q. Mar. Plantagenet doth quit Plantagenet,
Edward for Edward pays a dying debt.
Q. Eliz. Wilt thou, O God, fly from such gentle lambs,
And throw them in the entrails of the wolf?
When didst thou sleep, when such a deed was done?
Q. Mar. When holy Harry died, and my sweet son.
Duch. Dead life, blind sight, poor mortal-living ghost,
Woe's scene, world's shame, grave's due by life usurp'd,
Brief abstract and record of tedious days,
Rest thy unrest on England's lawful earth, [*Sitting down.*
Unlawfully made drunk with innocent blood!
Q. Eliz. Ah, that thou would'st as soon afford a grave,
As thou canst yield a melancholy seat;
Then would I hide my bones, not rest them here!
Ah, who hath any cause to mourn, but we? [*Sitting down by her.*

Q. Mar. If ancient sorrow be most reverent,
Give mine the benefit of seniory,
And let my griefs frown on the upper hand.
If sorrow can admit society, [*Sitting down with them.*
Tell o'er your woes again by viewing mine:—
I had an Edward, till a Richard kill'd him;
I had a husband, till a Richard kill'd him:
Thou hadst an Edward, till a Richard kill'd him.
Thou hadst a Richard, till a Richard kill'd him.
Duch. I had a Richard too, and thou didst kill him;
I had a Rutland too, thou holp'st to kill him.
Q. Mar. Thou hadst a Clarence too, and Richard kill'd him;
From forth the kennel of thy womb hath crept
A hell hound, that doth hunt us all to death:
That dog, that had his teeth before his eyes,
To worry lambs, and lap their gentle blood;
That foul defacer of God's handy work;
That excellent grand tyrant of the earth,
That reigns in galled eyes of weeping souls,
Thy womb let loose, to chase us to our graves.—
O upright, just, and true disposing God,
How do I thank thee, that this carnal cur
Preys on the issue of his mother's body,
And makes her pew-fellow with others' moan!
Duch. O Harry's wife, triumph not in my woes;
God witness with me, I have wept for thine.
Q. Mar. Bear with me, I am hungry for revenge,
And now I cloy me with beholding it.
Thy Edward he is dead, that kill'd my Edward;
Thy other Edward dead, to quit my Edward;
Young York he is but boot, because both they
Match not the high perfection of my loss.
Thy Clarence he is dead, that stabb'd my Edward;
And the beholders of this tragic play,
The adulterate Hastings, Rivers, Vaughan, Grey,
Untimely smother'd in their dusky graves.
Richard yet lives, hell's black intelligencer;
Only reserv'd their factor, to buy souls,
And send them thither: But at hand, at hand,
Ensues his piteous and unpitied end:
Earth gapes, hell burns, fiends roar, saints pray,
To have him suddenly convey'd from hence:—
Cancel his bond of life, dear God, I pray,
That I may live to say, The dog is dead!
Q. Eliz. O, thou didst prophesy, the time would come,
That I should wish for thee to help me curse
That bottled spider, that foul bunch-back'd toad.
Q. Mar. I call'd thee then, vain flourish of my fortune;
I call'd thee then, poor shadow, painted queen;
The presentation of but what I was,
The flattering index of a direful pageant,
One heav'd a high, to be hurl'd down below:
A mother only mock'd with two fair babes;
A dream of what thou wast; a garish flag,
To be the aim of every dangerous shot;
A sign of dignity, a breath, a bubble;
A queen in jest, only to fill the scene.
Where is thy husband now? where be thy brothers?
Where be thy two sons? wherein dost thou joy?
Who sues, and kneels, and says—God save the queen?
Where be the bending peers that flatter'd thee?
Where be the thronging troops that follow'd thee?
Decline all this, and see what now thou art.
For happy wife, a most distressed widow;
For joyful mother, one that wails the name;
For one being sued to, one that humbly sues;
For queen, a very caitiff crown'd with care;
For one that scorn'd at me, now scorn'd of me;
For one being fear'd of all, now fearing one;
For one commanding all, obey'd of none.
Thus hath the course of justice wheel'd about,
And left thee but a very prey to time;
Having no more but thought of what thou wert,
To torture thee the more, being what thou art.
Thou didst usurp my place. And dost thou not
Usurp the just proportion of my sorrow?
Now thy proud neck bears half my burden'd yoke;
From which even here I slip my wearied head,
And leave the burden of it all on thee.
Farewell, York's wife,—and queen of sad mischance,—
These English woes shall make me smile in France.
Q. Eliz. O thou well skill'd in curses, stay a while,
And teach me how to curse mine enemies.
Q. Mar. Forbear to sleep the night, and fast the day;
Compare dead happiness with living woe:
Think that thy babes were fairer than they were,
And he, that slew them, fouler than he is:
Bettering thy loss makes the bad causer worse;
Revolving this will teach thee how to curse.
Q. Eliz. My words are dull, O, quicken them with thine!
Q. Mar. Thy woes will make them sharp, and pierce like mine. [*Exit* Q. MARGARET.
Duch. Why should calamity be full of words?
Q. Eliz. Windy attorneys to their client woes,
Airy succeeders of intestate joys,
Poor breathing orators of miseries!
Let them have scope: though what they do impart
Help nothing else, yet do they ease the heart.
Duch. If so, then be not tongue-ty'd: go with me,
And in the breath of bitter words let's smother
My damned son, that thy two sweet sons smother'd. [*Drum within.*
I hear his drum,—be copious in exclaims.

Enter KING RICHARD, *and his* Train, *marching.*

K. Rich. Who intercepts me in my expedition?
Duch. O, she, that might have intercepted thee,
By strangling thee in her accursed womb,
From all the slaughters, wretch, that thou hast done.
Q. Eliz. Hid'st thou that forehead with a golden crown,
Where should be branded, if that right were right,
The slaughter of the prince that ow'd that crown,
And the dire death of my poor sons, and brothers?
Tell me, thou villain slave, where are my children?
Duch. Thou toad, thou toad, where is thy brother Clarence?
And little Ned Plantagenet, his son?
Q. Eliz. Where is the gentle Rivers, Vaughan, Grey?
Duch. Where is kind Hastings?
K. Rich. A flourish, trumpets!—strike alarum, drums!
Let not the heavens hear these tell-tale women
Rail on the Lord's anointed:—Strike, I say.— [*Flourish. Alarums.*
Either be patient and entreat me fair,
Or with the clamorous report of war
Thus will I drown your exclamations.
Duch. Art thou my son?
K. Rich. Ay; I thank God, my father, and yourself.
Duch. Then patiently hear my impatience.
K. Rich. Madam, I have a touch of your condition,
That cannot brook the accent of reproof.
Duch. O, let me speak.
K. Rich. Do, then; but I'll not hear.
Duch. I will be mild and gentle in my words.
K. Rich. And brief, good mother: for I am in haste.
Duch. Art thou so hasty? I have staid for thee,
God knows, in torment and in agony.

K. Rich. And came I not at last to comfort you?
Duch. No, by the holy rood, thou know'st it well,
Thou cam'st on earth to make the earth my hell.
A grievous burden was thy birth to me;
Tetchy and wayward was thy infancy;
Thy school-days, frightful, desperate, wild, and furious;
Thy prime of manhood, daring, bold, and venturous;
Thy age confirm'd, proud, subtle, sly, and bloody,
More mild, but yet more harmful, kind in hatred:
What comfortable hour canst thou name,
That ever grac'd me in thy company?
K. Rich. 'Faith, none, but Humphrey Hour, that call'd your grace
To breakfast once, forth of my company.
If I be so disgracious in your sight,
Let me march on, and not offend you, madam.—
Strike up the drum.
Duch. I pr'ythee, hear me speak.
K. Rich. You speak too bitterly.
Duch. Hear me a word;
For I shall never speak to thee again.
K. Rich. So.
Duch. Either thou wilt die, by God's just ordinance,
Ere from this war thou turn a conqueror;
Or I with grief and extreme age shall perish,
And never look upon thy face again.
Therefore take with thee my most heavy curse;
Which, in the day of battle, tire thee more,
Than all the complete armour that thou wear'st!
My prayers on the adverse party fight;
And there the little souls of Edward's children
Whisper the spirits of thine enemies,
And promise them success and victory.
Bloody thou art, bloody will be thy end;
Shame serves thy life, and doth thy death attend. [*Exit.*
Q. Eliz. Though far more cause, yet much less spirit to curse
Abides in me; I say amen to her. [*Going.*
K. Rich. Stay, madam, I must speak a word with you.
Q. Eliz. I have no more sons of the royal blood,
For thee to murder: for my daughters, Richard,—
They shall be praying nuns, not weeping queens;
And therefore level not to hit their lives.
K. Rich. You have a daughter call'd—Elizabeth,
Virtuous and fair, royal and gracious.
Q. Eliz. And must she die for this? O, let her live,
And I'll corrupt her manners, stain her beauty;
Slander myself, as false to Edward's bed;
Throw over her the veil of infamy:
So she may live unscarr'd of bleeding slaughter,
I will confess she was not Edward's daughter.
K. Rich. Wrong not her birth, she is of royal blood.
Q. Eliz. To save her life, I'll say—she is not so.
K. Rich. Her life is safest only in her birth.
Q. Eliz. And only in that safety died her brothers.
K. Rich. Lo, at their births, good stars were opposite.
Q. Eliz. No, to their lives bad friends were contrary.
K. Rich. All unavoided is the doom of destiny.
Q. Eliz. True, when avoided grace make destiny:
My babes were destin'd to a fairer death,
If grace had bless'd thee with a fairer life.
K. Rich. You speak, as if that I had slain my cousins.
Q. Eliz. Cousins, indeed; and by their uncle cozen'd
Of comfort, kingdom, kindred, freedom, life.
Whose hands soever lanc'd their tender hearts,
Thy head, all indirectly, gave direction:
No doubt the murderous knife was dull and blunt,
Till it was whetted on thy stone-hard heart,
To revel in the entrails of my lambs.
But that still use of grief makes wild grief tame,
My tongue should to thy ears not name my boys,
Till that my nails were anchor'd in thine eyes:
And I, in such a desperate bay of death,
Like a poor bark, of sails and tackling reft,
Rush all to pieces on thy rocky bosom.
K. Rich. Madam, so thrive I in my enterprise,
And dangerous success of bloody wars,
As I intend more good to you and yours,
Than ever you or yours by me were harm'd!
Q. Eliz. What good is cover'd with the face of heaven,
To be discover'd, that can do me good?
K. Rich. The advancement of your children, gentle lady.
Q. Eliz. Up to some scaffold, there to lose their heads?
K. Rich. No, to the dignity and height of fortune,
The high imperial type of this earth's glory.
Q. Eliz. Flatter my sorrows with report of it;
Tell me, what state, what dignity, what honour,
Canst thou demise to any child of mine?
K. Rich. Even all I have; ay, and myself and all,
Will I withal endow a child of thine;
So in the Lethe of thy angry soul
Thou drown the sad remembrance of those wrongs,
Which, thou supposest, I have done to thee.
Q. Eliz. Be brief, lest that the process of thy kindness
Last longer telling than thy kindness' date.
K. Rich. Then know, that from my soul, I love thy daughter.
Q. Eliz. My daughter's mother thinks it with her soul.
K. Rich. What do you think?
Q. Eliz. That thou dost love my daughter, from thy soul:
So, from thy soul's love, didst thou love her brothers:
And from my heart's love, I do thank thee for it.
K. Rich. Be not so hasty to confound my meaning;
I mean, that with my soul I love thy daughter,
And do intend to make her queen of England.
Q. Eliz. Well then, who dost thou mean shall be her king?
K. Rich. Even he, that makes her queen: Who else should be?
Q. Eliz. What, thou?
K. Rich. Even so: What think you of it, madam?
Q. Eliz. How canst thou woo her?
K. Rich. That I would learn of you,
As one being best acquainted with her humour.
Q. Eliz. And wilt thou learn of me?
K. Rich. Madam, with all my heart.
Q. Eliz. Send to her, by the man that slew her brothers,
A pair of bleeding hearts; thereon engrave,
Edward, and York; then, haply, will she weep:
Therefore present to her,—as sometime Margaret
Did to thy father, steep'd in Rutland's blood,—
A handkerchief; which, say to her, did drain
The purple sap from her sweet brother's body,
And bid her wipe her weeping eyes withal.
If this inducement move her not to love,
Send her a letter of thy noble deeds;
Tell her, thou mad'st away her uncle Clarence,
Her uncle Rivers; ay, and, for her sake,
Mad'st quick conveyance with her good aunt Anne.
K. Rich. You mock me, madam; this is not the way
To win your daughter.

Q. Eliz. There is no other way;
Unless thou could'st put on some other shape,
And not be Richard that hath done all this.
K. Rich. Say, that I did all this for love of her?
Q. Eliz. Nay, then indeed, she cannot choose but hate thee,
Having bought love with such a bloody spoil.
K. Rich. Look, what is done cannot be now amended;
Men shall deal unadvisedly sometimes,
Which after hours give leisure to repent.
If I did take the kingdom from your sons,
To make amends, I'll give it to your daughter.
If I have kill'd the issue of your womb,
To quicken your increase, I will beget
Mine issue of your blood upon your daughter.
A grandam's name is little less in love,
Than is the doting title of a mother;
They are as children, but one step below,
Even of your mettle, of your very blood;
Of all one pain,—save for a night of groans
Endur'd of her, for whom you bid like sorrow.
Your children were vexation to your youth,
But mine shall be a comfort to your age.
The loss, you have, is but—a son being king,
And, by that loss, your daughter is made queen.
I cannot make you what amends I would,
Therefore accept such kindness as I can.
Dorset, your son, that, with a fearful soul,
Leads discontented steps in foreign soil,
This fair alliance quickly shall call home
To high promotions and great dignity:
The king, that calls your beauteous daughter,—wife,
Familiarly shall call thy Dorset—brother;
Again shall you be mother to a king,
And all the ruins of distressful times
Repair'd with double riches of content.
What! we have many goodly days to see:
The liquid drops of tears that you have shed,
Shall come again, transform'd to orient pearl:
Advantaging their loan with interest
Of ten times double gain of happiness.
Go then, my mother, to thy daughter go;
Make bold her bashful years with your experience;
Prepare her ears to hear a wooer's tale;
Put in her tender heart the aspiring flame
Of golden sovereignty; acquaint the princess
With the sweet silent hours of marriage joys:
And when this arm of mine hath chastised
The petty rebel, dull-brain'd Buckingham,
Bound with triumphant garlands will I come,
And lead thy daughter to a conqueror's bed;
To whom I will retail my conquest won,
And she shall be sole victress, Cæsar's Cæsar.
Q. Eliz. What were I best to say? her father's brother
Would be her lord? Or shall I say, her uncle?
Or, he that slew her brothers, and her uncles?
Under what title shall I woo for thee,
That God, the law, my honour, and her love,
Can make seem pleasing to her tender years?
K. Rich. Infer fair England's peace by this alliance.
Q. Eliz. Which she shall purchase with still lasting war.
K. Rich. Tell her, the king, that may command, entreats.
Q. Eliz. That at her hands, which the king's King forbids.
K. Rich. Say, she shall be a high and mighty queen.
Q. Eliz. To wail the title, as her mother doth.
K. Rich. Say, I will love her everlastingly.
Q. Eliz. But how long shall that title, ever, last?
K. Rich. Sweetly in force unto her fair life's end.
Q. Eliz. But how long fairly shall her sweet life last?
K. Rich. As long as heaven, and nature, lengthens it.
Q. Eliz. As long as hell, and Richard, likes of it.
K. Rich. Say, I, her sovereign, am her subject low.
Q. Eliz. But she, your subject, loaths such sov'reignty.
K. Rich. Be eloquent in my behalf to her.
Q. Eliz. An honest tale speeds best, being plainly told.
K. Rich. Then in plain terms tell her my loving tale.
Q. Eliz. Plain, and not honest, is too harsh a style.
K. Rich. Your reasons are too shallow and too quick.
Q. Eliz. O, no, my reasons are too deep and dead;—
Too deep and dead, poor infants, in their graves,
K. Rich. Harp not on that string, madam; that is past.
Q. Eliz. Harp on it still shall I, till heartstrings break.
K. Rich. Now, by my George, my garter, and my crown,—
Q. Eliz. Profan'd, dishonour'd, and the third usurp'd.
K. Rich. I swear.
Q. Eliz. By nothing; for this is no oath.
Thy George, profan'd, hath lost his holy honour;
Thy garter, blemish'd, pawn'd his knightly virtue;
Thy crown, usurp'd, disgrac'd his kingly glory:
If something thou would'st swear to be believ'd,
Swear then by something that thou hast not wrong'd.
K. Rich. Now by the world,—
Q. Eliz. 'Tis full of thy foul wrongs.
K. Rich. My father's death,—
Q. Eliz. Thy life hath that dishonour'd.
K. Rich. Then, by myself,—
Q. Eliz. Thyself is self misus'd.
K. Rich. Why then, by God,—
Q. Eliz. God's wrong is most of all.
If thou hadst fear'd to break an oath by him,
The unity, the king thy brother made,
Had not been broken, nor my brother slain.
If thou hadst fear'd to break an oath by him,
The imperial metal circling now thy head,
Had grac'd the tender temples of my child;
And both the princes had been breathing here,
Which now, two tender bedfellows for dust,
Thy broken faith hath made a prey for worms.
What canst thou swear by now?
K. Rich. By the time to come.
Q. Eliz. That thou hast wronged in the time o'erpast;
For I myself have many tears to wash
Hereafter time, for time past, wrong'd by thee.
The children live, whose parents thou hast slaughter'd,
Ungovern'd youth, to wail it in their age:
The parents live, whose children thou hast butcher'd!
Old barren plants, to wail it with their age.
Swear not by time to come; for that thou hast
Misus'd ere used, by times ill us'd o'erpast.
K. Rich. As I intend to prosper, and repent!
So thrive I in my dangerous attempt
Of hostile arms! myself myself confound!
Heaven, and fortune, bar me happy hours!
Day, yield me not thy light; nor, night, thy rest!
Be opposite all planets of good luck
To my proceeding, if, with pure heart's love,
Immaculate devotion, holy thoughts,
I tender not thy beauteous princely daughter!
In her consists my happiness, and thine:
Without her, follows to myself, and thee,
Herself, the land, and many a christian soul,
Death, desolation, ruin, and decay:
It cannot be avoided but by this;
It will not be avoided, but by this.
Therefore, dear mother (I must call you so),
Be the attorney of my love to her.
Plead what I will be, not what I have been;

Not my deserts, but what I will deserve:
Urge the necessity and state of times,
And be not peevish found in great designs.

Q. Eliz. Shall I be tempted of the devil thus?

K. Rich. Ay, if the devil tempt thee to do good.

Q. Eliz. Shall I forget myself, to be myself?

K. Rich. Ay, if yourself's remembrance wrong yourself.

Q. Eliz. But thou didst kill my children.

K. Rich. But in your daughter's womb I bury them:
Where, in that nest of spicery, they shall breed
Selves of themselves, to your recomforture.

Q. Eliz. Shall I go win my daughter to thy will?

K. Rich. And be a happy mother by the deed.

Q. Eliz. I go.—Write to me very shortly,
And you shall understand from me her mind.

K. Rich. Bear her my true love's kiss, and so farewell.
[*Kissing her. Exit* Q. ELIZABETH.
Relenting fool, and shallow, changing—woman!
How now? what news?

Enter RATCLIFF; CATESBY *following.*

Rat. Most mighty sovereign, on the western coast
Rideth a puissant navy; to the shore
Throng many doubtful hollow-hearted friends,
Unarm'd, and unresolv'd to beat them back:
'Tis thought, that Richmond is their admiral;
And there they hull, expecting but the aid
Of Buckingham, to welcome them ashore.

K. Rich. Some lightfoot friend post to the duke of Norfolk:
Ratcliff, thyself,—or Catesby; where is he?

Cate. Here, my good lord.

K. Rich. Catesby, fly to the duke.

Cate. I will, my lord, with all convenient haste.

K. Rich. Ratcliff, come hither: Post to Salisbury;
When thou com'st thither,—Dull unmindful villain, [*To* CATESBY.
Why stay'st thou here, and go'st not to the duke?

Cate. First, mighty liege, tell me your highness' pleasure,
What from your grace I shall deliver to him.

K. Rich. O, true, good Catesby;—Bid him levy straight
The greatest strength and power he can make,
And meet me suddenly at Salisbury.

Cate. I go. [*Exit.*

Rat. What, may it please you, shall I do at Salisbury?

K. Rich. Why, what would'st thou do there, before I go?

Rat. Your highness told me, I should post before.

Enter STANLEY.

K. Rich. My mind is chang'd.—Stanley, what news with you?

Stan. None good, my liege, to please you with the hearing;
Nor none so bad, but well may be reported.

K. Rich. Heyday, a riddle! neither good nor bad!
What need'st thou run so many miles about,
When thou may'st tell thy tale the nearest way?
Once more, what news?

Stan. Richmond is on the seas.

K. Rich. There let him sink, and be the seas on him!
White liver'd runagate, what doth he there?

Stan. I know not, mighty sovereign, but by guess.

K. Rich. Well, as you guess?

Stan. Stirr'd up by Dorset, Buckingham, and Morton,
He makes for England, here to claim the crown.

K. Rich. Is the chair empty? is the sword unsway'd?
Is the king dead, the empire unpossess'd?
What heir of York is there alive, but we?
And who is England's king, but great York's heir?
Then, tell me, what makes he upon the seas?

Stan. Unless for that, my liege, I cannot guess.

K. Rich. Unless for that he comes to be your liege,
You cannot guess wherefore the Welshman comes.
Thou wilt revolt and fly to him, I fear.

Stan. No, mighty liege; therefore mistrust me not.

K. Rich. Where is thy power then, to beat him back?
Where be thy tenants, and thy followers?
Are they not now upon the western shore,
Safe-conducting the rebels from their ships?

Stan. No, my good lord, my friends are in the north.

K. Rich. Cold friends to me: what do they in the north,
When they should serve their sovereign in the west?

Stan. They have not been commanded, mighty king:
Pleaseth your majesty to give me leave,
I'll muster up my friends; and meet your grace,
Where, and what time, your majesty shall please.

K. Rich. Ay, ay, thou would'st be gone to join with Richmond:
I will not trust you, sir.

Stan. Most mighty sovereign,
You have no cause to hold my friendship doubtful;
I never was, nor never will be false.

K. Rich. Well, go, muster men. But, hear you, leave behind
Your son, George Stanley: look, your heart be firm,
Or else his head's assurance is but frail.

Stan. So deal with him, as I prove true to you.
[*Exit* STANLEY.

Enter a Messenger.

Mess. My gracious sovereign, now in Devonshire,
As I by friends am well advertised,
Sir Edward Courteney, and the haughty prelate,
Bishop of Exeter, his elder brother,
With many more confederates, are in arms.

Enter another Messenger.

2 *Mess.* In Kent, my liege, the Guilfords are in arms;
And every hour more competitors
Flock to the rebels, and their power grows strong.

Enter another Messenger.

3 *Mess.* My lord, the army of great Buckingham—

K. Rich. Out on ye, owls! nothing but songs of death? [*He strikes him.*
There, take thou that, till thou bring better news.

3 *Mess.* The news I have to tell your majesty,
Is,—that, by sudden floods and fall of waters,
Buckingham's army is dispers'd and scatter'd;
And he himself wander'd away alone,
No man knows whither.

K. Rich. O, I cry you mercy:
There is my purse to cure that blow of thine.
Hath any well advised friend proclaim'd
Reward to him that brings the traitor in?

3 *Mess.* Such proclamation hath been made, my liege.

Enter another Messenger.

4 *Mess.* Sir Thomas Lovel, and lord marquis Dorset,
'Tis said, my liege, in Yorkshire are in arms.
But this good comfort bring I to your highness,—
The Bretagne navy is dispers'd by tempest:
Richmond, in Dorsetshire, sent out a boat
Unto the shore, to ask those on the banks,

If they were his assistants, yea, or no;
Who answer'd him, they came from Buckingham
Upon his party: he, mistrusting them,
Hois'd sail, and made his course again for Bretagne.

K. Rich. March on, march on, since we are up in arms;
If not to fight with foreign enemies,
Yet to beat down these rebels here at home.

Enter CATESBY.

Cate. My liege, the duke of Buckingham is taken,
That is the best news; That the earl of Richmond
Is with a mighty power landed at Milford,
Is colder news, but yet they must be told.

K. Rich. Away towards Salisbury; while we reason here,
A royal battle might be won and lost:—
Some one take order, Buckingham be brought
To Salisbury;—the rest march on with me. [*Exeunt.*

SCENE V. *A Room in* Lord Stanley's *House.*

Enter STANLEY *and* SIR CHRISTOPHER URSWICK.

Stan. Sir Christopher, tell Richmond this from me:—
That in the sty of this most bloody boar,
My son George Stanley is frank'd up in hold;
If I revolt, off goes young George's head;
The fear of that withholds my present aid.
But, tell me, where is princely Richmond now?

Chris. At Pembroke, or at Ha'rford-west, in Wales.

Stan. What men of name resort to him?

Chris. Sir Walter Herbert, a renowned soldier;
Sir Gilbert Talbot, Sir William Stanley;
Oxford, redoubted Pembroke, Sir James Blunt,
And Rice ap Thomas, with a valiant crew;
And many other of great fame and worth:
And towards London do they bend their course,
If by the way they be not fought withal.

Stan. Well, hie thee to thy lord; commend me to him;
Tell him, the queen hath heartily consented
He shall espouse Elizabeth her daughter.
These letters will resolve him of my mind.
Farewell. [*Gives papers to* SIR CHRISTOPHER.
[*Exeunt.*

ACT V.

SCENE I. Salisbury. *An open Place.*

Enter the Sheriff, *and* Guard, *with* BUCKINGHAM, *led to execution.*

Buck. Will not King Richard let me speak with him?

Sher. No, my good lord; therefore be patient.

Buck. Hastings, and Edward's children, Rivers, Grey,
Holy King Henry, and thy fair son Edward,
Vaughan, and all that have miscarried
By underhand corrupted foul injustice;
If that your moody discontented souls
Do through the clouds behold this present hour,
Even for revenge mock my destruction!
This is All-Souls' day, fellows, is it not?

Sher. It is, my lord.

Buck. Why, then All-Souls' day is my body's doomsday.
This is the day, which, in King Edward's time,
I wish'd might fall on me, when I was found
False to his children, or his wife's allies:
This is the day, wherein I wish'd to fall
By the false faith of him whom most I trusted;
This, this, All-Souls' day to my fearful soul,
Is the determin'd respite of my wrongs.
That high All-seer which I dallied with,
Hath turned my feigned prayer on my head,
And given in earnest what I begg'd in jest.
Thus doth he force the swords of wicked men
To turn their own points on their masters' bosoms;
Thus Margaret's curse falls heavy on my neck,—
When he, quoth she, *shall split thy heart with sorrow,*
Remember Margaret was a prophetess.—
Come, sirs, convey me to the block of shame;
Wrong hath but wrong, and blame the due of blame. [*Exeunt* BUCKINGHAM, *&c.*

SCENE II. *Plain near* Tamworth.

Enter with drum and colours, RICHMOND, OXFORD, SIR JAMES BLUNT, SIR WALTER HERBERT, *and Others, with* Forces, *marching.*

Richm. Fellows in arms, and my most loving friends,
Bruis'd underneath the yoke of tyranny,
Thus far into the bowels of the land
Have we march'd on without impediment;
And here receive we from our father Stanley
Lines of fair comfort and encouragement.
The wretched, bloody, and usurping boar,
That spoil'd your summer fields, and fruitful vines,
Swills your warm blood like wash, and makes his trough
In your embowell'd bosoms, this foul swine
Lies now even in the centre of this isle,
Near to the town of Leicester, as we learn:
From Tamworth thither, is but one day's march.
In God's name, cheerly on, courageous friends,
To reap the harvest of perpetual peace
By this one bloody trial of sharp war.

Oxf. Every man's conscience is a thousand swords,
To fight against that bloody homicide.

Herb. I doubt not, but his friends will turn to us.

Blunt. He hath no friends, but who are friends for fear;
Which, in his dearest need, will fly from him.

Richm. All for our vantage. Then, in God's name, march:
True hope is swift, and flies with swallow's wings,
Kings it makes gods, and meaner creatures kings. [*Exeunt.*

SCENE III. Bosworth Field.

Enter KING RICHARD, *and* Forces; *the* DUKE OF NORFOLK, EARL OF SURREY, *and Others.*

K. Rich. Here pitch our tents, even here in Bosworth field.—
My lord of Surrey, why look you so sad?

Sur. My heart is ten times lighter than my looks.

K. Rich. My lord of Norfolk,——

Nor. Here, most gracious liege.

K. Rich. Norfolk, we must have knocks: Ha! must we not?

Nor. We must both give and take, my loving lord.

K. Rich. Up with my tent: Here will I lie to-night;
[Soldiers *begin to set up the* King's *Tent.*
But where to-morrow?—Well, all's one for that—
Who hath descried the number of the traitors?

Nor. Six or seven thousand is their utmost power.

K. Rich. Why, our battalia trebles that account:
Besides, the king's name is a tower of strength,
Which they upon the adverse faction want.
Up with the tent—Come, noble gentlemen,
Let us survey the vantage of the ground;—
Call for some men of sound direction:—
Let's want no discipline, make no delay;
For, lords, to-morrow is a busy day. [*Exeunt.*

Enter, on the other side of the Field, RICHMOND, SIR WILLIAM BRANDON, OXFORD, *and other* Lords. *Some of the* Soldiers *pitch* RICHMOND'S *Tent.*

Richm. The weary sun hath made a golden set,
And, by the bright track of his fiery car,
Gives token of a goodly day to-morrow.—
Sir William Brandon, you shall bear my standard.—
Give me some ink and paper in my tent;—
I'll draw the form and model of our battle,
Limit each leader to his several charge,
And part in just proportion our small power.
My lord of Oxford, you, Sir William Brandon,—
And you, Sir Walter Herbert, stay with me:
The earl of Pembroke keeps his regiment;—
Good Captain Blunt, bear my good night to him,
And by the second hour in the morning
Desire the earl to see me in my tent:
Yet one thing more, good captain, do for me;
Where is Lord Stanley quarter'd, do you know?

Blunt. Unless I have mista'en his colours much
(Which, well I am assur'd, I have not done),
His regiment lies half a mile at least
South from the mighty power of the king.

Richm. If without peril it be possible,
Sweet Blunt, make some good means to speak with him,
And give him from me this most needful note.

Blunt. Upon my life, my lord, I'll undertake it;
And so, God give you quiet rest to-night!

Richm. Good night, good captain Blunt. Come, gentlemen,
Let us consult upon to-morrow's business;
In to my tent, the air is raw and cold.
[*They withdraw into the Tent.*

Enter, to his Tent, KING RICHARD, NORFOLK, RATCLIFF, *and* CATESBY.

K. Rich. What is't o' clock?

Cate. It's supper time, my lord:
It's nine o' clock.

K. Rich. I will not sup to-night.—
Give me some ink and paper.—
What, is my beaver easier than it was?—
And all my armour laid into my tent?

Cate. It is, my liege; and all things are in readiness.

K. Rich. Good Norfolk, hie thee to thy charge;
Use careful watch, choose trusty sentinels.

Nor. I go, my lord.

K. Rich. Stir with the lark to-morrow, gentle Norfolk.

Nor. I warrant you, my lord. [*Exit.*

K. Rich. Ratcliff,——

Rat. My lord?

K. Rich. Send out a pursuivant at arms
To Stanley's regiment; bid him bring his power
Before sun-rising, lest his son George fall
Into the blind cave of eternal night.—
Fill me a bowl of wine.—Give me a watch:—
[*To* CATESBY.
Saddle white Surrey for the field to-morrow.—
Look that my staves be sound, and not too heavy.
Ratcliff,——

Rat. My lord?

K. Rich. Saw'st thou the melancholy Lord Northumberland?

Rat. Thomas the earl of Surrey, and himself,
Much about cock-shut time, from troop to troop,
Went through the army, cheering up the soldiers.

K. Rich. So, I am satisfied. Give me a bowl of wine:
I have not that alacrity of spirit,
Nor cheer of mind, that I was wont to have.—
Set it down.—Is ink and paper ready?

Rat. It is, my lord.

K. Rich. Bid my guard watch; leave me.
About the mid of night come to my tent,
And help to arm me.—Leave me, I say.
[KING RICHARD *retires into his Tent.*
Exeunt RATCLIFF *and* CATESBY.

RICHMOND'S *Tent opens, and discovers him, and his* Officers, *&c.*

Enter STANLEY.

Stan. Fortune and victory sit on thy helm!

Richm. All comfort that the dark night can afford,
Be to thy person, noble father-in-law!
Tell me how fares our loving mother?

Stan. I, by attorney, bless thee from thy mother,
Who prays continually for Richmond's good:
So much for that.—The silent hours steal on,
And flaky darkness breaks within the east.
In brief, for so the season bids us be,
Prepare thy battle early in the morning;
And put thy fortune to the arbitrement
Of bloody strokes, and mortal-staring war.
I, as I may (that which I would, I cannot),
With best advantage will deceive the time,
And aid thee in this doubtful shock of arms:
But on thy side I may not be too forward,
Lest, being seen, thy brother tender George
Be executed in his father's sight:
Farewell: The leisure and the fearful time
Cuts off the ceremonious vows of love,
And ample interchange of sweet discourse,
Which so long sunder'd friends should dwell upon;
God give us leisure for these rites of love:
Once more, adieu:—Be valiant, and speed well!

Richm. Good lords, conduct him to his regiment:
I'll strive with troubled thoughts, to take a nap;
Lest leaden slumber peise me down to-morrow,
When I should mount with wings of victory:
Once more, good night, kind lords and gentlemen. [*Exeunt* Lords, *&c. with* STANLEY.
O Thou! whose captain I account myself,
Look on my forces with a gracious eye;
Put in their hands thy bruising irons of wrath,
That they may crush down with a heavy fall
The usurping helmets of our adversaries!
Make us thy ministers of chastisement,
That we may praise thee in thy victory!
To thee I do commend my watchful soul,
Ere I let fall the windows of mine eyes;
Sleeping, and waking, O, defend me still!
[*Sleeps.*

The Ghost *of* Prince Edward, *Son to* Henry the Sixth, *rises between the two Tents.*

Ghost. Let me sit heavy on thy soul to-morrow!
[*To* KING RICHARD.
Think, how thou stab'dst me in my prime of youth
At Tewksbury; Despair therefore, and die!—
Be cheerful, Richmond; for the wronged souls
Of butcher'd princes fight in thy behalf:
King Henry's issue, Richmond, comforts thee.

The Ghost *of* King Henry the Sixth *rises.*

Ghost. When I was mortal, my anointed body
[*To* KING RICHARD.
By thee was punched full of deadly holes:
Think on the Tower, and me; Despair, and die;
Harry the Sixth bids thee despair and die.—
Virtuous and holy, be thou conqueror!
[*To* RICHMOND.
Harry, that prophesy'd thou should'st be king,
Doth comfort thee in thy sleep; Live, and flourish!

The Ghost *of* Clarence *rises.*

Ghost. Let me sit heavy on thy soul to-morrow!
[*To* KING RICHARD.
I, that was wash'd to death with fulsome wine,
Poor Clarence, by thy guile betray'd to death!
To-morrow in the battle think on me,
And fall thy edgeless sword; Despair, and die!—
Thou offspring of the house of Lancaster,
[*To* RICHMOND.
The wronged heirs of York do pray for thee;
Good angels guard thy battle! Live, and flourish!

The Ghosts *of* Rivers, Grey, *and* Vaughan, *rise.*

Riv. Let me sit heavy on thy soul to-morrow, [*To* King Richard.
Rivers, that died at Pomfret! Despair, and die!

Grey. Think upon Grey, and let thy soul despair! [*To* King Richard.

Vaugh. Think upon Vaughan; and, with guilty fear,
Let fall thy lance! Despair, and die!— [*To* King Richard.

All. Awake! and think, our wrongs in Richard's bosom [*To* Richmond.
Will conquer him;—awake, and win the day!

The Ghost *of* Hastings *rises.*

Ghost. Bloody and guilty, guiltily awake; [*To* King Richard.
And in a bloody battle end thy days!
Think on Lord Hastings; and despair, and die!—
Quiet untroubled soul, awake, awake! [*To* Richmond.
Arm, fight, and conquer, for fair England's sake!

The Ghosts *of the two young* Princes *rise.*

Ghosts. Dream on thy cousins smother'd in the Tower;
Let us be lead within thy bosom, Richard,
And weigh thee down to ruin, shame, and death!
Thy nephews' souls bid thee despair, and die.—
Sleep, Richmond, sleep in peace, and wake in joy;
Good angels guard thee from the boar's annoy!
Live, and beget a happy race of kings!
Edward's unhappy sons do bid thee flourish.

The Ghost *of* Queen Anne *rises.*

Ghost. Richard, thy wife, that wretched Anne thy wife,
That never slept a quiet hour with thee,
Now fills thy sleep with perturbations:
To-morrow in the battle think on me,
And fall thy edgeless sword; Despair, and die!—
Thou, quiet soul, sleep thou a quiet sleep; [*To* Richmond.
Dream of success and happy victory;
Thy adversary's wife doth pray for thee.

The Ghost *of* Buckingham *rises.*

Ghost. The first was I, that help'd thee to the crown; [*To* King Richard.
The last was I that felt thy tyranny:
O, in the battle think on Buckingham,
And die in terror of thy guiltiness!
Dream on, dream on, of bloody deeds and death!
Fainting, despair; despairing, yield thy breath!—
I died for hope, ere I could lend thee aid: [*To* Richmond.
But cheer thy heart, and be thou not dismay'd:
God, and good angels, fight on Richmond's side;
And Richard falls in height of all his pride.

[*The* Ghosts *vanish.* King Richard *starts out of his dream.*

K. Rich. Give me another horse,—bind up my wounds,—
Have mercy, Jesu!—Soft; I did but dream.—
O coward conscience, how dost thou afflict me!—
The lights burn blue.—It is now dead midnight.
Cold fearful drops stand on my trembling flesh.
What do I fear? myself? there's none else by:
Richard loves Richard: that is, I am I.
Is there a murderer here? No;—Yes; I am:
Then fly,—What, from myself? Great reason: Why?
Lest I revenge. What? Myself on myself?
I love myself. Wherefore? for any good,
That I myself have done unto myself?
O, no: alas, I rather hate myself,
For hateful deeds committed by myself.
I am a villain: Yet I lie, I am not.
Fool, of thyself speak well:—Fool, do not flatter.
My conscience hath a thousand several tongues,
And every tongue brings in a several tale,
And every tale condemns me for a villain.
Perjury, perjury, in the high'st degree,
Murder, stern murder, in the dir'st degree;
All several sins, all us'd in each degree,
Throng to the bar, crying all—Guilty! guilty!
I shall despair.—There is no creature loves me!
And, if I die, no soul will pity me:—
Nay, wherefore should they? since that I myself
Find in myself no pity to myself.
Methought, the souls of all that I had murder'd
Came to my tent: and every one did threat
To-morrow's vengeance on the head of Richard.

Enter Ratcliff.

Rat. My lord,——

K. Rich. Who's there?

Rat. Ratcliff, my lord; 'tis I. The early village cock
Hath twice done salutation to the morn:
Your friends are up, and buckle on their armour.

K. Rich. O, Ratcliff, I have dream'd a fearful dream!
What thinkest thou? will our friends prove all true?

Rat. No doubt, my lord.

K. Rich. Ratcliff, I fear, I fear,—

Rat. Nay, good my lord, be not afraid of shadows.

K. Rich. By the apostle Paul, shadows to-night
Have struck more terror to the soul of Richard,
Than can the substance of ten thousand soldiers,
Armed in proof, and led by shallow Richmond.
It is not yet near day. Come, go with me!
Under our tents I'll play the eaves-dropper,
To hear, if any mean to shrink from me.

[*Exeunt* King Richard *and* Ratcliff.

Richmond *wakes. Enter* Oxford *and Others.*

Lords. Good morrow, Richmond.

Richm. 'Cry mercy, lords, and watchful gentlemen,
That you have ta'en a tardy sluggard here.

Lords. How have you slept, my lord?

Richm. The sweetest sleep, and fairest-boding dreams,
That ever enter'd in a drowsy head,
Have I since your departure had, my lords.
Methought, their souls, whose bodies Richard murder'd,
Came to my tent, and cried—On! victory!
I promise you, my heart is very jocund
In the remembrance of so fair a dream.
How far into the morning is it, lords?

Lords. Upon the stroke of four.

Richm. Why then 'tis time to arm, and give direction.— [*He advances to the* Troops.
More than I have said, loving countrymen,
The leisure and enforcement of the time
Forbids to dwell on: Yet remember this,—
God, and our good cause, fight upon our side:
The prayers of holy saints, and wronged souls,
Like high rear'd bulwarks, stand before our faces;
Richard except, those whom we fight against,
Had rather have us win, than him they follow.
For what is he they follow? truly, gentlemen,
A bloody tyrant, and a homicide;
One rais'd in blood, and one in blood establish'd;
One that made means to come by what he hath,
And slaughter'd those that were the means to help him;
A base foul stone, made precious by the foil
Of England's chair, where he is falsely set;
One that hath ever been God's enemy:
Then, if you fight against God's enemy,
God will, in justice, ward you as his soldiers;
If you do sweat to put a tyrant down,
You sleep in peace, the tyrant being slain;
If you do fight against your country's foes,
Your country's fat shall pay your pains the hire;
If you do fight in safeguard of your wives,
Your wives shall welcome home the conquerors;
If you do free your children from the sword,

Your children's children quit it in your age.
Then, in the name of God, and all these rights,
Advance your standards, draw your willing swords;
For me, the ransome of my bold attempt
Shall be this cold corpse on the earth's cold face;
But if I thrive, the gain of my attempt
The least of you shall share his part thereof.
Sound, drums and trumpets, boldly and cheerfully;
God, and Saint George! Richmond, and victory! [*Exeunt.*

Re-enter KING RICHARD, RATCLIFF, Attendants, *and* Forces.

K. Rich. What said Northumberland, as touching Richmond?

Rat. That he was never trained up in arms.

K. Rich. He said the truth: And what said Surrey then?

Rat. He smil'd and said, the better for our purpose.

K. Rich. He was i' the right; and so, indeed, it is. [*Clock strikes.*
Tell the clock there.—Give me a calendar.—
Who saw the sun to-day?

Rat. Not I, my lord.

K. Rich. Then he disdains to shine; for, by the book,
He should have brav'd the east an hour ago:
A black day will it be to somebody.—
Ratcliff,——

Rat. My lord?

K. Rich. The sun will not be seen to-day;
The sky doth frown and lour upon our army.
I would, these dewy tears were from the ground.
Not shine to-day! Why, what is that to me,
More than to Richmond? for the self-same heaven,
That frowns on me, looks sadly upon him.

Enter NORFOLK.

Nor. Arm, arm, my lord; the foe vaunts in the field.

K. Rich. Come, bustle, bustle;—Caparison my horse;—
Call up Lord Stanley, bid him bring his power:—
I will lead forth my soldiers to the plain,
And thus my battle shall be ordered.
My foreward shall be drawn out all in length,
Consisting equally of horse and foot;
Our archers shall be placed in the midst:
John duke of Norfolk, Thomas earl of Surrey,
Shall have the leading of this foot and horse.
They thus directed, we ourself will follow
In the main battle; whose puissance on either side
Shall be well winged with our chiefest horse.
This, and Saint George to boot!—What think'st thou, Norfolk?

Nor. A good direction, warlike sovereign.—
This found I on my tent this morning. [*Giving a scrowl.*

K. Rich. *Jocky of Norfolk, be not too bold,* [reads.
For Dickon thy master is bought and sold.
A thing devised by the enemy.—
Go, gentlemen, every man unto his charge:
Let not our babbling dreams affright our souls;
Conscience is but a word that cowards use,
Devis'd at first to keep the strong in awe;
Our strong arms be our conscience, swords our law.
March on, join bravely, let us to't pell-mell;
If not to heaven, then hand in hand to hell.——
What shall I say more than I have inferr'd?
Remember whom you are to cope withal;—
A sort of vagabonds, rascals, and runaways,
A scum of Bretagnes, and base lackey peasants,
Whom their o'er-cloyed country vomits forth
To desperate ventures and assur'd destruction.
You sleeping safe, they bring you to unrest;
You having lands, and bless'd with beauteous wives,
They would restrain the one, distain the other.
And who doth lead them, but a paltry fellow,
Long kept in Bretagne at our mother's cost?
A milk-sop, one that never in his life
Felt so much cold as over shoes in snow?
Let's whip these stragglers o'er the seas again;
Lash hence these over-weening rags of France,
These famish'd beggars, weary of their lives;
Who, but for dreaming on this fond exploit,
For want of means, poor rats, had hang'd themselves:
If we be conquer'd, let men conquer us,
And not these bastard Bretagnes; whom our fathers
Have in their own land beaten, bobb'd and thump'd,
And, on record, left them the heirs of shame.
Shall these enjoy our lands? lie with our wives?
Ravish our daughters?—Hark, I hear their drum. [*Drum afar off.*
Fight, gentlemen of England! fight, bold yeomen!
Draw, archers, draw your arrows to the head!
Spur your proud horses hard, and ride in blood;
Amaze the welkin with your broken staves!

Enter a Messenger.

What says Lord Stanley? will he bring his power?

Mess. My lord, he doth deny to come.

K. Rich. Off instantly with his son George's head.

Nor. My lord, the enemy is pass'd the marsh;
After the battle let George Stanley die.

K. Rich. A thousand hearts are great within my bosom:
Advance our standards, set upon our foes;
Our ancient word of courage, fair Saint George,
Inspire us with the spleen of fiery dragons!
Upon them! Victory sits on our helms. [*Exeunt.*

SCENE IV. *Another part of the Field.*

Alarum. Excursions. Enter NORFOLK, *and* Forces; *to him* CATESBY.

Cate. Rescue, my lord of Norfolk, rescue, rescue!
The king enacts more wonders than a man,
Daring an opposite to every danger;
His horse is slain, and all on foot he fights,
Seeking for Richmond in the throat of death:
Rescue, fair lord, or else the day is lost!

Alarum. Enter KING RICHARD.

K. Rich. A horse! a horse! my kingdom for a horse!

Cate. Withdraw, my lord, I'll help you to a horse.

K. Rich. Slave, I have set my life upon a cast,
And I will stand the hazard of the die:
I think, there be six Richmonds in the field;
Five have I slain to-day, instead of him:—
A horse! a horse! my kingdom for a horse! [*Exeunt.*

Alarums. Enter KING RICHARD *and* RICHMOND; *and exeunt fighting. Retreat, and flourish. Then enter* RICHMOND, STANLEY *bearing the Crown, with divers other* Lords, *and* Forces.

Richm. God, and your arms, be prais'd, victorious friends;
The day is ours, the bloody dog is dead.

Stan. Courageous Richmond, well hast thou acquit thee!
Lo, here, this long usurped royalty,
From the dead temples of this bloody wretch
Have I pluck'd off, to grace thy brows withal,
Wear it, enjoy it, and make much of it.

Richm. Great God of heaven, say, amen, to all!—
But, tell me first, is young George Stanley living?

Stan. He is, my lord, and safe in Leicester town;
Whither, if it please you, we may now withdraw [us.

Richm. What men of name are slain on either side?

Stan. John Duke of Norfolk, Walter Lord [Ferrers,
Sir Robert Brakenbury, and Sir William Brandon.

Richm. Inter their bodies as becomes their births.
Proclaim a pardon to the soldiers fled,
That in submission will return to us;
And then, as we have ta'en the sacrament,
We will unite the white rose with the red:—
Smile heaven upon this fair conjunction,
That long hath frown'd upon their enmity!—
What traitor hears me, and says not,—amen?
England hath long been mad, and scarr'd herself;
The brother blindly shed the brother's blood,
The father rashly slaughter'd his own son,
The son, compell'd, been butcher to the sire;
All this divided York and Lancaster,
Divided, in their dire division.—
O, now, let Richmond and Elizabeth,
The true succeeders of each royal house,
By God's fair ordinance conjoin together!
And let their heirs (God, if thy will be so),
Enrich the time to come with smooth-fac'd peace,
With smiling plenty, and fair prosperous days!
Abate the edge of traitors, gracious Lord,
That would reduce these bloody days again!
And make poor England weep in streams of blood!
Let them not live to taste this land's increase,
That would with treason wound this fair land's peace!
Now civil wounds are stopp'd, peace lives again;
That she may long live here, God say—Amen.
[*Exeunt.*

KING HENRY THE EIGHTH.

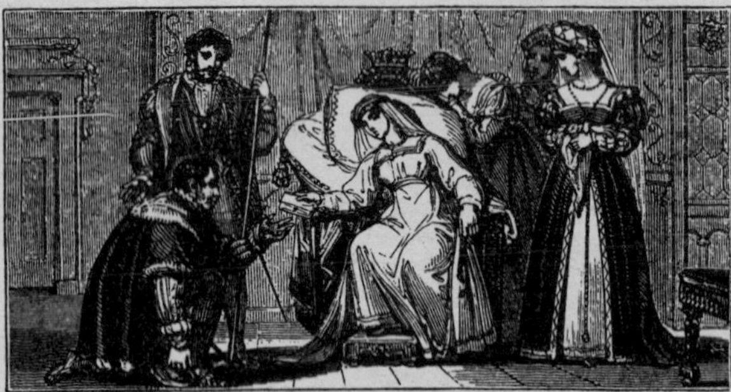

PERSONS REPRESENTED.

KING HENRY THE EIGHTH.
CARDINAL WOLSEY. CARDINAL CAMPEIUS.
CAPUCIUS, *Ambassador from the* Emp. Charles V.
CRANMER, Archbishop *of* Canterbury.
DUKE OF NORFOLK. DUKE OF BUCKINGHAM.
DUKE OF SUFFOLK. EARL OF SURREY.
LORD CHAMBERLAIN. LORD CHANCELLOR.
GARDINER, Bishop *of* Winchester.
BISHOP OF LINCOLN.
LORD ABERGAVENNY. LORD SANDS.
SIR HENRY GUILDFORD. SIR THOMAS LOVELL.
SIR ANTHONY DENNY. SIR NICHOLAS VAUX.
Secretaries *to* Wolsey.
CROMWELL, *Servant to* Wolsey.
GRIFFITH, *Gentleman Usher to* Queen Katharine.
Three other Gentlemen.
DOCTOR BUTTS, *Physician to the* King.
Garter, *King at Arms.*
Surveyor *to the* Duke *of* Buckingham.
BRANDON, *and a* Sergeant at Arms.
Door-keeper *of the Council Chamber.*
Porter, *and his* Man.
Page *to* Gardiner. *A* Crier.

QUEEN KATHARINE, *Wife to* King Henry, *afterwards divorced.*
ANNE BULLEN, *her Maid of Honour; afterwards* Queen.
An old Lady, *Friend to* Anne Bullen.
PATIENCE, *Woman to* Queen Catharine.

Several Lords *and* Ladies *in the Dumb Shows:* Women *attending upon the* Queen; Spirits, *which appear to her*; Scribes, Officers, Guards, *and other* Attendants.

SCENE—*chiefly in* London *and* Westminster: *once, at* Kimbolton.

PROLOGUE.

I COME no more to make you laugh; things now,
That bear a weighty and a serious brow,
Sad, high, and working, full of state and woe,
Such noble scenes as draw the eye to flow,
We now present. Those that can pity, here
May, if they think it well, let fall a tear;
The subject will deserve it. Such, as give
Their money out of hope they may believe,
May here find truth too. Those, that come to see
Only a show or two, and so agree,
The play may pass; if they be still, and willing,
I'll undertake, may see away their shilling
Richly in two short hours. Only they,
That come to hear a merry, bawdy play,
A noise of targets; or to see a fellow
In a long motley coat, guarded with yellow,
Will be deceived: for, gentle hearers, know,
To rank our chosen truth with such a show

As fool and fight is, beside forfeiting
Our own brains, and the opinion that we bring,
(To make that only true we now intend),
Will leave us never an understanding friend.
Therefore, for goodness' sake, and as you are known
The first and happiest hearers of the town,
Be sad, as we would make you: Think, ye see
The very persons of our noble story,
As they were living; think you see them great,
And follow'd with the general throng, and sweat,
Of thousand friends; then in a moment, see
How soon this mightiness meets misery!
And, if you can be merry then, I'll say,
A man may weep upon his wedding day.

ACT I.

SCENE I. London. *An Antechamber in the Palace.*

Enter the DUKE OF NORFOLK, *at one door: at the other, the* DUKE OF BUCKINGHAM, *and the* LORD ABERGAVENNY.

Buck. Good morrow, and well met. How have you done,
Since last we saw in France?

Nor. I thank your grace:
Healthful; and ever since a fresh admirer
Of what I saw there.

Buck. An untimely ague
Stay'd me a prisoner in my chamber, when
Those suns of glory, those two lights of men,
Met in the vale of Arde.

Nor. 'Twixt Guynes and Arde:
I was then present, saw them salute on horseback;
Beheld them, when they lighted, how they clung
In their embracement, as they grew together;
Which had they, what four thron'd ones could have weigh'd
Such a compounded one?

Buck. All the whole time
I was my chamber's prisoner.

Nor. Then you lost
The view of earthly glory: Men might say,
Till this time, pomp was single: but now married
To one above itself. Each following day
Became the next day's master, till the last
Made former wonders it's: To-day, the French,
All clinquant, all in gold, like heathen gods,
Shone down the English: and, to-morrow, they
Made Britain, India: every man, that stood,
Show'd like a mine. Their dwarfish pages were
As cherubins, all gilt: the madams too,
Not us'd to toil, did almost sweat to bear
The pride upon them, that their very labour
Was to them as a painting: now this mask
Was cry'd incomparable; and the ensuing night
Made it a fool and beggar. These two kings,
Equal in lustre, were now best, now worst,
As presence did present them; him in eye,
Still him in praise: and, being present both,
'Twas said, they saw but one; and no discerner
Durst wag his tongue in censure. When these suns
(For so they phrase them) by their heralds challeng'd
The noble spirits to arms, they did perform
Beyond thought's compass; that former fabulous story,
Being now seen possible enough, got credit,
That Bevis was believ'd.

Buck. O, you go far.

Nor. As I belong to worship, and affect
In honour honesty, the tract of every thing
Would by a good discourser lose some life,
Which action's self was tongue to. All was royal;
To the disposing of it nought rebell'd,
Order gave each thing view; the office did
Distinctly his full function.

Buck. Who did guide,
I mean, who set the body and the limbs
Of this great sport together, as you guess?

Nor. One, certes, that promises no element
In such a business.

Buck. I pray you, who, my lord?

Nor. All this was order'd by the good discretion
Of the right reverend cardinal of York.

Buck. The devil speed him! no man's pie is free'd
From his ambitious finger. What had he
To do in these fierce vanities? I wonder,
That such a keech can with his very bulk
Take up the rays o' the beneficial sun,
And keep it from the earth.

Nor. Surely, sir,
There's in him stuff that puts him to these ends;
For, being not propp'd by ancestry (whose grace
Chalks successors their way), nor call'd upon
For high feats done to the crown; neither allied
To eminent assistants, but, spider-like,
Out of his self-drawing web, he gives us note,
The force of his own merit makes his way;
A gift that heaven gives for him, which buys
A place next to the king.

Aber. I cannot tell
What heaven hath given him, let some graver eye
Pierce into that; but I can see his pride
Peep through each part of him: Whence has he that?
If not from hell, the devil is a niggard;
Or has given all before, and he begins
A new hell in himself.

Buck. Why the devil,
Upon this French going-out, took he upon him,
Without the privity o' the king, to appoint
Who should attend on him? He makes up the file
Of all the gentry; for the most part such
Too, whom as great a charge as little honour
He meant to lay upon; and his own letter,
The honourable board of council out,
Must fetch him in he papers.

Aber. I do know
Kinsmen of mine, three at the least, that have
By this so sicken'd their estates, that never
They shall abound as formerly.

Buck. O, many
Have broke their backs with laying manors on them
For this great journey. What did this vanity,
But minister communication of
A most poor issue?

Nor. Grievingly I think,
The peace between the French and us not values
The cost that did conclude it.

Buck. Every man,
After the hideous storm that follow'd, was
A thing inspir'd: and, not consulting, broke
Into a general prophecy,—That this tempest,
Dashing the garment of this peace, aboded
The sudden breach on 't.

Nor. Which is budded out;
For France hath flaw'd the league, and hath attach'd
Our merchants' goods at Bourdeaux.

Aber. Is it therefore
The ambassador is silenc'd?

Nor. Marry, is 't.

Aber. A proper title of a peace, and purchas'd
At a superfluous rate!

Buck. Why, all this business
Our reverend cardinal carried.

Nor. Like it your grace,
The state takes notice of the private difference
Betwixt you and the cardinal. I advise you
(And take it from a heart that wishes towards you
Honour and plenteous safety), that you read
The cardinal's malice and his potency
Together: to consider further, that

What his high hatred would effect, wants not
A minister in his power: You know his nature,
That he's revengeful; and I know, his sword
Hath a sharp edge: it's long, and, it may be said,
It reaches far; and where 'twill not extend,
Thither he darts it. Bosom up my counsel,
You'll find it wholesome. Lo, where comes that rock,
That I advise your shunning.

Enter CARDINAL WOLSEY, (*the purse borne before him*), *certain of the* Guard, *and two* Secretaries *with papers. The* CARDINAL *in his passage fixeth his eye on* BUCKINGHAM, *and* BUCKINGHAM *on him, both full of disdain.*

Wol. The duke of Buckingham's surveyor? ha?
Where's his examination?
1 *Secr.* Here, so please you.
Wol. Is he in person ready?
1 *Secr.* Ay, please your grace.
Wol. Well, we shall then know more; and Buckingham
Shall lessen his big look.
[*Exeunt* WOLSEY *and* Train.
Buck. This butcher's cur is venom-mouth'd, and I
Have not the power to muzzle him; therefore, best
Not wake him in his slumber. A beggar's book
Out-worths a noble's blood.
Nor. What, are you chaf'd?
Ask God for temperance; that's the appliance only,
Which your disease requires.
Buck. I read in his looks
Matter against me: and his eye revil'd
Me, as his abject object: at this instant
He bores me with some trick: He's gone to the king;
I'll follow, and outstare him.
Nor. Stay, my lord,
And let your reason with your choler question
What 'tis you go about: To climb steep hills,
Requires slow pace at first: Anger is like
A full hot horse; who, being allow'd his way,
Self-mettle tires him. Not a man in England
Can advise me like you: be to yourself
As you would to your friend.
Buck. I'll to the king;
And from a mouth of honour quite cry down
This Ipswich fellow's insolence; or proclaim,
There's difference in no persons.
Nor. Be advis'd;
Heat not a furnace for your foe so hot
That it do singe yourself: We may outrun,
By violent swiftness, that which we run at,
And lose by overrunning. Know you not,
The fire, that mounts the liquor till it run o'er,
In seeming to augment it, wastes it? Be advis'd:
I say again, there is no English soul
More stronger to direct you than yourself;
If with the sap of reason you would quench,
Or but allay, the fire of passion.
Buck. Sir,
I am thankful to you; and I'll go along
By your prescription:—but this top-proud fellow,
(Whom from the flow of gall, I name not, but
From sincere motions), by intelligence,
And proofs as clear as founts in July, when
We see each grain of gravel, I do know
To be corrupt and treasonous.
Nor. Say not, treasonous.
Buck. To the king I'll say't; and make my vouch as strong
As shore of rock. Attend. This holy fox,
Or wolf, or both (for he is equal ravenous,
As he is subtle; and as prone to mischief,
As able to perform it: his mind and place
Infecting one another, yea reciprocally),
Only to show his pomp as well in France
As here at home, suggests the king our master
To this last costly treaty, the interview,
That swallow'd so much treasure, and like a glass
Did break i' the rinsing.
Nor. 'Faith, and so it did.
Buck. Pray, give me favour, sir. This cunning cardinal
The articles o' the combination drew,
As himself pleas'd; and they were ratified,
As he cried, Thus let be: to as much end,
As give a crutch to the dead: But our count cardinal
Has done this, and 'tis well: for worthy Wolsey,
Who cannot err, he did it. Now this follows
(Which, as I take it, is a kind of puppy
To the old dam treason),—Charles the emperor,
Under pretence to see the queen his aunt,
(For 'twas, indeed, his colour; but he came
To whisper Wolsey), here makes visitation:
His fears were, that the interview, betwixt
England and France, might, through their amity,
Breed him some prejudice; for from this league
Peep'd harms that menac'd him: He privily
Deals with our cardinal; and, as I trow,
Which I do well; for, I am sure, the emperor
Paid ere he promis'd; whereby his suit was granted,
Ere it was ask'd;—but when the way was made,
And pav'd with gold, the emperor thus desir'd;—
That he would please to alter the king's course,
And break the foresaid peace. Let the king know
(As soon he shall by me), that thus the cardinal
Does buy and sell his honour as he pleases,
And for his own advantage.
Nor. I am sorry
To hear this of him; and could wish, he were
Something mistaken in 't.
Buck. No, not a syllable;
I do pronounce him in that very shape,
He shall appear in proof.

Enter BRANDON; *a* Sergeant at Arms *before him, and two or three of the* Guard.

Bran. Your office, sergeant; execute it.
Serg. Sir,
My lord the duke of Buckingham, and earl
Of Hereford, Stafford, and Northampton, I
Arrest thee of high treason, in the name
Of our most sovereign king.
Buck. Lo, you, my lord,
The net has fall'n upon me; I shall perish
Under device and practice.
Bran. I am sorry
To see you ta'en from liberty, to look on
The business present. 'Tis his highness' pleasure,
You shall to the Tower.
Buck. It will help me nothing,
To plead mine innocence; for that dye is on me,
Which makes my whitest part black. The will of heaven
Be done in this and all things!—I obey.—
O my lord Aberga'ny, fare you well.
Bran. Nay, he must bear you company:—The king [*To* ABERGAVENNY.
Is pleas'd, you shall to the Tower, till you know
How he determines further.
Aber. As the duke said,
The will of heaven be done, and the king's pleasure
By me obey'd.
Bran. Here is a warrant from
The king, to attach Lord Montacute, and the bodies
Of the duke's confessor, John de la Car,
One Gilbert Peck, his chancellor,—
Buck. So, so;
These are the limbs of the plot: no more, I hope.
Bran. A monk o' the Chartreux.
Buck. O, Nicholas Hopkins?
Bran. He.
Buck. My surveyor is false, the o'ergreat cardinal

Hath show'd him gold: my life is spann'd already:
I am the shadow of poor Buckingham;
Whose figure even this instant cloud puts out,
By dark'ning my clear sun.—My lord, farewell.
[*Exeunt.*

SCENE II. *The Council Chamber.*

Cornets. Enter KING HENRY, CARDINAL WOLSEY, *the* Lords *of the* Council, SIR THOMAS LOVELL, Officers, *and* Attendants. *The* King *enters, leaning on the* Cardinal's *shoulder.*

K. Hen. My life itself, and the best heart of it,
Thanks you for this great care: I stood i' the level
Of a full charg'd confederacy, and give thanks
To you that chok'd it.—Let be call'd before us
That gentleman of Buckingham's: in person
I'll hear him his confessions justify;
And point by point the treasons of his master
He shall again relate.

The King *takes his state. The* Lords *of the* Council *take their several places. The* Cardinal *places himself under the* King's *feet, on his right side.*

A noise within, crying, Room for the Queen. *Enter the* Queen, *ushered by the* DUKES OF NORFOLK *and* SUFFOLK: *she kneels. The* King *riseth from his state, takes her up, kisses, and placeth her by him.*

Q. Kath. Nay, we must longer kneel: I am a suitor.
K. Hen. Arise, and take place by us:—Half your suit
Never name to us; you have half our power:
The other moiety, ere you ask, is given;
Repeat your will, and take it.
Q. Kath. Thank your majesty.
That you would love yourself; and, in that love,
Not unconsider'd leave your honour, nor
The dignity of your office, is the point
Of my petition.
K. Hen. Lady mine, proceed.
Q. Kath. I am solicited, not by a few,
And those of true condition, that your subjects
Are in great grievance: there have been commissions
Sent down among them, which have flaw'd the heart
Of all their loyalties:—wherein, although,
My good lord cardinal, they vent reproaches
Most bitterly on you, as putter on
Of these exactions, yet the king our master
(Whose honour heaven shield from soil!) even he escapes not
Language unmannerly, yea, such which breaks
The sides of loyalty, and almost appears
In loud rebellion.
Nor. Not almost appears,
It doth appear; for, upon these taxations,
The clothiers all, not able to maintain
The many to them 'longing, have put off
The spinsters, carders, fullers, weavers, who,
Unfit for other life, compell'd by hunger
And lack of other means, in desperate manner
Daring the event to the teeth, are all in uproar,
And Danger serves among them.
K. Hen. Taxation!
Wherein? and what taxation?—My lord Cardinal,
You that are blam'd for it alike with us,
Know you of this taxation?
Wol. Please you, sir,
I know but of a single part, in aught
Pertains to the state; and front but in that file
Where others tell steps with me.
Q. Kath. No, my lord,
You know no more than others: but you frame
Things, that are known alike; which are not wholesome [must
To those which would not know them, and yet
Perforce be their acquaintance. These exactions,
Whereof my sovereign would have note, they are
Most pestilent to the hearing; and, to bear them,
The back is sacrifice to the load. They say,
They are devis'd by you; or else you suffer
Too hard an exclamation.
K. Hen. Still exaction!
The nature of it? In what kind, let's know,
Is this exaction?
Q. Kath. I am much too venturous
In tempting of your patience; but am bolden'd
Under your promis'd pardon. The subject's grief
Comes through commissions, which compel from each
The sixth part of his substance, to be levied
Without delay: and the pretence for this
Is nam'd, your wars in France: This makes bold mouths:
Tongues spit their duties out, and cold hearts freeze
Allegiance in them; their curses now
Live where their prayers did; and it's come to pass,
That tractable obedience is a slave
To each incensed will. I would, your highness
Would give it quick consideration, for
There is no primer business.
K. Hen. By my life,
This is against our pleasure.
Wol. And for me,
I have no farther gone in this, than by
A single voice; and that not pass'd me, but
By learned approbation of the judges. If I am
Traduc'd by ignorant tongues, which neither know
My faculties, nor person, yet will be
The chronicles of my doing,—let me say,
'Tis but the fate of place, and the rough brake
That virtue must go through. We must not stint
Our necessary actions, in the fear
To cope malicious censurers; which ever,
As ravenous fishes, do a vessel follow
That is new trimm'd; but benefit no further
Than vainly longing. What we oft do best,
By sick interpreters, once weak ones, is
Not ours, or not allow'd; what worst, as oft,
Hitting a grosser quality, is cried up
For our best act. If we shall stand still,
In fear, our motion will be mock'd or carp'd at,
We should take root here where we sit, or sit
State statues only.
K. Hen. Things done well,
And with a care, exempt themselves from fear:
Things done without example, in their issue
Are to be fear'd. Have you a precedent
Of this commission? I believe, not any.
We must not rend our subjects from our laws,
And stick them in our will. Sixth part of each?
A trembling contribution! Why, we take,
From every tree, lop, bark, and part o' the timber;
And, though we leave it with a root, thus hack'd,
The air will drink the sap. To every county,
Where this is question'd, send our letters, with
Free pardon to each man that has denied
The force of this commission; Pray look to't;
I put it to your care.
Wol. A word with you.
[*To the* Secretary.
Let there be letters writ to every shire,
Of the king's grace and pardon. The griev'd commons
Hardly conceive of me; let it be nois'd,
That, through our intercession, this revokement
And pardon comes: I shall anon advise you
Further in the proceeding. [*Exit* Secretary.

Enter Surveyor.

Q. Kath. I am sorry, that the duke of Buckingham
Is run in your displeasure.
K. Hen. It grieves many:
The gentleman is learn'd, and a most rare speaker,
To nature none more bound; his training such,
That he may furnish and instruct grave teachers,

And never seek for aid out of himself.
Yet see
When these so noble benefits shall prove
Not well dispos'd, the mind growing once corrupt,
They turn to vicious forms, ten times more ugly
Than ever they were fair. This man so complete,
Who was enroll'd 'mongst wonders, and when we,
Almost with ravish'd list'ning, could not find
His hour of speech a minute; he, my lady,
Hath into monstrous habits put the graces
That once were his, and is become as black
As if besmear'd in hell. Sit by us; you shall hear
(This was his gentleman in trust) of him
Things to strike honour sad.—Bid him recount
The fore-recited practices; whereof
We cannot feel too little, hear too much.

Wol. Stand forth; and with bold spirit relate what you,
Most like a careful subject, have collected
Out of the Duke of Buckingham.

K. Hen. Speak freely.

Serv. First, it was usual with him, every day
It would infect his speech, That if the king
Should without issue die, he'd carry it so
To make the sceptre his: These very words
I have heard him utter to his son-in-law,
Lord Aberga'ny; to whom by oath he menac'd
Revenge upon the cardinal.

Wol. Please your highness, note
This dangerous conception in this point.
Not friended by his wish, to your high person
His will is most malignant; and it stretches
Beyond you, to your friends.

Q. Kath. My learn'd lord cardinal,
Deliver all with charity.

K. Hen. Speak on:
How grounded he his title to the crown,
Upon our fail? to this point hast thou heard him
At any time speak aught?

Surv. He was brought to this
By a vain prophecy of Nicholas Hopkins.

K. Hen. What was that Hopkins?

Surv. Sir, a Chartreux friar,
His confessor; who fed him every minute
With words of sovereignty.

K. Hen. How know'st thou this?

Surv. Not long before your highness sped to France,
The duke being at the Rose, within the parish
Saint Lawrence Poultney, did of me demand
What was the speech amongst the Londoners
Concerning the French journey: I replied,
Men fear'd, the French would prove perfidious,
To the king's danger. Presently the duke
Said, 'Twas the fear indeed; and that he doubted,
'Twould prove the verity of certain words
Spoke by a holy monk: *That oft*, says he,
Hath sent to me, wishing me to permit
John de la Court, my chaplain, a choice hour
To hear from him a matter of some moment:
Whom after under the confession's seal
He solemnly had sworn, that, what he spoke,
My chaplain, to no creature living, but
To me, should utter, with demure confidence
This pausingly ensued,—Neither the king, nor his heirs
(Tell you the duke), shall prosper: bid him strive
To gain the love of the commonalty; the duke
Shall govern England.

Q. Kath. If I know you well,
You were the duke's surveyor, and lost your office
On the complaint o' the tenants: Take good heed,
You charge not in your spleen a noble person,
And spoil your nobler soul! I say, take heed;
Yes, heartily beseech you.

K. Hen. Let him on:—
Go forward.

Surv. On my soul, I'll speak but truth.
I told my lord the duke, By the devil's illusions
The monk might be deceiv'd; and that 'twas dang'rous for him
To ruminate on this so far, until
It forg'd him some design, which, being believ'd,
It was much like to do: He answer'd, *Tush!*
It can do me no damage: adding further,
That, had the king in his last sickness fail'd,
The cardinal's and Sir Thomas Lovell's heads
Should have gone off.

K. Hen. Ha! what, so rank? Ah, ha!
There's mischief in this man:——Canst thou say further?

Surv. I can, my liege.

K. Hen. Proceed.

Surv. Being at Greenwich,
After your highness had reprov'd the duke
About Sir William Blomer,—

K. Hen. I remember,
Of such a time:—Being my servant sworn,
The duke retain'd him his.——But on; What hence?

Surv. *If*, quoth he, *I for this had been committed,*
As, to the Tower, I thought,—I would have play'd
The part my father meant to act upon
The usurper Richard: who, being at Salisbury,
Made suit to come in his presence; which if granted,
As he made semblance of his duty, would
Have put his knife into him.

K. Hen. A giant traitor!

Wol. Now, madam, may his highness live in freedom,
And this man out of prison?

Q. Kath. God mend all!

K. Hen. There's something more would out of thee; What say'st?

Surv. After—*the duke his father*,—with *the knife*,—
He stretch'd him, and, with one hand on his dagger,
Another spread on his breast, mounting his eyes,
He did discharge a horrible oath; whose tenour
Was,—Were he evil us'd, he would outgo
His father, by as much as a performance
Does an irresolute purpose.

K. Hen. There's his period,
To sheath his knife in us. He is attach'd;
Call him to present trial: if he may
Find mercy in the law, 'tis his; if none,
Let him not seek 't of us: By day and night,
He's traitor to the height. [*Exeunt.*

SCENE III. *A Room in the Palace.*

Enter the Lord Chamberlain, *and* LORD SANDS.

Cham. Is it possible, the spells of France should juggle
Men into such strange mysteries?

Sands. New customs,
Though they be never so ridiculous,
Nay, let them be unmanly, yet are follow'd.

Cham. As far as I see, all the good our English
Have got by the late voyage, is but merely
A fit or two o' the face; but they are shrewd ones;
For when they hold them, you would swear directly,
Their very noses had been counsellors
To Pepin, or Clotharius, they keep state so.

Sands. They have all new legs, and lame ones; one would take it,
That never saw them pace before, the spavin,
A springhalt reign'd among them.

Cham. Death! my lord,
Their clothes are after such a pagan cut too,
That, sure, they have worn out christendom.
How now?
What news, Sir Thomas Lovell?

Enter SIR THOMAS LOVELL.

Lov. 'Faith, my lord,
I hear of none, but the new proclamation
That's clapp'd upon the court gate.

Cham. What is 't for?

Lov. The reformation of our travell'd gallants,
That fill the court with quarrels, talk, and tailors.

Cham. I am glad, 'tis there: now I would pray our monsieurs
To think an English courtier may be wise,
And never see the Louvre.

Lov. They must either
(For so run the conditions) leave these remnants
Of fool, and feather, that they got in France,
With all their honourable points of ignorance,
Pertaining thereunto (as fights, and fireworks;
Abusing better men than they can be,
Out of a foreign wisdom), renouncing clean
The faith they have in tennis, and tall stockings,
Short blister'd breeches, and those types of travel,
And understand again like honest men;
Or pack to their old playfellows: there, I take it,
They may, *cum privilegio*, wear away
The lag end of their lewdness, and be laugh'd at.
Sands. 'Tis time to give them physick, their diseases
Are grown so catching.
Cham. What a loss our ladies
Will have of these trim vanities!
Lov. Ay, marry,
There will be woe indeed, lords; the sly whoresons
Have got a speeding trick to lay down ladies;
A French song, and a fiddle, has no fellow.
Sands. The devil fiddle them! I am glad, they're going
(For, sure, there's no converting of them): now
An honest country lord, as I am, beaten
A long time out of play, may bring his plain song,
And have an hour of hearing; and, by'r lady,
Held current musick too.
Cham. Well said, Lord Sands:
Your colt's tooth is not cast yet.
Sands. No, my lord;
Nor shall not, while I have a stump.
Cham. Sir Thomas,
Whither were you a going?
Lov. To the cardinal's;
Your lordship is a guest too.
Cham. O, 'tis true:
This night he makes a supper, and a great one,
To many lords and ladies; there will be
The beauty of this kingdom, I'll assure you.
Lov. That churchman bears a bounteous mind indeed,
A hand as fruitful as the land that feeds us;
His dews fall every where.
Cham. No doubt, he's noble;
He had a black mouth, that said other of him.
Sands. He may, my lord, he has wherewithal; in him,
Sparing would show a worse sin than ill doctrine:
Men of his way should be most liberal,
They are set here for examples.
Cham. True, they are so:
But few now give so great ones. My barge stays;
Your lordship shall along:—Come, good Sir Thomas,
We shall be late else: which I would not be,
For I was spoke to, with Sir Henry Guildford,
This night to be comptrollers.
Sands. I am your lordship's.
[*Exeunt.*

SCENE IV.

The Presence Chamber in York Place.

Hautboys. A small table under a state for the Cardinal, *a longer table for the guests. Enter at one door* ANNE BULLEN, *and divers* Lords, Ladies, *and* Gentlewomen, *as guests; at another door, enter* SIR HENRY GUILDFORD.

Guild. Ladies, a general welcome from his grace
Salutes ye all: This night he dedicates
To fair content, and you: none here, he hopes,
In all this noble bevy, has brought with her
One care abroad: he would have all as merry
As first-good company, good wine, good welcome,
Can make good people.——O, my lord, you are tardy;

Enter Lord Chamberlain, LORD SANDS, *and* SIR THOMAS LOVELL.

The very thought of this fair company
Clapp'd wings to me.
Cham. You are young, Sir Harry Guildford.
Sands. Sir Thomas Lovell, had the cardinal
But half my lay-thoughts in him, some of these
Should find a running banquet ere they rested,
I think, would better please them: By my life,
They are a sweet society of fair ones.
Lov. O, that your lordship were but now confessor
To one or two of these!
Sands. I would, I were;
They should find easy penance.
Lov. 'Faith, how easy?
Sands. As easy as a down bed would afford it.
Cham. Sweet ladies, will it please you sit? Sir Harry,
Place you that side, I'll take the charge of this:
His grace is ent'ring.—Nay, you must not freeze;
Two women plac'd together makes cold weather:—
My Lord Sands, you are one will keep them waking;
Pray, sit between these ladies.
Sands. By my faith,
And thank your lordship.—By your leave, sweet ladies:
[*Seats himself between* ANNE BULLEN *and another* Lady.
If I chance to talk a little wild, forgive me;
I had it from my father.
Anne. Was he mad, sir?
Sands. O, very mad, exceeding mad, in love too:
But he would bite none; just as I do now,
He would kiss you twenty with a breath.
[*Kisses her.*
Cham. Well said, my lord.—
So, now you are fairly seated:—Gentlemen,
The penance lies on you, if these fair ladies
Pass away frowning.
Sands. For my little cure,
Let me alone.

Hautboys. Enter CARDINAL WOLSEY, *attended; and takes his state.*

Wol. You are welcome, my fair guests; that noble lady,
Or gentleman, that is not freely merry,
Is not my friend: This, to confirm my welcome;
And to you all good health. [*Drinks.*
Sands. Your grace is noble;—
Let me have such a bowl may hold my thanks,
And save me so much talking.
Wol. My Lord Sands,
I am beholden to you: cheer your neighbours.—
Ladies, you are not merry;—Gentlemen,
Whose fault is this?
Sands. The red wine first must rise
In their fair cheeks, my lord; then we shall have them
Talk us to silence.
Anne. You are a merry gamester, my Lord Sands.
Sands. Yes, if I make my play.——
Here's to your ladyship: and pledge it, madam,
For 'tis to such a thing,—
Anne. You cannot show me.
Sands. I told your grace, they would talk anon.
[*Drum and trumpets within: Chambers discharged.*
Wol. What's that?
Cham. Look out there, some of you.
[*Exit a* Servant.
Wol. What warlike voice?
And to what end is this?—Nay, ladies, fear not;
By all the laws of war you are privileg'd.

Re-enter Servant.

Cham. How now? what is't?
Serv. A noble troop of strangers,

For so they seem: they have left their barge, and landed:
And hither make, as great ambassadors
From foreign princes.
Wol. Good lord chamberlain,
Go, give them welcome, you can speak the French tongue;
And, pray, receive them nobly, and conduct them
Into our presence, where this heaven of beauty
Shall shine at full upon them:—Some attend him.—
[*Exit* Chamberlain, *attended. All arise, and Tables removed.*
You have now a broken banquet; but we'll mend it.
A good digestion to you all: and, once more,
I shower a welcome on you;—Welcome all.

Hautboys. Enter the King, *and twelve Others, as Maskers, habited like Shepherds, with sixteen Torchbearers: ushered by the* Lord Chamberlain. *They pass directly before the* Cardinal, *and gracefully salute him.*

A noble company! what are their pleasures?
Cham. Because they speak no English, thus they pray'd
To tell your grace;—That, having heard by fame
Of this so noble and so fair assembly
This night to meet here, they could do no less,
Out of the great respect they bear to beauty,
But leave their flocks; and under your fair conduct,
Crave leave to view these ladies, and entreat
An hour of revels with them.
Wol. Say, lord chamberlain,
They have done my poor house grace; for which I pay them
A thousand thanks, and pray them take their pleasures.
[Ladies *chosen for the dance. The* King *chooses* Anne Bullen.
K. Hen. The fairest hand I ever touch'd! O, beauty,
Till now I never knew thee. [*Musick. Dance.*
Wol. My lord,——
Cham. Your grace?
Wol. Pray, tell them thus much from me:
There should be one amongst them, by his person,
More worthy this place than myself; to whom,
If I but knew him, with my love and duty
I would surrender it.
Cham. I will, my lord.
[Chamberlain *goes to the company, and returns.*
Wol. What say they?
Cham. Such a one, they all confess,
There is, indeed; which they would have your grace
Find out, and he will take it.
Wol. Let me see then.—
[*Comes from his state.*
By all your good leaves, gentlemen;—Here I'll make
My royal choice.
K. Hen. You have found him, cardinal:
[*Unmasking.*
You hold a fair assembly; you do well, lord:
You are a churchman, or, I'll tell you, cardinal,
I should judge now unhappily.
Wol. I am glad,
Your grace is grown so pleasant.
K. Hen. My lord chamberlain,
Pr'ythee, come hither: What fair lady's that?
Cham. An 't please your grace, Sir Thomas Bullen's daughter,
The Viscount Rochford, one of her highness' women.
K. Hen. By heaven, she is a dainty one.—Sweetheart,
I were unmannerly, to take you out,
And not to kiss you.—A health, gentlemen,
Let it go round.
Wol. Sir Thomas Lovell, is the banquet ready
I' the privy chamber?
Lov. Yes, my lord.
Wol. Your grace,
I fear, with dancing is a little heated.
K. Hen. I fear, too much.
Wol. There's fresher air, my lord,
In the next chamber.
K. Hen. Lead in your ladies, every one.—Sweet partner,
I must not yet forsake you:—Let's be merry;—
Good my lord cardinal, I have half a dozen healths
To drink to these fair ladies, and a measure
To lead them once again; and then let's dream
Who's best in favour.—Let the musick knock it.
[*Exeunt, with trumpets.*

ACT II.

SCENE I. *A Street.*

Enter two Gentlemen, *meeting.*

1 Gent. Whither away so fast?
2 Gent. O,—God save you!
Even to the hall, to hear what shall become
Of the great duke of Buckingham.
1 Gent. I'll save you
That labour, sir. All's now done, but the ceremony
Of bringing back the prisoner.
2 Gent. Were you there?
1 Gent. Yes, indeed, was I.
2 Gent. Pray, speak, what has happen'd?
1 Gent. You may guess quickly what.
2 Gent. Is he found guilty?
1 Gent. Yes, truly is he, and condemn'd upon it.
2 Gent. I am sorry for't.
1 Gent. So are a number more.
2 Gent. But, pray, how pass'd it?
1 Gent. I'll tell you in a little. The great duke
Came to the bar; where, to his accusations,
He pleaded still, not guilty, and alleg'd
Many sharp reasons to defeat the law.
The king's attorney, on the contrary,
Urg'd on the examinations, proofs, confessions
Of divers witnesses; which the duke desir'd
To have brought, *viva voce*, to his face:
At which appear'd against him, his surveyor;
Sir Gilbert Peck his chancellor; and John Court,
Confessor to him; with that devil-monk,
Hopkins, that made this mischief.
2 Gent. That was he,
That fed him with his prophecies?
1 Gent. The same.
All these accus'd him strongly; which he fain
Would have flung from him, but, indeed he could not:
And so his peers, upon this evidence,
Have found him guilty of high treason. Much
He spoke, and learnedly, for life: but all
Was either pitied in him, or forgotten.
2 Gent. After all this, how did he bear himself?
1 Gent. When he was brought again to the bar,—to hear
His knell rung out, his judgment,—he was stirr'd
With such an agony, he sweat extremely,
And something spoke in choler, ill, and hasty:
But he fell to himself again, and, sweetly,
In all the rest show'd a most noble patience.
2 Gent. I do not think, he fears death.
1 Gent. Sure, he does not,
He never was so womanish; the cause
He may a little grieve at.
2 Gent. Certainly,
The cardinal is the end of this.
1 Gent. 'Tis likely,
By all conjectures: First, Kildare's attainder,

Then deputy of Ireland; who remov'd,
Earl Surrey was sent thither, and in haste too,
Lest he should help his father.

2 Gent. That trick of state
Was a deep envious one.

1 Gent. At his return,
No doubt, he will requite it. This is noted,
And generally: whoever the king favours,
The cardinal instantly will find employment,
And far enough from court too.

2 Gent. All the commons
Hate him perniciously, and, o' my conscience,
Wish him ten fathom deep: this duke as much
They love and dote on; call him bounteous Buckingham,
The mirror of all courtesy;—

1 Gent. Stay there, sir,
And see the noble ruin'd man you speak of.

Enter BUCKINGHAM *from his arraignment; Tipstaves before him, the axe with the edge towards him; halberds on each side: with him,* SIR THOMAS LOVELL, SIR NICHOLAS VAUX, SIR WILLIAM SANDS, *and common* People.

2 Gent. Let's stand close, and behold him.

Buck. All good people,
You that thus far have come to pity me,
Hear what I say, and then go home and lose me.
I have this day receiv'd a traitor's judgment,
And by that name must die; Yet, heaven bear witness,
And, if I have a conscience, let it sink me,
Even as the axe falls, if I be not faithful!
The law I bear no malice for my death,
It has done, upon the premises, but justice:
But those, that sought it, I could wish more christians:
Be what they will, I heartily forgive them:
Yet let them look they glory not in mischief,
Nor build their evils on the graves of great men;
For then my guiltless blood must cry against them.
For further life in this world I ne'er hope,
Nor will I sue, although the king have mercies
More than I dare make faults. You few that lov'd me,
And dare be bold to weep for Buckingham,
His noble friends, and fellows, whom to leave
Is only bitter to him, only dying,
Go with me, like good angels, to my end;
And, as the long divorce of steel falls on me,
Make of your prayers one sweet sacrifice,
And lift my soul to heaven.—Lead on, o' God's name.

Lov. I do beseech your grace, for charity,
If ever any malice in your heart
Were hid against me, now to forgive me frankly.

Buck. Sir Thomas Lovell, I as free forgive you,
As I would be forgiven: I forgive all;
There cannot be those numberless offences
'Gainst me, I can't take peace with: no black envy
Shall make my grave.—Commend me to his grace;
And, if he speak of Buckingham, pray, tell him
You met him half in heaven: my vows and prayers
Yet are the king's; and, till my soul forsake me,
Shall cry for blessings on him: May he live
Longer than I have time to tell his years!
Ever belov'd, and loving, may his rule be!
And, when old time shall lead him to his end,
Goodness and he fill up one monument!

Lov. To the water side I must conduct your grace;
Then give my charge up to Sir Nicholas Vaux,
Who undertakes you to your end.

Vaux. Prepare there,
The duke is coming: see, the barge be ready;
And fit it with such furniture, as suits
The greatness of his person.

Buck. Nay, Sir Nicholas,
Let it alone; my state now will but mock me.
When I came hither, I was lord high constable,
And duke of Buckingham; now, poor Edward Bohun:
Yet I am richer than my base accusers,
That never knew what truth meant: I now seal it;
And with that blood will make them one day groan for't.
My noble father, Henry of Buckingham,
Who first rais'd head against usurping Richard,
Flying for succour to his servant Banister,
Being distress'd, was by that wretch betray'd,
And without trial fell; God's peace be with him!
Henry the Seventh, succeeding, truly pitying
My father's loss, like a most royal prince,
Restor'd me to my honours, and, out of ruins,
Made my name once more noble. Now his son,
Henry the Eighth, life, honour, name, and all
That made me happy, at one stroke has taken
For ever from the world. I had my trial,
And, must needs say, a noble one; which makes me
A little happier than my wretched father:
Yet thus far we are one in fortunes,—Both
Fell by our servants, by those men we lov'd most;
A most unnatural and faithless service!
Heaven has an end in all: Yet, you that hear me,
This from a dying man receive as certain:
Where you are liberal of your loves, and counsels,
Be sure, you be not loose; for those you make friends,
And give your hearts to, when they once perceive
The least rub in your fortunes, fall away
Like water from ye, never found again
But where they mean to sink ye. All good people,
Pray for me! I must now forsake ye; the last hour
Of my long weary life is come upon me.
Farewell:
And when you would say something that is sad,
Speak how I fell.—I have done; and God forgive me! [*Exeunt* BUCKINGHAM *and* Train.

1 Gent. O, this is full of pity!—Sir, it calls,
I fear, too many curses on their heads,
That were the authors.

2 Gent. If the duke be guiltless,
'Tis full of woe: yet I can give you inkling
Of an ensuing evil; if it fall,
Greater than this.

1 Gent. Good angels keep it from us!
Where may it be? You do not doubt my faith, sir.

2 Gent. This secret is so weighty, 'twill require
A strong faith to conceal it.

1 Gent. Let me have it.
I do not talk much.

2 Gent. I am confident:
You shall, sir: Did you not of late days hear
A buzzing, of a separation
Between the king and Katharine?

1 Gent. Yes, but it held not:
For when the king once heard it, out of anger
He sent command to the lord mayor, straight
To stop the rumour, and allay those tongues
That durst disperse it.

2 Gent. But that slander, sir,
Is found a truth now; for it grows again
Fresher than e'er it was; and held for certain,
The king will venture at it. Either the cardinal,
Or some about him near, have, out of malice
To the good queen, possess'd him with a scruple
That will undo her: To confirm this too,
Cardinal Campeius is arriv'd, and lately;
As all think, for this business.

1 Gent. 'Tis the cardinal;
And merely to revenge him on the emperor,
For not bestowing on him, at his asking,
The archbishoprick of Toledo, this is purpos'd.

2 Gent. I think you have hit the mark: But is't not cruel,
That she should feel the smart of this? The cardinal
Will have his will, and she must fall.

1 Gent. 'Tis woful.
We are too open here to argue this;
Let's think in private more. [*Exeunt.*

SCENE II. *An Antechamber in the Palace.*

Enter the Lord Chamberlain, *reading a Letter.*

Cham. *My lord,—The horses your lordship sent for, with all the care I had, I saw well chosen, ridden, and furnished. They were young, and handsome: and of the best breed in the north. When they were ready to set out for London, a man of my lord cardinal's, by commission, and main power, took 'em from me; with this reason,—His master would be served before a subject, if not before the king: which stopped our mouths, sir.*

I fear, he will, indeed: Well, let him have them:
He will have all, I think.

Enter the Dukes of Norfolk *and* Suffolk.

Nor. Well met, my good lord chamberlain.
Cham. Good day to both your graces.
Suff. How is the king employ'd?
Cham. I left him private,
Full of sad thoughts and troubles.
Nor. What's the cause?
Cham. It seems, the marriage with his brother's wife
Has crept too near his conscience.
Suff. No, his conscience
Has crept too near another lady.
Nor. 'Tis so;
This is the cardinal's doing, the king-cardinal;
That blind priest, like the eldest son of fortune,
Turns what he lists. The king will know him one day.
Suff. Pray God, he do! he'll never know himself else.
Nor. How holily he works in all his business!
And with what zeal! For, now he has crack'd the league
Between us and the emperor, the queen's great nephew,
He dives into the king's soul; and there scatters
Dangers, doubts, wringing of the conscience,
Fears, and despairs, and all these for his marriage:
And, out of all these to restore the king,
He counsels a divorce; a loss of her,
That, like a jewel, has hung twenty years
About his neck, yet never lost her lustre;
Of her, that loves him with that excellence
That angels love good men with; even of her
That, when the greatest stroke of fortune falls,
Will bless the king: And is not this course pious?
Cham. Heaven keep me from such counsel! 'Tis most true,
These news are every where; every tongue speaks them,
And every true heart weeps for't: All, that dare
Look into these affairs, see this main end,—
The French king's sister: Heaven will one day open
The king's eyes, that so long have slept upon
This bold bad man.
Suff. And free us from his slavery.
Nor. We had need pray,
And heartily, for our deliverance;
Or this imperious man will work us all
From princes into pages: all men's honours
Lie in one lump before him, to be fashion'd
Into what pitch he please.
Suff. For me, my lords,
I love him not, nor fear him, there's my creed:
As I am made without him, so I'll stand,
If the king please; his curses and his blessings
Touch me alike, they are breath I not believe in.
I knew him, and I know him; so I leave him
To him, that made him proud, the pope.
Nor. Let's in;
And, with some other business, put the king
From these sad thoughts, that work too much upon him:—
My lord, you'll bear us company?
Cham. Excuse me;
The king hath sent me other-where: besides,
You'll find a most unfit time to disturb him:
Health to your lordships.
Nor. Thanks, my good lord chamberlain.
[*Exit* Lord Chamberlain.

Norfolk *opens a folding door. The* King *is discovered sitting, and reading pensively.*

Suff. How sad he looks! sure, he is much afflicted.
K. Hen. Who is there? ha?
Nor. 'Pray God, he be not angry.
K. Hen. Who's there, I say? How dare you thrust yourselves
Into my private meditations?
Who am I? ha?
Nor. A gracious king, that pardons all offences
Malice ne'er meant; our breach of duty, this way,
Is business of estate; in which, we come
To know your royal pleasure.
K. Hen. You are too bold;
Go to; I'll make ye know your times of business:
Is this an hour for temporal affairs? ha?—

Enter Wolsey *and* Campeius.

Who's there? my good lord cardinal?—O, my Wolsey,
The quiet of my wounded conscience,
Thou art a cure fit for a king.—You're welcome,
[*To* Campeius.
Most learned reverend sir, into our kingdom;
Use us, and it:—My good lord, have great care
I be not found a talker. [*To* Wolsey.
Wol. Sir, you cannot.
I would, your grace would give us but an hour
Of private conference.
K. Hen. We are busy; go.
[*To* Norfolk *and* Suffolk.
Nor. This priest has no pride in him?
Suff. Not to speak of;
I would not be so sick though, for his place:
But this cannot continue.
Nor. If it do,
I'll venture one have at him.
Suff. I another. } *Aside.*
[*Exeunt* Norfolk *and* Suffolk.
Wol. Your grace has given a precedent of wisdom
Above all princes, in committing freely
Your scruple to the voice of Christendom:
Who can be angry now? what envy reach you?
The Spaniard, tied by blood and favour to her,
Must now confess, if they have any goodness,
The trial just and noble. All the clerks,
I mean, the learned ones, in Christian kingdoms,
Have their free voices; Rome, the nurse of judgment,
Invited by your noble self, hath sent
One general tongue unto us, this good man,
This just and learned priest, Cardinal Campeius;
Whom, once more, I present unto your highness.
K. Hen. And, once more, in mine arms I bid him welcome,
And thank the holy conclave for their loves;
They have sent me such a man I would have wish'd for.
Cam. Your grace must needs deserve all strangers' loves,
You are so noble: To your highness' hand
I tender my commission; by whose virtue,
(The court of Rome commanding),—you, my lord
Cardinal of York, are join'd with me their servant,
In the unpartial judging of this business.
K. Hen. Two equal men. The queen shall be acquainted
Forthwith, for what you come:—Where's Gardiner?
Wol. I know, your majesty has always lov'd her

So dear in heart, not to deny her that
A woman of less place might ask by law,
Scholars, allow'd freely to argue for her.
K. Hen. Ay, and the best, she shall have; and my favour
To him that does best; God forbid else. Cardinal,
Pr'ythee, call Gardiner to me, my new secretary;
I find him a fit fellow. [*Exit* WOLSEY.

Re-enter WOLSEY, *with* GARDINER.

Wol. Give me your hand: much joy and favour to you;
You are the king's now.
Gard. But to be commanded
For ever by your grace, whose hand has rais'd me. [*Aside.*
K. Hen. Come hither, Gardiner. [*They converse apart.*
Cam. My lord of York, was not one Doctor Pace
In this man's place before him?
Wol. Yes, he was.
Cam. Was he not held a learned man?
Wol. Yes, surely.
Cam. Believe me, there's an ill opinion spread then
Even of yourself, lord cardinal.
Wol. How! of me?
Cam. They will not stick to say, you envied him;
And, fearing he would rise, he was so virtuous,
Kept him a foreign man still; which so griev'd him,
That he ran mad, and died.
Wol. Heaven's peace be with him!
That's Christian care enough: for living murmurers,
There's places of rebuke. He was a fool;
For he would needs be virtuous: That good fellow,
If I command him, follows my appointment;
I will have none so near else. Learn this, brother,
We live not to be grip'd by meaner persons.
K. Hen. Deliver this with modesty to the queen. [*Exit* GARDINER.
The most convenient place that I can think of,
For such receipt of learning, is Black-Friars;
There ye shall meet about this weighty business:—
My Wolsey, see it furnish'd.—O, my lord,
Would it not grieve an able man, to leave
So sweet a bedfellow? But, conscience, conscience,—
O, 'tis a tender place, and I must leave her. [*Exeunt.*

SCENE III.

An Antechamber in the Queen's *Apartments.*

Enter ANNE BULLEN, *and an old* Lady.

Anne. Not for that neither;—Here's the pang that pinches:
His highness having liv'd so long with her: and she
So good a lady, that no tongue could ever
Pronounce dishonour of her,—by my life,
She never knew harm-doing;—O now, after
So many courses of the sun enthron'd,
Still growing in a majesty and pomp,—the which
To leave is a thousand-fold more bitter, than
'Tis sweet at first to acquire,—after this process,
To give her the avaunt! it is a pity
Would move a monster.
Old L. Hearts of most hard temper
Melt and lament for her.
Anne. O, God's will! much better,
She ne'er had known pomp: though it be temporal,
Yet, if that quarrel, fortune, do divorce
It from the bearer, 'tis a sufferance, panging
As soul and body's severing.
Old L. Alas, poor lady!
She's a stranger now again.
Anne. So much the more
Must pity drop upon her. Verily,
I swear, 'tis better to be lowly born,
And range with humble livers in content,
Than to be perk'd up in a glistering grief,
And wear a golden sorrow.
Old L. Our content
Is our best having.
Anne. By my troth, and maidenhead,
I would not be a queen.
Old L. Beshrew me, I would,
And venture maidenhead for't; and so would you,
For all this spice of your hypocrisy:
You, that have so fair parts of woman on you,
Have too a woman's heart; which ever yet
Affected eminence, wealth, sovereignty;
Which, to say sooth, are blessings: and which gifts
(Saving your mincing) the capacity
Of your soft cheveril conscience would receive,
If you might please to stretch it.
Anne. Nay, good troth,—
Old L. Yes, troth, and troth,—You would not be a queen?
Anne. No, not for all the riches under heaven.
Old L. 'Tis strange; a threepence bowed would hire me,
Old as I am, to queen it: But, I pray you,
What think you of a duchess? have you limbs
To bear that load of title?
Anne. No, in truth.
Old L. Then you are weakly made: Pluck off a little;
I would not be a young count in your way,
For more than blushing comes to: if your back
Cannot vouchsafe this burden, 'tis too weak
Ever to get a boy.
Anne. How you do talk!
I swear again, I would not be a queen
For all the world.
Old L. In faith, for little England
You'd venture an emballing: I myself
Would for Carnarvonshire, although there 'long'd
No more to the crown but that. Lo, who comes here?

Enter the Lord Chamberlain.

Cham. Good morrow, ladies. What wer't worth to know
The secret of your conference?
Anne. My good lord,
Not your demand; it values not your asking:
Our mistress' sorrows we were pitying.
Cham. It was a gentle business, and becoming
The action of good women: there is hope,
All will be well.
Anne. Now I pray God, amen!
Cham. You bear a gentle mind, and heavenly blessings
Follow such creatures. That you may, fair lady,
Perceive I speak sincerely, and high note's
Ta'en of your many virtues, the king's majesty
Commends his good opinion to you, and
Does purpose honour to you no less flowing
Than marchioness of Pembroke; to which title
A thousand pound a year, annual support,
Out of his grace he adds.
Anne. I do not know,
What kind of my obedience I should tender;
More than my all is nothing: nor my prayers
Are not words duly hallow'd, nor my wishes
More worth than empty vanities; yet prayers, and wishes,
Are all I can return. 'Beseech your lordship,
Vouchsafe to speak my thanks, and my obedience,
As from a blushing handmaid, to his highness;
Whose health, and royalty, I pray for.
Cham. Lady,
I shall not fail to approve the fair conceit,

The king hath of you.—I have perus'd her well. [*Aside.*
Beauty and honour in her are so mingled,
That they have caught the king: and who knows yet,
But from this lady may proceed a gem,
To lighten all this isle?—I'll to the king,
And say, I spoke with you.

Anne. My honour'd lord.

[*Exit* Lord Chamberlain.

Old L. Why, this it is; see, see!
I have been begging sixteen years in court
(Am yet a courtier beggarly), nor could
Come pat betwixt too early and too late,
For any suit of pounds: and you, (O fate!)
A very fresh-fish here, (fye, fye upon
This compell'd fortune!) have your mouth fill'd up,
Before you open it.

Anne. This is strange to me.

Old L. How tastes it? is it bitter? forty pence, no.
There was a lady once ('tis an old story),
That would not be a queen, that would she not,
For all the mud in Egypt:—Have you heard it?

Anne. Come, you are pleasant.

Old L. With your theme, I could
O'ermount the lark. The marchioness of Pembroke!
A thousand pounds a year! for pure respect;
No other obligation: By my life,
That promises more thousands: Honour's train
Is longer than his foreskirt. By this time,
I know, your back will bear a duchess;—Say,
Are you not stronger than you were?

Anne. Good lady,
Make yourself mirth with your particular fancy,
And leave me out on't. 'Would I had no being,
If this salute my blood a jot; it faints me,
To think what follows.
The queen is comfortless, and we forgetful
In our long absence: Pray, do not deliver
What here you have heard, to her.

Old L. What do you think me?

[*Exeunt.*

SCENE IV. *A Hall in* Black-Friars.

Trumpets sennet, and cornets. Enter two Vergers, *with short silver wands; next them, two* Scribes, *in the habits of doctors; after them, the* Archbishop *of* Canterbury, *alone; after him the* Bishops *of* Lincoln, Ely, Rochester, *and* Saint Asaph; *next them, with some small distance, follows a* Gentleman *bearing the purse, with the great seal, and a cardinal's hat; then two* Priests, *bearing each a silver cross; then a* Gentleman Usher *bareheaded, accompanied with a* Sergeant at Arms, *bearing a silver mace; then two* Gentlemen, *bearing two great silver pillars; after them, side by side, the two* Cardinals, Wolsey *and*, Campeius; *two* Noblemen *with the sword and mace. Then enter the* King *and* Queen, *and their* Trains. *The* King *takes place under the cloth of state; the two* Cardinals *sit under him as judges. The* Queen *takes place at some distance from the* King. *The* Bishops *place themselves on each side the court, in manner of a consistory; between them, the* Scribes. *The* Lords *sit next the* Bishops. *The* Crier *and the rest of the* Attendants *stand in convenient order about the stage.*

Wol. Whilst our commission from Rome is read,
Let silence be commanded.

K. Hen. What's the need?
It hath already publickly been read,
And on all sides the authority allow'd;
You may then spare that time.

Wol. Be't so;—Proceed.

Scribe. Say, Henry king of England, come into the court.

Crier. Henry king of England, &c.

K. Hen. Here.

Scribe. Say, Katharine queen of England, come into court.

Crier. Katharine queen of England, &c.

[*The* Queen *makes no answer, rises out of her chair, goes about the court, comes to the* King, *and kneels at his feet; then speaks.*]

Q. Kath. Sir, I desire you, do me right and justice;
And to bestow your pity on me: for
I am a most poor woman, and a stranger,
Born out of your dominions; having here
No judge indifferent, nor no more assurance
Of equal friendship and proceeding. Alas, sir,
In what have I offended you? what cause
Hath my behaviour given to your displeasure,
That thus you should proceed to put me off,
And take your good grace from me? Heaven witness,
I have been to you a true and humble wife,
At all times to your will conformable:
Ever in fear to kindle your dislike,
Yea, subject to your countenance; glad, or sorry,
As I saw it inclin'd. When was the hour,
I ever contradicted your desire,
Or made it not mine too? Or which of your friends
Have I not strove to love, although I knew
He were mine enemy? what friend of mine
That had to him deriv'd your anger, did I
Continue in my liking? nay, gave notice
He was from thence discharg'd? Sir, call to mind
That I have been your wife, in this obedience,
Upward of twenty years, and have been blest
With many children by you: If, in the course
And process of this time, you can report,
And prove it too, against mine honour aught,
My bond to wedlock, or my love and duty,
Against your sacred person, in God's name,
Turn me away; and let the foul'st contempt
Shut door upon me, and so give me up
To the sharpest kind of justice. Please you, sir,
The king, your father, was reputed for
A prince most prudent, of an excellent
And unmatch'd wit and judgment: Ferdinand,
My father, king of Spain, was reckon'd one
The wisest prince, that there had reign'd by many
A year before: It is not to be question'd
That they had gather'd a wise council to them
Of every realm, that did debate this business,
Who deem'd our marriage lawful: Wherefore I humbly
Beseech you, sir, to spare me, till I may
Be by my friends in Spain advis'd; whose counsel
I will implore: if not; i' the name of God,
Your pleasure be fulfill'd!

Wol. You have here, lady,
(And of your choice), these reverend fathers; men
Of singular integrity and learning,
Yea, the elect of the land, who are assembled
To plead your cause: It shall be therefore bootless,
That longer you desire the court; as well
For your own quiet, as to rectify
What is unsettled in the king.

Cam. His grace
Hath spoken well, and justly: Therefore, madam,
It's fit this royal session do proceed;
And that, without delay, their arguments
Be now produc'd, and heard.

Q. Kath. Lord cardinal,—
To you I speak.

Wol. Your pleasure, madam?

Q. Kath. Sir,
I am about to weep; but, thinking that
We are a queen (or long have dream'd so), certain,

The daughter of a king, my drops of tears
I'll turn to sparks of fire.

Wol. Be patient yet.

Q. Kath. I will, when you are humble; nay, before,
Or God will punish me. I do believe,
Induc'd by potent circumstances, that
You are mine enemy; and make my challenge,
You shall not be my judge: for it is you
Have blown this coal betwixt my lord and me,—
Which God's dew quench!—Therefore, I say again,
I utterly abhor, yea, from my soul,
Refuse you for my judge; whom, yet once more,
I hold my most malicious foe, and think not
At all a friend to truth.

Wol. I do profess,
You speak not like yourself; who ever yet
Have stood to charity, and display'd the effects
Of disposition gentle, and of wisdom
O'ertopping woman's power. Madam, you do me wrong:
I have no spleen against you; nor injustice
For you, or any: how far I have proceeded,
Or how far further shall, is warranted
By a commission from the consistory,
Yea, the whole consistory of Rome. You charge me,
That I have blown this coal: I do deny it:
The king is present: if it be known to him,
That I gainsay my deed, how may he wound,
And worthily, my falsehood? yea, as much
As you have done my truth. But if he know
That I am free of your report, he knows,
I am not of your wrong. Therefore in him
It lies, to cure me; and the cure is, to
Remove these thoughts from you: The which before
His highness shall speak in, I do beseech
You, gracious madam, to unthink your speaking,
And to say so no more.

Q. Kath. My lord, my lord,
I am a simple woman, much too weak
To oppose your cunning. You are meek, and humble mouth'd;
You sign your place and calling, in full seeming,
With meekness and humility; but your heart
Is cramm'd with arrogancy, spleen, and pride.
You have, by fortune, and his highness' favours,
Gone slightly o'er low steps; and now are mounted
Where powers are your retainers: and your wards,
Domesticks to you, serve your will, as 't please
Yourself pronounce their office. I must tell you,
You tender more your person's honour, than
Your high profession spiritual: That again
I do refuse you for my judge; and here,
Before you all, appeal unto the pope,
To bring my whole cause 'fore his holiness,
And to be judg'd by him.

[*She curtsies to the* King, *and offers to depart.*

Cam. The queen is obstinate,
Stubborn to justice, apt to accuse it, and
Disdainful to be try'd by it; 'tis not well.
She's going away.

K. Hen. Call her again.

Crier. Katharine queen of England, come into the court.

Grif. Madam, you are call'd back.

Q. Kath. What need you note it? pray you, keep your way:
When you are call'd, return.—Now the Lord help,
They vex me past my patience!—pray you, pass on:
I will not tarry: no, nor ever more,
Upon this business, my appearance make
In any of their courts.

[*Exeunt* Queen, GRIF. *and her other* Attendants.

K. Hen. Go thy ways, Kate:
That man i' the world, who shall report he has
A better wife, let him in nought be trusted,
For speaking false in that: Thou art, alone,
(If thy rare qualities, sweet gentleness,
Thy meekness saint-like, wife-like government,—
Obeying in commanding,—and thy parts
Sovereign and pious else, could speak thee out),
The queen of earthly queens:—She is noble born;
And, like her true nobility, she has
Carried herself towards me.

Wol. Most gracious sir,
In humblest manner I require your highness,
That it shall please you to declare, in hearing
Of all these ears (for where I am robb'd and bound,
There must I be unloos'd; although not there
At once and fully satisfied), whether ever I
Did broach this business to your highness; or
Laid any scruple in your way, which might
Induce you to the question on 't? or ever
Have to you,—but with thanks to God for such
A royal lady,—spake one the least word, might
Be to the prejudice of her present state,
Or touch of her good person?

K. Hen. My lord cardinal,
I do excuse you; yea, upon mine honour
I free you from 't. You are not to be taught
That you have many enemies, that know not
Why they are so, but, like to village curs,
Bark when their fellows do: by some of these
The queen is put in anger. You are excus'd:
But will you be more justified? you ever
Have wish'd the sleeping of this business; never
Desir'd it to be stirr'd; but oft have hinder'd; oft
The passages made toward it:—on my honour,
I speak my good lord cardinal to this point,
And thus far clear him. Now, what mov'd me to 't,—
I will be bold with time, and your attention:—
Then mark the inducement. Thus it came;—give heed to 't:
My conscience first receiv'd a tenderness,
Scruple, and prick, on certain speeches utter'd
By the bishop of Bayonne, then French ambassador;
Who had been hither sent on the debating
A marriage, 'twixt the duke of Orleans and
Our daughter Mary: I' the progress of this business,
Ere a determinate resolution, he
(I mean, the bishop) did require a respite;
Wherein he might the king his lord advertise
Whether our daughter were legitimate,
Respecting this our marriage with the dowager,
Sometimes our brother's wife. This respite shook
The bosom of my conscience, enter'd me,
Yea, with a splitting power, and made to tremble
The region of my breast; which forc'd such way,
That many maz'd considerings did throng,
And press'd in with this caution. First, methought,
I stood not in the smile of heaven; who had
Commanded nature, that my lady's womb,
If it conceiv'd a male child by me, should
Do no more offices of life to 't, than
The grave does to the dead: for her male issue
Or died where they were made, or shortly after
This world had air'd them: Hence I took a thought,
This was a judgment on me; that my kingdom,
Well worthy the best heir o' the world, should not
Be gladded in 't by me: Then follows, that
I weigh'd the danger which my realms stood in
By this my issue's fail; and that gave to me
Many a groaning throe. Thus hulling in
The wild sea of my conscience, I did steer
Toward this remedy, whereupon we are
Now present here together; that's to say,
I meant to rectify my conscience,—which
I then did feel full sick, and yet not well,—
By all the reverend fathers of the land,

And doctors learn'd,—First, I began in private
With you, my lord of Lincoln; you remember
How under my oppression I did reek,
When I first mov'd you.

Lin. Very well, my liege.

K. Hen. I have spoke long; be pleas'd yourself to say
How far you satisfied me.

Lin. So please your highness,
The question did at first so stagger me,—
Bearing a state of mighty moment in't,
And consequence of dread,—that I committed
The daring'st counsel which I had, to doubt;
And did entreat your highness to this course,
Which you are running here.

K. Hen. I then mov'd you,
My lord of Canterbury; and got your leave
To make this present summons:—Unsolicited
I left no reverend person in this court;
But by particular consent proceeded,
Under your hands and seals. Therefore, go on:
For no dislike i' the world against the person
Of the good queen, but the sharp thorny points
Of my alleged reasons, drive this forward:
Prove but our marriage lawful, by my life,
And kingly dignity, we are contented
To wear our mortal state to come, with her,
Katharine our queen, before the primest creature
That's paragon'd o' the world.

Cam. So please your highness,
The queen being absent, 'tis a needful fitness
That we adjourn this court till further day:
Mean while must be an earnest motion
Made to the queen, to call back her appeal
She intends unto his holiness.
[*They rise to depart.*

K. Hen. I may perceive, [*Aside.*
These cardinals trifle with me: I abhor
This dilatory sloth, and tricks of Rome.
My learn'd and well beloved servant, Cranmer,
Pr'ythee return! with thy approach, I know,
My comfort comes along. Break up the court:
I say, set on. [*Exeunt, in manner as they entered.*

ACT III.

SCENE I. *Palace at* Bridewell.

A Room in the Queen's *Apartment.*

The Queen, *and some of her* Women, *at work.*

Q. Kath. Take thy lute, wench: my soul grows sad with troubles;
Sing, and disperse them, if thou canst: leave working.

SONG.

Orpheus with his lute made trees,
And the mountain tops, that freeze,
Bow themselves, when he did sing:
To his musick, plants, and flowers,
Ever sprung; as sun, and showers,
There had been a lasting spring.

Every thing that heard him play,
Even the billows of the sea,
Hung their heads, and then lay by.
In sweet musick is such art;
Killing care, and grief of heart,
Fall asleep, or hearing, die.

Enter a Gentleman.

Q. Kath. How now?

Gent. An't please your grace, the two great cardinals
Wait in the presence.

Q. Kath. Would they speak with me?

Gent. They will'd me say so, madam.

Q. Kath. Pray their graces
To come near. [*Exit* Gent.] What can be their business
With me, a poor weak woman, fallen from favour?
I do not like their coming, now I think on't.
They should be good men; their affairs as righteous:
But all hoods make not monks.

Enter Wolsey *and* Campeius.

Wol. Peace to your highness!

Q. Kath. Your graces find me here part of a housewife;
I would be all, against the worst may happen.
What are your pleasures with me, reverend lords?

Wol. May it please you, noble madam, to withdraw
Into your private chamber, we shall give you
The full cause of our coming.

Q. Kath. Speak it here;
There's nothing I have done yet, o' my conscience,
Deserves a corner: 'Would, all other women
Could speak this with as free a soul as I do!
My lords, I care not (so much I am happy
Above a number), if my actions
Were tried by every tongue, every eye saw them,
Envy and base opinion set against them,
I know my life so even: If your business
Seek me out, and that way I am wife in,
Out with it boldly; Truth loves open dealing.

Wol. *Tanta est erga te mentis integritas, regina serenissima,—*

Q. Kath. O, good my lord, no Latin;
I am not such a truant since my coming,
As not to know the language I have liv'd in:
A strange tongue makes my cause more strange, suspicious;
Pray, speak in English: here are some will thank you,
If you speak truth, for their poor mistress' sake;
Believe me, she has had much wrong: Lord cardinal,
The willing'st sin I ever yet committed,
May be absolv'd in English.

Wol. Noble lady,
I am sorry, my integrity should breed
(And service to his majesty and you)
So deep suspicion, where all faith was meant.
We come not by the way of accusation,
To taint that honour every good tongue blesses;
Nor to betray you any way to sorrow;
You have too much, good lady: but to know
How you stand minded in the weighty difference
Between the king and you; and to deliver,
Like free and honest men, our just opinions,
And comforts to your cause.

Cam. Most honour'd madam,
My lord of York,—out of his noble nature,
Zeal and obedience he still bore your grace;
Forgetting, like a good man, your late censure
Both of his truth and him (which was too far),—
Offers, as I do, in a sign of peace,
His service and his counsel.

Q. Kath. To betray me.
[*Aside.*
My lords, I thank you both for your good wills,
Ye speak like honest men, (pray God, ye prove so!)
But how to make you suddenly an answer,
In such a point of weight, so near mine honour
(More near my life, I fear,) with my weak wit,
And to such men of gravity and learning,
In truth, I know not. I was set at work
Among my maids; full little, God knows, looking
Either for such men, or such business.
For her sake that I have been (for I feel
The last fit of my greatness), good your graces,
Let me have time, and counsel, for my cause;
Alas! I am a woman, friendless, hopeless.

Wol. Madam, you wrong the king's love with these fears;
Your hopes and friends are infinite.

Q. Kath. In England,
But little for my profit: Can you think, lords,

That any Englishman dare give me counsel?
Or be a known friend, 'gainst his highness' pleasure
(Though he be grown so desperate to be honest),
And live a subject? Nay, forsooth my friends,
They that must weigh out my afflictions,
They that my trust must grow to, live not here;
They are, as all my other comforts, far hence,
In mine own country, lords.

Cam. I would, your grace
Would leave your griefs, and take my counsel.

Q. Kath. How, sir?

Cam. Put your main cause into the king's protection;
He's loving, and most gracious; 'twill be much
Both for your honour better, and your cause;
For, if the trial of the law o'ertake you,
You'll part away disgrac'd.

Wol. He tells you rightly.

Q. Kath. Ye tell me what ye wish for both, my ruin:
Is this your Christian counsel? out upon ye!
Heaven is above all yet; there sits a judge,
That no king can corrupt.

Cam. Your rage mistakes us.

Q. Kath. The more shame for ye; holy men I thought ye,
Upon my soul, two reverend cardinal virtues:
But cardinal sins, and hollow hearts, I fear ye;
Mend them for shame, my lords. Is this your comfort?
The cordial that ye bring a wretched lady?
A woman lost among ye, laugh'd at, scorn'd?
I will not wish ye half my miseries,
I have more charity: But say, I warn'd ye;
Take heed, for heaven's sake, take heed, lest at once
The burden of my sorrows fall upon ye.

Wol. Madam, this is a mere distraction;
You turn the good we offer into envy.

Q. Kath. Ye turn me into nothing; Woe upon ye,
And all such false professors! Would ye have me
(If you have any justice, any pity;
If ye be any thing but churchmen's habits)
Put my sick cause into his hands that hates me?
Alas! he has banish'd me his bed already;
His love too long ago: I am old, my lords,
And all the fellowship I hold now with him
Is only my obedience. What can happen
To me, above this wretchedness? all your studies
Make me a curse like this.

Cam. Your fears are worse.

Q. Kath. Have I liv'd thus long—(let me speak myself,
Since virtue finds no friends),—a wife, a true one?
A woman (I dare say, without vainglory),
Never yet branded with suspicion?
Have I, with all my full affections
Still met the king? lov'd him next heaven? obey'd him?
Been, out of fondness, superstitious to him?
Almost forgot my prayers to content him?
And am I thus rewarded? 'tis not well, lords.
Bring me a constant woman to her husband,
One that ne'er dream'd a joy beyond his pleasure;
And to that woman, when she has done most,
Yet will I add an honour,—a great patience.

Wol. Madam, you wander from the good we aim at.

Q. Kath. My lord, I dare not make myself so guilty,
To give up willingly that noble title
Your master wed me to: nothing but death
Shall e'er divorce my dignities.

Wol. 'Pray, hear me.

Q. Kath. 'Would I had never trod this English earth,
Or felt the flatteries that grow upon it!
Ye have angels' faces, but heaven knows your hearts.
What will become of me now, wretched lady?
I am the most unhappy woman living.—
Alas! poor wenches, where are now your fortunes? [*To her* Women.
Shipwreck'd upon a kingdom, where no pity,
No friends, no hope; no kindred weep for me,
Almost, no grave allow'd me:—Like the lily,
That once was mistress of the field, and flourish'd,
I'll hang my head, and perish.

Wol. If your grace
Could but be brought to know, our ends are honest,
You'd feel more comfort: why should we, good lady,
Upon what cause, wrong you? alas! our places,
The way of our profession is against it;
We are to cure such sorrows, not to sow them.
For goodness' sake, consider what you do;
How you may hurt yourself, ay, utterly
Grow from the king's acquaintance, by this carriage.
The hearts of princes kiss obedience,
So much they love it; but to stubborn spirits,
They swell, and grow as terrible as storms.
I know, you have a gentle, noble temper,
A soul, as even as a calm; Pray, think us
Those we profess, peace-makers, friends, and servants.

Cam. Madam, you'll find it so. You wrong your virtues
With these weak women's fears. A noble spirit,
As yours was put into you, ever casts
Such doubts, as false coin, from it. The king loves you;
Beware, you lose it not: For us, if you please
To trust us in your business, we are ready
To use our utmost studies in your service.

Q. Kath. Do what ye will, my lords: And pray, forgive me,
If I have us'd myself unmannerly;
You know, I am a woman, lacking wit
To make a seemly answer to such persons.
Pray, do my service to his majesty:
He has my heart yet; and shall have my prayers,
While I shall have my life. Come, reverend fathers,
Bestow your counsels on me: she now begs,
That little thought, when she set footing here,
She should have bought her dignities so dear.
[*Exeunt.*

SCENE II.

Antechamber to the King's *Apartment.*

Enter the Duke of Norfolk, *the* Duke of Suffolk, *the* Earl of Surrey, *and the* Lord Chamberlain.

Nor. If you will now unite in your complaints,
And force them with a constancy, the cardinal
Cannot stand under them: If you omit
The offer of this time, I cannot promise,
But that you shall sustain more new disgraces,
With these you bear already.

Sur. I am joyful
To meet the least occasion, that may give me
Remembrance of my father-in-law, the duke,
To be reveng'd on him.

Suff. Which of the peers
Have uncontemn'd gone by him, or at least
Strangely neglected? when did he regard
The stamp of nobleness in any person,
Out of himself?

Cham. My lord, you speak your pleasures:
What he deserves of you and me, I know;
What we can do to him (though now the time
Gives way to us), I much fear. If you cannot
Bar his access to the king, never attempt
Any thing on him; for he hath a witchcraft
Over the king in his tongue.

Nor. O, fear him not;
His spell in that is out: the king hath found
Matter against him, that for ever mars
The honey of his language. No, he's settled,
Not to come off in his displeasure.

Sur. Sir,
I should be glad to hear such news as this
Once every hour.
Nor. Believe it, this is true.
In the divorce, his contrary proceedings
Are all unfolded; wherein he appears,
As I could wish mine enemy.
Sur. How came
His practices to light?
Suff. Most strangely.
Sur. O, how, how?
Suff. The cardinal's letter to the pope miscarried, [read,
And came to the eye o' the king: wherein was
How that the cardinal did entreat his holiness
To stay the judgment o' the divorce: for if
It did take place, *I do*, quoth he, *perceive*
My king is tangled in affection to
A creature of the queen's, Lady Anne Bullen.
Sur. Has the king this?
Suff. Believe it.
Sur. Will this work?
Cham. The king in this perceives him, how he coasts,
And hedges, his own way. But in this point
All his tricks founder, and he brings his physick
After his patient's death; the king already
Hath married the fair lady.
Sur. 'Would he had!
Suff. May you be happy in your wish, my lord!
For, I profess, you have it.
Sur. Now all my joy
Trace the conjunction!
Suff. My amen to't!
Nor. All men's.
Suff. There's order given for her coronation:
Marry, this is yet but young, and may be left
To some ears unrecounted.—But, my lords,
She is a gallant creature, and complete
In mind and feature: I persuade me, from her
Will fall some blessing to this land, which shall
In it be memoriz'd.
Sur. But, will the king
Digest this letter of the cardinal's?
The Lord forbid!
Nor. Marry, amen!
Suff. No, no;
There be more wasps that buz about his nose,
Will make this sting the sooner. Cardinal Campeius
Is stolen away to Rome; hath ta'en no leave;
Has left the cause o' the king unhandled; and
Is posted, as the agent of our cardinal,
To second all his plot. I do assure you
The king cried, ha! at this.
Cham. Now, God incense him,
And let him cry ha, louder!
Nor. But, my lord,
When returns Cranmer?
Suff. He is return'd, in his opinions; which
Have satisfied the king for his divorce,
Together with all famous colleges
Almost in Christendom: shortly, I believe,
His second marriage shall be publish'd, and
Her coronation. Katharine no more
Shall be call'd, queen; but princess dowager,
And widow to Prince Arthur.
Nor. This same Cranmer's
A worthy fellow, and hath ta'en much pain
In the king's business.
Suff. He has: and we shall see him
For it, an archbishop.
Nor. So I hear.
Suff. 'Tis so.
The cardinal—

Enter WOLSEY *and* CROMWELL.

Nor. Observe, observe, he's moody.
Wol. The packet, Cromwell, gave it you the king?
Crom. To his own hand, in his bedchamber.
Wol. Look'd he o' the inside of the paper?
Crom. Presently
He did unseal them; and the first he view'd,
He did it with a serious mind; a heed
Was in his countenance: You, he bade
Attend him here this morning.
Wol. Is he ready
To come abroad?
Crom. I think, by this he is.
Wol. Leave me awhile. [*Exit* CROMWELL.
It shall be to the duchess of Alençon,
The French king's sister: he shall marry her.—
Anne Bullen! No, I'll no Anne Bullens for him:
There is more in it than fair visage.—Bullen!
No, we'll no Bullens.—Speedily I wish
To hear from Rome.—The marchioness of Pembroke!
Nor. He's discontented.
Suff. May be, he hears the king
Does whet his anger to him.
Sur. Sharp enough,
Lord, for thy justice!
Wol. The late queen's gentlewoman; a knight's daughter,
To be her mistress' mistress! the queen's queen!—
This candle burns not clear: 'tis I must snuff it;
Then, out it goes.—What though I know her virtuous,
And well deserving? yet I know her for
A spleeny Lutheran; and not wholesome to
Our cause, that she should lie i' the bosom of
Our hard-rul'd king. Again, there is sprung up
An heretick, an arch one, Cranmer; one
Hath crawl'd into the favour of the king,
And is his oracle.
Nor. He's vex'd at something.
Suff. I would 'twere something that would fret the string,
The master-cord of his heart!

Enter the King, *reading a Schedule; and* LOVELL.

Suff. The king, the king.
K. Hen. What piles of wealth hath he accumulated
To his own portion! and what expense by the hour
Seems to flow from him! How, i' the name of thrift,
Does he rake this together!—Now, my lords;
Saw you the cardinal?
Nor. My lord, we have
Stood here observing him: Some strange commotion
Is in his brain: he bites his lip, and starts;
Stops on a sudden, looks upon the ground,
Then lays his finger on his temple; straight,
Springs out into fast gait; then stops again,
Strikes his breast hard; and anon, he casts
His eye against the moon: in most strange postures
We have seen him set himself.
K. Hen. It may well be;
There is a mutiny in his mind. This morning
Papers of state he sent me to peruse,
As I requir'd: and, wot you what I found
There; on my conscience, put unwittingly?
Forsooth, an inventory, thus importing,—
The several parcels of his plate, his treasure,
Rich stuffs, and ornaments of household; which
I find at such proud rate, that it outspeaks
Possession of a subject.
Nor. It's heaven's will;
Some spirit put this paper in the packet,
To bless your eye withal.
K. Hen. If we did think
His contemplation were above the earth,
And fix'd on spiritual object, he should still
Dwell in his musings: but, I am afraid,
His thinkings are below the moon, not worth
His serious considering.
[*He takes his seat, and whispers* LOVELL, *who goes to* WOLSEY.

Wol. Heaven forgive me!
Ever God bless your highness!
K. Hen. Good my lord,
You are full of heavenly stuff, and bear the inventory
Of your best graces in your mind; the which
You were now running o'er; you have scarce time
To steal from spiritual leisure a brief span,
To keep your earthly audit: Sure, in that
I deem you an ill husband; and am glad
To have you therein my companion.
Wol. Sir,
For holy offices I have a time; a time
To think upon the part of business, which
I bear i' the state; and nature does require
Her times of preservation, which, perforce,
I her frail son, amongst my brethren mortal,
Must give my tendance to.
K. Hen. You have said well.
Wol. And ever may your highness yoke together,
As I will lend you cause, my doing well
With my well saying!
K. Hen. 'Tis well said again;
And 'tis a kind of good deed to say well:
And yet words are no deeds. My father lov'd you:
He said, he did; and with his deed did crown
His word upon you. Since I had my office,
I have kept you next my heart; have not alone
Employ'd you where high profits might come home,
But par'd my present havings, to bestow
My bounties upon you.
Wol. What should this mean?
Sur. The lord increase this business! [*Aside.*
K. Hen. Have I not made you
The prime man of the state? I pray you, tell me,
If what I now pronounce, you have found true:
And, if you may confess it, say, withal,
If you are bound to us or no. What say you?
Wol. My sovereign, I confess, your royal graces,
Shower'd on me daily, have been more than could
My studied purposes requite; which went
Beyond all man's endeavours;—my endeavours
Have ever come too short of my desires,
Yet, fil'd with my abilities: Mine own ends
Have been mine so, that evermore they pointed
To the good of your most sacred person, and
The profit of the state. For your great graces
Heap'd upon me, poor undeserver, I
Can nothing render but allegiant thanks;
My prayers to heaven for you; my loyalty,
Which ever has, and ever shall be growing,
Till death, that winter, kill it.
K. Hen. Fairly answer'd;
A loyal and obedient subject is
Therein illustrated: The honour of it
Does pay the act of it: as, i' the contrary,
The foulness is the punishment. I presume,
That, as my hand has open'd bounty to you,
My heart dropp'd love, my power rain'd honour, more
On you, than any; so your hand and heart,
Your brain, and every function of your power,
Should, notwithstanding that your bond of duty,
As 'twere in love's particular, be more
To me, your friend, than any.
Wol. I do profess,
That for your highness' good I ever labour'd
More than mine own; that am, have, and will be.
Though all the world should crack their duty to you,
And throw it from their soul; though perils did
Abound, as thick as thought could make them, and
Appear in forms more horrid; yet my duty,
As doth a rock against the chiding flood,
Should the approach of this wild river break,
And stand unshaken yours.
K. Hen. 'Tis nobly spoken:
Take notice, lords, he has a loyal breast,
For you have seen him open't.—Read o'er this;
[*Giving him papers.*
And, after, this: and then to breakfast, with
What appetite you have.
[*Exit* King, *frowning upon* CARDINAL WOLSEY: *the* Nobles *throng after him, smiling, and whispering.*
Wol. What should this mean?
What sudden anger's this? how have I reap'd it?
He parted frowning from me, as if ruin
Leap'd from his eyes: So looks the chafed lion
Upon the daring huntsman that has gall'd him;
Then makes him nothing. I must read this paper;
I fear, the story of his anger.—'Tis so;
This paper has undone me:—'Tis the account
Of all that world of wealth I have drawn together
For mine own ends; indeed, to gain the popedom,
And fee my friends in Rome. O negligence,
Fit for a fool to fall by! What cross devil
Made me put this main secret in the packet
I sent the king? Is there no way to cure this?
No new device to beat this from his brains?
I know, 'twill stir him strongly: Yet I know
A way, if it take right, in spite of fortune
Will bring me off again. What's this—*To the Pope?*
The letter, as I live, with all the business
I writ to his holiness. Nay, then, farewell!
I have touch'd the highest point of all my greatness;
And, from that full meridian of my glory,
I haste now to my setting: I shall fall
Like a bright exhalation in the evening,
And no man see me more.

Re-enter the DUKES OF NORFOLK *and* SUFFOLK, *the* EARL OF SURREY, *and the* Lord Chamberlain.

Nor. Hear the king's pleasure, cardinal: who commands you
To render up the great seal presently
Into our hands; and to confine yourself
To Asher-house, my lord of Winchester's,
Till you hear further from his highness.
Wol. Stay,
Where's your commission, lords? words cannot carry
Authority so weighty.
Suff. Who dare cross them?
Bearing the king's will from his mouth expressly?
Wol. Till I find more than will, or words to do it,
(I mean your malice), know, officious lords,
I dare and must deny it. Now I feel
Of what course metal ye are moulded,—envy.
How eagerly ye follow my disgraces,
As if it fed ye? and how sleek and wanton
Ye appear in every thing may bring my ruin!
Follow your envious courses, men of malice;
You have Christian warrant for them, and, no doubt,
In time will find their fit rewards. That seal
You ask with such a violence, the king
(Mine, and your master) with his own hand gave me:
Bade me enjoy it, with the place and honours,
During my life; and, to confirm his goodness,
Tied it by letters patents: Now, who'll take it?
Sur. The king that gave it.
Wol. It must be himself then.
Sur. Thou art a proud traitor, priest.
Wol. Proud lord, thou liest;
Within these forty hours Surrey durst better
Have burnt that tongue than said so.
Sur. Thy ambition,
Thou scarlet sin, robb'd this bewailing land
Of noble Buckingham, my father-in-law;

The heads of all thy brother cardinals
(With thee, and all thy best parts bound together)
Weigh'd not a hair of his. Plague of your policy!
You sent me deputy for Ireland;
Far from his succour, from the king, from all
That might have mercy on the fault thou gav'st him;
Whilst your great goodness, out of holy pity,
Absolv'd him with an axe.

Wol. This, and all else
This talking lord can lay upon my credit,
I answer, is most false. The duke by law
Found his deserts: how innocent I was
From any private malice in his end,
His noble jury and foul cause can witness.
If I lov'd many words, lord, I should tell you,
You have as little honesty as honour;
That I, in the way of loyalty and truth
Toward the king, my ever royal master,
Dare mate a sounder man than Surrey can be,
And all that love his follies.

Sur. By my soul,
Your long coat, priest, protects you; thou should'st feel
My sword i' the life-blood of thee else.—My lords,
Can ye endure to hear this arrogance?
And from this fellow? If we live thus tamely,
To be thus jaded by a piece of scarlet,
Farewell nobility; let his grace go forward,
And dare us with his cap, like larks.

Wol. All goodness
Is poison to thy stomach.

Sur. Yes, that goodness
Of gleaning all the land's wealth into one,
Into your own hands, cardinal, by extortion;
The goodness of your intercepted packets,
You writ to the pope, against the king: your goodness,
Since you provoke me, shall be most notorious.—
My lord of Norfolk, as you are truly noble,
As you respect the common good, the state
Of our despis'd nobility, our issues,
Who, if he live, will scarce be gentlemen,—
Produce the grand sum of his sins, the articles
Collected from his life;—I'll startle you
Worse than the sacring bell, when the brown wench
Lay kissing in your arms, lord cardinal.

Wol. How much, methinks, I could despise this man,
But that I am bound in charity against it!

Nor. Those articles, my lord, are in the king's hand:
But, thus much, they are foul ones.

Wol. So much fairer,
And spotless, shall mine innocence arise,
When the king knows my truth.

Sur. This cannot save you;
I thank my memory, I yet remember
Some of these articles; and out they shall.
Now, if you can blush, and cry guilty, cardinal,
You'll show a little honesty.

Wol. Speak on, sir:
I dare your worst objections: if I blush,
It is, to see a nobleman want manners.

Sur. I'd rather want those, than my head. Have at you.
First, that without the king's assent, or knowledge,
You wrought to be a legate; by which power
You maim'd the jurisdiction of all bishops.

Nor. Then, that, in all you writ to Rome, or else
To foreign princes, *Ego et Rex meus*
Was still inscrib'd; in which you brought the king
To be your servant.

Suff. Then, that, without the knowledge
Either of king or council, when you went
Ambassador to the emperor, you made bold
To carry into Flanders the great seal.

Sur. Item, you sent a large commission
To Gregory de Cassalis, to conclude,
Without the king's will, or the state's allowance,
A league between his highness and Ferrara.

Suff. That, out of mere ambition, you have caus'd
Your holy hat to be stamp'd on the king's coin.

Sur. Then, that you have sent innumerable substance
(By what means got, I leave to your own conscience),
To furnish Rome, and to prepare the ways
You have for dignities; to the mere undoing
Of all the kingdom. Many more there are;
Which, since they are of you, and odious,
I will not taint my mouth with.

Cham. O my lord,
Press not a falling man too far; 'tis virtue:
His faults lie open to the laws; let them,
Not you, correct him. My heart weeps to see him
So little of his great self.

Sur. I forgive him.

Suff. Lord Cardinal, the king's further pleasure is,—
Because all those things, you have done of late
By your power legatine within this kingdom,
Fall into compass of a *præmunire*,—
That therefore such a writ be sued against you;
To forfeit all your goods, lands, tenements,
Chattels, and whatsoever, and to be
Out of the king's protection:—this is my charge.

Nor. And so we'll leave you to your meditations
How to live better. For your stubborn answer,
About the giving back the great seal to us,
The king shall know it, and, no doubt, shall thank you.
So fare you well, my little good lord cardinal.

[*Exeunt all but* WOLSEY.

Wol. So farewell to the little good you bear me.
Farewell, a long farewell to all my greatness!
This is the state of man; To-day he puts forth
The tender leaves of hope, to-morrow blossoms,
And bears his blushing honours thick upon him:
The third day comes a frost, a killing frost;
And,—when he thinks, good easy man, full surely
His greatness is a ripening,—nips his root,
And then he falls, as I do. I have ventur'd,
Like little wanton boys that swim on bladders,
This many summers in a sea of glory;
But far beyond my depth; my high-blown pride
At length broke under me; and now has left me,
Weary, and old with service, to the mercy
Of a rude stream, that must for ever hide me.
Vain pomp, and glory of this world, I hate ye;
I feel my heart new open'd: O, how wretched
Is that poor man, that hangs on princes' favours!
There is, betwixt that smile we would aspire to,
That sweet aspect of princes, and their ruin,
More pangs and fears than wars or women have;
And when he falls, he falls like Lucifer,
Never to hope again.—

Enter CROMWELL, *amazedly.*

Why, how now, Cromwell?

Crom. I have no power to speak, sir.

Wol. What, amaz'd
At my misfortunes? can thy spirit wonder,
A great man should decline? Nay, an you weep,
I am fallen indeed.

Crom. How does your grace?

Wol. Why, well;
Never so truly happy, my good Cromwell.
I know myself now; and I feel within me
A peace above all earthly dignities,
A still and quiet conscience. The king has cur'd me,
I humbly thank his grace; and from these shoulders,
These ruin'd pillars, out of pity, taken

A load would sink a navy, too much honour:
O, 'tis a burden, Cromwell, 'tis a burden,
Too heavy for a man that hopes for heaven.
Crom. I am glad, your grace has made that right use of it.
Wol. I hope, I have: I am able now methinks
(Out of a fortitude of soul I feel),
To endure more miseries, and greater far,
Than my weak-hearted enemies dare offer.
What news abroad?
Crom. The heaviest, and the worst,
Is your displeasure with the king.
Wol. God bless him!
Crom. The next is, that Sir Thomas More is chosen
Lord Chancellor in your place.
Wol. That's somewhat sudden:
But he's a learned man. May he continue
Long in his highness' favour, and do justice
For truth's sake, and his conscience; that his bones,
When he has run his course, and sleeps in blessings,
May have a tomb of orphans' tears wept on 'em!
What more?
Crom. That Cranmer is return'd with welcome,
Install'd lord archbishop of Canterbury.
Wol. That's news indeed.
Crom. Last, that the Lady Anne,
Whom the king hath in secrecy long married,
This day was view'd in open, as his queen,
Going to chapel; and the voice is now
Only about her coronation.
Wol. There was the weight that pull'd me down. O Cromwell,
The king has gone beyond me, all my glories
In that one woman I have lost for ever:
No sun shall ever usher forth mine honours,
Or gild again the noble troops that waited
Upon my smiles. Go, get thee from me, Cromwell;
I am a poor fallen man, unworthy now
To be thy lord and master: Seek the king;
That sun, I pray, may never set! I have told him
What, and how true thou art: he will advance thee;
Some little memory of me will stir him
(I know his noble nature) not to let
Thy hopeful service perish too: Good Cromwell,
Neglect him not; make use now, and provide
For thine own future safety.
Crom. O, my lord,
Must I then leave you? Must I needs forego
So good, so noble, and so true a master?
Bear witness, all that have not hearts of iron,
With what a sorrow Cromwell leaves his lord.—
The king shall have my service; but my prayers
For ever, and for ever, shall be yours.
Wol. Cromwell, I did not think to shed a tear
In all my miseries; but thou hast forc'd me
Out of thy honest truth to play the woman.
Let's dry our eyes: and thus far hear me, Cromwell;
And,—when I am forgotten, as I shall be;
And sleep in dull cold marble, where no mention
Of me more must be heard of,—say, I taught thee;
Say, Wolsey,—that once trod the ways of glory,
And sounded all the depths and shoals of honour,—
Found thee a way, out of his wreck, to rise in;
A sure and safe one, though thy master miss'd it.
Mark but my fall, and that that ruin'd me.
Cromwell, I charge thee, fling away ambition;
By that sin fell the angels, how can man then,
The image of his Maker, hope to win by't?
Love thyself last: cherish those hearts that hate thee;
Corruption wins not more than honesty;
Still in thy right hand carry gentle peace,
To silence envious tongues. Be just, and fear not:
Let all the ends, thou aim'st at, be thy country's,
Thy God's, and truth's; then if thou fall'st, O Cromwell,
Thou fall'st a blessed martyr. Serve the king;
And,—Pr'ythee, lead me in:
There take an inventory of all I have,
To the last penny: 'tis the king's: my robe,
And my integrity to heaven, is all
I dare now call mine own. O Cromwell, Cromwell,
Had I but serv'd my God with half the zeal
I serv'd my king, he would not in mine age
Have left me naked to mine enemies.
Crom. Good sir, have patience.
Wol. So I have. Farewell
The hopes of court! my hopes in heaven do dwell.
[*Exeunt.*

ACT IV.

SCENE I. *A Street in* Westminster.

Enter two Gentlemen, *meeting.*

1 *Gent.* You are well met once again.
2 *Gent.* And so are you.
1 *Gent.* You come to take your stand here, and behold
The Lady Anne pass from her coronation?
2 *Gent.* 'Tis all my business. At our last encounter,
The duke of Buckingham came from his trial.
1 *Gent.* 'Tis very true: but that time offer'd sorrow;
This, general joy.
2 *Gent.* 'Tis well: The citizens,
I am sure, have shown at full their royal minds,
(As, let them have their rights, they are ever forward)
In celebration of this day with shows,
Pageants, and sights of honour.
1 *Gent.* Never greater,
Nor, I'll assure you, better taken, sir.
2 *Gent.* May I be bold to ask what that contains,
That paper in your hand?
1 *Gent.* Yes; 'tis the list
Of those that claim their offices this day,
By custom of the coronation.
The duke of Suffolk is the first, and claims
To be high steward; next, the duke of Norfolk,
He to be earl marshal: you may read the rest.
2 *Gent.* I thank you, sir; had I not known those customs,
I should have been beholden to your paper.
But, I beseech you, what's become of Katharine,
The princess dowager? how goes her business?
1 *Gent.* That I can tell you too. The archbishop
Of Canterbury, accompanied with other
Learned and reverend fathers of his order,
Held a late court at Dunstable, six miles off
From Ampthill, where the princess lay; to which
She oft was cited by them, but appear'd not:
And, to be short, for not appearance, and
The king's late scruple, by the main assent
Of all these learned men she was divorc'd,
And the late marriage made of none effect:
Since which, she was removed to Kimbolton,
Where she remains now, sick.
2 *Gent.* Alas, good lady!—
[*Trumpets.*
The trumpets sound: stand close, the queen is coming.

THE ORDER OF THE PROCESSION.

A lively flourish of Trumpets; then, enter

1. *Two Judges.*
2. *Lord Chancellor, with the purse and mace before him.*
3. *Choristers singing.* [Musick.
4. *Mayor of London, bearing the mace. Then Garter, in his coat of arms, and on his head a gilt copper crown.*

5. *Marquis Dorset, bearing a sceptre of gold, on his head a demi-coronal of gold. With him, the Earl of Surrey, bearing the rod of silver with the dove, crowned with an earl's coronet. Collars of SS.*
6. *Duke of Suffolk, in his robe of estate, his coronet on his head, bearing a long white wand, as high-steward. With him, the Duke of Norfolk, with the rod of marshalship, a coronet on his head. Collars of SS.*
7. *A canopy borne by four of the Cinque-ports; under it, the Queen in her robe; in her hair richly adorned with pearl, crowned. On each side of her, the Bishops of London and Winchester.*
8. *The old Duchess of Norfolk, in a coronal of gold, wrought with flowers, bearing the Queen's train.*
9. *Certain Ladies or Countesses, with plain circlets of gold without flowers.*

2 *Gent.* A royal train, believe me.—These I know;—
Who's that, that bears the sceptre?
1 *Gent.* Marquis Dorset:
And that the earl of Surrey with the rod.
2 *Gent.* A bold brave gentleman: And that should be
The duke of Suffolk.
1 *Gent.* 'Tis the same; high steward.
2 *Gent.* And that my lord of Norfolk?
1 *Gent.* Yes.
2 *Gent.* Heaven bless thee;
[*Looking on the* Queen.
Thou hast the sweetest face I ever look'd on.—
Sir, as I have a soul, she is an angel;
Our king has all the Indies in his arms,
And more, and richer, when he strains that lady;
I cannot blame his conscience.
1 *Gent.* They, that bear
The cloth of honour over her, are four barons
Of the Cinque-ports.
2 *Gent.* Those men are happy; and so are all, are near her,
I take it, she that carries up the train,
Is that old noble lady, duchess of Norfolk.
1 *Gent.* It is; and all the rest are countesses.
2 *Gent.* Their coronets say so. These are stars indeed;
And, sometimes, falling ones.
1 *Gent.* No more of that.
[*Exit Procession, with a great flourish of Trumpets.*

Enter a third Gentleman.

God save you, sir! Where have you been broiling?
3 *Gent.* Among the crowd i'the abbey; where a finger
Could not be wedg'd in more; and I am stifled
With the mere rankness of their joy.
2 *Gent.* You saw
The ceremony?
3 *Gent.* That I did.
1 *Gent.* How was it?
3 *Gent.* Well worth the seeing.
2 *Gent.* Good sir, speak it to us.
3 *Gent.* As well as I am able. The rich stream
Of lords, and ladies, having brought the queen
To a prepar'd place in the choir, fell off
A distance from her; while her grace sat down
To rest a while, some half an hour, or so,
In a rich chair of state, opposing freely
The beauty of her person to the people.
Believe me, sir, she is the goodliest woman
That ever lay by man: which when the people
Had the full view of, such a noise arose
As the shrouds make at sea in a stiff tempest,
As loud, and to as many tunes: hats, cloaks
(Doublets, I think) flew up; and had their faces
Been loose, this day they had been lost. Such joy
I never saw before. Great-bellied women,
That had not half a week to go, like rams
In the old time of war, would shake the press,
And make them reel before them. No man living
Could say, *This is my wife*, there; all were woven
So strangely in one piece.
2 *Gent.* But, pray, what follow'd?
3 *Gent.* At length her grace rose, and with modest paces
Came to the altar; where she kneel'd, and, saint-[like,
Cast her fair eyes to heaven, and pray'd devoutly.
Then rose again, and bow'd her to the people:
When by the archbishop of Canterbury
She had all the royal makings of a queen;
As holy oil, Edward Confessor's crown,
The rod, and bird of peace, and all such emblems
Laid nobly on her: which perform'd, the choir,
With all the choicest musick of the kingdom,
Together sung *Te Deum.* So she parted,
And with the same full state pac'd back again,
To York Place, where the feast is held.
1 *Gent.* Sir, you
Must no more call it York Place, that is past:
For, since the cardinal fell, that title's lost;
'Tis now the king's, and call'd—Whitehall.
3 *Gent.* I know it;
But 'tis so lately altered, that the old name
Is fresh about me.
2 *Gent.* What two reverend bishops
Were those that went on each side of the queen?
3 *Gent.* Stokesly and Gardiner; the one, of Winchester
(Newly preferr'd from the king's secretary),
The other, London.
2 *Gent.* He of Winchester
Is held no great good lover of the archbishop's,
The virtuous Cranmer.
3 *Gent.* All the land knows that:
However, yet there's no great breach; when it comes,
Cranmer will find a friend will not shrink from him.
2 *Gent.* Who may that be, I pray you?
3 *Gent.* Thomas Cromwell;
A man in much esteem with the king, and truly
A worthy friend.—The king
Has made him master o'the jewel-house,
And one, already, of the privy council.
2 *Gent.* He will deserve more.
3 *Gent.* Yes, without all doubt.
Come, gentlemen, ye shall go my way, which
Is to the court, and there ye shall be my guests;
Something I can command. As I walk thither,
I'll tell ye more.
Both. You may command us, sir.
[*Exeunt.*

SCENE II. Kimbolton.

Enter KATHARINE, *Dowager, sick; led between* GRIFFITH *and* PATIENCE.

Grif. How does your grace?
Kath. O, Griffith, sick to death:
My legs, like loaden branches, bow to the earth,
Willing to leave their burden: Reach a chair;—
So,—now, methinks, I feel a little ease.
Didst thou not tell me, Griffith, as thou led'st me,
That the great child of honour, cardinal Wolsey,
Was dead?
Grif. Yes, madam; but, I think, your grace,
Out of the pain you suffer'd, gave no ear to't.
Kath. Pr'ythee good Griffith, tell me how he died:
If well, he stepp'd before me, happily,
For my example.
Grif. Well, the voice goes, madam:
For after the stout Earl Northumberland
Arrested him at York, and brought him forward
(As a man sorely tainted) to his answer,
He fell sick suddenly, and grew so ill,
He could not sit his mule.
Kath. Alas! poor man!
Grif. At last, with easy roads, he came to Leicester,
Lodg'd in the Abbey; where the reverend abbot,
With all his convent, honourably receiv'd him;
To whom he gave these words,—*O father abbot,*

An old man, broken with the storms of state,
Is come to lay his weary bones among ye;
Give him a little earth for charity!
So went to bed: where eagerly his sickness
Pursu'd him still; and, three nights after this,
About the hour of eight (which he himself
Foretold, should be his last), full of repentance,
Continual meditations, tears, and sorrows,
He gave his honours to the world again,
His blessed part to heaven, and slept in peace.

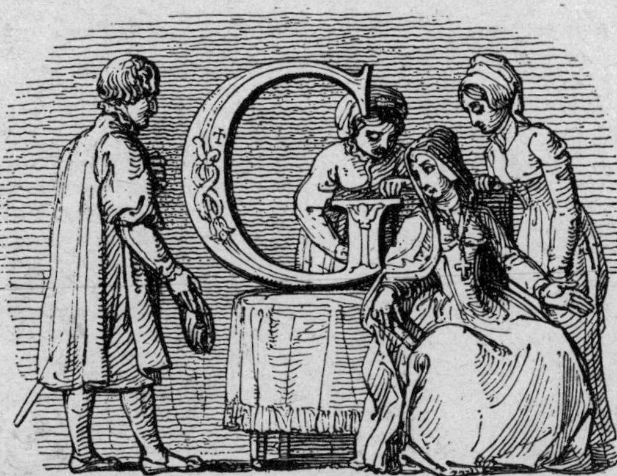

Kath. So may he rest; his faults lie gently on him!
Yet thus far, Griffith, give me leave to speak him,
And yet with charity,—He was a man
Of an unbounded stomach, ever ranking
Himself with princes; one, that by suggestion
Ty'd all the kingdom: simony was fair play;
His own opinion was his law: I' the presence
He would say untruths; and be ever double,
Both in his words and meaning: He was never,
But where he meant to ruin, pitiful:
His promises were, as he then was, mighty;
But his performance, as he is now, nothing.
Of his own body he was ill, and gave
The clergy ill example.
Grif. Noble madam,
Men's evil manners live in brass; their virtues
We write in water. May it please your highness
To hear me speak his good now?
Kath. Yes, good Griffith;
I were malicious else.
Grif. This cardinal,
Though from an humble stock, undoubtedly
Was fashion'd to much honour from his cradle.
He was a scholar, and a ripe, and good one;
Exceeding wise, fair spoken, and persuading:
Lofty, and sour, to them that lov'd him not;
But, to those men that sought him, sweet as summer.
And though he were unsatisfied in getting
(Which was a sin), yet, in bestowing, madam,
He was most princely; Ever witness for him
Those twins of learning, that he rais'd in you,
Ipswich, and Oxford! one of which fell with him.
Unwilling to outlive the good that did it;
The other, though unfinish'd, yet so famous,
So excellent in art, and still so rising,
That Christendom shall ever speak his virtue.
His overthrow heap'd happiness upon him;
For then, and not till then, he felt himself,
And found the blessedness of being little:
And, to add greater honours to his age
Than man could give him, he died, fearing God.
Kath. After my death I wish no other herald,
No other speaker of my living actions,
To keep mine honour from corruption,
But such an honest chronicler as Griffith.
Whom I most hated living, thou hast made me,
With thy religious truth, and modesty,
Now in his ashes honour: Peace be with him!—
Patience, be near me still; and set me lower:
I have not long to trouble thee.—Good Griffith,
Cause the musicians play me that sad note
I nam'd my knell, whilst I sit meditating
On that celestial harmony I go to.

Sad and solemn musick.

Grif. She is asleep: Good wench, let's sit down quiet,
For fear we wake her;—Softly, gentle Patience.

The Vision. Enter, solemnly tripping one after another, six Personages, clad in white robes, wearing on their heads garlands of bays, and golden vizards on their faces; branches of bays, or palm in their hands. They first congee unto her, then dance; and at certain changes, the first two hold a spare garland over her head; at which, the other four make reverend court'sies; then the two that held the garland, deliver the same to the other next two, who observe the same order in their changes, and holding the garland over her head: which done, they deliver the same garland to the last two, who likewise observe the same order: at which (as it were by inspiration) she makes in her sleep signs of rejoicing, and holdeth up her hands to heaven: and so in their dancing they vanish, carrying the garland with them. The musick continues.

Kath. Spirits of peace, where are ye? Are ye all gone?
And leave me here in wretchedness behind ye?
Grif. Madam, we are here.
Kath. It is not you I call for:
Saw ye none enter, since I slept?
Grif. None, madam.
Kath. No? Saw you not, even now, a blessed troop
Invite me to a banquet; whose bright faces
Cast thousand beams upon me, like the sun?
They promis'd me eternal happiness;
And brought me garlands, Griffith, which I feel
I am not worthy yet to wear: I shall,
Assuredly.
Grif. I am most joyful, madam, such good dreams
Possess your fancy.
Kath. Bid the musick leave,
They are harsh and heavy to me.
[*Musick ceases.*
Pat. Do you note,
How much her grace is alter'd on the sudden?

How long her face is drawn? How pale she looks,
And of an earthly cold? Mark you her eyes?
Grif. She is going, wench; pray, pray.
Pat. Heaven comfort her!

Enter a Messenger.

Mess. An't like your grace,—
Kath. You are a saucy fellow:
Deserve we no more reverence?
Grif. You are to blame,
Knowing, she will not lose her wonted greatness,
To use so rude behaviour: go to, kneel.
Mess. I humbly do entreat your highness' pardon;
My haste made me unmannerly: There is staying
A gentleman, sent from the king, to see you.
Kath. Admit him entrance, Griffith: But this fellow
Let me ne'er see again.
[*Exeunt* GRIFFITH *and* Messenger.

Re-enter GRIFFITH, *with* CAPUCIUS.

If my sight fail not,
You should be lord ambassador from the emperor,
My royal nephew, and your name Capucius.
Cap. Madam, the same, your servant.
Kath. O my lord,
The times, and titles, now are alter'd strangely
With me, since first you knew me. But, I pray you,
What is your pleasure with me?
Cap. Noble lady,
First, mine own service to your grace; the next,
The king's request that I would visit you;
Who grieves much for your weakness, and by me
Sends you his princely commendations,
And heartily entreats you take good comfort.
Kath. O my good lord, that comfort comes too late;
'Tis like a pardon after execution:
That gentle physick, given in time, had cured me;
But now I am past all comforts here, but prayers.
How does his highness?
Cap. Madam, in good health.
Kath. So may he ever do! and ever flourish,
When I shall dwell with worms, and my poor name
Banish'd the kingdom!—Patience, is that letter,
I caus'd you write, yet sent away?
Pat. No, madam.
[*Giving it to* KATHARINE.
Kath. Sir, I most humbly pray you to deliver
This to my lord the king.
Cap. Most willing, madam.
Kath. In which I have commended to his goodness
The model of our chaste loves, his young daughter:—
The dews of heaven fall thick in blessings on her!—
Beseeching him, to give her virtuous breeding
(She is young, and of a noble modest nature;
I hope, she will deserve well); and a little
To love her for her mother's sake, that lov'd him,
Heaven knows how dearly. My next poor petition
Is that his noble grace would have some pity
Upon my wretched women, that so long,
Have follow'd both my fortunes faithfully;
Of which there is not one, I dare avow
(And now I should not lie), but will deserve,
For virtue, and true beauty of the soul,
For honesty, and decent carriage,
A right good husband, let him be a noble;
And, sure, those men are happy that shall have them.
The last is, for my men: they are the poorest,
But poverty could never draw them from me;—
That they may have their wages duly paid them,
And something over to remember me by;
If heaven had pleas'd to have given me longer life,
And able means, we had not parted thus.
These are the whole contents;—And, good my lord,
By that you love the dearest in this world,
As you wish christian peace to souls departed,
Stand these poor people's friend, and urge the king
To do me this last right.
Cap. By heaven, I will;
Or let me lose the fashion of a man!
Kath. I thank you, honest lord. Remember me
In all humility unto his highness;
Say, his long trouble now is passing
Out of this world: tell him, in death I bless'd him,
For so I will.—Mine eyes grow dim.—Farewell,
My lord.—Griffith, farewell.—Nay, Patience,
You must not leave me yet. I must to bed;
Call in more women.—When I am dead, good wench,
Let me be us'd with honour; strew me over
With maiden flowers, that all the world may know
I was a chaste wife to my grave: embalm me,
Then lay me forth: although unqueen'd, yet like
A queen, and daughter to a king, inter me.
I can no more.—— [*Exeunt, leading* KATHARINE.

ACT V.

SCENE I. *A Gallery in the Palace.*

Enter GARDINER, Bishop *of* Winchester, *a* Page *with a Torch before him, met by* SIR THOMAS LOVELL.

Gar. It's one o'clock, boy, is't not?
Boy. It hath struck.
Gar. These should be hours for necessities,
Not for delights: times to repair our nature
With comforting repose, and not for us
To waste these times.—Good hour of night, Sir Thomas!
Whither so late?
Lov. Came you from the king, my lord?
Gar. I did, Sir Thomas; and left him at primero
With the duke of Suffolk.
Lov. I must to him too,
Before he go to bed. I'll take my leave.
Gar. Not yet, Sir Thomas Lovell. What's the matter?
It seems, you are in haste: an if there be
No great offence belongs to't, give your friend
Some touch of your late business: Affairs, that walk
(As they say, spirits do) at midnight, have
In them a wilder nature, than the business
That seeks despatch by day.
Lov. My lord, I love you;
And durst commend a secret to your ear
Much weightier than this work. The queen's in labour,
They say, in great extremity; and fear'd,
She'll with the labour end.
Gar. The fruit, she goes with,
I pray for heartily; that it may find
Good time, and live; but for the stock, Sir Thomas,
I wish it grubb'd up now.
Lov. Methinks, I could
Cry the amen; and yet my conscience says
She's a good creature, and, sweet lady, does
Deserve our better wishes.
Gar. But, sir, sir,—
Hear me, Sir Thomas: You are a gentleman
Of mine own way; I know you wise, religious,
And, let me tell you, it will ne'er be well,—
'Twill not, Sir Thomas Lovell, take't of me,
Till Cranmer, Cromwell, her two hands, and she,
Sleep in their graves.

Lov. Now, sir, you speak of two,
The most remark'd i' the kingdom. As for Cromwell,—
Beside that of the jewel-house, he's made master
O' the rolls, and the king's secretary: further, sir,
Stands in the gap and trade of more preferments,
With which the time will load him: The archbishop
Is the king's hand and tongue; and who dare speak
One syllable against him?

Gar. Yes, yes, Sir Thomas,
There are that dare; and I myself have ventur'd
To speak my mind of him: and, indeed, this day,
Sir (I may tell it you), I think, I have
Incensed the lords o' the council, that he is
(For so I know he is, they know he is)
A most arch heretick, a pestilence
That does infect the land: with which they moved,
Have broken with the king; who hath so far
Given ear to our complaint (of his great grace
And princely care; foreseeing those fell mischiefs
Our reasons laid before him), he hath commanded
To-morrow morning to the council board
He be convented. He's a rank weed, Sir Thomas,
And we must root him out. From your affairs,
I hinder you too long: good night, Sir Thomas.

Lov. Many good nights, my lord: I rest your servant. [*Exeunt* GARDINER *and* Page.

As LOVELL *is going out, enter the* King, *and the* DUKE OF SUFFOLK.

K. Hen. Charles, I will play no more to-night;
My mind's not on 't, you are too hard for me.

Suff. Sir, I did never win of you before.

K. Hen. But little, Charles;
Nor shall not, when my fancy's on my play.—
Now, Lovell, from the queen what is the news?

Lov. I could not personally deliver to her
What you commanded me, but by her woman
I sent your message; who return'd her thanks
In the greatest humbleness, and desir'd your highness
Most heartily to pray for her.

K. Hen. What say'st thou? ha!
To pray for her? what, is she crying out?

Lov. So said her woman; and that her sufferance made
Almost each pang a death.

K. Hen. Alas, good lady!

Suff. God safely quit her of her burden, and
With gentle travail, to the gladding of
Your highness with an heir!

K. Hen. 'Tis midnight, Charles,
Pr'ythee, to bed; and in thy prayers remember
The estate of my poor queen. Leave me alone;
For I must think of that, which company
Would not be friendly to.

Suff. I wish your highness
A quiet night, and my good mistress will
Remember in my prayers.

K. Hen. Charles, good night.— [*Exit* SUFFOLK.

Enter SIR ANTONY DENNY.

Well, sir, what follows?

Den. Sir, I have brought my lord the archbishop,
As you commanded me.

K. Hen. Ha! Canterbury?

Den. Ay, my good lord.

K. Hen. 'Tis true: Where is he, Denny?

Den. He attends your highness' pleasure.

K. Hen. Bring him to us. [*Exit* DENNY.

Lov. This is about that which the bishop spake:
I am happily come hither. [*Aside.*

Re-enter DENNY, *with* CRANMER.

K. Hen. Avoid the gallery. [LOVELL *seems to stay.*
Ha!—I have said.—Be gone.
What!— [*Exeunt* LOVELL *and* DENNY.

Cran. I am fearful:—Wherefore frowns he thus?
'Tis his aspect of terror. All's not well.

K. Hen. How now, my lord? You do desire to know
Wherefore I sent for you.

Cran. It is my duty
To wait your highness' pleasure.

K. Hen. 'Pray you, arise,
My good and gracious lord of Canterbury.
Come, you and I must walk a turn together;
I have news to tell you: Come, come, give me your hand.
Ah, my good lord, I grieve at what I speak,
And am right sorry to repeat what follows:
I have, and most unwillingly, of late
Heard many grievous, I do say, my lord,
Grievous complaints of you: which, being consider'd,
Have mov'd us and our council, that you shall
This morning come before us; where, I know,
You cannot with such freedom purge yourself,
But that, till further trial, in those charges
Which will require your answer, you must take
Your patience to you, and be well contented
To make your house our Tower: You a brother of us,
It fits we thus proceed, or else no witness
Would come against you.

Cran. I humbly thank your highness:
And am right glad to catch this good occasion
Most thoroughly to be winnow'd, where my chaff
And corn shall fly asunder: for, I know,
There's none stands under more calumnious tongues,
Than I myself, poor man.

K. Hen. Stand up, good Canterbury;
Thy truth, and thy integrity, is rooted
In us, thy friend: Give me thy hand, stand up;
Pr'ythee, let's walk. Now, by my holy dame,
What manner of man are you? My lord, I look'd
You would have given me your petition, that
I should have ta'en some pains to bring together
Yourself and your accusers; and to have heard you
Without indurance, further.

Cran. Most dread liege,
The good I stand on is my truth, and honesty;
If they shall fail, I, with mine enemies,
Will triumph o'er my person; which I weigh not,
Being of those virtues vacant. I fear nothing
What can be said against me.

K. Hen. Know you not how
Your state stands i' the world, with the whole world?
Your enemies are many, and not small; their practices
Must bear the same proportion: and not ever
The justice and the truth o' the question carries
The due o' the verdict with it: At what ease
Might corrupt minds procure knaves as corrupt
To swear against you? such things have been done.
You are potently opposed; and with a malice
Of as great size. Ween you of better luck,
I mean, in perjur'd witness, than your master,
Whose minister you are, whiles here he liv'd
Upon this naughty earth? Go to, go to;
You take a precipice for no leap of danger,
And woo your own destruction.

Cran. God, and your majesty,
Protect mine innocence, or I fall into
The trap is laid for me!

K. Hen. Be of good cheer;
They shall no more prevail, than we give way to.
Keep comfort to you; and this morning see
You do appear before them; if they shall chance,
In charging you with matters, to commit you,
The best persuasions to the contrary
Fail not to use, and with what vehemency

The occasion shall instruct you: if entreaties
Will render you no remedy, this ring
Deliver them, and your appeal to us
There make before them.—Look, the good man weeps!
He's honest, on mine honour. God's blest mother!
I swear, he is true hearted; and a soul
None better in my kingdom.—Get you gone,
And do as I have bid you.—[*Exit* CRANMER.]
He has strangled
His language in his tears.

Enter an old Lady.

Gent. [*Within.*] Come back; What mean you?
Lady. I'll not come back: the tidings that I bring
Will make my boldness manners.—Now, good angels
Fly o'er thy royal head, and shade thy person
Under their blessed wings!
K. Hen. Now, by thy looks
I guess thy message. Is the queen deliver'd?
Say, ay; and of a boy.
Lady. Ay, ay, my liege;
And of a lovely boy: The God of heaven
Both now and ever bless her!—'tis a girl,
Promises boys hereafter. Sir, your queen
Desires your visitation, and to be
Acquainted with this stranger; 'tis as like you,
As cherry is to cherry.
K. Hen. Lovell,—

Enter LOVELL.

Lov. Sir,
K. Hen. Give her an hundred marks. I'll to the queen. [*Exit* King.
Lady. An hundred marks! By this light I'll have more.
An ordinary groom is for such payment.
I will have more, or scold it out of him.
Said I for this, the girl is like to him?
I will have more, or else unsay't: and now
While it is hot, I'll put it to the issue. [*Exeunt.*

SCENE II. *Lobby before the Council Chamber.*

Enter CRANMER; Servants, Doorkeeper, *&c. attending.*

Cran. I hope, I am not too late; and yet the gentleman,
That was sent to me from the council, pray'd me
To make great haste. All fast? what means this?—Hoa!
Who waits there?—Sure you know me?
D. Keep. Yes, my lord;
But yet I cannot help you.
Cran. Why?
D. Keep. Your grace must wait till you be call'd for.

Enter DOCTOR BUTTS.

Cran. So.
Butts. This is a piece of malice. I am glad,
I came this way so happily. The king
Shall understand it presently. [*Exit* BUTTS.
Cran. [*Aside.*] 'Tis Butts,
The king's physician; As he past along,
How earnestly he cast his eyes upon me!
Pray heaven, he sound not my disgrace! For certain,
This is of purpose lay'd by some that hate me
(God turn their hearts! I never sought their malice),
To quench mine honour: they would shame to make me
Wait else at door; a fellow counsellor,
Among boys, grooms, and lackeys. But their pleasures
Must be fulfilled, and I attend with patience.

Enter, at a Window above, the King *and* BUTTS.

Butts. I'll show your grace the strangest sight,—
K. Hen. What's that, Butts?
Butts. I think, your highness saw this many a day.
K. Hen. Body o' me, where is it?
Butts. There, my lord:
The high promotion of his grace of Canterbury;
Who holds his state at door, 'mongst pursuivants,
Pages, and footboys.
K. Hen. Ha! 'Tis he, indeed:
Is this the honour they do one another?
'Tis well, there's one above them yet. I had thought
They had parted so much honesty among them
(At least, good manners) as not thus to suffer
A man of his place, and so near our favour,
To dance attendance on their lordships' pleasures,
And at the door too, like a post with packets.
By holy Mary, Butts, there's knavery:
Let them alone, and draw the curtain close;
We shall hear more anon.— [*Exeunt.*

THE COUNCIL CHAMBER.

Enter the Lord Chancellor, *the* DUKE OF SUFFOLK, EARL OF SURREY, Lord Chamberlain, GARDINER, *and* CROMWELL. *The* Chancellor *places himself at the upper end of the table on the left hand; a seat being left void above him, as for the* ARCHBISHOP OF CANTERBURY. *The rest seat themselves in order on each side.* CROMWELL *at the lower end, as Secretary.*

Chan. Speak to the business, master secretary:
Why are we met in council?
Crom. Please your honours,
The chief cause concerns his grace of Canterbury.
Gar. Has he had knowledge of it?
Crom. Yes.
Nor. Who waits there?
D. Keep. Without, my noble lords?
Gar. Yes.
D. Keep. My lord archbishop;
And has done half an hour, to know your pleasures.
Chan. Let him come in.
D. Keep. Your grace may enter now.
[CRANMER *approaches the Council-table.*
Chan. My good lord archbishop, I am very sorry
To sit here at this present, and behold
That chair stand empty: But we all are men,
In our own natures frail, and capable
Of our flesh, few are angels: out of which frailty,
And want of wisdom, you, that best should teach us,
Have misdemean'd yourself, and not a little,
Toward the king first, then his laws, in filling
The whole realm, by your teaching, and your chaplains
(For so we are inform'd), with new opinions,
Divers, and dangerous; which are heresies,
And, not reform'd, may prove pernicious.
Gar. Which reformation must be sudden too,
My noble lords: for those that tame wild horses,
Pace them not in their hands to make them gentle;
But stop their mouths with stubborn bits, and spur them,
Till they obey the manage. If we suffer
(Out of our easiness, and childish pity
To one man's honour) this contagious sickness,
Farewell, all physick: And what follows then?
Commotions, uproars, with a general taint
Of the whole state: as of late days our neighbours,
The upper Germany, can dearly witness,
Yet freshly pitied in our memories.
Cran. My good lords, hitherto, in all the progress
Both of my life and office, I have labour'd,
And with no little study, that my teaching,
And the strong course of my authority,
Might go one way, and safely! and the end
Was ever, to do well: nor is there living

(I speak it with a single heart, my lords)
A man, that more detests, more stirs against,
Both in his private conscience, and his place,
Defacers of a public peace, than I do.
'Pray heaven, the king may never find a heart
With less allegiance in it! Men, that make
Envy and crooked malice, nourishment,
Dare bite the best. I do beseech your lordships,
That in this case of justice, my accusers,
Be what they will, may stand forth face to face
And freely urge against me.

Suff. Nay, my lord,
That cannot be; you are a counsellor,
And, by that virtue, no man dare accuse you.

Gar. My lord, because we have business of more moment,
We will be short with you. 'Tis his highness' pleasure,
And our consent, for better trial of you,
From hence you be committed to the Tower;
Where, being but a private man again,
You shall know many dare accuse you boldly,
More than, I fear, you are provided for.

Cran. Ah, my good lord of Winchester, I thank you,
You are always my good friend; if you will pass;
I shall both find your lordship judge and juror,
You are so merciful: I see your end,
'Tis my undoing: Love, and meekness, lord,
Become a churchman better than ambition;
Win straying souls with modesty again,
Cast none away. That I shall clear myself,
Lay all the weight ye can upon my patience,
I make as little doubt, as you do conscience,
In doing daily wrongs. I could say more,
But reverence to your calling makes me modest.

Gar. My lord, my lord, you are a sectary,
That's the plain truth; your painted gloss discovers,
To men that understand you, words and weakness.

Crom. My lord of Winchester, you are a little,
By your good favour, too sharp; men so noble,
However faulty, yet should find respect
For what they have been: 'tis a cruelty,
To load a falling man.

Gar. Good master secretary,
I cry your honour mercy; you may, worst
Of all this table, say so.

Crom. Why, my lord?

Gar. Do not I know you for a favourer
Of this new sect? ye are not sound.

Crom. Not sound?

Gar. Not sound, I say.

Crom. 'Would you were half so honest;
Men's prayers then would seek you, not their fears.

Gar. I shall remember this bold language.

Crom. Do.
Remember your bold life too.

Chan. This is too much;
Forbear, for shame, my lords.

Gar. I have done.

Crom. And I.

Chan. Then thus for you, my lord,—It stands agreed,
I take it, by all voices, that forthwith
You be convey'd to the Tower a prisoner;
There to remain, till the king's further pleasure
Be known unto us: Are you all agreed, lords?

All. We are.

Cran. Is there no other way of mercy,
But I must needs to the Tower, my lords?

Gar. What other
Would you expect? You are strangely troublesome!
Let some of the guard be ready there.

Enter Guard.

Cran. For me?
Must I go like a traitor thither?

Gar. Receive him,
And see him safe i' the Tower.

Cran. Stay, good my lords,
I have a little yet to say. Look there, my lords;
By virtue of that ring, I take my cause
Out of the gripes of cruel men, and give it
To a most noble judge, the king my master.

Chan. This is the king's ring.

Sur. 'Tis no counterfeit.

Suff. 'Tis the right ring, by heaven: I told ye all,
When we first put this dangerous stone a rolling,
'Twould fall upon ourselves.

Nor. Do you think, my lords,
The king will suffer but the little finger
Of this man to be vex'd?

Chan. 'Tis now too certain:
How much more is his life in value with him?
'Would I were fairly out on't.

Crom. My mind gave me,
In seeking tales, and informations,
Against this man, (whose honesty the devil
And his disciples only envy at),
Ye blew the fire that burns ye: Now have at ye.

Enter the King, *frowning on them; takes his seat.*

Gar. Dread sovereign, how much are we bound to heaven
In daily thanks, that gave us such a prince;
Not only good and wise, but most religious:
One that, in all obedience, makes the church
The chief aim of his honour; and, to strengthen
That holy duty, out of dear respect,
His royal self in judgment comes to hear
The cause betwixt her and this great offender.

K. Hen. You were ever good at sudden commendations,
Bishop of Winchester. But know, I come not
To hear such flattery now, and in my presence;
They are too thin and bare to hide offences.
To me you cannot reach, you play the spaniel,
And think with wagging of your tongue to win me!
But, whatsoe'er thou tak'st me for, I am sure,
Thou hast a cruel nature, and a bloody.—
Good man, [*To* CRANMER.] sit down. Now let me see the proudest
He, that dares most, but wag his finger at thee:
By all that's holy, he had better starve,
Than but once think his place becomes thee not.

Sur. May it please your grace,—

K. Hen. No, sir, it does not please me.
I had thought, I had had men of some understanding
And wisdom of my council; but I find none.
Was it discretion, lords, to let this man,
This good man (few of you deserve that title),
This honest man, wait like a lousy footboy
At chamber door? and one as great as you are?
Why, what a shame was this? Did my commission
Bid ye so far forget yourselves? I gave ye
Power as he was a counsellor to try him,
Not as a groom; There's some of ye, I see,
More out of malice than integrity,
Would try him to the utmost, had ye mean;
Which ye shall never have, while I live.

Chan. Thus far,
My most dread sovereign, may it like your grace
To let my tongue excuse all. What was purpos'd
Concerning his imprisonment, was rather
(If there be faith in men) meant for his trial,
And fair purgation to the world, than malice;
I am sure, in me.

K. Hen. Well, well, my lords, respect him;
Take him, and use him well, he's worthy of it.
I will say thus much for him, If a prince
May be beholden to a subject, I
Am, for his love and service, so to him.
Make me no more ado, but all embrace him:
Be friends for shame, my lords.—My lord of Canterbury,
I have a suit which you must not deny me;
That is, a fair young maid that yet wants baptism,
You must be godfather, and answer for her.

Cran. The greatest monarch now alive may glory
In such an honour; how may I deserve it,
That am a poor and humble subject to you?

K. Hen. Come, come, my lord, you'd spare your spoons; you shall have
Two noble partners with you; the old duchess of Norfolk,
And lady marquis Dorset; Will these please you?
Once more, my lord of Winchester, I charge you,
Embrace, and love this man.

Gar. With a true heart,
And brother-love, I do it.

Cran. And let heaven
Witness how dear I hold this confirmation.

K. Hen. Good man, those joyful tears show thy true heart.
The common voice, I see, is verified
Of thee, which says thus, *Do my lord of Canterbury*
A shrewd turn, and he is your friend for ever.—
Come, lords, we trifle time away; I long
To have this young one made a christian.
As I have made ye one, lords, one remain;
So I grow stronger, you more honour gain. [*Exeunt.*

SCENE III. *The Palace Yard.*

Noise and tumult within. Enter Porter *and his* Man.

Port. You'll leave your noise anon, ye rascals; Do you take the court for Paris-garden? ye rude slaves, leave your gaping.

[*Within.*] Good master porter I belong to the larder.

Port. Belong to the gallows, and be hanged, you rogue: Is this a place to roar in?—Fetch me a dozen crab-tree staves, and strong ones; these are but switches to them.—I'll scratch your heads: You must be seeing christenings? Do you look for ale and cakes here, you rude rascals?

Man. Pray, sir, be patient; 'tis as much impossible
(Unless we sweep them from the door with cannons),
To scatter them, as 'tis to make them sleep
On May-day morning; which will never be:
We may as well push against Paul's, as stir them.

Port. How got they in, and be hang'd?

Man. Alas, I know not; How gets the tide in?
As much as one sound cudgel of four foot
(You see the poor remainder) could distribute,
I made no spare, sir.

Port. You did nothing, sir.

Man. I am not Samson, nor Sir Guy, nor Colbrand, to mow them down before me: but, if I spared any, that had a head to hit, either young or old, he or she, cuckold, or cuckold-maker, let me never hope to see a chine again; and that I would not for a cow, God save her.

[*Within.*] Do you hear, master Porter?

Port. I shall be with you presently, good master puppy.—Keep the door close, sirrah.

Man. What would you have me do?

Port. What should you do, but knock them down by the dozens? Is this Moorfields to muster in? or have we some strange Indian with the great tool come to court, the women so besiege us? Bless me, what a fry of fornication is at door! On my Christian conscience, this one christening will beget a thousand; here will be father, godfather, and all together.

Man. The spoons will be the bigger, sir. There is a fellow somewhat near the door, he should be a brazier by his face, for, o' my conscience, twenty of the dog-days now reign in 's nose: all that stand about him are under the line, they need no other penance: That fire-drake did I hit three times on the head, and three times was his nose discharged against me: he stands there, like a mortar-piece, to blow us. There was a haberdasher's wife of small wit near him, that railed upon me till her pink'd porringer fell off her head, for kindling such a combustion in the state. I miss'd the meteor once, and hit that woman, who cried out, *clubs!* when I might see from far some forty truncheoneers draw to her succour, which were the hope of the Strand, where she was quarter'd. They fell on; I made good my place; at length they came to the broomstaff with me, I defied them still; when suddenly a file of boys behind them, loose shot, delivered such a shower of pebbles, that I was fain to draw mine honour in, and let them win the work. The devil was amongst them, I think, surely.

Port. These are the youths that thunder at a playhouse, and fight for bitten apples; that no audience, but the Tribulation of Tower-hill, or the limbs of Limehouse, their dear brothers, are able to endure. I have some of them in *Limbo Patrum*, and there they are like to dance these three days; besides the running banquet of two beadles, that is to come.

Enter the Lord Chamberlain.

Cham. Mercy o' me, what a multitude are here!
They grow still too, from all parts they are coming,
As if we kept a fair here! Where are these porters,
These lazy knaves?—Ye have made a fine hand, fellows.
There's a trim rabble let in: Are all these
Your faithful friends o' the suburbs? We shall have
Great store of room, no doubt, left for the ladies,
When they pass back from the christening.

Port. An't please your honour
We are but men; and what so many may do,
Not being torn a pieces, we have done:
An army cannot rule them.

Cham. As I live,
If the king blame me for't, I'll lay ye all
By the heels, and suddenly; and on your heads
Clap round fines, for neglect: You are lazy knaves;
And here ye lie baiting of bombards, when
Ye should do service. Hark, the trumpets sound;
They are come already from the christening:
Go, break among the press, and find a way out
To let the troop pass fairly; or, I'll find
A Marshalsea, shall hold you play these two months.

Port. Make way there for the princess.

Man. You great fellow, stand close up, or I'll make your head ake.

Port. You i' the camblet, get up o' the rail; I'll pick you o'er the pales else. [*Exeunt.*

SCENE IV. *The Palace.*

Enter Trumpets, sounding; then two Aldermen, Lord Mayor, Garter, CRANMER, DUKE OF NORFOLK, *with his Marshal staff,* DUKE OF SUFFOLK, *two* Noblemen *bearing great standing-bowls for the christening gifts; then four* Noblemen *bearing a canopy, under which the* DUCHESS OF NORFOLK, *godmother, bearing the* Child *richly habited in a mantle, &c. Train borne by a* Lady; *then follows the* MARCHIONESS OF DORSET, *the other godmother, and Ladies. The* Troop *pass once about the stage, and* Garter *speaks.*

Gart. Heaven, from thy endless goodness, send prosperous life, long, and ever happy, to the high and mighty princess of England, Elizabeth.

Flourish. Enter King, *and* Train.

Cran. [*Kneeling.*] And to your royal grace, and the good queen,
My noble partners, and myself, thus pray:
All comfort, joy, in this most gracious lady,
Heaven ever laid up to make parents happy,
May hourly fall upon ye!

K. Hen. Thank you, good lord archbishop;
What is her name?
Cran. Elizabeth.
K. Hen. Stand up, lord.—
[*The* King *kisses the* Child.
With this kiss take my blessing: God protect thee!
Into whose hands I give thy life.
Cran. Amen.
K. Hen. My noble gossips, ye have been too prodigal:
I thank ye heartily; so shall this lady,
When she has so much English.
Cran. Let me speak, sir,
For heaven now bids me; and the words I utter
Let none think flattery, for they'll find them truth.
This royal infant (heaven still move about her!)
Though in her cradle, yet now promises
Upon this land a thousand thousand blessings,
Which time shall bring to ripeness: She shall be
(But few now living can behold that goodness),
A pattern to all princes living with her,
And all that shall succeed: Sheba was never
More covetous of wisdom, and fair virtue,
Than this pure soul shall be: all princely graces,
That mould up such a mighty piece as this is,
With all the virtues that attend the good,
Shall still be doubled on her: truth shall nurse her,
Holy and heavenly thoughts still counsel her:
She shall be lov'd, and fear'd: Her own shall bless her:
Her foes shake like a field of beaten corn,
And hang their heads with sorrow: Good grows with her:
In her days, every man shall eat in safety
Under his own vine, what he plants; and sing
The merry songs of peace to all his neighbours:
God shall be truly known; and those about her
From her shall read the perfect ways of honour,
And by those claim their greatness, not by blood.
[Nor shall this peace sleep with her: But as when
The bird of wonder dies, the maiden phœnix,
Her ashes new create another heir,
As great in admiration as herself:
So shall she leave her blessedness to one,
(When heaven shall call her from this cloud of darkness),
Who, from the sacred ashes of her honour,
Shall star-like rise, as great in fame as she was,
And so stand fix'd: Peace, plenty, love, truth, terror,
That were the servants to this chosen infant,
Shall then be his, and like a vine grow to him;
Wherever the bright sun of heaven shall shine,
His honour and the greatness of his name
Shall be, and make new nations: He shall flourish,
And, like a mountain cedar, reach his branches
To all the plains about him;——Our children's children
Shall see this, and bless heaven.
K. Hen. Thou speakest wonders.]
Cran. She shall be, to the happiness of England,
An aged princess; many days shall see her,
And yet no day without a deed to crown it.
'Would I had known no more! but she must die,
She must, the saints must have her; yet a virgin,
A most unspotted lily shall she pass
To the ground, and all the world shall mourn her.
K. Hen. O lord archbishop,
Thou hast made me now a man; never, before
This happy child, did I get any thing:
This oracle of comfort has so pleas'd me,
That, when I am in heaven, I shall desire
To see what this child does, and praise my Maker.—
I thank ye all,—To you, my good lord mayor,
And your good brethren, I am much beholden;
I have received much honour by your presence,
And ye shall find me thankful. Lead the way, lords;—
Ye must all see the queen, and she must thank ye,
She will be sick else. This day, no man think
He has business at his house; for all shall stay,
This little one shall make it holiday. [*Exeunt.*

EPILOGUE.

'Tis ten to one this play can never please
All that are here: Some come to take their ease,
And sleep an act or two; but those, we fear,
We have frighted with our trumpets; so, 'tis clear,
They'll say, 'tis naught: others, to hear the city
Abus'd extremely, and to cry,—*that's witty!*
Which we have not done neither: that, I fear
All the expected good we are like to hear
For this play at this time, is only in
The merciful construction of good women;
For such a one we show'd them; If they smile,
And say, 'twill do, I know, within a while
All the best men are ours; for 'tis ill hap,
If they hold, when their ladies bid them clap.

TROILUS AND CRESSIDA.

PERSONS REPRESENTED.

PRIAM, King *of* Troy.
HECTOR, TROILUS, PARIS, DEIPHOBUS, HELENUS, } *his Sons.*
ÆNEAS, ANTENOR, } Trojan *Commanders.*
CALCHAS, *a* Trojan *Priest, taking part with the* Greeks.
PANDARUS, *Uncle to* Cressida.
MARGARELON, *a bastard Son of* Priam.

AGAMEMNON, *the* Grecian *General.*
MENELAUS, *his Brother.*
ACHILLES, *a* Grecian *Commander.*
AJAX, ULYSSES, NESTOR, DIOMEDES, PATROCLUS. } Grecian *Commanders.*
THERSITES, *a deformed and scurrilous* Grecian.
ALEXANDER, *Servant to* Cressida.
Servant *to* Troilus; Servant *to* Paris; Servant *to* Diomedes.

HELEN, *Wife to* Menelaus.
ANDROMACHE, *Wife to* Hector.
CASSANDRA, *Daughter to* Priam; *a Prophetess.*
CRESSIDA, *Daughter to* Calchas.

Trojan *and* Greek Soldiers, *and* Attendants.

SCENE—Troy, *and the* Grecian *Camp before it.*

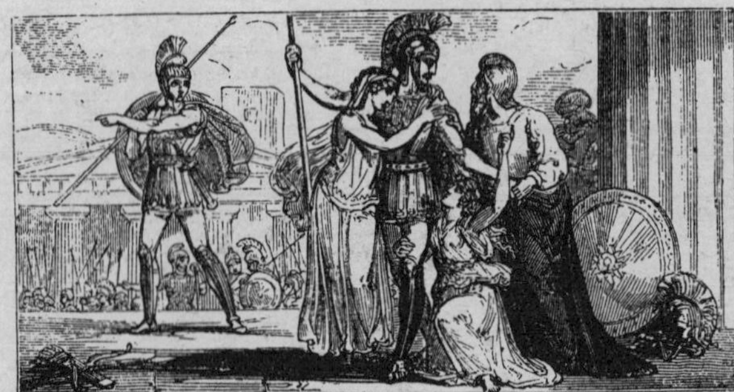

PROLOGUE.

IN Troy, there lies the scene. From isles of Greece
The princes orgulous, their high blood chaf'd,
Have to the port of Athens sent their ships,
Fraught with the ministers and instruments
Of cruel war: Sixty and nine, that wore
Their crownets regal, from the Athenian bay
Put forth toward Phrygia: and their vow is made,
To ransack Troy; within whose strong immures
The ravish'd Helen, Menelaus' queen,
With wanton Paris sleeps; and that's the quarrel.
To Tenedos they come;
And the deep-drawing barks do there disgorge
Their warlike fraughtage: Now on Dardan plains
The fresh and yet unbruised Greeks do pitch
Their brave pavilions: Priam's six-gated city,
Dardan, and Tymbria, Ilias, Chetas, Trojan,
And Antenorides, with massy staples,
And corresponsive and fulfilling bolts,
Sperr up the sons of Troy.
Now expectation, tickling skittish spirits,
On one and other side, Trojan and Greek,
Sets all on hazard:—And hither am I come
A prologue arm'd, but not in confidence
Of aúthor's pen, or actor's voice, but suited
In like conditions as our argument,—
To tell you, fair beholders, that our play
Leaps o'er the vaunt and firstlings of those broils,
'Ginning in the middle; starting thence away
To what may be digested in a play.
Like, or find fault; do as your pleasures are;
Now good, or bad, 'tis but the chance of war.

ACT I.

SCENE I. Troy. *Before* Priam's *Palace.*

Enter TROILUS *armed, and* PANDARUS.

Tro. Call here my varlet, I'll unarm again:
Why should I war without the walls of Troy,
That find such cruel battle here within?
Each Trojan, that is master of his heart,
Let him to field; Troilus, alas! hath none.

Pan. Will this geer ne'er be mended?

Tro. The Greeks are strong, and skilful to their strength,
Fierce to their skill, and to their fierceness valiant;
But I am weaker than a woman's tear,
Tamer than sleep, fonder than ignorance;
Less valiant than the virgin in the night,
And skill-less as unpractis'd infancy.

Pan. Well, I have told you enough of this: for my part, I'll not meddle nor make no further. He that will have a cake out of the wheat, must tarry the grinding.

Tro. Have I not tarried?

Pan. Ay, the grinding; but you must tarry the bolting.

Tro. Have I not tarried?

Pan. Ay, the bolting; but you must tarry the leavening.

Tro. Still have I tarried.

Pan. Ay, to the leavening: but here's yet in the word—hereafter, the kneading, the making of the cake, the heating of the oven, and the baking; nay, you must stay the cooling too, or you may chance to burn your lips.

Tro. Patience herself, what goddess e'er she be,
Doth lesser blench at sufferance than I do.
At Priam's royal table do I sit;
And when fair Cressid comes into my thoughts,—
So, traitor!—when she comes!—When is she thence?

Pan. Well, she look'd yesternight fairer than ever I saw her look, or any woman else.

Tro. I was about to tell thee,—When my heart,
As wedged with a sigh, would rive in twain;
Lest Hector, or my father should perceive me,
I have, (as when the sun doth light a storm),
Bury'd this sigh in wrinkle of a smile:
But sorrow, that is couch'd in seeming gladness,
Is like that mirth fate turns to sudden sadness.

Pan. An her hair were not somewhat darker than Helen's (well, go to), there were no more comparison between the women,—But, for my part, she is my kinswoman; I would not, as they term it, praise her,—But I would somebody had heard her talk yesterday, as I did. I will not dispraise your sister Cassandra's wit; but—

Tro. O Pandarus! I tell thee, Pandarus,—
When I do tell thee, There my hopes lie drown'd,
Reply not in how many fathoms deep
They lie indrench'd. I tell thee, I am mad
In Cressid's love: Thou answer'st, She is fair;
Pour'st in the open ulcer of my heart
Her eyes, her hair, her cheek, her gait, her voice,
Handlest in thy discourse;—O, that her hand!
In whose comparison all whites are ink,
Writing their own reproach; To whose soft seizure
The cygnet's down is harsh, and spirit of sense
Hard as the palm of ploughman! This, thou tell'st me,
As true thou tell'st me, when I say, I love her;
But, saying, thus, instead of oil and balm,
Thou lay'st in every gash that love hath given me
The knife that made it.

Pan. I speak no more than truth.

Tro. Thou dost not speak so much.

Pan. 'Faith, I'll not meddle in't. Let her be as she is: if she be fair, 'tis the better for her; an she be not, she has the mends in her own hands.

Tro. Good Pandarus! How now, Pandarus?

Pan. I have had my labour for my travel; ill-thought on of her, and ill-thought on of you; gone between and between, but small thanks for my labour.

Tro. What, art thou angry, Pandarus! what, with me?

Pan. Because she is kin to me, therefore, she's not so fair as Helen: an she were not kin to me, she would be as fair on Friday, as Helen is on Sunday. But what care I? I care not, an she were a black-a-moor; 'tis all one to me.

Tro. Say I, she is not fair?

Pan. I do not care whether you do or no. She's a fool to stay behind her father; let her to the Greeks; and so I'll tell her the next time I see her: for my part, I'll meddle nor make no more in the matter.

Tro. Pandarus,—

Pan. Not I.

Tro. Sweet Pandarus,—

Pan. Pray you, speak no more to me; I will leave all as I found it, and there an end.

[*Exit* PANDARUS. *An Alarum.*

Tro. Peace, you ungracious clamours! peace, rude sounds!
Fools on both sides! Helen must needs be fair,
When with your blood you daily paint her thus.
I cannot fight upon this argument;
It is too starv'd a subject for my sword.
But Pandarus—O Gods, how do you plague me!
I cannot come to Cressid, but by Pandar;
And he's as tetchy to be woo'd to woo,
As she is stubborn-chaste against all suit.
Tell me, Apollo, for thy Daphne's love,
What Cressid is, what Pandar, and what we?
Her bed is India; there she lies, a pearl:
Between our Ilium, and where she resides,
Let it be call'd the wild and wandering flood;
Ourself the merchant; and this sailing Pandar,
Our doubtful hope, our convoy, and our bark.

Alarum. *Enter* ÆNEAS.

Æne. How now, Prince Troilus? wherefore not afield?

Tro. Because not there; This woman's answer sorts,
For womanish it is to be from thence.
What news, Æneas, from the field to-day?

Æne. That Paris is returned home, and hurt.

Tro. By whom, Æneas?

Æne. Troilus, by Menelaus.

Tro. Let Paris bleed: 'tis but a scar to scorn;
Paris is gor'd with Menelaus horn. [*Alarum.*

Æne. Hark! what good sport is out of town to-day!

Tro. Better at home, if *would I might*, were *may.*—
But, to the sport abroad;—Are you bound thither?

Æne. In all swift haste.

Tro. Come, go we then together. [*Exeunt.*

SCENE II. *The same. A Street.*

Enter CRESSIDA *and* ALEXANDER.

Cres. Who were those went by?

Alex. Queen Hecuba, and Helen.

Cres. And whither go they?

Alex. Up to the eastern tower,
Whose height commands as subject all the vale,
To see the battle. Hector, whose patience
Is, as a virtue, fix'd, to-day was mov'd:
He chid Andromache, and struck his armourer;
And, like as there were husbandry in war,
Before the sun rose, he was harness'd light,
And to the field goes he; where every flower
Did, as prophet, weep what it foresaw
In Hector's wrath.

Cres. What was his cause of anger?

Alex. The noise goes, this: There is among the Greeks
A lord of Trojan blood, nephew to Hector;
They call him, Ajax.

Cres. Good; And what of him?

Alex. They say he is a very man *per se*,
And stands alone.

Cres. So do all men; unless they are drunk, sick, or have no legs.

Alex. This man, lady, hath robb'd many beasts of their particular additions; he is as valiant as the lion, churlish as the bear, slow as the elephant, a man into whom nature hath so crowded humours that his valour is crushed into folly, his folly sauced with discretion: there is no man hath a virtue that he hath not a glimpse of; nor any man an attaint, but he carries some stain of it: he is melancholy without cause, and merry against the hair: He hath the joints of every thing; but every thing so out of joint, that he is a gouty Briareus, many hands and no use; or purblind Argus, all eyes and no sight.

Cres. But how should this man, that makes me smile, make Hector angry?

Alex. They say, he yesterday coped Hector in the battle, and struck him down; the disdain and shame whereof hath ever since kept Hector fasting and waking.

Enter PANDARUS.

Cres. Who comes here?

Alex. Madam, your uncle Pandarus.

Cres. Hector's a gallant man.

Alex. As may be in the world, lady.

Pan. What's that? what's that?

Cres. Good morrow, uncle Pandarus.

Pan. Good morrow, cousin Cressid: What do you talk of?—Good morrow, Alexander.—How do you, cousin? When were you at Ilium?

Cres. This morning, uncle.

Pan. What were you talking of, when I came? Was Hector armed, and gone, ere ye came to Ilium? Helen was not up, was she?

Cres. Hector was gone; but Helen was not up.

Pan. E'en so; Hector was stirring early.

Cres. That were we talking of, and of his anger.

Pan. Was he angry?

Cres. So he says here.

Pan. True, he was so; I know the cause too: he'll lay about him to-day, I can tell them that; and there is Troilus will not come far behind him; let them take heed of Troilus; I can tell them that too.

Cres. What, is he angry too?

Pan. Who, Troilus? Troilus is the better man of the two.

Cres. O, Jupiter! there's no comparison.

Pan. What, not between Troilus and Hector? Do you know a man if you see him?

Cres. Ay, if I ever saw him before, and knew him.

Pan. Well, I say, Troilus is Troilus.

Cres. Then you say as I say; for I am sure, he is not Hector.

Pan. No, nor Hector is not Troilus, in some degrees.

Cres. 'Tis just to each of them; he is himself.

Pan. Himself? Alas, poor Troilus! I would, he were,——

Cres. So he is.

Pan. ——Condition, I had gone barefoot to India.

Cres. He is not Hector.

Pan. Himself? no, he's not himself—'Would 'a were himself! Well, the Gods are above; Time must friend or end: Well, Troilus, well, —I would, my heart were in her body!—No, Hector is not a better man than Troilus.

Cres. Excuse me.

Pan. He is elder.

Cres. Pardon me, pardon me.

Pan. The other's not come to't; you shall tell me another tale when the other's come to't. Hector shall not have his wit this year.

Cres. He shall not need it, if he have his own.

Pan. Nor his qualities;—

Cres. No matter.

Pan. Nor his beauty.

Cres. 'Twould not become him, his own's better.

Pan. You have no judgment, neice: Helen herself swore the other day, that Troilus, for a brown favour (for so 'tis, I must confess),—Not brown neither.

Cres. No, but brown.

Pan. 'Faith, to say truth, brown and not brown.

Cres. To say the truth, true and not true.

Pan. She prais'd his complexion above Paris.

Cres. Why, Paris hath colour enough.

Pan. So he has.

Cres. Then, Troilus should have too much: if she praised him above, his complexion is higher than his; he having colour enough, and the other higher, is too flaming a praise for a good complexion. I had as lief, Helen's golden tongue had commended Troilus for a copper nose.

Pan. I swear to you, I think Helen loves him better than Paris.

Cres. Then she's a merry Greek, indeed.

Pan. Nay, I am sure she does. She came to him the other day into a compass'd window,—and, you know, he has not pass'd three or four hairs on his chin.

Cres. Indeed a tapster's arithmetick may soon bring his particulars therein to a total.

Pan. Why, he is very young: and yet will he, within three pound, lift as much as his brother Hector.

Cres. Is he so young a man, and so old a lifter?

Pan. But, to prove to you that Helen loves him;—she came, and puts me her white hand to his cloven chin,—

Cres. Juno have mercy!—How came it cloven?

Pan. Why, you know, 'tis dimpled: I think, his smiling becomes him better than any man in all Phrygia.

Cres. O, he smiles valiantly.

Pan. Does he not?

Cres. O yes, an 'twere a cloud in autumn.

Pan. Why, go to then:—But to prove to you that Helen loves Troilus,——

Cres. Troilus will stand to the proof, if you'll prove it so.

Pan. Troilus? why, he esteems her no more than I esteem an addle egg.

Cres. If you love an addle egg as well as you love an idle head, you would eat chickens i' the shell.

Pan. I cannot choose but laugh to think how she tickled his chin;—Indeed, she has a marvellous white hand, I must needs confess.

Cres. Without the rack.

Pan. And she takes upon her to spy a white hair on his chin.

Cres. Alas poor chin, many a wart is richer.

Pan. But there was such laughing:—Queen Hecuba laughed, that her eyes ran o'er.

Cres. With mill-stones.

Pan. And Cassandra laughed.

Cres. But there was a more temperate fire under the pot of her eyes;—Did her eyes run o'er too?

Pan. And Hector laughed.

Cres. At what was all this laughing?

Pan. Marry, at the white hair that Helen spied on Troilus' chin.

Cres. An't had been a green hair, I should have laughed too.

Pan. They laughed not so much at the hair, as at his pretty answer.

Cres. What was his answer?

Pan. Quoth she, *Here's but one and fifty hairs on your chin, and one of them is white.*

Cres. This is her question.

Pan. That's true; make no question of that. *One and fifty hairs*, quoth he, *and one white: That white hair is my father, and all the rest are his sons.* Jupiter! quoth she, *which of these hairs is Paris my husband? The forked one*, quoth he; *pluck it out, and give it him.* But, there was such laughing! and Helen so blushed, and Paris so chafed, and all the rest so laughed, that it passed.

Cres. So let it now; for it has been a great while going by.

Pan. Well, cousin, I told you a thing yesterday; think on't.

Cres. So I do.

Pan. I'll be sworn, 'tis true; he will weep you, an 'twere a man born in April.

Cres. And I'll spring up in his tears, an 'twere a nettle against May. [*A Retreat sounded.*

Pan. Hark, they are coming from the field: Shall we stand up here, and see them, as they pass toward Ilium? good niece, do; sweet niece Cressida.

Cres. At your pleasure.

Pan. Here, here, here's an excellent place; here we may see most bravely: I'll tell you them all by their names, as they pass by; but mark Troilus above the rest.

ÆNEAS *passes over the stage.*

Cres. Speak not so loud.

Pan. That's Æneas; Is not that a brave man? he's one of the flowers of Troy, I can tell you; But mark Troilus; you shall see anon.

Cres. Who's that?

ANTENOR *passes over.*

Pan. That's Antenor: he has a shrewd wit, I can tell you; and he's a man good enough: he's one o' the soundest judgments in Troy, whosoever, and a proper man of person:—

When comes Troilus?—I'll show you Troilus anon; if he see me, you shall see him nod at me.

Cres. Will he give you the nod?

Pan. You shall see.

Cres. If he do, the rich shall have more.

HECTOR *passes over.*

Pan. That's Hector, that, that, look you, that; There's a fellow!—Go thy way, Hector;—There's a brave man, niece. O brave Hector!—Look, how he looks! there's a countenance: Is't not a brave man?

Cres. O, a brave man!

Pan. Is 'a not? It does a man's heart good—Look you what hacks are on his helmet? look you yonder, do you see? look you there! There's no jesting: there's laying on; take't off who will, as they say: there be hacks!

Cres. Be those with swords?

PARIS *passes over.*

Pan. Swords? any thing, he cares not: an the devil come to him, it's all one: By god's lid, it does one's heart good:—Yonder comes Paris, yonder comes Paris: look ye yonder, niece; Is't not a gallant man too, is't not?—Why, this is brave now.—Who said he came hurt home to-day? he's not hurt: why this will do Helen's heart good now. Ha! would I could see Troilus now!—you shall see Troilus anon.

Cres. Who's that?

HELENUS *passes over.*

Pan. That's Helenus,—I marvel where Troilus is:—That's Helenus;—I think he went not forth to-day:—That's Helenus.

Cres. Can Helenus fight, uncle?

Pan. Helenus? no:—yes, he'll fight indifferent well:—I marvel, where Troilus is!—Hark; do you not hear the people cry, Troilus?—Helenus is a priest.

Cres. What sneaking fellow comes yonder?

TROILUS *passes over.*

Pan. Where? yonder? that's Deiphobus: 'Tis Troilus! there's a man, niece!—Hem!—Brave Troilus! the prince of chivalry!

Cres. Peace, for shame, peace!

Pan. Mark him; Note him;—O brave Troilus!—look well upon him, niece; look you, how his sword is bloodied, and his helm more hacked than Hector's: And how he looks, and how he goes!—O admirable youth! he ne'er saw three and twenty. Go thy way, Troilus, go thy way; had I a sister were a grace, or a daughter a goddess, he should take his choice. O admirable man! Paris?—Paris is dirt to him; and, I warrant, Helen, to change, would give an eye to boot.

Forces *pass over the stage.*

Cres. Here come more.

Pan. Asses, fools, dolts! chaff and bran, chaff and bran! porridge after meat! I could live and die i'the eyes of Troilus. Ne'er look, ne'er look; the eagles are gone; crows and daws, crows and daws! I had rather be such a man as Troilus, than Agamemnon and all Greece.

Cres. There is among the Greeks, Achilles; a better man than Troilus.

Pan. Achilles? a drayman, a porter, a very camel.

Cres. Well, well.

Pan, Well, well?—Why, have you any discretion? have you any eyes? Do you know what a man is? Is not birth, beauty, good shape, discourse, manhood, learning, gentleness, virtue, youth, liberality, and such like, the spice and salt that season a man?

Cres. Ay, a minced man: and then to be baked with no date in the pie,—for then the man's date is out.

Pan. You are such a woman! one knows not at what ward you lie.

Cres. Upon my back, to defend my belly; upon my wit to defend my wiles; upon my secrecy, to defend mine honesty; my mask, to defend my beauty; and you, to defend all these: and at all these wards I lie, at a thousand watches.

Pan. Say one of your watches.

Cres. Nay, I'll watch you for that; and that's one of the chiefest of them too; if I cannot ward what I would not have hit, I can watch you for telling how I took the blow; unless it swell past hiding, and then it is past watching.

Pan. You are such another!

Enter Troilus' Boy.

Boy. Sir, my lord would instantly speak with you.

Pan. Where?

Boy. At your own house; there he unarms him.

Pan. Good boy, tell him I come: [*Exit* Boy.
I doubt he be hurt.—Fare ye well, good niece.

Cres. Adieu, uncle.

Pan. I'll be with you, niece, by and by.

Cres. To bring, uncle,——

Pan. Ay, a token from Troilus.

Cres. By the same token—you are a bawd.—
[*Exit* PANDARUS.

Words, vows, griefs, tears, and love's full sacrifice,
He offers in another's enterprise:
But more in Troilus thousand fold I see
Than in the glass of Pandar's praise may be;
Yet hold I off. Women are angels wooing:
Things won are done, joy's soul lies in the doing:
That she belov'd knows nought, that knows not this,—
Men prize the thing ungain'd more than it is:
That she was never yet, that ever knew
Love got so sweet, as when desire did sue:
Therefore this maxim out of love I teach,—
Achievement is command; ungain'd, beseech:
Then though my heart's content firm love doth bear,
Nothing of that shall from mine eyes appear.
[*Exit.*

SCENE III.

The Grecian *Camp. Before* Agamemnon's *Tent.*

Trumpets. Enter AGAMEMNON, NESTOR, ULYSSES, MENELAUS, *and Others.*

Agam. Princes,
What grief hath set the jaundice on your cheeks?
The ample proposition, that hope makes
In all designs begun on earth below,
Fails in the promis'd largeness; checks and disasters
Grow in the veins of actions highest rear'd:
As knots, by the conflux of meeting sap,
Infect the sound pine, and divert his grain
Tortive and errant from his course of growth.
Nor, princes, is it matter new to us,
That we come short of our suppose so far,
That, after seven years' siege, yet Troy walls stand;
Sith every action that hath gone before,
Whereof we have record, trial did draw
Bias and thwart, not answering the aim,
And that unbodied figure of the thought
That gav'st surmised shape. Why then, you princes,
Do you with cheeks abash'd behold our works;
And think them shames, which are, indeed, nought else
But the protractive trials of great Jove,
To find persistive constancy in men?
The fineness of which metal is not found
In fortune's love: for then, the bold and coward,
The wise and fool, the artist and unread,
The hard and soft, seem all affin'd and kin:
But, in the wind and tempest of her frown,
Distinction, with a broad and powerful fan,
Puffing at all, winnows the light away;

And what hath mass, or matter by itself
Lies rich in virtue, and unmingled.
Nest. With due observance of thy godlike seat,
Great Agamemnon, Nestor shall apply
Thy latest words. In the reproof of chance
Lies the true proof of men: The sea being smooth,
How many shallow bauble boats dare sail
Upon her patient breast, making their way
With those of nobler bulk;
But let the ruffian Boreas once enrage
The gentle Thetis, and, anon, behold
The strong-ribb'd bark through liquid mountains cut,
Bounding between the two moist elements,
Like Perseus' horse: Where's then the saucy boat,
Whose weak untimber'd sides but even now
Co-rival'd greatness? either to harbour fled,
Or made a toast for Neptune. Even so
Doth valour's show, and valour's worth divide,
In storms of fortune: For, in her ray and brightness,
The herd hath more annoyance by the brize,
Than by the tiger: but when the splitting wind
Makes flexible the knees of knotted oaks,
And flies fled under shade, Why, then, the thing of courage,
As rous'd with rage, with rage doth sympathise,
And, with an accent tun'd in self-same key,
Returns to chiding fortune.
Ulyss. Agamemnon,—
Thou great commander, nerve and bone of Greece,
Heart of our numbers, soul and only spirit,
In whom the tempers and the minds of all
Should be shut up,—hear what Ulysses speaks.
Besides the applause and approbation,
The which,—most mighty for thy place and sway,— [*To* AGAMEMNON.
And thou most reverend for thy stretch'd-out life,— [*To* NESTOR.
I give to both your speeches,—which were such,
As Agamemnon and the hand of Greece
Should hold up high in brass; and such again,
As venerable Nestor, hatch'd in silver,
Should with a bond of air (strong as the axletree
On which heaven rides) knit all the Greekish ears
To his experienc'd tongue,—yet let it please both,—
Thou great and wise,—to hear Ulysses speak.
Agam. Speak, prince of Ithaca; and be't of less expect
That matter needless, of importless burden,
Divide thy lips; than we are confident,
When rank Thersites opes his mastiff jaws,
We shall hear musick, wit, and oracle.
Ulyss. Troy, yet upon his basis, had been down,
And the great Hector's sword had lack'd a master,
But for these instances.
The specialty of rule hath been neglected:
And, look, how many Grecian tents do stand
Hollow upon this plain, so many hollow factions.
When that the general is not like the hive,
To whom the foragers shall all repair,
What honey is expected? Degree being visarded,
The unworthiest shows as fairly in the mask.
The heavens themselves, the planets, and this centre,
Observe degree, priority, and place,
Insisture, course, proportion, season, form,
Office, and custom, in all line of order:
And therefore is the glorious planet, Sol,
In noble eminence enthron'd and spher'd
Amidst the other; whose med'cinable eye
Corrects the ill aspects of planets evil,
And posts, like the commandment of a king,
Sans check, to good and bad: But when the planets,
In evil mixture, to disorder wander,
What plagues, and what portents? what mutiny?
What raging of the sea? shaking of earth?
Commotion in the winds? frights, changes, horrors,
Divert and crack, rend and deracinate
The unity and married calm of states
Quite from their fixture? O, when degree is shak'd,
Which is the ladder of all high designs,
The enterprise is sick! How could communities,
Degrees in schools, and brotherhoods in cities,
Peaceful commerce from dividable shores,
The primogenitive and due of birth,
Prerogative of age, crowns, sceptres, laurels,
But by degree, stand in authentick place?
Take but degree away, untune that string,
And, hark, what discord follows! each thing meets
In mere oppugnancy: The bounded waters
Should lift their bosoms higher than the shores,
And make a sop of all this solid globe:
Strength should be lord of imbecility,
And the rude son should strike his father dead:
Force should be right; or rather right and wrong
(Between whose endless jar justice resides),
Should lose their names, and so should justice too.
Then every thing includes itself in power,
Power into will, will into appetite;
And appetite, an universal wolf,
So doubly seconded with will and power,
Must make perforce an universal prey,
And, last, eat up himself. Great Agamemnon,
This chaos, when degree is suffocate,
Follows the choking.
And this neglection of degree it is,
That by a pace goes backward, with a purpose
It hath to climb. The general's disdain'd
By him one step below; he, by the next;
That next, by him beneath: so every step,
Exampled by the first pace that is sick
Of his superior, grows to an envious fever
Of pale and bloodless emulation;
And 'tis this fever that keeps Troy on foot,
Not her own sinews. To end a tale of length,
Troy in our weakness stands, not in her strength.
Nest. Most wisely hath Ulysses here discover'd
The fever whereof all our power is sick.
Agam. The nature of the sickness found, Ulysses,
What is the remedy?
Ulyss. The great Achilles,—whom opinion crowns
The sinew and the forehead of our host,—
Having his ear full of his airy fame,
Grows dainty of his worth, and in his tent
Lies mocking our designs: With him, Patroclus,
Upon a lazy bed the livelong day
Breaks scurril jests;
And with ridiculous and awkward action
(Which, slanderer, he imitation calls)
He pageants us. Sometime, great Agamemnon,
Thy topless deputation he puts on;
And like a strutting player,—whose conceit
Lies in his hamstring, and doth think it rich
To hear the wooden dialogue and sound
'Twixt his stretch'd footing and the scaffoldage,
Such to-be-pitied and o'er-wrested seeming
He acts thy greatness in: and when he speaks,
'Tis like a chime a mending; with terms unsquar'd,
Which, from the tongue of roaring Typhon dropp'd,
Would seem hyperboles. At this fusty stuff,
The large Achilles, on his press'd bed lolling,
From his deep chest laughs out a loud applause;
Cries—*Excellent!—'tis* Agamemnon *just.*—
Now play me Nestor;—*hem, and stroke thy beard,*
As he, being drest to some oration.
That's done;—as near as the extremest ends
Of parallels; as like as Vulcan and his wife:
Yet good Achilles still cries, *Excellent!*

'Tis Nestor *right! Now play him me,* Patroclus,
Arming to answer in a night alarm.
And then, forsooth, the faint defects of age
Must be the scene of mirth; to cough, and spit,
And, with a palsy-fumbling on his gorget,
Shake in and out the rivet:—and at this sport
Sir Valour dies; cries, *O! enough,* Patroclus;—
Or give me ribs of steel! I shall split all
In pleasure of my spleen. And in this fashion,
All our abilities, gifts, natures, shapes,
Severals and generals of grace exact,
Achievements, plots, orders, preventions,
Excitements to the field, or speech for truce,
Success, or loss, what is, or is not, serves
As stuff for these two to make paradoxes.

Nest. And in the imitation of these twain
(Whom, as Ulysses says, opinion crowns
With an imperial voice) many are infect.
Ajax is grown self-will'd; and bears his head
In such a rein, in full as proud a place
As broad Achilles: keeps his tent like him:
Makes factious feasts; rails on our state of war,
Bold as an oracle: and sets Thersites
(A slave, whose gall coins slanders like a mint)
To match us in comparisons with dirt;
To weaken and discredit our exposure,
How rank soever rounded in with danger.

Ulyss. They tax our policy, and call it cowardice;
Count wisdom as no member of the war;
Forestall prescience, and esteem no act
But that of hand: the still and mental parts,—
That do contrive how many hands shall strike,
When fitness calls them on; and know by measure
Of their observant toil, the enemies' weight,—
Why, this hath not a finger's dignity:
They call this—bed-work, mappery, closet-war:
So that the ram, that batters down the wall,
For the great swing and rudeness of his poise,
They place before his hand that made the engine;
Or those, that with the fineness of their souls
By reason guide his execution.

Nest. Let this be granted, and Achilles' horse
Makes many Thetis' sons. [*Trumpet sounds.*

Agam. What trumpet? look, Menelaus.

Enter ÆNEAS.

Men. From Troy.

Agam. What would you 'fore our tent?

Æne. Is this
Great Agamemnon's tent, I pray?

Agam. Even this.

Æne. May one, that is a herald and a prince,
Do a fair message to his kingly ears?

Agam. With surety stronger than Achilles' arm
'Fore all the Greekish heads, which with one voice
Call Agamemnon head and general.

Æne. Fair leave, and large security. How may
A stranger to those most imperial looks
Know them from eyes of other mortals?

Agam. How?

Æne. Ay;
I ask, that I might waken reverence,
And bid the cheek be ready with a blush
Modest as morning when she coldly eyes
The youthful Phœbus:
Which is that god in office, guiding men?
Which is the high and mighty Agamemnon?

Agam. This Trojan scorns us; or the men of Troy
Are ceremonious courtiers.

Æne. Courtiers as free, as debonair, unarm'd,
As bending angels; that's their fame in peace:
But when they would seem soldiers, they have galls,
Good arms, strong joints, true swords; and, Jove's accord:—
Nothing so full of heart. But peace, Æneas,
Peace, Trojan; lay thy finger on thy lips!
The worthiness of praise distains his worth,
If that the prais'd himself bring the praise forth:
But what the repining enemy commends,
That breath fame blows; that praise, sole pure, transcends.

Agam. Sir, you of Troy, call you yourself Æneas?

Æne. Ay, Greek, that is my name.

Agam. What's your affair, I pray you?

Æne. Sir, pardon; 'tis for Agamemnon's ears.

Agam. He hears nought privately that comes from Troy.

Æne. Nor I from Troy come not to whisper him:
I bring a trumpet to awake his ear;
To set his sense on the attentive bent,
And then to speak.

Agam. Speak frankly as the wind;
It is not Agamemnon's sleeping hour:
That thou shalt know, Trojan, he is awake,
He tells thee so himself.

Æne. Trumpet, blow loud,
Send thy brass voice through all these lazy tents;—
And every Greek of mettle, let him know,
What Troy means fairly, shall be spoke aloud.
[*Trumpet sounds.*
We have, great Agamemnon, here in Troy
A prince call'd Hector (Priam is his father),
Who in this dull and long continued truce
Is rusty grown; he bade me take a trumpet,
And to this purpose speak. Kings, princes, lords!
If there be one among the fairest of Greece,
That holds his honour higher than his ease;
That seeks his praise more than he fears his peril;
That knows his valour, and knows not his fear;
That loves his mistress more than in confession
(With truant vows to her own lips he loves),
And dare avow her beauty and her worth,
In other arms than hers,—to him this challenge,
Hector, in view of Trojans and of Greeks,
Shall make it good, or do his best to do it,
He hath a lady, wiser, fairer, truer,
Than ever Greek did compass in his arms;
And will to-morrow with his trumpet call,
Mid-way between your tents and walls of Troy,
To rouse a Grecian that is true in love:
If any come, Hector shall honour him;
If none, he'll say in Troy, when he retires,
The Grecian dames are sun-burn'd, and not worth
The splinter of a lance. Even so much.

Agam. This shall be told our lovers, lord Æneas:
If none of them have soul in such a kind,
We left them all at home: But we are soldiers:
And may that soldier a mere recreant prove,
That means not, hath not, or is not in love!
If then one is, or hath, or means to be,
That one meets Hector; if none else, I am he.

Nest. Tell him of Nestor, one that was a man
When Hector's grandsire suck'd: He is old now;
But, if there be not in our Grecian host
One noble man, that hath one spark of fire
To answer for his love, Tell him from me,—
I'll hide my silver beard in a gold beaver,
And in my vantbrace put this wither'd brawn;
And, meeting him, will tell him that my lady
Was fairer than his grandame, and as chaste
As may be in the world: His youth in flood,
I'll prove this truth with my three drops of blood.

Æne. Now heaven forbid such scarcity of youth!

Ulyss. Amen.

Agam. Fair lord Æneas, let me touch your hand;
To our pavilion shall I lead you, sir.
Achilles shall have word of this intent;
So shall each lord of Greece, from tent to tent:
Yourself shall feast with us before you go,
And find the welcome of a noble foe.
[*Exeunt all but* ULYSSES *and* NESTOR.

Ulyss. Nestor,——

Nest. What says Ulysses?

Ulyss. I have a young conception in my brain,
Be you my time to bring it to some shape.
Nest. What is't?
Ulyss. This 'tis:
Blunt wedges rive hard knots: The seeded pride
That hath to this maturity blown up
In rank Achilles, must or now be cropp'd,
Or, shedding, breed a nursery of like evil,
To overbulk us all.
Nest. Well, and how?
Ulyss. This challenge that the gallant Hector sends,
However it is spread in general name,
Relates in purpose only to Achilles.
Nest. The purpose is perspicuous even as substance,
Whose grossness little characters sum up:
And in the publication make no strain,
But that Achilles, were his brain as barren
As banks of Libya,—though Apollo knows,
'Tis dry enough,—will with great speed of judgment,
Ay, with celerity, find Hector's purpose
Pointing on him.
Ulyss. And wake him to the answer, think you?
Nest. Yes,
It is most meet; Whom may you else oppose,
That can from Hector bring those honours off,
If not Achilles? Though't be a sportful combat,
Yet in the trial much opinion dwells;
For here the Trojans taste our dear'st repute
With their fin'st palate: And trust to me, Ulysses,
Our imputation shall be oddly pois'd
In this wild action: for the success,
Although particular, shall give a scantling
Of good or bad unto the general;
And in such indexes, although small pricks
To their subsequent volumes, there is seen
The baby figure of the giant mass
Of things to come at large. It is suppos'd,
He, that meets Hector, issues from our choice:
And choice, being mutual act of all our souls,
Makes merit her election; and doth boil,
As 'twere from forth us all, a man distill'd
Out of our virtues; Who miscarrying,
What heart receives from hence a conquering part,
To steel a strong opinion to themselves?
Which entertain'd, limbs are his instruments,
In no less working, than are swords and bows
Directive by the limbs.
Ulyss. Give pardon to my speech;—
Therefore 'tis meet, Achilles meet not Hector.
Let us, like merchants, show our foulest wares,
And think, perchance, they'll sell; if not,
The lustre of the better shall exceed,
By showing the worse first. Do not consent,
That ever Hector and Achilles meet;
For both our honour and our shame, in this,
Are dogg'd with two strange followers.
Nest. I see them not with my old eyes; what are they?
Ulyss. What glory our Achilles shares from Hector,
Were he not proud, we all should share with him:
But he already is too insolent;
And we were better parch in Africk sun,
Than in the pride and salt scorn of his eyes,
Should he 'scape Hector fair: if he were foil'd,
Why, then we did our main opinion crush
In taint of our best man. No, make a lottery;
And, by device, let blockish Ajax draw
The sort to fight with Hector: Among ourselves,
Give him allowance for the better man,
For that will physick the great Myrmidon,
Who broils in loud applause; and make him fall
His crest, that prouder than blue Iris bends.
If the dull brainless Ajax come safe off,
We'll dress him up in voices; If he fail,
Yet go we under our opinion still
That we have better men. But, hit or miss,
Our project's life this shape of sense assumes,—
Ajax, employ'd, plucks down Achilles' plumes.
Nest. Ulysses,
Now I begin to relish thy advice:
And I will give a taste of it forthwith
To Agamemnon: go we to him straight.
Two curs shall tame each other: Pride alone
Must tarre the mastiffs on, as 'twere their bone.
[*Exeunt.*

ACT II.

SCENE I. *Another part of the* Grecian *Camp.*

Enter AJAX *and* THERSITES.

Ajax. Thersites,——

Ther. Agamemnon—how if he had boils? full, all over, generally?

Ajax. Thersites,—

Ther. And those boils did run?—Say so,—did not the general run then? were not that a botchy core?

Ajax. Dog,——

Ther. Then would come some matter from him; I see none now.

Ajax. Thou bitch-wolf's son, canst thou not hear?
Feel then. [*Strikes him.*

Ther. The plague of Greece upon thee, thou mongrel beef-witted lord!

Ajax. Speak then, thou unsalted leaven, speak!
I will beat thee into handsomeness.

Ther. I shall sooner rail thee into wit and holiness: but, I think, thy horse will sooner con an oration, than thou learn a prayer without book. Thou canst strike, canst thou? a red murrain o'thy jade's tricks!

Ajax. Toads-stool, learn me the proclamation.

Ther. Dost thou think, I have no sense, thou strikest me thus?

Ajax. The proclamation,—

Ther. Thou art proclaimed a fool, I think.

Ajax. Do not, porcupine, do not; my fingers itch.

Ther. I would, thou didst itch from head to foot, and I had the scratching of thee; I would make thee the loathsomest scab in Greece. When thou art forth in the incursions, thou strikest as slow as another.

Ajax. I say, the proclamation,——

Ther. Thou grumblest and railest every hour on Achilles; and thou art as full of envy at his greatness, as Cerberus is at Proserpina's beauty, ay, that thou barkest at him.

Ajax. Mistress Thersites!

Ther. Thou shouldst strike him.

Ajax. Cobloaf!

Ther. He would pun thee into shivers with his fist, as a sailor breaks a biscuit.

Ajax. You whoreson cur! [*Beating him.*

Ther. Do, do.

Ajax. Thou stool for a witch!

Ther. Ay, do do; thou sodden witted lord! thou hast no more brain than I have in mine elbows: an assinico may tutor thee: Thou scurvy valiant ass! thou art here put to thrash Trojans; and thou art bought and sold among those of any wit, like a Barbarian slave. If thou use to beat me, I will begin at thy heel, and tell what thou art by inches, thou thing of no bowels, thou!

Ajax. You dog!

Ther. You scurvy lord!

Ajax. You cur! [*Beating him.*

Ther. Mars his idiot! do, rudeness; do, camel; do, do.

Enter ACHILLES *and* PATROCLUS.

Achil. Why, how now, Ajax? wherefore do you thus?
How, now, Thersites? what's the matter, man,

Ther. You see him there, do you?
Achil. Ay; what's the matter?
Ther. Nay, look upon him.
Achil. So I do; what's the matter?
Ther. Nay, but regard him well.
Achil. Well, why I do so.
Ther. But yet you look not well upon him: for, whosoever you take him to be, he is Ajax.
Achil. I know that, fool.
Ther. Ay, but that fool knows not himself.
Ajax. Therefore I beat thee.
Ther. Lo, lo, lo, lo, what modicums of wit he utters! his evasions have ears thus long. I have bobbed his brain, more than he has beat my bones: I will buy nine sparrows for a penny, and his *pia mater* is not worth the ninth part of a sparrow. This, lord Achilles, Ajax,—who wears his wit in his belly, and his guts in his head,—I'll tell you what I say of him.
Achil. What?
Ther. I say, this Ajax——
Achil. Nay, good Ajax.
[AJAX *offers to strike him*, ACHILLES *interposes.*
Ther. Has not so much wit——
Achil. Nay, I must hold you.
Ther. As will stop the eye of Helen's needle, for whom he comes to fight.
Achil. Peace, fool!
Ther. I would have peace and quietness, but the fool will not: he there; that he; look you there.
Ajax. O thou damned cur! I shall——
Achil. Will you set your wit to a fool's?
Ther. No, I warrant you: for a fool's will shame it.
Patr. Good words, Thersites.
Achil. What's the quarrel?
Ajax. I bade the vile owl, go learn me the tenour of the proclamation, and he rails upon me.
Ther. I serve thee not.
Ajax. Well, go to, go to.
Ther. I serve here voluntary.
Achil. Your last service was sufferance, 'twas not voluntary; no man is beaten voluntary: Ajax was here the voluntary, and you as under an impress.
Ther. Even so?—a great deal of your wit too lies in your sinews, or else there be liars. Hector shall have a great catch, if he knock out either of your brains; a' were as good crack a fusty nut with no kernel.
Achil. What, with me too, Thersites?
Ther. There's Ulysses, and old Nestor,—whose wit was mouldy ere your grandsires had nails on their toes,—yoke you like draught oxen, and make you plough up the wars.
Achil. What, what?
Ther. Yes, good sooth; To, Achilles! to, Ajax! to!
Ajax. I shall cut out your tongue.
Ther. 'Tis no matter; I shall speak as much as thou afterwards.
Patr. No more words, Thersites; peace.
Ther. I will hold my peace when Achilles' brach bids me, shall I?
Achil. There's for you, Patroclus.
Ther. I will see you hanged, like clotpoles, ere I come any more to your tents; I will keep where there is wit stirring, and leave the faction of fools. [*Exit.*
Patr. A good riddance.
Achil. Marry this, sir, is proclaimed through all our host:
That Hector, by the first hour of the sun,
Will, with a trumpet, 'twixt our tents and Troy,
To-morrow morning call some knight to arms,
That hath a stomach; and such a one, that dare
Maintain—I know not what; 'tis trash: Farewell.
Ajax. Farewell. Who shall answer him?
Achil. I know not, it is put to lottery: otherwise,
He knew his man.
Ajax. O, meaning you:—I'll go learn more of it. [*Exeunt.*

SCENE II. Troy. *A Room in* Priam's *Palace.*

Enter PRIAM, HECTOR, TROILUS, PARIS, *and* HELENUS.

Pri. After so many hours, lives, speeches spent,
Thus once again says Nestor from the Greeks;
Deliver Helen, and all damage else—
As honour, loss of time, travel expense,
Wounds, friends, and what else dear that is consum'd
In hot digestion of this cormorant war,
Shall be struck off:—Hector, what say you to't?
Hect. Though no man lesser fears the Greeks than I,
As far as toucheth my particular, yet,
Dread Priam,
There is no lady of more softer bowels,
More spungy to suck in the sense of fear,
More ready to cry out—*Who knows what follows?*
Than Hector is: The wound of peace is surety,
Surety secure; but modest doubt is called
The beacon of the wise, the tent that searches
To the bottom of the worst. Let Helen go:
Since the first sword was drawn about this question,
Every tithe soul, 'mongst many thousand dismes,
Hath been as dear as Helen; I mean of ours:
If we have lost so many tenths of ours,
To guard a thing not ours; not worth to us,
Had it our name, the value of one ten;
What merit's in that reason, which denie
The yielding of her up?
Tro. Fye, fye, my brother!
Weigh you the worth and honour of a king,
So great as our dread father, in a scale
Of common ounces? will you with counters sum
The past-proportion of his infinite?
And buckle-in a waist most fathomless,
With spans and inches so diminutive
As fears and reasons? fye, for godly shame!
Hel. No marvel, though you bite so sharp at reasons,
You are so empty of them. Should not our father
Bear the great sway of his affairs with reasons,
Because your speech hath none, that tells him so?
Tro. You are for dreams and slumbers, brother priest,
You fur your gloves with reason. Here are your reasons:
You know, an enemy intends you harm;
You know, a sword employ'd is perilous,
And reason flies the object of all harm;
Who marvels then, when Helenus beholds
A Grecian and his sword, if he do set
The very wings of reason to his heels;
And fly like chidden Mercury from Jove,
Or like a star disorb'd?—Nay, if we talk of reason,
Let's shut our gates, and sleep: Manhood and honour
Should have hare hearts, would they but fat their thoughts
With this cramm'd reason: reason and respect
Make livers pale and lustlihood deject.
Hect. Brother, she is not worth what she doth cost
The holding.
Tro. What is aught, but as 'tis valued?
Hect. But value dwells not in particular will;
It holds his estimate and dignity
As well wherein 'tis precious of itself
As in the prizer: 'tis mad idolatry,
To make the service greater than the god;
And the will dotes, that is attributive
To what infectiously itself affects,
Without some image of the affected merit.
Tro. I take to-day a wife, and my election
Is led on in the conduct of my will;
My will enkindled by mine eyes and ears,
Two traded pilots 'twixt the dangerous shores
Of will and judgment: How may I avoid,
Although my will distaste what it elected,
The wife I chose? there can be no evasion

To blench from this, and to stand firm by honour:
We turn not back the silks upon the merchant,
When we have soil'd them; nor the remainder viands
We do not throw in unrespective sieve,
Because we now are full. It was thought meet,
Paris should do some vengeance on the Greeks:
Your breath with full consent bellied his sails;
The seas and winds (old wranglers) took a truce,
And did him service! he touch'd the ports desir'd;
And, for an old aunt, whom the Greeks held captive,
He brought a Grecian queen, whose youth and freshness
Wrinkles Apollo's, and makes pale the morning.
Why keep we her? the Grecians keep our aunt:
Is she worth keeping? why, she is a pearl,
Whose price hath launch'd above a thousand ships,
And turn'd crown'd kings to merchants.
If you'll avouch, 'twas wisdom Paris went
(As you must needs, for you all cry'd—*Go, go*),
If you'll confess, he brought home noble prize,
(As you must needs, for you all clapp'd your hands,
And cry'd—*Inestimable!*) why do you now
The issue of your proper wisdoms rate;
And do a deed that fortune never did,
Beggar the estimation which you priz'd
Richer than sea and land? O theft most base;
That we have stolen what we do fear to keep!
But, thieves, unworthy of a thing so stolen,
That in their country did them that disgrace,
We fear to warrant in our native place!

Cas. [*Within.*] Cry, Trojans, cry!

Pri. What noise? what shriek is this?

Tro. 'Tis our mad sister, I do know her voice.

Cas. [*Within.*] Cry, Trojans!

Hect. It is Cassandra.

Enter CASSANDRA, *raving.*

Cas. Cry, Trojans, cry! lend me ten thousand eyes,
And I will fill them with prophetick tears.

Hect. Peace, sister, peace.

Cas. Virgins and boys, mid-age and wrinkled elders,
Soft infancy, that nothing canst but cry,
Add to my clamours! let us pay betimes
A moiety of that mass of moan to come.
Cry, Trojans, cry! practise your eyes with tears!
Troy must not be, nor goodly Ilion stand;
Our firebrand brother, Paris, burns us all.
Cry, Trojans, cry! a Helen, and a woe:
Cry, cry! Troy burns, or else let Helen go. [*Exit.*

Hect. Now, youthful Troilus, do not these high strains
Of divination in our sister work
Some touches of remorse? or is your blood
So madly hot, that no discourse of reason,
Nor fear of bad success in a bad cause,
Can qualify the same?

Tro. Why, brother Hector,
We may not think the justness of each act
Such and no other than event doth form it;
Nor once deject the courage of our minds
Because Cassandra's mad: her brainsick raptures
Cannot distaste the goodness of a quarrel,
Which hath our several honours all engag'd
To make it gracious. For my private part,
I am no more touch'd than all Priam's sons:
And Jove forbid, there should be done amongst us
Such things as might offend the weakest spleen
To fight for and maintain!

Par. Else might the world convince of levity
As well my undertakings, as your counsels:
But I attest the gods, your full consent
Gave wings to my propension, and cut off
All fears attending on so dire a project.
For what, alas! can these my single arms?
What propugnation is in one man's valour,
To stand the push and enmity of those
This quarrel would excite? Yet I protest,
Were I alone to pass the difficulties,
And had as ample power as I have will,
Paris should ne'er retract what he hath done,
Nor faint in the pursuit.

Pri. Paris, you speak
Like one besotted on your sweet delights:
You have the honey still, but these the gall;
So to be valiant is no praise at all.

Par. Sir, I propose not merely to myself
The pleasures such a beauty brings with it;
But I would have the soil of her fair rape
Wip'd off, in honourable keeping her.
What treason were it to the ransack'd queen,
Disgrace to your great worths, and shame to me,
Now to deliver her possession up,
On terms of base compulsion? Can it be,
That so degenerate a strain as this
Should once set footing in your generous bosoms?
There's not the meanest spirit on our party,
Without a heart to dare, or sword to draw,
When Helen is defended; nor none so noble,
Whose life were ill bestow'd, or death unfam'd,
Where Helen is the subject: then, I say,
Well may we fight for her, whom we know well,
The world's large spaces cannot parallel.

Hect. Paris, and Troilus, you have both said well:
And on the cause and question now in hand
Have gloz'd,—but superficially; not much
Unlike young men, whom Aristotle thought
Unfit to hear moral philosophy:
The reasons, you allege, do more conduce
To the hot passion of distemper'd blood,
Than to make up a free determination
'Twixt right and wrong; For pleasure, and revenge,
Have ears more deaf than adders to the voice
Of any true decision. Nature craves,
All dues be render'd to their owners; Now
What nearer debt in all humanity,
Than wife is to the husband? if this law
Of nature be corrupted through affection;
And that great minds, of partial indulgence
To their benumbed wills, resist the same;
There is a law in each well order'd nation,
To curb those raging appetites that are
Most disobedient and refractory.
If Helen then be wife to Sparta's king,—
As it is known she is,—these moral laws
Of nature, and of nations, speak aloud
To have her back return'd: Thus to persist
In doing wrong, extenuates not wrong,
But makes it much more heavy. Hector's opinion
Is this, in way of truth: yet, ne'ertheless,
My spritely brethren, I propend to you
In resolution to keep Helen still;
For 'tis a cause that hath no mean dependance
Upon our joint and several dignities.

Tro. Why, there you touch'd the life of our design:
Were it not glory that we more affected
Than the performance of our heaving spleens,
I would not wish a drop of Trojan blood
Spent more in her defence. But, worthy Hector,
She is a theme of honour and renown;
A spur to valiant and magnanimous deeds;
Whose present courage may beat down our foes,
And fame, in time to come, canonize us:
For, I presume, brave Hector would not lose
So rich advantage of a promis'd glory,
As smiles upon the forehead of this action,
For the wide world's revenue.

Hect. I am yours,
You valiant offspring of great Priamus.—
I have a roisting challenge sent amongst

The dull and factious nobles of the Greeks,
Will strike amazement to their drowsy spirits:
I was advertis'd, their great general slept,
Whilst emulation in the army crept;
This, I presume, will wake him. [*Exeunt.*

SCENE III.

The Grecian *Camp. Before* Achilles' *Tent.*

Enter THERSITES.

Ther. How now, Thersites? what, lost in the labyrinth of thy fury? Shall the elephant Ajax carry it thus? he beats me, and I rail at him: O worthy satisfaction! 'would, it were otherwise; that I could beat him, whilst he railed at me: 'Sfoot, I'll learn to conjure and raise devils, but I'll see some issue of my spiteful execrations. Then there's Achilles, a rare engineer. If Troy be not taken till these two undermine it, the walls will stand till they fall of themselves. O thou great thunder-darter of Olympus, forget that thou art Jove the king of gods; and, Mercury, lose all the serpentine craft of thy *Caduceus;* if ye take not that little little less-than-little wit from them that they have! which short-armed ignorance itself knows is so abundant scarce, it will not in circumvention deliver a fly from a spider, without drawing their massy irons, and cutting the web. After this, the vengeance on the whole camp! or, rather, the bone-ache! for that, methinks, is the curse dependant on those that war for a placket. I have said my prayers; and devil, envy, say Amen. What, ho! my lord Achilles!

Enter PATROCLUS.

Patr. Who's there? Thersites? Good Thersites, come in and rail.

Ther. If I could have remembered a gilt counterfeit, thou wouldest not have slipped out of my contemplation: but it is no matter; Thyself upon thyself! The common curse of mankind, folly and ignorance, be thine in great revenue! heaven bless thee from a tutor, and discipline come not near thee! Let thy blood be thy direction till thy death! then if she, that lays thee out, says—thou art a fair corse, I'll be sworn and sworn upon 't, she never shrouded any but lazars. Amen.—Where's Achilles?

Patr. What, art thou devout? wast thou in prayer?

Ther. Ay; the heavens hear me!

Enter ACHILLES.

Achil. Who's there?

Patr. Thersites, my lord.

Achil. Where, where?—Art thou come? Why, my cheese, my digestion, why hast thou not served thyself in to my table so many meals? Come, what's Agamemnon?

Ther. Thy commander, Achilles;—Then tell me, Patroclus, what's Achilles?

Patr. Thy lord, Thersites; Then tell me, I pray thee, what's thyself?

Ther. Thy knower, Patroclus; Then tell me, Patroclus, what art thou?

Patr. Thou mayest tell, that knowest.

Achil. O, tell, tell.

Ther. I'll decline the whole question. Agamemnon commands Achilles; Achilles is my lord; I am Patroclus' knower; and Patroclus is a fool.

Patr. You rascal!

Ther. Peace, fool; I have not done.

Achil. He is a privileged man.—Proceed, Thersites.

Ther. Agamemnon is a fool; Achilles is a fool; Thersites is a fool; and, as aforesaid, Patroclus is a fool.

Achil. Derive this; come.

Ther. Agamemnon is a fool to offer to command Achilles; Achilles is a fool to be commanded of Agamemnon; Thersites is a fool to serve such a fool; and Patroclus is a fool positive.

Patr. Why am I a fool?

Ther. Make that demand of the prover.—It suffices me, thou art. Look you, who comes here?

Enter AGAMEMNON, ULYSSES, NESTOR, DIOMEDES, *and* AJAX.

Achil. Patroclus, I'll speak with nobody:—
Come in with me, Thersites. [*Exit.*

Ther. Here is such patchery, such juggling, and such knavery! all the argument is, a cuckold, and a whore; a good quarrel, to draw emulous factions, and bleed to death upon! Now the dry *serpigo* on the subject! and war, and lechery, confound all! [*Exit.*

Agam. Where is Achilles?

Patr. Within his tent; but ill dispos'd, my lord.

Agam. Let it be known to him, that we are here.
He shent our messengers; and we lay by
Our appertainments, visiting of him:
Let him be told so; lest, perchance, he think
We dare not move the question of our place,
Or know not what we are.

Patr. I shall say so to him. [*Exit.*

Ulyss. We saw him at the opening of his tent;
He is not sick.

Ajax. Yes, lion-sick, sick of proud heart; you may call it melancholy, if you will favour the man; but, by my head, 'tis pride: But why, why? let him show us a cause.—A word, my lord. [*Takes* AGAMEMNON *aside.*

Nest. What moves Ajax thus to bay at him?

Ulyss. Achilles hath inveigled his fool from him.

Nest. Who? Thersites?

Ulyss. He.

Nest. Then will Ajax lack matter, if he have lost his argument.

Ulyss. No; you see he is his argument, that has his argument; Achilles.

Nest. All the better; their fraction is more our wish, than their faction: But it was a strong composure, a fool could disunite.

Ulyss. The amity that wisdom knits not, folly may easily untie. Here comes Patroclus.

Re-enter PATROCLUS.

Nest. No Achilles with him.

Ulyss. The elephant hath joints, but none for courtesy: his legs are legs for necessity, not for flexure.

Patr. Achilles bids me say—he is much sorry,
If any thing more than your sport and pleasure
Did move your greatness, and this noble state,
To call upon him; he hopes it is no other,
But, for your health and your digestion sake,
An after-dinner's breath.

Agam. Hear you, Patroclus;—
We are too well acquainted with these answers;
But his evasion, wing'd thus swift with scorn,
Cannot outfly our apprehensions.
Much attribute he hath; and much the reason
Why we ascribe it to him; yet all his virtues,—
Not virtuously on his own part beheld,—
Do, in our eyes, begin to lose their gloss;
Yea, like fair fruit in an unwholesome dish,
Are like to rot untasted. Go and tell him,
We come to speak with him: And you shall not sin,
If you do say—We think him over-proud,
And under-honest; in self-assumption greater,
That in the note of judgment; and worthier than himself
Here tend the savage strangeness he puts on;
Disguise the holy strength of their command,
And underwrite in an observing kind
His humorous predominance; yea, watch
His pettish lunes, his ebbs, his flows, as if
The passage and whole carriage of this action

Rode on his tide. Go, tell him this; and ad
That, if he overhold his price so much,
We'll none of him; but let him, like an engine
Not portable, lie under this report—
Bring action hither, this cannot go to war:
A stirring dwarf we do allowance give
Before a sleeping giant:—Tell him so.

Patr. I shall; and bring his answer presently. [*Exit.*

Agam. In second voice we'll not be satisfied,
We come to speak with him.—Ulysses, enter. [*Exit* ULYSSES.

Ajax. What is he more than another?

Agam. No more than what he thinks he is.

Ajax. Is he so much? Do you not think, he thinks himself a better man than I am?

Agam. No question.

Ajax. Will you subscribe his thought, and say—he is?

Agam. No, noble Ajax; you are as strong, as valiant, as wise, no less noble, much more gentle, and altogether more tractable.

Ajax. Why should a man be proud? How doth pride grow? I know not what pride is.

Agam. Your mind's the clearer, Ajax, and your virtues the fairer. He that is proud, eats up himself: pride is his own glass, his own trumpet, his own chronicle: and whatever praises itself but in the deed, devours the deed in the praise.

Ajax. I do hate a proud man, as I hate the engendering of toads.

Nest. And yet he loves himself: Is it not strange? [*Aside.*

Re-enter ULYSSES.

Ulyss. Achilles will not to the field to-morrow.

Agam. What's his excuse?

Ulyss. He doth rely on none;
But carries on the stream of his dispose,
Without observance or respect of any,
In will peculiar and in self-admission.

Agam. Why will he not, upon our fair request,
Untent his person, and share the air with us?

Ulyss. Things small as nothing, for request's sake only,
He makes important: Possess'd he is with greatness;
And speaks not to himself, but with a pride
That quarrels at self-breath: imagin'd worth
Holds in his blood such swoln and hot discourse,
That, 'twixt his mental and his active parts,
Kingdom'd Achilles in commotion rages,
And batters down himself: What should I say?
He is so plaguy proud, that the death tokens of it
Cry—*No recovery.*

Agam. Let Ajax go to him.—
Dear lord, go you and greet him in his tent:
'Tis said he holds you well: and will be led,
At your request, a little from himself.

Ulyss. O Agamemnon, let it not be so!
We'll consecrate the steps that Ajax makes
When they go from Achilles; Shall the proud lord,
That bastes his arrogance with his own seam;
And never suffers matter of the world
Enter his thoughts,—save such as do revolve
And ruminate himself,—shall he be worship'd
Of that we hold an idol more than he?
No, this thrice worthy and right valiant lord
Must not so stale his palm, nobly acquir'd;
Nor, by my will, assubjugate his merit,
As amply titled as Achilles is,
By going to Achilles:
That were to enlard his fat-already pride;
And add more coals to Cancer, when he burns
With entertaining great Hyperion.
This lord go to him! Jupiter forbid,
And say in thunder—*Achilles, go to him.*

Nest. O, this is well; he rubs the vein of him. [*Aside.*

Dio. And how his silence drinks up this applause! [*Aside.*

Ajax. If I go to him, with my arm'd fist I'll pash him
Over the face.

Agam. O, no, you shall not go.

Ajax. An he be proud with me, I'll pheeze his pride:
Let me go to him.

Ulyss. Not for the worth that hangs upon our quarrel.

Ajax. A paltry, insolent fellow!——

Nest. How he describes
Himself! [*Aside.*

Ajax. Can he not be sociable?

Ulyss. The raven
Chides blackness. [*Aside.*

Ajax. I will let his humours blood.

Agam. He'll be the physician, that should be the patient. [*Aside.*

Ajax. An all men
Were o' my mind,—

Ulyss. Wit would be out of fashion. [*Aside.*

Ajax. He should not bear it so,
He should eat swords first: Shall pride carry it?

Nest. An 'twould, you'd carry half. [*Aside.*

Ulyss. He'd have ten shares. [*Aside.*

Ajax. I'll knead him, I will make him supple:—

Nest. He's not yet thorough warm: force him with praises:
Pour in, pour in; his ambition is dry. [*Aside.*

Ulyss. My lord, you feed too much on this dislike. [*To* AGAMEMNON.

Nest. O noble general, do not do so.

Dio. You must prepare to fight without Achilles.

Ulyss. Why, 'tis this naming of him does him harm.
Here is a man—But 'tis before his face;
I will be silent.

Nest. Wherefore should you so?
He is not emulous, as Achilles is.

Ulyss. Know the whole world, he is as valiant.

Ajax. A whoreson dog, that shall palter thus with us!
I would, he were a Trojan!

Nest. What a vice
Were it in Ajax now——

Ulyss. If he were proud?

Dio. Or covetous of praise?

Ulyss. Ay, or surly borne?

Dio. Or strange, or self-affected?

Ulyss. Thank the heavens, lord, thou art of sweet composure;
Praise him that got thee, she that gave thee suck:
Fam'd be thy tutor, and thy parts of nature
Thrice-fam'd, beyond all erudition:
But he that disciplin'd thy arms to fight,
Let Mars divide eternity in twain,
And give him half: and, for thy vigour,
Bull-bearing Milo his addition yield
To sinewy Ajax. I will not praise thy wisdom,
Which, like a bourn, a pale, a shore confines
Thy spacious and dilated parts: Here's Nestor,—
Instructed by the antiquary times,
He must, he is, he cannot but be wise;—
But pardon, father Nestor, were your days
As green as Ajax', and your brain so temper'd,
You should not have the eminence of him,
But be as Ajax.

Ajax. Shall I call you father?

Nest. Ay, my good son.

Dio. Be rul'd by him, lord Ajax.

Ulyss. There is no tarrying here: the hart Achilles
Keeps thicket. Please it our great general
To call together all his state of war;
Fresh kings are come to Troy: To-morrow,
We must with all our main of power stand fast:

And here's a lord,—come knights from east to west,
And cull their flower, Ajax shall cope the best.

Agam. Go we to council. Let Achilles sleep:
Light boats sail swift, though greater hulks draw deep. [*Exeunt.*

ACT III.

SCENE I. Troy. *A Room in* Priam's *Palace.*

Enter PANDARUS *and a* Servant.

Pan. Friend! you; pray you, a word: Do not you follow the young lord Paris?

Serv. Ay, sir, when he goes before me.

Pan. You do depend upon him, I mean?

Serv. Sir, I do depend upon the lord.

Pan. You do depend upon a noble gentleman; I must needs praise him.

Serv. The lord be praised!

Pan. You know me, do you not?

Serv. 'Faith, sir, superficially.

Pan. Friend, know me better; I am the lord Pandarus.

Serv. I hope, I shall know your honour better.

Pan. I do desire it.

Serv. You are in the state of grace. [*Musick within.*

Pan. Grace! not so, friend; honour and lordship are my titles:—What musick is this?

Serv. I do but partly know, sir; it is musick in parts.

Pan. Know you the musicians?

Serv. Wholly, sir.

Pan. Who play they to?

Serv. To the hearers, sir.

Pan. At whose pleasure, friend?

Serv. At mine, sir, and theirs that love musick.

Pan. Command, I mean, friend.

Serv. Who shall I command, sir?

Pan. Friend, we understand not one another; I am too courtly, and thou art too cunning: At whose request do these men play?

Serv. That's to 't, indeed, sir: Marry, sir, at the request of Paris, my lord, who is there in person; with him, the mortal Venus, the heart-blood of beauty, love's invisible soul,—

Pan. Who, my cousin Cressida?

Serv. No, sir, Helen: Could you not find out that by her attributes?

Pan. It should seem, fellow, that thou hast not seen the lady Cressida. I come to speak with Paris from the prince Troilus; I will make a complimental assault upon him, for my business seeths.

Serv. Sodden business! there's a stewed phrase, indeed!

Enter PARIS *and* HELEN, *attended.*

Pan. Fair be to you, my lord, and to all this fair company! fair desires, in all fair measure, fairly guide them! especially to you, fair queen! fair thoughts be your fair pillow!

Helen. Dear lord, you are full of fair words.

Pan. You speak your fair pleasure, sweet queen.—Fair prince, here is good broken musick.

Par. You have broke it, cousin: and, by my life, you shall make it whole again; you shall piece it out with a piece of your performance:—Nell, he is full of harmony.

Pan. Truly, lady, no.

Helen. O, sir,——

Pan. Rude, in sooth; in good sooth, very rude.

Par. Well said, my lord! well, you say so in fits.

Pan. I have business to my lord, dear queen:—My lord, will you vouchsafe me a word?

Helen. Nay, this shall not hedge us out: we'll hear you sing, certainly.

Pan. Well, sweet queen, you are pleasant with me.—But (marry) thus, my lord,—My dear lord, and most esteemed friend, your brother Troilus—

Helen. My lord Pandarus; honey-sweet lord,—

Pan. Go to, sweet queen, go to:—commends himself most affectionately to you.

Helen. You shall not bob us out of our melody; If you do, our melancholy upon your head!

Pan. Sweet queen, sweet queen; that's a sweet queen, i' faith.

Helen. And to make a sweet lady sad, is a sour offence.

Pan. Nay, that shall not serve your turn; that shall it not, in truth, la. Nay, I care not for such words; no, no.—And, my lord, he desires you, that, if the king call for him at supper, you will make his excuse.

Helen. My lord Pandarus,——

Pan. What says my sweet queen,—my very very sweet queen?

Par. What exploit's in hand? where sups he to-night?

Helen. Nay, but my lord,——

Pan. What says my sweet queen?—My cousin will fall out with you. You must not know where he sups.

Par. I'll lay my life, with my disposer Cressida.

Pan. No, no, no such matter, you are wide; come, your disposer is sick.

Par. Well, I'll make excuse.

Pan. Ay, good my lord. Why should you say —Cressida? no, your poor disposer's sick.

Par. I spy.

Pan. You spy! what do you spy?—Come, give me an instrument.—Now, sweet queen.

Helen. Why, this is kindly done.

Pan. My niece is horribly in love with a thing you have, sweet queen.

Helen. She shall have it, my lord, if it be not my lord Paris.

Pan. He! no, she'll none of him: they two are twain.

Helen. Falling in, after falling out, may make them three.

Pan. Come, come, I'll hear no more of this; I'll sing you a song now.

Helen. Ay, ay, pr'ythee now. By my troth, sweet lord, thou hast a fine forehead.

Pan. Ay, you may, you may.

Helen. Let thy song be love; this love will undo us all. O, Cupid, Cupid, Cupid!

Pan. Love! ay, that it shall, i' faith.

Par. Ay, good now, love, love, nothing but love.

Pan. In good troth, it begins so:

Love, love, nothing but love, still more!
For oh, love's bow
Shoots buck and doe:
The shaft confounds,
Not that it wounds,
But tickles still the sore.

These lovers cry—Oh! Oh! they die!
Yet that which seems the wound to kill,
Doth turn oh! oh! to ha! ha! he!
So dying love lives still:
Oh! oh! awhile, but ha! ha! ha!
Oh! oh! groans out for ha! ha! ha!

Hey ho!

Helen. In love, i' faith, to the very tip of the nose.

Par. He eats nothing but doves, love; and that breeds hot blood, and hot blood begets hot thoughts, and hot thoughts beget hot deeds, and hot deeds is love.

Pan. Is this the generation of love? hot blood, hot thoughts, and hot deeds?—Why, they are vipers: Is love a generation of vipers? Sweet lord, who's a-field to-day?

Par. Hector, Deiphobus, Helenus, Antenor, and all the gallantry of Troy: I would fain have armed to-night, but my Nell would not have it so. How chance my brother Troilus went not?

Helen. He hangs the lip at something;—you know all, lord Pandarus.

Pan. Not I, honey-sweet queen.—I long to hear how they sped to-day.—You'll remember your brother's excuse?

Par. To a hair.

Pan. Farewell, sweet queen.

Helen. Commend me to your niece.

Pan. I will, sweet queen. [*Exit.*

[*A Retreat sounded.*

Par. They are come from field: let us to Priam's hall,
To greet the warriors. Sweet Helen, I must woo you
To help unarm our Hector: his stubborn buckles,
With these your white enchanting fingers touch'd,
Shall more obey, than to the edge of steel,
Or force of Greekish sinews; you shall do more
Than all the island kings, disarm great Hector.

Helen. 'Twill make us proud to be his servant, Paris:
Yea, what he shall receive of us in duty,
Give us more palm in beauty than we have;
Yea, overshines ourself.

Par. Sweet, above thought I love thee.

[*Exeunt.*

SCENE II. *The same.* Pandarus' *Orchard.*

Enter PANDARUS *and a* Servant, *meeting.*

Pan. How now? where's thy master? at my cousin Cressida's?

Serv. No, sir; he stays for you to conduct him thither.

Enter TROILUS.

Pan. O, here he comes.—How now, how now?

Tro. Sirrah, walk off. [*Exit* Servant.

Pan. Have you seen my cousin?

Tro. No, Pandarus: I stalk about her door,
Like a strange soul upon the Stygian banks
Staying for waftage. O, be thou my Charon,
And give me swift transportance to those fields,
Where I may wallow in the lily beds
Propos'd for the deserver! O gentle Pandarus,
From Cupid's shoulder pluck his painted wings,
And fly with me to Cressid!

Pan. Walk here i' the orchard, I'll bring her straight. [*Exit* PANDARUS.

Tro. I am giddy: expectation whirls me round.
The imaginary relish is so sweet
That it enchants my sense; What will it be,
When that the watry palate tastes indeed
Love's thrice-reputed nectar; death, I fear me;
Swooning destruction; or some joy too fine,
Too subtle potent, tun'd too sharp in sweetness,
For the capacity of my ruder powers:
I fear it much; and I do fear besides,
That I shall lose distinction in my joys;
As doth a battle, when they charge on heaps
The enemy flying.

Re-enter PANDARUS.

Pan. She's making her ready, she'll come straight: you must be witty now. She does so blush, and fetches her wind so short, as if she were frayed with a sprite; I'll fetch her. It is the prettiest villain: she fetches her breath as short as a new-ta'en sparrow. [*Exit* PANDARUS.

Tro. Even such a passion doth embrace my bosom:
My heart beats thicker than a feverous pulse;
And all my powers do their bestowing lose,
Like vassalage at unawares encount'ring
The eye of majesty.

Enter PANDARUS *and* CRESSIDA.

Pan. Come, come, what need you blush? shame's a baby.—Here she is now: swear the oaths now to her, that you have sworn to me.—What, are you gone again? you must be watched ere you be made tame, must you? Come your ways, come your ways; an you draw backward, we'll put you i' the fills.—Why do you not speak to her?—Come, draw this curtain, and let's see your picture. Alas the day, how loath you are to offend daylight! an 'twere dark, you'd close sooner. So, so; rub on, and kiss the mistress. How now, a kiss in fee-farm! build there carpenter: the air is sweet. Nay, you shall fight your hearts out, ere I part you. The falcon as the tercel, for all the ducks i' the river: go to, go to.

Tro. You have bereft me of all words, lady.

Pan. Words pay no debts, give her deeds: but she'll bereave you of the deeds too, if she call your activity in question. What, billing again? Here's—*In witness whereof the parties interchangeably*—Come in, come in; I'll go get a fire. [*Exit* PANDARUS.

Cres. Will you walk in, my lord?

Tro. O, Cressida, how often have I wished me thus?

Cres. Wished, my lord?—The gods grant!—O my lord!

Tro. What should they grant? what makes this pretty abruption? What too curious dreg espies my sweet lady in the fountain of our love?

Cres. More dregs than water, if my fears have eyes.

Tro. Fears make devils cherubims: they never see truly.

Cres. Blind fear, that seeing reason leads, finds safer footing than blind reason stumbling without fear: To fear the worst, oft cures the worst.

Tro. O, let my lady apprehend no fear: in all Cupid's pageant there is presented no monster.

Cres. Nor nothing monstrous neither?

Tro. Nothing, but our undertakings; when we vow to weep seas, live in fire, eat rocks, tame tigers; thinking it harder for our mistress to devise imposition enough, than for us to undergo any difficulty imposed. This is the monstruosity in love, lady—that the will is infinite, and the execution confined; that the desire is boundless, and the act a slave to limit.

Cres. They say, all lovers swear more performance than they are able, and yet reserve an ability that they never perform; vowing more than the perfection of ten, and discharging less than the tenth part of one. They that have the voice of lions, and the act of hares, are they not monsters?

Tro. Are there such? such are not we: Praise us as we are tasted, allow us as we prove; our head shall go bare, till merit crown it: no perfection in reversion shall have a praise in present: we will not name desert, before his birth; and, being born, his addition shall be humble. Few words to fair faith: Troilus shall be such to Cressid, as what envy can say worst, shall be a mock for his truth; and what truth can speak truest, not truer than Troilus.

Cres. Will you walk in, my lord?

Re-enter PANDARUS.

Pan. What, blushing still? have you not done talking yet?

Cres. Well, uncle, what folly I commit I dedicate to you.

Pan. I thank you for that; if my lord get a boy of you, you'll give him me: Be true to my lord: if he flinch, chide me for it.

Tro. You know now your hostages; your uncle's word, and my firm faith.

Pan. Nay, I'll give my word for her too; our kindred, though they be long ere they are wooed, they are constant, being won: they are burs, I can tell you: they'll stick where they are thrown.

Cres. Boldness comes to me now, and brings me heart:—
Prince Troilus, I have lov'd you night and day
For many weary months.

Tro. Why was my Cressid then so hard to win?
Cres. Hard to seem won; but I was won, my lord,
With the first glance that ever—Pardon me;—
If I confess much, you will play the tyrant.
I love you now; but not, till now, so much
But I might master it:—in faith, I lie;
My thoughts were like unbridled children, grown
Too headstrong for their mother: See, we fools!
Why have I blabb'd? who shall be true to us,
When we are so unsecret to ourselves?
But, though I lov'd you well, I woo'd you not;
And yet, good faith, I wish'd myself a man;
Or that we women had men's privilege
Of speaking first. Sweet, bid me hold my tongue;
For, in this rapture, I shall surely speak
The thing I shall repent. See, see, your silence,
Cunning in dumbness, from my weakness draws
My very soul of counsel: Stop my mouth.
Tro. And shall, albeit sweet musick issues thence.
Pan. Pretty, i' faith.
Cres. My lord, I do beseech you pardon me!
'Twas not my purpose, thus to beg a kiss:
I am asham'd;—O heavens! what have I done?—
For this time will I take my leave, my lord.
Tro. Your leave, sweet Cressid?
Pan. Leave! an you take leave till to-morrow morning,——
Cres. Pray you, content you.
Tro. What offends you, lady?
Cres. Sir, mine own company.
Tro. You cannot shun
Yourself.
Cres. Let me go and try:
I have a kind of self resides with you;
But an unkind self, that itself will leave,
To be another's fool. I would be gone:
Where is my wit? I know not what I speak.
Tro. Well know they what they speak, that speak so wisely.
Cres. Perchance, my lord, I show more craft than love;
And fell so roundly to a large confession,
To angle for your thoughts: But you are wise;
Or else you love not; For to be wise, and love,
Exceeds man's might; that dwells with gods above.
Tro. O, that I thought it could be in a woman,
(As, if it can, I will presume in you),
To feed for aye her lamp and flames of love;
To keep her constancy in plight and youth,
Outliving beauty's outward, with a mind
That doth renew swifter than blood decays!
Or, that persuasion could but thus convince me,—
That my integrity and truth to you
Might be affronted with the match and weight
Of such a winnow'd purity in love;
How were I then uplifted! but alas,
I am as true as truth's simplicity,
And simpler than the infancy of truth.
Cres. In that I'll war with you.
Tro. O virtuous fight,
When right with right wars who shall be most right!
True swains in love shall, in the world to come,
Approve their truths by Troilus: when their rhymes,
Full of protest, of oath, and big compare,
Want similes of truth, tir'd with iteration,—
As true as steel, as plantage to the moon,
As sun to day, as turtle to her mate,
As iron to adamant, as earth to the centre,—
Yet, after all comparisons of truth,
As truth's authentick author to be cited,
As true as Troilus shall crown up the verse,
And sanctify the numbers.
Cres. Prophet may you be!
If I be false, or swerve a hair from truth,
When time is old and hath forgot itself,
When waterdrops have worn the stones of Troy,
And blind oblivion swallow'd cities up,
And mighty states characterless are grated
To dusty nothing; yet let memory,
From false to false, among false maids in love,
Upbraid my falsehood! when they have said—as false
As air, as water, wind, or sandy earth,
As fox to lamb, as wolf to heifer's calf,
Pard to the hind, or stepdame to her son;
Yea, let them say, to stick the heart of falsehood,
As false as Cressid.
Pan. Go to, a bargain made: seal it, seal it: I'll be the witness.—Here I hold your hand; here, my cousin's. If ever you prove false one to another, since I have taken such pains to bring you together, let all pitiful goers-between be called to the world's end after my name, call them all—Pandars; let all constant men be Troiluses, all false women Cressids, and all brokers-between Pandars! say, amen.
Tro. Amen.
Cres. Amen.
Pan. Amen. Whereupon I will show you a chamber and a bed, which bed, because it shall not speak of your pretty encounters, press it to death: away.
And Cupid grant all tongue-tied maidens here,
Bed, chamber, Pandar to provide this geer!
[*Exeunt.*

SCENE III. *The Grecian Camp.*

Enter AGAMEMNON, ULYSSES, DIOMEDES, NESTOR, AJAX, MENELAUS, *and* CALCHAS.

Cal. Now, princes, for the service I have done you,
The advantage of the time prompts me aloud
To call for recompense. Appear it to your mind,
That, through the sight I bear in things, to Jove
I have abandon'd Troy, left my possession,
Incurr'd a traitor's name; expos'd myself,
From certain and possess'd conveniences,
To doubtful fortunes: sequest'ring from me all
That time, acquaintance, custom, and condition,
Made tame and most familiar to my nature;
And here, to do you service, am become
As new into the world, strange, unacquainted:
I do beseech you, as in way of taste,
To give me now a little benefit,
Out of those many register'd in promise,
Which you say, live to come in my behalf.
Agam. What would'st thou of us, Trojan? make demand.
Cal. You have a Trojan prisoner, call'd Antenor,
Yesterday took; Troy holds him very dear.
Oft have you (often have you thanks therefore),
Desir'd my Cressid in right great exchange,
Whom Troy hath still denied: But this Antenor,
I know, is such a wrest in their affairs,
That their negotiations all must slack,
Wanting his manage; and they will almost
Give us a prince of blood, a son of Priam,
In change of him: let him be sent, great princes,
And he shall buy my daughter; and her presence
Shall quite strike off all service I have done,
In most accepted pain.
Agam. Let Diomedes bear him,
And bring us Cressid hither; Calchas shall have
What he requests of us.—Good Diomed,
Furnish you fairly for this interchange:
Withal, bring word—if Hector will to-morrow
Be answer'd in his challenge: Ajax is ready.
Dio. This shall I undertake; and 'tis a burden
Which I am proud to bear.
[*Exeunt* DIOMEDES *and* CALCHAS

Enter ACHILLES *and* PATROCLUS, *before their Tent.*

Ulyss. Achilles stands i' the entrance of his tent:—
Please it our general to pass strangely by him,
As if he were forgot; and princes all,
Lay negligent and loose regard upon him:
I will come last: 'Tis like, he'll question me

Why such unplausive eyes are bent, why turn'd on him:
If so, I have derision med'cinable,
To use between your strangeness and his pride,
Which his own will shall have desire to drink;
It may do good: pride hath no other glass
To show itself, but pride; for supple knees
Feed arrogance, and are the proud man's fees.

Agam. We'll execute your purpose, and put on
A form of strangeness as we pass along;
So do each lord; and either greet him not,
Or else disdainfully which shall shake him more
Than if not look'd on. I will lead the way.

Achil. What, comes the general to speak with me?
You know my mind, I'll fight no more 'gainst Troy.

Agam. What says Achilles? would he aught with us?

Nest. Would you, my lord, aught with the general?

Achil. No.

Nest. Nothing, my lord.

Agam. The better.

[*Exeunt* AGAMEMNON *and* NESTOR.

Achil. Good day, good day.

Men. How do you? how do you?

[*Exit* MENELAUS.

Achil. What, does the cuckold scorn me?

Ajax. How now, Patroclus?

Achil. Good morrow, Ajax.

Ajax. Ha?

Achil. Good morrow.

Ajax. Ay, and good next day too.

[*Exit* AJAX.

Achil. What mean these fellows? Know they not Achilles?

Patr. They pass by strangely: they were us'd to bend,
To send their smiles before them to Achilles;
To come as humbly, as they us'd to creep
To holy altars.

Achil. What, am I poor of late?
'Tis certain, greatness, once fallen out with fortune,
Must fall out with men too: What the declin'd is,
He shall as soon read in the eyes of others,
As feel in his own fall: for men, like butterflies,
Show not their mealy wings, but to the summer;
And not a man, for being simply man,
Hath any honour; but honour for those honours
That are without him, as place, riches, favour,
Prizes of accident as oft as merit:
Which when they fall, as being slippery standers,
The love that lean'd on them as slippery too,
Do one pluck down another, and together
Die in the fall. But 'tis not so with me:
Fortune and I are friends; I do enjoy
At ample point all that I did possess,
Save these men's looks: who do, methinks, find out
Something not worth in me such rich beholding
As they have often given. Here is Ulysses;
I'll interrupt his reading.—
How now, Ulysses?

Ulyss. Now, great Thetis' son?

Achil. What are you reading?

Ulyss. A strange fellow here
Writes me, That man—how dearly ever parted,
How much in having, or without, or in,—
Cannot make boast to have that which he hath,
Nor feels not what he owes, but by reflection;
As when his virtues shining upon others
Heat them, and they retort that heat again
To the first giver.

Achil. This is not strange, Ulysses.
The beauty that is borne here in the face
The bearer knows not, but commends itself
To others' eyes: nor doth the eye itself
(That most pure spirit of sense), behold itself,
Not going from itself; but eye to eye oppos'd
Salutes each other with each other's form.
For speculation turns not to itself,
Till it hath travell'd, and is married there
Where it may see itself: this is not strange at all.

Ulyss. I do not strain at the position,
It is familiar; but at the author's drift:
Who, in his circumstance, expressly proves—
That no man is the lord of any thing
(Though in and of him there be much consisting),
Till he communicate his parts to others:
Nor doth he of himself know them for aught
Till he behold them form'd in the applause
Where they are extended; which, like an arch, reverberates
The voice again: or like a gate of steel
Fronting the sun, receives and renders back
His figure and his heat. I was much rapt in this;
And apprehended here immediately
The unknown Ajax.
Heavens, what a man is there! a very horse;
That has he knows not what. Nature, what things there are,
Most abject in regard, and dear in use!
What things again most dear in the esteem,
And poor in worth! Now shall we see to-morrow,
An act that very chance doth throw upon him,—
Ajax renown'd. O heavens, what some men do,
While some men leave to do!
How some men creep in skittish fortune's hall,
Whiles others play the idiots in her eyes!
How one man eats into another's pride,
While pride is fasting in his wantonness!
To see these Grecian lords!—why, even already
They clap the lubber Ajax on the shoulder;
As if his foot were on brave Hector's breast,
And great Troy shrinking.

Achil. I do believe it: for they passed by me,
As misers do by beggars: neither gave to me
Good word, nor look: What, are my deeds forgot?

Ulyss. Time hath, my lord, a wallet at his back,
Wherein he puts alms for oblivion,
A great-sized monster of ingratitudes:
Those scraps are good deeds past: which are devour'd
As fast as they are made, forgot as soon
As done: Perseverance, dear my lord,
Keeps honour bright: To have done, is to hang
Quite out of fashion, like a rusty mail
In monumental mockery. Take the instant way;
For honour travels in a strait so narrow,
Where one but goes abreast: keep then the path;
For emulation hath a thousand sons,
That one by one pursue: If you give way,
Or hedge aside from the direct forthright,
Like to an enter'd tide, they all rush by,
And leave you hindmost:—
Or, like a gallant horse fallen in first rank,
Lie there for pavement to the abject rear,
O'errun and trampled on: Then what they do in present,
Though less than yours in past, must o'ertop yours:
For time is like a fashionable host,
That slightly shakes his parting guest by the hand;
And with his arms outstretch'd, as he would fly,
Grasps in the comer: Welcome ever smiles,
And farewell goes out sighing. O, let not virtue seek
Remuneration for the thing it was;
For beauty, wit,
High birth, vigour of bone, desert in service,
Love, friendship, charity, are subjects all
To envious and calumniating time
One touch of nature makes the whole world kin,—
That all, with one consent, praise new-born gawds,
Though they are made and moulded of things past;
And give to dust, that is a little gilt,
More laud than gilt o'er-dusted.
The present eye praises the present object:
Then marvel not, thou great and complete man,
That all the Greeks begin to worship Ajax;
Since things in motion sooner catch the eye,

Than what not stirs. The cry went once on thee,
And still it might; and yet it may again,
If thou would'st not entomb thyself alive,
And case thy reputation in thy tent;
Whose glorious deeds, but in these fields of late,
Made emulous missions 'mongst the gods themselves,
And drave great Mars to faction.

Achil. Of this my privacy
I have strong reasons.

Ulyss. But 'gainst your privacy
The reasons are more potent and heroical:
'Tis known, Achilles, that you are in love
With one of Priam's daughters.

Achil. Ha! known?

Ulyss. Is that a wonder?
The providence that's in a watchful state,
Knows almost every grain of Plutus' gold;
Finds bottom in the uncomprehensive deeps;
Keeps place with thought, and almost, like the gods,
Does thoughts unveil in their dumb cradles.
There is a mystery (with whom relation
Durst never meddle) in the soul of state;
Which hath an operation more divine,
Than breath or pen can give expressure to:
All the commerce that you have had with Troy,
As perfectly is ours, as yours, my lord;
And better would it fit Achilles much,
To throw down Hector, than Polyxena:
But it must grieve young Pyrrhus now at home,
When fame shall in our islands sound her trump;
And all the Greekish girls shall tripping sing,—
Great Hector's sister did Achilles win;
But our great Ajax bravely beat down him.
Farewell, my lord: I as your lover speak;
The fool slides o'er the ice that you should break. [*Exit.*

Patr. To this effect, Achilles, have I mov'd you:
A woman impudent and mannish grown
Is not more loath'd than an effeminate man
In time of action. I stand condemn'd for this;
They think, my little stomach to the war,
And your great love to me, restrains you thus:
Sweet, rouse yourself; and the weak wanton Cupid
Shall from your neck unloose his amorous fold,
And, like a dewdrop from the lion's mane,
Be shook to air.

Achil. Shall Ajax fight with Hector?

Patr. Ay; and, perhaps, receive much honour by him.

Achil. I see my reputation is at stake;
My fame is shrewdly gor'd.

Patr. O, then beware;
Those wounds heal ill, that men do give themselves:
Omission to do what is necessary
Seals a commission to a blank of danger;
And danger, like an ague, subtly taints
Even then when we sit idly in the sun.

Achil. Go call Thersites hither, sweet Patroclus:
I'll send the fool to Ajax, and desire him
To invite the Trojan lords, after the combat,
To see us here unarm'd: I have a woman's longing,
An appetite that I am sick withal,
To see great Hector in his weeds of peace;
To talk with him, and to behold his visage,
Even to my full of view. A labour sav'd!

Enter THERSITES.

Ther. A wonder!

Achil. What?

Ther. Ajax goes up and down the field, asking for himself.

Achil. How so?

Ther. He must fight singly to-morrow with Hector; and is so prophetically proud of an heroical cudgelling, that he raves in saying nothing.

Achil. How can that be?

Ther. Why, he stalks up and down like a peacock, a stride, and a stand: ruminates, like an hostess, that hath no arithmetick but her brain to set down her reckoning: bites his lip with a politick regard, as who should say—there were wit in this head, an 'twould out; and so there is; but it lies as coldly in him as fire in a flint, which will not show without knocking. The man's undone for ever: for if Hector break not his neck i' the combat, he'll break it himself in vainglory. He knows not me: I said, *Good-morrow*, Ajax; and he replies, *Thanks*, Agamemnon. What think you of this man, that takes me for the general? He is grown a very land-fish, languageless, a monster. A plague of opinion! a man may wear it on both sides, like a leather jerkin.

Achil. Thou must be my ambassador to him, Thersites.

Ther. Who, I? why, he'll answer nobody; he professes not answering; speaking is for beggars; he wears his tongue in his arms. I will put on his presence; let Patroclus make demands to me, you shall see the pageant of Ajax.

Achil. To him, Patroclus: Tell him,—I humbly desire the valiant Ajax, to invite the most valorous Hector to come unarmed to my tent; and to procure safe conduct for his person, of the magnanimous, and most illustrious, six-or-seven-times-honoured captain-general of the Grecian army, Agamemnon. Do this.

Patr. Jove bless great Ajax.

Ther. Humph!

Patr. I come from the worthy Achilles,——

Ther. Ha!

Patr. Who most humbly desires you to invite Hector to his tent!——

Ther. Humph!

Patr. And to procure safe conduct from Agamemnon.

Ther. Agamemnon?

Patr. Ay, my lord.

Ther. Ha!

Patr. What say you to't?

Ther. God be wi' you, with all my heart.

Patr. Your answer, sir.

Ther. If to-morrow be a fair day, by eleven o'clock it will go one way or other: howsoever, he shall pay for me ere he has me.

Patr. Your answer, sir.

Ther. Fare you well, with all my heart.

Achil. Why, but he is not in this tune, is he?

Ther. No, but he's out o' tune thus. What musick will be in him when Hector has knocked out his brains, I know not: But, I am sure, none; unless the fiddler Apollo get his sinews to make catlings on.

Achil. Come, thou shalt bear a letter to him straight.

Ther. Let me bear another to his horse; for that's the more capable creature.

Achil. My mind is troubled, like a fountain stirr'd:
And I myself see not the bottom of it.
[*Exeunt* ACHILLES *and* PATROCLUS.

Ther. 'Would the fountain of your mind were clear again, that I might water an ass at it! I had rather be a tick in a sheep, than such a valiant ignorance. [*Exit.*

ACT IV.

SCENE I. Troy. *A Street.*

Enter, at one side, ÆNEAS, *and* Servant *with a Torch; at the other,* PARIS, DEIPHOBUS, ANTENOR, DIOMEDES, *and Others, with Torches.*

Par. See, ho! who's that there?

Dei. 'Tis the lord Æneas.

Æne. Is the prince there in person?—

Had I so good occasion to lie long,
As you, prince Paris, nothing but heavenly business
Should rob my bed-mate of my company.
Dio. That's my mind too.—Good morrow, lord Æneas.
Par. A valiant Greek, Æneas; take his hand;
Witness the process of your speech, wherein
You told—how Diomed, a whole week by days,
Did haunt you in the field.
Æne. Health to you, valiant sir,
During all question of the gentle truce:
But when I meet you arm'd, as black defiance,
As heart can think, or courage execute.
Dio. The one and other Diomed embraces.
Our bloods are now in calm; and, so long, health:
But when contention and occasion meet,
By Jove, I'll play the hunter for thy life,
With all my force, pursuit, and policy.
Æne. And thou shalt hunt a lion, that will fly
With his face backward.—In humane gentleness,
Welcome to Troy! now, by Anchises' life,
Welcome, indeed! By Venus' hand I swear,
No man alive can love, in such a sort,
The thing he means to kill more excellently.
Dio. We sympathise:—Jove, let Æneas live,
If to my sword his fate be not the glory,
A thousand complete courses of the sun!
But, in mine emulous honour, let him die,
With every joint a wound; and, that to-morrow!
Æne. We know each other well.
Dio. We do; and long to know each other worse.
Par. This is the most despiteful gentle greeting,
The noblest hateful love, that e'er I heard of.—
What business, lord, so early?
Æne. I was sent for to the king; but why, I know not.
Par. His purpose meets you: 'Twas to bring this Greek
To Calchas' house; and there to render him,
For the enfreed Antenor, the fair Cressid:
Let's have your company; or, if you please,
Haste there before us: I constantly do think
(Or, rather, call my thoughts a certain knowledge),
My brother Troilus lodges there to-night;
Rouse him, and give him note of our approach,
With the whole quality wherefore: I fear,
We shall be much unwelcome.
Æne. That I assure you;
Troilus had rather Troy were borne to Greece,
Than Cressid borne from Troy.
Par. There is no help;
The bitter disposition of the time
Will have it so. On, lord; we'll follow you.
Æne. Good morrow, all. [*Exit.*
Par. And tell me, noble Diomed; 'faith, tell me true,
Even in the soul of sound good-fellowship,—
Who, in your thoughts, merits fair Helen best,
Myself, or Menelaus?
Dio. Both alike:
He merits well to have her, that doth seek her
(Not making any scruple of her soilure),
With such a hell of pain, and world of charge;
And you as well to keep her, that defend her
(Not palating the taste of her dishonour)
With such a costly loss of wealth and friends:
He, like a puling cuckold, would drink up
The lees and dregs of a flat tamed piece:
You, like a lecher, out of whorish loins
Are pleas'd to breed out your inheritors:
Both merits pois'd, each weighs nor less nor more;
But he as he, the heavier for a whore.
Par. You are too bitter to your countrywoman.
Dio. She's bitter to her country: Hear me, Paris,—
For every false drop in her bawdy veins
A Grecian's life hath sunk; for every scruple
Of her contaminated carrion weight,
A Trojan hath been slain: since she could speak,
She hath not given so many good words breath,
As for her Greeks and Trojans suffer'd death.
Par. Fair Diomed, you do as chapmen do,
Dispraise the thing that you desire to buy:
But we in silence hold this virtue well,—
We'll not commend what we intend to sell.
Here lies our way. [*Exeunt.*

SCENE II.

The same. Court before the House of Pandarus.

Enter TROILUS *and* CRESSIDA.

Tro. Dear, trouble not yourself; the morn is cold.
Cres. Then, sweet my lord, I'll call mine uncle down;
He shall unbolt the gates.
Tro. Trouble him not;
To bed, to bed: Sleep kill those pretty eyes,
And give as soft attachment to thy senses,
As infants' empty of all thought!
Cres. Good morrow then.
Tro. 'Pr'ythee now, to bed.
Cres. Are you aweary of me?
Tro. O Cressida! but that the busy day,
Wak'd by the lark, hath rous'd the ribald crows,
And dreaming night will hide our joys no longer,
I would not from thee.
Cres. Night hath been too brief.
Tro. Beshrew the witch! with venomous wights she stays,
As tediously as hell; but flies the grasps of love,
With wings more momentary-swift than thought.
You will catch cold, and curse me.
Cres. Pr'ythee, tarry;—
You men will never tarry.——
O foolish Cressid!—I might have still held off,
And then you would have tarried. Hark! there's one up.
Pan. [*Within.*] What, are all the doors open here?
Tro. It is your uncle.

Enter PANDARUS.

Cres. A pestilence on him! now will he be mocking:
I shall have such a life,——
Pan. How now, how now? how go maidenheads?—Here, you maid! where's my cousin Cressid?
Cres. Go hang yourself, you naughty mocking uncle!
You bring me to do, and then you flout me too.
Pan. To do what? to do what?—let her say what: what have I brought you to do?
Cres. Come, come; beshrew your heart! you'll ne'er be good,
Nor suffer others.
Pan. Ha, ha! Alas, poor wretch! a poor capocchia—hast not slept to-night? would he not, a naughty man, let it sleep? a bugbear take him! [*Knocking.*
Cres. Did I not tell you?—'would he were knock'd o' the head!
Who's that at door? good uncle, go and see.—
My lord, come you again into my chamber:
You smile, and mock me, as if I meant naughtily.
Tro. Ha, ha!
Cres. Come, you are deceiv'd, I think of no such thing. [*Knocking.*
How earnestly they knock!—pray you, come in.
I would not for half Troy have you seen here.
[*Exeunt* TROILUS *and* CRESSIDA.
Pan. [*Going to the door.*] Who's there? what's the matter? will you beat down the door? How now? what's the matter?

Enter ÆNEAS.

Æne. Good morrow, lord, good morrow.
Pan. Who's there? my Lord Æneas? By my

truth, I knew you not: what news with you so early?

Æne. Is not Prince Troilus here?

Pan. Here! what should he do here?

Æne. Come, he is here, my lord, do not deny him;
It doth import him much, to speak with me.

Pan. Is he here, say you? 'tis more than I know,
I'll be sworn:—For my own part, I came in late:
What should he do here?

Æne. Who!—nay, then:—Come, come, you'll do him wrong ere you are 'ware: you'll be so true to him, to be false to him: Do not you know of him? yet go fetch him hither; go.

As PANDARUS *is going out, enter* TROILUS.

Tro. How now? what's the matter?

Æne. My lord, I scarce have leisure to salute you,
My matter is so rash: There is at hand
Paris your brother, and Deiphobus,
The Grecian Diomed, and our Antenor
Deliver'd to us; and for him forthwith,
Ere the first sacrifice, within this hour,
We must give up to Diomedes' hand
The lady Cressida.

Tro. Is it so concluded?

Æne. By Priam, and the general state of Troy:
They are at hand, and ready to effect it.

Tro. How my achievements mock me!
I will go meet them; and, my Lord Æneas,
We met by chance; you did not find me here.

Æne. Good, good, my lord: the secrets of nature
Have not more gift in taciturnity.

[*Exeunt* TROILUS *and* ÆNEAS.

Pan. Is't possible? no sooner got, but lost? The devil take Antenor! the young prince will go mad. A plague upon Antenor! I would they had broke's neck!

Enter CRESSIDA.

Cres. How now? What is the matter? Who was here?

Pan. Ah, ah!

Cres. Why sigh you so profoundly? where's my lord gone?
Tell me, sweet uncle, what's the matter?

Pan. 'Would I were as deep under the earth as I am above!

Cres. O the gods!—what's the matter?

Pan. Pr'ythee, get thee in; 'Would thou hadst ne'er been born! I knew, thou would'st be his death:—O poor gentleman!—A plague upon Antenor!

Cres. Good uncle, I beseech you on my knees,
I beseech you, what's the matter?

Pan. Thou must be gone, wench, thou must be gone: thou art changed for Antenor: thou must to thy father, and be gone from Troilus; 'twill be his death; 'twill be his bane: he cannot bear it.

Cres. O you immortal gods!—I will not go.

Pan. Thou must.

Cres. I will not, uncle: I have forgot my father;
I know no touch of consanguinity;
No kin, no love, no blood, no soul so near me,
As the sweet Troilus.—O you gods divine!
Make Cressid's name the very crown of falsehood,
If ever she leave Troilus! Time, force, and death,
Do to this body what extremes you can;
But the strong base and building of my love
Is as the very centre of the earth,
Drawing all things to it.—I'll go in, and weep;—

Pan. Do, do.

Cres. Tear my bright hair, and scratch my praised cheeks,
Crack my clear voice with sobs, and break my heart
With sounding Troilus. I will not go from Troy.

[*Exeunt.*

SCENE III. *The same. Before* Pandarus' *House.*

Enter PARIS, TROILUS, ÆNEAS, DEIPHOBUS, ANTENOR, *and* DIOMEDES.

Par. It is great morning; and the hour prefix'd
Of her delivery to this valiant Greek
Comes fast upon:—Good my brother Troilus,
Tell you the lady what she is to do,
And haste her to the purpose.

Tro. Walk in to her house;
I'll bring her to the Grecian presently:
And to his hand when I deliver her,
Think it an altar; and thy brother Troilus
A priest, there offering to it his own heart.

[*Exit.*

Par. I know what 'tis to love;
And 'would, as I shall pity, I could help!—
Please you, walk in, my lords. [*Exeunt.*

SCENE IV.

The same. A Room in Pandarus' *House.*

Enter PANDARUS *and* CRESSIDA.

Pan. Be moderate, be moderate.

Cres. Why tell you me of moderation?
The grief is fine, full, perfect, that I taste,
And violenteth in a sense as strong
As that which causeth it: How can I moderate it?
If I could temporize with my affection,
Or brew it to a weak and colder palate,
The like allayment could I give my grief:
My love admits no qualifying dross:
No more my grief, in such a precious loss.

Enter TROILUS.

Pan. Here, here, here he comes.—Ah sweet ducks!

Cres. O Troilus! Troilus! [*Embracing him.*

Pan. What a pair of spectacles is here! Let me embrace too: *O heart,*—as the goodly saying is——

——— *O heart, O heavy heart,*
Why sigh'st thou without breaking?

where he answers again,

Because thou canst not ease thy smart,
By friendship, nor by speaking.

There never was a truer rhyme. Let us cast away nothing, for we may live to have need of such a verse; we see it, we see it.—How now, lambs?

Tro. Cressid, I love thee in so strain'd a purity,
That the blest gods—as angry with my fancy,
More bright in zeal than the devotion which
Cold lips blow to their deities—take thee from me.

Cres. Have the gods envy?

Pan. Ay, ay, ay, ay; 'tis too plain a case.

Cres. And is it true, that I must go from Troy?

Tro. A hateful truth.

Cres. What, and from Troilus too?

Tro. From Troy, and Troilus.

Cres. Is it possible?

Tro. And suddenly; where injury of chance
Puts back leave-taking, justles roughly by
All time of pause, rudely beguiles our lips
Of all rejoindure, forcibly prevents
Our lock'd embrasures, strangles our dear vows
Even in the birth of our own labouring breath:
We two, that with so many thousand sighs
Did buy each other, must poorly sell ourselves
With the rude brevity and discharge of one.
Injurious time now, with a robber's haste,
Crams his rich thievery up, he knows not how:
As many farewells as be stars in heaven,
With distinct breath and consign'd kisses to them,
He fumbles up into a loose adieu;
And scants us with a single famish'd kiss,
Distasted with the salt of broken tears.

Æne. [*Within.*] My lord! is the lady ready?

Tro. Hark! you are call'd: Some say, the Genius so

Cries, *Come!* to him that instantly must die.—
Bid them have patience; she shall come anon.

Pan. Where are my tears? rain, to lay this wind, or my heart will be blown up by the root!
[*Exit* PANDARUS.

Cres. I must then to the Greeks?

Tro. No remedy.

Cres. A woful Cressid 'mongst the merry Greeks!
When shall we see again?

Tro. Hear me, my love: Be thou but true of heart,——

Cres. I true! how now? what wicked deem is this?

Tro. Nay, we must use expostulation kindly,
For it is parting from us:
I speak not, *be thou true*, as fearing thee;
For I will throw my glove to death himself,
That there's no maculation in thy heart:
But *be thou true*, say I, to fashion in
My sequent protestation; be thou true,
And I will see thee.

Cres. O, you shall be expos'd, my lord, to dangers
As infinite as imminent! but, I'll be true.

Tro. And I'll grow friend with danger. Wear this sleeve.

Cres. And you this glove. When shall I see you?

Tro. I will corrupt the Grecian sentinels,
To give thee nightly visitation.
But yet, be true.

Cres. O heavens! be true again?

Tro. Hear why I speak it, love;
The Grecian youths are full of quality;
They're loving, well compos'd, with gifts of nature flowing,
And swelling o'er with arts and exercise;
How novelty may move, and parts with person,
Alas, a kind of godly jealousy
(Which I beseech you, call a virtuous sin)
Makes me afeard.

Cres. O heavens! you love me not.

Tro. Die I a villain then!
In this I do not call your faith in question,
So mainly as my merit: I cannot sing,
Nor heel the high lavolt, nor sweeten talk,
Nor play at subtle games; fair virtues all,
To which the Grecians are most prompt and pregnant:
But I can tell, that in each grace of these
There lurks a still and dumb-discoursive devil,
That tempts most cunningly: but be not tempted.

Cres. Do you think I will?

Tro. No.
But something may be done, that we will not:
And sometimes we are devils to ourselves,
When we will tempt the frailty of our powers,
Presuming on their changeful potency.

Æne. [*Within.*] Nay, good my lord,——

Tro. Come, kiss; and let us part.

Par. [*Within.*] Brother Troilus!

Tro. Good brother, come you hither;
And bring Æneas, and the Grecian, with you.

Cres. My lord, will you be true?

Tro. Who I? alas, it is my vice, my fault:
While others fish with craft for great opinion,
I with great truth catch mere simplicity;
Whilst some with cunning gild their copper crowns,
With truth and plainness I do wear mine bare.
Fear not my truth; the moral of my wit
Is—plain, and true,—there's all the reach of it.

Enter ÆNEAS, PARIS, ANTENOR, DEIPHOBUS, *and* DIOMEDES.

Welcome, Sir Diomed! here is the lady,
Which for Antenor we deliver you:
At the port, lord, I'll give her to thy hand;
And, by the way, possess thee what she is.
Entreat her fair; and, by my soul, fair Greek,
If e'er thou stand at mercy of my sword,
Name Cressid, and thy life shall be as safe
As Priam is in Ilion.

Dio. Fair lady Cressid,
So please you, save the thanks this prince expects:
The lustre in your eye, heaven in your cheek,
Pleads your fair usage; and to Diomed
You shall be mistress, and command him wholly.

Tro. Grecian, thou dost not use me courteously,
To shame the zeal of my petition to thee,
In praising her: I tell thee, lord of Greece,
She is as far high-soaring o'er thy praises,
As thou unworthy to be call'd her servant.
I charge thee, use her well, even for my charge;
For, by the dreadful Pluto, if thou dost not,
Though the great bulk Achilles be thy guard,
I'll cut thy throat.

Dio. O, be not mov'd, Prince Troilus;
Let me be privileg'd by my place, and message,
To be a speaker free; when I am hence,
I'll answer to my lust: And know you, lord,
I'll nothing do on charge: To her own worth
She shall be priz'd; but that you say—be 't so,
I'll speak it in my spirit and honour,—no.

Tro. Come, to the port.—I tell thee, Diomed,
This brave shall oft make thee to hide thy head.—
Lady, give me your hand; and, as we walk,
To our own selves bend we our needful talk.
[*Exeunt* TROILUS, CRESSIDA, *and* DIOMED.
[*Trumpet heard.*

Par. Hark! Hector's trumpet.

Æne. How have we spent this morning!
The prince must think me tardy and remiss,
That swore to ride before him to the field.

Par. 'Tis Troilus' fault: Come, come, to field with him.

Dei. Let us make ready straight.

Æne. Yea, with a bridegroom's fresh alacrity,
Let us address to tend on Hector's heels:
The glory of our Troy doth this day lie,
On his fair worth and single chivalry. [*Exeunt.*

SCENE V. *The* Grecian *Camp. Lists set out.*

Enter AJAX, *armed;* AGAMEMNON, ACHILLES, PATROCLUS, MENELAUS, ULYSSES, NESTOR, *and Others.*

Agam. Here art thou in appointment fresh and fair,
Anticipating time with starting courage.
Give with thy trumpet a loud note to Troy,
Thou dreadful Ajax; that the appalled air
May pierce the head of the great combatant,
And hale him hither.

Ajax. Thou, trumpet, there's my purse.
Now crack thy lungs, and split thy brazen pipe:
Blow, villain, till thy sphered bias-cheek
Outswell the colick of puff'd Aquilon:
Come, stretch thy chest, and let thy eyes spout blood;
Thou blow'st for Hector. [*Trumpet sounds.*

Ulyss. No trumpet answers.

Achil. 'Tis but early days.

Agam. Is not yon Diomed, with Calchas' daughter?

Ulyss. 'Tis he, I ken the manner of his gait;
He rises on the toe: that spirit of his
In aspiration lifts him from the earth.

Enter DIOMED, *with* CRESSIDA.

Agam. Is this the lady Cressid?

Dio. Even she.

Agam. Most dearly welcome to the Greeks, sweet lady.

Nest. Our general doth salute you with a kiss.

Ulyss. Yet is the kindness but particular;
'Twere better she were kiss'd in general.

Nest. And very courtly counsel: I'll begin.—
So much for Nestor.

Achil. I'll take that winter from your lips, fair lady:
Achilles bids you welcome.

Men. I had good argument for kissing once.
Patr. But that's no argument for kissing now:
For thus popp'd Paris in his hardiment;
And parted thus you and your argument.
Ulyss. O deadly gall, and theme of all our scorns!
For which we lose our heads, to gild his horns.
Patr. The first was Menelaus' kiss;—this, mine;
Patroclus kisses you.
Men. O, this is trim!
Patr. Paris, and I, kiss evermore for him.
Men. I'll have my kiss, sir:—Lady, by your leave.
Cres. In kissing do you render or receive?
Patr. Both take and give.
Cres. I'll make my match to live,
The kiss you take is better than you give;
Therefore no kiss.
Men. I'll give you boot, I'll give you three for one.
Cres. You're an odd man; give even, or give none.
Men. An odd man, lady? every man is odd.
Cres. No, Paris is not; for, you know, 'tis true,
That you are odd, and he is even with you.
Men. You fillip me o' the head.
Cres. No, I'll be sworn.
Ulyss. It were no match, your nail against his horn.—
May I, sweet lady, beg a kiss of you.
Cres. You may.
Ulyss. I do desire it.
Cres. Why, beg then.
Ulyss. Why then, for Venus' sake, give me a kiss,
When Helen is a maid again, and his.
Cres. I am your debtor, claim it when tis due.
Ulyss. Never's my day, and then a kiss of you.
Dio. Lady, a word;—I'll bring you to your father. [DIOMED *leads out* CRESSIDA.
Nest. A woman of quick sense.
Ulyss. Fye, fye upon her!
There's language in her eye, her cheek, her lip,
Nay, her foot speaks; her wanton spirits look out
At every joint and motive of her body.
O, these encounterers, so glib of tongue,
That give a coasting welcome ere it comes,
And wide unclasp the tables of their thoughts
To every ticklish reader! set them down
For sluttish spoils of opportunity,
And daughters of the game. [*Trumpet within.*
All. The Trojan's trumpet.
Agam. Yonder comes the troop.

Enter HECTOR, *armed;* ÆNEAS, TROILUS, *and other* Trojans, *with* Attendants.

Æne. Hail, all the state of Greece! what shall be done
To him that victory commands? Or do you purpose,
A victor shall be known? will you, the knights
Shall to the edge of all extremity
Pursue each other: or shall they be divided
By any voice or order of the field?
Hector bade ask.
Agam. Which way would Hector have it?
Æne. He cares not, he'll obey conditions.
Achil. 'Tis done like Hector; but securely done,
A little proudly, and great deal misprizing
The knight oppos'd.
Æne. If not Achilles, sir,
What is your name?
Achil. If not Achilles, nothing.
Æne. Therefore Achilles: But, whate'er, know this;—
In the extremity of great and little,
Valour and pride excel themselves in Hector;
The one almost as infinite as all,
The other blank as nothing. Weigh him well,
And that, which looks like pride, is courtesy.
This Ajax is half made of Hector's blood:
In love whereof, half Hector stays at home;
Half heart, half hand, half Hector comes to seek
This blended knight, half Trojan, and half Greek.
Achil. A maiden battle then?—O, I perceive you.

Re-enter DIOMED.

Agam. Here is Sir Diomed;—Go, gentle knight,
Stand by our Ajax: as you and lord Æneas
Consent upon the order of their fight,
So be it; either to the uttermost,
Or else a breath: the combatants being kin,
Half stints their strife before their strokes begin. [AJAX *and* HECTOR *enter the lists.*
Ulyss. They are oppos'd already.
Agam. What Trojan is that same that looks so heavy?
Ulyss. The youngest son of Priam, a true knight:
Not yet mature, yet matchless: firm of word;
Speaking in deeds, and deedless in his tongue;
Not soon provok'd, nor, being provoked, soon calm'd:
His heart and hand both open, and both free;
For what he has, he gives, what thinks, he shows;
Yet gives he not till judgment guide his bounty,
Nor dignifies an impair thought with breath:
Manly as Hector, but more dangerous;
For Hector, in his blaze of wrath, subscribes
To tender objects; but he, in heat of action,
Is more vindicative than jealous love;
They call him Troilus; and on him erect
A second hope, as fairly built as Hector.
Thus says Æneas; one that knows the youth
Even to his inches, and, with private soul,
Did in great Ilion thus translate him to me.
[*Alarum.* HECTOR *and* AJAX *fight.*
Agam. They are in action.
Nest. Now, Ajax, hold thine own!
Tro. Hector, thou sleep'st;
Awake thee!
Agam. His blows are well dispos'd:—there, Ajax!
Dio. You must no more. [*Trumpets cease.*
Æne. Princes, enough, so please you.
Ajax. I am not warm yet, let us fight again.
Dio. As Hector pleases.
Hect. Why then, will I no more:—
Thou art, great lord, my father's sister's son,
A cousin-german to great Priam's seed;
The obligation of our blood forbids
A gory emulation 'twixt us twain:
Were thy commixtion Greek, and Trojan so,
That thou could'st say—*This hand is Grecian all,*
And this is Trojan; the sinews of this leg
All Greek, and this all Troy; my mother's blood
Runs on the dexter cheek, and this sinister
Bounds-in my father's; By Jove multipotent,
Thou should'st not bear from me a Greekish member
Wherein my sword had not impressure made
Of our rank feud; But the just gods gainsay,
That any drop thou borrow'st from thy mother,
My sacred aunt, should by my mortal sword
Be drain'd! Let me embrace thee, Ajax:
By him that thunders, thou hast lusty arms;
Hector would have them fall upon him thus:
Cousin, all honour to thee!
Ajax. I thank thee, Hector:
Thou art too gentle, and too free a man:
I came to kill thee, cousin, and bear hence
A great addition earned in thy death.
Hect. Not Neoptolemus so mirable
(On whose bright crest Fame with her loud'st O yes
Cries, *This is he,*) could promise to himself
A thought of added honour torn from Hector.

Æne. There is expectance here from both the sides,
What further you will do.
Hect. We'll answer it;
The issue is embracement:—Ajax, farewell.
Ajax. If I might in entreaties find success
(As seld I have the chance), I would desire
My famous cousin to our Grecian tents.
Dio. 'Tis Agamemnon's wish: and great Achilles
Doth long to see unarm'd the valiant Hector.
Hect. Æneas, call my brother Troilus to me:
And signify this loving interview
To the expecters of our Trojan part;
Desire them home.—Give me thy hand, my cousin;
I will go eat with thee, and see your knights.
Ajax. Great Agamemnon comes to meet us here.
Hect. The worthiest of them tell me name by name;
But for Achilles, my own searching eyes
Shall find him by his large and portly size.
Agam. Worthy of arms! as welcome as to one
That would be rid of such an enemy;
But that's no welcome: Understand more clear,
What's past, and what's to come, is strew'd with husks
And formless ruin of oblivion;
But in this extant moment, faith and troth,
Strain'd purely from all hollow bias-drawing,
Bids thee, with most divine integrity,
From heart of very heart, great Hector, welcome.
Hect. I thank thee, most imperious Agamemnon.
Agam. My well-fam'd lord of Troy, no less to you. [*To* TROILUS.
Men. Let me confirm my princely brother's greeting;—
You brace of warlike brothers, welcome hither.
Hect. Whom must we answer?
Men. The noble Menelaus.
Hect. O you, my lord? by Mars his gauntlet, thanks!
Mock not, that I affect the untraded oath;
Your *quondam* wife swears still by Venus' glove:
She's well, but bade me not commend her to you.
Men. Name her not now, sir; she's a deadly theme.
Hect. O, pardon; I offend.
Nest. I have, thou gallant Trojan, seen thee oft,
Labouring for destiny, make cruel way
Through ranks of Greekish youth: and I have seen thee,
As hot as Perseus, spur thy Phrygian steed,
Despising many forfeits and subduements,
When thou hast hung thy advanced sword i' the air,
Not letting it decline on the declin'd;
That I have said to some my standers-by,
Lo, Jupiter is yonder, dealing life!
And I have seen thee pause, and take thy breath,
When that a ring of Greeks have hemm'd thee in,
Like an Olympian wrestling: this have I seen;
But this thy countenance, still lock'd in steel,
I never saw till now. I knew thy grandsire,
And once fought with him: he was a soldier good;
But, by great Mars, the captain of us all,
Never like thee: Let an old man embrace thee;
And, worthy warrior, welcome to our tents.
Æne. 'Tis the old Nestor.
Hect. Let me embrace thee, good old chronicle,
That hast so long walk'd hand in hand with time:—
Most reverend Nestor, I am glad to clasp thee.
Nest. I would, my arms could match thee in contention,
As they contend with thee in courtesy.
Hect. I would they could.
Nest. Ha!
By this white beard, I'd fight with thee to-morrow.
Well, welcome, welcome! I have seen the time—
Ulyss. I wonder now how yonder city stands,
When we have here her base and pillar by us.
Hect. I know your favour, Lord Ulysses, well,
Ah, sir, there's many a Greek and Trojan dead,
Since first I saw yourself and Diomed
In Ilion, on your Greekish embassy.
Ulyss. Sir, I foretold you then what would ensue:
My prophecy is but half his journey yet;
For yonder walls, that pertly front your town,
Yon towers, whose wanton tops do buss the clouds,
Must kiss their own feet.
Hect. I must not believe you;
There they stand yet; and modestly I think,
The fall of every Phrygian stone will cost
A drop of Grecian blood: The end crowns all;
And that old common arbitrator, time,
Will one day end it.
Ulyss. So to him we leave it.
Most gentle, and most valiant Hector, welcome:
After the general, I beseech you next
To feast with me, and see me at my tent.
Achil. I shall forestall thee, Lord Ulysses, thou!—
Now, Hector, I have fed mine eyes on thee;
I have with exact view perus'd thee, Hector,
And quoted joint by joint.
Hect. Is this Achilles?
Achil. I am Achilles.
Hect. Stand fair, I pray thee: let me look on thee.
Achil. Behold thy fill.
Hect. Nay, I have done already.
Achil. Thou art too brief; I will the second time,
As I would buy thee, view thee limb by limb.
Hect. O, like a book of sport thou'lt read me o'er;
But there's more in me than thou understand'st.
Why dost thou so oppress me with thine eye?
Achil. Tell me, you heavens, in which part of his body
Shall I destroy him? whether there, there, or there?
That I may give the local wound a name;
And make distinct the very breach whereout
Hector's great spirit flew: Answer me, heavens!
Hect. It would discredit the bless'd gods, proud man,
To answer such a question: Stand again:
Think'st thou to catch my life so pleasantly,
As to prenominate in nice conjecture,
Where thou wilt hit me dead?
Achil. I tell thee, yea.
Hect. Wert thou an oracle to tell me so,
I'd not believe thee. Henceforth guard thee well;
For I'll not kill thee there, nor there, nor there;
But, by the forge that stithied Mars his helm,
I'll kill thee every where, yea, o'er and o'er.—
You wisest Grecians, pardon me this brag,
His insolence draws folly from my lips;
But I'll endeavour deeds to match these words,
Or may I never——
Ajax. Do not chafe thee, cousin;
And you Achilles, let these threats alone,
Till accident, or purpose, bring you to't:
You may have every day enough of Hector,
If you have stomach; the general state, I fear,
Can scarce entreat you to be odd with him.
Hect. I pray you, let us see you in the field;
We have had pelting wars, since you refus'd
The Grecians' cause.
Achil. Dost thou entreat me, Hector?
To-morrow, do I meet thee, fell as death;
To-night, all friends.
Hect. Thy hand upon that match.

Agam. First, all you peers of Greece, go to my tent;
There in the full convive we: afterwards,
As Hector's leisure and your bounties shall
Concur together, severally entreat him.—
Beat loud the tabourines, let the trumpets blow,
That this great soldier may his welcome know.
[*Exeunt all but* TROILUS *and* ULYSSES.

Tro. My Lord Ulysses, tell me, I beseech you,
In what place of the field doth Calchas keep?

Ulyss. At Menelaus' tent, most princely Troilus:
There Diomed doth feast with him to-night:
Who neither looks upon the heaven, nor earth,
But gives all gaze and bent of amorous view
On the fair Cressid.

Tro. Shall I, sweet lord, be bound to you so much,
After we part from Agamemnon's tent,
To bring me thither?

Ulyss. You shall command me, sir.
As gentle tell me, of what honour was
This Cressida in Troy? Had she no lover there
That wails her absence?

Tro. O, sir, to such as boasting show their scars,
A mock is due. Will you walk on, my lord?
She was belov'd, she lov'd; she is, and doth:
But, still, sweet love is food for fortune's tooth.
[*Exeunt.*

ACT V.

SCENE I. *The* Grecian *Camp.* *Before* Achilles' *Tent.*

Enter ACHILLES *and* PATROCLUS.

Achil. I'll heat his blood with Greekish wine to-night,
Which with my scimitar I'll cool to-morrow.—
Patroclus, let us feast him to the height.

Patr. Here comes Thersites.

Enter THERSITES.

Achil. How now, thou core of envy?
Thou crusty batch of nature, what's the news?

Ther. Why, thou picture of what thou seemest, and idol of idiot-worshippers, here's a letter for thee.

Achil. From whence, fragment?

Ther. Why, thou full dish of fool, from Troy.

Patr. Who keeps the tent now?

Ther. The surgeon's box, or the patient's wound.

Patr. Well said, Adversity! and what need these tricks?

Ther. 'Pr'ythee be silent, boy; I profit not by thy talk: thou art thought to be Achilles' male varlet.

Patr. Male varlet, you rogue! what's that?

Ther. Why, his masculine whore. Now the rotten diseases of the south, the guts-griping, ruptures, catarrhs, loads o' gravel i' the back, lethargies, cold palsies, raw eyes, dirt-rotten livers, wheezing lungs, bladders full of imposthume, sciaticas, limekilns i' the palm, incurable bone-ach, and the rivelled fee-simple of the tetter, take and take again such preposterous discoveries!

Patr. Why thou damnable box of envy, thou, what meanest thou to curse thus?

Ther. Do I curse thee?

Patr. Why, no, you ruinous butt; you whoreson indistinguishable cur, no.

Ther. No? why art thou then exasperate, thou idle immaterial skein of sleave silk, thou green sarcenet flap for a sore eye, thou tassel of a prodigal's purse, thou? Ah, how the poor world is pestered with such water-flies: diminutives of nature!

Patr. Out, gall!

Ther. Finch egg!

Achil. My sweet Patroclus, I am thwarted quite
From my great purpose in to-morrow's battle.
Here is a letter from queen Hecuba:
A token from her daughter, my fair love;
Both taxing me, and gaging me to keep
An oath that I have sworn. I will not break it:
Fall, Greeks; fail, fame; honour, or go, or stay,
My major vow lies here, this I'll obey.——
Come, come, Thersites, help to trim my tent;
This night in banqueting must all be spent.
Away, Patroclus. [*Exeunt* ACHIL. *and* PATR.

Ther. With too much blood and too little brain, these two may run mad; but if with too much brain, and too little blood, they do, I'll be a curer of madmen. Here's Agamemnon,—an honest fellow enough, and one that loves quails; but he has not so much brain as earwax. And the goodly transformation of Jupiter there, his brother, the bull,—the primitive statue, and oblique memorial of cuckolds; a thrifty shoeing-horn in a chain, hanging at his brother's leg,—to what form, but that he is, should wit larded with malice, and malice forced with wit, turn him to? To an ass, were nothing: he is both ass and ox: to an ox were nothing: he is both ox and ass. To be a dog, a mule, a cat, a fitchew, a toad, a lizard, an owl, a puttock, or a herring without a roe, I would not care: but to be Menelaus,—I would conspire against destiny. Ask me not what I would be, if I were not Thersites; for I care not to be the louse of a lazar, so I were not Menelaus.—Hey-day! spirits and fires!

Enter HECTOR, TROILUS, AJAX, AGAMEMNON, ULYSSES, NESTOR, MENELAUS, *and* DIOMED, *with Lights.*

Agam. We go wrong, we go wrong.

Ajax. No, yonder 'tis;
There, where we see the lights.

Hect. I trouble you.

Ajax. No, not a whit.

Ulyss. Here comes himself to guide you.

Enter ACHILLES.

Achil. Welcome, brave Hector; welcome, princes all.

Agam. So now, fair prince of Troy, I bid good night.
Ajax commands the guard to tend on you.

Hect. Thanks, and good night, to the Greeks' general.

Men. Good night, my lord.

Hect. Good night, sweet lord Menelaus.

Ther. Sweet draught: Sweet, quoth 'a! sweet sink, sweet sewer.

Achil. Good night,
And welcome, both to those that go, and tarry.

Agam. Good night.
[*Exeunt* AGAMEMNON *and* MENELAUS.

Achil. Old Nestor tarries; and you too, Diomed,
Keep Hector company an hour or two.

Dio. I cannot, lord; I have important business,
The tide whereof is now.—Good night, great Hector.

Hect. Give me your hand.

Ulyss. Follow his torch, he goes
To Calchas' tent; I'll keep you company.
[*Aside to* TROILUS.

Tro. Sweet sir, you honour me.

Hect. And so good night.
[*Exit* DIO.; ULYSS. *and* TROI. *following*.

Achil. Come, come, enter my tent.
[*Exeunt* ACHIL. HECT. AJAX, *and* NEST.

Ther. That same Diomed's a false-hearted rogue, a most unjust knave; I will no more trust him when he leers, than I will a serpent when he hisses: he will spend his mouth, and promise, like Brabler the hound; but when he performs, astronomers foretell it; it is prodigious, there will come some change; the sun borrows of the moon, when Diomed keeps his word. I will rather leave to see Hector, than not to dog him: they say, he keeps a Trojan drab, and uses the traitor Calchas' tent: I'll after.—Nothing but lechery! all incontinent varlets! [*Exit.*

SCENE II. *The same. Before* Calchas' *Tent.*

Enter DIOMEDES.

Dio. What are you up here, ho? speak.
Cal. [*Within.*] Who calls?
Dio. Diomed.—Calchas, I think,—Where's your daughter?
Cal. [*Within.*] She comes to you.

Enter TROILUS *and* ULYSSES, *at a distance; after them* THERSITES.

Ulyss. Stand where the torch may not discover us.

Enter CRESSIDA.

Tro. Cressid comes forth to him!
Dio. How now, my charge?
Cres. Now, my sweet guardian!—Hark! a word with you. [*Whispers.*
Tro. Yea, so familiar!
Ulyss. She will sing any man at first sight.
Ther. And any man may sing her, if he can take her cliff; she's noted.
Dio. Will you remember?
Cres. Remember? yes.
Dio. Nay, but do then;
And let your mind be coupled with your words.
Tro. What should she remember?
Ulyss. List!
Cres. Sweet honey Greek, tempt me no more [to folly.
Ther. Roguery!
Dio. Nay, then,—
Cres. I'll tell you what:
Dio. Pho! pho! come, tell a pin: You are forsworn.—
Cres. In faith, I cannot: What would you have me do?
Ther. A juggling trick, to be—secretly open.
Dio. What did you swear you would bestow on me?
Cres. I pr'ythee, do not hold me to mine oath?
Bid me do any thing but that, sweet Greek.
Dio. Good night.
Tro. Hold, patience!
Ulyss. How, now, Trojan?
Cres. Diomed,——
Dio. No, no, good night: I'll be your fool no more.
Tro. Thy better must.
Cres. Hark! one word in your ear.
Tro. O plague and madness!
Ulyss. You are mov'd, prince; let us depart, I pray you,
Lest your displeasure should enlarge itself
To wrathful terms: this place is dangerous;
The time right deadly; I beseech you, go.
Tro. Behold, I pray you!
Ulyss. Now, good my lord, go off;
You flow to great destruction; come, my lord.
Tro. I pr'ythee, stay.
Ulyss. You have not patience; come.
Tro. I pray you, stay; by hell, and all hell's torments,
I will not speak a word.
Dio. And so, good night.
Cres. Nay, but you part in anger.
Tro. Doth that grieve thee?
O wither'd truth!
Ulyss. Why, how now, lord!
Tro. By Jove,
I will be patient.
Cres. Guardian!—why, Greek!
Dio. Pho, pho! adieu; you palter.
Cres. In faith, I do not; come hither once again.
Ulyss. You shake, my lord, at something; will you go?
You will break out.
Tro. She strokes his cheek!
Ulyss. Come, come.
Tro. Nay, stay; by Jove, I will not speak a word:
There is between my will and all offences
A guard of patience:—stay a little while.
Ther. How the devil luxury, with his fat rump, and potatoe finger, tickles these together! Fry, lechery, fry!
Dio. But will you then?
Cres. In faith, I will, la; never trust me else.
Dio. Give me some token for the surety of it.
Cres. I'll fetch you one. [*Exit.*
Ulyss. You have sworn patience.
Tro. Fear me not, my lord;
I will not be myself, nor have cognition
Of what I feel; I am all patience.

Re-enter CRESSIDA.

Ther. Now the pledge; now, now, now!
Cres. Here, Diomed, keep this sleeve.
Tro. O beauty! where's thy faith!
Ulyss. My lord,——
Tro. I will be patient; outwardly I will.
Cres. You look upon that sleeve; Behold it well.—
He loved me—O false wench!—Give't me again.
Dio. Who was't?
Cres. No matter, now I hav't again.
I will not meet with you to-morrow night:
I pr'ythee, Diomed, visit me no more.
Ther. Now she sharpens:—Well said, whet-[stone.
Dio. I shall have it.
Cres. What, this?
Dio. Ay, that.
Cres. O, all you gods!—O pretty pretty pledge,
Thy master now lies thinking in his bed
Of thee, and me; and sighs, and takes my glove,
And gives memorial dainty kisses to it,
As I kiss thee.—Nay, do not snatch it from me;
He, that takes that, must take my heart withal.
Dio. I had your heart before, this follows it.
Tro. I did swear patience.
Cres. You shall not have it, Diomed; 'faith you shall not;
I'll give you something else.
Dio. I will have this; Whose was it?
Cres. 'Tis no matter.
Dio. Come, tell me whose it was.
Cres. 'Twas one's that loved me better than you will.
But, now you have it, take it.
Dio. Whose was it?
Cres. By all Diana's waiting-women yonder,
And by herself, I will not tell you whose.
Dio. To-morrow will I wear it on my helm;
And grieve his spirit that dares not challenge it.
Tro. Wert thou the devil, and wor'st it on thy horn,
It should be challeng'd.
Cres. Well, well, 'tis done, 'tis past,—And yet it is not;
I will not keep my word.
Dio. Why then, farewell;
Thou never shalt mock Diomed again.
Cres. You shall not go:—One cannot speak a word,
But it straight starts you.
Dio. I do not like this fooling.
Ther. Nor I, by Pluto: but that that likes not you, pleases me best.
Dio. What, shall I come? the hour?
Cres. Ay, come:—O Jove!—
Do come:—I shall be plagu'd.
Dio. Farewell till then.
Cres. Good night. I pr'ythee, come.—
[*Exit* DIOMEDES.
Troilus, farewell! one eye yet looks on thee;
But with my heart the other eye doth see.
Ah! poor our sex! this fault in us I find,
The error of our eye directs our mind:

What error leads, must err; O then conclude,
Minds, sway'd by eyes, are full of turpitude.
[*Exit* CRESSIDA.

Ther. A proof of strength she could not publish more,
Unless she said, My mind is now turn'd whore.

Ulyss. All's done, my lord.

Tro. It is.

Ulyss. Why stay we then?

Tro. To make a recordation to my soul
Of every syllable that here was spoke.
But, if I tell how these two did co-act,
Shall I not lie in publishing a truth?
Sith yet there is a credence in my heart,
An esperance so obstinately strong,
That doth invert the attest of eyes and ears;
As if those organs had deceptious functions,
Created only to calumniate.
Was Cressid here?

Ulyss. I cannot conjure, Trojan.

Tro. She was not, sure.

Ulyss. Most sure she was.

Tro. Why, my negation hath no taste of madness.

Ulyss. Nor mine, my lord: Cressid was here but now.

Tro. Let it not be believ'd for womanhood!
Think, we had mothers; do not give advantage
To stubborn criticks—apt, without a theme,
For depravation,—to square the general sex
By Cressid's rule: rather think this not Cressid.

Ulyss. What hath she done, prince, that can soil our mothers?

Tro. Nothing at all, unless that this were she.

Ther. Will he swagger himself out on's own eyes?

Tro. This she? no, this is Diomed's Cressida:
If beauty have a soul, this is not she;
If souls guide vows, if vows be sanctimony,
If sanctimony be the gods' delight,
If there be rule in unity itself,
This was not she. O madness of discourse,
That cause sets up with and against itself!
Bi-fold authority! where reason can revolt
Without perdition, and loss assume all reason
Without revolt: this is, and is not, Cressid!
Within my soul there doth commence a fight
Of this strange nature, that a thing inseparate
Divides more wider than the sky and earth;
And yet the spacious breadth of this division
Admits no orifice for a point, as subtle
As Ariachne's broken woof, to enter.
Instance, O instance! strong as Pluto's gates;
Cressid is mine, tied with the bonds of heaven:
Instance, O instance! strong as heaven itself;
The bonds of heaven are slipp'd, dissolv'd, and loos'd;
And with another knot, five-finger-tied,
The fractions of her faith, orts of her love,
The fragments, scraps, the bits, and greasy reliques
Of her o'er-eaten faith, are bound to Diomed.

Ulyss. May worthy Troilus be half attach'd
With that which here his passion doth express?

Tro. Ay, Greek; and that shall be divulged well
In characters as red as Mars his heart
Inflam'd with Venus: never did young man fancy
With so eternal and so fix'd a soul.
Hark, Greek;—As much as I do Cressid love,
So much by weight hate I her Diomed;
That sleeve is mine, that he'll bear on his helm;
Were it a casque compos'd by Vulcan's skill,
My sword should bite it: not the dreadful spout,
Which shipmen do the hurricano call
Constring'd in mass by the almighty sun,
Shall dizzy with more clamour Neptune's ear
In his descent, than shall my prompted sword
Falling on Diomed.

Ther. He'll tickle it for his concupy.

Tro. O Cressid! O false Cressid; false, false, false!
Let all untruths stand by thy stained name,
And they'll seem glorious.

Ulyss. O, contain yourself;
Your passion draws ears hither.

Enter ÆNEAS.

Æne. I have been seeking you this hour, my lord:
Hector, by this, is arming him in Troy;
Ajax your guard, stays to conduct you home.

Tro. Have with you, prince:—My courteous lord, adieu:
Farewell, revolted fair!—and, Diomed,
Stand fast, and wear a castle on thy head!

Ulyss. I'll bring you to the gates.

Tro. Accept distracted thanks.
[*Exeunt* TROILUS, ÆNEAS, *and* ULYSSES.

Ther. 'Would, I could meet that rogue Diomed! I would croak like a raven; I would bode, I would bode. Patroclus will give me any thing for the intelligence of this whore: the parrot will not do more for an almond, than he for a commodious drab. Lechery, lechery; still, wars and lechery; nothing else holds fashion: A burning devil take them! [*Exit.*

SCENE III. Troy. *Before* Priam's *Palace.*

Enter HECTOR *and* ANDROMACHE.

And. When was my lord so much ungently temper'd,
To stop his ears against admonishment?
Unarm, unarm, and do not fight to-day.

Hect. You train me to offend you; get you in:
By all the everlasting gods, I'll go.

And. My dreams will, sure, prove ominous to the day.

Hect. No more, I say.

Enter CASSANDRA.

Cas. Where is my brother Hector?

And. Here, sister; arm'd, and bloody in intent;
Consort with me in loud and dear petition,
Pursue we him on knees; for I have dream'd
Of bloody turbulence, and this whole night
Hath nothing been but shapes and forms of slaughter.

Cas. O, it is true.

Hect. Ho! bid my trumpet sound!

Cas. No notes of sally, for the heavens, sweet brother.

Hect. Begone, I say: the gods have heard me swear.

Cas. The gods are deaf to hot and peevish vows;
They are polluted offerings, more abhorr'd
Than spotted livers in the sacrifice.

And. O! be persuaded: Do not count it holy
To hurt by being just: it is as lawful,
For we would give much, to use violent thefts,
And rob in the behalf of charity.

Cas. It is the purpose that makes strong the vow;
But vows to every purpose must not hold:
Unarm, sweet Hector.

Hect. Hold you still, I say;
Mine honour keeps the weather of my fate:
Life every man holds dear; but the dear man
Holds honour far more precious-dear than life.—

Enter TROILUS.

How now, young man? mean'st thou to fight to-day?

And. Cassandra, call my father to persuade.
[*Exit* CASSANDRA.

Hect. No, faith, young Troilus; doff thy harness, youth;
I am to-day i' the vein of chivalry:
Let grow thy sinews till their knots be strong,
And tempt not yet the brushes of the war.
Unarm thee, go; and doubt thou not, brave boy,
I'll stand to-day, for thee, and me, and Troy.

Tro. Brother, you have a vice of mercy in you,
Which better fits a lion than a man.

Hect. What vice is that, good Troilus? chide me for it.
Tro. When many times the captive Grecians fall,
Even in the fan and wind of your fair sword,
You bid them rise and live.
Hect. O, 'tis fair play.
Tro. Fool's play, by heaven, Hector.
Hect. How now? how now?
Tro. For the love of all the gods,
Let's leave the hermit Pity with our mother;
And when we have our armours buckled on,
The venom'd vengeance ride upon our swords;
Spur them to ruthful work, rein them from ruth.
Hect. Fye, savage, fye!
Tro. Hector, then 'tis wars.
Hect. Troilus, I would not have you fight to-day.
Tro. Who should withhold me?
Not fate, obedience, nor the hand of Mars
Beckoning with fiery truncheon my retire;
Not Priamus and Hecuba on knees,
Their eyes o'ergalled with recourse of tears;
Nor you, my brother, with your true sword drawn,
Oppos'd to hinder me, should stop my way,
But by my ruin.

Re-enter CASSANDRA, *with* PRIAM.

Cas. Lay hold upon him, Priam, hold him fast:
He is thy crutch; now if thou lose thy stay,
Thou on him leaning, and all Troy on thee,
Fall all together.
Pri. Come, Hector, come, go back:
Thy wife hath dream'd; thy mother hath had visions;
Cassandra doth foresee; and I myself
Am like a prophet suddenly enrapt,
To tell thee—that this day is ominous:
Therefore, come back.
Hect. Æneas is afield;
And I do stand engag'd to many Greeks,
Even in the faith of valour, to appear
This morning to them.
Pri. But thou shalt not go.
Hect. I must not break my faith.
You know me dutiful; therefore, dear sir,
Let me not shame respect; but give me leave
To take that course by your consent and voice,
Which you do here forbid me, royal Priam.
Cas. O Priam, yield not to him.
And. Do not, dear father.
Hect. Andromache, I am offended with you:
Upon the love you bear me, get you in.
[*Exit* ANDROMACHE.
Tro. This foolish, dreaming, superstitious girl,
Makes all these bodements.
Cas. O farewell, dear Hector.
Look, how thou diest! look, how thy eye turns pale!
Look, how thy wounds do bleed at many vents!
Hark, how Troy roars! how Hecuba cries out!
How poor Andromache shrills her dolours forth!
Behold, destruction, frenzy, and amazement,
Like witless anticks, one another meet,
And all cry—Hector! Hector's dead! O Hector!
Tro. Away!—Away!
Cas. Farewell.—Yet, soft:—Hector, I take my leave:
Thou dost thyself and all our Troy deceive.
[*Exit.*
Hect. You are amaz'd, my liege, at her exclaim:
Go in, and cheer the town: we'll forth, and fight;
Do deeds worth praise, and tell you them at night.
Pri. Farewell; the gods with safety stand about thee!
[*Exeunt severally* PRI. *and* HECT. *Alarums.*
Tro. They are at it; hark! Proud Diomed, believe,
I come to lose my arm, or win my sleeve.

As TROILUS *is going out, enter, from the other side,* PANDARUS.

Pan. Do you hear, my lord? do you hear?
Tro. What now?
Pan. Here's a letter from yon' poor girl.
Tro. Let me read.
Pan. A whoreson ptisick, a whoreson rascally ptisick so troubles me, and the foolish fortune of this girl; and what one thing, what another, that I shall leave you one o' these days: And I have a rheum in mine eyes too; and such an ache in my bones, that, unless a man were cursed, I cannot tell what to think on't.—What says she there?
Tro. Words, words, mere words, no matter from the heart; [*Tearing the letter.*
The effect doth operate another way.
Go, wind, to wind, there turn and change together.—
My love with words and errors still she feeds;
But edifies another with her deeds.
[*Exeunt severally.*

SCENE IV.

Between Troy *and the* Grecian *Camp.*

Alarums: Excursions. Enter THERSITES.

Ther. Now they are clapper-clawing one another; I'll go look on. That dissembling abominable varlet, Diomed, has got that same scurvy doting foolish young knave's sleeve of Troy there, in his helm; I would fain see them meet; that that same young Trojan ass, that loves the whore there, might send that Greekish whoremasterly villain, with the sleeve, back to the dissembling luxurious drab, on a sleeveless errand. O' the other side, The policy of those crafty swearing rascals,—that stale old mouse-eaten dry cheese, Nestor; and that same dog-fox, Ulysses,—is not proved worth a blackberry:—They set me up, in policy, that mongrel cur, Ajax, against that dog of as bad a kind, Achilles; and now is the cur Ajax prouder than the cur Achilles, and will not arm to-day: whereupon the Grecians begin to proclaim barbarism, and policy grows into an ill opinion. Soft! here comes sleeve, and t'other.

Enter DIOMEDES, TROILUS *following.*

Tro. Fly not; for, shouldst thou take the river Styx,
I would swim after.
Dio. Thou dost miscall retire:
I do not fly; but advantageous care
Withdrew me from the odds of multitude:
Have at thee!
Ther. Hold thy whore, Grecian!—now for thy whore, Trojan!—now the sleeve, now the sleeve!
[*Exeunt* TROILUS *and* DIOMEDES, *fighting.*

Enter HECTOR.

Hect. What art thou, Greek? art thou for Hector's match?
Art thou of blood, and honour?
Ther. No, no:—I am a rascal; a scurvy railing knave; a very filthy rogue.
Hect. I do believe thee:—live. [*Exit.*
Ther. God-a-mercy, that thou wilt believe me; But a plague break thy neck, for frighting me! What's become of the wenching rogues? I think, they have swallowed one another; I would laugh at that miracle. Yet, in a sort, lechery eats itself. I'll seek them. [*Exit.*

SCENE V. *The same.*

Enter DIOMEDES *and a* Servant.

Dio. Go, go, my servant, take thou Troilus' horse;
Present the fair steed to my lady Cressid:
Fellow, commend my service to her beauty;
Tell her, I have chastis'd the amorous Trojan,
And am her knight by proof.
Serv. I go, my lord. [*Exit* Servant.

Enter AGAMEMNON.

Agam. Renew, renew! The fierce Polydamus
Hath beat down Menon: bastard Margarelon
Hath Doreus prisoner:
And stands colossus-wise, waving his beam,
Upon the pashed corses of the kings
Epistrophus and Cedius: Polixenes is slain;
Amphimachus, and Thoas, deadly hurt;
Patroclus ta'en, or slain; and Palamedes
Sore hurt and bruised: the dreadful Sagittary
Appals our numbers; haste we, Diomed,
To reinforcement, or we perish all.

Enter NESTOR.

Nest. Go, bear Patroclus' body to Achilles;
And bid the snail-pac'd Ajax arm for shame.—
There is a thousand Hectors in the field:
Now here he fights on Galathe his horse,
And there lacks work; anon, he's there afoot,
And there they fly, or die, like scaled sculls
Before the belching whale; then is he yonder,
And there the strawy Greeks, ripe for his edge,
Fall down before him, like the mower's swath:
Here, there, and every where, he leaves, and takes;
Dexterity so obeying appetite,
That what he will, he does; and does so much,
That proof is call'd impossibility.

Enter ULYSSES.

Ulyss. O, courage, courage, princes! great Achilles
Is arming, weeping, cursing, vowing vengeance:
Patroclus' wounds have rous'd his drowsy blood,
Together with his mangled myrmidons,
That noseless, handless, hack'd and chipp'd, come to him,
Crying on Hector. Ajax hath lost a friend,
And foams at mouth, and he is arm'd, and at it,
Roaring for Troilus; who hath done to-day
Mad and fantastic execution;
Engaging and redeeming of himself,
With such a careless force, and forceless care,
As if that luck, in very spite of cunning,
Bade him win all.

Enter AJAX.

Ajax. Troilus! thou coward Troilus! [*Exit.*
Dio. Ay, there, there.
Nest. So, so, we draw together.

Enter ACHILLES.

Achil. Where is this Hector?
Come, come, thou boy-queller, show thy face;
Know what it is to meet Achilles angry.
Hector! where's Hector? I will none but Hector.
[*Exeunt.*

SCENE VI. *Another part of the Field.*

Enter AJAX.

Ajax. Troilus, thou coward Troilus, show thy head!

Enter DIOMEDES.

Dio. Troilus, I say, where's Troilus?
Ajax. What would'st thou?
Dio. I would correct him.
Ajax. Were I the general, thou should'st have my office
Ere that correction:—Troilus, I say! what, Troilus!

Enter TROILUS.

Tro. O traitor Diomed!—turn thy false face, thou traitor,
And pay thy life thou ow'st me for my horse!
Dio. Ha! art thou there?
Ajax. I'll fight with him alone: stand, Diomed.
Dio. He is my prize, I will not look upon.
Tro. Come both, you cogging Greeks; have at you both. [*Exeunt, fighting.*

Enter HECTOR.

Hect. Yea, Troilus? O, well fought, my youngest brother!

Enter ACHILLES.

Achil. Now do I see thee; Ha!—Have at thee, Hector.
Hect. Pause, if thou wilt.
Achil. I do disdain thy courtesy, proud Trojan.
Be happy, that my arms are out of use:
My rest and negligence befriend thee now,
But thou anon shalt hear of me again;
Till when, go seek thy fortune. [*Exit.*
Hect. Fare thee well:—
I would have been much more a fresher man,
Had I expected thee.—How now, my brother?

Re-enter TROILUS.

Tro. Ajax hath ta'en Æneas; Shall it be?
No, by the flame of yonder glorious heaven,
He shall not carry him; I'll be taken, too,
Or bring him off:—Fate, hear me what I say!
I reck not though I end my life to-day. [*Exit.*

Enter One in sumptuous Armour.

Hect. Stand, stand, thou Greek; thou art a goodly mark:—
No? wilt thou not?—I like thy armour well;
I'll frush it, and unlock the rivets all,
But I'll be master of it:—Wilt thou not, beast, abide?
Why then, fly on, I'll hunt thee for thy hide.
[*Exeunt.*

SCENE VII. *The same.*

Enter ACHILLES, *with* Myrmidons.

Achil. Come here about me, you my Myrmidons;
Mark what I say.—Attend me where I wheel:
Strike not a stroke, but keep yourselves in breath;
And when I have the bloody Hector found,
Empale him with your weapons round about;
In fellest manner execute your arms.
Follow me, sirs, and my proceedings eye!
It is decreed—Hector the great must die.
[*Exeunt.*

SCENE VIII. *The same.*

Enter MENELAUS *and* PARIS, *fighting; then* THERSITES.

Ther. The cuckold, and the cuckold-maker are at it: Now, bull! now, dog! 'Loo, Paris, 'loo! now, my double-henned sparrow! 'loo, Paris, 'loo! The bull has the game:—'ware horns, ho! [*Exeunt* PARIS *and* MENELAUS.

Enter MARGARELON.

Mar. Turn, slave, and fight.
Ther. What art thou?
Mar. A bastard son of Priam's.
Ther. I am a bastard too; I love bastards: I am a bastard begot, bastard instructed, bastard in mind, bastard in valour, in every thing illegitimate. One bear will not bite another, and wherefore should one bastard? Take heed, the quarrel's most ominous to us: if the son of a whore fight for a whore, he tempts judgment: Farewell, bastard.
Mar. The devil take thee, coward! [*Exeunt.*

SCENE IX. *Another part of the Field.*

Enter HECTOR.

Hect. Most putrified core, so fair without,
Thy goodly armour thus hath cost thy life.
Now is my day's work done; I'll take good breath:
Rest, sword; thou hast thy fill of blood and death!
[*Puts off his helmet, and hangs his shield behind him.*

Enter ACHILLES *and* Myrmidons.

Achil. Look, Hector, how the sun begins to set;
How ugly night comes breathing at his heels:
Even with the vail and dark'ning of the sun,
To close the day up, Hector's life is done.

Hect. I am unarm'd; forego this vantage, Greek.

Achil. Strike, fellows, strike; this is the man I seek. [HECTOR *falls.*

So, Ilion, fall thou next! now, Troy, sink down:
Here lies thy heart, thy sinews, and thy bone.—
On, Myrmidons; and cry you all amain,
Achilles hath the mighty Hector slain.

[*A Retreat sounded.*

Hark! a retreat upon our Grecian part.

Myr. The Trojan trumpets sound the like my lord.

Achil. The dragon wing of night o'erspreads the earth,
And, stickler like, the armies separates,
My half-supp'd sword, that frankly would have fed,
Pleas'd with this dainty bit, thus goes to bed.—

[*Sheathes his sword.*

Come, tie his body to my horse's tail;
Along the field I will the Trojan trail. [*Exeunt.*

SCENE X. *The same.*

Enter AGAMEMNON, AJAX, MENELAUS, NESTOR, DIOMEDES, *and Others, marching. Shouts within.*

Agam. Hark! hark! what shout is that?

Nest. Peace, drums.

[*Within.*] Achilles!
Achilles! Hector's slain! Achilles!

Dio. The bruit is—Hector's slain, and by Achilles.

Ajax. If it be so, yet bragless let it be;
Great Hector was as good a man as he.

Agam. March patiently along:—Let one be sent
To pray Achilles see us at our tent.—
If in his death the gods have us befriended,
Great Troy is ours, and our sharp wars are ended.

[*Exeunt, marching.*

SCENE XI. *Another part of the Field.*

Enter ÆNEAS *and* Trojans.

Æne. Stand, ho! yet are we masters of the field:
Never go home; here starve we out the night.

Enter TROILUS.

Tro. Hector is slain.

All. Hector?—The gods forbid!

Tro. He's dead; and at the murderer's horse's tail,
In beastly sort, dragg'd through the shameful field.—
Frown on, you heavens, effect your rage with speed!
Sit, gods, upon your thrones, and smile at Troy!
I say, at once let your brief plagues be mercy,
And linger not our sure destructions on!

Æne. My lord, you do discomfort all the host.

Tro. You understand me not, that tell me so;
I do not speak of flight, of fear, of death;
But dare all imminence, that gods and men,
Address their dangers in. Hector is gone!
Who shall tell Priam so, or Hecuba?
Let him that will a screech-owl aye be call'd,
Go in to Troy, and say there—Hector's dead:
There is a word will Priam turn to stone;
Make wells and Niobes of the maids and wives,
Cold statues of the youth; and, in a word,
Scare Troy out of itself. But, march, away:
Hector is dead; there is no more to say.
Stay yet;—You vile abominable tents,
Thus proudly pight upon our Phrygian plains,
Let Titan rise as early as he dare,
I'll through and through you!—And thou, great-siz'd coward!
No space of earth shall sunder our two hates;
I'll haunt thee like a wicked conscience still,
That mouldeth goblins swift as frenzy thoughts.—
Strike a free march to Troy!—with comfort go:
Hope of revenge shall hide our inward woe.

[*Exeunt* ÆNEAS *and* Trojans.

As TROILUS *is going out, enter, from the other side,* PANDARUS.

Pan. But hear you, hear you!

Tro. Hence, broker lackey! ignomy and shame
Pursue thy life, and live aye with thy name!

[*Exit* TROILUS.

Pan. A goodly med'cine for my aching bones!—O world! world! world! thus is the poor agent despised! O traitors and bawds, how earnestly are you set a' work, and how ill requited! Why should our endeavour be so loved, and the performance so loathed? what verse for it? what instance for it?—Let me see:—

Full merrily the humble bee doth sing,
Till he hath lost his honey, and his sting:
And being once subdued in armed tail,
Sweet honey, and sweet notes together fail.—

Good traders in the flesh, set this in your painted cloths.

As many as be here of Pandar's hall,
Your eyes, half out, weep out at Pandar's fall:
Or, if you cannot weep, yet give some groans,
Though not for me, yet for your aching bones.
Brethren, and sisters, of the hold-door trade,
Some two months hence my will shall here be made:
It should be now, but that my fear is this,—
Some galled goose of Winchester would hiss:
Till then I'll sweat, and seek about for eases;
And, at that time, bequeath you my diseases.

[*Exit.*

TIMON OF ATHENS.

PERSONS REPRESENTED.

TIMON, *a noble* Athenian.
LUCIUS, LUCULLUS, SEMPRONIUS, *Lords, and Flatterers of* Timon.
VENTIDIUS, *one of* Timon's *false Friends.*
APEMANTUS, *a churlish Philosopher.*
ALCIBIADES, *an* Athenian *General.*
FLAVIUS, *Steward to* Timon.
FLAMINIUS, LUCILIUS, SERVILIUS, Timon's *Servants.*
CAPHIS, PHILOTUS, *Servants to* Timon's *Creditors.*
TITUS, LUCIUS, HORTENSIUS, *Servants to* Timon's *Creditors.*
Two Servants *of* Varro, *and the* Servant *of* Isidore; *two of* Timon's *Creditors.*
CUPID *and* Maskers. *Three* Strangers.
Poet, Painter, Jeweller, *and* Merchant.
An old Athenian. *A* Page. *A* Fool.
PHRYNIA, TIMANDRA, *Mistresses to* Alcibiades.
Other Lords, Senators, Officers, Soldiers, Thieves, *and* Attendants.

SCENE—Athens; *and the Woods adjoining.*

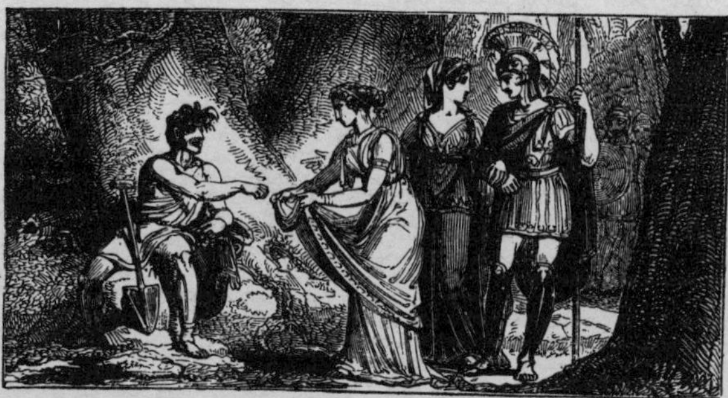

ACT I.

SCENE I. Athens. *A Hall in* Timon's *House.*

Enter Poet, Painter, Jeweller, Merchant, *and Others, at several Doors.*

Poet. GOOD day, sir.
Pain. I am glad you are well.
Poet. I have not seen you long; How goes the world?
Pain. It wears, sir, as it grows.
Poet. Ay, that's well known:
But what particular rarity? what strange,
Which manifold record not matches? See,
Magic of bounty! all these spirits thy power
Hath conjur'd to attend. I know the merchant.
Pain. I know them both; t'other's a jeweller.
Mer. O, 'tis a worthy lord!
Jew. Nay, that's most fix'd.
Mer. A most incomparable man; breath'd, as it were,
To an untirable and continuate goodness:
He passes.
Jew. I have a jewell here.
Mer. O, pray, let's see't: For the Lord Timon, sir?
Jew. If he will touch the estimate: But, for that——
Poet. *When we for recompence have prais'd the vile,*
It stains the glory in that happy verse
Which aptly sings the good.
Mer. 'Tis a good form.
[*Looking at the Jewel.*
Jew. And rich: here is a water, look you.
Pain. You are rapt, sir, in some work, some dedication
To the great lord.
Poet. A thing slipp'd idly from me.
Our poesy is as a gum, which oozes
From whence 'tis nourished: The fire i'the flint
Shows not, till it be struck; our gentle flame
Provokes itself, and, like the current, flies
Each bound it chafes. What have you there?
Pain. A picture, sir.—And when comes your book forth?
Poet. Upon the heels of my presentment, sir.
Let's see your piece.
Pain. 'Tis a good piece.
Poet. So 'tis: this comes off well and excellent.
Pain. Indifferent.
Poet. Admirable: How this grace
Speaks his own standing! what a mental power
This eye shoots forth! how big imagination
Moves in this lip! to the dumbness of the gesture
One might interpret.
Pain. It is a pretty mocking of the life.
Here is a touch; Is't good?
Poet. I'll say of it,
It tutors nature: artificial strife
Lives in these touches, livelier than life.

Enter certain Senators, *and pass over.*

Pain. How this lord's follow'd!
Poet. The senators of Athens:—Happy men!
Pain. Look, more!
Poet. You see this confluence, this great flood of visitors.
I have, in this rough work, shap'd out a man,
Whom this beneath world doth embrace and hug

With amplest entertainment: My free drift
Halts not particularly, but moves itself
In a wide sea of wax: no level'd malice
Infects one comma in the course I hold;
But flies an eagle flight, bold, and forth on,
Leaving no tract behind.

Pain. How shall I understand you?

Poet. I'll unbolt to you.
You see how all conditions, how all minds
(As well of glib and slippery creatures, as
Of grave and austere quality), tender down
Their services to Lord Timon: his large fortune,
Upon his good and gracious nature hanging,
Subdues and properties to his love and tendance
All sorts of hearts; yea, from the glass-fac'd flatterer
To Apemantus, that few things loves better
Than to abhor himself: even he drops down
The knee before him, and returns in peace
Most rich in Timon's nod.

Pain. I saw them speak together.

Poet. Sir, I have upon a high and pleasant hill,
Feign'd Fortune to be thron'd: The base o' the mount
Is rank'd with all deserts, all kind of natures,
That labour on the bosom of this sphere
To propagate their states: amongst them all,
Whose eyes are on this sovereign lady fix'd,
One do I personate of Lord Timon's frame,
Whom Fortune with her ivory hand wafts to her:
Whose present grace to present slaves and servants
Translates his rivals.

Pain. 'Tis conceiv'd to scope.
This throne, this Fortune, and this hill, methinks,
With one man beckon'd from the rest below,
Bowing his head against the steepy mount
To climb his happiness, would be well express'd
In our condition.

Poet. Nay, sir, but hear me on:
All those which were his fellows, but of late
(Some better than his value), on the moment
Follow his strides, his lobbies fill with tendance,
Rain sacrificial whisperings in his ear,
Make sacred even his stirrop, and through him
Drink the free air.

Pain. Ay, marry, what of these?

Poet. When Fortune, in her shift and change of mood,
Spurns down her late belov'd, all his dependants,
Which labour'd after him to the mountain's top,
Even on their knees and hands, let him slip down,
Not one accompanying his declining foot.

Pain. 'Tis common:
A thousand moral paintings I can show,
That shall demonstrate these quick blows of fortune
More pregnantly than words. Yet you do well,
To show Lord Timon, that mean eyes have seen
The foot above the head.

Trumpets sound. Enter TIMON, *attended: the* Servant *of* VENTIDIUS *talking with him.*

Tim. Imprison'd is he, say you?

Ven. Serv. Ay, my good lord: five talents is his debt;
His means most short, his creditors most strait:
Your honourable letter he desires
To those have shut him up; which failing to him,
Periods his comfort.

Tim. Noble Ventidius! Well;
I am not of that feather to shake off
My friend when he must need me. I do know him
A gentleman, that well deserves a help,
Which he shall have: I'll pay the debt, and free him.

Ven. Serv. Your lordship ever binds him.

Tim. Commend me to him: I will send his ransome;
And, being enfranchis'd, bid him come to me;—
'Tis not enough to help the feeble up,
But to support him after.—Fare you well.

Ven. Serv. All happiness to your honour! [*Exit.*

Enter an old Athenian.

Old Ath. Lord Timon, hear me speak.

Tim. Freely, good father.

Old Ath. Thou hast a servant nam'd Lucilius.

Tim. I have so: What of him?

Old Ath. Most noble Timon, call the man before thee.

Tim. Attends he here, or no? Lucilius!

Enter LUCILIUS.

Luc. Here, at your lordship's service.

Old Ath. This fellow here, Lord Timon, this thy creature,
By night frequents my house. I am a man
That from my first have been inclin'd to thrift;
And my estate deserves an heir more rais'd,
Than one which holds a trencher.

Tim. Well: what further?

Old Ath. One only daughter have I, no kin else,
On whom I may confer what I have got:
The maid is fair, o' the youngest for a bride,
And I have bred her at my dearest cost,
In qualities of the best. This man of thine
Attempts her love: I pr'ythee, noble lord,
Join with me to forbid him her resort;
Myself have spoke in vain.

Tim. The man is honest.

Old Ath. Therefore he will be, Timon:
His honesty rewards him in itself,
It must not bear my daughter.

Tim. Does she love him?

Old Ath. She is young, and apt:
Our own precedent passions do instruct us
What levity's in youth.

Tim. [*To* LUCILIUS.] Love you the maid?

Luc. Ay, my good lord, and she accepts of it.

Old Ath. If in her marriage my consent be missing,
I call the gods to witness, I will choose
Mine heir from forth the beggars of the world,
And dispossess her all.

Tim. How shall she be endow'd,
If she be mated with an equal husband?

Old Ath. Three talents, on the present; in future, all.

Tim. This gentleman of mine hath serv'd me long;
To build his fortune, I will strain a little,
For 'tis a bond in men. Give him thy daughter:
What you bestow, in him I'll counterpoise,
And make him weigh with her.

Old Ath. Most noble lord,
Pawn me to this your honour, she is his.

Tim. My hand to thee; mine honour on my promise.

Luc. Humbly I thank your lordship: Never may
That state or fortune fall into my keeping,
Which is not ow'd to you!

[*Exeunt* LUCILIUS *and old* Athenian.

Poet. Vouchsafe my labour, and long live your lordship!

Tim. I thank you; you shall hear from me anon;
Go not away.—What have you there, my friend?

Pain. A piece of painting, which I do beseech
Your lordship to accept.

Tim. Painting is welcome.
The painting is almost the natural man;
For since dishonour trafficks with man's nature,
He is but outside: These pencil'd figures are
Even such as they give out. I like your work;
And you shall find, I like it: wait attendance
Till you hear further from me.

Pain. The gods preserve you!

Tim. Well fare you, gentlemen: Give me your hand;

We must needs dine together.—Sir, your jewel
Hath suffer'd under praise.

Jew. What, my lord? dispraise?

Tim. A meer satiety of commendations.
If I should pay you for't as 'tis extoll'd,
It would unclew me quite.

Jew. My lord, 'tis rated
As those, which sell, would give: But you well know,
Things of like value, differing in the owners,
Are prized by their masters: believe't, dear lord,
You mend the jewel by wearing it.

Tim. Well mock'd.

Mer. No, my good lord; he speaks the common tongue.
Which all men speak with him.

Tim. Look, who comes here. Will you be chid?

Enter APEMANTUS.

Jew. We will bear, with your lordship.

Mer. He'll spare none.

Tim. Good morrow to thee, gentle Apemantus!

Apem. Till I be gentle, stay for thy good morrow;
When thou art Timon's dog, and these knaves honest.

Tim. Why dost thou call them knaves? thou know'st them not.

Apem. Are they not Athenians?

Tim. Yes.

Apem. Then I repent not.

Jew. You know me, Apemantus.

Apem. Thou knowest, I do; I call thee by thy name.

Tim. Thou art proud, Apemantus.

Apem. Of nothing so much, as that I am not like Timon.

Tim. Whither art going?

Apem. To knock out an honest Athenian's brains.

Tim. That's a deed thou'lt die for.

Apem. Right, if doing nothing be death by the law.

Tim. How likest thou this picture, Apemantus?

Apem. The best for the innocence.

Tim. Wrought he not well, that painted it?

Apem. He wrought better that made the painter; and yet he's but a filthy piece of work.

Pain. You are a dog.

Apem. Thy mother's of my generation; What's she, if I be a dog.

Tim. Wilt dine with me, Apemantus?

Apem. No; I eat not lords.

Tim. An thou shouldst, thou'dst anger ladies.

Apem. O, they eat lords; so they come by great bellies.

Tim. That's a lascivious apprehension.

Apem. So thou apprehend'st it; Take it for thy labour.

Tim. How dost thou like this jewel, Apemantus?

Apem. Not so well as plain dealing, which will not cost a man a doit.

Tim. What dost thou think 'tis worth?

Apem. Not worth my thinking.—How now, poet?

Poet. How now, philosopher?

Apem. Thou liest.

Poet. Art not one?

Apem. Yes.

Poet. Then I lie not.

Apem. Art not a poet?

Poet. Yes.

Apem. Then thou liest: look in thy last work, where thou hast feign'd him a worthy fellow.

Poet. That's not feign'd, he is so.

Apem. Yes, he is worthy of thee, and to pay thee for thy labour: He, that loves to be flattered, is worthy o' the flatterer. Heavens, that I were a lord!

Tim. What would'st do then, Apemantus?

Apem. Even as Apemantus does now, hate a lord with my heart.

Tim. What, thyself?

Apem. Ay.

Tim. Wherefore?

Apem. That I had no angry wit to be a lord.—
Art not thou a merchant?

Mer. Ay, Apemantus.

Apem. Traffick confound thee, if the gods will not!

Mer. If traffick do it, the gods do it.

Apem. Traffick's thy god, and thy god confound thee!

Trumpets sound. Enter a Servant.

Tim. What trumpet's that?

Serv. 'Tis Alcibiades, and
Some twenty horse, all of companionship.

Tim. 'Pray, entertain them; give them guide to us.— [*Exeunt some* Attendants.
You must needs dine with me:—Go not you hence,
Till I have thank'd you; and, when dinner's done,
Show me this piece.—I am joyful of your sights.—

Enter ALCIBIADES, *with his* Company.

Most welcome, sir! [*They salute.*

Apem. So, so; there!—
Aches contract and starve your supple joints!—
That there should be small love 'mongst these sweet knaves,
And all this court'sy! The strain of man's bred out
Into baboon and monkey.

Alcib. Sir, you have sav'd my longing, and I feed
Most hungrily on your sight.

Tim. Right welcome, sir:
Ere we depart, we'll share a bounteous time
In different pleasures. 'Pray yet, let us in.
[*Exeunt all but* APEMANTUS.

Enter two Lords.

1 *Lord.* What time a day is't, Apemantus?

Apem. Time to be honest.

1 *Lord.* That time serves still.

Apem. The most accursed thou, that still omit'st it.

2 *Lord.* Thou art going to Lord Timon's feast.

Apem. Ay; to see meat fill knaves, and wine heat fools.

2 *Lord.* Fare thee well, fare thee well.

Apem. Thou art a fool to bid me farewell twice.

2 *Lord.* Why, Apemantus?

Apem. Shouldst have kept one to thyself, for I mean to give thee none.

1 *Lord.* Hang thyself.

Apem. No, I will do nothing at thy bidding; make thy requests to thy friend.

2 *Lord.* Away, unpeaceable dog, or I'll spurn thee hence.

Apem. I will fly, like a dog, the heels of the ass. [*Exit.*

1 *Lord.* He's opposite to humanity. Come, shall we in,
And taste Lord Timon's bounty? he outgoes
The very heart of kindness.

2 *Lord.* He pours it out; Plutus, the god of gold,
Is but his steward: no meed, but he repays
Sevenfold above itself; no gift to him,
But breeds the giver a return exceeding
All use of quittance.

1 *Lord.* The noblest mind he carries,
That ever govern'd man.

2 *Lord.* Long may he live in fortunes! Shall we in?

1 *Lord.* I'll keep you company. [*Exeunt.*

SCENE II.

The same. A Room of State in Timon's *House.*

Hautboys playing loud musick. A great banquet served in; FLAVIUS *and others attending; then enter* TIMON, ALCIBIADES, LUCIUS, LUCULLUS, SEMPRONIUS, *and other* Athenian Senators, *with* VENTIDIUS, *and* Attendants. *Then comes dropping after all,* APEMANTUS, *discontentedly.*

Ven. Most honour'd Timon, 't hath pleas'd the gods to remember
My father's age, and call him to long peace.
He is gone happy, and has left me rich:
Then, as in grateful virtue I am bound
To your free heart, I do return those talents,
Doubled, with thanks, and service, from whose help
I deriv'd liberty.

Tim. O, by no means,
Honest Ventidius: you mistake my love;
I gave it freely ever; and there's none
Can truly say, he gives, if he receives:
If our betters play at that game, we must not dare
To imitate them; Faults that are rich, are fair.

Ven. A noble spirit.

[*They all stand ceremoniously looking on* TIMON.

Tim. Nay, my lords, ceremony
Was but devis'd at first, to set a gloss
On faint deeds, hollow welcomes,
Recanting goodness, sorry ere 'tis shown;
But where there is true friendship, there needs none.
'Pray, sit; more welcome are ye to my fortunes,
Than my fortunes to me. [*They sit.*

1 *Lord.* My lord, we always have confess'd it.

Apem. Ho, ho, confess'd it? hang'd it, have you not?

Tim. O, Apemantus! you are welcome.

Apem. No,
You shall not make me welcome:
I come to have thee thrust me out of doors.

Tim. Fie, thou art a churl: you have got a humour there
Does not become a man, 'tis much to blame:—
They say, my lords, that *ira furor brevis est*,
But yond' man's ever angry.
Go, let him have a table by himself;
For he does neither affect company,
Nor is he fit for it, indeed.

Apem. Let me stay at thine apperil, Timon;
I come to observe; I give thee warning on't.

Tim. I take no heed of thee; thou art an Athenian; therefore welcome: I myself would have no power: 'pr'ythee, let my meat make thee silent.

Apem. I scorn thy meat; 'twould choke me, for I should
Ne'er flatter thee.—O you gods; what a number
Of men eat Timon, and he sees them not!
It grieves me, to see so many dip their meat
In one man's blood; and all the madness is,
He cheers them up too.
I wonder, men dare trust themselves with men:
Methinks they should invite them without knives;
Good for their meat, and safer for their lives.
There's much example for't; the fellow, that
Sits next him now, parts bread with him, and pledges
The breath of him in a divided draught,
Is the readiest man to kill him; it has been prov'd.
If I
Were a huge man, I should fear to drink at meals;
Lest they should spy my windpipe's dangerous notes:
Great men should drink with harness on their throats.

Tim. My lord, in heart; and let the health go round.

Lord. Let it flow this way, my good lord.

Apem. Flow this way!
A brave fellow!—he keeps his tides well. Timon,
Those healths will make thee, and thy state, look ill.
Here's that, which is too weak to be a sinner,
Honest water, which ne'er left man i'the mire:
This, and my food, are equals; there's no odds.
Feasts are too proud to give thanks to the gods.

APEMANTUS'S GRACE.

Immortal gods, I crave no pelf;
I pray for no man, but myself:
Grant I may never prove so fond
To trust man on his oath or bond;
Or a harlot, for her weeping;
Or a dog, that seems a sleeping:
Or a keeper, with my freedom;
Or my friends, if I should need 'em.
Amen. So fall to't:
Rich men sin, and I eat root.

[*Eats and drinks.*

Much good dich thy good heart, Apemantus!

Tim. Captain Alcibiades, your heart's in the field now.

Alcib. My heart is ever at your service, my lord.

Tim. You had rather be at a breakfast of enemies, than a dinner of friends.

Alcib. So they were bleeding new, my lord, there's no meat like them; I could wish my best friend at such a feast.

Apem. 'Would all those flatterers were thine enemies then; that then thou might'st kill 'em, and bid me to 'em.

1 *Lord.* Might we but have that happiness, my lord, that you would once use our hearts, whereby we might express some part of our zeals, we should think ourselves for ever perfect.

Tim. O, no doubt, my good friends, but the gods themselves have provided that I shall have much help from you: How had you been my friends else? why have you that charitable title from thousands, did you not chiefly belong to my heart? I have told more of you to myself, than you can with modesty speak in your own behalf; and thus far I confirm you. O, you gods, think I, what need we have any friends, if we should never have need of them? they were the most needless creatures living, should we ne'er have use for them: and would most resemble sweet instruments hung up in cases, that keep their sounds to themselves. Why, I have often wished myself poorer, that I might come nearer to you. We are born to do benefits: and what better or properer can we call our own, than the riches of our friends? O, what a precious comfort 'tis to have so many, like brothers, commanding one another's fortunes! O joy, e'en made away ere it can be born! Mine eyes cannot hold out water, methinks: to forget their faults, I drink to you.

Apem. Thou weepest to make them drink, Timon.

2 *Lord.* Joy had the like conception in our eyes,
And, at that instant, like a babe sprung up.

Apem. Ho, ho! I laugh to think that babe a bastard.

3 *Lord.* I promise you, my lord, you mov'd me much.

Apem. Much! [*Tucket sounded.*

Tim. What means that trump?—How now?

Enter a Servant.

Serv. Please you, my lord, there are certain ladies most desirous of admittance.

Tim. Ladies? what are their wills?

Serv. There comes with them a forerunner, my lord, which bears that office, to signify thier pleasures.

Tim. I pray, let them be admitted.

Enter CUPID.

Cup. Hail to thee, worthy Timon;—and to all
That of his bounties taste!—The five best senses
Acknowledge thee their patron; and come freely
To gratulate thy plenteous bosom: The ear,
Taste, touch, smell, all pleas'd from thy table rise;
They only now come but to feast thine eyes.

Tim. They are welcome all; let them have kind admittance:
Musick, make their welcome. [*Exit* CUPID.

1 Lord. You see, my lord, how ample you are belov'd.

Musick. Re-enter CUPID, *with a masque of* Ladies *as Amazons, with lutes in their hands, dancing and playing.*

Apem. Hey-day, what a sweep of vanity comes this way!
They dance! they are mad women.
Like madness is the glory of this life,
As this pomp shows to a little oil, and root.
We make ourselves fools, to disport ourselves;
And spend our flatteries, to drink those men,
Upon whose age we void it up again,
With poisonous spite, and envy. Who lives, that's not
Depraved, or depraves? who dies, that bears
Not one spurn to their graves of their friends' gift?
I should fear, those, that dance before me now,
Would one day stamp upon me: It has been done;
Men shut their doors against a setting sun.

The Lords *rise from table, with much adoring of* TIMON; *and, to show their loves, each singles out an* Amazon, *and all dance, men with women, a lofty strain or two to the hautboys, and cease.*

Tim. You have done our pleasures much grace, fair ladies,
Set a fair fashion on our entertainment,
Which was not half so beautiful and kind;
You have added worth unto't, and lively lustre,
And entertain'd me with mine own device;
I am to thank you for it.

1 Lady. My lord, you take us even at the best.

Apem. 'Faith, for the worst is filthy; and would not hold taking, I doubt me.

Tim. Ladies, there is an idle banquet
Attends you: Please you to dispose yourselves.

All Lad. Most thankfully, my lord.
[*Exeunt* CUPID *and* Ladies.

Tim. Flavius,—

Flav. My lord.

Tim. The little casket bring me hither.

Flav. Yes, my lord.—More jewels yet!
There is no crossing him in his humour; [*Aside.*
Else I should tell him,—Well,—i'faith, I should,
When all's spent, he'd be cross'd then, an he could.
'Tis pity, bounty had not eyes behind;
That man might ne'er be wretched for his mind.
[*Exit, and returns with the casket.*

1 Lord. Where be our men?

Serv. Here, my lord, in readiness.

2 Lord. Our horses.

Tim. O, my friends,
I have one word to say to you: Look, my good lord,
I must entreat you honour me so much,
As to advance this jewel; accept and wear it,
Kind my lord.

1 Lord. I am so far already in your gifts,—

All. So are we all.

Enter a Servant.

Serv. My lord, there are certain nobles of the senate
Newly alighted, and come to visit you.

Tim. They are fairly welcome.

Flav. I beseech your honour,
Vouchsafe me a word; it does concern you near.

Tim. Near? why then another time I'll hear thee:
I pr'ythee, let us be provided
To show them entertainment.

Flav. I scarce know how. [*Aside.*

Enter another Servant.

2 Serv. May it please your honour, the Lord Lucius,
Out of his free love, hath presented to you
Four milk-white horses, trapp'd in silver.

Tim. I shall accept them fairly: let the presents

Enter a third Servant.

Be worthily entertain'd.—How now, what news?

3 Serv. Please you, my lord, that honourable gentleman, Lord Lucullus, entreats your company to-morrow to hunt with him; and has sent your honour two brace of greyhounds.

Tim. I'll hunt with him; and let them be receiv'd,
Not without fair reward.

Flav. [*Aside.*] What will this come to?
He commands us to provide, and give
Great gifts, and all out of an empty coffer.
Nor will he know his purse; or yield me this,
To show him what a beggar his heart is,
Being of no power to make his wishes good;
His promises fly so beyond his state,
That what he speaks is all in debt, he owes
For every word; he is so kind, that he now
Pays interest for't; his land's put to their books.
Well, 'would I were gently put out of office,
Before I were forc'd out!
Happier is he that has no friend to feed,
Than such as do even enemies exceed.
I bleed inwardly for my lord. [*Exit.*

Tim. You do yourselves
Much wrong, you bate too much of your own merits:—
Here, my lord, a trifle of our love.

2 Lord. With more than common thanks I will receive it.

3 Lord. O, he is the very soul of bounty!

Tim. And now I remember me, my lord, you gave
Good words the other day of a bay courser
I rode on: it is yours, because you lik'd it.

2 Lord. I beseech you, pardon me, my lord, in that.

Tim. You may take my word, my lord; I know, no man
Can justly praise, but what he does affect:
I weigh my friend's affection with mine own;
I'll tell you true. I'll call on you.

All Lords. None so welcome.

Tim. I take all and your several visitations
So kind to heart, 'tis not enough to give;
Methinks, I could deal kingdoms to my friends,
And ne'er be weary.—Alcibiades,
Thou art a soldier, therefore seldom rich,
It comes in charity to thee: for all thy living
Is 'mongst the dead: and all the lands thou hast
Lie in a pitch'd field.

Alcib. Ay, defiled land, my lord.

1 Lord. We are so virtuously bound,——

Tim. And so
Am I to you.

2 Lord. So infinitely endeared,——

Tim. All to you.—Lights, more lights.

1 Lord. The best of happiness,
Honour, and fortunes, keep with you, Lord Timon!

Tim. Ready for his friends.
[*Exeunt* ALCIBIADES, Lords, *&c.*

Apem. What a coil's here!
Serving of becks, and jutting out of bums!
I doubt whether their legs be worth the sums
That are given for 'em. Friendship's full of dregs:

Methinks, false hearts should never have sound legs.
Thus honest fools lay out their wealth on court'sies.

Tim. Now, Apemantus, if thou wert not sullen, I'd be good to thee.

Apem. No, I'll nothing: for, if I should be brib'd too, there would be none left to rail upon thee; and then thou would'st sin the faster. Thou givest so long, Timon, I fear me, thou wilt give away thyself in paper shortly: What need these feasts, pomps, and vainglories?

Tim. Nay, an you begin to rail on society once, I am sworn, not to give regard to you. Farewell; and come with better musick. [*Exit.*

Apem. So;—thou'lt not hear me now,—thou shalt not then, I'll lock thy heaven from thee. O, that men's ears should be
To counsel deaf, but not to flattery! [*Exit.*

ACT II.

SCENE I.

Athens. *A Room in a* Senator's *House.*

Enter a Senator, *with papers in his hand.*

Sen. And late, five thousand to Varro; and to Isidore
He owes nine thousand; besides my former sum,
Which makes it five and twenty.—Still in motion
Of raging waste? It cannot hold; it will not.
If I want gold, steal but a beggar's dog,
And give it Timon, why, the dog coins gold:
If I would sell my horse, and buy twenty more
Better than he, why, give my horse to Timon,
Ask nothing, give it him, it foals me, straight,
And able horses: No porter at his gate;
But rather one that smiles, and still invites
All that pass by. It cannot hold; no reason
Can sound his state in safety. Caphis, ho!
Caphis, I say!

Enter CAPHIS.

Caph. Here, sir; What is your pleasure?

Sen. Get on your cloak, and haste you to Lord Timon;
Importune him for my monies; be not ceas'd
With slight denial; nor then silenc'd, when—
Commend me to your master—and the cap
Plays in the right hand, thus:—but tell him, sirrah,
My uses cry to me, I must serve my turn
Out of mine own; his days and times are past,
And my reliances on his fracted dates
Have smit my credit; I love, and honour him;
But must not break my back, to heal his finger:
Immediate are my needs; and my relief
Must not be toss'd and turn'd to me in words,
But find supply immediate. Get you gone:
Put on a most importunate aspect,
A visage of demand; for, I do fear,
When every feather sticks in his own wing,
Lord Timon will be left a naked gull,
Which flashes now a phœnix. Get you gone.

Caph. I go, sir.

Sen. I go, sir?—take the bonds along with you,
And have the dates in compt.

Caph. I will sir.

Sen. Go.
[*Exeunt.*

SCENE II.

The same. A Hall in Timon's *House.*

Enter FLAVIUS, *with many Bills in his hand.*

Flav. No care, no stop! so senseless of expense,
That he will neither know how to maintain it,
Nor cease his flow of riot: Takes no account
How things go from him; nor resumes no care
Of what is to continue; Never mind
Was to be so unwise, to be so kind.
What shall be done? He will not hear, till feel:
I must be round with him now he comes from hunting.
Fye, fye, fye, fye!

Enter CAPHIS, *and the* Servants *of* Isidore *and* Varro.

Caph. Good even, Varro: What,
You come for money?

Var. Serv. Is't not your business too?

Caph. It is;—And yours too, Isidore?

Isid. Serv. It is so.

Caph. 'Would we were all discharg'd!

Var. Serv. I fear it.

Caph. Here comes the lord.

Enter TIMON, ALCIBIADES, *and* Lords, *&c.*

Tim. So soon as dinner's done, we'll forth again,
My Alcibiades.—With me? What's your will?

Caph. My lord, here is a note of certain dues.

Tim. Dues? Whence are you?

Caph. Of Athens, here, my lord.

Tim. Go to my steward.

Caph. Please it your lordship, he hath put me off
To the succession of new days this month:
My master is awak'd by great occasion,
To call upon his own; and humbly prays you,
That with your other noble parts you'll suit,
In giving him his right.

Tim. Mine honest friend,
I pr'ythee, but repair to me next morning.

Caph. Nay, good my lord,——

Tim. Contain thyself, good friend.

Var. Serv. One Varro's servant, my good lord,—

Isid. Serv. From Isidore;
He humbly prays your speedy payment,——

Caph. If you did know, my lord, my master's wants,——

Var. Serv. 'Twas due on forfeiture, my lord, six weeks,
And past,——

Isid. Serv. Your steward puts me off, my lord;
And I am sent expressly to your lordship.

Tim. Give me breath,——
I do beseech you, good my lords, keep on;
[*Exeunt* ALCIBIADES *and* Lords.
I'll wait upon you instantly.—Come hither, pray you; [*To* FLAVIUS.
How goes the world, that I am thus encounter'd
With clamorous demands of date-broke bonds,
And the detention of long-since due debts,
Against my honour?

Flav. Please you, gentlemen,
The time is unagreeable to this business:
Your importunacy cease, till after dinner:
That I may make his lordship understand
Wherefore you are not paid.

Tim. Do so, my friends:
See them well entertain'd. [*Exit* TIMON.

Flav. I pray, draw near.
[*Exit* FLAVIUS.

Enter APEMANTUS *and a* Fool.

Caph. Stay, stay, here comes the fool with Apemantus; let's have some sport with 'em.

Var. Serv. Hang him, he'll abuse us.

Isid. Serv. A plague upon him, dog!

Var. Serv. How dost, fool?

Apem. Dost dialogue with thy shadow?

Var. Serv. I speak not to thee.

Apem. No; 'tis to thyself,—Come away.
[*To the* Fool.

Isid. Serv. [*To* Var. Serv.] There's the fool hangs on your back already.

Apem. No, thou stand'st single, thou art not on him yet.

Caph. Where's the fool now?

Apem. He last ask'd the question.—Poor rogues, and usurers' men! bawds between gold and want!

All Serv. What are we, Apemantus?

Apem. Asses.

All Serv. Why?

Apem. That you ask me what you are, and do not know yourselves.—Speak to 'em, fool.

Fool. How do you, gentlemen?

All Serv. Gramercies, good fool: How does your mistress?

Fool. She's e'en setting on water to scald such chickens as you are. 'Would, we could see you at Corinth.

Apem. Good! gramercy.

Enter Page.

Fool. Look you, here comes my mistress' page.

Page. [*To the* Fool.] Why, how now, captain? what do you in this wise company?—How dost thou, Apemantus?

Apem. Would I had a rod in my mouth, that I might answer thee profitably.

Page. Pr'ythee, Apemantus, read me the superscription of these letters; I know not which is which.

Apem. Canst not read?

Page. No.

Apem. There will little learning die then, that day thou art hanged. This is to Lord Timon; this to Alcibiades. Go: thou wast born a bastard, and thou'lt die a bawd.

Page. Thou wast whelped a dog; and thou shalt famish, a dog's death. Answer not, I am gone. [*Exit* Page.

Apem. Even so thou out-run'st grace. Fool, I will go with you to Lord Timon's.

Fool. Will you leave me there?

Apem. If Timon stay at home.—You three serve three usurers?

All Serv. Ay; 'would they served us!

Apem. So would I, as good a trick as ever hangman served thief.

Fool. Are you three usurers' men?

All Serv. Ay, fool.

Fool. I think, no usurer but has a fool to his servant: My mistress is one, and I am her fool. When men come to borrow of your masters, they approach sadly, and go away merry; but they enter my mistress' house merrily, and go away sadly: The reason of this?

Var. Serv. I could render one.

Apem. Do it then, that we may account thee a whoremaster, and a knave; which notwithstanding, thou shalt be no less esteemed.

Var. Serv. What is a whoremaster, fool?

Fool. A fool in good clothes, and something like thee. 'Tis a spirit: sometime, it appears like a lord; sometime, like a lawyer; sometime, like a philosopher, with two stones more than his artificial one: He is very often like a knight; and, generally in all shapes, that man goes up and down in, from fourscore to thirteen, this spirit walks in.

Var. Serv. Thou art not altogether a fool.

Fool. Nor thou altogether a wise man: as much foolery as I have, so much wit thou lackest.

Apem. That answer might have become Apemantus.

All Serv. Aside, aside; here comes Lord Timon.

Re-enter TIMON *and* FLAVIUS.

Apem. Come with me, fool, come.

Fool. I do not always follow lover, elder brother, and woman; sometime, the philosopher. [*Exeunt* APEMANTUS *and* Fool.

Flav. 'Pray you, walk near; I'll speak with you anon. [*Exeunt* Servants.

Tim. You make me marvel: wherefore, ere this time,
Had you not fully laid my state before me;
That I might so have rated my expense,
As I had leave of means?

Flav. You would not hear me,
At many leisures I propos'd.

Tim. Go to:
Perchance, some single vantages you took,
When my indisposition put you back;
And that unaptness made your minister,
Thus to excuse yourself.

Flav. O my good lord!
At many times I brought in my accounts,
Laid them before you; you would throw them off,
And say, you found them in mine honesty.
When, for some trifling present, you have bid me
Return so much, I have shook my head, and wept;
Yea, 'gainst the authority of manners, pray'd you
To hold your hand more close; I did endure
Not seldom, nor no slight checks; when I have
Prompted you, in the ebb of your estate,
And your great flow of debts. My dear-lov'd lord,
Though you hear now (too late!) yet now's a time,
The greatest of your having lacks a half
To pay your present debts.

Tim. Let all my land be sold.

Flav. 'Tis all engag'd, some forfeited and gone:
And what remains will hardly stop the mouth
Of present dues: the future comes apace:
What shall defend the interim? and at length
How goes our reckoning?

Tim. To Lacedæmon did my land extend.

Flav. O my good lord, the world is but a word;
Were it all yours to give it in a breath,
How quickly were it gone?

Tim. You tell me true.

Flav. If you suspect my husbandry, or falsehood,
Call me before the exactest auditors,
And set me on the proof. So the gods bless me,
When all our offices have been oppress'd
With riotous feeders; when our vaults have wept
With drunken spilth of wine; when every room
Hath blaz'd with lights, and bray'd with minstrelsy:
I have retir'd me to a wasteful cock,
And set mine eyes at flow.

Tim. Pr'ythee, no more.

Flav. Heavens, have I said, the bounty of this lord!
How many prodigal bits have slaves, and peasants,
This night englutted! Who is not Timon's?
What heart, head, sword, force, means, but is Lord Timon's?
Great Timon, noble, worthy, royal Timon?
Ah! when the means are gone that buy this praise,
The breath is gone whereof this praise is made:
Feast-won, fast-lost; one cloud of winter showers,
These flies are couch'd.

Tim. Come, sermon me no further;
No villanous bounty yet hath pass'd my heart;
Unwisely, not ignobly, have I given.
Why dost thou weep? Canst thou the conscience lack,
To think I shall lack friends? Secure thy heart;
If I would broach the vessels of my love,
And try the argument of hearts by borrowing,
Men, and men's fortunes, could I frankly use,
As I can bid thee speak.

Flav. Assurance bless your thoughts!

Tim. And, in some sort, these wants of mine are crown'd,
That I account them blessings; for by these
Shall I try friends; You shall perceive, how you
Mistake my fortunes; I am wealthy in my friends.
Within there, ho!—Flaminius! Servilius!

Enter FLAMINIUS, SERVILIUS, *and other* Servants.

Serv. My lord, my lord.——

Tim. I will despatch you severally.—You, to Lord Lucius,—

To Lord Lucullus you; I hunted with his
Honour to-day;—You to Sempronius;
Commend me to their loves; and, I am proud, say,
That my occasions have found time to use them
Toward a supply of money: let the request
Be fifty talents.

Flam. As you have said, my lord.

Flav. Lord Lucius, and Lord Lucullus? humph! [*Aside.*

Tim. Go you, sir [*To another* Serv.], to the senators
(Of whom, even to the state's best health, I have
Deserv'd this hearing), bid 'em send o' the instant,
A thousand talents to me.

Flav. I have been bold
(For that I knew it the most general way),
To them to use your signet, and your name;
But they do shake their heads, and I am here
No richer in return.

Tim. Is't true? can it be?

Flav. They answer, in a joint and corporate voice,
That now they are at fall, want treasure, cannot
Do what they would; are sorry—you are honourable,—
But yet they could have wish'd—they know not —but
Something hath been amiss—a noble nature
May catch a wrench—would all were well—'tis pity—
And so, intending other serious matters,
After distasteful looks, and these hard fractions,
With certain half-caps, and cold moving nods,
They froze me into silence.

Tim. You gods, reward them!—
I pr'ythee, man, look cheerly; These old fellows
Have their ingratitude in them hereditary:
Their blood is cak'd, 'tis cold, it seldom flows;
Tis lack of kindly warmth, they are not kind;
And nature, as it grows again toward earth,
Is fashion'd for the journey, dull, and heavy.—
Go to Ventidius, [*To a* Serv.]—'Pr'ythee, [*To* FLAVIUS], be not sad,
Thou art true, and honest; ingeniously I speak,
No blame belongs to thee;—[*To* Serv.] Ventidius lately
Buried his father; by whose death, he's stepp'd
Into a great estate: when he was poor,
Imprison'd, and in scarcity of friends,
I clear'd him with five talents; Greet him from me;
Bid him suppose, some good necessity
Touches his friend, which craves to be remember'd
With those five talents:—that had,—[*To* FLAV.] give it these fellows
To whom 'tis instant due. Ne'er speak, or think,
That Timon's fortunes 'mong his friends can sink.

Flav. I would, I could not think it; That thought is bounty's foe;
Being free itself, it thinks all others so. [*Exeunt.*

ACT III.

SCENE I. Athens. *A Room in* Lucullus's *House.*

FLAMINIUS *waiting. Enter a* Servant *to him.*

Serv. I have told my lord of you, he is coming down to you.

Flam. I thank you, sir.

Enter LUCULLUS.

Serv. Here's my lord.

Lucul. [*Aside.*] One of Lord Timon's men? a gift, I warrant. Why, this hits right; I dreamt of a silver bason and ewer to-night. Flaminius, honest Flaminius; you are very respectively welcome, sir.—Fill me some wine.—[*Exit* Servant.]—And how does that honourable, complete, free-hearted gentleman of Athens, thy very bountiful good lord and master?

Flam. His health is well, sir,

Lucul. I am right glad that his health is well, sir: And what hast thou there under thy cloak, pretty Flaminius?

Flam. 'Faith, nothing but an empty box, sir; which, in my lord's behalf, I come to entreat your honour to supply; who, having great and instant occasion to use fifty talents, hath sent to your lordship to furnish him; nothing doubting your present assistance therein.

Lucul. La, la, la, la,—nothing doubting, says he? alas, good lord! a noble gentleman 'tis, if he would not keep so good a house. Many a time and often I have dined with him, and told him on't; and come again to supper to him, of purpose to have him spend less: and yet he would embrace no counsel, take no warning by my coming. Every man has his fault, and honesty is his; I have told him on't, but I could never get him from it.

Re-enter Servant, *with wine.*

Serv. Please your lordship, here is the wine.

Lucul. Flaminius, I have noted thee always wise.
Here's to thee.

Flam. Your lordship speaks your pleasure.

Lucul. I have observed thee always for a towardly prompt spirit,—give thee thy due,—and one that knows what belongs to reason: and canst use the time well, if the time use thee well: good parts in thee.—Get you gone, sirrah.—[*To the* Servant, *who goes out.*]—Draw nearer, honest Flaminius. Thy lord's a bountiful gentleman: but thou art wise; and thou knowest well enough, although thou comest to me, that this is no time to lend money; especially upon bare friendship, without security. Here's three solidares for thee; good boy, wink at me, and say, thou saw'st me not. Fare thee well.

Flam. Is't possible, the world should so much differ;
And we alive, that liv'd? Fly, damned baseness,
To him that worships thee.
[*Throwing the money away.*

Lucul. Ha! Now I see, thou art a fool, and fit for thy master. [*Exit* LUCULLUS.

Flam. May these add to the number that may scald thee!
Let molten coin be thy damnation,
Thou disease of a friend, and not himself!
Has friendship such a faint and milky heart,
It turns in less than two nights? O you gods,
I feel my master's passion! This slave
Unto his honour, has my lord's meat in him:
Why should it thrive, and turn to nutriment,
When he is turn'd to poison?
O, may diseases only work upon't!
And, when he is sick to death, let not that part of nature
Which my lord paid for, be of any power
To expel sickness, but prolong his hour! [*Exit.*

SCENE II. *The same. A public place.*

Enter LUCIUS, *with three* Strangers.

Luc. Who, the Lord Timon? he is my very good friend, and an honourable gentleman.

1 Stran. We know him for no less, though we are but strangers to him. But I can tell you one thing, my lord, and which I hear from common rumours; now Lord Timon's happy hours are done and past, and his estate shrinks from him.

Luc. Fye no, do not believe it; he cannot want for money.

2 Stran. But believe you this, my lord, that, not long ago, one of his men was with the Lord Lucullus, to borrow so many talents; nay, urged extremely for't, and showed what necessity belonged to't, and yet was denied.

Luc. How?

2 *Stran.* I tell you, denied, my lord.

Luc. What a strange case was that? now, before the gods, I am ashamed on't. Denied that honourable man? there was very little honour showed in't. For my own part, I must needs confess, I have received some small kindnesses from him, as money, plate, jewels, and such like trifles, nothing comparing to his; yet had he mistook him, and sent to me, I should ne'er have denied his occasion so many talents.

Enter SERVILIUS.

Ser. See, by good hap, yonder's my lord; I have sweat to see his honour.—My honoured lord,— [*To* LUCIUS.

Luc. Servilius! you are kindly met, sir. Fare thee well:—Commend me to thy honourable-virtuous lord, my very exquisite friend.

Ser. May it please your honour, my lord hath sent——

Luc. Ha! what has he sent? I am so much endeared to that lord; he's ever sending: How shall I thank him, thinkest thou? And what has he sent now?

Ser. He has only sent his present occasion now, my lord; requesting your lordship to supply his instant use with so many talents.

Luc. I know, his lordship is but merry with me;
He cannot want fifty-five hundred talents.

Ser. But in the mean time he wants less, my lord.
If his occasion were not virtuous,
I should not urge it half so faithfully.

Luc. Dost thou speak seriously, Servilius?

Ser. Upon my soul, 'tis true, sir.

Luc. What a wicked beast was I, to disfurnish myself against such a good time, when I might have shown myself honourable! how unluckily it happened, that I should purchase the day before for a little part, and undo a great deal of honour!—Servilius, now before the gods, I am not able to do't; the more beast, I say:—I was sending to use Lord Timon myself, these gentlemen can witness; but I would not, for the wealth of Athens, I had done it now. Commend me bountifully to his good lordship: and I hope, his honour will conceive the fairest of me, because I have no power to be kind: And tell him this from me, I count it one of my greatest afflictions, say, that I cannot pleasure such an honourable gentleman. Good Servilius, will you befriend me so far, as to use mine own words to him?

Ser. Yes, sir, I shall.

Luc. I will look you out a good turn, Servilius.— [*Exit* SERVILIUS.
True, as you said, Timon is shrunk, indeed;
And he, that's once denied, will hardly speed.
[*Exit* LUCIUS.

1 *Stran.* Do you observe this, Hostilius?

2 *Stran.* Ay, too well.

1 *Stran.* Why, this
Is the world's soul; and just of the same piece
Is every flatterer's spirit. Who can call him
His friend, that dips in the same dish? for, in
My knowing, Timon has been this lord's father,
And kept his credit with his purse:
Supported his estate; nay, Timon's money
Has paid his men their wages: He ne'er drinks,
But Timon's silver treads upon his lip;
And yet (O, see the monstrousness of man
When he looks out in an ungrateful shape!)
He does deny him, in respect of his,
What charitable men afford to beggars.

3 *Stran.* Religion groans at it.

1 *Stran.* For mine own part,
I never tasted Timon in my life,
Nor came any of his bounties over me,
To mark me for his friend; yet, I protest,
For his right noble mind, illustrious virtue,
And honourable carriage,
Had his necessity made use of me,
I would have put my wealth into donation,
And the best half should have return'd to him,
So much I love his heart: But, I perceive,
Men must learn now with pity to dispense:
For policy sits above conscience. [*Exeunt.*

SCENE III.

The same. A Room in Sempronius's *House.*

Enter SEMPRONIUS, *and a* Servant *of* Timon's.

Sem. Must he needs trouble me in't? Humph!
'Bove all others?
He might have tried Lord Lucius, or Lucullus;
And now Ventidius is wealthy too,
Whom he redeem'd from prison: all these three
Owe their estates unto him.

Serv. O my lord,
They have all been touch'd, and found base metal; for
They have all denied him.

Sem. How! have they denied him?
Has Ventidius and Lucullus denied him?
And does he send to me? Three? humph!—
It shows but little love or judgment in him.
Must I be his last refuge? His friends, like physicians,
Thrive, give him over; Must I take the cure upon me?—
He has much disgrac'd me in't; I am angry at him,
That might have known my place: I see no sense for't,
But his occasions might have woo'd me first;
For, in my conscience, I was the first man
That e'er received gift from him:
And does he think so backwardly of me now,
That I'll requite it last? No: So it may prove
An argument of laughter to the rest,
And I amongst the lords be thought a fool.
I had rather than the worth of thrice the sum,
He had sent to me first, but for my mind's sake;
I had such a courage to do him good. But now return,
And with their faint reply this answer join;
Who bates mine honour, shall not know my coin.
[*Exit.*

Serv. Excellent! Your lordship's a goodly villain. The devil knew not what he did, when he made man politick; he crossed himself by't: and I cannot think, but, in the end, the villanies of man will set him clear. How fairly this lord strives to appear foul! takes virtuous copies to be wicked; like those that, under hot ardent zeal, would set whole realms on fire.
Of such a nature is his politick love.
This was my lord's best hope; now all are fled,
Save the gods only: Now his friends are dead,
Doors, that were ne'er acquainted with their wards
Many a bounteous year, must be employ'd
Now to guard sure their master.
And this is all a liberal course allows;
Who cannot keep his wealth, must keep his house. [*Exit.*

SCENE IV. *The same. A Hall in* Timon's *House.*

Enter two Servants *of* Varro, *and the* Servant *of* Lucius, *meeting* TITUS, HORTENSIUS, *and other* Servants *to* Timon's *Creditors, waiting his coming out.*

Var. Serv. Well met; good-morrow, Titus and Hortensius.

Tit. The like to you, kind Varro.

Hor. Lucius?
What, do we meet together?

Luc. Serv. Ay, and, I think,
One business does command us all; for mine
Is money.

Tit. So is theirs and ours.

Enter PHILOTUS.

Luc. Serv. And sir Philotus too!

Phi. Good day at once.

Luc. Serv. Welcome, good brother. What do you think the hour?

Phi. Labouring for nine.

Luc. Serv. So much?

Phi. Is not my lord seen yet?

Luc. Serv. Not yet.

Phi. I wonder on't; he was wont to shine at seven.

Luc. Serv. Ay, but the days are waxed shorter with him:
You must consider that a prodigal course
Is like the sun's; but not, like his, recoverable.
I fear,
'Tis deepest winter in Lord Timon's purse;
That is, one may reach deep enough, and yet
Find little.

Phi. I am of your fear for that.

Tit. I'll show you how to observe a strange event.
Your lord sends now for money.

Hor. Most true, he does.

Tit. And he wears jewels now of Timon's gift,
For which you wait for money.

Hor. It is against my heart.

Luc. Serv. Mark, how strange it shows,
Timon in this should pay more than he owes:
And e'en as if your lord should wear rich jewels,
And send for money for 'em.

Hor. I am weary of this charge, the gods can witness:
I know, my lord hath spent of Timon's wealth,
And now ingratitude makes it worse than stealth.

1 *Var. Serv.* Yes, mine's three thousand crowns: What's yours?

Luc. Serv. Five thousand mine.

1 *Var. Serv.* 'Tis much deep: and it should seem by the sum,
Your master's confidence was above mine;
Else, surely, his had equall'd.

Enter FLAMINIUS.

Tit. One of Lord Timon's men.

Luc. Serv. Flaminius! sir, a word: 'Pray, is my lord ready to come forth?

Flam. No, indeed, he is not.

Tit. We attend his lordship; 'pray, signify so much.

Flam. I need not tell him that; he knows, you are too diligent. [*Exit* FLAMINIUS.

Enter FLAVIUS *in a cloak, muffled.*

Luc. Serv. Ha! is not that his steward muffled so.
He goes away in a cloud: call him, call him.

Tit. Do you hear, sir?

1 *Var. Serv.* By your leave, sir,——

Flav. What do you ask of me, my friend?

Tit. We wait for certain money here, sir.

Flav. Ay,
If money were as certain as your waiting,
'Twere sure enough. Why then preferr'd you not
Your sums and bills, when your false masters eat
Of my lord's meat? Then they could smile and fawn
Upon his debts, and take down th' interest
Into their gluttonous maws. You do yourselves but wrong,
To stir me up; let me pass quietly:
Believe't, my lord and I have made an end;
I have no more to reckon, he to spend.

Luc. Serv. Ay, but this answer will not serve.

Flav. If 'twill not,
'Tis not so base as you; for you serve knaves. [*Exit.*

1 *Var. Ser.* How! what does his cashier'd worship mutter?

2 *Var. Serv.* No matter what; he's poor, and that's revenge enough. Who can speak broader than he that has no house to put his head in? such may rail against great buildings.

Enter SERVILIUS.

Tit. O, here's Servilius; now we shall know some answer.

Ser. If I might beseech you, gentlemen, to repair some other hour, I should derive much from it: for, take it on my soul, my lord leans wondrously to discontent. His comfortable temper has forsook him; he is much out of health, and keeps his chamber.

Luc. Serv. Many do keep their chambers, are not sick:
And, if it be so far beyond his health,
Methinks he should the sooner pay his debts,
And make a clear way to the gods.

Ser. Good gods!

Tit. We cannot take this for an answer, sir.

Flam. [*Within.*] Servilius, help!—my lord! my lord!—

Enter TIMON, *in a rage;* FLAMINIUS *following.*

Tim. What, are my doors oppos'd against my passage?
Have I been ever free, and must my house
Be my retentive enemy, my gaol?
The place, which I have feasted, does it now,
Like all mankind, show me an iron heart?

Luc. Serv. Put in now, Titus.

Tit. My lord, here is my bill.

Luc. Serv. Here's mine.

Hor. Serv. And mine, my lord.

Both Var. Serv. And ours, my lord.

Phi. All our bills.

Tim. Knock me down with 'em: cleave me to the girdle.

Luc. Serv. Alas! my lord,——

Tim. Cut my heart in sums.

Tit. Mine fifty talents.

Tim. Tell out my blood.

Luc. Serv. Five thousand crowns, my lord.

Tim. Five thousand drops pays that.—
What yours?—and yours?

1 *Var. Serv.* My lord,——

2 *Var. Serv.* My lord,——

Tim. Tear me, take me, and the gods fall upon you! [*Exit.*

Hor. 'Faith, I perceive our masters may throw their caps at their money; these debts may well be called desperate ones, for a madman owes 'em. [*Exeunt.*

Re-enter TIMON *and* FLAVIUS.

Tim. They have e'en put my breath from me, the slaves:
Creditors!—devils.

Flav. My dear lord,——

Tim. What if it should be so?

Flav. My lord,——

Tim. I'll have it so:—My steward!

Flav. Here, my lord.

Tim. So fitly? Go, bid all my friends again,
Lucius, Lucullus, and Sempronius; all:
I'll once more feast the rascals.

Flav. O, my lord,
You only speak from your distracted soul;
There is not so much left, to furnish out
A moderate table.

Tim. Be't not in thy care; go,
I charge thee; invite them all: let in the tide
Of knaves once more; my cook and I'll provide. [*Exeunt.*

SCENE V. *The same. The Senate House.*

The Senate *sitting.* *Enter* ALCIBIADES, *attended.*

1 *Sen.* My lord, you have my voice to't; the fault's
Bloody; 'tis necessary he should die:
Nothing emboldens sin so much as mercy.

2 *Sen.* Most true; the law shall bruise him.

Alcib. Honour, health, and compassion to the senate!

1 *Sen.* Now, captain?
Alcib. I am an humble suitor to your virtues;
For pity is the virtue of the law,
And none but tyrants use it cruelly.
It pleases time, and fortune, to lie heavy
Upon a friend of mine, who in hot blood,
Hath stepp'd into the law, which is past depth
To those that, without heed, do plunge into it.
He is a man, setting his fate aside,
Of comely virtues:
Nor did he soil the fact with cowardice
(An honour in him, which buys out his fault);
But, with a noble fury, and fair spirit,
Seeing his reputation touch'd to death,
He did oppose his foe:
And with such sober and unnoted passion
He did behave his anger, ere 'twas spent,
As if he had but prov'd an argument.
1 *Sen.* You undergo too strict a paradox,
Striving to make an ugly deed look fair:
Your words have took such pains, as if they labour'd
To bring manslaughter into form, set quarrelling
Upon the head of valour; which, indeed,
Is valour misbegot, and came into the world
When sects and factions were newly born:
He's truly valiant, that can wisely suffer
The worst that man can breathe; and make his wrongs
His outsides; wear them like his raiment, carelessly;
And ne'er prefer his injuries to his heart,
To bring it into danger.
If wrongs be evils, and enforce us kill,
What folly 'tis to hazard life for ill!
Alcib. My lord,——
1 *Sen.* You cannot make gross sins look clear;
To revenge is no valour, but to bear.
Alcib. My lords, then, under favour, pardon me,
If I speak like a captain.—
Why do fond men expose themselves to battle,
And not endure all threatenings? sleep upon it,
And let the foes quietly cut their throats,
Without repugnancy? but if there be
Such valour in the bearing, what make we
Abroad? why then, women are more valiant,
That stay at home, if bearing carry it;
And th' ass more captain than the lion; the felon,
Loaden with irons, wiser than the judge,
If wisdom be in suffering. O my lords,
As you are great, be pitifully good:
Who cannot condemn rashness in cold blood?
To kill, I grant, is sin's extremest gust;
But, in defence, by mercy, 'tis most just.
To be in anger is impiety;
But who is man, that is not angry?
Weigh but the crime with this.
2 *Sen.* You breathe in vain.
Alcib. In vain! his service done
At Lacedæmon, and Byzantium,
Were a sufficient briber for his life.
1 *Sen.* What's that?
Alcib. Why, I say, my lords, h' as done fair service,
And slain in fight many of your enemies:
How full of valour did he bear himself
In the last conflict, and made plenteous wounds?
2 *Sen.* He has made too much plenty with 'em, he
Is a sworn rioter, h' as a sin that often
Drowns him, and takes his valour prisoner:
If there were no foes, that were enough alone
To overcome him: in that beastly fury
He has been known to commit outrages,
And cherish factions: 'Tis inferr'd to us,
His days are foul, and his drink dangerous.
1 *Sen.* He dies.
Alcib. Hard fate! he might have died in war.
My lords, if not for any parts in him
(Though his right arm might purchase his own time,
And be in debt to none), yet, more to move you,
Take my deserts to his, and join them both:
And, for I know your reverend ages love
Security, I'll pawn my victories, all
My honour to you, upon his good returns.
If by this crime he owes the law his life,
Why, let the war receive 't in valiant gore;
For law is strict, and war is nothing more.
1 *Sen.* We are for law, he dies; urge it no more,
On height of our displeasure: Friend or brother,
He forfeits his own blood, that spills another.
Alcib. Must it be so? it must not be. My lords,
I do beseech you, know me.
2 *Sen.* How?
Alcib. Call me to your remembrances.
3 *Sen.* What?
Alcib. I cannot think, but your age has forgot me;
It could not else be, I should prove so base,
To sue, and be denied such common grace:
My wounds ache at you.
1 *Sen.* Do you dare our anger?
'Tis in few words, but spacious in effect;
We banish thee for ever.
Alcib. Banish me?
Banish your dotage; banish usury,
That makes the senate ugly.
1 *Sen.* If, after two days shine, Athens contain thee,
Attend our weightier judgment. And, not to swell our spirit,
He shall be executed presently.
[*Exeunt* Senators.
Alcib. Now the gods keep you old enough; that you may live
Only in bone, that none may look on you!
I am worse than mad: I have kept back their foes,
While they have told their money, and let out
Their coin upon large interest; I myself,
Rich only in large hurts;—All those, for this?
Is this the balsam, that the usuring senate
Pours into captains' wounds? ha! banishment?
It comes not ill; I hate not to be banish'd;
It is a cause worthy my spleen and fury,
That I may strike at Athens. I'll cheer up
My discontented troops, and lay for hearts.
'Tis honour, with most lands to be at odds;
Soldiers should brook as little wrongs, as gods.
[*Exit.*

SCENE VI.

A magnificent Room in Timon's *House.*

Musick. Tables set out; Servants *attending. Enter divers* Lords, *at several doors.*

1 *Lord.* The good time of day to you, sir.

2 *Lord.* I also wish it to you. I think, this honourable lord did but try us this other day.

1 *Lord.* Upon that were my thoughts tiring, when we encountered: I hope, it is not so low with him, as he made it seem in the trial of his several friends.

2 *Lord.* It should not be, by the persuasion of his new feasting.

1 *Lord.* I should think so: He hath sent me an earnest inviting, which many my near occasions did urge me to put off; but he hath conjured me beyond them, and I must needs appear.

2 *Lord.* In like manner was I in debt to my importunate business, but he would not hear my excuse. I am sorry, when he sent to borrow of me, that my provision was out.

1 *Lord.* I am sick of that grief too, as I understand how all things go.

2 *Lord.* Every man here's so. What would he have borrowed of you?

1 *Lord.* A thousand pieces.

2 *Lord.* A thousand pieces!

1 *Lord.* What of you?

3 *Lord.* He sent to me, sir,—Here he comes.

Enter TIMON, *and* Attendants.

Tim. With all my heart, gentlemen both:—
And how fare you?

1 *Lord.* Ever at the best, hearing well of your lordship.

2 *Lord.* The swallow follows not summer more willing, than we your lordship.

Tim. [*Aside.*] Nor more willingly leaves winter; such summer-birds are men.—Gentlemen, our dinner will not recompense this long stay: feast your ears with the musick awhile; if they will fare so harshly on the trumpet's sound: we shall to 't presently.

1 *Lord.* I hope, it remains not unkindly with your lordship, that I returned you an empty messenger.

Tim. O, sir, let it not trouble you.

2 *Lord.* My noble lord,——

Tim. Ah, my good friend! what cheer?

[*The Banquet brought in.*

2 *Lord.* My most honourable lord, I am e'en sick of shame, that, when your lordship this other day sent to me, I was so unfortunate a beggar.

Tim. Think not on 't, sir.

2 *Lord.* If you had sent but two hours before,—

Tim. Let it not cumber your better remembrance.—Come, bring in all together.

2 *Lord.* All covered dishes!

1 *Lord.* Royal cheer, I warrant you.

3 *Lord.* Doubt not that, if money, and the season, can yield it.

1 *Lord.* How do you? What's the news?

3 *Lord.* Alcibiades is banished; Hear you of it?

1 & 2 *Lord.* Alcibiades banished!

3 *Lord.* 'Tis so, be sure of it.

1 *Lord.* How? how?

2 *Lord.* I pray you, upon what?

Tim. My worthy friends, will you draw near?

3 *Lord.* I'll tell you more anon. Here's a noble feast toward.

2 *Lord.* This is the old man still.

3 *Lord.* Will't hold? will't hold?

2 *Lord.* It does: but time will—and so—

3 *Lord.* I do conceive.

Tim. Each man to his stool, with that spur as he would to the lip of his mistress: your diet shall be in all places alike. Make not a city feast of it, to let the meat cool ere we can agree upon the first place: Sit, sit. The gods require our thanks.

You great benefactors, sprinkle our society with thankfulness. For your own gifts, make yourselves praised: but reserve still to give, lest your deities be despised. Lend to each man enough, that one need not lend to another: for, were your godheads to borrow of men, men would forsake the gods. Make the meat be beloved, more than the man that gives it. Let no assembly of twenty be without a score of villains: If there sit twelve women at the table, let a dozen of them be—as they are.—The rest of your lees, O gods,—the senators of Athens, together with the common lag of people,—what is amiss in them, you gods, make suitable for destruction. For these my present friends,—as they are to me nothing, so in nothing bless them, and to nothing they are welcome.

Uncover, dogs, and lap.

[*The dishes uncovered are full of warm water.*

Some speak. What does his lordship mean?

Some other. I know not.

Tim. May you a better feast never behold,
You knot of mouth-friends! smoke, and lukewarm water
Is your perfection. This is Timon's last;
Who stuck and spangled you with flatteries,
Washes it off, and sprinkles in your faces

[*Throwing water in their faces.*

Your reeking villany. Live loath'd, and long,
Most smiling, smooth, detested parasites,
Courteous destroyers, affable wolves, meek bears,
You fools of fortune, trencher-friends, time's flies,
Cap and knee slaves, vapours, and minute-jacks!
Of man, and beast, the infinite malady
Crust you quite o'er!—What, dost thou go?
Soft, take thy physick first—thou too,—and thou;—

[*Throws the dishes at them, and drives them out.*

Stay, I will lend thee money, borrow none.—
What, all in motion? Henceforth be no feast,
Whereat a villain's not a welcome guest.
Burn, house; sink, Athens! henceforth hated be
Of Timon, man, and all humanity! [*Exit.*

Re-enter the Lords, *with other* Lords *and* Senators.

1 *Lord.* How now, my lords?

2 *Lord.* Know you the quality of Lord Timon's fury?

3 *Lord.* Pish! did you see my cap?

4 *Lord.* I have lost my gown.

3 *Lord.* He's but a mad lord, and nought but humour sways him. He gave me a jewel the other day, and now he has beat it out of my hat:—Did you see my jewel?

4 *Lord.* Did you see my cap?

2 *Lord.* Here 'tis.

4 *Lord.* Here lies my gown.

1 *Lord.* Let's make no stay.

2 *Lord.* Lord Timon's mad.

3 *Lord.* I feel't upon my bones.

4 *Lord.* One day he gives us diamonds, next day stones. [*Exeunt.*

ACT IV.

SCENE I. *Without the Walls of* Athens.

Enter TIMON.

Tim. Let me look back upon thee, O thou wall,
That girdlest in those wolves! Dive in the earth,
And fence not Athens! Matrons, turn incontinent;
Obedience fail in children! slaves, and fools,
Pluck the grave wrinkled senate from the bench,
And minister in their steads! to general filths
Convert o' the instant, green virginity!
Do't in your parents' eyes; bankrupts, hold fast;
Rather than render back, out with your knives,
And cut your trusters' throats! bound servants, steal!
Large handed robbers your grave masters are,
And pill by law: maid, to thy master's bed;
Thy mistress is o' the brothel! son of sixteen,
Pluck the lin'd crutch from the old limping sire,
With it beat out his brains! piety, and fear,
Religion to the gods, peace, justice, truth,
Domestick awe, night-rest, and neighbourhood,
Instruction, manners, mysteries, and trades,
Degrees, observances, customs, and laws,
Decline to your confounding contraries,
And yet confusion live!—Plagues, incident to men,
Your potent and infectious fevers heap
On Athens, ripe for stroke! thou cold sciatica,
Cripple our senators, that their limbs may halt
As lamely as their manners! lust and liberty
Creep in the minds and marrows of our youth;
That 'gainst the stream of virtue they may strive,
And drown themselves in riot! itches, blains,
Sow all the Athenian bosoms; and their crop
Be general leprosy! breath infect breath;
That their society, as their friendship, may
Be merely poison! Nothing I'll bear from thee,
But nakedness, thou detestable town!
Take thou that too, with multiplying banns!
Timon will to the woods; where he shall find
The unkindest beast more kinder than mankind.
The gods confound (hear me, you good gods all),
The Athenians both within and out that wall!
And grant, as Timon grows, his hate may grow
To the whole race of mankind, high and low!
Amen. [*Exit.*

SCENE II. Athens. *A Room in* Timon's *House.*

Enter FLAVIUS, *with two or three* Servants.

1 *Serv.* Hear you, master steward, where's our master?
Are we undone? cast off? nothing remaining?

Flav. Alack, my fellows, what should I say to you?
Let me be recorded by the righteous gods,
I am as poor as you.

1 *Serv.* Such a house broke!
So noble a master fallen! All gone! and not
One friend, to take his fortune by the arm,
And go along with him!

2 *Serv.* As we do turn our backs
From our companion, thrown into his grave;
So his familiars to his buried fortunes
Slink all away; leave their false vows with him,
Like empty purses pick'd: and his poor self,
A dedicated beggar to the air,
With his disease of all-shunn'd poverty,
Walks, like contempt, alone.—More of our fellows.

Enter other Servants.

Flav. All broken implements of a ruin'd house.

3 *Serv.* Yet do our hearts wear Timon's livery,
That see I by our faces; we are fellows still,
Serving alike in sorrow: Leak'd is our bark;
And we, poor mates, stand on the dying deck,
Hearing the surges threat: we must all part
Into this sea of air.

Flav. Good fellows all,
The latest of my wealth, I'll share amongst you.
Wherever we shall meet, for Timon's sake,
Let's yet be fellows; let's shake our heads, and say,
As 'twere a knell unto our master's fortunes,
We have seen better days. Let's each take some;
[*Giving them money.*
Nay, put out all your hands. Not one word more:
Thus part we rich in sorrow, parting poor.
[*Exeunt* Servants.
O, the fierce wretchedness that glory brings us!
Who would not wish to be from wealth exempt,
Since riches point to misery and contempt?
Who'd be so mock'd with glory? or to live
But in a dream of friendship?
To have his pomp, and all what state compounds,
But only painted, like his varnish'd friends?
Poor honest lord, brought low by his own heart;
Undone by goodness! Strange, unusual blood,
When man's worst sin is, he does too much good!
Who then dares to be half so kind again?
For bounty, that makes gods, does still mar men.
My dearest lord,—bless'd, to be most accurs'd,
Rich, only to be wretched;—thy great fortunes
Are made thy chief afflictions. Alas, kind lord!
He's flung in rage from this ungrateful seat
Of monstrous friends: nor has he with him to
Supply his life, or that which can command it.
I'll follow, and inquire him out:
I'll ever serve his mind with my best will;
Whilst I have gold, I'll be his steward still.
[*Exit.*

SCENE III. *The Woods.*

Enter TIMON.

Tim. O blessed breeding sun, draw from the earth
Rotten humidity; below thy sister's orb
Infect the air! Twinn'd brothers of one womb,—
Whose procreation, residence, and birth,
Scarce is dividant,—touch them with several fortunes;
The greater scorns the lesser. Not nature,
To whom all sores lay siege, can bear great fortune,
But by contempt of nature:
Raise me this beggar, and deny't that lord;
The senator shall bear contempt hereditary,
The beggar native honour.
It is the pasture lards the brother's sides,
The want that makes him lean. Who dares, who dares,
In purity of manhood stand upright,
And say, *This man's a flatterer?* if one be,
So are they all; for every grize of fortune
Is smooth'd by that below: the learned pate
Ducks to the golden fool: All is oblique;
There's nothing level in our cursed natures,
But direct villany. Therefore, be abhorr'd
All feasts, societies, and throngs of men!
His semblable, yea, himself, Timon disdains:
Destruction fang mankind!—Earth, yield me roots!
[*Digging.*
Who seeks for better of thee, sauce his palate
With thy most operant poison! What is here?
Gold? yellow, glittering, precious gold? No, gods,
I am no idle votarist. Roots, you clear heavens!
Thus much of this, will make black, white; foul, fair;
Wrong, right; base, noble; old, young; coward, valiant.
Ha, you gods! why this? What this, you gods? Why this
Will lug your priests and servants from your sides;
Pluck stout men's pillows from below their heads:
This yellow slave
Will knit and break religions; bless the accurs'd;
Make the hoar leprosy ador'd; place thieves,
And give them title, knee, and approbation,
With senators on the bench: this is it,
That makes the wappen'd widow wed again;
She, whom the spital-house, and ulcerous sores
Would cast the gorge at, this embalms and spices
To the April day again. Come, damned earth,
Thou common whore of mankind, that put'st odds
Among the rout of nations, I will make thee
Do thy right nature.—[*March afar off.*]—Ha! a drum?—Thou'rt quick,
But yet I'll bury thee: Thou'lt go, strong thief,
When gouty keepers of thee cannot stand:—
Nay, stay thou out for earnest.
[*Keeping some gold.*

Enter ALCIBIADES, *with drum and fife, in warlike manner;* PHRYNIA *and* TIMANDRA.

Alcib. What art thou there?
Speak.

Tim. A beast, as thou art. The canker gnaw thy heart,
For showing me again the eyes of man!

Alcib. What is thy name? Is man so hateful to thee,
That art thyself a man!

Tim. I am *misanthropos*, and hate mankind.
For thy part, I do wish thou wert a dog,
That I might love thee something.

Alcib. I know thee well;
But in thy fortunes am unlearn'd and strange.

Tim. I know thee too; and more, than that I know thee,
I not desire to know. Follow thy drum;
With man's blood paint the ground, gules, gules:
Religious canons, civil laws are cruel;
Then what should war be? This fell whore of thine
Hath in her more destruction than thy sword,
For all her cherubin look.

Phry. Thy lips rot off!

Tim. I will not kiss thee; then the rot returns
To thine own lips again.

Alcib. How came the noble Timon to this change?

Tim. As the moon does, by wanting light to give:
But then renew I could not, like the moon;
There were no suns to borrow of.

Alcib. Noble Timon,
What friendship may I do thee?
Tim. None, but to
Maintain my opinion.
Alcib. What is it, Timon?
Tim. Promise me friendship, but perform none: If
Thou wilt not promise, the gods plague thee, for
Thou art a man! if thou dost perform, confound thee,
For thou'rt a man!
Alcib. I have heard in some sort of thy miseries.
Tim. Thou saw'st them, when I had prosperity.
Alcib. I see them now; then was a blessed time.
Tim. As thine is now, held with a brace of harlots.
Timan. Is this the Athenian minion, whom the world
Voic'd so regardfully?
Tim. Art thou Timandra?
Timan. Yes.
Tim. Be a whore still! they love thee not, that use thee;
Give them diseases, leaving with thee their lust.
Make use of thy salt hours: season the slaves
For tubs, and baths; bring down rose-cheeked youth
To the tub-fast, and the diet.
Timan. Hang thee, monster!
Alcib. Pardon him, sweet Timandra; for his wits
Are drown'd and lost in his calamities.—
I have but little gold of late, brave Timon,
The want whereof doth daily make revolt
In my penurious band: I have heard, and griev'd,
How cursed Athens, mindless of thy worth,
Forgetting thy great deeds, when neighbour states,
But for thy sword and fortune, trod upon them,—
Tim. I pr'ythee, beat thy drum, and get thee gone.
Alcib. I am thy friend, and pity thee, dear Timon.
Tim. How dost thou pity him, whom thou dost trouble?
I had rather be alone.
Alcib. Why, fare thee well:
Here's some gold for thee.
Tim. Keep't, I cannot eat it.
Alcib. When I have laid proud Athens on a heap,——
Tim. Warr'st thou 'gainst Athens?
Alcib. Ay, Timon, and have cause.
Tim. The gods confound them all i' thy conquest; and
Thee after, when thou hast conquer'd?
Alcib. Why me, Timon?
Tim. That,
By killing villains, thou wast born to conquer
My country.
Put up thy gold; Go on,—here's gold,—go on;
Be as a planetary plague, when Jove
Will o'er some high-vic'd city hang his poison
In the sick air: Let not thy sword skip one:
Pity not honour'd age for his white beard,
He's an usurer: Strike me the counterfeit matron;
It is her habit only that is honest,
Herself's a bawd: Let not the virgin's cheek
Make soft thy trenchant sword: for those milk-paps,
That through the window-bars bore at men's eyes,
Are not within the leaf of pity writ,
But set them down horrible traitors: Spare not the babe,
Whose dimpled smiles from fools exhaust their mercy:
Think it a bastard, whom the oracle
Hath doubtfully pronounc'd thy throat shall cut,
And mince it sans remorse: Swear against objects;
Put armour on thine ears, and on thine eyes;
Whose proof, nor yells of mothers, maids, nor babes,
Nor sight of priests in holy vestments bleeding,
Shall pierce a jot. There's gold to pay thy soldiers:
Make large confusion; and, thy fury spent,
Confounded be thyself! Speak not, be gone.
Alcib. Hast thou gold yet? I'll take the gold thou giv'st me,
Not all thy counsel.
Tim. Dost thou, or dost thou not, heaven's curse upon thee!
Phry. & Timan. Give us some gold, good Timon: Hast thou more?
Tim. Enough to make a whore forswear her trade,
And to make whores, a bawd. Hold up, you sluts,
Your aprons mountant: You are not oathable,—
Although, I know, you'll swear, terribly swear,
Into strong shudders, and to heavenly agues,
The immortal gods that hear you,—spare your oaths,
I'll trust to your conditions: Be whores still;
And he whose pious breath seeks to convert you,
Be strong in whore, allure him, burn him up;
Let your close fire predominate his smoke,
And be no turncoats: Yet may your pains, six months,
Be quite contrary: And thatch your poor thin roofs
With burdens of the dead;—some that were hang'd,
No matter:—wear them, betray with them: whore still;
Paint till a horse may mire upon your face:
A pox of wrinkles!
Phry. & Timan. Well, more gold;—What then?—
Believe't, that we'll do any thing for gold.
Tim. Consumptions sow
In hollow bones of man; strike their sharp shins,
And mar men's spurring. Crack the lawyer's voice,
That he may never more false title plead,
Nor sound his quillets shrilly: hoarse the flamen,
That scolds against the quality of flesh,
And not believes himself: down with the nose,
Down with it flat; take the bridge quite away
Of him, that his particular to foresee,
Smells from the general weal: make curl'd-pate ruffians bald;
And let the unscarr'd braggarts of the war
Derive some pain from you: Plague all;
That your activity may defeat and quell
The source of all erection.—There's more gold:—
Do you damn others, and let this damn you,
And ditches grave you all!
Phry. & Timan. More counsel with more money, bounteous Timon.
Tim. More whore, more mischief first; I have given you earnest.
Alcib. Strike up the drum towards Athens. Farewell, Timon;
If I thrive well, I'll visit thee again.
Tim. If I hope well, I'll never see thee more.
Alcib. I never did thee harm.
Tim. Yes, thou spok'st well of me.
Alcib. Call'st thou that harm?
Tim. Men daily find it such. Get thee away,
And take thy beagles with thee.
Alcib. We but offend him.—
Strike. [*Drum beats. Exeunt* ALCIBIADES, PHRYNIA, *and* TIMANDRA.
Tim. That nature, being sick of man's unkindness,
Should yet be hungry!—Common mother, thou, [*Digging.*
Whose womb unmeasurable, and infinite breast,

Teems and feeds all; whose self-same mettle,
Whereof thy proud child, arrogant man, is puff'd,
Engenders the black toad, and adder blue,
The gilded newt, and eyeless venom'd worm,
With all the abhorred births below crisp heaven
Whereon Hyperion's quickening fire doth shine;
Yield him, who all thy human sons doth hate,
From forth thy plenteous bosom, one poor root!
Ensear thy fertile and conceptious womb,
Let it no more bring out ingrateful man!
Go great with tigers, dragons, wolves, and bears;
Teem with new monsters, whom thy upward face
Hath to the marbled mansions all above
Never presented!—O, a root,—Dear thanks!
Dry up thy marrows, vines, and plough-torn leas;
Whereof ingrateful man, with liquorish draughts,
And morsels unctuous, greases his pure mind,
That from it all consideration slips!

Enter APEMANTUS.

More man? Plague! plague!

Apem. I was directed hither: Men report,
Thou dost affect my manners, and dost use them.

Tim. 'Tis then, because thou dost not keep a dog
Whom I would imitate. Consumption catch [thee!

Apem. This is in thee a nature but affected;
A poor unmanly melancholy, sprung
From change of fortune. Why this spade? this place?
This slavelike habit? and these looks of care?
Thy flatterers yet wear silk, drink wine, lie soft;
Hug their diseas'd perfumes, and have forgot
That ever Timon was. Shame not these woods,
By putting on the cunning of a carper.
Be thou a flatterer now, and seek to thrive
By that which has undone thee: hinge thy knee,
And let his very breath, whom thou'lt observe,
Blow off thy cap; praise his most vicious strain,
And call it excellent: Thou wast told thus;
Thou gav'st thine ears, like tapsters, that bid welcome,
To knaves, and all approachers: 'Tis most just,
That thou turn rascal; hadst thou wealth again,
Rascals should have't. Do not assume my likeness.

Tim. Were I like thee, I'd throw away myself.

Apem. Thou hast cast away thyself, being like thyself;
A madman so long, now a fool; What, think'st
That the bleak air, thy boisterous chamberlain,
Will put thy shirt on warm? Will these moss'd trees,
That have outliv'd the eagle, page thy heels,
And skip when thou point'st out? Will the cold brook,
Candied with ice, caudle thy morning taste,
To cure thy o'ernight's surfeit? call the creatures,—
Whose naked natures live in all the spite
Of wreakful heaven; whose bare unhoused trunks,
To the conflicting elements expos'd,
Answer mere nature,—bid them flatter thee;
O! thou shalt find——

Tim. A fool of thee: Depart.

Apem. I love thee better now than e'er I did.

Tim. I hate thee worse.

Apem. Why?

Tim. Thou flatter'st misery.

Apem. I flatter not; but say, thou art a caitiff.

Tim. Why dost thou seek me out?

Apem. To vex thee.

Tim. Always a villain's office, or a fool's.
Dost please thyself in't?

Apem. Ay.

Tim. What! a knave too?

Apem. If thou didst put this sour cold habit on
To castigate thy pride, 'twere well: but thou
Dost it enforcedly; thou'dst courtier be again,
Wert thou not beggar. Willing misery
Outlives incertain pomp, is crown'd before:
The one is filling still, never complete;
The other, at high wish: Best state, contentless,
Hath a distracted and most wretched being,
Worse than the worst, content.
Thou should'st desire to die, being miserable.

Tim. Not by his breath, that is more miserable.
Thou art a slave, whom Fortune's tender arm
With favour never clasp'd: but bred a dog.
Hadst thou, like us, from our first swath, proceeded
The sweet degrees that this brief world affords
To such as may the passive drugs of it
Freely command, thou would'st have plunged thyself
In general riot: melted down thy youth
In different beds of lust; and never learn'd
The icy precepts of respect, but follow'd
The sugar'd game before thee. But myself,
Who had the world as my confectionary;
The mouths, the tongues, the eyes, and hearts of men
At duty, more than I could frame employment;
That numberless upon me stuck, as leaves
Do on the oak, have with one winter's brush
Fell from their boughs, and left me open, bare
For every storm that blows;—I, to bear this,
That never knew but better, is some burden:
Thy nature did commence in sufferance, time
Hath made thee hard in 't. Why should'st thou hate men?
They never flatter'd thee: What hast thou given?
If thou wilt curse,—thy father, that poor rag,
Must be thy subject: who, in spite, put stuff
To some she beggar, and compounded thee
Poor rogue hereditary. Hence! be gone!—
If thou hadst not been born the worst of men,
Thou hadst been a knave, and flatterer.

Apem. Art thou proud yet?

Tim. Ay, that I am not thee.

Apem. I, that I was
No prodigal.

Tim. I, that I am one now;
Were all the wealth I have, shut up in thee,
I'd give thee leave to hang it. Get thee gone.—
That the whole life of Athens were in this!
Thus would I eat it. [*Eating a root.*

Apem. Here; I will mend thy feast. [*Offering him something.*

Tim. First mend my company, take away thyself.

Apem. So I shall mend mine own, by the lack [of thine.

Tim. 'Tis not well mended so, it is but botch'd:
If not, I would it were.

Apem. What would'st thou have to Athens?

Tim. Thee, thither in a whirlwind. If thou wilt,
Tell them there I have gold; look, so I have.

Apem. Here is no use for gold.

Tim. The best, and truest:
For here it sleeps, and does no hired harm.

Apem. Where ly'st o' nights, Timon?

Tim. Under that's above me.
Where feed'st thou o' days, Apemantus?

Apem. Where my stomach finds meat; or, rather, where I eat it.

Tim. 'Would poison were obedient, and knew my mind!

Apem. Where would'st thou send it?

Tim. To sauce thy dishes.

Apem. The middle of humanity thou never knewest, but the extremity of both ends: When thou wast in thy gilt, and thy perfume, they mocked thee for too much curiosity; in thy rags thou knowest none, but art despised for the contrary. There's a medlar for thee, eat it.

Tim. On what I hate, I feed not.

Apem. Dost hate a medlar?

Tim. Ay, though it look like thee.

Apem. An thou hadst hated medlers sooner, thou should'st have loved thyself better now. What man didst thou ever know unthrift, that was beloved after his means?

Tim. Who without those means thou talk'st of, didst thou ever know beloved?

Apem. Myself.

Tim. I understand thee; thou hadst some means to keep a dog.

Apem. What things in the world canst thou nearest compare to thy flatterers?

Tim. Women nearest; but men, men are the things themselves. What would'st thou do with the world, Apemantus, if it lay in thy power?

Apem. Give it the beasts, to be rid of the men.

Tim. Would'st thou have thyself fall in the confusion of men, and remain a beast with the beasts.

Apem. Ay, Timon.

Tim. A beastly ambition, which the gods grant thee to attain to! If thou wert the lion, the fox would beguile thee: if thou wert the lamb, the fox would eat thee: if thou wert the fox, the lion would suspect thee, when, peradventure, thou wert accused by the ass: if thou wert the ass, thy dullness would torment thee; and still thou livedst but as a breakfast to the wolf: if thou wert the wolf, thy greediness would afflict thee, and oft thou should'st hazard thy life for thy dinner: wert thou the unicorn, pride and wrath would confound thee, and make thine own self the conquest of thy fury: wert thou a bear, thou would'st be kill'd by the horse: wert thou a horse, thou would'st be seized by the leopard: wert thou a leopard, thou wert german to the lion, and the spots of thy kindred were jurors on thy life: all thy safety were remotion, and thy defence, absence. What beast could'st thou be, that were not subject to a beast? and what a beast art thou already, that seest not thy loss in transformation?

Apem. If thou could'st please me with speaking to me, thou might'st have hit upon it here: The commonwealth of Athens is become a forest of beasts.

Tim. How has the ass broke the wall, that thou art out of the city?

Apem. Yonder comes a poet, and a painter: The plague of company light upon thee! I will fear to catch it, and give way: When I know not what els to do, I'll see thee again.

Tim. When there is nothing living but thee, thou shalt be welcome. I had rather be a beggar's dog, than Apemantus.

Apem. Thou art the cap of all the fools alive.

Tim. 'Would thou wert clean enough to spit upon.

Apem. A plague on thee, thou art too bad to curse.

Tim. All villains, that do stand by thee, are pure.

Apem. There is no leprosy but what thou speak'st.

Tim. If I name thee,—
I'll beat thee,—but I should infect my hands.

Apem. I would, my tongue could rot them off!

Tim. Away, thou issue of a mangy dog!
Choler does kill me, that thou art alive;
I swoon to see thee.

Apem. 'Would thou would'st burst!

Tim. Away,
Thou tedious rogue! I am sorry I shall lose
A stone by thee. [*Throws a stone at him.*

Apem. Beast!

Tim. Slave!

Apem. Toad!

Tim. Rogue, rogue, rogue!

[APEMANTUS *retreats backward, as going.*

I am sick of this false world; and will love nought
But even the mere necessities upon it.
Then, Timon, presently prepare thy grave;
Lie where the light foam of the sea may beat
Thy grave-stone daily: make thine epitaph,
That death in me at other's lives may laugh.
O thou sweet king-killer, and dear divorce
[*Looking on the gold.*
'Twixt natural son and sire! thou bright defiler
Of Hymen's purest bed! thou valiant Mars!
Thou ever young, fresh, lov'd, and delicate wooer,
Whose blush doth thaw the consecrated snow
That lies on Dian's lap! thou visible god,
That solder'st close impossibilities,
And mak'st them kiss! that speak'st with every tongue,
To every purpose! O thou touch of hearts!
Think, thy slave man rebels; and by thy virtue
Set them into confounding odds, that beasts
May have the world in empire!

Apem. 'Would 'twere so;—
But not till I am dead!—I'll say, thou hast gold:
Thou wilt be throng'd to shortly.

Tim. Throng'd to?

Apem. Ay.

Tim. Thy back, I pr'ythee.

Apem. Live, and love thy misery!

Tim. Long live so, and so die!—I am quit.—
[*Exit* APEMANTUS.
More things like men?—Eat, Timon, and abhor them.

Enter Thieves.

1 *Thief.* Where should he have this gold? It is some poor fragment, some slender ort of his remainder: The mere want of gold, and the falling-from of his friends, drove him into this melancholy.

2 *Thief.* It is noised, he hath a mass of treasure.

3 *Thief.* Let us make the assay upon him; if he care not for't, he will supply us easily; If he covetously reserve it, how shall's get it?

2 *Thief.* True; for he bears it not about him, 'tis hid.

1 *Thief.* Is not this he?

Thieves. Where?

2 *Thief.* 'Tis his description.

3 *Thief.* He; I know him.

Thieves. Save thee, Timon.

Tim. Now, thieves?

Thieves. Soldiers, not thieves.

Tim. Both too; and women's sons.

Thieves. We are not thieves, but men that much do want.

Tim. Your greatest want is, you want much of men.
Why should you want? Behold the earth hath roots;
Within this mile break forth a hundred springs:
The oaks bear mast, the briars scarlet hips:
The bounteous housewife, nature, on each bush
Lays her full mess before you. Want? why want?

1 *Thief.* We cannot live on grass, on berries, water,
As beasts, and birds, and fishes.

Tim. Nor on the beasts themselves, the birds, and fishes;
You must eat men. Yet thanks I must you con,
That you are thieves profess'd; that you work not
In holier shapes: for there is boundless theft
In limited professions. Rascal thieves,
Here's gold: Go, suck the subtle blood of the grape
Till the high fever seeth your blood to froth,
And so 'scape hanging: trust not the physician;
His antidotes are poison, and he slays
More than you rob: take wealth and lives together;
Do villany, do, since you profess to do't,
Like workmen. I'll example you with thievery:
The sun's a thief, and with his great attraction
Robs the vast sea: the moon's an arrant thief,
And her pale fire she snatches from the sun:
The sea's a thief, whose liquid surge resolves
The moon into salt tears: the earth's a thief,
That feeds, and breeds by a composture stol'n
From general excrement: each thing's a thief;
The laws, your curb and whip, in their rough power
Have uncheck'd theft. Love not yourselves: away;

Rob one another. There's more gold: Cut throats;
All that you meet are thieves: To Athens, go,
Break open shops; for nothing can you steal,
But thieves do lose it: Steal not less, for this
I give you; and gold confound you howsoever!
Amen. [TIMON *retires to his Cave.*

3 *Thief.* He has almost charmed me from my profession, by persuading me to it.

1 *Thief.* 'Tis in the malice of mankind, that he thus advises us; not to have us thrive in our mystery.

2 *Thief.* I'll believe him as an enemy, and give over my trade.

1 *Thief.* Let us first see peace in Athens: There is no time so miserable, but a man may be true. [*Exeunt* Thieves.

Enter FLAVIUS.

Flav. O you gods!
Is yon despis'd and ruinous man my lord?
Full of decay and failing? O monument
And wonder of good deeds evilly bestow'd!
What an alteration of honour has
Desperate want made!
What viler thing upon the earth, than friends,
Who can bring noblest minds to basest ends!
How rarely does it meet with this time's guise,
When man was wish'd to love his enemies:
Grant I may ever love, and rather woo
Those that would mischief me, than those that do!
He has caught me in his eye: I will present
My honest grief unto him: and, as my lord,
Still serve him with my life.—My dearest master!

TIMON *comes forward from his Cave.*

Tim. Away! what art thou?
Flav. Have you forgot me, sir?
Tim. Why dost ask that? I have forgot all men;
Then, if thou grant'st thou'rt a man, I have forgot thee.
Flav. An honest poor servant of yours.
Tim. Then
I know thee not: I ne'er had honest man
About me, I; all that I kept were knaves,
To serve in meat to villains.
Flav. The gods are witness,
Ne'er did poor steward wear a truer grief
For his undone lord, than mine eyes for you.
Tim. What, dost thou weep?—Come nearer;—then I love thee,
Because thou art a woman, and disclaim'st
Flinty mankind; whose eyes do never give,
But thorough lust, and laughter. Pity's sleeping;
Strange times that weep with laughing, not with weeping!
Flav. I beg of you to know me, good my lord,
To accept my grief, and, whilst this poor wealth lasts,
To entertain me as your steward still.
Tim. Had I a steward so true, so just, and now
So comfortable? It almost turns
My dangerous nature mild. Let me behold
Thy face.—Surely this man was born of woman.—
Forgive my general and exceptless rashness,
You perpetual-sober gods? I do proclaim
One honest man,—mistake me not,—but one;
No more, I pray,—and he is a steward.—
How fain would I have hated all mankind,
And thou redeem'st thyself: But all, save thee,
I fell with curses.
Methinks thou art more honest now than wise;
For, by oppressing and betraying me,
Thou might'st have sooner got another service:
For many so arrive at second masters,
Upon their first lord's neck. But tell me true
(For I must ever doubt, though ne'er so sure),
Is not thy kindness subtle, covetous,
If not a usuring kindness; and as rich men deal gifts,
Expecting in return twenty for one?
Flav. No, my most worthy master, in whose breast
Doubt and suspect, alas, are plac'd too late:
You should have fear'd false times, when you did feast:
Suspect still comes where an estate is least.
That which I show, heaven knows, is merely love,
Duty and zeal to your unmatched mind,
Care of your food and living: and, believe it,
My most honour'd lord,
For any benefit that points to me,
Either in hope, or present, I'd exchange
For this one wish, That you had power and wealth
To requite me, by making rich yourself.
Tim. Look thee, 'tis so!—Thou singly honest man,
Here, take:—the gods out of my misery
Have sent thee treasure. Go, live rich, and happy:

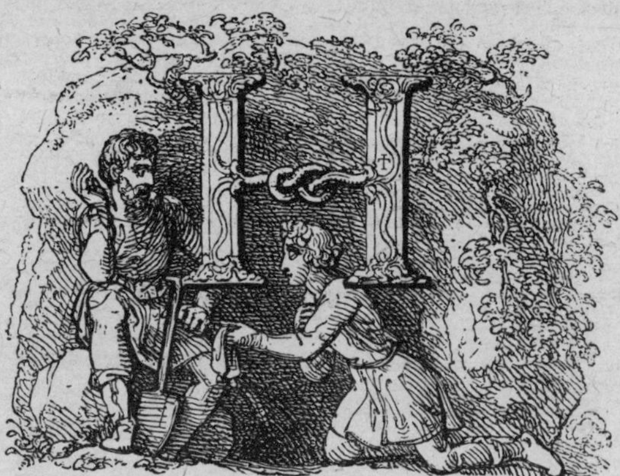

But thus condition'd; Thou shalt build from men;
Hate all, curse all: show charity to none;
But let the famish'd flesh slide from the bone,
Ere thou relieve the beggar: give to dogs
What thou deny'st to men; let prisons swallow them,
Debts wither them: Be men like blasted woods

And may diseases lick up their false bloods!
And so farewell, and thrive.

Flav. O, let me stay,
And comfort you, my master.

Tim. If thou hat'st
Curses, stay not; fly whilst thou art bless'd and free:
Ne'er see thou man, and let me ne'er see thee.
[*Exeunt severally.*

ACT V.

SCENE I. *The same. Before* Timon's *Cave.*

Enter Poet *and* Painter; TIMON *behind, unseen.*

Pain. As I took note of the place, it cannot be far where he abides.

Poet. What's to be thought of him? Does the rumour hold for true, that he is so full of gold?

Pain. Certain: Alcibiades reports it; Phrynia and Timandra had gold of him: he likewise enriched poor straggling soldiers with great quantity: 'Tis said, he gave unto his steward a mighty sum.

Poet. Then this breaking of his has been but a try for his friends.

Pain. Nothing else; you shall see him a palm in Athens again, and flourish with the highest. Therefore, 'tis not amiss, we tender our loves to him, in this supposed distress of his: it will show honestly in us; and is very likely to load our purposes with what they travel for, if it be a just and true report that goes of his having.

Poet. What have you now to present unto him?

Pain. Nothing at this time but my visitation: only I will promise him an excellent piece.

Poet. I must serve him so too; tell him of an intent that's coming toward him.

Pain. Good as the best. Promising is the very air o'the time: it opens the eyes of expectation; performance is ever the duller for his act; and, but in the plainer and simpler kind of people, the deed of saying is quite out of use. To promise is most courtly and fashionable: performance is a kind of will or testament, which argues a great sickness in his judgment that makes it.

Tim. Excellent workman! Thou canst not paint a man so bad as thyself.

Poet. I am thinking, what I shall say I have provided for him: It must be a personating of himself: a satire against the softness of prosperity; with a discovery of the infinite flatteries that follow youth and opulency.

Tim. Must thou needs stand for a villain in thine own work? Wilt thou whip thine own faults in other men? Do so, I have gold for thee.

Poet. Nay, let's seek him:
Then do we sin against our own estate,
When we may profit meet, and come too late.

Pain. True;
When the day serves before black-corner'd night,
Find what thou want'st by free and offer'd light.
Come.

Tim. I'll meet you at the turn. What a god's gold,
That he is worship'd in a baser temple,
Than where swine feed!
'Tis thou that rigg'st the bark, and plough'st the foam;
Settlest admired reverence in a slave:
To thee be worship! and thy saints for aye
Be crown'd with plagues, that thee alone obey!
'Fit I do meet them. [*Advancing.*

Poet. Hail, worthy Timon!

Pain. Our late noble master.

Tim. Have I once liv'd to see two honest men?

Poet. Sir,
Having often of your open bounty tasted,
Hearing you were retir'd, your friends fall'n off,
Whose thankless natures—O abhorred spirits!
Not all the whips of heaven are large enough—
What! to you!
Whose starlike nobleness gave life and influence
To their whole being! I am rapt, and cannot cover
The monstrous bulk of this ingratitude
With any size of words.

Tim. Let it go naked, men may see't the better:
You, that are honest, by being what you are,
Make them best seen, and known.

Pain. He, and myself,
Have travell'd in the great shower of your gifts,
And sweetly felt it.

Tim. Ay, you are honest men.

Pain. We are hither come to offer you our service.

Tim. Most honest men! Why, how shall I requite you?
Can you eat roots, and drink cold water? no.

Both. What we can do, we'll do, to do you service.

Tim. You are honest men: You have heard that I have gold:
I am sure you have: Speak truth, you are honest men.

Pain. So it is said, my noble lord: but therefore
Came not my friend, nor I.

Tim. Good honest men:—thou draw'st a counterfeit
Best in all Athens: thou art, indeed, the best;
Thou counterfeit'st most lively.

Pain. So, so, my lord.

Tim. Even so, sir, as I say:—And, for thy fiction, [*To the* Poet.
Why, thy verse swells with stuff so fine and smooth,
That thou art even natural in thine art.—
But, for all this, my honest natur'd friends,
I must needs say you have a little fault:
Marry, 'tis not monstrous in you: neither wish I,
You take much pains to mend.

Both. Beseech your honour,
To make it known to us.

Tim. You'll take it ill.

Both. Most thankfully, my lord.

Tim. Will you, indeed?

Both. Doubt it not, worthy lord.

Tim. There's ne'er a one of you but trusts a knave,
That mightily deceives you.

Both. Do we, my lord?

Tim. Ay, and you hear him cog, see him dissemble,
Know his gross patchery, love him, feed him,
Keep in your bosom: yet remain assur'd,
That he's a made-up villain.

Pain. I know none such, my lord.

Poet. Nor I.

Tim. Look you, I love you well: I'll give you gold,
Rid me these villains from your companies:
Hang them, or stab them, drown them in a draught,
Confound them by some course, and come to me,
I'll give you gold enough.

Both. Name them, my lord, let's know them.

Tim. You that way, and you this, but two in company:—
Each man apart, all single and alone,
Yet an arch villain keeps him company.
If, where thou art, two villains shall not be,
[*To the* Painter.
Come not near him.—If thou wouldst not reside
[*To the* Poet.
But where one villain is, then him abandon.—
Hence! pack! there's gold, ye came for gold, ye slaves:
You have done work for me, there's payment: Hence!
You are an alchymist, make gold of that:—
Out, rascal dogs!
[*Exit, beating and driving them out.*

SCENE II. *The same.*

Enter FLAVIUS *and two* Senators.

Flav. It is in vain that you would speak with Timon;
For he is set so only to himself,
That nothing but himself, which looks like man,
Is friendly with him.

1 Sen. Bring us to his cave:
It is our part, and promise to the Athenians,
To speak with Timon.

2 Sen. At all times alike
Men are not still the same: 'Twas time, and griefs,
That fram'd him thus: time, with his fairer hand,
Offering the fortunes of his former days,
The former man may make him: Bring us to him,
And chance it as it may.

Flav. Here is his cave.—
Peace and content be here! Lord Timon! Timon!
Look out, and speak to friends: The Athenians,
By two of their most reverend senate, greet thee:
Speak to them, noble Timon.

Enter TIMON.

Tim. Thou sun, that comfort'st, burn!—Speak, and be hang'd:
For each true word, a blister! and each false
Be as a caut'rizing to the root o' the tongue,
Consuming it with speaking!

1 Sen. Worthy Timon—

Tim. Of none but such as you, and you of Timon.

2 Sen. The senators of Athens greet thee, Timon.

Tim. I thank them; and would send them back the plague,
Could I but catch it for them.

1 Sen. O, forget
What we are sorry for ourselves in thee.
The senators, with one consent of love,
Entreat thee back to Athens; who have thought
On special dignities, which vacant lie
For thy best use and wearing.

2 Sen. They confess,
Toward thee, forgetfulness too general, gross:
Which now the publick body,—which doth seldom
Play the recanter,—feeling in itself
A lack of Timon's aid, hath sense withal
Of its own fall, restraining aid to Timon;
And send forth us, to make their sorrowed render,
Together with a recompense more fruitful
Than their offence can weigh down by the dram:
Ay, even such heaps and sums of love and wealth,
As shall to thee blot out what wrongs were theirs,
And write in thee the figures of their love,
Ever to read them thine.

Tim. You witch me in it;
Surprise me to the very brink of tears:
Lend me a fool's heart, and a woman's eyes,
And I'll beweep these comforts, worthy senators.

1 Sen. Therefore, so please thee to return with us,
And of our Athens (thine, and ours) to take
The captainship, thou shalt be met with thanks,
Allow'd with absolute power, and thy good name
Live with authority:—so soon we shall drive back
Of Alcibiades the approaches wild;
Who, like a boar too savage, doth root up
His country's peace.

2 Sen. And shakes his threatening sword
Against the walls of Athens.

1 Sen. Therefore, Timon,—

Tim. Well, sir, I will; therefore, I will, sir; Thus,—
If Alcibiades kill my countrymen,
Let Alcibiades know this of Timon,
That—Timon knows not. But if he sack fair Athens,
And take our goodly aged men by the beards,
Giving our holy virgins to the stain
Of contumelious, beastly, mad-brain'd war;
Then, let him know,—and tell him Timon speaks it,
In pity of our aged, and our youth,
I cannot choose but tell him, that—I care not,
And let him tak't at worst; for their knives care not,
While you have throats to answer; for myself,
There's not a whittle in the unruly camp,
But I do prize it at my love, before
The reverend'st throat in Athens. So I leave you
To the protection of the prosperous gods,
As thieves to keepers.

Flav. Stay not, all's in vain.

Tim. Why, I was writing of my epitaph,
It will be seen to-morrow; my long sickness
Of health, and living, now begins to mend,
And nothing brings me all things. Go, live still;
Be Alcibiades your plague, you his.
And last so long enough!

1 Sen. We speak in vain.

Tim. But yet I love my country; and am not
One that rejoices in the common wreck,
As common bruit doth put it.

1 Sen. That's well spoke.

Tim. Commend me to my loving countrymen—

1 Sen. These words become your lips as they pass through them.

2 Sen. And enter in our ears, like great triumphers
In their applauding gates.

Tim. Commend me to them;
And tell them that, to ease them of their griefs,
Their fears of hostile strokes, their aches, losses,
Their pangs of love, with other incident throes
That nature's fragile vessel doth sustain
In life's uncertain voyage, I will some kindness do them:
I'll teach them to prevent wild Alcibiades' wrath.

2 Sen. I like this well, he will return again.

Tim. I have a tree, which grows here in my close,
That mine own use invites me to cut down,
And shortly must I fell it; Tell my friends,
Tell Athens, in the sequence of degree,
From high to low throughout, that whoso please
To stop affliction, let him take his haste,
Come hither, ere my tree hath felt the axe,
And hang himself:—I pray you, do my greeting.

Flav. Trouble him no further, thus you still shall find him.

Tim. Come not to me again; but say to Athens,
Timon hath made his everlasting mansion
Upon the beached verge of the salt flood;
Which once a day with his embossed froth
The turbulent surge shall cover; thither come,
And let my grave-stone be your oracle.—
Lips, let sour words go by, and language end:
What is amiss, plague and infection mend!
Graves only be men's works; and death their gain!
Sun, hide thy beams! Timon hath done his reign.
[*Exit* TIMON.

1 Sen. His discontents are unremovably
Coupled to nature.

2 Sen. Our hope in him is dead; let us return,
And strain what other means is left unto us
In our dear peril.

1 Sen. It requires swift foot.
[*Exeunt.*

SCENE III. *The Walls of* Athens.

Enter two Senators, *and a* Messenger.

1 Sen. Thou hast painfully discover'd; are his files
As full as thy report?

Mess. I have spoke the least:

Besides, his expedition promises
Present approach.

2 *Sen.* We stand much hazard, if they bring not Timon.

Mess. I met a courier, one, mine ancient friend:—
Whom, though in general part we were oppos'd,
Yet our old love made a particular force,
And made us speak like friends:—this man was riding
From Alcibiades to Timon's cave,
With letters of entreaty, which imported
His fellowship i'the cause against your city,
In part for his sake mov'd.

Enter Senators *from* Timon.

1 *Sen.* Here come our brothers.

3 *Sen.* No talk of Timon, nothing of him expect.—
The enemies' drum is heard, and fearful scouring
Doth choke the air with dust; in and prepare;
Ours is the fall, I fear, our foes the snare. [*Exeunt.*

SCENE IV.

The Woods. Timon's *Cave, and a Tombstone seen.*

Enter a Soldier, *seeking* Timon.

Sol. By all description this should be the place
Who's here? speak, ho!—No answer? What is this?
Timon is dead, who hath outstretch'd his span:
Some beast rear'd this; there does not live a man.
Dead, sure; and this his grave.—
What's on this tomb I cannot read; the character
I'll take with wax.
Our captain hath in every figure skill;
An ag'd interpreter, though young in days:
Before proud Athens he's set down by this,
Whose fall the mark of his ambition is. [*Exit.*

SCENE V. *Before the Walls of* Athens.

Trumpets sound. Enter ALCIBIADES *and* Forces.

Alcib. Sound to this coward and lascivious town
Our terrible approach. [*A parley sounded.*

Enter Senators *on the Walls.*

Till now you have gone on, and fill'd the time
With all licentious measure, making your wills
The scope of justice; till now, myself, and such
As slept within the shadow of your power,
Have wander'd with our travers'd arms, and, breath'd
Our sufferance vainly: Now the time is flush,
When crouching marrow, in the bearer strong,
Cries of itself, *No more:* now breathless wrong
Shall sit and pant in your great chairs of ease;
And pursy insolence shall break his wind,
With fear and horrid flight.

1 *Sen.* Noble and young,
When thy first griefs were but a mere conceit,
Ere thou hadst power, or we had cause of fear,
We sent to thee; to give thy rages balm,
To wipe out our ingratitude with loves
Above their quantity.

2 *Sen.* So did we woo
Transformed Timon to our city's love,
By humble message, and by promis'd means;
We were not all unkind, nor all deserve
The common stroke of war.

1 *Sen.* These walls of ours
Were not erected by their hands, from whom
You have receiv'd your griefs: nor are they such,
That these great towers, trophies, and schools should fall
For private faults in them.

2 *Sen.* Nor are they living,
Who were the motives that you first went out;
Shame that they wanted cunning, in excess
Hath broke their hearts. March, noble lord,
Into our city with thy banners spread:
By decimation, and a tithed death
(If thy revenges hunger for that food,
Which nature loathes), take thou the destin'd tenth;
And by the hazard of the spotted die,
Let die the spotted.

1 *Sen.* All have not offended:
For those that were, it is not square, to take,
On those that are, revenges: crimes like lands,
Are not inherited. Then, dear countryman,
Bring in thy ranks, but leave without thy rage:
Spare thy Athenian cradle, and those kin,
Which in the bluster of thy wrath, must fall
With those that have offended: like a shepherd,
Approach the fold, and cull the infected forth,
But kill not all together.

2 *Sen.* What thou wilt,
Thou rather shalt enforce it with thy smile,
Than hew to 't with thy sword.

1 *Sen.* Set but thy foot
Against our rampir'd gates, and they shall ope;
So thou wilt send thy gentle heart before,
To say, thou'lt enter friendly.

2 *Sen.* Throw thy glove;
Or any token of thine honour else,
That thou wilt use the wars as thy redress,
And not as our confusion, all thy powers
Shall make their harbour in our town, till we
Have seal'd thy full desire.

Alcib. Then there's my glove;
Descend, and open your uncharged ports;
Those enemies of Timon's, and mine own,
Whom you yourself shall set out for reproof,
Fall, and no more: and, to atone your fears
With my more noble meaning,—not a man
Shall pass his quarter, or offend the stream
Of regular justice in your city's bounds,
But shall be remedied to your public laws
At heaviest answer.

Both. 'Tis most nobly spoken.

Alcib. Descend, and keep your words.

The Senators *descend, and open the Gates.*

Enter a Soldier.

Sol. My noble general, Timon is dead:
Entomb'd upon the very hem o' the sea:
And on his gravestone, this insculpture; which
With wax I brought away, whose soft impression
Interprets for my poor ignorance.

Alcib. [Reads.] *Here lies a wretched corse, of wretched soul bereft:*
Seek not my name: A plague consume you wicked caitiffs left!
Here lie I Timon; who, alive, all living men did hate:
Pass by, and curse thy fill; but pass, and stay not here thy gait.

These well express in thee thy latter spirits:
Though thou abhorr'dst in us our human griefs,
Scorn'dst our brain's flow, and those our droplets which
From niggard nature fall, yet rich conceit
Taught thee to make vast Neptune weep for aye
On thy low grave, on faults forgiven. Dead
Is noble Timon; of whose memory
Hereafter more.—Bring me into your city,
And I will use the olive with my sword:
Make war breed peace; make peace stint war; make each
Prescribe to other, as each other's leech.
Let our drums strike. [*Exeunt.*

CORIOLANUS.

PERSONS REPRESENTED.

CAIUS MARCIUS CORIOLANUS, *a noble* Roman.
TITUS LARTIUS, } *Generals against the* Volcians.
COMINIUS, }
MENENIUS AGRIPPA, *Friend to* Coriolanus.
SICINIUS VELUTUS, } *Tribunes of the People.*
JUNIUS BRUTUS, }
Young MARCIUS, *Son to* Coriolanus.
A Roman Herald.
TULLUS AUFIDIUS, *General of the* Volcians.
Lieutenant *to* Aufidius.
Conspirators *with* Aufidius.

A Citizen *of* Antium.
Two Volcian Guards.

VOLUMNIA, *Mother to* Coriolanus.
VIRGILIA, *Wife to* Coriolanus.
VALERIA, *Friend to* Virgilia.
Gentlewoman, *attending* Virgilia.

Roman *and* Volcian Senators, Patricians, Ædiles, Lictors, Soldiers, Citizens, Messengers, Servants *to* Aufidius, *and other* Attendants.

SCENE—*partly in* Rome; *and partly in the Territories of the* Volcians *and* Antiates.

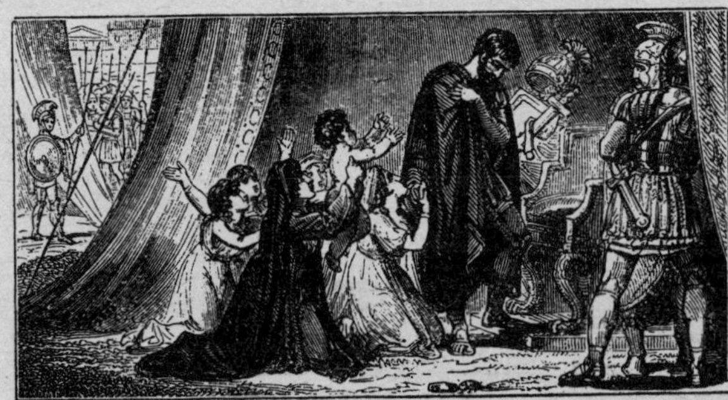

ACT I.

SCENE I. Rome. *A Street.*

Enter a Company of mutinous Citizens, *with Staves, Clubs, and other Weapons.*

1 *Cit.* BEFORE we proceed any further, hear me speak.

Cit. Speak, speak. [*Several speaking at once.*

1 *Cit.* You are all resolved rather to die, than to famish?

Cit. Resolved, resolved.

1 *Cit.* First you know, Caius Marcius is chief enemy to the people.

Cit. We know't, we know't.

1 *Cit.* Let us kill him, and we'll have corn at our own price. Is't a verdict?

Cit. No more talking on't; let it be done: away, away.

2 *Cit.* One word, good citizens.

1 *Cit.* We are accounted poor citizens; the patricians, good; What authority surfeits on, would relieve us; If they would yield us but the superfluity, while it were wholesome, we might guess, they relieved us humanely; but they think, we are too dear: the leanness that afflicts us, the object of our misery, is as an inventory to particularize their abundance: our sufferance is a gain to them.—Let us revenge this with our pikes, ere we become rakes: for the gods know, I speak this in hunger for bread, not in thirst for revenge.

2 *Cit.* Would you proceed especially against Caius Marcius?

Cit. Against him first; he's a very dog to the commonalty.

2 *Cit.* Consider you what services he has done for his country?

1 *Cit.* Very well; and could be content to give him good report for't, but that he pays himself with being proud.

2 *Cit.* Nay, but speak not maliciously.

1 *Cit.* I say unto you, what he hath done famously, he did it to that end: though soft conscienc'd men can be content to say, it was for his country, he did it to please his mother, and to be partly proud; which he is, even to the altitude of his virtue.

2 *Cit.* What he cannot help in his nature, you account a vice in him: You must in no way say, he is covetous.

1 *Cit.* If I must not, I need not be barren of accusations; he hath faults, with surplus, to tire in repetition. [*Shouts within.*] What shouts are these? The other side o'the city is risen: Why stay we prating here? To the Capitol.

Cit. Come, come.

1 *Cit.* Soft; who comes here?

Enter MENENIUS AGRIPPA.

2 *Cit.* Worthy Menenius Agrippa; one that hath always loved the people.

1 *Cit.* He's one honest enough; 'Would, all the rest were so!

Men. What work's, my countrymen, in hand? Where go you
With bats and clubs? The matter? Speak, I [pray you.

1 *Cit.* Our business is not unknown to the senate; they have had inkling, this fortnight, what we intend to do, which now we'll show 'em in deeds. They say, poor suitors have strong breaths; they shall know, we have strong arms too.

Men. Why, masters, my good friends, mine honest neighbours,
Will you undo yourselves?

1 *Cit.* We cannot, sir, we are undone already.

Men. I tell you, friends, most charitable care
Have the patricians of you. For your wants,
Your suffering in this dearth, you may as well
Strike at the heaven with your staves, as lift them
Against the Roman state; whose course will on
The way it takes, cracking ten thousand curbs
Of more strong link asunder, than can ever
Appear in your impediment: For the dearth,
The gods, not the patricians, make it; and
Your knees to them, not arms, must help. Alack,
You are transported by calamity
Thither where more attends you; and you slander
The helms o'the state, who care for you like fathers,
When you curse them as enemies.

1 *Cit.* Care for us!—True, indeed!—They ne'er cared for us yet. Suffer us to famish, and their store-houses crammed with grain: make edicts for usury, to support usurers: repeal daily any wholesome act established against the rich; and provide more piercing statutes daily to chain up and restrain the poor. If the wars eat us not up, they will; and there's all the love they bear us.

Men. Either you must
Confess yourselves wondrous malicious,
Or be accus'd of folly. I shall tell you
A pretty tale; it may be, you have heard it;
But, since it serves my purpose, I will venture
To stale't a little more.

1 *Cit.* Well, I'll hear it, sir: yet you must not think to fob off our disgrace with a tale: but an't please you, deliver.

Men. There was a time, when all the body's members
Rebell'd against the belly; thus accus'd it:—
That only like a gulf it did remain
I' the midst o' the body, idle and inactive,
Still cupboarding the viand, never bearing
Like labour with the rest; where the other instruments
Did see, and hear, devise, instruct, walk, feel,
And, mutually participate, did minister
Unto the appetite and affection common
Of the whole body. The belly answered,—

1 *Cit.* Well, sir, what answer made the belly?

Men. Sir, I shall tell you.—With a kind of smile,
Which ne'er came from the lungs, but even thus
(For, look you, I may make the belly smile,
As well as speak,) it tauntingly replied
To the discontented members, the mutinous parts
That envied his receipt; even so most fitly
As you malign our senators, for that
They are not such as you.

1 *Cit.* Your belly's answer: What?

Men. The kingly crowned head, the vigilant eye,
The counsellor heart, the arm our soldier,
Our steed the leg, the tongue our trumpeter
With other muniments and petty helps
In this our fabrick, if that they——

1 *Cit.* What then?—

Men. 'Fore me this fellow speaks!—what then? what then?
Should by the cormorant belly be restrain'd,
Who is the sink o'the body,—

1 *Cit.* Well, what then?
The former agents, if they did complain,
What could the belly answer?

Men. I will tell you;
If you'll bestow a small (of what you have little),
Patience, a while, you'll hear the belly's answer.

1 *Cit.* You are long about it.

Men. Note me this, good friend;
Your most grave belly was deliberate,
Not rash like his accusers, and thus answer'd:
True it is, my incorporate friends, quoth he,
That I receive the general food at first,
Which you do live upon: and fit it is;
Because I am the store-house, and the shop
Of the whole body: But if you do remember,
I send it through the rivers of your blood,
Even to the court, the heart,—to the seat o'the brain:
And, through the cranks and offices of man,
The strongest nerves, and small inferior veins,
From me receive that natural competency
Whereby they live: And though that all at once,
You, my good friends (this says the belly), mark me,—

1 *Cit.* Ay, sir; well, well.

Men. *Though all at once cannot*
See what I do deliver out to each;
Yet I can make my audit up, that all
From me do back receive the flower of all,
And leave me but the bran. What say you to't?

1 *Cit.* It was an answer: How apply you this?

Men. The senators of Rome are this good belly,
And you the mutinous members: For examine
Their counsels, and their cares; digest things rightly,
Touching the weal of the common; you shall find,
No public benefit which you receive,
But it proceeds, or comes, from them to you,
And no way from yourselves.—What do you think?
You the great toe of this assembly?—

1 *Cit.* I the great toe? Why the great toe?

Men. For that being one o' the lowest, basest, poorest,
Of this most wise rebellion, thou go'st foremost:
Thou rascal, that art worst in blood, to run
Lead'st first, to win some vantage.—
But make you ready your stiff bats and clubs;
Rome and her rats are at the point of battle,
The one side must have bale. Hail, noble Marcius!

Enter Caius Marcius.

Mar. Thanks.—What's the matter, you dissentious rogues,
That rubbing the poor itch of your opinion,
Make yourselves scabs?

1 *Cit.* We have ever your good word.

Mar. He that will give good words to thee, will flatter
Beneath abhorring.—What would you have, you curs,
That like nor peace nor war? the one affrights you,
The other makes you proud. He that trusts you,
Where he should find you lions, finds you hares;
Where foxes, geese: You are no surer, no,
Than is the coal of fire upon the ice,
Or hailstone in the sun. Your virtue is,
To make him worthy, whose offence subdues him,
And curse that justice did it. Who deserves greatness,
Deserves your hate: and your affections are
A sick man's appetite, who desires most that
Which would increase his evil. He that depends
Upon your favours, swims with fins of lead,
And hews down oaks with rushes. Hang ye! Trust ye?
With every minute you do change a mind;
And call him noble that was now your hate,
Him vile, that was your garland. What's the matter,
That in these several places of the city
You cry against the noble senate, who,
Under the gods, keep you in awe, which else
Would feed on one another?—What's their seeking?

Men. For corn at their own rates: whereof, they say,
The city is well stor'd.

Mar. Hang 'em! They say?
They'll sit by the fire, and presume to know
What's done i' the Capitol: who's like to rise,
Who thrives, and who declines: side factions, and give out

Conjectural marriages; making parties strong,
And feebling such as stand not in their liking,
Below their cobbled shoes. They say, there's grain enough?
Would the nobility lay aside their ruth,
And let me use my sword, I'd make a quarry
With thousands of these quarter'd slaves, as high
As I could pick my lance.

Men. Nay, these are almost thoroughly persuaded;
For though abundantly they lack discretion,
Yet are they passing cowardly. But I beseech you,
What says the other troop?

Mar. They are dissolved: Hang 'em!
They said, they were an hungry; sigh'd forth proverbs;—
That, hunger broke stone walls; that, dogs must eat;
That meat was made for mouths; that, the gods sent not
Corn for the rich men only:—With these shreds
They vented their complainings; which being answer'd,
And a petition granted them, a strange one
(To break the heart of generosity,
And make bold power look pale), they threw their caps
As they would hang them on the horns o' the moon,
Shouting their emulation.

Men. What is granted them?

Mar. Five tribunes to defend their vulgar wisdoms,
Of their own choice: One's Junius Brutus,
Sicinius Velutus, and I know not—'Sdeath!
The rabble should have first unroof'd the city,
Ere so prevail'd with me: it will in time
Win upon power, and throw forth greater themes
For insurrection's arguing.

Men. This is strange.

Mar. Go, get you home, you fragments!

Enter a Messenger.

Mess. Where's Caius Marcius?

Mar. Here: What's the matter?

Mess. The news is, sir, the Volces are in arms.

Mar. I am glad on't; then we shall have means to vent
Our musty superfluity:—See, our best elders.

Enter COMINIUS, TITUS LARTIUS, *and other* Senators; JUNIUS BRUTUS, *and* SICINIUS VELUTUS.

1 *Sen.* Marcius, 'tis true, that you have lately told us;
The Volces are in arms.

Mar. They have a leader,
Tullus Aufidius that will put you to't.
I sin in envying his nobility:
And were I any thing but what I am,
I would wish me only he.

Com. You have fought together.

Mar. Were half to half the world by the ears, and he
Upon my party, I'd revolt, to make
Only my wars with him: he is a lion
That I am proud to hunt.

1 *Sen.* Then, worthy Marcius,
Attend upon Cominius to these wars.

Com. It is your former promise.

Mar. Sir, it is;
And I am constant.—Titus Lartius, thou
Shalt see me once more strike at Tullus' face:
What, art thou stiff? stand'st out?

Tit. No, Caius Marcius:
I'll lean upon one crutch, and fight with the other,
Ere stay behind this business.

Men. O, true bred!

1 *Sen.* Your company to the Capitol; where, I know,
Our greatest friends attend us.

Tit. Lead you on:
Follow, Cominius; we must follow you;
Right worthy you priority.

Com. Noble Lartius!

1 *Sen.* Hence! To your homes, be gone. [*To the* Citizens.

Mar. Nay, let them follow:
The Volces have much corn; take these rats thither,
To gnaw their garners:—Worshipful mutineers,
Your valour puts well forth: pray, follow.

[*Exeunt* Senators, COM. MAR. TIT. *and* MENEN. Citizens *steal away*.

Sic. Was ever man so proud as is this Marcius?

Bru. He has no equal.

Sic. When we were chosen tribunes for the people,——

Bru. Mark'd you his lip, and eyes?

Sic. Nay, but his taunts.

Bru. Being mov'd, he will not spare to gird the gods.

Sic. Be-mock the modest moon.

Bru. The present wars devour him: he is grown
Too proud to be so valiant.

Sic. Such a nature,
Tickled with good success, disdains the shadow
Which he treads on at noon: But I do wonder,
His insolence can brook to be commanded
Under Cominius.

Bru. Fame, at the which he aims,—
In whom already he is well grac'd,—cannot
Better be held, nor more attain'd, than by
A place below the first: for what miscarries
Shall be the general's fault, though he perform
To the utmost of a man; and giddy censure
Will then cry out of Marcius, *O, if he
Had borne the business!*

Sic. Besides, if things go well,
Opinion, that so sticks on Marcius, shall
Of his demerits rob Cominius.

Bru. Come:
Half all Cominius' honours are to Marcius,
Though Marcius earn'd them not; and all his faults
To Marcius shall be honours, though, indeed,
In aught he merit not.

Sic. Let's hence, and hear,
How the despatch is made; and in what fashion,
More than in singularity, he goes
Upon his present action.

Bru. Let's along. [*Exeunt.*

SCENE II. Corioli. *The Senate-House.*

Enter TULLUS AUFIDIUS, *and certain* Senators.

1 *Sen.* So your opinion is, Aufidius,
That they of Rome are enter'd in our counsels,
And know how we proceed.

Auf. Is it not yours?
What ever hath been thought on in this state,
That could be brought to bodily act ere Rome
Had circumvention! 'Tis not four days gone,
Since I heard thence; these are the words: I think,
I have the letter here; yes, here it is: [*Reads.*
*They have prest a power, but it is not known
Whether for east, or west: The dearth is great;
The people mutinous: and it is rumour'd,*
Cominius, Marcius, *your old enemy,
(Who is of Rome worse hated than of you),
And* Titus Lartius, *a most valiant Roman,
These three lead on this preparation
Whither 'tis bent: most likely, 'tis for you:
Consider of it.*

1 *Sen.* Our army's in the field:
We never yet made doubt but Rome was ready
To answer us.

Auf. Nor did you think it folly,
To keep your great pretences veil'd, till when
They needs must show themselves; which in the hatching,
It seem'd, appear'd to Rome. By the discovery,
We shall be shorten'd in our aim; which was,
To take in many towns, ere, almost, Rome
Should know we were afoot.

2 *Sen.* Noble Aufidius,

Take your commission; hie you to your bands:
Let us alone to guard Corioli:
If they set down before us, for the remove
Bring up your army; but I think you'll find
They have not prepar'd for us.

Auf. O, doubt not that;
I speak from certainties. Nay, more,
Some parcels of their powers are forth already,
And only hitherward. I leave your honours.
If we and Caius Marcius chance to meet,
'Tis sworn between us, we shall never strike
Till one can do no more.

All. The gods assist you!

Auf. And keep your honours safe!

1 Sen. Farewell.

2 Sen. Farewell.

All. Farewell. [*Exeunt.*

SCENE III.

Rome. *An Apartment in* Marcius' *House.*

Enter VOLUMNIA, *and* VIRGILIA: *They sit down on two low stools, and sew.*

Vol. I pray you, daughter, sing; or express yourself in a more comfortable sort: If my son were my husband, I should freelier rejoice in that absence wherein he won honour, than in the embracements of his bed, where he would show most love. When yet he was but tender-bodied, and the only son of my womb; when youth with comeliness plucked all gaze his way; when, for a day of kings' entreaties, a mother should not sell him an hour from her beholding; I,—considering how honour would become such a person; that it was no better than picture-like to hang by the wall, if renown made it not stir, —was pleased to let him seek danger where he was like to find fame. To a cruel war I sent him; from whence he returned, his brows bound with oak. I tell thee, daughter,—I sprang not more in joy at first hearing he was a man-child, than now in first seeing he had proved himself a man.

Vir. But had he died in the business, madam? how then?

Vol. Then his good report should have been my son; I therein would have found issue. Hear me profess sincerely: Had I a dozen sons, —each in my love alike, and none less dear than thine and my good Marcius,—I had rather had eleven die nobly for their country, than one voluptuously surfeit out of action.

Enter a Gentlewoman.

Gent. Madam, the lady Valeria is come to visit you.

Vir. 'Beseech you, give me leave to retire myself.

Vol. Indeed, you shall not.
Methinks, I hear hither your husband's drum;
See him pluck Aufidius down by the hair;
As children from a bear, the Volces shunning him:
Methinks, I see him stamp thus, and call thus,—
Come on, you cowards, you were got in fear,
Though you were born in Rome: His bloody brow
With his mail'd hand then wiping, forth he goes;
Like to a harvest-man, that's task'd to mow
Or all, or lose his hire.

Vir. His bloody brow! O, Jupiter, no blood!

Vol. Away, you fool! it more becomes a man,
Than gilt his trophy: The breasts of Hecuba,
When she did suckle Hector, look'd not lovelier
Than Hector's forehead, when it spit forth blood
At Grecian swords' contending.—Tell Valeria,
We are fit to bid her welcome. [*Exit* Gent.

Vir. Heavens bless my lord from fell Aufidius!

Vol. He'll beat Aufidius' head below his knee,
And tread upon his neck.

Re-enter Gentlewoman, *with* VALERIA *and her* Usher.

Val. My ladies both, good day to you.

Vol. Sweet madam,——

Vir. I am glad to see your ladyship.

Val. How do you both? you are manifest housekeepers. What, are you sewing here? A fine spot, in good faith.—How does your little son?

Vir. I thank your ladyship; well, good madam.

Vol. He had rather see the swords, and hear a drum, than look upon his schoolmaster.

Val. O' my word, the father's son: I'll swear, 'tis a very pretty boy. O' my troth, I looked upon him o' Wednesday half an hour together: he has such a confirmed countenance. I saw him run after a gilded butterfly; and when he caught it, he let it go again; and after it again; and over and over he comes, and up again; catched it again: or whether his fall enraged him, or how 'twas, he did so set his teeth, and tear it; O, I warrant, how he mammocked it!

Vol. One of his father's moods.

Val. Indeed la, 'tis a noble child.

Vir. A crack, madam.

Val. Come, lay aside your stitchery; I must have you play the idle huswife with me this afternoon.

Vir. No, good madam; I will not out of doors.

Val. Not out of doors!

Vol. She shall, she shall.

Vir. Indeed, no, by your patience: I will not over the threshold, till my lord return from the wars.

Val. Fye, you confine yourself most unreasonably; Come, you must go visit the good lady that lies in.

Vir. I will wish her speedy strength, and visit her with my prayers; but I cannot go thither.

Vol. Why, I pray you?

Vir. 'Tis not to save labour, nor that I want love.

Val. You would be another Penelope: yet they say, all the yarn she spun, in Ulysses' absence, did but fill Ithaca full of moths. Come; I would, your cambrick were sensible as your finger, that you might leave pricking it for pity. Come, you shall go with us.

Vir. No, good madam, pardon me; indeed, I will not forth.

Val. In truth, la, go with me; and I'll tell you excellent news of your husband.

Vir. O, good madam, there can be none yet.

Val. Verily, I do not jest with you; there came news from him last night.

Vir. Indeed, madam?

Val. In earnest, it's true; I heard a senator speak it. Thus it is:—The Volces have an army forth; against whom Cominius the general is gone, with one part of our Roman power: your lord, and Titus Lartius, are set down before their city Corioli; they nothing doubt prevailing, and to make it brief wars. This is true, on mine honour; and so, I pray, go with us.

Vir. Give me excuse, good madam; I will obey you in every thing hereafter.

Vol. Let her alone, lady; as she is now, she will but disease our better mirth.

Val. In troth, I think she would:—Fare you well then.—Come, good sweet lady.—Pr'ythee, Virgilia, turn thy solemness out o'door, and go along with us.

Vir. No: at a word, madam; indeed, I must not. I wish you much mirth.

Val. Well, then farewell. [*Exeunt.*

SCENE IV. *Before* Corioli.

Enter, with Drums and Colours, MARCIUS, TITUS LARTIUS, Officers, *and* Soldiers. *To them a* Messenger.

Mar. Yonder comes news:—A wager they have met.

Lart. My horse to yours, no.

Mar. 'Tis done.

Lart. Agreed,

Mar. Say, has our general met the enemy?

Mess. They lie in view; but have not spoke as yet.
Lart. So, the good horse is mine.
Mar. I'll buy him of you.
Lart. No, I'll nor sell, nor give him: lend you him, I will,
For half a hundred years.—Summon the town.
Mar. How far off lie these armies?
Mess. Within this mile and half.
Mar. Then shall we hear their larum, and they ours.
Now, Mars, I pr'ythee make us quick in work;
That we with smoking swords may march from hence,
To help our fielded friends!—Come, blow thy blast.

They sound a parley. Enter, on the walls, some Senators, *and Others.*

Tullus Aufidius, is he within your walls?
1 Sen. No, nor a man that fears you less than he,
That's lesser than a little. Hark, our drums
[*Alarums afar off.*
Are bringing forth our youth: We'll break our walls,
Rather than they shall pound us up: our gates,
Which yet seem shut, we have but pinn'd with rushes;
They'll open of themselves. Hark you, far off;
[*Other Alarums.*
There is Aufidius; list, what work he makes
Amongst your cloven army.
Mar. O, they are at it!
Lart. Their noise be our instruction.—Ladders, ho!

The Volces *enter and pass over the Stage.*

Mar. They fear us not, but issue forth their city.
Now put your shields before your hearts, and fight
With hearts more proof than shields.—Advance, brave Titus:
They do disdain us much beyond our thoughts,
Which makes me sweat with wrath.—Come on, my fellows;
He that retires, I'll take him for a Volce,
And he shall feel mine edge.

Alarum, and exeunt Romans *and* Volces, *fighting. The* Romans *are beaten back to their trenches. Re-enter* MARCIUS.

Mar. All the contagion of the south light on you,
You shames of Rome! you herd of,——Boils and plagues
Plaster you o'er; that you may be abhorr'd
Further than seen, and one infect another
Against the wind a mile! You souls of geese,
That bear the shapes of men, how have you run
From slaves that apes would beat? Pluto and hell!
All hurt behind; backs red, and faces pale
With flight and argued fear! Mend, and charge home,
Or, by the fires of heaven, I'll leave the foe,
And make my wars on you: look to't: Come on;
If you'll stand fast, we'll beat them to their wives,
As they us to our trenches followed.

Another Alarum. The Volces *and* Romans *re-enter, and the fight is renewed. The* Volces *retire into* Corioli, *and* MARCIUS *follows them to the gates.*

So, now the gates are ope:—Now prove good seconds:
'Tis for the followers fortune widens them,
Not for the fliers: mark me, and do the like.
[*He enters the gates, and is shut in.*
1 Sol. Fool-hardiness; not I.
2 Sol. Nor I.
3 Sol. See, they
Have shut him in. [*Alarum continues.*
All. To the pot, I warrant him.

Enter TITUS LARTIUS.

Lart. What is become of Marcius?
All. Slain, sir, doubtless.
1 Sol. Following the fliers at the very heels,
With them he enters: who, upon the sudden,
Clapp'd-to their gates; he is himself alone,
To answer all the city.
Lart. O noble fellow!
Who, sensible, outdares his senseless sword,
And, when it bows, stands up! Thou art left, Marcius:
A carbuncle entire, as big as thou art,
Were not so rich a jewel. Thou wast a soldier
Even to Cato's wish, not fierce and terrible
Only in strokes; but with thy grim looks, and
The thunder-like percussion of thy sounds,
Thou mad'st thine enemies shake, as if the world
Were feverous, and did tremble.

Re-enter MARCIUS *bleeding, assaulted by the enemy.*

1 Sol. Look sir,
Lart. 'Tis Marcius:
Let's fetch him off, or make remain alike.
[*They fight, and all enter the city.*

SCENE V. *Within the Town. A Street.*

Enter certain Romans, *with spoils.*

1 Rom. This will I carry to Rome.
2 Rom. And I this.
3 Rom. A murrain on't! I took this for silver.
[*Alarum continues still afar off.*

Enter MARCIUS, *and* TITUS LARTIUS, *with a Trumpet.*

Mar. See here these movers, that do prize their hours
At a crack'd drachm! Cushions, leaden spoons,
Irons of a doit, doublets that hangmen would
Bury with those that wore them, these base slaves,
Ere yet the fight be done, pack up:—Down with them.—
And hark, what noise the general makes!—To him:—
There is the man of my soul's hate, Aufidius,
Piercing our Romans: Then, valiant Titus, take
Convenient numbers to make good the city;
Whilst I, with those that have the spirit, will haste
To help Cominius.
Lart. Worthy sir, thou bleed'
Thy exercise hath been too violent for
A second course of fight.
Mar. Sir, praise me not
My work hath yet not warm'd me: Fare you well.
The blood I drop is rather physical
Than dangerous to me: To Aufidius thus
I will appear, and fight.
Lart. Now the fair goddess, Fortune,
Fall deep in love with thee; and her great charms
Misguide thy opposers' swords? Bold gentleman,
Prosperity be thy page!
Mar. Thy friend no less
Than those she placeth highest! So, farewell.
Lart. Thou worthiest Marcius!—
[*Exit* MARCIUS.
Go, sound thy trumpet in the market-place;
Call thither all the officers of the town,
Where they shall know our mind. Away.
[*Exeunt.*

SCENE VI. *Near the Camp of* Cominius.

Enter COMINIUS *and* Forces, *retreating.*

Com. Breathe you, my friends; well fought: we are come off
Like Romans, neither foolish in our stands,
Nor cowardly in retire: believe me, sirs,
We shall be charg'd again. Whiles we have struck,
By interims, and conveying gusts, we have heard
The charges of our friends:—The Roman gods,

Lead their successes as we wish our own;
That both our powers, with smiling fronts encountering,

Enter a Messenger.

May give you thankful sacrifice!—Thy news?
Mess. The citizens of Corioli have issued,
And given to Lartius and to Marcius battle:
I saw our party to their trenches driven,
And then I came away.
Com. Though thou speak'st truth,
Methinks thou speak'st not well. How long is't since?
Mess. Above an hour, my lord.
Com. 'Tis not a mile; briefly we heard their drums:
How could'st thou in a mile confound an hour,
And bring thy news so late?
Mess. Spies of the Volces
Held me in chase, that I was forc'd to wheel
Three or four miles about; else had I, sir,
Half an hour since brought my report.

Enter MARCIUS.

Com. Who's yonder,
That does appear as he were flay'd? O gods!
He has the stamp of Marcius; and I have
Before-time seen him thus.
Mar. Come I too late?
Com. The shepherd knows not thunder from a tabor,
More than I know the sound of Marcius' tongue,
From every meaner man's.
Mar. Come I too late?
Com. Ay, if you come not in the blood of others,
But mantled in your own.
Mar. O! let me clip you
In arms as sound, as when I woo'd; in heart
As merry, as when our nuptial day was done,
And tapers burn'd to bedward.
Com. Flower of warriors,
How is't with Titus Lartius?
Mar. As with a man busied about decrees:
Condemning some to death, and some to exile;
Ransoming him, or pitying, threat'ning the other;
Holding Corioli in the name of Rome,
Even like a fawning greyhound in the leash,
To let him slip at will.
Com. Where is that slave,
Which told me they had beat you to your trenches?
Where is he? Call him hither.
Mar. Let him alone,
He did inform the truth: But for our gentlemen,
The common file (A plague!—Tribunes for them!)
The mouse ne'er shunn'd the cat, as they did budge
From rascals worse than they.
Com. But how prevail'd you?
Mar. Will the time serve to tell? I do not think—
Where is the enemy? Are you lords o' the field?
If not, why cease you till you are so?
Com. Marcius,
We have at disadvantage fought, and did
Retire, to win our purpose.
Mar. How lies their battle? Know you on which side
They have plac'd their men of trust?
Com. As I guess, Marcius,
Their bands in the vaward are the Antiates,
Of their best trust: o'er them Aufidius,
Their very heart of hope.
Mar. I do beseech you,
By all the battles wherein we have fought,
By the blood we have shed together, by the vows
We have made to endure friends, that you directly
Set me against Aufidius, and his Antiates:
And that you not delay the present; but,
Filling the air with swords advanc'd, and darts,
We prove this very hour.
Com. Though I could wish
You were conducted to a gentle bath,
And balms applied to you, yet dare I never
Deny your asking; take your choice of those
That best can aid your action.
Mar. Those are they
That most are willing;—If any such be here
(As it were sin to doubt), that love this painting
Wherein you see me smear'd; if any fear
Lesser his person than an ill report;
If any think, brave death outweighs bad life,
And that his country's dearer than himself;
Let him, alone, or so many, so minded,
Wave thus, [*waving his hand*], to express his disposition,
And follow Marcius.
[*They all shout, and wave their swords; take him up in their arms, and cast up their caps.*
O me, alone! Make you a sword of me?
If these shows be not outward, which of you
But is four Volces? None of you but is
Able to bear against the great Aufidius
A shield as hard as his. A certain number,
Though thanks to all, must I select from all: the rest
Shall bear the business in some other fight,
As cause will be obey'd. Please you to march;
And four shall quickly draw out my command,
Which men are best inclin'd.
Com. March on, my fellows:
Make good this ostentation, and you shall
Divide in all with us. [*Exeunt.*

SCENE VII. *The Gates of* Corioli.

TITUS LARTIUS, *having set a guard upon* Corioli, *going with a drum and trumpet toward* Cominius *and* Caius Marcius, *enters with a* Lieutenant, *a Party of* Soldiers, *and a* Scout.

Lart. So, let the ports be guarded. keep your duties,
As I have set them down. If I do send, despatch
Those centuries to our aid; the rest will serve
For a short holding: If we lose the field,
We cannot keep the town.
Lieu. Fear not our care, sir.
Lart. Hence, and shut your gates upon us.—
Our guider, come; to the Roman camp conduct us. [*Exeunt.*

SCENE VIII.

A Field of Battle between the Roman *and the* Volcian *Camps.*

Alarum. Enter MARCIUS *and* AUFIDIUS.

Mar. I'll fight with none but thee; for I do hate thee
Worse than a promise-breaker.
Auf. We hate alike;
Not Africk owns a serpent, I abhor
More than thy fame and envy: Fix thy foot.
Mar. Let the first budger die the other's slave,
And the gods doom him after!
Auf. If I fly, Marcius,
Halloo me like a hare.
Mar. Within these three hours, Tullus,
Alone I fought in your Corioli walls,
And made what work I pleas'd; 'Tis not my blood,
Wherein thou seest me mask'd; for thy revenge
Wrench up thy power to the highest.
Auf. Wert thou the Hector,
That was the whip of your bragg'd progeny,
Thou should'st not scape me here.—
[*They fight, and certain* Volces *come to the aid of* AUFIDIUS.
Officious, and not valiant—you have sham'd me
In your condemned seconds.
[*Exeunt fighting, driven in by* MARCIUS.

SCENE IX. *The* Roman *Camp.*

Alarum. A Retreat is sounded. Flourish. Enter at one side, COMINIUS *and* Romans; *at the other side,* MARCIUS, *with his arm in a scarf, and other* Romans.

Com. If I should tell thee o'er this thy day's work,
Thou'lt not believe thy deeds: but I'll report it,
Where senators shall mingle tears with smiles;
Where great patricians shall attend, and shrug,
I' the end, admire; where ladies shall be frighted,
And, gladly quak'd, hear more; where the dull tribunes,
That, with the fusty plebeians, hate thine honours,
Shall say, against their hearts—*We thank the gods, Our Rome hath such a soldier!*—
Yet cam'st thou to a morsel of this feast,
Having fully dined before.

Enter TITUS LARTIUS, *with his* Power, *from the pursuit.*

Lart. O general,
Here is the steed, we the caparison:
Hadst thou beheld——

Mar. 'Pray now, no more: my mother,
Who has a charter to extol her blood,
When she does praise me, grieves me. I have done,
As you have done; that's what I can; induc'd
As you have been; that's for my country:
He, that has but effected his good will,
Hath overta'en mine act.

Com. You shall not be
The grave of your deserving; Rome must know
The value of her own: 'twere a concealment
Worse than a theft, no less than a traducement,
To hide your doings; and to silence that,
Which, to the spire and top of praises vouch'd,
Would seem but modest: Therefore, I beseech you
(In sign of what you are, not to reward
What you have done), before our army hear me.

Mar. I have some wounds upon me, and they smart
To hear themselves remember'd.

Com. Should they not,
Well might they fester 'gainst ingratitude,
And tent themselves with death. Of all the horses
(Whereof we have ta'en good, and good store), of all
The treasure, in this field achiev'd, and city,
We render you the tenth; to be ta'en forth,
Before the common distribution, at
Your only choice.

Mar. I thank you, general;
But cannot make my heart consent to take
A bribe to pay my sword: I do refuse it;
And stand upon my common part with those
That have beheld the doing.

[*A long flourish. They all cry,* Marcius! Marcius! *cast up their caps and lances:* COMINIUS *and* LARTIUS *stand bare.*

Mar. May these same instruments, which you profane,
Never sound more! When drums and trumpets shall
I' the field prove flatterers, let courts and cities be
Made all of false-fac'd soothing: When steel grows
Soft as the parasite's silk, let him be made
An overture for the wars! No more, I say;
For that I have not wash'd my nose that bled,
Or foil'd some debile wretch,—which, without note,
Here's many else have done,—you shout me forth
In acclamations hyperbolical;
As if I lov'd my little should be dieted
In praises sauc'd with lies.

Com. Too modest are you;
More cruel to your good report, than grateful
To us that give you truly: by your patience,
If 'gainst yourself you be incens'd, we'll put you
(Like one that means his proper harm) in manacles,
Then reason safely with you.—Therefore, be it known,
As to us, to all the world, that Caius Marcius
Wears this war's garland: in token of the which
My noble steed, known to the camp, I give him,
With all his trim belonging; and, from this time,
For what he did before Corioli, call him,
With all the applause and clamour of the host,
CAIUS MARCIUS CORIOLANUS.—
Bear the addition nobly ever!

[*Flourish. Trumpets sound, and Drums.*

All. Caius Marcius Coriolanus!

Cor. I will go wash;
And when my face is fair, you shall perceive
Whether I blush, or no: Howbeit, I thank you:—
I mean to stride your steed; and, at all times,
To undercrest your good addition,
To the fairness of my power.

Com. So, to our tent:
Where, ere we do repose us, we will write
To Rome of our success.—You, Titus Lartius,
Must to Corioli back: send us to Rome
The best with whom we may articulate
For their own good, and ours.

Lart. I shall, my lord.

Cor. The gods begin to mock me. I that now
Refus'd most princely gifts, am bound to beg
Of my lord general.

Com. Take it: 'tis yours.—What is 't?

Cor. I sometime lay, here in Corioli,
At a poor man's house; he us'd me kindly:
He cried to me; I saw him prisoner;
But then Aufidius was within my view,
And wrath o'erwhelm'd my pity: I request you
To give my poor host freedom.

Com. O, well begg'd!
Were he the butcher of my son, he should
Be free, as is the wind. Deliver him, Titus.

Lart. Martius, his name?

Cor. By Jupiter, forgot:—
I am weary; yea, my memory is tir'd.—
Have we no wine here?

Com. Go we to our tent:
The blood upon your visage dries: 'tis time
It should be look'd to: come. [*Exeunt.*

SCENE X. *The Camp of the* Volces.

A Flourish. Cornets. Enter TULLUS AUFIDIUS, *bloody, with two or three* Soldiers.

Auf. The town is ta'en.

1 *Sol.* 'Twill be deliver'd back on good condition.

Auf. Condition?—
I would, I were a Roman; for I cannot,
Being a Volce, be that I am.—Condition!—
What good condition can a treaty find
I' the part that is at mercy? Five times, Marcius,
I have fought with thee; so often hast thou beat me;
And would'st do so, I think, should we encounter
As often as we eat.—By the elements,
If e'er again I meet him beard to beard,
He is mine, or I am his: Mine emulation
Hath not that honour in 't, it had; for where
I thought to crush him in an equal force
(True sword to sword), I'll potch at him some way;
Or wrath, or craft, may get him.

1 *Sol.* He's the devil.

Auf. Bolder, though not so subtle: My valour's poison'd,
With only suffering stain by him; for him
Shall fly out of itself: nor sleep, nor sanctuary,
Being naked, sick: nor fane, nor Capitol,
The prayers of priests, nor times of sacrifice,
Embarquements all of fury, shall lift up
Their rotten privilege and custom 'gainst
My hate to Marcius: where I find him, were it

At home, upon my brother's guard, even there
Against the hospitable canon, would I
Wash my fierce hand in his heart. Go you to the city;
Learn, how 'tis held; and what they are that must
Be hostages for Rome.

1 *Sol.* Will not you go?

Auf. I am attended at the cypress grove:
I pray you
('Tis south the city mills), bring me word thither
How the world goes; that to the pace of it
I may spur on my journey.

1 *Sol.* I shall, sir. [*Exeunt.*

ACT II.

SCENE I. Rome. *A Publick Place.*

Enter MENENIUS, SICINIUS, *and* BRUTUS.

Men. The augurer tells me, we shall have news to-night.

Bru. Good or bad?

Men. Not according to the prayer of the people, for they love not Marcius.

Sic. Nature teaches beasts to know their friends.

Men. 'Pray you, who does the wolf love?

Sic. The lamb.

Men. Ay, to devour him; as the hungry plebeians would the noble Marcius.

Bru. He's a lamb indeed, that baes like a bear.

Men. He's a bear indeed, that lives like a lamb. You two are old men; tell me one thing that I shall ask you.

Both Trib. Well, sir.

Men. In what enormity is Marcius poor, that you two have not in abundance?

Bru. He's poor in no one fault, but stored with all.

Sic. Especially, in pride.

Bru. And topping all others in boasting.

Men. This is strange now: Do you two know how you are censured here in the city, I mean of us o' the right hand file? Do you?

Both Trib. Why, how are we censured?

Men. Because you talk of pride now,—Will you not be angry?

Both Trib. Well, well, sir, well.

Men. Why, 'tis no great matter; for a very little thief of occasion will rob you of a great deal of patience: give your disposition the reins, and be angry at your pleasures; at the least, if you take it as a pleasure to you, in being so. You blame Marcius for being proud!

Bru. We do it not alone, sir.

Men. I know you can do very little alone: for your helps are many; or else your actions would grow wondrous single: your abilities are too infantlike, for doing much alone. You talk of pride: O, that you could turn your eyes towards the napes of your necks, and make but an interior survey of your good selves! O, that you could!

Bru. What then, sir?

Men. Why, then you should discover a brace of unmeriting, proud, violent, testy magistrates (alias fools), as any in Rome.

Sic. Menenius, you are known well enough too.

Men. I am known to be a humorous patrician, and one that loves a cup of hot wine with not a drop of allaying Tyber in 't; said to be something imperfect, in favouring the first complaint: hasty, and tinder-like, upon too trivial motion: one that converses more with the buttock of the night, than with the forehead of the morning. What I think, I utter; and spend my malice in my breath: Meeting two such weals-men as you are (I cannot call you Lycurguses), if the drink you give me, touch my palate adversely, I make a crooked face at it. I cannot say, your worships have delivered the matter well, when I find the ass in compound with the major part of your syllables: and though I must be content to bear with those that say you are reverend grave men; yet they lie deadly, that tell, you have good faces. If you see this in the map of my microcosm, follows it, that I am known well enough too? What harm can your bisson conspectuities glean out of this character, if I be known well enough too?

Bru. Come, sir, come, we know you well enough.

Men. You know neither me, yourselves, nor any thing. You are ambitious for poor knaves' caps and legs; you wear out a good wholesome forenoon, in hearing a cause between an orange-wife and a fosset-seller; and then rejourn the controversy of three-pence to a second day of audience.—When you are hearing a matter between party and party, if you chance to be pinched with the colick, you make faces like mummers; set up the bloody flag against all patience; and, in roaring for a chamber-pot, dismiss the controversy bleeding, the more entangled by your hearing: all the peace you make in their cause, is, calling both the parties knaves: You are a pair of strange ones.

Bru. Come, come, you are well understood to be a perfecter giber for the table, than a necessary bencher in the Capitol.

Men. Our very priests must become mockers, if they shall encounter such ridiculous subjects as you are. When you speak best unto the purpose, it is not worth the wagging of your beards; and your beards deserve not so honourable a grave, as to stuff a botcher's cushion, or to be entombed in an ass's pack-saddle. Yet you must be saying, Marcius is proud; who, in a cheap estimation, is worth all your predecessors, since Deucalion; though peradventure, some of the best of them were hereditary hangmen. Good e'en to your worships; more of your conversation would infect my brain, being the herdsmen of the beastly plebeians: I will be bold to take my leave of you.

[BRU. *and* SIC. *retire to the back of the Scene.*

Enter VOLUMNIA, VIRGILIA, *and* VALERIA, *&c.*

How now, my as fair as noble ladies (and the moon, were she earthly, no nobler), whither do you follow your eyes so fast?

Vol. Honourable Menenius, my boy Marcius approaches; for the love of Juno, let's go.

Men. Ha! Marcius coming home!

Vol. Ay, worthy Menenius; and with most prosperous approbation.

Men. Take my cap, Jupiter, and I thank thee:—Hoo! Marcius coming home!

Two Ladies. Nay, 'tis true.

Vol. Look, here's a letter from him; the state hath another, his wife another: and, I think, there's one at home for you.

Men. I will make my very house reel to-night:—A letter for me?

Vir. Yes, certain, there's a letter for you; I saw it.

Men. A letter for me? It gives me an estate of seven years' health; in which time I will make a lip at the physician: the most sovereign prescription in Galen is but empiricutick, and, to this preservative, of no better report than a horse-drench. Is he not wounded? he was wont to come home wounded.

Vir. O, no, no, no.

Vol. O, he is wounded, I thank the gods for't.

Men. So do I too, if it be not too much:—Brings 'a victory in his pocket?—The wounds become him.

Vol. On's brows, Menenius: he comes the third time home with the oaken garland.

Men. Has he disciplined Aufidius soundly?

Vol. Titus Lartius writes,—they fought together, but Aufidius got off.

Men. And 'twas time for him too, I'll warrant him that: an he had staid by him, I would not have been so fidiused for all the chests in Corioli, and the gold that's in them. Is the senate possessed of this?

Vol. Good ladies, let's go:—Yes, yes, yes: the senate has letters from the general, wherein he gives my son the whole name of the war: he hath in this action outdone his former deeds doubly.

Val. In troth, there's wondrous things spoke of him.

Men. Wondrous? ay, I warrant you, and not without his true purchasing.

Vir. The gods grant them true!

Vol. True? pow, wow.

Men. True? I'll be sworn they are true:—Where is he wounded? God save your good worships! [*To the Tribunes, who come forward.*] Marcius is coming home: he has more cause to be proud.—Where is he wounded?

Vol. I' the shoulder, and i' the left arm: There will be large cicatrices to show the people, when he shall stand for his place. He received in the repulse of Tarquin, seven hurts i' the body.

Men. One in the neck, and two in the thigh,—there's nine that I know.

Vol. He had, before this last expedition, twenty-five wounds upon him.

Men. Now it's twenty-seven: every gash was an enemy's grave: [*A Shout and Flourish.*] Hark! the trumpets.

Vol. These are the ushers of Marcius: before him
He carries noise, and behind him he leaves tears;
Death, that dark spirit, in's nervy arm doth lie;
Which being advanc'd, declines; and then men die.

A Sennet. Trumpets sound. Enter COMINIUS *and* TITUS LARTIUS; *between them,* CORIOLANUS, *crowned with an oaken garland; with* Captains, Soldiers, *and a* Herald.

Her. Know, Rome, that all alone Marcius did fight
Within Corioli' gates; where he hath won,
With fame, a name to Caius Marcius; these
In honour follows, Coriolanus:
Welcome to Rome, renowned Coriolanus! [*Flourish.*

All. Welcome to Rome, renowned Coriolanus!

Cor. No more of this, it does offend my heart;
Pray now, no more.

Com. Look, sir, your mother,——

Cor. O!
You have, I know, petition'd all the gods
For my prosperity. [*Kneels.*

Vol. Nay, my good soldier, up;
My gentle Marcius, worthy Caius, and
By deed-achieving honour newly nam'd,
What is it? Coriolanus, must I call thee?
But O, thy wife,——

Cor. My gracious silence, hail!
Would'st thou have laugh'd, had I come coffin'd home,
That weep'st to see me triumph? Ah, my dear,
Such eyes the widows in Corioli wear,
And mothers that lack sons.

Men. Now the gods crown thee!

Cor. And live you yet?—O my sweet lady, pardon. [*To* VALERIA.

Val. I know not where to turn:—O welcome home;
And welcome, general;—And you are welcome all.

Men. A hundred thousand welcomes: I could weep,
And I could laugh: I am light, and heavy: Welcome:
A curse begin at very root of his heart,
That is not glad to see thee!—You are three,
That Rome should dote on: yet, by the faith of men,
We have some old crab-trees here at home, that will not
Be grafted to your relish. Yet welcome, warriors:
We call a nettle, but a nettle; and
The faults of fools, but folly.

Com. Ever right.

Cor. Menenius, ever, ever.

Her. Give way there, and go on.

Cor. Your hand, and yours:
[*To his Wife and Mother.*
Ere in our own house I do shade my head,
The good patricians must be visited;
From whom I have receiv'd not only greetings,
But with them change of honours.

Vol. I have lived
To see inherited my very wishes,
And the buildings of my fancy: only there
Is one thing wanting, which I doubt not, but
Our Rome will cast upon thee.

Cor. Know, good mother,
I had rather be their servant in my way,
Than sway with them in theirs.

Com. On to the Capitol.
[*Flourish. Cornets. Exeunt in state as before. The* Tribunes *remain.*

Bru. All tongues speak of him, and the bleared sights
Are spectacled to see him: Your prattling nurse
Into a rapture lets her baby cry,
While she chats him: the kitchen malkin pins
Her richest lockram 'bout her reechy neck,
Clambering the walls to eye him: stalls, bulks, windows,
Are smother'd up, leads fill'd, and ridges hors'd
With variable complexions; all agreeing
In earnestness to see him: seld-shown flamens
Do press among the popular throngs, and puff
To win a vulgar station; our veil'd dames
Commit the war of white and damask, in
Their nicely gawded cheeks, to the wanton spoil
Of Phœbus' burning kisses: such a pother,
As if that whatsoever god, who leads him,
Were slily crept into his human powers,
And gave him graceful posture.

Sic. On the sudden,
I warrant him consul.

Bru. Then our office may,
During his power, go sleep.

Sic. He cannot temperately transport his honours
From where he should begin, and end; but will
Lose those that he hath won.

Bru. In that there's comfort.

Sic. Doubt not, the commoners, for whom we stand,
But they, upon their ancient malice, will
Forget, with the least cause, these his new honours;
Which that he'll give them, make as little question
As he is proud to do 't.

Bru. I heard him swear,
Were he to stand for consul, never would he
Appear i' the market-place, nor on him put
The napless vesture of humility;
Nor, showing (as the manner is) his wounds
To the people, beg their stinking breaths.

Sic. 'Tis right.

Bru. It was his word: O, he would miss it, rather
Than carry it, but by the suit o' the gentry to him,
And the desire of the nobles.

Sic. I wish no better,
Than have him hold that purpose, and to put it
In execution.

Bru. 'Tis most like, he will.

Sic. It shall be to him then, as our good wills;
A sure destruction.

Bru. So it must fall out
To him, or our authorities. For an end,
We must suggest the people, in what hatred

He still hath held them: that, to his power, he would
Have made them mules, silenc'd their pleaders, and
Dispropertied their freedoms; holding them,
In human action and capacity,
Of no more soul, nor fitness for the world,
Than camels in their war; who have their provand
Only for bearing burdens, and sore blows
For sinking under them.

Sic. This, as you say, suggested
At some time when his soaring insolence
Shall teach the people (which time shall not want,
If he be put upon 't; and that's as easy,
As to set dogs on sheep), will be his fire
To kindle their dry stubble; and their blaze
Shall darken him for ever.

Enter a Messenger.

Bru. What's the matter?

Mess. You are sent for to the Capitol. 'Tis thought,
That Marcius shall be consul: I have seen
The dumb men throng to see him, and the blind
To hear him speak: The matrons flung their gloves,
Ladies and maids their scarfs and handkerchiefs,
Upon him as he pass'd; the nobles bended,
As to Jove's statue; and the commons made
A shower, and thunder, with their caps, and shouts:
I never saw the like.

Bru. Let's to the Capitol;
And carry with us ears and eyes for the time,
But hearts for the event.

Sic. Have with you. [*Exeunt.*

SCENE II. *The same. The Capitol.*

Enter two Officers, *to lay Cushions.*

1 *Off.* Come, come, they are almost here: How many stand for consulships?

2 *Off.* Three, they say: but 'tis thought of every one, Coriolanus will carry it.

1 *Off.* That's a brave fellow: but he's vengeance proud, and loves not the common people.

2 *Off.* 'Faith, there have been many great men that have flatter'd the people, who ne'er loved them; and there be many that they have loved, they know not wherefore: so that if they love they know not why, they hate upon no better a ground: Therefore, for Coriolanus neither to care whether they love or hate him, manifests the true knowledge he has in their disposition; and, out of his noble carelessness, lets them plainly see't.

1 *Off.* If he did not care whether he had their love, or no, he waved indifferently 'twixt doing them neither good, nor harm; but he seeks their hate with greater devotion than they can render it him: and leaves nothing undone, that may fully discover him their opposite. Now to seem to affect the malice and displeasure of the people, is as bad as that which he dislikes, to flatter them for their love.

2 *Off.* He hath deserved worthily of his country: And his ascent is not by such easy degrees as those, who having been supple and courteous to the people, bonneted, without any further deed to have them at all into their estimation and report: but he hath so planted his honours in their eyes, and his actions in their hearts, that for their tongues to be silent, and not confess so much, were a kind of ingrateful injury; to report otherwise were a malice, that, giving itself the lie, would pluck reproof and rebuke from every ear that heard it.

1 *Off.* No more of him; he is a worthy man: Make way, they are coming.

A Sennet. Enter, with Lictors *before them,* COMINIUS *the* Consul, MENENIUS, CORIOLANUS, *many other* Senators, SICINIUS, *and* BRUTUS. *The* Senators *take their places; the* Tribunes *take theirs also by themselves.*

Men. Having determin'd of the Volces, and
To send for Titus Lartius, it remains,
As the main point of this our after-meeting,
To gratify his noble service, that
Hath thus stood for his country: Therefore, please you,
Most reverend and grave elders, to desire
The present consul, and last general
In our well found successes, to report
A little of that worthy work perform'd
By Caius Marcius Coriolanus; whom
We meet here, both to thank, and to remember
With honours like himself.

1 *Sen.* Speak, good Cominius:
Leave nothing out for length, and make us think,
Rather our state's defective for requital,
Then we to stretch it out. Masters o' the people,
We do request your kindest ears: and, after,
Your loving motion toward the common body,
To yield what passes here.

Sic. We are convented
Upon a pleasing treaty; and have hearts
Inclinable to honour and advance
The theme of our assembly.

Bru. Which the rather
We shall be bless'd to do, if he remember
A kinder value of the people, than
He hath hereto priz'd them at.

Men. That's off, that's off;
I would you rather had been silent: Please you
To hear Cominius speak?

Bru. Most willingly:
But yet my caution was more pertinent,
Than the rebuke you give it.

Men. He loves your people:
But tie him not to be their bedfellow.
Worthy Cominius, speak.—Nay, keep your place. [COR. *rises, and offers to go away.*

1 *Sen.* Sit, Coriolanus: never shame to hear
What you have nobly done.

Cor. Your honours' pardon;
I had rather have my wounds to heal again,
Than hear say how I got them.

Bru. Sir, I hope,
My words disbench'd you not.

Cor. No, sir: yet oft,
When blows have made me stay, I fled from words.
You sooth'd not, therefore hurt not: But, your people,
I love them as they weigh.

Men. Pray now, sit down.

Cor. I had rather have one scratch my head i' the sun,
When the alarum were struck, than idly sit
To hear my nothings monster'd. [*Exit* COR.

Men. Masters o' the people,
Your multiplying spawn how can he flatter
(That's thousand to one good one), when you now see,
He had rather venture all his limbs for honour,
Than one of his ears to hear it?—Proceed, Cominius,

Com. I shall lack voice: the deeds of Coriolanus
Should not be utter'd feebly.—It is held,
That valour is the chiefest virtue, and
Most dignifies the haver: if it be,
The man I speak of cannot in the world
Be singly counterpois'd. At sixteen years,
When Tarquin made a head for Rome, he fought
Beyond the mark of others: our then dictator,
Whom with all praise I point at, saw him fight,
When with his Amazonian chin he drove
The bristled lips before him: he bestrid
An o'erpress'd Roman, and i' the consul's view
Slew three opposers: Tarquin's self he met,

And struck him on his knee: in that day's feats,
When he might act the woman in the scene,
He prov'd best man i' the field, and for his meed
Was brow-bound with the oak. His pupil age
Man-entered thus, he waxed like a sea;
And, in the brunt of seventeen battles since,
He lurch'd all swords o' the garland. For this last,
Before and in Corioli, let me say,
I cannot speak him home: He stopp'd the fliers;
And, by his rare example, made the coward
Turn terror into sport: as waves before
A vessel under sail, so men obey'd,
And fell below his stem: his sword (death's stamp)
Where it did mark, it took; from face to foot
He was a thing of blood, whose every motion
Was tim'd with dying cries: alone he enter'd
The mortal gate o' the city, which he painted
With shunless destiny, aidless came off,
And with a sudden reenforcement struck
Corioli, like a planet: now all's his:
When by and by the din of war 'gan pierce
His ready sense: then straight his doubled spirit
Requicken'd what in flesh was fatigate,
And to the battle came he; where he did
Run reeking o'er the lives of men, as if
'Twere a perpetual spoil: and, till we call'd
Both field and city ours, he never stood
To ease his breast with panting.

Men. Worthy man!

1 *Sen.* He cannot but with measure fit the honours
Which we devise him.

Com. Our spoils he kick'd at;
And look'd upon things precious, as they were
The common muck o' the world; he covets less
Than misery itself would give; rewards
His deeds with doing them; and is content
To spend the time, to end it.

Men. He's right noble;
Let him be call'd for.

1 *Sen.* Call Coriolanus.

Off. He doth appear.

Re-enter CORIOLANUS.

Men. The senate, Coriolanus, are well pleas'd
To make thee consul.

Cor. I do owe them still
My life, and services.

Men. It then remains,
That you do speak to the people.

Cor. I do beseech you,
Let me o'erleap that custom; for I cannot
Put on the gown, stand naked, and entreat them,
For my wounds' sake, to give their suffrage: please you,
That I may pass this doing.

Sic. Sir, the people
Must have their voices: neither will they bate
One jot of ceremony.

Men. Put them not to't:
Pray you go fit you to the custom: and
Take to you, as your predecessors have,
Your honour with your form.

Cor. It is a part
That I shall blush in acting, and might well
Be taken from the people.

Bru. Mark you that?

Cor. To brag unto them,—Thus I did, and thus;—
Show them the unaching scars which I should hide,
As if I had receiv'd them for the hire
Of their breath only:—

Men. Do not stand upon 't.—
We recommend to you, tribunes of the people,
Our purpose to them; and to our noble consul
Wish we all joy and honour.

Sen. To Coriolanus come all joy and honour!
[*Flourish. Then exeunt* Senators.

Bru. You see how he intends to use the people.

Sic. May they perceive his intent! He will require them,
As if he did contemn what he requested
Should be in them to give.

Bru. Come, we'll inform them
Of our proceedings here: on the market-place,
I know, they do attend us. [*Exeunt.*

SCENE III. *The same. The* Forum.

Enter several Citizens.

1 *Cit.* Once, if he do require our voices, we ought not to deny him.

2 *Cit.* We may, sir, if we will.

3 *Cit.* We have power in ourselves to do it, but it is a power that we have no power to do; for if he show us his wounds, and tell us his deeds, we are to put our tongues into those wounds, and speak for them; so, if he tell us his noble deeds, we must also tell him our noble acceptance of them. Ingratitude is monstrous: and for the multitude to be ingrateful, were to make a monster of the multitude; of the which, we being members, should bring ourselves to be monstrous members.

1 *Cit.* And to make us no better thought of, a little help will serve: for once we stood up about the corn, he himself stuck not to call us the many-headed multitude.

3 *Cit.* We have been called so of many; not that our heads are some brown, some black, some auburn, some bald, but that our wits are so diversely coloured: and truly I think, if all our wits were to issue out of one scull, they would fly east, west, north, south; and their consent of one direct way should be at once to all points o' the compass.

2 *Cit.* Think you so? Which way, do you judge, my wit would fly?

3 *Cit.* Nay, your wit will not so soon out as another man's will, 'tis strongly wedged up in a blockhead: but if it were at liberty, 'twould, sure, southward.

2 *Cit.* Why that way?

3 *Cit.* To lose itself in a fog; where being three parts melted away with rotten dews, the fourth would return for conscience sake, to help to get thee a wife.

2 *Cit.* You are never without your tricks:— You may, you may.

3 *Cit.* Are you all resolved to give your voices? But that's no matter, the greater part carries it. I say, if he would incline to the people, there was never a worthier man.

Enter CORIOLANUS *and* MENENIUS.

Here he comes, and in the gown of humility; mark his behaviour. We are not to stay altogether, but to come by him where he stands, by ones, by twos, and by threes. He's to make his requests by particulars: wherein every one of us has a single honour, in giving him our own voices with our own tongues: therefore follow me, and I'll direct you how you shall go by him.

All. Content, content. [*Exeunt.*

Men. O sir, you are not right: have you not known
The worthiest men have done it?

Cor. What must I say?—
I pray, sir,—Plague upon't! I cannot bring
My tongue to such a pace:——Look, sir!——my wounds!
I got them in my country's service, when
Some certain of your brethren roar'd, and ran
From the noise of our own drums.

Men. O me, the gods!
You must not speak of that; you must desire them
To think upon you.

Cor. Think upon me? Hang 'em!
I would they would forget me, like the virtues
Which our divines lose by them.

Men. You'll mar all;
I'll leave you: 'Pray you, speak to them, I pray you,
In wholesome manner. [*Exit.*

Enter two Citizens.

Cor. Bid them wash their faces,
And keep their teeth clean.—So, here comes a brace.
You know the cause, sir, of my standing here.

1 Cit. We do, sir; tell us what hath brought you to't.

Cor. Mine own desert.

2 Cit. Your own desert?

Cor. Ay, not
Mine own desire.

1 Cit. How! not your own desire?

Cor. No, sir:
'Twas never my desire yet,
To trouble the poor with begging.

1 Cit. You must think, if we give you any thing,
We hope to gain by you.

Cor. Well, then, I pray, your price o'the consulship?

1 Cit. The price is, sir, to ask it kindly.

Cor. Kindly?
Sir, I pray, let me ha't: I have wounds to show you,
Which shall be yours in private.—Your good voice, sir;
What say you?

2 Cit. You shall have it, worthy sir.

Cor. A match, sir:—
There is in all two worthy voices begg'd:
I have your alms; adieu.

1 Cit. But this is something odd.

2 Cit. An 'twere to give again,—But 'tis no matter. [*Exeunt two* Citizens.

Enter two other Citizens.

Cor. 'Pray you now, if it may stand with the tune of your voices, that I may be consul, I have here the customary gown.

3 Cit. You have deserved nobly of your country, and you have not deserved nobly.

Cir. Your enigma?

3 Cit. You have been a scourge to her enemies, you have been a rod to her friends: you have not, indeed, loved the common people.

Cor. You should account me the more virtuous, that I have not been common in my love. I will, sir, flatter my sworn brother the people, to earn a dearer estimation of them; 'tis a condition they account gentle: and since the wisdom of their choice is rather to have my hat than my heart, I will practise the insinuating nod, and be off to them most counterfeitly: that is, sir, I will counterfeit the bewitchment of some popular man, and give it bountifully to the desirers. Therefore, beseech you, I may be consul.

4 Cit. We hope to find you our friend; and therefore give you our voices heartily.

3 Cit. You have received many wounds for your country.

Cor. I will not seal your knowledge with showing them. I will make much of your voices, and so trouble you no further.

Both Cit. The gods give you joy, sir, heartily! [*Exeunt.*

Cor. Most sweet voices!—
Better it is to die, better to starve,
Than crave the hire which first we do deserve.
Why in this wolvish gown should I stand here,
To beg of Hob and Dick, that do appear,
Their needless vouches? Custom calls me to't:—
What custom wills, in all things should we do't,
The dust on antique time would lie unswept,
And mountainous error be too highly heap'd
For truth to overpeer.—Rather than fool it so,
Let the high office and the honour go
To one that would do thus.—I am half through:
The one part suffer'd, the other will I do.

Enter three other Citizens.

Here come more voices,—
Your voices: for your voices I have fought;
Watch'd for your voices; for your voices, bear
Of wounds two dozen odd; battles thrice six
I have seen, and heard of; for your voices, have
Done many things, some less, some more: your voices;
Indeed, I would be consul.

5 Cit. He has done nobly, and cannot go without any honest man's voice.

6 Cit. Therefore let him be consul: The gods give him joy, and make him good friend to the people!

All. Amen, Amen.——
God save thee, noble consul! [*Exeunt* Citizens.

Cor. Worthy voices!

Re-enter MENENIUS, *with* BRUTUS, *and* SICINIUS.

Men. You have stood your limitation; and the tribunes
Endue you with the people's voice; Remains,
That, in the official marks invested, you
Anon do meet the senate.

Cor. Is this done?

Sic. The custom of request you have discharg'd:
The people do admit you; and are summon'd
To meet anon, upon your approbation.

Cor. Where? at the senate-house?

Sic. There, Coriolanus.

Cor. May I change these garments?

Sic. You may, sir.

Cor. That I'll straight do; and, knowing myself again,
Repair to the senate-house.

Men. I'll keep you company.—Will you along?

Bru. We stay here for the people.

Sic. Fare you well.
[*Exeunt* CORIOL. *and* MENEN.
He has it now; and by his looks, methinks,
'Tis warm at his heart.

Bru. With a proud heart he wore
His humble weeds: Will you dismiss the people?

Re-enter Citizens.

Sic. How now, my masters? have you chose this man?

1 Cit. He has our voices, sir.

Bru. We pray the gods, he may deserve your loves.

2 Cit. Amen, sir: To my poor unworthy notice,
He mock'd us, when he begg'd our voices.

3 Cit. Certainly,
He flouted us downright.

1 Cit. No, 'tis his kind of speech, he did not mock us.

2 Cit. Not one amongst us, save yourself, but says,
He us'd us scornfully: he should have show'd us
His marks of merit, wounds receiv'd for his country.

Sic. Why, so he did, I am sure.

Cit. No: no man saw 'em.
[*Several speak.*

3 Cit. He said, he had wounds, which he could show in private;
And with his hat, thus waving it in scorn,
I would be consul, says he: *aged custom,*
But by your voices, will not so permit me;
Your voices therefore: When we granted that,
Here was,—*I thank you for your voices,—thank you,—*
Your most sweet voices:—now you have left your voices,
I have no further with you:——Was not this mockery?

Sic. Why, either, were you ignorant to see't?

Or, seeing it, of such childish friendliness
To yield your voices?

Bru. Could you not have told him,
As you were lesson'd,—When he had no power,
But was a petty servant to the state,
He was your enemy; ever spake against
Your liberties, and the charters that you bear
I' the body of the weal: and now, arriving
A place of potency, and sway o' the state,
If he should still malignantly remain
Fast foe to the plebeii, your voices might
Be curses to yourselves? You should have said,
That, as his worthy deeds did claim no less
Than what he stood for; so his gracious nature
Would think upon you for your voices, and
Translate his malice towards you into love,
Standing your friendly lord.

Sic. Thus to have said,
As you were fore-advis'd, had touch'd his spirit,
And try'd his inclination; from him pluck'd
Either his gracious promise, which you might,
As cause had call'd you up, have held him to;
Or else it would have gall'd his surly nature,
Which easily endures not article
Tying him to aught; so, putting him to rage,
You should have ta'en the advantage of his choler,
And pass'd him unelected.

Bru. Did you perceive,
He did solicit you in free contempt,
When he did need your loves; and do you think
That his contempt shall not be bruising to you,
When he hath power to crush? Why, had your bodies
No heart among you? Or had you tongues, to cry
Against the rectorship of judgment?

Sic. Have you,
Ere now, deny'd the asker? and, now again,
On him, that did not ask, but mock, bestow
Your su'd-for tongues?

3 *Cit.* He's not confirm'd, we may deny him yet.

2 *Cit.* And will deny him:
I'll have five hundred voices of that sound.

1 *Cit.* I twice five hundred, and their friends to piece 'em.

Bru. Get you hence instantly; and tell those friends,—
They have chose a consul, that will from them take
Their liberties; make them of no more voice
Than dogs, that are as often beat for barking,
As therefore kept to do so.

Sic. Let them assemble;
And, on a safer judgment, all revoke
Your ignorant election: Enforce his pride,
And his old hate unto you: besides, forget not
With what contempt he wore the humble weed:
How in his suit he scorn'd you: but your loves,
Thinking upon his services, took from you
The apprehension of his present portance,
Which most gibingly, ungravely he did fashion
After the inveterate hate he bears you.

Bru. Lay
A fault on us, your tribunes; that we labour'd
(No impediment between) but that you must
Cast your election on him.

Sic. Say, you chose him
More after our commandment, than as guided
By your own true affections: and that, your minds
Preoccupy'd with what you rather must do,
Than what you should, made you against the grain
To voice him consul: Lay the fault on us.

Bru. Ay, spare us not. Say, we read lectures to you,
How youngly he began to serve his country,
How long continued: and what stock he springs of,
The noble house o'the Marcians; from whence came
That Ancus Marcius, Numa's daughter's son,
Who, after great Hostilius, here was king:
Of the same house Publius and Quintus were,
That our best water brought by conduits hither;
And Censorinus darling of the people,
And nobly nam'd so, being censor twice,
Was his great ancestor.

Sic. One thus descended,
That hath beside well in his person wrought
To be set high in place, we did commend
To your remembrances: but you have found,
Scaling his present bearing with his past,
That he's your fixed enemy, and revoke
Your sudden approbation.

Bru. Say, you ne'er had done't
(Harp on that still), but by our putting on:
And presently, when you have drawn your number,
Repair to the Capitol.

Cit. We will so: almost all [*Several speak.*
Repent in their election. [*Exeunt* Citizens.

Bru. Let them go on;
This mutiny were better put in hazard,
Than stay, past doubt, for greater:
If, as his nature is, he fall in rage
With their refusal, both observe and answer
The vantage of his anger.

Sic. To the Capitol:
Come; we'll be there before the stream o' the people;
And this shall seem, as partly 'tis, their own,
Which we have goaded onward. [*Exeunt.*

ACT III.

SCENE I. *The same. A Street.*

Cornets. Enter CORIOLANUS, MENENIUS, COMINIUS, TITUS LARTIUS, Senators, *and* Patricians.

Cor. Tullus Aufidius then had made new head?

Lart. He had, my lord; and that it was, which caus'd
Our swifter composition.

Cor. So then the Volces stand but as at first;
Ready, when time shall prompt them, to make road
Upon us again.

Com. They are worn, lord consul, so,
That we shall hardly in our ages see
Their banners wave again.

Cor. Saw you Aufidius?

Lart. On safeguard he came to me; and did curse
Against the Volces, for they had so vilely
Yielded the town: he is retir'd to Antium.

Cor. Spoke he of me?

Lart. He did, my lord.

Cor. How? what?

Lart. How often he had met you, sword to sword:
That, of all things upon the earth, he hated
Your person most: That he would pawn his fortunes
To hopeless restitution, so he might
Be call'd your vanquisher.

Cor. At Antium lives he?

Lart. At Antium.

Cor. I wish, I had a cause to seek him there,
To oppose his hatred fully.—Welcome home.
[*To* LARTIUS.

Enter SICINIUS *and* BRUTUS.

Behold! these are the tribunes of the people,
The tongues o' the common mouth. I do despise them;
For they do prank them in authority,
Against all noble sufferance.

Sic. Pass no further.

Cor. Ha! what is that?

Bru. It will be dangerous to
Go on: no further.

Cor. What makes this change?
Men. The matter?
Com. Hath he not pass'd the nobles, and the commons?
Bru. Cominius, no.
Cor. Have I had children's voices?
1 *Sen.* Tribunes, give way; he shall to the market-place.
Bru. The people are incens'd against him.
Sic. Stop,
Or all will fall in broil.
Cor. Are these your herd?—
Must these have voices, that can yield them now,
And straight disclaim their tongues?—What are your offices?
You being their mouths, why rule you not their teeth?
Have you not set them on?
Men. Be calm, be calm.
Cor. It is a purpos'd thing, and grows by plot,
To curb the will of the nobility:—
Suffer it, and live with such as cannot rule,
Nor ever will be rul'd.
Bru. Call't not a plot:
The people cry, you mock'd them: and, of late,
When corn was given them gratis, you repin'd;
Scandal'd the suppliants for the people; call'd them
Time-pleasers, flatterers, foes to nobleness.
Cor. Why, this was known before.
Bru. Not to them all.
Cor. Have you inform'd them since?
Bru. How! I inform them!
Cor. You are like to do such business.
Bru. Not unlike,
Each way to better yours.
Cor. Why then should I be consul? By yon clouds,
Let me deserve so ill as you, and make me
Your fellow tribune.
Sic. You show too much of that,
For which the people stir: If you will pass
To where you are bound, you must inquire your way,
Which you are out of, with a gentler spirit;
Or never be so noble as a consul,
Nor yoke with him for tribune.
Men. Let's be calm.
Com. The people are abus'd:—Set on.—This palt'ring
Becomes not Rome; nor has Coriolanus
Deserv'd this so dishonour'd rub, laid falsely
I' the plain way of his merit.
Cor. Tell me of corn!
This was my speech, and I will speak't again;—
Men. Not now, not now.
1 *Sen.* Not in this heat, sir, now.
Cor. Now, as I live, I will.—My nobler friends,
I crave their pardons:—
For the mutable, rank-scented many, let them
Regard me as I do not flatter, and
Therein behold themselves: I say again,
In soothing them, we nourish 'gainst our senate
The cockle of rebellion, insolence, sedition,
Which we ourselves have plough'd for, sow'd and scatter'd,
By mingling them with us, the honour'd number;
Who lack not virtue, no, nor power, but that
Which they have given to beggars.
Men. Well, no more.
1 *Sen.* No more words, we beseech you.
Cor. How, no more?
As for my country I have shed my blood,
Not fearing outward force, so shall my lungs
Coin words till their decay, against those meazels,
Which we disdain should tetter us, yet sought
The very way to catch them.
Bru. You speak o' the people,
As if you were a god to punish, not
A man of their infirmity.
Sic. 'Twere well,
We let the people know't.
Men. What, what? his choler?
Cor. Choler!
Were I as patient as the midnight sleep,
By Jove, 'twould be my mind.
Sic. It is a mind,
That shall remain a poison where it is,
Not poison any further.
Cor. Shall remain!—
Hear you this Triton of the minnows? mark you
His absolute *shall?*
Com. 'Twas from the canon.
Cor. *Shall!*
O good, but most unwise patricians, why,
You grave, but reckless senators, have you thus
Given Hydra here to choose an officer,
That with his peremptory *shall*, being but
The horn and noise o' the monsters, wants not spirit
To say, he'll turn your current in a ditch,
And make your channel his; If he have power,
Then vail your ignorance: if none, awake
Your dangerous lenity. If you are learned,
Be not as common fools; if you are not,
Let them have cushions by you. You are plebeians,
If they be senators: and they are no less,
When, both your voices blended, the greatest taste
Most palates theirs. They choose their magistrate;
And such a one as he, who puts his *shall*,
His popular *shall*, against a graver bench
Than ever frown'd in Greece! By Jove himself,
It makes the consuls base: and my soul akes,
To know, when two authorities are up,
Neither supreme, how soon confusion
May enter 'twixt the gap of both, and take
The one by the other.
Com. Well—on to the market-place.
Cor. Whoever gave that counsel, to give forth
The corn o' the storehouse gratis, as 'twas us'd
Sometime in Greece,——
Men. Well, well, no more of that.
Cor. (Though there the people had more absolute power)
I say, they nourish'd disobedience, fed
The ruin of the state.
Bru. Why, shall the people give
One, that speaks thus, their voice?
Cor. I'll give my reasons,
More worthier than their voices. They know, the corn
Was not our recompense; resting well assur'd
They ne'er did service for't: Being press'd to the war,
Even when the navel of the state was touch'd,
That would not thread the gates: this kind of service
Did not deserve corn gratis: being i' the war,
Their mutinies and revolts, wherein they show'd
Most valour, spoke not for them: The accusation
Which they have often made against the senate,
All cause unborn, could never be the native
Of our so frank donation. Well, what then?
How shall this bosom multiplied digest
The senate's courtesy? Let deeds express
What's like to be their words:—*We did request it:*
We are the greater poll, and in true fear
They gave us our demands:—Thus we debase
The nature of our seats, and make the rabble
Call our cares, fears: which will in time break ope
The locks o' the senate, and bring in the crows
To peck the eagles.—
Men. Come, enough.
Bru. Enough, with overmeasure.
Cor. No, take more:
What may be sworn by, both divine and human,
Seal what I end withal!—This double worship,—
Where one part does disdain with cause, the other

Insult without all reason; where gentry, title, wisdom
Cannot conclude, but by the yea and no
Of general ignorance,—it must omit
Real necessities, and give way the while
To unstable slightness: purpose so barr'd, it follows,
Nothing is done to purpose: Therefore, beseech you,—
You that will be less fearful than discreet;
That love the fundamental part of state,
More than you doubt the change of't; that prefer
A noble life before a long, and wish
To jump a body with a dangerous physick
That's sure of death without it,—at once pluck out
The multitudinous tongue, let them not lick
The sweet which is their poison: your dishonour
Mangles true judgment, and bereaves the state
Of that integrity which should become it;
Not having the power to do the good it would,
For the ill which doth control it.

Bru. He has said enough.

Sic. He has spoken like a traitor, and shall answer
As traitors do.

Cor. Thou wretch! despite o'erwhelm thee!—
What should the people do with these bald tribunes?
On whom depending, their obedience fails
To the greater bench: In a rebellion,
When what's not meet, but what must be, was law,
Then were they chosen; in a better hour
Let what is meet, be said it must be meet,
And throw their power i' the dust.

Bru. Manifest treason.

Sic. This a consul? no.

Bru. The Ædiles, ho!—Let him be apprehended.

Sic. Go, call the people; [*Exit* BRUTUS.] in whose name, myself
Attach thee, as a traitorous innovator,
A foe to the public weal: Obey, I charge thee,
And follow to thine answer.

Cor. Hence, old goat!

Sen. & Pat. We'll surety him.

Com. Aged sir, hands off.

Cor. Hence, rotten thing, or I shall shake thy bones
Out of thy garments.

Sic. Help, ye citizens.

Re-enter BRUTUS, *with the* Ædiles, *and a Rabble of* Citizens.

Men. On both sides more respect.

Sic. Here's he, that would
Take from you all your power.

Bru. Seize him, Ædiles.

Cit. Down with him, down with him!
[*Several speak.*

2 *Sen.* Weapons, weapons, weapons!
[*They all bustle about* CORIOLANUS.
Tribunes, patricians, citizens!—what ho!—
Sicinius, Brutus, Coriolanus, citizens!

Cit. Peace, peace, peace; stay, hold, peace!

Men. What is about to be?—I am out of breath;
Confusion's near: I cannot speak:—You, tribunes
To the people,—Coriolanus, patience:
Speak, good Sicinius.

Sic. Hear me, people;—Peace.

Cit. Let's hear our tribune:—Peace. Speak, speak, speak.

Sic. You are at point to lose your liberties:
Marcius would have all from you; Marcius,
Whom late you have nam'd for consul.

Men. Fye, fye, fye!
This is the way to kindle, not to quench.

1 *Sen.* To unbuild the city, and to lay all flat.

Sic. What is the city, but the people?

Cit. True,
The people are the city.

Bru. By the consent of all, we were establish'd
The people's magistrates.

Cit. You so remain.

Men. And so are like to do.

Cor. That is the way to lay the city flat;
To bring the roof to the foundation;
And bury all, which yet distinctly ranges,
In heaps and piles of ruin.

Sic. This deserves death.

Bru. Or let us stand to our authority,
Or let us lose it:—We do here pronounce,
Upon the part o' the people, in whose power
We were elected theirs, Marcius is worthy
Of present death.

Sic. Therefore lay hold of him;
Bear him to the rock Tarpeian, and from thence
Into destruction cast him.

Bru. Ædiles, seize him.

Cit. Yield, Marcius, yield.

Men. Hear me one word.
Beseech you, tribunes, hear me but a word.

Ædi. Peace, peace.

Men. Be that you seem, truly your country's friend,
And temperately proceed to what you would
Thus violently redress.

Bru. Sir, those cold ways,
That seem like prudent helps, are very poisonous
Where the disease is violent:—Lay hands upon him,
And bear him to the rock.

Cor. No; I'll die here.
[*Drawing his Sword.*
There's some among you have beheld me fighting;
Come, try upon yourselves what you have seen me.

Men. Down with that sword;—Tribunes, withdraw awhile.

Bru. Lay hands upon him.

Men. Help, help Marcius! help,
You that be noble; help him, young, and old!

Cit. Down with him, down with him!
[*In this Mutiny, the* Tribunes, *the* Ædiles, *and the* People, *are all beat in.*

Men. Go, get you to your house; be gone, away,
All will be naught else.

2 *Sen.* Get you gone.

Cor. Stand fast;
We have as many friends as enemies.

Men. Shall it be put to that?

1 *Sen.* The gods forbid!
I pr'ythee, noble friend, home to thy house;
Leave us to cure this cause.

Men. For 'tis a sore upon us,
You cannot tent yourself: Begone, 'beseech you.

Com. Come, sir, along with us.

Cor. I would they were barbarians (as they are,
Though in Rome litter'd), not Romans (as they are not,
Though calv'd i' the porch o' the Capitol)—

Men. Be gone;
Put not your worthy rage into your tongue;
One time will owe another.

Cor. On fair ground
I could beat forty of them.

Men. I could myself
Take up a brace of the best of them; yea, the two tribunes.

Com. But now 'tis odds beyond arithmetick;
And manhood is call'd foolery, when it stands
Against a falling fabrick.—Will you hence,
Before the tag return? whose rage doth rend
Like interrupted waters, and o'erbear
What they are used to bear.

Men. 'Pray you, be gone:
I'll try whether my old wit be in request
With those that have but little; this must be patch'd
With cloth of any colour.

Com. Nay, come away.
[*Exeunt* COR. COM. *and Others.*

1 *Pat.* This man has marr'd his fortune.
Men. His nature is too noble for the world;
He would not flatter Neptune for his trident,
Or Jove for his power to thunder. His heart's his mouth;
What his breast forges, that his tongue must vent;
And, being angry, does forget that ever
He heard the name of death. [*A noise within.*
Here's goodly work!
2 *Pat.* I would they were abed!
Men. I would they were in Tyber!—What, the vengeance,
Could he not speak them fair?

Re-enter BRUTUS *and* SICINIUS, *with the* Rabble.

Sic. Where is this viper,
That would depopulate the city, and
Be every man himself?
Men. You worthy tribunes,—
Sic. He shall be thrown down the Tarpeian rock
With rigorous hands; he hath resisted law,
And therefore law shall scorn him further trial
Than the severity of the public power,
Which he so sets at nought.
1 *Cit.* He shall well know,
The noble tribunes are the people's mouths,
And we their hands.
Cit. He shall, sure on 't.
[*Several speak together.*
Men. Sir,—
Sic. Peace.
Men. Do not cry, havock, where you should but hunt
With modest warrant.
Sic. Sir, how comes it that you
Have holp to make this rescue?
Men. Hear me speak:—
As I do know the consul's worthiness,
So can I name his faults:—
Sic. Consul!—What consul?
Men. The consul Coriolanus.
Bru. He a consul!
Cit. No, no, no, no, no.
Men. If, by the tribunes' leave, and yours, good people,
I may be heard, I'd crave a word or two;
The which shall turn you to no further harm,
Than so much loss of time.
Sic. Speak briefly then;
For we are peremptory, to despatch
This viperous traitor: to eject him hence,
Were but one danger; and, to keep him here,
Our certain death; therefore it is decreed,
He dies to-night.
Men. Now the good gods forbid,
That our renowned Rome, whose gratitude
Towards her deserved children is enroll'd
In Jove's own book, like an unnatural dam
Should now eat up her own!
Sic. He's a disease, that must be cut away.
Men. O, he's a limb, that has but a disease;
Mortal, to cut it off; to cure it, easy.
What has he done to Rome, that's worthy death?
Killing our enemies? The blood he hath lost
(Which, I dare vouch, is more than that he hath,
By many an ounce), he dropp'd it for his country:
And, what is left, to lose it by his country,
Were to us all, that do 't, and suffer it,
A brand to the end o' the world.
Sic. This is clean kam.
Bru. Merely awry: when he did love his country,
It honour'd him.
Men. The service of the foot
Being once gangren'd, is not then respected
For what before it was?
Bru. We'll hear no more:—
Pursue him to his house, and pluck him thence;
Lest his infection, being of catching nature,
Spread further.
Men. One word more, one word.
This tiger-footed rage, when it shall find
The harm of unscann'd swiftness, will, too late,
Tie leaden pounds to his heels. Proceed, by process;
Lest parties (as he is belov'd) break out,
And sack great Rome with Romans.
Bru. If it were so,—
Sic. What do ye talk?
Have we not had a taste of his obedience?
Our Ædiles smote? ourselves resisted?—
Come:—
Men. Consider this;—He has been bred i' the wars
Since he could draw a sword, and is ill school'd
In boulted language: meal and bran together
He throws without distinction. Give me leave,
I'll go to him, and undertake to bring him
Where he shall answer, by a lawful form
(In peace), to his utmost peril.
1 *Sen.* Noble tribunes,
It is the humane way: the other course
Will prove too bloody; and the end of it
Unknown to the beginning.
Sic. Noble Menenius,
Be you then as the people's officer:
Masters, lay down your weapons.
Bru. Go not home.
Sic. Meet on the market-place:—We'll attend you there:
Where, if you bring not Marcius, we'll proceed
In our first way.
Men. I'll bring him to you:
Let me desire your company. [*To the* Senators.]
He must come,
Or what is worst will follow.
1 *Sen.* 'Pray you, let's to him.
[*Exeunt.*

SCENE II. *A Room in* Coriolanus's *House.*

Enter CORIOLANUS, *and* Patricians.

Cor. Let them pull all about mine ears; present me
Death on the wheel, or at wild horses' heels;
Or pile ten hills on the Tarpeian rock,
That the precipitation might down stretch
Below the beam of sight, yet will I still
Be thus to them.

Enter VOLUMNIA.

1 *Pat.* You do the nobler.
Cor. I muse, my mother
Does not approve me further, who was wont
To call them woollen vassals, things created
To buy and sell with groats; to show bare heads
In congregations, to yawn, be still, and wonder,
When one but of my ordinance stood up
To speak of peace, or war. I talk of you;
[*To* VOLUMNIA.
Why did you wish me milder? Would you have me
False to my nature? Rather say, I play
The man I am.
Vol. O, sir, sir, sir,
I would have had you put your power well on,
Before you had worn it out.
Cor. Let go.
Vol. You might have been enough the man you are,
With striving less to be so: Lesser had been
The thwartings of your dispositions, if
You had not show'd them how you were dispos'd
Ere they lack'd power to cross you.
Cor. Let them hang.
Vol. Ay, and burn too.

Enter MENENIUS, *and* Senators.

Men. Come, come, you have been too rough, something too rough;
You must return, and mend it.
1 *Sen.* There's no remedy;
Unless, by not so doing, our good city
Cleave in the midst, and perish.

Vol. Pray be counsell'd:
I have a heart as little apt as yours,
But yet a brain, that leads my use of anger,
To better vantage.
Men. Well said, noble woman:
Before he should thus stoop to the herd, but that
The violent fit o' the time craves it as physick
For the whole state, I would put mine armour on,
Which I can scarcely bear.
Cor. What must I do?
Men. Return to the tribunes.
Cor. Well,
What then? what then?
Men. Repent what you have spoke.
Cor. For them?—I cannot do it to the gods;
Must I then do't to them?
Vol. You are too absolute;
Though therein you can never be too noble,
But when extremities speak. I have heard you say,
Honour and policy, like unsever'd friends,
I' the war do grow together: Grant that, and tell me,
In peace, what each of them by th' other lose,
That they combine not there.
Cor. Tush, tush!
Men. A good demand.
Vol. If it be honour, in your wars, to seem
The same you are not (which, for your best ends,
You adopt your policy), how is it less, or worse,
That it shall hold companionship in peace
With honour, as in war; since that to both
It stands in like request?
Cor. Why force you this?
Vol. Because that now it lies you on to speak
To the people; not by your own instruction,
Nor by the matter which your heart prompts you to,
But with such words that are but roted in
Your tongue, though but bastards, and syllables
Of no allowance to your bosom's truth.
Now, this no more dishonours you at all,
Than to take in a town with gentle words,
Which else would put you to your fortune, and
The hazard of much blood.—
I would dissemble with my nature, where
My fortunes, and my friends, at stake, requir'd,
I should do so in honour: I am in this,
Your wife, your son, these senators, the nobles;
And you will rather show our general lowts
How you can frown, then spend a fawn upon them,
For the inheritance of their loves, and safeguard
Of what that want might ruin.
Men. Noble lady!—
Come, go with us; speak fair: you may salve so,
Not what is dangerous present, but the loss
Of what is past.
Vol. I pr'ythee now, my son,
Go to them, with this bonnet in thy hand;
And thus far having stretch'd it (here be with them),
Thy knee bussing the stones (for in such business
Action is eloquence, and the eyes of the ignorant
More learned than the ears), waving thy head,
Which often, thus, correcting thy stout heart,
Now humble, as the ripest mulberry,
That will not hold the handling: Or, say to them,
Thou art their soldier, and being bred in broils,
Hast not the soft way, which, thou dost confess,
Were fit for thee to use, as they to claim,
In asking their good loves; but thou wilt frame
Thyself, forsooth, hereafter theirs, so far
As thou hast power, and person.
Men. This but done,
Even as she speaks, why, their hearts were yours:
For they have pardons, being ask'd, as free
As words to little purpose.
Vol. Pr'ythee now,
Go, and be rul'd: although, I know, thou hadst rather
Follow thine enemy in a fiery gulf,
Than flatter him in a bower. Here is Cominius.

Enter COMINIUS.

Com. I have been i' the market-place: and, sir, 'tis fit
You make strong party, or defend yourself
By calmness, or by absence; all's in anger.
Men. Only fair speech.
Com. I think, 'twill serve, if he
Can thereto frame his spirit.
Vol. He must, and will:—
Pr'ythee, now, say, you will, and go about it.
Cor. Must I go show them my unbarb'd sconce? Must I
With my base tongue, give to my noble heart
A lie, that it must bear? Well, I will do't:
Yet were there but this single plot to lose,
This mould of Marcius, they to dust should grind it,
And throw it against the wind.—To the market-place:—
You have put me now to such a part, which never
I shall discharge to the life.
Com. Come, come, we'll prompt you.
Vol. I pr'ythee now, sweet son; as thou hast said,
My praises made thee first a soldier, so,
To have my praise for this, perform a part
Thou hast not done before.
Cor. Well, I must do't:
Away, my disposition, and possess me
Some harlot's spirit! My throat of war be turn'd,
Which quired with my drum, into a pipe
Small as an eunuch, or the virgin voice
That babies lulls asleep! The smiles of knaves
Tent in my cheeks; and schoolboys' tears take up
The glasses of my sight! A beggar's tongue
Make motion through my lips; and my arm'd knees,
Who bow'd but in my stirrup, bend like his
That hath receiv'd an alms!—I will not do't:
Lest I surcease to honour mine own truth,
And, by my body's action, teach my mind
A most inherent baseness.
Vol. At thy choice then:
To beg of thee, it is my more dishonour,
Than thou of them. Come all to ruin; let
Thy mother rather feel thy pride, than fear
Thy dangerous stoutness; for I mock at death
With as big heart as thou. Do as thou list.
Thy valiantness was mine, thou suck'dst it from me;
But owe thy pride thyself.
Cor. 'Pray, be content;
Mother, I am going to the market-place;
Chide me no more. I'll mountebank their loves,
Cog their hearts from them, and come home belov'd
Of all the trades in Rome. Look, I am going:
Commend me to my wife. I'll return consul;
Or never trust to what my tongue can do
I' the way of flattery, further.
Vol. Do your will. [*Exit.*
Com. Away, the tribunes do attend you: arm yourself
To answer mildly; for they are prepar'd
With accusations, as I hear, more strong
Than are upon you yet.
Cor. The word is, mildly:—'Pray you, let us go;
Let them accuse me by invention, I
Will answer in mine honour.
Men. Ay, but mildly.
Cor. Well, mildly be it then; mildly.
[*Exeunt.*

SCENE III. *The same. The Forum.*

Enter SICINIUS *and* BRUTUS.

Bru. In this point charge him home, that he affects
Tyrannical power: If he evade us there,
Enforce him with his envy to the people;

And that the spoil, got on the Antiates,
Was ne'er distributed.—

Enter an Ædile.

What, will he come?
Æd. He's coming.
Bru. How accompanied?
Æd. With old Menenius, and those senators
That always favoured him.
Sic. Have you a catalogue
Of all the voices that we have procur'd,
Set down by the poll?
Æd. I have; 'tis ready, here.
Sic. Have you collected them by tribes?
Æd. I have.
Sic. Assemble presently the people hither:
And when they hear me say, *It shall be so
I' the right and strength o' the commons*, be it either
For death, for fine, or banishment, then let them,
If I say, fine, cry *fine*; if death, cry *death*;
Insisting on the old prerogative
And power, i' the truth o' the cause.
Æd. I shall inform them.
Bru. And when such time they have begun to cry,
Let them not cease, but with a din confus'd
Enforce the present execution
Of what we chance to sentence.
Æd. Very well.
Sic. Make them be strong, and ready for this hint,
When we shall hap to give 't them.
Bru. Go about it.—
[*Exit* Ædile.
Put him to choler straight: He hath been us'd
Ever to conquer, and to have his worth
Of contradiction: Being once chaf'd, he cannot
Be rein'd again to temperance; then he speaks
What's in his heart; and that is there, which looks
With us to break his neck.

Enter Coriolanus, Menenius, Cominius, Senators, *and* Patricians.

Sic. Well, here he comes.
Men. Calmly, I do beseech you.
Cor. Ay, as an ostler, that for the poorest piece
Will bear the knave by the volume.—The honour'd gods
Keep Rome in safety, and the chairs of justice
Supplied with worthy men! plant love among us!
Throng our large temples with the shows of peace,
And not our streets with war!
1 Sen. Amen, amen!
Men. A noble wish.

Re-enter Ædile, *with* Citizens.

Sic. Draw near, ye people.
Æd. List to your tribunes; audience: Peace, I say.
Cor. First, hear me speak.
Both Tri. Well, say.—Peace, ho.
Cor. Shall I be charg'd no further than this present?
Must all determine here?
Sic. I do demand,
If you submit you to the people's voices,
Allow their officers, and are content
To suffer lawful censure for such faults
As shall be prov'd upon you?
Cor. I am content.
Men. Lo, citizens, he says he is content:
The warlike service he has done, consider;
Think on the wounds his body bears, which show
Like graves i' the holy churchyard.
Cor. Scratches with briars,
Scars to move laughter only.
Men. Consider further,
That when he speaks not like a citizen,
You find him like a soldier: Do not take
His rougher accents for malicious sounds,
But, as I say, such as become a soldier,
Rather than envy you.
Com. Well, well, no more.
Cor. What is the matter,
That being pass'd for consul with full voice,
I am so dishonour'd, that the very hour
You take it off again?
Sic. Answer to us.
Cor. Say then: 'tis true, I ought so.
Sic. We charge you, that you have contriv'd to take
From Rome all season'd office, and to wind
Yourself into a power tyrannical:
For which, you are a traitor to the people.
Cor. How! Traitor?
Men. Nay; temperately; Your promise.
Cor. The fires i' the lowest hell fold in the people!
Call me their traitor!—Thou injurious tribune;
Within thine eyes sat twenty thousand deaths,
In thy hands clutch'd as many millions, in
Thy lying tongue both numbers, I would say,
Thou liest, unto thee, with a voice as free
As I do pray the gods.
Sic. Mark you this, people?
Cit. To the rock; to the rock with him!
Sic. Peace.
We need not put new matter to his charge:
What you have seen him do, and heard him speak,
Beating your officers, cursing yourselves,
Opposing laws with strokes, and here defying
Those whose great power must try him; even this,
So criminal, and in such capital kind,
Deserves the extremest death.
Bru. But since he hath
Serv'd well for Rome,——
Cor. What do you prate of service?
Bru. I talk of that that know it.
Cor. You?
Men. Is this
The promise that you made your mother?
Com. Know,
I pray you,——
Cor. I'll know no further:
Let them pronounce the steep Tarpeian death,
Vagabond exile, flaying: Pent to linger
But with a grain a day, I would not buy
Their mercy at the price of one fair word;
Nor check my courage for what they can give,
To have 't with saying, Good morrow.
Sic. For that he has
(As much as in him lies) from time to time
Envied against the people, seeking means
To pluck away their power as now at last
Given hostile strokes, and that not in the presence
Of dreaded justice, but on the ministers
That do distribute it; In the name o' the people,
And in the power of us the tribunes, we,
Even from this instant, banish him our city:
In peril of precipitation
From off the rock Tarpeian, never more
To enter our Rome gates: I' the people's name,
I say, it shall be so.
Cit. It shall be so, it shall be so; let him away:
He's banish'd, and it shall be so.
Com. Hear me, my masters, and my common friends;——
Sic. He's sentenc'd: no more hearing.
Com. Let me speak:
I have been consul, and can show from Rome,
Her enemies' marks upon me. I do love
My country's good, with a respect more tender,
More holy, and profound, that mine own life,
My dear wife's estimate, her womb's increase,
And treasure of my loins; then if I would
Speak that——
Sic. We know your drift: Speak what?
Bru. There's no more to be said, but he is banish'd,
As enemy to the people, and his country:
It shall be so.

Cit. It shall be so, it shall be so.
Cor. You common cry of curs! whose breath I hate
As reek o' the rotten fens, whose loves I prize
As the dead carcasses of unburied men
That do corrupt my air, I banish you;
And here remain with your uncertainty!
Let every feeble rumour shake your hearts!
Your enemies, with nodding of their plumes,
Fan you into despair! Have the power still
To banish your defenders; till at length,
Your ignorance (which finds not till it feels),
Making but reservation of yourselves,
(Still your own foes), deliver you, as most
Abated captives, to some nation
That won you without blows! Despising,
For you, the city, thus I turn my back:
There is a world elsewhere.
[*Exeunt* CORIOLANUS, COMINIUS, MENENIUS, Senators, *and* Patricians.
Æd. The people's enemy is gone, is gone!
Cit. Our enemy's banish'd! he is gone! Hoo hoo!
[*The* People *shout, and throw up their Caps.*
Sic. Go, see him out at gates, and follow him,
As he hath follow'd you, with all despite;
Give him deserv'd vexation. Let a guard
Attend us through the city.
Cit. Come, come, let us see him out at gates: come:—
The gods preserve our noble tribunes!—Come.
[*Exeunt.*

ACT IV.

SCENE I. *The same. Before a Gate of the City.*

Enter CORIOLANUS, VOLUMNIA, VIRGILIA, MENENIUS, COMINIUS, *and several young* Patricians.

Cor. Come, leave your tears: a brief farewell:—the beast
With many heads butts me away.—Nay, mother,
Where is your ancient courage? you were us'd
To say, extremity was the trier of spirits;
That common chances common men could bear;
That, when the sea was calm, all boats alike
Show'd mastership in floating: fortune's blows,
When most struck home, being gentle wounded, craves
A noble cunning: you were us'd to load me
With precepts, that would make invincible
The heart that conn'd them.
Vir. O heavens! O heavens!
Cor. Nay, I pr'ythee, woman,—
Vol. Now the red pestilence strike all trades in Rome,
And occupations perish!
Cor. What, what, what!
I shall be lov'd when I am lack'd. Nay, mother,
Resume that spirit, when you were wont to say,
If you had been the wife of Hercules,
Six of his labours you'd have done, and sav'd
Your husband so much sweat.—Cominius,
Droop not; adieu:—Farewell, my wife! my mother!
I'll do well yet.—Thou old and true Menenius,
Thy tears are salter than a younger man's,
And venomous to thine eyes.—My sometime general,
I have seen thee stern, and thou hast oft beheld
Heart-hard'ning spectacles; tell these sad women,
'Tis fond to wail inevitable strokes,
As 'tis to laugh at them.—My mother, you wot well,
My hazards still have been your solace: and
Believe't not lightly (though I go alone
Like to a lonely dragon, that his fen
Makes fear'd, and talk'd of more than seen), your son
Will, or exceed the common, or be caught
With cautelous baits and practice.
Vol. My first son,
Whither wilt thou go? Take good Cominius
With thee a while: Determine on some course,
More than a wild exposture to each chance
That starts i' the way before thee.
Cor. O the gods!
Com. I'll follow thee a month, devise with thee
Where thou shalt rest, that thou may'st hear of us,
And we of thee: so, if the time thrust forth
A cause for thy repeal, we shall not send
O'er the vast world, to seek a single man;
And lose advantage, which doth ever cool
I' the absence of the needer.
Cor. Fare ye well;—
Thou hast years upon thee; and thou art too full
Of the wars' surfeits, to go rove with one
That's yet unbruis'd: bring me but out at gate.—
Come, my sweet wife, my dearest mother, and
My friends of noble touch, when I am forth,
Bid me farewell and smile. I pray you, come.
While I remain above the ground, you shall
Hear from me still; and never of me aught
But what is like me formerly.
Men. That's worthily
As any ear can hear. Come, let's not weep.—
If I could shake off but one seven years
From these old arms and legs, by the good gods,
I'd with thee every foot.
Cor. Give me thy hand:
Come. [*Exeunt.*

SCENE II. *The same. A Street near the Gate.*

Enter SICINIUS, BRUTUS, *and an* Ædile.

Sic. Bid them all home: he's gone, and we'll no further.—
The nobility are vex'd, who, we see, have sided
In his behalf.
Bru. Now we have shown our power,
Let us seem humbler after it is done,
Than when it was a doing.
Sic. Bid them home:
Say, their great enemy is gone, and they
Stand in their ancient strength.
Bru. Dismiss them home.
[*Exit* Ædile.

Enter VOLUMNIA, VIRGILIA, *and* MENENIUS.

Here comes his mother.
Sic. Let's not meet her.
Bru. Why?
Sic. They say, she's mad.
Bru. They have ta'en note of us:
Keep on your way.
Vol. O you're well met: The hoarded plague o' the gods
Requite your love!
Men. Peace, peace: be not so loud.
Vol. If that I could for weeping, you should hear,—
Nay, and you shall hear some.—Will you be gone? [*To* BRUTUS.
Vir. You shall stay too: [*To* SIC.] I would, I had the power
To say so to my husband.
Sic. Are you mankind?
Vol. Ay, fool; is that a shame?—Note but this fool.—
Was not a man my father? Hadst thou foxship
To banish him that struck more blows for Rome,
Than thou hast spoken words?
Sic. O blessed heavens!
Vol. More noble blows, than ever thou wise words;
And for Rome's good.—I'll tell thee what:—Yet go:—
Nay, but thou shalt stay too:—I would, my son
Were in Arabia, and thy tribe before him,
His good sword in his hand.

Sic. What then?
Vir. What then?
He'd make an end of thy posterity.
Vol. Bastards, and all.—
Good man, the wounds that he does bear for Rome!
Men. Come, come, peace.
Sic. I would, he had continu'd to his country,
As he began; and not unknit himself
The noble knot he made.
Bru. I would he had.
Vol. I would he had! 'Twas you incens'd the rabble;
Cats, that can judge as fitly of his worth,
As I can of those mysteries which heaven
Will not have earth to know.
Bru. Pray, let us go.
Vol. Now, pray sir, get you gone:
You have done a brave deed. Ere you go, hear this:
As far as doth the Capitol exceed
The meanest house in Rome: so far my son
(This lady's husband here, this, do you see),
Whom you have banish'd, does exceed you all.
Bru. Well, well, we'll leave you.
Sic. Why stay we to be baited
With one that wants her wits?
Vol. Take my prayers with you.—
I would the gods had nothing else to do,
[*Exeunt* Tribunes.
But to confirm my curses! Could I meet them
But once a day, it would unclog my heart
Of what lies heavy to 't.
Men. You have told them home,
And, by my troth, you have cause. You'll sup with me?
Vol. Anger's my meat; I sup upon myself,
And so shall starve with feeding.—Come, let's go;
Leave this faint puling, and lament as I do,
In anger, Juno-like. Come, come, come.
Men. Fye, fye, fye! [*Exeunt.*

SCENE III.

A Highway between Rome *and* Antium.

Enter a Roman *and a* Volce, *meeting.*

Rom. I know you well, sir, and you know me: your name, I think, is Adrian.

Vol. It is so sir: truly, I have forgot you.

Rom. I am a Roman; and my services are, as you are, against them: Know you me yet?

Vol. Nicanor? No.

Rom. The same, sir.

Vol. You had more beard, when I last saw you; but your favour is well appayed by your tongue. What's the news in Rome? I have a note from the Volcian state, to find you out there: You have well saved me a day's journey.

Rom. There hath been in Rome strange insurrection: the people against the senators, patricians, and nobles.

Vol. Hath been! Is it ended then? Our state thinks not so; they are in a most warlike preparation, and hope to come upon them in the heat of their division.

Rom. The main blaze of it is past, but a small thing would make it flame again. For the nobles receive so to heart the banishment of that worthy Coriolanus, that they are in a ripe aptness, to take all power from the people, and to pluck from them their tribunes for ever. This lies glowing, I can tell you, and is almost mature for the violent breaking out.

Vol. Coriolanus banished?

Rom. Banished, sir.

Vol. You will be welcome with this intelligence, Nicanor.

Rom. The day serves well for them now. I have heard it said, the fittest time to corrupt a man's wife, is when she's fallen out with her husband. Your noble Tullus Aufidius will appear well in these wars, with his great opposer, Coriolanus, being now in no request of his country.

Vol. He cannot choose. I am most fortunate, thus accidentally to encounter you: You have ended my business, and I will merrily accompany you home.

Rom. I shall, between this and supper, tell you most strange things from Rome; all tending to the good of their adversaries. Have you an army ready, say you?

Vol. A most royal one: the centurions, and their charges, distinctly billeted, already in the entertainment, and to be on foot at an hour's warning.

Rom. I am joyful to hear of their readiness, and am the man, I think, that shall set them in present action. So, sir, heartily well met, and most glad of your company.

Vol. You take my part from me, sir; I have the most cause to be glad of yours.

Rom. Well, let us go together. [*Exeunt.*

SCENE IV. Antium. *Before* Aufidius's *House.*

Enter CORIOLANUS, *in mean Apparel, disguised and muffled.*

Cor. A goodly city is this Antium: City,
'Tis I that made thy widows; many an heir
Of these fair edifices 'fore my wars
Have I heard groan and drop: then know me not;
Lest that thy wives with spits, and boys with stones,
Enter a Citizen.
In puny battle slay me.—Save you, sir.
Cit. And you.
Cor. Direct me, if it be your will,
Where great Aufidius lies: Is he in Antium?
Cit. He is, and feasts the nobles of the state,
At his house this night.
Cor. Which is his house, 'beseech you?
Cit. This, here, before you.
Cor. Thank you, sir, farewell.
[*Exit* Citizen.
O, world, thy slippery turns! Friends now fast sworn,
Whose double bosoms seem to wear one heart,
Whose hours, whose bed, whose meal, and exercise,
Are still together, who twin as twere in love
Unseparable, shall within this hour,
On a dissension of a doit, break out
To bitterest enmity; So fellest foes,
Whose passions and whose plots have broke their sleep
To take the one the other, by some chance,
Some trick not worth an egg, shall grow dear friends,
And interjoin their issues. So with me:—
My birth-place hate I, and my love's upon
This enemy town.—I'll enter: if he slay me,
He does fair justice; if he give me way,
I'll do his country service. [*Exit.*

SCENE V.

The same. A Hall in Aufidius's *House.*

Musick within. Enter a Servant.

1 *Serv.* Wine, wine, wine! What service is here! I think our fellows are asleep. [*Exit.*

Enter another Servant.

2 *Serv.* Where's Cotus? my master calls for him. Cotus! [*Exit.*

Enter CORIOLANUS.

Cor. A goodly house: The feast smells well: but I
Appear not like a guest.

Re-enter the first Servant.

1 *Serv.* What would you have, friend? Whence are you? Here's no place for you: Pray, go to the door.

Cor. I have deserv'd no better entertainment,
In being Coriolanus.

Re-enter second Servant.

2 *Serv.* Whence are you, sir? Has the porter his eyes in his head, that he gives entrance to such companions? Pray, get you out.

Cor. Away!

2 *Serv.* Away? Get you away.

Cor. Now thou art troublesome.

2 *Serv.* Are you so brave? I'll have you talked with anon.

Enter a third Servant. *The first meets him.*

3 *Serv.* What fellow's this?

1 *Serv.* A strange one as ever I look'd on: I cannot get him out o'the house; Pr'ythee, call my master to him.

3 *Serv.* What have you to do here, fellow? Pray you, avoid the house.

Cor. Let me but stand; I will not hurt your hearth.

3 *Serv.* What are you?

Cor. A gentleman.

3 *Serv.* A marvellous poor one.

Cor. True, so I am.

3 *Serv.* Pray you, poor gentleman, take up some other station; here's no place for you; pray you, avoid; come.

Cor. Follow your function, go!
And batten on cold bits. [*Pushes him away.*

3 *Serv.* What, will you not? Pr'ythee, tell my master what a strange guest he has here.

2 *Serv.* And I shall. [*Exit.*

3 *Serv.* Where dwellest thou?

Cor. Under the canopy.

3 *Serv.* Under the canopy?

Cor. Ay.

3 *Serv.* Where's that?

Cor. I' the city of kites and crows.

3 *Serv.* I' the city of kites and crows?—What an ass it is!—Then thou dwellest with daws too?

Cor. No, I serve not thy master.

3 *Serv.* How, sir! Do you meddle with my master?

Cor. Ay; 'tis an honester service than to meddle with thy mistress:
Thou prat'st, and prat'st: serve with thy trencher, hence! [*Beats him away.*

Enter AUFIDIUS *and the second* Servant.

Auf. Where is this fellow?

2 *Serv.* Here, sir; I'd have beaten him like a dog, but for disturbing the lords within.

Auf. Whence comest thou? what wouldest thou? Thy name?
Why speak'st not? Speak, man: What's thy name?

Cor. If, Tullus, [*Unmuffling.*
Not yet thou know'st me, and seeing me, dost not
Think me for the man I am, necessity
Commands me name myself.

Auf. What is thy name?
[Servants *retire.*

Cor. A name unmusical to the Volcians' ears,
And harsh in sound to thine.

Auf. Say, what's thy name?
Thou hast a grim appearance, and thy face
Bears a command in't; though thy tackle's torn,
Thou show'st a noble vessel: What's thy name?

Cor. Prepare thy brow to frown: Know'st thou me yet?

Auf. I know thee not: Thy name?

Cor. My name is Caius Marcius, who hath done
To thee particularly, and to all the Volces,
Great hurt and mischief; thereto witness may
My surname, Coriolanus: The painful service,
The extreme dangers, and the drops of blood
Shed for my thankless country, are requited
But with that surname; a good memory,
And witness of the malice and displeasure
Which thou should'st bear me; only that name remains;
The cruelty and envy of the people,
Permitted by our dastard nobles, who
Have all forsook me, hath devour'd the rest;
And suffered me by the voice of slaves to be
Whoop'd out of Rome. Now this extremity
Hath brought me to thy hearth; Not out of hope,
Mistake me not, to save my life; for if
I had fear'd death, of all the men i' the world
I would have 'voided thee: but in mere spite,
To be full quit of those my banishers,
Stand I before thee here. Then if thou hast
A heart of wreak in thee, that will revenge
Thine own particular wrongs, and stop those maims
Of shame seen through thy country, speed thee straight,
And make my misery serve thy turn: so use it,
That my revengeful services may prove
As benefits to thee: for I will fight
Against my canker'd country with the spleen
Of all the under fiends. But if so be
Thou dar'st not this, and that to prove more fortunes
Thou art tir'd, then, in a word, I also am
Longer to live most weary, and present
My throat to thee, and to thy ancient malice:
Which not to cut, would show thee but a fool;
Since I have ever follow'd thee with hate,
Drawn tuns of blood out of thy country's breast,
And cannot live but to thy shame, unless
It be to do thee service.

Auf. O, Marcius, Marcius,
Each word thou hast spoke hath weeded from my heart
A root of ancient envy. If Jupiter
Should from yon cloud speak divine things, and say,
'*Tis true;* I'd not believe them more than thee,
All noble Marcius.—O, let me twine
Mine arms about that body, where against
My grained ash an hundred times hath broke,
And scarr'd the moon with splinters! Here I clip
The anvil of my sword; and do contest
As hotly and as nobly with thy love,
As ever in ambitious strength I did
Contend against thy valour. Know thou first,
I loved the maid I married: never man
Sigh'd truer breath; but that I see thee here,
Thou noble thing! more dances my rapt heart,
Than when I first my wedded mistress saw
Bestride my threshold. Why, thou Mars! I tell thee,
We have a power on foot; and I had purpose
Once more to hew thy target from thy brawn,
Or lose mine arm for't: Thou hast beat me out
Twelve several times, and I have nightly since
Dreamt of encounters 'twixt thyself and me:
We have been down together in my sleep,
Unbuckling helms, fisting each other's throat,
And wak'd half dead with nothing. Worthy Marcius,
Had we no other quarrel else to Rome, but that
Thou art thence banish'd, we would muster all
From twelve to seventy; and pouring war
Into the bowels of ungrateful Rome,
Like a bold flood o'er-beat. O, come, go in,
And take our friendly senators by the hands;
Who now are here, taking their leaves of me,
Who am prepar'd against your territories,
Though not for Rome itself.

Cor. You bless me, gods!

Auf. Therefore, most absolute sir, if thou wilt have
The leading of thine own revenges, take
The one half of my commission; and set down,—
As best thou art experienc'd, since thou know'st
Thy country's strength and weakness,—thine own ways:
Whether to knock against the gates of Rome,
Or rudely visit them in parts remote,
To fright them, ere destroy. But come in:
Let me commend thee first to those, that shall

Say, *yea*, to thy desires. A thousand welcomes!
And more a friend than e'er an enemy;
Yet, Marcius, that was much. Your hand; Most welcome! [*Exeunt* COR. *and* AUF.

1 *Serv.* [*Advancing.*] Here's a strange alteration!

2 *Serv.* By my hand, I had thought to have strucken him with a cudgel; and yet my mind gave me, his clothes made a false report of him.

1 *Serv.* What an arm he has! He turned me about with his finger and his thumb, as one would set up a top.

2 *Serv.* Nay, I knew by his face that there was something in him: He had, sir, a kind of face, methought,—I cannot tell how to term it.

1 *Serv.* He had so: looking as it were,——'Would I were hanged, but I thought there was more in him than I could think.

2 *Serv.* So did I, I'll be sworn: He is simply the rarest man i' the world.

1 *Serv.* I think, he is: but a greater soldier than he, you wot one.

2 *Serv.* Who? my master?

1 *Serv.* Nay, it's no matter for that.

2 *Serv.* Worth six of him.

1 *Serv.* Nay, not so neither; but I take him to be the greater soldier.

2 *Serv.* 'Faith, look you, one cannot tell how to say that: for the defence of a town, our general is excellent.

1 *Serv.* Ay, and for an assault too.

Re-enter third Servant.

3 *Serv.* O, slaves, I can tell you news; news, you rascals.

1, 2 *Serv.* What, what, what? let's partake.

3 *Serv.* I would not be a Roman, of all nations; I had as lieve be a condemned man.

1, 2 *Serv.* Wherefore? wherefore?

3 *Serv.* Why, here's he that was wont to thwack our general,—Caius Marcius.

1 *Serv.* Why do you say, thwack our general?

3 *Serv.* I do not say, thwack our general; but he was always good enough for him.

2 *Serv.* Come, we are fellows, and friends: he was ever too hard for him; I have heard him say so himself.

1 *Serv.* He was too hard for him directly, to say the truth on't: before Corioli, he scotched him and notched him like a carbonado.

2 *Serv.* An he had been cannibally given, he might have broiled and eaten him too.

1 *Serv.* But, more of thy news?

3 *Serv.* Why, he is so made on here within, as if he were son and heir to Mars: set at upper end o' the table: no question asked him by any of the senators, but they stand bald before him: Our general himself makes a mistress of him; sanctifies himself with's hand, and turns up the white o' the eye to his discourse. But the bottom of the news is, our general is cut i' the middle, and but one half of what he was yesterday; for the other has half, by the entreaty and grant of the whole table. He'll go, he says, and sowle the porter of Rome gates by the ears: He will mow down all before him, and leave his passage polled.

2 *Serv.* And he's as like to do't, as any man I can imagine.

3 *Serv.* Do't? he will do't: For, look you, sir, he has as many friends as enemies: which friends, sir (as it were), durst not (look you, sir) show themselves (as we term it) his friends, whilst he's in directitude.

1 *Serv.* Directitude! what's that?

3 *Serv.* But when they shall see, sir, his crest up again, and the man in blood, they will out of their burrows, like conies after rain, and revel all with him.

1 *Serv.* But when goes this forward?

3 *Serv.* To-morrow; to-day; presently. You shall have the drum struck up this afternoon: 'tis, as it were, a parcel of their feast, and to be executed ere they wipe their lips.

2 *Serv.* Why, then we shall have a stirring world again. This peace is nothing, but to rust iron, increase tailors, and breed ballad-makers.

1 *Serv.* Let me have war, say I; it exceeds peace, as far as day does night; it's sprightly, waking, audible, and full of vent. Peace is a very apoplexy, lethargy; mulled, deaf, sleepy, insensible; a getter of more bastard children, than wars a destroyer of men.

2 *Serv.* 'Tis so: and as wars, in some sort, may be said to be a ravisher; so it cannot be denied, but peace is a great maker of cuckolds.

1 *Serv.* Ay, and it makes men hate one another.

3 *Serv.* Reason, because they then less need one another. The wars for my money. I hope to see Romans as cheap as Volcians. They are rising, they are rising.

All. In, in, in, in. [*Exeunt.*

SCENE VI. Rome. *A publick Place.*

Enter SICINIUS *and* BRUTUS.

Sic. We hear not of him, neither need we fear him;
His remedies are tame i' the present peace
And quietness o' the people, which before
Were in wild hurry. Here do we make his friends
Blush, that the world goes well; who rather had,
Though they themselves did suffer by't, behold
Dissentious numbers pestering streets, than see
Our tradesmen singing in their shops, and going
About their functions friendly.

Enter MENENIUS.

Bru. We stood to't in good time. Is this Menenius?

Sic. 'Tis he, 'tis he: O, he is grown most kind
Of late.—Hail, sir!

Men. Hail to you both!

Sic. Your Coriolanus, sir, is not much miss'd,
But with his friends: the commonwealth doth stand;
And so would do, were he more angry at it.

Men. All's well; and might have been much better, if
He could have temporiz'd.

Sic. Where is he, hear you?

Men. Nay, I hear nothing; his mother and his wife
Hear nothing from him.

Enter Three or Four Citizens.

Cit. The gods preserve you both!

Sic. Good e'en, our neighbours.

Bru. Good e'en to you all, good e'en to you all.

1 *Cit.* Ourselves, our wives, and children, on our knees,
Are bound to pray for you both.

Sic. Live, and thrive!

Bru. Farewell, kind neighbours; we wish'd Coriolanus
Had lov'd you as we did.

Cit. Now the gods keep you!

Both Tri. Farewell, farewell. [*Exeunt* Citizens.

Sic. This is a happier and more comely time,
Than when these fellows ran about the streets,
Crying, Confusion.

Bru. Caius Marcius was
A worthy officer i' the war; but insolent,
O'ercome with pride, ambitious past all thinking,
Self-loving,——

Sic. And affecting one sole throne,
Without assistance.

Men. I think not so.

Sic. We should by this, to all our lamentation,
If he had gone forth consul, found it so.

Bru. The gods have well prevented it, and Rome
Sits safe and still without him.

Enter Ædile.

Æd. Worthy tribunes,
There is a slave, whom we have put in prison,
Reports,—the Volces with two several powers
Are enter'd in the Roman territories;
And with the deepest malice of the war
Destroy what lies before them.

Men. 'Tis Aufidius,
Who, hearing of our Marcius' banishment,
Thrusts forth his horns again into the world:
Which were inshell'd, when Marcius stood for Rome
And durst not once peep out.

Sic. Come, what talk you
Of Marcius?

Bru. Go see this rumourer whipp'd.—It cannot be,
The Volces dare break with us.

Men. Cannot be!
We have record, that very well it can;
And three examples of the like have been
Within my age. But reason with the fellow,
Before you punish him, where he heard this:
Lest you should chance to whip your information,
And beat the messenger who bids beware
Of what is to be dreaded.

Sic. Tell not me:
I know, this cannot be.

Bru. Not possible.

Enter a Messenger.

Mess. The nobles, in great earnestness, are going
All to the senate-house: some news is come,
That turns their countenances.

Sic. 'Tis this slave;—
Go whip him 'fore the people's eyes:—his raising!
Nothing but his report!

Mess. Yes, worthy sir,
The slave's report is seconded; and more,
More fearful is deliver'd.

Sic. What more fearful?

Mess. It is spoke freely out of many mouths
(How probable I do not know), that Marcius,
Join'd with Aufidius, leads a power 'gainst Rome;
And vows revenge as spacious, as between
The young'st and oldest thing.

Sic. This is most likely!

Bru. Rais'd only, that the weaker sort may wish
Good Marcius home again.

Sic. The very trick on't.

Men. This is unlikely:
He and Aufidius can no more atone,
Than violentest contrariety.

Enter another Messenger.

Mess. You are sent for to the senate:
A fearful army, led by Caius Marcius,
Associated with Aufidius, rages
Upon our territories; and have already,
O'erborne their way, consum'd with fire, and [took
What lay before them.

Enter COMINIUS.

Com. O, you have made good work!

Men. What news? what news?

Com. You have holp to ravish your own daughters, and
To melt the city leads upon your pates;
To see your wives dishonour'd to your noses;——

Men. What's the news? what's the news?

Com. Your temples burned in their cement; and
Your franchises, whereon you stood, confin'd
Into an augre's bore.

Men. Pray now, your news?—
You have made fair work, I fear me:—Pray, your news?
If Marcius should be join'd with Volcians,——

Com. If!
He is their god; he leads them like a thing
Made by some other deity than nature,
That shapes man better: and they follow him,
Against us brats, with no less confidence,
Than boys pursuing summer butterflies,
Or butchers killing flies.

Men. You have made good work,
You, and your apron men; you that stood so much
Upon the voice of occupation, and
The breath of garlick-eaters!

Com. He will shake
Your Rome about your ears.

Men. As Hercules
Did shake down mellow fruit: You have made fair work!

Bru. But is this true, sir?

Com. Ay; and you'll look pale
Before you find it other. All the regions
Do smilingly revolt, and, who resist,
Are only mock'd for valiant ignorance,
And perish constant fools. Who is't can blame him?
Your enemies, and his, find something in him.

Men. We are all undone, unless
The noble man have mercy.

Com. Who shall ask it?
The tribunes cannot do't for shame; the people
Deserve such pity of him, as the wolf
Does of the shepherds: for his best friends, if they
Should say, *Be good to Rome*, they charg'd him even
As those should do that had deserv'd his hate,
And therein show'd like enemies.

Men. 'Tis true:
If he were putting to my house the brand
That should consume it, I have not the face
To say, '*Beseech you, cease.*—You have made fair hands,
You, and your crafts! you have crafted fair!

Com. You have brought
A trembling upon Rome, such as was never
So incapable of help.

Tri. Say not, we brought it.

Men. How! Was it we? We lov'd him; but, like beasts,
And cowardly nobles, gave way to your clusters,
Who did hoot him out o' the city.

Com. But, I fear
They'll roar him in again. Tullus Aufidius,
The second name of men, obeys his points
As if he were his officer:—Desperation
Is all the policy, strength, and defence,
That Rome can make against them.

Enter a Troop of Citizens.

Men. Here come the clusters.—
And is Aufidius with him?—You are they
That made the air unwholesome, when you cast
Your stinking, greasy caps, in hooting at
Coriolanus' exile. Now he's coming;
And not a hair upon a soldier's head,
Which will not prove a whip: as many coxcombs,
As you threw caps up will he tumble down,
And pay you for your voices. 'Tis no matter;
If he could burn us all into one coal,
We have deserv'd it.

Cit. 'Faith, we hear fearful news.

1 *Cit.* For mine own part,
When I said, banish him, I said, 'twas pity.

2 *Cit.* And so did I.

3 *Cit.* And so did I; and, to say the truth, so did very many of us; That we did, we did for the best: and though we willingly consented to his banishment, yet it was against our will.

Com. You are goodly things, you voices!

Men. You have made
Good work, you and your cry!—Shall us to the Capitol?

Com. O, ay; what else?

[*Exeunt* COMINIUS *and* MENENIUS.

Sic. Go, masters, get you home, be not dismay'd;
These are a side, that would be glad to have
This true, which they so seem to fear. Go home,
And show no sign of fear.

1 *Cit.* The gods be good to us! Come, masters, let's home. I ever said, we were i' the wrong, when we banished him.

2 *Cit.* So did we all. But come, let's home.

[*Exeunt* Citizens.

Bru. I do not like this news.

Sic. Nor I.

Bru. Let's to the Capitol:—Would, half my wealth
Would buy this for a lie!

Sic. Pray, let us go.

[*Exeunt.*

SCENE VII.

A Camp; at a small distance from Rome.

Enter AUFIDIUS, *and his* Lieutenant.

Auf. Do they still fly to the Roman?

Lieu. I do not know what witchcraft's in him; but
Your soldiers use him as the grace 'fore meat,
Their talk at table, and their thanks at end;
And you are darken'd in this action, sir,
Even by your own.

Auf. I cannot help it now;
Unless by using means, I lame the foot
Of our design. He bears himself more proudlier
Even to my person, than I thought he would,
When first I did embrace him: Yet his nature
In that's no changeling; and I must excuse
What cannot be amended.

Lieu. Yet I wish, sir,
(I mean for your particular), you had not
Join'd in commission with him: but either
Had borne the action of yourself, or else
To him had left it solely.

Auf. I understand thee well; and be thou sure,
When he shall come to his account, he knows not
What I can urge against him. Although it seems,
And so he thinks, and is no less apparent
To the vulgar eye, that he bears all things fairly,
And shows good husbandry for the Volcian state;
Fights dragon-like, and does achieve as soon
As draw his sword: yet he hath left undone
That, which shall break his neck, or hazard mine,
Whene'er we come to our account.

Lieu. Sir, I beseech you, think you he'll carry Rome?

Auf. All places yield to him ere he sits down;
And the nobility of Rome are his:
The senators, and patricians, love him too:
The tribunes are no soldiers; and their people
Will be as rash in the repeal, as hasty
To expel him thence. I think, he'll be to Rome,
As is the osprey to the fish, who takes it
By sovereignty of nature. First he was
A noble servant to them; but he could not
Carry his honours even: whether 'twas pride,
Which out of daily fortune ever taints
The happy man; whether defect of judgment,
To fail in the disposing of those chances
Which he was lord of; or whether nature,
Not to be other than one thing, not moving
From the casque to the cushion, but commanding peace
Even with the same austerity and garb
As he controll'd the war: but, one of these
(As he hath spices of them all, not all,
For I dare so far free him), made him fear'd,
So hated, and so banish'd: But he has a merit,
To choke it in the utterance. So our virtues
Lie in the interpretation of the time:
And power, unto itself most commendable,
Hath not a tomb so evident as a hair
To extol what it hath done.
One fire drives out one fire; one nail, one nail;
Rights by rights fouler, strength by strengths do fail.
Come let's away. When, Caius, Rome is thine,
Thou art poor'st of all; then shortly art thou mine.

[*Exeunt.*

ACT V.

SCENE I. Rome. *A publick Place.*

Enter MENENIUS, COMINIUS, SICINIUS, BRUTUS, *and Others.*

Men. No, I'll not go: you hear, what he hath said,
Which was sometime his general; who loved him
In a most dear particular. He call'd me, father:
But what o' that? Go, you that banish'd him,
A mile before his tent fall down, and kneel
The way into his mercy: Nay, if he coy'd
To hear Cominius speak, I'll keep at home.

Com. He would not seem to know me.

Men. Do you hear?

Com. Yet one time he did call me by my name:
I urg'd our old acquaintance, and the drops
That we have bled together. Coriolanus
He would not answer to: forbad all names;
He was a kind of nothing, titleless,
Till he had forg'd himself a name i' the fire
Of burning Rome.

Men. Why so: you have made good work:
A pair of tribunes that have rack'd for Rome,
To make coals cheap: A noble memory!

Com. I minded him how royal 'twas to pardon
When it was less expected: he replied,
It was a bare petition of a state
To one whom they had punish'd.

Men. Very well:
Could he say less?

Com. I offer'd to awaken his regard
For his private friends: His answer to me was,
He could not stay to pick them in a pile
Of noisome, musty chaff: He said, 'twas folly,
For one poor grain or two, to leave unburnt,
And still to nose the offence.

Men. For one poor grain
Or two? I am one of those; his mother, wife,
His child, and this brave fellow too, we are the grains:
You are the musty chaff; and you are smelt
Above the moon: We must be burnt for you.

Sic. Nay, pray, be patient: If you refuse your aid
In this so never-heeded help, yet do not
Upbraid us with our distress. But, sure, if you
Would be your country's pleader, your good tongue,
More than the instant army we can make,
Might stop our countryman.

Men. No; I'll not meddle.

Sic. Pray you, go to him.

Men. What should I do?

Bru. Only make trial what your love can do
For Rome, towards Marcius.

Men. Well, and say that Marcius
Return me, as Cominius is return'd,
Unheard; what then?—
But as a discontented friend, grief-shot
With his unkindness? Say't be so?

Sic. Yet your good will
Must have that thanks from Rome, after the measure
As you intended well.

Men. I'll undertake it:
I think, he'll hear me. Yet to bite his lip,
And hum at good Cominius, much unhearts me.
He was not taken well; he had not din'd:
The veins unfill'd, our blood is cold, and then
We pout upon the morning, are unapt
To give or to forgive; but when we have stuff'd
These pipes and these conveyances of our blood

With wine and feeding, we have suppler souls
Than in our priest-like fasts: therefore I'll watch
Till he be dieted to my request, [him
And then I'll set upon him.

Bru. You know the very road into his kindness,
And cannot lose your way.

Men. Good faith, I'll prove him,
Speed how it will. I shall ere long have knowledge
Of my success. [*Exit.*

Com. He'll never hear him.

Sic. Not?

Com. I tell you, he does sit in gold, his eye
Red as 'twould burn Rome; and his injury
The gaoler to his pity. I kneel'd before him;
'Twas very faintly he said, *Rise;* dismiss'd me
Thus, with his speechless hand; What he would do,
He sent in writing after me; what he would not,
Bound with an oath, to yield to his conditions:
So, that all hope is vain,
Unless his noble mother, and his wife;
Who, as I hear, mean to solicit him
For mercy to his country. Therefore, let's hence,
And with our fair entreaties haste them on.
[*Exeunt.*

SCENE II.

An advanced Post of the Volcian *Camp before* Rome. *The* Guard *at their Stations.*

Enter to them, MENENIUS.

1 G. Stay: Whence are you?

2 G. Stand, and go back.

Men. You guard like men; 'tis well: But, by your leave,
I am an officer of state, and come
To speak with Coriolanus.

1 G. From whence?

Men. From Rome.

1 G. You may not pass, you must return: our general
Will no more hear from thence.

2 G. You'll see your Rome embrac'd with fire, before
You'll speak with Coriolanus.

Men. Good my friends,
If you have heard your general talk of Rome,
And of his friends there, it is lots to blanks,
My name hath touch'd your ears: it is Menenius.

1 G. Be it so; go back: the virtue of your name
Is not here passable.

Men. I tell thee, fellow,
Thy general is my lover: I have been
The book of his good acts, whence men have read
His fame unparallel'd, haply, amplified;
For I have ever verified my friends
(Of whom he's chief), with all the size that verity
Would without lapsing suffer: nay, sometimes,
Like to a bowl upon a subtle ground,
I have tumbled past the throw; and in his praise
Have, almost, stamp'd the leasing: Therefore, fellow,
I must have leave to pass.

1 G. 'Faith, sir, if you had told as many lies in his behalf, as you have uttered words in your own, you should not pass here: no, though it were as virtuous to lie, as to live chastly. Therefore, go back.

Men. Pr'ythee, fellow, remember my name is Menenius, always factionary on the party of your general.

2 G. Howsoever you have been his liar (as you say, you have), I am one that, telling true under him, must say, you cannot pass. Therefore, go back.

Men. Has he dined, canst thou tell? for I would not speak with him till after dinner.

1 G. You are a Roman, are you?

Men. I am as thy general is.

1 G. Then you should hate Rome as he does. Can you, when you have pushed out your gates the very defender of them, and, in a violent popular ignorance, given your enemy your shield, think to front his revenges with the easy groans of old women, the virginal palms of your daughters, or with the palsied intercession of such a decayed dotant as you seem to be? Can you think to blow out the intended fire your city is ready to flame in, with such weak breath as this? No, you are deceived; therefore, back to Rome, and prepare for your execution: you are condemned, our general has sworn you out of reprieve and pardon.

Men. Sirrah, If thy captain knew I were here, he would use me with estimation.

2 G. Come, my captain knows you not.

Men. I mean, thy general.

1 G. My general cares not for you. Back, I say, go, lest I let forth your half pint of blood;—back,—that's the utmost of your having:—back.

Men. Nay, but fellow, fellow,——

Enter CORIOLANUS *and* AUFIDIUS.

Cor. What's the matter?

Men. Now, you companion, I'll say an errand for you; you shall know now that I am in estimation; you shall perceive that a jack guardant cannot office me from my son Coriolanus: guess, but by my entertainment with him, if thou stand'st not i' the state of hanging, or of some death more long in spectatorship, and crueller in suffering; behold now presently, and swoon for what's to come upon thee.—The glorious gods sit in hourly synod about thy particular prosperity, and love thee no worse than thy old father Menenius does! O, my son! my son! thou art preparing fire for us; look thee here's water to quench it. I was hardly moved to come to thee; but being assured, none but myself could move thee, I have been blown out of your gates with sighs; and conjure thee to pardon Rome, and thy petitionary countrymen. The good gods assuage thy wrath, and turn the dregs of it upon this varlet here; this, who, like a block, hath denied my access to thee.

Cor. Away!

Men. How! away?

Cor. Wife, mother, child, I know not. My affairs
Are servanted to others: Though I owe
My revenge properly, my remission lies
In Volcian breasts. That we have been familiar,
Ingrate forgetfulness shall poison, rather
Than pity note how much.—Therefore, be gone.
Mine ears against your suits are stronger, than
Your gates against my force. Yet, for I lov'd thee,
Take this along; I writ it for thy sake,
[*Gives a Letter.*
And would have sent it. Another word, Menenius,
I will not hear thee speak.—This man, Aufidius,
Was my beloved in Rome: yet thou behold'st——

Auf. You keep a constant temper.
[*Exeunt* CORIOLANUS *and* AUFIDIUS.

1 G. Now, sir, is your name Menenius?

2 G. 'Tis a spell, you see, of much power: You know the way home again.

1 G. Do you hear how we are shent for keeping your greatness back?

2 G. What cause do you think, I have to swoon?

Men. I neither care for the world, nor your general: for such things as you, I can scarce think there's any, you are so slight. He that hath a will to die by himself, fears it not from another. Let your general do his worst. For you, be that you are, long; and your misery increase with your age! I say to you, as I was said to, Away! [*Exit.*

1 G. A noble fellow, I warrant him.

2 G. The worthy fellow is our general: He is the rock, the oak not to be wind-shaken.
[*Exeunt.*

SCENE III. *The Tent of* Coriolanus.

Enter CORIOLANUS, AUFIDIUS, *and Others.*

Cor. We will before the walls of Rome to-morrow
Set down our host.—My partner in this action,
You must report to the Volcian lords, how plainly
I have borne this business.

Auf. Only their ends
You have respected; stopp'd your ears against
The general suit of Rome; never admitted
A private whisper, no, not with such friends
That thought them sure of you.

Cor. This last old man,
Whom with a crack'd heart I have sent to Rome,
Loved me above the measure of a father;
Nay, godded me, indeed. Their latest refuge
Was to send him: for whose old love, I have
(Though I show'd sourly to him), once more offer'd
The first conditions, which they did refuse,
And cannot now accept, to grace him only,
That thought he could do more; a very little
I have yielded to: Fresh embassies, and suits,
Nor from the state, nor private friends, hereafter
Will I lend ear to.—Ha! what shout is this?
[*Shout within.*
Shall I be tempted to infringe my vow
In the same time 'tis made? I will not.—

Enter, in mourning habits, VIRGILIA, VOLUMNIA, *leading young* MARCIUS, VALERIA, *and* Attendants.

My wife comes foremost: then the honour'd mould
Wherein this trunk was fram'd, and in her hand
The grandchild to her blood. But, out, affection!
All bond and privilege of nature, break!
Let it be virtuous, to be obstinate.—
What is that curt'sy worth; or those doves' eyes,
Which can make gods forsworn?—I melt, and am not
Of stronger earth than others.—My mother bows;
As if Olympus to a molehill should
In supplication nod: and my young boy
Hath an aspect of intercession, which
Great nature cries, *Deny not.*—Let the Volces
Plough Rome, and harrow Italy; I'll never
Be such a gosling to obey instinct; but stand,
As if a man were author of himself,
And knew no other kin.

Vir. My lord and husband!

Cor. These eyes are not the same I wore in Rome.

Vir. The sorrow, that delivers us thus chang'd,
Makes you think so.

Cor. Like a dull actor now,
I have forgot my part, and I am out,
Even to a full disgrace. Best of my flesh,
Forgive my tyranny; but do not say,
For that, *Forgive our Romans.*—O, a kiss
Long as my exile, sweet as my revenge!
Now by the jealous queen of heaven, that kiss
I carried from thee, dear; and my true lip
Hath virgin'd it e'er since. You gods! I prate,
And the most noble mother of the world
Leave unsaluted: Sink, my knee, i' the earth;
[*Kneels.*
Of thy deep duty more impression show
Than that of common sons.

Vol. O, stand up bless'd!
Whilst, with no softer cushion than the flint,
I kneel before thee; and unproperly
Show duty, as mistaken all the while
Between the child and parent. [*Kneels.*

Cor. What is this?
Your knees to me? to your corrected son?
Then let the pebbles on the hungry beach
Fillip the stars; then let the mutinous winds
Strike the proud cedars 'gainst the fiery sun;
Murd'ring impossibility, to make
What cannot be, slight work.

Vol. Thou art my warrior;
I holp to frame thee. Do you know this lady?

Cor. The noble sister of Publicola,
The moon of Rome; chaste as the icicle,
That's curded by the frost from purest snow,
And hangs on Dian's temple: Dear Valeria!

Vol. This is a poor epitome of yours,
Which by the interpretation of full time
May show like all yourself.

Cor. The god of soldiers,
With the consent of supreme Jove, inform
Thy thoughts with nobleness; that thou may'st prove
To shame unvulnerable, and stick i'the wars
Like a great seamark, standing every flaw,
And saving those that eye thee!

Vol. Your knee, sirrah.

Cor. That's my brave boy.

Vol. Even he, your wife, this lady, and myself,
Are suitors to you.

Cor. I beseech you, peace:
Or, if you'd ask, remember this before;
The things, I have forsworn to grant, may never
Be held by you denials. Do not bid me
Dismiss my soldiers, or capitulate
Again with Rome's mechanicks:—Tell me not
Wherein I seem unnatural: Desire not
To allay my rages and revenges, with
Your colder reasons.

Vol. O, no more, no more!
You have said, you will not grant us any thing;
For we have nothing else to ask, but that
Which you deny already: Yet we will ask;
That, if you fail in our request, the blame
May hang upon your hardness: therefore hear us.

Cor. Aufidius, and you Volces, mark; for we'll
Hear nought from Rome in private.—Your request?

Vol. Should we be silent and not speak, our raiment,
And state of bodies, would bewray what life
We have led since thy exile. Think with thyself,
How more unfortunate than all living women
Are we come hither: since that thy sight, which should
Make our eyes flow with joy, hearts dance with comforts,
Constrains them weep, and shake with fear and sorrow;
Making the mother, wife, and child, to see
The son, the husband, and the father, tearing
His country's bowels out. And to poor we,
Thine enmity's most capital: thou barr'st us
Our prayers to the gods, which is a comfort
That all but we enjoy: For how can we,
Alas! how can we for our country pray,
Whereto we are bound; together with thy victory,
Whereto we are bound? Alack! or we must lose
The country, our dear nurse; or else thy person,
Our comfort in the country. We must find
An evident calamity, though we had
Our wish, which side should win: for either thou
Must, as a foreign recreant, be led
With manacles through our streets, or else
Triumphantly tread on thy country's ruin;
And bear the palm, for having bravely shed
Thy wife and children's blood. For myself, son,
I purpose not to wait on fortune, till
These wars determine: if I cannot persuade thee
Rather to show a noble grace to both parts,
Than seek the end of one, thou shalt no sooner
March to assault thy country, than to tread
(Trust to't, thou shalt not) on thy mother's womb,
That brought thee to this world.

Vir. Ay, and on mine,
That brought you forth this boy, to keep your name
Living to time.

Boy. He shall not tread on me;
I'll run away, till I am bigger, but then I'll fight.
Cor. Not of a woman's tenderness to be,
Requires nor child nor woman's face to see.
I have sat too long. [*Rising.*
Vol. Nay, go not from us thus.
If it were so, that our request did tend
To save the Romans, thereby to destroy
The Volces whom you serve, you might condemn us,
As poisonous of your honour; No; our suit
Is, that you reconcile them; while the Volces
May say, *This mercy we have show'd;* the Romans,
This we receiv'd; and each in either side
Give the all-hail to thee, and cry, *Be bless'd
For making up this peace!* Thou know'st, great son,
The end of war's uncertain; but this certain,
That, if thou conquer Rome, the benefit
Which thou shalt thereby reap, is such a name,
Whose repetition will be dogg'd with curses:
Whose chronicle thus writ,—*The man was noble,
But with his last attempt he wip'd it out:
Destroy'd his country; and his name remains
To the ensuing age abhorr'd.* Speak to me, son:
Thou hast affected the fine strains of honour,
To imitate the graces of the gods;
To tear with thunder the wide cheeks o' the air,
And yet to charge thy sulphur with a bolt
That should but rive an oak. Why dost not speak?
Think'st thou it honourable for a noble man
Still to remember wrongs?—Daughter, speak you:
He cares not for your weeping.—Speak thou, boy:
Perhaps, thy childishness will move him more
Than can our reasons.—There is no man in the world
More bound to his mother; yet here he lets me prate
Like one i' the stocks. Thou hast never in thy life
Show'd thy dear mother any courtesy;
When she (poor hen!) fond of no second brood,
Has cluck'd thee to the wars, and safely home,
Loaden with honour. Say, my request's unjust,
And spurn me back: But if it be not so,
Thou art not honest; and the gods will plague thee,
That thou restrain'st from me the duty, which
To a mother's part belongs.—He turns away:
Down, ladies; let us shame him with our knees.
To his surname Coriolanus 'longs more pride,
Than pity to our prayers. Down; an end:
This is the last;—So we will home to Rome,
And die among our neighbours.—Nay, behold us:
This boy, that cannot tell what he would have,
But kneels, and holds up hands, for fellowship,
Does reason our petition with more strength
Than thou hast to deny't.—Come, let us go:
This fellow had a Volcian to his mother;
His wife is in Corioli, and his child
Like him by chance:—Yet give us our despatch;
I am hush'd until our city be afire,
And then I'll speak a little.
Cor. O mother, mother!
[*Holding* VOLUMNIA *by the Hands, silent.*
What have you done? Behold, the heavens do ope,
The gods look down, and this unnatural scene
They laugh at. O my mother, mother! O!
You have won a happy victory to Rome:
But, for your son,—believe it, O, believe it,
Most dangerously you have with him prevail'd,
If not most mortal to him. But, let it come:—
Aufidius, though I cannot make true wars,
I'll frame convenient peace. Now, good Aufidius,
Were you in my stead, say, would you have heard
A mother less? or granted less, Aufidius?
Auf. I was mov'd withal.
Cor. I dare be sworn, you were:
And, sir, it is no little thing, to make
Mine eyes to sweat compassion. But, good sir,
What peace you'll make, advise me: For my part,
I'll not to Rome, I'll back with you; and pray [you,
Stand to me in this cause.—O mother! wife!
Auf. I am glad thou hast set thy mercy and thy honour
At difference in thee: out of that I'll work
Myself a former fortune. [*Aside.*
[*The Ladies make signs to* CORIOLANUS.
Cor. Ay, by and by;
[*To* VOLUMNIA, VIRGILIA, *&c.*
But we will drink together; and you shall bear
A better witness back than words, which we,
On like conditions, will have counterseal'd.
Come enter with us. Ladies, you deserve
To have a temple built you: all the swords
In Italy, and her confederate arms,
Could not have made this peace. [*Exeunt.*

SCENE IV. Rome. *A publick Place.*

Enter MENENIUS *and* SICINIUS.

Men. See you yond' coign o' the Capitol: yond' corner stone?

Sic. Why, what of that?

Men. If it be possible for you to displace it with your little finger, there is some hope the ladies of Rome, especially his mother, may prevail with him. But I say, there is no hope in't; our throats are sentenced, and stay upon execution.

Sic. Is't possible, that so short a time can alter the condition of a man?

Men. There is differency between a grub and a butterfly; yet your butterfly was a grub. This Marcius is grown from man to dragon; he has wings; he's more than a creeping thing.

Sic. He loved his mother dearly.

Men. So did he me: and he no more remembers his mother now, than an eight year old horse. The tartness of his face sours ripe grapes. When he walks, he moves like an engine, and the ground shrinks before his treading. He is able to pierce a corslet with his eye; talks like a knell, and his hum is a battery. He sits in his state, as a thing made for Alexander. What he bids be done, is finished with his bidding. He wants nothing of a god but eternity, and a heaven to throne in.

Sic. Yes, mercy, if you report him truly.

Men. I paint him in the character. Mark what mercy his mother shall bring from him: There is no more mercy in him, than there is milk in a male tiger; that shall our poor city find: and all this is 'long of you.

Sic. The gods be good unto us!

Men. No, in such a case the gods will not be good unto us. When we banished him, we respected not them; and, he returning to break our necks, they respect not us.

Enter a Messenger.

Mess. Sir, if you'd save your life, fly to your house;
The plebeians have got your fellow tribune,
And hale him up and down; all swearing, if
The Roman ladies bring not comfort home,
They'll give him death by inches.

Enter another Messenger.

Sic. What's the news?
Mess. Good news, good news:—The ladies have prevail'd,
The Volces are dislodg'd, and Marcius gone:
A merrier day did never yet greet Rome,
No, not the expulsion of the Tarquins.
Sic. Friend,
Art thou certain this is true? Is it most certain?
Mess. As certain as I know the sun is fire;

Where have you lurk'd, that you make doubt of it?
Ne'er through an arch so hurried the blown tide,
As the recomforted through the gates. Why, hark you;
[*Trumpets and Hautboys sounded, and Drums beaten, all together. Shouting also within.*
The trumpets, suckbuts, psalteries, and fifes,
Tabors, and cymbals, and the shouting Romans,
Make the sun dance. Hark you!
[*Shouting again.*
Men. This is good news:
I will go meet the ladies. This Volumnia
Is worth of consuls, senators, patricians,
A city full; of tribunes, such as you,
A sea and land full: You have pray'd well to-day;
This morning, for ten thousand of your throats
I'd not have given a doit. Hark, how they joy!
[*Shouting and Musick.*
Sic. First, the gods bless you for your tidings; next,
Accept my thankfulness.
Mess. Sir, we have all
Great cause to give great thanks.
Sic. They are near the city?
Mess. Almost at point to enter.
Sic. We will meet them,
And help the joy. [*Going.*

Enter the Ladies, *accompanied by* Senators, Patricians, *and* People. *They pass over the Stage.*

1 *Sen.* Behold our patroness, the life of Rome;
Call all your tribes together, praise the gods,
And make triumphant fires; strew flowers before them;
Unshout the noise that banish'd Marcius,
Repeal him with the welcome of his mother;
Cry,—Welcome, ladies, welcome!—
All. Welcome, ladies!
Welcome! [*A Flourish with Drums and Trumpets.*
[*Exeunt.*

SCENE V. Antium. *A publick Place.*

Enter TULLUS AUFIDIUS, *with* Attendants.

Auf. Go tell the lords of the city, I am here:
Deliver them this paper: having read it,
Bid them repair to the market-place; where I,
Even in theirs, and in the common's ears,
Will vouch the truth of it. Him I accuse,
The city ports by this hath enter'd, and
Intends to appear before the people, hoping
To purge himself with words: Despatch.
[*Exeunt* Attendants.

Enter Three or Four Conspirators *of* Aufidius' *Faction.*

Most welcome!
1 *Con.* How is it with our general?
Auf. Even so,
As with a man by his own alms empoison'd,
And with his charity slain.
2 *Con.* Most noble sir,
If you do hold the same intent wherein
You wish'd us parties, we'll deliver you
Of your great danger.
Auf. Sir, I cannot tell;
We must proceed, as we do find the people.
3 *Con.* The people will remain uncertain, whilst
'Twixt you there's difference; but the fall of either
Makes the survivor heir of all.
Auf. I know it;
And my pretext to strike at him admits
A good construction. I rais'd him, and I pawn'd
Mine honour for his truth: Who being so heighten'd,
He water'd his new plants with dews of flattery,
Seducing so my friends: and, to this end,
He bow'd his nature, never known before
But to be rough, unswayable, and free.
3 *Con.* Sir, his stoutness,
When he did stand for consul, which he lost
By lack of stooping,——
Auf. That I would have spoke of:
Being banish'd for't, he came unto my hearth;
Presented to my knife his throat: I took him;
Made him joint servant with me; gave him way
In all his own desires: nay, let him choose
Out of my files, his projects to accomplish,
My best and freshest men; serv'd his designments
In mine own person; holp to reap the fame,
Which he did end all his; and took some pride
To do myself this wrong: till, at the last,
I seem'd his follower, not partner; and
He wag'd me with his countenance, as if
I had been mercenary.
1 *Con.* So he did, my lord:
The army marvell'd at it. And, in the last,
When he had carried Rome; and that we look'd
For no less spoil, than glory,—
Auf. There was it:—
For which my sinews shall be stretch'd upon him.
At a few drops of women's rheum, which are
As cheap as lies, he sold the blood and labour
Of our great action; Therefore shall he die,
And I'll renew me in his fall. But, hark!
[*Drums and Trumpets sound, with great Shouts of the People.*
1 *Con.* Your native town you enter'd like a post,
And had no welcomes home; but he returns,
Splitting the air with noise.
2 *Con.* And patient fools,
Whose children he hath slain, their base throats tear,
With giving him glory.
3 *Con.* Therefore, at your vantage,
Ere he express himself, or move the people
With what he would say, let him feel your sword,
Which we will second. When he lies along,
After your way his tale pronounc'd shall bury
His reasons with his body.
Auf. Say no more;
Here come the lords.

Enter the Lords *of the City.*

Lords. You are most welcome home.
Auf. I have not deserv'd it;
But, worthy lords, have you with heed perus'd
What I have written to you?
Lords. We have.
1 *Lord.* And grieve to hear it.
What faults he made before the last, I think,
Might have found easy fines: but there to end
Where he was to begin; and give away
The benefit of our levies, answering us
With our own charge: making a treaty, where
There was a yielding; This admits no excuse.
Auf. He approaches, you shall hear him.

Enter CORIOLANUS, *with Drums and Colours; a Crowd of* Citizens *with him.*

Cor. Hail, lords! I am return'd your soldier,
No more infected with my country's love,
Than when I parted hence, but still subsisting
Under your great command. You are to know,
That prosperously I have attempted, and
With bloody passage, led your wars, even to
The gates of Rome. Our spoils we have brought home,
Do more than counterpoise, a full third part,
The charges of the action. We have made peace
With no less honour to the Antiates,
Than shame to the Romans: And we here deliver,
Subscrib'd by the consuls and patricians,
Together with the seal o' the senate, what
We have compounded on.
Auf. Read it not, noble lords:
But tell the traitor, in the highest degree
He hath abus'd your powers.

Cor. Traitor?—How now!
Auf. Ay, traitor Marcius.
Cor. Marcius!
Auf. Ay, Marcius, Caius Marcius; Dost thou think
I'll grace thee with that robbery, thy stol'n name
Coriolanus in Corioli?—
You lords and heads of the state, perfidiously
He has betray'd your business, and given up,
For certain drops of salt, your city Rome
(I say, your city), to his wife and mother:
Breaking his oath and resolution, like
A twist of rotten silk; never admitting
Counsel o' the war; but at his nurse's tears
He whin'd and roar'd away your victory:
That pages blush'd at him, and men of heart
Look'd wondering each at other.
Cor. Hear'st thou, Mars?
Auf. Name not the god, thou boy of tears,—
Cor. Ha!
Auf. No more.
Cor. Measureless liar, thou hast made my heart
Too great for what contains it. Boy! O slave!—
Pardon me, lords, 'tis the first time that ever
I was forc'd to scold. Your judgments, my grave lords,
Must give this cur the lie: and his own notion
(Who wears my stripes impress'd on him; that must bear
My beating to his grave) shall join to thrust
The lie unto him.
1 Lord. Peace, both, and hear me speak.
Cor. Cut me to pieces, Volces; men and lads,
Stain all your edges on me.—Boy! False hound!
If you have writ your annals true, 'tis there,
That like an eagle in a dovecote, I
Flutter'd your Volces in Corioli:
Alone I did it.—Boy!
Auf. Why, noble lords,
Will you be put in mind of his blind fortune,
Which was your shame, by this unholy braggart,
'Fore your own eyes and ears?
Con. Let him die for't. [*Several speak at once.*
Cit. [*Speaking promiscuously.*] Tear him to pieces, do it presently. He killed my son;—my daughter;—He killed my cousin Marcus;—He killed my father.
2 Lord. Peace, ho;—no outrage;—peace.
The man is noble, and his fame folds in
This orb o' the earth. His last offence to us
Shall have judicious hearing.—Stand, Aufidius,
And trouble not the peace.
Cor. O, that I had him,
With six Aufidiuses, or more, his tribe,
To use my lawful sword!
Auf. Insolent villain!
Con. Kill, kill, kill, kill, kill him.
[AUFIDIUS *and the* Conspirators *draw, and kill* CORIOLANUS, *who falls, and* AUFIDIUS *stands on him.*
Lords. Hold, hold, hold, hold.
Auf. My noble masters, hear me speak.
1 Lord. O Tullus!—
2 Lord. Thou hast done a deed whereat valour will weep.
3 Lord. Tread not upon him.—Masters all, be quiet;
Put up your swords.
Auf. My lords, when you shall know (as in this rage,
Provok'd by him, you cannot) the great danger
Which this man's life did owe you, you'll rejoice
That he is thus cut off. Please it your honours
To call me to your senate, I'll deliver
Myself your loyal servant, or endure
Your heaviest censure.
1 Lord. Bear from hence his body,
And mourn you for him: let him be regarded
As the most noble corse, that ever herald
Did follow to his urn.
2 Lord. His own impatience
Takes from Aufidius a great part of blame.
Let's make the best of it.
Auf. My rage is gone,
And I am struck with sorrow.—Take him up:
Help, three o'the chiefest soldiers; I'll be one.—
Beat thou the drum that it speak mournfully:
Trail your steel pikes.—Though in this city he
Hath widow'd and unchilded many a one,
Which to this hour bewail the injury,
Yet he shall have a noble memory.—
Assist.
[*Exeunt, bearing the body of* Coriolanus. *A dead March sounded.*

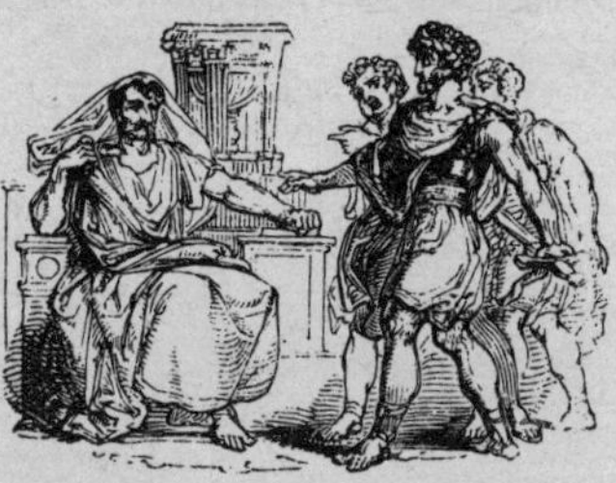

JULIUS CÆSAR.

PERSONS REPRESENTED.

JULIUS CÆSAR.
OCTAVIUS CÆSAR, MARCUS ANTONIUS, M. ÆMIL. LEPIDUS, } *Triumvirs after the Death of* Julius Cæsar.
CICERO, PUBLIUS, POPILIUS LENA, *Senators.*
MARCUS BRUTUS, CASSIUS, CASCA, TREBONIUS, LIGARIUS, DECIUS BRUTUS, METELLUS CIMBER, CINNA, } *Conspirators against* Julius Cæsar.
FLAVIUS *and* MARULLUS, *Tribunes.*
ARTEMIDORUS, *a Sophist of* Cnidos.
A Soothsayer.
CINNA, *a Poet.* *Another* Poet.
LUCILIUS, TITINIUS, MESSALA, *young* CATO, *and* VOLUMNIUS, *Friends to* Brutus *and* Cassius.
VARRO, CLITUS, CLAUDIUS, STRATO, LUCIUS, DARDANIUS, *Servants to* Brutus.
PINDARUS, *Servant to* Cassius.

CALPHURNIA, *Wife to* Cæsar.
PORTIA, *Wife to* Brutus.

Senators, Citizens, Guards, Attendants, *&c.*

SCENE—*during a great part of the Play, at* Rome; *afterwards at* Sardis; *and near* Philippi.

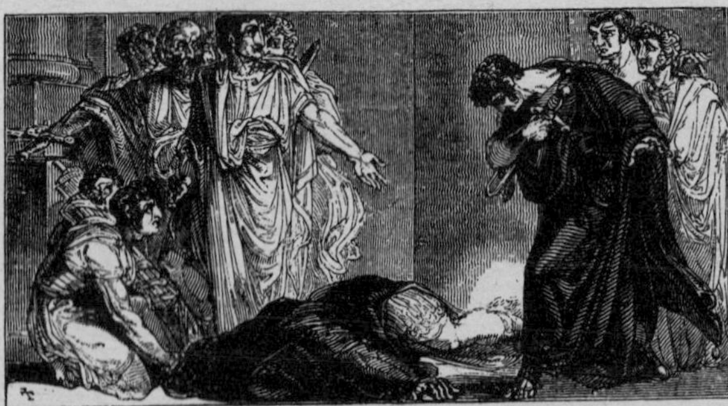

ACT I.

SCENE I. Rome. *A Street.*

Enter FLAVIUS, MARULLUS, *and a Rabble of* Citizens.

Flav. HENCE; home, you idle creatures, get you home;
Is this a holiday? What! know you not,
Being mechanical, you ought not walk,
Upon a labouring day, without the sign
Of your profession?—Speak, what trade art thou?

1 *Cit.* Why, sir, a carpenter.

Mar. Where is thy leather apron, and thy rule?
What dost thou with thy best apparel on?—
You, sir; what trade are you?

2 *Cit.* Truly, sir, in respect of a fine workman, I am but, as you would say, a cobbler.

Mar. But what trade art thou? Answer me directly.

2 *Cit.* A trade, sir, that, I hope, I may use with a safe conscience: which is, indeed, sir, a mender of bad soals.

Mar. What trade, thou knave; thou naughty knave, what trade?

2 *Cit.* Nay, I beseech you, sir, be not out with me: yet, if you be out, sir, I can mend you.

Mar. What mean'st thou by that? Mend me, thou saucy fellow?

2 *Cit.* Why, sir, cobble you.

Flav. Thou art a cobbler, art thou?

2 *Cit.* Truly, sir, all that I live by is, with the awl: I meddle with no tradesman's matters, nor women's matters, but with awl. I am, indeed, sir, a surgeon to old shoes; when they are in great danger, I recover them. As proper men as ever trod upon neat's leather, have gone upon my handy work.

Flav. But wherefore art not in thy shop to-day?
Why dost thou lead these men about the streets?

2 *Cit.* Truly, sir, to wear out their shoes, to get myself into more work. But, indeed, sir, we make holiday, to see Cæsar, and to rejoice in his triumph.

Mar. Wherefore rejoice? What conquest brings he home?
What tributaries follow him to Rome,
To grace in captive bonds his chariot wheels?
You blocks, you stones, you worse than senseless things!
O, you hard hearts, you cruel men of Rome,
Knew you not Pompey? Many a time and oft
Have you climb'd up to walls and battlements,
To towers and windows, yea, to chimney tops,
Your infants in your arms, and there have sat
The live-long day, with patient expectation,
To see great Pompey pass the streets of Rome;
And when you saw his chariot but appear,
Have you not made an universal shout,
That Tyber trembled underneath her banks,
To hear the replication of your sounds,
Made in her concave shores?
And do you now put on your best attire?
And do you now cull out a holiday?
And do you now strew flowers in his way,
That comes in triumph over Pompey's blood?
Be gone;
Run to your houses, fall upon your knees,

Pray to the gods to intermit the plague
That needs must light on this ingratitude.
Flav. Go, go, good countrymen, and, for this fault,
Assemble all the poor men of your sort;
Draw them to Tyber banks, and weep your tears
Into the channel, till the lowest stream
Do kiss the most exalted shores of all.
[*Exeunt* Citizens.
See, whe'r their basest metal be not mov'd:
They vanish tongue-tied in their guiltiness.
Go you down that way towards the Capitol:
This way will I: Disrobe the images,
If you do find them deck'd with ceremonies.
Mar. May we do so?
You know it is the feast of Lupercal.
Flav. It is no matter; let no images
Be hung with Cæsar's trophies. I'll about,
And drive away the vulgar from the streets:
So do you too, where you perceive them thick.
These growing feathers pluck'd from Cæsar's wing,
Will make him fly an ordinary pitch;
Who else would soar above the view of men,
And keep us all in servile fearfulness. [*Exeunt.*

SCENE II. *The same. A publick Place.*

Enter, in Procession, with Musick, CÆSAR; ANTONY, *for the course;* CALPHURNIA, PORTIA, DECIUS, CICERO, BRUTUS, CASSIUS, *and* CASCA, *a great Crowd following, among them a* Soothsayer.

Cæs. Calphurnia,—
Casca. Peace, ho! Cæsar speaks.
[*Musick ceases.*
Cæs. Calphurnia,—
Cal. Here, my lord.
Cæs. Stand you directly in Antonius' way,
When he doth run his course.—Antonius.
Ant. Cæsar, my lord.
Cæs. Forget not, in your speed, Antonius,
To touch Calphurnia: for our elders say,
The barren, touched in this holy chase,
Shake off their steril curse.
Ant. I shall remember:
When Cæsar says, *Do this,* it is perform'd.
Cæs. Set on; and leave no ceremony out.
[*Musick.*
Sooth. Cæsar.
Cæs. Ha! who calls?
Casca. Bid every noise be still:—Peace yet again. [*Musick ceases.*
Cæs. Who is it in the press, that calls on me?
I hear a tongue, shriller than all the musick,
Cry, Cæsar: Speak; Cæsar is turn'd to hear.
Sooth. Beware the ides of March.
Cæs. What man is that?
Bru. A soothsayer, bids you beware the ides of March.
Cæs. Set him before me, let me see his face.
Cas. Fellow, come from the throng: Look upon Cæsar.
Cæs. What say'st thou to me now? Speak once again.
Sooth. Beware the ides of March.
Cæs. He is a dreamer; let us leave him;—pass.
[*Sennet. Exeunt all but* BRU. *and* CAS.
Cas. Will you go see the order of the course?
Bru. Not I.
Cas. I pray you, do.
Bru. I am not gamesome; I do lack some part
Of that quick spirit that is in Antony.
Let me not hinder, Cassius, your desires;
I'll leave you.
Cas. Brutus, I do observe you now of late:
I have not from your eyes that gentleness,
And show of love, as I was wont to have:
You bear too stubborn and too strange a hand
Over your friend that loves you.
Bru. Cassius,
Be not deceiv'd: if I have veil'd my look,
I turn the trouble of my countenance
Merely upon myself. Vexed I am,
Of late, with passions of some difference,
Conceptions only proper to myself,
Which give some soil, perhaps, to my behaviours:
But let not therefore my good friends be griev'd
(Among which number, Cassius, be you one);
Nor construe any further my neglect,
Than that poor Brutus, with himself at war,
Forgets the shows of love to other men.
Cas. Then, Brutus, I have much mistook your passion,
By means whereof, this breast of mine hath buried
Thoughts of great value, worthy cogitations.
Tell me, good Brutus, can you see your face?
Bru. No, Cassius; for the eye sees not itself,
But by reflection, by some other things.
Cas. 'Tis just:
And it is very much lamented, Brutus,
That you have no such mirrors, as will turn
Your hidden worthiness into your eye,
That you might see your shadow. I have heard,
Where many of the best respect in Rome
(Except immortal Cæsar), speaking of Brutus,
And groaning underneath this age's yoke,
Have wish'd that noble Brutus had his eyes.
Bru. Into what dangers would you lead me, Cassius,
That you would have me seek into myself
For that which is not in me?
Cas. Therefore, good Brutus, be prepar'd to hear:
And, since you know you cannot see yourself
So well as by reflection, I, your glass,
Will modestly discover to yourself
That of yourself which you yet know not of.
And be not jealous of me, gentle Brutus:
Were I a common laugher, or did use
To stale with ordinary oaths my love
To every new protester: if you know
That I do fawn on men, and hug them hard,
And after scandal them; or if you know
That I profess myself in banqueting
To all the rout, then hold me dangerous.
[*Flourish and Shout.*
Bru. What means this shouting? I do fear, the people
Choose Cæsar for their king.
Cas. Ay, do you fear it?
Then must I think you would not have it so.
Bru. I would not, Cassius; yet I love him well:—
But wherefore do you hold me here so long?
What is it that you would impart to me?
If it be aught toward the general good,
Set honour in one eye, and death i' the other,
And I will look on both indifferently:
For, let the gods so speed me, as I love
The name of honour more than I fear death.
Cas. I know that virtue to be in you, Brutus,
As well as I do know your outward favour.
Well, honour is the subject of my story.—
I cannot tell what you and other men
Think of this life; but, for my single self,
I had as lief not be, as live to be
In awe of such a thing as I myself.
I was born free as Cæsar; so were you:
We both have fed as well: and we can both
Endure the winter's cold, as well as he.
For once, upon a raw and gusty day,
The troubled Tyber chafing with her shores,
Cæsar said to me, *Dar'st thou,* Cassius, *now
Leap in with me into this angry flood,
And swim to yonder point?* Upon the word,
Accoutred as I was, I plunged in,
And bade him follow: so, indeed, he did.
The torrent roar'd; and we did buffet it
With lusty sinews; throwing it aside
And stemming it with hearts of controversy.
But ere we could arrive the point propos'd,
Cæsar cry'd, *Help me,* Cassius, *or I sink.*

I, as Æneas, our great ancestor,
Did from the flames of Troy upon his shoulder
The old Anchises bear, so, from the waves of Tyber
Did I the tired Cæsar: And this man
Is now become a god; and Cassius is
A wretched creature, and must bend his body,
If Cæsar carelessly but nod on him.
He had a fever when he was in Spain,
And, when the fit was on him, I did mark
How he did shake: 'tis true, this god did shake:
His coward lips did from their colour fly;
And that same eye, whose bend doth awe the world,
Did lose his lustre: I did hear him groan:
Ay, and that tongue of his, that bade the Romans
Mark him, and write his speeches in their books,
Alas! it cried, *Give me some drink*, Titinius,
As a sick girl. Ye gods, it doth amaze me,
A man of such a feeble temper should
So get the start of the majestick world,
And bear the palm alone. [*Shout. Flourish.*

Bru. Another general shout!
I do believe, that these applauses are
For some new honours that are heap'd on Cæsar.

Cas. Why, man, he doth bestride the narrow world,
Like a Colossus; and we petty men
Walk under his huge legs, and peep about
To find ourselves dishonourable graves.
Men at some time are masters of their fates:
The fault, dear Brutus, is not in our stars,
But in ourselves, that we are underlings.
Brutus, and Cæsar: What should be in that Cæsar?
Why should that name be sounded more than yours?
Write them together, yours is as fair a name;
Sound them, it doth become the mouth as well;
Weigh them, it is as heavy; conjure with them,
Brutus will start a spirit as soon as Cæsar. [*Shout.*
Now in the names of all the gods at once,
Upon what meat doth this our Cæsar feed,
That he is grown so great? Age, thou art sham'd:
Rome, thou hast lost the breed of noble bloods!
When went there by an age, since the great flood,
But it was fam'd with more than with one man?
When could they say, till now, that talk'd of Rome,
That her wide walks encompass'd but one man?
Now is it Rome indeed, and room enough,
When there is in it but one only man.
O! you and I have heard our fathers say,
There was a Brutus once, that would have brook'd
The eternal devil to keep his state in Rome,
As easily as a king.

Bru. That you do love me, I am nothing jealous;
What you would work me to, I have some aim;
How I have thought of this, and of these times,
I shall recount hereafter; for this present,
I would not, so with love I might entreat you,
Be any further mov'd. What you have said,
I will consider; what you have to say,
I will with patience hear: and find a time
Both meet to hear, and answer, such high things.
Till then, my noble friend, chew upon this;
Brutus had rather be a villager,
Than to repute himself a son of Rome
Under these hard conditions as this time
Is like to lay upon us.

Cas. I am glad that my weak words
Have struck but thus much show of fire from Brutus.

Re-enter CÆSAR, *and his* Train.

Bru. The games are done, and Cæsar is returning.

Cas. As they pass by, pluck Casca by the sleeve:
And he will, after his sour fashion, tell you
What hath proceeded, worthy note, to-day.

Bru. I will do so:—But, look you, Cassius,
The angry spot doth glow on Cæsar's brow,
And all the rest look like a chidden train:
Calphurnia's cheek is pale; and Cicero
Looks with such ferret and such fiery eyes,
As we have seen him in the Capitol,
Being cross'd in conference by some senators.

Cas. Casca will tell us what the matter is.

Cæs. Antonius.

Ant. Cæsar.

Cæs. Let me have men about me that are fat;
Sleek-headed men, and such as sleep o'nights:
Yond' Cassius has a lean and hungry look;
He thinks too much: such men are dangerous.

Ant. Fear him not, Cæsar, he's not dangerous:
He's a noble Roman, and well given.

Cæs. 'Would he were fatter:—But I fear him not:
Yet if my name were liable to fear,
I do not know the man I should avoid
So soon as that spare Cassius. He reads much;
He is a great observer, and he looks
Quite through the deeds of men: he loves no plays,
As thou dost, Antony; he hears no musick:
Seldom he smiles; and smiles in such a sort,
As if he mock'd himself, and scorn'd his spirit
That could be mov'd to smile at any thing.
Such men as he be never at heart's ease,
Whiles they behold a greater than themselves;
And therefore are they very dangerous.
I rather tell thee what is to be fear'd,
Than what I fear, for always I am Cæsar.
Come on my right hand, for this ear is deaf,
And tell me truly what thou think'st of him.

[*Exeunt* CÆSAR *and his* Train. CASCA *stays behind.*

Casca. You pull'd me by the cloak; Would you speak with me?

Bru. Ay, Casca; tell us what hath chanc'd to-day,
That Cæsar looks so sad.

Casca. Why you were with him, were you not?

Bru. I should not then ask Casca what hath chanc'd.

Casca. Why, there was a crown offer'd him; and being offer'd him, he put it by with the back of his hand, thus; and then the people fell a' shouting.

Bru. What was the second noise for?

Casca. Why, for that too.

Cas. They shouted thrice? What was the last cry for?

Casca. Why, for that too.

Bru. Was the crown offered him thrice?

Casca. Ay, marry, was't, and he put it by thrice, every time gentler than other; and at every putting by, mine honest neighbours shouted.

Cas. Who offered him the crown?

Casca. Why, Antony.

Bru. Tell us the manner of it, gentle Casca.

Casca. I can as well be hanged, as tell the manner of it: it was mere foolery. I did not mark it. I saw Mark Antony offer him a crown;—yet 'twas not a crown neither, 'twas one of these coronets;—and, as I told you, he put it by once; but, for all that, to my thinking, he would fain have had it. Then he offered it to him again; then he put it by again: but, to my thinking, he was very loath to lay his fingers off it. And then he offered it the third time; he put it the third time by: and still as he refused it, the rabblement hooted, and clapped their chopped hands, and threw up their sweaty night-caps, and uttered such a deal of stinking breath because Cæsar refused the crown, that it had almost choked Cæsar; for he swooned, and fell down at it: And for mine own part, I durst not laugh, for fear of opening my lips, and receiving the bad air.

Cas. But, soft, I pray you; What? did Cæsar swoon?

Casca. He fell down in the market-place, and foamed at mouth, and was speechless.

Bru. 'Tis very like: he hath the falling sickness.

Cas. No, Cæsar hath it not; but you, and I,
And honest Casca, we have the falling sickness.

Casca. I know not what you mean by that; but, I am sure, Cæsar fell down. If the tag-rag people did not clap him, and hiss him, according as he pleased, and displeased them, as they use to do the players in the theatre, I am no true man.

Bru. What said he, when he came unto himself?

Casca. Marry, before he fell down, when he perceiv'd the common herd was glad he refused the crown, he plucked me ope his doublet, and offered them his throat to cut.—An I had been a man of any occupation, if I would not have taken him at a word, I would I might go to hell among the rogues:—and so he fell. When he came to himself again, he said, If he had done, or said any thing amiss, he desired their worships to think it was his infirmity. Three or four wenches, where I stood, cried, *Alas, good soul!*—and forgave him with all their hearts: But there's no heed to be taken of them; if Cæsar had stabbed their mothers, they would have done no less.

Bru. And after that, he came, thus sad, away?

Casca. Ay.

Cas. Did Cicero say any thing?

Casca. Ay, he spoke Greek.

Cas. To what effect?

Casca. Nay, an I tell you that, I'll ne'er look you i'the face again: But those, that understood him, smiled at one another, and shook their heads; but, for mine own part, it was Greek to me. I could tell you more news too: Marullus and Flavius, for pulling scarfs off Cæsar's images, are put to silence. Fare you well. There was more foolery yet, if I could remember it.

Cas. Will you sup with me to-night, Casca?

Casca. No, I am promised forth.

Cas. Will you dine with me to-morrow?

Casca. Ay, if I be alive, and your mind hold, and your dinner worth the eating.

Cas. Good; I will expect you.

Casca. Do so; Farewell, both. [*Exit* CASCA.

Bru. What a blunt fellow is this grown to be?
He was quick mettle, when he went to school.

Cas. So he is now, in execution
Of any bold or noble enterprise,
However he puts on this tardy form.
This rudeness is a sauce to his good wit,
Which gives men stomach to digest his words
With better appetite.

Bru. And so it is. For this time I will leave you:
To-morrow, if you please to speak with me,
I will come home to you: or, if you will,
Come home to me, and I will wait for you.

Cas. I will do so:—till then, think of the world.
[*Exit* BRUTUS.
Well, Brutus, thou art noble; yet, I see,
Thy honourable metal may be wrought
From that it is disposed: Therefore 'tis meet
That noble minds keep ever with their likes:
For who so firm, that cannot be seduc'd?
Cæsar doth bear me hard; but he loves Brutus:
If I were Brutus now, and he were Cassius,
He should not humour me. I will this night,
In several hands, in at his windows throw,
As if they came from several citizens,
Writings all tending to the great opinion
That Rome holds of his name: wherein obscurely
Cæsar's ambition shall be glanced at:
And, after this, let Cæsar seat him sure;
For we will shake him, or worse days endure.
[*Exit.*

SCENE III. *The same. A Street.*

Thunder and Lightning. Enter, from opposite sides, CASCA, *with his sword drawn, and* CICERO.

Cic. Good even, Casca: Brought you Cæsar home?
Why are you breathless? and why stare you so?

Casca. Are not you mov'd, when all the sway of earth
Shakes, like a thing unfirm? O Cicero,
I have seen tempests, when the scolding winds
Have riv'd the knotty oaks; and I have seen
The ambitious ocean swell, and rage, and foam,
To be exalted with the threat'ning clouds:
But never till to-night, never till now,
Did I go through a tempest dropping fire.
Either there is a civil strife in heaven;
Or else the world, too saucy with the gods,
Incenses them to send destruction.

Cic. Why, saw you any thing more wonderful?

Casca. A common slave (you know him well by sight),
Held up his left hand, which did flame and burn
Like twenty torches join'd; and yet his hand,
Not sensible of fire, remain'd unscorch'd.
Besides (I have not since put up my sword),
Against the Capitol I met a lion,
Who glar'd upon me, and went surly by,
Without annoying me! And there were drawn
Upon a heap a hundred ghastly women,
Transformed with their fear: who swore, they saw
Men, all in fire, walk up and down the streets.
And yesterday, the bird of night did sit,
Even at noon-day, upon the market-place,
Hooting and shrieking. When these prodigies
Do so conjointly meet, let not men say,
These are their reasons,—They are natural;
For, I believe, they are portentous things
Unto the climate that they point upon.

Cic. Indeed, it is a strange-disposed time:
But men may construe things after their fashion,
Clean from the purpose of the things themselves.
Comes Cæsar to the Capitol to-morrow?

Casca. He doth; for he did bid Antonius
Send word to you, he would be there to-morrow.

Cic. Good night then, Casca: this disturbed sky
Is not to walk in.

Casca. Farewell, Cicero.
[*Exit* CICERO.

Enter CASSIUS.

Cas. Who's there?

Casca. A Roman.

Cas. Casca, by your voice.

Casca. Your ear is good. Cassius, what night is this?

Cas. A very pleasing night to honest men.

Casca. Who ever knew the heavens menace so?

Cas. Those, that have known the earth so full of faults.
For my part, I have walk'd about the streets,
Submitting me unto the perilous night:
And, thus unbraced, Casca, as you see,
Have bar'd my bosom to the thunder stone:
And, when the cross blue lightning seem'd to open
The breast of heaven, I did present myself
Even in the aim and very flash of it.

Casca. But wherefore did you so much tempt the heavens?
It is the part of men to fear and tremble,
When the most mighty gods, by tokens, send
Such dreadful heralds to astonish us.

Cas. You are dull, Casca; and those sparks of life
That should be in a Roman, you do want,
Or else you use not: You look pale, and gaze,
And put on fear, and cast yourself in wonder,
To see the strange impatience of the heavens:
But if you would consider the true cause,
Why all these fires, why all these gliding ghosts,

Why birds, and beasts, from quality and kind;
Why old men, fools, and children calculate;
Why all these things change, from their ordinance,
Their natures, and preformed faculties,
To monstrous quality; why, you shall find,
That heaven hath infus'd them with these spirits,
To make them instruments of fear, and warning,
Unto some monstrous state. Now, could I, Casca,
Name to thee a man most like this dreadful night;
That thunders, lightens, opens graves, and roars
As doth the lion in the Capitol:
A man no mightier than thyself, or me,
In personal action; yet prodigious grown
And fearful, as these strange eruptions are.

Casca. 'Tis Cæsar that you mean: Is it not, Cassius?

Cas. Let it be who it is: for Romans now
Have thewes and limbs like to their ancestors;
But, woe the while! our fathers' minds are dead,
And we are govern'd with our mothers' spirits;
Our yoke and sufferance show us womanish.

Casca. Indeed, they say, the senators to-morrow
Mean to establish Cæsar as a king:
And he shall wear his crown by sea and land,
In every place, save here in Italy.

Cas. I know where I will wear this dagger then;
Cassius from bondage will deliver Cassius:
Therein, ye gods, you make the weak most strong;
Therein, ye gods, you tyrants do defeat:
Nor stony tower, nor walls of beaten brass,
Nor airless dungeon, nor strong links of iron,
Can be retentive to the strength of spirit;
But life, being weary of these worldly bars,
Never lacks power to dismiss itself.
If I know this, know all the world besides,
That part of tyranny, that I do bear,
I can shake off at pleasure.

Casca. So can I:
So every bondman in his own hand bears
The power to cancel his captivity.

Cas. And why should Cæsar be a tyrant then?
Poor man! I know, he would not be a wolf,
But that he sees the Romans are but sheep:
He were no lion, were not Romans hinds.
Those that with haste will make a mighty fire,
Begin it with weak straws: What trash is Rome,
What rubbish, and what offal, when it serves
For the base matter to illuminate
So vile a thing as Cæsar? But, O, grief!
Where hast thou led me? I, perhaps, speak this
Before a willing bondman: then I know
My answer must be made: But I am arm'd,
And dangers are to me indifferent.

Casca. You speak to Casca; and to such a man,
That is no fleering tell-tale. Hold my hand:
Be factious for redress of all these griefs;
And I will set this foot of mine as far,
As who goes farthest.

Cas. There's a bargain made.
Now know you, Casca, I have mov'd already
Some certain of the noblest-minded Romans,
To undergo, with me, an enterprise
Of honourable-dangerous consequence:
And I do know, by this, they stay for me
In Pompey's porch; for now, this fearful night,
There is no stir, or walking in the streets:
And the complexion of the element,
In favour's, like the work we have in hand,
Most bloody, fiery, and most terrible.

Enter CINNA.

Casca. Stand close awhile, for here comes one in haste.

Cas. 'Tis Cinna, I do know him by his gait:
He is a friend.—Cinna, where haste you so?

Cin. To find out you: Who's that? Metellus Cimber?

Cas. No, it is Casca; one incorporate
To our attempts. Am I not staid for, Cinna?

Cin. I am glad on't. What a fearful night is this!
There's two or three of us have seen strange sights.

Cas. Am I not staid for, Cinna? Tell me.

Cin. Yes,
You are. O, Cassius, if you could but win
The noble Brutus to our party——

Cas. Be you content: Good Cinna, take this paper,
And look you lay it in the prætor's chair,
Where Brutus may but find it; and throw this
In at his window: set this up with wax
Upon old Brutus' statue: all this done,
Repair to Pompey's porch, where you shall find us.
Is Decius Brutus, and Trebonius, there?

Cin. All but Metellus Cimber; and he's gone
To seek you at your house. Well, I will hie,
And so bestow these papers as you bade me.

Cas. That done, repair to Pompey's theatre.
[*Exit* CINNA.
Come, Casca, you and I will, yet, ere day,
See Brutus at his house: three parts of him
Is ours already; and the man entire,
Upon the next encounter, yields him ours.

Casca. O, he sits high in all the people's hearts:
And that, which would appear offence in us,
His countenance, like richest alchymy,
Will change to virtue, and to worthiness.

Cas. Him, and his worth, and our great need of him,
You have right well conceited. Let us go,
For it is after midnight; and, ere day,
We will awake him, and be sure of him.
[*Exeunt.*

ACT II.

SCENE I. *The same.* Brutus's *Orchard.*

Enter BRUTUS.

Bru. What, Lucius! ho!—
I cannot, by the progress of the stars,
Give guess how near to day.—Lucius, I say!—
I would it were my fault to sleep so soundly.—
When, Lucius, when? Awake, I say: What, Lucius!

Enter LUCIUS.

Luc. Call'd you, my lord?

Bru. Get me a taper in my study, Lucius:
When it is lighted, come and call me here.

Luc. I will, my lord. [*Exit.*

Bru. It must be by his death: and, for my part,
I know no personal cause to spurn at him,
But for the general. He would be crown'd:—
How that might change his nature, there's the question.
It is the bright day that brings forth the adder;
And that craves wary walking. Crown him?—That;—
And then, I grant, we put a sting in him,
That at his will he may do danger with.
The abuse of greatness is, when it disjoins
Remorse from power: And to speak truth of Cæsar,
I have not known when his affections sway'd
More than his reason. But 'tis a common proof,
That lowliness is young ambition's ladder,
Whereto the climber-upward turns his face:
But when he once attains the utmost round,
He then unto the ladder turns his back,
Looks in the clouds, scorning the base degrees
By which he did ascend: So Cæsar may;
Then, lest he may, prevent. And, since the quarrel
Will bear no colour for the thing he is,
Fashion it thus; that what he is, augmented,
Would run to these, and these extremities:

And therefore think him as a serpent's egg,
Which, hatch'd, would, as his kind, grow mischievous,
And kill him in the shell.

Re-enter LUCIUS.

Luc. The taper burneth in your closet, sir.
Searching the window for a flint, I found
This paper, thus seal'd up; and, I am sure,
It did not lie there, when I went to bed.
Bru. Get you to bed again, it is not day.
Is not to-morrow, boy, the ides of March?
Luc. I know not, sir.
Bru. Look in the calendar, and bring me word.
Luc. I will, sir. [*Exit.*
Bru. The exhalations, whizzing in the air,
Give so much light, that I may read by them.
[*Opens the Letter, and reads.*
Brutus, thou sleep'st; awake, and see thyself.
Shall Rome, &c. Speak, strike, redress!
Brutus, thou sleep'st; awake,——
Such instigations have been often dropp'd
Where I have took them up.
Shall Rome, &c. Thus, must I piece it out;
Shall Rome stand under one man's awe? What! Rome?
My ancestors did from the streets of Rome
The Tarquin drive, when he was call'd a king.
Speak, strike, redress!—Am I entreated
To speak, and strike? O Rome! I make thee promise,
If the redress will follow, thou receivest
Thy full petition at the hand of Brutus!

Re-enter LUCIUS.

Luc. Sir, March is wasted fourteen days.
[*Knock within.*
Bru. 'Tis good. Go to the gate; somebody knocks. [*Exit* LUCIUS.
Since Cassius first did whet me against Cæsar,
I have not slept.
Between the acting of a dreadful thing
And the first motion, all the interim is
Like a phantasma, or a hideous dream:
The genius, and the mortal instruments,
Are then in council; and the state of man,
Like to a little kingdom, suffers then
The nature of an insurrection.

Re-enter LUCIUS.

Luc. Sir, 'tis your brother Cassius at the door,
Who doth desire to see you.
Bru. Is he alone?
Luc. No, sir; there are more with him.
Bru. Do you know them?
Luc. No, sir; their hats are pluck'd about their ears,
And half their faces buried in their cloaks,
That by no means I may discover them
By any mark of favour.
Bru. Let them enter.
[*Exit* LUCIUS.
They are the faction. O conspiracy!
Sham'st thou to show thy dangerous brow by night,
When evils are most free? O, then, by day,
Where wilt thou find a cavern dark enough
To mask thy monstrous visage? Seek none, conspiracy;
Hide it in smiles, and affability:
For if thou path, thy native semblance on,
Not Erebus itself were dim enough
To hide thee from prevention.

Enter CASSIUS, CASCA, DECIUS, CINNA, METELLUS CIMBER, *and* TREBONIUS.

Cas. I think we are too bold upon your rest;
Good morrow, Brutus: Do we trouble you?
Bru. I have been up this hour; awake, all night.
Know I these men, that come along with you?
Cas. Yes, every man of them; and no man here,
But honours you: and every one doth wish,
You had but that opinion of yourself,
Which every noble Roman bears of you.
This is Trebonius.
Bru. He is welcome hither.
Cas. This Decius Brutus.
Bru. He is welcome too.
Cas. This, Casca; this, Cinna;
And this, Metellus Cimber.
Bru. They are all welcome.
What watchful cares do interpose themselves
Betwixt your eyes and night?
Cas. Shall I entreat a word? [*They whisper.*
Dec. Here lies the east: Doth not the day break here?
Casca. No.
Cin. O, pardon, sir, it doth; and yon gray lines,
That fret the clouds, are messengers of day.
Casca. You shall confess, that you are both deceiv'd.
Here, as I point my sword, the sun arises;
Which is a great way growing on the south,
Weighing the youthful season of the year.
Some two months hence, up higher toward the north
He first presents his fire; and the high east
Stands as the Capitol, directly here.
Bru. Give me your hands all over, one by one.
Cas. And let us swear our resolution.
Bru. No, not an oath: If not the face of men,
The sufferance of our souls, the time's abuse,—
If these be motives weak, break off betimes,
And every man hence to his idle bed;
So let high-sighted tyranny range on,
Till each man drop by lottery. But if these,
As I am sure they do, bear fire enough
To kindle cowards, and to steel with valour
The melting spirits of women; then, countrymen,
What need we any spur but our own cause,
To prick us to redress? what other bond,
Than secret Romans, that have spoke the word,
And will not palter? and what other oath,
Than honesty to honesty engag'd,
That this shall be, or we will fall for it?
Swear priests, and cowards, and men cautelous,
Old feeble carrions, and such suffering souls
That welcome wrongs; unto bad causes swear
Such creatures as men doubt: but do not stain
The even virtue of our enterprise,
Nor the insuppressive metal of our spirits,
To think, that, or our cause, or our performance,
Did need an oath; when every drop of blood,
That every Roman bears, and nobly bears,
Is guilty of a several bastardy,
If he do break the smallest particle
Of any promise that hath pass'd from him.
Cas. But what of Cicero? Shall we sound him?
I think, he will stand very strong with us.
Casca. Let us not leave him out.
Cin. No, by no means.
Met. O let us have him; for his silver hairs
Will purchase us a good opinion,
And buy men's voices to commend our deeds:
It shall be said, his judgment rul'd our hands;
Our youths, and wildness, shall no whit appear,
But all be buried in his gravity.
Bru. O, name him not; let us not break with him;
For he will never follow any thing
That other men begin.
Cas. Then leave him out.
Casca. Indeed, he is not fit.
Dec. Shall no man else be touch'd but only Cæsar?
Cas. Decius, well urg'd:—I think it is not meet,
Mark Antony, so well belov'd of Cæsar,
Should outlive Cæsar: We shall find of him
A shrewd contriver; and, you know, his means,
If he improve them, may well stretch so far,
As to annoy us all: which to prevent,
Let Antony, and Cæsar, fall together.
Bru. Our course will seem too bloody, Caius Cassius,

To cut the head off, and then hack the limbs;
Like wrath in death, and envy afterwards:
For Antony is but a limb of Cæsar.
Let us be sacrificers, but no butchers, Caius.
We all stand up against the spirit of Cæsar;
And in the spirit of men there is no blood:
O, that we then could come by Cæsar's spirit,
And not dismember Cæsar! But, alas,
Cæsar must bleed for it! And, gentle friends,
Let's kill him boldly, but not wrathfully;
Let's carve him as a dish fit for the gods,
Not hew him as a carcass fit for hounds:
And let our hearts, as subtle masters do,
Stir up their servants to an act of rage,
And after seem to chide them. This shall make
Our purpose necessary, and not envious:
Which so appearing to the common eyes,
We shall be call'd purgers, not murderers.
And for Mark Antony, think not of him;
For he can do no more than Cæsar's arm,
When Cæsar's head is off.

Cas. Yet I do fear him:
For in the ingrafted love he bears to Cæsar,——

Bru. Alas, good Cassius, do not think of him:
If he love Cæsar, all that he can do
Is to himself; take thought, and die for Cæsar:
And that were much he should; for he is given
To sports, to wildness, and much company.

Treb. There is no fear in him; let him not die;
For he will live, and laugh at this hereafter.
[*Clock strikes.*

Bru. Peace, count the clock.

Cas. The clock hath stricken three.

Treb. 'Tis time to part.

Cas. But it is doubtful yet,
Whe'r Cæsar will come forth to-day, or no:
For he is superstitious grown of late;
Quite from the main opinion he held once
Of fantasy, of dreams, and ceremonies:
It may be these apparent prodigies,
The unaccustom'd terror of this night,
And the persuasion of his augurers,
May hold him from the Capitol to-day.

Dec. Never fear that: If he be so resolv'd,
I can o'ersway him: for he loves to hear,
That unicorns may be betray'd with trees,
And bears with glasses, elephants with holes,
Lions with toils, and men with flatterers:
But, when I tell him, he hates flatterers,
He says, he does; being then most flattered.
Let me work:
For I can give his humour the true bent;
And I will bring him to the Capitol.

Cas. Nay, we will all of us be there to fetch him.

Bru. By the eighth hour: Is that the uttermost?

Cin. Be that the uttermost, and fail not then.

Met. Caius Ligarius doth bear Cæsar hard,
Who rated him for speaking well of Pompey:
I wonder, none of you have thought of him.

Bru. Now, good Metellus, go along by him:
He loves me well, and I have given him reasons;
Send him but hither, and I'll fashion him.

Cas. The morning comes upon us: We'll leave you, Brutus:—
And, friends, disperse yourselves: but all remember
What you have said, and show yourselves true Romans.

Bru. Good gentlemen, look fresh and merrily;
Let not our looks put on our purposes;
But bear it as our Roman actors do,
With untir'd spirits, and formal constancy:
And so, good-morrow to you every one.
[*Exeunt all but* BRUTUS.
Boy! Lucius!—Fast asleep?—It is no matter;
Enjoy the honey-heavy dew of slumber:
Thou hast no figures, nor no fantasies,
Which busy care draws in the brains of men;
Therefore thou sleep'st so sound.

Enter PORTIA.

Por. Brutus, my lord!

Bru. Portia, what mean you? Wherefore rise you now?
It is not for your health, thus to commit
Your weak condition to the raw cold morning.

Por. Nor for yours neither. You have ungently, Brutus,
Stole from my bed: And yesternight, at supper,
You suddenly arose, and walk'd about,
Musing, and sighing, with your arms across:
And when I ask'd you what the matter was,
You star'd upon me with ungentle looks:
I urg'd you further: then you scratch'd your head,
And too impatiently stamp'd with your foot:
Yet I insisted, yet you answer'd not;
But with an angry wafture of your hand,
Gave sign for me to leave you: So I did;
Fearing to strengthen that impatience,
Which seem'd too much enkindled; and, withal,
Hoping it was but an effect of humour,
Which sometime hath his hour with every man.
It will not let you eat, nor talk, nor sleep;
And, could it work so much upon your shape;
As it hath much prevail'd on your condition,
I should not know you, Brutus. Dear my lord,
Make me acquainted with your cause of grief.

Bru. I am not well in health, and that is all.

Por. Brutus is wise, and were he not in health,
He would embrace the means to come by it.

Bru. Why, so I do:—Good Portia, go to bed.

Por. Is Brutus sick? and is it physical
To walk unbraced, and suck up the humours
Of the dank morning? What, is Brutus sick;
And will he steal out of his wholesome bed,
To dare the vile contagion of the night!
And tempt the rheumy and unpurged air
To add unto his sickness? No, my Brutus;
You have some sick offence within your mind,
Which, by the right and virtue of my place,
I ought to know of: And, upon my knees,
I charm you, by my once commended beauty,
By all your vows of love, and that great vow
Which did incorporate and make us one,
That you unfold to me, yourself, your half,
Why you are heavy; and what men to-night
Have had resort to you: for here have been
Some six or seven, who did hide their faces
Even from darkness.

Bru. Kneel not, gentle Portia.

Por. I should not need, if you were gentle Brutus.
Within the bond of marriage, tell me, Brutus,
Is it expected, I should know no secrets
That appertain to you? Am I yourself,
But, as it were, in sort, or limitation:
To keep with you at meals, comfort your bed,
And talk to you sometimes? Dwell I but in the suburbs
Of your good pleasure? If it be no more,
Portia is Brutus' harlot, not his wife.

Bru. You are my true and honourable wife;
As dear to me, as are the ruddy drops
That visit my sad heart.

Por. If this were true, then should I know this secret.
I grant, I am a woman: but, withal,
A woman that Lord Brutus took to wife:
I grant, I am a woman; but, withal,
A woman well reputed; Cato's daughter.
Think you, I am no stronger than my sex,
Being so father'd, and so husbanded?
Tell me your counsels, I will not disclose them:
I have made strong proof of my constancy,
Giving myself a voluntary wound
Here, in the thigh: Can I bear that with patience,
And not my husband's secrets?

Bru. O ye gods,
Render me worthy of this noble wife!
[*Knocking within.*

Hark, hark! one knocks: Portia, go in a while;
And by and by thy bosom shall partake
The secrets of my heart.
All my engagements I will construe to thee,
All the charactery of my sad brows:—
Leave me with haste. [*Exit* PORTIA.

Enter LUCIUS *and* LIGARIUS.

Lucius, who is that knocks?
Luc. Here is a sick man, that would speak with you.
Bru. Caius Ligarius, that Metellus spake of.—
Boy, stand aside.—Caius Ligarius! how?
Lig. Vouchsafe good morrow from a feeble tongue.
Bru. O, what a time have you chose out, brave Caius,
To wear a kerchief? 'Would, you were not sick!
Lig. I am not sick, if Brutus have in hand
Any exploit worthy the name of honour.
Bru. Such an exploit have I in hand, Ligarius,
Had you a healthful ear to hear of it.
Lig. By all the gods that Romans bow before,
I here discard my sickness. Soul of Rome!
Brave son, deriv'd from honourable loins!
Thou, like an exorcist, hast conjur'd up
My mortified spirit. Now bid me run,
And I will strive with things impossible;
Yea, get the better of them. What's't to do?
Bru. A piece of work, that will make sick men whole.
Lig. But are not some whole, that we must make sick?
Bru. That must we also. What it is, my Caius,
I shall unfold to thee, as we are going
To whom it must be done.
Lig. Set on your foot;
And, with a heart new fir'd, I follow you,
To do I know not what: but it sufficeth,
That Brutus leads me on.
Bru. Follow me then.
[*Exeunt.*

SCENE II.

The same. A Room in Cæsar's *Palace.*

Thunder and Lightning. Enter CÆSAR, *in his Nightgown.*

Cæs. Nor heaven, nor earth, have been at peace to-night:
Thrice hath Calphurnia in her sleep cried out,
Help, ho! they murder Cæsar!—Who's within?

Enter a Servant.

Serv. My lord?
Cæs. Go bid the priests do present sacrifice,
And bring me their opinions of success.
Serv. I will, my lord. [*Exit.*

Enter CALPHURNIA.

Cal. What mean you, Cæsar? Think you to walk forth?
You shall not stir out of your house to-day.
Cæs. Cæsar shall forth: The things that threaten'd me,
Ne'er look'd but on my back; when they shall see
The face of Cæsar, they are vanished.
Cal. Cæsar, I never stood on ceremonies,
Yet now they fright me. There is one within,
Besides the things that we have heard and seen,
Recounts most horrid sights seen by the watch.
A lioness hath whelped in the streets;
And graves have yawn'd, and yielded up their dead:
Fierce fiery warriors fight upon the clouds,
In ranks, and squadrons, and right form of war,
Which drizzled blood upon the Capitol:
The noise of battle hurtled in the air,
Horses did neigh, and dying men did groan;
And ghosts did shriek, and squeal about the streets.
O Cæsar! these things are beyond all use,
And I do fear them.
Cæs. What can be avoided,
Whose end is purpos'd by the mighty gods?
Yet Cæsar shall go forth; for these predictions
Are to the world in general, as to Cæsar.
Cal. When beggars die, there are no comets seen;
The heavens themselves blaze forth the death of princes.
Cæs. Cowards die many times before their deaths;
The valiant never taste of death but once.
Of all the wonders that I yet have heard,
It seems to me most strange that men should fear;
Seeing that death, a necessary end,
Will come, when it will come.

Re-enter a Servant.

What say the augurers?
Serv. They would not have you to stir forth to-day.
Plucking the entrails of an offering forth,
They could not find a heart within the beast.
Cæs. The gods do this in shame of cowardice:
Cæsar should be a beast without a heart,
If he should stay at home to-day for fear.
No, Cæsar shall not: Danger knows full well,
That Cæsar is more dangerous than he.
We were two lions litter'd in one day,
And I the elder and more terrible;
And Cæsar shall go forth.
Cal. Alas, my lord,
Your wisdom is consum'd in confidence.
Do not go forth to-day: Call it my fear,
That keeps you in the house, and not your own.
We'll send Mark Antony to the senate-house;
And he shall say, you are not well to-day:
Let me, upon my knee, prevail in this.
Cæs. Mark Antony shall say, I am not well;
And, for thy humour, I will stay at home.

Enter DECIUS.

Here's Decius Brutus, he shall tell them so.
Dec. Cæsar, all hail! Good morrow, worthy Cæsar:
I come to fetch you to the senate-house.
Cæs. And you are come in very happy time,
To bear my greeting to the senators,
And tell them, that I will not come to-day:
Cannot is false; and that I dare not, falser;
I will not come to-day: Tell them so, Decius.
Cal. Say, he is sick.
Cæs. Shall Cæsar send a lie?
Have I in conquest stretch'd mine arm so far,
To be afeard to tell gray-beards the truth?
Decius, go tell them, Cæsar will not come.
Dec. Most mighty Cæsar, let me know some cause,
Lest I be laugh'd at, when I tell them so.
Cæs. The cause is in my will, I will not come;
That is enough to satisfy the senate.
But, for your private satisfaction,
Because I love you, I will let you know;
Calphurnia here, my wife, stays me at home:
She dreamt to-night she saw my stutua,
Which, like a fountain, with a hundred spouts,
Did run pure blood: and many lusty Romans
Came smiling, and did bathe their hands in it.
And these doth she apply for warnings, portents,
And evils imminent; and on her knee
Hath begg'd, that I will stay at home to-day.
Dec. This dream is all amiss interpreted;
It was a vision, fair and fortunate:
Your statue spouting blood in many pipes,
In which so many smiling Romans bath'd,
Signifies that from you great Rome shall suck
Reviving blood: and that great men shall press
For tinctures, stains, relicks, and cognizance.
This by Calphurnia's dream is signified.
Cæs. And this way have you well expounded it.
Dec. I have, when you have heard what I can say:

And know it now: The senate have concluded
To give, this day, a crown to mighty Cæsar.
If you shall send them word, you will not come,
Their minds may change. Besides, it were a mock
Apt to be render'd, for some one to say,
Break up the senate till another time,
When Cæsar's wife shall meet with better dreams.
If Cæsar hide himself, shall they not whisper,
Lo, Cæsar is afraid?
Pardon me, Cæsar; for my dear, dear love
To your proceeding bids me tell you this;
And reason to my love is liable.

Cæs. How foolish do your fears seem now, Calphurnia?
I am ashamed I did yield to them.—
Give me my robe, for I will go:—

Enter PUBLIUS, BRUTUS, LIGARIUS, METELLUS, CASCA, TREBONIUS, *and* CINNA.

And look where Publius is come to fetch me.

Pub. Good morrow, Cæsar.

Cæs. Welcome, Publius.—
What, Brutus, are you stirr'd so early too?—
Good morrow, Casca.—Caius Ligarius,
Cæsar was ne'er so much your enemy,
As that same ague which hath made you lean.—
What is't o'clock?

Bru. Cæsar, 'tis strucken eight.

Cæs. I thank you for your pains and courtesy.

Enter ANTONY.

See! Antony, that revels long o'nights,
Is notwithstanding up:—
Good morrow, Antony.

Ant. So to most noble Cæsar.

Cæs. Bid them prepare within:—
I am to blame to be thus waited for.—
Now, Cinna:—Now, Metellus:—What, Trebonius!
I have an hour's talk in store for you:
Remember that you call on me to-day;
Be near me, that I may remember you.

Treb. Cæsar, I will:—and so near will I be, [*Aside.*
That your best friends shall wish I had been further.

Cæs. Good friends, go in, and taste some wine with me;
And we, like friends, will straightway go together.

Bru. That every like is not the same, O Cæsar,
The heart of Brutus yearns to think upon! [*Exeunt.*

SCENE III.

The same. A Street near the Capitol.

Enter ARTEMIDORUS, *reading a Paper.*

Art. Cæsar, *beware of* Brutus; *take heed of* Cassius; *come not near* Casca; *have an eye to* Cinna; *trust not* Trebonius; *mark well* Metellus Cimber; Decius Brutus *loves thee not; thou hast wronged* Caius Ligarius. *There is but one mind in all these men, and it is bent against* Cæsar. *If thou be'st not immortal, look about you: Security gives way to conspiracy. The mighty gods defend thee! Thy lover.*
ARTEMIDORUS.

Here will I stand, till Cæsar pass along,
And as a suitor will I give him this.
My heart laments that virtue cannot live
Out of the teeth of emulation.
If thou read this, O Cæsar, thou may'st live;
If not, the fates with traitors do contrive. [*Exit.*

SCENE IV.

The same. Another Part of the same Street, before the House of Brutus.

Enter PORTIA *and* LUCIUS.

Por. I pr'ythee, boy, run to the senate-house,
Stay not to answer me, but get thee gone:
Why dost thou stay?

Luc. To know my errand, madam.

Por. I would have had thee there, and here again,
Ere I can tell thee what thou should'st do there.—
O constancy, be strong upon my side!
Set a huge mountain 'tween my heart and tongue!
I have a man's mind, but a woman's might.
How hard it is for women to keep counsel!—
Art thou here yet?

Luc. Madam, what should I do?
Run to the Capitol, and nothing else?
And so return to you, and nothing else?

Por. Yes, bring me word, boy, if thy lord look well,
For he went sickly forth: And take good note,
What Cæsar doth, what suitors press to him.
Hark, boy! what noise is that?

Luc. I hear none, madam.

Por. Pr'ythee, listen well;
I heard a bustling rumour, like a fray,
And the wind brings it from the Capitol.

Luc. Sooth, madam, I hear nothing.

Enter Soothsayer.

Por. Come hither, fellow:
Which way hast thou been?

Sooth. At mine own house, good lady.

Por. What is't o'clock?

Sooth. About the ninth hour, lady.

Por. Is Cæsar yet gone to the Capitol?

Sooth. Madam, not yet; I go to take my stand,
To see him pass on to the Capitol?

Por. Thou hast some suit to Cæsar, hast thou not?

Sooth. That I have, lady: if it will please Cæsar
To be so good to Cæsar, as to hear me,
I shall beseech him to befriend himself.

Por. Why, know'st thou any harm's intended towards him?

Sooth. None that I know will be, much that I fear may chance.
Good morrow to you. Here the street is narrow:
The throng that follows Cæsar at the heels,
Of senators, of prætors, common suitors,
Will crowd a feeble man almost to death:
I'll get me to a place more void, and there
Speak to great Cæsar as he comes along. [*Exit.*

Por. I must go in.—Ah me! how weak a thing
The heart of woman is! O Brutus!
The heavens speed thee in thine enterprise!
Sure, the boy heard me:—Brutus hath a suit,
That Cæsar will not grant.—O, I grow faint:—
Run, Lucius, and commend me to my lord;
Say, I am merry: come to me again,
And bring me word what he doth say to thee.
[*Exeunt.*

ACT III.

SCENE I.

The same. The Capitol; the Senate sitting.

A Crowd of People *in the Street leading to the Capitol; among them* ARTEMIDORUS, *and the* Soothsayer. *Flourish. Enter* CÆSAR, BRUTUS, CASSIUS, CASCA, DECIUS, METELLUS, TREBONIUS, CINNA, ANTONY, LEPIDUS, POPILIUS, PUBLIUS, *and Others.*

Cæs. The ides of March are come.

Sooth. Ay, Cæsar; but not gone.

Art. Hail, Cæsar! Read this schedule.

Dec. Trebonius doth desire you to o'er-read,
At your best leisure, this his humble suit.

Art. O, Cæsar, read mine first; for mine's a suit
That touches Cæsar nearer: Read it, great Cæsar.

Cæs. What touches us ourself, shall be last serv'd.

Art. Delay not, Cæsar; read it instantly.

Cæs. What, is the fellow mad?

Pub. Sirrah, give place.

Cæs. What, urge you your petitions in the street?
Come to the Capitol.

CÆSAR *enters the* Capitol, *the rest following. All the* Senators *rise.*

Pop. I wish, your enterprise to-day may thrive.
Cas. What enterprise, Popilius?
Pop. Fare you well.
[*Advances to* CÆSAR.
Bru. What said Popilius Lena?
Cas. He wish'd, to-day our enterprise might thrive.
I fear our purpose is discover'd.
Bru. Look, how he makes to Cæsar: Mark him.
Cas. Casca, be sudden, for we fear prevention.—
Brutus, what shall be done? If this be known,
Cassius or Cæsar never shall turn back,
For I will slay myself.
Bru. Cassius, be constant:
Popilius Lena speaks not of our purposes;
For, look, he smiles, and Cæsar doth not change.
Cas. Trebonius knows his time: for, look you, Brutus,
He draws Mark Antony out of the way.
[*Exeunt* ANTONY *and* TREBONIUS. CÆSAR *and the* Senators *take their seats.*
Dec. Where is Metellus Cimber? Let him go,
And presently prefer his suit to Cæsar.
Bru. He is address'd: press near, and second him.
Cin. Casca, you are the first that rears your hand.
Cæs. Are we all ready? what is now amiss,
That Cæsar and his senate must redress?
Met. Most high, most mighty, and most puissant Cæsar,
Metellus Cimber throws before thy seat
An humble heart:— [*Kneeling.*
Cæs. I must prevent thee, Cimber.
These couchings, and these lowly courtesies,
Might fire the blood of ordinary men;
And turn pre-ordinance, and first decree,
Into the law of children. Be not fond,
To think that Cæsar bears such rebel blood,
That will be thaw'd from the true quality
With that which melteth fools; I mean, sweet words,
Low crooked curt'sies, and base spaniel fawning.
Thy brother by decree is banished;
If thou dost bend, and pray, and fawn for him,
I spurn thee like a cur out of my way.
Know, Cæsar doth not wrong; nor without cause
Will he be satisfied.
Met. Is there no voice more worthy than my own,
To sound more sweetly in great Cæsar's ear,
For the repealing of my banish'd brother?
Bru. I kiss thy hand, but not in flattery, Cæsar;
Desiring thee, that Publius Cimber may
Have an immediate freedom of repeal.
Cæs. What, Brutus!
Cas. Pardon, Cæsar: Cæsar, pardon:
As low as to thy foot doth Cassius fall,
To beg enfranchisement for Publius Cimber.
Cæs. I could be well mov'd, if I were as you;
If I could pray to move, prayers would move me:
But I am constant as the northern star,
Of whose true-fix'd, and resting quality,
There is no fellow in the firmament.
The skies are painted with unnumber'd sparks,
They are all fire, and every one doth shine;
But there's but one in all doth hold his place:
So, in the world; 'Tis furnish'd well with men,
And men are flesh and blood, and apprehensive;
Yet, in the number, I do know but one
That unassailable holds on his rank,
Unshak'd of motion; and, that I am he,
Let me a little show it, even in this;
That I was constant, Cimber should be banish'd,
And constant do remain to keep him so.
Cin. O Cæsar,——
Cæs. Hence! Wilt thou lift up Olympus?
Dec. Great Cæsar,——
Cæs. Doth not Brutus bootless kneel?
Casca. Speak, hands, for me.
[CASCA *stabs* CÆSAR *in the Neck.* CÆSAR *catches hold of his Arm. He is then stabbed by several other* Conspirators, *and at last by* MARCUS BRUTUS.
Cæs. Et tu, Brute?—Then, fall, Cæsar.
[*Dies. The* Senators *and* People *retire in confusion.*
Cin. Liberty! Freedom! Tyranny is dead!—
Run hence, proclaim, cry it about the streets.
Cas. Some to the common pulpits, and cry out,
Liberty, freedom, and enfranchisement!
Bru. People, and senators! be not affrighted;
Fly not; stand still:—ambition's debt is paid.
Casca. Go to the pulpit, Brutus.
Dec. And Cassius too.
Bru. Where's Publius?
Cin. Here, quite confounded with this mutiny.
Met. Stand fast together, lest some friend of Cæsar's
Should chance——
Bru. Talk not of standing;—Publius, good cheer;
There is no harm intended to your person,
Nor to no Roman else: so tell them, Publius.
Cas. And leave us, Publius; lest that the people,
Rushing on us, should do your age some mischief.
Bru. Do so;—and let no man abide this deed,
But we the doers.

Re-enter TREBONIUS.

Cas. Where's Antony?
Tre. Fled to his house amaz'd:
Men, wives, and children, stare, cry out, and run,
As it were doomsday.
Bru. Fates! we will know your pleasures:—
That we shall die, we know; 'tis but the time,
And drawing days out, that men stand upon.
Cas. Why, he that cuts off twenty years of life,
Cuts off so many years of fearing death.
Bru. Grant that, and then is death a benefit:
So are we Cæsar's friends, that have abridg'd
His time of fearing death.—Stoop, Romans, stoop,
And let us bathe our hands in Cæsar's blood
Up to the elbows, and besmear our swords:
Then walk we forth, even to the market-place;
And, waving our red weapons o'er our heads,
Let's all cry, Peace! Freedom! and Liberty!
Cas. Stoop then, and wash. How many ages hence,
Shall this our lofty scene be acted over,
In states unborn, and accents yet unknown?
Bru. How many times shall Cæsar bleed in sport,
That now on Pompey's basis lies along,
No worthier than the dust?
Cas. So oft as that shall be,
So often shall the knot of us be call'd
The men that gave our country liberty.
Dec. What, shall we forth?
Cas. Ay, every man away:
Brutus shall lead; and we will grace his heels
With the most boldest and best hearts of Rome.

Enter a Servant.

Bru. Soft, who comes here? A friend of Antony's.
Serv. Thus, Brutus, did my master bid me kneel;
Thus did Mark Antony bid me fall down:
And, being prostrate, thus he bade me say:
Brutus is noble, wise, valiant, and honest;
Cæsar was mighty, bold, royal, and loving:
Say, I love Brutus, and I honour him;
Say, I fear'd Cæsar, honour'd him, and lov'd him.
If Brutus will vouchsafe, that Antony

May safely come to him, and be resolv'd
How Cæsar hath deserv'd to lie in death,
Mark Antony shall not love Cæsar dead
So well as Brutus living; but will follow
The fortunes and affairs of noble Brutus,
Thorough the hazards of this untrod state,
With all true faith. So says my master Antony.

Bru. Thy master is a wise and valiant Roman;
I never thought him worse.
Tell him, so please him come unto this place,
He shall be satisfied; and, by my honour,
Depart untouch'd.

Serv. I'll fetch him presently.
[*Exit* Servant.

Bru. I know, that we shall have him well to friend.

Cas. I wish, we may: but yet have I a mind,
That fears him much; and my misgiving still
Falls shrewdly to the purpose.

Re-enter ANTONY.

Bru. But here comes Antony.—Welcome, Mark Antony.

Ant. O mighty Cæsar! Dost thou lie so low?
Are all thy conquests, glories, triumphs, spoils,
Shrunk to this little measure?—Fare thee well.—
I know not, gentlemen, what you intend,
Who else must be let blood, who else is rank:
If I myself, there is no hour so fit
As Cæsar's death's hour! nor no instrument
Of half that worth, as those your swords, made rich
With the most noble blood of all this world.
I do beseech you, if you bear me hard,
Now, whilst your purpled hands do reek and smoke,
Fulfil your pleasure. Live a thousand years,
I shall not find myself so apt to die:
No place will please me so, no mean of death,
As here by Cæsar, and by you cut off,
The choice and master spirits of this age.

Bru. O Antony! beg not your death of us.
Though now we must appear bloody and cruel,
As, by our hands, and this our present act,
You see we do; yet see you but our hands,
And this the bleeding business they have done:
Our hearts you see not, they are pitiful;
And pity to the general wrong of Rome
(As fire drives out fire, so pity, pity),
Hath done this deed on Cæsar. For your part,
To you our swords have leaden points, Mark Antony:
Our arms, in strength of malice, and our hearts,
Of brothers' temper, do receive you in
With all kind love, good thoughts, and reverence.

Cas. Your voice shall be as strong as any man's,
In the disposing of new dignities.

Bru. Only be patient, till we have appeas'd
The multitude, beside themselves with fear,
And then we will deliver you the cause,
Why I, that did love Cæsar when I struck him,
Have thus proceeded.

Ant. I doubt not of your wisdom.
Let each man render me his bloody hand:
First, Marcus Brutus, will I shake with you:—
Next, Caius Cassius, do I take your hand;—
Now, Decius Brutus, yours;—Now yours, Metellus;
Yours, Cinna;—and, my valiant Casca, yours;—
Though last, not least in love, yours, good Trebonius.
Gentlemen all,—alas! what shall I say?
My credit now stands on such slippery ground,
That one of two bad ways you must conceit me,
Either a coward or a flatterer.—
That I did love thee, Cæsar, O, 'tis true:—
If then thy spirit look upon us now,
Shall it not grieve thee, dearer than thy death,
To see thy Antony making his peace,
Shaking the bloody fingers of thy foes,
Most noble! in the presence of thy corse?
Had I as many eyes as thou hast wounds,
Weeping as fast as they stream forth thy blood,
It would become me better, than to close
In terms of friendship with thine enemies.
Pardon me, Julius!—Here wast thou bay'd, brave hart:
Here didst thou fall; and here thy hunters stand,
Sign'd in thy spoil, and crimson'd in thy lethe.
O world! thou wast the forest to this hart;
And this, indeed, O world, the heart of thee.—
How like a deer, stricken by many princes,
Dost thou here lie!

Cas. Mark Antony,——

Ant. Pardon me, Caius Cassius:
The enemies of Cæsar shall say this;
Then, in a friend, it is cold modesty.

Cas. I blame you not for praising Cæsar so;
But what compact mean you to have with us?
Will you be prick'd in number of our friends;
Or shall we on, and not depend on you?

Ant. Therefore I took your hands; but was, indeed,
Sway'd from the point, by looking down on Cæsar.
Friends am I with you all, and love you all;
Upon this hope, that you shall give me reasons,
Why, and wherein, Cæsar was dangerous.

Bru. Or else were this a savage spectacle:
Our reasons are so full of good regard,
That were you, Antony, the son of Cæsar,
You should be satisfied.

Ant. That's all I seek:
And am moreover suitor, that I may
Produce his body to the market-place;
And in the pulpit, as becomes a friend,
Speak in the order of his funeral.

Bru. You shall, Mark Antony.

Cas. Brutus, a word with you.—
You know not what you do: Do not consent,
[*Aside.*
That Antony speak in his funeral:
Know you how much the people may be mov'd
By that which he will utter?

Bru. By your pardon;
I will myself into the pulpit first,
And show the reason of our Cæsar's death:
What Antony shall speak, I will protest
He speaks by leave and by permission;
And that we are contented, Cæsar shall
Have all true rites, and lawful ceremonies.
It shall advantage more, than do us wrong.

Cas. I know not what may fall; I like it not.

Bru. Mark Antony, here, take you Cæsar's body.
You shall not in your funeral speech blame us,
But speak all good you can devise of Cæsar;
And say, you do't by our permission;
Else shall you not have any hand at all
About his funeral: and you shall speak
In the same pulpit whereto I am going,
After my speech is ended.

Ant. Be it so;
I do desire no more.

Bru. Prepare the body then, and follow us.
[*Exeunt all but* ANTONY.

Ant. O, pardon me, thou bleeding piece of earth,
That I am meek and gentle with these butchers!
Thou art the ruins of the noblest man,
That ever lived in the tide of times.
Woe to the hand that shed this costly blood!
Over thy wounds now do I prophesy,—
Which, like dumb mouths, do ope their ruby lips,
To beg the voice and utterance of my tongue!—
A curse shall light upon the limbs of men;
Domestick fury, and fierce civil strife,
Shall cumber all the parts in Italy:
Blood and destruction shall be so in use,
And dreadful objects so familiar,
That mothers shall but smile, when they behold
Their infants quarter'd with the hands of war;
All pity chok'd with custom of fell deeds:
And Cæsar's spirit, ranging for revenge,

With Ate by his side, come hot from hell,
Shall in these confines, with a monarch's voice,
Cry *Havock*, and let slip the dogs of war;
That this foul deed shall smell above the earth
With carrion men, groaning for burial.

Enter a Servant.

You serve Octavius Cæsar, do you not?
Serv. I do, Mark Antony.
Ant. Cæsar did write for him to come to Rome.
Serv. He did receive his letters, and is coming:
And bid me say to you by word of mouth,—
O Cæsar!— [*Seeing the Body.*
Ant. Thy heart is big, get thee apart and weep.
Passion, I see, is catching; for mine eyes,
Seeing those beads of sorrow stand in thine,
Began to water. Is thy master coming?
Serv. He lies to-night within seven leagues of Rome.
Ant. Post back with speed, and tell him what hath chanc'd:
Here is a mourning Rome, a dangerous Rome,
No Rome of safety for Octavius yet;
Hie hence, and tell him so. Yet stay a while;
Thou shalt not back, till I have borne this corse
Into the market-place: there shall I try,
In my oration, how the people take
The cruel issue of these bloody men;
According to the which, thou shalt discourse
To young Octavius of the state of things.
Lend me your hand. [*Exeunt with* Cæsar's *Body.*

SCENE II. *The same. The* Forum.

Enter BRUTUS *and* CASSIUS, *and a throng of* Citizens.

Cit. We will be satisfied; let us be satisfied.
Bru. Then follow me, and give me audience, friends.—
Cassius, go you into the other street,
And part the numbers.—
Those that will hear me speak, let them stay here;
Those that will follow Cassius, go with him;
And publick reasons shall be rendered
Of Cæsar's death.
1 Cit. I will hear Brutus speak.
2 Cit. I will hear Cassius; and compare their reasons,
When severally we hear them rendered.
[*Exit* CASSIUS, *with some of the* Citizens.
BRUTUS *goes into the Rostrum.*
3 Cit. The noble Brutus is ascended: Silence!
Bru. Be patient till the last.
Romans, countrymen, and lovers! hear me for my cause; and be silent, that you may hear: believe me for mine honour; and have respect to mine honour, that you may believe: censure me in your wisdom; and awake your senses, that you may the better judge. If there be any in this assembly, any dear friend of Cæsar's, to him I say, that Brutus' love to Cæsar was no less than his. If then that friend demand, why Brutus rose against Cæsar, this is my answer,—Not that I loved Cæsar less, but that I loved Rome more. Had you rather Cæsar were living, and die all slaves; than that Cæsar were dead, to live all free men? As Cæsar loved me, I weep for him; as he was fortunate, I rejoice at it; as he was valiant, I honour him: but, as he was ambitious, I slew him: There is tears, for his love; joy, for his fortune; honour, for his valour; and death, for his ambition. Who is here so base, that would be a bondman? If any, speak; for him have I offended. Who is here so rude, that would not be a Roman? If any, speak; for him have I offended. Who is here so vile, that will not love his country? If any, speak; for him have I offended. I pause for a reply.
Cit. None, Brutus, none.
[*Several speaking at once.*
Bru. Then none have I offended. I have done no more to Cæsar, than you should do to Brutus. The question of his death is enrolled in the Capitol: his glory not extenuated, wherein he was worthy; nor his offences enforced, for which he suffered death.

Enter ANTONY *and Others, with* Cæsar's *Body.*

Here comes his body, mourned by Mark Antony: who, though he had no hand in his death, shall receive the benefit of his dying, a place in the commonwealth; As which of you shall not? With this I depart; That as I slew my best lover for the good of Rome, I have the same dagger for myself, when it shall please my country to need my death.
Cit. Live, Brutus, live! live!
1 Cit. Bring him with triumph home unto his house.
2 Cit. Give him a statue with his ancestors.
3 Cit. Let him be Cæsar.
4 Cit. Cæsar's better parts
Shall now be crown'd in Brutus.
1 Cit. We'll bring him to his house with shouts and clamours.
Bru. My countrymen,——
2 Cit. Peace; silence! Brutus speaks.
1 Cit. Peace, ho!
Bru. Good countrymen, let me depart alone,
And for my sake, stay here with Antony:
Do grace to Cæsar's corpse, and grace his speech
Tending to Cæsar's glories; which Mark Antony,
By our permission, is allow'd to make.
I do entreat you, not a man depart,
Save I alone, till Antony have spoke. [*Exit.*
1 Cit. Stay, ho! and let us hear Mark Antony.
3 Cit. Let him go up into the publick chair;
We'll hear him:—Noble Antony, go up.
Ant. For Brutus' sake, I am beholden to you.
4 Cit. What does he say of Brutus?
3 Cit. He says, for Brutus' sake,
He finds himself beholden to us all.
4 Cit. 'Twere best he speak no harm of Brutus here.
1 Cit. This Cæsar was a tyrant.
3 Cit. Nay, that's certain;
We are bless'd, that Rome is rid of him.
2 Cit. Peace; let us hear what Antony can say.
Ant. You gentle Romans,——
Cit. Peace, ho! let us hear him.
Ant. Friends, Romans, countrymen, lend me your ears;
I come to bury Cæsar, not to praise him.
The evil, that men do, lives after them;
The good is oft interred with their bones;
So let it be with Cæsar. The noble Brutus
Hath told you, Cæsar was ambitious:
If it were so, it was a grievous fault;
And grievously hath Cæsar answer'd it.
Here, under leave of Brutus, and the rest
(For Brutus is an honourable man;
So are they all; all honourable men),
Come I to speak in Cæsar's funeral.
He was my friend, faithful and just to me:
But Brutus says, he was ambitious,
And Brutus is an honourable man.
He hath brought many captives home to Rome,
Whose ransoms did the general coffers fill:
Did this in Cæsar seem ambitious?
When that the poor have cried, Cæsar hath wept:
Ambition should be made of sterner stuff:
Yet Brutus says, he was ambitious;
And Brutus is an honourable man.
You all did see, that on the Lupercal,
I thrice presented him a kingly crown,
Which he did thrice refuse. Was this ambition?
Yet Brutus says, he was ambitious;
And sure, he is an honourable man.
I speak not to disprove what Brutus spoke,
But here I am to speak what I do know.
You all did love him once, not without cause;
What cause withholds you then to mourn for him?

O judgment, thou art fled to brutish beasts,
And men have lost their reason!—Bear with me;
My heart is in the coffin there with Cæsar,
And I must pause till it come back to me.

1 *Cit.* Methinks, there is much reason in his sayings.

2 *Cit.* If thou consider rightly of the matter,
Cæsar had great wrong.

3 *Cit.* Has he, masters?
I fear, there will a worse come in his place.

4 *Cit.* Mark'd ye his words? he would not take the crown;
Therefore, 'tis certain, he was not ambitious.

1 *Cit.* If it be found so, some will dear abide it.

2 *Cit.* Poor soul! his eyes are red as fire with weeping.

3 *Cit.* There's not a nobler man in Rome, than Antony.

4 *Cit.* Now mark him, he begins again to speak.

Ant. But yesterday, the word of Cæsar might
Have stood against the world: now lies he there,
And none so poor to do him reverence.
O masters! if I were dispos'd to stir
Your hearts and minds to mutiny and rage,
I should do Brutus wrong, and Cassius wrong,
Who, you all know, are honourable men:
I will not do them wrong; I rather choose
To wrong the dead, to wrong myself, and you,
Than I will wrong such honourable men.
But here's a parchment, with the seal of Cæsar,
I found it in his closet, 'tis his will:
Let but the commons hear this testament
(Which, pardon me, I do not mean to read),
And they would go and kiss dead Cæsar's wounds,
And dip their napkins in his sacred blood;
Yea, beg a hair of him for memory,
And, dying, mention it within their wills,
Bequeathing it as a rich legacy,
Unto their issue.

4 *Cit.* We'll hear the will: Read it, Mark Antony.

Cit. The will, the will; we will hear Cæsar's will.

Ant. Have patience, gentle friends, I must not read it;
It is not meet you know how Cæsar lov'd you.
You are not wood, you are not stones, but men;
And, being men, hearing the will of Cæsar,
It will inflame you, it will make you mad:
'Tis good you know not that you are his heirs;
For if you should, O, what would come of it!

4 *Cit.* Read the will; we will hear it, Antony;
You shall read us the will; Cæsar's will.

Ant. Will you be patient? Will you stay a while?
I have o'ershot myself, to tell you of it.
I fear, I wrong the honourable men,
Whose daggers have stabb'd Cæsar; I do fear it.

4 *Cit.* They were traitors: Honourable men!

Cit. The will! the testament!

2 *Cit.* They were villains, murderers: The will! read the will!

Ant. You will compel me then to read the will?
Then make a ring about the corpse of Cæsar,
And let me show you him that made the will.
Shall I descend? And will you give me leave?

Cit. Come down.

2 *Cit.* Descend. [*He comes down from the Pulpit.*

3 *Cit.* You shall have leave.

4 *Cit.* A ring; stand round.

1 *Cit.* Stand from the hearse, stand from the body.

2 *Cit.* Room for Antony;—most noble Antony.

Ant. Nay, press not so upon me; stand far off.

Cit. Stand back! room! bear back!

Ant. If you have tears, prepare to shed them now.
You all do know this mantle: I remember
The first time ever Cæsar put it on;
'Twas on a summer's evening, in his tent;
That day he overcame the Nervii:—
Look! in this place, ran Cassius' dagger through:
See, what a rent the envious Casca made:
Through this, the well beloved Brutus stabb'd;
And, as he pluck'd his cursed steel away,
Mark how the blood of Cæsar follow'd it;
As rushing out of doors, to be resolv'd
If Brutus so unkindly knock'd, or no;
For Brutus, as you know, was Cæsar's angel:
Judge, O you gods, how dearly Cæsar lov'd him!
This was the most unkindest cut of all:
For when the noble Cæsar saw him stab,
Ingratitude, more strong than traitors' arms,
Quite vanquish'd him: then burst his mighty heart;
And, in his mantle muffling up his face,
Even at the base of Pompey's statua,
Which all the while ran blood, great Cæsar fell.
O, what a fall was there, my countrymen!
Then I, and you, and all of us fell down,
Whilst bloody treason flourish'd over us.
O, now you weep; and, I perceive, you feel
The dint of pity: these are gracious drops.
Kind souls, what, weep you, when you but behold
Our Cæsar's vesture wounded? Look you here,
Here is himself, marr'd, as you see, with traitors.

1 *Cit.* O piteous spectacle!

2 *Cit.* O noble Cæsar!

3 *Cit.* O woful day!

4 *Cit.* O traitors, villains!

1 *Cit.* O most bloody sight!

2 *Cit.* We will be revenged:—revenge: about,—seek,—burn,—fire,—kill,—slay!—let not a traitor live.

Ant. Stay, countrymen.

1 *Cit.* Peace there;—Hear the noble Antony.

2 *Cit.* We'll hear him, we'll follow him, we'll die with him.

Ant. Good friends, sweet friends, let me not stir you up
To such a sudden flood of mutiny.
They, that have done this deed, are honourable;
What private griefs they have, alas, I know not,
That made them do it; they are wise and honourable,
And will, no doubt, with reasons answer you.
I come not, friends, to steal away your hearts;
I am no orator, as Brutus is:
But, as you know me all, a plain blunt man,
That love my friend; and that they know full well
That gave me publick leave to speak of him.
For I have neither wit, nor words, nor worth,
Action, nor utterance, nor the power of speech,
To stir men's blood: I only speak right on;
I tell you that, which you yourselves do know;
Show you sweet Cæsar's wounds, poor, poor dumb mouths,
And bid them speak for me; But were I Brutus,
And Brutus Antony, there were an Antony
Would ruffle up your spirits, and put a tongue
In every wound of Cæsar, that should move
The stones of Rome to rise and mutiny.

Cit. We'll mutiny.

1 *Cit.* We'll burn the house of Brutus.

3 *Cit.* Away then, come, seek the conspirators.

Ant. Yet hear me, countrymen; yet hear me speak.

Cit. Peace, ho! Hear Antony, most noble Antony.

Ant. Why, friends, you go to do you know not what:
Wherein hath Cæsar thus deserv'd your loves?
Alas, you know not:—I must tell you then:
You have forgot the will I told you of.

Cit. Most true;—the will;—let's stay, and hear the will.

Ant. Here is the will, and under Cæsar's seal.
To every Roman Citizen he gives,
To every several man, seventy five drachmas.

2 *Cit.* Most noble Cæsar! we'll revenge his death.
3 *Cit.* O royal Cæsar!
Ant. Hear me with patience.
Cit. Peace, ho!
Ant. Moreover, he hath left you all his walks,
His private arbours, and new planted orchards,
On this side Tyber; he hath left them you,
And to your heirs for ever; common pleasures,
To walk abroad, and recreate yourselves.
Here was a Cæsar: When comes such another?
1 *Cit.* Never, never:—Come, away, away:
We'll burn his body in the holy place,
And with the brands fire the traitors' houses.
Take up the body.
2 *Cit.* Go, fetch fire.
3 *Cit.* Pluck down benches.
4 *Cit.* Pluck down forms, windows, any thing.
[*Exeunt* Citizens, *with the Body.*
Ant. Now let it work: Mischief, thou art afoot.
Take thou what course thou wilt!—How now, fellow?

Enter a Servant.

Serv. Sir, Octavius is already come to Rome.
Ant. Where is he?
Serv. He and Lepidus are at Cæsar's house.
Ant. And thither will I straight to visit him:
He comes upon a wish. Fortune is merry,
And in this mood will give us any thing.
Serv. I heard him say, Brutus and Cassius
Are rid like madmen through the gates of Rome.
Ant. Belike, they had some notice of the people,
How I had mov'd them. Bring me to Octavius.
[*Exeunt.*

SCENE III. *The same. A Street.*

Enter CINNA, *the Poet.*

Cin. I dreamt to-night, that I did feast with Cæsar,
And things unluckily charge my fantasy:
I have no will to wander forth of doors,
Yet something leads me forth.

Enter Citizens.

1 *Cit.* What is your name?
2 *Cit.* Whither are you going?
3 *Cit.* Where do you dwell?
4 *Cit.* Are you a married man, or a bachelor?
2 *Cit.* Answer every man directly.
1 *Cit.* Ay, and briefly.
4 *Cit.* Ay, and wisely.
3 *Cit.* Ay, and truly, you were best.

Cin. What is my name? Whither am I going? Where do I dwell? Am I a married man, or a bachelor? Then to answer every man directly, and briefly, wisely, and truly. Wisely I say, I am a bachelor.

2 *Cit.* That's as much as to say, they are fools that marry:—You'll bear me a bang for that, I fear. Proceed; directly.

Cin. Directly, I am going to Cæsar's funeral.
1 *Cit.* As a friend, or an enemy?
Cin. As a friend.
2 *Cit.* That matter is answered directly.
4 *Cit.* For your dwelling,—briefly.
Cin. Briefly, I dwell by the Capitol.
3 *Cit.* Your name, sir, truly.
Cin. Truly, my name is Cinna.
1 *Cit.* Tear him to pieces, he's a conspirator.
Cin. I am Cinna the poet, I am Cinna the poet.

4 *Cit.* Tear him for his bad verses, tear him for his bad verses.

2 *Cit.* It is no matter, his name's Cinna; pluck but his name out of his heart, and turn him going.

3 *Cit.* Tear him, tear him. Come, brands, ho! firebrands. To Brutus', to Cassius'; burn all. Some to Decius' house, and some to Casca's; some to Ligarius': away; go. [*Exeunt.*

ACT IV.

SCENE I.

The same. A Room in Antony's *House.*

ANTONY, OCTAVIUS, *and* LEPIDUS, *seated at a Table.*

Ant. These many then shall die; their names are prick'd.
Oct. Your brother too must die; Consent you, Lepidus?
Lep. I do consent.
Oct. Prick him down, Antony.
Lep. Upon condition Publius shall not live,
Who is your sister's son, Mark Antony.
Ant. He shall not live; look, with a spot I damn him.
But, Lepidus, go you to Cæsar's house;
Fetch the will hither, and we will determine
How to cut off some charge in legacies.
Lep. What, shall I find you here?
Oct. Or here, or at
The Capitol. [*Exit* LEPIDUS.
Ant. This is a slight unmeritable man,
Meet to be sent on errands: Is it fit,
The threefold world divided, he should stand
One of the three to share it?
Oct. So you thought him;
And took his voice who should be prick'd to die,
In our black sentence and proscription.
Ant. Octavius, I have seen more days than you:
And though we lay these honours on this man,
To ease ourselves of divers slanderous loads,
He shall but bear them as the ass bears gold.
To groan and sweat under the business,
Either led or driven, as we point the way;
And having brought our treasure where we will,
Then take we down his load, and turn him off,
Like to the empty ass, to shake his ears,
And graze in commons.
Oct. You may do your will:
But he's a tried and valiant soldier.
Ant. So is my horse, Octavius; and, for that,
I do appoint him store of provender.
It is a creature that I teach to fight,
To wind, to stop, to run directly on;
His corporal motion govern'd by my spirit.
And, in some taste, is Lepidus but so;
He must be taught, and train'd, and bid go forth:
A barren-spirited fellow; one that feeds
On objects, arts, and imitations;
Which, out of use, and stal'd by other men,
Begin his fashion. Do not talk of him,
But as a property. And now, Octavius,
Listen great things.—Brutus and Cassius
Are levying powers: we must straight make head:
Therefore, let our alliance be combin'd,
Our best friends made, and our best means stretch'd out,
And let us presently go sit in council,
How covert matters may be best disclos'd,
And open perils surest answered.
Oct. Let us do so; for we are at the stake,
And bay'd about with many enemies;
And some, that smile, have in their hearts, I fear,
Millions of mischiefs. [*Exeunt.*

SCENE II.

Before Brutus' *Tent, in the Camp near* Sardis.

Drum. Enter BRUTUS, LUCILIUS, LUCIUS, *and* Soldiers: TITINIUS *and* PINDARUS *meeting them.*

Bru. Stand ho!
Luc. Give the word, ho! and stand.
Bru. What now, Lucilius? is Cassius near?
Luc. He is at hand; and Pindarus is come
To do you salutation from his master.
[PINDARUS *gives a Letter to* BRUTUS.
Bru. He greets me well.—Your master, Pindarus,
In his own change, or by ill officers,

Hath given me some worthy cause to wish
Things done, undone: but, if he be at hand,
I shall be satisfied.

Pin. I do not doubt,
But that my noble master will appear
Such as he is, full of regard and honour.

Bru. He is not doubted.—A word, Lucilius:
How he receiv'd you, let me be resolv'd.

Luc. With courtesy, and with respect enough;
But not with such familiar instances,
Nor with such free and friendly conference,
As he hath used of old.

Bru. Thou hast describ'd
A hot friend cooling: Ever note, Lucilius,
When love begins to sicken and decay,
It useth an enforced ceremony.
There are no tricks in plain and simple faith:
But hollow men, like horses hot at hand,
Make gallant show and promise of their mettle:
But when they should endure the bloody spur,
They fall their crests, and, like deceitful jades,
Sink in the trial. Comes his army on?

Luc. They mean this night in Sardis to be quarter'd;
The greater part, the horse in general,
Are come with Cassius. [*March within.*

Bru. Hark, he is arriv'd:—
March gently on to meet him.

Enter Cassius *and* Soldiers.

Cas. Stand, ho!

Bru. Stand, ho! Speak the word along.

Within. Stand.

Within. Stand.

Within. Stand.

Cas. Most noble brother, you have done me wrong.

Bru. Judge me, you gods! Wrong I mine [enemies?
And, if not so, how should I wrong a brother?

Cas. Brutus, this sober form of yours hides wrongs;
And when you do them——

Bru. Cassius, be content,
Speak your griefs softly,—I do know you well:—
Before the eyes of both our armies here,
Which should perceive nothing but love from us,
Let us not wrangle: Bid them move away;
Then in my tent, Cassius, enlarge your griefs,
And I will give you audience.

Cas. Pindarus,
Bid our commanders lead their charges off
A little from this ground.

Bru. Lucilius, do you the like; and let no man
Come to our tent, till we have done our conference.
Let Lucius and Titinius guard our door.
[*Exeunt.*

SCENE III. *Within the Tent of* Brutus.

Lucius *and* Titinius *at some distance from it.*

Enter Brutus *and* Cassius.

Cas. That you have wrong'd me, doth appear in this:
You have condemn'd and noted Lucius Pella,
For taking bribes here of the Sardians;
Wherein, my letters, praying on his side,
Because I knew the man, were slighted off.

Bru. You wrong'd yourself, to write in such a case.

Cas. In such a time as this, it is not meet
That every nice offence should bear his comment.

Bru. Let me tell you, Cassius, you yourself
Are much condemn'd to have an itching palm;
To sell and mart your offices for gold,
To undeservers.

Cas. I an itching palm?
You know, that you are Brutus that speak this,
Or, by the gods, this speech were else your last.

Bru. The name of Cassius honours this corruption,
And chastisement doth therefore hide his head.

Cas. Chastisement!

Bru. Remember March, the ides of March remember!
Did not great Julius bleed for justice sake?
What villain touch'd his body, that did stab,
And not for justice? What, shall one of us,
That struck the foremost man of all this world,
But for supporting robbers; shall we now
Contaminate our fingers with base bribes?
And sell the mighty space of our large honours,
For so much trash, as may be grasped thus?—
I had rather be a dog, and bay the moon,
Than such a Roman.

Cas. Brutus, bay not me,
I'll not endure it: you forget yourself,
To hedge me in; I am a soldier, I,
Older in practice, abler than yourself
To make conditions.

Bru. Go to; you're not, Cassius.

Cas. I am.

Bru. I say, you are not.

Cas. Urge me no more, I shall forget myself;
Have mind upon your health, tempt me no further.

Bru. Away, slight man!

Cas. Is 't possible?

Bru. Hear me, for I will speak.
Must I give way and room to your rash choler?
Shall I be frighted, when a madman stares?

Cas. O ye gods! ye gods! Must I endure all this?

Bru. All this? ay, more: Fret, till your proud heart break;
Go, show your slaves how cholerick you are,
And make your bondmen tremble. Must I budge?
Must I observe you? Must I stand and crouch
Under your testy humour? By the gods,
You shall digest the venom of your spleen,
Though it do split you: for, from this day forth,
I'll use you for my mirth, yea, for my laughter,
When you are waspish.

Cas. Is it come to this?

Bru. You say, you are a better soldier:
Let it appear so; make your vaunting true,
And it shall please me well: For mine own part,
I shall be glad to learn of noble men.

Cas. You wrong me every way, you wrong me, Brutus;
I said, an elder soldier, not a better:
Did I say, better?

Bru. If you did, I care not.

Cas. When Cæsar liv'd, he durst not thus have mov'd me.

Bru. Peace, peace; you durst not so have tempted him.

Cas. I durst not?

Bru. No.

Cas. What? durst not tempt him?

Bru. For your life you durst not.

Cas. Do not presume too much upon my love,
I may do that I shall be sorry for.

Bru. You have done that you should be sorry for.
There is no terror, Cassius, in your threats;
For I am arm'd so strong in honesty,
That they pass by me as the idle wind,
Which I respect not. I did send to you
For certain sums of gold, which you denied me;—
For I can raise no money by vile means:
By heaven, I had rather coin my heart,
And drop my blood for drachmas, than to wring
From the hard hands of peasants their vile trash,
By any indirection. I did send
To you for gold to pay my legions,
Which you denied me: Was that done like Cassius?
Should I have answer'd Caius Cassius so?
When Marcus Brutus grows so covetous,
To lock such rascal counters from his friends,
Be ready, gods, with all your thunderbolts,
Dash him to pieces!

Cas. I denied you not.
Bru. You did.
Cas. I did not; he was but a fool
That brought my answer back.—Brutus hath riv'd my heart:
A friend should bear his friend's infirmities,
But Brutus makes mine greater than they are.
Bru. I do not, till you practise them on me.
Cas. You love me not.
Bru. I do not like your faults.
Cas. A friendly eye could never see such faults.
Bru. A flatterer's would not, though they do appear
As huge as high Olympus.
Cas. Come, Antony, and young Octavius, come,
Revenge yourselves alone on Cassius,
For Cassius is aweary of the world:
Hated by one he loves; brav'd by his brother;
Check'd like a bondman; all his faults observ'd,
Set in a note-book, learn'd, and conn'd by rote,
To cast into my teeth. O, I could weep
My spirit from mine eyes!—There is my dagger,
And here my naked breast; within, a heart
Dearer than Plutus' mine, richer than gold:
If that thou be'st a Roman, take it forth;
I, that denied thee gold, will give my heart:
Strike as thou didst at Cæsar; for, I know,
When thou didst hate him worst, thou lov'dst him better
Than ever thou lov'dst Cassius.
Bru. Sheath your dagger:
Be angry when you will, it shall have scope;
Do what you will, dishonour shall be humour.
O Cassius, you are yoked with a lamb
That carries anger, as the flint bears fire;
Who, much enforced, shows a hasty spark,
And straight is cold again.
Cas. Hath Cassius liv'd
To be but mirth and laughter to his Brutus,
When grief, and blood ill temper'd, vexeth him?
Bru. When I spoke that, I was ill temper'd too.
Cas. Do you confess so much? Give me your hand.
Bru. And my heart too.
Cas. O Brutus!—
Bru. What's the matter?
Cas. Have you not love enough to bear with me,
When that rash humour, which my mother gave me,
Makes me forgetful?
Bru. Yes, Cassius; and, from henceforth,
When you are over earnest with your Brutus,
He'll think your mother chides, and leave you so.
[*Noise within.*
Poet. [*Within.*] Let me go in to see the generals;
There is some grudge between them, 'tis not meet
They be alone.
Luc. [*Within.*] You shall not come to them.
Poet. [*Within.*] Nothing but death shall stay me.

Enter Poet.

Cas. How now? What's the matter?
Poet. For shame, you generals; What do you mean?
Love, and be friends, as two such men should be;
For I have seen more years, I am sure, than ye.
Cas. Ha, ha; how vilely doth this cynick rhyme!
Bru. Get you hence, sirrah; saucy fellow, hence.
Cas. Bear with him, Brutus; 'tis his fashion.
Bru. I'll know his humour, when he knows his time:
What should the wars do with these jigging fools?
Companion, hence.
Cas. Away, away, be gone. [*Exit* Poet.

Enter LUCILIUS *and* TITINIUS.

Bru. Lucilius and Titinius, bid the commanders
Prepare to lodge their companies to-night.
Cas. And come yourselves, and bring Messala with you
Immediately to us.
[*Exeunt* LUCILIUS *and* TITINIUS.
Bru. Lucius, a bowl of wine.
Cas. I did not think you could have been so angry.
Bru. O Cassius, I am sick of many griefs.
Cas. Of your philosophy you make no use,
If you give place to accidental evils.
Bru. No man bears sorrow better:—Portia is dead.
Cas. Ha! Portia?
Bru. She is dead.
Cas. How scap'd I killing, when I cross'd you so?—
O insupportable and touching loss!—
Upon what sickness?
Bru. Impatient of my absence;
And grief, that young Octavius with Mark Antony
Have made themselves so strong;—for with her death
That tidings came;—With this she fell distract,
And, her attendants absent, swallow'd fire.
Cas. And died so?
Bru. Even so.
Cas. O ye immortal gods!

Enter LUCIUS, *with Wine and Tapers.*

Bru. Speak no more of her.—Give me a bowl of wine:—
In this I bury all unkindness, Cassius. [*Drinks.*
Cas. My heart is thirsty for that noble pledge:—
Fill, Lucius, till the wine o'erswell the cup;
I cannot drink too much of Brutus' love.
[*Drinks.*

Re-enter TITINICS, *with* MESSALA.

Bru. Come in, Titinius:—Welcome, good Messala.—
Now sit we close about this taper here,
And call in question our necessities.
Cas. Portia, art thou gone?
Bru. No more, I pray you.—
Messala, I have here received letters,
That young Octavius, and Mark Antony,
Come down upon us with a mighty power,
Bending their expedition toward Philippi.
Mes. Myself have letters of the selfsame tenour.
Bru. With what addition?
Mes. That by proscription, and bills of outlawry,
Octavius, Antony, and Lepidus,
Have put to death an hundred senators.
Bru. Therein our letters do not well agree;
Mine speak of seventy senators, that died
By their proscriptions, Cicero being one.
Cas. Cicero one?
Mes. Ay, Cicero is dead,
And by that order of proscription.—
Had you your letters from your wife, my lord?
Bru. No, Messala.
Mes. Nor nothing in your letters writ of her?
Bru. Nothing, Messala.
Mes. That, methinks, is strange.
Bru. Why ask you? Hear you aught of her in yours?
Mes. No, my lord.
Bru. Now, as you are a Roman, tell me true.
Mes. Then like a Roman bear the truth I tell:
For certain she is dead, and by strange manner.
Bru. Why, farewell, Portia.—We must die, Messala:
With meditating that she must die once,
I have the patience to endure it now.
Mes. Even so great men great losses should endure.
Cas. I have as much of this in art as you,
But yet my nature could not bear it so.
Bru. Well, to our work alive. What do you think
Of marching to Philippi presently?

Cas. I do not think it good.
Bru. Your reason?
Cas. This it is:
'Tis better that the enemy seek us:
So shall he waste his means, weary his soldiers,
Doing himself offence; whilst we, lying still,
Are full of rest, defence, and nimbleness.
Bru. Good reasons must, of force, give place to better.
The people 'twixt Philippi and this ground,
Do stand but in a forc'd affection;
For they have grudg'd us contribution:
The enemy, marching along by them,
By them shall make a fuller number up,
Come on refresh'd, new added, and encourag'd;
From which advantage shall we cut him off,
If at Philippi we do face him there,
These people at our back.
Cas. Hear me, good brother.
Bru. Under your pardon.—You must note beside,
That we have tried the utmost of our friends,
Our legions are brim full, our cause is ripe:
The enemy increaseth every day,
We at the height, are ready to decline.
There is a tide in the affairs of men,
Which, taken at the flood, leads on to fortune;
Omitted, all the voyage of their life
Is bound in shallows, and in miseries.
On such a full sea are we now afloat;
And we must take the current when it serves,
Or lose our ventures.
Cas. Then, with your will, go on;
We'll along ourselves, and meet them at Philippi.
Bru. The deep of night is crept upon our talk,
And nature must obey necessity;
Which we will niggard with a little rest.
There is no more to say?
Cas. No more. Good night;
Early to-morrow will we rise, and hence.
Bru. Lucius, my gown. [*Exit* LUCIUS.] Farewell, good Messala;—
Good night, Titinius:—Noble, noble Cassius,
Good night, and good repose.
Cas. O my dear brother!
This was an ill beginning of the night:
Never come such division 'tween our souls!
Let it not, Brutus.
Bru. Every thing is well.
Cas. Good night, my lord.
Bru. Good night, good brother.
Tit. Mes. Good night, Lord Brutus.
Bru. Farewell, every one.
[*Exeunt* CAS. TIT. *and* MES.

Re-enter LUCIUS, *with the Gown.*

Give me the gown. Where is thy instrument?
Luc. Here in the tent.
Bru. What, thou speak'st drowsily?
Poor knave, I blame thee not: thou art o'er-watch'd.
Call Claudius, and some other of my men;
I'll have them sleep on cushions in my tent.
Luc. Varro, and Claudius!

Enter VARRO *and* CLAUDIUS.

Var. Calls my lord?
Bru. I pray you, sirs, lie in my tent, and sleep;
It may be, I shall raise you by and by
On business to my brother Cassius.
Var. So please you, we will stand, and watch your pleasure.
Bru. I will not have it so: lie down, good sirs;
It may be, I shall otherwise bethink me.
Look, Lucius, here's the book I sought for so;
I put it in the pocket of my gown.
[Servants *lie down.*
Luc. I was sure, your lordship did not give it me.
Bru. Bear with me, good boy, I am much forgetful.
Canst thou hold up thy heavy eyes awhile,
And touch thy instrument a strain or two?
Luc. Ay, my lord, an it please you.
Bru. It does, my boy:
I trouble thee too much, but thou art willing.
Luc. It is my duty, sir.
Bru. I should not urge thy duty past thy might;
I know, young bloods look for a time of rest.
Luc. I have slept, my lord, already.
Bru. It is well done; and thou shalt sleep again;
I will not hold thee long: if I do live,
I will be good to thee. [*Musick, and a Song.*
This is a sleepy tune: O murd'rous slumber!
Lay'st thou thy leaden mace upon my boy,
That plays the musick?—Gentle knave, good night!
I will not do thee so much wrong to wake thee.
If thou dost nod, thou break'st thy instrument;
I'll take it from thee; and, good boy, good night.
Let me see, let me see; Is not the leaf turn'd down,
Where I left reading? Here it is, I think.
[*He sits down.*

Enter the Ghost *of* Cæsar.

How ill this taper burns!—Ha! who comes here?
I think, it is the weakness of mine eyes,
That shapes this monstrous apparition.
It comes upon me:—Art thou any thing?
Art thou some god, some angel, or some devil,
That mak'st my blood cold, and my hair to stare?
Speak to me, what thou art.
Ghost. Thy evil spirit, Brutus.
Bru. Why com'st thou?
Ghost. To tell thee, thou shalt see me at Philippi.
Bru. Well;
Then I shall see thee again?
Ghost. Ay, at Philippi.
[Ghost *vanishes.*
Bru. Why, I will see thee at Philippi then.—
Now I have taken heart, thou vanishest:
Ill spirit, I would hold more talk with thee.—
Boy! Lucius!—Varro! Claudius! Sirs, awake!—
Claudius!
Luc. The strings, my lord, are false.
Bru. He thinks, he still is at his instrument.—
Lucius, awake.
Luc. My lord!
Bru. Didst thou dream, Lucius, that thou so cry'dst out?
Luc. My lord, I do not know that I did cry.
Bru. Yes, that thou didst: Didst thou see any thing?
Luc. Nothing, my lord.
Bru. Sleep again, Lucius.—Sirrah, Claudius!
Fellow thou! awake.
Var. My lord.
Clau. My lord.
Bru. Why did you so cry out, sirs, in your sleep?
Var. Clau. Did we, my lord?
Bru. Ay; Saw you any thing?
Var. No, my lord, I saw nothing.
Clau. Nor I, my lord.
Bru. Go, and commend me to my brother Cassius;
Bid him set on his powers betimes before,
And we will follow.
Var. Clau. It shall be done, my lord.
[*Exeunt.*

ACT V.

SCENE I. *The Plains of* Philippi.

Enter OCTAVIUS, ANTONY, *and their* Army.

Oct. Now, Antony, our hopes are answered:
You said, the enemy would not come down,
But keep the hills and upper regions;
It proves not so: their battles are at hand;
They mean to warn us at Philippi here,
Answering before we do demand of them.

Ant. Tut, I am in their bosoms, and I know
Wherefore they do it: they could be content
To visit other places; and come down
With fearful bravery, thinking, by this face,
To fasten in our thoughts that they have courage;
But 'tis not so.

Enter a Messenger.

Mess. Prepare you, generals:
The enemy comes on in gallant show,
Their bloody sign of battle is hung out,
And something to be done immediately.
Ant. Octavius, lead your battle softly on,
Upon the left hand of the even field.
Oct. Upon the right hand I, keep thou the left.
Ant. Why do you cross me in this exigent?
Oct. I do not cross you; but I will do so. [*March.*

Drum. Enter BRUTUS, CASSIUS, *and their* Army; LUCILIUS, TITINIUS, MESSALA, *and Others.*

Bru. They stand, and would have parley.
Cas. Stand fast, Titinius: We must out and talk.
Oct. Mark Antony, shall we give sign of battle?
Ant. No, Cæsar, we will answer on their charge.
Make forth, the generals would have some words.
Oct. Stir not until the signal.
Bru. Words before blows: Is it so, countrymen?
Oct. Not that we love words better, as you do.
Bru. Good words are better than bad strokes, Octavius.
Ant. In your bad strokes, Brutus, you give good words:
Witness the hole you made in Cæsar's heart.
Crying, *Long live! hail, Cæsar.*
Cas. Antony,
The posture of your blows are yet unknown:
But for your words, they rob the Hybla bees,
And leave them honeyless.
Ant. Not stingless too.
Bru. O, yes, and soundless too;
For you have stol'n their buzzing, Antony,
And, very wisely, threat before you sting.
Ant. Villains, you did not so, when your vile daggers
Hack'd one another in the sides of Cæsar:
You show'd your teeth like apes, and fawn'd like hounds,
And bow'd like bondmen, kissing Cæsar's feet;
Whilst damned Casca, like a cur, behind,
Struck Cæsar on the neck. O flatterers!
Cas. Flatterers!—Now, Brutus, thank yourself:
This tongue had not offended so to-day,
If Cassius might have rul'd.
Oct. Come, come, the cause: If arguing make us sweat,
The proof of it will turn to redder drops,
Look;
I draw a sword against conspirators:
When think you that the sword goes up again?—
Never, till Cæsar's three and twenty wounds
Be well aveng'd; or till another Cæsar
Have added slaughter to the sword of traitors.
Bru. Cæsar, thou canst not die by traitors,
Unless thou bring'st them with thee.
Oct. So I hope;
I was not born to die on Brutus' sword.
Bru. O, if thou wert the noblest of thy strain,
Young man, thou could'st not die more honourable.
Cas. A peevish schoolboy, worthless of such honour,
Join'd with a masker and a reveller.
Ant. Old Cassius still!
Oct. Come, Antony; away.—
Defiance, traitors, hurl we in your teeth;
If you dare fight to-day, come to the field;
If not, when you have stomachs.
[*Exeunt* OCTAVIUS, ANTONY, *and their* Army.
Cas. Why now, blow, wind; swell, billow; and swim, bark!
The storm is up, and all is on the hazard.
Bru. Ho!
Lucilius; hark, a word with you.
Luc. My lord.
[BRUTUS *and* LUCILIUS *converse apart.*
Cas. Messala.
Mess. What says my general?
Cas. Messala,
This is my birth-day; as this very day
Was Cassius born. Give me thy hand, Messala;
Be thou my witness, that against my will,
As Pompey was, am I compell'd to set
Upon one battle all our liberties.
You know, that I held Epicurus strong,
And his opinion: now I change my mind,
And partly credit things that do presage.
Coming from Sardis, on our former ensign
Two mighty eagles fell, and there they perch'd,
Gorging and feeding from our soldiers' hands;
Who to Philippi here consorted us;
This morning are they fled away, and gone;
And in their steads, do ravens, crows, and kites,
Fly o'er our heads, and downward look on us,
As we were sickly prey; their shadows seem
A canopy most fatal, under which
Our army lies, ready to give up the ghost.
Mess. Believe not so.
Cas. I but believe it partly;
For I am fresh of spirit, and resolv'd
To meet all perils very constantly.
Bru. Even so, Lucilius.
Cas. Now, most noble Brutus,
The gods to-day stand friendly; that we may,
Lovers in peace, lead on our days to age!
But, since the affairs of men rest still uncertain,
Let's reason with the worst that may befall.
If we do lose this battle, then is this
The very last time we shall speak together:
What are you then determined to do?
Bru. Even by the rule of that philosophy,
By which I did blame Cato for the death
Which he did give himself:—I know not how,
But I do find it cowardly and vile,
For fear of what might fall, so to prevent
The time of life:—arming myself with patience,
To stay the providence of some high powers,
That govern us below.
Cas. Then, if we lose this battle,
You are contented to be led in triumph
Thorough the streets of Rome?
Bru. No, Cassius, no: think not, thou noble Roman,
That ever Brutus will go bound to Rome;
He bears too great a mind. But this same day
Must end that work, the ides of March begun;
And whether we shall meet again, I know not.
Therefore our everlasting farewell take:—
For ever, and for ever, farewell, Cassius!
If we do meet again, why we shall smile;
If not, why then this parting was well made.
Cas. For ever, and for ever, farewell, Brutus!
If we do meet again, we'll smile indeed:
If not, 'tis true, this parting was well made.
Bru. Why, then, lead on.—O, that a man might know
The end of this day's business, ere it come!
But it sufficeth, that the day will end,
And then the end is known.—Come, ho! away!
[*Exeunt.*

SCENE II. *The same. The field of Battle.*

Alarum. Enter BRUTUS *and* MESSALA.

Bru. Ride, ride, Messala, ride, and give these bills
Unto the legions on the other side:
[*Loud Alarum.*
Let them set on at once; for I perceive

But cold demeanour in Octavius' wing,
And sudden push gives them the overthrow.
Ride, ride, Messala; let them all come down.
[*Exeunt.*

SCENE III.

The same. Another Part of the Field.

Alarum. Enter CASSIUS *and* TITINIUS.

Cas. O, look, Titinius, look, the villains fly!
Myself have to mine own turn'd enemy:
This ensign here of mine was turning back;
I slew the coward, and did take it from him.
Tit. O Cassius, Brutus gave the word too early;
Who having some advantage on Octavius,
Took it too eagerly; his soldiers fell to spoil,
Whilst we by Antony are all enclos'd.

Enter PINDARUS.

Pin. Fly further off, my lord, fly further off;
Mark Antony is in your tents, my lord!
Fly, therefore, noble Cassius, fly far off.
Cas. this hill is far enough. Look, look, Titinius;
Are those my tents, where I perceive the fire?
Tit. They are, my lord.
Cas. Titinius, if thou lov'st me,
Mount thou my horse, and hide thy spurs in him,
Till he have brought thee up to yonder troops,
And here again: that I may rest assur'd,
Whether yond' troops are friends or enemy.
Tit. I will be here again, even with a thought.
[*Exit.*
Cas. Go, Pindarus, get higher on that hill:
My sight was ever thick; Regard Titinius,
And tell me what thou not'st about the field.—
[*Exit* PINDARUS.
This day I breathed first; time is come round,
And where I did begin, there shall I end;
My life is run his compass.—Sirrah, what news?
Pin. [*Above.*] O my lord!
Cas. What news?
Pin. Titinius is enclosed round about
With horsemen, that make to him on the spur;—
Yet he spurs on.—Now they are almost on him;
Now, Titinius!—now some 'light;—Oh, he 'lights too:—he's ta'en;—
And hark! [*shout*] they shout for joy.
Cas. Come down, behold no more.—
O, coward that I am, to live so long,
To see my best friend ta'en before my face!

Enter PINDARUS.

Come hither, sirrah:
In Parthia did I take thee prisoner;
And then I swore thee, saving of thy life,
That whatsoever I did bid thee do,
Thou should'st attempt it. Come now, keep thine oath!
Now be a freeman; and with this good sword,
That ran through Cæsar's bowels, search this bosom.
Stand not to answer: Here, take thou the hilts;
And, when my face is cover'd as 'tis now,
Guide thou the sword.—Cæsar, thou art reveng'd,
Even with the sword that kill'd thee. [*Dies.*
Pin. So, I am free; yet would not so have been,
Durst I have done my will. O Cassius!
Far from this country Pindarus shall run,
Where never Roman shall take note of him.
[*Exit.*

Re-enter TITINIUS, *with* MESSALA.

Mes. It is but change, Titinius; for Octavius
Is overthrown by noble Brutus' power,
As Cassius' legions are by Antony.
Tit. These tidings will well comfort Cassius.
Mes. Where did you leave him?
Tit. All disconsolate,
With Pindarus his bondman on this hill.
Mes. Is not that he, that lies upon the ground?
Tit. He lies not like the living. O my heart!
Mes. Is not that he?
Tit. No, this was he, Messala,
But Cassius is no more.—O setting sun!
As in thy red rays thou dost sink to-night,
So in his red blood Cassius's day is set;
The sun of Rome is set! Our day is gone;
Clouds, dews, and dangers come; our deeds are done!
Mistrust of my success hath done this deed.
Mes. Mistrust of good success hath done this deed.
O hateful error, melancholy's child!
Why dost thou show to the apt thoughts of men
The things that are not? O error, soon conceiv'd,
Thou never com'st unto a happy birth,
But kill'st the mother that engender'd thee.
Tit. What, Pindarus; Where art thou, Pindarus?
Mes. Seek him, Titinius: whilst I go to meet
The noble Brutus, thrusting this report
Into his ears: I may say, thrusting it;
For piercing steel, and darts envenomed,
Shall be as welcome to the ears of Brutus,
As tidings of this sight.
Tit. Hie you, Messala,
And I will seek for Pindarus the while.
[*Exit* MESSALA.
Why didst thou send me forth, brave Cassius?
Did I not meet thy friends? and did not they
Put on my brows this wreath of victory,
And bid me give 't thee? Didst thou not hear their shouts?
Alas, thou hast misconstrued every thing.
But hold thee, take this garland on thy brow;
Thy Brutus bid me give it thee, and I
Will do his bidding.—Brutus, come apace,
And see how I regarded Caius Cassius.—
By your leave, gods:—This is a Roman's part:
Come, Cassius' sword, and find Titinius' heart.
[*Dies.*

Alarum. Re-enter MESSALA, *with* BRUTUS, *young* CATO, STRATO, VOLUMNIUS, *and* LUCILIUS.

Bru. Where, where, Messala, doth his body lie?
Mes. Lo, yonder; and Titinius mourning it.
Bru. Titinius' face is upward.
Cato. He is slain.
Bru. O Julius Cæsar, thou art mighty yet!
Thy spirit walks abroad, and turns our swords
In our own proper entrails. [*Loud alarums.*
Cato. Brave Titinius!
Look, whe'r he have not crown'd dead Cassius!
Bru. Are yet two Romans living such as these?—
The last of all the Romans, fare thee well!
It is impossible, that ever Rome
Should breed thy fellow.—Friends, I owe more tears
To this dead man, than you shall see me pay.—
I shall find time, Cassius, I shall find time.—
Come, therefore, and to Thassos send his body;
His funeral shall not be in our camp,
Lest it discomfort us.—Lucilius, come;—
And come, young Cato; let us to the field.—
Labeo, and Flavius, set our battles on:—
'Tis three o'clock; and, Romans, yet ere night
We shall try fortune in a second fight. [*Exeunt.*

SCENE IV. *Another Part of the Field.*

Alarum. Enter fighting, Soldiers *of both Armies; then* BRUTUS, CATO, LUCILIUS, *and Others.*

Bru. Yet countrymen, O, yet hold up your heads!
Cato. What bastard doth not? Who will go with me?
I will proclaim my name about the field:—
I am the son of Marcus Cato, ho!

A foe to tyrants, and my country's friend:
I am the son of Marcus Cato, ho!
[*Charges the* Enemy.
Bru. And I am Brutus, Marcus Brutus, I;
Brutus, my country's friend: know me for Brutus. [*Exit, charging the* Enemy. CATO *is overpowered, and falls.*
Luc. O young and noble Cato, art thou down?
Why, now thou diest as bravely as Titinius;
And may'st be honour'd being Cato's son.
1 *Sold.* Yield, or thou diest.
Luc. Only I yield to die;
There is so much, that thou wilt kill me straight;
[*Offering money.*
Kill Brutus, and be honour'd in his death.
1 *Sold.* We must not—A noble prisoner!
2 *Sold.* Room, ho! Tell Antony, Brutus is ta'en.
1 *Sold.* I'll tell the news.—Here comes the general:—

Enter ANTONY.

Brutus is ta'en, Brutus is ta'en, my lord.
Ant. Where is he?
Luc. Safe, Antony; Brutus is safe enough:
I dare assure thee, that no enemy
Shall ever take alive the noble Brutus:
The gods defend him from so great a shame!
When you do find him, or alive or dead,
He will be found like Brutus, like himself.
Ant. This is not Brutus, friend; but I assure you,
A prize no less in worth: keep this man safe,
Give him all kindness: I had rather have
Such men my friends, than enemies. Go on,
And see whe'r Brutus be alive, or dead:
And bring us word, unto Octavius' tent,
How every thing is chanc'd. [*Exeunt.*

SCENE V. *Another Part of the Field.*

Enter BRUTUS, DARDANIUS, CLITUS, STRATO, *and* VOLUMNIUS.

Bru. Come, poor remains of friends, rest on this rock.
Cli. Statilius show'd the torch-light: but, my lord,
He came not back; he is or ta'en or slain.
Bru. Sit thee down, Clitus: Slaying is the word;
It is a deed in fashion. Hark thee, Clitus.—
[*Whispering.*
Cli. What, I, my lord? No, not for all the world.
Bru. Peace then, no words.
Cli. I'll rather kill myself.
Bru. Hark thee, Dardanius! [*Whispers him.*
Dar. I do such a deed?
Cli. O, Dardanius!
Dar. O, Clitus!
Cli. What ill request did Brutus make to thee?
Dar. To kill him, Clitus: Look, he meditates.
Cli. Now is that noble vessel full of grief,
That it runs over even at his eyes.
Bru. Come hither, good Volumnius: list a word.
Vol. What says my lord?
Bru. Why, this, Volumnius;
The ghost of Cæsar hath appear'd to me
Two several times by night: at Sardis once;
And, this last night, here in Philippi' fields.
I know, my hour is come.
Vol. Not so, my lord.
Bru. Nay, I am sure it is, Volumnius.
Thou seest the world, Volumnius, how it goes:
Our enemies have beat us to the pit:
It is more worthy to leap in ourselves,
Than tarry till they push us. Good Volumnius,
Thou know'st, that we two went to school together:
Even for that our love of old, I pray thee,
Hold thou my sword-hilts, whilst I run on it.
Vol. That's not an office for a friend, my lord.
[*Alarum still.*
Cli. Fly, fly, my lord; there is no tarrying here.
Bru. Farewell to you;—and you;—and you, Volumnius.—
Strato, thou hast been all this while asleep;
Farewell to thee too, Strato.—Countrymen,
My heart doth joy, that yet, in all my life,
I found no man, but he was true to me.
I shall have glory by this losing day,
More than Octavius, and Mark Antony,
By this vile conquest shall attain unto.
So fare you well, at once; for Brutus' tongue
Hath almost ended his life's history:
Night hangs upon mine eyes; my bones would rest,
That have but labour'd to attain this hour.
[*Alarum. Cry within;* Fly, fly, fly.
Cli. Fly, my lord, fly.
Bru. Hence; I will follow.
[*Exeunt* CLITUS, DARDANIUS, *and* VOLUMNIUS.
I pr'ythee, Strato, stay thou by thy lord:
Thou art a fellow of a good respect;
Thy life hath had some smatch of honour in it:
Hold then my sword, and turn away thy face,
While I do run upon it. Wilt thou, Strato?
Stra. Give me your hand first: Fare you well, my lord.
Bru. Farewell, good Strato.—Cæsar, now be still:
I kill'd not thee with half so good a will.
[*He runs on his Sword and dies.*

Alarum. Retreat. Enter OCTAVIUS, ANTONY, MESSALA, LUCILIUS, *and their* Army.

Oct. What man is this?
Mes. My master's man.—Strato, where is thy master?
Stra. Free from the bondage you are in, Messala;
The conquerors can but make a fire of him;
For Brutus only overcame himself,
And no man else hath honour by his death.
Luc. So Brutus should be found.—I thank thee, Brutus,
That thou hast prov'd Lucilius' saying true.
Oct. All that serv'd Brutus, I will entertain them.
Fellow, wilt thou bestow thy time with me?
Stra. Ay, if Messala will prefer me to you.
Oct. Do so, Messala.
Mes. How died my master, Strato?
Stra. I held the sword, and he did run on it.
Mes. Octavius, then take him to follow thee,
That did the latest service to my master.
Ant. This was the noblest Roman of them all:
All the conspirators, save only he,
Did that they did in envy of great Cæsar;
He, only, in a general honest thought,
And common good to all, made one of them.
His life was gentle; and the elements
So mix'd in him, that Nature might stand up,
And say to all the world, *This was a man!*
Oct. According to his virtue let us use him,
With all respect and rites of burial.
Within my tent his bones to-night shall lie,
Most like a soldier, order'd honourably.—
So, call the field to rest: and let's away,
To part the glories of this happy day. [*Exeunt.*

ANTONY AND CLEOPATRA.

PERSONS REPRESENTED.

M. ANTONY, OCTAVIUS CÆSAR, M. ÆMIL. LEPIDUS, — *Triumvers.*
SEXTUS POMPEIUS.
DOMITIUS ENOBARBUS, VENTIDIUS, EROS, SCARUS, DERCETAS, DEMETRIUS, PHILO, — *Friends of* Antony.
MECÆNAS, AGRIPPA, DOLABELLA, PROCULEIUS, THYREUS, GALLUS, — *Friends of* Cæsar.
MENAS, MENECRATES, VARRIUS, — *Friends of* Pompey.
TAURUS, *Lieutenant-General to* Cæsar.
CANIDIUS, *Lieutenant-General to* Antony.
SILIUS, *an Officer in* Ventidius's *Army.*
EUPHRONIUS, *an Ambassador from* Antony *to* Cæsar.
ALEXAS, MARDIAN, SELEUCUS, *and* DIOMEDES, *Attendants on* Cleopatra.
A Soothsayer. *A* Clown.

CLEOPATRA, Queen *of* Egypt.
OCTAVIA, *Sister to* Cæsar, *and Wife to* Antony.
CHARMIAN, *and* IRAS, *Attendants on* Cleopatra.

Officers, Soldiers, Messengers, *and other* Attendants.

SCENE—*dispersed in several Parts of the* Roman *Empire.*

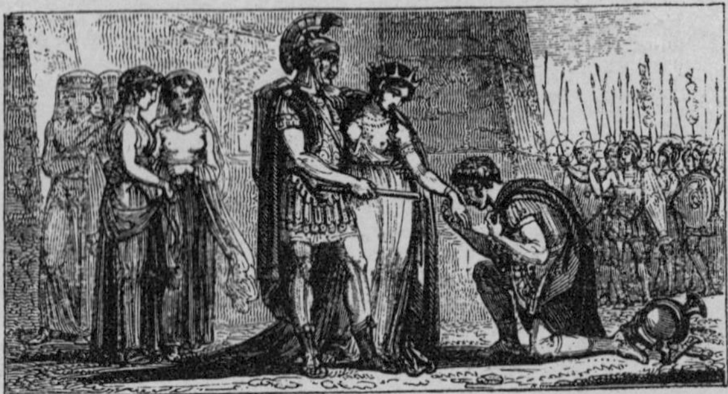

ACT I.

SCENE I. Alexandria. *A Room in* Cleopatra's *Palace.*

Enter DEMETRIUS *and* PHILO.

Phi. NAY, but this dotage of our general's
O'erflows the measure: those his goodly eyes,
That o'er the files and musters of the war
Have glow'd like plated Mars, now bend, now turn,
The office and devotion of their view
Upon a tawny front: his captain's heart,
Which in the scuffles of great fights hath burst
The buckles on his breast, reneges all temper:
And is become the bellows, and the fan,
To cool a gipsy's lust. Look, where they come!

Flourish. Enter ANTONY *and* CLEOPATRA, *with their* Trains; Eunuchs *fanning her.*

Take but good note, and you shall see in him
The triple pillar of the world transform'd
Into a strumpet's fool: behold and see.
Cleo. If it be love indeed, tell me how much.
Ant. There's beggary in the love that can be reckon'd.
Cleo. I'll set a bourn how far to be belov'd.
Ant. Then must thou needs find out new heaven, new earth.

Enter an Attendant.

Att. News, my good lord, from Rome.
Ant. Grates me:—The sum.
Cleo. Nay, hear them, Antony:
Fulvia, perchance, is angry; Or, who knows
If the scarce-bearded Cæsar have not sent
His powerful mandate to you, *Do this, or this:*
Take in that kingdom, and enfranchise that;
Perform't, or else we damn thee.
Ant. How, my love!
Cleo. Perchance,—nay, and most like,
You must not stay here longer, your dismission
Is come from Cæsar; therefore hear it, Antony.—
Where's Fulvia's process? Cæsar's, I would say?—Both?—
Call in the messengers.—As I am Egypt's queen,
Thou blushest, Antony; and that blood of thine
Is Cæsar's homager: else so thy cheek pays shame,
When shrill-tongu'd Fulvia scolds.—The messengers.
Ant. Let Rome in Tyber melt! and the wide arch
Of the rang'd empire fall! Here is my space;
Kingdoms are clay: our dungy earth alike
Feeds beast as man: the nobleness of life
Is, to do thus; when such a mutual pair, [*Embracing.*
And such a twain can do't, in which, I bind,
On pain of punishment, the world to weet,
We stand up peerless.
Cleo. Excellent falsehood!
Why did he marry Fulvia, and not love her?—
I'll seem the fool I am not; Antony
Will be himself.

Ant. But stirr'd by Cleopatra.—
Now, for the love of Love, and her soft hours,
Let's not confound the time with conference harsh:
There's not a minute of our lives should stretch
Without some pleasure now: What sport to-night?
Cleo. Hear the ambassadors.
Ant. Fye, wrangling queen!
Whom every thing becomes, to chide, to laugh,
To weep; whose every passion fully strives
To make itself, in thee, fair and admir'd!
No messenger; but thine and all alone,
To-night, we'll wander through the streets, and note
The qualities of people. Come, my queen;
Last night you did desire it:—Speak not to us.
[*Exeunt* ANT. *and* CLEO. *with their* Train.
Dem. Is Cæsar with Antonius priz'd so slight?
Phi. Sir, sometimes, when he is not Antony,
He comes too short of that great property
Which still should go with Antony.
Dem. I'm full sorry,
That he approves the common liar, who
Thus speaks of him at Rome: But I will hope
Of better deeds to-morrow. Rest you happy!
[*Exeunt.*

SCENE II. *The same. Another Room.*

Enter CHARMIAN, IRAS, ALEXAS, *and a* Soothsayer.

Char. Lord Alexas, sweet Alexas, most any thing Alexas, almost most absolute Alexas, where's the soothsayer that you praised so to the queen? O, that I knew this husband, which, you say, must charge his horns with garlands!
Alex. Soothsayer.
Sooth. Your will?
Char. Is this the man?—Is't you, sir, that know things?
Sooth. In nature's infinite book of secrecy,
A little I can read.
Alex. Show him your hand.

Enter ENOBARBUS.

Eno. Bring in the banquet quickly; wine enough,
Cleopatra's health to drink.
Char. Good sir, give me good fortune.
Sooth. I make not, but foresee.
Char. Pray then, foresee me one.
Sooth. You shall be yet far fairer than you are.
Char. He means, in flesh.
Iras. No, you shall paint when you are old.
Char. Wrinkles forbid!
Alex. Vex not his prescience; be attentive.
Char. Hush!
Sooth. You shall be more beloving, than beloved.
Char. I had rather heat my liver with drinking.
Alex. Nay, hear him.
Char. Good now, some excellent fortune! Let me be married to three kings in a forenoon, and widow them all: let me have a child at fifty, to whom Herod of Jewry may do homage: find me to marry me with Octavius Cæsar, and companion me with my mistress.
Sooth. You shall outlive the lady whom you serve.
Char. O excellent! I love long life better than figs.
Sooth. You have seen and proved a fairer former fortune
Than that which is to approach.
Char. Then, belike, my children shall have no names: Pr'ythee, how many boys and wenches must I have?
Sooth. If every of your wishes had a womb,
And fertile every wish, a million.
Char. Out, fool; I forgive thee for a witch.
Alex. You think none but your sheets are privy to your wishes.
Char. Nay, come, tell Iras hers.
Alex. We'll know all our fortunes.
Eno. Mine, and most of our fortunes, to-night, shall be—drunk to bed.
Iras. There's a palm presages chastity, if nothing else.
Char. Even as the o'erflowing Nilus presageth famine.
Iras. Go, you wild bedfellow, you cannot soothsay.
Char. Nay, if an oily palm be not a fruitful prognostication, I cannot scratch mine ear.—Pry'thee, tell her but a worky-day fortune.
Sooth. Your fortunes are alike.
Iras. But how, but how? give me particulars.
Sooth. I have said.
Iras. Am I not an inch of fortune better than she?
Char. Well, if you were but an inch of fortune better than I, where would you choose it?
Iras. Not in my husband's nose.
Char. Our worser thoughts heavens mend! Alexas,—come, his fortune, his fortune.—O, let him marry a woman that cannot go, sweet Isis, I beseech thee! And let her die too, and give him a worse! and let worse follow worse, till the worst of all follow him laughing to his grave, fifty-fold a cuckold! Good Isis, hear me this prayer, though thou deny me a matter of more weight; good Isis, I beseech thee!
Iras. Amen. Dear goddess, hear that prayer of the people? for, as it is a heart-breaking to see a handsome man loose-wived, so it is a deadly sorrow to behold a foul knave uncuckolded; Therefore, dear Isis, keep decorum, and fortune him accordingly!
Char. Amen.
Alex. Lo, now! if it lay in their hands to make me a cuckold, they would make themselves whores, but they'd do't.
Eno. Hush! here comes Antony.
Char. Not he, the queen.

Enter CLEOPATRA.

Cleo. Saw you my lord?
Eno. No, lady,
Cleo. Was he not here?
Char. No, madam.
Cleo. He was dispos'd to mirth; but on the sudden
A Roman thought hath struck him.—Enobarbus,—
Eno. Madam.
Cleo. Seek him, and bring him hither. Where's Alexas?
Alex. Here, madam, at your service.—My lord approaches.

Enter ANTONY, *with a* Messenger *and* Attendants.

Cleo. We will not look upon him: Go with us.
[*Exeunt* CLEO. ENO. ALEX. IRAS, CHAR. Soothsayer, *and* Attendants.
Mess. Fulvia thy wife first came into the field.
Ant. Against my brother Lucius?
Mess. Ay:
But soon that war had end, and the time's state
Made friends of them, jointing their force 'gainst Cæsar;
Whose better issue in the war, from Italy,
Upon the first encounter, drave them.
Ant. Well,
What worst?
Mess. The nature of bad news infects the teller.
Ant. When it concerns the fool or coward.—On:
Things, that are past, are done, with me.—'Tis thus;
Who tells me true, though in his tale lie death,
I hear him as he flatter'd.
Mess. Labienus
(This is stiff news) hath, with his Parthian force,
Extended Asia from Euphrates;
His conquering banner shook, from Syria

To Lydia, and to Ionia;
Whilst——

Ant. Antony, thou would'st say,—

Mess. O, my lord!

Ant. Speak to me home, mince not the general tongue;
Name Cleopatra as she's call'd in Rome:
Rail thou in Fulvia's phrase: and taunt my faults
With such full licence, as both truth and malice
Have power to utter. O, then we bring forth weeds,
When our quick minds lie still: and our ills told us,
Is as our earing. Fare thee well awhile.

Mess. At your noble pleasure. [*Exit.*

Ant. From Sicyon how the news? Speak there.

1 *Att.* The man from Sicyon.—Is there such a one?

2 *Att.* He stays upon your will.

Ant. Let him appear,—
These strong Egyptian fetters I must break.

Enter another Messenger.

Or lose myself in dotage.—What are you?

2 *Mess.* Fulvia thy wife is dead.

Ant. Where died she?

2 *Mess.* In Sicyon:
Her length of sickness, with what else more serious
Importeth thee to know, this bears. [*Gives a letter.*

Ant. Forbear me.— [*Exit* Messenger.
There's a great spirit gone: Thus did I desire it:
What our contempts do often hurl from us,
We wish it ours again; the present pleasure,
By revolution lowering, does become
The opposite of itself: she's good, being gone;
The hand could pluck her back, that shov'd her on,
I must from this enchanting queen break off;
Ten thousand harms, more than the ills I know,
My idleness doth hatch.—How now! Enobarbus!

Enter ENOBARBUS.

Eno. What's your pleasure, sir?

Ant. I must with haste from hence.

Eno. Why, then, we kill all our women: We see how mortal an unkindness is to them: if they suffer our departure, death's the word.

Ant. I must be gone.

Eno. Under a compelling occasion, let women die: It were pity to cast them away for nothing; though, between them and a great cause, they should be esteemed nothing. Cleopatra, catching but the least noise of this, dies instantly; I have seen her die twenty times upon far poorer moment: I do think there is mettle in death, which commits some loving act upon her, she hath such a celerity in dying.

Ant. She is cunning past man's thought.

Eno. Alack, sir, no; her passions are made of nothing but the finest part of pure love: We cannot call her winds and waters, sighs and tears; they are greater storms and tempests than almanacks can report: this cannot be cunning in her; if it be, she makes a shower of rain as well as Jove.

Ant. 'Would, I had never seen her!

Eno. O, sir, you had then left unseen a wonderful piece of work: which not to have been blessed withal, would have discredited your travel.

Ant. Fulvia is dead.

Eno. Sir?

Ant. Fulvia is dead.

Eno. Fulvia?

Ant. Dead.

Eno. Why, sir, give the gods a thankful sacrifice. When it pleaseth their deities to take the wife of a man from him, it shows to man the tailors of the earth; comforting therein, that when old robes are worn out, there are members to make new. If there were no more women but Fulvia, then had you indeed a cut, and the case to be lamented; this grief is crowned with consolation; your old smock brings forth a new petticoat:—and, indeed, the tears live in an onion, that should water this sorrow.

Ant. The business she hath broached in the state,
Cannot endure my absence.

Eno. And the business you have broached here cannot be without you; especially that of Cleopatra's, which wholly depends on your abode.

Ant. No more light answers. Let our officers
Have notice what we purpose. I shall break
The cause of our expedience to the queen,
And get her love to part. For not alone
The death of Fulvia, with more urgent touches,
Do strongly speak to us; but the letters too
Of many our contriving friends in Rome
Petition us at home: Sextus Pompeius
Hath given the dare to Cæsar, and commands
The empire of the sea: our slippery people
(Whose love is never link'd to the deserver,
Till his deserts are past), begin to throw
Pompey the Great, and all his dignities,
Upon his son: who, high in name and power,
Higher than both in blood and life, stands up
For the main soldier: whose quality, going on,
The sides o' the world may danger: Much is breeding,
Which, like the courser's hair, hath yet but life,
And not a serpent's poison. Say, our pleasure,
To such whose place is under us, requires
Our quick remove from hence.

Eno. I shall do't. [*Exeunt.*

SCENE III.

Enter CLEOPATRA, CHARMIAN, IRAS, *and* ALEXAS.

Cleo. Where is he?

Char. I did not see him since.

Cleo. See where he is, who's with him, what he does:—
I did not send you;—If you find him sad,
Say, I am dancing: if in mirth, report
That I am sudden sick: Quick, and return. [*Exit* ALEXAS.

Char. Madam, methinks, if you did love him dearly,
You do not hold the method to enforce
The like from him.

Cleo. What should I do, I do not?

Char. In each thing give him way, cross him in nothing.

Cleo. Thou teachest like a fool: the way to lose him.

Char. Tempt him not so too far: I wish, forbear;
In time we hate that which we often fear.

Enter ANTONY.

But here comes Antony.

Cleo. I am sick, and sullen.

Ant. I am sorry to give breathing to my purpose,—

Cleo. Help me away, dear Charmian, I shall fall;
It cannot be thus long, the sides of nature
Will not sustain it.

Ant. Now, my dearest queen,—

Cleo. 'Pray you, stand further from me.

Ant. What's the matter?

Cleo. I know, by that same eye, there's some good news.
What says the married woman?—You may go;
'Would, she had never given you leave to come!
Let her not say, 'tis I that keep you here,
I have no power upon you; hers you are.

Ant. The gods best know,—

Cleo. O, never was there queen
So mightily betray'd! Yet, at the first,
I saw the treasons planted.

Ant. Cleopatra,—
Cleo. Why should I think you can be mine, and true,
Though you in swearing shake the throned gods,
Who have been false to Fulvia? Riotous madness,
To be entangled with those mouth-made vows,
Which break themselves in swearing!
Ant. Most sweet queen,—
Cleo. Nay, pray you, seek no colour for your going.
But bid farewell, and go: when you sued staying,
Then was the time for words:—No going then;—
Eternity was in our lips and eyes;
Bliss in our brows' bent; none our parts so poor,
But was a race of heaven: They are so still,
Or thou, the greatest soldier of the world,
Art turn'd the greatest liar.
Ant. How now, lady!
Cleo. I would, I had thy inches; thou should'st know,
There were a heart in Egypt.
Ant. Hear me, queen;
The strong necessity of time commands
Our services a while; but my full heart
Remains in use with you. Our Italy
Shines o'er with civil swords: Sextus Pompeius
Makes his approaches to the port of Rome:
Equality of two domestic powers
Breeds scrupulous faction: The hated, grown to strength,
Are newly grown to love: the condemn'd Pompey,
Rich in his father's honour, creeps apace
Into the hearts of such as have not thriv'd
Upon the present state, whose numbers threaten;
And quietness, grown sick of rest, would purge
By any desperate change: My more particular,
And that which most with you should safe my going,
Is Fulvia's death.
Cleo. Though age from folly could not give me freedom,
It does from childishness:—Can Fulvia die?
Ant. She's dead, my queen:
Look here, and, at thy sovereign leisure, read
The garboils she awak'd; at the last, best:
See, when, and where she died.
Cleo. O most false love!
Where be the sacred vials thou should'st fill
With sorrowful water? I see, I see,
In Fulvia's death, how mine receiv'd shall be.
Ant. Quarrel no more, but be prepar'd to know
The purposes I bear; which are, or cease,
As you shall give the advice; by the fire,
That quickens Nilus' slime, I go from hence,
Thy soldier, servant; making peace, or war,
As thou affect'st.
Cleo. Cut my lace, Charmian, come;—
But let it be.—I am quickly ill, and well:
So Antony loves.
Ant. My precious queen, forbear;
And give true evidence to his love, which stands
An honourable trial.
Cleo. So Fulvia told me.
I pr'ythee, turn aside, and weep for her;
Then bid adieu to me, and say, the tears
Belong to Egypt: Good now, play one scene
Of excellent dissembling; and let it look
Like perfect honour.
Ant. You'll heat my blood; no more.
Cleo. You can do better yet; but this is meetly.
Ant. Now, by my sword,—
Cleo. And target,—still he mends;
But this is not the best: Look, pr'ythee, Charmian,
How this Herculean Roman does become
The carriage of his chafe.
Ant. I'll leave you, lady.
Cleo. Courteous lord, one word.
Sir, you and I must part,—but that's not it:
Sir, you and I have lov'd,—but there's not it;
That you know well: Something it is I would,—
O, my oblivion is a very Antony,
And I am all forgotten.
Ant. But that your royalty
Holds idleness your subject, I should take you
For idleness itself.
Cleo. 'Tis sweating labour,
To bear such idleness so near the heart
As Cleopatra this. But, sir, forgive me;
Since my becomings kill me, when they do not
Eye well to you: Your honour calls you hence;
Therefore be deaf to my unpitied folly,
And all the gods go with you! upon your sword
Sit laurel'd victory! and smooth success
Be strew'd before your feet!
Ant. Let us go. Come;
Our separation so abides, and flies,
That thou, residing here, go'st yet with me,
And I, hence fleeting, here remain with thee.
Away. [*Exeunt.*

SCENE IV.

Rome. *An Apartment in* Cæsar's *House.*

Enter OCTAVIUS CÆSAR, LEPIDUS, *and* Attendants.

Cæs. You may see, Lepidus, and henceforth know,
It is not Cæsar's natural vice to hate
Our great competitor: From Alexandria
This is the news; He fishes, drinks, and wastes
The lamps of night in revel: is not more manlike
Than Cleopatra; nor the queen of Ptolemy
More womanly than he: hardly gave audience, or
Vouchsaf'd to think he had partners: You shall find there
A man, who is the abstract of all faults
That all men follow.
Lep. I must not think, there are
Evils enough to darken all his goodness:
His faults, in him, seem as the spots of heaven,
More fiery by night's blackness; hereditary,
Rather than purchas'd; what he cannot change,
Than what he chooses.
Cæs. You are too indulgent: Let us grant it is not
Amiss to tumble on the bed of Ptolemy;
To give a kingdom for a mirth; to sit
And keep the turn of tipling with a slave;
To reel the streets at noon, and stand the buffet
With knaves that smell of sweat; say, this becomes him,
(As his composure must be rare indeed,
Whom these things cannot blemish), yet must Antony
No way excuse his soils, when we do bear
So great weight in his lightness. If he fill'd
His vacancy with his voluptuousness,
Full surfeits, and the dryness of his bones,
Call on him for't: but to confound such time,
That drums him from his sport, and speaks as loud
As his own state, and ours,—'tis to be chid
As we rate boys; who, being mature in knowledge,
Pawn their experience to their present pleasure,
And so rebel to judgment.

Enter a Messenger.

Lep. Here's more news.
Mess. Thy biddings have been done: and every hour,
Most noble Cæsar, shalt thou have report
How 'tis abroad. Pompey is strong at sea;
And it appears, he is belov'd of those
That only have fear'd Cæsar: to the ports
The discontents repair, and men's reports
Give him much wrong'd.
Cæs. I should have known no less:—
It hath been taught us from the primal state,
That he, which is, was wish'd until he were;

And the ebb'd man ne'er lov'd, till ne'er worth love,
Comes dear'd, by being lack'd. This common body,
Like a vagabond flag upon the stream,
Goes to, and back, lackeying the varying tide,
To rot itself with motion.

Mess. Cæsar, I bring thee word,
Menecrates and Menas, famous pirates
Make the sea serve them: which they ear and wound
With keels of every kind: Many hot inroads
They make in Italy: the borders maritime
Lack blood to think on't, and flush youth revolt:
No vessel can peep forth, but 'tis as soon
Taken as seen! for Pompey's name strikes more,
Than could his war resisted.

Cæs. Antony,
Leave thy lascivious wassals. When thou once
Wast beaten from Modena, where thou slew'st
Hirtius and Pansa, consuls, at thy heel
Did famine follow; whom thou fought'st against,
Though daintily brought up, with patience more
Than savages could suffer: Thou didst drink
The stale of horses, and the gilded puddle
Which beasts would cough at: thy palate then did deign
The roughest berry on the rudest hedge;
Yea, like the stag, when snow the pasture sheets,
The barks of trees thou browsed'st; on the Alps
It is reported, thou didst eat strange flesh,
Which some did die to look on: And all this
(It wounds thine honour, that I speak it now),
Was borne so like a soldier, that thy cheek
So much as lank'd not.

Lep. 'Tis pity of him.

Cæs. Let his shames quickly
Drive him to Rome: 'Tis time we twain
Did show ourselves i'the field; and, to that end,
Assemble we immediate council: Pompey
Thrives in our idleness.

Lep. To-morrow, Cæsar,
I shall be furnish'd to inform you rightly
Both what by sea and land I can be able,
To 'front this present time.

Cæs. Till which encounter,
It is my business too. Farewell.

Lep. Farewell, my lord: What you shall know mean time
Of stirs abroad, I shall beseech you, sir,
To let me be partaker.

Cæs. Doubt not, sir;
I knew it for my bond. [*Exeunt.*

SCENE V.

Alexandria. *A Room in the Palace.*

Enter CLEOPATRA, CHARMIAN, IRAS, *and* MARDIAN.

Cleo. Charmian,—

Char. Madam.

Cleo. Ha, ha!
Give me to drink mandragora.

Char. Why, madam?

Cleo. That I might sleep out this great gap of time,
My Antony is away.

Char. You think of him
Too much.

Cleo. O, 'tis treason!

Char. Madam, I trust, not so.

Cleo. Thou, eunuch, Mardian!

Mar. What's your highness' pleasure?

Cleo. Not now to hear thee sing; I take no pleasure
In aught a eunuch has: 'Tis well for thee,
That, being unseminar'd, thy freer thoughts
May not fly forth of Egypt. Hast thou affections?

Mar. Yes, gracious madam.

Cleo. Indeed?

Mar. Not in deed, madam; for I can do nothing
But what in deed is honest to be done:
Yet I have fierce affections, and think,
What Venus did with Mars.

Cleo. O Charmian,
Where think'st thou he is now? Stands he, or sits he?
Or does he walk? or is he on his horse?
O happy horse, to bear the weight of Antony!
Do bravely, horse! for wot'st thou whom thou mov'st?
The demi-Atlas of this earth, the arm
And burgonet of men.—He's speaking now,
Or murmuring, *Where's my serpent of old Nile?*
For so he calls me: Now I feed myself
With most delicious poison:—Think on me,
That am with Phœbus' amorous pinches black,
And wrinkled deep in time? Broad-fronted Cæsar,
When thou wast here above the ground, I was
A morsel for a monarch: and great Pompey
Would stand, and make his eyes grow in my brow;
There would he anchor his aspect, and die
With looking on his life.

Enter ALEXAS.

Alex. Sovereign of Egypt, hail!

Cleo. How much unlike art thou Mark Antony!
Yet, coming from him, that great medicine hath
With his tinct gilded thee.—
How goes it with my brave Mark Antony?

Alex. Last thing he did, dear queen,
He kiss'd,—the last of many doubled kisses,
This orient pearl:—His speech sticks in my heart.

Cleo. Mine ear must pluck it thence.

Alex. Good friend, quoth he,
Say, *The firm Roman to great Egypt sends*
This treasure of an oyster; at whose foot
To mend the petty present, I will piece
Her opulent throne with kingdoms; All the east,
Say thou, *shall call her mistress.* So he nodded,
And soberly did mount a termagant steed,
Who neigh'd so high, that what I would have spoke
Was beastly dumb'd by him.

Cleo. What, was he sad, or merry?

Alex. Like to the time o' the year, between the extremes
Of heat and cold; he was nor sad, nor merry.

Cleo. O well-divided disposition!—Note him,
Note him, good Charmian, 'tis the man; but note him;
He was not sad; for he would shine on those
That make their looks by his: he was not merry,
Which seem'd to tell them, his remembrance lay
In Egypt with his joy: but between both;
O heavenly mingle!—be'st thou sad, or merry,
The violence of either thee becomes;
So does it no man else.—Met'st thou my posts?

Alex. Ay, madam, twenty several messengers:
Why do you send so thick?

Cleo. Who's born that day
When I forget to send to Antony,
Shall die a beggar.—Ink and paper, Charmian.—
Welcome, my good Alexas.—Did I, Charmian,
Ever love Cæsar so?

Char. O that brave Cæsar!

Cleo. Be chok'd with such another emphasis!
Say, the brave Antony.

Char. The valiant Cæsar!

Cleo. By Isis, I will give thee bloody teeth,
If thou with Cæsar paragon again
My man of men.

Char. By your most gracious pardon,
I sing but after you.

Cleo. My sallad days:
When I was green in judgment:—Cold in blood,
To say, as I said then!—But, come, away:
Get me ink and paper: he shall have every day
A several greeting, or I'll unpeople Egypt.
[*Exeunt.*

ACT II.

SCENE I.

Messina. *A Room in* Pompey's *House.*

Enter POMPEY, MENECRATES, *and* MENAS.

Pom. If the great gods be just, they shall assist
The deeds of justest men.
Mene. Know, worthy Pompey,
That what they do delay, they not deny.
Pom. Whiles we are suitors to their throne, decays
The thing we sue for.
Mene. We, ignorant of ourselves,
Beg often our own harms; which the wise powers
Deny us for our good; so find we profit,
By losing of our prayers.
Pom. I shall do well:
The people love me, and the sea is mine;
My power's a crescent, and my auguring hope
Says, it will come to the full. Mark Antony
In Egypt sits at dinner, and will make
No wars without doors; Cæsar gets money, where
He loses hearts: Lepidus flatters both,
Of both is flatter'd; but he neither loves,
Nor either cares for him.
Men. Cæsar and Lepidus
Are in the field; a mighty strength they carry.
Pom. Where have you this? 'tis false.
Men. From Silvius, sir.
Pom. He dreams; I know, they are in Rome together,
Looking for Antony: But all the charms of love
Salt Cleopatra, soften thy wan'd lip!
Let witchcraft join with beauty, lust with both!
Tie up the libertine in a field of feasts,
Keep his brain fuming: Epicurean cooks,
Sharpen with cloyless sauce his appetite;
That sleep and feeding may prorogue his honour,
Even till a Lethe'd dulness.—How now, Varrius?

Enter VARRIUS.

Var. This is most certain that I shall deliver:
Mark Antony is every hour in Rome
Expected; since he went from Egypt, 'tis
A space for further travel.
Pom. I could have given less matter
A better ear.—Menas, I did not think,
This amorous surfeiter would have don'd his helm
For such a petty war: his soldiership
Is twice the other twain: But let us rear
The higher our opinion, that our stirring
Can from the lap of Egypt's widow pluck
The ne'er lust-wearied Antony.
Men. I cannot hope,
Cæsar and Antony shall well greet together:
His wife, that's dead, did trespasses to Cæsar;
His brother warr'd upon him; although, I think,
Not mov'd by Antony.
Pom. I know not, Menas,
How lesser enmities may give way to greater.
Were't not that we stand up against them all,
'Twere pregnant they should square between themselves;
For they have entertained cause enough
To draw their swords: but how the fear of us
May cement their divisions, and bind up
The petty difference, we yet not know.
Be it as our gods will have it! It only stands
Our lives upon, to use our strongest hands.
Come, Menas. [*Exeunt.*

SCENE II.

Rome. *A Room in the House of* Lepidus.

Enter ENOBARBUS *and* LEPIDUS.

Lep. Good Enobarbus, 'tis a worthy deed,
And shall become you well, to entreat your captain
To soft and gentle speech.
Eno. I shall entreat him
To answer like himself: if Cæsar move him,
Let Antony look over Cæsar's head,
And speak as loud as Mars. By Jupiter,
Were I the wearer of Antonius' beard,
I would not shav't to-day.
Lep. 'Tis not a time
For private stomaching.
Eno. Every time
Serves for the matter that is then born in it.
Lep. But small to greater matters must give way.
Eno. Not if the small come first.
Lep. Your speech is passion:
But, pray you, stir no embers up. Here comes
The noble Antony.

Enter ANTONY *and* VENTIDIUS.

Eno. And yonder, Cæsar.

Enter CÆSAR, MECÆNAS, *and* AGRIPPA.

Ant. If we compose well here, to Parthia:
Hark you, Ventidius.
Cæs. I do not know,
Mecænas; ask Agrippa.
Lep. Noble friends,
That which combin'd us was most great, and let not
A leaner action rend us. What's amiss,
May it be gently heard: When we debate
Our trivial difference loud, we do commit
Murder in healing wounds: Then, noble partners
(The rather, for I earnestly beseech),
Touch you the sourest points with sweetest terms,
Nor curstness grow to the matter.
Ant. 'Tis spoken well:
Were we before our armies, and to fight,
I should do thus.
Cæs. Welcome to Rome.
Ant. Thank you.
Cæs. Sit.
Ant. Sit, sir!
Cæs. Nay,
Then—
Ant. I learn, you take things ill, which are not so;
Or, being, concern you not.
Cæs. I must be laughed at,
If, or for nothing, or a little, I
Should say myself offended; and with you
Chiefly i' the world: more laugh'd at, that I should
Once name you derogately, when to sound your name
It not concern'd me.
Ant. My being in Egypt, Cæsar,
What was't to you?
Cæs. No more than my residing here at Rome
Might be to you in Egypt: Yet, if you there
Did practise on my state, your being in Egypt
Might be my question.
Ant. How intend you, practis'd?
Cæs. You may be pleas'd to catch at mine intent,
By what did here befall me. Your wife, and brother,
Made wars upon me: and their contestation
Was theme for you, you were the word of war.
Ant. You do mistake your business; my brother never
Did urge me in his act: I did inquire it;
And have my learning from some true reports,
That drew their swords with you. Did he not rather
Discredit my authority with yours;
And make the wars alike against my stomach,
Having alike your cause? Of this, my letters
Before did satisfy you. If you'll patch a quarrel,
As matter whole you have not to make it with,
It must not be with this.
Cæs. You praise yourself
By laying defects of judgment to me; but
You patch'd up your excuses.

Ant. Not so, not so;
I know you could not lack, I am certain on't,
Very necessity of this thought, that I,
Your partner in the cause 'gainst which he fought,
Could not with graceful eyes attend those wars
Which fronted mine own peace. As for my wife,
I would you had her spirit in such another:
The third o' the world is yours; which with a snaffle,
You may pace easy, but not such a wife.

Eno. 'Would we had all such wives, that the men might go to wars with the women!

Ant. So much uncurable, her garboils, Cæsar,
Made out of her impatience (which not wanted
Shrewdness of policy too), I grieving grant,
Did you too much disquiet: for that you must
But say, I could not help it.

Cæs. I wrote to you,
When rioting in Alexandria; you
Did pocket up my letters, and with taunts
Did gibe my missive out of audience.

Ant. Sir,
He fell upon me, ere admitted; then
Three kings I had newly feasted, and did want
Of what I was i'the morning; but, next day,
I told him of myself: which was as much,
As to have ask'd him pardon: Let this fellow
Be nothing of our strife; if we contend,
Out of our question wipe him.

Cæs. You have broken
The article of your oath; which you shall never
Have tongue to charge me with.

Lep. Soft, Cæsar.

Ant. No, Lepidus, let him speak;
The honour's sacred which he talks on now,
Supposing that I lack'd it: But on, Cæsar:
The article of my oath,—

Cæs. To lend me arms, and aid, when I requir'd them;
The which you both denied.

Ant. Neglected, rather;
And then, when poison'd hours have bound me up
From mine own knowledge. As nearly as I may,
I'll play the penitent to you: but mine honesty
Shall not make poor my greatness, nor my power
Work without it: Truth is, that Fulvia,
To have me out of Egypt, made wars here;
For which myself, the ignorant motive, do
So far ask pardon, as befits mine honour
To stoop in such a case.

Lep. 'Tis nobly spoken.

Mec. If it might please you, to enforce no further
The griefs between ye: to forget them quite,
Were to remember that the present need
Speaks to atone you.

Lep. Worthily spoke, Mecænas.

Eno. Or, if you borrow one another's love for the instant, you may, when you hear no more words of Pompey, return it again: you shall have time to wrangle in, when you have nothing else to do.

Ant. Thou art a soldier only; speak no more.

Eno. That truth should be silent, I had almost forgot.

Ant. You wrong this presence, therefore speak no more.

Eno. Go to then; your considerate stone.

Cæs. I do not much dislike the matter, but
The manner of his speech: for it cannot be,
We shall remain in friendship, our conditions
So differing in their acts. Yet, if I knew
What hoop should hold us stanch, from edge to edge
O' the world I would pursue it.

Agr. Give me leave, Cæsar,—

Cæs. Speak, Agrippa.

Agr. Thou hast a sister by the mother's side,
Admir'd Octavia: great Mark Antony
Is now a widower.

Cæs. Say not so, Agrippa;
If Cleopatra heard you, your reproof
Were well deserv'd of rashness.

Ant. I am not married, Cæsar: let me hear
Agrippa further speak.

Agr. To hold you in perpetual amity,
To make you brothers, and to knit your hearts
With an unslipping knot, take Antony
Octavia to his wife: whose beauty claims
No worse a husband than the best of men;
Whose virtue, and whose general graces, speak
That which none else can utter. By this marriage,
All little jealousies, which now seem great,
And all great fears, which now import their dangers,
Would then be nothing: truths would be tales,
Where now half tales be truths: her love to both,
Would, each to other, and all loves to both,
Draw after her. Pardon what I have spoke;
For 'tis a studied, not a present thought,
By duty ruminated.

Ant. Will Cæsar speak?

Cæs. Not till he hears how Antony is touch'd
With what is spoke already.

Ant. What power is in Agrippa,
If I would say, *Agrippa, be it so,*
To make this good?

Cæs. The power of Cæsar, and
His power unto Octavia.

Ant. May I never
To this good purpose, that so fairly shows,
Dream of impediment:—Let me have thy hand:
Further this act of grace; and, from this hour,
The heart of brothers govern in our loves,
And sway our great designs!

Cæs. There is my hand.
A sister I bequeath you, whom no brother
Did ever love so dearly: Let her live
To join our kingdoms, and our hearts: and never
Fly off our loves again!

Lep. Happily, amen!

Ant. I did not think to draw my sword 'gainst Pompey:
For he hath laid strange courtesies, and great,
Of late upon me: I must thank him only,
Lest my remembrance suffer ill report;
At heel of that, defy him.

Lep. Time calls upon us:
Of us must Pompey presently be sought,
Or else he seeks out us.

Ant. And where lies he?

Cæs. About the Mount Misenum.

Ant. What's his strength
By land?

Cæs. Great, and increasing: but by sea
He is an absolute master.

Ant. So is the fame.
'Would, we had spoke together! Haste we for it:
Yet, ere we put ourselves in arms, despatch we
The business we have talk'd of.

Cæs. With most gladness;
And do invite you to my sister's view,
Whither straight I will lead you.

Ant. Let us, Lepidus,
Not lack your company.

Lep. Noble Antony,
Not sickness should detain me.

[*Flourish. Exeunt* CÆS. ANT. *and* LEP.

Mec. Welcome from Egypt, sir.

Eno. Half the heart of Cæsar, worthy Mecænas!—my honourable friend, Agrippa!—

Agr. Good Enobarbus!

Mec. We have cause to be glad, that matters are so well digested. You stayed well by it in Egypt.

Eno. Ay, sir; we did sleep day out of countenance, and made the night light with drinking.

Mec. Eight wild boars roasted whole at a breakfast, and but twelve persons there; Is this true?

Eno. This was but as a fly by an eagle: we had much more monstrous matter of feasts, which worthily deserved noting.

Mec. She's a most triumphant lady, if report be square to her.

Eno. When she first met Mark Antony, she pursed up his heart upon the river of Cydnus.

Agr. There she appeared indeed; or my reporter devised well for her.

Eno. I will tell you:
The barge she sat in, like a burnish'd throne,
Burn'd on the water: the poop was beaten gold:
Purple the sails, and so perfumed, that
The winds were lovesick with them: the oars were silver;
Which to the tune of flutes kept stroke, and made
The water, which they beat, to follow faster,
As amorous of their strokes. For her own person,
It beggar'd all description: she did lie
In her pavilion (cloth of gold, of tissue),
O'er-picturing that Venus, where we see,
The fancy outwork nature: on each side her,
Stood pretty dimpled boys, like smiling Cupids,
With diverse-colour'd fans, whose wind did seem
To glow the delicate cheeks which they did cool,
And what they undid, did.

Agr. O, rare for Antony!

Eno. Her gentlewomen, like the Nereides,
So many mermaids, tended her i' the eyes,
And made their bends adornings: at the helm
A seeming mermaid steers; the silken tackle
Swell with the touches of those flower-soft hands,
That yarely frame the office. From the barge
A strange invisible perfume hits the sense
Of the adjacent wharfs. The city cast
Her people out upon her; and Antony,
Enthron'd in the market-place, did sit alone,
Whistling to the air; which, but for vacancy,
Had gone to gaze on Cleopatra too,
And made a gap in nature.

Agr. Rare Egyptian!

Eno. Upon her landing, Antony sent to her,
Invited her to supper: she replied,
It should be better, he became her guest;
Which she entreated; Our courteous Antony,
Whom ne'er the word of *No* woman heard speak,
Being barber'd ten times o'er, goes to the feast;
And, for his ordinary, pays his heart,
For what his eyes eat only.

Agr. Royal wench!
She made great Cæsar lay his sword to bed;
He plough'd her, and she cropp'd.

Eno. I saw her once
Hop forty paces through the publick street:
And having lost her breath, she spoke, and panted,
That she did make defect, perfection,
And, breathless, power breathe forth.

Mec. Now Antony must leave her utterly.

Eno. Never; he will not;
Age cannot wither her, nor custom stale
Her infinite variety: Other women
Cloy th' appetites they feed; but she makes hungry
Where most she satisfies. For vilest things
Become themselves in her; that the holy priests
Bless her, when she is riggish.

Mec. If beauty, wisdom, modesty, can settle
The heart of Antony, Octavia is
A blessed lottery to him.

Agr. Let us go.—
Good Enobarbus, make yourself my guest,
Whilst you abide here.

Eno. Humbly, sir, I thank you. [*Exeunt.*

SCENE III.

The same. A Room in Cæsar's House.

Enter CÆSAR, ANTONY, OCTAVIA *between them;* Attendants, *and a* Soothsayer.

Ant. The world, and my great office, will sometimes
Divide me from your bosom.

Octa. All which time
Before the gods my knee shall bow my prayers
To them for you.

Ant. Good night, sir.—My Octavia,
Read not my blemishes in the world's report:
I have not kept my square: but that to come
Shall all be done by the rule. Good night, dear lady.—

Octa. Good night, sir.

Cæs. Good night. [*Exeunt* CÆS. *and* OCTA.

Ant. Now, sirrah! you do wish yourself in Egypt?

Sooth. 'Would, I had never come from thence, nor you
Thither!

Ant. If you can, your reason?

Sooth. I see't in
My motion, have it not in my tongue: But yet
Hie you again to Egypt.

Ant. Say to me,
Whose fortunes shall rise higher, Cæsar's, or mine?

Sooth. Cæsar's.
Therefore, O Antony, stay not by his side:
Thy dæmon, that's thy spirit which keeps thee, is
Noble, courageous, high, unmatchable,
Where Cæsar's is not; but, near him, thy angel
Becomes a Fear, as being o'erpower'd; therefore
Make space enough between you.

Ant. Speak this no more.

Sooth. To none but thee; no more, but when to thee.
If thou dost play with him at any game,
Thou art sure to lose; and of that natural luck,
He beats thee 'gainst the odds: thy lustre thickens,
When he shines by: I say again, thy spirit
Is all afraid to govern thee near him;
But, he away, 'tis noble.

Ant. Get thee gone:
Say to Ventidius, I would speak with him: [*Exit* Soothsayer.
He shall to Parthia.—Be it art or hap,
He hath spoken true: The very dice obey him:
And, in our sports, my better cunning faints
Under his chance: if we draw lots, he speeds:
His cocks do win the battle still of mine,
When it is all to nought; and his quails ever
Beat mine, inhoop'd, at odds. I will to Egypt:
And though I make this marriage for my peace,

Enter VENTIDIUS.

I' the east my pleasure lies:—O, come, Ventidius,
You must to Parthia; your commission's ready:
Follow me, and receive it. [*Exeunt.*

SCENE IV. *The same. A Street.*

Enter LEPIDUS, MECÆNAS, *and* AGRIPPA.

Lep. Trouble yourselves no further: pray you, hasten
Your generals after.

Agr. Sir, Mark Antony
Will e'en but kiss Octavia, and we'll follow.

Lep. Till I shall see you in your soldier's dress,
Which will become you both, farewell.

Mec. We shall,
As I conceive the journey, be at mount
Before you, Lepidus.

Lep. Your way is shorter,
My purposes do draw me much about;
You'll win two days upon me.

Mec. Agr. Sir, good success!

Lep. Farewell. [*Exeunt.*

SCENE V. Alexandria. *A Room in the Palace.*

Enter CLEOPATRA, CHARMIAN, IRAS, *and* ALEXAS.

Cleo. Give me some musick; musick, moody food
Of us that trade in love.

Attend. The musick, ho!

Enter MARDIAN.

Cleo. Let it alone; let us to billiards:
Come, Charmian.

Char. My arm is sore, best play with Mardian.
Cleo. As well a woman with an eunuch play'd,
As with a woman;—Come, you'll play with me, sir?
Mar. As well as I can, madam.
Cleo. And when good will is show'd, though it come too short,
The actor may plead pardon. I'll none now:—
Give me mine angle,—We'll to the river: there,
My musick playing far off, I will betray
Tawny-finn'd fishes; my bended hook shall pierce
Their slimy jaws; and, as I draw them up,
I'll think them every one an Antony,
And say, Ah, ha! you're caught.
Char. 'Twas merry, when
You wager'd on your angling; when your diver
Did hang a salt fish on his hook, which he
With fervency drew up.
Cleo. That time!—O times!—
I laugh'd him out of patience; and that night
I laugh'd him into patience! and next morn,
Ere the ninth hour, I drunk him to his bed;
Then put my tires and mantles on him, whilst
I wore his sword Philippan. O! from Italy;

Enter a Messenger.

Ram thou thy fruitful tidings in mine ears,
That long time have been barren.
Mess. Madam, madam,—
Cleo. Antony's dead?—
If thou say so, villain, thou kill'st thy mistress:
But well and free,
If thou so yield him, there is gold, and here
My bluest veins to kiss; a hand that kings
Have lipp'd, and trembled kissing.
Mess. First, madam, he's well.
Cleo. Why, there's more gold. But, sirrah, mark; We use
To say, the dead are well: bring it to that,
The gold I give thee, will I melt, and pour
Down thy ill-uttering throat.
Mess. Good madam, hear me.
Cleo. Well, go to, I will;
But there's no goodness in thy face: If Antony
Be free, and healthful,—why so tart a favour
To trumpet such good tidings? If not well,
Thou should'st come like a fury crown'd with snakes,
Not like a formal man.
Mess. Will't please you hear me?
Cleo. I have a mind to strike thee, ere thou speak'st:
Yet, if thou say, Antony lives, is well,
Or friends with Cæsar, or not captive to him,
I'll set thee in a shower of gold, and hail
Rich pearls upon thee.
Mess. Madam, he's well,
Cleo. Well said.
Mess. And friends with Cæsar.
Cleo. Thou'rt an honest man.
Mess. Cæsar and he are greater friends than ever.
Cleo. Make thee a fortune from me.
Mess. But yet, madam,—
Cleo. I do not like *but yet*, it does allay
The good precedence; fye upon *but yet:*
But yet is as a gaoler to bring forth
Some monstrous malefactor. Pr'ythee, friend,
Pour out the pack of matter to mine ear,
The good and bad together: He's friends with Cæsar;
In state of health, thou say'st; and, thou say'st, free.
Mess. Free, madam! no; I made no such report:
He's bound unto Octavia.
Cleo. For what good turn?
Mess. For the best turn i' the bed.
Cleo. I am pale, Charmian.
Mess. Madam, he's married to Octavia.
Cleo. The most infectious pestilence upon thee!
[*Strikes him down.*
Mess. Good madam, patience.
Cleo. What say you?—Hence,
[*Strikes him again.*
Horrible villain! or I'll spurn thine eyes
Like balls before me; I'll unhair thy head;
[*She hales him up and down.*
Thou shalt be whipp'd with wire, and stew'd in brine,
Smarting in ling'ring pickle.
Mess. Gracious madam,
I, that do bring the news, made not the match.
Cleo. Say, tis not so, a province I will give thee,
And make thy fortunes proud: the blow thou hadst
Shall make thy peace, for moving me to rage;
And I will boot thee with what gift beside
Thy modesty can beg.
Mess. He's married, madam.
Cleo. Rogue, thou hast liv'd too long.
[*Draws a Dagger.*
Mess. Nay, then I'll run:—
What mean you, madam? I have made no fault.
[*Exit.*
Char. Good madam, keep yourself within yourself;
The man is innocent.
Cleo. Some innocents 'scape not the thunderbolt.—
Melt Egypt into Nile! and kindly creatures
Turn all to serpents!—Call the slave again:
Though I am mad, I will not bite him:—Call.
Char. He is afeard to come.
Cleo. I will not hurt him:—
These hands do lack nobility, that they strike
A meaner than myself; since I myself
Have given myself the cause.—Come hither, sir.

Re-enter Messenger.

Though it be honest, it is never good
To bring bad news: Give to a gracious message
An host of tongues; but let ill tidings tell
Themselves, when they be felt.
Mess. I have done my duty.
Cleo. Is he married?
I cannot hate thee worser than I do,
If thou again say, Yes.
Mess. He is married, madam.
Cleo. The gods confound thee! dost thou hold there still?
Mess. Should I lie, madam?
Cleo. O, I would, thou didst;
So half my Egypt were submerg'd, and made
A cistern for scal'd snakes! Go, get thee hence;
Hadst thou Narcissus in thy face, to me
Thou would'st appear most ugly. He is married?
Mess. I crave your highness' pardon.
Cleo. He is married?
Mess. Take no offence, that I would not offend you:
To punish me for what you make me do,
Seems much unequal: He is married to Octavia.
Cleo. O, that his fault should make a knave of thee,
That art not!—What? thou'rt sure of't——Get thee hence:
The merchandise which thou hast brought from Rome,
Are all too dear for me; Lie they upon thy hand,
And be undone by 'em! [*Exit* Messenger.
Char. Good your highness, patience.
Cleo. In praising Antony, I have disprais'd Cæsar.
Char. Many times, madam.
Cleo. I am paid for't now.
Lead me from hence,
I faint; O Iras, Charmian,—'Tis no matter;—
Go to the fellow, good Alexas; bid him
Report the feature of Octavia, her years,
Her inclination, let him not leave out
The colour of her hair:—bring me word quickly.— [*Exit* ALEXAS.
Let him for ever go:—Let him not—Charmian,

Though he be painted one way like a Gorgon,
The other way he's a Mars:—Bid you Alexas [*To* MARDIAN.
Bring me word, how tall she is.—Pity me, Charmian,
But do not speak to me.—Lead me to my chamber. [*Exeunt.*

SCENE VI. *Near* Misenum.

Enter POMPEY *and* MENAS, *at one side, with Drum and Trumpet; at another,* CÆSAR, LEPIDUS, ANTONY, ENOBARBUS, MECÆNAS, *with* Soldiers *marching.*

Pom. Your hostages I have, so have you mine;
And we shall talk before we fight.
Cæs. Most meet
That first we come to words; and therefore have we
Our written purposes before us sent;
Which, if thou hast consider'd, let us know
If 'twill tie up thy discontented sword;
And carry back to Sicily much tall youth,
That else must perish here.
Pom. To you all three,
The senators alone of this great world,
Chief factors for the gods,—I do not know,
Wherefore my father should revengers want,
Having a son and friends: since Julius Cæsar,
Who at Philippi the good Brutus ghosted,
There saw you labouring for him. What was it,
That mov'd pale Cassius to conspire? And what
Made the all-honour'd, honest Roman Brutus,
With the arm'd rest, courtiers of beauteous freedom,
To drench the Capitol; but that they would
Have one man but a man! And that is it,
Hath made me rig my navy: at whose burden
The anger'd ocean foams; with which I meant
To scourge the ingratitude that despiteful Rome
Cast on my noble father.
Cæs. Take your time.
Ant. Thou canst not fear us, Pompey, with thy sails,
We'll speak with thee at sea: at land, thou know'st
How much we do o'ercount thee.
Pom. At land, indeed,
Thou dost o'ercount me of my father's house:
But, since the cuckoo builds not for himself,
Remain in't as thou may'st.
Lep. Be pleas'd to tell us
(For this is from the present), how you take
The offers we have sent you.
Cæs. There's the point.
Ant. Which do not be entreated to, but weigh
What it is worth embrac'd.
Cæs. And what may follow,
To try a larger fortune.
Pom. You have made me offer
Of Sicily, Sardinia; and I must
Rid all the sea of pirates; then, to send
Measures of wheat to Rome: This 'greed upon,
To part with unhack'd edges, and bear back
Our targe undinted.
Cæs. Ant. Lep. That's our offer.
Pom. Know then,
I came before you here, a man prepar'd
To take this offer: But Mark Antony
Put me to some impatience:—Though I lose
The praise of it by telling, You must know,
When Cæsar and your brothers were at blows,
Your mother came to Sicily, and did find
Her welcome friendly.
Ant. I have heard it, Pompey;
And am well studied for a liberal thanks,
Which I do owe you.
Pom. Let me have your hand:
I did not think sir, to have met you here.
Ant. The beds i' the east are soft; and thanks to you,
That call'd me, timelier than my purpose, hither;
For I have gain'd by it.
Cæs. Since I saw you last,
There is a change upon you.
Pom. Well, I know not
What counts harsh fortune casts upon my face;
But in my bosom shall she never come,
To make my heart her vassal.
Lep. Well met here.
Pom. I hope so, Lepidus.—Thus we are agreed:
I crave, our composition may be written,
And seal'd between us.
Cæs. That's the next to do.
Pom. We'll feast each other, ere we part; and let us
Draw lots who shall begin.
Ant. That will I, Pompey.
Pom. No, Antony, take the lot: but, first,
Or last, your fine Egyptian cookery
Shall have the fame. I have heard, that Julius Cæsar
Grew fat with feasting there.
Ant. You have heard much.
Pom. I have fair meanings, sir.
Ant. And fair words to them.
Pom. Then so much have I heard:—
And I have heard, Apollodorus carried—
Eno. No more of that:—he did so.
Pom. What, I pray you?
Eno. A certain queen to Cæsar in a mattress.
Pom. I know thee now;—How far'st thou, soldier?
Eno. Well;
And well am like to do; for, I perceive,
Four feasts are toward.
Pom. Let me shake thy hand;
I never hated thee: I have seen thee fight,
When I have envied thy behaviour.
Eno. Sir,
I never lov'd you much: but I have prais'd you,
When you have well deserv'd ten times as much
As I have said you did.
Pom. Enjoy thy plainness,
It nothing ill becomes thee.—
Aboard my galley I invite you all:
Will you lead, lords?
Cæs. Ant. Lep. Show us the way, sir.
Pom. Come.
[*Exeunt* POMPEY, CÆSAR, ANTONY, LEPIDUS, Soldiers, *and* Attendants.

Men. Thy father, Pompey, would ne'er have made this treaty.—[*Aside.*]—You and I have known, sir.

Eno. At sea, I think.

Men. We have, sir.

Eno. You have done well by water.

Men. And you by land.

Eno. I will praise any man that will praise me: though it cannot be denied what I have done by land.

Men. Nor what I have done by water.

Eno. Yes, something you can deny for your own safety: you have been a great thief by sea.

Men. And you by land.

Eno. There I deny my land service. But give me your hand, Menas: If our eyes had authority, here they might take two thieves kissing.

Men. All men's faces are true, whatsoe'er their hands are.

Eno. But there is never a fair woman has a true face.

Men. No slander; they steal hearts.

Eno. We came hither to fight with you.

Men. For my part, I am sorry it is turned to a drinking. Pompey doth this day laugh away his fortune.

Eno. If he do, sure he cannot weep it back again.

Men. You have said, sir. We looked not for Mark Antony here; Pray you, is he married to Cleopatra?

Eno. Cæsar's sister is call'd Octavia.

Men. True, sir; she was the wife of Caius Marcellus,

Eno. But she is now the wife of Marcus Antonius.

Men. Pray you, sir?

Eno. 'Tis true.

Men. Then is Cæsar, and he, for ever knit together.

Eno. If I were bound to divine of this unity, I would not prophesy so.

Men. I think, the policy of that purpose made more in the marriage, than the love of the parties.

Eno. I think so too. But you shall find, the band that seems to tie their friendship together, will be the very strangler of their amity; Octavia is of a holy, cold, and still conversation.

Men. Who would not have his wife so?

Eno. Not he, that himself is not so; which is Mark Antony. He will to his Egyptian dish again: then shall the sighs of Octavia blow the fire up in Cæsar; and, as I said before, that which is the strength of their amity, shall prove the immediate author of their variance. Antony will use his affection where it is; he married but his occasion here.

Men. And thus it may be. Come, sir, will you aboard? I have a health for you.

Eno. I shall take it, sir: we have used our throats in Egypt.

Men. Come; let's away. [*Exeunt.*

SCENE VII.

On Board Pompey's *Galley, lying near* Misenum.

Musick. Enter two or three Servants, *with a Banquet.*

1 *Serv.* Here they'll be, man: Some o' their plants are ill rooted already, the least wind i' the world will blow them down.

2 *Serv.* Lepidus is high-coloured.

1 *Serv.* They have made him drink almsdrink.

2 *Serv.* As they pinch one another by the disposition, he cries out, *no more;* reconciles them to his entreaty, and himself to the drink.

1 *Serv.* But it raises the greater war between him and his discretion.

2 *Serv.* Why, this it is to have a name in great men's fellowship: I had as lief have a reed that will do me no service, as a partisan I could not heave.

1 *Serv.* To be called into a huge sphere, and not to be seen to move in't, are the holes where eyes should be, which pitifully disaster the cheeks.

A Sennet sounded. Enter CÆSAR, ANTONY, POMPEY, LEPIDUS, AGRIPPA, MECÆNAS, ENOBARBUS, MENAS, *with other* Captains.

Ant. Thus do they, sir: [*To* CÆSAR.] They take the flow o' the Nile
By certain scales i' the pyramid; they know,
By the height, the lowness, or the mean, if dearth,
Or foizon, follow: The higher Nilus swells,
The more it promises: as it ebbs, the seedsman
Upon the slime and ooze scatters his grain,
And shortly comes to harvest.

Lep. You have strange serpents there.

Ant. Ay, Lepidus.

Lep. Your serpent of Egypt is bred now of your mud by the operation of your sun: so is your crocodile.

Ant. They are so.

Pom. Sit,—and some wine.—A health to Lepidus.

Lep. I am not so well as I should be, but I'll ne'er out.

Eno. Not till you have slept: I fear me, you'll be in, till then.

Lep. Nay, certainly, I have heard, the Ptolemies' pyramises are very goodly things; without contradiction, I have heard that.

Men. Pompey, a word. [*Aside.*

Pom. Say in mine ear: What is't?

Men. Forsake thy seat, I do beseech thee, captain, [*Aside.*
And hear me speak a word.

Pom. Forbear me till anon.—
This wine for Lepidus.

Lep. What manner o' thing is your crocodile?

Ant. It is shaped, sir, like itself; and it is as broad as it hath breadth; it is just so high as it is, and moves with its own organs: it lives by that which nourisheth it; and the elements once out of it, it transmigrates.

Lep. What colour is it of?

Ant. Of its own colour too.

Lep. 'Tis a strange serpent.

Ant. 'Tis so. And the tears of it are wet.

Cæs. Will this description satisfy him?

Ant. With the health that Pompey gives him, else he is a very epicure.

Pom. [*To* MENAS *aside.*] Go, hang, sir, hang! Tell me of that? away!
Do as I bid you.—Where's this cup I call'd for?

Men. If for the sake of merit thou wilt hear me,
Rise from thy stool. [*Aside.*

Pom. I think, thou'rt mad. The matter?
[*Rises, and walks aside.*

Men. I have ever held my cap off to thy fortunes.

Pom. Thou hast serv'd me with much faith: What's else to say?
Be jolly, lords.

Ant. These quicksands, Lepidus,
Keep off them, for you sink.

Men. Wilt thou be lord of all the world?

Pom. What say'st thou?

Men. Wilt thou be lord of the whole world? That's twice.

Pom. How should that be?

Men. But entertain it, and,
Although thou think me poor, I am the man
Will give thee all the world.

Pom. Hast thou drunk well?

Men. No, Pompey, I have kept me from the cup.
Thou art, if thou dar'st be, the earthly Jove:
Whate'er the ocean pales, or sky inclips,
Is thine, if thou wilt have't.

Pom. Show me which way.

Men. These three world-sharers, these competitors,
Are in thy vessel: Let me cut the cable;
And, when we are put off, fall to their throats:
All there is thine.

Pom. Ah, this thou should'st have done,
And not have spoke on't! In me, 'tis villany;
In thee, it had been good service. Thou must know,
'Tis not my profit that does lead mine honour;
Mine honour, it. Repent, that e'er thy tongue
Hath so betray'd thine act: Being done unknown,
I should have found it afterwards well done;
But must condemn it now. Desist, and drink.

Men. For this, [*Aside.*
I'll never follow thy pall'd fortunes more,—
Who seeks, and will not take, when once 'tis offer'd,
Shall never find it more.

Pom. This health to Lepidus.

Ant. Bear him ashore.—I'll pledge it for him, Pompey.

Eno. Here's to thee, Menas.

Men. Enobarbus, welcome.

Pom. Fill, till the cup be hid.

Eno. There's a strong fellow, Menas.
[*Pointing to the* Attend. *who carries off* LEP.

Men. Why?

Eno. He bears
The third part of the world, man; Seest not?

Men. The third part then is drunk: 'Would it were all,
That it might go on wheels!

Eno. Drink thou; increase the reels.

Men. Come.
Pom. This is not yet an Alexandrian feast.
Ant. It ripens towards it.—Strike the vessels, ho!
Here is to Cæsar.
Cæs. I could well forbear it.
It's monstrous labour when I wash my brain,
And it grows fouler.
Ant. Be a child o' the time.
Cæs. Possess it, I'll make answer: but I had rather fast
From all, four days, than drink so much in one.
Eno. Ha! my brave emperor! [*To* ANTONY.
Shall we dance now the Egyptian Bacchanals,
And celebrate our drink?
Pom. Let's ha 't, good soldier.
Ant. Come, let us all take hands;
Till that the conquering wine hath steep'd our sense
In soft and delicate Lethe.
Eno. All take hands.—
Make battery to our ears with the loud musick;—
The while, I'll place you: Then the boy shall sing;
The holding every man shall bear, as loud
As his strong sides can volley.
[*Musick plays.* ENOBARBUS *places them hand in hand.*

SONG.

Come, thou monarch of the vine,
Plumpy Bacchus, with pink eyne:
In thy vats our cares be drown'd;
With thy grapes our hairs be crown'd;
Cup us, till the world go round;
Cup us, till the world go round!

Cæs. What would you more?—Pompey, good night. Good brother,
Let me request you off: our graver business
Frowns at this levity.—Gentle lords, let's part;
You see, we have burnt our cheeks: strong Enobarbe
Is weaker than the wine; and mine own tongue
Splits what it speaks: the wild disguise hath almost
Antick'd us all. What needs more words? Good night.—
Good Antony, your hand.
Pom. I'll try you o' the shore.
Ant. And shall, sir: give's your hand.
Pom. O, Antony,
You have my father's house,—But what? we are friends:
Come, down into the boat.
Eno. Take heed you fall not.—
[*Exeunt* POM. CÆS. ANT. *and* Attendants.
Menas, I'll not on shore.
Men. No, to my cabin.—
These drums!—these trumpets, flutes! what!—
Let Neptune hear me bid a loud farewell
To these great fellows: Sound, and be hang'd, sound out.
[*A Flourish of Trumpets, with Drums.*
Eno. Ho, says 'a!—There's my cap.
Men. Ho!—noble captain!
Come. [*Exeunt.*

ACT III.

SCENE I. *A Plain in* Syria.

Enter VENTIDIUS, *as after Conquest, with* SILIUS, *and other* Romans, Officers, *and* Soldiers; *the dead Body of* Pacorus *borne before him.*

Ven. Now, darting Parthia, art thou struck; and now
Pleas'd fortune does of Marcus Crassus' death
Make me revenger.—Bear the king's son's body
Before our army:—Thy Pacorus, Orodes,
Pays this for Marcus Crassus.
Sil. Noble Ventidius,
Whilst yet with Parthian blood thy sword is warm,
The fugitive Parthians follow; spur through Media,
Mesopotamia, and the shelters whither
The routed fly: so thy grand captain Antony
Shall set thee on triumphant chariots, and
Put garlands on thy head.
Ven. O Silius, Silius,
I have done enough: A lower place, note well,
May make too great an act: For learn this, Silius;
Better to leave undone, than by our deed
Acquire too high a fame, when him we serve's away.
Cæsar, and Antony, have ever won
More in their officer, than person: Sossius,
One of my place in Syria, his lieutenant,
For quick accumulation of renown,
Which he achiev'd by the minute, lost his favour.
Who does i' the wars more than his captain can,
Becomes his captain's captain: and ambition,
The soldier's virtue, rather makes choice of loss,
Than gain, which darkens him.
I could do more to do Antonius good,
But 'twould offend him; and in his offence
Should my performance perish.
Sil. Thou hast, Ventidius, that
Without the which a soldier, and his sword,
Grants scarce distinction. Thou wilt write to Antony?
Ven. I'll humbly signify what in his name,
That magical word of war, we have effected;
How, with his banners, and his well paid ranks,
The ne'er-yet-beaten horse of Parthia
We have jaded out o' the field.
Sil. Where is he now?
Ven. He purposeth to Athens: whither with what haste
The weight we must convey with us will permit,
We shall appear before him.—On, there; pass along. [*Exeunt.*

SCENE II.

Rome. *An Antechamber in* Cæsar's *House.*

Enter AGRIPPA, *and* ENOBARBUS, *meeting.*

Agr. What, are the brothers parted?
Eno. They have despatch'd with Pompey, he is gone;
The other three are sealing. Octavia weeps
To part from Rome: Cæsar is sad; and Lepidus,
Since Pompey's feast, as Menas says, is troubled
With the green-sickness.
Agr. 'Tis a noble Lepidus.
Eno. A very fine one: O, how he loves Cæsar!
Agr. Nay, but how dearly he adores Mark Antony!
Eno. Cæsar? Why, he's the Jupiter of men.
Agr. What's Antony? The god of Jupiter.
Eno. Spake you of Cæsar? How? the nonpareil!
Agr. O Antony! O thou Arabian bird!
Eno. Would you praise Cæsar, say,—Cæsar;—go no further.
Agr. Indeed, he ply'd them both with excellent praises.
Eno. But he loves Cæsar best;—Yet he loves Antony:
Ho! hearts, tongues, figures, scribes, bards, [poets, cannot
Think, speak, cast, write, sing, number, ho, his love
To Antony. But as for Cæsar,
Kneel down, kneel down, and wonder.
Agr. Both he loves.
Eno. They are his shards, and he their beetle.
So,— [*Trumpets.*
This is to horse.—Adieu, noble Agrippa.
Agr. Good fortune, worthy soldier; and farewell.

Enter CÆSAR, ANTONY, LEPIDUS, *and* OCTAVIA.

Ant. No further, sir.
Cæs. You take from me a great part of myself;

Use me well in it.—Sister, prove such a wife
As my thoughts make thee, and as my furthest band
Shall pass on thy approof.—Most noble Antony,
Let not the piece of virtue, which is set
Betwixt us, as the cement of our love,
To keep it builded, be the ram, to batter
The fortress of it: for better might we
Have loved without this mean, if on both parts
This be not cherish'd.

Ant. Make me not offended
In your distrust.

Cæs. I have said.

Ant. You shall not find,
Though you be therein curious, the least cause
For what you seem to fear: So, the gods keep you,
And make the hearts of Romans serve your ends!
We will here part.

Cæs. Farewell, my dearest sister, fare thee well;
The elements be kind to thee, and make
Thy spirits all of comfort! fare thee well.

Octa. My noble brother!—

Ant. The April's in her eyes: it is love's spring,
And these the showers to bring it on.—Be cheerful.

Octa. Sir, look well to my husband's house; and—

Cæs. What,
Octavia?

Octa. I'll tell you in your ear.

Ant. Her tongue will not obey her heart, nor can
Her heart inform her tongue: the swan's down feather,
That stands upon the swell at full of tide,
And neither way inclines.

Eno. Will Cæsar weep? [*Aside to* AGRIPPA.

Agr. He has a cloud in's face.

Eno. He were the worse for that, were he a horse;
So is he, being a man.

Agr. Why, Enobarbus?
When Antony found Julius Cæsar dead,
He cried almost to roaring: and he wept
When at Philippi he found Brutus slain.

Eno. That year, indeed, he was troubled with a rheum;
What willingly he did confound, he wail'd:
Believe it, till I weep too.

Cæs. No, sweet Octavia,
You shall hear from me still; the time shall not
Outgo my thinking on you.

Ant. Come, sir, come;
I'll wrestle with you in my strength of love:
Look, here I have you; thus I let you go,
And give you to the gods.

Cæs. Adieu; be happy!

Lep. Let all the number of the stars give light
To thy fair way!

Cæs. Farewell, farewell! [*Kisses* OCTAVIA.

Ant. Farewell!

[*Trumpets sound. Exeunt.*

SCENE III. Alexandria. *A Room in the Palace.*

Enter CLEOPATRA, CHARMIAN, IRAS, *and* ALEXAS.

Cleo. Where is the fellow?

Alex. Half afeard to come.

Cleo. Go to, go to:—Come hither, sir.

Enter a Messenger.

Alex. Good majesty,
Herod of Jewry dare not look upon you,
But when you are well pleas'd.

Cleo. That Herod's head
I'll have: But how? when Antony is gone
Through whom I might command it.—Come thou near.

Mess. Most gracious majesty,—

Cleo. Didst thou behold
Octavia?

Mess. Ay, dread queen.

Cleo. Where?

Mess. Madam, in Rome
I look'd her in the face; and saw her led
Between her brother and Mark Antony.

Cleo. Is she as tall as me?

Mess. She is not, madam.

Cleo. Didst hear her speak? Is she shrill-tongu'd, or low?

Mess. Madam, I heard her speak; she is low-voic'd.

Cleo. That's not so good:—he cannot like her long.

Char. Like her? O Isis! 'tis impossible.

Cleo. I think so, Charmian: Dull of tongue, and dwarfish!—
What majesty is in her gait? Remember,
If e'er thou look'dst on majesty.

Mess. She creeps;
Her motion and her station are as one:
She shows a body rather than a life;
A statue, than a breather.

Cleo. Is this certain?

Mess. Or I have no observance.

Char. Three in Egypt
Cannot make better note.

Cleo. He's very knowing,
I do perceive't:—There's nothing in her yet:—
The fellow has good judgment.

Char. Excellent.

Cleo. Guess at her years, I pr'ythee.

Mess. Madam,
She was a widow.

Cleo. Widow?—Charmian, hark.

Mess. And I do think, she's thirty.

Cleo. Bear'st thou her face in mind? is't long, or round?

Mess. Round even to faultiness.

Cleo. For the most part too, they are foolish that are so.——
Her hair, what colour?

Mess. Brown, madam: And her forehead
As low as she would wish it.

Cleo. There is gold for thee.
Thou must not take my former sharpness ill:—
I will employ thee back again; I find thee
Most fit for business: Go, make thee ready;
Our letters are prepar'd. [*Exit* Messenger.

Char. A proper man.

Cleo. Indeed, he is so: I repent me much,
That I so harry'd him. Why, methinks, by him,
This creature's no such thing.

Char. Nothing, madam.

Cleo. The man hath seen some majesty, and should know.

Char. Hath he seen majesty? Isis else defend,
And serving you so long!

Cleo. I have one thing more to ask him yet, good Charmian:—
But 'tis no matter; thou shalt bring him to me
Where I will write: All may be well enough.

Char. I warrant you, madam. [*Exeunt.*

SCENE IV. Athens. *A Room in* Antony's *House.*

Enter ANTONY *and* OCTAVIA.

Ant. Nay, nay, Octavia, not only that,—
That were excusable, that, and thousands more
Of semblable import,—but he hath wag'd
New wars 'gainst Pompey: made his will, and read it
To publick ear:
Spoke scantly of me; when perforce he could not
But pay me terms of honour, cold and sickly
He vented them; most narrow measure lent me:
When the best hint was given him, he not took't,
Or did it from his teeth.

Oct. O my good lord,
Believe not all: or, if you must believe,
Stomach not all. A more unhappy lady,
If this division chance, ne'er stood between,
Praying for both parts: the good gods will mock me presently,

When I shall pray, *O bless my lord and husband!*
Undo that prayer, by crying out as loud,
O, bless my brother! Husband win, win brother,
Prays, and destroys the prayer; no midway
'Twixt these extremes at all.
Ant. Gentle Octavia,
Let your best love draw to that point, which seeks
Best to preserve it: If I lose mine honour,
I lose myself: better I were not yours,
Than yours so branchless. But, as you requested,
Yourself shall go between us; The mean time, lady,
I'll raise the preparation of a war
Shall stain your brother; Make your soonest haste;
So your desires are yours.
Oct. Thanks to my lord.
The Jove of power make me most weak, most weak,
Your reconciler! Wars 'twixt you twain would be
As if the world should cleave, and that slain men
Should solder up the rift.
Ant. When it appears to you where this begins,
Turn your displeasure that way; for our faults
Can never be so equal, that your love
Can equally move with them. Provide your going;
Choose your own company, and command what cost
Your heart has mind to. [*Exeunt.*

SCENE V. *The same. Another Room in the same.*

Enter ENOBARBUS *and* EROS, *meeting.*

Eno. How now, friend Eros?
Eros. There's strange news come, sir.
Eno. What, man?
Eros. Cæsar and Lepidus have made wars upon Pompey.
Eno. This is old; What is the success?
Eros. Cæsar, having made use of him in the wars 'gainst Pompey, presently denied him rivality; would not let him partake in the glory of the action: and not resting here, accuses him of letters he had formerly wrote to Pompey; upon his own appeal, seizes him: So the poor third is up, till death enlarge his confine.
Eno. Then, world, thou hast a pair of chaps, no more;
And throw between them all the food thou hast,
They'll grind the one the other. Where's Antony?
Eros. He's walking in the garden—thus; and spurns
The rush that lies before him; cries, *Fool, Lepidus!*
And threats the throat of that his officer,
That murder'd Pompey.
Eno. Our great navy's rigged.
Eros. For Italy, and Cæsar. More, Domitius;
My lord desires you presently: my news
I might have told hereafter.
Eno. 'Twill be naught:
But let it be.—Bring me to Antony.
Eros. Come, sir. [*Exeunt.*

SCENE VI. Rome. *A Room in* Cæsar's *House.*

Enter CÆSAR, AGRIPPA, *and* MECÆNAS.

Cæs. Contemning Rome, he has done all this: And more;
In Alexandria,—here's the manner of it,—
I' the market-place, on a tribunal silver'd,
Cleopatra and himself in chairs of gold
Were publickly enthron'd: at the feet, sat
Cæsarion, whom they call my father's son;
And all the unlawful issue, that their lust
Since then hath made between them. Unto her
He gave the 'stablishment of Egypt; made her
Of lower Syria, Cyprus, Lydia,
Absolute queen.
Mec. This in the publick eye?
Cæs. I' the common show-place, where they exercise.
His sons he there proclaim'd, The kings of kings:
Great Media, Parthia, and Armenia,
He gave to Alexander; to Ptolemy he assign'd
Syria, Cilicia, and Phœnicia: She
In the habiliments of the goddess Isis
That day appear'd; and oft before gave audience
As 'tis reported, so.
Mec. Let Rome be thus
Inform'd.
Agr. Who, queasy with his insolence
Already, will their good thoughts call from him.
Cæs. The people know it: and have now receiv'd
His accusations.
Agr. Whom does he accuse?
Cæs. Cæsar: and that, having in Sicily
Sextus Pompeius spoil'd, we had not rated him
His part o' the isle: then does he say, he lent me
Some shipping unrestor'd: lastly, he frets,
That Lepidus of the triumvirate
Should be depos'd; and, being, that we detain
All his revenue.
Agr. Sir, this should be answer'd.
Cæs. 'Tis done already, and the messenger gone.
I have told him, Lepidus was grown too cruel;
That he his high authority abus'd,
And did deserve his change; for what I have conquer'd,
I grant him part; but then, in his Armenia,
And other of his conquer'd kingdoms, I
Demand the like.
Mec. He'll never yield to that.
Cæs. Nor must not then be yielded to in this.

Enter OCTAVIA.

Oct. Hail, Cæsar, and my lord! hail, most dear Cæsar!
Cæs. That ever I should call thee, cast-away!
Oct. You have not call'd me so, nor have you cause.
Cæs. Why have you stol'n upon us thus? You come not
Like Cæsar's sister: The wife of Antony
Should have an army for an usher, and
The neighs of horse to tell of her approach,
Long ere she did appear; the trees by the way,
Should have borne men; and expectation fainted,
Longing for what it had not: nay, the dust
Should have ascended to the roof of heaven,
Rais'd by your populous troops: But you are come
A market-maid to Rome; and have prevented
The ostentation of our love, which, left unshown
Is often left unlov'd: we should have met you
By sea, and land; supplying every stage
With an augmented greeting.
Oct. Good my lord,
To come thus was I not constrain'd, but did it
On my free-will. My lord, Mark Antony
Hearing that you prepar'd for war, acquainted
My grieved ear withal; whereon, I begg'd
His pardon for return.
Cæs. Which soon he granted,
Being an obstruct 'tween his lust and him.
Oct. Do not say so, my lord.
Cæs. I have eyes upon him,
And his affairs come to me on the wind.
Where is he now?
Oct. My lord, in Athens.
Cæs. No, my most wronged sister; Cleopatra
Hath nodded him to her. He hath given his empire
Up to a whore; who now are levying
The kings o' the earth for war: He hath assembled
Bocchus, the king of Libya; Archelaus,
Of Cappadocia; Philadelphos, king
Of Paphlagonia; the Thracian king, Adallas:
King Malchus of Arabia; king of Pont;

Herod of Jewry; Mithridates, king
Of Comagene; Polemon and Amintas,
The kings of Mede, and Lycaonia, with a
More larger list of sceptres.

Oct. Ah me, most wretched,
That have my heart parted betwixt two friends,
That do afflict each other!

Cæs. Welcome hither:
Your letters did withhold our breaking forth;
Till we perceiv'd, both how you were wrong led,
And we in negligent danger. Cheer your heart:
Be you not troubled with the time, which drives
O'er your content these strong necessities;
But let determin'd things to destiny
Hold unbewail'd their way. Welcome to Rome:
Nothing more dear to me. You are abus'd
Beyond the mark of thought: and the high gods,
To do you justice, make them ministers
Of us, and those that love you. Best of comfort!
And ever welcome to us.

Agr. Welcome, lady.

Mec. Welcome, dear madam.
Each heart in Rome does love and pity you:
Only the adulterous Antony, most large
In his abominations, turns you off;
And gives his potent regiment to a trull,
That noises it against us.

Oct. Is it so, sir?

Cæs. Most certain. Sister, welcome. 'Pray you,
Be ever known to patience: My dearest sister!
[*Exeunt.*

SCENE VII.

Antony's *Camp, near to the Promontory of* Actium.

Enter CLEOPATRA *and* ENOBARBUS.

Cleo. I will be even with thee, doubt it not.

Eno. But why, why, why?

Cleo. Thou hast forespoke my being in these wars;
And say'st, it is not fit.

Eno. Well, is it, is it?

Cleo. Is't not denounc'd against us? Why should not we
Be there in person?

Eno. [*Aside.*] Well, I could reply:—
If we should serve with horse and mares together,
The horse were merely lost; the mares would bear
A soldier, and his horse.

Cleo. What is't you say?

Eno. Your presence needs must puzzle Antony;
Take from his heart, take from his brain, from his time,
What should not then be spar'd. He is already
Traduc'd for levity; and 'tis said in Rome,
That Photinus, a eunuch, and your maids,
Manage this war.

Cleo. Sink Rome; and their tongues rot,
That speak against us! A charge we bear i' the war,
And, as the president of my kingdom, will
Appear there for a man. Speak not against it;
I will not stay behind.

Eno. Nay, I have done:
Here comes the emperor.

Enter ANTONY *and* CANIDIUS.

Ant. Is't not strange, Canidius,
That from Tarentum, and Brundusium,
He could so quickly cut the Ionian sea,
And take in Toryne?—You have heard on't, sweet?

Cleo. Celerity is never more admir'd,
Than by the negligent.

Ant. A good rebuke,
Which might have well becom'd the best of men,
To taunt at slackness.—Canidius, we
Will fight with him by sea.

Cleo. By sea! What else?

Can. Why will my lord do so?

Ant. For that he dares us to't.

Eno. So hath my lord dar'd him to single fight.

Can. Ay, and to wage this battle at Pharsalia,
Where Cæsar fought with Pompey: But these offers,
Which serve not for his vantage, he shakes off;
And so should you.

Eno. Your ships are not well mann'd;
Your mariners are muleteers, reapers, people
Ingross'd by swift impress; in Cæsar's fleet
Are those, that often have 'gainst Pompey fought:
Their ships are yare; yours, heavy. No disgrace
Shall fall you for refusing him at sea,
Being prepar'd for land.

Ant. By sea, by sea.

Eno. Most worthy sir, you therein throw away
The absolute soldiership you have by land;
Distract your army, which doth most consist
Of war-mark'd footmen; leave unexecuted
Your own renowned knowledge; quite forego
The way which promises assurance; and
Give up yourself merely to chance and hazard,
From firm security.

Ant. I'll fight at sea.

Cleo. I have sixty sails, Cæsar none better.

Ant. Our overplus of shipping will we burn;
And, with the rest full-mann'd, from the head of Actium
Beat the approaching Cæsar. But if we fail,

Enter a Messenger.

We then can do't at land.—Thy business?

Mess. The news is true, my lord; he is descried;
Cæsar has taken Toryne.

Ant. Can he be there in person? 'tis impossible;
Strange, that his power should be.—Canidius,
Our nineteen legions thou shalt hold by land,
And our twelve thousand horse:—We'll to our ship:

Enter a Soldier.

Away, my Thetis!—How now, worthy soldier?

Sold. O noble emperor, do not fight by sea;
Trust not to rotten planks: do you misdoubt
This sword, and these my wounds? Let the Egyptians,
And the Phœnicians, go a ducking: we
Have used to conquer, standing on the earth,
And fighting foot to foot.

Ant. Well, well, away.
[*Exeunt* ANT. CLEO. *and* ENO.

Sold. By Hercules, I think, I am i' the right.

Can. Soldier, thou art: but his whole action grows
Not in the power on't: So our leader's led,
And we are women's men.

Sold. You keep by land
The legions and the horse whole, do you not?

Can. Marcus Octavius, Marcus Justeius,
Publicola, and Cælius, are for sea:
But we keep whole by land. This speed of Cæsar's
Carries beyond belief.

Sold. While he was yet in Rome,
His power went out in such distractions, as
Beguil'd all spies.

Can. Who's his lieutenant, hear you?

Sold. They say, one Taurus.

Can. Well I know the man.

Enter a Messenger.

Mess. The emperor calls Canidius.

Can. With news the time's with labour; and throes forth,
Each minute, some. [*Exeunt.*

SCENE VIII. *A Plain near* Actium.

Enter CÆSAR, TAURUS, Officers, *and Others.*

Cæs. Taurus,—

Taur. My lord.

Cæs. Strike not by land; keep whole;
Provoke not battle, till we have done at sea.

Do not exceed the prescript of this scroll:
Our fortune lies upon this jump. [*Exeunt.*

Enter ANTONY *and* ENOBARBUS.

Ant. Set we our squadrons on yon side o'the hill,
In eye of Cæsar's battle; from which place
We may the number of the ships behold,
And so proceed accordingly. [*Exeunt.*

Enter CANIDIUS, *marching with his* Land Army *one Way over the Stage*; *and* TAURUS, *the Lieutenant of* Cæsar, *the other Way. After their going in, is heard the Noise of a Sea-fight.*

Alarum. Re-enter ENOBARBUS.

Eno. Naught, naught, all naught! I can behold no longer;
The Antoniad, the Egyptian admiral,
With all their sixty, fly, and turn the rudder;
To see't, mine eyes are blasted.

Enter SCARUS.

Scar. Gods and goddesses,
All the whole synod of them!

Eno. What's thy passion?

Scar. The greater cantle of the world is lost
With very ignorance; we have kiss'd away
Kingdoms and provinces.

Eno. How appears the fight?

Scar. On our side like the token'd pestilence,
Where death is sure. Yon' ribaudred hag of Egypt,
Whom leprosy o'ertake! i' the midst o' the fight,—
When vantage like a pair of twins appear'd,
Both as the same, or rather ours the elder,—
The brize upon her, like a cow in June,
Hoists sails, and flies.

Eno. That I beheld:
Mine eyes did sicken at the sight, and could not
Endure a further view.

Scar. She once being loof'd,
The noble ruin of her magick, Antony,
Claps on his sea-wing, and like a doting mallard,
Leaving the fight in height, flies after her:
I never saw an action of such shame;
Experience, manhood, honour, ne'er before
Did violate so itself.

Eno. Alack, alack!

Enter CANIDIUS.

Can. Our fortune on the sea is out of breath,
And sinks most lamentably. Had our general
Been what he knew himself, it had gone well:
O, he has given example for our flight,
Most grossly, by his own.

Eno. Ay, are you thereabouts? Why then, good night
Indeed. [*Aside.*

Can. Towards Peloponnesus are they fled.

Scar. 'Tis easy to't; and there I will attend
What further comes.

Can. To Cæsar will I render
My legions, and my horse; six kings already
Show me the way of yielding.

Eno. I'll yet follow
The wounded chance of Antony, though my reason
Sits in the wind against me. [*Exeunt.*

SCENE IX. Alexandria. *A Room in the Palace.*

Enter ANTONY *and* Attendants.

Ant. Hark, the land bids me tread no more upon't,
It is asham'd to bear me!—Friends, come hither.
I am so lated in the world, that I
Have lost my way for ever:—I have a ship
Laden with gold; take that, divide it; fly,
And make your peace with Cæsar.

Att. Fly! not we.

Ant. I have fled myself; and have instructed cowards
To run, and show their shoulders.—Friends, be gone;
I have myself resolv'd upon a course,
Which has no need of you; be gone:
My treasure's in the harbour, take it.—O,
I follow'd that I blush to look upon:
My very hairs do mutiny; for the white
Reprove the brown for rashness, and they them
For fear and doting.—Friends, be gone; you shall
Have letters from me to some friends, that will
Sweep your way for you. 'Pray you, look not sad,
Nor make replies of loathness: take the hint
Which my despair proclaims: let that be left
Which leaves itself: to the seaside straightway:
I will possess you of that ship and treasure.
Leave me, I pray, a little: 'pray you now:—
Nay, do so; for, indeed, I have lost command,
Therefore I pray you;—I'll see you by and by. [*Sits down.*

Enter EROS, *and* CLEOPATRA, *led by* CHARMIAN *and* IRAS.

Eros. Nay, gentle madam, to him;—Comfort him.

Iras. Do, most dear queen.

Char. Do! why, what else?

Cleo. Let me sit down. O Juno!

Ant. No, no, no, no, no.

Eros. See you here, sir?

Ant. O fye, fye, fye.

Char. Madam,—

Iras. Madam; O good empress!—

Eros. Sir, sir,—

Ant. Yes, my lord, yes;—He, at Philippi, kept
His sword e'en like a dancer: while I struck
The lean and wrinkled Cassius: and 'twas I,
That the mad Brutus ended: he alone
Dealt on lieutenantry, and no practice had
In the brave squares of war; Yet now—No matter.

Cleo. Ah, stand by.

Eros. The queen, my lord, the queen.

Iras. Go to him, madam, speak to him;
He is unqualitied with very shame.

Cleo. Well then,—Sustain me:—Oh!

Eros. Most noble sir, arise; the queen approaches;
Her head's declin'd, and death will seize her; but
Your comfort makes the rescue.

Ant. I have offended reputation:
A most unnoble swerving.

Eros. Sir, the queen.

Ant. O, whither hast thou led me, Egypt? See,
How I convey my shame out of thine eyes
By looking back on what I have left behind
'Stroy'd in dishonour.

Cleo. O my lord, my lord!
Forgive my fearful sails! I little thought,
You would have follow'd.

Ant. Egypt, thou knew'st too well,
My heart was to thy rudder tied by the strings,
And thou should'st tow me after; O'er my spirit
Thy full supremacy thou knew'st; and that
Thy beck might from the bidding of the gods
Command me.

Cleo. O, my pardon.

Ant. Now I must
To the young man send humble treaties, dodge
And palter in the shifts of lowness; who
With half the bulk o' the world play'd as I pleas'd,
Making and marring fortunes. You did know,
How much you were my conqueror; and that
My sword, made weak by my affection, would
Obey it on all cause.

Cleo. O pardon, pardon.

Ant. Fall not a tear, I say; one of them rates
All that is won and lost: Give me a kiss;

Even this repays me.—We sent our schoolmaster,
Is he come back?—Love, I am full of lead :—
Some wine, within there, and our viands:—
Fortune knows,
We scorn her most, when most she offers blows.
[*Exeunt.*

SCENE X. Cæsar's *Camp, in* Egypt.

Enter CÆSAR, DOLABELLA, THYREUS, *and Others.*

Cæs. Let him appear that's come from Antony.—
Know you him?

Dol. Cæsar, 'tis his schoolmaster:
An argument that he is pluck'd, when hither
He sends so poor a pinion of his wing,
Which had superfluous kings for messengers,
Not many moons gone by.

Enter EUPHRONIUS.

Cæs. Approach, and speak.

Eup. Such as I am, I come from Antony:
I was of late as petty to his ends,
As is the morn-dew on the myrtle leaf
To his grand sea.

Cæs. Be it so; Declare thine office.

Eup. Lord of his fortunes he salutes thee, and
Requires to live in Egypt: which not granted,
He lessens his requests; and to thee sues
To let him breathe between the heavens and earth,
A private man in Athens: This for him.
Next Cleopatra does confess thy greatness;
Submits her to thy might; and of thee craves
The circle of the Ptolemies for her heirs,
Now hazarded to thy grace.

Cæs. For Antony,
I have no ears to his request. The queen
Of audience, nor desire, shall fail: so she
From Egypt drive her all-disgraced friend,
Or take his life there: This if she perform,
She shall not sue unheard. So to them both.

Eup. Fortune pursue thee!

Cæs. Bring him through the bands.
[*Exit* EUPHRONIUS.
To try thy eloquence, now 'tis time: Despatch;
From Antony win Cleopatra: promise,
[*To* THYREUS.
And in our name, what she requires; add more,
From thine invention, offers: women are not,
In their best fortunes, strong: but want will perjure
The ne'er-touch'd vestal: Try thy cunning, Thyreus;
Make thine own edict for thy pains, which we
Will answer as a law.

Thyr. Cæsar, I go.

Cæs. Observe how Antony becomes his flaw;
And what thou think'st his very action speaks
In every power that moves.

Thyr. Cæsar, I shall. [*Exeunt.*

SCENE XI. Alexandria. *A Room in the Palace.*

Enter CLEOPATRA, ENOBARBUS, CHARMIAN, *and* IRAS.

Cleo. What shall we do, Enobarbus?

Eno. Think, and die.

Cleo. Is Antony, or we, in fault for this?

Eno. Antony only, that would make his will
Lord of his reason. What though you fled
From that great face of war, whose several ranges
Frighted each other? why should he follow?
The itch of his affection should not then
Have nick'd his captainship; at such a point,
When half to half the world oppos'd, he being
The mered question: 'Twas a shame no less
Than was his loss, to course your flying flags,
And leave his navy gazing.

Cleo. 'Pr'ythee, peace.

Enter ANTONY, *with* EUPHRONIUS.

Ant. Is this his answer?

Eup. Ay, my lord.

Ant. The queen shall then have courtesy, so she
Will yield us up.

Eup. He says so.

Ant. Let her know it.—
To the boy Cæsar send this grizzled head,
And he will fill thy wishes to the brim
With principalities.

Cleo. That head, my lord?

Ant. To him again; Tell him, he wears the rose
Of youth upon him; from which the world should note
Something particular: his coin, ships, legions
May be a coward's; whose ministers would prevail
Under the service of a child, as soon
As i' the command of Cæsar: I dare him therefore
To lay his gay comparisons apart,
And answer me declin'd; sword against sword,
Ourselves alone; I'll write it; follow me.
[*Exeunt* ANTONY *and* EUPHRONIUS.

Eno. Yes, like enough, high-battled Cæsar will
Unstate his happiness, and be stag'd to the show,
Against a sworder.—I see, men's judgments are
A parcel of their fortunes; and things outward
Do draw the inward quality after them,
To suffer all alike. That he should dream,
Knowing all measures, the full Cæsar will
Answer his emptiness!—Cæsar thou hast subdu'd
His judgment too.

Enter an Attendant.

Att. A messenger from Cæsar.

Cleo. What, no more ceremony?—See, my women!—
Against the blown rose may they stop their nose,
That kneel'd unto the buds.—Admit him, sir,

Eno. Mine honesty, and I begin to square.
[*Aside.*
The loyalty, well held to fools, does make
Our faith mere folly:—Yet he, that can endure
To follow with allegiance a fallen lord,
Does conquer him that did his master conquer,
And earns a place i' the story.

Enter THYREUS.

Cleo. Cæsar's will.

Thyr. Hear it apart.

Cleo. None but friends; say boldly.

Thyr. So, haply, are they friends to Antony.

Eno. He needs as many, sir, as Cæsar has:
Or needs not us. If Cæsar please, our master
Will leap to be his friend: For us, you know,
Whose he is, we are; and that's Cæsar's.

Thyr. So.—
Thus then, thou most renown'd; Cæsar entreats,
Not to consider in what case thou stand'st,
Further than he is Cæsar.

Cleo. Go on: Right royal.

Thyr. He knows that you embrace not Antony
As you did love, but as you fear'd him.

Cleo. O!

Thyr. The scars upon your honour, therefore, he
Does pity, as constrained blemishes,
Not as deserv'd.

Cleo. He is a god, and knows
What is most right: Mine honour was not yielded,
But conquer'd merely.

Eno. To be sure of that,
[*Aside.*
I will ask Antony.—Sir, sir, thou'rt so leaky,
That we must leave thee to thy sinking, for
Thy dearest quit thee. [*Exit* ENOBARBUS.

Thyr. Shall I say to Cæsar,
What you require of him? for he partly begs
To be desir'd to give. It much would please him
That of his fortunes you should make a staff
To lean upon: but it would warm his spirits,
To hear from me you had left Antony,
And put yourself under his shroud,
The universal landlord.

Cleo. What's your name?
Thyr. My name is Thyreus.
Cleo. Most kind messenger,
Say to great Cæsar this in disputation,
I kiss his conqu'ring hand: tell him I am prompt
To lay my crown at his feet, and there to kneel:
Tell him, from his all-obeying breath I hear
The doom of Egypt.
Thyr. 'Tis your noblest course,
Wisdom and fortune combating together,
If that the former dare but what it can,
No chance may shake it. Give me grace to lay
My duty on your hand.
Cleo. Your Cæsar's father
Oft, when he hath mus'd of taking kingdoms in,
Bestow'd his lips on that unworthy place,
As it rain'd kisses.

Re-enter ANTONY *and* ENOBARBUS.

Ant. Favours, by Jove that thunders!—
What art thou, fellow?
Thyr. One, that but performs
The bidding of the fullest man, and worthiest
To have command obey'd.
Eno. You will be whipp'd.
Ant. Approach, there:—Ay, you kite;—Now gods and devils!
Authority melts from me: Of late, when I cried, *ho!*
Like boys unto a muss, kings would start forth,
And cry, *Your will?* Have you no ears? I am

Enter Attendants.

Antony yet. Take hence this Jack, and whip him.
Eno. 'Tis better playing with a lion's whelp,
Than with an old one dying.
Ant. Moon and stars!
Whip him:—Were't twenty of the greatest tributaries
That do acknowledge Cæsar, should I find them
So saucy with the hand of she here (What's her name,
Since she was Cleopatra?)—Whip him, fellows,
Till, like a boy, you see him cringe his face,
And whine aloud for mercy: Take him hence.
Thyr. Mark Antony,—
Ant. Tug him away: being whipp'd,
Bring him again:—This Jack of Cæsar's shall
Bear us an errand to him.—
[*Exeunt* Attendants *with* THYREUS.
You were half blasted ere I knew you:—Ha!
Have I my pillow left unpress'd in Rome,
Forborne the getting of a lawful race,
And by a gem of women, to be abus'd
By one that looks on feeders.
Cleo. Good my lord,—
Ant. You have been a boggler ever:
But when we in our viciousness grow hard,
(O misery on't!) the wise gods seel our eyes;
In our own filth drop our clear judgments; make us
Adore our errors; laugh at us, while we strut
To our confusion.
Cleo. O, is it come to this?
Ant. I found you as a morsel, cold upon
Dead Cæsar's trencher: nay, you were a fragment
Of Cneius Pompey's; besides what hotter hours,
Unregister'd in vulgar fame, you have
Luxuriously pick'd out:—For, I am sure,
Though you can guess what temperance should be,
You know not what it is.
Cleo. Wherefore is this?
Ant. To let a fellow that will take rewards,
And say, *God quit you!* be familiar with
My playfellow, your hand; this kingly seal
And plighter of high hearts!—O, that I were
Upon the hill of Basan, to outroar
The horned herd! for I have savage cause;
And to proclaim it civilly, were like
A halter'd neck, which does the hangman thank
For being yare about him.—Is he whipp'd?

Re-enter Attendants *with* THYREUS.

1 *Att.* Soundly, my lord.
Ant. Cried he? and begg'd he pardon?
1 *Att.* He did ask favour.
Ant. If that thy father live, let him repent
Thou wast not made his daughter; and be thou sorry
To follow Cæsar in his triumph, since
Thou hast been whipp'd for following him: henceforth,
The white hand of a lady fever thee,
Shake thou to look on't.—Get thee back to Cæsar,
Tell him thy entertainment: Look, thou say,
He makes me angry with him: for he seems
Proud and disdainful; harping on what I am;
Not what he knew I was: He makes me angry;
And at this time most easy 'tis to do't;
When my good stars, that were my former guides,
Have empty left their orbs, and shot their fires
Into the abism of hell. If he mislike
My speech, and what is done; tell him, he has
Hipparchus, my enfranchis'd bondman, whom
He may at pleasure whip, or hang, or torture,
As he shall like, to quit me: Urge it thou:
Hence, with thy stripes, begone.
[*Exit* THYREUS.
Cleo. Have you done yet?
Ant. Alack, our terrene moon
Is now eclips'd; and it portends alone
The fall of Antony!
Cleo. I must stay his time.
Ant. To flatter Cæsar would you mingle eyes
With one that ties his points?
Cleo. Not know me yet?
Ant. Cold-hearted toward me?
Cleo. Ah, dear, if I be so,
From my cold heart let heaven engender hail,
And poison it in the source; and the first stone
Drop in my neck: as it determines, so
Dissolve my life! The next Cæsarion smite!
Till, by degrees, the memory of my womb,
Together with my brave Egyptians all,
By the discandying of this pelleted storm,
Lie graveless; till the flies and gnats of Nile
Have buried them for prey!
Ant. I am satisfied.
Cæsar sits down in Alexandria; where
I will oppose his fate. Our force by land
Hath nobly held; our sever'd navy too
Have knit again, and fleet, threat'ning most sealike.
Where hast thou been, my heart?—Dost thou hear, lady?
If from the field I shall return once more
To kiss these lips, I will appear in blood;
I and my sword will earn our chronicle;
There is hope in it yet.
Cleo. That's my brave lord!
Ant. I will be treble-sinew'd, hearted, breath'd,
And fight maliciously: for when mine hours
Were nice and lucky, men did ransome lives
Of me for jests; but now, I'll set my teeth,
And send to darkness all that stop me.—Come,
Let's have one other gaudy night: call to me
All my sad captains, fill our bowls; once more
Let's mock the midnight bell.
Cleo. It is my birthday:
I had thought, to have held it poor; but, since my lord
Is Antony again, I will be Cleopatra.
Ant. We'll yet do well.
Cleo. Call all his noble captains to my lord.
Ant. Do so, we'll speak to them; and to-night I'll force
The wine peep through their scars.—Come on my queen;
There's sap in't yet.—The next time I do fight,
I'll make death love me; for I will contend
Even with his pestilent scythe.
[*Exeunt* ANT. CLEO. *and* Attendants.

Eno. Now he'll out-stare the lightning. To be furious,
Is, to be frighted out of fear: and in that mood,
The dove will peck the estridge; and I see still,
A diminution in our captain's brain
Restores his heart: When valour preys on reason,
It eats the sword it fights with. I will seek
Some way to leave him. [*Exit.*

ACT IV.

SCENE I. Cæsar's *Camp at* Alexandria.

Enter CÆSAR, *reading a Letter;* AGRIPPA, MECÆNAS, *and Others.*

Cæs. He calls me boy; and chides, as he had power
To beat me out of Egypt: my messenger
He hath whipp'd with rods; dares me to personal combat,
Cæsar to Antony: Let the old ruffian know,
I have many other ways to die; mean time,
Laugh at his challenge.
Mec. Cæsar must think,
When one so great begins to rage, he's hunted
Even to falling. Give him no breath, but now
Make boot of his distraction: Never anger
Made good guard for itself.
Cæs. Let our best heads
Know, that to-morrow the last of many battles
We mean to fight:—Within our files there are
Of those that serv'd Mark Antony but late,
Enough to fetch him in. See it be done;
And feast the army: we have store to do't,
And they have earn'd the waste. Poor Antony!
[*Exeunt.*

SCENE II. Alexandria. *A Room in the Palace.*

Enter ANTONY, CLEOPATRA, ENOBARBUS, CHARMIAN, IRAS, ALEXAS, *and Others.*

Ant. He will not fight with me, Domitius.
Eno. No.
Ant. Why should he not?
Eno. He thinks, being twenty times of better fortune,
He is twenty men to one.
Ant. To-morrow, soldier,
By sea and land I'll fight: or I will live,
Or bathe my dying honour in the blood
Shall make it live again. Woo't thou fight well?
Eno. I'll strike; and cry, *Take all.*
Ant. Well said; come on.—
Call forth my household servants; let's to-night

Enter Servants.

Be bounteous at our meal.—Give me thy hand,
Thou hast been rightly honest;—so hast thou;—
And thou,—and thou,—and thou:—you have serv'd me well,
And kings have been your fellows.
Cleo. What means this?
Eno. 'Tis one of those odd tricks, which sorrow shoots [*Aside.*
Out of the mind.
Ant. And thou art honest too.
I wish, I could be made so many men;
And all of you clapp'd up together in
An Antony, that I might do you service,
So good as you have done.
Serv. The gods forbid!
Ant. Well, my good fellows, wait on me to-night:
Scant not my cups; and make as much of me,
As when mine empire was your fellow too,
And suffer'd my command.
Cleo. What does he mean?
Eno. To make his followers weep.
Ant. Tend me to-night;
May be, it is the period of your duty:
Haply, you shall not see me more; or if,
A mangled shadow: perchance to-morrow
You'll serve another master. I look on you,
As one that takes his leave. Mine honest friends,
I turn you not away; but, like a master
Married to your good service, stay till death:
Tend me to-night two hours, I ask no more,
And the gods yield you for't!
Eno. What mean you, sir,
To give them this discomfort? Look, they weep;
And I, an ass, am onion-ey'd; for shame,
Transform us not to women.
Ant. Ho, ho, ho!
Now the witch take me, if I meant it thus!
Grace grow where those drops fall! My hearty friends,
You take me in too dolorous a sense:
I spake to you for your comfort: did desire you
To burn this night with torches: Know, my hearts,
I hope well of to-morrow; and will lead you,
Where rather I'll expect victorious life,
Than death and honour. Let's to supper; come,
And drown consideration. [*Exeunt.*

SCENE III. *The same. Before the Palace.*

Enter Two Soldiers, *to their Guard.*

1 *Sold.* Brother, good night: to-morrow is the day.
2 *Sold.* It will determine one way: fare you well.
Heard you of nothing strange about the streets?
1 *Sold.* Nothing: what news?
2 *Sold.* Belike, 'tis but a rumour:
Good night to you.
1 *Sold.* Well, sir, good night.

Enter Two other Soldiers.

2 *Sold.* Soldiers,
Have careful watch.
3 *Sold.* And you: Good night, good night.
[*The first Two place themselves at their Posts.*
4 *Sold.* Here we: [*They take their Posts.*] and if to-morrow
Our navy thrive, I have an absolute hope
Our landmen will stand up.
3 *Sold.* 'Tis a brave army,
And full of purpose.
[*Musick of Hautboys under the Stage.*
4 *Sold.* Peace, what noise?
1 *Sold.* List, list!
2 *Sold.* Hark!
1 *Sold.* Musick i' the air.
3 *Sold.* Under the earth.
4 *Sold.* It signs well,
Does't not?
3 *Sold.* No.
1 *Sold.* Peace, I say. What should this mean?
2 *Sold.* 'Tis the god Hercules, whom Antony lov'd,
Now leaves him.
1 *Sold.* Walk; let's see if other watchmen
Do hear what we do.
[*They advance to another Post.*
2 *Sold.* How now, masters?
Sold. How now?
How now? do you hear this?
[*Several speaking together.*
1 *Sold.* Ay; Is't not strange?
3 *Sold.* Do you hear, masters? do you hear?
1 *Sold.* Follow the noise so far as we have quarter;
Let's see how't will give off.
Sold. [*Several speaking.*] Content: 'Tis strange.
[*Exeunt.*

SCENE IV. *The same. A Room in the Palace.*

Enter ANTONY *and* CLEOPATRA; CHARMIAN *and Others attending.*

Ant. Eros! mine armour, Eros!
Cleo. Sleep a little.
Ant. No, my chuck.—Eros, come; mine armour, Eros!

Enter EROS, *with Armour.*

Come, good fellow, put thine iron on:—
If fortune be not ours to-day, it is
Because we brave her.—Come.

Cleo. Nay, I'll help too.
What's this for?

Ant. Ah, let be, let be! thou art
The armourer of my heart:—False, false; this, this.

Cleo. Sooth, la, I'll help: Thus it must be.

Ant. Well, well;
We shall thrive now.—Seest thou, my good fellow?
Go, put on thy defences.

Eros. Briefly, sir.

Cleo. Is not this buckled well?

Ant. Rarely, rarely:
He that unbuckles this, till we do please
To doff't for our repose, shall hear a storm.—
Thou fumblest, Eros; and my queen's a squire
More tight at this, than thou: Despatch.—O love,
That thou could'st see my wars to-day, and knew'st
The royal occupation; thou should'st see

Enter an Officer, *armed.*

A workman in't.—Good morrow to thee; welcome:
Thou look'st like him that knows a warlike charge:
To business that we love, we rise betime,
And go to it with delight.

1 *Off.* A thousand, sir,
Early though it be, have on their riveted trim,
And at the port expect you.

[*Shout. Trumpets. Flourish.*

Enter other Officers, *and* Soldiers.

2 *Off.* The morn is fair.—Good morrow, general.

All. Good morrow, general.

Ant. 'Tis well blown, lads.
This morning, like the spirit of a youth
That means to be of note, begins betimes.—
So, so; come, give me that: this way; well said.
Fare thee well, dame, whate'er becomes of me:
This is a soldier's kiss; rebukable, [*Kisses her.*
And worthy shameful check it were, to stand
On more mechanic compliment; I'll leave thee
Now, like a man of steel.—You, that will fight,
Follow me close; I'll bring you to't.—Adieu.

[*Exeunt* ANT. EROS, Officers, *and* Soldiers.

Char. Please you, retire to your chamber?

Cleo. Lead me,
He goes forth gallantly. That he and Cæsar might
Determine this great war in single fight:
Then, Antony,—But now,—Well, on. [*Exeunt.*

SCENE V. Antony's *Camp near* Alexandria.

Trumpets sound. Enter ANTONY *and* EROS; *a* Soldier *meeting them.*

Sold. The gods make this a happy day to Antony!

Ant. 'Would, thou and those thy scars had once prevail'd
To make me fight at land!

Sold. Hadst thou done so,
The kings that have revolted, and the soldier
That has this morning left thee, would have still
Follow'd thy heels.

Ant. Who's gone this morning?

Sold. Who?
One ever near thee; Call for Enobarbus,
He shall not hear thee; or from Cæsar's camp
Say, *I am none of thine.*

Ant. What say'st thou?

Sold. Sir,
He is with Cæsar.

Eros. Sir, his chests and treasure
He has not with him.

Ant. Is he gone?

Sold. Most certain;

Ant. Go, Eros, send his treasure after; do it.
Detain no jot, I charge thee: write to him
(I will subscribe) gentle adieus, and greetings:
Say, that I wish he never find more cause
To change a master.—O, my fortunes have
Corrupted honest men:—Despatch:—Enobarbus! [*Exeunt.*

SCENE VI. Cæsar's *Camp before* Alexandria.

Flourish. Enter CÆSAR, *with* AGRIPPA, ENOBARBUS, *and Others.*

Cæs. Go forth, Agrippa, and begin the fight:
Our will is, Antony be took alive;
Make it so known.

Agr. Cæsar, I shall. [*Exit* AGRIPPA.

Cæs. The time of universal peace is near:
Prove this a prosperous day, the three-nook'd world
Shall bear the olive freely.

Enter a Messenger.

Mess. Antony
Is come into the field.

Cæs. Go, charge Agrippa,
Plant those that have revolted in the van,
That Antony may seem to spend his fury
Upon himself. [*Exeunt* CÆSAR *and his* Train.

Eno. Alexas did revolt; and went to Jewry,
On affairs of Antony; there did persuade
Great Herod to incline himself to Cæsar,
And leave his master Antony: for his pains,
Cæsar hath hang'd him. Canidius, and the rest
That fell away, have entertainment, but
No honourable trust. I have done ill,
Of which I do accuse myself so sorely,
That I will joy no more.

Enter a Soldier *of* Cæsar's.

Sold. Enobarbus, Antony
Hath after thee sent all thy treasure, with
His bounty overplus: The messenger
Came on my guard; and at thy tent is now,
Unloading of his mules.

Eno. I give it you.

Sold. Mock me not, Enobarbus.
I tell you true: Best that you saf'd the bringer
Out of the host; I must attend mine office,
Or would have don't myself. Your emperor
Continues still a Jove. [*Exit* Soldier.

Eno. I am alone the villain of the earth,
And feel I am so most. O Antony,
Thou mine of bounty, how would'st thou have paid
My better service, when my turpitude
Thou dost so crown with gold! This blows my heart:
If swift thought break it not, a swifter mean
Shall outstrike thought: but thought will do't, I feel.
I fight against thee!—No! I will go seek
Some ditch, wherein to die; the foul'st best fits
My latter part of life. [*Exit.*

SCENE VII. *Field of Battle between the Camps.*

Alarum. Drums and Trumpets. Enter AGRIPPA, *and Others.*

Agr. Retire, we have engag'd ourselves too far;
Cæsar himself has work, and our oppression
Exceeds what we expected. [*Exeunt.*

Alarum. Enter ANTONY *and* SCARUS, *wounded.*

Scar. O my brave emperor, this is fought, indeed!
Had we done so at first, we had driven them home
With clouts about their heads.

Ant. Thou bleed'st apace

Scar. I had a wound here that was like a T,
But now 'tis made an H.

Ant. They do retire.

Scar. We'll beat 'em into bench-holes; I have yet
Room for six scotches more.

Enter EROS.

Eros. They are beaten, sir; and our advantage serves
For a fair victory.

Scar. Let us score their backs,
And snatch 'em up, as we take hares, behind;
'Tis sport to maul a runner.

Ant. I will reward thee
Once for thy spritely comfort, and tenfold
For thy good valour. Come thee on.

Scar. I'll halt after. [*Exeunt.*

SCENE VIII. *Under the Walls of* Alexandria.

Alarum. Enter ANTONY, *marching;* SCARUS, *and* Forces.

Ant. We have beat him to his camp; Run one before,
And let the queen know of our guests.—To-morrow,
Before the sun shall see us, we'll spill the blood
That has to-day escaped. I thank you all;
For doughty-handed are you: and have fought
Not as you served the cause, but as it had been
Each man's like mine; you have shown all Hectors.
Enter the city, clip your wives, your friends,
Tell them your feats; whilst they with joyful tears
Wash the congealment from your wounds, and kiss
The honour'd gashes whole.—Give me thy hand;
[*To* SCARUS.

Enter CLEOPATRA, *attended.*

To this great fairy I'll commend thy acts,
Make her thanks bless thee.—O thou day o' the world,
Chain mine arm'd neck; leap thou, attire and all,
Through proof of harness to my heart, and there
Ride on the pants triumphing.

Cleo. Lord of lords!
O infinite virtue! com'st thou smiling from
The world's great snare uncaught?

Ant. My nightingale,
We have beat them to their beds. What, girl? though gray
Do something mingle with our younger brown; yet have we
A brain that nourishes our nerves, and can
Get goal for goal of youth. Behold this man;
Commend unto his lips thy favouring hand;—
Kiss it, my warrior:—He hath fought to-day,
As if a god, in hate of mankind, had
Destroy'd in such a shape.

Cleo. I'll give thee, friend,
An armour all of gold: it was a king's.

Ant. He has deserv'd it; were it carbuncled
Like holy Phœbus' car.—Give me thy hand;
Through Alexandria make a jolly march;
Bear our hack'd targets like the men that owe them:
Had our great palace the capacity
To camp this host, we all would sup together;
And drink carouses to the next day's fate,
Which promises royal peril.—Trumpeters,
With brazen din blast you the city's ear;
Make mingle with our rattling tabourines;
That heaven and earth may strike their sounds together,
Applauding our approach. [*Exeunt.*

SCENE IX. Cæsar's *Camp.*

Sentinels *on their Post. Enter* ENOBARBUS.

1 Sold. If we be not reliev'd within this hour,
We must return to the court of guard: The night
Is shiny; and, they say, we shall embattle
By the second hour i' the morn.

2 Sold. This last day was
A shrewd one to us.

Eno. O, bear me witness, night,—

3 Sold. What man is this?

2 Sold. Stand close, and list him.

Eno. Be witness to me, O thou blessed moon,
When men revolted shall upon record
Bear hateful memory, poor Enobarbus did
Before thy face repent!—

1 Sold. Enobarbus!

3 Sold. Peace;
Hark further.

Eno. O sovereign mistress of true melancholy,
The poisonous damp of night dispunge upon me;
That life, a very rebel to my will,
May hang no longer on me: Throw my heart
Against the flint and hardness of my fault;
Which, being dried with grief, will break to powder,
And finish all foul thoughts. O Antony,
Nobler than my revolt is infamous,
Forgive me in thine own particular;
But let the world rank me in register
A master-leaver, and a fugitive:
O Antony! O Antony! [*Dies.*

2 Sold. Let's speak
To him.

1 Sold. Let's hear him, for the things he speaks
May concern Cæsar.

3 Sold. Let's do so. But he sleeps.

1 Sold. Swoons rather; for so bad a prayer as his
Was never yet for sleep.

2 Sold. Go we to him.

3 Sold. Awake, awake, sir; speak to us.

2 Sold. Hear you, sir?

1 Sold. The hand of death hath raught him.
Hark, the drums [*Drums afar off.*
Demurely wake the sleepers. Let us bear him
To the court of guard; he is of note: our hour
Is fully out.

3 Sold. Come on then;
He may recover yet. [*Exeunt with the Body.*

SCENE X. *Between the two Camps.*

Enter ANTONY *and* SCARUS, *with* Forces, *marching.*

Ant. Their preparation is to-day by sea;
We please them not by land.

Scar. For both, my lord.

Ant. I would, they'd fight i'the fire, or in the air;
We'd fight there too. But this it is; Our foot
Upon the hills adjoining to the city,
Shall stay with us: order for sea is given;
They have put forth the haven: Let's seek a spot,
Where their appointment we may best discover,
And look on their endeavour. [*Exeunt.*

Enter CÆSAR, *and his* Forces, *marching.*

Cæs. But being charg'd, we will be still by land,
Which, as I tak't, we shall; for his best force
Is forth to man his galleys. To the vales,
And hold our best advantage. [*Exeunt.*

Re-enter ANTONY *and* SCARUS.

Ant. Yet they're not join'd: Where yonder pine does stand,
I shall discover all: I'll bring thee word
Straight, how 'tis like to go. [*Exit.*

Scar. Swallows have built
In Cleopatra's sails their nests: the auguries
Say, they know not,—they cannot tell;—look grimly,
And dare not speak their knowledge. Antony
Is valiant, and dejected; and, by starts,
His fretted fortunes give him hope, and fear,
Of what he has, and has not.

Alarum afar off, as at a Sea-Fight. Re-enter ANTONY.

Ant. All is lost;
This foul Egyptian hath betrayed me:
My fleet hath yielded to the foe: and yonder

They cast their caps up, and carouse together
Like friends long lost.—Triple-turn'd whore! 'tis thou
Hast sold me to this novice; and my heart
Makes only wars on thee.—Bid them all fly;
For when I am reveng'd upon my charm,
I have done all:—Bid them all fly, begone.
[*Exit* SCARUS.
O sun, thy uprise shall I see no more:
Fortune and Antony part here; even here
Do we shake hands.—All come to this?—The hearts
That spaniel'd me at heels, to whom I gave
Their wishes, do discandy, melt their sweets
On blossoming Cæsar; and this pine is bark'd,
That overtopp'd them all. Betray'd I am:
O this false soul of Egypt! this grave charm,
Whose eye beck'd forth my wars, and call'd them home;
Whose bosom was my crownet, my chief end,
Like a right gipsy, hath, at fast and loose,
Beguil'd me to the very heart of loss,—
What, Eros, Eros!

Enter CLEOPATRA.

Ah, thou spell! Avaunt.
Cleo. Why is my lord enrag'd against his love?
Ant. Vanish; or I shall give thee thy deserving,
And blemish Cæsar's triumph. Let him take thee,
And hoist thee up to the shouting plebeians:
Follow his chariot, like the greatest spot
Of all thy sex: most monster-like, be shown
For poor'st diminutives, for doits; and let
Patient Octavia plough thy visage up
With her prepared nails. [*Exit* CLEO.] 'Tis well thou'rt gone,
If it be well to live: But better 'twere
Thou fell'st into my fury, for one death
Might have prevented many.—Eros, ho!—
The shirt of Nessus is upon me: Teach me,
Alcides, thou mine ancestor, thy rage:
Let me lodge Lichas on the horns o' the moon;
And with those hands, that grasp'd the heaviest club,
Subdue my worthiest self. The witch shall die;
To the Roman boy she hath sold me, and I fall
Under this plot: she dies for't.—Eros, ho!
[*Exit.*

SCENE XI. Alexandria. *A Room in the Palace.*

Enter CLEOPATRA, CHARMIAN, IRAS, *and* MARDIAN.

Cleo. Help me, my women! O, he is more mad
Than Telamon for his shield; the boar of Thessaly
Was never so emboss'd.
Char. To the monument;
There lock yourself, and send him word you are dead.
The soul and body rive not more in parting,
Than greatness going off.
Cleo. To the monument:—
Mardian, go tell him I have slain myself;
Say, that the last I spoke was, Antony,
And word it, pr'ythee, piteously: Hence,
Mardian; and bring me how he takes my death.—
To the monument. [*Exeunt.*

SCENE XII. *The same. Another Room.*

Enter ANTONY *and* EROS.

Ant. Eros, thou yet behold'st me?
Eros. Ay, noble lord.
Ant. Sometime, we see a cloud that's dragonish;
A vapour, sometime like a bear, or lion,
A tower'd citadel, a pendent rock,
A forked mountain, or blue promontory
With trees upon't, that nod unto the world,
And mock our eyes with air: Thou hast seen these signs;
They are black vesper's pageants.
Eros. Ay, my lord.
Ant. That which is now a horse, even with a thought,
The rack dislimns, and makes it indistinct,
As water is in water.
Eros. It does, my lord.
Ant. My good knave, Eros, now thy captain is
Even such a body: here I am Antony;
Yet cannot hold this visible shape, my knave.
I made these wars for Egypt; and the queen,—
Whose heart, I thought, I had, for she had mine;
Which, whilst it was mine, had annex'd unto 't
A million more, now lost,—she, Eros, has
Pack'd cards with Cæsar, and false play'd my glory
Unto an enemy's triumph.—
Nay, weep not, gentle Eros; there is left us
Ourselves to end ourselves.—O, thy vile lady!

Enter MARDIAN.

She has robb'd me of my sword.
Mar. No, Antony;
My mistress lov'd thee, and her fortunes mingled
With thine entirely.
Ant. Hence, saucy eunuch; peace;
She hath betray'd me, and shall die the death.
Mar. Death of one person can be paid but once;
And that she has discharg'd: What thou would'st do,
Is done unto thy hand; the last she spake
Was Antony! most noble Antony!
Then in the midst a tearing groan did break
The name of Antony; it was divided
Between her heart and lips: she render'd life,
Thy name so buried in her.
Ant. Dead then?
Mar. Dead.
Ant. Unarm, Eros; the long day's task is done.
And we must sleep:—That thou depart'st hence safe,
Does pay thy labour richly; Go.—Off, pluck off;— [*Exit* MARDIAN.
The sevenfold shield of Ajax cannot keep
The battery from my heart. O, cleave my sides!
Heart, once be stronger than thy continent,
Crack thy frail case!—Apace, Eros, apace.—
No more a soldier:—Bruised pieces, go;
You have been nobly borne.—From me a while.— [*Exit* EROS.
I will o'ertake thee, Cleopatra, and
Weep for my pardon. So it must be, for now
All length is torture:—Since the torch is out,
Lie down, and stray no further: Now all labour
Mars what it does; yea, very force entangles
Itself with strength: Seal then, and all is done.—
Eros!—I come, my queen:—Eros!—Stay for me:
Where souls do couch on flowers, we'll hand in hand,
And with our sprightly port make the ghosts gaze:
Dido and her Æneas shall want troops,
And all the haunt be ours.—Come, Eros, Eros!

Re-enter EROS.

Eros. What would my lord?
Ant. Since Cleopatra died,
I have liv'd in such dishonour, that the gods
Detest my baseness. I, that with my sword
Quarter'd the world, and o'er green Neptune's back
With ships made cities, condemn myself to lack
The courage of a woman; less noble mind
Than she, which, by her death, our Cæsar tells,
I am conqueror of myself. Thou art sworn, Eros,
That, when the exigent should come (which now
Is come, indeed), when I should see behind me
The inevitable prosecution of
Disgrace and horror, that, on my command,
Thou then would'st kill me: do't; the time is come:
Thou strik'st not me, 'tis Cæsar thou defeat'st.
Put colour in thy cheek.

Eros. The gods withhold me!
Shall I do that, which all the Parthian darts,
Though enemy, lost aim, and could not?
Ant. Eros,
Would'st thou be window'd in great Rome, and see
Thy master thus with pleach'd arms, bending down
His corrigible neck, his face subdued
To penetrative shame; whilst the wheel'd seat
Of fortunate Cæsar, drawn before him, branded
His baseness that ensu'd?
Eros. I would not see 't.
Ant. Come then; for with a wound I must be cur'd.
Draw that thy honest sword, which thou hast worn
Most useful for thy country.
Eros. O, sir, pardon me.
Ant. When I did make thee free, swor'st thou not then
To do this when I bade thee? Do it at once;
Or thy precedent services are all
But accidents unpurpos'd. Draw, and come.
Eros. Turn from me then that noble countenance,
Wherein the worship of the whole world lies.
Ant. Lo thee. [*Turning from him.*
Eros. My sword is drawn.
Ant. Then let it do at once
The thing why thou hast drawn it.
Eros. My dear master,
My captain, and my emperor! let me say,
Before I strike this bloody stroke, farewell.
Ant. 'Tis said, man; and farewell.
Eros. Farewell, great chief. Shall I strike now?
Ant. Now, Eros.
Eros. Why, there then:—[*Falls on his Sword.*]
Thus do I escape the sorrow
Of Antony's death. [*Dies.*
Ant. Thrice nobler than myself!
Thou teachest me, O valiant Eros, what
I should, and thou could'st not. My queen and Eros
Have, by their brave instruction, got upon me
A nobleness in record: But I will be
A bridegroom in my death, and run into 't
As to a lover's bed. Come then; and, Eros,
Thy master dies thy scholar: to do thus
[*Falling on his Sword.*
I learn'd of thee. How! not dead? not dead?—
The guard!—ho!—O, despatch me.

Enter DERCETAS *and* Guard.

1 *Guard.* What's the noise?
Ant. I have done my work ill, friends; O make an end
Of what I have begun.
2 *Guard.* The star is fallen.
1 *Guard.* And time is at his period.
All. Alas, and woe!
Ant. Let him that loves me, strike me dead.
1 *Guard.* Not I.
2 *Guard.* Nor I.
3 *Guard.* Nor any one. [*Exeunt* Guard.
Der. Thy death and fortunes bid thy followers fly.
This sword but shown to Cæsar, with this tidings,
Shall enter me with him.

Enter DIOMEDES.

Dio. Where's Antony?
Der. There, Diomed, there.
Dio. Lives he?
Wilt thou not answer, man? [*Exit* DERCETAS.
Ant. Art thou there, Diomed? Draw thy sword, and give me
Sufficing strokes for death.
Dio. Most absolute lord,
My mistress Cleopatra sent me to thee.
Ant. When did she send thee?
Dio. Now, my lord.
Ant. Where is she?
Dio. Lock'd in her monument. She had a prophesying fear
Of what hath come to pass: for when she saw
(Which never shall be found) you did suspect
She had dispos'd with Cæsar, and that your rage
Would not be purg'd, she sent you word she was dead;
But, fearing since how it might work, hath sent
Me to proclaim the truth; and I am come,
I dread, too late.
Ant. Too late, good Diomed:—Call my guard, I pr'ythee.
Dio. What, ho! the emperor's guard! The guard, what, ho!
Come, your lord calls.

Enter some of the Guard.

Ant. Bear me, good friends, where Cleopatra bides;
'Tis the last service that I shall command you.
1 *Guard.* Woe, woe are we, sir, you may not live to wear
All your true followers out.
All. Most heavy day!
Ant. Nay, good my fellows, do not please sharp fate
To grace it with your sorrows: bid that welcome
Which comes to punish us, and we punish it
Seeming to bear it lightly. Take me up:
I have led you oft; carry me now, good friends
And have my thanks for all.
[*Exeunt, bearing* ANTONY

SCENE XIII. *The same. A Monument.*

Enter above, CLEOPATRA, CHARMIAN, *and* IRAS.

Cleo. O Charmian, I will never go from hence.
Char. Be comforted, dear madam.
Cleo. No, I will not;
All strange and terrible events are welcome,
But comforts we despise; our size of sorrow,
Proportion'd to our cause, must be as great

Enter DIOMEDES.

As that which makes it.—How now? is he dead?
Dio. His death's upon him, but not dead.
Look out o' the other side your monument,
His guard have brought him thither.

Enter ANTONY, *borne by the* Guard.

Cleo. O thou sun,
Burn the great sphere thou mov'st in!—darkling stand
The varying shore o' th' world. O Antony, Antony, Antony!
Help, Charmian; help, Iras, help: help, friends
Below, let's draw him hither.
Ant. Peace:
Not Cæsar's valour hath o'erthrown Antony,
But Antony's hath triumphed on itself.
Cleo. So it should be, that none but Antony
Should conquer Antony; but woe, 'tis so!
Ant. I am dying, Egypt, dying; only
I here importune death a while, until
Of many thousand kisses the poor last
I lay upon thy lips.—
Cleo. I dare not, dear
(Dear my lord, pardon), I dare not,
Lest I be taken: not the imperious show
Of the full-fortun'd Cæsar ever shall
Be brooch'd with me; if knife, drugs, serpents, have
Edge, sting, or operation, I am safe:
Your wife Octavia, with her modest eyes,
And still conclusion, shall acquire no honour
Demuring upon me.—But come, come, Antony,—
Help me, my women,—we must draw thee up;—
Assist, good friends.
Ant. O, quick, or I am gone.
Cleo. Here's sport, indeed!—How heavy weighs my lord!
Our strength is all gone into heaviness,
That makes the weight: Had I great Juno's power,
The strong-wing'd Mercury should fetch thee up,
And set thee by Jove's side. Yet come a little.—
Wishers were ever fools;—O, come, come, come; [*They draw* ANTONY *up.*

And welcome, welcome! die, where thou hast liv'd:
Quicken with kissing; had my lips that power,
Thus would I wear them out.

All. A heavy sight!

Ant. I am dying, Egypt, dying;
Give me some wine, and let me speak a little.

Cleo. No, let me speak; and let me rail so high,
That the false housewife Fortune break her wheel,
Provok'd by my offence.

Ant. One word, sweet queen:
Of Cæsar seek your honour with your safety.—O!

Cleo. They do not go together.

Ant. Gentle, hear me:
None about Cæsar trust, but Proculeius.

Cleo. My resolution, and my hands, I'll trust;
None about Cæsar.

Ant. The miserable change now at my end,
Lament nor sorrow at: but please your thoughts,
In feeding them with those my former fortunes
Wherein I liv'd, the greatest prince o' the world,
The noblest: and do now not basely die,
Nor cowardly; put off my helmet to
My countryman, a Roman, by a Roman
Valiantly vanquish'd. Now, my spirit is going;
I can no more. [*Dies.*

Cleo. Noblest of men, woo't die?
Hast thou no care of me? shall I abide
In this dull world, which in thy absence is
No better than a sty?—O, see, my women,
The crown o'the earth doth melt:—My lord!—
O, wither'd is the garland of the war,
The soldier's pole is fallen; young boys and girls,
Are level now with men: the odds is gone,
And there is nothing left remarkable
Beneath the visiting moon. [*She faints.*

Char. O, quietness, lady!

Iras. She is dead too, our sovereign.

Char. Lady,—

Iras. Madam,—

Char. O madam, madam, madam!

Iras. Royal Egypt!
Empress!

Char. Peace, peace, Iras.

Cleo. No more, but e'en a woman; and commanded
By such poor passion as the maid that milks,
And does the meanest chares.—It were for me
To throw my sceptre at the injurious gods,
To tell them, that this world did equal theirs,
Till they had stolen our jewel. All's but naught;
Patience is sottish; and impatience does
Become a dog that's mad: Then is it sin,
To rush into the secret house of death,
Ere death dare come to us?—How do you, women?
What, what? good cheer! Why, how now, Charmian?
My noble girls!—Ah, women, women! look,
Our lamp is spent, it's out:—Good sirs, take heart:— [*To the Guard below.*
We'll bury him: and then what's brave, what's noble,
Let's do it after the high Roman fashion,
And make death proud to take us. Come, away:
This case of that huge spirit now is cold.
Ah women, women! come; we have no friend
But resolution, and the briefest end.

[*Exeunt; those above bearing off* Antony's *Body.*

ACT V.

SCENE I. Cæsar's *Camp before* Alexandria.

Enter CÆSAR, AGRIPPA, DOLABELLA, MECÆNAS, GALLUS, PROCULEIUS, *and Others.*

Cæs. Go to him, Dolabella, bid him yield;
Being so frustrate, tell him, he mocks us by
The pauses that he makes.

Dol. Cæsar, I shall. [*Exit.*

Enter DERCETAS, *with the Sword of* ANTONY.

Cæs. Wherefore is that? and what art thou, that dar'st
Appear thus to us?

Der. I am call'd Dercetas;
Mark Antony I serv'd: who best was worthy
Best to be serv'd: whilst he stood up, and spoke,
He was my master; and I wore my life,
To spend upon his haters: If thou please
To take me to thee, as I was to him
I'll be to Cæsar; If thou pleasest not,
I yield thee up my life.

Cæs. What is't thou say'st?

Der. I say, O Cæsar, Antony is dead.

Cæs. The breaking of so great a thing should make
A greater crack: The round world should have shook
Lions into civil streets,
And citizens to their dens:—The death of Antony
Is not a single doom; in the name lay
A moiety of the world.

Der. He is dead, Cæsar;
Not by a publick minister of justice,
Nor by a hir'd knife; but that self hand,
Which writ his honour in the acts it did,
Hath, with the courage which the heart did lend it,
Splitted the heart.—This is his sword,
I robb'd his wound of it; behold it stain'd
With his most noble blood.

Cæs. Look you sad, friends?
The gods rebuke me, but it is tidings
To wash the eyes of kings.

Agr. And strange it is,
That nature must compel us to lament
Our most persisted deeds.

Mec. His taints and honours
Waged equal with him.

Agr. A rarer spirit never
Did steer humanity: but you, gods, will give us
Some faults to make us men. Cæsar is touch'd.

Mec. When such a spacious mirror's set before him,
He needs must see himself.

Cæs. O Antony!
I have follow'd thee to this;—But we do lance
Diseases in our bodies: I must perforce
Have shown to thee such a declining day,
Or look on thine; we could not stall together
In the whole world: But yet let me lament,
With tears as sovereign as the blood of hearts,
That thou, my brother, my competitor
In top of all design, my mate in empire,
Friend and companion in the front of war,
The arm of mine own body, and the heart
Where mine his thoughts did kindle,—that our stars,
Unreconcilable, should divide
Our equalness to this.—Hear me, good friends,—
But I will tell you at some meeter season;

Enter a Messenger.

The business of this man looks out of him,
We'll hear him what he says.—Whence are you?

Mess. A poor Egyptian yet. The queen, my mistress,
Confin'd in all she has, her monument,
Of thy intents desires instruction;
That she preparedly may frame herself
To the way she's forced to.

Cæs. Bid her have good heart;
She soon shall know of us, by some of ours,
How honourable and how kindly we
Determine for her: for Cæsar cannot live
To be ungentle.

Mess. So the gods preserve thee! [*Exit.*

Cæs. Come hither, Proculeius; Go, and say,
We purpose her no shame: give her what comforts
The quality of her passion shall require;
Lest, in her greatness, by some mortal stroke
She do defeat us: for her life in Rome
Would be eternal in our triumph: Go,
And, with your speediest, bring us what she says,
And how you find of her.

Pro. Cæsar, I shall. [*Exit* PRO.

Cæs. Gallus, go you along.—Where's Dolabella,
To second Proculeius? [*Exit* GALLUS.
Agr. Mec. Dolabella!
Cæs. Let him alone, for I remember now
How he's employed; he shall in time be ready.
Go with me to my tent; where you shall see
How hardly I was drawn into this war;
How calm and gentle I proceeded still
In all my writings: Go with me, and see
What I can show in this. [*Exeunt.*

SCENE II.

Alexandria. *A Room in the Monument.*

Enter CLEOPATRA, CHARMIAN, *and* IRAS.

Cleo. My desolation does begin to make
A better life: 'Tis paltry to be Cæsar;
Not being fortune, he's but fortune's knave,
A minister of her will; And it is great
To do that thing that ends all other deeds;
Which shackles accidents, and bolts up change;
Which sleeps, and never palates more the dung;
The beggar's nurse and Cæsar's.

Enter, to the Gates of the Monument, PROCULEIUS, GALLUS, *and* Soldiers.

Pro. Cæsar sends greeting to the queen of Egypt;
And bids thee study on what fair demands
Thou mean'st to have him grant thee.
Cleo. [*Within.*] What's thy name?
Pro. My name is Proculeius.
Cleo. [*Within.*] Antony
Did tell me of you, bade me trust you; but
I do not greatly care to be deceiv'd,
That have no use for trusting. If your master
Would have a queen his beggar, you must tell [him,
That majesty, to keep decorum, must
No less beg than a kingdom: if he please
To give me conquer'd Egypt for my son,
He gives me so much of mine own, as I
Will kneel to him with thanks.
Pro. Be of good cheer;
You are fallen into a princely hand, fear nothing:
Make your full reference freely to my lord,
Who is so full of grace, that it flows over
On all that need: Let me report to him
Your sweet dependancy; and you shall find
A conqueror, that will pray in aid for kindness,
Where he for grace is kneel'd to.
Cleo. [*Within.*] Pray you, tell him
I am his fortune's vassal, and I send him
The greatness he has got. I hourly learn
A doctrine of obedience; and would gladly
Look him i' the face.
Pro. This I'll report, dear lady.
Have comfort; for, I know, your plight is pitied
Of him that caus'd it.
Gal. You see how easily she may be surpris'd.
[*Here* PROCULEIUS, *and two of the* Guard, *ascend the Monument by a Ladder placed against a Window, and having descended, come behind* CLEOPATRA. *Some of the* Guard *unbar and open the Gates.*
Guard her till Cæsar come.
[*To* PROCULEIUS *and the* Guard. *Exit* GALLUS.
Iras. Royal queen!
Char. O Cleopatra! thou art taken, queen!—
Cleo. Quick, quick, good hands.
[*Drawing a Dagger.*
Pro. Hold, worthy lady, hold:
[*Seizes and disarms her.*
Do not yourself such wrong, who are in this
Reliev'd, but not betray'd.
Cleo. What, of death too
That rids our dogs of languish?
Pro. Cleopatra,
Do not abuse my master's bounty, by
The undoing of yourself: let the world see
His nobleness well acted, which your death
Will never let come forth.
Cleo. Where art thou, death?
Come hither, come! come, come, and take a [queen
Worth many babes and beggars!
Pro. O, temperance, lady!
Cleo. Sir, I will eat no meat, I'll not drink, sir
(If idle talk will once be necessary);
I'll not sleep neither: This mortal house I'll ruin,
Do Cæsar what he can. Know, sir, that I
Will not wait pinion'd at your master's court;
Nor once be chastis'd with the sober eye
Of dull Octavia. Shall they hoist me up,
And show me to the shouting varletry
Of censuring Rome? Rather a ditch in Egypt
Be gentle grave to me! rather on Nilus' mud
Lay me stark naked, and let the water-flies
Blow me into abhorring! rather make
My country's high pyramides my gibbet,
And hang me up in chains!
Pro. You do extend
These thoughts of horror further than you shall
Find cause in Cæsar.

Enter DOLABELLA.

Dol. Proculeius,
What thou hast done thy master Cæsar knows,
And he hath sent for thee: as for the queen,
I'll take her to my guard.
Pro. So, Dolabella,
It shall content me best: be gentle to her.—
To Cæsar I will speak what you shall please,
[*To* CLEOPATRA.
If you'll employ me to him.
Cleo. Say, I would die.
[*Exeunt* PROCULEIUS, *and* Soldiers.
Dol. Most noble empress, you have heard of me?
Cleo. I cannot tell.
Dol. Assuredly, you know me.
Cleo. No matter, sir, what I have heard, or known.
You laugh, when boys, or women, tell their [dreams;
Is't not your trick?
Dol. I understand not, madam.
Cleo. I dream'd there was an emperor Antony;—
O, such another sleep, that I might see
But such another man!
Dol. If it might please you,—
Cleo. His face was as the heavens; and therein stuck
A sun, and moon; which kept their course, and lighted
The little O, the earth.
Dol. Most sovereign creature,—
Cleo. His legs bestrid the ocean: his rear'd arm
Crested the world: his voice was propertied
As all the tuned spheres, and that to friends;
But when he meant to quail and shake the orb,
He was as rattling thunder. For his bounty,
There was no winter in't; an autumn 'twas,
That grew the more by reaping: His delights
Were dolphin-like: they show'd his back above
The element they liv'd in: In his livery
Walk'd crowns and crownets; realms and islands were
As plates dropp'd from his pocket.
Dol. Cleopatra,—
Cleo. Think you, there was, or might be, such a man
As this I dream'd of?
Dol. Gentle madam, no.
Cleo. You lie, up to the hearing of the gods.
But, if there be, or ever were one such,
It's past the size of dreaming: Nature wants stuff
To vie strange forms with fancy; yet, to imagine
An Antony, were nature's piece 'gainst fancy,
Condemning shadows quite.
Dol. Hear me, good madam:
Your loss is as yourself, great; and you bear it
As answering to the weight: 'Would, I might never
O'ertake pursu'd success, but I do feel,
By the rebound of yours, a grief that shoots
My very heart at root.
Cleo. I thank you, sir,
Know you, what Cæsar means to do with me?

Dol. I am loath to tell you what I would you knew.
Cleo. Nay, pray you, sir,—
Dol. Though he be honourable,—
Cleo. He'll lead me then in triumph?
Dol. Madam, he will;
I know it.
Within. Make way there,—Cæsar.

Enter CÆSAR, GALLUS, PROCULEIUS, MECÆNAS, SELEUCUS, *and* Attendants.

Cæs. Which is the queen
Of Egypt?
Dol. 'Tis the emperor, madam.
[CLEOPATRA *kneels.*
Cæs. Arise,
You shall not kneel:—
I pray you, rise; rise, Egypt.
Cleo. Sir, the gods
Will have it thus; my master and my lord
I must obey.
Cæs. Take to you no hard thoughts:
The record of what injuries you did us,
Though written in our flesh, we shall remember
As things but done by chance.
Cleo. Sole sir o' the world,
I cannot project mine own cause so well
To make it clear; but do confess, I have
Been laden with like frailties, which before
Have often sham'd our sex.
Cæs. Cleopatra, know,
We will extenuate, rather than enforce:
If you apply yourself to our intents
(Which towards you are most gentle), you shall find
A benefit in this change; but if you seek
To lay on me a cruelty, by taking
Antony's course, you shall bereave yourself
Of my good purposes, and put your children
To that destruction which I'll guard them from,
If thereon you rely. I'll take my leave.
Cleo. And may, through all the world: 'tis yours: and we
Your 'scutcheons, and your signs of conquest, shall
Hang in what place you please. Here, my good lord.
Cæs. You shall advise me in all for Cleopatra.
Cleo. This is the brief of money, plate, and jewels,
I am possess'd of: 'tis exactly valued;
Not petty things admitted.—Where's Seleucus?
Sel. Here, madam.
Cleo. This is my treasurer; let him speak, my lord,
Upon his peril, that I have reserv'd
To myself nothing. Speak the truth, Seleucus.
Sel. Madam,
I had rather seel my lips, than, to my peril,
Speak that which is not.
Cleo. What have I kept back?
Sel. Enough to purchase what you have made known.
Cæs. Nay, blush not, Cleopatra! I approve
Your wisdom in the deed.
Cleo. See, Cæsar! O, behold
How pomp is follow'd! mine will now be yours;
And, should we shift estates, yours would be mine.
The ingratitude of this Seleucus does
Even make me wild:—O slave, of no more trust
Than love that's hir'd!—What, go'st thou back? thou shalt
Go back, I warrant thee; but I'll catch thine eyes,
Though they had wings: Slave, soul-less villain, dog!
O rarely base!
Cæs. Good queen, let us entreat you.
Cleo. O Cæsar, what a wounding shame is this:
That thou, vouchsafing here to visit me,
Doing the honour of thy lordliness
To one so meek, that mine own servant should
Parcel the sum of my disgraces by
Addition of his envy! Say, good Cæsar,
That I some lady trifles have reserv'd
Immoment toys, things of such dignity
As we greet modern friends withal: and say,
Some nobler token I have kept apart
For Livia, and Octavia, to induce
Their mediation; must I be unfolded
With one that I have bred? The gods! it smites me
Beneath the fall I have. 'Pr'ythee, go hence;
[*To* SELEUCUS.
Or I shall show the cinders of my spirits
Through the ashes of my chance.—Wert thou a man,
Thou would'st have mercy on me.
Cæs. Forbear, Seleucus.
[*Exit* SELEUCUS.
Cleo. Be it known that we, the greatest, are misthought
For things that others do; and, when we fall,
We answer others' merits in our name,
Are therefore to be pitied.
Cæs. Cleopatra,
Not what you have reserv'd, nor what acknowledg'd,
Put we i' the roll of conquest: still be it yours,
Bestow it at your pleasure; and believe,
Cæsar's no merchant, to make prize with you
Of things that merchants sold. Therefore be cheer'd;
Make not your thoughts your prisons: no, dear queen;
For we intend so to dispose you, as
Yourself shall give us counsel. Feed, and sleep,
Our care and pity is so much upon you,
That we remain your friend; and so adieu.
Cleo. My master, and my lord!
Cæs. Not so: Adieu.
[*Exeunt* CÆSAR, *and his* Train.
Cleo. He words me, girls, he words me, that I should not
Be noble to myself: but hark thee, Charmian.
[*Whispers* CHARMIAN.
Iras. Finish, good lady: the bright day is done,
And we are for the dark.
Cleo. Hie thee again:
I have spoke already, and it is provided;
Go, put it to the haste.
Char. Madam, I will.

Re-enter DOLABELLA.

Dol. Where is the queen?
Char. Behold, sir. [*Exit* CHARMIAN.
Cleo. Dolabella?
Dol. Madam, as thereto sworn by your command,
Which my love makes religion to obey,
I tell you this: Cæsar through Syria
Intends his journey; and, within three days,
You with your children will he send before:
Make your best use of this: I have perform'd
Your pleasure, and my promise.
Cleo. Dolabella,
I shall remain your debtor.
Dol. I your servant.
Adieu, good queen: I must attend on Cæsar.
Cleo. Farewell, and thanks. [*Exit* DOL.] Now, Iras, what think'st thou?
Thou, an Egyptian puppet, shall be shown
In Rome, as well as I: mechanick slaves
With greasy aprons, rules, and hammers, shall
Uplift us to the view; in their thick breaths,
Rank of gross diet, shall we be enclouded,
And forc'd to drink their vapour.
Iras. The gods forbid!
Cleo. Nay, 'tis most certain, Iras: Saucy lictors
Will catch at us, like strumpets; and scald rhymers
Ballad us out o' tune: the quick comedians
Extemporally will stage us, and present
Our Alexandrian revels; Antony
Shall be brought drunken forth, and I shall see

Some squeaking Cleopatra boy my greatness
I' the posture of a whore.

Iras. O the good gods!

Cleo. Nay, that is certain.

Iras. I'll never see it; for, I am sure, my nails
Are stronger than mine eyes.

Cleo. Why, that's the way
To fool their preparation, and to conquer
Their most absurd intents.—Now, Charmian?—

Enter CHARMIAN.

Show me, my women, like a queen;—Go fetch
My best attires;—I am again for Cydnus,
To meet Mark Antony:—Sirrah, Iras, go.—
Now, noble Charmian, we'll despatch indeed:
And, when thou hast done this chare, I'll give thee leave
To play till doomsday.—Bring our crown and all:
Wherefore's this noise?

[*Exit* IRAS. *A Noise within.*

Enter one of the Guard.

Guard. Here is a rural fellow,
That will not be denied your highness' presence;
He brings you figs.

Cleo. Let him come in. How poor an instrument [*Exit* Guard.
May do a noble deed! he brings me liberty.
My resolution's plac'd, and I have nothing
Of woman in me: Now from head to foot
I am marble constant: now the fleeting moon
No planet is of mine.

Re-enter Guard, *with a* Clown, *bringing a Basket.*

Guard. This is the man.

Cleo. Avoid, and leave him. [*Exit* Guard.
Hast thou the pretty worm of Nilus there,
That kills and pains not?

Clown. Truly I have him: but I would not be the party that should desire you to touch him, for his biting is immortal; those, that do die of it, do seldom or never recover.

Cleo. Remember'st thou any that have died on't?

Clown. Very many, men and women too. I heard of one of them no longer than yesterday: a very honest woman, but something given to lie; as a woman should not do, but in the way of honesty:—how she died of the biting of it, what pain she felt.—Truly, she makes a very good report o' the worm: But he that will believe all that they say, shall never be saved by half that they do. But this is most fallible, the worm's an odd worm.

Cleo. Get thee hence; farewell.

Clown. I wish you all joy of the worm.

Cleo. Farewell. [Clown *sets down the Basket.*

Clown. You must think this, look you, that the worm will do his kind.

Cleo. Ay, ay; farewell.

Clown. Look you, the worm is not to be trusted, but in the keeping of wise people; for, indeed, there is no goodness in the worm.

Cleo. Take thou no care; it shall be heeded.

Clown. Very good: give it nothing, I pray you, for it is not worth the feeding.

Cleo. Will it eat me?

Clown. You must not think I am so simple, but I know the devil himself will not eat a woman: I know that a woman is a dish for the gods, if the devil dress her not. But, truly, these same whoreson devils do the gods great harm in their women; for in every ten that they make, the devils mar five.

Cleo. Well, get thee gone; farewell.

Clown. Yes, forsooth; I wish you joy of the worm. [*Exit.*

Re-enter IRAS, *with a Robe, Crown, &c.*

Cleo. Give me my robe, put on my crown; I have
Immortal longings in me: now no more
The juice of Egypt's grape shall moist this lip:—
Yare, yare, good Iras; quick.—Methinks, I hear
Antony call; I see him rouse himself
To praise my noble act; I hear him mock
The luck of Cæsar, which the gods give men
To excuse their after wrath: Husband, I come:
Now to that name my courage prove my title!
I am fire, and air; my other elements
I give to baser life.—So,—have you done?
Come then, and take the last warmth of my lips.
Farewell, kind Charmian:—Iras, long farewell.

[*Kisses them.* IRAS *falls and dies.*

Have I the aspick in my lips? Dost fall?
If thou and nature can so gently part,
The stroke of death is as a lover's pinch,
Which hurts, and is desir'd. Dost thou lie still?
If thus thou vanishest, thou tell'st the world
It is not worth leave-taking.

Char. Dissolve, thick cloud, and rain; that I may say,
The gods themselves do weep!

Cleo. This proves me base:
If she first meet the curled Antony,
He'll make demand of her; and spend that kiss,
Which is my heaven to have. Come, mortal wretch,

[*To the Asp, which she applies to her Breast.*

With thy sharp teeth this knot intrinsicate
Of life at once untie; poor venomous fool,
Be angry, and despatch. O, could'st thou speak!
That I might hear thee call great Cæsar, ass
Unpolicied!

Char. O eastern star!

Cleo. Peace, peace!
Dost thou not see my baby at my breast,
That sucks the nurse asleep?

Char. O, break! O, break!

Cleo. As sweet as balm, as soft as air, as gentle,—
O Antony!—Nay, I will take thee too:—

[*Applying another Asp to her Arm.*

What should I stay— [*Falls on a Bed, and dies.*

Char. In this wild world?—So fare thee well.—
Now boast thee, death! in thy possession lies
A lass unparallel'd.—Downy windows, close;
And golden Phœbus never be beheld
Of eyes again so royal! Your crown's awry;
I'll mend it, and then play.

Enter the Guard, *rushing in.*

1 *Guard.* Where is the queen?

Char. Speak softly, wake her not.

1 *Guard.* Cæsar hath sent—

Char. Too slow a messenger.

[*Applies the Asp.*

O, come; apace, despatch; I partly feel thee.

1 *Guard.* Approach, ho! All's not well: Cæsar's beguil'd.

2 *Guard.* There's Dolabella sent from Cæsar:—call him.

1 *Guard.* What work is here?—Charmian, is this well done?

Char. It is well done, and fitting for a princess
Descended of so many royal kings.
Ah, soldier! [*Dies.*

Enter DOLABELLA.

Dol. How goes it here?

2 *Guard.* All dead.

Dol. Cæsar, thy thoughts
Touch their effects in this: Thyself art coming
To see perform'd the dreaded act, which thou
So sought'st to hinder.

Within. A way there, a way for Cæsar!

Enter CÆSAR, *and* Attendants.

Dol. O, sir, you are too sure an augurer;
That you did fear, is done.

Cæs. Bravest at the last:
She levell'd at our purposes, and, being royal,

Took her own way.—The manner of their deaths?
I do not see them bleed.

Dol. Who was last with them?

1 *Guard.* A simple countryman, that brought her figs;
This was his basket.

Cæs. Poison'd then.

1 *Guard.* O Cæsar,
This Charmian lived but now; she stood, and spake:
I found her trimming up the diadem
On her dead mistress; tremblingly she stood,
And on the sudden dropp'd.

Cæs. O noble weakness!—
If they had swallow'd poison, 'twould appear
By external swelling; but she looks like sleep,
As she would catch another Antony
In her strong toil of grace.

Dol. Here, on her breast,
There is a vent of blood, and something blown:
The like is on her arm.

1 *Guard.* This is an aspick's trail: and these fig-leaves
Have slime upon them, such as the aspick leaves
Upon the caves of Nile.

Cæs. Most probable,
That so she died; for her physician tells me,
She hath pursu'd conclusions infinite
Of easy ways to die.—Take up her bed;
And bear her women from the monument:—
She shall be buried by her Antony:
No grave upon the earth shall clip in it
A pair so famous. High events as these
Strike those that make them: and their story is
No less in pity, than his glory, which
Brought them to be lamented. Our army shall,
In solemn show, attend this funeral;
And then to Rome.—Come, Dolabella, see
High order in this great solemnity. [*Exeunt.*

CYMBELINE.

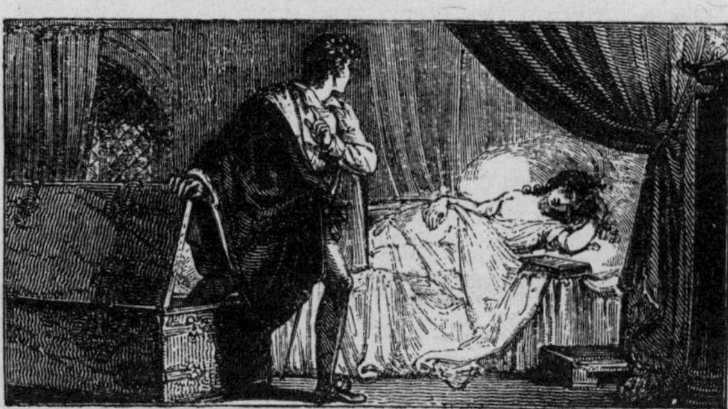

PERSONS REPRESENTED.

CYMBELINE, King *of* Britain.
CLOTEN, *Son to the* Queen *by a former Husband.*
LEONATUS POSTHUMUS, *a Gentleman, Husband to* Imogen.
BELARIUS, *a banished Lord, disguised under the name of* Morgan.
GUIDERIUS, ARVIRAGUS, } *Sons to* Cymbeline, *disguised under the names of* Polydore, *and* Cadwal, *supposed Sons to* Belarius.
PHILARIO, *Friend to* Posthumus, IACHIMO, *Friend to* Philario, } Italians.
A French Gentleman, *Friend to* Philario.
CAIUS LUCIUS, *General of the* Roman Forces.
A Roman Captain. *Two* British Captains.
PISANIO, *Servant to* Posthumus.
CORNELIUS, *a Physician.*
Two Gentlemen.
Two Gaolers.

Queen, *Wife to* Cymbeline.
IMOGEN, *Daughter to* Cymbeline *by a former Queen.*
HELEN, *Woman to* Imogen.

Lords, Ladies, Roman Senators, Tribunes, Apparitions, *a* Soothsayer, *a* Dutch Gentleman, *a* Spanish Gentleman, Musicians, Officers, Captains, Soldiers, Messengers, *and other* Attendants.

SCENE—*sometimes in* Britain; *sometimes in* Italy.

ACT I.

SCENE I. Britain. *The Garden behind* Cymbeline's *Palace.*

Enter Two Gentlemen.

1 *Gent.* You do not meet a man but frowns: our bloods
No more obey the heavens, than our courtiers;
Still seem, as does the king's.

2 *Gent.* But what's the matter?

1 *Gent.* His daughter, and the heir of his kingdom, whom
He purpos'd to his wife's sole son (a widow
That late he married), hath referr'd herself
Unto a poor but worthy gentleman: She's wedded;
Her husband banish'd; she imprison'd: all
Is outward sorrow; though, I think, the king
Be touch'd at very heart.

2 *Gent.* None but the king?

1 *Gent.* He, that hath lost her, too: so is the queen,
That most desir'd the match: But not a courtier,
Although they wear their faces to the bent
Of the king's looks, hath a heart that is not
Glad at the thing they scowl at.

2 *Gent.* And why so?

1 *Gent.* He that hath miss'd the princess, is a thing
Too bad for bad report: and he that hath her,
(I mean, that married her,—alack, good man!—
And therefore banish'd) is a creature such
As, to seek through the regions of the earth
For one his like, there would be something failing
In him that should compare. I do not think,
So fair an outward, and such stuff within,
Endows a man but he.
2 *Gent.* You speak him far.
1 *Gent.* I do extend him, sir, within himself;
Crush him together, rather than unfold
His measure duly.
2 *Gent.* What's his name, and birth?
1 *Gent.* I cannot delve him to the root: His father
Was call'd Sicilius, who did join his honour
Against the Romans, with Cassibelan;
But had his titles by Tenantius, whom
He serv'd with glory and admir'd success:
So gain'd the sur-addition, Leonatus:
And had, besides this gentleman in question,
Two other sons, who, in the wars o' the time,
Died with their swords in hand; for which their father
(Then old and fond of issue) took such sorrow,
That he quit being; and his gentle lady,
Big of this gentleman, our theme, deceas'd
As he was born. The king, he takes the babe
To his protection; calls him Posthumus:
Breeds him, and makes him of his bedchamber:
Puts him to all the learnings that his time
Could make him the receiver of: which he took,
As we do air, fast as 'twas minister'd; and
In his spring became a harvest: Liv'd in court
(Which rare it is to do) most prais'd, most lov'd:
A sample to the youngest; to the more mature
A glass that feated them; and to the graver,
A child that guided dotards; to his mistress,
For whom he now is banish'd,—her own price
Proclaims how she esteem'd him and his virtue;
By her election may be truly read,
What kind of man he is.
2 *Gent.* I honour him
Even out of your report. But, 'pray you, tell me,
Is she sole child to the king?
1 *Gent.* His only child.
He had two sons (if this be worth your hearing,
Mark it), the eldest of them at three years old,
I' the swathing clothes the other, from their nursery
Were stolen: and to this hour, no guess in knowledge
Which way they went.
2 *Gent.* How long is this ago?
1 *Gent.* Some twenty years.
2 *Gent.* That a king's children should be so convey'd!
So slackly guarded! And the search so slow,
That could not trace them!
1 *Gent.* Howsoe'er 'tis strange,
Or that the negligence may well be laugh'd at,
Yet is it true, sir.
2 *Gent.* I do well believe you.
1 *Gent.* We must forbear: Here comes the queen and princess. [*Exeunt.*

SCENE II. *The same.*

Enter the Queen, POSTHUMUS, *and* IMOGEN.

Queen. No, be assur'd, you shall not find me, daughter,
After the slander of most step-mothers,
Evil-eyed unto you: you are my prisoner, but
Your gaoler shall deliver you the keys
That lock up your restraint. For you, Posthumus,
So soon as I can win the offended king,
I will be known your advocate: marry, yet
The fire of rage is in him: and 'twere good,
You lean'd unto his sentence, with what patience
Your wisdom may inform you.
Post. Please your highness,
I will from hence to-day.
Queen. You know the peril:—
I'll fetch a turn about the garden, pitying
The pangs of barr'd affections: though the king
Hath charg'd you should not speak together.
[*Exit* Queen.
Imo. O
Dissembling courtesy! How fine this tyrant
Can tickle where she wounds!—My dearest husband,
I something fear my father's wrath: but nothing
(Always reserv'd my holy duty), what
His rage can do on me: You must be gone;
And I shall here abide the hourly shot
Of angry eyes: not comforted to live,
But that there is this jewel in the world,
That I may see again.
Post. My queen! my mistress!
O, lady, weep no more; lest I give cause
To be suspected of more tenderness
Than doth become a man! I will remain
The loyal'st husband that did e'er plight troth.
My residence in Rome, at one Philario's;
Who to my father was a friend, to me
Known but by letter: thither write, my queen,
And with mine eyes I'll drink the words you send,
Though ink be made of gall.

Re-enter Queen.

Queen. Be brief, I pray you:
If the king come, I shall incur I know not
How much of his displeasure:—Yet I'll move him [*Aside.*
To walk this way: I never do him wrong,
But he does buy my injuries, to be friends:
Pays dear for my offences. [*Exit.*
Post. Should we be taking leave
As long a term as yet we have to live,
The loathness to depart would grow: Adieu!
Imo. Nay, stay a little:
Were you but riding forth to air yourself,
Such parting were too petty. Look here, love;
This diamond was my mother's: take it, heart;
But keep it till you woo another wife,
When Imogen is dead.
Post. How! how! another?—
You gentle gods, give me but this I have,
And sear up my embracements from a next
With bonds of death!—Remain, remain thou here [*Putting on the Ring.*
While sense can keep it on! And sweetest, fairest,
As I my poor self did exchange for you,
To your so infinite loss; so, in our trifles
I still win of you: For my sake, wear this;
It is a manacle of love; I'll place it
Upon this fairest prisoner.
[*Putting a Bracelet on her Arm.*
Imo. O, the gods!
When shall we see again?

Enter CYMBELINE *and* Lords.

Post. Alack, the king!
Cym. Thou basest thing, avoid! hence, from my sight!
If, after this command, thou fraught the court
With thy unworthiness, thou diest: Away!
Thou art poison to my blood.
Post. The gods protect you!
And bless the good remainders of the court!
I am gone. [*Exit.*
Imo. There cannot be a pinch in death
More sharp than this is.
Cym. O disloyal thing,
That should'st repair my youth; thou heapest
A year's age on me!
Imo. I beseech you, sir,
Harm not yourself with your vexation: I
Am senseless of your wrath; a touch more rare
Subdues all pangs, all fears.

Cym. Past grace? obedience?
Imo. Past hope, and in despair; that way, past grace.
Cym. That might'st have had the sole son of my queen!
Imo. O bless'd, that I might not! I chose an eagle,
And did avoid a puttock.
Cym. Thou took'st a beggar; would'st have made my throne
A seat for baseness.
Imo. No; I rather added
A lustre to it.
Cym. O thou vile one!
Imo. Sir,
It is your fault that I have lov'd Posthumus:
You bred him as my playfellow; and he is
A man, worth any woman: overbuys me
Almost the sum he pays.
Cym. What!—art thou mad?
Imo. Almost, sir: Heaven restore me!—'Would I were
A neat-herd's daughter! and my Leonatus
Our neighbour shepherd's son!

Re-enter Queen.

Cym. Thou foolish thing!—
They were again together: you have done [*To the* Queen.
Not after our command. Away with her,
And pen her up.
Queen. 'Beseech your patience:—Peace,
Dear lady daughter, peace; Sweet sovereign,
Leave us to ourselves; and make yourself some comfort
Out of your best advice.
Cym. Nay, let her languish
A drop of blood a day; and, being aged,
Die of this folly! [*Exit.*

Enter PISANIO.

Queen. Fye!—you must give way:
Here is your servant.—How now, sir? What news?
Pis. My lord your son drew on my master.
Queen. Ha!
No harm, I trust, is done?
Pis. There might have been,
But that my master rather play'd than fought,
And had no help of anger: they were parted
By gentlemen at hand.
Queen. I am very glad on't.
Imo. Your son's my father's friend: he takes his part.—
To draw upon an exile!—O brave sir!—
I would they were in Africk both together;
Myself by with a needle, that I might prick
The goer back.—Why came you from your master?
Pis. On his command: He would not suffer me
To bring him to the haven: left these notes
Of what commands I should be subject to,
When it pleas'd you to employ me.
Queen. This hath been
Your faithful servant: I dare lay mine honour,
He will remain so.
Pis. I humbly thank your highness.
Queen. Pray, walk a while.
Imo. About some half hour hence,
I pray you, speak with me: you shall, at least,
Go see my lord aboard: for this time, leave me. [*Exeunt.*

SCENE III. *A publick Place.*

Enter CLOTEN, *and Two* Lords.

1 *Lord.* Sir, I would advise you to shift a shirt; the violence of action hath made you reek as a sacrifice: Where air comes out, air comes in: there's none abroad so wholesome as that you vent.
Clo. If my shirt were bloody, then to shift it—Have I hurt him?
2 *Lord.* No, faith; not so much as his patience. [*Aside.*
1 *Lord.* Hurt him? his body's a passable carcass, if he be not hurt: it is a thoroughfare for steel, if it be not hurt.
2 *Lord.* His steel was in debt; it went o' the backside the town. [*Aside.*
Clo. The villain would not stand me.
2 *Lord.* No; but he fled forward still, toward your face. [*Aside.*
1 *Lord.* Stand you! you have land enough of your own: but he added to your having; gave you some ground.
2 *Lord.* As many inches as you have oceans: Puppies! [*Aside.*
Clo. I would, they had not come between us.
2 *Lord.* So would I, till you had measured how long a fool you were upon the ground. [*Aside.*
Clo. And that she should love this fellow, and refuse me!
2 *Lord.* If it be a sin to make a true election, she is damned. [*Aside.*
1 *Lord.* Sir, as I told you always, her beauty and her brain go not together: She's a good sign, but I have seen small reflection of her wit.
2 *Lord.* She shines not upon fools, lest the reflection should hurt her. [*Aside.*
Clo. Come, I'll to my chamber: 'Would there had been some hurt done!
2 *Lord.* I wish not so; unless it had been the fall of an ass, which is no great hurt. [*Aside.*
Clo. You'll go with us?
1 *Lord.* I'll attend your lordship.
Clo. Nay, come, let's go together.
2 *Lord.* Well, my lord. [*Exeunt.*

SCENE IV. *A Room in* Cymbeline's *Palace.*

Enter IMOGEN *and* PISANIO.

Imo. I would thou grew'st unto the shores o' the haven,
And question'dst every sail: if he should write,
And I not have it, 'twere a paper lost
As offer'd mercy is. What was the last
That he spake to thee?
Pis. 'Twas, *His queen, his queen!*
Imo. Then wav'd his handkerchief?
Pis. And kiss'd it, madam.
Imo. Senseless linen! happier therein than I!—
And that was all?
Pis. No, madam; for so long
As he could make me with this eye or ear
Distinguish him from others, he did keep
The deck, with glove, or hat, or handkerchief,
Still waving, as the fits and stirs of his mind
Could best express how slow his soul sail'd on,
How swift his ship.
Imo. Thou should'st have made him
As little as a crow, or less, ere left
To after-eye him.
Pis. Madam, so I did.
Imo. I would have broke mine eye-strings; crack'd them, but
To look upon him; till the diminution
Of space had pointed him sharp as my needle:
Nay, follow'd him, till he had melted from
The smallness of a gnat to air; and then
Have turn'd mine eye, and wept.—But, good Pisanio,
When shall we hear from him?
Pis. Be assur'd, madam,
With his next vantage.
Imo. I did not take my leave of him, but had
Most pretty things to say: ere I could tell him,
How I would think on him, at certain hours,
Such thoughts, and such; or I could make him swear
The shes of Italy should not betray
Mine interest, and his honour; or have charg'd him,
At the sixth hour of morn, at noon, at midnight
To encounter me with orisons, for then

I am in heaven for him: or ere I could
Give him that parting kiss, which I had set
Betwixt two charming words, comes in my father,
And, like the tyrannous breathing of the north,
Shakes all our buds from growing.

Enter a Lady.

Lady. The queen, madam,
Desires your highness' company.

Imo. Those things I bid you do, get them despatch'd.—
I will attend the queen.

Pis. Madam, I shall.
[*Exeunt.*

SCENE V.

Rome. *An Apartment in* Philario's *House.*

Enter PHILARIO, IACHIMO, *a* Frenchman, *a* Dutchman, *and a* Spaniard.

Iach. Believe it, sir: I have seen him in Britain: he was then of a crescent note, expected to prove so worthy, as since he hath been allowed the name of: but I could then have looked on him without the help of admiration: though the catalogue of his endowments had been tabled by his side, and I to peruse him by items.

Phi. You speak of him when he was less furnished, than now he is, with that which makes him both without and within.

French. I have seen him in France: we had very many there, could behold the sun with as firm eyes as he.

Iach. This matter of marrying his king's daughter (wherein he must be weighed rather by her value, than his own), words him, I doubt not, a great deal from the matter.

French. And then his banishment:—

Iach. Ay, and the approbation of those, that weep this lamentable divorce, under her colours are wonderfully to extend him; be it but to fortify her judgment, which else an easy battery might lay flat, for taking a beggar without more quality. But how comes it, he is to sojourn with you? How creeps acquaintance?

Phi. His father and I were soldiers together; to whom I have been often bound for no less than my life:——

Enter POSTHUMUS.

Here comes the Briton: Let him be so entertained amongst you, as suits, with gentlemen of your knowing, to a stranger of his quality.—I beseech you all, be better known to this gentleman; whom I commend to you, as a noble friend of mine: How worthy he is, I will leave to appear hereafter, rather than story him in his own hearing.

French. Sir, we have known together in Orleans.

Post. Since when I have been debtor to you for courtesies, which I will be ever to pay, and yet pay still.

French. Sir, you o'er-rate my poor kindness: I was glad I did atone my countryman and you; it had been pity, you should have been put together with so mortal a purpose, as then each bore, upon importance of so slight and trivial a nature.

Post. By your pardon, sir, I was then a young traveller: rather shunn'd to go even with what I heard, than in my every action to be guided by others' experiences: but, upon my mended judgment (if I offend not to say it is mended), my quarrel was not altogether slight.

French. 'Faith, yes, to be put to the arbitrement of swords; and by such two, that would, by all likelihood, have confounded one the other, or have fallen both.

Iach. Can we, with manners, ask what was the difference?

French. Safely, I think: 'twas a contention in publick, which may, without contradiction, suffer the report. It was much like an argument that fell out last night, where each of us fell in praise of our country mistresses: This gentleman at that time vouching (and upon warrant of bloody affirmation), his to be more fair, virtuous, wise, chaste, constant-qualified, and less attemptible, than any the rarest of our ladies in France.

Iach. That lady is not now living; or this gentleman's opinion, by this, worn out.

Post. She holds her virtue still, and I my mind.

Iach. You must not so far prefer her 'fore ours of Italy.

Post. Being so far provoked as I was in France, I would abate her nothing; though I profess myself her adorer, not her friend.

Iach. As fair, and as good (a kind of hand-in-hand comparison), had been something too fair, and too good, for any lady in Britany. If she went before others I have seen, as that diamond of yours out-lustres many I have beheld, I could not but believe she excelled many: but I have not seen the most precious diamond that is, nor you the lady.

Post. I praised her, as I rated her: so do I my stone.

Iach. What do you esteem it at?

Post. More than the world enjoys.

Iach. Either your unparagoned mistress is dead, or she's outpriz'd by a trifle.

Post. You are mistaken: the one may be sold, or given; if there were wealth enough for the purchase, or merit for the gift: the other is not a thing for sale, and only the gift of the gods.

Iach. Which the gods have given you?

Post. Which, by their graces, I will keep.

Iach. You may wear her in title yours: but, you know, strange fowl light upon neighbouring ponds. Your ring may be stolen too: so, of your brace of unprizeable estimations, the one is but frail, and the other casual: a cunning thief, or a that-way accomplished courtier, would hazard the winning both of first and last.

Post. Your Italy contains none so accomplished a courtier, to convince the honour of my mistress; if, in the holding or loss of that, you term her frail. I do nothing doubt, you have store of thieves; notwithstanding I fear not my ring.

Phi. Let us leave here, gentlemen.

Post. Sir, with all my heart. This worthy signior, I thank him, makes no stranger of me: we are familiar at first.

Iach. With five times so much conversation, I should get ground of your fair mistress: make her go back, even to the yielding; had I admittance, and opportunity to friend.

Post. No, no.

Iach. I dare, thereupon, pawn the moiety of my estate to your ring; which, in my opinion, o'er-values it something: But I make my wager rather against your confidence, than her reputation: and, to bar your offence herein too, I durst attempt it against any lady in the world.

Post. You are a great deal abused in too bold a persuasion; and I doubt not you sustain what you're worthy of, by your attempt.

Iach. What's that?

Post. A repulse: Though your attempt, as you call it, deserve more; a punishment too.

Phi. Gentlemen, enough of this: it came in too suddenly; let it die as it was born, and, I pray you, be better acquainted.

Iach. 'Would I had put my estate, and my neighbour's, on the approbation of what I have spoke.

Post. What lady would you choose to assail?

Iach. Yours; whom in constancy, you think, stands so safe. I will lay you ten thousand ducats to your ring, that, commend me to the court where your lady is, with no more advantage than the opportunity of a second conference, and I will bring from thence that honour of hers, which you imagine so reserved.

Post. I will wage against your gold, gold to it: my ring I hold dear as my finger; 'tis part of it.

Iach. You are a friend, and therein the wiser. If you buy ladies' flesh at a million a dram, you cannot preserve it from tainting: But, I see, you have some religion in you, that you fear.

Post. This is but a custom in your tongue; you bear a graver purpose, I hope.

Iach. I am the master of my speeches; and would undergo what's spoken, I swear.

Post. Will you?—I shall but lend my diamond till your return:—Let there be covenants drawn between us: My mistress exceeds in goodness the hugeness of your unworthy thinking: I dare you to this match: here's my ring.

Phi. I will have it no lay.

Iach. By the gods it is one: If I bring you no sufficient testimony that I have enjoyed the dearest bodily part of your mistress, my ten thousand ducats are yours; so is your diamond too. If I come off, and leave her in such honour as you have trust in, she your jewel, this your jewel, and my gold are yours:—provided, I have your commendation, for my more free entertainment.

Post. I embrace these conditions; let us have articles betwixt us:—only, thus far you shall answer. If you make your voyage upon her, and give me directly to understand you have prevailed, I am no further your enemy, she is not worth our debate: if she remain unseduced (you not making it appear otherwise), for your ill opinion, and the assault you have made to her chastity, you shall answer me with your sword.

Iach. Your hand; a covenant: We will have these things set down by lawful counsel, and straight away for Britain; lest the bargain should catch cold and starve: I will fetch my gold, and have our two wagers recorded.

Post. Agreed. [*Exeunt* POST. *and* IACH.

French. Will this hold, think you?

Phi. Signior Iachimo will not from it. Pray, let us follow 'em. [*Exeunt.*

SCENE VI.

Britain. *A Room in* Cymbeline's *Palace.*

Enter Queen, Ladies, *and* CORNELIUS.

Queen. Whiles yet the dew's on ground, gather those flowers;
Make haste: Who has the note of them?

1 Lady. I, madam.

Queen. Despatch.—— [*Exeunt* Ladies.
Now, master doctor; have you brought those drugs?

Cor. Pleaseth your highness, ay: here they are, madam: [*Presenting a small Box.*
But I beseech your grace (without offence;
My conscience bids me ask); wherefore you have
Commanded of me these most poisonous compounds,
Which are the movers of a languishing death;
But, though slow, deadly?

Queen. I do wonder, doctor,
Thou ask'st me such a question: Have I not been
Thy pupil long? Hast thou not learn'd me how
To make perfumes? distil? preserve? yea, so,
That our great king himself doth woo me oft
For my confections? Having thus far proceeded
(Unless thou think'st me devilish), is't not meet
That I did amplify my judgment in
Other conclusions? I will try the forces
Of these thy compounds on such creatures as
We count not worth the hanging (but none human),
To try the vigour of them, and apply
Allayments to their act; and by them gather
Their several virtues, and effects.

Cor. Your highness
Shall from this practice but make hard your heart:
Besides, the seeing these effects will be
Both noisome and infectious.

Queen. O, content thee.—

Enter PISANIO.

Here comes a flattering rascal; upon him [*Aside.*
Will I first work: he's for his master,
And enemy to my son.—How now, Pisanio?—
Doctor, your service for this time is ended;
Take your own way.

Cor. I do suspect you, madam;
But you shall do no harm. [*Aside.*

Queen. Hark thee, a word.— [*To* PISANIO.

Cor. [*Aside.*] I do not like her. She doth think she has
Strange lingering poisons: I do know her spirit,
And will not trust one of her malice with
A drug of such damn'd nature: Those, she has,
Will stupify and dull the sense awhile:
Which first, perchance, she'll prove on cats, and dogs;
Then afterward up higher: but there is
No danger in what show of death it makes,
More than the locking up the spirits a time,
To be more fresh, reviving. She is fool'd
With a most false effect; and I the truer,
So to be false with her.

Queen. No further service, doctor,
Until I send for thee.

Cor. I humbly take my leave. [*Exit.*

Queen. Weeps she still, say'st thou? Dost thou think, in time
She will not quench; and let instructions enter
Where folly now possesses? Do thou work;
When thou shalt bring me word, she loves my son,
I'll tell thee, on the instant, thou art then
As great as is thy master; greater; for
His fortunes all lie speechless, and his name
Is at last gasp: Return he cannot, nor
Continue where he is; to shift his being,
Is to exchange one misery with another;
And every day, that comes, comes to decay
A day's work in him: What shalt thou expect,
To be depender on a thing that leans?
Who cannot be new built; nor has no friends,
[*The* Queen *drops a Box:* PISANIO *takes it up.*
So much as but to prop him?—Thou tak'st up
Thou know'st not what; but take it for thy labour:
It is a thing I made, which hath the king
Five times redeem'd from death: I do not know
What is more cordial:—Nay, I pr'ythee, take it;
It is an earnest of a further good
That I mean to thee. Tell thy mistress how
The case stands with her; do't, as from thyself.
Think what a chance thou changest on; but think
Thou hast thy mistress still; to boot, my son,
Who shall take notice of thee; I'll move the king
To any shape of thy preferment, such
As thou'lt desire; and then myself, I chiefly,
That set thee on to this desert, am bound
To load thy merit richly. Call my women:
Think on my words. [*Exit* PISA.]—A sly and constant knave;
Not to be shak'd: the agent for his master;
And the remembrancer of her, to hold
The hand fast to her lord.—I have given him that,
Which, if he take, shall quite unpeople her
Of liegers for her sweet; and which she, after,
Except she bend her humour, shall be assur'd

Re-enter PISANIO, *and* Ladies.

To taste of too.—So, so;—well done, well done:
The violets, cowslips, and the primroses,
Bear to my closet:—Fare thee well, Pisanio;
Think on my words.
[*Exeunt* Queen *and* Ladies.

Pis. And shall do:
But when to my good lord I prove untrue,
I'll choke myself; there's all I'll do for you.
[*Exit.*

SCENE VII. *Another Room in the same.*

Enter IMOGEN.

Imo. A father cruel, and a step-dame false;
A foolish suitor to a wedded lady,
That hath her husband banish'd;—O, that husband!
My supreme crown of grief! and those repeated
Vexations of it! Had I been thief-stolen,
As my two brothers, happy! but most miserable
Is the desire that's glorious: Blessed be those,
How mean soe'er, that have their honest wills,
Which seasons comfort.—Who may this be? Fye!

Enter PISANIO *and* IACHIMO.

Pis. Madam, a noble gentleman of Rome;
Comes from my lord with letters.
Iach. Change you, madam?
The worthy Leonatus is in safety,
And greets your highness dearly.
[*Presents a Letter.*
Imo. Thanks, good sir:
You are kindly welcome.
Iach. All of her, that is out of door, most rich!
[*Aside.*
If she be furnish'd with a mind so rare,
She is alone the Arabian bird; and I
Have lost the wager. Boldness be my friend!
Arm me, audacity, from head to foot!
Or, like the Parthian, I shall flying fight:
Rather, directly fly.
Imo. [Reads.]—*He is one of the noblest note, to whose kindnesses I am most infinitely tied. Reflect upon him accordingly, as you value your truest*
LEONATUS.
So far I read aloud:
But even the very middle of my heart
Is warm'd by the rest, and takes it thankfully.—
You are as welcome, worthy sir, as I
Have words to bid you; and shall find it so,
In all that I can do.
Iach. Thanks, fairest lady.—
What! are men mad? Hath nature given them eyes
To see this vaulted arch, and the rich crop
Of sea and land, which can distinguish 'twixt
The fiery orbs above, and the twinn'd stones
Upon the number'd beach? and can we not
Partition make with spectacles so precious
'Twixt fair and foul?
Imo. What makes your admiration?
Iach. It cannot be i' the eye; for apes and monkeys
'Twixt two such she's, would chatter this way, and
Contemn with mows the other: Nor i'the judgment;
For idiots, in this case of favour, would
Be wisely definite: Nor i' the appetite;
Sluttery to such neat excellence oppos'd
Should make desire vomit emptiness,
Not so allur'd to feed.
Imo. What is the matter, trow?
Iach. The cloyed will
(That satiate yet unsatisfied desire,
That tub both fill'd and running), ravening first
The lamb, longs after for the garbage.
Imo. What, dear sir,
Thus raps you? Are you well?
Iach. Thanks, madam; well:—'Beseech you, sir, desire [*To* PISANIO.
My man's abode where I did leave him: he
Is strange and peevish.
Pis. I was going, sir,
To give him welcome. [*Exit* PISANIO.
Imo. Continues well my lord? His health, beseech you?
Iach. Well, madam.
Imo. Is he dispos'd to mirth? I hope, he is.
Iach. Exceeding pleasant: none a stranger there
So merry and so gamesome: he is call'd
The Briton reveller.
Imo. When he was here,
He did incline to sadness; and oft-times
Not knowing why.
Iach. I never saw him sad.
There is a Frenchman his companion, one
An eminent monsieur, that, it seems, much loves
A Gallian girl at home: he furnaces
The thick sighs from him; whiles the jolly Briton
(Your lord, I mean), laughs from's free lungs, cries, *O!*
Can my sides hold, to think, that man,—who knows
By history, report, or his own proof,
What woman is, yea, what she cannot choose
But must be,—will his free hours languish for
Assured bondage?
Imo. Will my lord say so?
Iach. Ay, madam; with his eyes in flood with laughter.
It is a recreation to be by,
And hear him mock the Frenchman: But, heavens know,
Some men are much to blame.
Imo. Not he, I hope.
Iach. Not he: But yet heaven's bounty towards him might
Be us'd more thankfully. In himself, 'tis much;
In you,—which I count his, beyond all talents,—
Whilst I am bound to wonder, I am bound
To pity too.
Imo. What do you pity, sir?
Iach. Two creatures, heartily.
Imo. Am I one, sir?
You look on me; What wreck discern you in me,
Deserves your pity?
Iach. Lamentable! What!
To hide me from the radiant sun, and solace
I' the dungeon by a snuff?
Imo. I pray you, sir,
Deliver with more openness your answers
To my demands. Why do you pity me?
Iach. That others do,
I was about to say, enjoy your——But
It is an office of the gods to venge it,
Not mine to speak on't.
Imo. You do seem to know
Something of me, or what concerns me; 'Pray you
(Since doubting things go ill, often hurts more
Than to be sure they do: For certainties
Either are past remedies; or, timely knowing,
The remedy then born), discover to me
What both you spur and stop.
Iach. Had I this cheek
To bathe my lips upon; this hand, whose touch,
Whose every touch, would force the feeler's soul
To the oath of loyalty; this object, which
Takes prisoner the wild motion of mine eye,
Fixing it only here: should I (damn'd then),
Slaver with lips as common as the stairs
That mount the Capitol; join gripes with hands
Made hard with hourly falsehood (falsehood, as
With labour); then lie peeping in an eye,
Base and unlustrous as the smoky light
That's fed with stinking tallow; it were fit,
That all the plagues of hell should at one time
Encounter such revolt.
Imo. My lord, I fear,
Has forgot Britain.
Iach. And himself. Not I,
Inclin'd to this intelligence, pronounce
The beggary of his change; but 'tis your graces
That, from my mutest conscience, to my tongue,
Charms this report out.
Imo. Let me hear no more.
Iach. O dearest soul! your cause doth strike my heart

With pity, that doth make me sick. A lady
So fair, and fasten'd to an empery,
Would make the great'st king double! to be partner'd
With tomboys, hired with that self-exhibition
Which your own coffers yield! with diseas'd ventures,
That play with all infirmities for gold
Which rottenness can lend nature; such boil'd stuff,
As well might poison poison! Be reveng'd;
Or she, that bore you, was no queen, and you
Recoil from your great stock.

Imo. Reveng'd!
How should I be reveng'd? If this be true
(As I have such a heart, that both mine ears
Must not in haste abuse), if it be true,
How should I be reveng'd?

Iach. Should he make me
Live like Diana's priest, betwixt cold sheets;
Whiles he is vaulting variable ramps,
In your despite, upon your purse? Revenge it.
I dedicate myself to your sweet pleasure;
More noble than that runagate to your bed;
And will continue fast to your affection,
Still close, as sure.

Imo. What ho, Pisanio!

Iach. Let me my service tender on your lips.

Imo. Away!—I do condemn mine ears, that have
So long attended thee.—If thou wert honourable,
Thou would'st have told this tale for virtue, not
For such an end thou seek'st; as base, as strange.
Thou wrong'st a gentleman, who is as far
From thy report, as thou from honour; and
Solicit'st here a lady, that disdains
Thee and the devil alike.—What ho, Pisanio!—
The king my father shall be made acquainted
Of thy assault: if he shall think it fit,
A saucy stranger, in his court, to mart
As in a Romish stew, and to expound
His beastly mind to us; he hath a court
He little cares for, and a daughter whom
He not respects at all.—What ho, Pisanio!—

Iach. O happy Leonatus! I may say;
The credit, that thy lady hath of thee,
Deserves thy trust! and thy most perfect goodness
Her assur'd credit!—Blessed live you long!
A lady to the worthiest sir, that ever
Country call'd his! and you his mistress, only
For the most worthiest fit! Give me your pardon.
I have spoke this, to know if your affiance
Were deeply rooted; and shall make your lord,
That which he is, new o'er: And he is one
The truest manner'd; such a holy witch,
That he enchants societies unto him:
Half all men's hearts are his.

Imo. You make amends.

Iach. He sits 'mongst men, like a descended god:
He hath a kind of honour sets him off,
More than a mortal seeming. Be not angry,
Most mighty princess, that I have adventur'd
To try your taking of a false report; which hath
Honour'd with confirmation your great judgment
In the election of a sir so rare,
Which you know, cannot err: The love I bear him
Made me to fan you thus; but the gods made you,
Unlike all others, chaffless. 'Pray your pardon.

Imo. All's well, sir; Take my power i' the court for yours.

Iach. My humble thanks. I had almost forgot
To entreat your grace but in a small request,
And yet of moment too, for it concerns
Your lord; myself, and other noble friends,
Are partners in the business.

Imo. 'Pray, what is't?

Iach. Some dozen Romans of us, and your lord
(The best feather of our wing), have mingled sums,
To buy a present for the emperor;
Which I, the factor for the rest, have done
In France: 'Tis plate, of rare device; and jewels,
Of rich and exquisite form; their values great;
And I am something curious, being strange,
To have them in safe stowage; May it please you
To take them in protection?

Imo. Willingly;
And pawn mine honour for their safety: since
My lord hath interest in them, I will keep them
In my bed-chamber.

Iach. They are in a trunk,
Attended by my men: I will make bold
To send them to you, only for this night;
I must aboard to-morrow.

Imo. O no, no.

Iach. Yes, I beseech; or I shall short my word,
By length'ning my return. From Gallia
I cross'd the seas on purpose, and on promise
To see your grace.

Imo. I thank you for your pains;
But not away to-morrow?

Iach. O, I must, madam:
Therefore, I shall beseech you, if you please
To greet your lord with writing, do't to-night:
I have outstood my time; which is material
To the tender of our present.

Imo. I will write.
Send your trunk to me; it shall safe be kept,
And truly yielded you: You are very welcome,
[*Exeunt.*

ACT II.

SCENE I. *Court before* Cymbeline's *Palace.*

Enter CLOTEN, *and Two* Lords.

Clo. Was there ever man had such luck! when I kissed the jack upon an upcast, to be hit away! I had a hundred pound on't: And then a whoreson jackanapes must take me up for swearing; as if I borrowed mine oaths of him, and might not spend them at my pleasure.

1 *Lord.* What got he by that? You have broke his pate with your bowl.

2 *Lord.* If his wit had been like him that broke it, it would have ran all out. [*Aside.*

Clo. When a gentleman is disposed to swear, it is not for any standers by to curtail his oaths: Ha?

2 *Lord.* No, my lord; nor [*aside*] crop the ears of them.

Clo. Whoreson dog!—I give him satisfaction? 'Would, he had been one of my rank!

2 *Lord.* To have smelt like a fool. [*Aside.*

Clo. I am not more vexed at any thing in the earth,—A pox on't! I had rather not be so noble as I am; they dare not fight with me, because of the queen my mother: every jack-slave hath his belly full of fighting, and I must go up and down like a cock that nobody can match.

2 *Lord.* You are a cock and capon too: and you crow, cock, with your comb on. [*Aside.*

Clo. Sayest thou?

1 *Lord.* It is not fit, your lordship should undertake every companion that you give offence to.

Clo. No, I know that: but it is fit, I should commit offence to my inferiors.

2 *Lord.* Ay, it is fit for your lordship only.

Clo. Why, so I say.

1 *Lord.* Did you hear of a stranger, that's come to court to-night?

Clo. A stranger! and I not know on't!

2 *Lord.* He's a strange fellow himself, and knows it not. [*Aside.*

1 *Lord.* There's an Italian come; and, 'tis thought, one of Leonatus' friends.

Clo. Leonatus! a banished rascal; and he's

another, whatsoever he be. Who told you of this stranger?

1 *Lord*. One of your lordship's pages.

Clo. Is it fit, I went to look upon him? Is there no derogation in't?

1 *Lord*. You cannot derogate, my lord.

Clo. not easily, I think.

2 *Lord*. You are a fool granted; therefore your issues being foolish, do not derogate. [*Aside*.

Clo. Come, I'll go see this Italian: What I have lost to-day at bowls, I'll win to-night of him. Come, go.

2 *Lord*. I'll attend your lordship.

[*Exeunt* CLOTEN *and first* Lord.

That such a crafty devil as is his mother
Should yield the world this ass! a woman, that
Bears all down with her brain; and this her son
Cannot take two from twenty for his heart,
And leave eighteen. Alas, poor princess,
Thou divine Imogen, what thou endur'st!
Betwixt a father by thy step-dame govern'd;
A mother hourly coining plots; a wooer,
More hateful than the foul expulsion is
Of thy dear husband, than that horrid act
Of the divorce he'd make! The heavens hold firm
The walls of thy dear honour; keep unshak'd
That temple, thy fair mind; that thou may'st stand,
To enjoy thy banish'd lord, and this great land!

[*Exit*.

SCENE II.

A Bedchamber; in one Part of it a Trunk.

IMOGEN *reading in her Bed; a* Lady *attending*.

Imo. Who's there? my woman Helen?

Lady. Please you, madam.

Imo. What hour is it?

Lady. Almost midnight, madam.

Imo. I have read three hours then; mine eyes are weak:—
Fold down the leaf where I have left: To bed:
Take not away the taper, leave it burning;
And if thou canst awake by four o'the clock,
I pr'ythee, call me. Sleep hath seiz'd me wholly. [*Exit* Lady.
To your protection I commend me, gods!
From fairies, and the tempters of the night,
Guard me, beseech ye!

[*Sleeps*. IACHIMO, *from the Trunk*.

Iach. The crickets sing, and man's o'erlabour'd sense
Repairs itself by rest: Our Tarquin thus
Did softly press the rushes, ere he waken'd
The chastity he wounded.—Cytherea,
How bravely thou becom'st thy bed! fresh lily!
And whiter than the sheets! That I might touch!
But kiss; one kiss!—Rubies unparagon'd,
How dearly they do't!—'Tis her breathing that
Perfumes the chamber thus: The flame o'the taper
Bows toward her; and would underpeep her lids,
To see the enclosed lights, now canopied
Under these windows: White and azure, lac'd
With blue of heaven's own tinct.—But my design?
To note the chamber:—I will write all down:—
Such, and such, pictures:—There the window:—Such
The adornment of her bed:—The arras, figures,
Why, such, and such:—And the contents o'the story,—
Ay, but some natural notes about her body,
Above ten thousand meaner moveables
Would testify, to enrich mine inventory:
O sleep, thou ape of death, lie dull upon her!
And be her sense but as a monument,
Thus in a chapel lying!—Come off, come off;—

[*Taking off her Bracelet*.

As slippery, as the Gordian knot was hard!—
'Tis mine; and this will witness outwardly,
As strongly as the conscience does within,
To the madding of her lord. On her left breast
A mole cinque-spotted, like the crimson drops
I' the bottom of a cowslip: Here's a voucher,
Stronger than ever law could make: this secret
Will force him think I have pick'd the lock, and ta'en
The treasure of her honour. No more.—To what end?
Why should I write this down, that's riveted,
Screw'd to my memory? She hath been reading late
The tale of Tereus; here the leaf's turn'd down,
Where Philomel gave up;—I have enough:
To the trunk again, and shut the spring of it.
Swift, swift, you dragons of the night!—that dawning
May bear the raven's eye: I lodge in fear;
Though this a heavenly angel, hell is here.

[*Clock strikes*.

One, two, three,—Time, time!

[*Goes into the Trunk. The Scene closes*.

SCENE III.

An Ante-Chamber adjoining Imogen's *Apartment*.

Enter CLOTEN *and* Lords.

1 *Lord*. Your lordship is the most patient man in loss, the most coldest that ever turn'd up ace.

Clo. It would make any man cold to lose.

1 *Lord*. But not every man patient, after the noble temper of your lordship; You are most hot, and furious, when you win.

Clo. Winning would put any man into courage: If I could get this foolish Imogen, I should have gold enough: It's almost morning, is't not?

1 *Lord*. Day, my lord.

Clo. I would this musick would come: I am advised to give her musick o'mornings; they say, it will penetrate.

Enter Musicians.

Come on; tune: If you can penetrate her with your fingering, so; we'll try with tongue too: if none will do, let her remain; but I'll never give o'er. First, a very excellent good-conceited thing; after, a wonderful sweet air, with admirable rich words to it,—and then let her consider.

SONG.

Hark! hark! the lark at heaven's gate sings,
And Phœbus 'gins arise,
His steeds to water at those springs
On chalic'd flowers that lies;
And winking Mary-buds begin
To ope their golden eyes;
With every thing that pretty bin:
My lady sweet, arise;
Arise, arise.

So, get you gone: If this penetrate, I will consider your musick the better: if it do not, it is a vice in her ears, which horse-hairs, and cats-guts, nor the voice of unpaved eunuch to boot, can never amend. [*Exeunt* Musicians.

Enter CYMBELINE *and* Queen.

2 *Lord*. Here comes the king.

Clo. I am glad, I was up so late: for that's the reason I was up so early: He cannot choose but take this service I have done, fatherly.—Good morrow to your majesty, and to my gracious mother.

Cym. Attend you here the door of our stern daughter?
Will she not forth?

Clo. I have assailed her with musick, but she vouchsafes no notice.

Cym. The exile of her minion is too new;
She hath not yet forgot him: some more time
Must wear the print of his remembrance out,
And then she's yours.

Queen. You are most bound to the king:

Who lets go by no vantages, that may
Prefer you to his daughter: Frame yourself
To orderly solicits; and be friended
With aptness of the season: make denials
Increase your services: so seem, as if
You were inspir'd to do those duties which
You tender to her; that you in all obey her,
Save when command to your dismission tends,
And therein you are senseless.

Clo. Senseless? not so.

Enter a Messenger.

Mess. So like you, sir, embassadors from Rome;
The one is Caius Lucius.

Cym. A worthy fellow,
Albeit he comes on angry purpose now;
But that's no fault of his: We must receive him
According to the honour of his sender;
And towards himself his goodness forespent on us
We must extend our notice.—Our dear son,
When you have given good morning to your mistress,
Attend the queen, and us; we shall have need
To employ you towards this Roman.—Come, our queen.

[*Exeunt* CYM. Queen, Lords, and Mess.

Clo. If she be up, I'll speak with her; if not,
Let her lie still, and dream.—By your leave ho!—

[*Knocks.*

I know her women are about her; What
If I do line one of their hands? 'Tis gold
Which buys admittance; oft it doth; yea, and makes
Diana's rangers false themselves, yield up
Their deer to the stand of the stealer; and 'tis gold
Which makes the true man kill'd, and saves the thief;
Nay, sometime, hangs both thief and true man: What
Can it not do, and undo? I will make
One of her women lawyer to me; for
I yet not understand the case myself.
By your leave. [*Knocks.*

Enter a Lady.

Lady. Who's there, that knocks?

Clo. A gentleman.

Lady. No more?

Clo. Yes, and a gentlewoman's son.

Lady. That's more
Than some, whose tailors are as dear as yours,
Can justly boast of: What's your lordship's pleasure?

Clo. Your lady's person: Is she ready?

Lady. Ay,
To keep her chamber.

Clo. There's gold for you; sell me your good report.

Lady. How! my good name? or to report of you
What I shall think is good?—The princess——

Enter IMOGEN.

Clo. Good morrow, fairest sister: Your sweet hand.

Imo. Good morrow, sir: You lay out too much pains
For purchasing but trouble: the thanks I give,
Is telling you that I am poor of thanks,
And scarce can spare them.

Clo. Still, I swear, I love you.

Imo. If you but said so, 'twere as deep with me:
If you swear still, your recompense is still
That I regard it not.

Clo. This is no answer.

Imo. But that you shall not say I yield, being silent,
I would not speak. I pray you, spare me i' faith,
I shall unfold equal discourtesy
To your best kindness; one of your great knowing
Should learn, being taught, forbearance.

Clo. To leave you in your madness, 'twere my sin:
I will not.

Imo. Fools are not mad folks.

Clo. Do you call me fool?

Imo. As I am mad, I do:
If you'll be patient, I'll no more be mad;
That cures us both. I am much sorry, sir,
You put me to forget a lady's manners,
By being so verbal: and learn now, for all,
That I, which know my heart, do here pronounce,
By the very truth of it, I care not for you;
And am so near the lack of charity
(To accuse myself), I hate you: which I had rather
You felt, than make't my boast.

Clo. You sin against
Obedience, which you owe your father. For
The contract you pretend with that base wretch
(One, bred of alms, and foster'd with cold dishes,
With scraps o' the court), it is no contract, none:
And though it be allow'd in meaner parties,
(Yet who, than he, more mean?) to knit their souls
(On whom there is no more dependency
But brats and beggary) in self-figur'd knot;
Yet you are curb'd from that enlargement by
The consequence o' the crown; and must not soil
The precious note of it with a base slave,
A hilding for a livery, a squire's cloth,
A pantler, not so eminent.

Imo. Profane fellow!
Wert thou the son of Jupiter, and no more,
But what thou art, besides, thou wert too base
To be his groom: thou wert dignified enough,
Even to the point of envy, if 'twere made
Comparative for your virtues, to be styl'd
The under-hangman of his kingdom; and hated
For being preferr'd so well.

Clo. The south-fog rot him!

Imo. He never can meet more mischance than come
To be but nam'd of thee. His meanest garment,
That ever hath but clipp'd his body, is dearer,
In my respect, than all the hairs above thee,
Were they all made such men.—How now, Pisanio?

Enter PISANIO.

Clo. His garment? Now, the devil——

Imo. To Dorothy my woman hie thee presently:—

Clo. His garment?

Imo. I am sprighted with a fool;
Frighted, and anger'd worse:—Go, bid my woman
Search for a jewel, that too casually
Hath left mine arm; it was thy master's: 'shrew me,
If I would lose it for a revenue
Of any king's in Europe. I do think,
I saw't this morning: Confident I am,
Last night 'twas on mine arm; I kiss'd it:
I hope, it be not gone, to tell my lord
That I kiss aught but he.

Pis. 'Twill not be lost.

Imo. I hope so: go, and search. [*Exit* PISANIO.

Clo. You have abus'd me:—
His meanest garment?

Imo. Ay; I said so, sir.
If you will make't an action, call witness to't.

Clo. I will inform your father.

Imo. Your mother too:
She's my good lady; and will conceive, I hope,
But the worst of me. So I leave you, sir,
To the worst of discontent. [*Exit.*

Clo. I'll be reveng'd:—
His meanest garment?—Well. [*Exit.*

SCENE IV.

Rome. *An Apartment in* Philario's *House.*

Enter POSTHUMUS *and* PHILARIO.

Post. Fear it not, sir: I would, I were so sure
To win the king, as I am bold, her honour
Will remain hers.
Phi. What means do you make to him?
Post. Not any; but abide the change of time;
Quake in the present winter's state, and wish
That warmer days would come: in these fear'd hopes,
I barely gratify your love; they failing,
I must die much your debtor.
Phi. Your very goodness, and your company,
O'erpays all I can do. By this, your king
Hath heard of great Augustus: Caius Lucius
Will do his commission throughly: And I think,
He'll grant the tribute, send the arrearages,
Or look upon our Romans, whose remembrance
Is yet fresh in their grief.
Post. I do believe
(Statist though I am none, nor like to be),
That this will prove a war; and you shall hear
The legions now in Gallia, sooner landed
In our not-fearing Britain, than have tidings
Of any penny tribute paid. Our countrymen
Are men more order'd, than when Julius Cæsar
Smil'd at their lack of skill, but found their courage
Worthy his frowning at: Their discipline
(Now mingled with their courages) will make known
To their approvers, they are people, such
That mend upon the world.

Enter IACHIMO.

Phi. See! Iachimo?
Post. The swiftest harts have posted you by land:
And winds of all the corners kiss'd your sails,
To make your vessel nimble.
Phi. Welcome, sir.
Post. I hope, the briefness of your answer made
The speediness of your return.
Iach. Your lady
Is one the fairest that I have look'd upon.
Post. And, therewithal, the best; or let her beauty
Look through a casement to allure false hearts,
And be false with them.
Iach. Here are letters for you.
Post. Their tenour good, I trust.
Iach. 'Tis very like.
Phi. Was Caius Lucius in the Britain court,
When you were there?
Iach. He was expected then,
But not approach'd.
Post. All is well yet.—
Sparkles this stone as it was wont? or is't not
Too dull for your good wearing?
Iach. If I have lost it,
I should have lost the worth of it in gold.
I'll make a journey twice as far, to enjoy
A second night of such sweet shortness, which
Was mine in Britain; for the ring is won.
Post. The stone's too hard to come by.
Iach. Not a whit,
Your lady being so easy.
Post. Make, not sir,
Your loss your sport: I hope, you know that we
Must not continue friends.
Iach. Good sir, we must,
If you keep covenant: Had I not brought
The knowledge of your mistress home, I grant
We were to question further: but I now
Profess myself the winner of her honour,
Together with your ring; and not the wronger
Of her, or you, having proceeded but
By both your wills.
Post. If you can make't apparent
That you have tasted her in bed, my hand,
And ring is yours: if not, the foul opinion
You had of her pure honour, gains, or loses,
Your sword, or mine; or masterless leaves both
To who shall find them.
Iach. Sir, my circumstances
Being so near the truth, as I will make them,
Must first induce you to believe: whose strength
I will confirm with oath; which, I doubt not,
You'll give me leave to spare, when you shall find
You need it not.
Post. Proceed.
Iach. First, her bed-chamber
(Where, I confess, I slept not; but, profess,
Had that was well worth watching), It was hang'd
With tapestry of silk and silver; the story
Proud Cleopatra, when she met her Roman,
And Cydnus swell'd above the banks, or for
The press of boats, or pride: a piece of work
So bravely done, so rich, that it did strive
In workmanship, and value: which, I wonder'd,
Could be so rarely and exactly wrought,
Since the true life on't was——
Post. This is true;
And this you might have heard of here, by me,
Or by some other.
Iach. More particulars
Must justify my knowledge.
Post. So they must,
Or do your honour injury.
Iach. The chimney
Is south the chamber; and the chimney-piece,
Chaste Dian, bathing: never saw I figures
So likely to report themselves: the cutter
Was as another nature, dumb; outwent her,
Motion and breath left out.
Post. This is a thing,
Which you might from relation likewise reap;
Being, as it is, much spoke of.
Iach. The roof o' the chamber
With golden cherubins is fretted. Her andirons
(I had forgot them), were two winking Cupids
Of silver, each on one foot standing, nicely
Depending on their brands.
Post. This is her honour!—
Let it be granted, you have seen all this (and praise
Be given to your remembrance), the description
Of what is in her chamber, nothing saves
The wager you have laid.
Iach. Then, if you can,
[*Pulling out the Bracelet.*
Be pale; I beg but leave to air this jewel: See!—
And now 'tis up again: it must be married
To that your diamond; I'll keep them.
Post. Jove!—
Once more let me behold it: Is it that
Which I left with her?
Iach. Sir (I thank her), that:
She stripp'd it from her arm; I see her yet;
Her pretty action did outsell her gift,
And yet enrich'd it too: She gave it me, and said,
She priz'd it once.
Post. May be, she pluck'd it off,
To send it me.
Iach. She writes so to you? doth she?
Post. O, no, no, no; 'tis true. Here, take this too; [*Gives the Ring.*
It is a basilisk unto mine eye,
Kills me to look on't:—Let there be no honour,
Where there is beauty; truth, where semblance; love,
Where there's another man: The vows of women
Of no more bondage be, to where they are made,
Than they are to their virtues: which is nothing:—
O, above measure false!
Phi. Have patience, sir,
And take your ring again; 'tis not yet won:
It may be probable, she lost it; or,
Who knows if one of her women, being corrupted,
Hath stolen it from her.

Post. Very true;
And so, I hope, he came by't;—Back my ring;—
Render to me some corporal sign about her,
More evident than this; for this was stolen.

Iach. By Jupiter, I had it from her arm.

Post. Hark you, he swears; by Jupiter he swears.
'Tis true;—nay keep the ring—'tis true:—I am sure,
She would not lose it: her attendants are
All sworn and honourable:—They induc'd to steal it!
And by a stranger?—No, he hath enjoy'd her.
The cognizance of her incontinency
Is this,—she hath bought the name of whore thus dearly.—
There, take thy hire: and all the fiends of hell
Divide themselves between you!

Phi. Sir, be patient:
This is not strong enough to be believ'd
Of one persuaded well of——

Post. Never talk on't;
She hath been colted by him.

Iach. If you seek
For further satisfying, under her breast
Worthy the pressing, lies a mole, right proud
Of that most delicate lodging: By my life,
I kiss'd it: and it gave me present hunger
To feed again, though full. You do remember
This stain upon her?

Post. Ay, and it doth confirm
Another stain, as big as hell can hold,
Were there no more but it.

Iach. Will you hear more?

Post. Spare your arithmetick; never count the turns;
Once, and a million;

Iach. I'll be sworn,——

Post. No swearing.
If you will swear you have not done't, you lie;
And I will kill thee, if thou dost deny
Thou hast made me cuckold.

Iach. I will deny nothing.

Post. O, that I had her here, to tear her limb-meal!
I will go there, and do't; i' the court; before
Her father:—I'll do something—— [*Exit.*

Phi. Quite besides
The government of patience!—You have won:
Let's follow him, and pervert the present wrath
He hath against himself.

Iach. With all my heart. [*Exeunt.*

SCENE V. *The same. Another Room in the same.*

Enter POSTHUMUS.

Post. Is there no way for men to be, but women
Must be half-workers? We are bastards all;
And that most venerable man, which I
Did call my father, was I know not where
When I was stamp'd; some coiner with his tools
Made me a counterfeit: Yet my mother seem'd
The Dian of that time: so doth my wife
The nonpareil of this.—O vengeance, vengeance!
Me of my lawful pleasure she restrain'd,
And pray'd me, oft, forbearance: did it with
A pudency so rosy, the sweet view on't
Might well have warm'd old Saturn; that I thought her
As chaste as unsunn'd snow;—O, all the devils!—
This yellow Iachimo, in an hour,—was't not?—
Or less,—at first: Perchance he spoke not; but,
Like a full-acorn'd boar, a German one,
Cry'd, *oh!* and mounted: found no opposition
But what he look'd for should oppose, and she
Should from encounter guard. Could I find out
The woman's part in me! For there's no motion
That tends to vice in man, but I affirm
It is the woman's part: Be it lying, note it,
The woman's; flattering, hers; deceiving, hers;
Lust and rank thoughts, hers, hers; revenges, hers;
Ambitions, covetings, change of prides, disdain,
Nice longings, slanders, mutability,
All faults that may be nam'd, nay, that hell knows,
Why, hers, in part, or all; but, rather, all:
For ev'n to vice
They are not constant, but are changing still
One vice, but of a minute old, for one
Not half so old as that. I'll write against them,
Detest them, curse them: Yet 'tis greater skill
In a true hate to pray they have their will:
The very devils cannot plague them better. [*Exit.*

ACT III.

SCENE I.

Britain. *A Room of State in* Cymbeline's *Palace.*

Enter CYMBELINE, Queen, CLOTEN, *and* Lords, *at one Door; and at another,* CAIUS LUCIUS, *and* Attendants.

Cym. Now say, what would Augustus Cæsar with us?

Luc. When Julius Cæsar (whose remembrance yet
Lives in men's eyes; and will to ears, and tongues,
Be theme, and hearing ever), was in this Britain,
And conquer'd it, Cassibelan, thine uncle
(Famous in Cæsar's praises, no whit less
Than in his feats deserving it), for him,
And his succession, granted Rome a tribute,
Yearly three thousand pounds; which by thee lately
Is left untender'd.

Queen. And, to kill the marvel,
Shall be so ever.

Clo. There be many Cæsars,
Ere such another Julius. Britain is
A world by itself; and we will nothing pay,
For wearing our own noses.

Queen. That opportunity,
Which then they had to take from us, to resume
We have again.—Remember, sir, my liege,
The kings your ancestors; together with
The natural bravery of your isle; which stands
As Neptune's park, ribbed and paled in
With rocks unscaleable, and roaring waters;
With sands, that will not bear your enemies' boats,
But suck them up to the top-mast. A kind of conquest
Cæsar made here; but made not here his brag
Of, *came*, and *saw*, and *overcame;* with shame
(The first that ever touch'd him), he was carried
From off our coast, twice beaten; and his shipping,
(Poor ignorant baubles!) on our terrible seas,
Like egg-shells mov'd upon their surges, crack'd
As easily 'gainst our rocks: for joy whereof,
The fam'd Cassibelan, who was once at point
(O, giglot fortune!) to master Cæsar's sword,
Made Lud's town with rejoicing fires bright,
And Britons strut with courage.

Clo. Come, there's no more tribute to be paid: Our kingdom is stronger than it was at that time; and, as I said, there is no more such Cæsars: other of them may have crooked noses: but, to owe such straight arms, none.

Cym. Son, let your mother end.

Clo. We have yet many among us can gripe as hard as Cassibelan: I do not say, I am one; but I have a hand.—Why tribute? why should we pay tribute? If Cæsar can hide the sun from us with a blanket, or put the moon in his pocket, we will pay him tribute for light; else, sir, no more tribute, pray you now.

Cym. You must know,

Till the injurious Romans did extort
This tribute from us, we were free: Cæsar's ambition
(Which swell'd so much, that it did almost stretch
The sides o' the world), against all colour, here
Did put the yoke upon us; which to shake off,
Becomes a warlike people, whom we reckon
Ourselves to be. We do say then to Cæsar,
Our ancestor was that Mulmutius, which
Ordain'd our laws; whose use the sword of Cæsar
Hath too much mangled; whose repair, and franchise,
Shall, by the power we hold, be our good deed,
(Though Rome be therefore angry); Mulmutius,
Who was the first of Britain, which did put
His brows within a golden crown, and call'd
Himself a king.

Luc. I am sorry, Cymbeline,
That I am to pronounce Augustus Cæsar
(Cæsar, that hath more kings his servants, than
Thyself domestick officers), thine enemy:
Receive it from me, then:—War, and confusion,
In Cæsar's name pronounce I 'gainst thee: look
For fury not to be resisted:—Thus defied,
I thank thee for myself.

Cym. Thou art welcome, Caius.
Thy Cæsar knighted me; my youth I spent
Much under him; of him I gather'd honour;
Which he, to seek of me again, perforce,
Behoves me keep at utterance; I am perfect,
That the Pannonians and Dalmatians, for
Their liberties are now in arms: a precedent
Which, not to read, would show the Britons cold:
So Cæsar shall not find them.

Luc. Let proof speak.

Clo. His majesty bids you welcome. Make pastime with us a day, or two, longer: If you seek us afterwards in other terms, you shall find us in our salt-water girdle: if you beat us out of it, it is yours; if you fall in the adventure, our crows shall fare the better for you; and there's an end.

Luc. So, sir.

Cym. I know your master's pleasure, and he mine:
All the remain is, welcome. [*Exeunt.*

SCENE II. *Another Room in the same.*

Enter PISANIO.

Pis. How! of adultery? wherefore write you not
What monster's her accuser?—Leonatus!
O, master! what a strange infection
Is fallen into thy ear? What false Italian
(As poisonous tongu'd, as handed) hath prevail'd
On thy too ready hearing?—Disloyal? No:
She's punish'd for her truth; and undergoes,
More goddess-like than wife-like, such assaults
As would take in some virtue.—O, my master!
Thy mind to her is now as low, as were
Thy fortunes.—How! that I should murder her?
Upon the love, and truth, and vows, which I
Have made to thy command?—I, her?—her blood?
If it be so to do good service, never
Let me be counted serviceable. How look I,
That I should seem to lack humanity,
So much as this fact comes to? *Do't: The letter* [Reading.
That I have sent her, by her own command
Shall give thee opportunity.—O damn'd paper!
Black as the ink that's on thee! Senseless bauble,
Art thou a feodary for this act, and look'st
So virgin-like without? Lo, here she comes.

Enter IMOGEN.

I am ignorant in what I am commanded.

Imo. How now, Pisanio?

Pis. Madam, here is a letter from my lord.

Imo. Who? thy lord? that is my lord? Leonatus?
O, learn'd indeed were that astronomer,
That knew the stars, as I his characters;
He'd lay the future open.—You good gods,
Let what is here contain'd relish of love,
Of my lord's health, of his content,—yet not,
That we two are asunder, let that grieve him,—
(Some griefs are med'cinable;) that is one of them,
For it doth physick love;—of his content,
All but in that!—Good wax, thy leave:—Bless'd be,
You bees, that make these locks of counsel! Lovers,
And men in dangerous bonds, pray not alike;
Though forfeiters you cast in prison, yet
You clasp young Cupid's tables.—Good news, gods! [*Reads.*

Justice, and your father's wrath, should he take me in his dominion, could not be so cruel to me as you, O the dearest of creatures, would not even renew me with your eyes. Take notice, that I am in Cambria, at Milford-Haven. What your own love will, out of this, advise you, follow. So, he wishes you all happiness, that remains loyal to his vow, and your, increasing in love, LEONATUS POSTHUMUS.

O, for a horse with wings!—Hear'st thou, Pisanio?
He is at Milford Haven: Read, and tell me
How far 'tis thither. If one of mean affairs
May plod it in a week, why may not I
Glide thither in a day?—Then, true Pisanio,
(Who long'st, like me, to see thy lord; who long'st,—
O, let me 'bate,—but not like me;—yet long'st,—
But in a fainter kind:—O, not like me;
For mine's beyond beyond) say, and speak thick;
(Love's counsellor should fill the bores of hearing,
To the smothering of the sense), how far it is
To this same blessed Milford: And, by the way,
Tell me how Wales was made so happy, as
To inherit such a haven: But, first of all,
How we may steal from hence; and, for the gap
That we shall make in time, from our hence-going,
And our return, to excuse: but first, how get hence:
Why should excuse be born or e'er begot?
We'll talk of that hereafter. Pr'ythee, speak,
How many score of miles may we well ride
'Twixt hour and hour?

Pis. One score, 'twixt sun and sun,
Madam, 's enough for you; and too much too.

Imo. Why, one that rode to his execution, man,
Could never go so slow: I have heard of riding wagers,
Where horses have been nimbler than the sands
That run i' the clock's behalf:——But this is foolery:—
Go, bid my woman feign a sickness; say
She'll home to her father: and provide me, presently,
A riding suit; no costlier than would fit
A franklin's housewife.

Pis. Madam, you're best consider.

Imo. I see before me, man, nor here, nor here,
Nor what ensues; but have a fog in them,
That I cannot look through. Away, I pr'ythee;
Do as I bid thee: There's no more to say;
Accessible is none but Milford way. [*Exeunt.*

SCENE III.

Wales. *A mountainous Country, with a Cave.*

Enter BELARIUS, GUIDERIUS, *and* ARVIRAGUS.

Bel. A goodly day not to keep house, with such
Whose roof's as low as ours! Stoop, boys: This gate
Instructs you how to adore the heavens; and bows you

To morning's holy office: The gates of monarchs
Are arch'd so high, that giants may jet through
And keep their impious turbans on, without
Good morrow to the sun.—Hail, thou fair heaven!
We house i'the rock, yet use thee not so hardly
As prouder livers do.
Gui. Hail, heaven!
Arv. Hail, heaven!
Bel. Now, for our mountain sport: Up to yon hill,
Your legs are young; I'll tread these flats. Consider,
When you above perceive me like a crow,
That it is place which lessens, and sets off.
And you may then revolve what tales I have told you,
Of courts, of princes, of the tricks in war:
This service is not service, so being done,
But being so allow'd: To apprehend thus,
Draws us a profit from all things we see:
And often to our comfort shall we find
The sharded beetle in a safer hold
Than is the full-wing'd eagle. O, this life
Is nobler, than attending for a check:
Richer, than doing nothing for a brabe;
Prouder, than rustling in unpaid-for silk:
Such gain the cap of him, that makes him fine,
Yet keeps his book uncross'd: no life to ours.
Gui. Out of your proof you speak: we, poor unfledg'd,
Have never wing'd from view o' the nest; nor know not
What air's from home. Haply, this life is best,
If quiet life be best; sweeter to you,
That have a sharper known: well corresponding
With your stiff age; but, unto us, it is
A cell of ignorance; travelling abed;
A prison for a debtor, that not dares
To stride a limit.
Arv. What should we speak of,
When we are old as you? when we shall hear
The rain and wind beat dark December, how,
In this our pinching cave, shall we discourse
The freezing hours away? We have seen nothing:
We are beastly; subtle as the fox, for prey;
Like warlike as the wolf, for what we eat:
Our valour is, to chase what flies; our cage
We make a quire, as doth the prison bird,
And sing our bondage freely.
Bel. How you speak!
Did you but know the city's usuries,
And felt them knowingly: the art o' the court,
As hard to leave, as keep; whose top to climb
Is certain falling, or so slippery, that
The fear's as bad as falling: the toil of the war,
A pain that only seems to seek out danger
I' the name of fame, and honour; which dies i' the search;
And hath as oft a slanderous epitaph,
As record of fair act; nay, many times,
Doth ill deserve by doing well; what's worse,
Must court'sey at the censure:—O, boys, this story
The world may read in me: My body's mark'd
With Roman swords: and my report was once
First with the best of note: Cymbeline lov'd me;
And when a soldier was the theme, my name
Was not far off: Then was I as a tree,
Whose boughs did bend with fruit: but in one night,
A storm, or robbery, call it what you will,
Shook down my mellow hangings, nay, my leaves,
And left me bare to weather.
Gui. Uncertain favour!
Bel. My fault being nothing (as I have told you oft),
But that two villains, whose false oaths prevail'd
Before my perfect honour, swore to Cymbeline,
I was confederate with the Romans; so,
Follow'd my banishment; and, this twenty years,
This rock, and these demesnes, have been my world:
Where I have liv'd at honest freedom; paid
More pious debts to heaven, than in all
The fore-end of my time.—But, up to the mountains;
This is not hunters' language:—He, that strikes
The venison first, shall be the lord o' the feast;
To him the other two shall minister;
And we will fear no poison, which attends
In place of greater state. I'll meet you in the valleys. [*Exeunt* GUI. *and* ARV.
How hard it is, to hide the sparks of nature!
These boys know little, they are sons to the king;
Nor Cymbeline dreams that they are alive.
They think, they are mine: and, though train'd up thus meanly
I' the cave, wherein they bow, their thoughts do hit
The roofs of palaces; and nature prompts them,
In simple and low things, to prince it, much
Beyond the trick of others. This Polydore,
The heir of Cymbeline and Britain, whom
The king his father call'd Guiderius,—Jove!
When on my three-foot stool I sit, and tell
The warlike feats I have done, his spirits fly out
Into my story: say,—*Thus mine enemy fell;*
And thus I set my foot on his neck; even then
The princely blood flows in his cheek, he sweats,
Strains his young nerves, and puts himself in posture
That acts my words. The younger brother, Cadwal
(Once Arviragus), in as like a figure,
Strikes life into my speech, and shows much more
His own conceiving. Hark! the game is rous'd!—
O Cymbeline! heaven, and my conscience, knows,
Thou didst unjustly banish me: whereon,
At three, and two years old, I stole these babes;
Thinking to bar thee of succession, as
Thou reft'st me of my lands. Euriphile,
Thou wast their nurse; they took thee for their mother,
And every day do honour to her grave:
Myself, Belarius, that am Morgan call'd,
They take for natural father. The game is up. [*Exit.*

SCENE IV. *Near* Milford Haven.

Enter PISANIO *and* IMOGEN.

Imo. Thou told'st me, when we came from horse, the place
Was near at hand:—Ne'er long'd my mother so
To see me first, as I have now:—Pisanio! Man!
Where is Posthumus? What is in thy mind,
That makes thee stare thus? Wherefore breaks that sigh
From the inward of thee? One, but painted thus,
Would be interpreted a thing perplex'd
Beyond self-explication: Put thyself
Into a haviour of less fear, ere wildness
Vanquish my staider senses. What's the matter?
Why tender'st thou that paper to me, with
A look untender? If it be summer news,
Smile to 't before: if winterly, thou need'st
But keep that countenance still.—My husband's hand!
That drug-damn'd Italy hath out-craftied him,
And he's at some hard point.—Speak, man; thy tongue
May take off some extremity, which to read
Would be even mortal to me.
Pis. Please you, read;
And you shall find me, wretched man, a thing
The most disdain'd of fortune.
Imo. [Reads.] *Thy mistress,* Pisanio, *hath played the strumpet in my bed; the testimonies whereof lie*

bleeding in me. I speak not out of weak surmises; but from proof as strong as my grief, and as certain as I expect my revenge. That part, thou, Pisanio, *must act for me, if thy faith be not tainted with the breach of hers. Let thine own hands take away her life: I shall give thee opportunities at* Milford Haven: *she hath my letter for the purpose; Where, if thou fear to strike, and to make me certain it is done, thou art the pander to her dishonour, and equally to me disloyal.*

Pis. What shall I need to draw my sword? the paper
Hath cut her throat already.—No, 'tis slander;
Whose edge is sharper than the sword; whose tongue
Outvenoms all the worms of Nile; whose breath
Rides on the posting winds, and doth belie
All corners of the world: kings, queens, and states,
Maids, matrons, nay, the secrets of the grave
This viperous slander enters.—What cheer, madam?

Imo. False to his bed! What is it, to be false?
To lie in watch there, and to think on him?
To weep 'twixt clock and clock? if sleep charge nature,
To break it with a fearful dream of him,
And cry myself awake? that's false to his bed?
Is it?

Pis. Alas, good lady!

Imo. I false? Thy conscience witness:—Iachimo,
Thou didst accuse him of incontinency;
Thou then look'dst like a villain; now, methinks,
Thy favour's good enough.—Some jay of Italy,
Whose mother was her painting, hath betray'd him:
Poor I am stale, a garment out of fashion;
And, for I am richer than to hang by the walls,
I must be ripp'd:—to pieces with me!—O,
Men's vows are women's traitors! All good seeming,
By thy revolt, O husband, shall be thought
Put on for villany; not born, where 't grows;
But worn, a bait for ladies.

Pis. Good madam, hear me.

Imo. True honest men being heard, like false Æneas,
Were, in his time, thought false: and Sinon's weeping
Did scandal many a holy tear: took pity
From most true wretchedness: So, thou, Posthumus,
Wilt lay the leaven on all proper men;
Goodly, and gallant, shall be false and perjur'd,
From thy great fail.—Come, fellow, be thou honest:
Do thou thy master's bidding: when thou seest him,
A little witness my obedience: Look!
I draw the sword myself: take it; and hit
The innocent mansion of my love, my heart:
Fear not: 'tis empty of all things, but grief:
Thy master is not there; who was, indeed,
The riches of it: Do his bidding; strike.
Thou may'st be valiant in a better cause;
But now thou seem'st a coward.

Pis. Hence, vile instrument!
Thou shalt not damn my hand.

Imo. Why, I must die;
And if I do not by thy hand, thou art
No servant of thy master's: Against self-slaughter
There is a prohibition so divine,
That cravens my weak hand. Come, here's my heart;
Something's afore 't:—Soft, soft; we'll no defence;
Obedient as the scabbard.—What is here?
The scriptures of the loyal Leonatus,
All turn'd to heresy? Away, away,
Corrupters of my faith! you shall no more
Be stomachers to my heart! Thus may poor fools
Believe false teachers! Though those that are betray'd
Do feel the treason sharply, yet the traitor
Stands in worse case of woe.
And thou, Posthumus, thou that didst set up
My disobedience 'gainst the king my father,
And make me put into contempt the suits
Of princely fellows, shalt hereafter find
It is no act of common passage, but
A strain of rareness: and I grieve myself,
To think, when thou shalt be disedg'd by her
That now thou tir'st on, how thy memory
Will then be pang'd by me.—Pr'ythee, despatch:
The lamb entreats the butcher: Where's thy knife?
Thou art too slow to do thy master's bidding,
When I desire it too.

Pis. O gracious lady,
Since I receiv'd command to do this business,
I have not slept one wink.

Imo. Do 't, and to bed then.

Pis. I'll wake mine eyeballs blind first.

Imo. Wherefore then
Didst undertake it? Why hast thou abus'd
So many miles with a pretence? this place?
Mine action, and thine own? our horses' labour?
The time inviting thee? the perturb'd court,
For my being absent; whereunto I never
Purpose return? Why hast thou gone so far,
To be unbent, when thou hast ta'en thy stand,
The elected deer before thee?

Pis. But to win time
To lose so bad employment: in the which
I have consider'd of a course; Good lady,
Hear me with patience.

Imo. Talk thy tongue weary; speak:
I have heard, I am a strumpet: and mine ear,
Therein false struck, can take no greater wound,
Nor tent to bottom that. But speak.

Pis. Then, madam,
I thought you would not back again.

Imo. Most like;
Bringing me here to kill me.

Pis. Not so, neither:
But if I were as wise as honest, then
My purpose would prove well. It cannot be,
But that my master is abus'd:
Some villain, ay, and singular in his art,
Hath done you both this cursed injury.

Imo. Some Roman courtezan.

Pis. No, on my life.
I'll give but notice you are dead, and send him
Some bloody sign of it; for 'tis commanded
I should do so: You shall be miss'd at court,
And that will well confirm it.

Imo. Why, good fellow,
What shall I do the while? Where bide? How live?
Or in my life what comfort, when I am
Dead to my husband?

Pis. If you'll back to the court,—

Imo. No court, no father; nor no more ado
With that harsh, noble, simple, nothing:
That Cloten, whose love-suit hath been to me
As fearful as a siege.

Pis. If not at court,
Then not in Britain must you bide.

Imo. Where then?
Hath Britain all the sun that shines? Day, night,
Are they not but in Britain? I'the world's volume
Our Britain seems as of it, but not in it;
In a great pool, a swan's nest; Pr'ythee, think
There's livers out of Britain.

Pis. I am most glad
You think of other place. The embassador
Lucius the Roman, comes to Milford Haven
To-morrow: Now, if you could wear a mind
Dark as your fortune is; and but disguise
That, which, to appear itself, must not yet be,
But by self-danger; you should tread a course
Pretty, and full of view; yea, haply near
The residence of Posthumus: so nigh, at least,
That though his actions were not visible, yet

Report should render him hourly to your ear,
As truly as he moves.
Imo. O, for such means!
Though peril to my modesty, not death on 't,
I would adventure.
Pis. Well then, here's the point:
You must forget to be a woman; change
Command into obedience; fear and niceness
(The handmaids of all women, or, more truly,
Woman its pretty self) into a waggish courage;
Ready in gibes, quick-answer'd, saucy, and
As quarrelous as the weasel: nay, you must
Forget that rarest treasure of your cheek,
Exposing it (but, O, the harder heart!
Alack no remedy!) to the greedy touch
Of common-kissing Titan! and forget
Your laboursome and dainty trims, wherein
You made great Juno angry.
Imo. Nay, be brief:
I see into thy end, and am almost
A man already.
Pis. First, make yourself but like one.
Fore-thinking this, I have already fit
('Tis in my cloak-bag) doublet, hat, hose, all
That answer to them: Would you, in their serving,
And with what imitation you can borrow
From youth of such a season, 'fore noble Lucius
Present yourself, desire his service, tell him
Wherein you are happy (which you'll make him know,
If that his head have ear in musick), doubtless,
With joy he will embrace you; for he's honourable,
And, doubling that, most holy. Your means abroad
You have me, rich; and I will never fail
Beginning, nor supplyment.
Imo. Thou art all the comfort
The gods will diet me with. Pr'ythee, away:
There's more to be consider'd; but we'll even
All that good time will give us: This attempt
I am soldier to, and will abide it with
A prince's courage. Away, I pr'ythee.
Pis. Well, madam, we must take a short farewell;
Lest, being miss'd, I be suspected of
Your carriage from the court. My noble mistress,
Here is a box; I had it from the queen;
What's in 't is precious; if you are sick at sea,
Or stomach-qualm'd at land, a dram of this
Will drive away distemper.—To some shade,
And fit you to your manhood:—May the gods
Direct you to the best!
Imo. Amen: I thank thee.
[*Exeunt.*

SCENE V. *A Room in* Cymbeline's *Palace.*

Enter CYMBELINE, Queen, CLOTEN, LUCIUS, *and* Lords.

Cym. Thus far; and so farewell.
Luc. Thanks, royal sir.
My emperor hath wrote; I must from hence;
And am right sorry, that I must report ye
My master's enemy.
Cym. Our subjects, sir,
Will not endure his yoke: and for ourself
To show less sovereignty than they, must needs
Appear unkinglike.
Luc. So, sir, I desire of you
A conduct over land, to Milford Haven.—
Madam, all joy befall your grace, and you!
Cym. My lords, you are appointed for that office;
The due of honour in no point omit:—
So, farewell, noble Lucius.
Luc. Your hand, my lord.
Clo. Receive it friendly: but from this time forth
I wear it as your enemy.
Luc. Sir, the event
Is yet to name the winner; Fare you well.
Cym. Leave not the worthy Lucius, good my lords,
Till he have cross'd the Severn.—Happiness!
[*Exeunt* LUCIUS, *and* Lords.
Queen. He goes hence frowning: but it honours us,
That we have given him cause.
Clo. 'Tis all the better;
Your valiant Britons have their wishes in it.
Cym. Lucius hath wrote already to the emperor
How it goes here. It fits us therefore, ripely,
Our chariots and our horsemen be in readiness:
The powers that he already hath in Gallia
Will soon be drawn to head, from whence he moves
His war for Britain.
Queen. 'Tis not sleepy business;
But must be look'd to speedily, and strongly.
Cym. Our expectation that it would be thus,
Hath made us forward. But, my gentle queen,
Where is our daughter? She hath not appear'd
Before the Roman, nor to us hath tender'd
The duty of the day: She looks us like
A thing more made of malice, than of duty:
We have noted it.—Call her before us; for
We have been too slight in sufferance.
[*Exit an* Attendant.
Queen. Royal sir,
Since the exile of Posthumus, most retir'd
Hath her life been; the cure whereof, my lord,
'Tis time must do. 'Beseech your majesty,
Forbear sharp speeches to her: she's a lady
So tender of rebukes, that words are strokes,
And strokes death to her.

Re-enter an Attendant.

Cym. Where is she, sir? How
Can her contempt be answer'd?
Atten. Please you, sir,
Her chambers are all lock'd; and there's no answer
That will be given to the loud'st of noise we make.
Queen. My lord, when last I went to visit her,
She pray'd me to excuse her keeping close;
Whereto constrain'd by her infirmity,
She should that duty leave unpaid to you,
Which daily she was bound to proffer: this
She wish'd me to make known; but our great court
Made me to blame in memory.
Cym. Her doors lock'd?
Not seen of late? Grant, heavens, that which I
Fear prove false! [*Exit.*
Queen. Son, I say, follow the king.
Clo. That man of hers, Pisanio, her old servant,
I have not seen these two days.
Queen. Go, look after.—
[*Exit* CLOTEN.
Pisanio, thou that stand'st so for Posthumus!—
He hath a drug of mine: I pray, his absence
Proceed by swallowing that; for he believes
It is a thing most precious. But for her,
Where is she gone? Haply, despair hath seized her;
Or, wing'd with fervour of her love, she's flown
To her desir'd Posthumus: Gone she is
To death, or to dishonour; and my end
Can make good use of either: She being down,
I have the placing of the British crown.

Re-enter CLOTEN.

How now, my son?
Clo. 'Tis certain, she is fled;
Go in, and cheer the king; he rages; none
Dare come about him.
Queen. All the better; May
This night forestall him of the coming day!
[*Exit* Queen.
Clo. I love, and hate her; for she's fair and royal;
And that she hath all courtly parts more exquisite
Than lady, ladies, woman; from every one

The best she hath, and she, of all compounded,
Outsells them all: I love her therefore; But,
Disdaining me, and throwing favours on
The low Posthumus, slanders so her judgment,
That what's else rare, is chok'd; and, in that point,
I will conclude to hate her, nay, indeed,
To be reveng'd upon her. For, when fools

Enter PISANIO.

Shall—Who is here? What! are you packing, sirrah?
Come hither: Ah, you precious pander! Villain,
Where is thy lady? In a word; or else
Thou art straightway with the fiends.

Pis. O, good my lord!

Clo. Where is thy lady? or, by Jupiter
I will not ask again. Close villain,
I'll have this secret from thy heart, or rip
Thy heart to find it. Is she with Posthumus?
From whose so many weights of baseness cannot
A dram of worth be drawn.

Pis. Alas, my lord,
How can she be with him? When was she miss'd?
He is in Rome.

Clo. Where is she, sir? Come nearer;
No further halting: satisfy me home,
What is become of her?

Pis. O, my all-worthy lord!

Clo. All-worthy villain!
Discover where thy mistress is, at once,
At the next word,—No more of worthy lord,—
Speak, or thy silence on the instant is
Thy condemnation and thy death.

Pis. Then, sir,
This paper is the history of my knowledge
Touching her flight. [*Presenting a Letter.*

Clo. Let's see 't:—I will pursue her
Even to Augustus' throne.

Pis. Or this, or perish.
She's far enough; and what he learns by this,
May prove his travel, not her danger. } *Aside.*

Clo. Humph!

Pis. I'll write to my lord she's dead. O Imogen,
Safe may'st thou wander, safe return again!
[*Aside.*

Clo. Sirrah, is this letter true?

Pis. Sir, as I think.

Clo. It is Posthumus' hand; I know't,—Sirrah, if thou would'st not be a villain, but do me true service; undergo those employments, wherein I should have cause to use thee, with a serious industry,—that is, what villainy soe'er I bid thee do, to perform it, directly and truly,—I would think thee an honest man: thou shouldest neither want my means for thy relief, nor my voice for thy preferment.

Pis. Well, my good lord.

Clo. Wilt thou serve me? For since patiently and constantly thou hast stuck to the bare fortune of that beggar Posthumus, thou canst not in the course of gratitude but be a diligent follower of mine. Wilt thou serve me?

Pis. Sir, I will.

Clo. Give me thy hand, here's my purse. Hast any of thy late master's garments in thy possession?

Pis. I have my lord, at my lodging, the same suit he wore when he took leave of my lady and mistress.

Clo. The first service thou dost me, fetch that suit hither: let it be thy first service; go.

Pis. I shall, my lord. [*Exit.*

Clo. Meet thee at Milford Haven:—I forgot to ask him one thing; I'll remember't anon:—Even there, thou villain, Posthumus, will I keep thee.—I would these garments were come. She said upon a time (the bitterness of it I now belch from my heart), that she held the very garment of Posthumus in more respect than my noble and natural person, together with the adornment of my qualities. With that suit upon my back, will I ravish her: First kill him, and in her eyes; there shall she see my valour, which will then be a torment to her contempt. He on the ground, my speech of insultment ended on his dead body,—and when my lust hath dined (which, as I say, to vex her, I will execute in the clothes that she so praised), to the court I'll knock her back, foot her home again. She hath despised me rejoicingly, and I'll be merry in my revenge.

Re-enter PISANIO, *with the Clothes.*

Be those the garments?

Pis. Ay, my noble lord.

Clo. How long is 't since she went to Milford Haven?

Pis. She can scarce be there yet.

Clo. Bring this apparel to my chamber; that is the second thing that I have commanded thee: the third is, that thou wilt be a voluntary mute to my design. Be but duteous, and true preferment shall tender itself to thee.—My revenge is now at Milford; 'Would, I had wings to follow it!—Come, and be true. [*Exit.*

Pis. Thou bidd'st me to my loss: for, true to thee,
Were to prove false, which I will never be,
To him that is most true.—To Milford go,
And find not her whom thou pursu'st. Flow, flow,
You heavenly blessings, on her! this fool's speed
Be cross'd with slowness; labour be his meed!
[*Exit.*

SCENE VI. *Before the Cave of* Belarius.

Enter IMOGEN, *in Boy's Clothes.*

Imo. I see, a man's life is a tedious one;
I have tired myself; and for two nights together
Have made the ground my bed. I should be sick,
But that my resolution helps me.—Milford,
When from the mountain-top Pisanio show'd thee,
Thou wast within a ken: O Jove! I think
Foundations fly the wretched: such, I mean,
Where they should be reliev'd. Two beggars told me,
I could not miss my way: Will poor folks lie,
That have affliction on them; knowing 'tis
A punishment, or trial? Yes; no wonder,
When rich ones scarce tell true: To lapse in fulness
Is sorer, than to lie for need; and falsehood
Is worse in kings, than beggars.—My dear lord!
Thou art one o' the false ones: Now I think on thee,
My hunger's gone; but even before, I was
At point to sink for food.—But what is this?
Here is a path to it: 'Tis some savage hold:
I were best not call; I dare not call: yet famine,
Ere clean it o'erthrow nature, makes it valiant.
Plenty, and peace, breeds cowards; hardness ever
Of hardiness is mother.—Ho! who's here?
If any thing that's civil, speak; if savage,
Take, or lend.—Ho!—No answer? then I'll enter.
Best draw my sword; and if mine enemy
But fear the sword like me, he'll scarcely look on't.
Such a foe, good heavens!
[*She goes into the Cave.*

Enter BELARIUS, GUIDERIUS, *and* ARVIRAGUS.

Bel. You, Polydore, have prov'd best woodman, and
Are master of the feast: Cadwal, and I,
Will play the cook and servant; 'tis our match.
The sweat of industry would dry, and die,
But for the end it works to. Come; our stomachs
Will make what's homely, savoury: Weariness
Can snore upon the flint, when restie sloth

Finds the down pillow hard.—Now, peace be here,
Poor house, that keep'st thyself!

Gui. I am thoroughly weary.

Arv. I am weak with toil, yet strong in appetite.

Gui. There is cold meat i' the cave; we'll browze on that,
Whilst what we have kill'd be cook'd.

Bel. Stay; come not in: [*Looking in.*
But that it eats our victuals, I should think
Here were a fairy.

Gui. What's the matter, sir?

Bel. By Jupiter, an angel! or, if not,
An earthly paragon!—Behold divineness
No elder than a boy!

Enter IMOGEN.

Imo. Good masters, harm me not:
Before I enter'd here, I call'd: and thought
To have begg'd, or bought, what I have took: Good troth,
I have stolen nought; nor would not, though I had found
Gold strew'd o'the floor. Here's money for my meat:
I would have left it on the board, so soon
As I had made my meal; and parted
With prayers for the provider.

Gui. Money, youth?

Arv. All gold and silver rather turn to dirt!
As 'tis no better reckon'd, but of those
Who worship dirty gods.

Imo. I see, you are angry:
Know, if you kill me for my fault, I should
Have died, had I not made it.

Bel. Whither bound?

Imo. To Milford Haven.

Bel. What is your name?

Imo. Fidele, sir: I have a kinsman, who
Is bound to Italy; he embark'd at Milford;
To whom being going, almost spent with hunger,
I am fallen in this offence.

Bel. 'Pr'ythee, fair youth,
Think us no churls; nor measure our good minds
By this rude place we live in. Well encounter'd!
'Tis almost night: you shall have better cheer
Ere you depart; and thanks to stay and eat it.—
Boys, bid him welcome.

Gui. Were you a woman, youth,
I should woo hard, but be your groom.—In honesty,
I bid for you, as I'd buy.

Arv. I'll mak't my comfort,
He is a man; I'll love him as my brother:—
And such a welcome as I'd give to him,
After long absence, such is yours:—Most welcome!
Be sprightly, for you fall 'mongst friends.

Imo. 'Mong'st friends!
If brothers?—'Would, it had been so, that they
Had been my father's sons! then had my prize
Been less; and so more equal ballasting
To thee, Posthumus. [*Aside.*

Bel. He wrings at some distress.

Gui. 'Would, I could free't!

Arv. Or I; whate'er it be,
What pain it cost, what danger! Gods!

Bel. Hark, boys. [*Whispering.*

Imo. Great men,
That had a court no bigger than this cave,
That did attend themselves, and had the virtue
Which their own conscience seal'd them (laying by
That nothing gift of differing multitudes),
Could not out-peer these twain. Pardon me, gods!
I'd change my sex to be companion with them,
Since Leonatus false.

Bel. It shall be so:
Boys, we'll go dress our hunt.—Fair youth, come in:
Discourse is heavy, fasting; when we have supp'd,
We'll mannerly demand thee of thy story,
So far as thou wilt speak it.

Gui. Pray draw near.

Arv. The night to the owl, and morn to the lark, less welcome.

Imo. Thanks, sir.

Arv. I pray, draw near. [*Exeunt.*

SCENE VII. Rome.

Enter Two Senators *and* Tribunes.

1 *Sen.* This is the tenour of the emperor's writ;
That since the common men are now in action
'Gainst the Pannonians and Dalmatians;
And that the legions now in Gallia are
Full weak to undertake our wars against
The fallen off Britons; that we do incite
The gentry to this business: He creates
Lucius pro-consul: and to you the tribunes,
For this immediate levy, he commands
His absolute commission. Long live Cæsar!

Tri. Is Lucius general of the forces?

2 *Sen.* Ay.

Tri. Remaining now in Gallia?

1 *Sen.* With those legions
Which I have spoke of, whereunto your levy
Must be supplyant: The words of your commission
Will tie you to the numbers, and the time
Of their despatch.

Tri. We will discharge our duty. [*Exeunt.*

ACT IV.

SCENE I. *The Forest, near the Cave.*

Enter CLOTEN.

Clo. I am near to the place where they should meet, if Pisanio have mapped it truly. How fit his garments serve me! Why should his mistress, who was made by him that made the tailor, not be fit too? the rather (saving reverence of the word) for 'tis said, a woman's fitness comes by fits. Therein I must play the workman. I dare speak it to myself (for it is not vainglory, for a man and his glass to confer; in his own chamber, I mean), the lines of my body are as well drawn as his; no less young, more strong, not beneath him in fortunes, beyond him in the advantage of the time, above him in birth, alike conversant in general services, and more remarkable in single oppositions: yet this imperseverant thing loves him in my despite. What mortality is! Posthumus, thy head, which now is growing upon thy shoulders, shall within this hour be off; thy mistress enforced; thy garments cut to pieces before thy face: and all this done, spurn her home to her father: who may, haply, be a little angry for my so rough usage: but my mother, having power of his testiness, shall turn all into my commendations. My horse is tied up safe: Out, sword, and to a sore purpose! Fortune, put them into my hand! This is the very description of their meeting-place; and the fellow dares not deceive me. [*Exit.*

SCENE II. *Before the Cave.*

Enter, from the Cave, BELARIUS, GUIDERIUS, ARVIRAGUS, *and* IMOGEN.

Bel. You are not well [*To* IMOGEN]: remain here in the cave:
We'll come to you after hunting.

Arv. Brother, stay here: [*To* IMO.
Are we not brothers?

Imo. So man and man should be;
But clay and clay differs in dignity,
Whose dust is both alike. I am very sick.
Gui. Go you to hunting. I'll abide with him.
Imo. So sick I am not; yet I am not well:
But not so citizen a wanton, as
To seem to die, ere sick: So please you leave me;
Stick to your journal course; the breach of custom
Is breach of all. I am ill; but your being by me
Cannot amend me: Society is no comfort
To one not sociable: I am not very sick,
Since I can reason of it. Pray you, trust me here:
I'll rob none but myself; and let me die,
Stealing so poorly.
Gui. I love thee; I have spoke it:
How much the quantity, the weight as much,
As I do love my father.
Bel. What? how? how?
Arv. If it be sin to say so, sir, I yoke me
In my good brother's fault: I know not why
I love this youth; and I have heard you say,
Love's reason's without reason; the bier at door,
And a demand who is't shall die, I'd say,
My father, not this youth.
Bel. O noble strain! [*Aside.*
O worthiness of nature! breed of greatness!
Cowards father cowards, and base things sire base:
Nature hath meal, and bran; contempt, and grace.
I am not their father: yet who this should be,
Doth miracle itself, lov'd before me.—
'Tis the ninth hour o' the morn.
Arv. Brother, farewell.
Imo. I wish ye sport.
Arv. You health.—So please you, sir.
Imo. [*Aside.*] These are kind creatures. Gods, what lies I have heard!
Our courtiers say, all's savage, but at court:
Experience, O, thou disprov'st report!
The imperious seas breed monsters; for the dish,
Poor tributary rivers as sweet fish.
I am sick still; heart-sick:—Pisanio,
I'll now taste of thy drug.
Gui. I could not stir him;
He said, he was gentle, but unfortunate;
Dishonestly afflicted, but yet honest.
Arv. Thus did he answer me: yet said, hereafter
I might know more.
Bel. To the field, to the field:—
We'll leave you for this time; go in, and rest.
Arv. We'll not be long away.
Bel. Pray, be not sick,
For you must be our housewife.
Imo. Well, or ill,
I am bound to you.
Bel. And so shalt be ever. [*Exit* Imo.
This youth, howe'er distress'd, appears, he hath had
Good ancestors.
Arv. How angel-like he sings!
Gui. But his neat cookery! He cut our roots in characters:
And sauc'd our broths, as Juno had been sick,
And he her dieter.
Arv. Nobly he yokes
A smiling with a sigh: as if the sigh
Was that it was, for not being such a smile;
The smile mocking the sigh, that it would fly
From so divine a temple, to commix
With winds that sailors rail at.
Gui. I do note,
That grief and patience, rooted in him both,
Mingle their spurs together.
Arv. Grow, patience!
And let the stinking elder, grief, untwine
His perishing root, with the increasing vine!
Bel. It is great morning. Come; away.—who's there?

Enter Cloten.

Clo. I cannot find those runagates; that villain
Hath mock'd me: I am faint.
Bel. Those runagates!
Means he not us? I partly know him; 'tis
Cloten, the son o'the queen. I fear some ambush.
I saw him not these many years, and yet
I know 'tis he:—We are held as outlaws:—Hence.
Gui. He is but one: You and my brother search
What companies are near: pray you, away:
Let me alone with him.
[*Exeunt* Belarius *and* Arviragus.
Clo. Soft! What are you
That fly me thus? some villain mountaineers?
I have heard of such. What slave art thou?
Gui. A thing
More slavish did I ne'er, than answering
A slave, without a knock.
Clo. Thou art a robber,
A law-breaker, a villain: Yield thee, thief.
Gui. To who? to thee? What art thou? Have not I
An arm as big as thine? a heart as big?
Thy words, I grant, are bigger; for I wear not
My dagger in my mouth. Say, what thou art;
Why I should yield to thee?
Clo. Thou villain base,
Know'st me not by my clothes?
Gui. No, nor thy tailor, rascal,
Who is thy grandfather; he made those clothes,
Which, as it seems, make thee.
Clo. Thou precious varlet,
My tailor made them not.
Gui. Hence then, and thank
The man that gave them thee. Thou art some fool;
I am loath to beat thee.
Clo. Thou injurious thief,
Hear but my name, and tremble.
Gui. What's thy name?
Clo. Cloten, thou villain.
Gui. Cloten, thou double villain, be thy name,
I cannot tremble at it; were't toad, or adder, spider,
'Twould move me sooner.
Clo. To thy further fear,
Nay, to thy mere confusion, thou shalt know
I'm son to the queen.
Gui. I'm sorry for't; not seeming
So worthy as thy birth.
Clo. Art not afeard?
Gui. Those that I reverence, those I fear; the wise;
At fools I laugh, not fear them.
Clo. Die the death:
When I have slain thee with my proper hand,
I'll follow those that even now fled hence,
And on the gates of Lud's town set your heads:
Yield, rustick mountaineer. [*Exeunt, fighting.*

Enter Belarius *and* Arviragus.

Bel. No company's abroad.
Arv. None in the world: You did mistake him, sure.
Bel. I cannot tell: Long is it since I saw him,
But time hath nothing blurr'd those lines of favour
Which then he wore; the snatches in his voice,
And burst of speaking, were as his: I am absolute,
'Twas very Cloten.
Arv. In this place we left them:
I wish my brother make good time with him,
You say he is so fell.
Bel. Being scarce made up,
I mean, to man, he had not apprehension
Of roaring terrors; for defect of judgment
Is oft the cure of fear: But see, thy brother.

Re-enter Guiderius, *with* Cloten's *Head.*

Gui. This Cloten was a fool: an empty purse,
There was no money in't: not Hercules

Could have knock'd out his brains, for he had none:
Yet I not doing this, the fool had borne
My head, as I do his.

Bel. What hast thou done?

Gui. I am perfect, what: cut off one Cloten's head.
Son to the queen, after his own report;
Who call'd me traitor, mountaineer: and swore,
With his own single hand he'd take us in,
Displace our heads, where (thank the gods!) they grow,
And set them on Lud's town.

Bel. We are all undone.

Gui. Why, worthy father, what have we to lose,
But, that he swore to take, our lives? The law
Protects not us: Then why should we be tender
To let an arrogant piece of flesh threat us;
Play judge, and executioner, all himself;
For we do fear the law? What company
Discover you abroad?

Bel. No single soul
Can we set eye on, but, in all safe reason,
He must have some attendants. Though his humour
Was nothing but mutation; ay, and that
From one bad thing to worse; not frenzy, not
Absolute madness could so far have rav'd,
To bring him here alone: Although, perhaps,
It may be heard at court, that such as we
Cave here, hunt here, are outlaws, and in time
May make some stronger head: the which he hearing
(As it is like him), might break out, and swear
He'd fetch us in; yet is't not probable
To come alone, either he so undertaking,
Or they so suffering: then on good ground we fear,
If we do fear this body hath a tail
More perilous than the head.

Arv. Let ordinance
Come as the gods foresay it: howsoe'er,
My brother hath done well.

Bel. I had no mind
To hunt this day: the boy Fidele's sickness
Did make my way long forth.

Gui. With his own sword,
Which he did wave against my throat, I have ta'en
His head from him: I'll throw't into the creek
Behind our rock; and let it to the sea,
And tell the fishes, he's the queen's son, Cloten:
That's all I reck. [*Exit.*

Bel. I fear, 'twill be reveng'd:
'Would, Polydore, thou had'st not done't! though valour
Becomes thee well enough.

Arv. 'Would, I had done't,
So the revenge alone pursued me!—Polydore,
I love thee brotherly; but envy much,
Thou hast robb'd me of this deed: I would, revenges,
That possible strength might meet, would seek us through,
And put us to our answer.

Bel. Well, 'tis done:—
We'll hunt no more to-day, nor seek for danger
Where there's no profit. I pr'ythee, to our rock;
You and Fidele play the cooks: I'll stay
Till hasty Polydore return, and bring him
To dinner presently.

Arv. Poor sick Fidele!
I'll willingly to him: To gain his colour,
I'd let a parish of such Clotens blood,
And praise myself for charity. [*Exit.*

Bel. O thou goddess,
Thou divine Nature, how thyself thou blazon'st
In these two princely boys! They are as gentle
As zephyrs, blowing below the violet,
Not wagging his sweet head: and yet as rough,
Their royal blood enchaf'd, as the rud'st wind,
That by the top doth take the mountain pine,
And make him stoop to the vale. 'Tis wonderful,
That an invisible instinct should frame them
To royalty unlearn'd; honour untaught;
Civility not seen from other; valour,
That wildly grows in them, but yields a crop
As if it had been sow'd! Yet still it's strange
What Cloten's being here to us portends;
Or what his death will bring us.

Re-enter GUIDERIUS.

Gui. Where's my brother?
I have sent Cloten's clotpoll down the stream,
In embassy to his mother; his body's hostage
For his return. [*Solemn Musick.*

Bel. My ingenious instrument!
Hark, Polydore, it sounds! But what occasion
Hath Cadwal now to give it motion! Hark!

Gui. Is he at home?

Bel. He went hence even now.

Gui. What does he mean? since death of my dear'st mother
It did not speak before. All solemn things
Should answer solemn accidents. The matter?
Triumphs for nothing, and lamenting toys,
Is jollity for apes, and grief for boys,
Is Cadwal mad?

Re-enter ARVIRAGUS, *bearing* IMOGEN, *as dead, in his Arms.*

Bel. Look, here he comes,
And brings the dire occasion in his arms,
Of what we blame him for!

Arv. The bird is dead,
That we have made so much on. I had rather
Have skipp'd from sixteen years of age to sixty,
To have turn'd my leaping time into a crutch,
Than have seen this.

Gui. O sweetest, fairest lily!
My brother wears thee not the one half so well,
As when thou grew'st thyself.

Bel. O, melancholy;
Who ever yet could sound thy bottom? find
The ooze, to show what coast thy sluggish crare
Might easiliest harbour in?—Thou blessed thing!
Jove knows what man thou might'st have made? but I,
Thou diedst, a most rare boy, of melancholy!—
How found you him?

Arv. Stark, as you see:
Thus smiling, as some fly had tickled slumber,
Not as death's dart, being laugh'd at; his right cheek
Reposing on a cushion.

Gui. Where?

Arv. O' the floor;
His arms thus leagu'd: I thought, he slept: and put
My clouted brogues from off my feet, whose rudeness
Answer'd my steps too loud.

Gui. Why, he but sleeps:
If he be gone, he'll make his grave a bed;
With female fairies will his tomb be haunted,
And worms will not come to thee.

Arv. With fairest flowers,
Whilst summer lasts, and I live here, Fidele,
I'll sweeten thy sad grave: Thou shalt not lack
The flower, that's like thy face, pale primrose; nor
The azur'd harebell, like thy veins; no, nor
The leaf of eglantine, whom not to slander,
Out-sweeten'd not thy breath: the ruddock would,
With charitable bill (O bill, sore-shaming
Those rich-left heirs, that let their fathers lie
Without a monument!) bring thee all this;
Yea, and furr'd moss besides, when flowers are none,
To winter-ground thy corse.

Gui. 'Pr'ythee, have done;
And do not play in wench like words with that
Which is so serious. Let us bury him,

And not protract with admiration what
Is now due debt.—To the grave.

Arv. Say, where shall's lay him?

Gui. By good Euriphile, our mother.

Arv. Be't so:
And let us, Polydore, though now our voices
Have got the mannish crack, sing him to the ground,
As once our mother; use like note, and words,
Save that Euriphile must be Fidele.

Gui. Cadwal,
I cannot sing: I'll weep, and word it with thee:
For notes of sorrow, out of tune, are worse
Than priests and fanes that lie.

Arv. We'll speak it then.

Bel. Great griefs, I see, medicine the less: for Cloten
Is quite forgot. He was a queen's son, boys:
And, though he came our enemy, remember,
He was paid for that: Though mean and mighty, rotting
Together, have one dust: yet reverence
(That angel of the world), doth make distinction
Of place 'tween high and low. Our foe was princely;
And though you took his life, as being our foe,
Yet bury him as a prince.

Gui. Pray you, fetch him hither.
Thersites' body is as good as Ajax,
When neither are alive.

Arv. If you'll go fetch him,
We'll say our song the whilst.—Brother, begin.
[*Exit* Belarius.

Gui. Nay, Cadwal, we must lay his head to the east;
My father hath a reason for't.

Arv. 'Tis true.

Gui. Come on then, and remove him.

Arv. So,—begin.

SONG.

Gui. *Fear no more the heat o' the sun,*
Nor the furious winter's rages;
Thou thy worldly task hast done,
Home art gone, and ta'en thy wages:
Golden lads and girls all must,
As chimney-sweepers, come to dust.

Arv. *Fear no more the frown o' the great,*
Thou art past the tyrant's stroke;
Care no more to clothe, and eat;
To thee the reed is as the oak:
The sceptre, learning, physick, must
All follow this, and come to dust.

Gui. *Fear no more the lightning-flash,*
Arv. *Nor the all-dreaded thunder-stone;*
Gui. *Fear not slander, censure rash;*
Arv. *Thou hast finish'd joy and moan:*
Both. *All lovers young, all lovers must*
Consign to thee, and come to dust.

Gui. *No exorciser harm thee!*
Arv. *Nor no witchcraft charm thee!*
Gui. *Ghost unlaid forbear thee!*
Arv. *Nothing ill come near thee!*
Both. *Quiet consummation have;*
And renowned be thy grave!

Re-enter Belarius, *with the Body of* Cloten.

Gui. We have done our obsequies: Come, lay him down.

Bel. Here's a few flowers, but about midnight, more:
The herbs, that have on them cold dew o' the night,
Are strewing fitt'st for graves.—Upon their faces:
You were as flowers, now wither'd: even so
These herb'lets shall, which we upon you strow.—
Come on, away: apart upon our knees.
The ground, that gave them first, has them again;
Their pleasures here are past, so is their pain.
[*Exeunt* Bel. Gui. *and* Arv.

Imo. [*Awaking.*] Yes, sir, to Milford Haven; Which is the way?—
I thank you.—By yon bush?—Pray, how far thither?
'Ods pittikins!—can it be six miles yet?
I have gone all night:—'Faith, I'll lay down and sleep.
But, soft! no bedfellow:—O, gods and goddesses!
[*Seeing the Body.*
These flowers are like the pleasures of the world;
This bloody man, the care on't.—I hope, I dream;
For, so, I thought I was a cave-keeper,
And cook to honest creatures: But 'tis not so;
'Twas but a bolt of nothing, shot at nothing,
Which the brain makes of fumes. Our very eyes
Are sometimes like our judgments, blind. Good faith,
I tremble still with fear: But if there be
Yet left in heaven as small a drop of pity
As a wren's eye, fear'd gods, a part of it!
The dream's here still; even when I wake, it is
Without me, as within me; not imagin'd, felt.
A headless man!—The garments of Posthumus!
I know the shape of his leg; this is his hand;
His foot Mercurial; his Martial thigh;
The brawns of Hercules: but his Jovial face—
Murder in heaven?—How?—'Tis gone.—Pisanio,
All curses madded Hecuba gave the Greeks,
And mine to boot, be darted on thee! Thou,
Conspir'd with that irregulous devil, Cloten,
Hast here cut off my lord.—To write and read,
Be henceforth treacherous!—damn'd Pisanio
Hath with his forged letters,—damn'd Pisanio—
From this most bravest vessel of the world
Struck the main-top!—O, Posthumus! alas,
Where is thy head? where's that? Ah me! where's that?
Pisanio might have kill'd thee at the heart,
And left this head on.—How should this be? Pisanio?
'Tis he, and Cloten: malice and lucre in them
Have laid this woe here. O, 'tis pregnant, pregnant!
The drug he gave me, which, he said, was precious
And cordial to me, have I not found it
Murd'rous to the senses? That confirms it home:
This is Pisanio's deed, and Cloten's! O!—
Give colour to my pale cheek with thy blood,
That we the horrider may seem to those
Which chance to find us: O, my lord, my lord!

Enter Lucius, *a* Captain, *and other* Officers, *and a* Soothsayer.

Cap. To them the legions garrison'd in Gallia,
After your will, have cross'd the sea; attending
You here at Milford Haven, with your ships:
They are here in readiness.

Luc. But what from Rome?

Cap. The senate hath stirr'd up the confiners,
And gentlemen of Italy; most willing spirits,
That promise noble service: and they come
Under the conduct of bold Iachimo,
Sienna's brother.

Luc. When expect you them?

Cap. With the next benefit o' the wind.

Luc. This forwardness
Makes our hopes fair. Command, our present numbers
Be muster'd; bid the captains look to't.—Now, sir,
What have you dream'd, of late, of this war's purpose?

Sooth. Last night the very gods show'd me a vision:
(I fast, and pray'd, for their intelligence), Thus:—
I saw Jove's bird, the Roman eagle, wing'd
From the spungy south to this part of the west,
There vanish'd in the sunbeams: which portends
(Unless my sins abuse my divination),
Success to the Roman host.

Luc. Dream often so,
And never false.—Soft, ho! what trunk is here,
Without his top? The ruin speaks, that sometime
It was a worthy building.—How! a page;
Or dead, or sleeping on him? But dead, rather:
For nature doth abhor to make his bed
With the defunct, or sleep upon the dead.—
Let's see the boy's face.

Cap. He is alive, my lord.

Luc. He'll then instruct us of this body.—Young one,
Inform us of thy fortunes: for it seems,
They crave to be demanded: who is this,
Thou mak'st thy bloody pillow? or who was he,
That, otherwise than noble nature did,
Hath alter'd that good picture? What's thy interest
In this sad wreck? How came it? Who is it?
What art thou?

Imo. I am nothing: or if not,
Nothing to be were better. This was my master,
A very valiant Briton, and a good,
That here by mountaineers lies slain:—Alas!
There are no more such masters: I may wander
From east to occident, cry out for service,
Try many, all good, serve truly, never
Find such another master.

Luc. 'Lack, good youth!
Thou mov'st no less with thy complaining, than
Thy master in bleeding: Say his name, good friend.

Imo. Richard du Champ. If I do lie, and do
No harm by it, though the gods hear, I hope [*Aside.*
They'll pardon it. Say you, sir?

Luc. Thy name!

Imo. Fidele, sir.

Luc. Thou dost approve thyself the very same:
Thy name well fits thy faith; thy faith, thy name.
Wilt take thy chance with me? I will not say,
Thou shalt be so well master'd; but, be sure,
No less belov'd. The Roman emperor's letters,
Sent by a consul to me, should not sooner
Than thine own worth prefer thee: Go with me.

Imo. I'll follow, sir. But first, an't please the gods,
I'll hide my master from the flies, as deep
As these poor pickaxes can dig: and when
With wild wood-leaves and weeds I have strew'd his grave,
And on it said a century of prayers,
Such as I can, twice o'er, I'll weep, and sigh;
And, leaving so his service, follow you,
So please you entertain me.

Luc. Ay, good youth;
And rather father thee, than master thee.—
My friends,
The boy hath taught us manly duties: Let us
Find out the prettiest daisied plot we can,
And make him with our pikes and partizans
A grave: Come, arm him.—Boy, he is preferr'd
By thee to us; and he shall be interr'd,
As soldiers can. Be cheerful; wipe thine eyes:
Some falls are means the happier to arise.
[*Exeunt.*

SCENE III. *A Room in* Cymbeline's *Palace.*

Enter CYMBELINE, *Lords, and* PISANIO.

Cym. Again; and bring me word, how 'tis with her.
A fever with the absence of her son:
A madness, of which her life's in danger:—Heavens,
How deeply you at once do touch me! Imogen,
The great part of my comfort, gone: my queen
Upon a desperate bed; and in a time
When fearful wars point at me; her son gone,
So needful for this present: It strikes me, past
The hope of comfort.—But for thee, fellow,
Who needs must know of her departure, and
Dost seem so ignorant, we'll enforce it from thee
By a sharp torture.

Pis. Sir, my life is yours,
I humbly set it at your will: But, for my mistress,
I nothing know where she remains, why gone,
Nor when she purposes return. 'Beseech your highness,
Hold me your loyal servant.

1 Lord. Good, my liege,
The day that she was missing, he was here:
I dare be bound he's true, and shall perform
All parts of his subjection loyally.
For Cloten,—
There wants no diligence in seeking him,
And will, no doubt, be found.

Cym. The time's troublesome:
We'll slip you for a season; but our jealousy
[*To* PISANIO.
Does yet depend.

1 Lord. So please your majesty,
The Roman legions, all from Gallia drawn,
Are landed on your coast; with a supply
Of Roman gentlemen, by the senate sent.

Cym. Now for the counsel of my son, and queen;—
I am amaz'd with matter.

1 Lord. Good my liege,
Your preparation can affront no less
Than what you hear of: come more, for more you're ready:
The want is, but to put those powers in motion,
That long to move.

Cym. I thank you: Let's withdraw;
And meet the time, as it seeks us. We fear not
What can from Italy annoy us; but
We grieve at chances here.—Away. [*Exeunt.*

Pis. I heard no letter from my master, since
I wrote him, Imogen was slain: 'Tis strange:
Nor hear I from my mistress, who did promise
To yield me often tidings; Neither know I
What is betid to Cloten; but remain
Perplex'd in all. The heavens still must work:
Wherein I am false, I am honest; not true, to be true.
These present wars shall find I love my country,
Even to the note o' the king, or I'll fall in them.
All other doubts, by time let them be clear'd:
Fortune brings in some boats, that are not steer'd.
[*Exit.*

SCENE IV. *Before the Cave.*

Enter BELARIUS, GUIDERIUS, *and* ARVIRAGUS.

Gui. The noise is round about us.

Bel. Let us from it.

Arv. What pleasure, sir, find we in life, to lock it
From action and adventure?

Gui. Nay, what hope
Have we in hiding us? this way, the Romans
Must or for Britons slay us; or receive us
For barbarous and unnatural revolts
During their use, and slay us after.

Bel. Sons,
We'll higher to the mountains; there secure us.
To the king's party there's no going; newness
Of Cloten's death (we being not known, not muster'd
Among the bands) may drive us to a render
Where we have liv'd; and so extort from us
That which we've done, whose answer would be death
Drawn on with torture.

Gui. This is, sir, a doubt,
In such a time, nothing becoming you,
Nor satisfying us.

Arv. It is not likely,
That when they hear the Roman horses neigh,
Behold their quarter'd fires, have both their eyes
And ears so cloy'd importantly as now,
That they will waste their time upon our note,
To know from whence we are.

Bel. O, I am known

Of many in the army: many years,
Though Cloten then but young, you see, not wore him
From my remembrance. And, besides, the king
Hath not deserv'd my service, nor your loves;
Who find in my exile the want of breeding,
The certainty of this hard life; aye hopeless
To have the courtesy your cradle promis'd,
But to be still hot summer's tanlings, and
The shrinking slaves of winter.

Gui. Than be so,
Better to cease to be. Pray, sir, to the army:
I and my brother are not known; yourself,
So out of thought, and thereto so o'ergrown,
Cannot be question'd.

Arv. By this sun that shines,
I'll thither: What thing is it, that I never
Did see man die? scarce ever look'd on blood,
But that of coward hares, hot goats, and venison?
Never bestrid a horse, save one, that had
A rider like myself, who ne'er wore rowel
Nor iron on his heel? I am asham'd
To look upon the holy sun, to have
The benefit of his bless'd beams, remaining
So long a poor unknown.

Gui. By heavens, I'll go:
If you will bless me, sir, and give me leave,
I'll take the better care; but if you will not,
The hazard therefore due fall on me, by
The hands of Romans!

Arv. So say I; Amen.

Bel. No reason I, since on your lives you set
So slight a valuation, should reserve
My crack'd one to more care. Have with you, boys;
If in your country wars you chance to die,
That is my bed too, lads, and there I'll lie:
Lead, lead.—The time seems long; their blood thinks scorn, [*Aside.*
Till it fly out, and show them princes born.
[*Exeunt.*

ACT V.

SCENE I. *A Field between the* British *and* Roman *Camps.*

Enter POSTHUMUS, *with a bloody Handkerchief.*

Post. Yea, bloody cloth, I'll keep thee; for I wish'd
Thou should'st be colour'd thus. You married ones,
If each of you would take this course, how many
Must murder wives much better than themselves,
For wrying but a little?—O, Pisanio!
Every good servant does not all commands:
No bond, but to do just ones.—Gods! if you
Should have ta'en vengeance on my faults, I never
Had liv'd to put on this: so had you saved
The noble Imogen to repent; and struck
Me, wretch, more worth your vengeance. But, alack,
You snatch some hence for little faults; that's love,
To have them fall no more: you some permit
To second ills with ills, each elder worse;
And make them dread it to the doer's shrift.
But Imogen is your own: Do your best wills,
And make me bless'd to obey!—I am brought hither
Among the Italian gentry, and to fight
Against my lady's kingdom: 'Tis enough
That, Britain, I have kill'd thy mistress; peace!
I'll give no wound to thee. Therefore, good heavens,
Hear patiently my purpose: I'll disrobe me
Of these Italian weeds, and suit myself
As does a Briton peasant: so I'll fight
Against the part I come with; so I'll die
For thee, O Imogen, even for whom my life
Is, every breath, a death: and thus, unknown,
Pitied, nor hated, to the face of peril
Myself I'll dedicate. Let me make men know
More valour in me, than my habits show.
Gods put the strength o' the Leonati in me!
To shame the guise o' the world, I will begin
The fashion, less without, and more within.
[*Exit.*

SCENE II. *The same.*

Enter at one side LUCIUS, IACHIMO, *and the* Roman Army; *at the other side, the* British Army; LEONATUS POSTHUMUS *following it, like a poor Soldier. They march over, and go out. Alarums. Then enter again in skirmish,* IACHIMO *and* POSTHUMUS: *he vanquisheth and disarmeth* IACHIMO, *and then leaves him.*

Iach. The heaviness and guilt within my bosom
Takes off my manhood: I have belied a lady,
The princess of this country, and the air on't
Revengingly enfeebles me; Or could this carl,
A very drudge of nature's, have subdu'd me,
In my profession? Knighthoods and honours, borne
As I wear mine, are titles but of scorn.
If that thy gentry, Britain, go before
This lout, as he exceeds our lords, the odds
Is, that we scarce are men, and you are gods.
[*Exit.*

The Battle continues; the Britons *fly;* CYMBELINE *is taken: then enter to his rescue,* BELARIUS, GUIDERIUS, *and* ARVIRAGUS.

Bel. Stand, stand! We have the advantage of the ground;
The lane is guarded: nothing routs us, but
The villany of our fears.

Gui. Arv. Stand, stand, and fight!

Enter POSTHUMUS, *and seconds the* Britons: *They rescue* CYMBELINE, *and exeunt. Then, enter* LUCIUS, IACHIMO, *and* IMOGEN.

Luc. Away, boy, from the troops, and save thyself:
For friends kill friends, and the disorder's such
As war were hood-wink'd.

Iach. 'Tis their fresh supplies.

Luc. It is a day turn'd strangely: or betimes
Let's reinforce, or fly. [*Exeunt.*

SCENE III. *Another Part of the Field.*

Enter POSTHUMUS *and a* British Lord.

Lord. Cam'st thou from where they made the stand?

Post. I did:
Though you, it seems, come from the fliers.

Lord. I did.

Post. No blame be to you, sir; for all was lost,
But that the heavens fought: The king himself
Of his wings destitute, the army broken,
And but the backs of Britons seen, all flying
Through a strait lane; the enemy full-hearted,
Lolling the tongue with slaughtering, having work
More plentiful than tools to do 't, struck down
Some mortally, some slightly touch'd, some falling
Merely through fear; that the strait pass was damm'd
With dead men, hurt behind, and cowards living
To die with lengthen'd shame.

Lord. Where was this lane?

Post. Close by the battle, ditch'd, and wall'd with turf;
Which gave advantage to an ancient soldier,—
An honest one, I warrant; who deserv'd
So long a breeding, as his white beard came to,
In doing this for his country;—athwart the lane,
He, with two striplings (lads more like to run
The country base, than to commit such slaughter;
With faces fit for masks, or rather fairer
Than those for preservation cas'd, or shame),

Made good the passage; cry'd to those that fled,
Our Britain's *harts die flying, not our men:*
To darkness fleet, souls that fly backwards! Stand!
Or we are Romans, *and will give you that*
Like beasts, which you shun beastly; and may save,
But to look back in frown; stand, stand.—These three,
Three thousand confident, in act as many
(For three performers are the file, when all
The rest do nothing), with this word, *stand, stand,*
Accommodated by the place, more charming,
With their own nobleness (which could have turn'd
A distaff to a lance), gilded pale looks,
Part, shame, part, spirit renew'd; that some, turn'd coward
But by example (O, a sin in war,
Damn'd in the first beginners!) 'gan to look
The way that they did, and to grin like lions
Upon the pikes o' the hunters. Then began
A stop i' the chaser, a retire; anon,
A rout, confusion thick: Forthwith they fly
Chickens, the way which they stoop'd eagles; slaves,
The strides they victors made: and now our cowards
(Like fragments in hard voyages), became
The life o' the need; having found the back-door open
Of the unguarded hearts, Heavens, how they wound!
Some, slain before; some, dying; some, their friends
O'erborne i' the former wave: ten, chas'd by one,
Are now each one the slaughter-man of twenty:
Those, that would die or ere resist, are grown
The mortal bugs o' the field.

Lord. This was strange chance:
A narrow lane! an old man, and two boys!

Post. Nay, do not wonder at it: You are made
Rather to wonder at the things you hear,
Than to work any. Will you rhyme upon 't,
And vent it for a mockery? Here is one:
Two boys, an old man twice a boy, a lane,
Preserv'd the Britons, was the Romans' bane.

Lord. Nay, be not angry, sir.

Post. 'Lack, to what end?
Who dares not stand his foe, I'll be his friend:
For if he'll do, as he is made to do,
I know, he'll quickly fly my friendship too.
You have put me into rhyme.

Lord. Farewell, you are angry. [*Exit.*

Post. Still going?—This is a lord! O noble misery!
To be i' the field, and ask, what news, of me!
To-day how many would have given their honours
To have sav'd their carcasses? took heel to do 't,
And yet died too? I, in mine own woe charm'd,
Could not find death, where I did hear him groan;
Nor feel him, where he struck: Being an ugly monster,
'Tis strange, he hides him in fresh cups, soft beds,
Sweet words; or hath more ministers than we
That draw his knives i' the war.—Well, I will find him:
For being now a favourer to the Roman,
No more a Briton, I have resum'd again
The part I came in: Fight I will no more,
But yield me to the veriest hind, that shall
Once touch my shoulder. Great the slaughter is
Here made by the Roman; great the answer be
Britons must take; For me, my ransome's death;
On either side I come to spend my breath;
Which neither here I'll keep, nor bear again,
But end it by some means for Imogen.

Enter Two British Captains, *and* Soldiers.

1 *Cap.* Great Jupiter be prais'd! Lucius is taken:
Tis thought, the old man and his sons were angels.

2 *Cap.* There was a fourth man, in a silly habit,
That gave the affront with them.

1 *Cap.* So 'tis reported:
But none of them can be found.—Stand! who is there?

Post. A Roman;
Who had not now been drooping here, if seconds
Had answer'd him.

2 *Cap.* Lay hands on him; a dog!
A leg of Rome shall not return to tell
What crows have peck'd them here. He brags his service
As if he were of note: bring him to the king.

Enter CYMBELINE, *attended:* BELARIUS, GUIDERIUS, ARVIRAGUS, PISANIO, *and* Roman Captives. *The* Captains *present* POSTHUMUS *to* CYMBELINE, *who delivers him over to a* Gaoler: *after which, all go out.*

SCENE IV. *A Prison.*

Enter POSTHUMUS, *and Two* Gaolers.

1 *Gaol.* You shall not now be stolen, you have locks upon you;
So graze, as you find pasture.

2 *Gaol.* Ay, or a stomach. [*Exeunt* Gaolers.

Post. Most welcome, bondage! for thou art a way,
I think, to liberty: Yet am I better
Than one that's sick o' the gout: since he had rather
Groan so in perpetuity, than be cur'd
By the sure physician, death; who is the key
To unbar these locks. My conscience! thou art fetter'd
More than my shanks, and wrists: You good gods, give me
The penitent instrument, to pick that bolt,
Then, free for ever! Is 't enough, I am sorry?
So children temporal fathers do appease;
Gods are more full of mercy. Must I repent?
I cannot do it better than in gyves,
Desir'd, more than constrain'd: to satisfy,
If of my freedom 'tis the main part, take
No stricter render of me, than my all.
I know, you are more clement than vile men,
Who of their broken debtors take a third,
A sixth, a tenth, letting them thrive again
On their abatement; that's not my desire:
For Imogen's dear life, take mine; and though
'Tis not so dear, yet 'tis a life; you coin'd it:
'Tween man and man they weigh not every stamp;
Though light, take pieces for the figure's sake:
You rather mine, being yours: and so, great powers,
If you will take this audit, take this life,
And cancel these cold bonds. O Imogen!
I'll speak to thee in silence. [*He sleeps.*

Solemn Musick. Enter, as an Apparition, SICILIUS LEONATUS, *Father to* Posthumus, *an old Man, attired like a Warrior; leading in his hand an ancient* Matron, *his Wife, and Mother to* Posthumus, *with Musick before them. Then, after other Musick, follow the Two young* Leonati, *Brothers to* Posthumus, *with wounds, as they died in the Wars. They circle* POSTHUMUS *round, as he lies sleeping.*

Sici. No more, thou thunder-master, show
Thy spite on mortal flies:
With Mars fall out, with Juno chide,
That thy adulteries
Rates and revenges.
Hath my poor boy done aught but well,
Whose face I never saw?
I died, whilst in the womb he stay'd
Attending Nature's law.
Whose father then (as men report,
Thou orphans' father art),
Thou should'st have been, and shielded him
From this earth-vexing smart.

Moth. Lucina lent not me her aid,
But took me in my throes;
That from me was Posthumus ript,
Came crying 'mongst his foes,
A thing of pity!
Sici. Great nature, like his ancestry,
Moulded the stuff so fair,
That he deserv'd the praise o' the world,
As great Sicilius' heir.
1 *Bro.* When once he was mature for man,
In Britain where was he
That could stand up his parallel;
Or fruitful object be
In eye of Imogen, that best
Could deem his dignity?
Moth. With marriage wherefore was he mock'd,
To be exil'd and thrown
From Leonati' seat, and cast
From her his dearest one,
Sweet Imogen?
Sici. Why did you suffer Iachimo,
Slight thing of Italy,
To taint his nobler heart and brain
With needless jealousy:
And to become the geck and scorn
O' the other's villany?
2 *Bro.* For this, from stiller seats we came,
Our parents, and us twain,
That, striking in our country's cause,
Fell bravely, and were slain;
Our fealty, and Tenantius' right,
With honour to maintain.
1 *Bro.* Like hardiment Posthumus hath
To Cymbeline perform'd:
Then Jupiter, thou king of gods,
Why hast thou thus adjourn'd
The graces for his merits due;
Being all to dolours turn'd?
Sici. Thy crystal window ope; look out;
No longer exercise,
Upon a valiant race, thy harsh
And potent injuries:
Moth. Since, Jupiter, our son is good,
Take off his miseries.
Sici. Peep through thy marble mansion; help!
Or we poor ghosts will cry
To the shining synod of the rest,
Against thy deity.
2 *Bro.* Help, Jupiter; or we appeal,
And from thy justice fly.

JUPITER *descends in Thunder and Lightning, sitting upon an Eagle: he throws a Thunder-bolt. The* Ghosts *fall on their knees.*

Jup. No more, you petty spirits of region low,
Offend our hearing; hush!—How dare you, ghosts,
Accuse the thunderer, whose bolt, you know,
Sky-planted, batters all rebelling coasts?
Poor shadows of Elysium, hence; and rest
Upon your never withering banks of flowers:
Be not with mortal accidents opprest;
No care of yours it is, you know, 'tis ours.
Whom best I love, I cross; to make my gift,
The more delay'd, delighted. Be content;
Your low-laid son our godhead will uplift:
His comforts thrive, his trials well are spent.
Our Jovial star reign'd at his birth, and in
Our temple was he married.—Rise, and fade!—
He shall be lord of lady Imogen,
And happier much by his affliction made.
This tablet lay upon his breast; wherein
Our pleasure his full fortune doth confine;
And so, away: no further with your din
Express impatience, lest you stir up mine.—
Mount, eagle, to my palace crystalline.
[*Ascends.*
Sici. He came in thunder; his celestial breath
Was sulphurous to smell: the holy eagle
Stoop'd, as to foot us: his ascension is
More sweet than our bless'd fields; his royal bird
Prunes the immortal wing, and cloys his beak,
As when his god is pleas'd.
All. Thanks, Jupiter!
Sici. The marble pavement closes, he is enter'd
His radiant roof:—Away! and, to be blest,
Let us with care perform his great behest.
[Ghosts *vanish.*
Post. [*Waking.*] Sleep, thou hast been a grandsire, and begot
A father to me: and thou hast created
A mother and two brothers: But (O scorn!)
Gone! they went hence so soon as they were born.
And so I am awake.—Poor wretches that depend
On greatness' favour, dream as I have done;
Wake, and find nothing.—But, alas, I swerve:
Many dream not to find, neither deserve,
And yet are steep'd in favours; so am I
That have this golden chance, and know not why.
What fairies haunt this ground? A book? O, rare one!
Be not, as is our fangled world, a garment
Nobler than that it covers: let thy effects
So follow, to be most unlike our courtiers,
As good as promise.

[Reads.] *When as a lion's whelp shall, to himself unknown, without seeking find, and be embraced by a piece of tender air: and when from a stately cedar shall be lopped branches, which, being dead many years, shall after revive, be jointed to the old stock, and freshly grow; then shall* Posthumus *end his miseries,* Britain *be fortunate, and flourish in peace and plenty.*

'Tis still a dream; or else such stuff as madmen
Tongue, and brain not: either both, or nothing:
Or senseless speaking, or a speaking such
As sense cannot untie. Be what it is,
The action of my life is like it, which
I'll keep, if but for sympathy.

Re-enter Gaolers.

Gaol. Come, sir, are you ready for death?

Post. Over-roasted, rather: ready long ago.

Gaol. Hanging is the word, sir; if you be ready for that, you are well cooked.

Post. So, if I prove a good repast to the spectators, the dish pays the shot.

Gaol. A heavy reckoning for you, sir: But the comfort is, you shall be called to no more payments, fear no more tavern bills; which are often the sadness of parting, as the procuring of mirth: you come in faint for want of meat, depart reeling with too much drink; sorry that you have paid too much, and sorry that you are paid too much; purse and brain both empty: the brain the heavier for being too light, the purse too light, being drawn of heaviness: O! of this contradiction you shall now be quit.—O the charity of a penny cord! it sums up thousands in a trice: you have no true debitor and creditor but it; of what's past, is, and to come, the discharge:—Your neck, sir, is pen, book, and counters; so the acquittance follows.

Post. I am merrier to die, than thou art to live.

Gaol. Indeed, sir, he that sleeps feels not the tooth-ach: But a man that were to sleep your sleep, and a hangman to help him to bed, I think, he would change places with his officer: for, look you, sir, you know not which way you shall go.

Post. Yes, indeed, do I, fellow.

Gaol. Your death has eyes in's head then; I have not seen him so pictured: you must either be directed by some that take upon them to know; or take upon yourself that, which I am sure you do not know; or jump the after-inquiry on your own peril: and how you shall speed in your journey's end, I think you'll never return to tell one.

Post. I tell thee, fellow, there are none want eyes to direct them the way I am going, but such as wink, and will not use them.

Gaol. What an infinite mock is this, that a man should have the best use of eyes, to see the way of blindness! I am sure, hanging's the way of winking.

Enter a Messenger.

Mess. Knock off his manacles; bring your prisoner to the king.

Post. Thou bringest good news;—I am called to be made free.

Gaol. I'll be hanged then.

Post. Thou shalt be then freer than a gaoler; no bolts for the dead.

[*Exeunt* POSTHUMUS *and* Messenger.

Gaol. Unless a man would marry a gallows, and beget young gibbets, I never saw one so prone. Yet, on my conscience, there are verier knaves desire to live, for all he be a Roman: and there be some of them too, that die against their wills; so should I, if I were one. I would we were all of one mind, and one mind good; O, there were desolation of gaolers, and gallowses! I speak against my present profit; but my wish hath a preferment in 't. [*Exeunt.*

SCENE V. Cymbeline's *Tent.*

Enter CYMBELINE, BELARIUS, GUIDERIUS, ARVIRAGUS, PISANIO, Lords, Officers, *and* Attendants.

Cym. Stand by my side, you whom the gods have made
Preservers of my throne. Woe is my heart,
That the poor soldier, that so richly fought,
Whose rags sham'd gilded arms, whose naked breast
Stepp'd before targe of proof, cannot be found:
He shall be happy that can find him, if
Our grace can make him so.

Bel. I never saw
Such noble fury in so poor a thing;
Such precious deeds in one that promis'd nought
But beggary and poor looks.

Cym. No tidings of him?

Pis. He hath been search'd among the dead and living,
But no trace of him.

Cym. To my grief, I am
The heir of his reward; which I will add
To you, the liver, heart, and brain of Britain,
[*To* BELARIUS, GUIDERIUS, *and* ARVIRAGUS.
By whom, I grant, she lives; 'Tis now the time
To ask of whence you are:—report it.

Bel. Sir,
In Cambria are we born, and gentlemen:
Further to boast, were neither true nor modest,
Unless I add, we are honest.

Cym. Bow your knees:
Arise, my knights o' the battle: I create you
Companions to our person, and will fit you
With dignities becoming your estates.

Enter CORNELIUS *and* Ladies.

There's business in these faces.—Why so sadly
Greet you our victory? you look like Romans,
And not o' the court of Britain.

Cor. Hail, great king!
To sour your happiness, I must report
The queen is dead.

Cym. Whom worse than a physician
Would this report become? But I consider,
By medicine life might be prolong'd, yet death
Will seize the doctor too.—How ended she?

Cor. With horror, madly dying, like her life;
Which, being cruel to the world, concluded
Most cruel to herself. What she confess'd,
I will report, so please you; These her women
Can trip me, if I err: who, with wet cheeks,
Were present when she finish'd.

Cym. Pr'ythee, say.

Cor. First, she confess'd she never lov'd you; only
Affected greatness got by you, not you:
Married your royalty, was wife to your place;
Abhorr'd your person.

Cym. She alone knew this:
And but she spoke it dying, I would not
Believe her lips in opening it. Proceed.

Cor. Your daughter, whom she bore in hand to love
With such integrity, she did confess
Was as a scorpion to her sight; whose life,
But that her flight prevented it, she had
Ta'en off by poison.

Cym. O most delicate fiend!
Who is 't can read a woman?—Is there more?

Cor. More, sir, and worse. She did confess, she had
For you a mortal mineral: which, being took,
Should by the minute feed on life, and, ling'ring,
By inches waste you: In which time she purpos'd,
By watching, weeping, tendance, kissing, to
O'ercome you with her show: yes, and in time
(When she had fitted you with her craft), to work
Her son into the adoption of the crown.
But failing of her end by his strange absence,
Grew shameless desperate; open'd in despite
Of heaven and men, her purposes; repented
The evils she hatch'd, were not effected: so,
Despairing, died.

Cym. Heard you all this, her women?

Lady. We did, so please your highness.

Cym. Mine eyes
Were not in fault, for she was beautiful;
Mine ears, that heard her flattery; nor my heart,
That thought her like her seeming; it had been vicious,
To have mistrusted her: yet, O my daughter!
That it was folly in me, thou may'st say,
And prove it in thy feeling. Heaven mend all!

Enter LUCIUS, IACHIMO, *the* Soothsayer, *and other* Roman Prisoners, *guarded;* POSTHUMUS *behind, and* IMOGEN.

Thou com'st not, Caius, now for tribute; that
The Britons have raz'd out, though with the loss
Of many a bold one; whose kinsmen have made suit,
That their good souls may be appeas'd with slaughter
Of you their captives, which ourself have granted;
So, think of your estate.

Luc. Consider, sir, the chance of war: the day
Was yours by accident; had it gone with us,
We should not, when the blood was cool, have threaten'd
Our prisoners with the sword. But since the gods
Will have it thus, that nothing but our lives
May be call'd ransome, let it come: sufficeth,
A Roman with a Roman's heart can suffer:
Augustus lives to think on 't: And so much
For my peculiar care. This one thing only
I will entreat; My boy, a Briton born,
Let him be ransom'd: never master had
A page so kind, so duteous, diligent,
So tender over his occasions, true,
So feat, so nurselike: let his virtue join
With my request, which I'll make bold, your highness
Cannot deny; he hath done no Briton harm,
Though he have serv'd a Roman: save him, sir,
And spare no blood beside.

Cym. I have surely seen him:
His favour is familiar to me.—
Boy, thou hast look'd thyself into my grace,
And art mine own.—I know not why, nor wherefore,
To say, live, boy: ne'er thank thy master; live:
And ask of Cymbeline what boon thou wilt,
Fitting my bounty, and thy state, I'll give it;
Yea, though thou do demand a prisoner,
The noblest ta'en.

Imo. I humbly thank your highness.

Luc. I do not bid thee beg my life, good lad;
And yet, I know, thou wilt.

Imo. No, no; alack,

There's other work in hand: I see a thing
Bitter to me as death: your life, good master,
Must shuffle for itself.

Luc. The boy disdains me,
He leaves me, scorns me: Briefly die their joys,
That place them on the truth of girls and boys?—
Why stands he so perplex'd?

Cym. What would'st thou, boy?
I love thee more and more; think more and more
What's best to ask. Know'st him thou look'st on? speak,
Wilt have him live? Is he thy kin? thy friend?

Imo. He is a Roman; no more kin to me,
Than I to your highness; who, being born your vassal,
Am something nearer.

Cym. Wherefore ey'st him so?

Imo. I'll tell you, sir, in private, if you please
To give me hearing.

Cym. Ay, with all my heart,
And lend my best attention. What's thy name?

Imo. Fidele, sir.

Cym. Thou art my good youth, my page;
I'll be thy master: Walk with me; speak freely.
[CYMBELINE *and* IMOGEN *converse apart.*

Bel. Is not this boy reviv'd from death?

Arv. One sand another
Not more resembles: That sweet rosy lad,
Who died, and was Fidele:—What think you?

Gui. The same dead thing alive.

Bel. Peace, peace! see further; he eyes us not; forbear;
Creatures may be alike: were't he, I am sure
He would have spoke to us.

Gui. But we saw him dead.

Bel. Be silent; let's see further.

Pis. It is my mistress: [*Aside.*
Since she is living, let the time run on,
To good, or bad. [CYM. *and* IMO. *come forward.*

Cym. Come, stand thou by our side;
Make thy demand aloud.—Sir, [*To* IACH.] step you forth;
Give answer to this boy, and do it freely;
Or, by our greatness, and the grace of it,
Which is our honour, bitter torture shall
Winnow the truth from falsehood.—On, speak to him.

Imo. My boon is, that this gentleman may render
Of whom he had this ring.

Post. What's that to him? [*Aside.*

Cym. That diamond upon your finger, say,
How came it yours?

Iach. Thou'lt torture me to leave unspoken that
Which, to be spoke, would torture thee.

Cym. How! me?

Iach. I am glad to be constrain'd to utter that which
Torments me to conceal. By villany
I got this ring: 'twas Leonatus' jewel:
Whom thou didst banish; and (which more may grieve thee,
As it doth me), a nobler sir ne'er liv'd
'Twixt sky and ground. Wilt thou hear more, my lord?

Cym. All that belongs to this.

Iach. That paragon, thy daughter,—
For whom my heart drops blood, and my false spirits
Quail to remember,—Give me leave: I faint.

Cym. My daughter! what of her? Renew thy strength:
I had rather thou should'st live while nature will,
Than die ere I hear more: strive man, and speak.

Iach. Upon a time (unhappy was the clock
That struck the hour!) it was in Rome (accurs'd
The mansion where?) 'twas at a feast, (O 'would
Our viands had been poison'd! or, at least,
Those which I heav'd to head!) the good Posthumus,
(What should I say? he was too good, to be
Where ill men were; and was the best of all
Amongst the rar'st of good ones), sitting sadly,
Hearing us praise our loves of Italy
For beauty that made barren the swell'd boast
Of him that best could speak: for feature, laming
The shrine of Venus, or straight pight Minerva,
Postures beyond brief nature; for condition,
A shop of all the qualities that man
Loves woman for; besides, that hook of wiving,
Fairness which strikes the eye:——

Cym. I stand on fire:
Come to the matter.

Iach. All too soon I shall,
Unless thou would'st grieve quickly.—This Posthumus
(Most like a noble lord in love, and one
That had a royal lover), took his hint;
And, not dispraising whom we prais'd (therein
He was as calm as virtue), he began
His mistress picture; which by his tongue being made,
And then a mind put in't, either our brags
Were crack'd of kitchen trulls, or his description
Prov'd us unspeaking sots.

Cym. Nay, nay, to the purpose.

Iach. Your daughter's chastity—there it begins.
He spake of her as Dian had hot dreams,
And she alone were cold: Whereat, I, wretch!
Made scruple of his praise; and wager'd with him
Pieces of gold, 'gainst this which then he wore
Upon his honour'd finger, to attain
In suit the place of his bed, and win this ring
By hers and mine adultery: he, true knight,
No lesser of her honour confident
Than I did truly find her, stakes this ring;
And would so, had it been a carbuncle
Of Phœbus' wheel; and might so safely, had it
Been all the worth of his car. Away to Britain
Post I in this design: Well may you, sir,
Remember me at court, where I was taught
Of your chaste daughter the wide difference
'Twixt amorous and villanous. Being thus quench'd
Of hope, not longing, mine Italian brain
'Gan in your duller Britain operate
Most vilely; for my vantage excellent;
And, to be brief, my practice so prevail'd,
That I return'd with similar proof enough
To make the noble Leonatus mad,
By wounding his belief in her renown
With tokens thus, and thus; averring notes
Of chamber-hanging, pictures, this her bracelet,
(O, cunning, how I got it!) nay, some marks
Of secret on her person, that he could not
But think her bond of chastity quite crack'd,
I having ta'en the forfeit. Whereupon,—
Methinks, I see him now,—

Post. Ay, so thou dost, [*Coming forward.*
Italian fiend!—Ah me, most credulous fool,
Egregious murderer, thief, any thing
That's due to all the villains past, in being,
To come!—O give me cord, or knife, or poison,
Some upright justicer! Thou king, send out
For torturers ingenious: it is I
That all the abhorred things o'the earth amend,
By being worse than they. I am Posthumus,
That kill'd thy daughter:—villain-like, I lie;
That caus'd a lesser villain than myself,
A sacrilegious thief, to do't:—the temple
Of virtue was she; yea, and she herself.
Spit, and throw stones, cast mire upon me, set
The dogs o' the street to bay me: every villain
Be call'd Posthumus Leonatus: and
Be villany less than 'twas!—O Imogen!
My queen, my life, my wife! O Imogen,
Imogen, Imogen!

Imo. Peace, my lord; hear, hear—

Post. Shall's have a play of this? Thou scornful page,
There lie thy part. [*Striking her; she falls.*

Pis. O, gentlemen, help, help

Mine, and your mistress:—O, my lord Posthumus!
You ne'er kill'd Imogen till now:—Help, help!—
Mine honour'd lady!

Cym. Does the world go round?

Post. How come these staggers on me?

Pis. Wake, my mistress!

Cym. If this be so, the gods do mean to strike me
To death with mortal joy.

Pis. How fares my mistress?

Imo. O get thee from my sight;
Thou gav'st me poison: dangerous fellow, hence!
Breathe not where princes are.

Cym. The tune of Imogen!

Pis. Lady,
The gods throw stones of sulphur on me, if
That box I gave you was not thought by me
A precious thing; I had it from the queen.

Cym. New matter still?

Imo. It poison'd me.

Cor. O gods!
I left out one thing which the queen confess'd,
Which must approve thee honest: If Pisanio
Have, said she, given his mistress that confection
Which I gave him for a cordial, she is serv'd
As I would serve a rat.

Cym. What's this, Cornelius?

Cor. The queen, sir, very oft importun'd me
To temper poisons for her; still pretending
The satisfaction of her knowledge, only
In killing creatures vile, as cats and dogs
Of no esteem: I, dreading that her purpose
Was of more danger, did compound for her
A certain stuff, which, being ta'en, would cease
The present power of life; but, in short time,
All offices of nature should again
Do their due functions.—Have you ta'en of it?

Imo. Most like I did, for I was dead.

Bel. My boys,
There was our error.

Gui. This is sure, Fidele.

Imo. Why did you throw your wedded lady from you?
Think, that you are upon a rock; and now
Throw me again. [*Embracing him.*

Post. Hang there, like fruit, my soul,
Till the tree die!

Cym. How now, my flesh, my child?
What, mak'st thou me a dullard in this act?
Wilt thou not speak to me?

Imo. Your blessing, sir. [*Kneeling.*

Bel. Though you did love this youth, I blame ye not;
You had a motive for't. [*To* GUI. *and* ARV.

Cym. My tears that fall,
Prove holy water on thee! Imogen,
Thy mother's dead.

Imo. I am sorry for't, my lord.

Cym. O, she was naught; and long of her it was,
That we meet here so strangely: But her son
Is gone, we know not how, nor where.

Pis. My lord,
Now fear is from me, I'll speak troth. Lord Cloten,
Upon my lady's missing, came to me
With his sword drawn; foam'd at the mouth, and swore,
If I discover'd not which way she was gone,
It was my instant death: By accident,
I had a feigned letter of my master's
Then in my pocket; which directed him
To seek her on the mountains near to Milford;
Where, in a frenzy, in my master's garments,
Which he inforc'd from me, away he posts
With unchaste purpose, and with oath to violate
My lady's honour: what became of him,
I further know not.

Gui. Let me end the story:
I slew him there.

Cym. Marry, the gods forefend!
I would not thy good deeds should from my lips
Pluck a hard sentence: pr'ythee, valiant youth,
Deny't again.

Gui. I have spoke it, and I did it.

Cym. He was a prince.

Gui. A most uncivil one: The wrongs he did me
Were nothing princelike; for he did provoke me
With language that would make me spurn the sea,
If it could so roar to me: I cut off's head;
And am right glad he is not standing here
To tell this tale of mine.

Cym. I am sorry for thee:
By thine own tongue thou art condemn'd, and must
Endure our law: Thou art dead.

Imo. That headless man
I thought had been my lord.

Cym. Bind the offender,
And take him from our presence.

Bel. Stay, sir king:
This man is better than the man he slew,
As well descended as thyself; and hath
More of thee merited, than a band of Clotens
Had ever scar for.—Let his arms alone;
[*To the Guard.*
They were not born for bondage.

Cym. Why, old soldier,
Wilt thou undo the worth thou art unpaid for,
By tasting of our wrath? How of descent
As good as we?

Arv. In that he spake too far.

Cym. And thou shalt die for't.

Bel. We will die all three:
But I will prove, that two of us are as good
As I have given out him.—My sons, I must,
For mine own part, unfold a dangerous speech,
Though, haply, well for you.

Arv. Your danger is
Ours.

Gui. And our good his.

Bel. Have at it then.—
By leave;—Thou hadst, great king, a subject, who
Was call'd Belarius.

Cym. What of him? he is
A banish'd traitor.

Bel. He it is, that hath
Assum'd this age: indeed, a banish'd man;
I know not how, a traitor.

Cym. Take him hence;
The whole world shall not save him.

Bel. Not too hot;
First pay me for the nursing of thy sons;
And let it be confiscate all, so soon
As I have receiv'd it.

Cym. Nursing of my sons!

Bel. I am too blunt and saucy: Here's my knee;
Ere I arise, I will prefer my sons;
Then, spare not the old father. Mighty sir,
These two young gentlemen, that call me father,
And think they are my sons, are none of mine;
They are the issue of your loins, my liege,
And blood of your begetting.

Cym. How! my issue?

Bel. So sure as you your father's. I, old Morgan,
Am that Belarius whom you sometime banish'd:
Your pleasure was my mere offence, my punishment
Itself, and all my treason; that I suffer'd,
Was all the harm I did. These gentle princes
(For such, and so they are) these twenty years
Have I train'd up: those arts they have, as I
Could put into them; my breeding was, sir, as
Your highness knows. Their nurse, Euriphile,
Whom for the theft I wedded, stole these children
Upon my banishment: I mov'd her to't;
Having receiv'd the punishment before,
For that which I did then: Beaten for loyalty,
Excited me to treason; Their dear loss,
The more of you 'twas felt, the more it shap'd

Unto my end of stealing them. But, gracious sir,
Here are your sons again; and I must lose
Two of the sweet'st companions in the world:—
The benediction of these covering heavens
Fall on their heads like dew! for they are worthy
To inlay heaven with stars.

Cym. Thou weep'st, and speak'st.
The service, that you three have done, is more
Unlike than this thou tell'st: I lost my children;
If these be they, I know not how to wish
A pair of worthier sons.

Bel. Be pleas'd awhile.—
This gentleman whom I call Polydore,
Most worthy prince, as yours, is true Guiderius;
This gentleman, my Cadwal, Arviragus,
Your younger princely son: he, sir, was lapp'd
In a most curious mantle, wrought by the hand
Of his queen mother, which for more probation,
I can with ease produce.

Cym. Guiderius had
Upon his neck a mole, a sanguine star:
It was a mark of wonder.

Bel. This is he;
Who hath upon him still that natural stamp;
It was wise nature's end in the donation,
To be his evidence now.

Cym. O, what am I
A mother to the birth of three? Ne'er mother
Rejoic'd deliverance more:—Bless'd may you be,
That after this strange starting from your orbs,
You may reign in them now!—O Imogen,
Thou hast lost by this a kingdom.

Imo. No, my lord;
I have got two worlds by't.—O my gentle brothers,
Have we thus met? O never say hereafter,
But I am truest speaker: you call'd me brother,
When I was but your sister; I you brothers,
When you were so indeed.

Cym. Did you e'er meet?

Arv. Ay, my good lord.

Gui. And at first meeting lov'd;
Continued so, until we thought he died.

Cor. By the queen's dram she swallow'd.

Cym. O rare instinct!
When shall I hear all through? This fierce abridgment
Hath to it circumstantial branches, which
Distinction should be rich in.—Where, how liv'd you?
And when came you to serve our Roman captive?
How parted with your brothers? how first met them?
Why fled you from the court? and whither? These,
And your three motives to the battle, with
I know not how much more, should be demanded;
And all the other by-dependancies,
From chance to chance; but nor the time, nor place,
Will serve our long intergatories. See,
Posthumus anchors upon Imogen;
And she, like harmless lightning, throws her eye
On him, her brothers, me, her master; hitting
Each object with a joy; the counterchange
Is severally in all. Let's quit this ground,
And smoke the temple with our sacrifices.—
Thou art my brother; So we'll hold thee ever.
[*To* BELARIUS.

Imo. You are my father too; and did relieve me,
To see this gracious season.

Cym. All o'erjoy'd,
Save these in bonds; let them be joyful too,
For they shall taste our comfort.

Imo. My good master,
I will yet do you service.

Luc. Happy be you!

Cym. The forlorn soldier, that so nobly fought,
He would have well becom'd this place, and grac'd
The thankings of a king.

Post. I am, sir,
The soldier that did accompany these three
In poor beseeming; 'twas a fitment for
The purpose I then follow'd;—That I was he,
Speak, Iachimo; I had you down, and might
Have made you finish.

Iach. I am down again: [*Kneeling.*
But now my heavy conscience sinks my knee,
As then your force did. Take that life, 'beseech you,
Which I so often owe: but, your ring first;
And here the bracelet of the truest princess,
That ever swore her faith.

Post. Kneel not to me:
The power that I have on you, is to spare you;
The malice towards you, to forgive you: Live,
And deal with others better.

Cym. Nobly doom'd:
We'll learn our freeness of a son-in-law;
Pardon's the word to all.

Arv. You holp us, sir,
As you did mean indeed to be our brother;
Joy'd are we, that you are.

Post. Your servant, princes.—Good my lord of Rome,
Call forth your soothsayer: As I slept, methought,
Great Jupiter, upon his eagle back,
Appear'd to me, with other spritely shows
Of mine own kindred; when I wak'd, I found
This label on my bosom; whose containing
Is so from sense in hardness, that I can
Make no collection of it; let him show
His skill in the construction.

Luc. Philarmonus,—

Sooth. Here, my good lord.

Luc. Read, and declare the meaning.

Sooth. [Reads.] *When as a lion's whelp shall, to himself unknown, without seeking find, and be embraced by a piece of tender air; and when from a stately cedar shall be lopped branches, which, being dead many years shall after revive, be jointed to the old stock, and freshly grow; then shall* Posthumus *end his miseries,* Britain *be fortunate, and flourish in peace and plenty.*
Thou, Leonatus, art the lion's whelp;
The fit and apt construction of thy name,
Being Leo-natus, doth import so much:
The piece of tender air, thy virtuous daughter,
[*To* CYMBELINE.
Which we call *mollis aer;* and *mollis aer*
We term it *mulier:* which *mulier* I divine,
Is this most constant wife: who, even now,
Answering the letter of the oracle,
Unknown to you, unsought, were clipp'd about
With this most tender air.

Cym. This hath some seeming.

Sooth. The lofty cedar, royal Cymbeline,
Personates thee: and thy lopp'd branches point
Thy two sons forth: who, by Belarius stolen,
For many years thought dead, are now reviv'd,
To the majestic cedar join'd; whose issue
Promises Britain peace and plenty.

Cym. Well,
My peace we will begin:—And, Caius Lucius,
Although the victor, we submit to Cæsar,
And to the Roman empire: promising
To pay our wonted tribute, from the which
We were dissuaded by our wicked queen;
Whom heavens, in justice (both on her and hers),
Have laid most heavy hand.

Sooth. The fingers of the powers above do tune
The harmony of this peace. The vision
Which I made known to Lucius, ere the stroke
Of this yet scarce-cold battle, at this instant
Is full accomplish'd: For the Roman eagle,
From south to west on wing soaring aloft,
Lessen'd herself, and in the beams o' the sun
So vanish'd: which foreshow'd our princely eagle,
The imperial Cæsar, should again unite
His favour with the radiant Cymbeline,
Which shines here in the west.

Cym. Laud we the gods;
And let our crooked smokes climb to their nostrils
From our bless'd altars! Publish we this peace
To all our subjects. Set we forward: Let
A Roman and a British ensign wave
Friendly together: so through Lud's town march:
And in the temple of great Jupiter
Our peace we'll ratify; seal it with feasts.—
Set on there:—Never was a war did cease,
Ere bloody hands were wash'd, with such a peace. [*Exeunt.*

A SONG,

SUNG BY GUIDERIUS AND ARVIRAGUS OVER FIDELE, SUPPOSED TO BE DEAD.

BY MR. WILLIAM COLLINS.

To fair Fidele's *grassy tomb,*
Soft maids and village hinds shall bring
Each opening sweet, of earliest bloom,
And rifle all the breathing spring.

No wailing ghost shall dare appear
To vex with shrieks this quiet grove;
But shepherd lads assemble here,
And melting virgins own their love.

No wither'd witch shall here be seen,
No goblins lead their nightly crew:
The female fays shall haunt the green,
And dress thy grave with pearly dew.

The redbreast oft at evening hours
Shall kindly lend his little aid,
With hoary moss, and gather'd flowers,
To deck the ground where thou art laid.

When howling winds, and beating rain,
In tempests shake the silvan cell;
Or midst the chase on every plain,
The tender thought on thee shall dwell.

Each lonely scene shall thee restore;
For thee the tear be duly shed;
Belov'd till life could charm no more;
And mourn'd till pity's self be dead.

TITUS ANDRONICUS.

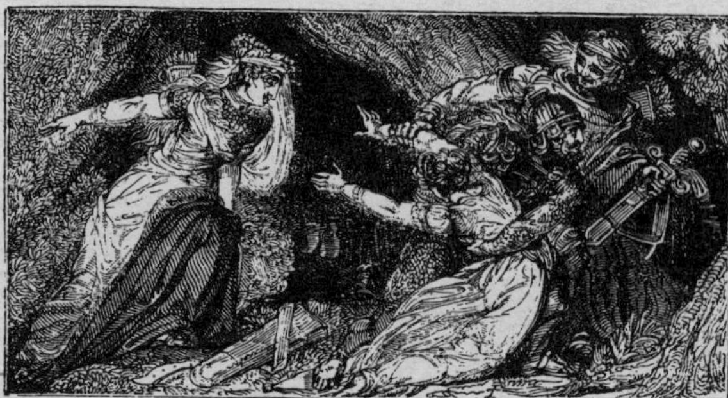

PERSONS REPRESENTED.

SATURNINUS, *Son to the late* Emperor *of* Rome, *and afterwards declared* Emperor *himself.*
BASSIANUS, *Brother to* Saturninus; *in love with* Lavinia.
TITUS ANDRONICUS, *a noble* Roman, *General against the* Goths.
MARCUS ANDRONICUS, *Tribune of the People; and Brother to* Titus.
LUCIUS, QUINTUS, MARTIUS, MUTIUS, } *Sons to* Titus Andronicus.
Young LUCIUS, *a Boy, Son to* Lucius.
PUBLIUS, *Son to* Marcus *the Tribune.*
ÆMILIUS, *a noble* Roman.
ALARBUS, CHIRON, DEMETRIUS, } *Sons to* Tamora.
AARON, *a Moor, beloved by* Tamora.
A Captain, Tribune, Messenger, *and* Clown Romans.
Goths, *and* Romans.
TAMORA, Queen *of the* Goths.
LAVINIA, *Daughter to* Titus Andronicus.
A Nurse, *and a black* Child.
Kinsmen *of* Titus, Senators, Tribunes, Officers, Soldiers, *and* Attendants.

SCENE—Rome; *and the Country near it.*

ACT I.

SCENE I. Rome. *Before the* Capitol.

The Tomb of the Andronici *appearing; the* Tribunes *and* Senators *aloft, as in the Senate. Enter, below,* SATURNINUS *and his* Followers, *on one side; and* BASSIANUS *and his* Followers *on the other; with Drum and Colours.*

Sat. NOBLE patricians, patrons of my right,
Defend the justice of my cause with arms;
And, countrymen, my loving followers,
Plead my successive title with your swords:
I am his first-born son, that was the last
That ware the imperial diadem of Rome;
Then let my father's honours live in me,
Nor wrong mine age with this indignity.

Bas. Romans,—friends, followers, favourers of my right,—
If ever Bassianus, Cæsar's son,
Were gracious in the eyes of royal Rome,
Keep then this passage to the Capitol;
And suffer not dishonour to approach
The imperial seat, to virtue consecrate,

To justice, continence, and nobility:
But let desert in pure election shine;
And, Romans, fight for freedom in your choice.

Enter MARCUS ANDRONICUS, *aloft, with the Crown.*

Mar. Princes—that strive by factions, and by friends,
Ambitiously for rule and empery,— [stand
Know, that the people of Rome, for whom we
A special party, have, by common voice,
In election for the Roman empery,
Chosen Andronicus, surnamed Pius,
For many good and great deserts to Rome;
A nobler man, a braver warrior,
Lives not this day within the city walls:
He by the senate is accited home,
From weary wars against the barbarous Goths;
That, with his sons, a terror to our foes,
Hath yok'd a nation strong, train'd up in arms.
Ten years are spent, since first he undertook
This cause of Rome, and chastised with arms
Our enemies' pride: Five times he hath return'd
Bleeding to Rome, bearing his valiant sons
In coffins from the field;
And now at last, laden with honour's spoils,
Returns the good Andronicus to Rome,
Renowned Titus, flourishing in arms.
Let us entreat,—By honour of his name,
Whom, worthily, you would have now succeed,
And in the Capitol and senate's right,
Whom you pretend to honour and adore,—
That you withdraw you, and abate your strength;
Dismiss your followers, and, as suitors should,
Plead your deserts in peace and humbleness.

Sat. How fair the tribune speaks to calm my thoughts!

Bas. Marcus Andronicus, so I do affy
In thy uprightness and integrity,
And so I love and honour thee and thine,
Thy nobler brother Titus, and his sons,
And her to whom my thoughts are humbled all,
Gracious Lavinia, Rome's rich ornament,
That I will here dismiss my loving friends;
And to my fortunes, and the people's favour,
Commit my cause in balance to be weigh'd.
[*Exeunt the* Followers *of* Bassianus.

Sat. Friends, that have been thus forward in my right,
I thank you all, and here dismiss you all;
And to the love and favour of my country
Commit myself, my person, and the cause.
[*Exeunt the* Followers *of* Saturninus.
Rome, be as just and gracious unto me,
As I am confident and kind to thee.—
Open the gates, and let me in.

Bas. Tribunes! and me, a poor competitor.
[SAT. *and* BAS. *go into the Capitol, and exeunt with* Senators, MARCUS, *&c.*

SCENE II. *The same.*

Enter a Captain, *and Others.*

Cap. Romans, make way; The good Andronicus,
Patron of virtue, Rome's best champion,
Successful in the battles that he fights,
With honour and with fortune is return'd,
From where he circumscribed with his sword,
And brought to yoke, the enemies of Rome.

Flourish of Trumpets, &c. Enter MUTIUS *and* MARTIUS; *after them* Two Men *bearing a Coffin covered with black; then* QUINTUS *and* LUCIUS. *After them,* TITUS ANDRONICUS; *and then* TAMORA, *with* ALARBUS, CHIRON, DEMETRIUS, AARON, *and other* Goths, *prisoners*; Soldiers *and* People *following. The* Bearers *set down the Coffin, and* TITUS *speaks.*

Tit. Hail, Rome, victorious in thy mourning weeds!
Lo, as the bark that hath discharg'd her fraught,
Returns with precious lading to the bay,
From whence at first she weigh'd her anchorage,
Cometh Andronicus, bound with laurel boughs,
To resalute his country with his tears:
Tears of true joy for his return to Rome.—
Thou great defender of this Capitol,
Stand gracious to the rights that we intend!—
Romans, of five and twenty valiant sons,
Half of the number that king Priam had,
Behold the poor remains alive, and dead!
These, that survive, let Rome reward with love;
These, that I bring unto their latest home,
With burial amongst their ancestors:
Here Goths have given me leave to sheath my sword.
Titus, unkind, and careless of thine own,
Why suffer'st thou thy sons, unburied yet,
To hover on the dreadful shore of Styx?—
Make way to lay them by their brethren.
[*The Tomb is opened.*
There greet in silence, as the dead are wont,
And sleep in peace, slain in your country's wars!
O sacred receptacle of my joys,
Sweet cell of virtue and nobility,
How many sons of mine hast thou in store,
That thou wilt never render to me more?

Luc. Give us the proudest prisoner of the Goths,
That we may hew his limbs, and, on a pile,
Ad manes fratrum sacrifice his flesh,
Before this earthly prison of their bones;
That so the shadows be not unappeas'd,
Nor we disturb'd with prodigies on earth.

Tit. I give him you; the noblest that survives,
The eldest son of this distressed queen.

Tam. Stay, Roman brethren;—Gracious conqueror,
Victorious Titus, rue the tears I shed,
A mother's tears in passion for her son:
And, if thy sons were ever dear to thee,
O, think my son to be as dear to me.
Sufficeth not, that we are brought to Rome,
To beautify thy triumphs, and return,
Captive to thee, and to thy Roman yoke;
But must my sons be slaughter'd in the streets,
For valiant doings in their country's cause?
O! if to fight for king and commonweal
Were piety in thine, it is in these.
Andronicus, stain not thy tomb with blood:
Wilt thou draw near the nature of the gods?
Draw near them then in being merciful:
Sweet mercy is nobility's true badge;
Thrice-noble Titus, spare my first-born son.

Tit. Patient yourself, madam, and pardon me.
These are their brethren, whom you Goths beheld
Alive, and dead; and for their brethren slain,
Religiously they ask a sacrifice:
To this your son is mark'd; and die he must,
To appease their groaning shadows that are gone.

Luc. Away with him! and make a fire straight;
And with our swords, upon a pile of wood,
Let's hew his limbs, till they be clean consum'd.
[*Exeunt* LUCIUS, QUINTUS, MARTIUS, *and* MUTIUS, *with* ALARBUS.

Tam. O cruel, irreligious piety!

Chi. Was ever Scythia half so barbarous?

Dem. Oppose not Scythia to ambitious Rome.
Alarbus goes to rest; and we survive
To tremble under Titus' threatening look.
Then, madam, stand resolv'd; but hope withal,
The selfsame gods that arm'd the queen of Troy
With opportunity of sharp revenge
Upon the Thracian tyrant in his tent,
May favour Tamora, the queen of Goths
(When Goths were Goths, and Tamora was queen),
To quit the bloody wrongs upon her foes.

Re-enter LUCIUS, QUINTUS, MARTIUS, *and* MUTIUS, *with their swords bloody.*

Luc. See, lord and father, how we have perform'd
Our Roman rites: Alarbus' limbs are lopp'd,

And entrails feed the sacrificing fire,
Whose smoke, like incense, doth perfume the sky.
Remaineth nought, but to inter our brethren,
And with loud 'larums welcome them to Rome.
Tit. Let it be so, and let Andronicus
Make this his latest farewell to their souls.
[*Trumpets sounded, and the Coffin laid in the Tomb.*
In peace and honour rest you here, my sons;
Rome's readiest champions, repose you here in rest,
Secure from worldly chances and mishaps!
Here lurks no treason, here no envy swells,
Here grow no damned grudges; here are no storms,
No noise, but silence and eternal sleep:

Enter LAVINIA.

In peace and honour rest you here, my sons!
Lav. In peace and honour live Lord Titus long;
My noble lord and father, live in fame!
Lo! at this tomb my tributary tears
I render, for my brethren's obsequies;
And at thy feet I kneel with tears of joy
Shed on the earth, for thy return to Rome:
O, bless me here with thy victorious hand,
Whose fortunes Rome's best citizens applaud.
Tit. Kind Rome, thou hast thus lovingly reserv'd
The cordial of mine age to glad my heart!—
Lavinia, live; outlive thy father's days,
And fame's eternal date, for virtue's praise!

Enter MARCUS ANDRONICUS, SATURNINUS, BASSIANUS, *and Others.*

Mar. Long live Lord Titus, my beloved brother,
Gracious triumpher in the eyes of Rome!
Tit. Thanks, gentle tribune, noble brother Marcus.
Mar. And welcome, nephews, from successful wars,
You that survive, and you that sleep in fame.
Fair lords, your fortunes are alike in all,
That in your country's service drew your swords:
But safer triumph is this funeral pomp,
That hath aspir'd to Solon's happiness,
And triumphs over chance, in honour's bed.—
Titus Andronicus, the people of Rome,
Whose friend in justice thou hast ever been,
Send thee by me, their tribune, and their trust,
This palliament of white and spotless hue;
And name thee in election for the empire,
With these our late deceased emperor's sons:
Be *candidatus* then, and put it on,
And help to set a head on headless Rome.
Tit. A better head her glorious body fits,
Than his, that shakes for age and feebleness;
What? should I don this robe, and trouble you?
Be chosen with proclamations to-day;
To-morrow, yield up rule, resign my life,
And set abroad new business for you all?
Rome, I have been thy soldier forty years,
And buried one and twenty valiant sons,
Knighted in field, slain manfully in arms,
In right and service of their noble country:
Give me a staff of honour for mine age,
But not a sceptre to control the world:
Upright he held it, lords, that held it last.
Mar. Titus, thou shalt obtain and ask the empery.
Sat. Proud and ambitious tribune, canst thou tell,—
Tit. Patience, Prince Saturnine.
Sat. Romans, do me right;—
Patricians, draw your swords, and sheath them not
Till Saturninus be Rome's emperor:—
Andronicus, 'would thou wert shipp'd to hell,
Rather than rob me of the people's hearts.
Luc. Proud Saturnine, interrupter of the good
That noble-minded Titus means to thee!
Tit. Content thee, prince; I will restore to thee
The people's hearts, and wean them from themselves.
Bas. Andronicus, I do not flatter thee,
But honour thee, and will do till I die;
My faction if thou strengthen with thy friends,
I will most thankful be: and thanks, to men
Of noble minds, is honourable meed.
Tit. People of Rome, and people's tribunes here,
I ask your voices, and your suffrages;
Will you bestow them friendly on Andronicus?
Trib. To gratify the good Andronicus,
And gratulate his safe return to Rome,
The people will accept whom he admits.
Tit. Tribunes, I thank you; and this suit I make,
That you create your emperor's eldest son,
Lord Saturnine; whose virtues will, I hope,
Reflect on Rome, as Titan's rays on earth,
And ripen justice in this commonweal:
Then if you will elect, by my advice,
Crown him, and say,—*Long live our emperor!*
Mar. With voices and applause of every sort,
Patricians and plebeians, we create
Lord Saturninus, Rome's great emperor;
And say, *Long live our emperor Saturnine!*
[*A long Flourish.*
Sat. Titus Andronicus, for thy favours done
To us in our election this day,
I give thee thanks in part of thy deserts,
And will with deeds requite thy gentleness;
And, for an onset, Titus, to advance
Thy name, and honourable family,
Lavinia will I make my empress,
Rome's royal mistress, mistress of my heart,
And in the sacred Pantheon her espouse:
Tell me, Andronicus, doth this motion please thee?
Tit. It doth, my worthy lord; and, in this match,
I hold me highly honour'd of your grace:
And here, in sight of Rome, to Saturnine,—
King and commander of our commonweal,
The wide world's emperor,—do I consecrate
My sword, my chariot, and my prisoners;
Presents well worthy Rome's imperial lord:
Receive them then, the tribute that I owe,
Mine honour's ensign's humbled at thy feet.
Sat. Thanks, noble Titus, father of my life!
How proud I am of thee, and of thy gifts,
Rome shall record; and, when I do forget
The least of these unspeakable deserts,
Romans, forget your fealty to me.
Tit. Now, madam, are you prisoner to an emperor; [*To* TAMORA.
To him, that for your honour and your state,
Will use you nobly, and your followers.
Sat. A goodly lady, trust me; of the hue
That I would choose, were I to choose anew.—
Clear up, fair queen, that cloudy countenance;
Though chance of war hath wrought this change of cheer,
Thou com'st not to be made a scorn in Rome:
Princely shall be thy usage every way.
Rest on my word, and let not discontent
Daunt all your hopes: Madam, he comforts you,
Can make you greater than the queen of Goths.—
Lavinia, you are not displeas'd with this?
Lav. Not I, my lord; sith true nobility
Warrants these words in princely courtesy.
Sat. Thanks, sweet Lavinia.—Romans, let us go:
Ransomeless here we set our prisoners free:
Proclaim our honours, lords, with trump and drum.
Bas. Lord Titus, by your leave, this maid is mine. [*Seizing* LAVINIA.
Tit. How, sir? Are you in earnest then, my lord?

Bas. Ay, noble Titus; and resolv'd withal,
To do myself this reason and this right.
[*The* Emperor *courts* TAMORA *in dumb show.*
Mar. *Suum cuique* is our Roman justice:
This prince in justice seizeth but his own.
Luc. And that he will, and shall, if Lucius live.
Tit. Traitors, avaunt! Where is the emperor's guard?
Treason, my lord; Lavinia is surpris'd.
Sat. Surpris'd, by whom?
Bas. By him that justly may
Bear his betroth'd from all the world away.
[*Exeunt* MARCUS *and* BASSIANUS, *with* LAVINIA.
Mut. Brothers, help to convey her hence away,
And with my sword I'll keep this door safe.
[*Exeunt* LUCIUS, QUINTUS, *and* MARTIUS.
Tit. Follow, my lord, and I'll soon bring her back.
Mut. My lord, you pass not here.
Tit. What, villain boy!
Barr'st me my way in Rome?
[TITUS *kills* MUTIUS.
Mut. Help, Lucius, help.

Re-enter LUCIUS.

Luc. My lord, you are unjust: and, more than so,
In wrongful quarrel you have slain your son.
Tit. Nor thou, nor he, are any sons of mine:
My sons would never so dishonour me;
Traitor, restore Lavinia to the emperor.
Luc. Dead, if you will: but not to be his wife,
That is another's lawful promis'd love. [*Exit.*
Sat. No, Titus, no; the emperor needs her not,
Nor her, nor thee, nor any of thy stock:
I'll trust, by leisure, him that mocks me once;
Thee never, nor thy traitorous haughty sons,
Confederates all thus to dishonour me.
Was there none else in Rome to make a stale of,
But Saturnine? Full well, Andronicus,
Agree these deeds with that proud brag of thine,
That said'st, I begg'd the empire at thy hands.
Tit. O monstrous! what reproachful words are these?
Sat. But go thy ways; go, give that changing piece
To him that flourish'd for her with his sword:
A valiant son-in-law thou shalt enjoy;
One fit to bandy with thy lawless sons,
To ruffle in the commonwealth of Rome.
Tit. These words are razors to my wounded heart.
Sat. And therefore, lovely Tamora, queen of Goths,—
That, like the stately Phœbe 'mongst her nymphs,
Dost overshine the gallant'st dames of Rome,—
If thou be pleas'd with this my sudden choice,
Behold, I choose thee, Tamora, for my bride,
And will create thee empress of Rome.
Speak, queen of Goths, dost thou applaud my choice?
And here I swear by all the Roman gods,—
Sith priest and holy water are so near,
And tapers burn so bright, and every thing
In readiness for Hymeneus stand,—
I will not resalute the streets of Rome,
Or climb my palace, till from forth this place
I lead espous'd my bride along with me.
Tam. And here, in sight of heaven, to Rome I swear,
If Saturnine advance the queen of Goths,
She will a handmaid be to his desires,
A loving nurse, a mother to his youth.
Sat. Ascend, fair queen, Pantheon:—Lords, accompany
Your noble emperor, and his lovely bride,
Sent by the heavens for prince Saturnine,
Whose wisdom hath her fortune conquered:
There shall we consummate our spousal rites.
[*Exeunt* SATURNINUS, *and his* Followers; TAMORA, *and her* Sons; AARON, *and* Goths.

Tit. I am not bid to wait upon this bride;—
Titus, when wert thou wont to walk alone,
Dishonour'd thus, and challenged of wrongs?

Re-enter MARCUS, LUCIUS, QUINTUS, *and* MARTIUS.

Mar. O, Titus, see, O, see, what thou hast done!
In a bad quarrel slain a virtuous son.
Tit. No, foolish tribune, no; no son of mine,—
Nor thou, nor these confederates in the deed
That hath dishonour'd all our family;
Unworthy brother, and unworthy sons!
Luc. But let us give him burial, as becomes;
Give Mutius burial with our brethren.
Tit. Traitors, away! he rests not in this tomb.
This monument five hundred years hath stood,
Which I have sumptuously re-edified:
Here none but soldiers, and Rome's servitors,
Repose in fame; none basely slain in brawls:—
Bury him where you can, he comes not here.
Mar. My lord, this is impiety in you:
My nephew Mutius' deeds do plead for him;
He must be buried with his brethren.
Quin. Mart. And shall, or him we will accompany.
Tit. And shall? What villain was it spoke that word?
Quin. He that would vouch't in any place but here.
Tit. What, would you bury him in my despite?
Mar. No, noble Titus; but entreat of thee
To pardon Mutius, and to bury him.
Tit. Marcus, even thou hast struck upon my crest,
And, with these boys, mine honour thou hast wounded:
My foes I do repute you every one;
So trouble me no more, but get you gone.
Mart. He is not with himself: let us withdraw.
Quin. Not I, till Mutius' bones be buried.
[MARCUS *and the* Sons *of* Titus *kneel.*
Mar. Brother, for in that name doth nature plead.
Quin. Father, and in that name doth nature speak.
Tit. Speak thou no more, if all the rest will speed.
Mar. Renowned Titus, more than half my soul,—
Luc. Dear father, soul and substance of us all,—
Mar. Suffer thy brother Marcus to inter
His noble nephew here in virtue's nest,
That died in honour and Lavinia's cause.
Thou art a Roman, be not barbarous.
The Greeks, upon advice, did bury Ajax
That slew himself; and wise Laertes' son
Did graciously plead for his funerals.
Let not young Mutius then, that was thy joy,
Be barr'd his entrance here.
Tit. Rise, Marcus, rise:—
The dismal'st day is this, that e'er I saw,
To be dishonour'd by my sons in Rome!—
Well, bury him, and bury me the next.
[MUTIUS *is put into the Tomb.*
Luc. There lie thy bones, sweet Mutius, with thy friends,
Till we with trophies do adorn thy tomb!—
All. No man shed tears for noble Mutius;
He lives in fame that died in virtue's cause.
Mar. My lord,—to step out of these dreary dumps,—
How comes it, that the subtle queen of Goths
Is of a sudden thus advanc'd in Rome?
Tit. I know not, Marcus; but, I know, it is;
Whether by device, or no, the heavens can tell:
Is she not then beholden to the man
That brought her for this high good turn so far?
Yes, and will nobly him remunerate.

Flourish. Re-enter at one side, SATURNINUS, *attended;* TAMORA, CHIRON, DEMETRIUS, *and* AARON: *at the other,* BASSIANUS, LAVINIA, *and Others.*

Sat. So, Bassianus, you have play'd your prize;
God give you joy, sir, of your gallant bride.

Bas. And you of yours, my lord: I say no more,
Nor wish no less; and so I take my leave.
Sat. Traitor, if Rome have law, or we have power,
Thou and thy faction shall repent this rape.
Bas. Rape, call you it, my lord, to seize my own,
My true betrothed love, and now my wife?
But let the laws of Rome determine all;
Mean while I am possess'd of that is mine.
Sat. 'Tis good, sir: You are very short with us;
But, if we live, we'll be as sharp with you.
Bas. My lord, what I have done, as best I may,
Answer I must, and shall do with my life.
Only thus much I give your grace to know,
By all the duties that I owe to Rome,
This noble gentleman, Lord Titus here,
Is in opinion, and in honour, wrong'd;
That, in the rescue of Lavinia,
With his own hand did slay his youngest son,
In zeal to you, and highly mov'd to wrath
To be control'd in that he frankly gave:
Receive him then to favour, Saturnine;
That hath express'd himself, in all his deeds,
A father, and a friend, to thee, and Rome.
Tit. Prince Bassianus, leave to plead my deeds;
'Tis thou, and those, that have dishonour'd me:
Rome and the righteous heavens be my judge,
How I have lov'd and honour'd Saturnine!
Tam. My worthy lord, if ever Tamora
Were gracious in those princely eyes of thine,
Then hear me speak indifferently for all;
And at my suit, sweet, pardon what is past.
Sat. What! madam! be dishonour'd openly,
And basely put it up without revenge?
Tam. Not so, my lord; the gods of Rome forefend,
I should be author to dishonour you!
But, on mine honour, dare I undertake
For good Lord Titus' innocence in all,
Whose fury not dissembled, speaks his griefs:
Then, at my suit, look graciously on him;
Lose not so noble a friend on vain suppose,
Nor with sour looks afflict his gentle heart.
My lord, be rul'd by me, be won at last,
Dissemble all your griefs and discontents:
You are but newly planted in your throne;
Lest then the people, and patricians too,
Upon a just survey, take Titus' part,
And so supplant us for ingratitude
(Which Rome reputes to be a heinous sin),
Yield at entreats, and then let me alone:
I'll find a day to massacre them all,
And raze their faction, and their family,
The cruel father, and his traitorous sons,
To whom I sued for my dear son's life;
And make them know, what 'tis to let a queen
Kneel in the streets, and beg for grace in vain. *Aside.*
Come, come, sweet emperor,—Come, Andronicus,
Take up this good old man, and cheer the heart
That dies in tempest of thy angry frown.
Sat. Rise, Titus, rise, my empress hath prevail'd.
Tit. I thank your majesty, and her, my lord:
These words, these looks, infuse new life in me.
Tam. Titus, I am incorporate in Rome,
A Roman now adopted happily,
And must advise the emperor for his good.
This day all quarrels die, Andronicus;—
And let it be mine honour, good my lord,
That I have reconcil'd your friends and you.—
For you, Prince Bassianus, I have pass'd
My word and promise to the emperor,
That you will be more mild and tractable.—
And fear not, lords,—and you, Lavinia,
By my advice, all humbled on your knees,
You shall ask pardon of his majesty.
Luc. We do; and vow to heaven, and to his highness,
That, what we did, was mildly, as we might,
Tend'ring our sister's honour, and our own.
Mar. That on mine honour here I do protest.
Sat. Away, and talk not; trouble us no more.—
Tam. Nay, nay, sweet emperor, we must all be friends:
The tribune and his nephews kneel for grace;
I will not be denied. Sweet heart, look back.
Sat. Marcus, for thy sake, and thy brother's here,
And at my lovely Tamora's entreats,
I do remit these young men's heinous faults.
Stand up.
Lavinia, though you left me like a churl,
I found a friend; and sure as death I swore,
I would not part a bachelor from the priest.
Come, if the emperor's court can feast two brides,
You are my guest, Lavinia, and your friends:
This day shall be a love-day, Tamora.
Tit. To-morrow, an it please your majesty,
To hunt the panther and the hart with me,
With horn and hound, we'll give your grace *bon jour*.
Sat. Be it so, Titus, and gramercy too.
[*Exeunt.*

ACT II.

SCENE I. Rome. *Before the Palace.*

Enter AARON.

Aar. Now climbeth Tamora Olympus' top,
Safe out of fortune's shot: and sits aloft,
Secure of thunder's crack, or lightning's flash;
Advanc'd above pale envy's threat'ning reach.
As when the golden sun salutes the morn,
And, having gilt the ocean with his beams,
Gallops the zodiack in his glistering coach,
And overlooks the highest-peering hills;
So Tamora.——
Upon her wit doth earthly honour wait,
And virtue stoops and trembles at her frown.
Then, Aaron, arm thy heart, and fit thy thoughts
To mount aloft with thy imperial mistress,
And mount her pitch; whom thou in triumph long
Hast prisoner held, fetter'd in amorous chains;
And faster bound to Aaron's charming eyes,
Than is Prometheus tied to Caucasus.
Away with slavish weeds, and servile thoughts!
I will be bright, and shine in pearl and gold,
To wait upon this new-made emperess.
To wait, said I? to wanton with this queen,
This goddess, this Semiramis:—this nymph,
This siren, that will charm Rome's Saturnine,
And see his shipwreck, and his commonweal's.
Holloa! what storm is this?

Enter CHIRON *and* DEMETRIUS, *braving.*

Dem. Chiron, thy years want wit, thy wit wants edge,
And manners, to intrude where I am grac'd:
And may, for aught thou know'st, affected be.
Chi. Demetrius, thou dost overween in all:
And so in this to bear me down with braves.
'Tis not the difference of a year, or two,
Makes me less gracious, thee more fortunate:
I am as able, and as fit, as thou,
To serve, and to deserve my mistress' grace;
And that my sword upon thee shall approve,
And plead my passions for Lavinia's love.
Aar. Clubs, clubs! these lovers will not keep the peace.
Dem. Why, boy, although our mother, unadvis'd,
Gave you a dancing-rapier by your side,
Are you so desperate grown, to threat your friends?

Go to; have your lath glued within your sheath,
Till you know better how to handle it.
Chi. Meanwhile, sir, with the little skill I have,
Full well shalt thou perceive how much I dare.
Dem. Ay, boy, grow ye so brave? [*They draw.*
Aar. Why, how now, lords?
So near the emperor's palace dare you draw,
And maintain such a quarrel openly?
Full well I wot the ground of all this grudge;
I would not for a million of gold,
The cause were known to them it most concerns:
Nor would your noble mother, for much more,
Be so dishonour'd in the court of Rome.
For shame, put up.
Dem. Not I: till I have sheath'd
My rapier in his bosom, and, withal,
Thrust these reproachful speeches down his throat,
That he hath breath'd in my dishonour here.
Chi. For that I am prepar'd and full resolv'd,—
Foul spoken coward! that thunder'st with thy tongue,
And with thy weapon nothing dar'st perform.
Aar. Away, I say.—
Now by the gods, that warlike Goths adore,
This petty brabble will undo us all.—
Why, lords,—and think you not how dangerous
It is to jut upon a prince's right?
What, is Lavinia then become so loose,
Or Bassianus so degenerate,
That for her love such quarrels may be broach'd,
Without controlment, justice, or revenge?
Young lords, beware!—an should the empress know
This discord's ground, the musick would not please.
Chi. I care not, I, knew she and all the world;
I love Lavinia more than all the world.
Dem. Youngling, learn thou to make some meaner choice:
Lavinia is thine elder brother's hope.
Aar. Why, are ye mad? or know ye not, in Rome
How furious and impatient they be,
And cannot brook competitors in love?
I tell you, lords, you do but plot your deaths
By this device.
Chi. Aaron, a thousand deaths
Would I propose, to achieve her whom I love.
Aar. To achieve her!—How?
Dem. Why mak'st thou it so strange?
She is a woman, therefore may be woo'd;
She is a woman, therefore may be won;
She is Lavinia, therefore must be lov'd.
What, man! more water glideth by the mill
Than wots the miller of; and easy it is
Of a cut loaf to steal a shive, we know:
Though Bassianus be the emperor's brother,
Better than he have yet worn Vulcan's badge.
Aar. Ay, and as good as Saturninus may. [*Aside.*
Dem. Then why should he despair, that knows to court it
With words, fair looks, and liberality?
What, hast thou not full often struck a doe,
And borne her cleanly by the keeper's nose?
Aar. Why then, it seems, some certain snatch, or so,
Would serve your turns.
Chi. Ay, so the turn were serv'd.
Dem. Aaron, thou hast hit it.
Aar. 'Would you had hit it too;
Then should not we be tir'd with this ado.
Why, hark ye, hark ye,—And are you such fools,
To square for this? Would it offend you then
That both should speed?
Chi. I' faith, not me.
Dem. Nor me,
So I were one.
Aar. For shame, be friends; and join for that you jar.
'Tis policy and stratagem must do
That you affect; and so must you resolve;
That what you cannot, as you would, achieve,
You must perforce accomplish as you may.
Take this of me, Lucrece was not more chaste
Than this Lavinia, Bassianus' love.
A speedier course than lingering languishment
Must we pursue, and I have found the path.
My lords, a solemn hunting is in hand;
There will the lovely Roman ladies troop:
The forest walks are wide and spacious;
And many unfrequented plots there are,
Fitted by kind for rape and villany:
Single you thither then this dainty doe,
And strike her home by force, if not by words:
This way, or not at all, stand you in hope.
Come, come, our empress, with her sacred wit,
To villany and vengeance consecrate,
Will we acquaint with all that we intend;
And she shall file our engines with advice,
That will not suffer you to square yourselves,
But to your wishes' height advance you both.
The emperor's court is like the house of fame,
The palace full of tongues, of eyes, of ears:
The woods are ruthless, dreadful, deaf, and dull;
There speak, and strike, brave boys, and take your turns:
There serve your lust, shadow'd from heaven's eye,
And revel in Lavinia's treasury.
Chi. Thy counsel, lad, smells of no cowardice.
Dem. *Sit fas aut nefas*, till I find the stream
To cool this heat, a charm to calm these fits,
Per Styga, per manes vehor. [*Exeunt.*

SCENE II.

A Forest near Rome. *A Lodge seen at a distance. Horns, and cry of Hounds heard.*

Enter TITUS ANDRONICUS, *with* Hunters, *&c.* MARCUS, LUCIUS, QUINTUS, *and* MARTIUS.

Tit. The hunt is up, the morn is bright and gray,
The fields are fragrant, and the woods are green:
Uncouple here, and let us make a bay,
And wake the emperor and his lovely bride,
And rouse the prince; and ring a hunter's peal,
That all the court may echo with the noise.
Sons, let it be your charge, as it is ours,
To tend the emperor's person carefully:
I have been troubled in my sleep this night,
But dawning day new comfort hath inspir'd.

Horns wind a Peal. Enter SATURNINUS, TAMORA, BASSIANUS, LAVINIA, CHIRON, DEMETRIUS, *and* Attendants.

Tit. Many good morrows to your majesty;—
Madam, to you as many and as good!—
I promised your grace a hunter's peal.
Sat. And you have rung it lustily, my lords,
Somewhat too early for new married ladies.
Bas. Lavinia, how say you?
Lav. I say, no;
I have been broad awake two hours and more.
Sat. Come on then, horse and chariots let us have,
And to our sport:—Madam, now shall ye see
Our Roman hunting. [*To* TAMORA.
Mar. I have dogs, my lord,
Will rouse the proudest panther in the chase,
And climb the highest promontory top.
Tit. And I have horse will follow where the game
Makes way, and run like swallows o'er the plain.
Dem. Chiron, we hunt not, we, with horse nor hound,
But hope to pluck a dainty doe to ground. [*Exeunt.*

SCENE III. *A desert Part of the Forest.*

Enter AARON, *with a Bag of Gold.*

Aar. He, that had wit, would think that I had none,
To bury so much gold under a tree,
And never after to inherit it.

Let him, that thinks of me so abjectly,
Know, that this gold must coin a stratagem;
Which, cunningly effected, will beget
A very excellent piece of villany;
And so repose, sweet gold, for their unrest, [*Hides the Gold.*
That have their alms out of the empress' chest.

Enter TAMORA.

Tam. My lovely Aaron, wherefore look'st thou sad,
When every thing doth make a gleeful boast?
The birds chant melody on every bush;
The snake lies rolled in the cheerful sun;
The green leaves quiver with the cooling wind,
And make a chequer'd shadow on the ground:
Under their sweet shade, Aaron, let us sit,
And—whilst the babbling echo mocks the hounds,
Replying shrilly to the well tun'd horns,
As if a double hunt were heard at once,—
Let us sit down, and mark their yelling noise:
And—after conflict, such as was suppos'd
The wandering prince and Dido once enjoy'd,
When with a happy storm they were surpris'd,
And curtain'd with a counsel-keeping cave,—
We may, each wreathed in the other's arms,
Our pastimes done, possess a golden slumber;
While hounds, and horns, and sweet melodious birds,
Be unto us, as is a nurse's song
Of lullaby, to bring her babe asleep.

Aar. Madam, though Venus govern your desires,
Saturn is dominator over mine:
What signifies my deadly standing eye,
My silence, and my cloudy melancholy?
My fleece of woolly hair that now uncurls,
Even as an adder, when she doth unroll
To do some fatal execution?
No, madam, these are no venereal signs;
Vengeance is in my heart, death in my hand,
Blood and revenge are hammering in my head.
Hark, Tamora,—the empress of my soul,
Which never hopes more heaven than rest in thee,
This is the day of doom for Bassianus;
His Philomel must lose her tongue to-day:
Thy sons make pillage of her chastity,
And wash their hands in Bassianus' blood.
Seest thou this letter? take it up, I pray thee,
And give the king this fatal-plotted scroll:—
Now question me no more, we are espied;
Here comes a parcel of our hopeful booty,
Which dreads not yet their lives' destruction.

Tam. Ah, my sweet Moor, sweeter to me than life!

Aar. No more, great empress, Bassianus comes:
Be cross with him; and I'll go fetch thy sons
To back thy quarrels, whatsoe'er they be. [*Exit.*

Enter BASSIANUS *and* LAVINIA.

Bas. Who have we here? Rome's royal empress,
Unfurnish'd of her well beseeming troop?
Or is it Dian, habited like her;
Who hath abandoned her holy groves,
To see the general hunting in this forest?

Tam. Saucy controller of our private steps!
Had I the power, that, some say, Dian had,
Thy temples should be planted presently
With horns, as was Actæon's; and the hounds
Should drive upon thy new transformed limbs,
Unmannerly intruder as thou art!

Lav. Under your patience, gentle empress,
'Tis thought you have a goodly gift in horning;
And to be doubted, that your Moor and you
Are singled forth to try experiments:
Jove shield your husband from his hounds to-day!
'Tis pity, they should take him for a stag.

Bas. Believe me, queen, your swarth Cimmerian
Doth make your honour of his body's hue,
Spotted, detested, and abominable.
Why are you sequester'd from all your train?
Dismounted from your snow-white goodly steed,
And wander'd hither to an obscure plot,
Accompanied with a barbarous Moor,
If foul desire had not conducted you?

Lav. And, being intercepted in your sport,
Great reason that my noble lord be rated
For sauciness.—I pray you, let us hence,
And let her 'joy her raven-colour'd love;
This valley fits the purpose passing well.

Bas. The king, my brother, shall have note of this.

Lav. Ay, for these slips have made him noted long:
Good king! to be so mightily abus'd!

Tam. Why have I patience to endure all this?

Enter CHIRON *and* DEMETRIUS.

Dem. How now, dear sovereign, and our gracious mother,
Why doth your highness look so pale and wan?

Tam. Have I not reason, think you, to look pale?
These two have tic'd me hither to this place,
A barren detested vale, you see, it is:
The trees, though summer, yet forlorn and lean,
O'ercome with moss, and baleful misletoe.
Here never shines the sun, here nothing breeds,
Unless the nightly owl, or fatal raven.
And, when they show'd me this abhorred pit,
They told me, here, at dead time of the night,
A thousand fiends, a thousand hissing snakes,
Ten thousand swelling toads, as many urchins,
Would make such fearful and confused cries,
As any mortal body, hearing it,
Should straight fall mad, or else die suddenly.
No sooner had they told this hellish tale,
But straight they told me, they would bind me here
Unto the body of a dismal yew;
And leave me to this miserable death.
And then they call'd me, foul adulteress,
Lascivious Goth, and all the bitterest terms
That ever ear did hear to such effect.
And, had you not by wondrous fortune come,
This vengeance on me had they executed:
Revenge it, as you love your mother's life,
Or be ye not henceforth call'd my children.

Dem. This is a witness that I am thy son. [*Stabs* BASSIANUS.

Chi. And this for me, struck home to show my strength. [*Stabbing him likewise.*

Lav. Ay, come, Semiramis,—nay, barbarous Tamora!
For no name fits thy nature but thy own!

Tam. Give me thy poniard; you shall know, my boys,
Your mother's hand shall right your mother's wrong.

Dem. Stay, madam, here is more belongs to her;
First, thrash the corn, then after burn the straw:
This minion stood upon her chastity,
Upon her nuptial vow, her loyalty,
And with that painted hope braves your mightiness:
And shall she carry this unto her grave?

Chi. An if she do, I would I were a eunuch.
Drag hence her husband to some secret hole,
And make his dead trunk pillow to our lust.

Tam. But when you have the honey you desire,
Let not this wasp outlive, us both to sting.

Chi. I warrant you, madam; we will make that sure.—
Come, mistress, now, perforce, we will enjoy
That nice-preserved honesty of yours.

Lav. O Tamora! thou bear'st a woman's face,—

Tam. I will not hear her speak; away with her.
Lav. Sweet Lords, entreat her hear me but a word.
Dem. Listen, fair madam: Let it be your glory
To see her tears: but be your heart to them,
As unrelenting flint to drops of rain.
Lav. When did the tiger's young ones teach the dam?
O, do not learn her wrath; she taught it thee:
The milk, thou suck'dst from her, did turn to marble;
Even at thy teat thou hadst thy tyranny.—
Yet every mother breeds not sons alike;
Do thou entreat her show a woman pity. [*To* CHIRON.
Chi. What! would'st thou have me prove myself a bastard?
Lav. 'Tis true: the raven doth not hatch a lark;
Yet I have heard (O could I find it now!)
The lion mov'd with pity, did endure
To have his princely paws par'd all away.
Some say that ravens foster forlorn children,
The whilst their own birds famish in their nests;
O, be to me, though thy hard heart say no,
Nothing so kind, but something pitiful!
Tam. I know not what it means; away with [her.
Lav. O, let me teach thee: for my father's sake,
That gave thee life, when well he might have slain thee,
Be not obdurate, open thy deaf ears.
Tam. Had thou in person ne'er offended me,
Even for his sake am I pitiless:—
Remember, boys, I pour'd forth tears in vain,
To save your brother from the sacrifice;
But fierce Andronicus would not relent.
Therefore away with her, and use her as you will;
The worse to her, the better lov'd of me.
Lav. O Tamora, be call'd a gentle queen,
And with thine own hands kill me in this place:
For 'tis not life, that I have begg'd so long;
Poor I was slain, when Bassianus died.
Tam. What begg'st thou then? fond woman, let me go.
Lav. 'Tis present death I beg; and one thing more,
That womanhood denies my tongue to tell:
O, keep me from their worse than killing lust,
And tumble me into some loathsome pit;
Where never man's eye may behold my body:
Do this, and be a charitable murderer.
Tam. So should I rob my sweet sons of their fee:
No, let them satisfy their lust on thee.
Dem. Away, for thou hast staid us here too long.
Lav. No grace? no womanhood? Ah, beastly creature!
The blot and enemy to our general name!
Confusion fall——
Chi. Nay, then I'll stop your mouth:—Bring thou her husband: [*Dragging off* LAVINIA.
This is the hole where Aaron bid us hide him. [*Exeunt.*
Tam. Farewell, my sons; see that you make her sure:
Ne'er let my heart know merry cheer indeed,
Till all the Andronici be made away.
Now will I hence, to seek my lovely Moor,
And let my spleenful sons this trull deflower. [*Exit.*

SCENE IV. *The same.*

Enter AARON, *with* QUINTUS *and* MARTIUS.

Aar. Come on, my lords; the better foot before:
Straight will I bring you to the loathsome pit,
Where I espy'd the panther fast asleep.
Quin. My sight is very dull, whate'er it bodes.
Mart. And mine, I promise you; wer't not for shame,
Well could I leave our sport to sleep awhile. [MARTIUS *falls into the Pit.*
Quin. What, art thou fallen? What subtle hole is this,
Whose mouth is cover'd with rude-growing [briars;
Upon whose leaves are drops of new-shed blood,
As fresh as morning's dew distill'd on flowers?
A very fatal place it seems to me:—
Speak, brother hast thou hurt thee with the fall?
Mart. O, brother, with the dismall'st object
That ever eye, with sight, made heart lament.
Aar. [*Aside.*] Now will I fetch the king to find them here:
That he thereby may give a likely guess,
How these were they that made away his brother. [*Exit* AARON.
Mart. Why dost not comfort me, and help me out
From this unhallow'd and blood-stain'd hole?
Quin. I am surprised with an uncouth fear:
A chilling sweat o'erruns my trembling joints;
My heart suspects more than mine eye can see.
Mart. To prove thou hast a true divining heart,
Aaron and thou look down into this den,
And see a fearful sight of blood and death.
Quin. Aaron is gone; and my compassionate heart
Will not permit mine eyes once to behold
The thing, whereat it trembles by surmise:
O, tell me how it is; for ne'er till now
Was I a child, to fear I know not what.
Mart. Lord Bassianus lies embrewed here,
All on a heap like to a slaughter'd lamb,
In this detested, dark, blood-drinking pit.
Quin. If it be dark, how dost thou know 'tis he?
Mart. Upon his bloody finger he doth wear
A precious ring, that lightens all the hole,
Which, like a taper in some monument,
Doth shine upon the dead man's earthy cheeks,
And shows the ragged entrails of this pit:
So pale did shine the moon on Pyramus,
When he by night lay bath'd in maiden blood.
O brother, help me with thy fainting hand,—
If fear hath made thee faint, as me it hath,—
Out of this fell devouring receptacle,
As hateful as Cocytus' misty mouth.
Quin. Reach me thy hand, that I may help thee out;
Or, wanting strength to do thee so much good,
I may be pluck'd into the swallowing womb
Of this deep pit, poor Bassianus' grave.
I have no strength to pluck thee to the brink.
Mart. Nor I no strength to climb without thy help.
Quin. Thy hand once more; I will not loose [again,
Till thou art here aloft, or I below:
Thou canst not come to me, I come to thee. [*Falls in.*

Enter SATURNINUS *and* AARON.

Sat. Along with me:—I'll see what hole is here,
And what he is, that now is leap'd into it.
Say, who art thou, that lately didst descend
Into this gaping hollow of the earth?
Mart. The unhappy son of old Andronicus;
Brought hither in a most unlucky hour,
To find thy brother Bassianus dead.
Sat. My brother dead? I know, thou dost but [jest:
He and his lady both are at the lodge,
Upon the north side of this pleasant chase;
'Tis not an hour since I left him there.
Mart. We know not where you left him all alive,
But, out alas! here have we found him dead.

Enter TAMORA, *with* Attendants; TITUS ANDRONICUS, *and* LUCIUS.

Tam. Where is my lord, the king?
Sat. Here, Tamora; though griev'd with killing grief.
Tam. Where is thy brother Bassianus?
Sat. Now to the bottom dost thou search my wound;
Poor Bassianus here lies murdered.

Tam. Then all too late I bring this fatal writ.
[*Giving a Letter.*
The complot of this timeless tragedy:
And wonder greatly, that man's face can fold
In pleasing smiles such murderous tyranny.

Sat. [Reads.] *An if we miss to meet him handsomely,—*
Sweet huntsman, Bassianus 'tis we mean,—
Do thou so much as dig the grave for him;
Thou know'st our meaning: Look for thy reward
Among the nettles at the elder tree,
Which overshades the mouth of that same pit,
Where we decreed to bury Bassianus.
Do this, and purchase us thy lasting friends.
O, Tamora; was ever heard the like?
This is the pit, and this the elder tree:
Look, sirs, if you can find the huntsman out,
That should have murder'd Bassianus here.

Aar. My gracious lord, here is the bag of gold.
[*Showing it.*

Sat. Two of thy whelps, [*To* TIT.] fell curs of bloody kind,
Have here bereft my brother of his life:—
Sirs, drag them from the pit unto the prison;
There let them bide, until we have devis'd
Some never-heard-of torturing pain for them.

Tam. What, are they in this pit? O wondrous thing!
How easily murder is discovered!

Tit. High emperor, upon my feeble knee
I beg this boon, with tears not lightly shed,
That this fell fault of my accursed sons,
Accursed, if the fault be prov'd in them,——

Sat. If it be prov'd! you see, it is apparent.—
Who found this letter? Tamora, was it you?

Tam. Andronicus himself did take it up.

Tit. I did, my lord: yet let me be their bail:
For by my father's reverend tomb, I vow,
They shall be ready at your highness' will,
To answer their suspicion with their lives.

Sat. Thou shalt not bail them: see, thou follow me.
Some bring the murder'd body, some the murderers:
Let them not speak a word, the guilt is plain;
For, by my soul, were there worse end than death,
That end upon them should be executed.

Tam. Andronicus, I will entreat the king;
Fear not thy sons, they shall do well enough.

Tit. Come, Lucius, come: stay not to talk with them. [*Exeunt severally.*

SCENE V. *The same.*

Enter DEMETRIUS *and* CHIRON, *with* LAVINIA, *ravished; her Hands cut off, and her Tongue cut out.*

Dem. So, now go tell, an if thy tongue can speak,
Who 'twas that cut thy tongue, and ravish'd thee.

Chi. Write down thy mind, bewray thy meaning so;
And, if thy stumps will let thee, play the scribe.

Dem. See, how with signs and tokens she can scowl.

Chi. Go home, call for sweet water, wash thy hands.

Dem. She hath no tongue to call, nor hands to wash:
And so let's leave her to her silent walks.

Chi. An 'twere my case, I should go hang myself.

Dem. If thou hadst hands to help thee knit the cord. [*Exeunt* DEM. *and* CHI.

Enter MARCUS.

Mar. Who's this,—my niece, that flies away so fast?
Cousin, a word; Where is your husband?—
If I do dream, would all my wealth would wake me!
If I do wake, some planet strike me down,
That I may slumber in eternal sleep!—
Speak, gentle niece, what stern ungentle hands
Have lopp'd, and hew'd, and made thy body bare
Of her two branches? those sweet ornaments,
Whose circling shadows kings have sought to sleep in;
And might not gain so great a happiness,
As half thy love? Why dost not speak to me?—
Alas, a crimson river of warm blood,
Like to a bubbling fountain stirr'd with wind,
Doth rise and fall between thy rosed lips,
Coming and going with thy honey breath.
But, sure, some Tereus hath deflour'd thee;
And, lest thou should'st detect him, cut thy tongue.
Ah, now thou turn'st away thy face for shame!
And, notwithstanding all this loss of blood,—
As from a conduit with three issuing spouts,—
Yet do thy cheeks look red as Titan's face,
Blushing to be encounter'd with a cloud.
Shall I speak for thee? shall I say, 'tis so?
O, that I knew thy heart; and knew the beast
That I might rail at him to ease my mind!
Sorrow concealed, like an oven stopp'd,
Doth burn the heart to cinders where it is.
Fair Philomela, she but lost her tongue,
And in a tedious sampler sew'd her mind;
But, lovely niece, that mean is cut from thee;
A craftier Tereus, cousin, hast thou met,
And he hath cut those pretty fingers off,
That could have better sew'd than Philomel.
O, had the monster seen those lily hands
Tremble, like aspen leaves, upon a lute,
And make the silken strings delight to kiss them;
He would not then have touch'd them for his life:
Or, had he heard the heavenly harmony,
Which that sweet tongue hath made,
He would have dropp'd his knife, and fell asleep,
As Cerberus at the Thracian poet's feet.
Come, let us go, and make thy father blind:
For such a sight will blind a father's eye:
One hour's storm will drown the fragrant meads;
What will whole months of tears thy father's eyes?
Do not draw back, for we will mourn with thee;
O, could our mourning ease thy misery?
[*Exeunt.*

ACT III.

SCENE I. Rome. *A Street.*

Enter Senators, Tribunes, *and* Officers *of* Justice, *with* MARTIUS *and* QUINTUS, *bound, passing on to the Place of Execution:* TITUS *going before, pleading.*

Tit. Hear me, grave fathers! noble tribunes, stay!
For pity of mine age, whose youth was spent
In dangerous wars, whilst you securely slept;
For all my blood in Rome's great quarrel shed;
For all the frosty nights that I have watch'd;
And for these bitter tears, which now you see
Filling the aged wrinkles in my cheeks;
Be pitiful to my condemned sons,
Whose souls are not corrupted as 'tis thought!
For two and twenty sons I never wept,
Because they died in honour's lofty bed.
For these, good tribunes, in the dust I write
[*Throwing himself on the Ground.*
My heart's deep languor, and my soul's sad tears.
Let my tears stanch the earth's dry appetite;
My sons' sweet blood will make it shame and blush. [*Exeunt* Senators, Tribunes, *&c. with the* Prisoners.
O earth, I will befriend thee more with rain,
That shall distil from these two ancient urns,
Than youthful April shall with all his showers:
In summer's drought, I'll drop upon thee still;
In winter, with warm tears I'll melt the snow,
And keep eternal spring-time on thy face,
So thou refuse to drink my dear sons' blood.

Enter LUCIUS, *with his Sword drawn.*

O, reverend tribunes! gentle aged men!
Unbind my sons, reverse the doom of death;
And let me say, that never wept before,
My tears are now prevailing orators.

Luc. O, noble father, you lament in vain;
The tribunes hear you not, no man is by,
And you recount your sorrows to a stone.

Tit. Ah, Lucius, for thy brothers let me plead;
Grave tribunes, once more I entreat of you.

Luc. My gracious lord, no tribune hears you speak.

Tit. Why, 'tis no matter, man: if they did hear,
They would not mark me; or if they did mark,
They would not pity me; yet plead I must,
All bootless unto them.
Therefore I tell my sorrows to the stones;
Who, though they cannot answer my distress,
Yet in some sort they're better than the tribunes,
For that they will not intercept my tale;
When I do weep, they humbly at my feet
Receive my tears, and seem to weep with me;
And, were they but attired in grave weeds,
Rome could afford no tribune like to these.
A stone is soft as wax, tribunes more hard than stones:
A stone is silent, and offendeth not;
And tribunes with their tongues doom men to death.
But wherefore stand'st thou with thy weapon drawn?

Luc. To rescue my two brothers from their death:
For which attempt, the judges have pronounc'd
My everlasting doom of banishment.

Tit. O happy man! they have befriended thee.
Why, foolish Lucius, dost thou not perceive,
That Rome is but a wilderness of tigers?
Tigers must prey; and Rome affords no prey,
But me and mine: How happy art thou then,
From these devourers to be banished?
But who comes with our brother Marcus here?

Enter MARCUS *and* LAVINIA.

Mar. Titus, prepare thy aged eyes to weep;
Or, if not so, thy noble heart to break;
I bring consuming sorrow to thine age.

Tit. Will it consume me? let me see it then.

Mar. This was thy daughter.

Tit. Why, Marcus, so she is.

Luc. Ah me! this object kills me!

Tit. Faint-hearted boy, arise, and look upon her:—
Speak, my Lavinia, what accursed hand
Hath made thee handless in thy father's sight?
What fool hath added water to the sea?
Or brought a faggot to bright burning Troy?
My grief was at the height before thou cam'st,
And now, like Nilus, it disdaineth bounds.—
Give me a sword, I'll chop off my hands too;
For they have fought for Rome, and all in vain;
And they have nurs'd this woe, in feeding life;
In bootless prayer have they been held up,
And they have serv'd me to effectless use;
Now, all the service I require of them
Is, that the one will help to cut the other.—
'Tis well, Lavinia, that thou hast no hands;
For hands, to do Rome service, are but vain.

Luc. Speak, gentle sister, who hath martyr'd thee?

Mar. O, that delightful engine of her thoughts,
That blabb'd them with such pleasing eloquence,
Is torn from forth that pretty hollow cage;
Where like a sweet melodious bird, it sung
Sweet varied notes, enchanting every ear!

Luc. O, say thou for her, who hath done this deed?

Mar. O, thus I found her, straying in the park,
Seeking to hide herself, as doth the deer,
That hath receiv'd some unrecuring wound.

Tit. It was my deer: and he, that wounded her,
Hath hurt me more, than had he kill'd me dead:
For now I stand as one upon a rock,
Environ'd with a wilderness of sea;
Who marks the waxing tide grow wave by wave,
Expecting ever when some envious surge
Will in his brinish bowels swallow him.
This way to death my wretched sons are gone;
Here stands my other son, a banish'd man;
And here, my brother, weeping at my woes;
But that, which gives my soul the greatest spurn,
Is dear Lavinia, dearer than my soul.—
Had I but seen thy picture in this plight,
It would have madded me: What shall I do
Now I behold thy lively body so?
Thou hast no hands, to wipe away thy tears;
Nor tongue, to tell me who hath martyr'd thee:
Thy husband he is dead: and, for his death,
Thy brothers are condemn'd, and dead by this:—
Look, Marcus! ah, son Lucius, look on her:
When I did name her brothers, then fresh tears
Stood on her cheeks; as doth the honey dew
Upon a gather'd lily almost wither'd.

Mar. Perchance, she weeps because they kill'd her husband:
Perchance, because she knows them innocent.

Tit. If they did kill thy husband, then be joyful
Because the law hath ta'en revenge on them.—
No, no, they would not do so foul a deed;
Witness the sorrow that their sister makes.—
Gentle Lavinia, let me kiss thy lips;
Or make some sign how I may do thee ease:
Shall thy good uncle, and thy brother Lucius,
And thou, and I, sit round about some fountain;
Looking all downwards, to behold our cheeks
How they are stain'd? like meadows, yet not dry
With miry slime left on them by a flood?
And in the fountain shall we gaze so long,
Till the fresh taste be taken from that clearness,
And made a brine pit with our bitter tears?
Or shall we cut away our hands, like thine?
Or shall we bite our tongues, and in dumb shows
Pass the remainder of our hateful days?
What shall we do? let us, that have our tongues,
Plot some device of further misery,
To make us wonder'd at in time to come.

Luc. Sweet father, cease your tears; for, at your grief,
See, how my wretched sister sobs and weeps.

Mar. Patience, dear niece:—good Titus, dry thine eyes.

Tit. Ah, Marcus, Marcus! brother, well I wot,
Thy napkin cannot drink a tear of mine,
For thou, poor man, hast drown'd it with thine own.

Luc. Ah, my Lavinia, I will wipe thy cheeks.

Tit. Mark, Marcus, mark! I understand her signs:
Had she a tongue to speak, now would she say
That to her brother, which I said to thee;
His napkin with his true tears all bewet,
Can do no service on her sorrowful cheeks,
O, what a sympathy of woe is this!
As far from help as limbo is from bliss!

Enter AARON.

Aar. Titus Andronicus, my lord the emperor
Sends thee this word.—That, if thou love thy sons,
Let Marcus, Lucius, or thyself, old Titus,
Or any one of you, chop off your hand,
And send it to the king: he, for the same,
Will send thee hither both thy sons alive;
And that shall be the ransome for their fault.

Tit. O, gracious emperor! O, gentle Aaron!
Did ever raven sing so like a lark,
That gives sweet tidings of the sun's uprise?
With all my heart, I'll send the emperor
My hand:
Good Aaron, wilt thou help to chop it off?

Luc. Stay, father; for that noble hand of thine,
That hath thrown down so many enemies,
Shall not be sent: my hand will serve the turn:

My youth can better spare my blood than you:
And therefore mine shall save my brothers' lives.
Mar. Which of your hands hath not defended Rome,
And rear'd aloft the bloody battleaxe,
Writing destruction on the enemy's castle?
O, none of both but are of high desert:
My hand hath been but idle; let it serve
To ransome my two nephews from their death;
Then have I kept it to a worthy end.
Aar. Nay, come agree, whose hand shall go along,
For fear they die before their pardon come.
Mar. My hand shall go.
Luc. By heaven, it shall not go.
Tit. Sirs, strive no more; such wither'd herbs as these
Are meet for plucking up, and therefore mine.
Luc. Sweet father, if I shall be thought thy son,
Let me redeem my brothers both from death.
Mar. And, for our father's sake, and mother's care,
Now let me show a brother's love to thee.
Tit. Agree between you; I will spare my hand.
Luc. Then I'll go fetch an axe.
Mar. But I will use the axe.
[*Exeunt* LUCIUS *and* MARCUS.
Tit. Come, hither, Aaron; I'll deceive them both;
Lend me thy hand, and I will give thee mine.
Aar. If that be call'd deceit, I will be honest,
And never, whilst I live, deceive men so:—
But I'll deceive you in another sort,
And that you'll say, ere half an hour can pass.
[*Aside. He cuts off* TITUS'S *Hand.*

Enter LUCIUS *and* MARCUS.

Tit. Now, stay your strife: what shall be, is despatch'd.—
Good Aaron, give his majesty my hand:
Tell him it was a hand that warded him
From thousand dangers; bid him bury it;
More hath it merited, that let it have.
As for my sons, say, I account of them
As jewels purchas'd at an easy price;
And yet dear too, because I bought mine own.
Aar. I go, Andronicus: and for thy hand,
Look by and by to have thy sons with thee:—
Their heads, I mean.—O, how this villany [*Aside.*
Doth fat me with the very thoughts of it!
Let fools do good, and fair men call for grace,
Aaron will have his soul black like his face.
[*Exit.*
Tit. O, here I lift this one hand up to heaven,
And bow this feeble ruin to the earth:
If any power pities wretched tears,
To that I call:—What, wilt thou kneel with me?
[*To* LAVINIA.
Do then, dear heart; for heaven shall hear our prayers;
Or with our sighs we'll breathe the welkin dim,
And stain the sun with fog, as sometime clouds,
When they do hug him in their melting bosoms.
Mar. O! brother, speak with possibilities,
And do not break into these deep extremes.
Tit. Is not my sorrow deep, having no bottom?
Then be my passions bottomless with them.
Mar. But yet let reason govern thy lament.
Tit. If there were reason for these miseries,
Then into limits could I bind my woes:
When heaven doth weep, doth not the earth o'erflow?
If the winds rage, doth not the sea wax mad,
Threat'ning the welkin with his big-swoln face?
And wilt thou have a reason for this coil?
I am the sea; hark, how her sighs do blow:
She is the weeping welkin, I the earth:
Then must my sea be moved with her sighs;
Then must my earth with her continual tears
Become a deluge, overflow'd and drown'd:
For why? my bowels cannot hide her woes,
But like a drunkard must I vomit them.
Then give me leave; for losers will have leave
To ease their stomachs with their bitter tongues.

Enter a Messenger, *with Two Heads and a Hand.*

Mess. Worthy Andronicus, ill art thou repaid
For that good hand thou sent'st the emperor.
Here are the heads of thy two noble sons;
And here's thy hand, in scorn to thee sent back;
Thy griefs their sports, thy resolution mock'd:
That woe is me to think upon thy woes,
More than remembrance of my father's death.
[*Exit.*
Mar. Now let hot Ætna cool in Sicily,
And be my heart an ever burning hell!
These miseries are more than may be borne!
To weep with them that weep doth ease some deal,
But sorrow flouted at is double death.
Luc. Ah, that this sight should make so deep a wound,
And yet detested life not shrink thereat!
That ever death should let life bear his name,
Where life hath no more interest but to breathe?
[LAVINIA *kisses him.*
Mar. Alas, poor heart, that kiss is comfortless,
As frozen water to a starved snake.
Tit. When will this fearful slumber have an end?
Mar. Now, farewell, flattery: Die, Andronicus;
Thou dost not slumber: see, thy two sons' heads;
Thy warlike hand: thy mangled daughter here;
Thy other banish'd son, with this dear sight
Struck pale and bloodless; and thy brother, I,
Even like a stony image, cold and numb.
Ah! now no more will I control thy griefs:
Rent off thy silver hair, thy other hand
Gnawing with thy teeth; and be this dismal sight
The closing up of our most wretched eyes!
Now is a time to storm; why art thou still?
Tit. Ha, ha, ha!
Mar. Why dost thou laugh? it fits not with this hour.
Tit. Why, I have not another tear to shed:
Besides this sorrow is an enemy,
And would usurp upon my watry eyes,
And make them blind with tributary tears;
Then which way shall I find revenge's cave?
For these two heads do seem to speak to me;
And threat me, I shall never come to bliss,
Till all these mischiefs be return'd again,
Even in their throats that have committed them.
Come, let me see what task I have to do.—
You heavy people, circle me about;
That I may turn me to each one of you,
And swear unto my soul to right your wrongs.
The vow is made.—Come, brother, take a head;
And in this hand the other will I bear:
Lavinia, thou shalt be employed in these things;
Bear thou my hand, sweet wench, between thy teeth.
As for thee, boy, go, get thee from my sight;
Thou art an exile, and thou must not stay:
Hie to the Goths, and raise an army there:
And, if you love me, as I think you do,
Let's kiss and part, for we have much to do.
[*Exeunt* TITUS, MARCUS, *and* LAVINIA.
Luc. Farewell, Andronicus, my noble father;
The woful'st man that ever liv'd in Rome!
Farewell, proud Rome! till Lucius come again,
He leaves his pledges dearer than his life.
Farewell, Lavinia, my noble sister!
O, 'would, thou wert as thou 'tofore hast been!
But now nor Lucius, nor Lavinia lives,
But in oblivion, and hateful griefs,
If Lucius live, he will requite your wrongs;
And make proud Saturninus and his empress
Beg at the gates, like Tarquin and his queen.
Now will I to the Goths, and raise a power,
To be reveng'd on Rome and Saturnine. [*Exit.*

SCENE II.

A Room in Titus's *House. A Banquet set out.*

Enter TITUS, MARCUS, LAVINIA, *and young* LUCIUS, *a Boy.*

Tit. So, so; now sit: and look, you eat no more
Than will preserve just so much strength in us
As will revenge these bitter woes of ours.
Marcus, unknit that sorrow-wreathen knot;
Thy niece and I, poor creatures, want our hands
And cannot passionate our tenfold grief
With folded arms. This poor right hand of mine
Is left to tyrannize upon my breast;
And when my heart, all mad with misery,
Beats in this hollow prison of my flesh,
Then thus I thump it down.—
Thou map of woe, that thus dost talk in signs!
[*To* LAVINIA.
When thy poor heart beats with outrageous beating,
Thou canst not strike it thus to make it still.
Wound it with sighing, girl; kill it with groans;
Or get some little knife between thy teeth,
And just against thy heart make thou a hole;
That all the tears that thy poor eyes let fall,
May run into that sink, and, soaking in,
Drown the lamenting fool in sea-salt tears.

Mar. Fye, brother, fye! teach her not thus to lay
Such violent hands upon her tender life.

Tit. How now! has sorrow made thee dote already?
Why, Marcus, no man should be mad but I.
What violent hands can she lay on her life?
Ah, wherefore dost thou urge the name of hands;—
To bid Æneas tell the tale twice o'er,
How Troy was burnt, and he made miserable?
O, handle not the theme to talk of hands;
Lest we remember still, that we have none.—
Fye, fye, how franticly I square my talk!
As if we should forget we had no hands,
If Marcus did not name the word of hands!—
Come, let's fall to: and, gentle girl, eat this:—
Here is no drink! Hark, Marcus, what she says;—
I can interpret all her martyr'd signs,—
She says, she drinks no other drink but tears,
Brew'd with her sorrows, mesh'd upon her cheeks:—
Speechless complainer, I will learn thy thought;
In thy dumb action will I be as perfect
As begging hermits in their holy prayers:
Thou shalt not sigh, nor hold thy stumps to heaven,
Nor wink, nor nod, nor kneel, nor make a sign,
But I, of these, will wrest an alphabet,
And, by still practice, learn to know thy meaning.

Boy. Good grandsire, leave these bitter deep laments:
Make my aunt merry with some pleasing tale.

Mar. Alas, the tender boy, in passion mov'd,
Doth weep to see his grandsire's heaviness.

Tit. Peace, tender sapling: thou art made of tears,
And tears will quickly melt thy life away.—
[MARCUS *strikes the Dish with a knife.*
What dost thou strike at, Marcus, with thy knife?

Mar. At that that I have kill'd, my lord; a fly.

Tit. Out on thee, murderer! thou kill'st my heart;
Mine eyes are cloy'd with view of tyranny:
A deed of death, done on the innocent,
Becomes not Titus' brother: Get thee gone;
I see, thou art not for my company.

Mar. Alas, my lord, I have but kill'd a fly.

Tit. But how, if that fly had a father and mother?
How would he hang his slender gilded wings,
And buz lamenting doings in the air?
Poor harmless fly!
That, with his pretty buzzing melody,
Came here to make us merry; and thou hast kill'd him.

Mar. Pardon me, sir; 'twas a black ill favour'd fly,
Like to the empress' Moor; therefore I kill'd him.

Tit. O, O, O,
Then pardon me for reprehending thee,
For thou hast done a charitable deed.
Give me thy knife, I will insult on him;
Flattering myself, as if it were the Moor,
Come hither purposely to poison me.—
There's for thyself, and that's for Tamora.—
Ah, sirrah!—
Yet I do think we are not brought so low,
But that, between us, we can kill a fly,
That comes in likeness of a coal-black Moor.

Mar. Alas, poor man! grief has so wrought on him,
He takes false shadows for true substances.

Tit. Come, take away.—Lavinia, go with me:
I'll to thy closet; and go read with thee
Sad stories, chanced in the times of old.—
Come, boy, and go with me; thy sight is young,
And thou shalt read, when mine begins to dazzle.
[*Exeunt.*

ACT IV.

SCENE I. *The same. Before* Titus's *House.*

Enter TITUS *and* MARCUS. *Then enter Young* LUCIUS, LAVINIA *running after him.*

Boy. Help, grandsire, help! my aunt Lavinia
Follows me every where, I know not why:—
Good uncle Marcus, see how swift she comes!
Alas, sweet aunt, I know not what you mean.

Mar. Stand by me, Lucius; do not fear thine aunt.

Tit. She loves thee, boy, too well to do thee harm.

Boy. Ay, when my father was in Rome, she did.

Mar. What means my niece Lavinia by these signs?

Tit. Fear her not, Lucius:—Somewhat doth she mean:
See, Lucius, see, how much she makes of thee:
Somewhither would she have thee go with her.
Ah, boy, Cornelia never with more care
Read to her sons, than she hath read to thee,
Sweet poetry, and Tully's Orator.
Canst thou not guess wherefore she plies thee thus?

Boy. My lord, I know not, I, nor can I guess,
Unless some fit or frenzy do possess her:
For I have heard my grandsire say full oft,
Extremity of griefs would make men mad;
And I have read that Hecuba of Troy
Ran mad through sorrow: That made me to fear;
Although, my lord, I know, my noble aunt
Loves me as dear as e'er my mother did,
And would not, but in fury, fright my youth:
Which made me down to throw my books, and fly;
Causeless, perhaps: But pardon me, sweet aunt:
And, madam, if my uncle Marcus go,
I will most willingly attend your ladyship.

Mar. Lucius, I will.
[LAVINIA *turns over the Books which* LUCIUS *has let fall.*

Tit. How now, Lavinia?—Marcus, what means this?
Some book there is that she desires to see:—
Which is it, girl, of these?—Open them, boy.—
But thou art deeper read, and better skill'd;
Come, and take choice of all my library,
And so beguile thy sorrow, till the heavens
Reveal the damn'd contriver of this deed.—
Why lifts she up her arms in sequence thus?

Mar. I think, she means, that there was more than one

Confederate in the fact:—Ay, more there was:—
Or else to heaven she heaves them for revenge.

Tit. Lucius, what book is that she tosseth so?

Boy. Grandsire, 'tis Ovid's Metamorphosis;
My mother gave 't me.

Mar. For love of her that's gone,
Perhaps she cull'd it from among the rest.

Tit. Soft! see, how busily she turns the leaves!
Help her:—
What would she find?—Lavinia, shall I read?
This is the tragick tale of Philomel,
And treats of Tereus' treason, and his rape;
And rape, I fear, was root of thine annoy.

Mar. See, brother, see; note how she quotes the leaves.

Tit. Lavinia, wert thou thus surpris'd, sweet girl,
Ravish'd and wrong'd, as Philomela was,
Forc'd in the ruthless, vast, and gloomy woods?—
See, see!——
Ay, such a place there is, where we did hunt,
(O, had we never, never, hunted there!)
Pattern'd by that the poet here describes,
By nature made for murders, and for rapes.

Mar. O, why should nature build so foul a den,
Unless the gods delight in tragedies!

Tit. Give signs, sweet girl,—for here are none but friends,—
What Roman lord it was durst do the deed?
Or slunk not Saturnine, as Tarquin erst,
That left the camp to sin in Lucrece' bed?

Mar. Sit down, sweet niece;—brother, sit down by me.—
Apollo, Pallas, Jove, or Mercury,
Inspire me, that I may this treason find!—
My lord, look here;—Look here, Lavinia:
This sandy plot is plain; guide, if thou canst,
This after me, when I have writ my name
Without the help of any hand at all.

[*He writes his Name with his Staff, and guides it with his Feet and Mouth.*

Curs'd be that heart, that forc'd us to this shift!—
Write thou, good niece: and here display, at last,
What God will have discover'd for revenge!
Heaven guide thy pen to print thy sorrows plain,
That we may know the traitors, and the truth!

[*She takes the Staff in her Mouth, and guides it with her Stumps, and writes.*

Tit. O, do you read, my lord, what she hath writ?
Stuprum—Chiron—Demetrius.

Mar. What, what!—the lustful sons of Tamora
Performers of this heinous, bloody deed?

Tit. *Magne Dominator poli,*
Tam lentus audis scelera? tam lentus vides?

Mar. O, calm thee, gentle lord! although, I know,
There is enough written upon this earth,
To stir a mutiny in the mildest thoughts,
And arm the minds of infants to exclaims.
My lord, kneel down with me: Lavinia, kneel;
And kneel, sweet boy, the Roman Hector's hope;
And swear with me,—as with the woful feere,
And father, of that chaste dishonour'd dame,
Lord Junius Brutus sware for Lucrece' rape,—
That we will prosecute, by good advice,
Mortal revenge upon these traitorous Goths,
And see their blood, or die with this reproach.

Tit. 'Tis sure enough, an you knew how,
But if you hurt these bear-whelps, then beware:
The dam will wake; and, if she wind you once,
She's with the lion deeply still in league,
And lulls him whilst she playeth on her back,
And, when he sleeps, will she do what she list.
You're a young huntsman, Marcus: let it alone;
And, come, I will go get a leaf of brass,
And with a gad of steel will write these words,
And lay it by: the angry northern wind
Will blow these sands, like Sibyl's leaves, abroad,
And where's your lesson then?—Boy, what say you?

Boy. I say, my lord, that if I were a man,
Their mother's bed-chamber should not be safe
For these bad bondmen to the yoke of Rome.

Mar. Ay, that's my boy! thy father hath full oft
For this ungrateful country done the like.

Boy. And, uncle, so will I, an if I live.

Tit. Come, go with me into mine armoury;
Lucius, I'll fit thee; and withal, my boy
Shall carry from me to the empress' sons
Presents, that I intend to send them both:
Come, come; thou'lt do thy message, wilt thou not?

Boy. Ay, with my dagger in their bosoms, grandsire.

Tit. No, boy, not so; I'll teach thee another course.
Lavinia, come:—Marcus, look to my house;
Lucius and I'll go brave it at the court;
Ay, marry, will we, sir: and we'll be waited on.

[*Exeunt* TITUS, LAVINIA, *and* BOY.

Mar. O heavens, can you hear a good man groan,
And not relent, or not compassion him?
Marcus, attend him in his ecstasy;
That hath more scars of sorrow in his heart,
Than foemen's marks upon his batter'd shield:
But yet so just, that he will not revenge:—
Revenge the heavens for old Andronicus! [*Exit.*

SCENE II. *The same. A Room in the Palace.*

Enter AARON, CHIRON, *and* DEMETRIUS, *at one Door; at another Door, Young* LUCIUS, *and an* Attendant, *with a Bundle of Weapons, and Verses writ upon them.*

Chi. Demetrius, here's the son of Lucius;
He hath some message to deliver to us.

Aar. Ay, some mad message from his mad grandfather.

Boy. My lords, with all the humbleness I may,
I greet your honours from Andronicus;—
And pray the Roman gods confound you both. [*Aside.*

Dem. Gramercy, lovely Lucius; What's the news?

Boy. That you are both decipher'd, that's the news,
For villains mark'd with rape. [*Aside.*] May it please you,
My grandsire, well advis'd, hath sent by me
The goodliest weapons of his armoury,
To gratify your honourable youth,
The hope of Rome; for so he bade me say;
And so I do, and with his gifts present
Your lordships, that whenever you have need,
You may be armed and appointed well:
And so I leave you both, [*aside*] like bloody villains. [*Exeunt* Boy *and* Attendant.

Dem. What's here? A scroll; and written round about?
Let's see;
Integer vitæ, scelerisque purus,
Non eget Mauri jaculis, nec arcu.

Chi. O, 'tis a verse in Horace; I know it well:
I read it in the grammar long ago.

Aar. Ay, just!—a verse in Horace:—right, you have it.
Now, what a thing it is to be an ass!
Here's no sound jest! the old man hath found their guilt;
And sends the weapons wrapp'd about with lines,
That wound beyond their feeling to the quick.
But were our witty empress well a-foot,
She would applaud Andronicus' conceit.
But let her rest in her unrest awhile.— [*Aside.*]
And now, young lords, was 't not a happy star
Led us to Rome, strangers, and more than so,
Captives, to be advanced to this height?
It did me good, before the palace gate
To brave the tribune in his brother's hearing.

Dem. But me more good, to see so great a lord
Basely insinuate, and send us gifts.
Aar. Had he not reason, Lord Demetrius?
Did you not use his daughter very friendly?
Dem. I would, we had a thousand Roman dames
At such a bay, by turn to serve our lust.
Chi. A charitable wish, and full of love.
Aar. Here lacks but your mother for to say amen.
Chi. And that would she for twenty thousand more.
Dem. Come, let us go; and pray to all the gods
For our beloved mother in her pains.
Aar. Pray to the devils; the gods have given us o'er. [*Aside. Flourish.*
Dem. Why do the emperor's trumpets flourish thus?
Chi. Belike, for joy the emperor hath a son.
Dem. Soft: who comes here?

Enter a Nurse, *with a black-a-moor* Child *in her Arms.*

Nur. Good morrow, lords:
O, tell me, did you see Aaron the moor?
Aar. Well, more, or less, or ne'er a whit at all,
Here Aaron is: and what with Aaron now?
Nur. O gentle Aaron, we are all undone!
Now help, or woe betide thee evermore!
Aar. Why, what a caterwauling dost thou keep?
What dost thou wrap and fumble in thine arms?
Nur. O, that which I would hide from heaven's eye,
Our empress' shame, and stately Rome's disgrace;—
She is deliver'd, lords, she is deliver'd.
Aar. To whom?
Nur. I mean, she's brought to bed.
Aar. Well, God
Give her good rest! What hath he sent her?
Nur. A devil.
Aar. Why, then she's the devil's dam; a joyful issue.
Nur. A joyless, dismal, black, and sorrowful issue:
Here is the babe, as loathsome as a toad
Amongst the fairest breeders of our clime.
The empress sends it thee, thy stamp, thy seal,
And bids thee christen it with thy dagger's point.
Aar. Out, out, you whore! is black so base a hue?
Sweet blowse, you are a beauteous blossom, sure.
Dem. Villain, what hast thou done?
Aar. Done! that which thou
Canst not undo.
Chi. Thou hast undone our mother.
Aar. Villain, I have done thy mother.
Dem. And therein, hellish dog, thou hast undone.
Woe to her chance, and damn'd her loathed choice!
Accurs'd the offspring of so foul a fiend!
Chi. It shall not live.
Aar. It shall not die,
Nur. Aaron, it must: the mother wills it so.
Aar. What, must it, nurse? then let no man but I
Do execution on my flesh and blood.
Dem. I'll broach the tadpole on my rapier's point;
Nurse, give it me; my sword shall soon despatch it.
Aar. Sooner this sword shall plough thy bowels up,
[*Takes the* Child *from the* Nurse, *and draws.*
Stay, murderous villains! will you kill your brother?
Now, by the burning tapers of the sky,
That shone so brightly when this boy was got,
He dies upon my scimitar's sharp point
That touches this my first-born son and heir!
I tell you, younglings, not Enceladus,
With all his threat'ning band of Typhon's brood,
Nor great Alcides, nor the god of war,
Shall seize this prey out of his father's hands.
What, what; ye sanguine, shallow-hearted boys!
Ye white-lim'd walls! ye alehouse painted signs!
Coal black is better than another hue,
In that it scorns to bear another hue:
For all the water in the ocean
Can never turn a swan's black legs to white,
Although she lave them hourly in the flood.
Tell the empress from me, I am of age
To keep mine own; excuse it how she can.
Dem. Wilt thou betray thy noble mistress thus?
Aar. My mistress is my mistress! this, myself;
The vigour, and the picture of my youth:
This, before all the world, do I prefer;
This, maugre all the world, will I keep safe,
Or some of you shall smoke for it in Rome.
Dem. By this our mother is for ever sham'd.
Chi. Rome will despise her for this foul escape.
Nur. The emperor, in his rage, will doom her death.
Chi. I blush to think upon this ignomy.
Aar. Why, there's the privilege your beauty bears:
Fye, treacherous hue! that will betray with blushing
The close enacts and counsels of the heart!
Here's a young lad fram'd of another leer:
Look, how the black slave smiles upon the father;
As who should say, *Old lad, I am thine own.*
He is your brother, lords; sensibly fed
Of that self-blood that first gave life to you;
And, from that womb, where you imprison'd were,
He is enfranchised and come to light:
Nay, he's your brother by the surer side,
Although my seal be stamped in his face.
Nur. Aaron, what shall I say unto the empress?
Dem. Advise thee, Aaron, what is to be done,
And we will all subscribe to thy advice;
Save thou the child, so we may all be safe.
Aar. Then sit we down, and let us all consult.
My son and I will have the wind of you:
Keep there: Now talk at pleasure of your safety.
[*They sit on the Ground.*
Dem. How many women saw this child of his?
Aar. Why, so, brave lords; When we all join in league,
I am a lamb: but if you brave the Moor,
The chafed bear, the mountain lioness,
The ocean swells not so as Aaron storms.—
But, say again, how many saw the child?
Nur. Cornelia the midwife, and myself,
And no one else, but the deliver'd empress.
Aar. The emperess, the midwife, and yourself:
Two may keep counsel, when the third's away:
Go to the empress; tell her, this I said:—
[*Stabbing her.*
Weke, weke!—so cries a pig, prepar'd to the spit.
Dem. What mean'st thou, Aaron? Wherefore didst thou this?
Aar. O, lord, sir, 'tis a deed of policy:
Shall she live to betray this guilt of ours?
A long-tongu'd babbling gossip? no, lords, no.
And now be it known to you my full intent.
Not far, one Muliteus lives, my countryman,
His wife but yesternight was brought to bed;
His child is like to her, fair as you are:
Go pack with him, and give the mother gold,
And tell them both the circumstance of all;
And how by this their child shall be advanc'd
And be received for the emperor's heir.
And substituted in the place of mine,
To calm this tempest whirling in the court;
And let the emperor dandle him for his own.

Hark ye, lords, ye see, that I have given her physick, [*Pointing to the* Nurse.
And you must needs bestow her funeral;
The fields are near, and you are gallant grooms:
This done, see that you take no longer days,
But send the midwife presently to me.
The midwife, and the nurse, well made away,
Then let the ladies tattle what they please.
Chi. Aaron, I see, thou wilt not trust the air
With secrets.
Dem. For this care of Tamora,
Herself, and hers, are highly bound to thee.
[*Exeunt* DEM. *and* CHI. *bearing off the* Nurse.
Aar. Now to the Goths, as swift as swallow flies;
There to dispose this treasure in mine arms,
And secretly to greet the empress' friends.—
Come on, you thick-lipp'd slave, I'll bear you hence;
For it is you that puts us to our shifts:
I'll make you feed on berries, and on roots,
And feed on curds and whey, and suck the goat,
And cabin in a cave; and bring you up
To be a warrior, and command a camp. [*Exit.*

SCENE III. *The same. A publick Place.*

Enter TITUS, *bearing Arrows, with Letters at the ends of them; with him,* MARCUS, *Young* LUCIUS, *and other* Gentlemen, *with bows.*

Tit. Come, Marcus, come;—Kinsmen, this is the way:—
Sir boy, now let me see your archery;
Look ye draw home enough, and 'tis there straight;
Terras Astræa reliquit:
Be you remember'd, Marcus, she's gone, she's fled.
Sir, take you to your tools. You, cousins, shall
Go sound the ocean, and cast your nets;
Happily you may find her in the sea;
Yet there's as little justice as at land:—
No; Publius and Sempronius, you must do it;
'Tis you must dig with mattock, and with spade,
And pierce the inmost centre of the earth:
Then, when you come to Pluto's region,
I pray you, deliver him this petition:
Tell him, it is for justice, and for aid:
And that it comes from old Andronicus,
Shaken with sorrows in ungrateful Rome.—
Ah, Rome!—Well, well; I made thee miserable,
What time I threw the people's suffrages
On him that thus doth tyrannize o'er me.—
Go, get you gone; and pray be careful all,
And leave you not a man of war unsearch'd;
This wicked emperor may have shipp'd her hence,
And, kinsmen, then we may go pipe for justice.
Mar. O, Publius, is not this a heavy case,
To see thy noble uncle thus distract?
Pub. Therefore, my lord, it highly us concerns,
By day and night to attend him carefully;
And feed his humour kindly as we may,
Till time beget some careful remedy.
Mar. Kinsmen, his sorrows are past remedy.
Join with the Goths; and with revengeful war
Take wreak on Rome for this ingratitude,
And vengeance on the traitor Saturnine.
Tit. Publius, how now? how now, my masters? What,
Have you met with her?
Pub. No, my good lord: but Pluto sends you word
If you will have revenge from hell, you shall:
Marry, for Justice she is so employ'd,
He thinks, with Jove in heaven, or some where else,
So that perforce you must needs stay a time.
Tit. He doth me wrong to feed me with delays.
I'll dive into the burning lake below,
And pull her out of Acheron by the heels.—
Marcus, we are but shrubs, no cedars we;
No big-bon'd men, fram'd of the Cyclops' size:
But metal, Marcus, steel to the very back;
Yet wrung with wrongs, more than our backs can bear:
And sith there is no justice in earth nor hell,
We will solicit heaven; and move the gods,
To send down justice for to wreak our wrongs:
Come, to this gear. You are a good archer, Marcus. [*He gives them the Arrows.*
Ad Jovem, that's for you:—Here, *ad Apollinem.*—
Ad Martem, that's for myself;—
Here, boy, to Pallas:—Here, to Mercury:
To Saturn, Caius, not to Saturnine,—
You were as good to shoot against the wind.
To it, boy. Marcus, loose you when I bid:
O' my word, I have written to effect;
There's not a god left unsolicited.
Mar. Kinsmen, shoot all your shafts into the court:
We will afflict the emperor in his pride.
Tit. Now, masters, draw. [*They shoot.*] O, well said, Lucius!
Good boy, in Virgo's lap; give it Pallas.
Mar. My lord, I aim a mile beyond the moon;
Your letter is with Jupiter by this.
Tit. Ha! Publius, Publius, what hast thou done?
See, see, thou hast shot off one of Taurus' horns.
Mar. This was the sport, my lord: when Publius shot,
The bull being gall'd, gave Aries such a knock,
That down fell both the ram's horns in the court;
And who should find them but the empress' villain?
She laugh'd, and told the moor, he should not choose
But give them to his master for a present.
Tit. Why, there it goes: God give your lordship joy.

Enter a Clown, *with a Basket and two Pigeons.*

News, news from heaven! Marcus, the post is come.
Sirrah, what tidings? have you any letters?
Shall I have justice? what says Jupiter?
Clo. Ho! the gibbet maker? he says, that he hath taken them down again, for the man must not be hang'd till the next week.
Tit. But what says Jupiter, I ask thee?
Clo. Alas, sir, I know not Jupiter; I never drank with him in all my life.
Tit. Why, villain, art not thou the carrier?
Clo. Ay, of my pigeons, sir; nothing else.
Tit. Why, didst thou not come from heaven?
Clo. From heaven? alas, sir, I never came there; God forbid, I should be so bold to press to heaven in my young days. Why, I am going with my pigeons to the tribunal plebs, to take up a matter of brawl betwixt my uncle and one of the emperial's men.
Mar. Why, sir, that is as fit as can be, to serve for your oration; and let him deliver the pigeons to the emperor from you.
Tit. Tell me, can you deliver an oration to the emperor with a grace?
Clo. Nay, truly, sir, I could never say grace in all my life.
Tit. Sirrah, come hither: make no more ado,
But give your pigeons to the emperor:
By me thou shalt have justice at his hands.
Hold, hold;—mean while, here's money for thy charges.
Give me a pen and ink.
Sirrah, can you with a grace deliver a supplication?
Clo. Ay, sir.
Tit. Then here is a supplication for you. And when you come to him, at the first approach, you must kneel; then kiss his foot; then deliver up your pigeons; and then look for your reward. I'll be at hand, sir; see you do it bravely.
Clo. I warrant you, sir; let me alone.
Tit. Sirrah, hast thou a knife? Come, let me see it.
Here, Marcus, fold it in the oration;

For thou hast made it like an humble suppliant:—
And when thou hast given it to the emperor,
Knock at my door, and tell me what he says.

Clo. God be with you, sir; I will.

Tit. Come, Marcus, let's go:—Publius, follow me. [*Exeunt.*

SCENE IV. *The same. Before the Palace.*

Enter SATURNINUS, TAMORA, CHIRON, DEMETRIUS, Lords, *and Others;* SATURNINUS *with the Arrows in his Hand that* TITUS *shot.*

Sat. Why, lords, what wrongs are these? Was ever seen
An emperor of Rome thus overborne,
Troubled, confronted thus: and, for the extent
Of egal justice, us'd in such contempt?
My lords, you know, as do the mightful gods,
However these disturbers of our peace
Buz in the people's ears, there nought hath pass'd,
But even with law, against the wilful sons
Of old Andronicus. And what an if
His sorrows have so overwhelm'd his wits,
Shall we be thus afflicted in his wreaks,
His fits, his frenzy, and his bitterness?
And now he writes to heaven for his redress:
See, here's to Jove, and this to Mercury;
This to Apollo; this to the god of war:
Sweet scrolls to fly about the streets of Rome!
What's this, but libelling against the senate,
And blazoning our injustice every where?
A goodly humour, is it not, my lords?
As who would say, in Rome no justice were.
But, if I live, his feigned ecstasies
Shall be no shelter to these outrages:
But he and his shall know, that justice lives
In Saturninus' health; whom, if she sleep,
He'll so awake, as she in fury shall
Cut off the proud'st conspirator that lives.

Tam. My gracious lord, my lovely Saturnine,
Lord of my life, commander of my thoughts,
Calm thee, and bear the faults of Titus' age,
The effects of sorrow for his valiant sons,
Whose loss hath pierc'd him deep and scarr'd his heart;
And rather comfort his distressed plight,
Than prosecute the meanest, or the best,
For these contempts. Why, thus it shall become
High-witted Tamora to gloze with all: [*Aside.*
But, Titus, I have touch'd thee to the quick,
Thy life-blood out: if Aaron now be wise,
Then is all safe, the anchor's in the port.—

Enter Clown.

How now, good fellow? would'st thou speak with us?

Clo. Yes, forsooth, an your mistership be imperial.

Tam. Empress I am, but yonder sits the emperor.

Clo. 'Tis he.—God, and Saint Stephen, give you good den:—I have brought you a letter, and a couple of pigeons here.

[SATURNINUS *reads the Letter.*

Sat. Go, take him away, and hang him presently.

Clo. How much money must I have?

Tam. Come, sirrah, you must be hang'd.

Clo. Hang'd! By'r lady, then I have brought up a neck to a fair end. [*Exit, guarded.*

Sat. Despiteful and intolerable wrongs!
Shall I endure this monstrous villany?
I know from whence this same device proceeds;
May this be borne?—as if his traitorous sons,
That died by law for murder of our brother,
Have by my means been butcher'd wrongfully.—
Go, drag the villain hither by the hair;
Nor age, nor honour, shall shape privilege:
For this proud mock, I'll be thy slaughterman;
Sly frantick wretch, that holp'st to make me great,
In hope thyself should govern Rome and me.

Enter ÆMILIUS.

What news with thee, Æmilius?

Æmil. Arm, arm, my lords; Rome never had more cause!
The Goths have gather'd head; and with a power
Of high-resolved men, bent to the spoil,
They hither march amain, under conduct
Of Lucius, son to old Andronicus;
Who threats, in course of this revenge, to do
As much as ever Coriolanus did.

Sat. Is warlike Lucius general of the Goths?
These tidings nip me; and I hang the head
As flowers with frost, or grass beat down with storms.
Ay, now begin our sorrows to approach:
'Tis he the common people love so much;
Myself hath often overheard them say
(When I have walked like a private man),
That Lucius' banishment was wrongfully,
And they have wish'd that Lucius were their emperor.

Tam. Why should you fear? is not your city strong?

Sat. Ay, but the citizens favour Lucius:
And will revolt from me, to succour him.

Tam. King, be thy thoughts imperious, like thy name.
Is the sun dimm'd, that gnats do fly in it?
The eagle suffers little birds to sing,
And is not careful what they mean thereby;
Knowing that, with the shadow of his wings,
He can at pleasure stint their melody:
Even so may'st thou the giddy men of Rome.
Then cheer thy spirit; for know, thou emperor,
I will enchant the old Andronicus,
With words more sweet, and yet more dangerous,
Than baits to fish, or honey-stalks to sheep;
When as the one is wounded with the bait,
The other rotted with delicious feed.

Sat. But he will not entreat his son for us.

Tam. If Tamora entreat him, then he will:
For I can smooth and fill his aged ear
With golden promises; that were his heart
Almost impregnable, his old ears deaf,
Yet should both ear and heart obey my tongue.—
Go thou before, be our embassador; [*To* ÆMILIUS.
Say, that the emperor requests a parley
Of warlike Lucius, and appoint the meeting,
Even at his father's house, the old Andronicus.

Sat. Æmilius, do this message honourably:
And if he stand on hostage for his safety,
Bid him demand what pledge will please him best.

Æmil. Your bidding shall I do effectually. [*Exit* ÆMILIUS.

Tam. Now will I to that old Andronicus;
And temper him with all the art I have,
To pluck proud Lucius from the warlike Goths.
And now, sweet emperor, be blithe again,
And bury all thy fear in my devices.

Sat. Then go successfully, and plead to him. [*Exeunt.*

ACT V.

SCENE I. *Plains near* Rome.

Enter LUCIUS, *and* Goths, *with Drum and Colours.*

Luc. Approved warriors, and my faithful friends,
I have received letters from great Rome,
Which signify, what hate they bear their emperor,
And how desirous of our sight they are.
Therefore, great lords, be, as your titles witness,
Imperious, and impatient of your wrongs;
And, wherein Rome hath done you any scath,
Let him make treble satisfaction.

1 *Goth.* Brave slip, sprung from the great Andronicus,

Whose name was once our terror, now our comfort;
Whose high exploits, and honourable deeds,
Ingrateful Rome requites with foul contempt,
Be bold in us: we'll follow where thou lead'st,—
Like stinging bees in hottest summer's day,
Led by their master to the flower'd fields,—
And be aveng'd on cursed Tamora.

Goths. And, as he saith, so say we all with him.

Luc. I humbly thank him, and I thank you all.
But who comes here, led by a lusty Goth?

Enter a Goth, *leading* AARON, *with his* Child *in his Arms.*

2 *Goth.* Renowned Lucius, from our troops I stray'd,
To gaze upon a ruinous monastery;
And as I earnestly did fix mine eye
Upon the wasted building, suddenly
I heard a child cry underneath a wall:
I made unto the noise; when soon I heard
The crying babe controll'd with this discourse:
Peace, tawny slave; half me, and half thy dam!
Did not thy hue bewray whose brat thou art,
Had nature lent thee but thy mother's look,
Villain, thou might'st have been an emperor:
But where the bull and cow are both milk-white,
They never do beget a coal-black calf.
Peace, villain, peace!—even thus he rates the babe,—
For I must bear thee to a trusty Goth;
Who, when he knows thou art the empress' babe,
Will hold thee dearly for thy mother's sake.
With this, my weapon drawn, I rush'd upon him,
Surpris'd him suddenly; and brought him hither,
To use as you think needful of the man.

Luc. O worthy Goth! this is the incarnate devil,
That robb'd Andronicus of his good hand:
This is the pearl that pleas'd your empress' eye;
And here's the base fruit of his burning lust.—
Say, wall-ey'd slave, whither would'st thou convey
This growing image of thy fiend-like face?
Why dost not speak? What! deaf? No; not a word?
A halter, soldiers; hang him on this tree,
And by his side his fruit of bastardy.

Aar. Touch not the boy, he is of royal blood.

Luc. Too like the sire for ever being good.—
First, hang the child, that he may see it sprawl;
A sight to vex the father's soul withal.
Get me a ladder.

[*A Ladder is brought, which* AARON *is obliged to ascend.*

Aar. Lucius, save the child;
And bear it from me to the empress.
If thou do this, I'll show thee wondrous things,
That highly may advantage thee to hear:
If thou wilt not, befall what may befall,
I'll speak no more; But vengeance rot you all!

Luc. Say on; and if it please me which thou speak'st,
Thy child shall live, and I will see it nourish'd.

Aar. An if it please thee? why, assure thee, Lucius,
'Twill vex thy soul to hear what I shall speak;
For I must talk of murders, rapes, and massacres,
Acts of black night, abominable deeds,
Complots of mischief, treason; villanies
Ruthful to hear, yet piteously perform'd:
And this shall all be buried by my death,
Unless thou swear to me, my child shall live.

Luc. Tell on thy mind; I say, thy child shall live.

Aar. Swear, that he shall, and then I will begin.

Luc. Who should I swear by? thou believ'st no god;
That granted, how canst thou believe an oath?

Aar. What if I do not? as, indeed, I do not:
Yet, for I know thou art religious,
And hast a thing within thee, called conscience;
With twenty popish tricks and ceremonies,
Which I have seen thee careful to observe,—
Therefore I urge thy oath:—For that, I know,
An idiot holds his bauble for a god,
And keeps the oath, which by that god he swears;
To that I'll urge him:—Therefore, thou shalt vow
By that same god, what god soe'er it be,
That thou ador'st and hast in reverence,—
To save my boy, to nourish, and bring him up;
Or else I will discover nought to thee.

Luc. Even by my god, I swear to thee, I will.

Aar. First know thou, I begot him on the empress.

Luc. O most insatiate, luxurious woman!

Aar. Tut, Lucius! this was but a deed of charity,
To that which thou shalt hear of me anon:
'Twas her two sons that murder'd Bassianus;
They cut thy sister's tongue, and ravish'd her,
And cut her hands; and trimm'd her as thou saw'st.

Luc. O, detestable villain! call'st thou that [trimming?

Aar. Why, she was wash'd, and cut, and trimm'd; and 'twas
Trim sport for them that had the doing of it.

Luc. O, barbarous, beastly villains, like thyself!

Aar. Indeed, I was their tutor to instruct them!
That codding spirit had they from their mother,
As sure a card as ever won the set:
That bloody mind, I think, they learn'd of me,
As true a dog as ever fought at head.—
Well, let my deeds be witness of my worth.
I train'd thy brethren to that guileful hole,
Where the dead corpse of Bassianus lay:
I wrote the letter that thy father found,
And hid the gold within the letter mention'd,
Confederate with the queen, and her two sons;
And what not done, that thou hast cause to rue,
Wherein I had no stroke of mischief in it?
I play'd the cheater for thy father's hand;
And, when I had it, drew myself apart,
And almost broke my heart with extreme laughter.
I pry'd me through the crevice of a wall,
When, for his hand, he had his two sons' heads;
Beheld his tears, and laugh'd so heartily,
That both mine eyes were rainy like to his;
And when I told the empress of this sport,
She swounded almost at my pleasing tale,
And, for my tidings, gave me twenty kisses.

Goth. What! canst thou say all this, and never blush?

Aar. Ay, like a black dog, as the saying is.

Luc. Art thou not sorry for these heinous deeds?

Aar. Ay, that I had not done a thousand more.
Even now I curse the day (and yet, I think,
Few come within the compass of my curse),
Wherein I did not some notorious ill;
As kill a man, or else devise his death;
Ravish a maid, or plot the way to do it;
Accuse some innocent, and forswear myself:
Set deadly enmity between two friends;
Make poor men's cattle break their necks;
Set fire on barns and haystacks in the night,
And bid the owners quench them with their tears.
Oft have I digg'd up dead men from their graves,
And set them upright at their dear friends' doors,
Even when their sorrows almost were forgot;
And on their skins, as on the bark of trees,
Have with my knife carved, in Roman letters,
Let not your sorrow die, though I am dead.
Tut, I have done a thousand dreadful things,
As willingly as one would kill a fly:
And nothing grieves me heartily indeed,
But that I cannot do ten thousand more.

Luc. Bring down the devil; for he must not die
So sweet a death, as hanging presently.

Aar. If there be devils, 'would I were a devil,

To live and burn in everlasting fire;
So I might have your company in hell,
But to torment you with my bitter tongue!
Luc. Sirs, stop his mouth, and let him speak no more.

Enter a Goth.

Goth. My lord, there is a messenger from Rome,
Desires to be admitted to your presence.
Luc. Let him come near.—

Enter ÆMILIUS.

Welcome, Æmilius, what's the news from Rome?
Æmil. Lord Lucius, and you princes of the Goths,
The Roman emperor greets you all by me:
And, for he understands you are in arms,
He craves a parley at your father's house,
Willing you to demand your hostages,
And they shall be immediately deliver'd.
I *Goth.* What says our general?
Luc. Æmilius, let the emperor give his pledges
Unto my father and my uncle Marcus,
And we will come.—March away. [*Exeunt.*

SCENE II. Rome. *Before* Titus's *House.*

Enter TAMORA, CHIRON, *and* DEMETRIUS, *disguised.*

Tam. Thus, in this strange and sad habiliment,
I will encounter with Andronicus;
And, say, I am Revenge, sent from below,
To join with him, and right his heinous wrongs.
Knock at his study, where, they say, he keeps,
To ruminate strange plots of dire revenge;
Tell him, Revenge is come to join with him,
And work confusion on his enemies.
[*They knock.*

Enter TITUS, *above.*

Tit. Who doth molest my contemplation?
Is it your trick, to make me ope the door;
That so my sad decrees may fly away,
And all my study be to no effect?
You are deceiv'd: for what I mean to do,
See here, in bloody lines I have set down;
And what is written shall be executed.
Tam. Titus, I come to talk with thee.
Tit. No! not a word: How can I grace my talk,
Wanting a hand to give it action?
Thou hast the odds of me, therefore no more.
Tam. If thou didst know me, thou would'st talk with me.
Tit. I am not mad; I know thee well enough,
Witness this wretched stump, these crimson lines;
Witness these trenches, made by grief and care:
Witness the tiring day, and heavy night;
Witness all sorrow, that I know thee well
For our proud empress, mighty Tamora:
Is not thy coming for my other hand?
Tam. Know thou, sad man, I am not Tamora;
She is thy enemy, and I thy friend:
I am Revenge; sent from the infernal kingdom,
To ease the gnawing vulture of thy mind,
By working wreakful vengeance on thy foes.
Come down, and welcome me to this world's light;
Confer with me of murder and of death:
There's not a hollow cave, or lurking place,
No vast obscurity, or misty vale,
Where bloody murder, or detested rape,
Can couch for fear, but I will find them out;
And in their ears tell them my dreadful name,
Revenge, which makes the foul offender quake.
Tit. Art thou Revenge? and art thou sent to me,
To be a torment to mine enemies?
Tam. I am; therefore come down, and welcome me.
Tit. Do me some service, ere I come to thee.
Lo, by thy side where Rape, and Murder, stands;
Now give some 'surance that thou art Revenge,
Stab them, or tear them on thy chariot wheels;
And then I'll come, and be thy waggoner,
And whirl along with thee about the globes.
Provide thee proper palfreys, black as jet,
To hale thy vengeful waggon swift away,
And find out murderers in their guilty caves:
And, when thy car is loaden with their heads,
I will dismount, and by the waggon wheel
Trot, like a servile footman, all day long;
Even from Hyperion's rising in the east,
Until his very downfal in the sea.
And day by day I'll do this heavy task,
So thou destroy Rapine and Murder there.
Tam. These are my ministers, and come with me.
Tit. Are they thy ministers? what are they call'd?
Tam. Rapine, and Murder; therefore call'd so,
'Cause they take vengeance of such kind of men.
Tit. Good lord, how like the empress' sons they are!
And you the empress! But we worldly men
Have miserable, mad, mistaking eyes.
O sweet Revenge, now do I come to thee:
And, if one arm's embracement will content thee,
I will embrace thee in it by and by.
[*Exit* TITUS, *from above.*
Tam. This closing with him fits his lunacy:
Whate'er I forge, to feed his brain-sick fits,
Do you uphold and maintain in your speeches.
For now he firmly takes me for Revenge;
And, being credulous in this mad thought,
I'll make him send for Lucius, his son;
And, whilst I at a banquet hold him sure,
I'll find some cunning practice out of hand,
To scatter and disperse the giddy Goths,
Or, at the least, make them his enemies.
See, here he comes, and I must ply my theme.

Enter TITUS.

Tit. Long have I been forlorn, and all for thee:
Welcome, dread fury to my woful house;
Rapine, and Murder, you are welcome too:—
How like the empress and her sons you are!
Well are you fitted, had you but a Moor:—
Could not all hell afford you such a devil?—
For, well I wot, the empress never wags,
But in her company there is a Moor:
And, would you represent our queen aright,
It were convenient you had such a devil:
But welcome, as you are. What shall we do?
Tam. What would'st thou have us do, Andronicus?
Dem. Show me a murderer, I'll deal with him.
Chi. Show me a villain that hath done a rape,
And I am sent to be reveng'd on him.
Tam. Show me a thousand, that have done thee wrong,
And I will be revenged on them all.
Tit. Look round about the wicked streets of Rome;
And when thou find'st a man that's like thyself,
Good Murder, stab him; he's a murderer.—
Go thou with him; and when it is thy hap,
To find another that is like to thee,
Good Rapine, stab him; he is a ravisher.—
Go thou with them; and in the emperor's court
There is a queen, attended by a Moor:
Well may'st thou know her by thy own proportion,
For up and down she doth resemble thee;
I pray thee, do on them some violent death,
They have been violent to me and mine.
Tam. Well hast thou lesson'd us; this shall we do.
But would it please thee, good Andronicus,
To send for Lucius, thy thrice valiant son,
Who leads towards Rome a band of warlike Goths,
And bid him come and banquet at thy house:
When he is here, even at thy solemn feast,
I will bring in the empress and her sons,

The emperor himself, and all thy foes;
And at thy mercy shall they stoop and kneel,
And on them shalt thou ease thy angry heart.
What says Andronicus to this device?

Tit. Marcus, my brother!—'tis sad Titus calls.

Enter MARCUS.

Go, gentle Marcus, to thy nephew Lucius;
Thou shalt inquire him out among the Goths:
Bid him repair to me, and bring with him
Some of the chiefest princes of the Goths;
Bid him encamp his soldiers where they are:
Tell him, the emperor and the empress too
Feast at my house: and he shall feast with them.
This do thou for my love; and so let him,
As he regards his aged father's life.

Mar. This will I do, and soon return again. [*Exit.*

Tam. Now will I hence about thy business,
And take my ministers along with me.

Tit. Nay, nay, let Rape and Murder stay with me;
Or else I'll call my brother back again,
And cleave to no revenge but Lucius.

Tam. What say you, boys? will you abide with him,
Whiles I go tell my lord the emperor,
How I have govern'd our determin'd jest?
Yield to his humour, smooth and speak him fair, [*Aside.*
And tarry with him, till I come again.

Tit. I know them all, though they suppose me mad;
And will o'erreach them in their own devices,
A pair of cursed hell-hounds, and their dam. [*Aside.*

Dem. Madam, depart at pleasure, leave us here. [goes

Tam. Farewell, Andronicus: Revenge now
To lay a complot to betray thy foes. [*Exit.*

Tit. I know, thou dost; and, sweet Revenge, farewell.

Chi. Tell us, old man, how shall we be employ'd?

Tit. Tut, I have work enough for you to do.—
Publius, come hither, Caius, and Valentine!

Enter PUBLIUS, *and Others.*

Pub. What's your will?

Tit. Know you these two?

Pub. Th' empress' sons,
I take them, Chiron and Demetrius.

Tit. Fye, Publius, fye! thou art too much deceiv'd;
The one is Murder, Rape is the other's name:
And therefore bind them, gentle Publius;
Caius, and Valentine, lay hands on them:
Oft have you heard me wish for such an hour,
And now I find it; therefore bind them sure;
And stop their mouths, if they begin to cry.

[*Exit* TITUS.—PUBLIUS, *&c. lay hold on* CHIRON *and* DEMETRIUS.

Chi. Villains, forbear: we are the empress' sons.

Pub. And therefore do we what we are commanded.—
Stop close their mouths, let them not speak a word:
Is he sure bound? look, that you bind them fast.

Re-enter TITUS ANDRONICUS, *with* LAVINIA; *she bearing a Bason, and he a Knife.*

Tit. Come, come, Lavinia; look, thy foes are bound;—
Sirs, stop their mouths, let them not speak to me;
But let them hear what fearful words I utter.—
O villains, Chiron and Demetrius!
Here stands the spring whom you have stain'd with mud;
This goodly summer with your winter mix'd.
You kill'd her husband; and for that vile fault,
Two of her brothers were condemn'd to death:
My hand cut off, and made a merry jest:
Both her sweet hands, her tongue, and that, more dear
Than hands or tongue, her spotless chastity,
Inhuman traitors, you constrain'd and forc'd.
What would you say, if I should let you speak?
Villains, for shame you could not beg for grace.
Hark, wretches, how I mean to martyr you.
This one hand yet is left to cut your throats;
Whilst that Lavinia 'tween her stumps doth hold
The bason, that receives your guilty blood.
You know your mother means to feast with me,
And calls herself Revenge, and thinks me mad,—
Hark, villains; I will grind your bones to dust,
And with your blood and it, I'll make a paste;
And of the paste a coffin I will rear,
And make two pasties of your shameful heads;
And bid that strumpet, your unhallow'd dam,
Like to the earth, swallow her own increase.
This is the feast that I have bid her to,
And this the banquet she shall surfeit on;
For worse than Philomel you us'd my daughter,
And worse than Progne I will be reveng'd:
And now prepare your throats.—Lavinia, come, [*He cuts their Throats.*
Receive the blood: and, when that they are dead,
Let me go grind their bones to powder small,
And with this hateful liquor temper it;
And in that paste let their vile heads be bak'd.
Come, come, be every one officious
To make this banquet; which I wish may prove
More stern and bloody than the Centaur's feast.
So, now bring them in, for I will play the cook,
And see them ready 'gainst their mother comes.

[*Exeunt, bearing the dead Bodies.*

SCENE III.

The same. A Pavilion with Tables, &c.

Enter LUCIUS, MARCUS, *and* Goths, *with* AARON, *Prisoner.*

Luc. Uncle Marcus, since 'tis my father's mind,
That I repair to Rome, I am content.

1 Goth. And ours with thine, befall what fortune will.

Luc. Good uncle, take you in this barbarous Moor,
This ravenous tiger, this accursed devil;
Let him receive no sustenance, fetter him,
Till he be brought unto the empress' face,
For testimony of her foul proceedings:
And see the ambush of our friends be strong:
I fear, the emperor means no good to us.

Aar. Some devil whisper curses in mine ear,
And prompt me, that my tongue may utter forth
The venomous malice of my swelling heart!

Luc. Away, inhuman dog! unhallow'd slave!—
Sirs, help our uncle to convey him in.—

[*Exeunt* Goths, *with* AARON. *Flourish.*

The trumpets show the emperor is at hand.

Enter SATURNINUS *and* TAMORA, *with* Tribunes, Senators, *and Others.*

Sat. What, hath the firmament more suns than one?

Luc. What boots it thee, to call thyself a sun?

Mar. Rome's emperor, and nephew, break the parle;
These quarrels must be quietly debated.
The feast is ready, which the careful Titus
Hath ordain'd to an honourable end,
For peace, for love, for league, and good to Rome:
Please you, therefore, draw nigh, and take your places.

Sat. Marcus, we will.

[*Hautboys sound. The* Company *sit down at Table.*

Enter TITUS, *dressed like a Cook,* LAVINIA, *veiled, young* LUCIUS, *and Others.* TITUS *places the Dishes on the Table.*

Tit. Welcome, my gracious lord: welcome, dread queen;
Welcome, ye warlike Goths; welcome, Lucius;

And welcome, all: although the cheer be poor,
'Twill fill your stomachs; please you eat of it.
Sat. Why art thou thus attir'd, Andronicus?
Tit. Because I would be sure to have all well,
To entertain your highness and your empress.
Tam. We are beholden to you, good Andronicus.
Tit. An if your highness knew my heart, you were.
My lord the emperor, resolve me this;
Was it well done of rash Virginius,
To slay his daughter with his own right hand,
Because she was enforc'd, stain'd, and deflour'd?
Sat. It was, Andronicus.
Tit. Your reason, mighty lord!
Sat. Because the girl should not survive her shame,
And by her presence still renew his sorrows.
Tit. A reason mighty, strong, and effectual;
A pattern, precedent, and lively warrant,
For me, most wretched, to perform the like:—
Die, die, Lavinia, and thy shame with thee;
[*He kills* LAVINIA.
And, with thy shame, thy father's sorrow die!
Sat. What hast thou done, unnatural and unkind?
Tit. Kill'd her, for whom my tears have made me blind.
I am as woful as Virginius was:
And have a thousand times more cause than he
To do this outrage;—and it is now done.
Sat. What, was she ravish'd? tell, who did the deed.
Tit. Will't please you eat? will't please your highness feed?
Tam. Why hast thou slain thine only daughter thus?
Tit. Not I; 'twas Chiron, and Demetrius:
They ravish'd her, and cut away her tongue,
And they, 'twas they, that did her all this wrong.
Sat. Go, fetch them hither to us presently.
Tit. Why, there they are both, baked in that pie;
Whereof their mother daintily hath fed,
Eating the flesh that she herself hath bred.
'Tis true, 'tis true; witness my knife's sharp point. [*Killing* TAMORA.
Sat. Die, frantick wretch, for this accursed deed. [*Killing* TITUS.
Luc. Can the son's eye behold his father bleed?
There's meed for meed, death for a deadly deed.
[*Kills* SATURNINUS. *A great Tumult. The* People *in confusion disperse.* MARCUS, LUCIUS, *and their* Partisans *ascend the Steps before* Titus's *House.*
Mar. You sad-fac'd men, people and sons of Rome,
By uproar sever'd, like a flight of fowl
Scatter'd by winds and high tempestuous gusts,
O, let me teach you how to knit again
This scatter'd corn into one mutual sheaf,
These broken limbs again into one body.
Sen. Lest Rome herself be bane unto herself;
And she, whom mighty kingdoms court'sy to,
Like a forlorn and desperate castaway,
Do shameful execution on herself.
But if my frosty signs, and chaps of age,
Grave witnesses of true experience,
Cannot induce you to attend my words,—
Speak, Rome's dear friend; [*To* LUCIUS.] as erst our ancestor,
When with his solemn tongue he did discourse
To lovesick Dido's sad attending ear,
The story of that baleful burning night,
When subtle Greeks surpris'd King Priam's Troy;
Tell us, what Sinon hath bewitch'd our ears,
Or who hath brought the fatal engine in,
That gives our Troy, our Rome, the civil wound.—
My heart is not compact of flint, nor steel;
Nor can I utter all our bitter grief,
But floods of tears will drown my oratory,
And break my very utterance; even i' the time
When it should move you to attend me most,
Lending your kind commiseration:
Here is a captain, let him tell the tale;
Your hearts will throb and weep to hear him speak.
Luc. Then, noble auditory, be it known to you,
That cursed Chiron and Demetrius
Were they that murdered our emperor's brother;
And they it were that ravished our sister:
For their fell faults our brothers were beheaded;
Our father's tears despis'd; and basely cozen'd
Of that true hand, that fought Rome's quarrel out,
And sent her enemies unto the grave.
Lastly, myself unkindly banished,
The gates shut on me, and turn'd weeping out,
To beg relief among Rome's enemies;
Who drown'd their enmity in my true tears,
And op'd their arms to embrace me as a friend:
And I am the turn'd-forth, be it known to you
That have preserv'd her welfare in my blood:
And from her bosom took the enemy's point,
Sheathing the steel in my advent'rous body.
Alas! you know, I am no vaunter, I;
My scars can witness, dumb although they are,
That my report is just, and full of truth.
But, soft; methinks, I do digress too much,
Citing my worthless praise: O, pardon me;
For when no friends are by, men praise themselves.
Mar. Now is my turn to speak; Behold this child,
[*Pointing to the* Child *in the arms of an* Attendant.
Of this was Tamora delivered;
The issue of an irreligious Moor,
Chief architect and plotter of these woes;
The villain is alive in Titus' house,
Damn'd as he is, to witness this is true.
Now judge, what cause had Titus to revenge
These wrongs, unspeakable, past patience,
Or more than any living man could bear.
Now you have heard the truth, what say you, Romans?
Have we done aught amiss? Show us wherein,
And, from the place where you behold us now,
The poor remainder of Andronici
Will, hand in hand, all headlong cast us down,
And on the ragged stones beat forth our brains,
And make a mutual closure of our house.
Speak, Romans, speak; and, if you say, we shall,
Lo, hand in hand, Lucius and I will fall.
Æmil. Come, come, thou reverend man of Rome,
And bring our emperor gently in thy hand,
Lucius, our emperor; for well I know,
The common voice do cry, it shall be so.
Rom. [*Several speak.*] Lucius, all hail; Rome's royal emperor!

LUCIUS, *&c. descend.*

Mar. Go, go into old Titus' sorrowful house;
[*To an* Attendant.
And hither hale that misbelieving Moor,
To be adjudg'd some direful slaughtering death,
As punishment for his most wicked life.
Rom. [*Several speak.*] Lucius, all hail: Rome's gracious governor!
Luc. Thanks, gentle Romans; May I govern so,
To heal Rome's harms, and wipe away her woe!
But, gentle people, give me aim awhile,—
For nature puts me to a heavy task;—
Stand all aloof,—but, uncle, draw you near,
To shed obsequious tears upon this trunk:—
O, take this warm kiss on thy pale cold lips,
[*Kisses* TITUS.
These sorrowful drops upon thy blood-stain'd face,
The last true duties of thy noble son!
Mar. Tear for tear, and loving kiss for kiss,
Thy brother Marcus tenders on thy lips:
O, were the sum of these that I should pay
Countless and infinite, yet would I pay them!

Luc. Come hither, boy; come, come, and learn of us
To melt in showers: Thy grandsire lov'd thee well:
Many a time he danc'd thee on his knee,
Sung thee asleep, his loving breast thy pillow;
Many a matter hath he told to thee,
Meet, and agreeing with thine infancy;
In that respect then, like a loving child,
Shed yet some small drops from thy tender spring,
Because kind nature doth require it so:
Friends should associate friends in grief and woe:
Bid him farewell; commit him to the grave;
Do him that kindness, and take leave of him.

Boy. O grandsire, grandsire! even with all my heart
Would I were dead, so you did live again!—
O lord, I cannot speak to him for weeping;
My tears will choke me, if I ope my mouth.

Enter Attendants, *with* AARON.

1 *Rom.* You sad Andronici, have done with woes;
Give sentence on this execrable wretch,
That hath been breeder of these dire events.

Luc. Set him breast-deep in earth, and famish him;
There let him stand, and rave and cry for food:
If any one relieves or pities him,
For the offence he dies. This is our doom:
Some stay, to see him fasten'd in the earth.

Aar. O, why should wrath be mute, and fury dumb?
I am no baby, I, that, with base prayers,
I should repent the evils I have done;
Ten thousand, worse than ever yet I did,
Would I perform, if I might have my will;
If one good deed in all my life I did,
I do repent it from my very soul.

Luc. Some loving friends convey the emperor hence,
And give him burial in his father's grave:
My father, and Lavinia, shall forthwith
Be closed in our household's monument.
As for that heinous tiger, Tamora,
No funeral rite, nor man in mournful weeds,
No mournful bell shall ring her burial;
But throw her forth to beasts, and birds of prey:
Her life was beast-like, and devoid of pity;
And, being so, shall have like want of pity.
See justice done to Aaron, that damn'd Moor,
By whom our heavy haps had their beginning:
Then, afterwards, to order well the state;
That like events may ne'er it ruinate. [*Exeunt.*

PERICLES, PRINCE OF TYRE.

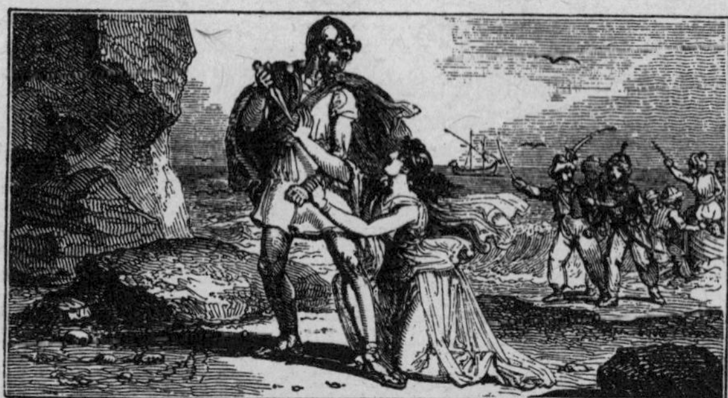

PERSONS REPRESENTED.

ANTIOCHUS, King *of* Antioch.
PERICLES, Prince *of* Tyre.
HELICANUS, ESCANES, } *two* Lords *of* Tyre.
SIMONIDES, King *of* Pentapolis.
CLEON, Governor *of* Tharsus.
LYSIMACHUS, Governor *of* Mitylene.
CERIMON, *a* Lord *of* Ephesus.
THALIARD, *a* Lord *of* Antioch.
PHILEMON, *Servant to* Cerimon.
LEONINE, *Servant to* Dionyza. Marshal.
A Pandar, *and his* Wife. BOULT, *their Servant.*
GOWER, *as Chorus.*

The Daughter *of* Antiochus.
DIONYZA, *Wife to* Cleon.
THAISA, *Daughter to* Simonides.
MARINA, *Daughter to* Pericles *and* Thaisa.
LYCHORIDA, *Nurse to* Marina. DIANA.

Lords, Ladies, Knights, Gentlemen, Sailors, Pirates, Fishermen, *and* Messengers, *&c.*

SCENE—*dispersedly in various Countries.*

ACT I.

Enter GOWER.

Before the Palace of Antioch.

To sing a song of old was sung,
From ashes ancient Gower is come;
Assuming man's infirmities,
To glad your ear, and please your eyes.
It hath been sung at festivals,
On ember-eves, and holy ales;
And lords and ladies of their lives
Have read it for restoratives:
The purchase is to make men glorious;
Et bonum quo antiquius, eo melius.
If you, born in these latter times,
When wit's more ripe, accept my rhymes,
And that to hear an old man sing,
May to your wishes pleasure bring,
I life would wish, and that I might
Waste it for you, like taper-light.—
This city then, Antiochus the Great
Built up this city for his chiefest seat;

The fairest in all Syria;
(I tell you what mine authors say:)
This king unto him took a pheere,
Who died and left a female heir,
So buxom, blithe, and full of face,
As heaven had lent her all his grace;
With whom the father liking took,
And her to incest did provoke:
Bad father! to entice his own
To evil, should be done by none.
By custom, what they did begin,
Was, with long use, account no sin.
The beauty of this sinful dame
Made many princes thither frame,
To seek her as a bed-fellow,
In marriage-pleasures play-fellow:
Which to prevent, he made a law
(To keep her still, and men in awe),
That whoso ask'd her for his wife,
His riddle told not, lost his life:
So for her many a wight did die,
As yon grim looks do testify.
What now ensues, to the judgment of your eye
I give, my cause who best can justify. [*Exit.*

SCENE I. Antioch. *A Room in the Palace.*

Enter ANTIOCHUS, PERICLES, *and* Attendants.

Ant. Young prince of Tyre, you have at large receiv'd
The danger of the task you undertake.

Per. I have, Antiochus, and with a soul
Embolden'd with the glory of her praise,
Think death no hazard, in this enterprise. [*Musick.*

Ant. Bring in our daughter, clothed like a bride,
For the embracements even of Jove himself;
At whose conception (till Lucina reign'd,
Nature this dowry gave, to glad her presence),
The senate-house of planets all did sit,
To knit in her their best perfections.

Enter the Daughter *of* Antiochus.

Per. See, where she comes, apparell'd like the spring,
Graces her subjects, and her thoughts the king
Of every virtue gives renown to men!
Her face, the book of praises, where is read
Nothing but curious pleasures, as from thence
Sorrow were ever ras'd, and testy wrath
Could never be her mild companion.
Ye gods that made me man, and sway in love,
That have inflam'd desire in my breast,
To taste the fruit of yon celestial tree,
Or die in the adventure, be my helps,
As I am son and servant to your will,
To compass such a boundless happiness!

Ant. Prince Pericles,——

Per. That would be son to great Antiochus.

Ant. Before thee stands this fair Hesperides,
With golden fruit, but dangerous to be touch'd;
For death-like dragons here affright thee hard:
Her face, like heaven, enticeth thee to view
Her countless glory, which desert must gain:
And which, without desert, because thine eye
Presumes to reach, all thy whole heap must die.
Yon sometime famous princes, like thyself,
Drawn by report, advent'rous by desire,
Tell thee with speechless tongues, and semblance pale,
That without covering, save yon field of stars,
They here stand martyrs, slain in Cupid's wars;
And with dead cheeks advise thee to desist,
For going on death's net, whom none resist.

Per. Antiochus, I thank thee, who hath taught
My frail mortality to know itself,
And by those fearful objects to prepare
This body, like to them, to what I must:
For death remember'd, should be like a mirror,
Who tells us, life's but breath; to trust it, error.
I'll make my will then; and as sick men do,
Who know the world, see heaven, but feeling woe,
Gripe not at earthly joys, as erst they did;
So I bequeath a happy peace to you,
And all good men, as every prince should do;
My riches to the earth from whence they came;
But my unspotted fire of love to you.
[*To the* Daughter *of* Antiochus.
Thus ready for the way of life or death,
I wait the sharpest blow, Antiochus,
Scorning advice.

Ant. Read the conclusion then;
Which read and not expounded, 'tis decreed,
As these before thee, thou thyself shalt bleed.

Daugh. In all, save that, may'st thou prove prosperous!
In all, save that, I wish thee happiness!

Per. Like a bold champion, I assume the lists,
Nor ask advice of any other thought
But faithfulness, and courage.

[He reads the Riddle.]

I am no viper, yet I feed
On mother's flesh, which did me breed:
I sought a husband, in which labour,
I found that kindness in a father.
He's father, son, and husband mild,
I mother, wife, and yet his child.
How they may be, and yet in two,
As you will live, resolve it you.

Sharp physick is the last: but O you powers!
That give heaven countless eyes to view men's acts,
Why cloud they not their sights perpetually,
If this be true, which makes me pale to read it?
Fair glass of light, I lov'd you, and could still,
[*Takes hold of the Hand of the* Princess.
Were not this glorious casket stor'd with ill:
But I must tell you,—now, my thoughts revolt;
For he's no man on whom perfections wait,
That knowing sin within, will touch the gate.
You're a fair viol, and your sense the strings:
Who, finger'd to make man his lawful musick,
Would draw heaven down, and all the gods to hearken;
But, being play'd upon before your time,
Hell only danceth at so harsh a chime:
Good sooth, I care not for you.

Ant. Prince Pericles, touch not, upon thy life,
For that's an article within our law,
As dangerous as the rest. Your time's expir'd;
Either expound now, or receive your sentence.

Per. Great king,
Few love to hear the sins they love to act;
'Twould 'braid yourself too near for me to tell it.
Who has a book of all that monarchs do,
He's more secure to keep it shut, than shown;
For vice repeated, is like the wand'ring wind,
Blows dust in others' eyes, to spread itself;
And yet the end of all is bought thus dear,
The breath is gone, and the sore eyes see clear:
To stop the air would hurt them. The blind mole casts
Copp'd hills towards heaven, to tell, the earth is throng'd
By man's oppression; and the poor worm doth die for't.
Kings are earth's gods: in vice their law's their will;
And if Jove stray, who dares say, Jove doth ill?
It is enough you know; and it is fit,
What being more known grows worse, to smother it.
All love the womb that their first beings bred,
Then give my tongue like leave to love my head.

Ant. Heaven, that I had thy head! he has found the meaning;—
But I will gloze with him. [*Aside.*] Young prince of Tyre,
Though by the tenour of our strict edict,
Your exposition misinterpreting,
We might proceed to cancel of your days;
Yet hope, succeeding from so fair a tree
As your fair self, doth tune us otherwise:
Forty days longer we do respite you;

If by which time our secret be undone,
This mercy shows, we'll joy in such a son:
And until then, your entertain shall be,
As doth befit our honour, and your worth.
[*Exeunt* ANT. *his* Daughter, *and* Attendants.
Per. How courtesy would seem to cover sin!
When what is done is like a hypocrite,
The which is good in nothing but in sight.
If it be true that I interpret false,
Then were it certain, you were not so bad,
As with foul incest to abuse your soul;
Where now you're both a father and a son,
By your untimely claspings with your child
(Which pleasure fits a husband, not a father);
And she an eater of her mother's flesh,
By the defiling of her parent's bed;
And both like serpents are, who though they feed
On sweetest flowers, yet they poison breed.
Antioch, farewell! for wisdom sees, those men
Blush not in actions blacker than the night,
Will shun no course to keep them from the light.
One sin, I know, another doth provoke;
Murder's as near to lust, as flame to smoke.
Poison and treason are the hands of sin,
Ay, and the targets, to put off the shame:
Then, lest my life be cropp'd to keep you clear,
By flight I'll shun the danger which I fear.
[*Exit.*

Re-enter ANTIOCHUS.

Ant. He hath found the meaning, for the which we mean
To have his head.
He must not live to trumpet forth my infamy,
Nor tell the world, Antiochus doth sin
In such a loathed manner:
And therefore instantly this prince must die;
For by his fall my honour must keep high.
Who attends on us there?

Enter THALIARD.

Thal. Doth your highness call?
Ant. Thaliard, you're of our chamber, and our mind
Partakes her private actions to your secrecy;
And for your faithfulness we will advance you.
Thaliard, behold, here's poison, and here's gold;
We hate the prince of Tyre, and thou must kill him;
It fits thee not to ask the reason why,
Because we bid it. Say, is it done?
Thal. My lord,
'Tis done.

Enter a Messenger.

Ant. Enough.
Let your breath cool yourself, telling your haste.
Mess. My lord, Prince Pericles is fled.
[*Exit* Messenger.
Ant. As thou
Wilt live, fly after: and, as an arrow, shot
From a well experienc'd archer, hits the mark
His eye doth level at, so ne'er return,
Unless thou say, Prince Pericles is dead.
Thal. My lord, if I
Can get him once within my pistol's length,
I'll make him sure; so farewell to your highness.
[*Exit.*
Ant. Thaliard, adieu! till Pericles be dead,
My heart can lend no succour to my head.
[*Exit.*

SCENE II. Tyre. *A Room in the Palace.*

Enter PERICLES, HELICANUS, *and other* Lords.

Per. Let none disturb us: Why should this change of thought?
The sad companion, dull-ey'd melancholy,
By me so us'd a guest is, not an hour,
In the day's glorious walk, or peaceful night
(The tomb where grief should sleep), can breed me quiet!
Here pleasures court mine eyes, and mine eyes shun them,
And danger, which I feared, is at Antioch,
Whose arm seems far too short to hit me here:
Yet neither pleasure's art can joy my spirits,
Nor yet the other's distance comfort me.
Then it is thus: the passions of the mind,
That have their first conception by misdread,
Have after-nourishment and life by care;
And what was first but fear what might be done,
Grows elder now, and cares it be not done.
And so with me;—the great Antiochus
('Gainst whom I am too little to contend,
Since he's so great, can make his will his act),
Will think me speaking, though I swear to silence;
Nor boots it me to say, I honour him,
If he suspect I may dishonour him:
And what may make him blush in being known;
He'll stop the course by which it might be known;
With hostile forces he'll o'erspread the land,
And with the ostent of war will look so huge,
Amazement shall drive courage from the state;
Our men be vanquish'd, ere they do resist,
And subjects punish'd, that ne'er thought offence:
Which care of them, not pity of myself
(Who am no more but as the tops of trees,
Which fence the roots they grow by, and defend them),
Makes both my body pine, and soul to languish,
And punish that before that he would punish.
1 *Lord.* Joy and all comfort in your sacred breast!
2 *Lord.* And keep your mind, till you return to us,
Peaceful and comfortable!
Hel. Peace, peace, my lords, and give experience tongue.
They do abuse the king, that flatter him:
For flattery is the bellows blows up sin;
The thing the which is flatter'd, but a spark,
To which that breath gives heat and stronger glowing;
Whereas reproof, obedient, and in order,
Fits kings, as they are men, for they may err.
When Signior Sooth here does proclaim a peace,
He flatters you, makes war upon your life:
Prince, pardon me, or strike me, if you please;
I cannot be much lower than my knees.
Per. All leave us else; but let your cares o'erlook
What shipping, and what lading's in our haven,
And then return to us. [*Exeunt* Lords.] Helicanus, thou
Hast moved us: what seest thou in our looks?
Hel. An angry brow, dread lord.
Per. If there be such a dart in princes' frowns,
How durst thy tongue move anger to our face?
Hel. How dare the plants look up to heaven, from whence
They have their nourishment?
Per. Thou know'st I have power
To take thy life.
Hel. [*Kneeling.*] I have ground the axe myself;
Do you but strike the blow.
Per. Rise, pr'ythee rise;
Sit down, sit down; thou art no flatterer:
I thank thee for it; and high heaven forbid,
That kings should let their ears hear their faults hid!
Fit counsellor, and servant for a prince,
Who by thy wisdom mak'st a prince thy servant,
What would'st thou have me do?
Hel. With patience bear
Such griefs as you do lay upon yourself.
Per. Thou speak'st like a physician, Helicanus;
Who minister'st a potion unto me,
That thou would'st tremble to receive thyself.
Attend me then: I went to Antioch,
Where, as thou know'st, against the face of death,
I sought the purchase of a glorious beauty,
From whence an issue I might propagate,

Are arms to princes, and bring to subjects joys.
Her face was to mine eye beyond all wonder;
The rest (hark in thine ear), as black as incest;
Which by my knowledge found, the sinful father
Seem'd not to strike, but smooth: but thou know'st this,
'Tis time to fear, when tyrants seem to kiss.
Which fear so grew in me, I hither fled,
Under the covering of a careful night,
Who seem'd my good protector; and being here,
Bethought me what was past, what might succeed.
I knew him tyrannous; and tyrants' fears
Decrease not, but grow faster than their years:
And should he doubt it (as no doubt he doth),
That I should open to the listening air,
How many worthy princes' bloods were shed,
To keep his bed of blackness unlaid ope,—
To lop that doubt, he'll fill this land with arms,
And make pretence of wrong that I have done him;
When all, for mine, if I may call't offence,
Must feel war's blow, who spares not innocence:
Which love to all (of which thyself art one,
Who now reprov'st me for it)——

Hel. Alas, sir!

Per. Drew sleep out of mine eyes, blood from my cheeks,
Musings into my mind, a thousand doubts
How I might stop this tempest, ere it came;
And finding little comfort to relieve them,
I thought it princely charity to grieve them.

Hel. Well, my lord, since you have given me leave to speak,
Freely I'll speak. Antiochus you fear,
And justly too, I think, you fear the tyrant,
Who, either by public war, or private treason,
Will take away your life.
Therefore, my lord, go travel for a while,
Till that his rage and anger be forgot,
Or Destinies do cut his thread of life.
Your rule direct to any; if to me,
Day serves not light more faithful than I'll be.

Per. I do not doubt thy faith;
But should he wrong my liberties in absence—

Hel. We'll mingle bloods together in the earth,
From whence we had our being and our birth.

Per. Tyre, I now look from thee then, and to Tharsus
Intend my travel, where I'll hear from thee:
And by whose letters I'll dispose myself.
The care I had and have of subjects' good,
On thee I lay, whose wisdom's strength can bear it.
I'll take thy word for faith, not ask thine oath;
Who shuns not to break one, will sure crack both:
But in our orbs we'll live so round and safe,
That time of both this truth shall ne'er convince,
Thou show'dst a subject's shine, I a true prince.
[*Exeunt.*

SCENE III.

Tyre. *An Ante-Chamber in the Palace.*

Enter THALIARD.

Thal. So, this is Tyre, and this is the court. Here must I kill king Pericles; and if I do not, I am sure to be hang'd at home: 'tis dangerous.—Well, I perceive he was a wise fellow, and had good discretion, that being bid to ask what he would of the king, desired he might know none of his secrets. Now do I see he had some reason for it: for if a king bid a man be a villain, he is bound by the indenture of his oath to be one.—Hush, here come the lords of Tyre.

Enter HELICANUS, ESCANES, *and other* Lords.

Hel. You shall not need, my fellow peers of Tyre,
Further to question of your king's departure.
His seal'd commission, left in trust with me,
Doth speak sufficiently, he's gone to travel.

Thal. How! the king gone! [*Aside.*

Hel. If further yet you will be satisfied,
Why, as it were unlicens'd of your loves,
He would depart, I'll give some light unto you.
Being at Antioch——

Thal. What from Antioch? [*Aside.*

Hel. Royal Antiochus (on what cause I know not),
Took some displeasure at him; at least he judg'd so:
And doubting lest that he had err'd or sinn'd,
To show his sorrow, would correct himself;
So puts himself unto the shipman's toil,
With whom each minute threatens life or death.

Thal. Well, I perceive [*Aside.*
I shall not be hang'd now, although I would;
But since he's gone, the king it sure must please,
He scap'd the land, to perish on the seas.—
But I'll present me. Peace to the lords of Tyre!

Hel. Lord Thaliard from Antiochus is welcome.

Thal. From him I come
With message unto princely Pericles;
But, since my landing, as I have understood
Your lord has took himself to unknown travels,
My message must return from whence it came.

Hel. We have no reason to desire it, since
Commended to our master, not to us:
Yet, ere you shall depart, this we desire,—
As friends to Antioch, we may feast in Tyre.
[*Exeunt.*

SCENE IV.

Tharsus. *A Room in the Governor's House.*

Enter CLEON, DIONYZA, *and* Attendants.

Cle. My Dionyza, shall we rest us here,
And by relating tales of others' griefs,
See if 'twill teach us to forget our own?

Dio. That were to blow at fire, in hope to quench it;
For who digs hills because they do aspire,
Throws down one mountain, to cast up a higher.
O my distressed lord, even such our griefs;
Here they're but felt, and seen with mistful eyes,
But like to groves, being topp'd, they higher rise.

Cle. O Dionyza,
Who wanteth food, and will not say he wants it,
Or can conceal his hunger, till he famish?
Our tongues and sorrows do sound deep our woes
Into the air; our eyes do weep, till lungs
Fetch breath that may proclaim them louder; that,
If the Gods slumber, while their creatures want,
They may awake their helps to comfort them.
I'll then discourse our woes, felt several years,
And wanting breath to speak, help me with tears.

Dio. I'll do my best, sir.

Cle. This Tharsus, o'er which I have government,
A city on whom plenty held full hand
(For riches strew'd herself even in the streets);
Whose towers bore heads so high, they kiss'd the clouds,
And strangers ne'er beheld, but wonder'd at;
Whose men and dames so jetted and adorn'd,
Like one another's glass to trim them by:
Their tables were stor'd full, to glad the sight,
And not so much to feed on, as delight;
All poverty was scorn'd, and pride so great,
The name of help grew odious to repeat.

Dio. O, 'tis too true.

Cle. But see what heaven can do! By this our change,
These mouths, whom but of late, earth, sea, and air,
Were all too little to content and please,
Although they gave their creatures in abundance,
As houses are defil'd for want of use,
They are now starv'd for want of exercise:
Those palates, who not yet two summers younger,

Must have inventions to delight the taste,
Would now be glad of bread, and beg for it;
Those mothers who, to nousle up their babes,
Thought nought too curious, are ready now,
To eat those little darlings whom they lov'd.
So sharp are hunger's teeth, that man and wife
Draw lots, who first shall die to lengthen life:
Here stands a lord, and there a lady weeping;
Here many sink, yet those which see them fall,
Have scarce strength left to give them burial.
Is not this true?

Dio. Our cheeks and hollow eyes do witness it.

Cle. O, let those cities, that of Plenty's cup
And her prosperities so largely taste,
With their superfluous riots, hear these tears!
The misery of Tharsus may be theirs.

Enter a Lord.

Lord. Where's the lord governor?

Cle. Here. [haste,
Speak out thy sorrows which thou bring'st, in
For comfort is too far for us to expect.

Lord. We have descried, upon our neighbouring shore,
A portly sail of ships make hitherward.

Cle. I thought as much.
One sorrow never comes, but brings an heir,
That may succeed as his inheritor;
And so in ours: some neighbouring nation,
Taking advantage of our misery,
Hath stuff'd these hollow vessels with their power,
To beat us down, the which are down already;
And make a conquest of unhappy me,
Whereas no glory's got to overcome.

Lord. That's the least fear: for by the semblance
Of their white flags display'd, they bring us peace,
And come to us, as favourers, not as foes.

Cle. Thou speak'st like him untutor'd to repeat,
Who makes the fairest show means most deceit.
But bring they what they will, what need we fear?
The ground's the low'st, and we are half way there.
Go tell their general, we attend him here,
To know for what he comes, and whence he comes,
And what he craves.

Lord. I go, my lord. [*Exit.*

Cle. Welcome is peace, if he on peace consist;
If wars, we are unable to resist.

Enter PERICLES, *with* Attendants.

Per. Lord governor, for so we hear you are,
Let not our ships, and number of our men,
Be, like a beacon fir'd, to amaze your eyes.
We have heard your miseries as far as Tyre,
And see the desolation of your streets!
Nor come we to add sorrow to your tears,
But to relieve them of their heavy load;
And these our ships you happily may think
Are, like the Trojan horse, war-stuff'd within,
With bloody views, expecting overthrow,
Are stor'd with corn, to make your needy bread,
And give them life, who are hunger-starv'd, half dead.

All. The gods of Greece protect you!
And we'll pray for you.

Per. Rise, I pray you, rise;
We do not look for reverence, but for love.
And harbourage for ourself, our ships, and men.

Cle. The which when any shall not gratify,
Or pay you with unthankfulness in thought,
Be it our wives, our children, or ourselves,
The curse of heaven and men succeed their evils!
Till when (the which, I hope, shall ne'er be seen),
Your grace is welcome to our town and us.

Per. Which welcome we'll accept; feast here a while,
Until our stars that frown, lend us a smile.
[*Exeunt.*

ACT II.

Enter GOWER.

Gow. Here have you seen a mighty king
His child, I wis, to incest bring;
A better prince, and benign lord,
Prove awful both in deed and word.
Be quiet then, as men should be,
Till he hath pass'd necessity.
I'll show you those in trouble's reign,
Losing a mite, a mountain gain.
The good in conversation
(To whom I give my benizon),
Is still at Tharsus, where each man
Thinks all is writ he spoken can:
And, to remember what he does,
Gild his statue to make it glorious:
But tidings to the contrary
Are brought your eyes; what need speak I?

Dumb Show.

Enter at one door PERICLES, *talking with* CLEON; *all the* Train *with them. Enter at another door, a* Gentleman *with a Letter to* PERICLES; PERICLES *shows the Letter to* CLEON; *then gives the* Messenger *a reward, and knights him. Exeunt* PERICLES, CLEON, *&c. severally.*

Gow. Good Helicane, that staid at home
(Not to eat honey, like a drone,
From others' labours; for though he strive
To killen bad, keep good alive;
And, to fulfil his prince' desire),
Sends word of all that haps in Tyre:
How Thaliard came full bent with sin,
And hid intent, to murder him;
And that in Tharsus was not best
Longer for him to make his rest:
He knowing so, put forth to seas,
Where when men been, there's seldom ease;
For now the wind begins to blow;
Thunder above, and deeps below,
Make such unquiet, that the ship
Should house him safe, is wreck'd and split;
And he, good prince, having all lost,
By waves from coast to coast is tost:
All perishen of man, of pelf,
Ne aught escapen but himself;
Till fortune, tir'd with doing bad,
Threw him ashore, to give him glad:
And here he comes: what shall be next,—
Pardon old Gower; this 'longs the text.
[*Exit.*

SCENE I.

Pentapolis. *An open Place by the Sea Side.*

Enter PERICLES, *wet.*

Per. Yet cease your ire, ye angry stars of heaven!
Wind, rain, and thunder, remember, earthly man
Is but a substance that must yield to you;
And I, as fits my nature, do obey you;
Alas, the sea hath cast me on the rocks,
Wash'd me from shore to shore, and left me breath
Nothing to think on, but ensuing death:
Let it suffice the greatness of your powers,
To have bereft a prince of all his fortunes;
And having thrown him from your watery grave,
Here to have death in peace, is all he'll crave.

Enter Three Fishermen.

1 *Fish.* What, ho, Pilche!

2 *Fish.* Ho! come, and bring away the nets.

1 *Fish.* What, Patch breech, I say!

3 *Fish.* What say you, master?

1 *Fish.* Look how thou stirrest now! come away, or I'll fetch thee with a wannion.

3 *Fish.* 'Faith, master, I am thinking of the poor men that were cast away before us, even now.

1 *Fish.* Alas, poor souls, it griev'd my heart to hear what pitiful cries they made to us, to

help them, when, well-a-day, we could scarce help ourselves.

3 *Fish.* Nay, master, said not I as much, when I saw the porpus, how he bounced and tumbled? they say, they are half fish, half flesh: a plague on them, they ne'er come, but I look to be wash'd. Master, I marvel how the fishes live in the sea.

1 *Fish.* Why, as men do a-land; the great ones eat up the little ones: I can compare our rich misers to nothing so fitly as to a whale; 'a plays and tumbles, driving the poor fry before him, and at last devours them all at a mouthful. Such whales have I heard on a' the land, who never leave gaping, till they've swallow'd the whole parish, church, steeple, bells and all.

Per. A pretty moral.

3 *Fish.* But, master, if I had been the sexton, I would have been that day in the belfry.

2 *Fish.* Why, man?

3 *Fish.* Because he should have swallow'd me too: and when I had been in his belly, I would have kept such a jangling of the bells, that he should never have left, till he cast bells, steeple, church, and parish, up again. But if the good king Simonides were of my mind——

Per. Simonides?

3 *Fish.* We would purge the land of these drones, that rob the bee of her honey.

Per. How from the finny subject of the sea
These fishers tell the infirmities of men;
And from their watery empire recollect
All that may men approve, or men detect!—
Peace be at your labour, honest fishermen.

2 *Fish.* Honest! good fellow, what's that? if it be a day fits you, scratch it out of the calendar, and no body will look after it.

Per. Nay, see, the sea hath cast upon your coast—

2 *Fish.* What a drunken knave was the sea, to cast thee in our way!

Per. A man whom both the waters and the wind,
In that vast tennis-court, hath made the ball
For them to play upon, entreats you pity him;
He asks of you, that never us'd to beg.

1 *Fish.* No, friend, cannot you beg? here's them in our country of Greece, gets more with begging, than we can do with working.

2 *Fish.* Canst thou catch any fishes then?

Per. I never practis'd it.

2 *Fish.* Nay, then thou wilt starve sure: for here's nothing to be got nowadays, unless thou canst fish for't.

Per. What I have been, I have forgot to know;
But what I am, want teaches me to think on;
A man shrunk up with cold: my veins are chill,
And have no more of life than may suffice
To give my tongue that heat, to ask your help;
Which if you shall refuse, when I am dead,
For I am a man, pray see me buried.

1 *Fish.* Die quoth-a? Now gods forbid! I have a gown here; come, put it on; keep thee warm. Now, afore me, a handsome fellow! Come, thou shalt go home, and we'll have flesh for holidays, fish for fasting-days, and moreo'er puddings and flap-jacks, and thou shalt be welcome.

Per. I thank you, sir.

2 *Fish.* Hark you, my friend, you said you could not beg.

Per. I did but crave.

2 *Fish.* But crave? Then I'll turn craver too, and so I shall 'scape whipping.

Per. Why, are all your beggars whipped then?

2 *Fish.* O, not all, my friend, not all; for if all your beggars were whipp'd, I would wish no better office, than to be beadle. But, master, I'll go draw up the net.

[*Exeunt two of the* Fishermen.

Per. How well this honest mirth becomes their labour!

1 *Fish.* Hark you, sir! do you know where you are?

Per. Not well.

1 *Fish.* Why, I'll tell you: this is called Pentapolis, and our king, the good Simonides.

Per. The good king Simonides, do you call him?

1 *Fish.* Ay, sir; and he deserves to be so call'd, for his peaceable reign, and good government.

Per. He is a happy king, since he gains from his subjects the name of good, by his government. How far is his court distant from this shore?

1 *Fish.* Marry, sir, half a day's journey; and I'll tell you, he hath a fair daughter, and to-morrow is her birth-day; and there are princes and knights come from all parts of the world, to just and tourney for her love.

Per. Were my fortunes equal to my desires, I could wish to make one there.

1 *Fish.* O, sir, things must be as they may; and what a man cannot get, he may lawfully deal for—his wife's soul.

Re-enter the Two Fishermen, *drawing up a net.*

2 *Fish.* Help, master, help; here's a fish hangs in the net, like a poor man's right in the law; 'twill hardly come out. Ha! bots on't, tis come at last, and 'tis turn'd to a rusty armour.

Per. An armour, friends! I pray you, let me see it.
Thanks, fortune, yet, that after all my crosses,
Thou giv'st me somewhat to repair myself;
And, though it was mine own, part of mine heritage,
Which my dead father did bequeath to me,
With this strict charge (even as he left his life),
Keep it, my Pericles, it hath been a shield
'Twixt me and death (and pointed to this brace):
For that it sav'd me, keep it: in like necessity,
The which the gods protect thee from! it may defend thee.
It kept where I kept, I so dearly lov'd it;
Till the rough seas, that spare not any man,
Took it in rage, though calm'd, have given it again.
I thank thee for't; my shipwreck's now no ill,
Since I have here my father's gift by will.

1 *Fish.* What mean you, sir?

Per. To beg of you, kind friends, this coat of worth,
For it was sometime target to a king;
I know it by this mark. He lov'd me dearly,
And for his sake, I wish the having of it;
And that you'd guide me to your sovereign's court,
Where with 't I may appear a gentleman;
And if that ever my low fortunes better,
I'll pay your bounties; till then, rest your debtor.

1 *Fish.* Why, wilt thou tourney for the lady?

Per. I'll show the virtue I have borne in arms.

1 *Fish.* Why, do you take it, and the gods give thee good on't!

2 *Fish.* Ay, but hark you, my friend; 'twas we that made up this garment through the rough seams of the waters: there are certain condolements, certain vails. I hope, sir, if you thrive, you'll remember from whence you had it.

Per. Believe 't, I will.
Now, by your furtherance, I am cloth'd in steel;
And spite of all the rupture of the sea,
This jewel holds his biding on my arm;
Unto thy value will I mount myself
Upon a courser, whose delightful steps
Shall make the gazer joy to see him tread.—
Only, my friend, I yet am unprovided
Of a pair of bases.

2 *Fish.* We'll sure provide: thou shalt have my best gown to make thee a pair; and I'll bring thee to the court myself.

Per. Then honour be but a goal to my will;
This day I'll rise, or else add ill to ill. [*Exeunt.*

SCENE II.

The same. A publick Way, or Platform, leading to the Lists. A Pavilion by the side of it, for the reception of the King, Princess, Lords, *&c.*

Enter SIMONIDES, THAISA, Lords, *and* Attendants.

Sim. Are the knights ready to begin the triumph?

1 *Lord.* They are, my liege;
And stay your coming to present themselves.

Sim. Return them, we are ready; and our daughter,
In honour of whose birth these triumphs are,
Sits here, like beauty's child, whom nature gat
For men to see, and seeing wonder at.
[*Exit a* Lord.

Thai. It pleaseth you, my father, to express
My commendations great, whose merit's less.

Sim. 'Tis fit it should be so; for princes are
A model, which heaven makes like to itself:
As jewels lose their glory, if neglected,
So princes their renown, if not respected.
'Tis now your honour, daughter, to explain
The labour of each knight, in his device.

Thai. Which, to preserve mine honour, I'll perform.

Enter a Knight: *he passes over the Stage, and his* Squire *presents his Shield to the* Princess.

Sim. Who is the first that doth prefer himself?

Thai. A knight of Sparta, my renowned father;
And the device he bears upon his shield
Is a black Æthiop, reaching at the sun;
The word, *Lux tua vita mihi.*

Sim. He loves you well, that holds his life of you. [*The second* Knight *passes.*
Who is the second, that presents himself?

Thai. A prince of Macedon, my royal father;
And the device he bears upon his shield
Is an arm'd knight, that's conquer'd by a lady:
The motto thus, in Spanish, *Piu per dulcura que per fuerca.* [*The third* Knight *passes.*

Sim. And what's the third?

Thai. The third, of Antioch;
And his device, a wreath of chivalry:
The word, *Me pompæ provexit apex.*
[*The fourth* Knight *passes.*

Sim. What is the fourth?

Thai. A burning torch, that's turned upside down;
The word, *Quod me alit, me extinguit.*

Sim. Which shows that beauty hath his power and will,
Which can as well inflame, as it can kill.
[*The fifth* Knight *passes.*

Thai. The fifth, an hand environed with clouds;
Holding out gold, that's by the touchstone tried:
The motto thus, *Sic spectanda fides.*
[*The sixth* Knight *passes.*

Sim. And what's the sixth and last, which the knight himself
With such a graceful courtesy deliver'd?

Thai. He seems to be a stranger; but his present is
A wither'd branch, that's only green at top;
The motto, *In hac spe vivo.*

Sim. A pretty moral;
From the dejected state wherein he is,
He hopes by you his fortunes yet may flourish.

1 *Lord.* He had need mean better than his outward show
Can any way speak in his just commend:
For, by his rusty outside, he appears
To have practis'd more the whipstock, than the lance.

2 *Lord.* He well may be a stranger, for he comes
To an honour'd triumph, strangely furnished.

3 *Lord.* And on set purpose let his armour rust
Until this day, to scour it in the dust.

Sim. Opinion's but a fool, that makes us scan
The outward habit by the inward man.
But stay, the knights are coming; we'll withdraw
Into the gallery. [*Exeunt.*
[*Great shouts, and all cry,* The mean knight.

SCENE III.

The same. A Hall of State.—A Banquet prepared.

Enter SIMONIDES, THAISA, Lords, Knights, *and* Attendants.

Sim. Knights,
To say you are welcome, were superfluous.
To place upon the volume of your deeds,
As in a title-page, your worth in arms,
Were more than you expect, or more than's fit,
Since every worth in show commends itself.
Prepare for mirth, for mirth becomes a feast:
You are my guests.

Thai. But you, my knight and guest;
To whom this wreath of victory I give,
And crown you king of this day's happiness.

Per. 'Tis more by fortune, lady, than my merit.

Sim. Call it by what you will, the day is yours;
And here, I hope, is none that envies it.
In framing artists, art hath thus decreed,
To make some good, but others to exceed;
And you're her labour'd scholar. Come, queen o' the feast
(For, daughter, so you are), here take your place:
Marshal the rest, as they deserve their grace.

Knights. We are honour'd much by good Simonides.

Sim. Your presence glads our days; honour we love,
For who hates honour, hates the gods above.

Marsh. Sir, yond's your place.

Per. Some other is more fit.

1 *Knight.* Contend not, sir: for we are gentlemen,
That neither in our hearts, nor outward eyes,
Envy the great, nor do the low despise.

Per. You are right courteous knights.

Sim. Sit, sit, sir; sit.

Per. By Jove, I wonder, that is king of thoughts,
These cates resist me, be not thought upon.

Thai. By Juno, that is queen
Of marriage, all the viands that I eat
Do seem unsavoury, wishing him my meat;
Sure he's a gallant gentleman.

Sim. He's but
A country gentleman;
He has done no more than other knights have done;
Broken a staff, or so; so let it pass.

Thai. To me he seems like diamond to glass.

Per. Yon king's to me, like to my father's picture,
Which tells me, in that glory once he was;
Had princes sit, like stars, about his throne,
And he the sun, for them to reverence.
None that beheld him, but, like lesser lights,
Did vail their crowns to his supremacy;
Where now his son's a glowworm in the night,
The which hath fire in darkness, none in light;
Whereby I see that time's the king of men,
For he's their parent, and he is their grave,
And gives them what he will, not what they crave.

Sim. What, are you merry knights?

1 *Knight.* Who can be other, in this royal presence?

Sim. Here, with a cup that's stor'd unto the brim
(As you do love, fill to your mistress' lips),
We drink this health to you.

Knights. We thank your grace.

Sim. Yet pause a while;
Yon knight, methinks, doth sit too melancholy,
As if the entertainment in our court
Had not a show might countervail his worth.
Note it not you, Thaisa?

Thai. What is it
To me, my father?
Sim. O, attend, my daughter;
Princes, in this, should live like gods above,
Who freely give to every one that comes
To honour them: and princes, not doing so,
Are like to gnats, which make a sound, but kill'd
Are wonder'd at.
Therefore to make's entrance more sweet
Here say, we drink this standing-bowl of wine to him.
Thai. Alas, my father, it befits not me
Unto a stranger knight to be so bold;
He may my proffer take for an offence,
Since men take women's gifts for impudence.
Sim. How!
Do as I bid you, or you'll move me else.
Thai. Now, by the gods, he could not please me better. [*Aside.*
Sim. And further tell him, we desire to know,
Of whence he is, his name, and parentage.
Thai. The king, my father, sir, has drunk to you.
Per. I thank him.
Thai. Wishing it so much blood unto your life.
Per. I thank both him and you, and pledge him freely.
Thai. And further he desires to know of you,
Of whence you are, your name and parentage.
Per. A gentleman of Tyre—(my name, Pericles;
My education being in arts and arms);—
Who looking for adventures in the world,
Was by the rough seas reft of ships and men,
And, after shipwreck, driven upon this shore.
Thai. He thanks your grace; names himself Pericles,
A gentleman of Tyre, who only by
Misfortune of the seas has been bereft
Of ships and men, and cast upon this shore.
Sim. Now by the gods, I pity his misfortune,
And will awake him from his melancholy.
Come, gentlemen, we sit too long on trifles,
And waste the time, which looks for other revels.
Even in your armours, as you are address'd,
Will very well become a soldier's dance.
I will not have excuse, with saying, this
Loud musick is too harsh for ladies' heads;
Since they love men in arms, as well as beds.
[*The* Knights *dance.*
So, this was well ask'd, 'twas so well perform'd.
Come, sir;
Here is a lady that wants breathing too:
And I have often heard, you knights of Tyre
Are excellent in making ladies trip:
And that their measures are as excellent.
Per. In those that practise them, they are, my lord.
Sim. O, that's as much, as you would be denied [*The* Knights *and* Ladies *dance.*
Of your fair courtesy.—Unclasp, unclasp;
Thanks, gentlemen, to all; all have done well;
But you the best. [*To* PERICLES]. Pages and lights, conduct
These knights unto their several lodgings: Yours, sir,
We have given order to be next our own.
Per. I am at your grace's pleasure.
Sim. Princes, it is too late to talk of love,
For that's the mark I know you level at:
Therefore each one betake him to his rest;
To-morrow, all for speeding do their best.
[*Exeunt.*

SCENE IV.

Tyre. *A Room in the* Governor's *House.*

Enter HELICANUS *and* ESCANES.

Hel. No, no, my Escanes; know this of me,—
Antiochus from incest liv'd not free;
For which, the most high gods not minding longer
To withhold the vengeance that they had in store,
Due to this heinous capital offence,
Even in the height and pride of all his glory,
When he was seated, and his daughter with him,
In a chariot of inestimable value,
A fire from heaven came, and shrivel'd up
Their bodies, even to loathing; for they so stunk,
That all those eyes ador'd them ere their fall,
Scorn now their hand should give them burial.
Esca. 'Twas very strange.
Hel. And yet but just; for though
This king were great, his greatness was no guard
To bar heaven's shaft; but sin had his reward.
Esca. 'Tis very true.

Enter Three Lords.

1 *Lord.* See, not a man in private conference,
Or council, has respect with him but he.
2 *Lord.* It shall no longer grieve without reproof.
3 *Lord.* And curst be he that will not second it.
1 *Lord.* Follow me then: Lord Helicane, a word.
Hel. With me? and welcome: Happy day, my lords.
1 *Lord.* Know, that our griefs are risen to the top,
And now at length they overflow their banks.
Hel. Your griefs, for what? wrong not the prince you love.
1 *Lord.* Wrong not yourself then, noble Helicane;
But if the prince do live, let us salute him,
Or know what ground's made happy by his breath.
If in the world he live, we'll seek him out;
If in his grave he rest, we'll find him there;
And be resolv'd, he lives to govern us,
Or dead, gives cause to mourn his funeral,
And leaves us to our free election.
2 *Lord.* Whose death's, indeed, the strongest in our censure:
And knowing this kingdom, if without a head
(Like goodly buildings left without a roof),
Will soon to ruin fall, your noble self,
That best know'st how to rule, and how to reign,
We thus submit unto,—our sovereign.
All. Live, noble Helicane!
Hel. Try, honour's cause, forbear your suffrages:
If that you love prince Pericles, forbear.
Take I your wish, I leap into the seat,
Where's hourly trouble for a minute's ease.
A twelvemonth longer, let me then entreat you
To forbear choice i' the absence of your king;
If in which time expir'd, he not return,
I shall with aged patience bear your yoke.
But if I cannot win you to this love,
Go search like noblemen, like noble subjects,
And in your search spend your adventurous worth;
Whom if you find, and win unto return,
You shall like diamonds sit about his crown.
1 *Lord.* To wisdom he's a fool that will not yield;
And, since Lord Helicane enjoineth us,
We with our travels will endeavour it.
Hel. Then you love us, we you, and we'll clasp hands;
When peers thus knit, a kingdom ever stands.
[*Exeunt.*

SCENE V. Pentapolis. *A Room in the Palace.*

Enter SIMONIDES, *reading a Letter; the* Knights *meet him.*

1 *Knight.* Good morrow to the good Simonides.
Sim. Knights, from my daughter this I let you know,
That for this twelvemonth, she'll not undertake
A married life.

Her reason to herself is only known,
Which from herself by no means can I get.
2 *Knight.* May we not get access to her, my lord?
Sim. 'Faith, by no means; she hath so strictly tied her
To her chamber, that it is impossible.
One twelve moons more she'll wear Diana's livery;
This by the eye of Cynthia hath she vow'd,
And on her virgin honour will not break it.
3 *Knight.* Though loath to bid farewell, we take our leaves. [*Exeunt.*
Sim. So
They're well despatch'd; now to my daughter's letter:
She tells me here, she'll wed the stranger knight,
Or never more to view nor day nor light.
Mistress, 'tis well, your choice agrees with mine;
I like that well:—nay, how absolute she's in't,
Not minding whether I dislike or no!
Well, I commend her choice;
And will no longer have it be delay'd.
Soft, here he comes:—I must dissemble it.

Enter PERICLES.

Per. All fortune to the good Simonides!
Sim. To you as much, sir! I am beholden to you,
For your sweet musick this last night: my ears,
I do protest, were never better fed
With such delightful pleasing harmony.
Per. It is your grace's pleasure to commend;
Not my desert.
Sim. Sir, you are musick's master.
Per. The worst of all her scholars, my good lord.
Sim. Let me ask one thing. What do you think, sir, of
My daughter?
Per. As of a most virtuous princess.
Sim. And she is fair too, is she not?
Per. As a fair day in summer; wondrous fair.
Sim. My daughter, sir, thinks very well of you;
Ay, so well, sir, that you must be her master,
And she'll your scholar be; therefore look to it.
Per. Unworthy I to be her schoolmaster.
Sim. She thinks not so; peruse this writing else.
Per. What's here?
A letter, that she loves the knight of Tyre?
'Tis the king's subtilty, to have my life. [*Aside.*
O, seek not to entrap, my gracious lord,
A stranger, and distressed gentleman,
That never aim'd so high, to love your daughter.
But bent all offices to honour her.
Sim. Thou hast bewitch'd my daughter, and thou art
A villain.
Per. By the gods, I have not, sir.
Never did thought of mine levy offence;
Nor never did my actions yet commence
A deed might gain her love, or your displeasure.
Sim. Traitor, thou liest.
Per. Traitor!
Sim. Ay, traitor, sir.
Per. Even in his throat (unless it be the king),
That calls me traitor, I return the lie.
Sim. Now, by the gods, I do applaud his courage. [*Aside.*
Per. My actions are as noble as my thoughts,
That never relish'd of a base descent.
I came unto your court, for honour's cause,
And not to be a rebel to her state;
And he that otherwise accounts of me,
This sword shall prove he's honour's enemy.
Sim. No!—
Here comes my daughter, she can witness it.

Enter THAISA.

Per. Then, as you are as virtuous as fair,
Resolve your angry father, if my tongue
Did e'er solicit, or my hand subscribe
To any syllable that made love to you?
Thai. Why, sir, say if you had,
Who takes offence at that would make me glad?
Sim. Yea, mistress, are you so peremptory?—
I am glad of it with all my heart. [*Aside.*] I'll tame you;
I'll bring you in subjection.—
Will you, not having my consent, bestow
Your love and your affections on a stranger?
(Who, for aught I know to the contrary,
Or think, may be as great in blood as I.) [*Aside.*
Hear therefore, mistress; frame your will to mine,—
And you, sir, hear you.—Either be rul'd by me,
Or I will make you—man and wife.—
Nay, come; your hands and lips must seal it too.—
And being join'd, I'll thus your hopes destroy;—
And for a further grief,—God give you joy!
What, are you both pleas'd?
Thai. Yes, if you love me, sir.
Per. Even as my life, my blood that fosters it.
Sim. What, are you both agreed?
Both. Yes, please your majesty.
Sim. It pleaseth me so well, I'll see you wed;
Then, with what haste you can, get you to bed. [*Exeunt.*

ACT III.

Enter GOWER.

Gow. Now sleep yslaked hath the rout;
No din but snores, the house about,
Made louder by the o'er-fed breast
Of this most pompous marriage-feast.
The cat, with eyne of burning coal,
Now couches 'fore the mouse's hole;
And crickets sing at th' oven's mouth,
As the blither for their drouth.
Hymen hath brought the bride to bed,
Where, by the loss of maidenhead,
A babe is moulded;—Be attent,
And time that is so briefly spent,
With your fine fancies quaintly eche;
What's dumb in show, I'll plain with speech.

Dumb Show.

Enter PERICLES *and* SIMONIDES *at one door, with* Attendants: *a* Messenger *meets them, kneels, and gives* PERICLES *a Letter.* PERICLES *shows it to* SIMONIDES; *the* Lords *kneel to the former. Then enter* THAISA *with child, and* LYCHORIDA. SIMONIDES *shows his* Daughter *the Letter; she rejoices: she and* PERICLES *take leave of her* Father, *and depart. Then* SIMONIDES, *&c. retire.*

Gow. By many a dearn and painful perch,
Of Pericles the careful search
By the four opposing coignes,
Which the world together joins,
Is made, with all due diligence,
That horse, and sail, and high expense,
Can stead the quest. At last from Tyre
(Fame answering the most strong inquire),
To the court of King Simonides
Are letters brought; the tenour these:
Antiochus and his daughter's dead;
The men of Tyrus, on the head
Of Helicanus would set on
The crown of Tyre, but he will none:
The mutiny there he hastes t' oppress;
Says to them, if King Pericles
Come not home, in twice six moons,
He, obedient to their dooms,
Will take the crown. The sum of this,
Brought hither to Pentapolis,
Y-ravished the regions round,
And every one with claps 'gan sound,
Our heir apparent is a king:
Who dream'd, who thought of such a thing?
Brief, he must hence depart to Tyre:
His queen, with child, makes her desire

(Which who shall cross?) along to go
(Omit we all their dole and woe);
Lychorida, her nurse, she takes,
And so to sea. Their vessel shakes
On Neptune's billow; half the flood
Hath their keel cut; but fortune's mood
Varies again; the grizzled north
Disgorges such a tempest forth,
That, as a duck for life that dives,
So up and down the poor ship drives.
The lady shrieks, and, well-a-near!
Doth fall in travail with her fear:
And what ensues in this fell storm,
Shall, for itself, itself perform.
I nill relate; action may
Conveniently the rest convey:
Which might not what by me is told.
In your imagination hold
This stage, the ship, upon whose deck
The sea-tost prince appears to speak. [*Exit.*

SCENE I.

Enter PERICLES, *on a Ship at Sea.*

Per. Thou God of this great vast, rebuke these surges,
Which wash both heaven and hell; and thou, that hast
Upon the winds command, bind them in brass,
Having call'd them from the deep! O still thy deaf'ning,
Thy dreadful thunders; gently quench thy nimble
Sulphureous flashes!—O how, Lychorida,
How does my queen!—Thou storm, thou! venomously
Wilt thou spit all thyself?—The seaman's whistle
Is as a whisper in the ears of death,
Unheard.—Lychorida!—Lucina, O
Divinest patroness, and midwife, gentle
To those that cry by night, convey thy deity
Aboard our dancing boat; make swift the pangs
Of my queen's travails!—Now, Lychorida——

Enter LYCHORIDA, *with an* Infant.

Lyc. Here is a thing
Too young for such a place, who if it had
Conceit would die as I am like to do.
Take in your arms this piece of your dead queen.

Per. How! how, Lychorida!

Lyc. Patience, good sir; do not assist the storm.
Here's all that is left living of your queen,—
A little daughter; for the sake of it,
Be manly, and take comfort.

Per. O you gods!
Why do you make us love your goodly gifts,
And snatch them straight away? We, here below,
Recall not what we give, and therein may
Vie honour with yourselves.

Lyc. Patience, good sir,
Even for this charge.

Per. Now, mild may be thy life!
For a more blust'rous birth had never babe:
Quiet and gentle thy conditions!
For thou art the rudeliest welcom'd to this world,
That e'er was prince's child. Happy what follows!
Thou hast as chiding a nativity,
As fire, air, water, earth, and heaven can make,
To herald thee from the womb: even at the first,
Thy loss is more than can thy portage quit,
With all thou canst find here.—Now the good gods
Throw their best eyes upon it!

Enter Two Sailors.

1 *Sail.* What courage, sir? God save you.

Per. Courage enough: I do not fear the flaw;
It hath done to me the worst. Yet, for the love
Of this poor infant, this fresh-new sea-farer,
I would, it would be quiet.

1 *Sail.* Slack the bolins there; thou wilt not, wilt thou? Blow and split thyself.

2 *Sail.* But sea-room, an the brine and cloudy billow kiss the moon, I care not.

1 *Sail.* Sir, your queen must overboard; the sea works high, the wind is loud, and will not lie till the ship be cleared of the dead.

Per. That's your superstition.

1 *Sail.* Pardon us, sir; with us at sea it still hath been observed; and we are strong in custom. Therefore briefly yield her; for she must overboard straight.

Per. Be it as you think meet.—Most wretched queen!

Lyc. Here she lies, sir.

Per. A terrible child-bed hast thou had, my dear,
No light, no fire; the unfriendly elements
Forgot thee utterly; nor have I time
To give thee hallow'd to thy grave, but straight
Must cast thee, scarcely coffin'd, in the ooze;
Where, for a monument upon thy bones,
And aye-remaining lamps, the belching whale,
And humming water must o'erwhelm thy corpse,
Lying with simple shells. Lychorida,
Bid Nestor bring me spices, ink, and paper,
My casket and my jewels; and bid Nicander
Bring me the satin coffer: lay the babe
Upon the pillow: hie thee, whiles I say
A priestly farewell to her: suddenly, woman.
[*Exit* LYCHORIDA.

2 *Sail.* Sir, we have a chest beneath the hatches, caulk'd and bitumed ready.

Per. I thank thee. Mariner, say what coast is this?

2 *Sail.* We are near Tharsus.

Per. Thither, gentle mariner,
Alter thy course for Tyre. When canst thou reach it?

2 *Sail.* By break of day, if the wind cease.

Per. O make for Tharsus.
There will I visit Cleon, for the babe
Cannot hold out to Tyrus; there I'll leave it
At careful nursing. Go thy ways, good mariner;
I'll bring the body presently. [*Exeunt.*

SCENE II.

Ephesus. *A Room in* Cerimon's *House.*

Enter CERIMON, *a* Servant, *and some* Persons *who have been shipwrecked.*

Cer. Philemon, ho!

Enter PHILEMON.

Phil. Doth my lord call?

Cer. Get fire and meat for these poor men;
It has been a turbulent and stormy night.

Serv. I have been in many; but such a night as this,
Till now I ne'er endur'd.

Cer. Your master will be dead ere you return;
There's nothing can be minister'd to nature,
That can recover him. Give this to the 'pothecary,
And tell me how it works. [*To* PHILEMON.
[*Exeunt* PHILEMON, Servant, *and those who had been shipwrecked.*

Enter Two Gentlemen.

1 *Gent.* Good morrow, sir.

2 *Gent.* Good morrow to your lordship.

Cer. Gentlemen,
Why do you stir so early?

1 *Gent.* Sir,
Our lodging, standing bleak upon the sea,
Shook, as the earth did quake;
The very principals did seem to rend,
And all to topple; pure surprise and fear
Made me to quit the house.

2 *Gent.* That is the cause we trouble you so early;
'Tis not our husbandry.

Cer. O, you say well.

1 *Gent.* But I much marvel that your lordship, having

Rich tire about you, should at these early hours
Shake off the golden slumber of repose.
It is most strange,
Nature should be so conversant with pain,
Being thereto not compell'd.
Cer. I held it ever,
Virtue and cunning were endowments greater
Than nobleness and riches; careless heirs
May the two latter darken and expend;
But immortality attends the former,
Making a man a god. 'Tis known, I ever
Have studied physick, through which secret art,
By turning o'er authorities, I have
(Together with my practice), made familiar
To me and to my aid, the blest infusions
That dwell in vegetives, in metals, stones;
And I can speak of the disturbances
That nature works, and of her cures; which gives me
A more content in course of true delight
Than to be thirsty after tottering honour,
Or tie my treasure up in silken bags,
To please the fool and death.
2 Gent. Your honour has through Ephesus pour'd forth
Your charity, and hundreds call themselves
Your creatures, who by you have been restor'd:
And not your knowledge, personal pain, but even
Your purse, still open, hath built Lord Cerimon
Such strong renown as time shall never——

Enter Two Servants *with a Chest.*

Serv. So; lift there.
Cer. What is that?
Serv. Sir, even now
Did the sea toss upon our shore this chest;
'Tis of some wreck.
Cer. Set 't down, let's look on it.
2 Gent. 'Tis like a coffin, sir.
Cer. Whate'er it be,
'Tis wondrous heavy. Wrench it open straight;
If the sea's stomach be o'ercharg'd with gold,
It is a good constraint of fortune, that
It belches upon us.
2 Gent. 'Tis so, my lord.
Cer. How close 'tis caulk'd and bitum'd!—
Did the sea cast it up?
Serv. I never saw so huge a billow, sir,
As toss'd it upon shore.
Cer. Come, wrench it open;
Soft, soft!—it smells most sweetly in my sense.
2 Gent. A delicate odour.
Cer. As ever hit my nostril; so,—up with it.
O you most potent gods! what's here? a corse!
1 Gent. Most strange!
Cer. Shrouded in cloth of state; balm'd and entreasur'd
With bags of spices full! A passport too!
Apollo, perfect me i' the characters!
[*Unfolds a Scroll.*

Here I give to understand [Reads.
(If e'er this coffin drive a land),
I, king Pericles, have lost
This queen, worth all our mundane cost.
Who finds her, give her burying,
She was the daughter of a king:
Besides this treasure for a fee,
The gods requite his charity!

If thou liv'st, Pericles, thou hast a heart
That even cracks for woe!—This chanc'd to-[night.
2 Gent. Most likely, sir.
Cer. Nay, certainly to-night;
For look, how fresh she looks!—They were too rough,
That threw her in the sea. Make fire within;
Fetch hither all the boxes in my closet.
Death may usurp on nature many hours,
And yet the fire of life kindle again
The overpressed spirits. I have heard
Of an Egyptian, had nine hours lien dead,
By good appliance was recover'd.

Enter a Servant, *with Boxes, Napkins, and Fire.*

Well said, well said; the fire and the cloths.—
The rough and woful music that we have,
Cause it to sound, 'beseech you.
The vial once more;—How thou stirr'st, thou block!—
The musick there.—I pray you, give her air:—
Gentlemen,
This queen will live: nature awakes; a warmth
Breathes out of her; she hath not been entranc'd
Above five hours. See, how she 'gins to blow
Into life's flower again!
1 Gent. The heavens, sir,
Through you, increase our wonder, and set up
Your fame for ever.
Cer. She is alive; behold,
Her eyelids, cases to those heavenly jewels
Which Pericles hath lost,
Begin to part their fringes of bright gold;
The diamonds of a most praised water
Appear, to make the world twice rich. O live,
And make us weep to hear your fate, fair creature,
Rare as you seem to be! [*She moves.*
Thai. O dear Diana,
Where am I? Where's my lord? What world is this?
2 Gent. Is not this strange?
1 Gent. Most rare.
Cer. Hush, gentle neighbours;
Lend me your hands: to the next chamber bear her.
Get linen; now this matter must be look'd to,
For her relapse is mortal. Come, come, come;
And Æsculapius guide us!
[*Exeunt, carrying* THAISA *away.*

SCENE III. Tharsus. *A Room in* Cleon's *House.*

Enter PERICLES, CLEON, DIONYZA, LYCHORIDA, *and* MARINA.

Per. Most honour'd Cleon, I must needs be gone;
My twelve months are expir'd, and Tyrus stands
In a litigious peace. You, and your lady,
Take from my heart all thankfulness! The gods
Make up the rest upon you!
Cle. Your shafts of fortune, though they hurt you mortally,
Yet glance full wand'ringly on us.
Dion. O your sweet queen!
That the strict fates had pleas'd you had brought her hither,
To have bless'd mine eyes!
Per. We cannot but obey
The powers above us. Could I rage and roar
As doth the sea she lies in, yet the end
Must be as 'tis. My babe Marina (whom,
For she was born at sea, I have nam'd so) here
I charge your charity withal, and leave her
The infant of your care; beseeching you
To give her princely training, that she may be
Manner'd as she is born.
Cle. Fear not, my lord, but think
Your grace, that fed my country with your corn
(For which the people's prayers still fall upon you),
Must in your child be thought on. If neglection
Should therein make me vile, the common body,
By you reliev'd, would force me to my duty:
But if to that my nature need a spur,
The gods revenge it upon me and mine,
To the end of generation!
Per. I believe you;
Your honour and your goodness teach me credit,
Without your vows. Till she be married, madam,
By bright Diana, whom we honour all,
Unscissar'd shall this hair of mine remain,
Though I show will in 't. So I take my leave.
Good madam, make me blessed in your care
In bringing up my child.
Dion. I have one myself,

Who shall not be more dear to my respect,
Than yours, my lord.
Per. Madam, my thanks and prayers.
Cle. We'll bring your grace e'en to the edge o' the shore;
Then give you up to the mask'd Neptune; and
The gentlest winds of heaven.
Per. I will embrace
Your offer. Come, dear'st madam.—O, no tears,
Lychorida, no tears:
Look to your little mistress, on whose grace
You may depend hereafter.—Come, my lord.
[*Exeunt.*

SCENE IV.

Ephesus. *A Room in* Cerimon's *House.*

Enter CERIMON *and* THAISA.

Cer. Madam, this letter, and some certain jewels,
Lay with you in your coffer; which are now
At your command. Know you the character?
Thai. It is my lord's.
That I was shipp'd at sea, I well remember,
Even on my eaning time; but whether there
Delivered or no, by the holy gods,
I cannot rightly say: But since King Pericles,
My wedded lord, I ne'er shall see again,
A vestal livery will I take me to,
And never more have joy.
Cer. Madam, if this you purpose as you speak,
Diana's temple is not distant far,
Where you may 'bide until your date expire.
Moreover, if you please, a niece of mine
Shall there attend you.
Thai. My recompense is thanks, that's all:
Yet my good will is great, though the gift small.
[*Exeunt.*

ACT IV.

Enter GOWER.

Gow. Imagine Pericles arriv'd at Tyre,
Welcom'd and settled to his own desire.
His woful queen leave at Ephesus,
Unto Diana there a votaress.
Now to Marina bend your mind,
Whom our fast growing scene must find
At Tharsus, and by Cleon train'd
In musick, letters; who hath gain'd
Of education all the grace,
Which makes her both the heart and place
Of general wonder. But alack!
That monster envy, oft the wrack
Of earned praise, Marina's life
Seeks to take off by treason's knife.
And in this kind hath our Cleon
One daughter, and a wench full grown,
Even ripe for marriage fight; this maid
Hight Philoten: and it is said
For certain in our story, she
Would ever with Marina be:
Be't when she weav'd the sleided silk
With fingers long, small, white as milk;
Or when she would with sharp neeld wound
The cambrick, which she made more sound
By hurting it; or when to the lute
She sung, and made the night-bird mute,
That still records with moan; or when
She would with rich and constant pen
Vail to her mistress Dian; still
This Philoten contends in skill
With absolute Marina: so
With the dove of Paphos might the crow
Vie feathers white. Marina gets
All praises, which are paid as debts,
And not as given. This so darks
In Philoten all graceful marks,
That Cleon's wife, with envy rare,
A present murderer does prepare
For good Marina, that her daughter
Might stand peerless by this slaughter.
The sooner her vile thoughts to stead,
Lychorida, our nurse, is dead;
And cursed Dionyza hath
The pregnant instrument of wrath
Prest for this blow. The unborn event
I do commend to your content:
Only I carry winged time
Post on the lame feet of my rhyme;
Which never could I so convey,
Unless your thoughts went on my way.—
Dionyza does appear,
With Leonine, a murderer. [*Exit.*

SCENE I.

Tharsus. *An open Place near the Seashore.*

Enter DIONYZA *and* LEONINE.

Dion. Thy oath remember; thou hast sworn to do it;
'Tis but a blow, which never shall be known.
Thou canst not do a thing i' the world so soon,
To yield thee so much profit. Let not conscience,
Which is but cold, inflaming love, thy bosom
Inflame too nicely; nor let pity, which
Even women have cast off, melt thee, but be
A soldier to thy purpose.
Leon. I'll do't; but yet she is a goodly creature.
Dion. The fitter then the gods should have her. Here
Weeping she comes for her old nurse's death.
Thou art resolv'd?
Leon. I am resolv'd.

Enter MARINA, *with a Basket of Flowers.*

Mar. No, no, I will rob Tellus of her weed,
To strew thy green with flowers: the yellows, blues,
The purple violets, and marigolds,
Shall, as a chaplet, hang upon thy grave,
While summer days do last. Ah me! poor maid,
Born in a tempest, when my mother died,
This world to me is like a lasting storm,
Whirring me from my friends.
Dion. How now, Marina! why do you keep alone!
How chance my daughter is not with you? Do not
Consume your blood with sorrowing: you have
A nurse of me. Lord! how your favour's chang'd
With this unprofitable woe! Come, come;
Give me your wreath of flowers. Ere the sea mar it,
Walk forth with Leonine; the air is quick there,
Piercing, and sharpens well the stomach. Come;—
Leonine, take her by the arm, walk with her.
Mar. No, I pray you;
I'll not bereave you of your servant.
Dion. Come, come;
I love the king your father, and yourself,
With more than foreign heart. We every day
Expect him here: when he shall come, and find
Our paragon to all reports, thus blasted,
He will repent the breadth of his great voyage;
Blame both my lord and me, that we have ta'en
No care to your best courses. Go, I pray you,
Walk, and be cheerful once again; reserve
That excellent complexion, which did steal
The eyes of young and old. Care not for me;
I can go home alone.
Mar. Well, I will go;
But yet I have no desire to it.
Dion. Come, come, I know 'tis good for you,
Walk half an hour, Leonine, at the least;
Remember what I have said.
Leon. I warrant you, madam.
Dion. I'll leave you, my sweet lady, for a while;
Pray you walk softly, do not heat your blood:
What! I must have a care of you.
Mar. Thanks, sweet madam.—
[*Exit* DIONYZA.
Is this wind westerly that blows?
Leon. South-west.

Mar. When I was born, the wind was north.
Leon. Was 't so?
Mar. My father, as nurse said, did never fear,
But cry'd, *Good seamen!* to the sailors, galling
His kingly hands with hauling of the ropes;
And, clasping to the mast, endur'd a sea
That almost burst the deck.
Leon. When was this?
Mar. When I was born:
Never was waves nor wind more violent;
And from the ladder-tackle washes off
A canvass-climber. *Ha!* says one, *wilt out?*
And with a dropping industry they skip
From stem to stern: the boatswain whistles, and
The master calls, and trebles their confusion.
Leon. Come, say your prayers.
Mar. What mean you?
Leon. If you require a little space for prayer,
I grant it: Pray! but be not tedious,
For the gods are quick of ear, and I am sworn
To do my work with haste.
Mar. Why will you kill me?
Leon. To satisfy my lady.
Mar. Why would she have me kill'd?
Now, as I can remember, by my troth,
I never did her hurt in all my life;
I never spake bad word, nor did ill turn
To any living creature: believe me, la,
I never kill'd a mouse, nor hurt a fly:
I trod upon a worm against my will,
But I wept for it. How have I offended,
Wherein my death might yield her profit, or
My life imply her danger?
Leon. My commission
Is not to reason of the deed, but do it.
Mar. You will not do't for all the world, I hope.
You are well favour'd, and your looks foreshow
You have a gentle heart. I saw you lately,
When you caught hurt in parting two that fought:
Good sooth, it show'd well in you: do so now:
Your lady seeks my life: come you between,
And save poor me, the weaker.
Leon. I am sworn,
And will despatch.

Enter Pirates, *whilst* MARINA *is struggling.*

1 *Pirate.* Hold, villain! [LEONINE *runs away.*
2 *Pirate.* A prize! a prize!
3 *Pirate.* Half-part, mates, half-part. Come, let's have her aboard suddenly.
[*Exeunt* Pirates *with* MARINA.

SCENE II. *The same.*

Re-enter LEONINE.

Leon. These roving thieves serve the great pirate Valdes;
And they have seiz'd Marina. Let her go:
There's no hope she'll return. I'll swear she's dead,
And thrown into the sea.—But I'll see further;
Perhaps they will but please themselves upon her,
Not carry her aboard. If she remain,
Whom they have ravish'd, must by me be slain.
[*Exit.*

SCENE III. Mitylene. *A Room in a Brothel.*

Enter PANDER, Bawd, *and* BOULT.

Pand. Boult.
Boult. Sir.
Pand. Search the market narrowly; Mitylene is full of gallants. We lost too much money this mart, by being too wenchless.
Bawd. We were never so much out of creatures. We have but poor three, and they can do no more than they can do; and with continual action are even as good as rotten.
Pand. Therefore let's have fresh ones, whate'er we pay for them. If there be not a conscience to be us'd in every trade, we shall never prosper.
Bawd. Thou say'st true; 'tis not the bringing up of poor bastards, as I think I have brough up some eleven——
Boult. Ay, to eleven, and brought them down again. But shall I search the market?
Bawd. What else, man? The stuff we have, a strong wind will blow it to pieces, they are so pitifully sodden.
Pand. Thou say'st true; they are too unwholesome o' conscience. The poor Transilvanian is dead, that lay with the little baggage.
Boult. Ay, she quickly pooped him; she made him roast meat for worms:—but I'll go search the market. [*Exit* BOULT.
Pand. Three or four thousand chequins were as pretty a proportion to live quietly, and so give over.
Bawd. Why, to give over, I pray you? is it a shame to get when we are old?
Pand. O, our credit comes not in like the commodity: nor the commodity wages not with the danger; therefore, if in our youths we could pick up some pretty estate, 'twere not amiss to keep our door hatch'd. Besides, the sore terms we stand upon with the gods, will be strong with us for giving over.
Bawd. Come, other sorts offend as well as we.
Pand. As well as we! ay, and better too; we offend worse. Neither is our profession any trade; it's no calling:—but here comes Boult.

Enter the Pirates, *and* BOULT, *dragging in* MARINA.

Boult. Come your ways. [*To* MARINA.]—My masters, you say she's a virgin?
1 *Pirate.* O, sir, we doubt it not.
Boult. Master, I have gone thorough for this piece, you see: if you like her, so; if not, I have lost my earnest.
Bawd. Boult, has she any qualities?
Boult. She has a good face, speaks well, and has excellent good clothes; there's no further necessity of qualities can make her be refused.
Bawd. What's her price, Boult?
Boult. I cannot be bated one doit of a thousand pieces.
Pand. Well, follow me, my masters; you shall have your money presently. Wife, take her in; instruct her what she has to do, that she may not be raw in her entertainment.
[*Exeunt* Pander *and* Pirates.
Bawd. Boult, take you the marks of her; the colour of her hair, complexion, height, age, with warrant of her virginity; and cry, *He that will give most, shall have her first.* Such a maidenhead were no cheap thing, if men were as they have been. Get this done as I command you.
Boult. Performance shall follow.
[*Exit* BOULT.
Mar. Alack, that Leonine was so slack, so slow!
(He should have struck, not spoke;) or that these pirates
(Not enough barbarous) had not overboard
Thrown me, to seek my mother!
Bawd. Why lament you, pretty one?
Mar. That I am pretty.
Bawd. Come, the gods have done their part in you.
Mar. I accuse them not.
Bawd. You are lit into my hands, where you are like to live.
Mar. The more my fault,
To 'scape his hands, where I was like to die.
Bawd. Ay, and you shall live in pleasure.
Mar. No.
Bawd. Yes, indeed, shall you, and taste gentlemen of all fashions. You shall fare well; you shall have the difference of all complexions. What! do you stop your ears?
Mar. Are you a woman?
Bawd. What would you have me be, an I be not a woman?
Mar. An honest woman, or not a woman.

Bawd. Marry, whip thee, gosling: I think I shall have something to do with you. Come, you are a young foolish sapling, and must be bowed as I would have you.

Mar. The gods defend me!

Bawd. If it please the gods to defend you by men, then men must comfort you, men must feed you, men must stir you up.—Boult's returned.

Enter BOULT.

Now, sir, hast thou cried her through the market?

Boult. I have cried her almost to the number of her hairs; I have drawn her picture with my voice.

Bawd. And I pr'ythee tell me, how dost thou find the inclination of the people, especially of the younger sort?

Boult. 'Faith, they listen'd to me, as they would have hearken'd to their father's testament. There was a Spaniard's mouth so watered, that he went to bed to her very description.

Bawd. We shall have him here to-morrow with his best ruff on.

Boult. To-night, to-night. But, mistress, do you know the French knight that cowers i' the hams?

Bawd. Who? Monsieur Veroles?

Boult. Ay; he offered to cut a caper at the proclamation; but he made a groan at it, and swore he would see her to-morrow.

Bawd. Well, well; as for him, he brought his disease hither: here he does but repair it. I know, he will come in our shadow, to scatter his crowns in the sun.

Boult. Well, if we had of every nation a traveller, we should lodge them with this sign.

Bawd. Pray you come hither awhile. You have fortunes coming upon you. Mark me; you must seem to do that fearfully, which you commit willingly; to despise profit, where you have most gain. To weep that you live as you do, makes pity in your lovers: Seldom, but that pity begets you a good opinion, and that opinion a mere profit.

Mar. I understand you not.

Boult. O, take her home, mistress, take her home: these blushes of hers must be quenched with some present practice.

Bawd. Thou say'st true, i'faith, so they must: for your bride goes to that with shame, which is her way to go with warrant.

Boult. 'Faith, some do, and some do not. But, mistress, if I have bargained for the joint,——

Bawd. Thou may'st cut a morsel off the spit.

Boult. I may so.

Bawd. Who should deny it? Come, young one, I like the manner of your garments well.

Boult. Ay, by my faith, they shall not be changed yet.

Bawd. Boult, spend thou that in the town: report what a sojourner we have: you'll lose nothing by custom. When nature framed this piece, she meant thee a good turn; therefore say what a paragon she is, and thou hast the harvest out of thine own report.

Boult. I warrant you, mistress, thunder shall not so awake the beds of eels, as my giving out her beauty stir up the lewdly-inclined. I'll bring home some to-night.

Bawd. Come your ways; follow me.

Mar. If fires be hot, knives sharp, or waters deep,
Untied I still my virgin knot will keep.
Diana, aid my purpose!

Bawd. What have we to do with Diana? Pray you, will you go with us? [*Exeunt.*

SCENE IV. Tharsus. *A Room in* Cleon's *House.*

Enter CLEON *and* DIONYZA.

Dion. Why, are you foolish? Can it be undone?

Cle. O Dionyza, such a piece of slaughter
The sun and moon ne'er look'd upon!

Dion. I think
You'll turn a child again.

Cle. Were I chief lord of all the spacious world,
I'd give it to undo the deed. O lady,
Much less in blood than virtue, yet a princess
To equal any single crown o' the earth,
I' the justice of compare! O villain Leonine,
Whom thou hast poison'd too!
If thou had'st drunk to him, it had been a kindness
Becoming well thy feat: what canst thou say,
When noble Pericles shall demand his child?

Dion. That she is dead. Nurses are not the fates,
To foster it, nor ever to preserve.
She died at night; I'll say so. Who can cross it?
Unless you play the impious innocent,
And for an honest attribute, cry out,
She died by foul play.

Cle. O, go to. Well, well,
Of all the faults beneath the heavens, the gods
Do like this worst.

Dion. Be one of those, that think
The pretty wrens of Tharsus will fly hence,
And open this to Pericles. I do shame
To think of what a noble strain you are,
And of how coward a spirit.

Cle. To such proceeding
Who ever but his approbation added,
Though not his pre-consent, he did not flow
From honourable courses.

Dion. Be it so then:
Yet none does know, but you, how she came dead,
Nor none can know, Leonine being gone.
She did disdain my child, and stood between
Her and her fortunes: None would look on her,
But cast their gazes on Marina's face;
Whilst ours was blurted at, and held a malkin,
Not worth the time of day. It pierced me thorough;
And though you call my course unnatural,
You not your child well loving, yet I find,
It greets me as an enterprise of kindness,
Perform'd to your sole daughter.

Cle. Heavens forgive it!

Dion. And as for Pericles,
What should he say? We wept after her hearse,
And even yet we mourn; her monument
Is almost finish'd, and her epitaphs
In glittering golden characters express
A general praise to her, and care in us
At whose expense 'tis done.

Cle. Thou art like the harpy,
Which, to betray, doth wear thine angel's face,
Seize with thine eagle's talons.

Dion. You are like one, that superstitiously
Doth swear to the gods, that winter kills the flies;
But yet I know you'll do as I advise. [*Exeunt.*

Enter GOWER, *before the Monument of* Marina *at* Tharsus.

Gow. Thus time we waste, and longest leagues make short;
Sail seas in cockles, have, and wish but for't;
Making (to take your imagination),
From bourn to bourn, region to region.
By you being pardon'd, we commit no crime
To use one language, in each several clime,
Where our scenes seem to live. I do beseech you,
To learn of me, who stand i' the gaps to teach you
The stages of our story. Pericles
Is now again thwarting the wayward seas
(Attended on by many a lord and knight),
To see his daughter, all his life's delight.
Old Escanes, whom Helicanus late
Advanc'd in time to great and high estate,
Is left to govern. Bear you it in mind,
Old Helicanus goes along behind.
Well sailing ships, and bounteous winds, have brought
This king to Tharsus (think this pilot-thought;

So with his steerage shall your thoughts grow on),
To fetch his daughter home, who first is gone.
Like motes and shadows see them move awhile;
Your ears unto your eyes I'll reconcile.

Dumb Show.

Enter at one door, PERICLES, *with his* Train; CLEON *and* DIONYZA *at the other.* CLEON *shows* PERICLES *the Tomb of* Marina; *whereat* PERICLES *makes lamentation, puts on Sackcloth, and in a mighty passion departs. Then* CLEON *and* DIONYZA *retire.*

Gow. See how belief may suffer by foul show!
This borrow'd passion stands for true old woe;
And Pericles, in sorrow all devour'd,
With sighs shot through, and biggest tears o'er-shower'd,
Leaves Tharsus, and again embarks. He swears
Never to wash his face, nor cut his hairs;
He puts on sackcloth, and to sea. He bears
A tempest, which his mortal vessel tears,
And yet he rides it out. Now please you wit
The epitaph is for Marina writ
By wicked Dionyza.

[*Reads the Inscription on* Marina's *Monument.*

The fairest, sweet'st, and best, lies here,
Who wither'd in her spring of year.
She was of Tyrus, the king's daughter,
On whom foul death hath made this slaughter:
Marina was she call'd; and at her birth,
Thetis, being proud, swallow'd some part o' the earth:
Therefore the earth, fearing to be o'erflow'd,
Hath Thetis birth-child on the heavens bestow'd:
Wherefore she does (and swears she'll never stint),
Make raging battery upon shores of flint.
No visor does become black villany,
So well as soft and tender flattery.
Let Pericles believe his daughter's dead,
And bear his courses to be ordered
By lady fortune; while our scenes display
His daughter's woe and heavy well-a-day,
In her unholy service. Patience then,
And think you now are all in Mitylen. [*Exit.*

SCENE V. Mitylene. *A Street before the Brothel.*

Enter, from the Brothel, Two Gentlemen.

1 *Gent.* Did you ever hear the like?

2 *Gent.* No, nor never shall do in such a place as this, she being once gone.

1 *Gent.* But to have divinity preached there! did you ever dream of such a thing?

2 *Gent.* No, no. Come, I am for no more bawdy-houses: shall we go hear the vestals sing?

1 *Gent.* I'll do any thing now that is virtuous; but I am out of the road of rutting, for ever. [*Exeunt.*

SCENE VI. *The same. A Room in the Brothel.*

Enter PANDER, Bawd, *and* BOULT.

Pand. Well, I had rather than twice the worth of her, she had ne'er come here.

Bawd. Fye, fye upon her: she is able to freeze the god Priapus, and undo a whole generation. We must either get her ravished, or be rid of her. When she should do for clients her fitment, and do me the kindness of our profession, she has me her quirks, her reasons, her master reasons, her prayers, her knees; that she would make a puritan of the devil, if he should cheapen a kiss of her.

Boult. 'Faith, I must ravish her, or she'll disfurnish us of all our cavaliers, and make all our swearers priests.

Pand. Now, the pox upon her green-sickness for me!

Bawd. 'Faith, there's no way to be rid on't, but by the way to the pox. Here comes the Lord Lysimachus, disguised.

Boult. We should have both lord and lown, if the peevish baggage would but give way to customers.

Enter LYSIMACHUS.

Lys. How now? How a dozen of virginities?

Bawd. Now, the gods to-bless your honour!

Boult. I am glad to see your honour in good health.

Lys. You may so; 'tis the better for you that your resorters stand upon sound legs. How now, wholesome iniquity? Have you that a man may deal withal, and defy the surgeon?

Bawd. We have here one, sir, if she would —but there never came her like in Mitylene.

Lys. If she'd do the deeds of darkness, thou would'st say.

Bawd. Your honour knows what 'tis to say well enough.

Lys. Well; call forth, call forth.

Boult. For flesh and blood, sir, white and red, you shall see a rose; and she were a rose indeed, if she had but——

Lys. What, pr'ythee?

Boult. O, sir, I can be modest.

Lys. That dignifies the renown of a bawd, no less than it gives a good report to an anchor to be chaste.

Enter MARINA.

Bawd. Here comes that which grows to the stalk;—never plucked yet, I can assure you. Is she not a fair creature?

Lys. 'Faith, she would serve after a long voyage at sea. Well, there's for you;—leave us.

Bawd. I beseech your honour, give me leave: a word, and I'll have done presently.

Lys. I beseech you, do.

Bawd. First, I would have you note, this is an honourable man.

[*To* MARINA, *whom she takes aside.*

Mar. I desire to find him so, that I may worthily note him.

Bawd. Next, he's the governor of this country, and a man whom I am bound to.

Mar. If he govern the country, you are bound to him indeed; but how honourable he is in that, I know not.

Bawd. 'Pray you, without any more virginal fencing, will you use him kindly? He will line your apron with gold.

Mar. What he will do graciously, I will thankfully receive.

Lys. Have you done?

Bawd. My lord, she's not paced yet; you must take some pains to work her to your manage. Come, we will leave his honour and her together. [*Exeunt* Bawd, PANDER, *and* BOULT.

Lys. Go thy ways.—Now, pretty one, how long have you been at this trade?

Mar. What trade, sir?

Lys. What I cannot name but I shall offend.

Mar. I cannot be offended with my trade. Please you to name it.

Lys. How long have you been of this profession?

Mar. Ever since I can remember.

Lys. Did you go to it so young? Were you a gamester at five, or at seven?

Mar. Earlier too, sir, if now I be one.

Lys. Why, the house you dwell in, proclaims you to be a creature of sale.

Mar. Do you know this house to be a place of such resort, and will come into it? I hear say, you are of honourable parts, and are the governor of this place.

Lys. Why, hath your principal made known unto you who I am?

Mar. Who is my principal?

Lys. Why, your herb-woman; she that sets seeds and roots of shame and iniquity. O, you have heard something of my power, and so stand aloof for more serious wooing. But I protest to thee, pretty one, my authority shall not see thee, or else, look friendly upon thee. Come, bring me to some private place. Come, come.

Mar. If you were born to honour, show it now;

If put upon you, make the judgment good
That thought you worthy of it.

Lys. How's this? how's this?—Some more; —be sage.

Mar. For me,
That am a maid, though most ungentle fortune
Hath placed me here within this loathsome stie,
Where, since I came, diseases have been sold
Dearer than physick,—O that the good gods
Would set me free from this unhallow'd place,
Though they did change me to the meanest bird
That flies i' the purer air!

Lys. I did not think
Thou could'st have spoke so well; ne'er dream'd thou could'st.
Had I brought hither a corrupted mind,
Thy speech had alter'd it. Hold, here's gold for thee:
Persever still in that clear way thou goest,
And the gods strengthen thee!

Mar. The gods preserve you!

Lys. For me, be you thoughten
That I came with no ill intent; for to me
The very doors and windows savour vilely.
Farewell. Thou art a piece of virtue, and
I doubt not but thy training hath been noble.—
Hold; here's more gold for thee.—
A curse upon him, die he like a thief,
That robs thee of thy goodness! If thou hear'st
It shall be for thy good. [from me,

[*As* LYSIMACHUS *is putting up his Purse,* BOULT *enters.*

Boult. I beseech your honour, one piece for me.

Lys. Avaunt, thou damned door-keeper! Your house,
But for this virgin that doth prop it up,
Would sink, and overwhelm you all. Away!
[*Exit* LYSIMACHUS.

Boult. How's this! We must take another course with you. If your peevish chastity, which is not worth a breakfast in the cheapest country under the cope, shall undo a whole household, let me be gelded like a spaniel. Come your ways.

Mar. Whither would you have me?

Boult. I must have your maidenhead taken off, or the common hangman shall execute it. Come your way. We'll have no more gentlemen driven away. Come your ways, I say.

Re-enter Bawd.

Bawd. How now! what's the matter?

Boult. Worse and worse, mistress; she has here spoken holy words to the Lord Lysimachus.

Bawd. O abominable!

Boult. She makes our profession as it were to stink afore the face of the gods.

Bawd. Marry, hang her up for ever!

Boult. The nobleman would have dealt with her like a nobleman, and she sent him away as cold as a snowball; saying his prayers too.

Bawd. Boult, take her away; use her at thy pleasure: crack the glass of her virginity, and make the rest malleable.

Boult. An if she were a thornier piece of ground than she is, she shall be ploughed.

Mar. Hark, hark, you gods!

Bawd. She conjures: away with her. 'Would, she had never come within my doors! Marry, hang you! She's born to undo us. Will you not go the way of womankind? Marry come up, my dish of chastity with rosemary and bays! [*Exit* Bawd.

Boult. Come, mistress; come your way with me.

Mar. Whither would you have me?

Boult. To take from you the jewel you hold so dear.

Mar. 'Pr'ythee tell me one thing first.

Boult. Come now, your one thing.

Mar. What canst thou wish thine enemy to be?

Boult. Why, I could wish him to be my master, or rather, my mistress.

Mar. Neither of these are yet so bad as thou art,
Since they do better thee in their command.
Thou hold'st a place, for which the pained'st fiend
Of hell would not in reputation change:
Thou'rt the damn'd door-keeper to every coystrel
That hither comes inquiring for his tib;
To the choleric fisting of each rogue thy ear
Is liable; thy very food is such
As hath been belch'd on by infected lungs.

Boult. What would you have me? go to the wars, would you? where a man may serve seven years for the loss of a leg, and have not money enough in the end to buy him a wooden one?

Mar. Do any thing but this thou doest. Empty
Old receptacles, common sewers, of filth;
Serve by indenture to the common hangman;
Any of these ways are better yet than this:
For that which thou professest, a baboon,
Could he but speak, would own a name too dear.
O that the gods would safely from this place
Deliver me! Here, here is gold for thee.
If that thy master would gain aught by me,
Proclaim that I can sing, weave, sew, and dance,
With other virtues, which I'll keep from boast;
And I will undertake all these to teach.
I doubt not but this populous city will
Yield many scholars.

Boult. But can you teach all this you speak of?

Mar. Prove that I cannot, take me home again,
And prostitute me to the basest groom
That doth frequent your house.

Boult. Well, I will see what I can do for thee; if I can place thee, I will.

Mar. But, amongst honest women?

Boult. 'Faith, my acquaintance lies little amongst them. But since my master and mistress have bought you, there's no going but by their consent: therefore I will make them acquainted with your purpose, and I doubt not but I shall find them tractable enough. Come, I'll do for thee what I can; come your ways.
[*Exeunt.*

ACT V.

Enter GOWER.

Gow. Marina thus the brothel scapes, and chances
Into an honest house, our story says.
She sings like one immortal, and she dances
As goddess-like to her admired lays:
Deep clerks she dumbs, and with her neeld composes
Nature's own shape, of bud, bird, branch, or berry;
That even her art sisters the natural roses:
Her inkle silk, twin with the rubied cherry:
That pupils lacks she none of noble race,
Who pour their bounty on her; and her gain
She gives the cursed bawd. Here we her place;
And to her father turn our thoughts again,
Where we left him, on the sea. We there him lost:
Whence driven before the winds, he is arriv'd
Here where his daughter dwells: and on this coast
Suppose him now at anchor. The city striv'd
God Neptune's annual feast to keep; from whence
Lysimachus our Tyrian ship espies,
His banners sable, trimm'd with rich expense;
And to him in his barge with fervour hies.
In your supposing once more put your sight;
Of heavy Pericles think this the bark;
Where, what is done in action, more, if might,
Shall be discover'd; please you, sit, and hark.
[*Exit.*

SCENE I.

On board Pericles' *Ship, off* Mitylene. *A close Pavilion on deck, with a Curtain before it;* PERICLES *within it, reclined on a Couch. A Barge lying beside the* Tyrian *Vessel.*

Enter Two Sailors, *one belonging to the* Tyrian *Vessel, the other to the Barge; to them* HELICANUS.

Tyr. Sail. Where's the Lord Helicanus? he can resolve you. [*To the* Sailor *of* Mitylene.
O here he is.——
Sir, there's a barge put off from Mitylene,
And in it is Lysimachus the governor,
Who craves to come aboard. What is your will?
Hel. That he have his. Call up some gentlemen.
Tyr. Sail. Ho, gentlemen! my lord calls.

Enter Two Gentlemen.

1 *Gent.* Doth your lordship call?
Hel. Gentlemen,
There is some of worth would come aboard; I pray you,
To greet them fairly.
[*The* Gentlemen *and the Two* Sailors *descend, and go on board the Barge.*

Enter, from thence LYSIMACHUS *and* Lords; *the* Tyrian Gentlemen, *and the Two* Sailors.

Tyr. Sail. Sir,
This is the man that can, in aught you would,
Resolve you.
Lys. Hail, reverend sir! the gods preserve you!
Hel. And you, sir, to outlive the age I am,
And die as I would do.
Lys. You wish me well.
Being on shore, honouring of Neptune's triumphs,
Seeing this goodly vessel ride before us,
I made to it, to know of whence you are.
Hel. First, sir, what is your place?
Lys. I am governor of this place you lie before.
Hel. Sir,
Our vessel is of Tyre, in it the king:
A man, who for this three months hath not spoken
To any one, nor taken sustenance,
But to prorogue his grief.
Lys. Upon what ground is his distemperature?
Hel. Sir, it would be too tedious to repeat;
But the main grief of all springs from the loss
Of a beloved daughter and a wife.
Lys. May we not see him, then?
Hel. You may indeed, sir,
But bootless is your sight; he will not speak
To any.
Lys. Yet, let me obtain my wish.
Hel. Behold him, sir: [PERICLES *discovered.*] this was a goodly person,
Till the disaster, that, one mortal night,
Drove him to this.
Lys. Sir, king, all hail! the gods preserve you! Hail,
Hail, royal sir!
Hel. It is in vain; he will not speak to you.
1 *Lord.* Sir, we have a maid in Mitylene, I durst wager,
Would win some words of him.
Lys. 'Tis well bethought.
She, questionless, with her sweet harmony
And other choice attractions, would allure
And make a battery through his deafen'd parts,
Which now are midway stopp'd:
She is all happy as the fairest of all,
And, with her fellow maids, is now upon
The leafy shelter that abuts against
The island's side.
[*He whispers one of the attendant* Lords.—
Exit Lord, *in the Barge of* LYSIMACHUS.
Hel. Sure all's effectless; yet nothing we'll omit
That bears recovery's name. But, since your kindness,
We have stretch'd thus far, let us beseech you further,
That for our gold we may provision have,
Wherein we are not destitute for want,
But weary for the staleness.
Lys. O, sir, a courtesy
Which if we should deny, the most just God
For every graff would send a caterpillar,
And so inflict our province.—Yet once more
Let me entreat to know at large the cause
Of your king's sorrow.
Hel. Sit, sir, I will recount it;—
But see, I am prevented.

Enter, from the Barge, Lord, MARINA, *and a young* Lady.

Lys. O, here is
The lady that I sent for. Welcome, fair one!
Is't not a goodly presence?
Hel. A gallant lady.
Lys. She's such, that were I well assur'd she came
Of gentle kind, and noble stock, I'd wish
No better choice, and think me rarely wed.
Fair one, all goodness that consists in bounty
Expect even here, where is a kingly patient:
If that thy prosperous-artificial feat
Can draw him but to answer thee in aught,
Thy sacred physick shall receive such pay
As thy desires can wish.
Mar. Sir, I will use
My utmost skill in his recovery,
Provided none but I and my companion
Be suffer'd to come near him.
Lys. Come, let us leave her,
And the gods make her prosperous!
[MARINA *sings.*
Lys. Mark'd he your musick?
Mar. No, nor look'd on us.
Lys. See, she will speak to him.
Mar. Hail, sir! my lord, lend ear:——
Per. Hum! ha!
Mar. I am a maid,
My lord, that ne'er before invited eyes,
But have been gaz'd on, comet-like: she speaks,
My lord, that may be, hath endur'd a grief
Might equal yours, if both were justly weigh'd.
Though wayward fortune did malign my state,
My derivation was from ancestors
Who stood equivalent with mighty kings:
But time hath rooted out my parentage,
And to the world and awkward casualties
Bound me in servitude.—I will desist;
But there is something glows upon my cheek,
And whispers in mine ear, *Go not till he speak.*
[*Aside.*
Per. My fortunes—parentage—good parentage—
To equal mine!—was it not thus? what say you?
Mar. I said, my lord, if you did know my parentage,
You would not do me violence.
Per. I do think so.
I pray you, turn your eyes again upon me.—
You are like something that—What countrywoman?
Here of these shores?
Mar. No, nor of any shores:
Yet I was mortally brought forth, and am
No other than I appear.
Per. I am great with woe, and shall deliver weeping.
My dearest wife was like this maid, and such a one
My daughter might have been: my queen's square brows;
Her stature to an inch; as wand-like straight;
As silver voic'd; her eyes as jewel-like,
And cas'd as richly: in pace another Juno;

Who starves the ears she feeds, and makes them hungry,
The more she gives them speech.—Where do you live?
Mar. Where I am but a stranger: from the deck
You may discern the place.
Per. Where were you bred?
And how achiev'd you these endowments, which
You make more rich to owe?
Mar. Should I tell my history,
'Twould seem like lies disdain'd in the reporting.
Per. 'Pr'ythee speak;
Falseness cannot come from thee, for thou look'st
Modest as justice, and thou seem'st a palace
For the crown'd truth to dwell in; I'll believe thee,
And make my senses credit thy relation.
To points that seem impossible; for thou look'st
Like one I lov'd indeed. What were thy friends?
Didst thou not say, when I did push thee back
(Which was when I perceiv'd thee), that thou cam'st
From good descending?
Mar. So indeed I did.
Per. Report thy parentage. I think thou said'st
Thou hadst been toss'd from wrong to injury,
And that thou thought'st thy griefs might equal mine,
If both were open'd.
Mar. Some such thing indeed
I said, and said no more but what my thoughts
Did warrant me was likely.
Per. Tell thy story;
If thine consider'd prove the thousandth part
Of my endurance, thou art a man, and I
Have suffer'd like a girl: yet thou dost look
Like Patience, gazing on king's graves, and smiling
Extremity out of act. What were thy friends?
How lost thou them? Thy name, my most kind virgin?
Recount, I do beseech thee; come, sit by me.
Mar. My name, sir, is Marina.
Per. O, I am mock'd,
And thou by some incensed god sent hither
To make the world laugh at me.
Mar. Patience, good sir,
Or here I'll cease.
Per. Nay, I'll be patient;
Thou little know'st how thou dost startle me,
To call thyself Marina.
Mar. The name Marina
Was given me by one that had some power;
My father, and a king.
Per. How! a king's daughter?
And call'd Marina?
Mar. You said you would believe me;
But, not to be a troubler of your peace,
I will end here.
Per. But are you flesh and blood?
Have you a working pulse? and are no fairy?
No motion? Well; speak on. Where were you born?
And wherefore call'd Marina?
Mar. Call'd Marina,
For I was born at sea.
Per. At sea? thy mother?
Mar. My mother was the daughter of a king;
Who died the very minute I was born,
As my good nurse Lychorida hath oft
Deliver'd weeping.
Per. O, stop there a little!
This is the rarest dream that e'er dull sleep
Did mock sad fools withal: this cannot be.
My daughter's buried. [*Aside.*] Well:—where were you bred?
I'll hear you more, to the bottom of your story,
And never interrupt you.
Mar. You'll scarce believe me; 'twere best I did give o'er.
Per. I will believe you by the syllable
Of what you shall deliver. Yet, give me leave:—
How came you in these parts? where were you bred?
Mar. The king, my father, did in Tharsus leave me;
Till cruel Cleon, with his wicked wife,
Did seek to murder me: and having woo'd
A villain to attempt it, who having drawn,
A crew of pirates came and rescued me;
Brought me to Mitylene. But now, good sir,
Whither will you have me? Why do you weep?
It may be,
You think me an impostor; no, good faith;
I am the daughter to king Pericles,
If good king Pericles be.
Per. Ho, Helicanus!
Hel. Calls my gracious lord?
Per. Thou art a grave and noble counsellor,
Most wise in general: Tell me, if thou canst,
What this maid is, or what is like to be,
That thus hath made me weep?
Hel. I know not; but
Here is the regent, sir, of Mitylene,
Speaks nobly of her.
Lys. She would never tell
Her parentage; being demanded that,
She would sit still and weep.
Per. O Helicanus, strike me, honour'd sir;
Give me a gash, put me to present pain;
Lest this great sea of joys rushing upon me,
O'erbear the shores of my mortality,
And drown me with their sweetness. O, come hither,
Thou that beget'st him that did thee beget;
Thou that wast born at sea, buried at Tharsus,
And found at sea again! O Helicanus,
Down on thy knees, thank the holy gods, as loud
As thunder threatens us; This is Marina.—
What was thy mother's name? tell me but that,
For truth can never be confirm'd enough,
Though doubts did ever sleep.
Mar. First, sir, I pray,
What is your title?
Per. I am Pericles of Tyre: but tell me now
My drown'd queen's name (as in the rest thou hast
Been godlike perfect), thou'rt the heir of kingdoms,
And another life to Pericles thy father.
Mar. Is it no more to be your daughter, than
To say, my mother's name was Thaisa?
Thaisa was my mother, who did end,
The minute I began.
Per. Now, blessing on thee, rise; thou art my child.
Give me fresh garments. Mine own, Helicanus
(Not dead at Tharsus, as she should have been,
By savage Cleon), she shall tell thee all;
When thou shalt kneel and justify in knowledge,
She is thy very princess.—Who is this?
Hel. Sir, 'tis the governor of Mitylene,
Who, hearing of your melancholy state,
Did come to see you.
Per. I embrace you, sir.
Give me my robes; I am wild in my beholding.
O heavens bless my girl! But hark, what musick?—
Tell Helicanus, my Marina, tell him
O'er point by point, for yet he seems to doubt,
How sure you are my daughter.—But what musick?
Hel. Hy lord, I hear none.
Per. None?
The musick of the spheres: list, my Marina.
Lys. It is not good to cross him; give him way.
Per. Rarest sounds!
Do ye not hear?
Lys. Musick? my lord, I hear—
Per. Most heavenly musick:
It nips me unto list'ning, and thick slumber
Hangs on mine eyelids; let me rest. [*He sleeps.*

Lys. A pillow for his head;
[*The Curtain before the Pavilion of* PERICLES *is closed.*
So leave him all.—Well, my companion-friends,
If this but answer to my just belief,
I'll well remember you.
[*Exeunt* LYSIMACHUS, HELICANUS, MARINA, *and attendant* Lady.

SCENE II. *The same.*

PERICLES *on the Deck asleep;* DIANA *appearing to him as in a Vision.*

Dia. My temple stands in Ephesus; hie thee thither,
And do upon mine altar sacrifice.
There, when my maiden priests are met together,
Before the people all,
Reveal how thou at sea didst lose thy wife;
To mourn thy crosses, with thy daughter's, call,
And give them repetition to the life.
Perform my bidding, or thou liv'st in woe:
Do 't, and be happy, by my silver bow.
Awake, and tell thy dream. [DIANA *disappears.*

Per. Celestial Dian, goddess argentine,
I will obey thee!—Helicanus!

Enter LYSIMACHUS, HELICANUS, *and* MARINA.

Hel. Sir.

Per. My purpose was for Tharsus, there to strike
The inhospitable Cleon; but I am
For other service first: toward Ephesus
Turn our blown sails; eftsoons I'll tell thee why.— [*To* HELICANUS.
Shall we refresh us, sir, upon your shore,
And give you gold for such provision
As our intents will need?

Lys. With all my heart, sir; and when you come ashore,
I have another suit.

Per. You shall prevail,
Were it to woo my daughter; for it seems
You have been noble towards her.

Lys. Sir, lend your arm.

Per. Come, my Marina. [*Exeunt.*

Enter GOWER, *before the Temple of* Diana *at* Ephesus.

Gow. Now our sands are almost run;
More a little, and then done.
This, as my last boon, give me
(For such kindness must relieve me),
That you aptly will suppose
What pageantry, what feats, what shows,
What minstrelsy, and pretty din,
The regent made in Mitylin,
To greet the king. So he has thriv'd,
That he is promis'd to be wiv'd
To fair Marina; but in no wise
Till he had done his sacrifice,
As Dian bade: whereto being bound,
The interim, pray you, all confound.
In feather'd briefness sails are fill'd,
And wishes fall out as they're will'd.
At Ephesus, the temple see,
Our king, and all his company.
That he can hither come so soon,
Is by your fancy's thankful boon. [*Exit.*

SCENE III.

The Temple of Diana *at* Ephesus: THAISA *standing near the Altar, as High Priestess; a number of* Virgins *on each side;* CERIMON *and other* Inhabitants *of* Ephesus *attending.*

Enter PERICLES, *with his* Train; LYSIMACHUS, HELICANUS, MARINA, *and a* Lady.

Per. Hail Dian! to perform thy just command,
I here confess myself the king of Tyre;
Who, frighted from my country, did wed
The fair Thaisa, at Pentapolis.
At sea in childbed died she, but brought forth
A maid-child call'd Marina; who, O goddess,
Wears yet thy silver livery. She at Tharsus
Was nurs'd with Cleon; whom at fourteen years
He sought to murder: but her better stars
Brought her to Mitylene: against whose shore
Riding, her fortunes brought the maid aboard us,
Where, by her own most clear remembrance, she
Made known herself my daughter.

Thai. Voice and favour!—
You are—you are—O royal Pericles!— [*She faints.*

Per. What means the woman? she dies! help, gentlemen!

Cer. Noble sir,
If you have told Diana's altar true,
This is your wife.

Per. Reverend appearer, no;
I threw her overboard with these very arms.

Cer. Upon this coast, I warrant you.

Per. 'Tis most certain.

Cer. Look to the lady;—O, she's but o'erjoy'd!
Early, one blust'ring morn, this lady was
Thrown on this shore. I op'd the coffin, and
Found there rich jewels; recover'd her, and plac'd her
Here in Diana's temple.

Per. May we see them?

Cer. Great sir, they shall be brought you to my house,
Whither I invite you. Look! Thaisa is
Recover'd.

Thai. O, let me look!
If he be none of mine, my sanctity
Will to my sense bend no licentious ear,
But curb it, spite of seeing. O, my lord,
Are you not Pericles? Like him you speak,
Like him you are: Did you not name a tempest,
A birth, and death?

Per. The voice of dead Thaisa!

Thai. That Thaisa am I, supposed dead,
And drown'd.

Per. Immortal Dian!

Thai. Now I know you better.
When we with tears parted Pentapolis,
The king, my father, gave you such a ring. [*Shows a Ring.*

Per. This, this; no more, you gods! your present kindness
Makes my past miseries sport: You shall do well,
That on the touching of her lips, I may
Melt, and no more be seen. O come, be buried
A second time within these arms.

Mar. My heart
Leaps to be gone into my mother's bosom. [*Kneels to* THAISA.

Per. Look, who kneels here! Flesh of thy flesh, Thaisa;
Thy burden at the sea, and call'd Marina,
For she was yielded there.

Thai. Bless'd and mine own!

Hel. Hail, madam, and my queen!

Thai. I know you not.

Per. You have heard me say, when I did fly from Tyre,
I left behind an ancient substitute.
Can you remember what I call'd the man?
I have nam'd him oft.

Thai. 'Twas Helicanus then.

Per. Still confirmation:
Embrace him, dear Thaisa: this is he.
Now do I long to hear how you were found;
How possibly preserv'd; and whom to thank,
Besides the gods, for this great miracle.

Thai. Lord Cerimon, my lord; this man
Through whom the gods have shown their power; that can
From first to last resolve you.

Per. Reverend sir,
The gods can have no mortal officer
More like a god than you. Will you deliver
How this dead queen relives?

Cer. I will, my lord.
Beseech you, first go with me to my house,

Where shall be shown you all was found with her;
How she came placed here within the temple;
No needful thing omitted.

Per. Pure Diana!
I bless thee for thy vision, and will offer
My night oblations to thee. Thaisa,
This prince, the fair-betrothed of your daughter,
Shall marry her at Pentapolis. And now,
This ornament that makes me look so dismal,
Will I, my lov'd Marina, clip to form;
And what this fourteen years no razor touch'd,
To grace thy marriage-day, I'll beautify.

Thai. Lord Cerimon hath letters of good credit,
Sir, that my father's dead.

Per. Heavens make a star of him! Yet there, my queen,
We'll celebrate their nuptials, and ourselves
Will in that kingdom spend our following days;
Our son and daughter shall in Tyrus reign.
Lord Cerimon, we do our longing stay,
To hear the rest untold.—Sir, lead the way.
[*Exeunt.*

Enter GOWER.

Gow. In Antioch, and his daughter, you have heard
Of monstrous lust the due and just reward:
In Pericles, his queen and daughter, seen
(Although assail'd with fortune fierce and keen),
Virtue preserv'd from fell destruction's blast,
Led on by heaven, and crown'd with joy at last.
In Helicanus may you well descry
A figure of truth, of faith, of loyalty:
In reverend Cerimon there well appears,
The worth that learned charity aye wears.
For wicked Cleon and his wife, when fame
Had spread their cursed deed, and honour'd name
Of Pericles, to rage the city turn;
That him and his they in his palace burn.
The gods for murder seemed so content
To punish them; although not done, but meant.
So on your patience evermore attending,
New joy wait on you! Here our play has ending.
[*Exeunt.*

KING LEAR.

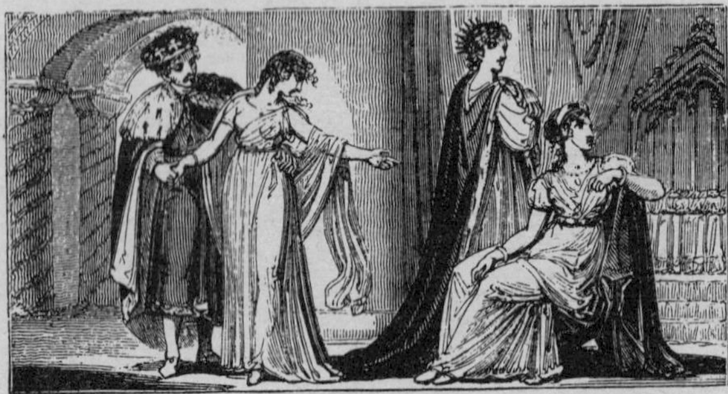

PERSONS REPRESENTED.

LEAR, King *of* Britain.
KING OF FRANCE.
DUKE OF BURGUNDY.
DUKE OF CORNWALL.
DUKE OF ALBANY.
EARL OF KENT.
EARL OF GLOSTER.
EDGAR, *Son to* Gloster.
EDMUND, *Bastard Son to* Gloster.
CURAN, *a Courtier.*
Old Man, *Tenant to* Gloster.
Physician.
Fool.
OSWALD, *Steward to* Goneril.
An Officer, *employed by* Edmund.
Gentleman, *Attendant on* Cordelia.
A Herald.
Servants *to* Cornwall.

GONERIL, REGAN, CORDELIA, } *Daughters to* Lear.

Knights *attending on the* King, Officers, Messengers, Soldiers, *and* Attendants.

SCENE—Britain.

ACT I.

SCENE I. *A Room of State in* King Lear's *Palace.*

Enter KENT, GLOSTER, *and* EDMUND.

Kent. I THOUGHT the king had more affected the duke of Albany, than Cornwall.

Glo. It did always seem so to us: but now, in the division of the kingdom, it appears not which of the dukes he values most; for equalities are so weigh'd, that curiosity in neither can make choice of either's moiety.

Kent. Is not this your son, my lord?

Glo. His breeding, sir, hath been at my charge: I have so often blush'd to acknowledge him, that now I am brazed to it.

Kent. I cannot conceive you.

Glo. Sir, this young fellow's mother could: whereupon she grew round-wombed; and had, indeed, sir, a son for her cradle, ere she had a husband for her bed. Do you smell a fault?

Kent. I cannot wish the fault undone, the issue of it being so proper.

Glo. But I have, sir, a son by order of law, some year elder than this, who yet is no dearer in my account: though this knave came somewhat saucily into the world before he was sent for, yet was his mother fair; there was good sport at his making, and the whoreson must be acknowledged.—Do you know this noble gentleman, Edmund?

Edm. No, my lord.

Glo. My lord of Kent: remember him hereafter as my honourable friend.

Edm. My services to your lordship.

Kent. I must love you, and sue to know you better.

Edm. Sir, I shall study deserving.

Glo. He hath been out nine years, and away he shall again:—The king is coming.

[*Trumpets sound within.*

Enter LEAR, CORNWALL, ALBANY, GONERIL, REGAN, CORDELIA, *and* Attendants.

Lear. Attend the lords of France and Burgundy, Gloster.

Glo. I shall, my liege.

[*Exeunt* GLOSTER *and* EDMUND.

Lear. Mean time we shall express our darker purpose.
Give me the map there.—Know, that we have divided,
In three, our kingdom; and 'tis our fast intent
To shake all cares and business from our age;
Conferring them on younger strengths, while we
Unburden'd crawl toward death.—Our son of Cornwall,
And you, our no less loving son of Albany,
We have this hour a constant will to publish
Our daughters' several dowers, that future strife
May be prevented now. The princes, France and Burgundy,
Great rivals in our youngest daughter's love,
Long in our court have made their amorous sojourn,
And here are to be answer'd.—Tell me, my daughters
(Since now we will divest us, both of rule,
Interest of territory, cares of state),
Which of you, shall we say, doth love us most?
That we our largest bounty may extend
Where merit doth most challenge it.—Goneril,
Our eldest-born, speak first.

Gon. Sir, I
Do love you more than words can wield the matter,
Dearer than eye-sight, space, and liberty;
Beyond what can be valued, rich or rare;
No less than life, with grace, health, beauty, honour:
As much as child e'er lov'd, or father found.
A love that makes breath poor, and speech unable:
Beyond all manner of so much I love you.

Cor. What shall Cordelia do? Love, and be silent. [*Aside.*

Lear. Of all these bounds, even from this line to this,
With shadowy forests and with champains rich'd,
With plenteous rivers and wide-skirted meads,
We make thee lady: To thine and Albany's issue
Be this perpetual.—What says our second daughter,
Our dearest Regan, wife to Cornwall? Speak.

Reg. I am made of that self metal as my sister,
And prize me at her worth. In my true heart
I find, she names my very deed of love;
Only she comes too short,—that I profess
Myself an enemy to all other joys,
Which the most precious square of sense possesses;
And find, I am alone felicitate
In your dear highness' love.

Cor. Then poor Cordelia!
[*Aside.*
And yet not so; since, I am sure, my love's
More richer than my tongue.

Lear. To thee, and thine, hereditary ever,
Remain this ample third of our fair kingdom;
No less in space, validity, and pleasure,
Than that conferr'd on Goneril.—Now, our joy,
Although the last, not least: to whose young love
The vines of France, and milk of Burgundy,
Strive to be interess'd: what can you say, to draw
A third more opulent than your sisters? Speak.

Cor. Nothing, my lord.

Lear. Nothing?

Cor. Nothing.

Lear. Nothing can come of nothing: speak again.

Cor. Unhappy that I am, I cannot heave
My heart into my mouth: I love your majesty
According to my bond; nor more, nor less.

Lear. How, how, Cordelia? mend your speech a little,
Lest it may mar your fortunes.

Cor. Good my lord,
You have begot me, bred me, lov'd me: I
Return those duties back as are right fit,
Obey you, love you, and most honour you.
Why have my sisters husbands, if they say,
They love you, all? Haply, when I shall wed,
That lord, whose hand must take my plight, shall carry
Half my love with him, half my care, and duty:
Sure, I shall never marry like my sisters,
To love my father all.

Lear. But goes this with thy heart?

Cor. Ay, good my lord.

Lear. So young, and so untender?

Cor. So young, my lord, and true.

Lear. Let it be so,—Thy truth then be thy dower:
For, by the sacred radiance of the sun:
The mysteries of Hecate, and the night;
By all the operations of the orbs,
From whom we do exist, and cease to be;
Here I disclaim all my paternal care,
Propinquity and property of blood,
And as a stranger to my heart and me
Hold thee, from this, for ever. The barbarous Scythian,
Or he that makes his generation messes
To gorge his appetite, shall to my bosom
Be as well neighbour'd, pitied, and reliev'd,
As thou my sometime daughter.

Kent. Good my liege,—

Lear. Peace, Kent!
Come not between the dragon and his wrath:
I lov'd her most, and thought to set my rest
On her kind nursery.—Hence, and avoid my sight!— [*To* CORDELIA.
So be my grave my peace, as here I give
Her father's heart from her!—Call France;—Who stirs?
Call Burgundy.—Cornwall, and Albany,
With my two daughters' dowers digest this third:
Let pride, which she calls plainness, marry her.
I do invest you jointly with my power,
Pre-eminence, and all the large effects
That troop with majesty.—Ourself, by monthly course,
With reservation of a hundred knights,
By you to be sustain'd, shall our abode
Make with you by due turns. Only we still retain
The name, and all the additions to a king;
The sway,
Revenue, execution of the rest,
Beloved sons, be yours: which to confirm,
This coronet part between you.

[*Giving the Crown.*

Kent. Royal Lear,
Whom I have ever honour'd as my king,
Lov'd as my father, as my master follow'd,
As my great patron thought on in my prayers,—

Lear. The bow is bent and drawn, make from the shaft.

Kent. Let it fall rather, though the fork invade
The region of my heart: be Kent unmannerly

When Lear is mad. What would'st thou do, old man?
Think'st thou, that duty shall have dread to speak,
When power to flattery bows? To plainness honour's bound,
When majesty stoops to folly. Reverse thy doom;
And, in thy best consideration, check
This hideous rashness: answer my life my judgment,
Thy youngest daughter does not love thee least;
Nor are those empty hearted, whose low sound
Reverbs no hollowness.

Lear. Kent, on thy life, no more.

Kent. My life I never held but as a pawn
To wage against thine enemies, nor fear to lose it,
Thy safety being the motive.

Lear. Out of my sight!

Kent. See better, Lear, and let me still remain
The true blank of thine eye.

Lear. Now, by Apollo,—

Kent. Now, by Apollo, king,
Thou swear'st thy gods in vain.

Lear. O, vassal! miscreant!
[*Laying his Hand on his Sword.*

Alb. Corn. Dear sir, forbear.

Kent. Do;
Kill thy physician, and the fee bestow
Upon the foul disease. Revoke thy gift;
Or, whilst I can vent clamour from my throat,
I'll tell thee, thou dost evil.

Lear. Hear me, recreant!
On thine allegiance hear me!—
Since thou hast sought to make us break our vow,
(Which we durst never yet), and, with strain'd pride,
To come betwixt our sentence and our power
(Which nor our nature nor our place can bear);
Our potency made good, take thy reward.
Five days we do allot thee, for provision
To shield thee from diseases of the world;
And, on the sixth, to turn thy hated back
Upon our kingdom: if, on the tenth day following,
Thy banish'd trunk be found in our dominions,
The moment is thy death. Away! By Jupiter,
This shall not be revok'd.

Kent. Fare thee well, king: since thus thou wilt appear,
Freedom lives hence, and banishment is here.—
The gods to their dear shelter take thee, maid,
[*To* CORDELIA.
That justly think'st, and hast most rightly said!—
And your large speeches may your deeds approve, [*To* REGAN *and* GONERIL.
That good effects may spring from words of love.—
Thus Kent, O princes, bids you all adieu:
He'll shape his old course in a country new.
[*Exit.*

Re-enter GLOSTER; *with* FRANCE, BURGUNDY, *and* Attendants.

Glo. Here's France and Burgundy, my noble lord.

Lear. My lord of Burgundy,
We first address towards you, who with this king
Hath rivall'd for our daughter; What, in the least,
Will you require in present dower with her,
Or cease your quest of love?

Bur. Most royal majesty,
I crave no more than hath your highness offer'd,
Nor will you tender less.

Lear. Right noble Burgundy,
When she was dear to us, we did hold her so;
But now her price is fall'n: Sir, there she stands;
If aught within that little, seeming substance,
Or all of it, with our displeasure piec'd,
And nothing more, may fitly like your grace,
She's there, and she is yours.

Bur. I know no answer.

Lear. Sir,
Will you, with those infirmities she owes,
Unfriended, new-adopted to our hate,
Dower'd with our curse, and stranger'd with our oath,
Take her, or leave her?

Bur. Pardon me, royal sir;
Election makes not up on such conditions.

Lear. Then leave her, sir; for, by the power that made me,
I tell you all her wealth.—For you, great king,
[*To* FRANCE.
I would not from your love make such a stray,
To match you where I hate; therefore beseech you
To avert your liking a more worthier way,
Than on a wretch whom nature is asham'd
Almost to acknowledge hers.

France. This is most strange!
That she, that even but now was your best object,
The argument of your praise, balm of your age,
Most best, most dearest, should in this trice of time
Commit a thing so monstrous, to dismantle
So many folds of favour! Sure, her offence
Must be of such unnatural degree,
That monsters it, or your fore-vouch'd affection
Fall into taint: which to believe of her,
Must be a faith, that reason without miracle
Could never plant in me.

Cor. I yet beseech your majesty
(If for I want that glib and oily art,
To speak and purpose not; since what I well intend,
I'll do't before I speak), that you make known
It is no vicious blot, murder, or foulness,
No unchaste action, or dishonour'd step,
That hath depriv'd me of your grace and favour:
But even for want of that, for which I am richer;
A still-soliciting eye, and such a tongue
That I am glad I have not, though not to have it,
Hath lost me in your liking.

Lear. Better thou
Hadst not been born, than not to have pleas'd me better.

France. Is it but this? a tardiness in nature,
Which often leaves the history unspoke,
That it intends to do?—My lord of Burgundy,
What say you to the lady? Love is not love,
When it is mingled with respects, that stand
Aloof from the entire point. Will you have her?
She is herself a dowry.

Bur. Royal Lear,
Give but that portion which yourself propos'd,
And here I take Cordelia by the hand,
Duchess of Burgundy.

Lear. Nothing: I have sworn; I am firm.

Bur. I am sorry then, you have so lost a father,
That you must lose a husband.

Cor. Peace be with Burgundy!
Since that respects of fortune are his love,
I shall not be his wife.

France. Fairest Cordelia, that art most rich, being poor!
Most choice, forsaken; and most lov'd, despis'd!
Thee and thy virtues here I seize upon:
Be it lawful, I take up what's cast away.
Gods, gods! 'tis strange, that from their cold'st neglect
My love should kindle to inflam'd respect.—
Thy dowerless daughter, king, thrown to my chance,
Is queen of us, of ours, and our fair France:
Not all the dukes of wat'rish Burgundy
Shall buy this unpriz'd precious maid of me.—
Bid them farewell, Cordelia, though unkind:
Thou losest here, a better where to find.

Lear. Thou hast her, France: let her be thine; for we
Have no such daughter, nor shall ever see
That face of hers again:—Therefore be gone,

Without our grace, our love, our benizon.—
Come, noble Burgundy.
[*Flourish. Exeunt* LEAR, BUR. CORN. ALB. GLO. *and* Attendants.

France. Bid farewell to your sisters.

Cor. The jewels of our father, with wash'd eyes
Cordelia leaves you; I know you what you are:
And, like a sister, am most loath to call
Your faults, as they are nam'd. Use well our father;
To your professed bosoms I commit him:
But yet, alas! stood I within his grace,
I would prefer him to a better place.
So farewell to you both.

Gon. Prescribe not us our duties.

Reg. Let your study
Be, to content your lord; who hath receiv'd you
At fortune's alms. You have obedience scanted,
And well are worth the want that you have wanted.

Cor. Time shall unfold what plaited cunning hides;
Who cover faults, at last shame them derides.
Well may you prosper!

France. Come, my fair Cordelia.
[*Exeunt* FRANCE *and* CORDELIA.

Gon. Sister, it is not a little I have to say, of what most nearly appertains to us both. I think, our father will hence to-night.

Reg. That's most certain, and with you; next month with us.

Gon. You see how full of changes his age is; the observation we have made of it hath not been little: he always loved our sister most; and with what poor judgment he hath now cast her off, appears too grossly.

Reg. 'Tis the infirmity of his age: yet he hath ever but slenderly known himself.

Gon. The best and soundest of his time hath been but rash; then must we look to receive from his age, not alone the imperfections of long-engrafted condition, but therewithal, the unruly waywardness that infirm and cholerick years bring with them.

Reg. Such unconstant starts are we like to have from him, as this of Kent's banishment.

Gon. There is further compliment of leave-taking between France and him. 'Pray you, let us hit together: If our father carry authority with such dispositions as he bears, this last surrender of his will but offend us.

Reg. We shall further think of it.

Gon. We must do something, and i' the heat.
[*Exeunt.*

SCENE II. *A Hall in the* Earl *of* Gloster's *Castle.*

Enter EDMUND, *with a Letter.*

Edm. Thou, nature, art my goddess; to thy law
My services are bound; Wherefore should I
Stand in the plague of custom; and permit
The curiosity of nations to deprive me,
For that I am some twelve or fourteen moonshines
Lag of a brother? Why bastard? wherefore base?
When my dimensions are as well compact,
My mind as generous, and my shape as true,
As honest madam's issue? Why brand they us
With base? with baseness? bastardy? base, base?
Who, in the lusty stealth of nature, take
More composition and fierce quality,
Than doth, within a dull, stale, tired bed,
Go to the creating a whole tribe of fops,
Got 'tween asleep and wake?—Well then,
Legitimate Edgar, I must have your land:
Our father's love is to the bastard Edmund,
As to the legitimate: Fine word,—legitimate!
Well, my legitimate, if this letter speed,
And my invention thrive, Edmund the base
Shall top the legitimate. I grow; I prosper:—
Now, gods, stand up for bastards!

Enter GLOSTER.

Glo. Kent banish'd thus! And France in choler parted!
And the king gone to-night! subscrib'd his power!
Confin'd to exhibition! All this done
Upon the gad!——Edmund! How now? what news?

Edm. So please your lordship, none.
[*Putting up the Letter.*

Glo. Why so earnestly seek you to put up that letter?

Edm. I know no news, my lord.

Glo. What paper were you reading?

Edm. Nothing, my lord.

Glo. No? What needed then that terrible despatch of it into your pocket? the quality of nothing hath not such need to hide itself. Let's see: Come, if it be nothing, I shall not need spectacles.

Edm. I beseech you, sir, pardon me: it is a letter from my brother, that I have not all o'er-read; for so much as I have perused, I find it not fit for your over-looking.

Glo. Give me the letter, sir.

Edm. I shall offend, either to detain or give it. The contents, as in part I understand them, are to blame.

Glo. Let's see, let's see.

Edm. I hope, for my brother's justification, he wrote this but as an essay or taste of my virtue.

Glo. [Reads.] *This policy, and reverence of age, makes the world bitter to the best of our times; keeps our fortunes from us, till our oldness cannot relish them. I begin to find an idle and fond bondage in the oppression of aged tyranny; who sways, not as it hath power, but as it is suffered. Come to me, that of this I may speak more. If our father would sleep till I waked him, you should enjoy half his revenue for ever, and live the beloved of your brother,* Edgar! —Humph—Conspiracy!—*Sleep till I waked him —you should enjoy half his revenue,*—My son Edgar!—Had he a hand to write this? a heart and brain to breed it in?—When came this to you? Who brought it?

Edm. It was not brought me, my lord, there's the cunning of it; I found it thrown in at the casement of my closet.

Glo. You know the character to be your brother's?

Edm. If the matter were good, my lord, I durst swear it were his; but, in respect of that, I would fain think it were not.

Glo. It is his.

Edm. It is his hand, my lord; but, I hope, his heart is not in the contents.

Glo. Hath he never heretofore sounded you in this business?

Edm. Never, my lord: But I have often heard him maintain it to be fit, that, sons at perfect age, and fathers declining, the father should be as ward to the son, and the son manage his revenue.

Glo. O villain, villain!—His very opinion in the letter!—Abhorred villain! Unnatural, detested, brutish villain! worse than brutish!—Go, sirrah, seek him; I'll apprehend him:—Abominable villain!—Where is he?

Edm. I do not well know, my lord. If it shall please you to suspend your indignation against my brother, till you can derive from him better testimony of his intent, you shall run a certain course; where, if you violently proceed against him, mistaking his purpose, it would make a great gap in your own honour, and shake in pieces the heart of his obedience. I dare pawn down my life for him, that he hath writ this to feel my affection to your honour, and to no other pretence of danger.

Glo. Think you so?

Edm. If your honour judge it meet, I will

place you where you shall hear us confer of this, and by an auricular assurance have your satisfaction; and that without any further delay than this very evening.

Glo. He cannot be such a monster.

Edm. Nor is not, sure.

Glo. To his father, that so tenderly and entirely loves him.—Heaven and earth!—Edmund, seek him out; wind me into him, I pray you: frame the business after your own wisdom: I would unstate myself, to be in a due resolution.

Edm. I will seek him, sir, presently; convey the business as I shall find means, and acquaint you withal.

Glo. These late eclipses in the sun and moon portend no good to us: Though the wisdom of nature can reason it thus and thus, yet nature finds itself scourged by the sequent effects: love cools, friendship falls off, brothers divide: in cities, mutinies; in countries, discord; in palaces, treason: and the bond cracked between son and father. This villain of mine comes under the prediction; there's son against father: the king falls from bias of nature; there's father against child. We have seen the best of our time: Machinations, hollowness, treachery, and all ruinous disorders, follow us disquietly to our graves!—Find out this villain, Edmund, it shall lose thee nothing; do it carefully:—And the noble and true-hearted Kent banished! his offence, honesty!—Strange! strange! [*Exit.*

Edm. This is the excellent foppery of the world! that, when we are sick in fortune (often the surfeit of our own behaviour), we make guilty of our disasters, the sun, the moon, and the stars: as if we were villains by necessity: fools, by heavenly compulsion; knaves, thieves, and treachers, by spherical predominance; drunkard, liars, and adulterers, by an enforced obedience of planetary influence: and all that we are evil in, by a divine thrusting on: An admirable evasion of whoremaster man, to lay his goatish disposition to the charge of a star; My father compounded with my mother under the dragon's tail; and my nativity was under *ursa major*; so that it follows, I am rough and lecherous.—Tut, I should have been that I am, had the maidenliest star in the firmament twinkled on my bastardizing. Edgar—

Enter EDGAR.

and pat he comes, like the catastrophe of the old comedy: My cue is villanous melancholy, with a sigh like Tom o' Bedlam.—O, these eclipses do portend these divisions! fa, sol, la, mi.

Edg. How now, brother Edmund? What serious contemplation are you in?

Edm. I am thinking, brother, of a prediction I read this other day, what should follow these eclipses.

Edg. Do you busy yourself with that?

Edm. I promise you, the effects he writes of, succeed unhappily: as of unnaturalness between the child and the parent; death, dearth, dissolutions of ancient amities; divisions in state, menaces and maledictions against king and nobles; needless diffidences, banishment of friends, dissipation of cohorts, nuptial breaches, and I know not what.

Edg. How long have you been a sectary astronomical?

Edm. Come, come; when saw you my father last?

Edg. Why, the night gone by.

Edm. Spake you with him?

Edg. Ay, two hours together.

Edm. Parted you in good terms? Found you no displeasure in him, by word or countenance?

Edg. None at all.

Edm. Bethink yourself, wherein you may have offended him: and at my entreaty, forbear his presence, till some little time hath qualified the heat of his displeasure; which at this instant so rageth in him, that with the mischief of your person it would scarcely allay.

Edg. Some villain hath done me wrong.

Edm. That's my fear. I pray you, have a continent forbearance, till the speed of his rage goes slower; and, as I say, retire with me to my lodging, from whence I will fitly bring you to hear my lord speak: Pray you, go; there's my key;—If you do stir abroad, go armed.

Edg. Armed, brother?

Edm. Brother, I advise you to the best: go armed; I am no honest man, if there be any good meaning towards you: I have told you what I have seen and heard, but faintly; nothing like the image and horror of it: 'Pray you, away.

Edg. Shall I hear from you anon?

Edm. I do serve you in this business.— [*Exit* EDGAR.

A credulous father, and a brother noble,
Whose nature is so far from doing harms,
That he suspects none; on whose foolish honesty
My practices ride easy!—I see the business.—
Let me, if not by birth, have lands by wit:
All with me's meet, that I can fashion fit. [*Exit.*

SCENE III.

A Room in the Duke *of* Albany's *Palace.*

Enter GONERIL *and* Steward.

Gon. Did my father strike my gentleman for chiding of his fool?

Stew. Ay, madam.

Gon. By day and night! he wrongs me; every hour
He flashes into one gross crime or other,
That sets us all at odds: I'll not endure it:
His knights grow riotous, and himself upbraids us
On every trifle;—When he returns from hunting,
I will not speak with him: say, I am sick:—
If you come slack of former services,
You shall do well; the fault of it I'll answer.

Stew. He's coming, madam; I hear him. [*Horns within.*

Gon. Put on what weary negligence you please,
You and your fellows; I'd have it come to question:
If he dislike it, let him to my sister,
Whose mind and mine, I know, in that are one,
Not to be overrul'd. Idle old man,
That still would manage those authorities,
That he hath given away!—Now, by my life,
Old fools are babes again; and must be us'd
With checks, as flatteries,—when they are seen abus'd.
Remember what I have said.

Stew. Very well, madam.

Gon. And let his knights have colder looks among you;
What grows of it, no matter; advise your fellows so:
I would breed from hence occasions, and I shall,
That I may speak:—I'll write straight to my sister,
To hold my very course:—Prepare for dinner. [*Exeunt.*

SCENE IV. *A Hall in the same.*

Enter KENT, *disguised.*

Kent. If but as well I other accents borrow,
That can my speech diffuse, my good intent
May carry through itself to that full issue
For which I raz'd my likeness.—Now, banish'd Kent,
If thou canst serve where thou dost stand condemn'd,

(So may it come!) thy master, whom thou lov'st,
Shall find thee full of labours.

Horns within. Enter LEAR, Knights, *and* Attendants.

Lear. Let me not stay a jot for dinner: go, get it ready. [*Exit an* Attendant.] How now, what art thou?

Kent. A man, sir.

Lear. What dost thou profess? What would'st thou with us?

Kent. I do profess to be no less than I seem; to serve him truly, that will put me in trust; to love him that is honest; to converse with him that is wise, and says little; to fear judgment; to fight, when I cannot choose: and to eat no fish.

Lear. What art thou?

Kent. A very honest-hearted fellow, and as poor as the king.

Lear. If thou be as poor for a subject, as he is for a king, thou art poor enough. What would'st thou?

Kent. Service.

Lear. Who would'st thou serve?

Kent. You.

Lear. Dost thou know me, fellow?

Kent. No, sir; but you have that in your countenance, which I would fain call master.

Lear. What's that?

Kent. Authority.

Lear. What services canst thou do?

Kent. I can keep honest counsel, ride, run, mar a curious tale in telling it, and deliver a plain message bluntly: that which ordinary men are fit for, I am qualified in; and the best of me is diligence.

Lear. How old art thou?

Kent. Not so young, sir, to love a woman for singing; nor so old, to dote on her for any thing: I have years on my back forty-eight.

Lear. Follow me; thou shalt serve me; if I like thee no worse after dinner, I will not part from thee yet.—Dinner, ho, dinner!—Where's my knave? my fool? Go you, and call my fool hither:

Enter Steward.

You, you, sirrah, where's my daughter?

Stew. So please you,— [*Exit.*

Lear. What says the fellow there? Call the clotpoll back.—Where's my fool, ho?—I think the world's asleep.—How now? where's that mongrel?

Knight. He says, my lord, your daughter is not well.

Lear. Why came not the slave back to me, when I call'd him?

Knight. Sir, he answer'd me in the roundest manner, he would not.

Lear. He would not!

Knight. My lord, I know not what the matter is; but, to my judgment, your highness is not entertain'd with that ceremonious affection as you were wont; there's a great abatement of kindness appears, as well in the general dependants, as in the duke himself also, and your daughter.

Lear. Ha! say'st thou so?

Knight. I beseech you, pardon me, my lord, if I be mistaken; for my duty cannot be silent, when I think your highness is wrong'd.

Lear. Thou but remember'st me of mine own conception; I have perceived a most faint neglect of late; which I have rather blamed as mine own jealous curiosity, than as a very pretence and purpose of unkindness: I will look further into't.—But where's my fool? I have not seen him this two days.

Knight. Since my young lady's going into France, sir, the fool hath much pined away.

Lear. No more of that; I have noted it well.—Go you, and tell my daughter I would speak with her.—Go you, and call hither my fool.—

Re-enter Steward.

O, you sir, you sir, come you hither: Who am I, sir?

Stew. My lady's father.

Lear. My lady's father! my lord's knave: you whoreson dog! you slave! you cur!

Stew. I am none of this, my lord; I beseech you, pardon me.

Lear. Do you bandy looks with me, you rascal? [*Striking him.*

Stew. I'll not be struck, my lord.

Kent. Nor tripped neither; you base foot-ball player. [*Tripping up his heels.*

Lear. I thank thee, fellow; thou servest me, and I'll love thee.

Kent. Come, sir, arise, away: I'll teach you differences: away, away: If you will measure your lubber's length again, tarry: but away: go to: Have you wisdom? so. [*Pushes the* Steward *out.*

Lear. Now, my friendly knave, I thank thee: there's earnest of thy service. [*Giving* KENT *Money.*

Enter Fool.

Fool. Let me hire him too;—Here's my coxcomb. [*Giving* KENT *his Cap.*

Lear. How now, my pretty knave? how dost thou?

Fool. Sirrah, you were best take my coxcomb.

Kent. Why, fool?

Fool. Why? For taking one's part that is out of favour: Nay, an thou canst not smile as the wind sits, thou'lt catch cold shortly. There, take my coxcomb: Why, this fellow has banish'd two of his daughters, and did the third a blessing against his will: if thou follow him, thou must needs wear my coxcomb.—How now, nuncle? 'Would, I had two coxcombs, and two daughters!

Lear. Why, my boy?

Fool. If I gave them all my living, I'd keep my coxcombs myself: There's mine; beg another of thy daughters.

Lear. Take heed, sirrah; the whip.

Fool. Truth's a dog that must to kennel? he must be whipped out, when Lady, the brach, may stand by the fire, and stink.

Lear. A pestilent gall to me!

Fool. Sirrah, I'll teach thee a speech.

Lear. Do.

Fool. Mark it, nuncle:—

Have more than thou showest,
Speak less than thou knowest,
Lend less than thou owest,
Ride more than thou goest,
Learn more than thou trowest,
Set less than thou throwest,
Leave thy drink and thy whore,
And keep in-a-door,
And thou shalt have more
Than two tens to a score.

Lear. This is nothing, fool.

Fool. Then 'tis like the breath of an unfee'd lawyer; you gave me nothing for't; Can you make no use of nothing, nuncle?

Lear. Why, no, boy; nothing can be made out of nothing.

Fool. 'Pr'ythee, tell him, so much the rent of his land comes to; he will not believe a fool. [*To* KENT.

Lear. A bitter fool!

Fool. Dost thou know the difference, my boy, between a bitter fool and a sweet fool?

Lear. No, lad; teach me.

Fool. That lord that counsel'd thee
To give away thy land,
Come place him here by me,—
Or do thou for him stand:
The sweet and bitter fool
Will presently appear;
The one in motley here,
The other found out there.

Lear. Dost thou call me fool, boy?

Fool. All thy other titles thou hast given away; that thou wast born with.

Kent. This is not altogether fool, my lord.

Fool. No, 'faith, lords and great men will not let me; if I had a monopoly out, they would have part on 't: and ladies too, they will not let me have all fool to myself; they'll be snatching.—Give me an egg, nuncle, and I'll give thee two crowns.

Lear. What two crowns shall they be?

Fool. Why, after I have cut the egg i'the middle, and eat up the meat, the two crowns of the egg. When thou clovest thy crown i' the middle, and gavest away both parts, thou borest thine ass on thy back over the dirt: Thou had'st little wit in thy bald crown, when thou gavest thy golden one away. If I speak like myself in this, let him be whipp'd that first finds it so.

Fools had ne'er less grace in a year; [Singing.
For wise men are grown foppish;
And know not how their wits to wear,
Their manners are so apish.

Lear. When were you wont to be so full of songs, sirrah?

Fool. I have used it, nuncle, ever since thou madest thy daughters thy mother: for when thou gavest them the rod, and put'st down thine own breeches,

Then they for sudden joy did weep, [Singing.
And I for sorrow sung,
That such a king should play bo-peep,
And go the fools among.

Pr'ythee, nuncle, keep a schoolmaster that can teach thy fool to lie; I would fain learn to lie.

Lear. If you lie sirrah, we'll have you whipp'd.

Fool. I marvel, what kin thou and thy daughters are: they'll have me whipp'd for speaking true, thou'lt have me whipp'd for lying; and, sometimes, I am whipp'd for holding my peace. I had rather be any kind of thing, than a fool: and yet I would not be thee, nuncle; thou hast pared thy wit o' both sides, and left nothing in the middle: Here comes one o' the parings.

Enter GONERIL.

Lear. How now, daughter! what makes that frontlet on? Methinks, you are too much of late i' the frown.

Fool. Thou wast a pretty fellow, when thou had'st no need to care for her frowning; now thou art an O without a figure: I am better than thou art now; I am a fool, thou art nothing.—Yes, forsooth, I will hold my tongue! so your face [*To* GON.] bids me, though you say nothing. Mum, mum,
He that keeps nor crust nor crum,
Weary of all, shall want some.
That's a shealed peascod. [*Pointing to* LEAR.

Gon. Not only, sir, this your all-licens'd fool,
But other of your insolent retinue
Do hourly carp and quarrel; breaking forth
In rank and not-to-be-endured riots. Sir,
I had thought, by making this well known unto you,
To have found a safe redress, but now grow fearful,
By what yourself too late have spoke and done,
That you protect this course, and put it on
By your allowance; which if you should, the fault
Would not 'scape censure, nor the redresses sleep;
Which in the tender of a wholesome weal,
Might in their working do you that offence,
Which else were shame, that then necessity
Will call discreet proceeding.

Fool. For you trow, nuncle,
The hedge sparrow fed the cuckoo so long,
That it had its head bit off by its young.
So, out went the candle, and we were left darkling.

Lear. Are you our daughter?

Gon. Come, sir, I would, you would make use of that good wisdom whereof I know you are fraught; and put away these dispositions, which of late transform you from what you rightly are.

Fool. May not an ass know when the cart draws the horse? Whoop, Jug! I love thee.

Lear. Does any here know me?—Why this is not Lear: does Lear walk thus? speak thus? Where are his eyes? Either his notion weakens, or his discernings are lethargied.—Sleeping or waking?—Ha! sure 'tis not so.—Who is it that can tell me who I am?

Fool. Lear's shadow,—

Lear. I would learn that; for by the marks of sovereignty, knowledge, and reason, I should be false persuaded I had daughters.

Fool.—Which they will make an obedient father.

Lear. Your name, fair gentlewoman?

Gon. Come, sir;
This admiration is much o' the favour
Of other your new pranks. I do beseech you
To understand my purposes aright:
As you are old and reverend, you should be wise:
Here do you keep a hundred knights and squires;
Men so disorder'd, so debauch'd and bold,
That this our court, infected with their manners,
Shows like a riotous inn: epicurism and lust
Make it more like a tavern or a brothel,
Than a grac'd palace. The shame itself doth speak
For instant remedy: Be then desir'd
By her, that else will take the thing she begs,
A little to disquantity your train:
And the remainder, that shall still depend
To be such men as may besort your age,
And know themselves and you.

Lear. Darkness and devils!—
Saddle my horses; call my train together.—
Degenerate bastard! I'll not trouble thee;
Yet have I left a daughter.

Gon. You strike my people; and your disorder'd rabble
Make servants of their betters.

Enter ALBANY.

Lear. Woe, that too late repents,—O, sir, are you come?
Is it your will? [*To* ALB.] Speak, sir.—Prepare my horses.
Ingratitude! thou marble-hearted fiend,
More hideous, when thou show'st thee in a child,
Than the sea-monster!

Alb. 'Pray, sir, be patient.

Lear. Detested kite! thou liest: [*To* GON.
My train are men of choice and rarest parts,
That all particulars of duty know:
And in the most exact regard support
The worships of their name.—O most small fault,
How ugly didst thou in Cordelia show!
Which, like an engine, wrench'd my frame of nature
From the fix'd place: drew from my heart all love,
And added to the gall. O Lear, Lear, Lear!
Beat at this gate that let thy folly in.
[*Striking his Head.*
And thy dear judgment out.—Go, go, my people.

Alb. My lord, I am guiltless, as I am ignorant
Of what hath mov'd you.

Lear. It may be so, my lord.—Hear, nature, hear;
Dear goddess hear! Suspend thy purpose, if
Thou didst intend to make this creature fruitful!
Into her womb convey sterility!
Dry up in her the organs of increase;
And from her derogate body never spring
A babe to honour her! If she must teem,
Create her child of spleen; that it may live,

And be a thwart disnatur'd torment to her!
Let it stamp wrinkles in her brow of youth;
With cadent tears fret channels in her cheeks:
Turn all her mother's pains, and benefits,
To laughter and contempt; that she may feel
How sharper than a serpent's tooth it is
To have a thankless child!—Away, away! [*Exit.*

Alb. Now, gods, that we adore, whereof comes this?

Gon. Never afflict yourself to know the cause;
But let his disposition have that scope
That dotage gives it.

Re-enter LEAR.

Lear. What, fifty of my followers, at a clap!
Within a fortnight?

Alb. What's the matter, sir?

Lear. I'll tell thee;—Life and death! I am asham'd
That thou hast power to shake my manhood thus: [*To* GONERIL.
That these hot tears, which break from me perforce,
Should make thee worth them.—Blasts and fogs upon thee!
The untented woundings of a father's curse
Pierce every sense about thee!—Old fond eyes,
Beweep this cause again, I'll pluck you out;
And cast you, with the waters that you lose,
To temper clay.—Ha! is it come to this?
Let it be so:—Yet have I left a daughter,
Who, I am sure, is kind and comfortable;
When she shall hear this of thee, with her nails
She'll flay thy wolfish visage. Thou shalt find,
That I'll resume the shape which thou dost think
I have cast off for ever; thou shalt, I warrant thee. [*Exeunt* LEAR, KENT, *and* Attend.

Gon. Do you mark that, my lord?

Alb. I cannot be so partial, Goneril,
To the great love I bear you.—

Gon. 'Pray you, content.—What, Oswald, ho!
You, sir, more knave than fool, after your master. [*To the* Fool.

Fool. Nuncle Lear, nuncle Lear, tarry, and take the fool with thee.

A fox when one has caught her,
And such a daughter,
Should sure to the slaughter,
If my cap would buy a halter;
So the fool follows after. [*Exit.*

Gon. This man hath had good counsel:—A hundred knights!
'Tis politick, and safe, to let him keep
At point, a hundred knights. Yes, that on every dream,
Each buz, each fancy, each complaint, dislike,
He may enguard his dotage with their powers,
And hold our lives in mercy. Oswald, I say!—

Alb. Well, you may fear too far.

Gon. Safer than trust:
Let me still take away the harms I fear,
Not fear still to be taken. I know his heart:
What he hath utter'd, I have writ my sister;
If she sustain him and his hundred knights,
When I have show'd the' unfitness,—How now, Oswald?

Enter Steward.

What, have you writ that letter to my sister?

Stew. Ay, madam.

Gon. Take you some company, and away to horse:
Inform her full of my particular fear;
And thereto add such reasons of your own,
As may compact it more. Get you gone;
And hasten your return. [*Exit* Stew.] No, no, my lord,
This milky gentleness, and course of yours,
Though I condemn it not, yet, under pardon,
You are much more attask'd for want of wisdom,
Than prais'd for harmful mildness.

Alb. How far your eyes may pierce, I cannot tell;
Striving to better, oft we mar what's well.

Gon. Nay, then—

Alb. Well, well; the event. [*Exeunt.*

SCENE V. *Court before the same.*

Enter LEAR, KENT, *and* Fool.

Lear. Go you before to Gloster with these letters: acquaint my daughter no further with any thing you know, than comes from her demand out of the letter: If your diligence be not speedy, I shall be there before you.

Kent. I will not sleep, my lord, till I have delivered your letter. [*Exit.*

Fool. If a man's brains were in his heels, were't not in danger of kibes?

Lear. Ay, boy.

Fool. Then, I pr'ythee, be merry; thy wit shall not go slip-shod.

Lear. Ha, ha, ha!

Fool. Shalt see, thy other daughter will use thee kindly; for though she's as like this as a crab is like an apple, yet I can tell what I can tell.

Lear. Why, what canst thou tell, my boy?

Fool. She will taste as like this, as a crab does to a crab. Thou canst tell, why one's nose stands i' the middle of his face?

Lear. No.

Fool. Why, to keep his eyes on either side his nose; that what a man cannot smell out, he may spy into.

Lear. I did her wrong:—

Fool. Can'st tell how an oyster makes his shell?

Lear. No.

Fool. Nor I neither; but I can tell why a snail has a house.

Lear. Why?

Fool. Why, to put his head in; not to give it away to his daughters, and leave his horns without a case.

Lear. I will forget my nature.—So kind a father!—Be my horses ready?

Fool. Thy asses are gone about 'em. The reason why the seven stars are no more than seven, is a pretty reason.

Lear. Because they are not eight?

Fool. Yes, indeed: Thou wouldest make a good fool.

Lear. To take it again perforce!—Monster, ingratitude!

Fool. If thou wert my fool, nuncle, I'd have thee beaten for being old before thy time.

Lear. How's that?

Fool. Thou should'st not have been old, before thou hadst been wise.

Lear. O let me not be mad, not mad, sweet heaven!
Keep me in temper; I would not be mad!—

Enter Gentleman.

How now! Are the horses ready?

Gent. Ready, my lord.

Lear. Come, boy.

Fool. She that is maid now, and laughs at my departure,
Shall not be a maid long, unless things be cut shorter. [*Exeunt.*

ACT II.

SCENE I. *A Court within the Castle of the* Earl *of* Gloster.

Enter EDMUND *and* CURAN, *meeting.*

Edm. Save thee, Curan.

Cur. And you, sir. I have been with your father; and given him notice, that the Duke of Cornwall, and Regan his duchess, will be here with him to-night.

Edm. How comes that?

Cur. Nay, I know not: You have heard of the news abroad; I mean, the whispered ones, for they are yet but ear-kissing arguments?

Edm. Not I; 'Pray you, what are they?

Cur. Have you heard of no likely wars toward, 'twixt the Dukes of Cornwall and Albany?

Edm. Not a word.

Cur. You may then, in time. Fare you well, sir. [*Exit.*

Edm. The duke be here to-night? The better! Best!
This weaves itself perforce into my business!
My father hath set guard to take my brother;
And I have one thing, of a queasy question,
Which I must act:—Briefness, and fortune, work!—
Brother, a word; descend:—Brother, I say;

Enter EDGAR.

My father watches:—O sir, fly this place;
Intelligence is given where you are hid;
You have now the good advantage of the night:—
Have you not spoken 'gainst the duke of Cornwall?
He's coming hither; now, i' the night, i' the haste,
And Regan with him; Have you nothing said
Upon his party 'gainst the duke of Albany?
Advise yourself.

Edg. I am sure on't, not a word.

Edm. I hear my father coming,—Pardon me:—
In cunning, I must draw my sword upon you:—
Draw: Seem to defend yourself: Now quit you well.
Yield:—come before my father;—Light, ho, here!—
Fly, brother;—Torches! torches!—So, farewell.— [*Exit* EDGAR.
Some blood drawn on me would beget opinion [*Wounds his Arm.*
Of my more fierce endeavour: I have seen drunkards
Do more than this in sport.—Father! Father!
Stop, stop! No help?

Enter GLOSTER, *and* Servants *with Torches.*

Glo. Now, Edmund, where's the villain?

Edm. Here stood he in the dark, his sharp sword out,
Mumbling of wicked charms, conjuring the moon
To stand his auspicious mistress:—

Glo. But where is he?

Edm. Look, sir, I bleed.

Glo. Where is the villain, Edmund?

Edm. Fled this way, sir. When by no means he could—

Glo. Pursue him, ho!—Go after.—[*Exit* Serv.] By no means,—what?

Edm. Persuade me to the murder of your lordship;
But that I told him, the revenging gods
'Gainst parricides did all their thunders bend;
Spoke, with how manifold and strong a bond
The child was bound to the father;—Sir, in fine,
Seeing how loathly opposite I stood
To his unnatural purpose, in fell motion,
With his prepared sword, he charges home
My unprovided body, lanc'd mine arm:
But when he saw my best alarum'd spirits,
Bold in the quarrel's right, rous'd to the encounter,
Or whether gasted by the noise I made,
Full suddenly he fled.

Glo. Let him fly far:
Not in this land shall he remain uncaught;
And found—Despatch.—The noble duke my master,
My worthy arch and patron, comes to-night:
By his authority I will proclaim it,
That he, which finds him, shall deserve our thanks,
Bringing the murderous coward to the stake;
He, that conceals him, death.

Edm. When I dissuaded him from his intent,
And found him pight to do it, with curst speech;
I threaten'd to discover him: He replied,
Thou unpossessing bastard! dost thou think
If I would stand against thee, would the reposal
Of any trust, virtue, or worth, in thee
Make thy words faith'd! No: what I should deny,
(As this I would; ay, though thou didst produce
My very character), I'd turn it all
To thy suggestion, plot, and damned practice:
And thou must make a dullard of the world,
If they not thought the profits of my death
Were very pregnant and potential spurs
To make thee seek it.

Glo. Strong and fasten'd villain;
Would he deny his letter?—I never got him. [*Trumpets within.*
Hark, the duke's trumpets! I know not why he comes:—
All ports I'll bar; the villain shall not 'scape;
The duke must grant me that: besides, his picture
I will send far and near, that all the kingdom
May have due note of him; and of my land,
Loyal and natural boy, I'll work the means
To make thee capable.

Enter CORNWALL, REGAN, *and* Attendants.

Corn. How now, my noble friend? since I came hither
(Which I can call but now), I have heard strange news.

Reg. If it be true, all vengeance comes too short,
Which can pursue the offender. How dost, my lord?

Glo. O, madam, my old heart is crack'd, is crack'd!

Reg. What, did my father's godson seek your life?
He whom my father nam'd? your Edgar?

Glo. O lady, lady, shame would have it hid!

Reg. Was he not companion with the riotous knights
That tend upon my father?

Glo. I know not, madam:
It is too bad, too bad.—

Edm. Yes, madam, he was.

Reg. No marvel then, though he were ill affected;
'Tis they have put him on the old man's death,
To have the waste and spoil of his revenues.
I have this present evening from my sister
Been well inform'd of them; and with such cautions,
That, if they come to sojourn at my house,
I'll not be there.

Corn. Nor I, assure thee, Regan.—
Edmund, I hear that you have shown your father
A child-like office.

Edm. 'Twas my duty, sir.

Glo. He did bewray his practice, and receiv'd
This hurt you see, striving to apprehend him.

Corn. Is he pursued?

Glo. Ay, my good lord, he is.

Corn. If he be taken, he shall never more
Be fear'd of doing harm: make your own purpose,
How in my strength you please.—For you, Edmund,
Whose virtue and obedience doth this instant
So much commend itself, you shall be ours;
Natures of such deep trust we shall much need;
You we first seize on.

Edm. I shall serve you, sir,
Truly, however else.

Glo. For him I thank your grace.

Corn. You know not why we came to visit you,—

Reg. Thus out of season; threading dark-ey'd night.

Occasions, noble Gloster, of some poize,
Wherein we must have use of your advice:—
Our father he hath writ, so hath our sister,
Of differences, which I best thought it fit
To answer from our home; the several messengers
From hence attend despatch. Our good old friend,
Lay comforts to your bosom; and bestow
Your needful counsel to our business,
Which craves the instant use.

Glo. I serve you, madam:
Your graces are right welcome. [*Exeunt.*

SCENE II. *Before* Gloster's *Castle.*

Enter KENT *and* Steward, *severally.*

Stew. Good dawning to thee, friend: Art of the house?

Kent. Ay.

Stew. Where may we set our horses?

Kent. I' the mire.

Stew. 'Pr'ythee, if thou love me, tell me.

Kent. I love thee not.

Stew. Why, then I care not for thee.

Kent. If I had thee in Lipsbury pinfold, I would make thee care for me.

Stew. Why dost thou use me thus? I know thee not.

Kent. Fellow, I know thee.

Stew. What dost thou know me for?

Kent. A knave; a rascal, an eater of broken meats; a base, proud, shallow, beggarly, three-suited, hundred-pound, filthy worsted-stocking knave; a lily-liver'd, action-taking knave; a whorson, glass-gazing, superserviceable, finical rogue; one-trunk-inheriting slave; one that would'st be a bawd, in way of good-service, and art nothing but the composition of a knave, beggar, coward, pander, and the son and heir of a mongrel bitch: one whom I will beat into clamorous whining, if thou deny'st the least syllable of thy addition.

Stew. Why, what a monstrous fellow art thou, thus to rail on one, that is neither known of thee, nor knows thee?

Kent. What a brazen-faced varlet art thou, to deny thou know'st me? Is it two days ago, since I tripp'd up thy heels, and beat thee, before the king? Draw, you rogue: for though it be night, the moon shines; I'll make a sop o' the moonshine of you: Draw, you whorson cullionly barber-monger, draw. [*Drawing his Sword.*

Stew. Away; I have nothing to do with thee.

Kent. Draw, you rascal: you come with letters against the king; and take vanity the puppet's part, against the royalty of her father: Draw, you rogue, or I'll so carbonado your shanks:—draw, you rascal: come your ways.

Stew. Help ho! murder! help!

Kent. Strike, you slave; stand, rogue, stand; you neat slave, strike. [*Beating him.*

Stew. Help, ho! murder! murder!

Enter EDMUND, CORNWALL, REGAN, GLOSTER, *and* Servants.

Edm. How now? What's the matter? Part.

Kent. With you, goodman boy, if you please; come, I'll flesh you; come on, young master.

Glo. Weapons! arms! What's the matter here?

Corn. Keep peace, upon your lives;
He dies, that strikes again: What is the matter?

Reg. The messengers from our sister and the king.

Corn. What is your difference? speak.

Stew. I am scarce in breath, my lord.

Kent. No marvel, you have so bestirr'd your valour. You cowardly rascal, nature disclaims in thee; a tailor made thee.

Corn. Thou art a strange fellow: a tailor make a man?

Kent. Ay, a tailor, sir; a stone-cutter, or a painter, could not have made him so ill, though they had been but two hours at the trade.

Corn. Speak yet, how grew your quarrel?

Stew. This ancient ruffian, sir, whose life I have spar'd,
At suit of his gray beard,—

Kent. Thou whorson zed! thou unnecessary letter!—My lord, if you will give me leave, I will tread this unbolted villain into mortar, and daub the wall of a jakes with him.—Spare my gray beard, you wagtail?

Corn. Peace, sirrah!
You beastly knave, know you no reverence?

Kent. Yes, sir; but anger has a privilege.

Corn. Why art thou angry?

Kent. That such a slave as this should wear a sword,
Who wears no honesty. Such smiling rogues as these,
Like rats, oft bite the holy cords atwain
Which are too intrinse t' unloose: smooth every passion
That in the natures of their lords rebels;
Bring oil to fire, snow to their colder moods;
Renege, affirm, and turn their halcyon beaks
With every gale and vary of their masters,
As knowing nought, like dogs, but following.—
A plague upon your epileptick visage!
Smile you my speeches, as I were a fool?
Goose, if I had you upon Sarum plain,
I'd drive ye cackling home to Camelot.

Corn. What, art thou mad, old fellow?

Glo. How fell you out?
Say that.

Kent. No contraries hold more antipathy,
Than I and such a knave.

Corn. Why dost thou call him knave? What's his offence?

Kent. His countenance likes me not.

Corn. No more, perchance, does mine, or his, or hers.

Kent. Sir, 'tis my occupation to be plain;
I have seen better faces in my time,
Than stands on any shoulder that I see
Before me at this instant.

Corn. This is some fellow,
Who, having been prais'd for bluntness, doth affect
A saucy roughness; and constrains the garb,
Quite from his nature; He cannot flatter, he!—
An honest mind and plain,—he must speak truth:
An they will take it, so; if not, he's plain.
These kind of knaves I know, which in this plainness
Harbour more craft, and more corrupter ends,
Than twenty silly ducking observants,
That stretch their duties nicely.

Kent. Sir, in good sooth, in sincere verity,
Under the allowance of your grand aspect,
Whose influence, like the wreath of radiant fire
On flickering Phœbus' front,—

Corn. What mean'st by this?

Kent. To go out of my dialect, which you discommend so much. I know, sir, I am no flatterer: he that beguiled you, in a plain accent, was a plain knave; which, for my part, I will not be, though I should win your displeasure to entreat me to it.

Corn. What was the offence you gave him?

Stew. Never any:
It pleas'd the king his master, very late,
To strike at me, upon his misconstruction:
When he, conjunct, and flattering his displeasure,
Tripp'd me behind; being down, insulted, rail'd,
And put upon him such a deal of man,
That worthy'd him, got praises of the king
For him attempting who was self subdu'd;
And, in the fleshment of this dread exploit,
Drew on me here.

Kent. None of these rogues, and cowards,
But Ajax is their fool.

Corn. Fetch forth the stocks, ho!
You stubborn ancient knave, you reverend braggart,
We'll teach you—

Kent. Sir, I am too old to learn:
Call not your stocks for me: I serve the king;
On whose employment I was sent to you:
You shall do small respect, show too bold malice
Against the grace and person of my master,
Stocking his messenger.

Corn. Fetch forth the stocks:
As I've life and honour, there shall he sit till noon.

Reg. Till noon! till night, my lord; and all night too.

Kent. Why, madam, if I were your father's dog,
You should not use me so.

Reg. Sir, being his knave, I will.
[*Stocks brought out.*

Corn. This is a fellow of the selfsame colour
Our sister speaks of:—Come, bring away the stocks.

Glo. Let me beseech your grace not to do so:
His fault is much, and the good king his master
Will check him for't: your purpos'd low correction
Is such, as basest and contemned'st wretches,
For pilferings and most common trespasses,
Are punish'd with: the king must take it ill,
That he,—so slightly valu'd in his messenger,
—Should have him thus restrain'd.

Corn. I'll answer that.

Reg. My sister may receive it much more worse,
To have her gentleman abus'd, assaulted,
For following her affairs.—Put in his legs.—
[KENT *is put in the Stocks.*
Come, my good lord; away.
[*Exeunt* REGAN *and* CORNWALL.

Glo. I am sorry for thee, friend; 'tis the duke's pleasure,
Whose disposition, all the world well knows,
Will not be rubb'd, nor stopp'd; I'll entreat for thee.

Kent. 'Pray, do not, sir: I have watch'd, and travell'd hard;
Some time I shall sleep out, the rest I'll whistle.
A good man's fortune may grow out at heels:
Give you good morrow!

Glo. The duke's to blame in this; 'twill be ill taken. [*Exit.*

Kent. Good king, that must approve the common saw!
Thou out of heaven's benediction com'st
To the warm sun!
Approach, thou beacon to this under globe,
That by thy comfortable beams I may
Peruse this letter!—Nothing almost sees miracles,
But misery;—I know 'tis from Cordelia;
Who hath most fortunately been inform'd
Of my obscured course; and shall find time
From this enormous state,—seeking,—to give
Losses their remedies:—All weary and o'erwatch'd,
Take vantage, heavy eyes, not to behold
This shameful lodging.
Fortune, good night; smile once more; turn thy wheel! [*He sleeps.*

SCENE III. *A Part of the Heath.*

Enter EDGAR.

Edg. I heard myself proclaim'd;
And, by the happy hollow of a tree,
Escap'd the hunt. No port is free; no place,
That guard, and most unusual vigilance,
Does not attend my taking. While I may scape,
I will preserve myself: and am bethought
To take the basest and most poorest shape,
That ever penury, in contempt of man,
Brought near to beast: my face I'll grime with filth;
Blanket my loins; elf all my hair in knots;
And with presented nakedness outface
The winds, and persecutions of the sky.
The country gives me proof and precedent
Of Bedlam beggars, who, with roaring voices,
Strike in their numb'd and mortified bare arms
Pins, wooden pricks, nails, sprigs of rosemary;
And with this horrible object, from low farms,
Poor pelting villages, sheep-cotes and mills,
Sometime with lunatick bans, sometime with prayers,
Enforce their charity.—Poor Turlygood! poor Tom!
That's something yet; Edgar I nothing am.
[*Exit.*

SCENE IV. *Before* Gloster's *Castle.*

Enter LEAR, Fool, *and* Gentleman.

Lear. 'Tis strange, that they should so depart from home,
And not send back my messenger.

Gent. As I learn'd,
The night before there was no purpose in them
Of this remove.

Kent. Hail to thee, noble master!

Lear. How!
Mak'st thou this shame thy pastime?

Kent. No, my lord.

Fool. Ha, ha; look! he wears cruel garters! Horses are tied by the heads; dogs, and bears, by the neck; monkeys by the loins, and men by the legs: when a man is over-lusty at legs, then he wears wooden nether-stocks.

Lear. What's he, that hath so much thy place mistook
To set thee here?

Kent. It is both he and she,
Your son and daughter.

Lear. No.

Kent. Yes.

Lear. No, I say.

Kent. I say, yea.

Lear. No, no; they would not.

Kent. Yes, they have.

Lear. By Jupiter, I swear, no.

Kent. By Juno, I swear, ay.

Lear. They durst not do't;
They could not, would not do't; 'tis worse than murder,
To do, upon respect, such violent outrage:
Resolve me, with all modest haste, which way
Thou might'st deserve, or they impose, this usage,
Coming from us.

Kent. My lord, when at their home
I did commend your highness' letters to them,
Ere I was risen from the place that show'd
My duty kneeling, came there a reeking post,
Stew'd in his haste, half breathless, panting forth,
From Goneril his mistress, salutations:
Deliver'd letters, spite of intermission,
Which presently they read; on whose contents,
They summon'd up their meiny, straight took horse;
Commanded me to follow, and attend
The leisure of their answer; gave me cold looks:
And meeting here the other messenger,
Whose welcome, I perceiv'd, had poison'd mine
(Being the very fellow that of late
Display'd so saucily against your highness),
Having more man than wit about me, drew;
He rais'd the house with loud and coward cries:
Your son and daughter found this trespass worth
The shame which here it suffers.

Fool. Winter's not gone yet, if the wild geese fly that way.

Fathers, that wear rags,
Do make their children blind;
But fathers, that bear bags,
Shall see their children kind.
Fortune, that arrant whore,
Ne'er turns the key to the poor.—

But, for all this, thou shalt have as many dolours for thy daughters, as thou canst tell in a year.

Lear. O, how this mother swells up toward my heart!
Hysterica passio! down, thou climbing sorrow,
Thy element's below!—Where is this daughter?

Kent. With the earl, sir, here within.

Lear. Follow me not;
Stay here. [*Exit.*

Gent. Made you no more offence than what you speak of?

Kent. None.
How chance the king comes with so small a train?

Fool. An thou hadst been set i' the stocks for that question, thou hadst well deserved it.

Kent. Why, fool?

Fool. We'll set thee to school to an ant, to teach thee there's no labouring in the winter. All that follow their noses are led by their eyes, but blind men; and there's not a nose among twenty, but can smell him that's stinking. Let go thy hold, when a great wheel runs down a hill, lest it break thy neck with following it; but the great one that goes up the hill, let him draw thee after. When a wise man gives thee better counsel, give me mine again: I would have none but knaves follow it, since a fool gives it.

That, sir, which serves and seeks for gain,
And follows but for form,
Will pack, when it begins to rain,
And leave thee in the storm.
But I will tarry, the fool will stay,
And let the wise man fly:
The knave turns fool, that runs away;
The fool no knave, perdy.

Kent. Where learn'd you this, fool?

Fool. Not i' the stocks, fool.

Re-enter LEAR, *with* GLOSTER.

Lear. Deny to speak with me? They are sick? they are weary?
They have travell'd hard to-night? Mere fetches;
The images of revolt and flying off!
Fetch me a better answer.

Glo. My dear lord,
You know the fiery quality of the duke;
How unremoveable and fix'd he is
In his own course.

Lear. Vengeance! plague! death! confusion!—
Fiery? what quality? Why, Gloster, Gloster,
I'd speak with the duke of Cornwall, and his wife.

Glo. Well, my good lord, I have inform'd them so.

Lear. Inform'd them! Dost thou understand me, man?

Glo. Ay, my good lord.

Lear. The king would speak with Cornwall; the dear father
Would with his daughter speak, commands her service:
Are they inform'd of this?——My breath and blood!—
Fiery? the fiery duke?—Tell the hot duke, that—
No, but not yet:—may be, he is not well:
Infirmity doth still neglect all office,
Whereto our health is bound; we are not ourselves,
When nature, being oppress'd, commands the mind
To suffer with the body: I'll forbear;
And am fallen out with my more headier will,
To take the indispos'd and sickly fit
For the sound man. Death on my state! wherefore [*Looking on* KENT.
Should he sit here? This act persuades me,
That this remotion of the duke and her
Is practice only. Give me my servant forth:
Go, tell the duke and his wife, I'd speak with them,
Now, presently: bid them come forth and hear me,
Or at their chamber door I'll beat the drum,
Till it cry—*Sleep to death.*

Glo. I'd have all well betwixt you. [*Exit.*

Lear. O me, my heart, my rising heart!—but, down.

Fool. Cry to it, nuncle, as the cockney did to the eels, when she put them i' the paste alive; she rapp'd 'em o' the coxcombs with a stick, and cry'd, *Down, wantons, down:* 'Twas her brother, that in pure kindness to his horse, butter'd his hay.

Enter CORNWALL, REGAN, GLOSTER, *and* Servants.

Lear. Good morrow to you both.

Corn. Hail to your grace!
[KENT *is set at liberty.*

Reg. I am glad to see your highness.

Lear. Regan, I think you are; I know what reason
I have to think so: if thou should'st not be glad,
I would divorce me from thy mother's tomb,
Sepulchring an adultress.—O, are you free?
[*To* KENT.
Some other time for that.—Beloved Regan,
Thy sister's naught: O Regan, she hath tied
Sharp-tooth'd unkindness, like a vulture here,—
[*Points to his heart.*
I can scarce speak to thee; thou'lt not believe,
Of how deprav'd a quality——O Regan!

Reg. I pray you, sir, take patience; I have hope,
You less know how to value her desert,
Than she to scant her duty.

Lear. Say, how is that?

Reg. I cannot think, my sister in the least
Would fail her obligation: If, sir, perchance,
She have restrain'd the riots of your followers,
'Tis on such ground, and to such wholesome end,
As clears her from all blame.

Lear. My curses on her!

Reg. O, sir, you are old;
Nature in you stands on the very verge
Of her confine: you should be rul'd, and led
By some discretion, that discerns your state
Better than you yourself: Therefore, I pray you,
That to our sister you do make return;
Say, you have wrong'd her, sir.

Lear. Ask her forgiveness?
Do you but mark how this becomes the house:
Dear daughter, I confess that I am old;
Age is unnecessary: on my knees I beg,
[Kneeling.
That you'll vouchsafe me raiment, bed, and food.

Reg. Good sir, no more; these are unsightly tricks:
Return you to my sister.

Lear. Never, Regan:
She hath abated me of half my train;
Look'd black upon me: struck me with her tongue,
Most serpentlike, upon the very heart:—
All the stor'd vengeances of heaven fall
On her ingrateful top! Strike her young bones,
You taking airs, with lameness!

Corn. Fye, fye, fye!

Lear. You nimble lightnings, dart your blinding flames
Into her scornful eyes! Infect her beauty,
You fen-suck'd fogs, drawn by the powerful sun,
To fall and blast her pride!

Reg. O the blest gods!
So will you wish on me, when the rash mood is on.

Lear. No, Regan, thou shalt never have my curse;
Thy tender-hefted nature shall not give
Thee o'er to harshness; her eyes are fierce, but thine
Do comfort, and not burn: 'Tis not in thee
To grudge my pleasures, to cut off my train,
To bandy hasty words, to scant my sizes,
And, in conclusion, to oppose the bolt
Against my coming in: thou better know'st
The offices of nature, bond of childhood,
Effects of courtesy, dues of gratitude;
Thy half o' the kingdom hast thou not forgot,
Wherein I thee endow'd.

Reg. Good sir, to the purpose.
[*Trumpets within.*

Lear. Who put my man i' the stocks?

Corn. What trumpet's that?

Enter Steward.

Reg. I know't, my sister's; this approves her letter,
That she would soon be here.—Is your lady come?

Lear. This is a slave, whose easy-borrow'd pride
Dwells in the fickle grace of her he follows:—
Out, varlet, from my sight!

Corn. What means your grace?

Lear. Who stock'd my servant? Regan, I have good hope
Thou didst not know of 't.—Who comes here? O heavens,

Enter GONERIL.

If you do love old men, if your sweet sway
Allow obedience, if yourselves are old,
Make it your cause; send down, and take my part!—
Art not asham'd to look upon this beard?—
[*To* GONERIL.
O, Regan, wilt thou take her by the hand?

Gon. Why not by the hand, sir? How have I offended?
All's not offence, that indiscretion finds,
And dotage terms so.

Lear. O, sides, you are too tough!
Will you yet hold?—How came my man i' the stocks?

Corn. I set him there, sir: but his own disorders
Deserv'd much less advancement.

Lear. You! did you?

Reg. I pray you, father, being weak, seem so.
If, till the expiration of your month,
You will return and sojourn with my sister,
Dismissing half your train, come then to me;
I am now from home, and out of that provision
Which shall be needful for your entertainment.

Lear. Return to her, and fifty men dismiss'd?
No, rather I abjure all roofs, and choose
To wage against the enmity o' the air;
To be a comrade with the wolf and owl,—
Necessity's sharp pinch!—Return with her?
Why, the hot-blooded France, that dowerless took
Our youngest born, I could as well be brought
To knee his throne, and, squirelike, pension beg
To keep base life afoot;—Return with her?
Persuade me rather to be slave and sumpter
To this detested groom.
[*Looking on the* Steward.

Gon. At your choice, sir.

Lear. I pr'ythee, daughter, do not make me mad;
I will not trouble thee, my child; farewell:
We'll no more meet, no more see one another:—
But yet thou art my flesh, my blood, my daughter;
Or rather a disease that's in my flesh,
Which I must needs call mine: thou art a boil,
A plague-sore, an embossed carbuncle,
In my corrupted blood. But I'll not chide thee;
Let shame come when it will, I do not call it:
I do not bid the thunder-bearer shoot,
Nor tell tales of thee to high-judging Jove:
Mend, when thou canst; be better at thy leisure:
I can be patient; I can stay with Regan,
I, and my hundred knights.

Reg. Not altogether so, sir;
I look'd not for you yet, nor am provided
For your fit welcome: Give ear, sir, to my sister;
For those that mingle reason with your passion,
Must be content to think you old, and so—
But she knows what she does.

Lear. Is this well spoken now?

Reg. I dare avouch it, sir: what, fifty followers?
Is it not well? What should you need of more?
Yea, or so many? sith that both charge and danger
Speak 'gainst so great a number? How, in one house,
Should many people, under two commands,
Hold amity? 'Tis hard; almost impossible.

Gon. Why might not you, my lord, receive attendance
From those that she calls servants, or from mine?

Reg. Why not, my lord? If then they chanc'd to slack you,
We could control them: If you will come to me
(For now I spy a danger), I entreat you
To bring but five and twenty; to no more
Will I give place or notice.

Lear. I gave you all—

Reg. And in good time you gave it.

Lear. Made you my guardians, my depositaries;
But kept a reservation to be follow'd
With such a number: What, must I come to you
With five and twenty, Regan? said you so?

Reg. And speak it again, my lord; no more with me.

Lear. Those wicked creatures yet do look well favour'd,
When others are more wicked; not being the worst,
Stands in some rank of praise:—I'll go with thee;
[*To* GONERIL.
Thy fifty yet doth double five and twenty,
And thou art twice her love.

Gon. Hear me, my lord;
What need you five and twenty, ten, or five,
To follow in a house, where twice so many
Have a command to tend you?

Reg. What need one?

Lear. O, reason not the need: our basest beggars
Are in the poorest things superfluous:
Allow not nature more than nature needs,
Man's life is cheap as beast's: thou art a lady;
If only to go warm were gorgeous,
Why, nature needs not what thou gorgeous wear'st,
Which scarcely keeps thee warm.—But, for true need,—
You heavens, give me that patience, patience I need!
You see me here, you gods, a poor old man,
As full of grief as age; wretched in both!
If it be you that stir these daughters' hearts
Against their father, fool me not so much
To bear it tamely; touch me with noble anger!
O, let not women's weapons, water-drops,
Stain my man's cheeks!—No, you unnatural hags,
I will have such revenges on you both,
That all the world shall—I will do such things,—
What they are, yet I know not; but they shall be
The terrors of the earth. You think, I'll weep;
No, I'll not weep:—
I have full cause of weeping; but this heart

Shall break into a hundred thousand flaws,
Or ere I'll weep:—O, fool, I shall go mad!

[*Exeunt* LEAR, GLOSTER, KENT, *and* Fool.

Corn. Let us withdraw, 'twill be a storm.

[*Storm heard at a distance.*

Reg. This house
Is little; the old man and his people cannot
Be well bestow'd.

Gon. 'Tis his own blame; he hath put
Himself from rest, and must needs taste his folly.

Reg. For his particular, I'll receive him gladly,
But not one follower.

Gon. So am I purpos'd.
Where is my lord of Gloster?

Re-enter GLOSTER.

Corn. Follow'd the old man forth:—he is return'd.

Glo. The king is in high rage.

Corn. Whither is he going?

Glo. He calls to horse; but will I know not whither.

Corn. 'Tis best to give him way; he leads himself.

Gon. My lord, entreat him by no means to stay.

Glo. Alack, the night comes on, and the bleak winds
Do sorely ruffle; for many miles about
There's scarce a bush.

Reg. O, sir, to wilful men,
The injuries, that they themselves procure,
Must be their schoolmasters: Shut up your doors;
He is attended with a desperate train;
And what they may incense him to, being apt
To have his ear abus'd, wisdom bids fear.

Corn. Shut up your doors, my lord: 'tis a wild night;
My Regan counsels well; come out o' the storm.

[*Exeunt.*

ACT III.

SCENE I. *A Heath.*

A Storm is heard, with Thunder and Lightning.

Enter KENT, *and a* Gentleman, *meeting.*

Kent. Who's here, beside foul weather?

Gent. One minded like the weather, most unquietly.

Kent. I know you; Where's the king?

Gent. Contending with the fretful element:
Bids the wind blow the earth into the sea,
Or swell the curled waters 'bove the main,
That things might change, or cease: tears his white hair;
Which the impetuous blasts, with eyeless rage,
Catch in their fury, and make nothing of:
Strives in his little world of man to out-scorn
The to-and-fro-conflicting wind and rain.
This night, wherein the cub-drawn bear would couch,
The lion and the belly-pinched wolf
Keep their fur dry, unbonneted he runs,
And bids what will take all.

Kent. But who is with him?

Gent. None but the fool; who labours to outjest
His heart-struck injuries.

Kent. Sir, I do know you;
And dare upon the warrant of my art,
Commend a dear thing to you. There is division,
Although as yet the face of it be cover'd
With mutual cunning, 'twixt Albany and Cornwall;
Who have (as who have not, that their great stars
Thron'd and set high?) servants, who seem no less;
Which are to France the spies and speculations
Intelligent of our state; what hath been seen,
Either in snuffs and packings of the dukes;
Or the hard rein which both of them have borne
Against the old kind king; or something deeper,
Whereof, perchance, these are but furnishings:—
But, true it is, from France there comes a power
Into this scatter'd kingdom; who already
Wise in our negligence, have secret feet
In some of our best ports, and are at point
To show their open banner.—Now to you:
If on my credit you dare build so far
To make your speed to Dover, you shall find
Some that will thank you, making just report
Of how unnatural and bemadding sorrow
The king hath cause to plain.
I am a gentleman of blood and breeding;
And, from some knowledge and assurance, offer
This office to you.

Gent. I will talk further with you.

Kent. No, do not.
For confirmation that I am much more
Than my out wall, open this purse, and take
What it contains: If you shall see Cordelia
(As fear not but you shall), show her this ring;
And she will tell you who your fellow is
That yet you do not know. Fye on this storm!
I will go seek the king.

Gent. Give me your hand: Have you no more to say?

Kent. Few words, but, to effect, more than all yet;
That, when we have found the king (in which your pain
That way; I'll this); he that first lights on him,
Holloa the other. [*Exeunt severally.*

SCENE II.

Another Part of the Heath. Storm continues.

Enter LEAR *and* Fool.

Lear. Blow, wind, and crack your cheeks! rage! blow!
You cataracts, and hurricanoes, spout
Till you have drench'd our steeples, drown'd the cocks!
You sulphurous and thought-executing fires,
Vaunt-couriers to oak-cleaving thunderbolts,
Singe my white head! And thou, all-shaking thunder,
Strike flat the thick rotundity o' the world!
Crack nature's moulds, all germens spill at once,
That make ingrateful man!

Fool. O nuncle, court holy-water in a dry house is better than this rain-water out o' door. Good nuncle, in, and ask thy daughter's blessing! Here's a night pities neither wise men nor fools.

Lear. Rumble thy bellyful! Spit, fire! spout, rain!
Nor rain, wind, thunder, fire, are my daughters;
I tax not you, you elements, with unkindness,
I never gave you kingdom, call'd you children,
You owe me no subscription; why, then let fall
Your horrible pleasure; here I stand, your slave,
A poor, infirm, weak, and despis'd old man:—
But yet I call you servile ministers,
That have with two pernicious daughters join'd
Your high engender'd battles, 'gainst a head
So old and white as this. O! O! 'tis foul!

Fool. He that has a house to put his head in, has a good head-piece.

The cod-piece that will house,
Before the head has any,
The head and he shall louse;
So beggars marry many.
The man that makes his toe
What he his heart should make
Shall of a corn cry woe,
And turn his sleep to wake.

—for there was never yet fair woman, but she made mouths in a glass.

Enter KENT.

Lear. No, I will be the pattern of all patience,
I will say nothing.

Kent. Who's there?

Fool. Marry, here's grace, and a cod-piece; that's a wise man, and a fool.

Kent. Alas, sir, are you here? things that love night,
Love not such nights as these; the wrathful skies
Gallow the very wanderers of the dark,
And make them keep their caves: Since I was man,
Such sheets of fire, such bursts of horrid thunder,
Such groans of roaring wind and rain, I never
Remember to have heard: man's nature cannot carry
The affliction, nor the fear.

Lear. Let the great gods,
That keep this dreadful pother o'er our heads,
Find out their enemies now. Tremble, thou wretch,
That hast within thee undivulged crimes,
Unwhipp'd of justice: Hide thee, thou bloody hand;
Thou perjur'd, and thou simular man of virtue
That art incestuous: Caitiff, to pieces shake,
That under covert and convenient seeming
Hast practised on man's life!—Close pent-up guilts,
Rive your concealing continents, and cry
These dreadful summoners grace. I am a man,
More sinn'd against, than sinning.

Kent. Alack, bare-headed!
Gracious, my lord, hard by here is a hovel;
Some friendship will it lend you 'gainst the tempest;
Repose you there: while I to this hard house,
(More hard than is the stone whereof 'tis rais'd;
Which even but now, demanding after you,
Denied me to come in), return, and force
Their scanted courtesy.

Lear. My wits begin to turn,—
Come on, my boy: How dost, my boy? Art cold?
I am cold myself.—Where is this straw, my fellow?
The art of our necessities is strange,
That can make vile things precious. Come, your hovel,
Poor fool and knave, I have one part in my heart
That's sorry yet for thee.

Fool. *He that has a little tiny wit,—*
With a heigh, ho, the wind and the rain,—
Must make content with his fortunes fit;
For the rain it raineth every day.

Lear. True, my good boy.—Come, bring us to this hovel. [*Exeunt* LEAR *and* KENT.

Fool. This is a brave night to cool a courtesan.
—I'll speak a prophecy ere I go:
When priests are more in word than matter;
When brewers mar their malt with water;
When nobles are their tailors' tutors;
No hereticks burn'd, but wenches' suitors:
When every case in law is right;
No squire in debt, nor no poor knight;
When slanders do not live in tongues;
Nor cutpurses come not to throngs;
When usurers tell their gold i' the field;
And bawds and whores do churches build:—
Then shall the realm of Albion
Come to great confusion.
Then comes the time, who lives to see't,
That going shall be us'd with feet.
This prophecy Merlin shall make; for I live before his time. [*Exit.*

SCENE III. *A Room in* Gloster's *Castle.*

Enter GLOSTER *and* EDMUND.

Glo. Alack, alack, Edmund, I like not this unnatural dealing: When I desired their leave that I might pity him, they took from me the use of mine own house; charged me, on pain of their perpetual displeasure, neither to speak of him, entreat for him, nor any way sustain him.

Edm. Most savage, and unnatural!

Glo. Go to; say you nothing: There is division between the dukes; and a worse matter than that: I have received a letter this night;—'tis dangerous to be spoken:—I have locked the letter in my closet: these injuries the king now bears will be revenged home; there is part of a power already footed: we must incline to the king. I will seek him, and privily relieve him: go you, and maintain talk with the duke, that my charity be not of him perceived: If he ask for me, I am ill, and gone to bed. If I die for it, as no less is threatened me, the king my old master must be relieved. There is some strange things toward, Edmund: pray you, be careful. [*Exit.*

Edm. This courtesy, forbid thee, shall the duke
Instantly know; and of that letter too:—
This seems a fair deserving, and must draw me
That which my father loses; no less than all:
The younger rises, when the old doth fall. [*Exit.*

SCENE IV. *A Part of the Heath, with a Hovel.*

Enter LEAR, KENT, *and* Fool.

Kent. Here is the place, my lord; good my lord, enter:
The tyranny of the open night's too rough
For nature to endure. [*Storm still.*

Lear. Let me alone.

Kent. Good my lord, enter here.

Lear. Wilt break my heart?

Kent. I'd rather break mine own: Good my lord, enter.

Lear. Thou think'st 'tis much, that this contentious storm
Invades us to the skin: so 'tis to thee;
But where the greater malady is fix'd,
The lesser is scarce felt. Thou'dst shun a bear;
But if thy flight lay toward the raging sea,
Thou'dst meet the bear i'the mouth. When the mind's free,
The body's delicate: the tempest in my mind
Doth from my senses take all feeling else,
Save what beats there.—Filial ingratitude!
Is it not as this mouth should tear this hand,
For lifting food to't?—But I will punish home:—
No, I will weep no more.—In such a night
To shut me out!—Pour on; I will endure:—
In such a night as this! O Regan, Goneril!—
Your old kind father, whose frank heart gave all,—
O, that way madness lies; let me shun that;
No more of that,—

Kent. Good, my lord, enter here.

Lear. 'Pr'ythee, go in thyself; seek thine own ease;
This tempest will not give me leave to ponder
On things would hurt me more.—But I'll go in:
In, boy; go first.—[*To the* Fool.] You houseless poverty,—
Nay, get thee in. I'll pray, and then I'll sleep.— [Fool *goes in.*
Poor naked wretches, wheresoe'er you are,
That bide the pelting of this pitiless storm,
How shall your houseless heads, and unfed sides,
Your loop'd and window'd raggedness, defend you
From seasons, such as these? O, I have ta'en
Too little care of this! Take physick, pomp;
Expose thyself to feel what wretches feel;
That thou may'st shake the superflux to them,
And show the heavens more just.

Edg. [*Within.*] Fathom and half, fathom and half! Poor Tom!

[*The* Fool *runs out from the Hovel.*

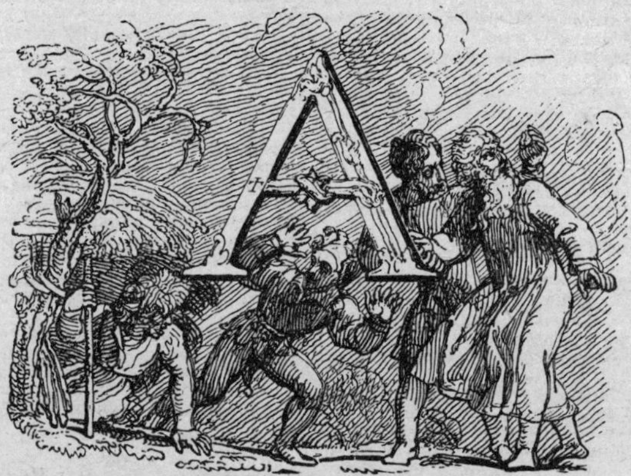

Fool. Come not in here, nuncle, here's a spirit. Help me, help me!

Kent. Give me thy hand.—Who's there?

Fool. A spirit, a spirit; he says his name's poor Tom.

Kent. What art thou that dost grumble there i' the straw?
Come forth.

Enter EDGAR, *disguised as a Madman.*

Edg. Away! the foul fiend follows me:—
Through the sharp hawthorn blows the cold wind.—
Humph! go to thy cold bed, and warm thee.

Lear. Hast thou given all to thy two daughters?
And art thou come to this?

Edg. Who gives any thing to poor Tom? whom the foul fiend hath led through fire and through flame, through ford and whirlpool, over bog and quagmire, that hath laid knives under his pillow, and halters in his pew; set ratsbane by his porridge; made him proud of heart, to ride on a bay trotting-horse over four-inched bridges, to course his own shadow for a traitor:—Bless thy five wits! Tom's a-cold.—O, do de, do de, do de.—Bless thee from whirlwinds, star-blasting, and taking! Do poor Tom some charity, whom the foul fiend vexes: There could I have him now,—and there,—and there, and there again, and there. [*Storm continues.*

Lear. What, have his daughters brought him to this pass?—
Could'st thou save nothing? Did'st thou give them all?

Fool. Nay, he reserved a blanket, else we had been all shamed.

Lear. Now, all the plagues that in the pendulous air
Hang fated o'er men's faults, light on thy daughters!

Kent. He hath no daughters, sir.

Lear. Death, traitor! nothing could have subdu'd nature
To such a lowness, but his unkind daughters.—
Is it the fashion, that discarded fathers
Should have thus little mercy on their flesh?
Judicious punishment! 'Twas this flesh begot
Those pelican daughters.

Edg. Pillicock sat on pillicock's-hill;—
Halloo, halloo, loo, loo!

Fool. This cold night will turn us all to fools and madmen.

Edg. Take heed o' the foul fiend: Obey thy parents; keep thy word justly; swear not; commit not with man's sworn spouse; set not thy sweetheart on proud array: Tom's a-cold.

Lear. What hast thou been?

Edg. A serving-man, proud in heart and mind; that curled my hair; wore gloves in my cap; served the lust of my mistress' heart, and did the act of darkness with her; swore as many oaths as I spake words, and broke them in the sweet face of heaven: one, that slept in the contriving of lust, and waked to do it: Wine loved I deeply; dice dearly; and in woman, out-paramoured the Turk: False of heart, light of ear, bloody of hand; Hog in sloth, fox in stealth, wolf in greediness, dog in madness, lion in prey. Let not the creaking of shoes, nor the rustling of silks, betray thy poor heart to women: Keep thy foot out of brothels, thy hand out of plackets, thy pen from lenders' books, and defy the foul fiend.—Still through the hawthorn blows the cold wind; Says suum, mun, ha no nonny, dolphin my boy, my boy, sessa; let him trot by. [*Storm still continues.*

Lear. Why, thou wert better in thy grave, than to answer with thy uncovered body this extremity of the skies.—Is man no more than this? Consider him well. Thou owest the worm no silk, the beast no hide, the sheep no wool, the cat no perfume:—Ha! there's three of us are sophisticated!—Thou art the thing itself:—unaccommodated man is no more but such a poor, bare, forked animal as thou art.—Off, off, you lendings:—Come; unbutton here.
[*Tearing off his Clothes.*

Fool. 'Pr'ythee, nuncle, be contented; this is a naughty night to swim in.—Now a little fire in a wild field were like an old lecher's heart; a small spark, all the rest of his body cold.—Look, here comes a walking fire.

Edg. This is the foul fiend Flibbertigibbet: he begins at curfew, and walks till the first cock: he gives the web and the pin, squints the eye, and makes the hare-lip; mildews the white wheat, and hurts the poor creatures of earth.

Saint Withold footed thrice the wold;
He met the night-mare and her nine-fold;
Bid her alight,
And her troth plight,
And, aroint thee, witch, aroint thee!

Kent. How fares your grace?

Enter GLOSTER, *with a Torch.*

Lear. What's he?

Kent. Who's there? What is't you seek?

Glo. What are you there? Your names?

Edg. Poor Tom; that eats the swimming frog,

the toad, the tadpole, the wall-newt, and the water: that in the fury of his heart, when the foul fiend rages, eats cow-dung for sallets; swallows the old rat, and the ditch-dog; drinks the green mantle of the standing pool; who is whipped from tything to tything, and stocked, punished, and imprisoned; who hath had three suits to his back, six shirts to his body, horse to ride, and weapon to wear,—

But mice and rats, and such small deer,
Have been Tom's food for seven long year.

Beware my follower: Peace, Smolkin; peace, thou fiend!

Glo. What, hath your grace no better company?

Edg. The prince of darkness is a gentleman;
Modo he's call'd, and Mahu.

Glo. Our flesh and blood, my lord, is grown so vile,
That it doth hate what gets it.

Edg. Poor Tom's a-cold.

Glo. Go in with me; my duty cannot suffer
To obey in all your daughter's hard commands:
Though their injunction be to bar my doors,
And let this tyrannous night take hold upon you,
Yet have I ventured to come seek you out,
And bring you where both fire and food is ready.

Lear. First let me talk with this philosopher:—
What is the cause of thunder?

Kent. Good my lord, take his offer;
Go into the house.

Lear. I'll talk a word with this same learned Theban:
What is your study?

Edg. How to prevent the fiend, and to kill vermin.

Lear. Let me ask you one word in private.

Kent. Importune him once more to go, my lord,
His wits begin to unsettle.

Glo. Canst thou blame him?
His daughters seek his death:—Ah, that good Kent!—
He said it would be thus:—Poor banish'd man!—
Thou say'st, the king grows mad; I'll tell thee, friend,
I am almost mad myself; I had a son,
Now outlaw'd from my blood; he sought my life,
But lately, very late; I lov'd him, friend,—
No father his son dearer: true to tell thee, [*Storm continues.*
The grief hath craz'd my wits. What a night's this!
I do beseech your grace,—

Lear. O, cry you mercy,
Noble philosopher, your company.

Edg. Tom's a-cold.

Glo. In, fellow, there, to the hovel; keep thee warm.

Lear. Come, let's in all.

Kent. This way, my lord.

Lear. With him;
I will keep still with my philosopher.

Kent. Good my lord, sooth him: let him take the fellow.

Glo. Take him you on.

Kent. Sirrah, come on; go along with us.

Lear. Come, good Athenian.

Glo. No words, no words:
Hush.

Edg. *Child Rowland to the dark tower came,*
His word was still,—Fie, foh, and fum,
I smell the blood of a British man.
[*Exeunt.*

SCENE V. *A Room in* Gloster's *Castle.*

Enter CORNWALL *and* EDMUND.

Corn. I will have my revenge, ere I depart his house.

Edm. How, my lord, I may be censured, that nature thus gives way to loyalty, something fears me to think of.

Corn. I now perceive, it was not altogether your brother's evil disposition made him seek his death; but a provoking merit, set a-work by a reprovable badness in himself.

Edm. How malicious is my fortune, that I must repent to be just! This is the letter he spoke of, which approves him an intelligent party to the advantages of France. O heavens! that this treason were not, or not I the detector!

Corn. Go with me to the duchess.

Edm. If the matter of this paper be certain, you have mighty business in hand.

Corn. True, or false, it hath made thee earl of Gloster. Seek out where thy father is, that he may be ready for our apprehension.

Edm. [*Aside.*] If I find him comforting the king, it will stuff his suspicion more fully.—I will persevere in my course of loyalty, though the conflict be sore between that and my blood.

Corn. I will lay trust upon thee; and thou shalt find a dearer father in my love. [*Exeunt.*

SCENE VI.

A Chamber in a Farm-House, adjoining the Castle.

Enter GLOSTER, LEAR, KENT, Fool, *and* EDGAR.

Glo. Here is better than the open air; take it thankfully; I will piece out the comfort with what addition I can: I will not be long from you.

Kent. All the power of his wits has given way to his impatience;—The gods reward your kindness! [*Exit* GLOSTER.

Edg. Frateretto calls me; and tells me Nero is an angler in the lake of darkness. Pray, innocent, and beware the foul fiend.

Fool. 'Pr'ythee, nuncle, tell me, whether a madman be a gentleman, or a yeoman?

Lear. A king, a king!

Fool. No; he's a yeoman, that has a gentleman to his son; for he's a mad yeoman, that sees his son a gentleman before him.

Lear. To have a thousand with red burning spits
Come hissing in upon them:—

Edg. The foul fiend bites my back.

Fool. He's mad, that trusts in the tameness of a wolf, a horse's heels, a boy's love, or a whore's oath.

Lear. It shall be done, I will arraign them straight:—
Come, sit thou here, most learned justicer:—— [*To* EDGAR.
Thou, sapient sir, sit here. [*To the* Fool]—Now, you she foxes!—

Edg. Look, where he stands and glares!—
Wantest thou eyes at trial, madam?

Come o'er the bourn, Bessy, to me:—

Fool. *Her boat hath a leak.*
And she must not speak
Why she dares not come over to thee.

Edg. The foul fiend haunts poor Tom in the voice of a nightingale. *Hopdance* cries in Tom's belly for two white herrings. Croak not, black angel; I have no food for thee.

Kent. How do you, sir? Stand you not so amaz'd:
Will you lie down and rest upon the cushions?

Lear. I'll see their trial first:—Bring in the evidence—
Thou robed man of justice, take thy place; [*To* EDGAR.
And thou, his yoke-fellow of equity, [*To the* Fool.
Bench by his side:—You are of the commission,
Sit you too. [*To* KENT.

Edg. Let us deal justly.

Sleepest, or wakest thou, jolly shepherd?
Thy sheep be in the corn;
And for one blast of thy minikin mouth,
Thy sheep shall take no harm.

Pur! the cat is gray.

Lear. Arraign her first; 'tis Goneril. I here take my oath before this honourable assembly, she kicked the poor king her father.

Fool. Come hither, mistress; Is your name Goneril?

Lear. She cannot deny it.

Fool. Cry you mercy, I took you for a joint-stool.

Lear. And here's another, whose warp'd looks proclaim
What store her heart is made of.—Stop her there!
Arms, arms, sword, fire!—Corruption in the place!
False justicer, why hast thou let her 'scape?

Edg. Bless thy five-wits!

Kent. O pity!—Sir, where is the patience now,
That you so oft have boasted to retain?

Edg. My tears begin to take his part so much,
They'll mar my counterfeiting. [*Aside.*

Lear. The little dogs and all,
Tray, Blanch, and Sweet-heart, see, they bark at me.

Edg. Tom will throw his head at them:—
Avaunt, you curs!
Be thy mouth or black or white,
Tooth that poisons if it bite;
Mastiff, greyhound, mongrel grim,
Hound, or spaniel, brach, or lym;
Or bobtail tike, or trundle-tail;
Tom will make them weep and wail:
For, with throwing thus my head,
Dogs leap the hatch, and all are fled.
Do de, de de. Sessa. Come, march to wakes and fairs, and market towns:—Poor Tom, thy horn is dry.

Lear. Then let them anatomize Regan, see what breeds about her heart: Is there any cause in nature, that makes these hard hearts?—You, sir, I entertain you for one of my hundred; only I do not like the fashion of your garments: you will say, they are Persian attire! but let them be changed. [*To* EDGAR.

Kent. Now, good my lord, lie here, and rest awhile.

Lear. Make no noise, make no noise; draw the curtains: So, so, so: We'll go to supper i' the morning: So, so, so.

Fool. And I'll go to bed at noon.

Re-enter GLOSTER.

Glo. Come hither, friend: Where is the king my master?

Kent. Here, sir; but trouble him not, his wits are gone.

Glo. Good friend, I pr'ythee take him in thy arms;
I have o'erheard a plot of death upon him:
There is a litter ready; lay him in't,
And drive towards Dover, friend, where thou shalt meet
Both welcome and protection. Take up thy master:
If thou should'st dally half an hour, his life,
With thine, and all that offer to defend him,
Stand in assured loss: Take up, take up;
And follow me, that will to some provision
Give thee quick conduct.

Kent. Oppress'd nature sleeps:—
This rest might yet have balm'd thy broken senses,
Which, if convenience will not allow,
Stand in hard cure.—Come, help to bear thy master;
Thou must not stay behind. [*To the* Fool.

Glo. Come, come, away.
[*Exeunt* KENT, GLOSTER, *and the* Fool, *bearing off the* King.

Edg. When we our betters see bearing our woes,
We scarcely think our miseries our foes.
Who alone suffers, suffers most i' the mind;
Leaving free things, and happy shows, behind:
But then the mind much sufferance doth o'erskip,
When grief hath mates, and bearing fellowship.
How light and portable my pain seems now,
When that, which makes me bend, makes the king bow;
He childed, as I father'd!—Tom, away:
Mark the high noises: and thyself bewray,
When false opinion, whose wrong thought defiles thee,
In thy just proof, repeals, and reconciles thee.
What will hap more to-night, safe scape the king!
Lurk, lurk. [*Exit.*

SCENE VII. *A Room in* Gloster's *Castle.*

Enter CORNWALL, REGAN, GONERIL, EDMUND, *and* Servants.

Corn. Post speedily to my lord your husband; show him this letter;—the army of France is landed:—Seek out the villain Gloster.
[*Exeunt some of the* Servants.

Reg. Hang him instantly.

Gon. Pluck out his eyes.

Corn. Leave him to my displeasure.—Edmund, keep you our sister company; the revenges we are bound to take upon your traitorous father, are not fit for your beholding. Advise the duke, where you are going, to a most festinate preparation; we are bound to the like. Our post shall be swift, and intelligent betwixt us. Farewell, dear sister;—farewell, my lord of Gloster.

Enter Steward.

How now? Where's the king?

Stew. My lord of Gloster hath convey'd him hence:
Some five or six and thirty of his knights
Hot questrists after him, met him at gate;
Who with some other of the lord's dependants,
Are gone with him towards Dover; where they boast
To have well armed friends.

Corn. Get horses for your mistress.

Gon. Farewell, sweet lord, and sister.
[*Exeunt* GONERIL *and* EDMUND.

Corn. Edmund, farewell.—Go, seek the traitor Gloster,
Pinion him like a thief, bring him before us.
[*Exeunt other* Servants.
Though well we may not pass upon his life
Without the form of justice; yet our power
Shall do a courtesy to our wrath, which men
May blame, but not control. Who's there? The traitor?

Re-enter Servants, *with* GLOSTER.

Reg. Ingrateful fox! 'tis he.

Corn. Bind fast his corky arms.

Glo. What mean your graces?——Good my friends, consider
You are my guests: do me no foul play, friends.

Corn. Bind him, I say. [Servants *bind him.*

Reg. Hard, hard:—O filthy traitor.

Glo. Unmerciful lady as you are, I am none.

Corn. To this chair bind him:—Villain, thou shalt find— [REGAN *plucks his Beard.*

Glo. By the kind gods, 'tis most ignobly done,
To pluck me by the beard.

Reg. So white, and such a traitor!

Glo. Naughty lady,
These hairs, which thou dost ravish from my chin,
Will quicken and accuse thee: I am your host;
With robbers' hands, my hospitable favours
You should not ruffle thus. What will you do?

Corn. Come, sir, what letters had you late from France?

Reg. Be simple answer'd, for we know the truth.

Corn. And what confederacy have you with the traitors
Late footed in the kingdom?

Reg. To whose hands have you sent the lunatick king?
Speak.
Glo. I have a letter guessingly set down,
Which came from one that's of a neutral heart,
And not from one oppos'd.
Corn. Cunning.
Reg. And false.
Corn. Where hast thou sent the king?
Glo. To Dover.
Reg. Wherefore
To Dover? Wast thou not charg'd at thy peril—
Corn. Wherefore to Dover? Let him first answer that.
Glo. I am tied to the stake, and I must stand the course.
Reg. Wherefore to Dover?
Glo. Because I would not see thy cruel nails
Pluck out his poor old eyes; nor thy fierce sister
In his anointed flesh stick boarish fangs.
The sea, with such a storm as his bare head
In hell-black night endur'd, would have buoy'd up,
And quench'd the stelled fires: yet, poor old heart,
He holp the heavens to rain.
If wolves had at thy gate howl'd that stern time,
Thou should'st have said, *Good porter, turn the key;*
All cruel's else subscrib'd:—But I shall see
The winged vengeance overtake such children.
Corn. See it shalt thou never:—Fellows, hold the chair:
Upon these eyes of thine I'll set my foot.
[GLOSTER *is held down in his Chair, while* CORNWALL *plucks out one of his Eyes, and sets his Foot on it.*
Glo. He, that will think to live till he be old,
Give me some help:—O cruel! O ye gods!
Reg. One side will mock another; the other too.
Corn. If you see vengeance,—
Serv. Hold your hand, my lord:
I have serv'd you ever since I was a child;
But better service have I never done you,
Than now to bid you hold.
Reg. How now, you dog?
Serv. If you did wear a beard upon your chin,
I'd shake it on this quarrel; What do you mean?
Corn. My villain! [*Draws, and runs at him.*
Serv. Nay, then come on, and take the chance of anger.
[*Draws. They fight.* CORN. *is wounded.*
Reg. Give me thy sword.—[*To another* Serv.]
A peasant stand up thus!
[*Snatches a Sword, comes behind him, and stabs him.*
Serv. O, I am slain!—My lord, you have one eye left
To see some mischief on him:—O! [*Dies.*
Corn. Lest it see more, prevent it:—Out, vile jelly!
Where is thy lustre now?
[*Tears out* GLOSTER'*s other eye, and throws it on the ground.*
Glo. All dark and comfortless.—Where's my son Edmund?
Edmund, enkindle all the sparks of nature,
To quit this horrid act.
Reg. Out, treacherous villain!
Thou call'st on him that hates thee: it was he
That made the overture of thy treasons to us;
Who is too good to pity thee.
Glo. O my follies!
Then Edgar was abus'd.—
Kind gods, forgive me that, and prosper him!
Reg. Go, thrust him out at gates, and let him smell
His way to Dover.—How is't, my lord? How look you?
Corn. I have receiv'd a hurt:—Follow me, lady.—
Turn out that eyeless villain;—throw this slave
Upon the dunghill.—Regan, I bleed apace:
Untimely comes this hurt: Give me your arm.
[*Exit* CORNWALL, *led by* REGAN;—*Servants unbind* GLOSTER, *and lead him out.*
1 *Serv.* I'll never care what wickedness I do,
If this man come to good.
2 *Serv.* If she live long,
And, in the end, meet the old course of death,
Women will all turn monsters.
1 *Serv.* Let's follow the old earl, and get the Bedlam
To lead him where he would; his roguish madness
Allows itself to any thing.
2 *Serv.* Go thou; I'll fetch some flax, and whites of eggs,
To apply to his bleeding face. Now, heaven help him! [*Exeunt severally.*

ACT IV.

SCENE I. *The Heath.*

Enter EDGAR.

Edg. Yet better thus, and known to be contemn'd,
Than still contemn'd and flatter'd. To be worst,
The lowest and most dejected thing of fortune,
Stands still in esperance, lives not in fear:
The lamentable change is from the best;
The worst returns to laughter. Welcome then,
Thou unsubstantial air, that I embrace!
The wretch, that thou hast blown unto the worst,
Owes nothing to thy blasts.—But who comes here?—

Enter GLOSTER, *led by an old Man.*

My father, poorly led?—World, world, O world!
But that thy strange mutations make us hate thee,
Life would not yield to age.
Old Man. O my good lord, I have been your tenant, and your father's tenant, these fourscore years.
Glo. Away, get thee away; good friend, be gone:
Thy comforts can do me no good at all,
Thee they may hurt.
Old Man. Alack, sir, you cannot see your way.
Glo. I have no way, and therefore want no eyes;
I stumbled when I saw: Full oft 'tis seen,
Our mean secures us, and our mere defects
Prove our commodities.—Ah, dear son, Edgar,
The food of thy abused father's wrath?
Might I but live to see thee in my touch,
I'd say, I had eyes again!
Old Man. How now? Who's there?
Edg. [*Aside.*] O gods! Who is't can say, *I am at the worst?*
I am worse than e'er I was.
Old Man. 'Tis poor mad Tom.
Edg. [*Aside.*] And worse I may be yet; The worst is not,
So long as we can say, *This is the worst.*
Old Man. Fellow, where goest?
Glo. Is it a beggar man?
Old Man. Madman and beggar too.
Glo. He has some reason, else he could not beg,
I'the last night's storm I such a fellow saw;
Which made me think a man a worm: My son
Came then into my mind; and yet my mind
Was then scarce friends with him: I have heard more since:
As flies to wanton boys, are we to the gods;
They kill us for their sport.
Edg. How should this be?—
Bad is the trade must play the fool to sorrow,
Ang'ring itself and others. [*Aside.*]—Bless thee, master!
Glo. Is that the naked fellow?
Old Man. Ay, my lord.
Glo. Then, 'pr'ythee, get thee gone: if, for my sake

Thou wilt o'ertake us, hence a mile or twain,
I' the way to Dover, do it for ancient love;
And bring some covering for this naked soul,
Whom I'll entreat to lead me.

Old Man. Alack, sir, he's mad.

Glo. 'Tis the time's plague, when madmen lead the blind.
Do as I bid thee, or rather do thy pleasure;
Above the rest, be gone.

Old Man. I'll bring him the best 'parel that I have,
Come on't what will. [*Exit.*

Glo. Sirrah, naked fellow.

Edg. Poor Tom's a cold.—I cannot daub it further. [*Aside.*

Glo. Come hither, fellow.

Edg. [*Aside.*] And yet I must.—Bless thy sweet eyes, they bleed.

Glo. Know'st thou the way to Dover?

Edg. Both stile and gate, horse-way, and foot-path. Poor Tom hath been scared out of his good wits: Bless the good man from the foul fiend! Five fiends have been in poor Tom at once; of lust, as *Obidicut; Hobbididance*, prince of dumbness; *Mahu*, of stealing; *Modo*, of murder; and *Flibbertigibbet*, of mopping and mowing; who since possesses chambermaids and waitingwomen. So, bless thee, master!

Glo. Here take this purse, thou whom the heaven's plagues
Have humbled to all strokes: that I am wretched,
Makes thee the happier:—Heavens, deal so still!
Let the superfluous, and lust-dieted man,
That slaves your ordinance, that will not see
Because he doth not feel, feel your power quickly;
So distribution should undo excess,
And each man have enough.—Dost thou know Dover?

Edg. Ay, master.

Glo. There is a cliff, whose high and bending head
Looks fearfully in the confined deep:
Bring me but to the very brim of it,
And I'll repair the misery thou dost bear,
With something rich about me: from that place
I shall no leading need.

Edg. Give me thy arm;
Poor Tom shall lead thee. [*Exeunt.*

SCENE II. *Before the* Duke *of* Albany's *Palace.*

Enter GONERIL *and* EDMUND; Steward *meeting them.*

Gon. Welcome, my lord: I marvel, our mild husband
Not met us on the way:—Now, where's your master?

Stew. Madam, within; but never man so chang'd:
I told him of the army that was landed;
He smil'd at it: I told him, you were coming;
His answer was, *The worse:* of Gloster's treachery,
And of the loyal service of his son,
When I inform'd him, then he call'd me sot;
And told me, I had turn'd the wrong side out:—
What most he should dislike, seems pleasant to him;
What like, offensive.

Gon. Then shall you go no further. [*To* EDMUND.
It is the cowish terror of his spirit,
That dares not undertake: he'll not feel wrongs,
Which tie him to an answer: Our wishes on the way,
May prove effects. Back, Edmund, to my brother;
Hasten his musters, and conduct his powers:
I must change arms at home, and give the distaff
Into my husband's hands. This trusty servant
Shall pass between us: ere long you are like to hear,
If you dare venture in your own behalf,
A mistress's command. Wear this; spare speech;
[*Giving a Favour.*
Decline your head: this kiss, if it durst speak,
Would stretch thy spirits up into the air;—
Conceive, and fare thee well.

Edm. Yours in the ranks of death.

Gon. My most dear Gloster!
[*Exit* EDMUND.
O, the difference of man, and man!
To thee a woman's services are due;
My fool usurps my bed.

Stew. Madam, here comes my lord.
[*Exit* Steward.

Enter ALBANY.

Gon. I have been worth the whistle.

Alb. O Goneril!
You are not worth the dust which the rude wind
Blows in your face—I fear your disposition:
That nature, which contemns its origin,
Cannot be border'd certain in itself;
She that herself will sliver and disbranch
From her material sap, perforce must wither,
And come to deadly use.

Gon. No more; the text is foolish.

Alb. Wisdom and goodness to the vile seem vile:
Filths savour but themselves. What have you done?
Tigers, not daughters, what have you perform'd?
A father, and a gracious aged man,
Whose reverence the head-lugg'd bear would lick,
Most barbarous, most degenerate! have you madded.
Could my good brother suffer you to do it?
A man, a prince, by him so benefited?
If that the heavens do not their visible spirits
Send quickly down to tame these vile offences,
'Twill come,
Humanity must perforce prey on itself,
Like monsters of the deep.

Gon. Milk-liver'd man!
That bear'st a cheek for blows, a head for wrongs;
Who hast not in thy brows an eye discerning
Thine honour from thy suffering; that not know'st,
Fools do those villains pity, who are punish'd
Ere they have done their mischief. Where's thy drum?
France spreads his banners in our noiseless land;
With plumed helm thy slayer begins threats;
Whilst thou, a moral fool, sit'st still, and cry'st,
Alack! why does he so?

Alb. See thyself, devil!
Proper deformity seems not in the fiend
So horrid, as in woman.

Gon. O vain fool!

Alb. Thou changed and self-cover'd thing, for shame,
Be-monster not thy feature. Were it my fitness
To let these hands obey my blood,
They are apt enough to dislocate and tear
Thy flesh and bones;—Howe'er thou art a fiend,
A woman's shape doth shield thee.

Gon. Marry, your manhood now!

Enter a Messenger.

Alb. What news?

Mess. O, my good lord, the Duke of Cornwall's dead;
Slain by his servant, going to put out
The other eye of Gloster.

Alb. Gloster's eyes!

Mess. A servant that he bred, thrill'd with remorse,
Oppos'd against the act, bending his sword
To his great master; who, thereat enrag'd,
Flew on him, and amongst them fell'd him dead:
But not without that harmful stroke, which since
Hath pluck'd him after.

Alb. This shows you are above,
You justicers, that these our nether crimes
So speedily can venge!—But, O poor Gloster!
Lost he his other eye?

Mess. Both, both, my lord.—
This letter, madam, craves a speedy answer;
'Tis from your sister.

Gon. [*Aside.*] One way I like this well;
But being widow, and my Gloster with her,
May all the building in my fancy pluck
Upon my hateful life: Another way,
The news is not so tart.—I'll read and answer. [*Exit.*

Alb. Where was his son, when they did take his eyes?

Mess. Come with my lady hither.

Alb. He is not here.

Mess. No, my good lord; I met him back again.

Alb. Knows he the wickedness?

Mess. Ay, my good lord; 'twas he inform'd against him;
And quit the house on purpose, that their punishment
Might have the freer course.

Alb. Gloster, I live
To thank thee for the love thou show'dst the king,
And to revenge thine eyes.—Come hither, friend;
Tell me what more thou knowest. [*Exeunt.*

SCENE III. *The* French *Camp near* Dover.

Enter KENT, *and a* Gentleman.

Kent. Why the King of France is so suddenly gone back know you the reason?

Gent. Something he left imperfect in the state,
Which since his coming forth is thought of; which
Imports to the kingdom so much fear and danger,
That his personal return was most required,
And necessary.

Kent. Who hath he left behind him, general?

Gent. The Mareschal of France, Monsieur le Fer.

Kent. Did your letters pierce the queen to any demonstration of grief?

Gent. Ay, sir, she took them, read them in my presence;
And now and then an ample tear trill'd down
Her delicate cheek: it seem'd, she was a queen
Over her passion; who, most rebel-like,
Sought to be king o'er her.

Kent. O, then it mov'd her.

Gent. Not to a rage: patience and sorrow strove
Who should express her goodliest. You have seen
Sunshine and rain at once; her smiles and tears
Were like;—a better way. Those happy smiles,
That play'd on her ripe lip, seem'd not to know
What guests were in her eyes; which parted thence,
As pearls from diamonds dropp'd.—In brief, sorrow
Would be a rarity most belov'd, if all
Could so become it.

Kent. Made she no verbal question?

Gent. 'Faith, once, or twice, she heav'd the name of *father*
Pantingly forth, as if it press'd her heart;
Cried, *Sisters! sisters!—Shame of ladies! sisters!*
Kent! father! sisters! What? i' the storm? i' the night?
Let pity not be believed!—There she shook
The holy water from her heavenly eyes,
And clamour moisten'd: then away she started
To deal with grief alone.

Kent. It is the stars,
The stars above us, govern our conditions;
Else one self mate and mate could not beget
Such different issues. You spoke not with her since?

Gent. No.

Kent. Was this before the king return'd?

Gent. No, since.

Kent. Well, sir; The poor distress'd Lear is i' the town:
Who sometime, in his better tune, remembers
What we are come about, and by no means
Will yield to see his daughter.

Gent. Why, good sir?

Kent. A sovereign shame so elbows him: his own unkindness,
That stripp'd her from his benediction, turn'd her
To foreign casualties, gave her dear rights
To his dog-hearted daughters,—these things sting
His mind so venomously, that burning shame
Detains him from Cordelia.

Gent. Alack, poor gentleman!

Kent. Of Albany's and Cornwall's powers you heard not!

Gent. 'Tis so, they are afoot.

Kent. Well, sir, I'll bring you to our master [Lear,
And leave you to attend him: some dear cause
Will in concealment wrap me up awhile;
When I am known aright, you shall not grieve
Lending me this acquaintance. I pray you, go
Along with me. [*Exeunt.*

SCENE IV. *The same. A Tent.*

Enter CORDELIA, Physician, *and* Soldiers.

Cor. Alack, 'tis he; why, he was met e'en now
As mad as the vex'd sea: singing aloud;
Crown'd with rank fumiter, and furrow weeds,
With harlocks, hemlock, nettles, cuckoo-flowers,
Darnel, and all the idle weeds that grow
In our sustaining corn.—A century send forth;
Search every acre in the high grown field,
And bring him to our eye. [*Exit an* Officer.]—
What can man's wisdom do,
In the restoring of his bereaved sense?
He, that helps him, take all my outward worth.

Phy. There is means, madam:
Our foster-nurse of nature is repose,
The which he lacks; that to provoke in him,
Are many simples operative, whose power
Will close the eye of anguish.

Cor. All bless'd secrets,
All you unpublish'd virtues of the earth,
Spring with my tears! be aidant, and remediate,
In the good man's distress!—Seek, seek for him;
Lest his ungovern'd rage dissolve the life
That wants the means to lead it.

Enter a Messenger.

Mess. Madam, news;
The British powers are marching hitherward.

Cor. 'Tis known before; our preparation stands
In expectation of them.—O dear father,
It is thy business that I go about;
Therefore great France
My mourning, and important tears, hath pitied.
No blown ambition doth our arms incite,
But love, dear love, and our ag'd father's right;
Soon may I hear, and see him. [*Exeunt.*

SCENE V. *A Room in* Gloster's *Castle.*

Enter REGAN *and* Steward.

Reg. But are my brother's powers set forth?

Stew. Ay, madam,

Reg. Himself
In person there?

Stew. Madam, with much ado:
Your sister is the better soldier.

Reg. Lord Edmund spake not with your lord at home?

Stew. No, madam.

Reg. What might import my sister's letter to him?

Stew. I know not, lady.

Reg. 'Faith, he is posted hence on serious matter.
It was great ignorance, Gloster's eyes being out,

To let him live; where he arrives, he moves
All hearts against us; Edmund, I think, is gone,
In pity of his misery, to despatch
His nighted life; moreover, to descry
The strength o' the enemy.

Stew. I must needs after him, madam, with my letter.

Reg. Our troops set forth to-morrow; stay with us;
The ways are dangerous.

Stew. I may not, madam;
My lady charg'd my duty in this business.

Reg. Why should she write to Edmund? Might not you
Transport her purposes by word? Belike,
Something—I know not what:—I'll love thee much,
Let me unseal the letter.

Stew. Madam, I had rather—

Reg. I know, your lady does not love her husband;
I am sure of that: and, at her late being here,
She gave strange œiliads, and most speaking looks
To noble Edmund: I know, you are of her bosom.

Stew. I, madam?

Reg. I speak in understanding; you are, I know it:
Therefore, I do advise you, take this note:
My lord is dead; Edmund and I have talk'd;
And more convenient is he for my hand,
Than for your lady's:—You may gather more.
If you do find him, pray you, give him this;
And when your mistress hears thus much from you,
I pray, desire her call her wisdom to her.
So, fare you well.
If you do chance to hear of that blind traitor,
Preferment falls on him that cuts him off.

Stew. 'Would, I could meet him, madam! I would show
What party I do follow.

Reg. Fare thee well. [*Exeunt.*

SCENE VI. *The Country near* Dover.

Enter GLOSTER, *and* EDGAR, *dressed like a Peasant.*

Glo. When shall we come to the top of that same hill?

Edg. You do climb up it now: look, how we labour.

Glo. Methinks the ground is even.

Edg. Horrible steep:
Hark, do you hear the sea?

Glo. No, truly.

Edg. Why, then your other senses grow imperfect
By your eyes' anguish.

Glo. So may it be, indeed:
Methinks, thy voice is alter'd; and thou speak'st
In better phrase, and matter, than thou didst.

Edg. You are much deceiv'd; in nothing am I chang'd,
But in my garments.

Glo. Methinks, you are better spoken.

Edg. Come on, sir; here's the place:—stand still.—How fearful
And dizzy 'tis, to cast one's eyes so low!
The crows, and choughs, that wing the midway air,
Show scarce so gross as beetles: Half way down
Hangs one that gathers samphire; dreadful trade!
Methinks, he seems no bigger than his head:
The fishermen, that walk upon the beach,
Appear like mice; and yon' tall anchoring bark,
Diminish'd to her cock; her cock, a buoy
Almost too small for sight: The murmuring surge,
That on the unnumber'd idle pebbles chafes,
Cannot be heard so high;—I'll look no more;
Lest my brain turn, and the deficient sight
Topple down headlong.

Glo. Set me where you stand.

Edg. Give me your hand: You are now within a foot
Of the extreme verge: for all beneath the moon
Would I not leap upright.

Glo. Let go my hand.
Here, friend, is another purse; in it a jewel
Well worth a poor man's taking: Fairies, and gods,
Prosper it with thee! Go thou further off;
Bid me farewell, and let me hear thee going.

Edg. Now fare you well, good sir. [*Seems to go.*

Glo. With all my heart.

Edg. Why I do trifle thus with his despair,
Is done to cure it.

Glo. O you mighty gods!
This world I do renounce; and, in your sights,
Shake patiently my great affliction off:
If I could bear it longer, and not fall
To quarrel with your great opposeless wills,
My snuff, and loathed part of nature, should
Burn itself out. If Edgar live, O bless him!—
Now, fellow, fare thee well.
[*He leaps, and falls along.*

Edg. Gone, sir? farewell.—
And yet I know not how conceit may rob
The treasury of life, when life itself
Yields to the theft: Had he been where he thought,
By this, had thought been past.—Alive, or dead?
Ho, you sir! friend!—Hear you, sir?—speak!
Thus might he pass indeed:—Yet he revives:
What are you, sir?

Glo. Away, and let me die.

Edg. Had'st thou been aught but gossomer, feathers, air,
So many fathom down precipitating,
Thou had'st shiver'd like an egg: but thou dost breathe;
Hast heavy substance; bleed'st not; speak'st; art sound.
Ten masts at each make not the altitude,
Which thou hast perpendicularly fell;
Thy life's a miracle: Speak yet again.

Glo. But have I fallen, or no?

Edg. From the dread summit of this chalky bourn:
Look up a-height;—the shrill-gorg'd lark so far
Cannot be seen or heard: do but look up.

Glo. Alack, I have no eyes.—
Is wretchedness depriv'd that benefit,
To end itself by death? 'Twas yet some comfort,
When misery could beguile the tyrant's rage,
And frustrate his proud will.

Edg. Give me your arm:
Up:—So;—How is't? Feel you your legs? You stand.

Glo. Too well, too well.

Edg. This is above all strangeness.
Upon the crown o' the cliff, what thing was that
Which parted from you?

Glo. A poor unfortunate beggar.

Edg. As I stood here below, methought, his eyes
Were two full moons; he had a thousand noses,
Horns welk'd, and wav'd like the enridged sea;
It was some fiend: therefore, thou happy father,
Think that the clearest gods, who make them honours
Of men's impossibilities, have preserv'd thee.

Glo. I do remember now; henceforth I'll bear
Affliction, till it do cry out itself,
Enough, enough, and, *die.* That thing you speak of,
I took it for a man; often 'twould say,
The fiend, the fiend: he led me to that place.

Edg. Bear free and patient thoughts.—But who comes here?

Enter LEAR, *fantastically dressed up with Flowers.*

The safer sense will ne'er accommodate
His master thus.

Lear. No, they cannot touch me for coining; I am the king himself.

Edg. O thou side-piercing sight!

Lear. Nature's above art in that respect.—There's your press-money. That fellow handles his bow like a crow-keeper: draw me a clothier's yard.—Look, look, a mouse! Peace, peace;—this piece of toasted cheese will do 't.—There's my gauntlet; I'll prove it on a giant.—Bring up the brown bills.—O, well flown, bird!—i' the clout, i' the clout; hewgh!—Give the word.

Edg. Sweet marjoram.

Lear. Pass.

Glo. I know that voice.

Lear. Ha! Goneril!—with a white beard!—They flatter'd me like a dog; and told me, I had white hairs in my beard, ere the black ones were there. To say, *ay*, and *no*, to every thing I said!—Ay and no too was no good divinity. When the rain came to wet me once, and the wind to make me chatter; when the thunder would not peace at my bidding; there I found them, there I smelt them out. Go to, they are not men o' their words: they told me I was every thing: 'tis a lie; I am not ague-proof.

Glo. The trick of that voice I do well remember:
Is 't not the king?

Lear. Ay, every inch a king:
When I do stare, see, how the subject quakes.
I pardon that man's life: what was thy cause?—
Adultery!—
Thou shalt not die; die for adultery! No:
The wren goes to 't, and the small gilded fly
Does lecher in my sight.
Let copulation thrive, for Gloster's bastard son
Was kinder to his father, than my daughters
Got 'tween the lawful sheets.
To 't luxury, pell-mell, for I lack soldiers.—
Behold yon simpering dame,
Whose face between her forks presageth snow;
That minces virtue, and does shake the head
To hear of pleasure's name;
The fitchew, nor the soiled horse, goes to 't
With a more riotous appetite.
Down from the waist they are centaurs,
Though women all above;
But to the girdle do the gods inherit,
Beneath is all the fiends'; there's hell, there's darkness,
There is the sulphurous pit, burning, scalding, stench, consumption;—Fye, fye, fye; pah; pah! Give me an ounce of civet, good apothecary, to sweeten my imagination; there's money for thee.

Glo. O, let me kiss that hand!

Lear. Let me wipe it first; it smells of mortality.

Glo. O ruin'd piece of nature! This great world
Shall so wear out to nought.—Dost thou know me?

Lear. I remember thine eyes well enough. Dost thou squiny at me? No, do thy worst, blind Cupid; I'll not love.—Read thou this challenge; mark but the penning of it.

Glo. Were all the letters suns, I could not see one.

Edg. I would not take this from report;—it is,
And my heart breaks at it.

Lear. Read.

Glo. What, with the case of eyes?

Lear. O, ho, are you there with me? No eyes in your head, nor no money in your purse? Your eyes are in a heavy case, your purse in a light: Yet you see how this world goes.

Glo. I see it feelingly.

Lear. What, art mad? A man may see how this world goes, with no eyes. Look with thine ears: see how yon' justice rails upon yon' simple thief. Hark, in thine ear: Change places; and, handy-dandy, which is the justice, which is the thief?—Thou hast seen a farmer's dog bark at a beggar?

Glo. Ay, sir.

Lear. And the creature run from the cur? There thou might'st behold the great image of authority: a dog's obey'd in office.
Thou rascal beadle, hold thy bloody hand:
Why dost thou lash that whore? Strip thine own back;
Thou hotly lust'st to use her in that kind
For which thou whipp'st her. The usurer hangs the cozener.
Through tatter'd clothes small vices do appear;
Robes, and furr'd gowns, hide all. Plate sin with gold,
And the strong lance of justice hurtless breaks:
Arm it in rags, a pigmy's straw doth pierce it.
None does offend, none, I say, none; I'll able 'em:
Take that of me, my friend, who have the power
To seal the accuser's lips. Get thee glass eyes;
And, like a scurvy politician, seem
To see the things thou dost not.—Now, now, now, now:
Pull off my boots:—harder, harder; so.

Edg. O, matter and impertinency mix'd!
Reason in madness!

Lear. If thou wilt weep my fortunes, take my eyes.
I know thee well enough; thy name is Gloster:
Thou must be patient; we came crying hither,
Thou know'st, the first time that we smell the air,
We wawl, and cry:—I will preach to thee; mark me.

Glo. Alack, alack the day!

Lear. When we are born, we cry, that we are come
To this great stage of fools;——This a good block?
It were a delicate stratagem, to shoe
A troop of horse with felt: I'll put it in proof;
And when I have stolen upon these sons-in-law,
Then, kill, kill, kill, kill, kill, kill.

Enter a Gentleman, *with* Attendants.

Gent. O, here he is, lay hand upon him.—Sir,
Your most dear daughter——

Lear. No rescue? What, a prisoner? I am even
The natural fool of fortune.—Use me well;
You shall have ransome. Let me have a surgeon,
I am cut to the brains.

Gent. You shall have any thing.

Lear. No seconds? All myself?
Why, this would make a man, a man of salt,
To use his eyes for garden water-pots,
Ay, and for laying autumn's dust.

Gent. Good sir,—

Lear. I will die bravely, like a bridegroom: What?
I will be jovial; come, come; I am a king,
My masters, know you that!

Gent. You are a royal one, and we obey you.

Lear. Then there's life in it. Nay, an you get it, you shall get it by running. Sa, sa, sa, sa.

[*Exit, running;* Attendants *follow.*

Gent. A sight most pitiful in the meanest wretch;
Past speaking of in a king!—Thou hast one daughter,
Who redeems nature from the general curse
Which twain have brought her to.

Edg. Hail, gentle sir.

Gent. Sir, speed you: What's your will?

Edg. Do you hear aught, sir, of a battle toward?

Gent. Most sure, and vulgar: every one hears that,
Which can distinguish sound.

Edg. But, by your favour,
How near's the other army?

Gent. Near, and on speedy foot, the main descry
Stands on the hourly thought.

Edg. I thank you, sir: that's all.

Gent. Though that the queen on special cause is here,
Her army is mov'd on.
Edg. I thank you, sir.
[*Exit* Gentleman.
Glo. You ever-gentle gods, take my breath from me;
Let not my worser spirit tempt me again
To die before you please!
Edg. Well pray you, father.
Glo. Now, good sir, what are you?
Edg. A most poor man, made lame by fortune's blows:
Who, by the art of known and feeling sorrows,
Am pregnant to good pity. Give me your hand,
I'll lead you to some biding.
Glo. Hearty thanks:
The bounty and the benizon of heaven
To boot, and boot!

Enter Steward.

Stew. A proclaim'd prize! Most happy!
That eyeless head of thine was first fram'd flesh
To raise my fortunes.—Thou old unhappy traitor,
Briefly thyself remember:—The sword is out
That must destroy thee.
Glo. Now let thy friendly hand
Put strength enough to it. [EDGAR *opposes.*
Stew. Wherefore, bold peasant,
Dar'st thou support a publish'd traitor? Hence;
Lest that the infection of his fortune take
Like hold on thee. Let go his arm.
Edg. Ch'ill not let go, zir, without vurther 'casion.
Stew. Let go, slave, or thou diest.
Edg. Good gentleman, go your gait, and let poor volk pass. And ch'ud ha' been zwagger'd out of my life, 'twould not ha' been zo long as 'tis by a vortnight. Nay, come not near the old man; keep out, che vor'ye, or ise try whether your costard or my bat be the harder: Ch'ill be plain with you.
Stew. Out, dunghill!
Edg. Ch'ill pick your teeth, zir; Come; no matter vor your foins.
[*They fight; and* EDGAR *knocks him down.*
Stew. Slave, thou hast slain me:—Villain, take my purse;
If ever thou wilt thrive, bury my body;
And give the letters, which thou find'st about me,
To Edmund, earl of Gloster; seek him out
Upon the British party:——O, untimely death!
[*Dies.*
Edg. I know thee well: A serviceable villain;
As duteous to the vices of thy mistress,
As badness would desire.
Glo. What, is he dead?
Edg. Sit you down, father; rest you.—
Let's see his pockets; these letters, that he speaks of,
May be my friends.—He's dead: I am only sorry
He had no other deathsman.—Let us see:
Leave, gentle wax; and, manners, blame us not:
To know our enemies' minds, we'd rip their hearts;
Their papers, is more lawful.
[Reads.] *Let our reciprocal vows be remembered. You have many opportunities to cut him off: if your will want not, time and place will be fruitfully offered. There is nothing done, if he return the conqueror: Then am I the prisoner, and his bed my gaol; from the loathed warmth whereof deliver me, and supply the place for your labour.*
Your wife (so I would say), and your affectionate servant,
GONERIL.
O undistinguish'd space of woman's will!—
A plot upon her virtuous husband's life;
And the exchange, my brother!—Here, in the sands,
Thee I'll rake up, the post unsanctified
Of murderous lechers: and, in the mature time,
With this ungracious paper strike the sight
Of the death-practis'd duke: for him 'tis well,
That of thy death and business I can tell.
[*Exit* EDGAR, *dragging out the Body.*
Glo. The king is mad: How stiff is my vile sense,
That I stand up, and have ingenious feeling
Of my huge sorrows! Better I were distract:
So should my thoughts be sever'd from my griefs;
And woes, by wrong imaginations, lose
The knowledge of themselves.

Re-enter EDGAR.

Edg. Give me your hand:
Far off, methinks, I hear the beaten drum.
Come, father, I'll bestow you with a friend.
[*Exeunt.*

SCENE VII.

A Tent in the French *Camp.* LEAR *on a Bed, asleep:* Physician, Gentleman, *and Others attending: Enter* CORDELIA *and* KENT.

Cor. O thou good Kent, how shall I live, and work,
To match thy goodness? My life will be too short,
And every measure fail me.
Kent. To be acknowledg'd, madam, is o'erpaid.
All my reports go with the modest truth;
Nor more, nor clipp'd, but so.
Cor. Be better suited:
These weeds are memories of those worser hours;
I pr'ythee put them off.
Kent. Pardon me, dear madam;
Yet to be known, shortens my made intent:
My boon I make it, that you know me not,
Till time and I think meet.
Cor. Then be it so, my good lord.—How does the king? [*To the* Physician.
Phys. Madam, sleeps still.
Cor. O you kind gods,
Cure this great breach in his abused nature!
The untun'd and jarring senses, O, wind up
Of this child-changed father!
Phys. So please your majesty,
That we may wake the king? he hath slept long.
Cor. Be govern'd by your knowledge, and proceed
I' the sway of your own will. Is he array'd?
Gent. Ay, madam; in the heaviness of his sleep,
We put fresh garments on him.
Phys. Be by, good madam, when we do awake him;
I doubt not of his temperance.
Cor. Very well.
Phys. Please you, draw near.—Louder the musick there.
Cor. O my dear father! Restoration, hang
Thy medicine upon my lips; and let this kiss
Repair those violent harms, that my two sisters
Have in thy reverence made!
Kent. Kind and dear princess!
Cor. Had you not been their father, these white flakes
Had challeng'd pity of them. Was this a face
To be expos'd against the warring winds?
To stand against the deep dread-bolted thunder?
In the most terrible and nimble stroke
Of quick, cross lightning? to watch (poor perdu!)
With this thin helm? Mine enemy's dog,
Though he had bit me, should have stood that night
Against my fire; And wast thou fain, poor father,
To hovel thee with swine, and rogues forlorn,
In short and musty straw? Alack, alack!
'Tis wonder, that thy life and wits at once
Had not concluded all.—He wakes; speak to him.
Phys. Madam, do you; 'tis fittest.
Cor. How does my royal lord? How fares your majesty?
Lear. You do me wrong, to take me out o' the grave:—
Thou art a soul in bliss; but I am bound

Upon a wheel of fire, that mine own tears
Do scald like molten lead.
Cor. Sir, do you know me?
Lear. You are a spirit, I know; When did you die?
Cor. Still, still, far wide!
Phys. He's scarce awake; let him alone awhile.
Lear. Where have I been?—Where am I?—
Fair day light?—
I am mightily abus'd.—I should even die with pity,
To see another thus.—I know not what to say.—
I will not swear, these are my hands:—let's see;
I feel this pin prick. 'Would, I were assur'd
Of my condition.
Cor. O, look upon me, sir,
And hold your hands in benediction o'er me;—
No, sir, you must not kneel.
Lear. Pray, do not mock me:
I am a very foolish fond old man,
Fourscore and upward; and, to deal plainly,
I fear, I am not in my perfect mind.
Methinks, I should know you, and know this man:
Yet I am doubtful: for I am mainly ignorant
What place this is; and all the skill I have
Remembers not these garments; nor I know not
Where I did lodge last night: Do not laugh at me;
For, as I am a man, I think this lady
To be my child Cordelia.
Cor. And so I am, I am.
Lear. Be your tears wet? Yes, 'faith. I pray, weep not:
If you have poison for me, I will drink it.
I know you do not love me; for your sisters
Have, as I do remember, done me wrong:
You have some cause, they have not.
Cor. No cause, no cause.
Lear. Am I in France?
Kent. In your own kingdom, sir.
Lear. Do not abuse me.
Phys. Be comforted, good madam: the great rage,
You see, is cur'd in him: and yet it is danger
To make him even o'er the time he has lost.
Desire him to go in; trouble him no more,
Till further settling.
Cor. Will't please your highness walk?
Lear. You must bear with me:
'Pray now, forget and forgive: I am old, and foolish.
[*Exeunt* LEAR, COR. Phy. *and* Attendants.
Gent. Holds it true, sir,
That the Duke of Cornwall was so slain?
Kent. Most certain, sir.
Gent. Who is conductor of his people?
Kent. As 'tis said,
The bastard son of Gloster.
Gent. They say, Edgar,
His banish'd son, is with the Earl of Kent
In Germany.
Kent. Report is changeable.
'Tis time to look about; the powers o'the kingdom
Approach apace.
Gent. The arbitrement is like to be a bloody.
Fare you well, sir. [*Exit.*
Kent. My point and period will be thoroughly wrought,
Or well, or ill, as this day's battle's fought.
[*Exit.*

ACT V.

SCENE I. *The Camp of the* British Forces, *near* Dover.

Enter, with Drums and Colours, EDMUND, REGAN, Officers, Soldiers, *and Others.*

Edm. Know of the Duke, if his last purpose hold;
Or, whether since he is advis'd by aught
To change the course: He's full of alteration,
And self-reproving:—bring his constant pleasure. [*To an* Officer, *who goes out.*
Reg. Our sister's man is certainly miscarried.
Edm. 'Tis to be doubted, madam.
Reg. Now, sweet lord,
You know the goodness I intend upon you:
Tell me,—but truly,—but then speak the truth,
Do you not love my sister?
Edm. In honour'd love.
Reg. But have you never found my brother's way
To the forefended place?
Edm. That thought abuses you.
Reg. I am doubtful that you have been conjunct
And bosom'd with her, as far as we call hers.
Edm. No, by mine honour, madam.
Reg. I never shall endure her: Dear my lord,
Be not familiar with her.
Edm. Fear me not:——
She, and the duke her husband,——

Enter ALBANY, GONERIL, *and* Soldiers.

Gon. I had rather lose the battle, than that sister
Should loosen him and me. [*Aside.*
Alb. Our very loving sister, well be met.—
Sir, this I hear,—The king is come to his daughter,
With others, whom the rigour of our state
Forc'd to cry out. Where I could not be honest,
I never yet was valiant: for this business,
It toucheth us as France invades our land,
Not bolds the king; with others, whom, I fear,
More just and heavy causes make oppose.
Edm. Sir, you speak nobly.
Reg. Why is this reason'd?
Gon. Combine together 'gainst the enemy:
For these domestick and particular broils
Are not to question here.
Alb. Let us then determine
With the ancient of war on our proceedings.
Edm. I shall attend you presently at your tent.
Reg. Sister, you'll go with us?
Gon. No.
Reg. 'Tis most convenient; 'pray you, go with us.
Gon. O, ho, I know the riddle: [*Aside.*] I will go.

As they are going out, Enter EDGAR, *disguised.*

Edg. If e'er your grace had speech with man so poor,
Hear me one word.
Alb. I'll overtake you.—Speak.
[*Exeunt* EDMUND, REGAN, GONERIL, Officers, Soldiers, *and* Attendants.
Edg. Before you fight the battle, ope this letter.
If you have victory, let the trumpet sound
For him that brought it: wretched though I seem,
I can produce a champion, that will prove
What is avouched there: If you miscarry,
Your business of the world hath so an end,
And machination ceases. Fortune love you!
Alb. Stay till I have read the letter.
Edg. I was forbad it.
When time shall serve, let but the herald cry,
And I'll appear again. [*Exit.*
Alb. Why, fare thee well; I will o'erlook thy paper.

Re-enter EDMUND.

Edm. The enemy's in view, draw up your powers,
Here is the guess of their true strength and forces
By diligent discovery;—but your haste
Is now urg'd on you.
Alb. We will greet the time. [*Exit.*
Edm. To both these sisters have I sworn my love:
Each jealous of the other, as the stung
Are of the adder. Which of them shall I take?
Both? one? or neither? Neither can be enjoy'd,
If both remain alive; To take the widow,
Exasperates, makes mad her sister Goneril;
And hardly shall I carry out my side,

Her husband being alive. Now then, we'll use
His countenance for the battle: which being done,
Let her, who would be rid of him, devise
His speedy taking off. As for the mercy
Which he intends to Lear, and to Cordelia,—
The battle done, and they within our power,
Shall never see his pardon: for my state
Stands on me to defend, not to debate. [*Exit.*

SCENE II. *A Field between the two Camps.*

Alarum within. Enter, with Drum, and Colours, LEAR, CORDELIA, *and their* Forces; *and exeunt.*

Enter EDGAR *and* GLOSTER.

Edg. Here, father, take the shadow of this tree
For your good host; pray that the right may thrive:
If ever I return to you again,
I'll bring you comfort.
Glo. Grace go with you, sir!
[*Exit* EDGAR.

Alarums; afterwards a Retreat. Re-enter EDGAR.

Edg. Away, old man, give me thy hand, away;
King Lear hath lost, he and his daughter ta'en:
Give me thy hand, come on.
Glo. No further, sir; a man may rot even here.
Edg. What, in ill thoughts again? Men must endure
Their going hence, even as their coming hither:
Ripeness is all: Come on.
Glo. And that's true too.
[*Exeunt.*

SCENE III. *The* British *Camp near* Dover.

Enter, in Conquest, with Drum and Colours, EDMUND; LEAR *and* CORDELIA, *as Prisoners;* Officers, Soldiers, *&c.*

Edm. Some officers take them away; good guard;
Until their greater pleasures first be known
That are to censure them.
Cor. We are not the first,
Who, with best meaning, have incurr'd the worst.
For thee, oppressed king, am I cast down;
Myself could else outfrown false fortune's frown.
Shall we not see these daughters, and these sisters?
Lear. No, no, no, no! Come, let's away to prison:
We two alone will sing like birds i' the cage:
When thou dost ask me blessing, I'll kneel down,
And ask of thee forgiveness: So we'll live,
And pray, and sing, and tell old tales, and laugh
At gilded butterflies, and hear poor rogues
Talk of court news; and we'll talk with them too,
Who loses, and who wins; who's in, who's out;—
And take upon us the mystery of things,
As if we were God's spies: And we'll wear out,
In a wall'd prison, packs and sects of great ones,
That ebb and flow by the moon.
Edm. Take them away.
Lear. Upon such sacrifices, my Cordelia,
The gods themselves throw incense. Have I caught thee?
He, that parts us, shall bring a brand from heaven,
And fire us hence, like foxes. Wipe thine eyes;
The goujeers shall devour them, flesh and fell,
Ere they shall make us weep: we'll see them starve first.
Come. [*Exeunt* LEAR *and* CORDELIA, *guarded.*
Edm. Come hither, captain; hark.
Take thou this note; [*Giving a Paper.*] go, follow them to prison:
One step I have advanc'd thee; if thou dost
As this instructs thee, thou dost make thy way
To noble fortunes: Know thou this,—that men
Are as the time is: to be tender-minded
Does not become a sword:—Thy great employment
Will not bear question: either say, thou'lt do't,
Or thrive by other means.
Off. I'll do't, my lord.
Edm. About it; and write happy, when thou hast done.
Mark,—I say instantly; and carry it so,
As I have set it down.
Off. I cannot draw a cart, nor eat dried oats:
If it be man's work, I will do it. [*Exit* Officer.

Flourish. Enter ALBANY, GONERIL, REGAN, Officers, *and* Attendants.

Alb. Sir, you have shown to-day your valiant strain,
And fortune led you well: You have the captives
Who were the opposites of this day's strife:
We do require them of you; so to use them,
As we shall find their merits and our safety
May equally determine.
Edm. Sir, I thought it fit
To send the old and miserable king
To some retention, and appointed guard;
Whose age has charms in it, whose title more,
To pluck the common bosom on his side,
And turn our impress'd lances in our eyes
Which do command them. With him I sent the queen;
My reason all the same; and they are ready
To-morrow, or at further space, to appear
Where you shall hold your session. At this time
We sweat and bleed: the friend hath lost his friend:
And the best quarrels, in the heat, are curs'd
By those that feel their sharpness:—
The question of Cordelia, and her father,
Requires a fitter place.
Alb. Sir, by your patience,
I hold you but a subject of this war,
Not as a brother.
Reg. That's as we list to grace him.
Methinks our pleasure might have been demanded,
Ere you had spoke so far. He led our powers;
Bore the commission of my place and person;
The which immediacy may well stand up,
And call itself your brother.
Gon. Not so hot:
In his own grace he doth exalt himself,
More than in your advancement.
Reg. In my rights,
By me invested, he compeers the best.
Gon. That were the most, if he should husband you.
Reg. Jesters do oft prove prophets.
Gon. Holla, holla!
That eye, that told you so, look'd but a-squint.
Reg. Lady, I am not well; else I should answer
From a full flowing stomach.—General,
Take thou my soldiers, prisoners, patrimony;
Dispose of them, of me; the walls are thine:
Witness the world, that I create thee here
My lord and master.
Gon. Mean you to enjoy him?
Alb. The let alone lies not in your good will.
Edm. Nor in thine, lord.
Alb. Half-blooded fellow, yes.
Reg. Let the drum strike, and prove my title thine. [*To* EDMUND.
Alb. Stay yet; hear reason:—Edmund, I arrest thee
On capital treason; and, in thine, attaint
This gilded serpent: [*Pointing to* GON.]—for your claim, fair sister,
I bar it in the interest of my wife;
'Tis she is subcontracted to this lord,
And I, her husband, contradict your bans.
If you will marry, make your love to me,
My lady is bespoke.
Gon. An interlude!
Alb. Thou art arm'd, Gloster:—Let the trumpet sound:

If none appear to prove upon thy person,
Thy heinous, manifest, and many treasons,
There is my pledge; [*Throwing down a Glove.*]
I'll prove it on thy heart,
Ere I taste bread, thou art in nothing less
Than I have here proclaim'd thee.

Reg. Sick, O, sick!

Gon. If not, I'll ne'er trust poison. [*Aside.*

Edm. There's my exchange: [*Throwing down a Glove.*] what in the world he is
That names me traitor, villain-like he lies:
Call by thy trumpet: he that dares approach,
On him, on you, (who not?) I will maintain
My truth and honour firmly.

Alb. A herald, ho!

Edm. A herald, ho, a herald!

Alb. Trust to thy single virtue; for thy soldiers,
All levied in my name, have in my name
Took their discharge.

Reg. This sickness grows upon me.

Enter a Herald.

Alb. She is not well; convey her to my tent.
[*Exit* REGAN, *led.*
Come hither, herald.—Let the trumpet sound,—
And read out this.

Off. Sound, trumpet. [*A Trumpet sounds.*

Herald *reads.*

If any man of quality, or degree, within the lists of the army, will maintain upon Edmund, *supposed earl of* Gloster, *that he is a manifold traitor, let him appear at the third sound of the trumpet: He is bold in his defence.*

Edm. Sound. [1 *Trumpet.*

Her. Again. [2 *Trumpet.*

Her. Again. [3 *Trumpet.*

[*Trumpet answers within.*

Enter EDGAR, *armed, preceded by a Trumpet.*

Alb. Ask him his purposes, why he appears
Upon this call o' the trumpet.

Her. What are you?
Your name, your quality? and why you answer
This present summons?

Edg. Know, my name is lost;
By treason's tooth bare-gnawn, and canker-bit:
Yet am I noble as the adversary
I come to cope withal.

Alb. Which is that adversary?

Edg. What's he, that speaks for Edmund earl of Gloster?

Edm. Himself;—What say'st thou to him?

Edg. Draw thy sword;
That, if my speech offend a noble heart,
Thy arm may do thee justice: here is mine.
Behold, it is the privilege of mine honours,
My oath, and my profession: I protest,—
Maugre thy strength, youth, place, and eminence,
Despite thy victor sword, and fire-new fortune,
Thy valour, and thy heart,—thou art a traitor:
False to thy gods, thy brother, and thy father;
Conspirant 'gainst this high illustrious prince;
And, from the extremest upward of thy head,
To the descent and dust beneath thy feet,
A most toad-spotted traitor. Say thou, *No,*
This sword, this arm, and my best spirits, are bent
To prove upon thy heart, whereto I speak,
Thou liest.

Edm. In wisdom, I should ask thy name;
But, since thy outside looks so fair and warlike,
And that thy tongue some 'say of breeding breathes,
What safe and nicely I might well delay
By rule of knighthood, I disdain and spurn:
Back do I toss these treasons to thy head;
With the hell-hated lie o'erwhelm thy heart;
Which, (for they yet glance by, and scarcely bruise),
This sword of mine shall give them instant way,
Where they shall rest for ever.—Trumpets, speak. [*Alarums. They fight,* EDM. *falls.*

Alb. O save him, save him!

Gon. This is mere practice, Gloster.
By the law of arms, thou wast not bound to answer
An unknown opposite; thou art not vanquish'd,
But cozen'd and beguil'd.

Alb. Shut your mouth, dame,
Or with this paper shall I stop it:—Hold, sir:—
Thou worse than any name, read thine own evil:—
No tearing, lady; I perceive you know it.
[*Gives the Letter to* EDMUND.

Gon. Say, if I do; the laws are mine, not thine:
Who shall arraign me for't?

Alb. Most monstrous!
Know'st thou this paper?

Gon. Ask me not what I know. [*Exit.*

Alb. Go after her; she's desperate; govern her.
[*To an* Officer, *who goes out.*

Edm. What you have charg'd me with, that have I done;
And more, much more; the time will bring it out:
'Tis past, and so am I: But what art thou,
That hast this fortune on me? If thou art noble,
I do forgive thee.

Edg. Let's exchange charity.
I am no less in blood than thou art, Edmund;
If more, the more thou hast wrong'd me.
My name is Edgar, and thy father's son.
The gods are just, and of our pleasant vices
Make instruments to scourge us:
The dark and vicious place where thee he got,
Cost him his eyes.

Edm. Thou hast spoken right, 'tis true;
The wheel is come full circle; I am here.

Alb. Methought, thy very gait did prophesy
A royal nobleness:—I must embrace thee;
Let sorrow split my heart, if ever I
Did hate thee, or thy father!

Edg. Worthy prince, I know't.

Alb. Where have you hid yourself?
How have you known the miseries of your father?

Edg. By nursing them, my lord.—List a brief tale:
And, when 'tis told, O, that my heart would burst!
The bloody proclamation to escape,
That follow'd me so near (O our lives' sweetness!
That with the pain of death we'd hourly die,
Rather than die at once!) taught me to shift
Into a madman's rags; to assume a semblance
That very dogs disdain'd: and in this habit
Met I my father with his bleeding rings,
Their precious stones new lost; became his guide,
Led him, begg'd for him, sav'd him from despair;
Never (O fault!) reveal'd myself unto him,
Until some half hour past, when I was arm'd,
Not sure, though hoping, of this good success,
I ask'd his blessing, and from first to last
Told him my pilgrimage: But his flaw'd heart
(Alack, too weak the conflict to support!)
'Twixt two extremes of passion, joy and grief,
Burst smilingly.

Edm. This speech of yours hath moved me,
And shall, perchance, do good: but speak you on;
You look as you had something more to say.

Alb. If there be more, more woful, hold it in;
For I am almost ready to dissolve,
Hearing of this.

Edg. This would have seem'd a period
To such as love not sorrow, but another,
To amplify too much, would make much more,
And top extremity.
Whilst I was big in clamour, came there a man,
Who having seen me in my worst estate,
Shunn'd my abhorr'd society; but then, finding
Who 'twas that so endur'd, with his strong arms
He fasten'd on my neck, and bellow'd out
As he'd burst heaven: threw him on my father;
Told the most piteous tale of Lear and him,
That ever ear receiv'd: which in recounting
His grief grew puissant, and the strings of life
Began to crack: Twice then the trumpet sounded,
And there I left him tranc'd.

Alb. But who was this?
Edg. Kent, sir, the banish'd Kent; who in disguise
Follow'd his enemy king, and did him service
Improper for a slave.

Enter a Gentleman *hastily, with a bloody Knife.*

Gent. Help! help! O help!
Edg. What kind of help?
Alb. Speak, man.
Edg. What means that bloody knife?
Gent. 'Tis hot, it smokes;
It came even from the heart of—
Alb. Who, man? speak.
Gent. Your lady, sir, your lady: and her sister
By her is poison'd; she hath confess'd it.
Edm. I was contracted to them both; all three
Now marry in an instant.
Alb. Produce their bodies, be they alive or dead!
This judgment of the heavens, that makes us tremble,
Touches us not with pity. [*Exit* Gentleman.

Enter KENT.

Edg. Here comes Kent, sir.
Alb. O! it is he.
The time will not allow the compliment,
Which very manners urges.
Kent. I am come
To bid my king and master aye good night;
Is he not here?
Alb. Great thing of us forgot!—
Speak, Edmund, where's the king? and where's Cordelia?—
Seest thou this object, Kent?
[*The Bodies of* GON. *and* REG. *are brought in.*
Kent. Alack, why thus?
Edm. Yet Edmund was belov'd:
The one the other poison'd for my sake,
And after slew herself.
Alb. Even so.—Cover their faces.
Edm. I pant for life:—Some good I mean to do,
Despite of mine own nature. Quickly send,—
Be brief in it,—to the castle, for my writ
Is on the life of Lear, and on Cordelia:—
Nay, send in time.
Alb. Run, run, O run—
Edg. To who, my lord?—Who has the office? send
Thy token of reprieve.
Edm. Well thought on; take my sword,
Give it the captain.
Alb. Haste thee, for thy life. [*Exit* EDGAR.
Edm. He hath commission from thy wife and me
To hang Cordelia in the prison, and
To lay the blame upon her own despair,
That she fordid herself.
Alb. The gods defend her! Bear him hence awhile. [EDMUND *is borne off.*

Enter LEAR, *with* CORDELIA *dead in his Arms;* EDGAR, Officer, *and Others.*

Lear. Howl, howl, howl, howl!—O, you are men of stones;
Had I your tongues and eyes, I'd use them so
That heaven's vault should crack:—O, she is gone for ever!—
I know when one is dead, and when one lives;
She's dead as earth:—Lend me a looking glass;
If that her breath will mist or stain the stone,
Why, then she lives.
Kent. Is this the promis'd end?
Edg. Or image of that horror?
Alb. Fall, and cease!
Lear. This feather stirs; she lives! if it be so,
It is a chance that does redeem all sorrows
That ever I have felt.
Kent. O my good master! [*Kneeling.*
Lear. 'Pr'ythee, away.
Edg. 'Tis noble Kent, your friend.
Lear. A plague upon you, murderers, traitors all!
I might have sav'd her; now she's gone for ever!—
Cordelia, Cordelia, stay a little. Ha!
What is't thou say'st?—Her voice was ever soft,
Gentle, and low; an excellent thing in woman:
I kill'd the slave that was a hanging thee.
Off. 'Tis true, my lords, he did.
Lear. Did I not, fellow?
I have seen the day, with my good biting falchion
I would have made them skip: I am old now,
And these same crosses spoil me.—Who are you?
Mine eyes are none o' the best:—I'll tell you straight.
Kent. If fortune brag of two she lov'd and hated,
One of them we behold.
Lear. This is a dull sight: Are you not Kent?
Kent. The same;
Your servant Kent: Where is your servant Caius?
Lear. He's a good fellow, I can tell you that;
He'll strike, and quickly too:—He's dead and rotten.
Kent. No, my good lord, I am the very man;—
Lear. I'll see that straight.
Kent. That from your first of difference and decay,
Have follow'd your sad steps.
Lear. You are welcome hither.
Kent. Nor no man else; all's cheerless, dark, and deadly.—
Your eldest daughters have fore-doom'd themselves,
And desperately are dead.
Lear. Ay, so I think.
Alb. He knows not what he says; and vain it is
That we present us to him.
Edg. Very bootless.

Enter an Officer.

Off. Edmund is dead, my lord.
Alb. That's but a trifle here.—
You lords, and noble friends, know our intent.
What comfort to this great decay may come,
Shall be applied; for us, we will resign,
During the life of this old majesty,
To him our absolute power:—You, to your rights; [*To* EDGAR *and* KENT.
With boot, and such addition as your honours
Have more than merited:—All friends shall taste
The wages of their virtue, and all foes
The cup of their deservings.—O, see, see!
Lear. And my poor fool is hang'd! No, no, no life:
Why should a dog, a horse, a rat, have life,
And thou no breath at all? O, thou wilt come no more,
Never, never, never, never, never!—
'Pray you, undo this button: Thank you, sir.—
Do you see this?—Look on her,—look,—her lips,—
Look there, look there!— [*He dies.*
Edg. He faints!—My lord, my lord,—
Kent. Break, heart; I pr'ythee, break!
Edg. Look up, my lord.
Kent. Vex not his ghost: O, let him pass! he hates him,
That would upon the rack of this tough world
Stretch him out longer.
Edg. O, he is gone indeed.
Kent. The wonder is, he hath endur'd so long:
He but usurp'd his life.
Alb. Bear them from hence.—Our present business
Is general woe. Friends of my soul, you twain
[*To* KENT *and* EDGAR.
Rule in this realm, and the gor'd state sustain.
Kent. I have a journey, sir, shortly to go;
My master calls, and I must not say, no.
Alb. The weight of this sad time we must obey;
Speak what we feel, not what we ought to say.
The oldest hath borne most; we, that are young,
Shall never see so much, nor live so long.
[*Exeunt, with a dead March.*

ROMEO AND JULIET.

PERSONS REPRESENTED.

ESCALUS, Prince *of* Verona.
PARIS, *a young Nobleman, Kinsman to the* Prince.
MONTAGUE, } *Heads of Two Houses at variance with*
CAPULET, } *each other.*
An old Man, *Uncle to* Capulet.
ROMEO, *Son to* Montague.
MERCUTIO, *Kinsman to the* Prince, *and Friend to* Romeo.
BENVOLIO, *Nephew to* Montague, *and Friend to* Romeo.
TYBALT, *Nephew to* Lady Capulet.
FRIAR LAURENCE, *a Franciscan.*
FRIAR JOHN, *of the same Order.*
BALTHAZAR, *Servant to* Romeo.
SAMPSON, *Servant to* Capulet.
GREGORY, *Servant to* Capulet.
ABRAM, *Servant to* Montague.
An Apothecary.
Three Musicians.
Chorus. Boy. Page *to* Paris.
PETER. *An* Officer.

LADY MONTAGUE, *Wife to* Montague.
LADY CAPULET, *Wife to* Capulet.
JULIET, *Daughter to* Capulet.
Nurse *to* Juliet.

Citizens *of* Verona; *several* Men *and* Women, *Relations to both Houses;* Maskers, Guards, Watchmen, *and* Attendants.

SCENE—*during the greater Part of the Play, in* Verona: *once, in the Fifth Act, at* Mantua.

PROLOGUE.

Two households, both alike in dignity,
In fair Verona, where we lay our scene,
From ancient grudge, break to new mutiny,
Where civil blood makes civil hands unclean.
From forth the fatal loins of these two foes
A pair of star-cross'd lovers take their life;
Whose misadventur'd piteous overthrows
Do, with their death, bury their parents' strife.
The fearful passage of their death-mark'd love,
And the continuance of their parents' rage,
Which, but their children's end, nought could remove,
Is now the two hours' traffick of our stage;
The which if you with patient ears attend,
What here shall miss, our toil shall strive to mend.

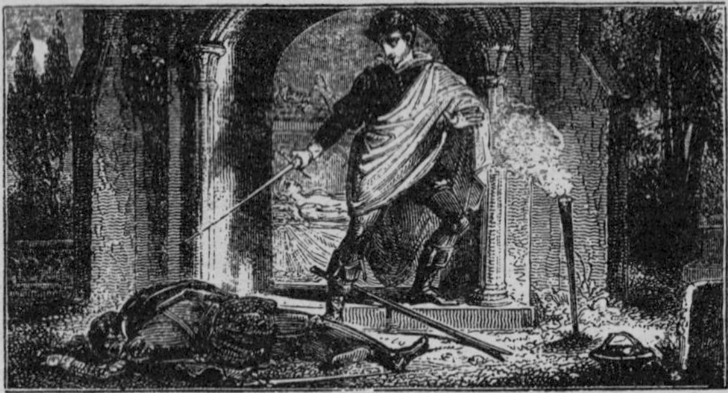

ACT I.

SCENE I. *A public Place.*

Enter SAMPSON *and* GREGORY, *armed with Swords and Bucklers.*

Sam. GREGORY, o' my word, we'll not carry coals.

Gre. No, for then we should be colliers.

Sam. I mean, an we be in choler, we'll draw.

Gre. Ay, while you live, draw your neck out of the collar.

Sam. I strike quickly, being moved.

Gre. But thou art not quickly moved to strike.

Sam. A dog of the house of Montague moves me.

Gre. To move, is—to stir; and to be valiant, is—to stand to it:—therefore, if thou art mov'd, thou run'st away.

Sam. A dog of that house shall move me to stand: I will take the wall of any man or maid of Montague's.

Gre. That shows thee a weak slave; for the weakest goes to the wall.

Sam. True; and therefore women, being the weaker vessels, are ever thrust to the wall:—therefore I will push Montague's men from the wall, and thrust his maids to the wall.

Gre. The quarrel is between our masters, and us their men.

Sam. 'Tis all one, I will show myself a tyrant: when I have fought with the men, I will be cruel with the maids; I will cut off their heads.

Gre. The heads of the maids?

Sam. Ay, the heads of the maids, or their maidenheads; take it in what sense thou wilt.

Gre. They must take it in sense, that feel it.

Sam. Me they shall feel, while I am able to stand: and, 'tis known, I am a pretty piece of flesh.

Gre. 'Tis well, thou art not fish; if thou hadst, thou hadst been poor John. Draw thy tool; here comes two of the house of the Montagues.

Enter ABRAM *and* BALTHAZAR.

Sam. My naked weapon is out; quarrel, I will back thee.

Gre. How? turn thy back, and run?

Sam. Fear me not.

Gre. No, marry: I fear thee!

Sam. Let us take the law of our sides; let them begin.

Gre. I will frown, as I pass by; and let them take it as they list.

Sam. Nay, as they dare. I will bite my thumb at them; which is a disgrace to them, if they bear it.

Abr. Do you bite your thumb at us, sir?

Sam. I do bite my thumb, sir.

Abr. Do you bite your thumb at us, sir?

Sam. Is the law on our side, if I say—ay?

Gre. No.

Sam. No, sir, I do not bite my thumb at you, sir; but I bite my thumb, sir.

Gre. Do you quarrel, sir?

Abr. Quarrel, sir? no, sir.

Sam. If you do, sir, I am for you: I serve as good a man as you.

Abr. No better.

Sam. Well, sir.

Enter BENVOLIO, *at a distance.*

Gre. Say—better; here comes one of my master's kinsmen.

Sam. Yes, better, sir.

Abr. You lie.

Sam. Draw, if you be men.—Gregory, remember thy swashing blow. [*They fight.*

Ben. Part, fools; put up your swords; you know not what you do.

[*Beats down their Swords.*

Enter TYBALT.

Tyb. What, art thou drawn among these heartless hinds?
Turn thee, Benvolio, look upon thy death.

Ben. I do but keep the peace: put up thy sword,
Or manage it to part these men with me.

Tyb. What, drawn, and talk of peace? I hate the word,
As I hate hell, all Montagues, and thee:
Have at thee, coward. [*They fight.*

Enter several Partisans *of both Houses, who join the Fray; then enter* Citizens, *with Clubs.*

1 *Cit.* Clubs, bills, and partisans! strike! beat them down!
Down with the Capulets! down with the Montagues!

Enter CAPULET, *in his Gown; and* LADY CAPULET.

Cap. What noise is this?—Give me my long sword, ho!

La. Cap. A crutch, a crutch!—Why call you for a sword?

Cap. My sword, I say!—Old Montague is come,
And flourishes his blade in spite of me.

Enter MONTAGUE *and* LADY MONTAGUE.

Mon. Thou villain Capulet,—Hold me not, let me go.

La. Mon. Thou shalt not stir one foot to seek a foe.

Enter Prince, *with* Attendants.

Prin. Rebellious subjects, enemies to peace,
Profaners of this neighbour-stained steel,—
Will they not hear?—what ho! you men, you beasts,—
That quench the fire of your pernicious rage
With purple fountains issuing from your veins,
On pain of torture, from those bloody hands
Throw your mistemper'd weapons to the ground,
And hear the sentence of your moved prince.—
Three civil brawls, bred of an airy word,
By thee, old Capulet and Montague,
Have thrice disturb'd the quiet of our streets;
And made Verona's ancient citizens
Cast by their grave beseeming ornaments,
To wield old partisans, in hands as old,
Canker'd with peace, to part your canker'd hate:
If ever you disturb our streets again,
Your lives shall pay the forfeit of the peace.
For this time, all the rest depart away:
You, Capulet, shall go along with me;
And, Montague, come you this afternoon,
To know our further pleasure in this case,
To old Free-town, our common judgment-place.
Once more, on pain of death, all men depart.

[*Exeunt* Prince, *and* Attendants; CAPULET, LA. CAP. TYBALT, Citizens, *and* Servants.

Mon. Who set this ancient quarrel new abroach?
Speak, nephew, were you by, when it began?

Ben. Here were the servants of your adversary,
And yours, close fighting ere I did approach:
I drew to part them; in the instant came
The fiery Tybalt, with his sword prepar'd;
Which, as he breathed defiance to my ears,
He swung about his head, and cut the winds,
Who, nothing hurt withal, hiss'd him in scorn:
While we were interchanging thrusts and blows,
Came more and more, and fought on part and part,
Till the prince came, who parted either part.

La. Mon. O, where is Romeo?—saw you him to-day?
Right glad I am, he was not at this fray.

Ben. Madam, an hour before the worship'd sun
Peer'd forth the golden window of the east,
A troubled mind drave me to walk abroad;
Where, underneath the grove of sycamore,
That westward rooteth from the city's side,—
So early walking did I see your son:
Towards him I made; but he was 'ware of me,
And stole into the covert of the wood:
I, measuring his affections by my own,—
That most are busied when they are most alone,—
Pursu'd my humour, not pursuing his,
And gladly shunn'd who gladly fled from me.

Mon. Many a morning hath he there been seen,
With tears augmenting the fresh morning's dew,
Adding to clouds more clouds with his deep sighs:
But all so soon as the all-cheering sun
Should in the further east begin to draw
The shady curtains from Aurora's bed,
Away from light steals home my heavy son,
And private in his chamber pens himself;
Shuts up his windows, locks fair daylight out,
And makes himself an artificial night:
Black and portentous must this humour prove,
Unless good counsel may the cause remove.

Ben. My noble uncle, do you know the cause?

Mon. I neither know it, nor can learn of him.

Ben. Have you importun'd him by any means?

Mon. Both by myself, and many other friends:
But he, his own affection's counsellor,
Is to himself—I will not say, how true—
But to himself so secret and so close,
So far from sounding and discovery,
As is the bud bit with an envious worm,
Ere he can spread his sweet leaves to the air,
Or dedicate his beauty to the sun.
Could we but learn from whence his sorrows grow,
We would as willingly give cure, as know.

Enter ROMEO, *at a distance.*

Ben. See, where he comes: So please you, step aside;
I'll know his grievance, or be much denied.

Mon. I would, thou wert so happy by thy stay,
To hear true shrift.—Come, madam, let's away.
[*Exeunt* MONTAGUE *and* Lady.

Ben. Good morrow, cousin.
Rom. Is the day so young?
Ben. But new struck nine.
Rom. Ah me! sad hours seem long.
Was that my father that went hence so fast?
Ben. It was:—What sadness lengthens Romeo's hours?
Rom. Not having that, which having makes them short.
Ben. In love?
Rom. Out—
Ben. Of love?
Rom. Out of her favour, where I am in love.
Ben. Alas, that love, so gentle in his view,
Should be so tyrannous and rough in proof!
Rom. Alas, that love, whose view is muffled still,
Should, without eyes, see pathways to his will!
Where shall we dine?—O me!—What fray was here?
Yet tell me not, for I have heard it all.
Here's much to do with hate, but more with love:—
Why then, O brawling love! O loving hate!
O any thing, of nothing first create!
O heavy lightness, serious vanity!
Misshapen Chaos of well-seeming forms!
Feather of lead, bright smoke, cold fire, sick health!
Still waking sleep, that is not what it is!—
This love feel I, that feel no love in this.
Dost thou not laugh?
Ben. No, coz, I rather weep.
Rom. Good heart, at what?
Ben. At thy good heart's oppression.
Rom. Why, such is love's transgression.—
Griefs of mine own lie heavy in my breast;
Which thou wilt propagate, to have it prest
With more of thine: this love, that thou hast shown,
Doth add more grief to too much of mine own.
Love is a smoke rais'd with the fume of sighs;
Being urg'd, a fire sparkling in lovers' eyes;
Being vex'd, a sea nourish'd with lovers' tears:
What is it else? a madness most discreet,
A choking gall, and a preserving sweet.
Farewell, my coz. [*Going.*
Ben. Soft, I will go along;
And if you leave me so, you do me wrong.
Rom. Tut, I have lost myself; I am not here;
This is not Romeo, he's some other where.
Ben. Tell me in sadness, whom she is you love.
Rom. What, shall I groan, and tell thee?
Ben. Groan? why, no;
But sadly tell me who.
Rom. Bid a sick man in sadness make his will:—
Ah, word ill urg'd to one that is so ill!
In sadness, cousin, I do love a woman.
Ben. I aim'd so near, when I suppos'd you lov'd.
Rom. A right good marksman!—And she's fair I love.
Ben. A right fair mark, fair coz, is soonest hit.
Rom. Well, in that hit, you miss: she'll not be hit
With Cupid's arrow, she hath Dian's wit;
And, in strong proof of chastity well arm'd,
From love's weak childish bow she lives unharm'd.
She will not stay the siege of loving terms,
Nor bide the encounter of assailing eyes,
Nor ope her lap to saint-seducing gold:
O, she is rich in beauty; only poor,
That, when she dies, with beauty dies her store.
Ben. Then she hath sworn, that she will still live chaste?
Rom. She hath, and in that sparing makes huge waste;
For beauty, starv'd with her severity,
Cuts beauty off from all posterity.
She is too fair, too wise; wisely too fair,
To merit bliss by making me despair:
She hath forsworn to love; and, in that vow,
Do I live dead, that live to tell it now.
Ben. Be rul'd by me, forget to think of her.
Rom. O, teach me how I should forget to think.
Ben. By giving liberty unto thine eyes;
Examine other beauties.
Rom. 'Tis the way
To call hers, exquisite, in question more:
These happy masks, that kiss fair ladies' brows,
Being black, put us in mind they hide the fair;
He, that is strucken blind, cannot forget
The precious treasure of his eyesight lost:
Show me a mistress that is passing fair,
What doth her beauty serve, but as a note
Where I may read, who pass'd that passing fair?
Farewell; thou canst not teach me to forget.
Ben. I'll pay that doctrine, or else die in debt. [*Exeunt.*

SCENE II. *A Street.*

Enter CAPULET, PARIS, *and* Servant.

Cap. And Montague is bound as well as I,
In penalty alike; and 'tis not hard, I think,
For men so old as we to keep the peace.
Par. Of honourable reckoning are you both;
And pity 'tis, you liv'd at odds so long.
But now, my lord, what say you to my suit?
Cap. By saying o'er what I have said before:
My child is yet a stranger in the world,
She hath not seen the change of fourteen years;
Let two more summers wither in their pride,
Ere we may think her ripe to be a bride.
Par. Younger than she are happy mothers made.
Cap. And too soon marr'd are those so early made.
The earth hath swallow'd all my hopes but she,
She is the hopeful lady of my earth:
But woo her, gentle Paris, get her heart,
My will to her consent is but a part;
An she agree, within her scope of choice
Lies my consent and fair according voice.
This night I hold an old accustom'd feast,
Whereto I have invited many a guest,
Such as I love; and you, among the store,
One more, most welcome, makes my number more.
At my poor house, look to behold this night
Earth-treading stars, that make dark heaven light:
Such comfort, as do lusty young men feel
When well apparell'd April on the heel
Of limping winter treads, even such delight
Among fresh female buds shall you this night
Inherit at my house; hear all, all see,
And like her most, whose merit most shall be:
Which, on more view of many, mine being one,
May stand in number, though in reckoning none.
Come, go with me;—Go, sirrah; trudge about
Through fair Verona; find those persons out,
Whose names are written there [*gives a Paper*], and to them say,
My house and welcome on their pleasure stay.
[*Exeunt* CAPULET *and* PARIS.

Serv. Find them out, whose names are written here? It is written—that the shoemaker should meddle with his yard,—and the tailor with his last, the fisher with his pencil, and the painter with his nets; but I am sent to find those persons, whose names are here writ, and can never find what names the writing person hath here writ. I must to the learned:—In good time.

Enter BENVOLIO *and* ROMEO.

Ben. Tut, man! one fire burns out another's burning,
One pain is lessen'd by another's anguish;
Turn giddy, and be holp by backward turning;
One desperate grief cures with another's languish:

Take thou some new infection to the eye,
And the rank poison of the old will die.
Rom. Your plantain leaf is excellent for that.
Ben. For what, I pray thee?
Rom. For your broken shin.
Ben. Why, Romeo, art thou mad?
Rom. Not mad, but bound more than a madman is:
Shut up in prison, kept without my food,
Whipp'd, and tormented, and—Good-e'en, good fellow.
Serv. God gi' good e'en.—I pray, sir, can you read?
Rom. Ay, mine own fortune in my misery.
Serv. Perhaps you have learn'd it without book: But, I pray, can you read any thing you see?
Rom. Ay, if I know the letters, and the language.
Serv. Ye say honestly; Rest you merry!
Rom. Stay, fellow; I can read. [*Reads.*
Signior Martino, *and his wife and daughters; County* Anselme, *and his beauteous sisters; The lady widow of* Vitruvio; *Signior* Placentio, *and his lovely nieces;* Mercutio, *and his brother* Valentine; *Mine uncle* Capulet, *his wife and daughters; My fair niece,* Rosaline; Livia; *Signior* Valentio, *and his cousin* Tybalt; Lucio, *and the lively* Helena.
A fair assembly; [*Gives back the Note*]. Whither should they come?
Serv. Up.
Rom. Whither?
Serv. To supper; to our house.
Rom. Whose house?
Serv. My master's.
Rom. Indeed, I should have asked you that before.
Serv. Now I'll tell you without asking: My master is the great rich Capulet; and if you be not of the house of Montagues, I pray, come and crush a cup of wine. Rest you merry. [*Exit.*
Ben. At this same ancient feast of Capulet's
Sups the fair Rosaline, whom thou so lov'st;
With all the admired beauties of Verona.
Go thither; and, with unattainted eye,
Compare her face with some that I shall show,
And I will make thee think thy swan a crow.
Rom. When the devout religion of mine eye
Maintains such falsehood, then turn tears to fires!
And these,—who, often drown'd, could never die,—
Transparent heretics, be burnt for liars!
One fairer than my love! the all-seeing sun
Ne'er saw her match, since first the world begun.
Ben. Tut! you saw her fair, none else being by,
Herself pois'd with herself in either eye:
But in those crystal scales, let there be weigh'd
Your lady's love against some other maid
That I will show you, shining at this feast,
And she shall scant show well, that now shows best.
Rom. I'll go along, no such sight to be shown,
But to rejoice in splendour of mine own. [*Exeunt.*

SCENE III. *A Room in* Capulet's *House.*

Enter LADY CAPULET *and* Nurse.

La. Cap. Nurse, where's my daughter? call her forth to me,
Nurse. Now, by my maidenhead,—at twelve year old,—
I bade her come.—What, lamb? what, lady-bird!—
God forbid!—where's this girl?—what, Juliet!

Enter JULIET.

Jul. How now, who calls?
Nurse. Your mother.
Jul. Madam, I am here,
What is your will?
La. Cap. This is the matter:—Nurse, give leave awhile,
We must talk in secret.—Nurse, come back again;
I have remember'd me, thou shalt hear our counsel,
Thou know'st my daughter's of a pretty age.
Nurse. 'Faith, I can tell her age unto an hour.
La. Cap. She's not fourteen.
Nurse. I'll lay fourteen of my teeth,
And yet, to my teen be it spoken, I have but four,—
She is not fourteen: How long is it now
To Lammas-tide?
La. Cap. A fortnight, and odd days.
Nurse. Even or odd, of all days in the year,
Come Lammas-eve at night, shall she be fourteen.
Susan and she,—God rest all Christian souls!—
Were of an age.—Well, Susan is with God;
She was too good for me: But, as I said,
On Lammas eve at night shall she be fourteen;
That shall she, marry; I remember it well.
'Tis since the earthquake now eleven years;
And she was wean'd,—I never shall forget it,—
Of all the days of the year, upon that day;
For I had then laid wormwood to my dug,
Sitting in the sun under the dove-house wall,
My lord and you were then at Mantua:—
Nay, I do bear a brain:—but, as I said,
When it did taste the wormwood on the nipple
Of my dug, and felt it bitter, pretty fool!
To see it tetchy, and fall out with the dug.
Shake, quoth the dove-house: 'twas no need, I trow,
To bid me trudge.
And since that time it is eleven years:
For then she could stand alone; nay, by the rood,
She could have run and waddled all about.
For even the day before, she broke her brow:
And then my husband—God be with his soul!
'A was a merry man;—took up the child:
Yea, quoth he, *dost thou fall upon thy face?*
Thou wilt fall backward, when thou hast more wit;
Wilt thou not, Jule? and, by my holy-dam,
The pretty wretch left crying, and said—*Ay:*
To see now, how a jest shall come about!
I warrant, an I should live a thousand years,
I never should forget it; *Wilt thou not, Jule?* quoth he:
And, pretty fool, it stinted, and said—*Ay.*
La. Cap. Enough of this; I pray thee, hold thy peace.
Nurse. Yes, madam; Yet I cannot choose but laugh,
To think it should leave crying, and say—*Ay:*
And yet, I warrant, it had upon its brow
A bump as big as a young cockrel's stone;
A parlous knock; and it cried bitterly.
Yea, quoth my husband, *fall'st upon thy face;*
Thou wilt fall backward, when thou com'st to age;
Wilt thou not, Jule? it stinted, and said—*Ay.*
Jul. And stint thou too, I pray thee, nurse, say I.
Nurse. Peace, I have done. God mark thee to his grace!
Thou wast the prettiest babe that e'er I nurs'd:
An I might live to see thee married once,
I have my wish.
La. Cap. Marry, that marry is the very theme
I came to talk of:—Tell me, daughter Juliet,
How stands your disposition to be married?
Jul. It is an honour that I dream not of.
Nurse. An honour! were not I thine only nurse,
I'd say, thou hadst suck'd wisdom from thy teat.
La. Cap. Well, think of marriage now; younger than you,
Here in Verona, ladies of esteem,
Are made already mothers: by my count,
I was your mother much upon these years

That you are now a maid. Thus then, in brief;—
The valiant Paris seeks you for his love.

Nurse. A man, young lady! lady, such a man,
As all the world—Why, he's a man of wax.

La. Cap. Verona's summer hath not such a flower.

Nurse. Nay, he's a flower; in faith, a very flower.

La. Cap. What say you? can you love the gentleman?
This night you shall behold him at our feast;
Read o'er the volume of young Paris' face,
And find delight writ there with beauty's pen;
Examine every married lineament,
And see how one another lends content:
And what obscur'd in this fair volume lies,
Find written in the margin of his eyes.
This precious book of love, this unbound lover,
To beautify him, only lacks a cover:
The fish lives in the sea; and 'tis much pride,
For fair without the fair within to hide:
That book in many's eyes doth share the glory,
That in gold clasps locks in the golden story;
So shall you share all that he doth possess,
By having him, making yourself no less.

Nurse. No less? nay, bigger; women grow by men.

La. Cap. Speak briefly, can you like of Paris' love?

Jul. I'll look to like, if looking liking move:
But no more deep will I endart mine eye,
Than your consent gives strength to make it fly.

Enter a Servant.

Serv. Madam, the guests are come, supper served up, you called, my young lady asked for, the nurse cursed in the pantry, and every thing in extremity. I must hence to wait; I beseech you, follow straight.

La. Cap. We follow thee.—Juliet the county stays.

Nurse. Go, girl, seek happy nights to happy days. [*Exeunt.*

SCENE IV. *A Street.*

Enter Romeo, Mercutio, Benvolio, *with five or six* Maskers, Torch-bearers, *and Others.*

Rom. What, shall this speech be spoke for our excuse?
Or shall we on without apology?

Ben. The date is out of such prolixity.
We'll have no cupid hood-wink'd with a scarf,
Bearing a Tartar's painted bow of lath,
Scaring the ladies like a crow-keeper;
Nor no without-book prologue, faintly spoke
After the prompter, for our entrance:
But, let them measure us by what they will,
We'll measure them a measure, and be gone.

Rom. Give me a torch,—I am not for this ambling;
Being heavy, I will bear the light.

Mer. Nay, gentle Romeo, we must have you dance.

Rom. Not I, believe me: you have dancing shoes,
With nimble soles: I have a soul of lead,
So stakes me to the ground, I cannot move.

Mer. You are a lover; borrow Cupid's wings,
And soar with them above a common bound.

Rom. I am too sore enpierced with his shaft,
To soar with his light feathers; and so bound,
I cannot bound a pitch above dull woe:
Under love's heavy burden do I sink.

Mer. And, to sink in it, should you burden love,
Too great oppression for a tender thing.

Rom. Is love a tender thing? it is too rough,
Too rude, too boist'rous; and it pricks like thorn.

Mer. If love be rough with you, be rough with love;
Prick love for pricking, and you beat love down.—
Give me a case to put my visage in:
[*Putting on a Mask.*
A visor for a visor!—what care I,
What curious eye doth quote deformities?
Here are the beetle-brows shall blush for me.

Ben. Come, knock, and enter: and no sooner in,
But every man betake him to his legs.

Rom. A torch for me: let wantons, light of heart,
Tickle the senseless rushes with their heels;
For I am proverb'd with a grandsire phrase,—
I'll be a candle-holder, and look on,—
The game was ne'er so fair, and I am done.

Mer. Tut! dun's the mouse, the constable's own word:
If thou art dun, we'll draw thee from the mire
Of this (save reverence) love, wherein thou stick'st
Up to the ears.—Come, we burn day-light, ho.

Rom. Nay, that's not so.

Mer. I mean, sir, in delay
We waste our lights in vain, like lamps by day.
Take our good meaning; for our judgment sits
Five times in that, ere once in our five wits.

Rom. And we mean well, in going to this mask.
But 'tis no wit to go.

Mer. Why, may one ask?

Rom. I dreamt a dream to-night.

Mer. And so did I.

Rom. Well, what was yours?

Mer. That dreamers often lie.

Rom. In bed asleep, while they do dream things true.

Mer. O, then, I see queen Mab hath been with you.
She is the fairies' midwife; and she comes
In shape no bigger than an agate-stone
On the forefinger of an alderman,
Drawn with a team of little atomies
Athwart men's noses as they lie asleep:
Her waggon-spokes made of long spinners' legs;
The cover, of the wings of grasshoppers;
The traces, of the smallest spider's web;
The collars, of the moonshine's watery beams:
Her whip of cricket's bone; the lash of film:
Her waggoner a small gray-coated gnat,
Not half so big as a round little worm
Prick'd from the lazy finger of a maid:
Her chariot is an empty hazel-nut,
Made by the joiner squirrel, or old grub,
Time out of mind the fairies' coach-makers.
And in this state she gallops night by night
Through lovers' brains, and then they dream of love:
On courtiers' knees, that dream on court'sies straight:
O'er lawyers' fingers, who straight dream on fees:
O'er ladies' lips, who straight on kisses dream;
Which oft the angry Mab with blisters plagues,
Because their breaths with sweet-meats tainted are.
Sometime she gallops o'er a courtier's nose,
And then dreams he of smelling out a suit:
And sometimes comes she with a tithe-pig's tail,
Tickling a parson's nose as a' lies asleep,
Then dreams he of another benefice:
Sometime she driveth o'er a soldier's neck,
And then dreams he of cutting foreign throats,
Of breaches, ambuscadoes, Spanish blades,
Of healths five fathom deep: and then anon
Drums in his ear; at which he starts, and wakes;
And, being thus frighted, swears a prayer or two,
And sleeps again. This is that very Mab,
That plats the manes of horses in the night:
And bakes the elf-locks in foul sluttish hairs,
Which, once untangled, much misfortune bodes.
This is the hag, when maids lie on their backs,
That presses them, and learns them first to bear,
Making them women of good carriage.
This, this is she—

Rom. Peace, peace, Mercutio, peace;
Thou talk'st of nothing.

Mer. True, I talk of dreams;
Which are the children of an idle brain,
Begot of nothing but vain fantasy;
Which is as thin of substance as the air;
And more inconstant than the wind, who woos
Even now the frozen bosom of the north,
And, being anger'd, puffs away from thence,
Turning his face to the dew-dropping south.
Ben. This wind, you talk of, blows us from ourselves;
Supper is done, and we shall come too late.
Rom. I fear, too early; for my mind misgives,
Some consequence, yet hanging in the stars,
Shall bitterly begin his fearful date
With this night's revels; and expire the term
Of a despised life, clos'd in my breast,
By some vile forfeit of untimely death:
But He, that hath the steerage of my course,
Direct my sail!—On, lusty gentlemen.
Ben. Strike, drum. [*Exeunt.*

SCENE V. *A Hall in* Capulet's *House.*

Musicians waiting. Enter Servants.

1 *Serv.* Where's Potpan, that he helps not to take away? he shift a trencher! he scrape a trencher!
2 *Serv.* When good manners shall lie all in one or two men's hands, and they unwashed too, 'tis a foul thing.
1 *Serv.* Away with the joint-stools, remove the court cupboard, look to the plate:—good thou, save me a piece of marchpane; and, as thou lovest me, let the porter let in Susan Grindstone, and Nell.—Antony! and Potpan!
2 *Serv.* Ay, boy; ready.
1 *Serv.* You are looked for, and called for, asked for, and sought for, in the great chamber.
2 *Serv.* We cannot be here and there too.—Cheerly, boys; be brisk a while, and the longer liver take all. [*They retire behind.*

Enter CAPULET, *&c. with the* Guests *and the* Maskers.

Cap. Gentlemen, welcome! ladies, that have their toes
Unplagu'd with corns, will have a bout with you.
Ah ha, my mistresses! which of you all
Will now deny to dance? she that makes dainty, she,
I'll swear, hath corns; Am I come near you now?
You are welcome, gentlemen! I have seen the day,
That I have worn a visor; and could tell
A whispering tale in a fair lady's ear,
Such as would please;—'tis gone, 'tis gone, 'tis gone:
You are welcome, gentlemen!—Come, musicians, play.
A hall! a hall! give room, and foot it, girls.
[*Musick plays, and they dance.*
More lights, ye knaves; and turn the tables up,
And quench the fire, the room is grown too hot.—
Ah, sirrah, this unlook'd-for sport comes well.
Nay, sit, nay, sit, good cousin Capulet;
For you and I are past our dancing days:
How long is't now, since last yourself and I
Were in a mask?
2 *Cap.* By'r lady, thirty years.
1 *Cap.* What, man! 'tis not so much, 'tis not so much:
'Tis since the nuptial of Lucentio,
Come pentecost as quickly as it will,
Some five and twenty years; and then we mask'd.
2 *Cap.* 'Tis more, 'tis more: his son is elder, sir:
His son is thirty.
1 *Cap.* Will you tell me that?
His son was but a ward two years ago.

Rom. What lady's that which doth enrich the hand
Of yonder knight?
Serv. I know not, sir.
Rom. O, she doth teach the torches to burn bright!
It seems she hangs upon the cheek of night
Like a rich jewel in an Ethiop's ear:
Beauty too rich for use, for earth too dear!
So shows a snowy dove trooping with crows,
As yonder lady o'er her fellows shows,
The measure done, I'll watch her place of stand,
And, touching hers, make happy my rude hand.
Did my heart love till now? forswear it, sight!
For I ne'er saw true beauty till this night.
Tyb. This, by his voice, should be a Montague:—
Fetch me my rapier, boy:—What! dares the slave
Come hither, cover'd with an antick face,
To fleer and scorn at our solemnity:
Now, by the stock and honour of my kin,
To strike him dead I hold it not a sin.
1 *Cap.* Why, how now, kinsman? wherefore storm you so?
Tyb. Uncle, this is a Montague, our foe;
A villain, that is hither come in spite,
To scorn at our solemnity this night.
1 *Cap.* Young Romeo is't?
Tyb. 'Tis he, that villain Romeo.
1 *Cap.* Content thee, gentle coz, let him alone,
He bears him like a portly gentleman:
And, to say truth, Verona brags of him,
To be a virtuous and well govern'd youth:
I would not for the wealth of all this town,
Here in my house, do him disparagement:
Therefore be patient, take no note of him,
It is my will; the which if thou respect,
Show a fair presence, and put off these frowns,
An ill beseeming semblance for a feast.
Tyb. It fits, when such a villain is a guest;
I'll not endure him.
1 *Cap.* He shall be endur'd;
What, goodman boy?—I say, he shall;—Go to:—
Am I the master here, or you? go to.
You'll not endure him!—God shall mend my soul—
You'll make a mutiny among my guests!
You will set cock-a-hoop! you'll be the man!
Tyb. Why, uncle, 'tis a shame.
1 *Cap.* Go to, go to.
You are a saucy boy:—Is't so, indeed?
This trick may chance to scath you:—I know what.
You must contrary me! marry, 'tis time—
Well said, my hearts:—You are a princox; go:—
Be quiet, or—More light, more light, for shame!—
I'll make you quiet; What!—Cheerly, my hearts.
Tyb. Patience perforce with wilful choler meeting
Makes my flesh tremble in their different greeting.
I will withdraw: but this intrusion shall,
Now seeming sweet, convert to bitter gall.
[*Exit.*
Rom. If I profane with my unworthy hand
[*To* JULIET.
This holy shrine, the gentle fine is this—
My lips, two blushing pilgrims, ready stand
To smooth that rough touch with a tender kiss.
Jul. Good pilgrim, you do wrong your hand too much,
Which mannerly devotion shows in this;
For saints have hands that pilgrims' hands do touch,
And palm to palm is holy palmers' kiss.
Rom. Have not saints lips, and holy palmers too?
Jul. Ay, pilgrim, lips that they must use in prayer.

Rom. O then, dear saint, let lips do what hands do;
They pray, grant thou, lest faith turn to despair.
Jul. Saints do not move, though grant for prayers' sake.
Rom. Then move not, while my prayer's effect I take.
Thus from my lips, by yours, my sin is purg'd.
[*Kissing her.*
Jul. Then have my lips the sin that they have took.
Rom. Sin from my lips? O trespass sweetly urg'd!
Give me my sin again.
Jul. You kiss by the book.
Nurse. Madam, your mother craves a word with you.
Rom. What is her mother?
Nurse. Marry, bachelor!
Her mother is the lady of the house,
And a good lady, and a wise and virtuous:
I nurs'd her daughter, that you talk'd withal:
I tell you,—he, that can lay hold of her,
Shall have the chinks.
Rom. Is she a Capulet?
O dear account! my life is my foe's debt.
Ben. Away, begone; the sport is at the best.
Rom. Ay, so I fear; the more is my unrest.
1 *Cap.* Nay, gentlemen, prepare not to be gone;
We have a trifling foolish banquet towards.—
Is it e'en so? Why, then I thank you all;
I thank you, honest gentlemen; good night:—
More torches here!—Come on, then let's to bed.
Ah, sirrah [*To* 2 *Cap.*], by my fay, it waxes late;
I'll to my rest.
[*Exeunt all but* JULIET *and* Nurse.
Jul. Come hither, nurse: What is yon gentleman?
Nurse. The son and heir of old Tiberio.
Jul. What's he, that now is going out of door?
Nurse. Marry, that, I think, be young Petruchio.
Jul. What's he, that follows there, that would not dance?
Nurse. I know not.
Jul. Go, ask his name: if he be married,
My grave is like to be my wedding bed.
Nurse. His name is Romeo, and a Montague;
The only son of your great enemy.
Jul. My only love sprung from my only hate!
Too early seen unknown, and known too late!
Prodigious birth of love it is to me,
That I must love a loathed enemy.
Nurse. What's this? what's this?
Jul. A rhyme I learn'd even now
Of one I danc'd withal.
[*One calls within,* Juliet.
Nurse. Anon, anon:—
Come, let's away; the strangers all are gone.
[*Exeunt.*

Enter CHORUS.

Now old desire doth in his deathbed lie,
And young affection gapes to be his heir;
That fair, which love groan'd for, and would die,
With tender Juliet match'd is now not fair.
Now Romeo is belov'd, and loves again,
Alike bewitched by the charm of looks;
But to his foe suppos'd he must complain,
And she steal love's sweet bait from fearful hooks:
Being held a foe, he may not have access
To breathe such vows as lovers use to swear;
And she as much in love, her means much less
To meet her new-beloved any where:
But passion lends them power, time means to meet,
Temp'ring extremities with extreme sweet.
[*Exit.*

ACT II.

SCENE I. *An open Place, adjoining* Capulet's *Garden.*

Enter ROMEO.

Rom. Can I go forward, when my heart is here?
Turn back, dull earth, and find thy centre out.
[*He climbs the Wall, and leaps down within it.*

Enter BENVOLIO *and* MERCUTIO.

Ben. Romeo! my cousin Romeo!
Mer. He is wise;
And, on my life, hath stolen him home to bed.
Ben. He ran this way, and leap'd this orchard wall:
Call, good Mercutio.
Mer. Nay, I'll conjure too.—
Romeo! humours! madman! passion! lover!
Appear thou in the likeness of a sigh,
Speak but one rhyme, and I am satisfied;
Cry but—Ah me! pronounce but—love and dove;
Speak to my gossip Venus one fair word,
One nickname for her purblind son and heir,
Young Adam Cupid, he that shot so trim,
When king Cophetua lov'd the beggar-maid.—
He heareth not, he stirreth not, he moveth not;
The ape is dead, and I must conjure him.—
I conjure thee by Rosaline's bright eyes,
By her high forehead, and her scarlet lip,
By her fine foot, straight leg, and quivering thigh,
And the demesnes that there adjacent lie,
That in thy likeness thou appear to us.
Ben. An if he hear thee, thou wilt anger him.
Mer. This cannot anger him: 'twould anger him
To raise a spirit in his mistress' circle
Of some strange nature, letting it there stand
Till she had laid it, and conjur'd it down;
That were some spite: my invocation
Is fair and honest, and, in his mistress' name,
I conjure only but to raise up him.
Ben. Come, he hath hid himself among those trees,
To be consorted with the humorous night:
Blind is his love, and best befits the dark.
Mer. If love be blind, love cannot hit the mark.
Now will he sit under a medlar tree,
And wish his mistress were that kind of fruit,
As maids call medlars, when they laugh alone.—
Romeo, good night;—I'll to my truckle-bed;
This field-bed is too cold for me to sleep:
Come, shall we go?
Ben. Go, then; for 'tis in vain
To seek him here, that means not to be found.
[*Exeunt.*

SCENE II. Capulet's *Garden.*

Enter ROMEO.

Rom. He jests at scars, that never felt a wound.—
[JULIET *appears above, at a Window.*
But, soft! what light through yonder window breaks?
It is the east, and Juliet is the sun!—
Arise, fair sun, and kill the envious moon,
Who is already sick and pale with grief,
That thou her maid art far more fair than she:
Be not her maid, since she is envious;
Her vestal livery is but sick and green,
And none but fools do wear it; cast it off.—
It is my lady; O, it is my love:
O, that she knew she were!—
She speaks, yet she says nothing; What of that?
Her eye discourses, I will answer it.
I am too bold, 'tis not to me she speaks:
Two of the fairest stars in all the heaven,
Having some business, do entreat her eyes
To twinkle in their spheres till they return.
What if her eyes were there, they in her head?

The brightness of her cheek would shame those stars,
As daylight doth a lamp; her eye in heaven
Would through the airy region stream so bright,
That birds would sing, and think it were not night.
See, how she leans her cheek upon her hand!
O, that I were a glove upon that hand,
That I might touch that cheek!

Jul. Ah me!

Rom. She speaks:—
O, speak again, bright angel! for thou art
As glorious to this sight, being o'er my head,
As is a winged messenger of heaven
Unto the white-upturned wond'ring eyes
Of mortals, that fall back to gaze on him,
When he bestrides the lazy-pacing clouds,
And sails upon the bosom of the air.

Jul. O Romeo, Romeo! wherefore art thou Romeo?
Deny thy father, and refuse thy name:
Or, if thou wilt not, be but sworn my love,
And I'll no longer be a Capulet.

Rom. Shall I hear more, or shall I speak at this? [*Aside.*

Jul. 'Tis but thy name, that is my enemy;—
Thou art thyself though, not a Montague.
What's Montague? it is nor hand, nor foot,
Nor arm, nor face, nor any other part
Belonging to a man. O, be some other name!
What's in a name? that which we call a rose,
By any other name would smell as sweet;
So Romeo would, were he not Romeo call'd,
Retain that dear perfection which he owes,
Without that title:—Romeo, doff thy name:
And for that name, which is no part of thee,
Take all myself.

Rom. I take thee at thy word:
Call me but love, and I'll be new baptiz'd;
Henceforth I never will be Romeo.

Jul. What man art thou, that, thus bescreen'd in night,
So stumblest on my counsel?

Rom. By a name
I know not how to tell thee who I am:
My name, dear saint, is hateful to myself,
Because it is an enemy to thee;
Had I it written, I would tear the word.

Jul. My ears have not yet drunk a hundred words
Of that tongue's utterance, yet I know the sound;
Art thou not Romeo, and a Montague?

Rom. Neither, fair saint, if either thee dislike.

Jul. How cam'st thou hither, tell me? and wherefore?
The orchard walls are high, and hard to climb;
And the place death, considering who thou art,
If any of my kinsmen find thee here.

Rom. With love's light wings did I o'er-perch these walls;
For stony limits cannot hold love out:
And what love can do, that dares love attempt;
Therefore thy kinsmen are no let to me.

Jul. If they do see thee, they will murder thee.

Rom. Alack! there lies more peril in thine eye,
Than twenty of their swords; look thou but sweet,
And I am proof against their enmity.

Jul. I would not for the world they saw thee here.

Rom. I have night's cloak to hide me from their sight;
And, but thou love me, let them find me here:
My life were better ended by their hate,
Than death prorogued, wanting of thy love.

Jul. By whose direction found'st thou out this place?

Rom. By love, who first did prompt me to inquire:
He lent me counsel, and I lent him eyes.
I am no pilot; yet, wert thou as far
As that vast shore wash'd with the furthest sea,
I would adventure for such merchandise.

Jul. Thou know'st, the mask of night is on my face;
Else would a maiden blush bepaint my cheek,
For that which thou hast heard me speak to-night.
Fain would I dwell on form, fain, fain deny
What I have spoke; But farewell compliment!
Dost thou love me? I know, thou wilt say—Ay;
And I will take thy word: yet, if thou swear'st,
Thou mayst prove false; at lovers' perjuries,
They say, Jove laughs. O, gentle Romeo,
If thou dost love, pronounce it faithfully:—
Or if thou think'st I am too quickly won,
I'll frown, and be perverse, and say thee nay,
So thou wilt woo: but, else, not for the world.
In truth, fair Montague, I am too fond;
And therefore thou may'st think my haviour light:
But trust me, gentleman, I'll prove more true
Than those that have more cunning to be strange.
I should have been more strange, I must confess,
But that thou overheard'st, ere I was ware,
My true love's passion: therefore pardon me;
And not impute this yielding to light love,
Which the dark night hath so discovered.

Rom. Lady, by yonder blessed moon I swear,
That tips with silver all these fruit-tree tops,—

Jul. O, swear not by the moon, the inconstant moon
That monthly changes in her circled orb,
Lest that thy love prove likewise variable.

Rom. What shall I swear by?

Jul. Do not swear at all;
Or, if thou wilt, swear by thy gracious self,
Which is the god of my idolatry,
And I'll believe thee.

Rom. If my heart's dear love—

Jul. Well, do not swear: although I joy in thee,
I have no joy of this contract to-night:
It is too rash, too unadvis'd, too sudden;
Too like the lightning, which doth cease to be,
Ere one can say—It lightens. Sweet, good night!
This bud of love, by summer's ripening breath,
May prove a beauteous flower when next we meet.
Good night, good night! as sweet repose and rest
Come to thy heart, as that within my breast!

Rom. O, wilt thou leave me so unsatisfied?

Jul. What satisfaction canst thou have to-night?

Rom. The exchange of thy love's faithful vow for mine.

Jul. I gave thee mine before thou didst request it:
And yet I would it were to give again.

Rom. Would'st thou withdraw it? for what purpose, love?

Jul. But to be frank, and give it thee again.
And yet I wish but for the thing I have:
My bounty is as boundless as the sea,
My love as deep; the more I give to thee,
The more I have, for both are infinite.
[Nurse *calls within.*
I hear some noise within; Dear love, adieu!
Anon, good nurse!—Sweet Montague, be true.
Stay, but a little, I will come again. [*Exit.*

Rom. O blessed, blessed night! I am afeard,
Being in night, all this is but a dream,
Too flattering-sweet to be substantial.

Re-enter JULIET, *above.*

Jul. Three words, dear Romeo, and good night, indeed.
If that thy bent of love be honourable,
Thy purpose marriage, send me word to-morrow,
By one that I'll procure to come to thee,
Where, and what time, thou wilt perform the rite;
And all my fortunes at thy foot I'll lay,
And follow thee my lord throughout the world:

Nurse. [*Within.*] Madam.

Jul. I come anon:—But if thou mean'st not well,
I do beseech thee,—
Nurse. [*Within.*] Madam.
Jul. By and by, I come:—
So cease thy suit, and leave me to my grief:
To-morrow will I send.
Rom. So thrive my soul,—
Jul. A thousand times good night! [*Exit.*
Rom. A thousand times the worse, to want thy light.—
Love goes toward love, as school-boys from their books;
But love from love, toward school with heavy looks. [*Retiring slowly.*

Re-enter JULIET, *above.*

Jul. Hist! Romeo, hist!—O, for a falconer's voice,
To lure this tassel-gentle back again!
Bondage is hoarse, and may not speak aloud;
Else would I tear the cave where echo lies,
And make her airy tongue more hoarse than mine
With repetition of my Romeo's name.
Rom. It is my soul, that calls upon my name;
How silver-sweet sound lovers' tongues by night,
Like softest musick to attending ears!
Jul. Romeo!
Rom. My sweet!
Jul. At what o' clock to-morrow
Shall I send to thee?
Rom. At the hour of nine.
Jul. I will not fail; 'tis twenty years till then.
I have forgot why I did call thee back.
Rom. Let me stand here till thou remember it.
Jul. I shall forget, to have thee still stand there,
Rememb'ring how I love thy company.
Rom. And I'll still stay, to have thee still forget,
Forgetting any other home but this.
Jul. 'Tis almost morning, I would have thee gone;
And yet no further than a wanton's bird;
Who lets it hop a little from her hand,
Like a poor prisoner in his twisted gyves,
And with a silk thread plucks it back again,
So loving-jealous of his liberty.
Rom. I would, I were thy bird.
Jul. Sweet, so would I;
Yet I should kill thee with much cherishing.
Good night, good night! parting is such sweet sorrow,
That I shall say—good night, till it be morrow. [*Exit.*
Rom. Sleep dwell upon thine eyes, peace in thy breast!—
'Would, I were sleep and peace, so sweet to rest!
Hence will I to my ghostly father's cell;
His help to crave, and my dear hap to tell. [*Exit.*

SCENE III. Friar Laurence's *Cell.*

Enter FRIAR LAURENCE, *with a Basket.*

Fri. The gray-ey'd morn smiles on the frowning night,
Checkering the eastern clouds with streaks of light;
And flecked darkness like a drunkard reels
From forth day's path-way, made by Titan's wheels:
Now, ere the sun advance his burning eye,
The day to cheer, and night's dank dew to dry,
I must fill up this osier cage of ours,
With baleful weeds, and precious-juiced flowers.
The earth, that's nature's mother, is her tomb;
What is her burying grave, that is her womb:
And from her womb children of divers kind
We sucking on her natural bosom find;
Many for many virtues excellent,
None but for some, and yet all different.
O, mickle is the powerful grace, that lies
In herbs, plants, stones, and their true qualities:
For nought so vile that on the earth doth live,
But to the earth some special good doth give;
Nor aught so good, but, strain'd from that fair use,
Revolts from true birth, stumbling on abuse:
Virtue itself turns vice, being misapplied;
And vice sometime's by action dignified.
Within the infant rind of this small flower
Poison hath residence, and med'cine power:
For this, being smelt, with that part cheers each part;
Being tasted, slays all senses with the heart.
Two such opposed foes encamp them still
In man as well as herbs, grace, and rude will;
And, where the worser is predominant,
Full soon the canker death eats up that plant.

Enter ROMEO.

Rom. Good morrow, father!
Fri. *Benedicite!*
What early tongue so sweet saluteth me?—
Young son, it argues a distemper'd head,
So soon to bid good morrow to thy bed:
Care keeps his watch in every old man's eye,
And where care lodges, sleep will never lie;
But where unbruised youth with unstuff'd brain
Doth couch his limbs, there golden sleep doth reign:
Therefore thy earliness doth me assure,
Thou art uprous'd by some distemp'rature;
Or if not so, then here I hit it right—
Our Romeo hath not been in bed to-night.
Rom. That last is true, the sweeter rest was mine.
Fri. God pardon sin! wast thou with Rosaline?
Rom. With Rosaline, my ghostly father? no;
I have forgot that name, and that name's woe.
Fri. That's my good son: But where hast thou been then?
Rom. I'll tell thee, ere thou ask it me again.
I have been feasting with mine enemy;
Where on a sudden, one hath wounded me,
That's by me wounded; both our remedies
Within thy help and holy physick lies:
I bear no hatred, blessed man; for, lo,
My intercession likewise steads my foe.
Fri. Be plain, good son, and homely in thy drift;
Riddling confession finds but riddling shrift.
Rom. Then plainly know, my heart's dear love is set
On the fair daughter of rich Capulet:
As mine on hers, so hers is set on mine:
And all combin'd, save what thou must combine
By holy marriage: When, and where, and how,
We met, we woo'd, and made exchange of vow,
I'll tell thee as we pass; but this I pray,
That thou consent to marry us this day.
Fri. Holy Saint Francis! what a change is here!
Is Rosaline, whom thou didst love so dear,
So soon forsaken? Young men's love then lies
Not truly in their hearts, but in their eyes.
Jesu Maria! what a deal of brine
Hath wash'd thy sallow cheeks for Rosaline!
How much salt water thrown away in waste,
To season love, that of it doth not taste!
The sun not yet thy sighs from heaven clears,
Thy old groans ring yet in my ancient ears;
Lo, here upon thy cheek the stain doth sit
Of an old tear that is not wash'd off yet:
If e'er thou wast thyself, and these woes thine,
Thou and these woes were all for Rosaline;
And art thou chang'd? pronounce this sentence then—
Women may fall, when there's no strength in men.
Rom. Thou chid'st me oft for loving Rosaline.
Fri. For doting, not for loving, pupil mine.
Rom. And bad'st me bury love.
Fri. Not in a grave,
To lay one in, another out to have.

Rom. I pray thee, chide not: she whom I love now,
Doth grace for grace, and love for love allow;
The other did not so.
Fri. O, she knew well,
Thy love did read by rote; and could not spell.
But come, young waverer, come go with me,
In one respect I'll thy assistant be;
For this alliance may so happy prove,
To turn your household's rancour to pure love.
Rom. O, let us hence; I stand on sudden haste.
Fri. Wisely, and slow; they stumble, that run fast. [*Exeunt.*

SCENE IV. *A Street.*

Enter BENVOLIO *and* MERCUTIO.

Mer. Where the devil should this Romeo be?—
Came he not home to-night?
Ben. Not to his father's; I spoke with his man.
Mer. Ah, that same pale hard-hearted wench, that Rosaline,
Torments him so, that he will sure run mad.
Ben. Tybalt, the kinsman of old Capulet,
Hath sent a letter to his father's house.
Mer. A challenge, on my life.
Ben. Romeo will answer it.
Mer. Any man, that can write, may answer a letter.
Ben. Nay, he will answer the letter's master, how he dares, being dared.
Mer. Alas, poor Romeo, he is already dead! stabbed with a white wench's black eye; shot thorough the ear with a love-song; the very pin of his heart cleft with the blind bow-boy's butt-shaft: And is he a man to encounter Tybalt?
Ben. Why, what is Tybalt?
Mer. More than prince of cats, I can tell you. O, he is the courageous captain of compliments. He fights as you sing prick-song, keeps time, distance, and proportion; rests me his minim rest, one, two, and the third in your bosom: the very butcher of a silk button, a duellist, a duellist; a gentleman of the very first house,—of the first and second cause: Ah, the immortal passado! the punto reverso! the hay!
Ben. The what?
Mer. The pox of such antick, lisping, affecting fantasticoes; these new tuners of accents!—*By Jesu, a very good blade!—a very tall man!—a very good whore!*—Why is not this a lamentable thing, grandsire, that we should be thus afflicted with these strange flies, these fashion-mongers, these *pardonnez-moys*, who stand so much on the new form, that they cannot sit at ease on the old bench? O, their *bons*, their *bons!*

Enter ROMEO.

Ben. Here comes Romeo, here comes Romeo.
Mer. Without his roe, like a dried herring;—O, flesh, flesh, how art thou fishified!—Now is he for the numbers that Petrarch flowed in: Laura, to his lady, was but a kitchen wench;—marry, she had a better love to be-rhyme her: Dido, a dowdy; Cleopatra, a gipsy; Helen and Hero, hildings and harlots; Thisbe, a gray eye or so, but not to the purpose.—Signior Romeo, *bon jour!* there's a French salutation to your French slop. You gave us the counterfeit fairly last night.
Rom. Good morrow to you both. What counterfeit did I give you?
Mer. The slip, sir, the slip: Can you not conceive?
Rom. Pardon, good Mercutio, my business was great; and, in such a case as mine, a man may strain courtesy.
Mer. That's as much as to say—such a case as yours constrains a man to bow in the hams.
Rom. Meaning—to court'sy.
Mer. Thou hast most kindly hit it.
Rom. A most courteous exposition.
Mer. Nay, I am the very pink of courtesy.
Rom. Pink for flower.
Mer. Right.
Rom. Why, then is my pump well flowered.
Mer. Well said: Follow me this jest now, till thou hast worn out thy pump; that, when the single sole of it is worn, the jest may remain, after the wearing, solely singular.
Rom. O single-soled jest, solely singular for the singleness.
Mer. Come between us, good Benvolio; my wits fail.
Rom. Switch and spurs, switch and spurs; or I'll cry a match.
Mer. Nay, if thy wits run the wild-goose chase, I have done; for thou hast more of the wild-goose in one of thy wits, than, I am sure, I have in my whole five: Was I with you there for the goose?
Rom. Thou wast never with me for any thing, when thou wast not there for the goose.
Mer. I will bite thee by the ear for that jest.
Rom. Nay, good goose, bite not.
Mer. Thy wit is a very bitter sweeting; it is a most sharp sauce.
Rom. And is it not well served in to a sweet goose?
Mer. O, here's a wit of cheveril, that stretches from an inch narrow to an ell broad!
Rom. I stretch it out for that word—broad: which added to the goose, proves thee far and wide a broad goose.
Mer. Why, is not this better now than groaning for love? now art thou sociable, now art thou Romeo; now art thou what thou art, by art as well as by nature: for this drivelling love is like a great natural, that runs lolling up and down to hide his bauble in a hole.
Ben. Stop there, stop there.
Mer. Thou desirest me to stop in my tale against the hair.
Ben. Thou would'st else have made thy tale large.
Mer. O, thou art deceiv'd, I would have made it short: for I was come to the whole depth of my tale: and meant, indeed, to occupy the argument no longer.
Rom. Here's goodly geer!

Enter NURSE *and* PETER.

Mer. A sail, a sail, a sail!
Ben. Two, two; a shirt, and a smock.
Nurse. Peter!
Peter. Anon?
Nurse. My fan, Peter.
Mer. 'Pr'ythee, do, good Peter, to hide her face; for her fan's the fairer of the two.
Nurse. God ye good morrow, gentlemen.
Mer. God ye good den, fair gentlewoman.
Nurse. Is it good den?
Mer. 'Tis no less, I tell you; for the bawdy hand of the dial is now upon the prick of noon.
Nurse. Out upon you! what a man are you?
Rom. One, gentlewoman, that God hath made himself to mar.
Nurse. By my troth, it is well said;—For himself to mar, quoth'a?—Gentlemen, can any of you tell me where I may find the young Romeo?
Rom. I can tell you; but young Romeo will be older when you have found him, than he was when you sought him: I am the youngest of that name, for 'fault of a worse.
Nurse. You say well.
Mer. Yea, is the worst well? very well took, i' faith; wisely, wisely.
Nurse. If you be he, sir, I desire some confidence with you.
Ben. She will indite him to some supper.
Mer. A bawd, a bawd, a bawd! So ho!
Rom. What hast thou found?
Mer. No hare, sir; unless a hare, sir, in a

lenten pie, that is something stale and hoar ere it be spent,

An old hare hoar,
And an old hare hoar,
Is very good meat in lent:
But a hare that is hoar,
Is too much for a score,
When it hoars ere it be spent.—

Romeo, will you come to your father's? we'll to dinner thither.

Rom. I will follow you.

Mer. Farewell, ancient lady; farewell, lady, lady, lady.

[*Exeunt* MERCUTIO *and* BENVOLIO.

Nurse. Marry, farewell! I pray you, sir, what saucy merchant was this, that was so full of his ropery?

Rom. A gentleman, nurse, that loves to hear himself talk; and will speak more in a minute, than he will stand to in a month.

Nurse. An 'a speak any thing against me, I'll take him down an 'a were lustier than he is, and twenty such Jacks; and if I cannot, I'll find those that shall. Scurvy knave! I am none of his flirt-gills; I am none of his skains-mates:— And thou must stand by too, and suffer every knave to use me at his pleasure?

Pet. I saw no man use you at his pleasure; if I had, my weapon should quickly have been out, I warrant you: I dare draw as soon as another man, if I see occasion in a good quarrel, and the law on my side.

Nurse. Now, afore God, I am so vexed, that every part about me quivers. Scurvy knave!— 'Pray you, sir, a word: and as I told you, my young lady bade me inquire you out; what she bade me say, I will keep to myself: but first let me tell ye, if ye should lead her into a fool's paradise, as they say, it were a very gross kind of behaviour, as they say: for the gentlewoman is young; and, therefore, if you should deal double with her, truly, it were an ill thing to be offered to any gentlewoman, and very weak dealing.

Rom. Nurse, commend me to thy lady and mistress. I protest unto thee,—

Nurse. Good heart! and, i'faith, I will tell her as much: Lord, lord, she will be a joyful woman.

Rom. What wilt thou tell her, nurse? thou dost not mark me.

Nurse. I will tell her, sir,—that you do protest; which, as I take it, is a gentlemanlike offer.

Rom. Bid her devise some means to come to shrift
This afternoon;
And there she shall at friar Laurence' cell
Be shriv'd, and married. Here is for thy pains.

Nurse. No, truly, sir; not a penny.

Rom. Go to; I say, you shall.

Nurse. This afternoon, sir? well, she shall be there.

Rom. And stay, good nurse, behind the abbey-wall:
Within this hour my man shall be with thee;
And bring thee cords made like a tackled stair,
Which to the high top-gallant of my joy
Must be my convoy in the secret night.
Farewell!—Be trusty, and I'll quit thy pains.
Farewell!—Commend me to thy mistress.

Nurse. Now God in heaven bless thee!—Hark you, sir.

Rom. What say'st thou, my dear nurse?

Nurse. Is your man secret? Did you ne'er hear say—
Two may keep counsel, putting one away?

Rom. I warrant thee; my man's as true as steel.

Nurse. Well, sir; my mistress is the sweetest lady,—lord, lord!—when 'twas a little prating thing,—O, there's a nobleman in town, one Paris, that would fain lay knife aboard: but she, good soul, had as lieve see a toad, a very toad, as see him. I anger her sometimes, and tell her that Paris is the properer man: but, I'll warrant you, when I say so, she looks as pale as any clout in the varsal world. Doth not rosemary and Romeo begin both with a letter?

Rom. Ay, nurse; What of that? both with an R.

Nurse. Ah, mocker! that's the dog's name. R is for the dog. No; I know it begins with some other letter: and she hath the prettiest sententious of it, of you and rosemary, that it would do you good to hear it.

Rom. Commend me to thy lady. [*Exit.*

Nurse. Ay, a thousand times.—Peter!

Pet. Anon?

Nurse. Peter, take my fan, and go before. [*Exeunt.*

SCENE V. Capulet's *Garden.*

Enter JULIET.

Jul. The clock struck nine, when I did send the nurse;
In half an hour she promis'd to return.
Perchance, she cannot meet him: that's not so.—
O, she is lame! love's heralds should be thoughts,
Which ten times faster glide than the sun's beams,
Driving back shadows over louring hills:
Therefore do nimble-pinion'd doves draw love,
And therefore hath the wind-swift Cupid wings.
Now is the sun upon the highmost hill
Of this day's journey; and from nine till twelve
Is three long hours,—yet she is not come.
Had she affections, and warm youthful blood,
She'd be as swift in motion as a ball;
My words would bandy her to my sweet love,
And his to me:
But old folks, many feign as they were dead;
Unwieldy, slow, heavy and pale as lead.

Enter Nurse *and* PETER.

O God, she comes!—O honey nurse, what news?
Hast thou met with him? Send thy man away.

Nurse. Peter, stay at the gate. [*Exit* PETER.

Jul. Now, good sweet nurse,—O lord! why look'st thou sad?
Though news be sad, yet tell them merrily;
If good, thou sham'st the musick of sweet news
By playing it to me with so sour a face.

Nurse. I am weary, give me leave awhile;—
Fye, how my bones ache! What a jaunt have I had!

Jul. I would, thou hadst my bones, and I thy news:
Nay, come, I pray thee, speak;—good, good nurse, speak.

Nurse. Jesu, what haste? can you not stay awhile?
Do you not see, that I am out of breath?

Jul. How art thou out of breath, when thou hast breath
To say to me—that thou art out of breath?
The excuse, that thou dost make in this delay,
Is longer than the tale thou dost excuse.
Is thy news good, or bad? answer to that;
Say either, and I'll stay the circumstance:
Let me be satisfied, Is't good or bad?

Nurse. Well, you have made a simple choice; you know not how to choose a man: Romeo! no, not he; though his face be better than any man's, yet his leg excels all men's; and for a hand, and a foot, and a body,—though they be not to be talked on, yet they are past compare: He is not the flower of courtesy,—but, I'll warrant him, as gentle as a lamb.—Go thy ways, wench; serve God.—What, have you dined at home?

Jul. No, no: But all this did I know before;
What says he of our marriage? what of that?

Nurse. Lord, how my head akes! what a head have I?
It beats as it would fall in twenty pieces.
My back o't'other side,—O, my back, my back!—

Beshrew your heart, for sending me about,
To catch my death with jaunting up and down!

Jul. I'faith, I am sorry that thou art not well:
Sweet, sweet, sweet nurse, tell me, what says my love?

Nurse. Your love says like an honest gentleman,
And a courteous, and a kind, and a handsome,
And, I warrant, a virtuous:—Where is your mother?

Jul. Where is my mother?—why, she is within;
Where should she be? How oddly thou repliest!
Your love says like an honest gentleman,—
Where is your mother?

Nurse. O, God's lady dear!
Are you so hot? Marry, come up, I trow;
Is this the poultice for my aking bones?
Henceforward do your messages yourself.

Jul. Here's such a coil,—come, what says Romeo?

Nurse. Have you got leave to go to shrift to-day?

Jul. I have.

Nurse. Then hie you hence to friar Laurence' cell,
There stays a husband to make you a wife:
Now comes the wanton blood up in your cheeks,
They'll be in scarlet straight at any news.
Hie you to church; I must another way,
To fetch a ladder, by the which your love
Must climb a bird's nest soon, when it is dark:
I am the drudge, and toil in your delight;
But you shall bear the burden soon at night.
Go, I'll to dinner; hie you to the cell.

Jul. Hie to high fortune!—honest nurse, farewell. [*Exeunt.*

SCENE VI. Friar Laurence's *Cell.*

Enter FRIAR LAURENCE *and* ROMEO.

Fri. So smile the heavens upon this holy act,
That after-hours with sorrow chide us not!

Rom. Amen, amen! but come what sorrow can,
It cannot countervail the exchange of joy
That one short minute gives me in her sight:
Do thou but close our hands with holy words,
Then love-devouring death do what he dare,
It is enough I may but call her mine.

Fri. These violent delights have violent ends,
And in their triumph die! like fire and powder,
Which, as they kiss, consume: The sweetest honey
Is loathsome in his own deliciousness,
And in the taste confounds the appetite:
Therefore, love moderately: long love doth so;
Too swift arrives as tardy as too slow.

Enter JULIET.

Here comes the lady:—O, so light a foot
Will ne'er wear out the everlasting flint:
A lover may bestride the gossomers
That idle in the wanton summer air,
And yet not fall; so light is vanity.

Jul. Good even to my ghostly confessor.

Fri. Romeo shall thank thee, daughter, for us both.

Jul. As much to him, else are his thanks too much.

Rom. Ah, Juliet, if the measure of thy joy
Be heap'd like mine, and that thy skill be more
To blazon it, then sweeten with thy breath
This neighbour air, and let rich musick's tongue
Unfold the imagin'd happiness that both
Receive in either by this dear encounter.

Jul. Conceit, more rich in matter than in words,
Brags of his substance, not of ornament:
They are but beggars that can count their worth;
But my true love is grown to such excess,
I cannot sum up half my sum of wealth.

Fri. Come, come with me, and we will make short work;
For, by your leaves, you shall not stay alone,
Till holy church incorporate two in one. [*Exeunt.*

ACT III.

SCENE I. *A public Place.*

Enter MERCUTIO, BENVOLIO, Page, *and* Servants.

Ben. I pray thee, good Mercutio, let's retire:
The day is hot, the Capulets abroad,
And, if we meet, we shall not 'scape a brawl;
For now, these hot days, is the mad blood stirring.

Mer. Thou art like one of those fellows, that when he enters the confines of a tavern, claps me his sword upon the table, and says, *God send me no need of thee!* and, by the operation of the second cup, draws it on the drawer, when, indeed, there is no need.

Ben. Am I like such a fellow?

Mer. Come, come, thou art as hot a Jack in thy mood as any in Italy; and as soon moved to be moody, and as soon moody to be moved.

Ben. And what to?

Mer. Nay, an there were two such, we should have none shortly, for one would kill the other. Thou! why thou wilt quarrel with a man that hath a hair more, or a hair less, in his beard, than thou hast. Thou wilt quarrel with a man for cracking nuts, having no other reason but because thou hast hazel eyes: What eye, but such an eye, would spy out such a quarrel? Thy head is as full of quarrels, as an egg is full of meat; and yet thy head hath been beaten as addle as an egg, for quarrelling. Thou hast quarrelled with a man for coughing in the street, because he hath wakened thy dog that hath lain asleep in the sun. Didst thou not fall out with a tailor for wearing his new doublet before Easter? with another, for tying his new shoes with old riband? and yet thou wilt tutor me from quarrelling!

Ben. An I were so apt to quarrel as thou art, any man should buy the fee simple of my life for an hour and a quarter.

Mer. The fee simple? O simple!

Enter TYBALT, *and Others.*

Ben. By my head, here come the Capulets.

Mer. By my heel, I care not.

Tyb. Follow me close, for I will speak to them.—
Gentlemen, good den: a word with one of you.

Mer. And but one word with one of us? Couple it with something; make it a word and a blow.

Tyb. You will find me apt enough to that, sir, if you will give me occasion.

Mer. Could you not take some occasion without giving?

Tyb. Mercutio, thou consortest with Romeo,—

Mer. Consort! what, dost thou make us minstrels? an thou make minstrels of us, look to hear nothing but discords; here's my fiddlestick; here's that shall make you dance. 'Zounds, consort!

Ben. We talk here in the public haunt of men:
Either withdraw into some private place,
Or reason coldly of your grievances,
Or else depart; here all eyes gaze on us.

Mer. Men's eyes were made to look, and let them gaze;
I will not budge for no man's pleasure, I.

Enter ROMEO.

Tyb. Well, peace be with you, sir! here comes my man.

Mer. But I'll be hanged, sir, if he wear your livery:
Marry, go before to field, he'll be your follower;
Your worship, in that sense, may call him—man.

Tyb. Romeo, the hate I bare thee can afford
No better term than this—Thou art a villain.

Rom. Tybalt, the reason that I have to love thee
Doth much excuse the appertaining rage

To such a greeting:—Villain am I none;
Therefore, farewell; I see, thou know'st me not.
Tyb. Boy, this shall not excuse the injuries
That thou hast done me; therefore turn, and draw.
Rom. I do protest, I never injured thee;
But love thee better than thou canst devise,
Till thou shalt know the reason of my love:
And so, good Capulet,—which name I tender
As dearly as mine own,—be satisfied.
Mer. O calm, dishonourable, vile submission!
A la stoccata carries it away. [*Draws.*
Tybalt, you rat catcher, will you walk?
Tyb. What would'st thou have with me?
Mer. Good king of cats, nothing but one of your nine lives; that I mean to make bold withal, and, as you shall use me hereafter, dry-beat the rest of the eight. Will you pluck your sword out of his pilcher by the ears? make haste, lest mine be about your ears ere it be out.
Tyb. I am for you. [*Drawing.*
Rom. Gentle Mercutio, put thy rapier up.
Mer. Come, sir, your passado. [*They fight.*
Rom. Draw, Benvolio:
Beat down their weapons:—Gentlemen, for shame
Forbear this outrage;—Tybalt—Mercutio—
The prince expressly hath forbid this bandying
In Verona streets:—hold, Tybalt;—good Mercutio. [*Exeunt* TYBALT *and his* Partisans.
Mer. I am hurt;—
A plague o' both the houses!—I am sped:—
Is he gone, and hath nothing?
Ben. What, art thou hurt?
Mer. Ay, ay, a scratch, a scratch; marry, 'tis enough.—
Where is my page?—go, villain, fetch a surgeon. [*Exit* Page.
Rom. Courage, man; the hurt cannot be much.
Mer. No, 'tis not so deep as a well, nor so wide as a church door; but 'tis enough, 'twill serve: ask for me to-morrow, and you shall find me a grave man. I am peppered, I warrant, for this world:—A plague o' both your houses!—Zounds, a dog, a rat, a mouse, a cat, to scratch a man to death! a braggart, a rogue, a villain, that fights by the book of arithmetic!—Why, the devil, came you between us? I was hurt under your arm.
Rom. I thought all for the best.
Mer. Help me into some house, Benvolio,
Or I shall faint.—A plague o' both your houses!
They have made worm's meat of me:
I have it, and soundly too:—Your houses!
[*Exeunt* MERCUTIO *and* BENVOLIO.
Rom. This gentleman, the prince's near ally,
My very friend, hath got his mortal hurt
In my behalf; my reputation stain'd
With Tybalt's slander, Tybalt, that an hour
Hath been my kinsman:—O sweet Juliet,
Thy beauty hath made me effeminate,
And in my temper soften'd valour's steel.

Re-enter BENVOLIO.

Ben. O Romeo, Romeo, brave Mercutio's dead;
That gallant spirit hath aspir'd the clouds,
Which too untimely here did scorn the earth.
Rom. This day's black fate on more days doth depend;
This but begins the woe, others must end.

Re-enter TYBALT.

Ben. Here comes the furious Tybalt back again.
Rom. Alive! in triumph! and Mercutio slain!
Away to heaven, respective lenity,
And fire-ey'd fury be my conduct now!—
Now, Tybalt, take the *villain* back again,
That late thou gav'st me; for Mercutio's soul
Is but a little way above our heads,
Staying for thine to keep him company;
Either thou, or I, or both, must go with him.
Tyb. Thou, wretched boy, that didst consort him here,
Shalt with him hence.
Rom. This shall determine that.
[*They fight;* TYBALT *falls.*
Ben. Romeo, away, be gone!
The citizens are up, and Tybalt slain:
Stand not amaz'd:—the prince will doom thee death,
If thou art taken:—hence!—be gone!—away!
Rom. O! I am fortune's fool!
Ben. Why dost thou stay?
[*Exit* ROMEO.

Enter Citizens, *&c.*

1 *Cit.* Which way ran he, that kill'd Mercutio?
Tybalt, that murderer, which way ran he?
Ben. There lies that Tybalt.
1 *Cit.* Up, sir, go with me;
I charge thee in the prince's name, obey.

Enter Prince, *attended;* MONTAGUE, CAPULET, *their* Wives, *and Others.*

Prin. Where are the vile beginners of this fray?
Ben. O noble prince, I can discover all
The unlucky manage of this fatal brawl:
There lies the man, slain by young Romeo,
That slew thy kinsman, brave Mercutio.
La. Cap. Tybalt, my cousin!—O my brother's child!
Unhappy sight! ah me, the blood is spill'd
Of my dear kinsman!—Prince, as thou art true,
For blood of ours, shed blood of Montague.
O cousin, cousin!
Prin. Benvolio, who began this bloody fray?
Ben. Tybalt, here slain, whom Romeo's hand did slay;
Romeo that spoke him fair, bade him bethink
How nice the quarrel was, and urg'd withal
Your high displeasure:—All this—uttered
With gentle breath, calm look, knees humbly bow'd,—
Could not take truce with the unruly spleen
Of Tybalt deaf to peace, but that he tilts
With piercing steel at bold Mercutio's breast;
Who, all as hot, turns deadly point to point,
And, with a martial scorn, with one hand beats
Cold death aside, and with the other sends
It back to Tybalt, whose dexterity
Retorts it: Romeo he cries aloud,
Hold, friends! friends, part! and, swifter than his tongue,
His agile arm beats down their fatal points,
And 'twixt them rushes; underneath whose arm
An envious thrust from Tybalt hit the life
Of stout Mercutio, and then Tybalt fled:
But by and by comes back to Romeo,
Who had but newly entertain'd revenge,
And to't they go like lightning; for, ere I
Could draw to part them, was stout Tybalt slain;
And, as he fell, did Romeo turn and fly;
This is the truth, or let Benvolio die.
La. Cap. He is a kinsman to the Montague.
Affection makes him false; he speaks not true:
Some twenty of them fought in this black strife,
And all those twenty could but kill one life:
I beg for justice, which thou, prince, must give;
Romeo slew Tybalt, Romeo must not live.
Prin. Romeo slew him, he slew Mercutio;
Who now the price of his dear blood doth owe?
Mon. Not Romeo, prince, he was Mercutio's friend;
His fault concludes but, what the law should end,
The life of Tybalt.
Prin. And, for that offence,
Immediately we do exile him hence:
I have an interest in your hates' proceeding,
My blood for your rude brawls doth lie a bleeding:
But I'll amerce you with so strong a fine,
That you shall all repent the loss of mine:
I will be deaf to pleading and excuses;
Nor tears, nor prayers, shall purchase out abuses,

Therefore use none: let Romeo hence in haste,
Else, when he's found, that hour is his last.
Bear hence his body, and attend our will:
Mercy but murders, pardoning those that kill.
[*Exeunt.*

SCENE II. *A Room in* Capulet's *House.*

Enter JULIET.

Jul. Gallop apace, you fiery-footed steeds,
Towards Phœbus' mansion; such a waggoner
As Phaeton, would whip you to the west,
And bring in cloudy night immediately.—
Spread thy close curtain, love-performing night!
That run-away's eyes may wink; and Romeo
Leap to these arms, untalk'd of, and unseen!—
Lovers can see to do their amorous rites
By their own beauties: or, if love be blind,
It best agrees with night.—Come, civil night,
Thou sober-suited matron, all in black,
And learn me how to lose a winning match,
Play'd for a pair of stainless maidenhoods:
Hood my unmann'd blood bating in my cheeks,
With thy black mantle; till strange love, grown bold,
Think true love acted, simple modesty.
Come, night!—Come, Romeo! come, thou day in night!
For thou wilt lie upon the wings of night
Whiter than new snow on a raven's back.—
Come, gentle night; come, loving, black-brow'd night,
Give me my Romeo; and, when he shall die,
Take him and cut him out in little stars,
And he will make the face of heaven so fine,
That all the world will be in love with night,
And pay no worship to the garish sun.—
O, I have bought the mansion of a love,
But not possess'd it; and, though I am sold,
Not yet enjoy'd: So tedious is this day,
As is the night before some festival,
To an impatient child, that hath new robes,
And may not wear them. O, here comes my nurse,

Enter Nurse, *with Cords.*

And she brings news: and every tongue, that speaks
But Romeo's name, speaks heavenly eloquence—
Now, nurse, what news? What hast thou there, the cords,
That Romeo bade thee fetch?
Nurse. Ay, ay, the cords.
[*Throws them down.*
Jul. Ah me! what news! why dost thou wring thy hands?
Nurse. Ah well-a-day! he's dead, he's dead, he's dead!
We are undone, lady, we are undone;
Alack the day!—he's gone, he's kill'd, he's dead!
Jul. Can heaven be so envious?
Nurse. Romeo can,
Though heaven cannot:—O Romeo! Romeo!—
Who ever would have thought it?—Romeo!
Jul. What devil art thou, that dost torment me thus?
This torture should be roar'd in dismal hell.
Hath Romeo slain himself? say thou but *I*,
And that bare vowel *I* shall poison more
Than the death-darting eye of cockatrice:
I am not I, if there be such an *I*;
Or those eyes shut, that make thee answer, *I.*
If he be slain, say—*I*; or if not, no:
Brief sounds determine of my weal, or woe.
Nurse. I saw the wound, I saw it with mine eyes,—
God save the mark!—here on his manly breast:
A piteous corse, a bloody piteous corse;
Pale, pale as ashes, all bedaub'd in blood,
All in gore blood; I swounded at the sight.
Jul. O break, my heart!—poor bankrupt, break at once!
To prison, eyes! ne'er look on liberty!
Vile earth, to earth resign; end motion here;
And thou, and Romeo, press one heavy bier!
Nurse. O Tybalt, Tybalt, the best friend I had!
O courteous Tybalt! honest gentleman!
That ever I should live to see thee dead!
Jul. What storm is this, that blows so contrary?
Is Romeo slaughter'd: and is Tybalt dead?
My dear-lov'd cousin, and my dearer lord?
Then dreadful trumpet, sound the general doom!
For who is living, if those two are gone?
Nurse. Tybalt is gone, and Romeo banished;
Romeo, that kill'd him, he is banished.
Jul. O God!—did Romeo's hand shed Tybalt's blood?
Nurse. It did, it did; alas the day! it did.
Jul. O serpent heart, hid with a flow'ring face!
Did ever dragon keep so fair a cave?
Beautiful tyrant! fiend angelical!
Dove-feather'd raven! wolvish-ravening lamb!
Despised substance of divinest show!
Just opposite to what thou justly seem'st,
A damned saint, an honourable villain!—
O, nature! what hadst thou to do in hell,
When thou didst bower the spirit of a fiend
In mortal paradise of such sweet flesh?
Was ever book, containing such vile matter,
So fairly bound? O, that deceit should dwell
In such a gorgeous palace!
Nurse. There's no trust,
No faith, no honesty in men; all perjur'd,
All forsworn, all naught, all dissemblers.—
Ah, where's my man? give me some *aqua vitæ*:—
These griefs, these woes, these sorrows make me old.
Shame come to Romeo!
Jul. Blister'd be thy tongue,
For such a wish! he was not born to shame:
Upon his brow shame is asham'd to sit;
For 'tis a throne where honour may be crown'd
Sole monarch of the universal earth.
O, what a beast was I to chide at him!
Nurse. Will you speak well of him that kill'd your cousin?
Jul. Shall I speak ill of him that is my husband?
Ah, poor my lord, what tongue shall smooth thy name,
When I, thy three-hours wife, have mangled it?—
But wherefore, villain, didst thou kill my cousin?
That villain cousin would have kill'd my husband:
Back, foolish tears, back to your native spring;
Your tributary drops belong to woe,
Which you, mistaking, offer up to joy.
My husband lives, that Tybalt would have slain;
And Tybalt's dead, that would have slain my husband:
All this is comfort: Wherefore weep I then?
Some word there was, worser than Tybalt's death,
That murder'd me; I would forget it fain;
But, O! it presses to my memory,
Like damned guilty deeds to sinners' minds;
Tybalt is dead, and Romeo—banished:
That—*banished*, that one word—*banished*,
Hath slain ten thousand Tybalts. Tybalt's death
Was woe enough, if it had ended there:
Or,—if sour woe delights in fellowship,
And needly will be rank'd with other griefs,—
Why follow'd not, when she said—Tybalt's dead,
Thy father, or thy mother, nay, or both,
Which modern lamentation might have mov'd?
But, with a rear-ward following Tybalt's death,
Romeo is banished,—to speak that word,
Is father, mother, Tybalt, Romeo, Juliet,
All slain, all dead:—*Romeo is banished*,—
There is no end, no limit, measure, bound,

In that word's death; no words can that woe sound.—
Where is my father, and my mother, nurse?

Nurse. Weeping and wailing over Tybalt's corse:
Will you go to them? I will bring you thither.

Jul. Wash they his wounds with tears? mine shall be spent,
When theirs are dry, for Romeo's banishment.
Take up those cords:—Poor ropes, you are beguil'd,
Both you and I; for Romeo is exil'd:
He made you for a highway to my bed;
But I, a maid, die maiden-widowed.
Come, cords; come, nurse; I'll to my wedding bed;
And death, not Romeo, take my maidenhead!

Nurse. Hie to your chamber: I'll find Romeo
To comfort you:—I wot well where he is.
Hark ye, your Romeo will be here at night;
I'll to him; he is hid at Laurence' cell.

Jul. O find him! give this ring to my true knight,
And bid him come to take his last farewell.
[*Exeunt.*

SCENE III. Friar Laurence's *Cell.*

Enter FRIAR LAURENCE *and* ROMEO.

Fri. Romeo, come forth; come forth, thou fearful man;
Affliction is enamour'd of thy parts,
And thou art wedded to calamity.

Rom. Father, what news? what is the prince's doom?
What sorrow craves acquaintance at my hand,
That I yet know not?

Fri. Too familiar
Is my dear son with such sour company:
I bring thee tidings of the prince's doom.

Rom. What less than dooms-day is the prince's doom?

Fri. A gentler judgment vanish'd from his lips,
Not body's death, but body's banishment.

Rom. Ha! banishment? be merciful, say—death:
For exile hath more terror in his look,
Much more than death: do not say—banishment.

Fri. Hence from Verona art thou banished:
Be patient, for the world is broad and wide.

Rom. There is no world without Verona walls,
But purgatory, torture, hell itself.
Hence-banished is banish'd from the world,
And world's exile is death:—then banishment
Is death misterm'd: calling death—banishment,
Thou cut'st my head off with a golden axe,
And smil'st upon the stroke that murders me.

Fri. O deadly sin! O rude unthankfulness!
Thy fault our law calls death; but the kind prince,
Taking thy part, hath rush'd aside the law,
And turn'd that black word death to banishment:
This is dear mercy, and thou seest it not.

Rom. 'Tis torture, and not mercy: heaven is here,
Where Juliet lives; and every cat, and dog,
And little mouse, every unworthy thing,
Live here in heaven, and may look on her,
But Romeo may not.—More validity,
More honourable state, more courtship lives
In carrion flies, than Romeo: they may seize
On the white wonder of dear Juliet's hand,
And steal immortal blessing from her lips;
Who, even in pure and vestal modesty,
Still blush, as thinking their own kisses sin;
But Romeo may not; he is banished:
Flies may do this, when I from this must fly:
They are free men, but I am banished.
And say'st thou yet, that exile is not death?
Hadst thou no poison mix'd, no sharp-ground knife,
No sudden mean of death, though ne'er so mean,
But—banished—to kill me; banished?
O friar, the damned use that word in hell;
Howlings attend it: How hast thou the heart,
Being a divine, a ghostly confessor,
A sin-absolver, and my friend profess'd,
To mangle me with that word—banishment?

Fri. Thou fond mad man, hear me but speak a word.

Rom. O, thou wilt speak again of banishment.

Fri. I'll give thee armour to keep off that word;
Adversity's sweet milk, philosophy,
To comfort thee, though thou art banished.

Rom. Yet banished?—Hang up philosophy!
Unless philosophy can make a Juliet,
Displant a town, reverse a prince's doom;
It helps not, it prevails not, talk no more.

Fri. O, then I see that madmen have no ears.

Rom. How should they, when that wise men have no eyes?

Fri. Let me dispute with thee of thy estate.

Rom. Thou canst not speak of what thou dost not feel:
Wert thou as young as I, Juliet thy love,
An hour but married, Tybalt murdered,
Doting like me, and like me banished,
Then might'st thou speak, then might'st thou tear thy hair,
And fall upon the ground, as I do now,
Taking the measure of an unmade grave.

Fri. Arise; one knocks; good Romeo, hide thyself. [*Knocking within.*

Rom. Not I; unless the breath of heart-sick groans,
Mistlike, infold me from the search of eyes.
[*Knocking.*

Fri. Hark, how they knock!—Who's there?—Romeo, arise;
Thou wilt be taken:—Stay awhile: stand up;
[*Knocking.*
Run to my study:—By and by:—God's will!
What wilfulness is this?—I come, I come.
[*Knocking.*
Who knocks so hard? whence come you? what's your will?

Nurse. [*Within.*] Let me come in, and you shall know my errand;
I come from Lady Juliet.

Fri. Welcome then.

Enter Nurse.

Nurse. O holy friar, O tell me, holy friar,
Where is my lady's lord, where's Romeo?

Fri. There on the ground, with his own tears made drunk.

Nurse. O, he is even in my mistress' case,
Just in her case!

Fri. O woful sympathy!
Piteous predicament!

Nurse. Even so lies she,
Blubbering and weeping, weeping and blubbering:—
Stand up, stand up; stand, an you be a man:
For Juliet's sake, for her sake, rise and stand;
Why should you fall into so deep an O?

Rom. Nurse!

Nurse. Ah sir! ah sir;—Well, death's the end of all.

Rom. Spak'st thou of Juliet? how is it with her?
Doth she not think me an old murderer,
Now I have stain'd the childhood of our joy
With blood remov'd but little from her own?
Where is she? and how doth she? and what says
My conceal'd lady to our cancell'd love?

Nurse. O, she says nothing, sir, but weeps and weeps;
And now falls on her bed; and then starts up,
And Tybalt calls; and then on Romeo cries,
And then falls down again.

Rom. As if that name,
Shot from the deadly level of a gun,
Did murder her; as that name's cursed hand
Murder'd her kinsman.—O tell me, friar, tell me,

In what vile part of this anatomy
Doth my name lodge? tell me, that I may sack
The hateful mansion. [*Drawing his Sword.*

Fri. Hold thy desperate hand:
Art thou a man? thy form cries out, thou art;
Thy tears are womanish; thy wild acts denote
The unreasonable fury of a beast:
Unseemly woman, in a seeming man!
Or ill beseeming beast, in seeming both!
Thou hast amaz'd me: by my holy order,
I thought thy disposition better temper'd.
Hast thou slain Tybalt? wilt thou slay thyself?
And slay thy lady too that lives in thee,
By doing damned hate upon thyself?
Why rail'st thou on thy birth, the heaven, and earth?
Since birth, and heaven, and earth, all three do meet
In thee at once; which thou at once would'st lose.
Fye, fye! thou sham'st thy shape, thy love, thy wit;
Which, like a usurer, abound'st in all,
And usest none in that true use indeed
Which should bedeck thy shape, thy love, thy wit.
Thy noble shape is but a form of wax,
Digressing from the valour of a man:
Thy dear love, sworn, but hollow perjury,
Killing that love which thou hast vow'd to cherish:
Thy wit, that ornament to shape and love,
Misshapen in the conduct of them both,
Like powder in a skill-less soldier's flask,
Is set on fire by thine own ignorance,
And thou dismember'd with thine own defence.
What, rouse thee, man! thy Juliet is alive,
For whose dear sake thou wast but lately dead;
There art thou happy: Tybalt would kill thee,
But thou slew'st Tybalt; there art thou happy too:
The law, that threaten'd death, becomes thy friend,
And turns it to exile; there art thou happy:
A pack of blessings lights upon thy back;
Happiness courts thee in her best array;
But, like a misbehav'd and sullen wench,
Thou pout'st upon thy fortune and thy love:
Take heed, take heed, for such die miserable.
Go, get thee to thy love, as was decreed,
Ascend her chamber, hence and comfort her;
But, look, thou stay not till the watch be set,
For then thou canst not pass to Mantua;
Where thou shalt live, till we can find a time
To blaze your marriage, reconcile your friends,
Beg pardon of the prince, and call thee back
With twenty hundred thousand times more joy
Than thou went'st forth in lamentation.—
Go before, nurse: commend me to thy lady;
And bid her hasten all the house to bed,
Which heavy sorrow makes them apt unto:
Romeo is coming.

Nurse. O Lord, I could have staid here all the night,
To hear good counsel: O, what learning is!—
My lord, I'll tell my lady you will come.

Rom. Do so, and bid my sweet prepare to chide.

Nurse. Here, sir, a ring she bid me give you, sir:
Hie you, make haste, for it grows very late.
[*Exit* Nurse.

Rom. How well my comfort is reviv'd by this!

Fri. Go hence: Good night! and here stands all your state;
Either be gone before the watch be set,
Or by the break of day disguis'd from hence:
Sojourn in Mantua; I'll find out your man,
And he shall signify from time to time
Every good hap to you, that chances here:
Give me thy hand; 'tis late: farewell; good night.

Rom. But that a joy past joy calls out on me,
It were a grief, so brief to part with thee;
Farewell. [*Exeunt.*

SCENE IV. *A Room in* Capulet's *House.*

Enter CAPULET, LADY CAPULET, *and* PARIS.

Cap. Things have fallen out, sir, so unluckily,
That we have had no time to move our daughter;
Look you, she lov'd her kinsman Tybalt dearly,
And so did I;—Well, we were born to die.—
'Tis very late, she'll not come down to-night:
I promise you, but for your company,
I would have been a-bed an hour ago.

Par. These times of woe afford no time to woo;
Madam, good night: commend me to your daughter.

La. Cap. I will, and know her mind early to-morrow:
To-night she's mew'd up to her heaviness.

Cap. Sir Paris, I will make a desperate tender
Of my child's love: I think, she will be rul'd
In all respects by me; nay more, I doubt it not.
Wife, go you to her ere you go to bed;
Acquaint her here of my son Paris' love;
And bid her, mark you me, on Wednesday next—
But, soft; What day is this?

Par. Monday, my lord.

Cap. Monday? ha! ha! Well Wednesday is too soon,
O' Thursday let it be;—o' Thursday, tell her,
She shall be married to this noble earl:—
Will you be ready? do you like this haste?
We'll keep no great ado;—a friend, or two:—
For hark you, Tybalt being slain so late,
It may be thought we held him carelessly,
Being our kinsman, if we revel much:
Therefore we'll have some half a dozen friends,
And there an end. But what say you to Thursday?

Par. My lord, I would that Thursday were to-morrow.

Cap. Well, get you gone:—O' Thursday be it then:—
Go you to Juliet ere you go to bed,
Prepare her, wife, against this wedding-day.—
Farewell, my lord.—Light to my chamber, ho!
Afore me, it is so very late, that we
May call it early by and by:—Good night.
[*Exeunt.*

SCENE V. Juliet's *Chamber.*

Enter ROMEO *and* JULIET.

Jul. Wilt thou be gone? it is not yet near day.
It was the nightingale, and not the lark,
That pierc'd the fearful hollow of thine ear;
Nightly she sings on yon pomegranate tree:
Believe me, love, it was the nightingale.

Rom. It was the lark, the herald of the morn,
No nightingale: look, love, what envious streaks
Do lace the severing clouds in yonder east:
Night's candles are burnt out, and jocund day
Stands tiptoe on the misty mountain tops;
I must be gone and live, or stay and die.

Jul. Yon light is not daylight, I know it, I:
It is some meteor that the sun exhales,
To be to thee this night a torch-bearer,
And light thee on thy way to Mantua:
Therefore stay yet, thou need'st not to be gone.

Rom. Let me be ta'en, let me be put to death;
I am content, so thou wilt have it so.
I'll say, yon gray is not the morning's eye,
'Tis but the pale reflex of Cynthia's brow;
Nor that is not the lark, whose notes do beat
The vaulty heaven so high above our heads;
I have more care to stay, than will to go;
Come, death, and welcome! Juliet wills it so.—
How is't, my soul? let's talk, it is not day.

Jul. It is, it is, hie hence, be gone, away:
It is the lark that sings so out of tune,
Straining harsh discords, and unpleasing sharps.
Some say, the lark makes sweet division;
This doth not so, for she divideth us:
Some say the lark and loathed toad chang'd eyes;
O, now I would they had chang'd voices too!

Since arm from arm that voice doth us affray,
Hunting thee hence with hunts-up to the day.
O, now be gone; more light and light it grows.

Rom. More light and light?—more dark and dark our woes.

Enter Nurse.

Nurse. Madam!

Jul. Nurse?

Nurse. Your lady mother's coming to your chamber:
The day is broke; be wary, look about.
[*Exit* Nurse.

Jul. Then, window, let day in, and let life out.

Rom. Farewell, farewell! one kiss, and I'll descend. [ROMEO *descends.*

Jul. Art thou gone so? my love! my lord! my friend!
I must hear from thee every day i' the hour,
For in a minute there are many days:
O, by this count I shall be much in years,
Ere I again behold my Romeo.

Rom. Farewell! I will omit no opportunity
That may convey my greetings, love, to thee.

Jul. O, think'st thou, we shall ever meet again?

Rom. I doubt it not; and all these woes shall serve
For sweet discourses in our time to come.

Jul. O God! I have an ill-divining soul:
Methinks, I see thee, now thou art below,
As one dead in the bottom of a tomb:
Either my eyesight fails, or thou look'st pale.

Rom. And trust me, love, in my eyes so do you:
Dry sorrow drinks our blood. Adieu! adieu!
[*Exit* ROMEO.

Jul. O fortune, fortune! all men call thee fickle:
If thou art fickle, what dost thou with him
That is renown'd for faith? Be fickle, fortune;
For then, I hope, thou wilt not keep him long,
But send him back.

La. Cap. [*Within.*] Ho, daughter! are you up?

Jul. Who is't that calls? is it my lady mother?
Is she not down so late, or up so early?
What unaccustom'd cause procures her hither?

Enter LADY CAPULET.

La. Cap. Why, how now, Juliet?

Jul. Madam, I am not well.

La. Cap. Evermore weeping for your cousin's death?
What, wilt thou wash him from his grave with tears?
An if thou could'st, thou could'st not make him live;
Therefore, have done: Some grief shows much of love:
But much of grief shows still some want of wit.

Jul. Yet let me weep for such a feeling loss.

La. Cap. So shall you feel the loss, but not the friend
Which you weep for.

Jul. Feeling so the loss,
I cannot choose but ever weep the friend.

La. Cap. Well, girl, thou weep'st not so much for his death,
As that the villain lives which slaughter'd him.

Jul. What villain, madam?

La. Cap. That same villain, Romeo.

Jul. Villain and he are many miles asunder.
God pardon him! I do with all my heart;
And yet no man, like he, doth grieve my heart.

La. Cap. That is, because the traitor murderer lives.

Jul. Ay, madam, from the reach of these my hands.
'Would, none but I might venge my cousin's death!

La. Cap. We will have vengeance for it, fear thou not:
Then weep no more. I'll send to one in Mantua,—
Where that same banish'd runagate doth live,—
That shall bestow on him so sure a draught,
That he shall soon keep Tybalt company:
And then, I hope, thou wilt be satisfied.

Jul. Indeed, I never shall be satisfied
With Romeo, till I behold him—dead—
Is my poor heart so for a kinsman vex'd:—
Madam, if you could find out but a man
To bear a poison, I would temper it;
That Romeo should, upon receipt thereof,
Soon sleep in quiet.—O, how my heart abhors
To hear him nam'd,—and cannot come to him,—
To wreak the love I bore my cousin Tybalt
Upon his body that hath slaughter'd him!

La. Cap. Find thou the means, and I'll find such a man.
But now I'll tell thee joyful tidings, girl.

Jul. And joy comes well in such a needful time:
What are they, I beseech your ladyship?

La. Cap. Well, well, thou hast a careful father, child:
One, who, to put thee from thy heaviness,
Hath sorted out a sudden day of joy,
That thou expect'st not, nor I look'd not for.

Jul. Madam, in happy time, what day is that?

La. Cap. Marry, my child, early next Thursday morn,
The gallant, young, and noble gentleman,
The county Paris, at Saint Peter's church,
Shall happily make thee there a joyful bride.

Jul. Now, by Saint Peter's church, and Peter too,
He shall not make me there a joyful bride.
I wonder at this haste; that I must wed
Ere he, that should be husband, comes to woo.
I pray you, tell my lord and father, madam,
I will not marry yet; and when I do, I swear,
It shall be Romeo, whom you know I hate,
Rather than Paris:—These are news indeed!

La. Cap. Here comes your father; tell him so yourself,
And see how he will take it at your hands.

Enter CAPULET *and* Nurse.

Cap. When the sun sets the air doth drizzle dew;
But for the sunset of my brother's son,
It rains downright.—
How now, a conduit, girl? what, still in tears?
Ever more showering? In one little body
Thou counterfeit'st a bark, a sea, a wind:
For still thy eyes, which I may call the sea,
Do ebb and flow with tears; the bark thy body is,
Sailing in this salt flood; the winds, thy sighs;
Who, raging with thy tears, and they with them,—
Without a sudden calm will overset
Thy tempest-tossed body.—How now, wife?
Have you deliver'd to her our decree?

La. Cap. Ay, sir; but she will none, she gives you thanks.
I would, the fool were married to her grave!

Cap. Soft, take me with you, take me with you, wife.
How! will she none? doth she not give us thanks?
Is she not proud? doth she not count her bless'd,
Unworthy as she is, that we have wrought
So worthy a gentleman to be her bridegroom?

Jul. Not proud, you have; but thankful, that you have;
Proud can I never be of what I hate;
But thankful even for hate, that is made love.

Cap. How now! how now, chop-logick! What is this?
Proud,—and, I thank you,—and, I thank you not;
And yet not proud;—Mistress minion, you,
Thank me no thankings, nor proud me no prouds,
But settle your fine joints 'gainst Thursday next,
To go with Paris to Saint Peter's church,
Or I will drag thee on a hurdle thither.
Out, you green sickness carrion! out, you baggage!
You tallow face!

La. Cap. Fye, fye! what are you mad?
Jul. Good father, I beseech you on my knees,
Hear me with patience but to speak a word.
Cap. Hang thee, young baggage! disobedient wretch!
I tell thee what,—get thee to church o' Thursday,
Or never after look me in the face:
Speak not, reply not, do not answer me:
My fingers itch.—Wife, we scarce thought us bless'd,
That God had sent us but this only child;
But now I see this one is one too much,
And that we have a curse in having her:
Out on her, hilding!
Nurse. God in heaven bless her!—
You are to blame, my lord, to rate her so.
Cap. And why, my lady wisdom? hold your tongue,
Good prudence; smatter with your gossips, go.
Nurse. I speak no treason.
Cap. O, God ye good den!
Nurse. May not one speak?
Cap. Peace, you mumbling fool!
Utter your gravity o'er a gossip's bowl,
For here we need it not.
La. Cap. You are too hot.
Cap. God's bread! it makes me mad: Day, night, late, early,
At home, abroad, alone, in company,
Waking, or sleeping, still my care hath been
To have her match'd: and having now provided
A gentleman of princely parentage,
Of fair demesnes, youthful, and nobly train'd,
Stuff'd (as they say,) with honourable parts,
Proportion'd as one's heart could wish a man,—
And then to have a wretched puling fool,
A whining mammet, in her fortune's tender,
To answer—*I'll not wed,—I cannot love,*
I am too young,—I pray you, pardon me;—
But, an you will not wed, I'll pardon you;
Graze where you will, you shall not house with me;
Look to't, think on't, I do not use to jest.
Thursday is near; lay hand on heart, advise:
An you be mine, I'll give you to my friend;
An you be not, hang, beg, starve, die i'the streets,
For, by my soul, I'll ne'er acknowledge thee,
Nor what is mine shall never do thee good:
Trust to't, bethink you, I'll not be forsworn. [*Exit.*
Jul. Is there no pity sitting in the clouds,
That sees into the bottom of my grief?
O, sweet my mother, cast me not away!
Delay this marriage for a month, a week;
Or, if you do not, make the bridal bed
In that dim monument where Tybalt lies.
La. Cap. Talk not to me, for I'll not speak a word;
Do as thou wilt, for I have done with thee. [*Exit.*
Jul. O God!—O nurse! how shall this be prevented?
My husband is on earth, my faith in heaven;
How shall that faith return again to earth,
Unless that husband send it me from heaven
By leaving earth?—comfort me, counsel me.—
Alack, alack, that heaven should practise stratagems
Upon so soft a subject as myself?—
What say'st thou? hast thou not a word of joy?
Some comfort, nurse.
Nurse. 'Faith, here 'tis: Romeo
Is banished; and all the world to nothing,
That he dares ne'er come back to challenge you;
Or, if he do, it needs must be by stealth.
Then, since the case so stands as now it doth,
I think it best you married with the county.
O, he's a lovely gentleman!
Romeo's a dishclout to him; an eagle, madam,
Hath not so green, so quick, so fair an eye,
As Paris hath. Beshrew my very heart,
I think you are happy in this second match,
For it excels your first: or if it did not,
Your first is dead: or 'twere as good he were,
As living here, and you no use of him.
Jul. Speakest thou from thy heart?
Nurse. From my soul too;
Or else beshrew them both.
Jul. Amen!
Nurse. To what?
Jul. Well, thou hast comforted me marvellous much.
Go in; and tell my lady I am gone,
Having displeas'd my father, to Laurence' cell,
To make confession, and to be absolv'd.
Nurse. Marry, I will; and this is wisely done. [*Exit.*
Jul. Ancient damnation! O most wicked fiend!
Is it more sin—to wish me thus forsworn,
Or to dispraise my lord with that same tongue
Which she hath prais'd him with above compare
So many thousand times?—Go, counsellor;
Thou and my bosom henceforth shall be twain.—
I'll to the friar, to know his remedy;
If all else fail, myself have power to die. [*Exit.*

ACT IV.

SCENE I. Friar Laurence's *Cell.*

Enter FRIAR LAURENCE *and* PARIS.

Fri. On Thursday, sir? the time is very short.
Par. My father Capulet will have it so;
And I am nothing slow, to slack his haste.
Fri. You say, you do not know the lady's mind;
Uneven is the course, I like it not.
Par. Immoderately she weeps for Tybalt's death,
And therefore have I little talk'd of love;
For Venus smiles not in a house of tears.
Now, sir, her father counts it dangerous,
That she doth give her sorrow so much sway;
And, in his wisdom, hastes our marriage,
To stop the inundation of her tears;
Which, too much minded by herself alone,
May be put from her by society:
Now do you know the reason of this haste.
Fri. I would, I knew not why it should be slow'd. [*Aside.*
Look, sir, here comes the lady towards my cell.

Enter JULIET.

Par. Happily met, my lady, and my wife!
Jul. That may be, sir, when I may be a wife.
Par. That may be, must be, love, on Thursday next.
Jul. What must be shall be.
Fri. That's a certain text.
Par. Come you to make confession to this father?
Jul. To answer that, were to confess to you.
Par. Do not deny to him, that you love me.
Jul. I will confess to you, that I love him.
Par. So will you, I am sure, that you love me.
Jul. If I do so, it will be of more price,
Being spoke behind your back, than to your face.
Par. Poor soul, thy face is much abus'd with tears.
Jul. The tears have got small victory by that;
For it was bad enough before their spite.
Par. Thou wrong'st it, more than tears, with that report.
Jul. That is no slander, sir, that is a truth;
And what I spake, I spake it to my face.
Par. Thy face is mine, and thou hast slander'd it.
Jul. It may be so, for it is not mine own.—
Are you at leisure, holy father, now;
Or shall I come to you at evening mass?
Fri. My leisure serves me, pensive daughter, now:—
My lord, we must entreat the time alone.
Par. God shield, I should disturb devotion:—
Juliet, on Thursday early will I rouse you:
Till then, adieu! and keep this holy kiss. [*Exit.*

Jul. O, shut the door! and when thou hast done so,
Come weep with me; Past hope, past cure, past help!

Fri. Ah, Juliet, I already know thy grief;
It strains me past the compass of my wits:
I hear thou must, and nothing must prorogue it,
On Thursday next be married to this county.

Jul. Tell me not, friar, that thou hear'st of this,
Unless thou tell me how I may prevent it:
If, in thy wisdom, thou canst give no help,
Do thou but call my resolution wise,
And with this knife I'll help it presently.
God join'd my heart and Romeo's, thou our hands;
And ere this hand, by thee to Romeo seal'd,
Shall be the label to another deed,
Or my true heart with treacherous revolt
Turn to another, this shall slay them both:
Therefore, out of thy long-experienc'd time,
Give me some present counsel; or, behold
'Twixt my extremes and me this bloody knife
Shall play the umpire; arbitrating that
Which the commission of thy years and art
Could to no issue of true honour bring.
Be not so long to speak; I long to die,
If what thou speak'st speak not of remedy.

Fri. Hold, daughter; I do spy a kind of hope,
Which craves as desperate an execution
As that is desperate which we would prevent.
If, rather than to marry county Paris,
Thou hast the strength of will to slay thyself;
Then is it likely, thou wilt undertake
A thing like death to chide away this shame,
That cop'st with death himself to scape from it;
And, if thou dar'st, I'll give thee remedy.

Jul. O, bid me leap, rather than marry Paris,
From off the battlements of yonder tower;
Or walk in thievish ways; or bid me lurk
Where serpents are; chain me with roaring bears;
Or shut me nightly in a charnel-house,
O'er-cover'd quite with dead men's rattling bones,
With reeky shanks, and yellow chapless sculls;
Or bid me go into a new made grave,
And hide me with a dead man in his shroud;
Things that, to hear them told, have made me tremble;
And I will do it without fear or doubt,
To live an unstain'd wife to my sweet love.

Fri. Hold, then; go home, be merry, give consent
To marry Paris: Wednesday is to-morrow;
To-morrow night look that thou lie alone,
Let not thy nurse lie with thee in thy chamber;
Take thou this phial, being then in bed,
And this distilled liquor drink thou off;
When presently, through all thy veins shall run
A cold and drowsy humour, which shall seize
Each vital spirit; for no pulse shall keep
His natural progress, but surcease to beat:
No warmth, no breath, shall testify thou liv'st;
The roses in thy lips and cheeks shall fade
To paly ashes; thy eyes' windows fall,
Like death, when he shuts up the day of life;
Each part depriv'd of supple government,
Shall, stiff, and stark, and cold, appear like death:
And in this borrow'd likeness of shrunk death
Thou shalt remain full two and forty hours,
And then awake as from a pleasant sleep.
Now when the bridegroom in the morning comes
To rouse thee from thy bed, there art thou dead:
Then (as the manner of our country is)
In thy best robes uncover'd on the bier,
Thou shalt be borne to that same ancient vault,
Where all the kindred of the Capulets lie.
In the mean time against thou shalt awake,
Shall Romeo by my letters know our drift;
And hither shall he come; and he and I
Will watch thy waking, and that very night
Shall Romeo bear thee hence to Mantua.
And this shall free thee from this present shame;
If no unconstant toy, or womanish fear,
Abate thy valour in the acting it.

Jul. Give me, O give me! tell me not of fear.

Fri. Hold; get you gone, be strong and prosperous
In this resolve: I'll send a friar with speed
To Mantua, with my letters to thy lord.

Jul. Love, give me strength! and strength shall help afford.
Farewell, dear father! [*Exeunt.*

SCENE II. *A Room in* Capulet's *House.*

Enter CAPULET, LADY CAPULET, Nurse, *and* Servants.

Cap. So many guests invite as here are writ.— [*Exit* Servant.
Sirrah, go hire me twenty cunning cooks.

2 Serv. You shall have none ill, sir; for I'll try if they can lick their fingers.

Cap. How canst thou try them so?

2 Serv. Marry sir, 'tis an ill cook that cannot lick his own fingers: therefore he, that cannot lick his fingers, goes not with me.

Cap. Go, begone.— [*Exit* Servant.
We shall be much unfurnished for this time.—
What, is my daughter gone to friar Laurence?

Nurse. Ay, forsooth.

Cap. Well, he may chance to do some good on her:
A peevish self-will'd harlotry it is.

Enter JULIET.

Nurse. See, where she comes from shrift with merry look.

Cap. How now, my headstrong? where have you been gadding?

Jul. Where I have learn'd me to repent the sin
Of disobedient opposition
To you, and your behests; and am enjoin'd
By holy Laurence to fall prostrate here,
And beg your pardon:—Pardon, I beseech you!
Henceforward I am ever rul'd by you.

Cap. Send for the county: go tell him of this;
I'll have this knot knit up to-morrow morning.

Jul. I met the youthful lord at Laurence' cell;
And gave him what becomed love I might,
Not stepping o'er the bounds of modesty.

Cap. Why, I am glad on't; this is well,—stand up:
This is as't should be.—Let me see the county;
Ay, marry, go, I say, and fetch him hither.—
Now, afore God, this reverend holy friar,
All our whole city is much bound to him.

Jul. Nurse, will you go with me into my closet,
To help me sort such needful ornaments
As you think fit to furnish me to-morrow?

La. Cap. No, not till Thursday; there is time enough.

Cap. Go, nurse, go with her:—we'll to church to-morrow. [*Exeunt* JULIET *and* Nurse.

La. Cap. We shall be short in our provision;
'Tis now near night.

Cap. Tush! I will stir about,
And all things shall be well, I warrant thee, wife:
Go thou to Juliet, help to deck up her;
I'll not to bed to-night;—let me alone;
I'll play the housewife for this once.—What, ho!
They are all forth: Well, I will walk myself
To county Paris, to prepare him up
Against to-morrow: my heart is wondrous light,
Since this same wayward girl is so reclaim'd.
[*Exeunt.*

SCENE III. Juliet's *Chamber.*

Enter JULIET *and* Nurse.

Jul. Ay, those attires are best:—But, gentle nurse,
I pray thee, leave me to myself to night;
For I have need of many orisons

To move the heavens to smile upon my state,
Which, well thou know'st, is cross and full of sin.

Enter LADY CAPULET.

La. Cap. What, are you busy? do you need my help?

Jul. No, madam; we have cull'd such necessaries
As are behoveful for our state to-morrow;
So please you, let me now be left alone,
And let the nurse this night sit up with you;
For, I am sure, you have your hands full all,
In this so sudden business.

La. Cap. Good night!
Get thee to bed, and rest; for thou hast need.
[*Exeunt* LADY CAPULET *and* Nurse.

Jul. Farewell!—God knows, when we shall meet again.
I have a faint cold fear thrills through my veins
That almost freezes up the heat of life:
I'll call them back again to comfort me:—
Nurse!—What should she do here?
My dismal scene I needs must act alone.—
Come, phial.—
What if this mixture do not work at all?
Must I of force be married to the county?—
No, no;—this shall forbid it:—lie thou there.—
[*Laying down a Dagger.*
What if it be a poison, which the friar
Subtly hath minister'd to have me dead;
Lest in this marriage he should be dishonour'd,
Because he married me before to Romeo?
I fear, it is: and yet, methinks, it should not,
For he hath still been tried a holy man:
I will not entertain so bad a thought.—
How if, when I am laid into the tomb,
I wake before the time that Romeo
Come to redeem me? there's a fearful point!
Shall I not then be stifled in the vault,
To whose foul mouth no healthsome air breathes in,
And there die strangled ere my Romeo comes?
Or, if I live, is it not very like,
The horrible conceit of death and night,
Together with the terror of the place,—
As in a vault, an ancient receptacle,
Where, for these many hundred years, the bones
Of all my buried ancestors are pack'd;
Where bloody Tybalt, yet but green in earth,
Lies fest'ring in his shroud; where, as they say,
At some hours in the night spirits resort;—
Alack, alack! is it not like, that I,
So early waking,—what with loathsome smells,
And shrieks like mandrakes torn out of the earth,
That living mortals hearing them run mad;—
O! if I wake, shall I not be distraught,
Environed with all these hideous fears?
And madly play with my forefathers' joints?
And pluck the mangled Tybalt from his shroud?
And, in this rage, with some great kinsman's bone,
As with a club, dash out my desperate brains?
O, look! methinks, I see my cousin's ghost
Seeking out Romeo, that did spit his body
Upon a rapier's point:—Stay, Tybalt, stay!—
Romeo, I come! this do I drink to thee.
[*She throws herself on the Bed.*

SCENE IV. Capulet's *Hall.*

Enter LADY CAPULET *and* Nurse.

La. Cap. Hold, take these keys, and fetch more spices, nurse.

Nurse. They call for dates and quinces in the pastry. [*Exit* Nurse.

Enter CAPULET.

Cap. Come, stir, stir, stir! the second cock hath crow'd,
The curfew bell hath rung, 'tis three o'clock:—
Look to the bak'd meats, good Angelica:
Spare not for cost.

La. Cap. Go, go, you cot-quean, go,
Get you to bed; 'faith, you'll be sick to-morrow
For this night's watching.

Cap. No, not a whit; What! I have watch'd ere now
All night for lesser cause, and ne'er been sick.

La. Cap. Ay, you have been a mouse-hunt in your time;
But I will watch you from such watching now.
[*Exit* LADY CAPULET.

Cap. A jealous-hood, a jealous-hood!—Now, fellow,
What's there?

Enter Servants, *with Spits, Logs, and Baskets.*

1 *Serv.* Things for the cook, sir; but I know not what.

Cap. Make haste, make haste. [*Exit* 1 Serv.
—Sirrah, fetch drier logs;
Call Peter, he will show thee where they are.

2 *Serv.* I have a head, sir, that will find out logs,
And never trouble Peter for the matter. [*Exit.*

Cap. 'Mass, and well said; A merry whoreson! ha,
Thou shalt be logger-head.—Good faith, 'tis day:
The county will be here with musick straight.
[*Musick within.*
For so he said he would. I hear him near:—
Nurse!—Wife!—what ho!—what, nurse, I say!

Enter Nurse.

Go, waken Juliet, go, and trim her up;
I'll go and chat with Paris:—Hie, make haste,
Make haste! the bridegroom he is come already:
Make haste, I say! [*Exeunt.*

SCENE V. Juliet's *Chamber;* JULIET *on the Bed.*

Enter Nurse.

Nurse. Mistress!—what, mistress!—Juliet!—fast, I warrant her, she:—
Why, lamb! why, lady;—fye, you slug-a-bed!—
Why, love, I say!—madam! sweet-heart; why, bride!
What, not a word?—you take your pennyworths now;
Sleep for a week; for the next night, I warrant,
The county Paris hath set up his rest,
That you shall rest but little.—God forgive me,
(Marry and amen!) how sound is she asleep!
I needs must wake her:—Madam, madam, madam!
Ay, let the county take you in your bed;
He'll fright you up, i'faith.—Will it not be?
What, drest! and in your clothes! and down again!
I must needs wake you: Lady! lady! lady!
Alas! alas!—Help! help! my lady's dead!—
O, well-a-day, that ever I was born!—
Some aqua-vitæ, ho!—my lord! my lady!

Enter LADY CAPULET.

La. Cap. What noise is here?

Nurse. O lamentable day!

La. Cap. What is the matter?

Nurse. Look, look! O heavy day!

La. Cap. O me, O me!—my child, my only life,
Revive, look up, or I will die with thee!—
Help, help!—call help.

Enter CAPULET.

Cap. For shame, bring Juliet forth; her lord is come.

Nurse. She's dead, deceas'd, she's dead; alack the day!

La. Cap. Alack the day! she's dead, she's dead, she's dead.

Cap. Ha! let me see her:—Out, alas! she's cold;
Her blood is settled; and her joints are stiff;
Life and these lips have long been separated:
Death lies on her, like an untimely frost
Upon the sweetest flower of all the field.
Accursed time! unfortunate old man!

Nurse. O lamentable day!

La. Cap. O woful time!

Cap. Death, that hath ta'en her hence to make me wail,
Ties up my tongue, and will not let me speak.

Enter FRIAR LAURENCE *and* PARIS, *with* Musicians.

Fri. Come, is the bride ready to go to church?
Cap. Ready to go, but never to return:
O son, the night before thy wedding-day
Hath death lain with thy bride:—See, there she lies,
Flower as she was, deflowered by him.
Death is my son-in-law, death is my heir;
My daughter he hath wedded! I will die,
And leave him all; life leaving, all is death's.
Par. Have I thought long to see this morning's face,
And doth it give me such a sight as this?
La. Cap. Accurs'd, unhappy, wretched, hateful day!
Most miserable hour that e'er time saw
In lasting labour of his pilgrimage!
But one, poor one, one poor and loving child,
But one thing to rejoice and solace in,
And cruel death hath catch'd it from my sight.
Nurse. O woe! O woful, woful, woful day!
Most lamentable day! most woful day,
That ever, ever, I did yet behold!
O day! O day! O day! O hateful day!
Never was seen so black a day as this:
O woful day, O woful day!
Par. Beguil'd, divorced, wronged, spited, slain,
Most detestable death by thee beguil'd,
By cruel, cruel thee quite overthrown!—
O love! O life!—not life, but love in death!
Cap. Despis'd, distressed, hated, martyr'd, kill'd!—
Uncomfortable time! why cam'st thou now
To murder murder our solemnity?—
O child! O child!—my soul, and not my child!—
Dead art thou, dead!—alack! my child is dead;
And, with my child, my joys are buried!
Fri. Peace, ho, for shame! confusion's cure lives not
In these confusions. Heaven and yourself
Had part in this fair maid; now heaven hath all,
And all the better is it for the maid:
Your part in her you could not keep from death;
But heaven keeps his part in eternal life.
The most you sought was—her promotion;
For 'twas your heaven, she should be advanc'd:
And weep ye now, seeing she is advanc'd,
Above the clouds, as high as heaven itself?
O, in this love, you love your child so ill,
That you run mad, seeing that she is well:
She's not well married, that lives married long;
But she's best married, that dies married young.
Dry up your tears, and stick your rosemary
On this fair corse; and, as the custom is,
In all her best array bear her to church:
For though fond nature bids us all lament,
Yet nature's tears are reason's merriment.
Cap. All things that we ordained festival,
Turn from their office to black funeral;
Our instruments, to melancholy bells;
Our wedding cheer, to a sad burial feast;
Our solemn hymns to sullen dirges change;
Our bridal flowers serve for a buried corse,
And all things change them to the contrary.
Fri. Sir, go you in,—and, madam, go with him;—
And go, sir Paris;—every one prepare
To follow this fair corse unto her grave:
The heavens do lour upon you, for some ill;
Move them no more, by crossing their high will.
[*Exeunt* CAP. LADY CAP. PARIS, *and* Friar.

1 *Mus.* 'Faith, we may put up our pipes, and be gone.
Nurse. Honest good fellows, ah, put up; put up:
For, well you know, this is a pitiful case. [*Exit.*

1 *Mus.* Ay, by my troth, the case may be amended.

Enter PETER.

Pet. Musicians, O, musicians, *Heart's ease, heart's ease;* O, an you will have me live, play —*heart's ease.*
1 *Mus.* Why *heart's ease?*
Pet. O, musicians, because my heart itself plays—*My heart is full of woe.* O, play me some merry dump, to comfort me.
2 *Mus.* Not a dump we; 'tis no time to play now.
Pet. You will not then?
Mus. No.
Pet. I will then give it you soundly.
1 *Mus.* What will you give us?
Pet. No money, on my faith; but the gleek: I will give you the minstrel.
1 *Mus.* Then will I give you the serving-creature.
Pet. Then will I lay the serving-creature's dagger on your pate. I will carry no crotchets: I'll *re* you, I'll *fa* you; Do you note me?
1 *Mus.* An you *re* us, and *fa* us, you note us.
2 *Mus.* 'Pray you, put up your dagger, and put out your wit.
Pet. Then have at you with my wit; I will dry-beat you with an iron wit, and put up my iron dagger:—Answer me like men:

When griping grief the heart doth wound,
And doleful dumps the mind oppress,
Then musick with her silver sound—

Why, *silver sound?* why, *musick with her silver sound?*
What say you, Simon Catling?
1 *Mus.* Marry, sir, because silver hath a sweet sound.
Pet. Pretty! What say you, Hugh Rebeck?
2 *Mus.* I say—*silver sound,* because musicians sound for silver.
Pet. Pretty too!—What say you, James Soundpost?
3 *Mus.* 'Faith, I know not what to say.
Pet. O, I cry you mercy! you are the singer: I will say for you. It is—*musick with her silver sound,* because such fellows as you have seldom gold for sounding:—

Then musick with her silver sound
With speedy help doth lend redress.
[*Exit, singing.*

1 *Mus.* What a pestilent knave is this same!
2 *Mus.* Hang him, Jack! Come, we'll in here; tarry for the mourners, and stay dinner.
[*Exeunt.*

ACT V.

SCENE I. Mantua. *A Street.*

Enter ROMEO.

Rom. If I may trust the flattering eye of sleep,
My dreams presage some joyful news at hand:
My bosom's lord sits lightly in his throne;
And, all this day, an unaccustom'd spirit
Lifts me above the ground with cheerful thoughts.
I dreamt, my lady came and found me dead
(Strange dream! that gives a dead man leave to think);
And breath'd such life with kisses in my lips,
That I reviv'd, and was an emperor.
Ah me! how sweet is love itself possess'd,
When but love's shadows are so rich in joy!

Enter BALTHASAR.

News from Verona!—How now, Balthasar?
Dost thou not bring me letters from the friar?
How doth my lady? Is my father well?
How fares my Juliet? That I ask again;
For nothing can be ill, if she be well.
Bal. Then she is well, and nothing can be ill;

Her body sleeps in Capel's monument,
And her immortal part with angels lives;
I saw her laid low in her kindred's vault,
And presently took post to tell it you;
O pardon me for bringing these ill news,
Since you did leave it for my office, sir.

Rom. Is it even so? then I defy you, stars!—
Thou know'st my lodging: get me ink and paper,
And hire post-horses; I will hence to-night.

Bal. Pardon me, sir, I will not leave you thus:
Your looks are pale and wild, and do import
Some misadventure.

Rom. Tush, thou art deceiv'd;
Leave me, and do the thing I bid thee do;
Hast thou no letters to me from the friar?

Bal. No, my good lord.

Rom. No matter: get thee gone,
And hire those horses; I'll be with thee straight.
[*Exit* BALTHASAR.

Well, Juliet, I will lie with thee to-night.
Let's see for means:—O, mischief! thou art swift
To enter in the thoughts of desperate men!
I do remember an apothecary,—
And hereabouts he dwells,—whom late I noted
In tatter'd weeds, with overwhelming brows,
Culling of simples; meagre were his looks,
Sharp misery had worn him to the bones:
And in his needy shop a tortoise hung,
An alligator stuff'd, and other skins
Of ill shap'd fishes; and about his shelves
A beggarly account of empty boxes,
Green earthen pots, bladders, and musty seeds,
Remnants of packthread, and old cakes of roses,
Were thinly scatter'd, to make up a show.
Noting this penury, to myself I said—
And if a man did need a poison now,
Whose sale is present death in Mantua,
Here lives a caitiff wretch would sell it him.
O, this same thought did but forerun my need;
And this same needy man must sell it me.
As I remember, this should be the house;
Being holiday, the beggar's shop is shut,—
What, ho! apothecary!

Enter Apothecary.

Ap. Who calls so loud?

Rom. Come hither, man.—I see, that thou art poor;
Hold, there is forty ducats; let me have
A dram of poison; such soon-speeding geer
As will disperse itself through all the veins,
That the life-weary taker may fall dead;
And that the trunk may be discharg'd of breath
As violently, as hasty powder fir'd
Doth hurry from the fatal cannon's womb.

Ap. Such mortal drugs I have; but Mantua's law
Is death, to any he that utters them.

Rom. Art thou so bare, and full of wretchedness,
And fear'st to die? famine is in thy cheeks,
Need and oppression stareth in thy eyes,
Upon thy back hangs ragged misery,
The world is not thy friend, nor the world's law:
The world affords no law to make thee rich;
Then be not poor, but break it, and take this.

Ap. My poverty, but not my will, consents.

Rom. I pay thy poverty, and not thy will.

Ap. Put this in any liquid thing you will,
And drink it off; and, if you had the strength
Of twenty men, it would despatch you straight.

Rom. There is thy gold, worse poison to men's souls,
Doing more murders in this loathsome world,
Than these poor compounds that thou may'st not sell:
I sell thee poison, thou hast sold me none.
Farewell; buy food, and get thyself in flesh.—
Come, cordial, and not poison; go with me
To Juliet's grave, for there must I use thee.
[*Exeunt.*

SCENE II. Friar Laurence's *Cell.*

Enter FRIAR JOHN.

John. Holy Franciscan friar! brother, ho!

Enter FRIAR LAURENCE.

Lau. This same should be the voice of Friar John.—
Welcome from Mantua; What says Romeo?
Or, if his mind be writ, give me his letter.

John. Going to find a barefoot brother out,
One of our order to associate me,
Here in this city visiting the sick,
And finding him, the searchers of the town,
Suspecting that we both were in a house
Where the infectious pestilence did reign,
Seal'd up the doors, and would not let us forth;
So that my speed to Mantua there was stay'd.

Lau. Who bare my letter then to Romeo?

John. I could not send it,—here it is again,—
Nor get a messenger to bring it thee,
So fearful were they of infection.

Lau. Unhappy fortune! by my brotherhood,
The letter was not nice, but full of charge,
Of dear import; and the neglecting it
May do much danger: Friar John, go hence;
Get me an iron crow, and bring it straight
Unto my cell.

John. Brother, I'll go and bring it thee.
[*Exit.*

Lau. Now must I to the monument alone;
Within this three hours will fair Juliet wake;
She will beshrew me much, that Romeo
Hath had no notice of these accidents:
But I will write again to Mantua,
And keep her at my cell till Romeo come;
Poor living corse, clos'd in a dead man's tomb!
[*Exit.*

SCENE III.

A Church Yard: in it a Monument belonging to the Capulets.

Enter PARIS, *and his* Page, *bearing Flowers and a Torch.*

Par. Give me thy torch, boy: Hence, and stand aloof;—
Yet put it out, for I would not be seen.
Under yon yew-trees lay thee all along,
Holding thine ear close to the hollow ground;
So shall no foot upon the churchyard tread
(Being loose, unfirm, with digging up of graves),
But thou shalt hear it: whistle then to me,
As signal that thou hear'st something approach.
Give me those flowers. Do as I bid thee, go.

Page. I am almost afraid to stand alone
Here in the churchyard; yet I will adventure.
[*Retires.*

Par. Sweet flower, with flowers I strew thy bridal bed:
Sweet tomb, that in thy circuit dost contain
The perfect model of eternity;
Fair Juliet, that with angels dost remain,
Accept this latest favour at my hands;
That living honour'd thee, and, being dead,
With funeral praises do adorn thy tomb!
[*The* Boy *whistles.*

The boy gives warning, something doth approach.
What cursed foot wanders this way to-night,
To cross my obsequies, and true-love's rights?
What, with a torch!—muffle me, night, a while.
[*Retires.*

Enter ROMEO *and* BALTHASAR, *with a Torch, Mattock, &c.*

Rom. Give me that mattock, and the wrenching iron.
Hold, take this letter; early in the morning
See thou deliver it to my lord and father.
Give me the light: Upon thy life I charge thee,
Whate'er thou hear'st, or seest, stand all aloof,
And do not interrupt me in my course.

Why I descend into this bed of death,
Is, partly, to behold my lady's face:
But, chiefly, to take thence from her dead finger
A precious ring; a ring that I must use
In dear employment: therefore hence, be gone:—
But if thou, jealous, dost return to pry
In what I further shall intend to do,
By heaven, I will tear thee joint by joint,
And strew this hungry churchyard with thy limbs:
The time and my intents are savage wild;
More fierce, and more inexorable far,
Than empty tigers, or the roaring sea.

Bal. I will be gone, sir, and not trouble you.

Rom. So shalt thou show me friendship.—take thou that:
Live, and be prosperous; and farewell, good fellow.

Bal. For all this same, I'll hide me hereabout:
His looks I fear, and his intents I doubt. [*Retires.*

Rom. Thou detestable maw, thou womb of death,
Gorg'd with the dearest morsel of the earth,
Thus I enforce thy rotten jaws to open,
[*Breaking open the Door of the Monument.*
And, in despite, I'll cram thee with more food!

Par. This is that banish'd haughty Montague,
That murder'd my love's cousin;—with which grief,
It is supposed the fair creature died,—
And here is come to do some villanous shame
To the dead bodies: I will apprehend him.— [*Advances.*
Stop thy unhallow'd toil, vile Montague;
Can vengeance be pursu'd further than death?
Condemned villain, I do apprehend thee:
Obey, and go with me; for thou must die.

Rom. I must, indeed; and therefore came I hither.—
Good gentle youth, tempt not a desperate man;
Fly hence and leave me;—think upon these gone;
Let them affright thee.—I beseech thee, youth,
Heap not another sin upon my head,
By urging me to fury:—O, be gone!
By heaven, I love thee better than myself:
For I come hither arm'd against myself:
Stay not, begone;—live, and hereafter say—
A madman's mercy bade thee run away.

Par. I do defy thy conjurations,
And do attach thee as a felon here.

Rom. Wilt thou provoke me? then have at thee, boy. [*They fight.*

Page. O lord! they fight; I will go call the watch. [*Exit* Page.

Par. O, I am slain! [*Falls.*]—If thou be merciful,
Open the tomb, lay me with Juliet. [*Dies.*

Rom. In faith, I will:—Let me peruse this face;
Mercutio's kinsman, noble county Paris;
What said my man when my betossed soul
Did not attend him as we rode? I think,
He told me, Paris should have married Juliet:
Said he not so? or did I dream it so?
Or am I mad, hearing him talk of Juliet,
To think it was so?—O, give me thy hand,
One writ with me in sour misfortune's book!
I'll bury thee in a triumphant grave,—
A grave? O, no; a lantern, slaughter'd youth,
For here lies Juliet, and her beauty makes
This vault a feasting presence full of light.
Death, lie thou there, by a dead man interr'd.
[*Laying* Paris *in the Monument.*
How oft when men are at the point of death
Have they been merry? which their keepers call
A lightning before death: O, how may I
Call this a lightning?—O, my love! my wife!
Death, that hath suck'd the honey of thy breath,
Hath had no power yet upon thy beauty:
Thou art not conquer'd; beauty's ensign yet
Is crimson in thy lips, and in thy cheeks,
And death's pale flag is not advanced there.—
Tybalt, liest thou there in thy bloody sheet?
O, what more favour can I do to thee,
Than with that hand that cut thy youth in twain;
To sunder his that was thine enemy?
Forgive me, cousin!—Ah, dear Juliet,
Why art thou yet so fair? Shall I believe
That unsubstantial death is amorous;
And that the lean abhorred monster keeps
Thee here in dark to be his paramour?
For fear of that, I will still stay with thee;
And never from this palace of dim night
Depart again; here, here will I remain
With worms that are thy chambermaids; O, here
Will I set up my everlasting rest;
And shake the yoke of inauspicious stars
From this world-wearied flesh.—Eyes, look your last!
Arms, take your last embrace! and lips, O you
The doors of breath, seal with a righteous kiss
A dateless bargain to engrossing death!—
Come, bitter conduct, come, unsavoury guide!
Thou desperate pilot, now at once run on
The dashing rocks thy seasick weary bark!
Here's to my love! [*Drinks.*]—O, true apothecary!
Thy drugs are quick.—Thus with a kiss I die. [*Dies.*

Enter at the other end of the Churchyard, Friar Laurence, *with a Lantern, Crow, and Spade.*

Fri. Saint Francis be my speed! how oft to-night
Have my old feet stumbled at graves?—Who's there?
Who is it that consorts, so late, the dead?

Bal. Here's one, a friend, and one that knows you well.

Fri. Bliss be upon you! Tell me, good my friend,
What torch is yond' that vainly lends his light
To grubs and eyeless sculls? as I discern,
It burneth in the Capels' monument.

Bal. It doth so, holy sir; and there's my master,
One that you love.

Fri. Who is it?

Bal. Romeo.

Fri. How long hath he been there?

Bal. Full half an hour.

Fri. Go with me to the vault.

Bal. I dare not, sir:
My master knows not, but I am gone hence,
And fearfully did menace me with death,
If I did stay to look on his intents.

Fri. Stay then, I'll go alone;—Fear comes upon me:
O, much I fear some ill unlucky thing.

Bal. As I did sleep under this yew-tree here,
I dreamt my master and another fought,
And that my master slew him.

Fri. Romeo? [*Advances.*
Alack, alack, what blood is this, which stains
The stony entrance of this sepulchre?—
What mean these masterless and gory swords
To lie discolour'd by this place of peace?
[*Enters the Monument.*
Romeo! O, pale!—Who else? what, Paris too?
And steep'd in blood?—Ah, what an unkind hour
Is guilty of this lamentable chance!—
The lady stirs. [Juliet *wakes and stirs.*

Jul. O comfortable friar! where is my lord?
I do remember well where I should be,
And there I am:—Where is my Romeo?
[*Noise within.*

Fri. I hear some noise.—Lady, come from that nest
Of death, contagion, and unnatural sleep;
A greater Power than we can contradict
Hath thwarted our intents; come, come away:

Thy husband in thy bosom there lies dead;
And Paris too; come, I'll dispose of thee
Among a sisterhood of holy nuns:
Stay not to question, for the watch is coming;
Come, go, good Juliet,—[*Noise again.*] I dare stay no longer. [*Exit.*

Jul. Go, get thee hence, for I will not away.—
What's here? a cup, clos'd in my true love's hand?
Poison, I see, hath been his timeless end:—
O churl! drink all; and leave no friendly drop,
To help me after?—I will kiss thy lips;
Haply, some poison yet doth hang on them,
To make me die with a restorative.
[*Kisses him.*
Thy lips are warm!

1 *Watch.* [*Within.*] Lead, boy:—Which way?

Jul. Yea, noise?—then I'll be brief.—O happy dagger! [*Snatching* ROMEO'S *Dagger.*
This is thy sheath [*Stabs herself*]; there rust, and let me die.
[*Falls on* ROMEO'S *Body, and dies.*

Enter Watch, *with the* Page *of* Paris.

Page. This is the place; there, where the torch doth burn.

1 *Watch.* The ground is bloody; Search about the churchyard:
Go, some of you, whoe'er you find, attach.
[*Exeunt some.*
Pitiful sight! here lies the county slain;
And Juliet bleeding; warm, and newly dead,
Who here hath lain these two days buried.—
Go, tell the prince,—run to the Capulets,—
Raise up the Montagues,—some others search;—
[*Exeunt other* Watchmen.
We see the ground whereon these woes do lie;
But the true ground of all these piteous woes
We cannot without circumstance descry.

Enter some of the Watch, *with* BALTHASAR.

2 *Watch.* Here's Romeo's man, we found him in the churchyard.

1 *Watch.* Hold him in safety, till the prince come hither.

Enter another Watchman, *with* FRIAR LAURENCE.

3 *Watch.* Here is a friar, that trembles, sighs, and weeps:
We took this mattock and this spade from him,
As he was coming from this churchyard side.

1 *Watch.* A great suspicion; Stay the friar too.

Enter the Prince *and* Attendants.

Prince. What misadventure is so early up,
That calls our person from our morning's rest?

Enter CAPULET, LADY CAPULET, *and Others.*

Cap. What should it be, that they so shriek abroad?

La. Cap. The people in the street cry—Romeo,
Some—Juliet, and some—Paris; and all run,
With open outcry toward our monument.

Prince. What fear is this which startles in our ears?

1 *Watch.* Sovereign, here lies the county Paris slain;
And Romeo dead; and Juliet, dead before,
Warm and new kill'd.

Prince. Search, seek, and know how this foul murder comes.

1 *Watch.* Here is a friar, and slaughter'd Romeo's man,
With instruments upon them, fit to open
These dead men's tombs.

Cap. O heavens!—O, wife! look how our daughter bleeds!
This dagger hath mista'en,—for lo! this house
Is empty on the back of Montague,—
And is missheathed in my daughter's bosom.

La. Cap. O me, this sight of death is as a bell,
That warns my old age to a sepulchre.

Enter MONTAGUE *and Others.*

Prince. Come, Montague, for thou art early up,
To see thy son and heir more early down.

Mon. Alas, my liege, my wife is dead to-night;
Grief of my son's exile hath stopp'd her breath;
What further woe conspires against mine age?

Prince. Look, and thou shalt see.

Mon. O thou untaught! what manners is in this,
To press before thy father to a grave?

Prince. Seal up the mouth of outrage for a while,
'Till we can clear these ambiguities,
And know their spring, their head, their true descent;
And then will I be general of your woes,
And lead you even to death: Mean time forbear,
And let mischance be slave to patience.—
Bring forth the parties of suspicion.

Fri. I am the greatest, able to do least,
Yet most suspected, as the time and place
Doth make against me, of this direful murder;
And here I stand, both to impeach and purge
Myself condemned and myself excus'd.

Prince. Then say at once what thou dost know in this.

Fri. I will be brief, for my short date of breath
Is not so long as is a tedious tale.
Romeo, there dead, was husband to that Juliet;
And she, there dead, that Romeo's faithful wife:
I married them; and their stolen marriage-day
Was Tybalt's doomsday, whose untimely death
Banish'd the new made bridegroom from this city;
For whom, and not for Tybalt, Juliet pin'd.
You—to remove that siege of grief from her,—
Betroth'd, and would have married her perforce,
To county Paris:—Then comes she to me;
And, with wild looks, bid me devise some means
To rid her from this second marriage,
Or, in my cell there would she kill herself.
Then gave I her, so tutor'd by my art,
A sleeping potion; which so took effect
As I intended, for it wrought on her
The form of death: meantime I writ to Romeo,
That he should hither come as this dire night,
To help to take her from her borrow'd grave,
Being the time the potion's force should cease.
But he which bore my letter, Friar John,
Was staid by accident; and yesternight
Return'd my letter back: Then all alone,
At the prefixed hour of her waking,
Came I to take her from her kindred's vault;
Meaning to keep her closely at my cell,
Till I conveniently could send to Romeo:
But, when I came (some minute ere the time
Of her awakening), here untimely lay
The noble Paris, and true Romeo, dead.
She wakes; and I entreated her come forth,
And bear this work of heaven with patience:
But then a noise did scare me from the tomb;
And she, too desperate, would not go with me,
But (as it seems) did violence on herself.
All this I know: and to the marriage
Her nurse is privy: And, if aught in this
Miscarried by my fault, let my old life
Be sacrific'd, some hour before his time,
Unto the rigour of severest law.

Prince. We still have known thee for a holy man.—
Where's Romeo's man? what can he say in this?

Bal. I brought my master news of Juliet's death?
And then in post he came from Mantua,
To this same place, to this same monument.
This letter he early bid me give his father;
And threaten'd me with death, going in the vault,
If I departed not, and left him there.

Prince. Give me the letter, I will look on it.—
Where is the county's page, that rais'd the watch?
Sirrah, what made your master in this place?

Page. He came with flowers to strew his lady's grave;
And bid me stand aloof, and so I did;
Anon, comes one with light to ope the tomb;
And, by and by, my master drew on him;
And then I ran away to call the watch.

Prince. This letter doth make good the friar's words,
Their course of love, the tidings of her death:
And here he writes—that he did buy a poison
Of a poor 'pothecary, and therewithal
Came to this vault to die, and lie with Juliet.—
Where be these enemies? Capulet! Montague!—
See, what a scourge is laid upon your hate,
That heaven finds means to kill your joys with love!
And I, for winking at your discords too,
Have lost a brace of kinsmen:—all are punish'd.

Cap. O, brother Montague, give me thy hand;
This is my daughter's jointure, for no more
Can I demand.

Mon. But I can give thee more:
For I will raise her statue in pure gold;
That, while Verona by that name is known,
There shall no figure at such rate be set,
As that of true and faithful Juliet.

Cap. As rich shall Romeo by his lady lie;
Poor sacrifices of our enmity!

Prince. A glooming peace this morning with it brings:
The sun for sorrow will not show his head:
Go hence, to have more talk of these sad things;
Some shall be pardoned, and some punished;
For never was a story of more woe,
Than this of Juliet and her Romeo. [*Exeunt.*

HAMLET, PRINCE OF DENMARK.

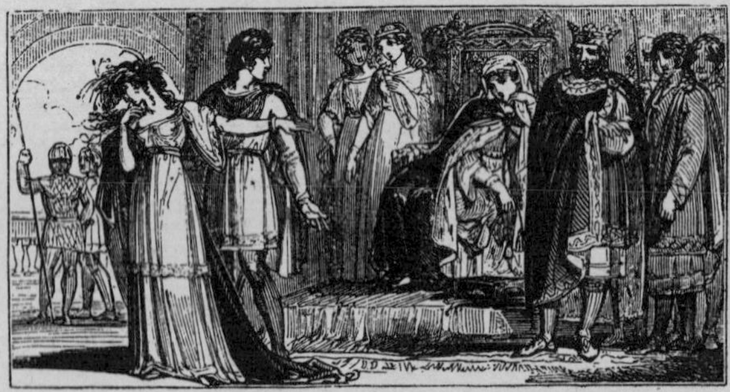

PERSONS REPRESENTED.

CLAUDIUS, King *of* Denmark.
HAMLET, *Son to the former, and Nephew to the present* King.
POLONIUS, *Lord Chamberlain.*
HORATIO, *Friend to* Hamlet.
LAERTES, *Son to* Polonius.
VOLTIMAND, CORNELIUS, ROSENCRANTZ, GUILDENSTERN, *Courtiers.*
OSRIC, *a Courtier.*
Another Courtier.
A Priest.
MARCELLUS, *an Officer.*
BERNARDO, *an Officer.*
FRANCISCO, *a Soldier.*
REYNALDO, *Servant to* Polonius.
A Captain. *An* Ambassador.
Ghost *of* Hamlet's Father.
FORTINBRAS, Prince *of* Norway.

GERTRUDE, Queen *of* Denmark, *and Mother to* Hamlet.
OPHELIA, *Daughter to* Polonius.

Lords, Ladies, Officers, Soldiers, Players, Grave-diggers, Sailors, Messengers, *and other* Attendants.

SCENE—Elsinore.

ACT I.

SCENE I. Elsinore. *A Platform before the Castle.*

FRANCISCO *on his Post. Enter to him* BERNARDO.

Ber. WHO's there?

Fran. Nay, answer me; stand, and unfold
Yourself.

Ber. Long live the king!

Fran. Bernardo?

Ber. He.

Fran. You come most carefully upon your hour.

Ber. 'Tis now struck twelve; get thee to bed, Francisco.

Fran. For this relief, much thanks: 'tis bitter cold,
And I am sick at heart.

Ber. Have you had quiet guard?

Fran. Not a mouse stirring.

Ber. Well, good night.
If you do meet Horatio and Marcellus,
The rivals of my watch, bid them make haste.

Enter HORATIO *and* MARCELLUS.

Fran. I think, I hear them.—Stand, ho! Who is there?

Hor. Friends to this ground.

Mar. And liegemen to the Dane.

Fran. Give you good night.

Mar. O, farewell, honest soldier:
Who hath reliev'd you?

Fran. Bernardo hath my place.
Give you good night. [*Exit* FRANCISCO.
Mar. Holla! Bernardo!
Ber. Say.
What, is Horatio there?
Hor. A piece of him.
Ber. Welcome, Horatio; welcome, good Marcellus.
Hor. What, has this thing appear'd again tonight?
Ber. I have seen nothing.
Mar. Horatio says, 'tis but our fantasy;
And will not let belief take hold of him,
Touching this dreaded sight, twice seen of us;
Therefore I have entreated him along,
With us to watch the minutes of this night;
That, if again this apparition come,
He may approve our eyes, and speak to it.
Hor. Tush! tush! 'twill not appear.
Ber. Sit down awhile;
And let us once again assail your ears,
That are so fortified against our story,
What we two nights have seen.
Hor. Well, sit we down,
And let us hear Bernardo speak of this.
Ber. Last night of all,
When yon same star, that's westward from the pole,
Had made his course to illume that part of heaven
Where now it burns, Marcellus, and myself,
The bell then beating one,—
Mar. Peace, break thee off; look, where it comes again!

Enter Ghost.

Ber. In the same figure like the king that's dead.
Mar. Thou art a scholar, speak to it, Horatio.
Ber. Looks it not like the king? mark it, Horatio.
Hor. Most like:—it harrows me with fear, and wonder.
Ber. It would be spoke to.
Mar. Speak to it, Horatio.
Hor. What art thou, that usurp'st this time of night,
Together with that fair and warlike form
In which the majesty of buried Denmark
Did sometimes march? by heaven I charge thee, speak.
Mar. It is offended.
Ber. See! it stalks away.

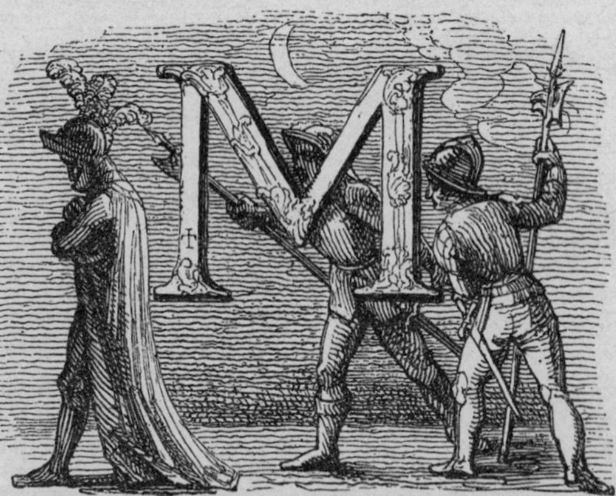

Hor. Stay; speak: speak I charge thee, speak.
[*Exit* Ghost.
Mar. 'Tis gone, and will not answer.
Ber. How now, Horatio? you tremble, and look pale:
Is not this something more than fantasy?
What think you of it?
Hor. Before my God, I might not this believe,
Without the sensible and true avouch
Of mine own eyes.
Mar. Is it not like the king?
Hor. As thou art to thyself:
Such was the very armour he had on,
When he the ambitious Norway combated;
So frown'd he once, when in an angry parle,
He smote the sledded Polack on the ice.
'Tis strange.
Mar. Thus, twice before, and jump at this dead hour,
With martial stalk hath he gone by our watch.
Hor. In what particular thought to work, I know not;
But, in the gross and scope of mine opinion,
This bodes some strange eruption to our state.
Mar. Good now, sit down, and tell me, he that knows,
Why this same strict and most observant watch
So nightly toils the subject of the land?
And why such daily cast of brazen cannon,
And foreign mart for implements of war;
Why such impress of shipwrights, whose sore task
Does not divide the Sunday from the week:
What might be toward, that this sweaty haste
Doth make the night joint-labourer with the day;
Who is't, that can inform me?
Hor. That can I;
At least, the whisper goes so. Our last king,
Whose image even but now appear'd to us,
Was, as you know, by Fontinbras of Norway,
Thereto prick'd on by a most emulate pride,
Dar'd to the combat; in which our valiant Hamlet
(For so this side of our known world esteem'd him),
Did slay this Fortinbras; who, by a seal'd compact,
Well ratified by law and heraldry,
Did forfeit with his life, all those his lands,
Which he stood seiz'd of, to the conqueror:
Against the which, a moiety competent
Was gaged by our king: which had return'd
To the inheritance of Fortinbras,
Had he been vanquisher; as, by the same comart,
And carriage of the article design'd,
His fell to Hamlet: Now, sir, young Fortinbras
Of unimproved mettle hot and full,
Hath in the skirts of Norway, here and there,
Shark'd up a list of landless resolutes,

For food and diet, to some enterprise
That hath a stomach in't: which is no other
(As it doth well appear unto our state),
But to recover of us, by strong hand,
And terms compulsatory, those 'foresaid lands
So by his father lost: And this, I take it,
Is the main motive of our preparations;
The source of this our watch; and the chief head
Of this post-haste and romage in the land.

Ber. I think, it be no other, but even so:
Well may it sort, that this portentous figure
Comes armed through our watch: so like the king
That was, and is, the question of these wars.

Hor. A mote it is, to trouble the mind's eye.
In the most high and palmy state of Rome,
A little ere the mightiest Julius fell,
The graves stood tenantless, and the sheeted dead
Did squeak and gibber in the Roman streets.

* * * * * * * * * * *

As stars with trains of fire and dews of blood,
Disasters in the sun; and the moist star,
Upon whose influence Neptune's empire stands,
Was sick almost to doomsday with eclipse.
And even the like precurse of fierce events,—
As harbingers preceding still the fates,
And prologue to the omen coming on,
Have heaven and earth together demonstrated
Unto our climatures and countrymen.—

Re-enter Ghost.

But, soft; behold! lo, where it comes again!
I'll cross it, though it blast me.—Stay, illusion!
If thou hast any sound, or use of voice,
Speak to me:
If there be any good thing to be done,
That may to thee do ease, and grace to me,
Speak to me:
If thou art privy to thy country's fate,
Which, happily, foreknowing, may avoid,
O, speak!
Or, if thou hast uphoarded in thy life
Extorted treasure in the womb of earth,
For which, they say, you spirits oft walk in death,
[*Cock crows.*
Speak of it:—stay, and speak.—Stop it, Marcellus.

Mar. Shall I strike at it with my partisan?

Hor. Do, if it will not stand.

Ber. 'Tis here!

Hor. 'Tis here!

Mar. 'Tis gone! [*Exit* Ghost.
We do it wrong, being so majestical,
To offer it the show of violence;
For it is, as the air, invulnerable,
And our vain blows malicious mockery.

Ber. It was about to speak, when the cock crew.

Hor. And then it started like a guilty thing
Upon a fearful summons. I have heard,
The cock, that is the trumpet to the morn,
Doth with his lofty and shrill-sounding throat
Awake the god of day: and at his warning,
Whether in sea or fire, in earth or air,
The extravagant and erring spirit hies
To his confine: and of the truth herein
This present object made probation.

Mar. It faded on the crowing of the cock.
Some say, that ever 'gainst that season comes
Wherein our Saviour's birth is celebrated,
This bird of dawning singeth all night long:
And then they say no spirit dares stir abroad;
The nights are wholesome: then no planets strike,
No fairy takes, nor witch hath power to charm,
So hallow'd and so gracious is the time.

Hor. So have I heard, and do in part believe it.
But, look, the morn, in russet mantle clad,
Walks o'er the dew of yon high eastern hill:
Break we our watch up; and, by my advice,
Let us impart what we have seen to-night
Unto young Hamlet: for, upon my life,
This spirit, dumb to us, will speak to him:
Do you consent we shall acquaint him with it,
As needful in our loves, fitting our duty?

Mar. Let's do't, I pray; and I this morning know
Where we shall find him most convenient.
[*Exeunt.*

SCENE II.

The same. A Room of State in the same.

Enter the King, Queen, HAMLET, POLONIUS, LAERTES, VOLTIMAND, CORNELIUS, Lords, *and* Attendants.

King. Though yet of Hamlet our dear brother's death
The memory be green: and that it us befitted
To bear our hearts in grief, and our whole kingdom
To be contracted in one brow of woe;
Yet so far hath discretion fought with nature,
That we with wisest sorrow think on him,
Together with remembrance of ourselves.
Therefore our sometime sister, now our queen,
The imperial jointress of this warlike state,
Have we, as 'twere, with a defeated joy,—
With one auspicious, and one dropping eye;
With mirth in funeral, and with dirge in marriage,
In equal scale weighing delight and dole,—
Taken to wife: nor have we herein barr'd
Your better wisdoms, which have freely gone
With this affair along:—For all, our thanks.
Now follows, that you know, young Fortinbras,—
Holding a weak supposal of our worth;
Or thinking, by our late dear brother's death,
Our state to be disjoint and out of frame,
Colleagued with this dream of his advantage,
He hath not fail'd to pester us with message,
Importing the surrender of those lands
Lost by his father, with all bands of law,
To our most valiant brother.—So much for him.
Now for ourself, and for this time of meeting.
Thus much the business is: We have here writ
To Norway, uncle of young Fortinbras,—
Who, impotent and bed-rid, scarcely hears
Of this his nephew's purpose,—to suppress
His further gait herein; in that the levies,
The lists, and full proportions, are all made
Out of his subject:—and we here despatch
You, good Cornelius, and you, Voltimand,
For bearers of this greeting to old Norway;
Giving to you no further personal power
To business with the king, more than the scope
Of these related articles allow.
Farewell; and let your haste commend your duty.

Cor. Vol. In that, and all things, will we show our duty.

King. We doubt it nothing; heartily farewell.
[*Exeunt* VOLTIMAND *and* CORNELIUS.
And now, Laertes, what's the news with you?
You told us of some suit; What is't, Laertes?
You cannot speak of reason to the Dane,
And lose your voice: What would'st thou beg, Laertes,
That shall not be my offer, not thy asking?
The head is not more native to the heart,
The hand more instrumental to the mouth,
Than is the throne of Denmark to thy father.
What would'st thou have, Laertes?

Laer. My dread lord,
Your leave and favour to return to France;
From whence though willingly I came to Denmark,
To show my duty in your coronation;
Yet now, I must confess, that duty done,
My thoughts and wishes bend again toward France,
And bow them to your gracious leave and pardon.

King. Have you your father's leave? What says Polonius?
Pol. He hath, my lord, wrung from me my slow leave,
By laboursome petition; and, at last,
Upon his will I seal'd my hard consent:
I do beseech you, give him leave to go.
King. Take thy fair hour, Laertes; time be thine,
And thy best graces spend it at thy will.—
But now, my cousin Hamlet, and my son,——
Ham. A little more than kin, and less than kind. [*Aside*.
King. How is it that the clouds still hang on you?
Ham. Not so, my lord, I am too much i'the sun.
Queen. Good Hamlet, cast thy nighted colour off,
And let thine eye look like a friend on Denmark,
Do not, for ever, with thy vailed lids
Seek for thy noble father in the dust:
Thou know'st, 'tis common; all, that live, must die,
Passing through nature to eternity.
Ham. Ay, madam, it is common.
Queen. If it be,
Why seems it so particular with thee?
Ham. Seems, madam! nay, it is; I know not seems.
'Tis not alone my inky cloak, good mother,
Nor customary suits of solemn black,
Nor windy suspiration of forc'd breath,
No, nor the fruitful river in the eye,
Nor the dejected haviour of the visage,
Together with all forms, modes, shows of grief,
That can denote me truly: These, indeed, seem,
For they are actions that a man might play;
But I have that within, which passeth show;
These, but the trappings and the suits of woe.
King. 'Tis sweet and commendable in your nature, Hamlet,
To give these mourning duties to your father:
But you must know your father lost a father;
That father lost, lost his; and the survivor bound
In filial obligation for some term
To do obsequious sorrow. But to persever
In obstinate condolement is a course
Of impious stubbornness; 'tis unmanly grief:
It shows a will most incorrect to heaven;
A heart unfortified, or mind impatient;
An understanding simple and unschool'd:
For what, we know, must be, and is as common
As any the most vulgar thing to sense,
Why should we, in our peevish opposition,
Take it to heart? Fye! 'tis a fault to heaven,
A fault against the dead, a fault to nature,
To reason most absurd; whose common theme
Is death of fathers, and who still hath cried,
From the first corse, till he that died to-day,
This must be so. We pray you, throw to earth
This unprevailing woe; and think of us
As of a father: for let the world take note,
You are the most immediate to our throne;
And with no less nobility of love,
Than that which dearest father bears his son,
Do I impart toward you. For your intent
In going back to school in Wittenberg,
It is most retrograde to our desire:
And, we beseech you, bend you to remain
Here, in the cheer and comfort of our eye,
Our chiefest courtier, cousin, and our son.
Queen. Let not thy mother lose her prayers, Hamlet;
I pray thee, stay with us, go not to Wittenberg.
Ham. I shall in all my best obey you, madam.
King. Why, 'tis a loving and a fair reply;
Be as ourself in Denmark.—Madam, come;
This gentle and unforc'd accord of Hamlet
Sits smiling to my heart: in grace whereof
No jocund health, that Denmark drinks to-day,
But the great cannon to the clouds shall tell;
And the king's rouse the heaven shall bruit again,
Respeaking earthly thunder. Come away.
[*Exeunt* King, Queen, Lords, *&c*. POLONIUS, *and* LAERTES.
Ham. O, that this too too solid flesh would melt,
Thaw, and resolve itself into a dew!
Or that the Everlasting had not fix'd
His canon 'gainst self-slaughter! O God! O God!
How weary, stale, flat, and unprofitable
Seem to me all the uses of this world!
Fye on't! O fye! 'tis an unweeded garden
That grows to seed; things rank, and gross in nature,
Possess it merely. That it should come to this!
But two months dead!—nay, not so much, not two:
So excellent a king; that was, to this,
Hyperion to a satyr: so loving to my mother,
That he might not beteem the winds of heaven
Visit her face too roughly. Heaven and earth!
Must I remember? why, she would hang on him,
As if increase of appetite had grown
By what it fed on: And yet, within a month,—
Let me not think on't;—Frailty, thy name is woman!—
A little month; or ere those shoes were old,
With which she follow'd my poor father's body,
Like Niobe, all tears;—why she, even she,—
O heaven! a beast, that wants discourse of reason,
Would have mourn'd longer,—married with my uncle,
My father's brother; but no more like my father,
Than I to Hercules: Within a month;
Ere yet the salt of most unrighteous tears
Had left the flushing in her galled eyes,
She married:—O most wicked speed, to post
With such dexterity to incestuous sheets!
It is not, nor it cannot come to, good;
But break, my heart: for I must hold my tongue!

Enter HORATIO, BERNARDO, *and* MARCELLUS.

Hor. Hail to your lordship!
Ham. I am glad to see you well;
Horatio,—or I do forget myself.
Hor. The same, my lord, and your poor servant ever.
Ham. Sir, my good friend; I'll change that name with you.
And what make you from Wittenberg, Horatio?—
Marcellus?
Mar. My good lord,——
Ham. I am very glad to see you; good even, sir.—
But what, in faith, make you from Wittenberg?
Hor. A truant disposition, good my lord.
Ham. I would not hear your enemy say so:
Nor shall you do mine ear that violence,
To make it truster of your own report
Against yourself: I know you are no truant.
But what is your affair in Elsinore?
We'll teach you to drink deep ere you depart.
Hor. My lord, I came to see your father's funeral.
Ham. I pray thee, do not mock me, fellow student;
I think, it was to see my mother's wedding.
Hor. Indeed, my lord, it follow'd hard upon.
Ham. Thrift, thrift, Horatio! the funeral bak'd meats
Did coldly furnish forth the marriage tables.
'Would, I had met my dearest foe in heaven
Or ever I had seen that day, Horatio!
My father,—Methinks, I see my father.
Hor. Where,
My lord?
Ham. In my mind's eye, Horatio.
Hor. I saw him once, he was a goodly king.
Ham. He was a man take him for all in all,
I shall not look upon his like again.

Hor. My lord, I think I saw him yesternight.
Ham. Saw! who?
Hor. My lord, the king your father.
Ham. The king my father?
Hor. Season your admiration for a while
With an attent ear; till I may deliver,
Upon the witness of these gentlemen,
This marvel to you.
Ham. For God's love, let me hear.
Hor. Two nights together had these gentlemen,
Marcellus and Bernardo, on their watch,
In the dead waste and middle of the night,
Been thus encounter'd. A figure like your father,
Armed at point, exactly, cap-a-pe,
Appears before them, and, with solemn march,
Goes slow and stately by them: thrice he walk'd
By their oppress'd and fear-surprised eyes,
Within his truncheon's length; whilst they, distill'd
Almost to jelly with the act of fear,
Stand dumb, and speak not to him. This to me
In dreadful secrecy impart they did;
And I with them, the third night kept the watch;
Where, as they had deliver'd, both in time,
Form of the thing, each word made true and good,
The apparition comes; I knew your father;
These hands are not more like.
Ham. But where was this?
Hor. My lord, upon the platform where we watch'd.
Ham. Did you not speak to it?
Hor. My lord, I did:
But answer made it none: yet once, methought,
It lifted up its head, and did address
Itself to motion, like as it would speak;
But, even then, the morning cock crew loud;
And at the sound it shrunk in haste away,
And vanish'd from our sight.
Ham. 'Tis very strange.
Hor. As I do live, my honour'd lord, 'tis true;
And we did think it writ down in our duty,
To let you know of it.
Ham. Indeed, indeed, sirs, but this troubles me.
Hold you the watch to-night?
All. We do, my lord.
Ham. Arm'd, say you?
All. Arm'd, my lord.
Ham. From top to toe?
All. My lord, from head to foot.
Ham. Then saw you not
His face.
Hor. O, yes, my lord; he wore his beaver up.
Ham. What, look'd he frowningly?
Hor. A countenance more
In sorrow than in anger.
Ham. Pale, or red?
Hor. Nay, very pale.
Ham. And fix'd his eyes upon you?
Hor. Most constantly.
Ham. I would, I had been there.
Hor. It would have much amaz'd you.
Ham. Very like,
Very like: Stay'd it long?
Hor. While one with moderate haste might tell a hundred.
Mar. Ber. Longer, longer.
Hor. Not when I saw it.
Ham. His beard was grizzl'd? no?
Hor. It was, as I have seen it in his life,
A sable silver'd.
Ham. I will watch to-night;
Perchance, 'twill walk again.
Hor. I warrant, it will.
Ham. If it assume my noble father's person,
I'll speak to it, though hell itself should gape,
And bid me hold my peace. I pray you all,
If you have hitherto conceal'd this sight,
Let it be tenable in your silence still;
And whatsoever else shall hap to-night,
Give it an understanding, but no tongue;
I will requite your loves: So, fare you well:
Upon the platform, 'twixt eleven and twelve,
I'll visit you.
All. Our duty to your honour.
Ham. Your loves, as mine to you: Farewell.
[*Exeunt* HOR. MAR. *and* BER.
My father's spirit in arms! all is not well;
I doubt some foul play: 'would, the night were come!
Till then sit still, my soul: Foul deeds will rise,
Though all the earth o'erwhelm them, to men's eyes. [*Exit.*

SCENE III. *A Room in* Polonius' *House.*

Enter LAERTES *and* OPHELIA.

Laer. My necessaries are embark'd; farewell:
And, sister, as the winds give benefit,
And convoy is assistant, do not sleep,
But let me hear from you.
Oph. Do you doubt that?
Laer. For Hamlet, and the trifling of his favour,
Hold it a fashion, and a toy in blood;
A violet in the youth of primy nature,
Forward, not permanent, sweet, not lasting,
The perfume and suppliance of a minute;
No more.
Oph. No more but so?
Laer. Think it no more:
For nature, crescent, does not grow alone
In thews, and bulk; but, as this temple waxes,
The inward service of the mind and soul
Grows wide withal. Perhaps, he loves you now;
And now no soil, nor cautel, doth besmirch
The virtue of his will: but, you must fear,
His greatness weigh'd, his will is not his own;
For he himself is subject to his birth:
He may not, as unvalued persons do,
Carve for himself; for on his choice depends
The safety and health of the whole state;
And therefore must his choice be circumscribed
Unto the voice and yielding of that body,
Whereof he is the head: Then if he says he loves you,
It fits your wisdom so far to believe it,
As he in his particular act and place
May give his saying deed; which is no further,
Than the main voice of Denmark goes withal.
Then weigh what loss your honour may sustain,
If with too credent ear you list his songs;
Or lose your heart; or your chaste treasure open
To his unmaster'd importunity.
Fear it, Ophelia, fear it, my dear sister;
And keep you in the rear of your affection,
Out of the shot and danger of desire.
The chariest maid is prodigal enough,
If she unmask her beauty to the moon:
Virtue itself scapes not calumnious strokes:
The canker galls the infants of the spring,
Too oft before their buttons be disclos'd;
And in the morn and liquid dew of youth
Contagious blastments are most imminent.
Be wary then: best safety lies in fear;
Youth to itself rebels, though none else near.
Oph. I shall the effect of this good lesson keep,
As watchman to my heart; But, good my brother,
Do not, as some ungracious pastors do,
Show me the steep and thorny way to heaven;
Whilst, like a puff'd and reckless libertine,
Himself the primrose path of dalliance treads,
And recks not his own read.
Laer. O fear me not.
I stay too long;—But here my father comes.

Enter POLONIUS.

A double blessing is a double grace;
Occasion smiles upon a second leave.
Pol. Yet here, Laertes! aboard, aboard, for shame;
The wind sits in the shoulder of your sail,
And you are staid for: There,—my blessing with you; [*Laying his Hand on* LAERTES' *Head.*
And these few precepts in thy memory

Look thou character. Give thy thoughts no tongue,
Nor any unproportion'd thought his act.
Be thou familiar, but by no means vulgar.
The friends thou hast, and their adoption tried,
Grapple them to thy soul with hooks of steel;
But do not dull thy palm with entertainment
Of each new hatch'd, unfledg'd comrade. Beware
Of entrance to a quarrel: but, being in,
Bear it that the opposer may beware of thee.
Give every man thine ear, but few thy voice:
Take each man's censure, but reserve thy judgment.
Costly thy habit as thy purse can buy,
But not express'd in fancy; rich, not gaudy:
For the apparel oft proclaims the man:
And they in France, of the best rank and station,
Are most select and generous, chief in that.
Neither a borrower, nor a lender be:
For loan oft loses both itself and friend;
And borrowing dulls the edge of husbandry.
This above all,—To thine ownself be true;
And it must follow, as the night the day,
Thou canst not then be false to any man.
Farewell; my blessing season this in thee!

Laer. Most humbly do I take my leave, my lord.

Pol. The time invites you; go, your servants tend.

Laer. Farewell, Ophelia; and remember well
What I have said to you.

Oph. 'Tis in my memory lock'd,
And you yourself shall keep the key of it.

Laer. Farewell. [*Exit* LAERTES.

Pol. What is't, Ophelia, he hath said to you?

Oph. So please you, something touching the lord Hamlet.

Pol. Marry, well bethought:
'Tis told me he hath very oft of late
Given private time to you; and you yourself
Have of your audience been most free and bounteous:
If it be so (as so 'tis put on me,
And that in way of caution), I must tell you,
You do not understand yourself so clearly,
As it behoves my daughter, and your honour:
What is between you? give me up the truth.

Oph. He hath, my lord, of late, made many tenders
Of his affection to me.

Pol. Affection? puh! you speak like a green girl,
Unsifted in such perilous circumstance.
Do you believe his tenders, as you call them?

Oph. I do not know, my lord, what I should think.

Pol. Marry, I'll teach you: think yourself a baby;
That you have ta'en these tenders for true pay,
Which are not sterling. Tender yourself more dearly;
Or (not to crack the wind of the poor phrase,
Wronging it thus), you'll tender me a fool.

Oph. My lord, he hath importun'd me with love,
In honourable fashion.

Pol. Ay, fashion you may call it; go to, go to.

Oph. And hath given countenance to his speech, my lord,
With almost all the holy vows of heaven.

Pol. Ay, springes to catch woodcocks. I do know,
When the blood burns, how prodigal the soul
Lends the tongue vows: these blazes, daughter,
Giving more light than heat,—extinct in both,
Even in their promise, as it is a making,—
You must not take for fire. From this time,
Be somewhat scanter of your maiden presence;
Set your entreatments at a higher rate,
Than a command to parley. For lord Hamlet,
Believe so much in him, That he is young;
And with a larger tether may he walk,
Than may be given you: In few, Ophelia,
Do not believe his vows: for they are brokers,
Not of that dye which their investments show,
But mere implorators of unholy suits,
Breathing like sanctified and pious bonds,
The better to beguile. This is for all,—
I would not, in plain terms, from this time forth,
Have you so slander any moment's leisure,
As to give words or talk with the Lord Hamlet.
Look to 't, I charge you; come your ways.

Oph. I shall obey, my lord. [*Exeunt.*

SCENE IV. *The Platform.*

Enter HAMLET, HORATIO, *and* MARCELLUS.

Ham. The air bites shrewdly; it is very cold.

Hor. It is a nipping and an eager air.

Ham. What hour now?

Hor. I think it lacks of twelve.

Mar. No, it is struck.

Hor. Indeed? I heard it not; it then draws near the season,
Wherein the spirit held his wont to walk.
[*A Flourish of Trumpets, and Ordnance shot off, within.*
What does this mean, my lord?

Ham. The king doth wake to-night, and takes his rouse,
Keeps wassel, and the swaggering up-spring reels;
And, as he drains his draughts of Rhenish down,
The kettledrum and trumpet thus bray out
The triumph of his pledge.

Hor. Is it a custom?

Ham. Ay, marry, is 't:
But to my mind,—though I am native here,
And to the manner born,—it is a custom
More honour'd in the breach than the observance.
This heavy-headed revel, east and west,
Makes us traduc'd, and tax'd of other nations:
They clepe us, drunkards, and, with swinish phrase
Soil our addition; and, indeed it takes
From our achievements, though perform'd at height,
The pith and marrow of our attribute.
So, oft it chances in particular men,
That, for some vicious mole of nature in them,
As, in their birth (wherein they are not guilty,
Since nature cannot choose his origin),
By the o'ergrowth of some complexion,
Oft breaking down the pales and forts of reason;
Or by some habit, that too much o'erleavens
The form of plausive manners;—that these men,—
Carrying, I say, the stamp of one defect;
Being nature's livery, or fortune's star,—
Their virtues else (be they as pure as grace,
As infinite as man may undergo,)
Shall in the general censure take corruption
From that particular fault: The dram of base
Doth all the noble substance often doubt
To his own scandal.

Enter Ghost.

Hor. Look, my lord, it comes!

Ham. Angels and ministers of grace, defend us!—
Be thou a spirit of health, or goblin damn'd,
Bring with thee airs from heaven, or blasts from hell,
Be thy intents wicked, or charitable,
Thou com'st in such a questionable shape,
That I will speak to thee: I'll call thee, Hamlet,
King, father, royal Dane: O, answer me:
Let me not burst in ignorance! but tell,
Why thy canoniz'd bones, hearsed in death,
Have burst their cerements! why the sepulchre,
Wherein we saw thee quietly in-urn'd,
Hath op'd his ponderous and marble jaws,
To cast thee up again! What may this mean,
That thou, dead corse, again, in complete steel

Revisit'st thus the glimpses of the moon,
Making night hideous; and we fools of nature,
So horribly to shake our disposition,
With thoughts beyond the reaches of our souls?
Say, why is this? wherefore? what should we do?
Hor. It beckons you to go away with it,
As if it some impartment did desire
To you alone.
Mar. Look, with what courteous action
It waves you to a more removed ground:
But do not go with it.
Hor. No, by no means.
Ham. It will not speak; then I will follow it.
Hor. Do not, my lord.
Ham. Why, what should be the fear?
I do not set my life at a pin's fee;
And, for my soul, what can it do to that,
Being a thing immortal as itself?
It waves me forth again;—I'll follow it.
Hor. What, if it tempt you toward the flood, my lord,
Or to the dreadful summit of the cliff,
That beetles o'er his base into the sea?
And there assume some other horrible form,
Which might deprive your sovereignty of reason,
And draw you into madness? think of it:
The very place puts toys of desperation,
Without more motive, into every brain,
That looks so many fathoms to the sea,
And hears it roar beneath.
Ham. It waves me still.—
Go on, I'll follow thee.
Mar. You shall not go, my lord.
Ham. Hold off your hands.
Hor. Be rul'd, you shall not go.
Ham. My fate cries out,
And makes each petty artery in this body
As hardy as the Nemean lion's nerve.— [Ghost *beckons.*
Still am I call'd;—unhand me, gentlemen;— [*Breaking from them.*
By heaven, I'll make a ghost of him that lets me:—
I say, away:—Go on, I'll follow thee. [*Exeunt* Ghost *and* HAMLET.
Hor. He waxes desperate with imagination.
Mar. Let's follow; 'tis not fit thus to obey him.
Hor. Have after:—To what issue will this come?
Mar. Something is rotten in the state of Denmark.
Hor. Heaven will direct it.
Mar. Nay, let's follow him. [*Exeunt.*

SCENE V. *A more remote Part of the Platform.*

Re-enter Ghost *and* HAMLET.

Ham. Whither wilt thou lead me? speak, I'll go no further.
Ghost. Mark me.
Ham. I will.
Ghost. My hour is almost come,
When I to sulphurous and tormenting flames
Must render up myself.
Ham. Alas, poor ghost!
Ghost. Pity me not, but lend thy serious hearing
To what I shall unfold.
Ham. Speak, I am bound to hear.
Ghost. So art thou to revenge, when thou shalt hear.
Ham. What?
Ghost. I am thy father's spirit;
Doom'd for a certain term to walk the night;
And, for the day, confin'd to fast in fires,
Till the foul crimes, done in my days of nature,
Are burnt and purg'd away. But that I am forbid
To tell the secrets of my prison house,
I could a tale unfold, whose lightest word
Would harrow up thy soul; freeze thy young blood;
Make thy two eyes, like stars, start from their spheres;
Thy knotted and combined locks to part,
And each particular hair to stand on end,
Like quills upon the fretful porcupine:
But this eternal blazon must not be
To ears of flesh and blood.—List, list, O list!—
If thou didst ever thy dear father love,——
Ham. O heaven!
Ghost. Revenge his foul and most unnatural murder.
Ham. Murder?
Ghost. Murder most foul, as in the best it is;
But this most foul, strange, and unnatural.
Ham. Haste me to know it; that I, with wings as swift
As meditation, or the thoughts of love,
May sweep to my revenge.
Ghost. I find thee apt;
And duller should'st thou be than the fat weed
That roots itself in ease on Lethe wharf,
Would'st thou not stir in this. Now, Hamlet, hear:
'Tis given out, that sleeping in mine orchard,
A serpent stung me; so the whole ear of Denmark
Is by a forged process of my death
Rankly abus'd: but know, thou noble youth,
The serpent that did sting thy father's life,
Now wears his crown.
Ham. O, my prophetick soul! my uncle!
Ghost. Ay, that incestuous, that adulterate beast,
With witchcraft of his wit, with traitorous gifts,
(O wicked wit, and gifts, that have the power
So to seduce!) won to his shameful lust
The will of my most seeming virtuous queen:
O, Hamlet, what a falling-off was there!
From me, whose love was of that dignity,
That it went hand in hand even with the vow
I made to her in marriage; and to decline
Upon a wretch, whose natural gifts were poor
To those of mine!
But virtue, as it never will be mov'd,
Though lewdness court it in a shape of heaven;
So lust, though to a radiant angel link'd,
Will sate itself in a celestial bed,
And prey on garbage.
But soft! methinks, I scent the morning air;
Brief let me be:—Sleeping within mine orchard,
My custom always of the afternoon,
Upon my secure hour thy uncle stole,
With juice of cursed hebenon in a vial,
And in the porches of mine ears did pour
The leperous distilment: whose effect
Holds such an enmity with blood of man,
That, swift as quicksilver, it courses through
The natural gates and alleys of the body;
And with a sudden vigour, it doth posset
And curd, like eager droppings into milk,
The thin and wholesome blood: so did it mine;
And a most instant tetter bark'd about,
Most lazar-like with vile and loathsome crust,
All my smooth body.
Thus was I, sleeping, by a brother's hand,
Of life, of crown, of queen, at once despatch'd;
Cut off even in the blossoms of my sin,
Unhousel'd, disappointed, unanel'd;
No reckoning made, but sent to my account
With all my imperfections on my head:
O, horrible! O, horrible! most horrible!
If thou hast nature in thee, bear it not;
Let not the royal bed of Denmark be
A couch for luxury and damned incest.
But, howsoever thou pursu'st this act,
Taint not thy mind, nor let thy soul contrive
Against thy mother aught; leave her to heaven,
And to those thorns that in her bosom lodge,
To prick and sting her. Fare thee well at once!
The glowworm shows the matin to be near,
And 'gins to pale his uneffectual fire;
Adieu, adieu, adieu! remember me. [*Exit.*
Ham. O all you host of heaven! O earth! What else?
And shall I couple hell?—O fye!—Hold, hold my heart!

And you, my sinews, grow not instant old,
But bear me stiffly up!—Remember thee?
Ay, thou poor ghost, while memory holds a seat
In this distracted globe. Remember thee?
Yea, from the table of my memory
I'll wipe away all trivial fond records,
All saws of books, all forms, all pressures past,
That youth and observation copied there;
And thy commandment all alone shall live
Within the book and volume of my brain,
Unmix'd with baser matter: yes, by heaven.
O most pernicious woman!
O villain, villain, smiling, damned villain!
My tables,—meet it is, I set it down,
That one may smile, and smile, and be a villain;
At least, I am sure, it may be so in Denmark:
[*Writing.*
So, uncle, there you are. Now to my word;
It is, *Adieu, adieu! remember me.*
I have sworn 't.

Hor. [*Within.*] My lord, my lord,——
Mar. [*Within.*] Lord Hamlet,——
Hor. [*Within.*] Heaven secure him!
Ham. So be it!
Mar. [*Within.*] Illo, ho, ho, my lord!
Ham. Hillo, ho, ho, boy! come, bird, come.

Enter HORATIO *and* MARCELLUS.

Mar. How is 't, my noble lord?
Hor. What news, my lord?
Ham. O wonderful!
Hor. Good my lord, tell it.
Ham. No;
You will reveal it.
Hor. Not I, my lord, by heaven.
Mar. Nor I, my lord.
Ham. How say you then; would heart of man once think it?
But you'll be secret,——
Hor. Mar. Ay, by heaven, my lord.
Ham. There's ne'er a villain, dwelling in all Denmark,
But he's an arrant knave.
Hor. There needs no ghost, my lord, come from the grave,
To tell us this.
Ham. Why, right; you are in the right;
And so, without more circumstance at all,
I hold it fit, that we shake hands, and part:
You, as your business, and desire, shall point you;—
For every man hath business, and desire,
Such as it is,—and, for my own poor part,
Look you, I will go pray.
Hor. These are but wild and whirling words, my lord.
Ham. I am sorry they offend you, heartily;
'Faith, heartily. [yes,
Hor. There's no offence, my lord.
Ham. Yes, by Saint Patrick, but there is, Horatio,
And much offence too. Touching this vision here,—
It is an honest ghost, that let me tell you:
For your desire to know what is between us,
O'ermaster it as you may. And now, good friends,
As you are friends, scholars, and soldiers,
Give me one poor request.
Hor. What is 't, my lord?
We will.
Ham. Never make known what you have seen to-night.
Hor. Mar. My lord, we will not.
Ham. Nay, but swear 't.
Hor. In faith,
My lord, not I.
Mar. Nor I, my lord, in faith.
Ham. Upon my sword.
Mar. We have sworn, my lord, already.
Ham. Indeed, upon my sword, indeed.
Ghost. [*Beneath.*] Swear.
Ham. Ha, ha, boy! say'st thou so? art thou there, true-penny?
Come on,—you hear this fellow in the cellarage,—
Consent to swear.
Hor. Propose the oath, my lord.
Ham. Never to speak of this that you have seen,
Swear by my sword.
Ghost. [*Beneath.*] Swear.
Ham. *Hic et ubique!* then we'll shift our ground:—
Come hither, gentlemen,
And lay your hands again upon my sword:
Swear by my sword,
Never to speak of this that you have heard.
Ghost. [*Beneath.*] Swear by his sword.
Ham. Well said, old mole! canst work i' the earth so fast?
A worthy pioneer!—Once more remove, good friends.
Hor. O day and night, but this is wondrous strange!
Ham. And therefore as a stranger give it welcome.
There are more things in heaven and earth, Horatio,
Than are dreamt of in your philosophy.
But come;—
Here, as before, never, so help you mercy!
How strange or odd soe'er I bear myself,
As I, perchance, hereafter shall think meet
To put an antick disposition on,—
That you, at such times seeing me, never shall,
With arms encumber'd thus, or this head-shake,
Or by pronouncing of some doubtful phrase,
As, *Well, well, we know*;—or, *We could, an if we would*;—or, *If we list to speak*;—or, *There be, an if they might*;—
Or such ambiguous giving out, to note
That you know aught of me:—This not to do, swear;
So grace and mercy at your most need help you!
Ghost. [*Beneath.*] Swear.
Ham. Rest, rest, perturbed spirit! So, gentlemen,
With all my love I do commend me to you:
And what so poor a man as Hamlet is
May do, to express his love and friending to you,
God willing, shall not lack. Let us go in together;
And still your fingers on your lips, I pray.
The time is out of joint;—O cursed spite!
That ever I was born to set it right!
Nay, come, let's go together. [*Exeunt.*

ACT II.

SCENE I. *A Room in* Polonius' *House.*

Enter POLONIUS *and* REYNALDO.

Pol. Give him this money, and these notes, Reynaldo.
Rey. I will, my lord.
Pol. You shall do marvellous wisely, good Reynaldo,
Before you visit him, to make inquiry
Of his behaviour.
Rey. My lord, I did intend it.
Pol. Marry, well said: very well said. Look you, sir,
Inquire me first what Danskers are in Paris;
And how, and who, what means, and where they keep,
What company, at what expense; and finding,
By this encompassment and drift of question,
That they do know my son, come you more nearer
Than your particular demands will touch it;

Take you, as 'twere, some distant knowledge of him;
As thus,—*I know his father, and his friends,*
And, in part, him;—Do you mark this, Reynaldo?

Rey. Ay, very well, my lord.

Pol. *And, in part, him;—but,* you may say, *not well:*
But, if't be he I mean, he's very wild;
Addicted so and so;—and there put on him
What forgeries you please; marry, none so rank
As may dishonour him; take heed of that;
But, sir, such wanton, wild, and usual slips,
As are companions noted and most known
To youth and liberty.

Rey. As, gaming, my lord.

Pol. Ay, or drinking, fencing, swearing, quarrelling,
Drabbing:—You may go so far.

Rey. My lord, that would dishonour him.

Pol. 'Faith, no; as you may season it in the charge.
You must not put another scandal on him,
That he is open to incontinency;
That's not my meaning: but breathe his faults so quaintly,
That they may seem the taints of liberty;
The flash and outbreak of a fiery mind;
A savageness in unreclaimed blood,
Of general assault.

Rey. But, my good lord,——

Pol. Wherefore should you do this?

Rey. Ay, my lord,
I would know that.

Pol. Marry, sir, here's my drift;
And, I believe, it is a fetch of warrant:
You laying these slight sullies on my son,
As 'twere a thing a little soil'd i'the working,
Mark you,
Your party in converse, him you would sound,
Having ever seen in the prenominate crimes,
The youth you breathe of, guilty, be assur'd,
He closes with you in this consequence;
Good sir, or so; or *friend,* or *gentleman,*—
According to the phrase, or the addition,
Of man, and country.

Rey. Very good, my lord.

Pol. And then, sir, does he this,—He does—
What was I about to say?—By the mass, I was about to say something:—Where did I leave?

Rey. At, closes in the consequence.

Pol. At, closes in the consequence,—*Ay, marry;*
He closes with you thus:—*I know the gentleman;*
I saw him yesterday, or t'other day,
Or then, or then; with such, or such; and, as you say,
There was he gaming; there o'ertook in his rouse;
There falling out at tennis: or, perchance,
I saw him enter such a house of sale
(*Videlicet,* a brothel), *or so forth.*
See you now;
Your bait of falsehood takes this carp of truth:
And thus do we of wisdom and of reach,
With windlaces, and with assays of bias,
By indirections find directions out;
So, by my former lecture and advice,
Shall you my son: You have me, have you not?

Rey. My lord, I have.

Pol. God be wi' you; fare you well.

Rey. Good my lord,——

Pol. Observe his inclination in yourself.

Rey. I shall, my lord.

Pol. And let him ply his musick.

Rey. Well, my lord. [*Exit.*

Enter OPHELIA.

Pol. Farewell!—How now, Ophelia? what's the matter?

Oph. O, my lord, my lord, I have been so affrighted!

Pol. With what, in the name of heaven?

Oph. My lord, as I was sewing in my closet,
Lord Hamlet,—with his doublet all unbrac'd;
No hat upon his head; his stockings foul'd,
Ungarter'd, and down-gyved to his ancle;
Pale as his shirt; his knees knocking each other;
And with a look so piteous in purport,
As if he had been loosed out of hell,
To speak of horrors,—he comes before me.

Pol. Mad for thy love?

Oph. My lord, I do not know;
But, truly, I do fear it.

Pol. What said he?

Oph. He took me by the wrist, and held me hard;
Then goes he to the length of all his arm;
And, with his other hand thus o'er his brow,
He falls to such perusal of my face,
As he would draw it. Long stay'd he so;
At last,—a little shaking of mine arm,
And thrice his head thus waving up and down,—
He rais'd a sigh so piteous and profound,
As it did seem to shatter all his bulk,
And end his being: That done, he let's me go:
And, with his head over his shoulder turn'd,
He seem'd to find his way without his eyes;
For out o' doors he went without their help,
And, to the last, bended their light on me.

Pol. Come, go with me; I will go seek the king.
This is the very ecstasy of love;
Whose violent property foredoes itself,
And leads the will to desperate undertakings,
As oft as any passion under heaven,
That does afflict our natures. I am sorry,—
What, have you given him any hard words of late?

Oph. No, my good lord; but, as you did command,
I did repel his letters, and denied
His access to me.

Pol. That hath made him mad.
I am sorry, that with better heed and judgment,
I had not quoted him: I fear'd, he did but trifle,
And meant to wreck thee; but, beshrew my jealousy!
It seems, it is as proper to our age
To cast beyond ourselves in our opinions,
As it is common for the younger sort
To lack discretion. Come, go we to the king:
This must be known; which, being kept close, might move
More grief to hide, than hate to utter love.
Come. [*Exeunt.*

SCENE II. *A Room in the Castle.*

Enter King, Queen, ROSENCRANTZ, GUILDENSTERN, *and* Attendants.

King. Welcome, dear Rosencrantz, and Guildenstern!
Moreover that we much did long to see you,
The need, we have to use you, did provoke
Our hasty sending. Something have you heard
Of Hamlet's transformation; so I call it,
Since not the exterior nor the inward man
Resembles that it was: What it should be,
More than his father's death, that thus hath put him
So much from the understanding of himself,
I cannot dream of: I entreat you both,
That,—being of so young days brought up with him;
And, since, so neighbour'd to his youth and humour,—
That you vouchsafe your rest here in our court
Some little time: so by your companies
To draw him on to pleasures; and to gather,
So much as from occasion you may glean,
Whether aught, to us unknown, afflicts him thus,
That, open'd, lies within our remedy.

Queen. Good gentlemen, he hath much talk'd of you;
And, sure I am, two men there are not living,
To whom he more adheres. If it will please you

To show us so much gentry, and good will,
As to expend your time with us awhile,
For the supply and profit of our hope,
Your visitation shall receive such thanks
As fits a king's remembrance.

Ros. Both your majesties
Might, by the sovereign power you have of us,
Put your dread pleasures more into command
Than to entreaty.

Guil. But we both obey;
And here give up ourselves, in the full bent,
To lay our service freely at your feet,
To be commanded.

King. Thanks, Rosencrantz, and gentle Guildenstern:

Queen. Thanks, Guildenstern, and gentle Rosencrantz;
And I beseech you instantly to visit
My too much changed son.—Go, some of you,
And bring these gentlemen where Hamlet is.

Guil. Heavens make our presence, and our practices,
Pleasant and helpful to him!

Queen. Ay, amen!

[*Exeunt* ROS. GUIL. *and some* Attendants.

Enter POLONIUS.

Pol. The embassadors from Norway, my good lord,
Are joyfully return'd.

King. Thou still hast been the father of good news.

Pol. Have I, my lord? Assure you, my good liege,
I hold my duty, as I hold my soul,
Both to my God, and to my gracious king;
And I do think (or else this brain of mine
Hunts not the trail of policy so sure
As it hath us'd to do) that I have found
The very cause of Hamlet's lunacy.

King. O, speak of that; that do I long to hear.

Pol. Give first admittance to the embassadors;
My news shall be the fruit to that great feast.

King. Thyself do grace to them, and bring them in. [*Exit* POLONIUS.
He tells me, my dear Gertrude, he hath found
The head and source of all your son's distemper.

Queen. I doubt, it is no other but the main;
His father's death, and our o'erhasty marriage.

Re-enter POLONIUS, *with* VOLTIMAND *and* CORNELIUS.

King. Well, we shall sift him.—Welcome my good friends!
Say, Voltimand, what from our brother Norway?

Vol. Most fair return of greetings and desires.
Upon our first, he sent out to suppress
His nephew's levies; which to him appear'd
To be a preparation 'gainst the Polack;
But, better look'd into, he truly found
It was against your highness: Whereat griev'd,—
That so his sickness, age, and impotence,
Was falsely borne in hand,—sends out arrests
On Fortinbras; which he, in brief, obeys;
Receives rebuke from Norway; and, in fine,
Makes vow before his uncle, never more
To give the assay of arms against your majesty.
Whereon old Norway, overcome with joy,
Gives him three thousand crowns in annual fee;
And his commission, to employ those soldiers,
So levied as before, against the Polack:
With an entreaty, herein further shown,
[*Gives a Paper.*
That it might please you to give quiet pass
Through your dominions for this enterprise;
On such regards of safety and allowance.
As therein are set down.

King. It likes us well:
And, at our more consider'd time, we'll read,
Answer, and think upon this business.
Mean time, we thank you for your well-took labour:
Go to your rest; at night we'll feast together:
Most welcome home!

[*Exeunt* VOLTIMAND *and* CORNELIUS.

Pol. This business is well ended.
My liege, and madam, to expostulate
What majesty should be, what duty is,
Why day is day, night, night, and time is time,
Were nothing but to waste night, day, and time.
Therefore,—since brevity is the soul of wit,
And tediousness the limbs and outward flourishes,—
I will be brief: Your noble son is mad:
Mad call I it: for, to define true madness,
What is't, but to be nothing else but mad:
But let that go.

Queen. More matter, with less art,

Pol. Madam, I swear, I use no art at all.
That he is mad, 'tis true: 'tis true, 'tis pity;
And pity 'tis, 'tis true: a foolish figure;
But farewell it, for I will use no art.
Mad let us grant him then: and now remains,
That we find out the cause of this effect;
Or, rather say, the cause of this defect;
For this effect, defective, comes by cause:
Thus it remains, and the remainder thus.
Perpend.
I have a daughter; have, while she is mine;
Who, in her duty and obedience, mark,
Hath given me this: Now gather and surmise.
—*To the celestial, and my soul's idol, the most beautified Ophelia.*——
That's an ill phrase, a vile phrase; *beautified* is a vile phrase; but you shall hear.—Thus:
In her excellent white bosom, these, &c.

Queen. Came this from Hamlet to her?

Pol. Good madam, stay awhile; I will be faithful.—

Doubt thou the stars are fire, [Reads.
Doubt, that the sun doth move,
Doubt truth to be a liar;
But never doubt I love.

O dear Ophelia, *I am ill at these numbers; I have not art to reckon my groans; but that I love thee best, O most best, believe it. Adieu.*

Thine evermore, most dear lady, whilst this machine is to him, Hamlet.

This, in obedience, hath my daughter shown me:
And more above, hath his solicitings,
As they fell out by time, by means, and place,
All given to mine ear.

King. But how hath she
Receiv'd his love?

Pol. What do you think of me?

King. As of a man faithful and honourable.

Pol. I would fain prove so. But what might you think,
When I had seen this hot love on the wing
(As I perceiv'd it, I must tell you that,
Before my daughter told me), what might you,
Or my dear majesty your queen here, think,
If I had play'd the desk, or table-book;
Or given my heart a winking, mute and dumb;
Or look'd upon this love with idle sight;
What might you think? no, I went round to work,
And my young mistress thus did I bespeak;
Lord Hamlet is a prince out of thy star;
This must not be: and then I precepts gave her,
That she should lock herself from his resort,
Admit no messengers, receive no tokens.
Which done, she took the fruits of my advice;
And he, repulsed (a short tale to make),
Fell into a sadness; then into a fast;
Thence to a watch; thence into a weakness;
Thence to a lightness; and, by this declension,
Into the madness wherein now he raves,
And all we mourn for.

King. Do you think, 'tis this?

Queen. It may be, very likely.

Pol. Hath there been such a time (I'd fain know that),

That I have positively said, *'Tis so,*
When it prov'd otherwise?

King. Not that I know.

Pol. Take this from this, if this be otherwise:
[*Pointing to his Head and Shoulder.*
If circumstances lead me, I will find
Where truth is hid, though it were hid indeed
Within the centre.

King. How may we try it further?

Pol. You know, sometimes he walks four hours together,
Here in the lobby.

Queen. So he does, indeed.

Pol. At such a time I'll loose my daughter to him:
Be you and I behind an arras then;
Mark the encounter: if he love her not,
And be not from his reason fallen thereon,
Let me be no assistant for a state,
But keep a farm, and carters.

King. We will try it.

Enter HAMLET, *reading.*

Queen. But, look, where sadly the poor wretch comes reading.

Pol. Away, I do beseech you, both away;
I'll board him presently:—O, give me leave.—
[*Exeunt* KING, QUEEN, *and* Attendants.
How does my good Lord Hamlet?

Ham. Well, god-'a-mercy.

Pol. Do you know me, my lord?

Ham. Excellent well; you are a fishmonger.

Pol. Not I, my lord.

Ham. Then I would you were so honest a man.

Pol. Honest, my lord?

Ham. Ay, sir; to be honest, as this world goes, is to be one man picked out of ten thousand.

Pol. That's very true, my lord.

Ham. For if the sun breed maggots in a dead dog, being a god, kissing carrion,——Have you a daughter?

Pol. I have, my lord.

Ham. Let her not walk i'the sun: conception is a blessing; but as your daughter may conceive,—friend, look to't.

Pol. How say you by that? [*Aside.*] Still harping on my daughter:—yet he knew me not at first; he said, I was a fishmonger: He is far gone, far gone: and, truly in my youth I suffered much extremity for love; very near this. I'll speak to him again.—What do you read, my lord?

Ham. Words, words, words!

Pol. What is the matter, my lord?

Ham. Between who?

Pol. I mean, the matter that you read, my lord.

Ham. Slanders, sir: for the satirical rogue says here, that old men have gray beards: that their faces are wrinkled; their eyes purging thick amber, and plum-tree gum; and that they have a plentiful lack of wit, together with most weak hams: All of which, sir, though I most powerfully and potently believe, yet I hold it not honesty to have it thus set down; for yourself, sir, should be as old as I am, if, like a crab, you could go backward.

Pol. Though this be madness, yet there's method in it. [*Aside.*] Will you walk out of the air, my lord?

Ham. Into my grave?

Pol. Indeed, that is out o' the air.—How pregnant sometimes his replies are! a happiness that often madness hits on, which reason and sanity could not so prosperously be delivered of. I will leave him, and suddenly contrive the means of meeting between him and my daughter.—My honourable lord, I will most humbly take my leave of you.

Ham. You cannot, sir, take from me any thing that I will more willingly part withal; except my life, except my life, except my life.

Pol. Fare you well, my lord.

Ham. Those tedious old fools!

Enter ROSENCRANTZ *and* GUILDENSTERN.

Pol. You go to seek the Lord Hamlet; there he is.

Ros. God save you, sir! [*To* POLONIUS.
[*Exit* POLONIUS.

Guil. My honour'd lord!—

Ros. My most dear lord!—

Ham. My excellent good friends! How dost thou, Guildenstern? Ah, Rosencrantz! Good lads, how do ye both?

Ros. As the indifferent children of the earth.

Guil. Happy, in that we are not overhappy;
On fortune's cap we are not the very button.

Ham. Nor the soles of her shoe?

Ros. Neither, my lord.

Ham. Then you live about her waist, or in the middle of her favours?

Guil. 'Faith, her privates we.

Ham. In the secret paths of fortune? O, most true; she is a strumpet. What news?

Ros. None, my lord; but that the world is grown honest.

Ham. Then is doomsday near: But your news is not true. Let me question more in particular: What have you, my good friends, deserved at the hands of fortune, that she sends you to prison hither?

Guil. Prison, my lord!

Ham. Denmark's a prison.

Ros. Then is the world one.

Ham. A goodly one; in which there are many confines, wards, and dungeons; Denmark being one of the worst.

Ros. We think not so, my lord.

Ham. Why, then 'tis none to you; for there is nothing either good or bad, but thinking makes it so: to me it is a prison.

Ros. Why, then your ambition makes it one; 'tis too narrow for your mind.

Ham. O God! I could be bounded in a nutshell, and count myself a king of infinite space; were it not that I have bad dreams.

Guil. Which dreams, indeed, are ambition; for the very substance of the ambitious is merely the shadow of a dream.

Ham. A dream itself is but a shadow.

Ros. Truly, and I hold ambition of so airy and light a quality, that it is but a shadow's shadow.

Ham. Then are our beggars, bodies; and our monarchs, and outstretch'd heroes, the beggars' shadows: Shall we to the court? for, by my fay, I cannot reason.

Ros. Guil. We'll wait upon you.

Ham. No such matter: I will not sort you with the rest of my servants; for, to speak to you like an honest man, I am most dreadfully attended. But, in the beaten way of friendship, what make you at Elsinore?

Ros. To visit you, my lord; no other occasion.

Ham. Beggar that I am, I am even poor in thanks; but I thank you; and sure, dear friends, my thanks are too dear, a halfpenny. Were you not sent for? Is it your own inclining? Is it a free visitation? Come, come; deal justly with me: come, come; nay, speak.

Guil. What should we say, my lord?

Ham. Any thing—but to the purpose. You were sent for; and there is a kind of confession in your looks, which your modesties have not craft enough to colour: I know, the good king and queen have sent for you.

Ros. To what end, my lord?

Ham. That you must teach me. But let me conjure you by the rights of our fellowship, by the consonancy of our youth, by the obligation of our ever-preserved love, and by what more dear a better proposer could charge you withal, be even and direct with me, whether you were sent for, or no?

Ros. What say you? [*To* GUILDENSTERN.

Ham. Nay, then I have an eye of you; [*Aside.*] —if you love me, hold not off.

Guil. My lord, we were sent for.

Ham. I will tell you why; so shall my anticipation prevent your discovery, and your secrecy to the king and queen moult no feather. I have of late (but, wherefore, I know not,) lost all my mirth, forgone all custom of exercises: and, indeed, it goes so heavily with my disposition, that this goodly frame, the earth, seems to me a steril promontory; this most excellent canopy, the air, look you, this brave o'erhanging firmament, this majestical roof fretted with golden fire, why, it appears no other thing to me, than a foul and pestilent congregation of vapours. What a piece of work is a man! How noble in reason! how infinite in faculties! in form, and moving, how express and admirable! in action, how like an angel! in apprehension, how like a god! the beauty of the world! the paragon of animals; And yet, to me, what is this quintessence of dust? man delights not me, no, nor woman neither; though, by your smiling, you seem to say so.

Ros. My lord, there is no such stuff in my thoughts.

Ham. Why did you laugh then when I said, *Man delights not me?*

Ros. To think, my lord, if you delight not in man, what lenten entertainment the players shall receive from you: we coted them on the way; and hither are they coming, to offer you service.

Ham. He that plays the king, shall be welcome; his majesty shall have tribute of me: the adventurous knight shall use his foil, and target: the lover shall not sigh gratis; the humorous man shall end his part in peace: the clown shall make those laugh, whose lungs are tickled o' the sere; and the lady shall say her mind freely, or the blank verse shall halt for't. —What players are they?

Ros. Even those you were wont to take such delight in, the tragedians of the city.

Ham. How chances it, they travel? their residence, both in reputation and profit, was better both ways.

Ros. I think, their inhibition comes by the means of the late innovation.

Ham. Do they hold the same estimation they did when I was in the city? Are they so followed?

Ros. No, indeed, they are not.

Ham. How comes it? Do they grow rusty?

Ros. Nay, their endeavour keeps in the wonted pace: But there is, sir, an aiery of children, little eyases, that cry out on the top of question, and are most tyrannically clapped for't; these are now the fashion; and so berattle the common stages (so they call them), that many, wearing rapiers, are afraid of goose quills, and dare scarce come thither.

Ham. What, are they children? who maintains them? how are they escoted? Will they pursue the quality, no longer than they can sing? will they not say afterwards, if they should grow themselves to common players (as it is most like, if their means are no better,) their writers do them wrong, to make them exclaim against their own succession?

Ros. 'Faith, there has been much to do on both sides; and the nation holds it no sin, to tarre them on to controversy: there was, for a while, no money bid for argument, unless the poet and the player went to cuffs in the question.

Ham. Is it possible?

Guil. O, there has been much throwing about of brains.

Ham. Do the boys carry it away?

Ros. Ay, that they do, my lord; Hercules and his load too.

Ham. It is not very strange: for my uncle is King of Denmark, and those, that would make mouths at him while my father lived, give twenty, forty, fifty, a hundred ducats a piece, for his picture in little. 'Sblood, there is something it this more than natural, if philosophy could find it out. [*Flourish of Trumpets within.*

Guil. There are the players.

Ham. Gentlemen, you are welcome to Elsinore. Your hands. Come then: the appurtenance of welcome is fashion and ceremony: let me comply with you in this garb; lest my extent to the players, which, I tell you, must show fairly outward, should more appear like entertainment than yours. You are welcome: but my uncle-father, and aunt-mother, are deceived.

Guil. In what, my dear lord?

Ham. I am but mad north-north west; when the wind is southerly, I know a hawk from a hand-saw.

Enter POLONIUS.

Pol. Well be with you, gentlemen!

Ham. Hark you, Guildenstern;—and you too;—at each ear a hearer: that great baby, you see there, is not yet out of his swaddling-clouts.

Ros. Happily, he's the second time come to them; for, they say, an old man is twice a child.

Ham. I will prophesy, he comes to tell me of the players; mark it.—You say right, sir: o'Monday morning; 'twas then, indeed.

Pol. My lord, I have news to tell you.

Ham. My lord, I have news to tell you; When Roscius was an actor in Rome,——

Pol. The actors are come hither, my lord.

Ham. Buz, buz!

Pol. Upon my honour,——

Ham. *Then came each actor on his ass,*——

Pol. The best actors in the world, either for tragedy, comedy, history, pastoral, pastoral-comical, historical-pastoral, tragical-historical, tragical-comical-historical-pastoral, scene individable, or poem unlimited:—Seneca cannot be too heavy, nor Plautus too light for the law of writ, and the liberty:—these are the only men.

Ham. *O Jephthah, judge of Israel,*—what a treasure hadst thou!

Pol. What a treasure had he, my lord?

Ham. Why—*One fair daughter, and no more,*
The which he loved passing well.

Pol. Still on my daughter. [*Aside.*

Ham. Am I not i' the right, old Jephthah?

Pol. If you call me Jephthah, my lord, I have a daughter that I love passing well.

Ham. Nay, that follows not.

Pol. What follows then, my lord?

Ham. Why, *As by lot, God wot,* and then, you know, *It came to pass, As most like it was,*—The first row of the pious chanson will show you more; for look, my abridgment comes.

Enter Four or Five Players.

You are welcome, masters; welcome, all:—I am glad to see thee well:—welcome, good friends.—O, old friend! Why, thy face is valanced since I saw thee last; Com'st thou to beard me in Denmark?—What! my young lady and mistress! By-'r-lady, your ladyship is nearer to heaven, than when I saw you last, by the altitude of a chopine. 'Pray God, your voice, like a piece of uncurrent gold, be not cracked within the ring.—Masters, you are all welcome. We'll e'en to't like French falconers, fly at any thing we see: We'll have a speech straight: Come, give us a taste of your quality; come, a passionate speech.

1 *Play.* What speech, my lord?

Ham. I heard thee speak me a speech once, —but it was never acted; or, if it was, not above once: for the play, I remember, pleased not the million; 'twas caviare to the general: but it was (as I received it, and others, whose judgments, in such matters, cried in the top of mine), an excellent play: well digested in the scenes, set down with as much modesty as cunning. I remember, one said, there were no sallets in the lines, to make the matter savoury: nor no matter in the phrase, that might indite the author of affection; but called it, an honest method, as wholesome as sweet, and by very much more handsome than fine. One speech in it I chiefly loved: 'twas Æneas' tale to Dido; and thereabout of it especially, where he speaks of Priam's slaughter: If it live in your memory, begin at this line; let me see, let me see;—

The rugged Pyrrhus, like the Hyrcanian beast,—

'tis not so; it begins with Pyrrhus.

The rugged Pyrrhus, he whose sable arms,
Black as his purpose, did the night resemble,
When he lay couched in the ominous horse,
Hath now his dread and black complexion smear'd
With heraldry more dismal; head to foot
Now is he total gules; horridly trick'd
With blood of fathers, mothers, daughters, sons;
Bak'd and impasted with the parching streets,
That lend a tyrannous and a damned light
To their lord's murder: Roasted in wrath, and fire,
And thus o'er-sized with coagulate gore,
With eyes like carbuncles, the hellish Pyrrhus
Old grandsire Priam seeks;—So proceed you.

Pol. 'Fore God, my lord, well spoken: with good accent, and good discretion.

1 Play. *Anon he finds him*
Striking too short at Greeks; his antique sword,
Rebellious to his arm, lies where it falls,
Repugnant to command: Unequal match'd,
Pyrrhus at Priam drives; in rage, strikes wide;
But with the whiff and wind of his fell sword
The unnerved father falls. Then senseless Ilium,
Seeming to feel this blow, with flaming top
Stoops to his base; and with a hideous crash
Takes prisoner Pyrrhus' ear: for, lo! his sword
Which was declining on the milky head
Of reverend Priam, seem'd i' the air to stick:
So, as a painted tyrant, Pyrrhus stood;
And, like a neutral to his will and matter,
Did nothing.
But as we often see, against some storm,
A silence in the heavens, the rack stand still,
The bold winds speechless, and the orb below
As hush as death: anon the dreadful thunder
Doth rend the region: So, after Pyrrhus' pause,
A roused vengeance sets him new a work;
And never did the Cyclops' hammers fall
On Mars's armour, forg'd for proof eterne
With less remorse than Pyrrhus' bleeding sword
Now falls on Priam.—
Out, out, thou strumpet, Fortune! All you gods,
In general synod, take away her power;
Break all the spokes and fellies from her wheel,
And bowl the round nave down the hill of heaven,
As low as to the fiends!

Pol. This is too long.

Ham. It shall to the barber's, with your beard. —'Pr'ythee, say on:—He's for a jig, or a tale of bawdry, or he sleeps:—say on: come to Hecuba.

1 Play. *But who, ah woe! had seen the mobled queen*——

Ham. The mobled queen?

Pol. That's good; mobled queen is good.

1 Play. *Run barefoot up and down, threat'ning the flames*
With bisson rheum; a clout upon that head,
Where late the diadem stood; and, for a robe,
About her lank and all o'er-teemed loins,
A blanket, in the alarm of fear caught up;
Who this had seen, with tongue in venom steep'd,
'Gainst fortune's state would treason have pronounc'd:
But if the gods themselves did see her then,
When she saw Pyrrhus make malicious sport
In mincing with his sword her husband's limbs:
The instant burst of clamour that she made
(Unless things mortal move them not at all),
Would have made milch the burning eye of heaven,
And passion in the gods.

Pol. Look, whether he has not turn'd his colour, and has tears in's his eyes.—'Pr'ythee, no more.

Ham. 'Tis well; I'll have thee speak out the rest of this soon.—Good my lord, will you see the players well bestowed? Do you hear, let them be well used; for they are the abstract, and brief chronicles, of the time: After your death you were better have a bad epitaph, than their ill report while you live.

Pol. My lord, I will use them according to their desert.

Ham. Odd's bodikin, man, much better: Use every man after his desert, and who shall 'scape whipping? Use them after your own honour and dignity: The less they deserve, the more merit is in your bounty. Take them in.

Pol. Come, sirs.

[*Exit* POLONIUS, *with some of the* Players.

Ham. Follow him, friends: we'll hear a play to-morrow.—Dost thou hear me, old friend; can you play the murder of Gonzago?

1 *Play.* Ay, my lord.

Ham. We'll have it to-morrow night. You could, for a need, study a speech of some dozen or sixteen lines, which I would set down, and insert in't? could you not?

1 *Play.* Ay, my lord.

Ham. Very well.—Follow that lord; and look you mock him not. [*Exit* Player.] My good friends [*To* Ros. *and* Guil.] I'll leave you till night: you are welcome to Elsinore.

Ros. Good my lord!

[*Exeunt* ROSENCRANTZ *and* GUILDENSTERN.

Ham. Ay, so, God be wi' you:—Now I am alone.
O what a rogue and peasant slave am I!
Is it not monstrous that this player here,
But in a fiction, in a dream of passion,
Could force his soul so to his own conceit,
That from her working, all his visage wann'd;
Tears in his eyes, distraction in's aspect,
A broken voice, and his whole function suiting
With forms to his conceit? And all for nothing!
For Hecuba!
What's Hecuba to him, or he to Hecuba,
That he should weep for her? What would he do,
Had he the motive and the cue for passion,
That I have? He would drown the stage with tears,
And cleave the general ear with horrid speech;
Make mad the guilty, and appal the free,
Confound the ignorant, and amaze, indeed,
The very faculties of eyes and ears.
Yet I,
A dull and muddy-mettled rascal, peak,
Like John a-dreams, unpregnant of my cause,
And can say nothing; no not for a king,
Upon whose property, and most dear life,
A damn'd defeat was made. Am I a coward?
Who calls me villain? breaks my pate across?
Plucks off my beard, and blows it in my face?
Tweaks me by the nose? gives me the lie i' the throat,
As deep as to the lungs? Who does me this?
Ha!
Why, I should take it: for it cannot be,
But I am pigeon-liver'd, and lack gall
To make oppression bitter; or, ere this,
I should have fatted all the region kites
With this slave's offal: Bloody, bawdy villain!
Remorseless, treacherous, lecherous, kindless villain!
Why, what an ass am I? This is most brave;
That I, the son of a dear father murder'd,
Prompted to my revenge by heaven and hell,
Must, like a whore, unpack my heart with words,

And fall a cursing like a very drab,
A scullion!
Fye upon't! foh! About my brains! Humph! I have heard,
That guilty creatures, sitting at a play,
Have, by the very cunning of the scene,
Been struck so to the soul, that presently
They have proclaim'd their malefactions;
For murder, though it have no tongue, will speak
With most miraculous organ. I'll have these players
Play something like the murder of my father,
Before mine uncle; I'll observe his looks;
I'll tent him to the quick; if he do blench,
I know my course. The spirit, that I have seen,
May be a devil: and the devil hath power
To assume a pleasing shape; yea, and, perhaps,
Out of my weakness, and my melancholy
(As he is very potent with such spirits),
Abuses me to damn me: I'll have grounds
More relative than this: The play's the thing,
Wherein I'll catch the conscience of the king.
[*Exit.*

ACT III.

SCENE I. *A Room in the Castle.*

Enter King, Queen, POLONIUS, OPHELIA, ROSENCRANTZ, *and* GUILDENSTERN.

King. And can you, by no drift of conference
Get from him why he puts on this confusion;
Grating so harshly all his days of quiet
With turbulent and dangerous lunacy?

Ros. He does confess, he feels himself distracted;
But from what cause he will by no means speak.

Guil. Nor do we find him forward to be sounded;
But, with a crafty madness, keeps aloof,
When we would bring him on to some confession
Of his true state.

Queen. Did he receive you well?

Ros. Most like a gentleman.

Guil. But with much forcing of his disposition.

Ros. Niggard of question; but, of our demands,
Most free in his reply.

Queen. Did you assay him
To any pastime?

Ros. Madam, it so fell out, that certain players
We o'er-raught on the way: of these we told him;
And there did seem in him a kind of joy
To hear of it: They are about the court;
And, as I think, they have already order
This night to play before him.

Pol. 'Tis most true:
And he beseech'd me to entreat your majesties,
To hear and see the matter.

King. With all my heart; and it doth much content me
To hear him so inclin'd.
Good gentlemen, give him a further edge,
And drive his purpose on to these delights.

Ros. We shall, my lord.
[*Exeunt* ROSENCRANTZ *and* GUILDENSTERN.

King. Sweet Gertrude, leave us too:
For we have closely sent for Hamlet hither;
That he, as 'twere by accident, may here
Affront Ophelia:
Her father, and myself (lawful espials),
Will so bestow ourselves, that, seeing, unseen,
We may of their encounter frankly judge;
And gather by him, as he is behav'd,
If't be the affliction of his love, or no,
That thus he suffers for.

Queen. I shall obey you:
And, for your part, Ophelia, I do wish,
That your good beauties be the happy cause
Of Hamlet's wildness: so shall I hope, your virtues
Will bring him to his wonted way again,
To both your honours.

Oph. Madam, I wish it may.
[*Exit* Queen.

Pol. Ophelia, walk you here:—Gracious, so please you,
We will bestow ourselves:—Read on this book;
[*To* OPHELIA.
That show of such an exercise may colour
Your loneliness.—We are oft to blame in this,—
'Tis too much prov'd,—that, with devotion's visage,
And pious action, we do sugar o'er
The devil himself.

King. O, 'tis too true! how smart
A lash that speech doth give my conscience!
The harlot's cheek, beautied with plast'ring art,
Is not more ugly to the thing that helps it,
Than is my deed to my most painted word:
O heavy burden! [*Aside.*

Pol. I hear him coming; let's withdraw, my lord. [*Exeunt* King *and* POLONIUS.

Enter HAMLET.

Ham. To be, or not to be, that is the question:—
Whether 'tis nobler in the mind, to suffer
The slings and arrows of outrageous fortune;
Or to take arms against a sea of troubles,
And, by opposing, end them?—To die,—to sleep,—
No more;—and, by a sleep, to say we end
The heart-ach, and the thousand natural shocks
That flesh is heir to,—'tis a consummation
Devoutly to be wish'd. To die;—to sleep;—
To sleep! perchance to dream;—ay, there's the rub;
For in that sleep of death what dreams may come,
When we have shuffled off this mortal coil,
Must give us pause: There's the respect,
That makes calamity of so long life:
For who would bear the whips and scorns of time,
The oppressor's wrong, the proud man's contumely,
The pangs of despis'd love, the law's delay,
The insolence of office, and the spurns
That patient merit of the unworthy takes,
When he himself might his quietus make
With a bare bodkin? who would fardels bear,
To grunt and sweat under a weary life;
But that the dread of something after death,—
The undiscover'd country, from whose bourn
No traveller returns,—puzzles the will;
And makes us rather bear those ills we have,
Than fly to others that we know not of?
Thus conscience does make cowards of us all;
And thus the native hue of resolution
Is sicklied o'er with the pale cast of thought;
And enterprises of great pith and moment,
With this regard, their currents turn awry,
And lose the name of action.—Soft you, now!
The fair Ophelia:—Nymph, in thy orisons
Be all my sins remember'd.

Oph. Good my lord,
How does your honour for this many a day?

Ham. I humbly thank you; well.

Oph. My lord, I have remembrances of yours,
That I have longed long to redeliver;
I pray you, now receive them.

Ham. No, not I;
I never gave you aught.

Oph. My honour'd lord, you know right well, you did:
And, with them, words of so sweet breath compos'd
As made the things more rich: their perfume lost,
Take these again; for to the noble mind,
Rich gifts wax poor, when givers prove unkind.
There, my lord.

Ham. Ha, ha! are you honest?

Oph. My lord?

Ham. Are you fair?

Oph. What means your lordship?

Ham. That if you be honest, and fair, your honesty should admit no discourse to your beauty.

Oph. Could beauty, my lord, have better commerce than with honesty?

Ham. Ay, truly; for the power of beauty will sooner transform honesty from what it is to a bawd, than the force of honesty can translate beauty into his likeness; this was some time a paradox, but now the time gives it proof. I did love you once.

Oph. Indeed, my lord, you made me believe so.

Ham. You should not have believed me; for virtue cannot so inoculate our old stock, but we shall relish of it: I loved you not.

Oph. I was the more deceived.

Ham. Get thee to a nunnery; Why would'st thou be a breeder of sinners? I am myself indifferent honest; but yet I could accuse me of such things, that it were better, my mother had not borne me: I am very proud, revengeful, ambitious; with more offences at my beck, than I have thoughts to put them in, imagination to give them shape, or time to act them in; What should such fellows as I do crawling between earth and heaven! We are arrant knaves, all; believe none of us: Go thy ways to a nunnery. Where's your father?

Oph. At home, my lord.

Ham. Let the doors be shut upon him; that he may play the fool no where but in's own house. Farewell.

Oph. O, help him, you sweet heavens!

Ham. If thou dost marry, I'll give thee this plague for thy dowry; Be thou as chaste as ice, as pure as snow, thou shalt not escape calumny. Get thee to a nunnery; farewell: Or, if thou wilt needs marry, marry a fool; for wise men know well enough, what monsters you make of them. To a nunnery, go; and quickly too. Farewell.

Oph. Heavenly powers restore him!

Ham. I have heard of your paintings too, well enough; God hath given you one face, and you make yourselves another: you jig, you amble, and you lisp, and nickname God's creatures, and make your wantonness your ignorance; Go to; I'll no more of it: it hath made me mad. I say, we will have no more marriages: those that are married already, all but one, shall live; the rest shall keep as they are. To a nunnery, go. [*Exit* HAMLET.

Oph. O, what a noble mind is here o'erthrown!
The courtier's, soldier's, scholar's eye, tongue, sword:
The expectancy and rose of the fair state,
The glass of fashion, and the mould of form,
The observ'd of all observers! quite, quite down,
And I, of ladies most deject and wretched,
That suck'd the honey of his musick vows,
Now see that noble and most sovereign reason,
Like sweet bells jangled, out of tune and harsh;
That unmatch'd form and feature of blown youth,
Blasted with ecstasy: O, woe is me!
To have seen what I have seen, see what I see!

Re-enter KING *and* POLONIUS.

King. Love! his affections do not that way tend;
Nor what he spake, though it lack'd form a little,
Was not like madness. There's something in his soul,
O'er which his melancholy sits on brood;
And, I do doubt, the hatch and the disclose
Will be some danger: Which for to prevent,
I have, in quick determination,
Thus set it down; He shall with speed to England,
For the demand of our neglected tribute:
Haply, the seas, and countries different,
With variable objects, shall expel
This something-settled matter in his heart;
Whereon his brains still beating, puts him thus
From fashion of himself. What think you on't?

Pol. It shall do well: But yet, I do believe,
The origin and commencement of his grief
Sprung from neglected love.—How now, Ophelia?
You need not tell us what lord Hamlet said;
We heard it all.—My lord, do as you please;
But, if you hold it fit after the play,
Let his queen mother all alone entreat him
To show his grief; let her be round with him;
And I'll be plac'd, so please you, in the ear
Of all their conference; If she find him not,
To England send him; or confine him, where
Your wisdom best shall think.

King. It shall be so:
Madness in great ones must not unwatch'd go. [*Exeunt.*

SCENE II. *A Hall in the same.*

Enter HAMLET, *and certain* Players.

Ham. Speak the speech, I pray you, as I pronounced it to you, trippingly on the tongue: but if you mouth it, as many of our players do, I had as lief the town crier spoke my lines. Nor do not saw the air too much with your hand, thus; but use all gently: for in the very torrent, tempest, and (as I may say) whirlwind of your passion, you must acquire and beget a temperance, that may give it smoothness. O, it offends me to the soul, to hear a robustious periwig-pated fellow tear a passion to tatters, to very rags, to split the ears of the groundlings: who, for the most part, are capable of nothing but inexplicable dumb shows, and noise: I would have such a fellow whipped for o'erdoing Termagant; it out-herods Herod: 'Pray you, avoid it.

1 *Play.* I warrant your honour.

Ham. Be not too tame neither, but let your own discretion be your tutor: suit the action to the word, the word to the action: with this special observance, that you o'erstep not the modesty of nature: for any thing so overdone is from the purpose of playing, whose end, both at the first, and now, was, and is, to hold, as 'twere, the mirrour up to nature; to show virtue her own feature, scorn her own image, and the very age and body of the time, his form and pressure. Now this, overdone, or come tardy off, though it make the unskilful laugh, cannot but make the judicious grieve; the censure of which one, must, in your allowance, o'erweigh a whole theatre of others. O, there be players, that I have seen play,—and heard others praise, and that highly,—not to speak it profanely, that, neither having the accent of Christians, nor the gait of Christian, pagan, nor man, have so strutted, and bellowed, that I have thought some of nature's journeymen had made men, and not made them well, they imitated humanity so abominably.

1 *Play.* I hope, we have reformed that indifferently with us.

Ham. O, reform it altogether. And let those, that play your clowns, speak no more than is set down for them: for there be of them, that will themselves laugh, to set on some quantity of barren spectators to laugh too; though, in the mean time, some necessary question of the play be then to be considered: that's villanous; and shows a most pitiful ambition in the fool that uses it. Go, make you ready — [*Exeunt* Players.

Enter POLONIUS, ROSENCRANTZ, *and* GUILDENSTERN.

How now, my lord? will the king hear this piece of work?

Pol. And the queen too, and that presently.

Ham. Bid the players make haste.—
[*Exit* POLONIUS.
Will you two help to hasten them?
Both. Ay, my lord.
[*Exeunt* ROSENCRANTZ *and* GUILDENSTERN.
Ham. What, ho; Horatio!

Enter HORATIO.

Hor. Here, sweet lord, at your service.
Ham. Horatio, thou art e'en as just a man
As e'er my conversation cop'd withal.
Hor. O, my dear lord,——
Ham. Nay, do not think I flatter:
For what advancement may I hope from thee,
That no revenue hast, but thy good spirits,
To feed, and clothe thee? Why should the poor be flatter'd?
No, let the candied tongue lick absurd pomp;
And crook the pregnant hinges of the knee,
Where thrift may follow fawning. Dost thou hear?
Since my dear soul was mistress of her choice,
And could of men distinguish her election,
She hath seal'd thee for herself: for thou hast been
As one, in suffering all, that suffers nothing;
A man, that fortune's buffets and rewards
Hast ta'en with equal thanks; and bless'd are those,
Whose blood and judgment are so well co-mingled,
That they are not a pipe for fortune's finger
To sound what stop she please: Give me that man
That is not passion's slave, and I will wear him
In my heart's core, ay, in my heart of heart,
As I do thee.—Something too much of this.—
There is a play to-night before the king;
One scene of it comes near the circumstance,
Which I have told thee of my father's death.
I pr'ythee, when thou seest that act afoot,
Even with the very comment of thy soul
Observe my uncle: if his occulted guilt
Do not itself unkennel in one speech,
It is a damned ghost that we have seen;
And my imaginations are as foul
As Vulcan's stithy. Give him heedful note:
For I mine eyes will rivet to his face;
And, after, we will both our judgments join
In censure of his seeming.
Hor. Well, my lord:
If he steal aught, the whilst this play is playing,
And scape detecting, I will pay the theft.
Ham. They are coming to the play; I must be idle:
Get you a place.

Danish March. A Flourish. Enter King, Queen, POLONIUS, OPHELIA, ROSENCRANTZ, GUILDENSTERN, *and Others.*

King. How fares our cousin Hamlet?
Ham. Excellent, i'faith; of the chameleon's dish: I eat the air, promise-crammed; you cannot feed capons so.
King. I have nothing with this answer, Hamlet; these words are not mine.
Ham. No, nor mine now. My lord,—you played once in the university, you say?
[*To* POLONIUS.
Pol. That did I, my lord; and was accounted a good actor.
Ham. And what did you enact?
Pol. I did enact Julius Cæsar: I was killed i'the Capitol; Brutus killed me.
Ham. It was a brute part of him, to kill so capital a calf there.—Be the players ready?
Ros. Ay, my lord; they stay upon your patience.
Queen. Come hither, my dear Hamlet, sit by me.
Ham. No, good mother, here's metal more attractive.
Pol. O ho! do you mark that? [*To the* King.
Ham. Lady, shall I lie in your lap?
[*Lying down at* OPHELIA'S *Feet.*
Oph. No, my lord.
Ham. I mean, my head upon your lap?
Oph. Ay, my lord.
Ham. Do you think, I meant country matters?
Oph. I think nothing, my lord.
Ham. That's a fair thought to lie between maids' legs.
Oph. What is, my lord.
Ham. Nothing.
Oph. You are merry, my lord.
Ham. Who, I?
Oph. Ay, my lord.
Ham. O! your only jig-maker. What should a man do, but be merry? for, look you, how cheerfully my mother looks, and my father died within these two hours.
Oph. Nay, 'tis twice two months, my lord.
Ham. So long? Nay, then let the devil wear black, for I'll have a suit of sables. O heavens! die two months ago, and not forgotten yet? Then there's hope, a great man's memory may outlive his life half a year: But, by'r-lady, he must build churches then: or else shall he suffer not thinking on, with the hobby-horse; whose epitaph is, *For, O, for, O, the hobby horse is forgot.*

Trumpets sound. The Dumb Show follows.

Enter a King *and a* Queen, *very lovingly: the* Queen *embracing him, and he her. She kneels, and makes show of protestation unto him. He takes her up, and declines his head upon her neck: lays him down upon a bank of flowers; she, seeing him asleep, leaves him. Anon comes in a* Fellow, *takes off his crown, kisses it, and pours poison in the* King's *ears, and exit. The* Queen *returns; finds the* King *dead, and makes passionate action. The* Poisoner, *with some two or three* Mutes, *comes in again, seeming to lament with her. The dead body is carried away. The* Poisoner *woos the* Queen *with gifts; she seems loath and unwilling awhile; but, in the end accepts his love.*
[Exeunt.

Oph. What means this, my lord?
Ham. Marry, this is miching malicho; it means mischief.
Oph. Belike, this show imports the argument of the play.

Enter Prologue.

Ham. We shall know by this fellow: the players cannot keep counsel; they'll tell all.
Oph. Will he tell us what this show meant?
Ham. Ay, or any show that you'll show him: Be not you ashamed to show, he'll not shame to tell you what it means.
Oph. You are naught, you are naught; I'll mark the play.
Pro. *For us, and for our tragedy,*
Here stooping to your clemency,
We beg your hearing patiently.
Ham. Is this a prologue, or the posy of a ring?
Oph. 'Tis brief, my lord.
Ham. As woman's love.

Enter a King *and a* Queen.

P. King. Full thirty times hath Phœbus' cart gone round
Neptune's salt wash, and Tellus' orbed ground;
And thirty dozen moons, with borrow'd sheen,
About the world have times twelve thirties been;
Since love our hearts, and Hymen did our hands,
Unite commutual in most sacred bands.
P. Queen. So many journeys may the sun and moon
Make us again count o'er, ere love be done!
But, woe is me, you are so sick of late,
So far from cheer, and from your former state,
That I distrust you. Yet, though I distrust,
Discomfort you, my lord, it nothing must:
For women fear too much, even as they love;
And women's fear and love hold quantity;

In neither aught, or in extremity.
Now, what my love is, proof hath made you know;
And as my love is siz'd, my fear is so.
Where love is great, the littlest doubts are fear;
Where little fears grow great, great love grows there.

P. King. 'Faith, I must leave thee, love, and shortly too;
My operant powers their functions leave to do;
And thou shalt live in this fair world behind,
Honour'd, belov'd; and, haply, one as kind
For husband shalt thou——

P. Queen. O, confound the rest!
Such love must needs be treason in my breast;
In second husband let me be accurst!
None wed the second, but who kill'd the first.

Ham. That's wormwood.

P. Queen. The instances, that second marriage move,
Are base respects of thrift, but none of love;
A second time I kill my husband dead,
When second husband kisses me in bed.

P. King. I do believe, you think what now you speak;
But, what we do determine, oft we break.
Purpose is but the slave to memory;
Of violent birth, but poor validity:
Which now, like fruit unripe, sticks on the tree;
But fall, unshaken, when they mellow be.
Most necessary 'tis, that we forget
To pay ourselves what to ourselves is debt:
What to ourselves in passion we propose,
The passion ending, doth the purpose lose.
The violence of either grief or joy
Their own enactures, with themselves destroy;
Where joy most revels, grief doth most lament;
Grief joys, joy grieves, on slender accident.
This world is not for aye; nor 'tis not strange,
That even our loves should with our fortunes change;
For 'tis a question left us yet to prove,
Whether love lead fortune, or else fortune love.
The great man down, you mark his favourite flies;
The poor advanc'd makes friends of enemies.
And hitherto doth love on fortune tend:
For who not needs, shall never lack a friend;
And who in want a hollow friend doth try,
Directly seasons him his enemy.
But, orderly to end where I begun,—
Our wills, and fates, do so contrary run,
That our devices still are overthrown;
Our thoughts are ours, their ends none of our own:
So think thou wilt no second husband wed;
But die thy thoughts, when thy first lord is dead.

P. Queen. Nor earth to me give food, nor heaven light!
Sport and repose lock from me, day, and night!
To desperation turn my trust and hope!
An anchor's cheer in prison be my scope!
Each opposite, that blanks the face of joy,
Meet what I would have well, and it destroy!
Both here, and hence, pursue me lasting strife,
If, once a widow, ever I be wife!

Ham. If she should break it now,—— [*To* OPHELIA.

P. King. 'Tis deeply sworn. Sweet, leave me here a while;
My spirits grow dull, and fain I would beguile
The tedious day with sleep. [*Sleeps.*

P. Queen. Sleep rock thy brain;
And never come mischance between us twain! [*Exit.*

Ham. Madam, how like you this play?

Queen. The lady doth protest too much, methinks.

Ham. O, but she'll keep her word.

King. Have you heard the argument? Is there no offence in't?

Ham. No, no, they do but jest, poison in jest; no offence i' the world.

King. What do you call the play?

Ham. The mouse-trap. Marry, how? Tropically. This play is the image of a murder done in Vienna: Gonzago is the duke's name, his wife, Baptista: you shall see anon; 'tis a knavish piece of work: But what of that? your majesty, and we that have free souls, it touches us not: Let the galled jade wince, our withers are unwrung.—

Enter LUCIANUS.

This is one Lucianus, nephew to the king,

Oph. You are as good as a chorus, my lord.

Ham. I could interpret between you and your love, if I could see the puppets dallying.

Oph. You are keen, my lord, you are keen.

Ham. It would cost you a groaning, to take off my edge.

Oph. Still better, and worse.

Ham. So you mistake your husbands.—Begin, murderer; leave thy damnable faces, and begin. Come;——
——The croaking raven
Doth bellow for revenge.

Luc. Thoughts black, hands apt, drugs fit, and time agreeing;
Confederate season, else no creature seeing;
Thou mixture rank, of midnight weeds collected,
With Hecat's ban thrice blasted, thrice infected,
Thy natural magick and dire property,
On wholesome life usurp immediately.
[*Pours the Poison into the Sleeper's Ears.*

Ham. He poisons him i' the garden for his estate. His name's Gonzago: the story is extant, and written in very choice Italian: You shall see anon, how the murderer gets the love of Gonzago's wife

Oph. The king rises.

Ham. What! frighted with false fire!

Queen. How fares my lord?

Pol. Give o'er the play.

King. Give me some light:—away!

Pol. Lights, lights, lights!
[*Exeunt all but* HAMLET *and* HORATIO.

Ham. Why let the strucken deer go weep,
The hart ungalled play:
For some must watch, while some must sleep;
Thus runs the world away.—
Would not this, sir, and a forest of feathers (if the rest of my fortunes turn Turk with me,) with two provincial roses on my razed shoes, get me a fellowship in a cry of players, sir?

Hor. Half a share.

Ham. A whole one, I.
For thou dost know, O Damon dear,
This realm dismantled was
Of Jove himself; and now reigns here
A very, very—peacock.

Hor. You might have rhymed.

Ham. O good Horatio, I'll take the ghost's word for a thousand pound. Didst perceive?

Hor. Very well, my lord.

Ham. Upon the talk of the poisoning,——

Hor. I did very well note him.

Ham. Ah, ha!—Come, some musick; come, the recorders.—
For if the king like not the comedy,
Why then, belike,—he likes it not, perdy.

Enter ROSENCRANTZ *and* GUILDENSTERN.

Come, some musick.

Guil. Good my lord, vouchsafe me a word with you.

Ham. Sir, a whole history.

Guil. The king, sir,——

Ham. Ay, sir, what of him?

Guil. Is, in his retirement, marvellous distempered.

Ham. With drink, sir?

Guil. No, my lord, with choler.

Ham. Your wisdom should show itself more richer, to signify this to the doctor; for, for me to put him to his purgation, would, perhaps, plunge him into more choler.

Guil. Good my lord, put your discourse into some frame, and start not so wildly from my affair.

Ham. I am tame, sir:—pronounce.

Guil. The queen, your mother, in most great affliction of spirit, hath sent me to you.

Ham. You are welcome.

Guil. Nay, good my lord, this courtesy is not of the right breed. If it shall please you to make me a wholesome answer, I will do your mother's commandment: if not, your pardon, and my return shall be the end of my business.

Ham. Sir, I cannot.

Guil. What, my lord?

Ham. Make you a wholesome answer; my wit's diseased: But, sir, such answer as I can make, you shall command; or, rather, as you say, my mother: therefore no more, but to the matter; My mother, you say,——

Ros. Then thus she says: Your behaviour hath struck her into amazement and admiration.

Ham. O wonderful son, that can so astonish a mother!—But is there no sequel at the heels of this mother's admiration? impart.

Ros. She desires to speak with you in her closet, ere you go to bed.

Ham. We shall obey, were she ten times our mother. Have you any further trade with us?

Ros. My lord, you once did love me.

Ham. And do still, by these pickers and stealers.

Ros. Good my lord, what is your cause of distemper? you do, surely, but bar the door upon your own liberty, if you deny your griefs to your friend.

Ham. Sir, I lack advancement.

Ros. How can that be, when you have the voice of the king himself for your succession in Denmark?

Ham. Ay, sir, but *While the grass grows*,—the proverb is something musty.

Enter the Players, *with* Recorders.

O, the recorders:—let me see one.—To withdraw with you.—Why do you go about to recover the wind of me, as if you would drive me into a toil?

Guil. O, my lord, if my duty be too bold, my love is too unmannerly.

Ham. I do not well understand that. Will you play upon this pipe?

Guil. My, lord, I cannot.

Ham. I pray you.

Guil. Believe me, I cannot.

Ham. I do beseech you.

Guil. I know no touch of it, my lord.

Ham. 'Tis as easy as lying: govern these ventages with your fingers and thumb, give it breath with your mouth, and it will discourse most eloquent musick. Look you, these are the stops.

Guil. But these cannot I command to any utterance of harmony; I have not the skill.

Ham. Why, look you now, how unworthy a thing you make of me? You would play upon me; you would seem to know my stops; you would pluck out the heart of my mystery; you would sound me from my lowest note to the top of my compass: and there is much musick, excellent voice, in this little organ; yet cannot you make it speak. 'Sblood, do you think, I am easier to be played on than a pipe? Call me what instrument you will, though you can fret me, you cannot play upon me.

Enter Polonius.

God bless you, sir!

Pol. My lord, the queen would speak with you, and presently.

Ham. Do you see yonder cloud, that's almost in shape of a camel?

Pol. By the mass, and tis like a camel, indeed.

Ham. Methinks, it is like a weasel.

Pol. It is backed like a weasel.

Ham. Or, like a whale?

Pol. Very like a whale.

Ham. Then will I come to my mother by and by.—They fool me to the top of my bent. I will come by and by.

Pol. I will say so. [*Exit* Polonius.

Ham. By and by is easily said.—Leave me, friends. [*Exeunt* Ros. Guil. Hor. *&c.*
'Tis now the very witching time of night;
When churchyards yawn, and hell itself breathes out
Contagion to this world: Now could I drink hot blood,
And do such bitter business as the day
Would quake to look on. Soft; now to my mother,—
O heart, lose not thy nature; let not ever
The soul of Nero enter this firm bosom:
Let me be cruel, not unnatural:
I will speak daggers to her, but use none;
My tongue and soul in this be hypocrites:
How in my words soever she be shent,
To give them seals never, my soul, consent! [*Exit.*

SCENE III. *A Room in the same.*

Enter King, Rosencrantz, *and* Guildenstern.

King. I like him not; nor stands it safe with us,
To let his madness range. Therefore, prepare you;
I your commission will forthwith despatch,
And he to England shall along with you:
The terms of our estate may not endure
Hazard so near us, as doth hourly grow
Out of his lunes.

Guil. We will ourselves provide:
Most holy and religious fear it is,
To keep those many, many bodies safe,
That live, and feed, upon your majesty.

Ros. The single and peculiar life is bound,
With all the strength and armour of the mind,
To keep itself from 'noyance; but much more
That spirit, upon whose weal depend and rest
The lives of many. The cease of majesty
Dies not alone; but, like a gulf, doth draw
What's near it, with it: it is a massy wheel,
Fix'd on the summit of the highest mount,
To whose huge spokes ten thousand lesser things
Are mortis'd and adjoin'd; which, when it falls,
Each small annexment, petty consequence,
Attends the boist'rous ruin. Never alone
Did the king sigh, but with a general groan.

King. Arm you, I pray you, to this speedy voyage;
For we will fetters put upon this fear,
Which now goes too free-footed.

Ros. Guil. We will haste us.
[*Exeunt* Ros. *and* Guil.

Enter Polonius.

Pol. My lord, he's going to his mother's closet:
Behind the arras I'll convey myself,
To hear the process; I'll warrant, she'll tax him home;
And, as you said, and wisely was it said,
'Tis meet, that some more audience, than a mother,
Since nature makes them partial, should o'erhear
The speech, of vantage. Fare you well, my liege;
I'll call upon you ere you go to bed.
And tell you what I know.

King. Thanks, dear my lord.
[*Exit* Polonius.
O, my offence is rank, it smells to heaven;
It hath the primal eldest curse upon't,
A brother's murder!—Pray can I not,
Though inclination be as sharp as will;

My stronger guilt defeats my strong intent;
And, like a man to double business bound,
I stand in pause where I shall first begin,
And both neglect. What if this cursed hand
Were thicker than itself with brother's blood?
Is there not rain enough in the sweet heavens,
To wash it white as snow? Whereto serves mercy,
But to confront the visage of offence?
And what's in prayer, but this two-fold force,—
To be forestalled, ere we come to fall,
Or pardon'd, being down? Then I'll look up;
My fault is past. But, O, what form of prayer
Can serve my turn? Forgive me my foul murder!—
That cannot be; since I am still possess'd
Of those effects for which I did the murder,
My crown, mine own ambition, and my queen.
May one be pardon'd, and retain the offence?
In the corrupted currents of this world,
Offence's gilded hand may shove by justice;
And oft 'tis seen, the wicked prize itself
Buys out the law: But 'tis not so above:
There is no shuffling, there the action lies
In his true nature: and we ourselves compell'd,
Even to the teeth and forehead of our faults,
To give in evidence. What then? what rests?
Try what repentance can: What can it not?
Yet what can it, when one cannot repent?
O wretched state! O bosom, black as death!
O limed soul; that struggling to be free,
Art more engag'd! Help, angels, make assay!
Bow, stubborn knees! and, heart, with strings of steel,
Be soft as sinews of the new-born babe;
All may be well! [*Retires and kneels.*

Enter HAMLET.

Ham. Now might I do it, pat, now he is praying;
And now I'll do't; and so he goes to heaven:
And so am I reveng'd? That would be scann'd:
A villain kills my father; and, for that,
I, his sole son, do this same villain send
To heaven.
Why, this is hire and salary, not revenge.
He took my father grossly full of bread;
With all his crimes broad blown, as flush as May;
And, how his audit stands, who knows, save heaven?
But, in our circumstance and course of thought,
'Tis heavy with him: And am I then reveng'd,
To take him in the purging of his soul,
When he is fit and season'd for his passage?
No.
Up, sword; and know thou a more horrid hent:
When he is drunk, asleep, or in his rage;
Or in the incestuous pleasures of his bed;
At gaming, swearing; or about some act
That has no relish of salvation in't:
Then trip him, that his heels may kick at heaven:
And that his soul may be as damn'd, and black,
As hell, whereto it goes. My mother stays:
This physick but prolongs thy sickly days.
[*Exit.*

The King *rises and advances.*

King. My words fly up, my thoughts remain below:
Words, without thoughts, never to heaven go.
[*Exit.*

SCENE IV. *Another Room in the same.*

Enter Queen *and* POLONIUS.

Pol. He will come straight. Look, you lay home to him:
Tell him, his pranks have been too broad to bear with;
And that your grace hath screen'd and stood between
Much heat and him. I'll silence me e'en here.
'Pray you, be round with him.

Queen. I'll warrant you;
Fear me not:—withdraw, I hear him coming.
[POLONIUS *hides himself.*

Enter HAMLET.

Ham. Now, mother; what's the matter?
Queen. Hamlet, thou hast thy father much offended.
Ham. Mother, you have my father much offended.
Queen. Come, come, you answer with an idle tongue.
Ham. Go, go, you question with a wicked tongue.
Queen. Why, how now, Hamlet?
Ham. What's the matter now?
Queen. Have you forgot me?
Ham. No, by the rood, not so:
You are the queen, your husband's brother's wife;
And,—'would it were not so!—you are my mother.
Queen. Nay, then I'll set those to you that can speak.
Ham. Come, come, and sit you down; you shall not budge;
You go not, till I set you up a glass
Where you may see the inmost part of you.
Queen. What wilt thou do? thou wilt not murder me?
Help, help, ho!
Pol. [*Behind.*] What, ho! help!
Ham. How now! a rat? [*Draws.*
Dead, for a ducat, dead.
[HAMLET *makes a pass through the Arras.*
Pol. [*Behind.*] O, I am slain.
[*Falls, and dies.*
Queen. O me, what hast thou done?
Ham. Nay, I know not:
Is it the king?
[*Lifts up the Arras, and draws forth* POLONIUS.
Queen. O, what a rash and bloody deed is this!
Ham. A bloody deed; almost as bad, good mother,
As kill a king, and marry with his brother.
Queen. As kill a king!
Ham. Ay, lady, 'twas my word.—
Thou wretched, rash, intruding fool, farewell!
[*To* POLONIUS.
I took thee for thy better; take thy fortune:
Thou find'st to be too busy, is some danger.—
Leave wringing of your hands; Peace; sit you down,
And let me wring your heart: for so I shall,
If it be made of penetrable stuff:
If damned custom have not braz'd it so,
That it be proof and bulwark against sense.
Queen. What have I done, that thou dar'st wag thy tongue
In noise so rude against me?
Ham. Such an act,
That blurs the grace and blush of modesty;
Calls virtue, hypocrite; takes off the rose
From the fair forehead of an innocent love,
And sets a blister there; makes marriage vows
As false as dicers' oaths: O, such a deed
As from the body of contraction plucks
The very soul; and sweet religion makes
A rhapsody of words: Heaven's face doth glow;
Yea, this solidity and compound mass,
With tristful visage, as against the doom,
Is thought-sick at the act.
Queen. Ah me, what act,
That roars so loud, and thunders in the index?
Ham. Look here upon this picture, and on this;
The counterfeit presentment of two brothers.
See, what a grace was seated on this brow:
Hyperion's curls; the front of Jove himself;
An eye like Mars, to threaten and command;
A station like the herald Mercury,
New-lighted on a heaven-kissing hill;
A combination, and a form, indeed,

Where every god did seem to set his seal,
To give the world assurance of a man:
This was your husband.—Look you now, what follows:
Here is your husband; like a mildew'd ear,
Blasting his wholesome brother. Have you eyes?
Could you on this fair mountain leave to feed,
And batten on this moor? Ha! have you eyes?
You cannot call it, love: for, at your age,
The hey-day in the blood is tame, it's humble,
And waits upon the judgment; And what judgment
Would step from this to this? Sense, sure you [have,
Else could you not have motion: But, sure, that sense
Is apoplex'd: for madness would not err;
Nor sense to ecstasy was ne'er so thrall'd,
But it reserv'd some quantity of choice,
To serve in such a difference. What devil was't
That thus hath cozen'd you at hoodman-blind?
Eyes without feeling, feeling without sight,
Ears without hands or eyes, smelling sans all,
Or but a sickly part of one true sense
Could not so mope.
O shame! where is thy blush? Rebellious hell,
If thou canst mutine in a matron's bones,
To flaming youth let virtue be as wax,
And melt in her own fire; proclaim no shame,
When the compulsive ardour gives the charge;
Since frost itself as actively doth burn,
And reason panders will.

Queen. O Hamlet, speak no more:
Thou turn'st mine eyes into my very soul;
And there I see such black and grained spots
As will not leave their tinct.

Ham. Nay, but to live
In the rank sweat of an enseamed bed;
Stew'd in corruption; honeying, and making love
Over the nasty sty;——

Queen. O, speak to me no more;
These words, like daggers, enter in mine ears:
No more, sweet Hamlet.

Ham. A murderer, and a villain;
A slave, that is not twentieth part the tithe
Of your precedent lord:—a vice of kings:
A cutpurse of the empire and the rule;
That from a shelf the precious diadem stole,
And put it in his pocket!

Queen. No more.

Enter Ghost.

Ham. A king
Of shreds and patches:—
Save me, and hover o'er me with your wings,
You heavenly guards!—What would your gracious figure?

Queen. Alas, he's mad.

Ham. Do you not come your tardy son to chide,
That, laps'd in time and passion, let's go by
The important acting of your dread command?
O, say!

Ghost. Do not forget: This visitation
Is but to whet thy almost blunted purpose.
But, look! amazement on thy mother sits:
O, step between her and her fighting soul;
Conceit in weakest bodies strongest works;
Speak to her, Hamlet.

Ham. How is it with you, lady?

Queen. Alas, how is't with you?
That you do bend your eye on vacancy,
And with the incorporal air do hold discourse?
Forth at your eyes your spirits wildly peep;
And, as the sleeping soldiers in the alarm,
Your bedded hair, like life in excrements,
Starts up, and stands on end. O gentle son,
Upon the heat and flame of thy distemper
Sprinkle cool patience. Whereon do you look?

Ham. On him! on him!—Look you, how pale he glares!
His form and cause conjoin'd, preaching to stones,
Would make them capable.—Do not look upon me;
Lest, with this piteous action, you convert
My stern affects: then what I have to do
Will want true colour; tears, perchance, for blood.

Queen. To whom do you speak this?

Ham. Do you see nothing there?

Queen. Nothing at all; yet all, that is, I see.

Ham. Nor did you nothing hear?

Queen. No, nothing, but ourselves.

Ham. Why, look you there! look, how it steals away!
My father, in his habit as he liv'd!
Look, where he goes, even now, out at the portal!
[*Exit* Ghost.

Queen. This is the very coinage of your brain:
This bodiless creation ecstasy
Is very cunning in.

Ham. Ecstasy!
My pulse, as yours, doth temperately keep time,
And makes as healthful musick: It is not madness,
That I have utter'd: bring me to the test,
And I the matter will reword; which madness
Would gambol from. Mother, for love of grace,
Lay not that flattering unction to your soul,
That not your trespass, but my madness speaks:
It will but skin and film the ulcerous place;
Whiles rank corruption, mining all within,
Infects unseen. Confess yourself to heaven;
Repent what's past; avoid what is to come;
And do not spread the compost on the weeds,
To make them ranker. Forgive me this my virtue:
For in the fatness of these pursy times,
Virtue itself of vice must pardon beg:
Yea, curb and woo, for leave to do him good.

Queen. O, Hamlet! thou hast cleft my heart in twain.

Ham. O, throw away the worser part of it,
And live the purer with the other half.
Good night: but go not to my uncle's bed;
Assume a virtue, if you have it not.
That monster, custom, who all sense doth eat
Of habit's devil, is angel yet in this;
That to the use of actions fair and good
He likewise gives a frock, or livery,
That aptly is put on: Refrain to-night;
And that shall lend a kind of easiness
To the next abstinence: the next more easy:
For use almost can change the stamp of nature,
And either curb the devil, or throw him out
With wondrous potency. Once more, good night!
And when you are desirous to be bless'd,
I'll blessing beg of you.—For this same lord,
[*Pointing to* POLONIUS.
I do repent: But heaven hath pleas'd it so,—
To punish me with this, and this with me,
That I must be their scourge and minister.
I will bestow him, and will answer well
The death I gave him. So, again, good night!—
I must be cruel, only to be kind:
Thus bad begins, and worse remains behind.—
But one word more, good lady.

Queen. What shall I do?

Ham. Not this, by no means, that I bid you do:
Let the bloat king tempt you again to bed;
Pinch wanton on your cheek; call you his mouse;
And let him, for a pair of reechy kisses,
Or padling in your neck with his damn'd fingers,
Make you to ravel all this matter out,
That I essentially am not in madness,
But mad in craft. 'Twere good you let him know;
For who, that's but a queen, fair, sober, wise,
Would from a paddock, from a bat, a gib,
Such dear concernings hide? who would do so?
No, in despite of sense, and secrecy,
Unpeg the basket on the house's top,
Let the birds fly; and, like the famous ape,

To try conclusions, in the basket creep,
And break your own neck down.

Queen. Be thou assur'd, if words be made of breath,
And breath of life, I have no life to breathe
What thou hast said to me.

Ham. I must to England; you know that?

Queen. Alack,
I had forgot; 'tis so concluded on.

Ham. There's letters seal'd: and my two schoolfellows,—
Whom I will trust, as I will adders fang'd,—
They bear the mandate; they must sweep my way,
And marshal me to knavery: Let it work;
For 'tis the sport, to have the engineer
Hoist with his own petar: and it shall go hard,
But I will delve one yard below their mines,
And blow them at the moon: O, 'tis most sweet,
When in one line two crafts directly meet.—
This man shall set me packing.
I'll lug the guts into the neighbour room:
Mother, good night.—Indeed, this counsellor
Is now most still, most secret, and most grave,
Who was in life a foolish prating knave.
Come, sir, to draw toward an end with you:—
Good night, mother.

[*Exeunt severally;* HAM. *dragging in* POL.

ACT IV.

SCENE I. *The same.*

Enter King, Queen, ROSENCRANTZ, *and* GUILDENSTERN.

King. There's matter in these sighs; these profound heaves:
You must translate: 'tis fit we understand them:
Where is your son?

Queen. Bestow this place on us a little while.—
[*To* ROS. *and* GUIL. *who go out.*
Ah, my good lord, what have I seen to-night!

King. What, Gertrude? How does Hamlet?

Queen. Mad as the sea, and wind, when both contend
Which is the mightier: In his lawless fit,
Behind the arras hearing something stir,
Whips out his rapier, cries, *A rat! a rat!*
And, in this brainish apprehension, kills
The unseen good old man.

King. O heavy deed!
It had been so with us, had we been there:
His liberty is full of threats to all;
To you yourself, to us, to every one.
Alas! how shall this bloody deed be answer'd?
It will be laid to us, whose providence
Should have kept short, restrain'd, and out of haunt,
This mad young man: but, so much was our love,
We would not understand what was most fit;
But, like the owner of a foul disease,
To keep it from divulging, let it feed
Even on the pith of life. Where is he gone?

Queen. To draw apart the body he hath kill'd:
O'er whom his very madness, like some ore,
Among a mineral of metals base,
Shows itself pure; he weeps for what is done.

King. O, Gertrude, come away!
The sun no sooner shall the mountains touch,
But we will ship him hence: and this vile deed
We must, with all our majesty and skill,
Both countenance and excuse.—Ho! Guildenstern!

Enter ROSENCRANTZ *and* GUILDENSTERN.

Friends both, go join with you some further aid:
Hamlet in madness hath Polonius slain,
And from his mother's closet hath he dragg'd him:
Go, seek him out; speak fair, and bring the body
Into the chapel. I pray you, haste in this.
[*Exeunt* ROS. *and* GUIL.
Come, Gertrude, we'll call up our wisest friends;
And let them know, both what we mean to do,
And what's untimely done: so, haply, slander,—
Whose whisper o'er the world's diameter,
As level as the cannon to his blank,
Transports his poison'd shot, may miss our name,
And hit the woundless air.—O, come away!
My soul is full of discord, and dismay.
[*Exeunt.*

SCENE II. *Another Room in the same.*

Enter HAMLET.

Ham.——Safely stowed,—[Ros. *&c. within.* Hamlet! Lord Hamlet!] But soft!—what noise? who calls on Hamlet? O, here they come.

Enter ROSENCRANTZ *and* GUILDENSTERN.

Ros. What have you done, my lord, with the dead body?

Ham. Compounded it with dust, whereto 'tis kin.

Ros. Tell us where 'tis; that we may take it thence,
And bear it to the chapel.

Ham. Do not believe it.

Ros. Believe what?

Ham. That I can keep your counsel, and not mine own. Besides, to be demanded of a sponge!—what replication should be made by the son of a king?

Ros. Take you me for a sponge, my lord?

Ham. Ay, sir; that soaks up the king's countenance, his rewards, his authorities. But such officers do the king best service in the end. He keeps them, like an ape doth nuts, in the corner of his jaw; first mouthed, to be last swallowed: When he needs what you have gleaned, it is but squeezing you, and, sponge, you shall be dry again.

Ros. I understand you not, my lord.

Ham. I am glad of it: A knavish speech sleeps in a foolish ear.

Ros. My lord, you must tell us where the body is, and go with us to the king.

Ham. The body is with the king, but the king is not with the body. The king is a thing——

Guil. A thing, my lord?

Ham. Of nothing: bring me to him. Hide fox, and all after. [*Exeunt.*

SCENE III. *Another Room in the same.*

Enter King, *attended.*

King. I have sent to seek him, and to find the body.
How dangerous is it, that this man goes loose!
Yet must not we put the strong law on him:
He's lov'd of the distracted multitude,
Who like not in their judgment, but their eyes;
And, where 'tis so, the offender's scourge is weigh'd,
But never the offence. To bear all smooth and even,
This sudden sending him away must seem
Deliberate pause: Diseases, desperate grown,
By desperate appliance are relieved,

Enter ROSENCRANTZ.

Or not at all.—How now? what hath befallen?

Ros. Where the dead body is bestow'd, my lord,
We cannot get from him.

King. But where is he?

Ros. Without, my lord; guarded, to know your pleasure.

King. Bring him before us.

Ros. Ho, Guildenstern! bring in my lord.

Enter HAMLET *and* GUILDENSTERN.

King. Now, Hamlet, where's Polonius?

Ham. At supper.

King. At supper? Where?

Ham. Not where he eats, but where he is eaten: a certain convocation of politick worms are e'en at him. Your worm is your only emperor for diet: we fat all creatures else, to fat us; and we fat ourselves for maggots; Your fat king, and your lean beggar, is but variable service; two dishes, but to one table; that's the end.

King. Alas, alas!

Ham. A man may fish with the worm that hath eat of a king; and eat of the fish that hath fed of that worm.

King. What dost thou mean by this?

Ham. Nothing, but to show you how a king may go a progress through the guts of a beggar.

King. Where is Polonius?

Ham. In heaven; send thither to see: if your messenger find him not there, seek him i' the other place yourself. But, indeed, if you find him not within this month, you shall nose him as you go up the stairs into the lobby.

King. Go seek him there. [*To some* Attendants.

Ham. He will stay till you come. [*Exeunt* Attendants.

King. Hamlet, this deed, for thine especial safety,—
Which we do tender, as we dearly grieve
For that which thou hast done,—must send thee hence
With fiery quickness: Therefore prepare thyself;
The bark is ready, and the wind at help,
The associates tend, and every thing is bent
For England.

Ham. For England?

King. Ay, Hamlet.

Ham. Good.

King. So is it, if thou knew'st our purposes.

Ham. I see a cherub, that sees them.—But, come; for England!—Farewell, dear mother.

King. Thy loving father, Hamlet.

Ham. My mother: Father and mother is man and wife; man and wife is one flesh; and so, my mother. Come, for England. [*Exit.*

King. Follow him at foot: tempt him with speed aboard:
Delay it not, I'll have him hence to-night;
Away; for every thing is seal'd and done
That else leans on the affair: 'Pray you, make haste. [*Exeunt* ROS. *and* GUIL.
And, England, if my love thou hold'st at aught,
(As my great power thereof may give thee sense;
Since yet thy cicatrice looks raw and red
After the Danish sword, and thy free awe
Pays homage to us,) thou may'st not coldly set
Our sovereign process; which imports at full,
By letters conjuring to that effect,
The present death of Hamlet. Do it, England;
For like the hectick in my blood he rages,
And thou must cure me: Till I know 'tis done,
Howe'er my haps, my joys will ne'er begin.
[*Exit.*

SCENE IV. *A Plain in* Denmark.

Enter FORTINBRAS, *and* Forces, *marching.*

For. Go, captain, from me greet the Danish king;
Tell him, that, by his licence, Fortinbras
Claims the conveyance of a promis'd march
Over his kingdom. You know the rendezvous.
If that his majesty would aught with us,
We shall express our duty in his eye.
And let him know so.

Cap. I will do't, my lord.

For. Go softly on.
[*Exeunt* FORTINBRAS *and* Forces.

Enter HAMLET, ROSENCRANTZ, GUILDENSTERN, *&c.*

Ham. Good sir, whose powers are these?

Cap. They are of Norway, sir.

Ham. How purpos'd, sir,
I pray you?

Cap. Against some part of Poland.

Ham. Who
Commands them, sir?

Cap. The nephew to old Norway, Fortinbras.

Ham. Goes it against the main of Poland, sir,
Or for some frontier?

Cap. Truly to speak, sir, and with no addition,
We go to gain a little patch of ground,
That hath in it no profit but the name.
To pay five ducats, five, I would not farm it;
Nor will it yield to Norway, or the Pole,
A ranker rate, should it be sold in fee.

Ham. Why, then the Polack never will defend [it.

Cap. Yes, 'tis already garrison'd.

Ham. Two thousand souls, and twenty thousand ducats,
Will not debate the question of this straw:
This is the imposthume of much wealth and peace;
That inward breaks, and shows no cause without
Why the man dies.—I humbly thank you, sir.

Cap. God be wi' you, sir. [*Exit* Captain.

Ros. Will't please you go, my lord?

Ham. I will be with you straight. Go a little before. [*Exeunt* ROS. *and* GUIL.
How all occasions do inform against me,
And spur my dull revenge! What is a man,
If his chief good, and market of his time,
Be but to sleep, and feed? a beast, no more.
Sure, he, that made us with such large discourse,
Looking before, and after, gave us not
That capability and godlike reason
To fust in us unus'd. Now, whether it be
Bestial oblivion, or some craven scruple
Of thinking too precisely on the event,—
A thought, which, quarter'd, hath but one part wisdom,
And, ever, three parts coward,—I do not know
Why yet I live to say, *This thing's to do:*
Sith I have cause, and will, and strength, and means,
To do't. Examples, gross as earth, exhort me:
Witness, this army of such mass, and charge,
Led by a delicate and tender prince;
Whose spirit, with divine ambition puff'd,
Makes mouths at the invisible event;
Exposing what is mortal, and unsure,
To all that fortune, death, and danger, dare,
Even for an egg-shell. Rightly to be great,
Is, not to stir without great argument;
But greatly to find quarrel in a straw,
When honour's at the stake. How stand I then,
That have a father kill'd, a mother stain'd,
Excitements of my reason, and my blood,
And let all sleep? while, to my shame, I see
The imminent death of twenty thousand men,
That, for a fantasy, and trick of fame,
Go to their graves like beds: fight for a plot
Whereon the numbers cannot try the cause,
Which is not tomb enough, and continent,
To hide the slain!—O, from this time forth,
My thoughts be bloody, or be nothing worth!
[*Exit.*

SCENE V. Elsinore. *A Room in the Castle.*

Enter Queen *and* HORATIO.

Queen. ——I will not speak with her.

Hor. She is importunate; indeed, distract;
Her mood will needs be pitied.

Queen. What would she have?

Hor. She speaks much of her father; says, she hears,
There's tricks i' the world; and hems, and beats her heart;
Spurns enviously at straws; speaks things in doubt,
That carry but half sense: her speech is nothing,
Yet the unshaped use of it doth move
The hearers to collection; they aim at it,
And botch the words up fit to their own thoughts;
Which, as her winks and nods, and gestures yield them,

Indeed would make one think, there might be thought,
Though nothing sure, yet much unhappily.

Queen. 'Twere good, she were spoken with; for she may strew
Dangerous conjectures in ill-breeding minds:
Let her come in. [*Exit* HORATIO.
To my sick soul, as sin's true nature is,
Each toy seems prologue to some great amiss:
So full of artless jealousy is guilt,
It spills itself in fearing to be spilt.

Re-enter HORATIO, *with* OPHELIA.

Oph. Where is the beauteous majesty of Denmark?

Queen. How now, Ophelia?

Oph. *How should I your true love know,*
From another one?
By his cockle hat and staff,
And his sandal shoon. [Singing.

Queen. Alas, sweet lady, what imports this song?

Oph. Say you? nay; 'pray you, mark.
He is dead and gone, lady, [Sings.
He is dead and gone;
At his head a grass-green turf,
At his heels a stone.
O, ho!

Queen. Nay, but, Ophelia,——

Oph. 'Pray you, mark.
White his shroud as the mountain snow. [Sings.

Enter King.

Queen. Alas, look here, my lord.

Oph. *Larded all with sweet flowers;*
Which bewept to the grave did go,
With true love showers.

King. How do you, pretty lady?

Oph. Well, God'ield you! They say, the owl was a baker's daughter. Lord, we know what we are, but know not what we may be. God be at your table!

King. Conceit upon her father.

Oph. 'Pray, let us have no words of this; but when they ask you, what it means, say you this:

Good morrow, 'tis Saint Valentine's day,
All in the morning betime,
And I a maid at your window,
To be your Valentine:

Then up he rose, and don'd his clothes,
And dupp'd the chamber door;
Let in the maid, that out a maid
Never departed more.

King. Pretty Ophelia!

Oph. Indeed, without an oath, I'll make an end on't:

By Gis, and by Saint Charity,
Alack, and fye for shame!
Young men will do't, if they come to't;
By cock, they are to blame.

Quoth she, before you tumbled me,
You promised me to wed.
[He answers.]
So would I ha' done, by yonder sun,
An thou hadst not come to my bed.

King. How long hath she been thus?

Oph. I hope, all will be well. We must be patient: but I cannot choose but weep, to think, they should lay him i' the cold ground: My brother shall know of it, and so I thank you for your good counsel. Come, my coach! Good night, ladies; good night, sweet ladies: good night, good night. [*Exit.*

King. Follow her close! give her good watch, I pray you. [*Exit* HORATIO.
O! this is the poison of deep grief; it springs
All from her father's death: And now behold,
O Gertrude, Gertrude,
When sorrows come, they come not single spies,
But in battalions! First, her father slain;
Next, your son gone; and he most violent author
Of his own just remove: The people muddied,
Thick and unwholesome in their thoughts and whispers,
For good Polonius' death; and we have done but greenly,
In hugger-mugger to inter him: Poor Ophelia
Divided from herself, and her fair judgment;
Without the which we are pictures, or mere beasts.
Last, and as much containing as all these,
Her brother is in secret come from France:
Feeds on his wonder, keeps himself in clouds,
And wants not buzzers to infect his ear
With pestilent speeches of his father's death;
Wherein necessity, of matter beggar'd,
Will nothing stick our person to arraign
In ear and ear. O my dear Gertrude, this,
Like to a murdering piece, in many places
Gives me superfluous death! [*A noise within.*

Queen. Alack! what noise is this?

Enter a Gentleman.

King. Attend.
Where are my Switzers? Let them guard the door:
What is the matter?

Gent. Save yourself, my lord;
The ocean, overpeering of his list,
Eats not the flats with more impetuous haste,
Than young Laertes, in a riotous head,
O'erbears your officers! The rabble call him lord;
And, as the world were now but to begin,
Antiquity forgot, custom not known,
The ratifiers and props of every word,
They cry, *Choose we; Laertes shall be king!*
Caps, hands, and tongues, applaud it to the clouds,
Laertes shall be king, Laertes king!

Queen. How cheerfully on the false trail they cry!
O, this is counter, you false Danish dogs.

King. The doors are broke. [*Noise within.*

Enter LAERTES, *armed;* Danes *following.*

Laer. Where is this king?—Sirs, stand you all without.

Dan. No, let's come in.

Laer. I pray you, give me leave.

Dan. We will, we will.
[*They retire without the door.*

Laer. I thank you:—keep the door.—O thou vile king,
Give me my father.

Queen. Calmly, good Laertes.

Laer. That drop of blood, that's calm, proclaims me bastard;
Cries, cuckold, to my father; brands the harlot
Even here, between the chaste unsmirched brow
Of my true mother.

King. What is the cause, Laertes,
That thy rebellion looks so giant-like?—
Let him go, Gertrude; do not fear our person;
There's such divinity doth hedge a king,
That treason can but peep to what it would,
Acts little of his will.—Tell me, Laertes,
Why thou art thus incens'd;—Let him go, Gertrude;—
Speak, man.

Laer. Where is my father?

King. Dead.

Queen. But not by him.

King. Let him demand his fill.

Laer. How came he dead? I'll not be juggled with:
To hell, allegiance! vows, to the blackest devil!
Conscience, and grace, to the profoundest pit!
I dare damnation: To this point I stand,—
That both the worlds I give to negligence,
Let come what comes; only I'll be reveng'd
Most thoroughly for my father.

King. Who shall stay you?

Laer. My will, not all the world's:

And, for my means, I'll husband them so well,
They shall go far with little.
King. Good Laertes,
If you desire to know the certainty
Of your dear father's death, is't writ in your revenge,
That, sweepstake, you will draw both friend and foe,
Winner and loser?
Laer. None but his enemies.
King. Will you know them then?
Laer. To his good friends thus wide I'll ope my arms;
And like the kind life-rendering pelican,
Repast them with my blood.
King. Why, now you speak
Like a good child, and a true gentleman.
That I am guiltless of your father's death,
And am most sensibly in grief for it,
It shall as level to your judgment pierce
As day does to your eye.
Danes. [*Within.*] Let her come in.
Laer. How now! What noise is that?

Enter OPHELIA, *fantastically dressed with Straws and Flowers.*

O heat, dry up my brains! tears seven times salt,
Burn out the sense and virtue of mine eye!—
By heaven, thy madness shall be paid with weight,
Till our scale turn the beam. O rose of May!
Dear maid, kind sister, sweet Ophelia!
O heavens! is't possible, a young maid's wits
Should be as mortal as an old man's life?
Nature is fine in love; and, where 'tis fine,
It sends some precious instance of itself
After the thing it loves.
Oph. *They bore him barefac'd on the bier;*
Hey no nonny, nonny hey nonny:
And in his grave rain'd many a tear;—
Fare you well, my dove!
Laer. Hadst thou thy wits, and didst persuade revenge,
It could not move thus.
Oph. You must sing, *Down-a-down, an you call him a-down-a.* O, how the wheel becomes it! it is the false steward, that stole his master's daughter.
Laer. This nothing's more than matter.
Oph. There's rosemary, that's for remembrance; 'pray you, love, remember: and there is pansies, that's for thoughts.
Laer. A document in madness; thoughts and remembrance fitted.
Oph. There's fennel for you, and columbines: —there's rue for you; and here's some for me: —we may call it, herb of grace o' Sundays:— you may wear your rue with a difference.— There's a daisy;—I would give you some violets; but they withered all, when my father died:—They say, he made a good end,——
For bonny sweet Robin is all my joy,— [Sings.
Laer. Thought and affliction, passion, hell itself,
She turns to favour and to prettiness.
Oph. *And will he not come again?* [Sings.
And will he not come again?
No, no, he is dead,
Go to thy death-bed,
He never will come again.

His beard was as white as snow,
All flaxen was his poll:
He is gone, he is gone,
And we cast away moan;
God 'a mercy on his soul!
And of all christian souls! I pray God. God be wi' you! [*Exit* OPHELIA.
Laer. Do you see this? O God!
King. Laertes, I must commune with your grief,
Or you deny me right. Go but apart,
Make choice of whom your wisest friends you will,
And they shall hear and judge 'twixt you and me:
If by direct or by collateral hand
They find us touch'd, we will our kingdom give,
Our crown, our life, and all that we call ours,
To you in satisfaction; but, if not
Be you content to lend your patience to us,
And we shall jointly labour with your soul
To give it due content.
Laer. Let this be so;
His means of death, his obscure funeral,—
No trophy, sword, nor hatchment, o'er his bones,
No noble rite, nor formal ostentation,—
Cry to be heard, as 'twere from heaven to earth,
That I must call't in question.
King. So you shall;
And where the offence is, let the great axe fall.
I pray you, go with me. [*Exeunt.*

SCENE VI. *Another Room in the same.*

Enter HORATIO *and a* Servant.

Hor. What are they that would speak with me?
Serv. Sailors, sir;
They say, they have letters for you.
Hor. Let them come in.— [*Exit* Servant.
I do not know from what part of the world
I should be greeted, if not from Lord Hamlet.

Enter Sailors.

1 *Sail.* God bless you, sir.
Hor. Let him bless thee to.
1 *Sail.* He shall, sir, an't please him. There's a letter for you, sir: it comes from the ambassador that was bound for England; if your name be Horatio, as I am let to know it is.
Hor. [*Reads.*] Horatio, *when thou shalt have overlooked this, give these fellows some means to the king; they have letters for him. Ere we were two days old at sea, a pirate of very warlike appointment gave us chase: Finding ourselves too slow of sail, we put on a compelled valour; and in the grapple I boarded them: on the instant, they got clear of our ship: so I alone became their prisoner. They have dealt with me like thieves of mercy; but they knew what they did; I am to do a good turn for them. Let the king have the letters I have sent; and repair thou to me with as much haste as thou would'st fly death. I have words to speak in thine ear, will make thee dumb; yet are they much too light for the bore of the matter. These good fellows will bring thee where I am.* Rosencrantz *and* Guildenstern *hold their course for England: of them I have much to tell thee. Farewell.*
He that thou knowest thine, Hamlet.
Come, I will give you way for these your letters;
And do't the speedier, that you may direct me
To him from whom you brought them. [*Exeunt.*

SCENE VII. *Another Room in the same.*

Enter King *and* LAERTES.

King. Now must your conscience my acquittance seal,
And you must put me in your heart for friend;
Sith you have heard, and with a knowing ear,
That he, which hath your noble father slain,
Pursu'd my life.
Laer. It well appears:—But tell me,
Why you proceeded not against these feats,
So crimeful and so capital in nature,
As by your safety, greatness, wisdom, all things else,
You mainly were stirr'd up.
King. O, for two special reasons;
Which may to you, perhaps, seem much unsinew'd,
But yet to me they are strong. The queen, his mother,

Lives almost by his looks; and for myself,
(My virtue, or my plague, be it either which),
She is so conjunctive to my life and soul,
That, as the star moves not but in his sphere,
I could not but by her. The other motive,
Why to a publick count I might not go,
Is, the great love the general gender bear him:
Who, dipping all his faults in their affection,
Would, like the spring that turneth wood to stone,
Convert his gyves to graces; so that my arrows,
Too slightly timber'd for so loud a wind,
Would have reverted to my bow again,
And not where I had aim'd them.

Laer. And so have I a noble father lost;
A sister driven into desperate terms;
Whose worth, if praises may go back again,
Stood challenger on mount of all the age
For her perfections:—But my revenge will come.

King. Break not your sleeps for that: you must not think,
That we are made of stuff so flat and dull,
That we can let our beard be shook with danger,
And think it pastime. You shortly shall hear more:
I loved your father, and we love ourself;
And that, I hope, will teach you to imagine,—
How now? what news?

Enter a Messenger.

Mess. Letters, my lord, from Hamlet:
This to your majesty; this to the queen.

King. From Hamlet! who brought them?

Mess. Sailors, my lord, they say: I saw them not;
They were given me by Claudio, he received them
Of him that brought them.

King. Laertes, you shall hear them:—
Leave us. [*Exit* Messenger.

[Reads.] *High and mighty, you shall know, I am set naked on your kingdom. To-morrow shall I beg leave to see your kingly eyes: when I shall, first asking your pardon thereunto, recount the occasion of my sudden and more strange return.* Hamlet.

What should this mean? Are all the rest come back?
Or is it some abuse, and no such thing?

Laer. Know you the hand?

King. 'Tis Hamlet's character. *Naked,*—
And, in a postscript here, he says, *alone:*
Can you advise me?

Laer. I am lost in it, my lord. But let him come;
It warms the very sickness in my heart,
That I shall live and tell him to his teeth,
Thus diddest thou.

King. If it be so, Laertes,
As how should it be so? how otherwise?—
Will you be rul'd by me?

Laer. Ay, my lord;
So you will not o'errule me to a peace.

King. To thine own peace. If he be now return'd,—
As checking at his voyage, and that he means
No more to undertake it,—I will work him
To an exploit, now ripe in my device,
Under the which he shall not choose but fall:
And for his death no wind of blame shall breathe;
But even his mother shall uncharge the practice,
And call it, accident.

Laer. My lord, I will be rul'd;
The rather, if you could devise it so,
That I might be the organ.

King. It falls right.
You have been talk'd of since your travel much,
And that in Hamlet's hearing, for a quality
Wherein, they say, you shine: your sum of parts
Did not together pluck such envy from him,
As did that one; and that, in my regard,
Of the unworthiest siege.

Laer. What part is that, my lord?

King. A very riband in the cap of youth,
Yet needful too; for youth no less becomes
The light and careless livery that it wears,
Than settled age his sables and his weeds,
Importing health and graveness.—Two months since,
Here was a gentleman of Normandy,—
I have seen myself, and serv'd against the French,
And they can well on horseback: but this gallant
Had witchcraft in 't; he grew unto his seat;
And to such wondrous doing brought his horse,
As he had been incorps'd and demi-natur'd
With the brave beast: so far he topp'd my thought,
That I, in forgery of shapes and tricks,
Come short of what he did.

Laer. A Norman was 't?

King. A Norman.

Laer. Upon my life, Lamord.

King. The very same.

Laer. I know him well: he is the brooch indeed,
And gem of all the nation.

King. He made confession of you;
And gave you such a masterly report,
For art and exercise in your defence,
And for your rapier most especial,
That he cried out, 'twould be a sight indeed,
If one could match you: the scrimers of their nation,
He swore, had neither motion, guard, nor eye,
If you oppos'd them: Sir, this report of his
Did Hamlet so envenom with his envy,
That he could nothing do, but wish and beg
Your sudden coming o'er, to play with you.
Now, out of this,——

Laer. What out of this, my lord?

King. Laertes, was your father dear to you?
Or are you like the painting of a sorrow,
A face without a heart?

Laer. Why ask you this?

King. Not that I think, you did not love your father;
But that I know, love is begun by time;
And that I see, in passages of proof,
Time qualifies the spark and fire of it.
There lives within the very flame of love
A kind of wick, or snuff, that will abate it;
And nothing is at a like goodness still;
For goodness, growing to a plurisy,
Dies in his own too-much: That we would do,
We should do when we would; for this *would* changes,
And hath abatements and delays as many,
As there are tongues, are hands, are accidents;
And then this *should* is like a spendthrift's sigh,
That hurts by easing. But, to the quick o' the ulcer:
Hamlet comes back; What would you undertake,
To show yourself in deed your father's son
More than in words?

Laer. To cut his throat i' the church.

King. No place, indeed, should murder sanctuarize;
Revenge should have no bounds. But, good Laertes,
Will you do this, keep close within your chamber:
Hamlet, return'd, shall know you are come home:
We'll put on those shall praise your excellence,
And set a double varnish on the fame
The Frenchman gave you; bring you, in fine, together,
And wager o'er your heads: he, being remiss,
Most generous and free from all contriving,
Will not peruse the foils; so that, with ease,
Or with a little shuffling you may choose
A sword unbated, and, in a pass of practice,
Requite him for your father.

Laer. I will do 't:

And, for the purpose, I'll anoint my sword.
I bought an unction of a mountebank,
So mortal, that but dip a knife in it,
Where it draws blood no cataplasm so rare,
Collected from all simples that have virtue
Under the moon, can save the thing from death,
That is but scratch'd withal: I'll touch my point
With this contagion; that, if I gall him slightly,
It may be death.

King. Let's further think of this;
Weigh, what convenience, both of time and means,
May fit us to our shape: If this should fail,
And that our drift look through our bad performance,
'Twere better not assay'd: therefore this project
Should have a back, or second, that might hold,
If this should blast in proof. Soft;—let me see:—
We'll make a solemn wager on your cunnings,
I ha't:
When in your motion you are hot and dry,
(As make your bouts more violent to that end,)
And that he calls for drink, I'll have prepar'd him
A chalice for the nonce; whereon but sipping,
If he by chance escape your venom'd stuck,
Our purpose may hold there. But stay, what noise?

Enter Queen.

How now, sweet queen?

Queen. One woe doth tread upon another's heel,
So fast they follow:—Your sister's drown'd, Laertes.

Laer. Drown'd! O, where?

Queen. There is a willow grows ascaunt the brook,
That shows his hoar leaves in the glassy stream:
Therewith fantastick garlands did she make
Of crow-flowers, nettles, daisies, and long purples,
That liberal shepherds give a grosser name,
But our cold maids do dead men's fingers call them:
There on the pendent boughs her coronet weeds
Clambering to hang, an envious sliver broke;
When down her weedy trophies, and herself,
Fell in the weeping brook. Her clothes spread wide;
And, mermaid-like, awhile they bore her up:
Which time, she chanted snatches of old tunes;
As one incapable of her own distress,
Or like a creature native and indu'd
Unto that element: but long it could not be,
Till that her garments, heavy with their drink,
Pull'd the poor wretch from her melodious lay
To muddy death.

Laer. Alas then, she is drown'd?

Queen. Drown'd, drown'd.

Laer. Too much of water hast thou, poor Ophelia,
And therefore I forbid my tears: But yet
It is our trick; nature her custom holds,
Let shame say what it will: when these are gone,
The woman will be out.—Adieu, my lord!
I have a speech of fire, that fain would blaze,
But that this folly drowns it. [*Exit.*

King. Let's follow, Gertrude:
How much I had to do to calm his rage!
Now fear I, this will give it start again;
Therefore, let's follow. [*Exeunt.*

ACT V.

SCENE I. *A Church Yard.*

Enter Two Clowns, *with Spades, &c.*

1 *Clo.* Is she to be buried in christian burial, that wilfully seeks her own salvation?

2 *Clo.* I tell thee, she is; therefore make her grave straight: the crowner hath set on her, and finds it christian burial.

1 *Clo.* How can that be, unless she drowned herself in her own defence?

2 *Clo.* Why, 'tis found so.

1 *Clo.* It must be *se offendendo;* it cannot be else. For here lies the point: If I drown myself wittingly, it argues an act; and an act hath three branches; it is, to act, to do, and to perform; Argal, she drowned herself wittingly.

2 *Clo.* Nay, but hear you, goodman delver.

1 *Clo.* Give me leave. Here lies the water: good; here stands the man; good: If the man go to this water, and drown himself, it is, will he, nill he, he goes; mark you that: but if the water come to him, and drown him, he drowns not himself: Argal, he, that is not guilty of his death, shortens not his own life.

2 *Clo.* But is this law?

1 *Clo.* Ay, marry is't; crowner's-quest law.

2 *Clo.* Will you ha' the truth on't? If this had not been a gentlewoman, she should have been buried out of christian burial.

1 *Clo.* Why there thou say'st: And the more pity; that great folks shall have countenance in this world to drown or hang themselves more than their even-christian. Come, my spade. There is no ancient gentlemen but gardeners, ditchers, and grave-makers: they hold up Adam's profession.

2 *Clo.* Was he a gentleman?

1 *Clo.* He was the first that ever bore arms.

2 *Clo.* Why, he had none.

1 *Clo.* What, art a heathen? How dost thou understand the scripture? The scripture says, Adam digged: Could he dig without arms? I'll put another question to thee,: if thou answerest me not to the purpose, confess thyself——

2 *Clo.* Go to.

1 *Clo.* What is he, that builds stronger than either the mason, the shipwright, or the carpenter?

2 *Clo.* The gallows-maker, for that frame outlives a thousand tenants.

1 *Clo.* I like thy wit well, in good faith; the gallows does well: But how does it well? it does well to those that do ill: now thou dost ill, to say, the gallows is built stronger than the church: argal, the gallows may do well to thee. To't again: come.

2 *Clo.* Who builds stronger than a mason, a shipwright, or a carpenter?

1 *Clo.* Ay, tell me that, and unyoke.

2 *Clo.* Marry, now I can tell.

1 *Clo.* To't.

2 *Clo.* Mass, I cannot tell.

Enter HAMLET *and* HORATIO, *at a distance.*

1 *Clo.* Cudgel thy brains no more about it; for your dull ass will not mend his pace with beating: and, when you are asked this question next, say, a grave-maker; the houses that he makes, last till doomsday. Go, get thee to Yaughan, and fetch me a stoup of liquor. [*Exit* 2 Clown.

1 Clown digs, and sings.

In youth, when I did love, did love,
Methought, it was very sweet,
To contract, O, the time, for, ah, my behove
O, methought, there was nothing meet.

Ham. Has this fellow no feeling of his business? he sings at grave-making.

Hor. Custom hath made it in him a property of easiness.

Ham. 'Tis e'en so: the hand of little employment hath the daintier sense.

1 Clo. *But age, with his stealing steps,*
Hath claw'd me in his clutch,
And hath shipped me into the land,
As if I had never been such.
[Throws up a scull.

Ham. That scull had a tongue in it, and could sing once: How the knave jowls it to the ground, as if it were Cain's jawbone, that did the first murder! This might be the pate of a politician, which this ass now o'erreaches; one that would circumvent God, might it not?

Hor. It might, my lord.

Ham. Or of a courtier; which could say, *Good-morrow, sweet lord! How dost thou, good lord?* This might be my lord such-a-one, that praised my lord such-a-one's horse, when he meant to beg it; might it not?

Hor. Ay, my lord.

Ham. Why, e'en so: and now my lady Worm's; chapless, and knocked about the mazzard with a sexton's spade: Here's fine revolution, an we had the trick to see't. Did these bones cost no more the breeding, but to play at loggarts with them? mine ache to think on't.

1 Clo. *A pickaxe and a spade, a spade,* [Sings.
For—and a shrouding sheet:
O, a pit of clay for to be made
For such a guest is meet.
[Throws up a scull.

Ham. There's another: Why may not that be the scull of a lawyer? Where be his quiddits now, his quillets, his cases, his tenures, and his tricks? why does he suffer this rude knave now to knock him about the sconce with a dirty shovel, and will not tell him of his action of battery? Humph! This fellow might be in's time a great buyer of land, with his statutes, his recognizances, his fines, his double vouchers, his recoveries: Is this the fine of his fines, and the recovery of his recoveries, to have his fine pate full of fine dirt? will his vouchers vouch him no more of his purchases, and double ones too, than the length and breadth of a pair of indentures? The very conveyances of his lands will hardly lie in this box; and must the inheritor himself have no more? ha?

Hor. Not a jot more, my lord.

Ham. Is not parchment made of sheep-skins?

Hor. Ay, my lord, and of calves-skins too.

Ham. They are sheep, and calves, which seek out assurance in that. I will speak to this fellow:—Whose grave's this, sirrah?

1 *Clo.* Mine, sir.—
O, a pit of clay for to be made [Sings.
For such a guest is meet.

Ham. I think it be thine, indeed, for thou liest in't.

1 *Clo.* You lie out on't, sir, and therefore it is not yours: for my part, I do not lie in't, yet it is mine.

Ham. Thou dost lie in't, to be in't, and say it is thine: 'tis for the dead, not for the quick; therefore thou liest.

1 *Clo.* 'Tis a quick lie, sir; 'twill away, again, from me to you.

Ham. What man dost thou dig it for?

1 *Clo.* For no man, sir.

Ham. What woman then?

1 *Clo.* For none neither.

Ham. Who is to be buried in't?

1 *Clo.* One, that was a woman, sir; but, rest her soul, she's dead.

Ham. How absolute the knave is! we must speak by the card, or equivocation will undo us. By the lord, Horatio, these three years I have taken note of it; the age is grown so picked, that the toe of the peasant comes so near the heel of the courtier, he galls his kibe. —How long hast thou been a grave-maker?

1 *Clo.* Of all the days i'the year, I came to't that day that our last king Hamlet overcame Fortinbras.

Ham. How long's that since?

1 *Clo.* Cannot you tell that? every fool can tell that: It was that very day that young Hamlet was born: he that is mad, and sent into England.

Ham. Ay, marry, why was he sent into England?

1 *Clo.* Why, because he was mad: he shall recover his wits there; or, if he do not, 'tis no great matter there.

Ham. Why?

1 *Clo.* 'Twill not be seen in him there; there the men are as mad as he.

Ham. How came he mad?

1 *Clo.* Very strangely, they say.

Ham. How strangely?

1 *Clo.* 'Faith, e'en with losing his wits.

Ham. Upon what ground?

1 *Clo.* Why, here in Denmark; I have been sexton here, man, and boy, thirty years.

Ham. How long will a man lie i' the earth ere he rot?

1 *Clo.* 'Faith, if he be not rotten before he die (as we have many pocky corses nowadays, that will scarce hold the laying in), he will last you some eight year, or nine year; a tanner will last you nine year.

Ham. Why he more than another?

1 *Clo.* Why, sir, his hide is so tanned with his trade, that he will keep out water a great while; and your water is a sore decayer of your whoreson dead body. Here's a scull now hath lain you i'the earth three-and-twenty years.

Ham. Whose was it?

1 *Clo.* A whoreson mad fellow's it was; Whose do you think it was?

Ham. Nay, I know not.

1 *Clo.* A pestilence on him for a mad rogue, he poured a flagon of Rhenish on my head once. This same scull, sir, was Yorick's scull, the king's jester.

Ham. This? [*Takes the Scull.*

1 *Clo.* E'en that.

Ham. Alas, poor Yorick!—I knew him, Horatio; a fellow of infinite jest, of most excellent fancy: he hath borne me on his back a thousand times; and now, how abhorred in my imagination it is! my gorge rises at it. Here hung those lips, that I have kissed I know not how oft. Where be your gives now? your gambols? your songs? your flashes of merriment, that were wont to set the table on a roar? Not one now, to mock your own grinning? quite chapfallen? Now get you to my lady's chamber, and tell her, let her paint an inch thick, to this favour she must come; make her laugh at that. —'Pr'ythee, Horatio, tell me one thing.

Hor. What's that, my lord?

Ham. Dost thou think, Alexander look'd o' this fashion i' the earth?

Hor. E'en so.

Ham. And smelt so? pah!
[*Throws down the Skull.*

Hor. E'en so, my lord.

Ham. To what base uses we may return, Horatio! Why may not imagination trace the noble dust of Alexander, till he find it stopping a bunghole?

Hor. 'Twere to consider too curiously, to consider so.

Ham. No, faith, not a jot; but to follow him thither with modesty enough, and likelihood to lead it: As thus; Alexander died, Alexander was buried, Alexander returneth to dust; the dust is earth; of earth we make loam: And why of that loam, whereto he was converted, might they not stop a beer barrel?

Imperious Cæsar, dead, and turn'd to clay,
Might stop a hole to keep the wind away:
O, that the earth, which kept the world in awe,
Should patch a wall to expel the winter's flaw!
But soft! but soft! aside:—Here comes the king,

Enter Priests, *&c. in Procession; the Corpse of* Ophelia, LAERTES, *and* Mourners, *following*; King, Queen, *their* Trains, *&c.*

The queen, the courtiers! Who is this they follow?
And with such maimed rites! This doth betoken,

The corse, they follow, did with desperate hand
Fordo its own life. 'Twas of some estate.
Couch we awhile, and mark.
[*Retiring with* HORATIO.

Laer. What ceremony else?

Ham. That is Laertes;
A very noble youth: Mark.

Laer. What ceremony else?

1 *Priest.* Her obsequies have been as far enlarg'd
As we have warranty: her death was doubtful;
And, but that great command o'ersways the order,
She should in ground unsanctified have lodg'd
Till the last trumpet; for charitable prayers,
Shards, flints, and pebbles, should be thrown on her,
Yet here she is allow'd her virgin crants,
Her maiden strewments, and the bringing home
Of bell, and burial.

Laer. Must there no more be done?

1 *Priest.* No more be done!
We should profane the service of the dead,
To sing a *requiem*, and such rest to her
As to peace-parted souls.

Laer. Lay her i' the earth;—
And from her fair and unpolluted flesh,
May violets spring!—I tell thee, churlish priest,
A minist'ring angel shall my sister be,
When thou liest howling.

Ham. What, the fair Ophelia!

Queen. Sweets to the sweet: Farewell!
[*Scattering Flowers.*
I hop'd, thou should'st have been my Hamlet's wife;
I thought, thy bride-bed to have deck'd, sweet maid,
And not have strew'd thy grave.

Laer. O treble woe
Fall ten times treble on that cursed head,
Whose wicked deed thy most ingenious sense
Depriv'd thee of!—Hold off the earth awhile,
Till I have caught her once more in mine arms.
[*Leaps into the Grave.*
Now pile your dust upon the quick and dead;
Till of this flat a mountain you have made
To o'ertop old Pelion, or the skyish head
Of blue Olympus.

Ham. [*Advancing.*] What is he, whose grief
Bears such an emphasis? whose phrase of sorrow
Conjures the wand'ring stars, and makes them stand
Like wonder-wounded hearers? this is I,
Hamlet the Dane. [*Leaps into the Grave.*

Laer. The devil take thy soul!
[*Grappling with him.*

Ham. Thou pray'st not well.
I pr'ythee, take thy fingers from my throat;
For, though I am not splenetive and rash,
Yet have I in me something dangerous,
Which let thy wisdom fear: Hold off thy hand.

King. Pluck them asunder.

Queen. Hamlet, Hamlet!

All. Gentlemen,——

Hor. Good my lord, be quiet.
[*The* Attendants *part them, and they come out of the Grave.*

Ham. Why, I will fight with him upon this theme,
Until my eyelids will no longer wag.

Queen. O my son! what theme?

Ham. I lov'd Ophelia; forty thousand brothers
Could not, with all their quantity of love,
Make up my sum.—What wilt thou do for her?

King. O, he is mad, Laertes.

Queen. For love of God, forbear him.

Ham. Zounds, show me what thou'lt do:
Woo't weep? woo't fight? woo't fast? woo't tear thyself?
Woo't drink up Esile, eat a crocodile?
I'll do't.—Dost thou come here to whine?
To outface me with leaping in her grave?
Be buried quick with her, and so will I:
And, if thou prate of mountains, let them throw
Millions of acres on us; till our ground,
Singeing his pate against the burning zone,
Make Ossa like a wart! Nay, an thou'lt mouth,
I'll rant as well as thou.

Queen. This is mere madness:
And thus a while the fit will work on him;
Anon, as patient as the female dove,
When that her golden couplets are disclosed,
His silence will sit drooping.

Ham. Hear you, sir;
What is the reason that you use me thus?
I lov'd you ever: But it is no matter;
Let Hercules himself do what he may,
The cat will mew, the dog will have his day.
[*Exit.*

King. I pray thee, good Horatio, wait upon him.— [*Exit* HORATIO.
Strengthen your patience in our last night's speech; [*To* LAERTES.
We'll put the matter to the present push.—
Good Gertrude, set some watch over your son.—
This grave shall have a living monument:
An hour of quiet shortly shall we see;
Till then, in patience our proceeding be.
[*Exeunt.*

SCENE II. *A Hall in the Castle.*

Enter HAMLET *and* HORATIO.

Ham. So much for this, sir; now shall you see the other;
You do remember all the circumstance?

Hor. Remember it, my lord!

Ham. Sir, in my heart there was a kind of fighting,
That would not let me sleep: methought, I lay
Worse than the mutines in the bilboes. Rashly,
And prais'd be rashness for't,—Let us know,
Our indiscretion sometimes serves us well,
When our deep plots do pall: and that should teach us,
There's a divinity that shapes our ends,
Rough-hew them how we will.

Hor. That is most certain.

Ham. Up from my cabin,
My sea-gown scarf'd about me, in the dark
Grop'd I to find out them: had my desire;
Finger'd their packet: and, in fine, withdrew
To mine own room again: making so bold,
My fears forgetting manners, to unseal
Their grand commission; where I found, Horatio,
A royal knavery; an exact command,—
Larded with many several sorts of reasons,—
Importing Denmark's health, and England's too,
With, ho! such bugs and goblins in my life,—
That on the supervise, no leisure bated,
No, not to stay the grinding of the axe,
My head should be struck off.

Hor. Is't possible?

Ham. Here's the commission; read it at more leisure.
But wilt thou hear now how I did proceed?

Hor. Ay, 'beseech you.

Ham. Being thus benetted round with villanies,
Or I could make a prologue to my brains,
They had begun the play;—I sat me down;
Devis'd a new commission; wrote it fair:
I once did hold it, as our statists do,
A baseness to write fair, and labour'd much
How to forget that learning; but, sir, now
It did me yeoman's service: Wilt thou know
The effect of what I wrote?

Hor. Ay, good my lord.

Ham. An earnest conjuration from the king,—
As England was his faithful tributary;
As love between them like the palm might flourish;
As peace should still her wheaten garland wear,

And stand a comma 'tween their amities;
And many such like ases of great charge,—
That, on the view and knowing of these contents,
Without debatement further, more, or less,
He should the bearers put to sudden death,
Not shriving-time allow'd.

Hor. How was this seal'd?

Ham. Why, even in that was heaven ordinant;
I had my father's signet in my purse,
Which was the model of that Danish seal:
Folded the writ up in form of the other;
Subscrib'd it; gave't the impression; plac'd it safely,
The changeling never known: Now, the next day
Was our sea-fight; and what to this was sequent
Thou know'st already.

Hor. So Guildenstern and Rosencrantz go to't.

Ham. Why, man, they did make love to this employment;
They are not near my conscience; their defeat
Does by their own insinuation grow:
'Tis dangerous, when the baser nature comes
Between the pass and fell incensed points
Of mighty opposites.

Hor. Why, what a king is this!

Ham. Does it not, think thee, stand me now upon?
He that hath kill'd my king, and whor'd my mother;
Popp'd in between the election and my hopes;
Thrown out his angle for my proper life,
And with such cozenage; is't not perfect conscience,
To quit him with this arm; and is't not to be damn'd,
To let this canker of our nature come
In further evil?

Hor. It must be shortly known to him from England,
What is the issue of the business there.

Ham. It will be short: the interim is mine;
And a man's life no more than to say, one.
But I am very sorry, good Horatio,
That to Laertes I forgot myself;
For by the image of my cause, I see
The portraiture of his: I'll count his favours:
But, sure, the bravery of his grief did put me
Into a towering passion.

Hor. Peace: who comes here?

Enter OSRIC.

Osr. Your lordship is right welcome back to Denmark.

Ham. I humbly thank you, sir.—Dost know this water-fly?

Hor. No, my good lord.

Ham. Thy state is the more gracious; for 'tis a vice to know him: He hath much land, and fertile; let a beast be lord of beasts, and his crib shall stand at the king's mess: 'Tis a chough; but, as I say, spacious in the possession of dirt.

Osr. Sweet lord, if your lordship were at leisure, I should impart a thing to you from his majesty.

Ham. I will receive it, sir, with all diligence of spirit: Your bonnet to his right use; 'tis for the head.

Osr. I thank your lordship, 'tis very hot.

Ham. No, believe me, 'tis very cold: the wind is northerly.

Osr. It is indifferent cold, my lord, indeed.

Ham. But yet, methinks, it is very sultry and hot; or my complexion——

Osr. Exceedingly, my lord; it is very sultry,—as 'twere,—I cannot tell how—My lord, his majesty bade me signify to you, that he has laid a great wager on your head: Sir, this is the matter,—

Ham. I beseech you, remember——

[HAMLET *moves him to put on his Hat.*

Osr. Nay, good my lord; for my ease, in good faith. Sir, here is newly come to court, Laertes: believe me, an absolute gentleman, full of most excellent differences, of very soft society, and great showing: Indeed, to speak feelingly of him, he is the card or calendar of gentry, for you shall find in him the continent of what part a gentleman would see.

Ham. Sir, his definement suffers no perdition in you;—though, I know, to divide him inventorially, would dizzy the arithmetick of memory; and yet but raw neither, in respect of his quick sail. But in the verity of extolment, I take him to be a soul of great article; and his infusion of such dearth and rareness, as, to make true diction of him, his semblable is his mirrour; and, who else would trace him, his umbrage, nothing more.

Osr. Your lordship speaks most infallibly of him.

Ham. The concernancy, sir? why do we wrap the gentleman in our more rawer breath?

Osr. Sir?

Hor. Is't not possible to understand in another tongue? You will do't, sir, really.

Ham. What imports the nomination of this gentleman?

Osr. Of Laertes?

Hor. His purse is empty already; all his golden words are spent.

Ham. Of him, sir.

Osr. I know, you are not ignorant——

Ham. I would, you did, sir; yet, in faith, if you did, it would not much approve me.—Well, sir.

Osr. You are not ignorant of what excellence Laertes is——

Ham. I dare not confess that, lest I should compare with him in excellence; but, to know a man well, were to know himself.

Osr. I mean, sir, for his weapon; but in the imputation laid on him by them, in his meed he's unfellowed.

Ham. What's his weapon?

Osr. Rapier and dagger.

Ham. That's two of his weapons: but, well.

Osr. The king, sir, hath wagered with him six Barbary horses: against the which he hath impawned, as I take it, six French rapiers and poniards, with their assigns, as girdle, hangers, and so: Three of the carriages, in faith, are very dear to fancy, very responsive to the hilts, most delicate carriages, and of very liberal conceit.

Ham. What call you the carriages?

Hor. I knew, you must be edified by the margent, ere you had done.

Osr. The carriages, sir, are the hangers.

Ham. The phrase would be more german to the matter, if we could carry a cannon by our sides; I would, it might be hangers till then. But, on: Six Barbary horses against six French swords, their assigns, and three liberal conceited carriages: that's the French bet against the Danish: Why is this impawned, as you call it?

Osr. The king, sir, hath laid, that in a dozen passes between yourself and him, he shall not exceed you three hits: he hath laid on twelve for nine; and it would come to immediate trial, if your lordship would vouchsafe the answer.

Ham. How, if I answer, no?

Osr. I mean, my lord, the opposition of your person in trial.

Ham. Sir, I will walk here in the hall: If it please his majesty, it is the breathing time of day with me: let the foils be brought, the gentleman willing, and the king hold his purpose, I will win for him, if I can; if not, I will gain nothing but my shame, and the odd hits.

Osr. Shall I deliver you so?

Ham. To this effect, sir; after what flourish your nature will.

Osr. I commend my duty to your lordship.

[*Exit.*

Ham. Yours, yours.—He does well to commend it himself; there are no tongues else for's turn.

Hor. This lapwing runs away with the shell on his head.

Ham. He did comply with his dug, before he sucked it. Thus has he (and many more of the same bevy, that, I know, the drossy age dotes on), only got the tune of the time, and outward habit of encounter; a kind of yesty collection, which carries them through and through the most fanned and winnowed opinions; and do but blow them to their trial, the bubbles are out.

Enter a Lord.

Lord. My lord, his majesty commended him to you by young Osric, who brings back to him, that you attend him in the hall: He sends to know, if your pleasure hold to play with Laertes, or that you will take longer time.

Ham. I am constant to my purposes, they follow the king's pleasure: if his fitness speaks, mine is ready; now, or whensoever, provided I be so able as now.

Lord. The king, and queen, and all are coming down.

Ham. In happy time.

Lord. The queen desires you, to use some gentle entertainment to Laertes, before you fall to play.

Ham. She well instructs me. [*Exit* Lord.

Hor. You will lose this wager, my lord.

Ham. I do not think so; since he went into France, I have been in continual practice; I shall win at the odds. But thou would'st not think, how ill all's here about my heart: but it is no matter.

Hor. Nay, good my lord,——

Ham. It is but foolery; but it is such a kind of gain-giving, as would, perhaps, trouble a woman.

Hor. If your mind dislike any thing, obey it: I will forestall their repair hither, and say, you are not fit.

Ham. Not a whit, we defy augury; there is a special providence in the fall of a sparrow. If it be now, 'tis not to come; if it be not to come, it will be now; if it be not now, yet it will come: the readiness is all: Since no man, of aught he leaves,—knows;—what is't to leave betimes. Let be.

Enter King, Queen, LAERTES, Lords, OSRIC, *and* Attendants, *with Foils, &c.*

King. Come, Hamlet, come, and take this hand from me.

[*The* King *puts the hand of* LAERTES *into that of* HAMLET.

Ham. Give me your pardon, sir: I have done you wrong;
But pardon it, as you are a gentleman.
This presence knows, and you must needs have heard,
How I am punish'd with a sore distraction.
What I have done,
That might your nature, honour, and exception,
Roughly awake, I here proclaim was madness.
Was't Hamlet wrong'd Laertes? Never, Hamlet:
If Hamlet from himself be ta'en away,
And, when he's not himself, does wrong Laertes,
Then Hamlet does it not, Hamlet denies it.
Who does it then? His madness: If't be so,
Hamlet is of the faction that is wrong'd;
His madness is poor Hamlet's enemy.
Sir, in this audience,
Let my disclaiming from a purpos'd evil
Free me so far in your most generous thoughts,
That I have shot my arrow o'er the house,
And hurt my brother.

Laer. I am satisfied in nature,
Whose motive, in this case, should stir me most
To my revenge: but in my terms of honour,
I stand aloof; and will no reconcilement,
Till by some elder masters, of known honour,
I have a voice and precedent of peace,
To keep my name ungor'd: But till that time,
I do receive your offer'd love like love,
And will not wrong it.

Ham. I embrace it freely;
And will this brother's wager frankly play.—
Give us the foils; come on.

Laer. Come, one for me.

Ham. I'll be your foil, Laertes; in mine ignorance
Your skill shall, like a star i' the darkest night,
Stick fiery off indeed.

Laer. You mock me, sir.

Ham. No, by this hand.

King. Give them the foils, young Osric.—Cousin Hamlet,
You know the wager?

Ham. Very well, my lord;
Your grace hath laid the odds o' the weaker side.

King. I do not fear it: I have seen you both:—
But since he's better'd, we have therefore odds.

Laer. This is too heavy, let me see another.

Ham. This likes me well: These foils have all a length? [*They prepare to play.*

Osr. Ay, my good lord.

King. Set me the stoups of wine upon that table:—
If Hamlet give the first or second hit,
Or quit in answer of the third exchange,
Let all the battlements their ordnance fire:
The king shall drink to Hamlet's better breath;
And in the cup an union shall he throw,
Richer than that which four successive kings
In Denmark's crown have worn; Give me the cups;
And let the kettle to the trumpet speak,
The trumpet to the cannoneer without,
The cannons to the heavens, the heaven to earth,
Now the king drinks to Hamlet.—Come, begin;—
And you, the judges, bear a wary eye.

Ham. Come on, sir.

Laer. Come, my lord. [*They play.*

Ham. One.

Laer. No.

Ham. Judgment.

Osr. A hit, a very palpable hit.

Laer. Well,—again.

King. Stay, give me drink: Hamlet, this pearl is thine;
Here's to thy health.—Give him the cup.

[*Trumpets sound; and Cannons shot off within.*

Ham. I'll play this bout first, set it by awhile.
Come.—Another hit; What say you?

[*They play.*

Laer. A touch, a touch, I do confess.

King. Our son shall win.

Queen. He's fat, and scant of breath.—
Here, Hamlet, take my napkin, rub thy brows:
The queen carouses to thy fortune, Hamlet.

Ham. Good madam,——

King. Gertrude, do not drink.

Queen. I will, my lord;—I pray you pardon me.

King. It is the poison'd cup; it is too late.

[*Aside.*

Ham. I dare not drink yet, madam; by and by.

Queen. Come, let me wipe thy face.

Laer. My lord, I'll hit him now.

King. I do not think it.

Laer. And yet it is almost against my conscience. [*Aside.*

Ham. Come, for the third, Laertes: You do but dally;
I pray you, pass with your best violence;
I am afeard, you make a wanton of me.

Laer. Say you so? come on. [*They play.*

Osr. Nothing neither way.

Laer. Have at you now.

[LAERTES *wounds* HAMLET; *then in scuffling, they change Rapiers, and* HAMLET *wounds* LAERTES.

King. Part them, they are incens'd.

Ham. Nay, come again. [*The* Queen *falls.*

Osr. Look to the queen there, ho!
Hor. They bleed on both sides;—How is it, my lord?
Osr. How is't, Laertes?
Laer. Why, as a woodcock to mine own springe, Osric;
I am justly kill'd with mine own treachery.
Ham. How does the queen?
King. She swoons to see them bleed.
Queen. No, no, the drink, the drink,—O my dear Hamlet!
The drink, the drink;—I am poison'd! [*Dies.*
Ham. O villany!—Ho! let the door be lock'd:
Treachery! seek it out. [LAERTES *falls.*
Laer. It is here, Hamlet: Hamlet, thou art slain;
No medicine in the world can do thee good,
In thee there is not half an hour's life;
The treacherous instrument is in thy hand,
Unbated, and envenom'd: the foul practice
Hath turn'd itself on me: lo, here I lie,
Never to rise again: Thy mother's poison'd;
I can no more; the king, the king's to blame.
Ham. The point
Envenom'd too!—Then, venom, to thy work.
[*Stabs the* King.
Osr. & Lords. Treason! treason!
King. O, yet defend me, friends, I am but hurt.
Ham. Here, thou incestuous, murd'rous, damned Dane,
Drink off this potion:—Is the union here?
Follow my mother. [King *dies.*
Laer. He is justly serv'd;
It is a poison temper'd by himself.—
Exchange forgiveness with me, noble Hamlet:
Mine and my father's death come not upon thee;
Nor thine on me! [*Dies.*
Ham. Heaven make thee free of it! I follow thee.
I am dead, Horatio:—Wretched queen, adieu!—
You that look pale and tremble at this chance,
That are but mutes or audience to this act,
Had I but time (as this fell sergeant, death,
Is strict in his arrest), O, I could tell you,—
But let it be:—Horatio, I am dead;
Thou liv'st; report me and my cause aright
To the unsatisfied.
Hor. Never believe it;
I am more an antique Roman than a Dane,
Here's yet some liquor left.
Ham. As thou'rt a man,—
Give me the cup; let go; by heaven, I'll have it.—
O God!—Horatio, what a wounded name,
Things standing thus unknown, shall live behind me?
If thou didst ever hold me in thy heart,
Absent thee from felicity awhile,
And in this harsh world draw thy breath in pain,
To tell my story.—
[*March afar off, and Shot within.*
What warlike noise is this?
Osr. Young Fortinbras, with conquest come from Poland,
To the ambassadors of England gives
This warlike volley.
Ham. O, I die, Horatio;
The potent poison quite o'ercrows my spirit;
I cannot live to hear the news from England:
But I do prophesy the election lights
On Fortinbras; he has my dying voice;
So tell him, with the occurrents, more or less,
Which have solicited,—The rest is silence.
[*Dies.*
Hor. Now cracks a noble heart;—Good night, sweet prince;
And flights of angels sing thee to thy rest!
Why does the drum come hither?
[*March within.*

Enter FORTINBRAS, *the* English Ambassadors, *and Others.*

Fort. Where is this sight?
Hor. What is it, you would see?
If aught of woe, or wonder, cease your search.
Fort. This quarry cries on havock!—O proud death!
What feast is toward in thine eternal cell,
That thou so many princes, at a shot,
So bloodily hast struck?
1 *Amb.* The sight is dismal;
And our affairs from England come too late:
The ears are senseless, that should give us hearing,
To tell him, his commandment is fulfill'd,
That Rosencrantz and Guildenstern are dead:
Where should we have our thanks?
Hor. Not from his mouth,
Had it the ability of life to thank you;
He never gave commandment for their death.
But since, so jump upon this bloody question,
You from the Polack wars, and you from England,
Are here arriv'd; give order, that these bodies
High on a stage be placed to the view;
And let me speak, to the yet unknowing world,
How these things came about: So shall you hear
Of carnal, bloody, and unnatural acts;
Of accidental judgments, casual slaughters;
Of deaths put on by cunning, and forc'd cause;
And, in this upshot, purposes mistook
Fall'n on the inventors' heads: all this can I
Truly deliver.
Fort. Let us haste to hear it.
And call the noblest to the audience.
For me, with sorrow I embrace my fortune;
I have some rights of memory in this kingdom,
Which now to claim my vantage doth invite me.
Hor. Of that I shall have also cause to speak,
And from his mouth whose voice will draw on more:
But let this same be presently perform'd,
Even while men's minds are wild; lest more mischance,
On plots and errors, happen.
Fort. Let four captains
Bear Hamlet, like a soldier, to the stage;
For he was likely, had he been put on,
To have prov'd most royally: and, for his passage,
The soldier's musick, and the rites of war,
Speak loudly for him.—
Take up the bodies:—Such a sight as this
Becomes the field, but here shows much amiss.
Go, bid the soldiers shoot. [*A dead march.*
[*Exeunt, bearing off the dead Bodies; after which, a Peal of Ordnance is shot off.*

OTHELLO, THE MOOR OF VENICE.

PERSONS REPRESENTED.

DUKE OF VENICE.
BRABANTIO, *a Senator.*
Two other Senators.
GRATIANO, *Brother to* Brabantio.
LODOVICO, *Kinsman to* Brabantio.
OTHELLO, *the Moor:*
CASSIO, *his Lieutenant;*
IAGO, *his Ancient.*
RODERIGO, *a* Venetian *Gentleman.*
MONTANO, Othello's *Predecessor in the Government of* Cyprus.
Clown, *Servant to* Othello.
Herald.

DESDEMONA, *Daughter to* Brabantio, *and Wife to* Othello.
EMILIA, *Wife to* Iago.
BIANCA, *a Courtesan, Mistress to* Cassio.

Officers, Gentlemen, Messengers, Musicians, Sailors, Attendants, *&c.*

SCENE—*for the first Act, in* Venice; *during the rest of the Play, at a Seaport in* Cyprus.

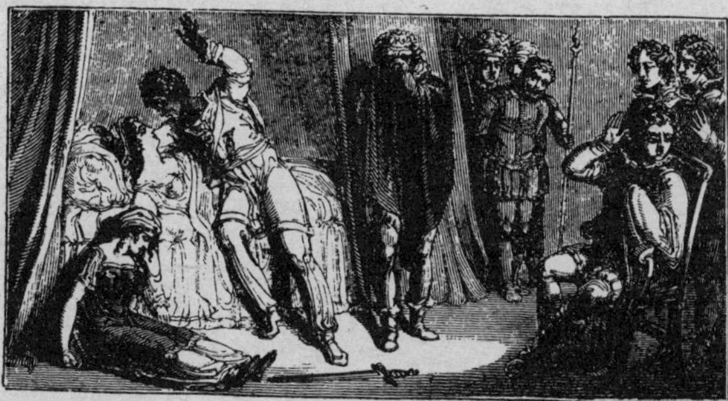

ACT I.

SCENE I. Venice. *A Street.*

Enter RODERIGO *and* IAGO.

Rod. TUSH, never tell me, I take it much unkindly,
That thou, Iago,—who hast had my purse,
As if the strings were thine,—should'st know of this.

Iago. 'Sblood, but you will not hear me:—
If ever I did dream of such a matter,
Abhor me.

Rod. Thou told'st me, thou did'st hold him in thy hate.

Iago. Despise me, if I do not. Three great ones of the city,
In personal suit to make me his lieutenant,
Oft capp'd to him;—and, by the faith of man,
I know my price, I am worth no worse a place:
But he, as loving his own pride and purposes,
Evades them, with a bombast circumstance,
Horribly stuff'd with epithets of war;
And, in conclusion, nonsuits
My mediators; *for, certes,* says he,
I have already chose my officer.
And what was he?
Forsooth, a great arithmetician,
One Michael Cassio, a Florentine,
A fellow almost damn'd in a fair wife;
That never set a squadron in the field,
Nor the division of a battle knows
More than a spinster; unless the bookish theorick,
Wherein the toged consuls can propose
As masterly as he: mere prattle, without practice,
Is all his soldiership. But, he, sir, had the election:
And I,—of whom his eyes had seen the proof,
At Rhodes, at Cyprus; and on other grounds
Christian and heathen,—must be be-lee'd and calm'd
By debitor and creditor, this counter-caster;
He, in good time, must his lieutenant be,
And I (God bless the mark!) his Moorship's ancient.

Rod. By heaven, I rather would have been his hangman.

Iago. But there's no remedy, 'tis the curse of service;
Preferment goes by letter, and affection,
Not by the old gradation, where each second
Stood heir to the first. Now, sir, be judge yourself,
Whether I in any just term am affin'd
To love the Moor.

Rod. I would not follow him then.

Iago. O, sir, content you;
I follow him to serve my turn upon him:
We cannot all be masters, nor all masters
Cannot be truly follow'd. You shall mark
Many a duteous and knee-crooking knave,
That, doting on his own obsequious bondage,
Wears out his time, much like his master's ass,
For nought but provender; and, when he's old, cashier'd;
Whip me such honest knaves: Others there are,
Who, trimm'd in forms and visages of duty,
Keep yet their hearts attending on themselves;
And, throwing but shows of service on their lords,
Do well thrive by them, and, when they have lin'd their coats,

Do themselves homage: these fellows have some soul;
And such a one do I profess myself.
For, sir,
It is as sure as you are Roderigo,
Were I the Moor, I would not be Iago:
In following him, I follow but myself:
Heaven is my judge, not I for love and duty,
But seeming so, for my peculiar end:
For when my outward action doth demonstrate
The native act and figure of my heart
In compliment extern, 'tis not long after
But I will wear my heart upon my sleeve
For daws to peck at: I am not what I am.

Rod. What a full fortune does the thick-lips owe,
If he can carry't thus!

Iago. Call up her father,
Rouse him: make after him, poison his delight,
Proclaim him in the streets; incense her kinsmen,
And, though he in a fertile climate dwell,
Plague him with flies: though that his joy be joy,
Yet throw such changes of vexation on't,
As it may lose some colour.

Rod. Here is her father's house: I'll call aloud.

Iago. Do; with like timorous accent, and dire yell,
As when, by night and negligence, the fire
Is spied in populous cities.

Rod. What ho! Brabantio! signior Brabantio! ho!

Iago. Awake! what ho! Brabantio! thieves! thieves! thieves!
Look to your house, your daughter, and your bags!
Thieves! thieves!

BRABANTIO, *above, at a Window.*

Bra. What is the reason of this terrible summons?
What is the matter there?

Rod. Signior, is all your family within?

Iago. Are your doors lock'd?

Bra. Why? wherefore ask you this?

Iago. 'Zounds, sir, you are robb'd; for shame, put on your gown:
Your heart is burst, you have lost half your soul;
Even now, very now, an old black ram
Is tupping your white ewe. Arise, arise;
Awake the snorting citizens with the bell,
Or else the devil will make a grandsire of you:
Arise, I say.

Bra. What, have you lost your wits?

Rod. Most reverend signior, do you know my voice?

Bra. Not I; What are you?

Rod. My name is—Roderigo.

Bra. The worse welcome:
I have charg'd thee, not to haunt about my doors;
In honest plainness thou hast heard me say,
My daughter is not for thee; and now, in madness,
Being full of supper, and distempering draughts,
Upon malicious bravery, dost thou come
To start my quiet.

Rod. Sir, sir, sir, sir,——

Bra. But thou must needs be sure,
My spirit, and my place, have in them power
To make this bitter to thee.

Rod. Patience, good sir.

Bra. What tell'st thou me of robbing? this is Venice;
My house is not a grange.

Rod. Most grave Brabantio,
In simple and pure soul I come to you.

Iago. 'Zounds, sir, you are one of those, that will not serve God, if the devil bid you. Because we come to do you service, you think we are ruffians: You'll have your daughter covered with a Barbary horse; you'll have your nephews neigh to you: you'll have coursers for cousins, and gennets for germans.

Bra. What profane wretch art thou?

Iago. I am one, sir, that comes to tell you, your daughter and the Moor are now making the beast with two backs.

Bra. Thou art a villain.

Iago. You are—a senator.

Bra. This thou shalt answer: I know thee, Roderigo.

Rod. Sir, I will answer any thing. But I beseech you,
If't be your pleasure, and most wise consent,
(As partly I find, it is), that your fair daughter,
At this odd-even and dull watch o'the night,
Transported—with no worse nor better guard,
But with a knave of common hire, a gondolier,—
To the gross clasps of a lascivious Moor,—
If this be known to you, and your allowance,
We then have done you bold and saucy wrongs;
But if you know not this, my manners tell me,
We have your wrong rebuke. Do not believe,
That, from the sense of all civility,
I thus would play and trifle with your reverence:
Your daughter,—if you have not given her leave,—
I say again, hath made a gross revolt;
Tying her duty, beauty, wit, and fortunes,
In an extravagant and wheeling stranger,
Of here and every where: Straight satisfy yourself:
If she be in her chamber, or your house,
Let loose on me the justice of the state
For thus deluding you.

Bra. Strike on the tinder, ho!
Give me a taper;—call up all my people:—
This accident is not unlike my dream,
Belief of it oppresses me already:—
Light, I say! light! [*Exit, from above.*

Iago. Farewell; for I must leave you:
It seems not meet, nor wholesome to my place,
To be produc'd (as, if I stay, I shall),
Against the Moor: For, I do know, the state,—
However this may gall him with some check,—
Cannot with safety cast him; for he's embark'd
With such loud reason to the Cyprus' wars
(Which even now stand in act), that, for their souls,
Another of his fathom they have not,
To lead their business: in which regard,
Though I do hate him as I do hell pains,
Yet, for necessity of present life,
I must show out a flag and sign of love,
Which is indeed but sign. That you shall surely find him,
Lead to the Sagittary the rais'd search;
And there will I be with him. So, farewell.
[*Exit.*

Enter below, BRABANTIO, *and* Servants, *with Torches.*

Bra. It is too true an evil: gone she is:
And what's to come of my despised time,
Is nought but bitterness.—Now, Roderigo,
Where didst thou see her?—O, unhappy girl!—
With the Moor, say'st thou?—Who would be a father?—
How didst thou know 'twas she? O, thou deceiv'st me
Past thought!—What said she to you?—Get more tapers;
Raise all my kindred.—Are they married, think [you?

Rod. Truly, I think, they are.

Bra. O heaven!—How got she out?—O treason of the blood!—
Fathers, from hence trust not your daughters' minds,
By what you see them act.—Are there not charms,
By which the property of youth and maidhood
May be abus'd? Have you not read, Roderigo,
Of some such thing?

Rod. Yes, sir, I have indeed.
Bra. Call up my brother.—O, that you had had her!—
Some one way, some another.—Do you know
Where we may apprehend her and the Moor?
Rod. I think, I can discover him; if you please,
To get good guard, and go along with me.
Bra. 'Pray you, lead on. At every house I'll call;
I may command at most;—Get weapons, ho!
And raise some special officers of night.—
On, good Roderigo;—I'll deserve your pains.
[*Exeunt.*

SCENE II. *The same. Another Street.*

Enter OTHELLO, IAGO, *and* Attendants.

Iago. Though in the trade of war I have slain men,
Yet do I hold it very stuff o' the conscience,
To do no contriv'd murder; I lack iniquity
Sometimes, to do me service: Nine or ten times
I had bethought to have yerk'd him here under the ribs,
Oth. 'Tis better as it is.
Iago. Nay, but he prated,
And spoke such scurvy and provoking terms
Against your honour,
That, with the little godliness I have,
I did full hard forbear him. But, I pray, sir,
Are you fast married? for, be sure of this,—
That the magnifico is much beloved;
And hath, in his effect, a voice potential
As double as the duke's; he will divorce you;
Or put upon you what restraint and grievance
The law (with all his might, to enforce it on),
Will give him cable.
Oth. Let him do his spite:
My services which I have done the signiory,
Shall out-tongue his complaints. 'Tis yet to know,
(Which, when I know that boasting is an honour,
I shall promulgate), I fetch my life and being
From men of royal siege; and my demerits
May speak, unbonneted, to as proud a fortune
As this that I have reach'd: For know, Iago,
But that I love the gentle Desdemona,
I would not my unhoused free condition
Put into circumscription and confine
For the sea's worth. But, look! what lights come yonder?

Enter CASSIO, *at a distance, and certain* Officers *with Torches.*

Iago. These are the raised father, and his friends:
You were best go in.
Oth. Not I: I must be found;
My parts, my title, and my perfect soul,
Shall manifest me rightly. Is it they?
Iago. By Janus, I think no.
Oth. The servants of the duke, and my lieutenant.
The goodness of the night upon you, friends!
What is the news?
Cas. The duke does greet you, general;
And he requires your haste, post-haste, appearance,
Even on the instant.
Oth. What is the matter, think you?
Cas. Something from Cyprus, as I may divine
It is a business of some heat; the galleys
Have sent a dozen sequent messengers
This very night at one another's heels;
And many of the consuls, rais'd, and met,
Are at the duke's already: You have been hotly call'd for;
When, being not at your lodging to be found,
The senate hath sent about three several quests,
To search you out.
Oth. 'Tis well I am found by you.
I will but spend a word here in the house,
And go with you. [*Exit.*
Cas. Ancient, what makes he here?
Iago. 'Faith, he to-night hath boarded a land carrack;
If it prove lawful prize, he's made for ever.
Cas. I do not understand.
Iago. He's married.
Cas. To who?

Re-enter OTHELLO.

Iago. Marry, to—Come, captain, will you go?
Oth. Have with you.
Cas. Here comes another troop to seek for you.

Enter BRABANTIO, RODERIGO, *and* Officers *of Night, with Torches and Weapons.*

Iago. It is Brabantio:—general, be advis'd;
He comes to bad intent.
Oth. Hola! stand there!
Rod. Signior, it is the Moor.
Bra. Down with him, thief!
[*They draw on both sides.*
Iago. You, Roderigo! come, sir, I am for you.
Oth. Keep up your bright swords, for the dew will rust them.—
Good signior, you shall more command with years,
Than with your weapons.
Bra. O thou foul thief, where hast thou stow'd my daughter?
Damn'd as thou art, thou hast enchanted her:
For I'll refer me to all things of sense,
If she in chains of magick were not bound,
Whether a maid—so tender, fair, and happy;
So opposite to marriage, that she shunn'd
The wealthy curled darlings of our nation,
Would ever have, to incur a general mock,
Run from her guardage to the sooty bosom
Of such a thing as thou: to fear, not to delight.
Judge me the world, if 'tis not gross in sense,
That thou hast practis'd on her with foul charms,
Abus'd her delicate youth with drugs, or minerals,
That waken motion:—I'll have it disputed on;
'Tis probable, and palpable to thinking.
I therefore apprehend and do attach thee,
For an abuser of the world, a practiser
Of arts inhibited and out of warrant:—
Lay hold upon him; if he do resist,
Subdue him at his peril.
Oth. Hold your hands,
Both you of my inclining, and the rest:
Were it my cue to fight, I should have known it
Without a prompter.—Where will you that I go
To answer this your charge?
Bra. To prison: till fit time
Of law, and course of direct session,
Call thee to answer.
Oth. What if I do obey?
How may the duke be therewith satisfied;
Whose messengers are here about my side,
Upon some present business of the state,
To bring me to him?
Off. 'Tis true, most worthy signior,
The duke's in council; and your noble self,
I am sure, is sent for.
Bra. How! the duke in council!
In this time of the night!—Bring him away:
Mine's not an idle cause: the duke himself,
Or any of my brothers of the state,
Cannot but feel this wrong, as 'twere their own:
For if such actions may have passage free,
Bond-slaves, and pagans, shall our statesmen be.
[*Exeunt.*

SCENE III. *The same. A Council Chamber.*

The Duke, *and* Senators, *sitting at a Table;* Officers *attending.*

Duke. There is no composition in these news,
That gives them credit.
1 Sen. Indeed, they are disproportion'd;
My letters say, a hundred and seven galleys.
Duke. And mine, a hundred and forty.

2 Sen. And mine, two hundred:
But though they jump not on a just account,
(As in these cases, where the aim reports,
'Tis oft with difference), yet do they all confirm
A Turkish fleet, and bearing up to Cyprus.
Duke. Nay, it is possible enough to judgment;
I do not so secure me in the error,
But the main article I do approve
In fearful sense.
Sailor. [*Within.*] What ho! what ho! what ho!

Enter an Officer, *with a* Sailor.

Off. A messenger from the galleys.
Duke. Now? the business?
Sailor. The Turkish preparation makes for Rhodes;
So was I bid report here to the state,
By signior Angelo.
Duke. How say you by this change?
1 Sen. This cannot be,
By no assay of reason; 'tis a pageant,
To keep us in false gaze: When we consider
The importancy of Cyprus to the Turk;
And let ourselves again but understand,
That, as it more concerns the Turk than Rhodes,
So may he with more facile question bear it,
For that it stands not in such warlike brace,
But altogether lacks the abilities
That Rhodes is dress'd in:—if we make thought of this,
We must not think, the Turk is so unskilful,
To leave that latest which concerns him first;
Neglecting an attempt of ease, and gain,
To wake, and wage, a danger profitless.
Duke. Nay, in all confidence, he's not for Rhodes.
Off. Here is more news.

Enter a Messenger.

Mess. The Ottomites, reverend and gracious,
Steering with due course toward the isles of Rhodes,
Have there injointed them with an after fleet.
1 Sen. Ay, so I thought:—How many, as you guess?
Mess. Of thirty sail: and now do they restem
Their backward course, bearing with frank appearance
Their purposes toward Cyprus.—Signior Montano,
Your trusty and most valiant servitor,
With his free duty recommends you thus,
And prays you to believe him.
Duke. 'Tis certain then for Cyprus,—
Marcus Lucchese, is he not in town?
1 Sen. He's now in Florence.
Duke. Write from us; wish him post-post-haste: despatch.
1 Sen. Here comes Brabantio, and the valiant Moor.

Enter BRABANTIO, OTHELLO, IAGO, RODERIGO, *and* Officers.

Duke. Valiant Othello, we must straight employ you
Against the general enemy Ottoman.
I did not see you; welcome, gentle signior; [*To* BRABANTIO.
We lack'd your counsel and your help to-night.
Bra. So did I yours: Good your grace, pardon me;
Neither my place, nor aught I heard of business,
Hath rais'd me from my bed; nor doth the general care
Take hold on me; for my particular grief
Is of so flood-gate and o'erbearing nature,
That it engluts and swallows other sorrows,
And it is still itself.
Duke. Why, what's the matter?
Bra. My daughter! O, my daughter!
Sen. Dead?
Bra. Ay, to me;
She is abus'd, stol'n from me, and corrupted
By spells and medicines bought of mountebanks:
For nature so preposterously to err,
Being not deficient, blind, or lame of sense,
Sans witchcraft could not——
Duke. Whoe'er he be, that, in this foul proceeding,
Hath thus beguil'd your daughter of herself,
And you of her, the bloody book of law
You shall yourself read in the bitter letter,
After your own sense; yea, though our proper son
Stood in your action.
Bra. Humbly I thank your grace.
Here is the man, this Moor; whom now, it seems,
Your special mandate, for the state affairs,
Hath hither brought.
Duke & Sen. We are very sorry for it.
Duke. What, in your own part, can you say to this? [*To* OTHELLO.
Bra. Nothing, but this is so.
Oth. Most potent, grave, and reverend signiors,
My very noble and approved good masters,
That I have ta'en away this old man's daughter,
It is most true; true, I have married her;
The very head and front of my offending
Hath this extent, no more. Rude am I in my speech,
And little bless'd with the set phrase of peace;
For since these arms of mine had seven years' pith,
Till now some nine moons wasted, they have us'd
Their dearest action in the tented field;
And little of this great world can I speak,
More than pertains to feats of broil and battle;
And therefore little shall I grace my cause,
In speaking for myself: Yet, by your gracious patience,
I will a round unvarnish'd tale deliver
Of my whole course of love! what drugs, what charms,
What conjuration, and what mighty magick
(For such proceeding I am charg'd withal),
I won his daughter with.
Bra. A maiden never bold;
Of spirit so still and quiet, that her motion
Blush'd at herself; And she,—in spite of nature,
Of years, of country, credit, every thing,—
To fall in love with what she fear'd to look on?
It is a judgment maim'd, and most imperfect,
That will confess—perfection so could err
Against all rules of nature; and must be driven
To find out practises of cunning hell,
Why this should be. I therefore vouch again,
That with some mixtures powerful o'er the blood,
Or with some dram conjur'd to this effect,
He wrought upon her.
Duke. To vouch this, is no proof;
Without more certain and more overt test,
Than these thin habits, and poor likelihoods
Of modern seeming, do prefer against him.
1 Sen. But, Othello, speak:—
Did you by indirect and forced courses
Subdue and poison this young maid's affections?
Or came it by request, and such fair question
As soul to soul affordeth?
Oth. I do beseech you,
Send for the lady to the Sagittary,
And let her speak of me before her father:
If you do find me foul in her report,
The trust, the office, I do hold of you,
Not only take away, but let your sentence
Even fall upon my life.
Duke. Fetch Desdemona hither.
Oth. Ancient, conduct them; you best know the place.— [*Exeunt* IAGO *and* Attendants.
And, till she come, as truly as to heaven
I do confess the vices of my blood,
So justly to your grave ears I'll present
How I did thrive in this fair lady's love,
And she in mine.
Duke. Say it, Othello.

Oth. Her father lov'd me; oft invited me;
Still question'd me the story of my life,
From year to year; the battles, sieges, fortunes,
That I have pass'd.
I ran it through, even from my boyish days,
To the very moment that he bade me tell it.
Wherein I spoke of most disastrous chances,
Of moving accidents, by flood, and field:
Of hair-breadth scapes i' the imminent deadly breach;
Of being taken by the insolent foe,
And sold to slavery; of my redemption thence,
And portance in my travel's history:
Wherein of antres vast, and deserts wild,
Rough quarries, rocks, and hills whose heads touch heaven,
It was my hint to speak, such was the process;
And of the cannibals that each other eat,
The anthropophagi, and men whose heads
Do grow beneath their shoulders. These things to hear,
Would Desdemona seriously incline:
But still the house affairs would draw her thence;
Which ever as she could with haste despatch,
She'd come again, and with a greedy ear
Devour up my discourse: Which I observing,
Took once a pliant hour; and found good means
To draw from her a prayer of earnest heart,
That I would all my pilgrimage dilate,
Whereof by parcels she had something heard,
But not intentively: I did consent;
And often did beguile her of her tears,
When I did speak of some distressful stroke,
That my youth suffer'd. My story being done,
She gave me for my pains a world of sighs:
She swore,—In faith, 'twas strange, 'twas passing strange;
'Twas pitiful, 'twas wondrous pitiful:
She wish'd, she had not heard it; yet she wish'd
That heaven had made her such a man; she thank'd me;
And bade me, if I had a friend that lov'd her,
I should but teach him how to tell my story,
And that would woo her. Upon this hint, I spake:
She lov'd me for the dangers I had pass'd;
And I lov'd her, that she did pity them.
This only is the witchcraft I have us'd;
Here comes the lady, let her witness it.

Enter DESDEMONA, IAGO, *and* Attendants.

Duke. I think, this tale would win my daughter too.—
Good Brabantio,
Take up this mangled matter at the best:
Men do their broken weapons rather use,
Than their bare hands.
Bra. I pray you, hear her speak;
If she confess, that she was half the wooer,
Destruction on my head, if my bad blame
Light on the man!—Come hither, gentle mistress;
Do you perceive in all this noble company,
Where most you owe obedience?
Des. My noble father,
I do perceive here a divided duty:
To you, I am bound for life, and education;
My life, and education, both do learn me
How to respect you; you are the lord of duty,
I am hitherto your daughter: But here's my husband;
And so much duty as my mother show'd
To you, preferring you before her father,
So much I challenge that I may profess
Due to the Moor, my lord.
Bra. God be with you!—I have done:—
Please it your grace, on to the state affairs;
I had rather to adopt a child, than get it.—
Come hither, Moor:
I here do give thee that with all my heart,
Which, but thou hast already, with all my heart
I would keep from thee.—For your sake, jewel,
I am glad at soul I have no other child;
For thy escape would teach me tyranny,
To hang clogs on them.—I have done, my lord.
Duke. Let me speak like yourself; and lay a sentence,
Which, as a grise, or step, may help these lovers
Into your favour.
When remedies are past, the griefs are ended,
By seeing the worst, which late on hopes depended.
To mourn a mischief that is past and gone,
Is the next way to draw new mischief on.
What cannot be preserv'd when fortune takes,
Patience her injury a mockery makes.
The robb'd, that smiles, steals something from the thief;
He robs himself, that spends a bootless grief.
Bra. So let the Turk of Cyprus us beguile;
We lose it not, so long as we can smile.
He bears the sentence well, that nothing bears
But the free comfort which from thence he hears;
But he bears both the sentence and the sorrow,
That, to pay grief, must of poor patience borrow,
These sentences, to sugar, or to gall,
Being strong on both sides, are equivocal:
But words are words; I never yet did hear,
That the bruis'd heart was pierced through the ear.
I humbly beseech you, proceed to the affairs of state.

Duke. The Turk with a most mighty preparation makes for Cyprus:—Othello, the fortitude of the place is best known to you: And though we have there a substitute of most allowed sufficiency, yet opinion, a sovereign mistress of effects, throws a more safer voice on you; you must therefore be content to slubber the gloss of your new fortunes with this more stubborn and boisterous expedition.

Oth. The tyrant custom, most grave senators,
Hath made the flinty and steel couch of war
My thrice-driven bed of down: I do agnize
A natural and prompt alacrity,
I find in hardness; and do undertake
These present wars against the Ottomites.
Most humbly therefore bending to your state,
I crave fit disposition for my wife;
Due reference of place, and exhibition,
With such accommodation, and besort,
As levels with her breeding.
Duke. If you please,
Be't at her father's.
Bra. I'll not have it so.
Oth. Nor I.
Des. Nor I; I would not there reside,
To put my father in impatient thoughts,
By being in his eye. Most gracious duke,
To my unfolding lend a gracious ear;
And let me find a charter in your voice,
To assist my simpleness.
Duke. What would you, Desdemona?
Des. That I did love the Moor to live with him,
My downright violence and storm of fortunes
May trumpet to the world; my heart's subdued
Even to the very quality of my lord:
I saw Othello's visage in his mind;
And to his honours, and his valiant parts,
Did I my soul and fortunes consecrate.
So that, dear lords, if I be left behind,
A moth of peace, and he go to the war,
The rites, for which I love him, are bereft me,
And I a heavy interim shall support
By his dear absence: Let me go with him.
Oth. Your voices, lords—'beseech you, let her will
Have a free way.
Vouch with me, heaven; I therefore beg it not,
To please the palate of my appetite;
Nor to comply with heat (the young affects,
In me defunct) and proper satisfaction;
But to be free and bounteous to her mind:

And heaven defend your good souls, that you think
I will your serious and great business scant,
For she is with me: No, when light-wing'd toys
Of feather'd Cupid seel with wanton dulness
My speculative and active instruments,
That my disports corrupt and taint my business,
Let housewives make a skillet of my helm,
And all indign and base adversities
Make head against my estimation;

Duke. Be it as you shall privately determine
Either for her stay, or going: the affair cries—haste,
And speed must answer it; you must hence to-night.

Des. To-night, my lord?

Duke. This night.

Oth. With all my heart.

Duke. At nine i'the morning here we'll meet again.
Othello, leave some officer behind,
And he shall our commission bring to you:
With such things else of quality and respect,
As doth import you.

Oth. Please your grace, my ancient;
A man he is of honesty and trust:
To his conveyance I assign my wife,
With what else needful your good grace shall think
To be sent after me.

Duke. Let it be so.—
Good night to every one.—And, noble signior, [*To* BRABANTIO.
If virtue no delighted beauty lack,
Your son-in-law is far more fair than black.

1 *Sen.* Adieu, brave Moor! use Desdemona well.

Bra. Look to her, Moor; have a quick eye to see;
She has deceiv'd her father, and may thee.
[*Exeunt* Duke, Senators, Officers, *&c.*

Oth. My life upon her faith.—Honest Iago,
My Desdemona must I leave to thee:
I pr'ythee, let thy wife attend on her;
And bring them after in the best advantage.—
Come, Desdemona; I have but an hour
Of love, of worldly matters and direction,
To spend with thee: we must obey the time.
[*Exeunt* OTHELLO *and* DESDEMONA.

Rod. Iago.

Iago. What say'st thou, noble heart?

Rod. What will I do, thinkest thou?

Iago. Why, go to bed, and sleep.

Rod. I will incontinently drown myself.

Iago. Well, if thou dost, I shall never love thee after it. Why, thou silly gentleman!

Rod. It is silliness to live, when to live is a torment: and then have we a prescription to die, when death is our physician.

Iago. O villanous! I have looked upon the world for four times seven years! and since I could distinguish between a benefit and an injury, I never found a man that knew how to love himself. Ere I would say, I would drown myself for the love of a Guinea-hen, I would change my humanity with a baboon.

Rod. What should I do? I confess, it is my shame to be so fond: but it is not in virtue to amend it.

Iago. Virtue? a fig? 'tis in ourselves, that we are thus, or thus. Our bodies are our gardens; to the which, our wills are gardeners: so that if we will plant nettles, or sow lettuce; set hyssop, and weed up thyme; supply it with one gender of herbs, or distract it with many; either to have it steril with idleness, or manured with industry: why, the power and corrigible authority of this lies in our wills. If the balance of our lives had not one scale of reason to poise another of sensuality, the blood and baseness of our natures would conduct us to most preposterous conclusions: But we have reason to cool our raging motions, our carnal stings, our unbitted lusts; whereof I take this, that you call—love, to be a sect, or scion.

Rod. It cannot be.

Iago. It is merely a lust of the blood, and a permission of the will. Come, be a man: Drown thyself? drown cats, and blind puppies. I have professed me thy friend, and I confess me knit to thy deserving with cables of perdurable toughness; I could never better stead thee than now. Put money in thy purse; follow these wars; defeat thy favour with an usurped beard; I say, put money in thy purse. It cannot be, that Desdemona should long continue her love to the Moor,—put money in thy purse;—nor he his to her: it was a violent commencement, and thou shalt see an answerable sequestration;—put but money in thy purse.—These Moors are changeable in their wills:—fill thy purse with money: the food that to him now is as luscious as locusts, shall be to him shortly as bitter as coloquintida. She must change for youth; when she is sated with his body, she will find the error of her choice.—She must have change, she must; therefore put money in thy purse.—If thou wilt needs damn thyself, do it a more delicate way than drowning. Make all the money thou canst: If sanctimony and a frail vow, betwixt an erring barbarian and a supersubtle Venetian, be not too hard for my wits, and all the tribe of hell, thou shalt enjoy her; therefore make money. A pox of drowning thyself! it is clean out of the way: seek thou rather to be hanged in compassing thy joy, than to be drowned and go without her.

Rod. Wilt thou be fast to my hopes, if I depend on the issue?

Iago. Thou art sure of me;—Go, make money:—I have told thee often, and I retell thee again and again, I hate the Moor: My cause is hearted: thine hath no less reason: Let us be conjunctive in our revenge against him: if thou canst cuckold him, thou dost thyself a pleasure, and me a sport. There are many events in the womb of time, which will be delivered. Traverse; go: provide thy money. We will have more of this to-morrow.—Adieu.

Rod. Where shall we meet i' the morning?

Iago. At my lodging.

Rod. I'll be with thee betimes.

Iago. Go to; farewell. Do you hear, Roderigo?

Rod. What say you?

Iago. No more of drowning, do you hear.

Rod. I am changed. I'll sell all my land.

Iago. Go to; farewell: put money enough in your purse. [*Exit* RODERIGO.
Thus do I ever make my fool my purse:
For I mine own gain'd knowledge should profane,
If I would time expend with such a snipe,
But for my sport and profit. I hate the Moor;
And it is thought abroad, that 'twixt my sheets
He has done my office: I know not if 't be true;
But I, for mere suspicion in that kind,
Will do, as if for surety. He holds me well;
The better shall my purpose work on him.
Cassio's a proper man: Let me see now;
To get his place, and to plume up my will;
A double knavery,—How? how?—Let me see—
After some time, to abuse Othello's ear,
That he is too familiar with his wife:
He hath a person; and a smooth dispose
To be suspected; fram'd to make women false,
The Moor is of a free and open nature,
That thinks men honest, that but seem to be so;
And will as tenderly be led by the nose,
As asses are.
I have't;—it is engender'd:—Hell and night
Must bring this monstrous birth to the world's light. [*Exit.*

ACT II.

SCENE I. *A Seaport Town in* Cyprus. *A Platform.*

Enter MONTANO *and Two* Gentlemen.

Mon. What from the cape can you discern at sea?

1 Gent. Nothing at all: it is a high-wrought flood;
I cannot, 'twixt the heaven and the main,
Descry a sail.

Mon. Methinks, the wind hath spoke aloud at land;
A fuller blast ne'er shook our battlements:
If it hath ruffian'd so upon the sea,
What ribs of oak, when mountains melt on them,
Can hold the mortise? what shall we hear of this?

2 Gent. A segregation of the Turkish fleet:
For do but stand upon the foaming shore,
The chiding billow seems to pelt the clouds;
The wind-shak'd surge, with high and monstrous main,
Seems to cast water on the burning bear,
And quench the guards of the ever-fixed pole:
I never did like molestation view
On the' enchafed flood.

Mon. If that the Turkish fleet
Be not enshelter'd and embay'd, they are drown'd;
It is impossible they bear it out.

Enter a third Gentleman.

3 Gent. News, lords! our wars are done:
The desperate tempest hath so bang'd the Turks,
That their designment halts: A noble ship of Venice
Hath seen a grievous wreck and sufferance
On most part of their fleet.

Mon. How! is this true?

3 Gent. The ship is here put in,
A Veronese; Michael Cassio,
Lieutenant to the warlike Moor, Othello,
Is come on shore: the Moor himself's at sea,
And is in full commission here for Cyprus.

Mon. I am glad on't; 'tis a worthy governor.

3 Gent. But this same Cassio,—though he speak of comfort,
Touching the Turkish loss,—yet he looks sadly,
And prays the Moor be safe; for they were parted
With foul and violent tempest.

Mon. 'Pray heaven, he be;
For I have serv'd him, and the man commands
Like a full soldier. Let's to the seaside, ho!
As well to see the vessel that's come in,
As to throw out our eyes for brave Othello;
Even till we make the main, and the aerial blue,
An indistinct regard.

3 Gent. Come, let's do so;
For every minute is expectancy
Of more arrivance.

Enter CASSIO.

Cas. Thanks to the valiant of this warlike isle,
That so approve the Moor; O, let the heavens
Give him defence against the elements,
For I have lost him on a dangerous sea!

Mon. Is he well shipp'd?

Cas. His bark is stoutly timber'd, and his pilot
Of very expert and approv'd allowance;
Therefore my hopes, not surfeited to death,
Stand in bold cure.

[*Within.*] A sail, a sail, a sail!

Enter another Gentleman.

Cas. What noise?

4 Gent. The town is empty; on the brow o'the sea
Stand ranks of people, and they cry—a sail.

Cas. My hopes do shape him for the governor.

2 Gent. They do discharge their shot of courtesy.
Our friends, at least. [*Guns heard.*

Cas. I pray you, sir, go forth,
And give us truth who 'tis that is arriv'd.

2 Gent. I shall. [*Exit.*

Mon. But, good lieutenant, is your general wiv'd?

Cas. Most fortunately: he hath achiev'd a maid
That paragons description, and wild fame;
One that excels the quirks of blazoning pens,
And in the essential vesture of creation,
Does bear all excellency.—How now? who has put in?

Re-enter second Gentleman.

2 Gent. 'Tis one Iago, ancient to the general.

Cas. He has had most favourable and happy speed:
Tempests themselves, high seas, and howling winds,
The gutted rocks, and congregated sands,—
Traitors ensteep'd to clog the guiltless keel,
As having sense of beauty, do omit
Their mortal natures, letting go safely by
The divine Desdemona.

Mon. What is she?

Cas. She that I spake of, our great captain's captain,
Left in the conduct of the bold Iago;
Whose footing here anticipates our thoughts,
A se'nnight's speed.—Great Jove, Othello guard,
And swell his sail with thine own powerful breath;
That he may bless this bay with his tall ship,
Make love's quick pants in Desdemona's arms,
Give renew'd fire to our extincted spirits,
And bring all Cyprus comfort!—O, behold,

Enter DESDEMONA, EMILIA, IAGO, RODERIGO, *and* Attendants.

The riches of the ship is come on shore!
Ye men of Cyprus, let her have your knees:—
Hail to thee, lady! and the grace of heaven,
Before, behind thee, and on every hand,
Enwheel thee round!

Des. I thank you, valiant Cassio.
What tidings can you tell me of my lord?

Cas. He is not yet arriv'd; nor know I aught
But that he's well, and will be shortly here.

Des. O, but I fear;—How lost you company?

Cas. The great contention of the sea and skies
Parted our fellowship: But, hark! a sail.
[*Cry within,* A sail, a sail! *Then guns heard.*

2 Gent. They give their greeting to the citadel;
This likewise is a friend.

Cas. See for the news.— [*Exit* Gentleman.
Good ancient, you are welcome;—Welcome, mistress:— [*To* EMILIA.
Let it not gall your patience, good Iago,
That I extend my manners; 'tis my breeding
That gives me this bold show of courtesy. [*Kissing her.*

Iago. Sir, would she give you so much of her lips
As of her tongue she oft bestows on me,
You'd have enough.

Des. Alas, she has no speech.

Iago. In faith, too much;
I find it still, when I have list to sleep:
Marry, before your ladyship, I grant,
She puts her tongue a little in her heart,
And chides with thinking.

Emil. You have little cause to say so.

Iago. Come on, come on; you are pictures out of doors,
Bells in your parlours, wild cats in your kitchens,
Saints in your injuries, devils being offended,
Players in your housewifery, and housewives in your beds.

Des. O, fye upon thee, slanderer!

Iago. Nay, it is true, or else I am a Turk;
You rise to play, and go to bed to work.

Emil. You shall not write my praise.

Iago. No, let me not.

Des. What would'st thou write of me, if thou should'st praise me?

Iago. O gentle lady, do not put me to't;
For I am nothing, if not critical.

Des. Come on, assay:—There's one gone to the harbour?

Iago. Ay, madam.

Des. I am not merry; but I do beguile
The thing I am, by seeming otherwise.—
Come, how would'st thou praise me?

Iago. I am about it; but, indeed, my invention
Comes from my pate, as birdlime does from frize,
It plucks out brains and all: But my muse labours,
And thus she is deliver'd.
If she be fair and wise,—fairness, and wit,
The one's for use, the other useth it.

Des. Well prais'd! How if she be black and witty?

Iago. If she be black, and thereto have a wit,
She'll find a white that shall her blackness fit.

Des. Worse and worse.

Emil. How, if fair and foolish?

Iago. She never yet was foolish that was fair;
For even her folly help'd her to an heir.

Des. These are old fond paradoxes, to make fools laugh i' the alehouse. What miserable praise hast thou for her that's foul and foolish?

Iago. There's none so foul, and foolish thereunto,
But does foul pranks which fair and wise ones do.

Des. O heavy ignorance!—thou praisest the worst best. But what praise could'st thou bestow on a deserving woman indeed? one, that, in the authority of her merit, did justly put on the vouch of very malice itself?

Iago. She that was ever fair, and never proud;
Had tongue at will, and yet was never loud;
Never lack'd gold, and yet went never gay;
Fled from her wish, and yet said,—*now I may;*
She that, being anger'd, her revenge being nigh,
Bade her wrong stay, and her displeasure fly:
She, that in wisdom never was so frail,
To change the cod's head for the salmon's tail;
She that could think, and ne'er disclose her mind,
See suitors following, and not look behind;
She was a wight,—if ever such wight were,—

Des. To do what?

Iago. To suckle fools, and chronicle small beer.

Des. O most lame and impotent conclusion!—Do not learn of him, Emilia, though he be thy husband.—How say you, Cassio? is he not a most profane and liberal counsellor?

Cas. He speaks home, madam; you may relish him more in the soldier, than in the scholar.

Iago. [*Aside.*] He takes her by the palm: Ay, well said, whisper: with as little a web as this, will I ensnare as great a fly as Cassio. Ay, smile upon her, do; I will gyve thee in thine own courtship. You say true; 'tis so indeed: if such tricks as these strip you out of your lieutenantry, it had been better you had not kissed your three fingers so oft, which now again you are most apt to play the sir in. Very good; well kissed! an excellent courtesy! 'tis so, indeed. Yet again your fingers to your lips? 'would, they were clyster-pipes for your sake!
——[*Trumpet.*] The Moor, I know his trumpet.

Cas. 'Tis truly so.

Des. Let's meet him, and receive him.

Cas. Lo, where he comes!

Enter OTHELLO, *and* Attendants.

Oth. O my fair warrior!

Des. My dear Othello!

Oth. It gives me wonder great as my content,
To see you here before me. O my soul's joy!
If after every tempest come such calms,
May the winds blow till they have waken'd death!
And let the labouring bark climb hills of seas,
Olympus-high; and duck again as low
As hell's from heaven! If it were now to die,
'Twere now to be most happy; for, I fear,
My soul hath her content so absolute,
That not another comfort like to this
Succeeds in unknown fate.

Des. The heavens forbid,
But that our loves and comforts should increase,
Even as our days do grow!

Oth. Amen to that, sweet powers!—
I cannot speak enough of this content,
It stops me here; it is too much of joy:
And this, and this, the greatest discords be, [*Kissing her.*
That e'er our hearts shall make!

Iago. O, you are well tun'd now!
But I'll set down the pegs that make this musick,
As honest as I am. [*Aside.*

Oth. Come, let's to the castle.—
News, friends; our wars are done, the Turks are drown'd.
How do our old acquaintance of this isle?—
Honey, you shall be well desir'd in Cyprus,
I have found great love amongst them. O my sweet,
I prattle out of fashion, and I dote
In mine own comforts.—I pr'ythee, good Iago,
Go to the bay, and disembark my coffers:
Bring thou the master to the citadel;
He is a good one, and his worthiness
Does challenge much respect.—Come, Desdemona,
Once more well met at Cyprus.

[*Exeunt* OTH. DES. *and* Attendants.

Iago. Do thou meet me presently at the harbour. Come hither. If thou be'st valiant as (they say) base men, being in love, have then a nobility in their natures more than is native to them,—list me. The lieutenant to-night watches on the court of guard:—First, I must tell thee this—Desdemona is directly in love with him.

Rod. With him! why, 'tis not possible.

Iago. Lay thy finger—thus, and let thy soul be instructed. Mark me with what violence she first loved the Moor, but for bragging, and telling her fantastical lies: And will she love him still for prating? let not thy discreet heart think it. Her eye must be fed; and what delight shall she have to look on the devil? When the blood is made dull with the act of sport, there should be,—again to inflame it, and to give satiety a fresh appetite,—loveliness in favour; sympathy in years, manners, and beauties; all which the Moor is defective in: Now, for want of these required conveniences, her delicate tenderness will find itself abused, begin to heave the gorge, disrelish and abhor the Moor; very nature will instruct her in it, and compel her to some second choice. Now, sir, this granted (as it is a most pregnant and unforced position), who stands so eminently in the degree of this fortune, as Cassio does? a knave very voluble, no further conscionable, than in putting on the mere form of civil and humane seeming, for the better compassing of his salt and most hidden loose affection? why, none; why, none: A slippery and subtle knave; a finder out of occasions; that has an eye can stamp and counterfeit advantages, though true advantage never present itself: A devilish knave! besides the knave is handsome, young; and hath all those requisites in him, that folly and green minds look after: A pestilent complete knave; and the woman hath found him already.

Rod. I cannot believe that in her; she is full of most blessed condition.

Iago. Blessed fig's end! the wine she drinks is made of grapes: if she had been blessed, she would never have loved the Moor; Blessed pudding! Didst thou not see her paddle with the palm of his hand? didst not mark that?

Rod. Yes, that I did; but that was but courtesy.

Iago. Lechery, by this hand; an index, and

obscure prologue to the history of lust and foul thoughts. They met so near with their lips, that their breaths embraced together. Villanous thoughts, Roderigo! when these mutualities so marshal the way, hard at hand comes the master and main exercise, the incorporate conclusion: Pish!—But, sir, be you ruled by me: I have brought you from Venice. Watch you to-night; for the command, I'll lay't upon you: Cassio knows you not;—I'll not be far from you: Do you find some occasion to anger Cassio, either by speaking too loud, or tainting his discipline; or from what other course you please, which the time shall more favourably minister.

Rod. Well.

Iago. Sir, he is rash, and very sudden in choler; and, haply, with his truncheon may strike at you: Provoke him, that he may: for, even out of that, will I cause these of Cyprus to mutiny; whose qualification shall come into no true taste again, but by the displanting of Cassio. So shall you have a shorter journey to your desires, by the means I shall then have to prefer them; and the impediment most profitably removed, without the which there were no expectation of our prosperity.

Rod. I will do this, if I can bring it to any opportunity.

Iago. I warrant thee. Meet me by and by at the citadel: I must fetch his necessaries ashore. Farewell.

Rod. Adieu. [*Exit.*

Iago. That Cassio loves her, I do well believe it.
That she loves him, 'tis apt, and of great credit:
The Moor—howbeit that I endure him not,—
Is of a constant, loving, noble nature;
And, I dare think, he'll prove to Desdemona
A most dear husband. Now I do love her too;
Not out of absolute lust (though, peradventure,
I stand accountant for as great a sin),
But partly led to diet my revenge,
For that I do suspect the lusty Moor
Hath leap'd into my seat: the thought whereof
Doth, like a poisonous mineral, gnaw my inwards;
And nothing can or shall content my soul,
Till I am even with him, wife for wife;
Or, failing so, yet that I put the Moor
At least into a jealousy so strong
That judgment cannot cure. Which thing to do,—
If this poor trash of Venice, whom I trace
For his quick hunting, stand the putting on,
I'll have our Michael Cassio on the hip;
Abuse him to the Moor in the rank garb,
For I fear Cassio with my nightcap too;
Make the Moor thank me, love me, and reward me,
For making him egregiously an ass,
And practising upon his peace and quiet
Even to madness. 'Tis here, but yet confus'd;
Knavery's plain face is never seen till us'd.
[*Exit.*

SCENE II. *A Street.*

Enter a Herald, *with a Proclamation;* People *following.*

Her. It is Othello's pleasure, our noble and valiant general, that, upon certain tidings now arrived, importing the mere perdition of the Turkish fleet, every man put himself into triumph; some to dance, some to make bonfires, each man to what sport and revels his addiction leads him; for, besides these beneficial news, it is the celebration of his nuptials: So much was his pleasure should be proclaimed. All offices are open; and there is full liberty of feasting, from this present hour of five, till the bell hath told eleven. Heaven bless the isle of Cyprus, and our noble general Othello.
[*Exeunt.*

SCENE III. *A Hall in the Castle.*

Enter OTHELLO, DESDEMONA, CASSIO, *and* Attendants.

Oth. Good Michael, look you to the guard to-night:
Let's teach ourselves that honourable stop,
Not to outsport discretion.

Cas. Iago hath direction what to do;
But, notwithstanding, with my personal eye
Will I look to't.

Oth. Iago is most honest.
Michael, good night: To-morrow, with our earliest,
Let me have speech with you.—Come, my dear [love,
The purchase made, the fruits are to ensue;
[*To* DESDEMONA.
That profit's yet to come 'twixt me and you.—
Good night. [*Exeunt* OTH. DES. *and* Attend.

Enter IAGO.

Cas. Welcome, Iago: We must to the watch.

Iago. Not this hour, lieutenant; 'tis not yet ten o' clock: Our general cast us thus early, for the love of his Desdemona; whom let us not therefore blame; he hath not yet made wanton the night with her: and she is sport for Jove.

Cas. She's a most exquisite lady.

Iago. And, I'll warrant her, full of game.

Cas. Indeed, she is a most fresh and delicate creature.

Iago. What an eye she has! methinks it sounds a parley of provocation.

Cas. An inviting eye; and yet methinks right modest.

Iago. And, when she speaks, is it not an alarm to love?

Cas. She is, indeed, perfection.

Iago. Well, happiness to their sheets! Come, lieutenant, I have a stoop of wine; and here without are a brace of Cyprus gallants, that would fain have a measure to the health of the black Othello.

Cas. Not to-night, good Iago; I have very poor and unhappy brains for drinking; I could well wish courtesy would invent some other custom of entertainment.

Iago. O, they are our friends; but one cup; I'll drink for you.

Cas. I have drunk but one cup to-night, and that was craftily qualified too, and, behold, what innovation it makes here: I am unfortunate in the infirmity, and dare not task my weakness with any more.

Iago. What, man! 'tis a night of revels; the gallants desire it.

Cas. Where are they?

Iago. Here at the door; I pray you, call them in.

Cas. I'll do't; but it dislikes me. [*Exit.*

Iago. If I can fasten but one cup upon him,
With that which he hath drunk to-night already,
He'll be as full of quarrel and offence
As my young mistress' dog. Now, my sick fool, Roderigo,
Whom love has turn'd almost the wrong side outward,
To Desdemona hath to-night carous'd
Potations pottle deep; and he's to watch:
Three lads of Cyprus,—noble swelling spirits,
That hold their honours in a wary distance,
The very elements of this warlike isle,
Have I to-night fluster'd with flowing cups,
And they watch too. Now, 'mongst this flock of drunkards,
Am I to put our Cassio in some action
That may offend the isle: But here they come:
If consequence do but approve my dream,
My boat sails freely, both with wind and stream.

Re-enter CASSIO, *with him* MONTANO, *and* Gentlemen.

Cas. 'Fore heaven, they have given me a rouse already.

Mon. Good faith, a little one; not past a pint, as I am a soldier.

Iago. Some wine, ho!

And let me the canakin clink, clink; [Sings.
And let me the canakin clink:
A soldier's a man;
A life's but a span;
Why then, let a soldier drink.

Some wine, boys. [*Wine brought in.*

Cas. 'Fore heaven, an excellent song.

Iago. I learned it in England, where (indeed) they are most potent in potting: your Dane, your German, and your swag-bellied Hollander,—Drink, ho!—are nothing to your English.

Cas. Is your Englishman so expert in his drinking?

Iago. Why, he drinks you, with facility, your Dane dead drunk; he sweats not to overthrow your Almain; he gives your Hollander a vomit, ere the next pottle can be filled.

Cas. To the health of our general.

Mon. I am for it, lieutenant; and I'll do you justice.

Iago. O sweet England!

King Stephen *was a worthy peer,*
His breeches cost him but a crown;
He held them sixpence all too dear,
With that he call'd the tailor—lown.
He was a wight of high renown,
And thou art but of low degree:
'Tis pride that pulls the country down:
Then take thine auld cloak about thee.

Some wine, ho!

Cas. Why, this is a more exquisite song than the other.

Iago. Will you hear it again?

Cas. No; for I hold him to be unworthy of his place, that does those things.—Well, Heaven's above all: and there be souls that must be saved, and there be souls must not be saved.

Iago. It's true, good lieutenant.

Cas. For mine own part,—no offence to the general, or any man of quality,—I hope to be saved.

Iago. And so do I too, lieutenant.

Cas. Ay, but by your leave, not before me: the lieutenant is to be saved before the ancient. Let's have no more of this; let's to our affairs.—Forgive us our sins!—Gentlemen, let's look to our business. Do not think, gentlemen, I am drunk; this is my ancient;—this is my right hand, and this is my left hand;—I am not drunk now; I can stand well enough, and speak well enough.

All. Excellent well.

Cas. Why, very well, then; you must not think that I am drunk. [*Exit.*

Mon. To the platform, masters; come, let's set the watch.

Iago. You see this fellow, that is gone before;
He is a soldier, fit to stand by Cæsar
And give direction: and do but see his vice;
'Tis to his virtue a just equinox,
The one as long as the other: 'tis pity of him.
I fear, the trust Othello puts him in,
On some odd time of his infirmity
Will shake this island.

Mon. But is he often thus?

Iago. 'Tis evermore the prologue to his sleep:
He'll watch the horologe a double set,
If drink rock not his cradle.

Mon. It were well,
The general were put in mind of it.
Perhaps, he sees it not; or his good nature
Prizes the virtue that appears in Cassio,
And looks not on his evils; Is not this true?

Enter RODERIGO.

Iago. How now, Roderigo? [*Aside.*
I pray you, after the lieutenant; go. [*Exit* ROD.

Mon. And 'tis great pity, that the noble Moor
Should hazard such a place, as his own second,
With one of an ingraft infirmity;
It were an honest action, to say
So to the Moor.

Iago. Not, for this fair island:
I do love Cassio well; and would do much
To cure him of this evil. But hark! what noise?
[*Cry within*—Help! help!

Re-enter CASSIO, *driving in* RODERIGO.

Cas. You rogue! you rascal!

Mon. What's the matter, lieutenant?

Cas. A knave!—teach me my duty!
I'll beat the knave into a twiggen bottle.

Rod. Beat me!

Cas. Dost thou prate, rogue?
[*Striking* RODERIGO.

Mon. Nay, good lieutenant;
[*Staying him.*
I pray you, sir, hold your hand.

Cas. Let me go, sir,
Or I'll knock you o'er the mazzard.

Mon. Come, come, you're drunk.

Cas. Drunk! [*They fight.*

Iago. Away, I say! go out, and cry—a mutiny.
[*Aside to* ROD. *who goes out.*
Nay, good lieutenant,—alas, gentlemen,—
Help, ho!—Lieutenant,—sir,—Montano,—sir;—
Help, masters!—Here's a goodly watch, indeed! [*Bell rings.*
Who's that that rings the bell?—Diablo, ho!
The town will rise; God's will, lieutenant, hold;
You will be sham'd for ever.

Enter OTHELLO *and* Attendants.

Oth. What it the matter here?

Mon. I bleed still, I am hurt to the death;—he dies.

Oth. Hold, for your lives.

Iago. Hold, hold, lieutenant, sir, Montano,—gentlemen,—
Have you forgot all sense of place and duty?
Hold, hold! the general speaks to you; hold, for shame!

Oth. Why, how now, ho! from whence ariseth this?
Are we turn'd Turks; and to ourselves do that,
Which heaven hath forbid the Ottomites?
For christian shame, put by this barbarous brawl:
He that stirs next to carve for his own rage,
Holds his soul light; he dies upon his motion.—
Silence that dreadful bell, it frights the isle
From her propriety.—What is the matter, masters?—
Honest Iago, that look'st dead with grieving,
Speak, who began this? on thy love, I charge thee.

Iago. I do not know;—friends all but now, even now,
In quarter, and in terms like bride and groom
Devesting them for bed: and then, but now,
(As if some planet had unwitted men),
Swords out, and tilting one at other's breast,
In opposition bloody. I cannot speak
Any beginning to this peevish odds;
And 'would, in action glorious I had lost
These legs, that brought me to a part of it!

Oth. How comes it, Michael, you are thus forgot?

Cas. I pray you, pardon me, I cannot speak.

Oth. Worthy Montano, you were wont be civil;
The gravity and stillness of your youth
The world hath noted, and your name is great
In mouths of wisest censure; What's the matter,
That you unlace your reputation thus,
And spend your rich opinion, for the name
Of a night brawler? give me answer to it.

Mon. Worthy Othello, I am hurt to danger;
Your officer, Iago, can inform you—

While I spare speech, which something now offends me :—
Of all that I do know ; nor know I aught
By me that's said or done amiss this night :
Unless self-charity be sometime a vice ;
And to defend ourselves it be a sin,
When violence assails us.

Oth. Now, by heaven,
My blood begins my safer guides to rule:
And passion, having my best judgment collied,
Assays to lead the way: If I once stir,
Or do but lift this arm, the best of you
Shall sink in my rebuke. Give me to know
How this foul rout began, who set it on ;
And he that is approv'd in this offence,
Though he had twinn'd with me, both at a birth,
Shall lose me.—What! in a town of war,
Yet wild, the people's hearts brimful of fear,
To manage private and domestick quarrel,
In night, and on the court of guard and safety !
'Tis monstrous.—Iago, who began it?

Mon. If partially affin'd, or leagu'd in office,
Thou dost deliver more or less than truth,
Thou art no soldier.

Iago. Touch me not so near:
I had rather have this tongue cut from my mouth.
Than it should do offence to Michael Cassio ;
Yet, I persuade myself, to speak the truth
Shall nothing wrong him.—Thus it is, general.
Montano and myself being in speech,
There comes a fellow, crying out for help ;
And Cassio following with determin'd sword,
To execute upon him : Sir, this gentleman
Steps in to Cassio, and entreats his pause;
Myself the crying fellow did pursue,
Lest, by his clamour (as it so fell out),
The town might fall in fright: he, swift of foot,
Outran my purpose ; and I return'd the rather
For that I heard the clink and fall of swords,
And Cassio high in oath ; which, till to-night,
I ne'er might say before: when I came back
(For this was brief) I found them close together,
At blow, and thrust ; even as again they were,
When you yourself did part them.
More of this matter can I not report :—
But men are men ; the best sometimes forget :—
Though Cassio did some little wrong to him,—
As men in rage strike those that wish them best,—
Yet, surely, Cassio, I believe, receiv'd,
From him that fled, some strange indignity,
Which patience could not pass.

Oth. I know, Iago,
Thy honesty and love doth mince this matter,
Making it light to Cassio :—Cassio, I love thee ;
But never more be officer of mine.—

Enter DESDEMONA, *attended.*

Look, if my gentle love be not rais'd up ;—
I'll make thee an example.

Des. What's the matter, dear?

Oth. All's well now, sweeting; Come away to bed.
Sir, for your hurts,
Myself will be your surgeon ; Lead him off.
[*To* MONTANO, *who is led off.*
Iago, look with care about the town ;
And silence those whom this vile brawl distracted.—
Come, Desdemona ; 'tis the soldier's life,
To have their balmy slumbers wak'd with strife.
[*Exeunt all but* IAGO *and* CASSIO.

Iago. What, are you hurt, lieutenant?

Cas. Ay, past all surgery.

Iago. Marry, heaven forbid !

Cas. Reputation, reputation, reputation ! O, I have lost my reputation ! I have lost the immortal part, sir, of myself, and what remains is bestial.—My reputation, Iago, my reputation.

Iago. As I am an honest man, I thought you had received some bodily wound ; there is more offence in that, than in reputation. Reputation is an idle and most false imposition ; oft got without merit, and lost without deserving : You have lost no reputation at all, unless you repute yourself such a loser. What, man ! there are ways to recover the general again : You are but now cast in his mood, a punishment more in policy than in malice ; even so as one would beat his offenceless dog, to affright an imperious lion: sue to him again, and he's yours.

Cas. I will rather sue to be despised, than to deceive so good a commander, with so slight, so drunken, and so indiscreet an officer. Drunk? and speak parrot? and squabble? swagger? swear? and discourse fustian with one's own shadow?—O thou invisible spirit of wine, if thou hast no name to be known by, let us call thee—devil.

Iago. What was he that you followed with your sword? What had he done to you?

Cas. I know not.

Iago. Is it possible?

Cas. I remember a mass of things, but nothing distinctly ; a quarrel, but nothing wherefore.—O, that men should put an enemy in their mouths, to steal away their brains! that we should, with joy, revel, pleasure, and applause, transform ourselves into beasts!

Iago. Why, but you are now well enough: How came you thus recovered?

Cas. It hath pleased the devil drunkenness, to give place to the devil, wrath: one unperfectness shows me another, to make me frankly despise myself.

Iago. Come, you are too severe a moraler: As the time, the place, and the condition of this country stands, I could heartily wish this had not befallen ; but, since it is as it is, mend it for your own good.

Cas. I will ask him for my place again ; he shall tell me, I am a drunkard ! Had I as many mouths as Hydra, such an answer would stop them all. To be now a sensible man, by and by a fool, and presently a beast! O strange!—Every inordinate cup is unblessed, and the ingredient is a devil.

Iago. Come, come, good wine is a good familiar creature, if it be well used ; exclaim no more against it. And, good lieutenant, I think, you think I love you.

Cas. I have well approved it, sir,—I drunk !

Iago. You, or any man living, may be drunk at some time, man. I'll tell you what you shall do. Our general's wife is now the general; —I may say so in this respect, for that he hath devoted and given up himself to the contemplation, mark, and denotement of her parts and graces :—confess yourself freely to her : importune her ; she'll help to put you in your place again ; she is of so free, so kind, so apt, so blessed a disposition, that she holds it a vice in her goodness, not to do more than she is requested ; This broken joint between you and her husband, entreat her to splinter ; and, my fortunes against any lay worth naming, this crack of your love shall grow stronger than it was before.

Cas. You advise me well.

Iago. I protest, in the sincerity of love, and honest kindness.

Cas. I think it freely ; and, betimes in the morning, I will beseech the virtuous Desdemona to undertake for me : I am desperate of my fortunes, if they check me here.

Iago. You are in the right. Good night, lieutenant ; I must to the watch.

Cas. Good night, honest Iago. [*Exit* CAS.

Iago. And what's he then, that says,—I play the villain?
When this advice is free, I give, and honest,
Probal to thinking, and (indeed) the course
To win the Moor again ? For, 'tis most easy
The inclining Desdemona to subdue
In any honest suit ! she's fram'd and fruitful

As the free elements. And then for her
To win the Moor,—were't to renounce his baptism,
All seals and symbols of redeemed sin,—
His soul is so enfetter'd to her love,
That she may make, unmake, do what she list,
Even as her appetite shall play the god
With his weak function. How am I then a villain,
To counsel Cassio to this parallel course,
Directly to his good? Divinity of hell!
When devils will their blackest sins put on,
They do suggest at first with heavenly shows,
As I do now: For while this honest fool
Plies Desdemona to repair his fortunes,
And she for him pleads strongly to the Moor,
I'll pour this pestilence into his ear,—
That she repeals him for her body's lust;
And, by how much she strives to do him good,
She shall undo her credit with the Moor.
So will I turn her virtue into pitch;
And out of her own goodness make the net,
That shall enmesh them all.—How now, Roderigo?

Enter RODERIGO.

Rod. I do follow here in the chase, not like a hound that hunts, but one that fills up the cry. My money is almost spent; I have been to-night exceedingly well cudgelled; and, I think, the issue will be—I shall have so much experience for my pains: and so, with no money at all, and a little more wit, return to Venice.

Iago. How poor are they, that have not patience!—
What wound did ever heal, but by degrees?
Thou know'st we work by wit, and not by witchcraft?
And wit depends on dilatory time.
Does't not go well? Cassio hath beaten thee,
And thou, by that small hurt, hath cashier'd Cassio;
Though other things grow fair against the sun,
Yet fruits, that blossom first, will first be ripe;
Content thyself awhile.—By the mass, 'tis morning;
Pleasure, and action, make the hours seem short.—
Retire thee; go where thou art billeted:
Away, I say; thou shalt know more hereafter:
Nay, get thee gone. [*Exit* ROD.] Two things are to be done,—
My wife must move for Cassio to her mistress;
I'll set her on;
Myself, the while, to draw the Moor apart,
And bring him jump when he may Cassio find
Soliciting his wife; Ay, that's the way;
Dull not device by coldness and delay. [*Exit.*

ACT III.

SCENE I. *Before the Castle.*

Enter CASSIO *and some* Musicians.

Cas. Masters, play here, I will content your pains,
Something that's brief; and bid—good morrow, general. [*Musick.*

Enter Clown.

Clo. Why, masters, have your instruments been at Naples, that they speak i'the nose thus?

1 *Mus.* How, sir, how!

Clo. Are these, I pray you, called wind instruments?

1 *Mus.* Ay, marry, are they, sir.

Clo. O, thereby hangs a tail.

1 *Mus.* Whereby hangs a tale, sir?

Clo. Marry, sir, by many a wind instrument that I know. But masters, here's money for you; and the general so likes your musick, that he desires you, of all loves, to make no more noise with it.

1 *Mus.* Well, sir, we will not.

Clo. If you have any musick that may not be heard, to't again: but, as they say, to hear musick, the general does not greatly care.

1 *Mus.* We have none such, sir.

Clo. Then put up your pipes in your bag, for I'll away: Go; vanish into air; away. [*Exeunt* Musicians.

Cas. Dost thou hear, my honest friend?

Clo. No, I hear not your honest friend; I hear you.

Cas. Pr'ythee keep up thy quillets. There's a poor piece of gold for thee: if the gentlewoman that attends the general's wife be stirring, tell her, there's one Cassio entreats her a little favour of speech: Wilt thou do this?

Clo. She is stirring, sir; if she will stir hither, I shall seem to notify unto her. [*Exit.*

Enter IAGO.

Cas. Do, good my friend.—In happy time, Iago.

Iago. You have not been abed then?

Cas. Why, no; the day had broke
Before we parted. I have made bold, Iago,
To send into your wife: My suit to her
Is, that she will to virtuous Desdemona
Procure me some access.

Iago. I'll send her to you presently;
And I'll devise a mean to draw the Moor
Out of the way, that your converse and business
May be more free. [*Exit.*

Cas. I humbly thank you for't. I never knew
A Florentine more kind and honest.

Enter EMILIA.

Emil. Good morrow, good lieutenant: I am sorry
For your displeasure; but all will soon be well.
The general, and his wife, are talking of it;
And she speaks for you stoutly: The Moor replies,
That he, you hurt, is of great fame in Cyprus,
And great affinity; and that, in wholesome wisdom,
He might not but refuse you: but, he protests, he loves you;
And needs no other suitor, but his likings,
To take the saf'st occasion by the front,
To bring you in again.

Cas. Yet, I beseech you,—
If you think fit, or that it may be done,
Give me advantage of some brief discourse
With Desdemona alone.

Emil. 'Pray you, come in;
I will bestow you where you shall have time
To speak your bosom freely.

Cas. I am much bound to you. [*Exeunt.*

SCENE II. *A Room in the Castle.*

Enter OTHELLO, IAGO, *and* Gentlemen.

Oth. These letters give, Iago, to the pilot;
And, by him, do my duties to the state:
That done, I will be walking on the works,
Repair there to me.

Iago. Well, my good lord, I'll do't.

Oth. This fortification, gentlemen,—shall we see't?

Gent. We'll wait upon your lordship. [*Exeunt.*

SCENE III. *Before the Castle.*

Enter DESDEMONA, CASSIO, *and* EMILIA.

Des. Be thou assur'd, good Cassio, I will do
All my abilities in thy behalf.

Emil. Good madam, do; I know, it grieves my husband,
As if the case were his.

Des. O, that's an honest fellow.—Do not doubt, Cassio,

But I will have my lord and you again
As friendly as you were.
Cas. Bounteous madam,
Whatever shall become of Michael Cassio,
He's never any thing but your true servant.
Des. O, sir, I thank you: You do love my lord,
You have known him long; and be you well assur'd,
He shall in strangeness stand no further off
Than in a politick distance.
Cas. Ay, but, lady,
That policy may either last so long,
Or feed upon such nice and waterish diet,
Or breed itself so out of circumstance,
That, I being absent, and my place supplied,
My general will forget my love and service.
Des. Do not doubt that; before Emilia here,
I give thee warrant of thy place: assure thee,
If I do vow a friendship, I'll perform it
To the last article: my lord shall never rest;
I'll watch him tame, and talk him out of patience;
His bed shall seem a school, his board a shrift;
I'll intermingle every thing he does
With Cassio's suit: Therefore be merry, Cassio;
For thy solicitor shall rather die,
Than give thy cause away.

Enter OTHELLO, *and* IAGO, *at a distance.*

Emil. Madam, here comes
My lord.
Cas. Madam, I'll take my leave.
Des. Why, stay,
And hear me speak.
Cas. Madam, not now; I am very ill at ease,
Unfit for mine own purposes.
Des. Well, well,
Do your discretion. [*Exit* CASSIO.
Iago. Ha! I like not that.
Oth. What dost thou say?
Iago. Nothing, my lord: or if—I know not what.
Oth. Was not that Cassio, parted from my wife?
Iago. Cassio, my lord? No, sure, I cannot think it,
That he would steal away so guiltylike,
Seeing you coming.
Oth. I do believe 'twas he.
Des. How now, my lord?
I have been talking with a suitor here,
A man that languishes in your displeasure.
Oth. Who is't you mean?
Des. Why, your lieutenant Cassio. Good my lord,
If I have any grace or power to move you,
His present reconciliation take;
For, if he be not one that truly loves you,
That errs in ignorance, and not in cunning,
I have no judgment in an honest face:
I pr'ythee call him back.
Oth. Went he hence now?
Des. Ay, sooth; so humbled,
That he hath left part of his grief with me;
I suffer with him. Good love, call him back.
Oth. Not now, sweet Desdemona; some other time.
Des. But shall't be shortly?
Oth. The sooner, sweet, for you.
Des. Shall't be to-night at supper?
Oth. No, not to-night.
Des. To-morrow dinner then?
Oth. I shall not dine at home;
I meet the captains at the citadel.
Des. Why then, to-morrow night; or Tuesday morn;
Or Tuesday noon, or night; or Wednesday morn;—
I pray thee, name the time; but let it not
Exceed three days: in faith, he's penitent;
And yet his trespass, in our common reason
(Save that, they say, the wars must make examples
Out of their best), is not almost a fault
To incur a private check: When shall he come?
Tell me, Othello. I wonder in my soul,
What you could ask me, that I should deny,
Or stand so mammering on. What! Michael Cassio,
That came a wooing with you; and many a time,
When I have spoke of you dispraisingly,
Hath ta'en your part; to have so much to do
To bring him in! Trust me, I could do much,—
Oth. 'Pry'thee, no more: let him come when he will;
I will deny thee nothing.
Des. Why, this is not a boon:
'Tis as I should entreat you wear your gloves,
Or feed on nourishing dishes, or keep you warm;
Or sue to you to do peculiar profit
To your own person: Nay, when I have a suit,
Wherein I mean to touch your love indeed,
It shall be full of poize and difficulty,
And fearful to be granted.
Oth. I will deny thee nothing:
Whereon, I do beseech thee, grant me this,
To leave me but a little to myself.
Des. Shall I deny you? no: Farewell, my lord.
Oth. Farewell, my Desdemona: I will come to thee straight.
Des. Emilia, come:—Be it as your fancies teach you;
Whate'er you be, I am obedient.
[*Exit with* EMILIA.
Oth. Excellent wretch! Perdition catch my soul,
But I do love thee! and when I love thee not,
Chaos is come again.
Iago. My noble lord,——
Oth. What dost thou say, Iago?
Iago. Did Michael Cassio, when you woo'd my lady,
Know of your love?
Oth. He did, from first to last: Why dost thou ask?
Iago. But for a satisfaction of my thought;
No further harm.
Oth. Why of thy thought, Iago?
Iago. I did not think he had been acquainted with her.
Oth. O, yes; and went between us very oft.
Iago. Indeed?
Oth. Indeed! ay, indeed:—Discern'st thou aught in that?
Is he not honest?
Iago. Honest, my lord?
Oth. Ay, honest.
Iago. My lord, for aught I know.
Oth. What dost thou think?
Iago. Think, my lord?
Oth. Think, my lord!
By heaven, he echoes me,
As if there were some monster in his thought
Too hideous to be shown.—Thou dost mean something:
I heard thee say but now,—Thou lik'dst not that,
When Cassio left my wife; What didst not like?
And, when I told thee—he was of my counsel
In my whole course of wooing, thou cry'dst, *Indeed?*
And didst contract and purse thy brow together,
As if thou then had'st shut up in thy brain
Some horrible conceit: If thou dost love me,
Show me thy thought.
Iago. My lord, you know I love you.
Oth. I think, thou dost:
And,—for I know thou art full of love and honesty,
And weigh'st thy words before thou giv'st them breath,—
Therefore these stops of thine fright me the more:
For such things, in a false disloyal knave,
Are tricks of custom; but, in a man that's just,

They are close denotements, working from the heart,
That passion cannot rule.

Iago. For Michael Cassio,—
I dare be sworn, I think that he is honest.

Oth. I think so too.

Iago. Men should be what they seem;
Or, those that be not, 'would they might seem none!

Oth. Certain, men should be what they seem.

Iago. Why then, I think Cassio's an honest man.

Oth. Nay, yet there's more in this:
I pray thee, speak to me as to thy thinkings,
As thou dost ruminate; and give thy worst of thoughts
The worst of words.

Iago. Good my lord, pardon me;
Though I am bound to every act of duty,
I am not bound to that all slaves are free to.
Utter my thoughts? Why, say, they are vile and false,—
As where's that palace, whereinto foul things
Sometimes intrude not? who has a breast so pure,
But some uncleanly apprehensions
Keep leets, and law-days, and in session sit
With meditations lawful?

Oth. Thou dost conspire against thy friend, Iago,
If thou but think'st him wrong'd, and mak'st his [ear
A stranger to thy thoughts.

Iago. I do beseech you,—
Though I, perchance, am vicious in my guess,
As, I confess, it is my nature's plague
To spy into abuses: and, oft, my jealousy
Shapes faults that are not,—I entreat you then,
From one that so imperfectly conjects,
You'd take no notice; nor build yourself a trouble
Out of his scattering and unsure observance:
It were not for your quiet, nor your good,
Nor for my manhood, honesty, or wisdom,
To let you know my thoughts.

Oth. What dost thou mean?

Iago. Good name, in man, and woman, dear my lord,
Is the immediate jewel of their souls:
Who steals my purse, steals trash; 'tis something, nothing;
'Twas mine, 'tis his, and has been slave to thousands;
But he that filches from me my good name,
Robs me of that, which not enriches him,
And makes me poor indeed.

Oth. By heaven, I'll know thy thought.

Iago. You cannot, if my heart were in your hand;
Nor shall not, whilst 'tis in my custody.

Oth. Ha!

Iago. O, beware, my lord, of jealousy;
It is the green-ey'd monster, which doth make
The meat it feeds on: That cuckold lives in bliss,
Who, certain of his fate, loves not his wronger;
But, O, what damned minutes tells he o'er,
Who dotes, yet doubts; suspects, yet strongly loves!

Oth. O misery!

Iago. Poor, and content, is rich, and rich enough;
But riches, fineless, is as poor as winter,
To him that ever fears he shall be poor:—
Good heaven, the souls of all my tribe defend
From jealousy!

Oth. Why! why is this?
Think'st thou, I'd make a life of jealousy,
To follow still the changes of the moon
With fresh suspicions? No: to be once in doubt,
Is—once to be resolv'd: Exchange me for a goat,
When I shall turn the business of my soul
To such exsufflicate and blown surmises,
Matching thy inference. 'Tis not to make me jealous,
To say—my wife is fair, feeds well, loves company,
Is free of speech, sings, plays, and dances well;
Where virtue is, these are more virtuous:
Nor from mine own weak merits will I draw
The smallest fear, or doubt of her revolt;
For she had eyes, and chose me: No, Iago;
I'll see, before I doubt; when I doubt, prove;
And, on the proof, there is no more but this,—
Away at once with love, or jealousy.

Iago. I am glad of this, for now I shall have reason
To show the love and duty that I bear you
With franker spirit: therefore, as I am bound,
Receive it from me:—I speak not yet of proof.
Look to your wife; observe her well with Cassio;
Wear your eye—thus, not jealous, nor secure:
I would not have your free and noble nature,
Out of self-bounty, be abus'd; look to't:
I know our country disposition well;
In Venice they do let heaven see the pranks
They dare not show their husbands; their best conscience
Is—not to leave undone, but keep unknown.

Oth. Dost thou say so?

Iago. She did deceive her father, marrying you;
And, when she seem'd to shake, and fear your looks,
She lov'd them most.

Oth. And so she did.

Iago. Why, go to, then;
She that, so young, could give out such a seeming,
To seal her father's eyes up, close as oak,—
He thought, 'twas witchcraft:—But I am much to blame;
I humbly do beseech you of your pardon,
For too much loving you.

Oth. I am bound to thee for ever.

Iago. I see, this hath a little dash'd your spirits.

Oth. Not a jot, not a jot.

Iago. Trust me, I fear it has.
I hope, you will consider, what is spoke
Comes from my love;—But, I do see you are mov'd:—
I am to pray you, not to strain my speech
To grosser issues, nor to larger reach,
Than to suspicion

Oth. I will not.

Iago. Should you do so, my lord,
My speech should fall into such vile success
As my thoughts aim not at. Cassio's my worthy friend:—
My lord, I see you are mov'd.

Oth. No, not much mov'd:—
I do not think but Desdemona's honest.

Iago. Long live she so! and long live you to think so!

Oth. And yet, how nature erring from itself,—

Iago. Ay, there's the point:—As,—to be bold with you,—
Not to affect many proposed matches,
Of her own clime, complexion, and degree;
Whereto, we see, in all things nature tends:
Foh! one may smell, in such, a will most rank,
Foul disproportion, thoughts unnatural.—
But pardon me; I do not, in position,
Distinctly speak of her: though I may fear,
Her will, recoiling to her better judgment,
May fall to match you with her country forms,
And (happily) repent.

Oth. Farewell, farewell:
If more thou dost perceive, let me know more;
Set on thy wife to observe: Leave me, Iago.

Iago. My lord, I take my leave. [*Going.*

Oth. Why did I marry?—This honest creature, doubtless,
Sees and knows more, much more than he unfolds.

Iago. My lord, I would, I might entreat your honour

To scan this thing no further; leave it to time:
And though it be fit that Cassio have his place
(For, sure, he fills it up with great ability),
Yet, if you please to hold him off a while,
You shall by that perceive him and his means:
Note, if your lady strain his entertainment
With any strong or vehement importunity;
Much will be seen in that. In the mean time,
Let me be thought too busy in my fears
(As worthy cause I have to fear—I am)
And hold her free, I do beseech your honour.

Oth. Fear not my government.

Iago. I once more take my leave. [*Exit.*

Oth. This fellow's of exceeding honesty,
And knows all qualities, with a learned spirit,
Of human dealings: If I do prove her haggard,
Though that her jesses were my dear heart-strings,
I'd whistle her off, and let her down the wind,
To prey at fortune. Haply, for I am black;
And have not those soft parts of conversation
That chamberers have:—Or, for I am declin'd
Into the vale of years;—yet that's not much;—
She's gone; I am abus'd; and my relief
Must be to loathe her. O curse of marriage,
That we can call these delicate creatures ours,
And not their appetites! I had rather be a toad,
And live upon the vapour of a dungeon,
Than keep a corner in the thing I love,
For others' uses. Yet, 'tis the plague of great ones;
Prerogativ'd are they less than the base;
'Tis destiny unshunnable, like death;
Even then this forked plague is fated to us,
When we do quicken. Desdemona comes:

Enter DESDEMONA *and* EMILIA.

If she be false, O, then heaven mocks itself!—
I'll not believe it.

Des. How now, my dear Othello?
Your dinner, and the generous islanders
By you invited, do attend your presence.

Oth. I am to blame.

Des. Why is your speech so faint? are you not well?

Oth. I have a pain upon my forehead here.

Des. 'Faith, that's with watching; 'twill away again:
Let me but bind it hard, within this hour
It will be well.

Oth. Your napkin is too little;
[*He puts the Handkerchief from him, and it drops.*
Let it alone. Come, I'll go in with you.

Des. I am very sorry that you are not well.
[*Exeunt* OTHELLO *and* DESDEMONA.

Emil. I am glad I have found this napkin;
This was her first remembrance from the Moor:
My wayward husband hath a hundred times
Woo'd me to steal it; but she so loves the token
(For he conjur'd her, she would ever keep it),
That she reserved it ever more about her,
To kiss and talk to. I'll have the work ta'en out,
And give 't Iago:
What he'll do with it, heaven knows, not I;
I nothing, but to please his fantasy.

Enter IAGO.

Iago. How now! what do you here alone?

Emil. Do not you chide; I have a thing for you.

Iago. A thing for me?—it is a common thing.

Emil. Ha!

Iago. To have a foolish wife.

Emil. O, is that all? What will you give me now
For that same handkerchief?

Iago. What handkerchief?

Emil. What handkerchief?
Why, that the Moor first gave to Desdemona;
That which so often you did bid me steal.

Iago. Hast stolen it from her?

Emil. No, 'faith; she let it drop by negligence;
And to the advantage, I, being here, took 't up.
Look, here it is.

Iago. A good wench; give it me.

Emil. What will you do with it, that you have been so earnest
To have me filch it?

Iago. Why, what's that to you? [*Snatching it.*

Emil. If it be not for some purpose of import,
Give it me again: Poor lady, she'll run mad,
When she shall lack it.

Iago. Be not you known of't; I have use for it.
Go, leave me. [*Exit* EMILIA.
I will in Cassio's lodging lose this napkin,
And let him find it: Trifles, light as air,
Are, to the jealous, confirmations strong
As proofs of holy writ. This may do something.
The Moor already changes with my poison:
Dangerous conceits are, in their natures, poisons,
Which, at the first, are scarce found to distaste;
But, with a little act upon the blood,
Burn like the mines of sulphur.—I did say so:

Enter OTHELLO.

Look, where he comes! Not poppy, nor mandragora,
Nor all the drowsy sirups of the world,
Shall ever medicine thee to that sweet sleep
Which thou ow'dst yesterday.

Oth. Ha! ha! false to me?
To me?

Iago. Why, how now, general? no more of that.

Oth. Avaunt! be gone! thou hast set me on the rack:—
I swear, 'tis better to be much abus'd,
Than but to know a little.

Iago. How now, my lord?

Oth. What sense had I of her stolen hours of lust?
I saw it not, thought it not, it harm'd not me:
I slept the next night well, was free and merry;
I found not Cassio's kisses on her lips:
He that is robb'd, not wanting what is stolen,
Let him not know it, and he's not robb'd at all.

Iago. I am sorry to hear this.

Oth. I had been happy, if the general camp,
Pioneers and all, had tasted her sweet body,
So I had nothing known: O now, for ever,
Farewell the tranquil mind! farewell content!
Farewell the plumed troop, and the big wars,
That make ambition virtue! O, farewell!
Farewell the neighing steed, and the shrill trump,
The spirit-stirring drum, the ear-piercing fife,
The royal banner; and all quality,
Pride, pomp, and circumstance of glorious war!
And, O, you mortal engines, whose rude throats
The immortal Jove's dread clamours counterfeit,
Farewell! Othello's occupation's gone!

Iago. Is it possible!—my lord,——

Oth. Villain, be sure thou prove my love a whore;
Be sure of it; give me the ocular proof;
[*Taking him by the Throat.*
Or, by the worth of mine eternal soul,
Thou hadst been better have been born a dog,
Than answer my wak'd wrath.

Iago. Is it come to this?

Oth. Make me to see it; or (at the least) so prove it,
That the probation bear no hinge, nor loop,
To hang a doubt on: or, woe upon thy life!

Iago. My noble lord,——

Oth. If thou dost slander her, and torture me,
Never pray more: abandon all remorse;
On horror's head horrors accumulate:
Do deeds to make heaven weep, all earth amaz'd,
For nothing canst thou to damnation add,
Greater than that.

Iago. O grace! O heaven, defend me!
Are you a man? have you a soul or sense?—
God be wi' you; take mine office.—O wretched fool,

That liv'st to make thine honesty, a vice!—
O monstrous world! Take note, take note, O world,
To be direct and honest, is not safe.—
I thank you for this profit; and, from hence,
I'll love no friend, since love breeds such offence.

Oth. Nay, stay:—Thou should'st be honest.

Iago. I should be wise; for honesty's a fool,
And loses that it works for.

Oth. By the world,
I think my wife be honest, and think she is not;
I think that thou art just, and think thou art not;
I'll have some proof: Her name, that was as fresh
As Dian's visage, is now begrim'd and black
As mine own face.—If there be cords, or knives,
Poison, or fire, or suffocating streams,
I'll not endure it.—'Would I were satisfied!

Iago. I see, sir, you are eaten up with passion:
I do repent me, that I put it to you.
You would be satisfied?

Oth, Would? nay, I will.

Iago. And may: but how? how satisfied, my lord?
Would you, the supervisor, grossly gape on?
Behold her tupp'd?

Oth. Death and damnation! O!

Iago. It were a tedious difficulty, I think,
To bring them to that prospect: Damn them then,
If ever mortal eyes do see them bolster,
More than their own! What then? how then?
What shall I say? Where's satisfaction?
It is impossible you should see this,
Were they as prime as goats, as hot as monkeys,
As salt as wolves in pride, and fools as gross
As ignorance made drunk. But yet, I say,
If imputation, and strong circumstances,—
Which lead directly to the door of truth,—
Will give you satisfaction, you may have it.

Oth. Give me a living reason she's disloyal.

Iago. I do not like the office:
But, sith I am enter'd in this cause so far,—
Prick'd to it by foolish honesty and love,—
I will go on. I lay with Cassio lately;
And, being troubled with a raging tooth,
I could not sleep,
There are a kind of men so loose of soul,
That in their sleeps will mutter their affairs;
One of this kind is Cassio:
In sleep I heard him say,—*Sweet Desdemona,*
Let us be wary, let us hide our loves!
And then, sir, would he gripe and wring my hand,
Cry,—*O, sweet creature!* and then kiss me hard,
As if he pluck'd up kisses by the roots,
That grew upon my lips: then laid his leg
Over my thigh, and sigh'd, and kiss'd; and then
Cried,—*Cursed fate, that gave thee to the Moor!*

Oth. O monstrous! monstrous!

Iago. Nay, this was but his dream.

Oth. But this denoted a foregone conclusion;
'Tis a shrewd doubt, though it be but a dream.

Iago. And this may help to thicken other proofs,
That do demonstrate thinly.

Oth. I'll tear her all to pieces.

Iago. Nay, but be wise: yet we see nothing done;
She may be honest yet. Tell me but this,—
Have you not sometimes seen a handkerchief,
Spotted with strawberries, in your wife's hand?

Oth. I gave her such a one; 'twas my first gift.

Iago. I know not that: but such a handkerchief
(I am sure it was your wife's), did I to-day
See Cassio wipe his beard with.

Oth. If it be that,—

Iago. If it be that, or any that was hers,
It speaks against her with the other proofs.

Oth. O, that the slave had forty thousand lives;
One is too poor, too weak for my revenge!
Now do I see 'tis true.—Look here, Iago;
All my fond love thus do I blow to heaven:
'Tis gone.—
Arise, black vengeance, from thy hollow cell!
Yield up, O love, thy crown and hearted throne,
To tyrannous hate! swell bosom, with thy fraught;
For 'tis of aspicks' tongues!

Iago. Pray, be content.

Oth. O, blood, Iago, blood!

Iago. Patience, I say; your mind, perhaps, may change.

Oth. Never, Iago. Like to the Pontick sea,
Whose icy current and compulsive course
Ne'er feels retiring ebb, but keeps due on
To the Propontick, and the Hellespont;
Even so my bloody thoughts, with violent pace,
Shall ne'er look back, ne'er ebb to humble love,
Till that a capable and wide revenge
Swallow them up.—Now, by yond' marble heaven,
In the due reverence of a sacred vow [*Kneels.*
I here engage my words.

Iago. Do not rise yet.— [*Kneels.*
Witness, you ever-burning lights above!
You elements that clip us round about!
Witness, that here Iago doth give up
The execution of his wit, hands, heart,
To wrong'd Othello's service! let him command,
And to obey shall be in me remorse,
What bloody work soever.

Oth. I greet thy love,
Not with vain thanks, but with acceptance bounteous,
And will upon the instant put thee to 't:
Within these three days let me hear thee say,
That Cassio's not alive.

Iago. My friend is dead; 'tis done, at your request:
But let her live.

Oth. Damn her, lewd minx; O, damn her!
Come, go with me apart; I will withdraw,
To furnish me with some swift means of death
For the fair devil. Now art thou my lieutenant.

Iago. I am your own for ever. [*Exeunt.*

SCENE IV. *The same.*

Enter DESDEMONA, EMILIA, *and* Clown.

Des. Do you know, sirrah, where lieutenant Cassio lies?

Clo. I dare not say, he lies any where.

Des. Why, man?

Clo. He's a soldier; and for me to say a soldier lies, is stabbing.

Des. Go to; Where lodges he?

Clo. To tell you where he lodges, is to tell you where I lie.

Des. Can any thing be made of this?

Clo. I know not where he lodges; and for me to devise a lodging, and say—he lies here, or he lies there, were to lie in my own throat.

Des. Can you inquire him out, and be edified by report?

Clo. I will catechise the world for him; that is, make questions, and by them answer.

Des. Seek him, bid him come hither: tell him, I have moved my lord in his behalf, and hope, all will be well.

Clo. To do this, is within the compass of man's wit; and therefore I will attempt the doing it. [*Exit.*

Des. Where should I lose that handkerchief, Emilia?

Emil. I know not, madam.

Des. Believe me, I had rather have lost my purse
Full of crusadoes. And, but my noble Moor
Is true of mind, and made of no such baseness
As jealous creatures are, it were enough
To put him to ill thinking.

Emil. Is he not jealous?

Des. Who, he? I think, the sun, where he was born,
Drew all such humours from him.

Emil. Look, where he comes.

Des. I will not leave him now, till Cassio
Be call'd to him.—How is't with you, my lord?

Enter OTHELLO.

Oth. Well, my good lady.—[*Aside.*] O, hardness to dissemble!—
How do you, Desdemona?

Des. Well, my good lord.

Oth. Give me your hand: This hand is moist, my lady.

Des. It yet has felt no age, nor known no sorrow.

Oth. This argues fruitfulness, and liberal heart;—
Hot, hot, and moist; This hand of yours requires
A sequester from liberty, fasting and prayer,
Much castigation, exercise devout;
For here's a young and sweating devil here,
That commonly rebels. 'Tis a good hand,
A frank one.

Des. You may, indeed, say so;
For 'twas that hand that gave away my heart.

Oth. A liberal hand: The hearts of old, gave hands;
But our new heraldry is—hands, not hearts.

Des. I cannot speak of this. Come now your promise.

Oth. What promise, chuck?

Des. I have sent to bid Cassio come speak with you.

Oth. I have a salt and sullen rheum offends me;
Lend me thy handkerchief.

Des. Here, my lord.

Oth. That which I gave you.

Des. I have it not about me.

Oth. Not?

Des. No, indeed, my lord.

Oth. That is a fault:
That handkerchief
Did an Egyptian to my mother give;
She was a charmer, and could almost read
The thoughts of people: she told her, while she kept it,
'Twould make her amiable, and subdue my father
Entirely to her love; but if she lost it,
Or made a gift of it, my father's eye
Should hold her loathly, and his spirits should hunt
After new fancies: She, dying, gave it me:
And bid me, when my fate would have me wive,
To give it her. I did so: and take heed of't,
Make it a darling like your precious eye;
To lose or give't away, were such perdition,
As nothing else could match.

Des. Is it possible?

Oth. 'Tis true: there's magic in the web of it:
A sibyl, that had number'd in the world
The sun to make two hundred compasses,
In her prophetick fury sew'd the work;
The worms were hallow'd, that did breed the silk;
And it was dyed in mummy, which the skilful
Conserv'd of maidens' hearts.

Des. Indeed! is't true?

Oth. Most veritable; therefore look to't well.

Des. Then 'would to heaven, that I had never seen it.

Oth. Ha! wherefore?

Des. Why do you speak so startingly and rash?

Oth. Is't lost? is't gone? speak, is it out of the way?

Des. Heaven bless us!

Oth. Say you?

Des. It is not lost: But what an if it were?

Oth. Ha!

Des. I say it is not lost.

Oth. Fetch't, let me see it.

Des. Why, so I can, sir, but I will not now;
This is a trick, to put me from my suit;
I pray, let Cassio be receiv'd again.

Oth. Fetch me that handkerchief: my mind misgives.

Des. Come, come;
You'll never meet a more sufficient man.

Oth. The handkerchief,—

Des. I pray, talk me of Cassio.

Oth. The handkerchief,—

Des. A man that, all his time,
Hath founded his good fortune on your love,
Shar'd dangers with you;—

Oth. The handkerchief,—

Des. In sooth,
You are to blame.

Oth. Away! [*Exit* OTHELLO.

Emil. Is not this man jealous?

Des. I ne'er saw this before.
Sure, there's some wonder in this handkerchief:
I am most unhappy in the loss of it.

Emil. 'Tis not a year or two shows us a man:
They are all but stomachs, and we all but food;
They eat us hungerly, and when they are full,
They belch us. Look you! Cassio, and my husband.

Enter IAGO *and* CASSIO.

Iago. There's no other way; 'tis she must do't;
And, lo, the happiness! go, and importune her.

Des. How now, good Cassio? what's the news with you?

Cas. Madam, my former suit: I do beseech you,
That, by your virtuous means, I may again
Exist, and be a member of his love,
Whom I, with all the duty of my heart,
Entirely honour; I would not be delay'd
If my offence be of such mortal kind,
That neither service past, nor present sorrows,
Nor purpos'd merit in futurity,
Can ransome me into his love again,
But to know so must be my benefit;
So shall I clothe me in a forc'd content,
And shut myself up in some other course,
To fortune's alms.

Des. Alas! thrice gentle Cassio,
My advocation is not now in tune;
My lord is not my lord; nor should I know him,
Were he in favour, as in humour, alter'd.
So help me, every spirit sanctified,
As I have spoken for you all my best;
And stood within the blank of his displeasure,
For my free speech! You must awhile be patient:
What I can do, I will; and more I will,
Than for myself I dare; let that suffice you.

Iago. Is my lord angry?

Emil. He went hence but now,
And, certainly, in strange unquietness.

Iago. Can he be angry? I have seen the cannon,
When it hath blown his ranks into the air;
And, like the devil, from his very arm
Puff'd his own brother;—And can he be angry?
Something of moment, then: I will go meet him;
There's matter in't indeed, if he be angry.

Des. I pr'ythee, do so.—Something, sure, of state,— [*Exit* IAGO.
Either from Venice; or some unhatch'd practice,
Made demonstrable here in Cyprus to him,—
Hath puddled his clear spirit: and, in such cases,
Men's natures wrangle with inferior things,
Though great ones are their object. 'Tis even so:
For let our finger ache, and it indues
Our other healthful members ev'n to that sense
Of pain: Nay, we must think men are not gods;
Nor of them look for such observances
As fit the bridal.—Beshrew me much, Emilia,
I was (unhandsome warrior as I am),
Arraigning his unkindness with my soul;
But now I find, I had suborn'd the witness,
And he's indited falsely.

Emil. Pray heaven, it be state matters, as you think;

And no conception, nor no jealous toy,
Concerning you.

Des. Alas, the day! I never gave him cause.

Emil. But jealous souls will not be answer'd so;
They are not ever jealous for the cause,
But jealous for they are jealous: 'tis a monster,
Begot upon itself, born on itself.

Des. Heaven keep that monster from Othello's mind!

Emil. Lady, amen.

Des. I will go seek him.—Cassio, walk hereabout:
If I do find him fit, I'll move your suit,
And seek to effect it to my uttermost.

Cas. I humbly thank your ladyship.

[*Exeunt* DESDEMONA *and* EMILIA.

Enter BIANCA.

Bian. Save you, friend Cassio!

Cas. What make you from home?
How is it with you, my most fair Bianca?
I' faith, sweet love, I was coming to your house.

Bian. And I was going to your lodging, Cassio.
What! keep a week away? seven days and nights?
Eight score eight hours? and lovers' absent hours,
More tedious than the dial eight score times?
O weary reckoning!

Cas. Pardon me, Bianca;
I have this while with leaden thoughts been press'd;
But I shall, in a more continuate time,
Strike off this score of absence. Sweet Bianca,
[*Giving her* Desdemona's *Handkerchief.*
Take me this work out.

Bian. O, Cassio, whence came this?
This is some token from a newer friend.
To the felt absence now I feel a cause:
Is it come to this? Well, well.

Cas. Go to! woman,
Throw your vile guesses in the devil's teeth,
From whence you have them. You are jealous now,
That this is from some mistress, some remembrance:
No, in good troth, Bianca.

Bian. Why, whose is it?

Cas. I know not, sweet: I found it in my chamber.
I like the work well; ere it be demanded,
(As like enough, it will), I'd have it copied:
Take it, and do't; and leave me for this time.

Bian. Leave you! wherefore?

Cas. I do attend here on the general;
And think it no addition, nor my wish,
To have him see me woman'd.

Bian. Why, I pray you.

Cas. Not that I love you not.

Bian. But that you do not love me.
I pray you, bring me on the way a little;
And say, if I shall see you soon at night.

Cas. 'Tis but a little way, that I can bring you,
For I attend here: but I'll see you soon.

Bian. 'Tis very good; I must be circumstanc'd.
[*Exeunt.*

ACT IV.

SCENE I. *Before the Castle.*

Enter OTHELLO *and* IAGO.

Iago. Will you think so?

Oth. Think so, Iago?

Iago. What,
To kiss in private?

Oth. An unauthoris'd kiss.

Iago. Or to be naked with her friend abed,
An hour, or more, not meaning any harm?

Oth. Naked abed, Iago, and not mean harm?
It is hypocrisy against the devil:
They that mean virtuously, and yet do so,
The devil their virtue tempts, and they tempt heaven.

Iago. So they do nothing, 'tis a venial slip:
But if I give my wife a handkerchief,——

Oth. What then?

Iago. Why then 'tis hers, my lord; and, being hers,
She may, I think, bestow't on any man.

Oth. She is protectress of her honour too;
May she give that?

Iago. Her honour is an essence that's not seen;
They have it very oft, that have it not:
But, for the handkerchief,——

Oth. By heaven, I would most gladly have forgot it:—
Thou said'st,—O, it comes o'er my memory,
As doth the raven o'er the infected house,
Boding to all,—he had my handkerchief.

Iago. Ay, what of that?

Oth. That's not so good, now.

Iago. What, if I had said, I had seen him do you wrong?
Or heard him say,—As knaves be such abroad,
Who, having, by their own importunate suit,
Or voluntary dotage of some mistress,
Convinced or supplied them, cannot choose
But they must blab——

Oth. Hath he said any thing?

Iago. He hath, my lord; but be you well assur'd,
No more than he'll unswear.

Oth. What hath he said?

Iago. 'Faith, that he did,—I know not what he did.

Oth. What? what?

Iago. Lie—

Oth. With her?

Iago. With her, on her; what you will.

Oth. Lie with her! lie on her!—We say, lie on her, when they belie her: Lie with her! that's fulsome.—Handkerchief,—confessions,—handkerchief.—To confess and be hang'd for his labour.—First to be hanged, and then to confess:—I tremble at it. Nature would not invest herself in such shadowing passion, without some instruction. It is not words, that shake me thus:—Pish!—Noses, ears, and lips:—Is it possible?—Confess!—Handkerchief!—O devil!— [*Falls in a Trance.*

Iago. Work on,
My medicine, work! Thus credulous fools are caught;
And many worthy and chaste dames, even thus,
All guiltless meet reproach.—What, ho! my lord!

Enter CASSIO.

My lord, I say! Othello!—How now, Cassio?

Cas. What is the matter?

Iago. My lord is fallen into an epilepsy;
This is his second fit; he had one yesterday.

Cas. Rub him about the temples.

Iago. No, forbear:
The lethargy must have his quiet course:
If not, he foams at mouth; and, by and by,
Breaks out to savage madness. Look, he stirs:
Do you withdraw yourself a little while,
He will recover straight; when he is gone,
I would on great occasion speak with you.—
[*Exit* CASSIO.
How is it, general? have you not hurt your head?

Oth. Dost thou mock me?

Iago. I mock you! no, by heaven:
'Would you would bear your fortunes like a man.

Oth. A horned man's a monster, and a beast.

Iago. There's many a beast then in a populous city,
And many a civil monster.

Oth. Did he confess it?

Iago. Good sir, be a man;
Think, every bearded fellow, that's but yok'd,

May draw with you; there's millions now alive,
That nightly lie in those unproper beds,
Which they dare swear peculiar; your case is better.
O, 'tis the spite of hell, the fiend's arch-mock,
To lip a wanton in a secure couch,
And to suppose her chaste! No, let me know;
And, knowing what I am, I know what she shall be.

Oth. O, thou art wise; 'tis certain.

Iago. Stand you awhile apart;
Confine yourself but in a patient list.
Whilst you were here, ere while mad with your grief
(A passion most unsuiting such a man),
Cassio came hither: I shifted him away,
And laid good 'scuse upon your ecstasy;
Bade him anon return, and here speak with me;
The which he promis'd. Do but encave yourself,
And mark the fleers, the gibes, and notable scorns,
That dwell in every region of his face;
For I will make him tell the tale anew,—
Where, how, how oft, how long ago, and when
He hath, and is again to cope your wife:
I say, but mark his gesture. Marry, patience;
Or I shall say, you are all in all in spleen,
And nothing of a man.

Oth. Dost thou hear, Iago?
I will be found most cunning in my patience;
But (dost thou hear?) most bloody.

Iago. That's not amiss;
But yet keep time in all. Will you withdraw?
[OTHELLO *withdraws.*
Now will I question Cassio of Bianca,
A housewife, that, by selling her desires,
Buys herself bread and clothes: it is a creature,
That dotes on Cassio,—as 'tis the strumpet's plague,
To beguile many, and be beguil'd by one;
He, when he hears of her, cannot refrain
From the excess of laughter!—Here he comes!—

Re-enter CASSIO.

As he shall smile, Othello shall go mad;
And his unbookish jealousy must construe
Poor Cassio's smiles, gestures, and light behaviour,
Quite in the wrong.—How do you now, lieutenant?

Cas. The worser, that you give me the addition,
Whose want even kills me.

Iago. Ply Desdemona well, and you are sure of't.
Now, if this suit lay in Bianca's power,
[*Speaking lower.*
How quickly should you speed?

Cas. Alas, poor caitiff!

Oth. Look, how he laughs already! [*Aside.*

Iago. I never knew a woman love man so.

Cas. Alas, poor rogue! I think i'faith she loves me.

Oth. Now he denies it faintly, and laughs it out.
[*Aside.*

Iago. Do you hear, Cassio?

Oth. Now he importunes him
To tell it o'er: Go to; well said, well said.
[*Aside.*

Iago. She gives it out, that you shall marry her:
Do you intend it?

Cas. Ha, ha, ha!

Oth. Do you triumph, Roman? do you triumph? [*Aside.*

Cas. I marry her!—what? a customer! I pr'ythee, bear some charity to my wit; do not think it so unwholesome. Ha, ha, ha!

Oth. So, so, so, so: They laugh that win.
[*Aside.*

Iago. 'Faith, the cry goes, that you shall marry her.

Cas. Pr'ythee, say true.

Iago. I am a very villain else.

Oth. Have you scored me? Well. [*Aside.*

Cas. This is the monkey's own giving out: she is persuaded I will marry her, out of her own love and flattery, not out of my promise.

Oth. Iago beckons me; now he begins the story.
[*Aside.*

Cas. She was here even now: she haunts me in every place. I was, the other day, talking on the seabank with certain Venetians; and thither comes this bauble; by this hand, she falls thus about my neck;——

Oth. Crying, O dear Cassio! as it were: his gesture imports it. [*Aside.*

Cas. So hangs, and lolls, and weeps upon me; so hales, and pulls me: ha, ha, ha!—

Oth. Now he tells, how she pluck'd him to my chamber: O, I see that nose of yours, but not that dog I shall throw it to. [*Aside.*

Cas. Well, I must leave her company.

Iago. Before me! look where she comes.

Enter BIANCA.

Cas. 'Tis such another fitchew! marry, a perfumed one.—What do you mean by this haunting of me?

Bian. Let the devil and his dam haunt you! What did you mean by that same handkerchief, you gave me even now? I was a fine fool to take it. I must take out the whole work?—A likely piece of work, that you should find it in your chamber, and not know who left it there! This is some minx's token, and I must take out the work! There,—give it your hobby-horse: wheresoever you had it, I'll take out no work on't.

Cas. How now, my sweet Bianca? how now? how now?

Oth. By heaven, that should be my handkerchief. [*Aside.*

Bian. An you'll come to supper to-night, you may: an you will not, come when you are next prepared for. [*Exit.*

Iago. After her, after her.

Cas. 'Faith, I must, she'll rail in the street else.

Iago. Will you sup there?

Cas. 'Faith, I intend so.

Iago. Well, I may chance to see you; for I would very fain speak with you.

Cas. Pr'ythee, come; Will you?

Iago. Go to: say no more. [*Exit* CASSIO.

Oth. How shall I murder him, Iago?

Iago. Did you perceive how he laughed at his vice?

Oth. O, Iago!

Iago. And did you see the handkerchief?

Oth. Was that mine?

Iago. Yours, by this hand: and to see how he prizes the foolish woman, your wife! she gave it him, and he hath given it his whore.

Oth. I would have him nine years a killing:—A fine woman! a fair woman! a sweet woman!

Iago. Nay, you must forget that.

Oth. Ay, let her rot, and perish, and be damned to-night; for she shall not live: No, my heart is turned to stone; I strike it, and it hurts my hand. O, the world hath not a sweeter creature: she might lie by an emperor's side, and command him tasks.

Iago. Nay, that's not your way.

Oth. Hang her! I do but say what she is:—So delicate with her needle!—An admirable musician! O, she will sing the savageness out of a bear!—Of so high and plenteous wit and invention!—

Iago. She's the worse for all this.

Oth. O, a thousand, a thousand times:—And then, of so gentle a condition!

Iago. Ay, too gentle.

Oth. Nay, that's certain: But yet the pity of it, Iago!—O, Iago, the pity of it, Iago!

Iago. If you are so fond over her iniquity, give her patent to offend; for, if it touch not you, it comes near nobody.

Oth. I will chop her into messes!—Cuckold me!

Iago. O, 'tis foul in her.

Oth. With mine officer!

Iago. That's fouler.

Oth. Get me some poison, Iago; this night:—I'll not expostulate with her, lest her body and beauty unprovide my mind again: this night, Iago.

Iago. Do it not with poison, strangle her in her bed, even the bed she hath contaminated.

Oth. Good, good: the justice of it pleases; very good.

Iago. And, for Cassio,—let me be his undertaker: you shall hear more by midnight. [*A Trumpet within.*

Oth. Excellent good.—What trumpet is that same?

Iago. Something from Venice, sure. 'Tis Lodovico,
Come from the duke: and, see, your wife is with him.

Enter Lodovico, Desdemona, *and* Attendants.

Lod. 'Save you, worthy general!

Oth. With all my heart, sir.

Lod. The duke and senators of Venice greet you. [*Gives him a Packet.*

Oth. I kiss the instrument of their pleasures. [*Opens the Packet and reads.*

Des. And what's the news, good cousin Lodovico?

Iago. I am very glad to see you, signior;
Welcome to Cyprus.

Lod. I thank you: How does lieutenant Cassio?

Iago. Lives, sir.

Des. Cousin, there's fallen between him and my lord
An unkind breach: but you shall make all well.

Oth. Are you sure of that?

Des. My lord?

Oth. *This fail you not to do, as you will—* [*Reads.*

Lod. He did not call; he's busy in the paper.
Is there division 'twixt thy lord and Cassio?

Des. A most unhappy one; I would do much
To atone them, for the love I bear to Cassio.

Oth. Fire and brimstone!

Des. My lord?

Oth. Are you wise?

Des. What, is he angry?

Lod. May be, the letter mov'd him;
For, as I think, they do command him home,
Deputing Cassio in his government.

Des. By my troth, I am glad on't.

Oth. Indeed.

Des. My lord?

Oth. I am glad to see you mad.

Des. How, sweet Othello?

Oth. Devil! [*Striking her.*

Des. I have not deserv'd this.

Lod. My lord, this would not be believ'd in Venice,
Though I should swear I saw it; 'Tis very much;
Make her amends, she weeps.

Oth. O devil, devil!
If that the earth could teem with woman's tears,
Each drop she falls would prove a crocodile;—
Out of my sight!

Des. I will not stay to offend you. [*Going.*

Lod. Truly, an obedient lady:—
I do beseech your lordship, call her back.

Oth. Mistress,——

Des. My lord?

Oth. What would you with her, sir?

Lod. Who, I, my lord?

Oth. Ay; you did wish, that I would make her turn;
Sir, she can turn, and turn, and yet go on,
And turn again; and she can weep, sir, weep;
And she's obedient, as you say,—obedient,—
Very obedient:—Proceed you in your tears.—
Concerning this, sir,—O well painted passion!
I am commanded home:—Get you away;
I'll send for you anon.—Sir, I obey the mandate,
And will return to Venice;—Hence, avaunt! [*Exit* Desdemona.
Cassio shall have my place. And,—sir,—to-night,
I do entreat that we may sup together.
You are welcome, sir, to Cyprus.—Goats and monkeys! [*Exit.*

Lod. Is this the noble Moor whom our full senate
Call—all-in-all sufficient?—This the noble nature
Whom passion could not shake? whose solid virtue
The shot of accident, nor dart of chance,
Could neither graze, nor pierce?

Iago. He is much chang'd.

Lod. Are his wits safe? is he not light of brain?

Iago. He is that he is; I may not breathe my censure.
What he might be,—if what he might, he is not,—
I would to heaven, he were.

Lod. What, strike his wife!

Iago. 'Faith, that was not so well; Yet, 'would I knew,
That stroke would prove the worst.

Lod. Is it his use?
Or did the letters work upon his blood,
And new create this fault?

Iago. Alas, alas!
It is not honesty in me, to speak
What I have seen and known. You shall observe him;
And his own courses will denote him so,
That I may save my speech: Do but go after,
And mark how he continues.

Lod. I am sorry, that I am deceiv'd in him. [*Exeunt.*

SCENE II. *A Room in the Castle.*

Enter Othello *and* Emilia.

Oth. You have seen nothing then?

Emil. Nor ever heard; nor ever did suspect.

Oth. Yes, you have seen Cassio and she together.

Emil. But then I saw no harm: and then I heard
Each syllable that breath made up between them.

Oth. What, did they never whisper?

Emil. Never, my lord.

Oth. Nor send you out o'the way?

Emil. Never.

Oth. To fetch her fan, her gloves, her mask, nor nothing?

Emil. Never, my lord.

Oth. That's strange.

Emil. I durst, my lord, to wager she is honest,
Lay down my soul at stake: if you think other,
Remove your thought; it doth abuse your bosom.
If any wretch hath put this in your head,
Let heaven requite it with the serpent's curse!
For, if she be not honest, chaste, and true,
There's no man happy; the purest of their wives
Is foul as slander.

Oth. Bid her come hither:—go.— [*Exit* Emilia.
She says enough:—yet she's a simple bawd,
That cannot say as much. This is a subtle whore,
A closet-lock-and-key of villanous secrets:
And yet she'll kneel, and pray: I have seen her do't.

Re-enter Emilia, *with* Desdemona.

Des. My lord, what is your will?

Oth. 'Pray, chuck, come hither.

Des. What is your pleasure?
Oth. Let me see your eyes;
Look in my face.
Des. What horrible fancy's this?
Oth. Some of your function, mistress;
[*To* EMILIA.
Leave procreants alone, and shut the door;
Cough, or cry—hem, if any body come:
Your mystery, your mystery;—nay, despatch.
[*Exit* EMILIA.
Des. Upon my knees, what doth your speech import?
I understand a fury in your words,
But not the words.
Oth. Why, what art thou?
Des. Your wife, my lord; your true
And loyal wife.
Oth. Come, swear it, damn thyself:
Lest, being like one of heaven, the devils themselves
Should fear to seize thee: therefore be double damn'd,
Swear—thou art honest.
Des. Heaven doth truly know it.
Oth. Heaven truly knows, that thou art false as hell.
Des. To whom, my lord? with whom? How am I false?
Oth. O Desdemona!—away! away! away!
Des. Alas, the heavy day!—Why do you weep?
Am I the occasion of these tears, my lord?
If, haply, you my father do suspect,
An instrument of this your calling back,
Lay not your blame on me; if you have lost him,
Why, I have lost him too.
Oth. Had it pleas'd heaven
To try me with affliction; had he rain'd
All kinds of sores, and shames, on my bare head;
Steep'd me in poverty to the very lips;
Given to captivity me and my utmost hopes;
I should have found in some part of my soul
A drop of patience: but (alas!) to make me
A fixed figure, for the time of scorn
To point his slow unmoving finger at,—
O! O!
Yet could I bear that too; well, very well:
But there, where I have garner'd up my heart;
Where either I must live or bear no life;
The fountain from the which my current runs,
Or else dries up; to be discarded thence!
Or keep it as a cistern, for foul toads
To knot and gender in!—turn thy complexion there!
Patience, thou young and rose-lipp'd cherubim;
Ay, there, look grim as hell!
Des. I hope, my noble lord esteems me honest.
Oth. O, ay; as summer flies are in the shambles,
That quicken even with blowing. O thou weed,
Who art so lovely fair, and smell'st so sweet,
That the sense aches at thee.—'Would, thou had'st ne'er been born!
Des. Alas, what ignorant sin have I committed?
Oth. Was this fair paper, this most goodly book,
Made to write whore upon? What committed!
Committed!—O thou public commoner!
I should make very forges of my cheeks,
That would to cinders burn up modesty,
Did I but speak thy deeds.—What committed?
Heaven stops the nose at it, and the moon winks;
The bawdy wind, that kisses all it meets,
Is hush'd within the hollow mine of earth,
And will not hear it: What committed!—
Impudent strumpet!
Des. By heaven, you do me wrong.
Oth. Are not you a strumpet?
Des. No, as I am a Christian:
If to preserve this vessel for my lord,
From any other foul unlawful touch,
Be—not to be a strumpet, I am none.
Oth. What, not a whore?
Des. No, as I shall be saved.
Oth. Is it possible?
Des. O, heaven forgive us!
Oth. I cry you mercy, then;
I took you for that cunning whore of Venice,
That married with Othello.—You, mistress,

Re-enter EMILIA.

That have the office opposite to Saint Peter,
And keep the gate of hell; You! you! ay, you!
We have done our course; there's money for your pains;
I pray you, turn the key, and keep our counsel.
[*Exit.*
Emil. Alas, what does this gentleman conceive?—
How do you, madam? how do you, my good lady?
Des. 'Faith, half asleep.
Emil. Good madam, what's the matter with my lord?
Des. With who?
Emil. Why, with my lord, madam.
Des. Who is thy lord?
Emil. He that is yours, sweet lady.
Des. I have none: Do not talk to me, Emilia;
I cannot weep; nor answer I have none,
But what should go by water. 'Pr'ythee, to-night
Lay on my bed my wedding sheets,—remember;—
And call thy husband hither.
Emil. Here is a change, indeed! [*Exit.*
Des. 'Tis meet I should be us'd so, very meet.
How have I been behav'd, that he might stick
The small'st opinion on my great'st abuse?

Re-enter EMILIA, *with* IAGO.

Iago. What is your pleasure, madam! How is it with you?
Des. I cannot tell. Those, that do teach young babes,
Do it with gentle means, and easy tasks:
He might have chid me so; for, in good faith,
I am a child to chiding.
Iago. What's the matter, lady?
Emil. Alas, Iago, my lord hath so bewhor'd her,
Thrown such despite and heavy terms upon her,
As true hearts cannot bear.
Des. Am I that name, Iago?
Iago. What name, fair lady?
Des. Such as, she says, my lord did say I was.
Emil. He call'd her, whore; a beggar, in his drink,
Could not have laid such terms upon his callet.
Iago. Why did he so?
Des. I do not know; I am sure, I am none such.
Iago. Do not weep, do not weep; Alas, the day!
Emil. Has she forsook so many noble matches,
Her father, and her country, and her friends,
To be call'd—whore? would it not make one weep?
Des. It is my wretched fortune.
Iago. Beshrew him for it!
How comes this trick upon him?
Des. Nay, heaven doth know.
Emil. I will be hang'd, if some eternal villain,
Some busy and insinuating rogue,
Some cogging cozening slave, to get some office,
Have not devis'd this slander; I'll be hang'd else.
Iago. Fye, there is no such man; it is impossible.
Des. If any such there be, heaven pardon him!
Emil. A halter pardon him! and hell gnaw his bones!
Why should he call her, whore? who keeps her company?

What place? what time? what form? what likelihood!
The Moor's abus'd by some most villanous knave,
Some base notorious knave, some scurvy fellow:—
O, heaven, that such companions thoud'st unfold;
And put in every honest hand a whip,
To lash the rascal naked through the world,
Even from the east to the west!

Iago. Speak within door.

Emil. O, fye upon him! some such squire he was,
That turn'd your wit the seamy side without,
And made you to suspect me with the Moor.

Iago. You are a fool; go to.

Des. O good Iago,
What shall I do to win my lord again?
Good friend, go to him; for, by this light of heaven,
I know not how I lost him. Here I kneel:—
If e'er my will did trespass 'gainst his love,
Either in discourse of thought, or actual deed;
Or that mine eyes, mine ears, or any sense,
Delighted them in any other form;
Or that I do not yet, and ever did,
And ever will,—though he do shake me off
To beggarly divorcement,—love him dearly,
Comfort forswear me! Unkindness may do much;
And his unkindness may defeat my life,
But never taint my love. I cannot say, whore;
It does abhor me, now I speak the word;
To do the act that might the addition earn,
Not the world's mass of vanity could make me.

Iago. I pray you, be content; 'tis but his humour;
The business of the state does him offence,
And he does chide with you.

Des. If 'twere no other,—

Iago. It is but so, I warrant you. [*Trumpets.*
Hark, how these instruments summon to supper!
And the great messengers of Venice stay:
Go in, and weep not; all things shall be well.
[*Exeunt* DESDEMONA *and* EMILIA.

Enter RODERIGO.

How now, Roderigo?

Rod. I do not find, that thou deal'st justly with me.

Iago. What in the contrary?

Rod. Every day thou doff'st me with some device, Iago; and rather (as it seems to me now), keep'st from me all conveniency, than suppliest me with the least advantage of hope. I will, indeed, no longer endure it: Nor am I yet persuaded, to put up in peace what already I have foolishly suffered.

Iago. Will you hear me, Roderigo?

Rod. 'Faith, I have heard too much; for your words, and performances, are no kin together.

Iago. You charge me most unjustly.

Rod. With nought but truth. I have wasted myself out of my means. The jewels you have had from me, to deliver to Desdemona, would half have corrupted a votarist: You have told me—she has received them, and returned me expectations and comforts of sudden respect and acquittance; but I find none.

Iago. Well; go to; very well.

Rod. Very well! go to! I cannot go to, man; nor 'tis not very well: By this hand, I say, it is very scurvy; and begin to find myself fobbed in it.

Iago. Very well.

Rod. I tell you, 'tis not very well. I will make myself known to Desdemona: If she will return me my jewels, I will give over my suit, and repent my unlawful solicitation; if not, assure yourself, I will seek satisfaction of you.

Iago. You have said now.

Rod. Ay, and I have said nothing, but what I protest intendment of doing.

Iago. Why, now I see there's mettle in thee; and even, from this instant, do build on thee a better opinion than ever before. Give me thy hand, Roderigo: Thou hast taken against me a most just exception; but, yet I protest, I have dealt most directly in thy affair.

Rod. It hath not appeared.

Iago. I grant, indeed, it hath not appeared: and your suspicion is not without wit and judgment. But, Roderigo, if thou hast that within thee indeed, which I have greater reason to believe now than ever,—I mean, purpose, courage, and valour,—this night show it: if thou the next night following enjoyest not Desdemona, take me from this world with treachery, and devise engines for my life.

Rod. Well, what is it? is it within reason, and compass?

Iago. Sir, there is especial commission come from Venice, to depute Cassio in Othello's place.

Rod. Is that true? why, then Othello and Desdemona return again to Venice.

Iago. O, no; he goes into Mauritania, and takes away with him the fair Desdemona, unless his abode be lingered here by some accident; wherein none can be so determinate, as the removing of Cassio.

Rod. How do you mean—removing of him?

Iago. Why, by making him uncapable of Othello's place; knocking out his brains.

Rod. And that you would have me do?

Iago. Ay; if you dare do yourself a profit, and a right. He sups to-night with a harlot, and thither will I go to him;—he knows not yet of his honourable fortune: if you will watch his going thence (which I will fashion to fall out between twelve and one), you may take him at your pleasure; I will be near to second your attempt, and he shall fall between us. Come, stand not amazed at it, but go along with me; I will show you such a necessity in his death, that you shall think yourself bound to put it on him. It is now high supper-time, and the night grows to waste: about it.

Rod. I will hear further reason for this.

Iago. And you shall be satisfied. [*Exeunt.*

SCENE III. *Another Room in the Castle.*

Enter OTHELLO, LODOVICO, DESDEMONA, EMILIA, *and* Attendants.

Lod. I do beseech you, sir, trouble yourself no further.

Oth. O, pardon me; 'twill do me good to walk.

Lod. Madam, good night; I humbly thank your ladyship.

Des. Your honour is most welcome.

Oth. Will you walk, sir?—
O,—Desdemona,——

Des. My lord?

Oth. Get you to bed on the instant, I will be returned forthwith: dismiss your attendant there; look, it be done.

Des. I will, my lord.
[*Exeunt* OTH. LOD. *and* Attendants.

Emil. How goes it now? he looks gentler than he did.

Des. He says he will return incontinent;
He hath commanded me to go to bed,
And bade me to dismiss you.

Emil. Dismiss me!

Des. It was his bidding; therefore, good Emilia,
Give me my nightly wearing, and adieu:
We must not now displease him.

Emil. I would, you had never seen him!

Des. So would not I; my love doth so approve him,
That even his stubbornness, his checks, and frowns,—

'Pr'ythee, unpin me,—have grace and favour in them.

Emil. I have laid those sheets you bade me on the bed.

Des. All's one:—Good father! how foolish are our minds!—
If I do die before thee, 'pr'ythee, shroud me
In one of those same sheets.

Emil. Come, come, you talk.

Des. My mother had a maid call'd—Barbara:
She was in love; and he, she lov'd, prov'd mad,
And did forsake her: she had a song of—willow,
An old thing 'twas, but it express'd her fortune,
And she died singing it: That song, to-night,
Wil not go from my mind; I have much to do,
But to go hang my head all at one side,
And sing it like poor Barbara. 'Pr'ythee, despatch.

Emil. Shall I go fetch your night-gown?

Des. No, unpin me here.—
This Lodovico is a proper man.

Emil. A very handsome man.

Des. And he speaks well.

Emil. I know a lady in Venice, who would have walked barefoot to Palestine, for a touch of his nether lip.

I.

Des. *The poor soul sat sighing by a sycamore tree,*
Sing all a green willow; [Singing.
Her hand on her bosom, her head on her knee,
Sing willow, willow, willow:
The fresh streams ran by her, and murmur'd her moans;
Sing willow, &c.
Her salt tears fell from her, and soften'd the stones;
Lay by these:
Sing willow, willow, willow;
'Pr'ythee, hie thee; he'll come anon.—
Sing all a green willow must be my garland.

II.

Let nobody blame him, his scorn I approve,—
Nay, that's not next.—Hark! who is it that knocks?

Emil. It is the wind.

Des. *I call'd my love, false love; but what said he then?*
Sing willow, &c.
If I court mo women, you'll couch with mo men.
So, get thee gone; good night. Mine eyes do itch;
Doth that bode weeping?

Emil. 'Tis neither here nor there.

Des. I have heard it said so.—O, these men, these men!—
Dost thou in conscience think,—tell me, Emilia,—
That there be women do abuse their husbands
In such gross kind?

Emil. There be some such, no question.

Des. Would'st thou do such a deed for all the world?

Emil. Why, would not you?

Des. No, by this heavenly light!

Emil. Nor I neither by this heavenly light;
I might do't as well i'the dark.

Des. Would'st thou do such a deed for all the world?

Emil. The world is a huge thing: 'Tis a great price
For a small vice.

Des. Good troth, I think thou would'st not.

Emil. By my troth, I think I should; and undo't, when I had done. Marry, I would not do such a thing for a joint ring; nor for measures of lawn; nor for gowns, petticoats, nor caps, nor any petty exhibition: but, for the whole world,—Why, who would not make her husband a cuckold, to make him a monarch? I should venture purgatory for't.

Des. Beshrew me, if I would do such a wrong for the whole world.

Emil. Why, the wrong is but a wrong i'the world, and having the world for your labour, 'tis a wrong in your own world, and you might quickly make it right.

Des. I do not think there is any such woman.

Emil. Yes, a dozen; and as many
To the vantage, as would store the world they play'd for.
But, I do think, it is their husbands' faults,
If wives do fall: Say, that they slack their duties,
And pour our treasures into foreign laps;
Or else break out in peevish jealousies,
Throwing restraint upon us; or, say, they strike us,
Or scant our former having in despite:
Why, we have galls; and, though we have some grace,
Yet we have some revenge. Let husbands know,
Their wives have sense like them: they see, and smell,
And have their palates both for sweet and sour,
As husbands have. What is it that they do,
When they change us for others? Is it sport?
I think it is; And doth affection breed it?
I think, it doth? Is't frailty, that thus errs?
It is so too: And have not we affections?
Desires for sport? and frailty, as men have?
Then, let them use us well; else, let them know,
The ills we do, their ills instruct us to.

Des. Good night, good night; Heaven me such usage send,
Not to pick bad from bad; but, by bad, mend!
[*Exeunt.*

ACT V.

SCENE I. *A Street.*

Enter IAGO *and* RODERIGO.

Iago. Here, stand behind this bulk; straight will he come;
Wear thy good rapier bare, and put it home;
Quick, quick: fear nothing; I'll be at thy elbow:
It makes us, or it mars us; think on that,
And fix most firm thy resolution.

Rod. Be near at hand; I may miscarry in't.

Iago. Here, at thy hand; be bold, and take thy sword. [*Retires to a little distance.*

Rod. I have no great devotion to the deed;
And yet he has given me satisfying reasons:—
'Tis but a man gone:—forth, my sword; he dies.
[*Goes to his stand.*

Iago. I have rubb'd this young quat almost to the sense,
And he grows angry. Now, whether he kill Cassio,
Or Cassio him, or each do kill the other,
Every way makes my gain: Live, Roderigo,
He calls me to a restitution large
Of gold, and jewels, that I bobb'd from him,
As gifts to Desdemona;
It must not be: if Cassio do remain,
He hath a daily beauty in his life,
That makes me ugly; and besides, the Moor
May unfold me to him; there stand I in much peril:
No, he must die:—But so, I hear him coming.

Enter CASSIO.

Rod. I know his gait, 'tis he:—Villain, thou diest.
[*Rushes from his post, and makes a pass at* CASSIO.

Cas. That thrust had been mine enemy indeed,

But that my coat is better than thou think'st;
I will make proof of thine.
[*Draws, and wounds* RODERIGO.

Rod. O, I am slain!

[IAGO *rushes from his post, and cuts* CASSIO *behind in the Leg, and exit.*

Cas. I am maim'd for ever:—Help, ho! murder! murder! [*Falls.*

Enter OTHELLO, *at a distance.*

Oth. The voice of Cassio:—Iago keeps his word.

Rod. O, villain that I am!

Oth. Hark! 'tis even so.

Cas. O, help! ho! light; a surgeon!

Oth. 'Tis he;—O brave Iago, honest, and just,
That hast such noble sense of thy friend's wrong!
Thou teachest me,—Minion, your dear lies dead,
And your fate hies apace;—Strumpet, I come;
Forth of my heart those charms, thine eyes, are blotted;
Thy bed, lust stain'd, shall with lust's blood be spotted. [*Exit* OTHELLO.

Enter LODOVICO *and* GRATIANO, *at a distance.*

Cas. What ho! no watch! no passage? murder! murder!

Gra. 'Tis some mischance; the cry is very direful.

Cas. O, help!

Lod. Hark!

Rod. O wretched villain!

Lod. Two or three groans:—it is a heavy night:
These may be counterfeits; let's think't unsafe
To come into the cry, without more help.

Rod. Nobody come? then shall I bleed to death.

Enter IAGO, *with a Light.*

Lod. Hark!

Gra. Here's one comes in his shirt, with light and weapons.

Iago. Who's there? whose noise is this, that cries on murder?

Lod. We do not know.

Iago. Did you not hear a cry?

Cas. Here, here; for heaven's sake, help me.

Iago. What's the matter?

Gra. This is Othello's ancient, as I take it.

Lod. The same, indeed; a very valiant fellow.

Iago. What are you here that cry so grievously?

Cas. Iago? O, I am spoil'd, undone by villains?
Give me some help.

Iago. O me, lieutenant! what villains have done this?

Cas. I think, that one of them is hereabout,
And cannot make away.

Iago. O treacherous villains!—
What are you there? come in, and give some help. [*To* LODOVICO *and* GRATIANO.

Rod. O, help me here!

Cas. That's one of them.

Iago. O murderous slave! O villain!
[IAGO *stabs* RODERIGO.

Rod. O damn'd Iago! O inhuman dog!—
O! O! O!

Iago. Kill men i' the dark!—Where be these bloody thieves?
How silent is this town!—Ho! murder! murder!
What may you be? are you of good, or evil?

Lod. As you shall prove us, praise us.

Iago. Signior Lodovico?

Lod. He, sir.

Iago. I cry you mercy; Here's Cassio hurt
By villains.

Gra. Cassio?

Iago. How is it, brother?

Cas. My leg is cut in two.

Iago. Marry, heaven forbid!—
Light, gentlemen; I'll bind it with my shirt.

Enter BIANCA.

Bian. What is the matter, ho? who is it that cry'd?

Iago. Who is't that cry'd?

Bian. O my dear Cassio! my sweet Cassio!
O Cassio! Cassio! Cassio!

Iago. O notable strumpet!—Cassio, may you suspect
Who they should be, that have thus mangled you?

Cas. No.

Gra. I am sorry, to find you thus: I have been to seek you.

Iago. Lend me a garter: So.—O, for a chair,
To bear him easily hence!

Bian. Alas, he faints:—O Cassio! Cassio! Cassio!

Iago. Gentlemen all, I do suspect this trash
To be a party in this injury.
Patience awhile, good Cassio.—Come, come;
Lend me a light.—Know we this face, or no?
Alas! my friend, and my dear countryman,
Roderigo? no:—Yes, sure; O heaven! Roderigo.

Gra. What, of Venice?

Iago. Even he, sir; did you know him?

Gra. Know him, ay.

Iago. Signior Gratiano? I cry you gentle pardon;
These bloody accidents must excuse my manners,
That so neglected you.

Gra. I am glad to see you.

Iago. How do you, Cassio?—O, a chair, a chair!

Gra. Roderigo?

Iago. He, he, 'tis he:—O, that's well said;—the chair:— [*A Chair brought in.*
Some good man bear him carefully from hence;
I'll fetch the general's surgeon.—For you, mistress, [*To* BIANCA.
Save you your labour. He that lies slain here, Cassio,
Was my dear friend: What malice was between you?

Cas. None in the world; nor do I know the man.

Iago. [*To* BIAN.] What, look you pale?—O, bear him out o' the air.—
[CASSIO *and* RODERIGO *are borne off.*
Stay you, good gentlemen:—Look you pale, mistress?
Do you perceive the ghastness of her eye?—
Nay, if you stare, we shall hear more anon:
Behold her well; I pray you, look upon her;
Do you see, gentlemen? nay, guiltiness will speak,
Though tongues were out of use.

Enter EMILIA.

Emil. 'Las, what's the matter; what's the matter, husband?

Iago. Cassio hath here been set on in the dark,
By Roderigo, and fellows that are 'scap'd;
He's almost slain, and Roderigo dead.

Emil. Alas, good gentleman! alas, good Cassio!

Iago. This is the fruit of whoring.—'Pr'ythee, Emilia,
Go know of Cassio where he supp'd to-night:—
What, do you shake at that?

Bian. He supp'd at my house; but I therefore shake not.

Iago. O, did he so? I charge you, go with me.

Emil. Fye, fye upon thee, strumpet!

Bian. I am no strumpet; but of life as honest,
As you that thus abuse me.

Emil. As I? foh! fye upon thee!

Iago. Kind gentlemen, let's go see poor Cassio dress'd:—
Come, mistress, you must tell us another tale.—
Emilia, run you to the citadel,

And tell my lord and lady what has happ'd.—
Will you go on, I pray;—This is the night, [*Aside.*
That either makes me, or fordoes me quite. [*Exeunt.*

SCENE II. *A Bedchamber:* DESDEMONA *in Bed asleep. A Light burning.*

Enter OTHELLO.

Oth. It is the cause, it is the cause, my soul,
Let me not name it to you, you chaste stars!—
It is the cause.—Yet I'll not shed her blood;
Nor scar that whiter skin of her's than snow,
And smooth as monumental alabaster. [*Takes off his sword.*
Yet she must die, else she'll betray more men.
Put out the light, and then—Put out the light!
If I quench thee, thou flaming minister,
I can again thy former light restore,
Should I repent me:—but once put out thine,
Thou cunning'st pattern of excelling nature,
I know not where is that Promethean heat,
That can thy light relume. When I have pluck'd thy rose,
I cannot give it vital growth again,
It needs must wither:—I'll smell it on the tree.— [*Kissing her.*
O balmy breath, that dost almost persuade
Justice to break her sword!—One more, one more.—
Be thus when thou art dead, and I will kill thee,
And love thee after:—One more, and this the last:
So sweet was ne'er so fatal. I must weep,
But they are cruel tears; this sorrow's heavenly;
It strikes where it doth love.—She wakes—
Des. Who's there? Othello?
Oth. Ay, Desdemona.
Des. Will you come to bed, my lord?
Oth. Have you pray'd to-night, Desdemona?
Des. Ay, my lord.
Oth. If you bethink yourself of any crime,
Unreconcil'd as yet to heaven and grace,
Solicit for it straight.
Des. Alas, my lord, what may you mean by that?
Oth. Well, do it, and be brief; I will walk by:
I would not kill thy unprepared spirit;
No,—Heaven forefend!—I would not kill thy soul.
Des. Talk you of killing?
Oth. Ay, I do.
Des. Then, heaven
Have mercy on me!
Oth. Amen, with all my heart!
Des. If you say so, I hope you will not kill me.
Oth. Humph!
Des. And yet I fear you: for you are fatal then,
When your eyes roll so: Why I should fear, I know not,
Since guiltiness I know not; but yet I feel, I fear.
Oth. Think on thy sins.
Des. They are loves I bear to you.
Oth. Ay, and for that thou diest.
Des. That death's unnatural, that kills for loving.—
Alas, why gnaw you so your nether lip?
Some bloody passion shakes your very frame:
These are portents; but yet, I hope, I hope,
They do not point on me.
Oth. Peace, and be still!
Des. I will so: What's the matter?
Oth. That handkerchief, which I so lov'd, and gave thee,
Thou gav'st to Cassio.
Des. No, by my life and soul;
Send for the man, and ask him.
Oth. Sweet soul, take heed,
Take heed of perjury; thou'rt on thy death-bed.
Des. Ay, but not yet to die.
Oth. Yes, presently:
Therefore confess thee freely of thy sin;
For to deny each article with oath,
Cannot remove, nor choke, the strong conception,
That I do groan withal. Thou art to die.
Des. Then, Lord have mercy on me!
Oth. I say, amen.
Des. And have you mercy too! I never did
Offend you in my life; never lov'd Cassio,
But with such general warranty of heaven
As I might love: I never gave him token.
Oth. By heaven, I saw my handkerchief in his hand.
O perjur'd woman! thou dost stone my heart,
And mak'st me call what I intend to do,—
(A murder which I thought,)—a sacrifice:
I saw the handkerchief.
Des. He found it then;
I never gave it him:—Send for him hither,
And let him confess a truth.
Oth. He hath confess'd.
Des. What, my lord?
Oth. That he hath—us'd thee.
Des. How? unlawfully?
Oth. Ay.
Des. He'll not say so.
Oth. No, his mouth is stopp'd;
Honest Iago hath ta'en order for't.
Des. My fear interprets then,—What, is he dead?
Oth. Had all his hairs been lives, my great revenge
Had stomach for them all.
Des. Alas! he is betray'd, and I undone.
Oth. Out, strumpet! Weep'st thou for him to my face?
Des. O, banish me, my lord, but kill me not.
Oth. Down, strumpet!
Des. Kill me to-morrow, let me live to-night.
Oth. Nay, if you strive,——
Des. But half an hour.
Oth. Being done,
There is no pause.
Des. But while I say one prayer.
Oth. It is too late. [*He smothers her.*
Emil. [*Within.*] My lord, my lord! what ho! my lord! my lord!
Oth. What noise is this? Not dead! not yet quite dead?
I, that am cruel, am yet merciful;
I would not have thee linger in thy pain.—
So, so.
Emil. [*Within.*] What ho! my lord, my lord!
Oth. Who's there?
Emil. [*Within.*] O, good my lord, I would speak a word with you.
Oth. Yes;—'tis Emilia:—by and by.—She's dead.
'Tis like she comes to speak of Cassio's death:
The noise was high.—Ha! no more moving?
Still as the grave. She shall come in? Were't good?
I think she stirs again:—No.—What's the best?
If she come in, she'll sure speak to my wife:
My wife! my wife! what wife?—I have no wife:
O insupportable! O heavy hour!
Methinks it should be now a huge eclipse
Of sun and moon; and that the affrighted globe
Should yawn at alteration.
Emil. [*Within.*] I do beseech you I may speak with you,
O, good my lord!
Oth. I had forgot thee: O, come in, Emilia:—
Soft,—by and by:—Let me the curtains draw.—
Where art thou? What's the matter with thee now? [*Unlocks the door.*

Enter EMILIA.

Emil. O, good my lord, yonder's foul murder done.
Oth. What? now?
Emil. But now, my lord!

Oth. It is the very error of the moon;
She comes more near the earth than she was wont;
And makes men mad.
Emil. Cassio, my lord, has kill'd a young Venetian,
Call'd—Roderigo.
Oth. Roderigo kill'd!
And Cassio kill'd?
Emil. No, Cassio is not kill'd.
Oth. Not Cassio kill'd? Then murder's out of tune,
And sweet revenge grows harsh.
Des. O, falsely, falsely murder'd!
Emil. Alas! what cry is that?
Oth. That! what?
Emil. Out, and alas! that was my lady's voice:—
Help! help! ho! help!—O lady, speak again!
Sweet Desdemona! O, sweet mistress, speak!
Des. A guiltless death I die.
Emil. O, who hath done
This deed?
Des. Nobody; I myself; farewell:
Commend me to my kind lord; O, farewell. [*Dies.*
Oth. Why, how should she be murder'd?
Emil. Alas, who knows?
Oth. You heard her say herself, it was not I.
Emil. She said so; I must needs report the truth.
Oth. She's, like a liar, gone to burning hell;
'Twas I that kill'd her.
Emil. O, the more angel she,
And you the blacker devil!
Oth. She turn'd to folly, and she was a whore.
Emil. Thou dost belie her, and thou art a devil.
Oth. She was false as water.
Emil. Thou art rash as fire, to say
That she was false; O, she was heavenly true!
Oth. Cassio did tup her; ask thy husband else.
O, I were damn'd beneath all depth in hell,
But that I did proceed upon just grounds
To this extremity; Thy husband knew it all.
Emil. My husband?
Oth. Thy husband.
Emil. That she was false to wedlock?
Oth. Ay, with Cassio.
Nay, had she been true,
If heaven would make me such another world
Of one entire and perfect chrysolite,
I'd not have sold her for it.
Emil. My husband?
Oth. Ay, 'twas he that told me first;
An honest man he is, and hates the slime
That sticks on filthy deeds.
Emil. My husband?
Oth. What needs this iterance, woman? I say, thy husband.
Emil. O mistress, villany hath made mocks with love!—
My husband say, that she was false?
Oth. He, woman.
I say, thy husband: Dost understand the word?
My friend, thy husband, honest, honest Iago.
Emil. If he say so, may his pernicious soul
Rot half a grain a day! he lies to the heart;
She was too fond of her most filthy bargain.
Oth. Ha!
Emil. Do thy worst:
This deed of thine is no more worthy heaven,
Than thou wast worthy her.
Oth. Peace, you were best.
Emil. Thou hast not half the power to do me harm,
As I have to be hurt. O gull! O dolt!
As ignorant as dirt! thou hast done a deed,—
I care not for thy sword; I'll make thee known,
Though I lost twenty lives:—Help! help, ho! help!
The Moor has kill'd my mistress: Murder! murder!

Enter MONTANO, GRATIANO, *and* IAGO.

Mon. What is the matter?—How now, general?
Emil. O, are you come, Iago? you have done well,
That men must lay their murders on your neck.
Gra. What is the matter?
Emil. Disprove this villain, if thou beest a man:
He says, thou told'st him that his wife was false:
I know, thou didst not, thou'rt not such a villain;
Speak, for my heart is full.
Iago. I told him what I thought; and told no more
Than what he found himself was apt and true.
Emil. But did you ever tell him, she was false?
Iago. I did.
Emil. You told a lie; an odious damned lie;
Upon my soul, a lie; a wicked lie:—
She false with Cassio!—Did you say with Cassio?
Iago. With Cassio, mistress; Go to, charm your tongue.
Emil. I will not charm my tongue; I am bound to speak;
My mistress here lies murder'd in her bed.
All. O heavens forefend!
Emil. And your reports have set the murder on.
Oth. Nay, stare not, masters; it is true, indeed.
Gra. 'Tis a strange truth.
Mon. O monstrous act!
Emil. Villany, villany, villany!—
I think upon't,—I think,—I smell't;—O villany!
I thought so then;—I'll kill myself for grief.—
O villany, villany!
Iago. What, are you mad? I charge you, get you home.
Emil. Good gentlemen, let me have leave to speak;
'Tis proper I obey him, but not now:—
Perchance, Iago, I will ne'er go home.
Oth. O! O! O! [*Hanging over his wife.*
Emil. Nay, lay thee down and roar;
For thou hast kill'd the sweetest innocent,
That e'er did lift up eye.
Oth. O, she was foul!— [*Rising.*
I scarce did know you, uncle: There lies your niece,
Whose breath indeed, these hands have newly stopp'd:
I know, this act shows horrible and grim.
Gra. Poor Desdemona! I am glad thy father's dead;
Thy match was mortal to him, and pure grief
Shore his old thread in twain: did he live now,
This sight would make him do a desperate turn,
Yea, curse his better angel from his side,
And fall to reprobation.
Oth. 'Tis pitiful: but yet Iago knows,
That she with Cassio hath the act of shame
A thousand times committed; Cassio confess'd it:
And she did gratify his amorous works
With that recognizance and pledge of love
Which I first gave her; I saw it in his hand;
It was a handkerchief, an antique token
My father gave my mother.
Emil. O heaven! O heavenly powers!
Iago. Come, hold your peace.
Emil. 'Twill out, 'twill out;—I hold my peace, sir? no;
No, I will speak as liberal as the air;
Let heaven, and men, and devils, let them all,
All, all, cry shame against me, yet I'll speak.
Iago. Be wise, and get you home.
Emil. I will not.
[IAGO *offers to stab his wife.*
Gra. Fye!
Your sword upon a woman?
Emil. O thou dull Moor! that handkerchief thou speak'st of,
I found by fortune, and did give my husband;

For often, with a solemn earnestness
(More than, indeed, belong'd to such a trifle,)
He begg'd of me to steal it.

Iago. Villanous whore!

Emil. She give it Cassio! no, alas; I found it,
And I did give't my husband.

Iago. Filth, thou liest.

Emil. By heaven, I do not; I do not, gentlemen:
O murd'rous coxcomb! what should such a fool
Do with so good a wife?

[IAGO *stabs* EMILIA, *then runs out.*

Oth. Are there no stones in heaven,
But what serve for the thunder?—Precious villain?

Gra. The woman falls; sure, he has kill'd his wife.

Emil. Ay, ay; O, lay me by my mistress' side!

Gra. He's gone, but his wife's kill'd.

Mon. 'Tis a notorious villain. Take you this weapon,
Which I have here recover'd from the Moor:
Come, guard the door without: let him not pass,
But kill him rather; I'll after that same villain,
For 'tis a damned slave.

[*Exeunt* MONTANO *and* GRATIANO.

Oth. I am not valiant neither,
But every puny whipster gets my sword:—
But why should honour outlive honesty?
Let it go all.

Emil. What did thy song bode, lady?
Hark, canst thou hear me? I will play the swan,
And die in musick;—*Willow, willow, willow.*—
Moor, she was chaste; she lov'd thee, cruel Moor;
So come my soul to bliss, as I speak true;
So speaking as I think, I die,—I die. [*Dies.*

Oth. I have another weapon in this chamber,
It is a sword of Spain, the ice-brook's temper!
O, here it is:—Uncle, I must come forth.

Gra. [*Within.*] If thou attempt it, it will cost thee dear;
Thou hast no weapon, and perforce must suffer.

Oth. Look in upon me then, and speak with me,
Or, naked as I am, I will assault thee.

Re-enter GRATIANO.

Gra. What is the matter?

Oth. Behold! I have a weapon;
A better never did itself sustain
Upon a soldier's thigh: I have seen the day,
That, with this little arm, and this good sword,
I have made my way through more impediments
Than twenty times your stop:—But, O vain boast!
Who can control his fate? 'tis not so now.—
Be not afraid, though you do see me weapon'd;
Here is my journey's end, here is my butt,
And very seamark of my utmost sail.
Do you go back dismay'd? 'tis a lost fear;
Man but a rush against Othello's breast,
And he retires;—Where should Othello go?—
Now, how dost thou look now? O ill-starr'd wench!
Pale as thy smock! when we shall meet at compt,
This look of thine will hurl my soul from heaven,
And fiends will snatch at it. Cold, cold, my girl?
Even like thy chastity.—
O cursed, cursed slave!—Whip me, ye devils,
From the possession of this heavenly sight!
Blow me about in winds! roast me in sulphur!
Wash me in steep-down gulfs of liquid fire!—
O Desdemona! Desdemona! dead?
Dead? O! O! O!

Enter LODOVICO, MONTANO, CASSIO, *carried in a Chair, and* Officers, *with* IAGO, *prisoner.*

Lod. Where is this rash and most unfortunate man?

Oth. That's he, that was Othello; here I am.

Lod. Where is that viper? bring the villain forth.

Oth. I look down towards his feet—but that's a fable;
If that thou be'st a devil, I cannot kill thee.

[OTHELLO *wounds* IAGO.

Lod. Wrench his sword from him.

Iago. I bleed, sir; but not kill'd.

Oth. I am not sorry neither; I'd have thee live;
For, in my sense, 'tis happiness to die.

Lod. O thou Othello, that wast once so good,
Fall'n in the practice of a cursed slave.
What shall be said to thee?

Oth. Why, any thing:
An honourable murderer, if you will;
For nought I did in hate, but all in honour.

Lod. This wretch hath part confess'd his villany:
Did you and he consent in Cassio's death?

Oth. Ay.

Cas. Dear general, I never gave you cause.

Oth. I do believe it, and I ask your pardon.
Will you, I pray you, demand that demi-devil,
Why he hath thus ensnar'd my soul and body?

Iago. Demand me nothing: What you know, you know:
From this time forth I never will speak word.

Lod. What! not to pray?

Gra. Torments will ope your lips.

Oth. Well, thou dost best.

Lod. Sir, you shall understand what hath befall'n,
Which, as I think, you know not: Here is a letter,
Found in the pocket of the slain Roderigo;
And here, another: the one of them imports
The death of Cassio to be undertook
By Roderigo.

Oth. O villain!

Cas. Most heathenish, and most gross!

Lod. Now here's another discontented paper,
Found in his pocket too: and this, it seems,
Roderigo meant to have sent this damned villain;
But that belike, Iago, in the interim,
Came in and satisfied him.

Oth. O the pernicious caitiff!—
How came you, Cassio, by that handkerchief
That was my wife's?

Cas. I found it in my chamber:
And he himself confess'd, but even now,
That there he dropp'd it, for a special purpose,
Which wrought to his desire.

Oth. O fool! fool! fool!

Cas. There is, besides, in Roderigo's letter,—
How he upbraids Iago, that he made him
Brave me upon the watch; whereon it came
That I was cast; And even but now he spake,
After long seeming dead,—Iago hurt him,
Iago set him on.

Lod. You must forsake this room, and go with us;
Your power and your command is taken off,
And Cassio rules in Cyprus. For this slave,—
If there be any cunning cruelty,
That can torment him much, and hold him long,
It shall be his: You shall close prisoner rest,
Till that the nature of your fault be known
To the Venetian state:—Come, bring him away.

Oth. Soft you; a word or two, before you go.
I have done the state some service, and they know it;
No more of that;—I pray you, in your letters,
When you shall these unlucky deeds relate,
Speak of me as I am; nothing extenuate,
Nor set down aught in malice: then must you speak
Of one, that lov'd not wisely, but too well;
Of one not easily jealous, but, being wrought,
Perplex'd in the extreme; of one, whose hand,
Like the base Judean, threw a pearl away,
Richer than all his tribe; of one, whose subdu'd eyes,
Albeit unused to the melting mood,
Drop tears as fast as the Arabian trees

Their medicinal gum. Set you down this:
And say, besides,—that in Aleppo once,
Where a malignant and a turban'd Turk
Beat a Venetian, and traduc'd the state,
I took by the throat the circumcised dog,
And smote him—thus. [*Stabs himself.*

Lod. O bloody period!

Gra. All, that's spoke, is marr'd.

Oth. I kiss'd thee, ere I kill'd thee;—No way but this, [*Falling upon* DESDEMONA.
Killing myself, to die upon a kiss. [*Dies.*

Cas. This did I fear, but thought he had no weapon;
For he was great of heart.

Lod. O Spartan dog,
More fell than anguish, hunger, or the sea!
Look on the tragick loading of this bed; [*To* IAGO.
This is thy work: the object poisons sight;—
Let it be hid. Gratiano, keep the house,
And seize upon the fortunes of the Moor,
For they succeed to you.—To you, lord governor,
Remains the censure of this hellish villain;
The time, the place, the torture,—O enforce it!
Myself will straight aboard! and, to the state,
This heavy act with heavy heart relate. [*Exeunt.*

THE END.

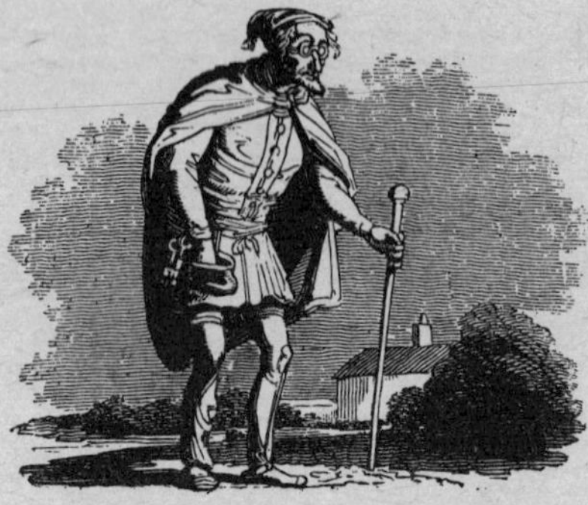

VENUS AND ADONIS

'Vilia miretur vulgus; mihi flavus Apollo
Pocula Castalia plena ministret aqua.'

TO THE

RIGHT HONOURABLE HENRY WRIOTHESLY,

EARL OF SOUTHAMPTON, AND BARON
OF TICHFIELD.

Right Honourable,

I know not how I shall offend in dedicating my unpolished lines to your lordship, nor how the world will censure me for choosing so strong a prop to support so weak a burden: only, if your honour seem but pleased, I account myself highly praised, and vow to take advantage of all idle hours, till I have honoured you with some graver labour. But if the first heir of my invention prove deformed, I shall be sorry it had so noble a god-father, and never after ear so barren a land, for fear it yield me still so bad a harvest. I leave it to your honourable survey, and your honour to your heart's content; which I wish may always answer your own wish and the world's hopeful expectation.

Your honour's in all duty,

William Shakespeare.

Even as the sun with purple-colour'd face
Had ta'en his last leave of the weeping morn,
Rose-cheek'd Adonis hied him to the chase;
Hunting he loved, but love he laugh'd to scorn;
  Sick-thoughted Venus makes amain unto him,
  And like a bold-faced suitor 'gins to woo him.

'Thrice-fairer than myself,' thus she began,
'The field's chief flower, sweet above compare,
Stain to all nymphs, more lovely than a man,
More white and red than doves or roses are;
  Nature that made thee, with herself at strife,
  Saith that the world hath ending with thy life.

'Vouchsafe, thou wonder, to alight thy steed,
And rein his proud head to the saddle-bow;
If thou wilt deign this favour, for thy meed
A thousand honey secrets shalt thou know:
  Here come and sit, where never serpent hisses;
  And being set, I'll smother thee with kisses:

'And yet not cloy thy lips with loathed satiety,
But rather famish them amid their plenty,
Making them red and pale with fresh variety;
Ten kisses short as one, one long as twenty:
  A summer's day will seem an hour but short,
  Being wasted in such time-beguiling sport.'

With this she seizeth on his sweating palm,
The precedent of pith and livelihood,
And trembling in her passion, calls it balm,
Earth's sovereign salve to do a goddess good:
  Being so enraged, desire doth lend her force
  Courageously to pluck him from his horse.

Over one arm the lusty courser's rein,
Under her other was the tender boy,
Who blush'd and pouted in a dull disdain,
With leaden appetite, unapt to toy;
  She red and hot as coals of glowing fire,
  He red for shame, but frosty in desire.

The studded bridle on a ragged bough
Nimbly she fastens; O! how quick is love:
The steed is stalled up, and even now
To tie the rider she begins to prove:
  Backward she push'd him, as she would be thrust,
  And govern'd him in strength, though not in lust.

So soon was she along, as he was down,
Each leaning on their elbows and their hips:
Now doth she stroke his cheek, now doth he frown,
And 'gins to chide, but soon she stops his lips;
  And kissing speaks, with lustful language broken,
  'If thou wilt chide, thy lips shall never open.'

He burns with bashful shame; she with her tears
Doth quench the maiden burning of his cheeks;

Then with her windy sighs and golden hairs
To fan and blow them dry again she seeks:
He saith she is immodest, blames her miss;
What follows more she murders with a kiss.

Even as an empty eagle, sharp by fast,
Tires with her beak on feathers, flesh and bone,
Shaking her wings, devouring all in haste,
Till either gorge be stuff'd or prey be gone;
Even so she kiss'd his brow, his cheek, his chin,
And where she ends she doth anew begin.

Forced to content, but never to obey,
Panting he lies, and breatheth in her face;
She feedeth on the steam as on a prey,
And calls it heavenly moisture, air of grace;
Wishing her cheeks were gardens full of flowers,
So they were dew'd with such distilling showers.

Look! how a bird lies tangled in a net,
So fasten'd in her arms Adonis lies;
Pure shame and awed resistance made him fret,
Which bred more beauty in his angry eyes:
Rain added to a river that is rank
Perforce will force it overflow the bank.

Still she entreats, and prettily entreats,
For to a pretty ear she tunes her tale;
Still is he sullen, still he lours and frets,
'Twixt crimson shame and anger ashy-pale;
Being red, she loves him best; and being white,
Her best is better'd with a more delight.

Look how he can, she cannot choose but love;
And by her fair immortal hand she swears,
From his soft bosom never to remove,
Till he take truce with her contending tears,
Which long have rain'd, making her cheeks all wet;
And one sweet kiss shall pay this countless debt.

Upon this promise did he raise his chin,
Like a dive-dapper peering through a wave,
Who, being look'd on, ducks as quickly in;
So offers he to give what she did crave;
But when her lips were ready for his pay,
He winks, and turns his lips another way.

Never did passenger in summer's heat
More thirst for drink than she for this good turn.
Her help she sees, but help she cannot get;
She bathes in water, yet her fire must burn:
'O! pity,' 'gan she cry, 'flint-hearted boy:
'T is but a kiss I beg; why art thou coy?

'I have been woo'd, as I entreat thee now,
Even by the stern and direful god of war,
Whose sinewy neck in battle ne'er did bow,
Who conquers where he comes in every jar;
Yet hath he been my captive and my slave,
And begg'd for that which thou unask'd shalt have.

'Over my altars hath he hung his lance,
His batter'd shield, his uncontrolled crest,
And for my sake hath learn'd to sport and dance,
To toy, to wanton, dally, smile and jest;
Scorning his churlish drum and ensign red,
Making my arms his field, his tent my bed.

'Thus he that overruled I oversway'd,
Leading him prisoner in a red-rose chain:
Strong-temper'd steel his stronger strength obey'd,
Yet was he servile to my coy disdain.
O! be not proud, nor brag not of thy might,
For mastering her that foil'd the god of fight.

'Touch but my lips with those fair lips of thine,
Though mine be not so fair, yet are they red,
The kiss shall be thine own as well as mine.
What seest thou in the ground? hold up thy head:
Look in mine eyeballs, there thy beauty lies;
Then why not lips on lips, since eyes in eyes?

'Art thou ashamed to kiss? then wink again,
And I will wink; so shall the day seem night;
Love keeps his revels where there are but twain;
Be bold to play, our sport is not in sight:
These blue-vein'd violets whereon we lean
Never can blab, nor know not what we mean.

'The tender spring upon thy tempting lip
Shows thee unripe, yet may'st thou well be tasted.
Make use of time, let not advantage slip;
Beauty within itself should not be wasted:
Fair flowers that are not gather'd in their prime
Rot and consume themselves in little time.

'Were I hard-favour'd, foul, or wrinkled-old,
Ill-nurtured, crooked, churlish, harsh in voice,
O'erworn, despised, rheumatic, and cold,
Thick-sighted, barren, lean, and lacking juice,
Then might'st thou pause, for then I were not for thee;
But having no defects, why dost abhor me?

'Thou canst not see one wrinkle in my brow;
Mine eyes are grey and bright, and quick in turning;
My beauty as the spring doth yearly grow;
My flesh is soft and plump, my marrow burning;
My smooth moist hand, were it with thy hand felt,
Would in thy palm dissolve, or seem to melt.

'Bid me discourse, I will enchant thine ear,
Or like a fairy trip upon the green,
Or like a nymph, with long dishevell'd hair,
Dance on the sands, and yet no footing seen:
Love is a spirit all compact of fire,
Not gross to sink, but light, and will aspire.

'Witness this primrose bank whereon I lie;
These forceless flowers like sturdy trees support me;
Two strengthless doves will draw me through the sky,
From morn till night, even where I list to sport me:
Is love so light, sweet boy, and may it be
That thou shouldst think it heavy unto thee?

'Is thine own heart to thine own face affected?
Can thy right hand seize love upon thy left?
Then woo thyself, be of thyself rejected
Steal thine own feeedom, and complain on theft.
Narcissus so himself himself forsook,
And died to kiss his shadow in the brook.

'Torches are made to light, jewels to wear,
Dainties to taste, fresh beauty for the use,
Herbs for their smell, and sappy plants to bear;
Things growing to themselves are growth's abuse:
Seeds spring from seeds, and beauty breedeth beauty;
Thou wast begot; to get it is thy duty.

'Upon the earth's increase why should'st thou feed,
Unless the earth with thy increase be fed?
By law of nature thou art bound to breed,
That thine may live when thou thyself art dead;
And so in spite of death thou dost survive,
In that thy likeness still is left alive.'

By this the love-sick queen began to sweat,
For where they lay the shadow had forsook them,
And Titan, tired in the mid-day heat,
With burning eye did hotly overlook them;
Wishing Adonis had his team to guide,
So he were like him and by Venus' side.

And now Adonis, with a lazy spright,
And with a heavy, dark, disliking eye,
His louring brows o'erwhelming his fair sight,
Like misty vapours when they blot the sky,
Souring his cheeks, cries 'Fie! no more of love:
The sun doth burn my face; I must remove.'

'Ay me!' quoth Venus, 'young and so unkind?
What bare excuses makest thou to be gone;
I'll sigh celestial breath, whose gentle wind
Shall cool the heat of this descending sun:
I'll make a shadow for thee of my hairs;
If they burn too, I'll quench them with my tears.

'The sun that shines from heaven shines but warm,
And, lo! I lie between that sun and thee:
The heat I have from thence doth little harm,
Thine eye darts forth the fire that burneth me;
And were I not immortal, life were done
Between this heavenly and earthly sun.

'Art thou obdurate, flinty, hard as steel?
Nay, more than flint, for stone at rain relenteth.
Art thou a woman's son, and canst not feel
What 't is to love? how want of love tormenteth?
O! had thy mother borne so hard a mind,
She had not brought forth thee, but died unkind.

'What am I, that thou should'st contemn me this?
Or what great danger dwells upon my suit?
What were thy lips the worse for one poor kiss?
Speak, fair; but speak fair words, or else be mute:
Give me one kiss, I'll give it thee again,
And one for interest, if thou wilt have twain.

'Fie! lifeless picture, cold and senseless stone,
Well-painted idol, image dull and dead,
Statue contenting but the eye alone,
Thing like a man, but of no woman bred:
Thou art no man, though of a man's complexion,
For men will kiss even by their own direction.'

This said, impatience chokes her pleading tongue,
And swelling passion doth provoke a pause;
Red cheeks and fiery eyes blaze forth her wrong;
Being judge in love, she cannot right her cause:
And now she weeps, and now she fain would speak,
And now her sobs do her intendments break.

Sometimes she shakes her head, and then his hand;
Now gazeth she on him, now on the ground;
Sometimes her arms infold him like a band:
She would, he will not in her arms be bound;
And when from thence he struggles to be gone,
She locks her lily fingers one in one.

'Fondling,' she saith, 'since I have hemm'd thee here
Within the circuit of this ivory pale,
I'll be a park, and thou shalt be my deer;
Feed where thou wilt, on mountain or in dale:
Graze on my lips, and if those hills be dry,
Stray lower, where the pleasant fountains lie.

'Within this limit is relief enough,
Sweet bottom-grass and high delightful plain,
Round rising hillocks, brakes obscure and rough,
To shelter thee from tempest and from rain:
Then be my deer, since I am such a park;
No dog shall rouse thee, though a thousand bark.'

At this Adonis smiles as in disdain,
That in each cheek appears a pretty dimple:
Love made those hollows, if himself were slain,
He might be buried in a tomb so simple;
Foreknowing well, if there he came to lie,
Why, there Love lived and there he could not die.

These lovely caves, these round enchanting pits,
Open'd their mouths to swallow Venus' liking.
Being mad before, how doth she now for wits?
Struck dead at first, what needs a second striking?
Poor Queen of love, in thine own law forlorn,
To love a cheek that smiles at thee in scorn!

Now which way shall she turn? what shall she say?
Her words are done, her woes the more increasing;
The time is spent, her object will away,
And from her twining arms doth urge releasing.
'Pity!' she cries, 'some favour, some remorse!'
Away he springs, and hasteth to his horse.

But, lo! from forth a copse that neighbours by,
A breeding jennet, lusty, young, and proud,

Adonis' trampling courser doth espy,
And forth she rushes, snorts and neighs aloud:
  The strong-neck'd steed, being tied unto a tree,
  Breaketh his rein, and to her straight goes he.

Imperiously he leaps, he neighs, he bounds,
And now his woven girths he breaks asunder;
The bearing earth with his hard hoof he wounds,
Whose hollow womb resounds like heaven's thunder;
  The iron bit he crusheth 'tween his teeth,
  Controlling what he was controlled with.

His ears up-prick'd; his braided hanging mane
Upon his compass'd crest now stand on end;
His nostrils drink the air, and forth again,
As from a furnace, vapours doth he send:
  His eye, which scornfully glisters like fire,
  Shows his hot courage and his high desire.

Sometime he trots, as if he told the steps,
With gentle majesty and modest pride;
Anon he rears upright, curvets and leaps,
As who should say 'Lo! thus my strength is tried;
  And this I do to captivate the eye
  Of the fair breeder that is standing by.'

What recketh he his rider's angry stir,
His flattering holla, or his 'Stand, I say'?
What cares he now for curb or pricking spur,
For rich caparisons or trapping gay?
  He sees his love, and nothing else he sees,
  For nothing else with his proud sight agrees.

Look, when a painter would surpass the life,
In limning out a well-proportion'd steed,
His art with nature's workmanship at strife,
As if the dead the living should exceed;
  So did this horse excel a common one,
  In shape, in courage, colour, pace and bone.

Round-hoof'd, short-jointed, fetlocks shag and long,
Broad breast, full eye, small head, and nostril wide,
High crest, short ears, straight legs and passing strong,
Thin mane, thick tail, broad buttock, tender hide:
  Look, what a horse should have he did not lack,
  Save a proud rider on so proud a back.

Sometime he scuds far off, and there he stares;
Anon he starts at stirring of a feather;
To bid the wind a base he now prepares,
And whe'r he run or fly they know not whether;
  For through his mane and tail the high wind sings,
  Fanning the hairs, who wave like feather'd wings.

He looks upon his love, and neighs unto her;
She answers him as if she knew his mind;
Being proud, as females are, to see him woo her,
She puts on outward strangeness, seems unkind,
  Spurns at his love and scorns the heat he feels,
  Beating his kind embracements with her heels.

Then, like a melancholy malecontent,
He vails his tail that, like a falling plume,
Cool shadow to his melting buttock lent:
He stamps, and bites the poor flies in his fume.
  His love, perceiving how he is enraged,
  Grew kinder, and his fury was assuaged.

His testy master goeth about to take him;
When, lo! the unback'd breeder, full of fear,
Jealous of catching, swiftly doth forsake him,
With her the horse, and left Adonis there.
  As they were mad, unto the wood they hie them,
  Out-stripping crows that strive to over-fly them.

All swoln with chafing, down Adonis sits,
Banning his boisterous and unruly beast:
And now the happy season once more fits,
That love-sick Love by pleading may be blest;
  For lovers say, the heart hath treble wrong
  When it is barr'd the aidance of the tongue.

An oven that is stopp'd, or river stay'd,
Burneth more hotly, swelleth with more rage:
So of concealed sorrow may be said;
Free vent of words love's fire doth assuage;
  But when the heart's attorney once is mute,
  The client breaks, as desperate in his suit.

He sees her coming, and begins to glow,
Even as a dying coal revives with wind,
And with his bonnet hides his angry brow;
Looks on the dull earth with disturbed mind,
  Taking no notice that she is so nigh,
  For all askance he holds her in his eye.

O! what a sight it was, wistly to view
How she came stealing to the wayward boy;
To note the fighting conflict of her hue,
How white and red each other did destroy:
  But now her cheek was pale, and by and by
  It flash'd forth fire, as lightning from the sky.

Now was she just before him as he sat,
And like a lowly lover down she kneels;
With one fair hand she heaveth up his hat,
Her other tender hand his fair cheek feels:
  His tenderer cheek receives her soft hand's print,
  As apt as new-fall'n snow takes any dint.

O! what a war of looks was then between them;
Her eyes petitioners to his eyes suing;
His eyes saw her eyes as they had not seen them;
Her eyes woo'd still, his eyes disdain'd the wooing:
  And all this dumb play had his acts made plain
  With tears, which, chorus-like, her eyes did rain.

Full gently now she takes him by the hand,
A lily prison'd in a gaol of snow,
Or ivory in an alabaster band;
So white a friend engirts so white a foe:
  This beauteous combat, wilful and unwilling,
  Show'd like two silver doves that sit a-billing.

Once more the engine of her thoughts began:
'O fairest mover on this mortal round,
Would thou wert as I am, and I a man,
My heart all whole as thine, thy heart my wound;

For one sweet look thy help I would assure thee,
Though nothing but my body's bane would cure thee.'

'Give me my hand,' saith he, 'why dost thou feel it?'
'Give me my heart,' saith she, 'and thou shalt have it;
O! give it me, lest thy hard heart do steel it,
And being steel'd, soft sighs can never grave it:
Then love's deep groans I never shall regard,
Because Adonis' heart hath made mine hard.'

'For shame!' he cries, 'let go, and let me go;
My day's delight is past, my horse is gone,
And 't is your fault I am bereft him so:
I pray you hence, and leave me here alone:
For all my mind, my thought, my busy care,
Is how to get my palfrey from the mare.'

Thus she replies: 'Thy palfrey, as he should,
Welcomes the warm approach of sweet desire:
Affection is a coal that must be cool'd;
Else, suffer'd, it will set the heart on fire.
The sea hath bounds, but deep desire hath none;
Therefore no marvel though thy horse be gone.

'How like a jade he stood, tied to the tree,
Servilely master'd with a leathern rein!
But when he saw his love, his youth's fair fee,
He held such petty bondage in disdain;
Throwing the base thong from his bending crest,
Enfranchising his mouth, his back, his breast.

'Who sees his true-love in her naked bed,
Teaching the sheets a whiter hue than white,
But, when his glutton eye so full hath fed,
His other agents aim at like delight?
Who is so faint, that dare not be so bold
To touch the fire, the weather being cold?

'Let me excuse thy courser, gentle boy,
And learn of him, I heartily beseech thee,
To take advantage on presented joy;
Though I were dumb, yet his proceedings teach thee.
O! learn to love; the lesson is but plain,
And once made perfect, never lost again.'

'I know not love,' quoth he, 'nor will not know it,
Unless it be a boar, and then I chase it;
'T is much to borrow, and I will not owe it;
My love to love is love but to disgrace it;
For I have heard it is a life in death,
That laughs, and weeps, and all but with a breath.

'Who wears a garment shapeless and unfinish'd?
Who plucks the bud before one leaf put forth?
If springing things be any jot diminish'd,
They wither in their prime, prove nothing worth:
The colt that 's back'd and burden'd being young
Loseth his pride and never waxeth strong.

You hurt my hand with wringing; let us part,
and leave this idle theme, this bootless chat:
Remove your siege from my unyielding heart;
To love's alarms it will not ope the gate:
Dismiss your vows, your feigned tears, your flattery;
For where a heart is hard, they make no battery.'

'What! canst thou talk?' quoth she, 'hast thou a tongue?
O! would thou hadst not, or I had no hearing;
Thy mermaid's voice hath done me double wrong;
I had my load before, now press'd with bearing:
Melodious discord, heavenly tune harsh-sounding,
Ear's deep-sweet music, and heart's deep-sore wounding.

'Had I no eyes but ears, my ears would love
That inward beauty and invisible;
Or were I deaf, thy outward parts would move
Each part in me that were but sensible:
Though neither eyes nor ears, to hear nor see,
Yet should I be in love by touching thee.

'Say, that the sense of feeling were bereft me,
And that I could not see, nor hear, nor touch,
And nothing but the very smell were left me,
Yet would my love to thee be still as much;
For from the still'tory of thy face excelling
Comes breath perfumed that breedeth love by smelling.

'But O! what banquet wert thou to the taste,
Being nurse and feeder of the other four;
Would they not wish the feast might ever last,
And bid Suspicion double-lock the door,
Lest Jealousy, that sour unwelcome guest,
Should, by his stealing in, disturb the feast?'

Once more the ruby-colour'd portal open'd,
Which to his speech did honey passage yield;
Like a red morn, that ever yet betoken'd
Wreck to the seaman, tempest to the field,
Sorrow to shepherds, woe unto the birds,
Gusts and foul flaws to herdmen and to herds.

This ill presage advisedly she marketh:
Even as the wind is hush'd before it raineth,
Or as the wolf doth grin before he barketh,
Or as the berry breaks before it staineth,
Or like the deadly bullet of a gun,
His meaning struck her ere his words begun.

And at his look she flatly falleth down,
For looks kill love and love by looks reviveth;
A smile recures the wounding of a frown;
But blessed bankrupt, that by love so thriveth!
The silly boy, believing she is dead,
Claps her pale cheek, till clapping makes it red;

And all amazed brake off his late intent,
For sharply he did think to reprehend her,
Which cunning love did wittily prevent:
Fair fall the wit that can so well defend her!
For on the grass she lies as she were slain,
Till his breath breatheth life in her again.

He wrings her nose, he strikes her on the cheeks,
He bends her fingers, holds her pulses hard,
He chafes her lips; a thousand ways he seeks
To mend the hurt that his unkindness marr'd:
He kisses her; and she, by her good will,
Will never rise, so he will kiss her still.

The night of sorrow now is turn'd to day:
Her two blue windows faintly she up-heaveth,
Like the fair sun, when in his fresh array
He cheers the morn and all the earth relieveth:
And as the bright sun glorifies the sky,
So is her face illumined with her eye;

Whose beams upon his hairless face are fix'd,
As if from thence they borrow'd all their shine.
Were never four such lamps together mixed,
Had not his clouded with his brow's repine;
But hers, which through the crystal tears gave light,
Shone like the moon in water seen by night.

'O! where am I?' quoth she, 'in earth or heaven,
Or in the ocean drench'd, or in the fire?
What hour is this? or morn or weary even?
Do I delight to die, or life desire?
But now I lived, and life was death's annoy;
But now I died, and death was lively joy.

'O! thou didst kill me; kill me once again:
Thy eyes' shrewd tutor, that hard heart of thine,
Hath taught them scornful tricks and such disdain
That they have murder'd this poor heart of mine;
And these mine eyes, true leaders to their queen,
But for thy piteous lips no more had seen.

'Long may they kiss each other for this cure!
O! never let their crimson liveries wear;
And as they last, their verdure still endure,
To drive infection from the dangerous year:
That the star-gazers, having writ on death,
May say, the plague is banish'd by thy breath.

'Pure lips, sweet seals in my soft lips imprinted,
What bargains may I make, still to be sealing?
To sell myself I can be well contented,
So thou wilt buy and pay and use good dealing;
Which purchase if thou make, for fear of slips
Set thy seal-manual on my wax-red lips.

'A thousand kisses buys my heart from me;
And pay them at thy leisure, one by one.
What is ten hundred touches unto thee?
Are they not quickly told and quickly gone?
Say, for non-payment that the debt should double,
Is twenty hundred kisses such a trouble?'

'Fair queen,' quoth he, 'if any love you owe me,
Measure my strangeness with my unripe years:
Before I know myself, seek not to know me;
No fisher but the ungrown fry forbears:
The mellow plum doth fall, the green sticks fast,
Or being early pluck'd is sour to taste.

'Look! the world's comforter, with weary gait,
His day's hot task hath ended in the west;
The owl, night's herald, shrieks 't is very late;
The sheep are gone to fold, birds to their nest,
And coal-black clouds that shadow heaven's light
Do summon us to part and bid good night.

'Now let me say good night, and so say you;
If you will say so, you shall have a kiss.'
'Good night,' quoth she; and ere he says adieu,
The honey fee of parting tender'd is:
Her arms do lend his neck a sweet embrace;
Incorporate then they seem, face grows to face.

Till, breathless, he disjoin'd, and backward drew
The heavenly moisture, that sweet coral mouth,
Whose precious taste her thirsty lips well knew,
Whereon they surfeit, yet complain on drouth:
He with her plenty press'd, she faint with dearth,
Their lips together glued, fall to the earth.

Now quick desire hath caught the yielding prey,
And glutton-like she feeds, yet never filleth;
Her lips are conquerors, his lips obey,
Paying what ransom the insulter willeth;
Whose vulture thought doth pitch the price so high,
That she will draw his lips' rich treasure dry.

And having felt the sweetness of the spoil,
With blindfold fury she begins to forage;
Her face doth reek and smoke, her blood doth boil,
And careless lust stirs up a desperate courage;
Planting oblivion, beating reason back,
Forgetting shame's pure blush and honour's wrack.

Hot, faint, and weary, with her hard embracing,
Like a wild bird being tamed with too much handling,
Or as the fleet-foot roe that's tired with chasing,
Or like the froward infant still'd with dandling,
He now obeys, and now no more resisteth,
While she takes all she can, not all she listeth.

What wax so frozen but dissolves with tempering,
And yields at last to every light impression?
Things out of hope are compass'd oft with venturing,
Chiefly in love, whose leave exceeds commission:
Affection faints not like a pale-faced coward,
But then woos best when most his choice is froward.

When he did frown, O! had she then gave over,
Such nectar from his lips she had not suck'd.
Foul words and frowns must not repel a lover;
What though the rose have prickles, yet 't is pluck'd:
Were beauty under twenty locks kept fast,
Yet love breaks through and picks them all at last.

For pity now she can no more detain him;
The poor fool prays her that he may depart:
She is resolved no longer to restrain him,
Bids him farewell, and look well to her heart,
The which, by Cupid's bow she doth protest,
He carries thence incaged in his breast.

'Sweet boy,' she says, 'this night I'll waste in sorrow,
For my sick heart commands mine eyes to watch.
Tell me, Love's master, shall we meet to-morrow?
Say, shall we? shall we? wilt thou make the match?'
He tells her, no; to-morrow he intends
To hunt the boar with certain of his friends.

'The boar!' quoth she; whereat a sudden pale,
Like lawn being spread upon the blushing rose,
Usurps her cheek, she trembles at his tale,
And on his neck her yoking arms she throws:
She sinketh down, still hanging by his neck,
He on her belly falls, she on her back.

Now is she in the very lists of love,
Her champion mounted for the hot encounter:
All is imaginary she doth prove,
He will not manage her, although he mount her;
That worse than Tantalus' is her annoy,
To clip Elysium and to lack her joy.

Even as poor birds, deceived with painted grapes,
Do surfeit by the eye and pine the maw,
Even so she languisheth in her mishaps,
As those poor birds that helpless berries saw.
The warm effects which she in him finds missing,
She seeks to kindle with continual kissing.

But all in vain; good queen, it will not be:
She hath assay'd as much as may be proved;
Her pleading hath deserved a greater fee;
She's Love, she loves, and yet she is not loved.
'Fie, fie!' he says, 'you crush me; let me go;
You have no reason to withhold me so.'

'Thou hadst been gone,' quoth she, 'sweet boy, ere this,
But that thou told'st me thou wouldst hunt the boar.
O! be advised; thou know'st not what it is
With javelin's point a churlish swine to gore,
Whose tushes never sheathed he whetteth still,
Like to a mortal butcher, bent to kill.

'On his bow-back he hath a battle set
Of bristly pikes, that ever threat his foes;
His eyes like glow-worms shine when he doth fret;
His snout digs sepulchres where'er he goes;
Being moved, he strikes whate'er is in his way,
And whom he strikes his cruel tushes slay.

His brawny sides, with hairy bristles arm'd,
Are better proof than thy spear's point can enter;
His short thick neck cannot be easily harm'd;
Being ireful, on the lion he will venture:
The thorny brambles and embracing bushes,
As fearful of him, part, through whom he rushes.

'Alas! he nought esteems that face of thine,
To which Love's eyes pay tributary gazes;
Nor thy soft hands, sweet lips, and crystal eyne,
Whose full perfection all the world amazes;
But having thee at vantage, wondrous dread!
Would root these beauties as he roots the mead.

'O! let him keep his loathsome cabin still;
Beauty hath nought to do with such foul fiends:
Come not within his danger by thy will;
They that thrive well take counsel of their friends.
When thou didst name the boar, not to dissemble,
I fear'd thy fortune, and my joints did tremble.

'Didst thou not mark my face? was it not white?
Saw'st thou not signs of fear lurk in mine eye?
Grew I not faint? and fell I not downright?
Within my bosom, whereon thou dost lie,
My boding heart pants, beats, and takes no rest,
But, like an earthquake, shakes thee on my breast.

'For where Love reigns, disturbing Jealousy
Doth call himself Affection's sentinel;
Gives false alarms, suggesteth mutiny,
And in a peaceful hour doth cry "Kill, kill!"
Distempering gentle Love in his desire,
As air and water do abate the fire.

'This sour informer, this bate-breeding spy,
This canker that eats up Love's tender spring,
This carry-tale, dissentious Jealousy,
That sometime true news, sometime false doth bring,
Knocks at my heart, and whispers in mine ear
That if I love thee, I thy death should fear:

'And more than so, presenteth to mine eye
The picture of an angry-chafing boar,
Under whose sharp fangs on his back doth lie
An image like thyself, all stain'd with gore;
Whose blood upon the fresh flowers being shed
Doth make them droop with grief and hang the head.

'What should I do, seeing thee so indeed,
That tremble at the imagination?
The thought of it doth make my faint heart bleed,
And fear doth teach it divination:
I prophesy thy death, my living sorrow,
If thou encounter with the boar to-morrow.

'But if thou needs wilt hunt, be ruled by me;
Uncouple at the timorous flying hare,
Or at the fox which lives by subtlety,
Or at the roe which no encounter dare:
Pursue these fearful creatures o'er the downs,
And on thy well-breath'd horse keep with thy hounds.

'And when thou hast on foot the purblind hare,
Mark the poor wretch, to overshoot his troubles
How he outruns the wind, and with what care
He cranks and crosses with a thousand doubles:
The many musets through the which he goes
Are like a labyrinth to amaze his foes.

'Sometime he runs among a flock of sheep,
To make the cunning hounds mistake their smell

And sometime where earth-delving conies keep,
To stop the loud pursuers in their yell,
And sometime sorteth with a herd of deer;
Danger deviseth shifts; wit waits on fear:

'For there his smell with others being mingled,
The hot scent-snuffing hounds are driven to doubt,
Ceasing their clamorous cry till they have singled
With much ado the cold fault cleanly out;
Then do they spend their mouths: Echo replies,
As if another chase were in the skies.

'By this, poor Wat, far off upon a hill,
Stands on his hinder legs with listening ear,
To hearken if his foes pursue him still:
Anon their loud alarums he doth hear;
And now his grief may be compared well
To one sore sick that hears the passing-bell.

'Then shalt thou see the dew-bedabbled wretch
Turn, and return, indenting with the way;
Each envious briar his weary legs doth scratch,
Each shadow makes him stop, each murmur stay:
For misery is trodden on by many,
And being low never relieved by any.

'Lie quietly, and hear a little more;
Nay, do not struggle, for thou shalt not rise:
To make thee hate the hunting of the boar,
Unlike myself thou hear'st me moralize,
Applying this to that, and so to so;
For love can comment upon every woe.

'Where did I leave?' 'No matter where,' quoth he;
'Leave me, and then the story aptly ends:
The night is spent.' 'Why, what of that?' quoth she.
'I am,' quoth he, 'expected of my friends;
And now 't is dark, and going I shall fall.'
'In night,' quoth she, 'desire sees best of all.

'But if thou fall, O! then imagine this,
The earth, in love with thee, thy footing trips,
And all is but to rob thee of a kiss.
Rich preys make true men thieves; so do thy lips
Make modest Dian cloudy and forlorn,
Lest she should steal a kiss and die forsworn.

'Now of this dark night I perceive the reason:
Cynthia for shame obscures her silver shine,
Till forging Nature be condemn'd of treason,
For stealing moulds from heaven that were divine;
Wherein she framed thee in high heaven's despite,
To shame the sun by day and her by night.

'And therefore hath she bribed the Destinies
To cross the curious workmanship of nature,
To mingle beauty with infirmities,
And pure perfection with impure defeature;
Making it subject to the tyranny
Of mad mischances and much misery;

'As burning fevers, agues pale and faint,
Life-poisoning pestilence and frenzies wood,
The marrow-eating sickness, whose attaint
Disorder breeds by heating of the blood;
Surfeits, imposthumes, grief, and damn'd despair,
Swear Nature's death for framing thee so fair.

'And not the least of all these maladies
But in one minute's fight brings beauty under:
Both favour, savour, hue, and qualities,
Whereat the impartial gazer late did wonder,
Are on the sudden wasted, thaw'd and done,
As mountain-snow melts with the mid-day sun.

'Therefore, despite of fruitless chastity,
Love-lacking vestals and self-loving nuns,
That on the earth would breed a scarcity,
And barren dearth of daughters and of sons,
Be prodigal: the lamp that burns by night
Dries up his oil to lend the world his light.

'What is thy body but a swallowing grave,
Seeming to bury that posterity
Which by the rights of time thou needs must have,
If thou destroy them not in dark obscurity?
If so, the world will hold thee in disdain,
Sith in thy pride so fair a hope is slain.

So in thyself thyself art made away;
A mischief worse than civil home-bred strife,
Or theirs whose desperate hands themselves do slay,
Or butcher-sire that reaves his son of life.
Foul-cankering rust the hidden treasure frets,
But gold that 's put to use more gold begets.'

'Nay then,' quoth Adon, 'you will fall again
Into your idle over-handled theme;
The kiss I gave you is bestow'd in vain,
And all in vain you strive against the stream;
For by this black-faced night, desire's foul nurse,
Your treatise makes me like you worse and worse.

'If love have lent you twenty thousand tongues,
And every tongue more moving than your own,
Bewitching like the wanton mermaid's songs,
Yet from mine ear the tempting tune is blown;
For know, my heart stands armed in mine ear,
And will not let a false sound enter there;

'Lest the deceiving harmony should run
Into the quiet closure of my breast;
And then my little heart were quite undone,
In his bedchamber to be barr'd of rest.
No, lady, no; my heart longs not to groan,
But soundly sleeps, while now it sleeps alone.

'What have you urged that I cannot reprove?
The path is smooth that leadeth on to danger;
I hate not love, but your device in love,
That lends embracements unto every stranger.
You do it for increase: O strange excuse!
When reason is the bawd to lust's abuse.

'Call it not love, for Love to heaven is fled,
Since sweating Lust on earth usurp'd his name;
Under whose simple semblance he hath fed
Upon fresh beauty, blotting it with blame;

Which the hot tyrant stains and soon bereaves,
As caterpillars do the tender leaves.

'Love comforteth like sunshine after rain,
But Lust's effect is tempest after sun;
Love's gentle spring doth always fresh remain,
Lust's winter comes ere summer half be done.
Love surfeits not, Lust like a glutton dies;
Love is all truth, Lust full of forged lies.

'More I could tell, but more I dare not say;
The text is old, the orator too green.
Therefore, in sadness, now I will away;
My face is full of shame, my heart of teen:
Mine ears, that to your wanton talk attended,
Do burn themselves for having so offended.'

With this he breaketh from the sweet embrace
Of those fair arms which bound him to her breast,
And homeward through the dark laund runs apace;
Leaves Love upon her back deeply distress'd.
Look, how a bright star shooteth from the sky,
So glides he in the night from Venus' eye;

Which after him she darts, as one on shore
Gazing upon a late-embarked friend,
Till the wild waves will have him seen no more,
Whose ridges with the meeting clouds contend:
So did the merciless and pitchy night
Fold in the object that did feed her sight.

Whereat amazed, as one that unaware
Hath dropp'd a precious jewel in the flood,
Or 'stonish'd as night-wanderers often are,
Their light blown out in some mistrustful wood;
Even so confounded in the dark she lay,
Having lost the fair discovery of her way.

And now she beats her heart, whereat it groans,
That all the neighbour caves, as seeming troubled,
Make verbal repetition of her moans;
Passion on passion deeply is redoubled:
'Ay me!' she cries, and twenty times 'Woe, woe!'
And twenty echoes twenty times cry so.

She marking them begins a wailing note,
And sings extemporally a woeful ditty;
How love makes young men thrall and old men dote;
How love is wise in folly, foolish-witty:
Her heavy anthem still concludes in woe,
And still the choir of echoes answer so.

Her song was tedious, and outwore the night,
For lovers' hours are long, though seeming short.
If pleased themselves, others, they think, delight
In such-like circumstance, with such-like sport:
Their copious stories, oftentimes begun,
End without audience, and are never done.

For who hath she to spend the night withal,
But idle sounds resembling parasites,
Like shrill-tongued tapsters answering every call,
Soothing the humour of fantastic wits?
She says ''T is so:' they answer all ''T is so;'
And would say after her, if she said 'No.'

Lo! here the gentle lark, weary of rest,
From his moist cabinet mounts up on high,
And wakes the morning, from whose silver breast
The sun ariseth in his majesty;
Who doth the world so gloriously behold,
That cedar-tops and hills seem burnish'd gold.

Venus salutes him with this fair good-morrow:
'O thou clear god, and patron of all light,
From whom each lamp and shining star doth borrow
The beauteous influence that makes him bright,
There lives a son that suck'd an earthly mother,
May lend thee light, as thou dost lend to other.

This said, she hasteth to a myrtle grove,
Musing the morning is so much o'erworn,
And yet she hears no tidings of her love;
She hearkens for his hounds and for his horn:
Anon she hears them chant it lustily,
And all in haste she coasteth to the cry.

And as she runs, the bushes in the way
Some catch her by the neck, some kiss her face,
Some twine about her thigh to make her stay:
She wildly breaketh from their strict embrace,
Like a milch doe, whose swelling dugs do ache,
Hasting to feed her fawn hid in some brake.

By this she hears the hounds are at a bay;
Whereat she starts, like one that spies an adder
Wreathed up in fatal folds just in his way,
The fear whereof doth make him shake and shudder;
Even so the timorous yelping of the hounds
Appals her senses, and her spirit confounds.

For now she knows it is no gentle chase,
But the blunt boar, rough bear, or lion proud,
Because the cry remaineth in one place,
Where fearfully the dogs exclaim aloud:
Finding their enemy to be so curst,
They all strain courtesy who shall cope him first.

This dismal cry rings sadly in her ear,
Through which it enters to surprise her heart;
Who, overcome by doubt and bloodless fear,
With cold-pale weakness numbs each feeling part;
Like soldiers, when their captain once doth yield,
They basely fly and dare not stay the field.

Thus stands she in a trembling ecstacy,
Till, cheering up her senses all dismay'd,
She tells them 't is a causeless fantasy,
And childish error, that they are afraid;

Bids them leave quaking, bids them fear no more:
And with that word she spied the hunted boar,

Whose frothy mouth bepainted all with red,
Like milk and blood being mingled both together,
A second fear through all her sinews spread,
Which madly hurries her she knows not whither:
This way she runs, and now she will no further,
But back retires to rate the boar for murther.

A thousand spleens bear her a thousand ways,
She treads the path that she untreads again;
Her more than haste is mated with delays,
Like the proceedings of a drunken brain,
Full of respects, yet nought at all respecting,
In hand with all things, nought at all effecting.

Here kennell'd in a brake she finds a hound,
And asks the weary caitiff for his master,
And there another licking of his wound,
'Gainst venom'd sores the only sovereign plaster;
And here she meets another sadly scowling,
To whom she speaks, and he replies with howling.

When he hath ceased his ill-resounding noise,
Another flap-mouth'd mourner, black and grim,
Against the welkin volleys out his voice;
Another and another answer him,
Clapping their proud tails to the ground below,
Shaking their scratch'd ears, bleeding as they go

Look, how the world's poor people are amazed
At apparitions, signs, and prodigies,
Whereon with fearful eyes they long have gazed,
Infusing them with dreadful prophecies;
So she at these sad signs draws up her breath,
And sighing it again, exclaims on Death.

'Hard-favour'd tyrant, ugly, meagre, lean,
Hateful divorce of love,' thus chides she Death,
'Grim-grinning ghost, earth's worm, what dost thou mean
To stifle beauty and to steal his breath,
Who when he lived, his breath and beauty set
Gloss on the rose, smell to the violet?

'If he be dead, O no! it cannot be,
Seeing his beauty, thou should'st strike at it;
O yes! it may; thou hast no eyes to see,
But hatefully at random dost thou hit.
Thy mark is feeble age, but thy false dart
Mistakes that aim and cleaves an infant's heart.

'Had'st thou but bid beware, then he had spoke,
And hearing him thy power had lost his power.
The Destinies will curse thee for this stroke;
They bid thee crop a weed, thou pluck'st a flower.
Love's golden arrow at him should have fled,
And not Death's ebon dart, to strike him dead.

Dost thou drink tears, that thou provokest such weeping?
That may a heavy groan advantage thee?
Why hast thou cast into eternal sleeping
Those eyes that taught all other eyes to see?
Now Nature cares not for thy mortal vigour,
Since her best work is ruin'd with thy rigour.'

Here overcome, as one full of despair,
She vail'd her eyelids, who, like sluices, stopp'd
The crystal tide that from her two cheeks fair
In the sweet channel of her bosom dropp'd;
But through the flood-gates breaks the silver rain,
And with his strong course opens them again.

O! how her eyes and tears did lend and borrow;
Her eyes seen in the tears, tears in her eye;
Both crystals, where they view'd each other's sorrow,
Sorrow that friendly sighs sought still to dry;
But like a stormy day, now wind, now rain,
Sighs dry her cheeks, tears make them wet again.

Variable passions throng her constant woe,
As striving who should best become her grief;
All entertain'd, each passion labours so,
That every present sorrow seemeth chief,
But none is best; then join they altogether,
Like many clouds consulting for foul weather.

By this, far off she hears some huntsman holla;
A nurse's song ne'er pleased her babe so well:
The dire imagination she did follow
This sound of hope doth labour to expel;
For now reviving joy bids her rejoice,
And flatters her it is Adonis' voice.

Whereat her tears began to turn their tide,
Being prison'd in her eye, like pearls in glass;
Yet sometimes falls an orient drop beside,
Which her cheek melts, as scorning it should pass,
To wash the foul face of the sluttish ground,
Who is but drunken when she seemeth drown'd.

O hard-believing love! how strange it seems
Not to believe, and yet too credulous;
Thy weal and woe are both of them extremes;
Despair and hope make thee ridiculous:
The one doth flatter thee in thoughts unlikely,
In likely thoughts the other kills thee quickly.

Now she unweaves the web that she hath wrought,
Adonis lives, and Death is not to blame;
It was not she that call'd him all to naught,
Now she adds honours to his hateful name;
She clepes him king of graves, and grave for kings,
Imperious supreme of all mortal things.

'No, no,' quoth she, 'sweet Death, I did but jest;
Yet pardon me I felt a kind of fear
Whenas I met the boar, that bloody beast,
Which knows no pity, but is still severe;
Then, gentle shadow, truth I must confess,
I rail'd on thee, fearing my love's decease.

''T is not my fault: the boar provoked my tongue;
Be wreak'd on him, invisible commander;

'T is he, foul creature, that hath done thee wrong;
I did but act, he 's author of thy slander.
Grief hath two tongues, and never woman yet
Could rule them both without ten women's wit.'

Thus hoping that Adonis is alive,
Her rash suspect she doth extenuate;
And that his beauty may the better thrive,
With Death she humbly doth insinuate;
Tells him of trophies, statues, tombs, and stories
His victories, his triumphs, and his glories.

'O Jove!' quoth she, 'how much a fool was I
To be of such a weak and silly mind
To wail his death who lives and must not die
Till mutual overthrow of mortal kind;
For he being dead, with him is beauty slain,
And, beauty dead, black chaos comes again.

'Fie, fie, fond love! thou art so full of fear
As one with treasure laden, hemm'd with thieves;
Trifles, unwitnessed with eye or ear,
Thy coward heart with false bethinking grieves.'
Even at this word she hears a merry horn,
Whereat she leaps that was but late forlorn.

As falcon to the lure, away she flies;
The grass stoops not, she treads on it so light;
And in her haste unfortunately spies
The foul boar's conquest on her fair delight;
Which seen, her eyes, as murder'd with the view,
Like stars ashamed of day, themselves withdrew:

Or, as the snail, whose tender horns being hit,
Shrinks backward in his shelly cave with pain,
And there, all smother'd up, in shade doth sit,
Long after fearing to creep forth again;
So, at his bloody view, her eyes are fled
Into the deep dark cabins of her head:

Where they resign their office and their light
To the disposing of her troubled brain;
Who bids them still consort with ugly night,
And never wound the heart with looks again;
Who, like a king perplexed in his throne,
By their suggestion gives a deadly groan;

Whereat each tributary subject quakes;
As when the wind, imprison'd in the ground,
Struggling for passage, earth's foundation shakes,
Which with cold terror doth men's minds confound.
This mutiny each part doth so surprise
That from their dark beds once more leap her eyes;

And, being open'd, threw unwilling light
Upon the wide wound that the boar had trench'd
In his soft flank; whose wonted lily white
With purple tears, that his wound wept, was drench'd:
No flower was nigh, no grass, herb, leaf, or weed,
But stole his blood and seem'd with him to bleed.

This solemn sympathy poor Venus noteth,
Over one shoulder doth she hang her head,
Dumbly she passions, franticly she doteth;
She thinks he could not die, he is not dead:
Her voice is stopp'd, her joints forget to bow,
Her eyes are mad that they have wept till now.

Upon his hurt she looks so steadfastly,
That her sight dazzling makes the wound seem three;
And then she reprehends her mangling eye,
That makes more gashes where no breach should be:
His face seems twain, each several limb is doubled;
For oft the eye mistakes, the brain being troubled.

'My tongue cannot express my grief for one,
And yet,' quoth she, 'behold two Adons dead!
My sighs are blown away, my salt tears gone,
Mine eyes are turn'd to fire, my heart to lead:
Heavy heart's lead, melt at mine eyes' red fire!
So shall I die by drops of hot desire.

'Alas! poor world, what treasure hast thou lost?
What face remains alive that 's worth the viewing?
Whose tongue is music now? what canst thou boast
Of things long since, or any thing ensuing?
The flowers are sweet, their colours fresh and trim;
But true-sweet beauty lived and died with him.

'Bonnet nor veil henceforth no creature wear!
Nor sun nor wind will ever strive to kiss you:
Having no fair to lose, you need not fear;
The sun doth scorn you, and the wind doth hiss you:
But when Adonis lived, sun and sharp air
Lurk'd like two thieves, to rob him of his fair:

'And therefore would he put his bonnet on,
Under whose brim the gaudy sun would peep;
The wind would blow it off, and, being gone,
Play with his locks: then would Adonis weep;
And straight, in pity of his tender years,
They both would strive who first should dry his tears.

'To see his face the lion walk'd along
Behind some hedge, because he would not fear him;
To recreate himself when he hath sung,
The tiger would be tame and gently hear him;
If he had spoke, the wolf would leave his prey
And never fright the silly lamb that day.

'When he beheld his shadow in the brook,
The fishes spread on it their golden gills;
When he was by, the birds such pleasure took,
That some would sing, some other in their bills
Would bring him mulberries and ripe-red cherries;
He fed them with his sight, they him with berries.

'But this toul, grim, and urchin-snouted boar,
Whose downward eye still looketh for a grave,
Ne'er saw the beauteous livery that he wore;
Witness the entertainment that he gave:
If he did see his face, why then I know
He thought to kiss him, and hath kill'd him so.

''T is true, 't is true; thus was Adonis slain:
He ran upon the boar with his sharp spear,
Who did not whet his teeth at him again,
But by a kiss thought to persuade him there;
And nuzzling in his flank, the loving swine
Sheathed unaware the tusk in his soft groin.

'Had I been tooth'd like him, I must confess,
With kissing him I should have kill'd him first;
But he is dead, and never did he bless
My youth with his; the more am I accurst.'
With this she falleth in the place she stood,
And stains her face with his congealed blood.

She looks upon his lips, and they are pale;
She takes him by the hand, and that is cold;
She whispers in his ears a heavy tale,
As if they heard the woeful words she told;
She lifts the coffer-lids that close his eyes,
Where, lo! two lamps, burnt out, in darkness lies;

Two glasses, where herself herself beheld
A thousand times, and now no more reflect;
Their virtue lost, wherein they late excell'd,
And every beauty robb'd of his effect:
'Wonder of time,' quoth she, 'this is my spite,
That, thou being dead, the day should yet be light.

'Since thou art dead, lo! here I prophesy,
Sorrow on love hereafter shall attend:
It shall be waited on with jealousy,
Find sweet beginning, but unsavoury end;
Ne'er settled equally, but high or low;
That all love's pleasure shall not match his woe.

'It shall be fickle, false, and full of fraud,
Bud and be blasted in a breathing-while;
The bottom poison, and the top o'erstraw'd
With sweets that shall the truest sight beguile:
The strongest body shall it make most weak,
Strike the wise dumb and teach the fool to speak.

'It shall be sparing and too full of riot,
Teaching decrepit age to tread the measures;
The staring ruffian shall it keep in quiet,
Pluck down the rich, enrich the poor with treasures;
It shall be raging mad, and silly mild,
Make the young old, the old become a child.

'It shall suspect where is no cause of fear;
It shall not fear where it should most mistrust;
It shall be merciful, and too severe,
And most deceiving when it seems most just;
Perverse it shall be, where it shows most toward,
Put fear to valour, courage to the coward.

'It shall be cause of war and dire events,
And set dissension 'twixt the son and sire;
Subject and servile to all discontents,
As dry combustious matter is to fire:
Sith in his prime Death doth my love destroy,
They that love best their loves shall not enjoy.'

By this, the boy that by her side lay kill'd
Was melted like a vapour from her sight,
And in his blood that on the ground lay spill'd,
A purple flower sprung up, chequer'd with white;
Resembling well his pale cheeks, and the blood
Which in round drops upon their whiteness stood.

She bows her head, the new sprung flower to smell,
Comparing it to her Adonis' breath,
And says within her bosom it shall dwell,
Since he himself is reft from her by death:
She crops the stalk, and in the breach appears
Green dropping sap, which she compares to tears.

'Poor flower,' quoth she, 'this was thy father's guise,
Sweet issue of a more sweet-smelling sire,
For every little grief to wet his eyes:
To grow unto himself was his desire,
And so 't is thine; but know, it is as good
To wither in my breast as in his blood.

'Here was thy father's bed, here in my breast;
Thou art the next of blood, and 't is thy right:
Lo! in this hollow cradle take thy rest,
My throbbing heart shall rock thee day and night:
There shall not be one minute in an hour
Wherein I will not kiss my sweet love's flower.'

Thus weary of the world, away she hies,
And yokes her silver doves; by whose swift aid
Their mistress mounted through the empty skies
In her light chariot quickly is convey'd;
Holding their course to Paphos, where their queen
Means to immure herself and not be seen.

THE RAPE OF LUCRECE

TO THE

RIGHT HONOURABLE HENRY WRIOTHESLY,

EARL OF SOUTHAMPTON AND BARON
OF TICHFIELD.

The love I dedicate to your lordship is without end; whereof this pamphlet, without beginning, is but a superfluous moiety. The warrant I have of your honourable disposition, not the worth of my untutored lines, makes it assured of acceptance. What I have done is yours; what I have to do is yours; being part in all I have, devoted yours. Were my worth greater, my duty would show greater; meantime, as it is, it is bound to your lordship, to whom I wish long life, still lengthened with all happiness.

Your lordship's in all duty,

WILLIAM SHAKESPEARE.

THE ARGUMENT.

Lucius Tarquinius, for his excessive pride surnamed Superbus, after he had caused his own father-in-law Servius Tullius to be cruelly murdered, and, contrary to the Roman laws and customs, not requiring or staying for the people's suffrages, had possessed himself of the kingdom, went, accompanied with his sons and other noblemen of Rome, to besiege Ardea. During which siege the principal men of the army meeting one evening at the tent of Sextus Tarquinius, the king's son, in their discourses after supper every one commended the virtues of his own wife: among whom Collatinus extolled the incomparable chastity of his wife Lucretia. In that pleasant humour they all posted to Rome; and intending, by their secret and sudden arrival, to make trial of that which every one had before avouched, only Collatinus finds his wife, though it were late in the night, spinning amongst her maids: the other ladies were all found dancing and revelling, or in several disports. Whereupon the noblemen yielded Collatinus the victory, and his wife the fame. At that time Sextus Tarquinius being inflamed with Lucrece' beauty, yet smothering his passions for the present, departed with the rest back to the camp; from whence he shortly after privily withdrew himself, and was, according to his estate, royally entertained and lodged by Lucrece at Collatium. The same night he treacherously stealeth into her chamber, violently ravished her, and early in the morning speedeth away. Lucrece, in this lamentable plight, hastily dispatcheth messengers, one to Rome for her father, another to the camp for Collatine. They came, the one accompanied with Junius Brutus, the other with Publius Valerius; and finding Lucrece attired in mourning habit, demanded the cause of her sorrow. She, first taking an oath of them for her revenge, revealed the actor, and whole manner of his dealing, and withal suddenly stabbed herself. Which done, with one consent they all vowed to root out the whole hated family of the Tarquins; and bearing the dead body to Rome, Brutus acquainted the people with the doer and manner of the vile deed, with a bitter invective against the tyranny of the king: wherewith the people were so moved, that with one consent and a general acclamation the Tarquins were all exiled, and the state government changed from kings to consuls.

From the besieged Ardea all in post,
Borne by the trustless wings of false desire,
Lust-breathed Tarquin leaves the Roman host,
And to Collatium bears the lightless fire
Which, in pale embers hid, lurks to aspire,
  And girdle with embracing flames the waist
  Of Collatine's fair love, Lucrece the chaste.

Haply that name of 'chaste' unhappily set
This bateless edge on his keen appetite;
When Collatine unwisely did not let
To praise the clear unmatched red and white
Which triumph'd in that sky of his delight,
  Where mortal stars, as bright as heaven's beauties,
  With pure aspects did him peculiar duties.

For he the night before, in Tarquin's tent,
Unlock'd the treasure of his happy state;
What priceless wealth the heavens had him lent

In the possession of his beauteous mate;
Reckoning his fortune at such high-proud rate,
That kings might be espoused to more fame,
But king nor peer to such a peerless dame.

O happiness enjoy'd but of a few!
And, if possess'd, as soon decay'd and done
As is the morning's silver-melting dew
Against the golden splendour of the sun;
An expired date, cancell'd ere well begun:
Honour and beauty, in the owner's arms,
Are weakly fortress'd from a world of harms.

Beauty itself doth of itself persuade
The eyes of men without an orator;
What needeth then apologies be made
To set forth that which is so singular?
Or why is Collatine the publisher
Of that rich jewel he should keep unknown
From thievish ears, because it is his own?

Perchance his boast of Lucrece' sovereignty
Suggested this proud issue of a king;
For by our ears our hearts oft tainted be:
Perchance that envy of so rich a thing,
Braving compare, disdainfully did sting
His high-pitch'd thoughts, that meaner men should vaunt
That golden hap which their superiors want.

But some untimely thought did instigate
His all-too-timeless speed, if none of those:
His honour, his affairs, his friends, his state,
Neglected all, with swift intent he goes
To quench the coal which in his liver glows.
O! rash false heat, wrapp'd in repentant cold,
Thy hasty spring still blasts, and ne'er grows old.

When at Collatium this false lord arrived,
Well was he welcomed by the Roman dame,
Within whose face beauty and virtue strived
Which of them both should underprop her fame:
When virtue bragg'd, beauty would blush for shame;
When beauty boasted blushes, in despite
Virtue would stain that or with silver white.

But beauty, in that white intituled,
From Venus' doves doth challenge that fair field;
Then virtue claims from beauty beauty's red,
Which virtue gave the golden age to gild
Their silver cheeks, and call'd it then their shield;
Teaching them thus to use it in the fight,
When shame assail'd, the red should fence the white.

This heraldry in Lucrece' face was seen,
Argued by beauty's red and virtue's white:
Of either's colour was the other queen,
Proving from world's minority their right:
Yet their ambition makes them still to fight;
The sovereignty of either being so great,
That oft they interchange each other's seat.

This silent war of lilies and of roses,
Which Tarquin view'd in her fair face's field,
In their pure ranks his traitor eye encloses;
Where, lest between them both it should be kill'd,
The coward captive vanquished doth yield
To those two armies that would let him go,
Rather than triumph in so false a foe.

Now thinks he that her husband's shallow tongue,
The niggard prodigal that praised her so,
In that high task hath done her beauty wrong,
Which far exceeds his barren skill to show:
Therefore that praise which Collatine doth owe
Enchanted Tarquin answers with surmise,
In silent wonder of still-gazing eyes.

This earthly saint, adored by this devil,
Little suspecteth the false worshipper;
For unstain'd thoughts do seldom dream on evil,
Birds never limed no secret bushes fear:
So guiltless she securely gives good cheer
And reverent welcome to her princely guest,
Whose inward ill no outward harm express'd:

For that he colour'd with his high estate,
Hiding base sin in plaits of majesty;
That nothing in him seem'd inordinate,
Save sometime too much wonder of his eye,
Which, having all, all could not satisfy;
But, poorly rich, so wanteth in his store,
That, cloy'd with much, he pineth still for more.

But she, that never coped with stranger eyes,
Could pick no meaning from their parling looks,
Nor read the subtle-shining secrecies
Writ in the glassy margents of such books.
She touch'd no unknown baits, nor fear'd no hooks;
Nor could she moralize his wanton sight,
More than his eyes were open'd to the light.

He stories to her ears her husband's fame,
Won in the fields of fruitful Italy;
And decks with praises Collatine's high name,
Made glorious by his manly chivalry
With bruised arms and wreaths of victory:
Her joy with heaved-up hand she doth express,
And, wordless, so greets heaven for his success.

Far from the purpose of his coming thither,
He makes excuses for his being there:
No cloudy show of stormy blustering weather
Doth yet in his fair welkin once appear;
Till sable Night, mother of Dread and Fear,
Upon the world dim darkness doth display,
And in her vaulty prison stows the Day.

For then is Tarquin brought unto his bed,
Intending weariness with heavy spright;
For after supper long he questioned
With modest Lucrece, and wore out the night;
Now leaden slumber with life's strength doth fight,
And every one to rest themselves betake,
Save thieves, and cares, and troubled minds that wake.

As one of which doth Tarquin lie revolving
The sundry dangers of his will's obtaining;
Yet ever to obtain his will resolving,
Though weak-built hopes persuade him to abstaining:
Despair to gain doth traffic oft for gaining;
  And when great treasure is the meed proposed,
  Though death be adjunct, there's no death supposed.

Those that much covet are with gain so fond,
That what they have not, that which they possess
They scatter and unloose it from their bond,
And so, by hoping more, they have but less;
Or, gaining more, the profit of excess
  Is but to surfeit, and such griefs sustain,
  That they prove bankrupt in this poor-rich gain.

The aim of all is but to nurse the life
With honour, wealth, and ease, in waning age;
And in this aim there is such thwarting strife,
That one for all, or all for one we gage;
As life for honour in fell battle's rage;
  Honour for wealth; and oft that wealth doth cost
  The death of all, and all together lost.

So that in venturing ill we leave to be
The things we are for that which we expect;
And this ambitious foul infirmity,
In having much, torments us with defect
Of that we have: so then we do neglect
  The thing we have; and, all for want of wit,
  Make something nothing by augmenting it.

Such hazard now must doting Tarquin make,
Pawning his honour to obtain his lust,
And for himself himself he must forsake:
Then where is truth, if there be no self-trust?
When shall he think to find a stranger just,
  When he himself himself confounds, betrays
  To slanderous tongues and wretched hateful days?

Now stole upon the time the dead of night,
When heavy sleep had closed up mortal eyes;
No comfortable star did lend his light,
No noise but owls' and wolves' death-boding cries;
Now serves the season that they may surprise
  The silly lambs; pure thoughts are dead and still,
  While lust and murder wake to stain and kill.

And now this lustful lord leap'd from his bed,
Throwing his mantle rudely o'er his arm;
Is madly toss'd between desire and dread;
Th' one sweetly flatters, th' other feareth harm;
But honest fear, bewitch'd with lust's foul charm,
  Doth too too oft betake him to retire,
  Beaten away by brain-sick rude desire.

His falchion on a flint he softly smiteth,
That from the cold stones sparks of fire do fly;
Whereat a waxen torch forthwith he lighteth,
Which must be lode-star to his lustful eye;
And to the flame thus speaks advisedly:
  'As from this cold flint I enforced this fire,
  So Lucrece must I force to my desire.'

Here pale with fear he doth premeditate
The dangers of his loathsome enterprise,
And in his inward mind he doth debate
What following sorrow may on this arise:
Then looking scornfully, he doth despise
  His naked armour of still-slaughter'd lust,
  And justly thus controls his thoughts unjust:

'Fair torch, burn out thy light, and lend it not
To darken her whose light excelleth thine;
And die, unhallow'd thoughts, before you blot
With your uncleanness that which is divine;
Offer pure incense to so pure a shrine:
  Let fair humanity abhor the deed
  That spots and stains love's modest snow-white weed.

'O shame to knighthood and to shining arms!
O foul dishonour to my household's grave!
O impious act, including all foul harms!
A martial man to be soft fancy's slave!
True valour still a true respect should have;
  Then my digression is so vile, so base,
  That it will live engraven in my face.

'Yea, though I die, the scandal will survive,
And be an eye-sore in my golden coat;
Some loathsome dash the herald will contrive,
To cipher me how fondly I did dote;
That my posterity, shamed with the note,
  Shall curse my bones, and hold it for no sin
  To wish that I their father had not been.

'What win I if I gain the thing I seek?
A dream, a breath, a froth of fleeting joy.
Who buys a minute's mirth to wail a week?
Or sells eternity to get a toy?
For one sweet grape who will the vine destroy?
  Or what fond beggar, but to touch the crown,
  Would with the sceptre straight be strucken down?

'If Collatinus dream of my intent,
Will he not wake, and in a desperate rage
Post hither, this vile purpose to prevent?
This siege that hath engirt his marriage,
This blur to youth, this sorrow to the sage,
  This dying virtue, this surviving shame,
  Whose crime will bear an ever-during blame?

'O! what excuse can my invention make,
When thou shalt charge me with so black a deed?
Will not my tongue be mute, my frail joints shake,
Mine eyes forgo their light, my false heart bleed?
The guilt being great, the fear doth still exceed;
  And extreme fear can neither fight nor fly,
  But coward-like with trembling terror die.

'Had Collatinus kill'd my son or sire,
Or lain in ambush to betray my life,
Or were he not my dear friend, this desire
Might have excuse to work upon his wife,
As in revenge or quittal of such strife:

But as he is my kinsman, my dear friend,
The shame and fault finds no excuse nor end.

'Shameful it is; ay, if the fact be known:
Hateful it is; there is no hate in loving:
I'll beg her love; but she is not her own:
The worst is but denial and reproving:
My will is strong, past reason's weak removing.
Who fears a sentence, or an old man's saw,
Shall by a painted cloth be kept in awe.'

Thus, graceless, holds he disputation
'Tween frozen conscience and hot-burning will,
And with good thoughts makes dispensation,
Urging the worser sense for vantage still;
Which in a moment doth confound and kill
All pure effects, and doth so far proceed.
That what is vile shows like a virtuous deed.

Quoth he, 'She took me kindly by the hand,
And gazed for tidings in my eager eyes,
Fearing some hard news from the war-like band,
Where her beloved Collatinus lies.
O! how her fear did make her colour rise:
First red as roses that on lawn we lay,
Then white as lawn, the roses took away.

'And how her hand, in my hand being lock'd,
Forced it to tremble with her loyal fear!
Which struck her sad, and then it faster rock'd
Until her husband's welfare she did hear;
Whereat she smiled with so sweet a cheer,
That had Narcissus seen her as she stood,
Self-love had never drown'd him in the flood.

'Why hunt I then for colour or excuses?
All orators are dumb when beauty pleadeth;
Poor wretches have remorse in poor abuses;
Love thrives not in the heart that shadows dreadeth;
Affection is my captain, and he leadeth;
And when his gaudy banner is display'd,
The coward fights and will not be dismay'd.

'Then, childish fear, avaunt! debating, die!
Respect and reason, wait on wrinkled age!
My heart shall never countermand mine eye:
Sad pause and deep regard beseem the sage;
My part is youth, and beats these from the stage.
Desire my pilot is, beauty my prize;
Then who fears sinking where such treasure lies?'

As corn o'ergrown by weeds, so heedful fear
Is almost choked by unresisted lust.
Away he steals with open listening ear,
Full of foul hope and full of fond mistrust;
Both which, as servitors to the unjust,
So cross him with their opposite persuasion,
That now he vows a league, and now invasion.

Within his thought her heavenly image sits,
And in the self-same seat sits Collatine:
That eye which looks on her confounds his wits;
That eye which him beholds, as more divine,
Unto a view so false will not incline;
But with a pure appeal seeks to the heart,
Which once corrupted takes the worser part;

And therein heartens up his servile powers,
Who, flatter'd by their leader's jocund show,
Stuff up his lust, as minutes fill up hours;
And as their captain, so their pride doth grow,
Paying more slavish tribute than they owe.
By reprobate desire thus madly led,
The Roman lord marcheth to Lucrece' bed.

The locks between her chamber and his will,
Each one by him enforced, retires his ward;
But as they open they all rate his ill,
Which drives the creeping thief to some regard:
The threshold grates the door to have him heard:
Night-wandering weasels shriek to see him there;
They fright him, yet he still pursues his fear.

As each unwilling portal yields him way,
Through little vents and crannies of the place
The wind wars with his torch to make him stay,
And blows the smoke of it into his face,
Extinguishing his conduct in this case;
But his hot heart, which fond desire doth scorch,
Puffs forth another wind that fires the torch:

And being lighted, by the light he spies
Lucretia's glove, wherein her needle sticks:
He takes it from the rushes where it lies,
And griping it, the neeld his finger pricks;
As who should say, 'This glove to wanton tricks
Is not inured; return again in haste;
Thou see'st our mistress' ornaments are chaste.'

But all these poor forbiddings could not stay him;
He in the worst sense construes their denial:
The doors, the wind, the glove, that did delay him,
He takes for accidental things of trial;
Or as those bars which stop the hourly dial,
Who with a ling'ring stay his course doth let,
Till every minute pays the hour his debt.

'So, so,' quoth he, 'these lets attend the time,
Like little frosts that sometime threat the spring,
To add a more rejoicing to the prime,
And give the sneaped birds more cause to sing.
Pain pays the income of each precious thing;
Huge rocks, high winds, strong pirates, shelves and sands,
The merchant fears, ere rich at home he lands.'

Now is he come unto the chamber door,
That shuts him from the heaven of his thought,
Which with a yielding latch, and with no more,
Hath barr'd him from the blessed thing he sought.
So from himself impiety hath wrought,
That for his prey to pray he doth begin,
As if the heavens should countenance his sin.

But in the midst of his unfruitful prayer,
Having solicited the eternal power
That his foul thoughts might compass his fair fair,
And they would stand auspicious to the hour,
Even there he starts: quoth he, 'I must deflower:

The powers to whom I pray abhor this fact,
How can they then assist me in the act?

'Then Love and Fortune be my gods, my guide!
My will is back'd with resolution:
Thoughts are but dreams till their effects be tried;
The blackest sin is clear'd with absolution;
Against love's fire fear's frost hath dissolution.
The eye of heaven is out, and misty night
Covers the shame that follows sweet delight.'

This said, his guilty hand pluck'd up the latch,
And with his knee the door he opens wide.
The dove sleeps fast that this night-owl will catch:
Thus treason works ere traitors be espied.
Who sees the lurking serpent steps aside;
But she, sound sleeping, fearing no such thing,
Lies at the mercy of his mortal sting.

Into the chamber wickedly he stalks,
And gazeth on her yet unstained bed.
The curtains being close, about he walks,
Rolling his greedy eyeballs in his head:
By their high treason is his heart misled;
Which gives the watch-word to his hand full soon,
To draw the cloud that hides the silver moon.

Look, as the fair and fiery-pointed sun,
Rushing from forth a cloud, bereaves our sight;
Even so, the curtain drawn, his eyes begun
To wink, being blinded with a greater light:
Whether it is that she reflects so bright,
That dazzleth them, or else some shame supposed,
But blind they are, and keep themselves enclosed.

O! had they in that darksome prison died,
Then had they seen the period of their ill;
Then Collatine again, by Lucrece' side,
In his clear bed might have reposed still:
But they must ope, this blessed league to kill,
And holy-thoughted Lucrece to their sight
Must sell her joy, her life, her world's delight.

Her lily hand her rosy cheek lies under,
Cozening the pillow of a lawful kiss;
Who, therefore angry, seems to part in sunder,
Swelling on either side to want his bliss;
Between whose hills her head entombed is:
Where, like a virtuous monument, she lies,
To be admired of lewd unhallow'd eyes.

Without the bed her other fair hand was,
On the green coverlet; whose perfect white
Show'd like an April daisy on the grass,
With pearly sweat, resembling dew of night.
Her eyes, like marigolds, had sheathed their light,
And canopied in darkness sweetly lay,
Till they might open to adorn the day.

Her hair, like golden threads, play'd with her breath;
O modest wantons! wanton modesty!
Showing life's triumph in the map of death,
And death's dim look in life's mortality:
Each in her sleep themselves so beautify,
As if between them twain there were no strife,
But that life lived in death, and death in life.

Her breasts, like ivory globes circled with blue,
A pair of maiden worlds unconquered,
Save of their lord no bearing yoke they knew,
And him by oath they truly honoured.
These worlds in Tarquin new ambition bred;
Who, like a foul usurper, went about
From this fair throne to heave the owner out.

What could he see but mightily he noted?
What did he note but strongly he desired?
What he beheld, on that he firmly doted,
And in his will his wilful eye he tired.
With more than admiration he admired
Her azure veins, her alabaster skin,
Her coral lips, her snow-white dimpled chin.

As the grim lion fawneth o'er his prey,
Sharp hunger by the conquest satisfied,
So o'er this sleeping soul doth Tarquin stay,
His rage of lust by gazing qualified;
Slack'd, not suppress'd; for standing by her side,
His eye, which late this mutiny restrains,
Unto a greater uproar tempts his veins:

And they, like straggling slaves for pillage fighting,
Obdurate vassals fell exploits effecting,
In bloody death and ravishment delighting,
Nor children's tears nor mothers' groans respecting,
Swell in their pride, the onset still expecting:
Anon his beating heart, alarum striking,
Gives the hot charge and bids them do their liking.

His drumming heart cheers up his burning eye,
His eye commends the leading to his hand;
His hand, as proud of such a dignity,
Smoking with pride, march'd on to make his stand
On her bare breast, the heart of all her land;
Whose ranks of blue veins, as his hand did scale,
Left their round turrets destitute and pale.

They, mustering to the quiet cabinet
Where their dear governess and lady lies,
Do tell her she is dreadfully beset,
And fright her with confusion of their cries:
She, much amazed, breaks ope her lock'd-up eyes,
Who, peeping forth this tumult to behold,
Are by his flaming torch dimm'd and controll'd.

Imagine her as one in dead of night
From forth dull sleep by dreadful fancy waking,
That thinks she hath beheld some ghastly sprite,
Whose grim aspect sets every joint a-shaking;
What terror 't is! but she, in worser taking,
From sleep disturbed, heedfully doth view
The sight which makes supposed terror true.

Wrapp'd and confounded in a thousand fears,
Like to a new-kill'd bird she trembling lies;

She dares not look; yet, winking, there appears
Quick-shifting anticks, ugly in her eyes:
Such shadows are the weak brain's forgeries;
  Who, angry that the eyes fly from their lights,
  In darkness daunts them with more dreadful sights.

His hand, that yet remains upon her breast,
Rude ram to batter such an ivory wall!
May feel her heart, poor citizen, distress'd,
Wounding itself to death, rise up and fall,
Beating her bulk, that his hand shakes withal.
  This moves in him more rage and lesser pity,
  To make the breach and enter this sweet city.

First, like a trumpet, doth his tongue begin
To sound a parley to his heartless foe;
Who o'er the white sheet peers her whiter chin,
The reason of this rash alarm to know,
Which he by dumb demeanour seeks to show;
  But she with vehement prayers urgeth still,
  Under what colour he commits this ill.

Thus he replies: 'The colour in thy face,
That even for anger makes the lily pale,
And the red rose blush at her own disgrace,
Shall plead for me and tell my loving tale;
Under that colour am I come to scale
  Thy never-conquer'd fort; the fault is thine,
  For those thine eyes betray thee unto mine.

'Thus I forestall thee, if thou mean to chide:
Thy beauty hath ensnar'd thee to this night,
Where thou with patience must my will abide,
My will that marks thee for my earth's delight,
Which I to conquer sought with all my might;
  But as reproof and reason beat it dead,
  By thy bright beauty was it newly bred.

'I see what crosses my attempt will bring;
I know what thorns the growing rose defends;
I think the honey guarded with a sting;
All this, beforehand, counsel comprehends:
But will is deaf and hears no heedful friends;
  Only he hath an eye to gaze on beauty,
  And dotes on what he looks, 'gainst law or duty.

'I have debated, even in my soul,
What wrong, what shame, what sorrow I shall breed;
But nothing can affection's course control,
Or stop the headlong fury of his speed.
I know repentant tears ensue the deed,
  Reproach, disdain, and deadly enmity;
  Yet strive I to embrace mine infamy.'

This said, he shakes aloft his Roman blade,
Which like a falcon towering in the skies,
Coucheth the fowl below with his wings' shade,
Whose crooked beak threats if he mount he dies:
So under his insulting falchion lies
  Harmless Lucretia, marking what he tells
  With trembling fear, as fowl hear falcon's bells.

'Lucrece,' quoth he, 'this night I must enjoy thee:
If thou deny, then force must work my way,
For in thy bed I purpose to destroy thee:
That done, some worthless slave of thine I'll slay,
To kill thine honour with thy life's decay;
  And in thy dead arms do I mean to place him,
  Swearing I slew him, seeing thee embrace him.

'So thy surviving husband shall remain
The scornful mark of every open eye;
Thy kinsmen hang their heads at this disdain,
Thy issue blurr'd with nameless bastardy:
And thou, the author of their obloquy,
  Shalt have thy trespass cited up in rhymes,
  And sung by children in succeeding times.

'But if thou yield, I rest thy secret friend:
The fault unknown is as a thought unacted;
A little harm done to a great good end
For lawful policy remains enacted.
The poisonous simple sometimes is compacted
  In a pure compound; being so applied,
  His venom in effect is purified.

'Then for thy husband and thy children's sake,
Tender my suit: bequeath not to their lot
The shame that from them no device can take,
The blemish that will never be forgot;
Worse than a slavish wipe or birth-hour's blot:
  For marks descried in men's nativity
  Are nature's faults, not their own infamy.'

Here with a cockatrice' dead-killing eye
He rouseth up himself and makes a pause;
While she, the picture of pure piety,
Like a white hind under the gripe's sharp claws,
Pleads in a wilderness where are no laws,
  To the rough beast that knows no gentle right,
  Nor aught obeys but his foul appetite.

But when a black-faced cloud the world doth threat
In his dim mist the aspiring mountains hiding,
From earth's dark womb some gentle gust doth get,
Which blows these pitchy vapours from their biding,
Hindering their present fall by this dividing;
  So his unhallow'd haste her words delays,
  And moody Pluto winks while Orpheus plays.

Yet, foul night-waking cat, he doth but dally,
While in his hold-fast foot the weak mouse panteth:
Her sad behaviour feeds his vulture folly,
A swallowing gulf that even in plenty wanteth:
His ear her prayers admits, but his heart granteth
  No penetrable entrance to her plaining:
  Tears harden lust though marble wear with raining.

Her pity-pleading eyes are sadly fix'd
In the remorseless wrinkles of his face;
Her modest eloquence with sighs is mix'd,
Which to her oratory adds more grace.
She puts the period often from his place;
  And midst the sentence so her accent breaks,
  That twice she doth begin ere once she speaks.

She conjures him by high almighty Jove,
By knighthood, gentry, and sweet friendship's oath,
By her untimely tears, her husband's love,
By holy human law, and common troth,
By heaven and earth, and all the power of both,
  That to his borrow'd bed he make retire,
  And stoop to honour, not to foul desire.

Quoth she, 'Reward not hospitality
With such black payment as thou hast pretended;
Mud not the fountain that gave drink to thee;
Mar not the thing that cannot be amended;
End thy ill aim before thy shoot be ended;
  He is no woodman that doth bend his bow
  To strike a poor unseasonable doe.

'My husband is thy friend, for his sake spare me;
Thyself art mighty, for thine own sake leave me;
Myself a weakling, do not then ensnare me;
Thou look'st not like deceit, do not deceive me;
My sighs, like whirlwinds, labour hence to heave thee.
  If ever man were moved with woman's moans,
  Be moved with my tears, my sighs, my groans:

'All which together, like a troubled ocean,
Beat at thy rocky and wreck-threatening heart,
To soften it with their continual motion;
For stones dissolved to water do convert.
O! if no harder than a stone thou art,
  Melt at my tears and be compassionate;
  Soft pity enters at an iron gate.

'In Tarquin's likeness I did entertain thee;
Hast thou put on his shape to do him shame?
To all the host of heaven I complain me,
Thou wrong'st his honour, wound'st his princely name:
Thou art not what thou seem'st; and if the same,
  Thou seem'st not what thou art, a god, a king;
  For kings like gods should govern every thing.

'How will thy shame be seeded in thine age,
When thus thy vices bud before thy spring!
If in thy hope thou darest do such outrage,
What darest thou not when once thou art a king?
O! be remember'd; no outrageous thing
  From vassal actors can be wiped away;
  Then kings' misdeeds cannot be hid in clay.

'This deed will make thee only loved for fear;
But happy monarchs still are fear'd for love:
With foul offenders thou perforce must bear,
When they in thee the like offences prove:
If but for fear of this, thy will remove;
  For princes are the glass, the school, the book,
  Where subjects' eyes do learn, do read, do look.

'And wilt thou be the school where lust shall learn?
Must he in thee read lectures of such shame?
Wilt thou be glass wherein it shall discern
Authority for sin, warrant for blame,
To privilege dishonour in thy name?
  Thou back'st reproach against long-living laud,
  And makest fair reputation but a bawd.

'Hast thou command! by him that gave it thee,
From a pure heart command thy rebel will:
Draw not thy sword to guard iniquity,
For it was lent thee all that brood to kill.
Thy princely office how canst thou fulfil,
  When, pattern'd by thy fault, foul sin may say,
  He learn'd to sin, and thou didst teach the way?

'Think but how vile a spectacle it were,
To view thy present trespass in another.
Men's faults do seldom to themselves appear;
Their own transgressions partially they smother:
This guilt would seem death-worthy in thy brother.
  O! how are they wrapp'd in with infamies
  That from their own misdeeds askance their eyes.

'To thee, to thee, my heav'd-up hands appeal,
Not to seducing lust, thy rash relier;
I sue for exiled majesty's repeal;
Let him return, and flattering thoughts retire:
His true respect will prison false desire,
  And wipe the dim mist from thy doting eyne,
  That thou shalt see thy state and pity mine.'

'Have done,' quoth he; 'my uncontrolled tide
Turns not, but swells the higher by this let.
Small lights are soon blown out, huge fires abide,
And with the wind in greater fury fret:
The petty streams that pay a daily debt
  To their salt sovereign, with their fresh falls haste
Add to his flow, but alter not his taste.'

'Thou art,' quoth she, 'a sea, a sovereign king;
And, lo! there falls into thy boundless flood
Black lust, dishonour, shame, misgoverning,
Who seek to stain the ocean of thy blood.
If all these petty ills shall change thy good,
  Thy sea within a puddle's womb is hearsed,
  And not the puddle in thy sea dispersed.

'So shall these slaves be king, and thou their slave;
Thou nobly base, they basely dignified;
Thou their fair life, and they thy fouler grave;
Thou loathed in their shame, they in thy pride:
The lesser thing should not the greater hide;
  The cedar stoops not to the base shrub's foot,
  But low shrubs wither at the cedar's root.

'So let thy thoughts, low vassals to thy state'—
'No more,' quoth he; 'by heaven, I will not hear thee:
Yield to my love; if not, enforced hate,
Instead of love's coy touch, shall rudely tear thee;
That done, despitefully I mean to bear thee
  Unto the base bed of some rascal groom,
  To be thy partner in this shameful doom.'

This said, he sets his foot upon the light,
For light and lust are deadly enemies:
Shame folded up in blind concealing night,
When most unseen, then most doth tyrannize.
The wolf hath seized his prey, the poor lamb cries;
  Till with her own white fleece her voice controll'd
  Entombs her outcry in her lips' sweet fold:

For with the nightly linen that she wears
He pens her piteous clamours in her head,
Cooling his hot face in the chastest tears
That ever modest eyes with sorrow shed.
O! that prone lust should stain so pure a bed:
  The spots whereof could weeping purify,
  Her tears should drop on them perpetually.

But she hath lost a dearer thing than life,
And he hath won what he would lose again;
This forced league doth force a further strife;
This momentary joy breeds months of pain;
This hot desire converts to cold disdain:
  Pure chastity is rifled of her store,
  And Lust, the thief, far poorer than before.

Look! as the full-fed hound or gorged hawk,
Unapt for tender smell or speedy flight,
Make slow pursuit, or altogether balk
The prey wherein by nature they delight;
So surfeit-taking Tarquin fares this night:
  His taste delicious, in digestion souring,
  Devours his will, that lived by foul devouring.

O! deeper sin than bottomless conceit
Can comprehend in still imagination;
Drunken Desire must vomit his receipt,
Ere he can see his own abomination.
While Lust is in his pride, no exclamation
  Can curb his heat or rein his rash desire,
  Till like a jade Self-will himself doth tire.

And then with lank and lean discolour'd cheek,
With heavy eye, knit brow, and strengthless pace,
Feeble Desire, all recreant, poor, and meek,
Like to a bankrupt beggar wails his case:
The flesh being proud, Desire doth fight with Grace,
  For there it revels; and when that decays,
  The guilty rebel for remission prays.

So fares it with this faultful lord of Rome,
Who this accomplishment so hotly chased;
For now against himself he sounds this doom,
That through the length of times he stands disgraced:
Besides, his soul's fair temple is defaced;
  To whose weak ruins muster troops of cares,
  To ask the spotted princess how she fares.

She says, her subjects with foul insurrection
Have batter'd down her consecrated wall,
And by their mortal fault brought in subjection
Her immortality, and made her thrall
To living death and pain perpetual:
  Which in her prescience she controlled still,
  But her foresight could not forestall their will.

Even in this thought through the dark night he stealeth,
A captive victor that hath lost in gain;
Bearing away the wound that nothing healeth,
The scar that will despite of cure remain;
Leaving his spoil perplex'd in greater pain.
  She bears the load of lust he left behind,
  And he the burden of a guilty mind.

He like a thievish dog creeps sadly thence,
She like a wearied lamb lies panting there;
He scowls and hates himself for his offence,
She desperate with her nails her flesh doth tear;
He faintly flies, sweating with guilty fear,
  She stays, exclaiming on the direful night;
  He runs, and chides his vanish'd, loathed delight.

He thence departs a heavy convertite,
She there remains a hopeless castaway;
He in his speed looks for the morning light,
She prays she never may behold the day;
'For day,' quoth she, 'night's scapes doth open lay,
  And my true eyes have never practised how
  To cloak offences with a cunning brow.

'They think not but that every eye can see
The same disgrace which they themselves behold;
And therefore would they still in darkness be,
To have their unseen sin remain untold;
For they their guilt with weeping will unfold,
  And grave, like water that doth eat in steel,
  Upon my cheeks what helpless shame I feel.'

Here she exclaims against repose and rest,
And bids her eyes hereafter still be blind.
She wakes her heart by beating on her breast,
And bids it leap from thence where it may find
Some purer chest to close so pure a mind.
  Frantic with grief thus breathes she forth her spite
  Against the unseen secrecy of night:

'O comfort-killing Night, image of hell!
Dim register and notary of shame!
Black stage for tragedies and murders fell!
Vast sin-concealing chaos! nurse of blame!
Blind muffled bawd! dark harbour for defame!
  Grim cave of death! whispering conspirator
  With close-tongued treason and the ravisher!

'O hateful, vaporous, and foggy Night!
Since thou art guilty of my cureless crime,
Muster thy mists to meet the eastern light,
Make war against proportion'd course of time;
Or if thou wilt permit the sun to climb
  His wonted height, yet ere he go to bed,
  Knit poisonous clouds about his golden head.

'With rotten damps ravish the morning air;
Let their exhaled unwholesome breaths make sick
The life of purity, the supreme fair,
Ere he arrive his weary noontide prick;
And let thy misty vapours march so thick,
  That in their smoky ranks his smother'd light
  May set at noon and make perpetual night.

'Were Tarquin Night, as he is but Night's child,
The silver-shining queen he would distain;
Her twinkling handmaids too, by him defiled,
Through Night's black bosom should not peep again:
So should I have co-partners in my pain;
  And fellowship in woe doth woe assuage,
  As palmers' chat makes short their pilgrimage.

'Where now I have no one to blush with me,
To cross their arms and hang their heads with mine,
To mask their brows and hide their infamy;
But I alone alone must sit and pine,
Seasoning the earth with showers of silver brine,
Mingling my talk with tears, my grief with groans,
Poor wasting monuments of lasting moans.

'O Night! thou furnace of foul-reeking smoke,
Let not the jealous Day behold that face
Which underneath thy black all-hiding cloak
Immodestly lies martyr'd with disgrace:
Keep still possession of thy gloomy place,
That all the faults which in thy reign are made
May likewise be sepulchred in thy shade.

'Make me not object to the tell-tale Day!
The light will show, character'd in my brow,
The story of sweet chastity's decay,
The impious breach of holy wedlock vow:
Yea, the illiterate, that know not how
To cipher what is writ in learned books,
Will quote my loathsome trespass in my looks.

'The nurse, to still her child, will tell my story,
And fright her crying babe with Tarquin's name;
The orator, to deck his oratory,
Will couple my reproach to Tarquin's shame;
Feast-finding minstrels, tuning my defame,
Will tie the hearers to attend each line,
How Tarquin wronged me, I Collatine.

'Let my good name, that senseless reputation,
For Collatine's dear love be kept unspotted:
If that be made a theme for disputation,
The branches of another root are rotted,
And undeserved reproach to him allotted
That is as clear from this attaint of mine,
As I ere this was pure to Collatine.

'O unseen shame! invisible disgrace!
O unfelt sore! crest-wounding, private scar!
Reproach is stamp'd in Collatinus' face,
And Tarquin's eye may read the mot afar,
How he in peace is wounded, not in war.
Alas! how many bear such shameful blows,
Which not themselves, but he that gives them knows.

'If, Collatine, thine honour lay in me,
From me by strong assault it is bereft.
My honey lost, and I, a drone-like bee,
Have no perfection of my summer left,
But robb'd and ransack'd by injurious theft:
In thy weak hive a wandering wasp hath crept,
And suck'd the honey which thy chaste bee kept.

'Yet am I guilty of thy honour's wrack;
Yet for thy honour did I entertain him;
Coming from thee, I could not put him back,
For it had been dishonour to disdain him:
Besides, of weariness he did complain him,
And talk'd of virtue: O! unlook'd-for evil,
When virtue is profaned in such a devil.

'Why should the worm intrude the maiden bud?
Or hateful cuckoos hatch in sparrows' nests?
Or toads infect fair founts with venom mud?
Or tyrant folly lurk in gentle breasts?
Or kings be breakers of their own behests?
But no perfection is so absolute,
That some impurity doth not pollute.

'The aged man that coffers-up his gold
Is plagued with cramps and gouts and painful fits;
And scarce hath eyes his treasure to behold,
But like still-pining Tantalus he sits,
And useless barns the harvest of his wits;
Having no other pleasure of his gain
But torment that it cannot cure his pain.

'So then he hath it when he cannot use it,
And leaves it to be master'd by his young;
Who in their pride do presently abuse it:
Their father was too weak, and they too strong,
To hold their cursed-blessed fortune long.
The sweets we wish for turn to loathed sours
Even in the moment that we call them ours.

'Unruly blasts wait on the tender spring;
Unwholesome weeds take root with precious flowers;
The adder hisses where the sweet birds sing;
What virtue breeds iniquity devours:
We have no good that we can say is ours,
But ill-annexed Opportunity
Or kills his life, or else his quality.

'O Opportunity! thy guilt is great,
'T is thou that executest the traitor's treason;
Thou sett'st the wolf where he the lamb may get;
Whoever plots the sin, thou point'st the season;
'T is thou that spurn'st at right, at law, at reason;
And in thy shady cell, where none may spy him,
Sits Sin to seize the souls that wander by him.

'Thou makest the vestal violate her oath;
Thou blow'st the fire when temperance is thaw'd;
Thou smother'st honesty, thou murder'st troth;
Thou foul abettor! thou notorious bawd!
Thou plantest scandal and displacest laud:
Thou ravisher, thou traitor, thou false thief,
Thy honey turns to gall, thy joy to grief!

'Thy secret pleasure turns to open shame,
Thy private feasting to a public fast,
Thy smoothing titles to a ragged name,
Thy sugar'd tongue to bitter wormwood taste:
Thy violent vanities can never last.
How comes it then, vile Opportunity,
Being so bad, such numbers seek for thee?

'When wilt thou be the humble suppliant's friend,
And bring him where his suit may be obtain'd?
When wilt thou sort an hour great strifes to end?
Or free that soul which wretchedness hath chain'd?
Give physic to the sick, ease to the pain'd?
The poor, lame, blind, halt, creep, cry out for thee;
But they ne'er meet with Opportunity.

'The patient dies while the physician sleeps;
The orphan pines while the oppressor feeds;
Justice is feasting while the widow weeps;
Advice is sporting while infection breeds:
Thou grant'st no time for charitable deeds:
Wrath, envy, treason, rape, and murder's rages,
Thy heinous hours wait on them as their pages.

'When Truth and Virtue have to do with thee,
A thousand crosses keep them from thy aid:
They buy thy help; but Sin ne'er gives a fee,
He gratis comes; and thou art well appaid
As well to hear as grant what he hath said.
My Collatine would else have come to me
When Tarquin did, but he was stay'd by thee.

'Guilty thou art of murder and of theft,
Guilty of perjury and subornation,
Guilty of treason, forgery, and shift,
Guilty of incest, that abomination;
An accessary by thine inclination
To all sins past, and all that are to come,
From the creation to the general doom.

'Misshapen Time, copesmate of ugly Night,
Swift subtle post, carrier of grisly care,
Eater of youth, false slave to false delight,
Base watch of woes, sin's pack-horse, virtue's snare;
Thou nursest all, and murder'st all that are;
O! hear me then, injurious, shifting Time,
Be guilty of my death, since of my crime.

'Why hath thy servant, Opportunity,
Betray'd the hours thou gavest me to repose?
Cancell'd my fortunes, and enchained me
To endless date of never-ending woes?
Time's office is to fine the hate of foes;
To eat up errors by opinion bred,
Not spend the dowry of a lawful bed.

'Time's glory is to calm contending kings,
To unmask falsehood and bring truth to light,
To stamp the seal of time in aged things,
To wake the morn and sentinel the night,
To wrong the wronger till he render right,
To ruinate proud buildings with thy hours,
And smear with dust their glittering golden towers;

'To fill with worm-holes stately monuments,
To feed oblivion with decay of things,
To blot old books and alter their contents,
To pluck the quills from ancient ravens' wings,
To dry the old oak's sap and cherish springs,
To spoil antiquities of hammer'd steel,
And turn the giddy round of Fortune's wheel;

'To show the beldam daughters of her daughter,
To make the child a man, the man a child,
To slay the tiger that doth live by slaughter,
To tame the unicorn and lion wild,
To mock the subtle in themselves beguiled,
To cheer the ploughman with increaseful crops,
And waste huge stones with little water-drops.

'Why work'st thou mischief in thy pilgrimage,
Unless thou couldst return to make amends?
One poor retiring minute in an age
Would purchase thee a thousand thousand friends,
Lending him wit, that to bad debtors lends:
O! this dread night, wouldst thou one hour come back,
I could prevent this storm and shun thy wrack.

'Thou ceaseless lackey to eternity,
With some mischance cross Tarquin in his flight:
Devise extremes beyond extremity,
To make him curse this cursed crimeful night:
Let ghastly shadows his lewd eyes affright,
And the dire thought of his committed evil
Shape every bush a hideous shapeless devil.

'Disturb his hours of rest with restless trances,
Afflict him in his bed with bedrid groans;
Let there bechance him pitiful mischances
To make him moan, but pity not his moans;
Stone him with harden'd hearts, harder than stones;
And let mild women to him lose their mildness,
Wilder to him than tigers in their wildness.

'Let him have time to tear his curled hair,
Let him have time against himself to rave,
Let him have time of Time's help to despair,
Let him have time to live a loathed slave,
Let him have time a beggar's orts to crave,
And time to see one that by alms doth live
Disdain to him disdained scraps to give.

'Let him have time to see his friends his foes,
And merry fools to mock at him resort;
Let him have time to mark how slow time goes
In time of sorrow, and how swift and short
His time of folly and his time of sport;
And ever let his unrecalling crime
Have time to wail the abusing of his time.

'O Time! thou tutor both to good and bad,
Teach me to curse him that thou taught'st this ill;
At his own shadow let the thief run mad,
Himself himself seek every hour to kill:
Such wretched hands such wretched blood should spill;
For who so base would such an office have
As slanderous deathsman to so base a slave?

'The baser is he, coming from a king,
To shame his hope with deeds degenerate:
The mightier man, the mightier is the thing
That makes him honour'd, or begets him hate;
For greatest scandal waits on greatest state.
The moon being clouded presently is miss'd,
But little stars may hide them when they list.

'The crow may bathe his coal-black wings in mire,
And unperceived fly with the filth away;
But if the like the snow-white swan desire,
The stain upon his silver down will stay.
Poor grooms are sightless night, kings glorious day,
Gnats are unnoted wheresoe'er they fly,
But eagles gazed upon with every eye.

'Out, idle words! servants to shallow fools,
Unprofitable sounds, weak arbitrators!
Busy yourselves in skill-contending schools;
Debate where leisure serves with dull debaters;
To trembling clients be you mediators:
For me, I force not argument a straw,
Since that my case is past the help of law.

'In vain I rail at Opportunity,
At Time, at Tarquin, and uncheerful Night;
In vain I cavil with mine infamy,
In vain I spurn at my confirm'd despite;
This helpless smoke of words doth me no right.
The remedy indeed to do me good
Is to let forth my foul-defiled blood.

'Poor hand, why quiverest thou at this decree?
Honour thyself to rid me of this shame;
For if I die, my honour lives in thee,
But if I live, thou livest in my defame;
Since thou couldst not defend thy loyal dame,
And wast afeard to scratch her wicked foe,
Kill both thyself and her for yielding so.'

This said, from her be-tumbled couch she starteth,
To find some desperate instrument of death;
But this no slaughterhouse, no tool imparteth
To make more vent for passage of her breath;
Which, thronging through her lips, so vanisheth
As smoke from Ætna, that in air consumes,
Or that which from discharged cannon fumes.

'In vain,' quoth she, 'I live, and seek in vain
Some happy mean to end a hapless life:
I fear'd by Tarquin's falchion to be slain,
Yet for the self-same purpose seek a knife:
But when I fear'd I was a loyal wife:
So am I now: O no! that cannot be;
Of that true type hath Tarquin rifled me.

'O! that is gone for which I sought to live,
And therefore now I need not fear to die.
To clear this spot by death, at least I give
A badge of fame to slander's livery;
A dying life to living infamy.
Poor helpless help, the treasure stol'n away,
To burn the guiltless casket where it lay!

'Well, well, dear Collatine, thou shalt not know
The stained taste of violated troth;
I will not wrong thy true affection so,
To flatter thee with an infringed oath;
This bastard graff shall never come to growth:
He shall not boast who did thy stock pollute
That thou art doting father of his fruit.

'Nor shall he smile at thee in secret thought,
Nor laugh with his companions at thy state;
But thou shalt know thy interest was not bought
Basely with gold, but stol'n from forth thy gate.
For me, I am the mistress of my fate,
And with my trespass never will dispense,
Till life to death acquit my forced offence.

'I will not poison thee with my attaint,
Nor fold my fault in cleanly-coin'd excuses;
My sable ground of sin I will not paint,
To hide the truth of this false night's abuses:
My tongue shall utter all; mine eyes, like sluices,
As from a mountain-spring that feeds a dale,
Shall gush pure streams to purge my impure tale.'

By this, lamenting Philomel had ended
The well-tuned warble of her nightly sorrow,
And solemn night with slow sad gait descended
To ugly hell; when, lo! the blushing morrow
Lends light to all fair eyes that light will borrow:
But cloudy Lucrece shames herself to see,
And therefore still in night would cloister'd be.

Revealing day through every cranny spies,
And seems to point her out where she sits weeping;
To whom she sobbing speaks: 'O eye of eyes!
Why pry'st thou through my window? leave thy peeping;
Mock with thy tickling beams eyes that are sleeping;
Brand not my forehead with thy piercing light,
For day hath nought to do what's done by night.'

Thus cavils she with every thing she sees:
True grief is fond and testy as a child,
Who wayward once, his mood with nought agrees:
Old woes, not infant sorrows, bear them mild;
Continuance tames the one; the other wild,
Like an unpractised swimmer plunging still,
With too much labour drowns for want of skill.

So she, deep-drenched in a sea of care,
Holds disputation with each thing she views,
And to herself all sorrow doth compare;
No object but her passion's strength renews,
And as one shifts, another straight ensues:
Sometime her grief is dumb and hath no words;
Sometime 't is mad and too much talk affords.

The little birds that tune their morning's joy
Make her moans mad with their sweet melody:
For mirth doth search the bottom of annoy;
Sad souls are slain in merry company;
Grief best is pleased with grief's society:
True sorrow then is feelingly sufficed
When with like semblance it is sympathized.

'T is double death to drown in ken of shore;
He ten times pines that pines beholding food;
To see the salve doth make the wound ache more;
Great grief grieves most at that would do it good;
Deep woes roll forward like a gentle flood,
Who, being stopp'd, the bounding banks o'erflows;
Grief dallied with nor law nor limit knows.

'You mocking birds,' quoth she, 'your tunes entomb
Within your hollow-swelling feather'd breasts,
And in my hearing be you mute and dumb:
My restless discord loves no stops nor rests;
A woeful hostess brooks not merry guests:

Relish your nimble notes to pleasing ears;
Distress likes dumps when time is kept with tears.

'Come, Philomel, that sing'st of ravishment,
Make thy sad grove in my dishevell'd hair:
As the dank earth weeps at thy languishment,
So I at each sad strain will strain a tear,
And with deep groans the diapason bear;
For burden-wise I'll hum on Tarquin still,
While thou on Tereus descant'st better skill.

'And whiles against a thorn thou bear'st thy part
To keep thy sharp woes waking, wretched I,
To imitate thee well, against my heart
Will fix a sharp knife to affright mine eye,
Who, if it wink, shall thereon fall and die.
These means, as frets upon an instrument,
Shall tune our heart-strings to true languishment.

'And for, poor bird, thou sing'st not in the day,
As shaming any eye should thee behold,
Some dark deep desert, seated from the way,
That knows not parching heat nor freezing cold,
Will we find out; and there we will unfold
To creatures stern sad tunes, to change their kinds:
Since men prove beasts, let beasts bear gentle minds.'

As the poor frighted deer, that stands at gaze,
Wildly determining which way to fly,
Or one encompass'd with a winding maze,
That cannot tread the way out readily;
So with herself is she in mutiny,
To live or die which of the twain were better,
When life is shamed, and death reproach's debtor.

'To kill myself,' quoth she, 'alack! what were it,
But with my body my poor soul's pollution?
They that lose half with greater patience bear it
Than they whose whole is swallow'd in confusion.
That mother tries a merciless conclusion,
Who, having two sweet babes, when death takes one
Will slay the other and be nurse to none.

'My body or my soul, which was the dearer,
When the one pure, the other made divine?
Whose love of either to myself was nearer,
When both were kept for heaven and Collatine?
Ay me! the bark peel'd from the lofty pine,
His leaves will wither and his sap decay;
So must my soul, her bark being peel'd away.

Her house is sack'd, her quiet interrupted,
Her mansion batter'd by the enemy;
Her sacred temple spotted, spoil'd, corrupted,
Grossly engirt with daring infamy:
Then let it not be call'd impiety,
If in this blemish'd fort I make some hole
Through which I may convey this troubled soul.

'Yet die I will not, till my Collatine
Have heard the cause of my untimely death;
That he may vow, in that sad hour of mine,
Revenge on him that made me stop my breath.
My stained blood to Tarquin I'll bequeath,
Which by him tainted shall for him be spent
And as his due writ in my testament.

'My honour I'll bequeath unto the knife
That wounds my body so dishonoured.
'T is honour to deprive dishonour'd life;
The one will live, the other being dead:
So of shame's ashes shall my fame be bred;
For in my death I murder shameful scorn:
My shame so dead, mine honour is new-born.

'Dear lord of that dear jewel I have lost,
What legacy shall I bequeath to thee?
My resolution, love, shall be thy boast,
By whose example thou revenged mayst be.
How Tarquin must be used, read it in me:
Myself, thy friend, will kill myself, thy foe,
And for my sake serve thou false Tarquin so.

'This brief abridgement of my will I make:
My soul and body to the skies and ground;
My resolution, husband, do thou take;
Mine honour be the knife's that makes my wound;
My shame be his that did my fame confound;
And all my fame that lives disbursed be
To those that live, and think no shame of me.

'Thou, Collatine, shalt oversee this will;
How was I overseen that thou shalt see it!
My blood shall wash the slander of mine ill;
My life's foul deed, my life's fair end shall free it.
Faint not, faint heart, but stoutly say "So be it":
Yield to my hand; my hand shall conquer thee:
Thou dead, both die, and both shall victors be.'

This plot of death when sadly she had laid,
And wiped the brinish pearl from her bright eyes,
With untuned tongue she hoarsely calls her maid,
Whose swift obedience to her mistress hies;
For fleet-wing'd duty with thought's feathers flies.
Poor Lucrece' cheeks unto her maid seem so
As winter meads when sun doth melt their snow.

Her mistress she doth give demure good-morrow,
With soft slow tongue, true mark of modesty,
And sorts a sad look to her lady's sorrow,
For why her face wore sorrow's livery;
But durst not ask of her audaciously
Why her two suns were cloud-eclipsed so,
Nor why her fair cheeks over-wash'd with woe.

But as the earth doth weep, the sun being set,
Each flower moisten'd like a melting eye;
Even so the maid with swelling drops 'gan wet
Her circled eyne, enforced by sympathy
Of those fair suns set in her mistress' sky,
Who in a salt-waved ocean quench their light,
Which makes the maid weep like the dewy night.

A pretty while these pretty creatures stand,
Like ivory conduits coral cisterns filling;
One justly weeps, the other takes in hand
No cause but company of her drops spilling;
Their gentle sex to weep are often willing,
Grieving themselves to guess at others' smarts,
And then they drown their eyes or break their hearts:

For men have marble, women waxen minds,
And therefore are they form'd as marble will;
The weak oppress'd, the impression of strange kinds
Is form'd in them by force, by fraud, or skill:
Then call them not the authors of their ill,
No more than wax shall be accounted evil
Wherein is stamp'd the semblance of a devil.

Their smoothness, like a goodly champaign plain,
Lays open all the little worms that creep;
In men, as in a rough-grown grove, remain
Cave-keeping evils that obscurely sleep:
Through crystal walls each little mote will peep:
Though men can cover crimes with bold stern looks,
Poor women's faces are their own faults'-books.

No man inveigh against the wither'd flower,
But chide rough winter that the flower hath kill'd:
Not that devour'd, but that which doth devour,
Is worthy blame. O! let it not be hild
For women's faults, that they are so fulfill'd
With men's abuses: those proud lords, to blame,
Make weak-made women tenants to their shame.

The precedent whereof in Lucrece view,
Assail'd by night with circumstances strong
Of present death, and shame that might ensue
By that her death, to do her husband wrong:
Such danger to resistance did belong,
That dying fear through all her body spread;
And who cannot abuse a body dead?

By this, mild patience bid fair Lucrece speak
To the poor counterfeit of her complaining:
'My girl,' quoth she, 'on what occasion break
Those tears from thee, that down thy cheeks are raining?
If thou dost weep for grief of my sustaining,
Know, gentle wench, it small avails my mood:
If tears could help, mine own would do me good.

'But tell me, girl, when went,' and there she stay'd
Till after a deep groan, 'Tarquin from hence?'
'Madam, ere I was up,' replied the maid,
'The more to blame my sluggard negligence:
Yet with the fault I thus far can dispense;
Myself was stirring ere the break of day,
And, ere I rose, was Tarquin gone away.

'But lady, if your maid may be so bold,
She would request to know your heaviness.'
'O! peace,' quoth Lucrece: 'if it should be told,
The repetition cannot make it less;
For more it is than I can well express:
And that deep torture may be call'd a hell,
When more is felt than one hath power to tell.

'Go, get me hither paper, ink, and pen:
Yet save that labour, for I have them here.
What should I say? One of my husband's men
Bid thou be ready by and by, to bear
A letter to my lord, my love, my dear:
Bid him with speed prepare to carry it;
The cause craves haste, and it will soon be writ.'

Her maid is gone, and she prepares to write,
First hovering o'er the paper with her quill:
Conceit and grief an eager combat fight;
What wit sets down is blotted straight with will;
This is too curious-good, this blunt and ill:
Much like a press of people at a door
Throng her inventions, which shall go before.

At last she thus begins: 'Thou worthy lord
Of that unworthy wife that greeteth thee,
Health to thy person! next vouchsafe t' afford,
If ever, love, thy Lucrece thou wilt see,
Some present speed to come and visit me.
So I commend me from our house in grief:
My woes are tedious, though my words are brief.'

Here folds she up the tenour of her woe,
Her certain sorrow writ uncertainly.
By this short schedule Collatine may know
Her grief, but not her grief's true quality:
She dares not thereof make discovery,
Lest he should hold it her own gross abuse,
Ere she with blood had stain'd her stain'd excuse.

Besides, the life and feeling of her passion
She hoards, to spend when he is by to hear her;
When sighs and groans and tears may grace the fashion
Of her disgrace, the better so to clear her
From that suspicion which the world might bear her.
To shun this blot, she would not blot the letter
With words, till action might become them better.

To see sad sights moves more than hear them told;
For then the eye interprets to the ear
The heavy motion that it doth behold,
When every part a part of woe doth bear:
'T is but a part of sorrow that we hear;
Deep sounds make lesser noise than shallow fords,
And sorrow ebbs, being blown with wind of words.

Her letter now is seal'd, and on it writ
'At Ardea to my lord, with more than haste.'
The post attends, and she delivers it,
Charging the sour-faced groom to hie as fast
As lagging fowls before the northern blast:

Speed more than speed but dull and slow she deems:
Extremity still urgeth such extremes.

The homely villain court'sies to her low;
And, blushing on her, with a steadfast eye
Receives the scroll without or yea or no,
And forth with bashful innocence doth hie:
But they whose guilt within their bosoms lie
Imagine every eye beholds their blame;
For Lucrece thought he blush'd to see her shame:

When, silly groom! God wot, it was defect
Of spirit, life, and bold audacity.
Such harmless creatures have a true respect
To talk in deeds, while others saucily
Promise more speed, but do it leisurely:
Even so this pattern of the worn-out age
Pawn'd honest looks but laid no words to gage.

His kindled duty kindled her mistrust,
That two red fires in both their faces blazed;
She thought he blush'd, as knowing Tarquin's lust,
And, blushing with him, wistly on him gazed;
Her earnest eye did make him more amazed:
The more she saw the blood his cheeks replenish,
The more she thought he spied in her some blemish.

But long she thinks till he return again,
And yet the duteous vassal scarce is gone.
The weary time she cannot entertain,
For now 't is stale to sigh, to weep, and groan:
So woe hath wearied woe, moan tired moan,
That she her plaints a little while doth stay,
Pausing for means to mourn some newer way.

At last she calls to mind where hangs a piece
Of skilful painting, made for Priam's Troy;
Before the which is drawn the power of Greece,
For Helen's rape the city to destroy,
Threat'ning cloud-kissing Ilion with annoy;
Which the conceited painter drew so proud,
As heaven, it seem'd, to kiss the turrets bow'd.

A thousand lamentable objects there,
In scorn of nature, art gave lifeless life;
Many a dry drop seem'd a weeping tear,
Shed for the slaughter'd husband by the wife:
The red blood reek'd, to show the painter's strife;
And dying eyes gleam'd forth their ashy lights,
Like dying coals burnt out in tedious nights.

There might you see the labouring pioner
Begrimed with sweat, and smeared all with dust;
And from the towers of Troy there would appear
The very eyes of men through loop-holes thrust,
Gazing upon the Greeks with little lust:
Such sweet observance in this work was had,
That one might see those far-off eyes look sad.

In great commanders grace and majesty
You might behold, triumphing in their faces;
In youth quick bearing and dexterity;
And here and there the painter interlaces
Pale cowards, marching on with trembling paces;
Which heartless peasants did so well resemble,
That one would swear he saw them quake and tremble.

In Ajax and Ulysses, O! what art
Of physiognomy might one behold;
The face of either cipher'd either's heart;
Their face their manners most expressly told:
In Ajax' eyes blunt rage and rigour roll'd;
But the mild glance that sly Ulysses lent
Show'd deep regard and smiling government.

There pleading might you see grave Nestor stand,
As 't were encouraging the Greeks to fight;
Making such sober action with his hand,
That it beguiled attention, charm'd the sight.
In speech, it seem'd, his beard, all silver white,
Wagg'd up and down, and from his lips did fly
Thin winding breath, which purl'd up to the sky.

About him were a press of gaping faces,
Which seem'd to swallow up his sound advice;
All jointly listening, but with several graces,
As if some mermaid did their ears entice,
Some high, some low, the painter was so nice;
The scalps of many, almost hid behind,
To jump up higher seem'd, to mock the mind

Here one man's hand lean'd on another's head,
His nose being shadow'd by his neighbour's ear;
Here one being throng'd bears back, all boll'n and red;
Another smother'd seems to pelt and swear;
And in their rage such signs of rage they bear,
As, but for loss of Nestor's golden words,
It seem'd they would debate with angry swords.

For much imaginary work was there;
Conceit deceitful, so compact, so kind,
That for Achilles' image stood his spear,
Griped in an armed hand; himself behind
Was left unseen, save to the eye of mind:
A hand, a foot, a face, a leg, a head,
Stood for the whole to be imagined.

And from the walls of strong-besieged Troy.
When their brave hope, bold Hector, march'd to field,
Stood many Trojan mothers, sharing joy
To see their youthful sons bright weapons wield;
And to their hope they such odd action yield,
That through their light joy seemed to appear,
Like bright things stain'd, a kind of heavy fear.

And from the strand of Dardan, where they fought,
To Simois' reedy banks the red blood ran,
Whose waves to imitate the battle sought
With swelling ridges; and their ranks began
To break upon the galled shore, and than
Retire again, till meeting greater ranks
They join and shoot their foam at Simois' banks.

To this well-painted piece is Lucrece come,
To find a face where all distress is stell'd.
Many she sees where cares have carved some,
But none where all distress and dolour dwell'd,
Till she despairing Hecuba beheld,
Staring on Priam's wounds with her old eyes,
Which bleeding under Pyrrhus' proud foot lies.

In her the painter had anatomized
Times ruin, beauty's wreck, and grim care's reign:
Her cheeks with chaps and wrinkles were disguised;
Of what she was no semblance did remain;
Her blue blood changed to black in every vein,
Wanting the spring that those shrunk pipes had fed,
Show'd life imprison'd in a body dead.

On this sad shadow Lucrece spends her eyes,
And shapes her sorrow to the beldam's woes,
Who nothing wants to answer her but cries,
And bitter words to ban her cruel foes:
The painter was no god to lend her those;
And therefore Lucrece swears he did her wrong,
To give her so much grief and not a tongue.

'Poor instrument,' quoth she, 'without a sound,
I 'll tune thy woes with my lamenting tongue,
And drop sweet balm in Priam's painted wound,
And rail on Pyrrhus that hath done him wrong,
And with my tears quench Troy that burns so long,
And with my knife scratch out the angry eyes
Of all the Greeks that are thine enemies.

'Show me the strumpet that began this stir,
That with my nails her beauty I may tear.
Thy heat of lust, fond Paris, did incur
This load of wrath that burning Troy doth bear:
Thine eye kindled the fire that burneth here;
And here in Troy, for trespass of thine eye,
The sire, the son, the dame, and daughter die.

'Why should the private pleasure of some one
Become the public plague of many moe?
Let sin, alone committed, light alone
Upon his head that hath transgressed so;
Let guiltless souls be freed from guilty woe:
For one's offence why should so many fall,
To plague a private sin in general?

'Lo! here weeps Hecuba, here Priam dies,
Here manly Hector faints, here Troilus swounds,
Here friend by friend in bloody channel lies,
And friend to friend gives unadvised wounds,
And one man's lust these many lives confounds:
Had doting Priam check'd his son's desire,
Troy had been bright with fame and not with fire.'

Here feelingly she weeps Troy's painted woes;
For sorrow, like a heavy-hanging bell,
Once set on ringing, with his own weight goes;
Then little strength rings out the doleful knell:
So Lucrece, set a-work, sad tales doth tell
To pencill'd pensiveness and colour'd sorrow;
She lends them words, and she their looks doth borrow.

She throws her eyes about the painting round,
And whom she finds forlorn she doth lament:
At last she sees a wretched image bound,
That piteous looks to Phrygian shepherds lent;
His face, though full of cares, yet show'd content;
Onward to Troy with the blunt swains he goes,
So mild, that Patience seem'd to scorn his woes.

In him the painter labour'd with his skill
To hide deceit, and give the harmless show
An humble gait, calm looks, eyes wailing still,
A brow unbent that seem'd to welcome woe;
Cheeks neither red nor pale, but mingled so
That blushing red no guilty instance gave,
Nor ashy pale the fear that false hearts have.

But, like a constant and confirmed devil,
He entertain'd a show so seeming-just,
And therein so ensconced his secret evil,
That jealousy itself could not mistrust
False-creeping craft and perjury should thrust
Into so bright a day such black-faced storms,
Or blot with hell-born sin such saint-like forms.

The well-skill'd workman this mild image drew
For perjured Sinon, whose enchanting story
The credulous old Priam after slew;
Whose words like wildfire burnt the shining glory
Of rich-built Ilion, that the skies were sorry,
And little stars shot from their fixed places,
When their glass fell wherein they view'd their faces.

This picture she advisedly perused,
And chid the painter for his wondrous skill,
Saying, some shape in Sinon's was abused;
So fair a form lodged not a mind so ill:
And still on him she gazed, and gazing still,
Such signs of truth in his plain face she spied,
That she concludes the picture was belied.

'It cannot be,' quoth she, 'that so much guile'—
She would have said 'can lurk in such a look';
But Tarquin's shape came in her mind the while,
And from her tongue 'can lurk' from 'cannot took:
'It cannot be' she in that sense forsook,
And turn'd it thus, 'It cannot be, I find,
But such a face should bear a wicked mind:

'For even as subtle Sinon here is painted,
So sober-sad, so weary, and so mild,
As if with grief or travail he had fainted,
To me came Tarquin armed; so beguiled
With outward honesty, but yet defiled
With inward vice: as Priam him did cherish,
So did I Tarquin; so my Troy did perish.

'Look, look, how listening Priam wets his eyes,
To see those borrow'd tears that Sinon sheds!
Priam, why art thou old and yet not wise?

For every tear he falls a Trojan bleeds:
His eye drops fire, no water thence proceeds;
Those round clear pearls of his, that move thy pity,
Are balls of quenchless fire to burn thy city.

'Such devils steal effects from lightless hell;
For Sinon in his fire doth quake with cold,
And in that cold hot-burning fire doth dwell;
These contraries such unity do hold,
Only to flatter fools and make them bold:
So Priam's trust false Sinon's tears doth flatter,
That he finds means to burn his Troy with water.'

Here, all enraged, such passion her assails,
That patience is quite beaten from her breast.
She tears the senseless Sinon with her nails,
Comparing him to that unhappy guest
Whose deed hath made herself herself detest:
At last she smilingly with this gives o'er;
'Fool! fool!' quoth she, 'his wounds will not be sore.'

Thus ebbs and flows the current of her sorrow,
And time doth weary time with her complaining.
She looks for night, and then she longs for morrow,
And both she thinks too long with her remaining:
Short time seems long in sorrow's sharp sustaining:
Though woe be heavy, yet it seldom sleeps;
And they that watch see time how slow it creeps.

Which all this time hath overslipp'd her thought,
That she with painted images hath spent;
Being from the feeling of her own grief brought
By deep surmise of others' detriment;
Losing her woes in shows of discontent.
It easeth some, though none it ever cured,
To think their dolour others have endured.

But now the mindful messenger, come back,
Brings home his lord and other company;
Who finds his Lucrece clad in mourning black;
And round about her tear-distained eye
Blue circles stream'd, like rainbows in the sky:
These water-galls in her dim element
Foretell new storms to those already spent.

Which when her sad-beholding husband saw,
Amazedly in her sad face he stares:
Her eyes, though sod in tears, look'd red and raw,
Her lively colour kill'd with deadly cares.
He hath no power to ask her how she fares:
Both stood like old acquaintance in a trance,
Met far from home, wondering each other's chance.

At last he takes her by the bloodless hand,
And thus begins: 'What uncouth ill event
Hath thee befall'n, that thou dost trembling stand?
Sweet love, what spite hath thy fair colour spent?
Why art thou thus attired in discontent?
Unmask, dear dear, this moody heaviness,
And tell thy grief, that we may give redress.'

Three times with sighs she gives her sorrow fire,
Ere once she can discharge one word of woe:
At length address'd to answer his desire,
She modestly prepares to let them know
Her honour is ta'en prisoner by the foe;
While Collatine and his consorted lords
With sad attention long to hear her words.

And now this pale swan in her watery nest
Begins the sad dirge of her certain ending.
'Few words,' quoth she, 'shall fit the trespass best,
Where no excuse can give the fault amending:
In me moe woes than words are now depending;
And my laments would be drawn out too long,
To tell them all with one poor tired tongue.

'Then be this all the task it hath to say:
Dear husband, in the interest of thy bed
A stranger came, and on that pillow lay
Where thou wast wont to rest thy weary head;
And what wrong else may be imagined
By foul enforcement might be done to me,
From that, alas! thy Lucrece is not free.

'For in the dreadful dead of dark midnight,
With shining falchion in my chamber came
A creeping creature, with a flaming light,
And softly cried "Awake, thou Roman dame,
And entertain my love; else lasting shame
On thee and thine this night I will inflict,
If thou my love's desire do contradict.

'"For some hard-favour'd groom of thine," quoth he,
"Unless thou yoke thy liking to my will,
I'll murder straight, and then I'll slaughter thee,
And swear I found you where you did fulfil
The loathsome act of lust, and so did kill
The lechers in their deed: this act will be
My fame, and thy perpetual infamy."

'With this I did begin to start and cry,
And then against my heart he set his sword,
Swearing, unless I took all patiently,
I should not live to speak another word;
So should my shame still rest upon record,
And never be forgot in mighty Rome
The adulterate death of Lucrece and her groom.

'Mine enemy was strong, my poor self weak,
And far the weaker with so strong a fear:
My bloody judge forbade my tongue to speak;
No rightful plea might plead for justice there:
His scarlet lust came evidence to swear
That my poor beauty had purloin'd his eyes;
And when the judge is robb'd the prisoner dies.

'O! teach me how to make mine own excuse,
Or at the least this refuge let me find;
Though my gross blood be stain'd with this abuse,
Immaculate and spotless is my mind;
That was not forced; that never was inclined
To accessary yieldings, but still pure
Doth in her poison'd closet yet endure.'

Lo! here the hopeless merchant of this loss,
With head declined, and voice damm'd up with woe,

With sad set eyes, and wretched arms across,
From lips new-waxen pale begins to blow
The grief away that stops his answer so:
But, wretched as he is, he strives in vain;
What he breathes out his breath drinks up again.

As through an arch the violent roaring tide
Outruns the eye that doth behold his haste,
Yet in the eddy boundeth in his pride
Back to the strait that forced him on so fast;
In rage sent out, recall'd in rage, being past:
Even so his sighs, his sorrows, make a saw,
To push grief on, and back the same grief draw.

Which speechless woe of his poor she attendeth,
And his untimely frenzy thus awaketh:
'Dear lord, thy sorrow to my sorrow lendeth
Another power; no flood by raining slaketh.
My woe too sensible thy passion maketh
More feeling-painful: let it then suffice
To drown one woe, one pair of weeping eyes.

'And for my sake, when I might charm thee so,
For she that was thy Lucrece, now attend me:
Be suddenly revenged on my foe,
Thine, mine, his own: suppose thou dost defend me
From what is past: the help that thou shalt lend me
Comes all too late, yet let the traitor die;
For sparing justice feeds iniquity.

'But ere I name him, you, fair lords,' quoth she,
Speaking to those that came with Collatine,
'Shall plight your honourable faiths to me,
With swift pursuit to venge this wrong of mine;
For 't is a meritorious fair design
To chase injustice with revengeful arms:
Knights, by their oaths, should right poor ladies' harms.'

At this request, with noble disposition
Each present lord began to promise aid,
As bound in knighthood to her imposition,
Longing to hear the hateful foe bewray'd:
But she, that yet her sad task hath not said,
The protestation stops. 'O! speak,' quoth she,
'How may this forced stain be wiped from me?

'What is the quality of mine offence,
Being constrain'd with dreadful circumstance?
May my pure mind with the foul act dispense,
My low-declined honour to advance?
May any terms acquit me from this chance?
The poison'd fountain clears itself again;
And why not I from this compelled stain?'

With this, they all at once began to say,
Her body's stain her mind untainted clears;
While with a joyless smile she turns away
The face, that map which deep impression bears
Of hard misfortune, carved in it with tears.
'No, no,' quoth she, 'no dame, hereafter living,
By my excuse shall claim excuse's giving.'

Here with a sigh, as if her heart would break,
She throws forth Tarquin's name: 'He, he,' she says,
But more than 'he' her poor tongue could not speak;
Till after many accents and delays,
Untimely breathings, sick and short assays,
She utters this, 'He, he, fair lords, 't is he,
That guides this hand to give this wound to me.

Even here she sheathed in her harmless breast
A harmful knife, that thence her soul unsheathed:
That blow did bail it from the deep unrest
Of that polluted prison where it breathed;
Her contrite sighs unto the clouds bequeathed
Her winged sprite, and through her wounds doth fly
Life's lasting date from cancell'd destiny.

Stone-still, astonish'd with this deadly deed,
Stood Collatine and all his lordly crew;
Till Lucrece' father, that beholds her bleed,
Himself on her self-slaughter'd body threw;
And from the purple fountain Brutus drew
The murderous knife, and, as it left the place,
Her blood, in poor revenge, held it in chase;

And bubbling from her breast, it doth divide
In two slow rivers, that the crimson blood
Circles her body in on every side,
Who like a late-sack'd island, vastly stood,
Bare and unpeopled in this fearful flood.
Some of her blood still pure and red remain'd,
And some look'd black, and that false Tarquin stain'd.

About the mourning and congealed face
Of that black blood a watery rigol goes,
Which seems to weep upon the tainted place:
And ever since, as pitying Lucrece' woes,
Corrupted blood some watery token shows;
And blood untainted still doth red abide,
Blushing at that which is so putrified.

'Daughter, dear daughter!' old Lucretius cries,
'That life was mine which thou hast here deprived.
If in the child the father's image lies,
Where shall I live now Lucrece is unlived?
Thou wast not to this end from me derived.
If children pre-decease progenitors,
We are their offspring, and they none of ours.

'Poor broken glass, I often did behold
In thy sweet semblance my old age new born:
But now that fair fresh mirror, dim and old,
Shows me a bare-bon'd death by time outworn.
O! from thy cheeks my image thou hast torn,
And shiver'd all the beauty of my glass,
That I no more can see what once I was.

'O time! cease thou thy course, and last no longer,
If they surcease to be that should survive.
Shall rotten death make conquest of the stronger,

And leave the faltering feeble souls alive?
The old bees die, the young possess their hive:
Then live, sweet Lucrece, live again and see
Thy father die, and not thy father thee.'

By this starts Collatine as from a dream,
And bids Lucretius give his sorrow place;
And then in key-cold Lucrece' bleeding stream
He falls, and bathes the pale fear in his face,
And counterfeits to die with her a space;
Till manly shame bids him possess his breath
And live to be revenged on her death.

The deep vexation of his inward soul
Hath served a dumb arrest upon his tongue;
Who, mad that sorrow should his use control,
Or keep him from heart-easing words so long,
Begins to talk; but through his lips do throng
Weak words so thick, come in his poor heart's aid,
That no man could distinguish what he said.

Yet sometime 'Tarquin' was pronounced plain,
But through his teeth, as if the name he tore.
This windy tempest, till it blow up rain,
Held back his sorrow's tide to make it more;
At last it rains, and busy winds give o'er:
Then son and father weep with equal strife
Who should weep most, for daughter or for wife.

The one doth call her his, the other his,
Yet neither may possess the claim they lay.
The father says 'She's mine.' 'O! mine she is,
Replies her husband; 'do not take away
My sorrow's interest; let no mourner say
He weeps for her, for she was only mine,
And only must be wail'd by Collatine.'

'O!' quoth Lucretius, 'I did give that life
Which she too early and too late hath spill'd.'
'Woe, woe!' quoth Collatine, 'she was my wife,
I owed her, and 't is mine that she hath kill'd.'
'My daughter' and 'my wife' with clamours fill'd
The dispersed air, who, holding Lucrece' life,
Answer'd their cries, 'my daughter' and 'my wife.'

Brutus, who pluck'd the knife from Lucrece' side,
Seeing such emulation in their woe,
Began to clothe his wit in state and pride,
Burying in Lucrece' wound his folly's show.
He with the Romans was esteemed so
As silly-jeering idiots are with kings,
For sportive words and uttering foolish things:

But now he throws that shallow habit by,
Wherein deep policy did him disguise;
And arm'd his long-hid wits advisedly,
To check the tears in Collatinus' eyes.
'Thou wronged lord of Rome,' quoth he, 'arise:
Let my unsounded self, supposed a fool,
Now set thy long-experienced wit to school.

'Why, Collatine, is woe the cure for woe?
Do wounds help wounds, or grief help grievous deeds?
Is it revenge to give thyself a blow
For his foul act by whom thy fair wife bleeds?
Such childish humour from weak minds proceeds:
Thy wretched wife mistook the matter so,
To slay herself, that should have slain her foe.

'Courageous Roman, do not steep thy heart
In such relenting dew of lamentations;
But kneel with me and help to bear thy part,
To rouse our Roman gods with invocations,
That they will suffer these abominations,
Since Rome herself in them doth stand disgraced,
By our strong arms from forth her fair streets chased.

'Now, by the Capitol that we adore,
And by this chaste blood so unjustly stain'd,
By heaven's fair sun that breeds the fat earth's store,
By all our country rights in Rome maintain'd,
And by chaste Lucrece' soul, that late complain'd
Her wrongs to us, and by this bloody knife,
We will revenge the death of this true wife.'

This said, he struck his hand upon his breast,
And kiss'd the fatal knife to end his vow;
And to his protestation urged the rest,
Who, wondering at him, did his words allow:
Then jointly to the ground their knees they bow;
And that deep vow which Brutus made before,
He doth again repeat, and that they swore.

When they had sworn to this advised doom,
They did conclude to bear dead Lucrece thence;
To show her bleeding body thorough Rome,
And so to publish Tarquin's foul offence:
Which being done with speedy diligence,
The Romans plausibly did give consent
To Tarquin's everlasting banishment.

SONNETS

TO THE ONLIE BEGETTER OF
THESE INSUING SONNETS
M^r^. W. H. ALL HAPPINESSE
AND THAT ETERNITIE
PROMISED
BY
OUR EVER-LIVING POET
WISHETH
THE WELL-WISHING
ADVENTURER IN
SETTING
FORTH.
T. T.

I.

From fairest creatures we desire increase,
That thereby beauty's rose might never die,
But as the riper should by time decease,
His tender heir might bear his memory:
But thou contracted to thine own bright eyes,
Feed'st thy light's flame with self-substantial fuel,
Making a famine where abundance lies,
Thyself thy foe, to thy sweet self too cruel.
Thou that art now the world's fresh ornament
And only herald to the gaudy spring,
Within thine own bud buriest thy content
And, tender churl, makest waste in niggarding.
  Pity the world, or else this glutton be,
  To eat the world's due, by the grave and thee.

II.

When forty winters shall besiege thy brow
And dig deep trenches in thy beauty's field,
The youth's proud livery, so gazed on now,
Will be a tatter'd weed, of small worth held:
Then being ask'd where all thy beauty lies,
Where all the treasure of thy lusty days,
To say, within thine own deep-sunken eyes,
Were an all-eating shame and thriftless praise.
How much more praise deserved thy beauty's use,
If thou could'st answer 'This fair child of mine
Shall sum my count and make my old excuse,'
Proving his beauty by succession thine!
  This were to be new made when thou art old,
  And see thy blood warm when thou feel'st it cold.

III.

Look in thy glass, and tell the face thou viewest
Now is the time that face should form another;
Whose fresh repair if now thou not renewest,
Thou dost beguile the world, unbless some mother.
For where is she so fair whose unear'd womb
Disdains the tillage of thy husbandry?
Or who is he so fond will be the tomb
Of his self-love, to stop posterity?
Thou art thy mother's glass, and she in thee
Calls back the lovely April of her prime;
So thou through windows of thine age shalt see,
Despite of wrinkles, this thy golden time.
  But if thou live, remember'd not to be,
  Die single, and thine image dies with thee.

IV.

Unthrifty lovliness, why dost thou spend
Upon thyself thy beauty's legacy?
Nature's bequest gives nothing, but doth lend,
And being frank, she lends to those are free:
Then, beauteous niggard, why dost thou abuse
The bounteous largess given thee to give?
Profitless usurer, why dost thou use
So great a sum of sums, yet canst not live?
For having traffic with thyself alone,
Thou of thyself thy sweet self dost deceive:
Then how, when Nature calls thee to be gone,
What acceptable audit canst thou leave?
  Thy unused beauty must be tomb'd with thee,
  Which, used, lives th' executor to be.

V.

Those hours, that with gentle work did frame
The lovely gaze where every eye doth dwell,
Will play the tyrants to the very same
And that unfair which fairly doth excel:
For never-resting time leads summer on
To hideous winter, and confounds him there;

Sap check'd with frost, and lusty leaves quite gone,
Beauty o'ersnow'd and bareness every where:
Then, were not summer's distillation left,
A liquid prisoner pent in walls of glass,
Beauty's effect with beauty were bereft,
Nor it, nor no remembrance what it was:
 But flowers distill'd, though they with winter meet,
 Leese but their show; their substance still lives sweet.

VI.

Then let not winter's ragged hand deface
In thee thy summer, ere thou be distill'd:
Make sweet some vial; treasure thou some place
With beauty's treasure, ere it be self-kill'd.
That use is not forbidden usury,
Which happies those that pay the willing loan;
That's for thyself to breed another thee,
Or ten times happier, be it ten for one;
Ten times thyself were happier than thou art,
If ten of thine ten times refigured thee:
Then what could death do, if thou should'st depart,
Leaving thee living in posterity?
 Be not self-will'd, for thou art much too fair
 To be death's conquest and make worms thine heir.

VII.

Lo! in the orient when the gracious light
Lifts up his burning head, each under eye
Doth homage to his new-appearing sight,
Serving with looks his sacred majesty;
And having climb'd the steep-up heavenly hill,
Resembling strong youth in his middle age,
Yet mortal looks adore his beauty still,
Attending on his golden pilgrimage;
But when from highmost pitch, with weary car,
Like feeble age, he reeleth from the day,
The eyes, 'fore duteous, now converted are
From his low tract, and look another way:
 So thou, thyself outgoing in thy noon,
 Unlook'd on diest, unless thou get a son.

VIII.

Music to hear, why hear'st thou music sadly?
Sweets with sweets war not, joy delights in joy:
Why lovest thou that which thou receivest not gladly,
Or else receivest with pleasure thine annoy?
If the true concord of well-tuned sounds,
By unions married, do offend thine ear,
They do but sweetly chide thee, who confounds
In singleness the parts that thou should'st bear.
Mark how one string, sweet husband to another,
Strikes each in each by mutual ordering;
Resembling sire and child and happy mother,
Who, all in one, one pleasing note do sing:
 Whose speechless song, being many, seeming one,
 Sings this to thee: 'Thou single wilt prove none.'

IX.

Is it for fear to wet a widow's eye
That thou consumest thyself in single life?
Ah! if thou issueless shalt hap to die,
The world will wail thee, like a makeless wife;
The world will be thy widow, and still weep
That thou no form of thee hast left behind,
When every private widow well may keep
By children's eyes her husband's shape in mind.
Look! what an unthrift in the world doth spend
Shifts but his place, for still the world enjoys it;
But beauty's waste hath in the world an end,
And, kept unused, the user so destroys it.
 No love toward others in that bosom sits
 That on himself such murderous shame commits

X.

For shame! deny that thou bear'st love to any,
Who for thyself art so unprovident.
Grant, if thou wilt, thou art beloved of many,
But that thou none lovest is most evident;
For thou art so possess'd with murderous hate
That 'gainst thyself thou stick'st not to conspire,
Seeking that beauteous roof to ruinate
Which to repair should be thy chief desire.
O! change thy thought, that I may change my mind:
Shall hate be fairer lodged than gentle love?
Be, as thy presence is, gracious and kind,
Or to thyself at least kind-hearted prove:
 Make thee another self, for love of me,
 That beauty still may live in thine or thee.

XI.

As fast as thou shalt wane, so fast thou grow'st
In one of thine, from that which thou departest;
And that fresh blood which youngly thou bestow'st
Thou may'st call thine when thou from youth convertest.
Herein lives wisdom, beauty and increase;
Without this, folly, age and cold decay:
If all were minded so, the times should cease
And threescore year would make the world away
Let those whom Nature hath not made for store,
Harsh, featureless and rude, barrenly perish:
Look, whom she best endow'd she gave the more;
Which bounteous gift thou should'st in bounty cherish:
 She carved thee for her seal, and meant thereby
 Thou should'st print more, nor let that copy die.

XII.

When I do count the clock that tells the time,
And see the brave day sunk in hideous night;
When I behold the violet past prime,
And sable curls all silver'd o'er with white;
When lofty trees I see barren of leaves,
Which erst from heat did canopy the herd,
And summer's green all girded up in sheaves,
Borne on the bier with white and bristly beard,
Then of thy beauty do I question make,
That thou among the wastes of time must go,
Since sweets and beauties do themselves forsake
And die as fast as they see others grow;
 And nothing 'gainst Time's scythe can make defence
 Save breed, to brave him when he takes thee hence.

XIII.

O! that you were yourself; but, love, you are
No longer yours than you yourself here live:
Against this coming end you should prepare,
And your sweet semblance to some other give:
So should that beauty which you hold in lease
Find no determination; then you were
Yourself again, after yourself's decease,
When your sweet issue your sweet form should bear.
Who lets so fair a house fall to decay,
Which husbandry in honour might uphold
Against the stormy gusts of winter's day
And barren rage of death's eternal cold?
O! none but unthrifts. Dear my love, you know
You had a father: let your son say so.

XIV.

Not from the stars do I my judgement pluck;
And yet methinks I have astronomy,
But not to tell of good or evil luck,
Of plagues, of dearths, or seasons' quality;
Nor can I fortune to brief minutes tell,
Pointing to each his thunder, rain and wind,
Or say with princes if it shall go well,
By oft predict that I in heaven find:
But from thine eyes my knowledge I derive,
And, constant stars, in them I read such art
As 'Truth and beauty shall together thrive,
If from thyself to store thou wouldst convert';
Or else of thee this I prognosticate:
'Thy end is truth's and beauty's doom and date.'

XV.

When I consider every thing that grows
Holds in perfection but a little moment,
That this huge stage presenteth nought but shows
Whereon the stars in secret influence comment;
When I perceive that men as plants increase,
Cheered and check'd even by the self-same sky,
Vaunt in their youthful sap, at height decrease,
And wear their brave state out of memory;
Then the conceit of this inconstant stay
Sets you most rich in youth before my sight,
Where wasteful Time debateth with Decay,
To change your day of youth to sullied night;
And all in war with Time for love of you,
As he takes from you, I engraft you new.

XVI.

But wherefore do not you a mightier way
Make war upon this bloody tyrant, Time?
And fortify yourself in your decay
With means more blessed than my barren rhyme?
Now stand you on the top of happy hours,
And many maiden gardens, yet unset,
With virtuous wish would bear your living flowers
Much liker than your painted counterfeit:
So should the lines of life that life repair,
Which this, Time's pencil, or my pupil pen,
Neither in inward worth nor outward fair,
Can make you live yourself in eyes of men.
To give away yourself keeps yourself still;
And you must live, drawn by your own sweet skill.

XVII.

Who will believe my verse in time to come,
If it were fill'd with your most high deserts?
Though yet, heaven knows, it is but as a tomb
Which hides your life and shows not half your parts.
If I could write the beauty of your eyes
And in fresh numbers number all your graces,
The age to come would say 'This poet lies;
Such heavenly touches ne'er touch'd earthly faces.'
So should my papers, yellow'd with their age,
Be scorn'd, like old men of less truth than tongue,
And your true rights be term'd a poet's rage
And stretched metre of an antique song:
But were some child of yours alive that time,
You should live twice; in it and in my rhyme.

XVIII.

Shall I compare thee to a summer's day?
Thou art more lovely and more temperate:
Rough winds do shake the darling buds of May,
And summer's lease hath all too short a date:
Sometime too hot the eye of heaven shines,
And often is his gold complexion dimm'd;
And every fair from fair sometime declines,
By chance or nature's changing course untrimm'd;
But thy eternal summer shall not fade,
Nor lose possession of that fair thou owest,
Nor shall death brag thou wander'st in his shade,
When in eternal lines to time thou growest;
So long as men can breathe, or eyes can see,
So long lives this, and this gives life to thee.

XIX.

Devouring Time, blunt thou the lion's paws,
And make the earth devour her own sweet brood;
Pluck the keen teeth from the fierce tiger's jaws,
And burn the long-lived phœnix in her blood;
Make glad and sorry seasons as thou fleets,
And do whate'er thou wilt, swift-footed Time,
To the wide world and all her fading sweets;
But I forbid thee one most heinous crime:
O! carve not with thy hours my love's fair brow,
Nor draw no lines there with thine antique pen;
Him in thy course untainted do allow
For beauty's pattern to succeeding men.
Yet do thy worst, old Time: despite thy wrong,
My love shall in my verse ever live young.

XX.

A woman's face with Nature's own hand painted
Hast thou, the master-mistress of my passion;
A woman's gentle heart, but not acquainted
With shifting change, as is false women's fashion;
An eye more bright than theirs, less false in rolling,
Gilding the object whereupon it gazeth;
A man in hue all hues in his controlling,
Which steals men's eyes and women's souls amazeth.
And for a woman wert thou first created;
Till Nature, as she wrought thee, fell a-doting,
And by addition me of thee defeated,
By adding one thing to my purpose nothing.
But since she prick'd thee out for women's pleasure,
Mine be thy love, and thy love's use their treasure.

XXI.

So is it not with me as with that Muse
Stirr'd by a painted beauty to his verse,
Who heaven itself for ornament doth use
And every fair with his fair doth rehearse,
Making a couplement of proud compare,
With sun and moon, with earth and sea's rich gems,
With April's first-born flowers, and all things rare
That heaven's air in this huge rondure hems.
O! let me, true in love, but truly write,
And then believe me, my love is as fair
As any mother's child, though not so bright
As those gold candles fix'd in heaven's air:
Let them say more that like of hear-say well;
I will not praise that purpose not to sell.

XXII.

My glass shall not persuade me I am old,
So long as youth and thou are of one date;
But when in thee time's furrows I behold,
Then look I death my days should expiate.
For all that beauty that doth cover thee
Is but the seemly raiment of my heart,
Which in thy breast doth live, as thine in me:
How can I then be elder than thou art?
O! therefore, love, be of thyself so wary
As I, not for myself, but for thee will;
Bearing thy heart, which I will keep so chary
As tender nurse her babe from faring ill.
Presume not on thy heart when mine is slain;
Thou gavest me thine, not to give back again.

XXIII.

As an unperfect actor on the stage,
Who with his fear is put besides his part,
Or some fierce thing replete with too much rage,
Whose strength's abundance weakens his own heart;
So I, for fear of trust, forget to say
The perfect ceremony of love's rite,
And in mine own love's strength seem to decay,
O'ercharged with burden of mine own love's might.
O! let my books be then the eloquence
And dumb presagers of my speaking breast,
Who plead for love, and look for recompense,
More than that tongue that more hath more express'd.
O! learn to read what silent love hath writ:
To hear with eyes belongs to love's fine wit.

XXIV.

Mine eye hath play'd the painter and hath stell'd
Thy beauty's form in table of my heart;
My body is the frame wherein 'tis held,
And perspective it is best painter's art.
For through the painter must you see his skill
To find where your true image pictured lies,
Which in my bosom's shop is hanging still,
That hath his windows glazed with thine eyes.
Now see what good turns eyes for eyes have done:
Mine eyes have drawn thy shape, and thine for me
Are windows to my breast, where-through the sun
Delights to peep, to gaze therein on thee;
Yet eyes this cunning want to grace their art,
They draw but what they see, know not the heart.

XXV.

Let those who are in favour with their stars
Of public honour and proud titles boast,
Whilst I, whom fortune of such triumph bars,
Unlook'd for joy in that I honour most.
Great princes' favourites their fair leaves spread
But as the marigold at the sun's eye,
And in themselves their pride lies buried,
For at a frown they in their glory die.
The painful warrior famoused for fight,
After a thousand victories once foil'd,
Is from the book of honour razed quite,
And all the rest forgot for which he toil'd:
Then happy I, that love and am beloved
Where I may not remove nor be removed.

XXVI.

Lord of my love, to whom in vassalage
Thy merit hath my duty strongly knit,
To thee I send this written ambassage,
To witness duty, not to show my wit:
Duty so great, which wit so poor as mine
May make seem bare, in wanting words to show it,
But that I hope some good conceit of thine
In thy soul's thought, all naked, will bestow it;
Till whatsoever star that guides my moving
Points on me graciously with fair aspect,
And puts apparel on my tatter'd loving,
To show me worthy of thy sweet respect:
Then may I dare to boast how I do love thee;
Till then not show my head where thou mayst prove me.

XXVII.

Weary with toil, I haste me to my bed,
The dear repose for limbs with travel tired;
But then begins a journey in my head
To work my mind, when body's work's expired:
For then my thoughts, from far where I abide,
Intend a zealous pilgrimage to thee,
And keep my drooping eyelids open wide,
Looking on darkness which the blind do see:
Save that my soul's imaginary sight
Presents thy shadow to my sightless view,
Which, like a jewel hung in ghastly night,
Makes black night beauteous and her old face new.
Lo! thus, by day my limbs, by night my mind,
For thee, and for myself no quiet find.

XXVIII.

How can I then return in happy plight,
That am debarr'd the benefit of rest?
When day's oppression is not eased by night,
But day by night, and night by day, oppressed;
And each, though enemies to either's reign,
Do in consent shake hands to torture me,
The one by toil, the other to complain
How far I toil, still farther off from thee?
I tell the day, to please him, thou art bright,
And dost him grace when clouds do blot the heaven:
So flatter I the swart-complexioned night;
When sparkling stars twire not thou glid'st the even.
But day doth daily draw my sorrows longer,
And night doth nightly make grief's length seem stronger.

XXIX.

When, in disgrace with fortune and men's eyes,
I all alone beweep my outcast state,
And trouble deaf heaven with my bootless cries,
And look upon thyself, and curse my fate,
Wishing me like to one more rich in hope,
Featured like him, like him with friends possess'd,
Desiring this man's art, and that man's scope,
With what I most enjoy contented least;
Yet in these thoughts myself almost despising,
Haply I think on thee, and then my state,
Like to the lark at break of day arising
From sullen earth, sings hymns at heaven's gate:
For thy sweet love rememb'red such wealth brings
That then I scorn to change my state with kings.

XXX.

When to the sessions of sweet silent thought
I summon up remembrance of things past,
I sigh the lack of many a thing I sought,
And with old woes new wail my dear time's waste:
Then can I drown an eye, unused to flow,
For precious friends hid in death's dateless night,
And weep afresh love's long since cancell'd woe,
And moan the expense of many a vanish'd sight:
Then can I grieve at grievances foregone,
And heavily from woe to woe tell o'er
The sad account of fore-bemoaned moan,
Which I new pay as if not paid before.
But if the while I think on thee, dear friend,
All losses are restored and sorrows end.

XXXI.

Thy bosom is endeared with all hearts,
Which I by lacking have supposed dead;
And there reigns Love, and all Love's loving parts,
And all those friends which I thought buried.
How many a holy and obsequious tear
Hath dear religious love stol'n from mine eye,
As interest of the dead, which now appear
But things removed that hidden in thee lie!
Thou art the grave where buried love doth live,
Hung with the trophies of my lovers gone,
Who all their parts of me to thee did give;
That due of many now is thine alone:
Their images I loved I view in thee,
And thou, all they, hast all the all of me.

XXXII.

If thou survive my well-contented day,
When that churl Death my bones with dust shall cover,
And shalt by fortune once more re-survey
These poor rude lines of thy deceased lover,
Compare them with the bettering of the time,
And though they be outstripp'd by every pen,
Reserve them for my love, not for their rhyme,
Exceeded by the height of happier men.
O! then vouchsafe me but this loving thought:
'Had my friend's Muse grown with this growing age,
A dearer birth than this his love had brought,
To march in ranks of better equipage:
But since he died, and poets better prove,
Theirs for their style I'll read, his for his love.'

XXXIII.

Full many a glorious morning have I seen
Flatter the mountain tops with sovereign eye,
Kissing with golden face the meadows green,
Gilding pale streams with heavenly alchemy;
Anon permit the basest clouds to ride
With ugly rack on his celestial face,
And from the forlorn world his visage hide,
Stealing unseen to west with this disgrace:
Even so my sun one early morn did shine
With all-triumphant splendour on my brow;
But, out, alack! he was but one hour mine,
The region cloud hath mask'd him from me now.
Yet him for this my love no whit disdaineth;
Suns of the world may stain when heaven's sun staineth.

XXXIV.

Why did'st thou promise such a beauteous day,
And make me travel forth without my cloak,
To let base clouds o'ertake me in my way,
Hiding thy bravery in their rotten smoke?
'Tis not enough that through the cloud thou break,
To dry the rain on my storm-beaten face,
For no man well of such a salve can speak
That heals the wound and cures not the disgrace:
Nor can thy shame give physic to my grief;
Though thou repent, yet I have still the loss:
The offender's sorrow lends but weak relief
To him that bears the strong offence's cross.
Ah! but those tears are pearl which thy love sheds,
And they are rich and ransom all ill deeds.

XXXV.

No more be grieved at that which thou hast done.
Roses have thorns, and silver fountains mud;
Clouds and eclipses stain both moon and sun,
And loathsome canker lives in sweetest bud.
All men make faults, and even I in this,
Authorizing thy trespass with compare,
Myself corrupting, salving thy amiss,
Excusing thy sins more than thy sins are;
For to thy sensual fault I bring in sense,
Thy adverse party is thy advocate,
And 'gainst myself a lawful plea commence:
Such civil war is in my love and hate,
That I an accessary needs must be
To that sweet thief which sourly robs from me.

XXXVI.

Let me confess that we two must be twain,
Although our undivided loves are one:
So shall those blots that do with me remain,
Without thy help, by me be borne alone.
In our two loves there is but one respect,
Though in our lives a separable spite,
Which, though it alter not love's sole effect,
Yet doth it steal sweet hours from love's delight.
I may not evermore acknowledge thee,
Lest my bewailed guilt should do thee shame,
Nor thou with public kindness honour me,
Unless thou take that honour from thy name:
But do not so; I love thee in such sort
As, thou being mine, mine is thy good report.

XXXVII.

As a decrepit father takes delight
To see his active child do deeds of youth,
So I, made lame by fortune's dearest spite,
Take all my comfort of thy worth and truth;
For whether beauty, birth, or wealth, or wit,
Or any of these all, or all, or more,
Entitled in thy parts do crowned sit,
I make my love engrafted to this store:
So then I am not lame, poor, nor despised,
Whilst that this shadow doth such substance give
That I in thy abundance am sufficed
And by a part of all thy glory live.
  Look, what is best, that best I wish in thee:
  This wish I have; then ten times happy me!

XXXVIII.

How can my Muse want subject to invent,
While thou dost breathe, that pour'st into my verse
Thine own sweet argument, too excellent
For every vulgar paper to rehearse?
O! give thyself the thanks, if aught in me
Worthy perusal stand against thy sight;
For who's so dumb that cannot write to thee,
When thou thyself dost give invention light?
Be thou the tenth Muse, ten times more in worth
Than those old nine which rhymers invocate;
And he that calls on thee, let him bring forth
Eternal numbers to outlive long date.
  If my slight Muse do please these curious days,
  The pain be mine, but thine shall be the praise.

XXXIX.

O! how thy worth with manners may I sing,
When thou art all the better part of me?
What can mine own praise to mine own self bring?
And what is't but mine own when I praise thee?
Even for this let us divided live,
And our dear love lose name of single one,
That by this separation I may give
That due to thee which thou deservest alone.
O absence! what a torment wouldst thou prove,
Were it not thy sour leisure gave sweet leave
To entertain the time with thoughts of love,
Which time and thoughts so sweetly doth deceive,
  And that thou teachest how to make one twain,
  By praising him here who doth hence remain.

XL.

Take all my loves, my love, yea, take them all;
What hast thou then more than thou hadst before?
No love, my love, that thou may'st true love call;
All mine was thine before thou hadst this more.
Then if for my love thou my love receivest,
I cannot blame thee for my love thou usest;
But yet be blamed, if thou thyself deceivest
By wilful taste of what thyself refusest.
I do forgive thy robbery, gentle thief,
Although thou steal thee all my poverty;
And yet love knows it is a greater grief
To bear love's wrong than hate's known injury.
  Lascivious grace, in whom all ill well shows,
  Kill me with spites; yet we must not be foes.

XLI.

Those pretty wrongs that liberty commits,
When I am sometime absent from thy heart,
Thy beauty and thy years full well befits,
For still temptation follows where thou art.
Gentle thou art, and therefore to be won,
Beauteous thou art, therefore to be assailed;
And when a woman woos, what woman's son
Will sourly leave her till she have prevailed?
Ay me! but yet thou might'st my seat forbear,
And chide thy beauty and thy straying youth,
Who lead thee in their riot even there
Where thou art forced to break a twofold truth;
  Hers, by thy beauty tempting her to thee,
  Thine, by thy beauty being false to me.

XLII.

That thou hast her, it is not all my grief,
And yet it may be said I loved her dearly;
That she hath thee, is of my wailing chief,
A loss in love that touches me more nearly.
Loving offenders, thus I will excuse ye:
Thou dost love her, because thou know'st I love her;
And for my sake even so doth she abuse me,
Suffering my friend for my sake to approve her.
If I lose thee, my loss is my love's gain,
And losing her, my friend hath found that loss;
Both find each other, and I lose both twain,
And both for my sake lay on me this cross:
  But here's the joy; my friend and I are one;
  Sweet flattery! then she loves but me alone.

XLIII.

When most I wink, then do mine eyes best see,
For all the day they view things unrespected;
But when I sleep, in dreams they look on thee,
And, darkly bright, are bright in dark directed.
Then thou, whose shadow shadows doth make bright,
How would thy shadow's form form happy show
To the clear day with thy much clearer light,
When to unseeing eyes thy shade shines so!
How would, I say, mine eyes be blessed made
By looking on thee in the living day,
When in dead night thy fair imperfect shade
Through heavy sleep on sightless eyes doth stay!
  All days are nights to see till I see thee,
  And nights bright days when dreams do show thee me.

XLIV.

If the dull substance of my flesh were thought,
Injurious distance should not stop my way;
For then, despite of space, I would be brought
From limits far remote, where thou dost stay.
No matter then although my foot did stand
Upon the furthest earth removed from thee;
For nimble thought can jump both sea and land,
As soon as think the place where he would be.
But, ah! thought kills me that I am not thought,
To leap large lengths of miles when thou art gone,
But that, so much of earth and water wrought,
I must attend time's leisure with my moan;
  Receiving nought by elements so slow
  But heavy tears, badges of either's woe.

XLV.

The other two, slight air and purging fire,
Are both with thee, wherever I abide;
The first my thought, the other my desire,
These present-absent with swift motion slide.
For when these quicker elements are gone
In tender embassy of love to thee,
My life, being made of four, with two alone
Sinks down to death, oppress'd with melancholy;
Until life's composition be recured
By those swift messengers return'd from thee,
Who even but now come back again, assured
Of thy fair health, recounting it to me:
  This told, I joy; but then no longer glad,
  I send them back again, and straight grow sad.

XLVI.

Mine eye and heart are at a mortal war,
How to divide the conquest of thy sight;
Mine eye my heart thy picture's sight would bar,
My heart mine eye the freedom of that right.
My heart doth plead that thou in him dost lie,
A closet never pierced with crystal eyes,
But the defendant doth that plea deny,
And says in him thy fair appearance lies.
To 'cide this title is impannelled
A quest of thoughts, all tenants to the heart;
And by their verdict is determined
The clear eye's moiety and the dear heart's part:
  As thus; mine eye's due is thine outward part,
  And my heart's right thine inward love of heart.

XLVII.

Betwixt mine eye and heart a league is took,
And each doth good turns now unto the other:
When that mine eye is famish'd for a look,
Or heart in love with sighs himself doth smother,
With my love's picture then my eye doth feast,
And to the painted banquet bids my heart;
Another time mine eye is my heart's guest,
And in his thoughts of love doth share a part:
So, either by thy picture or my love,
Thyself away art present still with me;
For thou not further than my thoughts canst move,
And I am still with them and they with thee;
  Or, if they sleep, thy picture in my sight
  Awakes my heart to heart's and eye's delight.

XLVIII.

How careful was I, when I took my way,
Each trifle under truest bars to thrust,
That to my use it might unused stay
From hands of falsehood, in sure wards of trust!
But thou, to whom my jewels trifles are,
Most worthy comfort, now my greatest grief,
Thou, best of dearest and mine only care,
Art left the prey of every vulgar thief.
Thee have I not lock'd up in any chest,
Save where thou art not, though I feel thou art,
Within the gentle closure of my breast,
From whence at pleasure thou mayst come and part;
  And even thence thou wilt be stol'n, I fear,
  For truth proves thievish for a prize so dear.

XLIX.

Against that time, if ever that time come,
When I shall see thee frown on my defects,
When as thy love hath cast his utmost sum,
Call'd to that audit by advised respects;
Against that time when thou shalt strangely pass,
And scarcely greet me with that sun, thine eye,
When love, converted from the thing it was,
Shall reasons find of settled gravity;
Against that time do I ensconce me here
Within the knowledge of mine own desert,
And this my hand against myself uprear,
To guard the lawful reasons on thy part:
  To leave poor me thou hast the strength of laws,
  Since why to love I can allege no cause.

L.

How heavy do I journey on the way,
When what I seek, my weary travel's end,
Doth teach that ease and that repose to say,
'Thus far the miles are measured from thy friend!'
The beast that bears me, tired with my woe,
Plods dully on, to bear that weight in me,
As if by some instinct the wretch did know
His rider loved not speed, being made from thee:
The bloody spur cannot provoke him on
That sometimes anger thrusts into his hide,
Which heavily he answers with a groan
More sharp to me than spurring to his side;
  For that same groan doth put this in my mind:
  My grief lies onward, and my joy behind.

LI.

Thus can my love excuse the slow offence
Of my dull bearer when from thee I speed:
From where thou art why should I haste me thence?
Till I return, of posting is no need.
O! what excuse will my poor beast then find,
When swift extremity can seem but slow?
Then should I spur, though mounted on the wind,
In winged speed no motion shall I know:
Then can no horse with my desire keep pace;
Therefore desire, of perfect'st love being made,
Shall neigh, no dull flesh in his fiery race;
But love, for love, thus shall excuse my jade;
  'Since from thee going he went wilful-slow,
  Towards thee I'll run and give him leave to go.'

LII.

So am I as the rich, whose blessed key
Can bring him to his sweet up-locked treasure,
The which he will not every hour survey,
For blunting the fine point of seldom pleasure.
Therefore are feasts so solemn and so rare,
Since, seldom coming, in the long year set,
Like stones of worth they thinly placed are,
Or captain jewels in the carcanet.
So is the time that keeps you as my chest,
Or as the wardrobe which the robe doth hide,
To make some special instant special blest,
By new unfolding his imprison'd pride.
  Blessed are you, whose worthiness gives scope,
  Being had, to triumph; being lack'd, to hope.

LIII.

What is your substance, whereof are you made,
That millions of strange shadows on you tend?
Since every one hath, every one, one shade,
And you, but one, can every shadow lend.
Describe Adonis, and the counterfeit
Is poorly imitated after you;
On Helen's cheek all art of beauty set,
And you in Grecian tires are painted new:
Speak of the spring and foison of the year,
The one doth shadow of your beauty show,
The other as your bounty doth appear;
And you in every blessed shape we know.
In all external grace you have some part,
But you like none, none you, for constant heart.

LIV.

O! how much more doth beauty beauteous seem
By that sweet ornament which truth doth give:
The rose looks fair, but fairer we it deem
For that sweet odour which doth in it live.
The canker-blooms have full as deep a dye
As the perfumed tincture of the roses,
Hang on such thorns, and play as wantonly
When summer's breath their masked buds discloses:
But, for their virtue only is their show,
They live unwoo'd and unrespected fade;
Die to themselves. Sweet roses do not so;
Of their sweet deaths are sweetest odours made:
And so of you, beauteous and lovely youth,
When that shall fade, by verse distils your truth.

LV.

Not marble, nor the gilded monuments
Of princes, shall outlive this powerful rhyme;
But you shall shine more bright in these contents
Than unswept stone, besmear'd with sluttish time.
When wasteful war shall statues overturn,
And broils root out the work of masonry,
Nor Mars his sword nor war's quick fire shall burn
The living record of your memory.
'Gainst death and all-oblivious enmity
Shall you pace forth; your praise shall still find room
Even in the eyes of all posterity
That wear this world out to the ending doom.
So, till the judgement that yourself arise,
You live in this, and dwell in lovers' eyes.

LVI.

Sweet love, renew thy force; be it not said
Thy edge should blunter be than appetite,
Which but to-day by feeding is allay'd,
To-morrow sharpened in his former might:
So, love, be thou; although to-day thou fill
Thy hungry eyes even till they wink with fulness,
To-morrow see again, and do not kill
The spirit of love with a perpetual dulness.
Let this sad interim like the ocean be
Which parts the shore, where two contracted new
Come daily to the banks, that, when they see
Return of love, more bless'd may be the view;
Or call it winter, which, being full of care,
Makes summer's welcome thrice more wish'd, more rare.

LVII.

Being your slave, what should I do but tend
Upon the hours and times of your desire?
I have no precious time at all to spend,
Nor services to do, till you require.
Nor dare I chide the world-without-end hour
Whilst I, my sovereign, watch the clock for you,
Nor think the bitterness of absence sour
When you have bid your servant once adieu;
Nor dare I question with my jealous thought
Where you may be, or your affairs suppose,
But, like a sad slave, stay and think of nought
Save, where you are how happy you make those.
So true a fool is love that in your will,
Though you do any thing, he thinks no ill.

LVIII.

That god forbid that made me first your slave,
I should in thought control your times of pleasure,
Or at your hand the account of hours to crave,
Being your vassal, bound to stay your leisure!
O! let me suffer, being at your beck,
The imprison'd absence of your liberty;
And patience, tame to sufferance, bide each check,
Without accusing you of injury.
Be where you list, your charter is so strong
That you yourself may privilege your time
To what you will; to you it doth belong
Yourself to pardon of self-doing crime.
I am to wait, though waiting so be hell,
Not blame your pleasure, be it ill or well.

LIX.

If there be nothing new, but that which is
Hath been before, how are our brains beguiled,
Which, labouring for invention, bear amiss
The second burthen of a former child!
O! that record could with a backward look,
Even of five hundred courses of the sun,
Show me your image in some antique book,
Since mind at first in character was done:
That I might see what the old world could say
To this composed wonder of your frame;
Whether we are mended, or whe'r better they,
Or whether revolution be the same.
O! sure I am, the wits of former days
To subjects worse have given admiring praise.

LX.

Like as the waves make towards the pebbled shore,
So do our minutes hasten to their end;
Each changing place with that which goes before,
In sequent toil all forwards do contend.
Nativity, once in the main of light,
Crawls to maturity, wherewith being crown'd,
Crooked eclipses 'gainst his glory fight,
And Time that gave doth now his gift confound.
Time doth transfix the flourish set on youth
And delves the parallels in beauty's brow,
Feeds on the rarities of nature's truth,
And nothing stands but for his scythe to mow:
And yet to times in hope my verse shall stand,
Praising thy worth, despite his cruel hand.

LXI.

Is it thy will thy image should keep open
My heavy eyelids to the weary night?
Dost thou desire my slumbers should be broken,
While shadows like to thee do mock my sight?
Is it thy spirit that thou send'st from thee
So far from home into my deeds to pry,
To find out shames and idle hours in me,
The scope and tenour of thy jealousy?
O, no! thy love, though much, is not so great:
It is my love that keeps mine eye awake;
Mine own true love that doth my rest defeat,
To play the watchman ever for thy sake:
For thee watch I whilst thou dost wake elsewhere,
From me far off, with others all too near.

LXII.

Sin of self-love possesseth all mine eye
And all my soul and all my every part;
And for this sin there is no remedy,
It is so grounded inward in my heart.
Methinks no face so gracious is as mine,
No shape so true, no truth of such account;
And for myself mine own worth do define,
As I all other in all worths surmount.
But when my glass shows me myself indeed,
Beated and chopp'd with tann'd antiquity,
Mine own self-love quite contrary I read;
Self so self-loving were iniquity.
'T is thee, myself, that for myself I praise,
Painting my age with beauty of thy days.

LXIII.

Against my love shall be, as I am now,
With Time's injurious hand crush'd and o'erworn;
When hours have drain'd his blood and fill'd his brow
With lines and wrinkles; when his youthful morn
Hath travell'd on to age's steepy night;
And all those beauties whereof now he 's king
Are vanishing or vanish'd out of sight,
Stealing away the treasure of his spring;
For such a time do I now fortify
Against confounding age's cruel knife,
That he shall never cut from memory
My sweet love's beauty, though my lover's life:
His beauty shall in these black lines be seen,
And they shall live, and he in them still green.

LXIV.

When I have seen by Time's fell hand defaced
The rich-proud cost of outworn buried age;
When sometime lofty towers I see down-razed,
And brass eternal slave to mortal rage;
When I have seen the hungry ocean gain
Advantage on the kingdom of the shore,
And the firm soil win of the watery main,
Increasing store with loss and loss with store;
When I have seen such interchange of state,
Or state itself confounded to decay;
Ruin hath taught me thus to ruminate,
That Time will come and take my love away.
This thought is as a death, which cannot choose
But weep to have that which it fears to lose.

LXV.

Since brass, nor stone, nor earth, nor boundless sea,
But sad mortality o'ersways their power,
How with this rage shall beauty hold a plea,
Whose action is no stronger than a flower?
O! how shall summer's honey breath hold out
Against the wreckful siege of battering days,
When rocks impregnable are not so stout,
Nor gates of steel so strong, but Time decays?
O fearful meditation! where, alack!
Shall Time's best jewel from Time's chest lie hid?
Or what strong hand can hold his swift foot back?
Or who his spoil of beauty can forbid?
O! none, unless this miracle have might,
That in black ink my love may still shine bright.

LXVI.

Tired with all these, for restful death I cry
As, to behold desert a beggar born,
And needy nothing trimm'd in jollity,
And purest faith unhappily forsworn,
And gilded honour shamefully misplaced,
And maiden virtue rudely strumpeted,
And right perfection wrongfully disgraced,
And strength by limping sway disabled,
And art made tongue-tied by authority,
And folly, doctor-like, controlling skill,
And simple truth miscall'd simplicity,
And captive good attending captain ill:
Tired with all these, from these would I be gone,
Save that, to die, I leave my love alone.

LXVII.

Ah! wherefore with infection should he live
And with his presence grace impiety,
That sin by him advantage should achieve
And lace itself with his society?
Why should false painting imitate his cheek,
And steal dead seeing of his living hue?
Why should poor beauty indirectly seek
Roses of shadow, since his rose is true?
Why should he live, now Nature bankrupt is,
Beggar'd of blood to blush through lively veins?
For she hath no exchequer now but his,
And, proud of many, lives upon his gains.
O! him she stores, to show what wealth she had
In days long since, before these last so bad.

LXVIII.

Thus is his cheek the map of days outworn,
When beauty lived and died as flowers do now,
Before these bastard signs of fair were born,
Or durst inhabit on a living brow;
Before the golden tresses of the dead,
The right of sepulchres, were shorn away,
To live a second life on second head;
Ere beauty's dead fleece made another gay:
In him those holy antique hours are seen,
Without all ornament, itself and true,
Making no summer of another's green,
Robbing no old to dress his beauty new;
And him as for a map doth Nature store,
To show false Art what beauty was of yore.

LXIX.

Those parts of thee that the world's eye doth view
Want nothing that the thought of hearts can mend;
All tongues, the voice of souls, give thee that due,
Uttering bare truth, even so as foes commend.
Thy outward thus with outward praise is crown'd;
But those same tongues, that give thee so thine own,
In other accents do this praise confound
By seeing further than the eye hath shown.
They look into the beauty of thy mind,
And that, in guess, they measure by thy deeds;
Then, churls, their thoughts, although their eyes were kind,
To thy fair flower and the rank smell of weeds:
But why thy odour matcheth not thy show,
The soil is this, that thou dost common grow.

LXX.

That thou art blamed shall not be thy defect,
For slander's mark was ever yet the fair;
The ornament of beauty is suspect,
A crow that flies in heaven's sweetest air.
So thou be good, slander doth but approve
Thy worth the greater, being woo'd of time;
For canker vice the sweetest buds doth love,
And thou present'st a pure, unstained prime.
Thou hast pass'd by the ambush of young days,
Either not assail'd, or victor being charged;
Yet this thy praise cannot be so thy praise,
To tie up envy evermore enlarged:
If some suspect of ill mask'd not thy show,
Then thou alone kingdoms of hearts shouldst owe.

LXXI.

No longer mourn for me when I am dead
Than you shall hear the surly sullen bell
Give warning to the world that I am fled
From this vile world, with vilest worms to dwell:
Nay, if you read this line, remember not
The hand that writ it; for I love you so,
That I in your sweet thoughts would be forgot,
If thinking on me then should make you woe.
O! if, I say, you look upon this verse
When I perhaps compounded am with clay,
Do not so much as my poor name rehearse,
But let your love even with my life decay;
Lest the wise world should look into your moan,
And mock you with me after I am gone.

LXXII.

O! lest the world should task you to recite
What merit lived in me, that you should love
After my death, dear love, forget me quite,
For you in me can nothing worthy prove;
Unless you would devise some virtuous lie,
To do more for me than mine own desert,
And hang more praise upon deceased I
Than niggard truth would willingly impart:
O! lest your true love may seem false in this,
That you for love speak well of me untrue,
My name be buried where my body is,
And live no more to shame nor me nor you.
For I am shamed by that which I bring forth,
And so should you, to love things nothing worth.

LXXIII.

That time of year thou mayst in me behold
When yellow leaves, or none, or few, do hang
Upon those boughs which shake against the cold,
Bare ruin'd choirs, where late the sweet birds sang.
In me thou see'st the twilight of such day
As after sunset fadeth in the west;
Which by and by black night doth take away,
Death's second self, that seals up all in rest.
In me thou see'st the glowing of such fire,
That on the ashes of his youth doth lie,
As the death-bed whereon it must expire,
Consumed with that which it was nourish'd by.
This thou perceivest, which makes thy love more strong,
To love that well which thou must leave ere long.

LXXIV.

But be contented: when that fell arrest
Without all bail shall carry me away,
My life hath in this line some interest,
Which for memorial still with thee shall stay.
When thou reviewest this, thou dost review
The very part was consecrate to thee:
The earth can have but earth, which is his due:
My spirit is thine, the better part of me:
So then thou hast but lost the dregs of life,
The prey of worms, my body being dead;
The coward conquest of a wretch's knife,
Too base of thee to be remembered.
The worth of that is that which it contains,
And that is this, and this with thee remains.

LXXV.

So are you to my thoughts as food to life,
Or as sweet-season'd showers are to the ground;
And for the peace of you I hold such strife
As 'twixt a miser and his wealth is found;
Now proud as an enjoyer, and anon
Doubting the filching age will steal his treasure;
Now counting best to be with you alone,
Then better'd that the world may see my pleasure:
Sometime, all full with feasting on your sight,
And by and by clean starved for a look;
Possessing or pursuing no delight,
Save what is had or must from you be took.
Thus do I pine and surfeit day by day,
Or gluttoning on all, or all away.

LXXVI.

Why is my verse so barren of new pride,
So far from variation or quick change?
Why with the time do I not glance aside
To new-found methods and to compounds strange?
Why write I still all one, ever the same,
And keep invention in a noted weed,
That every word doth almost tell my name,
Showing their birth and where they did proceed?
O! know, sweet love, I always write of you,
And you and love are still my argument;
So all my best is dressing old words new,
Spending again what is already spent:
For as the sun is daily new and old,
So is my lc e still telling what is told.

LXXVII.

Thy glass will show thee how thy beauties wear,
Thy dial how thy precious minutes waste;
The vacant leaves thy mind's imprint will bear,
And of this book this learning may'st thou taste.
The wrinkles which thy glass will truly show
Of mouthed graves will give thee memory;
Thou by thy dial's shady stealth may'st know
Time's thievish progress to eternity.
Look! what thy memory cannot contain
Commit to these waste blanks, and thou shalt find
Those children nursed, deliver'd from thy brain,
To take a new acquaintance of thy mind.
These offices, so oft as thou wilt look,
Shall profit thee and much enrich thy book.

LXXVIII.

So oft have I invoked thee for my Muse
And found such fair assistance in my verse
As every alien pen hath got my use
And under thee their poesy disperse.
Thine eyes, that taught the dumb on high to sing
And heavy ignorance aloft to fly,
Have added feathers to the learned's wing
And given grace a double majesty.
Yet be most proud of that which I compile,
Whose influence is thine and born of thee:
In others' works thou dost but mend the style,
And arts with thy sweet graces graced be;
But thou art all my art, and dost advance
As high as learning my rude ignorance.

LXXIX.

Whilst I alone did call upon thy aid,
My verse alone had all thy gentle grace;
But now my gracious numbers are decay'd,
And my sick Muse doth give another place.
I grant, sweet love, thy lovely argument
Deserves the travail of a worthier pen;
Yet what of thee thy poet doth invent
He robs thee of, and pays it thee again.
He lends thee virtue, and he stole that word
From thy behaviour; beauty doth he give,
And found it in thy cheek; he can afford
No praise to thee but what in thee doth live.
Then thank him not for that which he doth say,
Since what he owes thee thou thyself dost pay.

LXXX.

O! how I faint when I of you do write,
Knowing a better spirit doth use your name,
And in the praise thereof spends all his might,
To make me tongue-tied, speaking of your fame.
But since your worth, wide as the ocean is,
The humble as the proudest sail doth bear,
My saucy bark, inferior far to his,
On your broad main doth wilfully appear.
Your shallowest help will hold me up afloat,
Whilst he upon your soundless deep doth ride;
Or, being wreck'd, I am a worthless boat,
He of tall building and of goodly pride:
Then if he thrive and I be cast away,
The worst was this; my love was my decay.

LXXXI.

Or I shall live your epitaph to make,
Or you survive when I in earth am rotten;
From hence your memory death cannot take,
Although in me each part will be forgotten.
Your name from hence immortal life shall have,
Though I, once gone, to all the world must die:
The earth can yield me but a common grave,
When you entombed in men's eyes shall lie.
Your monument shall be my gentle verse,
Which eyes not yet created shall o'er-read;
And tongues to be your being shall rehearse,
When all the breathers of this world are dead;
You still shall live, such virtue hath my pen,
Where breath most breathes, even in the mouths of men.

LXXXII.

I grant thou wert not married to my Muse,
And therefore may'st without attaint o'erlook
The dedicated words which writers use
Of their fair subject, blessing every book.
Thou art as fair in knowledge as in hue,
Finding thy worth a limit past my praise;
And therefore art enforced to seek anew
Some fresher stamp of the time-bettering days.
And do so, love; yet when they have devised
What strained touches rhetoric can lend,
Thou truly fair wert truly sympathized
In true plain words by thy true-telling friend;
And their gross painting might be better used
Where cheeks need blood; in thee it is abused.

LXXXIII.

I never saw that you did painting need,
And therefore to your fair no painting set;
I found, or thought I found, you did exceed
The barren tender of a poet's debt:
And therefore have I slept in your report,
That you yourself, being extant, well might show
How far a modern quill doth come too short,
Speaking of worth, what worth in you doth grow.
This silence for my sin you did impute,
Which shall be most my glory, being dumb;
For I impair not beauty being mute,
When others would give life and bring a tomb.
There lives more life in one of your fair eyes
Than both your poets can in praise devise.

LXXXIV.

Who is it that says most? which can say more
Than this rich praise, that you alone are you?
In whose confine immured is the store
Which should example where your equal grew.
Lean penury within that pen doth dwell
That to his subject lends not some small glory;
But he that writes of you, if he can tell
That you are you, so dignifies his story,
Let him but copy what in you is writ,
Not making worse what nature made so clear,
And such a counterpart shall fame his wit,
Making his style admired every where.
You to your beauteous blessings add a curse,
Being fond on praise, which makes your praises worse.

LXXXV.

My tongue-tied Muse in manners holds her still,
While comments of your praise, richly compiled,
Reserve their character with golden quill,
And precious phrase by all the Muses filled.
I think good thoughts, whilst other write good words,
And, like unletter'd clerk, still cry 'Amen'
To every hymn that able spirit affords,
In polish'd form of well-refined pen.
Hearing you praised, I say ''T is so, 't is true,'
And to the most of praise add something more;
But that is in my thought, whose love to you,
Though words come hindmost, holds his rank before.
Then others for the breath of words respect,
Me for my dumb thoughts, speaking in effect.

LXXXVI.

Was it the proud full sail of his great verse,
Bound for the prize of all too precious you,
That did my ripe thoughts in my brain inhearse,
Making their tomb the womb wherein they grew?
Was it his spirit, by spirits taught to write
Above a mortal pitch, that struck me dead?
No, neither he, nor his compeers by night
Giving him aid, my verse astonished.
He, nor that affable familiar ghost
Which nightly gulls him with intelligence,
As victors, of my silence cannot boast;
I was not sick of any fear from thence:
But when your countenance fill'd up his line,
Then lack'd I matter; that enfeebled mine.

LXXXVII.

Farewell! thou art too dear for my possessing,
And like enough thou know'st thy estimate:
The charter of thy worth gives thee releasing;
My bonds in thee are all determinate.
For how do I hold thee but by thy granting?
And for that riches where is my deserving?
The cause of this fair gift in me is wanting,
And so my patent back again is swerving.
Thyself thou gavest, thy own worth then not knowing,
Or me, to whom thou gavest it, else mistaking;
So thy great gift, upon misprision growing,
Comes home again, on better judgement making.
Thus have I had thee, as a dream doth flatter,
In sleep a king, but waking no such matter.

LXXXVIII.

When thou shalt be disposed to set me light,
And place my merit in the eye of scorn,
Upon thy side against myself I'll fight,
And prove thee virtuous, though thou art forsworn.
With mine own weakness being best acquainted,
Upon thy part I can set down a story
Of faults concealed, wherein I am attainted;
That thou in losing me shalt win much glory:
And I by this will be a gainer too;
For bending all my loving thoughts on thee,
The injuries that to myself I do,
Doing thee vantage, double-vantage me.
Such is my love, to thee I so belong,
That for thy right myself will bear all wrong.

LXXXIX.

Say that thou didst forsake me for some fault,
And I will comment upon that offence:
Speak of my lameness, and I straight will halt,
Against thy reasons making no defence.
Thou canst not, love, disgrace me half so ill,
To set a form upon desired change,
As I'll myself disgrace; knowing thy will,
I will acquaintance strangle and look strange;
Be absent from thy walks; and in my tongue
Thy sweet beloved name no more shall dwell,
Lest I, too much profane, should do it wrong,
And haply of our old acquaintance tell.
For thee, against myself I'll vow debate,
For I must ne'er love him whom thou dost hate.

XC.

Then hate me when thou wilt; if ever, now;
Now, while the world is bent my deeds to cross,
Join with the spite of fortune, make me bow,
And do not drop in for an after-loss:
Ah! do not, when my heart hath 'scaped this sorrow,
Come in the rearward of a conquer'd woe;
Give not a windy night a rainy morrow,
To linger out a purposed overthrow.
If thou wilt leave me, do not leave me last,
When other petty griefs have done their spite,
But in the onset come: so shall I taste
At first the very worst of fortune's might;
And other strains of woe, which now seem woe,
Compar'd with loss of thee will not seem so.

XCI.

Some glory in their birth, some in their skill,
Some in their wealth, some in their body's force;
Some in their garments, though new-fangled ill;
Some in their hawks and hounds, some in their horse;
And every humour hath his adjunct pleasure,
Wherein it finds a joy above the rest:
But these particulars are not my measure;
All these I better in one general best.
Thy love is better than high birth to me,
Richer than wealth, prouder than garments' cost,
Of more delight than hawks or horses be;
And having thee, of all men's pride I boast:
Wretched in this alone, that thou may'st take
All this away and me most wretched make.

XCII.

But do thy worst to steal thyself away,
For term of life thou art assured mine;
And life no longer than thy love will stay,
For it depends upon that love of thine.
Then need I not to fear the worst of wrongs,
When in the least of them my life hath end.
I see a better state to me belongs
Than that which on thy humour doth depend:
Thou canst not vex me with inconstant mind,
Since that my life on thy revolt doth lie.
O! what a happy title do I find,
Happy to have thy love, happy to die:
But what's so blessed-fair that fears no blot?
Thou may'st be false, and yet I know it not.

XCIII.

So shall I live, supposing thou art true,
Like a deceived husband; so love's face
May still seem love to me, though alter'd new;
Thy looks with me, thy heart in other place:
For there can live no hatred in thine eye,
Therefore in that I cannot know thy change.
In many's looks the false heart's history
Is writ in moods and frowns and wrinkles strange,
But heaven in thy creation did decree
That in thy face sweet love should ever dwell;
Whate'er thy thoughts or thy heart's workings be,
Thy looks should nothing thence but sweetness tell.
How like Eve's apple doth thy beauty grow,
If thy sweet virtue answer not thy show!

XCIV.

They that have power to hurt and will do none,
That do not do the thing they most do show,
Who, moving others, are themselves as stone,
Unmoved, cold, and to temptation slow;
They rightly do inherit heaven's graces
And husband nature's riches from expense;
They are the lords and owners of their faces,
Others but stewards of their excellence.
The summer's flower is to the summer sweet,
Though to itself it only live and die,
But if that flower with base infection meet,
The basest weed outbraves his dignity:
For sweetest things turn sourest by their deeds;
Lilies that fester smell far worse than weeds.

XCV.

How sweet and lovely dost thou make the shame
Which, like a canker in the fragrant rose,
Doth spot the beauty of thy budding name!
O! in what sweets dost thou thy sins enclose;
That tongue that tells the story of thy days,
Making lascivious comments on thy sport,
Cannot dispraise but in a kind of praise;
Naming thy name blesses an ill report.
O! what a mansion have those vices got
Which for their habitation chose out thee,
Where beauty's veil doth cover every blot
And all things turn to fair that eyes can see.
Take heed, dear heart, of this large privilege;
The hardest knife ill-used doth lose his edge.

XCVI.

Some say, thy fault is youth, some wantonness;
Some say, thy grace is youth and gentle sport;
Both grace and faults are loved of more and less:
Thou makest faults graces that to thee resort.
As on the finger of a throned queen
The basest jewel will be well esteem'd,
So are those errors that in thee are seen
To truths translated and for true things deem'd.
How many lambs might the stern wolf betray,
If like a lamb he could his looks translate!
How many gazers might'st thou lead away,
If thou would'st use the strength of all thy state!
But do not so; I love thee in such sort,
As thou being mine, mine is thy good report.

XCVII.

How like a winter hath my absence been
From thee, the pleasure of the fleeting year!
What freezings have I felt, what dark days seen!
What old December's bareness every where!
And yet this time removed was summer's time;
The teeming autumn, big with rich increase,
Bearing the wanton burden of the prime,
Like widow'd wombs after their lords' decease:
Yet this abundant issue seem'd to me
But hope of orphans and unfather'd fruit;
For summer and his pleasures wait on thee,
And, thou away, the very birds are mute:
Or, if they sing 't is with so dull a cheer
The leaves look pale, dreading the winter 's near.

XCVIII.

From you have I been absent in the spring,
When proud-pied April, dress'd in all his trim,
Hath put a spirit of youth in every thing,
That heavy Saturn laugh'd and leap'd with him.
Yet nor the lays of birds, nor the sweet smell
Of different flowers in odour and in hue,
Could make me any summer's story tell,
Or from their proud lap pluck them where they grew:
Nor did I wonder at the lily's white,
Nor praise the deep vermilion in the rose;
They were but sweet, but figures of delight,
Drawn after you, you pattern of all those.
Yet seem'd it winter still, and, you away,
As with your shadow I with these did play.

XCIX.

The forward violet thus did I chide:
Sweet thief, whence didst thou steal thy sweet that smells,
If not from my love's breath? The purple pride
Which on thy soft cheek for complexion dwells
In my love's veins thou hast too grossly dyed.
The lily I condemned for thy hand,
And buds of marjoram had stol'n thy hair;
The roses fearfully on thorns did stand,
One blushing shame, another white despair;
A third, nor red nor white, had stol'n of both,
And to his robbery had annex'd thy breath;
But, for his theft, in pride of all his growth
A vengeful canker eat him up to death.
More flowers I noted, yet I none could see
But sweet or colour it had stol'n from thee.

C.

Where art thou, Muse, that thou forget'st so long
To speak of that which gives thee all thy might?
Spend'st thou thy fury on some worthless song,
Dark'ning thy power to lend base subjects light?
Return, forgetful Muse, and straight redeem
In gentle numbers time so idly spent;
Sing to the ear that doth thy lays esteem
And gives thy pen both skill and argument.
Rise, resty Muse, my love's sweet face survey
If Time have any wrinkle graven there;
If any, be a satire to decay,
And make Time's spoils despised every where.
Give my love fame faster than Time wastes life;
So thou prevent'st his scythe and crooked knife.

CI.

O truant Muse, what shall be thy amends
For thy neglect of truth in beauty dyed?
Both truth and beauty on my love depends;
So dost thou too, and therein dignified.
Make answer, Muse: wilt thou not haply say,
'Truth needs no colour, with his colour fix'd;
Beauty no pencil, beauty's truth to lay;
But best is best, if never intermix'd'?
Because he needs no praise, wilt thou be dumb?
Excuse not silence so; for't lies in thee
To make him much outlive a gilded tomb
And to be prais'd of ages yet to be.
Then do thy office, Muse; I teach thee how
To make him seem long hence as he shows now.

CII.

My love is strengthen'd, though more weak in seeming;
I love not less, though less the show appear:
That love is merchandised whose rich esteeming
The owner's tongue doth publish every where.
Our love was new, and then but in the spring,
When I was wont to greet it with my lays;
As Philomel in summer's front doth sing,
And stops her pipe in growth of riper days:
Not that the summer is less pleasant now
Than when her mournful hymns did hush the night,
But that wild music burthens every bough,
And sweets grown common lose their dear delight.
Therefore, like her, I sometime hold my tongue,
Because I would not dull you with my song.

CIII.

Alack! what poverty my Muse brings forth,
That having such a scope to show her pride,
The argument, all bare, is of more worth
Than when it hath my added praise beside.
O! blame me not, if I no more can write;
Look in your glass, and there appears a face
That over-goes my blunt invention quite,
Dulling my lines and doing me disgrace.
Were it not sinful then, striving to mend,
To mar the subject that before was well?
For to no other pass my verses tend
Than of your graces and your gifts to tell;
And more, much more, than in my verse can sit,
Your own glass shows you when you look in it.

CIV.

To me, fair friend, you never can be old,
For as you were when first your eye I eyed,
Such seems your beauty still. Three winters cold
Have from the forests shook three summers' pride,
Three beauteous springs to yellow autumn turn'd
In process of the seasons have I seen,
Three April perfumes in three hot Junes burn'd,
Since first I saw you fresh, which yet are green.
Ah! yet doth beauty, like a dial-hand,
Steal from his figure, and no pace perceived;
So your sweet hue, which methinks still doth stand,
Hath motion, and mine eye may be deceived:
For fear of which, hear this, thou age unbred:
Ere you were born was beauty's summer dead.

CV.

Let not my love be call'd idolatry,
Nor my beloved as an idol show,
Since all alike my songs and praises be
To one, of one, still such, and ever so.
Kind is my love to-day, to-morrow kind,
Still constant in a wondrous excellence;
Therefore my verse, to constancy confined,
One thing expressing, leaves out difference.
'Fair, kind, and true,' is all my argument,
'Fair, kind, and true,' varying to other words;
And in this change is my invention spent,
Three themes in one, which wondrous scope affords.
'Fair, kind, and true,' have often lived alone,
Which three till now never kept seat in one.

CVI.

When in the chronicle of wasted time
I see descriptions of the fairest wights,
And beauty making beautiful old rhyme
In praise of ladies dead and lovely knights,
Then, in the blazon of sweet beauty's best,
Of hand, of foot, of lip, of eye, of brow,
I see their antique pen would have express'd
Even such a beauty as you master now.
So all their praises are but prophecies
Of this our time, all you prefiguring;
And, for they look'd but with divining eyes,
They had not skill enough your worth to sing:
For we, which now behold these present days,
Have eyes to wonder, but lack tongues to praise.

CVII.

Not mine own fears, nor the prophetic soul
Of the wide world dreaming on things to come,
Can yet the lease of my true love control,
Supposed as forfeit to a confined doom.
The mortal moon hath her eclipse endured,
And the sad augurs mock their own presage;
Incertainties now crown themselves assured,
And peace proclaims olives of endless age.
Now with the drops of this most balmy time
My love looks fresh, and Death to me subscribes,
Since, spite of him, I'll live in this poor rhyme,
While he insults o'er dull and speechless tribes:
And thou in this shalt find thy monument,
When tyrants' crests and tombs of brass are spent.

CVIII.

What's in the brain, that ink may character,
Which hath not figured to thee my true spirit?
What's new to speak, what new to register,
That may express my love, or thy dear merit?
Nothing, sweet boy; but yet, like prayers divine,
I must each day say o'er the very same;
Counting no old thing old, thou mine, I thine,
Even as when first I hallow'd thy fair name.
So that eternal love in love's fresh case
Weighs not the dust and injury of age,
Nor gives to necessary wrinkles place,
But makes antiquity for aye his page;
Finding the first conceit of love there bred,
Where time and outward form would show it dead.

CIX.

O! never say that I was false of heart,
Though absence seem'd my flame to qualify.
As easy might I from myself depart
As from my soul, which in thy breast doth lie:
That is my home of love: if I have ranged,
Like him that travels, I return again;
Just to the time, not with the time exchanged,
So that myself bring water for my stain.
Never believe, though in my nature reign'd
All frailties that besiege all kinds of blood,
That it could so preposterously be stain'd,
To leave for nothing all thy sum of good;
For nothing this wide universe I call,
Save thou, my rose; in it thou art my all.

CX.

Alas! 't is true I have gone here and there,
And made myself a motley to the view,
Gored mine own thoughts, sold cheap what is most dear,
Made old offences of affections new;
Most true it is that I have look'd on truth
Askance and strangely; but, by all above,
These blenches gave my heart another youth,
And worse essays proved thee my best of love.
Now all is done, have what shall have no end:
Mine appetite I never more will grind
On newer proof, to try an older friend,
A god in love, to whom I am confined.
Then give me welcome, next my heaven the best,
Even to thy pure and most loving breast.

CXI.

O! for my sake do you with Fortune chide,
The guilty goddess of my harmful deeds,
That did not better for my life provide
Than public means which public manners breeds.
Thence comes it that my name receives a brand,
And almost thence my nature is subdued
To what it works in, like the dyer's hand:
Pity me then and wish I were renew'd;
Whilst, like a willing patient, I will drink
Potions of eisel, 'gainst my strong infection;
No bitterness that I will bitter think,
Nor double penance, to correct correction.
Pity me then, dear friend, and I assure ye
Even that your pity is enough to cure me.

CXII.

Your love and pity doth the impression fill
Which vulgar scandal stamp'd upon my brow;
For what care I who calls me well or ill,
So you o'er-green my bad, my good allow?
You are my all the world, and I must strive
To know my shames and praises from your tongue;
None else to me, nor I to none alive,
That my steel'd sense or changes right or wrong.
In so profound abysm I throw all care
Of others' voices, that my adder's sense
To critic and to flatterer stopped are.
Mark how with my neglect I do dispense:
You are so strongly in my purpose bred
That all the world besides methinks they're dead.

CXIII.

Since I left you mine eye is in my mind,
And that which governs me to go about
Doth part his function and is partly blind,
Seems seeing, but effectually is out;
For it no form delivers to the heart
Of bird, of flower, or shape, which it doth latch:
Of his quick objects hath the mind no part,
Nor his own vision holds what it doth catch;
For if it see the rudest or gentlest sight,
The most sweet favour or deformed'st creature,
The mountain or the sea, the day or night,
The crow or dove, it shapes them to your feature:
Incapable of more, replete with you,
My most true mind thus maketh mine untrue.

CXIV.

Or whether doth my mind, being crown'd with you,
Drink up the monarch's plague, this flattery?
Or whether shall I say, mine eye saith true,
And that your love taught it this alchemy,
To make of monsters and things indigest
Such cherubins as your sweet self resemble,
Creating every bad a perfect best,
As fast as objects to his beams assemble?
O! 't is the first; 't is flattery in my seeing,
And my great mind most kingly drinks it up:
Mine eye well knows what with his gust is 'greeing,
And to his palate doth prepare the cup:
If it be poison'd, 't is the lesser sin
That mine eye loves it and doth first begin.

CXV.

Those lines that I before have writ do lie,
Even those that said I could not love you dearer:
Yet then my judgement knew no reason why
My most full flame should afterwards burn clearer.
But reckoning Time, whose million'd accidents
Creep in 'twixt vows, and change decrees of kings,
Tan sacred beauty, blunt the sharp'st intents,
Divert strong minds to the course of altering things;
Alas! why, fearing of Time's tyranny,
Might I not then say 'Now I love you best,'
When I was certain o'er incertainty,
Crowning the present, doubting of the rest?
Love is a babe; then might I not say so,
To give full growth to that which still doth grow?

CXVI.

Let me not to the marriage of true minds
Admit impediments. Love is not love
Which alters when it alteration finds,
Or bends with the remover to remove:
O, no! it is an ever-fixed mark,
That looks on tempests and is never shaken;
It is the star to every wandering bark,
Whose worth's unknown, although his height be taken.
Love's not Time's fool, though rosy lips and cheeks
Within his bending sickle's compass come;
Love alters not with his brief hours and weeks,
But bears it out even to the edge of doom.
If this be error and upon me proved,
I never writ, nor no man ever loved.

CXVII.

Accuse me thus: that I have scanted all
Wherein I should your great deserts repay,
Forgot upon your dearest love to call,
Whereto all bonds do tie me day by day;
That I have frequent been with unknown minds,
And given to time your own dear-purchased right;
That I have hoisted sail to all the winds
Which should transport me furthest from your sight.
Book both my wilfulness and errors down,
And on just proof surmise accumulate;
Bring me within the level of your frown,
But shoot not at me in your waken'd hate;
Since my appeal says I did strive to prove
The constancy and virtue of your love.

CXVIII.

Like as, to make our appetites more keen,
With eager compounds we our palate urge;
As, to prevent our maladies unseen,
We sicken to shun sickness when we purge;
Even so, being full of your ne'er-cloying sweetness,
To bitter sauces did I frame my feeding;
And sick of welfare found a kind of meetness
To be diseased, ere that there was true needing.
Thus policy in love, to anticipate
The ills that were not, grew to faults assured,
And brought to medicine a healthful state,
Which, rank of goodness, would by ill be cured:
But thence I learn, and find the lesson true,
Drugs poison him that so fell sick of you.

CXIX.

What potions have I drunk of Siren tears,
Distill'd from limbecks foul as hell within,
Applying fears to hopes and hopes to fears,
Still losing when I saw myself to win!
What wretched errors hath my heart committed.
Whilst it hath thought itself so blessed never!
How have mine eyes out of their spheres been fitted,
In the distraction of this madding fever!
O benefit of ill! now I find true
That better is by evil still made better;
And ruin'd love, when it is built anew,
Grows fairer than at first, more strong, far greater.
So I return rebuked to my content,
And gain by ills thrice more than I have spent.

CXX.

That you were once unkind befriends me now,
And for that sorrow which I then did feel
Needs must I under my transgression bow,
Unless my nerves were brass or hammer'd steel.
For if you were by my unkindness shaken,
As I by yours, you've pass'd a hell of time;
And I, a tyrant, have no leisure taken
To weigh how once I suffer'd in your crime.
O! that our night of woe might have remember'd
My deepest sense, how hard true sorrow hits,
And soon to you, as you to me, then tender'd
The humble salve which wounded bosoms fits:
But that your trespass now becomes a fee;
Mine ransoms yours, and yours must ransom me.

CXXI.

'T is better to be vile than vile esteem'd,
When not to be receives reproach of being;
And the just pleasure lost, which is so deem'd
Not by our feeling, but by others' seeing:
For why should others' false adulterate eyes
Give salutation to my sportive blood?
Or on my frailties why are frailer spies,
Which in their wills count bad what I think good?
No, I am that I am, and they that level
At my abuses reckon up their own:
I may be straight, though they themselves be bevel;
By their rank thoughts my deeds must not be shown;
Unless this general evil they maintain,
All men are bad and in their badness reign.

CXXII.

Thy gift, thy tables, are within my brain
Full character'd with lasting memory,
Which shall above that idle rank remain,
Beyond all date, even to eternity:
Or, at the least, so long as brain and heart
Have faculty by nature to subsist;
Till each to razed oblivion yield his part
Of thee, thy record never can be miss'd.
That poor retention could not so much hold,
Nor need I tallies thy dear love to score;
Therefore to give them from me was I bold,
To trust those tables that receive thee more:
To keep an adjunct to remember thee
Were to import forgetfulness in me.

CXXIII.

No, Time, thou shalt not boast that I do change:
Thy pyramids built up with newer might
To me are nothing novel, nothing strange;
They are but dressings of a former sight.
Our dates are brief, and therefore we admire
What thou dost foist upon us that is old;
And rather make them born to our desire
Than think that we before have heard them told.
Thy registers and thee I both defy,
Not wondering at the present nor the past,
For thy records and what we see doth lie,
Made more or less by thy continual haste.
This I do vow, and this shall ever be,
I will be true, despite thy scythe and thee.

CXXIV.

If my dear love were but the child of state,
It might for Fortune's bastard be unfather'd,
As subject to Time's love or to Time's hate,
Weeds among weeds, or flowers with flowers gather'd.
No, it was builded far from accident;
It suffers not in smiling pomp, nor falls
Under the blow of thralled discontent,
Whereto the inviting time our fashion calls:
It fears not policy, that heretic,
Which works on leases of short number'd hours,
But all alone stands hugely politic,
That it nor grows with heat nor drowns with showers.

To this I witness call the fools of time,
Which die for goodness, who have lived for crime.

CXXV.

Were 't aught to me I bore the canopy,
With my extern the outward honouring,
Or laid great bases for eternity,
Which prove more short than waste or ruining?
Have I not seen dwellers on form and favour
Lose all, and more, by paying too much rent,
For compound sweet foregoing simple savour,
Pitiful thrivers, in their gazing spent?
No, let me be obsequious in thy heart,
And take thou my oblation, poor but free,
Which is not mix'd with seconds, knows no art
But mutual render, only me for thee.
Hence, thou suborn'd informer! a true soul
When most impeach'd stands least in thy control.

CXXVI.

O thou, my lovely boy, who in thy power
Dost hold Time's fickle glass, his sickle, hour;
Who hast by waning grown, and therein show'st
Thy lovers withering as thy sweet self grow'st;
If Nature, sovereign mistress over wrack,
As thou goest onwards, still will pluck thee back,
She keeps thee to this purpose, that her skill
May time disgrace and wretched minutes kill.
Yet fear her, O thou minion of her pleasure!
She may detain, but not still keep, her treasure:
Her audit, though delay'd, answer'd must be,
And her quietus is to render thee.

CXXVII.

In the old age black was not counted fair,
Or if it were, it bore not beauty's name;
But now is black beauty's successive heir,
And beauty slander'd with a bastard shame:
For since each hand hath put on nature's power,
Fairing the foul with art's false borrow'd face,
Sweet beauty hath no name, no holy bower,
But is profaned, if not lives in disgrace.
Therefore my mistress' eyes are raven black,
Her eyes so suited, and they mourners seem
At such who, not born fair, no beauty lack,
Sland'ring creation with a false esteem:
Yet so they mourn, becoming of their woe,
That every tongue says beauty should look so.

CXXVIII.

How oft, when thou, my music, music play'st
Upon that blessed wood whose motion sounds
With thy sweet fingers, whom thou gently sway'st
The wiry concord that mine ear confounds,
Do I envy those jacks that nimble leap
To kiss the tender inward of thy hand, [reap,
Whilst my poor lips, which should that harvest
At the wood's boldness by thee blushing stand!
To be so tickled, they would change their state
And situation with those dancing chips,
O'er whom thy fingers walk with gentle gait,
Making dead wood more bless'd than living lips.
Since saucy jacks so happy are in this,
Give them thy fingers, me thy lips to kiss.

CXXIX.

The expense of spirit in a waste of shame
Is lust in action; and till action, lust
Is perjured, murderous, bloody, full of blame,
Savage, extreme, rude, cruel, not to trust;
Enjoy'd no sooner but despised straight;
Past reason hunted; and no sooner had,
Past reason hated, as a swallow'd bait,
On purpose laid to make the taker mad:
Mad in pursuit, and in possession so;
Had, having, and in quest to have, extreme;
A bliss in proof, and proved, a very woe;
Before, a joy proposed; behind, a dream.
All this the world well knows; yet none knows well
To shun the heaven that leads men to this hell.

CXXX.

My mistress' eyes are nothing like the sun;
Coral is far more red than her lips' red:
If snow be white, why then her breasts are dun;
If hairs be wires, black wires grow on her head.
I have seen roses damask'd, red and white,
But no such roses see I in her cheeks;
And in some perfumes is there more delight
Than in the breath that from my mistress reeks.
I love to hear her speak, yet well I know
That music hath a far more pleasing sound:
I grant I never saw a goddess go,
My mistress, when she walks, treads on the ground:
And yet, by heaven, I think my love as rare
As any she belied with false compare.

CXXXI.

Thou art as tyrannous, so as thou art,
As those whose beauties proudly make them cruel
For well thou know'st to my dear doting heart
Thou art the fairest and most precious jewel.
Yet, in good faith, some say that thee behold,
Thy face hath not the power to make love groan:
To say they err I dare not be so bold,
Although I swear it to myself alone.
And to be sure that is not false I swear,
A thousand groans, but thinking on thy face,
One on another's neck, do witness bear
Thy black is fairest in my judgement's place.
In nothing art thou black save in thy deeds,
And thence this slander, as I think, proceeds.

CXXXII.

Thine eyes I love, and they, as pitying me,
Knowing thy heart torments me with disdain,
Have put on black and loving mourners be,
Looking with pretty ruth upon my pain.
And truly not the morning sun of heaven
Better becomes the gray cheeks of the east,
Nor that full star that ushers in the even
Doth half that glory to the sober west,
As those two mourning eyes become thy face:
O! let it then as well beseem thy heart
To mourn for me, since mourning doth thee grace,
And suit thy pity like in every part.
Then will I swear beauty herself is black,
And all they foul that thy complexion lack.

CXXXIII.

Beshrew that heart that makes my heart to groan
For that deep wound it gives my friend and me!
Is't not enough to torture me alone,
But slave to slavery my sweet'st friend must be?
Me from myself thy cruel eye hath taken,
And my next self thou harder hast engross'd:
Of him, myself, and thee, I am forsaken;
A torment thrice threefold thus to be cross'd.
Prison my heart in thy steel bosom's ward,
But then my friend's heart let my poor heart bail;
Whoe'er keeps me, let my heart be his guard;
Thou canst not then use rigour in my gaol:
And yet thou wilt; for I, being pent in thee,
Perforce am thine, and all that is in me.

CXXXIV.

So, now I have confess'd that he is thine,
And I myself am mortgaged to thy will,
Myself I'll forfeit, so that other mine
Thou wilt restore, to be my comfort still:
But thou wilt not, nor he will not be free,
For thou art covetous and he is kind;
He learn'd but surety-like to write for me,
Under that bond that him as fast doth bind.
The statute of thy beauty thou wilt take,
Thou usurer, that putt'st forth all to use,
And sue a friend came debtor for my sake;
So him I lose through my unkind abuse.
Him have I lost; thou hast both him and me:
He pays the whole, and yet am I not free.

CXXXV.

Whoever hath her wish, thou hast thy *Will*,
And *Will* to boot, and *Will* in overplus;
More than enough am I that vex thee still,
To thy sweet will making addition thus.
Wilt thou, whose will is large and spacious,
Not once vouchsafe to hide my will in thine?
Shall will in others seem right gracious,
And in my will no fair acceptance shine?
The sea, all water, yet receives rain still,
And in abundance addeth to his store;
So thou, being rich in *Will*, add to thy *Will*
One will of mine, to make thy large *Will* more.
Let no unkind, no fair beseechers kill;
Think all but one, and me in that one *Will*.

CXXXVI.

If thy soul check thee that I come so near,
Swear to thy blind soul that I was thy *Will*,
And will, thy soul knows, is admitted there;
Thus far for love, my love-suit, sweet, fulfil.
Will will fulfil the treasure of thy love,
Ay, fill it full with wills, and my will one.
In things of great receipt with ease we prove
Among a number one is reckon'd none:
Then in the number let me pass untold,
Though in thy store's account I one must be;
For nothing hold me, so it please thee hold
That nothing me, a something sweet to thee:
Make but my name thy love, and love that still,
And then thou lovest me, for my name is *Will*.

CXXXVII.

Thou blind fool, Love, what dost thou to mine eyes,
That they behold, and see not what they see?
They know what beauty is, see where it lies,
Yet what the best is take the worst to be.
If eyes, corrupt by over-partial looks,
Be anchor'd in the bay where all men ride,
Why of eyes' falsehood hast thou forged hooks,
Whereto the judgement of my heart is tied?
Why should my heart think that a several plot
Which my heart knows the wide world's common place?
Or mine eyes seeing this, say this is not,
To put fair truth upon so foul a face?
In things right true my heart and eyes have err'd,
And to this false plague are they now transferr'd.

CXXXVIII.

When my love swears that she is made of truth,
I do believe her, though I know she lies,
That she might think me some untutor'd youth,
Unlearned in the world's false subtleties.
Thus vainly thinking that she thinks me young,
Although she knows my days are past the best,
Simply I credit her false-speaking tongue:
On both sides thus is simple truth suppress'd.
But wherefore says she not she is unjust?
And wherefore say not I that I am old?
O! love's best habit is in seeming trust,
And age in love loves not to have years told:
Therefore I lie with her, and she with me,
And in our faults by lies we flatter'd be.

CXXXIX.

O! call not me to justify the wrong
That thy unkindness lays upon my heart;
Wound me not with thine eye, but with thy tongue;
Use power with power, and slay me not by art.
Tell me thou lovest elsewhere; but in my sight,
Dear heart, forbear to glance thine eye aside:
What need'st thou wound with cunning, when thy might
Is more than my o'erpress'd defence can bide?
Let me excuse thee: ah! my love well knows
Her pretty looks have been mine enemies;
And therefore from my face she turns my foes,
That they elsewhere might dart their injuries:
Yet do not so; but since I am near slain,
Kill me outright with looks, and rid my pain.

CXL.

Be wise as thou art cruel; do not press
My tongue-tied patience with too much disdain;
Lest sorrow lend me words, and words express
The manner of my pity-wanting pain.
If I might teach thee wit, better it were,
Though not to love, yet, love, to tell me so;
As testy sick men, when their deaths be near,
No news but health from their physicians know;
For, if I should despair, I should grow mad,
And in my madness might speak ill of thee:
Now this ill-wresting world is grown so bad,
Mad slanderers by mad ears believed be.
That I may not be so, nor thou belied,
Bear thine eyes straight, though thy proud heart go wide.

CXLI.

In faith, I do not love thee with mine eyes,
For they in thee a thousand errors note;
But 't is my heart that loves what they despise,
Who, in despite of view, is pleased to dote;
Nor are mine ears with thy tongue's tune delighted;
Nor tender feeling, to base touches prone,
Nor taste, nor smell, desire to be invited
To any sensual feast with thee alone:
But my five wits nor my five senses can
Dissuade one foolish heart from serving thee,
Who leaves unsway'd the likeness of a man,
Thy proud heart's slave and vassal wretch to be:
Only my plague thus far I count my gain,
That she that makes me sin awards me pain.

CXLII.

Love is my sin, and thy dear virtue hate,
Hate of my sin, grounded on sinful loving:
O! but with mine compare thou thine own state,
And thou shalt find it merits not reproving;
Or, if it do, not from those lips of thine,
That have profaned their scarlet ornaments
And seal'd false bonds of love as oft as mine,
Robb'd others' beds' revenues of their rents.
Be it lawful I love thee, as thou lovest those
Whom thine eyes woo as mine importune thee:
Root pity in thy heart, that, when it grows,
Thy pity may deserve to pitied be.
If thou dost seek to have what thou dost hide,
By self-example may'st thou be denied!

CXLIII.

Lo, as a careful housewife runs to catch
One of her feather'd creatures broke away,
Sets down her babe, and makes all swift dispatch
In pursuit of the thing she would have stay;
Whilst her neglected child holds her in chase,
Cries to catch her whose busy care is bent
To follow that which flies before her face,
Not prizing her poor infant's discontent:
So runn'st thou after that which flies from thee,
Whilst I thy babe chase thee afar behind;
But if thou catch thy hope, turn back to me,
And play the mother's part, kiss me, be kind:
So will I pray that thou may'st have thy *Will*,
If thou turn back and my loud crying still.

CXLIV.

Two loves I have of comfort and despair,
Which like two spirits do suggest me still:
The better angel is a man, right fair,
The worser spirit a woman, colour'd ill.
To win me soon to hell, my female evil
Tempteth my better angel from my side,
And would corrupt my saint to be a devil,
Wooing his purity with her foul pride.
And whether that my angel be turn'd fiend
Suspect I may, yet not directly tell;
But being both from me, both to each friend,
I guess one angel in another's hell:
Yet this shall I ne'er know, but live in doubt,
Till my bad angel fire my good one out.

CXLV.

Those lips that Love's own hand did make
Breathed forth the sound that said 'I hate,'
To me that languish'd for her sake:
But when she saw my woeful state,
Straight in her heart did mercy come,
Chiding that tongue that ever sweet
Was used in giving gentle doom;
And taught it thus anew to greet;
'I hate' she alter'd with an end,
That follow'd it as gentle day
Doth follow night, who, like a fiend,
From heaven to hell is flown away;
'I hate' from hate away she threw,
And saved my life, saying 'Not you.'

CXLVI.

Poor soul, the centre of my sinful earth,
. . . . . . these rebel powers that thee array,
Why dost thou pine within and suffer dearth,
Painting thy outward walls so costly gay?
Why so large cost, having so short a lease,
Dost thou upon thy fading mansion spend?
Shall worms, inheritors of this excess,
Eat up thy charge? Is this thy body's end?
Then, soul, live thou upon thy servant's loss,
And let that pine to aggravate thy store;
Buy terms divine in selling hours of dross;
Within be fed, without be rich no more:
So shalt thou feed on Death, that feeds on men,
And Death once dead, there's no more dying then.

CXLVII.

My love is as a fever, longing still
For that which longer nurseth the disease;
Feeding on that which doth preserve the ill,
The uncertain sickly appetite to please.
My reason, the physician to my love,
Angry that his prescriptions are not kept,
Hath left me, and I desperate now approve
Desire is death, which physic did except.
Past cure I am, now reason is past care,
And frantic-mad with evermore unrest;
My thoughts and my discourse as madmen's are,
At random from the truth, vainly express'd;
For I have sworn thee fair, and thought thee bright,
Who art as black as hell, as dark as night.

CXLVIII.

O me! what eyes hath Love put in my head,
Which have no correspondence with true sight;
Or, if they have, where is my judgement fled,
That censures falsely what they see aright?
If that be fair whereon my false eyes dote,
What means the world to say it is not so?
If it be not, then love doth well denote
Love's eye is not so true as all men's: no,
How can it? O! how can Love's eye be true,
That is so vex'd with watching and with tears?
No marvel then, though I mistake my view;
The sun itself sees not till heaven clears.
O cunning Love! with tears thou keep'st me blind,
Lest eyes well seeing thy foul faults should find

CXLIX.

Canst thou, O cruel! say I love thee not,
When I against myself with thee partake?
Do I not think on thee, when I forgot
Am of myself, all tyrant, for thy sake?
Who hateth thee that I do call my friend?
On whom frown'st thou that I do fawn upon?
Nay, if thou lour'st on me, do I not spend
Revenge upon myself with present moan?
What merit do I in myself respect,
That is so proud thy service to despise,
When all my best doth worship thy defect,
Commanded by the motion of thine eyes?
But, love, hate on, for now I know thy mind;
Those that can see thou lovest, and I am blind.

CL.

O! from what power hast thou this powerful might
With insufficiency my heart to sway?
To make me give the lie to my true sight,
And swear that brightness doth not grace the day?
Whence hast thou this becoming of things ill,
That in the very refuse of thy deeds
There is such strength and warrantise of skill,
That, in my mind, thy worst all best exceeds?
Who taught thee how to make me love thee more,
The more I hear and see just cause of hate?
O! though I love what others do abhor,
With others thou should'st not abhor my state:
If thy unworthiness raised love in me,
More worthy I to be beloved of thee.

CLI.

Love is too young to know what conscience is;
Yet who knows not conscience is born of love?
Then, gentle cheater, urge not my amiss,
Lest guilty of my faults thy sweet self prove:
For, thou betraying me, I do betray
My nobler part to my gross body's treason;
My soul doth tell my body that he may
Triumph in love; flesh stays no further reason,
But rising at thy name doth point out thee
As his triumphant prize. Proud of this pride,
He is contented thy poor drudge to be,
To stand in thy affairs, fall by thy side.
No want of conscience hold it that I call
Her 'love' for whose dear love I rise and fall.

CLII.

In loving thee thou know'st I am forsworn,
But thou art twice forsworn, to me love swearing;
In act thy bed-vow broke, and new faith torn,
In vowing new hate after new love bearing.
But why of two oaths' breach do I accuse thee,
When I break twenty? I am perjured most;
For all my vows are oaths but to misuse thee,
And all my honest faith in thee is lost:
For I have sworn deep oaths of thy deep kindness,
Oaths of thy love, thy truth, thy constancy;
And, to enlighten thee, gave eyes to blindness,
Or made them swear against the thing they see;
For I have sworn thee fair; more perjured I,
To swear against the truth so foul a lie!

CLIII.

Cupid laid by his brand and fell asleep:
A maid of Dian's this advantage found,
And his love-kindling fire did quickly steep
In a cold valley-fountain of that ground;
Which borrow'd from this holy fire of Love
A dateless lively heat, still to endure,
And grew a seething bath, which yet men prove
Against strange maladies a sovereign cure.
But at my mistress' eye Love's brand new-fired,
The boy for trial needs would touch my breast;
I, sick withal, the help of bath desired,
And thither hied, a sad distemper'd guest,
But found no cure: the bath for my help lies
Where Cupid got new fire, my mistress' eyes.

CLIV.

The little Love-god lying once asleep
Laid by his side his heart-inflaming brand,
Whilst many nymphs that vow'd chaste life to keep
Came tripping by; but in her maiden hand
The fairest votary took up that fire
Which many legions of true hearts had warm'd;
And so the general of hot desire
Was sleeping by a virgin hand disarm'd.
This brand she quenched in a cool well by,
Which from Love's fire took heat perpetual,
Growing a bath and healthful remedy
For men diseased; but I, my mistress' thrall,
Came there for cure, and this by that I prove,
Love's fire heats water, water cools not love.

A LOVER'S COMPLAINT

From off a hill whose concave womb re-worded
A plaintful story from a sistering vale,
My spirits to attend this double voice accorded,
And down I laid to list the sad-tuned tale;
Ere long espied a fickle maid full pale,
Tearing of papers, breaking rings a-twain,
Storming her world with sorrow's wind and rain.

Upon her head a platted hive of straw,
Which fortified her visage from the sun,
Whereon the thought might think sometime it saw
The carcass of a beauty spent and done:
Time had not scythed all that youth begun,
Nor youth all quit; but, spite of heaven's fell rage,
Some beauty peep'd through lattice of sear'd age.

Oft did she heave her napkin to her eyne,
Which on it had conceited characters,
Laundering the silken figures in the brine
That season'd woe had pelleted in tears,
And often reading what content it bears;
As often shrieking undistinguish'd woe
In clamours of all size, both high and low.

Sometimes her levell'd eyes their carriage ride,
As they did battery to the spheres intend;
Sometime, diverted, their poor balls are tied
To the orbed earth; sometimes they do extend
Their view right on; anon their gazes lend
To every place at once, and nowhere fix'd,
The mind and sight distractedly commix'd.

Her hair, nor loose nor tied in formal plat,
Proclaim'd in her a careless hand of pride;
For some, untuck'd, descended her sheav'd hat,
Hanging her pale and pined cheek beside;
Some in her threaden fillet still did bide,
And true to bondage would not break from thence
Though slackly braided in loose negligence.

A thousand favours from a maund she drew
Of amber, crystal, and of beaded jet,
Which one by one she in a river threw,
Upon whose weeping margent she was set;
Like usury, applying wet to wet,
Or monarchs' hands that let not bounty fall
Where want cries some, but where excess begs all.

Of folded schedules had she many a one,
Which she perused, sigh'd, tore, and gave the flood;
Crack'd many a ring of posied gold and bone,
Bidding them find their sepulchres in mud;
Found yet more letters sadly penn'd in blood,
With sleided silk feat and affectedly
Enswathed, and seal'd to curious secrecy.

These often bathed she in her fluxive eyes,
And often kiss'd, and often 'gan to tear;
Cried 'O false blood! thou register of lies,
What unapproved witness dost thou bear;
Ink would have seem'd more black and damned here.'
This said, in top of rage the lines she rents,
Big discontent so breaking their contents.

A reverend man that grazed his cattle nigh,
Sometime a blusterer, that the ruffle knew
Of court, of city, and had let go by
The swiftest hours, observed as they flew,
Towards this afflicted fancy fastly drew;
And, privileged by age, desires to know
In brief the grounds and motives of her woe.

So slides he down upon his grained bat,
And comely-distant sits he by her side;
When he again desires her, being sat,
Her grievance with his hearing to divide:
If that from him there may be aught applied
Which may her suffering ecstasy assuage,
'T is promised in the charity of age.

'Father,' she says, 'though in me you behold
The injury of many a blasting hour,
Let it not tell your judgement I am old;
Not age, but sorrow, over me hath power:
I might as yet have been a spreading flower,
Fresh to myself, if I had self-applied
Love to myself and to no love beside.

'But woe is me! too early I attended
A youthful suit, it was to gain my grace,
Of one by nature's outwards so commended,
That maidens' eyes stuck over all his face.
Love lack'd a dwelling, and made him her place;
And when in his fair parts she did abide,
She was new lodged and newly deified.

'His browny locks did hang in crooked curls,
And every light occasion of the wind
Upon his lips their silken parcels hurls.
What's sweet to do, to do will aptly find:
Each eye that saw him did enchant the mind,
For on his visage was in little drawn
What largeness thinks in Paradise was sawn.

'Small show of man was yet upon his chin;
His phœnix down began but to appear
Like unshorn velvet on that termless skin
Whose bare out-bragg'd the web it seem'd to wear;
Yet show'd his visage by that cost more dear,
And nice affections wavering stood in doubt
If best were as it was, or best without.

'His qualities were beauteous as his form,
For maiden-tongued he was, and thereof free;
Yet, if men moved him, was he such a storm
As oft 'twixt May and April is to see,
When winds breathe sweet, unruly though they be.
His rudeness so with his authorized youth
Did livery falseness in a pride of truth.

'Well could he ride, and often men would say
"That horse his mettle from his rider takes:
Proud of subjection, noble by the sway,
What rounds, what bounds, what course, what stop he makes!"
And controversy hence a question takes,
Whether the horse by him became his deed,
Or he his manage by the well-doing steed.

'But quickly on this side the verdict went:
His real habitude gave life and grace
To appertainings and to ornament,
Accomplish'd in himself, not in his case:
All aids, themselves made fairer by their place,
Came for additions; yet their purposed trim
Pieced not his grace, but were all graced by him.

'So on the tip of his subduing tongue
All kind of arguments and question deep,
All replication prompt, and reason strong,
For his advantage still did wake and sleep:
To make the weeper laugh, the laugher weep,
He had the dialect and different skill,
Catching all passions in his craft of will:

'That he did in the general bosom reign
Of young, of old; and sexes both enchanted,
To dwell with him in thoughts, or to remain
In personal duty, following where he haunted:
Consents bewitch'd, ere he desire, have granted;
And dialogued for him what he would say,
Ask'd their own wills, and made their wills obey.

'Many there were that did his picture get,
To serve their eyes, and in it put their mind;
Like fools that in the imagination set
The goodly objects which abroad they find
Of lands and mansions, theirs in thought assign'd;
And labouring in more pleasures to bestow them
Than the true gouty landlord which doth owe them.

'So many have, that never touch'd his hand,
Sweetly supposed them mistress of his heart.
My woeful self, that did in freedom stand,
And was my own fee-simple, not in part,
What with his art in youth, and youth in art,
Threw my affections in his charmed power,
Reserved the stalk and gave him all my flower.

'Yet did I not, as some my equals did,
Demand of him, nor being desired yielded;
Finding myself in honour so forbid,
With safest distance I mine honour shielded.
Experience for me many bulwarks builded
Of proofs new-bleeding, which remain'd the foil
Of this false jewel, and his amorous spoil.

'But, ah! who ever shunn'd by precedent
The destined ill she must herself assay?
Or forced examples, 'gainst her own content,
To put the by-pass'd perils in her way?
Counsel may stop awhile what will not stay;
For when we rage, advice is often seen
By blunting us to make our wits more keen.

'Nor gives it satisfaction to our blood,
That we must curb it upon others' proof;
To be forbod the sweets that seem so good,
For fear of harms that preach in our behoof.
O appetite! from judgement stand aloof;
The one a palate hath that needs will taste,
Though Reason weep, and cry "It is thy last."

'For further I could say "This man's untrue,"
And knew the patterns of his foul beguiling;
Heard where his plants in others' orchards grew
Saw how deceits were gilded in his smiling;
Knew vows were ever brokers to defiling;
Thought characters and words merely but art,
And bastards of his foul adulterate heart.

'And long upon these terms I held my city,
Till thus he 'gan besiege me: "Gentle maid,
Have of my suffering youth some feeling pity,
And be not of my holy vows afraid:
That's to ye sworn to none was ever said;
For feasts of love I have been call'd unto,
Till now did ne'er invite, nor never woo.

'"All my offences that abroad you see
Are errors of the blood, none of the mind;
Love made them not: with acture they may be,
Where neither party is nor true nor kind:
They sought their shame that so their shame did find,
And so much less of shame in me remains,
By how much of me their reproach contains.

'"Among the many that mine eyes have seen,
Not one whose flame my heart so much as warm'd,
Or my affection put to the smallest teen,
Or any of my leisures ever charm'd:
Harm have I done to them, but ne'er was harm'd;
Kept hearts in liveries, but mine own was free,
And reign'd, commanding in his monarchy.

'"Look here, what tributes wounded fancies sent me,
Of paled pearls and rubies red as blood;
Figuring that they their passions likewise lent me
Of grief and blushes, aptly understood
In bloodless white and the encrimson'd mood;
Effects of terror and dear modesty,
Encamp'd in hearts, but fighting outwardly.

'"And, lo! behold these talents of their hair,
With twisted metal amorously impleach'd,
I have received from many a several fair,
Their kind acceptance weepingly beseech'd,
With the annexions of fair gems enrich'd,
And deep-brain'd sonnets, that did amplify
Each stone's dear nature, worth, and quality.

'"The diamond; why 't was beautiful and hard,
Whereto his invised properties did tend;
The deep-green emerald, in whose fresh regard
Weak sights their sickly radiance do amend;
The heaven-hued sapphire and the opal blend
With objects manifold: each several stone,
With wit well blazon'd, smiled or made some moan.

'"Lo! all these trophies of affections hot,
Of pensived and subdued desires the tender,
Nature hath charged me that I hoard them not,
But yield them up where I myself must render,
That is, to you, my origin and ender;
For these, of force, must your oblations be,
Since I their altar, you enpatron me.

'"O! then, advance of yours that phraseless hand,
Whose white weighs down the airy scale of praise;
Take all these similes to your own command,
Hallow'd with sighs that burning lungs did raise;
What me your minister, for you obeys,
Works under you; and to your audit comes
Their distract parcels in combined sums.

'"Lo! this device was sent me from a nun,
Or sister sanctified, of holiest note;
Which late her noble suit in court did shun,
Whose rarest havings made the blossoms dote;
For she was sought by spirits of richest coat,
But kept cold distance, and did thence remove,
To spend her living in eternal love.

'"But, O my sweet! what labour is't to leave
The thing we have not, mastering what not strives,
Playing the place which did no form receive,
Playing patient sports in unconstrained gyves?
She that her fame so to herself contrives,
The scars of battle 'scapeth by the flight,
And makes her absence valiant, not her might.

'"O! pardon me, in that my boast is true;
The accident which brought me to her eye
Upon the moment did her force subdue,
And now she would the caged cloister fly;
Religious love put out religion's eye:
Not to be tempted, would she be immured,
And now, to tempt, all liberty procured.

'"How mighty then you are, O! hear me tell:
The broken bosoms that to me belong
Have emptied all their fountains in my well,
And mine I pour your ocean all among:
I strong o'er them, and you o'er me being strong,
Must for your victory us all congest,
As compound love to physic your cold breast.

'"My parts had power to charm a sacred nun,
Who, disciplined, ay, dieted in grace,
Believed her eyes when they to assail begun,
All vows and consecrations giving place.
O most potential love! vow, bond, nor space,
In thee hath neither sting, knot, nor confine,
For thou art all, and all things else are thine.

'"When thou impressest, what are precepts worth
Of stale example? When thou wilt inflame,
How coldly those impediments stand forth
Of wealth, of filial fear, law, kindred, fame
Love's arms are peace, 'gainst rule, 'gainst sense, 'gainst shame,
And sweetens, in the suffering pangs it bears,
The aloes of all forces, shocks, and fears.

'"Now all these hearts that do on mine depend,
Feeling it break, with bleeding groans they pine;
And supplicant their sighs to you extend,
To leave the battery that you make 'gainst mine,
Lending soft audience to my sweet design,
And credent soul to that strong-bonded oath
That shall prefer and undertake my troth."

'This said, his watery eyes he did dismount,
Whose sights till then were levell'd on my face;
Each cheek a river running from a fount
With brinish current downward flow'd apace.
O! how the channel to the stream gave grace;
Who glazed with crystal gate the glowing roses
That flame through water which their hue encloses.

'O father! what a hell of witchcraft lies
In the small orb of one particular tear,
But with the inundation of the eyes
What rocky heart to water will not wear?
What breast so cold that is not warmed here?
O cleft effect! cold modesty, hot wrath,
Both fire from hence and chill extincture hath.

'For, lo! his passion, but an art of craft,
Even there resolved my reason into tears;
There my white stole of chastity I daff'd,
Shook off my sober guards and civil fears;
Appear to him, as he to me appears,
All melting; though our drops this difference bore,
His poison'd me, and mine did him restore.

'In him a plenitude of subtle matter,
Applied to cautels, all strange forms receives,
Of burning blushes, or of weeping water,
Or swounding paleness; and he takes and leaves,
In either's aptness, as it best deceives,
To blush at speeches rank, to weep at woes,
Or to turn white and swoon at tragic shows:

'That not a heart which in his level came
Could 'scape the hail of his all-hurting aim,
Showing fair nature is both kind and tame;

And, veil'd in them, did win whom he would
maim:
Against the thing he sought he would exclaim;
When he most burn'd in heart-wish'd luxury,
He preach'd pure maid, and praised cold chastity.

'Thus merely with the garment of a Grace
The naked and concealed fiend he cover'd;
That the unexperient gave the tempter place,
Which like a cherubin above them hover'd.
Who, young and simple, would not be so lover'd?
Ay me! I fell; and yet do question make
What I should do again for such a sake.

'O! that infected moisture of his eye,
O! that false fire which in his cheek so glow'd,
O! that forced thunder from his heart did fly,
O! that sad breath his spongy lungs bestow'd,
O! all that borrow'd motion seeming owed,
Would yet again betray the fore-betray'd,
And new pervert a reconciled maid.'

THE PASSIONATE PILGRIM

I.

When my love swears that she is made of truth,
I do believe her, though I know she lies,
That she might think me some untutor'd youth,
Unskilful in the world's false forgeries.
Thus vainly thinking that she thinks me young,
Although I know my years be past the best,
I smiling credit her false-speaking tongue,
Outfacing faults in love with love's ill rest.
But wherefore says my love that she is young?
And wherefore say not I that I am old?
O! love's best habit is a soothing tongue,
And age, in love, loves not to have years told.
Therefore I'll lie with love, and love with me,
Since that our faults in love thus smother'd
be.

II.

Two loves I have of comfort and despair,
Which like two spirits do suggest me still;
The better angel is a man, right fair,
The worser spirit a woman, colour'd ill.
To win me soon to hell, my female evil
Tempteth my better angel from my side,
And would corrupt a saint to be a devil,
Wooing his purity with her fair pride:
And whether that my angel be turn'd fiend
Suspect I may, but not directly tell;
For being both to me, both to each friend,
I guess one angel in another's hell.
The truth I shall not know, but live in doubt,
Till my bad angel fire my good one out.

III.

Did not the heavenly rhetoric of thine eye,
'Gainst whom the world could not hold argument,
Persuade my heart to this false perjury?
Vows for thee broke deserve not punishment.
A woman I forswore; but I will prove,
Thou being a goddess, I forswore not thee:
My vow was earthly, thou a heavenly love;
Thy grace being gain'd cures all disgrace in me.
My vow was breath, and breath a vapour is;
Then thou, fair sun, that on this earth dost
shine,
Exhale this vapour vow; in thee it is:
If broken, then it is no fault of mine.
If by me broke, what fool is not so wise
To break an oath, to win a paradise?

IV.

Sweet Cytherea, sitting by a brook
With young Adonis, lovely, fresh, and green,
Did court the lad with many a lovely look,
Such looks as none could look but beauty's queen
She told him stories to delight his ear;
She show'd him favours to allure his eye;
To win his heart, she touch'd him here and there:
Touches so soft still conquer chastity.
But whether unripe years did want conceit,
Or he refused to take her figured proffer,
The tender nibbler would not touch the bait,
But smile and jest at every gentle offer:
Then fell she on her back, fair queen, and
toward:
He rose and ran away; ah! fool too froward.

V.

If love make me forsworn, how shall I swear to
love?
O! never faith could hold, if not to beauty vow'd:
Though to myself forsworn, to thee I'll constant
prove;
Those thoughts, to me like oaks, to thee like osiers
bow'd.
Study his bias leaves, and makes his book thine
eyes,
Where all those pleasures live that art can com-
prehend.
If knowledge be the mark, to know thee shall
suffice;
Well learned is that tongue that well can thee
commend;
All ignorant that soul that sees thee without
wonder;
Which is to me some praise, that I thy parts ad-
mire:
Thine eye Jove's lightning seems, thy voice his
dreadful thunder,
Which, not to anger bent, is music and sweet fire.
Celestial as thou art, O! do not love that wrong,
To sing heaven's praise with such an earthly
tongue.

VI.

Scarce had the sun dried up the dewy morn,
And scarce the herd gone to the hedge for shade,
When Cytherea, all in love forlorn,
A longing tarriance for Adonis made

Under an osier growing by a brook,
A brook where Adon used to cool his spleen:
Hot was the day; she hotter that did look
For his approach, that often there had been.
Anon he comes, and throws his mantle by,
And stood stark naked on the brook's green brim:
The sun look'd on the world with glorious eye,
Yet not so wistly as this queen on him:
He, spying her, bounced in, whereas he stood:
'O Jove,' quoth she, 'why was not I a flood!'

VII.

Fair is my love, but not so fair as fickle;
Mild as a dove, but neither true nor trusty;
Brighter than glass, and yet, as glass is, brittle;
Softer than wax, and yet, as iron, rusty:
A lily pale, with damask dye to grace her,
None fairer, nor none falser to deface her.

Her lips to mine how often hath she joined,
Between each kiss her oaths of true love swearing!
How many tales to please me hath she coined,
Dreading my love, the loss thereof still fearing!
Yet in the midst of all her pure protestings,
Her faith, her oaths, her tears, and all were jestings.

She burn'd with love, as straw with fire flameth;
She burn'd out love, as soon as straw out-burneth;
She framed the love, and yet she foil'd the framing;
She bade love last, and yet she fell a-turning.
Was this a lover, or a lecher whether?
Bad in the best, though excellent in neither.

VIII.

If music and sweet poetry agree,
As they must needs, the sister and the brother,
Then must the love be great 'twixt thee and me,
Because thou lovest the one, and I the other.
Dowland to thee is dear, whose heavenly touch
Upon the lute doth ravish human sense;
Spenser to me, whose deep conceit is such
As, passing all conceit, needs no defence.
Thou lovest to hear the sweet melodious sound
That Phœbus' lute, the queen of music, makes;
And I in deep delight am chiefly drown'd
Whenas himself to singing he betakes.
One god is god of both, as poets feign;
One knight loves both, and both in thee remain.

IX.

Fair was the morn when the fair queen of love,
* * * * * *
Paler for sorrow than her milk-white dove,
For Adon's sake, a youngster proud and wild;
Her stand she takes upon a steep-up hill:
Anon Adonis comes with horn and hounds;
She, silly queen, with more than love's good will,
Forbade the boy he should not pass those grounds.
'Once,' quoth she, 'did I see a fair sweet youth
Here in these brakes deep-wounded with a boar,
Deep in the thigh, a spectacle of ruth!
See, in my thigh,' quoth she, 'here was the sore.'
She showed hers; he saw more wounds than one,
And blushing fled, and left her all alone.

X.

Sweet rose, fair flower, untimely pluck'd, soon vaded,
Pluck'd in the bud, and vaded in the spring!
Bright orient pearl, alack! too timely shaded;
Fair creature, kill'd too soon by death's sharp sting!
Like a green plum that hangs upon a tree,
And falls, through wind, before the fall should be.

I weep for thee, and yet no cause I have;
For why thou left'st me nothing in thy will:
And yet thou left'st me more than I did crave;
For why I craved nothing of thee still:
O yes, dear friend, I pardon crave of thee,
Thy discontent thou didst bequeath to me.

XI.

Venus, with young Adonis sitting by her
Under a myrtle shade, began to woo him:
She told the youngling how god Mars did try her,
And as he fell to her, so fell she to him.
'Even thus,' quoth she, 'the war-like god embraced me,'
And then she clipp'd Adonis in her arms;
'Even thus,' quoth she, 'the war-like god unlaced me,'
As if the boy should use like loving charms.
'Even thus,' quoth she, 'he seized on my lips,'
And with her lips on his did act the seizure;
And as she fetched breath, away he skips,
And would not take her meaning nor her pleasure.
Ah! that I had my lady at this bay,
To kiss and clip me till I ran away.

XII.

Crabbed age and youth cannot live together:
Youth is full of pleasance, age is full of care;
Youth like summer morn, age like winter weather;
Youth like summer brave, age like winter bare.
Youth is full of sport, age's breath is short;
Youth is nimble, age is lame;
Youth is hot and bold, age is weak and cold;
Youth is wild, and age is tame.
Age, I do abhor thee; youth, I do adore thee;
O! my love, my love is young:
Age, I do defy thee: O! sweet shepherd, hie thee,
For methinks thou stay'st too long.

XIII.

Beauty is but a vain and doubtful good;
A shining gloss that vadeth suddenly;
A flower that dies when first it 'gins to bud;
A brittle glass that's broken presently:
A doubtful good, a gloss, a glass, a flower,
Lost, vaded, broken, dead within an hour.

And as goods lost are sold or never found,
As vaded gloss no rubbing will refresh,
As flowers dead lie wither'd on the ground,
As broken glass no cement can redress,
So beauty blemish'd once 's for ever lost,
In spite of physic, painting, pain, and cost.

XIV.

Good night, good rest. Ah! neither be my share:
She bade good night that kept my rest away;
And daff'd me to a cabin hang'd with care,
To descant on the doubts of my decay.
'Farewell,' quoth she, 'and come again to-morrow:'
Fare well I could not, for I supp'd with sorrow.

Yet at my parting sweetly did she smile,
In scorn or friendship, nill I construe whether:
'T may be, she joy'd to jest at my exile,
'T may be, again to make me wander thither:
'Wander,' a word for shadows like thyself,
As take the pain, but cannot pluck the pelf.

XV.

Lord! how mine eyes throw gazes to the east;
My heart doth charge the watch; the morning rise
Doth cite each moving sense from idle rest.
Not daring trust the office of mine eyes,
While Philomela sits and sings, I sit and mark,
And wish her lays were tuned like the lark;

For she doth welcome daylight with her ditty,
And drives away dark dismal-dreaming night:
The night so pack'd, I post unto my pretty;
Heart hath his hope, and eyes their wished sight;
Sorrow changed to solace, solace mix'd with sorrow;
For why, she sigh'd and bade me come to-morrow.

Were I with her, the night would post too soon;
But now are minutes added to the hours;
To spite me now, each minute seems a moon;
Yet not for me, shine sun to succour flowers!
Pack night, peep day; good day, of night now borrow:
Short, night, to-night, and length thyself to-morrow.

SONNETS TO SUNDRY NOTES OF MUSIC

I.

It was a lording's daughter, the fairest one of three,
That liked of her master as well as well might be,
Till looking on an Englishman, the fair'st that eye could see,
Her fancy fell a-turning.

Long was the combat doubtful that love with love did fight,
To leave the master loveless, or kill the gallant knight:
To put in practice either, alas! it was a spite
Unto the silly damsel.

But one must be refused; more mickle was the pain
That nothing could be used to turn them both to gain,
For of the two the trusty knight was wounded with disdain:
Alas! she could not help it.

Thus art with arms contending was victor of the day,
Which by a gift of learning did bear the maid away;
Then lullaby, the learned man hath got the lady gay;
For now my song is ended.

II.

On a day, alack the day!
Love, whose month was ever May,
Spied a blossom passing fair,
Playing in the wanton air:
Through the velvet leaves the wind,
All unseen, 'gan passage find;
That the lover, sick to death,
Wish'd himself the heaven's breath.
'Air,' quoth he, 'thy cheeks may blow;
Air, would I might triumph so!
But, alas! my hand hath sworn
Ne'er to pluck thee from thy thorn:
Vow, alack! for youth unmeet:
Youth, so apt to pluck a sweet.
Thou for whom Jove would swear
Juno but an Ethiope were;
And deny himself for Jove,
Turning mortal for thy love.'

III.

My flocks feed not,
My ewes breed not,
My rams speed not,
All is amiss:
Love's denying,
Faith's defying,
Heart's renying,
Causer of this.
All my merry jigs are quite forgot,
All my lady's love is lost, God wot:
Where her faith was firmly fix'd in love,
There a nay is placed without remove.
One silly cross
Wrought all my loss;
O! frowning Fortune, cursed, fickle dame
For now I see
Inconstancy
More in women than in men remain.

In black mourn I,
All fears scorn I,
Love hath forlorn me,
Living in thrall:
Heart is bleeding,
All help needing,
O! cruel speeding,
Fraughted with gall.
My shepherd's pipe can sound no deal,
My wether's bell rings doleful knell;
My curtal dog, that wont to have play'd.
Plays not at all, but seems afraid;
My sighs so deep
Procure to weep,
In howling wise, to see my doleful plight.
How sighs resound
Through heartless ground,
Like a thousand vanquish'd men in bloody fight!

Clear wells spring not,
Sweet birds sing not,
Green plants bring not
Forth their dye;
Herds stand weeping,
Flocks all sleeping,
Nymphs back peeping
Fearfully:
All our pleasure known to us poor swains,
All our merry meetings on the plains,
All our evening sport from us is fled,
All our love is lost, for Love is dead.
Farewell, sweet lass,
Thy like ne'er was
For a sweet content, the cause of all my moan:
Poor Corydon
Must live alone;
Other help for him I see that there is none.

IV.

Whenas thine eye hath chose the dame,
And stall'd the deer that thou should'st strike,
Let reason rule things worthy blame,
As well as fancy partial wight:
Take counsel of some wiser head,
Neither too young nor yet unwed.

And when thou comest thy tale to tell,
Smooth not thy tongue with filed talk,
Lest she some subtle practice smell;
A cripple soon can find a halt:
But plainly say thou lovest her well,
And set thy person forth to sell.

What though her frowning brows be bent,
Her cloudy looks will clear ere night;
And then too late she will repent
That thus dissembled her delight;
And twice desire, ere it be day,
That which with scorn she put away.

What though she strive to try her strength,
And ban and brawl, and say thee nay,
Her feeble force will yield at length,
When craft hath taught her thus to say,
'Had women been so strong as men,
In faith, you had not had it then.'

And to her will frame all thy ways;
Spare not to spend, and chiefly there
Where thy desert may merit praise,
By ringing in thy lady's ear:
The strongest castle, tower, and town,
The golden bullet beats it down.

Serve always with assured trust,
And in thy suit be humble true;
Unless thy lady prove unjust,
Seek never thou to choose anew.
When time shall serve, be thou not slack
To proffer, though she put thee back.

The wiles and guiles that women work,
Dissembled with an outward show,
The tricks and toys that in them lurk,
The cock that treads them shall not know.
Have you not heard it said full oft,
A woman's nay doth stand for nought?

Think, women love to match with men
And not to live so like a saint:
Here is no heaven; they holy then
Begin when age doth them attaint.
Were kisses all the joys in bed,
One woman would another wed.

But, soft! enough! too much, I fear,
For if my mistress hear my song,
She will not stick to ring my ear,
To teach my tongue to be so long:
Yet will she blush, here be it said,
To hear her secrets so bewray'd.

V.

Live with me, and be my love,
And we will all the pleasures prove
That hills and valleys, dales and fields,
And all the craggy mountains yields.

There will we sit upon the rocks,
And see the shepherds feed their flocks,
By shallow rivers, by whose falls
Melodious birds sing madrigals.

There will I make thee a bed of roses,
With a thousand fragrant posies,
A cap of flowers, and a kirtle
Embroider'd all with leaves of myrtle.

A belt of straw and ivy buds,
With coral clasps and amber studs;
And if these pleasures may thee move,
Then live with me and be my love.

LOVE'S ANSWER.

If that the world and love were young,
And truth in every shepherd's tongue,
These pretty pleasures might me move
To live with thee and be thy love.

VI.

As it fell upon a day
In the merry month of May,
Sitting in a pleasant shade
Which a grove of myrtles made,
Beasts did leap, and birds did sing,
Trees did grow, and plants did spring;
Every thing did banish moan,
Save the nightingale alone:
She, poor bird, as all forlorn,
Lean'd her breast up-till a thorn,
And there sung the dolefull'st ditty,
That to hear it was great pity:
'Fie, fie, fie!' now would she cry;
'Tereu, Tereu!' by and by;
That to hear her so complain,
Scarce I could from tears refrain;
For her griefs, so lively shown,
Made me think upon mine own.
Ah! thought I, thou mourn'st in vain,
None takes pity on thy pain:
Senseless trees they cannot hear thee,
Ruthless beasts they will not cheer thee:
King Pandion he is dead,
All thy friends are lapp'd in lead,
All thy fellow birds do sing
Careless of thy sorrowing.
Even so, poor bird, like thee,
None alive will pity me.
Whilst as fickle Fortune smiled,
Thou and I were both beguiled.
Every one that flatters thee
Is no friend in misery.
Words are easy, like the wind;
Faithful friends are hard to find:
Every man will be thy friend
Whilst thou hast wherewith to spend;
But if store of crowns be scant,
No man will supply thy want.
If that one be prodigal,
Bountiful they will him call,
And with such-like flattering,
'Pity but he were a king.'
If he be addict to vice,
Quickly him they will entice;
If to women he be bent,
They have him at commandement:
But if Fortune once do frown,
Then farewell his great renown;
They that fawn'd on him before
Use his company no more.
He that is thy friend indeed,
He will help thee in thy need:
If thou sorrow, he will weep;
If thou wake, he cannot sleep:
Thus of every grief in heart
He with thee does bear a part.
These are certain signs to know
Faithful friend from flattering foe.

GLOSSARY.

ABJECTS, the most servile and lowest of subjects.
Aby, to pay dear for, to suffer.
Abysm, abyss, from the French *abysme*, now *abime*.
Accite, to call or summons.
Aconitum, wolfsbane.
Adam, the name of an outlaw, noted for his skill in archery. *Much Ado.*
Adam Cupid, an allusion to the same person.
Addrest, ready, prepared.
Advertising, attentive.
Aery, or *Aiery*, a nest.
Affect the letter, to practise alliteration.
Affects, affections or passions.
Affeered, a law-term for confirmed.
Affied, betrothed.
Affined, joined by affinity.
Affront, sometimes, to face or confront.
Affy, to betroth in marriage.
Aglet-baby, a diminutive being, not exceeding in size the tag of a point; from *aiguillettes*.
Agnize, acknowledge, confess, avow.
Aiery, a hawk's or eagle's nest.
Airy fame, verbal eulogium.
Alder-liefest, preferred to all things; from *leve* or *lefe*, dear, and *alder*, of all.
A'life, at life.
Amazonian chin, a chin without a beard.
Ames-ace, the lowest chance of the dice.
Amort, sunk, dispirited.
Ancient, an ensign, or standard-bearer.
Angle, a fishing-rod.
Antres, caves and dens.
Appeach, to impeach.
Apple-John, species of apple that will keep for two years; in French, *deux-ans*.
Approof, approbation, or sometimes, proof, confirmation.
Aqua vitæ, probably, usquebaugh.
Arabian bird, the phœnix.
Argentine goddess, regent of the silver moon.
Argier, Algiers.
Argosies, ships of great burthen.
Aroint, avaunt, or be gone.
Ascapart, a giant.
Ascaunt, askew, aside, sideways.
Aspersion, sprinkling.
Assay, to take the assay, applied to those who tasted wine for princes.
Assinego, an ass driver, a foolish fellow.
Astringer, a gentleman falconer; from *austercus*, a goshawk.
At point, completely armed.
Atomies, minute particles discernible when the sun breaks into a darkened room.
Attasked, taken to task, censured.
Attent, attentive.

Baccare, a proverbial word, of doubtful meaning; perhaps from *baccalare*, arrogant.
Bale, bane, ruin, misfortune.
Baldrick, a belt.
Balked, either bathed, or piled up.
Bandog, i. e. band-dog, a village dog, or mastiff.
Bandy, a metaphor from tennis-playing, to exchange smartly.
Banning, cursing, commonly used in Scotland.
Bans, curses.
Barbason, the name of a dæmon.
Barbe, a kind of veil.
Barber-monger, one who consorts with barbers, a low fellow.
Barm, yeast; used in the midland counties, and in Ireland and Scotland.
Barnacles, a kind of shell-fish, growing on the bottom of ships.
Barne, a child.
Barrfull, full of impediments.
Bases, a kind of loose breeches.
Basta, 'tis enough.
Bate, strife or contention.
Batlet, the instrument with which washers beat their coarse clothes.
Batten, to grow fat.
Bavin, brushwood, which, fired, burns fiercely, but is soon out.
Bawcock, perhaps from *beau* and *coq*, a jolly cock, or cock of the game.
Baycurtal, a bay docked horse.
Bay windows, bow windows.
Beadsmen, chaplains, or persons maintained by charity to pray for their benefactor.
Bear a brain, to have a perfect remembrance.
Beck, a salutation made with the head; in the North, it means curtsying.
Becomed, becoming.
Behests, commands.
Behowl, to howl at.
Beldame, ancient mother.
Be-lee'd, becalmed.
Belongings, endowments.
Be-mete, bemeasure.
Bemoiled, bedraggled, bemired.
Besmirch, to foul or dirty.
Bestraught, distracted.
Beteem, to give or bestow, or to permit, deign, or suffer.
Bevy, a company, or number, originally applied to larks.
Bewray, betray, discover.
Bezonian, a term of reproach; from *bisognoso*, a needy person.
Bias cheek, swelling out like the bias of a bowl.
Bid the base, to challenge in a contest.
Biggin, a kind of cap, worn now only by children.
Bilberry, the whurtle-berry.
Bilbo, a Spanish blade, flexible and elastic; the best of which are made at Bilboa.
Bilboes, a bar of iron, with fetters annexed to it, by which mutinous sailors were anciently linked together; derived from Bilboa, which was famous for the manufacture of instruments of steel. The bilboes may be seen in the Tower of London, among the spoils of the Spanish armada.
Bill, articles of accusation.
Bill, the old weapon of English infantry, still used by the watchmen in some towns.
Bin, is.
Bird-bolt, a short thick arrow without a point, used to kill rooks, and shot from a crossbow.
Bisson, blind.
Black cornered night, night which is as obscure as a dark corner.
Blacks, mourning made of stuffs of different colours dyed black.
Blank, i. e. of the eye, the white, or the white mark at which arrows are discharged.
Blank and *level*, mark and aim, terms of gunnery.
Blaze, i. e. of youth, the spring of early life.
Blench, to start off, to fly off.
Blent, blended, mixed together.
Blind-worms, the Cæcilia, or slow-worm.
Block, the thing on which a hat is formed.
Blurted, or *blurt*, an expression of contempt.
Bobbed, fooled out of, cheated.
Bodge, to botch, or to budge.
Boitier, a box to hold salve, or simples.
Bolds, emboldens.
Boltered, bedaubed, begrimed.
Bolting-hutch, a wooden receptacle into which the meal is bolted.
Bombard, a barrel.
Bona-robas, ladies of pleasure.
Bores, stabs, or wounds.
Borne in hand, deceived, imposed upon.
Bosky, woody; bosky acres are fields divided by hedge-rows; from *boscus* and *bosquet*.
Bots, worms in the stomach of a horse.—*A bots light upon*, an imprecation.
Bottled spider, a large bloated, glossy spider.
Boulted, sifted, or refined.
Bourn, boundary, or rivulet dividing land.
Bow, yoke.
Bower, chamber.
Bowlins, or *bowlines*, ropes by which the sails of a ship are governed when the wind is unfavourable.
Bowling, or the smoothness of a bowling-green.
Bowstrings, i. e. *hold* or *cut*, at all events.
Brace, the armour for the arm: *warlike brace*, state of defence.
Brach, a kind of hound; or used as a term of contempt.
Brack, to salt.
Braid, crafty or deceitful.
Brain's flow, tears.
Brake, an instrument of torture, or a thicket or furze-bush.
Brands, a part of the andirons, on which the wood for the fire was supported.
Brasier, a manufacturer in brass, or a reservoir for charcoal.
Brave, to make fine; bravery was the old term for elegance of dress.
Bravely, splendidly, or gallantly.
Bravery, finery.
Brawl, a kind of dance.
Braying, an epithet applied to the sound of the trumpet, harsh, grating.
Break, to begin.
Break up, to carve.
Break with, to break the matter to.
Breast, voice.
Breath, speech, *K. John. Timon.* Exercise, *Troilus and Cres.* A slight exercise of arms, *ibid.*
Breathing-courtsy, verbal compliment.
Breeched, foully sheathed, or mired.
Breeching, liable to school discipline.
Bribe-buck, a buck sent for a bribe.
Bridal, a nuptial feast; a word yet used in the North.
Brief, a short account, a contract hastily performed.—*Now-born brief*, is the *breve originale* of the feudal times.
Bring, attend or accompany.
Bring out, bring forth.
Brize, the gad, or horse-fly.
Broach, to put on the spit, to transfix.
Brock, the badger.
Brogues, a kind of shoes.
Broken, communicated.
Broken mouth, a mouth that has lost part of its teeth.
Broken tears, tears which are interrupted.
Broker, a matchmaker, a procuress.
Broker, deals as a broker.
Brooch, a trinket with a pin fixed to it.
Brooched, adorned.
Brought, attended.
Brow, i. e. of youth, the height of youth.
Brown bill, a kind of battle-axe affixed to a stick.
Brownist, a follower of Brown, a sectarian.
Bruising irons, an allusion to the ancient mace.
Bruit, noise, or report.
Brush, i. e. of time, decay by time.
Buckle, to bend, or yield to pressure.
Bug, bugbear.
Bugle, hunting-horn.
Bulk, body.
Bumbard, a large vessel for holding drink.
Bung, a cut-purse.
Bunting, the name of a bird.
Burgonet, a helmet.
Burst, to break, or broken.
Busky, woody.
Butt-shaft, an arrow to shoot at butts with.
Buxom, under good command, obedient.

Caddis-garter, a kind of worsted garter.
Caddises, worsted lace.
Cade, a barrel.
Cadent, falling.
Cage, a prison.
Cain-coloured, yellow; Cain was represented of that colour in old pictures.
Caitiff, a prisoner, slave, or scoundrel.
Calculate, to foretell or prophesy.
Caliver, a light kind of musket.
Callet, a bad woman, or witch.
Calling, appellation.
Camelot, a place where king Arthur is supposed to have kept his court.
Canaries, the name of a brisk, light dance.
Canker, the canker-rose, dog-rose, or hip.
Canstick, candlestick.
Cantle, a corner, or piece of any thing.
Cantons, used for cantos.
Canvas-climber, one who climbs the mast to furl the canvas, a ship-boy.
Capped, saluted by taking off the cap.
Capable impressure, hollow mark.
Capocchia, a sot, or dull, heavy gull, from the Italian *capocchio*.
Capricious, lascivious.
Captious, for capacious.
Carack, a vessel of great bulk.
Caracts, characters.
Carbonado, a piece of meat cut crossways for the gridiron.
Card, sea-chart.
Carded, mixed.
Carieres, i. e. to pass the carieres, a military phrase. Means that the common bounds of good behaviour were overpassed.
Carkanet, a kind of necklace or chain.
Carl, clown, husbandman.

Carlot, a peasant or churl; from *carl*.
Carnal, sanguinary.
Carowses, drinks.
Carpet knight, a term of reproach, spoken of one knighted in time of peace, and on a carpet, on some festive occasion.
Carriage, import.
Case, skin, outside.
Case of lives, a set of lives, or pair of any thing.
Cased lion, a lion irritated by confinement.
Casques, helmets.
Cassock, a horseman's loose coat.
Cast, to empty, to throw or reject.
Cast lips, left-off lips.
Cast the water, to find out disorders by inspecting the urine.
Cataian, a liar; the first adventurers who visited Cataia, or China, were notorious liars, as Paulo and Mandeville.
Catling, a small lute-string made of catgut.
Cavalero-justice, a cant term.
Cavalero, an airy, sprightly, irregular fellow.
Caviare, too good for, or foreign to.
Caviare, a luxurious Russian dish made of the roe of the sturgeon.
Cautel, subtlety, or deceit.
Cautelous, artful, or insidious.
Cauterizing, burning, or blistering.
Cearment, the wrapping of an embalmed body.
Cease, decease, die.
Censer, brasiere.
Certes, certainly.
Cess, measure, tax, or subsidy.
Chaliced, i. e. flowers, with cups, from *calix*.
Challenge, law-term, the right of refusing a juryman.
Chamber, London was anciently called the king's chamber.
Chamber, a piece of ordnance.
Chamberers, men of intrigue.
Changeling, a child substituted for one stolen.
Channel, kennel.
Chantry, little chapel in a cathedral.
Character, hand-writing.
Characts, characters.
Charactery, the matter of which characters are made.
Chares, task-work.
Charge-house, free-school.
Chariest, from *chary*, the most cautious.
Chariness, caution.
Charles-wain, vulgar name for the constellation called the Bear.
Charneco, a kind of sweet wine.
Chases, a term in tennis.
Chaudron, entrails.
Cheater, for escheatour, an office in the Exchequer.
Check, command, control.
Cheer, countenance.
Cherry-pit, pitching cherry-stones into a little hole.
Cheveril, kid-skin, soft leather.
Chewet, or *chuet*, a pie, a noisy, chattering bird, or a fat pudding.
Chide, resound, reecho.
Child, sometimes applied to knights and heroes.
Childing, pregnant.
Choppine, a high shoe or clog.
Chopping, jabbering, talking glibly.
Chough, a bird of the jackdaw kind.
Christom, or *chrisom*, a christened child.
Chrystals, eyes.
Chuck, chicken, a term of endearment.
Chuffs, rich, avaricious people.
Circummured, walled round.
Circumstance, circumlocution.
Circumstanced, treated according to circumstances.
Cital, recital.
Clack-dish, a beggar's dish.
Clamour, when bells are at the height, in order to cease them the repetition of the strokes becomes much quicker than before, which is called *clamouring* them
Clap in, fall to.
Clapped i' the clout, hit the white mark.
Claw, to flatter.
Clean kam, awry.
Clearest, purest.
Clepe, to call.
Clerkly, like a scholar.
Cling, to dry or shrink up.
Clinquant, glittering, shining.
Clipt, twined around, embraced.
Clout, the white mark at which archers took their aim.
Clouted, strengthened with clout, or hobnails.
Clutch, to clasp, or grasp.
Coasting, conciliating, inviting.
Cob-loaf, a crusty, uneven, gibbous-loaf.
Cock and pye, a popular adjuration.
Cockshut-time, twilight.
Cockle, a weed which grows up with corn.
Cockled, like the fish called a cockle.
Cockle-hat, cockle-shell hat, such as pilgrims wore.
Cockney, a well-known term of reproach.
Codding, amorous.
Codpiece, a piece of dress.
Coffin, ancient term for the raised crust of a pie.
Cog, to falsify the dice, to lie.
Cogging, lying.
Coigne of vantage, convenient corner.
Coignes, corners.
Coil, bustle, stir.
Collection, consequence or corollary.
Collied, black, smutted with coal, discoloured.
Collier, a term of reproach, from the impositions of coal-dealers.
Comart, a bargain.
Combrinate, betrothed.
Comforting, abetting.
Commend, commit.
Committed, lain with.
Commodity, self-interest.
Commonty, a comedy.
Companies, companions.
Compassed, round.
Composture, composition.
C'oncupy, a cant word from concupiscence.
Conduct, conductor.
Coney-catched, deceived, cheated.
Conject, conjecture.
Consent, used sometimes for will.
Continent, that which contains or encloses.
Contraction, marriage, contract.
Control, confute.
Convents, agrees, is convenient.
Convented, summoned.
Convertite, a convert.
Convey, steal, conveyance, theft.
Conveyers, thieves.
Conveyed himself, derived his title.
Convicted, overpowered, baffled, destroyed.
Convive, to feast.
Copatain hat, a hat with a conical crown.
Copped, rising to a top or head.
Coragio, an exclamation of encouragement.
Corky, dry, or withered.
Corollary, surplus, one more than enough.
Corporal, corporeal.
Corrigible, corrected.
Costard, a head.
Coster-monger, a dealer in costers, or costards, a kind of apples.
Cote, to overtake.
Couch, to lie with.
Counter-caster, one who reckons by counters.
Countercheck, an old term in the game of chess.
Counterfeit, sometimes used for a *portrait*.
Counterpoints, counterpanes.
County, ancient term for a nobleman.
Courser's-hair, alluding to the notion that the hair of a horse, dropt into a corrupted water, will turn to an animal.
Courses, the mainsail and foresail.
Court-cupboard, sideboard.
Cowed, restrained, or made cowardly.
Cower, to sink by bending the hams.
Cowlstaff, a staff for carrying a large tub or basket with two handles.
Coyed, condescended reluctantly.
Coystril, a coward cock, a paltry fellow.
Cozier, a tailor, from *cousu*; or a cobbler, or sowter.
Crack, a child.
Crack of doom, dissolution of nature.
Cranking, *crankling*, applied to the rush of a river.
Cranks, windings.
Crare, a small trading vessel.
Crash, to be merry over.
Craven, a degenerate, dispirited cock. Cowardly, to make cowardly.
Credent, creditable, probable.
Cressets, a light set upon a beacon, from *croissette*.
Crisp, curling, winding; or for *crypt*, vaulted.
Crone, old worn-out woman.
Cross-gartered, an article of puritanical dress.
Crow-keeper, a scare-crow.
Crownet, last purpose.
Cruel, worsted. *Lear*, applied to garters.
Crush, to drink.
Crusado, a Portuguese coin.
Cry, a pack or troop.
Cub-drawn, i. e. bear, one whose dugs are drawn dry.
Cuisses, armour for the thighs, *cuisses*, *Fr.*
Cunning, knowing, skilful, in a good meaning.
Curb, to bend and truckle, from *courber*.
Curled, ostentatiously dressed.
Curious, scrupulous.
Currents, occurrences.
Curst, shrewd, mischievous.
Curtail-dog, one which misses the game.
Curtle axe, a cutlass, broad-sword.
Customer, a common woman. *Oth. &c.* or one who visits such.
Cut, horse.
Cut and long tail, a phrase from dogs, poor or rich.
Cuttle, a knife used by sharpers.

Daff, or *Doff*, to put off.
Damn, condemn.
Dank, wet, rotten.
Darkling, in the dark.
Darraign, range, put in order.
Dauberry, counterfeit, disguise.
Day-bed, a couch.
Dealt, fought by proxy.
Dear, sometimes means immediate, consequential.
Dearn, direful, lone, solitary.
Deboshed, debauched.
Dock, of cards, a pack.
Decked, sprinkled.
Decline, as in grammar, to run through from first to last.
Deem, opinion, surmise.
Default, (in the) at need.
Defeat, to free, to disembarrass.
Defeature, alteration of features.
Defence, the art of fencing.
Deftly, adroitly, dexterously.
Delighted, spirit, accustomed to delight.
Demise, grant.
Denay, denial.
Denayed, denied.
Denotements, indications, discoveries.
Denude, strip, divest.
Depart and *part*, often synonymous.
Deprive disinherit
Deracinate, force up by the roots.
Derogate, degraded.
Descant, a term in music, or to harangue upon.
Deserved, deserving.
Despatched, bereft.
Detected, suspected, or charged.
Determined, sometimes for *concluded*.
Dibble, an instrument in gardening.
Dickon, Richard.
Diet, to put under a regimen, to oblige to fast, or to loathe.
Diffused, wild, irregular, extravagant.
Digression, transgression.
Dildos, the burthen of a song.
Directitude, discreditude, or discredit.
Disable, undervalue.
Disappointed, unappointed, unprepared.
Discandy, to melt the sweets, to dissolve.
Discourse, reason.
Dishabited, dislodged.
Dismes, Fr. tenths.
Disnatured, wanting natural affection.
Dispark, to throw down the hedges.
Disperge, to sprinkle.
Dispose, to make terms.
Disputable, disputatious.
Dispute, talk over, reason upon, account for.
Disseat, displace.
Distained, unstained.
Distate, to corrupt.
Distemperature, perturbation.
Distraught, distracted.
Diverted, turned out of the course of nature.
Division, phrase in music, the parts of it.
Doff. See *Daff*.
Dole, alms, or distribution.
Don, to do on, put on.
Dout, do out, extinguish.
Dowl, a feather.
Down-gyved, hanging down like the loose cincture which confines the fetters round the ancle.
Draught, the jakes.
Draw, sometimes used for withdraw.
Drawn, swords drawn.
A drawn fox, one which is trailed over the ground, and deceives the hounds.
Dressings, semblances or habiliments of virtue.
Driven bed, one for which the feathers are selected by driving with a fan.
Drumble, to act as confused and stupid.
Ducdame, *duc ad me*, the supposed burthen of a song.
Dudgeon, the haft or handle of a dagger.
Dull, gentle soothing.
Dullard, a person stupidly unconcerned.
Dumbs, makes silent.
Dump, a mournful elegy.
Dung, an obscene word, probably part of a proverb.
Dungy, of dung, earthy.
Dupped, did up, put up, opened.
Durance, some lasting kind of stuff.

Eager, sour, harsh.
Eanlings, lambs just dropt.
Ear, to plough.
Ear-kissing, whispering.
Easy, slight, inconsiderable.
Eche, eke out.
Ecstasy, alienation of mind.
Edward shovel-boards, Edward VIth's shillings, used at shuffle-board.
Effects, affects, affections, *Mea. for Mea.* Actions, *Ham.*
Eftest, or *Deftest*, readiest.
Eld, old person or persons, *Mer. Wiv.* Decrepitude, *Mea. for Mea.*
Element, initiation, previous practice.
Elf, done by elves or fairies.

Elvish marked, marked by elves.
Emballing, being distinguished by the ball, the emblem of royalty.
Embare, expose, display to view.
Embarquements, impediments, hinderances.
Embossed, enclosed; when a deer is run hard, and foams at the mouth, he is said to be embossed. Swollen, puffy.
Empericutick, of an empirical kind, quackish.
Empery, dominion, sovereign command.
Emulous, often used in a bad sense for envious.
Enactures, laws.
Encave, hide.
End, still an end, generally.
Enfeoff, to invest with possession.
Engaged, delivered as a hostage.
Engross, to fatten or pamper.
Engrossments, accumulations.
Enkindle, or *kindle*, to stimulate.
Enmesh, enclose them all, from taking birds or fishes with meshes.
Enmew, to force to lie in cover; a term in falconry.
Enridged, bordered, or perhaps for *enraged*.
Ensconce, to secure in a safe place.
Enseamed, greasy.
Enshield, concealed, masked.
Ensteeped, immersed.
Entertainment, pay, *Cor. Oth.* Receive into service, *Jul. Cæs.*
Entreatments, favours, or objects of entreaty.
Envy, often used for aversion, malice.
Ephesian, a cant term, perhaps for a toper.
Erewhile, a little while ago.
Erring, wandering, errant.
Escape, illegitimate child.
Escoted, paid; from *escot*, shot, or reckoning.
Esil, or *Eisel*, a river.
Esperance, the motto of the Percy family.
Espials, spies.
Essential, real, existent.
Estimable, i.e. *wonder*, esteeming wonder, or esteem and wonder.
Estimate, the rate at which I value.
Estimation, conjecture.
Estridges, ostriches.
Eterne, eternal.
Even, to make even, or represent plain.
Even Christian, fellow Christian.
Evils, jakes.
Examined, disputed or doubted.
Excellent differences, distinguished excellencies.
Excrement, the beard.
Execute, sometimes for *to use*, or *employ*.
Executors, executioners.
Exempt, independent, not under the control of.
Exercise, exhortation, lecture.
Exhale, breathe your last.
Exhibition, allowance.
Exigent, end.
Exorcism, in Shakspeare, generally means the *raising* of spirits.
Expect, expectation.
Expedience, expedition.
Expedient, often for *expeditious*.
Expediently, expeditiously.
Expostulate, inquire or discuss.
Exsufflicate, bubble-like.
Extacy, a degree of madness.
Extend, to seize.
Extent, violence.
Extern, outward.
Extremity, calamity.
Eyas-musket, a troublesome puppy, infant Lilliputian.
Eyas and musket, are young hawks.
Eyases, young nestlings.

Eye, a shade.
Eyliads, eyes; from *œillades*. *Fr.*
Eyne, eyes.

Face-royal, a face not to be meddled with.
Faced, turned up with facings.
Facinorous, wicked.
Factious, active.
Faculty, exercise of power.
Fadge, to suit or fit.
Fadings, a dance.
Fain, fond.
Fair, sometimes for fairness, beauty.
Faitors, traitors, rascals.
Fall, often used as an active verb: *At fall*, at an ebb.
Falsing, a thing that's falsified, or false.
Falsely, illegally, illegitimately. *Mea. for Mea.* Dishonestly, treacherously.
Familiar, a demon.
Fancies and Goodnights, little poems so called.
Fancy, often used for *love*.
Fang, to seize, or gripe.
Fantastical, of fancy, or imagination.
Fantasticoes, affected, foolish fellows.
Fap, beaten, or drunk.
Far, extensively.
Far off guilty, guilty in a remote degree.
Farced, stuffed.
Farthel, or *fardel*, a bundle, a burthen.
Fashions, the farcens, or farcy.
Favour, often for countenance.
Favours, features.
Fear, sometimes to affright.
Fear, danger.
Feat, to form, to model.
Feat, ready, dexterous.
Federacy, a confederate.
Fee-farm, a kiss in fee-farm, a long and unbounded kiss, from a law phrase.
Feeders, low debauched servants. [tenance.
Feeding, substance, or main-
Feere, a companion, a husband.
Fell, skin.
Fell of hair, hairy part.
Fence, skill in fencing.
Feodary, an accomplice.
Festinately, hastily.
Festival terms, splendid phraseology.
Fet, fetched, derived.
Fico, a fig, or *figo*.
Fielded, in the field.
Fig, to insult.
File, a list.
Filed, defiled.
Finch egg, a term of reproach; a finch's egg is remarkably gaudy.
Fine, to make showy or specious.
Finer, for final.
Fine issues, great consequences.
Fineless, unbounded, endless.
Fire-drake, a serpent, a will-o'-the wisp, a firework.
Fire-new, just off the irons, quite new.
Firk, to chastise.
First house, chief branch of the family.
Firstlings, first produce.
Fit o' the face, grimace.
Fits o' the season, its disorders.
Fixure, position.
Flap-dragon, an inflammable substance swallowed by topers.
Flap-jack, a kind of pancake.
Flaw, a sudden gust of wind.
Flecked, spotted, dappled, streaked.
Fleet, for float.
Fleshment, performance. A young soldier fleshes his sword when he first draws blood with it.
Flewed, deep-mouthed, applied to hounds.
Flibbertigibbet, a fiend.
Flickering, fluttering, undulation, the motion of flame.
Flote, wave.
Flourish, to ornament, sanction.

Flout, to wave idly, to wave in mockery.
Flush youth, youth ripened to manhood.
Foeman, an enemy in war.
Foin, to make a thrust in fencing.
Foison, plenty.
Foison plenty, plenty, to the utmost abundance. *Fr.*
Fond, valued, prized, sometimes foolish, indiscreet.
Fond done, foolishly done.
Foot, to grasp.
Forage, to range abroad.
Fordone, overcome or destroyed. [doom.
Foredoomed, anticipated their
Forefended, prohibited, forbid.
Foreslow, to be dilatory.
Forgetive, from forge, inventive, imaginative.
Forked plague, an allusion to the cuckold's horns.
Formal capacity, not de-arranged, or out of form.
Former, sometimes for foremost.
Forspoken, contradicted, spoken against.
Forwearied, worn out.
Frampold, fretful, peevish.
Frank, a stye.
Franklin, a freeholder, a yeoman.
Frets, the stops of a musical instrument, which regulate the vibrations of a string.
Frippery, a shop where old clothes were sold.
Frontlet, part of a woman's headdress.
Frush, to break, or bruise.
Fulham, a cant term for false dice.
Fulsome, obscene.
Furnishings, colours, external pretences.
Fustilarian, from fusty, a cant name.

Gaberdine, the coarse frock of a peasant, or a loose cloak.
Gad, a sharp pointed instrument: *Done upon the Gad*, suddenly, capriciously.
Galliard, an ancient dance.
Galliasses, a kind of ships so called.
Gallimawfry, a confused heap of things together.
Gallow, to scare, or frighten.
Gallow-glasses, foot soldiers among the Irish.
Garboils, commotions.
Garish, gaudy, showy.
Garnered, treasured up.
Gasted, frighted.
Gaunt, thin, lean, or meagre.
Gawd, a bauble, or trifle.
Gear, a colloquial expression, for things or matters.
Geck, a fool.
Gennets, or *jennets*, Spanish horses.
German, a-kin.
Germins, seeds which have begun to germinate or sprout.
Gest, a stage, or journey.
Gib, a name for a cat.
Giglots, wanton wenches.
Gimmal, a ring.
Gimmal bit, a bit of which the parts played one with another.
Ging, an old word for *gang*.
Gird, a sarcasm, or gibe: *To gird*, to be sarcastical.
Glaire, a sword.
Glared, gazed upon, looked fiercely.
Gleek, to joke or scoff.
Glib, to lib, or geld.
Glooming, gloomy.
Gloze, to expound, or explain.
Glut, to swallow.
God'ild you, God yield you, or reward you.
God's sonties, the abbreviation of an ancient oath.
Gongarian, for Hungarian, used as a term of reproach.
Good den, good evening.
Good-jer, from *gougero*, what the pox!
Gorbellied, fat and corpulent.
Gospelled, of precise or puritan virtue.

Goss, furze.
Gossomer, the white exhalations which fly about in summer. [per.
Gougeers, the French distem-
Gourd, an instrument of gaming.
Gouts, drops. *Fr.*
Gramercy, grand merci, great thanks. *Fr.*
Grange, a solitary farm-house.
Gratulate, to be rejoiced in.
Grise, or *Grize*, a step.
Groundlings, the lower sort of people who stood or sat on the ground, in the old theatres.
Guerdon, reward.
Guerdoned, rewarded.
Gules, a term in heraldry, red.
Gust, to taste.
Gyve, to catch, to shackle.
Gyves, shackles.

Haggard, a kind of hawk.
Halcyon, a bird, otherwise called the king-fisher.
Hallidom, sentence at the day of judgment.
Handsaw, corrupted from *Hernshaw*.
Hangers, that part of the girdle or belt by which the sword was suspended.
Hardiment, hardiness, bravery, stoutness.
Harlocks, the name of a plant, probably the burdock.
Harlots, sometimes applied to cheats of the male sex.
Harlotry, vulgar, filthy.
Harness, armour.
Harrow, to conquer, to subdue
Harry, to hurt, to use roughly
Hatch, to cut, or engrave.
Having, estate or fortune.
Haught, haughty.
Hay, a term in fencing.
Hearted throne, the heart in which thou wast enthroned.
Hebenon, henbane.
Hefted, heaved, agitated.
Hefts, heavings.
Hell, a cant name for a dungeon in a prison.
Hence, henceforward.
Henchman, page of honour.
Hent, to seize or take possession, to take hold of.
Herb of grace, rue.
Hermits, beadsmen.
Hest, for behest, command.
Hight, called.
Hilding, or hilderling, a low wretch.
Hoar, hoary, mouldy.
Hob-nob, let it happen or not.
Hold, i.e. rumour, to believe it
Hold taking, bear handling.
Hoodman-blind, blind-man's buff.
Horologe, clock.
Hoxes, to hox, or hough, to cut the hamstring.
Hull, to drive to and fro upon the water, without sails or rudder.
Humming, overwhelming.
Hunt-counter, blunderer, worthless fellow, probably bailiff.
Hunts-up, a morning hunting tune.
Hurly, noise.
Hurtle, to dash, or push violently.
Hyen, hyæna.

Jauncing, jaunting.
Jay, a bad woman.
Ice-brook, i. e. temper, tempered by being plunged into an ice-brook.
Jesses, straps of leather tied about the foot of a hawk to hold her in hand.
Jet, to strut, to walk proudly.
Ignomy, ignominy.
Jig, a ludicrous dialogue in metre.
Imbare, to lay open, or expose.
Immanity, barbarity, savageness.
Immediacy, proximity without intervention.
Imp out, to supply the deficiency, a phrase from falconry.
Impair, unsuitable to the dignity.

Impawn, to engage; the modern word is to commit one's self.
Imperious, sometimes used for imperial.
Imperseverant, ill perseverent, or perseverant.
Impress, a device, or motto.
Incarnardine, stained of a flesh colour, or red.
Inclips, embraces.
Incony, fine, or pretty, a term of endearment.
Indent, to bargain, or article.
Indues, subdues.
Indued, inured, or formed by nature.
Indurance, delay, procrastination.
Inhibit, for inhabit, or to forbid, or decline, as a person refusing a challenge.
Inhooped, enclosed, confined.
Initiate, young, just initiated.
Ink-horn mate, a bookman.
Inkle, a species of tape, or worsted.
Insculped, engraved.
Insconce, to fortify.
Intention and *intentively*, for attention, attentively.
Interessed, interested.
Intrenchant, that which cannot be cut.
Intrinse, intricate, or intrinsecate, ravelled.
Inward, sometimes for an intimate.
Journal, daily.
Irk, to make uneasy.
Irregulous, lawless, licentious.
Iteration, citation, or repetition.
Jump, sometimes to agree with, to suit.
Justicer, a justice.
Juvenal, a young man.

Keech, a lump or mass of tallow.
Keel, to cool.
Kernes, light-armed soldiers. See *Gallow-glasses*.
Key-cold, as cold as iron, a key of which is used to stop small bleedings.
Kicksy-wicksy, a ludicrous name for a wife.
Kiln-hole, the place into which coals are put under a stove.
Kirtle, a sort of garment.
Knap, to break short.
Knotts, figures into which part of a garden was disposed.
Known, sometimes for been acquainted.

Laced mutton, cant name for a courtesan.
Lackeying, floating backwards and forwards.
Lag, the fag-end.
Lakin, ladykin, or little lady.
Lances, lance-men.
Land-damn, probably, to banish from the land.
Land-rakers, wanderers on foot.
Lapsed in time, having suffered time to slip.
Latch, to lay hold of.
Lated, belated, benighted.
Latten, lathy, thin.
Lavolt, a dance.
Laund, lawn.
Lay, a wager.
Leaguer, a name for a camp.
Leasing, falsehood.
Leavened, matured, prepared.
Leech, physician.
Leer, feature, complexion, or colour.
Leet, court-leet, a petty court of justice.
Leg, obeisance to my father.
Legerity, lightness, nimbleness.
Leiger, a resident, or resident-ambassador.
Leman, a lover, or mistress.
Lenten, short and spare.
L'envoy, a term borrowed from the old French poetry.
Lewd, sometimes means idle.
Libbard, leopard.
Liberty, for libertines, or libertinism.
Liefest, dearest.
Lifter, a thief.
Limbeck, a vessel to emit fumes and vapours.
Limbo-patrum, in confinement.
Limed, ensnared, as with birdlime.
Limits, estimates, or outlines, rough sketches.
Lined, delineated.
Line, genealogy.
Link, a torch, used to make old hats black.
Linstock, the staff to which the match is fixed, when ordnance is fired.
List, the bound or limit.
Lither, flexible, or yielding.
Loach, a very small fish, exceedingly prolific.
Lob, an epithet implying dullness and inactivity.
Lock, a particular lock of hair, called a love-lock.
Lockram, a kind of linen.
Lode-star, leading star, the pole-star.
Loggats, a game played with bowl and pins.
Longing, for longed, wished, or desired.
Longly, longingly.
Loofed, brought close to the wind.
Loon, a base fellow.
Looped, full of apertures.
Lop, the branches.
Lordings, the diminutive of lord.
Lover, sometimes used for mistress.
Lown, a sorry fellow.
Lowted, treated with contempt.
Lozel, a worthless fellow.
Lunes, lunacy, frenzy.
Lurch, to purloin, to deprive.
Lush, a dark full colour.
Lustic, cheerful, pleasant. *Dutch*.
Lym, or *lyme*, a bloodhound.

Mace, sceptre.
Magot-pie, magpie.
Magnifico, a chief man in Venice.
Mailed, wrapt up, bundled up, covered with mail.
Main descry, the main body is descried.
Male, male parent.
Malich, a wicked art. *Span.*
Malkin, a kitchen wench, or scullion, a trull.
Maltworms, tipplers.
Mammering, hesitating, stammering.
Mammocked, cut in pieces.
Mammets, puppets.
Manage, conduct, administration.
Mandragora, a plant of soporific virtue.
Mandrake, a root, supposed to have the shape of a man, and to groan when pulled from the ground.
Mankind, i. e. witch, a masculine witch.
Manner, with the manner, in the fact.
Marchpane, a kind of sweet confection, or biscuit.
Marches, borders, confines.
Martlemas, the latter spring.
Mated, confounded.
Meacock, timorous, dastardly.
Mealed, sprinkled, or mingled.
Mean, a tenor.
Measure, a solemn dance.
Meazels, lepers.
Medicin, physician.
Meditation, quickness of enthusiastic thought.
Meiney, people. *Fr.*
Mell, to meddle with.
Memory, sometimes used for memorial.
Mends, the means, the wherewithal.
Mere, sometimes for absolute, entire, total.
Mered question, the sole question.
Mewed, confined.
Micher, a truant.
Miching mallecho, a secret mischief.
Minute-jacks, Jack o'lantern.
Miscreate, illegitimate, spurious.
Misprised, mistaken.
Misprising, despising, contemning.
Missingly, at intervals, occasionally.
Missives, messengers.
Mistempered, angry, contentious.
Mistful, i. e. eyes ready to flow with tears.
Mobled, veiled or muffled.
Model, sometimes for mould.
Modern, sometimes for absurd, new-fangled.
Module, model.
Moe, to make mouths.
Moist star, the moon.
Mome, a dull, stupid, blockhead.
Momentary, short, momentary.
Monster, to make monstrous.
Moonish, variable.
Mope, to be stupid or foolish.
Mopes and *mowes*, wry faces and mockings.
Mort, i. e. of the deer, a tune on the death of the deer.
Mortal, abounding.
Mortified, religious, retired, peaceable.
Motion, sometimes for puppet; puppetshows were called motions.
Motive, sometimes for assistant, or mover.
Mouldwarp, the mole.
Moys, pieces of gold.
Much, sometimes an expression of admiration or disdain.
Muckwater, the drain of a dunghill.
Muffler, a part of the female head-dress.
Mulled, softened, dispirited.
Mummy, the liquor that runs from mummies.
Mundane, worldly.
Mure, wall.
Murky, dark.
Muss, a scramble.
Mutine, to mutiny, or a mutinous fellow.

Napless, threadbare.
Nayword, a watchword, or a byeword.
Neb, the mouth.
Neelds, needles.
Neglection, for neglect.
Neif, fist.
Nether-stocks, stockings.
Newt, the eft.
Next, sometimes for nearest.
Nice, sometimes for silly, trifling.
Nick, reckoning or count.
To nick, to set the mark of folly on.
Night-rule, frolic of the night.
Nill, shall not.
Nine men's morris, figures cut out in the turf for a game so called.
Noble touch, true metal unalloyed.
Nonce, for the *nonce*, on purpose.
Noon-tide prick, noontide point on the dial.
Nott-pated, round-headed, cropt.
Novum, a game at dice.
Nouzle, to nurstle a fondling.
Nowl, a head.
Nurture, education.
Nut hood, a catchpole.

Odd-even, the interval between twelve at night and one in the morning.
Od's pitikins, God's my pity.
Oeliads, glances of the eye. *Fr.*
Oes, circles.
Onyers, probably for owners.
Opal, a precious stone, of almost all colours.
Operant, active.
Opinion, sometimes for self-conceit.
Orbs, fairy circles.
Ordinance, rank.
Orgulous, proud. *Fr.*
Ostent, ostentation or demonstration.
Overcrows, overcomes, triumphs over.
Overscutched, whipt, or carted applied to low prostitutes.
Ouphes, fairies.
Ousel-cock, supposed the cock black-bird.
Out-vied, defeated, a term in the old game of gleek.
Owe, sometimes used for own.
Oxlip, the greater cowslip.

Pack, to make a bargain, or act collusively.
Packings, frauds.
Payed, beaten, drubbed. *Hen. IV. 1st. Part*, punished.
Pale, sometimes dominions, boundaries.
Pall, to wrap, or invest.
Palled, vapid, decayed.
Palmers, pilgrims who visited holy places.
Palmy, victorious.
Palter, to shuffle.
Paragoned, peerless, without comparison.
Parcell-bawd, half-bawd.
To parcell, sometimes to reckon.
Parcell-gilt, partly gilt.
Paritors, apparitors, officers of the spiritual court.
Parle, dispute by words.
Parlous, perilous, keen, shrewd.
Partizan, a pike.
Pash, head.
To pash, to butt, or strike with violence.
Passed, sometimes for surpassed all expression.
Passy-measure, a kind of dance.
Patch, a fool.
Path, to walk.
Patines, round broad plates.
Pavin, a kind of dance.
Paucas palabris, few words, corrupted from the Sp. *pocas palabras*.
Peat, pet, or darling, a spoiled child.
Peculiar, belonging to an individual.
Peer-out, appear out, or peep out.
Peevish, sometimes for foolish.
Peize, to weigh, to keep in suspense. *Fr.*
Pelting, sometimes for paltry.
Pennons, small flags.
Perdu, one of the forlorn hope. *Fr.*
Perdurable, lasting.
Perdy, a corruption of the French oath, *par Dieu*.
Perfect, sometimes used for certain, or well assured.
Periapts, charms worn about the neck.
Pew-fellow, a companion.
Pheere, a mate, or companion
Pheese, to plague, or tease.
I'll pheese you, I'll comb your head.
Pia Mater, the membrane that protects the substance of the brain.
Pick, sometimes for to pitch.
Pickers, hands.
Pick-thank, an officious parasite.
Piece, sometimes used as an epithet of contempt.
Pieled, shaved.
Pight, pitched, fixed.
Pilcher, leathern sheath.
Piled, that which has lost the hair.
Piled-esteemed, probably for vile-esteemed.
Pilled, pillaged.
Pinfold, a pound.
Pink eyne, red eyes.
Pinnace, anciently signified a ship of small burthen.
Pix, the box in which consecrated wafers were kept.
Placket, a petticoat.
Plague, for, to punish.
Plainly, openly, free from concealment.
Planched, made of boards or planks.
Plantage, plaintain, or any kind of plants subject to the influence of the moon.
Plants, feet; from the *Lat.*
Plates, silver money.
Platforms, plans or schemes.

Plausive, gracious, pleasing, popular.
Pleached, folded in each other.
Plot, a piece or portion.
Point, to point exactly, completely.
Point-devise, exactly. *Fr.*
Poize, weight or moment.
Polack, an inhabitant of Poland.
Politick regard, a sly look.
Polled, bared or cleared.
Pomander, a perfumed ball, worn in times of infection.
Pomewater, a species of apple.
Poor John, hake, dried and salted.
Popinjay, a parrot.
Port, show or appearance.
Portage, open space, or safe arrival at a port.
Portance, carriage.
Possess, sometimes for to make understand.
Potch, to push roughly or violently.
Potents, potentates.
Poulter, poulterer.
Pouncet box, a box cut with open work. *Fr.*
Prank, to adorn, to deck out.
Precisian, one who pretends to great sanctity.
Preeches, breeched, flogged.
Prenominate, already named.
Pricket, a buck of the second year.
Prig, to filch.
Prime, sprightliness of youth
Primer, more important.
Primero, a game at cards.
Princox, a coxcomb or pet
Probal, probable.
Proface, much good may it do you. *Ital.*
Profane, sometimes, free of speech, talkative.
Profession, end and purpose of coming.
Prolixious, coy, distant.
Prompture, suggestion, instigation.
Prone, humble or prompt.
Properties, the necessaries of a theatre.
Provand, provender.
Prune, sometimes for to plume.
Pugging, cant word for coveting, as a thief or sharper.
Puke, colour between russet and black.
Pun, to pound.
Pussel, a low wench.
Putter-out, one who puts out his money on interest or other advantage.
Puttock, a mean species of hawk.

Quail, to sink, to faint.
Quaint, fantastically dressed.
Quaked, thrown into trepidation.
Quarry, the game after it is killed.
Quart d'ecu, fourth part of a French crown.
Quat, a scab, an angry blockhead.
Queasy, suspicious, unsettled.
Quell, sometimes, to murder.
Queller, a murderer.
Quests, reports.
Quest, pursuit.
Question, sometimes, conversation.
Questrist, one who goes in search of another.
Quiddits, subtleties.
Quill, in the quill, written.
Quillets, evasion, chicanery.
Quintain, a post or butt set up.
Quips, hasty, passionate reproaches and scoffs.
Quired, played in concert.
Quit, sometimes to requite.
Quittance, return of injuries or favours.
Quiver, nimble, active.
Quote, sometimes, to observe or regard.

Rabato, an ornament for the neck.
Rabbit-sucker, a young rabbit.
Race of heaven, something descended from heaven, heavenly.
Race, a single root.
Rack, the last fleeting vestige of the highest clouds.
To rack, to harass by exactions.
Ram, for rain.
Rampallion, a ramping low creature.
Rapt, rapturously affected.
Rated sinew, a strength reckoned upon.
Ravin, to devour voraciously.
Raught, reached.
Rawly, without preparation, suddenly, hastily.
Rayed, bewrayed.
Raze, a bale.
Recheat, a horn, a tune to call the dogs back.
Reck, to care for.
Reckless, careless.
Recorders, a kind of flute.
Red-lattice phrases, alehouse conversation, from the form of the doors and windows.
Red plague, the erysipelas, St. Antony's fire.
Reechy, discoloured by smoke.
Reels, probably for wheels.
Refel, to confute.
Regreet, exchange of salutation.
Reguerdon, recompense, return.
Remorse, sometimes used for pity.
Remotion, removal from place to place, shifting.
Remues, journeys, stages.
Render, sometimes, to describe.
Renege, to renounce.
Repair, generally signifies to renovate.
Repeals, recalls.
Reports, reporters.
Reproof, confutation.
Repugn, to resist.
Reserve, to guard, to preserve carefully.
Resolve, sometimes for dissolve.
Respect, caution, regard to consequences.
Respective, respectful or respectable.
Respectively, respectfully.
Rest, what I am resolved on.
Retort, to refer back.
Reverbs, reverberates.
Revolt of mien, change of complexion.
Revolts, revolters.
Rheumatic, for capricious, humoursome.
Rib, to enclose.
Ribald, lewd fellow.
Rid, to destroy.
Rift, to split.
Riggish, wanton.
Rigol, a circle.
Rim, probably a cant word for money.
Ringed, encircled.
Rivage, the bank or shore.
Rivality, equal rank.
Rivals, equals.
Rive, to discharge or burst.
Romage, tumultuous hurry.
Ronyon, a scab, a despicable person.
Rood, the cross.
Rooky, abounding with rooks.
Ropetricks, roguish tricks, or abusive language.
Ropery, roguery.
Roundel, a circular dance.
Roundure, a circle.
Rouse, a draught of jollity, carousal.
Royal, or *real*, a coin of the value of ten shillings.
Royally attorneyed, nobly supplied by substitution of embassies.
Roynish, mangy, scurvy.
Ruddock, the redbreast.
Ruffle, to be noisy, disorderly.
Ruffling, bustling or rustling.
Rule, method of life.
Rump-fed, fed with offals.
Rush, for rush-ring.
Ruth, pity, compassion.

Sacarson, the name of a bear.
Sacring-bell, the bell which gives notice of the host approaching.
Sad ostent, grave appearance.
Sagg, to sink down.
Sallet, a helmet.
Saltiers, satyrs.
Samingo, San Domingo.
Sandied, of a sandy colour, the colour of the true bloodhound.
Saw, discourse.
Say, old word for silk.
Scale, to disperse, to spread.
Scaling, weighing.
Scall, a word of reproach, scab.
Scamble, to scramble.
Scanned, examined nicely.
Scandling, measure or proportion.
Scarfed, decorated with flags.
Scath, destruction, harm.
Sconce, the head, or a kind of fortification.
Scotch, to bruise or crush.
Scrimers, fencers. *Fr.*
Scroyles, scabby fellows.
Scrubbed, stunted, shrub-like, or short and dirty.
Sculls, shoals of fish.
Seam, lard.
Seamels, a bird.
Seamy side without, inside out.
Sear, dry.
Sear, to close up.
Seel, to sew up.
Seeling, blinding.
Seld, for seldom.
Semblably, in resemblance, alike.
Seniory, seniority.
Sennet, a flourish on cornets.
Sense, sometimes for reason and natural affection.
Septentrion, the North.
Sequence, of degree, methodically.
Sere, dry, withered.
Serpigo, a kind of tetter.
Sessa, from *cesser*, be quiet.
Set of wit, a term from tennis.
Sets up his rest, a term from the military exercise.
Setobos, a kind of god or devil.
Several, or *severell*, a field separated from others to bear corn and grass.
Sewer, the person who placed the dishes in order.
Shard borne, borne on shards or wings.
Shark up, to pick up without distinction.
Shaven Hercules, Samson.
Sheen, shining, bright, gay.
Sheer, pellucid, transparent.
Shent, scolded, roughly treated.
Sherris sack, sherry sack.
Shive, a slice.
Shog, to go off.
Shotten, projected.
Shove groat, a kind of game.
Shovel boards, shillings used at the game of shovel-board.
Shoughs, a species of dog.
Shoulder clapper, a bailiff.
Shrewd, sometimes for severe, bitter.
Shrift, confession.
Shrive, to call to confession.
Side, purpose or resolution.
Siege, a stool, or privy, or seat.
Sieve, a common voider.
Sightless, unsightly.
Sights, i. e. of steel, the perforated part of the helmet.
Single, sometimes for weak, little.
Sister, to imitate or re-echo.
Sith, and *sithence*, since.
Sizes, allowances.
Skain's mates, kin's mates.
Skill, reason.
Skills not, is of no importance.
Skinker, a tapster; from *Skink*, drink.
Skirr, to scour.
Slave, to treat with indignity.
Sleave, coarse, unwrought silk.
Sledded, carried on a sledge.
Sleided, untwisted.
Slights, arts.
Slip, a counterfeit piece of money.
Slips, a contrivance in leather, to start two dogs at the same time.
Slivered, sliced.
Slops, loose breeches or trowsers.
Slough, the skin which the serpent throws off annually.
Slowed, delayed.
Slubber, to obscure.
Smirched, soiled, obscured.
Sneap, rebuke, check.
Sneck up, a cant phrase, probably for, go hang yourself.
Snipe, an insignificant fellow.
Snuff, sometimes for anger.
Snuffs, dislikes.
Soft, i. e. conditions, gentle qualities of mind.
Soil, sometimes, turpitude, reproach.
Solidares, some species of coin.
Sooth, truth.
Sorer, a greater or heavier crime.
Sorel, a deer during his third year.
Sort, to choose out.
Sorts, different degrees or kinds.
Sort and suit, figure and rank
Sot, fool. *Fr.*
Souced gurnet, a gudgeon, a term of reproach.
Soud, sweet, or an exclamation denoting weariness.
Sowle, to drag down.
Sowter, the name of a hound.
Spanieled, dogged.
Speak parrot, to act childishly and foolishly.
Speak holiday, i.e. words, curiously and affectedly chosen.
Speculation, for sight.
Speculative instruments, the eyes.
Speed, fate or event.
Sperr, to stir.
Spill, to destroy.
Spleen, often for hurry, or tumultuous speed.
Spotted, wicked.
Sprag, ready, alert.
Sprighted, haunted.
Springhalt, a disease incident to horses.
Square, sometimes, to quarrel,
Squarer, a quarrelsome fellow.
Squash, an immature peascod.
Squiney, to look asquint.
Squire, sometimes for a rule or square.
Stage, to place conspicuously.
Staged, exhibited.
Staggers, a disorder peculiar to horses.
Stain, colour or tincture.
Stale, a decoy to catch birds.
Stannyel, the name of a kind of hawk; a stallion.
Stark, stiff.
State, sometimes for a chair of state.
Statists, statesmen.
Statua, statue, sometimes pronounced as three syllables.
Staves, the wood of the lances.
Stead, to help or befriend.
Sternage, the hinder part, close after.
Stickler, one who stood by to part the combatants, an umpire.
Stigmatical, marked or stigmatized.
Still, sometimes for constant, continual.
Stilly, gladly, lowly.
Stinted, stopped.
Stint, sometimes to stop.
Stithied, forged; from *stithy*, an anvil.
Stoccata, a thrust or stab. *Ital.*
Stock, sometimes for stocking.
Stomach, sometimes for stubborn resolution, pride, or haughtiness.
Stone-bow, a crossbow to shoot stones.
Stover, hay made of coarse ran grass, and used for thatching.
Strachy, or *thracky*, of Thrace.
Strait, narrow, avaricious.
Straited, put to difficulties.
Strange and *strangeness*, sometimes for shy and shyness.
Strangle, sometimes for to suppress.
Strawy, straying.
Striker, cant word for a borrower.
Stuck, or *stock*, for *stoccata*, a term in fencing.
Stuffed sufficiency, abilities more than enough.
Submerged, whelmed under water.
Subscribe, sometimes to yield or surrender.
Subtleties, disguised dishes.

Success, sometimes for succession.
Successive, i. e. title, title to the succession.
Suggest, sometimes, to tempt, to excite.
Suited, dressed.
Sumpter, either the horse or the package that conveys necessaries.
Superfluous, overclothed, *All's Well*. Living in abundance, *Lear*.
Surcease, cessation, stop.
Surreigned, overridden.
Swart, or *swarth*, black or dark brown.
Swashing, imposing, bullying.
Swath, the quantity of grass cut down by a single stroke of the scythe.
Sway, weight or momentum.
Sweltered, weltered.
Swinge-bucklers rakes or rioters.
Swounded, swooned.

Table, the palm of the hand extended, a picture.
Tables, books of ivory for memorandums.
Tabourines, small drums.
Ta'en order, taken measures.
Tag, the vulgar populace.
Taint, corruption or disgrace.
Take, i. e. a house, to go into a house.
Take, sometimes, to strike with lameness or disease.
Take in, to subdue.
Talent, often for *talon*.
Tarre, to stimulate, to set on.
Tasked, sometimes for taxed.
Tassel-gentle, or *tercel gentle*, a species of hawk.
Tawney coat, the dress of a summoner or apparitor.
Taxation, sometimes for *censure* or *satire*.
Teen, sorrow, grief, or trouble.
Temper, to mould like wax.
Temperance, temperature.
Tend, sometimes for *attend*.
Tender, to regard with affection.
Tent, to take up residence.
Tercel, the male hawk.
Terms, the technical language of courts.
Tested, attested, genuine.
Testerned, gratified with a tester, or sixpence.
Tetchy, touchy, peevish, fretful.
Tether, a string by which any animal is fastened.
Tharborough, third borough, a peace officer.
Theorick, theory.
Thews, muscular strength, or appearance of manhood.
Thick-pleached, thickly interwoven.
Thill, or *fill*, the shafts of a cart or waggon.
Thin helm, thin covering of hair.
Thought, sometimes for *melancholy*.
Thrasonical, insolently boasting; from *Thraso*, a braggadocio in Terence.
Thread, sometimes for to pass.
Three-pile, rich velvet.
Thrift, a state of prosperity.
Thrumbed, made of thrum, the end of the weaver's warp.
Tib, a nickname for a wanton.
Tickle, sometimes for ticklish.
Tickle-brain, the name of a strong liquor.
Tilley-valley, an interjection of contempt.
Time, a ripener.
Timeless, untimely.
Timely-parted, i. e. ghost, departed in the course of time and nature.
Tire, to fasten, to fix the talons.
Tire valiant, or *volant*, a kind of head-dress.
Tired, sometimes for adorned.
Tod, to produce a tod, a certain quantity of wool.
Toged, wearing their habits.
Tokened, spotted.
Tolling, taking toll.
Tomboy, a masculine, forward girl.
Too much, any sum, ever so much.
Topless, supreme, sovereign.
Topple, to tumble.
Touches, the features, the trait.
Toward and *towards*, sometimes, instead of readiness.
Toys, sometimes for whims, freaks.
Toze, to unravel, to close examine.
Trace, sometimes, to follow or succeed in.
Trail, the scent left by the passage of the game.
Trammel, to catch; *tremmel* is a species of net.
Tranect, probably some kind of ferry, dam, or sluice.
Translate, sometimes for to change or transform.
Trash, to cut away the superfluities, or to check; a phrase in hunting.
Traverse, an ancient military word of command.
Traversed, i. e. arms, arms across.
Tray-trip, a kind of game at tables or draughts.
Treachers, traitors.
Trenched, cut or carved. *Fr.*
Trick, sometimes for a peculiarity of feature.
Trick, to dress out.
Tricksy, clever, adroit.
Trigon, Aries, Leo, and Sagittarius.
Trip, to defeat or disappoint.
Triple, for third, or one of the three.
Triumphs, sometimes for shows, masks, revels.
Trol-my-dames, trou-madame, the game of nine holes.
Troll, to sing trippingly.
Trossers, probably for trowsers, or a kind of breeches.
Trot, a familiar address to a man.
Trow, to imagine or conceive; I trow.
True, sometimes for honest.
Trundle-tail, a species of dog.
Trusted, for *thrusted*.
Try conclusions, try experiments.
Tub-fast, the sweating process in the venereal disorder.
Tucket, toccata, a flourish on a trumpet. *Ital.*
Tupped, lien with; from *tup*, a ram.
Turlygood, for *turlupin*, a naked beggar.
Turquoise, a species of precious stone, supposed to be endued with extraordinary virtues.
Twangling Jack, a paltry musician.
Twiggen-bottle, a wickered bottle.
Tyed, limited, or circumscribed.

Vail, sometimes to cast down, to let fall down.
Valenced, fringed with a beard.
Validity, sometimes for value.
Vanity, an illusion.
Vantage, opportunity.
Vantbrace, armour for the arm. *Fr.*
Vast, sometimes for waste, dreary.
Vaunt, the avant, what went before, or the vanguard.
Vaward, the forepart.
Velure, velvet.
Venetian, admittance, a fashion admitted from Venice.
Venew, a bout at a fencing school.
Veneys, venews.
Vent, rumour, materials for discourse.
Ventages, the holes of a flute.
Verbal, verbose.
Verify, to bear witness.
Very, sometimes for immediate.
Vice, to draw or persuade.
Vice, a grasp. A mimic.
Vie, a term at cards, to brag.
Violenteth, probably rageth.
Virgin crants, maiden garlands. *Ger.*
Virginal, a kind of spinnet.
Virginal, belonging to a virgin.
Virtuous, sometimes for salutiferous.
Vizament, advisement.
Umber, a dusky, yellow-coloured earth.
Umbered, discoloured.
Unaneled, without extreme unction.
Unavoided, unavoidable.
Unbarbed, bare, uncovered, beardless.
Unbated, i. e. sword not blunted as foils are.
Unbitted, unbridled.
Unbonneted, without any addition from dignities.
Unbreathed, unexercised, unpractised.
Uncape, a term in hunting, to stop every hole before the fox is uncaped or turned out of the bag.
Uncharged, unattacked.
Unclew, to unwind, to ruin.
Uncoined, unrefined, unadorned.
Unconfirmed, unpractised in the ways of the world, not hardened.
Undercraft, a phrase from heraldry, to wear beneath the crest.
Uneffectual, i. e. fire, shining without heat.
Unexpressive, inexpressible.
Ungenitured, not having genitals. [ful.
Unhaired, unbearded, youth-
Unhappy, sometimes for mischievously waggish, unlucky.
Unhoused, free from domestic cares.
Unhouselled, without having the sacrament.
Unmastered, licentious.
Unproper, common.
Unqualitied, unmanned.
Unquestionable, averse to conversation.
Unrespective, inconsiderate.
Unrest, disquiet.
Unrough youths, beardless youths.
Unsisting, unresisting or unfeeling.
Unsmirched, clean, not defiled.
Unsquared, as stones, unadapted to their purposes.
Unstanched, incontinent.
Untempering, not softening.
Untented, not probed, virulent.
Untraded, singular, not in common use.
Unvalued, invaluable.
Upspring, upstart.
Use and *usance*, sometimes for usury.
Utis, a merry festival.
Utterance, the extremity of defiance.

Waft, to beckon.
Wage, sometimes, to hire or reward, to fight.
Wan'd, probably for waned, decayed, or in the wane.
Wanned, pale, made wan.
Wanton, sometimes for a man feeble and effeminate.
Wappened, probably decayed or diseased.
Ward, defence, a phrase in the art of defence.
Warder, a guard or sentinel.
Warden, a species of large pear.
Warn, sometimes, to summons.
Warp, to change from the natural state.
Wassel, a kind of drink, or intemperate drinking.
Wassel candle, candle used at feasts.
Waxen, to increase.
Waxen, soft, yielding, easily obliterated.
Web and the pin, diseases of the eye.
Wee, very little.
Ween, to think or imagine.
Weigh, sometimes, to value or esteem.
Weird, prophetic.
Welkin, the sky.
Welkin-eye, blue eye.
Well-a-near, well-a-day, lack-a-day.
Wend, to go.
Westward-hoe, the name of a play acted in Shakspeare's time.
Wether, used for ram.
Whelked, varied with protuberances; from *whelks*, protuberances, a small shell-fish.
Whe'r, often for whether.
Where, sometimes for whereas.
Whiffler, an officer who walked in processions.
Whiles, until.
Whipstock, the carter's whip.
Whirring, hurrying away.
Whist, being silent.
Whiting time, bleaching time.
Whitsters, bleachers of linen.
Whittle, a pocket clasp knife.
Whooping, measure and reckoning.
Wimpled, hooded, or veiled; from *wimple*, a hood.
Winchester goose, a strumpet; the stews were formerly licensed by the bishop of Winchester.
Winking-gates, gates hastily closed from fear or danger.
Winnowed, sifted, examined.
Wis, to know.
Wish, sometimes, to recommend or desire.
Wits, sometimes for senses.
Wittol-cuckold, one who knows himself a cuckold, and is contented.
Woe, to be sorry.
Wondered, able to perform wonders.
Wood, crazy.
Woolvish, giving an idea of a wolf in sheep's clothing.
Woolward, clothed in wool, or rather naked.
Worts, the ancient name of all kinds of cabbage.
Wot, to know.
Wreck, resentment.
Wrest, an instrument for drawing up the strings of a harp; a help.
Wrested pomp, pomp obtained by violence.
Writhled, wrinkled.
Wrought, worked, agitated.
Wrying, deviating.

Yare, handy, nimble.
Yearn, to grieve or vex.
Yerk, to kick.
Yesty, foaming, frothy.

Zany, a buffoon, a merry Andrew.
Zealous, pious, influenced by religion.
Zed, a term of contempt. The letter Z is not in any word originally Teutonic.